Evert Augustus Duyckinck, Geor

Cyclopaedia of American Literature

Vol. II

Evert Augustus Duyckinck, George Long Duyckinck

Cyclopaedia of American Literature

Vol. II

Reprint of the original, first published in 1856.

1st Edition 2024 | ISBN: 978-3-37517-722-5

Salzwasser Verlag is an imprint of Outlook Verlagsgesellschaft mbH.

Verlag (Publisher): Outlook Verlag GmbH, Zeilweg 44, 60439 Frankfurt, Deutschland
Vertretungsberechtigt (Authorized to represent): E. Roepke, Zeilweg 44, 60439 Frankfurt, Deutschland
Druck (Print): Books on Demand GmbH, In de Tarpen 42, 22848 Norderstedt, Deutschland

CYCLOPÆDIA

OF

AMERICAN LITERATURE;

EMBRACING

PERSONAL AND CRITICAL NOTICES OF AUTHORS,

AND SELECTIONS FROM THEIR WRITINGS.

FROM THE EARLIEST PERIOD TO THE PRESENT DAY·

WITH

PORTRAITS, AUTOGRAPHS, AND OTHER ILLUSTRATIONS.

EVERT A. DUYCKINCK AND GEORGE L. DUYCKINCK.

IN TWO VOLUMES.

VOL. II.

NEW YORK:
CHARLES SCRIBNER.

1856.

CONTENTS OF VOLUME II.

CYCLOPÆDIA

OF

AMERICAN LITERATURE.

JAMES KIRKE PAULDING,

J K Paulding

Is descended from one of the early pioneers of the State of New York, who appears in the ancient records of Ulster County, of which he was sheriff in the time of Governor Dongan, sometimes as Hendrick Pauldinck, sometimes as Heinrick Paulden, and at others Henry Pawling, which was probably his English name, being so written in a grant of four thousand acres of land in Dutchess County to his widow Eltje Pawling, by King William the Third. This confusion of names is to be partly traced to the struggle for ascendency between the Dutch and English languages, and partly to the carelessness of the writers, who were not much practised in orthography; so that from these causes it remains doubtful whether Henry Pawling was of English or Dutch extraction.

Subsequently to this grant of King William the family removed to Dutchess County, a township of which is still called after their name. The grandfather of the subject of this sketch, many years previous to the Revolution, settled in the county of Westchester, on a farm still in possession of his descendants. He always wrote his name Paulding, which has been ever since adopted by that branch of the family, though that of Pawling has been retained by the others. The residence of Paulding's father being "within the lines," that is in the district intervening between the British army at New York and the American forces in the Highlands, and he being a somewhat distinguished Whig of the good old revolutionary stamp, his family was exposed to the insults and depredations of the Jagars, the Tories, and the Cow Boys. He removed his family in consequence to Dutchess County, where he possessed some property. Here Paulding was born, August 22, 1779, at a place called Pleasant Valley. His father who, previous to the commencement of the Revolution, had acquired a competency, took a decided and active part in the preliminary struggles; was a leader of the Whig party in the county of Westchester; a member of the first Committee of Safety, and subsequently Commissary General of the New York Continental quota of troops. When, in consequence of the total extinction of the public credit, and the almost hopeless state of the good cause, it was sometimes impossible to procure the necessary supplies for the American army then occupying the highlands of the Hudson, he made use of his own credit with his neighbors, the farmers, and became responsible for large sums of money. At the conclusion of the war, on presenting his accounts to the Auditor-General, this portion of them was rejected on the ground that he was not authorized to make these pledges in behalf of government. He retired a ruined man, was thrown into a prison, which accidentally taking fire, he walked home and remained unmolested by his creditors. He could never be persuaded to renew his application to government; would never accept any office; and though he lived to a great age made no exertions whatever to retrieve his fortunes. His wife, who was the main stay of the family, and a woman of great energy, industry, and economy, survived him several years and died still more aged.

After the peace the family returned to their former abode in Westchester, where Paulding was educated at the village school, a log-house nearly two miles distant from his residence, in which he received all the learning he ever acquired from the tuition of others, so that he may be fairly considered a self-made man. Here he remained at home until he arrived at manhood, when he came to the city of New York. His first sojourn in the city was with the late Mr. William Irving, who had married his sister, a man of wit and genius, whose home was the familiar resort of a knot of young men of a similar stamp, who were members of the Calliopean Society, one of the first purely literary institutions established in the city.* He also became intimate at this time with Washington Irving, whose elder brother William married Paulding's sister, and in connexion with whom he made his first literary venture in the publication of the series of periodical essays entitled *Salmagundi; or the Whim-Whams and Opinions of Launcelot Langstaff and others*, which were issued by David Longworth, a respectable but whimsical bookseller of the times, who, in virtue of having a copy of Boydell's Shakespeare, the plates of which he exhibited in his second story, christened his shop the Shakespeare Gallery; sometimes, too, calling it on the title-pages of his publications the Sentimental Epicure's Ordinary. He was an extensive publisher of plays foreign and native, and became famous for his enterprise of the New York Directory.†

The first number of Salmagundi appeared Saturday, January 24, 1807, in an eighteenmo. of twenty pages. It closed with the issue of number twenty, January 25, 1808. It was the joint work of Paulding and Irving, with the exception of the poetical epistles and three or four of the prose articles, which were from the pen of William Irving. The work was a brilliant success from the start. The humors of the town were hit off with a freshness which is still unexhausted to the readers of an entirely different generation. It disclosed, too, the literary faculties of the writers, both very young men, with a rich promise for the future, in delicate shades of observation, the more pungent traits of satire, and a happy vein of description which grew out of an unaffected love of nature, and was enlivened by studies in the best school of English poetry. When the work was concluded its two chief authors pursued their literary career apart; but it is noticeable as an exhibition of their kindly character, that the early partnership in Salmagundi has never been dissolved by a division of the joint stock between the owners of the separate articles. The whole is included in the incomplete stereotype edition of Paulding's works. In 1819 a second series of the work was published, which was entirely from his hand. Though not unsuccessful, it was not received by the public as its predecessor. The "town" interest had diminished. More than ten years had elapsed; the writer was then engaged in official duties at Washington; his mind had assumed a graver cast, and the second series of Salmagundi is deficient in that buoyant spirit of vivacity which is one of the distinguishing features of the first.

About the period of the commencement of the second war with England, his feelings being strongly excited by the position of affairs of the times, he published *The Diverting History of John Bull and Brother Jonathan*, in the style of Arbuthnot, in which the United States and England are represented as private individuals, father and son engaged in a domestic feud. In this work the policy and conduct of England towards the United States is keenly but good-humoredly satirized, so much so that the whole was republished in numbers in one of the British journals. It passed through several editions, one of which is embellished with several capital illustrations by Jarvis, and was among the most successful of the author's productions. In the volume of Harpers' edition of this tale it is followed by another in the same vein called the *History of Uncle Sam and his Boys*.

The Diverting History was followed by a poem entitled *The Lay of the Scottish Fiddle*,* a free parody of the Lay of the Last Minstrel, which appeared anonymously, like most of Paulding's earlier writings. This production is principally devoted to satirizing the predatory warfare of the British on Chesapeake Bay, and, what is somewhat remarkable, was published in a very handsome style in London with a preface highly complimentary to the author. The hero is Admiral Cockburn, and the principal incident the burning and sacking the little town of Havre de Grace on the coast of Maryland. It had at that time what might be called the distinction of provoking a fierce review from the London Quarterly. It is clever as a parody, and contains many passages entirely original and of no inconsiderable beauty.

Paulding soon after published a pamphlet in prose, *The United States and England*, taking up the defence of the country against the attack of the London Quarterly in its famous review of Ingersoll's Inchiquin Letters. The sale of the work was interrupted by the failure of the publisher about the time of its publication. It however attracted the notice of President Madison, and paved the way for the subsequent political career of the author. The design of the work was to expose the unwarrantable course of the Quarterly in drawing general conclusions from solitary examples, and for this purpose the author cites instances from the newspapers of England and other

* One of the members of this society was Richard Bingham Davis, who was much admired for his poetical talents. In his appearance and manners he is said to have reminded his associates of Oliver Goldsmith. His person was clumsy, his manner awkward, his speech embarrassed, and his simplicity most remarkable in one who had been born and brought up in the midst of a crowd of his fellow creatures. He was born in New York, August 21, 1771, was educated at Columbia College, modestly pursued the business of his father, in carving or sculpture in wood, but was induced in 1796 to undertake the editorial department of the *Diary*, a daily gazette published in New York, for which he wrote during a year. He was too sensitive, and his literary tastes, which lay in the direction of the belles lettres, were too delicate for this pursuit. He next engaged in mercantile affairs. In 1799 he fell a victim to the yellow fever then prevailing in New York, carrying the seeds of the disease with him to New Brunswick, New Jersey, where he died in his twenty-eighth year. His poems were expressions of personal feeling and sentiment, and have a tinge of melancholy. They were collected by his friends of the Calliopean Society after his death and published by Swords in 1807, with a well written prefatory memoir from the pen of John T. Irving. An "Ode to Imagination" shows his earnestness, as a clever "Elegy on an Old Wig found in the street," does his humor. He was also a contributor to the Drone papers in the New York Magazine, where he drew a well written character of himself under the name of Martlet.

† "David Longworth, an eccentric bookseller, who had filled a large apartment with the valuable engravings of Boydell's Shakespeare Gallery, magnificently framed, and had nearly obscured the front of his house with a huge sign,—a colossal painting, in *chiaro scuro*, of the crowning of Shakespeare. Longworth had an extraordinary propensity to publish elegant works, to the great gratification of persons of taste, and the no small diminution of his own slender fortune."—Preface to Salmagundi. Paris edition. 1824.

* The Lay of the Scottish Fiddle; a Tale of Havre de Grace. Supposed to be written by Walter Scott, Esq. First American, from the fourth Edinburgh edition. New York: Inskeep and Bradford. 1813. 32mo. pp. 262.

sources to show that if these are to be assumed as the standard of national morality or manners the English are far in advance of the Americans in vulgarity, vice, and depravity.

This was followed up, in 1822, by *A Sketch of Old England by a New England Man*, purporting to be a narrative of a tour in that country. It commences with an account of various travelling incidents humorously narrated; but the writer soon passes to a discussion of the social, religious, and political points of difference between the two nations, which occupies the chief portion of the volumes. In 1824 he returned to this subject in a new satire on the English travellers, *John Bull in America; or the New Munchausen*, purporting to be a tour of a cockney English traveller in the United States. It exhibits a broad caricature of the ignorant blunders and homebred prejudices of this class of national libellers, equally provocative of laughter and contempt. The hero, through various chances, frequently encounters a shrewd little Frenchman wearing a white hat, draped in white dimity, with gold ear-rings, who, from meeting so continually, he is at length convinced is seeking an opportunity to rob, if not to murder him.

In 1815, after a tour through Virginia, he wrote *Letters from the South, by a Northern Man*, principally occupied with sketching the beauties of the scenery and the manners of the people of the "Ancient Dominion." The author digresses to various subjects, on which he delivers his opinions with his usual straightforward frankness.

In 1818 appeared his principal poetical production, *The Backwoodsman*, an American poem in sentiment, scenery, and incidents. It is in six books of some five hundred lines each, written in the heroic measure. Basil, the hero, appears at the opening as a rural laborer on the banks of the Hudson, reduced to poverty by being confined a whole winter by sickness. On the approach of spring he is attracted by reports of the fertility of the West, the cheapness of the land, and the prospect of improving his condition, and resolves to seek his fortune in that far distant paradise. He abandons his home, and proceeds on his adventure accompanied by his wife and family. The wanderer's farewell, as he turns a last look on the course of the Hudson through the Highlands, is a pleasant passage of description; and the journey through Jersey and Pennsylvania to the Ohio, presents various little incidents, as well as sketches of scenery evidently drawn from the life by a true lover of nature. Arrived at Pittsburg, he proceeds with a company of emigrants he finds collected there to his destination in one of those primitive vessels called Broadhorns, which have become almost obsolete since the introduction of steamers. Here the progress of an infant settlement is sketched, and the author, after seeing Basil comfortably housed, leaves him somewhat abruptly to plunge into the desert wild, and introduce his readers to the Indian prophet, who, in conjunction with some renegade whites, was at that time employed in stirring up the savages to take part in the approaching hostilities between the United States and England, and by whom the little settlement of Basil and his companions is subsequently ravaged and destroyed. War ensues; the backwoodsmen with Basil at their head pursue the savages, and finally overtake them; a bloody fight follows; the prophet falls by the hand of Basil, and the savages are completely routed. Basil returns home; peace is restored, and he passes the remainder of his life in prosperity and honor. The poem closes with a glowing apostrophe to the native land of the author.

The descriptive parts of this poem are perhaps the best portions of the work. The versification is in general vigorous and glowing, though there are not a few occasional exceptions, together with some inaccuracies of expression, which the author would probably now correct were a new edition called for. The Backwoodsman belongs to the old school of poetry, and met with but ordinary success at home, though translations of a portion were published and praised in a literary periodical of the time at Paris.

The scene of Paulding's first novel is laid among the early Swedish settlers on the Delaware. It was originally called *Konigsmark, or the Long Finne*, a name that occurs in our early records, but the title was changed in a subsequent edition to *Old Times in the New World*, for reasons set forth in the publisher's notice. It was divided into separate books, each preceded by an introductory chapter after the manner of Fielding's Tom Jones, and having little connexion with the story. They are for the most part satirical, and in the progress of the narrative the author parodies Norna of the Fitful Head in the person of Bombie of the Frizzled Head, an ancient colored virago.

In 1826 he wrote *Merry Tales of the Three Wise Men of Gotham*, prefaced by a grave dissertation on the existence and locality of that renowned city. This was a satire on Mr. Owen's system of Socialism, which then first began to attract attention in the United States, on Phrenology, and the legal maxim of *Caveat Emptor*, each exemplified in a separate story. The Three Wise Men are introduced at sea in the famous Bowl, relating in turn their experience with a view of dissipating the ennui of the voyage.

This was followed by *The Traveller's Guide*, which was mistaken for an actual itinerary, in consequence of which it was christened somewhat irreverently *The New Pilgrim's Progress*. It is a burlesque on the grandiloquence of the current Guide Books, and the works of English travellers in America. It exhibits many satirical sketches of fashionable life and manners, and will be a treasure to future antiquaries for its allusions to scenes and persons who flourished at the time when, as the writer avers, the dandy must never, under any temptation, extend his morning promenade westwardly, and step beyond the northwest corner of Chambers street, all beyond being vulgar *terra incognita* to the fashionable world. Union Square was then a diminutive Dismal Swamp, and Thirteenth street a lamentable resort of cockney sportsmen. This was in 1828, when to be mistress of a three-story brick house, with mahogany folding doors, and marble mantels, was the highest ambition of a fashionable belle. After exhausting New York, the tourist recommends one of those "sumptuous aquatic palaces," the safety barges, which it grieves him to see are almost deserted for the swifter steamers, most especially by those whose time being worth nothing, they are anxious to save as much of it as possible. In one of these he proceeds leisurely up the river to Albany, loitering by the way, noticing the various towns and other objects of interest, indulging in a variety of philosophical abstractions and opinions, now altogether consigned to the dark ages. Finally he arrives at Balston and Saratoga by stage-coach, where he makes himself merry with foibles of the élite, the manœuvres of discreet mothers, the innocent arts of their unsophisticated daughters, and the deplorable fate of all grey-whiskered bachelors, who seek their helpmates at fashionable watering-places. The remainder of the volume is occupied with rules for the behavior of young ladies, married people, and bachelors young and old, at the time-renowned springs. A number of short stories and sketches are interspersed through the volume, which is highly characteristic of the author's peculiar humors.

Tales of the Good Woman, by a Doubtful Gentleman, followed in sequence, and soon after appeared *The Book of St. Nicholas*, purporting to be a translation from some curious old Dutch legends of New Amsterdam, but emanating exclusively from the fertile imagination of the author. He commemorates most especially the few quaint old Dutch buildings, with the gable-ends to the streets, and steep roofs edged like the teeth of a saw, the last of which maintained its station in New street until within a few years past as a bakery famous for New Year Cakes, but at length fell a victim to the spirit of "progress."

The Dutchman's Fireside, a story founded on the manners of the old Dutch settlers, so charmingly sketched by Mrs. Grant* in the Memoirs of an American Lady, next made its appearance. It is written in the author's happiest vein, and was the most popular of all his productions. It went through six editions within the year; was republished in London, and translated into the French and Dutch languages. This work was succeeded by *Westward Ho!* the scene of which is principally laid in Kentucky, though the story is commenced in Virginia. The Dutchman's Fireside was published in Paris under the title of *Le Coin du Feu d'un Hollandais*. For each of these novels the author, as we are assured, received the then and still important sum of fifteen hundred dollars from the publishers on delivery of the manuscript.

A Life of Washington, principally prepared for the use of the more youthful class of readers, succeeded these works of imagination. It was originally published in two small volumes, and afterwards incorporated with Harpers' Family Library. Five thousand copies were contracted for with the publishers for distribution in the public schools. It is an admirable production, and shows conclusively that the author is equally qualified for a different sphere of literature from that to which he has principally devoted himself. Though written with a steady glow of patriotism, and a full perception of the exalted character and services of the Father of his country, it is pure from all approaches to inflation, exaggeration, and bombast. The style is characterized by simplicity combined with vigor; the narrative is clear and sufficiently copious without redundancy, comprising all the important events of the life of the hero, interspersed with various characteristic anecdotes which give additional interest to the work, without degrading it to mere gossip, and is strongly imbued with the nationality of the author. Being addressed to the youthful reader, he frequently pauses in his narrative to inculcate the example of Washington's private and public virtues on his readers. The character of Washington, as summed up at the conclusion, is one of the most complete we have ever met with.

In 1836, about the period that what is known as the Missouri Question was greatly agitating the country, both North and South, he published a review of the institution, under the title of *Slavery in the United States*, in which he regards the subject with strong southern sympathies. He considers slavery as the offspring of war; as an expedient of humanity to prevent the massacre of prisoners by savage and barbarous tribes and nations, who having no system for the exchange of prisoners, and no means of securing them, have in all time past been accustomed to put to death those whose services they did not require as slaves. He treats the subject with reference both to divine and human laws, and passing from theory to the practical question as applicable to the United States, places before his readers the consequences, first of universal emancipation, next of political and social equality, and lastly of amalgamation.

The last of Paulding's avowed publications are *The Old Continental, or the Price of Liberty*, a Revolutionary story, *The Puritan and his Daughter*, the scene of which is partly in England, partly in the United States, and a volume of American Plays,* in conjunction with his youngest son William Irving Paulding, then a youth under age. The plots of these pieces are defective, and the incidents not sufficiently dramatic, but the dialogue exhibits no inconsiderable degree of the *vis comica*.

This closes our catalogue of the chief productions of the author, which appeared at different intervals during a period of nearly half a century.

* Mrs. Grant was born in Glasgow in 1755, the daughter of Duncan M'Vickar, who came in her childhood to America as an officer in the British army. He resided at different parts of New York; for a time at Albany and at Oswego, visiting the frontier settlements. This residence afforded Mrs. Grant the material for the admirable descriptions which she afterwards wrote of manners in this state as they existed before the Revolution. In 1768 she returned to Scotland. In 1779 she was married to the Rev. James Grant, the minister of Laggan in the Highlands, becoming his widow in 1801. After this, she turned her thoughts to literature, first publishing a volume of Poems in 1803; then her Letters from the Mountains, being a selection from her correspondence from 1778 to 1804, in 1806. Her Memoirs of an American Lady was published in 1808; her Essays on the Superstitions of the Highlands in 1811; and a Poem, Eighteen Hundred and Thirteen, in 1814. During her latter years she was quite a celebrity in Edinburgh, figuring pleasantly in the Diary of Walter Scott, who drew up the memorial which secured her a pension of one hundred pounds from George IV. She died Nov. 7, 1838, at the age of eighty-three.

* American Comedies by J. K. Paulding and William Irving Paulding. Contents—The Bucktails, or Americans in England; The Noble Exile; Madmen All, or the Cure of Love; Antipathies, or the Enthusiasts by the Ears. The first of these was the only one by the father. It was written shortly after the conclusion of the War of 1812. The volume was published by Carey & Hart in Philadelphia, in 1847.

Most of them were republished in a uniform stereotyped edition by Harper and Brothers in 1835. They constitute, however, only a portion of his writings, which many of them appeared anonymously, and are dispersed through various periodicals and newspapers, among which are the New York Mirror, the Analectic, the Knickerbocker, and Graham's Magazine, Godey's Lady's Book, the Democratic Review, the United States Review, the Literary World, Wheaton's National Advocate, the National Intelligencer, the Southern Press, the Washington Union, &c., &c. He also contributed two articles to a volume by different hands edited by the late Robert C. Sands, whimsically entitled *Tales of the Glauber Spa*. These contributions were, *Childe Roeliff's Pilgrimage*, and *Selim the Friend of Mankind*. The former is a burlesque on fashionable tours, the latter exposes the indiscreet attempts of over-zealous philanthropists to benefit mankind. Most of these contributions were anonymous, and many of them gratuitous; to others he affixed his name, on the requisition of the publishers. The collection would form many volumes, comprising a great variety of subjects, and exhibiting almost every diversity of style "from grave to gay, from lively to severe."

A favorite mode of our author is that of embodying and exemplifying some sagacious moral in a brief story or allegory, either verse or prose, specimens of which may be seen in the Literary World under the caption of *Odds and Ends, by an Obsolete Author*, in the New York Mirror, Graham's Magazine, and other periodicals.

He has also occasionally amused himself with the composition of Fairy Tales, and is the author of an anonymous volume published in 1838 by Appleton, called *A Gift from Fairy Land*, beautifully illustrated by designs from Chapman. We are informed that only one thousand copies of this work were contracted for by its publisher, five hundred of which were taken by a London bookseller. It appeared subsequently to the stereotyped edition of Harper and Brothers, and is not included in the series, which has never been completed, owing, we are informed, to some difficulties between the author and his publishers, in consequence of which it is now extremely difficult to procure a complete set of his works.

In almost all the writings of Paulding there is occasionally infused a dash of his peculiar vein of humorous satire and keen sarcastic irony. To those not familiarized with his manner, such is the imposing gravity, that it is sometimes somewhat difficult to decide when he is jesting and when he is in earnest. This is on the whole a great disadvantage in an age when irony is seldom resorted to, and has occasionally subjected the author to censure for opinions which he does not sanction. His most prominent characteristic is, however, that of nationality. He found his inspiration at home at a time when American woods and fields, and American traits of society, were generally supposed to furnish little if any materials for originality. He not merely drew his nourishment from his native soil, but whenever "that mother of a mighty race" was assailed from abroad by accumulated injuries and insults, stood up manfully in defence of her rights and her honor. He has never on any occasion bowed to the supremacy of European example or European criticism; he is a stern republican in all his writings.

Fortunately he has lived to see a new era dawning on his country. He has seen his country become intellectually, as well as politically, independent, and strong in the result he labored and helped to achieve, he may now look back with calm equanimity on objects which once called for serious opposition, and laugh where the satirist once raged.

Though a literary man by profession, he has, ever since the commencement of the second war with England, turned his mind occasionally towards politics, though never as an active politician. His writings on this subject have been devoted to the support of those great principles which lie at the root of the republican system, and to the maintenance of the rights of his country whenever assailed from any quarter. His progress in life has been upwards. In 1814 or '15 he was appointed Secretary to the Board of Navy Commissioners, then first established. After holding this position for a few years, he resigned to take the office of Navy Agent for the port of New York, which he held twelve years under different administrations, and finally resigned on being placed at the head of the Navy Department by President Van Buren. We have heard him state with some little pride, that all these offices were bestowed without any solicitation on his part, or that of his friends, so far as he knew.

After presiding over the Navy Department nearly the entire term of Mr. Van Buren's administration, he, according to custom, resigned his office on the inauguration of President Harrison, and soon afterwards retired to a pleasant country residence on the east bank of the Hudson, in the county of Dutchess, where he now resides.

Paulding's Residence.

Here, in the midst of his grand-children, enjoying as much health as generally falls to the lot of threescore and fifteen, and still preserving in all their freshness those rural tastes acquired in his youth, nature has rewarded her early votary in the calm pursuits of agriculture, lettered ease, and retirement. In a late visit we paid him at Hyde Park, he informs us, he had visited the city but twice in the last ten years, and gave his daily routine in the following cheerful summary. "I smoke a little, read a little, write a little, ruminate a little, grumble a little, and sleep a great deal. I was once great at pulling up weeds, to which I have a mortal antipathy, especially bull's-eyes, wild carrots, and toad-flax—alias butter and eggs. But my working days are almost over. I find that carrying seventy-five years on my shoulders is pretty nearly equal to the same number of pounds, and instead of laboring myself, sit in the shade watching the labors of others, which I find quite sufficient exercise."

A RURAL LOVER—FROM AN EPISODE IN THE LAY OF THE SCOTTISH FIDDLE.

Close in a darksome corner sat
A scowling wight with old wool hat,
That dangled o'er his sun-burnt brow,
And many a gaping rent did show.
His beard in grim luxuriance grew;
His great-toe peep'd from either shoe;
His brawny elbow shone all bare;
All matted was his carrot hair;
And in his sad face you might see,
The withering look of poverty.
He seem'd all desolate of heart,
And in the revels took no part;
Yet those who watch'd his blood-shot eye,
As the light dancers flitted by,
Might jealousy and dark despair,
And love detect, all mingled there.

He never turn'd his eye away
From one fair damsel passing gay;
But ever in her airy round,
Watch'd her quick step and lightsome bound.
Wherever in the dance she turn'd,
He turn'd his eye, and that eye burn'd
With such fierce spleen, that, sooth to say,
It made the gazer turn away.
Who was the damsel passing fair,
That caus'd his eyeballs thus to glare?
It was the blooming Jersey maid,
That our poor wight's tough heart betray'd.

* * * * * * * * *

By Pompton's stream, that silent flows,
Where many a wild-flower heedless blows.
Unmark'd by any human eye,
Unpluck'd by any passer-by,
There stands a church, whose whiten'd side
Is by the traveller often spied,
Glittering among the branches fair
Of locust trees that flourish there.
Along the margin of the tide,
That to the eye just seems to glide,
And to the list'ning ear ne'er throws
A murmur to disturb repose,
The stately elm majestic towers,
The lord of Pompton's fairy bowers.
The willow, that its branches waves,
O'er neighborhood of rustic graves,
Oft when the summer south-wind blows,
Its thirsty tendrils, playful throws
Into the river rambling there,
The cooling influence to share
Of the pure stream, that bears imprest
Sweet nature's image in its breast.
Sometimes on sunny Sabbath day,
Our ragged wight would wend his way
To this fair church, and lounge about,
With many an idle sunburnt lout,
And stumble o'er the silent graves;
Or where the weeping-willow waves,
His listless length would lay him down.
And spell the legend on the stone.
'Twas here, as ancient matrons say,
His eye first caught the damsel gay,
Who, in the interval between
The *services*, oft tript the green,
And threw her witching eyes about,
To great dismay of bumpkin stout,
Who felt his heart rebellious beat,
Whene'er those eyes he chanced to meet.

As our poor wight all listless lay,
Dozing the vacant hours away,
Or watching with his half-shut eye
The buzzing flight of bee or fly,
The beauteous damsel pass'd along,
Humming a stave of sacred song.
She threw her soft blue eyes askance,
And gave the booby such a glance,
That quick his eyes wide open flew,
And his wide mouth flew open too.
He gaz'd with wonder and surprise,
At the mild lustre of her eyes,
Her cherry lips, her dimpled cheek,
Where Cupids play'd at hide and seek,
Whence many an arrow well, I wot,
Against the wight's tough heart was shot.

He follow'd her where'er she stray'd,
While every look his love betray'd;
And when her milking she would ply,
Sooth'd her pleas'd ear with Rhino-Die,
Or made the mountain echoes ring,
With the great feats of John Paulding;—
How he, stout moss-trooper bold,
Refus'd the proffer'd glittering gold,
And to the gallant youth did cry,
"One of us two must quickly die!"

On the rough meadow of his cheek,
The scythe he laid full twice a week,
Foster'd the honors of his head,
That wide as scruboak branches spread,
With grape-vine juice, and bear's-grease too,
And dangled it in eelskin queue.
In short, he tried each gentle art
To anchor fast her floating heart;
But still she scorn'd his tender tale,
And saw unmov'd his cheek grow pale,
Flouted his suit with scorn so cold,
And gave him oft the bag to hold.

AN EVENING WALK IN VIRGINIA—FROM THE LETTERS FROM THE SOUTH.

In truth, the little solitary nook into which I am just now thrown, bears an aspect so interesting, that it is calculated to call up the most touchingly pleasing exertions, in the minds of those who love to indulge in the contemplation of beautiful scenes. We are the sons of earth, and the indissoluble kindred between nature and man is demonstrated by our sense of her beauties. I shall not soon forget last evening, which Oliver and myself spent at this place. It was such as can never be described —I will therefore not attempt it; but it was still as the sleep of innocence—pure as ether, and bright as immortality. Having travelled only fourteen miles that day, I did not feel tired as usual; and after supper strolled out alone along the windings of a little stream about twenty yards wide, that skirts a narrow strip of green meadow, between the brook and the high mountain at a little distance.

You will confess my landscapes are well watered, for every one has a river. But such is the case in this region, where all the passes of the mountains are made by little rivers, that in process of time have laboured through, and left a space for a road on their banks. If nature will do these things, I can't help it—not I. In the course of the ramble the moon rose over the mountain to the eastward, which being just by, seemed to bring the planet equally near; and the bright eyes of the stars began to glisten, as if weeping the dews of evening. I knew not the name of one single star. But what of that? It is not necessary to be an astronomer, to contemplate with sublime emotions the glories of the sky at night, and the countless wonders of the universe.

> These earthly godfathers of heaven's lights,
> That give a name to every fixed star,
> Have no more profit of their living nights,
> Than those that walk and wot not what they are.

Men may be too wise to wonder at anything; as they may be too ignorant to see anything without wondering. There is reason also to believe, that astronomers may be sometimes so taken up with measuring the distances and magnitude of the stars, as to lose, in the intense minuteness of calculation, that noble expansion of feeling and intellect combined, which lifts from nature up to its great first cause. As respects myself, I know no more of the planets, than the man in the moon. I only contemplate them as unapproachable, unextinguishable fires, glittering afar off, in those azure fields whose beauty and splendour have pointed them out as the abode of the Divinity; as such, they form bright links in the chain of thought that leads directly to a contemplation of the Maker of heaven and earth. Nature is, indeed, the only temple worthy of the Deity. There is a mute eloquence in her smile; a majestic severity in her frown; a divine charm in her harmony; a speechless energy in her silence; a voice in her thunders, that no reflecting being can resist. It is in such scenes and seasons, that the heart is deepest smitten with the power and goodness of Providence, and that the soul demonstrates its capacity for maintaining an existence independent of matter, by abstracting itself from the body, and expatiating alone in the boundless regions of the past and the future.

As I continued strolling forward, there gradually came a perfect calm—and even the aspen-tree whispered no more. But it was not the deathlike calm of a winter's night, when the northwest wind grows quiet, and the frosts begin in silence to forge fetters for the running brooks, and the gentle current of life, that flows through the veins of the forest. The voice of man and beast was indeed unheard; but the river murmured, and the insects chirped in the mild summer evening. There is something sepulchral in the repose of a winter night; but in the genial seasons of the year, though the night is the emblem of repose, it is the repose of the couch—not of the tomb—nature still breathes in the buzz of insects, the whisperings of the forests, and the murmurs of the running brooks. We know she will awake in the morning, with her smiles, her bloom, her zephyrs, and warbling birds. "In such a night as this," if a man loves any human being in this wide world, he will find it out, for there will his thoughts first centre. If he has in store any sweet, or bitter, or bitter-sweet recollections, which are lost in the bustle of the world, they will come without being called. If, in his boyish days, he wrestled, and wrangled, and rambled with, yet loved, some chubby boy, he will remember the days of his childhood, its companions, cares, and pleasures. If, in his days of romance, he used to walk of evenings, with some blue-eyed, musing, melancholy maid, whom the ever-rolling wave of life dashed away from him for ever—he will recall her voice, her eye, and her form. If any heavy and severe disaster has fallen on his riper manhood, and turned the future into a gloomy and unpromising wilderness; he will feel it bitterly at such a time. Or if it chance that he is grown an old man, and lived to see all that owned his blood, or shared his affections, struck down to the earth like dead leaves in autumn; in such a night, he will call their dear shades around, and wish himself a shadow.

A TRIO OF FRENCHMEN—FROM THE SAME.

My good opinion of French people has not been weakened by experience. The bloody scenes of St. Domingo and of France, have, within the last few years, brought crowds of Frenchmen to this land of the exile, and they are to be met with in every part of the United States. Wherever they are, I have found them accommodating themselves with a happy versatility, to the new and painful vicissitudes they had to encounter; remembering and loving the land of their birth, but at the same time doing justice to the land which gave them refuge. They are never heard uttering degrading comparisons between their country and ours; nor signalizing their patriotism, either by sneering at the land they have honoured with their residence, or outdoing a native-born demagogue in clamorous declamation, at the poll of an election. Poor as many of them are, in consequence of the revolutions of property in their native country, they never become beggars. Those who have no money turn the accomplishments of gentlemen into the means of obtaining bread, and become the instruments of lasting benefit to our people. Others who have saved something from the wreck, either establish useful manufactures, or retire into the villages, where they embellish society, and pass quietly on to the grave.

In their amusements, or in their hours of relaxation, we never find them outraging the decencies of society by exhibitions of beastly drunkenness, or breaking its peace by ferocious and bloody brawls at taverns or in the streets. Their leisure hours are passed in a public garden or walk, where you will see them discussing matters with a vehemence which, in some people, would be the forerunner of blows, but which is only an ebullition of a national vivacity, which misfortune cannot repress, nor exile destroy. Or, if you find them not here, they are at some little evening assembly, to which they know how to communicate a gaiety and interest peculiar to French people. Whatever may be their poverty at home, they never exhibit it abroad in rags and dirtiness, but keep their wants to themselves, and give their spirits to others; thus making others happy, when they have ceased to be so themselves.

This subject recalls to my mind the poor *Chevalier*, as we used to call him, who, of all the men I ever saw, bore adversity the best. It is now fifteen years since I missed him at his accustomed walks—where, followed by his little dog, and dressed in his long blue surtout, old-fashioned cocked hat, long queue, and gold-headed cane, with the ribbon of some order at his button-hole, he carried his basket of cakes about every day, except Sunday, rain or shine. He never asked anybody to buy his cakes, nor did he look as if he wished to ask. I never, though I used often to watch him, either saw him smile, or heard him speak to a living soul; but year after year did he walk or sit in the same place, with the same coat, hat, cane, queue, and ribbon, and little dog. One day he disappeared; but whether he died, or got permission to go home to France, nobody knew, and nobody inquired; for, except the little dog, he seemed to have no friend in the wide world.

There was another I will recall to your mind, in this review of our old acquaintance. The queer little man we used to call the little duke, who first attracted our notice, I remember, by making his appearance in our great public walk, dressed in a full suit of white dimity, with a white hat, a little white dog, and a little switch in his hand. Here, of a sunny day, the little duke would ramble about with the lofty air of a man of clear estate, or lean against a tree, and scrutinize the ladies as they passed, with the recognizance of a thorough-bred connoisseur. Sometimes he would go to the circus—that is to say, you would see him lying most luxuriously over a fence just opposite, where, as the windows were open in the summer, he could hear the music, and see the shadow of the horses on the opposite wall, without its costing him a farthing.

In this way he lived, until the Corporation pulled down a small wooden building in the yard of what was then the government-house, when the duke and his dog scampered out of it like two rats. He had lived here upon a little bed of radishes; but now he and his dog were obliged to dissolve partnership, for his master could no longer support him. The dog I never saw again; but the poor duke gradually descended into the vale of poverty. His white dimity could not last for ever, and he gradually went to seed, and withered like a stately onion. In fine, he was obliged to work, and that ruined him—for nature had made him a gentleman.—And a gentleman is the *caput mortuum* of human nature, out of which you can make nothing, under heaven—but a gentleman. He first carried wild game about to sell; but this business not answering, he bought himself a buck and saw, and became a redoubtable sawyer. But he could not get over his old propensity—and whenever a lady passed where he was at work, the little man was always observed to stop his saw, lean his knee on the stick of wood, and gaze at her till she was quite out of sight. Thus, like Antony, he sacrificed the world for a woman—for he soon lost all employment—he was always so long about his work. The last time I saw him he was equipped in the genuine livery of poverty, leaning against a tree on the Battery, and admiring the ladies.

The last of the trio of Frenchmen, which erst attracted our boyish notice, was an old man, who had once been a naval officer, and had a claim of some kind or other, with which he went to Washington every session, and took the field against Amy Dardin's horse. Congress had granted him somewhere about five thousand, which he used to affirm was recognising the justice of the whole claim. The money produced him an interest of three hundred and fifty dollars a year, which he divided into three parts. One-third for his board, clothing, &c.; one for his pleasures, and one for the expenses of his journey to the seat of government. He travelled in the most economical style—eating bread and cheese by the way; and once was near running a fellow-passenger through the body, for asking him to eat dinner with him, and it should cost him nothing. He always dressed neatly—and sometimes of a remarkably fine day would equip himself in uniform, gird on his trusty and rusty sword, and wait upon his excellency the governor. There was an eccentric sort of chivalry about him, for he used to insult every member of Congress who voted against his claim; never put up with a slight of any kind from anybody, and never was known to do a mean action, or to run in debt. There was a deal of dignity, too, in his appearance and deportment, though of the same eccentric cast, so that whenever he walked the streets he attracted a kind of notice not quite amounting to admiration, and not altogether free from merriment. Peace to his claim and his ashes; for he and Amy Dardin's horse alike have run their race, and their claims have survived them.

CHARACTER OF WASHINGTON.

In analysing the character of Washington, there is nothing that strikes me as more admirable than its beautiful symmetry. In this respect it is consummate. His different qualities were so nicely balanced, so rarely associated, of such harmonious affinities, that no one seemed to interfere with another, or predominate over the whole. The natural ardour of his disposition was steadily restrained by a power of self-command which it dared not disobey. His caution never degenerated into timidity, nor his courage into imprudence or temerity. His memory was accompanied by a sound, unerring judgment, which turned its acquisitions to the best advantage; his industry and economy of time neither rendered him dull or unsocial; his dignity never was vitiated by pride or harshness, and his unconquerable firmness was free from obstinacy, or self-willed arrogance. He was gigantic, but at the same time he was well-proportioned and beautiful. It was this symmetry of parts that diminished the apparent magnitude of the whole; as in those fine specimens of Grecian architecture, where the size of the temple seems lessened by its perfection. There are plenty of men who become distinguished by the predominance of one single faculty, or the exercise of a solitary virtue; but few, very few, present to our contemplation such a combination of virtues unalloyed by a single vice; such a succession of actions, both public and private, in which even his enemies can find nothing to blame.

Assuredly he stands almost alone in the world. He occupies a region where there are, unhappily for mankind, but few inhabitants. The Grecian biographer could easily find parallels for Alexander and Cæsar, but were he living now, he would meet with great difficulty in selecting one for Washington. There seems to be an elevation of moral excellence, which, though possible to attain to, few ever approach. As in ascending the lofty peaks of the Andes, we at length arrive at a line where vegetation ceases, and the principle of life seems extinct; so in the gradations of human character, there is an elevation which is never attained by mortal man. A few have approached it, and none nearer than Washington.

He is eminently conspicuous as one of the great benefactors of the human race, for he not only gave liberty to millions, but his name now stands, and will for ever stand, a noble example to high and low. He is a great work of the almighty Artist, which none can study without receiving purer ideas and more lofty conceptions of the grace and beauty of the human character. He is one that all may copy at different distances, and whom none can contemplate without receiving lasting and salutary impressions of the sterling value, the inexpressible beauty of piety integrity, courage, and patriotism, associated with a clear, vigorous, and well-poised intellect.

Pure, and widely disseminated as is the fame of this great and good man, it is yet in its infancy. It is every day taking deeper root in the hearts of his countrymen, and the estimation of strangers, and spreading its branches wider and wider, to the air and the skies. He is already become the saint of liberty, which has gathered new honours by being associated with his name; and when men aspire to free nations, they must take him for their model. It is, then, not without ample reason that the suffrages of mankind have combined to place Washington at the head of his race. If we estimate him by the examples recorded in history, he stands without a parallel in the virtues he exhibited, and the vast, unprecedented consequences resulting from their exercise. The whole world was the theatre of his actions, and all mankind are destined to partake sooner or later in their results. He is a hero of a new species: he had no model; will he have any imitators? Time, which bears the thousands and thousands of common cut-throats to the ocean of oblivion, only adds new lustre to his fame, new force to his example, and new strength to the reverential affection of all good men. What a glorious fame is his, to be acquired without guilt, and enjoyed without envy; to be cherished by millions living, hundreds of millions yet unborn! Let the children of my country prove themselves worthy of his virtues, his labours, and his sacrifices, by reverencing his name and imitating his piety, integrity, industry, fortitude, patience, forbearance, and patriotism. So shall they become fitted to enjoy the blessings of freedom and the bounties of heaven.

THE MAN THAT WANTED BUT ONE THING; THE MAN THAT WANTED EVERYTHING; AND THE MAN THAT WANTED NOTHING.

Everybody, young and old, children and greybeards, has heard of the renowned Haroun Al Raschid, the hero of Eastern history and Eastern romance, and the most illustrious of the caliphs of Bagdad, that famous city on which the light of learning and science shone, long ere it dawned on the benighted regions of Europe, which has since succeeded to the diadem that once glittered on the brow of Asia. Though as the successor of the Prophet he exercised a despotic sway over the lives and fortunes of his subjects, yet did he not, like the eastern despots of more modern times, shut himself up within the walls of his palace, hearing nothing but the adulation of his dependents; seeing nothing but the shadows which surrounded him; and knowing nothing but what he received through the medium of interested deception or malignant falsehood. That he might see with his own eyes and hear with his own ears, he was accustomed to go about through the streets of Bagdad by night, in disguise, accompanied by Giafer the Barmecide, his grand vizier, and Mesrour, his executioner; one to give him his counsel, the other to fulfil his commands promptly, on all occasions. If he saw any commotion among the people he mixed with them and learned its cause; and if in passing a house he heard the moanings of distress or the complaints of suffering, he entered, for the purpose of administering relief. Thus he made himself acquainted with the condition of his subjects, and often heard those salutary truths which never reached his ears through the walls of his palace, or from the lips of the slaves that surrounded him.

On one of these occasions, as Al Raschid was thus perambulating the streets at night, in disguise, accompanied by his vizier and his executioner, in passing a splendid mansion, he overheard through the lattice of a window, the complaints of some one who seemed in the deepest distress, and silently approaching, looked into an apartment exhibiting all the signs of wealth and luxury. On a sofa of satin embroidered with gold, and sparkling with brilliant gems, he beheld a man richly dressed, in whom he recognised his favorite boon companion Bedreddin, on whom he had showered wealth and honors with more than eastern prodigality. He was stretched out on the sofa, slapping his forehead, tearing his beard, and moaning piteously, as if in the extremity of suffering. At length starting up on his feet, he exclaimed in tones of despair, "Oh, Allah! I beseech thee to relieve me from my misery, and take away my life."

The Commander of the Faithful, who loved Bedreddin, pitied his sorrows, and being desirous to know their cause, that he might relieve them, knocked at the door, which was opened by a black slave, who, on being informed that they were strangers in want of food and rest, at once admitted them, and informed his master, who called them into his presence, and bade them welcome. A plentiful feast was spread before them, at which the master of the house sat down with his guests, but of which he did not partake, but looked on, sighing bitterly all the while.

The Commander of the Faithful at length ventured to ask him what caused his distress, and why he refrained from partaking in the feast with his guests, in proof that they were welcome. "Has Allah afflicted thee with disease, that thou canst not enjoy the blessings he has bestowed? Thou art surrounded by all the splendor that wealth can procure; thy dwelling is a palace, and its apartments are adorned with all the luxuries which captivate the eye, or administer to the gratification of the senses. Why is it then, oh! my brother, that thou art miserable?"

"True, O stranger," replied Bedreddin. "I have all these. I have health of body; I am rich enough to purchase all that wealth can bestow, and if I required more wealth and honors, I am the favorite companion of the Commander of the Faithful, on whose head lie the blessing of Allah, and of whom I have only to ask, to obtain all I desire, save one thing only."

"And what is that?" asked the caliph.

"Alas! I adore the beautiful Zuleima, whose face is like the full moon, whose eyes are brighter and softer than those of the gazelle, and whose mouth is like the seal of Solomon. But she loves another, and all my wealth and honors are as nothing. The want of one thing renders the possession of every other of no value. I am the most wretched of men; my life is a burden, and my death would be a blessing."

"By the beard of the Prophet," cried the Caliph, "I swear thy case is a hard one. But Allah is great and powerful, and will, I trust, either deliver thee from thy burden or give thee strength to bear it." Then thanking Bedreddin for his hospitality, the Commander of the Faithful departed, with his companions.

Taking their way towards that part of the city inhabited by the poorer classes of people, the Caliph stumbled over something, in the obscurity of night, and was nigh falling to the ground; at the same moment a voice cried out, "Allah, preserve me! Am I not wretched enough already, that I must be trodden under foot by a wandering beggar like myself, in the darkness of night!"

Mezrour the executioner, indignant at this insult to the Commander of the Faithful, was preparing to cut off his head, when Al Raschid interposed, and inquired of the beggar his name, and why he was there sleeping in the streets, at that hour of the night.

"Mashallah," replied he, "I sleep in the street because I have nowhere else to sleep, and if I lie on a satin sofa my pains and infirmities would rob me of rest. Whether on divans of silk or in the dirt, all one to me, for neither by day nor by night do I know any rest. If I close my eyes for a moment, my dreams are of nothing but feasting, and I awake only to feel more bitterly the pangs of hunger and disease."

"Hast thou no home to shelter thee, no friends or kindred to relieve thy necessities, or administer to thy infirmities?"

"No," replied the beggar; "my house was consumed by fire; my kindred are all dead, and my friends have deserted me. Alas! stranger, I am in want of everything: health, food, clothing, home, kindred, and friends. I am the most wretched of mankind, and death alone can relieve me."

"Of one thing, at least, I can relieve thee," said the Caliph, giving him his purse. "Go and provide thyself food and shelter, and may Allah restore thy health."

The beggar took the purse, but instead of calling down blessings on the head of his benefactor exclaimed, "Of what use is money; it cannot cure disease?" and the Caliph again went on his way with Giafer his vizier, and Mezrour his executioner.

Passing from the abodes of want and misery, they at length reached a splendid palace, and seeing lights glimmering from the windows, the caliph approached, and looking through the silken curtains, beheld a man walking backwards and forwards, with languid step, as if oppressed with a load of cares. At length casting himself down on a sofa, he stretched out his limbs, and yawning desperately, exclaimed, "Oh! Allah, what shall I do; what will become of me! I am weary of life; it is nothing but a cheat, promising what it never purposes, and affording only hopes that end in disappointment, or, if realized, only in disgust."

The curiosity of the Caliph being awakened to know the cause of his despair, he ordered Mezrour to knock at the door, which being opened, they pleaded the privilege of strangers to enter, for rest and refreshments. Again, in accordance with the precepts of the Koran, and the customs of the East, the strangers were admitted to the presence of the lord of the palace, who received them with welcome, and directed refreshments to be brought. But though he treated his guests with kindness, he neither sat down with them nor asked any questions, nor joined in their discourse, walking back and forth languidly, and seeming oppressed with a heavy burden of sorrows.

At length the Caliph approached him reverently, and said: "Thou seemest sorrowful, O my brother! If thy suffering is of the body I am a physician, and peradventure can afford thee relief; for I have travelled into distant lands, and collected very choice remedies for human infirmity."

"My sufferings are not of the body, but of the mind," answered the other.

"Hast thou lost the beloved of thy heart, the friend of thy bosom, or been disappointed in the attainment of that on which thou hast rested all thy hopes of happiness?"

"Alas! no. I have been disappointed not in the means, but in the attainment of happiness. I want nothing but a want. I am cursed with the gratification of all my wishes, and the fruition of all my hopes. I have wasted my life in the acquisition of riches, that only awakened new desires, and honors that no longer gratify my pride or repay me for the labor of sustaining them. I have been cheated in the pursuit of pleasures that weary me in the enjoyment, and am perishing for lack of the excitement of some new want. I have everything I wish, yet enjoy nothing."

"Thy case is beyond my skill," replied the Caliph; and the man cursed with the fruition of all his desires turned his back on him in despair. The Caliph, after thanking him for his hospitality, departed with his companions, and when they had reached the street exclaimed—

"Allah preserve me! I will no longer fatigue myself in a vain pursuit, for it is impossible to confer happiness on such a perverse generation. I see it is all the same, whether a man wants one thing, everything, or nothing. Let us go home and sleep."

1853.

JOSEPH STORY.

Joseph Story was born at Marblehead, Mass., September 18, 1779. He was the eldest of eleven sons of Dr. Elisha Story, an active Whig of the Revolution, who was of the "Boston Tea Party," and served in the army during a portion of the war as a surgeon. He was a boy of an active mind, and when only a few years old delighted in visiting the barber's shop of the town to listen to the gossip about public affairs. He was a great favorite with his handsome florid face and long auburn ringlets, and would frequently sit upon the table to recite pieces from memory and make prayers for the amusement of the company. During his childhood he was saved from being burnt to death by his mother, who snatched him from his blazing bed at the cost of severe personal injury to herself. He was prepared for college in his native village, and entered Harvard in 1795. Dr. Channing was one of his classmates. He was a hard student during his collegiate course, and on its termination entered the office of Samuel Sewall, in Marblehead. He completed his studies at Salem, where he commenced practice. In 1804 he published *The Power of Solitude, a poem in two parts*, with a few fugitive verses appended. The author was at a subsequent period a merciless critic on his own performance, burning all the copies he could lay his hands upon. It is written in the ornate style of the time,

Joseph Story

with some incongruities which do not lead the reader to regret that the writer "took a lawyer's farewell of the muse." He published the same year a *Selection of Pleadings in Civil Actions*, and near its close married Miss Mary Lynde Oliver, who died on the 22d of June following. In 1808, he was married to Miss Sarah Waldo Wetmore.

Story's rise in his profession was rapid, and in 1810 he was appointed by Madison, Associate Justice of the Supreme Court. He accepted the office at a pecuniary sacrifice of his professional income exceeding the official salary of $3500 a year, some two thousand dollars. In 1827, he prepared an edition in three volumes of the Laws of the United States. In 1829, the Hon. Nathan Dane offered the sum of $10,000 to Harvard College, as the foundation of a law professorship, on the condition that his friend Story should consent to become its first incumbent. Story having as a friend of the college and of legal science accepted the appointment, delivered an inauguration *Address on the Value and Importance of the Study of Law*, which is regarded as one of his finest productions.

His instructions were of course delivered during the vacations of the Supreme Court. His biographer gives a pleasant picture of the interest taken by teacher and pupil in the subject matter before them.

For the benefit of the students he sold to the college his library at one half its value.

During the preparation of the Encyclopædia Americana by his friend Dr. Lieber, Justice Story contributed a number of articles on legal subjects, forming some hundred and twenty pages of the work. He was also a large contributor to the American Jurist.

In 1832, he published his *Commentaries on the Constitution* in three volumes, and in the following spring the *Abridgment* of the work, which is in general use throughout the country as a college text-book. The Commentaries were received with universal favor at home and abroad, where they were translated into French and German.

In 1834, he published his *Commentaries on the Conflict of Laws*. In 1835, a selection from his *Miscellaneous Writings*. In 1836, the first volume of his *Commentaries upon Equity Jurisprudence*, and in 1846, a work on *Promissory Notes*.

To these we must add the comprehensive reference to his miscellaneous writings made by his son.

When we review his public life, the amount of labor accomplished by him seems enormous. Its mere recapitulation is sufficient to appal an ordinary mind. The judgments delivered by him on his Circuits, comprehend thirteen volumes. The Reports of the Supreme Court during his judicial life occupy thirty-five volumes, of which he wrote a full share. His various treatises on legal subjects cover thirteen volumes, besides a volume of Pleadings. He edited and annotated three different treatises, with copious notes, and published a volume of Poems. He delivered and published eight discourses on literary and scientific subjects, before different societies. He wrote biographical sketches of ten of his contemporaries; six elaborate reviews for the North American; three long and learned memorials to Congress. He delivered many elaborate speeches in the Legislature of Massachusetts and the Congress of the United States. He also drew up many other papers of importance, among which are the argument before Harvard College, on the subject of the Fellows of the University; the Reports on Codification, and on the salaries of the Judiciary; several very important Acts of Congress, such as the Crimes Act, the Judiciary Act, the Bankrupt Act, besides many other smaller matters.

In quantity, all other authors in the English Law, and Judges, must yield to him the palm. The labors of Coke, Eldon, and Mansfield, among Judges, are not to be compared to his in amount. And no jurist, in the Common Law, can be measured with him, in extent and variety of labor.

In 1845, he determined to resign his judicial office and devote his entire attention to his favorite law school, which had prospered greatly under his care. It was his wish, however, before doing so to dispose of all the cases argued before him, and it was in consequence of the severe labor he imposed upon himself in the heat of summer to accomplish this object, that he became so utterly exhausted that his physical frame could offer slight resistance to the attacks of disease. In September, 1845, he was engaged in writing out the last of these opinions when he was taken with a cold followed by stricture, and the stoppage of the intestinal canal. He was relieved from this attack after great suffering for many hours, but his powers were too enfeebled to rally, and he sank into a torpor, "breathed the name of God, the last word that ever was heard from his lips," and a few hours after, on the evening of the tenth of September, died.

Every honor was paid his memory. Shops were closed and business suspended in Cambridge on the day of his funeral, which in accordance with his wishes was conducted in a simple manner, and a sum of money was soon after raised at the suggestion of the Trustees of Mount Auburn where he was buried, for the purpose of placing his statue in the chapel of that cemetery. The commission for the work was intrusted to the son of the deceased, Mr. William W. Story, who has since published in two large octavo volumes the "Life and Letters" of his distinguished father, and has thus contributed by the exercise of two of the most permanent in effect of human instruments, the pen and the chisel, to the perpetuation and extension of his fame.

Judge Story was an active student throughout life. It was his practice to keep interleaved copies of his works near at hand, and to add on the blank pages any decisions or information bearing upon their subject. The personal habits of one who accomplished so much were necessarily simple and temperate, but the detail may be read with interest as recorded by his son.

He arose at seven in summer, and at half past seven in winter,—never earlier. If breakfast was not ready, he went at once to his library and occupied the interval, whether it was five minutes or fifty, in writing. When the family assembled he was called, and breakfasted with them. After breakfast he sat in the drawing-room, and spent from a half to three quarters of an hour in reading the newspapers of the day. He then returned to his study and wrote until the bell sounded for his lecture at the Law School. After lecturing for two and sometimes three hours, he returned to his study and worked until two o'clock, when he was called to dinner. To his dinner (which, on his part, was always simple), he gave an hour, and then again betook himself to his study, where in the winter time he worked as long as the daylight lasted, unless called away by a visitor or obliged to attend a moot-court. Then he came down and joined the family, and work for the day was over. Tea came in about seven o'clock; and how lively and gay was he then, chatting over the most familiar topics of the day, or entering into deeper currents of conversation with equal ease. All of his law he left up stairs in the library; he was here the domestic man in his home. During the evening he received his friends, and he was rarely without company; but if alone, he read some new publication of the day,—the reviews, a novel, an English newspaper; sometimes corrected a proof-sheet, listened to music, or talked with the family, or, what was very common, played a game of backgammon with my mother. This was the only game of the kind that he liked. Cards and chess he never played.

In the summer afternoons he left his library towards twilight, and might always be seen by the passer-by sitting with his family under the portico, talking or reading some light pamphlet or newspaper, often surrounded by friends, and making the air ring with his gay laugh. This, with the interval occupied by tea, would last until nine o'clock. Generally, also, the summer afternoon was varied three or four times a week, in fair weather, by a drive with my mother of about an hour through the surrounding country in an open chaise. At about ten or half past ten he retired for the night, never varying a half hour from this time.

Story retained his early fondness for poetry throughout life, and sometimes amused his leisure moments even when on the bench by versifying "any casual thought suggested to him by the arguments of counsel." A few specimens of these rhymed reflections are given by his son.

It was my father's habit, while sitting on the Bench, to versify any casual thought suggested to him by the arguments of counsel, and in his note books of points and citations, several pages are generally devoted to memoranda in prose and verse, of facts, and thoughts, which interested him. In his memorandum-book of arguments before the Supreme Court in 1831 and 1832, I select the following fragments written on the fly-leaf:—

You wish the Court to hear, and listen too?
Then speak with point, be brief, be close, be true.
Cite well your cases; let them be in point;
Not learned rubbish, dark, and out of joint;—
And be your reasoning clear, and closely made,
Free from false taste, and verbiage, and parade.

Stuff not your speech with every sort of law,
Give us the grain, and throw away the straw.

Books should be read; but if you can't digest,
The same's the surfeit, take the worst or best.

Clear heads, sound hearts, full minds, with point may speak,
All else how poor in fact, in law how weak.

Who 's a great lawyer? He, who aims to say
The least his cause requires, not all he may.

Greatness ne'er grew from soils of spongy mould,
All on the surface dry; beneath all cold;
The generous plant from rich and deep must rise,
And gather vigor, as it seeks the skies.

Whoe'er in law desires to win his cause,
Must speak with point, not measure out "wise saws,"
Must make his learning apt, his reasoning clear,
Pregnant in matter, but in style severe;
But never drawl, nor spin the thread so fine,
That all becomes an evanescent line.

The following sketch was drawn at this time on the Bench, and apparently from life:—

With just enough of learning to confuse,—
With just enough of temper to abuse,—
With just enough of genius, when confest,
To urge the worst of passions for the best,—
With just enough of all that wins in life,
To make us hate a nature formed for strife,—
With just enough of vanity and spite,
To turn to all that's wrong from all that's right,—
Who would not curse the hour when first he saw
Just such a man, called learned in the law.

The legal writings of Judge Story from his own pen extend to thirteen volumes; the Reports of his decisions on Circuits to thirteen; and those of the Supreme Court while he occupied a seat on the Bench and contributed his full share to their contents, to thirty-five.

The style of Story, both in his Commentaries and in his Miscellanies, is that of the scholar and man of general reading, as well as the thoroughly practised lawyer. It is full, inclined to the rhetorical, but displays everywhere the results of laborious investigation and calm reflection. His law books have fairly brought what in the old volumes was considered a crabbed science to the appreciation and sympathy of the unprofessional reader. Chancellor Kent, on the receipt of his Miscellaneous Works in 1836, complimented the author on "the variety, exuberance, comprehensiveness, and depth of his moral, legal, and political wisdom. Every page and ordinary topic is replete with a copious and accurate display of principles, clothed in a powerful and eloquent style, and illustrated and recommended by striking analogies, and profuse and brilliant illustrations. You handle the topic of the mechanical arts, and the science on which they are founded, enlarged, adorned, and applied, with a mastery, skill, and eloquence, that is unequalled. As for jurisprudence, you have again and again, and on all occasions, laid bare its foundations, traced its histories, eulogized its noblest masters, and pressed its inestimable importance with a gravity, zeal, pathos, and beauty, that is altogether irresistible."* This was generously said, and though the language of eulogy, it points out with great distinctness the peculiar merits which gave the writings of Story their high reputation at home and abroad.

WASHINGTON ALLSTON.

It is a pleasing moral coincidence which has been remarked that two of the foremost names in our national literature and art should be associated with that of the great leader, in war and peace, of their country.

Washington Allston, the descendant of a family of much distinction in South Carolina, was born at Charleston, November 5, 1779. He was prepared for college at the school of Mr. Robert Rogers, of Newport, R. I.; entered Harvard in

* Story's Life, ii. 217.

1796, and on the completion of his course delivered a poem.

He returned to South Carolina; sold his property; sailed for England, and on his arrival in London became a student of the Royal Academy, then under the presidency of Benjamin West. Here he remained for three years, and then, after a sojourn at Paris, went to Rome, where he resided for four years, and became the intimate associate of Coleridge.

In 1809 he returned to America for a period of two years, which he passed in Boston, and at this time married the sister of the Rev. Dr. Channing. He also delivered a poem before the Phi Beta Kappa Society. In 1811 he commenced a second residence in London, where, in 1813, he published a small volume, *The Sylphs of the Seasons, and other Poems*, which was reprinted in Boston the same year. The date is also marked in his career by the death of his wife, an event which affected him deeply.

During this sojourn in Europe, which extended to 1818, several of his finest paintings were produced. On his return home he resumed his residence at Boston. In 1830 he married a sister of Richard H. Dana, and removed to Cambridgeport. His lectures on Art were commenced about the same period. It was his intention to prepare a course of six, to be delivered before a select audience in Boston, but four only were completed, and these did not appear until after his decease.

Washington Allston

In 1841 he published *Monaldi*, an Italian romance of moderate length, which had been written as early as 1821 when Dana published his Idle Man, and, but for the discontinuance of that work, would probably have appeared there. In the latter part of his life he was chiefly engaged on his great painting of Belshazzar's Feast. After a week's steady labor on this work, he retired late on Saturday night, July 8, 1843, from his studio to his family circle, and after a conversation of peculiar solemnity, sat down to his books and papers, which furnished the usual occupation of a great portion of his nights. It was while thus silently sitting alone near the dawning of Sunday, with scarce a struggle, he was called from the temporary repose of the holy day to the perpetual Sabbath of eternity. His remains were interred at the setting of the sun on the day of the funeral, in the tomb of the Dana family in the old Cambridge graveyard.

Had Mr. Allston been a less severe critic of his own productions he would have both painted more and written more. Nothing left his easel or his desk which was not the ripe product of his mind, which had cost not only labor but perplexity, from the frequent change to which his fastidiousness submitted all his productions. His Belshazzar's Feast, as it hangs in its incomplete state in the Boston Athenæum, shows a strange and grotesque combination of figures, of gigantic mingled with those of ordinary stature. It is owing to the artist's determination, when his work was nearly completed, to reconstruct the whole, and by the radical change we have mentioned, as well as others of composition, render his months of former labor null and void. Had his life been extended the work no doubt would have been completed, and have created the same feelings of awe and admiration which some of its single figures, that of the Queen for example, now excite; but as it stands, it is perhaps a more characteristic as well as impressive monument of the man.

With the exception of this work, Mr. Allston's productions are all complete.

In the Spring of 1839, Allston exhibited, with remarkable success, a gallery of his paintings at Boston. They were forty-five; brought together from various private and other sources. A letter was published at the time in the New York *Evening Post*, noticing the collection, which was understood to be written from Dana to his friend Bryant. It speaks of "the variety and contrast, not only in the subjects and thoughts, and emotions made visible, but in the style also," and finds in the apparent diversity "the related variety of one mind." Several of the more prominent subjects, and the influence breathing from them, are thus alluded to:—"Here, under the pain and confused sense of returning life lay the man who, when the bones of the prophet touched him, lived again. Directly opposite sat, with the beautiful and patiently expecting Baruch at his feet, the majestic announcer of the coming woes of Jerusalem, seeing through earthly things, as seeing them not, and looking off into the world of spirits and the vision of God. What sees he there? Wait! For the vision is closing, and he is about to speak! And there is Beatrice, absorbed in meditation, touched gently with sadness, and stealing so upon your heart, that curiosity is lost in sympathy—you forget to ask yourself what her thought? and look in silence till you become the very soul of meditation too. And Rosalie, born of music, her face yet tremulous with the last vibrations of those sweet sounds to which her inmost nature had been responding. What shall I say of the spiritual depth of those eyes? You look into them till you find yourself communing with her inmost life, with emotions beautiful, exquisite, almost to pain. Indeed, when you recollect yourself, you experience this effect to be true of nearly all these pictures, whether of living beings or of nature. After a little while you do not so much look upon them as commune with them, until you recover yourself, and are made aware that you had been lost in them. Herein is the spirit of art, the creative power—poetry. And the landscapes—spots in nature, fit dwelling-places for beings such as these!"

His poems, though few in number, are exquisite in finish, and in the fancies and thoughts which they embody. They are delicate, subtle, and philosophical. Thought and feeling are united in them, and the meditative eye

> which hath kept watch
> o'er man's mortality

broods over all. In *The Sylphs of the Seasons* he has pictured the successive delights of each quarter of the year with the joint sensibility of the poet and the artist, bringing before us a series of images of the imagination blended with the purest sentiment.

If the other poems may be described as occasional, it should be remarked they are the occasions not of a trifler or a man of the world, but of a philosopher and a Christian, whose powers were devoted to the sacred duties of life, to his art, to his friends, to the inner world of faith. In this view rather than as exercises of poetic rhetoric, they are to be studied. One of the briefer poems has a peculiar interest, that entitled Rosalie. It is the very reflection in verse of the ideal portrait which he painted, bearing that name.

His lectures on Art, published after his decease, in the volume edited by R. H. Dana, Jr., show the vigorous grasp, the intense love, the keen perception which we should naturally look for from such a master.

Monaldi is an Italian story of jealousy, murder, and madness. Monaldi is suspicious of his wife, kills her in revenge, and becomes a maniac. The work is entirely of a subjective character, dealing with thought, emotion, and passion, with a concentration and energy for which we are accustomed to look only to the greatest dramatists. The chief scene of the volume is the self-torturing jealousy of Monaldi, contrasted with the innocent calmness of his wife. We read it with shortened breath and a sense of wonder. Not less powerfully does the author carve out, as it were, in statuary, the preliminary events by which this noble heart falls from its steadfast truth-worshipping loyalty. We see the gradual process of disaffection, from the first rude physical health of the soul, when it is incapable of fear or suspicion, rejecting the poison of envy; then gradually admitting the idea as if some unconscious act of memory, a haunting reminiscence, then recurring wilfully to the thought, till poison becomes the food of the mind, and it lives on baleful jealousies, wrongs, and revenges: the high intellectual nature, so difficult to reach, but the height once scaled, how flauntingly they bear the banner of disloyalty; Monaldi, like Othello, then spurns all bounds; like Othello, wronged and innocent.

Those who had the privilege of a friendship or even an acquaintance with Allston, speak with enthusiasm of his conversational powers. He excelled not only in the matter but the manner of his speech. His fine eye, noble countenance, and graceful gesture were all unconsciously brought into play as he warmed with his subject, and he would hold his hearer by the hour as fixedly with a disquisition on morals as by a series of wild tales of Italian banditti. Allston gave his best to his friends as well as to the public, and some of his choicest literary composition is doubtless contained in the correspondence he maintained for many years with Coleridge, Wordsworth, Southey, Lamb, and others among the best men of his, and of all time.

In an enumeration of the published works of Mr. Allston, the volume of outline engravings from the sketches found in his studio after his decease should be especially commemorated, for it contains some of his most beautiful as well as most sublime conceptions; and as nearly all his paintings, with the exception of the Belshazzar, are the property of private individuals, forms almost the only opportunity accessible to the general public for the enjoyment of his artistic productions. His manner may there be learnt in its precision, strength, grandeur, and beauty.

Of the moral harmony of Allston's daily life, we have been kindly favored with a picture, filled with incident, warm, genial, and thoroughly appreciative, from the pen, we had almost said the pencil, of the artist's early friend in Italy, Washington Irving. It is taken from a happy period of his life, and our readers will thank the author for the reminiscence:—

"I first became acquainted," writes Washington Irving to us, "with Washington Allston, early in the spring of 1805. He had just arrived from France, I from Sicily and Naples. I was then not quite twenty-two years of age—he a little older. There was something, to me, inexpressibly engaging in the appearance and manners of Allston. I do not think I have ever been more completely captivated on a first acquaintance. He was of a light and graceful form, with large blue eyes and black silken hair, waving and curling round a pale expressive countenance. Everything about him bespoke the man of intellect and refinement. His conversation was copious, animated, and highly graphic; warmed by a genial sensibility and benevolence, and enlivened at times by a chaste and gentle humor. A young man's intimacy took place immediately between us, and we were much together during my brief sojourn at Rome. He was taking a general view of the place before settling himself down to his professional studies. We visited together some of the finest collections of paintings, and he taught me how to visit them to the most advantage, guiding me always to the masterpieces, and passing by the others without notice. 'Never attempt to enjoy every picture in a great collection,' he would say, 'unless you have a year to bestow upon it. You may as well attempt to enjoy every dish in a Lord Mayor's feast. Both mind and palate get confounded by a great variety and rapid succession, even of delicacies. The mind can only take in a certain number of images and impressions distinctly; by multiplying the number you weaken each, and render the whole confused and vague. Study the choice pieces in each collection; look upon none else, and you will afterwards find them hanging up in your memory.'

"He was exquisitely sensible to the graceful

and the beautiful, and took great delight in paintings which excelled in color; yet he was strongly moved and roused by objects of grandeur. I well recollect the admiration with which he contemplated the sublime statue of Moses by Michael Angelo, and his mute awe and reverence on entering the stupendous pile of St. Peter's. Indeed the sentiment of veneration so characteristic of the elevated and poetic mind was continually manifested by him. His eyes would dilate; his pale countenance would flush; he would breathe quick, and almost gasp in expressing his feelings when excited by any object of grandeur and sublimity.

"We had delightful rambles together about Rome and its environs, one of which came near changing my whole course of life. We had been visiting a stately villa, with its gallery of paintings, its marble halls, its terraced gardens set out with statues and fountains, and were returning to Rome about sunset. The blandness of the air, the serenity of the sky, the transparent purity of the atmosphere, and that nameless charm which hangs about an Italian landscape, had derived additional effect from being enjoyed in company with Allston, and pointed out by him with the enthusiasm of an artist. As I listened to him, and gazed upon the landscape, I drew in my mind a contrast between our different pursuits and prospects. He was to reside among these delightful scenes, surrounded by masterpieces of art, by classic and historic monuments, by men of congenial minds and tastes, engaged like him in the constant study of the sublime and beautiful. I was to return home to the dry study of the law, for which I had no relish, and, as I feared, but little talent.

"Suddenly the thought presented itself, 'Why might I not remain here, and turn painter?' I had taken lessons in drawing before leaving America, and had been thought to have some aptness, as I certainly had a strong inclination for it. I mentioned the idea to Allston, and he caught at it with eagerness. Nothing could be more feasible. We would take an apartment together. He would give me all the instruction and assistance in his power, and was sure I would succeed.

"For two or three days the idea took full possession of my mind; but I believe it owed its main force to the lovely evening ramble in which I first conceived it, and to the romantic friendship I had formed with Allston. Whenever it recurred to mind, it was always connected with beautiful Italian scenery, palaces, and statues, and fountains, and terraced gardens, and Allston as the companion of my studio. I promised myself a world of enjoyment in his society, and in the society of several artists with whom he had made me acquainted, and pictured forth a scheme of life, all tinted with the rainbow hues of youthful promise.

"My lot in life, however, was differently cast. Doubts and fears gradually clouded over my prospect; the rainbow tints faded away; I began to apprehend a sterile reality, so I gave up the transient but delightful prospect of remaining in Rome with Allston, and turning painter.

"My next meeting with Allston was in America, after he had finished his studies in Italy; but as we resided in different cities we saw each other only occasionally. Our intimacy was closer some years afterwards, when we were both in England. I then saw a great deal of him during my visits to London, where he and Leslie resided together. Allston was dejected in spirits from the loss of his wife, but I thought a dash of melancholy had increased the amiable and winning graces of his character. I used to pass long evenings with him and Leslie; indeed Allston, if any one would keep him company, would sit up until cock-crowing, and it was hard to break away from the charms of his conversation. He was an admirable story teller, for a ghost story none could surpass him. He acted the story as well as told it.

"I have seen some anecdotes of him in the public papers, which represent him in a state of indigence and almost despair, until rescued by the sale of one of his paintings.* This is an exaggeration. I subjoin an extract or two from his letters to me, relating to his most important pictures. The first, dated May 9, 1817, was addressed to me at Liverpool, where he supposed I was about to embark for the United States:—

"Your sudden resolution of embarking for America has quite thrown me, to use a sea phrase, all aback. I have so many things to tell you of, to consult you about, &c., and am such a sad correspondent, that before I can bring my pen to do its office, 'tis a hundred to one but the vexations for which your advice would be wished, will have passed and gone. One of these subjects (and the most important) is the large picture I talked of soon beginning: the Prophet Daniel interpreting the *hand-writing on the wall* before Belshazzar. I have made a highly finished sketch of it, and I wished much to have your remarks on it. But as your sudden departure will deprive me of this advantage, I must beg, should any hints on the subject occur to you during your voyage, that you will favor me with them, at the same time you let me know that you are again safe in our good country.

"I think the composition the best I ever made. It contains a multitude of figures and (if I may be allowed to say it) they are without confusion. Don't you think it a fine subject? I know not any that so happily unites the magnificent and the awful. A mighty sovereign surrounded by his whole court, intoxicated with his own state, in the midst of his revellings, palsied in a moment under the spell of a preternatural hand suddenly tracing his doom on the wall before him; his powerless limbs, like a wounded spider's, shrunk up to his body, while his heart, *compressed to a point*, is only kept from vanishing by the terrific suspense that animates it during the interpretation of his mysterious sentence. His less guilty but scarcely less agitated queen, the panic-struck courtiers and concubines, the splendid and deserted banquet table, the half arrogant, half astounded magicians, the holy vessels of the temple (shining as it were in triumph through the gloom), and the calm solemn contrast of the prophet, standing like an animated pillar in the midst, breathing forth the oracular destruction of the empire! The picture will be twelve feet high by seventeen feet long. Should I succeed in it to my wishes, I know not what may be its fate; but I leave the future to Providence. Perhaps I may send it to America.

"The next letter from Allston which remains in

---

* Anecdotes of Artists.

my possession, is dated London, 18th March, 1818. In the interim he had visited Paris, in company with Leslie and Newton; the following extract gives the result of the excitement caused by a study of the masterpieces in the Louvre.

"Since my return from Paris I have painted two pictures, in order to have something in the present exhibition at the British gallery; the subjects, the Angel Uriel in the Sun, and Elijah in the Wilderness. Uriel was immediately purchased (at the price I asked, 150 guineas) by the Marquis of Stafford, and the Directors of the British Institution moreover presented me a *donation* of a hundred and fifty pounds 'as a mark of their *approbation* of the talent evinced,' &c. The manner in which this was done was highly complimentary; and I can only say that it was full as gratifying as it was unexpected. As both these pictures together cost me but ten weeks, I do not regret having deducted that time from the Belshazzar, to whom I have since returned with redoubled vigour. I am sorry I did not exhibit Jacob's Dream. If I had dreamt of this success I certainly would have sent it there.

"Leslie, in a letter to me, speaks of the picture of Uriel seated in the Sun. 'The figure is colossal, the attitude and air very noble, and the form heroic, without being overcharged. In the color he has been equally successful, and with a very rich and glowing tone he has avoided *positive* colours, which would have made him too material. There is neither red, blue, nor yellow on the picture, and yet it possesses a harmony equal to the best pictures of Paul Veronese.'

"The picture made what is called 'a decided hit,' and produced a great sensation, being pronounced worthy of the old masters. Attention was immediately called to the artist. The Earl of Egremont, a great connoisseur and patron of the arts, sought him in his studio, eager for any production from his pencil. He found an admirable picture there, of which he became the glad possessor. The following is an extract from Allston's letter to me on the subject:—

"Leslie tells me he has informed you of the sale of Jacob's Dream. I do not remember if you have seen it. The manner in which Lord Egremont bought it was particularly gratifying—to say nothing of the price, which is no trifle to me at present. But Leslie having told you all about it I will not repeat it. Indeed, by the account he gives me of his letter to you, he seems to have puffed me off in grand style. Well—you know I don't *bribe* him to do it, and 'if they will buckle praise upon my back,' why, I can't help it! Leslie has just finished a very beautiful little picture of Anne Page inviting Master Slender into the house. Anne is exquisite, soft and feminine, yet arch and playful. She is all she should be. Slender also is very happy; he is a good parody on Milton's 'linked sweetness long drawn out.' Falstaff and Shallow are seen through a window in the background. The whole scene is very picturesque, and beautifully painted. 'Tis his best picture. You must not think this praise the 'return in kind.' I give it, because I really admire the picture, and I have not the smallest doubt that he will do great things when he is once freed from the necessity of painting portraits.*

"Lord Egremont was equally well pleased with the artist as with his works, and invited him to his noble seat at Petworth, where it was his delight to dispense his hospitalities to men of genius.

"The road to fame and fortune was now open to Allston; he had but to remain in England, and follow up the signal impression he had made.

"Unfortunately, previous to this recent success he had been disheartened by domestic affliction, and by the uncertainty of his pecuniary prospects, and had made arrangements to return to to America. I arrived in London a few days before his departure, full of literary schemes, and delighted with the idea of our pursuing our several arts in fellowship. It was a sad blow to me to have this day-dream again dispelled. I urged him to remain and complete his grand painting of Belshazzar's Feast, the study of which gave promise of the highest kind of excellence. Some of the best patrons of the art were equally urgent. He was not to be persuaded, and I saw him depart with still deeper and more painful regret than I had parted with him in our youthful days at Rome. I think our separation was a loss to both of us—to me a grievous one. The companionship of such a man was invaluable. For his own part, had he remained in England for a few years longer, surrounded by everything to encourage and stimulate him, I have no doubt he would have been at the head of his art. He appeared to me to possess more than any contemporary the spirit of the old masters; and his merits were becoming widely appreciated. After his departure he was unanimously elected a member of the Royal Academy.

"The next time I saw him was twelve years afterwards, on my return to America, when I visited him at his studio at Cambridge, in Massachusetts, and found him, in the grey evening of life, apparently much retired from the world; and his grand picture of Belshazzar's Feast yet unfinished.

"To the last he appeared to retain all those elevated, refined, and gentle qualities which first endeared him to me.

"Such are a few particulars of my intimacy with Allston; a man whose memory I hold in reverence and affection, as one of the purest, noblest, and most intellectual beings that ever honored me with his friendship."

AMERICA TO GREAT BRITAIN.

All hail! thou noble land,
Our Fathers' native soil!
O, stretch thy mighty hand,
Gigantic grown by toil,
O'er the vast Atlantic wave to our shore!
For thou with magic might
Canst reach to where the light
Of Phœbus travels bright
The world o'er!

The Genius of our clime,
From his pine-embattled steep,
Shall hail the guest sublime;
While the Tritons of the deep
With their conchs the kindred league shall proclaim.
Then let the world combine,—
O'er the main our naval line
Like the milky-way shall shine
Bright in fame!

* This picture was lately exhibited in the "Washington Gallery" in New York.

Though ages long have past
Since our Fathers left their home,
Their pilot in the blast,
O'er untravelled seas to roam,
Yet lives the blood of England in our veins!
And shall we not proclaim
That blood of honest fame
Which no tyranny can tame
By its chains!

While the language free and bold
Which the Bard of Avon sung,
In which our Milton told
How the vault of heaven rung
When Satan, blasted, fell with his host;—
While this, with reverence meet,
Ten thousand echoes greet,
From rock to rock repeat
Round our coast;—

While the manners, while the arts,
That mould a nation's soul,
Still cling around our hearts,—
Between let Ocean roll,
Our joint communion breaking with the Sun:
Yet still from either beach
The voice of blood shall reach,
More audible than speech,
"We are One." *

WINTER—FROM THE SYLPHS OF THE SEASONS.

And last the Sylph of Winter spake,
The while her piercing voice did shake
The castle vaults below:—
"O youth, if thou, with soul refined,
Hast felt the triumph pure of mind,
And learnt a secret joy to find
In deepest scenes of woe;

"If e'er with fearful ear at eve
Hast heard the wailing tempests grieve
Through chink of shattered wall,
The while it conjured o'er thy brain
Of wandering ghosts a mournful train,
That low in fitful sobs complain
Of death's untimely call;

"Or feeling, as the storm increased,
The love of terror nerve thy breast,
Didst venture to the coast,
To see the mighty war-ship leap
From wave to wave upon the deep,
Like chamois goat from steep to steep,
Till low in valley lost;

"When, glancing to the angry sky,
Behold the clouds with fury fly
The lurid moon athwart—
Like armies huge in battle, throng,
And pour in volleying ranks along,
While piping winds in martial song
To rushing war exhort:

"O, then to me thy heart be given,
To me, ordained by Him in heaven
Thy nobler powers to wake.
And, O! if thou with poet's soul,
High brooding o'er the frozen pole,
Hast felt beneath my stern control
The desert region quake;

"Or from old Hecla's cloudy height,
When o'er the dismal, half-year's night
He pours his sulphurous breath,
Hast known my petrifying wind
Wild ocean's curling billows bind,
Like bending sheaves by harvest hind,
Erect in icy death;

"Or heard adown the mountain's steep
The northern blast with furious sweep
Some cliff dissevered dash,
And seen it spring with dreadful bound,
From rock to rock, to gulf profound,
While echoes fierce from caves resound
The never-ending crash:

"If thus with terror's mighty spell
Thy soul inspired was wont to swell,
Thy heaving frame expand,
O, then to me thy heart incline;
For know, the wondrous charm was mine,
That fear and joy did thus combine
In magic union bland.

"Nor think confined my native sphere
To horrors gaunt, or ghastly fear,
Or desolation wild;
For I of pleasures fair could sing,
That steal from life its sharpest sting,
And man have made around it cling,
Like mother to her child.

"When thou, beneath the clear blue sky,
So calm no cloud was seen to fly,
Hast gazed on snowy plain,
Where Nature slept so pure and sweet,
She seemed a corse in winding-sheet,
Whose happy soul had gone to meet
The blest Angelic train;

"Or marked the sun's declining ray
In thousand varying colors play
O'er ice-incrusted heath,
In gleams of orange now, and green,
And now in red and azure sheen,
Like hues on dying dolphin seen,
Most lovely when in death;

"Or seen at dawn of eastern light
The frosty toil of Fays by night
On pane of casement clear,
Where bright the mimic glaciers shine,
And Alps, with many a mountain pine,
And armed knights from Palestine
In winding march appear:

"'T was I on each enchanting scene
The charm bestowed, that banished spleen
Thy bosom pure and light.
But still a *nobler* power I claim,—
That power allied to poet's fame,
Which language vain has dared to name,—
The soul's creative might.

"Though Autumn grave, and Summer fair,
And joyous Spring, demand a share
Of Fancy's hallowed power,
Yet these I hold of humbler kind,
To grosser means of earth confined,
Through mortal *sense* to reach the mind,
By mountain, stream, or flower.

"But mine, of purer nature still,
Is that which to thy secret will
Did minister unseen,
Unfelt, unheard, when every sense
Did sleep in drowsy indolence,
And silence deep and night intense
Enshrouded every scene;

* *Note by the Author.*—This alludes merely to the moral union of the two countries. The author would not have it supposed that the tribute of respect, offered in these stanzas to the land of his ancestors, would be paid by him, if at the expense of the independence of that which gave him birth.

"That o'er thy teeming brain did raise
The spirits of departed days
Through all the varying year,
And images of things remote,
And sounds that long had ceased to float,
With every hue, and every note,
As living now they were;

"And taught thee from the motley mass
Each harmonizing part to class
(Like Nature's self employed);
And then, as worked thy wayward will,
From these, with rare combining skill,
With new-created worlds to fill
Of space the mighty void.

"O, then to me thy heart incline;
To me, whose plastic powers combine
The harvest of the mind;
To me whose magic coffers bear
The spoils of all the toiling year,
That still in mental vision wear
A lustre more refined."

ROSALIE.

"O pour upon my soul again
That sad, unearthly strain,
That seems from other worlds to plain;
Thus falling, falling from afar,
As if some melancholy star
Had mingled with her light her sighs,
And dropped them from the skies!

"No,—never came from aught below
This melody of woe,
That makes my heart to overflow,
As from a thousand gushing springs,
Unknown before; that with it brings
This nameless light,—if light it be,—
That veils the world I see.

"For all I see around me wears
The hue of other spheres;
And something blent of smiles and tears
Comes from the very air I breathe.
O, nothing, sure, the stars beneath
Can mould a sadness like to this,—
So like angelic bliss."

So, at that dreamy hour of day
When the last lingering ray
Stops on the highest cloud to play,—
So thought the gentle Rosalie,
As on her maiden reverie
First fell the strain of him who stole
In music to her soul.

INVENTION IN ART IN OSTADE AND RAPHAEL—FROM THE LECTURES ON ART.

The interior of a Dutch cottage forms the scene of Ostade's work, presenting something between a kitchen and a stable. Its principal object is the carcass of a hog, newly washed and hung up to dry; subordinate to which is a woman nursing an infant; the accessories, various garments, pots, kettles, and other culinary utensils.

The bare enumeration of these coarse materials would naturally predispose the mind of one, unacquainted with the Dutch school, to expect any thing but pleasure; indifference, not to say disgust, would seem to be the only possible impression from a picture composed of such ingredients. And such, indeed, would be their effect under the hand of any but a real Artist. Let us look into the picture and follow Ostade's *mind*, as it leaves its impress on the several objects. Observe how he spreads his principal light, from the suspended carcass to the surrounding objects, moulding it, so to speak, into agreeable shapes, here by extending it to a bit of drapery, there to an earthen pot; then connecting it, by the flash from a brass kettle, with his second light, the woman and child; and again turning the eye into the dark recesses through a labyrinth of broken chairs, old baskets, roosting fowls, and bits of straw, till a glimpse of sunshine, from a half-open window, gleams on the eye, as it were, like an echo, and sending it back to the principal object, which now seems to act on the mind as the luminous source of all these diverging lights. But the magical whole is not yet completed; the mystery of color has been called in to the aid of light, and so subtly blends that we can hardly separate them; at least, until their united effect has first been felt, and after we have begun the process of cold analysis. Yet even then we cannot long proceed before we find the charm returning; as we pass from the blaze of light on the carcass, where all the tints of the prism seem to be faintly subdued, we are met on its borders by the dark harslet, glowing like rubies; then we repose awhile on the white cap and kerchief of the nursing mother; then we are roused again by the flickering strife of the antagonist colors on a blue jacket and red petticoat; then the strife is softened by the low yellow of a straw-bottomed chair; and thus with alternating excitement and repose do we travel through the picture, till the scientific explorer loses the analyst in the unresisting passiveness of a poetic dream. Now all this will no doubt appear to many if not absurd, at least exaggerated: but not so to those who have ever felt the sorcery of color. They, we are sure, will be the last to question the character of the feeling because of the ingredients which worked the spell, and, if true to themselves, they must call it poetry. Nor will they consider it any disparagement to the all-accomplished Raffaelle to say of Ostade that he also was an Artist.

We turn now to a work of the great Italian,—the Death of Ananias. The scene is laid in a plain apartment, which is wholly devoid of ornament, as became the hall of audience of the primitive Christians. The Apostles (then eleven in number) have assembled to transact the temporal business of the Church, and are standing together on a slightly elevated platform, about which, in various attitudes, some standing, others kneeling, is gathered a promiscuous assemblage of their new converts, male and female. This quiet assembly (for we still feel its quietness in the midst of the awful judgment) is suddenly roused by the sudden fall of one of their brethren; some of them turn and see him struggling in the agonies of death. A moment before he was in the vigor of life,—as his muscular limbs still bear evidence; but he had uttered a falsehood, and an instant after his frame is convulsed from head to foot. Nor do we doubt for a moment as to the awful cause: it is almost expressed in voice by those nearest to him, and, though varied by their different temperaments, by terror, astonishment, and submissive faith, this voice has yet but one meaning,—"Ananias has lied to the Holy Ghost." The terrible words, as if audible to the mind, now direct us to him who pronounced his doom, and the singly-raised finger of the Apostle marks him the judge; yet not of himself,—for neither his attitude, air, nor expression has any thing in unison with the impetuous Peter,—he is now the simple, passive, yet awful instrument of the Almighty: while another on the right, with equal calmness, though with more severity, by his elevated arm, as beckoning to judgment, anticipates the fate of the entering Sapphira. Yet all is not done; lest a question remain, the Apostle on the left confirms the judgment. No one can mistake what passes within him; like one transfixed in adoration, his uplifted eyes seem to ray out his soul, as if in recognition of the divine tribunal. But the overpowering thought of Omnipotence is now tempered by the human sympathy of his companion, whose open hands, connecting the past with the present, seem almost to articulate, "Alas, my brother!" By this exquisite turn, we are next brought to John, the gentle almoner of the Church, who is dealing out their portions to the needy brethren. And here, as most remote from the judged Ananias, whose suffering seems not yet to have reached it, we find a spot of repose,—not to pass by, but to linger upon, till we feel its quiet influence diffusing itself over the whole mind; nay, till, connecting it with the beloved Disciple, we find it leading us back through the exciting scene, modifying even our deepest emotions with a kindred tranquillity.

This is Invention; we have not moved a step through the picture but at the will of the Artist. He invented the chain which we have followed, link by link, through every emotion, assimilating many into one; and this is the secret by which he prepared us, without exciting horror, to contemplate the struggle of mortal agony.

This too is Art; and the highest art, when thus the awful power, without losing its character, is tempered, as it were, to our mysterious desires. In the work of Ostade, we see the same inventive power, no less effective, though acting through the medium of the humblest materials.

JOSEPH T. BUCKINGHAM.

Joseph T. Buckingham, one of the most prominent journalists of New England, is a descendant of Thomas Tinker, who came to Plymouth in the May Flower. His father, Nehemiah Tinker, resided at Windham, and ruined himself during the Revolutionary War by expending his whole property in the purchase of supplies for the army, for which he received pay in Continental currency, which rapidly depreciated, so that at his death, on the 17th of March, 1783, the several thousand dollars of paper money which he possessed, "would hardly pay for his winding sheet and coffin." He left a widow and ten children, the youngest of whom, Joseph, was born on the twenty-first of December, 1779. The widow endeavored to support the eight children dependent upon her by continuing her husband's business of tavern-keeping, but was obliged to abandon the establishment within a year, on account of ill health. She grew poorer and poorer, and her son records her thankfulness at receiving, on one occasion, the crusts cut from the bread prepared for the Holy Communion of the coming Sunday. She was at last compelled to solicit the aid of the selectmen of the town, and was supported in that manner for a winter. In the following year she received and accepted the offer of a home in the family of her friends, Mr. and Mrs. Lathrop, at Worthington, Mass. Her son, the subject of this sketch, was indentured at the same time by the selectmen to a farmer of the name of Welsh, until he attained the age of sixteen. He was kindly cared for in the family, and picked up a tolerable knowledge of reading, writing, and arithmetic. He devoured the few books he came across, and records his obligations to a set of Ames's Almanacs. At the expiration of his time he obtained a situation in the printing-office of David Carlisle, the publisher of the Farmer's Museum, at Walpole, N.H. The joviality of the wits who filled the columns of that famous sheet seems to have been shared in by the compositors who set up their articles, for they exhausted the poor boy's slender stock of cash by a demand for a treat, and then nearly choked him by forcing his own brandy down his throat. He remained only a few months with Carlisle, and then apprenticed himself in the office of the Greenfield (Mass.) Gazette. Here he exercised himself in grammar, by comparing the "copy" he had to set up with the rules he had learnt, and correcting it if wrong. In 1798 he lost his excellent mother. In 1803 he deserted the composing-stick for a few months, to fill the office of prompter to a company of comedians who played during the summer months at Salem and Providence. In 1806, having previously taken by act of legislature his mother's family name of Buckingham, he made his first essay as editor, by commencing a Monthly Magazine, *The Polyanthus*. The numbers contained seventy-two pages 18mo., with a portrait, each. It was suspended in September, 1807, and resumed in 1812, when two volumes of the original size and four in octavo appeared. In January, 1809, he commenced *The Ordeal*, a weekly, of sixteen octavo pages, which lasted six months. In 1817, he commenced, with Samuel L. Knapp, *The New England Galaxy and Masonic Magazine*. It was started without capital by its projector, who now had a wife and six children dependent on him, and frankly proposed to return a dollar and a half out of the three tendered by his first subscriber, on the plea that he did not believe he should be able to keep up the paper more than six months. By the aid of the Masonic Lodges it, however, became tolerably successful. Like his previous publications, it sided in politics with the Federal party.

In 1828, Mr. Buckingham sold the Galaxy, in order to devote his entire attention to the *Boston Courier*, a daily journal, which he had commenced on the second of March, 1824. The prominent idea of its founders was the advocacy of the "protective system." Mr. Buckingham continued to edit the Courier until June, 1848, when he sold out his interest. In July, 1831, he commenced with his son Edwin *The New England Magazine*, a monthly of ninety-six pages, and one of the best periodicals of its class which ever appeared in the United States. The number of July, 1833, contains a mention of the death of Edwin at sea, on a voyage to Smyrna, undertaken for the benefit of health. He was but twenty-three years of age. In November, 1834, the publication was transferred to Dr. Samuel G. Howe and John O. Sargent.

During the years 1828, 1831–3, 1836, 1838–9, Mr. Buckingham was a member of the Legislature, and in 1847–8, 1850–1, of the Senate of Massachusetts. He introduced a report in favor of the suppression of lotteries, and performed other valuable services during these periods.

Since his retirement from the press, Mr. Buckingham has published, *Specimens of Newspaper Literature, with Personal Memoirs, Anecdotes, and Reminiscences*, in two volumes duodecimo, which has passed through two editions; and *Personal Memoirs and Recollections of Editorial Life*, in two similar volumes. They contain a pleasant resumé of his career, with notices of the many persons with whom, at different periods, he has been connected.

MOSES STUART.

This eminent critic and philologist, the head of a school of Biblical learning in America, was born of honest but humble parentage in Wilton, Connecticut, March 26, 1780. He entered Yale at sixteen during the Presidency of Dwight, took his degree with the highest honors in 1799, then turned his attention to the law, to which he gave himself with earnestness, though he never practised the profession. From 1802 to 1804 he was tutor at Yale. In 1806, having in the meantime pursued the necessary preparation, he was ordained Pastor of the Centre Church in New Haven. His services at this time are thus spoken of by his thoughtful and eloquent friend and eulogist, Dr. Adams. "The fervor, fidelity, and success of his career as a pastor are still matters of grateful remembrance and distinct tradition. Distinguished as is the reputation which he subsequently acquired as a scholar, there are many who think that his best efforts were in the pulpit. The congregation over which he was ordained, accustomed for a third of a century to a style of discourse clear, cold, and philosophic, which deserves to be designated as 'diplomatic vagueness,' were startled from indifference by the short, simple, perspicuous sentences of their new pastor, and more than all by the unaffected earnestness and sincerity with which they were delivered."*

In 1810 Mr. Stuart attained the marked position of his life with which he was to be identified during the remainder of his career, extending over a period of well nigh half a century, in his appointment to the Professorship of Sacred Literature at the Theological Seminary at Andover, which had then recently been engrafted upon the academy founded by the Hon. John Phillips at that place. Mr. Stuart succeeded to the brief term of instruction of the Rev. Eliphalet Pearson, who had been Professor of the Hebrew and Oriental languages at Harvard from 1786 to 1806. It is noticeable that Stuart was chosen, "not because of extraordinary proficiency in Oriental languages, for his knowledge of Hebrew was at this time very limited. Two years' preparation for the ministry, and five years in the diligent prosecution of his profession, had not furnished large opportunities for exact and extensive study. Choice was fixed upon him because of the general qualities which designated him as one able and willing to furnish himself for any station; and upon that thorough qualification he entered, with characteristic enthusiasm, immediately upon his transfer to this new office."

The learned labors of Stuart began at once in his devotion to Hebrew studies, of which he knew nothing until after his arrival at Andover. His colleague, Dr. Woods, used to relate that he taught Stuart the Hebrew alphabet. He prepared at first a manuscript grammar of that language, which his pupils copied. When the requisite Oriental type for its publication was procured Stuart found no compositors ready for its use, and had to commence the work with his own hands. His first Hebrew Grammar, without points, was published in 1821. He soon became acquainted with the earlier labors of Gesenius, learning the German language for that purpose. His later Hebrew Grammar, with points, was first published in 1831, and rapidly became the text-book in general use for this study.* He also aided the study by his Hebrew Chrestomathy.

Having laid this foundation in the study of the rudiments of the language, Stuart next addressed himself to the philosophical interpretation of the text. In this he brought new life to the old dogmatic theology which prevailed at the beginning of his career. "Whatever could cast light upon the Holy Scriptures, or the languages in which they were contained, was to Professor Stuart a matter of exuberant delight. Whether it was a discussion by Middleton on the Greek article, or an essay by Wyttenbach on the mode of studying language, or the archæological researches of Jahn, or the journal of an intelligent traveller in the Egean, or Lane's book on Egypt, or the explorations of the French in the valley of the Nile,† or a Greek chorus, or a discovery of an inscription in Arabia Petrea, or exhumations in Nineveh—anything, from whatever source, which explained a difficult verse in the Bible, or illustrated an ancient custom of God's peculiar people, or led to a better comprehension of the three languages in which the name of our Lord was written upon his cross—all was hailed by this Christian student with unbounded satisfaction."‡ The application of his principles is thus characterized by the same pen. "After all the discriminations of Morus and Ernesti, republished by Professor Stuart, if I should undertake to condense his principles and practice concerning Biblical exegesis, aside from all technical phraseology, I should characterize it by *common sense*. Admit the distinctions as to literal and tropical language which are recognised in the ordinary conversation of ordinary men, and those modifications of language which are derived from local customs and use, and then let Scripture interpret Scripture. Compare spiritual things with spiritual, and let the *obvious meaning* of the Sacred Writings thus compared, be received as the true."§

With this exercise of the understanding, Stuart united the judgment of the heart, the verdict of a simple, earnest, spiritual faith, which reposed on the authority of the Bible. To this his learning

* A Discourse on the Life and Services of Professor Moses Stuart; delivered in the city of New York, Sabbath evening, January 25, 1852, by William Adams, Pastor of the Central Presbyterian Church; an able and judicious production, which we have closely followed as the best authority on the subject. It is understood that a Life of Professor Stuart is in preparation by his son-in-law, Professor Austin Phelps, of the Andover Theological Seminary.

* Dr. Adams records with just pride "the fourth edition of that Grammar was republished in England by Dr. Pusey, Regius Professor of Hebrew in the University of Oxford; and no small praise is it that a self-taught Professor in a Theological Seminary in a rural district of New England, should furnish text-books in oriental philology to the English universities, with their hereditary wealth of learned treasure and lordly provisions for literary leisure. The Hebrew Chrestomathy of Professor Stuart was reprinted in like manner at Oxford soon after its appearance. The Hebrew Grammar by Dr. Lee, of Cambridge University, England, did not appear till six years after the publication of Mr. Stuart's first edition."

† Greppo's Essay on Champollion was translated in his family.

‡ Dr. Adams's Discourse, pp. 29, 30.

§ Ibid. pp. 31, 32.

and argument were subsidiary. He showed how German learning might be employed and scriptural authority maintained. This was his service to the theology of his day and denomination. "The great merit," says an accomplished Oriental scholar, Mr. W. W. Turner, "of Professor Stuart, and one for which the gratitude and respect of American scholars must ever be his due, lies in the zeal and ability he has exhibited for a long series of years in bringing to the notice of the English-reading public the works of many of the soundest philologists and most enlightened and unprejudiced theologians of Germany; for to his exertions it is in a good degree owing that the names of Rosenmüller, Gesenius, Ewald, De Wette, Hupfield, Rödiger, Knobel, Hitzig, and others, are now familiar as household words to the present race of biblical students in this country, and to some extent in England."*

In 1827 appeared his *Commentary on the Epistle to the Hebrews*, vindicating the authenticity of the work, giving a new translation with full notes on the text, and an elucidation of the argument. This was followed in 1832 by a *Commentary on the Epistle to the Romans*, in which the same philological course is pursued. Other commentaries followed in due course, provoking more or less of criticism, on the Apocalypse, the Book of Daniel, of Ecclesiastes, of Proverbs, the last of which he had just completed at the time of his death.

Another series of works of Professor Stuart were his numerous articles in the periodicals, chiefly the *Biblical Repository* and *Bibliotheca Sacra*, as also his controversial writings, his *Letters to Channing* and others, of which he published a collection in a volume of *Miscellanies* in 1846.

One of his last productions, which excited much interest and some opposition at the time in New England, was his defence of the policy of Daniel Webster in his Essay on *Conscience and the Constitution*, an assertion of the principle of obedience to the Compromise act.

Stuart died at Andover, January 4, 1852. That he was industrious and energetic the bare enumeration of his works declares; but he also carried his enthusiasm of labor into the exercises with his classes, upon whom he impressed a hearty sympathy for his studies and his manner of pursuing them. Death found him at the age of seventy-two still active, still meditating new critical and learned labors in the inexhaustible field of biblical investigation.

A daughter of Dr. Stuart, Mrs. Elizabeth Phelps, the wife of Professor Austin Phelps of Andover, attained distinction in a popular field of literature by her felicitous sketches of New England society, in a series of tales by H. Trusta, an anagram of her maiden name. They are entitled *The Angel over the Right Shoulder; Sunny Side; Peep at Number Five* (a picture of clerical life); *Kitty Brown; Little Mary, or Talks and Tales for Children*, and *The Tell Tale; or Home Secrets told by Old Travellers.* The last was published in 1853, shortly after the death of the author. These tales have a well deserved popularity from their spirited style, and the life and character which they humorously portray.

* Literary World, No. 223.

WILLIAM ELLERY CHANNING

WAS born at Newport, Rhode Island, April 7, 1780. He was in the fourth generation from John Channing, who came to America from Dorsetshire, in England. His father was William Channing, a man of education, and distinguished as a lawyer in Newport; his grandfather on the mother's side was William Ellery, the signer of the Declaration. He has in one of his writings, the Discourse on *Christian Worship*, at the Dedication of the Unitarian Congregational Church at Newport in 1836, paid a tribute to the genial influences of his birth-place upon his youth. "I must bless God," said he, "for the place of my nativity; for as my mind unfolded, I became more and more alive to the beautiful scenery which now attracts strangers to our island. My first liberty was used in roaming over the neighbouring fields and shores; and amid this glorious nature, that love of liberty sprang up, which has gained strength within me to this hour. I early received impressions of the great and the beautiful, which I believe have had no small influence in determining my modes of thought and habits of life. In this town I pursued for a time my studies of theology. I had no professor or teacher to guide me; but I had two noble places of study. One was yonder beautiful edifice,* now so frequented and so useful as a public library, then so deserted that I spent day after day, and sometimes week after week, amidst its dusty volumes, without interruption from a single visitor. The other place was yonder beach, the roar of which has so often mingled with the worship of this place, my daily resort, dear to me in the sunshine, still more attractive in the storm. Seldom do I visit it now without thinking of the work, which there, in the sight of that beauty, in the sound of these waves, was carried on in my soul. No spot on earth has helped to form me so much as that beach. There I lifted up my voice in praise amidst the tempest; there, softened by beauty, I poured out my thanksgiving and contrite confessions. There, in reverential sympathy with the mighty power around me, I became conscious of power within. There, struggling thoughts and emotions broke forth, as if moved to utterance by nature's eloquence of the winds and waves. There began a happiness surpassing all worldly pleasures, all gifts of fortune, the happiness of communing with the works of God. Pardon me this reference to myself. I believe that the worship, of which I have this day spoken, was aided in my own soul by the scenes in which my early life was passed. Amidst these scenes, and in speaking of this worship, allow me to thank God that this beautiful island was the place of my birth." He completed his education at Harvard with the highest honors in 1798. He then engaged for a while as tutor to a family in Virginia, where his health became permanently enfeebled. He was ordained pastor of the Federal Street Church, Boston, June 1, 1803; visited Europe subse-

* The Redwood Library.

quently, and on his return continued alone in his charge till 1824.

Wm E. Channing

From that time for the remainder of his life he was connected with the same church, discharging its duties as his strength permitted; withdrawing, towards the close of his career, to strict retirement, husbanding his delicate health for his numerous literary efforts. In these he always exercised an important influence, and through them was as well known in England as in America. The collection of his works embraces six volumes, the larger portion of which is devoted to his theology, as a leader of the Unitarians. His *Moral Argument against Calvinism* appeared in the *Christian Disciple* for 1820. The first of his writings which brought him into the general field of literature, his *Remarks on the Character and Writings of John Milton*, was published in the *Christian Examiner* for 1826, followed by his articles on *Bonaparte*, during the next two years, in the same journal, and the winning article on *Fenelon* in 1829. The force, directness, and literary elegance of these papers attracted great attention, and the more from the bold challenge to popular discussion which was thrown out in his uncompromising estimate of Napoleon. Apart from his influence as a religious leader, he had now gained the ear of the public at large—an authority which he availed himself of to act upon the moral sentiment of the nation, which he addressed in his publications on Slavery, War, Temperance, and Education. His address on *Self Culture*, delivered at Boston in 1838, has been one of the most successful tracts of its kind ever published. Its direct appeal to whatever of character or manliness there may be in the young is almost irresistible. This is the prevailing trait of Channing's style, its single, moral energy. The titles of his publications indicate the man and his method. A general subject, as War, Temperance, Slavery, is proposed simply by itself, disconnected with any temporary associations or accidents of place that might limit it by conditions, and argued simply, clearly, forcibly on its own merits, according to the universal standard of truth and justice. Channing pushes at once to the centre of his subject, like a man who has business at the court of truth, and is not to be set aside by guards or courtiers. He has the ear of this royal mistress, and speaks from her side as with the voice of an oracle. Nothing can turn him "aside from the direct forthright." However deficient this course might be for the practical statesmanlike conduct of the world, and its circuitous progress to great ends, its influence on the mind of his own day, particularly on the young, is not to be questioned. Channing's moral vigor seemed to put new life into his readers. Notwithstanding the delicacy of his constitution, he appeared in public from time to time to within a short period of his death. His aspect was of great feebleness; small in person and fragile to excess, apparently contrasting with the vigor of his doctrines, but the well developed forehead, the full eye, the purity of expression, and the calm musical tone showed the concentration within. His oratory always charmed his audience, as in his winning tones he gained to his side the pride and powers of his hearers.

The last public effort of Channing was his address at Lenox, in Berkshire County, Mass., on the 1st of August, 1842, the anniversary of Emancipation in the West Indies. It shows no diminution of the acuteness of his mind or of his rare powers of expression.

Shortly after this time, while pursuing a mountain excursion, he was taken with typhus fever, and died at Bennington, Vermont, October 2, 1842.

MILITARY GENIUS—FROM THE ESSAY ON NAPOLEON.

Military talent, even of the highest order, is far from holding the first place among intellectual endowments. It is one of the lower forms of genius; for it is not conversant with the highest and richest objects of thought. We grant that a mind, which takes in a wide country at a glance, and understands, almost by intuition, the positions it affords for a successful campaign, is a comprehensive and vigorous one. The general, who disposes his forces so as to counteract a greater force; who supplies by skill, science, and invention, the want of numbers; who dives into the counsels of his enemy, and who gives unity, energy, and success to a vast variety of operations, in the midst of casualties and obstructions which no wisdom could foresee, manifests great power. But still the chief work of a general is to apply physical force; to remove physical obstructions; to avail himself of physical aids and advantages; to act on matter; to overcome rivers, ramparts, mountains, and human muscles; and these are not the highest objects of mind, nor do they demand intelligence of the highest order; and accordingly nothing is more common than to find men, eminent in this department, who are wanting in the noblest energies of the soul; in habits of profound and liberal thinking, in imagination and taste, in the capacity of enjoying works of genius, and in large and original views of human nature and society. The office of a great general does not differ widely from that of a great mechanician, whose business it is to frame new combinations of physical forces, to adapt them to new circumstances, and to remove new obstructions. Accordingly great generals, away from the camp, are often no greater men than the mechanician taken from his workshop. In conversation they are often dull. Deep and refined reasonings they cannot comprehend. We know that there are splendid exceptions. Such was Cesar, at once the greatest soldier and the most sagacious statesman of his age, whilst in eloquence and literature, he left behind him almost all, who had devoted themselves exclusively to these pursuits. But such cases are rare. The conqueror of Napoleon, the hero of Waterloo, possesses undoubtedly great military talents; but we do not understand, that his most partial admirers claim for him a place in the highest class of minds. We will not go down for illustration to such men as Nelson, a man great on the deck, but debased by gross vices, and who never pretended to enlargement of intellect. To institute a comparison in point of talent and genius between such men and Milton, Bacon, and Shakespeare, is almost an insult on these illustrious names. Who can think of these truly great intelligences; of the range of their minds through heaven and earth; of their deep intuition into the soul; of their new and glowing combinations of thought; of the energy with which they grasped, and subjected to their main purpose, the infinite materials of illustration which nature and life afford,—who can think of the forms of transcendent beauty and grandeur which they created, or which were rather emanations of their own minds; of the calm wisdom and fervid imagination which they conjoined; of the voice of power, in which "though dead, they still speak," and awaken intellect, sensibility, and genius in both hemispheres,—who can think of such men, and not feel the immense inferiority of the most gifted warrior, whose elements of thought are physical forces and physical obstructions, and whose employment is the combination of the lowest class of objects on which a powerful mind can be employed.

RELIGION AND LITERATURE—FROM THE ESSAY ON FENELON.

The truth is, that religion, justly viewed, surpasses all other principles, in giving a free and manifold action to the mind. It recognises in every faculty and sentiment the workmanship of God, and assigns a sphere of agency to each. It takes our whole nature under its guardianship, and with a parental love ministers to its inferior as well as higher gratifications. False religion mutilates the soul, sees evil in our innocent sensibilities, and rules with a tyrant's frown and rod. True religion is a mild and lawful sovereign, governing to protect, to give strength, to unfold all our inward resources. We believe, that, under its influence, literature is to pass its present limits, and to put itself forth in original forms of composition. Religion is of all principles most fruitful, multiform, and unconfined. It is sympathy with that Being, who seems to delight in diversifying the modes of his agency, and the products of his wisdom and power. It does not chain us to a few essential duties, or express itself in a few unchanging modes of writing. It has the liberality and munificence of nature, which not only produces the necessary root and grain, but pours forth fruits and flowers. It has the variety and bold contrasts of nature, which, at the foot of the awful mountain, scoops out the freshest, sweetest valleys, and embosoms, in the wild, troubled ocean, islands, whose vernal airs, and loveliness, and teeming fruitfulness, almost breathe the joys of Paradise. Religion will accomplish for literature what it most needs; that is, will give it depth, at the same time that it heightens its grace and beauty. The union of these attributes is most to be desired. Our literature is lamentably superficial, and to some the beautiful and the superficial even seem to be naturally conjoined. Let not beauty be so wronged. It resides chiefly in profound thoughts and feelings. It overflows chiefly in the writings of poets, gifted with a sublime and, piercing vision. A beautiful literature springs from the depth and fulness of intellectual and moral life, from an energy of thought and feeling, to which nothing, as we believe, ministers so largely as enlightened religion.

So far from a monotonous solemnity overspreading literature in consequence of the all-pervading influence of religion, we believe that the sportive and comic forms of composition, instead of being abandoned, will only be refined and improved. We know that these are supposed to be frowned upon by piety; but they have their root in the constitution which God has given us, and ought not therefore to be indiscriminately condemned. The propensity to wit and laughter does indeed, through excessive indulgence, often issue in a character of heartless levity, low mimicry, or unfeeling ridicule. It often seeks gratification in regions of impurity, throws a gaiety round vice, and sometimes even pours contempt on virtue. But, though often and mournfully perverted, it is still a gift of God, and may and ought to minister, not only to innocent pleasure, but to the intellect and the heart. Man was made for relaxation as truly as for labor; and by a law of his nature, which has not received the attention it deserves, he finds perhaps no relaxation so restorative, as that in which he reverts to his childhood, seems to forget his wisdom, leaves the imagination to exhilarate itself by sportive inventions, talks of amusing incongruities in conduct and events, smiles at the innocent eccentricities and odd mistakes of those whom he most esteems, allows himself in arch allusions or kind-hearted satire, and transports himself into a world of ludicrous combinations. We have said, that, on these occasions, the mind seems to put off its wisdom; but the truth is, that, in a pure mind, wisdom retreats, if we may so say, to its centre, and there, unseen, keeps guard over this transient folly, draws delicate lines which are never to be passed in the freest moments, and, like a judicious parent, watching the sports of childhood, preserves a stainless innocence of soul in the very exuberance of gaiety. This combination of moral power with wit and humor, with comic conceptions and irrepressible laughter, this union of mirth and virtue, belongs to an advanced stage of the character; and we believe, that, in proportion to the diffusion of an enlightened religion, this action of the mind will increase, and will overflow in compositions, which, joining innocence to sportiveness, will communicate unmixed delight. Religion is not at variance with occasional mirth. In the same character, the solemn thought and the sublime emotions of the improved Christian, may be joined with the unanxious freedom, buoyancy, and gaiety of early years.

We will add but one more illustration of our views. We believe, that the union of religion with genius will favor that species of composition to which it may seem at first to be least propitious. We refer to that department of literature, which has for its object the delineation of the stronger and more terrible and guilty passions. Strange as it may appear, these gloomy and appalling features of our nature may be best comprehended and portrayed by the purest and noblest minds. The common idea is, that overwhelming emotions, the more they are experienced, can the more effectually be described. We have one strong presumption against this doctrine. Tradition leads us to believe, that Shakespeare, though he painted so faithfully and fearfully the storms of passion, was a calm and cheerful man.

The passions are too engrossed by their objects to meditate on themselves; and none are more ignorant of their growth and subtile workings, than their own victims. Nothing reveals to us the secrets of our own souls like religion; and in disclosing to us, in ourselves, the tendency of passion to absorb every energy, and to spread its hues over every thought, it gives us a key to all souls; for, in all, human nature is essentially one, having the same spiritual elements, and the same grand features. No man, it is believed, understands the wild and irregular motions of the mind, like him in whom a principle of divine order has begun to establish peace. No man knows the horror of thick darkness which gathers over the slaves of vehement passion, like him who is rising into the light and liberty of virtue. There is indeed a selfish shrewdness, which is thought to give a peculiar and deep insight into human nature. But the knowledge, of which it boasts, is partial, distorted, and vulgar, and wholly unfit for the purposes of literature. We value it little. We believe, that no qualification avails so much to a knowledge of human nature in all its forms, in its good and evil manifestations, as that enlightened, celestial charity, which religion alone inspires; for this establishes sympathies between us and all men, and thus makes them intelligible to us. A man, imbued with this spirit, alone contemplates vice as it really exists, and as it ought always to be described. In the most depraved fellow-beings he sees partakers of his own nature. Amidst the terrible ravages of the passions, he sees conscience, though prostrate, not destroyed, nor wholly powerless. He sees the proofs of an unextinguished moral life, in inward struggles, in occasional relentings, in sighings for lost innocence, in reviving throbs of early affections, in the sophistry by which the guilty mind would become reconciled to itself, in remorse, in anxious forebodings, in despair, perhaps in studied recklessness and cherished self-forgetfulness. These conflicts, between the passions and the moral nature, are the most interesting subjects in the branch of literature to which we refer, and we believe, that to portray them with truth and power, the man of genius can find in nothing such effectual aid, as in the development of the moral and religious principles in his own breast.

HENRY T. FARMER.

Henry T. Farmer was a native of England, who emigrated to Charleston, S. C., where he was for some time engaged in commercial pursuits. He afterwards retired from business, and removed to New York for the purpose of studying medicine. He received the instructions of Drs. Francis and Hosack, was graduated at the College of Physicians and Surgeons, and licensed as a physician in 1821. During the progress of his studies he published *Imagination; the Maniac's Dream, and other Poems*, in a small volume. The collection is dedicated to Mrs. Charles Baring, the wife of the author's uncle. This lady was, during a portion of her career, an actress, and the author of *Virginia, The Royal Recluse, Zulaine*, and other dramas, which were performed with success. Several of the poems of the collection, as the *Essay on Taste*, which has an appeal to "Croaker," are addressed to Dr. Francis and others of the writer's friends.

Farmer returned to Charleston, where he practised medicine until his death, at the age of forty-six.

His verses show a ready pen, a taste for the poetry of his day, a kindly susceptibility, and occasionally sound with effect the louder notes of the lyre.

THE WOES OF MODERN GREECE. A PRIZE POEM.

There was a harp, that might thy woes rehearse,
In all the wild omnipotence of verse,
Imperial Greece! when wizard Homer's skill
Charm'd the coy muses from the woodland hill;
When nature, lavish of her boundless store,
Poured all her gifts, while art still showered more;
Thy classic chisel through each mountain rung,
Quick from its touch immortal labors sprung;
Truth vied with fancy in the grateful strife,
And rocks assumed the noblest forms of life.

Alas! thy land is now a land of wo;
Thy muse is crowned with Druid misletoe.
See the lorn virgin with dishevelled hair,
To distant climes in 'wildered haste repair;
Chill desolation seeks her favored bowers,
Neglect, that mildew, blasts her cherished flowers;
The spring may bid their foliage bloom anew,
The night may dress them in her fairy dew;
But what shall chase the winter-cloud of pain,
And bid her early numbers breathe again?
What spring shall bid her mental gloom depart?
'Tis always winter in a broken heart.

The aged Patriarch seeks the sea-beat strand,
To leave—for ever leave his native land;
No sun shall cheer him with so kind a beam,
No fountain bless him with so pure a stream;
Nay, should the exile through Elysium roam,
He leaves his heaven, when he leaves his home.
But, we may deeper, darker truth unfold,
Of matrons slaughtered, and of virgins sold,
Of shrines polluted by barbarian rage,
Of grey locks rifled from the head of age,
Of pilgrims murdered, and of chiefs defied,
Where Christians knelt, and Sparta's heroes died.
Once more thy chiefs their glittering arms resume,
For heaven, for vengeance, conquest or a tomb;
With fixed resolve to be for ever free,
Or leave all Greece one vast Thermopylæ.

Columbia, rise! A voice comes o'er the main,
To ask thy blessing, nor to ask in vain;
Stand forth in bold magnificence, and be
For classic Greece, what France was once for thee.
So shall the gods each patriot bosom sway,
And make each Greek the hero of his day.
But, should thy wisdom and thy valor stand
On neutral ground—oh! may thy generous hand
Assist her hapless warriors, and repair
Her altars, scath'd by sacrilege and care;
Hail all her triumphs, all her ills deplore,
Nor let old Homer's manes beg once more.

TIMOTHY FLINT.

Timothy Flint was born in Reading, Massachusetts, in the year 1780, and was graduated at Harvard in 1800. After two years of theological study, he was ordained pastor of the Congregational Church of Lunenburg, Worcester county, where he remained for twelve years. In October, 1815, in consequence of ill health, he left with his family for the west, in pursuit of a milder climate, and change of scene. Crossing the Alleganies, and descending the Ohio, he arrived at Cincinnati, where he passed the winter months. The following spring and summer were spent in travelling in Ohio, Indiana, and Illinois, and after a halt at St. Louis, where he was, so far as he could learn, the first

Protestant minister who ever administered the communion in the place, arrived at St. Charles on the Missouri. He here established himself as a missionary, and remained for three years thus employed in the town and surrounding country. He then removed to Arkansas, but returned after a few months to St. Charles. In 1822 he visited New Orleans, where he remained during the winter, and passed the next summer in Covington, Florida. Returning to New Orleans in the autumn, he removed to Alexandria on the Red River, in order to take charge of a school, but was forced by ill health, after a year's residence, to return to the North.

T. Flint.

In 1826 he published an account of these wanderings, and the scenes through which they had led him, in his *Recollections of the last Ten Years passed in occasional residences and journeyings in the Valley of the Mississippi, in a series of letters to the Rev. James Flint, of Salem, Mass.* It was successful, and was followed the same year by *Francis Berrian, or the Mexican Patriot*, a story of romantic adventure with the Comanches, and of military prowess in the Mexican struggle, resulting in the fall of Iturbide. The book has now become scarce. In its day it was better thought of by critics for its passages of description, than for its story, which involved many improbable and incongruous incidents. His third work, *The Geography and History of the Mississippi Valley*, appeared at Cincinnati in 1827, in two octavo volumes. It is arranged according to states, and gives ample information, in a plain style, on the subject comprised in its title.

In 1828 he published *Arthur Clenning*, a romantic novel, in which the hero and heroine are shipwrecked in the Southern Ocean, reach New Holland, and after various adventures settle down to rural felicity in Illinois. This was followed by *George Mason the Young Backwoodsman*, and in 1830 by the *Shoshonee Valley*, the scene of which is among the Indians of Oregon.

His next work, *Lectures upon Natural History, Geology, Chemistry, the Application of Steam, and Interesting Discoveries in the Arts*, was published in Boston in 1832.

On the retirement of Mr. C. F. Hoffman from the editorship of the Knickerbocker Magazine, Mr. Flint succeeded to his post for a few months in the year 1833. He translated about the same time *L'art d'être heureuse* by Droz, with additions of his own, and a novel entitled, *Celibacy Vanquished, or the Old Bachelor Reclaimed.* In 1834 he removed to Cincinnati, where he edited the *Western Monthly Magazine* for three years, contributing to it and to other periodicals as well, a number of tales and essays. In 1835 he furnished a series of *Sketches of the Literature of the United States* to the London Athenæum. He afterwards removed to Louisiana, and in May, 1840, returned to New England on a visit for the benefit of his health. Halting at Natchez on his way, he was for some hours buried in the ruins of a house thrown down, with many others, by the violence of a tornado. On his arrival at Reading his illness increased, and he wrote to his wife that his end would precede her reception of his letter, an announcement which hastened her own death and anticipated his own, by but a short time however, as he breathed his last on the eighteenth of August.

THE SHORES OF THE OHIO.

It was now the middle of November. The weather up to this time had been, with the exception of a couple of days of fog and rain, delightful. The sky has a milder and lighter azure than that of the northern states. The wide, clean sand-bars stretching for miles together, and now and then a flock of wild geese, swans, or sand-hill cranes, and pelicans, stalking along on them; the infinite varieties of form of the towering bluffs; the new tribes of shrubs and plants on the shores; the exuberant fertility of the soil, evidencing itself in the natural as well as cultivated vegetation, in the height and size of the corn, of itself alone a matter of astonishment to an inhabitant of the northern states, in the thrifty aspect of the young orchards, literally bending under their fruit, the surprising size and rankness of the weeds, and, in the enclosures where cultivation had been for a while suspended, the matted abundance of every kind of vegetation that ensued,—all these circumstances united to give a novelty and freshness to the scenery. The bottom forests everywhere display the huge sycamore, the king of the western forest, in all places an interesting tree, but particularly so here, and in autumn, when you see its white and long branches among its red and yellow fading leaves. You may add, that in all the trees that have been stripped of their leaves, you see them crowned with verdant tufts of the viscus or mistletoe, with its beautiful white berries, and their trunks entwined with grape-vines, some of them in size not much short of the human body. To add to this union of pleasant circumstances, there is a delightful temperature of the air, more easily felt than described. In New England, when the sky was partially covered with fleecy clouds, and the wind blew very gently from the southwest, I have sometimes had the same sensations from the temperature there. A slight degree of languor ensues; and the irritability that is caused by the rougher and more bracing air of the north, and which is more favourable to physical strength and activity than enjoyment, gives place to a tranquillity highly propitious to meditation. There is something, too, in the gentle and almost imperceptible motion, as you sit on the deck of the boat, and see the trees apparently moving by you, and new groups of scenery still opening upon your eye, together with the view of these ancient and magnificent forests, which the axe has not yet despoiled, the broad and beautiful river, the earth and the sky, which render such a trip at this season the very element of poetry. Let him that has within him the *bona indoles*, the poetic mania, as yet unwhipt of justice, not think to sail down the Ohio under such circumstances, without venting to the genius of the river, the rocks, and the woods, the swans, and perchance his distant beloved, his dolorous notes.

HENRY PICKERING.

Henry, the third son of Colonel Timothy Pickering and Rebecca Pickering, was born on the 8th of October, 1781, at Newburgh, in the Hasbrouck house, memorable as having been the headquarters of General Washington. Colonel Pickering was at the time quartermaster-general of the army of the Confederated States, and was absent with the commander-in-chief at the siege of Yorktown.

In 1801, after a long residence in Pennsylvania, Colonel Pickering returned with his family to his native state, Massachusetts; and subsequently Henry engaged in mercantile pursuits in Salem. In the course of a few years he acquired a moderate fortune, which he dispensed most liberally; among other things, contributing largely towards the support of his father's family and the education of its younger members. In 1825, in consequence of pecuniary losses, he removed from Salem to New York, in the hope of retrieving his affairs; but being unsuccessful in business, he retired from the city, and resided several years at Rondout, and other places on the banks of the Hudson, devoting much of his time to reading, and finding in poetical composition a solace for his misfortunes. His writings take occasionally a sombre tint from the circumstances which shaded the latter years of his life, although his natural temperament was cheerful. He was a lover of the beautiful, as well in art as in nature, and he numbered among his friends the most eminent poets and artists of our country. An amiable trait in his character was a remarkable fondness for children, to whom he was endeared by his attentions. The affection with which he regarded his mother was peculiarly strong; and he deemed himself highly blest in having parents, the one distinguished for ability, integrity, and public usefulness, the other, beautiful, pure, gentle, and loving.

H Pickering

The following just tribute to his memory appeared in the Salem Gazette, in May, 1838:—"Died in New York on the 8th instant Henry Pickering. . . . . . His remains were brought to this city on Friday last, and deposited at the side of the memorial which filial piety had erected to the memory of venerated parents—and amid the ancestral group which has been collecting since the settlement of the country.

"A devoted, affectionate, and liberal son and brother, he entwined around him the best and the warmest feelings of his family circle. To his friends and acquaintances he was courteous, delicate, and refined in his deportment. With a highly cultivated and tasteful mind he imparted pleasant instruction to all who held intercourse with him, while his unobtrusive manners silently forced themselves on the affections, and won the hearts of all who enjoyed his society."

The poems of Pickering are suggested by simple, natural subjects, and are in a healthy vein of reflection. A flower, a bird, a waterfall, childhood, maternal affection are his topics, with which he blends his own gentle moods. The *Buckwheat Cake*, which we print with his own corrections, first appeared in the New York Evening Post, and was published in an edition, now rare, in Boston, in 1831.

THE HOUSE IN WHICH I WAS BORN: ONCE THE HEADQUARTERS OF WASHINGTON.

I.

Square, and rough-hewn, and solid is the mass,
And ancient, if aught ancient here appear
Beside yon rock-ribb'd hills: but many a year
Hath into dim oblivion swept, alas!
Since bright in arms, the worthies of the land
Were here assembled. Let me reverent tread;
For now, meseems, the spirits of the dead
Are slowly gathering round, while I am fann'd
By gales unearthly. Ay, they hover near—
Patriots and Heroes—the august and great—
The founders of a young and mighty state,
Whose grandeur who shall tell? With holy fear,
While tears unbidden my dim eyes suffuse,
I mark them one by one, and marvelling, muse.

II.

I gaze, but they have vanish'd! and the eye,
Free now to roam from where I take my stand,
Dwells on the hoary pile. Let no rash hand
Attempt its desecration: for though I
Beneath the sod shall sleep, and memory's sigh
Be there for ever stifled in this breast,—
Yet all who boast them of a land so blest,
Whose pilgrim feet may some day hither hie,—
Shall melt, alike, and kindle at the thought
That these rude walls have echoed to the sound
Of *the great Patriot's voice!* that even the ground
I tread was trodden too by him who fought
To make us free; and whose unsullied name,
Still, like the sun, illustrious shines the same.

THE DISMANTLED CABINET.

Go, beautiful creations of the mind,
Fair forms of earth and heaven, and scenes as fair—
Where Art appears with Nature's loveliest air—
Go, glad the few upon whom Fortune kind
Yet lavishes her smiles. When calmly shin'd
My hours, ye did not fail a zest most rare
To add to life; and when oppress'd by care,
Or sadness twin'd, as she hath often twin'd,
With cypress wreath my brow, even then ye threw
Around enchantment. But though I deplore
The separation, in the mirror true
Of mind, I yet shall see you as before:
Then, go! like friends that vanish from our view,
Though ne'er to be forgot, we part to meet no more.

THE BUCKWHEAT CAKE.

But neither breath of morn, when she ascends
With charm of earliest birds; nor rising sun
On this delightful land; nor herb, fruit, flower,
Glistering with dew; nor fragrance after showers;
Nor grateful evening, without thee is sweet!

Muse, that upon the top of Pindus sitt'st,
And with the enchanting accents of thy lyre
Dost soothe the immortals, while thy influence sweet
Earth's favor'd bards confess, be present now;
Breathe through my soul, inspire thyself the song,
And upward bear me in the adventurous flight:
Lo the resistless theme—THE BUCKWHEAT CAKE.

Let others boastful sing the golden ear
Whose farinaceous treasures, by nice art
And sleight of hand, with store of milk and eggs,
Form'd into pancakes of an ample round,
Might please an epicure—and homebred bards
Delight to celebrate the tassell'd maize
Worn in the bosom of the Indian maid,
Who taught to make the hoe-cake, (dainty fare,
When butter'd well!) I envy not their joys.
How easier of digestion, and, beyond
Compare, more pure, more delicate, the cake
All other cakes above, queen of the whole,
And triumph of the culinary art—
The Buckwheat Cake! my passion when a boy,
And still the object of intensest love—
Love undivided, knowing no decline,
Immutable. My benison on thee,
Thou glorious Plant! that thus with gladness crown'dst
Life's spring-time, and beneath bright Summer's eye,
Lured'st me so oft to revel with the bee,
Among thy snow-white flowers: nay, that e'en yet
Propitious, amidst visions of the past
Which seem to make my day-dreams now of joy,
Giv'st me to triumph o'er the ills of time.
Thou, when the sun "pours down his sultry wrath,"
Scorching the earth and withering every flower,
Unlock'st, beneficent, thy fragrant cells,
And lavishest thy perfume on the air;
But when brown Autumn sweeps along the glebe,
Gathering the hoar-frost in her rustling train,
Thou captivat'st my heart! for thou dost then
Wear a rich purple tint, the sign most sure
That nature hath perform'd her kindly task,
Leaving the husbandman to sum his wealth,
And thank the bounteous Gods. O, now be wise,
Ye swains, and use the scythe most gently; else
The grain, plump and well-ripen'd, breaks the tie
Which slightly binds it to the parent stalk,
And falls in rattling showers upon the ground,
Mocking your futile toil; or, mingled straight
With earth, lies buried deep, with all the hopes
Of disappointed man! Soon as the scythe
Hath done its work, let the rake follow slow,
With caution gathering up into a swarth
The lusty corn; which the prompt teamster next,
Or to the barn floor clean transports, or heaps
Remorseless on the ground, there to be thresh'd—
Dull work, and most unmusical the flail!
And yet, if ponderous rollers smooth the soil,
The earth affords a substitute not mean
For the more polish'd plank; and they who boast
The texture of their meal—the sober race
That claim a peaceful founder for their state—
(Title worth all the kingdoms of the world!)
Do most affect the practice. But a point,
So subtile, others may debate: enough
For me, if, when envelop'd in a cloud
Of steam, hot from the griddle, I perceive,
On tasting, no rude mixture in the cake,
Gravel, or sandy particle, to the ear
Even painful, and most fearful in effect:
For should the jaws in sudden contact meet,
The while, within a luscious morsel hid,
Some pebble comes between, lo! as the gates
Of Hell, they "grate harsh thunder;" and the man
Aghast, writhing with pain, the table spurns,
And looks with loathing on the rich repast.

But now, his garners full, and the sharp air,
And fancy keener still, the appetite
Inspiriting, to the mill, perch'd near some crag
Down which the foamy torrent rushes loud,
The farmer bears his grist. And here I must
To a discovery rare, in time advert:
For the pure substance dense which is conceal'd
Within the husk, and which, by process quick
As simple, is transform'd to meal, should first
Be clean divested of its sombre coat:
The which effected, 'tween the whizzing stones
Descends the kernel, beauteous, and reduced
To dust impalpable, comes drifting out
In a white cloud. Let not the secret, thus
Divulg'd be lost on you, ye delicate!
Unless, in sooth, convinc'd ye should prefer
A sprinkling of the bran; for 'tis by some
Alleg'd that this a higher zest confers.
Who shall decide? Epicurean skill
I boast not, nor exactest taste; but if
I am to be the umpire, then I say,
As did the Baratarian king, of sleep—
My blessing on the man who first the art
Divine invented! Ay, let the pure flour
Be like the driven snow, bright to the eye,
And unadulterate. So jovial sons
Of Bacchus, with electric joy, behold
"The dancing ruby;" then, impatient, toss
The clear unsullied draught. But is there aught
In the inebriate cup, to be compar'd
To the attractive object of my love,
The Buckwheat Cake? Let those who list, still quaff
The madd'ning juice, and, in their height of bliss,
Believe that such, she of the laughing eye
And lip of rose, celestial Hebe, deals
Among the Gods; but O, ye Powers divine!
If e'er ye listen to a mortal's prayer,
Still give me my ambrosia. This confers
No "pains arthritic," racking every joint,
But leaves the body healthful, and the mind
Serene and imperturb'd.—A nicer art
Than all, remains yet to be taught; but dare
I venture on the theme? Ye Momus tribes,
Who laugh even wisdom into scorn—and ye,
Authoritative dames, who wave on high
Your sceptre-spit, away! and let the nymph
Whose smiles betoken pleasure in the task,
(If task it be,) bring forth the polish'd jar;
Or, wanting such, one of an humbler sort,
Earthen, but smooth within: although nor gold,
Nor silver vase, like those once used, in times
Remote, by the meek children of the Sun,
(Ere tyrant Spain had steep'd their land in gore,)
Were of too costly fabric. But, at once,
Obedient to the precepts of the muse,
Pour in the tepid stream, warm but not hot,
And pure as water from Castalian spring.
Yet interdicts she not the balmy tide
Which flows from the full udder, if preferr'd;
This, in the baking, o'er the luscious cake,
Diffuses a warm golden hue—but that
Frugality commends and Taste approves:
Though if the quantity of milk infus'd
Be not redundant, none can take offence.
Let salt the liquid mass impregnate next;
And then into the deep, capacious urn,
Adroitly sift the inestimable dust,
Stirring, meanwhile, with paddle firmly held,
The thickening fluid. Sage Discretion here
Can best determine the consistence fit,
Nor thin, nor yet too thick. Last add the barm—
The living spirit which throughout the whole
Shall quickly circulate, and airy, light,
Bear upward by degrees the body dull.

Be prudent now, nor let the appetite
Too keen, urge forward the last act of all.
Time, it is true, may move with languid wing,
And the impatient soul demand the cate
Delicious; yet would I advise to bear
A transient ill, and wait the award of Fate,

The sluggish mass must be indulg'd, till, wak'd
By the ethereal spirit, it shall mount
From its dark cell, and court the upper air;
For, bak'd too soon, the cake, compact and hard,
To the dissolving butter entrance free
Denies, while disappointment and disgust
Prey on the heart. Much less do thou neglect
The auspicious moment! Thee, nor business then
Must urgent claim, nor love the while engross:
For, ever to the skies aspiring still,
The fluid vivified anon ascends,
Disdains all bound, and o'er the vase's side
Flows awful! till, too late admonish'd, thou
The miserable waste shalt frantic see,
And, in the acid draff within, perceive
Thy hopes all frustrate. Thus Vesuvius in
Some angry hour, 'mid flames and blackening smoke,
From his infuriate crater pours profuse
The fiery lava—deluging the plains,
And burying in its course cities, and towns,
And fairest works of art! But, to avert
Catastrophe so dire, the griddle smooth,—
Like steely buckler of the heroic age,
Elliptical, or round—and for not less
Illustrious use design'd—make ready quick.
Rubb'd o'er the surface hot, a little sand
Will not be useless; this each particle
Adhesive of the previous batch removes,
And renders easy the important work,
To gracefully reverse the half-bak'd cake.
With like intent, the porker's salted rind,
Mov'd to and fro, must lubricate the whole:
And this perform'd, let the white batter stream
Upon the disk opaque, 'till silver'd o'er
Like Cynthia's, it enchants the thoughtful soul.
Impatient of restraint, the liquid spreads,
And, as it spreads, a thousand globules rise,
Glistening, but like the bubble joy, soon burst,
And disappear. Ah, seize the occasion fair,
Nor hesitate too long the cake to turn;
Which, of a truth, unsightly else must look,
And to the experienc'd, nicer palate, prove
Distasteful. See! 'tis done: and now, O now
The precious treat! spongy, and soft, and brown;
Exhaling, as it comes, a vapor bland:
While, all emboss'd with flowers, (to be dissolv'd,
Anon, as with the breath of the warm South,)
Upon the alluring board the butter gleams—
Not rancid, fit for appetite alone
Of coarsest gust, but delicate and pure,
And golden like the morn. Yet one thing more;—
The liquid amber which, untir'd, the bee
From many a bloom distils for thankless man;
For man, who, when her services are o'er,
The little glad purveyor of his board
Remorseless kills. But to the glorious feast!
Ye Gods! from your Olympian heights descend,
And share with me what ye, yourselves, shall own
Far dearer than ambrosia. That, indeed,
May haply give a zest to social mirth,
And, with the alternate cup, exhilarate
The sons of heaven: but my nepenthe rare,
Not only cheers the heart, but from the breast
Care, grief, and every nameless ill dispels—
Yielding a foretaste of immortal joy!

HENRY J. FINN.

HENRY J. FINN was born in the city of New York, in the year 1782. When a boy he sailed for England, on the invitation of a rich uncle resident there. The vessel sank at sea, and the passengers and crew were for many days exposed in small boats until they were picked up by a ship which landed them at Falmouth. Finn resided in London until the death of his uncle, who made no mention of him in his will. He then returned to New York in 1799, studied law for two years,—became tired of the profession, returned to London, and made his first appearance at the Haymarket Theatre "in the little part of Thomas in the Sleep Walker." He continued on the stage with success, and in 1811 returning to America made his first appearance at Montreal. He next performed in New York, and afterwards became a member of the stock company of the Federal Street Theatre, Boston. Here he remained for several years, and was at one time manager of the theatre. He was extremely successful here, and in every part of the country which he subsequently visited, as a comic actor, and accumulating a handsome fortune, retired in the intervals of his engagements to an elegant residence at Newport. He was on his way to his pleasant home, when with many others he met a sudden and awful death, in the conflagration of the steamboat Lexington on the night of January 13, 1840.

Finn was celebrated as a comic writer as well as a comic actor. He published a Comic Annual, and a number of articles in various periodicals. The bills of his benefit nights were, says Mr. Sargent, "usually made up of the most extraordinary and inconceivable puns, for which his own name furnished prolific materials."* He wrote occasional pathetic pieces, which possess much feeling and beauty, and left behind him a MS. tragedy, portions of which were published in the New York Mirror, to which he was a contributor in 1839. He also wrote a patriotic drama entitled *Montgomery, or the Falls of Montmorenci*, which was acted at Boston with success and published. He was a frequent versifier, and turned off a song with great readiness. He also possessed some ability as a miniature and landscape painter. Of his ingenious capacity in the art of punning, a paragraph from a sketch of May Day in New York in his "Comic Annual," may be taken as a specimen.

Then hogs have their essoine, the cart-horse is thrown upon the cart, and clothes-horses are broken upon the wheel. Old jugs, like old jokes, are cracked at their owners' expense, sofas lose their castors, and castors forsake their cruets, tumblers turn summersets, plates are dished; bellows, like bankrupts, can raise the wind no more, dog-irons go to pot, and pots go to the dogs; spiders are on the fly, the safe is not safe, the deuce is played with the tray, straw beds are down. It is the spring with cherry trees, but the fall with cherry tables, for they lose their leaves, and candlesticks their branches. The whole family of the brushes—hearth, hair, hat, clothes, flesh, tooth, nail, crumb, and blacking, are brushing off. Books, like ships, are outward bound; Scott's novels become low works, Old Mortality is in the dust, and Kenilworth is worthless in the kennel. Presidential pamphlets are paving the way for new candidates, medical tracts become treatises on the stone, naval tacticians descend to witness the novelty of American flags having been put down, and the advocates of liberality in thought, word, and deed, are gaining ground. Then wooden ware is every where. Pails are without the pale of preservation,

* Life by Epes Sargent, in Griswold's Biographical Annual. 1841.

and the tale of a tub, at which the washerwoman wrings her hands, in broken accents tells

> Of most disastrous chances,
> Of *moving* accidents by *flood* and field,
> That wind up the travel's history

of a New York comic annual celebration.

DANIEL WEBSTER.

DANIEL WEBSTER was born in the town of Salisbury, New Hampshire, Jan. 18, 1782. His father, a farmer, and according to the habit of the country and times an inn-keeper, a man of sterling character and intelligence, Major Ebenezer Webster, was a pioneer settler in the region on one of the townships* established after the conclusion of the old French War, in which he had served under Amherst at Ticonderoga. He was subsequently a soldier of the Revolution, with Stark at Bennington, and saw the surrender of Burgoyne at Saratoga. He closed his life in the honorable relation of Judge of the Court of Common Pleas in 1806, at the age of sixty-seven. His son, in one of his Franklin letters, describes him as "the handsomest man I ever saw, except my brother Ezekiel," and adds, "he had in him what I recollect to have been the character of some of the old Puritans. He was deeply religious, but not sour—on the contrary, good-humored, facetious—showing even in his age, with a contagious laugh, teeth, all as white as alabaster—gentle, soft, playful—and yet having a heart in him that he seemed to have borrowed from a lion."† Webster's first speech at the bar was while his father was on the bench; he never heard him again.

The future orator received his first education from his mother. In 1796 he was for a few months at Phillips (Exeter) Academy, under the charge of Dr. Benjamin Abbott,‡ making his preparations for college, which he completed under the Rev. Dr. Samuel Wood, of Boscawen, one of the trustees who facilitated his admission. He entered Dartmouth in 1797, and having overcome by his diligence the disadvantages of his hasty preparation, took his degree, with good reputation as a scholar, Aug. 26, 1801. In consequence of a difficulty with the Faculty respecting the appointments, he did not speak at the Commencement. There was a sharp feeling of competition growing out of the rival literary societies, which led him to resent the assignment of the chief post, the Latin Salutatory, to another; while the Faculty thought his fine talents in English composition might be better displayed in an oration on the fine arts or a poem.* He delivered a discourse the day previously, before the College Societies, on *The Influence of Opinion.* Subsequently, in 1806, he pronounced the Phi Beta Kappa College oration, on *The Patronage of Literature.*

While in College, in his nineteenth year, in 1800, he delivered a Fourth of July oration at the request of the citizens of Hanover, which was printed at the time. It is patriotic of course, and energetic, well stored with historical material, for Webster was not, even in a Fourth of July oration in youth, a sounder of empty words. A funeral oration, which he pronounced a short time before leaving college, on the death of Ephraim Simonds, a member of the Senior Class, has that dignity of enumeration which is noticeable in Webster's later orations of this description. "All of him that was mortal," he spoke, "now lies in the charnel of yonder cemetery. By the grass that nods over the mounds of Sumner, Merrill, and Cooke, now rests a fourth son of Dartmouth, constituting another monument of man's mortality. The sun, as it sinks to the ocean, plays its departing beams on his tomb, but they reanimate him not. The cold sod presses on his bosom; his hands hang down in weakness. The bird of the evening chants a melancholy air on the poplar, but her voice is stillness to his ears. While his pencil was drawing scenes of future felicity,—while his soul fluttered on the gay breezes of hope,—an unseen hand drew the curtain, and shut him from our view."†

Upon leaving college, Webster began the study of the law with Thomas W. Thompson, a lawyer of distinction, who was subsequently sent to the United States Senate, and presently left, to take charge, for a year, of the town academy at Fryeburg, in Maine, with a salary of three hundred and fifty dollars, which he was enabled to save by securing the post of Assistant to the Register of Deeds to the county, and with which he managed to provide something to support him in his legal studies, and for his brother Ezekiel's education. In 1802 he returned to the office of Thompson at Salisbury, and two years afterwards went to Boston, where he completed his legal studies with the Hon. Christopher Gore. He was admitted to the Suffolk bar in 1805. To be near his father he opened an office for the practice of his profession at Boscawen, N. H. After his father's death he removed to Portsmouth in his native state, where he maintained himself till 1816. In 1808 he had married the daughter of the Rev. Mr. Fletcher, of Hopkinton, N. H.‡

* It was in reference to this early habitation that Daniel Webster, in a speech at Saratoga in 1840, paid an elegant tribute to the memory of his father. He described the log-cabin in which his elder brothers and sisters were born, "raised amid the snow-drifts of New Hampshire, at a period so early, that when the smoke first rose from its rude chimney, and curled over the frozen hills, there was no similar evidence of a white man's habitation between it and the settlements on the rivers of Canada. Its remains still exist. I make to it an annual visit. I carry my children to it, to teach them the hardships endured by the generations which have gone before them. * * I weep to think that none of those who inhabited it are now among the living, and if ever I am ashamed of it, or if I ever fail in affectionate veneration for him who raised it and defended it against savage violence and destruction, cherished all the domestic virtues beneath its roof, and through the fire and blood of a seven years' revolutionary war, shrunk from no danger, no toil, no sacrifice to serve his country, and to raise his children to a condition better than his own, may my name and the name of my posterity, be blotted for ever from the memory of mankind."

† Letter of Webster, Franklin, May 3, 1846. Memorials (Appleton), ii. 243.

‡ This school was founded in 1778 by John Phillips, a graduate of Harvard, son of a pious minister of Andover, in conjunction with his brother, Samuel Phillips, of Andover. In 1789 John Phillips gave a further sum of $20,000, and bequeathed two thirds of his estate to the same object. He died in 1795. Dr. Abbott was the principal of this academy for fifty years, from 1789. At the close of that period he retired from his position, on which occasion a festival of the pupils was held, and speeches were made by Webster, Everett, and others. Among his pupils, of the public men of the country, had been Cass, Woodbury, the Everetts, Sparks, Bancroft.

* Prof. Sanborn, of Dartmouth. Eulogy on Webster before the Students of Phillips Academy, Andover.

† Lyman's Memorials of Webster, i. 246.

‡ This lady died in 1827, leaving four children—Grace, who died early; Fletcher, who survives his father; Julia, married to Mr. Appleton, of Boston, and since dead; and Edward, who

In 1812 he delivered a Fourth of July oration at Portsmouth, before the Washington Benevolent Society, on the ***Principal Maxims of Washington's Administration.***

In 1813 he was elected to the House of Representatives, and made his maiden speech on the Berlin and Milan decrees. In 1814 he was re-elected. In New Hampshire his legal course was sustained by association with Dexter, Story, Smith, and Mason. In Congress, he at once took his place with the solid and eloquent men of the House. In 1816 he removed to Boston, pursuing his profession with the highest distinction. In 1823 he again took his seat in the House of Representatives, and made his speech on the Greek Revolution, 19th Jan., 1824, a speech which added greatly to his reputation. He was re-elected—out of five thousand votes only ten being cast against him, and a similar event took place in 1826. The more prominent general addresses date from this period.

In December, 1820, while a member of the Convention to revise the Constitution of Massachusetts, he delivered his Plymouth oration on ***The First Settlement of New England.***

The first Bunker Hill speech was delivered June 17, 1825, when the corner-stone of the monument was laid; the second exactly eighteen years afterwards on its completion. His ***Discourse in Commemoration of Jefferson and Adams*** was pronounced at Faneuil Hall, August 2, 1826.

In 1827 he was elected to the Senate, where he continued for twelve years, during the administrations of Jackson and Van Buren. His brother, Ezekiel Webster, fell in court at Concord while pleading a cause, and died instantaneously, of disease of the heart, in 1829. In 1830, his celebrated oratorical passage with Col. Robert Y. Hayne, of South Carolina,* occurred, in reply to an attack upon New England, and an assertion of the nullification doctrines. The scene has been described both by pen and pencil, the artist Healy having made it the subject of a large historical picture. The contest embodied the antagonism for the time between the North and the South. Hayne, rich in elocution and energetic in bearing, was met by the cool argument and clear statement of Webster rising to his grand peroration, which still furnishes a national watchword of Union. It was observed, on this occasion, that Webster wore the colors of the Whig party of the Revolution, a blue coat and buff waistcoat, which was afterwards his not unusual oratorical costume. Webster's stalwart appearance, his fine olive complexion, his grave weighty look, his "cavernous eyes," which Miss Martineau and the newspaper writers celebrated, were no unimportant accessories to his oratory.

Danl Webster

Many of the speeches of Webster of this period were in opposition to the financial policy of the government. In the spring and summer of 1839 he visited England and France, and was received with the greatest distinction in both countries; where his reputation, personal and political, as a man and an orator was well established. He spoke on several public occasions, but the only instance in which his remarks have been preserved at length was his speech on his favorite topic of agriculture at the Triennial Celebration of the Royal Society of Agriculture at Oxford.* On his return he engaged in the presidential contest which resulted in the election of General Harrison, under whose administration he became Secretary of State in 1841. To complete the adjustment of the boundary question and other outstanding difficulties with England, he retained office under Tyler till 1843. In 1845, in the Presidency of Polk, he returned to his seat in the Senate, where he continued till he was called by Fillmore to the department of State again in 1850. He had previously sustained the Compromise Measures with the full weight of his ability, both in Congress and in numerous "Union" speeches throughout the country. He should have had the Whig nomination to the Presidency, but the availability of Scott interposed. The frequent engagements of Webster at Conventions and gatherings through the States, endeared him much in his latter days to the people. He spoke at the opening of the Erie Railroad in 1851; he delivered a discourse on his favorite books and studies before the New York Historical Society, in February, 1852; and in the same month presided at the Metropolitan Hall assembly, when Bryant read his eulogy on

fell a Major in the Mexican war. In 1830 Webster married a second time, Caroline, daughter of Herman Le Roy, of New York, by whom he had no children.

* Robert Y. Hayne was born in the parish of St. Paul, South Carolina, Nov. 10, 1791. His grandfather was a brother of the Revolutionary martyr, Col. Isaac Hayne. He was a law pupil of Langdon Cheves, and rose rapidly at the bar in Charleston. He began his political career in the state legislature in his twenty-third year, was soon Speaker of the House, and Attorney-General of the State. He took his seat in the United States Senate, in his thirty-first year, as soon as he was eligible for the office. He resigned his seat in 1832, to take the post of Governor of the State in the nullification days, when he issued a counter proclamation in reply to that of President Jackson. When the matter was adjusted he turned his attention to state improvement, in the midst of which he was taken with a mortal illness, and died in his forty-eighth year, Sept., 1839. Besides his speeches in the Senate, characterized by their ability and eloquence, he was the author of the papers in the old *Southern Review* on improvement of the navy, and the vindication of the memory of his relative, Col. Hayne.—Life, Character, and Speeches, of the late Robert Y. Hayne. Oct., 1845.

* July 18, 1839.

the novelist Cooper. In May he made his last great speech in Faneuil Hall to the men of Boston.

It was in office, the active service of the public, with scant intervals for recreation, and but a few months' travel away from his native land, that he had passed his life, and in the harness of office, as Secretary of State, he died. Since the deaths of Washington and Hamilton, no similar event had so deeply moved the country. The national heart throbbed with the pulsations of the telegraph which carried the news of his last moments through the land. Calmly, courageously, in the full exercise of his faculties, he discharged his last duties for his country, and watching the falling sands of life, discoursed with his friends of religion and immortality. The first intimation which the public received of his serious illness, was most touchingly conveyed in a newspaper article which appeared in the Boston *Courier* of the date of October 20, entitled, "Mr. Webster at Marshfield." Its author, who is understood to have been Professor C. C. Felton of Harvard College, after reviewing his recent political course, described the noble natural features of his farm, as a framework for a notice of its owner, to whom the writer passed by a masterly transition. "As you look down from these hills, your heart beats with the unspeakable emotion that such objects inspire; but the charm is heightened by the reflection that the capabilities of nature have been unfolded by the skill and taste of one whose fame fills the world; that an illustrious existence has here blended its activity with the processes of the genial earth, and breathed its power into the breath of heaven, and drawn its inspiration from the air, the sea, and the sky, and around and above; and that here, at this moment, the same illustrious existence is, for a time, struggling in doubtful contest with a foe to whom all men must, sooner or later, lay down their arms. * * Solemn thoughts exclude from his mind the inferior topics of the fleeting hour; and the great and awful themes of the future now seemingly opening before him—themes to which his mind has always and instinctively turned its profoundest meditations, now fill the hours won from the weary lassitude of illness, or from the public duties which sickness and retirement cannot make him forget or neglect. The eloquent speculations of Cicero on the immortality of the soul, and the admirable arguments against the Epicurean philosophy put into the mouth of one of the colloquists in the book of the Nature of the Gods, share his thoughts with the sure testimony of the Word of God." Two days after, the telegraph bore this brief announcement from Boston—"A special messenger from Marshfield arrived here this morning, with the melancholy intelligence that Daniel Webster cannot live through the day." From that moment, almost hourly, news was borne through the country to the end, between two and three o'clock on the morning of Sunday, October 24, 1852.

Among the last words which Webster listened to, and in which he expressed an interest, were some stanzas of Gray's Elegy, which he had endeavored to recall, and the sublime consolation of the Psalmist, repeated by his physician, Dr. Jeffries: —"Though I walk through the valley of the shadow of death I will fear no evil, for Thou art with me; Thy rod and thy staff they comfort me." The last words he uttered were, "I still live."*

Then it was felt how great a heart the mask of life had covered. Death, in the grand language of Bacon, had "opened the gate to good fame, and extinguished envy." Traits of the nobility of the man were called to mind. It was remembered how he had dwelt upon the simple universal ideas of the elements, the sea rolling before him at Marshfield; the starry heavens shining through the foliage of the elm at his door; the purpling of the dawn;† his admiration of the psalms and the prophets, and the primeval book of Job; his dying kindness to his friend Harvey,‡ and the friendly intercourse which he had sustained with the country people around, whose love for their rural occupations he had exalted; and how in his last days, when too feeble to leave his room, he had refreshed his mind with those favorite pursuits, by looking at the cattle, which he had caused to be driven to the window.

Funeral honors were paid to his memory in the chief cities of the Union by processions and orations. His interment took place at Marshfield on Friday the 29th October. His remains, dressed as when living, were conveyed from the library to a bier in front of the house, beneath his favorite elm. The funeral services were performed by the pastor of the neighboring church at South Marshfield, when the numerous procession, including delegates from various public bodies of several States, followed to the tomb, built for its new occupant, for his family and himself, on an elevation commanding a view of the country around, and of the sea. Here he rests. A marble block, since placed in front of the tomb, bears the legend: "Lord, I believe, help thou my unbelief."§

---

* It may be recalled that the poet Dwight, in his last hours, was consoled by the same text of Scripture; and that a similar expression was among the last which fell from the lips of Priestley.

An authentic account of Webster's illness and death was prepared by Mr. George Ticknor, and is published in the elegantly printed volume "A Memorial of Daniel Webster, from the city of Boston," published in 1853, which contains the obituary proceedings and orations of the courts and various societies, as well as Professor Felton's notice of "the last autumn at Marshfield."

† He took refuge in these remote starry suggestions, placing the temporizing politics of the hour at an infinite distance from him, when he was called up one night at Washington, by a crowd of citizens, to receive the news of Scott's nomination for the Presidency.—"Gentlemen: this is a serene and beautiful night. Ten thousand thousand of the lights of heaven illuminate the firmament. They rule the night. A few hours hence their glory will be extinguished.

> You meaner beauties of the night,
> Which poorly satisfy our eyes,
> What are you when the sun doth rise?

Gentlemen: There is not one among you who will sleep better to-night than I shall. If I wake I shall learn the hour from the constellations, and I shall rise in the morning, God willing, with the lark; and though the lark is a better songster than I am, yet he will not leave the dew and the daisies, and spring upward to greet the purpling east, with a more blithe and jocund spirit than I shall possess."

‡ The day before he died he called for his friend Peter Harvey, a merchant of Boston, whom he requested not to leave him till he was dead. He had shortly before written an order —"My son, take some piece of silver, let it be handsome, and put a suitable inscription on it, and give it, with my love, to Peter Harvey. Marshfield, Oct. 23, 1852."

§ With regard to Webster's religious views, he had probably no strongly defined system of observance. Early in life, it is said, he was a member of the Presbyterian church, latterly he was in communion with the Episcopal church.—Letter of the Hon. R. Barnwell Rhett, Charleston Mercury. Nov. 1852.

In his death, Webster remembered his love of country, and personal associations with the home of Marshfield. He left the property in the hands of trustees for the use of his son Fletcher, during his life, and after to his children, connecting, by provision, his books, pictures, plate, and furniture, with the building; "it being my desire and intention that they remain attached to the house, while it is occupied by any of my name and blood." His respect for his writings, which had been carefully arranged by his friend Edward Everett, was coupled with regard to his family and friends, to some of whom he dedicated separately each of the six volumes.* His literary executors, whom he left in charge of his papers by will, were Edward Everett, George Ticknor, Cornelius C. Felton, George T. Curtis.

The career of Webster remains as a study for his countrymen. Its lessons are not confined to oratory or political life. He was an example of manly American culture, such as is open to and may be shared by thousands through the land. His youth was one of New England self-denial and conscientious perseverance. Nature hardened her thriving son in a rugged soil of endurance.

The numerous anecdotes of his early life will pass to posterity as the type of a peculiar culture and form of civilization, which have made many men in America. There was a vein of the stout old Puritanic granite in his composition, which the corruptions of Washington life, the manners of cities and the arts of politics, never entirely overlaid.† To this he was true to the end. In whatever associations he might be placed there was always this show of strength and vigor. It was felt that whatever might appear otherwise was accidental and the effect of circumstances, while the substantive man, Daniel Webster, was a man of pith and moment, built up upon strong ever-during realities. And this is to be said of all human greatness, that it is but as the sun shining in glimpses through an obscured day of clouds and darkness. Clear and bright was that life at its rising; great warmth did it impart at its meridian; and a happy omen was the final Sabbath morn of strange purity and peace, with whose dawn its beams were at last blended.

Daniel Webster had completed the solemn allotment of three score and ten. It was his fortune at once to die at home, in the midst of the sanctities of his household, and in the almost instant discharge of his duties to the State. His public life to its close was identified with important questions of national concern and moment.

Of his capacities as an orator and writer—of his forensic triumphs and repute—of his literary skill and success much may be said. His speech had strength, force, and dignity; his composition was clear, rational, strengthened by a powerful imagination—in his great orations "the lightning of passion running along the iron links of argument."* The one lesson which they teach to the youth of America is self-respect, a manly consciousness of power, expressed simply and directly—to look for the substantial qualities of the thing, and utter them distinctly as they are felt intensely. This was the sum of the art which Webster used in his orations. There was no circumlocution or trick of rhetoric beyond the old Horatian recommendation, adopted by a generous nature:

Verbaque provisam rem non invita sequentur.

This habit of mind led Webster to the great masters of thought. He found his fertile nourishment in the books of the Bible, the simple energy of Homer, and the vivid grandeur of Milton. He has left traces of these studies on many a page.

There was about Webster a constant air of nobility of soul. Whatever subject he touched lost nothing of its dignity with him. The occasion rose in his hands, as he connected it with interests beyond those of the present moment or the passing object. Two grand ideas, capable of filling the soul to its utmost capacity, seem to have been ever present with him: the sense of nationality, of patriotism, with its manifold relations; and of the grand mutations of time. He lived for half a century in the public life of his country, with whose growth he grew, from the first generation of patriots, and in whose mould, as it was shaped over a continent, he was moulded. He seemed to be conscious himself of a certain historic element in his thoughts and actions. This will be remembered as a prevalent trait of his speeches and addresses, whether in the capitol or before a group of villagers. He recalled the generations which had gone before, the founders of states in colonial times on our western shores; the men of the days of Washington; our sires of the Revolution. He enumerated the yeomanry and peasantry; the names memorable in his youth, as they are recorded in the pages of the Iliad or the Æneid:—

Fortemque Gyan, fortemque Cloanthum,

or as imperishable history chronicles them in the sacred annals of Judea.

MORAL FORCE OF PUBLIC OPINION—FROM THE SPEECH ON THE REVOLUTION IN GREECE.

It may be asked, perhaps, Supposing all this to be true, what can *we* do? Are we to go to war? Are we to interfere in the Greek cause, or any other European cause? Are we to endanger our pacific relations? No, certainly not. What, then, the question recurs, remains for us? If we will not en-

---

* Works of Daniel Webster, with "Biographical Memoir of the Public Life," by Everett. Boston: Little and Brown. 1851.

† It is not to be denied that the associations and habits of Washington life detracted something from the position gained by the early manhood of Webster. His fortune broken by his separation from a lucrative practice, which he abandoned for public life, was afterwards too much dependent on the subscriptions of his mercantile friends. In his personal habits he became careless of expense, and in his financial affairs embarrassed. The intemperance of Webster became a popular notion, which was doubtless much exaggerated, as his friend Dr. Francis has demonstrated from physiological reasons, and Charles A. Stetson has shown in his vindication of him in this particular, in his remarks made at the celebration of his birth-day at the Astor House in 1854, and which he has since published. The use of stimulants appears, too, from the statement of his physicians (in the account of his illness and the autopsy in the American Medical Journal of Science for January, 1853), to have been resorted to as a sedative for physical pain and weakness.

* Address by George S. Hillard, at a meeting of citizens in Faneuil Hall, in honor of the memory of Webster. October 27, 1852.

danger our own peace, if we will neither furnish armies nor navies to the cause which we think the just one, what is there within our power?

Sir, this reasoning mistakes the age. The time has been, indeed, when fleets, and armies, and subsidies, were the principal reliances even in the best cause. But, happily for mankind, a great change has taken place in this respect. Moral causes come into consideration, in proportion as the progress of knowledge is advanced; and the public opinion of the civilized world is rapidly gaining an ascendency over mere brutal force. It is already able to oppose the most formidable obstruction to the progress of injustice and oppression; and as it grows more intelligent and more intense, it will be more and more formidable. It may be silenced by military power, but it cannot be conquered. It is elastic, irrepressible, and invulnerable to the weapons of ordinary warfare. It is that impassible, unextinguishable enemy of mere violence and arbitrary rule, which, like Milton's angels,

> Vital in every part, ...
> Cannot, but by annihilating, die.

Until this be propitiated or satisfied, it is vain for power to talk either of triumphs or of repose. No matter what fields are desolated, what fortresses surrendered, what armies subdued, or what provinces overrun. In the history of the year that has passed by us, and in the instance of unhappy Spain, we have seen the vanity of all triumphs in a cause which violates the general sense of justice of the civilized world. It is nothing, that the troops of France have passed from the Pyrenees to Cadiz; it is nothing that an unhappy and prostrate nation has fallen before them; it is nothing that arrests, and confiscation, and execution, sweep away the little remnant of national resistance. There is an enemy that still exists to check the glory of these triumphs. It follows the conqueror back to the very scene of his ovations; it calls upon him to take notice that Europe, though silent, is yet indignant; it shows him that the sceptre of his victory is a barren sceptre; that it shall confer neither joy nor honor, but shall moulder to dry ashes in his grasp. In the midst of his exaltation, it pierces his ear with the cry of injured justice; it denounces against him the indignation of an enlightened and civilized age; it turns to bitterness the cup of his rejoicing, and wounds him with the sting which belongs to the consciousness of having outraged the opinion of mankind.

THE UNION—PERORATION OF SECOND SPEECH ON FOOT'S RESOLUTION IN REPLY TO HAYNE.

Mr. President, I have thus stated the reasons of my dissent to the doctrines which have been advanced and maintained. I am conscious of having detained you and the Senate much too long. I was drawn into the debate with no previous deliberation, such as is suited to the discussion of so grave and important a subject. But it is a subject of which my heart is full, and I have not been willing to suppress the utterance of its spontaneous sentiments. I cannot, even now, persuade myself to relinquish it, without expressing once more my deep conviction, that, since it respects nothing less than the Union of the States, it is of most vital and essential importance to the public happiness. I profess, Sir, in my career hitherto, to have kept steadily in view the prosperity and honor of the whole country, and the preservation of our Federal Union. It is to that Union we owe our safety at home, and our consideration and dignity abroad. It is to that Union that we are chiefly indebted for whatever makes us most proud of our country. That Union we reached only by the discipline of our virtues in the severe school of adversity. It had its origin in the necessities of disordered finance, prostrate commerce, and ruined credit. Under its benign influences, these great interests immediately awoke, as from the dead, and sprang forth with newness of life. Every year of its duration has teemed with fresh proofs of its utility and its blessings; and although our territory has stretched out wider and wider, and our population spread farther and farther, they have not outrun its protection or its benefits. It has been to us all a copious fountain of national, social, and personal happiness.

I have not allowed myself, Sir, to look beyond the Union, to see what might lie hidden in the dark recess behind. I have not coolly weighed the chances of preserving liberty when the bonds that unite us together shall be broken asunder. I have not accustomed myself to hang over the precipice of disunion, to see whether, with my short sight, I can fathom the depth of the abyss below; nor could I regard him as a safe counsellor in the affairs of this government, whose thoughts should be mainly bent on considering, not how the Union may be best preserved, but how tolerable might be the condition of the people when it should be broken up and destroyed. While the Union lasts, we have high, exciting, gratifying prospects spread out before us, for us and our children. Beyond that I seek not to penetrate the veil. God grant that in my day, at least, that curtain may not rise! God grant that on my vision never may be opened what lies behind! When my eyes shall be turned to behold for the last time the sun in heaven, may I not see him shining on the broken and dishonored fragments of a once glorious Union; on States dissevered, discordant, belligerent; on a land rent with civil feuds, or drenched, it may be, in fraternal blood! Let their last feeble and lingering glance rather behold the gorgeous ensign of the republic, now known and honored throughout the earth, still full high advanced, its arms and trophies streaming in their original lustre, not a stripe erased or polluted, nor a single star obscured, bearing for its motto, no such miserable interrogatory as "What is all this worth?" nor those other words of delusion and folly, "Liberty first and Union afterwards;" but everywhere, spread all over in characters of living light, blazing on all its ample folds, as they float over the sea and over the land, and in every wind under the whole heavens, that other sentiment, dear to every true American heart,—Liberty *and* Union, now and for ever, one and inseparable!

THE SECRET OF MURDER—THE TRIAL OF KNAPP FOR THE MURDER OF WHITE.

He has done the murder. No eye has seen him, no ear has heard him. The secret is his own, and it is safe!

Ah! Gentlemen, that was a dreadful mistake. Such a secret can be safe nowhere. The whole creation of God has neither nook nor corner where the guilty can bestow it, and say it is safe. Not to speak of that eye which pierces through all disguises, and beholds every thing as in the splendor of noon, such secrets of guilt are never safe from detection, even by men. True it is, generally speaking, that "murder will out." True it is, that Providence hath so ordained, and doth so govern things, that those who break the great law of Heaven by shedding man's blood, seldom succeed in avoiding discovery. Especially, in a case exciting so much attention as this, discovery must come, and will come, sooner or later. A thousand eyes turn at once to explore every man, every thing, every circumstance, connected with the time and place; a thousand ears catch every whisper; a thousand excited minds intensely dwell on the scene, shedding all their light, and ready to kindle the slightest circumstance into a blaze of discovery. Meantime the guilty soul cannot keep its own secret. It is false to itself; or rather it feels an irresistible impulse of conscience to be true to itself. It labors under its guilty possession, and knows not what to do with it. The human heart was not made for the residence of such an inhabitant. It finds itself preyed on by a torment, which it dares not acknowledge to God or man. A vulture is devouring it, and it can ask no sympathy or assistance, either from heaven or earth. The secret which the murderer possesses soon comes to possess him; and, like the evil spirits of which we read, it overcomes him, and leads him whithersoever it will. He feels it beating at his heart, rising to his throat, and demanding disclosure. He thinks the whole world sees it in his face, reads it in his eyes, and almost hears its workings in the very silence of his thoughts. It has become his master. It betrays his discretion, it breaks down his courage, it conquers his prudence. When suspicions from without begin to embarrass him, and the net of circumstance to entangle him, the fatal secret struggles with still greater violence to burst forth. It must be confessed, it will be confessed; there is no refuge from confession but suicide, and suicide is confession.

FROM THE ADDRESS BEFORE THE NEW YORK HISTORICAL SOCIETY, 1852.

Unborn ages and visions of glory crowd upon my soul, the realization of all which, however, is in the hands and good pleasure of Almighty God, but, under his divine blessing, it will be dependent on the character and the virtues of ourselves, and of our posterity.

If classical history has been found to be, is now, and shall continue to be, the concomitant of free institutions, and of popular eloquence, what a field is opening to us for another Herodotus, another Thucydides, and another Livy! And let me say, Gentlemen, that if we, and our posterity, shall be true to the Christian religion, if we and they shall live always in the fear of God, and shall respect his commandments, if we, and they, shall maintain just, moral sentiments, and such conscientious convictions of duty as shall control the heart and life, we may have the highest hopes of the future fortunes of our country; and if we maintain those institutions of government and that political union, exceeding all praise as much as it exceeds all former examples of political associations, we may be sure of one thing, that, while our country furnishes materials for a thousand masters of the Historic Art, it will afford no topic for a Gibbon. It will have no Decline and Fall. It will go on prospering and to prosper. But, if we and our posterity reject religious instruction and authority, violate the rules of eternal justice, trifle with the injunctions of morality, and recklessly destroy the political constitution which holds us together, no man can tell, how sudden a catastrophe may overwhelm us, that shall bury all our glory in profound obscurity. Should that catastrophe happen, let it have no history! Let the horrible narrative never be written! Let its fate be like that of the lost books of Livy, which no human eye shall ever read, or the missing Pleiad, of which no man can ever know more, than that it is lost, and lost for ever!

LETTER ON THE MORNING.—TO MRS. J. W. PAIGE.

RICHMOND, VA.,
Five o'clock, A. M., April 29, 1852.

MY DEAR FRIEND:—Whether it be a favor or an annoyance, you owe this letter to my early habits of rising. From the hour marked at the top of the page, you will naturally conclude that my companions are not now engaging my attention, as we have not calculated on being early travellers to-day.

This city has a "pleasant seat." It is high; the James river runs below it, and when I went out, an hour ago, nothing was heard but the roar of the Falls. The air is tranquil and its temperature mild. It is morning, and a morning sweet and fresh, and delightful. Everybody knows the morning in its metaphorical sense, applied to so many occasions. The health, strength, and beauty of early years, lead us to call that period the "morning of life." Of a lovely young woman we say she is "bright as the morning," and no one doubts why Lucifer is called "son of the morning."

But the morning itself, few people, inhabitants of cities, know anything about. Among all our good people, no one in a thousand sees the sun rise once in a year. They know nothing of the morning; their idea of it is, that it is that part of the day which comes along after a cup of coffee and a beefsteak, or a piece of toast. With them morning is not a new issuing of light, a new bursting forth of the sun, a new waking up of all that has life from a sort of temporary death, to behold again the works of God, the heavens and the earth; it is only a part of the domestic day, belonging to reading the newspapers, answering notes, sending the children to school, and giving orders for dinner. The first streak of light, the earliest purpling of the east, which the lark springs up to greet, and the deeper and deeper coloring into orange and red, till at length the "glorious sun is seen, regent of the day"—this they never enjoy, for they never see it.

Beautiful descriptions of the morning abound in all languages, but they are the strongest perhaps in the East, where the sun is often an object of worship.

King David speaks of taking to himself the "wings of the morning." This is highly poetical and beautiful. The wings of the morning are the beams of the rising sun. Rays of light are wings. It is thus said that the sun of righteousness shall arise "with healing in his wings"—a rising sun that shall scatter life, health, and joy through the Universe.

Milton has fine descriptions of morning, but not so many as Shakespeare, from whose writings pages of the most beautiful imagery, all founded on the glory of morning, might be filled.

I never thought that Adam had much the advantage of us from having seen the world while it was new.

The manifestations of the power of God, like His mercies, are "new every morning," and fresh every moment.

We see as fine risings of the sun as ever Adam saw; and its risings are as much a miracle now as they were in his day, and I think a good deal more, because it is now a part of the miracle, that for thousands and thousands of years he has come to his appointed time, without the variation of a millionth part of a second. Adam could not tell how this might be. I know the morning—I am acquainted with it, and I love it. I love it fresh and sweet as it is—a daily new creation, breaking forth and calling all that have life and breath and being to new adoration, new enjoyments, and new gratitude.

DANIEL WEBSTER.

JOHN C. CALHOUN.

JOHN CALDWELL CALHOUN was born in Abbeville District, South Carolina, March 18, 1782. His father, Patrick Calhoun, was an Irishman by birth, who emigrated to Pennsylvania at an early age, removed to Western Virginia, and, after Braddock's defeat, to South Carolina. He was a man of a vigorous frame of mind as well as body, and was distinguished among his neighbors by his jealousy of the encroachments of government, carrying his principle so far as to oppose the adoption of the federal constitution on the ground that it gave other states the power of taxing his own. He married Miss Caldwell, of Charlotte County, Virginia.

The father's residence was situated in the wild, upper portion of the state, and was known as the Calhoun Settlement. The future senator was sent at the age of thirteen to the nearest academy, which was fifty miles distant. It was presided over by the Rev. Dr. Waddell, a Presbyterian, his brother-in-law. In consequence of the death of this gentleman's wife not long after, the school was broken up. Calhoun continued to reside with Mr. Waddell, who happened to have in charge the circulating library of the village. This small collection of books was eagerly devoured by the young student, whose tastes even then led him to the graver departments of literature. He read the histories of Rollin, Robertson, and Voltaire, with such assiduity, that in fourteen weeks he had despatched several volumes of these, with Cook's Voyages, and a portion of Locke on the Understanding. This intense application injured his eyes and his general health to such an extent that his mother interposed, and by a judicious course of out-door physical exercise, succeeded in restoring the natural vigor of his constitution, and giving him a taste for rural sports which was of service then, and afterwards, as a relief to his mental labors.

After four years spent at home, Calhoun en-

tered Yale College in 1802, on the completion of his course studied law at the celebrated school of Litchfield, and was admitted to practice in 1807. In 1808 he was elected to the Legislature of South Carolina, and in 1811 to the National House of Representatives. In 1817 he was appointed Secretary of War by President Monroe, an office which he held for seven years, introducing during his incumbency an order and vigor in its administration, which was of eminent service to the future operations of the department. In 1825 he was elected Vice-President, with Mr. Adams as President, and again in 1829. In 1831 he resigned the office, to take General Hayne's place, vacated by his election as Governor of South Carolina, in the Senate. He retired at the close of his term. During Mr. Tyler's administration, he was appointed Secretary of State. In 1845 he was again returned to the Senate, where he remained in active service until his death, which occurred at Washington, March 31, 1850.

Mr. Calhoun was a warm advocate of the war of 1812, of the nullification proceedings in his native state during General Jackson's administration, and was for many years the leading statesman of the Southern States. He took extreme ground in regard to State rights and the slavery question.

Webster, in his tribute in the Senate to Calhoun, noticed the qualities of his mind, and the simple, single pursuits of his life. "His eloquence was part of his intellectual character. It was plain, strong, terse, condensed, concise; sometimes impassioned, still always severe. Rejecting ornament, not often seeking far for illustration, his power consisted in the plainness of his propositions, in the closeness of his logic, and in the earnestness and energy of his manner"—adding, "I have known no man who wasted less of life in what is called recreation, or employed less of it in any pursuits not connected with the immediate discharge of his duty. He seemed to have no recreation but the pleasure of conversation with his friends."* Ingersoll, too, in his History of the Second War with England, condenses in a few vigorous words a striking picture of Calhoun as an orator, including the marked characteristics of the man:—"Speaking with aggressive aspect, flashing eye, rapid action and enunciation, unadorned argument, eccentricity of judgment, unbounded love of rule; impatient, precipitate in ambition, kind in temper; with conception, perception, and demonstration, quick and clear; with logical precision arguing paradoxes, and carrying home conviction beyond rhetorical illustration; his own impressions so intense, as to discredit, scarcely to listen to any other suggestions."

The publication of Calhoun's works, edited by Richard K. Cralle, under the direction of the General Assembly of the State of South Carolina, was commenced in Charleston in 1851, and shortly after transferred to the Messrs. Appleton of New York. Four volumes have been issued, and others are to follow. The first includes the posthumous work on which the author had been engaged in 1848 and 1849, *A Disquisition on Government, and a Discourse on the Constitution and Government of the United States*; the remainder are occupied with *Speeches delivered in the House of Representatives, and in the Senate of the United States*. His Documentary Writings and a Life are in preparation.

Calhoun's view of state rights is expressed in broad terms in his Disquisition on Government, in his theory of the right of the minority, which is the essence of the volume. This, like his other

* Remarks in the Senate, April 1, 1850.

views, even when they are pushed to excess, is handled in a straightforward manner, without concealment or subterfuge. It leads him in his theory to maintain the right of veto in a single member of a confederacy over the remaining associates—a proceeding which would practically stop the wheels of the national movement; and which is little likely to be adopted, however logically the argument may be drawn out in print.

In his personal conduct Calhoun was of great purity and simplicity of character. His mode of life on his plantation at Fort Hill was simple and unostentatious, but ever warm-hearted and hospitable. An inmate of his household, Miss Bates, for many years the governess of his children, bears honorable testimony to the purity and elevation of character of the great statesman in the private relations of the family. "Life with him," she says, "was solemn and earnest, and yet all about him was cheerful. I never heard him utter a jest; there was an unvarying dignity in his manner; and yet the playful child regarded him fearlessly and lovingly. Few men indulged their families in as free, confidential, and familiar intercourse as did this great statesman. Indeed, to those who had an opportunity of observing him in his own house, it was evident that his cheerful and happy home had attractions for him superior to those which any other place could offer."

He enjoyed the out-door supervision of his plantation at Fort Hill, and like Clay and Webster aimed at an agricultural reputation. His tastes were as simple as refined, and he carried his avoidance of personal luxury to a degree almost of abstemiousness.

His conversation was eagerly sought for its rare exhibition of logical power and philosophical acumen, especially in the range of government topics. Although he did not aim at brilliancy, his clear expression of deep thought, his extensive and thorough information, his readiness on every topic, his courtesy and sympathy with the mode of life and character of others, made his society a coveted enjoyment.

He cared little for what others said of him. Anonymous letters he never read, and those of mere abuse or flattery, after receiving a slight glance, shared the same neglect.*

STATE SOVEREIGNTY—FROM THE SPEECH ON THE FORCE BILL IN THE SENATE, FEBRUARY, 1833.

Notwithstanding all that has been said, I may say that neither the Senator from Delaware (Mr. Clayton), nor any other who has spoken on the same side, has directly and fairly met the great question at issue: Is this a federal union? a union of States, as distinct from that of individuals? Is the sovereignty in the several States, or in the American people in the aggregate? The very language which we are compelled to use when speaking of our political institutions, affords proof conclusive as to its real character. The terms union, federal, united, all imply a combination of sovereignties, a confederation of States. They are never applied to an association of individuals. Who ever heard of the United State of New York, of Massachusetts, or of Virginia? Who ever heard the term federal or union applied to the aggregation of individuals into one community? Nor is the other point less clear—that the sovereignty is in the several States, and that our system is a union of twenty-four sovereign powers, under a constitutional compact, and not of a divided sovereignty between the States severally and the United States. In spite of all that has been said, I maintain that sovereignty is in its nature indivisible. It is the supreme power in a State, and we might just as well speak of half a square, or half of a triangle, as of half a sovereignty. It is a gross error to confound the *exercise* of sovereign powers with *sovereignty* itself, or the *delegation* of such powers with the *surrender* of them. A sovereign may delegate his powers to be exercised by as many agents as he may think proper, under such conditions and with such limitations as he may impose; but to surrender any portion of his sovereignty to another is to annihilate the whole. The Senator from Delaware (Mr. Clayton) calls this metaphysical reasoning, which he says he cannot comprehend. If by metaphysics he means that scholastic refinement which makes distinctions without difference, no one can hold it in more utter contempt than I do; but if, on the contrary, he means the power of analysis and combination—that power which reduces the most complex idea into its elements, which traces causes to their first principle, and, by the power of generalization and combination, unites the whole in one harmonious system—then, so far from deserving contempt, it is the highest attribute of the human mind. It is the power which raises man above the brute—which distinguishes his faculties from mere sagacity, which he holds in common with inferior animals. It is this power which has raised the astronomer from being a mere gazer at the stars to the high intellectual eminence of a Newton or a Laplace, and astronomy itself from a mere observation of insulated facts into that noble science which displays to our admiration the system of the universe. And shall this high power of the mind, which has effected such wonders when directed to the laws which control the material world, be for ever prohibited, under a senseless cry of metaphysics, from being applied to the high purpose of political science and legislation? I hold them to be subject to laws as fixed as matter itself, and to be as fit a subject for the application of the highest intellectual power. Denunciation may, indeed, fall upon the philosophical inquirer into these first principles, as it did upon Galileo and Bacon when they first unfolded the great discoveries which have immortalized their names; but the time will come when truth will prevail in spite of prejudice and denunciation, and when politics and legislation will be considered as much a science as astronomy and chemistry.

In connexion with this part of the subject, I understood the Senator from Virginia (Mr. Rives) to say that sovereignty was divided, and that a portion remained with the States severally, and that the residue was vested in the Union. By Union, I suppose the Senator meant the United States. If such be his meaning—if he intended to affirm that the sovereignty was in the twenty-four States, in whatever light he may view them, our opinions will not disagree; but according to my conception, the whole sovereignty is in the several States, while the exercise of sovereign powers is divided—a part being exercised under compact, through this General Government, and the residue through the separate State Governments. But if the Senator from Virginia (Mr. Rives) means to assert that the twenty-four States form but one community, with a single sovereign power as to the objects of the Union, it will be but the revival of the old question, of whe-

* Oration on the Life, Character, and Services of John C. Calhoun, by J. H. Hammond: 1851. Homes of American Statesmen, pp. 397-415.

ther the Union is a union between States, as distinct communities, or a mere aggregate of the American people, as a mass of individuals; and in this light his opinions would lead directly to consolidation.

But to return to the bill. It is said that the bill ought to pass, because the law must be enforced. The law must be enforced! The imperial edict must be executed! It is under such sophistry, couched in general terms, without looking to the limitations which must ever exist in the practical exercise of power, that the most cruel and despotic acts ever have been covered. It was such sophistry as this that cast Daniel into the lion's den, and the three Innocents into the fiery furnace. Under the same sophistry the bloody edicts of Nero and Caligula were executed. The law must be enforced. Yes, the act imposing the "tea-tax must be executed." This was the very argument which impelled Lord North and his administration to that mad career which for ever separated us from the British crown. Under a similar sophistry, "that religion must be protected," how many massacres have been perpetrated? and how many martyrs have been tied to the stake? What! acting on this vague abstraction, are you prepared to enforce a law without considering whether it be just or unjust, constitutional or unconstitutional? Will you collect money when it is acknowledged that it is not wanted? He who earns the money, who digs it from the earth with the sweat of his brow, has a just title to it against the universe. No one has a right to touch it without his consent except his government, and this only to the extent of its legitimate wants; to take more is robbery, and you propose by this bill to enforce robbery by murder. Yes: to this result you must come, by this miserable sophistry, this vague abstraction of enforcing the law, without a regard to the fact whether the law be just or unjust, constitutional or unconstitutional.

In the same spirit, we are told that the Union must be preserved, without regard to the means. And how is it proposed to preserve the Union? By force! Does any man in his senses believe that this beautiful structure—this harmonious aggregate of States, produced by the joint consent of all—can be preserved by force? Its very introduction will be certain destruction to this Federal Union. No, no. You cannot keep the States united in their constitutional and federal bonds by force. Force may, indeed, hold the parts together, but such union would be the bond between master and slave—a union of exaction on one side and of unqualified *obedience* on the other. That *obedience* which, we are told by the Senator from Pennsylvania (Mr. Wilkins), is the Union! Yes, exaction on the side of the master; for this very bill is intended to collect what can be no longer called taxes—the voluntary contribution of a free people—but tribute—tribute to be collected under the mouths of the cannon! Your custom-house is already transferred to a garrison, and that garrison with its batteries turned, not against the enemy of your country, but on subjects (I will not say citizens), on whom you propose to levy contributions. Has reason fled from our borders? Have we ceased to reflect? It is madness to suppose that the Union can be preserved by force. I tell you plainly, that the bill, should it pass, cannot be enforced. It will prove only a blot upon your statute-book, a reproach to the year, and a disgrace to the American Senate. I repeat, it will not be executed; it will rouse the dormant spirit of the people, and open their eyes to the approach of despotism. The country has sunk into avarice and political corruption, from which nothing can arouse t but some measure, on the part of the Government, of folly and madness, such as that now under consideration.

Disguise it as you may, the controversy is one between power and liberty; and I tell the gentlemen who are opposed to me, that, as strong as may be the love of power on their side, the love of liberty is still stronger on ours. History furnishes many instances of similar struggles, where the love of liberty has prevailed against power under every disadvantage, and among them few more striking than that of our own Revolution; where, as strong as was the parent country, and feeble as were the colonies, yet, under the impulse of liberty, and the blessing of God, they gloriously triumphed in the contest. There are, indeed, many and striking analogies between that and the present controversy. They both originated substantially in the same cause—with this difference—in the present case, the power of taxation is converted into that of regulating industry; in the other, the power of regulating industry, by the regulation of commerce, was attempted to be converted into the power of taxation. Were I to trace the analogy further, we should find that the perversion of the taxing power, in the one case, has given precisely the same control to the Northern section over the industry of the Southern section of the Union, which the power to regulate commerce gave to Great Britain over the industry of the colonies in the other; and that the very articles in which the colonies were permitted to have a free trade, and those in which the mother-country had a monopoly, are almost identically the same as those in which the Southern States are permitted to have a free trade by the act of 1832, and in which the Northern States have, by the same act, secured a monopoly. The only difference is in the means. In the former, the colonies were permitted to have a free trade with all countries south of Cape Finisterre, a cape in the northern part of Spain; while north of that, the trade of the colonies was prohibited, except through the mother-country, by means of her commercial regulations. If we compare the products of the country north and south of Cape Finisterre, we shall find them almost identical with the list of the protected and unprotected articles contained in the act of last year. Nor does the analogy terminate here. The very arguments resorted to at the commencement of the American Revolution, and the measures adopted, and the motives assigned to bring on that contest (to enforce the law), are almost identically the same.

ROBERT WALSH.

ROBERT WALSH was born in the city of Baltimore in 1784. His father was by birth an Irishman, bearing the same name; his mother was of Quaker Pennsylvanian origin. He received his early education at the Catholic College at Baltimore, and the Jesuit College at Georgetown. He was sent to Europe after passing through the usual school course to complete his education, and remained abroad until his twenty-fifth year, when he returned, married, and commenced the practice of the law, having prosecuted his studies under the superintendence of Robert Goodloe Harper. Owing in part, probably, to his deafness, he soon abandoned this profession.

He commenced his literary career as a writer in the Port Folio, and in 1809 published *A Letter on the Genius and Disposition of the French Government, including a View of the Taxation of the French Empire*, in which he commented with severity on the measures of

Napoleon. It contained a large mass of information respecting the internal economy of the government of Napoleon, which was entirely new to English readers. The work was written with spirit, and was received with favor not only in his own country, but, what was then a rarity, in England, where it passed through four editions, and the Edinburgh gave a hearty endorsement to its merits in a leading article.

Robert Walsh

In 1811 he commenced with the year the publication of the first quarterly attempted in America, *The American Review of History and Politics.* Eight numbers appeared, carrying the work through two years. Most of the articles were from the pen of the editor.

In 1813 his *Correspondence with Robert Goodloe Harper respecting Russia** and *Essay on the Future State of Europe* appeared. He also furnished several biographical prefaces to an edition of the English poets, in fifty eighteenmo. volumes, then in course of publication in Philadelphia. In 1817 he became the editor of *The American Register*, a valuable statistical publication, which was continued for two years only. In 1818 he published, in *Delaplaine's Repository*, a long and elaborate biographical paper on Benjamin Franklin, which still remains one of the most interesting memoirs of the sage. In 1819 Mr. Walsh published *An Appeal from the Judgments of Great Britain respecting the United States of America. Part First, containing an Historical Outline of their Merits and Wrongs as Colonies, and Strictures upon the Calumnies of the British Writers.* This work, forming an octavo volume of five hundred and twelve closely printed pages, was called forth by the long-continued calumnies of the British press, and particularly of the Edinburgh and Quarterly Reviews, in their endorsements of the foolish and unfounded slanders set forth by hasty, ignorant, and irresponsible travellers through the United States. These reviews, representing the deliberate judgment of the two great political parties of their country, excited a resentment in American readers which has left its traces to the present day.

* Vide *ante*, vol. i. 688.

Mr. Walsh met these assailants with facts drawn from English testimony of undoubted authority, often from previous admissions of the assailants themselves. The work is divided into sections on the history of the British maladministration of the American colonies, "the hostilities of the British Reviews," and the topic of negro slavery. It is careful in its statements, calm in tone, and at the same time energetic. It was at once accepted as an able vindication by the Americans, and did much to mend the manners of the English journals.

In 1821 he commenced, with Mr. William Fry, the *National Gazette*, a small newspaper, published on alternate afternoons. It was soon enlarged, and published daily. Mr. Walsh remained connected with this journal for fifteen years, and during that period did much to enlarge the scope of the newspaper literature of the country by writing freely and fully upon books, science, and the fine arts, as well as politics, and by joining in his treatment of the latter topic a little of the *suaviter in modo*, which had hitherto been somewhat lacking in the American press, to the *fortiter in re*, which required no increase of intensity.

Mr. Walsh was also connected with the editorship of *The American Magazine of Foreign Literature*, the forerunner of the Museum and Living Age of Mr. Littell, but in 1822 resigned that charge for the more agreeable task of the resuscitation of his original Review. The first number of the American Review was published in March, 1827. It was continued with great ability for ten years, and among its many excellent qualities is to be commended for its frequent and thorough attention to home literature and other subjects of national interest.

In 1837, Mr. Walsh finding the Gazette was failing to furnish its former support, retired from it. He published, about the same time, two volumes selected from his contributions to its columns, and from articles still in manuscript, under the title of *Didactics*. He removed in the same year to Paris, where he has since resided, filling, until a few years since, the post of United States Consul. He has maintained a constant and prominent literary connexion with his country by his regular foreign correspondence to the National Intelligencer, and more recently to the New York Journal of Commerce.

No American abroad has enjoyed more intimate relations with the savans and politicians of Europe, or has traced with greater interest the progress of government and science.

SENTENCES—FROM DIDACTICS.

We should endeavour to poetize our existence; to keep it clear of the material and grosser world. Music, flowers, verse, beauty, and natural scenery, the abstractions of philosophy, the spiritual refinements of religion are all important to that end.

Liberty is a boon which few of the European nations are worthy to receive or able to enjoy When attempts to give it have been vainly made, let us, before we speak of them, inquire whether they were practicable.

We should keep acknowledged evil out of the way of youth and its fealty; as we would avert frost from the blossom, and protect vegetable or animal life of any kind in its immaturity, from perilous exposure.

Maxim for a Republic.—Let the cause of every single citizen be the cause of the whole; and the cause of the whole be that of every single citizen.

Real sympathy and gratitude show themselves, not in words and pageants, but acts, sacrifices, which directly afford "comfort and consolation."

Let none of us cherish or invoke the spirit of religious fanaticism:—the ally would be quite as pestilent as the enemy.

We should never inquire into the faith or profession, religious or political, of our acquaintance; we should be satisfied when we find usefulness, integrity, beneficence, tolerance, patriotism, cheerfulness, sense, and manners. We encounter every day really good men, practical Christians, and estimable citizens, belonging respectively to all the sects and classes.

There is nothing, however good in itself, which may not be converted into "stuff," by making a jumble of it, and interpolating trash; and there is no journalist who may not be represented as inconsistent, no allowance being made for difference of times and circumstances, and the just and vivid impressions of particular periods and events.

It is well observed that good morals are not the fruit of metaphysical subtleties; nor are good political constitutions or salutary government. Abstractions and refinements are far from being enough for human nature and human communities.

Truth should never be sacrificed to *nationality;* but it is a sort of treason to decry unjustly indigenous productions, exalting at the same time those of a foreign country, without due examination or real grounds—to pretend national mortification in cases to which the opposite sentiment is due. Good, instructive literature and general politics need, in our country, liberal treatment in every quarter. They are subject to obstacles and disadvantages enough, without precipitate, sweeping, quackish opinions.

The effusions of genius, or rather, the most successful manifestations of what is called talent, are often the effects of distempered nerves and complexional spleen, as pearls are morbid secretions. How much of his reputation for superiority of intellect did not Mr. J. Randolph owe to his physical ills and misanthropic spirit!

The more the heart is exercised in the domestic affections, the more likely it is to be sympathetic and active with regard to external objects.

There are some human tongues which have two sides, like those of certain quadrupeds—one, smooth; the other very rough.

Restraints laid by a people on itself are sacrifices made to liberty; and it often shows the greatest wisdom in imposing them.

Write as wisely as we may, we cannot fix the minds of men upon our writings, unless we take them gently by the ear.

Candour is to be always admired, and equivocation to be shunned; but there is such a thing as supererogation, and very bold and ingenuous avowals may do much more harm than good.

It is an old saying that it is no small consolation to any one who is obliged to work to see another voluntarily take a share in his labour: since it seems to remove the idea of the constraint.

It would be well to allow some things to remain, as the poet says, "behind eternity;—hid in the secret treasure of the past."

A prudent man ought to be guided by a demonstrated probability not less than by a demonstrated certainty.

Men of wit have not always the clearest judgment or the deepest reason.

The perusal of books of sentiment and of descriptive poetry, and the frequent survey of natural scenery, with a certain degree of feeling and fancy, must have a most beneficial effect upon the imagination and the heart.

The true Fortunatus's purse is the richness of the generous and tender affections, which are worth much more for felicity, than the highest powers of the understanding, or the highest favours of fortune.

HENRY WHEATON.

HENRY WHEATON was a descendant from Robert Wheaton, a Baptist clergyman who emigrated in the reign of Charles I. to Salem, and afterwards removed to Rhode Island. He was born in Providence, November, 1785, and entered Brown University at the age of thirteen. After the completion of his course he studied law, and in 1806 went to Europe, to complete his education.

H. Wheaton

He resided for several months at Poitiers, engaged in the study of the French language, and of the recently established Code Napoleon. He afterwards devoted some time to the study of English law in London, and was an intimate of the American minister, Mr. Monroe. On his return he was admitted to the bar, and practised at Providence until 1818, when, in the meanwhile having married his cousin, the daughter of Dr. Wheaton of the same city, he removed to New York. Before his departure, he delivered a fourth of July oration, chiefly devoted to a consideration of the wars then raging in Europe, of which he spoke with detestation. After his establishment in New York he became the editor of the *National Advocate*, which he conducted for two years with marked ability. During this period he was appointed Judge of the Marine Court, and held for a few months the office of Army Judge Advocate. In 1815 he resumed practice, and in the same year published a *Treatise on the Law of Maritime Captures and Prizes*, regarded as the best work which had then appeared on the subject. In 1816 he was appointed Reporter of the Supreme Court at Washington, a position which he retained until 1827, publishing during his incumbency twelve volumes of Reports. In 1821 he was elected a member of the Convention called to revise the Constitution of the State of New York, and in 1825 was appointed by the Legislature one of the commissioners to revise, upon a new and systematic plan, all the statute laws of the State, a work which engaged his attention until his appointment by President Adams, in 1827, as Chargé d'Affaires to Denmark. He resided at Copenhagen until 1835, when he was appointed Minister Resident to the court of Prussia by President Jackson. In 1837 he was made Minister Plenipotentiary to the same court by President Van Buren. He retained this position until 1846, when he was recalled by President Polk.

Mr. Wheaton had, previously to his departure for Europe, delivered an *Address before the New York Historical Society* in 1820, and in 1824 at the opening of the New York Athenæum, an institution afterwards merged into the Society Library. He also contributed to the North American Review, and in 1826 published the *Life of William Pinkney*, with whom he had become personally acquainted during his residence at Washington. He afterwards prepared an abridgment of the work for Sparks's American Biography. He also translated the Code Napoleon, the manuscript of which was unfortunately consumed by fire soon after its completion.

This valuable literary career, side by side with laborious professional and public services, was continued with still greater efficiency in Europe. In 1831 he published in London *The History of the Northmen*, a work of great research, and one of the first on its subject in the language. It was translated into French in 1842, and its author was engaged in preparing a new American edition at the time of his death. In 1836 his *Elements of International Law* appeared in England and the United States. It was republished in 1846 with additions. In 1841 he wrote a work in French, *Histoire du Droit des Gens depuis la Paix de Westphalie*, which was complimented by the French Institute, republished at Leipsic in 1844, and translated in New York, with the title of *History of the Law of Nations*. It is regarded as a standard authority, and has received the highest commendations throughout Europe. In 1842 he published in Philadelphia, *An Enquiry into the British Claim of a Right of Search of American Vessels.*

In 1843 Mr. Wheaton was made corresponding member of the Section of Moral and Political Sciences of the French Institute, and in 1844 of the Academy of Sciences in Berlin. He took great interest in these associations, and enjoyed the intimacy of their most eminent members.

In 1844 he signed a convention with Baron Bulow, the Prussian Minister of Foreign Affairs, regulating the commercial intercourse between the United States and the Zollverein, on which he had labored for several years. It was, greatly to his regret, rejected by the Senate.

The long residence of Mr. Wheaton at one of the leading courts of Europe, combined with his extensive studies in international law, caused him to be frequently consulted by the representatives of his country in other parts of Europe, and he thus rendered eminent public services beyond the range of his own mission. He was universally regarded as the head of our foreign diplomacy, and his recall was lamented by considerate men of all parties as a national misfortune.

After a few months' residence in Paris, he returned in May, 1847, to New York, where a public dinner was given him soon after his arrival. A similar honor was tendered him in Philadelphia, but declined. His native city had his portrait painted by Healy, and placed in her council hall. He delivered an address in September of the same year before the Phi Beta Kappa Society of Brown University, on *the Progress and Prospects of Germany*. He was about to commence his duties as Professor of International Law at Harvard University, to which he had been elected soon after his return, when he was attacked by a disease which closed his life, on the eleventh of March, 1848.

Robert, the second son of the Hon. Henry Wheaton, was born in New York, October 5, 1826. His childhood was passed in Copenhagen, whither his father removed as Chargé d'Affaires of the United States shortly after his birth. In 1836 the family removed to Berlin, and in 1838, Robert, after a careful course of preliminary mental training by his father, was placed at school at Paris. In 1840 he lost his only brother Edward, a bereavement which afflicted him deeply. In 1841 he left school, and devoted two years to the study of engineering with a private tutor. Owing, however, to apprehensions that his health was too delicate for the out-door exposure incident to the practical duties of the profession, he abandoned it in 1843, and entered the school of MM. Barbé and Masson at Paris. After a year spent in classical studies he attended lectures at the Sorbonne and the College de France. He was at the same time cultivating his fine musical taste, and became a proficient in the science. His summers were passed in visits to his family at Berlin, and to friends in a few other cities of central Europe. In April, 1847, after his father's recal, he returned with him to the United States, and in the following September entered the Cambridge law school. On the completion of his course in 1850, he became a student in the office of Messrs. Dana and Parker of Boston, and in July, 1851, was admitted to practice. In the September following, while on his way to visit his family at Providence, he took cold, owing to exposure in consequence of the cars running off the track. His illness rapidly increased, and on the ninth of October, 1851, he breathed his last.

A volume of *Selections from the Writings of Robert Wheaton* appeared in 1854. It contains a sympathetic memoir of his brief but interesting life, with extracts from his journals and correspondence, and articles on the Sources of the Divina Commedia, Jasmin, Coquerel's Experimental Christianity, the Revolutions in Prussia and Sicily, and on a few other subjects, from the North American Review, and other periodicals, all ably and thoughtfully written.

CHARLES J. INGERSOLL.

Charles J. Ingersoll was born at Philadelphia on the third of October, 1782. His father, Jared Ingersoll, though belonging to a family who for the most part adhered to the Royalists in the Revolutionary contest (his father, Jared Ingersoll, of Connecticut, being Stampmaster-General under the Act of Parliament which provoked the American Revolution), was an active advocate of the popular side, and a member of the Convention which formed the Federal Constitution. He early settled in Philadelphia.

Mr. Ingersoll received a liberal education, and on its conclusion visited Europe, where he travelled in company with Mr. King, the American minister to London.

In 1801, a tragedy from his pen, *Edwy and Elgiva*, was produced at the Philadelphia theatre, and published.

In 1808 he wrote a pamphlet on the *Rights and Wrongs, Power and Policy of the United States of America*, in defence of the commercial measures of Jefferson's administration.

In 1809 he published anonymously a work which created a sensation, *Inchiquin's Letters*.* The "Letters" are introduced by the ancient mystification of the purchase, at a bookseller's stall in Antwerp, of a broken packet of letters from America, which turn out to be sent from Washington by Inchiquin, a Jesuit, to his friends in Europe, who, in one or two introductory epistles, express the greatest anxiety touching his mission to a land of savages, with considerable curiosity respecting the natives. A burlesque letter from Caravan, a Greek at Washington, gives a ludicrous account of the perils of the capital, and the foreign minister hunting in its *woods*. Inchiquin describes the houses of Congress and their oratory; runs over the characters of the Presidents, from Washington to Madison; the literature of Barlow's Columbiad and Marshall's Washington; the stock and population of the country; its education, amusements, resources, and prospects. The Columbiad is shrewdly criticised. One remark will show the pretensions, at that time, of the author. "Critically speaking, Homer, Virgil, and Milton occupy exclusively the illustrious (epic) quarter of Parnassus, and time alone can determine whether Barlow shall be seated with them. The 'dearth of invention,' 'faintness of the characters,' 'lack of pathos,' and other 'constitutional defects,' are set off against the learned, benevolent, elegant style of the performance." The Abbé Raynal is quoted for a *maximum* calculation of the prospective population of America at ten millions. Among other patriotic hits there is a humorous account of the foreign prejudiced or disappointed travellers who, in those days, gave the world its impressions of America.

In 1812 Ingersoll was elected a member of the House of Representatives. He took his seat at the special session called in May, 1813, to provide for the conduct of the war. He was one of the youngest members of that body, and more youthful in appearance even than in years, so that at his first entrance the doorkeeper refused him admittance. He was an earnest advocate of every measure brought forward for the vigorous prosecution of the war. In 1814, in an elaborate speech, he proclaimed and enforced the American version of the law of nations, that "free ships make free goods," a doctrine which, now generally recognised as a great peace measure, had at that time few advocates. On the expiration of his term of service the same year he was not re-elected, but was soon after appointed by Madison District Attorney of the State of Pennsylvania, an office which he held for fourteen years, until his removal by General Jackson at the commencement of his first Presidential term. During his second term, his administration had the warm support of Mr. Ingersoll. In 1826, at a convention of the advocates of the internal improvements of his state, Ingersoll presented a resolution in favor of the introduction of railroads worked by steam-power, similar to those which had just made their appearance in England. The plan was rejected by a large majority. As a member of the Legislature, a few years after, in 1829–30, one of the first railroad bills in the United States was enacted on his motion and report.

In 1837, by a report on currency, presented to the convention for reforming the Constitution of Pennsylvania, he anticipated by some months President Van Buren's recommendation to Congress of the Independent Treasury. He was an active member of the House of Representatives from 1839 to 1849.

C J Ingersoll

In 1845 he published the first volume of his *Historical Sketch of the Second War between the United States of America and Great Britain, embracing the events of* 1812–13, completing the work in three volumes. A second series, of the events of 1814–1815, appeared in 1852. The style of his history is irregular and discursive, but vivid and energetic. Its general character is that of a book of memoirs, strongly influenced by the democratic partisan views of the narrator. It contains numerous details of the principles and measures of public policy in which he was an eminent participant, with many matters of a more strictly personal character, especially in his account of the Bonaparte family, of whom, from his long friendship with Joseph Bonaparte, he had

* Inchiquin the Jesuit's Letters, during a late residence in the United States of America: being a fragment of a Private Correspondence, accidentally discovered in Europe; containing a favorable view of the Manners, Literature, and State of Society of the United States, and a refutation of many of the aspersions cast upon this country by former residents and tourists. By some unknown foreigner. New York: J. Riley.

original sources of information. Some three hundred pages of the "History" are thus occupied with the fortunes of the Napoleon dynasty. One of the most noteworthy of the American topics discussed is the defence of the system of privateering which has been since substantially set forth by President Pierce, in his Message of 1854. There are also, among other personal anecdotes, some animated descriptions of Washington and of Jefferson.

Mr. Ingersoll is at present engaged on a History of the Territorial Acquisitions of the United States.

Joseph Reed Ingersoll, the brother of Charles J. Ingersoll, a distinguished lawyer, for many years a prominent Whig in the House of Representatives, is the author of a translation of Roccus's treatise *De Navibus et Nauto*, of an address delivered in 1837 before the Phi Beta Kappa Society of Bowdoin College on *The Advantages of Science and Literature*, which attracted much attention, and of several other discourses of a similar character.

Edward, a third brother of the same family, wrote poems on the times entitled *Horace in Philadelphia*, which appeared in the Port Folio, and was a writer on political subjects in Walsh's Gazette.

BOOK-MAKING TRAVELLERS IN AMERICA—FROM THE INCHIQUIN LETTERS.

The labors of this class of writing travellers in America have been seconded by those of another, who, as their writings are confined to bills of exchange and accounts current, have contented themselves with being oral haberdashers of small stories, and retailers of ribaldry. Swarms of noxious insects swept from the factories and spunging-houses of Europe, after enjoying a full harvest of emolument and importance in the cities of this country, return to their original insignificance at home, to buzz assertions through their "little platoons of society," and then come back again to bask in the sunshine they feign to slight. Apprentices and understrappers, mongrel abbés and *gens d'industrie*, in the course of their flight over the Atlantic, are transmuted into fine gentlemen and virtuosi, shocked at the barbarian customs of this savage republic; the hospitality of whose citizens they condescend to accept, while they commiserate and calumniate their hosts, and consider it their especial errand and office to vilify, disturb, and overturn the government. The time was when these sturdy beggars walked without knocking into every door, taking *the chief seats in the synagogue, and the uppermost rooms at feasts, devouring widows' houses*, reviling with impunity the food they fed on. But so many ludicrous and so many serious explosions have gone off of these transatlantic bubbles, so many individuals have been put to shame, so many respectable families to ruin, by their polluting contact, that the delusion is broke, and they begin to be seen in their essential hideousness. Persons of condition from abroad have so often proved to be hostlers and footmen, and men of learning mountebank doctors, that the Americans find it necessary to shake these foreign vermin from their skirts, and to assert a dignity and self-respect, which are the first steps to that consideration from others, hitherto by this excrescent usurpation repelled from their society.

Hic nigræ succus loliginis, hæc est
Ærugo mera——

At the inn, where I lodged on my first arrival, it was my fortune to be assorted at every meal with half a dozen agents from the manufacturing towns of England, some Frenchmen exiled from St. Domingo, a Dutch supercargo, a Chinese mandarin—as a caitiff from Canton entitled himself—the young Greek, a copy of one of whose letters I sent you some time ago, and a countryman of mine; all of whom, after a plentiful regale, and drinking each other's healths till their brains were addled with strong liquors, would almost every day chime into a general execration of the fare, climate, customs, people, and institutions of this nether region. One of the Englishmen, a native of Cornwall, who was never out of a mist in his life till he left the parish of his birth, complained of the variableness of the weather, another of the beef, and a third of the porter, alleviations, without which they pronounced existence insupportable, taking care to accompany their complaints with magnificent eulogiums on the clear sky, cheap living, and other equally unquestionable advantages of their own country, with occasional intimations thrown in of their personal importance at home. The Creole French, in a bastard dialect, declaimed at the dishonesty and fickleness of the Americans, the demureness of their manners, and provoking irregularity of the language; winding up their philippic with a rapturous recollection of the charms of Paris; where in all probability no one of them ever was, except to obtain passports for leaving the kingdom.

They talk of beauties that they never saw,
And fancy raptures that they never knew.

The Chinese, who never was free from a sweat till he doubled the Cape of Good Hope, and who, when in Canton, never forgot in his prayers to implore the blessings of a famine or pestilence, catching the contagion of the company, and mechanically imitative, though he could not speak so as to be understood, endeavored, by signs and shrugs, to show that he suffered from the heat, and gave us to understand that an annual plague must be inevitable in such a climate. The Irishman, who swallowed two bottles of claret with a meal, besides brandy and malt liquors, swore the intemperate weather gave him fevers. The Hollander smoked his phlegmatic pipe in silence, looking approbation; and the complying Greek nodded assent, while at table, to every syllable that was uttered, though he afterwards coincided with me in a contradiction of the whole. When I was formerly in America, I knew several foreigners, then well stricken in years, who had resided here since the peace of 1783, always grumbling over the privations of this country, and sighing as usual; but fat and satisfied, and indulging not the least expectation of ever exchanging their forlorn state here for their brilliant prospects elsewhere. Like a well-fed curate, they dwell for ever on the fascinations of futurity, as contrasted with the wretchedness of mortality, recommending all good men to hasten from the one to the other, but without any wish for themselves to leave this world of tribulation.

LEWIS CASS.

Lew Cass.

Lewis Cass, the son of Jonathan Cass, a soldier of the Revolution, was born at Exeter, New Hampshire, October 9, 1782. He was a schoolfellow of Daniel Webster. At the age of seventeen, after having received an ordinary English education in his native place, he crossed the Alleghanies on foot and settled in Marietta, Ohio. In 1807 he was elected a member of the state legislature, where he introduced a bill which led to the arrest of Colonel Burr and the defeat of his plans. He was appointed about the same time Marshal of the State by Jefferson, an office which he resigned in 1811 to take part as a volunteer to repel the attacks of the Indians on the northern frontier. In 1812 he entered the United States army. He served with distinction at Detroit, and afterwards at the Battle of the Thames, and was appointed Governor of the territory of Michigan in 1813 by Madison, a position which he held until his appointment as Secretary of War by General Jackson in 1831. In this period, in 1819 and 1820, he projected and was engaged in carrying into effect a scientific exploration of the upper region of the Mississippi, which has identified his name permanently with the geography of the country. In 1836 he was appointed Minister to France, where he rendered important service in opposing the admission of the right of search in the quintuple treaty for the suppression of the Slave Trade. In consequence of opposition to the treaty made with Great Britain on this subject in 1842, which he regarded as involving his official position, he requested a recall and returned home. He published, in 1840, a volume entitled *France, its King, Court, and Government*, of historic interest for its sketch of the travels of Louis Philippe in America, which the minister had listened to from the lips of the royal adventurer at the Tuileries. Mr. Cass also contributed to the Southern Literary Messenger several papers on Candia and Cyprus. In 1845 he was elected United States Senator from Michigan, but resigned his seat in May on his nomination as the candidate of the Democratic party for the Presidency. After the election of General Taylor he was in 1849 re-elected to the Senate for the unexpired portion of his term, and still remains a member of that body. In 1848 he delivered an address before the New England Society of Michigan at Detroit, which was published at the time. In this eloquent discourse he thus contrasts the past of the old world with the present and future of America.

The hardy emigrant is ascending the passes of the Rocky Mountains, and already the forest is giving way before the axe of the woodsman on the very shores that look out upon China and Japan. In many portions of the old world, and in the oldest too, time has done its work. History has closed its record. Their high places have a world-renown in human annals, but they are solitudes. The pilgrim from other lands may go up to visit them, but it is for what they have been, and not for what they are. It is not to survey a prosperous country and a happy people; but to meditate upon the instability of human power, where the foundations of power were the deepest and the broadest. I have seen the wandering Arab, the descendant of Ishmael, sitting upon the ruins of Baalbeck, himself a ruin, not less marked and melancholy than they. Think you that visions of far away splendor passed before his eyes, and shut out the prospect of that wretchedness, which has bowed down his race for centuries? Think you that such dreams, waking though they may be, can give back to him his vale of Cœlo-Syria, covered with green pastures and rich flocks and herds, as in the days of the Patriarch? No, it is better to look round on prosperity than back on glory. The events of ages elsewhere seem here to be compressed within the ordinary life of man. Our birth is of yesterday; our growth of to-day. We have no past. No monuments, that have come down to us, glorious in their ruins, telling the story of former magnificence in the very solitude, that tells the story of present decay. Sometimes the shadows of bygone days pass over me, and I awake as from a dream, asking myself, is this great country, north of the Ohio and west of these broad Lakes, teeming with life, liberty, and prosperity; is this the country I entered half a century ago, shut out from the light of heaven by the primitive forests that covered it? Is this the country, which then contained one territory, and which now contains five States of this Union; whose population then numbered a few thousands, and now numbers five millions of people? And these flourishing towns, animated with the busy hum of industry, where they are, can I have slept under gigantic trees, throwing their broad branches over an unbroken soil? And the railroad, does it follow the war path, where I have followed the Indian? And the church bell, which summons a Christian community to prayer and to praise in the house of God, how brief the interval, since the solitude was broken by the war drum and the war song? We are realizing the fictions of Eastern imagination, and a better genius than him of Aladdin's lamp, the genius of industry and enterprise, is doing that mighty work, whose ultimate issue it is not given to human sagacity to foretell.

THOMAS HART BENTON.

Thomas Hart Benton was born in Orange county, North Carolina, in 1783. He was educated, but did not complete the full course, at the college at Chapel Hill. After leaving this institution he studied law with Mr. St. George Tucker, entered the United States army in 1810, and in

Thomas H. Benton,

1811 commenced the practice of the law in

Nashville, Tenn. Following the example of his family, both on the father's and mother's side, who had been active in the promotion of western emigration, he soon afterwards removed to Missouri, where, in 1820, he was elected one of her first United States Senators. In the interval of a year between his election and the admission of the state, he devoted himself to the study of the Spanish language, and to a preparation for the vigorous fulfilment of his duties. He took his seat in the Senate August 10, 1821, and retained it, by constant re-election, for the long period of thirty years, during which he took a leading part in the discussion of the great questions which came before that body, and was especially prominent in the debates on the United States Bank and the Sub-Treasury, being a warm friend of the latter measure.

Colonel Benton's moderate course on the slavery question not being approved by the majority of the Senate of his state, and his independent course on various other questions having added to the number of his enemies as well as his friends, he lost his election to the Senate in 1851. He offered himself at the next popular election as a candidate for the House of Representatives, and was successful. In 1854 he was, however, defeated—members of the Democratic party having united with and elected the candidate of the Whigs. In 1853 Colonel Benton published the first volume of his autobiographic work, *Thirty Years' View; or a History of the Working of the American Government for Thirty Years, from* 1820 *to* 1850. The thirty years is the period of Mr. Benton's senatorship, extending from the Presidency of Madison to that of Fillmore. The plan of the work, giving to a great mass of material, simplicity and clearness, is simply to treat in chronological order, in one view, the leading epochs of each question, connecting it with some memorable personage or crisis of debate. This is done by a disposition of the matter, in short, well discriminated chapters, easily referred to in a table of contents; devoted mainly to the immediate proceedings of Congress, but relieved by such episodes of a personal character as obituaries, or retirement from office of eminent actors on the scene. Thus there are chapters on the Admission of Missouri, on the Panama Mission, the Retirement of Rufus King, the arrival of La Fayette, the Deaths of Adams and Jefferson. The book is thus a succession of historical tableaux. In one point of view it is highly commendable, for its clear succinct narrative—the ease and *bonhommie* of the style. It is fluent without being diffuse, and exhibits the result of a long habit of imparting important information in the readiest and most intelligible way.

In addition to the ordinary narrative of events, which might be looked for in a view of the times, the book has two specialities in the reprint of the author's speeches bearing on the subjects, or of such portions of them as he still chooses to adopt, and the use of the unpublished papers of General Jackson which are to be drawn upon.

Mr. Benton's opportunities as an actor and eye-witness, give him great advantages in this species of historical memoir—for such it is, neither exactly history nor biography. In his preface he quotes Macaulay, and justly claims the prestige of his experience in public affairs for his work. If Gibbon, and Fox, and Mackintosh, wrote better for being Parliament men, Mr. Benton can set forth as well for his story the *quorum pars magna fui*. "I was," says he, "in the Senate the whole time of which I write—an active, business member, attending and attentive—in the confidence of half the administrations, and a close observer of the others—had an inside view of transactions of which the public saw only the outside, and of many of which the two sides were very different—saw the secret springs and hidden machinery by which men and parties were to be moved, and measures promoted or thwarted—saw patriotism and ambition at their respective labors, and was generally able to discriminate between them."

While the second volume was in progress, early in 1855, Mr. Benton's house at Washington was destroyed by fire, and his library and manuscripts perished in the flames. A letter which he wrote to his publishers will show the prospects of the work, and the prominent characteristics of the man in energy and literary industry.

WASHINGTON CITY, *March* 2, 1855.

Messrs. D. Appleton & Co.:

Gentlemen: It is not necessary to tell you what has happened, *cela va sans dire.* The point is, the effect—and what is to be done. The answer is, *first*, it will more than double my labor; *next*, it will delay the second volume say six months, or until the spring of 1856; *third*, there are some things lost which cannot be replaced, but which were chiefly for a posthumous volume, not coming under our present agreement—most of it composed of correspondence, such as I had deemed worthy, both for the character of the writers and the matter, to go to posterity. For the rest, I go to work immediately (after my return from St. Louis), and work incessantly.

Yours truly
THOMAS H. BENTON.

Mr. Benton's style as an orator is calm, full, and dignified. He speaks with ease, displays his subject with practised art; is indefatigable in the collection of his material, and convincing in its use. His devotion of late to the advancement of discovery and civilization in the great West, coupled with the labors of his son-in-law Fremont, have added a general interest to his more strictly Congressional reputation. His advocacy of the Pacific Railroad, and other measures, connects his name with scientific progress.

CHARACTER OF NATHANIEL MACON—FROM THE THIRTY YEARS' VIEW.

Philosophic in his temperament and wise in his conduct, governed in all his actions by reason and judgment, and deeply embued with Bible images, this virtuous and patriotic man (whom Mr. Jefferson called "the last of the Romans") had long fixed the term of his political existence at the age which the Psalmist assigns for the limit of manly life: "The days of our years are threescore years and ten; and if by reason of strength they be fourscore years, yet is their strength labor and sorrow, for it is soon cut off, and we fly away." He touched that age in 1828; and true to all his purposes, he was true to his resolve in this, and executed it with the quietude and indifference of an ordinary transaction. He was in the middle of a third senatorial term, and in the full possession of all his faculties of mind and body; but his time for retirement had come—the time fixed by himself; but fixed upon conviction and for well considered reasons, and inexorable to him as if fixed by fate. To the friends who urged him to remain to the end of his term, and who insisted that his mind was as good as ever, he would answer, that it was good enough yet to let him know that he ought to quit office before his mind quit him, and that he did not mean to risk the fate of the Archbishop of Grenada. He resigned his senatorial honors as he had worn them—meekly, unostentatiously, in a letter of thanks and gratitude to the General Assembly of his State;—and gave to repose at home that interval of thought and quietude which every wise man would wish to place between the turmoil of life and the stillness of eternity. He had nine years of this tranquil enjoyment, and died without pain or suffering June 29th, 1837,—characteristic in death as in life. It was eight o'clock in the morning when he felt that the supreme hour had come, had himself full-dressed with his habitual neatness, walked in the room and lay upon the bed, by turns conversing kindly with those who were about him, and showing by his conduct that he was ready and waiting, but hurrying nothing. It was the death of Socrates, all but the hemlock, and in that full faith of which the Grecian sage had only a glimmering. He directed his own grave on the point of a sterile ridge (where nobody would wish to plough), and covered with a pile of rough flint-stone (which nobody would wish to build with), deeming this sterility and the uselessness of this rock the best security for that undisturbed repose of the bones which is still desirable to those who are indifferent to monuments.

In almost all strongly-marked characters there is usually some incident or sign, in early life, which shows that character, and reveals to the close observer the type of the future man. So it was with Mr. Macon. His firmness, his patriotism, his self-denial, his devotion to duty and disregard of office and emolument; his modesty, integrity, self-control, and subjection of conduct to the convictions of reason and the dictates of virtue, all so steadily exemplified in a long life, were all shown from the early age of eighteen, in the miniature representation of individual action, and only confirmed in the subsequent public exhibitions of a long, beautiful, and exalted career.

HENRY A. S. DEARBORN.

HENRY ALEXANDER SCAMMELL DEARBORN was born at Exeter, New Hampshire, in 1783. His father was Gen. Henry Dearborn, an officer in the American Revolution, the author of a MS. journal of his expedition to Canada, imprisonment in Quebec, expedition to Wyoming, and other adventures during the war, printed in his life by his son. H. A. S. Dearborn was educated at William and Mary College, studied law with Wirt and Story; practised in Portland, and established himself in Boston, where he succeeded his father as Collector of the Port in 1813. He took a prominent part in the military and political affairs of Massachusetts, was a member of the convention to revise the constitution of the state legislature, and from 1831 to 1833 was member of Congress from the Norfolk District. He was Mayor of Roxbury from 1847 till his death, July 29, 1851.

General Dearborn published, in 1819, a *Memoir on the Commerce of the Black Sea*, in two volumes 8vo., with a quarto volume of maps (Boston); in 1839, *Letters on the Internal Improvements and Commerce of the West* (Boston); and was also the author of a *Biography of Commodore Bainbridge*, and of his father. He left many manuscripts unpublished, among which are a Diary in forty-five volumes, a Memoir of his father-in-law, Col. Wm. R. Lee of Marblehead, and a History of the Battle of Bunker's Hill.*

JOHN SANDERSON,

THE author of the lively sketches of French society in that attractive book *The American in Paris*, was a native of Pennsylvania, born in Carlisle in 1783. He first studied the classics (favorite passages of which, at the close of his life, he interwove in his essays with happy effect) with a clergyman of his region, travelling some seven miles from home daily for his instruction. In 1806 he studied law at Philadelphia, but requiring a means of immediate support became a teacher in the Clermont Seminary, afterwards marrying the daughter of the principal, John T. Carré, and becoming a partner in the enterprise. He contributed to the *Port Folio*, and wrote occasionally for the *Aurora*. The *Lives of the Signers of the Declaration of Independence*, published in 1820, were written by himself and his brother. Our author's share of this work was the composition of the first and second volumes. In 1833 he defended his favorite classical literature, as a branch of study, in the letters signed *Robertjeot*, directed against a plan of education proposed for the Girard College. His health failing he embarked for Havre in the summer of 1835, and remained in Paris nearly a year, writing the series of descriptive papers which he afterwards published in 1838, entitled *Sketches of Paris: in Familiar Letters to his Friends, by an American Gentleman*. He also visited England before his return, of which he commenced a similar account in several papers in the *Knickerbocker Magazine*.

Returning to America he taught the Greek and Latin languages in the Philadelphia High-School. Though broken in health he maintained a habit of cheerfulness, exercising his talent in humor and sarcasm. Griswold, who saw him in his last days, speaks of his mirth and tenderness, and fondness for his daughter, and his cherished recollections of his departed wife.† He died at Philadelphia, April 5, 1844.

The peculiar merit of his Sketches of Paris consists in their light French tone of enjoyment. He caught the spirit of the place and admirably transfused it into the style of his letters, mingled with quotations from Ovid and Horace, and with an occasional freedom of expression borrowed from the gay memories of the capital of which he was writing.

THE PARISIAN "PENSION."

If a gentleman comes to Paris in the dog-days, when his countrymen are spread over Europe, at watering-places and elsewhere, and when every soul of a French man is out of town—if he is used to love his friends at home, and be loved by them, and to see them gather around him in the evenings—let

* Loring's Boston Orators, p. 360–4.
† Prose Writers of America.

him not set a foot in that unnatural thing, a bachelor's apartment in a furnished hotel, to live alone, to eat alone, and to sleep alone! If he does, let him take leave of his wife and children, and settle up his affairs. Nor let him seek company at the Tavern Ordinary; here the guest arrives just at the hour, hangs up his hat, sits down in his usual place, crosses his legs, runs his fingers through his hair, dines, and then disappears, all the year round, without farther acquaintance. But let him look out a "Pension," having an amiable landlady, or, which is the same, amiable lodgers. He will become domiciliated here after some time, and find some relief from one of the trying situations of life. You know nothing yet, happily, of the solitude, the desolation of a populous city to a stranger. How often did I wish, during the first three months, for a cot by the side of some hoar hill of the Mahonoy. Go to a "Pension," especially if you are a suckling child, like me, in the ways of the world; and the lady of the house, usually a pretty woman, will feel it enjoined upon her humanity to counsel and protect you, and comfort you, or she will manage an acquaintance between you and some countess or baroness, who lodges with her, or at some neighbor's. I live now with a most spiritual little creature; she tells me so many obliging lies, and no offensive truths, which I take to be the perfection of politeness in a landlady; and she admits me to her private parties—little family "re-unions"—where I play at loto with Madame Thomas, and her three amiable daughters, just for a little cider, or cakes, or chestnuts, to keep up the spirit of the play; and then we have a song, a solo on the violin, or harp, and then a dance; and finally, we play at little games, which inflict kisses, embraces, and other such penalties. French people are always so merry, whatever be the amusement; they never let conversation flag, and I don't see any reason it should. One, for example, begins to talk of Paris, then the Passage Panorama, then of Mrs. Alexander's fine cakes, and then the pretty girl that sits behind the counter, and then of pretty girls that sit anywhere; and so one just lets oneself run with the association of ideas, or one makes a digression from the main story, and returns or not, just as one pleases. A Frenchman is always a mimic, an actor, and all that nonsense which we suffer to go to waste in our country, he economises for the enjoyment of society.

I am settled down in the family; I am adopted; the lady gives me to be sure now and then "a chance," as she calls it, of a ticket in a lottery ("the only one left"), of some distinguished lady now reduced, or some lady who has had three children, and is likely for the fourth, where one never draws anything; or "a chance" of conducting her and a pretty cousin of hers, who has taken a fancy to me, who adores the innocency of American manners, and hates the dissipation of the French, to the play. Have you never felt the pleasure of letting yourself be duped? Have you never felt the pleasure of letting your little bark float down the stream when you knew the port lay the other way. I look upon all this as a cheap return for the kindnesses I have so much need of; I am anxious to be cheated, and the truth is, if you do not let a French landlady cheat you now and then, she will drop your acquaintance. Never dispute any small items overcharged in her monthly bill; or she that was smooth as the ermine will be suddenly bristled as the porcupine; and why, for the sake of limiting some petty encroachment upon your purse, should you turn the bright heaven of her pretty face into a hurricane? Your actions should always leave a suspicion you are rich, and then you are sure she will anticipate every want and wish you may have with the liveliest affection; she will be all ravishment at your successes; she will be in an abyss of chagrin at your disappointments. *Helas! oh, mon Dieu!* and if you cry, she will cry with you! We love money well enough in America, but we do not feel such touches of human kindness, and cannot work ourselves up into such fits of amiability, for those who have it. I do not say it is hypocrisy; a Frenchwoman really does love you if you have a long purse; and if you have not (I do not say it is hypocrisy neither), she really does hate you.

A great advantage to a French landlady is the sweetness and variety of her smile; a quality in which Frenchwomen excel universally. Our Madame Gibou keeps her little artillery at play during the whole of the dinner-time, and has brought her smile under such a discipline as to suit it exactly to the passion to be represented, or the dignity of the person with whom she exchanges looks. You can tell any one who is in arrears as if you were her private secretary, or the wealth and liberality of a guest better than his banker, by her smile. If it be a surly knave who counts the pennies with her, the little thing is strangled in its birth; and if one who owes his meals, it miscarries altogether; and for a mere visiter she lets off one worth only three francs and a half; but if a favorite, who never looks into the particulars of her bill and takes her lottery tickets, then you will see the whole heaven of her face in a blaze, and it does not expire suddenly, but like the fine twilight of a summer evening, dies away gently on her lips. Sometimes I have seen one flash out like a squib, and leave you at once in the dark; it had lit on the wrong person; and at other times I have seen one struggling long for its life; I have watched it while it was gasping its last; she has a way too of knocking a smile on the head; I observed one at dinner to-day, from the very height and bloom of health fall down and die without a kick.

SELLECK OSBORN.

SELLECK OSBORN was born at Trumbull, Fairfield County, Conn., in the year 1788. He received the rudiments of an ordinary English education, and at the age of twelve was placed in a newspaper printing-office at Danbury. During his apprenticeship he wrote several short poems, and shortly after its expiration, on his attaining the age of twenty-one, became the editor of a Jeffersonian paper called the *Witness*. The federalists were largely in the majority in the county, and the journal, which was conducted in a violent tone, had many enemies. One of these sued for an alleged libel which appeared in its columns. The editor was found guilty, and sentenced to pay a heavy fine. In default of payment he was confined in the Litchfield jail, greatly to the indignation of his political friends, who marched in procession to the place of his confinement. After his release he returned to his paper, which he edited for several years. About 1809 he married a lady of New Bedford, who died a few years after. During the war of 1812–14 he served as a captain in the United States army, and was stationed on the Canada frontier. After the peace he resumed the editorial profession at Bennington, Vermont, where he remained a number of years, and then removed to Wilmington, Delaware. He was for a short time during the year 1825 the editor of a paper devoted to the support of John C. Calhoun for the Presidency. He next removed to Philadelphia, where he died in October, 1826.

His small volume of *Poems, Moral, Sentimental, and Satirical*, published at Boston in 1823, is a selection of his fugitive pieces written at various periods, mostly in a feeble vein of morality, with some crude attempts at humor. A sketch of Thanksgiving Day, in a descriptive account of New England, has a homely air of reality.

NEW ENGLAND.

Nurse of my earliest hope, my ripest joy!
What theme more grateful could my verse employ?
Thy copious breast is bounteous, if not fair—
My heart unweaned, still clings and nestles there.
Though doomed to exile by stern Fate's decree,
Still memory and mind can visit thee.
Borne on Imagination's buoyant wings,
Again I view thy groves, thy hills, thy springs;
Thy coy, reluctant, but relenting soil,
Woo'd and subdued by persevering toil—
Thy various coast; where frowns the rocky shore,
Where the rude breakers beat with ceaseless roar;
Or where the lazy billows slowly reach
And gambol on the far extended beach—
Where islands in fantastic groups are seen,
And pigmy promontories, crowned with green;
Where rise the hulks that float on distant seas,
In tropic climes that scorch, or climes that freeze,
Whose prows, directed by each hardy crew,
The giant whale or valued cod pursue—
Where many a fearless tar was early bred,
The light of victory round our flag to spread:
To scan all climes and visit every realm—
And o'er earth's surface guide the subject helm.

WASHINGTON IRVING.

WASHINGTON IRVING was born April 3, 1783, in the city of New York,* the youngest son of a merchant, William Irving, a native of Scotland, who had married an English lady and been settled in his new country some twenty years. His early education was much influenced by the tastes of his brothers, who had occupied themselves with literature; and he fell in himself with a stock of the best old English authors, the study of which generously unfolded his happy natural disposition. Chaucer and Spenser were his early favorites. He had an ordinary school education, and at the age of sixteen commenced the study of the law. In 1802 he wrote for the *Morning Chronicle*, a New York paper, edited by his brother Dr. Peter Irving, a series of essays on the theatres, manners of the town, and kindred topics, with the signature of Jonathan Oldstyle. A pamphlet edition of these was published in 1824 without the sanction of the author. In 1804, led by some symptoms of ill health, apparently of a pulmonary affection, he visited the South of Europe, sailing from New York for Bordeaux in May, and travelling on his arrival by Nice to Genoa, where he passed two months, thence to Messina in Sicily, making a tour of that island, and crossing from Palermo to Naples. Thence through Italy and Switzerland to France, where he resided several months in Paris, and reached England through Flanders and Holland, gathering a stock of materials for his future writings. While at Rome on this journey he became acquainted with Washington Allston, and so far participated in his studies as to meditate for a time the profession of a painter, for which he has naturally a taste. In the reminiscences of Allston from Irving's pen, in previous pages of this work, will be found an interesting account of this episode of artistical life and distinguished friendship.*

After an absence of two years he returned to New York in March, 1806. He took up again the study of the law, and was admitted at the close of the year attorney-at-law. He, however, never practised the profession.

Salmagundi; or, the Whim-Whams and Opinions of Launcelot Langstaff, Esq., and others, was at that time projected, and the publication commenced in a series of small eighteenmo numbers, appearing about once a fortnight from the Shakespeare Gallery of Longworth. The first is dated January 24, 1807. It was continued for a year, through twenty numbers. Paulding wrote a good portion of this work, William Irving the poetry, and Washington Irving the remainder. The humors of the day are hit off in this squib in so agreeable a style that it is still read with interest, what was piquant gossip then being amusing history now. It was the intention of Irving to have extended these papers by carrying out the invention and marrying Will Wizard to the eldest Miss Cockloft—with, of course, a grand wedding at Cockloft Hall, the original of which mansion was a veritable edifice owned by Gouverneur Kemble on the Passaic, a favorite resort of Geoffrey Crayon in his youthful days. Among other originals of these sketches we have heard it mentioned that some of the peculiarities of Dennie, the author, were hit off in the character of Launcelot Langstaff. The well-defined picture of "My Uncle John" is understood to have been from the pen of Paulding; his, too, was the original sketch of the paper entitled "Autumnal Reflections," though extended and wrought up by Irving.

Knickerbocker's History of New York† was published in December, 1809. It was commenced by Washington Irving in company with his brother Peter Irving, with the idea of parodying a handbook, which had just appeared, entitled A Picture of New York. In emulation of an historical account in that production, it was to burlesque the local records, and describe in an amusing way the habits and statistics of the town. Dr. Irving departing for Europe, and leaving the work solely with his brother, the latter confined it to the historical part, which had grown in his hands into a long comic history. The humorous capabilities of the subject were turned to account in the happiest way, the fun being broad enough not to be confounded with the realities, though a venerable clergyman, who was on the lookout for a history upon that subject from a clerical brother, is said to have begun the work in good faith, and to have been only gradually warmed to a consciousness of the joke. The highest honor ever paid to the authentic history of Knickerbocker was the quotation from it—in good Latin

* The house in which he was born was next to the corner of Fulton street in William, now, by the widening of the former street, on the corner, and one of the Washington Stores.

* *Ante*, p. 14.

† A History of New York, from the Beginning of the World to the end of the Dutch Dynasty; containing, among many surprising and curious matters, the Unutterable Ponderings of Walter the Doubter; the Disastrous Projects of William the Testy; and the Chivalric Achievements of Peter the Headstrong; the three Dutch Governors of New Amsterdam: being the only Authentic History of the Times that ever hath been or ever will be published. By Diedrich Knickerbocker.

phrase—by Goeller, German annotator of Thucydides, in illustration of a passage of the Greek author: Addo locum Washingtonis Irvingii *Hist. Novi Eboraci*, lib. vii. cap. 5.* To humor the pleasantry preliminary advertisements were inserted before the publication in the *Evening Post*, calling for information of "a small elderly gentleman, dressed in an old black coat and cocked hat, by the name of *Knickerbocker*," etc., who had left his lodgings at the Columbian Hotel in Mulberry street; then a statement that the old gentleman had left "a very curious kind of a written book in his room," followed by the announcement of the actual book "in two volumes duodecimo, price three dollars," from the publishers Inskeep and Bradford—to pay the bill of his landlord.

To the last revised edition of this work in 1850, which contains some very pleasant additions, the author has prefixed an "Apology," which, however, offers little satisfaction to the irate families who have considered their honor aggrieved by the publication of this extravagant burlesque—for the incorrigible author insists upon it that he has brought the old Dutch manners and times into notice, as proved by the innumerable Knickerbocker hotels, steamboats, ice-carts, and other appropriations of the name; and has added not only to the general hilarity but to the harmony of the city, the popular traditions which he has set in vogue "forming a convivial currency; linking our whole community together in good humor and good fellowship; the rallying points of home feeling; the seasoning of civic festivities; the staple of local tales and local pleasantries."† We should attach little importance to the subject had it not been made a matter of comment in the New York Historical Society, in an address before which body it was gravely held up to reprehension. The truth of the matter is that the historians should have occupied the ground earlier, if possible, and not have given the first advantage to the humorist. We do not find, however, that the burlesque has at all damaged the subject in the hands of Mr. Brodhead, who has at length brought to bear a system of original investigation and historical inquiry upon the worthy Dutch settlers of New Amsterdam; or deteriorated a whit the learned labors of O'Callaghan, who has illustrated the early Dutch annals with faithful diligence. The style of *Knickerbocker* is of great felicity. There is just enough flavor of English classical reading to give the riant, original material, the highest gusto. The descriptions of nature and manners are occasionally very happy in a serious way, and the satire is, much of it, of that universal character which will bear transplantation to wider scenes and interests. The laughter-compelling humor is irresistible, and we may readily believe the story of that arch wag himself, Judge Brackenridge, exploding over a copy of the work, which he had smuggled with him to the bench.

In 1810 Irving wrote a biographical sketch of the poet Campbell, which was prefixed to an edition of the poet's works published in Philadelphia. The circumstance which led to this was Irving's acquaintance with Archibald Campbell, a brother of the author, who was then residing in New York, and who was desirous of finding a purchaser for an American edition of "O'Connor's Child," which he had just received from London. To facilitate this object Irving wrote the preliminary sketch from facts furnished by his brother. It afterwards led to a personal acquaintance between the two authors when Irving visited England. In 1850, after Campbell's death, when his "Life and Letters," edited by Dr. Beattie, were being republished by the Harpers in New York, Irving was applied to for a few preliminary words of introduction. He wrote a letter, prefixed to the volumes, in which he speaks gracefully and nobly of his acquaintance with Campbell, many of the virtues of whose private life were first disclosed to the public in Dr. Beattie's publication.

After the perpetration of the *Knickerbocker*, Irving engaged with two of his brothers in mercantile business, as a silent partner. The second war with Great Britain then broke out, when he took part in the spirit of the day; edited the *Analectic Magazine*, published at Philadelphia, by Moses Thomas, writing an eloquent series of biographies, accompanying portraits of the American Naval Captains; and, in 1814, joined the military staff of Governor Tompkins as aide-de-camp and military secretary, with the title of Colonel. When the war was ended the next year, he sailed for Liverpool in the month of May, made excursions into Wales, some of the finest counties of England, and to the Highlands of Scotland, intending to visit the continent. The commercial revulsions which followed the war overwhelmed the house with which he was connected, and he was thrown upon his resources as an author. Repairing to London his excursions and his observations on rural life and manners furnished materials for some of the most attractive portions of his *Sketch Book*. The publication of this was commenced in New York, in large octavo pamphlets, a style afterwards adopted by Dana in his "Idle Man," and Longfellow in his "Outre Mer." When the first volume had appeared in this form it attracted the notice of Jerdan, who received a copy brought over from America by a passenger, republished some of the papers in his *Literary Gazette*,* and a reprint of the whole was in prospect by some bookseller, when the author applied to Murray to undertake the work. The answer was civil, but the publisher declined it. Irving then addressed Sir Walter Scott, by whom he had previously been cordially received at Abbotsford, on his visit in 1819, of which he has given so agreeable an account in the paper in the Crayon Miscellany,† to secure his assistance with Constable. Scott, in the most friendly manner, promised his aid, and offered Irving the editorial chair of a weekly periodical to be established at Edinburgh, with a salary of five hundred pounds, but he had too vivid a sense of the toils and responsibilities of such an office to ac-

* Classical Museum, Oct., 1849.

† The author's Apology, preface to edition of Knickerbocker, 1848.

* Autobiography of William Jerdan, ii. 288.

† Scott had been an admirer of Irving's early writings, having received a copy of Knickerbocker, not long after its publication, through Mr. Henry Brevoort. Irving carried him a letter of introduction from Campbell, to whom Scott sent a message, thanking him for "one of the best and pleasantest acquaintances I have made this many a day."—Lockhart's Scott, ch. xxxix.

cept it. He put the first volume of the *Sketch Book* to press at his own expense, with John Miller, February, 1820; it was getting along tolerably, when the bookseller failed in the first month. Scott came to London at this time, reopened the matter with Murray, who issued the entire work, and thenceforward Irving had a publisher for his successive works, "conducting himself in all his dealings with that fair, open, and liberal spirit which had obtained for him the well merited appellation of the Prince of Booksellers."* Murray bought the copyright for two hundred pounds, which he subsequently increased to four hundred, with the success of the work.

Washington Irving

In 1820 Irving took up his residence for a year in Paris, where he became acquainted with the poet Moore, and enjoyed his intimacy with the best English society in the metropolis. In the spring of 1821, Moore speaks in his Diary of Irving's being hard at work writing his Bracebridge Hall, having in the course of ten days written about one hundred and thirty pages of the size of those in the Sketch Book, adding, "this is amazing rapidity." *Bracebridge Hall, or the Humourists*, is a series of sketches of English rural life, holiday customs, and refined village character of Sir Roger de Coverley portraiture, centring about a fine old establishment in Yorkshire. The characters of Master Simon, Jack Tibbetts, and General Harbottle do credit to the school of Goldsmith and Addison. The Stout Gentleman, the Village Choir, the delicate story of Annette Delarbre display the best powers of the author; while the episodes of the Dutch tales of Dolph Heyliger and the Storm Ship relieve the monotony of the English description.

The winter of 1822 was passed by Irving at Dresden. He returned to Paris in 1823, and in the December of the following year published his *Tales of a Traveller*, with the stories of the Nervous Gentleman, including that fine piece of animal spirits and picturesque description, the Bold Dragoon, the series of pictures of literary life in Buckthorne and his Friends—in which there is some of his happiest writing, blending humor, sentiment, and a kindly indulgence for the failures of life,—the romantic Italian Stories, and, as in the preceding work, a sequel of New World legends of Dutchmen and others, built upon the writer's invention in the expansion of the fertile theme of Captain Kidd, the well known piratical and money-concealing adventurer. For this work Moore tells us that Murray gave Irving fifteen hundred pounds, and "he might have had two thousand."* These books were still published in the old form in numbers in New York, simultaneously with their English appearance.

The following winter of 1825 was passed by Irving in the South of France, and early in the next year he went to Madrid, at the suggestion of Alexander H. Everett, then minister to Spain, for the purpose of translating the important series of new documents relating to the voyages of Columbus, just collected by Navarrete. For a translation was substituted the *History of the Life and Voyages of Christopher Columbus*,† to which the *Voyages and Discoveries of the Companions of Columbus* were afterwards added. The Columbus was published in 1828, and the English edition brought its author three thousand guineas. A tour to the South of Spain in this and the following year provided the materials for *A Chronicle of the Conquest of Grenada*, and *The Alhambra, or the New Sketch Book*. The latter is dedicated, May, 1832, to Wilkie, the artist, who was a companion with the author in some of his excursions. Irving spent three months in the old Moorish palace. He some time after in America, published his *Legends of the Conquest of Spain* (in 1835), which with his *Mahomet and his Successors* (1849–50) complete a series of Spanish and Moorish subjects, marked by the same genial and poetic treatment; the fancy of the writer evidently luxuriating in the personal freedom of movement of his heroes, their humor of individual character, and the warm oriental coloring of the theme.

In July, 1829, Irving left Spain for England, having been appointed Secretary of Legation to the American Embassy at London, when Mr. M'Lane was Minister. He retired on the arrival of Van Buren. The University of Oxford conferred on him in 1831 the degree of LL.D. He arrived in America on his return, May 21, 1832, after an absence of seventeen years, and his friends at New York commemorated his arrival by a public dinner, at which Chancellor Kent presided. A few months later, in the summer, Irving accompanied Mr. Ellsworth, one of the commissioners for removing the Indian tribes west of the Mississippi, in his journey, which he has described in his *Tour on the Prairies*, published in the *Crayon Miscellany* in 1835. His *Abbotsford and Newstead Abbey* formed another volume of the series. In 1836 he published his

* Author's Preface to the Revised Edition of Sketch Book, 1848.

* Diary, 17 June, 1824.

† The Columbus gained him a high honor in the receipt of one of the fifty-guinea gold medals, provided by George IV. for eminence in historical writing, its companion being assigned to Hallam.

Astoria, attracted to the subject by an early fondness for the character of the trappers and voyageurs whom he had seen in his youth in Canada. He was assisted in the preparation of this work by his nephew, Mr. Pierre M. Irving.*

Another undertaking of a similar character was his *Adventures of Captain Bonneville, U.S.A., in the Rocky Mountains and the Far West*, prepared from the MSS. of that traveller, but made an original work by the observation and style of the writer. From 1839, for two years, Irving contributed a series of papers monthly to the *Knickerbocker Magazine*. Among these tales and sketches are two narratives, *The Early Experiences of Ralph Ringwood*, and *Mountjoy, or some Passages out of the Life of a Castle Builder*. A number of these papers, with some others from the English Annuals and other sources, have been collected in 1855 in a volume, with the title of Wolfert's Roost.

In February, 1842, he was appointed Minister to Spain, an office which he occupied for the next four years. He then returned home, and has since

Sunnyside.

continued to reside at his cottage residence, "Sunnyside," near Tarrytown, on the banks of the Hudson, the very spot which he had described years before in the "Legend of Sleepy Hollow," as the castle of the Heer van Tassel, illuminated with the throng of country beauties, and that prodigality of "a genuine Dutch country tea-table," in the presence of which the mouth of the schoolmaster Ichabod watered, and his skin dilated as it embraced the ample cheer. Of this neighborhood, Irving also wrote in that tale of his youth:—"If ever I should wish for a retreat, whither I might steal from the world and its distractions, and dream quietly away the remainder of a troubled life, I know of none more promising than this little valley." At this retreat since his last return from Europe he has lived, in the midst of a family circle composed of his brother and his nieces, hospitably entertaining his friends, occasionally visiting different portions of the country, and employing his pen in the composition of his *Life of Washington*, the first volume of which, as we write, is in progress through the press. The preparation of this, the publication of *Oliver Goldsmith, a Biography*, an enlargement of a life which he had prefixed to an edition in Paris of that author's works, adapting the researches of Prior and Forster, and a revised edition of his own writings published by Putnam, of which several of the volumes have been published in a more costly form, enriched by the vigorous and refined designs of Darley, have been his latest literary productions.

In estimating the genius of Irving, we can hardly attach too high a value to the refined qualities and genial humor which have made his writings favorites wherever the English language is read. The charm is in the proportion, the keeping, the happy vein which inspires happiness in return. It is the felicity of but few authors, out of the vast stock of English literature, to delight equally young and old. The tales of Irving are the favorite authors of childhood, and their good humor and amenity can please where most literature is weariness, in the sick room of the convalescent. Every influence which breathes from these writings is good and generous. Their sentiment is always just and manly, without cant or affectation; their humor is always within the bounds of propriety. They have a fresh inspiration of American nature, which is not the less nature for the art with which it is adorned. The color of personality attaches us throughout to the author, whose humor of character is always to be felt. This happy art of presenting rude and confused objects in an orderly pleasurable aspect, everywhere to be met with in the pages of Irving, is one of the most beneficent in literature. The philosopher Hume said a turn for humor was worth to him ten thousand a year, and it is this gift which the writings of Irving impart. To this quality is allied an active fancy and poetic imagination, many of the choicest passages of Irving being interpenetrated by this vivifying power. On one or two occasions only, we believe, in some stanzas to the Passaic River, some delicate lines, descriptive of a painting by Gilbert Stuart Newton,* and a theatrical address, once pronounced by Cooper at the Park Theatre, has he ever put pen to verse; but he is an essential poet in prose, in many exquisite passages of vivid description from Westminster Abbey and English rural scenery to the waste beauties of the great region beyond the Mississippi. Parallel with the ruder but more

* An interesting communication from Irving on this subject, contradicting a story of Mr. Astor having paid him five thousand dollars to "take up the MSS." will be found in the Literary World for November 22, 1851. The only compensation Irving received was his share of the profits from his publisher.

* An old philosopher is reading, in this picture, from a folio, to a young beauty who is asleep in a chair on the other side of the table. It is a fine summer's day, and the warm atmosphere is let in through the open casement. These are the lines which Irving wrote at his friend Newton's request, as a description of the picture:—

THE DULL LECTURE.

Frostie age, frostie age,
  Vain all thy learning;
Drowsie page, drowsie page,
  Evermore turning.

Young head no lore will heed,
  Young heart's a reckless rover,
Young beauty, while you read,
  Sleeping dreams of absent lover.

robust and athletic writings of Cooper, the volumes of Irving improved American society, and rendered the national name beloved and respected abroad. Both, to the honor of the country, have never lacked admirers from the start; both have been followed by diligent schools of imitators, and their books will continue to be read together, with equal honor, as the complement of each other.

We may here properly introduce some notices of the elder brothers of Washington Irving, who, together with himself, established the family reputation in literature. They were four:—William, Peter, Ebenezer, and John Treat. All were engaged in literary or professional life except Ebenezer, who pursued a mercantile career.

WILLIAM IRVING was born in New York, August 15, 1766. He commenced life as an Indian trader, residing at Johnstown and Caughawaga on the Mohawk, from 1787 to 1791. He married a sister of the author, James K. Paulding, November 7, 1793. At the date of Salmagundi he was a merchant at New York, with the character of a man of wit and refinement, who had added to a natural genial temperament the extensive resources of observation, and a fresh experience of the world, gathered in his border life. The part which he took in Salmagundi was chiefly the contribution of the poetical pieces, which are mainly from his pen—the letters and proclamations, the humorous and sentimental verse, "from the mill of Pindar Cockloft." These poems are in a happy vein, and if separately published with the author's name, would have long since given him a distinct place in the collections of the American literati. In furtherance of the prevailing humor of the book, they celebrate the simpler manners of former days, and the eccentricities and scandals of the passing time. The satire is pungent and good-natured, and the numbers felicitous. A few stanzas will show how pleasantly Pindar Cockloft, Esq., blended mirth with sentiment.

VISION OF TWO SISTERS IN A BALL-ROOM.

How oft I breathe the inward sigh,
And feel the dew-drop in my eye,
When I behold some beauteous frame,
Divine in everything but name,
Just venturing, in the tender age,
On Fashion's late new-fangled stage!
Where soon the guileless heart shall cease
To beat in artlessness and peace;
Where all the flowers of gay delight
With which youth decks its prospects bright,
Shall wither 'mid the cares—the strife—
The cold realities of life!

Thus lately, in my careless mood,
As I the world of fashion viewed,
While celebrating *great and small*,
That grand *solemnity*—a ball,
My roving vision chanced to light
On two sweet forms, divinely bright;
Two sister nymphs, alike in face,
In mien, in loveliness and grace;
Twin rose-buds, bursting into bloom,
In all their brilliance and perfume;
Like those fair forms that often beam,
Upon the eastern poet's dream:
For Eden had each lovely maid
In native innocence arrayed,—
And heaven itself had almost shed
Its sacred halo round each head!

They seemed, just entering hand in hand,
To cautious tread this fairy land;
To take a timid hasty view,
Enchanted with a scene so new.
The modest blush, untaught by art,
Bespoke their purity of heart;
And every timorous act unfurled
Two souls unspotted by the world.

Oh, how these strangers joyed my sight,
And thrilled my bosom with delight!
They brought the visions of my youth
Back to my soul in all their truth,
Recalled fair spirits into day,
That time's rough hand had swept away!
Thus the bright natives from above,
Who come on messages of love,
Will bless, at rare and distant whiles,
Our sinful dwelling by their smiles!

Oh! my romance of youth is past,
Dear airy dreams too bright to last!
Yet when such forms as these appear,
I feel your soft remembrance here;
For, ah! the simple poet's heart,
On which fond love once played its part,
Still feels the soft pulsations beat,
As loth to quit their former seat.
Just like the harp's melodious wire,
Swept by a bard with heavenly fire,
Though ceased the loudly swelling strain,
Yet sweet vibrations long remain.

Full soon I found the lovely pair
Had sprung beneath a mother's care,
Hard by a neighbouring streamlet's side,
At once its ornament and pride.
The beauteous parent's tender heart
Had well fulfilled its pious part;
And, like the holy man of old,
As we're by sacred writings told,
Who, when he from his pupil sped,
Poured two-fold blessings on his head,—
So this fond mother had imprest
Her early virtues in each breast,
And as she found her stock enlarge,
Had stampt new graces on her charge.

The fair resigned the calm retreat,
Where first their souls in concert beat,
And flew on expectation's wing,
To sip the joys of life's gay spring;
To sport in fashion's splendid maze,
Where friendship fades, and love decays.
So two sweet wild flowers, near the side
Of some fair river's silver tide,
Pure as the gentle stream that laves
The green banks with its lucid waves,
Bloom beauteous in their native ground,
Diffusing heavenly fragrance round:
But should a venturous hand transfer
These blossoms to the gay parterre
Where, spite of artificial aid,
The fairest plants of nature fade;
Though they may shine supreme awhile,
Mid *pale ones* of the stranger soil,
The tender beauties soon decay,
And their sweet fragrance dies away.

Blest spirits! who enthroned in air,
Watch o'er the virtues of the fair,
And with angelic ken survey,
Their windings through life's chequered way;

Who hover round them as they glide
Down fashion's smooth deceitful tide,
And guard them o'er that stormy deep
Where Dissipation's tempests sweep:
Oh, make this inexperienced pair,
The objects of your tenderest care.
Preserve them from the languid eye,
The faded cheek—the long drawn sigh;
And let it be your constant aim
To keep the fair ones *still the same:*
Two sister hearts, unsullied, bright
As the first beam of lucid light,
That sparkled from the youthful sun,
When first his jocund race begun.
So when these hearts shall burst their shrine,
To wing their flight to realms divine,
They may to radiant mansions rise
Pure as when first they left the skies.

In his poem entitled *Tea*, which is "earnestly recommended to the attention of all maidens of a certain age," there is this introduction of the time-out-of-mind scandal associated with that beverage.

In harmless chit-chat an acquaintance they roast,
And serve up a friend, as they serve up a toast,
Some gentle *faux pas*, or some female *mistake*,
Is like sweetmeats delicious, or relished as cake;
A bit of broad scandal is like a dry crust,
It would stick in the throat, so they butter it first
With a little affected good-nature, and cry
"No body regrets the thing deeper than I."
Our young ladies nibble a good name in play,
As for pastime they nibble a biscuit away:
While with shrugs and surmises, the toothless old
dame,
As she mumbles a crust she will mumble a name;
And as the fell sisters astonished the Scot,
In predicting of Banquo's descendants the lot,
Making shadows of kings, amid flashes of light,
To appear in array and to frown in his sight;
So they conjure up spectres all hideous in hue,
Which, as shades of their neighbors, are passed in
review.

In the more concentrated social humors of that day, there was opportunity for much satirical pleasantry, which is now lost among the numerous interests of metropolitan life. The fops and belles were then notabilities and subjects to be cared for by men of wit and society. One of the clever pleasantries of William Irving of that now distant time, which has never before appeared in print, was recently called up for us by Washington Irving, who recited the lines from memory, and kindly furnished us with a copy. It is in a style formerly in vogue in the days of Pindar and Colman—a trifle in allusion to an absurdity in the whisker line of the fops in the early years of the century.

Sir! said a barber to a thing going by his shop,
Sir, said he, will you stop
And be shaved? for I see you are lathered already,
I've a sweet going razor, and a hand that is steady.
Sir! damme, said the creature standing stiff on two
feet,
Damme, Sir,—do you intend to bore one in the
street?
Don't you see that *à la mode de Cockney*, I am
shaved and drest?
Lord, Sir, said the barber, I protest,
I took that load of hair, and meal, and lard,
That lies about your mouth to be a lathered beard.
This fashion of lathered whiskers and a rat's tail
behind,
Is the most ojusest thing that you can find.
And what makes it more ojus to me, is that,
It's a sure sign of a Tory or a harry stuck cat.
For mark it when you will, I assert it before ye,
The larger the whisker the greater the tory.

To the prose of Salmagundi William Irving furnished occasional hints and sketches, which were worked up by his brother. Among these were the letters of Mustapha in numbers five and fourteen, the last of which is the amusing sketch of the political logocracy. Mr. Irving was in Congress from 1813 to 1819. He died in New York, November 9, 1821.

PETER IRVING, the second brother, was born October 30, 1771. He studied medicine, without, however, devoting himself to the profession, though it gave him the title of Doctor through life. He was proprietor and editor of the *Morning Chronicle* newspaper, the first number of which he published in New York, October 1, 1802. This paper was in the democratic interest, and for the time was a warm advocate of Burr. It had among its contributors, besides the editor's brothers, Washington and John T. Irving, Paulding, William A. Duer, and Rudolph Bunner. As a tender to the daily, a more convenient method of parrying the opposition, and serving a temporary purpose on the eve of an election, the *Corrector*, a weekly newspaper, the work of several hands, was issued anonymously in March and April, 1804. Dr. Irving would probably have returned the compliments of the articles which his brother Washington had published in his newspaper, by contributing to Salmagundi, but he was abroad travelling in Europe during the time that work was issued. He left in December, 1806, and returned in January, 1808. He then projected with his brother the work which afterwards grew in the hands of the latter into Knickerbocker's New York; but before it was written sailed for Europe at the beginning of 1809, and remained there until the spring of 1836, when he embarked for home. In this period a novel appeared from his pen in New York, from the press of Van Winkle in 1820. It was, as its title intimates, an adaptation from the French, though with extensive alterations, *Giovanni Sbogarro: A Venetian Tale [taken from the French], by Percival G———*. It is a stirring tale of piratical adventure, in a now somewhat exploded school of fiction, and is written in a happy style.

Dr. Irving did not long survive his return to America. He died at his residence in New York, June 27, 1838.

EBENEZER IRVING was born January 27, 1776. He has long since retired from mercantile life, and his residence with his brother is one of the pleasing associations of the family home at Sunnyside.

JOHN T. IRVING was born May 26, 1778. He studied the profession of the law, in which he acquired a reputation that secured him, on the creation of the Court of Common Pleas for the city and county of New York in 1821, the appointment of First Judge. He presided in this court for seventeen years, till his death. As a judge, he is worthily pronounced to have been "in many respects a model for imitation. To the strictest integrity and a strong love of justice, he united the most exact and methodical habits of business; attentive, careful, and painstaking, few judges in this state ever have been more accurate, or perhaps more generally correct in their decisions."* In his early days we have seen him a contributor to his brother's newspaper. He was fond of composition, had the family elegance of style, and wrote brilliant political verses in the party conflicts of his day. He died in New York, March 15, 1838.

Of the younger members of the family, John Treat Irving, son of Judge Irving, is the author of several works of distinguished literary merit. In 1835 he published *Indian Sketches*, a narrative of an expedition to the Pawnee Tribes, a book of lively, spirited description. He is also the author of two novels, remarkable for their striking pathetic and humorous qualities: *The Attorney*, and *Harry Harson, or the Benevolent Bachelor*. Both of these were first published in the Knickerbocker Magazine, with the signature of John Quod, the well known title to many a pleasant article in that journal. The locality is New York, and the interest of each turns upon passages of the author's profession, the law. With the graver themes of rascality are mingled the humors of low life, both sketched with a firm hand.

Theodore, the son of Ebenezer Irving, joined his uncle, Washington Irving, in Europe in 1828, and resided with him in Spain and England. From 1836 to 1849 he was Professor of History and Belles Lettres at Geneva College, and subsequently held a similar position in the Free Academy in New York. In 1835 he published an historical work, *The Conquest of Florida, by Hernando de Soto*, to the composition of which he was led by his studies in Spain. It is written with ease and elegance, and has been well received, having been recently reprinted in 1851. Mr. Irving is also the author of a devotional volume, *The Fountain of Living Waters*. In 1854 he received orders in the Protestant Episcopal Church.

THE STOUT GENTLEMAN—FROM BRACEBRIDGE HALL.

It was a rainy Sunday in the gloomy month of November. I had been detained, in the course of a journey, by a slight indisposition, from which I was recovering; but was still feverish, and obliged to keep within doors all day, in an inn of the small town of Derby. A wet Sunday in a country inn!—whoever has had the luck to experience one can alone judge of my situation. The rain pattered against the casements; the bells tolled for church with a melancholy sound. I went to the windows in quest of something to amuse the eye; but it seemed as if I had been placed completely out of the reach of all amusement. The windows of my bedroom looked out among tiled roofs and stacks of chimneys, while those of my sitting-room commanded a full view of the stable-yard. I know of nothing more calculated to make a man sick of this world than a stable-yard on a rainy day. The place was littered with wet straw that had been kicked about by travellers and stable-boys. In one corner was a stagnant pool of water, surrounding an island of muck; there were several half-drowned fowls crowded together under a cart, among which was a miserable, crest-fallen cock, drenched out of all life and spirit; his drooping tail matted, as it were, into a single feather, along which the water trickled from his back; near the cart was a half-dozing cow, chewing the cud, and standing patiently to be rained on, with wreaths of vapor rising from her reeking hide; a wall-eyed horse, tired of the loneliness of the stable, was poking his spectral head out of a window, with the rain dripping on it from the eaves; an unhappy cur, chained to a doghouse hard by, uttered something every now and then, between a bark and a yelp; a drab of a kitchen wench tramped backwards and forwards through the yard in pattens, looking as sulky as the weather itself; every thing, in short, was comfortless and forlorn, except a crew of hardened ducks, assembled like boon companions round a puddle, and making a riotous noise over their liquor.

I was lonely and listless, and wanted amusement. My room soon became insupportable. I abandoned it, and sought what is technically called the travellers'-room. This is a public room set apart at most inns for the accommodation of a class of wayfarers, called travellers, or riders; a kind of commercial knights-errant, who are incessantly scouring the kingdom in gigs, on horseback, or by coach. They are the only successors that I know of at the present day, to the knights-errant of yore. They lead the same kind of roving adventurous life, only changing the lance for a driving whip, the buckler for a pattern-card, and the coat of mail for an upper Benjamin. Instead of vindicating the charms of peerless beauty, they rove about, spreading the fame and standing of some substantial tradesman or manufacturer, and are ready at any time to bargain in his name; it being the fashion now-a-days to trade, instead of fight, with one another. As the room of the hostel, in the good old fighting times, would be hung round at night with the armor of way-worn warriors, such as coats of mail, falchions, and yawning helmets; so the travellers'-room is garnished with the harnessing of their successors, with box-coats, whips of all kinds, spurs, gaiters, and oil-cloth covered hats.

I was in hopes of finding some of these worthies to talk with, but was disappointed. There were, indeed, two or three in the room; but I could make nothing of them. One was just finishing his breakfast, quarrelling with his bread and butter, and huffing the waiter; another buttoned on a pair of gaiters, with many execrations at Boots for not having cleaned his shoes well; a third sat drumming on the table with his fingers and looking at the rain as it streamed down the window-glass; they all appeared infected by the weather, and disappeared, one after the other, without exchanging a word.

I sauntered to the window, and stood gazing at the people, picking their way to church, with petticoats hoisted midleg high, and dripping umbrellas. The bell ceased to toll, and the streets became silent. I then amused myself with watching the daughters of a tradesman opposite; who, being confined to the house for fear of wetting their Sunday finery, played off their charms at the front windows, to fascinate the chance tenants of the inn. They at length were summoned away by a vigilant vinegar-faced mother, and I had nothing further from without to amuse me.

What was I to do to pass away the long-lived day? I was sadly nervous and lonely; and everything about an inn seems calculated to make a dull day ten times duller. Old newspapers, smelling of beer and tobacco smoke, and which I had already read half a dozen times. Good for nothing books, that were worse than rainy weather. I bored myself to

* Daly's History of Judicial Tribunals of New York, p. 65.

death with an old volume of the Lady's Magazine. I read all the commonplaced names of ambitious travellers scrawled on the panes of glass; the eternal families of the Smiths, and the Browns, and the Jacksons, and the Johnsons, and all the other sons; and I deciphered several scraps of fatiguing in-window poetry which I have met with in all parts of the world.

The day continued lowering and gloomy; the slovenly, ragged, spongy clouds drifted heavily along; there was no variety even in the rain: it was one dull, continued, monotonous patter—patter—patter, excepting that now and then I was enlivened by the idea of a brisk shower, from the rattling of the drops upon a passing umbrella.

It was quite *refreshing* (if I may be allowed a hackneyed phrase of the day) when, in the course of the morning, a horn blew, and a stage-coach whirled through the street, with outside passengers stuck all over it, cowering under cotton umbrellas, and seethed together, and reeking with the steams of wet box-coats and upper Benjamins.

The sound brought out from their lurking-places a crew of vagabond boys, and vagabond dogs, and the carroty-headed hostler, and that nondescript animal yeleped Boots, and all the other vagabond race that infest the purlieus of an inn; but the bustle was transient; the coach again whirled on its way; and boy and dog, and hostler and Boots, all slunk back again to their holes; the street again became silent, and the rain continued to rain on. In fact, there was no hope of its clearing up; the barometer pointed to rainy weather: mine hostess's tortoise-shell cat sat by the fire washing her face, and rubbing her paws over her ears; and, on referring to the Almanac, I found a direful prediction stretching from the top of the page to the bottom through the whole month, "expect—much—rain—about—this—time!"

I was dreadfully hipped. The hours seemed as if they would never creep by. The very ticking of the clock became irksome. At length the stillness of the house was interrupted by the ringing of a bell. Shortly after I heard the voice of a waiter at the bar: "The stout gentleman in No. 13, wants his breakfast. Tea and bread and butter, with ham and eggs; the eggs not to be too much done."

In such a situation as mine every incident is of importance. Here was a subject of speculation presented to my mind, and ample exercise for my imagination. I am prone to paint pictures to myself, and on this occasion I had some materials to work upon. Had the guest up stairs been mentioned as Mr. Smith or Mr. Brown, or Mr. Jackson, or Mr. Johnson, or merely as "the gentleman in No. 13," it would have been a perfect blank to me. I should have thought nothing of it; but "The stout gentleman!"—the very name had something in it of the picturesque. It at once gave the size; it embodied the personage to my mind's eye, and my fancy did the rest.

He was stout, or, as some term it, lusty; in all probability, therefore, he was advanced in life, some people expanding as they grow old. By his breakfasting rather late, and in his own room, he must be a man accustomed to live at his ease, and above the necessity of early rising; no doubt a round, rosy, lusty old gentleman.

There was another violent ringing. The stout gentleman was impatient for his breakfast. He was evidently a man of importance; "well to do in the world;" accustomed to be promptly waited upon; of a keen appetite, and a little cross when hungry; "perhaps," thought I, "he may be some London Alderman; or who knows but he may be a Member of Parliament?"

The breakfast was sent up, and there was a short interval of silence; he was, doubtless, making the tea. Presently there was a violent ringing; and before it could be answered, another ringing still more violent. "Bless me! what a choleric old gentleman!" The waiter came down in a huff. The butter was rancid, the eggs were over-done, the ham was too salt:—the stout gentleman was evidently nice in his eating; one of those who eat and growl, and keep the waiter on the trot, and live in a state militant with the household.

The hostess got into a fume. I should observe that she was a brisk, coquettish woman: a little of a shrew, and something of a slammerkin, but very pretty withal; with a nincompoop for a husband, as shrews are apt to have. She rated the servants roundly for their negligence in sending up so bad a breakfast, but said not a word against the stout gentleman; by which I clearly perceived that he must be a man of consequence, entitled to make a noise and to give trouble at a country inn. Other eggs, and ham, and bread and butter were sent up. They appeared to be more graciously received; at least there was no further complaint.

I had not made many turns about the travellers'-room, when there was another ringing. Shortly afterwards there was a stir and an inquest about the house. The stout gentleman wanted the Times or the Chronicle newspaper. I set him down, therefore, for a whig; or rather, from his being so absolute and lordly where he had a chance, I suspected him of being a radical. Hunt, I had heard, was a large man; "who knows," thought I, "but it is Hunt himself!"

My curiosity began to be awakened. I inquired of the waiter who was this stout gentleman that was making all this stir; but I could get no information: nobody seemed to know his name. The landlords of bustling inns seldom trouble their heads about the names or occupations of their transient guests. The color of a coat, the shape or size of the person, is enough to suggest a travelling name. It is either the tall gentleman, or the short gentleman, or the gentleman in black, or the gentleman in snuff-color; or, as in the present instance, the stout gentleman. A designation of the kind once hit on answers every purpose, and saves all further inquiry.

Rain—rain—rain! pitiless, ceaseless rain! No such thing as putting a foot out of doors, and no occupation nor amusement within. By and by I heard some one walking over head. It was in the stout gentleman's room. He evidently was a large man by the heaviness of his tread; and an old man from his wearing such creaking soles. "He is doubtless," thought I, "some rich old square-toes of regular habits, and is now taking exercise after breakfast."

I now read all the advertisements of coaches and hotels that were stuck about the mantel-piece. The Lady's Magazine had become an abomination to me; it was as tedious as the day itself. I wandered out, not knowing what to do, and ascended again to my room. I had not been there long, when there was a squall from a neighboring bedroom. A door opened and slammed violently; a chambermaid, that I had remarked for having a ruddy, good-humored face, went down stairs in a violent flurry. The stout gentleman had been rude to her!

This sent a whole host of my deductions to the deuce in a moment. This unknown personage could not be an old gentleman; for old gentlemen are not apt to be so obstreperous to chambermaids. He could not be a young gentleman; for young gentlemen are not apt to inspire such indignation. He must be a middle-aged man, and confounded ugly into the bargain, or the girl would not have taken the matter in such terrible dudgeon. I confess I was sorely puzzled.

In a few minutes I heard the voice of my landlady. I caught a glance of her as she came tramping up stairs; her face glowing, her cap flaring, her tongue wagging the whole way. "She'd have no such doings in her house, she'd warrant. If gentlemen did spend money freely, it was no rule. She'd have no servant maid of hers treated in that way, when they were about their work, that's what she wouldn't."

As I hate squabbles, particularly with women, and above all with pretty women, I slunk back into my room, and partly closed the door, but my curiosity was too much excited not to listen. The landlady marched intrepidly to the enemy's citadel, and entered it with a storm: the door closed after her. I heard her voice in high windy clamor for a moment or two. Then it gradually subsided, like a gust of wind in a garret; then there was a laugh; then I heard nothing more.

After a little while my landlady came out with an odd smile on her face, adjusting her cap, which was a little on one side. As she went down stairs I heard the landlord ask her what was the matter; she said, "Nothing at all, only the girl's a fool."—I was more than ever perplexed what to make of this unaccountable personage, who could put a good-natured chambermaid in a passion, and send away a termagant landlady in smiles. He could not be so old, nor cross, nor ugly either.

I had to go to work at his picture again, and to paint him entirely different. I now set him down for one of those stout gentlemen that are frequently met with swaggering about the doors of country inns. Moist, merry fellows, in Belcher handkerchiefs, whose bulk is a little assisted by malt-liquors. Men who have seen the world, and been sworn at Highgate; who are used to tavern life; up to all the tricks of tapsters, and knowing in the ways of sinful publicans. Free-livers on a small scale; who are prodigal within the compass of a guinea; who call all the waiters by name, touzle the maids, gossip with the landlady at the bar, and prose over a pint of port, or a glass of negus, after dinner.

The morning wore away in forming these and similar surmises. As fast as I wove one system of belief, some movement of the unknown would completely overturn it, and throw all my thoughts again into confusion. Such are the solitary operations of a feverish mind. I was, as I have said, extremely nervous; and the continual meditation on the concerns of this invisible personage began to have its effect:—I was getting a fit of the fidgets.

Dinner-time came. I hoped the stout gentleman might dine in the travellers'-room, and that I might at length get a view of his person: but no—he had dinner served in his own room. What could be the meaning of this solitude and mystery? He could not be a radical; there was something too aristocratical in thus keeping himself apart from the rest of the world, and condemning himself to his own dull company throughout a rainy day. And then, too, he lived too well for a discontented politician. He seemed to expatiate on a variety of dishes, and to sit over his wine like a jolly friend of good living. Indeed, my doubts on this head were soon at an end; for he could not have finished his first bottle before I could faintly hear him humming a tune; and on listening, I found it to be "God save the King." 'Twas plain, then, he was no radical, but a faithful subject; one who grew loyal over his bottle, and was ready to stand by king and constitution, when he could stand by nothing else. But who could he be! My conjectures began to run wild. Was he not some personage of distinction travelling incog.? "God knows!" said I, at my wit's end; "it may be one of the royal family for aught I know, for they are all stout gentlemen!"

The weather continued rainy. The mysterious unknown kept his room, and, as far as I could judge, his chair, for I did not hear him move. In the meantime, as the day advanced, the travellers'-room began to be frequented. Some, who had just arrived, came in buttoned up in box-coats; others came home who had been dispersed about the town. Some took their dinners, and some their tea. Had I been in a different mood, I should have found entertainment in studying this peculiar class of men. There were two especially, who were regular wags of the road, and up to all the standing jokes of travellers. They had a thousand sly things to say to the waiting-maid, whom they called Louisa, and Ethelinda, and a dozen other fine names, changing the name every time, and chuckling amazingly at their own waggery. My mind, however, had become completely engrossed by the stout gentleman. He had kept my fancy in chase during a long day, and it was not now to be diverted from the scent.

The evening gradually wore away. The travellers read the papers two or three times over. Some drew round the fire and told long stories about their horses, about their adventures, their overturns, and breakings down. They discussed the credit of different merchants and different inns; and the two wags told several choice anecdotes of pretty chambermaids, and kind landladies. All this passed as they were quietly taking what they called their night-caps, that is to say, strong glasses of brandy and water and sugar, or some other mixture of the kind; after which they one after another rang for "Boots" and the chambermaid, and walked off to bed in old shoes cut down into marvellously uncomfortable slippers.

There was now only one man left; a short-legged, long-bodied, plethoric fellow, with a very large, sandy head. He sat by himself, with a glass of port wine negus, and a spoon; sipping and stirring, and meditating and sipping, until nothing was left but the spoon. He gradually fell asleep bolt upright in his chair, with the empty glass standing before him; and the candle seemed to fall asleep too, for the wick grew long, and black, and cabbaged at the end, and dimmed the little light that remained in the chamber. The gloom that now prevailed was contagious. Around hung the shapeless, and almost spectral, box-coats of departed travellers, long since buried in deep sleep. I only heard the ticking of the clock, with the deep-drawn breathings of the sleeping topers, and the drippings of the rain, drop—drop—drop, from the eaves of the house. The church bells chimed midnight. All at once the stout gentleman began to walk over head, pacing slowly backwards and forwards. There was something extremely awful in all this, especially to one in my state of nerves. These ghastly great-coats, these guttural breathings, and the creaking footsteps of this mysterious being. His steps grew fainter and fainter, and at length died away. I could bear it no longer. I was wound up to the desperation of a hero of romance. "Be he who or what he may," said I to myself, "I'll have a sight of him!" I seized a chamber candle, and hurried up to No. 13. The door stood ajar. I hesitated—I entered: the room was deserted. There stood a large, broad-bottomed elbow-chair at a table, on which was an empty tumbler, and a "Times" newspaper, and the room smelt powerfully of Stilton cheese.

The mysterious stranger had evidently but just retired. I turned off, sorely disappointed, to my room, which had been changed to the front of the house. As I went along the corridor, I saw a large pair of boots, with dirty, waxed tops, standing at the door of a bed-chamber. They doubtless belonged to the unknown; but it would not do to disturb so redoubtable a personage in his den; he might discharge a pistol, or something worse, at my head. I went to bed, therefore, and lay awake half the night in a terribly nervous state; and even when I fell asleep, I was still haunted in my dreams by the idea of the stout gentleman and his wax-topped boots.

I slept rather late the next morning, and was awakened by some stir and bustle in the house, which I could not at first comprehend; until getting more awake, I found there was a mail-coach starting from the door. Suddenly there was a cry from below, "The gentleman has forgot his umbrella! look for the gentleman's umbrella in No. 13!" I heard an immediate scampering of a chambermaid along the passage, and a shrill reply as she ran, "Here it is! here is the gentleman's umbrella!"

The mysterious stranger then was on the point of setting off. This was the only chance I should ever have of knowing him. I sprang out of bed, scrambled to the window, snatched aside the curtains, and just caught a glimpse of the rear of a person getting in at the coach-door. The skirts of a brown coat parted behind, and gave me a full view of the broad disk of a pair of drab breeches. The door closed—"all right!" was the word—the coach whirled off:—and that was all I ever saw of the stout gentleman!

THE BROKEN HEART—FROM THE SKETCH BOOK.

It is a common practice with those who have outlived the susceptibility of early feeling, or have been brought up in the gay heartlessness of dissipated life, to laugh at all love stories, and to treat the tales of romantic passion as mere fictions of novelists and poets. My observations on human nature have induced me to think otherwise. They have convinced me, that however the surface of the character may be chilled and frozen by the cares of the world, or cultivated into mere smiles by the arts of society, still there are dormant fires lurking in the depths of the coldest bosom, which, when once enkindled, become impetuous, and are sometimes desolating in their effects. Indeed, I am a true believer in the blind deity, and go to the full extent of his doctrines. Shall I confess it? I believe in broken hearts, and the possibility of dying of disappointed love. I do not, however, consider it a malady often fatal to my own sex; but I firmly believe that it withers down many a lovely woman into an early grave.

Man is the creature of interest and ambition. His nature leads him forth into the struggle and bustle of the world. Love is but the embellishment of his early life, or a song piped in the intervals of the acts. He seeks for fame, for fortune, for space in the world's thought, and dominion over his fellow men. But a woman's whole life is a history of the affections. Her heart is her world: it is there her ambition strives for empires; it is there her avarice seeks for hidden treasures. She sends forth her sympathies on adventures; she embarks her whole soul in the traffic of affection; and if shipwrecked, her case is hopeless—for it is a bankruptcy of the heart.

To a man the disappointment of love may occasion some bitter pangs: it wounds some feelings of tenderness—it blasts some prospects of felicity; but he is an active being—he may dissipate his thoughts in the whirl of varied occupation, or may plunge into the tide of pleasure; or, if the scene of disappointment be too full of painful associations, he can shift his abode at will, and taking as it were the wings of the morning, can "fly to the uttermost parts of the earth, and be at rest."

But woman's is comparatively a fixed, a secluded, and a meditative life. She is more the companion of her own thoughts and feelings; and if they are turned to ministers of sorrow, where shall she look for consolation? Her lot is to be wooed and won; and if unhappy in her love, her heart is like some fortress that has been captured and sacked, and abandoned and left desolate.

How many bright eyes grow dim—how many soft cheeks grow pale—how many lovely forms fade away into the tomb, and none can tell the cause that blighted their loveliness! As the dove will clasp its wings to its side, and cover and conceal the arrow that is preying on its vitals, so is it in the nature of women to hide from the world the pangs of wounded affection. The love of a delicate female is always shy and silent. Even when fortunate, she scarcely breathes it to herself; but when otherwise, she buries it in the recesses of her bosom, and there lets it cower and brood among the ruins of her peace. With her the desire of the heart has failed. The great charm of existence is at an end. She neglects all the cheerful exercises which gladden the spirits, quicken the pulses, and send the tide of life in healthful currents through the veins. Her rest is broken—the sweet refreshment of sleep is poisoned by melancholy dreams—"dry sorrow drinks her blood," until her enfeebled frame sinks under the slightest external injury. Look for her, after a little while, and you will find friendship weeping over her untimely grave, and wondering that one, who but lately glowed with all the radiance of health and beauty, should so speedily be brought down to "darkness and the worm." You will be told of some wintry chill, some casual indisposition, that laid her low;—but no one knows of the mental malady that previously sapped her strength, and made her so easy a prey to the spoiler.

She is like some tender tree, the pride and beauty of the grove; graceful in its form, bright in its foliage, but with the worm preying at its heart. We find it suddenly withering, when it should be most fresh and luxuriant. We see it drooping its branches to the earth, and shedding leaf by leaf; until, wasted and perished away, it falls even in the stillness of the forest; and, as we muse over the beautiful ruin, we strive in vain to recollect the blast or thunderbolt that could have smitten it with decay.

I have seen many instances of women running to waste and self-neglect, and disappearing gradually from the earth, almost as if they had been exhaled to heaven; and have repeatedly fancied that I could trace their death through the various declensions of consumption, cold, debility, languor, melancholy, until I reached the first symptom of disappointed love. But an instance of the kind was lately told to me; the circumstances are well known in the country where they happened, and I shall but give them in the manner they were related.

Every one must recollect the tragical story of young E——, the Irish patriot; it was too touching to be soon forgotten. During the troubles in Ireland he was tried, condemned, and executed, on a charge of treason. His fate made a deep impression on public sympathy. He was so young—so intelligent—so generous—so brave—so every thing that we are apt to like in a young man. His conduct under trial, too, was so lofty and intrepid. The noble indignation with which he repelled the charge of treason against his country—the eloquent vindication of his name—and his pathetic appeal to posterity, in the hopeless hour of condemnation—all these entered deeply into every generous bosom, and even his enemies lamented the stern policy that dictated his execution.

But there was one heart, whose anguish it would be impossible to describe. In happier days and fairer fortunes, he had won the affections of a beautiful and interesting girl, the daughter of a late celebrated Irish barrister. She loved him with the disinterested fervour of a woman's first and early love. When every worldly maxim arrayed itself against him; when blasted in fortune, and disgrace and danger darkened around his name, she loved him the more ardently for his very sufferings. If, then, his fate could awaken the sympathy even of his foes, what must have been the agony of her, whose whole soul was occupied by his image? Let those tell who have had the portals of the tomb suddenly closed between them and the being they most loved on earth—who have sat at its threshold, as one shut out in a cold and lonely world, from whence all that was most lovely and loving had departed.

But then the horrors of such a grave! so frightful, so dishonoured! There was nothing for memory to dwell on that could soothe the pang of separation—none of those tender, though melancholy circumstances, that endear the parting scene—nothing to melt sorrow into those blessed tears, sent, like the dews of heaven, to revive the heart in the parting hour of anguish.

To render her widowed situation more desolate, she had incurred her father's displeasure by her unfortunate attachment, and was an exile from the paternal roof. But could the sympathy and kind offices of friends have reached a spirit so shocked and driven in by horror, she would have experienced no want of consolation, for the Irish are a people of quick and generous sensibilities. The most delicate and cherishing attentions were paid her by families of wealth and distinction. She was led into society, and they tried by all kinds of occupation and amusement to dissipate her grief, and wean her from the tragical story of her love. But it was all in vain. There are some strokes of calamity that scathe and scorch the soul—that penetrate to the vital seat of happiness—and blast it, never again to put forth bud or blossom. She never objected to frequent the haunts of pleasure, but she was as much alone there as in the depths of solitude. She walked about in a sad reverie, apparently unconscious of the world around her. She carried with her an inward woe that mocked at all the blandishments of friendship, and "heeded not the song of the charmer, charm he never so wisely."

The person who told me her story had seen her at a masquerade. There can be no exhibition of far-gone wretchedness more striking and painful than to meet it in such a scene. To find it wandering like a spectre, lonely and joyless, where all around is gay—to see it dressed out in the trappings of mirth, and looking so wan and woe-begone, as if it had tried in vain to cheat the poor heart into a momentary forgetfulness of sorrow. After strolling through the splendid rooms and giddy crowd with an air of utter abstraction, she sat herself down on the steps of an orchestra, and looking about for some time with a vacant air, that showed her insensibility to the garish scene, she began, with the capriciousness of a sickly heart, to warble a little plaintive air. She had an exquisite voice; but on this occasion it was so simple, so touching, it breathed forth such a soul of wretchedness, that she drew a crowd mute and silent around her, and melted every one into tears.

The story of one so true and tender could not but excite great interest in a country remarkable for enthusiasm. It completely won the heart of a brave officer, who paid his addresses to her, and thought that one so true to the dead could not but prove affectionate to the living. She declined his attentions, for her thoughts were irrevocably engrossed by the memory of her former lover. He, however, persisted in his suit. He solicited not her tenderness, but her esteem. He was assisted by her conviction of his worth and her sense of her own destitute and dependent situation, for she was existing on the kindness of friends. In a word, he at length succeeded in gaining her hand, though with the solemn assurance that her heart was unalterably another's.

He took her with him to Sicily, hoping that a change of scene might wear out the remembrance of early woes. She was an amiable and exemplary wife, and made an effort to be a happy one; but nothing could cure the silent and devouring melancholy that had entered into her very soul. She wasted away in a slow but hopeless decline, and at length sunk into the grave, the victim of a broken heart.

DESCRIPTION OF THE POWERFUL ARMY ASSEMBLED AT THE CITY OF NEW AMSTERDAM—FROM KNICKERBOCKER'S NEW YORK.

While thus the enterprising Peter was coasting, with flowing sail, up the shores of the lordly Hudson, and arousing all the phlegmatic little Dutch settlements upon its borders, a great and puissant concourse of warriors was assembling at the city of New Amsterdam. And here that invaluable fragment of antiquity, the Stuyvesant manuscript, is more than commonly particular; by which means I am enabled to record the illustrious host that encamped itself in the public square, in front of the fort, at present denominated the Bowling Green.

In the centre then was pitched the tent of the men of battle of the Manhattoes; who, being the inmates of the metropolis, composed the life-guards of the governor. These were commanded by the valiant Stoffel Brinkerhoof, who whilome had acquired such immortal fame at Oyster Bay—they displayed as a standard, a beaver *rampant* on a field of orange; being the arms of the province, and denoting the persevering industry, and the amphibious origin of the Nederlanders.

On their right hand might be seen the vassals of that renowned Mynheer Michael Paw, who lorded it over the fair regions of ancient Pavonia, and the lands away south, even unto the Navesink mountains, and was moreover patroon of Gibbet Island. His standard was borne by his trusty squire, Cornelius Van Vorst; consisting of a huge oyster *recumbent* upon a sea green field; being the armorial bearings of his favourite metropolis, Communipaw. He brought to the camp a stout force of warriors, heavily armed, being each clad in ten pair of linsey-wolsey breeches, and overshadowed by broad-brimmed beavers, with short pipes twisted in their hatbands. These were the men who vegetated in the mud along the shores of Pavonia; being of the race of genuine copperheads, and were fabled to have sprung from oysters.

At a little distance was encamped the tribe of warriors who came from the neighbourhood of Hell-Gate. These were commanded by the Suy Dams, and the Van Dams, incontinent hard swearers, as their names betokened—they were terrible looking fellows, clad in broad-skirted gaberdines, of that curious coloured cloth called thunder and lightning; and bore as a standard three Devil's-darning-needles, *volant*, in a flame-coloured field.

Hard by was the tent of the men of battle from the marshy borders of the Wael-bogtig, and the country thereabouts—these were of a sour aspect, by reason that they lived on crabs, which abound in these parts: they were the first institutors of that honourable order of knighthood, called *Fly market shirks;* and if tradition speak true, did likewise introduce the far-famed step in dancing, called "double trouble." They were commanded by the fearless Jacobus Varra Vanger, and had, moreover, a jolly band of Breukelen ferrymen, who performed a brave concerto on conchshells.

But I refrain from pursuing this minute description, which goes on to describe the warriors of Bloemendael, and Wee-hawk, and Hoboken, and sundry other places, well known in history and song—for now does the sound of martial music alarm the people of New Amsterdam, sounding afar from beyond the walls of the city. But this alarm was in a little time relieved, for lo, from the midst of a vast cloud of dust, they recognized the brimstone-coloured breeches, and splendid silver leg of Peter Stuyvesant, glaring in the sunbeams; and beheld him approaching at the head of a formidable army, which he had mustered along the banks of the Hudson. And here the excellent but anonymous writer of the Stuyvesant manuscript breaks out into a brave and glorious description of the forces, as they defiled through the principal gate of the city that stood by the head of Wall Street.

First of all came the Van Bummels, who inhabit the pleasant borders of the Bronx. These were short fat men, wearing exceeding large trunk breeches, and are renowned for feats of the trencher; they were the first inventors of suppawn or mush and milk.—Close in their rear marched the Van Vlotens, of Kaats Kill, most horrible quaffers of new cider, and arrant braggarts in their liquor.—After them came the Van Pelts of Groodt Esopus, dexterous horsemen, mounted upon goodly switch-tailed steeds of the Esopus breed: these were mighty hunters of minks and musk rats, whence came the word *Peltry*.—Then the Van Nests of Kinderhoeck, valiant robbers of birds' nests, as their name denotes: to these, if report may be believed, are we indebted for the invention of slapjacks, or buckwheat cakes.—Then the Van Higginbottoms, of Wapping's Creek; these came armed with ferrules and birchen rods, being a race of schoolmasters, who first discovered the marvellous sympathy between the seat of honour and the seat of intellect, and that the shortest way to get knowledge into the head was to hammer it into the bottom.—Then the Van Grolls, of Anthony's Nose, who carried their liquor in fair round little pottles, by reason they could not bouse it out of their canteens, having such rare long noses.—Then the Gardeniers, of Hudson and thereabouts, distinguished by many triumphant feats, such as robbing watermelon patches, smoking rabbits out of their holes, and the like, and by being great lovers of roasted pigs' tails: these were the ancestors of the renowned congressman of that name.—Then the Van Hoesens, of Sing-Sing, great choristers and players upon the Jew's-harp: these marched two and two, singing the great song of St. Nicholas.—Then the Couenhovens, of Sleepy Hollow: these gave birth to a jolly race of publicans, who first discovered the magic artifice of conjuring a quart of wine into a pint bottle.—Then the Van Kortlands, who lived on the wild banks of the Croton, and were great killers of wild ducks, being much spoken of for their skill in shooting with the long bow.—Then the Van Bunschotens, of Nyack and Kakiat, who were the first that did ever kick with the left foot: they were gallant bush-whackers, and hunters of racoons by moonlight.—Then the Van Winkles, of Haerlem, potent suckers of eggs, and noted for running of horses, and running up of scores at taverns: they were the first that ever winked with both eyes at once.—Lastly, came the Knickerbockers, of the great town of Schahtikoke, where the folk lay stones upon the houses in windy weather, lest they should be blown away. These derive their name, as some say, from *Knicker*, to shake, and *Beker*, a goblet, indicating thereby that they were sturdy tosspots of yore; but, in truth, it was derived from *Knicker*, to nod, and *Boeken*, books, plainly meaning that they were great nodders or dozers over books: from them did descend the writer of this history.

Such was the legion of sturdy bush-beaters that poured in at the grand gate of New Amsterdam. The Stuyvesant manuscript, indeed, speaks of many more, whose names I omit to mention, seeing that it behoves me to hasten to matters of greater moment. Nothing could surpass the joy and martial pride of the lion-hearted Peter, as he reviewed this mighty host of warriors; and he determined no longer to defer the gratification of his much wished-for revenge upon the scoundrel Swedes at Fort Casimir.

But before I hasten to record those unmatchable events which will be found in the sequel of this faithful history, let me pause to notice the fate of Jacobus Von Poffenburgh, the discomfited commander-in-chief of the armies of the New Netherlands. Such is the inherent uncharitableness of human nature, that scarcely did the news become public of his deplorable discomfiture at Fort Casimir, than a thousand scurvy rumours were set afloat in New Amsterdam; wherein it was insinuated, that he had in reality a treacherous understanding with the Swedish commander; that he had long been in the practice of privately communicating with the Swedes; together with divers hints about "secret service money"—to all which deadly charges I do not give a jot more credit than I think they deserve.

Certain it is, that the general vindicated his character by the most vehement oaths and protestations, and put every man out of the ranks of honour who dared to doubt his integrity. Moreover, on returning to New Amsterdam, he paraded up and down the streets with a crew of hard swearers at his heels,—sturdy bottle companions, whom he gorged and fattened, and who were ready to bolster him through all the courts of justice—heroes of his own kidney, fierce-whiskered, broad-shouldered, Colbrand-looking swaggerers, not one of whom but looked as though he could eat up an ox, and pick his teeth with the horns. These life-guard men quarrelled all his quarrels, were ready to fight all his battles, and scowled at every man that turned up his nose at the general, as though they would devour him alive. Their conversation was interspersed with oaths like minute-guns, and every bombastic rhodomontado was rounded off by a thundering execration, like a patriotic toast honoured with a discharge of artillery.

All these valorous vapourings had a considerable effect in convincing certain profound sages, many of whom began to think the general a hero of unutterable loftiness and magnanimity of soul, particularly as he was continually protesting *on the honour of a soldier*,—a marvellously high-sounding asseveration. Nay, one of the members of the council went so far as to propose they should immortalise him by an imperishable statue of plaster of Paris.

But the vigilant Peter the Headstrong was not thus to be deceived. Sending privately for the commander-in-chief of all the armies, and having heard all his story, garnished with the customary pious oaths, protestations, and ejaculations,—"Harkee, comrade," cried he, "though by your own account you are the most brave, upright, and honourable man in the whole province, yet do you lie under the misfortune of being damnably traduced and immeasurably despised. Now though it is certainly hard to punish a man for his misfortunes, and though it is very possible you are totally innocent of the crimes laid to your charge; yet as heaven, at present, doubtless for some wise purpose, sees fit to withhold all proofs of your innocence, far be it from me to counteract its sovereign will. Beside, I cannot consent to venture my armies with a commander whom they despise, or to trust the welfare of my people to a champion whom they distrust. Retire therefore, my friend, from the irksome toils and cares of public life, with this comforting reflection—that if you be guilty, you are but enjoying your just reward—and if innocent, that you are not the first great and good man, who has most wrongfully been slandered and maltreated in this wicked world—doubtless to be better treated in a better world, where there shall neither be error, calumny, nor persecution. In the meantime let me never see your face again, for I have a horrid antipathy to the countenances of unfortunate great men like yourself."

DICKINSON COLLEGE.

This institution, situated at Carlisle, the capital of Cumberland county in Pennsylvania, one hundred and twenty-eight miles from Philadelphia, was founded in the year 1783, by the efforts of an association in the state, of which the Hon. John Dickinson, the eminent political writer, and Dr. Benjamin Rush were the most prominent members. It received its name, in the language of the charter, "in memory of the great and important services rendered to his country by His Excellency John Dickinson, Esq., president of the Supreme Executive Council," and in commemoration of his very liberal donation to the institution. Dickinson was made first president of its board, and so continued till his death. Land was secured in the borough of Carlisle, and some funds collected.

The neighboring college of New Jersey having then acquired great success under the presidency of Witherspoon, it was thought that the fortunes of the new enterprise would be secured by procuring another eminent Scottish divine, of similar social and learned standing, for its head. This was Dr. Charles Nisbet, long established as a clergyman at Montrose, and an influential member in the General Assembly, where his powers of wit and argument were keenly appreciated. He was at the age of forty-seven when he was urged by Dr. Rush, who painted the prospects of a collegiate residence in a then remote part of the country in his most glowing and somewhat credulous strains, to come to America. Friends warned and advised, but the divine was touched by the prospect, and yielded to the invitation. He arrived at Philadelphia in June, 1785, and the fourth of the following month, on the celebration of the National Independence, reached Carlisle. His first experience was that of the illness incident to a change of residence to a new country. He was dismayed by the attacks of fever and ague which he bore with his family, and not less by the unsettled state of the country and the want of discipline in the youth. His efforts with the Trustees for a proper system of education were unheeded, so that within the year of his arrival he resigned his situation, with the intention of returning to Scotland. The necessity of remaining during the winter gave him opportunity for reflection, and he determined to sustain the position. In May, 1786, he was re-elected, and soon entered vigorously on the prosecution of his duties, performing the extraordinary labor of delivering four concurrent series of lectures on logic, the philosophy of the mind, and the Belles Lettres, to which he even added a fifth, which attracted great attention, a course on systematic theology. In the last he was an old-fashioned Calvinist: in all, he brought the best fruits of the Scottish system of instruction to the American wilds. One of his pupils, the Rev. Dr. Brown, president of Jefferson College, Canonsburg, Pa., preserved reports of these lectures, which he characterizes as full, thorough, philosophical, and appositely illustrated by wit. In a letter contributed to Dr. Samuel Miller's admirable memoir of President Nisbet, he gives a specimen from one of his discourses on Logic, which fully sustains the last quality.*

Charles Nisbet.

The first Commencement of the College was held the following year, in 1787, with some success, but the difficulties of the position were too great, and the points of antagonism in the general condition of the country too many to Dr. Nisbet's strongly, and doubtless, for the most part, justly entertained opinions, to permit him to enjoy, as such a scholar should, the peaceful honors of learning. He worked hard, was badly paid, and struggled ineffectually to bring the education

* Memoir of Nisbet, p. 321. These lectures surely are worthy of being published.

Dickinson College.

of the times up to his standard. "You have come to the land of promise," said a friend to him; "Yes," he replied, "but it is not the land of performance." We may suppose him bitterly sarcastic on the rash encouragements of his zealous inviter, Rush, with whose opinions, as time went on, and that philosopher lent an ear to rapid schemes of education without the classics, and French dreams of government, he found himself in increasing antagonism. Having once accepted the post he should have made the best of it, and not have railed ineffectually at the world, as his letters show him to have done; but there was great provocation for his wit in the temper of the times, and Carlisle, with its crude pupils and non-paying parishioners, was a poor exchange for the solid society and support of the best people in Scotland, whom he had left behind. Honor should be done to his sacrifices and his services to American scholarship, and to what was sound in his conservative views of public affairs. He devoted himself for eighteen years to the service of the college, and died at his post at Carlisle, in 1804, having just completed his sixty-eighth year. He was a man of decided mark and ability, of humor equal to that of Witherspoon, though his inferior in soundness of judgment. Dr. Miller's account of his life does justice to his talents, and preserves many interesting memorials of his friends in Scotland.

Dr. Nisbet was a scholar of picked reading in the classics and modern European languages; and being possessed of an extraordinary memory as well as ready wit, used his copious stores to great advantage. He had that vein of humorous drollery and satire which Sidney Smith encouraged, and which his friend Witherspoon's published writings exhibit. His collection of books now rests with the Theological Seminary at Princeton, having been given to that institution by two of his grandchildren, the Right Rev. Bishop M'Coskry of Michigan and Henry C. Turnbull of Maryland.*

* Dr. Miller's Memoir, p. 301.

Dr. Nisbet was a polyglott, and a collector of odds and ends in all languages. There is probably no such *olla podrida* in America as the "Nisbet Library" of the Princeton Seminary, consisting wholly of the Doctor's books. Some of these are of the 16th, and even 15th, and many of the 17th century; and a few of them, though in tatters, are among the rarest specimens of antiquarian bibliography, in the way of Elzevirs, first editions, and originals in astrology, and other out-of-the-way subjects. They are in Hebrew, Greek, Latin, French, Italian, Spanish, German, and Dutch, and many of them show how sedulously their owner had conned them.

The associates of Dr. Nisbet in the work of education were James Ross, author of a Latin Grammar formerly known, professor of the Greek and Latin languages; Mr. Robert Johnston, professor of Mathematics, and the Rev. Robert Davidson, with a voluminous professorship of "history, chronology, rhetoric, and belles lettres."

On the death of Dr. Nisbet the last mentioned acted for more than five years as president, when the office having been offered to Dr. Samuel Miller of New York, and declined, the Rev. Jeremiah Atwater, D.D., of Middlebury College, Vt., was chosen. He delivered his inaugural address at the Commencement in 1809. New departments of study were introduced, and the college gained ground, but difficulties arising in its government in 1815, Dr. Atwater resigned the presidency. After this, various efforts and expedients of management were resorted to for the repair of the exhausted finances, and the college was closed for six years.

In 1822 the Rev. John M. Mason of New York was created president, and held the office for two years, but with failing health his great reputation could not repair the fortunes of the college. The Rev. Dr. William Neill succeeded him, and in 1829 resigned. The Rev. Dr. Samuel B. How of New Jersey was the last occupant prior to the transfer of the college interest to the control of the Methodist Episcopal Church in 1833. A new organization was effected; funds were raised, and the Rev. John P. Durbin elected president. An efficient grammar-school was at the same time set on foot. The course of study followed the general outline of the New England colleges. With Mr. Durbin were associated Professors Merritt; Caldwell, of mental philosophy; Robert Emory, of ancient languages; the Rev. John M'Clintock, of the exact sciences. At present the presidency is held by the Rev. Dr. Charles Collins.

The catalogue for 1854 exhibits one hundred and forty-eight students in the four classes.

JAMES T. AUSTIN.

James Trecothic Austin was born in Boston, January, 1784. He was educated at the Latin School and Harvard College, and on the completion of his course at the latter institution in 1802, studied and commenced the practice of the law. In 1806, he married a daughter of Elbridge Gerry, then Vice-President of the United States. He edited for a time a literary periodical entitled *The Emerald*, but his chief attention was given to his profession, in which he rapidly rose to eminence. He became the Town Advocate in 1809, was for twenty years Advocate of Suffolk County, and Attorney General of Massachusetts from 1832 to 1843. He was also a member of the Massachusetts Legislature. In 1815 he delivered a Fourth of July oration at Lexington, which was published, and in 1828 a Life of Elbridge Gerry.* This work is one of the best presentations of the Revolutionary worthies. It is written in an agreeable style, and in addition to its narrative of the many important public transactions in which Mr. Gerry was a prominent participant, gives us pleasant glimpses of the domestic life of the Revolution, as in the following passages from a chapter on the "Private Life of the Members of the Provincial Congress."

Among the members of the provincial congress, suspicion of levity in matters of religion—and everything was then supposed to have some connexion with this subject—would have been fatal to an individual's influence. There were, however, many members in that assembly who had been accustomed to the elegancies and refinement of polished society. The king's government in Massachusetts had not indeed been able to borrow the splendour of a court, but it had in some degree copied its etiquette and politeness, and possibly its less defensible manners. Distinctions existed in society not precisely consistent with republican equality, and a style of address and deportment distinguished those who considered themselves in the upper circle, which was visible long after the revolution had swept away all other relics of the royal government. This early habit induced some of the patriots at Watertown to indulge in a little more regard to dress than suited the economy of the stricter puritans, in a love for better horses, in a social party at dinner, or evening, in an attendance on balls and dancing parties, and in a fondness for female society of respectability and reputation.

* * * * * * * * *

Most men have their besetting sins. It might have been in vain that the necessity of reasonable relaxation was pleaded as an excuse for supposed frivolity. The examples of eminent men, their friends too, on the other side the Atlantic, would have been urged as an excuse equally ineffectual, when ample retaliation was taken by the offending members in finding some of the sternest of the irritated moralists drinking tea, and endeavouring to disguise this high crime and misdemeanour by having it made in a coffee pot! This indulgence of taste at the expense of patriotism, this worse than bacchanalian intemperance, prevented for a time any remarks on the "court imitations" of the backsliding brethren.

The members of the provincial congress lived in the families of the inhabitants of Watertown, and held their daily sessions in the meeting-house on the plain. The congress opened early, and adjourned for an hour to give the members time to dine at one o'clock. Two sessions were usually held every day, and committees were often engaged till midnight. The time, which could be caught from such fatiguing duty without neglecting it, might well be devoted to rational diversion.

A gentleman, who paid any attention to his toilet, would have his hair combed out, powdered and tied in a long queue, a plaited white stock, a shirt ruffled at the bosom and over the hands, and fastened at the wrist with gold sleeve buttons, a peach bloom coat and white buttons, lined with white silk, and standing off at the skirts with buckram, a figured silk vest divided at the bottom, so that the pockets extended on the thighs, black silk small clothes with large gold or silver knee buckles, white cotton or silk stockings, large shoes with short quarters and buckles to match. This dress, sketched from the wardrobe of a member, was not peculiarly appropriate to occasions of ceremony, but assumed with more or less exactness by the fashionable gentlemen of the day.

The full bottomed wig, the red roquelot, and the gold-headed cane, which are seen in some of our ancient pictures, belonged to an earlier period, and were at that time the appropriate habiliments of persons distinguished for their age and wealth. It is not many years since some examples of this antiquated fashion were recognised in venerable men, who belonged to those interesting times, and seemed to connect a past generation with the present. They have now, it is believed, ceased from any connexion with society, if indeed any of them still have a being on the earth.

Mr. Austin has also published Addresses delivered before the Massachusetts Society for Suppressing Intemperance and the Massachusetts Mechanic Association, Remarks on Channing's Discourse on Slavery, a Review of his Letter to Jonathan Phillips, in which he takes strong ground against agitation of the subject, and a number of documents on the Municipal Affairs of Boston, and on professional subjects. He has also contributed to the Christian Examiner, and on political topics in the newspapers.*

SAMUEL L. KNAPP.

Samuel Lorenzo Knapp, a voluminous and useful miscellaneous writer, and the author of numerous original biographical essays in American literature, was born at Newburyport, Massachusetts, in 1784. He was prepared for college at the Phillips Academy at Exeter; was graduated at Dartmouth in

* The Life of Elbridge Gerry. With Contemporary Letters, to the close of the American Revolution. Boston: Wells & Lilly, 1828. 8vo. pp. 520.

* Loring's Boston Orators, pp. 470-476.

1804; studied law in the office of Chief-justice Parsons, and practised the profession with success. During the war of 1812 he commanded a regiment of state militia stationed for the defence of the coast. In 1824 he became editor of the *Boston Gazette;* he also conducted the *Boston Monthly Magazine*, to which he contributed several articles. In 1826 he established the *National Republican*, on the failure of which, after an experiment of two years, he commenced the practice of law in New York city. In 1818 he published *The Travels of Ali Bey,** a small volume purporting to furnish the observations of an Oriental traveller on the society and literature of Boston and Cambridge. This was followed in 1821 by *Biographical Sketches of Eminent Lawyers, and Statesmen, and Men of Letters;* in 1828 by the *Genius of Free-Masonry, or a Defence of the Order;* and in 1829 by *Lectures on American Literature*,† in which he followed the subject, from its earliest sources, with warmth and interest. He was also the author of *Sketches of Public Characters drawn from the Living and the Dead*,‡ a series of letters giving brief sketches of the leading politicians, authors, and artists of the United States. *The Bachelor and Other Tales, founded on American Incident and Character*, appeared in 1836; and in 1832 a small volume, entitled *Advice in the Pursuits of Literature*.§ It is dedicated to the members of the New York Mercantile Library Association, and designed as a guide to the study of English literature for persons engaged in business. It contains a brief review of the leading English authors from Chaucer to the present time, with occasional extracts, and a concise survey of European history, as connected with literature and the progress of learning, from the days of Homer to the settlement of the present United States. In 1833 he published *American Biography, or Original Biographical Sketches of Distinguished Americans*, one of the most valuable of his many productions in this department of literature. The volume does not profess to furnish more than a selection from the many eminent names which have graced our annals, and in this selection the author has been guided, in many instances, rather by his individual tastes and preferences than by the actual eminence of the persons introduced. His sketches are anecdotical and spirited, drawing largely in many cases on his own fund of personal recollection, and the work forms an agreeable and varied miscellany. It is republished in the third volume of The Treasury of Knowledge and Library of Reference.* Mr. Knapp was also the author of separate biographies, in a condensed popular form, of Aaron Burr, Andrew Jackson, Daniel Webster, Thomas Eddy, and in 1843 of *Female Biography of Different Ages and Nations;*† a pleasant volume, having many points of resemblance to his collection of male celebrities.

In addition to these numerous and industriously prepared volumes, Mr. Knapp was the author of several addresses delivered on various public occasions. He died at Hopkinton, Mass., July 8, 1838.

* Extracts from a Journal of Travels in North America, consisting of an account of Boston and its vicinity. By Ali Bey, etc. Translated from the original manuscript. Boston: 1818. 18mo. pp. 124.

† Lectures on American Literature, with Remarks on some Passages of American History. New York: 1829.

‡ Sketches of Public Characters, drawn from the Living and the Dead, with Notices of other Matters, by Ignatius Loyola Robertson, LL.D., a resident of the United States. New York: 1830. 12mo. pp. 260.

§ Advice in the Pursuits of Literature, containing Historical, Biographical, and Critical Remarks. By Samuel L. Knapp. New York: 1832. 12mo. pp. 296.

* New York: C. C. Childs, 1850.

† Female Biography; containing Notices of Distinguished Women of Different Ages and Nations. By Samuel L. Knapp. Philadelphia: 1843. 12mo. pp. 504.

LEVI FRISBIE.

Levi Frisbie was born at Ipswich, Mass., in the year 1784, and was the son of a clergyman of the place. He was prepared for college at Andover Academy, and entered Harvard in 1798. During his collegiate course he supported himself by writing several hours a day as a clerk, and by teaching during the winter vacations. On the completion of his course in 1802, he passed a year at a school in Concord, and then commenced the study of the law, a pursuit which he was soon obliged to abandon on account of an affection of the eyes, from which he never entirely recovered, being for some years dependent on the kindness of friends who read to him in English and Latin, and to a writing apparatus which had been suggested for the use of the blind, for the means of literary employment.

In 1805, Frisbie accepted the post of Latin tutor in Harvard College, and in 1811 was promoted to the professorship of the same department. In 1817 he married a daughter of Mr. John Mellen of Cambridge, and in the same year entered upon the duties of the professorship of "Natural Religion, Moral Philosophy, and Civil Polity" prefacing his course by an *Inaugural Address*. In 1821 he was attacked by consumption, and sank in the gradual course of that disease to its fatal termination, July 9, 1822.

Frisbie's writings were collected and published by his friend and fellow professor, Andrews Norton, in 1823. The volume contains, in addition to the Address already mentioned, articles on *Tacitus* and *Adam Smith's Theory of Moral Sentiments* from the North American Review, *Remarks on the Right and Duty of Government to provide for the Support of Religion by Law*, from the "Christian Disciple," extracts from notes of his professional lectures, and a few poems including a version of Horace's epistle *Ad Julium Florum*, first published in the General Repository and Review. These remains show their author to have been a vigorous thinker and good writer. His chief literary labors are inadequately represented, as, owing to the weakness of his eyes, he was accustomed to note down merely the heads or occasional passages in his lectures, which he expanded orally when before his class.

One of his poems, a general favorite, *A Castle in the Air*, not included in the volume of his writings, first appeared in the Monthly Anthology.

A CASTLE IN THE AIR.

I'll tell you, friend, what sort of wife,
Whene'er I scan this scene of life,
Inspires my waking schemes,
And when I sleep, with form so light,
Dances before my ravished sight,
In sweet aerial dreams.

The rose its blushes need not lend,
Nor yet the lily with them blend,
To captivate my eyes.
Give me a cheek the heart obeys,
And, sweetly mutable, displays
Its feelings as they rise;

Features, where pensive, more than gay,
Save when a rising smile doth play,
The sober thought you see;
Eyes that all soft and tender seem,
And kind affections round them beam,
But most of all on me;

A form, though not of finest mould,
Where yet a something you behold
Unconsciously doth please;
Manners all graceful without art,
That to each look and word impart
A modesty and ease.

But still her air, her face, each charm,
Must speak a heart with feeling warm,
And mind inform the whole:
With mind her mantling cheek must glow,
Her voice, her beaming eye must show
An all-inspiring soul.

Ah! could I such a being find,
And were her fate to mine but joined
By Hymen's silken tie,
To her myself, my all I'd give,
For her alone delighted live,
For her consent to die.

Whene'er by anxious gloom oppressed,
On the soft pillow of her breast
My aching head I'd lay;
At her sweet smile each care should cease,
Her kiss infuse a balmy peace,
And drive my griefs away.

In turn, I'd soften all her care,
Each thought, each wish, each feeling share;
Should sickness e'er invade,
My voice should soothe each rising sigh,
My hand the cordial should supply;
I'd watch beside her bed.

Should gathering clouds our sky deform,
My arms should shield her from the storm;
And, were its fury hurled,
My bosom to its bolts I'd bare,
In her defence undaunted dare
Defy the opposing world.

Together should our prayers ascend,
Together humbly would we bend,
To praise the Almighty name;
And when I saw her kindling eye
Beam upwards to her native sky,
My soul should catch the flame.

Thus nothing should our hearts divide,
But on our years serenely glide,
And all to love be given;
And, when life's little scene was o'er,
We'd part to meet and part no more,
But live and love in heaven.*

JOSEPH S. BUCKMINSTER.

JOSEPH STEVENS BUCKMINSTER, an eminent clergyman and scholar of Boston, was born at Portsmouth, New Hampshire, May 26, 1784. His father the Rev. Joseph Buckminster, himself the son of a clergyman, was for thirty-three years pastor of the most considerable Congregational Society there, and died in 1812 at the age of sixty-one.

The younger Buckminster showed strongly marked intellectual tendencies from his earliest years. He loved books as soon as he could comprehend what they were. He was taught for his pastime to read a chapter in the Greek Testament before he could be taught the language itself. And when he was between eleven and thirteen years old—the period when, at Phillips Academy at Exeter, he was prepared for college—his literary curiosity was so eager that, beginning one day to read Boswell's Johnson, as he chanced to be leaning on a mantel-piece, he forgot himself so long and so completely, that he did not move, until he fainted from exhaustion.

In 1797, he was entered in Harvard College, and when he was graduated there in 1800, at the age of sixteen, his performance as the leading scholar of his class made an impression still fresh in the minds of the few that heard it, and now survive, and left a tradition not likely soon to be lost. In fact, his college course had attracted much notice, and he had already come to be regarded as the most remarkable young man who had appeared in New England for more than one generation.

The two next years were spent by him as a teacher in the academy at Exeter, devoting his leisure to such a thorough study of the ancient classics, as was at that time unknown among us; and then he gave three years more to an equally thorough study of theology, which had been his favorite purpose from childhood. This, of course, was followed by his public appearance as a candidate for the ministry; but he had preached only a few discourses when, early in 1805, he was settled over the society in Brattle-street, Boston;—then, and from the period before the Revolution, regarded as of metropolitan dignity among the congregations of New England.

But there were circumstances connected with this decisive event in his life, which should not be passed over, because they largely illustrate the position and opinions of the clergy with whom he was at the time associated, and had much influence on his own.

---

* The following additional stanza was written by a friend of the author on reading the poem:—

This Castle's fine, its structure good,
Materials best when understood
By reason's sober view;
Fixed on this base by my control,
No more aerial it shall roll,
A fortress made by you.

J. S. Buckminster

From the middle of the eighteenth century, the old Puritanism of the Pilgrim Fathers had become much relaxed in Boston and its neighborhood. Dr. Chauncy and his friends by no means acknowledged the authority of the Assembly's Shorter Catechism; and the stern power of Calvinism necessarily died out yet more, a little later, when men like Dr. Freeman and Dr. Kirkland were enjoying the highest consideration of the community in which they lived. Mr. Buckminster had been educated among the straitest of the sect, in which, so far as New Hampshire was concerned, his father was a leader. It was the old school divinity. But his own inquiries carried him in a different direction. One doctrine after another of the Calvinistic system was given up by him, until at last he abandoned it altogether, and associated himself with the class then called Liberal Christians;—the same, which, with some modifications, is now recognised under the less comprehensive name of Unitarians. It was a great sorrow to his father; and once or twice, the young man nearly abandoned his pursuit of the profession he had chosen, rather than run counter to the feelings of one he so much venerated. But, at last, the parental assent was given, and the elder Buckminster preached his son's Ordination sermon.

His health, however, was uncertain. For four or five years he had suffered from slight epileptic attacks, and his fond and admiring parish, alarmed by their recurrence, proposed a voyage to Europe. He went in 1806 and returned in 1807; but though the interval of relaxation thus afforded him refreshed his strength and increased both his resources and his earnestness to use them, no permanent improvement in his health followed. Nor did he misinterpret the sad signs of such a visitation. On the contrary, from memoranda found among his papers, as well as from letters to his father, it is plain that he understood the usual results of the terrible malady with which he was afflicted, and foresaw the probable decay and wreck of his brilliant powers. But, though he always felt that he was standing on the threshold of the most awful of human calamities, and that he might be required to linger out a life gloomier than the grave, he never lost his alacrity in the performance of labors however humble or however arduous, and walked firmly and gladly onward in the path of duty, as if neither danger nor darkness were before him.

But, at last, the summons came—not with the dreadful warning he had feared, but with a single, crushing blow. He died in Boston June 9, 1812, at noon, after only a few days of unconscious illness; and his father, who was then in Vermont journeying for his health, died the next morning, without the least knowledge on his own part, or on the part of those near him, that his son was even indisposed, but saying, almost with his last breath, "My son Joseph is dead!" adding when assured that he must have dreamed it; "No, I have not slept nor dreamed—he is dead;" a circumstance, which, however much men were persuaded that it was an accidental coincidence, produced an electric effect at the time, and will be remembered among the strangest of the few facts of its class that are recorded on unquestionable testimony.

Mr. Buckminster was only twenty-eight years old when he died. He was ordained as a clergyman before he was twenty-one, and having been absent in Europe eighteen months, the proper term of his public service was only about five years and a half. The period was certainly short; and when to this is added his youth, we may well be surprised at the large space he filled in the interests of the community while he lived, and the permanent results he produced as a scholar and public teacher.

As a scholar, he did more to revive and establish in New England a love for classical literature, than any man of his time. The period during which the study of the great Greek and Roman masters was in favor, and when such a book as the "Pietas et Gratulatio" of 1761 could be produced at Harvard College, was gone by. The Revolution, its trials and consequences, had impaired the authority of such studies, and they had well nigh died out. His essays and reviews, above forty in number, scattered through the Boston Monthly Anthology—a publication which did good service to the cause of letters between 1803 and 1811, and out of which, not without his efficient help, grew the Boston Athenæum,—show beyond all doubt his earnest efforts in this direction. When he was in Europe in 1806–7, he collected a larger and more choice library of the ancient classics than was then possessed by any other private individual in the United States, and thus set the decisive example which has since been so well followed. If we add to this, that he not only invited young scholars to the freest use of its treasures, but by his advice and example showed them how best to profit by his kindness, it will be understood why it is not too much to say, that the first impulse to that pursuit of classical accomplishments in Boston and its neighborhood, which is still recognised there, is due more to him and to his library, than to any other cause whatever.

His apparatus for the illustration of the Scriptures in their original languages, and for the study of Biblical criticism, constituted, however, the most important part of his collection of books. In this branch of knowledge, his discussions in the Anthology and General Repository led the way for that careful philological learning which now prevails so generally in our schools of divinity. As a foundation for this, Mr. Wm. Wells, at Mr. Buckminster's urgent desire, and under his superintendence, published in 1809 an edition of Griesbach's Manual Greek Testament;—the first instance of a Greek book printed with becoming care and accuracy in the United States,* and still we suppose the only instance of a Greek book ordered in considerable numbers from this side of the Atlantic, to supply the demand of British scholars, because it had not so early been published in England. It was he too, who, by the consent of all, was appointed as the first lecturer on the foundation laid in Harvard College by the elder Dexter, to promote a more critical knowledge of Sacred Literature—a duty for which he was just preparing himself when he was suddenly cut off by death. In short, it was he who first took the study of the New Testament from the old basis on which it had rested during the poor discussions and controversies of the latter half of the eighteenth century, when little more learning was asked for than was to be found in such books as Campbell's Gospels and Macknight's Epistles; and placed it on the solid foundation of the text of the New Testament, as settled by Mill, Wetstein, and Griesbach, and as elucidated by the labors of Michaelis, Marsh, and Rosenmuller, and by the safe and wise learning of Grotius, Leclerc, and Simon. It has been permitted to few persons to render so considerable a service to the cause of Christianity in our Western World.

But Mr. Buckminster's great popular success was as a public preacher. His personal appearance, and particularly the beauty of his countenance, beaming with intelligence and goodness; his voice remarkable for its sweetness and solemnity; and his gracious manner, natural almost to carelessness, but marked with great earnestness, especially in his devotional services—all these circumstances favored, no doubt, the effect of his discourses as they were delivered. But we now judge them only as compositions which the press has given to the world to be estimated according to their appropriateness to the purpose for which they were prepared, and according to their intrinsic literary merits. He published only four during his lifetime; a short address at the ordination of his friend the Rev. Charles Lowell, in 1806; a sermon on the death of Gov. Sullivan, who was his parishioner, in 1808; his brilliant Discourse before the Phi Beta Kappa Society, of Cambridge, in 1809; and in 1811, a sermon on the death of the Rev. Wm. Emerson, with whose religious society his own was much connected. But after his death twenty-four of his sermons were selected and published, in 1814, with a memoir of his life, by his friend the Rev. S. C. Thatcher, to which, in 1829, another volume was added, containing twenty-two; and in 1839, the whole, with some extracts from his MSS. that had previously appeared in a religious periodical, were published together in two volumes. They are all carefully written, or at least they seem to be so; and yet they were all prepared when he was between twenty and twenty-eight years old, as the hurried demands of duty called for them; and they were all necessarily given to the press without that final revision by their author, which is always so important.

Before his time, the sermons of New England had been chiefly doctrinal, and generally either dull or metaphysical; and, although a different style of preaching, one more practical and more marked with literary grace and religious sensibility, had begun to prevail in Boston and its neighborhood, before Mr. Buckminster appeared, yet only occasional discourses of the sort had been published; and the volume of his sermons printed in 1814 undoubtedly gave the decisive and the guiding impulse to the better manner that has prevailed since.*

DAVID HOFFMAN.

This distinguished jurist and scholar was a native of Maryland, born in the city of Baltimore Dec. 25, 1784, of a family eminent for its literary accomplishments. He early devoted himself to the study of the law, and was for a long time one of its leading practitioners in the state. Incited by a love of the profession and an ardent desire for its advancement, he spared neither labor nor means to advance its interests. The position which he held for nearly twenty years, from 1817 to 1836, as Professor of Law in the University of Maryland, enabled him to render his accomplishments as a scholar directly available in this direction. He illustrated the study of the law in a series of publications; the first of which, issued in 1817, was his *Course of Legal Study*, a work which secured the respect of the soundest legal judgments; Marshall, Kent, Story, and De Witt Clinton, and other eminent authorities at home and abroad, bestowing their commendations on it for the method and acumen of its conception and execution. This work re-appeared in an enlarged and improved form in 1836. His next publi-

* The first Greek type used in the United States was used in printing an original Greek ode and an original Greek elegy, both by Stephen Sewall, afterwards Professor of Hebrew in Harvard College. This was in 1761, at Boston.

* Mr. Buckminster's principal publications in the periodicals of his time are:—

1805 Review of Miller's Retrospect of the xviii. cent.; in the Cambridge Literary Miscellany—his first appearance as an author.

1805 Review of the Salem Sallust; the first ancient classic printed in the United States, with original Latin preface and notes. Boston Anthology, vol. ii.

1808 Review of Logan's Translation of Cicero's Cato Major, published by Dr. Franklin, Philadelphia, 1744—the first translation of an ancient classic made and printed in the United States. Three articles in the Boston Anthology, vol. v.

1808, 1809, 1811. Articles on Griesbach's New Testament in the Boston Anthology, vols. v. vi. and x., and in the General Repository and Review, Cambridge, vol. i.

1812 Translation from Schleusner's Lexicon, with notes. His last publication.

We are indebted for this notice of Buckminster to the pen of Mr. George Ticknor, of Boston. It has been reduced from a biographical review which he published in the Christian Examiner for September, 1849.

cation was the *Legal Outlines* in 1836, a succinct and elaborate exposition of the practice and study of the law. The next year Mr. Hoffman admitted the public to a participation of some of his individual moods and humors, the result of his study of books and the world, in his volume of Essays, entitled *Miscellaneous Thoughts on Men, Manners, and Things, by Anthony Grumbler, of Grumbleton Hall, Esq.* A second volume, which may be regarded as a sequel to this, followed in 1841, *Viator; or a Peep into my Note Book.* A passage from the dedication of the latter to Thomas D'Oyly, Esq., serjeant at law, London, will exhibit the author's motive and the general complexion of his thoughts. "It is one of a series on a great variety of topics; the whole being designed to be illustrative and somewhat corrective of what is called the new school, and to portray the unhappy influences of the present mania in literature over men, manners, and things, as they appear, chiefly on this side of the broad Atlantic—and also to recall readers to some retrospect of by-gone days; and finally, to contrast them with that fashionable ultraism so prevalent here, and which is no less obvious in our law, government, morals, and religion, than it manifestly is in our popular literature." Though in the form of light literature these books, in a pleasant way, contain various important discussions of law, art, religion, literature, in a style of popular philosophy. They are the productions of a lover of books and of men. The brief aphoristic essay was an especial favorite of the author. In the words of the motto of his Note Book, from Butler—

'Tis in books the chief
Of all perfections to be plain and brief.

In the preface of his "Introductory Letters" (1837) he mentions that "This volume, together with the two editions of the author's Course of Legal Study, and his Legal Outlines, as also his *Moot Court Decisions*, and Abridgment of *Lord Coke's* Reports, with Notes, will afford, as he hopes, sufficient evidence, were any needed, that in *breaking up* the law professorship, the trustees have done the author no little injustice, and themselves no great credit." The two last-named, "Moot Court Decisions" and "Coke's Reports," were prepared for the press, but never published. The manuscripts are now in possession of his family, by whom they may at some future time be given to the world.

In 1846 he published, in Philadelphia, *Legal Hints, being a condensation of the leading ideas as relating to Professional Deportment*, contained in "A Course of Legal Study," with the addition of "Some Counsel to Law Students." In the preface to this book, Mr. Hoffman says:—"It has been suggested to the author to publish separately, in a small manual, the following observations on Professional Deportment, which forms a division in the second volume of the work (Legal Study). This suggestion is acquiesced in from a deep conviction that the high tone of the bar has suffered some impairment, consequent upon its immense increase in this country within the last ten years—a *cause*, as well as *effect*, of the lamentable fact alluded to. Such a little 'Vade Mecum,' it is thought, might often prove useful, where the larger work might not be found; and with a sincere desire to do all the good to so noble a profession that may be in the author's humble competency, he now submits this little volume."

In this short space may be found a fair exposition of the ruling motives of the life of this amiable and accomplished gentleman. In all the excitements of professional contests, or in the privacy of social life, the same sentiments seem to have been breathed. To elevate, to refine, to bring into closer connexion those with whom he had business or social relation, was with him a great source of pleasure; and there is apparent, everywhere in his writings known to the public, and in his private correspondence, a sincere and earnest desire to soften and ameliorate in every possible way, the hard and forbidding aspect presented to the beginner in his struggle with the world.

After the termination of his law professorship, Mr. Hoffman, with a view to relaxation, visited England and the Continent, where he remained for about two years. Upon his return he entered into the political campaign then pending, favoring with great earnestness the election of General Harrison to the presidency, and was chosen one of the senatorial electors from the State of Maryland. Upon the conclusion of the contest he settled in Philadelphia, resuming the practice of the law, remaining in that city until 1847, in the fall of which year he again visited Europe, with a view to the completion of the great work of his life, entitled *Chronicles selected from the Originals of Cartaphilus, the Wandering Jew.* During his residence in London he wrote a number of able articles, explaining the political and social economy of the U. S. government and people, which were published in the *London Times*, and were highly esteemed as truthful and reliable expositions of the subjects which they treated. The first volumes of the Cartaphilus were published in London, in 1853, by Bosworth, in an original style. The design and object of the work was to represent, in as compact and interesting view as possible, the History of the World, from the time of our Lord to the present; at the same time leading the mind of the reader into a more full understanding and consideration of the position of the different nations, their modes of government, and many other interesting subjects,—but more particularly showing the condition of the different religious sects—their rise, causes, success, and the events which followed—altogether forming a view of the most important changes in the positions of the nations since the commencement of the Christian era. This end is supposed to have been attained through the agency of Cartaphilus (the Wandering Jew). The tradition is taken up by the author, and carried successfully through the whole work. The book was originally intended to occupy six quarto volumes, two of which, as before mentioned, had been published, and the third printed in proof save about one hundred and twenty pages, of which the manuscript was prepared and ready for the press at the time of the death of Mr. H. These three volumes include the *first* series, the second volume bringing the "chronicles" down to the year of grace 578.

Of the second series (of three volumes, making the six) a great portion of the manuscript had been prepared, but not corrected.

This work, which in extent of reading is worthy to rank with the folios of an earlier day, shows the curious tastes and literary diligence of the author. He was always a careful conservator of antiquity; nor did he neglect the present, as the valuable collections of his library, which at several instalments have been disposed of to the public, and are now gathered in various public and private libraries, have fully witnessed.

He returned to this country from England in December, 1853, and became engaged in the arrangement of his private affairs, which long absence from the country had made a source of some solicitude. In the proper forwarding of this purpose he was much occupied in travelling. While on a visit to New York, in 1854, he died suddenly of apoplexy, November 11th of that year. His remains were taken to Baltimore for interment.

Mr. Hoffman had received, during his life, a number of honorary degrees from different institutions of learning in this country and Europe, the principal of which were that of LL.D., from the University of Maryland; also a like degree from the University of Oxford, England; and that of Juris Utri. Doct. Gottingen, besides other honorary degrees from several societies of "*Savants*."

FAME AND AUTHORSHIP—FROM THE INTRODUCTION TO "VIATOR."

In the following pages my readers will find I have, in some degree, consulted the prevalent taste, by endeavouring, *occasionally*, to convey my moral, or instruction, as the case may be, in something after the fashion of a tale! and, when this is not the case, by imparting to each theme as much of life and ease as may consist with the nature of my topics—and of my own nature. And yet truly, I have never seen any reason why the gravest, nay, even the most recondite subjects, may not be popularly, and sometimes even sportively handled; and I believe that the writings of the philosophers, of the school-men, and even of the early fathers of the "mother church," might be thus dealt with, and profitably withal, yet without the least disparagement of their dignity—and that when so taken up, our *surface* readers may thus gain some knowledge of facts and opinions in forgotten literature and science, that otherwise might never have reached them! Be this as it may, I shall complete my series, in my own way, both as to matter and manner, justly hoping, but not ardently craving, that if in the present day and generation, very many should be disposed humourously to say of me—

> Our author thus with stuff'd sufficiency,
> Of all omnigenous omnisciency,
> Began (as who would not begin,
> That had, like him, so much within?)
> To let it out in books of all sorts,
> In duodecimos, large and small sorts!—

the generation after it may possibly exclaim, "Oh Vandal age, now gone by! it was not given to thee, whilst in the *cartilage*, to be nourished on the pith and marrow of that author; but we, who are now in the muscle and bone of maturity, profit by his counsels, and take just pride in his old-fashioned wisdom." And thus is it that authors do sometimes take comfort unto themselves, even at the moment that some Zoilus would deprive them of this most benign self-complacency.

But, you all remember how, some thirty centuries ago, a powerful monarch, and the wisest of men, thus chronicles a lesson of humility for all authors—one that is, and will be, equally true in all past, present, and future ages—"*my son be admonished*—OF MAKING BOOKS *there is no end—much study is a weariness of the flesh*." And yet it would seem strange that in his day, when printing, stereotypes, and steam-presses were wholly unknown, Solomon should have had reason to feel so strongly the vanity, and absolute nothingness of authorship! Where are now the works, nay even the names of the myriads who then toiled for fame, if, for a bubble so perishable, they did toil, which hath ever seemed to me a most unphilosophical libel against the whole fraternity of authors, from Solomon's to the present day! I cannot harbour the thought that the love of *fame* ever guided the pen of any author, be he a maker of primers or of folios, and whether he were a Parley or a Shakespeare, a Pinnock or a Milton, a Boz or a Bacon, a Jack Downing or a Newton!—but contrariwise, I do verily opine, that nearly every other conceivable motive, rather than the love of praise, either present or posthumous, has attended them throughout their labours of the pen! To recount the incitements that may prompt and nourish authorship, would itself require a volume, in which fame, however, would occupy but an insignificant section. Even in Lord Byron, it was the dread of *ennui*, an indomitable imagination, a partial misanthropy, or rather a disgust towards some men and things, a strong love of satire, an arrogant contempt of ignorance and of folly—and, in fine, a thousand other motives which stimulated his pen more constantly and fervently, than any regard for "golden opinions." And though the noble author has said,

> 'Tis pleasant sure to see one's name in print;
> A book's a book, although there's nothing in't;

yet all know the spirit with which this couplet was written, and that no one was less inclined than his lordship, to practise what he so much condemned in others. The truth is, fame is the *last* and *least* of all the motives that lead to authorship of any kind—and if the lives of Voltaire—of Lope de Vega—of Bacon—of Sir Walter Scott, nay of all other voluminous writers, be closely examined, I cannot but think it would be found that much stronger, and more numerous incitements, than the praises of men, led them on from small beginnings to great results, in authorship. Young, in his epistle to Pope, has recorded some of the motives; and he might have easily filled his poetical letter with them.

> Some write confin'd by physic; some by debt;
> Some, for 'tis Sunday; some because 'tis wet;
> Another writes because his father writ,
> And proves himself a bastard by his wit.

And I may add, some write because they are the merriest crickets that chirp; others, lest they should be drowned in their own gall, did they not periodically vent their spleen; some write from mere repletion of learning; others from doubts whether they possess any! With some, composition is scarce an intellectual toil, but affords them the highest mental gratification; with others, it is a labour essential to the fixation of their thoughts, and to the ascertainment of their own resources; some, without the least alloy of selfishness, are actuated solely by the hope of benefiting their readers; others are prompted by every other selfish consideration, save that of fame. Be the motive, however, what it may, no author, in our day, judging from the past, can repose with much confidence, on securing the grateful remembrance of future ages. Dr. Johnson was the idol of his day, and for half a generation after! but his Dictionary, which *made* him, now reposes on many shelves, as mere dead lumber; and even our scholars seem to delight in demonstrating his etymological ignorances! Who, of this nineteenth century, now reads the Rambler?—not one in ten thousand! Who, as in former days, now with delight pore over his truly admirable Lives of the Poets? Not one, in as many hundred—his poetry? one here and there—his Miscellaneous Works? scarce any! And so of Milton, Pope, Bolingbroke, Goldsmith, with the exception of his Vicar of Wakefield; and Hume, likewise, excepting his History of England. Who now reads Spenser—Chaucer—Ben Jonson—Davenant—Glover—Marvell—Daniel—Cartwright—Hurdis—Chamberlayne—Sir Philip Sidney—Sir John Suckling, or even the best among the early English dramatic writers?—few, very few! And, may we not with truth ask, are not the plays, even of the immortal bard of Avon, comparatively but little read, and still less often enacted; and have they not recently sought more genial realms, and become more familiar to German, than even to English ears? Well hath Spenser exclaimed—

How many great ones may remembered be,
Which in their days most famously did flourish,
Of whom no word we hear, nor sign now see,
But as things wip'd with sponge do perish!

GULIAN C. VERPLANCK.

GULIAN CROMMELIN VERPLANCK, a name which in itself indicated its owner's descent from the founders of the Empire State, was born in the city of New York. He was one of the class of 1801, of Columbia College, and afterwards devoted himself to the law.

After being admitted to the Bar, Mr. Verplanck passed several years in Europe. On his return, he became interested in politics, and was elected a member of the State Legislature. In 1818 he delivered the first of the series of public addresses on which his literary reputation is mainly founded. In this discourse, pronounced on the anniversary of the New York Historical Society, after lamenting the prevalent lack of interest in the history of the country manifested by his fellow citizens, he announces as his theme The Early European Friends of America. In pursuance of this subject he introduces well sketched portraits of Las Casas, Williams, Lord Baltimore, Penn, Locke, Oglethorpe, Berkeley, and Hollis. From these names he passes to a tribute to the virtues of the Dutch and the Huguenots, and an enforcement of their claims to American gratitude. The comment which this portion of the discourse occasioned, furnishes sufficient evidence of the popular ignorance on the subject, and the need of the orator's exertions to arouse his fellow-townsmen to an assertion of the at least equal claims of their progenitors to those of any other portion of the Union, to the honor of having established the principles and the prosperity, the wise theory and successful practice of our confederacy. Mr. Verplanck's address passed through several editions, and secured him the respect of the friends of American history throughout the land. In the following year a little volume of political verse, *The State Triumvirate, a Political Tale*, and *The Epistles of Brevet Major Pindar Puff*, appeared anonymously. Its authorship has never been claimed, but Mr. Verplanck has usually received the credit of having had the chief hand in its production. The satire is principally levelled at the laudation of De Witt Clinton by his party friends, and contains a close review of the governor's literary pretensions. The volume is plentifully garnished with prolegomena, notes, and other scholastic trimmings *by Scriblerus Busby, LL.D.* Among the squibs of the town wits of this period is a clever brochure, attributed to Verplanck, on the inauguration of Dr. Hosack as President of the New York Historical Society. It is entitled, *Procès Verbal of the Ceremony of Installation.* The distinguished political and other local celebrities of the day are introduced as a committee of arrangement, severally taking part in the grand ceremonial. General Jacob Morton, Dr. Valentine Mott, the learned Dr. Graham, and other city magnates, tender various addresses in doggrel Latin. Mr. Simpson, of the Park Theatre, acts as stage manager for the ceremony. At an important stage of the proceedings, after a course of applause, music, and punch, the oath of office is thus ludicrously administered in the investiture of the new incumbent, who was the successor of Clinton, upon whom much of the satire turns, in the office—

Juras Clinton adorare,
Piff—paff—puffere, et laudare.

To which the President shall reply,—

Juro Clinton adorare,
Piff—paff—puffere, et laudare.

This was printed anonymously, "for the use of the members," in 1820.* In the same year, Mr. Verplanck was chairman of the Committee on Education, in the legislature. He soon after accepted the professorship of the Evidences of Christianity in the General Protestant Episcopal Seminary, and, in 1824, published *Essays on the Nature and Uses of the Various Evidences of Revealed Religion.*†

In this work, in addition to the usual historical argument of the authenticity of the Scriptures from the testimony of mankind, the agreement of prophecy with the events which have occurred since its promulgation, the harmony of the four Evangelists, and other points of a like character, the author brings in evidence the adaptation of the Christian religion to the felt requirements of the mind of man, two lines of argument which have generally been separately urged, but which our author rightly regards as mutually aiding one another. This work, while close in its argument, is written in a fluent and elegant manner. It was followed in the succeeding year by *An Essay on the Doctrine of Contracts.*‡ The

* The clique of wits did not enjoy the joke entirely by themselves. A sharp volley had been previously fired into their camp in a pamphlet, also anonymous, from the other side, bearing the title, "An Account of Abimelech Coody and other Celebrated Writers of New York: in a Letter from a Traveller to his Friend in South Carolina." This bears date January, 1815. It was a defence of the grave and honorable pursuits of the members of the Historical and Literary and Philosophical Society, and of Clinton in particular, who was understood to be its author, and who had at least an equal talent with his opponents in the satirical line, as his newspaper management of the celebrated "forty thieves" witnessed.

† New York, Chas. Wiley. 1824. 8vo. pp. 267.

‡ An Essay on the Doctrine of Contracts; being an Inquiry how Contracts are Affected in Law and Morals by Concealment, Error, or Inadequate Price. By Gulian C. Verplanck. Quod SEMPER Æquum et Bonum, JUS dicitur. *Digest*, l. 11. *de Just. et Jure.* New York: G. & C. Carvill. 1825. 8vo. pp. 234.

author's object in this treatise is to settle, so far as may be, "the nature and degree of equality required in contracts of mutual interest, as well in reference to inadequacy of price, as to the more perplexing difficulty of inequality of knowledge." The usually received maxim of *caveat emptor* he conceives to be unsound, and urges that the laws regulating insurance, by which the owner of the property is bound to furnish the underwriter with the fullest information touching its character and hazards, should be extended to cases of bargain and sale, in which the avowed interest of both parties is to furnish an equivalent in value. In the sale of articles whose value is not determinable, or where the buyer receives no guarantee and purchases on that condition, such information is not obligatory on the seller, nor is he bound to refund in case of a sudden rise or fall in the article after the sale, which neither anticipated with certainty at the time. The essay was occasioned by a desire to check the spirit of speculation which has so often run riot over the American community, and the author, at its outset, makes special reference to a purchase of tobacco in New Orleans, by a party who had possession of the fact of a treaty of peace having been signed between the United States and Great Britain, at the depressed market price of the commodity. As soon as the news on which the purchaser traded was known to the seller, he brought suit to recover the property. The sale was finally pronounced valid by Chief-justice Marshall.

In 1825 Mr. Verplanck was elected Member of Congress from the city of New York. He remained in the House of Representatives for eight years, and, though seldom appearing as a speaker, was prominent in many measures of importance, and especially in the advocacy of the bill extending the term of copyright from twenty-eight to forty-two years. At the close of the session (that of 1830–1) in which this measure was passed, Mr. Verplanck received the well merited compliment of a public dinner from "a number of citizens distinguished for the successful cultivation of letters and the arts."* The theme of his speech on the occasion was *The Law of Literary Property*. It is included in his collected discourses. In this he maintains that the right in the product of intellectual is the same as in that of manual labor.

In 1827 Verplanck, Sands, and Bryant united in the production of an Annual, called *The Talisman*. It was illustrated with engravings from pictures by American artists, and continued for three successive years. In 1833 the volumes were republished with the title of *Miscellanies first published under the name of The Talisman*, by G. C. Verplanck, W. C. Bryant, and Robert C. Sands.† These volumes contain some of the choicest productions of their distinguished authors. Many have since appeared in the collected writings of Bryant and Sands. One of the pleasant papers which may be readily from subject and style traced to Verplanck's pen, is devoted to *Reminiscences of New York*, always an inviting theme in his hands. In 1833 a volume of *Discourses and Addresses on Subjects of American History, Arts, and Literature, by Gulian C. Verplanck*, appeared from the press of the Harpers.* It contains, in addition to the Addresses already spoken of, an eulogy of Lord Baltimore; an address on the Fine Arts; a Tribute to the Memory of Daniel H. Barnes a well known schoolmaster of New York, in which he does justice to the calling as well as the individual; an address at Columbia College on the distinguished graduates of that institution, among whom he particularizes Hamilton, Jay, Robert R. Livingston, De Witt Clinton,† Gouverneur Morris, and Dr. Mason. The volume closes with an address before the Mercantile Library Association, somewhat similar in purpose to a lecture delivered near the close of the same year before the Mechanics' Institute,‡ which contains an admirable enforcement of the mutual dependence of art and science, the toil of the brain and the toil of the muscle, on one another, and the importance to the business and working man of literature as a rational recreation as well as practical instructor in his career.

In 1833, Mr. Verplanck also delivered a discourse, *The Right Moral Influence and Use of Liberal Studies*, at the commencement of Geneva College, Aug. 7, 1833; and in 1834, on a similar occasion at Union College, spoke on the *Influence of Moral Causes upon Opinion, Science, and Literature*. In 1836, he delivered one of the most celebrated of his discourses, *The American Scholar*,§ at Union College. The object of this production is to show that the mental activity of America, the general dissemination of intelligence, the open path to every species of intellectual distinction, more than counterbalance the opportunities for scholastic retirement, in which the new is as yet inferior to the old world. The student is warned to build his career in reference to the sphere of its employment, and not risk his happiness and usefulness by an inordinate longing for, or imitation of, models formed under different circumstances of age, society, and soil.

In 1844, the first number of an edition of Shakespeare's Plays, edited by Mr. Verplanck,

* Note in Discourses and Addresses, by G. C. Verplanck, p. 216.

† 3 vols. 18mo. Elam Bliss: New York, 1833.

* 12mo. pp. 257.

† In his remarks on Clinton he has a handsome allusion to forgetfulness of old difficulties:—

"The memory of De Witt Clinton, the first graduate of our Alma Mater after the peace of 1783, is another brilliant and treasured possession of this college. After the numerous tributes which have so recently been paid to his memory, and especially that luminous view of his character as a scholar and a statesman, as the promoter of good education and useful improvement, contained in the discourse lately delivered from this place by Professor Renwick, anything I could now say on the same subject would be but useless repetition. Else would I gladly pay the homage due to his eminent and lasting services, and honour that lofty ambition which taught him to look to designs of grand utility, and to their successful execution, as his arts of gaining or redeeming the confidence of a generous and public-spirited people. For whatever of party animosity might have ever blinded me to his merits, had died away long before his death; and I could now utter his honest praises without the imputation of hollow pretence from others, or the mortifying consciousness in my own breast, of rendering unwilling and tardy justice to noble designs and great public service."

‡ Lecture Introductory to the Course of Scientific Lectures before the Mechanics' Institute of the City of New York, Nov. 27, 1833. By Gulian C. Verplanck. New York: 1833.

§ The Advantages and the Dangers of the American Scholar. A Discourse delivered on the day preceding the Annual Commencement of Union College, July 26, 1836. By Gulian C. Verplanck. New York: Wiley and Long, 1836.

appeared. The publication was completed in 1847, forming three large octavo volumes.* The object of the publishers was to combine in the pictorial department, the attractions of the careful historical drawings of scenes and costumes of Planché and Harvey with the imaginative designs of Kenny Meadows, which had recently appeared in the London editions of Knight and Tyas. Mr. Verplanck's labors consist of a revision of the text, in which he has, in some cases, introduced readings varying from those of the ordinary editions, of selections from the notes of former editors, and the addition of others from his own pen. An excellent and novel feature of the latter is found in the care with which he has pointed out in the text several of the colloquial expressions often called Americanisms, which, out of use in England, have been preserved in this country. Mr. Verplanck has also given original prefaces to the plays, which, like the notes, have the ease and finish common to all his productions. His comments are judicious, and he has drawn his information from the best sources.

Mr. Verplanck has for many years divided his time between the city of New York and his ancestral homestead at Fishkill Landing on the Hudson, a well preserved old mansion, in which the Society of the Cincinnati was founded. He is one of the Commissioners of Emigration of the city, a member of the vestry of Trinity church, and is the incumbent of many other positions of trust and usefulness. He preserves in a hale old age the clear ruddy complexion with the activity of youth.

THE MOTHER AND THE SCHOOLMASTER.†

Of what incalculable influence, for good or for evil upon the dearest interests of society, must be the estimate entertained for the character of the great body of teachers, and the consequent respectability of the individuals who compose it.

* * * * * * *

What else is there in the whole of our social system of such extensive and powerful operation on the national character? There is one other influence more powerful, and but one. It is that of the MOTHER. The forms of a free government, the provisions of wise legislation, the schemes of the statesman, the sacrifices of the patriot, are as nothing compared with these. If the future citizens of our republic are to be worthy of their rich inheritance, they must be made so principally through the virtue and intelligence of their Mothers. It is in the school of maternal tenderness that the kind affections must be first roused and made habitual—the early sentiment of piety awakened and rightly directed—the sense of duty and moral responsibility unfolded and enlightened. But next in rank and in efficacy to that pure and holy source of moral influence is that of the Schoolmaster. It is powerful already. What would it be if in every one of those School districts which we now count by annually increasing thousands, there were to be found one teacher well-informed without pedantry, religious without bigotry or fanaticism, proud and fond of his profession, and honoured in the discharge of its duties! How wide would be the intellectual, the moral influence of such a body of men! Many such we have already amongst us—men humbly wise and obscurely useful, whom poverty cannot depress, nor neglect degrade. But to raise up a body of such men, as numerous as the wants and the dignity of the country demand, their labours must be fitly remunerated, and themselves and their calling cherished and honoured.

The schoolmaster's occupation is laborious and ungrateful; its rewards are scanty and precarious. He may indeed be, and he ought to be, animated by the consciousness of doing good, that best of all consolations, that noblest of all motives. But that too must be often clouded by doubt and uncertainty. Obscure and inglorious as his daily occupation may appear to learned pride or worldly ambition, yet to be truly successful and happy, he must be animated by the spirit of the same great principles which inspired the most illustrious benefactors of mankind. If he bring to his task high talent and rich acquirement, he must be content to look into distant years for the proof that his labours have not been wasted —that the good seed which he daily scatters abroad does not fall on stony ground and wither away, or among thorns, to be choked by the cares, the delusions, or the vices of the world. He must solace his toils with the same prophetic faith that enabled the greatest of modern philosophers,* amidst the neglect or contempt of his own times, to regard himself as sowing the seeds of truth for posterity and the care of Heaven. He must arm himself against disappointment and mortification, with a portion of that same noble confidence which soothed the greatest of modern poets when weighed down by care and danger, by poverty, old age, and blindness, still

> ——In prophetic dream he saw
> The youth unborn, with pious awe,
> Imbibe each virtue from his sacred page.

He must know and he must love to teach his pupils, not the meagre elements of knowledge, but the secret and the use of their own intellectual strength, exciting and enabling them hereafter to raise for themselves the veil which covers the majestic form of Truth. He must feel deeply the reverence due to the youthful mind fraught with mighty though undeveloped energies and affections, and mysterious and eternal destinies. Thence he must have learnt to reverence himself and his profession, and to look upon its otherwise ill-requited toils as their own exceeding great reward.

If such are the difficulties and the discouragements—such, the duties, the motives, and the consolations of teachers who are worthy of that name and trust, how imperious then the obligation upon every enlightened citizen who knows and feels the value of such men to aid them, to cheer them, and to honour them!

SAMUEL WOODWORTH,

THE author of the *Old Oaken Bucket*, was the youngest son of a farmer and revolutionary soldier, and was born at Scituate, Mass., January 13, 1785. He had but few educational advantages, as, according to the memoir prefixed to his poems in 1816, no school was taught in the village, except during the three winter months; and as a mistaken idea of economy always governed the selection of a teacher, he was generally as ignorant as his pupils.

---

* Shakespeare's Plays: with his Life. Illustrated with many hundred Wood-cuts, executed by H. W. Hewet, after designs by Kenny Meadows, Harvey, and others. Edited by Gulian C. Verplanck, LL.D., with Critical Introduction, Notes, etc., original and selected. In 3 vols. Harper & Brothers. 1847.

† From the Tribute to the Memory of Daniel H. Barnes.

* Bacon. "*Serere posteris ac Deo immortali.*"

Some juvenile verses written by young Woodworth attracted the attention of the village clergyman, the Rev. Nehemiah Thomas, who gave him a winter's instruction in the classics, and endeavored to raise an amount sufficient to support him at college, but without success. He was soon after apprenticed to a printer, the trade of his choice, Benjamin Russell the editor and publisher of the Columbian Centinel, Boston. He remained with his employer a year after the expiration of his indentures, and then removed to New Haven, where he commenced a weekly paper called the *Belles Lettres Repository*, of which he was "editor, publisher, printer, and (more than once) carrier." The latter duty was probably one of the lightest, as the periodical, after exhausting the cash received in advance, was discontinued at the end of the second month.

S Woodworth

Several of Woodworth's poems first appeared in The Complete Coiffeur; or an Essay on the Art of Adorning Natural and of Creating Artificial Beauty. By J. B. M. D. Lafoy, Ladies' Hair Dresser, 1817. This is a small volume of about two hundred pages, one half being occupied with a French translation of the other. M. Lafoy was probably ambitious to follow in the footsteps of the illustrious Huggins, or perhaps regarded the affair as a shrewd mode of advertising. It is to be hoped he paid Woodworth well for this literary job.

Woodworth left New Haven, and after a brief sojourn in Baltimore, removed to New York in 1809. In 1810 he married. During the contest of 1812 he conducted a quarto weekly paper entitled *The War*, and a monthly Swedenborgian magazine, *The Halcyon Luminary and Theological Repository*. Both were unsuccessful. His next literary undertaking was a contract in 1816 "to write a history of the late war, in the style of a romance, to be entitled *The Champions of Freedom*." The work was commenced in March, and the two duodecimos were ready for delivery in the following October. It possesses little merit as history or novel.

In 1818, a small volume of Woodworth's poetical contributions to various periodicals was published in New York. A second collection appeared in 1826.

In 1823, he commenced with George P. Morris the publication of the *New York Mirror*, a periodical with which he remained connected for a year. He was a frequent contributor of occasional verses to the newspapers, and his patriotic songs on the victories of the war of 1812 -14, and on other occasions, were widely popular. He was the author of several dramatic pieces, mostly operatic, which were produced with success. One of these, *The Forest Rose*, keeps possession of the stage, by virtue of the amusing Yankee character who is one of the dramatis personæ.

In the latter years of his life he suffered from paralysis. A complimentary benefit was given to him at the National Theatre in Leonard street, at which W. E. Burton made his first appearance in New York. It produced a substantial result, a gift as acceptable as well deserved, his pecuniary resources being meagre.

He died on the 9th of December, 1842. "The Old Oaken Bucket" is by far the best of his numerous lyrics. It will hold its place among the choice songs of the country.

AUTUMNAL REFLECTIONS.

The season of flowers is fled,
  The pride of the garden decayed,
The sweets of the meadow are dead,
  And the blushing parterre disarrayed.

The blossom-decked garb of sweet May,
  Enamell'd with hues of delight,
Is exchanged for a mantle less gay,
  And spangled with colours less bright.

For sober Pomona has won
  The frolicsome Flora's domains,
And the work the gay goddess begun,
  The height of maturity gains.

But though less delightful to view,
  The charms of ripe autumn appear,
Than spring's richly varied hue,
  That infantile age of the year:

Yet now, and now only, we prove
  The uses by nature designed;
The seasons were sanctioned to move,
  To please less than profit mankind.

Regret the lost beauties of May,
  But the fruits of those beauties enjoy;
The blushes that dawn with the day,
  Noon's splendour will ever destroy.

How pleasing, how lovely appears
  Sweet infancy, sportive and gay;
Its prattle, its smiles, and its tears,
  Like spring, or the dawning of day!

But manhood's the season designed
  For wisdom, for works, and for use;
To ripen the fruits of the mind,
  Which the seeds sown in childhood produce.

Then infancy's pleasures regret,
  But the fruits of those pleasures enjoy;
Does spring autumn's bounty beget?
  So the Man is begun in the Boy.

THE PRIDE OF THE VALLEY.

The pride of the valley is lovely young Ellen,
  Who dwells in a cottage enshrined by a thicket,
Sweet peace and content are the wealth of her dwelling,
  And Truth is the porter that waits at the wicket.

The zephyr that lingers on violet-down pinion,
  With Spring's blushing honors delighted to dally,
Ne'er breathed on a blossom in Flora's dominion,
  So lovely as Ellen, the pride of the valley.

She's true to her Willie, and kind to her mother,
  Nor riches nor honors can tempt her from duty;
Content with her station, she sighs for no other,
  Though fortunes and titles have knelt to her beauty.

To me her affections and promise are plighted,
  Our ages are equal, our tempers will tally;
O moment of rapture, that sees me united
  To lovely young Ellen, the pride of the valley.

THE OLD OAKEN BUCKET.

How dear to this heart are the scenes of my childhood,
When fond recollection presents them to view;
The orchard, the meadow, the deep tangled wild wood,
And every loved spot which my infancy knew;
The wide spreading pond, and the mill which stood by it,
The bridge and the rock where the cataract fell;
The cot of my father, the dairy-house nigh it,
And e'en the rude bucket which hung in the well.
The old oaken bucket, the iron-bound bucket,
The moss-covered bucket which hung in the well.

That moss-covered vessel I hail as a treasure;
For often, at noon, when returned from the field,
I found it the source of an exquisite pleasure,
The purest and sweetest that nature can yield.
How ardent I seized it with hands that were glowing,
And quick to the white pebbled bottom it fell;
Then soon, with the emblem of truth overflowing,
And dripping with coolness, it rose from the well;
The old oaken bucket, the iron-bound bucket,
The moss-covered bucket arose from the well.

How sweet from the green mossy brim to receive it,
As, pois'd on the curb, it inclined to my lips!
Not a full blushing goblet could tempt me to leave it,
Though fill'd with the nectar that Jupiter sips.
And now far removed from the loved situation,
The tear of regret will intrusively swell,
As fancy reverts to my father's plantation,
And sighs for the bucket which hangs in the well;
The old oaken bucket, the iron-bound bucket,
The moss-covered bucket which hangs in his well.

JOHN PIERPONT.

THE REV. JOHN PIERPONT was born at Litchfield, Connecticut, April 6, 1785. He is a descendant of the Rev. James Pierpont, the second minister of New Haven and a founder of Yale College. His early years were watched over with great care by an excellent mother, to whom he warmly expressed his gratitude in his subsequent poems. Entering Yale College he completed his course in 1804, and passed the succeeding four years as a private tutor in the family of Col. William Allston of South Carolina. On his return home he studied law in the celebrated school of his native town, and was admitted to practice in 1812. About the same period, being called upon to address the Washington Benevolent Society, Newburyport, where he had removed, he delivered the poem entitled "The Portrait," which he afterwards published, and which is included in the collection of his "Patriotic and Political Pieces." He soon, in consequence of impaired health, and the unsettled state of affairs produced by the war, relinquished his profession and became a merchant, conducting his business at Boston and afterwards at Baltimore. He was unsuccessful, and after a few years retired. In 1816 he published the *Airs of Palestine*, at Baltimore. It was well received, and was twice reprinted in the course of the following year at Boston.

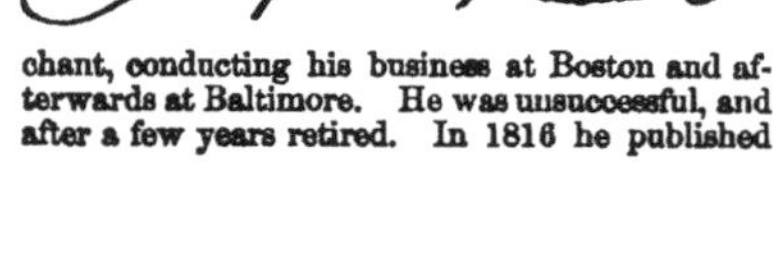

In 1819 Mr. Pierpont was ordained minister of the Hollis Street Unitarian church in Boston. He passed a portion of the years 1835–6 in Europe, and in 1840 published a choice edition of his poems.*

In 1851, on occasion of the centennial celebration at Litchfield, he delivered a poem of considerable length, with the mixture of pleasantry and sentiment called for in such recitations, and which contains, among other things, a humorous sketch of the Yankee character.

Besides his poems Mr. Pierpont has published several discourses.

Mr. Pierpont is erect and vigorous in appearance, with the healthy ruddiness in complexion of a youth. His style of speaking is energetic.

The chief poetical performances of Mr. Pierpont have been called forth for special occasions. Even his more matured poem, the Airs of Palestine, which first gave him reputation, was written for recitation at a charitable concert. Its design is to exhibit the associations of music combined with local scenery and national character in different countries of the world, the main theme being the sacred annals of Judea. It would bear as well the title The Power of Music. It is a succession of pleasing imagery, varied in theme and harmonious in numbers.

Most of the other poems of Pierpont are odes on occasional topics of religious, patriotic, or philanthropic celebrations. They are forcible and elevated, and have deservedly given the author a high reputation for this speciality.

INVITATIONS OF THE MUSE—FROM AIRS OF PALESTINE.

Here let us pause:—the opening prospect view:—
How fresh this mountain air!—how soft the blue,
That throws its mantle o'er the lengthening scene!
Those waving groves,—those vales of living green,—
Those yellow fields,—that lake's cerulean face,
That meets, with curling smiles, the cool embrace
Of roaring torrents, lulled by her to rest;—
That white cloud, melting on the mountain's breast:
How the wide landscape laughs upon the sky!
How rich the light that gives it to the eye!

Where lies our path?—though many a vista call.
We may admire, but cannot tread them all.
Where lies our path?—a poet, and inquire
What hills, what vales, what streams become the lyre?
See, there Parnassus lifts his head of snow;
See at his foot the cool Cephissus flow;
There Ossa rises; there Olympus towers;
Between them, Tempè breathes in beds of flowers,
For ever verdant; and there Peneus glides
Through laurels whispering on his shady sides.
Your theme is MUSIC:—Yonder rolls the wave,
Where dolphins snatched Arion from his grave,
Enchanted by his lyre:—Cithæron's shade
Is yonder seen, where first Amphion played
Those potent airs, that, from the yielding earth,
Charmed stones around him, and gave cities birth.
And fast by Hæmus, Thracian Hebrus creeps
O'er golden sands, and still for Orpheus weeps,
Whose gory head, borne by the stream along,
Was still melodious, and expired in song.

* Airs of Palestine and other Poems, by John Pierpont. Boston. Monroe & Co.

There Nereids sing, and Triton winds his shell;
There be thy path,—for there the Muses dwell.

No, no—a lonelier, lovelier path be mine:
Greece and her charms I leave, for Palestine.
There, purer streams through happier valleys flow,
And sweeter flowers on holier mountains blow.
I love to breathe where Gilead sheds her balm;
I love to walk on Jordan's banks of palm;
I love to wet my foot in Hermon's dews;
I love the promptings of Isaiah's muse;
In Carmel's holy grots I'll court repose,
And deck my mossy couch with Sharon's deathless rose.

AN ITALIAN SCENE.

On Arno's bosom, as he calmly flows,
And his cool arms round Vallombrosa throws,
Rolling his crystal tide through classic vales,
Alone,—at night,—the Italian boatman sails.
High o'er Mont' Alto walks, in maiden pride,
Night's queen;—he sees her image on that tide,
Now, ride the wave that curls its infant crest
Around his prow, then rippling sinks to rest;
Now, glittering dance around his eddying oar,
Whose every sweep is echoed from the shore;
Now, far before him, on a liquid bed
Of waveless water, rest her radiant head.
How mild the empire of that virgin queen!
How dark the mountain's shade! how still the scene!
Hushed by her silver sceptre, zephyrs sleep
On dewy leaves, that overhang the deep,
Nor dare to whisper through the boughs, nor stir
The valley's willow, nor the mountain's fir,
Nor make the pale and breathless aspen quiver,
Nor brush, with ruffling wing, that glassy river.

Hark!—'tis a convent's bell:—its midnight chime;
For music measures even the march of Time:—
O'er bending trees, that fringe the distant shore,
Gray turrets rise:—the eye can catch no more.
The boatman, listening to the tolling bell,
Suspends his oar:—a low and solemn swell,
From the deep shade, that round the cloister lies,
Rolls through the air, and on the water dies.
What melting song wakes the cold ear of Night?
A funeral dirge, that pale nuns, robed in white,
Chant round a sister's dark and narrow bed,
To charm the parting spirit of the dead.
Triumphant is the spell! with raptured ear,
That unchanged spirit hovering lingers near;—
Why should she mount? why pant for brighter bliss,
A lovelier scene, a sweeter song, than this!

DEDICATION HYMN.

Written for the Dedication of the new Congregational Church in Plymouth, built upon the Ground occupied by the earliest Congregational Church in America.

The winds and waves were roaring;
  The Pilgrims met for prayer;
And here, their God adoring,
  They stood, in open air.
When breaking day they greeted,
  And when its close was calm,
The leafless woods repeated
  The music of their psalm.

Not thus, O God, to praise thee,
  Do we, their children, throng;
The temple's arch we raise thee
  Gives back our choral song.
Yet, on the winds, that bore thee
  Their worship and their prayers,
May ours come up before thee
  From hearts as true as theirs!

What have we, Lord, to bind us
  To this, the Pilgrims' shore!—
Their hill of graves behind us,
  Their watery way before,
The wintry surge, that dashes
  Against the rocks they trod,
Their memory, and their ashes,—
  Be thou their guard, O God!

We would not, Holy Father,
  Forsake this hallowed spot,
Till on that shore we gather
  Where graves and griefs are not;
The shore where true devotion
  Shall rear no pillared shrine,
And see no other ocean
  Than that of love divine.

CENTENNIAL ODE.

Written for the Second Centennial Celebration of the Settlement of Boston, September 17th, 1830.

Break forth in song, ye trees,
As, through your tops, the breeze
  Sweeps from the sea!
For, on its rushing wings,
To your cool shades and springs,
That breeze a people brings,
  Exiled though free.

Ye sister hills, lay down
Of ancient oaks your crown,
  In homage due;—
These are the great of earth,
Great, not by kingly birth,
Great in their well proved worth,
  Firm hearts and true.

These are the living lights,
That from your bold, green heights,
  Shall shine afar,
Till they who name the name
Of Freedom, toward the flame
Come, as the Magi came
  Toward Bethlehem's star.

Gone are those great and good,
Who here, in peril, stood
  And raised their hymn.
Peace to the reverend dead!
The light, that on their head
Two hundred years have shed,
  Shall ne'er grow dim.

Ye temples, that to God
Rise where our fathers trod,
  Guard well your trust,—
The faith, that dared the sea,
The truth, that made them free,
Their cherished purity,
  Their garnered dust.

Thou high and holy ONE,
Whose care for sire and son
  All nature fills,
While day shall break and close,
While night her crescent shows,
O, let thy light repose
  On these our hills.

M. M. NOAH.

MORDECAI MANUEL NOAH, whose popular reputation, as a newspaper writer of ease and pleasantry, was extended through the greater part of a long life, was born in Philadelphia July 19, 1785. He was early apprenticed to a mechanical business, which he soon left, and engaged in the study of the law, mingling in politics and literature. He removed to Charleston, S. C., where he was busily engaged in politics of the day.

In 1813, under Madison, he was appointed U. S. consul to Morocco. The vessel in which he sailed from Charleston was taken by a British frigate, and he was carried to England and detained several weeks a prisoner, when he was allowed to proceed to his destination. After his return to America in 1819, he published a volume of his *Travels in England, France, Spain, and the Barbary States, from* 1813 *to* 1815. He had now established himself at New York, where he edited the *National Advocate*, a democratic journal. He was elected sheriff of the city and county. In a squib of the time he was taunted with his religion. "Pity," said his opponents, "that Christians are to be hereafter hung by a Jew." "Pretty Christians," replied the Major, as he was generally called, "to require hanging at all."

The *National Advocate* was discontinued in 1826, and Noah then commenced the publication of the *New York Enquirer*, which he conducted for a while till it was annexed to the *Morning Courier*, a union which gave rise to the present large commercial journal, *The Courier and Enquirer*. In 1834, in connexion with Thomas Gill, he established a popular daily newspaper, *The Evening Star*, which attained considerable reputation from the ready pen of Noah, who was considered the best newspaper paragraphist of his day. His style in these effusions well represented his character: facile, fluent, of a humorous turn, pleasing in expression, though sometimes ungrammatical, with a cheerful vein of moralizing, and a knowledge of the world. The *Star* was united to the *Times*, becoming the *Times and Star*, and was finally merged in the *Commercial Advertiser* in 1840. After this, in July, 1842, Noah originated the *Union*, a daily paper, illustrating a new phase of the Major's political life; and like all his other undertakings of the kind, enlivened by the editor's peculiar pleasantry. It was continued in his hands through the year, after which Noah, in conjunction with Messrs. Deans and Howard, established a Sunday newspaper, *The Times and Messenger*, for which he wrote weekly till within a few days of his death, by an attack of apoplexy, March 22, 1851.

There was no man better known in his day in New York than Major Noah. His easy manners, fund of anecdote, fondness for biographical and historical memoirs, acquaintance with the public characters, political and social, of half a century, with whom his newspaper undertakings had brought him in contact; his sympathy with the amusements of the town of all descriptions, actors, singers, and every class of performers, all of which were severally promoted by his benevolent disposition, made his company much sought and appreciated.

In 1845 Noah delivered *A Discourse on the Restoration of the Jews*, which was published—a fanciful speculation.

Some time before his death he published a little volume of his newspaper essays, entitled *Gleanings from a Gathered Harvest;* but they are of his more quiet and grave moralizings, and hardly indicate the shrewdness and satiric mirth which pointed his paragraphs against the follies of the times. In his way, too, the kindly Major had been something of a dramatist. He

M. M. Noah

has related the story of his accomplishments in this line in so characteristic a manner, in a letter to Dunlap, published in his "History of the American Theatre," that we may quote it at once as part of our history, and as a specimen of the style of the writer.

TO WILLIAM DUNLAP, ESQ.

NEW YORK, *July* 11, 1832.

DEAR SIR,

I am happy to hear that your work on the American Drama is in press, and trust that you may realize from it that harvest of fame and money to which your untiring industry and diversified labors give you an eminent claim. You desire me to furnish you a list of my dramatic productions; it will, my dear sir, constitute a sorry link in the chain of American writers—my plays have all been *ad captandum:* a kind of *amateur* performance, with no claim to the character of a settled, regular, or domiciliated writer for the green-room—a sort of volunteer supernumerary—a dramatic writer by "particular desire, and for this night only," as they say in the bills of the play; my "line," as you well know, has been in the more rugged paths of politics, a line in which there is more fact than poetry, more feeling than fiction; in which, to be sure, there are "exits and entrances"—where the "prompter's whistle" is constantly heard in the voice of the people; but which, in our popular government, almost disqualifies us for the more soft and agreeable translation of the lofty conceptions of tragedy, the pure diction of genteel comedy, or the wit, gaiety, and humor of broad farce.

I had an early hankering for the national drama, a kind of juvenile patriotism, which burst forth, for the first time, in a few sorry doggrels in the form of a prologue to a play, which a Thespian company, of which I was a member, produced in the South Street Theatre—the old American theatre in Philadelphia. The idea was probably suggested by the sign of the Federal Convention at the tavern opposite the theatre. You, no doubt, remember the picture and the motto: an excellent piece of painting of the kind, representing a group of venerable personages engaged in public discussions, with the following distich:

These thirty-eight great men have signed a powerful deed,
That better times to us shall very soon succeed.

The sign must have been painted soon after the adoption of the federal constitution, and I remember to have stood "many a time and oft," gazing, when a boy, at the assembled patriots, particularly the venerable head and spectacles of Dr. Franklin, always in conspicuous relief. In our Thespian corps, the honor of cutting the plays, substituting new passages, casting parts, and writing couplets at the exits, was divided between myself and a fellow of infinite wit and humor, by the name of Helmbold; who subsequently became the editor of a scandalous little paper, called the *Tickler:* he was a rare rascal, perpetrated all kinds of calumnies, was constantly mulcted in fines, sometimes imprisoned, was full of faults, which were forgotten in his conversational qualities and dry sallies of genuine wit, particularly his Dutch stories. After years of singular vicissitudes, Helmbold joined the army as a common soldier, fought bravely during the late war, obtained a commission, and died. Our little company soon dwindled away; the expenses were too heavy for our pockets; our writings and performances were sufficiently wretched, but as the audience was admitted without cost, they were too polite to express any disapprobation. We recorded all our doings in a little weekly paper, published, I believe, by Jemmy Riddle, at the corner of Chestnut and Third street, opposite the tavern kept by that sturdy old democrat, Israel Israel.

From a boy, I was a regular attendant of the Chestnut Street Theatre, during the management of Wignell and Reinagle, and made great efforts to compass the purchase of a season ticket, which I obtained generally of the treasurer, George Davis, for $18. Our habits through life are frequently governed and directed by our early steps. I seldom missed a night; and always retired to bed, after witnessing a good play, gratified and improved: and thus, probably, escaped the haunts of taverns, and the pursuits of depraved pleasures, which too frequently allure and destroy our young men; hence I was always the firm friend of the drama, and had an undoubted right to oppose my example through life to the horror and hostility expressed by sectarians to play and play-houses generally. Independent of several of your plays which had obtained possession of the stage, and were duly incorporated in the legitimate drama, the first call to support the productions of a fellow townsman, was, I think, Barker's opera of the "Indian Princess." Charles Ingersoll had previously written a tragedy, a very able production for a very young man, which was supported by all the "good society;" but Barker who was "one of us," an amiable and intelligent young fellow, who owed nothing to hereditary rank, though his father was a Whig, and a soldier of the Revolution, was in reality a fine spirited poet, a patriotic ode writer, and finally a gallant soldier of the late war. The managers gave Barker an excellent chance with all his plays, and he had merit and popularity to give them in return full houses.

About this time, I ventured to attempt a little melo-drama, under the title of *The Fortress of Sorrento*, which, not having money enough to pay for printing, nor sufficient influence to have acted, I thrust the manuscript in my pocket, and having occasion to visit New York, I called in at David Longworth's Dramatic Repository one day, spoke of the little piece, and struck a bargain with him, by giving him the manuscript in return for a copy of every play he had published, which at once furnished me with a tolerably large dramatic collection. I believe the play never was performed, and I was almost ashamed to own it; but it was my first regular attempt at dramatic composition.

In the year 1812, while in Charleston, S. C., Mr. Young requested me to write a piece for his wife's benefit. You remember her, no doubt; remarkable as she was for her personal beauty and amiable deportment, it would have been very ungallant to have refused, particularly as he requested that it should be a "*breeches part,*" to use a green-room term, though she was equally attractive in every character. Poor Mrs. Young! she died last year in Philadelphia. When she first arrived in New York, from London, it was difficult to conceive a more perfect beauty; her complexion was of dazzling whiteness, her golden hair and ruddy complexion, figure somewhat *embonpoint*, and graceful carriage, made her a great favorite. I soon produced the little piece, which was called *Paul and Alexis, or the Orphans of the Rhine.* I was, at that period, a very active politician, and my political opponents did me the honor to go to the theatre the night it was performed, for the purpose of hissing it, which was not attempted until the curtain fell, and the piece was successful. After three years' absence in Europe and Africa, I saw the same piece performed at the Park under the title of *The Wandering Boys*, which even now holds possession of the stage. It seems Mr. Young sent the manuscript to London, where the title was changed, and the bantling cut up, altered, and considerably improved.

About this time, John Miller, the American bookseller in London, paid us a visit. Among the passengers in the same ship was a fine English girl of great talent and promise, Miss Leesugg, afterwards Mrs. Hackett. She was engaged at the Park as a singer, and Phillips, who was here about the same period, fulfilling a most successful engagement, was decided and unqualified in his admiration of her talent. Every one took an interest in her success: she was gay, kind-hearted, and popular, always in excellent spirits, and always perfect. Anxious for her success, I ventured to write a play for her benefit, and in three days finished the patriotic piece of *She would be a Soldier, or the Battle of Chippewa*, which, I was happy to find, produced her an excellent house. Mrs. Hackett retired from the stage after her marriage, and lost six or seven years of profitable and unrivalled engagement.

"After this play, I became in a manner domiciliated in the green-room. My friends, Price and Simpson, who had always been exceedingly kind and liberal, allowed me to stray about the premises like one of the family, and always anxious for their success, I ventured upon another attempt for a holyday occasion, and produced *Marion, or the Hero of Lake George.* It was played on the 25th of November—Evacuation day, and I bustled about among my military friends, to raise a party in support of a military play, and what with generals, staff-officers, rank and file, the Park Theatre was so crammed, that not a word of the play was heard, which was a very fortunate affair for the author. The managers presented me with a pair of handsome silver pitchers, which I still retain as a memento of their good will and friendly consideration. You must bear in mind that while I was thus employed in occasional attempts at play-writing, I was engaged in editing a daily journal, and in all the fierce contests of political strife; I had, therefore, but little time to devote to all that study and reflection so essential to the success of dramatic composition.

My next piece, I believe, was written for the

benefit of a relative and friend, who wanted something to bring a house; and as the struggle for liberty in Greece was at that period the prevailing excitement, I finished the melo-drama of *The Grecian Captive*, which was brought out with all the advantages of good scenery and music. As a "good house" was of more consequence to the actor than fame to the author, it was resolved that the hero of the piece should make his appearance on an elephant, and the heroine on a camel, which were procured from a neighboring *menagerie*, and the *tout ensemble* was sufficiently imposing, only it happened that the huge elephant, in shaking his skin, so rocked the castle on his back, that the Grecian general nearly lost his balance, and was in imminent danger of coming down from his "high estate," to the infinite merriment of the audience. On this occasion, to use another significant phrase, a "gag" was hit upon of a new character altogether. The play was printed, and each auditor was presented with a copy gratis, as he entered the house. Figure to yourself a thousand people in a theatre, each with a book of the play in hand—imagine the turning over a thousand leaves simultaneously, the buzz and fluttering it produced, and you will readily believe that the actors entirely forgot their parts, and even the equanimity of the elephant and camel were essentially disturbed.

My last appearance as a dramatic writer was in another national piece, called *The Siege of Tripoli*, which the managers persuaded me to bring out for my own benefit, being my first attempt to derive any profit from dramatic efforts. The piece was elegantly got up—the house crowded with beauty and fashion—everything went off in the happiest manner; when a short time after the audience had retired, the Park Theatre was discovered to be on fire, and in a short time was a heap of ruins. This conflagration burnt out all my dramatic fire and energy, since which I have been, as you well know, peaceably employed in settling the affairs of the nation, and mildly engaged in the political differences and disagreements which are so fruitful in our great state.*

I still, however, retain a warm interest for the success of the drama, and all who are entitled to success engaged in sustaining it, and to none greater than to yourself, who has done more, in actual labor and successful efforts, than any man in America. That you may realize all you have promised yourself, and all that you are richly entitled to, is the sincere wish of

Dear sir,

Your friend and servant,

M. M. Noah.

Wm. Dunlap, Esq.

* The author does not add, which was the fact, that the proceeds of this fatal benefit evening which he received, amounting to the considerable sum of nearly two thousand dollars, were the next day given to the actors, and others, who had suffered by the fire.

FRANKLIN COLLEGE, GA.

Dr. Church, the president of this institution, which is situated at Athens, Georgia, in *A Discourse delivered before the Historical Society* of the state, has thus traced the progress of education in that region.

"The first constitution of Georgia was adopted the 5th of February, 1777, only a few months after the Declaration of Independence. The 54th section of this constitution declares, 'Schools shall be erected in each county, and supported at the general expense of the state.' This is an important record in the history of our education. On the 31st of July, 1783, the Legislature appropriated 1000 acres of land to each county for the support of free schools. In 1784, a few months after the ratification of the treaty of peace, by which our national independence was acknowledged, the legislature, again in session at Savannah, passed an act, appropriating 40,000 acres of land for the endowment of a college or university. This act commences with the remarkable preamble: 'Whereas, the encouragement of religion and learning is an object of great importance to any community, and must tend to the prosperity and advantage of the same.'

"In 1785, the charter of the university was granted, the preamble to which would do honor to any legislature, and will stand a monument to the wisdom and patriotism of those who framed, and of those who adopted it.

"'As it is the distinguishing happiness of free governments that civil order should be the result of choice and not necessity, and the common wishes of the people become the laws of the land, their public prosperity and even existence very much depends upon suitably forming the minds and morals of their citizens. When the minds of the people in general are viciously disposed and unprincipled, and their conduct disorderly, a free government will be attended with greater confusions, and evils more horrid than the wild uncultivated state of nature. It can only be happy where the public principles and opinions are properly directed and their manners regulated.

"'This is an influence beyond the stretch of laws and punishments, and can be claimed only by religion and education. It should, therefore, be among the first objects of those who wish well to the national prosperity, to encourage and support the principles of religion and morality; and early to place the youth under the forming hand of society, that, by instruction, they may be moulded to the love of virtue and good order. Sending them abroad to other countries for education will not answer the purposes, is too humiliating an acknowledgment of the ignorance or inferiority of our own, and will always be the cause of so great foreign attachments that, upon principles of policy, it is inadmissible.'

"In 1792, an act was passed appropriating one thousand pounds for the endowment of an Academy in each county.

"In 1798, a third constitution was adopted. The 13th section of the 4th article declares: 'The arts and sciences shall be patronized in one or more seminaries of learning.'

"In 1817, two hundred and fifty thousand dollars were appropriated to the support of poor schools. In 1818, every 10th and 100th lot of land in seven new counties were appropriated to the cause of education, and in 1821, two hundred and fifty thousand dollars were set apart for the support of county academies."*

The selection of the site for the university was peculiar. It was located on a tract of ground, on what was then the remote border of population on the north-western boundary of the territory, in reference to the future growth of the state

* A Discourse delivered before the Georgia Historical Society, on the occasion of its Sixth Anniversary, Feb. 12, 1845.

rather than present convenience. In addition to the forty thousand acres originally granted by the legislature for the support of the university, Governor Milledge generously presented to the institution, at an expense of four thousand dollars, a tract of land of seven hundred acres, better adapted for the site, on which Franklin College was established in 1801. It was some time before these endowments of land became available for the support of the institution. They have now provided an ample fund. In 1816 the lands of the original grant were sold, and one hundred thousand dollars were invested in bank stock, guaranteed by the state to yield an annual interest of eight per cent. From the lands purchased by Governor Milledge, the college has received, by the sale of lots at various times, some thirty thousand dollars, twenty thousand of which are invested as a permanent fund.

At the outset, the institution was embarrassed for want of ready pecuniary means; but its difficulties were met with spirit by the leading men of the state, among whom Dr. Church enumerates in his Discourse, Baldwin, Jackson, Milledge, Early, the Houstons, the Habershams, Clay, Few, Brownson, Taliaferro, Stephens, Walton, Jones, and Gov. Jackson.

The line of Presidents has been—the Rev. Dr. Josiah Meigs, from 1801 to 1811; the Rev. Dr. John Brown, from 1811 to 1816; the Rev. Dr. Robert Finley, who died after a year's incumbency, in 1817; the Rev. Dr. Moses Waddel, from 1819 to 1829; and the Rev. Dr. Alonzo Church, from that time. Dr. Meigs had been Professor of Natural Philosophy and Astronomy in Yale; Dr. Brown had held the chair of Moral Philosophy in Columbia College, South Carolina; Dr. Waddel, one of the most popular teachers of the South, was a native of North Carolina. He passed forty-five years as a teacher, dying in 1840 at the age of seventy.

Previously to the sale of the lands in 1816, the college was closed for three years, in consequence of the war and the want of funds. Its whole number of graduates to the close of 1852 appears by the catalogue to be six hundred and ninety-nine.

The college buildings have cost some eighty thousand dollars. The library consists of over twelve thousand volumes, and there is an excellent philosophical, chemical, and astronomical apparatus, with a valuable cabinet of minerals, and a neat botanic garden.

The college is under the charge of twenty-eight trustees, elected at first by the legislature, but all vacancies are filled by the trustees. The Senate of the State and Board of Trustees constitute the Senatus Academicus of the state, and all institutions of learning receiving funds from the state must report to the Senatus, of which the Governor of the State is president, at each meeting of the Legislature.

Of the other college institutions in the state, the Presbyterian institution of Oglethorpe University, situated near Milledgeville, was founded in 1837. It grew out of a manual labor school under the direction of the Rev. Dr. C. P. Beman, who became the first president of the college in 1838. On his retirement in 1840, he was succeeded by the present incumbent, the Rev. Dr. S. K. Talmage. The number of students by the catalogue of 1853–4 is sixty-four. Its alumni, from 1838 to 1853, have been one hundred and thirty-eight. The president is Professor of Ancient Languages and Belles Lettres.

Mercer University is a Baptist institution, situated at Penfield; and Emory College, at Oxford, is attached to the Methodist Church. The former has a theological course of instruction. It dates from 1838. Emory College was founded in 1837. Oxford, the town in which it is located, is a pleasant rural village with a permanent population of some six hundred persons, who have chosen that residence almost exclusively with reference to the college. The present head of Mercer is Dr. N. M. Crawford; of Emory, the Rev. Dr. P. S. Pierce.

In August 7, 1851, the semi-centennial anniversary of Franklin College was celebrated, and an address delivered in the college chapel at Athens before the Society of Alumni by the Hon. George R. Gilmer, who took for his subject "The Literary Progress of Georgia." In this discourse, which was printed at the time, will be found a genial picturesque narrative, with numerous anecdotes of the early days of Georgia, sketches of the character of her citizens and of their means of education, with the stray Ichabod Cranes who preceded the foundation of her academies and colleges, which have since become the distinguished ornaments of the state.

ST. JOHN'S COLLEGE, MARYLAND.

In 1782 an act of assembly in Maryland was passed for founding a seminary on the Eastern shore. The charter of incorporation required that a sum of money should be raised by contribution equal to five hundred pounds for each county in that region. Ten thousand pounds were thus collected in five months. The college went into operation at Chestertown, and took the name of Washington, who was one of the contributors to its funds. Its first annual Commencement was held May 16, 1783. Washington visited the college the next year. At the same time, in 1784, an act was passed for founding a college on the western shore, and constituting the same, together with Washington College, one institution. This was incorporated by the name of the Visitors and Governors of St. John's College, and a grant of seventeen hundred pounds "annually and for ever," was made by the legislature. There was also a subscription of ten thousand pounds, of which two thousand were subscribed by the Rector and Visitors of the Annapolis school. A board was organized, and its first meeting held in 1786. The joint institution was opened at Annapolis in 1789, and Dr. John McDowell was chosen as Professor of Mathematics, and afterwards as Principal. In 1792 six professors and teachers were constantly employed in the college, which was well attended, and sent forth numbers of the distinguished men of the state. In 1805, the legislature, by an illiberal act of economy, withdrew the annual fund solemnly granted at the founding of the college. This was for the time a virtual breaking up of the institution. Efforts were made for the restoration of the grant. In 1811 the legislature appropriated one thousand dollars, and in 1821 granted a lottery the proceeds of which were twenty thousand dollars. In 1832 two thousand dollars per annum were secured to the college by the legislature. In the meantime the succession of Principals had included, after Dr. McDowell, the Rev. Drs. Bethel Judd, Henry Lyon Davis, and William Rafferty. In 1831, about the time of the revival of the college affairs, the Rev. Dr. Hector Humphreys, the present incumbent, was elected Principal. The classes increased, new accommodation was required, and in 1835 a new college building was erected; an historical address being delivered at the ceremony of laying the corner-stone by John Johnson, one of the Visitors and Governors, who thus alluded to some of the advantages and associations of the site:—"If education is to be fostered in Mary-

St. John's College, Maryland.

land as its importance demands, no location more favorable for its cultivation could be selected than this. The building now existing, and that in the course of construction, are seated in a plain of great extent and unrivalled beauty. The climate of the place is unsurpassed for salubrity, and whilst the moral contamination incident to the vicinity of a large town is not to be dreaded, the presence of the seat of Government is full of advantages. Everything conspires to render St. John's a favorite of the State. It was built up by the purchasers of our freedom whilst the storms of the Revolution were yet rocking the battlements of the Republic. It has enrolled among its alumni some of the brightest ornaments of the nation, and continued its usefulness to the last, though frowned upon and discouraged by the parent which created it. It is endeared by its origin; venerable for its age; illustrious for the great minds nurtured within its walls, and entitled to our gratitude for yet striving to do good."

During the administration of Dr. Humphreys the prosperity of the college, in the number of students, has greatly increased. New departments of study have been opened, and new Professorships and college buildings projected.

C. S. RAFINESQUE.

C. S. Rafinesque was born, he informs us at the outset of his *Life of Travels and Researches*, at Galata, a suburb of Constantinople, in 1784. His father was a Levant merchant from Marseilles. While an infant he was taken to that city by sea, and says that it was owing to this early voyage that he was ever after exempt from sea-sickness. In his seventh year his father went to China, and on his return ran into Philadelphia to escape the English cruisers, where he died of yellow fever in 1793. Meanwhile the mother, terrified at the *sans-culottes*, removed with her children to Leghorn. After passing several years in various cities in the north of Italy, he was sent to the United States in 1802, with his brother. He landed at Philadelphia, visited Bartram and other naturalists, his botanical tastes having already developed themselves, and travelled a little in Pennsylvania and Delaware. He returned to Leghorn with a large stock of specimens in March, 1805, and in May of the same year sailed for Sicily, where he passed ten years in "residence and travels," engaged partly in botany, and partly in merchandise, during which he published a work, *The Analysis of Nature*, in the French language. In 1815 he sailed for New York, but was shipwrecked on the Long Island coast. "I lost," he says, "everything, my fortune, my share of the cargo, my collections and labors for twenty years past, my books, my manuscripts, my drawings, even my clothes—all that I possessed, except some scattered funds, and the insurance ordered in England for one third the value of my goods. The ship was a total wreck, and finally righted and sunk, after throwing up the confined air of the hold by an explosion."

He made his way to New York and presented himself to Dr. Mitchill, who introduced him to friends, and obtained a place for him as tutor to the family of Mr. Livingston on the Hudson. In 1818 he made a tour to the West, leaving the stage at Lancaster "to cross the Alleghanies on foot, as every botanist ought." He floated down the Ohio in an ark to Louisville, where he received an invitation to become Professor of Botany at Transylvania University, Lexington. After returning to Philadelphia to close his business affairs he removed to Lexington, and appears to have obtained the professorship, and performed its duties for some time. He still, however, continued his travels, lectured in various places, and endeavored to start a magazine and a botanic garden, but without success in either case. He finally established himself in Philadelphia, where he published *The Atlantic Journal and Friend of Knowledge, a Cyclopædic Journal and Review.* The first number is dated "Spring of 1832," and forms an octavo of thirty-six pages. "This journal," says the prospectus, "shall contain everything calculated to enlighten, instruct, and improve the mind." But eight numbers appeared. In 1836 he published *Life of Travels and Researches*, a brief narrative, furnishing little more than an itinerary of the places he visited during his almost uninterrupted peregrinations. In addition to these works he published several volumes on botany. Rafinesque died at Philadelphia, September 18, 1842.

DANIEL DRAKE—BENJAMIN DRAKE.

Daniel Drake was born at Plainfield, New Jersey, October 20, 1785; was taken while quite a youth to Mason county, Kentucky, and was brought up there. When a young man he went to Cincinnati, and studied medicine at the Medical School of the University of Pennsylvania, at Philadelphia, became a practitioner of medicine at Cincinnati, and attained high eminence in his profession. He was a professor and teacher of the medical science for the greater part of his life in the schools at Cincinnati, at Philadelphia, at Lexington, Kentucky, and at Louisville, Kentucky, where he was associated with the most distinguished men of his profession. Without excelling in any of the graces of the orator, he was a most effective and popular lecturer. An original thinker, zealous, energetic, a lover of truth, he delighted in acquiring and communicating knowledge. A philanthropist, a public-spirited citizen, a man of untiring industry and indomitable energy, he spent a long and active life in constant efforts to do good. Devoted to the interests of Cincinnati, he was a zealous and active promoter of every measure for the advancement of her prosperity, and especially for her moral and intellectual improvement. His time, his pen, his personal exertions, were at all times at the service of his profession, his country, his fellow-creatures. In a long life of uncommon industry, marked by a spirit and perseverance unattainable by ordinary men, the larger portion of his time was given to the public, to benevolence, and to science.

As a writer Dr. Drake is entitled to consideration in American literature, not from the style of his compositions, which had little to recommend it, but from their useful character and scientific value. Besides his acknowledged works, he was the author of a vast number of pamphlets and newspaper essays, written to promote useful objects, all marked by great vigor and conciseness of style, and singleness of purpose. His *Picture of Cincinnati*, under a modest title, embraced an admirable account of the whole Miami country, and was one of the first works to attract attention to the Ohio valley. His great work on the *Diseases of the Interior Valley of North America* occupied many years, and was perhaps in contemplation during the greater part of his professional life. It is a work of herculean labor,—of exertions of which few men would be capable. It covers the whole ground of the Mississippi and its tributaries, and nearly all of North America, and professes to treat of the diseases of that vast region. It is not compiled from books, nor could it be, for the subject is new. This vast mass of information is the result of the author's personal exploration, and of extensive correspondence with scientific men. During the vacations between the medical lectures, year after year, Dr. Drake travelled, taking one portion of country after another, and exploring each systematically and carefully, from the Canadian wilds to Florida and Texas. Dividing this vast region into districts, he gives a detailed topographical description of each, marking out distinctly its physical characteristics and peculiarities; he describes the climate, the productions, the cultivation, the habits of the people; he traces the rivers to their sources; points out the mountain ranges, the valleys, the plains—everything that could affect the health of man, as a local cause, is included in his survey. Then he gives the actual diseases which he found to be prevalent in each district, the peculiar phase of the disease, with the treatment, and other interesting facts.

Dr. Daniel Drake died at Cincinnati, November 5, 1852.*

Benjamin Drake, brother of Dr. Daniel Drake, was as marked for his benevolence and public spirit as for his literary tastes and abilities. He was born in Mason county, Kentucky, November 28, 1794, and died in Cincinnati, April 1, 1841. He was for many years editor of the *Cincinnati Chronicle*, a weekly literary newspaper published at Cincinnati, distinguished for its agreeable and sprightly articles, and for the courtesy, good taste, and common sense, with which it was conducted. It was particularly instrumental in promoting the prosperity of Cincinnati, by advocating all measures of improvement, and giving a public-spirited tone to public sentiment. As long as Drake lived this paper was very popular in the city and all the surrounding region. He was a most amiable, pure-minded man. His *Tales from the Queen City* are lively and very agreeable sketches of Western life, written with some ability, and much delicacy and taste. His *Life of Tecumseh* was written with great care from materials collected in Ohio and Indiana, where that distinguished warrior was well known, and is a valuable contribution to our national history.*

Charles D. Drake, of St. Louis, a son of Dr. Daniel Drake, born in Cincinnati, April 11, 1811, is the author of *A Treatise on the Law of Suits by Attachment in the United States*, an octavo volume, published in 1854.†

NICHOLAS BIDDLE.

Nicholas Biddle belonged to a family which furnished its quota to the service of the State. His father, Charles Biddle, was an active Revolutionary patriot, and held the post, at the time of his son's birth, of Vice-President of the Pennsylvania Commonwealth, when Franklin was president. His uncle, Edward Biddle, was the naval commodore who ended his career so gallantly in the affair of the Randolph.

The son and nephew, Nicholas, was born at Philadelphia, January 8, 1786. He was educated at the University of Pennsylvania, where he had

* The following is a list of books written by him, with the dates of their publication:—

1810. Notices concerning Cincinnati, pp. 64, 12mo.
1815. Picture of Cincinnati, pp. 250, 12mo.
1832. Practical Essays on Medical Education and the Medical Profession in the United States, pp. 104, 12mo.
1832. A Practical Treatise on the History, Prevention, and Treatment of Epidemic Cholera, designed both for the Profession and the People, pp. 180, 12mo.
1850. A Systematic Treatise, Historical, Etiological, and Practical, on the Principal Diseases of the Interior Valley of North America, as they appear in the Caucasian, African, Indian, and Esquimaux varieties of its population, pp. 878, 8vo.
1854. The second volume of the same, posthumously published, pp. 985., 8vo.

He edited, for many years, very ably and assiduously the Western Journal of Medical Science, published at Cincinnati, and contributed largely to its pages.

* The following is a complete list of his writings:—

1827. Cincinnati in 1826, by B. Drake and E. D. Mansfield, pp. 100, 12mo.
1830–33. Between these years he prepared a book on the subject of Agriculture, which was published anonymously. It was a compilation, and contained probably 300 pages, 12mo.
1838. The Life and Adventures of Black Hawk: with Sketches of Keokuk, the Sac and Fox Indians, and the late Black Hawk War, pp. 288, 12mo.
1838. Tales and Sketches from the Queen City, pp. 180, 12mo.
1840. Life of General William Henry Harrison, a small volume, of perhaps 250 pages, prepared jointly by B. Drake and Charles S. Todd.
1841. Life of Tecumseh, and his brother the Prophet, with a Historical Sketch of the Shawanoe Indians, pp. 285, 12mo.

† We are indebted for this notice of Drake and his family to Mr. James Hall of Cincinnati.

completed the round of studies at thirteen; when his youth led to a further course of study at Princeton, where, after two years and a half, he took his degree with distinguished honor, at a remarkably early age, in 1801. He then studied law in Philadelphia for three years, when his father's friend, General Armstrong, receiving the appointment of Minister to France, he embarked with him as his secretary, and resided till 1807 in Europe. They were the days of the Empire. At this time the payment of the indemnity for injuries to American commerce was going on, and young Biddle, at the age of eighteen, managed the details of the disbursements with the veterans of the French bureau. Leaving the legation he travelled through the greater part of the continent, and arriving in England, became secretary to Monroe, then minister at London. On a visit to Cambridge, the story is told of his delighting Monroe by the exhibition of his knowledge of modern Greek, picked up on his tour to the Mediterranean, when, in company with the English scholars, some question arose relating to the present dialect, with which they were unacquainted.

On his return to America in 1807 he engaged in the practice of the law, and filled up a portion of his time with literary pursuits. He became associated in the editorship of the Port Folio in 1813, and wrote much for it at different times. His papers on the Fine Arts, biographical and critical on the old masters, are written with elegance, and show a discriminating taste. He also penned various literary trifles, and wrote occasional verses, with the taste of the scholar and humorist. Among these light effusions a burlesque criticism of the nursery lines on Jack and Gill is a very pleasant specimen of his abilities in a line which the example of Canning and others has given something of a classic flavor.

When Lewis and Clarke were preparing the history of their American Exploration, the death of Lewis occurred suddenly, and the materials of the work were placed in the hands of Biddle, who wrote the narrative, and induced Jefferson to pen the preliminary memoir of Lewis. It was simply conducted through the press by Paul Allen, to whom the stipulated compensation was generously transferred; when the political engagements of Biddle rendered his further attention to it impracticable. He was in the State Legislature in 1810, advocating a system of popular education with views in advance of his times. It was not till 1836 that his ideas were carried out by legislative enactment. When the question of the renewal of the Charter of the old United States Bank was discussed in the session of 1811, he spoke in defence of the Institution in a speech which was widely circulated at the time, and gained the distinguished approval of Chief-justice Marshall.

From the Legislature he retired to his studies and agriculture, always a favorite pursuit with him. When the second war with England broke out, he was elected to the State Senate. He was now one of seven brothers, all his father's family engaged in the service of the country—in the navy, the army, and the militia. When the land was threatened with invasion, he proposed vigorous measures for the military defence of the State, which were in progress of discussion when peace intervened. At the close of the war, he met the attacks upon the Constitution of the Hartford Convention, by a Report on the questions at issue, adopted in the Pennsylvania Legislature. In the successive elections of 1818 and 1820, he received a large vote for Congress from the democratic party, but was defeated.

In 1819 he became director of the Bank of the United States, which was to exercise so unhappy an influence over his future career, on the nomination of President Monroe; who about the same time assigned to him the work, under a resolution of Congress, of collecting the laws and regulations of foreign countries relative to commerce, money, weights, and measures. These he arranged in an octavo volume, *The Commercial Digest*.

In 1823, on the retirement of Langdon Cheves from the Presidency of the Bank, he was elected his successor. His measures in the conduct of the institution belong to the financial and political history of the country. The veto of Jackson closed the affairs of the bank in 1836. The new state institution bearing the same name was immediately organized with Biddle at its head. He held the post for three years, till March, 1839. The failure of the bank took place in 1841. The loss was tremendous, and Biddle was personally visited as the cause of the disaster. He defended his course in a series of letters, and kept up his interest in public affairs, but death was busy at his heart; and not long after, the 26th February, 1844, at his residence of Andalusia on the Delaware, he died from a dropsical suffusion of that organ, having just completed his fifty-fourth year. He had entered upon active life early, and performed the work of three score and ten.

In addition to the pursuits already mentioned, requiring so large an amount of political force and sagacity, Biddle had distinguished himself through life by his tastes for literature. He delivered a eulogium on Jefferson before the Philosophical Society, and an Address on the Duties of the American to the Alumni of his college at Princeton. As a public speaker, he was polished and effective.

GARDINER SPRING.

Gardiner Spring was born at Newburyport, Massachusetts, February 24, 1785. He was the son of the Rev. Dr. Samuel Spring, one of the Chaplains of the Revolutionary Army, who accompanied Arnold in his attack on Quebec in 1775, and carried Burr, when wounded, off the field in his arms.

The son was prepared for college in the grammar-school of his native town, and under a private tutor in the office of Chief Justice Parsons. He entered Yale College, and delivered the valedictory oration at the conclusion of his course in 1805. After studying law in the office of Judge Daggett at New Haven, a por-

* Memoir by R. T. Conrad in the National Portrait Gallery. vol. iv. Ed. 1854.

tion of his time being occupied in teaching, he passed fifteen months in the island of Bermuda, where he established an English school. On his return he was admitted to the bar in December, 1808. He commenced the profession with good prospect of success, but was induced soon after, by the advice of his father and the effect of a sermon of the Rev. Dr. John M. Mason, from the text "To the poor the gospel is preached," to study theology. After a year passed at Andover, he was licensed to preach towards the close of 1809. In June, 1810, he accepted a call to the Brick church in the city of New York, where he has since remained, unmoved by invitations to the presidencies of Hamilton and Dartmouth Colleges, maintaining during nearly half a century a position as one of the most popular preachers and esteemed divines of the metropolis. He has for many years commemorated his long pastorate by an anniversary discourse.

Dr. Spring is the author of several works which have been published in uniform style, and now extend to eighteen octavo volumes. They have grown out of his duties as a pastor, and consist for the most part of courses of lectures on the duties and advantages of the Christian career. The edition of his works now in course of publication, embraces *The Attraction of the Cross*, designed to illustrate the leading Truths, Obligations, and Hopes of Christianity; *The Mercy-Seat*, Thoughts suggested by the Lord's Prayer; *First Things*, A Series of Lectures on the Great Facts and Moral Lessons first revealed to Mankind; *The Glory of Christ*, Illustrated in his Character and History, including the Last Things of His Mediatorial Government; *The Power of the Pulpit*, or, Plain Thoughts addressed to Christian Ministers and those who hear them, on the influence of a Preached Gospel; *Short Sermons for the People*, being a Series of short Discourses of a highly practical character; *The Obligations of the World to the Bible; Miscellanies*, including the Author's "Essays on the Distinguishing Traits of Christian Character," "The Church in the Wilderness," &c., &c. *The Contrast*, in press.

These volumes have passed through several editions, and have been in part reprinted and translated in Europe, and are held in well deserved repute.

In 1849 he published *Memoirs of the late Hannah L. Murray*, a lady of New York, distinguished in the wide circle of her friends for her benevolence and intellectual acquirements. She translated, with the aid of her sister, the whole of Tasso's Jerusalem Delivered, and many of the odes of Anacreon, into English verse, and was the author of a poem of five thousand lines in blank verse entitled The Restoration of Israel, an abstract of which, with other unpublished productions, is given by her biographer.

Dr. Spring is an eloquent, energetic preacher; his style direct and manly. As a characteristic specimen of his manner we give a passage from his volume, The Glory of Christ.

A POPULAR PREACHER.

Nor may the fact be overlooked, in the next place, that he was an *impressive and powerful preacher.* In the legitimate sense of the term, he was *popular*, and interested the multitude. He never preached to empty synagogues; and when he occupied the market or the mountain side, they were not hundreds that listened to his voice, but thousands. It is recorded of him, that "his fame went throughout all Syria;" and that "there followed him great multitudes of people from Decapolis, and from Jerusalem, and from Judea, and from beyond Jordan." On that memorable day when he went from the Mount of Olives to Judea, "a great multitude spread their garments in the way, and others cut down branches from the trees," and all cried "Hosannah to the Son of David!" After he uttered the parable of the vineyard, the rulers "sought to lay hold of him, but *feared the people*." When he "returned in the power of the Spirit into Galilee, there went out a fame of him throughout all the region round about," and he "was glorified of all, and great multitudes came together to hear him." So much was he, for the time, the idol of the people, that the chief priests and Pharisees were alarmed at his popularity, and said among themselves, "If we let him then alone, all men will believe on him; behold, *the world* is gone after him." He was the man of the people, and advocated the cause of the people. We are told that "the *common people* heard him gladly." He was "no respecter of persons." He was the preacher to man, as man. He never passed the door of poverty, and was not ashamed to be called "the friend of publicans and sinners." His gospel was and is the great and only bond of brotherhood; nor was there then, nor is there now, any other universal brotherhood, than that which consists in love and loyalty to him. He was the only safe reformer the world has seen, because he so well understood the checks and balances by which the masses are governed. His preaching, like his character, bold and uncompromising as it was, was also in the highest degree conservative. He taught new truths, and he was the great vindicator of those that were old. All these things made him a most impressive, powerful, and attractive preacher. His very instructiveness, prudence, and boldness, interested the people. They respected him for his acquaintance with the truth, and honored his discretion and fearlessness in proclaiming it. This is human nature; men love to be thus instructed; they come to the house of God for that purpose. A vapid and vapory preacher may entertain them for the hour; a smooth and flattering preacher may amuse them; a mere denunciatory preacher may produce a transient excitement; but such is the power of conscience, and such the power of God and the wants of men that, though their hearts naturally hate God's truth, they will crowd the sanctuaries where it is instructively and fearlessly, and discreetly urged, while ignorance, and error, and a coward preacher, put forth their voice to the listless and the few

ANDREWS NORTON.

ANDREWS NORTON was of the family of the celebrated John Norton of Ipswich, of the old age of Puritan divinity. He was born at Hingham, Mass., the last day of the year 1786. Fond of books from a child, at the age of eighteen he had completed his course at Harvard, where he remained a resident graduate, pursuing a course of literary and theological study. In October, 1809, he was appointed tutor in Bowdoin College. At the end of the year he returned to Cambridge, where in 1811 he was chosen tutor in mathematics in his college, where he remained till 1812, when he engaged in the conduct of *The General Repository*, a periodical work on the side of the new liberal school, as it was called, which took position at Harvard shortly after the beginning of the century. He had previously written for the Literary Miscellany, published at Cambridge, in 1804–5, several reviews and brief poetical translations, and had been a frequent contributor to the Monthly Anthology.

Andrews Norton

From 1813 to 1821 he was college librarian. In the former year he also commenced the course of instruction through which he gained his greatest distinction in his entrance upon the lectureship of Biblical Criticism and Interpretation, under the bequest of the Hon. Samuel Dexter, in which Buckminster and Channing were his predecessors. He discharged this duty till a similar professorship was created in 1819, when he became the new incumbent, holding the office till 1830. He then resigned it with the reputation of having performed its offices with industry, self-reliance, and a happy method of statement. He had in the meanwhile published several works. In 1814 he edited the Miscellaneous Writings of his friend Charles Eliot, whose early death he sincerely lamented, and in 1823 published a similar memoir of another friend and associate, the poet and professor Levi Frisbie. He wrote several tracts on the affairs of the college in 1824–5. At this time he was a contributor to the Christian Disciple of several articles on theological topics. In 1826 he edited an edition of the poems of Mrs. Hemans, of whom he was an earnest admirer, and in the following year in a visit to England was rewarded with her friendship in a personal acquaintance. In 1833 he published a theological treatise, *A Statement of Reasons for not believing the Doctrines of Trinitarians concerning the nature of God and the person of Christ.* In 1833–4 he edited, in connexion with his friend Charles Folsom, a quarterly publication, *The Select Journal of Foreign Periodical Literature,* which contained, among other original articles from his pen, papers on Goethe and Hamilton's Men and Manners in America.

In 1837 appeared the first volume of the most important of his publications, the *Genuineness of the Gospel,* followed by the second and third in 1844. It is devoted to the external historical evidence, and maintains a high character among theologians for its scholarship, and the pure medium of reasoning and style through which its researches are conveyed. He had also prepared a new translation of the Gospels, with critical and explanatory notes, which he left at the time of his death ready for the press. Besides these writings Mr. Norton was a frequent contributor to the Christian Examiner of articles on religious topics and others of a general literary interest, on the poetry of Mrs. Hemans and Pollok's Course of Time. He wrote for the North American Review on Franklin, Byron, Ware's Letters from Palmyra, and the Memoir of Mrs. Grant of Laggan.

His poems were few, but choicely expressed; and have been constant favorites with the public. They are the best indications of his temper, and of the fine devotional mood which pervades his writings.

Professor Norton died at Newport, which he had chosen for his residence in the failing health of his last years, Sunday evening, September 18, 1853.*

SCENE AFTER A SUMMER SHOWER.

The rain is o'er. How dense and bright
 Yon pearly clouds reposing lie!
Cloud above cloud, a glorious sight,
 Contrasting with the dark blue sky!

In grateful silence, earth receives
 The general blessing; fresh and fair,
Each flower expands its little leaves,
 As glad the common joy to share.

The softened sunbeams pour around
 A fairy light, uncertain, pale;
The wind flows cool; the scented ground
 Is breathing odors on the gale.

Mid yon rich clouds' voluptuous pile,
 Methinks some spirit of the air
Might rest, to gaze below awhile,
 Then turn to bathe and revel there.

The sun breaks forth; from off the scene
 Its floating veil of mist is flung;
And all the wilderness of green
 With trembling drops of light is hung.

Now gaze on Nature—yet the same—
 Glowing with life, by breezes fanned,
Luxuriant, lovely, as she came,
 Fresh in her youth, from God's own hand.

Hear the rich music of that voice,
 Which sounds from all below, above;
She calls her children to rejoice,
 And round them throws her arms of love.

Drink in her influence; low-born care,
 And all the train of mean desire,
Refuse to breathe this holy air,
 And 'mid this living light expire.

ON LISTENING TO A CRICKET.

I love, thou little chirping thing,
 To hear thy melancholy noise;
Though thou to Fancy's ear may sing
 Of summer past and fading joys.

Thou canst not now drink dew from flowers,
 Nor sport along the traveller's path,
But, through the winter's weary hours,
 Shalt warm thee at my lonely hearth.

And when my lamp's decaying beam
 But dimly shows the lettered page,
Rich with some ancient poet's dream,
 Or wisdom of a purer age,—

Then will I listen to thy sound,
 And, musing o'er the embers pale,
With whitening ashes strewed around,
 The forms of memory unveil;

Recall the many-colored dreams,
 That Fancy fondly weaves for youth,
When all the bright illusion seems
 The pictured promises of truth;

Perchance, observe the fitful light,
 And its faint flashes round the room,
And think some pleasures, feebly bright,
 May lighten thus life's varied gloom.

* We have followed closely in this account the authentic narrative article, published after Professor Norton's death, in the Christian Examiner for November, 1853.

I love the quiet midnight hour,
When Care, and Hope, and Passion sleep,
And Reason, with untroubled power,
Can her late vigils duly keep;—

I love the night: and sooth to say,
Before the merry birds, that sing
In all the glare and noise of day,
Prefer the cricket's grating wing.

But, see! pale Autumn strews her leaves,
Her withered leaves, o'er Nature's grave,
While giant Winter she perceives,
Dark rushing from his icy cave;

And in his train the sleety showers,
That beat upon the barren earth;
Thou, cricket, through these weary hours,
Shalt warm thee at my lonely hearth.

HYMN.

My God, I thank thee! may no thought
E'er deem thy chastisements severe;
But may this heart, by sorrow taught,
Calm each wild wish, each idle fear.

Thy mercy bids all nature bloom;
The sun shines bright, and man is gay;
Thine equal mercy spreads the gloom
That darkens o'er his little day.

Full many a throb of grief and pain
Thy frail and erring child must know,
But not one prayer is breathed in vain
Nor does one tear unheeded flow.

Thy various messengers employ;
Thy purposes of love fulfil;
And 'mid the wreck of human joy,
May kneeling faith adore thy will!

FUNERAL DIRGE.

He has gone to his God; he has gone to his home;
No more amid peril and error to roam;
His eyes are no longer dim;
His feet will no more falter;
No grief can follow him,
No pang his cheek can alter.

There are paleness, and weeping, and sighs below;
For our faith is faint, and our tears will flow;
But the harps of heaven are ringing;
Glad angels come to greet him;
And hymns of joy are singing,
While old friends press to meet him.

O honored, beloved, to earth unconfined,
Thou hast soared on high; thou hast left us behind;
But our parting is not for ever;
We will follow thee, by heaven's light,
Where the grave cannot dissever
The souls whom God will unite.

JOHN ENGLAND.

John England, the Roman Catholic Bishop of Charleston, was born in Cork, Ireland, September 23, 1786. He was educated in the schools of his native town, and at the age of fifteen, avowing his intention to become an ecclesiastic, was placed under the care of the Very Rev. Robert M'Carthy, by whom he was in two years fitted for the college of Carlow. During his connexion with this institution, he was instrumental in procuring the establishment of a female penitentiary in the town. On the ninth of October, 1808, he was ordained Deacon, and the following day Priest, and was appointed lecturer at the Cork Cathedral, an office which he discharged with great success. In May, 1809, he started a monthly periodical, *The Religious Repertory*, with the object of supplanting the corrupt literature current among the people, by a more healthy literary nutriment. He was also active in various charitable works, and indefatigable in his attendance on the victims of pestilence, and the inmates of prisons. In 1812 he took an active part, as a political writer, in the discussion of the subject of Catholic Emancipation. In 1817 he was appointed Parish Priest of Bandon, where he remained until made by the Pope, Bishop of the newly constituted See of Charleston, embracing the two Carolinas and Georgia. He was consecrated in Ireland, but refused to take the oath of allegiance to the British government customary on such occasions, declaring his intention to become naturalized in the United States. He arrived in Charleston, December 31, 1820.

One of his first acts was the establishment of a theological seminary, to which a preparatory school was attached. This led to corresponding exertions on the part of Protestants in the matter of education, which had hitherto been much neglected, and the first number of the Southern Review honored the bishop with the title of restorer of classical learning in Charleston. He was also instrumental in the formation of an "Anti-duelling Society," for the suppression of that barbarous and despicable form of manslaughter, of which General Thomas Pinckney was the first president. He also commenced a periodical, *The United States Catholic Miscellany*, to which he continued a constant contributor to the time of his death.

The bishop was greatly aided in his charitable endeavors, and in his social influence, by the arrival of his sister, Miss Joanna England. "She threw her little fortune into his poverty-stricken institutions. Her elegant taste presided over the literary department of the Miscellany. Her feminine tact would smoothe away whatever harshness his earnest temper might unconsciously infuse into his controversial writings. Her presence shed a magic charm around his humble dwelling, and made it the envied resort of the talented, the beautiful, and gay."* This estimable lady died in 1827.

In times of pestilence, Bishop England was fearless and untiring in his heroic devotion to the sick. He was so active in the discharge of his duties and in his ordinary movements, that on his visits to Rome, four of which occurred during his episcopate, he was called by the cardinals, *il vescovo a vapore*.

It was on his return from the last of these journeys, that in consequence of his exertions as priest and physician among the steerage passengers of the ship in which he sailed, he contracted the disease, dysentery, which was prevalent among them. He landed after a voyage of fifty-two days in Philadelphia, and instead of recruiting his strength, preached seventeen nights in succession. His health had been impaired some months previously, and although on his arrival at Charleston he became somewhat better, he died not

* Memoir of Bp. England prefixed to his works.

long after, on the eleventh of April, 1842, in the fifty-sixth year of his age.

The collected works of Bishop England* bear testimony to his literary industry, as well as ability. They extend to five large octavo volumes of some five hundred pages each, closely printed in double columns. They are almost entirely occupied by essays on topics of controversial theology, many of which are in the form of letters published during his lifetime in various periodicals. A portion of the fourth and fifth volumes is filled by the author's addresses before various college societies, and on other public occasions, including an oration on the character of Washington. These writings, like the discourses which in his lifetime attracted admiring crowds, are marked by force and elegance of style.

THOMAS SMITH GRIMKÉ

WAS born in Charleston, S. C., September 26, 1786. He was a descendant of the Huguenots. At the age of seventeen he was at Yale College, and travelled with Dr. Dwight during one of his vacations. Returning home, he studied law in the office of Mr. Langdon Cheves, and gradually attained distinction at the bar and in the politics of his state. His most noted legal effort was a speech on the constitutionality of the South Carolina "test oath" in 1834. As state senator from St. Philip's and St. Michael's in a speech on the Tariff in 1828, he supported the General Government and the Constitutional authority of the whole people. His literary efforts were chiefly orations and addresses illustrating topics of philanthropy and reform. Literature also employed his attention. He wrote several articles for the Southern Review. In a Fourth of July Oration at Charleston in 1809, by the appointment of the South Carolina State Society of Cincinnati, he supports union, and describes the horrors of civil war.

Thus should we see the objects of these States not only unanswered but supplanted by others. They had instituted the civic festival of peace, and beheld it changed for the triumph of war. They had crowned the eminent statesman with the olive of the citizen, and saw it converted into the laurels of the warrior. The old man who had walked exultingly in procession, to taste the waters of freedom from the fountain of a separate government, beheld the placid stream that flowed from it suddenly sink from his sight, and burst forth a dark and turbulent torrent.

His addresses on peace societies, Sunday schools, temperance and kindred topics, secured him the respect and sympathy of a large circle. He published and circulated gratuitously a large edition of Hancock on War, and at his death was republishing Dymond's Enquiry into the Accordance of War with the Principles of Christianity, for which he wrote an introductory essay. In 1827 he delivered an address on *The Character and Objects of Science* before the Literary and Philosophical Society of South Carolina; in 1830, an address before the Phi Beta Kappa of Yale, on *The Advantages to be derived from the Introduction of the Bible and of sacred literature as essential parts of all Education, in a literary point of view.* His oration on American education before the Western Literary Institute and College of Professional Teachers at Cincinnati, was delivered by him only a few days before his death, which occurred suddenly at the house of a gentleman by the roadside, from an attack of cholera, October 12, 1834, while on his way to Columbus, Ohio.

In a prefatory memorandum to this last address, the views of orthography which he had latterly adopted are clearly stated.

"Having been long satisfied that the orthography of the English language not only admitted but required a reform; and believing it my *duty* to act on this conviction, I hav publishd sevral pamphlets accordingly." These are his several propositions, which we give mostly in his words, following the exact spelling. 1. He omits the silent e in such classes of words as *disciplin, respit, believ, creativ, volly, &c.* 2. Introduces the apostrophe where the omission of the e might change the sound of the preceding vowel from long to short, as in *requir'd, refin'd, deriv'd.* 3. Nouns ending in y added an s to make the plural instead of changing y into ie, as *pluralitys, enmitys, &c.* 4. In verbs ending in y, instead of changing into ie and then adding an s or d, he retains the y and adds s or d: as in burys, buryd, varys, varyd, hurrys, hurryd. 5. In similar verbs where the y is long, I retain the y, omit the e, and substitute an apostrophe, as in multiply's, multiply'd, satisfy's, satisfy'd. 6. In such words as sceptre, battle, centre, I transpose the e, and write scepter, battel, center. 7. He suppresses one of two and the same consonants where the accent is *not* on *them;* as in *necesary, excelent, ilustrious, recomend, efectual, irresistible, worshipers.* 8. In such words as *honor, favor, savior, neighbor, savor,* the u is omitted. 9. In adjectives ending in y, instead of forming the comparativ and superlativ by changing y into ie and adding er and est, I hav retained the y, and simply added the er and est, as in *easyer, easyest, holyer, holyest, prettyer, prettyest.* In quotations and proper names, I hav not felt call'd upon to change the orthography.

This was not Grimké's only literary heresy. In his oration on the subject "that neither the classics nor the mathematics should form a part of a scheme of general education in our country," he condemns all existing schemes. "I think them radicaly defectiv in elements and modes." They are not "decidedly religious," neither are they "American." The latter, since the classics and mathematics being the same everywhere, are not of course distinctive to the country. "They do not fill the mind," he says, "with useful and entertaining knowledge." "As to valuable knowledge, except the first and most simple parts of arithmetic, I feel little hesitation in saying, as the result of my experience and observation, *that the whole body of the pure mathematics* is ABSOLUTELY USELESS to ninety-nine out of every hundred, who study them. Now, as to entertainment. Does more than one out of every hundred preserv his mathematical knowlege?"

"Ten thousand pockets," says he, "might be pick'd

* The Works of the Right Rev. John England, First Bishop of Charleston, collected and arranged under the advice and direction of his immediate successor, the Right Rev. Ignatius Aloysius Reynolds, and printed for him, in five volumes. Baltimore: John Murphy & Co. 1849.

without finding a dozen classics." "I ask boldly the question, what is there in the classics, that is realy instructiv and interesting?" He asks triumphantly —the ignorance is amazing,—"What orator ever prepared himself for parliamentary combat over the pages of Cicero or Demosthenes?" "Having dispos'd of the orators and historians, let us now attend to the classic poets, of what value are they? I answer of *none*, so far as useful knowlege is concerned; for all must admit, that none is to be found in this class of writers. It is plain that truth is a *very minor* concern, with writers of fiction. * * * I am strangely mistaken, if there be not more power, fidelity, and beauty in Walter Scott, than in a dozen Homers and Virgils. * * * Mrs. Hemans has written a greater number of charming little pieces, than are to be found in Horace and Anacreon."

The activity of Grimké's mind was sometimes in advance of his judgment. He was a happy man in his life,—his benevolence, and the ardor of his pursuits filling his heart. His death was received with every token of respect at Charleston, the preamble to the resolutions of the bar declaring "his mild face will no longer be seen among us, but the monuments of his public usefulness and benevolence are still with us, and the memory of his virtues will still dwell within our hearts."* The introduction of the Bible into schools was a favorite idea with him, which he urged in his Phi Beta address. He wrote occasional verses, and a descriptive poem on the Passaic, which is unpublished. As a speaker, he showed great readiness in a copious and fluent style.

A brother of the preceding, Frederick Grimké, is the author of a popular political text-book, entitled *The Nature and Tendency of Free Institutions*, published in Cincinnati in 1848.

* Collection of Addresses, &c., by Gr'mké, and Obituary Notices furnished by his family in the Boston Athenæum.

SAMUEL FARMAR JARVIS.

Samuel Farmar, the son of the Rev. Dr. Abraham Jarvis, afterwards bishop of the diocese of Connecticut, was born at Middletown in that State, January 20, 1787. He was educated under the care of his father, and entered the Sophomore class of Yale College in 1802. He was ordained deacon March 18, 1810, and priest April 5, 1811, by his father, and became, in 1813, the rector of St. Michael's Church, Bloomingdale, New York. In 1819 he was appointed Professor of Biblical Learning in the recently organized General Theological Seminary, a position he retained until his removal in 1820 to Boston, in acceptance of a call to the rectorship of St. Paul's church, where he remained until July, 1826, when he sailed for Europe. He remained abroad until 1835, pursuing his studies and collecting books connected with ecclesiastical history. Six of the nine years of his absence were passed in Italy. On his return he filled for two years the professorship of Oriental Literature in Washington College, Hartford. In 1837 he removed to Middletown to take charge, as rector, of Christ church in that place. He resigned this position in 1842, and devoted the remainder of his life to a work which he had commenced immediately after his return from Europe. This was a history of the church, a work especially intrusted to his hands by a vote of the General Convention of the dioceses of the United States, constituting him "Historiographer of the Church."

The first portion of his work published, appeared at New York, in 1845, in an octavo volume entitled, *A Chronological Introduction to the History of the Church, with an Original Harmony of the Four Gospels*.* A great portion of this learned volume is occupied with chronological tables, dissertations on the dates of our Lord's birth, which he places in the year of Rome 747, six years before the commonly received Christian era. In the Harmony of the Gospels the information the narratives contain is given in a consecutive form, embodying the facts but not the words of Scripture; while in four parallel columns at the side, reference is given to the chapter and verse of each of the Evangelists in which the event described is recorded.

The first volume of the history† itself was published in 1850. In it the author traces the course of the divine providence from the fall of Adam, the flood, the calling of Abraham, and the entire Jewish history, to the destruction of Jerusalem by Titus. While the same scrupulous regard to fact is manifested in this as in the introduction, the literary skill, for which no opportunity was afforded in the first, is used to good advantage in the second, the narrative being well written as well as accurate. In the author's own simile, the first volume is the rough stone-work of the foundation, the second is the elaborated superstructure which must satisfy, so far as it can, the eye of the artist as well as the mechanic.

In addition to his history, Dr. Jarvis published, in 1821, a discourse on *Regeneration*, with notes; in 1837, on *Christian Unity;* and in 1843, a collection of *Sermons on Prophecy*, a work of great research, forming a volume of about two hundred pages. In 1843 he also issued a pamphlet entitled, *No Union with Rome;* in 1846 a sermon, *The Colonies of Heaven;* and in 1847 a volume containing a *Reply to Dr. Milner's End of Religious Controversy*. He also contributed a number of learned and valuable articles to the Church Review. His progress in the History of the Church and the other useful labors of his life, was interrupted by his death, March 26, 1851.

Dr. Jarvis was a fine classical as well as biblical scholar. He also took a great interest in Art, and collected during his European residence a large gallery of old paintings, mostly of the Italian school, which were exhibited on his return for the benefit of a charitable association, and were again collected after his death in the city of New York to be dispersed by the auctioneer's hammer, with the large and valuable library, which included a number of volumes formerly owned by the historian Gibbon.

* A Chronological Introduction to the History of the Church, being a new inquiry into the True Dates of the Birth and Death of Our Lord and Saviour Jesus Christ; and containing an original Harmony of the Four Gospels, now first arranged in the order of time, by the Rev. S. F. Jarvis, D.D., LL.D. New York: Harper & Brothers. 1845. 8vo. pp. 618.

† The Church of the Redeemed, or the History of the Mediatorial Kingdom, 2 vols. containing the First Five Periods; from the Fall of Adam in Paradise to the Rejection of the Jews and the Calling of the Gentiles. By the Rev. S. F. Jarvis, D.D., LL.D. Boston: Charles Stimpson. 1850. 8vo. pp. 662.

WILLIAM CRAFTS.

William Crafts was born at Charleston, S. C., Jan. 24, 1787. "Owing," says his anonymous biographer,* somewhat grandiloquently, "to the precarious and evanescent character of the schools in Charleston," his early education suffered somewhat from the frequent change of teachers. He appears to have made up for juvenile disadvantages when in the course of education he reached Harvard, as he had a fair reputation there as a classical scholar, and judging from his advice subsequently to a younger brother, went still deeper into the ancient languages. "I hope," he writes, "that you will not treat the Hebrew tongue with that cold neglect and contemptuous disdain which it usually meets at Cambridge, and which is very much like the treatment a Jew receives from a Christian." His chief reputation among his fellows was as a wit and pleasant companion.

He returned to Charleston, was admitted in due course to practice, and the remainder of his life was passed in the duties of his profession and those of a member of the State Legislature, to which he was frequently elected. He was a ready speaker, and a large portion of the volume of his *Literary Remains*† consists of his orations on patriotic occasions. In 1817, he delivered the Phi Beta Kappa address at Harvard. These productions, as well as his prose essays, are somewhat too florid in style and deficient in substance for permanent recollection. Passages, however, occur of pleasing ornament and animation.

Wm Crafts

His poems are few and brief. The two longest are *Sullivan's Island*, a pleasant description of that ocean retreat, and *The Raciad*, in which the humors of the ring are depicted. An extract from "Kitty" follows, on the plea that "in New York they have Fanny, in Boston Sukey,‡ and why should we not have Kitty in Charleston!" There are also several agreeable lyrics. The *Monody on the Death of Decatur* was written immediately after the intelligence of the Commodore's death was received, and published the day following, a circumstance which should not be forgotten in a critical estimate. It is not included in the collection of his writings. He also wrote *The Sea Serpent; or Gloucester Hoax*, a dramatic jeu d'esprit in three acts, published in a pamphlet of 34 pages 12mo. Crafts was a constant writer for the Charleston Courier, and a number of his communications, some mere scraps, are printed in the volume of his "writings," but call for no especial remark.

Crafts died at Lebanon Springs, N. Y., Sept. 23, 1826.

MONODY ON THE DEATH OF DECATUR.

Sweet scented flowers on beauty's grave
We strew—but, for the honored brave,
The *fallen conqueror* of the wave—
Let ocean's flags adorn the bier,
And be the Pall of Glory there!

Tri-colored *France!* 'twas first with thee
He braved the battles of the sea;
And many a son of thine he gave
A resting-place beneath the wave.
Feared in the fight—beloved in peace
In death the feuds of valor cease.
Then let thy virgin lilies shed
Their fragrant whiteness o'er his head.
They grace a hero's form within,
As spotless—as unstained of sin.

Come, savage, from the Lybian shore,
Kneel at his grave, who—bathed in gore,
Avenged his brother's murder on your deck,
And drenched with coward blood the sinking wreck!
Lives in your mind that death-dispensing night,
The purple ambush and the sabred fight,—
The blazing frigate—and the cannon's roar,
That shamed your warriors flying to the shore:
Who, panic-stricken, plunged into the sea,
And found the death they vainly hoped to flee.

Now silent, cold, inanimate he lies,
Who sought the conflict and achieved the prize.
Here, savage, pause! The unresented worm
Revels on him—who ruled the battle storm.
His country's call—though bleeding and in tears—
Not e'en his country's call, the hero hears.
The floating streamers that his fame attest,
Repose in honored folds upon his breast,
And glory's lamp, with patriot sorrows fed,
Shall blaze eternal on Decatur's bed.

Britannia!—noble-hearted foe—
Hast thou no funeral flowers of woe
To grace his sepulchre—who ne'er again
Shall meet thy warriors on the purple main.
His pride to conquer—and his joy to save—
In triumph generous, as in battle brave—
Heroic—ardent—when a captive—great!
Feeling, as valiant—thou deplorest his fate.
And these thy sons who met him in the fray,
Shall weep with manly tears the hero passed away.

Fresh trophies graced his laurel-covered days,
His soil was danger—and his harvest, praise.
Still as he marched victorious o'er the flood,
It shook with thunder—and it streamed with blood.
He dimmed the baneful crescent of Algiers,
And taught the pirate penitence and tears.
The Christian stars on faithless shores revealed,
And lo! the slave is free—the robbers yield.
A Christian conqueror in the savage strife,
He gave his victims liberty and life.
Taught to relent—the infidel shall mourn,
And the pale crescent hover o'er his urn.

And thou, my country! young but ripe in grief!
Who shall console thee for the fallen *chief!*
Thou envied land, whom frequent foes assail,
Too often called to bleed or to prevail;
Doomed to deplore the gallant sons that save,
And follow from the triumph to—the grave.

Death seems enamoured of a glorious prize,
The chieftain conquers ere the victim dies.
Illustrious envoys—to some brighter sphere
They bear the laurels which they gathered here.

War slew thy Lawrence! Nor when blest with peace
Did then thy sufferings or thy sorrows cease:
The joyous herald, who the olive bore,
Sunk in the wave—to greet his home no more:
He sunk, alas!—blest with a triple wreath,
The modest Shubrick met the shaft of death.

* Life prefixed to his Remains.

† A Selection, in Prose and Poetry, from the Miscellaneous Writings of the late William Crafts, to which is prefixed a Memoir of his Life. Charleston. 1828.

‡ By William B. Walter.

For Blakely, slumbering in victorious sleep,
Rocked in the stormy cradle of the deep,
We yield alike the tribute and the tear,
The brave are always to their country dear.

Sorrow yet speaks in valor's eye,
Still heaves the patriot breast the sigh,
For Perry's early fate. O'er his cold brow
Where victory reigned sits death triumphant now.
Thou peerless youth, thou unassuming chief,
Thy country's blessing and thy country's grief,
Lord of the lake, and champion of the sea,
Long shall our nation boast—for ever mourn for thee.

Another hero meets his doom;
Such are the trophies of the tomb!
Ambitious death assails the high;
The shrub escapes, the cedars die.
The beacon turrets of the land
Submissive fall at Heaven's command,
While wondering, weeping mortals gaze,
In silent grief and agonized amaze.

Thou starry streamer! symbol of the brave,
Shining by day and night, on land and wave;
Sometimes obscured in battle, ne'er in shame,
The guide—the boast—the arbitress of fame!
Still wave in grateful admiration near,
And beam for ever on Decatur's bier;
And ye, blest stars of Heaven! responsive shed
Your pensive lustre on his lowly bed.

ELIZA LESLIE.

Eliza Leslie was born in Philadelphia, November 15, 1787. Her father was of Scotch descent, the family having emigrated to America about 1745, and was by profession a watchmaker. He was an excellent mathematician, and an intimate friend of Franklin and Jefferson, by the latter of whom he was made a member of the American Philosophical Society. He had five children, the eldest of whom is the subject of this sketch. Another is Charles R. Leslie, who has passed the greater portion of his life in England, and holds the foremost rank among the painters of that country, his line of art being somewhat analogous to that of his sister in literature, a like kindly and genuine humor and artistic finish pervading his cabinet pictures and her "Pencil Sketches." Her other brother is Major Thomas J. Leslie, U. S. A. When Miss Leslie was five years old she accompanied her parents to London, where they resided for six and a half years, her father being engaged in the exportation of clocks to this country. The death of his partner led to his return. On the voyage home the ship put into Lisbon, and remained at that port from November to March. They finally reached Philadelphia in May. The father died in 1803.

Miss Leslie early displayed a taste for books and drawing. She was educated for the most part at home by her parents.

"Like most authors," she says in an autobiographical letter to her friend Mrs. Neal, "I made my first attempts in *verse*. They were always songs, adapted to the popular airs of that time, the close of the last century. The subjects were chiefly soldiers, sailors, hunters, and nuns. I scribbled two or three in the pastoral line, but my father once pointing out to me a *real* shepherd, in a field somewhere in Kent, I made no farther attempt at Damons and Strephons playing on lutes and wreathing their brows with roses. My songs were, of course, foolish enough; but in justice to myself I will say, that, having a good ear, I was never guilty of a false quantity in any of my poetry—my lines never had a syllable too much or too little, and my rhymes always *did* rhyme. At thirteen or fourteen I began to despise my own poetry, and destroyed all I had."

Eliza Leslie

Miss Leslie did not appear in print until the year 1827, and then it was as the author of *Seventy-five Receipts for Pastry, Cakes, and Sweetmeats.* The collection had been commenced some time before, "when a pupil of Mrs. Goodfellow's cooking school, in Philadelphia," and was in such request in manuscript that an offer to publish was eagerly accepted. The book was successful, and the publisher suggesting a work of imagination, the author prepared *The Mirror*, a collection of juvenile stories. It was followed by *The Young Americans, Stories for Emma, Stories for Adelaide, Atlantic Tales, Stories for Helen, Birthday Stories*, and a compilation from Munchausen, Gulliver, and Sinbad, appropriately entitled *The Wonderful Traveller*, all volumes designed for children. *The American Girl's Book* was published in 1831, and has steadily maintained its position since.

Among the first of her stories for readers "of a larger growth" was *Mrs. Washington Potts*, written for a prize offered by the Lady's Book, which it was successful in obtaining. The author subsequently took three more prizes of a similar character, and at once became a constant and most popular contributor to "Godey and Graham." Miss Leslie also edited the Gift, one of the best of the American annuals. Her only story occupying a volume by itself, and approaching the ordinary dimensions of a novel, is *Amelia; or, A Young Lady's Vicissitudes.*

Miss Leslie's magazine tales have been collected in three volumes with the title of *Pencil Sketches.* She has also published *Althea Vernon, or the*

Embroidered Handkerchief, and *Henrietta Harrison, or the Blue Cotton Umbrella*, in one volume; and, each in a separate pamphlet, *Kitty's Relations*, *Leonilla Lynmore*, *The Maid of Canal Street*, and *The Dennings and their Beaux*.

During her career as a tale writer Miss Leslie has not forgotten the unctuous and delectable teachings of Mrs. Goodfellow, and has followed up the success of the seventy-five receipts by a much greater number, in *The Domestic Cookery Book*, 1837, of which over forty thousand copies have been sold; *The House Book*, 1840; and *The Lady's Receipt Book*, 1846, which have also had great success. In 1853 she published *The Behavior Book*, one of her pleasantest volumes, combining the solid good advice of her works on domestic duties with the happy vein of humor of her sketches.

THE MONTAGUES IN AMERICA—FROM MRS. WASHINGTON POTTS.

"Pray, sir," said Mrs. Quimby, "as you are from England, do you know anything of Betsey Dempsey's husband?"

"I have not the honor of being acquainted with that person," replied Mr. Montague, after a withering stare.

"Well, that's strange," pursued Aunt Quimby, "considering that she has been living in London at least eighteen years—or perhaps it is only seventeen! And yet I think it must be near eighteen, if not quite. May be seventeen and a half. Well, it's best to be on the safe side, so I'll say seventeen. Betsey Dempsey's mother was an old schoolmate of mine. Her father kept the Black Horse tavern. She was the only acquaintance I ever had that married an Englishman. He was a grocer, and in very good business; but he never liked America, and was always finding fault with it, and so he went home, and was to send for Betsey. But he never sent for her at all; for a very good reason, which was that he had another wife in England, as most of them have—no disparagement to you, sir."

Mrs. Marsden now came up, and informed Mrs. Potts in a whisper that the good old lady beside her was a distant relation or rather connexion of Mr. Marsden's, and that though a little primitive in appearance and manner, she had considerable property in bank-stock. To Mrs. Marsden's proposal that she should exchange her seat for a very pleasant one in the other room next to her old friend Mrs. Willis, Aunt Quimby replied nothing but "Thank you, I'm doing very well here."

Mrs. and Miss Montague, apparently heeding no one else, had talked nearly the whole evening to each other, but loudly enough to be heard by all around them. The young lady, though dressed as a child, talked like a woman, and she and her mother were now engaged in an argument whether the flirtation of the Duke of Risingham with Lady Georgiana Melbury would end seriously or not. "To my certain knowledge," said Miss Montague, "his Grace has never yet declared himself to Georgiana, or to any one else."

"I'll lay you two to one," said Mrs. Montague, "that he is married before we return to England."

"No," replied the daughter, "like all others of his sex he delights in keeping the ladies in suspense."

"What you say, Miss, is very true," said Aunt Quimby, leaning in her turn across Mr. Montague, "and considering how young you are you talk very sensibly. Men certainly have a way of keeping women in suspense, and an unwillingness to answer questions even when we ask them. There's my son-in-law Billy Fairfowl, that I live with. He married my daughter Mary eleven years ago, the 23d of last April. He's as good a man as ever breathed, and an excellent provider too. He always goes to market himself; and sometimes I can't help blaming him a little for his extravagance. But his greatest fault is his being so unsatisfactory. As far back as last March, as I was sitting at my knitting in the little front parlor with the door open (for it was quite warm weather for the time of year), Billy Fairfowl came home carrying in his hand a good-sized shad; and I called out to him to ask him what he gave for it, for it was the very beginning of the shad season; but he made not a word of answer; he had just passed on, and left the shad in the kitchen, and then went to his store. At dinner we had the fish, and a very nice one it was; and I asked him again how much he gave for it, but he still avoided answering, and began to talk about something else; so I thought I'd let it rest awhile. A week or two after, I again asked him; so then he actually said he had forgotten all about it. And to this day I don't know the price of that shad."

The Montagues looked at each other—almost laughed aloud, and drew back their chairs as far from Aunt Quimby as possible. So also did Mrs. Potts. Mrs. Marsden came up in an agony of vexation, and reminded her aunt in a low voice of the risk of renewing her rheumatism by staying so long between the damp newly-papered walls. The old lady answered aloud, "Oh! you need not fear, I am well wrapped up on purpose. And indeed considering that the parlors were only papered to-day, I think the walls have dried wonderfully (putting her hands on the paper)—I am sure nobody could find out the damp if they were not told."

"What!" exclaimed the Montagues; "only papered to-day (starting up and testifying all that prudent fear of taking cold, so characteristic of the English). How barbarous to inveigle us into such a place!"

"I thought I felt strangely chilly all the evening," says Mrs. Potts, whose fan had scarcely been at rest five minutes.

The Montagues proposed going away immediately, and Mrs. Potts declared she was *most* apprehensive for poor little Lafayette. Mrs. Marsden, who could not venture the idea of their departing till all the refreshments had been handed round (the best being yet to come), took great pains to persuade them that there was no real cause of alarm, as she had large fires all the afternoon. They held a whispered consultation, in which they agreed to stay for the oysters and chicken salad, and Mrs. Marsden went out to send them their shawls, with one for Lafayette.

By this time the secret of the newly-papered walls had spread round both rooms; the conversation now turned entirely on colds and rheumatisms; there was much shivering and considerable coughing, and the demand for shawls increased. However nobody actually went home in consequence.

"Papa," said Miss Montague, "let us all take French leave as soon as the oysters and chicken-salad have gone round."

Albina now came up to Aunt Quimby (gladly perceiving that the old lady looked tired), and proposed that she should return to her chamber, assuring her that waiters should be punctually sent up to her—"I do not feel quite ready to go yet," replied Mrs. Quimby. "I am very well. But you need not mind *me*. Go back to your company, and talk a little to those three poor girls in the yellow frocks that nobody has spoken to yet except Bromley Cheston. When I am ready to go I shall take French leave, as these English people call it."

But Aunt Quimby's idea of French leave was very different from the usual acceptation of the term; for having always heard that the French were a very polite people, she concluded that their manner of taking leave must be particularly respectful and ceremonious. Therefore, having paid her parting compliments to Mrs. Potts and the Montagues, she walked all round the room, courtesying to everybody and shaking hands, and telling them she had come to take French leave. To put an end to this ridiculous scene, Bromley Cheston (who had been on assiduous duty all the evening) now came forward, and, taking the old lady's arm in his, offered to escort her up stairs. Aunt Quimby was much flattered by this unexpected civility from the finest-looking young man in the room, and she smilingly departed with him, complimenting him on his politeness, and assuring him that he was a real gentleman, and trying also to make out the degree of relationship that existed between them.

"So much for Buckingham," said Cheston, as he ran down stairs after depositing the old lady at the door of her room. "Fools of all ranks and of all ages are to me equally intolerable. I never can marry into such a family."

The party went on.

"In the name of heaven, Mrs. Potts," said Mrs. Montague, "what induces you to patronize these people?"

"Why, they are the only tolerable persons in the neighborhood," answered Mrs. Potts, "and very kind and obliging in their way. I really think Albina a very sweet girl, very sweet, indeed; and Mrs. Marsden is rather amiable too, quite amiable. And they are so grateful for any little notice I take of them that it is really quite affecting. Poor things! how much trouble they have given themselves in getting up this party. They look as if they had had a hard day's work; and I have no doubt they will be obliged in consequence to pinch themselves for months to come: for I can assure you their means are very small, very small, indeed. As to this intolerable old aunt, I never saw her before, and as there is something rather genteel about Mrs. Marsden and her daughter—rather so, at least, about Albina—I did not suppose they had any such relations belonging to them. I think, in future, I must confine myself entirely to the aristocracy."

"We deliberated to the last moment," said Mrs. Montague, "whether we would come. But as Mr. Montague is going to write his tour when we return to England, he thinks it expedient to make some sacrifices for the sake of seeing the varieties of American society."

"Oh! these people are not in society," exclaimed Mrs. Potts, eagerly. "I can assure you these Marsdens have not the slightest pretensions to society. Oh! no; I beg of you not to suppose that Mrs. Marsden and her daughters are at all in society."

RICHARD HENRY DANA.

THE family of Mr. Dana is one of the oldest and most honored in Massachusetts. The first of the name who came to America was Richard Dana, in 1640; he settled at Cambridge, where six generations of the family have since resided.

The poet's grandfather on this side of the house, Richard, was a patriot of the times preceding the Revolution, and known at the bar as an eminent lawyer. His son was Francis Dana the Minister to Russia, and Chief Justice of the Supreme Court of Massachusetts, a man of honor, high personal sense of character, and of energetic eloquence. He married a daughter of William Ellery of Rhode Island, the signer of the Declaration of Independence, by which union his son and the celebrated Dr. Channing were cousins. Judge Ellery once described to his grandson, the poet, the aroused sense of honor which he witnessed in Francis Dana, in his rebuke of an impudent lawyer at the bar, who had charged him with an unfair management of the case. "In opening his reply to the jury," said Mr. Ellery, "he came down upon the creature; he did it in two or three minutes' time, and then dropped him altogether. I thought," added he, "I felt my hair rise and stand upright on my head while he did it."*

On the mother's side Dana's family runs up to the early poetess Anne Bradstreet, the daughter of Governor Dudley. His grandfather Ellery married the daughter of Judge Remington, who had married the daughter of that quaint disciple of Du Bartas. Dana's uncle, Judge Edmund Trowbridge, also married one of the Dudley family.

* The writer of the biographical notice of R. H. Dana, Jr., in Livingston's Sketches of Eminent American Lawyers (Part iv. 702), thus characterizes the old school of Federalism to which Francis Dana belonged.

"He possessed a large fortune for that day, chiefly in lands, and kept up, in his manner of life, the style of the olden time, which has almost passed out of the memory of our degenerate age. He used to ride to court in his coach, and would have thought it undignified to travel the circuits unattended by his private servant. In politics he was what would now be styled a high-toned Federalist of the old school—though the words imply far more than the mere adherence to certain political views, and siding with a particular political party. They have a much broader signification. The old Federal gentry of New England was chiefly composed of educated men, whose minds had been cultivated by the study of the eminent English lawyers, and who still retained some of the feelings of their own immediate ancestors. It must be confessed that they looked upon themselves less as the representatives, than as the temporal guardians of the people. They endeavoured to preserve what they conceived to be necessary distinctions in society, and in the municipal movements of government. They had a notion that the accidents of birth and education imposed upon them peculiar duties in the commonwealth—the duties of restraining the mass of the people by the force of dignity, and elevating them by their example. The honor of the state, the direction of its energies, the regulation of its manners, the security of its laws, and the solemnities of its religious observ-

Richard Henry Dana was born at Cambridge, November 15, 1787. His early years were passed at Newport, in the midst of the associations of the Revolution and the enjoyments of the fine sea views and atmosphere of the spot. He entered Harvard, which he left in 1807. He studied law in the office of his cousin Francis Dana Channing, the eldest brother of Dr. Channing. After admission to the Boston bar he spent about three months in the office of Robert Goodloe Harper at Baltimore, where he was admitted to practice. He returned home in 1811 and became a member of the legislature, where he found a better field for the exercise of his federal politics and opinions. His first literary public appearance was as an orator on the Fourth of July celebration of 1814.

The North American Review was commenced in 1815. It grew out of an association of literary gentlemen composing the Anthology Club who for eight years, from 1803 to 1811, had published the miscellany entitled *The Monthly Anthology*. Dana was a member of the club. The first editor of the Review was William Tudor, from whose hands it soon passed to the care of Willard Phillips, and then to the charge of an association of gentlemen for whom Mr. Sparks was the active editor. In 1818 Edward T. Channing became editor of the Review, and associated with him his cousin Richard H. Dana, who had left the law for the more congenial pursuits of literature.*

When Channing was made Boylston professor of Rhetoric and Oratory at Harvard he resigned the editorship of the Review, and Dana, who was considered too unpopular to succeed him, left the club. Dana wrote in the period of two years five papers, one an essay on "Old Times," the others on literary topics, chiefly poetical.† In 1824 Dana began the publication of *The Idle Man*, a periodical in which he communicated to the public his Tales and Essays. Six numbers of it were issued when it was discontinued; the author acquiring the experience hitherto not uncommon in the higher American literature, that if he would write as a poet and philosopher, and publish as a gentleman, he must pay as well as compose.

Bryant, with whom Dana had become acquainted in the conduct of the North American Review, was a contributor of several poems to the Idle Man; and when this publication was discontinued Dana wrote for his journal, the New York Review of 1825, and afterwards the United States Review of 1826–7. In the latter he published articles on Mrs. Radcliffe and the novels of Brockden Brown. From 1828 to 1831 he contributed four papers to The Spirit of the Pilgrims.* An Essay on *The Past and the Present* in the American Quarterly Observer for 1833; and another on *Law as suited to Man*, in the Biblical Repository for 1835, conclude the list of our author's contributions to periodical literature.

The first volume of Dana's Poems, containing *The Buccaneer*, was published in 1827. In 1833 he published at Boston a volume of *Poems and Prose Writings*, reprinting his first volume with additions, and including his papers in the Idle Man. In 1839 he delivered a course of eight lectures on Shakespeare at Boston and New York, which he has subsequently repeated in those cities and delivered at Philadelphia and elsewhere. In 1850 he published an edition of his writings in two volumes at New York, adding several essays and his review articles, with the exception of a notice of the historical romance of Yorktown, in Bryant's United States Review,† and the paper on Religious Controversy in the Spirit of the Pilgrims.‡

These are the last public incidents of Mr. Dana's literary career; but in private the influence of his tastes, conversation, and choice literary correspondence, embraces a liberal field of activity. He passes his time between his town residence at Boston and his country retirement at Cape Ann,

Mr. Dana's Residence.

where he enjoys a roof of his own in a neat marine villa, pleasantly situated in a niche of the rocky coast. Constant to the untiring love of nature, he is one of the first to seek this haunt in spring and the last to leave it in autumn.

His writings possess kindred qualities in prose and verse; thought and rhythm, speculation and imagination being borrowed by each from the other.

The Buccaneer is a philosophical poem; a tale of the heart and the conscience. The villany of the hero, though in remote perspective to the imagination, appeals on that account the more powerfully to our own consciousness. His remorse is touched with consummate art as the rude

---

ances, were committed to them. This was not confessedly, but pretty nearly in fact, their idea of their position and its consequent responsibilities."

* Edward Tyrrel Channing was Professor of Rhetoric and Oratory in Harvard College from 1819 to 1851, where the exactness of his instruction, his cultivated taste and highly disciplined mental powers gave him an eminent reputation with his pupils. His editorship of the North American Review extended over the seventh, eighth, and ninth volumes in 1818 and 1819. The following are among his articles in the Review: On Thomas Moore and Lalla Rookh, vol. vi.; Rob Roy, vol. vii.; Charles Brockden Browne's Life and Writings, vol. ix.; Southey's Life of Cooper, vol. xliv.; Prior's Life of Goldsmith, vol. xlv.; Sir Richard Steele's Life and Writings, vol. xlvi.; Lord Chesterfield's Letters to his Son, vol. l. These papers show the author's refined culture and vigorous pen. Professor Channing also wrote the life of his grandfather, William Ellery, in Sparks's American Biography, First Series, vol. vi. It is understood that he is about sending to the press a volume of Lectures read to the classes in Cambridge.

† They were "Old Times," 1817. Allston's Sylph of the Seasons, 1817. Edgeworth's Readings on Poetry, 1818. Hazlitt's English Poets, 1819. The Sketch Book, 1819.

* On Pollok's Course of Time, 1828. Pamphlets on Controversy, 1829. Natural History of Enthusiasm, 1830. Henry Martyn, 1831.

† January, 1827. ‡ ii. 198.

hard earthy nature steps into the region of the supernatural, and with unchanged rigidity embraces its new terrors. The machinery is at once objective and spiritual in the vision of the horse. The story is opened by glimpses to the reader in the only way in which modern art can attain, with cultivated minds, the effect of the old ballad directness. The visionary horror is relieved by simple touches of human feeling and sweet images, as in the opening, of the lovely, peaceful scenes of nature. The remaining poems are divided between the description of nature and a certain philosophical vein of thought which rises into the loftiest speculative region of religion, and is never long without indications of a pathetic sense of human life.

The prose of Dana has similar characteristics to his verse. It is close, elaborate, truthful in etymology; and, with a seeming plainness, musical in its expression. There is a rare use of figures, but when they occur they will be found inwrought with the life of the text; no sham or filigree work.

In the tales of *Tom Thornton* and *Paul Felton* there is much imaginative power in placing the mind on the extreme limits of sanity, under the influence of painful and engrossing passion. The story of the lovers, Edward and Mary, has its idyllic graces of the affections. In these writings the genius of our author is essentially dramatic.

The critical and philosophical essays, embracing the subtle and elaborate studies of human life in Shakespeare, show great skill in discrimination, guided by a certain logic of the heart and life, and not by mere artificial dialectics. They are not so much literary exercises as revelations of, and guides to character. This character is founded on calm reverence, a sleepless love of truth, a high sense of honor, and of individual worth. With these conditions are allied strong imagination, reaching to the ideal in art and virtue, and a corresponding sympathy with the humanity which falls short of it in life.

THE LITTLE BEACH BIRD.

I.

Thou little bird, thou dweller by the sea,
Why takest thou its melancholy voice?
And with that boding cry
Along the waves dost thou fly?
O! rather, Bird with me
Through the fair land rejoice!

II.

Thy flitting form comes ghostly dim and pale,
As driven by a beating storm at sea;
Thy cry is weak and scared,
As if thy mates had shared
The doom of us: Thy wail—
What does it bring to me?

III.

Thou call'st along the sand, and haunt'st the surge,
Restless and sad; as if, in strange accord
With the motion and the roar
Of waves that drive to shore,
One spirit did ye urge—
The Mystery—The Word.

IV.

Of the thousands, thou, both sepulchre and pall,
Old Ocean, art! A requiem o'er the dead,
From out thy gloomy cells
A tale of mourning tells—
Tells of man's woe and fall,
His sinless glory fled.

V.

Then turn thee, little bird, and take thy flight
Where the complaining sea shall sadness bring
Thy spirit never more.
Come, quit with me the shore,
For gladness and the light
Where birds of summer sing.

IMMORTALITY—FROM THE HUSBAND AND WIFE'S GRAVE.

And do our loves all perish with our frames?
Do those that took their root and put forth buds,
And their soft leaves unfolded in the warmth
Of mutual hearts, grow up and live in beauty,
Then fade and fall, like fair, unconscious flowers?
Are thoughts and passions that to the tongue give speech,
And make it send forth winning harmonies,—
That to the cheek do give its living glow,
And vision in the eye the soul intense
With that for which there is no utterance—
Are these the body's accidents?—no more?—
To live in it, and when that dies, go out
Like the burnt taper's flame?

O, listen, man!
A voice within us speaks the startling word,
"Man, thou shalt never die!" Celestial voices
Hymn it around our souls: according harps,
By angel fingers touched when the mild stars
Of morning sang together, sound forth still
The song of our great immortality:
Thick clustering orbs, and this our fair domain,
The tall, dark mountains, and the deep-toned seas,
Join in this solemn, universal song.
—O, listen ye, our spirits; drink it in
From all the air! 'T is in the gentle moonlight;
'T is floating in day's setting glories; Night,
Wrapt in her sable robe, with silent step
Comes to our bed and breathes it in our ears:
Night, and the dawn, bright day, and thoughtful eve,
All time, all bounds, the limitless expanse,
As one vast mystic instrument, are touched
By an unseen, living Hand, the conscious chords
Quiver with joy in this great jubilee:
—The dying hear it; and as sounds of earth
Grow dull and distant, wake their passing souls
To mingle in this heavenly harmony.

THE BUCCANEER.

Boy with thy blac berd,
I rede that thou blin,
And sone set the to shrive,
With sorrow of thi syn;

Ze met with the merchandes
And made them ful bare;
It es gude reason and right
That ze evill misfare.

For when ze stode in sowre strenkith,
Ze war all to stout.

LAURENCE MINOT.

The island lies nine leagues away.
Along its solitary shore,
Of craggy rock and sandy bay,
No sound but ocean's roar,
Save where the bold, wild sea-bird makes her home,
Her shrill cry coming through the sparkling foam.

But when the light winds lie at rest,
And on the glassy, heaving sea,
The black duck, with her glossy breast,
Sits swinging silently,—
How beautiful! no ripples break the reach,
And silvery waves go noiseless up the beach.

And inland rests the green, warm dell;
The brook comes tinkling down its side;
From out the trees the Sabbath bell
Rings cheerful, far and wide,
Mingling its sound with bleatings of the flocks,
That feed about the vale among the rocks.

Nor holy bell, nor pastoral bleat,
In former days within the vale;
Flapped in the bay the pirate's sheet;
Curses were on the gale;
Rich goods lay on the sand, and murdered men;
Pirate and wrecker kept their revels then.

But calm, low voices, words of grace,
Now slowly fall upon the ear;
A quiet look is in each face,
Subdued and holy fear;
Each motion gentle; all is kindly done.—
Come, listen how from crime the isle was won.

Twelve years are gone since Matthew Lee
Held in this isle unquestioned sway;
A dark, low, brawny man was he;
His law,—"It is my way."
Beneath his thick-set brows a sharp light broke
From small gray eyes; his laugh a triumph spoke.

Cruel of heart, and strong of arm,
Loud in his sport, and keen for spoil,
He little recked of good or harm,
Fierce both in mirth and toil;
Yet like a dog could fawn, if need there were;
Speak mildly, when he would, or look in fear.

Amid the uproar of the storm,
And by the lightning's sharp, red glare,
Were seen Lee's face and sturdy form;
His axe glanced quick in air.
Whose corpse at morn lies swinging in the sedge?
There's blood and hair, Matt, on thy axe's edge.

"Ask him who floats there; let him tell;
I make the brute, not man, my mark.
Who walks the cliffs, needs heed him well!
Last night was fearful dark.
Think ye the lashing waves will spare or feel?
An ugly gash!—These rocks—they cut like steel."

He wiped his axe; and turning round,
Said with a cold and hardened smile,
"The hemp is saved; the man is drowned.
We'll let him float awhile!
Or give him Christian burial on the strand?
He'll find his fellows peaceful under sand."

Lee's waste was greater than his gain.
"I'll try the merchant's trade," he thought,
"Though less the toil to kill than feign,—
Things sweeter robbed than bought.
But, then, to circumvent them at their arts!"
Ship manned, and spoils for cargo, Lee departs.

'Tis fearful, on the broad-backed waves,
To feel them shake, and hear them roar:
Beneath, unsounded, dreadful caves;
Around, no cheerful shore.
Yet 'mid this solemn world what deeds are done!
The curse goes up, the deadly sea-fight's won:—

And wanton talk, and laughter heard,
Where sounds a deep and awful voice.
There's awe from that lone ocean-bird:
Pray ye, when ye rejoice!
"Leave prayers to priests," cries Lee: "I'm ruler here!
These fellows know full well whom they should fear!"

The ship works hard; the seas run high;
Their white tops, flashing through the night,
Give to the eager, straining eye
A wild and shifting light.
"Hard at the pumps!—The leak is gaining fast!
Lighten the ship!—The devil rode that blast!"

Ocean has swallowed for its food
Spoils thou didst gain in murderous glee;
Matt, could its waters wash out blood,
It had been well for thee.
Crime fits for crime. And no repentant tear
Hast thou for sin?—Then wait thine hour of fear.

The sea has like a plaything tost
That heavy hull the livelong night.
The man of sin,—he is not lost:
Soft breaks the morning light.
Torn spars and sails,—her lading in the deep,—
The ship makes port with slow and labouring sweep.

Within a Spanish port she rides.
Angry and soured, Lee walks her deck.
"So, peaceful trade a curse betides?—
And thou, good ship, a wreck!
Ill luck in change!—Ho! cheer ye up, my men!
Rigged, and at sea, and then, old work again!"

A sound is in the Pyrenees!
Whirling and dark comes roaring down
A tide as of a thousand seas,
Sweeping both cowl and crown:
On field and vineyard, thick and red it stood;
Spain's streets and palaces are wet with blood.

And wrath and terror shake the land:
The peaks shine clear in watchfire lights;
Soon comes the tread of that stout band,—
Bold Arthur and his knights.
Awake ye, Merlin! Hear the shout from Spain!
The spell is broke!—Arthur is come again!—

Too late for thee, thou young, fair bride!
The lips are cold, the brow is pale,
That thou didst kiss in love and pride;
He cannot hear thy wail,
Whom thou didst lull with fondly murmured sound
His couch is cold and lonely in the ground.

He fell for Spain,—her Spain no more;
For he was gone who made it dear;
And she would seek some distant shore,
Away from strife and fear,
And wait amid her sorrows till the day
His voice of love should call her thence away.

Lee feigned him grieved, and bowed him low,
'Twould joy his heart, could he but aid
So good a lady in her woe,
He meekly, smoothly said.
With wealth and servants she is soon aboard,
And that white steed she rode beside her lord.

The sun goes down upon the sea;
The shadows gather round her home.
"How like a pall are ye to me!
My home, how like a tomb!
O, blow, ye flowers of Spain, above his head!
Ye will not blow o'er me when I am dead."

And now the stars are burning bright;
Yet still she's looking toward the shore
Beyond the waters black in night.
"I ne'er shall see thee more!
Ye're many, waves, yet lonely seems your flow;
And I'm alone,—scarce know I where I go."

Sleep, sleep, thou sad one on the sea!
The wash of waters lulls thee now;

His arm no more will pillow thee,
Thy fingers on his brow.
He is not near, to hush thee, or to save.
The ground is his, the sea must be thy grave.

The moon comes up; the night goes on.
Why, in the shadow of the mast,
Stands that dark, thoughtful man alone?
Thy pledge!—nay, keep it fast!
Bethink thee of her youth, and sorrows, Lee;
Helpless, alone,—and, then, her trust in thee.

When told the hardships thou hadst borne,
Her words to thee were like a charm.
With uncheered grief her heart is worn;
Thou wilt not do her harm?
He looks out on the sea that sleeps in light,
And growls an oath,—"It is too still to-night!"

He sleeps; but dreams of massy gold
And heaps of pearl,—stretches his hands;
But hears a voice,—"Ill man, withhold!"
A pale one near him stands.
Her breath comes deathly cold upon his cheek;
Her touch is cold; he hears a piercing shriek;—

He wakes!—But no relentings wake
Within his angered, restless soul.
"What, shall a dream Matt's purpose shake?
The gold will make all whole.
Thy merchant trade had nigh unmanned thee, lad!
What, balk my chance because a woman's sad!"

He cannot look on her mild eye;
Her patient words his spirit quell.
Within that evil heart there lie
The hates and fears of hell.
His speech is short; he wears a surly brow.
There's none will hear the shriek. What fear ye now?

The workings of the soul ye fear;
Ye fear the power that goodness hath;
Ye fear the Unseen One ever near,
Walking his ocean path.
From out the silent void there comes a cry,—
"Vengeance is mine! Thou, murderer, too, shalt die!"

Nor dread of ever-during woe,
Nor the sea's awful solitude,
Can make thee, wretch, thy crime forego.
Then, bloody hand,—to blood!
The scud is driving wildly overhead;
The stars burn dim; the ocean moans its dead.

Moan for the living; moan our sins,—
The wrath of man more fierce than thine.
Hark! still thy waves!—The work begins,—
Lee makes the deadly sign.
The crew glide down like shadows. Eye and hand
Speak fearful meanings through the silent band.

They're gone.—The helmsman stands alone;
And one leans idly o'er the bow.
Still as a tomb the ship keeps on;
Nor sound nor stirring now.
Hush, hark! as from the centre of the deep,
Shrieks, fiendish yells! They stab them in their sleep!

The scream of rage, the groan, the strife,
The blow, the gasp, the horrid cry,
The panting throttled prayer for life,
The dying's heaving sigh,
The murderer's curse, the dead man's fixed, still glare,
And fear's and death's cold sweat,—they all are there.

On pale, dead men, on burning cheek,
On quick, fierce eyes, brows hot and damp,
On hands that with the warm blood reek,
Shines the dim cabin lamp.
Lee looked. "They sleep so sound," he laughing, said,
"They'll scarcely wake for mistress or for maid."

A crash! They force the door,—and then
One long, long, shrill, and piercing scream
Comes thrilling 'bove the growl of men.
'Tis hers! O God, redeem
From worse than death thy suffering, helpless child!
That dreadful shriek again,—sharp, sharp, and wild!

It ceased.—With speed o' th' lightning's flash,
A loose-robed form, with streaming hair,
Shoots by.—A leap,—a quick, short splash!
'Tis gone!—and nothing there!
The waves have swept away the bubbling tide.
Bright-crested waves, how calmly on they ride!

She's sleeping in her silent cave,
Nor hears the loud, stern roar above,
Nor strife of man on land or wave.
Young thing! her home of love
She soon has reached! Fair, unpolluted thing!
They harmed her not!—Was dying suffering?

O no!—To live when joy was dead,
To go with one lone, pining thought,
To mournful love her being wed,
Feeling what death had wrought;
To live the child of woe, nor shed a tear,
Bear kindness, and yet share not joy or fear;

To look on man, and deem it strange
That he on things of earth should brood,
When all the thronged and busy range
To her was solitude,—
O, this was bitterness! Death came and pressed
Her wearied lids, and brought the sick heart rest.

Why look ye on each other so,
And speak no word?—Ay, shake the head!
She's gone where ye can never go.
What fear ye from the dead?
They tell no tales; and ye are all true men;—
But wash away that blood; then, home again!

'Tis on your souls; it will not out!
Lee, why so lost? 'Tis not like thee!
Come, where thy revel, oath, and shout?
"That pale one in the sea!—
I mind not blood.—But she,—I cannot tell!
A spirit was't?—It flashed like fires of hell!

"And when it passed there was no tread!
It leaped the deck.—Who heard the sound?
I heard none!—Say, what was it fled?
Poor girl! and is she drowned?—
Went down these depths? How dark they look, and cold!
She's yonder! stop her!—Now!—there!—hold her! hold!"

They gaze upon his ghastly face.
"What ails thee, Lee? and why that glare?"
"Look! ha! 'tis gone, and not a trace!
No, no, she was not there!—
Who of you said ye heard her when she fell?
'Twas strange!—I'll not be fooled!—Will no one tell?"

He paused. And soon the wildness passed.
Then came the tingling flush of shame.
Remorse and fear are gone as fast.
"The silly thing's to blame
To quit us so. 'Tis plain she loved us not;
Or she had stayed awhile, and shared my cot."

And then the ribald laughed. The jest,
Though old and foul, loud laughter drew;
And fouler yet came from the rest
Of that infernal crew.
Note, Heaven, their blasphemy, their broken trust!
Lust panders murder: murder panders lust!

Now slowly up they bring the dead
From out the silent, dim-lit room.
No prayer at their quick burial said;
No friend to weep their doom.
The hungry waves have seized them one by one;
And, swallowing down their prey, go roaring on.

Cries Lee, "We must not be betrayed;
'Tis but to add another corse!
Strange words, we're told, an ass once brayed:
I'll never trust a horse!
Out! throw him on the waves alive!—he'll swim;
For once a horse shall ride; we all ride him."

Such sound to mortal ear ne'er came
As rang far o'er the waters wide.
It shook with fear the stoutest frame:
The horse is on the tide!
As the waves leave, or lift him up, his cry
Comes lower now, and now is near and high.

And through the swift waves' yesty crown
His scared eyes shoot a fiendish light,
And fear seems wrath. He now sinks down,
Now heaves again to sight,
Then drifts away; and through the night they hear
Far off that dreadful cry.—But morn is near.

O, hadst thou known what deeds were done,
When thou wast shining far away,
Wouldst thou let fall, calm-coming sun,
Thy warm and silent ray?
The good are in their graves; thou canst not cheer
Their dark, cold mansions: Sin alone is here.

"The deed's complete! The gold is ours!
There, wash away that bloody stain!
Pray, who'd refuse what fortune showers?
Now, lads, we lot our gain!
Must fairly share, you know, what's fairly got?
A truly good night's work! Who says 'twas not?"

There's song, and oath, and gaming deep,
Hot words, and laughter, mad carouse;
There's naught of prayer, and little sleep;
The devil keeps the house!
"Lee cheats!" cried Jack. Lee struck him to the heart.
"That's foul!" one muttered.—"Fool! you take your part!

"The fewer heirs, the richer, man!
Hold forth your palm, and keep your prate!
Our life, we read, is but a span.
What matters soon or late?"
And when on shore, and asked, Did many die?
"Near half my crew, poor lads!" he'd say, and sigh.

Within the bay, one stormy night,
The isle-men saw boats make for shore,
With here and there a dancing light,
That flashed on man and oar.
When hailed, the rowing stopped, and all was dark.
"Ha! lantern-work!—We'll home! They're playing shark!"

Next day at noon, within the town,
All stare and wonder much to see
Matt and his men come strolling down;
Boys shouting, "Here comes Lee!"
"Thy ship, good Lee?" "Not many leagues from shore
Our ship by chance took fire."—They learned no more.

He and his crew were flush of gold.
"You did not lose your cargo, then?"
"Where all is fairly bought and sold,
Heaven prospers those true men.
Forsake your evil ways, as we forsook
Our ways of sin, and honest courses took!

"Would see my log-book? Fairly writ,
With pen of steel, and ink of blood!
How lightly doth the conscience sit!
Learn, truth's the only good."
And thus, with flout, and cold and impious jeer,
He fled repentance, if he scaped not fear.

Remorse and fear he drowns in drink.
"Come, pass the bowl, my jolly crew!
It thicks the blood to mope and think.
Here's merry days, though few!"
And then he quaffs.—So riot reigns within;
So brawl and laughter shake that house of sin.

Matt lords it now throughout the isle;
His hand falls heavier than before;
All dread alike his frown or smile.
None come within his door,
Save those who dipped their hands in blood with him;
Save those who laughed to see the white horse swim.

"To-night's our anniversary;
And, mind me, lads, we have it kept
With royal state and special glee!
Better with those who slept
Their sleep that night would he be now, who slinks!
And health and wealth to him who bravely drinks!"

The words they speak, we may not speak;
The tales they tell, we may not tell.
Mere mortal man, forbear to seek
The secrets of that hell!
Their shouts grow loud. 'Tis near mid-hour of night!
What means upon the waters that red light?

Not bigger than a star it seems.
And now 'tis like the bloody moon,
And now it shoots in hairy streams!
It moves!—'Twill reach us soon!
A ship! and all on fire!—hull, yard, and mast.
Her sails are sheets of flame!—she's nearing fast!

And now she rides upright and still,
Shedding a wild and lurid light,
Around the cove, on inland hill,
Waking the gloom of night.
All breathes of terror! men, in dumb amaze,
Gaze on each other in the horrid blaze.

It scares the sea-birds from their nests;
They dart and wheel with deafening screams;
Now dark,—and now their wings and breasts
Flash back disastrous gleams.
Fair Light, thy looks strange alteration wear;—
The world's great comforter,—why now its fear?

And what comes up above the wave,
So ghastly white? A spectral head!
A horse's head! (May Heaven save
Those looking on the dead,—
The waking dead!) There, on the sea he stands,—
The Spectre-Horse! He moves! he gains the sands;

And on he speeds! His ghostly sides
Are streaming with a cold blue light.
Heaven keep the wits of him who rides
The Spectre-Horse to-night!
His path is shining like a swift ship's wake.
Before Lee's door he gleams like day's gray break

The revel now is high within;
It bursts upon the midnight air

They little think, in mirth and din,
What spirit waits them there.
As if the sky became a voice, there spread
A sound to appal the living, stir the dead.

The Spirit steed sent up the neigh;
It seemed the living trump of hell,
Sounding to call the damned away,
To join the host that fell.
It rang along the vaulted sky: the shore
Jarred hard, as when the thronging surges roar.

It rang in ears that knew the sound;
And hot, flushed cheeks are blanched with fear.
Ha! why does Lee look wildly round?
Thinks he the drowned horse near?
He drops his cup,—his lips are stiff with fright.
Nay, sit thee down,—it is thy banquet night.

"I cannot sit;—I needs must go:
The spell is on my spirit now.
I go to dread,—I go to woe!"
O, who so weak as thou,
Strong man! His hoofs upon the door-stone, see,
The Shadow stands! His eyes are on thee, Lee!

Thy hair pricks up!—"O, I must bear
His damp, cold breath! It chills my frame!
His eyes,—their near and dreadful glare
Speaks that I must not name!"
Art mad to mount that Horse!—"A power within,
I must obey, cries, 'Mount thee, man of sin!'"

He's now upon the Spectre's back,
With rein of silk and curb of gold.
'Tis fearful speed!—the rein is slack
Within his senseless hold;
Borne by an unseen power, right on he rides,
Yet touches not the Shadow-Beast he strides.

He goes with speed; he goes with dread!
And now they're on the hanging steep!
And, now, the living and the dead,
They'll make the horrid leap!
The Horse stops short,—his feet are on the verge!
He stands, like marble, high above the surge.

And nigh, the tall ship's burning on,
With red hot spars, and crackling flame;
From hull to gallant, nothing's gone;—
She burns, and yet's the same!
Her hot, red flame is beating, all the night,
On man and Horse, in their cold, phosphor light.

Through that cold light the fearful man
Sits looking on the burning ship.
Wilt ever rail again, or ban?
How fast he moves the lip!
And yet he does not speak, or make a sound!
What see you, Lee? the bodies of the drowned?

"I look, where mortal man may not,—
Down to the chambers of the deep.
I see the dead, long, long forgot;
I see them in their sleep.
A dreadful power is mine, which none can know,
Save he who leagues his soul with death and woe."

Thou mild, sad mother, silent moon,
Thy last low, melancholy ray
Shines towards him. Quit him not so soon!
Mother, in mercy, stay!
Despair and death are with him; and canst thou,
With that kind, earthward look, go leave him now?

O, thou wast born for worlds of love;
Making more lovely in thy shine
Whate'er thou look'st on: hosts above,
In that soft light of thine,
Burn softer; earth, in silvery veil, seems heaven.
Thou'rt going down!—hast left him unforgiven!

The far, low west is bright no more.
How still it is! No sound is heard
At sea, or all along the shore,
But cry of passing bird.
Thou living thing,—and dar'st thou come so near
These wild and ghastly shapes of death and fear?

And long that thick, red light has shone
On stern, dark rocks, and deep, still bay,
On man and Horse that seem of stone,
So motionless are they.
But now its lurid fire less fiercely burns:
The night is going,—faint, gray dawn returns.

That Spectre-Steed now slowly pales,
Now changes like the moonlit cloud;
That cold, thin light now slowly fails,
Which wrapt them like a shroud.
Both ship and Horse are fading into air.
Lost, mazed, alone, see, Lee is standing there!

The morning air blows fresh on him;
The waves are dancing in his sight;
The sea-birds call, and wheel, and skim.
O blessed morning light!
He doth not hear their joyous call; he sees
No beauty in the wave, nor feels the breeze.

For he's accursed from all that's good;
He ne'er must know its healing power.
The sinner on his sin shall brood,
And wait, alone, his hour.
A stranger to earth's beauty, human love,—
No rest below for him, no hope above!

The sun beats hot upon his head.
He stands beneath the broad, fierce blaze,
As stiff and cold as one that's dead:
A troubled, dreamy maze
Of some unearthly horror, all he knows,—
Of some wild horror past, and coming woes.

The gull has found her place on shore;
The sun gone down again to rest;
And all is still but ocean's roar:
There stands the man unblest.
But, see, he moves,—he turns, as asking where
His mates:—Why looks he with that piteous stare?

Go, get ye home, and end your mirth!
Go, call the revellers again;
They're fled the isle; and o'er the earth
Are wanderers, like Cain.
As he his door-stone passed, the air blew chill.
The wine is on the board; Lee, take your fill!

"There's none to meet me, none to cheer:
The seats are empty,—lights burnt out;
And I, alone, must sit me here:
Would I could hear their shout!"
He ne'er shall hear it more,—more taste his wine!
Silent he sits within the still moonshine.

Day came again; and up he rose,
A weary man, from his lone board;
Nor merry feast, nor sweet repose,
Did that long night afford.
No shadowy-coming night, to bring him rest,—
No dawn, to chase the darkness of his breast!

He walks within the day's full glare,
A darkened man. Where'er he comes,
All shun him. Children peep and stare;
Then, frightened, seek their homes.
Through all the crowd a thrilling horror ran.
They point and say,—"There goes the wicked man!"

He turns, and curses in his wrath
Both man and child; then hastes away
Shoreward, or takes some gloomy path;
But there he cannot stay:

Terror and madness drive him back to men;
His hate of man to solitude again.

Time passes on, and he grows bold;
His eye is fierce; his oaths are loud;
None dare from Lee the hand withhold;
He rules and scoffs the crowd.
But still at heart there lies a secret fear;
For now the year's dread round is drawing near.

He laughs, but he is sick at heart;
He swears, but he turns deadly pale;
His restless eye and sudden start,—
They tell the dreadful tale
That will be told: it needs no words from thee,
Thou self-sold slave to fear and misery.

Bond-slave of sin! again the light!
"Ha! take me, take me from its blaze!"
Nay, thou must ride the Steed to-night!
But other weary days
And nights must shine and darken o'er thy head,
Ere thou shalt go with him to meet the dead.

Again the ship lights all the land;
Again Lee strides the Spectre-Beast;
Again upon the cliff they stand.
This once is he released!—
Gone ship and Horse; but Lee's last hope is o'er;
Nor laugh, nor scoff, nor rage, can help him more.

His spirit heard that Spirit say,
"Listen!—I twice have come to thee.
Once more,—and then a dreadful way!
And thou must go with me!"
Ay, cling to earth as sailor to the rock!
Sea-swept, sucked down in the tremendous shock,

He goes!—So thou must loose thy hold,
And go with Death; nor breathe the balm
Of early air, nor light behold,
Nor sit thee in the calm
Of gentle thoughts, where good men wait their close.
In life, or death, where look'st thou for repose?

Who's sitting on that long, black ledge,
Which makes so far out in the sea,
Feeling the kelp-weed on its edge?
Poor, idle Matthew Lee!
So weak and pale? A year and little more,
And bravely did he lord it round the shore.

And on the shingle now he sits,
And rolls the pebbles 'neath his hands;
Now walks the beach; now stops by fits,
And scores the smooth, wet sands;
Then tries each cliff, and cove, and jut, that bounds
The isle; then home from many weary rounds.

They ask him why he wanders so,
From day to day, the uneven strand?
"I wish, I wish that I might go!
But I would go by land;
And there's no way that I can find; I've tried
All day and night!"—He seaward looked, and sighed.

It brought the tear to many an eye,
That, once, his eye had made to quail.
"Lee, go with us; our sloop is nigh;
Come! help us hoist her sail."
He shook.—"You know the Spirit-Horse I ride!
He'll let me on the sea with none beside!"

He views the ships that come and go,
Looking so like to living things.
O! 'tis a proud and gallant show
Of bright and broad-spread wings,
Making it light around them, as they keep
Their course right onward through the unsounded deep.

And where the far-off sand-bars lift
Their backs in long and narrow line,
The breakers shout, and leap, and shift,
And toss the sparkling brine
Into the air; then rush to mimic strife:
Glad creatures of the sea, and full of life!—

But not to Lee. He sits alone;
No fellowship nor joy for him;
Borne down by woe,—but not a moan,—
Though tears will sometimes dim
That asking eye. O, how his worn thoughts crave—
Not joy again, but rest within the grave.

The rocks are dripping in the mist
That lies so heavy off the shore;
Scarce seen the running breakers;—list
Their dull and smothered roar!
Lee hearkens to their voice.—"I hear, I hear
You call.—Not yet!—I know my time is near!"

And now the mist seems taking shape,
Forming a dim gigantic ghost,—
Enormous thing! There's no escape;
'Tis close upon the coast.
Lee kneels, but cannot pray.—Why mock him so!
The ship has cleared the fog, Lee, see her go.

A sweet, low voice, in starry nights,
Chants to his ear a plaining song;
Its tones come winding up the heights,
Telling of woe and wrong;
And he must listen till the stars grow dim,
The song that gentle voice doth sing to him.

O, it is sad that aught so mild
Should bind the soul with bands of fear;
That strains to soothe a little child,
The man should dread to hear.
But sin hath broke the world's sweet peace,—unstrung
The harmonious chords to which the angels sung.

In thick dark nights he'd take his seat
High up the cliffs, and feel them shake,
As swung the sea with heavy beat
Below,—and hear it break
With savage roar, then pause and gather strength,
And, then, come tumbling in its swollen length.

But he no more shall haunt the beach,
Nor sit upon the tall cliff's crown,
Nor go the round of all that reach,
Nor feebly sit him down,
Watching the swaying weeds:—another day,
And he'll have gone far hence that dreadful way.

To-night the charmed number's told.
"Twice have I come for thee," it said.
"Once more, and none shall thee behold.
Come! live one!—to the dead."—
So hears his soul, and fears the gathering night;
Yet sick and weary of the soft, calm light.

Again he sits in that still room;
All day he leans at that still board;
None to bring comfort to his gloom,
Or speak a friendly word.
Weakened with fear, lone, haunted by remorse,
Poor, shattered wretch, there waits he that pale Horse.

Not long he waits. Where now are gone
Peak, citadel, and tower, that stood
Beautiful, while the west sun shone,
And bathed them in his flood
Of airy glory?—Sudden darkness fell;
And down they went, peak, tower, citadel.

The darkness, like a dome of stone,
Ceils up the heavens. 'Tis hush as death,—

All but the ocean's dull, low moan.
How hard he draws his breath!
He shudders as he feels the working Power.
Arouse thee, Lee! up! man thee for thine hour!

'Tis close at hand; for there, once more,
The burning ship. Wide sheets of flame
And shafted fire she showed before;—
Twice thus she hither came;—
But now she rolls a naked hulk, and throws
A wasting light; then settling, down she goes.

And where she sank, up slowly came
The Spectre-Horse from out the sea.
And there he stands! His pale sides flame.
He'll meet thee, shortly, Lee.
He treads the waters as a solid floor;
He's moving on. Lee waits him at the door.

They're met.—"I know thou com'st for me,"
Lee's spirit to the Spectre said;
"I know that I must go with thee:
Take me not to the dead.
It was not I alone that did the deed!"—
Dreadful the eye of that still, Spectral Steed!

Lee cannot turn. There is a force
In that fixed eye, which holds him fast.
How still they stand,—the man and Horse!
"Thine Hour is almost past."
"O, spare me," cries the wretch, "thou fearful One!"
"The time is come,—I must not go alone."

"I'm weak and faint. O, let me stay!"
"Nay, murderer, rest nor stay for thee!"
The Horse and man are on their way;
He bears him to the sea.
Hard breathes the Spectre through the silent night;
Fierce from his nostrils streams a deathly light.

He's on the beach; but stops not there;
He's on the sea,—that dreadful Horse!
Lee flings and writhes in wild despair.
In vain! The Spirit-Corse
Holds him by fearful spell; he cannot leap:
Within that horrid light he rides the deep.

It lights the sea around their track,—
The curling comb, and steel-dark wave:
And there sits Lee the Spectre's back;
Gone! gone! and none to save!
They're seen no more; the night has shut them in.
May heaven have pity on thee, man of sin!

The earth has washed away its stain;
The sealed-up sky is breaking forth,
Mustering its glorious hosts again,
From the far south and north;
The climbing moon plays on the rippling sea.
—O, whither on its waters rideth Lee?

EDMUND KEAN'S LEAR.—FROM THE PAPER ON KEAN'S ACTING.

It has been so common a saying, that Lear is the most difficult of characters to personate that we had taken it for granted no man could play it so as to satisfy us. Perhaps it is the hardest to represent. Yet the part which has generally been supposed the most difficult, the insanity of Lear, is scarcely more so than that of the choleric old king. Inefficient rage is almost always ridiculous; and an old man, with a broken-down body and a mind falling in pieces from the violence of its uncontrolled passions, is in constant danger of exciting, along with our pity, a feeling of contempt. It is a chance matter to which we may be most moved. And this it is which makes the opening of Lear so difficult.

We may as well notice here the objection which some make to the abrupt violence with which Kean begins in Lear. If this be a fault, it is Shakespeare, and not Kean, who is to blame; for, no doubt, he has conceived it according to his author. Perhaps, however, the mistake lies in this case, where it does in most others, with whose who put themselves into the seat of judgment to pass upon great men.

In most instances, Shakespeare has given us the gradual growth of a passion, with such little accompaniments as agree with it, and go to make up the whole man. In Lear, his object being to represent the beginning and course of insanity, he has properly enough gone but a little back of it, and introduced to us an old man of good feelings enough, but one who had lived without any true principle of conduct, and whose unruled passions had grown strong with age, and were ready, upon a disappointment, to make shipwreck of an intellect never strong. To bring this about, he begins with an abruptness rather unusual; and the old king rushes in before us, with his passions at their height, and tearing him like fiends.

Kean gives this as soon as the fitting occasion offers itself. Had he put more of melancholy and depression, and less of rage into the character, we should have been much puzzled at his so suddenly going mad. It would have required the change to have been slower; and besides, his insanity must have been of another kind. It must have been monotonous and complaining, instead of continually varying; at one time full of grief, at another playful, and then wild as the winds that roared about him, and fiery and sharp as the lightning that shot by him. The truth with which he conceived this was not finer than his execution of it. Not for a moment, in his utmost violence, did he suffer the imbecility of the old man's anger to touch upon the ludicrous, when nothing but the justest conception and feeling of the character could have saved him from it.

It has been said that Lear is a study for one who would make himself acquainted with the workings of an insane mind. And it is hardly less true, that the acting of Kean was an embodying of these workings. His eye, when his senses are first forsaking him, giving an inquiring look at what he saw, as if all before him was undergoing a strange and bewildering change which confused his brain,—the wandering, lost motions of his hands, which seemed feeling for something familiar to them, on which they might take hold and be assured of a safe reality,—the under monotone of his voice, as if he was questioning his own being, and what surrounded him,—the continuous, but slight, oscillating motion of the body,—all these expressed, with fearful truth, the bewildered state of a mind fast unsettling, and making vain and weak efforts to find its way back to its wonted reason. There was a childish, feeble gladness in the eye, and a half piteous smile about the mouth, at times, which one could scarce look upon without tears. As the derangement increased upon him, his eye lost its notice of objects about him, wandering over things as if he saw them not, and fastening upon the creatures of his crazed brain. The helpless and delighted fondness with which he clings to Edgar as an insane brother, is another instance of the justness of Kean's conceptions. Nor does he lose the air of insanity, even in the fine moralizing parts, and where he inveighs against the corruptions of the world: There is a madness even in his reason.

The violent and immediate changes of the passions in Lear, so difficult to manage without jarring upon us, are given by Kean with a spirit and with a fitness to nature which we had hardly thought possible. These are equally well done both before and after the loss of reason. The most difficult scene, in this respect, is the last interview between Lear and his daughters, Goneril and Regan,—(and how wonderfully does Kean carry it through!)—the scene which ends with the horrid shout and cry with which he runs out mad from their presence, as if his very brain had taken fire.

The last scene which we are allowed to have of Shakespeare's Lear, for the simply pathetic, was played by Kean with unmatched power. We sink down helpless under the oppressive grief. It lies like a dead weight upon our hearts. We are denied even the relief of tears; and are thankful for the shudder that seizes us when he kneels to his daughter in the deploring weakness of his crazed grief.

It is lamentable that Kean should not be allowed to show his unequalled powers in the last scene of Lear, as Shakespeare wrote it; and that this mighty work of genius should be profaned by the miserable, mawkish sort of by-play of Edgar's and Cordelia's loves: Nothing can surpass the impertinence of the man who made the change, but the folly of those who sanctioned it.

INFLUENCE OF HOME—FROM THE PAPER ON DOMESTIC LIFE.

Home gives a certain serenity to the mind, so that everything is well defined, and in a clear atmosphere, and the lesser beauties brought out to rejoice in the pure glow which floats over and beneath them from the earth and sky. In this state of mind afflictions come to us chastened; and if the wrongs of the world cross us in our door-path, we put them aside without anger. Vices are about us, not to lure us away, or make us morose, but to remind us of our frailty and keep down our pride. We are put into a right relation with the world; neither holding it in proud scorn, like the solitary man, nor being carried along by shifting and hurried feelings, and vague and careless notions of things, like the world's man. We do not take novelty for improvement, or set up vogue for a rule of conduct; neither do we despair, as if all great virtues had departed with the years gone by, though we see new vices, frailties, and follies taking growth in the very light which is spreading over the earth.

Our safest way of coming into communion with mankind is through our own household. For there our sorrow and regret at the failings of the bad are in proportion to our love, while our familiar intercourse with the good has a secretly assimilating influence upon our characters. The domestic man has an independence of thought which puts him at ease in society, and a cheerfulness and benevolence of feeling which seem to ray out from him, and to diffuse a pleasurable sense over those near him, like a soft, bright day. As domestic life strengthens a man's virtue, so does it help to a sound judgment and a right balancing of things, and gives an integrity and propriety to the whole character. God, in his goodness, has ordained that virtue should make its own enjoyment, and that wherever a vice or frailty is rooted out, something should spring up to be a beauty and delight in its stead. But a man of a character rightly cast, has pleasures at home, which, though fitted to his highest nature, are common to him as his daily food; and he moves about his house under a continued sense of them, and is happy almost without heeding it.

Women have been called angels, in love-tales and sonnets, till we have almost learned to think of angels as little better than woman. Yet a man who knows a woman thoroughly, and loves her truly,—and there are women who may be so known and loved,—will find, after a few years, that his relish for the grosser pleasures is lessened, and that he has grown into a fondness for the intellectual and refined without an effort, and almost unawares. He has been led on to virtue through his pleasures; and the delights of the eye, and the gentle play of that passion which is the most inward and romantic in our nature, and which keeps much of its character amidst the concerns of life, have held him in a kind of spiritualized existence: he shares his very being with one who, a creature of this world, and with something of the world's frailties, is

yet a Spirit still, and bright
With something of an angel light.

With all the sincerity of a companionship of feeling, cares, sorrows, and enjoyments, her presence is as the presence of a purer being, and there is that in her nature which seems to bring him nearer to a better world. She is, as it were, linked to angels, and in his exalted moments, he feels himself held by the same tie.

In the ordinary affairs of life, a woman has a greater influence over those near her than a man. While our feelings are, for the most part, as retired as anchorites, hers are in play before us. We hear them in her varying voice; we see them in the beautiful and harmonious undulations of her movements, in the quick shifting hues of her face, in her eye, glad and bright, then fond and suffused; her frame is alive and active with what is at her heart, and all the outward form speaks. She seems of a finer mould than we, and cast in a form of beauty, which, like all beauty, acts with a moral influence upon our hearts; and as she moves about us, we feel a movement within which rises and spreads gently over us, harmonizing us with her own. And can any man listen to this,—Can his eye, day after day, rest upon this, and he not be touched by it, and made better?

The dignity of a woman has its peculiar character; it awes more than that of man. His is more physical, bearing itself up with an energy of courage which we may brave, or a strength which we may struggle against; he is his own avenger, and we may stand the brunt. A woman's has nothing of this force in it; it is of a higher quality, and too delicate for mortal touch.

RICHARD DABNEY.

RICHARD DABNEY was born about 1787, in the county of Louisa, Virginia, of a family settled for several generations in that state, and which had, in early times of England, been *Daubeney*. Earlier still it is said to have been *D'Aubigny* or *D'Aubigné*, of France. His mother had been a Meriwether, aunt to Meriwether Lewis, who, with Captain Clarke, in Jefferson's presidency, explored the sources of the Missouri and the Rocky Mountains. Richard's father, Samuel Dabney, was a wealthy farmer and planter, with twelve children. None of them were regularly or thoroughly educated. Richard's instruction was but in the plainest rudiments of knowledge, till his sixteenth or eighteenth year, when he went to a school of Latin and Greek. In these languages he strode forward with great rapidity; learning in one or two years more than most boys learned in six. Afterwards he was an assistant teacher in a Richmond school. From the burning theatre of that city, in December, 1811, he barely escaped with life, receiving hurts which he bore with him to his grave.

In 1812, however, he published in Richmond a thin duodecimo volume of *Poems, Original and*

Translated, which, though of some merit, mortifyingly failed with the public, and he then endeavored to suppress the edition. Going to Philadelphia with general undefined views to literary pursuits, he published, through Mathew Carey, a much improved edition of his poems in 1815. This too was, as the publisher said, "quite a losing concern." Yet it had pieces remarkable for striking and vigorous thought; and the diversity of translation (from Grecian, Latin, and Italian poets) evinced ripeness of scholarship and correctness of taste. In the mechanical parts of poetry—in rhythm and in rhymes—he was least exact. Nearly half the volume consisted of translations. A short one from Sappho is not inelegant, or defective in versification:

I cannot——'tis in vain to try—
This tiresome talk for ever ply;
I cannot bear this senseless round,
To one dull course for ever bound;
I cannot, on the darkened page,
Con the deep maxims of the sage,
When all my thoughts perpetual swarm,
Around Eliza's blooming form.

Dabney was said to have written a large portion of Carey's "Olive Branch, or Faults on Both Sides," designed to show how flagrantly both of the great parties (*Federal* and *Republican*) had sinned against their country's good, and against their own respective principles, whenever party interests or party rage commanded.

In a few years more he returned to his native place, where his now widowed mother, with some of her children, lived upon her farm. Here he spent the rest of his life; in devouring such books and periodicals as he could find—in visits among a few of the neighboring farmers—and in such social enjoyments as rural Virginia then afforded, in which juleps and grog-drinking made a fearfully large part. Dabney had become an opium-eater, led on, it seems, by prescriptions of that poison for some of his injuries in the burning theatre. To this he added strong drink; and in his last years he was seldom sober when the means of intoxication were at hand. Some friends who desired to see his fine classical attainments turned to useful account, prevailed upon him to take a school of five or six boys, and that pursuit he continued nearly to the last.

During his country life, in 1818, was published a poem of much classic beauty, called "Rhododaphne, or the Thessalian Spell," which was attributed to Dabney by a Richmond Magazine, but he always denied the authorship; and Carey the publisher, in a letter dated 1827, says, "It was an English production, as my son informs me."

Dabney died in November, 1825, at the age of thirty-eight; prominent among the myriads to whom the *drinking usages* of America have made appropriate the deep self-reproach—

We might have won the meed of fame,
Essayed and reached a worthier aim—
Had more of wealth and less of shame,
Nor heard, as from a tongue of flame—
You might have been—you might have been!

The prevailing traits of his mind were memory and imagination. His excellence was only in literature. For mathematics and the sciences he had no strong taste. He was guileless, and had warm affections, which he too guardedly abstained from displaying, as he carried his dislike of courtliness and professions to the opposite extreme of cynicism.*

YOUTH AND AGE.

1.

As numerous as the stars of heaven,
Are the fond hopes to mortals given;
But two illume, with brighter ray,
The morn and eve of life's short day.

2.

Its glowing tints, on youth's fresh days,
The Lucifer of life displays,
And bids its opening joys declare
Their bloom of prime shall be so fair,
That all its minutes, all its hours
Shall breathe of pleasure's sweetest flowers.
But false the augury of that star—
The Lord of passion drives his car,
Swift up the middle line of heaven,
And blasts each flower that hope had given.
And care and woe, and pain and strife,
All mingle in the noon of life.

3.

Its gentle beams, on man's last days,
The Hesperus of life displays:
When all of passion's midday heat
Within the breast forgets to beat;
When calm and smooth our minutes glide,
Along life's tranquillizing tide;
It points with slow, receding light,
To the sweet rest of silent night;
And tells, when life's vain schemes shall end,
Thus will its closing light descend;
And as the eve-star seeks the wave,
Thus gently reach the quiet grave.

THE TRIBUTE.

When the dark shades of death dim the warrior's eyes,
When the warrior's spirit from its martial form flies,
The proud rites of pomp are performed at his grave,
And the pageants of splendor o'er its cold inmate wave;

Though that warrior's deeds were for tyrants performed,
And no thoughts of virtue that warrior's breast warmed,
Though the roll of his fame is the record of death,
And the tears of the widow are wet on his wreath.

What then are the rites that are due to be paid,
To the virtuous man's tomb, and the brave warrior's shade!
To him, who was firm to his country's love!
To him whom no might from stern virtue could move!

Be his requiem, the sigh of the wretched bereft;
Be his pageants, the tears of the friends he has left;
Such tears, as were late with impassioned grief shed,
On the grave that encloses our CARRINGTON† dead.

---

* We are indebted for this sketch of Richard Dabney to a gentleman of Virginia, Lucian Minor, Esq., of Louisa County.

† Col. E. Carrington, a revolutionary patriot, who died in the autumn of 1810, in Richmond, Virginia.

AN EPIGRAM, IMITATED FROM ARCHIAS.

——— Nos decebat
Lugere, ubi esset aliquis in lucem editus,
Humanæ vitæ varia reputantes mala;
At, qui labores morte finisset graves,
Omnes amicos laude et lætitia exequi.
Eurip. apud Tull.

O wise was the people that deeply lamented
The hour that presented their children to light,
And gathering around, all the mis'ries recounted,
That brood o'er life's prospects and whelm them in night.

And wise was the people that deeply delighted,
When death snatched its victim from life's cheerless day;
For then, all the clouds, life's views that benighted,
They believed, at his touch, vanished quickly away.

Life, faithless and treach'rous, is for ever presenting,
To our view, flying phantoms we never can gain;
Life, cruel and tasteless, is for ever preventing
All our joys, and involving our pleasure in vain.

Death, kind and consoling, comes calmly and lightly,
The balm of all sorrow, the cure of all ill,
And after a pang, that but thrills o'er us slightly,
All then becomes tranquil, all then becomes still.

NATHANIEL H. CARTER.

NATHANIEL H. CARTER was born at Concord, New Hampshire, September 17, 1787. He was educated at Exeter academy and Dartmouth College, and on the completion of his course became a teacher at Salisbury, New Hampshire, whence he soon after removed to take a similar charge at Portland, Maine. In 1817 he was appointed professor of languages in the University created by the state legislature at Dartmouth, where he remained until the institution was broken up by a decision of the Supreme Court, when he removed to New York. In 1819 he became editor of the Statesman, a newspaper of the Clintonian party. In 1824 he delivered a poem at Dartmouth College before the Phi Beta Kappa Society, entitled *The Pains of the Imagination.* In the following year he visited Europe, and wrote home letters descriptive of his travels to the Statesman, which were republished in other journals throughout the country. On his return in the spring of 1827 he published these letters, revised and enlarged, in two octavo volumes,* which were favorably received. In consequence of ill health he passed the following winter in Cuba, and on his return in the spring abandoned, for the same reason, the editorial profession. In the fall of 1829 he was invited by a friend residing in Marseilles to accompany him on a voyage to that place. While on shipboard, believing that his last hour was approaching, he wrote some lines entitled *The Closing Scene, or the Burial at Sea.* He survived, however, until a few days after his arrival, in December, 1829.

Mr. Carter's letters furnish a pleasing and somewhat minute account of the objects of interest in an ordinary European tour, at the period of its publication much more of a novelty than at present. His poems were written from time to time on incidents connected with his feelings, studies, and travels, and are for the most part simply reflective.

* Letters from Europe, comprising the Journal of a Tour through England, Scotland, France, Italy, and Switzerland, in the years 1825, '26, and '27. By N. H. Carter. New York: 1827. 2 vols. 8vo.

ISAAC HARBY.

ISAAC, the son of Solomon Harby, was the grandson of a lapidary of the Emperor of Morocco, who fled to England, and married an Italian lady. His son Solomon settled in Charleston, S. C., where Isaac was born in 1788. He was educated under the care of Dr. Best, a celebrated teacher of those days. He commenced, but soon abandoned the study of the law, and the support of his mother and the rest of his family falling upon him in consequence of the death of his father, he opened a school on Edisto Island, which met with success.

His taste for literature and facility in writing soon brought him in connexion with the press. He became the editor of a weekly journal, the "Quiver," and after its discontinuance of the "Investigator" newspaper, the title of which he changed to the "Southern Patriot," in which he supported the administration of Madison. He became widely and favorably known as a newspaper writer, especially in the department of theatrical criticism.

In 1807, his play of the *Gordian Knot, or Causes and Effects*, was produced at the Charleston Theatre, where he had previously offered another five act piece, *Alexander Severus*, which was declined. It was played but a few times. In 1819, *Alberti*, a five act play by the same author, appeared with better success. It was published soon after its performance.

In 1825 he delivered an address in Charleston, before the "Reformed Society of Israelites," advocating the addition of a sermon and services in English to the Hebrew worship of the Synagogue.

In June, 1828, Harby removed from Charleston to New York, his object being to secure a larger audience for his literary labors. He contributed to the Evening Post and other city periodicals, and was fast acquiring an influential position, when his career was interrupted by his death, on the fourteenth of November, 1828.

A selection from his writings was published at Charleston in the following year, in one volume octavo.* It contains his play of Alberti, Discourse before the Reformed Society of Israelites, and a number of political essays, with literary and theatrical criticisms, selected from his newspaper writings.

Alberti is founded upon the history of Lorenzo de Medici, and designed to vindicate his conduct from "the calumnies of Alfieri in his tragedy called The Conspiracy of the Pazzi." The drama is animated in action, and smooth in versification.

WILLIAM ELLIOTT.

WILLIAM ELLIOTT, the grandfather of the subject of our remarks, removed from Charleston nearly a century ago, sold his possessions in St. Paul's, and settled at Beaufort, where he intermarried with Mary Barnwell, grand-daughter of John Barnwell,

* A Selection from the Miscellaneous Writings of the late Isaac Harby, Esq., arranged and published by Henry L. Pinckney and Abraham Moise, for the benefit of his family. To which is prefixed a memoir of his life, by Abraham Moise.

distinguished first as the leader of the Tuscarora war, and afterwards as the agent of the colony in England, through whose representations the constitutions of Locke were abrogated, and the colony passed from the hands of the Lords Proprietors into those of the Crown.

From this marriage descended three sons—William, Ralph, and Stephen. Ralph died without surviving issue. Stephen is the naturalist and scholar, previously noticed.* William, the eldest, was born in 1761, received the rudiments of his education at Beaufort, and long before he had arrived at manhood joined in the patriotic struggle against the mother country, along with his uncles John, Edward, and Robert Barnwell. Enduring his full share of the hardships and perils of that period, he was dangerously wounded at the surprise on John's Island, was taken prisoner, and while yet a minor was held worthy of being immured in the prison-ship. His name will be found on the list of those worthies who signed the memorable letter to General Greene.

At the close of the war, Mr. Elliott applied himself to repair the losses suffered by his paternal estate, through the ravages of the enemy, and approved himself an able administrator. Of remarkable public spirit, he devoted his energy, and to a large extent his purse, to the promotion of various institutions of charity, education, and public improvement, served with honor in both branches of the legislature, and died in 1808, when Senator from his native parish,—thus closing at the age of forty-eight a life of patriotic devotion, of untiring usefulness, and spotless integrity.

He was married in 1787 to Phebe Waight, a lady of Beaufort, and their eldest son, William Elliott, the subject of this notice, was born in the same town on the 27th of April, 1788. The rudiments of his education were received in his native town. He there entered the Beaufort College (since merged into a grammar-school), whence he entered, ad eundem, after a two days' examination, the Sophomore Class at Cambridge. He was distinguished at that institution, having received the honor of an English oration at the Junior exhibition; and though forced to leave college at the end of that year from a dangerous attack of bronchitis, he received from the government the unsolicited compliment of an honorary degree. His father having died while he was at college, Mr. Elliott applied himself, on his return home, to the management of his estate. He was elected to the legislature, and served in both branches with credit; but from his liability to bronchial affections did not enter frequently into debate. In 1832, during the crisis of the Nullification fever, Mr. Elliott was a member of the Senate of South Carolina, and while unalterably opposed to a tariff of protection, as unequal and unjust to the Southern states, he denied that a nullification by a state was the proper remedy for the grievance. His constituents had come to think differently, and instructed him by a large majority to vote for the call of a convention, and in default of that, to vote for nullification of the tariff laws by the legislature. To this latter clause of their instructions Mr. Elliott excepted, as fatal to the union and subversive of the government, and, were it otherwise, impossible for him to carry out; because in his view contradictory to his oath of office, which bound him to maintain and defend the constitution of this State and of the United States. He contended that the tariff acts, however oppressive, sprang from a power clearly granted in the constitution, with one only condition annexed, that of uniformity; and that while that condition was inviolate, no palpable violation of the constitution could be pretended, and no state therefore, by the terms of "the Kentucky and Virginia resolutions," could be warranted in nullifying them. These exceptions were not satisfactory to his constituents, who, after hearing them, renewed their instructions, whereupon he resigned his office of Senator. From this time forward he has devoted himself to agricultural pursuits, to rural sports, varying the even tenor of his life by occasional inroads into the domain of letters, by essays on agriculture, controversial papers on political economy, addresses before Agricultural Societies, contributions to the Southern Review; by the essays of "Piscator" and "Venator," since enlarged and embodied in "Carolina Sports;" by a Tragedy in blank verse, printed, not published; and by occasional poems, of which a few have seen the light, and which serve to show what he might have accomplished in that department had the kindly spur of necessity been applied, or had other auspices attended his life.*

Mr. Elliott chose for the subject of his tragedy the Genoese conspiracy of Fiesco, in the management of which he has followed the narrative of DeRetz. He has handled the subject with freedom and spirit, in a mood of composition never lacking energy, though with more attention to eloquence than the finished accomplishments of verse. In one of the scenes with Fiesco, a conspirator is made to utter a glowing prediction of America.

> Not here look we for freedom:
> In that new world, by daring Colon given
> To the untiring gaze of pleased mankind;
> That virgin land, unstained as yet by crime,
> Insulted Freedom yet may rear her throne,
> And build perpetual altars.

The passage is continued with a closing allusion to the American Union.

> 'Gainst this rock
> The tempest of invasion harmless beats,
> While lurking treason, with envenomed tooth
> Still idly gnaws; till scorpion-like, he turns
> His disappointed rage upon himself,
> Strikes, and despairing dies.

Doria thus apostrophizes the city over which he ruled.

> Watchmen of Genoa! is the cry, all's well?
> The gath'ring mischief can no eye discern
> But mine, already dim, and soon to close
> In sleep eternal! Oh, thou fated city!

* *Ante*, vol. i. 601.

* Carolina Sports, by Land and Water; including Incidents of Devil Fishing, &c. By the Hon. Wm. Elliott of Beaufort, S. C. Charleston: 1856. 12mo. pp. 172.

Fiesco; a Tragedy, by an American. New York: Printed for the author. 1850. 12mo. pp. 64.

Address delivered by special request before the St. Paul's Agricultural Society, May, 1850. Published by the Society. Charleston: 1850.

(Cursed beyond all, but her who slew her lord,)
Must wars, seditions, desolations, be
Thy portion ever more? The Ostrogoth
Has mastered thee—the Saracen despoiled,
The Lombard pillaged thee. The Milanese
And the rude Switzer—each hath giv'n thee law,
The Frenchman bound thee to his galling yoke—
The Spaniard sacked and plundered thee! Alas!
Hast thou cast off the yoke of foreign foes
To feel the keener pang—the deadlier rage—
The agony of fierce domestic faction?
Rent were thy chains, and Freedom waved her wand
Over thy coasts, that straight like Eden bloomed!
And from the base of dark blue Appenine
Thy marble palaces looked brightly forth
Upon the sea, that mirrored them again,
Till the rough mariner forgot his helm
To gaze and wonder at thy loveliness!
The Moloch, Faction, enters, and in blood
Of brethren is this smiling Eden steeped!
Crumble the gilded spire, and gorgeous roof;
With one wide ruin they deform the land,
And mark the desolate shore, like monuments!
Staunched now, these cruel self-inflicted wounds;
Staunched is mine own hereditary feud;
Nor Doria, nor Spinola; Ghibeline,
Nor Guelph; disturb thee with new tragedies.
Th' Adorni and Fregoso—names that served
As rallying points to faction—are no more.
Now, that thou hail'st the dawn of liberty,
Say, Oh, my Country! shall a traitor mar,
With hellish spite, thy dearly purchased peace?

Mr. Elliott's prose sketches of the piscatory scenes of his ocean vicinity are clever Sporting Magazine papers, lively and picturesque; with a speciality of the author's own in the gigantic game with which he has identified himself of the Devil Fishing of Port Royal Sound. The following will show the quality of the sport.

I had left the cruising ground but a few days, when a party was formed, in July, 1844, to engage in this sport. Nath. Heyward, Jun., J. G. Barnwell, E. B. Means, and my son, Thos. R. S. Elliott, were respectively in command of a boat each, accompanied by several of their friends. While these boats were lying on their oars, expecting the approach of the fish, one showed himself far ahead, and they all started from their several stations in pursuit. It was my son's fortune to reach him first. His harpoon had scarcely pierced him, when the fish made a demivault in the air, and, in his descent, struck the boat violently with one of his wings. Had he fallen perpendicularly on the boat, it must have been crushed, to the imminent peril of all on board. As it happened, the blow fell aslant upon the bow,—and the effect was to drive her astern with such force, that James Cuthbert, Esq., of Pocotaligo, who was at the helm, was pitched forward at full length on the platform. Each oarsman was thrown forward beyond the seat he occupied; and my son, who was standing on the forecastle, was projected far beyond the bow of the boat. He fell, not into the sea, but directly upon the back of the Devil-fish, who lay in full sprawl on the surface. For some seconds Tom lay out of water, on this veritable Kraken, but happily made his escape without being entangled in the cordage, or receiving a parting salute from his formidable wings. My son was an expert swimmer, and struck off for the boat. The fish meantime had darted beneath, and was drawing her astern. My henchman Dick, who was the first to recover his wits, tossed overboard a coil of rope and extended an oar, the blade of which was seized by my son, who thus secured his retreat to the boat. He had no sooner gained footing in it, than, standing on the forecastle, he gave three hearty cheers, and thus assured his companions of his safety. They, meantime, from their several boats, had seen his perilous situation, without the chance of assisting him;—their oarsmen, when ordered to pull ahead, stood amazed or stupefied, and dropping their oars and jaws, cried out, "Great king! Mass Tom overboard!!" So intense was their curiosity to see how the affair would end, that they entirely forgot how much might depend on their own efforts. Could they have rowed and looked at the same time, it would have been all very well; but to turn their backs on such a pageant, every incident of which they were so keenly bent on observing, was expecting too much from African forethought and self-possession!

In a few minutes, my son found himself surrounded by his companions, whose boats were closely grouped around. They threw themselves into action, with a vivacity which showed that they were disposed to punish the fish for the insolence of his attack,—they allowed him but short time for shrift, and, forcing him to the surface, filled his body with their resentful weapons,—then, joining their forces, drew him rapidly to the shore, and landed him, amidst shouts and cheerings, at Mrs. Elliott's, Hilton Head. He measured sixteen feet across!

To this we may add the striking introduction of General Charles Cotesworth Pinckney's island residence in an account of another fishing excursion in the sound.

A third fishing-line was formerly drawn by placing the last pines on the Hilton Head beach in range with the mansion-house of Gen. C. C. Pinckney, on Pinckney Island. But this mansion no longer exists: it was swept away in one of the fearful hurricanes that vex our coast! To this spot, that sterling patriot and lion-hearted soldier retired from the arena of political strife, to spend the evening of his days in social enjoyment and literary relaxation. On a small island, attached to the larger one, which bears his name, and which, jutting out into the bay, afforded a delightful view of the ocean, he fixed his residence! *There*, in the midst of forests of oak, laurel and palmetto, the growth of centuries, his mansion-house was erected. There stood the laboratory, with its apparatus for chemical experiments,—the library, stored with works of science in various tongues; there bloomed the nursery for exotics; and there was found each other appliance, with which taste and intelligence surround the abodes of wealth. It is melancholy to reflect on the utter destruction that followed; even before the venerable proprietor had been gathered to his fathers! The ocean swallowed up everything: and it is literally true, that the sea monster now flaps his wings over the very spot where his hearth-stone was placed,—where the rites of an elegant hospitality were so unstintedly dispensed,—and where the delighted guest listened to many an instructive anecdote, and unrecorded yet significant incident of the revolutionary period, as they flowed from the cheerful lips of the patriot. It argues no defect of judgment in Gen. Pinckney, that he lavished such expense on a situation thus exposed. In strong practical sense he was surpassed by no man. It was, in truth, his characteristic. He built where trees of a century's growth gave promise of stability; but, in our Southern Atlantic borders, he who builds strongest, does not build on rock,—for among the shifting sands of our coast, old channels are closed, and new ones worn, by the prevailing winds and currents, through which the waters are poured, during the storms of the equinox, with a force that nothing can resist.

True to his antecedents, Mr. Elliott wielded in 1851, in his letters of "Agricola," the same effective pen against secession which he had so energetically pointed in 1831 against nullification.

SAMUEL JACKSON GARDNER.

Samuel Jackson Gardner was born at Brookline, near Boston, Massachusetts, the ninth day of July, 1788; a descendant of one of the early settlers of the name in New England, and on the mother's side from Edward Jackson, who came from England in 1642. He was educated at Harvard; pursued the practice of the law for several years; was elected more than once to the legislature of his native state, but manifested an early repugnance to public life. Since, he has resided in New York and has been a frequent contributor and (during the absence of Mr. Kinney, its editor, in Europe) the efficient conductor of the Newark Daily Advertiser. His essays, with the signature of "Decius," chiefly appearing in that journal, and occasionally in the Literary World, are written with ease and ingenuity on miscellaneous subjects, political economy topics, the principles of government, literature, manners; sometimes in a serious and moral, at other times in a critical, satirical, humorous vein. He has also written some fugitive poetry. His writings, always anonymous, have never been collected into a volume.

His son, Augustus K. Gardner, a physician in New York, is the author of a clever volume of sketches of Parisian life, published after a tour in France in 1848, with the title of *Old Wine in New Bottles.* He is also the author of several medical essays and tracts on civic hygiene.

WILLIAM J. GRAYSON

Was born in November, 1788, in Beaufort, S. C. His father, a descendant of one of the earliest settlers in that portion of the state in which the colonists under Sayle first landed, was an officer in the Continental army to the close of the Revolution. The son was educated at the South Carolina College; in 1813 was elected to the State House of Representatives, and was subsequently admitted to the bar at Charleston. In 1831 he was elected to the Senate of his state, and, in the controversy which then agitated the country on the subject of the tariff, took part with those who held that the reserved rights of the state gave it the power to determine when its grants for government to the federal authorities were violated, and how those violations should be arrested within its own limits. He was a temperate and moderate advocate of this view of the question in controversy, and never disposed to push it to the extreme of civil war, or a dissolution of the Union. In 1833 he was elected a member of Congress from the districts of Beaufort and Colleton, holding his seat for four years. In 1841 he was appointed collector of the port of Charleston by President Tyler, was re-appointed by President Polk, and removed by President Pierce from party considerations.

In 1850, at the height of the secession agitation, Mr. Grayson published in a pamphlet a *Letter to Governor Seabrook*, deprecating the threatened movement, and pointing out the greater evils of disunion.

Mr. Grayson is a lover and cultivator of literature. He has been for some years an occasional contributor to the Southern Review, and a frequent writer in the daily press. In 1854 he published a didactic poem entitled *The Hireling and the Slave*, the object of which is to compare the condition and advantages of the negro in his state of servitude at the South, with the frequent condition of the pauper laborer of Europe. This, however, though it gives name to the poem, is not its entire argument. It contains also an idyllic picture of rural life at the South as shared by the negro in his participation of its sports and enjoyments. This is handled in a pleasing manner; as the author describes the fishing and hunting scenes of his native region bordering on the coast. An episode introduces a sketch of General Charles Cotesworth Pinckney on his retirement at his "island home." From the descriptive portions we select this picture of

A SUNDAY SCENE AT THE SOUTH.

His too the Christian privilege to share
The weekly festival of praise and prayer;
For him the Sabbath shines with holier light,
The air is balmier, and the sky more bright;
Winter's brief suns with warmer radiance glow,
With softer breath the gales of autumn blow,
Spring with new flowers more richly strews the ground,
And summer spreads a fresher verdure round;
The early shower is past; the joyous breeze
Shakes pattering rain drops from the rustling trees,
And with the sun, the fragrant offerings rise,
From Nature's censers to the bounteous skies;
With cheerful aspect, in his best array,
To the far forest church he takes his way;
With kind salute the passing neighbour meets,
With awkward grace the morning traveller greets,
And joined by crowds, that gather as he goes,
Seeks the calm joy the Sabbath morn bestows.
There no proud temples to devotion rise,
With marble domes that emulate the skies;
But bosomed in primeval trees that spread,
Their limbs o'er mouldering mansions of the dead,
Moss-cinctured oaks and solemn pines between,
Of modest wood, the house of God is seen,
By shaded springs, that from the sloping land
Bubble and sparkle through the silver sand,
Where high o'erarching laurel blossoms blow,
Where fragrant bays breathe kindred sweets below,
And elm and ash their blended arms entwine
With the bright foliage of the mantling vine:
In quiet chat, before the hour of prayer,
Masters and Slaves in scattered groups appear;
Loosed from the carriage, in the shades around,
Impatient horses neigh and paw the ground;
No city discords break the silence here,
No sounds unmeet offend the listener's ear;
But rural melodies of flocks and birds,
The lowing, far and faint, of distant herds,
The mocking bird, with minstrel pride elate,
The partridge whistling for its absent mate,
The thrush's soft solitary notes prolong,
Bold, merry blackbirds swell the general song,
And cautious crows their harsher voices join,
In concert cawing, from the loftiest pine.

UNIVERSITY OF NORTH CAROLINA.

THE University of North Carolina was established by the Legislature of the state on the 11th of December, 1789. Forty of the most influential men of the state were incorporated as trustees, and held their first meeting in the town of Fayetteville in November of the next year, making it their earliest business to devise the means needful for the support of the Institution, and to determine upon a place for its location.

Immediately after the University was chartered, the Legislature granted to the trustees all escheated property, and all arrearages due to the state from receiving officers of the late and present governments up to Jan. 1, 1783, which grant was afterwards extended to Dec. 1799, together with all moneys in executors' and administrators' hands unclaimed by legatees. The site of the University, after much deliberation, was fixed at Chapel Hill in the county of Orange, about twenty-eight miles west of Raleigh. This place is central to the territory and population of the state, and is unrivalled for the beauty of its situation on an elevated range of hills, the purity of its air, and the healthfulness of its climate. Great interest in the welfare and prospects of the infant Institution was manifested throughout the community. Generous individuals gave large sums of money and valuable tracts of land for its support; and the ladies of the two principal towns of Raleigh and Newbern presented it with mathematical instruments, pledging themselves never to be indifferent to its objects and interests. Many gentlemen gave valuable books for the library; and the Legislature from time to time increased and renewed its properties and privileges.

The first college edifice being sufficiently completed in 1794 to accommodate students, its doors were opened and instruction commenced in February, 1795. The Rev. David Kerr, a graduate of Trinity College, Dublin, was the first professor, assisted in the preparatory department by Samuel A. Holmes. Shortly after, Charles W. Harris, a graduate of the College of New Jersey, was elected to the professorship of Mathematics, which chair he occupied for only one year. There was of necessity much to be done in devising, arranging, and carrying out the most practicable systems of instruction, and of prudential government—a work demanding much practical ability and unwavering devotion to the best interests of the University.

At this early crisis, Mr. Joseph Caldwell, then a young man but twenty-three years of age, was introduced to the notice of the trustees, having already acquired a high reputation for talents, scholarship, and success, in teaching. This gentleman was born in Lamington, New Jersey, April 21, 1773; entered the college at Princeton at the age of fourteen, and was graduated in 1791, having the Salutatory Oration in Latin assigned him. Having served his *alma mater* with much reputation as Tutor for several years, he was in 1796 elected to the principal professorship in the University of N. C. Thenceforward the history of his life becomes the history of the Institution. For nearly forty years he devoted his best energies to the promotion of its interests, and the cause of education generally throughout the state of his adoption; and to his administrative skill and untiring zeal, its present high position and prosperity are greatly owing. Under his care, the prospects of the University speedily brightened and flourished, and in 1804 the trustees signified their appreciation of his services by electing him president—the first who had filled that office. This chair he retained till the time of his death in 1835, with the exception of four years from 1812 to 1816, during which period he retired voluntarily to the professorship of Mathematics, for the sake of relief from cares and opportunity to prosecute the study of Theology. Meantime the presidential chair was filled by the Rev. Robert H. Chapman, D.D. Upon that gentleman's resignation in 1816, Mr. Caldwell was again elected to the presidency, at which time his *alma mater* conferred on him a Doctorate in Divinity, and he thenceforth took an elevated rank among scholars and divines of the Presbyterian church.

From the time of Dr. Caldwell's first connexion with the University, almost everything of interest in its progress and government was submitted to his consideration. He alone digested and made practicable the various plans of particular instruction, of internal policy and discipline. He raised the grade of scholarship and re-arranged the *curriculum* so as to embrace a period of four years with the usual division of classes. The first anniversary Commencement was in 1798, with a graduating class of nine. The greatest good of the University, and indeed the general progress and intellectual improvement of the state, were ever the most engrossing objects of Dr. Caldwell's care; and with untiring perseverance and fidelity, he presented the claims of education to the community, and appealed to their liberality for its support.

In 1821, the Board of Trustees was increased to sixty-five, the governor of the state being *ex officio* their President, and all vacancies occurring to be filled by a joint ballot of the two houses of Assembly. The actual government of the University, however, is vested in an executive committee of seven of the trustees, with the governor always as their presiding officer.

In 1824, Dr. Caldwell visited Europe for the purpose of increasing the Library, and forming cabinets, and procuring a very valuable philosophical apparatus constructed under his own inspection. To these has since been added a cabinet of minerals purchased in Vienna. On the death of Dr. Caldwell, January 28, 1835, for a few months the duties of the presidency were discharged by the senior professor, Dr. Mitchell, when the trustees elected to that office the Hon. David L. Swain, a native of Buncombe county, who, though comparatively a young man, had served the state with distinction in the Legislature and on the Superior Court bench, from which he was elected Governor for the years 1833, '34, '35. He entered on the office of the presidency of the University in January, 1836, and from that time to the present the Institution has been steadily advancing in reputation, influence, and numbers. It is a fortunate circumstance in the history of this University, that for a period of nearly sixty years its government has been administered by two incumbents both so well qualified for the office as Dr. Caldwell and Gov. Swain.

The number of students having greatly increased, additions have from time to time been made

University of North Carolina.

in the means of accommodation and instruction, and to the Faculty. The college buildings are now six in number, located on a beautiful and commanding site, so as to form a hollow square, inclosing a large area or lawn surrounded by groves of native growth. The grounds are tastefully disposed and ornamented with choice shrubs and flowers, and the lawn slopes gradually from the buildings, several hundred yards, to the main street of the village of Chapel Hill. A hall has lately been erected for the reception of the University Library, liberal appropriations having been made for valuable additions. The two literary societies belonging to the students are also accommodated with imposing edifices; and the number of volumes in their libraries, and that of the University together, amounts to about fifteen thousand.*

The College students now (1855) number two hundred and eighty-one from fifteen different states in the Union, as ascertained by the last annual catalogue; the whole number of graduates since 1795 is eleven hundred and fifty-five. The number of matriculates has been estimated to be nearly twice that of graduates. The executive Faculty number at present sixteen, of whom the senior professor, Dr. E. Mitchell, Professor of Chemistry, Geology, and Mineralogy, a native of Connecticut and graduate of Yale College, has been connected with the Institution for thirty-seven years; and Dr. Phillips, Professor of Mathematics and Natural Philosophy, a native of Essex county, England, has filled his present chair for twenty-nine years. Professorships of Civil Engineering and of Agricultural Chemistry have lately been established. The Department of Law is under the charge of the Hon. William H. Battle, one of the judges of the Supreme Court, and a regular course of lectures on international and constitutional Law is delivered to the Senior undergraduates towards the close of their second term by the president.

In 1837, the Trustees, with a liberality at that time without example, authorized the Faculty to admit gratuitously to the advantages of the Institution, all young men of fair character and ability who are natives of the state, and unable to defray the expenses incident to a college education. About fifteen have annually availed themselves of this liberality, many of whom now occupy with honor places of trust among their fellow citizens.

The number of Alumni who have attained distinction in public life will compare favorably with those who have gone forth from similar institutions in any part of the Union. At the last annual Commencement, six ex-Governors of this and other states were in the procession of the Alumni Association. Among numerous interesting incidents connected with the history of the University, which were presented in the course of a lecture delivered in the hall of the House of Commons since the beginning of the present session, it was remarked that among the alumni of the college were one of the late presidents, Polk, and one of the late vice-presidents of the United States, W. R. King; the present Secretary of the Navy, James C. Dobbin, and the Minister to France, John Y. Mason; the Governor, the Public Treasurer and Comptroller, two of the three Supreme and six of the seven Superior Court Judges, the Attorney-General, and nearly a fourth of the members of the General Assembly of the state of North Carolina.

It is not less noticeable that among the distinguished clergymen of various denominations who received their academical training in these Halls, and who are at present prominently before the public, the institution can refer to one whose reputation is established at home and abroad as a model of pulpit eloquence—the Rev. Francis L. Hawks, and to five Bishops of the Protestant Episcopal Church, with which he is connected—J. H. Otey of Tennessee, Leonidas Polk of Arkansas, Cicero S. Hawks of Missouri, W. M. Green of Mississippi, Thomas F. Davis of South Carolina.

* Our drawing of the College buildings and grounds has been kindly furnished by Miss Phillips, daughter of the venerable Mathematical professor of the Institution.

WILLIAM JAY.

William Jay, the second son of Chief-justice Jay, was born June 16, 1789. He studied the classics with the Rev. Thomas Ellison of Albany, the early friend of Bishop Chase, and at New Haven with the Rev. Mr. Davis, afterwards President of Hamilton College. After completing his course at Yale in 1808, he read law at Albany in the office of Mr. John B. Henry, until compelled by an affection of the eyes to abandon study, he retired to his father's country-seat at Bedford, with whom he resided until the death of the latter in 1829, when he succeeded to the estate, which has since been his principal residence. In 1812 he married the daughter of John McVickar, a New York merchant. He was appointed First Judge of the County of Westchester by Governor Tompkins, and successively reappointed by Clinton, Marcy, and Van Buren.

Judge Jay has throughout his life been a prominent opponent of slavery, and has, in this connexion, published numerous addresses and pamphlets, several of which have been collected by him in his *Miscellaneous Writings on Slavery*, published at Boston in 1854. He was one of the founders of the American Bible Society, has been President of the American Peace Society, is an active member of the Agricultural Society of Westchester, and of other associations of a similar character. In 1832 he published *The Life and Writings of John Jay*, in two volumes 8vo., a careful presentation of the career of his distinguished father with extracts from the correspondence and papers, which were bequeathed to the sons Peter A. and William Jay.

John Jay, the son of William Jay, born June 23, 1817, a graduate of Columbia College in 1836, is the author of several pamphlets on the Slavery question, and on the right of the delegates of churches composed of colored persons to seats in the convention of the Protestant Episcopal Church of the Diocese of New York.

RICHARD HENRY WILDE.

This fine scholar and delicate poet, who shared the accomplishments of literature with the active pursuits of legal and political life, was born in the city of Dublin, September 24, 1789. His mother's family, the Newitts, were strong Royalists. One of them, his uncle John Newitt, had been settled in America, and on the breaking out of the Revolutionary war had sold his flour mills upon the Hudson and returned to Ireland. His father, Richard Wilde, was a hardware merchant in Dublin, who, when he had resolved to come to America, thinking it possible that he might not like the new country and would return, left his business unclosed in the hands of a partner. He arrived at Baltimore in January, 1797, in a ship which he had freighted with goods on a joint venture with the captain, who owned the vessel. On landing, ship and cargo were seized as the property of the captain, and Mr. Wilde recovered his interest only after a long and expensive litigation. In addition to this misfortune, the rebellion of 1798 broke out at this time, when his Dublin partner was convicted of high treason and the property in his hands confiscated. Not long after this Richard Wilde died in 1802. His widow, the following year, removed to Augusta, Georgia, where she opened a small store to supply the necessities of the family, in which her son, Richard Henry, attended as clerk during the day, while he actively pursued his studies at night. In 1806 Mrs. Wilde visited Ireland with the hope of recovering some portion of the large fortune of her husband, but returned unsuccessful the same year. She died in 1815, but a few months before her son was elected to Congress.

It was to his mother that Wilde owed his early education, and from her he inherited his poetical talents. Many of her verses, remarkable for their vigor of thought and beauty of expression, are preserved among the papers of the family.

Wilde early directed his attention to the law while assisting his mother in Augusta. Delicate in constitution he studied laboriously, and before the age of twenty, by his solitary exertions, had qualified himself for admission to the bar in South Carolina. That his mother might not be mortified at his defeat, if he failed, he presented himself at the Green Superior Court, where he successfully passed a rigorous examination by Justice Early in the March term of 1809. He soon took an active part in his profession, and was elected Attorney-General of the State. In 1815 he was elected to the national House of Representatives, where he served for a single term. He was again in Congress from 1828 to 1835, maintaining the position of an independent thinker, well fortified in his opinions, though speaking but seldom. His course on the Force Bill of Jackson's administration, which he opposed, and in which he differed from the views of his constituents, led to his withdrawal from Congress.

Richard Henry Wilde

He next went abroad and passed five years, from 1835 to 1840, in Europe, residing most of the time in Florence, where he pursued to great advantage his favorite studies in Italian literature. He had free access to all the public libraries, besides the archives of the Medici family and the private collection of the Grand Duke, a favor seldom granted to a stranger. The large number of his manuscript notes and extracts from the Laurentian, Magliabecchian, and the library of the Reformagione, show how indefatigably his studies were pursued. His curious search was at length rewarded by the discovery of a number of documents connected with the life and times of Dante which had previously escaped attention. He was enabled also to set on foot an investigation which resulted in the discovery of an original painting by Giotto, of the author of the Divina Commedia. Having learnt, on the authority of an old biographer of the poet, that Giotto had once painted a portrait of Dante on the wall of the chapel of the Bargello, he communicated the fact to Mr. G. A. Bezzi, when a subscription was taken up among their friends for its recovery. After a sufficient sum was collected to begin the work, permission was obtained from the government to remove the whitewash with which the walls were covered, when, after a labor of some months, two sides of the room having been previously examined, upon the third the portrait was discovered. The government then took the enterprise in hand and completed the undertaking. Mr. Wilde commenced a life of Dante, one volume only of which was written and which remains in manuscript.

At Florence he had among his friends many of the most learned and distinguished men of the day, including Ciampi, Mannini, Capponi, Regio, and others.

Besides his investigation in the literature of Dante he made a special study of the vexed question connected with the life of Tasso. The result of this he gave to the public on his return to America in his *Conjectures and Researches concerning the Love, Madness, and Imprisonment of Torquato Tasso*,* a work of diligent scholarship, in which the elaborate argument is enlivened by the elegance of the frequent original translations of the sonnets. In this he maintains the sanity of Tasso, and traces the progress of the intrigue with the Princess Leonora D'Este as the key of the poet's difficulties.

Mr. Wilde removed to New Orleans, and was admitted to the bar in January, 1844, and on the organization of the Law Department of the University was appointed Professor of Common Law. He applied himself vigorously to the science of the civil law, became engaged in various important cases, and was rapidly acquiring a high position as a civilian at the time of his death, which occurred in the city of New Orleans, September 10, 1847.

In addition to the writings which have been mentioned, Mr. Wilde wrote for the *Southern Review* an article on Petrarch, was an occasional contributor of verses to the magazines, and left numerous choice and valuable manuscripts unpublished. Among the latter are various minor poems, a distinct finished poem of some four cantos entitled *Hesperia*, and a collection of Italian lyrics, which were to have been accompanied with lives of the poets from whom they were translated. The translations are nearly complete.

While abroad Mr. Wilde collected a large and valuable library of books and MSS., principally relating to Italian literature, many of which have numerous marginal notes from his pen. A memoir (to be accompanied by a collection of the author's poems) is understood to be on the eve of publication, from the pen of his eldest son William C. Wilde, a gentleman of literary tastes and cultivation, eminently qualified to do justice to his father's memory. To another son, John P. Wilde, a lawyer of New Orleans, we are indebted in advance of this publication for the interesting and authentic details which we have given.

These show a life of passionate earnestness, rising under great disadvantage to the honors of the most distinguished scholarship, and asserting an eminent position in public and professional life. In what was more peculiarly individual to the man, his exquisite tastes and sensibilities, the poetical extracts, the translations and original poems which we shall give, will speak for themselves.

* Two vols. 12mo. New York: A. V. Blake. 1842.

SONNETS TRANSLATED FROM TASSO.

To the Duchess of Ferrara who appeared masked at a fête.

'Twas Night, and underneath her starry vest
The prattling Loves were hidden, and their arts
Practised so cunningly on our hearts,
That never felt they sweeter scorn and jest:
Thousands of amorous thefts their skill attest—
All kindly hidden by the gloom from day,
A thousand visions in each trembling ray
Flitted around, in bright false splendor drest.
The clear pure moon rolled on her starry way
Without a cloud to dim her silver light,
And HIGH-BORN BEAUTY made our revels gay—
Reflecting back on heaven beams as bright,
Which even with the dawn fled not away—
When chased the SUN such lovely GHOSTS from Night.

On two Beautiful Ladies, one Gay and one Sad.

I saw two ladies once—illustrious, rare—
ONE a sad sun; her beauties at mid-day
In clouds concealed; the OTHER, bright and gay,
Gladdened, Aurora-like, earth, sea, and air;
One hid her light, lest men should call her fair,
And of her praises no reflected ray
Suffered to cross her own celestial way—
To charm and to be charmed, the other's care;
Yet *this* her loveliness veiled not so well,
But forth it broke. Nor could the other show
All HERS, which wearied mirrors did not tell;
Nor of *this* one could I be silent, though
Bidden in ire—nor *that* one's triumphs swell,
Since my tired verse, o'ertasked, refused to flow.

To Alphonso, Duke of Ferrara.

At thy loved name my voice grows loud and clear,
Fluent my tongue, as thou art wise and strong,
And soaring far above the clouds my song:
But soon it droops, languid and faint to hear;
And if thou conquerest not my fate, I fear,
Invincible ALPHONSO! FATE ere long
Will conquer me—freezing in DEATH my tongue
And closing eyes, now opened with a tear.
Nor dying merely grieves me, let me own,
But to die thus—with faith of dubious sound,
And buried name, to future times unknown,
In tomb or pyramid, of brass or stone,
For this, no consolation could be found;
My monument I sought in verse alone.

TO THE MOCKING-BIRD.

Wing'd mimic of the woods! thou motley fool!
 Who shall thy gay buffoonery describe?
Thine ever ready notes of ridicule
 Pursue thy fellows still with jest and gibe.
 Wit, sophist, songster, YORICK of thy tribe,
Thou sportive satirist of Nature's school;
 To thee the palm of scoffing we ascribe,
Arch-mocker and mad Abbot of Misrule!
 For such thou art by day—but all night long
Thou pour'st a soft, sweet, pensive, solemn strain,
 As if thou didst in this thy moonlight song
Like to the melancholy JACQUES complain,
 Musing on falsehood, folly, vice, and wrong,
And sighing for thy motley coat again.

STANZAS.

My life is like the summer rose
 That opens to the morning sky,
But ere the shades of evening close,
 Is scatter'd on the ground—to die!
Yet on the rose's humble bed
The sweetest dews of night are shed,
As if she wept the waste to see—
But none shall weep a tear for me!

My life is like the autumn leaf
 That trembles in the moon's pale ray,
Its hold is frail—its date is brief,
 Restless—and soon to pass away!
Yet, ere that leaf shall fall and fade,
The parent tree will mourn its shade,
The winds bewail the leafless tree,
But none shall breathe a sigh for me!

My life is like the prints, which feet
 Have left on Tampa's desert strand;
Soon as the rising tide shall beat,
 All trace will vanish from the sand;
Yet, as if grieving to efface
All vestige of the human race,
On that lone shore loud moans the sea,
But none, alas! shall mourn for me!

JAMES FENIMORE COOPER.

JAMES FENIMORE COOPER was born at Burlington, New Jersey, September 15, 1789. He was the descendant of an English family who settled at that place in 1679. His father, Judge William Cooper, was born in Pennsylvania, whither a portion of the family had removed, but in early life selected the old family home at Burlington as his residence. He was a man of high social position, and became possessed in 1785 of a large tract of land in the neighborhood of Otsego lake, in the State of New York. A settlement was formed to which he gave the name of Cooperstown, and in 1790 removed his family thither. He was the leading man of the place, and in 1795 and 1799 represented the district in Congress.

It was in this frontier home surrounded by noble scenery, and a population composed of adventurous settlers, hardy trappers, and the remnant of the noble Indian tribes who were once sole lords of the domain, that the novelist passed his boyhood to his thirteenth year. It was a good school for his future calling. At the age mentioned he entered Yale College, where he remained three years, maintaining notwithstanding his youth a good position in his class, when he obtained a midshipman's commission and entered the navy. The six following years of his life were passed in that service, and he was thus early and thoroughly familiarized with the second great field of his future literary career.

In 1811 he resigned his commission, married Miss De Lancey, a member of an old and leading family of the State of New York, and sister to the present bishop of its western diocese, and settled down to a home life in the village of Mamaroneck, near the city of New York. It was not long after that, almost accidentally, his literary career commenced. He had been reading an English novel to his wife, when, on laying aside the book, he remarked that he believed that he could write a better story himself. He forthwith proceeded to test the matter, and produced *Precaution*. The manuscript was completed, he informs us, without any intention of publication. He was, however, induced by the advice of his wife, and his friend Charles Wilkes, in whom he placed great confidence, to issue the work. It appeared, sadly deformed by misprints.

Precaution is a story on the old pattern of English rural life, the scene alternating between the hall, the parsonage, and other upper-class regions of a country town. A scene on the deck of a man-of-war, bringing her prizes into port, is almost the only indication of the writer's true strength. It is a respectable novel, offering little or no scope for comment, and was slightly valued then or afterwards by its author.

J. Fenimore Cooper

In 1821 he published *The Spy, a Tale of the Neutral Ground*, a region familiar to him by his residence within its borders. Harvey Birch, the spy, is a portrait from life of a revolutionary patriot, who was willing to risk his life and to subject his character to temporary suspicion for the service of his country. He appears in the novel as a pedlar, with a keen eye to trade as well as the movements of the enemy. The claim of Enoch Crosby, a native of Danbury, who was employed in this manner in the war, to be the original of this character, has been set forth with much show of probability by a writer, Captain H. L. Barnum, in a small volume entitled The Spy Unmasked, containing an interesting biography, but the matter has never been definitively settled, Cooper leaving the subject in doubt in the preface to the revised edition of the novel in 1849. The rugged, homely worth of Harvey Birch, his native shrewdness combined with heroic boldness, which develops itself in deeds, not in the heroic speeches which an ordinary novelist would have placed in his mouth, the dignified presentation of Washington in the slight disguise of the assumed name of Harper, the spirit of the battle scenes and hairbreadth escapes which abound in the narrative, the pleasant and truthful home scenes of the country mansion, place the Spy in the foremost rank of fiction. Its patriotic theme, a novelty at the time in the works of American romance, aided the impression made by its intrinsic merits.

It was followed, two years later, by *The Pioneers; or, the Sources of the Susquehanna, a Descriptive Tale.* In this the author drew on the early recollections of his life. He has described with minuteness the scenery which surrounded his father's residence, and probably some of its visitors and occupants. The best known character of the story is the world-renowned Leather-stocking, the noble pioneer, the chevalier of the woods. The author has aimed in this character at combining the heroic with the practical. Leather-stocking has the rude dialect of a backwoodsman, unformed, almost uneducated, by schools. He is before us in his native simplicity and native vigor, as free from the trickery of art as the trees which surround him. He was a new actor on the crowded stage of fiction, who at once commanded hearing and applause. The Pioneers well redeems its title of a descriptive tale, by its animated presentation of the vigorous and picturesque country life of its time and place, and its equally successful delineations of natural scenery.

The Pilot, the first of the sea novels, next appeared. It originated from a conversation of the author with his friend Wilkes on the naval inaccuracies of the recently published novel of the Pirate. Cooper's attention thus drawn to this field of composition, he determined to see how far he could meet his own requirements. The work extended its writer's reputation, not only by showing the new field of which he was master, but by its evidences, surpassing any he had yet given, of power and energy. The ships, with whose fortunes we have to do in this story, interest us like creatures of flesh and blood. We watch the chase and the fight like those who have a personal interest in the conflict, as if ourselves a part of the crew, with life and honor in the issue. Long Tom Coffin is probably the most widely-known sailor character in existence. He is an example of the heroic in action, like Leather-stocking losing not a whit of his individuality of body and mind in his nobleness of soul.

Lionel Lincoln, the next novel, was a second attempt in the revolutionary field of the Spy, which did not share in treatment or reception with its success.

It was followed in the same year by *The Last of the Mohicans, a Narrative of* 1757, in which we again meet Leather-stocking, in an early age of his career, and find the Indians, of whom we have had occasional glimpses in the Pioneers, in almost undisturbed possession of their hunting-grounds. In this story Cooper increased his hold on the young, the true public of the romantic novelist, by the spirit of his delineations of forest life. He has met objections which have been raised by maturer critics to his representations of the Aborigines in this and other works, in the following passage in the "Preface to the Leather-stocking Tales," published in 1850.

It has been objected to these books that they give a more favorable picture of the red man than he deserves. The writer apprehends that much of this objection arises from the habits of those who have made it. One of his critics, on the appearance of the first work in which Indian character was portrayed, objected that its "characters were Indians of the school of Heckewelder, rather than of the school of nature." These words quite probably contain the substance of the true answer to the objection. Heckewelder was an ardent, benevolent missionary, bent on the good of the red man, and seeing in him one who had the soul, reason, and characteristics of a fellow-being. The critic is understood to have been a very distinguished agent of the government, one very familiar with Indians, as they are seen at the councils to treat for the sale of their lands, where little or none of their domestic qualities come in play, and where indeed their evil passions are known to have the fullest scope. As just would it be to draw conclusions of the general state of American society from the scenes of the capital, as to suppose that the negotiating of one of these treaties is a fair picture of Indian life.

It is the privilege of all writers of fiction, more particularly when their works aspire to the elevation of romances, to present the *beau-ideal* of their characters to the reader. This it is which constitutes poetry, and to suppose that the red man is to be represented only in the squalid misery or in the degraded moral state that certainly more or less belongs to his condition, is, we apprehend, taking a very narrow view of an author's privileges. Such criticism would have deprived the world of even Homer.

In the same year Cooper visited Europe, having received a little before his departure the honor of a public dinner in the city of New York. He passed several years abroad, and was warmly welcomed in every country he visited, his works being already as well known, through translations, in foreign languages as in his own. He owed this wide-spread fame to his wisdom in the selection of topics. He was read by those who wished to learn something of the aboriginal and pioneer life of America, in the eyes of Europeans the characteristic features of the country; and it is a common remark of the educated class of German emigrants in this country, that they derived their first knowledge, and perhaps their first interest in their future home, from his pages.

Cooper's literary activity was not impaired by his change of scene. He published in 1827 *The Prairie.* Leather-stocking reappears and closes his career in its pages. "Pressed upon by time, he has ceased to be the hunter and the warrior, and has become a trapper of the great West. The sound of the axe has driven him from his beloved forests to seek a refuge, by a species of desperate resignation, on the denuded plains that stretch to the Rocky Mountains. Here he passes the few closing years of his life, dying as he had lived, a philosopher of the wilderness, with few of the failings, none of the vices, and all the nature and truth of his position."* The descriptions of natural scenery, the animated scenes with the Indians, and the rude vigor of the emigrant family, render this one of the most successful of the novelist's productions.

In the same year *The Red Rover* appeared, a second sea novel, which shared the success of the Pilot, a work which it fully equals in animation and perhaps surpasses in romantic interest.

In 1828 Cooper published *Notions of the Americans, by a Travelling Bachelor*. It purports to be a book of travels in the United States, and is designed to correct the many erroneous impressions which he found prevalent in English society, regarding his country. It is an able refutation of the slanders of the penny-a-line tourists who had so sorely tried the American temper, and contains a warm-hearted eulogy of the people and institutions of his country.

It was at the time of publication of this work that Halleck coupled a humorous reference to it with his noble tribute to the novelist, in the commencement of his poem of Red Jacket—

Cooper, whose name is with his country's woven,
First in her files, her PIONEER of mind—
A wanderer now in other climes, has proven
His love for the young land he left behind;

And throned her in the senate-hall of nations,
Robed like the deluge rainbow, heaven-wrought;
Magnificent as his own mind's creations,
And beautiful as its green world of thought;

And faithful to the Act of Congress, quoted
As law authority, it passed nem. con.:
He writes that we are, as ourselves have voted,
The most enlightened people ever known.

That all our week is happy as a Sunday
In Paris, full of song, and dance, and laugh;
And that, from Orleans to the Bay of Fundy,
There's not a bailiff or an epitaph.

And furthermore—in fifty years, or sooner,
We shall export our poetry and wine;
And our brave fleet, eight frigates and a schooner,
Will sweep the seas from Zembla to the Line.

His next novel, published in 1829, was *The Wept of Wish-ton-Wish*. He was in Paris at the breaking out of the Revolution of 1830, and suggested a plan to La Fayette, with whom he was very intimate,† that Henry V. should be recognised as King, and educated as a constitutional monarch, that the peerage should be abolished, and replaced by a senate to be elected by the general vote of the whole nation, the lower house being chosen by the departments—a scheme which combines the stability of an uninterrupted hereditary descent with a proper scope for political progress, two elements that have not as yet been united in the various governmental experiments of that country. This plan was first given to the public some years after in one of the author's volumes of Travels.

His next novel was the *Water Witch*, a sea tale, in which he has relied for a portion of its interest on the supernatural.

He, about the same time, undertook the defence of his country from a charge made in the *Revue Britannique*, that the government of the United States was one of the most expensive, and entailed as heavy a burden of taxation on those under its sway, as any in the world. He met this charge by a letter, which was translated into French, and published with a similar production by General Bertrand, whose long residence in America had rendered him familiar with the subject.

These letters, prepared and published at the suggestion of La Fayette, were in turn responded to, and the original slanders reiterated. Cooper, in reply, published a series of letters in the *National*, a leading daily paper of Paris, the last of which appeared May 2, 1832. In these he triumphantly established his position. It was during this discussion that he published *The Bravo*, which embodied to some extent the points at issue in the controversy. In the words of Bryant, "his object was to show how institutions, professedly created to prevent violence and wrong, become, when perverted from their natural destination, the instruments of injustice, and how, in every system which makes power the exclusive property of the strong, the weak are sure to be oppressed." The scene of this story is laid in Venice, a new field for his descriptive powers, to which he brings the same vigor and freshness which had characterized his scenes of forest life. The story is dramatic, the characters well contrasted, and in one, the daughter of the jailor, he presented one of the most perfect of his female delineations.

The Bravo was followed in 1832 by *The Heidenmauer*, and in 1833 by *The Headsman of Berne*, the scenes and incidents of both of which, as their titles suggest, were drawn from European history, their political purpose being similar to that of the Bravo.

Cooper's controversies in Europe attracted much attention at home, where his course found opponents as well as partisans; and many who, expressing no opinion on the points at issue, were disposed to regard him as having provoked a controversy for the gratification of his taste for discussion. It was during this divided state of public opinion that the novelist returned home in 1833. His first publication after his arrival was *A Letter to my Countrymen*, in which he gave a history of his controversy with a portion of the foreign press, and complained of the course pursued by that of his own country in relation thereto. Passing from this personal topic he censured the general deference to foreign criticism prevalent in the country, and entered with warmth into the discussion of various topics of the party politics of the day. He followed up this production by *The Monikins*, a political satire, and *The American Democrat*. "Had a suitable compound offered," he says in the preface to the latter, "the title of this book would have been something like 'Anti-Cant,' for such a term expresses the intention of the writer better, perhaps, than the one he has actually chosen. The work is written more in the spirit of censure than of praise, for its aim is correction; and virtues bring their own reward, while errors are dangerous."

This little volume embraces almost the entire

* Note to revised edition of the Prairie.

† He was one of the most active leaders in the demonstrations of welcome to La Fayette on his visit to the United States in 1824.—*Dr. Francis's Reminiscences of Cooper.*

range of topics connected with American government and society. It is a vigorous presentation of the author's opinions, and its spirit and independence may be best appreciated by the exhibition of one of its briefest but not least pungent sections.

"THEY SAY."

"They say," is the monarch of this country, in a social sense. No one asks "*who* says it," so long as it is believed that "*they* say it." Designing men endeavor to persuade the publick, that already "they say," what these designing men wish to be said, and the publick is only too much disposed blindly to join in the cry of "they say."

This is another consequence of the habit of deferring to the control of the publick, over matters in which the publick has no right to interfere.

Every well meaning man, before he yields his faculties and intelligence to this sort of dictation, should first ask himself "who" is "they," and on what authority "they say" utters its mandates.

These works, of course, furnished fruitful matter of comment to some of the newspaper editors of the day, who forgot good manners, and violently assailed the author's peculiarities. These asperities were heightened after the appearance of the novels of *Homeward Bound* and *Home as Found*, in 1838. In these the author introduced, with his usual force, and more than his usual humor, a portraiture of a newspaper editor. The newspapers, taking this humorous picture of the vices of a portion of their class as a slander on the entire body, retorted by nicknaming the author from a gentleman who forms one of the favored characters of these fictions, "the mild and gentlemanly Mr. Effingham."

The author now commenced his celebrated libel suits against the Commercial Advertiser and other influential journals. He followed up a tedious and vexatious litigation with his customary resolution and perseverance, bringing suit after suit, until the annoyance of which he complained was terminated. He thus sums up the issue of the affair in a sentence of a letter quoted by Mr. Bryant: "I have beaten every man I have sued who has not retracted his libels."

The accuracy of his *Naval History of the United States*, published in 1839 in two octavo volumes, was one of the matters which entered into this controversy, and in a suit brought on this issue Cooper appeared and defended in person his account of the Battle of Lake Erie with great ability. A lawyer, who was an auditor of its closing sentences, remarked to Mr. Bryant, who also characterizes its opening as "clear, skilful, and persuasive," "I have heard nothing like it since the days of Emmet."

The publication of the Naval History during this stormy period of the author's career, shows that controversy was far from occupying his entire attention. This work, as was to be expected from the author's mastery of the subject in another field of literature, was full of spirit. Its accuracy has been generally admitted, save on a few points, which still remain matter of discussion. It was the first attempt to fill an important and glorious portion of the record of the national progress, and still remains the chief authority on the subject, and from the finish and vigor of its battle-pieces, an American classic. During an earlier part of this same period, in 1836, Cooper issued his *Sketches of Switzerland* in four volumes, and in 1837 and 1838 his *Gleanings in Europe, France, and Italy*, each occupying two duodecimo volumes. The series forms a pleasant record of his wanderings, of the distinguished men whose friendship he enjoyed, and of the public events which he witnessed, and in some instances was himself participant, and contains ingenious criticism on the social and political characteristics of the several countries.

In 1840, while still in the midst of his libel suits, as if to re-assert his literary claims as well as personal rights, he returned to his old and strong field of literary exertion by the publication of *The Pathfinder*, a tale which introduces us again to the scenes, and many of the personages of *The Last of the Mohicans*. It was followed—the novel of *Mercedes of Castile* intervening—in 1841, by *The Deerslayer*. The scene of this fiction is laid on the Otsego lake and its vicinity in the middle of the last century. It abounds in fine descriptions of the scenery of the region, then in its primeval wildness, and succeeds admirably in making the reader at home in the life of the pioneer. Many of the incidents of the tale take place in the *ark* or floating habitation of Tom Hutter, the solitary white denizen of the region, who has constructed and adopted this floating fortress as a precaution against the Indians. His family consists of two daughters, Judith and Hetty, in whose characters the author has contrasted great mental vigor combined with lax moral principle, to enfeebled intellect strengthened by unswerving rectitude. These sisters are among the most successful of the author's female portraits. Deerslayer's course in the fiction is intended still further to enforce the same great truth of the strength afforded by a simple straightforward integrity. It is a noble picture of true manliness.

Deerslayer appears in this novel in early youth, and the work is, therefore, now that the Leather-stocking series is completed, to be regarded as that in which he commences his career. This character will always interest the world, both from its essential ingredients, and the novel circumstances in which it exhibits itself. It is the author's ideal of a chivalresque manhood, of the grace which is the natural flower of purity and virtue; not the stoic, but the Christian of the woods, the man of honorable act and sentiment, of courage and truth. Leather-stocking stands half way between savage and civilized life: he has the freshness of nature and the first fruits of Christianity, the seed dropped into the vigorous soil. These are the elements of one of the most original characters in fiction, in whom Cooper has transplanted all the chivalry ever feigned or practised in the middle ages, to the rivers, woods, and forests of the unbroken New World.

Deerslayer, in point of style, is one of Cooper's purest compositions. There are passages of Saxon in the dialogues and speeches which would do honor to the most admired pages of the romantic old Chroniclers. The language is as noble as the thought.

It is a singular proof of the extent to which the newspaper quarrels to which we have alluded had interfered with Cooper's position as a literary man, that the Pathfinder and the Deerslayer, two of the very best of his productions, attracted but little attention on their first appearance, for which we have the author's authority in his prefaces to the revised editions.

In 1842 Cooper issued two sea novels, *The Two Admirals*, and *Wing and Wing*, both spirited tales of naval conflict, in which the ships share the vitality in the reader's imagination of the "little Ariel" of the *Pilot*.

Wyandotte; or, the Hutted Knoll, appeared in 1843. In this tale Cooper again returns to the Otsego. It narrates the settlement of an English family in the vicinity of the lake about the commencement of the Revolution, and abounds in quiet scenes of sylvan beauty, and incidents of a calmer character than are usual in the author's fictions.

The *Autobiography of a Pocket-Handkerchief*, a short tale, originally published from month to month in Graham's Magazine, followed. *Ned Myers*, a more characteristic production, appeared about the same time. In this the author gives the veritable adventures of an old shipmate, taken down from his own lips. It abounds in striking scenes, which rival in intensity those of his professed fictions.

Cooper's novels followed in rapid succession during the latter period of his life. With his customary spirit he adapted himself to the publishing fashion introduced by the system of cheap reprints, and brought out his new works in twenty-five cent volumes.

Afloat and Ashore, and *Miles Wallingford*, its sequel, also tales of the sea, followed.

In 1844 the author published *A Review of the Mackenzie Case*, a severe comment on the course of the commander of the Somers.

His next novel, *Satanstoe*, published in 1845, was the first of a series avowedly written to denounce the anti-rent doctrines which then attracted much public notice. The scene of Satanstoe is laid in the district in which the outrages connected with this question took place, and the time of the action carries us back to the middle of the last century, and the early settlement of the region. In the second of the series, *The Chain Bearer*, we have the career of the Littlepage family carried down to the second generation at the close of the Revolution. In the third and concluding portion, *The Redskins; or, Indian and Ingin*, we come close upon the present day. The style of these fictions is energetic, but they fall short of his earlier productions in the delineation of character and interest. The treatment of the questions of law involved in the progress of the argument has been pronounced masterly by a competent authority.*

In 1846 Cooper published *Lives of Distinguished American Naval Officers*, a series of biographical sketches written for Graham's Magazine.

The Crater; or, Vulcan's Peak, followed in 1847. The scene of this story is on the shores of the Pacific. It has little to do with real life, the hero being wrecked on a reef, which, by supernatural machinery, is peopled with an Utopian community, giving the author an opportunity to exhibit his views of government.

Oak Openings; or, the Bee Hunter, a story of woodland life, appeared in the same year.

Jack Tier; or, the Florida Reef, was published in 1848, from the pages of Graham's Magazine; a story of the sea, resembling in its points of interest the *Water-Witch*.

The last of the long series of these ocean narratives, *The Sea Lions; or, the Lost Sealers*, opens on the coast of Suffolk county, Long Island, and transports us to the Antarctic Ocean, in whose "thrilling regions of thick-ribbed ice" the author finds ample scope for his descriptive powers. The two ships, the "Sea Lions," pass the winter locked in the ice, and their crews endure the usual mishaps and perils of the region, from which they escape in the following summer.

Cooper's last novel appeared in 1850. It was entitled *The Ways of the Hour*, and designed to exhibit the evils in the author's opinion of trial by jury.

Soon after the publication of this work, Cooper, whose personal appearance excited universal remark, from the robust strength and health it exhibited, was attacked by disease. This, while it wasted his frame, did not diminish his energy. He had in press an historical work on *The Towns of Manhattan*, and in contemplation a sixth Leather-stocking tale, when his disease, gaining strength, developed into a dropsy, which closed his life at his country estate at Cooperstown, September 14, 1851, on the eve of his sixty-second birthday.

A public meeting was held in honor of his memory in the city of New York, and as preliminary to the attempt to raise a fund for a monument for the same purpose, at Metropolitan Hall, Feb. 24, 1852. Daniel Webster presided, and made his last address to a New York assemblage. A discourse was read by Wm. C. Bryant, to which we have been largely indebted in the preparation of the present sketch.

Otsego Hall.

Mr. Cooper's residence at Otsego, to which he removed after his return from Europe, passed out of the hands of his family after his death, was converted into a hotel, and consumed by fire in the spring of 1853.

Cooper was the first American author who attained a wide popular reputation beyond the

* Bryant's Discourse, p. 66.

limits of his own language. His novels were translated as soon as they appeared in the principal countries of Europe, where the Indian tales especially were universal favorites. His delineation of the aboriginal character was a novelty which gained him a hearing, and the attention thus obtained was secured and extended by his vivid pictures of the forest and the frontier. These are topics akin in novel interest in the old world to ruined abbeys and castles in the new. Scott had worked the latter field to an extent that lessened the public interest in such scenes when treated by any but himself. Cooper wisely chose a new path, which he could make and hold as his own. He tried and succeeded.

The novels of Scott set the antiquaries to work rubbing the rust off old armor, and brushing the dust from many an old folio, and illustrating many a well-nigh forgotten chapter of history; and the productions of Cooper have rendered a like service. He has thrown a poetic atmosphere around the departing race of the Red men, which, if it cannot stay their destiny, will do much to fix their place in history.

In his personal character Cooper presents to us a manly resolute nature, of an independent mood, aggressive, fond of the attack; conscious of the strength which had led him to choose his own path in the world and triumph. He never exerted his power, however, but in some chivalrous cause. In Europe he battled for republicanism; in America he was punctilious for the personal virtues which grow up under an aristocracy. It would have been as well, perhaps, if he had sometimes been silent and waited for time to remedy the evils which he contended with; but this was not his nature. He had great powers, to which something should have been conceded by others, and it would have been better for the others as well as for him. The egotism of such a man, if not inevitable, is at least venial.

It was easy for those at a distance to sneer at alleged weaknesses; but those who knew him well, his family, his friends—and what noble men they were, in the highest stations of trust and confidence in the country—found new demands for sympathy and admiration in Cooper's society. With his intimates he was gay, frank, and warm-hearted; fond of the society of children; full of sport and merriment from his youth through life.

Miss Susan Cooper, the daughter of the novelist, is the author of two volumes of merit. *Rural Homes*, published in 1850, is a felicitous journal of country life, describing the scenery and character about her residence at Cooperstown, with minute observation, and with noticeable sincerity of style. *The Rhyme and Reason of Country Life*, published in 1854, is a choice collection of passages from the best authors, in prose and verse, who have treated rural themes, accompanied by just and sympathetic original comments.

CAPTURE OF A WHALE—FROM THE PILOT.

While the young cornet still continued gazing at the whale-boat (for it was the party from the schooner that he saw), the hour expired for the appearance of Griffith and his companions; and Barnstable reluctantly determined to comply with the letter of his instructions, and leave them to their own sagacity and skill to regain the Ariel. The boat had been suffered to ride in the edge of the surf, since the appearance of the sun; and the eyes of her crew were kept anxiously fixed on the cliffs, though in vain, to discover the signal that was to call them to the place of landing. After looking at his watch for the twentieth time, and as often casting glances of uneasy dissatisfaction towards the shore, the lieutenant exclaimed—

"A charming prospect, this, Master Coffin, but rather too much poetry in it for your taste; I believe you relish no land that is of a harder consistency than mud!"

"I was born on the waters, sir," returned the cockswain, from his snug abode, where he was bestowed with his usual economy of room, "and it's according to all things for a man to love his native soil. I'll not deny, Captain Barnstable, but I would rather drop my anchor on a bottom that won't broom a keel, though, at the same time, I harbour no great malice against dry land."

"I shall never forgive it, myself, if any accident has befallen Griffith in this excursion," rejoined the lieutenant; "his Pilot may be a better man on the water than on terra firma, long Tom."

The cockswain turned his solemn visage, with an extraordinary meaning, towards his commander, before he replied—

"For as long a time as I have followed the waters, sir, and that has been ever since I've drawn my rations, seeing that I was born while the boat was crossing Nantucket shoals, I've never known a Pilot come off in greater need, than the one we fell in with, when we made that stretch or two on the land, in the dogwatch of yesterday."

"Ay! the fellow has played his part like a man; the occasion was great, and it seems that he was quite equal to his work."

"The frigate's people tell me, sir, that he handled the ship like a top," continued the cockswain; "but she is a ship that is a nateral inimy of the bottom!"

"Can you say as much for this boat, Master Coffin?" cried Barnstable: "keep her out of the surf, or you'll have us rolling in upon the beach, presently, like an empty water-cask; you must remember that we cannot all wade, like yourself, in two-fathom water."

The cockswain cast a cool glance at the crests of foam that were breaking over the tops of the billows, within a few yards of where their boat was riding, and called aloud to his men—

"Pull a stroke or two; away with her into dark water."

The drop of the oars resembled the movements of a nice machine, and the light boat skimmed along the water like a duck, that approaches to the very brink of some imminent danger, and then avoids it, at the most critical moment, apparently without an effort. While this necessary movement was making, Barnstable arose, and surveyed the cliffs with keen eyes, and then turning once more in disappointment from his search, he said—

"Pull more from the land, and let her run down at an easy stroke to the schooner. Keep a look-out at the cliffs, boys; it is possible that they are stowed in some of the holes in the rocks, for it's no daylight business they are on."

The order was promptly obeyed, and they had glided along for nearly a mile in this manner, in the most profound silence, when suddenly the stillness was broken by a heavy rush of air, and a dash of water, seemingly at no great distance from them.

"By heaven, Tom," cried Barnstable, starting, "there is the blow of a whale!"

"Ay, ay, sir," returned the cockswain with undisturbed composure; "here is his spout not half a mile to seaward; the easterly gale has driven the creater to leeward, and he begins to find himself in shoal water. He's been sleeping, while he should have been working to windward!"

"The fellow takes it coolly, too! he's in no hurry to get an offing!"

"I rather conclude, sir," said the cockswain, rolling over his tobacco in his mouth, very composedly, while his little sunken eyes began to twinkle with pleasure at the sight, "the gentleman has lost his reckoning, and don't know which way to head to take himself back into blue water."

"'Tis a fin-back!" exclaimed the lieutenant; "he will soon make head-way, and be off."

"No, sir, 'tis a right whale," answered Tom; "I saw his spout; he threw up a pair of as pretty rainbows as a Christian would wish to look at. He's a raal oil-butt, that fellow!"

Barnstable laughed, turned himself away from the tempting sight, and tried to look at the cliffs; and then unconsciously bent his longing eyes again on the sluggish animal, who was throwing his huge carcass, at times, for many feet from the water, in idle gambols. The temptation for sport, and the recollection of his early habits, at length prevailed over his anxiety in behalf of his friends, and the young officer enquired of his cockswain—

"Is there any whale-line in the boat, to make fast to that harpoon which you bear about with you in fair weather or foul?"

"I never trust the boat from the schooner without part of a shot, sir," returned the cockswain; "there is something nateral in the sight of a tub to my old eyes."

Barnstable looked at his watch, and again at the cliffs, when he exclaimed, in joyous tones—

"Give strong way, my hearties! There seems nothing better to be done; let us have a stroke of a harpoon at that impudent rascal."

The men shouted spontaneously, and the old cockswain suffered his solemn visage to relax into a small laugh, while the whale-boat sprang forward like a courser for the goal. During the few minutes they were pulling towards their game, long Tom arose from his crouching attitude in the stern-sheets, and transferred his huge form to the bows of the boat, where he made such preparations to strike the whale as the occasion required. The tub, containing about half of a whale line, was placed at the feet of Barnstable, who had been preparing an oar to steer with in place of the rudder, which was unshipped, in order that, if necessary, the boat might be whirled round when not advancing.

Their approach was utterly unnoticed by the monster of the deep, who continued to amuse himself with throwing the water in two circular spouts high into the air, occasionally flourishing the broad flukes of his tail with a graceful but terrific force, until the hardy seamen were within a few hundred feet of him, when he suddenly cast his head downward, and, without an apparent effort, reared his immense body for many feet above the water, waving his tail violently, and producing a whizzing noise, that sounded like the rushing of winds.

The cockswain stood erect, poising his harpoon, ready for the blow; but when he beheld the creature assume this formidable attitude, he waved his hand to his commander, who instantly signed to his men to cease rowing. In this situation the sportsmen rested a few moments, while the whale struck several blows on the water in rapid succession, the noise of which re-echoed along the cliffs, like the hollow reports of so many cannon. After this wanton exhibition of his terrible strength, the monster sank again into his native element, and slowly disappeared from the eyes of his pursuers.

"Which way did he head, Tom?" cried Barnstable, the moment the whale was out of sight.

"Pretty much up and down, sir," returned the cockswain, whose eye was gradually brightening with the excitement of the sport; "he'll soon run his nose against the bottom if he stands long on that course, and will be glad to get another snuff of pure air; send her a few fathoms to starboard, sir, and I promise we shall not be out of his track."

The conjecture of the experienced old seaman proved true; for in a few moments the water broke near them, and another spout was cast into the air, when the huge animal rushed for half his length in the same direction, and fell on the sea with a turbulence and foam equal to that which is produced by the launching of a vessel, for the first time, into its proper element. After this evolution the whale rolled heavily, and seemed to rest from further efforts.

His slightest movements were closely watched by Barnstable and his cockswain, and when he was in a state of comparative rest, the former gave a signal to his crew to ply their oars once more. A few long and vigorous strokes sent the boat directly up to the broadside of the whale, with its bows pointing towards one of the fins, which was, at times, as the animal yielded sluggishly to the action of the waves, exposed to view. The cockswain poised his harpoon with much precision, and then darted it from him with a violence that buried the iron in the blubber of their foe. The instant the blow was made, long Tom shouted, with singular earnestness—

"Starn all!"

"Stern all!" echoed Barnstable; when the obedient seamen, by united efforts, forced the boat in a backward direction beyond the reach of any blow from their formidable antagonist. The alarmed animal, however, meditated no such resistance; ignorant of his own power, and of the insignificance of his enemies, he sought refuge in flight. One moment of stupid surprise succeeded the entrance of the iron, when he cast his huge tail into the air, with a violence that threw the sea around him into increased commotion, and then disappeared with the quickness of lightning, amid a cloud of foam.

"Snub him!" shouted Barnstable; "hold on, Tom; he rises already."

"Ay, ay, sir," replied the composed cockswain, seizing the line, which was running out of the boat with a velocity that rendered such a manœuvre rather hazardous, and causing it to yield more gradually round the large loggerhead that was placed in the bows of the boat for that purpose. Presently the line stretched forward, and rising to the surface with tremulous vibrations, it indicated the direction in which the animal might be expected to re-appear. Barnstable had cast the bows of the boat towards that point, before the terrified and wounded victim rose once more to the surface, whose time was, however, no longer wasted in his sports, but who cast the waters aside, as he forced his way, with prodigious velocity, along the surface. The boat was dragged violently in his wake, and cut through the billows with a terrific rapidity, that at moments appeared to bury the slight fabric in the ocean. When long Tom beheld his victim throwing his spouts on high again, he pointed with exultation to the jetting fluid, which was streaked with the deep red of blood, and cried—

"Ay! I've touched the fellow's life! it must be more than two foot of blubber that stops my iron from reaching the life of any whale that ever sculled the ocean!"

"I believe you have saved yourself the trouble of using the bayonet you have rigged for a lance," said his commander, who entered into the sport with all the ardour of one whose youth had been chiefly passed in such pursuits: "feel your line, Master Coffin; can we haul alongside of our enemy? I like not the course he is steering, as he tows us from the schooner."

"'Tis the creater's way, sir," said the cockswain; "you know they need the air in their nostrils, when they run, the same as a man; but lay hold, boys, and let's haul up to him."

The seamen now seized the whale-line, and slowly drew their boat to within a few feet of the tail of the fish, whose progress became sensibly less rapid, as he grew weak with the loss of blood. In a few minutes he stopped running, and appeared to roll uneasily on the water, as if suffering the agony of death.

"Shall we pull in, and finish him, Tom?" cried Barnstable; "A few sets from your bayonet would do it."

The cockswain stood examining his game with cool discretion, and replied to this interrogatory—

"No, sir, no—he's going into his flurry; there's no occasion for disgracing ourselves by using a soldier's weapon in taking a whale. Starn off, sir, starn off! the creater's in his flurry!"

The warning of the prudent cockswain was promptly obeyed, and the boat cautiously drew off to a distance, leaving to the animal a clear space, while under its dying agonies. From a state of perfect rest, the terrible monster threw its tail on high, as when in sport, but its blows were trebled in rapidity and violence, till all was hid from view by a pyramid of foam, that was deeply dyed with blood. The roarings of the fish were like the bellowing of a herd of bulls; and to one who was ignorant of the fact, it would have appeared as if a thousand monsters were engaged in deadly combat, behind the bloody mist that obstructed the view. Gradually, these effects subsided, and when the discoloured water again settled down to the long and regular swell of the ocean, the fish was seen, exhausted, and yielding passively to its fate. As life departed, the enormous black mass rolled to one side; and when the white and glistening skin of the belly became apparent, the seamen well knew that their victory was achieved.

"What's to be done now?" said Barnstable, as he stood and gazed with a diminished excitement at their victim; "he will yield no food, and his carcass will probably drift to land, and furnish our enemies with the oil."

"If I had but that creater in Boston Bay," said the cockswain, "it would prove the making of me; but such is my luck for ever! Pull up, at any rate, and let me get my harpoon and line—the English shall never get them while old Tom Coffin can blow."

THE PANTHER—FROM THE PIONEERS.

By this time they had gained the summit of the mountain, where they left the highway, and pursued their course under the shade of the stately trees that crowned the eminence. The day was becoming warm, and the girls plunged more deeply into the forest, as they found its invigorating coolness agreeably contrasted to the excessive heat they had experienced in the ascent. The conversation, as if by mutual consent, was entirely changed to the little incidents and scenes of their walk, and every tall pine, and every shrub or flower, called forth some simple expression of admiration.

In this manner they proceeded along the margin of the precipice, catching occasional glimpses of the placid Otsego, or pausing to listen to the rattling of wheels and the sounds of hammers, that rose from the valley, to mingle the signs of men with the scenes of nature, when Elizabeth suddenly started, and exclaimed—

"Listen! there are the cries of a child on this mountain! is there a clearing near us? or can some little one have strayed from its parents?"

"Such things frequently happen," returned Louisa. "Let us follow the sounds: it may be a wanderer starving on the hill."

Urged by this consideration, the females pursued the low, mournful sounds, that proceeded from the forest, with quick and impatient steps. More than once, the ardent Elizabeth was on the point of announcing that she saw the sufferer, when Louisa caught her by the arm, and pointing behind them, cried—

"Look at the dog!"

Brave had been their companion, from the time the voice of his young mistress lured him from his kennel, to the present moment. His advanced age had long before deprived him of his activity; and when his companions stopped to view the scenery, or to add to their bouquets, the mastiff would lay his huge frame on the ground, and await their movements, with his eyes closed, and a listlessness in his air that ill accorded with the character of a protector. But when, aroused by this cry from Louisa, Miss Temple turned, she saw the dog with his eyes keenly set on some distant object, his head bent near the ground, and his hair actually rising on his body, through fright or anger. It was most probably the latter, for he was growling in a low key, and occasionally showing his teeth, in a manner that would have terrified his mistress, had she not so well known his good qualities.

"Brave!" she said, "be quiet, Brave! what do you see, fellow?"

At the sounds of her voice, the rage of the mastiff, instead of being at all diminished, was very sensibly increased. He stalked in front of the ladies, and seated himself at the feet of his mistress, growling louder than before, and occasionally giving vent to his ire, by a short, surly barking.

"What does he see?" said Elizabeth: "there must be some animal in sight."

Hearing no answer from her companion, Miss Temple turned her head, and beheld Louisa, standing with her face whitened to the color of death, and her finger pointing upwards, with a sort of flickering, convulsed motion. The quick eye of Elizabeth glanced in the direction indicated by her friend, where she saw the fierce front and glaring eyes of a female panther, fixed on them in horrid malignity, and threatening to leap.

"Let us fly," exclaimed Elizabeth, grasping the arm of Louisa, whose form yielded like melting snow.

There was not a single feeling in the temperament of Elizabeth Temple that could prompt her to desert a companion in such an extremity. She fell on her knees, by the side of the inanimate Louisa, tearing from the person of her friend, with instinctive readiness, such parts of her dress as might obstruct her respiration, and encouraging their only safeguard, the dog, at the same time, by the sounds of her voice.

"Courage, Brave!" she cried, her own tones beginning to tremble, "courage, courage, good Brave!"

A quarter-grown cub, that had hitherto been unseen, now appeared, dropping from the branches of a sapling that grew under the shade of the beech which held its dam. This ignorant, but vicious creature, approached the dog, imitating the actions and sounds of its parent, but exhibiting a strange mixture of the playfulness of a kitten with the ferocity of its race. Standing on its hind legs, it would rend the bark of a tree with its fore paws, and play the antics of a cat; and then, by lashing itself with its tail, growling, and scratching the earth, it would attempt the manifestations of anger that rendered its parent so terrific.

All this time Brave stood firm and undaunted, his short tail erect, his body drawn backward on its haunches, and his eyes following the movements of both dam and cub. At every gambol played by the latter, it approached nigher to the dog, the growling of the three becoming more horrid at each moment, until the younger beast overleaping its intended bound, fell directly before the mastiff. There was a moment of fearful cries and struggles, but they ended almost as soon as commenced, by the cub appearing in the air, hurled from the jaws of Brave, with a violence that sent it against a tree so forcibly as to render it completely senseless.

Elizabeth witnessed the short struggle, and her blood was warming with the triumph of the dog, when she saw the form of the old panther in the air, springing twenty feet from the branch of the beech to the back of the mastiff. No words of ours can describe the fury of the conflict that followed. It was a confused struggle on the dry leaves, accompanied by loud and terrific cries. Miss Temple continued on her knees, bending over the form of Louisa, her eyes fixed on the animals, with an interest so horrid, and yet so intense, that she almost forgot her own stake in the result. So rapid and vigorous were the bounds of the inhabitant of the forest, that its active frame seemed constantly in the air, while the dog nobly faced his foe at each successive leap. When the panther lighted on the shoulders of the mastiff, which was its constant aim, old Brave, though torn with her talons, and stained with his own blood, that already flowed from a dozen wounds, would shake off his furious foe like a feather, and rearing on his hind legs, rush to the fray again, with jaws distended, and a dauntless eye. But age, and his pampered life, greatly disqualified the noble mastiff for such a struggle. In everything but courage, he was only the vestige of what he had once been. A higher bound than ever raised the wary and furious beast far beyond the reach of the dog, who was making a desperate but fruitless dash at her, from which she alighted in a favorable position, on the back of her aged foe. For a single moment only could the panther remain there, the great strength of the dog returning with a convulsive effort. But Elizabeth saw, as Brave fastened his teeth in the side of his enemy, that the collar of brass around his neck, which had been glittering throughout the fray, was of the color of blood, and directly, that his frame was sinking to the earth, where it soon lay prostrate and helpless. Several mighty efforts of the wild-cat to extricate herself from the jaws of the dog followed, but they were fruitless, until the mastiff turned on his back, his lips collapsed, and his teeth loosened, when the short convulsions and stillness that ensued, announced the death of poor Brave.

Elizabeth now lay wholly at the mercy of the beast. There is said to be something in the front of the image of the Maker that daunts the hearts of the inferior beings of his creation; and it would seem that some such power, in the present instance, suspended the threatened blow. The eyes of the monster and the kneeling maiden met for an instant, when the former stooped to examine her fallen foe; next to scent her luckless cub. From the latter examination, it turned, however, with its eyes apparently emitting flashes of fire, its tail lashing its sides furiously, and its claws projecting inches from her broad feet.

Miss Temple did not or could not move. Her hands were clasped in the attitude of prayer, but her eyes were still drawn to her terrible enemy—her cheeks were blanched to the whiteness of marble, and her lips were slightly separated with horror.

The moment seemed now to have arrived for the fatal termination, and the beautiful figure of Elizabeth was bowing meekly to the stroke, when a rustling of leaves behind seemed rather to mock the organs than to meet her ears.

"Hist! hist!" said a low voice, "steep lower, gal; your bonnet hides the creater's head."

It was rather the yielding of nature than a compliance with this unexpected order, that caused the head of our heroine to sink on her bosom; when she heard the report of the rifle, the whizzing of the bullet, and the enraged cries of the beast, who was rolling over on the earth biting its own flesh, and tearing the twigs and branches within its reach. At the next instant the form of the Leather-stocking rushed by her, and he called aloud—

"Come in, Hector, come in, old fool; 'tis a hard-lived animal, and may jump ag'in."

Natty fearlessly maintained his position in front of the females, notwithstanding the violent bounds and threatening aspect of the wounded panther, which gave several indications of returning strength and ferocity, until his rifle was again loaded, when he stepped up to the enraged animal, and placing the muzzle close to its head, every spark of life was extinguished by the discharge.

DEERSLAYER AT THE DEATH OF HIS SAVAGE FOE.

By this time the piece was reloaded, and Deerslayer, after tossing the tomahawk into the canoe, advanced to his victim, and stood over him, leaning on his rifle, in melancholy attention. It was the first instance in which he had seen a man fall in battle. It was the first fellow creature against whom he had ever seriously raised his own hand. The sensations were novel; and regret, with the freshness of our better feelings, mingled with his triumph. The Indian was not dead, though shot directly through the body. He lay on his back motionless, but his eyes, now full of consciousness, watched each action of his victor—as the fallen bird regards the fowler—jealous of every movement. The man probably expected the fatal blow which was to precede the loss of his scalp; or perhaps he anticipated that this latter act of cruelty would precede his death. Deerslayer read his thoughts; and he found a melancholy satisfaction in relieving the apprehensions of the helpless savage.

"No, no, red-skin," he said; "you've nothing more to fear from me. I am of a Christian stock, and scalping is not of my gifts. I'll just make sartain of your rifle, and then come back and do you what sarvice I can. Though here I can't stay much longer, as the crack of three rifles will be apt to bring some of your devils down upon me."

The close of this was said in a sort of soliloquy, as the young man went in quest of the fallen rifle. The piece was found where its owner had dropped it, and was immediately put into the canoe. Laying his own rifle at its side, Deerslayer then returned and stood over the Indian again.

"All inmity atween you and me's at an ind, red-skin," he said; "and you may set your heart at rest on the score of the scalp, or any further injury. My gifts are white, as I've told you; and I hope my conduct will be white also!"

Could looks have conveyed all they meant, it is probable Deerslayer's innocent vanity on the subject of color would have been rebuked a little; but he comprehended the gratitude that was expressed in the eyes of the dying savage, without in the least detecting the bitter sarcasm that struggled with the better feeling.

"Water!" ejaculated the thirsty and unfortunate creature; "give poor Injin water."

"Aye, water you shall have, if you drink the lake dry. I'll just carry you down to it, that you may take your fill. This is the way, they tell me, with all wounded people—water is their greatest comfort and delight."

So saying, Deerslayer raised the Indian in his arms, and carried him to the lake. Here he first helped him to take an attitude in which he could appease his burning thirst; after which he seated himself on a stone, and took the head of his wounded adversary in his own lap, and endeavored to soothe his anguish in the best manner he could.

"It would be sinful in me to tell you your time hadn't come, warrior," he commenced, "and therefore I'll not say it. You've passed the middle age already, and, considerin' the sort of lives ye lead, your days have been pretty well filled. The principal thing now, is to look forward to what comes next. Neither red-skin nor pale-face, on the whole, calculates much on sleepin' for ever; but both expect to live in another world. Each has his gifts, and will be judged by 'em, and I suppose, you've thought these matters over enough, not to stand in need of sarmons when the trial comes. You'll find your happy hunting-grounds, if you've been a just Injin; if an onjust, you'll meet your desarts in another way. I've my own idees about these things; but you're too old and exper'enced to need any explanations from one as young as I."

"Good!" ejaculated the Indian, whose voice retained its depth even as life ebbed away; "young head—ole wisdom!"

"It's sometimes a consolation, when the ind comes, to know that them we've harmed, or *tried* to harm, forgive us. I suppose natur' seeks this relief, by way of getting a pardon on 'arth: as we never can know whether He pardons, who is all in all, till judgment itself comes. It's soothing to know that *any* pardon at such times; and that, I conclude, is the secret. Now, as for myself, I overlook altogether your designs ag'in my life: first, because no harm came of 'em; next, because it's your gifts, and natur', and trainin', and I ought not to have trusted you at all; and, finally and chiefly, because I can bear no ill-will to a dying man, whether heathen or Christian. So put your heart at ease, so far as I'm consarned; you know best what other matters ought to trouble you, or what ought to give you satisfaction in so trying a moment."

It is probable that the Indian had some of the fearful glimpses of the unknown state of being which God in mercy seems at times to afford to all the human race; but they were necessarily in conformity with his habits and prejudices. Like most of his people, and like too many of our own, he thought more of dying in a way to gain applause among those he left than to secure a better state of existence hereafter. While Deerslayer was speaking his mind was a little bewildered, though he felt that the intention was good; and when he had done, a regret passed over his spirit that none of his own tribe were present to witness his stoicism, under extreme bodily suffering, and the firmness with which he met his end. With the high innate courtesy that so often distinguishes the Indian warrior before he becomes corrupted by too much intercourse with the worst class of the white men, he endeavored to express his thankfulness for the other's good intentions, and to let him understand that they were appreciated.

"Good!" he repeated, for this was an English word much used by the savages—"good—young head; young *heart*, too. *Old* heart tough; no shed tear. Hear Indian when he die, and no want to lie—what he call him?"

"Deerslayer is the name I bear now, though the Delawares have said that when I get back from this war-path, I shall have a more manly title, provided I can 'arn one."

"That good name for boy—poor name for warrior. He get better quick. No fear *there*"—the savage had strength sufficient, under the strong excitement he felt, to raise a hand and tap the young man on his breast—"eye sartain—finger lightning—aim, death—great warrior soon. No Deerslayer—Hawkeye—Hawkeye—Hawkeye. Shake hand."

Deerslayer—or Hawkeye, as the youth was then first named, for in after years he bore the appellation throughout all that region—Deerslayer took the hand of the savage, whose last breath was drawn in that attitude, gazing in admiration at the countenance of a stranger who had shown so much readiness, skill, and firmness, in a scene that was equally trying and novel. When the reader remembers it is the highest gratification an Indian can receive to see his enemy betray weakness, he will be better able to appreciate the conduct which had extorted so great a concession at such a moment.

"His spirit has fled!" said Deerslayer, in a suppressed, melancholy voice. "Ah's me! Well, to this we must all come, sooner or later; and he is happiest, let his skin be of what color it may, who is best fitted to meet it. Here lies the body of no doubt a brave warrior, and the soul is already flying towards its heaven or hell, whether that be a happy hunting-ground, a place scant of game; regions of glory, according to Moravian doctrine, or flames of fire! So it happens, too, as regards other matters! Here have old Hutter and Hurry Harry got themselves into difficulty, if they hav'n't got themselves into torment and death, and all for a bounty that luck offers to me in what many would think a lawful and suitable manner. But not a farthing of such money shall cross my hand. White I was born, and white will I die; clinging to color to the last, even though the King's Majesty, his governors, and all his councils, both at home and in the Colonies, forget from what they come, and where they hope to go, and all for a little advantage in warfare. No, no—warrior, hand of mine shall never molest your scalp, and so your soul may rest in peace on the point of making a decent appearance, when the body comes to join it, in your own land of spirits."

Deerslayer arose as soon as he had spoken. Then he placed the body of the dead man in a sitting posture, with its back against the little rock, taking the necessary care to prevent it from falling or in any way settling into an attitude that might be thought unseemly by the sensitive, though wild notions of a savage. When this duty was performed, the young man stood gazing at the grim countenance of his fallen foe, in a sort of melancholy abstraction.

JAMES A. HILLHOUSE.

The ancestors of James A. Hillhouse emigrated from the county Derry, Ireland, where the family had long held a high social position, to the colony of Connecticut in 1720. The grandfather and father of the poet were both men of standing and influence, the one having been employed for half a century in the public service of the colony, and the other having occupied a seat in both branches of the Federal Legislature, at periods not long after the Revolution. He married a daughter of Colonel Melancthon Woolsey, of Dosoris, Long Island, a lady of great refinement, beauty, and strength of mind and character. Their son, James, was born at New Haven, September 26, 1789. He was remarkable in his boyhood for his strength and dexterity in athletic exercises, and for the grace of his deportment. He entered Yale College in his fifteenth year, and maintained a high rank in his studies, and particularly in English composition. Upon taking his Master's degree, he delivered an oration on *The Education of a Poet*, which was so much admired that it obtained him an invitation to deliver a poem at the next anniversary of the Phi Beta Kappa Society. In fulfilment of this appointment he produced *The Judgment*, in 1812. Though a topic baffling all human intelligence, the poet treated its august incidents as they are portrayed in holy writ, with elevation, exercising his imagination on the allowable ground of the human emotions and the diverse gathering of the human race, with a truly poetic description of the last evening of the expiring world.

Soon after leaving College, Hillhouse passed three years in Boston, in preparation for a mercantile career. The war proving an interruption to his plans, he employed a period of enforced leisure in writing *Demetria*, *Percy's Masque*, and other dramatic compositions. After the peace he engaged in commerce in the city of New York, and in 1819 visited England, where he saw, among other distinguished men, Zachary Macaulay (the father of the historian), who afterwards spoke of him to his American friends as "the most accomplished young man with whom he was acquainted." During this visit he published "Percy's Masque," in London. It was at once reprinted in this country, and received with great favor on both sides of the Atlantic.

In 1822 he married Cornelia, the eldest daughter of Isaac Lawrence of New York, and soon after removed to a country seat near New Haven, which he called Sachem's Wood, and where, with the exception of an annual winter visit of a few months to New York, the remainder of his life was passed, in the cultivation and adornment of his beautiful home, and in literary pursuits and studies. These soon produced the ripe fruit of his mind, the drama of *Hadad*, written in 1824, and published in 1825.

In 1839, having carefully revised, he collected his previously published works, including several orations delivered on various occasions, and a domestic tragedy, *Demetria*, written twenty-six years before, in two volumes.* This settlement, so to speak, of his literary affairs, was to prove the precursor, at no remote interval, of the close of his earthly career. His friends had previously been alarmed by the symptoms of consumption which had impaired his former vigor, and this disease assuming a more aggravated form, and advancing with great rapidity, put an end to his life on the 4th of January, 1841.†

The prevalent character of the writings of Hillhouse is a certain spirit of elegance, which characterizes both his prose and poetry, and which is allied to the higher themes of passion and imagination. He felt deeply, and expressed his emotions naturally in the dramatic form. His conceptions were submitted to a laborious preparation, and took an artistical shape. Of his three dramatic productions, Demetria, an Italian tragedy, is a passionate story of perplexed love, jealousy, and intrigue; Hadad is a highly wrought dramatic poem, employing the agency of the supernatural; and Percy's Masque, suggested by an English ballad, Bishop Percy's Hermit of Warkworth, an historical romance, of much interest in the narrative, the plot being highly effective, at the expense somewhat of character, while the dialogue is filled with choice descriptions of the natural scenery in which the piece is cast, and tender sentiment of the lovers. That, however, which gained the author most repute with his contemporaries, and is the highest proof of his powers, is the twofold characterization of Hadad and Tamar; the supernatural fallen angel appearing as the sensual heathen lover, and the Jewish maiden. The dialogue in which these personages are displayed, abounds with rare poetical beauties; with lines and imagery worthy of the old Elizabethan drama. The description, in the conversation between Nathan and Tamar, of the associations of Hadad, who is "of the blood royal of Damascus," is in a rich imaginative vein.

Nathan. I think thou saidst he had surveyed the world.
Tamar. O, father, he can speak
Of hundred-gated Thebes, towered Babylon,
And mightier Nineveh, vast Palibothra,
Serendib anchored by the gates of morning,
Renowned Benares, where the Sages teach
The mystery of the soul, and that famed Ilium
Where fleets and warriors from Elishah's Isles
Besieged the Beauty, where great Memnon fell:—

* Dramas, Discourses and other Pieces, by James A. Hillhouse. 2 vols. Boston: Little & Brown.

† Everest's Poets of Connecticut, p. 169. An authentic family narrative from Bishop Kip, in Griswold's Poets of America.

Of pyramids, temples, and superstitious caves
Filled with strange symbols of the Deity;
Of wondrous mountains, desert-circled seas,
Isles of the ocean, lovely Paradises,
Set, like unfading emeralds, in the deep.

This being, who excites the revolt of Absalom, introduced to us at first at the court of David, as of an infidel race, practised in "arts inhibited and out of warrant," in the end displays his true nature in the spirit of the fiend, which has ruled the designs of the fair Syrian. The softness and confiding faith of the Hebrew girl, stronger in her religion than her love, triumph over the infidel spiritual assaults of Hadad; and in these passages of tenderness contrasted with the honeyed effrontery of the assailant, and mingled with scenes of revolt and battle, Hillhouse has displayed some of his finest graces. Perfection, in such a literary undertaking, would have tasked the powers of a Goethe. As a poetical and dramatic sketch of force and beauty, the author of Hadad has not failed in it. The conception is handled with dignity, and its defects are concealed in the general grace of the style, which is polished and refined.*

The descriptive poem of Sachem's Word is an enumeration of the points of historic interest and of family association connected with his place of residence, sketched in a cheerful vein of pleasantry.

Several fine prose compositions close the author's collection of his writings. They are a Phi Beta Kappa Discourse in 1826, at New Haven, *On Some of the Considerations which should influence an Epic or a Tragic Writer in the Choice of an Era;* a Discourse before the Brooklyn Lyceum, in 1836, *On the Relations of Literature to a Republican Government;* and a Discourse at New Haven, pronounced by request of the Common Council, August 19, 1834, in Commemoration of the Life and Services of General La Fayette.—all thoughtful, energetic, and polished productions.

It is pleasant to record the eulogy of one poet by another. Halleck, in his lines "To the Recorder," has thus alluded to Hillhouse:—

Hillhouse, whose music, like his themes,
Lifts earth to heaven—whose poet dreams
Are pure and holy as the hymn
Echoed from harps of seraphim,
By bards that drank at Zion's fountains
When glory, peace and hope were hers,
And beautiful upon her mountains
The feet of angel messengers.

Willis, too, paid a genial tribute to Hillhouse in his poem before the Linonian Society of Yale College, delivered a few months after the poet's death—in that passage where he celebrates the associations of the elm walk of the city.

LAST EVENING OF THE WORLD—FROM THE JUDGMENT.

By this, the sun his westering car drove low;
Round his broad wheel full many a lucid cloud
Floated, like happy isles, in seas of gold:
Along the horizon castled shapes were piled,
Turrets and towers whose fronts embattled gleamed
With yellow light: smit by the slanting ray,
A ruddy beam the canopy reflected;
With deeper light the ruby blushed; and thick
Upon the Seraphs' wings the glowing spots
Seemed drops of fire. Uncoiling from its staff
With fainter wave, the gorgeous ensign hung,
Or, swelling with the swelling breeze, by fits,
Cast off upon the dewy air huge flakes
Of golden lustre. Over all the hill,
The Heavenly legions, the assembled world,
Evening her crimson tint for ever drew.

* * * * *

Round I gazed
Where in the purple west, no more to dawn,
Faded the glories of the dying day.
Mild twinkling through a crimson-skirted cloud
The solitary star of Evening shone.
While gazing wistful on that peerless light
Thereafter to be seen no more, (as, oft,
In dreams strange images will mix,) sad thoughts
Passed o'er my soul. Sorrowing, I cried, "Farewell,
Pale, beauteous Planet, that displayest so soft
Amid yon glowing streak thy transient beam,
A long, a last farewell! Seasons have changed,
Ages and empires rolled, like smoke away,
But, thou, unaltered, beamest as silver fair
As on thy birthnight! Bright and watchful eyes,
From palaces and bowers, have hailed thy gem
With secret transport! Natal star of love,
And souls that love the shadowy hour of fancy,
How much I owe thee, how I bless thy ray!
How oft thy rising o'er the hamlet green,
Signal of rest, and social converse sweet,
Beneath some patriarchal tree, has cheered
The peasant's heart, and drawn his benison!
Pride of the West! beneath thy placid light
The tender tale shall never more be told,
Man's soul shall never wake to joy again:
Thou set'st for ever,—lovely Orb, farewell!"

INTERVIEW OF HADAD AND TAMAR.

The garden of ABSOLOM'S *house on Mount Zion, near the palace, overlooking the city.* TAMAR *sitting by a fountain.*

Tam. How aromatic evening grows! The flowers
And spicy shrubs exhale like onycha;
Spikenard and henna emulate in sweets.
Blest hour! which He, who fashioned it so fair,
So softly glowing, so contemplative,
Hath set, and sanctified to look on man.
And lo! the smoke of evening sacrifice
Ascends from out the tabernacle.—Heaven,
Accept the expiation, and forgive
This day's offences!—Ha! the wonted strain,
Precursor of his coming!—Whence can this—
It seems to flow from some unearthly hand—

Enter HADAD.

Had. Does beauteous Tamar view, in this clear fount,
Herself, or heaven?
Tam. Nay, Hadad, tell me whence
Those sad, mysterious sounds.
Had. What sounds, dear Princess?
Tam. Surely, thou know'st; and now I almost think
Some spiritual creature waits on thee.
Had. I heard no sounds, but such as evening sends
Up from the city to these quiet shades;
A blended murmur sweetly harmonizing
With flowing fountains, feathered minstrelsy,
And voices from the hills.
Tam. The sounds I mean,
Floated like mournful music round my head,
From unseen fingers.

* In a note to one of Coleridge's Lectures on the Personality of the Evil Being, &c. (Literary Remains, vol. i. p. 210, 1836), there is a passage given by him as written in a copy of Hadad, which offers some suggestion on the use of the "Fallen Spirits" in that poem.

Had. When?
Tam. Now, as thou camest.
Had. 'T is but thy fancy, wrought
To ecstasy; or else thy grandsire's harp
Resounding from his tower at eventide.
I 've lingered to enjoy its solemn tones,
Till the broad moon, that rose o'er Olivet,
Stood listening in the zenith; yea, have deemed
Viols and heavenly voices answer him.
Tam. But these—
Had. Were we in Syria, I might say
The Naiad of the fount, or some sweet Nymph,
The goddess of these shades, rejoiced in thee,
And gave thee salutations; but I fear
Judah would call me infidel to Moses.
Tam. How like my fancy! When these strains precede
Thy steps, as oft they do, I love to think
Some gentle being who delights in us
Is hovering near, and warns me of thy coming;
But they are dirge-like.
Had. Youthful fantasy,
Attuned to sadness, makes them seem so, lady,
So evening's charming voices, welcomed ever,
As signs of rest and peace;—the watchman's call,
The closing gates, the Levite's mellow trump,
Announcing the returning moon, the pipe
Of swains, the bleat, the bark, the housing-bell,
Send melancholy to a drooping soul.
Tam. But how delicious are the pensive dreams
That steal upon the fancy at their call!
Had. Delicious to behold the world at rest.
Meek labour wipes his brow, and intermits
The curse, to clasp the younglings of his cot;
Herdsmen and shepherds fold their flocks,—and hark!
What merry strains they send from Olivet!
The jar of life is still; the city speaks
In gentle murmurs; voices chime with lutes
Waked in the streets and gardens; loving pairs
Eye the red west in one another's arms;
And nature, breathing dew and fragrance, yields
A glimpse of happiness, which He, who formed
Earth and the stars, hath power to make eternal.

THE TEMPTATION.

ABSOLOM, the father of TAMAR, is slain, and HADAD entreats her to escape with him.

Tam. (*in alarm.*) What mean'st thou?
Had. Later witnesses report——
Alas!——
Tam. My father?—Gracious Heaven!—
Mean'st thou my father?—
Had. Dearest Tamar,—Israel's Hope—
Sleeps with the valiant of the years of old.
(TAMAR, *with convulsed cry, bursts into tears: HADAD seems to weep.*)
The bond is rent that knit thee to thy country.
Thy father's murderers triumph. Turn not there,
To see their mockery. Let us retire,
And, piously, on some far, peaceful shore,
With mingled tears embalm his memory.
Tam. (*clasping her hands.*) Am I an orphan?
Had. Nay, much-loved Princess, not while this
Fond heart——
Tam. Misguided father!—Hadst thou but listened,
Hadst thou believed——
Had. But now, what choice is left?
What refuge hast thou but thy faithful Hadad?
Tam. One—stricken—hoary head remains.
Had. The slayer of thy parent—Wouldst thou go
Where obloquy and shame and curses load him?
Hear him called rebel?
Tam. All is expiated now.
Had. Tamar,—wilt thou forsake me?
Tam. I must go to David.
Had. (*aside.*) Cursed thought!——
Think of your lot—neglect, reproach, and scorn,
For who will wed a traitor's offspring? All
The proud will slight thee, as a blasted thing.
Tam. O, wherefore this to me?——
Conduct me hence—Nay, instantly.
Had. (*in an altered tone.*) Hold! hold!
For thou must hear.—If deaf to love, thou 'rt not
To *fearful* ecstasy.
(TAMAR *startled:—he proceeds, but agitated and irresolute.*)
——Confide in me—
I can transport thee——O, to a paradise,
To which this Canaan is a darksome span;—
Beings shall welcome—serve thee—lovely as Angels;—
The Elemental Powers shall stoop—the Sea
Disclose her wonders, and receive thy feet
Into her sapphire chambers;—orbed clouds
Shall chariot thee from zone to zone, while earth,
A dwindled islet, floats beneath thee;—every
Season and clime shall blend for thee the garland—
The abyss of Time shall cast its secrets,—ere
The Flood marred primal nature,—ere this Orb
Stood in her station! Thou shalt know the stars,
The houses of Eternity, their names,
Their courses, destiny,—all marvels high.
Tam. Talk not so madly.
Had. (*vehemently.*) Speak—answer—
Wilt thou be mine, if mistress of them all?
Tam. Thy mien appals me;—I know not what I fear;—
Thou wouldst not wrong me,—reft and fatherless—
Confided to thee as a sacred trust—
Had. (*haughtily.*) My *power*
Is questioned. Whom dost thou imagine me?
Tam. Indeed, surpassed by nothing human.
Had. Bah!
Tam. O, Hadad, Hadad, what unhallow'd thought
So ruffles and transforms thee?
Had. Still, still,
Thou call'st me Hadad,—boy, worm, heritor
Of a poor, vanquished, tributary King!—
Then *know* me.
Tam. Seraphs hover round me!
Had. Woman!—(*Struggling, as with conflicting emotions.*)
What thou so dotest on—this form—was Hadad's—
But I—the Spirit—I, who speak through these
Clay lips, and glimmer through these eyes,—
Have challenged fellowship, equality,
With Deathless Ones—prescient Intelligences,—
Who scorn Man and his molehill, and esteem
The outgoing of the morning, yesterday!—
I, who commune with thee, have dared, proved, suffered,
In life—in death—and in *that* state whose bale
Is death's first issue! I could freeze thy blood
With mysteries too terrible——of Hades!—
Not there immured, for by my art I 'scaped
Those confines, and with beings dwelt of bright
Unbodied essence.—Canst thou *now* conceive
The love that could persuade me to these fetters?—
Abandoning my power—I, who could touch
The firmament, and plunge to darkest Sheol,
Bask in the sun's orb, fathom the green sea,
Even while I speak it—here to root and grow
In earth again, a mortal, abject thing,
To win and to enjoy thy love.
Tam. (*in a low voice of supplication.*) Heaven! Heaven!
Forsake me not!

THE EDUCATION OF MEN OF LEISURE—FROM THE RELATIONS OF LITERATURE TO A REPUBLICAN GOVERNMENT.

In casting about for the means of opposing the *sensual*, *selfish*, and *mercenary* tendencies of our nature (the real Hydra of free institutions), and of so elevating man, as to render it not chimerical to expect from him the safe ordering of his steps, no mere human agency can be compared with the resources laid up in the great TREASURE-HOUSE OF LITERATURE.—There, is collected the accumulated experience of ages,—the volumes of the historian, like lamps, to guide our feet;—there stand the heroic patterns of courage, magnanimity, and self-denying virtue:—there are embodied the gentler attributes, which soften and purify, while they charm the heart:—there lie the charts of those who have explored the deeps and shallows of the soul:—there the dear-bought testimony, which reveals to us the ends of the earth, and shows, that the girdle of the waters is nothing but their Maker's will:—there stands the Poet's harp, of mighty compass, and many strings:—there hang the deep-toned instruments through which patriot eloquence has poured its inspiring echoes over oppressed nations:—there, in the sanctity of their own self-emitted light, repose the Heavenly oracles. This glorious fane, vast, and full of wonders, has been reared and stored by the labors of Lettered Men; and *could* it be destroyed, mankind might relapse to the state of savages.

A restless, discontented, aspiring, immortal principle, placed in a material form, whose clamorous appetites, bitter pains, and final languishing and decay, are perpetually at war with the peace and innocence of the spiritual occupant: and have, moreover, power to jeopard its lasting welfare; is the mysterious combination of Human Nature! To *employ* the never-resting faculty; to *turn off* its desires from the dangerous illusions of the senses to the ennobling enjoyments of the mind; to place before the high-reaching principle, *objects* that will excite, and reward its efforts, and, at the same time, not unfit a thing immortal for the probabilities that await it when time shall be no more;—these are the legitimate aims of a *perfect education.*

Left to the scanty round of gratifications supplied by the senses, or eked by the frivolous gaieties which wealth mistakes for pleasure, the unfurnished mind becomes weary of all things and itself. With the capacity to feel its wretchedness, but without tastes or intellectual light to guide it to any avenue of escape, it gropes round its confines of clay, with the sensations of a caged wild beast. It riseth up, it moveth to and fro, it lieth down again. In the morning it says, Would God it were evening! in the evening it cries, Would God it were morning! Driven in upon itself, with passions and desires that madden for action, it grows desperate; its vision becomes perverted: and, at last, vice and ignominy seem preferable to what the great Poet calls "*the hell of the lukewarm.*" Such is the end of many a youth, to whom authoritative discipline and enlarged teaching might have early opened the interesting spectacle of man's past and prospective destiny. Instead of languishing,—his mind might have throbbed and burned, over the trials, the oppressions, the fortitude, the triumphs, of men and nations:—breathed upon by the life-giving lips of the Patriot, he might have discovered, that he had not only a country to love, but a head and a heart to serve her:—going out with Science, in her researches through the universe, he might have found, amidst the secrets of Nature, ever-growing food for reflection and delight:—ascending where the Muses sit, he might have gazed on transporting scenes, and transfigured beings; and snatched, through heaven's half-unfolded portals, glimpses unutterable of things beyond.

In view of these obvious considerations, one of the strangest misconceptions is that which blinds us to the policy, as well as duty, of educating in the most finished manner our youth of large expectations, expressly to meet the dangers and fulfil the duties of *men of leisure.* The mischievous, and truly American notion, that, to enjoy a respectable position, every man must *traffic*, or *preach*, or *practise*, or *hold an office*, brings to beggary and infamy, many who might have lived, under a juster estimate of things, usefully and happily; and cuts us off from a needful as well as ornamental, portion of society. The necessity of laboring for sustenance is, indeed, the great safeguard of the world, the *ballast*, without which the wild passions of men would bring communities to speedy wreck. But man will not labor without a *motive;* and successful accumulation, on the part of the parent, deprives the son of this impulse. Instead, then, of vainly contending against laws, as insurmountable as those of physics, and attempting to *drive* their children into lucrative industry, why do not men, who have made themselves opulent, open their eyes, at once, to the glaring fact, that the *cause*,—the cause itself,—which braced their own nerves to the struggle for fortune, does not *exist* for their offspring? *The father has taken from the son his motive!*—a motive confessedy important to happiness and virtue, in the present state of things. He is bound, therefore, by every consideration of prudence and humanity, neither to attempt to drag him forward without a cheering, animating principle of action,—nor recklessly to abandon him to his own guidance,—nor to poison him with the love of lucre for itself; but, under new circumstances,—with new prospects,—at a totally different starting-place from his own,—to supply *other motives*,—drawn from our sensibility to reputation,—from our natural desire to know,—from an enlarged view of our capacities and enjoyments,—and a more high and liberal estimate of our relations to society. Fearful, indeed, is the responsibility of leaving youth, without mental resources, to the temptations of splendid idleness! Men who have not considered this subject, while the objects of their affection yet surround their table, drop no seeds of generous sentiments, animate them with no discourse on the beauty of disinterestedness, the paramount value of the mind, and the dignity of that renown which is the echo of illustrious actions. Absorbed in one pursuit, their morning precept, their mid-day example, and their evening moral, too often conspire to teach a single maxim, and that in direct contradiction of the inculcation, so often and so variously repeated: "It is better to get wisdom than gold." Right views, a careful choice of agents, and the delegation, *betimes*, of strict authority, would insure the object. Only let the parent feel, and the son be early taught, that, with the command of money and leisure, to enter on manhood without having mastered every attainable accomplishment, is more disgraceful than threadbare garments, and we might have the happiness to see in the inheritors of paternal wealth, less frequently, idle, ignorant prodigals and heart-breakers, and more frequently, high-minded, highly educated young men, embellishing, if not called to public trusts, a private station.

JOHN W. FRANCIS.

DR. JOHN W. FRANCIS, whose long intimacy and association with two generations of American authors constitute an additional claim, with his own professional and literary reputation, upon honorable attention in any general memorial of American literature, was born in the city of New York, November 17, 1789. His father, Melchior Francis, was a native of Nuremberg, Germany, who came to America shortly after the establishment of American independence. He followed the business, in New York, of a grocer, and was known for his integrity and enterprise. He fell a victim to the yellow fever. Dr. Francis's mother was a lady of Philadelphia. Her maiden name was Sommers, of a family originally from Berne, in Switzerland. It is one of the favorite historical reminiscences of her son that she remembered when those spirits of the Revolution, Franklin, Rush, and Paine, passed her door in their daily associations, and the children of the neighborhood would cry out, "There go Poor Richard, Common Sense, and the Doctor." His association with Franklin is not merely a matter of fancy. In his youth Francis had chosen the calling of a printer, and was enlisted to the trade in the office of the strong-minded, intelligent, and ever-industrious George Long, who was also a prominent bookseller and publisher of the times, and who, emigrating from England by way of the Canadas, had carved out his own fortunes by his self-denial and perseverance. We have heard Mr. Long relate the anecdote of the hours stolen by the young Francis from meal-time and recreation, as, sitting under his frame, he partook of a frugal apple and cracker, and conned eagerly the Latin grammar; and of the pleasure with which he gave up his hold on the young scholar, that he might pursue the career to which his tastes and love of letters urged him. At this early period, while engaged in the art of printing, he was one of the few American subscribers to the English edition of Rees's Cyclopædia, which he devoured with the taste of a literary epicure; he afterwards became a personal friend and correspondent of the learned editor, and furnished articles for the London copy of that extensive and valuable work. His mother, who had been left in easy circumstances, had provided liberally for his education: first at a school of reputation, under the charge of the Rev. George Strebeck, and afterwards securing him the instructions in his classical studies of the Rev. John Conroy, a graduate of Trinity College, Dublin. He was thus enabled to enter an advanced class of Columbia College, and he pushed his advantages still further by commencing his medical studies during his undergraduate course.

He received his degree in 1809, and adopting the pursuit of medicine, became the pupil of the celebrated Dr. Hosack, then in the prime of life and height of his metropolitan reputation.

In 1811 Francis received his degree of M.D. from the College of Physicians and Surgeons, which had been established in 1807 under the presidency of Dr. Romayne, and which had been lately reorganized, with Dr. Bard at its head. Francis's name was the first recorded on the list of graduates of the new institution. The subject of his Essay on the occasion was *The Use of Mercury*, a topic which he handled not only with medical ability, but with a great variety of historical research. The paper was afterwards published in the *Medical and Philosophical Register*, and gained the author much distinction. He now became the medical partner of Hosack, an association which continued till 1820, and the fruits of which were not confined solely to his profession, as we find the names of the two united in many a scheme of literary and social advancement.

In compliment to his acquirements and personal accomplishments, Francis was appointed Lecturer on the Institutes of Medicine and the Materia Medica in the state college.

In 1813, when the medical faculty of Columbia College and of the "Physicians and Surgeons" were united, he received from the regents of the state the appointment of Professor of Materia Medica. With characteristic liberality he delivered his course of lectures without fees. His popularity gained him from the students the position of president of their Medico-Chirurgical Society, in which he succeeded Dr. Mitchill. At this time he visited Great Britain and a portion of the continent. In London he attended the lectures and enjoyed a friendly intercourse with Abernethy, to whom he carried the first American reprint of his writings. On receiving the volumes from the hands of Francis, satisfied with the compliment from the distant country, and not dreaming of copyright possibilities in those days, the eccentric physician grasped the books, ran his eye hastily over them, and set them on the mantelpiece of his study, with the exclamation, "Stay here, John Abernethy, until I remove you! Egad! this from America!" In Edinburgh, his acquaintance with Jameson, Playfair, John Bell, Gregory, Brewster, and the Duncans, gave him every facility of adding to the stores of knowledge. A residence of six months in London, and attendance on Abernethy and St. Bartholomew's Hospital, with the lectures of Pearson and Brande, increased these means; and in Paris, Gall, Denon, Dupuytren, were found accessible in the promotion of his scientific designs.

He returned to New York, bringing with him the foundation of a valuable library, since grown to one of the choicest private collections of the city. There were numerous changes in the administration of the medical institution to which he was attached, but Francis, at one time Professor of the Institutes of Medicine, at another of Medical Jurisprudence, and again of Obstetrics, held position in them all till his voluntary resignation with the rest of the faculty, in 1826; when he took part in the medical school founded in New York under the auspices of the charter of Rutgers College. Legislative enactments dissolved this school, which had, while in operation, a most successful career. But its existence was in nowise compatible with the interests of the state school. For about twenty years he was the assiduous and successful professor in several departments of medical science. With his retirement from this institution ceased his professorial career, though he was lately the first president of the New York Academy of Medicine, and is at present head of the Medical Board of the Bellevue Hospital. He has since been a leading practitioner in the city of New York, frequently consulted by his brethren of the faculty, and called to solve disputed points in the courts of medical jurisprudence.

In 1810 he founded, in conjunction with Hosack,

the *American Medical and Philosophical Register*, which he continued through four annual volumes. It was a very creditable enterprise, and now remains for historical purposes one of the most valuable journals of its class. Though dealing largely in the then engrossing topic of epidemics, its pages are by no means confined to medicine. It led the way with the discussion of steam and canal navigation, with papers from Fulton, Stevens, and Morris. Wilson's Ornithology, Livingston's merino sheep-shearing at Clermont, the biography of professional and other worthies, with the universalities of Mitchill, each had a share of its attention. It also contains a number of well executed original engravings; and for all these things it should not be forgotten there was, as usual in those times with such advances in the liberal arts, an unpaid expenditure of brain, and a decidedly unremunerating investment of money. Besides his contributions to this journal, his medical publications include his enlarged edition of Denman's Midwifery, which has several times been reprinted, Cases of Morbid Anatomy, On the Value of Vitriolic Emetics in the Membranous Stage of Croup, Facts and Inferences in Medical Jurisprudence, On the Anatomy of Drunkenness, and Death by Lightning, &c., essays on the cholera of New York in 1832, on the mineral waters of Avon, two discourses before the New York Academy of Medicine, and other minor performances. He

was also one of the editors, for some time, of the New York Medical and Physical Journal. He has been a prominent actor through the seasons of pestilence in New York for nearly fifty years; and was the first who awakened the attention of the medical faculty of the United States to the fact of the rare susceptibility of the human constitution to a second attack of the pestilential yellow fever, which he made known in his letter on Febrile Contagion, dated London, June, 1816.

In general literature, the productions of Francis, though the occupation of moments extorted from his overwrought profession, are numerous. He has largely added to our stock of biographical knowledge by many articles. His account of Franklin in New York has found its way into Valentine's Manual. He has delivered addresses before the New York Horticultural Society in 1829; the Philolexian Society of Columbia College in 1831, the topic of which is the biography of Chancellor Livingston; the discourse at the opening of the New Hall of the New York Lyceum of Natural History in 1836; several speeches at the Historical Society and the Typographical Society of New York, before which he read, at the anniversary in 1852, a paper of *Reminiscences of Printers, Authors, and Booksellers of New York*, which, as it was afterwards published at length,* constitutes an interesting addition to the literary history of the country. It is filled with vivid pictures of by-gone worthies, and might be readily enlarged from the published as well as conversational stores of the author to a large volume; for Francis has been a liberal contributor to the numerous labors of this kind of the Knapps, Dunlaps, Thachers, and others, from whose volumes he might reclaim many a fugitive page. His notices of Daniel Webster, called forth by the public proceedings after the death of that statesman, have been published by the Common Council of the city. His reminiscences of the novelist Cooper, with whom his relation had been one of long personal friendship, called forth by a similar occasion, appeared in the "Memorial" of the novelist, published in 1852. Dr. Francis is a member of many Medical and Philosophical Associations both abroad and in his native land. In 1850 he received the degree of LL.D. from Trinity College, Connecticut.

One of the latest and most characteristic of these biographical sketches is the paper on Christopher Colles, read in 1854† before the New York Historical Society, of which Dr. Francis has been, from an early date, a most efficient supporter. The subject was quaint and learned, with rare opportunities for picturesque description in the fortunes of a simple-minded, enthusiastic city reformer and philosopher, whose slender purse was out of all proportion with his enthusiasm and talent. His virtues were kindly dealt with, and his abilities intelligently set forth; while his "thin-spun life" was enriched by association with the memorable men and things of old New York in his day.

While thus inclined to dwell with the past, Dr. Francis, in his genial home, draws together the refined activities of the present. At his house in Bond street, enjoying the frankness and freedom of his warm, unobtrusive hospitality, may be met most of the literary and scientific celebrities of the time, who make their appearance in the metropolis. The humor and character of the host are universal solvents for all tastes and temperaments. Art, science, opera, politics, theology, and, above all, American history and antiquities, are handled, in that cheerful society, with zest and animation. If a dull argument or an

* In the International Mag. for Feb., 1852.

† It has been published in the Knickerbocker Gallery, 1855.

over-tedious tale is sometimes invaded by a shock of hearty Rabelaisian effrontery—truth does not suffer in the encounter. The cares and anxieties of professional life were never more happily relieved than in these intellectual recreations.

They were shared in lately by one whose early death has been sincerely mourned by many friends. In the beginning of 1855, the eldest son of Dr. Francis, bearing his father's name, at the early age of twenty-two, on the eve of taking his medical degree with high honor, fell by an attack of typhus fever, to which he had subjected himself in the voluntary charitable exercise of his profession. A memorial, privately printed since his death, contains numerous tributes to his virtues and talents, which gave earnest promise of important services to the public in philanthropy and literature.

CHRISTOPHER COLLES.

As Colles was an instructive representative of much of that peculiarity in the condition and affairs of New York, at the time in which he may be said to have flourished, I shall trespass a moment, by a brief exhibit of the circumstances which marked the period, in which he was, upon the whole, a prominent character. Everybody seemed to know him; no one spoke disparagingly of him. His enthusiasm, his restlessness, were familiar to the citizens at large. He, in short, was a part of our domestic history, and an extra word or two may be tolerated, the better to give him his fair proportions. Had I encountered Colles in any land, I would have been willing to have naturalized him to our soil and institutions. He had virtues, the exercise of which must prove profitable to any people. The biographer of Chaucer has seen fit, inasmuch as his hero was born in London, to give us a history and description of that city at the time of Chaucer's birth, as a suitable introduction to his work. I shall attempt no such task, nor shall I endeavor to make Colles a hero, much as I desire to swell his dimensions. I shall circumscribe him to a chap-book; he might be distended to a quarto. Yet the ardent and untiring man was so connected with divers affairs, even after he had domesticated himself among us, that every movement in which he took a part must have had a salutary influence on the masses of those days. He was a lover of nature, and our village city of that time gave him a fair opportunity of recreation among the lordly plane, and elm, and catalpa trees of Wall street, Broadwy, Pearl street, and the Bowery. The beautiful groves about Richmond Hill and Lispenard Meadows, and old Vauxhall, mitigated the dulness incident to his continuous toil. A trip to the scattered residences of Brooklyn awakened rural associations; a sail to Communipaw gave him the opportunity of studying marls and the bivalves. That divine principle of celestial origin, religious toleration, seems to have had a strong hold on the people of that day; and the persecuted Priestley, shortly after he reached our shores, held forth in the old Presbyterian Church in Wall street, doubtless favored in a measure by the friendship of old Dr. Rodgers, a convert to Whitefield, and a pupil of Witherspoon. This fact I received from John Pintard. Livingston and Rodgers, Moore and Provoost, supplied the best Christian dietetics his panting desires needed; while in the persons of Bayley and Kissam, and Hosack and Post, he felt secure from the misery of dislocations and fractures, and that alarming pest, the yellow fever. He saw the bar occupied with such advocates as Hamilton and Burr, Hoffman and Colden, and he dreaded neither the assaults of the lawless nor the chicanery of contractors. The old *Tontine* gave him more daily news than he had time to digest, and the *Argus* and *Minerva*, *Freneau's Time-Piece*, and *Swords' New York Magazine*, inspired him with increased zeal for liberty, and a fondness for belles-lettres. The city library had, even at that early day, the same tenacity of purpose which marks its career at the present hour. There were literary warehouses in abundance. Judah had decorated his with the portrait of Paine, and here Colles might study Common Sense and the Rights of Man, or he might stroll to the store of Duyckinck, the patron of books of piety, works on education, and Noah Webster; or join *tête-à-tête* with old Hugh Gaine, or James Rivington, and Philip Freneau; now all in harmony, notwithstanding the withering satire against those accommodating old tories, by the great bard of the revolutionary crisis.

The infantile intellect of those days was enlarged with Humpty-Dumpty and Hi-diddle-diddle. Shop-windows were stored with portraits of Paul Jones and Truxton, and the musical sentiment broke forth in ejaculations of Tally Ho! and old Towler in one part of the town, and, in softer accents, with Rousseau's Dream in another. Here and there, too, might be found a coterie gratified with the crescendo and diminuendo of Signor Trazetta: nearly thirty years elapsed from this period ere the arrival of the Garcia troupe, through the efforts of our lamented Almaviva, *Dominick Lynch*, the nonpareil of society, when the Italian opera, with its unrivalled claims, burst forth from the enchanting voice of that marvellous company. The years 1795–1800 were unquestionably the period in which the treasures of the German mind were first developed in this city by our exotic and indigenous writers. That learned orientalist, Dr. Kunze, now commenced the translations into English of the German Hymns, and Strebeck and Milledoler gave us the Catechism of the Lutherans. The Rev. Mr. Will, Charles Smith, and William Dunlap, now supplied novelties from the German dramatic school, and Kotzebue and Schiller were found on that stage where Shakespeare had made his first appearance in the New World in 1752. Colles had other mental resources, as the gaieties and gravities of life were dominant with him. The city was the home of many noble spirits of the Revolution; General Stevens of the Boston Tea-party was here, full of anecdote, Fish of Yorktown celebrity, and Gates of Saratoga, always accessible.

There existed in New York, about these times, a war of opinion, which seized even the medical faculty. The Bastile had been taken. French speculations looked captivating, and Genet's movements won admiration, even with grave men. In common with others, our schoolmasters partook of the prevailing mania; the tri-colored cockade was worn by numerous schoolboys, as well as by their seniors. The yellow-fever was wasting the population; but the patriotic fervor, either for French or English politics, glowed with ardor. With other boys I united in the enthusiasm. The Carmagnole was heard everywhere. I give a verse of a popular song echoed throughout the streets of our city, and heard at the Belvidere at that period.

America that lovely nation,
Once was bound, but now is free;
She broke her chain, for to maintain
The rights and cause of liberty.

Strains like this of the Columbian bards in those days of party-virulence emancipated the feelings of many a throbbing breast, even as now the songs, of pregnant simplicity and affluent tenderness, by Morris, afford delight to a community pervaded by a calmer spirit, and controlled by a loftier refinement. Moreover, we are to remember that in that early age of the Republic an author, and above all a poet, was not an every-day article. True, old Dr. Smith, the brother of the historian, and once a chemical professor in King's College, surcharged with learning and love, who found Delias and Daphnes everywhere, might be seen in the public ways, in his velvet dress, with his madrigals for the beautiful women of his select acquaintance; but the buds of promise of the younger Low (of a poetic family) were blighted by an ornithological error:

'Tis *morn*, and the landscape is lovely to view,
The *nightingale* warbles her song in the grove.

Weems had not yet appeared in the market with his Court of Hymen and his Nest of Love; Cliffton was pulmonary; Beach, recently betrothed to Thalia, was now dejected from dorsal deformity; Linn, *enceinte* with the Powers of Genius, had not yet advanced to a parturient condition; Townsend, sequestered amidst the rivulets and groves near Oyster Bay, had with ambitious effort struck the loud harp, but the Naiads and the Dryads were heedless of his melodious undulations; Wardell's declaration

To the tuneful Apollo I now mean to hollow!

was annunciatory—and nothing more; and Searson, exotic by birth, yet domesticated with us, having made vast struggles in his perilous journey towards Mount Parnassus, had already descended, with what feelings is left to conjecture, by the poet's closing lines of his Valedictory to his muse.

Poets like grasshoppers, sing till they die,
Yet, in this world, some laugh, some sing, some cry.

The Mohawk reviewers, as John Davis called the then critics of our city, thought, with the old saying, that "where there is so much smoke, there must be some fire." But it is no longer questionable, that our Castalian font was often dry, and when otherwise, its stream was rather a muddy rivulet than a spring of living waters. It needs our faithful Lossing to clear up the difficulties of that doubtful period of patriotism and of poetry.

ELIZA TOWNSEND.

ELIZA TOWNSEND was descended from an ancient and influential family, and was born in Boston in 1789. She was a contributor of poems to the Monthly Anthology, the Unitarian Miscellany, and the Port Folio, during the publication of those magazines, and to other periodicals. Her productions were anonymous, and the secret of their authorship was for some time preserved. They are almost entirely occupied with religious or moral reflection, are elevated in tone, and written in an animated and harmonious manner. They are not numerous, are all of moderate length, and have never been collected. The verses on *The Incomprehensibility of God; An Occasional Ode, written in June*, 1809, and published at the time in the Monthly Anthology, in which she comments with severity on the career of Napoleon, then at the summit of his greatness; *Lines to Robert Southey*, written in 1812; *The Rainbow*, published in the General Repository and Review, are her best known productions. She died at her residence in Boston, January 12, 1854.

Miss Townsend was much esteemed, not only for the high merit of her few literary productions but for the cultivation and vigor of her mind, her conversational powers, and her many amiable qualities.*

INCOMPREHENSIBILITY OF GOD.

"*I go forward, but he is not there; and backward, but I cannot perceive him.*"

Where art thou?—THOU! Source and Support of all
That is or seen or felt; Thyself unseen,
Unfelt, unknown,—alas! unknowable!
I look abroad among thy works—the sky,
Vast, distant, glorious with its world of suns,—
Life-giving earth,—and ever-moving main,—
And speaking winds,—and ask if these are Thee!
The stars that twinkle on, the eternal hills,
The restless tide's outgoing and return,
The omnipresent and deep-breathing air—
Though hailed as gods of old, and only less—
Are not the Power I seek; are thine, not Thee!
I ask Thee from the past; if in the years,
Since first intelligence could search its source,
Or in some former unremembered being,
(If such, perchance, were mine) did they behold Thee!
And next interrogate futurity—
So fondly tenanted with better things
Than e'er experience owned—but both are mute;
And past and future, vocal on all else,
So full of memories and phantasies,
Are deaf and speechless here! Fatigued, I turn
From all vain parley with the elements;
And close mine eyes, and bid the thought turn inward
From each material thing its anxious guest,
If, in the stillness of the waiting soul,
He may vouchsafe himself—Spirit to spirit!
O Thou, at once most dreaded and desired,
Pavilioned still in darkness, wilt thou hide thee?
What though the rash request be fraught with fate
Nor human eye may look on thine and live?
Welcome the penalty; let that come now,
Which soon or late must come. For light like this
Who would not dare to die?
Peace, my proud aim,
And hush the wish that knows not what it asks.
Await his will, who hath appointed this,
With every other trial. Be that will
Done now, as ever. For thy curious search,
And unprepared solicitude to gaze
On Him—the Unrevealed—learn hence, instead,
To temper highest hope with humbleness.
Pass thy novitiate in these outer courts,
Till rent the veil, no longer separating
The Holiest of all—as erst, disclosing
A brighter dispensation; whose results
Ineffable, interminable, tend
E'en to the perfecting thyself—thy kind
Till meet for that sublime beatitude,
By the firm promise of a voice from heaven
Pledged to the pure in heart!

THE RAINBOW.

Seen through the misty southern air,
What painted gleam of light is there
Luring the charmed eye?
Whose mellowing shades of different dyes,
In rich profusion gorgeous rise
And melt into the sky.

Higher and higher still it grows
Brighter and clearer yet it shows,
It widens, lengthens, rounds;

* Obituary Notice by the Rev. Convers Francis, D.D., of the Theological School of Harvard College; published in the Boston Daily Advertiser. Griswold's Female Poets of America.

And now that gleam of painted light,
A noble arch, compact to sight
Spans the empyreal bounds!

What curious mechanician wrought,
What viewless hands, as swift as thought,
Have bent this flexile bow?
What seraph-touch these shades could blend
Without beginning, without end?
What sylph such tints bestow?

If Fancy's telescope we bring
To scan withal this peerless thing,
The Air, the Cloud, the Water-King,
'Twould seem their treasures joined:
And the proud monarch of the day,
Their grand ally, his splendid ray
Of eastern gold combined.

Vain vision hence! That will revere
Which, in creation's infant year,
Bade, in compassion to our fear,
(Scarce spent the deluge rage)
Each elemental cause combine,
Whose rich effect should form this sign
Through every future age.

O Peace! the rainbow-emblemed maid,
Where have thy fairy footsteps strayed?
Where hides thy seraph form?
What twilight caves of ocean rest?
Or in what island of the blest
Sails it on gales of morn?

Missioned from heaven in early hour,
Designed through Eden's blissful bower
Delightedly to tread;
Till exiled thence in evil time,
Scared at the company of crime,
Thy startled pinions fled.

E'er since that hour, alas! the thought!
Like thine own dove, who vainly sought
To find a sheltered nest;
Still from the east, the south, the north,
Doomed to be driven a wanderer forth,
And find not where to rest.

Till, when the west its world displayed
Of hiding hills, and sheltering shade—
Hither thy weary flight was stayed,
Here fondly fixed thy seat;
Our forest glens, our desert caves,
Our wall of interposing waves
Deemed a secure retreat.

In vain—from this thy last abode,
(One pitying glance on earth bestowed)
We saw thee take the heavenward road
Where yonder cliffs arise;
Saw thee thy tearful features shroud
Till cradled on the conscious cloud,
That, to await thy coming, bowed,
We lost thee in the skies.

For now the maniac-demon War,
Whose ravings heard so long from far
Convulsed us with their distant jar,
Nearer and louder soars;
His arm, that death and conquest hurled
On all beside of all the world,
Claims these remaining shores.

What though the laurel leaves he tears
Proud round his impious brows to wear
A wreath that will not fade;
What boots him its perennial power—
Those laurels canker where they flower,
They poison where they shade.

But thou, around whose holy head
The balmy olive loves to spread,
Return, O nymph benign!
With buds that paradise bestowed,
Whence "healing for the nations" flowed,
Our bleeding temples twine.

For thee our fathers ploughed the strand,
For thee they left that goodly land,
The turf their childhood trod;
The hearths on which their infants played,
The tombs in which their sires were laid,
The altars of their God.

Then, by their consecrated dust
Their spirits, spirits of the just!
Now near their Maker's face,
By their privations and their cares,
Their pilgrim toils, their patriot prayers,
Desert thou not their race.

Descend to mortal ken confest,
Known by thy white and stainless vest,
And let us on the mountain crest
That snowy mantle see;
Oh let not here thy mission close,
Leave not the erring sons of those
Who left a world for thee!

Celestial visitant! again
Resume thy gentle golden reign,
Our honoured guest once more;
Cheer with thy smiles our saddened plain,
And let thy rainbow o'er the main
Tell that the storms are o'er!

January, 1818.

SARAH J. HALE.

Sarah Josepha Buell was born at the town of Newport, New Hampshire. Her education was principally directed by her mother and a brother in college, and was continued after her marriage by her husband, David Hale, an eminent lawyer and well read man. On his death in 1822, she was left dependent upon her own exertions for her support and that of her five children, the eldest of whom was but seven years old, and as a resource she turned to literature. A volume, *The Genius of Oblivion and other original poems*, was printed in Concord in 1823, for her benefit by the Freemasons, a body of which her husband had been a member. In 1827 she published *Northwood*, a novel in two volumes.

In 1828, she accepted an invitation to become editor of "The Ladies' Magazine," published at Boston, and removed in consequence to that city. In 1837 the magazine was united with the Lady's Book, a Philadelphia monthly, the literary charge of which was placed and still remains in her hands. She has published *Sketches of American Character; Traits of American Life; The Way to live well and to be well while we live; Grosvenor, a Tragedy* (founded on the Revolutionary story of the execution of Col. Isaac Hayne of South Carolina); *Alice Ray, a Romance in Rhyme; Harry Guy, the Widow's Son, a story of the sea* (also in verse); *Three Hours, or, the Vigil of Love, and other Poems.* Part of these have been reprinted from the magazines edited by her, which also contain a large number of tales and sketches in prose and verse from her pen not yet collected. Mrs. Hale's stories are brief, pleasant narratives, drawn generally from the every-day course of American life.

Her poems are for the most part narrative and reflective—and are written with force and elegance. One of the longest, *Three Hours, or the Vigil of Love*, is a story whose scene is laid in New England, and deals with the spiritual and material fears the early colonists were subjected to from their belief in witchcraft and the neighborhood of savage foes.

In 1853 Mrs. Hale published *Woman's Record, or Sketches of all Distinguished Women, from "the Beginning" till A.D.* 1850. In this work, which forms a large octavo volume of nine hundred and four pages, she has furnished biographical notices of the most distinguished of her sex in every period of history. Though many of the articles are necessarily brief, and much of it is a compilation from older cyclopædias, there are numerous papers of original value. The Record includes of course many distinguished in the field of authorship, and in these cases extracts are given from the productions which have gained eminence for their writers. The choice of names is wide and liberal, giving a fair representation of every field of female exertion.

Mrs. Hale has also prepared *A Complete Dictionary of Poetical Quotations, containing Selections from the Writings of the Poets of England and America*, in a volume of six hundred double column octavo pages, edited a number of annuals, written several books for children, and a volume on cookery.

IT SNOWS.

"It snows!" cries the school-boy—"hurrah!" and his shout
Is ringing through parlor and hall,
While swift as the wing of a swallow, he's out,
And his playmates have answered his call.
It makes the heart leap but to witness their joy,—
Proud wealth has no pleasures, I trow,
Like the rapture that throbs in the pulse of the boy,
As he gathers his treasures of snow;
Then lay not the trappings of gold on thine heirs,
While health, and the riches of Nature are theirs.

"It snows!" sighs the imbecile—"Ah!" and his breath
Comes heavy, as clogged with a weight;
While from the pale aspect of Nature in death
He turns to the blaze of his grate:
And nearer, and nearer, his soft cushioned chair
Is wheeled tow'rds the life-giving flame—
He dreads a chill puff of the snow-burdened air,
Lest it wither his delicate frame;
Oh! small is the pleasure existence can give,
When the fear we shall die only proves that we live!

"It snows!" cries the traveller—"Ho!" and the word
Has quickened his steed's lagging pace;
The wind rushes by, but its howl is unheard
Unfelt the sharp drift in his face;
For bright through the tempest his own home appeared—
Ay! though leagues intervened, he can see
There's the clear, glowing hearth, and the table prepared,
And his wife with their babes at her knee.
Blest thought! how it lightens the grief-laden hour,
That those we love dearest are safe from its power.

"It snows!" cries the Belle,—"Dear how lucky," and turns
From her mirror to watch the flakes fall;
Like the first rose of summer, her dimpled cheek burns
While musing on sleigh-ride and ball:
There are visions of conquest, of splendor, and mirth,
Floating over each drear winter's day;
But the tintings of Hope, on this storm-beaten earth,
Will melt, like the snowflakes, away;
Turn, turn thee to Heaven, fair maiden, for bliss
That world has a fountain ne'er opened in this.

"It snows!" cries the widow,—"Oh, God!" and her sighs
Have stifled the voice of her prayer,
Its burden ye'll read in her tear-swollen eyes,
On her cheek, sunk with fasting and care.
'Tis night—and her fatherless ask her for bread—
But "He gives the young ravens their food,"
And she trusts, till her dark hearth adds horror to dread,
And she lays on her last chip of wood.
Poor suff'rer! that sorrow thy God only knows—
'Tis a pitiful lot to be poor, when it snows!

* Woman's Record; or Sketches of all Distinguished Women, from "the Beginning" till A.D. 1850. Arranged in four eras. With selections from female writers of every age. By Sarah Josepha Hale. New York: 1853.

JOB DURFEE.

JOB DURFEE was born at Tiverton, Rhode Island, September 20, 1790. He entered Brown University in 1809, and on the conclusion of his academic course studied law and was licensed to practise. In 1814 he was elected a member of the state legislature, and six years afterwards of the national House of Representatives. He distinguished himself in Congress by his advocacy of the interests of his state in the bill providing for a new apportionment of representatives, and by his moderate course on the tariff. He remained in Congress during two terms. In 1826 he was re-elected to the state legislature, but after a service of two years declined a re-nomination, and retired to his farm, where he devoted himself to literature, and in 1832 published a small edition of his poem of *Whatcheer*.

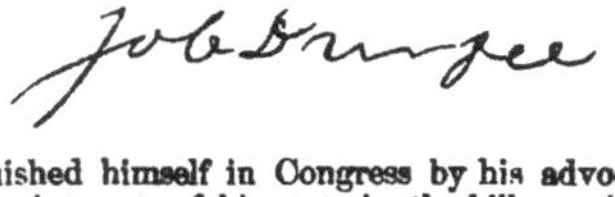

In 1833 he was appointed associate, and two years after chief-justice of the Supreme Court of the state. He continued in this office until his death, July 26, 1847. His works were collected in one octavo volume, with a memoir by his son, in 1849. They consist of his *Whatcheer* and a few juvenile verses, mostly of a fanciful character; a few historical addresses; an abstruse philosophical treatise, entitled *Panidea*, the object of which is to show the pervading influence and presence of the Deity throughout nature; and a few of his judicial charges.

Whatcheer is a poem of nine cantos, each containing some fifty or sixty eight-line stanzas. It is a versified account of Roger Williams's departure from Salem, his journey through the wilderness, interviews with the Indians, and the settlement of Rhode Island. It is written in a very plain manner, and makes no pretensions to high poetic merit, but many passages are impressive from their earnestness and simplicity. The versification is smooth and correct.

ROGER WILLIAMS IN THE FOREST.

Above his head the branches writhe and bend,
 Or in the mingled wreck the ruin flies—
The storm redoubles, and the whirlwinds blend
 The rising snow-drift with descending skies;
And oft the crags a friendly shelter lend
 His breathless bosom, and his sightless eyes;
But, when the transient gust its fury spends,
He through the storm again upon his journey wends.

Still truly does his course the magnet keep—
 No toils fatigue him, and no fears appal;
Oft turns he at the glimpse of swampy deep;
 Or thicket dense, or crag abrupt and tall,
Or backward treads to shun the headlong steep,
 Or pass above the tumbling waterfall;
Yet still he joys whene'er the torrents leap,
Or crag abrupt, or thicket dense, or swamp's far sweep

Assures him progress,—From gray morn till noon—
 Hour after hour—from that drear noon until
The evening's gathering darkness had begun
 To clothe with deeper glooms the vale and hill,
Sire Williams journeyed in the forest lone;
 And then night's thickening shades began to fill
His soul with doubt—for shelter had he none—
And all the out-stretched waste was clad with one

Vast mantle hoar. And he began to hear,
 At times, the fox's bark, and the fierce howl
Of wolf, sometimes afar—sometimes so near,
 That in the very glen they seemed to prowl
Where now he, wearied, paused—and then his ear
 Started to note some shaggy monster's growl,
That from his snow-clad, rocky den did peer.
 Shrunk with gaunt famine in that tempest drear,

And scenting human blood—yea, and so nigh,
 Thrice did our northern tiger seem to come,
He thought he heard the fagots crackling by,
 And saw, through driven snow and twilight gloom,
Peer from the thickets his fierce burning eye,
 Scanning his destined prey, and through the broom,
Thrice stealing on his ears, the whining cry
Swelled by degrees above the tempest high.

Wayworn he stood—and fast that stormy night
 Was gathering round him over hill and dale—
He glanced around, and by the lingering light
 Found he had paused within a narrow vale;
On either hand a snow-clad rocky height
 Ascended high, a shelter from the gale,
Whilst deep between them, in thick glooms bedight,
A swampy dingle caught the wanderer's sight.

Through the white billows thither did he wade,
 And deep within its solemn bosom trod;
There on the snow his oft repeated tread
 Hardened a flooring for his night's abode;
All there was calm, for the thick branches made
 A screen above, and round him closely stood
The trunks of cedars, and of pines arrayed
To the rude tempest, a firm barricade.

And now his hatchet, with resounding stroke,
 Hewed down the boscage that around him rose,
And the dry pine of brittle branches broke,
 To yield him fuel for the night's repose:
The gathered heap an ample store bespoke—
 He smites the steel—the tinder brightly glows,
And the fired match the kindled flame awoke,
And light upon night's seated darkness broke.

High branched the pines, and far the colonnade
 Of tapering trunks stood glimmering through the glen;
Then joyed our Father in this lonely glade,
 So far from haunts of persecuting men,
That he might break of honesty the bread,
 And blessings crave in his own way again—
Of the piled brush a seat and board he made,
Spread his plain fare, and piously he prayed.

"Father of mercies! thou the wanderer's guide,
 In this dire storm along the howling waste,
Thanks for the shelter thou dost here provide,
 Thanks for the mercies of the day that's past;
Thanks for the frugal fare thou hast supplied;
 And O! may still thy tender mercies last;
And may thy light on every falsehood shine,
Till man's freed spirit own no law save thine!

"Grant that thy humble instrument still shun
 His persecutors in their eager quest;
Grant the asylum yet to be begun,
 To persecution's exiles yield a rest;
Let ages after ages take the boon,
 And in soul-liberty fore'er be blest—
Grant that I live until this task be done,
And then, O Lord, receive me as thine own!"

LEVI WOODBURY.

LEVI WOODBURY was born at Francestown, New Hampshire, December 22, 1789. After receiving an excellent preliminary education, he entered Dartmouth College. On the completion of his course in 1809, he studied law at the celebrated Litchfield school, commenced practice in his native village, and rapidly rose to such eminence that in 1816 he was appointed one of the Judges of the Superior Court of his State.

In 1823 he was elected Governor, and in 1825 a member of the House of Representatives, where he was made Speaker, and soon after chosen Senator. In May, 1831, he was made Secretary of the Navy by President Jackson, and in 1834 Secretary of the Treasury. In 1841 he was a second time chosen Senator, and in 1845 became one of the Associated Judges of the Supreme Court. He died at his residence in Portsmouth, New Hampshire, September 4, 1851.

His political, judicial, and literary writings were collected in 1852 in three large octavo volumes, a volume being devoted to each, and a portion only of his productions of either class given. The first volume contains speeches and reports delivered in Congress as Governor, and in the deliberative assembly of his State, with "occasional letters and speeches on important topics." An Appendix furnishes us with specimens of his political addresses at popular meetings. The second volume is made up of Arguments and Charges. The third contains Addresses on the Importance of Science in the Arts, the Promotion and Uses of Science, the Remedies for Certain Defects in American Education; on Progress; on Historical Inquiries. The style in these is clear and efficient; the argument ingenious and practical.

MEANS AND MOTIVES IN AMERICAN EDUCATION—FROM THE ADDRESS ON THE REMEDIES FOR DEFECTS IN EDUCATION.

Print, if possible, beyond even the thirty sheets by a steam press now executed in the time one was formerly struck off. Go, also, beyond the present gain in their distribution over much of the world by improvements in the locomotive and the steamboat, so as to accomplish like results at far less than the former cost. Promote the discovery of still further materials than rags, bark, or straw, for the wonderful fabric of paper,—used, not merely as the ornament of our drawing-rooms, the preserver of history, the organ of intercourse between both distant places and distant ages, the medium of business, the evidence of property, the record of legislation, and in all ranks the faithful messenger of thought and affection; but, above all, the universal instrument of instruction. Reduce still further, by new inventions, the already low price of manufacturing paper. Render types also cheaper, as well as more durable. And, in short, set no boundaries and prostrate all barriers whatever to the enterprise of the human mind, in devising greater facilities for its own progress. Next to these considerations, new means might well be adopted to improve the quality of those books which are in most common use. This could be accomplished by greater attention to their practical tendency and suitableness to the times in which we live, and the public wants which exist under our peculiar institutions, whether social or political. The highest intellects might beneficially descend, at times, to labor in writing for the humblest spheres of letters and life. In cases of long and obvious deficiencies in books designed for particular branches of instruction, boards of education might well confer premiums for better compilations. Such boards might also, with advantage, strive to multiply institutions particularly intended to prepare more efficient teachers, female as well as male. In short, the fountains must always be watched, in order to insure pure streams; and the dew which descends nightly on every object, and in all places, however lowly, is more useful than a single shower confined to a limited range of country. We must take paternal care of the elements on which all at first feed; and if in these modes we seek with earnestness the improvement of the many, we help to protect the property and persons of the favoured few as much as we elevate the character and conduct of all situated in the more retired walks of society. There is another powerful motive for exertion, even by the higher classes, to advance the better education of the masses. It is this: the wealthy, for instance, can clearly foresee that, by the revolutions of fortune's wheel, their own children, or grandchildren, are in time likely to become indigent, so as to be the immediate recipients of favor under any system of free education, and thus may be assisted to attain once more rank and riches. Nor should the talented be parsimonious in like efforts, because a degeneracy of intellect, not unusual after high developments in a family, may plunge their posterity into ignorance and want, where some untaught Addison or "mute inglorious Milton" might, after a few generations, reappear, but never instruct or delight the age, unless assisted at first by opportunities and means furnished through a system like this. All which is thus bestowed will likewise prove, not only an inheritance for some of the offspring of the favored classes, but a more durable one than most of those honors and riches, endeavored so often, but fruitlessly, to be transmitted. It is true that vicissitudes seem impressed on almost everything human,—painful, heartrending vicissitudes,—which the fortunate dread, and would mitigate, if not able to avert. But they belong less to systems than to families or individuals, and can be obviated best by permanent plans to spread stores of intellectual wealth, constantly and freely, around all.

SAMUEL H. TURNER

WAS born in Philadelphia, January 23, 1790, the son of the Rev. Joseph Turner. He took his degree at the University of Pennsylvania in 1807. He was ordained deacon in the Protestant Episcopal Church by Bishop White in 1811, and the next year became settled in a parish in Chestertown, Kent county, Maryland. He returned to Philadelphia in 1817, and, October 7, 1818, was appointed Professor of Historic Theology in the General Theological Seminary at New York, where he has since resided, attached to that institution, with the exception of an interval in 1820 and 1821, which he passed at New Haven. In the last year he was appointed Professor of Biblical Learning and the Interpretation of Scripture, in the Seminary. In 1831 he was chosen Professor of the Hebrew Language and Literature in Columbia College.

His life has been almost exclusively passed in the occupations of a scholar engaged in the work of instruction: but he has also given the public numerous important books. He was one of the first to introduce into the country translations of the learned German critics and divines. In 1827 he prepared, with the joint assistance of Mr. (now Bishop) William R. Whittingham, of Maryland, a translation of *Jahn's Introduction to the Old Testament*, with notes, and, in 1834, a translation of *Planck's Introduction to Sacred Criticism and Interpretation*, with notes.

A third publication, in 1847, exhibits Dr. Turner on the ground of one of his favorite studies, the Rabbinical Literature, with which he is particularly conversant. It is entitled *Biographical Notices of Jewish Rabbies, with Translations and Notes.*

He is the author also of several theological writings; *Spiritual Things compared with Spiritual or Parallel References*, published in 1848; *Essay on our Lord's Discourse at Capernaum, in John* vi., in 1851; *Thoughts on Scriptural Prophecy*, 1852.

He has of late been engaged on a series of Critical Commentaries on the Epistles of the New Testament, of which the volumes on the *Hebrews* and the *Romans* severally appeared in 1852 and 1853.

Dr. Turner has, in addition, corrected and prepared for the press Mr. Jaeger's Translation of the Mythological Fictions of the Greeks and Romans, published in 1829 by Moritz.

Dr. Turner maintains a high rank for his exact critical scholarship and the fairness of his writings, which have received the approval of those who differ from him in theological opinions.

THE UNIVERSITY OF VERMONT.

IN the first organization of this state, when the country was for the most part a wilderness, the Constitution, in 1777, included a recommendation for the founding of a University. There was some delay while negotiations were going on with the neighboring Dartmouth College, which received a grant of land from Vermont in 1785. The home project was, however, fairly set on foot in 1789, when Ira Allen, of Colchester, made a liberal offer of lands, labor, and materials. Allen was the brother of Colonel Ethan Allen.

He was prominently connected with the early annals of Vermont, of which, in 1798, he published a history, and was always a zealous advocate of the interests of the College. His gift of land was liberal, and his selection of the position of the University clear-sighted. President Wheeler, in his College Historical Discourse in 1854, speaks of "his comprehensive mind and highly creative and philosophical spirit."

There was much agitation, as usual, respecting a site for the institution, but the various local claims were finally overcome in favor of Burlington, which, from its fine position on Lake Champlain, on the high road of travel, offered the most distinguished inducements. The University was chartered in 1791, but its officers were not appointed nor its building commenced till 1800. The Rev. Daniel C. Sanders, a graduate of Harvard of 1788, was elected the first president; of decided personal traits, in a stalwart figure, and mingled courage and courtesy, he was an efficient director of the youth under his charge. He performed his onerous duties for the first three years without an assistant. The class of 1804, we read, received all their instructions from him; and as the classes increased he often employed six, eight, and ten hours of the day in personal recitations. "He was not profound as a thinker," adds Dr. Wheeler, "nor severely logical as a reasoner, nor of a high form of classical elegance and accuracy as a writer; but he was lucid, fresh, and original in forms of expression, full of benignity and kindness in his sentiments, and was listened to with general admiration."* By the year 1807 a college building, including a chapel and a president's house, had been erected, and the commencement of a library and philosophical apparatus secured. The course of study embraced the usual topics, with the addition of anatomy; the Rev. Samuel Williams, the author of the Natural and Civil History of Vermont, first published in 1794, having delivered, for two years, lectures on astronomy and natural philosophy. As an illustration of the simple habits of the time and place, a calculation was made by the president, that "a poor scholar, by keeping school four months each winter, at the average price of sixteen dollars a month, could pay all his college bills and his board, and leave college with thirty-two dollars in his pocket."† The college asked only twelve dollars a year from each student. There was a moderate income from public lands, from which the president received a salary of six hundred dollars; a professor of mathematics less than three hundred and fifty, and a tutor three hundred. These simple receipts and expenditure required constant vigilance and self-denial in the management of the institution, which was shortly affected from without by the stoppage of the commerce of the town with Canada in consequence of the non-intercourse policy of Jefferson, by the rivalry of Middlebury College, which was chartered in 1800,‡ and by the interference of the legislature with the vested rights under the charter. The University outgrew these several difficulties. The war ended; it became strong enough to hold its own against all diversions; and the Dartmouth College legal decision having led to a better understanding of the rights of college property, the old charter was restored in its integrity. While under the more immediate control of the legislature the wants of the University were at least clearly indicated by a committee composed of the Hon. Royal Tyler and the Hon. W. C. Bradley, who reported in favor of the appointment of new professorships of the learned languages, of law, belles lettres, chemistry, and mineralogy. During the war the college exercises were suspended and the faculty broken up.

After the establishment of peace, the Rev. Samuel Austin was elected president in 1815. He was a native of Connecticut, born in 1760, a graduate of Yale, subsequently teacher of a grammar-school in New Haven, while he studied theology with the Rev. Dr. Jonathan Edwards then settled there, next a valued clergyman in Connecticut, and at the time of his call to the college settled in Worcester, Mass., where he had preached since 1790. He was a man of earnest religious devotion; and his reputation in this particular, no less than his especial labors, served the institution, which was thought in danger of lay influences, from the immediate control of the legislature of its affairs.

Dr. Austin resigned in 1821, despairing of reviving the college, which was now greatly pressed by financial embarrassments. The suspension of the college appeared at hand, when new vigor was infused, chiefly through the activity of Professor Arthur L. Porter, whose services were soon again required, on the destruction of the original college building by fire. The Rev. Daniel Haskell, a man of energy, was elected president, and was shortly succeeded, in 1825, by the Rev. Willard Preston, of an amiable character, who again, in the next year, gave place to the Rev. James Marsh, under whose auspices the fame of the institution was to be largely increased.

Jas. Marsh.

James Marsh, the scholar and philosopher, was born in Hartford, Vermont, July 19, 1794. His grandfather was one of the early settlers in the state, and its first lieutenant-governor. His father was a farmer; and it was amongst rural occupations, for which he ever after entertained a longing, that the first eighteen years of the life of the future professor were passed. He was brought up to the hardy labor of the farm, and it was only upon the withdrawal of his elder brother from

* Historical Discourse, p. 12.

† MSS of Sanders, quoted by President Wheeler.

‡ Middlebury College was encouraged by the success of the Addison County Grammar school, and the natural desire of the intelligent citizens of the district to take the lead in education. The Rev. Jeremiah Atwater, who had been connected with the school, was the first president. In 1805 there were sixteen graduates. Henry Davis, who had been professor of languages in Union College, succeeded to Atwater in 1810, and held the office till 1817. The Rev. Joshua Bates, of Dedham, Mass., was next chosen. He has since been succeeded by the Rev. Dr. Benjamin Labaree. The Institution has been well attended and has become enriched, from time to time, by various important donations and bequests.—Historical Sketch by Professor Fowler. Am. Quar. Reg. ix. 220-229.

the college opportunities tendered to him, that he turned his studies in that direction. He was admitted at Dartmouth in 1813, where he pursued the ancient languages and literature with diligence; and where, under the influence of a religious excitement which took place at the college, he became deeply devotional, which led to his entrance at the theological school at Andover. He passed a year there, and became a tutor in 1818 at Dartmouth. After two years profitably spent in this way he returned to Andover, taking a visit to Cambridge by the way, for the sake of a candid view of the studies he was prosecuting. His course at Andover was laborious. Abstemious in diet, and frugal of his physical resources and the claims of society, he devoted all his powers to learning. One of the first fruits of these studies was an article on *Ancient and Modern Poetry*, published in the North American Review for July, 1822, in which he exhibits the influences of Christianity upon the later literature. German literature had occupied much of his attention, and he prepared a translation of the work of Bellerman on the *Geography of the Scriptures*, as he afterwards employed himself upon a version of Hedgewisch on the *Elements of Chronology*. His most important work in this way was his translation of Herder's *Spirit of Hebrew Poetry*, published in two volumes at Burlington, in 1833.

From Andover he passed for awhile to the South, where he was engaged in the business of tuition in Hampden Sidney College, in Virginia, with Dr. Rice. He sometimes preached, though he had little fondness or aptitude for this "acting in public," as he called it at the time. Turning his thoughts to the North, an editorial connexion was planned with the *Christian Spectator*, a theological review at New Haven, a post for which he was well qualified, but the plan was not carried out. In 1824 he was formally appointed to a professorship in Hampden Sidney, and the same year was ordained a minister. His entire connexion with this college lasted but three years, when he was appointed to the presidency of the University of Vermont in 1826, a position which he entered upon and occupied till 1833, when he exchanged its duties for the professorship of Moral and Intellectual Philosophy in the same institution. He held this till his death, July 3, 1842, in the fifty-eighth year of his age.

It is by his college labors and the philosophical publications which they elicited, as well as by his noble personal influence upon his pupils, that Dr. Marsh is best known. He was one of the first to revive attention in the country to the sound Christian philosophy advocated by Coleridge, and illustrated in the writings of the old English divines, as distinguished from the later school of Locke. In the words of his faithful biographer, Professor Torrey,* "the prevailing doctrine of the day was, Understand, and then believe; while that which Mr. Marsh would set forth, not as anything new, but as the old doctrine of the church from the earliest times, was, "Believe, that ye may understand." "Such views," said Marsh, "may not indeed be learned from the superficial philosophy of the Paleian and Caledonian schools; but the higher and more spiritual philosophy of the great English divines of the seventeenth century abundantly teaches them, both by precept and practice." In accordance with these views he published in 1829 the first American edition of Coleridge's Aids to Reflection, as a book which answered his purpose, for which he wrote an able *Preliminary Essay*, addressed to "the earnest, single-hearted lovers" of Christian, spiritual, and moral truth. With the same view he edited a volume of Selections from the Old English Writers on Practical Theology, which contained Howe's Blessedness of the Righteous, and Bates's Four Last Things.

His views of college study and discipline were those of a liberal-minded reformer, and were to a considerable extent adopted by the institution over which he presided. He held that the admission to colleges might be extended with advantage to those who could avail themselves only of a partial course; that a paternal discipline, based on moral and social influence, might be employed; that the liberty of the powers of the individual might be preserved under a general system of training; that additional studies might be prosecuted by the enterprising: and that honors should be conferred on those only of real abilities and attainments. These were all liberal objects; and as they were pursued with warmth and candor by Dr. Marsh, they gained him the respect and affection of the best minds among his students, who have now carried his influence into the walks of active life.

In addition to the writings which we have mentioned, Dr. Marsh published in 1829 a series of papers in the *Vermont Chronicle*, signed "Philopolis," on Popular Education. He wrote also for the *Christian Spectator* a review of Professor Stuart's Commentary on the Hebrews, in which he did justice to the objects of the author. At the close of his life Dr. Marsh intrusted his manuscripts to Professor Torrey of the University of Vermont, by whom in 1843 a volume of Remains was published with a Memoir. It contains the author's college lectures on psychology, several philosophical essays, and theological discourses. He had projected and partially executed a System of Logic, and meditated a matured treatise on psychology.

In 1833, on the retirement of Dr. Marsh from the presidency, the Rev. John Wheeler, of Windsor, Vermont, was appointed president. A subscription which had been projected for the benefit of the college was now completed, and the sum of thirty thousand dollars obtained, which added largely to the practical efficiency of the institution. Other collections of funds have since been made, which have further secured its prosperity.

During the administration of Dr. Wheeler, Professor Torrey succeeded Dr. Marsh in his chair of moral and intellectual philosophy, the Rev. Calvin Pease was elected professor of the Latin and Greek languages, and the Rev. W. G. T. Shedd professor of English literature. In 1847 Professor George W. Benedict, a most active supporter of the college welfare, resigned his seat as professor of chemistry and natural history, after twenty-two years' services to the institution.

* Memoir prefixed to the Remains, p. 91.

President Wheeler resigned in 1848, and was succeeded by the present incumbent, the Rev. Worthington Smith, D.D., of St. Alban's, Vt.

On the 1st of August, 1854, the semi-centennial anniversary of the University was celebrated at Burlington.

A historical discourse was delivered by the former president, Dr. Wheeler, from which the materials of this narrative have been mostly drawn. An oration, "Our Lesson and our Work, or Spiritual Philosophy and Material Politics," was pronounced by Mr. James R. Spalding; a poem by the Rev. O. G. Wheeler; while the associations of the Institution were recalled in the after dinner festivities, with an honest pride in the favorite philosophy of the University.

In the course of the Historical Address Dr. Wheeler gave the following sketch of the course of study projected by Dr. Marsh and his associates, for the institution.

"The principal divisions or departments of a course of collegiate study are set forth in the laws of the University. They are four: first, the department of English literature; second, the department of languages; third, that of the mathematics and physics; fourth, that of political, moral, and intellectual philosophy. Every year, during my personal connexion with the University, the synopsis was carefully examined, always in reference to its practical execution, and commonly in reference also to its theoretic excellence. How much this means and involves, few can understand, who were not members of the faculty. If this course of study is carefully examined, it will be found to contain, perhaps, what no other course of collegiate study in the United States has so fully attempted. It seeks to give a coherence to the various studies in each department, so that its several parts shall present more or less the unity, not of an aggregation, nor of a juxtaposition, nor of a merely logical arrangement, but of a natural development, and a growth; and therefore the study of it, rightly pursued, would be a growing and enlarging process to the mind of the student. It was intended also, that these departments of study should have a coherence of greater or less practical use with each other. The highest department, that of philosophy, it was intended, should be, now the oscillating nerve, that should connect the various studies together, during the analytical instruction in each; and now the embosoming atmosphere that should surround and interpenetrate the whole and each in its synthetical teachings. In philosophy the course began with crystallography—the lowest form of organization—and discussed the laws of all forms, that is, the geometry of all material existence. It proceeded to the laws of vegetable life, as the next highest; to the laws of animal life, that is to physiology, as the next; thence to psychology, and the connexion of the senses with the intellect;—thence to the science of logic—the laws of the intellect,—in the acquisition and in the communication of knowledge, that is, the laws of universal thought, as seen in language and grammar; and thence to metaphysics, as the highest and last form of speculative reasoning, or of contemplation. Within this pale it considered the spiritual characteristics of humanity, as distinguished from all other existences. From this position moral science was seen to issue; the ground of the fine arts was examined and made intelligible; the principles of political science, as grounded in the truths of reason, but realized under the forms of the understanding, was unfolded, and natural and revealed religion was shown to open the path where reason had reached her termination, to glory, honor, and immortality."

CHARLES SPRAGUE

Was born in Boston, October 26, 1791. His father, a native of Hingham, Mass., where the family had lived for five generations, was one of those spirited Whigs of the Revolution who engaged in the adventure of throwing overboard the tea in Boston harbor. His mother, Joanna Thayer of Braintree, is spoken of for her original powers of mind and her influence in the development of her son's talents. The latter was educated at the Franklin school at Boston, where he had for one of his teachers, Lemuel Shaw, now the Chief-justice of Massachusetts. By an accident at this time he lost the use of his left eye. At thirteen, he entered a mercantile house engaged in the importation of dry-goods; and in 1816, at the age of twenty-five, formed a partnership with his employers, Messrs. Thayer and Hunt, which was continued till 1820, when he became a teller in the State Bank. On the establishment of the Globe Bank in 1825, he was chosen its cashier, an office, the duties of which he has discharged with exemplary fidelity to the present day.

Halleck, another poetical cashier by the way, has sighed over this "bank note world" and the visions of the romantic past, now that

Noble name and cultured land,
Palace and park and vassal band,
Are powerless to the notes of hand
Of Rothschild or the Barings.

Charles Sprague

But we may be contented with the change if bank offices produce many such poets.

Sprague, says his recent biographer, Mr. Loring,

"dares to acknowledge his homage to the Nine, in the very temple of the money changers; and enjoys, at the same time, the most favoring inspirations of the former, and the unlimited confidence of the latter. The Globe Bank has never failed to make a dividend; and its cashier has never failed to be at his station on the very day when the books were opened for the purpose to this period."*

The poetical writings of Mr. Sprague, of which there has been a recent edition, published by Ticknor in 1850, consist of a series of theatrical prize addresses which first gave the poet celebrity; a "Shakespeare Ode" delivered at the Boston theatre in 1823, at the exhibition of a pageant in honor of the great dramatist; his chief poem, *Curiosity*, delivered before the Phi Beta Kappa Society of Harvard, in 1829; a centennial ode the following year on the celebration of the settlement of Boston, and a number of poems chiefly on occasional topics, which the author's care and ability have rendered of permanent interest.

The dramatic odes are elegant polished compositions, and possess a certain chaste eloquence which is a characteristic of all the author's productions.

"Curiosity" is a succession of pleasing pictures illustrating this universal passion in the various means, low and elevated, taken for its gratification. The execution of the culprit, the pulpit, the fashionable preacher, the stage, the press, the learned pursuits of the antiquarian, the idle humors of the sick chamber, the scandal and gossip of social life; the incentives and delights of foreign travel; the earnest seeking of the eye of faith into the mysteries of the future world:—these all pass in review before the reader, and are touched with a skilful hand.

The *Centennial Ode* is a warm tribute to the virtues of the Pilgrim Fathers, with an animated sketch of the progress of national life since.

A civic Fourth of July Oration delivered in Boston in 1825, and an address in 1827, before the Massachusetts Society for the suppression of intemperance, are two vigorous prose compositions, published with the author's poetical writings.

PRIZE PROLOGUE—RECITED AT THE OPENING OF THE PARK THEATRE, 1821.

When mitred Zeal, in wild, unholy days,
Bared his red arm, and bade the fagot blaze,
Our patriot sires the pilgrim sail unfurled,
And Freedom pointed to a rival world.

Where prowled the wolf, and where the hunter roved,
Faith raised her altars to the God she loved;
Toil, linked with Art, explored each savage wild,
The lofty forest bowed, the desert smiled;
The startled Indian o'er the mountains flew,
The wigwam vanished, and the village grew;
Taste reared her domes, fair Science spread her page,
And Wit and Genius gathered round the Stage!

The Stage! where Fancy sits, creative queen,
And waves her sceptre o'er life's mimic scene;
Where young-eyed Wonder comes to feast his sight,
And quaff instruction while he drinks delight.—
The Stage!—that threads each labyrinth of the soul,
Wakes laughter's peal and bids the tear-drop roll;
That shoots at Folly, mocks proud Fashion's slave,
Uncloaks the hypocrite, and brands the knave.

The child of Genius, catering for the Stage,
Rifles the wealth of every clime and age.
He speaks! the sepulchre resigns her prey,
And crimson life runs through the sleeping clay.
The wave, the gibbet, and the battle-field,
At his command, their festering tenants yield.
Pale, bleeding Love comes weeping from the tomb
That kindred softness may bewail her doom;
Murder's dry bones, reclothed, desert the dust,
That after times may own his sentence just;
Forgotten Wisdom, freed from death's embrace,
Reads awful lessons to another race;
And the mad tyrant of some ancient shore
Here warns a world that he can curse no more.

May this fair dome, in classic beauty reared,
By Worth be honored, and by Vice be feared;
May chastened Wit here bend to Virtue's cause,
Reflect her image, and repeat her laws;
And Guilt, that slumbers o'er the sacred page
Hate his own likeness, shadowed from the Stage!

Here let the Guardian of the Drama sit,
In righteous judgment o'er the realms of wit.
Not his the shame, with servile pen to wait
On private friendship, or on private hate;
To flatter fools, or Satire's javelin dart,
Tipped with a lie, at proud Ambition's heart:
His be the nobler task to herald forth
Young, blushing Merit, and neglected Worth;
To brand the page where Goodness finds a sneer,
And lash the wretch that breathes the treason here!

Here shall bright Genius wing his eagle flight,
Rich dew-drops shaking from his plumes of light,
Till high in mental worlds, from vulgar ken
He soars, the wonder and the pride of men.
Cold Censure here to decent Mirth shall bow,
And Bigotry unbend his monkish brow.
Here Toil shall pause, his ponderous sledge thrown by,
And Beauty bless each strain with melting eye;
Grief, too, in fiction lost, shall cease to weep
And all the world's rude cares be laid to sleep.
Each polished scene shall Taste and Truth approve,
And the Stage triumph in the people's love.

ART.

An Ode written for the Sixth Triennial Festival of the Massachusetts Charitable Mechanic Association, 1824.

When, from the sacred garden driven,
  Man fled before his Maker's wrath,
An angel left her place in heaven,
  And crossed the wanderer's sunless path.
'Twas Art! sweet Art! new radiance broke
  Where her light foot flew o'er the ground,
And thus with seraph voice she spoke—
  "The Curse a Blessing shall be found."

She led him through the trackless wild,
  Where noontide sunbeam never blazed;
The thistle shrunk, the harvest smiled,
  And Nature gladdened as she gazed.
Earth's thousand tribes of living things,
  At Art's command, to him are given;
The village grows, the city springs,
  And point their spires of faith to heaven.

He rends the oak—and bids it ride,
  To guard the shores its beauty graced;
He smites the rock—upheaved in pride,
  See towers of strength and domes of taste.
Earth's teeming caves their wealth reveal,
  Fire bears his banner on the wave,
He bids the mortal poison heal,
  And leaps triumphant o'er the grave.

* Hundred Boston Orators, p. 418.

He plucks the pearls that stud the deep,
  Admiring Beauty's lap to fill;
He breaks the stubborn marble's sleep,
  And now mocks his Creator's skill.
With thoughts that swell his glowing soul,
  He bids the ore illume the page,
And, proudly scorning Time's control,
  Commerces with an unborn age.

In fields of air he writes his name,
  And treads the chambers of the sky;
He reads the stars, and grasps the flame
  That quivers round the Throne on high.
In war renowned, in peace sublime,
  He moves in greatness and in grace;
His power, subduing space and time,
  Links realm to realm, and race to race.

THE TRAVELLER—FROM CURIOSITY.

Withdraw yon curtain, look within that room,
Where all is splendor, yet where all is gloom:
Why weeps that mother? why, in pensive mood,
Group noiseless round, that little, lovely brood?
The battledoor is still, laid by each book,
And the harp slumbers in its customed nook.
Who hath done this? what cold, unpitying foe
Hath made this house the dwelling-place of woe?
'Tis he, the husband, father, lost in care,
O'er that sweet fellow in his cradle there:
The gallant bark that rides by yonder strand
Bears him to-morrow from his native land.
Why turns he, half unwilling, from his home,
To tempt the ocean, and the earth to roam?
Wealth he can boast a miser's sigh would hush,
And health is laughing in that ruddy blush;
Friends spring to greet him, and he has no foe—
So honored and so blessed, what bids him go?—
His eye must see, his foot each spot must tread,
Where sleeps the dust of earth's recorded dead;
Where rise the monuments of ancient time,
Pillar and pyramid in age sublime;
The Pagan's temple and the Churchman's tower,
War's bloodiest plain and Wisdom's greenest bower;
All that his wonder woke in school-boy themes,
All that his fancy fired in youthful dreams:
Where Socrates once taught he thirsts to stray,
Where Homer poured his everlasting lay;
From Virgil's tomb he longs to pluck one flower,
By Avon's stream to live one moonlight hour;
To pause where England "garners up" her great,
And drop a patriot's tear to Milton's fate;
Fame's living masters, too, he must behold,
Whose deeds shall blazon with the best of old;
Nations compare, their laws and customs scan,
And read, wherever spread, the book of Man;
For these he goes, self-banished from his hearth,
And wrings the hearts of all he loves on earth.

Yet say, shall not new joy those hearts inspire,
When, grouping round the future winter fire,
To hear the wonders of the world they burn,
And lose his absence in his glad return?—
Return?—alas! he shall return no more,
To bless his own sweet home, his own proud shore.
Look once again—cold in his cabin now,
Death's finger-mark is on his pallid brow;
No wife stood by, her patient watch to keep,
To smile on him, then turn away to weep;
Kind woman's place rough mariners supplied,
And shared the wanderer's blessing when he died.
Wrapped in the raiment that it long must wear,
His body to the deck they slowly bear;
Even there the spirit that I sing is true,
The crew look on with sad, but curious view;
The setting sun flings round his farewell rays,
O'er the broad ocean not a ripple plays;
How eloquent, how awful, in its power,
The silent lecture of death's sabbath-hour
One voice that silence breaks—the prayer is said,
And the last rite man pays to man is paid;
The plashing waters mark his resting-place,
And fold him round in one long, cold embrace;
Bright bubbles for a moment sparkle o'er,
Then break, to be, like him, beheld no more;
Down, countless fathoms down, he sinks to sleep,
With all the nameless shapes that haunt the deep.

THE BROTHERS.

We are but two—the others sleep
  Through Death's untroubled night;
We are but two—O, let us keep
  The link that binds us bright!

Heart leaps to heart—the sacred flood
  That warms us is the same;
That good old man—his honest blood
  Alike we fondly claim.

We in one mother's arms were locked—
  Long be her love repaid;
In the same cradle we were rocked,
  Round the same hearth we played.

Our boyish sports were all the same,
  Each little joy and woe;—
Let manhood keep alive the flame,
  Lit up so long ago.

We are but two—be that the band
  To hold us till we die;
Shoulder to shoulder let us stand,
  Till side by side we lie.

THE WINGED WORSHIPPERS.

Addressed to two Swallows that flew into the Chauncey Place Church during Divine Service.

    Gay, guiltless pair,
What seek ye from the fields of heaven?
    Ye have no need of prayer,
Ye have no sins to be forgiven.

    Why perch ye here,
Where mortals to their Maker bend?
    Can your pure spirits fear
The God ye never could offend?

    Ye never knew
The crimes for which we come to weep.
    Penance is not for you,
Blessed wanderers of the *upper deep*.

    To you 't is given
To wake sweet Nature's untaught lays;
    Beneath the arch of heaven
To chirp away a life of praise.

    Then spread each wing,
Far, far above, o'er the lakes and lands,
    And join the choirs that sing
In yon blue dome not reared with hands.

    Or, if ye stay,
To note the consecrated hour,
    Teach me the airy way,
And let me try your envied power.

    Above the crowd,
On upward wings could I but fly,
    I'd bathe in yon bright cloud,
And seek the stars that gem the sky.

    'Twere Heaven indeed
Through fields of trackless light to soar.
    On Nature's charms to feed,
And Nature's own great God adore.

Charles James Sprague, a son of the preceding, has also written verses in a delicate vein of sentiment. One of these is entitled—

THE EMPTY HOUSE.

"This house to let!"—so long the placard said,
  I went across to see
If it were dull, or dark, or comfortless,
  Or what the cause could be.

The parlor was a pleasant little room;
  The chambers snug and light,
The kitchen was quite neat and cheerful too,
  Although 'twas almost night.

My mind was somewhat in a thoughtful mood,
  So on a broken chair,
I sat me down to moralize awhile
  Upon the silence there.

How many changing scenes of life, thought I,
  This solitude recalls!
Joy's ringing laugh and sorrow's smothered moan,
  Have echoed from these walls!

Here in this parlor, jovial friends have met
  On many a winter's night!
Ripe ale has foamed, and this old rusty grate
  Sent forth a cheerful light.

Here stood the sofa, whereupon has wooed
  Some young and loving pair!
Here hung the clock that timed the last caress,
  And kiss upon the stair!

These chambers might relate a varied tale,
  Could the dumb walls find breath;
Of healthful slumber, and of wakeful pain—
  The birth-cry and the death.

Some crusty bachelor has here, perhaps,
  Crept grumbling into bed;
Some phrensied Caudle desperately sought
  To hide his aching head.

Some modest girl has here unrobed the charms
  Too pure for vulgar view;
Some bride has tasted here the sweets of love,—
  And curtain lectures, too.

This little studio has seen the toil
  Of some poor poet's brain,
His morn of hope, his disappointed day,
  And bitter night of pain.

Or else some well paid preacher has wrought out
  His hundredth paraphrase;
Or some old bookworm trimmed his lamp, to read
  The tale of other days.

And what are they to whom this was a home?
  How wide have they been cast,
Who gathered here around the social board,
  And sported in days past?

How many distant memories have turned
  To this deserted spot!
Recalling errors and reviving joys
  That cannot be forgot!

Young love may here have heaved its dying sigh,
  When angry words were spoken;
Domestic tyranny may here have reigned,
  And tender hearts have broken.

Perchance some mother, as she passes by,
  May cast a lingering gaze
Upon the scene of many a happier hour,
  The home of her young days.

And what are they who next will fill this void
  With busy, noisy life?
Will this become a home of happy peace,
  Or one of wretched strife?

In sober thought, I left the silent house.
  And gladly sought my own;
And when I passed next week, upon the door
  I saw the name of—Brown.

LYDIA H. SIGOURNEY.

Lydia Huntley, the daughter and only child of Ezekiel Huntley and Sophia Wentworth, was born at Norwich, Conn., September 1, 1791. Her father, who bore a part in the war of the Revolution, was a man of worth and benevolence. His wife possessed those well balanced, unobtrusive virtues of character which marked the New England lady of the olden time.

Among the happiest influences attending the childhood of their daughter, was the cultivated society of Madam Lathrop, the widow of Dr. Daniel Lathrop, and the daughter of the Hon. John Talcott, of Hartford, who held for a succession of years the office of Governor of Connecticut. Mr. Huntley, having charge of her estate, resided with his separate family under her roof, and in that fine old mansion their child was born. Her precocity was exhibited in reading fluently at the age of three, and composing simple verses at seven, smooth in rhythm, and of an invariable religious sentiment. As she grew older, she profited by the society of the distinguished visitors who sought the hospitable home; and received in addition every advantage of education which could then be obtained.

When Miss Huntley was fourteen, she had the misfortune to lose her venerable friend, who died at the ripe age of eighty-nine. She continued her studies until her nineteenth year, when she put into execution a plan she had long contemplated, of engaging in the work of instruction. Associating herself with her most intimate friend, Miss Ann Maria Hyde, who sympathized warmly in her scheme, a school was opened for young ladies, and conducted with great success for two years.

In 1814 Miss Huntley was induced to commence a select school at Hartford, under the auspices of influential relatives of her early friend, Mrs. Lathrop. Removing to that city, she became an inmate in the mansion of Mrs. Wadsworth, the widow of Colonel Jeremiah Wadsworth, a lady of high intellectual and moral worth. It was at the suggestion, and under the auspices of a son of this lady, Daniel Wadsworth, Esq., who had known Miss Huntley from her infancy, that a selection from her writings appeared in 1815. *Moral Pieces in Prose and Verse*, the title of Miss Huntley's volume, affords a good indication to its contents, almost all of the short poems which it contains having a direct moral purpose in view. The prose essays are introduced by the remark, that they were addressed to "a number of young ladies under her care," and the writer, throughout the volume, seems to have had her vocation of teacher in view. A poem on General St. Clair, "neglected and forgotten by his country, poor and in obscurity, on one of the Alleghany mountains," shows the sympathy with patriotic and national topics which has characterized her entire literary career. The volume was well received, and led to the author's engagement as a contributor to various periodicals.

In the summer of 1819 Miss Huntley became the wife of Mr. Charles Sigourney, a thoroughly educated and accomplished merchant of Hartford. They removed to a beautiful rural residence overlooking the city, where they resided for nearly twenty years.

Residence of Mrs. Sigourney.

In 1822 Mrs. Sigourney published *Traits of the Aborigines*, an historical poem, in five cantos. A collection of her miscellaneous poems was made about the same time in London, under the title of *Lays from the West*. In 1824 she published a volume in prose, *A Sketch of Connecticut Forty Years Since*. These were followed in rapid succession by *Letters to Young Ladies* and *Letters to Mothers*, a collection of poems* and of prose tales, and *Poetry for Children*. In 1836 *Zinzendorff and Other Poems*† appeared. The opening and chief production of the collection introduces us to the beautiful vale of Wyoming, and after an eloquent tribute to its scenery and historic fame, to the missionary Zinzendorff, doubly noble by ancestral rank and self-sacrificing labor, engaged in his missionary exertions among the Indians. We meet him striving to administer consolation by the couch of the dying chief; beneath the wide-spreading elm addressing the multitude on the subject of his mission, the welfare of their souls; at his quiet devotions in his tent, watched by assassins who shrank back from their purpose as they saw the rattlesnake glide past his feet unharming and unharmed, so calm and absorbed was the good man in his duty, the messengers of death returning to the grim savage prophet who had sent them on their errand, with the reply, that the stranger was a god. The poem closes with the departure of Zinzendorff at a later period from the infant city of Philadelphia, and an eloquent tribute to missionary labor, combined with an exhortation to Christian union.

The remaining poems are descriptive of natural scenery, commemorative of departed friends, versifications of scripture narratives, or inculcative of scripture truth. A warm sympathy with missionary effort, and with philanthropic labor of every description, is manifest in all.

In 1841 *Pocahontas and Other Poems*‡ appeared. The Pocahontas is one of the longest (extending to fifty-six stanzas of nine lines each) and also most successful of the author's productions. It opens with a beautiful picture of the vague and shadowy repose of nature, which the imagination conceives as the condition of the New World prior to the possession of its shores by the Eastern voyagers. We have then presented the landing at Jamestown, and the worship in the church quickly raised by the pious hands of the colonists. The music which formed a part of their daily service of common prayer attracts the ear of the Indian, and thus naturally and beautifully brings Powhatan and his daughter on the scene. The rescue of Captain Smith is but slightly alluded to, the writer preferring to dwell upon the less hackneyed if not equally picturesque scenes before her, in the life of her heroine. We have her visit of warning to the English, her baptism, reception in England, marriage, quiet domestic life, and early death, all presented in an animated and sympathetic manner, frequently interrupted by passages of reflection in Mrs. Sigourney's best vein. The remaining poems are similar in character to the contents of the volumes already noticed.

Pleasant Memories of Pleasant Lands, published in 1842,* is a volume of recollections in prose and poetry, of famous and picturesque scenes visited, and of hospitalities received during an European tour in 1840. The greater portion of the "Memories" are devoted to England and Scotland. The poems are descriptive, reflective, and occasionally in a sportive vein. During this sojourn in Europe, two volumes of Mrs. Sigourney's poems were published in London. Among the

gifts and tokens of kindness which greeted the author from various distinguished persons, was a splendid diamond bracelet from the Queen of the French.

Myrtis, with other Etchings and Sketches, ap-

* Philadelphia, 1834, 12mo., pp. 288.
† New York, 12mo., pp. 300.
‡ New York, 12mo., pp. 284.

* 12mo., pp. 368.

peared in 1846. In 1848 a choice edition of the author's miscellaneous poems was published, with illustrations from the pencil of Darley. In 1850, the death of her only son, and, with the exception of a daughter, only child, a youth of much promise, at the early age of nineteen, was followed by the publication of *The Faded Hope*, a touching and beautiful memento of her severe bereavement. Mrs. Sigourney has since published, *The Western Home, and Other Poems*, and a graceful volume of prose sketches entitled, *Past Meridian*.

Mrs. Sigourney has been one of the most voluminous of American female writers, having published from forty to fifty different volumes.*

Her most successful efforts are her occasional poems, which abound in passages of earnest, well expressed thought, and exhibit in their graver moods a pathos combined with hopeful resignation, characteristic of the mind trained by exercise in self-knowledge and self-control. They possess energy and variety. Mrs. Sigourney's wide and earnest sympathy with all topics of friendship and philanthropy is always at the service of these interests, while her command of versification enables her to present them with ease and fluency:

INDIAN NAMES.

"How can the red men be forgotten, while so many of our states and territories, bays, lakes, and rivers, are indelibly stamped by names of their giving?"

Ye say they all have passed away,
  That noble race and brave,
That their light canoes have vanished
  From off the crested wave;
That 'mid the forests where they roamed
  There rings no hunter's shout,
But their name is on your waters,
  Ye may not wash it out.

'Tis where Ontario's billow
  Like Ocean's surge is curled,
Where strong Niagara's thunders wake
  The echo of the world.
Where red Missouri bringeth
  Rich tribute from the west,
And Rappahannock sweetly sleeps
  On green Virginia's breast.

Ye say their cone-like cabins,
  That clustered o'er the vale,
Have fled away like withered leaves,
  Before the autumn gale,
But their memory liveth on your hills,
  Their baptism on your shore,
Your everlasting rivers speak
  Their dialect of yore.

Old Massachusetts wears it,
  Within her lordly crown,
And broad Ohio bears it,
  Amid his young renown;
Connecticut hath wreathed it
  Where her quiet foliage waves,
And bold Kentucky breathed it hoarse
  Through all her ancient caves.

Wachuset hides its lingering voise
  Within his rocky heart,
And Alleghany graves its tone
  Throughout his lofty chart;
Monadnock on his forehead hoar
  Doth seal the sacred trust,
Your mountains build their monument
  Though ye destroy their dust.

Ye call these red-browed brethren
  The insects of an hour,
Crushed like the noteless worm amid
  The regions of their power;
Ye drive them from their fathers' lands,
  Ye break of faith the seal,
But can ye from the court of Heaven
  Exclude their last appeal?

Ye see their unresisting tribes,
  With toilsome step and slow,
On through the trackless desert pass,
  A caravan of woe;
Think ye the Eternal's ear is deaf?
  His sleepless vision dim?
Think ye the *soul's blood* may not cry
  From that far land to him?

POETRY.

Morn on her rosy couch awoke,
  Enchantment led the hour,
And mirth and music drank the dews
  That freshened Beauty's flower,
Then from her bower of deep delight,
  I heard a young girl sing,
"Oh, speak no ill of poetry,
  For 'tis a holy thing."

The sun in noon-day heat rose high,
  And on with heaving breast,
I saw a weary pilgrim toil
  Unpitied and unblest,
Yet still in trembling measures flowed
  Forth from a broken string,
"Oh, speak no ill of poetry,
  For 'tis a holy thing."

'Twas night, and Death the curtains drew,
  'Mid agony severe,
While there a willing spirit went
  Home to a glorious sphere,
Yet still it sighed, even when was spread
  The waiting Angel's wing,
"Oh, speak no ill of poetry,
  For 'tis a holy thing."

JAMESTOWN CHURCH.

Yet, 'mid their cares, one hallowed dome they reared,
  To nurse devotion's consecrated flame;
And there a wondering world of forests heard,
  First borne in solemn chant, Jehovah's name;
First temple to his service, refuge dear
From strong affliction and the alien's tear,
  How swelled the sacred song, in glad acclaim;

* The following is a complete list of the titles of Mrs. Sigourney's works, in the order of their publication:—Moral Pieces in Prose and Verse; 1815. Biography and Writings of A. M. Hyde; 1816. Traits of the Aborigines: a Poem; 1822. Sketch of Connecticut; 1824. Poems; 1827. Biography of Females; 1829. Biography of Pious Persons; 1832. Evening Readings in History. Letters to Young Ladies. Memoir of Phebe Hammond. How to be Happy; 1833. Sketches and Tales. Poetry for Children. Select Poems. Tales and Essays for Children. Zinzendorff and Other Poems; 1834. History of Marcus Aurelius Antoninus; 1835. Olive Buds; 1836. Girl's Reading Book. Letters to Mothers; 1838. Boy's Reading Book; 1839. Religious Poems, Religious Souvenir, an annual, edited by Mrs. Sigourney, for 1839 and 1840. Pocahontas and Other Poems; 1841. Pleasant Memories of Pleasant Lands. Poems; 1842. Child's Book. Scenes in My Native Land; 1844. Poems for the Sea. Voice of Flowers. The Lovely Sisters; 1845. Myrtis and Other Sketches. Weeping Willow; 1846. Water Drops; 1847. Illustrated Poems; 1848. Whisper to a Bride; 1849. Letters to Pupils; 1850. Olive Leaves. Examples of Life and Death; 1851. The Faded Hope. Memoir of Mrs. Harriet Newell Cook; 1852. The Western Home and Other Poems. Past Meridian. Sayings of the Little Ones, and Poems for their Mothers; 1854.

England, sweet mother! many a fervent prayer
There poured its praise to Heaven for all thy love and care.

And they who 'neath the vaulted roof had bowed
Of some proud minster of the olden time,
Or where the vast cathedral towards the cloud
Reared its dark pile in symmetry sublime,
While through the storied pane the sunbeam played,
Tinting the pavement with a glorious shade,
Now breathed from humblest fane their ancient chime:
And learned they not, His presence sure might dwell
With every seeking soul, though bowed in lowliest cell?

Yet not quite unadorned their house of prayer:
The fragrant offspring of the genial morn
They duly brought; and fondly offered there
The bud that trembles ere the rose is born,
The blue clematis, and the jasmine pale,
The scarlet woodbine, waving in the gale,
The rhododendron, and the snowy thorn,
The rich magnolia, with its foliage fair,
High priestess of the flowers, whose censer fills the air.

Might not such incense please thee, Lord of love?
Thou, who with bounteous hand dost deign to show
Some foretaste of thy Paradise above,
To cheer the way-worn pilgrim here below?
Bidd'st thou 'mid parching sands the flow'ret meek
Strike its frail root and raise its tinted cheek,
And the slight pine defy the arctic snow,
That even the skeptic's frozen eye may see
On Nature's beauteous page what lines she writes of Thee?

What groups, at Sabbath morn, were hither led!
Dejected men, with disappointed frown,
Spoiled youths, the parents' darling and their dread,
From castles in the air hurled ruthless down,
The sea-bronzed mariner, the warrior brave,
The keen gold-gatherer, grasping as the grave;
Oft, 'mid these mouldering walls, which nettles crown,
Stern breasts have locked their purpose and been still,
And contrite spirits knelt, to learn their Maker's will.

Here, in his surplice white, the pastor stood,
A holy man, of countenance serene,
Who, 'mid the quaking earth or fiery flood
Unmoved, in truth's own panoply, had been
A fair example of his own pure creed;
Patient of error, pitiful to need,
Persuasive wisdom in his thoughtful mien,
And in that Teacher's heavenly meekness blessed,
Who laved his followers' feet with towel-girded vest.

Music upon the breeze! the savage stays
His flying arrow as the strain goes by;
He starts! he listens! lost in deep amaze,
Breath half-suppressed, and lightning in his eye.
Have the clouds spoken? Do the spirits rise
From his dead fathers' graves, with wildering melodies?
Oft doth he muse, 'neath midnight's solemn sky,
On those deep tones, which, rising o'er the sod,
Bore forth, from hill to hill, the white man's hymn to God.

LIFE'S EVENING.

"Abide with us, for it is now evening, and the day of life is far spent."

BISHOP ANDREWS.

The bright and blooming morn of youth
Hath faded from the sky,
And the fresh garlands of our hope
Are withered, sere, and dry;
O Thou, whose being hath no end,
Whose years can ne'er decay,
Whose strength and wisdom are our trust,
Abide with us, we pray.

Behold the noonday sun of life
Doth seek its western bound,
And fast the lengthening shadows cast
A heavier gloom around,
And all the glow-worm lamps are dead,
That, kindling round our way,
Gave fickle promises of joy—
Abide with us, we pray.

Dim eve draws on, and many a friend
Our early path that blessed,
Wrapped in the cerements of the tomb,
Have laid them down to rest;
But Thou, the Everlasting Friend,
Whose Spirit's glorious ray
Can gild the dreary vale of death,
Abide with us, we pray.

THE EARLY BLUE-BIRD.

Blue-bird! on yon leafless tree,
Dost thou carol thus to me,
"Spring is coming! Spring is here!"
Say'st thou so, my birdie dear?
What is that in misty shroud
Stealing from the darkened cloud?
Lo! the snow-flake's gathering mound
Settles o'er the whitened ground,
Yet thou singest, blithe and clear,
"Spring is coming! Spring is here!"

Strik'st thou not too bold a strain?
Winds are piping o'er the plain,
Clouds are sweeping o'er the sky,
With a black and threatening eye;
Urchins by the frozen rill
Wrap their mantles closer still;
Yon poor man, with doublet old,
Doth he shiver at the cold?
Hath he not a nose of blue?
Tell me, birdling—tell me true?

Spring's a maid of mirth and glee,
Rosy wreaths and revelry;
Hast thou wooed some winged love
To a nest in verdant grove?
Sung to her of greenwood bower,
Sunny skies that never lower?
Lured her with thy promise fair,
Of a lot that ne'er knows care?
Prithee, bird in coat of blue,
Though a lover—tell her true.

Ask her, if when storms are long,
She can sing a cheerful song?
When the rude winds rock the tree,
If she'll closer cling to thee?
Then, the blasts that sweep the sky,
Unappalled shall pass thee by;
Though thy curtained chamber show,
Siftings of untimely snow,
Warm and glad thy heart shall be,
Love shall make it spring for thee.

TALK WITH THE SEA.

I said with a moan, as I roamed alone,
By the side of the solemn sea,—
"Oh cast at my feet which thy billows meet
Some token to comfort me.
'Mid thy surges cold, a ring of gold
I have lost, with an amethyst bright,
Thou hast locked it so long, in thy casket strong,
That the rust must have quenched its light.

"Send a gift, I pray, on thy sheeted spray,
To solace my drooping mind,
For I'm sad and grieve, and ere long must leave
This rolling globe behind."
Then the Sea answered, "Spoils are mine,
From many an argosy,
And pearl-drops sleep in my bosom deep,
But naught have I there for thee!"

"When I mused before, on this rock-bound shore,
The beautiful walked with me,
She hath gone to her rest in the churchyard's breast
Since I saw thee last, thou sea!
Restore! restore! the smile she wore,
When her cheek to mine was pressed,
Give back the voice of the fervent soul
That could lighten the darkest breast!"

But the haughty Sea, in its majesty
Swept onward as before,
Though a surge in wrath from its rocky path,
Shrieked out to the sounding shore—
"Thou hast asked of our king, a harder thing
Than mortal e'er claimed before,
For never the wealth of a loving heart,
Could Ocean or Earth restore."

JONATHAN MAYHEW WAINWRIGHT.

J. M. WAINWRIGHT was born at Liverpool, England, February 24, 1792. His father, an Englishman by birth, had settled in America after the Revolution and married a daughter of Dr. Mayhew, the celebrated clergyman in Boston of that era. His residence in England, at the time of his son's birth, was not permanent, and the family not long after returned to America. The future Bishop graduated at Harvard in 1812, and subsequently was Tutor of Rhetoric and Oratory in that Institution. He early chose the Ministry of the Episcopal Church as his calling. When minister at Hartford, Ct., in 1819, he published *Chants, adapted to the Hymns in the Morning and Evening Service of the Protestant Episcopal Church*, and afterwards, in 1828, issued a volume of *Music of the Church*, and again, in 1851, in conjunction with Dr. Muhlenberg, *The Choir and Family Psalter;* a collection of the Psalms of David, with the Canticles of the Morning and Evening Prayer of the Episcopal service, arranged for chanting. He was always a devoted lover of music. When Malibran visited America, she sang on several occasions in the choir of Grace Church, with which Dr. Wainwright was long connected as pastor, in New York. His employments in the official duties of his church were various. He left New York for a time to be Rector of Trinity Church, in Boston. When he was chosen Provisional Bishop of New York in 1852, he was connected with Trinity Parish in the city. He would have been elected to that office in the previous year had he not cast his own vote against himself. He was indefatigable in the duties of his Bishopric during the severe heats of 1854, and in the autumn of that year, September 21, he died, prostrated by an attack of severe remittent fever. His chief literary works were two volumes of descriptive foreign travel, published in 1850 and the following year, after his return from a tour to the East. They bear the titles, *The Pathways and Abiding Places of Our Lord, illustrated in the Journal of a Tour through the Land of Promise and the Land of Bondage; its Ancient Monuments and Present Condition, being the Journal of a Tour in Egypt.* The style is pleasing and flowing, and the devotional sentiment uniformly maintained. Dr. W. also edited for Messrs. Appleton two illustrated volumes, *The Women of the Bible*, and *Our Saviour with Prophets and Apostles.*

Dr. Wainwright was engaged in a defence of Episcopacy, in a controversy with the Rev. Dr. Potts of the Presbyterian Church of New York, which grew out of a remark let fall by Rufus Choate, at the annual celebration of the New England Society, in New York, in 1843, in which the orator complimented a people who had planted "a state without a king, and a church without a bishop." At the dinner which followed, Dr. Wainwright, an invited guest, took exception to the saying, and was challenged to the controversy by Dr. Potts.

The discourses published by Dr. W. were few. In 1829 he published a thin octavo of *Sermons on Religious Education and Filial Duty.* His social influence was great. Courtly and easy in his manners, and taking part in the active interests of the day, he was universally known, and a general favorite in the city in which he resided. He assisted in the formation of the University of the city of New York. His reading in the Church services was much admired, his voice being finely modulated, with a delicate emphasis. As a preacher his style was finished in an ample rhetorical manner.

EDWIN C. HOLLAND.

EDWIN C. HOLLAND, a lawyer of Charleston, S. C., published in 1814 a volume of *Odes, Naval Songs*, and other occasional Poems, suggested for the most part by the war with England pending during their first publication in the Port Folio. His style is fluent, and occasionally somewhat too ornate and grandiloquent. One of the most spirited compositions is his prize poem—

THE PILLAR OF GLORY.

Hail to the heroes whose triumphs have brightened
The darkness which shrouded America's name;
Long shall their valour in battle that lightened,
Live in the brilliant escutcheons of fame:
Dark where the torrents flow,
And the rude tempests blow,
The stormy clad spirit of Albion raves;
Long shall she mourn the day,
When in the vengeful fray,
Liberty walked like a god on the waves.

The ocean, ye chiefs, (the region of glory,
Where fortune has destined Columbia to reign,)
Gleams with the halo and lustre of story,
That curl round the waves as the scene of her fame:
There, on its raging tide,
Shall her proud navy ride,
The bulwark of Freedom, protected by Heaven;

There shall her haughty foe
Bow to her prowess low,
There shall renown to her heroes be given.

The pillar of glory, the sea that enlightens,
Shall last till eternity rocks on its base;
The splendour of Fame, its waters that brightens,
Shall light the footsteps of Time in his race:
Wide o'er the stormy deep,
Where the rude surges sweep,
Its lustre shall circle the brows of the brave;
Honour shall give it light,
Triumph shall keep it bright,
Long as in battle we meet on the wave.

Already the storm of contention has hurled,
From the grasp of Old England, the trident of war;
The beams of our stars have illumined the world,
Unfurled our standard beats proud in the air:
Wild glares the eagle's eye,
Swift as he cuts the sky,
Marking the wake where our heroes advance;
Compassed with rays of light,
Hovers he o'er the fight;
Albion is heartless, and stoops to his glance.

WILLIAM H. TIMROD

WAS born in Charleston, South Carolina, in 1792. In straitened circumstances and of a limited education, and while following the trade of a mechanic, he wrote verses which were received with favor. His conversational abilities are also remembered by his friends with pleasure. In the year 1836 he went to St. Augustine as the captain of a militia corps of Charleston, which had volunteered to garrison that town for a certain period against the attacks of the Indians. In this expedition he contracted, from exposure, a disease which resulted in his death two years afterwards.

TO HARRY.

Harry! my little blue-eyed boy!
I love to hear thee playing near,
There's music in thy shouts of joy
To a fond father's ear.

I love to see the lines of mirth
Mantle thy cheek and forehead fair,
As if all pleasures of the earth
Had met to revel there.

For gazing on thee do I sigh
That these most happy hours will flee,
And thy full share of misery
Must fall in life to thee.

There is no lasting grief below,
My Harry, that flows not from guilt—
Thou can'st not read my meaning now,
In after times thou wilt.

Thou'lt read it when the churchyard clay
Shall lie upon thy father's breast,
And he, though dead, will point the way
Thou shalt be always blest.

They'll tell thee this terrestrial ball,
To man for his enjoyment given,
Is but a state of sinful thrall
To keep the soul from Heaven.

My boy! the verdure-crowned hills,
The vales where flowers innumerous blow,
The music of ten thousand rills,
Will tell thee 't is not so.

God is no tyrant who would spread
Unnumbered dainties to the eyes,
Yet teach the hungering child to dread
That touching them, he dies.

No! all can do his creatures good
He scatters round with hand profuse—
The only precept understood—
"Enjoy, but not abuse."

Henry Timrod, the son of the preceding, is a resident of the city of Charleston. His verses, which keep the promise of his father's reputation, have usually appeared in the *Southern Literary Messenger* with the signature "Aglaus."

THE PAST—A FRAGMENT.

To-day's most trivial act may hold the seed
Of future fruitfulness, or future dearth—
Oh, cherish always every word and deed,
The simplest record of thyself has worth.

If thou hast ever slighted one old thought,
Beware lest Grief enforce the truth at last—
The time must come wherein thou shalt be taught
The value and the beauty of the *Past*.

Not merely as a Warner and a Guide,
"A voice behind thee" sounding to the strife—
But something never to be put aside,
A part and parcel of thy present life.

Not as a distant and a darkened sky
Through which the stars peep, and the moonbeams glow—
But a surrounding atmosphere whereby
We live and breathe, sustained 'mid pain and woe.

A Fairy-land, where joy and sorrow kiss—
Each still to each corrective and relief—
Where dim delights are brightened into bliss,
And nothing wholly perishes but grief.

Ah me! not dies—no more than spirit dies—
But in a change like death is clothed with wings—
A serious angel with entranced eyes
Looking to far off and celestial things.

JOHN HOWARD PAYNE.

THE ancestors of JOHN HOWARD PAYNE were men of eminence. His paternal grandfather was a military officer and member of the Provincial Assembly of Massachusetts; and Dr. Osborn, the author of the celebrated whaling song, and Judge Paine, one of the signers of the Declaration of Independence, were of the family. His father was educated as a physician under General Warren, but soon abandoned the profession, owing to the unsettled state of affairs caused by the Revolution, and became a teacher, a calling in which he attained high eminence. Mr. Payne was the child of his second wife, the daughter of a highly respected inhabitant of the ancient village of East Hampton, Long Island, where his tombstone bears the simple epitaph, "An Israelite, indeed, in whom there was no guile." The oft-repeated story is first told of him, that sending a present of cranberries to a friend in England, he received, with the news of their arrival, the information that the fruit "had all turned sour upon the way." Payne's father, after an unsuccessful mercantile venture, became a resident of East Hampton, and the principal of the Clinton Academy, an institution of high reputation throughout the island, which owed its foundation to the reputation of Mr. Payne as a teacher. He afterwards removed to New York, where John Howard Payne was born June 9, 1792. He was one of

the eldest of nine children—seven sons and two daughters. One of the latter shared to some extent in his precocious fame. At the age of fourteen, after eight days' study of the Latin language, she underwent an examination by the classical professors of Harvard College, and displayed a remarkable skill in construing and parsing. She was afterwards highly distinguished as an amateur artist, and her literary compositions, none of which have been published, and correspondence, were said, by some of the best authorities of the country, to have been "among the most favorable specimens of female genius existing in America." Soon after Payne's birth, his father accepted the charge of a new educational establishment in Boston, and the family removed to that city. Here our author first came before the public as the leader of a military association of schoolboys who paraded the streets, and became the town-talk. On one occasion of general parade, when drawn up in the common near the regular troops, they were formally invited into the ranks, and reviewed by the commanding officer, Major-General Elliott. We soon after hear of him on a scene which was a nearer approach to that of his future fame. His father was highly celebrated as an elocutionist. A nervous complaint, by which the son was incapacitated for two or three years from severe study, was supposed to be benefited by exercises of this character. The pupil showed a remarkable aptitude, and soon became a leader in the school exhibitions in soliloquy and dialogue. A Boston actor, fresh from the performances of Master Betty in London, whose reputation was then world-wide, was so struck with the ability of Master Payne, that he urged his father to allow him to bring out the youth on the stage as the young American Roscius. The offer, much to the chagrin of its subject, was declined. He made his debut, however, in literature, becoming a contributor to a juvenile paper called the Fly, which was published by Samuel Woodworth, from the office where he worked as a printer's boy.

At this period, William Osborn, Payne's eldest brother, a partner in the mercantile house of Forbes and Payne, died, and partly with a view of weaning him from the stage, the would-be Roscius was set to "cramp his genius" among the folios of the counting-house of Mr. Forbes, who continued the business of the late firm, in the hope that Payne might ultimately fill the deceased brother's place. He was, however, no sooner installed in the new post in New York, than he commenced the publication of a little periodical, entitled *The Thespian Mirror.* One "Criticus" demurred to some of its statements and opinions, and the announcement in the Evening Post, that his communication would appear in the next newspaper, brought a letter to the editor from his juvenile contemporary, who, fearful of the anger of his relations, who were ignorant of his publication, besought the senior not to allow his incognito to be broken. Mr. Coleman invited Payne to call upon him, naturally interested in a boy of thirteen, who was a brother editor, and, as he states in his paper of Jan. 24, 1806, was much pleased with the interview. "His answers," he says, "were such as to dispel all doubts as to any imposition, and I found that it required an effort on my part to keep up the conversation in as choice a style as his own." Mr. Coleman's object in making the incident public, in spite of Payne's objections, was to call attention to his remarkable merits, and to create an interest in his career. In this he was so successful, that a benevolent gentleman of this city, Mr. John E. Seaman, volunteered to defray the youth's expenses at Union College. The offer was gladly accepted, and Payne took his departure for Albany in a sloop, in company with his friend and kind adviser, Charles Brockden Brown. He kept a journal of the tour, of which the following poetical fragment is all that has been preserved:—

On the deck of the slow-sailing vessel, alone,
As I silently sat, all was mute as the grave;
It was night—and the moon mildly beautiful shone,
Lighting up with her soft smile the quivering wave.

So bewitchingly gentle and pure was its beam,
In tenderness watching o'er nature's repose,
That I likened its ray to Christianity's gleam,
When it mellows and soothes without chasing our woes.

And I felt such an exquisite mildness of sorrow,
While entranced by the tremulous glow of the deep,
That I longed to prevent the intrusion of morrow,
And stayed there for ever to wonder and weep.

At college he started a periodical, called *The Pastime*, which became very popular among the students. The busybodies, who had pestered him with their advice after Mr. Coleman's publication in New York, continued their favors to him at Schenectady, especially after the publication of a Fourth of July ode, which was composed by Payne, and sung by the students in one of the churches. The author, as a joke, published an article in one of the Albany papers, berating himself, after the manner of his critics, in round terms. It produced a sensation among his associates, many of whom turned the cold shoulder upon him. The affair came to an issue at a supper party, where an individual gave as a toast "The Critics of Albany," and was, in common with the other carpers, satisfactorily nonplussed by Payne's quietly rising and returning thanks.

Soon after Payne's establishment at college, he lost his mother. The effect of this calamity on his father, already much broken by disease, was such as to incapacitate him for attention to his affairs, which had become involved, and his bankruptcy speedily followed. In this juncture, the son insisted upon trying the stage as a means of support, and obtaining the consent of his patron and parent, made his first appearance at

The Park Theatre.

the Park Theatre as Young Norval on the evening of February 24, 1809, in his sixteenth year. The performance, like those of the entire engagement, was highly successful. A writer, who had seen Garrick and all the great actors since his day, said, "I have seen Master Payne in Douglas, Zaphna, Solim, and Octavian, and may truly say, I think him superior to Betty in all. There was one scene of his Zaphna, which exhibited more taste and sensibility than I have witnessed since the days of Garrick. He has astonished everybody."

From New York Payne went to Philadelphia, and afterwards to Boston, performing with great success in both cities. He also appeared at Baltimore, Richmond, and Charleston, where Henry Placide, afterwards the celebrated comedian of the Park Theatre, gained his first success by a capital imitation of his style of acting.

On his return to New York, after these engagements, Payne yielded to the wishes of his family by retiring from the stage, and started a circulating library and reading-room, the Athenæum, which he designed to expand into a great public institution. Soon after this, George Frederick Cooke arrived in America. Payne, of course, became acquainted with him, and was very kindly treated by the great tragedian, who urged him to try his fortune on the London stage. They appeared once at the Park Theatre together, Payne playing Edgar to Cooke's Lear. Other joint performances were planned, but evaded by Cooke, whose pride was hurt at "having a boy called in to support him." The Athenæum speculation proving unprofitable, he returned to the stage. While playing an engagement at Boston, his father died. He afterwards played in Philadelphia and Baltimore. During his stay in the latter city, the printing-office of his friend Hanson, an editor, was attacked by a mob during the absence of its proprietor. He offered his services, and rendered essential aid to the paper at the crisis, and Mr. Hanson not only publicly acknowledged his services, but exerted himself in aiding his young friend to obtain the means to visit Europe. By the liberality of a few gentlemen of Baltimore this was effected, and Payne sailed from New York on the seventeenth of January, 1813, intending to be absent but one year. His first experience of England, where he arrived in February, was a brief imprisonment in Liverpool, the mayor of that city having determined to act with rigor in the absence of instructions from government respecting aliens.

On arriving in London, he spent several weeks in sight-seeing before applying to the managers. By the influence of powerful persons to whom he brought letters, he obtained a hearing from Mr. Whitbread of Drury Lane, and appeared at that theatre as Douglas, the performance being announced on the bills as by a young gentleman, "his first appearance," it being deemed advisable to obtain an unbiassed verdict from the audience. The debut was successful, and he was announced in the bills of his next night as "Mr. Payne, from the theatres of New York and Philadelphia." After playing a triumphant engagement, he made the circuit of the provinces, and, upon his return to London, visited Paris principally for the purpose of seeing Talma, by whom he was most cordially received. Bonaparte returned from Elba soon after his arrival, and he consequently remained in Paris during the Hundred Days. He then repaired to London, taking with him a translation of a popular French melodrama, *The Maid and the Magpie*, which he had made as an exercise in the study of the language without any view to representation. He was asked to play at Drury Lane, but by the influence of Mr. Kinnaird, one of the committee of stockholders who then conducted the management, his reappearance was postponed until a more favorable period of the theatrical season. Happening to be questioned about the famous new piece in Paris, Payne produced his version, and it was read by Mr. Kinnaird, who was so much pleased that he proposed to the translator to return to Paris for the purpose of watching the French stage, and sending over adaptations of the best pieces for the Drury Lane management, regretting, at the same time, that having engaged a translation of *The Maid and the Magpie*, it was impossible to produce Mr. Payne's superior version. He accepted the proposal, but before his departure, Mr. Harris, the rival manager of Covent Garden, purchased his manuscript of *The Maid and the Magpie* for one hundred and fifty pounds. Soon after his arrival, he sent over the play of *Accusation*, so carefully prepared for the stage, that it was performed six days after its reception, and was successful. Payne remained steadily at work for some months, sending over translations and drafts for cash to meet the heavy expenses incurred by his agency; but finding that the first were not produced, and the second not paid, returned to London to settle matters. Here the contract was repudiated by the management, on the ground that it was made by Mr. Kinnaird in his private capacity, and not as a member of the committee. In the midst of the controversy, Harris, the rival manager, stepped in and engaged Payne for Covent Garden at a salary of £300 for the season, to appear occasionally in leading parts, and look after the literary interests of the theatre, further remuneration being secured in the event of original pieces or translations from his pen being produced. The arrangement lasted but one season, difficulties springing up in the company with regard to the distribution of parts. Payne was repeatedly announced to appear in the tragedy of Adelgitha by Monk Lewis, in connexion with Miss O'Neil, and Messrs. Young and Macready, and was naturally desirous of taking part in so strong a cast, but the performance was postponed, as the appointed evening approached, by the "indisposition" of one or another of his colleagues. Towards the close of the season he sprained his ankle, and so was prevented from appearing. On his recovery he was offered the parts in which Charles Kemble had appeared, a proposal which, not wishing to bring himself into direct comparison with an established favorite, and incur the charge of presumption from the public, he declined. This led to a rupture, and the close of the engagement with Harris.

Released from this charge, Payne devoted himself to a tragedy, which he had long planned, on the subject of *Brutus*. It was designed for, and accepted by Kean, and produced by him at Drury Lane, December 4, 1818, with a success unexampled for years. In the height of its popularity, the printer of the theatre made the author an offer for the copyright, which was accepted. It was printed with the greatest expedition, the manuscript being taken, page by page, from the prompter during the performance, to a cellar under the stage, where the author descending to correct the proofs, found to his surprise that august body, the Roman senate, busy, with their togas thrown over their shoulders, "setting type." The hurry necessitated a brief preface, but in it the author made a distinct avowal of his obligations to the plays on the same subject, no less than seven in number, which had preceded his. "I have had no hesitation," he says in it, "in adopting the conceptions and language of my predecessors, wherever they seemed likely to strengthen the plan which I had prescribed." The play was published, and in spite of the avowal we have quoted, the cry of plagiarism was raised. A long discussion of the question ensued. "Æschylus" and "Vindex" maintained a long and angry controversy in the Morning Post, and many other periodicals were similarly occupied. Payne had been too long before the public not to have made enemies. He was assailed on all sides. One of the very proprietors who were making money out of the piece, told him that the owners of Cumberland's play of the Sybil, one of the seven predecessors of Brutus, intended to bring an action for the invasion of the copyright, and that an injunction on the performance of the play by the government, on the ground of the dangerous democratic sentiments it contained, was anticipated.

He promptly disposed of these charges by notes, which produced emphatic disclaimers of the alleged designs by the publisher of Cumberland's works, and Sir William Scott, who was said to have suggested the injunction to his brother the Lord Chancellor.

The dramatist met with as harsh and unfair treatment within as without the theatre. The proceeds of the benefits, which were the stipulated sources of his remuneration, were reduced on various pretences; and the leading performer, whose popularity had received a powerful impulse from the run of the piece, presented a gold snuff-box to the stage-manager, but made no acknowledgment of his indebtedness to the author. At the suggestion of the actor, the dramatist wrote and submitted a second classical play, *Virginius*, which was laid aside in favor of one on the same subject by a competitor, whose production was damned the first night. Annoyed by these and similar mishaps, Mr. Payne leased Sadlers' Wells, a theatre then on the outskirts of the city, and became a manager. He produced several new pieces, and appeared himself with success, but the situation and previous character of the house, and the interruption of the performances by deaths which occurred in the royal family, were obstacles which he could not surmount, and he retired at the end of the season sadly out of pocket.

His next play was *Therese, or the Orphan of Geneva*, adapted from a French original, and produced by Elliston, who had succeeded the committee of Drury Lane as manager of that theatre. It was very successful, but the author's profits were impaired by the production of a pirated copy, taken down in shorthand during the performance of the original, at a minor theatre, and a rival version at Covent Garden.

Payne next went to Paris, in the interests of Elliston. Here he was visited by one Burroughs, who made a similar contract for the Surrey Theatre. Both proved bad paymasters, and Payne is said to have suffered much from actual want.

Meanwhile, Charles Kemble became manager of Covent Garden, and applied, like his predecessors and rivals, to Payne for aid. He offered the new manager a number of manuscripts for £230. The odd thirty was the value set opposite the piece afterwards called *Clari*. Kemble closed with the offer, and produced this piece, which, at his request, the author had converted into an opera. It made the fortune of every one prominently connected with it, except the usual exception in these cases—the author. It gained for Miss M. Tree (the elder sister of Mrs. Charles Kean), who first sang "Home, sweet Home," a wealthy husband, and filled the house and the treasury.

HOME, SWEET HOME.

'Mid pleasures and palaces though we may roam,
Still, be it ever so humble, there's no place like home;
A charm from the skies seems to hallow it there,
Which, go through the world, you'll not meet elsewhere.

Home, home,
Sweet home!
There's no place like home—
There's no place like home.

An exile from home, pleasure dazzles in vain,
Ah! give me my lowly thatched cottage again;
The birds singing sweetly, that came to my call—
Give me them, and that peace of mind, dearer than
all.
Home, home, &c.

Upwards of one hundred thousand copies of the song were estimated in 1832 to have been sold by the original publishers, whose profits, within two years after it was issued, are said to have amounted to two thousand guineas. It is known all over the world, and doubtless, years after its composition, saluted its author's ears in far off Tunis. He not only lost the twenty-five pounds which was to have been paid for the copyright on the twentieth night of performance, but was not even complimented with a copy of his own song by the publisher. Author and actor soon after made a great hit in *Charles the Second.* It became one of Kemble's most favorite parts. The author sold the copyright for fifty pounds, one quarter of the average price paid for a piece of its length.

Soon after this, Payne returned to London, on a visit to superintend the production of his version of a French opera, *La Dame Blanche*, and started a periodical called *The Opera Glass.* Its publication was interrupted by a long and severe illness. On his recovery he found Stephen Price, with whom he had had difficulties in the Young Roscius days at the Park, vice Elliston, bankrupt. Price still showed Payne the cold shoulder, and soon followed Elliston, with his pockets in a similar condition. Charles Kemble held on, but with almost as much ill success. These gloomy theatrical prospects led to Payne's return home, in August, 1832. Soon after his return he issued the prospectus of a periodical, with the fanciful title, *Jam Jehan Nima*, meaning *the Goblet wherein you may behold the Universe.* "It is scarcely necessary to add," says the prospectus, "that the allusion is to that famous cup, supposed to possess the strange property of representing in it the whole world, and all the things which were then doing,—and celebrated as Jami Jemsheed, the cup of Jemshud, a very ancient king of Persia, and which is said to have been discovered in digging the foundations of Persepolis, filled with the elixir of immortality." The work was to appear simultaneously in England and the United States, and be contributed to by the best authors of both countries; to be the organ of American opinion in Europe, and of correct views of Europe in America. It was to be published in weekly numbers, of thirty-two octavo pages, at an annual subscription price of ten dollars. The affair never, however, got beyond a prospectus of eight pages, of unusually magnificent promise even among the hopeful productions of its class.

He contributed, in 1838, to the recently established Democratic Review, a number of prose papers, one of which contains his pleasant picture of East Hampton. During this period, while travelling in the southern states, he was arrested by some over-zealous soldiers belonging to the forces raised against the Seminoles, as a sympathizer with the enemy, and was not released until some days after. His amusing account of the occurrence went the rounds of the newspapers of the time.

He not long after received the appointment of Consul at Tunis, where he remained a few years, and then returned to the United States. After an ineffectual solicitation for a diplomatic post more in accordance with his wishes, he accepted a re-appointment to Tunis. He died soon after, in 1852.

At the time of Payne's return, in 1832, two long and interesting articles on his career were published in the New York Mirror, from the pen of his friend Theodore S. Fay. We are indebted to these for our full account of Payne's experiences with the London managers, a curious chapter of literary history, which could not, without injury to its interest, have been compressed in closer limits.

Our portrait is from an original and very beautifully executed miniature by Wood, and represents the young Roscius about the period of his first histrionic triumphs.

ODE.

For the Thirty-First Anniversary of American Independence.

Written as a College Exercise.

When erst our sires their sails unfurled,
To brave the trackless sea,
They boldly sought an unknown world,
Determined to be free!
They saw their homes recede afar,
The pale blue hills diverge,
And, Liberty their guiding star,
They ploughed the swelling surge!

No splendid hope their wand'rings cheered,
No lust of wealth beguiled;—
They left the towers that plenty reared
To seek the desert wild;
The climes where proud luxuriance shone,
Exchanged for forests drear;
The splendour of a Tyrant's throne,
For honest Freedom here!

Though hungry wolves the nightly prowl
Around their log-hut took;
Though savages with hideous howl
Their wild-wood shelter shook;
Though tomahawks around them glared,—
To Fear could such hearts yield?
No! God, for whom they danger dared,
In danger was their shield!

When giant Power, with blood-stained crest,
Here grasped his gory lance,
And dared the warriors of the West
Embattled to advance,—
Our young COLUMBIA sprang, alone
(In God her only trust),
And humbled, with a sling and stone,
This monster to the dust!

Thus nobly rose our greater Rome,
Bright daughter of the skies,—
Of Liberty the hallowed home,
Whose turrets proudly rise,—
Whose sails now whiten every sea,
On every wave unfurled;
Formed to be happy, great, and free,
The Eden of the world!

Shall we, the sons of valiant sires,
Such glories tamely stain?
Shall these rich vales, these splendid spires,
E'er brook a monarch's reign?
No! If the Despot's iron hand
Must here a sceptre wave,
Razed be those glories from the land,
And be the land our grave!

THE TOMB OF GENIUS.

Where the chilling north wind howls,
Where the weeds so wildly wave,
Mourned by the weeping willow,
Washed by the beating billow,
Lies the youthful Poet's grave.

Beneath yon little eminence,
Marked by the grass-green turf,
The winding-sheet his form encloses,
On the cold rock his head reposes—
Near him foams the troubled surf!

"Roars around" his tomb "the ocean,"
Pensive sleeps the moon-beam there!
Naiads love to wreathe his urn—
Dryads thither hie to mourn—
Fairy music melts in air!

O'er his tomb the village virgins
Love to drop the tribute tear;
Stealing from the groves around,
Soft they tread the hallowed ground,
And scatter wild flowers o'er his bier.

By the cold earth mantled—
All alone—
Pale and lifeless lies his form:
Batters on his grave the storm:
Silent now his tuneful numbers,
Here the son of Genius slumbers:
Stranger! mark his burial-stone!

The author, in a note, regrets that he has not space to insert the music composed for these verses by Miss Eleanor Augusta Johnson, who, at the tender age of fourteen, has thrown into her valued complement to the poetry, a skill and expressiveness which, for one so young, may be regarded as little less than miraculous.

JAMES HALL

Was born in Philadelphia August 19, 1793, and commenced the study of law in that city in 1811. At this period he saw something of military life. In 1813 he was one of a company of volunteers, the Washington Guards, commanded by Condy Raguet, Esq., afterwards United States Minister to Brazil, who entered the service of the United States and spent several months in camp, on the Delaware, watching the motions of a British fleet, performing all the duties of soldiers. At the close of that year he was commissioned a Third Lieutenant of Artillery, in the Second Regiment, commanded by Colonel Winfield Scott, who about that time became a Brigadier-General.

In the spring of 1814 he marched to the frontier with a company of artillery commanded by Captain Thomas Biddle, and joined the army at Buffalo under General Brown, in which Scott, Ripley, and Porter were Brigadiers. In the battle of Chippewa he commanded a detachment from his company, and had a full share of that brilliant affair. He was in the battle of Lundy's Lane (or Bridgewater), at Niagara, the siege of Fort Erie, and all the hard fighting and severe service of that campaign, and was commended afterwards officially, as having rendered "brave and meritorious services."

At the close of the war, unwilling to be inactive, Mr. Hall went to Washington and solicited a Midshipman's warrant in the Navy, in the hope of going out in Decatur's squadron against the Algerines, but without success. Subsequently it was decided to send out with that expedition a bomb-vessel and some mortars to be used in the bombardment of Algiers, under the command of Major Archer of the artillery; and our author had the honor of being selected as one of four young officers who accompanied him. He sailed in September, 1815, from Boston in the United States Brig Enterprise, commanded by Lieutenant Lawrence Kearney, now the veteran Commodore. The war with Algiers was a short one, and after a brief, but to him most delightful cruise in the Mediterranean, he returned at the close of the same year and was stationed at Newport, Rhode Island, and afterwards at various other ports until 1818, when he resigned, having previously resumed the study of law at Pittsburgh, Pennsylvania, where he was then stationed, and been admitted to the bar.

In the spring of 1820, having no dependence but his own exertions, with great ardor and hopefulness of spirit, and energy of purpose, he resolved to go to a new country to practise his profession where he could rise with the growth of the population; but allured in fact by a romantic disposition, a thirst for adventure, and a desire to see the rough scenes of the frontier, he went to Illinois, then recently admitted into the Union as a State, and commenced practice at Shawneetown, and edited a weekly newspaper, called the *Illinois Gazette*, for which he wrote a great deal. The next winter he was appointed Circuit Attorney, that is public prosecutor for a circuit containing ten counties.

In a reminiscence of these journeyings, which were to supply the author with that practical knowledge of the people of the west, and the scenes of genial humor which abound in his pages, he remarks—"Courts were held in these counties twice a year, and they were so arranged as to time that after passing through one circuit we went directly to the adjoining one, and thus proceeded to some twenty counties in succession. Thus we were kept on horseback and travelling over a very wide region the greater part of our time. There was no other way to travel but on horseback. There were but few roads for carriages, and we travelled chiefly by bridle-paths, through uncultivated wilds, fording rivers, and sometimes swimming creeks, and occasionally 'camping out.' There were few taverns, and we ate and slept chiefly at the log cabins of the settlers. The office of prosecuting in such a country is no *sinecure*. Several of the counties in my circuit were bounded by the Ohio river, which separated them from Kentucky, and afforded facilities to rogues and ruffians to change their jurisdictions, which allured them to settle among us in great gangs, such as could often defy the arm of the law. We had whole settlements of counterfeiters or horse thieves with their sympathizers, where rogues could change names, or pass from house to house, so skilfully as to elude detection, and where, if detected, the whole population were ready to rise to the rescue. There were other settlements of sturdy honest fellows, the regular backwoodsmen, in which rogues were not tolerated. There was, therefore, a continual struggle between these parties, the honest people trying to expel the others by the terrors of the law, and when that mode failed, forming *regulating* companies and driving them out by force. To be a public prosecutor among such a people requires much discretion and no small degree of courage. When the contest breaks out into violence, when arms are used, and a little civil war takes place, there are aggressions on both sides, and he is to avoid making himself a party with either; when called upon to prosecute either he is denounced and often threatened, and it required calmness, self-possession, and sometimes courage to enable him to do his duty, preserving his self-respect and the public confidence."*

In these cases Mr. Hall was a rigorous prosecutor, never flinching from duty, and on some occasions turning out himself and aiding in the arrest of notorious and bold villains. He served in that office four years, and obtained also a large practice on the civil side of the court. He was then elected by the legislature Judge of the Circuit Court, the court having general original jurisdiction, civil and criminal. He presided in that court three years, when a change in the judiciary system took place, the circuit courts were abolished, and all the judges repealed out of office. At the same session of the legislature he was elected State Treasurer, and removed to Vandalia, the seat of government. This office he held four years, in connexion with an extensive law practice, and in connexion also with the editorship of the *Illinois Intelligencer*, a weekly newspaper, and of the *Illinois Monthly Magazine*, which he established, published, owned, edited, and for which he wrote nearly all the matter—tale, poem, history, criticism, gossip.

In 1833 Mr. Hall removed to Cincinnati, his present residence, having lived in Illinois twelve years. He has since 1836 been engaged in financial pursuits, having been at first the cashier of the Commercial Bank, and since 1853 the president of another institution bearing the same name.

The series of Mr. Hall's numerous publications commenced with his contributions to the Port Folio during the editorship of his brother, who took charge of that work. In 1820, when descending the Ohio, and afterwards during the early part of his residence in Illinois, Mr. Hall wrote a series of *Letters from the West*, which were published in the Port Folio. They were written in the character of a youth travelling for amusement, giving the rein to a lively fancy, and indulging a vein of levity and rather extravagant fun. They were intended to be anonymous, but having been carried by a friend to England, unexpectedly to the author appeared from the London press ascribed to "the Hon. Judge Hall" on the title-page. The English reviews had their sport out of the apparent incongruity. They acknowledged a certain sort of ability about it, and confessed that the author wrote very good English;

James Hall

but sneered at the levities, and asked the English public what they would think of a learned judge who should lay aside the wig and robe of office, and roam about the land in quest of "black eyes" and "rosy cheeks," dancing at the cabins of the peasantry, and "kissing the pretty girls." The *venerable* Illinois Judge they pronounced to be a "sly rogue," and wondered if the learned gentleman was as funny on the bench, &c. &c. The author never allowed the book to be republished.

Mr. Hall's subsequent literary productions may be classed under the heads of periodical literature, books written to exhibit the political and social character and statistics of the West, and an extensive series of works of fiction illustrating the romance, adventure, and humor of the region. In 1829 he edited and secured the publication of the *Western Souvenir*, in imitation of the elegant annuals then in vogue. Half of the matter was written by himself. Though the appearance of the work suffered from mechanical defects, its spirit was admitted, and as a novelty it was quite successful.

In October, 1830, Mr. Hall published the first number of the *Illinois Monthly Magazine* at Vandalia, which was also a novelty, and judging from the numbers before us, quite a creditable one. In the worth and elegance of its matter it would not be out of place now in any of the leading cities of the country. Then it was a free-will offering of time, enthusiasm, and money (for the work was sustained by the author's purse as well as pen), to the cause of social improvement and refinement in a virgin state, the resources of which were as yet all to be developed. It was continued for two years, and served well its liberal purposes. This work was followed by the *Western Monthly Magazine*, published at Cincinnati for three years from 1833 to 1835, and sustained by a large subscription. Like the former it was not only diligently edited but mostly written by Mr. Hall.

A work of considerable magnitude, in which Mr. Hall soon engaged, involved vast labor and

* Mr. Hall has given a pleasant sketch of this time and region in the preface to his revised edition of the Legends of the West, published by Putnam in 1853.

original research. In connexion with Col. Thomas L. M'Kenney he undertook to edit and write *A History and Biography of the Indians of North America*. The work, a costly one, was to be illustrated by a series of portraits taken at Washington by King, who had formed a gallery in the War Department of the various celebrated chiefs who visited the capital. It was proposed by Col. M'Kenney, who had been Commissioner for Indian Affairs, to publish one hundred and twenty portraits, with a memoir of each of the chieftains. The work appeared easy, but it was soon found sufficiently difficult to task the energies of Mr. Hall, upon whom the toil of composition fell, to the extent even of his accustomed diligence and pliant pen. The material which had been supposed to exist in official and other documents at hand had to be sought personally from agents of government, old territorial governors, and such original authorities as Governor Cass, General Harrison, and others. With the exception of a few facts from the expeditions of Long, Pike, and Schoolcraft, nothing was compiled from books. The testimony of actors and eye-witnesses was sought and sifted, so that the work is not only full of new and interesting facts but of a reliable character.

The expensive style of this publication, a copy costing one hundred and twenty dollars, has confined it to the public libraries or to the collections of wealthy persons. From the failure of the first publishers, the change of others, and the expense of the work, Messrs. M'Kenney and Hall, who were to have received half the profits, got little or nothing.

In 1835 Mr. Hall published at Philadelphia two volumes of *Sketches of History, Life, and Manners in the West*, and subsequently at Cincinnati, another pair of volumes entitled *The West, its Soil, Surface, and Productions; Its Navigation and Commerce*. The "Sketches" illustrate the social, the others the material characteristics of this important region.

During the canvass between General Harrison and Van Buren in 1836 Mr. Hall published a life of the former, the materials of which he had prepared for the Sketches of the West.* It is a polished and interesting history.

The several volumes of Mr. Hall's tales include the separate publications, *The Legends of the West; The Border Tales; The Soldier's Bride and other Tales; Harpes Head, a Legend of Kentucky; The Wilderness and the War Path*. Many of these first appeared in magazines and annuals. They are characterized by a certain amenity and ease of narrative, a poetic appreciation of the beauties of nature, and the gentler moods of the affections; while the author's pleasing narrative has softened the rudeness without abating the interest of the wild border strife. The Indian subjects are handled with peculiar delicacy; the kindly sentiment of the author dwelling on their virtues, while his imagination is enkindled by their spiritual legends. His style, pure in sentiment and expression, may be aptly compared with the calm, tranquil aspect of his own Ohio river, occasionally darkened by wild bordering woods, but oftener reflecting the beauty of the azure heaven.

Several of Mr. Hall's family have engaged in literature. His mother, Mrs. Sarah Hall, the daughter of Dr. John Ewing, wrote *Conversations on the Bible*, which were republished abroad, and which have passed through several editions. She was a contributor to the Port Folio from the commencement and during the editorship of her son. A volume of her writings was edited and published by Harrison Hall in 1833, with a prefatory memoir by Judge Hall. She was born October 30, 1760, and died April 8, 1830.

John E. Hall, her eldest son, was born December, 1783. He was educated at Princeton, read law with Judge Hopkinson, was admitted to practice in 1805, and removed to Baltimore. He published the *American Law Journal* in Philadelphia from 1808 to 1817. He was elected Professor of Rhetoric and Belles Lettres in the University of Maryland. He collected and arranged an edition of the British Spy, to which he contributed several letters much to the gratification of Wirt the author. When the Baltimore riot broke out in 1811, he was one of the party of Federalists who aided in defending Hanson's house, and was one of the nine thrown on a heap as killed. He left Baltimore soon afterwards, removing to Philadelphia, where he assumed the editorship of the Port Folio in 1806. The memoirs of Anacreon in that journal were from his pen. They were a reproduction on this thread of narrative of Grecian manners and customs, supposed to be written by Critias of Athens, and the author was stimulated to their composition by the approval of the poet Moore, who was then creating a sensation in the literary circles of Philadelphia. Mr. Hall was the author of the life prefixed to the poems of his friend Dr. John Shaw, published in Baltimore in 1810. In 1827 he edited with biographical and critical notes, *The Philadelphia Souvenir*, a collection of fugitive pieces from the press of that city. The editor's part is written with spirit. In the same year was published in Philadelphia in an octavo volume, *Memoirs of Eminent Persons, with Portraits and Fac-Similes, written and in part selected by the Editor of the Port Folio*. In consequence of his declining health the Port Folio was discontinued in 1827. He died June 11, 1829. His brother, Harrison Hall, publisher of the Port Folio, is the author of a work on Distilling, first published in 1815, which has received the commendation of Dr. Hare and other scientific men of the day.

Dr. Thomas Mifflin Hall, a younger brother, contributed poetry and some scientific articles to the Port Folio. In 1828 he embarked on board of a South American ship of war to which he was appointed surgeon. The vessel was never heard of after.

SOLITUDE.

And what is solitude? Is it the shade
  Where nameless terrors brood—
The lonely dell, or haunted glade,
By gloomy phantasy arrayed?
  This is not solitude.

For I have dared alone to tread,
  In boyhood's truant mood,

* A Memoir of the Public Services of William Henry Harrison of Ohio. Philadelphia.

Among the mansions of the dead
By night, when others all had fled—
  Yet felt not solitude.

And I have travelled far and wide,
  And dared by field and flood;
Have slept upon the mountain side,
Or slumbered on the ocean tide,
  And known no solitude.

O'er prairies where the wild flowers bloom,
  Or through the silent wood,
Where weeds o'ershade the traveller's tomb,
It oft has been my fate to roam—
  Yet not in solitude.

For hope was mine, and friends sincere,
  The kindred of my blood;
And I could think of objects dear,
And tender images would cheer
  The gloom of solitude.

But when the friends of youth are gone,
  And the strong ties of blood
And sympathy, are riven one by one,
The heart, bewildered and alone,
  Desponds in solitude.

Though crowds may smile, and pleasures gleam,
  To chase its gloomy mood,
To that lone heart the world doth seem,
An idle and a frightful dream
  Of hopeless solitude.

Do any feel for it? They have the will
  To do a seeming good:
But strangers' kindness hath no skill
To touch the deeply seated ill
  Of the heart's solitude.

PIERRE, THE FRENCH BARBER'S INDIAN ADVENTURE—FROM THE DARK MAID OF ILLINOIS.*

[*Pierre, who is the butt of the village, and is anxious to see the wonders of the wilderness, marries an Indian bride and proposes a stroll.*]

When our inclinations prompt us strongly to a particular line of conduct, it is easy to find reasons enough to turn the scale. Indeed, it is most usual to adopt a theory first, and then to seek out arguments to support it. Pierre could now find a host of reasons urging him to instant wedlock with the Illinois maiden. And not the least were the advantages which would accrue to Father Francis, to the church, and to the cause of civilization. When he should become a prince, he could take the venerable priest under his patronage, encourage the spread of the true faith, cause his subjects to be civilized, and induce them to dress like Christians and feed like rational beings. He longed, with all the zeal of a reformer, to see them powder their hair, and abstain from the savage practice of eating roasted puppies.

So he determined to marry the lady; and, having thus definitely settled the question, thought it would be proper to take the advice of his spiritual guide. Father Francis was shocked at the bare mention of the affair. He admonished Pierre of the sin of marrying a heathen, and of the wickedness of breaking his plighted faith; and assured him, in advance, that such misconduct would bring down upon him the severe displeasure of the church. Pierre thanked him with the most humble appearance of conviction, and forthwith proceeded to gratify his own inclination—believing that, in the affair of wedlock, he knew what was for his own good quite as well as a holy monk, who, to the best of his judgment, could know very little about the matter.

On the following morning the marriage took place, with no other ceremony than the delivery of the bride into the hands of her future husband. Pierre was as happy as bridegrooms usually are—for his companion was a slender, pretty girl, with a mild black eye and an agreeable countenance. They were conducted to a wigwam, and installed at once into the offices of husband and wife, and into the possession of their future mansion. The females of the village assembled, and practised a good many jokes at the expense of the young couple: and Pierre, as well to get rid of these as to improve the earliest opportunity of examining into the mineral treasures of the country, endeavored, by signs, to invite his partner to a stroll—intimating, at the same time, that he would be infinitely obliged to her if she would have the politeness to show him a gold mine or two. The girl signified her acquiescence, and presently stole away through the forest, followed by the enamored hair-dresser.

As soon as they were out of sight of the village, Pierre offered her his arm, but the arch girl darted away, laughing, and shaking her black tresses, which streamed in the air behind her, as she leaped over the logs and glided through the thickets. Pierre liked her none the less for this evidence of coquetry, but gaily pursued his beautiful bride, for whom he began to feel the highest admiration. Her figure was exquisitely moulded, and the exercise in which she was now engaged displayed its gracefulness to the greatest advantage. There was a novelty, too, in the adventure, which pleased the gay-hearted Frenchman; and away they ran, mutually amused and mutually satisfied with each other.

Pierre was an active young fellow, and, for a while, followed the beautiful savage with a creditable degree of speed; but, unaccustomed to the obstacles which impeded the way, he soon became fatigued. His companion slackened her pace when she found him lingering behind; and, when the thicket was more than usually intricate, kindly guided him through the most practicable places,—always, however, keeping out of his reach; and whenever he mended his pace, or showed an inclination to overtake her, she would dart away, looking back over her shoulder, laughing, and coquetting, and inviting him to follow. For a time this was amusing enough, and quite to the taste of the merry barber; but the afternoon was hot, the perspiration flowed copiously, and he began to doubt the expediency of having to catch a wife, or win even a gold mine, by the sweat of his brow—especially in a new country. Adventurers to newly discovered regions expect to get things easily; the fruits of labor may be found at home.

On they went in this manner, until Pierre, wearied out, was about to give up the pursuit of his light-heeled bride, when they reached a spot where the ground gradually ascended, until, all at once, they stood upon the edge of an elevated and extensive plain. Our traveller had heretofore obtained partial glimpses of the prairies, but now saw one of these vast plains, for the first time, in its breadth and grandeur. Its surface was gently uneven; and, as he happened to be placed on one of the highest swells, he looked over a boundless expanse, where not a single tree intercepted the prospect, or relieved the monotony. He strained his vision forward, but the plain was boundless—marking the curved line of its profile on the far distant horizon. The effect was rendered more striking by the appearance of the setting sun, which had sunk to the level of the farthest edge of the prairie, and seemed like a globe of fire resting upon the ground. Pierre looked around him with admiration. The vast expanse—

* Published in the collection, The Wilderness and the War-Path.

destitute of trees, covered with tall grass, now dried by the summer's heat, and extending, as it seemed to him, to the western verge of the continent—excited his special wonder. Little versed in geography, he persuaded himself that he had reached the western boundary of the world, and beheld the very spot where the sun passed over the edge of the great terrestrial plane. There was no mistake. He had achieved an adventure worthy the greatest captain of the age. His form dilated, and his eye kindled, with a consciousness of his own importance. Columbus had discovered a continent, but *he* had travelled to the extreme verge of the earth's surface, beyond which nothing remained to be discovered. "Yes," he solemnly exclaimed, "there is the end of the world! How fortunate am I to have approached it by daylight, and with a guide; otherwise, I might have stepped over in the dark, and have fallen—I know not where!"

The Indian girl had seated herself on the grass, and was composedly waiting his pleasure, when he discovered large masses of smoke rolling upward in the west. He pointed towards this new phenomenon, and endeavored to obtain some explanation of its meaning; but the bride, if she understood his enquiry, had no means of reply. There is a language of looks which is sufficient for the purposes of love. The glance of approving affection beams expressively from the eye, and finds its way in silent eloquence to the heart. No doubt that the pair, whose bridal day we have described, had already learned, from each other's looks, the confession which they had no other common language to convey; but the intercourse of signs can go no further. It is perfectly inadequate to the interpretation of natural phenomena: and the Indian maid was unable to explain that singular appearance which so puzzled her lover. But discovering, from the direction to which he pointed, that his curiosity was strongly excited, the obliging girl rose and led the way towards the west. They walked for more than an hour. Pierre insensibly became grave and silent, and his sympathizing companion unconsciously fell into the same mood. He had taken her hand, which she now yielded without reluctance, and they moved slowly, side by side, over the plain—she with a submissive and demure air, and he alternately admiring his beautiful bride, and throwing suspicious glances at the novel scene around him. The sun had gone down, the breeze had subsided, and the stillness of death was hanging over the prairie. Pierre began to have awful sensations. Though bold and volatile, a something like fear crept over him, and he would have turned back; but the pride of a French gentleman, and a marquis in anticipation, prevented him. He felt mean—for no man of spirit ever becomes seriously alarmed without feeling a sense of degradation. There is something so unmanly in fear, that, although no bosom is entirely proof against it, we feel ashamed to acknowledge its influence even to ourselves. Our hero looked forward in terror, yet was too proud to turn back. Superstition was beginning to throw its misty visions about his fancy. He had taken a step contrary to the advice of his father confessor, and was in open rebellion against the church; and he began to fear that some evil spirit, under the guise of an Indian maid, was seducing him away to destruction. At all events, he determined not to go much further.

The shades of night had begun to close, when they again ascended one of those elevations which swells so gradually that the traveller scarcely remarks them until he reaches the summit, and beholds, from a commanding eminence, a boundless landscape spread before him. The veil of night, without concealing the scene, rendered it indistinct; the undulations of the surface were no longer perceptible; and the prairie seemed a perfect plain. One phenomenon astonished and perplexed him: before him the prairie was lighted up with a dim but supernatural brilliancy, like that of a distant fire, while behind was the blackness of darkness. An air of solitude reigned over that wild plain, and not a sound relieved the desolation of the scene. A chill crept over him as he gazed around, and not an object met his eye but that dark maid, who stood in mute patience by his side, as waiting his pleasure; but on whose features, as displayed by the uncertain light that glimmered on them, a smile of triumph seemed to play. He looked again, and the horizon gleamed brighter and brighter, until a fiery redness rose above its dark outline, while heavy, slow moving masses of cloud curled upward above it. It was evidently the intense reflection, and the voluminous smoke, of a vast fire. In another moment the blaze itself appeared, first shooting up at one spot, and then at another, and advancing, until the whole line of horizon was clothed in flames, that rolled around, and curled, and dashed upward, like the angry waves of a burning ocean. The simple Frenchman had never heard of the fires that sweep over our wide prairies in the autumn, nor did it enter into his head that a natural cause could produce an effect so terrific. The whole western horizon was clad in fire, and, as far as the eye could see, to the right and left, was one vast conflagration, having the appearance of angry billows of a fiery liquid, dashing against each other, and foaming, and throwing flakes of burning spray into the air. There was a roaring sound like that caused by the conflict of waves. A more terrific sight could scarcely be conceived; nor was it singular that an unpractised eye should behold in that scene a wide sea of flame, lashed into fury by some internal commotion.

Pierre could gaze no longer. A sudden horror thrilled his soul. His worse fears were realized in the tremendous landscape. He saw before him the lake of fire prepared for the devil and his angels. The existence of such a place of punishment he had never doubted; but, heretofore, it had been a mere dogma of faith, while now it appeared before him in its terrible reality. He thought he could plainly distinguish gigantic black forms dancing in the flames, throwing up their long misshapen arms, and writhing their bodies into fantastic shapes. Uttering a piercing shriek, he turned and fled with the swiftness of an arrow. Fear gave new vigor to the muscles which had before been relaxed with fatigue, and his feet, so lately heavy, now touched the ground with the light and springy tread of the antelope. Yet, to himself, his steps seemed to linger, as if his heels were lead.

The Indian girl clapped her hands and laughed aloud as she pursued him. That laugh, which, at an earlier hour of this eventful day, had enlivened his heart by its joyous tones, now filled him with terror. It seemed the yell of a demon—the triumphant scream of hellish delight over the downfall of his soul. The dark maid of Illinois, so lately an object of love, became, to his distempered fancy, a minister of vengeance—a fallen angel sent to tempt him to destruction. A supernatural strength and swiftness gave wings to his flight, as he bounded away with the speed of the ostrich of the desert; but he seemed, to himself, to crawl sluggishly, and, whenever he cast a glance behind, that mysterious girl of the prairie was laughing at his heels. He tried to invoke the saints, but, alas! in the confusion of his mind, he could not recollect the names of more than half a dozen, nor determine which was the most suitable one to be called upon in such an anomalous case. Arrived at the forest, he dashed headlong through its tangled thickets. Neither the darkness, nor any obstacle, checked his career; but scrambling over fallen timber, tearing through copse and briar, he held his way, bruised and bleeding, through the forest. At last he reached the village, staggered into a lodge which happened to be unoccupied, and sunk down insensible.

The sun was just rising above the eastern horizon when Pierre awoke. The Indian maid was bending over him with looks of tender solicitude. She had nursed him through the silent watches of the night, had pillowed his head upon the soft plumage of the swan, and covered him with robes of the finest fur. She had watched his dreamy sleep through the long hours, when all others were sleeping, and no eye witnessed her assiduous care—had bathed his throbbing temples with water from the spring, and passed her slender fingers through his ringlets, with the fondness of a young and growing affection, until she had soothed the unconscious object of her tenderness into a calm repose. It was her first love, and she had given her heart up to its influences with all the strength, and all the weakness, of female passion. Under other circumstances it might long have remained concealed in her own bosom, and have gradually become disclosed by the attentions of her lover, as the flower opens slowly to the sun. But she had been suddenly called to the discharge of the duties of a wife; and woman, when appealed to by the charities of life, gives full play to her affections, pouring out the treasures of her love in liberal profusion.

But her tenderness was thrown away upon the slumbering bridegroom, whose unusual excitement, both of body and mind, had been succeeded by a profound lethargy. No sooner did he open his eyes, than the dreadful images of the night became again pictured upon his imagination. Even that anxious girl, who had hung over him with sleepless solicitude throughout the night, and still watched, dejected, by his side, seemed to wear a malignant aspect, and to triumph in his anguish. He shrunk from the glance of her eye, as if its mild lustre would have withered him. She laid her hand upon his brow, and he writhed as if a serpent had crawled over his visage. The hope of escape suddenly presented itself to his mind. He rose, and rushed wildly to the shore. The boats were just leaving the bank; his companions had been grieved at his marriage, and were alarmed when they found he had left the village; but Father Francis, a rigid moralist, and a stern man, determined not to wait for him a moment, and the little barks were already shoved into the stream, when the haggard barber appeared, and plunged into the water. As he climbed the side of the nearest boat, he conjured his comrades, in tones of agony, to fly. Imagining he had discovered some treachery in their new allies, they obeyed; the oars were plied with vigor, and the vessels of the white strangers rapidly disappeared from the eyes of the astonished Illini, who were as much perplexed by the abrupt departure, as they had been by the unexpected visit of their eccentric guests.

Pierre took to his bed, and remained an invalid during the rest of the voyage. Nor did he set his foot on shore again in the new world. One glance at the lake of fire was enough for him, and he did not, like Orpheus, look back at the infernal regions from which he had escaped. The party descended the Mississippi to the gulf of Mexico, where, finding a ship destined for France, he took leave of his companions, from whom he had carefully concealed the true cause of his alarm. During the passage across the Atlantic he recovered his health, and, in some measure, his spirits; but he never regained his thirst for adventure, his ambition to be a marquis, or his desire to seek for gold. The fountain of rejuvenescence itself had no charms to allure him back to the dangerous wildernesses of the far west. On all these subjects he remained silent as the grave. One would have supposed that he had escaped the dominions of Satan under a pledge of secrecy.

WILLIAM L. STONE.

William Leete Stone was born at Esopus, in New York, in 1793, and was the son of the Rev. William Stone, a clergyman of the Presbyterian church. When quite young he removed to the western part of that state, where he assisted his father in the care of a farm, acquiring a fondness for agricultural pursuits which he always retained.

At the age of seventeen he left home; placed himself with Colonel Prentiss, the proprietor of the "Cooperstown Freeman's Journal," to learn the printing business; and from this time began to write newspaper paragraphs. In 1813 he became the editor of the "Herkimer American." He next edited a political newspaper at Hudson, then one at Albany, and then again one at Hartford in Connecticut. He at length, in the spring of 1821, succeeded Mr. Zachariah Lewis in the editorship of the "New York Commercial Advertiser," becoming at the same time one of its proprietors. He continued in charge of this till his death, which took place at Saratoga Springs, August 15, 1844.

W. L. Stone

Though an acknowledged political leader, Mr. Stone's attention, during his career as an editor, was very far from having been absorbed by the party contentions of the day. While residing at Hudson, besides the political journal, he edited a literary periodical styled the "Lounger," which was distinguished for sprightliness and frequent sallies of wit. Subsequently, he furnished a number of tales to the Annuals, some of which, with additions, he republished in 1834, under the title of *Tales and Sketches.* Many of the characters and incidents in these are historical, being founded on traditions respecting the revolutionary or colonial history of the United States.

In 1832, he published his *Letters on Masonry and Anti-Masonry;* then followed *Mathias and his Impostures*, a curious picture of an instance of gross but remarkable religious delusions, which occurred in the state of New York; and in 1836, a volume entitled *Ups and Downs in the Life of a Gentleman*, intended as a satire on the follies of the day, although the main facts stated actually occurred in the life of an individual well known to the author.

It has been stated that the parents of Mr. Stone, during his early childhood, removed to western New York. This section of country was at that time in fact, though not in name, an Indian Mission Station—so that in his very boyhood their son became well acquainted with the Indians of our forests, and his kindness of manner and offhand generosity won his way to their favor. To this it may be owing, that at an early period of his life he formed the purpose of gathering up and preserving what remained concerning the traits and character of the "Red Men" of America, intending to connect with an account of these, an authentic history of the life and times of the prominent individuals who figured immediately before the Revolution, more especially of Sir William Johnson.

The amount of labor thus bestowed, and the success with which he found his way to dusty MSS. or gained knowledge of the invaluable contents of old chests and rickety trunks stowed away as lumber in garrets, and almost forgotten by their owners, was remarkable. Still more noteworthy was the happy facility with which he would gain access to the hearts of hoary-headed and tottering old men, and bring them to live over again their early days of trial and hardships—gleaning quickly and pleasantly, desirable information from those who alone could communicate what he wished to hear. The result was an amount and variety of material which could scarcely be estimated, for he had the habit of systematizing the retentiveness of a powerful memory by a time-saving process entirely his own, and the very arrangement of his MSS. and books assisted this process, so that his library served him a double purpose.

In the course of these investigations he obtained an intimate acquaintance with the early annals of the country, and became a repository of facts in American and Revolutionary history.

His predilections in this particular department were doubtless cultivated by his father, who when a mere boy left college hall and classics to shoulder his musket, and fight the battles of his country.

While following out his main design, the materials collected enabled him to give to the public several works on the general subject with which they were connected. These were the *Memoirs of Joseph Brant*, in 1838; a *Memoir of Red Jacket*, in 1841; the *Life of Uncas*, and the *History of Wyoming*. He had completed the collection and arrangement of the materials for his more extended work, the history of Sir William Johnson, was ready to devote himself to its execution, and had already advanced to three hundred and fifty pages and upwards, when he was called to give up his earthly labor.

When it is remembered that the investigations just referred to, and the volumes which resulted, were accomplished at the same time with the editorship of a leading daily paper in our commercial metropolis, and that he acted up to his own exalted views of the power, influence, and responsibility of the press, as an organ of good or evil, it may be safely asserted that his industry was untiring.

The character of Mr. Stone could not be fully presented without mentioning his sympathy with those who were struggling in life, and how readily a word of kindness was written or spoken, or his purse opened for their assistance. The ingenuousness, transparency, and freshness of character, which he always retained, often shone forth with great beauty amid scenes and in circumstances little likely to elicit them.

From his early youth Mr. Stone's motives of action were elevated. He was a firm, decided, and consistent Christian. The religious enterprises and benevolent associations of the day commanded his earnest efforts in their behalf. The Colonization Society, from first to last, found in him a steadfast supporter. The cause of Education lay near his heart, and to it he gave his energies, and spared not even his decaying strength.

HENRY ROWE SCHOOLCRAFT

Is the descendant of a family identified with the early border life of America. His first ancestor in the country, James Calcraft, for so the name was written then, came from England fresh from the campaigns of Marlborough. He settled in Albany County, New York; was a land surveyor and schoolmaster, which latter vocation led to the popular change of his name. He died at the age of one-hundred-and-two in the Otter Creek region, in the present state of Vermont. His children were variously distributed in Canada, on the Susquehannah, and in the state of New York. One of them, John, was a soldier under the command of Sir William Johnson. His son Lawrence was in Fort Stanwix during the siege, and was the first volunteer to go forth to the relief of the brave Herkimer. He served through both wars with England, and died in 1840 at the age of eighty-four, with a high reputation for worth and integrity. His son, Henry Rowe Schoolcraft, was born in Albany county, 28th March, 1793. He received there, in the town of Guilderland, a good education from the schoolmasters of the region, but appears mainly to have instructed himself, his tastes leading him in his youth to a knowledge of poetry and languages, with which he connected the study of mineralogy. At fifteen he began writing for the newspapers. His first work was a treatise on *Vitreology*, published in Utica in 1817, a subject to which he was led by his father's superintendence of the glass manufacture. The next year he travelled to the Mississippi and made a mineralogical survey of the Lead Mines of Missouri, of which he published a report in 1819. His narrative or journal of this tour, published in 1820 in Van Winkle's *Belles Lettres Repository*

Henry R Schoolcraft.

at New York, is marked by a vein of unaffected simplicity and enthusiasm which has always been characteristic of the author. It was republished in London in Sir Richard Phillips's collection of Voyages and Travels; and has been lately reissued by the author in an enlarged form with the title, *Scenes and Adventures in the Semi-Alpine Region of the Ozark Mountains of Missouri and Arkansas, which were first traversed by DeSoto in* 1541. His next tour was in 1820, under the auspices of Monroe's administration, accompanying General Cass in his survey of the copper regions, and exploration of the Upper Mississippi. He published an account of this in a *Narrative Journal of Travels from Detroit to the Source of the Mississippi River.* In 1821 he journeyed to Chicago, examining the Wabash and Illinois Rivers, and published as the result his *Travels in the Central Portions of the Mississivpi Valley.* In 1822 he

Elmwood.

received the appointment of Agent for Indian Affairs on the North-west Frontiers, taking up his residence at Michilimackinack, where he continued to reside for nearly twenty years, occupying himself diligently with studying the Indian languages and history, and improving the condition of the tribes. He was a member of the Territorial Legislature from 1828 to 1832. He procured the incorporation of the Michigan Historical Society in 1828, and in 1832 founded the Algic Society at Detroit. The titles of his publications at this time will show his zeal in the promotion of his favorite topics, urged both in prose and verse.* He made a grammar of the Algonquin language. Mr. Du Ponceau translated two of his lectures before the Algic Society on the grammatical structure of the Indian language into French, for the National Institute of France.

In 1832 he was chosen by the Indian and War Department to conduct a second expedition into the region of the Upper Mississippi. This he accomplished successfully, establishing his lasting geographical reputation by the discovery of the head waters of the river in Itasca Lake. His account of the journey was published in an octavo volume by the Harpers in 1834; *Narrative of an Expedition to Itasca Lake, the actual source of the Mississippi River.* In 1839 his *Algic Researches* appeared in New York, a collection of Indian tales and legends, mythologic and allegoric. It is the working of one of the finest veins of the author's numerous aboriginal studies. The legends preserved in this and other of Mr. Schoolcraft's writings show the Indians to have possessed an unwritten literature of no little value in both a poetical and humorous aspect. There is much delicacy in the conception of many of these tales of the spirits of earth and air, with a genuine quaintness showing an affinity with the fairy stories of the northern races of Europe.

In bringing these curious traditions to light, valuable as an historical index to the character of the tribes, as well as for their invention, Mr. Schoolcraft is entitled to grateful recollection for his pioneer labors. He was the first to challenge attention to this department of national literature; and without his poetical interest in the subject very much of the material he has preserved would probably have perished. Mr. S., too, is a poet in his own right, the list of his writings numbering several productions in verse, chiefly relating to the Indians or the scenery of the west.

In 1841 Mr. Schoolcraft removed his residence to New York and took part in the proceedings of the Ethnological Society. The next year he visited England and the continent, and was present at the meeting of the British Association at Manchester. On his return he was employed by the legislature of New York, in 1845, to take a census of the Six Nations, the results of which investigation were published in his *Notes on the Iroquois*, an enlarged edition of which appeared in 1847. In 1845 Mr. S. commenced the publication of a collection of Indian literary material with the title, *Onéota, or Characteristics of the Red Race of America;* reissued in 1848 with the title, *The Indian in his Wigwam.*

* The Rise of the West, or a Prospect of the Mississippi Valley. A Poem. 1837. Detroit: G. L. Whitney; pp. 28.—Indian Melodies. New York: Elam Bliss, 1830; pp. 52, 8vo.—A Discourse before the Michigan Historical Society in 1831. Detroit. Whitney, pp. 59.—Outline of the Natural History of Michigan, a lecture delivered before the Detroit Lyceum in 1831. Detroit.—The Influence of Ardent Spirits on the Condition of North American Indians. *Ib.*—An Address before the Algic Society. *Ib.*—The Man of Bronze, or Portraitures of Indian Character, delivered before the Algic Society at its annual meeting in 1834.—Iosco, or the Vale of Norma. Detroit: 1838.—Report on Indian affairs in 1840. *Ib.*

One of the most interesting of the author's publications (in Philadelphia, 1851) is his *Personal Memoirs of a Residence of Thirty Years with the Indian Tribes on the American Frontiers; with brief notices of passing events, facts, and opinions*, 1812 to 1842.* This book is written in the form of a diary, and has the flavor of the time, with its motley incident on the frontier, with Indian chiefs, trappers, government employés, chance travellers, rising legislators, farmers, ministers of the gospel, all standing out with more or less of individuality in the formative period of the country. No man was, then and there, so humble or so insignificant as not to be of importance. With an instinct for the poetry of the past, and a vigilant eye for the present and the future, Mr. Schoolcraft has employed his pen in writing down legend, noting anecdotes of manners, chronicling personalities, recording adventure, and describing nature—the result of which is a picture which will grow more distinct and valuable with time, when the lineaments of this transition age—the closing period of the red man, the opening one of the white—will survive only in this and similar records.

The latest literary employment of Mr. Schoolcraft is his preparation, under a resolution of the government, of the series of five quarto volumes, printed in a style of great luxury, and illustrated by the pencil of Lieutenant Eastman, entitled *Ethnological Researches respecting the Red Man of America. Information respecting the History, Condition, and Prospects of the Indian Tribes of the United States.* The comprehensive plan of this work covers a wide range of subjects in the general history of the race; their traditions and associations with the whites; their special antiquities in the several departments of archæology in relation to the arts; their government, manners, and customs; their physiological and ethnological peculiarities as individuals and nations; their intellectual and moral cultivation; their statistics of population; their geographical position, past and present. The work, gigantic as it is, is mostly from the pen of Mr. Schoolcraft; but it also contains numerous important communications from government officials and others relating to the topics in hand.†

Mr. Schoolcraft has been twice married; in 1823 to a daughter of Mr. John Johnston, an Irish gentleman, who married the daughter of Wabojeeg, an Indian chief. This lady, with whom he passed the whole of his frontier residence in Michigan, died in 1842. In 1847 he married Miss Mary Howard of Beaufort, South Carolina. Being deprived by a partial paralysis of the ready use of his hand, his wife acts as his amanuensis. Beyond his confinement to his room this difficulty has not affected his health, while it has concentrated his attention, never relaxed, still more on his literary pursuits. It is satisfactory to see a pioneer in a branch of science and investigation not usually very highly rewarded by the public, thus pursuing—under the auspices and with the resources of Government—the studies commenced nearly half a century before.

THE WHITE STONE CANOE—FROM THE TALES OF A WIGWAM.

There was once a very beautiful young girl, who died suddenly on the day she was to have been married to a handsome young man. He was also brave, but his heart was not proof against this loss. From the hour she was buried, there was no more joy or peace for him. He went often to visit the spot where the women had buried her, and sat musing there, when, it was thought, by some of his friends, he would have done better to try to amuse himself in the chase, or by diverting his thoughts in the war-path. But war and hunting had both lost their charms for him. His heart was already dead within him. He pushed aside both his war-club and his bow and arrows.

He had heard the old people say, that there was a path that led to the land of souls, and he determined to follow it. He accordingly set out, one morning, after having completed his preparations for the journey. At first he hardly knew which way to go. He was only guided by the tradition that he must go south. For a while, he could see no change in the face of the country. Forests, and hills, and valleys, and streams had the same looks, which they wore in his native place. There was snow on the ground, when he set out, and it was sometimes seen to be piled and matted on the thick trees and bushes. At length, it began to diminish, and finally disappeared. The forest assumed a more cheerful appearance, the leaves put forth their buds, and before he was aware of the completeness of the change, he found himself surrounded by spring. He had left behind him the land of snow and ice. The air became mild, the dark clouds of winter had rolled away from the sky; a pure field of blue was above him, and as he went he saw flowers beside his path, and heard the songs of birds. By these signs he knew that he was going the right way, for they agreed with the traditions of his tribe. At length he spied a path. It led him through a grove, then up a long and elevated ridge, on the very top of which he came to a lodge. At the door stood an old man, with white hair, whose eyes, though deeply sunk, had a fiery brilliancy. He had a long robe of skins thrown loosely around his shoulders, and a staff in his hands.

The young Chippewayan began to tell his story; but the venerable chief arrested him, before he had proceeded to speak ten words. "I have expected you," he replied, "and had just risen to bid you welcome to my abode. She, whom you seek, passed here but a few days since, and being fatigued with her journey, rested herself here. Enter my lodge and be seated, and I will then satisfy your enquiries, and give you directions for your journey from this point." Having done this, they both issued forth to the lodge door. "You see yonder gulf," said he, "and the wide stretching blue plains beyond. It is the land of souls. You

* To this is prefixed "Sketches of the Life of Henry R. Schoolcraft:" a careful narrative, from which the facts of this notice have been derived.

† In addition to the works we have mentioned, Mr. Schoolcraft has published Cyclopædia Indiaensis, a specimen number. New York: Platt & Peers, 1842.—Alhalla, the Lord of Talladega. *Ib.* Wiley & Putnam. 1848. pp. 116.—Report on Aboriginal Names, and the Geographical Terminology of New York. *Ib.* Van Norden 1845, pp. 43.—An Address at Aurora, Cayuga County, New York, before an association of young men for investigating the Iroquois history. Auburn, 1846, pp. 35.—Historical Considerations on the Siege of Fort Stanwix in 1777, delivered before the New York Historical Society. New York: Van Norden. 1846, pp. 29. Plan for investigating American Ethnology. *Ib.* Jenkins. 1846, pp. 13.—An Address before the New York Historical Society on the Incentives to the study of the early period of American History. *Ib.* Van Norden. 1847, pp. 38.—Notices of Antique Earthen Vessels from Florida. *Ib.* 1847 pp. 15.—Literature of the Indian Languages. Washington: C. Alexander. 1849, pp. 28. Mr. S. has also been a contributor to most of the periodicals of the country, including Silliman's Journal, the North American Review, the Democratic Review. Helderbergia: or the apotheosis of the Heroes of the Anti-Rent War—a poem. Albany, N.Y. 1855. 8vo. pp. 54.

stand upon its borders, and my lodge is the gate of entrance. But you cannot take your body along. Leave it here with your bow and arrows, your bundle and your dog. You will find them safe on your return." So saying, he re-entered the lodge, and the freed traveller bounded forward, as if his feet had suddenly been endowed with the power of wings. But all things retained their natural colours and shapes. The woods and leaves, and streams and lakes, were only more bright and comely than he had ever witnessed. Animals bounded across his path, with a freedom and a confidence which seemed to tell him, there was no blood shed here. Birds of beautiful plumage inhabited the groves, and sported in the waters. There was but one thing, in which he saw a very unusual effect. He noticed that his passage was not stopped by trees or other objects. He appeared to walk directly through them. They were, in fact, but the souls or shadows of material trees. He became sensible that he was in a land of shadows. When he had travelled half a day's journey, through a country which was continually becoming more attractive, he came to the banks of a broad lake, in the centre of which was a large and beautiful island. He found a canoe of shining white stone, tied to the shore. He was now sure that he had come the right path, for the aged man had told him of this. There were also shining paddles. He immediately entered the canoe, and took the paddles in his hands, when to his joy and surprise, on turning round, he beheld the object of his search in another canoe, exactly its counterpart in every thing. She had exactly imitated his motions, and they were side by side. They at once pushed out from shore and began to cross the lake. Its waves seemed to be rising and at a distance looked ready to swallow them up; but just as they entered the whitened edge of them they seemed to melt away, as if they were but the images of waves. But no sooner was one wreath of foam passed, than another, more threatening still, rose up. Thus they were in perpetual fear; and what added to it, was the *clearness of the water*, through which they could see heaps of beings who had perished before, and whose bones lay strewed on the bottom of the lake. The Master of Life had, however, decreed to let them pass, for the actions of neither of them had been bad. But they saw many others struggling and sinking in the waves. Old men and young men, males and females of all ages and ranks were there; some passed, and some sank. It was only the little children whose canoes seemed to meet no waves. At length, every difficulty was gone, as in a moment, and they both leapt out on the happy island. They felt that the very air was food. It strengthened and nourished them. They wandered together over the blissful fields, where everything was formed to please the eye and the ear. There were no tempests—there was no ice, no chilly winds—no one shivered for the want of warm clothes: no one suffered for hunger—no one mourned for the dead. They saw no graves. They heard of no wars. There was no hunting of animals; for the air itself was their food. Gladly would the young warrior have remained there for ever, but he was obliged to go back for his body. He did not see the Master of Life, but he heard his voice in a soft breeze: "Go back," said this voice, "to the land from whence you came. Your time has not yet come. The duties for which I made you, and which you are to perform, are not yet finished. Return to your people, and accomplish the duties of a good man. You will be the ruler of your tribe for many days. The rules you must observe, will be told you by my messenger, who keeps the gate. When he surrenders back your body, he will tell you what to do. Listen to him, and you shall afterwards rejoin the spirit, which you must now leave behind. She is accepted and will be ever here, as young and as happy as she was when I first called her from the land of snows." When this voice ceased, the narrator awoke. It was the fancy work of a dream, and he was still in the bitter land of snows, and hunger, and tears.

WILLIAMS COLLEGE

Owes its name and original foundation to a soldier of the old French War, Colonel Ephraim Williams, once a valiant defender of the region in which it is situated. He was a native of the state, born in 1715 at Newton, and in early life was a sailor, making several voyages to Europe, and engrafting a knowledge of the world on his naturally vigorous powers of mind. He visited England, Spain, and Holland. In the war with France from 1740 to 1748 his attention was turned to military life, and he served as a captain in a New England company raised for the service against Canada. On the conclusion of peace he received from the General Court of Massachusetts a grant of two hundred acres of land in the town of Hoosac, with the command of the Forts Hoosac and Massachusetts, frontier posts, which then afforded protection from the Indians to the settlers of the fertile districts around and below.

On the breaking out of the war anew in 1755 he had command of a regiment for the general defence, which was ordered to join the forces then raising in New York by General Johnson against the French. On his way to the army he made, on the 22d July, 1755, his will at Albany, by which he bequeathed his property in Massachusetts as a foundation "for the support of a free-school in a township west of Fort Massachusetts; provided the said township fall within Massachusetts, after running the line between Massachusetts and New York, and provided the said township, when incorporated, be called Williamstown."

Proceeding with a large body of soldiers in the following autumn, September 8, 1755, to attack the advanced guard of Dieskau's invading force, the party was entrapped in an ambuscade in the neighborhood of Lake George, when Colonel Williams fell, mortally wounded by a musket ball in the head.

His bequest for the purposes of education seems to have grown out both of his respect for learning and his affection for the settlers, among whom his military life was passed. He was of a warm, generous disposition, with a winning ease and politeness; and though he was not much indebted to schools for his education, is said to have had a taste for books, and cultivated the society of men of letters.*

By the will of Colonel Williams his executors were directed to sell his lands, at their discretion, within five years after an established peace, and apply the interest of the proceeds, with that of certain bonds and notes, to the purposes of the free-school. The lands were sold, the money loaned, and the interest again invested till 1785, when an act of the legislature was procured incorporating a body of trustees "of the

* Mass. Hist. Coll., First Series, viii. 47.

donation of Ephraim Williams, for maintaining a free-school in Williamstown." William Williams was elected president, and the Rev. Seth Swift, treasurer.* Additional funds were solicited, and in 1788 a committee was appointed to erect a school-house, which, completed in 1790, is now the "West college" building of the institution. A good choice was made of a preceptor in the Rev. Ebenezer Fitch. This scholar and divine, who was to bear a prominent part in the establishment of the college, was born at Canterbury, Connecticut, September 26, 1756. He received his degree at Yale in 1777, and passed two years at New Haven as a resident graduate. He then was school teacher for a year in New Jersey, and from 1780 till 1783 was tutor in Yale College. An interval of mercantile business followed, in the course of which he visited London, again returning to Yale, as tutor, from 1786 to 1791, the year of his engagement at Williamstown. With this preparation he opened the free-school in October, with John Lester as assistant. Two departments were organized—a grammar-school or academy, with a college course of instruction, and an English free-school. In 1793 the school, by an act of the legislature, became Williams College, with a grant from the state treasury of four thousand dollars for the purchase of books and philosophical apparatus. To the old trustees were added the Rev. Dr. Stephen West, Henry Van Schaack, the Hon. Elijah Williams, Gen. Philip Schuyler, the Hon. Stephen Van Rensselaer, and the Rev. Job Swift, the charter allowing to the board seventeen members, including the college president. A grammar-school was at once provided for in connexion with the college, and the terms of admission to the latter required that the applicant "be able to accurately read, parse, and construe, to the satisfaction of the president and tutor, Virgil's Æneid, Tully's Orations, and the Evangelists in Greek; or, if he prefer to become acquainted with French, he must be able to read and pronounce, with a tolerable degree of accuracy and fluency, Hudson's French Scholar's Guide, Telemachus, or some other approved French author."

Mr. Fitch was unanimously elected president, and the first Commencement was held, a class of four, in 1795. The numbers rapidly increased with the resources of the college, which were augmented by a new grant of land from the state in 1796. Dr. Fitch held the presidency for twenty-one years, retiring from the office in 1815, after which he became pastor of a church in West Bloomfield, New York, where he died at the age of seventy-six in 1833.

The Rev. Zephaniah Swift Moore, then Professor of Languages at Dartmouth, was the successor of Dr. Fitch in the college presidency, and held the office from 1815 to 1821. The question was at this time discussed of the removal of the college to the banks of the Connecticut, an agitation which did not repair its fortunes. Dr. Moore, on his resignation, was chosen president of the collegiate institution at Amherst, which he had greatly favored, and which drew off many of the students from Williamstown.*

The Rev. Dr. Edward Dorr Griffin was then chosen president. He brought with him the prestige of an influential career in the ministry at Newark, New Jersey, and in the Park Street Church at Boston. He had also been professor of pulpit eloquence in the Theological Seminary at Andover. He was inaugurated president and professor of divinity at Williams College, November 14, 1821. His reputation and influence revived the college interests, which had become much depressed, and it was enabled to bear up successfully against the rivalry of Amherst. Various advantages of gifts and bequests, which gave the means of improvement and increase of the college library, apparatus, and buildings, were secured during Dr. Griffin's efficient presidency, which he was compelled to resign from ill health in 1836. He died at Newark, New Jersey, November 8 of the year following, at the age of sixty-eight.

The Rev. Dr. Mark Hopkins was inaugurated president of the college on the 15th of September, 1836. Dr. Hopkins is a native of Berkshire, Mass. He was born at Stockbridge, February 4, 1802; was educated at the college of which he is president; studied medicine, and received a medical degree in 1828. In 1830 he was elected professor of moral philosophy and rhetoric in Williams College, a position which he held at the time of his election to the presidency.

The college during his administration has increased steadily in its resources and the number of its students. It is due to his efficient exertions that astronomical and magnetical observatories have been erected and well supplied with scientific apparatus.

Dr. Hopkins has also rendered services to general literature by the publication of his *Lowell Lectures on the Evidences of Christianity* in 1846, and by the collection of his *Miscellaneous Essays and Discourses* the year following.

Among the papers preserved in the latter is the author's *Inaugural Discourse* at Williams College. Its review of the subject of education is sound in philosophy and practical in its suggestions. In a wise spirit he speaks of the principle now settled among all thinking men, that we are to regard the mind—

> not as a piece of iron to be laid upon the anvil and hammered into any shape, nor as a block of marble in which we are to find the statue by removing the rubbish, nor as a receptacle into which knowledge may be poured; but as a flame that is to be fed, as

* William Williams, Theodore Sedgwick, Woodbridge Little, John Bacon, Thompson J. Skinner, Israel Jones, David Noble, the Rev. Seth Swift, and the Rev. Daniel Collins, were the first body of trustees named in the act.

* Amherst College grew out of the academy at that place which was incorporated in 1812, and of which Noah Webster was one of the chief promoters. Further provision was required for the education of young men for the ministry. A college was resolved upon, and the question of union with Williams College agitated, in view of the removal of the latter. Dr. Moore was chosen the first president in 1821. He died two years after, when the Rev. Heman Humphrey was elected. A charter was obtained in 1825. Dr. Humphrey held the presidency till 1845, when he was succeeded by the Rev. Edward Hitchcock, who occupied the post till 1854, when the Rev. William A. Stearns was chosen in his place. The institution has preserved its distinct religious character in connexion with the Presbyterian Church. Its number of graduates, up to 1854, was over one thousand. It has a large charitable fund, from which the expenses of a numerous body of students preparing for the ministry are annually paid.—*Holland's History of Western Massachusetts*, i. 508-512.

Williams College.

an active being that must be strengthened to think and to feel—to dare, to do, and to suffer. It is as a germ, expanding under the influence certainly of air and sunlight and moisture, but yet only through the agency of an internal force; and external agency is of no value except as it elicits, and controls, and perfects the action of that force. He only who can rightly appreciate the force of this principle, and carry it out into all its consequences, in the spirit of the maxim, that nature is to be conquered only by obeying her laws, will do all that belongs to the office of a teacher.

With the same good sense he remarks:—

There is a strange slowness in assenting practically to that great law of nature, that the faculties are strengthened only by exercise. It is so with the body, and it is so with the mind. If a man would strengthen his intellectual faculties, he must exercise them; if he would improve his taste, he must employ it on the objects of taste; if he would improve his moral nature and make progress in goodness, he must perform acts of goodness. Nor will he improve his faculties by thinking about them and studying into their nature, unless by so doing he is enabled and induced to put them into more skilful and efficient action.

This practical mode of philosophizing, seeing moral and intellectual truth in connexion with its individual adaptations, is a marked habit of the author's mind, and admirably adapts him for the chair of the professor or the government of a college.

By the triennial catalogue of Williams College of 1853, it appears that there have been one thousand four hundred and forty-four alumni to that date: of whom four hundred and forty have followed the profession of divinity; three hundred and eighty-one the law; one hundred and seven medicine; and ninety-eight have become teachers.

Besides the usual branches of instruction, the physical sciences receive particular attention. Careful magnetic observations are made by the students; and the mineralogical and geological cabinets, prepared by Professor Ebenezer Emmons, eminent for his state geological surveys, afford full materials for study. The museum has also two colossal bas-reliefs from Nineveh, presented by Mr. Layard.

The bold and picturesque location of the college seems to invite to the study of natural phenomena. Seated at the foot of Saddleback, the grandest mountain elevation in the state, in a fair valley watered by the Hoosac, and at the northern termination of Berkshire, a county remarkable for its grandeur and beauty, the site is worthy to be associated with the choicest academic refinements of science and literature.*

EDWARD HITCHCOCK.

Edward Hitchcock was born at Deerfield, Massachusetts, May 24, 1793. In consequence of ill health, he was compelled to leave College before taking his degree. He commenced a literary career by the preparation of an almanac for four years, from 1815 to 1818; and by the publication of a tragedy extending to one hundred and eight pages, *The Downfall of Buonaparte*, in 1815. In 1816, he became principal of the Academy in Deerfield, where he remained for three years, when he was ordained minister of the Congregational

Edward Hitchcock

church at Conway, Mass. He resigned this post in 1825 to accept an appointment to the Professorship of Chemistry and Natural History in Amherst College, an institution which had been

* Sketches of Williams College, Williamstown, Mass., 1847. An interesting contribution to the history of the region, by D. A. Wells and S. H. Davis.

founded four years before. He continued his connexion with the college, having been appointed to the presidency, with the professorship of Natural Theology and Geology, in 1844, until his resignation in 1854.

In 1823, he published *Geology of the Connecticut Valley*, and in 1829 a *Catalogue of Plants within Twenty Miles of Amherst*. These works, with other scientific investigations, gave him such repute that, in 1830, he was appointed by the legislature to make a geological survey of the state of Massachusetts. He was re-appointed to the same service in 1837; and in 1850, commissioner to visit the Agricultural schools of Europe. In fulfilment of these trusts he published in 1832 a *First Report on the Economic Geology of Massachusetts;* in 1833, *Report on the Geology, Zoology, and Botany* of Massachusetts; in 1838, *Report on a Re-examination of the Geology of Massachusetts;* and in 1841, *Final Report on the Geology of Massachusetts;* and in 1851, *Report on the Agricultural Schools of Europe.*

He has also published *Elementary Geology*, 1840; *Fossil Footmarks in the United States*, 1848; and an *Outline of the Geology of the Globe*, in 1853.

In addition to these purely scientific volumes, President Hitchcock is the author of *The Religion of Geology and its Connected Sciences*, in 1851, and of *Religious Lectures on the Peculiar Phenomena of the Four Seasons;* works in which he has shown the harmony of science with the records of the Bible, and its religious uses in the increase of reverence for the Almighty consequent on the devout study of the wonders of creation, and its adaptation to the wants of man. These works have been largely circulated in this country and in England.

Dr. Hitchcock has also been a prominent writer on Dietetics. In 1830, he published in this connexion *Dyspepsia Forestalled and Resisted*, and *An Argument for Early Temperance.*

His other separate publications have been, *A Wreath for the Tomb*, 1839, and *Memoir of Mary Lyon.* He has contributed about forty scientific papers to Silliman's Journal; three elaborate articles on the connexion between Religion and Geology to the Biblical Repository, from 1835 to 1838. He is also the author of two Addresses delivered before the Mount Holyoke Female Seminary in 1848 and 1849; two before the Hampshire Hampden and Franklin Agricultural Society in 1827 and 1846; one on his inauguration as president in 1845; one before the Association of American Geologists and Naturalists (now the American Scientific Association) in 1841; one before the Mechanical Society of Andover in 1830; and one before the Porter Rhetorical Society in Andover in 1852—all of which were published.

He is also the author of several sermons, of four tracts—*Argument against the Manufacture and Sale of Ardent Spirits, Cars Ready, The Blind Slave in the Mines, Murderers of Fathers and Murderers of Mothers*—which have been issued by the American Tract Society, and of numerous contributions to the press.

The utilitarian writings of Dr. Hitchcock, and his peculiarly scientific labors, executed under conditions of the deepest public trust and confidence, speak for themselves. In his discussion of the relation of science with scripture he has shown a liberal appreciation of the necessities of the former, in a philosophical view, without derogating from the claims of the latter. As a writer on natural philosophy his works are not only stored with original research, but his observations are presented in a pleasing, animated style.

HENRY C. CAREY.

HENRY C. CAREY, one of the prominent writers on Political Economy of the day, is the son of Mathew Carey, and was born in Philadelphia in 1793. He was brought up in the business of his father, and succeeded him on his retirement in 1821. He conducted, with his partner Mr. Lea, one of the most extensive publishing houses in the United States, until 1838, when he retired, and devoted his leisure to the prosecution of authorship, a career he had commenced in 1835, by the publication of an *Essay on the Rate of Wages.* This was followed, in 1837–8–40, by three octavo volumes on the *Principles of Political Economy;* in 1838, *The Credit System in France, England, and the United States* appeared; and in 1848, *The Past, the Present, and the Future*, a further refutation of the statements of the ordinary school of political economists.

We may indicate the spirit of these volumes by two or three of their prominent theorems, which are in most marked contrast with the dogmas prevailing in Europe.

First, in time, was the demonstration that the progress of social wealth is in the normal order concomitant with and more rapid than that of population.

This proposition was connected with one even more adverse to the faith in the fixed demarkation of rank, class, and privilege, which the traditions of a social life founded on and adapted to military activity have sanctioned for so many ages, that it has grown into credence as a providential law. The doctrine to which we allude may be termed the law of Distribution, of a distribution, however, not mechanical, but organic, and as inseparable from growth as the distribution of sap in the branches, leaves, and buds, is from the life of a tree. It is, that in the natural growth of population and wealth, the share of the laborer in each successive increment increases, both relatively and absolutely, in proportion as well as in amount; while that of the capitalist, though increasing in amount, diminishes in proportion. In other words, there is in the growth of capital—the machinery by which man subordinates to his service the gratuitous powers and agencies of nature—a constant accelerating force, which, steadily increasing the productiveness of any given amount of toil, and therefore cheapening the result, or what in the converse is precisely equivalent, enhancing the *value* of labor, secures a product enlarged to the degree that a diminished proportion thereof gives a greater quantity than the capitalist formerly obtained from his large proportion of a smaller product. The enlarged proportion of an increased product provides the laborer an enhanced quantity, and not in spite, bnt in virtue, of increased cheapness to the consumer. This may be translated from the abstract into the concrete facts, patent upon the smallest examination of history, that commodities of all kinds are constantly falling in price while wages are rising, and that the rate of interest declines, while the mass of capital constantly receives larger accretions.

Mr. Carey has reached these vital conclusions while yet admitting the plausible hypothesis of Ricardo, that in the occupation and culture of the soil men pass from those of superior to those of progressively deteriorating fertility. If this hypothesis were well founded, there would be a diminishing product for the agricultural toil of each successive generation, and consequently an increasing proportion of laborers required to devote their energies for an ever declining remuneration. Mr. Carey has shown the existence of a power, in the growth of capital other than land, more than compensating the tendency to retrogression from the supposed decreasing productiveness of the soil. In 1848, however, he was led by the direct observation of facts to the discovery, that the course of individuals and communities in the occupation and culture of the soil, is diametrically opposite to that imagined by Ricardo; that men always, from the necessity of their unfurnished condition, subject the inferior lands to culture first, and constantly proceed as they acquire the power to those of superior fertility. In his Past, Present, and Future, he demonstrated the fact, historically, by the contrast of the same nation in its different stages, and geographically by the contrast of contemporary communities which now stand at the different grades of social progress. The question is treated in precisely the same method as any other question of natural history in respect to the habits and *habitats* of a plant or an animal would be treated. And herein is the first example of the distinctive method of his school, which, abandoning as fruitless the metaphysical idea of introspection into laws of human nature to find what man *would* do, aims at discovering the relations between man and physical nature, and the modes by which the former is to derive the greatest advantage from the latter—the field and problem of Political Economy—by studying the external world to learn what man *can* do, and following the same methods of investigation which have given certainty and the power of prediction in the positive sciences. The result of this discovery was to confirm and explain the law of Distribution, by absorbing it into a more general and comprehensive one. It is palpable, that the widest divergence must exist in the consequences flowing from this theory and that of Ricardo. The latter necessitates an increasing inequality of physical condition,—therefore of intellectual and moral culture, and of political privilege, between the classes of landowners, capitalists, and laborers. It is the firmest support of the hoary abuses of despotism; for it traces them to an imagined law of the all-beneficent Creator. The American system, on the contrary, shows them to be the result of tyrannous human interference with the divine economy. We leave the reader to seek in Mr. Carey's volumes the exposition of the differences on the minor questions of Political Economy, which must attend so profound a contradiction in the premises, methods, and main conclusions of the European and American systems.

Mr. Carey has also published several pamphlets on literary property, in which he takes a view of the subject opposed to the passage of an International Copyright Law.

HENRY COGSWELL KNIGHT

Was born at Newburyport, about the year 1788. He was early left with his brother an orphan, and found a home with his maternal grandfather, Dr. Nathaniel Cogswell, at the family seat in Rowley, Massachusetts, the beauties of which he has celebrated in one of his poems. Entering Brown University, he took his degree there in 1812, and prepared himself for the ministry of the Protestant Episcopal Church, in which he took orders. He began to preach, and published two volumes of sermons, but was never settled over a congregation. He was much occupied in literature. A collection of his youthful poems appeared in 1809. It is headed by *The Cypriad*, in two cantos, a celebration of the tender passion, which he subsequently worked over in his poem, *The Trophies of Love*. In 1815, he published at Philadelphia a volume of poems, with the title *The Broken Harp*, containing "Earl Kandorf and Rosabelle, a Harper's Tale," a number of grave and light pieces, and translations from the classical and modern Latin poets. A third collection of his poems, in two neat volumes, appeared from the press of Wells and Lilly, at Boston, in 1821.

We are not aware of any published account of Henry Knight's life. From the recently issued Memorial of his brother Frederick, to be noticed presently, it appears that he died early in life, and that he left behind him an Autobiographical Sketch, full of humor and character, which, judging from the specimens given, deserves to be published at length.

Mr. Knight's poems, if not always highly finished, are at least elegant and scholarlike performances. He took for his subjects, when he was not writing cantos on love, topics involving thought and reflection, though he handled them in a light vein. His "Crusade" has an elaborate "argument," setting forth the subtleties of theology. It is a playful satirical poem, on a serious theme. Another, "The Grave," is emulous of the didactic fervors of Cowper. In his "Sciences in Masquerade," an amusing illustration of the old theme of Sir Thomas More's "Praise of Folly," he sports gaily in a light rhyming measure. In his classical tastes he was fond of Horace, Ovid, the Epigrammatists, and such modern Latinists as Bonefonius. His muse was equally ready for the grave or gay—a sonnet or an epitaph.

THE COUNTRY OVEN.

I sing the Oven—glowing, fruitful theme.
Happy for me, that mad Achilles found,

And weak Ulysses erst, a servile bard,
That deigned their puny feats, else lost, to sing.
And happy that Æneas, feeble man!
Fell into hands of less emprise than mine;
Too mean the subject for a bard so high.
Not Dante, Ariosto, Tasso, dared
Sport their gross minds in such grand element.
Nor he, dame nature's master-journeyman,
Who nimbly wrought a comic tragedy,
As poet woos a muse, one Shakespeare called!
Nor Milton, who embattled Devils sung;
Nor bold Sir Blackmore, who an Epic built,
Quick as can mason rear a chimney-stack;
Nor later these, Klopstock and Wieland famed,
Who sung, this King of Elves, that King of Kings;
Dared the prolific Oven blaze in song.
  Expect not now of Furnaces to hear,
Where Æolus dilates the liquid glass;
Nor where the THREE, testing their God could save,
Walked barefoot thro' the lambent heat, unseared;
Nor where the Hollanders, in nests of tow,
With mimic nature, incubate their eggs;
For the Domestic Oven claims my powers.
  Come then, from kilns of flame, and tropic suns,
Each salamander Muse, and warm my brain.
  Need I describe?—Who hath a kitchen seen,
And not an arched concavity called Oven?
Grand farinaceous nourisher of life!
See hungry gapes its broad mouth for its food,
And hear the faggots crackling in its jaws,
Its palate glowing red with burning breath.
Do not approach too near; the ingulphing draught
Will drink your respiration ere you list.
  Glance now the fire-jambs round, and there observe
Utensils formed for culinary use.
Shovel and tongs, like ancient man and wife,
He, with his arms akimbo, she in hoops.
There, dangling sausages in chains hang down;
As Sciences and Arts, distinct, allied;
Or, as in Union bound, our sister States.
Here, flayed eels, strung pendent by the waist;
So swing aloof victims in heathen climes;
O Algier hearts! to mock at writhing pain.
And, high in smoke-wreaths, ponderous ham to cure;
So may each traitor to his country hang!
And, thick on nails, the housewife's herbs to dry;
Coltsfoot for pipe, and spearmint for a tea.
Upon the hearth, the shrill-lunged cricket chirps
Her serenade, not waiting to be prest,
And Sue, poking the cinders, smiles to point,
As fond associations cross the mind,
A gallant, ring, or ticket, fashioned there.
And purring puss, her pied-coat licked sleek,
Sits mousing for the crumbs, beside black Jack.
He, curious drone, with eyes and teeth of white,
And natural curl, who twenty Falls has seen,
And cannot yet count four!—nor ever can,
Tho' tasked to learn, until his nose be sharp.
'Tis marvel, if he thinks, but when he speaks;
Else, to himself, why mutter loud and strange,
And scold, and laugh, as half a score were by?
In shape, and parts, a seed of Caliban!
He now is roasting earth-nuts by the coals,
And hissing clams, like martyrs mocking pain;
And sizzing apples, air-lanced with a pin;
While in the embers hops the parching corn,
Crack! crack! disploding with the heat, like bombs.
Craunching, he squats, and grins, and gulps his mug,
And shows his pompion-shell, with eyes and mouth,
And candle fitted, for the tail of kite,
To scare the lasses in their evening walk—
For, next day, and Thanksgiving-Eve will come.
  Now turn we to the teeming Oven; while,
A skilful midwife, comes the aged Dame;
Her apron clean, and nice white cap of lawn.
With long lean arm, she lifts the griding slice,
And inward slides it, drawing slowly out,
In semi-globes, and frustums of the cone,
Tanned brown with heat, come, smoking, broad high loaves;
And drop-cakes, ranged like cocks round stack of hay;
Circles and segments, pies and turn-overs,
For children's children, who stand teasing round,
Scorching their mouths, and dance like juggler's apes,
Wishing the pie more cool, or they less keen.
Next, brown and wrinkled, like the good dame's brow,
Come russet-coated sweetings, pulp for milk;
A luscious dish—would one were brought me now!
And *kisses*, made by Sue for suitor's pun.
And when the morrow greets each smiling face,
And from the church, where grateful hearts have poured,
Led by the Man of God, their thanks and prayers,
To Him, who fills their granaries with good,
They hurry home, snuffing the spicy steams;
The pious matron, with full heart, draws forth
The spare-rib crisp—more savory from the spit!
Tall pots of pease and beans—vile, flatulent;
And puddings, smoking to the raftered walls;
And sweet cup-custards, part of the dessert.
These all, concreted some, some subtilized,
And by the generative heart matured,
A goodly birth, the welcome time brings forth.
  Illustrious Oven! warmest, heartiest friend!
Destroy but thee, and where were festive smiles?
We, cannibals, might torrify and seethe;
Or dry blood-reeking flesh in the cold sun;
Or, like the Arab, on his racing horse,
Beneath the saddle swelter it for food.
  And yet, ere thou give us, we must give thee.
Thus many an Oven barren is for life.
O poverty! how oft thy wishful eye
Rests on thine Oven, hungry as thyself!
Would I might load each Oven of the Poor,
With what each palate craves—a fruitless wish!
Yet seldom hear we Industry complain;
And no one should complain, who hath two eyes,
Two hands, and mind and body, sound and free.
And such, their powers to worthy ends applied,
Be pleased, indulgent Patroness, to feed.

FREDERICK KNIGHT, the younger brother of the preceding, and who for some time survived him, was born in Hampton, N. H., October 9, 1791. He shared with his brother the influences of the refined rural home of Rowley, and acquired a taste for the poetical beauties of nature, which became the solace of his disappointed career. He studied for a while at Harvard, but did not concentrate his attention sufficiently to pursue any settled plan of life. He was afterwards at the law school of Judges Reeve and Gould, at Litchfield, Conn. Subsequently he taught school for a while in the then partially settled region of the Penobscot, and pursued for a time the same vocation at Marblehead. His tastes and habits of retirement, however, constantly brought him back to the country-seat at Rowley, where he enjoyed a home with his amiable grandfather, Dr. Cogswell, an estimable physician, who retired from practice to the pleasures and pursuits of his farm. On the death of that relative, he was offered a situation with his uncle, Mr. Nathaniel Cogswell, an eminent merchant, who resided at one of the Canary Islands. Thither he went; but a passion for the beauties of the spot prevailed over the demands of business, and he failed in the objects of the journey. He returned to his beloved Rowley, where, upon the death of his grandmother and brother Henry, being left without resources, he accepted the offer of a home with Mrs. Sawyer, an aged widow of the neighborhood, who promised him the reversion of her cottage on her death. There, in a frugal mode of living, he passed the remainder of his days, cultivating his gentle tastes—for he was without vices—and penning numerous occasional poems addressed to his friends, or dedicated to his religious emotions. He died at Rowley, November 20, 1849, leaving his venerable friend in the cottage, his survivor, at the age of ninety-five. A memorial of this simple life has been lately published with the title, "Thorn Cottage, or the Poet's Home."* It contains numerous anecdotes of the simple-minded, sensitive man, who only lacked energy to have borne a more prominent part in the world, with many pleasing specimens of his poetical powers. One of these is a description of the furniture of the humble cottage.

Four windows—two in front to face the sun,
And in the south and western end, but one;
The fourth, o'ershadowed by a shed too near,
Lets in no golden beams to warm and cheer;
With crimson wainscots, dull and faded grown,
And time-worn curtains, deeply tinged with brown—
Thence to the ceiling, all the space between,
A hanging, traced with flowers and berries green.
Not quite like vernal bloom or autumn we,
A sort of ice-plant and a snow-ball tree.

A cherry dish—a kind of cottage shop,
With cups and mugs, and candlesticks on top;
A looking-glass; a dumb old-fashioned clock,
Like pale-faced nun, drest in her vesper frock:
Two ancient pictures, clouded by the smoke,
One, lifting Joseph, for the word he spoke,
From out the pit intended for his grave,
Whom God designed his chosen tribes to save:
The after-Joseph and his wondrous wife,
Between them leading the young Lord of Life;
Two smaller portraits, looking younger rather,
Good Flavel one—and one, good Cotton Mather.

Another is a touching expression of the religious feeling which cheered his broken fortunes.

FAITH.

Have faith—and thou shalt know its use;
Have faith—and thou wilt feel
'Tis this that fills the widow's cruse,
And multiplies her meal.

Have faith—and breaking from thy bound,
With eagles thou wilt rise,
And find thy cottage on the ground
A castle in the skies.

Have faith—and thou shalt hear the tread
Of horses in the air,
And see the chariot overhead
That's waiting for thee there.

Have faith—the earth will bloom beneath,
The sea divide before thee,
The air with odors round thee breathe,
And heaven wide open o'er thee.

Have faith—that purifies the heart;
And with thy flag unfurled,
Go forth without a spear or dart;
Thou'lt overcome the world.

Have faith—be on thy way:
Arise and trim thy light,
And shine, if not the orb of day,
Yet as a star of night.

Have faith—though threading lone and far
Through Pontine's deepest swamp,
When night has neither moon nor star,
Thou'lt need no staff nor lamp.

Have faith—go, roam with savage men,
And sleep with beasts of prey—
Go, sit with lions in their den,
And with the leopards play.

Have faith—on ocean's heaving breast
Securely thou may'st tread,
And make the billowy mountain's crest
Thy cradle and thy bed.

Have faith—around let thunders roar,
Let earth beneath thee rend—
The lightnings play, and deluge pour—
Thy pass-word is—a friend.

Have faith—in famine's sorest need,
When naked lie the fields,
Go forth and weeping sow the seed,
Then reap the sheaves it yields.

Have faith—in earth's most troubled scene,
In time's most trying hour,
Thy breast and brow shall be serene—
So soothing is its power.

Have faith—and say to yonder tree,
And mountain where it stands,
Be ye both buried in the sea—
They sink beneath its sands!

Have faith—upon the battle-field,
When facing foe to foe,
The shaft rebounding from thy shield,
Shall lay the archer low.

Have faith—the finest thing that flies,
On wings of golden ore,
That shines and melts along the skies,
Was but a worm before.

HEW AINSLIE.

Hew Ainslie was born on the fifth day of April, 1792, at Baugeny Mains, in the parish of Daily, Carrick District, Ayrshire, Scotland, on the estate of Sir Hew Dalrymple Hamilton, in whose service his father, George Ainslie, had been employed for many years. Hew received a good education, commenced under the care of a private tutor, who was supported by three or four families in the neighborhood, and continued at schools at Ballantrae and Ayr, until the age of twelve, when, in consequence of fears being entertained respecting his health, he was sent back to his native hills to recruit. Here he found Sir Hew, the landlord, engaged in an extensive plan for the improvement of his estate, under the direction of the celebrated landscape gardener White, and a number of young men from the South as assistants. Hew joined this company, and as the planters were all respectably educated, and, like

* Thorn Cottage, or the Poet's Home, a Memorial of Frederick Knight, Esq., of Rowley, Mass. Boston: Press of Crocker and Brewster. 1855. 12mo. pp. 108.

the mechanicals of Athens, sometimes "enacted plays," this new association aided him in the cultivation of literature as well as of mother earth.

In his seventeenth year, Ainslie was sent to Glasgow to study law in the office of a relation of his mother, but the pursuit proved uncongenial, and he soon rejoined his family, who had, in the meantime, removed to Roslin. He afterwards obtained a situation in the Register House, Edinburgh, which he retained until 1822, a portion of the time being passed at Kinniel House, as the amanuensis of Dugald Stewart, whose last work he copied for the press.

Ainslie married in 1812, and after his father's death in 1817, determined to remove to America, but was not able to put his plan in execution until 1822, when he crossed the ocean, landed at New York on the twenty-sixth of July, and purchased a small farm in Hoosick, Rensselaer county, New York.

In 1825 he removed to the West, tried Owen's settlement at New Harmony for a year, found it a failure, and settled down for a time as a brewer at Shippingport, Kentucky. In 1829, he built a brewery in Louisville, which was ruined by an inundation of the Ohio in 1832. He constructed a similar establishment the same year in New Albany, Indiana, which was destroyed by fire in 1834. Satisfied with these experiments, he has since employed himself in superintending the erection of breweries, mills, and distilleries, throughout the West, on account of others. He is at present a resident of Jersey City.

On the eve of his departure from Scotland, Ainslie published *A Pilgrimage to the Land of Burns*, a volume of notes interspersed with numerous songs and ballads, suggested by a visit to his early home in Ayrshire. He has recently collected these with his other *Songs, Ballads, and Poems*, published originally in various magazines, in a volume.*

Several of Ainslie's songs will be found in "Whistle-Binkie" and other collections of the lyric poetry of Scotland, and well deserve the popular reputation they have secured.

THE ABSENT FATHER.

The friendly greeting of our kind,
  Or gentler woman's smiling,
May soothe the weary wanderer's mind,
  His lonely hours beguiling;

May charm the restless spirit still,
  The pang of grief allaying;
But ah! the soul it cannot fill,
  Or keep the heart from straying.

O, how the fancy, when unbound,
  On wings of rapture swelling,
Will hurry to the holy ground,
  Where loves and friends are dwelling!

My lonely and my widowed wife,
  How oft to thee I wander!
Re-living those sweet hours o' life,
  When mutual love was tender.

And here with sickness lowly laid,
  All scenes to sadness turning,
Where will I find a breast like thine,
  To lay this brow that 's burning?

And how are all my pretty ones?
  How have the cherubs thriven,
Who cheered my leisure with their love,
  And made my home a heaven?

Does yet the rose array your cheek,
  As when in grief I blessed you?
O, are your cherry lips as sweet,
  As when in tears I kissed you?

Can your young broken prattle tell—
  Can your young memories gather
A thought of him who loves you well—
  Your weary wandering father?

O, I've had wants and wishes too,
  This world have checked and chilled;
But bless me but again with you,
  And half my prayer's fulfilled.

THE INGLE SIDE.

It's rare to see the morning bleeze,
  Like a bonfire frae the sea;
It's fair to see the burnie kiss
  The lip o' the flowery lea;
An' fine it is on green hill side,
  When hums the hinny bee;
But rarer, fairer, finer fair,
  Is the ingle side to me.

Glens may be gilt wi' gowans rare,
  The birds may fill the tree,
An' haughs hae a' the scented ware,
  That simmer's growth can gi'e;
But the cantie hearth where cronies meet,
  An' the darling o' our e'e;
That makes to us a warld complete,
  O, the ingle side's for me!

JOHN NEAL.

JOHN NEAL, as we learn from his own account of himself in Blackwood's Magazine,* is a native of Portland, Maine. He was born about 1794, and was of a Quaker family, but does not appear to have inherited any Quaker placidity of mind. In his boyhood he was "read out" of the drab fraternity for "knocking a man, who insulted him, head over heels; for paying a militia fine; for making a tragedy, and for desiring to be turned out, whether or no." He was brought up as a shop-boy, and when he became a man, became also a wholesale dry-goods dealer, in partnership with Pierpont, afterwards the poet. The concern failed, and Neal commenced the study of law, and with it the profession of literature, by an article on the poetry of Lord Byron, who had then just published the third canto of Childe Harold. Neal read through, and reviewed everything the poet had thus far written, in four days, producing an article long enough to make a small book, which appeared from month to month, until completed, in the *Portico*, a magazine published in Baltimore. He continued to write for this periodical "from the second up to the end of the fifth volume, being a large part of the whole, until he knocked it on the head, it is thought, by an article on Free Agency,"—no bad material, it must be admitted, for a literary slung-shot.

Next came *Keep Cool*, his first novel. "It was written chiefly for the discouragement of

* Scottish Songs, Ballads, and Poems. By Hew Ainslie. Redfield, New York. 1855.

* No. xvii. p. 190, Feb. 1825.

duelling—about which, as I was eternally in hot water, I began to entertain certain very tender, seasonable, talkative scruples of conscience. The hero is insulted, he fights under what anybody would call a justification—kills the insulter—and is never happy for an hour afterwards." The book was published in 1817. In Feb. 1825 it is thus summarily disposed of in the article from which our extracts have been taken. "Keep Cool is forgotten; or where it is known at all is looked upon as a disgrace to her literature."

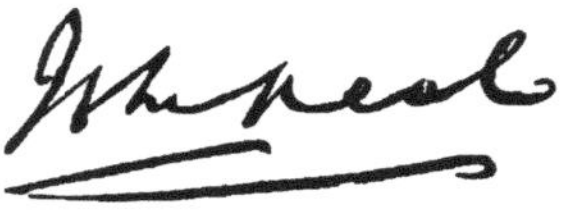

The Battle of Niagara, with other Poems, by Jehu O'Cataract, was published in 1818. This portentous *nom de plume* was a nickname given the author in a club to which he belonged, and intended to characterize his impetuosity. He had the good sense to drop it in a second edition of the poems, which appeared in 1819. *Otho*, a five act tragedy, was written about the same time. "Works," says Mr. Neal, "abounding throughout in absurdity, intemperance, affectation, extravagance—with continual but involuntary imitation: yet, nevertheless, containing altogether more sincere poetry, more exalted, *original*, pure poetry, than *all* the works of *all* the other authors that have ever appeared in America."

These poems possess vigor, spirit, and ease in versification. They consist of the "Battle of Niagara," which contains some fine passages of description of the scenes and conflict which supply its title; "Goldau, or the Maniac Harper," a narrative poem, suggested in part by the celebrated slide of the Rossberg, Switzerland, in 1806; an Ode delivered before the Delphians, a literary society of Baltimore, and a few brief miscellaneous pieces.

By way of a change of occupation after the composition of these poems, and probably as a somewhat safer means of gaining a little cash, he prepared an Index for Niles to his Register, which Niles was so much pleased with that, *mirabile dictu* for a publisher, or for anybody else, he gave nearly three times as much as he had promised for it.

He also wrote about a quarter of a History of the American Revolution, "by Paul Allen," who was a veritable flesh and blood man, but so inordinately lazy, that after announcing and receiving subscriptions for the work, it finally appeared from the pen of his friends Neal and Watkins, the preface only being by the nominal author.

Four novels followed these works in quick succession. Their chronology is thus given by their author:

"LOGAN—*begun*—— *ended* November 17, 1821.

"RANDOLPH—begun 26th November, 1821; 1st vol. finished 21st December, 1821; second, 8th January, 1822, with the interval of about a week between the two, when I wrote nothing—four English volumes in *thirty-six days.*

"ERRATA—begun (time uncertain) *after* the 8th of January, 1822; finished 16th February, 1822, four English volumes in less than *thirty-nine days.*

"SEVENTY-SIX—begun after February 16, 1822; finished 19th March, 1822, (with 4 days off, during which I did not see the MS.)—three English volumes in *twenty-seven days!*"

Meanwhile the author had studied law; been admitted, and was practising as energetically as he was writing.

"LOGAN," he goes on to say, "is a piece of *declamation;* SEVENTY-SIX, of *narrative;* RANDOLPH, *epistolary;* ERRATA, *colloquial.*"

Logan is a picture of Indian life, vigorous, picturesque, and in some of the set speeches at least, as the author confesses, declamatory.

Seventy-Six has the spirit and movement of the revolutionary era, when the youth of the country hurried to the field with the sufficient protection of the household musket and the paternal benediction. It is a lively presentation of the era.

In *Randolph*, a story of its own date, Neal introduces personal and critical sketches of the leading authors and public men of the day, including, as usual in his enumerations of this kind, himself. The remarks on William Pinckney excited the anger of his son, who challenged Neal as the presumed author, and on his refusal to fight posted him as a "craven." A history of the affair, in which just ground is taken on the subject of critical comment and the practice of duelling, appears in a letter signed by Neal, as a "postscript" to his next publication, *Errata.*

In *Errata*, also a story of modern times, his object was to show "that deformity of person does not of necessity imply deformity of heart; and that a dwarf in stature may be a giant in blood;" and to delineate the female character more in conformity with human nature than with the usual conventional type of the novelist. He has carried out this design in a tale of high dramatic interest. The preface to this work is in the author's happiest manner.

I have written this tale for the purpose of showing how people talk, when they are not talking for display; when they are telling a story of themselves familiarly; seated about their own fireside; with a plenty of apples and cider, in the depth of winter, with all their family, and one or two pleasant strangers lolling about, and the great house-dog with his nose in the ashes; or out under the green trees on a fine summer night, with all the faces that they love, coming and going like shadows, under the beautiful dim trees, and the red sky shining through them.

Reader—have you ever stood, with your hat in your hand, to look at a little dreamy light made by the moonshine, where it fell through the green leaves, and "*fermented*" in the wet turf?—or the starlight and water bubbles dancing together, under the willow trees? If you have, then you may form some notion of what I mean, by my love of Nature. Men go by her blossoming places, every hour, and never see them; her singing places, while there is a wedding in the grass, and trample upon them, without one thought of their beauty; and just so with the delicate beauties of conversation. They see nothing, hear nothing, until their attention be called to it. But they go out, where it is the fashion to be sentimental, and persuade themselves that their artificial rapture is the natural offspring of a warm heart and a pure taste. Pshaw!—people that do not love fine conversation and fine reading, beyond fine speaking and fine singing, have neither understanding nor taste.

The favorable reception of a portion of these novels in England, on their republication, induced their author to try his literary fortunes in that country. With his characteristic promptitude he closed up his business affairs, transferred his clients to a professional brother, borrowed cash, and was off in three weeks. He arrived in England in January, 1824, and remained three years, writing for Blackwood (where in 1824 and 1825 he published a series of articles on American writers, not forgetting, as we have already seen, himself) and other periodicals. He became acquainted with Jeremy Bentham, who asked him to dinner, and liked him so well, that he next invited him to reside in his house. He accepted the invitation, and passed the remainder of his time in London there, "with a glorious library at my elbow, a fine large comfortable study warmed by a steam-engine, exercise under ground, society, and retirement, all within my reach."*

In 1827, after a short tour in France, Neal returned to Portland, and commenced a weekly newspaper, *The Yankee.* It was after published at Boston, but change of air not improving its vitality, at the end of a year it was merged in "The New England Galaxy," and its late editor returned to Portland.

In 1828 he published *Rachel Dyer*, a story, in a single volume, the subject of which is "Salem Witchcraft." It is much more subdued in style than his earlier novels, and is a carefully prepared and historically correct picture of the period it presents. It was originally written for Blackwood's Magazine, as the first of a series of North American stories. It was accepted, paid for, and in type, when a misunderstanding occurring between the author and publisher, the former paid back the sum he had received, and withdrew the story, which he subsequently enlarged to its present form.

This was followed in 1830 by *Authorship, by a New Englander over the Sea.* It is a rambling narrative, whose interest is dependent on the mystery in which the reader is kept until near its close, respecting the character of the chief personages. The *Down Easters* and *Ruth Elder*, which have since appeared, close the series of Mr. Neal's novels.

There is a great deal of merit in the works we have mentioned; they are full of dramatic power and incident; but these virtues are well nigh overbalanced by their extravagance, and the jerking, out-of-breath style in which they are often written. "I do not pretend," he says, in the "unpublished preface to the *North American Stories*," prefixed to "Rachel Dyer," "to write English; that is, I do not pretend to write what the English themselves call English—I do not, and I hope to God—I say this reverently, although one of their reviewers may be again puzzled to determine 'whether I am swearing or praying,' when I say so—that I never shall write what is now worshipped under the name of *classical* English. It is no natural language—it never was—it never will be spoken alive on this earth, and therefore ought never to be written. We have dead languages enough now, but the deadest language I ever met with or heard of, was that in use among the writers of Queen Anne's day."

The vigor of the man, however, pervades everything he has produced. He sees and thinks as well as writes, after his own fashion, and neither fears nor follows criticism. It is to be regretted that he has not more fully elaborated his prose productions, as that process would probably have given them a firmer hold on public favor than they appear to have secured. There is much strong vigorous sense, independence in speaking of men and things; good, close thought; analysis of character, and clear description, which the public should not lose, in these pages.

Mr. Neal has written much for the periodicals, and some of his finest poems have appeared in this manner since the publication of his early volume. He announced, a few years since, that he was engaged upon a History of American Literature.

A WAR SONG OF THE REVOLUTION.

Men of the North! look up!
There's a tumult in your sky;
A troubled glory surging out,
Great shadows hurrying by.

Your strength—where is it now?
Your quivers—are they spent?
Your arrows in the rust of death,
Your fathers' bows unbent.

Men of the North! awake!
Ye're called to from the deep;
Trumpets in every breeze—
Yet there ye lie asleep.

A stir in every tree;
A shout from every wave;
A challenging on every side;
A moan from every grave:

A battle in the sky;
Ships thundering through the air—
Jehovah on the march—
Men of the North, to prayer!

Now, now—in all your strength;
There's that before your way,
Above, about you, and below,
Like armies in array.

Lift up your eyes, and see
The changes overhead;
Now hold your breath, and hear
The mustering of the dead.

See how the midnight air
With bright commotion burns,
Thronging with giant shape,
Banner and spear by turns.

The sea-fog driving in,
Solemnly and swift,
The moon afraid—stars dropping out—
The very skies adrift:

The Everlasting God:
Our Father—Lord of Love—
With cherubim and seraphim
All gathering above.

* Passage from the biography prefixed to the translation of the Principles of Legislation, from the French of Dumont.

Their stormy plumage lighted up
 As forth to war they go;
The shadow of the Universe,
 Upon our haughty foe!

THE BIRTH OF A POET.

On a blue summer night,
 While the stars were asleep,
 Like gems of the deep,
In their own drowsy light;
 While the newly mown hay
 On the green earth lay,
 And all that came near it went scented away.
From a lone woody place
There looked out a face,
With large blue eyes,
Like the wet warm skies,
 Brimful of water and light;
A profusion of hair
Flashing out on the air,
 And a forehead alarmingly bright:
'Twas the head of a poet! He grew
 As the sweet strange flowers of the wilderness grow,
In the dropping of natural dew,
 Unheeded—alone—
 Till his heart had blown—
 As the sweet strange flowers of the wilderness blow;
Till every thought wore a changeable stain,
Like flower-leaves wet with the sunset rain.
A proud and passionate boy was he,
Like all the children of Poesy;
With a haughty look and a haughty tread,
And something awful about his head;
 With wonderful eyes
 Full of woe and surprise,
Like the eyes of them that can see the dead.
 Looking about,
For a moment or two he stood
On the shore of the mighty wood;
 Then ventured out,
 With a bounding step and a joyful shout,
The brave sky bending o'er him!
The broad sea all before him!

ORVILLE DEWEY.

The Rev. Orville Dewey is the son of a farmer, of Sheffield, Berkshire, Massachusetts where he was born in the year 1794. He took his degree with distinction at Williams College in 1814, and afterwards passed some months in teaching school in his native village, and as a clerk in a dry-goods store in New York. In 1816 he entered Andover Theological Seminary. He completed his course of study in 1819, was ordained, and preached with success as a Presbyterian clergyman, but within a year connected himself with the Unitarian denomination. During the absence of Dr. Channing in Europe, Mr. Dewey was invited to supply his place. He was afterwards settled at New Bedford for ten years. He then in consequence of ill health went to Europe, remaining abroad for two years. On his return, in 1835, he published a volume of *Discourses on Various Subjects*, and about the same time became the pastor of the Unitarian Church of the Messiah in the city of New York. In 1836, he published *The Old World and the New; a Journal of Observations and Reflections made on a visit to Europe in* 1833 *and* 1834.

Dr. Dewey speedily became widely known as a pulpit orator, for his eloquent discussion of moral themes, and his adaptation of the religious essay to the pastoral wants and pursuits of the public. His church in Mercer-street having been destroyed by fire, was replaced by an edifice in Broadway of far greater value and architectural merit.

In 1838, Dr. Dewey followed out the spirit of a great portion of his professional labors by the publication of *Moral Views of Commerce, Society, and Politics*, in twelve Discourses. These were followed in 1841 by *Discourses on Human Life*, and in 1846 by *Discourses and Reviews on Questions relating to Controversial Theology and Practical Religion*. He has also published, separately, a number of sermons and addresses.

In 1844, all of the author's works which had then appeared were issued in London, in a closely printed octavo volume of about nine hundred pages.

In 1849, Dr. Dewey resigned his charge of the Church of the Messiah on account of ill health, and after a period of some months of relaxation, passed mostly in travel, accepted a call to Washington City. He has of late resided at his farm in Sheffield, in his native Berkshire.

As a preacher Dr. Dewey is grave and weighty; his manner conveying the idea of the man of thought, who draws his reflections from the depths of his own nature. He is ingenious and speculative, and impresses his audience as a philosophic teacher, whether from the pulpit or in the lecture hall.

STUDY—FROM A PHI BETA KAPPA ADDRESS AT CAMBRIDGE IN 1830.

The favorite idea of a genius among us, is of one who never studies, or who studies, nobody can tell when—at midnight, or at odd times and intervals—and now and then strikes out, *at a heat*, as the phrase is, some wonderful production. This is a character that has figured largely in the history of our literature, in the person of our Fieldings, our Savages, and our Steeles—"loose fellows about town," or loungers in the country, who slept in alehouses and wrote in bar-rooms, who took up the pen as a magician's wand to supply their wants, and when the pressure of necessity was relieved, resorted again to their carousals. Your real genius is an idle, irregular, vagabond sort of personage, who muses in the fields or dreams by the fire-side; whose strong impulses—that is the cant of it—must needs hurry him into wild irregularities or foolish eccentricity; who abhors order, and can bear no restraint, and eschews all labor: such an one, for instance, as Newton or Milton! What! they must have been irregular, else they were no geniuses.

"The young man," it is often said, "has genius enough, if he would only study." Now the truth is, as I shall take the liberty to state it, that genius will study, it is that in the mind which does study; that is the very nature of it. I care not to say that it will always use books. All study is not reading, any more than all reading is study. By study I mean—but let one of the noblest geniuses and hardest students of any age define it for me. "Studium," says Cicero, "est animi assidua et vehemens ad aliquam rem applicata magnâ cum voluntate occupatio, ut philosophiæ, poëticæ, geometriæ, literarum."* Such study, such intense mental

* De Inventione, Lib. i. c. 25.

action, and nothing else, is genius. And so far as there is any native predisposition about this enviable character of mind, it is a predisposition to that action. That is the only test of the original bias; and he who does not come to that point, though he may have shrewdness, and readiness, and parts, never had a genius. No need to waste regrets upon him, as that he never could be induced to give his attention or study to anything; he never had that which he is supposed to have lost. For attention it is, though other qualities belong to this transcendent power,—attention it is, that is the very soul of genius: not the fixed eye, not the poring over a book, but the fixed thought. It is, in fact, an action of the mind which is steadily concentrated upon one idea or one series of ideas,—which collects in one point the rays of the soul till they search, penetrate, and fire the whole train of its thoughts. And while the fire burns within, the outward man may indeed be cold, indifferent, negligent,—absent in appearance; he may be an idler, or a wanderer, apparently without aim or intent: but still the fire burns within. And what though "it bursts forth" at length, as has been said, "like volcanic fires, with spontaneous, original, native force!" It only shows the intenser action of the elements beneath. What though it breaks like lightning from the cloud! The electric fire had been collecting in the firmament through many a silent, calm, and clear day. What though the might of genius appears in one decisive blow, struck in some moment of high debate, or at the crisis of a nation's peril! That mighty energy, though it may have heaved in the breast of a Demosthenes, was once a feeble infant's thought. A mother's eye watched over its dawning. A father's care guarded its early growth. It soon trod with youthful steps the halls of learning, and found other fathers to wake and to watch for it,—even as it finds them here. It went on: but silence was upon its path, and the deep strugglings of the inward soul marked its progress, and the cherishing powers of nature silently ministered to it. The elements around breathed upon it and "touched it to finer issues." The golden ray of heaven fell upon it, and ripened its expanding faculties. The slow revolutions of years slowly added to its collected treasures and energies; till in its hour of glory, it stood forth embodied in the form of living, commanding, irresistible eloquence! The world wonders at the manifestation, and says, "Strange, strange, that it should come thus unsought, unpremeditated, unprepared!" But the truth is, there is no more a miracle in it, than there is in the towering of the preëminent forest tree, or in the flowing of the mighty and irresistible river, or in the wealth and the waving of the boundless harvest.

JARED SPARKS.

JARED SPARKS, whose numerous literary labors are so honorably connected with American history and biography, was born at Willington, in the state of Connecticut, about 1794. In his youth he worked on a farm, and in the intervals of occupation in a grist and saw-mill which he tended, became interested in a copy of Guthrie's Geography, which, in its way, encouraged his natural love of learning. He was a good student in such schools as a country town then afforded. He became apprenticed to a carpenter, with whom he remained some two years, when his employer, in deference to his love of study, relinquished his legal hold upon his time. Sparks became at once a village schoolmaster in the district of the town of Tolland, teaching in the winter, and returning for a livelihood to his trade in the summer. He attracted the attention of the clergyman of Willington, the Rev. Hubbel Loomis, who taught him mathematics and induced him to study Latin. In return for this instruction and residence in his friend's house, he turned his carpenter's knowledge to account, and shingled the minister's barn. The Rev. Abiel Abbot, lately of Peterborough, New Hampshire, extended the patronage which his brother clergyman had commenced. By his influence Sparks was secured a scholarship at the Phillips Exeter Academy, on a charitable foundation, which provided education and a home free of cost. He travelled to Mr. Abbot at Coventry, and thence on foot to Exeter. In 1809 he thus found himself at the celebrated institution then and long after under the care of Dr. Benjamin Abbot. He remained there two years, teaching a school one winter at Rochester in New Hampshire. He entered Harvard in 1811, and was assisted by his warm friend President Kirkland to a scholarship, the resources of which he eked out by district-school-keeping a portion of the year in New England, and an engagement in the first two years of his undergraduate course at a private school, as far off as Havre de Grace, in Maryland, to which he was recommended by President Dwight of Yale. While in this latter place it was invaded by the British troops in 1813. Before the assault he served in the militia, and remained to witness the conflagration of the town. He returned to Harvard to be a graduate with the class of 1815. He then taught a classical school at Lancaster, Massachusetts, and came back to Harvard to study divinity under Dr. Ware. The college, in 1817, appointed him a tutor in mathematics and natural philosophy, the duties of which he discharged for two years while he prosecuted his theological studies. He was one of the associates to whom Mr. Tudor assigned *The North American Review* at this time, and became its working editor. Two years afterwards, in May, 1819, he was ordained pastor of a new Unitarian Church at Baltimore, Maryland, Dr. Channing preaching on the occasion. It was the controversial period of Unitarianism, and Sparks took part in the discussion, publishing, in 1820, a volume of *Letters on the Ministry, Ritual, and Doctrines of the Protestant Episcopal Church*, in reply to a sermon levelled at his doctrines by the Rev. Dr. William E. Wyatt. In 1821, a proof of his position and standing, he was elected chaplain to the House of Representatives. The same year he commenced a monthly periodical, in duodecimo, entitled *The Unitarian Miscellany and Christian Monitor*. It was continued by him for two years during his stay at Baltimore. He wrote in it a series of letters to the Rev. Dr. Miller of Princeton, on the *Comparative Moral Tendency of Trinitarian and Unitarian Doctrines*, which he afterwards enlarged and published at Boston, in a volume, in 1823. He also commenced at Baltimore the publication of a *Collection of Essays and Tracts in Theology, from Various Authors, with Biographical and Critical Notices*, which was completed at Boston in 1826, in six duodecimo volumes. The plan was suggested by Bishop Watson's Collection of Tracts. It took a comprehensive range within the limits of practical Christianity and liberal inquiry, including such authors as Jeremy Taylor, Locke, Watts, William Penn, Bishop Hoadly, John Hales, and others of the English Church. It contained some translations from the French.

After four years of laborious ministerial duty at Baltimore, he retired from the position, and travelled in the western states for his health. Returning to Boston, he purchased *The North American Review* of its proprietors, and became its sole editor. In 1828, he published a *Life of John Ledyard, the American Traveller*, which passed through several editions, was translated into German by Dr. Michaelis, and published at Leipsic, and has since been included in the author's series of American Biography.

Jared Sparks

He had already undertaken an important work in his literary career, the collection for publication of the Writings of Washington. In pursuance of this work, in 1826, he had examined personally the revolutionary papers in the public offices of all the thirteen original States and the department at Washington, and afterwards, by arrangement with Judge Washington and Chief-justice Marshall, secured the possession of all the Washington papers at Mount Vernon. He further, in 1828, made a voyage to Europe for the purpose of transcribing documents in the state archives at London and Paris—which were now for the first time opened, for historical purposes, to his investigation, by the aid of Sir James Mackintosh, the Marquis of Lansdowne, and Lord Holland in England, and La Fayette and the Marquis de Marbois in France. At the end of a year he returned with a valuable stock of materials to America. After nine years of preparation the work appeared in successive volumes, from 1834 to 1837, bearing the title, *The Writings of George Washington; being his Correspondence, Addresses, Messages, and other Papers, official and private, selected and published from the original manuscripts, with a Life of the Author, Notes, and Illustrations.* The first volume was occupied with a *Life of Washington*, which has also been published separately. The whole was received with great favor at home and abroad, Mr. Everett reviewing the work in the North American, and Guizot, in France, editing a selection from the Correspondence, and prefixing to it his highly prized Introductory Discourse on the Character, Influence, and Public Career of Washington; while the German historian, Von Raumer, prepared an edition at Leipsic. During this period also, Mr. Sparks prepared, and with the aid of Congress published in 1829–30, a series of twelve octavo volumes of the *Diplomatic Correspondence of the American Revolution*, including, with occasional notes and comments, letters of Franklin, Adams, Jay, Deane, Lee, Dana, and other agents abroad, as well as of the French ministers, to Congress, during the period of the Revolution. These were derived from the American State Department, with omissions supplied from the editor's European and other collections.

In 1830, Mr. Sparks also originated what has formed one of the most valuable publications of the times, *The American Almanac and Repository of Useful Knowledge.* The first volume was edited by him. In 1832, he published another work of similar importance, *The Life of Gouverneur Morris, with Selections from his Correspondence and Miscellaneous Papers, detailing Events in the French Revolution and the Political History of the United States.* This also secured notice abroad, and was translated into French, in its chief portions, by M. Augustin Gandais, and published in two volumes at Paris. Another literary undertaking in which Mr. Sparks was not merely himself a pioneer, but the leader of a band of writers of influence, was his *Library of American Biography*, of which two series were published, the first of ten volumes from 1834 to 1838, the second of fifteen from 1844 to 1848. Of the sixty lives in this collection, eight were from the pen of Sparks, who contributed biographies of Ethan Allen, Benedict Arnold, Father Marquette, De la Salle, Count Pulaski, John Ribault, Charles Lee, and a reprint of the Ledyard volume. To these numerous and extended undertakings another, of parallel interest with the Washington Papers, was added in 1840, the ten volumes occupied with *The Works of Benjamin Franklin; containing several Political and Historical Tracts not included in any former edition, and many Letters, Official and Private, not hitherto published; with Notes and a Life of the Author.* The Life was a careful and elaborate supplement to the Autobiography, and the work was further enriched with many valuable facts and comments. As proof of the author's industry, two hundred and fifty-three of Franklin's Letters were there printed for the first time, and one hundred and fifty-four first brought together from scattered publications. The work also included numerous letters to Franklin, from his distinguished foreign correspondents.

A companion to the Washington Correspondence appeared at the beginning of 1854, *The Correspondence of the American Revolution, being*

Letters of Eminent Men to George Washington, from the time of his taking Command of the Army to the End of his Presidency. It was edited from the original MSS., which had been in Mr. Sparks's possession.

Besides these literary occupations, which have brought the libraries of the country an accession of no less than sixty-six volumes of national interest, Mr. Sparks has performed, at Harvard, the duties of the McLean Professorship of Ancient and Modern History, from 1839 to 1849; while from 1849 to 1852 he held the arduous office of President of that Institution, which he was compelled to relinquish from ill health. He has since resided at his home at Cambridge, still engaged upon the illustration of the history of his country, and with the preparation, it is currently reported, of a History of the American Revolution.

In his personal relations, the amiability of Mr. Sparks and the attachment of his friends are no less worthy of record than the hold which he has firmly secured upon the public gratitude by his numerous patriotic, carefully penned, and well directed literary labors.*

EDWARD ROBINSON.

DR. EDWARD ROBINSON, the eminent philologist and learned traveller and geographer of the Holy Land, was born April 10, 1794, in Southington, Conn., where his father, the Rev. William Robinson, was for forty-one years pastor of the Congregational church. The family are descended, through the Rev. John Robinson of Duxbury, Mass., from William Robinson of Dorchester. He was there in 1636; but there is no evidence that he was connected with John Robinson of Leyden. As the father's salary was small, less than $400 a year, he cultivated a farm; and the son was sent to the district-school in winter, and employed on the farm during summer. He had an early taste for reading, especially books of travels; for which his father's library, and a subscription library in the village, hardly afforded sufficient materials. In his fourteenth year he was placed, with several other boys, in the family and under the tuition of the Rev. I. B. Woodward of Wolcott, an adjacent town. Here he continued till early in 1810, having for a part of the time the poet Percival as a fellow-pupil. His studies were merely English with the elements of Latin; his father not purposing to send him to college, on account of his feeble constitution and infirm health. In March and April, 1810, he taught a district-school in East Haven, Conn., where a large portion of his pupils were older than himself. In the following May he was employed in the central district-school in Farmington, where he continued a year. The ensuing season, until May, 1812, he spent in a country store in Southington; in which it was his father's plan that he should become a partner. This, however, was not to his own taste; and in June, 1812, he went to Clinton, Oneida county, New York, where one maternal uncle, the Rev. A. S. Norton, D.D., was pastor of the village church; and another, Seth Norton, after having been for many years principal of the academy, had been appointed professor of languages in Hamilton College, then just chartered. Young Robinson joined that autumn the first Freshman class in the college, and graduated in 1816 with the highest honors. In college his inclination turned, perhaps, rather to mathematical than to philological pursuits. He enjoyed the confidence of the professors and of the president, Dr. Azel Backus, who died in the December after Mr. Robinson left. In February, 1817, Mr. Robinson entered the office of the late James Strong of Hudson, New York, afterwards member of Congress; but in October of that year was called as tutor to Hamilton College, where he remained a year, teaching mathematics and the Greek language. In the autumn of 1818 he married the youngest daughter of the Rev. Samuel Kirkland, former missionary to the Indians, sister of the late President Kirkland. She died in July of the following year; and Mr. Robinson continued to reside in Clinton, pursuing his studies, until September, 1821, when he returned for a short time to his father's house.

In December, 1821, he went to Andover, Mass., in order to print a work he had prepared for college instruction, containing the first books of the Iliad, with Latin notes, selected chiefly from Heyne. Here his attention was directed to theology, and he commenced the study of Hebrew; but without connecting himself with the seminary. A year afterwards, at the request of Professor Stuart, he was employed to correct the proofs of the second edition of his Hebrew Grammar (Andover, 1823), and soon became associated with him in the preparation of the work itself.

Edward Robinson

The same year (1823) Professor Stuart having gone on a foot-journey for his health, Mr. Robinson was employed to take charge of his class in the seminary. The same autumn he was appointed assistant instructor, and continued as such until the spring of 1826. In the meantime he translated from the German, in connexion with Professor Stuart, Winer's *Grammar of the New Testament;* and also by himself, from the Latin, Wahl's *Clavis Novi Testamenti* (Andover, 1825).

* We are indebted for the enumeration of facts in this notice to the new edition of 1854 of the American Portrait Gallery, which contains a clearly written and authentic summary of Mr. Sparks's literary career.

In June, 1826, Mr. Robinson sailed for Europe, and passed by way of Paris to the Rhine and Göttingen. Here he stayed some weeks; and then repaired to Halle, to profit by the instructions of Gesenius, Tholuck, Rödiger, and others. The winter was spent in hard labor, with the recreation of constant intercourse with the *savants* of the place and their families. In the summer of 1827 he travelled extensively, first in Northern Germany, Denmark, and Sweden; and afterwards in Southern Germany, through the Tyrol, and as far as to Vienna. The next winter was passed in Berlin in study, and in frequent intercourse with Neander, Hengstenberg, O. von Gerlach, and others. In August, 1828, Mr. Robinson married the youngest daughter of Professor Ludwig von Jakob of Halle. After making the tour of Switzerland, they spent the winter in Paris, and travelled in the spring of 1829 through Italy, as far as Naples. Returning to Halle, Mr. Robinson spent the next winter there in study, at the same time preparing a translation of Buttmann's *Greek Grammar*, which was afterwards published at Andover, 1833.

After his return home in 1830, Dr. Robinson was appointed professor extraordinary of sacred literature in the seminary at Andover. The department of Hebrew instruction fell mainly to him. Many circumstances combined to render this the palmiest period of the Andover Seminary, and classes numbering from sixty to eighty members were entered for several successive years. With the year 1831 Dr. Robinson commenced the publication of the *Biblical Repository*, of which he was the editor and principal contributor for four years. In 1833, his health having failed, he removed to Boston, where he spent the next three years in the preparation of a new *Lexicon of the Greek Testament;* carrying on at the same time his translation of the *Hebrew Lexicon* of Gesenius. Both these works were published at Boston in the autumn of 1836.

Early in 1837 Dr. Robinson was appointed professor of biblical literature in the Union Theological Seminary in the city of New York, the station which he still holds. He accepted it on condition of being permitted to visit Europe and Palestine, and thus carry out the plan he had laid five years before with the Rev. Eli Smith. Leaving his family in Germany, he proceeded to Egypt, where he was joined by Mr. Smith in February, 1838. They left Beyrout together in July of the same year, and after visiting Smyrna and Constantinople, returned by way of the Danube to Vienna; Mr. Smith having been commissioned to visit Leipzig in order to superintend the construction of new founts of Arabic type. At Vienna they were detained several weeks by the dangerous illness of Dr. Robinson, which brought him to the borders of the grave. After his recovery he fixed himself at Berlin, and devoted himself to the preparation of his *Biblical Researches in Palestine*. Here, in the unrestrained use of public and private libraries, with the constant counsel and aid of Ritter and Neander, as also occasionally of Humboldt, von Buch, and many others, two years fled rapidly away before his labors were completed. Dr. Robinson returned to New York in the autumn of 1840; and the work was published in three volumes in July, 1841, in Boston and London, as also in German at Halle, the same year. In reference to this work, the Royal Geographical Society of London awarded to the author one of their gold medals; and the theological faculty of the University of Halle conferred on him the honorary degree of doctor in theology. These volumes have become a standard authority in matters of biblical geography.

Notwithstanding the demands of his official duties upon his time and attention, Dr. Robinson established the *Bibliotheca Sacra*, of which one volume (1843) was issued under his supervision in New York. The work was then transferred to Andover. He also published in 1845 *A Harmony of the Four Gospels in Greek*, which was revised and stereotyped in 1851. An *English Harmony* was published by him first in 1846: it has been reprinted in London, and in French at Brussels. His principal labor, however, was connected with a new edition of the *Lexicon of the Greek Testament*, which appeared in 1850. The translation of Buttmann's *Greek Grammar*, revised from the latest edition of the original, was published in 1851. There have also issued from the press four later editions of the *Hebrew Lexicon*, the last one, finally completed from the Thesaurus, in 1854.*

In June, 1851, Dr. Robinson went with his family to Germany, and leaving them there, returned by way of Holland, England, and Scotland, in October. The directors of the Union Theological Seminary having kindly proffered him leave of absence in order to revisit Palestine, he went abroad again in December, and accomplished the journey in 1852, after an interval of fourteen years from his former visit, and mostly with the same companion, Dr. Eli Smith. This last journey was limited chiefly to Jerusalem and the country north. He returned home in October, 1852, and has since been occupied in preparing his new materials for the press. It is understood that the work is now nearly completed.

To no American scholar have the honors of learning been more generally awarded at home and abroad than to Dr. Robinson. The fidelity of his exact deductions in the topography of the Holy Land, based upon personal investigations, united with his studies of the original biblical literature, have given his works an authority not lightly to be disputed; while his labors in philology and the duties of his professor's chair have extended his influence in other walks of learning. His connexion with the Historical Society of New York, with the American Ethnological Society, and with the American Oriental Society, has added greatly to the honor and public usefulness of those bodies.

THERESE ALBERTINA LOUISE VON JAKOB, the wife of the Rev. Dr. Robinson, is the daughter of Ludwig von Jakob, professor of political economy at Halle, where she was born January 26, 1797. In 1806, after the suppression of the University of

* Of the Hebrew Lexicon about 10,000 copies have been disposed of altogether, chiefly in this country; and 9,000 copies of the Greek Lexicon of the New Testament have been sold here, besides three rival editions in England and Scotland. The Biblical Researches have been six or seven years out of print here, and much longer in England; of this work 5000 copies were printed in all.

Halle, her father removed to Charkow in Southern Russia, where he had been appointed professor, and afterwards to St. Petersburg, as member of the commission for revising the laws of the Russian Empire. In these removals his family accompanied him. His daughter, an earnest student even at that early age, made herself extensively acquainted with the Russo-Slavic languages and literature. In 1816 she returned with her father to Halle, where she acquired a knowledge of Latin. She published a number of tales, several of which were issued in 1825, in a volume entitled *Psyche*. These and her later works were put forth under the signature of *Talvi*, an anagram of the initials of her name. At this time the publication of the remarkable Servian popular songs by Wuk Stephanowitch led her to learn the Servian language; and encouraged by Wuk and Kopitar, she translated and published a large portion of them under the title of *Serbische Lieder*, "Servian Songs," in two volumes, Halle, 1826. A new edition, revised and enlarged, was issued by Brockhaus of Leipzig in 1853. This was a new field. The work was issued under the auspices of Goethe, and secured to the translator the friendship and correspondence of J. Grimm, Humboldt, Savigny, C. Ritter, Kopitar, and others.

In 1828 she married Professor Robinson, and accompanied him to America in 1830. Soon after her arrival she became interested in the study of the languages of the aborigines, and in 1834 published at Leipzig a German translation of Mr. Pickering's well known article on the *Indian Languages*. In the same year she prepared for the Biblical Repository, then edited by her husband, a series of articles on the *Slavic Languages and Literature*. These were enlarged, and issued in a volume, under the same title, in 1850. During her visit to Europe in 1838 she published a work in German on the *Popular Songs of the Nations of the Teutonic Race*, with remarks on those of other nations and races; and in 1840 a small work against the authenticity of the poems of Ossian. Of the first of these two works specimens had already appeared in various articles in the North American Review. In 1847 she published in German at Leipzig a *History of the Colonisation of New England*, of which a very defective translation into English appeared in London in 1851.

Mrs. Robinson has likewise given to the public the novels of *Heloise, or the Unrevealed Secret; Life's Discipline;* and *The Exiles*. These were published in both the English and German languages, at New York and Leipzig. The two former are romantic tales of the Eastern nations of Europe, with local historical accessories, though the psychological interest in the development of character and passion predominates. In the *Exiles* we have a picture of some of the prevalent influences and types of civilization visible in the settlement of America. Each of these books exhibits refined feeling, or original thought and acute observation, where these qualities are called for.

The style of Mrs. Robinson is simple and unexaggerated, well adapted to aid her learned accomplishments in the presentation of such a theme of literary history as her sketch of the Slavic poetry. There too she has the advantage of poetic culture, in the rendering of the original ballads into German or English verse at will.

EDWARD EVERETT.

Edward Everett was born in Dorchester, Mass., April 11, 1794. He was the son of Oliver Everett, a clergyman of Boston, who was afterwards Judge of the Court of Common Pleas for Norfolk. The family had furnished farmers and mechanics to the town of Dedham for two hundred years from the first settlement of the country. Everett received his early education in the free schools of Dorchester and Boston. He also attended a private school in the latter city kept by Ezekiel Webster, the brother of Daniel, and was at the public Latin school of Master Bigelow and at Dr. Abbott's Exeter Academy. He then entered Harvard about the age of thirteen in 1807, and took his degree in course. His Commencement speech had for its topic "Literary Evils;" and his Master of Arts oration "The Restoration of Greece."

In 1812 he was appointed tutor at Harvard, and the same year delivered the Phi Beta Kappa poem, taking for his topic "American Poets," whose opportunities and prospects he handled in the vein of mingled sentiment and humor which has grown habitual for such occasions. The points were neatly made, and it is upon the whole a pleasing poem. He notes the unpropitious toils of the first settlers, the comparative absence of wealth and of patronage or support, the want of association;—all well known and often pleaded discouragements of the American muse. Of the difficulties presented by American geography he says:

When the warm bard his country's worth would tell,
To Mas-sa-chu-setts' length his lines must swell.
Would he the gallant tales of war rehearse,
'Tis graceful Bunker fills the polished verse.
Sings he, dear land, those lakes and streams of thine,
Some mild Memphremagog murmurs in his line,
Some Ameriscoggin dashes by his way,
Or smooth Connecticut softens in his lay.
Would he one verse of easy movement frame,
The map will meet him with a hopeless name;
Nor can his pencil sketch one perfect act,
But vulgar history mocks him with a fact.

His presentation of the other side of the picture is warm and animated.

But yet in soberer mood, the time shall rise,
When bards will spring beneath our native skies:
Where the full chorus of creation swells,
And each glad spirit, but the poet, dwells,
Where whispering forests murmur notes of praise,
And headlong streams their voice in concert raise:
Where sounds each anthem, but the human tongue,
And nature blooms unrivalled, but unsung.
O yes! in future days, our western lyres,
Turned to new themes, shall glow with purer fires,
Clothed with the charms, to grace their later rhyme,
Of every former age and foreign clime.
Then Homer's arms shall ring in Bunker's shock,
And Virgil's wanderer land on Plymouth rock.
Then Dante's knights before Quebec shall fall,
And Charles's trump on trainband chieftains call.
Our mobs shall wear the wreaths of Tasso's Moors,
And Barbary's coast shall yield to Baltimore's.
Here our own bays some native Pope shall grace,

And lovelier beauties fill Belinda's place.
Here future hands shall Goldsmith's village rear,
And his tired traveller rest his wanderings here.
Hodeirah's son shall search our western plain,
And our own Gertrude visit us again.
Then Branksome's towers o'er Hudson's streams be
built,
And Marmion's blood on Monmouth's field be spilt.
Fitz-James's horn Niagara's echoes wake,
And Katrine's lady skim o'er Erie's lake.
Haste happy times, when through these wide domains,
Shall sound the concert of harmonious strains:
Through all the clime the softening notes be spread,
Sung in each grove and in each hamlet read.
Fair maids shall sigh, and youthful heroes glow,
At songs of valor and at tales of woe;
While the rapt poet strikes, along his lyre,
The virgin's beauty and the warrior's fire.
Thus each successive age surpass the old,
With happier bards to hail it, than foretold;
While poesy's star shall, like the circling sun,
Its orbit finish, where it first begun.

There is also a tribute to the Buckminsters, then recently deceased.

Everett was tutor at Harvard till 1814. It was his intention at first to have pursued the study of the law; but by the influence of his noble-minded friend Buckminster, he turned his attention to divinity while tutor, and on the death of that fine scholar and divine in 1813, succeeded to his ministry in the Brattle Street Church. This was at the early age of twenty. A memorial of his youthful divinity studies is preserved in the learned argument of his *Defence of Christianity against the work of George B. English,* entitled the Grounds of Christianity examined by comparing the New Testament with the Old*, which he published in Boston in 1814.

The same year having been invited to the new professorship of Greek literature in Harvard, with the privilege of further qualifying himself for its duties by a visit to Europe, he accepted the appointment and embarked for England—proceeding, on his arrival, to the University of Gottingen, where he passed more than two years chiefly engaged in study of the modern German and ancient classical literature. In the winter of 1817–18 he was in Paris, where he acquired a knowledge of the modern Greek language. In the spring he visited London, Cambridge, and Oxford, and became acquainted with many of the leading men of the country, enjoying the friendship of Scott, Byron, Jeffrey, Campbell, Mackintosh, Romilly, and Davy. Returning to the continent he divided the winter between Florence, Rome, and Naples, and made an extended journey to the East, in company with his friend Gen. Lyman,* the following season, visiting Athens and Constantinople; crossing the Balkan, he travelled through Wallachia and Hungary to Vienna. Returning to America in 1819, he at once engaged in the duties of his Professorship, to which he added the charge of the North American Review, which he conducted till 1824. A distinguishing feature of his editorship was his earnest defence of American manners and institutions, against the attacks or animadversions of British travellers. His reviews of Frances Wright, of Faux, of Schmidt and Gale, at this time, and afterwards his spirited article in the number for January, 1833, on Prince Puckler Muskau and Mrs. Trollope, attracted general attention. Sluggish readers who like the irritation of foreign abuse and the excitement of a stirring reply to warm their faculties, were stimulated. The national humor was gratified, while in the quiet walks of scholarship there was abundant provision for learned tastes in the editor's frequent articles on classical, scientific, and foreign continental topics. Mr. Everett, while editor, frequently wrote several articles for the same number of the review.†

In August, 1824, Everett acquired great reputation in a field of oratory and literature in which he has since been a leader, by the delivery of his

* The career of English deserves a note of admiration and warning. He was a native of Boston, a graduate of Harvard of 1807, where he was distinguished for his quickness and love of learning. He then studied law, became a theoretical reformer and disputant, and neglected its practice. From law he turned to theology, and while exhausting the Hebrew learning of Cambridge, contracted doubts of the Christian dispensation, and published his work attacking the New Testament while he supported the Old. This was the book answered by Everett. Before the reply reached him he was in Egypt, having in the meantime edited a country Western newspaper, then sought employment in the United States Marine Corps, and reaching Egypt in that capacity attached himself to the government of Ibrahim Pacha. He replied to Everett's book. He had an old taste for military affairs, and his new sovereign being then at war with the Abyssinians he projected a system of artillery service. He revived, in an experiment, the ancient scythe war chariot; but it was destroyed in an encounter with a stone wall in Cairo. His employment of camels in dragging cannon succeeded better, and he appears to have acquitted himself with success as General of Artillery in the War. He was cheated, however, out of his promised reward, and next became a kind of attaché of the American Government in the Levant. In 1827 he returned home and sought favor at Washington, which he did not live long to prosecute, dying the following year in that city. Samuel L. Knapp, who was his friend, has written of him with kindness, and composed an ingenious epitaph recounting the incidents of his life. His skill in languages was remarkable. An anecdote is told of his deceiving a Turkish ambassador at Marseilles, who doubted whether any foreigner could acquire his language, into the belief that he was a Turk. At Washington he once surprised a Cherokee delegation by remonstrating with them in their language against some harshness they had expressed in their own tongue. He had one of those minds which is wounded by its own sharpness. Knapp has a long article on him in his *American Biography*.

* Theodore Lyman (1792—1849) was a native of Boston. He was a man of education, and of political influence, having been elected to the state legislature and the mayoralty of Boston. He was active as a philanthropist. He published several works—"Political State of Italy," 1820; "Three Weeks in Paris," after a visit to that city; an account of the Hartford Convention, favorable to that body, in 1823; the "Diplomacy of the United States with Foreign Nations." 2 vols., 8vo. 1826. Loring's Boston Orators, pp. 391–2.

† The following among others were his contributions at this time:—

Prof. De Rossi,	Jan.	1820	
Canova and his Works,	April,	"	Vol. 10.
Walsh's Appeal,	"	"	
German Emigration to America,	July,	1820	
Tudor's Letters on the Eastern States,	"	"	Vol. 11.
Hope's Anastatius,	Oct.	"	
English Universities,	Jan.	1821	
History of Grecian Art,	"	"	
Italy,	"	"	Vol. 12.
Hartz Mountains,	"	"	
South America,	"	"	
England and America,	July,	"	Vol. 13.
Symmes' Voyage to the Internal World,	"	"	
Percival,	Jan.	1822	
Frances Wright,	"	"	
Aristophanes and Socrates,	April,	"	Vol. 14.
Herculaneum MSS.	"	"	
Simonds' Switzerland,	July,	1822	Vol. 15.
Alex. Humboldt's Works,	Jan.	1823	
Lord Bacon,	April,	"	Vol. 16.
Niebuhr's Rome,	"	"	
Schmidt and Gale on America,	July,	"	
Zodiac of Denderah,	Oct.	"	Vol. 17.
Say's Pol. Econ.	"	"	
Life of Ali Pacha,	Jan.	1824	Vol. 18.
Faux's Memorable Days in America,	July,	"	Vol. 19.

Edward Everett.

Phi Beta Kappa address on "The Circumstances Favorable to the Progress of Literature in America." These he found in the political organization of the country; the extent and uniformity of one great language; the rapid increase of population with the correspondent development of civilization. This combination of the philosophy of history with social and political statistics is a favorite method with Mr. Everett, who under various forms and at different times has often pursued the outlines of this his first mixed political and academic discourse. The oration closed with an eloquent address to Lafayette, who was present on the occasion. Ten years later, in 1834, at the request of the young men of Boston he delivered his admirable eulogy in memory of the departed hero, tracing his distinguished career with a patriotic fondness.

The occasional orations and addresses of Everett have become the permanent memorials of numerous important occasions of public interest from 1824 to the present time. There are historical orations pronounced at Plymouth, Concord, Charlestown, Lexington, and sites of colonial and revolutionary fame; eulogies of Washington, Adams, Jefferson, John Quincy Adams; anniversary discourses on the settlements of towns; addresses at agricultural gatherings and before mechanics' associations, and on social and philanthropic occasions. In all these the particular topic is handled at once with ease and dignity; there are similar traces of the scholar and the traveller; of the patriot and philosopher; with those personal reminiscences, original anecdotes, or "points" of observation interspersed, which relieve the attention of the audience, and coupled with the orator's skilful and polished delivery add so greatly to the pleasure of the hour.

In 1825 Mr. Everett took his seat in Congress as representative from Middlesex. For ten years he sat in the House of Representatives, bearing a prominent part in the debates, and for four successive years, from 1835 to 1839, was chosen Governor of Massachusetts. In the election for 1840 he lost the office by a single vote. He visited Europe again that year, and in 1841 was appointed Minister to England. Entering upon this new sphere of duty he was engaged in several international negotiations of delicacy and importance, as the arrangement of the North-Eastern Boundary, the affairs of McLeod and the Creole—which he conducted with signal ability. During this residence in England he delivered a number of occasional addresses at agricultural and other celebrations, which are preserved in the collection of his orations. The honorary degree of Doctor of Civil Law was conferred upon him by the Universities of Oxford and Cambridge.

In 1846, after his return to America, he was elected President of Harvard College, a position which he held till 1849. In November, 1852, he again entered public life, succeeding Daniel Webster as Secretary of State on the appointment of President Fillmore. He was chosen Senator in 1853, but was compelled by ill health to resign the following year.

Mr. Everett now passes his time in retirement, in the enjoyment of his ample friendships among the authors of his extensive library and the living actors of the times. He is an efficient member of the historical and other literary societies of the country, and his pen is ready for the service of every liberal interest. He is said to be employed in the composition of a Treatise on the Law of Nations. One of the latest and most elaborate productions of his pen is the valuable introductory memoir prefixed to the edition of the works of Webster, of whom he is one of the literary executors.

In 1822 Mr. Everett married Charlotte Gray, a daughter of the Hon. Peter C. Brooks, an elaborate memoir of whom, written by his son-in-law, has recently appeared.*

BENEFITS TO AMERICA OF ONE NATIONAL LITERATURE.†

This necessary connexion between the extent of a country and its intellectual progress, was, it is true, of more importance in antiquity than it is at the present day, because, at that period of the world, owing to political causes, on which we have not time to dwell, there was, upon the whole, but one civilized and cultivated people, at a time, upon the stage; and the mind of one nation found no sympathy, and derived no aid from the mind of another. Art and refinement followed in the train of political ascendency, from the East to Greece, and from Greece to Rome, declining in one region as they rose in another. In the modern world, a combination of political, intellectual, and even mechanical causes (for the art of printing is among the most powerful of them), has produced an extension of the highest civilization over a large family of states, existing contemporaneously in Europe and America. This circumstance might seem to mould the civilized portion of mankind into one republic of letters, and make it, comparatively, a matter of indifference to any individual mind, whether its lot was cast in a small or a large, a weak or a powerful, state. It must be freely admitted, that this is, to some extent, the case; and it is one of the great advantages of

* Art. on Everett by Felton, N. A. Rev. lxxi. Loring's Hundred Boston Orators. Men of the Time.

† From the Phi Beta Kappa Address on American Literature.

the modern over the ancient civilization. And yet a singular fatality immediately presents itself, to neutralize, in a great degree, the beneficial effects of this enlarged and diffused civilization on the progress of letters in any single state. It is true, that, instead of one sole country, as in antiquity, where the arts and refinements find a home, there are, in modern Europe, seven or eight, equally entitled to the general name of cultivated nations, and in each of which some minds of the first order have appeared. And yet, by the *multiplication of languages*, the powerful effect of international sympathy on the progress of letters has been greatly impaired. The muses of Shakespeare and Milton, of Camoens, of Lope de Vega and Calderon, of Corneille and Racine, of Dante and Tasso, of Goethe and Schiller, are comparative strangers to each other. Certainly it is not intended that these illustrious minds are unknown beyond the limits of the lands in which they were trained, and to which they spoke. But who is ignorant that not one of them finds a full and hearty response from any other people but his own, and that their writings must be, to some extent, a sealed book, except to those who read them in the mother tongue? There are other languages besides those alluded to, in which the works of a great writer would be still more effectually locked up. How few, even of well-educated foreigners, know anything of the literature of the Hungarian, Sclavonian, or Scandinavian races! to say nothing of the languages of the East.

This evil is so great and obvious, that for nearly two centuries after the revival of letters, the Latin language was adopted, as a matter of course, by the scholars of Europe, in works intended for general circulation. We see men like Luther, Calvin, Erasmus, Bacon, Grotius, and Leibnitz, who could scarce have written a line without exciting the admiration of their countrymen, driven to the use of a tongue which none but the learned could understand. For the sake of addressing the scholars of other countries, these great men, and others like them, in many of their writings, were willing to cut themselves off from all sympathy with the mass of those whom, as patriots, they must have wished most to instruct. In works of pure science and learned criticism, this is of the less consequence; for, being independent of sentiment, it matters less how remote from real life the symbols by which their ideas are conveyed. But, when we see a writer, like Milton, who, as much as any other that ever lived, was a master of the music of his native tongue; who, besides all the beauty of conception and imagery, knew better than most other men how to breathe forth his thoughts and images,

> In notes with many a winding bout
> Of linked sweetness long drawn out,
> With wanton heed and giddy cunning,
> The melting voice through mazes running,
> Untwisting all the chains that tie
> The hidden soul of harmony;

when we see a master of English eloquence, thus gifted, choosing a dead language,—the dialect of the closet, a tongue without an echo from the hearts of the people,—as the vehicle of his defence of that people's rights; asserting the cause of Englishmen in the language, as it may be truly called, of Cicero; we can only measure the incongruity, by reflecting what Cicero would himself have thought and felt, if compelled to defend the cause of Roman freedom, not in the language of the Roman citizen, but in that of the Grecian rhetorician, or the Punic merchant. And yet, Milton could not choose but employ this language; for he felt that in this, and this alone, he could speak the word "with which all Europe rang from side to side."

There is little doubt that the prevalence of the Latin language among modern scholars, was a great cause, not only of the slow progress of letters among the people at large, but of the stiffness and constraint of the vernacular style of most scholars themselves, in the sixteenth and seventeenth centuries. That the reformation in religion advanced with such rapidity is, in no small degree, to be attributed to the translations of the Scriptures and the use of liturgies in the modern tongues. The preservation, in legal acts, in England, of a foreign language,—I will not offend the majesty of Rome by calling it Latin,—down to so late a period as 1730, may be one reason why reform in the law did not keep pace with the progress of reform in some other departments. With the establishment of popular institutions under Cromwell, among various other legal improvements,* many of which were speedily adopted by our plain-dealing forefathers, the records of the law were ordered to be kept in English; "a novelty," says the learned commentator on the English laws, "which, at the restoration, was no longer continued, practisers having found it very difficult to express themselves so concisely or significantly in any other language but Latin."†

Nor are the other remedies for the evil of a multiplicity of tongues more efficacious. Something, of course, is done by translations, and something by the study of foreign languages. But that no effectual transfusion of the higher literature of a country can take place in the way of translation, need not be urged; and it is a remark of one of the few who could have courage to make such a remark, Madame de Stael, that it is impossible fully to comprehend the literature of a foreign tongue. The general preference, given till lately, to Young's Night Thoughts and Ossian, over all the other English poets, in many parts of the continent of Europe, confirms the justice of this observation. It is unnecessary, however, to repeat, that it is not intended to apply to works of exact science, or merely popular information.

There is, indeed, an influence of exalted genius, coëxtensive with the earth. Something of its power will be felt, in spite of the obstacles of different languages, remote regions, and other times. The minds of Dante and of Shakespeare have, no doubt, by indirect influence, affected thousands who never read a line of either. But the true empire of genius, its sovereign sway, must be at home, and over the hearts of kindred men. A charm, which nothing can borrow, and for which there is no substitute, dwells in the simple sound of our mother tongue. Not analysed, nor reasoned upon, it unites the simplest recollections of early life with the maturest conceptions of the understanding. The heart is willing to open all its avenues to the language in which its infantile caprices were soothed; and, by the curious efficacy of the principle of association, it is this echo from the faint dawn of intelligence, which gives to eloquence much of its manly power, and to poetry much of its divine charm.

What a noble prospect presents itself, in this way, for the circulation of thought and sentiment in our country! Instead of that multiplicity of dialect, by which mental communication and sympathy between different nations are restrained in the Old World, a continually expanding realm is opened to American intellect by the extension of one language over so large a portion of the Continent. The enginery of the press is here, for the first time, brought to bear with all its mighty power on the minds and hearts of men, in exchanging intelligence, and circu-

* See a number of them in Lord Somers's Tracts, vol. i.
† Blackstone's Commentaries, iii. 422.

lating opinions, unchecked by diversity of language, over an empire more extensive than the whole of Europe.

And this community of language, all important as it is, is but a part of the manifold brotherhood, which already unites the growing millions of America, with a most powerful influence on literary culture. In Europe, the work of international alienation, which begins in diversity of language, is consummated by diversity of race, institutions, and national prejudices. In crossing the principal rivers, channels, and mountains, in that quarter of the world, you are met, not only by new tongues, but by new forms of government, new associations of ancestry, new, and often hostile objects of national pride and attachment. While, on the other hand, throughout the vast regions included within the limits of our republic, not only the same language but the same national government, the same laws and manners, and common ancestral associations prevail. Mankind will here exist and act in a kindred mass, such as was scarcely ever before congregated on the earth's surface. What would be the effect on the intellectual state of Europe, at the present day, were all her nations and tribes amalgamated into one vast empire, speaking the same tongue, united into one political system, and that a free one, and opening one broad, unobstructed pathway, for the interchange of thought and feeling, from Lisbon to Archangel? If effects must bear a constant proportion to their causes; if the energy of thought is to be commensurate with the masses which prompt it, and the masses it must penetrate; if eloquence is to grow in fervor with the weight of the interests it is to plead, and the grandeur of the assemblies it addresses; in a word, if the faculties of the human mind are capable of tension and achievement altogether indefinite;

Nil actum reputans, dum quid superesset agendum;

then it is not too much to say, that a new era will open on the intellectual world, in the fulfilment of our country's prospects.

THE MEN AND DEEDS OF THE REVOLUTION.*

Often as it has been repeated, it will bear another repetition; it never ought to be omitted in the history of constitutional liberty; it ought especially to be repeated this day;—the various addresses, petitions, and appeals, the correspondence, the resolutions, the legislative and popular debates, from 1764 to the declaration of independence, present a maturity of political wisdom, a strength of argument, a gravity of style, a manly eloquence, and a moral courage, of which unquestionably the modern world affords no other example. This meed of praise, substantially accorded at the time by Lord Chatham in the British Parliament, may well be repeated by us. For most of the venerated men to whom it is paid, it is but a pious tribute to departed worth. The Lees and the Henrys, Otis, Quincy, Warren, and Samuel Adams, the men who spoke those words of thrilling power, which raised and directed the storm of resistance, and rang like the voice of fate across the Atlantic, are beyond the reach of our praise. To most of them it was granted to witness some of the fruits of their labors—such fruits as revolutions do not often bear. Others departed at an untimely hour, or nobly fell in the onset; too soon for this country, too soon for every thing but their own undying fame. But all are not gone; some still survive among us, to hail the jubilee of the independence they declared. Go back, fellow-citizens, to that day, when Jefferson and Adams composed the sub-committee who reported the Declaration of Independence. Think of the mingled sensations of that proud but anxious day, compared to the joy of this. What reward, what crown, what treasure, could the world and all its kingdoms afford, compared with the honor and happiness of having been united in that commission, and living to see its most wavering hopes turned into glorious reality! Venerable men, you have outlived the dark days which followed your more than heroic deed; you have outlived your own strenuous contention, who should stand first among the people whose liberty you had vindicated! You have lived to bear to each other the respect which the nation bears to you both; and each has been so happy as to exchange the honorable name of the leader of a party, for that more honorable one, the Father of his Country. While this our tribute of respect, on the jubilee of our independence, is paid to the grey hairs of the venerable survivor in our neighborhood (Adams), let it not less heartily be sped to him (Jefferson), whose hand traced the lines of that sacred charter, which, to the end of time, has made this day illustrious. And is an empty profession of respect all that we owe to the man who can show the original draught of the Declaration of the Independence of the United States of America, in his own handwriting? Ought not a title-deed like this to become the acquisition of the nation? Ought it not to be laid up in the public archives? Ought not the price at which it is bought to be a provision for the ease and comfort of the old age of him who drew it? Ought not he who, at the age of thirty, declared the independence of his country, at the age of eighty, to be secured by his country in the enjoyment of his own?

Nor would we, on the return of this eventful day, forget the men who, when the conflict of council was over, stood forward in that of arms. Yet let me not, by faintly endeavoring to sketch, do deep injustice to the story of their exploits. The efforts of a life would scarce suffice to draw this picture, in all its astonishing incidents, in all its mingled colors of sublimity and woe, of agony and triumph. But the age of commemoration is at hand. The voice of our fathers' blood begins to cry to us from beneath the soil which it moistened. Time is bringing forward, in their proper relief, the men and the deeds of that high-souled day. The generation of contemporary worthies is gone; the crowd of the unsignalized great and good disappears; and the leaders in war, as well as the cabinet, are seen, in fancy's eye, to take their stations on the mount of remembrance. They come from the embattled cliffs of Abraham; they start from the heaving sods of Bunker's Hill: they gather from the blazing lines of Saratoga and Yorktown, from the blood-dyed waters of the Brandywine, from the dreary snows of Valley Forge, and all the hard-fought fields of the war! With all their wounds and all their honors, they rise and plead with us for their brethren who survive; and command us, if indeed we cherish the memory of those who bled in our cause, to show our gratitude, not by sounding words, but by stretching out the strong arm of the country's prosperity, to help the veteran survivors gently down to their graves!

* From the Principles of the American Constitution, delivered at Cambridge, July 4, 1826.

HENRY WARE—HENRY WARE Jr.—JOHN WARE —WILLIAM WARE.

Henry Ware, the descendant in the fourth generation from Robert Ware, one of the early settlers of the town of Dedham in 1644, and the son of John Ware, a farmer, was born at Sherburne, Massachusetts, April 1, 1764. He was the youngest but one of a family of ten children, three of whom served in the Revolutionary war. He received a few weeks' schooling in the winter months, and was afterwards prepared for Harvard College by the village clergyman, the Rev. Elijah Brown, his elder brothers combining their means for his support during his studies. After completing his course in 1785, he took charge of the town school of Cambridge, in 1787 was ordained a clergyman, and in the same year received and accepted a call to the charge of the Congregational church of Hingham. He remained in this place, attaining high eminence as a preacher, for eighteen years, when he received the appointment of Hollis Professor of Divinity at Harvard. His election was a triumph of the Unitarian over the orthodox portion of the Congregationalists, and consequently excited much opposition from the latter. Dr. Ware took no part in the controversy which arose in this matter until the year 1820, when he published *Letters to Trinitarians and Calvinists, occasioned by Dr. Woods' Letters to Unitarians.* This was replied to by Dr. Woods in 1821. Dr. Ware put forth a second publication on the subject in 1822, and a *Postscript* in the year following.

He continued in the discharge of his professorship, largely extending its scope and efficiency, until 1840, when, in consequence of impaired sight, he resigned, and devoted himself entirely to the Divinity School founded in connexion with his professorship in 1826. An unsuccessful operation on his eyes soon after deprived him almost entirely of sight. He employed two years in carrying through the press a selection from one of his courses of lectures published in 1842 with the title of *An Inquiry into the Foundation, Evidences, and Truths of Religion.* The labor connected with this work impaired his previously enfeebled health, and the remaining years of his life were passed in retirement. He died July 12, 1845.

Dr. Ware married in 1789, and had a numerous family, his descendants (including the husbands and wives of his children) assembling on the twentieth of August, 1835, at his residence to the number of fifty.

Henry Ware, Jr., the fifth child and eldest son of the Rev. Henry Ware, was born at Hingham, April 21, 1794. He was educated under the charge of his cousin Ashur Ware, and passed the year previous to his admission to Harvard at the Phillips Academy, Andover. He employed a portion of one of the winters of his four years of college life in teaching school, as a discipline in his own education. At the close of his course in 1812 he became an assistant in the Academy at Exeter, where he passed two years. He entered the profession of divinity, and became pastor of the Second Church in Boston in 1816. He remained in this place for thirteen years with well deserved success as a preacher, when he was compelled to offer his resignation in consequence of ill health. In place of its acceptance a colleague was chosen to assist in the discharge of his duties. He about the same time accepted the Parkman Professorship of Pulpit Eloquence in the Divinity School of Harvard University. Before entering upon the duties of his office he passed seventeen months in Europe. On his return he resigned his pastoral charge and devoted himself entirely to his professorship, until forced, in 1842, by ill health to resign its duties. During this period he published in 1832 *The Life of the Saviour*, as the first volume of the Sunday Library, a series projected by him with the design of affording attractive and appropriate reading for young persons on that day. Three other volumes by different writers subsequently appeared, when the series was discontinued. In 1834 he prepared a *Memoir of the Rev. Dr. Parker*, of Portsmouth, to accompany a volume of sermons from the pen of that divine, who had recently died; and in 1835 a selection from the writings of Dr. Priestley, with a notice of his life and character. He also prepared a number of lectures and addresses delivered on various occasions, and numerous poems and essays for periodicals connected with his denomination. He died September 22, 1843. A selection from his writings by his friend and successor in his pastoral charge, the Rev. Chandler Robbins, was published in four volumes 12mo. in 1846. The first of these contains *The Recollections of Jotham Anderson, Minister of the Gospel*, a tale drawn in part from his personal experiences, with a few descriptive sketches, a number of poems prepared for recitation before the Phi Beta Kappa and other societies; *The Feast of Tabernacles*, a poem for music, prepared for an Oratorio; with several hymns and occasional verses suggested by the associations of travel or the incidents of life.

The second volume contains his Biographical Essays, a few addresses and controversial publications. The two remaining volumes are occupied by sermons.

These varied compositions are all well sustained in their appropriate spheres. Dr. Ware thought and wrote with energy, tempered by the care and reserve of the scholar. We select from the poetical portion of these volumes a sonnet.

SONNET ON THE COMPLETION OF NOYES'S TRANSLATION OF THE PROPHETS. November, 1837.

In rural life, by Jordan's fertile bed,
The holy prophets learned of yore to sing;
The sacred ointment bathed a ploughman's head,
The shepherd boy became the minstrel king.
And he who to our later ears would bring
The deep, rich fervors of their ancient lays,
Should dwell apart from man's too public ways,
And quaff pure thoughts from Nature's quiet spring.
Thus hath he chose his lot, whom city pride
And college hall might well desire to claim;
With sainted seers communing side by side,
And freshly honoring their illustrious name.
He hears them in the field at eventide,
And what their spirit speaks his lucid words proclaim.

A Memoir of the Life of Henry Ware, Jr., by his brother, John Ware, M.D., appeared in 1846 in two duodecimo volumes. It contains a selection from his letters, and presents a pleasant and satisfactory view of his life. Dr. Ware, the author of this work, has published a valuable series of medical lectures, and is also the author of a poem delivered before the Phi Beta Kappa Society of Harvard University, August 28, 1817. The topic was *Novel-writing*. He comments first on the Lydia Languish passion of young ladies for the perusal of romance, and on the absurdities of the fashionable life and Radcliffian schools of fiction then in vogue, and from thence passes to the proper scope and importance of fiction, maintaining throughout a lively and animated strain. The poem was printed in the North American Review for November, 1817.

Mary L. Ware, the wife of Henry Ware, Jr., survived her husband a few years, dying in April, 1849. She was a woman of great elevation of mind and active benevolence, qualities which have been commemorated in an admirable Biography by Edward B. Hall. This gentleman married a sister of Henry Ware, Jr., and holds a leading position among the Unitarian clergy.

WILLIAM, the brother of Henry Ware, Jr., was born at Hingham, August 3, 1797. He was fitted for college by Ashur Ware, the Rev. Dr. Allyne of Duxbury, and his father, and was graduated

W. Ware.

from Harvard in 1816. The following year was passed as an assistant teacher in the school of his native town. He next devoted three years to the study of theology at Cambridge. He commenced preaching at Northborough, Massachusetts, and was afterwards settled in Brooklyn, Connecticut; Burlington, Vermont; and in the city of New York, where he commenced his labors December 18, 1821. In 1823 he married Mary, daughter of Dr. Benjamin Waterhouse of Cambridge.

In March, 1836, he published in the Knickerbocker Magazine the first of the *Letters from Palmyra.* These letters, the style of which has the air of a literal rendering, purport to be written by a young nobleman of Rome, who visits Palmyra during the latter portion of the reign of Zenobia. They are among the most successful efforts to restore to the modern reader the every-day life of the Roman Empire, and place the author in the foremost rank as a classical scholar and classic author.

In the October following, he removed to Brookline, Massachusetts, where he took charge of a congregation during the winter, and prepared the letters which had appeared in the Magazine, with others, for publication. The work appeared in July, 1837. In June of the same year he removed to Waltham, and again removed in the following April to Jamaica Plain, where, although holding no parochial charge, he occasionally preached. In June, 1838, he published a sequel to his former work entitled *Probus*, in which we are introduced into the Imperial city during the last persecution of the Christians which preceded the accession of Constantine. The scenes of trial and martyrdom are depicted with energy and feeling, while the work shares in its classical keeping and vein of reflection, combined with vivid description, the merits of its predecessor. The Letters from Palmyra is now known as *Zenobia*, and Probus as *Aurelian*, changes of titles which the author adopted from the English reprints.

He became about the same time the editor and proprietor of the Christian Examiner, a position he retained until 1844. In July, 1839, he removed to Cambridge, and in 1841 published *Julian, or Scenes in Judea.* In this he has depicted many of the scenes of our Saviour's life, the work closing with the Crucifixion.

In 1844 he accepted a call to a church in West Cambridge, where he remained until compelled, in July, 1845, to resign his charge in consequence of ill health. He then returned to Cambridge, where he occasionally preached, and resided until April, 1848, when he sailed for Europe. He remained a little over a year abroad, passing most of the time in Italy, and on his return prepared, from letters written during his tour, a course of lectures on the cities he had visited, which were delivered in Boston, New York, and other places, and in 1851 published in a volume with the title, *Sketches of European Capitals.* They abound in choice reflection, criticism, and description. He next commenced the preparation of a course of lectures on the Works and Genius of Washington Allston, and after their completion was about making arrangements for their delivery, when he was seized by a third attack of epilepsy, a disease to which he had long been subject. He died, after lying a few days in an unconscious state, on the nineteenth of February, 1852.

The *Lectures on Allston* were soon after published. Mr. Ware claims in these the highest rank for Allston. He compares his landscapes with Salvator's, his female heads with Titian's, his Jeremiah with Michael Angelo's Prophets. It is, however, as the portrayer of ideal female beauty that he considers him to have worked most in harmony with his tastes, and to have achieved his most successful works. Among these he gives the preference to The Valentine (in the possession of Mr. George Ticknor of Boston). All of Mr. Allston's works are, however, passed in review, and full, yet discriminating, meed of praise dealt to each. One of the five lectures is principally devoted to the Belshazzar.

DEATH OF PROBUS—FROM AURELIAN.

The long peal of trumpets, and the shouts of the people without, gave note of the approach and entrance of the Emperor. In a moment more, with his swift step, he entered the amphitheatre, and strode to the place set apart for him, the whole multitude rising and saluting him with a burst of welcome that might have been heard beyond the walls of Rome. The Emperor acknowledged the salutation by rising from his seat and lifting the crown from his head. He was instantly seated again, and at a sign from him the herald made proclamation of the entertainments which were to follow. He who was named as the first to suffer was Probus.

When I heard his name pronounced, with the punishment which awaited him, my resolution to remain forsook me, and I turned to rush from the theatre. But my recollection of Probus's earnest entreaties that I would be there, restrained me, and I returned to my seat. I considered, that as I would attend the dying bed of a friend, so I was clearly bound to remain where I was, and wait for the last moments of this my more than Christian friend; and the circumstance that his death was to be shocking and harrowing to the friendly heart, was not enough to absolve me from the heavy obligation. I therefore kept my place, and awaited with patience the event.

I had waited not long when, from beneath that extremity of the theatre where I was sitting, Probus was led forth and conducted to the centre of the arena, where was a short pillar to which it was customary to bind the sufferers. Probus, as he entered, seemed rather like one who came to witness what was there, than to be himself the victim, so free was his step, so erect his form. In his face there might indeed be seen an expression, that could only dwell on the countenance of one whose spirit was already gone beyond the earth, and holding converse with things unseen. There is always much of this in the serene, uplifted face of this remarkable man; but it was now there written in lines so bold and deep, that there could have been few in that vast assembly but must have been impressed by it as never before by aught human. It must have been this which brought so deep a silence upon that great multitude—not the mere fact that an individual was about to be torn by lions—that is an almost daily pastime. For it was so, that when he first made his appearance, and, as he moved towards the centre, turned and looked round upon the crowded seats rising to the heavens, the people neither moved nor spoke, but kept their eyes fastened upon him as by some spell which they could not break.

When he had reached the pillar, and he who had conducted him was about to bind him to it, it was plain, by what at that distance we could observe, that Probus was entreating him to desist and leave him at liberty; in which he at length succeeded, for that person returned, leaving him alone and unbound. O sight of misery! he who for the humblest there present would have performed any office of love, by which the least good should redound to them, left alone and defenceless, they looking on and scarcely pitying his cruel fate!

When now he had stood there not many minutes, one of the doors of the vivaria was suddenly thrown back, and bounding forth with a roar that seemed to shake the walls of the theatre, a lion of huge dimensions leaped upon the arena. Majesty and power were inscribed upon his lordly limbs; and as he stood there where he had first sprung, and looked round upon the multitude, how did his gentle eye and noble carriage, with which no one for a moment could associate meanness, or cruelty, or revenge, cast shame upon the human monsters assembled to behold a solitary, unarmed man torn limb from limb! When he had in this way looked upon that cloud of faces, he then turned and moved round the arena through its whole circumference, still looking upwards upon those who filled the seats—not till he had come again to the point from which he started, so much as noticing him who stood, his victim, in the midst. Then, as if apparently for the first time becoming conscious of his presence, he caught the form of Probus; and moving slowly towards him, looked steadfastly upon him, receiving in return the settled gaze of the Christian. Standing there, still, awhile—each looking upon the other—he then walked round him, then approached nearer, making suddenly and for a moment those motions which indicate the roused appetite; but as it were in the spirit of self-rebuke, he immediately retreated a few paces and lay down in the sand, stretching out his head towards Probus, and closing his eyes as if for sleep.

The people, who had watched in silence, and with the interest of those who wait for their entertainment, were both amazed and vexed at what now appeared to be the dulness and stupidity of the beast. When, however, he moved not from his place, but seemed as if he were indeed about to fall into a quiet sleep, those who occupied the lower seats began both to cry out to him and shake at him their caps, and toss about their arms in the hope to rouse him. But it was all in vain; and at the command of the Emperor he was driven back to his den.

Again a door of the vivaria was thrown open, and another of equal size, but of a more alert and rapid step, broke forth, and, as if delighted with his sudden liberty and the ample range, coursed round and round the arena, wholly regardless both of the people and of Probus, intent only as it seemed upon his own amusement. And when at length he discovered Probus standing in his place, it was but to bound towards him as in frolic, and then wheel away in pursuit of a pleasure he esteemed more highly than the satisfying of his hunger.

At this, the people were not a little astonished, and many who were near me hesitated not to say, "that there might be some design of the gods in this." Others said plainly, but not with raised voices, "An omen! an omen!" At the same time Isaac turned and looked at me with an expression of countenance which I could not interpret. Aurelian meanwhile exhibited many signs of impatience; and when it was evident the animal could not be wrought up, either by the cries of the people, or of the keepers, to any act of violence, he too was taken away. But when a third had been let loose, and with no better effect, nay, with less—for he, when he had at length approached Probus, fawned upon him, and laid himself at his feet—the people, superstitious as you know beyond any others, now cried out aloud, "An omen! an omen!" and made the sign that Probus should be spared and removed.

Aurelian himself seemed almost of the same mind, and I can hardly doubt would have ordered him to be released, but that Fronto at that moment approached him, and by a few of those words, which, coming from him, are received by Aurelian as messages from Heaven, put within him a new and different mind; for rising quickly from his seat he ordered the keeper of the vivaria to be brought before him. When he appeared below upon the sands, Aurelian cried out to him,

"Why, knave, dost thou weary out our patience thus—letting forth beasts already over-fed? Do thus again, and thou thyself shalt be thrown to them. Art thou too a Christian?"

"Great Emperor," replied the keeper, "than those I have now let loose, there are not larger nor fiercer in the imperial dens, and since the sixth hour of yesterday they have tasted nor food nor drink. Why they have thus put off their nature 'tis hard to guess, unless the general cry be taken for the truth, 'that the gods have touched them.'"

Aurelian was again seen to waver, when a voice from the benches cried out,

"It is, O Emperor, but another Christian device! Forget not the voice from the temple! The Christians, who claim powers over demons, bidding them go and come at pleasure, may well be thought capable to change, by the magic imputed to them, the nature of a beast."

"I doubt not," said the Emperor, "but it is so. Slave! throw open now the doors of all thy vaults, and let us see whether both lions and tigers be not too much for this new necromancy. If it be the gods who interpose, they can shut the mouths of thousands as of one."

At those cruel words, the doors of the vivaria were at once flung open, and an hundred of their fierce tenants, maddened both by hunger and the goads that had been applied, rushed forth, and in the fury with which in a single mass they fell upon Probus—then kneeling upon the sands—and burying him beneath them, no one could behold his fate, nor, when that dark troop separated and ran howling about the arena in search of other victims, could the eye discover the least vestige of that holy man. I then fled from the theatre as one who flies from that which is worse than death.

Felix was next offered up, as I have learned, and after him more than fourscore of the Christians of Rome.

ZENOBIA, FAUSTA, AND PISO—FROM ZENOBIA.

A night scene on the Walls of Palmyra. Piso the narrator.

As Fausta said these words, we became conscious of the presence of a person at no great distance from us, leaning against the parapet of the wall, the upper part of the form just discernible.

"Who stands yonder?" said Fausta. "It has not the form of a sentinel—besides, the sentinel paces by us to and fro without pausing. It may be Calpurnius. His legion is in this quarter. Let us move towards him."

"No. He moves himself and comes towards us. How dark the night. I can make nothing of the form."

The figure passed us, and unchallenged by the sentinel whom it met. After a brief absence it returned, and stopping as it came before us—

"Fausta!" said a voice—once heard, not to be mistaken.

"Zenobia!" said Fausta, and forgetting dignity, embraced her as a friend.

"What makes you here?" inquired Fausta—"are there none in Palmyra to do your bidding, but you must be abroad at such an hour and such a place?"

"'Tis not so fearful quite," replied the Queen, "as a battle field, and there you trust me."

"Never, willingly."

"Then you do not love my honor?" said the Queen, taking Fausta's hand as she spoke.

"I love your safety better—no—no—what have I said—not better than your honor—and yet to what end is honor, if we lose the life in which it resides. I sometimes think we purchase human glory too dearly, at the sacrifice of quiet, peace, and security."

"But you do not think so long. What is a life of indulgence and sloth. Life is worthy only in what it achieves. Should I have done better to have sat over my embroidery, in the midst of my slaves, all my days, than to have spent them in building up a kingdom?"

"Oh, no—no—you have done right. Slaves can embroider. Zenobia cannot. This hand was made for other weapon than the needle."

"I am weary," said the Queen, "let us sit," and saying so, she placed herself upon the low stone block, upon which we had been sitting, and drawing Fausta near her, she threw her left arm round her, retaining the hand she held clasped in her own.

"I am weary," she continued, "for I have walked nearly the circuit of the walls. You ask what makes me here? No night passes but I visit these towers and battlements. If the governor of the ship sleeps, the men at the watch sleep. Besides, I love Palmyra too well to sleep while others wait and watch. I would do my share. How beautiful is this! The city girded by these strange fires! its ears filled with this busy music. Piso, it seems hard to believe an enemy, and such an enemy, is there, and that these sights and sounds are all of death."

"Would it were not so, noble Queen. Would it were not yet too late to move in the cause of peace. If even at the risk of life I"—

"Forbear, Piso," quickly rejoined the Queen, "it is to no purpose. You have my thanks, but your Emperor has closed the door of peace for ever. It is now war unto death. He may prove victor. It is quite possible. But I draw not back—no word of supplication goes from me. And every citizen of Palmyra—save a few sottish souls—is with me. It were worth my throne and my life, the bare suggestion of an embassy now to Aurelian. But let us not speak of this, but of things more agreeable. The day for trouble, the night for rest. Fausta, where is the quarter of Calpurnius? Methinks it is hereabouts."

"It is," replied Fausta, "just beyond the towers of the gate next to us; were it not for this thick night, we could see where at this time he is usually to be found doing, like yourself, an unnecessary task."

"He is a good soldier and a faithful—may he prove as true to you, my noble girl, as he has to me. Albeit I am myself a sceptic in love, I cannot but be made happier when I see hearts worthy of each other united by that bond. I trust that bright days are coming, when I may do you the honor I would. Piso, I am largely a debtor to your brother—and Palmyra as much. Singular fortune!—that while Rome thus oppresses me, to Romans I should owe so much—to one, twice my life, to another, my army. But where, Lucius Piso, was your heart, that it fell not into the snare that caught Calpurnius?"

"My heart," I replied, "has always been Fausta's—from childhood"—

"Our attachment," said Fausta, interrupting me, "is not less than love, but greater. It is the sacred tie of nature—if I may say so—of brother to sister—it is friendship."

"You say well," replied the Queen. "I like the sentiment. It is not less than love, but greater. Love is a delirium, a dream, a disease. It is full of disturbance. It is unequal—capricious—unjust; its felicity, when at the highest, is then nearest to deepest misery—a step—and it is into unfathomable gulfs of woe. While the object loved is as yet unattained—life is darker than darkest night. When it is attained, it is then oftener like the ocean heaving and tossing from its foundations, than the calm, peaceful lake, which mirrors friendship. And when lost—all is lost—the universe is nothing. Who will deny it the name of madness? Will love find entrance into Elysium? Will heaven know more than friendship? I trust not. It were an element of discord there where harmony should reign perpetual." After a pause in which she seemed buried in thought, she added musingly,—"What darkness rests upon the future. Life, like love, is itself but a dream—often a brief or a prolonged madness. Its light burns sometimes brightly, oftener obscurely, and with a flickering ray, and then goes out in smoke and darkness. How strange that creatures so exquisitely wrought as we are, capable of such thoughts and acts, rising by science, and art, and letters almost to the level of Gods, should be fixed here for so short a time, running our race with the unintelligent brute—living not so long as some, dying like all. Could I have ever looked out of this life into the possession of any other beyond it, I believe my aims would have been different. I should not so easily have been satisfied with glory and power. At least I think so—for who knows himself. I should then, I think, have reached after higher kinds of excellence, such, for example, as existing more in the mind itself could be of avail after death—could be carried out of the world—which power—riches—glory—cannot. The greatest service which any philosopher could perform for the human race, would be to demonstrate the certainty of a future existence, in the same satisfactory manner that Euclid demonstrates the truths of geometry. We cannot help believing Euclid if we would, and the truths he has established concerning lines and angles, influence us whether we will or not. Whenever the immortality of the soul shall be proved in like manner, so that men cannot help believing it, so that they shall draw it in with the first elements of all knowledge, then will mankind become a quite different race of beings. Men will be more virtuous and more happy. How is it possible to be either in a very exalted degree, dwelling as we do in the deep obscure—uncertain whether we are mere earth and water, or parts of the divinity—whether we are worms or immortals—men or Gods—spending all our days in, at best, miserable perplexity and doubt. Do you remember, Fausta and Piso, the discourse of Longinus in the garden, concerning the probability of a future life?"

"We do, very distinctly."

"And how did it impress you?"

"It seemed to possess much likelihood," replied Fausta, "but that was all."

"Yes," responded the Queen, sighing deeply, "that was indeed all. Philosophy, in this part of it, is a mere guess. Even Longinus can but conjecture. And what to his great and piercing intellect stands but in the strength of probability—to ours will, of necessity, address itself in the very weakness of fiction. As it is, I value life only for the brightest and best it can give now, and these to my mind are power and a throne. When these are lost I would fall unregarded into darkness and death."

"But," I ventured to suggest, "you derive great pleasure and large profit from study—from the researches of philosophy, from the knowledge of history, from contemplation of the beauties of art, and the magnificence of nature. Are not these things that give worth to life? If you reasoned aright, and probed the soul well, would you not find that from these, as from hidden springs, a great deal of all the best felicity you have tasted, has welled up? Then—still more, in acts of good and just government—in promoting the happiness of your subjects—from private friendship—from affections resting upon objects worthy to be loved—has no happiness come worth living for? And besides all this—from an inward consciousness of rectitude! Most of all this may still be yours, though you no longer sat upon a throne, and men held their lives but in your breath."

"From such sources," replied Zenobia, "some streams have issued, it may be, that have added to what I have enjoyed—but of themselves, they would have been nothing. The lot of earth, being of the low and common herd, is a lot too low and sordid to be taken if proffered. I thank the Gods mine has been better. It has been a throne—glory—renown—pomp and power—and I have been happy. Stripped of these, and without the prospect of immortality, and I would not live."

With these words she rose quickly from her seat, saying that she had a further duty to perform. Fausta entreated to be used as an agent or messenger, but could not prevail. Zenobia, darting from our side, was in a moment lost in the surrounding darkness. We returned to the house of Gracchus.

REPOSE—FROM THE LECTURES ON ALLSTON.

All the pictures to which I have just referred, and many others, to which I shall presently turn your attention, are examples of that peculiar charm in art, styled by the critics repose. There is hardly a work from the hand of Allston which is not, either in the whole, or in some considerable part, an instance in point. The word Repose alone, perhaps, with sufficient accuracy, describes the state of mind, and the outward aspect of nature intended by it. It describes the breathless silence and deep rest of a midsummer day, when not a leaf moves, and the shadows fall dark and heavy upon the face of the clear water, which repeats every object near it as in a mirror; the cow on the bank, half asleep, lazily chewing the cud, and flapping away the flies from her side; and the only sound to break the silence, the sleepy drone of the locust; while a warm, misty atmosphere, through which you just catch the roofs of the neighboring village, wraps all things in its purplish folds. Or, it describes the weary foot-traveller sitting upon a stone by the brook-side, as he rests, watching the sheep as they nibble the short grass, or the falling of the autumn leaves, as they alight upon those which had fallen before; these the only sounds, save the gurgling of the water among the pebbles, and the distant Sabbath bell that echoes among the hills. The poets understand this deep repose, and paint no picture oftener.

> Now fades the glimmering landscape on the sight,
> And all the air a solemn stillness holds,
> Save where the beetle wheels his drony flight,
> And drowsy tinklings lull the distant folds:
>
> Save that from yonder ivy-mantled tower
> The moping owl does to the moon complain
> Of such as, wandering near her secret bower,
> Molest her ancient, solitary reign.

And in the words of Bryant:

> For me, I lie
> Languidly in the shade, where the thick turf,
> Yet virgin from the kisses of the sun,
> Retains some freshness, and I woo the wind
> That still delays its coming.

And again:

> The massy rocks themselves,
> And the old and ponderous trunks of prostrate trees
> That lead from knoll to knoll a causey rude,
> Or bridge the sunken brook, and their dark roots,
> With all their earth upon them, twisting high,
> Breathe fixed tranquillity.

There is much that is closely kindred in the genius of Bryant and Allston. They both love, prefer, the calm, the thoughtful, the contemplative. Their pictures, in color and in verse, paint, oftener than any other theme, this silence, rest, deep repose of nature; the pictures of Allston full of poetry, the poems of Bryant gushing with life and truth.

As in these exquisite lines:

And now, when comes the calm mild day, as still such days will come,
To call the squirrel and the bee from out their winter home;
When the sound of dropping nuts is heard, though all the trees are still,
And twinkle in the smoky light the waters of the rill,
The south wind searches for the flowers whose fragrance late he bore,
And sighs to find them in the wood and by the stream no more.

Here are music, poetry, and painting—like Canova's Three Graces, embracing each other—bound together in indissoluble union; beautiful apart, beautiful always, but more beautiful when knit together by such a bond. I may add of this hymn of Bryant, that, like the Elegy of Gray, the one hardly less perfect than the other, the pathos and the beauty are too deep for any one to trust his voice to read aloud.

CAROLINE GILMAN.

This lady, the wife of the Rev. Samuel Gilman, of Charleston, is the daughter of Samuel Howard, a shipwright of Boston, in which city she was born October 8, 1794. Her father died in her infancy, when her mother took her to reside in various country towns of Massachusetts. The story of her early life and of her literary development has been told by herself in a pleasing chapter of Autobiography, in Hart's "Female Prose Writers of America." When she was ten years of age, she followed her mother's remains to the grave at North Andover. She has noticed the early influences of her life at Cambridge. "Either childhood," she writes,

is not the thoughtless period for which it is famed, or my susceptibility to suffering was peculiar. I remember much physical pain. I recollect, and I think Bunyan, the author of Pilgrim's Progress, describes the same, a deep horror at darkness, a suffocation, a despair, a sense of injury when left alone at night, that has since made me tender to this mysterious trial of youth. I recollect also my indignation after a chastisement for breaking some china, and in consequence I have always been careful never to express anger at children or servants for a similar misfortune.

In contrast to this, come the memories of chasing butterflies, launching chips for boats on sunny rills, dressing dolls, embroidering the glowing sampler, and the soft maternal mesmerism of my mother's hand, when, with my head reclined on her knee, she smoothed my hair, and sang the fine old song

In the downhill of life.

As Wordsworth says in his almost garrulous enthusiasm,

Fair seed-time had my soul, and I grew up,
Fostered alike by beauty and by fear;
Much favored in my birth-place.

I say birth-place, for true life is not stamped on the spot where our eyes first open, but our mind-birth comes from the varied associations of childhood, and therefore may I trace to the wild influences of nature, particularly to those of sweet Auburn, now the Cambridge Cemetery, the formation of whatever I may possess of the poetical temperament. Residing just at its entrance, I passed long summer mornings making thrones and couches of moss, and listening to the robins and blackbirds.

* * * * * * * * *

Our residence was nearly opposite Governor Gerry's, and we were frequent visiters there. One evening I saw a small book on the recessed window-seat of their parlor. It was Gesner's Death of Abel; I opened it, spelt out its contents, and soon tears began to flow. Eager to finish it, and ashamed of emotions so novel, I screened my little self so as to allow the light to fall only on the book, and, while forgotten by the group, I also forgetting the music and mirth that surrounded me, shed, at eight years, the first preluding tears over fictitious sorrow.

* * * * * * * * * *

I had seen scarcely any children's books except the Primer, and at the age of ten, no poetry adapted to my age; therefore, without presumption, I may claim some originality at an attempt at an acrostic on an infant, by the name of Howard, beginning—

How sweet is the half opened rose!
Oh, how sweet is the violet to view!
Who receives more pleasure from them—

Here it seems I broke down in the acrostic department, and went on—

Than the one who thinks them like you?
Yes, yes, you're a sweet little rose,
That will bloom like one awhile;
And then you will be like one still,
For I hope you will die without guile.

The Davidsons, at the same age, would I suppose have smiled at this poor rhyming, but in vindication of my ten-year-old-ship I must remark, that they were surrounded by the educational light of the present era, while I was in the dark age of 1805.

My education was exceedingly irregular, a perpetual passing from school to school, from my earliest memory. I drew a very little, and worked the "Babes in the Wood" on white satin, in floss silk; my teacher and my grandmother being the only persons who recognised in the remarkable individuals that issued from my hands, a likeness to those innocent sufferers.

I taught myself the English guitar at the age of fifteen from hearing a schoolmate take lessons, and ambitiously made a tune, which I doubt if posterity will care to hear. By depriving myself of some luxuries, I purchased an instrument, over which my whole soul was poured in joy and sorrow for many years. A dear friend, who shared my desk at school, was kind enough to work out all my sums for me (there were no black-boards then), while I wrote a novel in a series of letters, under the euphonious name of Eugenia Fitz Allen. The consequence is that, so far as arithmetic is concerned, I have been subject to perpetual mortification ever since, and shudder to this day when any one asks how much is seven times nine.

I never could remember the multiplication table, and, to heap coals of fire on its head in revenge, set it to rhyme. I wrote my school themes in rhyme, and instead of following "Beauty soon decays," and "Cherish no ill designs," in B and C, I surprised my teacher with Pope's couplet—

Beauties in vain their pretty eyes may roll,
Charms strike the sight, but merit wins the soul.

My teacher, who at that period was more ambitious for me than I was for myself, initiated me into Latin, a great step for that period.

* * * * * * * * *

About this period I walked four miles a week to Boston, to join a private class in French.

The religious feeling was always powerful within me. I remember, in girlhood, a passionate joy in lonely prayer, and a delicious elevation, when with upraised look, I trod my chamber floor, reciting or singing Watts's Sacred Lyrics. At sixteen I joined the Communion at the Episcopal Church in Cambridge.

At the age of eighteen I made another sacrifice in dress to purchase a Bible with a margin sufficiently large to enable me to insert a commentary. To this object I devoted several months of study, transferring to its pages my deliberate convictions.

I am glad to class myself with the few who first established the Sabbath School and Benevolent Society at Watertown, and to say that I have endeavored, under all circumstances, wherever my lot has fallen, to carry on the work of social love.

With such tastes and incentives, and a parallel development of the religious sentiment, Miss Howard commenced a literary career at the age of sixteen with a poetical composition, "Jepthah's Rash Vow." The *North American Review*, in its Miscellany, published her next verses, "Jairus's Daughter." In 1819 she was married to Samuel Gilman, and went to reside with him in Charleston, where he became pastor of the Unitarian Church. Dr. Gilman has a literary reputation outside of his profession, as the author of a pleasant volume of character, *The Memoirs of a New England Village Choir.*

Caroline Gilman

In 1832, Mrs. Gilman commenced the publication of the *Rose Bud*, a weekly juvenile newspaper, one of the earliest, if not the first of its kind in the country, which developed itself in the mature *Southern Rose*. From this periodical her writings have been collected. Her *Recollections of a New England Housekeeper*, and *of a Southern Matron*, have been much admired for their feminine simplicity and quiet humor; aiding the practical lessons of life in the most amiable spirit. The story in these is a slight vehicle for the facts. In her *Poetry of Travelling in the United States*, published in 1838, she has sketched the incidents of both a Northern and Southern Excursion with spirit. The volume also contains some pleasant papers by her friends. Mrs. Gilman's *Verses of a Lifetime* were published at Boston in 1849. *Tales and Ballads*, and *Ruth Raymond, or Love's Progress*, are other volumes from the same source. The *Oracles from the Poets*, and *The Sybil*, are passages of verse from the best poets, ingeniously arranged under appropriate classifications of fact or sentiment, to respond to numbers which are to be taken at random.

Mrs. Gilman has also edited the *Letters of Eliza Wilkinson during the Invasion of Charleston*, one of the most interesting personal memorials of the Revolutionary Era.*

The prose of Mrs. Gilman's books is natural and unaffected, with a cheerful vein of humor. Her poems are marked by their grace of expression, chiefly referring to nature, or the warm-hearted, home-cherishing affections. A description of a southern country home in the opening of a little poem entitled "The Plantation," is in a happy vein.

THE PLANTATION.

Farewell, awhile, the city's hum
  Where busy footsteps fall,
And welcome to my weary eye
  The planter's friendly hall.

Here let me rise at early dawn,
  And list the mockbird's lay,
That, warbling near our lowland home,
  Sits on the waving spray.

Then tread the shading avenue
  Beneath the cedar's gloom,
Or gum tree, with its flickered shade,
  Or chinquapen's perfume.

The myrtle tree, the orange wild,
  The cypress' flexile bough,
The holly with its polished leaves,
  Are all before me now.

There towering with imperial pride,
  The rich magnolia stands,
And here, in softer loveliness,
  The white-bloomed bay expands.

The long gray moss hangs gracefully,
  Idly I twine its wreaths,
Or stop to catch the fragrant air
  The frequent blossom breathes.

Life wakes around—the red bird darts
  Like flame from tree to tree;
The whip-poor-will complains alone,
  The robin whistles free.

The frightened hare scuds by my path,
  And seeks the thicket nigh;
The squirrel climbs the hickory bough,
  Thence peeps with careful eye.

The humming-bird, with busy wing,
  In rainbow beauty moves,
Above the trumpet-blossom floats,
  And sips the tube he loves.

Triumphant to yon withered pine,
  The soaring eagle flies,
There builds her eyry 'mid the clouds,
  And man and heaven defies.

The hunter's bugle echoes near,
  And see—his weary train,
With mingled howlings, scent the woods,
  Or scour the open plain.

Yon skiff is darting from the cove,
  And list the negro's song—
The theme, his owner and his boat—
  While glide the crew along.

* Mrs. Ellet's Women of the American Revolution, vol. I. pp. 222-236.

And when the leading voice is lost,
Receding from the shore,
His brother boatmen swell the strain,
In chorus with the oar.

The following is from the account of a visit to Quebec, in 1836, in *The Notes of a Traveller.*

TO THE URSULINES.

Oh pure and gentle ones, within your ark
Securely rest!
Blue be the sky above—your quiet bark—
By soft winds blest!

Still toil in duty and commune with heaven,
World-weaned and free;
God to his humblest creatures room has given,
And space to be.

Space for the eagle in the vaulted sky
To plume his wing—
Space for the ring-dove by her young to lie,
And softly sing.

Space for the sun-flower, bright with yellow glow
To court the sky—
Space for the violet, where the wild woods grow,
To live and die.

Space for the ocean in its giant might,
To swell and rave—
Space for the river, tinged with rosy light,
Where green banks wave.

Space for the sun, to tread his path in might,
And golden pride—
Space for the glow-worm, calling by her light,
Love to her side.

Then pure and gentle ones, within *your* ark
Securely rest!
Blue be the skies above, and your still bark
By kind winds blest.

Mrs. Caroline H. Glover, the daughter of the Rev. Dr. and Mrs. Gilman, has also acquired distinction in the popular literature of the Magazines, by a number of productions marked by their spirit and domestic sentiment. She was born in 1823, in Charleston; was married in 1840, and since the death of her husband in 1846, has resided with her parents.

Under the *nom de plume* of "Caroline Howard," her mother's maiden name, she has contributed largely to literature for children, and also written several poems and tales, which have appeared in many of the leading magazines of the day.

SPRING TIME.

God of the hours, God of these golden hours!
My heart o'erflows with love
To Thee, who giv'st with liberal hand these flowers;
To Thee, who sendest cool, delicious showers,
Fresh from the founts above.

God of the hours, the fleeting checkered time,
When Nature smiles and weeps,
Thou paintest sunset clouds with hues sublime,
Thou tunest bird-notes to the joyous chime
That all creation keeps.

Pale, emerald trees, how gracefully ye twine
Around your boughs a wreath;
Or does some angel hand with touch divine,
Bring from celestial bowers your verdure fine,
To deck the bowers beneath.

How silently your leaflets old and brown
On undulating wings,
In autumn months came floating, floating down,
To form a carpet, as they formed a crown
For you, ye forest kings.

Well may you bend with proud and haughty sweep,
For sunbeams love to lie
Upon your boughs, the breeze you captive keep,
And e'en the dew-drops which the night-clouds weep
Upon your leaflets, die.

Last eve the moon on modest twilight smiled,
And told the stars 'twas Spring!
She swept the wave, deliciously it gleamed,
She touched the birds, and woke them as they dreamed,
A few soft notes to sing.

God of the April flowers, how large thy gift—
The rainbow of the skies
That spans the changing clouds with footstep swift—
And rainbows of the earth, that meekly lift
To thee their glorious eyes.

Oh, not content with beauty rich and fair,
Thou givest perfume too,
That loads with burden sweet the tender air,
And comes to fill the heart with rapture rare,
Each blushing morn anew.

God of the Spring-time hours! what give we Thee,
When thus Thou bounteous art?
Thou owest us naught, we owe Thee all we see—
Enjoyment, hope, thought, health, eternity,
The life-beat of each heart.

This morn came birds on pinions bright and fleet,
A lullaby to sing
To Winter as he slept—but other voices sweet
The low dirge drowned, and warbled carol meet,
To greet the waking Spring.

Thus trees, and birds, and buds, and skies conspire
To speak unto the heart,
"Renew thy strength, be fresh, be pure, desire
To be new touched with purifying fire,
That evil's growth depart."

God of the Seasons! from our bosoms blow
The sin-leaves, and plant flowers
Bedewed by gentlest rains, that they may show,
That tended by thy love *alone they grow,*
God of these golden hours.

CARLOS WILCOX.

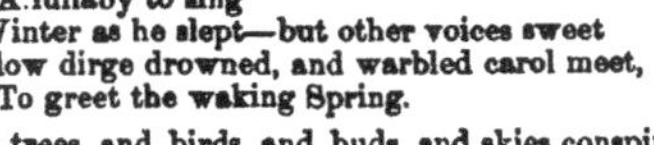

Carlos Wilcox was the son of a farmer of Newport, New Hampshire, where he was born, October 23, 1794. In his fourth year his parents removed to Orwell, Vermont. He entered Middlebury College soon after its organization, and on the completion of his course delivered the valedictory oration. He then went to Andover, where his studies were frequently interrupted by the delicate state of his health. He commenced preaching in 1818, but was obliged after a few months' trial to desist. The following two years were spent, with intervals of travelling, with a friend at Salisbury, Connecticut. His chief occupation was the composition of his poem, *The Age of Benevolence*, the first book of which he published at his own expense in 1822. In 1824 he accepted a call from the North Church at Hartford. He resigned this situation in 1826 on account of his health. This being somewhat re-established by travel during the summer months, he accepted a call to Danbury at the end of the year. Here he died on the 29th of the following May.

His *Remains** were published in 1828. The volume contains two poems, *The Age of Benevolence* and *The Religion of Taste*, delivered before the Phi Beta Kappa Society, and fourteen *Sermons*. Both of the poems are incomplete. It was the author's design that the first should extend to five books, of which he only lived to complete the first and portions of the three following. These are entitled, Benevolence, the Glory of Heaven; Benevolence on Earth, the resemblance of Heaven; the Need of Benevolence, and the Rewards of Benevolence. The second poem extends to one hundred and seven Spenserian stanzas.

The poems of Wilcox abound in passages of rural description of remarkable accuracy. The greater portion is, however, occupied with reflections on the power and beneficence of the Deity in the constitution of the material universe and the human mind. His verse always maintains correctness and dignity of expression, and often rises to passages of sublimity.

SPRING IN NEW ENGLAND—FROM THE AGE OF BENEVOLENCE.

The spring, made dreary by incessant rain,
Was well nigh gone, and not a glimpse appeared
Of vernal loveliness, but light-green turf
Round the deep bubbling fountain in the vale,
Or by the rivulet on the hill-side, near
Its cultivated base, fronting the south,
Where in the first warm rays of March it sprung
Amid dissolving snow:—save these mere specks
Of earliest verdure, with a few pale flowers,
In other years bright blowing soon as earth
Unveils her face, and a faint vermeil tinge
On clumps of maple of the softer kind,
Was nothing visible to give to May,
Though far advanced, an aspect more like her's
Than like November's universal gloom.
All day beneath the sheltering hovel stood
The drooping herd, or lingered near to ask
The food of winter. A few lonely birds,
Of those that in this northern clime remain
Throughout the year, and in the dawn of spring,
At pleasant noon, from their unknown retreat
Come suddenly to view with lively notes,
Or those that soonest to this clime return
From warmer regions, in thick groves were seen,
But with their feathers ruffled, and despoiled
Of all their glossy lustre, sitting mute,
Or only skipping, with a single chirp,
In quest of food. Whene'er the heavy clouds,
That half way down the mountain side oft hung,
As if o'erloaded with their watery store,
Were parted, though with motion unobserved,
Through their dark opening, white with snow appeared
Its lowest, e'en its cultivated, peaks.
With sinking heart the husbandman surveyed
The melancholy scene, and much his fears
On famine dwelt; when, suddenly awaked
At the first glimpse of daylight, by the sound,
Long time unheard, of cheerful martins, near
His window, round their dwelling chirping quick,
With spirits by hope enlivened up he sprung
To look abroad, and to his joy beheld
A sky without the remnant of a cloud.
From gloom to gayety and beauty bright
So rapid now the universal change,
The rude survey it with delight refined,
And e'en the thoughtless talk of thanks devout.
Long swoln in drenching rain, seeds, germs, and buds,
Start at the touch of vivifying beams.
Moved by their secret force, the vital lymph
Diffusive runs, and spreads o'er wood and field
A flood of verdure. Clothed, in one short week,
Is naked nature in her full attire.
On the first morn, light as an open plain
Is all the woodland, filled with sunbeams, poured
Through the bare tops, on yellow leaves below,
With strong reflection: on the last, 'tis dark
With full-grown foliage, shading all within.
In one short week the orchard buds and blooms;
And now, when steeped in dew or gentle showers,
It yields the purest sweetness to the breeze,
Or all the tranquil atmosphere perfumes.
E'en from the juicy leaves, of sudden growth,
And the rank grass of steaming ground, the air,
Filled with a watery glimmering receives
A grateful smell, exhaled by warming rays.
Each day are heard, and almost every hour,
New notes to swell the music of the groves.
And soon the latest of the feathered train
At evening twilight come;—the lonely snipe,
O'er marshy fields, high in the dusky air,
Invisible, but, with faint tremulous tones,
Hovering or playing o'er the listener's head;
And, in mid-air, the sportive night-hawk, seen
Flying awhile at random, uttering oft
A cheerful cry, attended with a shake
Of level pinions, dark, but when upturned
Against the brightness of the western sky,
One white plume showing in the midst of each,
Then far down diving with loud hollow sound;—
And, deep at first within the distant wood,
The whip-poor-will, her name her only song.
She, soon as children from the noisy sport
Of hooping, laughing, talking with all tones,
To hear the echoes of the empty barn,
Are by her voice diverted, and held mute,
Comes to the margin of the nearest grove;
And when the twilight deepened into night,
Calls them within, close to the house she comes,
And on its dark side, haply on the step
Of unfrequented door, lighting unseen,
Breaks into strains articulate and clear,
The closing sometimes quickened as in sport.
Now, animate throughout, from morn to eve
All harmony, activity, and joy,
Is lovely nature, as in her blest prime.
The robin to the garden, or green yard,
Close to the door repairs to build again
Within her wonted tree; and at her work
Seems doubly busy, for her past delay.
Along the surface of the winding stream,
Pursuing every turn, gay swallows skim;
Or round the borders of the spacious lawn
Fly in repeated circles, rising o'er
Hillock and fence, with motion serpentine,
Easy and light. One snatches from the ground
A downy feather, and then upward springs,
Followed by others, but oft drops it soon,
In playful mood, or from too slight a hold,
When all at once dart at the falling prize.
The flippant blackbird with light yellow crown,
Hangs fluttering in the air, and chatters thick
Till her breath fail, when, breaking off, she drops
On the next tree, and on its highest limb,
Or some tall flag, and gently rocking, sits,

* Remains of the Rev. Carlos Wilcox, late Pastor of the North Congregational Church in Hartford, with a Memoir of his Life. Hartford: Edward Hopkins, 1828. 8vo. pp. 430.

Her strain repeating. With sonorous notes
Of every tone, mixed in confusion sweet,
All chanted in the fulness of delight,
The forest rings:—where, far around enclosed
With bushy sides, and covered high above
With foliage thick, supported by bare trunks,
Like pillars rising to support a roof,
It seems a temple vast, the space within
Rings loud and clear with thrilling melody.
Apart, but near the choir, with voice distinct,
The merry mocking-bird together links
In one-continued song their different notes,
Adding new life and sweetness to them all.
Hid under shrubs, the squirrel that in fields
Frequents the stony wall and briery fence,
Here chirps so shrill that human feet approach
Unheard till just upon, when with cries
Sudden and sharp he darts to his retreat,
Beneath the mossy hillock or aged tree;
But oft a moment after re-appears,
First peeping out, then starting forth at once
With a courageous air, yet in his pranks
Keeping a watchful eye, nor venturing far
Till left unheeded. In rank pastures graze,
Singly and mutely, the contented herd;
And on the upland rough the peaceful sheep;
Regardless of the frolic lambs, that, close
Beside them, and before their faces prone,
With many an antic leap, and butting feint,
Try to provoke them to unite in sport,
Or grant a look, till tired of vain attempts;
When, gathering in one company apart,
All vigor and delight, away they run,
Straight to the utmost corner of the field
The fence beside; then, wheeling, disappear
In some small sandy pit, then rise to view;
Or crowd together up the heap of earth
Around some upturned root of fallen tree,
And on its top a trembling moment stand,
Then to the distant flock at once return.
Exhilarated by the general joy,
And the fair prospect of a fruitful year,
The peasant, with light heart, and nimble step,
His work pursues, as it were pastime sweet.
With many a cheering word, his willing team,
For labor fresh, he hastens to the field
Ere morning lose its coolness; but at eve
When loosened from the plough and homeward turned,
He follows slow and silent, stopping oft
To mark the daily growth of tender grain
And meadows of deep verdure, or to view
His scattered flock and herd, of their own will
Assembling for the night by various paths,
The old now freely sporting with the young,
Or laboring with uncouth attempts at sport.

WILLIAM CULLEN BRYANT

WAS born at Cummington, Hampshire County, Mass., November 3, 1794. His father, a physician, and a man of strength of character and literary culture, took pride in his son's early ability, and cherished the young poet with paternal affection. We have heard the anecdote of his reciting the poem "Thanatopsis" at the house of one of his friends, with tears in his eyes. "The father taught the son," we are told in a valuable notice of the poet's life and writings,* "the value of correctness and compression, and enabled him to distinguish between true poetic enthusiasm and fustian."

We may here quote the passage which follows in the article just referred to, for its personal details of the poet's family, and the apposite citations from his verse. "He who carefully reads the poems of the man, will see how largely the boy has profited by these early lessons—and will appreciate the ardent affection with which the son so beautifully repays the labor of the sire. The feeling and reverence with which Bryant cherishes the memory of his father, whose life was

Marked with some act of goodness every day,

is touchingly alluded to in several poems, and directly spoken of, with pathetic eloquence, in the *Hymn to Death*, written in 1825.

Alas! I little thought that the stern power
Whose fearful praise I sung, would try me thus
Before the strain was ended. It must cease—
For he is in his grave who taught my youth
The art of verse, and in the bud of life
Offered me to the Muses. Oh, cut off
Untimely! when thy reason in its strength,
Ripened by years of toil and studious search
And watch of Nature's silent lessons, taught
Thy hand to practise best the lenient art
To which thou gavest thy laborious days,
And, last, thy life. And, therefore, when the earth
Received thee, tears were in unyielding eyes,
And on hard cheeks, and they who deemed thy skill
Delayed their death-hour, shuddered and turned pale
When thou wert gone. This faltering verse, which thou
Shalt not, as wont, o'erlook, is all I have
To offer at thy grave—this—and the hope
To copy thy example.

Again, in *To the Past*, written in 1827, from which we quote:

Thou hast my better years,
Thou hast my earlier friends—the good—the kind,
Yielded to thee with tears—
The venerable form—the exalted mind.

My spirit yearns to bring
The lost ones back—yearns with desire intense,
And struggles hard to wring
Thy bolts apart, and pluck thy captives thence.

* * * * *

And then shall I behold
Him, by whose kind paternal side I sprung,
And her, who still and cold,
Fills the next grave—the beautiful and young.

"We have seen, too, while referring to his father, the devoted affection with which he speaks of her 'who fills the next grave.' The allusion is to his sister who died of consumption in 1824. In *The Death of the Flowers*, written in the autumn of 1825, we have another allusion to the memory of that sister:

And then I think of one who in her youthful beauty died,
The fair, meek blossom that grew up and faded by my side:

* * * *

——The gentle race of flowers
Are lying in their lowly beds, with the fair and good of ours.

"And in his volume there is a sonnet addressed to her, while sick she waited

* An article on Bryant, which appeared in the Southern Lit. Mess. for 1848. It is from the pen of Mr. James Lawson, an old friend of the poet.

Till the slow plague shall bring the fatal hour."

Bryant early displayed the poetical faculty, and fastened upon the genial influences of nature about him. He began to write verses at nine, and at ten composed a little poem to be spoken at a public school, which was published in a country newspaper. At the age of fourteen he prepared a collection of poems, which was published in Boston in 1809.* The longest of these is entitled the *Embargo*, a reflection in good set heroic measure of the prevalent New England anti-Jeffersonian Federalism of the times.† This was a second and enlarged edition of the "Embargo," which had appeared the year previous in a little pamphlet by itself. It is noticeable that never since that early publication, while actively engaged in public life, has the poet employed his muse upon the politics of the day, though the general topics of liberty and independence have given occasion to some of his finest poems. By the side of this juvenile production are an *Ode to Connecticut River*, and some verses entitled *Drought*, which show a characteristic observation of nature.

DROUGHT.

Plunged amid the limpid waters,
  Or the cooling shade beneath;
Let me fly the scorching sunbeams,
  And the south wind's sickly breath!

Sirius burns the parching meadows,
  Flames upon the embrowning hill;
Dries the foliage of the forest,
  And evaporates the rill.

Scarce is seen a lonely floweret,
  Save amid th' embowering wood;
O'er the prospect dim and dreary,
  Drought presides in sullen mood!

Murky vapours hung in æther,
  Wrap in gloom, the sky serene;
Nature pants distressful—silence
  Reigns o'er all the sultry scene.

Then amid the limpid waters,
  Or beneath the cooling shade;
Let me shun the scorching sunbeams,
  And the sickly breeze evade.

July, 1807.

Bryant studied at Williams College, which he left to prosecute the study of the law, a profession in which he was engaged in practice at Plainfield for one year, and afterwards for nine years at Great Barrington. In 1816 his poem of *Thanatopsis*, written in his nineteenth year, was published in the North American Review. Its sonorous blank verse created a marked sensation at the time, and the imitations of it have not ceased since.‡ In 1821 he delivered the Phi Beta Kappa poem at Harvard, his composition entitled the Ages, a didactic poem, viewing the past world's progress by the torch-light of liberty, and closing with a fair picture of American nature, and its occupation by the new race. This he published in that year with other poems at Cambridge. In 1825, abandoning the law for literature, he came to New York and edited a monthly periodical, the New York Review and Athenæum Magazine, which in 1826 was merged in a new work of a similar character, also conducted by him, the United States Review and Literary Gazette, which closed with its second volume in September of the following year. In these works appeared many just and forcible criticisms, and a number of his best known poems, including *The Death of the Flowers*, *The Disinterred Warrior*, *The African Chief*, *The Indian Girl's Lament*. These periodicals were supported by contributions from Richard H. Dana, the early friend of Bryant, who wrote both in prose and verse, by Sands, and by Halleck, whose Marco Bozzaris, Burns, and Wyoming appeared in their pages. Mr. Bryant was also a contributor of several prose articles to the early volumes of the North American Review.

In 1824 a number of his poems, *The Murdered Traveller*, *The Old Man's Funeral*, *The Forest Hymn*, *March*, and others, appeared in the United States Literary Gazette, a weekly review published at Boston, at first edited by Theophilus Parsons,* and afterwards by James G. Carter.

In 1826 Bryant became permanently connected with the Evening Post, a journal in which his clear, acute prose style has been constantly employed since; enforcing a pure and simple administration of the government within the confines of its legitimate powers, steadily opposing the corruptions of office, advocating the principles of free trade in political economy both in its foreign and domestic relations, generous and unwearied in support of the interests of art and literature, uncompromising in the rebuke of fraud and oppression of whatever clime or race.

On the completion of the half century of the Evening Post, Mr. Bryant published in that paper† a history of its career. Its first number was dated November 16, 1801, when it was founded by William Coleman, a barrister from

---

* The Embargo; or, Sketches of the Times. A Satire. The second edition, corrected and enlarged, together with the Spanish Revolution, and other Poems. By William Cullen Bryant. Boston: Printed for the Author by E. G. House, No. 5 Court street. 1809. 12mo., pp. 36.

† The poem received the following notice at the time from the Monthly Anthology for June, 1808:—"If the young bard has met with no assistance in the composition of this poem, he certainly bids fair, should he continue to cultivate his talent, to gain a respectable station on the Parnassian mount, and to reflect credit on the literature of his country."

‡ A story is told of the first publication of this poem in the Review, in connexion with Richard H. Dana, of which we are enabled to give the correct version. Dana was then a member of the club which conducted the Review, and received two poems, Thanatopsis and a Fragment, which now bears the title, "Inscription on the Entrance to a Wood." The first was somehow understood to be from the father; the other from the son. When Dana learnt the name, and that the author of Thanatopsis, Dr. Bryant, was a member of the State Legislature, he proceeded to the Senate-room to observe the new poet. He saw there a man of a dark complexion, with quite dark if not black hair, thick eyebrows, well developed forehead, well featured, with an uncommonly intellectual expression, though he could not discover in it the poetic faculty. He went away puzzled and mortified at his lack of discernment. When Bryant afterwards came to Cambridge to deliver the Phi Beta Kappa Poem, and Dana spoke of his father's Thanatopsis, the real author explained the matter, and became known as the writer of the two poems. In this innocent perplexity the acquaintance between these poets began.

* Mr. Theophilus Parsons, son of the eminent Judge Parsons, Dane Professor of Law at Cambridge, was also one of the early contributors to the North American Review under the editorship of Everett. He published a volume of "Essays" which reached a second edition in 1847. The subjects of these—Life, Providence, Correspondence, The Human Form, Religion, the New Jerusalem—indicate the Swedenborgian religious and philosophic views of the author. Mr. Carter, alluded to in the text, was much interested in the subject of Education, and took an active part in the introduction of normal schools into this country, in Massachusetts.

† No. for November 18, 1851.

Massachusetts, with the support of the leading members of the Federal party, to which, till the close of the war with England, it was a devoted adherent. In 1826 Mr. Bryant began to write for its columns. On the death of Coleman in 1829, William Leggett was employed as assistant editor, and remained with the paper till 1836, when he retired on the return of Mr. Bryant from Europe. It now remained in Mr. Bryant's sole editorial hands, assisted by various contributors, including the regular aid of his son-in-law, Mr. Parke Godwin, till the purchase by Mr. John Bigelow of a share of the paper in 1850, since which time he has been associated in the editorship.

In the first years of his engagement in these editorial duties, Bryant wrote, in conjunction with his friends Sands and Verplanck, *The Talisman*, in three annual volumes, 1827–29–30; the collection entitled, "Tales of the Glauber Spa," in 1832. His contributions to the "Talisman," besides a few poems, were an Adventure in the East Indies, The Cascade of Melsingah, Recollections of the South of Spain, A Story of the Island of Cuba, The Indian Spring, The Whirlwind, Phanette des Gaulelmes, and the Marriage Blunder. He also assisted in writing The Legend of the Devil's Pulpit, and Reminiscences of New York. For the Tales of the Glauber Spa, he wrote the Skeleton's Cave and Medfield. He has since from time to time published new poems in the periodicals of the day, which he has collected at intervals in new editions.* In the Evening Post have also appeared several series of Letters from Europe, the Southern States,

W. C. Bryant

and the West Indies, which mark the period of the author's travels at various times from 1834 to 1853. The last tour extended to the Holy Land. A collection of these papers has been published by Putnam, entitled *Letters of a Traveller; or, Notes of Things Seen in Europe and America.*

Among Mr. Bryant's separate publications should be mentioned his Eulogy of his friend Thomas Cole, the artist, delivered in New York in 1848, and a similar tribute to the genius of Cooper the novelist, in 1852. The style of these addresses, and of the author's other prose writings, is remarkable for its purity and clearness. Its truthfulness, in accuracy of thought and diction, is a constant charm to those who know the value of words, and have felt the poverty of exaggerated language. This extends to the daily articles written by the author in his newspaper, where no haste or interruptions are suffered to set aside his fastidious and jealous guardianship, not merely of sincere statement but of its pure expression. The style must have been formed at the outset by a vigorous nature, which can thus resist the usually pernicious influences of more than a quarter of a century of editorial wear and tear.

The poems of Bryant may be classed, with regard to their subjects:—those expressing a universal interest, relative to the great conditions of humanity, as *Thanatopsis*, *The Ages*, *Hymn to Death*, *The Past;* types of nature symbolical of these, as the Winds; poems of a national and patriotic sentiment, or expressive of the heroic in character, as the Song of Marion's Men, the Indian Poems, and some foreign subjects mingled with translations. Of these, probably the most enduring will be those which draw their vitality more immediately from the American soil. In these there is a purity of nature, and a certain rustic grace, which speak at once the nature of the poet and his subject. Mr. Bryant has been a close student of English poetry through its several periods, and while his taste would lead him to admire those who have minutely painted the scenes of nature, his fidelity to his own thoughts and experiences has preserved him from imitation of any.

Mr. Dana, in his preface to his reprint of his "Idle Man," speaks of a poetic influence in the early period of Bryant's career. "I shall never forget," says he, "with what feeling my friend Bryant, some years ago,* described to me the effect produced upon him by his meeting for the first time with Wordsworth's Ballads. He lived, when quite young, where but few works of poetry were to be had; at a period, too, when Pope was still the great idol of the Temple of Art. He said, that upon opening Wordsworth, a thousand springs seemed to gush up at once in his heart, and the face of nature, of a sudden, to change into a strange freshness and life." This may have been a seed sown in a generous nature, but the predetermined quality of the soil has marked the form and fragrance of the plant. It is American air we breathe, and American nature we see in his verses, and "the plain living and high thinking" of what should constitute American sentiment inspire them.

Bryant, whose songs are thoughts that bless
  The heart, its teachers, and its joy,

* The first general collection was published by Elam Bliss, a bookseller of great liberality and worth, a gentleman by nature, and a warm friend of the poet, in 1832; followed by another in Boston; others subsequently in New York from the press of the Harpers. In 1846 a richly illustrated edition, with engravings from original designs, by the painter Leutze, was published by Carey and Hart in Philadelphia. New editions of the poems, in three different forms, were published by the Appletons in New York, in 1855.

* This was written in 1833.

As mothers blend with their caress,
Lessons of truth and gentleness,
And virtue for the listening boy.
Spring's lovelier flowers for many a day,
Have blossomed on his wandering way,
Beings of beauty and decay,
They slumber in their autumn tomb;
But those that graced his own Green River,
And wreathed the lattice of his home,
Charmed by his song from mortal doom,
Bloom on, and will bloom on for ever.*

Bryant's Residence.

Mr. Bryant's country residence is at Roslyn, Long Island, a picturesquely situated village on the Sound, a few hours' journey from the city. There at a home, in the immediate vicinity of numerous fine land and water views, he finds retirement from the care and turmoil of metropolitan life, and there we may readily suppose his favorite woods and fields inspire the most genial moods of his poetic creations.

THANATOPSIS

To him who in the love of Nature holds
Communion with her visible forms, she speaks
A various language; for his gayer hours
She has a voice of gladness, and a smile
And eloquence of beauty, and she glides
Into his darker musings, with a mild
And healing sympathy, that steals away
Their sharpness ere he is aware. When thoughts
Of the last bitter hour come like a blight
Over thy spirit, and sad images
Of the stern agony, and shroud, and pall,
And breathless darkness, and the narrow house,
Make thee to shudder, and grow sick at heart;—
Go forth, under the open sky, and list
To Nature's teachings, while from all around—
Earth and her waters, and the depths of air,—
Comes a still voice—Yet a few days, and thee
The all-beholding sun shall see no more
In all his course; nor yet in the cold ground,
Where thy pale form was laid, with many tears,
Nor in the embrace of ocean, shall exist
Thy image. Earth, that nourished thee, shall claim
Thy growth, to be resolved to earth again,
And, lost each human trace, surrendering up
Thine individual being, shalt thou go
To mix for ever with the elements,
To be a brother to the insensible rock
And to the sluggish clod, which the rude swain
Turns with his share, and treads upon. The oak
Shall send his roots abroad, and pierce thy mould.

Yet not to thine eternal resting-place
Shalt thou retire alone,—nor couldst thou wish
Couch more magnificent. Thou shalt lie down
With patriarchs of the infant world—with kings,
The powerful of the earth—the wise, the good,
Fair forms, and hoary seers of ages past,
All in one mighty sepulchre. The hills
Rock-ribbed and ancient as the sun; the vales
Stretching in pensive quietness between;
The venerable woods; rivers that move
In majesty, and the complaining brooks
That make the meadows green; and, poured round all,
Old ocean's grey and melancholy waste,—
Are but the solemn decorations all
Of the great tomb of man. The golden sun
The planets, all the infinite host of heaven,
Are shining on the sad abodes of death,
Through the still lapse of ages. All that tread
The globe are but a handful to the tribes
That slumber in its bosom.—Take the wings
Of morning, traverse Barca's desert sands,
Or lose thyself in the continuous woods
Where rolls the Oregon, and hears no sound,
Save his own dashings—yet—the dead are there:
And millions in those solitudes, since first
The flight of years began, have laid them down
In their last sleep—the dead reign there alone.
So shalt thou rest, and what if thou withdraw
In silence from the living, and no friend
Take note of thy departure? All that breathe
Will share thy destiny. The gay will laugh
When thou art gone, the solemn brood of care
Plod on, and each one as before will chase
His favorite phantom; yet all these shall leave
Their mirth and their employments, and shall come,
And make their bed with thee. As the long train
Of ages glide away, the sons of men,
The youth in life's green spring, and he who goes
In the full strength of years, matron and maid,
And the sweet babe, and the grey-headed man,—
Shall one by one be gathered to thy side,
By those, who in their turn shall follow them.

So live, that when thy summons comes to join
The innumerable caravan, which moves
To that mysterious realm, where each shall take
His chamber in the silent halls of death,
Thou go not, like the quarry-slave at night,
Scourged to his dungeon, but, sustained and soothed
By an unfaltering trust, approach thy grave
Like one who wraps the drapery of his couch
About him, and lies down to pleasant dreams.

TO A WATERFOWL.

Whither, midst falling dew,
While glow the heavens with the last steps of day,
Far, through their rosy depths, dost thou pursue
Thy solitary way?

Vainly the fowler's eye
Might mark thy distant flight to do thee wrong,
As, darkly seen against the crimson sky,
Thy figure floats along.

Seek'st thou the plashy brink
Of weedy lake, or marge of river wide,
Or where the rocking billows rise and sin
On the chafed ocean side?

* Lines by Halleck, in his poem, "The Recorder."

There is a Power whose care
Teaches thy way along that pathless coast,—
The desert and illimitable air,—
Lone wandering, but not lost.

All day thy wings have fanned,
At that far height, the cold thin atmosphere,
Yet stoop not, weary, to the welcome land,
Though the dark night is near.

And soon that toil shall end;
Soon shalt thou find a summer home and rest,
And scream among thy fellows; reeds shall bend,
Soon, o'er thy sheltered nest.

Thou 'rt gone, the abyss of heaven
Hath swallowed up thy form; yet, on my heart
Deeply hath sunk the lesson thou hast given,
And shall not soon depart.

He who, from zone to zone,
Guides through the boundless sky thy certain flight,
In the long way that I must tread alone,
Will lead my steps aright.

JUNE.

I gazed upon the glorious sky
And the green mountains round;
And thought that when I came to lie
At rest within the ground,
'Twere pleasant, that in flowery June,
When brooks send up a cheerful tune,
And groves a joyous sound,
The sexton's hand, my grave to make,
The rich, green mountain turf should break.

A cell within the frozen mould,
A coffin borne through sleet,
And icy clods above it rolled,
While fierce the tempests beat—
Away!—I will not think of these—
Blue be the sky and soft the breeze,
Earth green beneath the feet,
And be the damp mould gently pressed
Into my narrow place of rest.

There through the long, long summer hours
The golden light should lie,
And thick young herbs and groups of flowers
Stand in their beauty by.
The oriole should build and tell
His love-tale close beside my cell;
The idle butterfly
Should rest him there, and there be heard
The housewife bee and humming-bird.

And what if cheerful shouts at noon
Come, from the village sent,
Or songs of maids, beneath the moon,
With fairy laughter blent?
And what if, in the evening light,
Betrothed lovers walk in sight
Of my low monument?
I would the lovely scene around
Might know no sadder sight or sound.

I know, I know I should not see
The season's glorious show;
Nor would its brightness shine for me,
Nor its wild music flow;
But if, around my place of sleep,
The friends I love should come to weep,
They might not haste to go.
Soft airs, and song, and light, and bloom,
Should keep them lingering by my tomb.

These to their softened hearts should bear
The thought of what has been,
And speak of one who cannot share
The gladness of the scene;
Whose part, in all the pomp that fills
The circuit of the summer hills,
Is—that his grave is green;
And deeply would their hearts rejoice
To hear again his living voice.

THE DEATH OF THE FLOWERS.

The melancholy days are come, the saddest of the year,
Of wailing winds and naked woods, and meadows brown and sere.
Heaped in the hollows of the grove, the autumn leaves lie dead;
They rustle to the eddying gust, and to the rabbit's tread.
The robin and the wren are flown, and from the shrubs the jay,
And from the wood-top calls the crow through all the gloomy day.

Where are the flowers, the fair young flowers, that lately sprang and stood
In brighter light, and softer airs, a beauteous sisterhood?
Alas! they all are in their graves, the gentle race of flowers
Are lying in their lowly beds, with the fair and good of ours.
The rain is falling where they lie, but the cold November rain
Calls not from out the gloomy earth the lovely ones again.

The wind-flower and the violet, they perished long ago,
And the brier-rose and the orchis died amid the summer glow;
But on the hill the golden-rod, and the aster in the wood,
And the yellow sun-flower by the brook in autumn beauty stood,
Till fell the frost from the clear cold heaven, as falls the plague on men,
And the brightness of their smile was gone from upland, glade, and glen.

And now, when comes the calm mild day, as still such days will come,
To call the squirrel and the bee from out their winter home;
When the sound of dropping nuts is heard, though all the trees are still,
And twinkle in the smoky light the waters of the rill,
The south wind searches for the flowers whose fragrance late he bore,
And sighs to find them in the wood and by the stream no more.

And then I think of one who in her youthful beauty died,
The fair meek blossom that grew up and faded by my side:
In the cold moist earth we laid her, when the forests cast the leaf,
And we wept that one so lovely should have a life so brief;
Yet not unmeet it was that one, like that young friend of ours,
So gentle and so beautiful, should perish with the flowers.

OH, FAIREST OF THE RURAL MAIDS.

Oh, fairest of the rural maids!
Thy birth was in the forest shades;
Green boughs, and glimpses of the sky,
Were all that met thine infant eye.

Thy sports, thy wanderings, when a child,
Were ever in the sylvan wild;
And all the beauty of the place
Is in thy heart and on thy face.

The twilight of the trees and rocks
Is in the light shade of thy locks;
Thy step is as the wind, that weaves
Its playful way among the leaves.

Thine eyes are springs, in whose serene
And silent waters heaven is seen;
Their lashes are the herbs that look
On their young figures in the brook.

The forest depths, by foot unpressed,
Are not more sinless than thy breast;
The holy peace that fills the air
Of those calm solitudes, is there.

TO THE EVENING WIND.

Spirit that breathest through my lattice, thou
That cool'st the twilight of the sultry day,
Gratefully flows thy freshness round my brow;
Thou hast been out upon the deep at play,
Riding all day the wild blue waves till now,
Roughening their crests, and scattering high their spray,
And swelling the white sail. I welcome thee
To the scorched land, thou wanderer of the sea!

Nor I alone—a thousand bosoms round
Inhale thee in the fulness of delight;
And languid forms rise up, and pulses bound
Livelier, at coming of the wind of night;
And, languishing to hear thy grateful sound,
Lies the vast inland stretched beyond the sight.
Go forth, into the gathering shade; go forth,
God's blessing breathed upon the fainting earth!

Go, rock the little wood-bird in his nest,
Curl the still waters, bright with stars, and rouse
The wide old wood from his majestic rest,
Summoning from the innumerable boughs
The strange, deep harmonies that haunt his breast:
Pleasant shall be thy way where meekly bows
The shutting flower, and darkling waters pass,
And where the o'ershadowing branches sweep the grass.

Stoop o'er the place of graves, and softly sway
The sighing herbage by the gleaming stone;
That they who near the churchyard willows stray,
And listen in the deepening gloom, alone,
May think of gentle souls that passed away,
Like thy pure breath, into the vast unknown,
Sent forth from heaven among the sons of men,
And gone into the boundless heaven again.*

The faint old man shall lean his silver head
To feel thee; thou shalt kiss the child asleep,
And dry the moistened curls that overspread
His temples, while his breathing grows more deep;
And they who stand about the sick man's bed
Shall joy to listen to thy distant sweep,
And softly part his curtains to allow
Thy visit, grateful to his burning brow.

Go—but the circle of eternal change,
Which is the life of nature, shall restore,
With sounds and scents from all thy mighty range,
Thee to thy birthplace of the deep once more;
Sweet odours in the sea-air, sweet and strange,
Shall tell the home-sick mariner of the shore;
And, listening to thy murmur, he shall deem
He hears the rustling leaf and running stream.

* This stanza is not included in the editions of Mr. Bryant's Poems. It appeared in "The Poets of America," published by Mr. John Keese, and illustrated by Chapman. The stanza is said to have been written at Mr. Keese's suggestion, to supply what is certainly an appropriate addition in keeping with the sentiment of the piece.

SONG OF MARION'S MEN.

Our band is few, but true and tried,
Our leader frank and bold;
The British soldier trembles
When Marion's name is told.
Our fortress is the good green wood,
Our tent the cypress-tree;
We know the forest round us,
As seamen know the sea.
We know its walls of thorny vines,
Its glades of reedy grass,
Its safe and silent islands
Within the dark morass.

Wo to the English soldiery
That little dread us near!
On them shall light at midnight
A strange and sudden fear:
When, waking to their tents on fire,
They grasp their arms in vain,
And they who stand to face us
Are beat to earth again;
And they who fly in terror deem
A mighty host behind,
And hear the tramp of thousands
Upon the hollow wind.

Then sweet the hour that brings release
From danger and from toil:
We talk the battle over,
And share the battle's spoil.
The woodland rings with laugh and shout,
As if a hunt were up,
And woodland flowers are gathered
To crown the soldier's cup.
With merry songs we mock the wind
That in the pine-top grieves,
And slumber long and sweetly,
On beds of oaken leaves.

Well knows the fair and friendly moon
The band that Marion leads—
The glitter of their rifles,
The scampering of their steeds.
'Tis life to guide our fiery barbs
Across the moonlight plains;
'Tis life to feel the night-wind
That lifts their tossing manes.
A moment in the British camp—
A moment—and away
Back to the pathless forest,
Before the peep of day.

Grave men there are by broad Santee,
Grave men with hoary hairs,
Their hearts are all with Marion,
For Marion are their prayers.
And lovely ladies greet our band,
With kindliest welcoming,
With smiles like those of summer,
And tears like those of spring.
For them we wear these trusty arms,
And lay them down no more
Till we have driven the Briton,
For ever, from our shore.

THE BATTLE-FIELD.

Once this soft turf, this rivulet's sands,
Were trampled by a hurrying crowd,
And fiery hearts and armed hands
Encountered in the battle cloud.

Ah! never shall the land forget
  How gushed the life-blood of her brave—
Gushed, warm with hope and courage yet,
  Upon the soil they fought to save.

Now all is calm, and fresh, and still,
  Alone the chirp of flitting bird,
And talk of children on the hill,
  And bell of wandering kine are heard.

No solemn host goes trailing by
  The black-mouthed gun and staggering wain;
Men start not at the battle-cry,
  Oh, be it never heard again!

Soon rested those who fought; but thou
  Who minglest in the harder strife
For truths which men receive not now,
  Thy warfare only ends with life.

A friendless warfare! lingering long
  Through weary day and weary year.
A wild and many-weaponed throng
  Hang on thy front, and flank, and rear.

Yet nerve thy spirit to the proof,
  And blench not at thy chosen lot.
The timid good may stand aloof,
  The sage may frown—yet faint thou not.

Nor heed the shaft too surely cast,
  The foul and hissing bolt of scorn;
For with thy side shall dwell, at last,
  The victory of endurance born.

Truth crushed to earth shall rise again;
  The eternal years of God are hers;
But Error wounded, writhes with pain,
  And dies among his worshippers.

Yea, though thou lie upon the dust,
  When they who helped thee flee in fear,
Die full of hope and manly trust,
  Like those who fell in battle here.

Another hand thy sword shall wield,
  Another hand the standard wave,
Till from the trumpet's mouth is pealed
  The blast of triumph o'er thy grave.

THE LAND OF DREAMS.

A mighty realm is the Land of Dreams,
  With steeps that hang in the twilight sky,
And weltering oceans and trailing streams,
  That gleam where the dusky valleys lie.

But over its shadowy border flow
  Sweet rays from the world of endless morn,
And the nearer mountains catch the glow,
  And flowers in the nearer fields are born.

The souls of the happy dead repair,
  From their bowers of light, to that bordering land,
And walk in the fainter glory there,
  With the souls of the living hand in hand.

One calm sweet smile, in that shadowy sphere,
  From eyes that open on earth no more—
One warning word from a voice once dear—
  How they rise in the memory o'er and o'er!

Far off from those hills that shine with day,
  And fields that bloom in the heavenly gales,
The Land of Dreams goes stretching away
  To dimmer mountains and darker vales.

There lie the chambers of guilty delight,
  There walk the spectres of guilty fear,
And soft low voices, that float through the night,
  Are whispering sin in the helpless ear.

Dear maid, in thy girlhood's opening flower,
  Scarce weaned from the love of childish play!
The tears on whose cheeks are but the shower
  That freshens the early blooms of May!

Thine eyes are closed, and over thy brow
  Pass thoughtful shadows and joyous gleams,
And I know, by thy moving lips, that now
  Thy spirit strays in the Land of Dreams.

Light-hearted maiden, oh, heed thy feet!
  O keep where that beam of Paradise falls,
And only wander where thou may'st meet
  The blessed ones from its shining walls.

So shalt thou come from the Land of Dreams,
  With love and peace to this world of strife;
And the light that over its border streams
  Shall lie on the path of thy daily life.

ROBERT OF LINCOLN.

Merrily swinging on brier and weed,
  Near to the nest of his little dame,
Over the mountain-side or mead,
  Robert of Lincoln is telling his name:
      Bob-o'-link, bob-o'-link,
      Spink, spank, spink;
Snug and safe is that nest of ours,
Hidden among the summer flowers.
      Chee, chee, chee.

Robert of Lincoln is gaily drest,
  Wearing a bright black wedding coat;
White are his shoulders and white his crest,
  Hear him call in his merry note:
      Bob-o'-link, bob-o'-link,
      Spink, spank, spink;
Look, what a nice new coat is mine,
Sure there was never a bird so fine.
      Chee, chee, chee.

Robert of Lincoln's Quaker wife,
  Pretty and quiet, with plain brown wings,
Passing at home a patient life,
  Broods in the grass while her husband sings:
      Bob-o'-link, bob-o'-link,
      Spink, spank, spink;
Brood, kind creature; you need not fear
Thieves and robbers while I am here.
      Chee, chee, chee.

Modest and shy as a nun is she:
  One weak chirp is her only note.
Braggart and prince of braggarts is he,
  Pouring boasts from his little throat:
      Bob-o'-link, bob-o'-link.
      Spink, spank, spink;
Never was I afraid of man;
Catch me, cowardly knaves, if you can.
      Chee, chee, chee.

Six white eggs on a bed of hay,
  Flecked with purple, a pretty sight!
There as the mother sits all day,
  Robert is singing with all his might:
      Bob-o'-link, bob-o'-link,
      Spink, spank, spink;
Nice good wife, that never goes out,
Keeping house while I frolic about.
      Chee, chee, chee.

Soon as the little ones chip the shell
  Six wide mouths are open for food;
Robert of Lincoln bestirs him well,
  Gathering seeds for the hungry brood.
      Bob-o'-link, bob-o'-link,
      Spink, spank, spink:
This new life is likely to be
Hard for a gay young fellow like me.
      Chee, chee, chee.

Robert of Lincoln at length is made
  Sober with work, and silent with care;
Off is his holiday garment laid,
  Half forgotten that merry air,
    Bob-o'-link, bob-o'-link,
    Spink, spank, spink;
Nobody knows but my mate and I
Where our nest and our nestlings lie.
    Chee, chee, chee.

Summer wanes; the children are grown;
  Fun and frolic no more he knows;
Robert of Lincoln's a humdrum crone;
  Off he flies, and we sing as he goes:
    Bob-o'-link, bob-o'-link,
    Spink, spank, spink;
When you can pipe that merry old strain,
Robert of Lincoln, come back again.
    Chee, chee, chee.

1855.

CORN-SHUCKING IN SOUTH CAROLINA—FROM THE LETTERS OF A TRAVELLER.

BARNWELL DISTRICT, South Carolina, *March* 29, 1843.

But you must hear of the corn-shucking. The one at which I was present was given on purpose that I might witness the humors of the Carolina negroes. A huge fire of *light-wood* was made near the corn-house. Light-wood is the wood of the long-leaved pine, and is so called, not because it is light, for it is almost the heaviest wood in the world, but because it gives more light than any other fuel. In clearing land, the pines are girdled and suffered to stand: the outer portion of the wood decays and falls off; the inner part, which is saturated with turpentine, remains upright for years, and constitutes the planter's provision of fuel. When a supply is wanted, one of these dead trunks is felled by the axe. The abundance of light-wood is one of the boasts of South Carolina. Wherever you are, if you happen to be chilly, you may have a fire extempore; a bit of light wood and a coal give you a bright blaze and a strong heat in an instant. The negroes make fires of it in the fields where they work; and, when the mornings are wet and chilly, in the pens where they are milking the cows. At a plantation, where I passed a frosty night, I saw fires in a small inclosure, and was told by the lady of the house that she had ordered them to be made to warm the cattle.

The light-wood-fire was made, and the negroes dropped in from the neighboring plantations, singing as they came. The driver of the plantation, a colored man, brought out baskets of corn in the husk, and piled it in a heap; and the negroes began to strip the husks from the ears, singing with great glee as they worked, keeping time to the music, and now and then throwing in a joke and an extravagant burst of laughter. The songs were generally of a comic character; but one of them was set to a singularly wild and plaintive air, which some of our musicians would do well to reduce to notation. These are the words:

Johnny come down de hollow.
    Oh hollow!
Johnny come down de hollow.
    Oh hollow!
De nigger-trader got me.
    Oh hollow!
De speculator bought me.
    Oh hollow!
I'm sold for silver dollars,
    Oh hollow!
Boys, go catch the pony.
    Oh hollow!
Bring him round the corner.
    Oh hollow!
I'm goin' away to Georgia.
    Oh hollow!
Boys, good-by forever!
    Oh hollow!

The song of "Jenny gone away," was also given, and another, called the monkey-song, probably of African origin, in which the principal singer personated a monkey, with all sorts of odd gesticulations, and the other negroes bore part in the chorus, "Dan, dan, who's the dandy?" One of the songs, commonly sung on these occasions, represents the various animals of the woods as belonging to some profession or trade. For example—

De cooter is de boatman—

The cooter is the terrapin, and a very expert boatman he is.

De cooter is de boatman.
    John John Crow.
De red-bird de soger.
    John John Crow.
De mocking-bird de lawyer.
    John John Crow.
De alligator sawyer
    John John Crow.

The alligator's back is furnished with a toothed ridge, like the edge of a saw, which explains the last line.

When the work of the evening was over the negroes adjourned to a spacious kitchen. One of them took his place as musician, whistling, and beating time with two sticks upon the floor. Several of the men came forward and executed various dances, capering, prancing, and drumming with heel and toe upon the floor, with astonishing agility and perseverance, though all of them had performed their daily tasks and had worked all the evening, and some had walked from four to seven miles to attend the corn-shucking. From the dances a transition was made to a mock military parade, a sort of burlesque of our militia trainings, in which the words of command and the evolutions were extremely ludicrous. It became necessary for the commander to make a speech, and confessing his incapacity for public speaking, he called upon a huge black man named Toby to address the company in his stead. Toby, a man of powerful frame, six feet high, his face ornamented with a beard of fashionable cut, had hitherto stood leaning against the wall, looking upon the frolic with an air of superiority. He consented, came forward, demanded a bit of paper to hold in his hand, and harangued the soldiery. It was evident that Toby had listened to stump-speeches in his day. He spoke of "de majority of Sous Carolina," "de interests of de state," "de honor of ole Ba'nwell district," and these phrases he connected by various expletives, and sounds of which we could make nothing. At length he began to falter, when the captain with admirable presence of mind came to his relief, and interrupted and closed the harangue with an hurrah from the company. Toby was allowed by all the spectators, black and white, to have made an excellent speech.

JOHN HOWARD BRYANT, the brother of the preceding, who has become known by his verses, chiefly descriptive of nature, was born at Cummington, July 22, 1807. His first poem, entitled *My Native Village*, appeared in 1826, in his brother's periodical, The United States Review. Having accomplished himself in various studies, in 1831 he emigrated to Illinois, where he established himself as a farmer, and where he has since occupied himself in agricultural life, occasionally writing poems, which have found their way to the public through the press. The following is a characteristic specimen of his muse:—

LINES ON FINDING A FOUNTAIN IN A SECLUDED PART OF A FOREST.

Three hundred years are scarcely gone,
Since, to the New World's virgin shore,
Crowds of rude men were pressing on,
To range its boundless regions o'er.

Some bore the sword in bloody hands,
And sacked its helpless towns for spoil;
Some searched for gold the river's sands,
Or trenched the mountain's stubborn soil.

And some with higher purpose sought,
Through forests wild and wastes uncouth,
Sought with long toil, yet found it not,
The fountain of eternal youth.

They said in some green valley where
The foot of man had never trod,
There gushed a fountain bright and fair
Up from the ever verdant sod.

There they who drank should never know
Age, with its weakness, pain, and gloom,
And from its brink the old should go,
With youth's light step and radiant bloom.

Is not this fount, so pure and sweet,
Whose stainless current ripples o'er
The fringe of blossoms at my feet,
The same those pilgrims sought of yore?

How brightly leap, 'mid glittering sands,
The living waters from below;
O let me dip these lean, brown hands,
Drink deep and bathe this wrinkled brow,

And feel, through every shrunken vein,
The warm, red stream flow swift and free—
Feel waking in my heart again,
Youth's brightest hopes, youth's wildest glee.

'Tis vain, for still the life-blood plays,
With sluggish course, through all my frame;
The mirror of the pool betrays
My wrinkled visage, still the same.

And the sad spirit questions still—
Must this warm frame—these limbs that yield
To each light motion of the will—
Lie with the dull clods of the field?

Has nature no renewing power
To drive the frost of age away?
Has earth no fount, or herb, or flower,
Which man may taste and live for aye?

Alas! for that unchanging state
Of youth and strength, in vain we yearn;
And only after death's dark gate
Is reached and passed, can youth return.

JOHN D. GODMAN.

John D. Godman was born at Annapolis, Maryland, December 20, 1794. Deprived in his second year of both his parents, he was left dependent on the care of an aunt, who discharged her duties towards him with great tenderness. He had the misfortune to lose this relative also at the early age of seven years.

Having lost by some fraudulent proceeding the small estate left him by his father, Godman, after the death of his aunt, by whom he had been placed at school, was apprenticed to a printer at Baltimore. Desirous of leading the life of a scholar he commenced and continued in this pursuit with reluctance.

In 1814, on the entrance of the British into Chesapeake Bay, he became a sailor in the navy, and was engaged in the bombardment of Fort McHenry.

In the following year he was invited by Dr. Luckey, who had become acquainted with the young printer while engaged in the study of his profession, to become an inmate of his residence at Elizabethtown. Gladly availing himself of this opening to the pursuit of the profession of his choice, Godman obtained a release from his indentures and devoted himself with ardor to study under the direction of his friend. Having thus passed a few months, he continued his course with Dr. Hall of Baltimore; and after attending lectures in that city, and in the latter part of his course filling the place of Professor Davidge during his temporary absence, he took his degree February 7, 1818.

After practising a short time in the villages of New Holland on the Susquehanna, in Ann Arundel county, and in the city of Philadelphia, he accepted the appointment of Professor of Anatomy in the recently established Medical College of Ohio, at Cincinnati, and entered upon his duties in October, 1821. Owing to difficulties "of which he was neither the cause nor the victim" he resigned his chair in a few months, and commenced a medical periodical, projected by Dr. Drake, entitled the Western Quarterly Reporter. Six numbers, of one hundred pages each, of this work were published.

In the autumn of 1822, he removed to Philadelphia, suffering much from exposure on the journey, owing to the lateness of the season and the delicacy of his constitution. He opened a room in the latter city under the auspices of the University, for private demonstrations in anatomy, a pursuit to which he devoted himself for some years with such assiduity as to still further impair his health.

In 1826, he removed to New York in acceptance of a call to the professorship of Anatomy in Rutgers Medical College. He delivered two courses of lectures with great success, but was then compelled to seek relief from exertion and a rigorous climate by passing a winter in the West Indies. After his return in the following summer, he settled at Germantown, where he remained, gradually sinking under a consumption, until his death, April 17, 1830.

His principal work, the *American Natural History*, was commenced in the spring of 1823, and completed in 1828, when it appeared in three volumes octavo. It is a work of much research, the author having journeyed many hundreds of miles as well as passed many months in his study in its preparation, and has been as much admired for its beauty of style as accuracy and fulness of information. Commencing with the aboriginal Indian, he pursues his inquiry through all the varieties of animal life, closing with an article on the Whale Fishery, and including the extinct Mastodon. Confining himself almost exclusively to description of the subject before him, we have little or no digression on the scenes in which his information was acquired, and the incidents connected with his researches. These themes he has touched upon in a later publication, *The Rambles of a Naturalist*, written with a frame enfeebled by disease, but with a mind still preserving its freshness, and in a style still vigorous. A portion of these essays first appeared in a weekly journal in Philadelphia. The series is incomplete, having been interrupted by the author's death.

Dr. Godman was for some time editor of the Philadelphia Journal of the Medical Sciences, and contributed largely to its pages until the close of his life. He was also the author of several articles in the American Quarterly Review, and of the notices of Natural History in the Encyclopædia Americana to the completion of the letter C. He translated and annotated many foreign medical works, and published a number of lectures and addresses delivered on various professional and public occasions, which were collected in a volume towards the close of his life.

At an early stage of his professional career, Dr. Godman adopted the atheistic views of some of the French naturalists. He retained these errors until the winter of 1827, when he was called to attend the death-bed of a student of medicine, who was possessed of "the comfort of a reasonable faith." His mind was so impressed by the scene, that he devoted himself to the study of the scriptures, and became a devoutly religious man.

The unremitting labor of Dr. Godman's career was sustained by the impetuosity and energy of his character. He knew no rest but in change of study, and no relaxation out of the range of his profession as a naturalist. In the directness, the simplicity and amiability of his character, he exhibited in an eminent degree the usual results of an enlightened communion with nature.

THE PINE FOREST.

Those who have only lived in forest countries, where vast tracts are shaded by a dense growth of oak, ash, chestnut, hickory, and other trees of deciduous foliage, which present the most pleasing varieties of verdure and freshness, can have but little idea of the effect produced on the feelings by aged forests of pine, composed in great degree of a single species, whose towering summits are crowned with one dark green canopy, which successive seasons find unchanged, and nothing but death causes to vary. Their robust and gigantic trunks rise a hundred or more feet high, in purely proportioned columns, before the limbs begin to diverge; and their tops, densely clothed with long bristling foliage, intermingle so closely as to allow of but slight entrance to the sun. Hence the undergrowth of such forests is comparatively slight and thin, since none but shrubs and plants that love the shade can flourish under this perpetual exclusion of the animating and invigorating rays of the great exciter of the vegetable world. Through such forests and by the merest footpaths in great part, it was my lot to pass many miles almost every day; and had I not endeavoured to derive some amusement and instruction from the study of the forest itself, my time would have been as fatiguing to me as it was certainly quiet and solemn. But wherever nature is, and under whatever form she may present herself, enough is always proffered to fix attention and produce pleasure, if we will condescend to observe with carefulness. I soon found that even a pine forest was far from being devoid of interest.

* * * * * * * * * *

A full grown pine forest is at all times a grand and majestic object to one accustomed to moving through it. Those vast and towering columns, sustaining a waving crown of deepest verdure; those robust and rugged limbs standing forth at a vast height overhead, loaded with the cones of various seasons; and the diminutiveness of all surrounding objects compared with these gigantic children of nature, cannot but inspire ideas of seriousness and even of melancholy. But how awful and even tremendous does such a situation become, when we hear the first wailings of the gathering storm, as it stoops upon the lofty summits of the pine, and soon increases to a deep hoarse roaring, as the boughs begin to wave in the blast, and the whole tree is forced to sway before its power!

In a short time the fury of the wind is at its height, the loftiest trees bend suddenly before it, and scarce regain their upright position ere they are again obliged to cower beneath its violence. Then the tempest literally howls, and amid the tremendous reverberations of thunder, and the blazing glare of the lightning, the unfortunate wanderer hears around him the crash of numerous trees hurled down by the storm, and knows not but the next may be precipitated upon him. More than once have I witnessed all the grandeur, dread, and desolation of such a scene, and have always found safety either by seeking as quickly as possible a spot where there were none but young trees, or if on the main road choosing the most open and exposed situation, out of the reach of the large trees. There, seated on my horse, who seemed to understand the propriety of such patience, I would quietly remain, however thoroughly drenched, until the fury of the wind was completely over. To say nothing of the danger from falling trees, the peril of being struck by the lightning, which so frequently shivers the loftiest of them, is so great as to render any attempt to advance, at such a time, highly imprudent.

Like the ox among animals, the pine tree may be looked upon as one of the most universally useful of the sons of the forest. For all sorts of building, for firewood, tar, turpentine, rosin, lampblack, and a vast variety of other useful products, this tree is invaluable to man. Nor is it a pleasing contemplation, to one who knows its usefulness, to observe to how vast an amount it is annually destroyed in this country, beyond the proportion that nature can possibly supply. However, we are not disposed to believe that this evil will ever be productive of very great injury, especially as coal fuel is becoming annually more extensively used. Nevertheless, were I the owner of a pine forest, I should exercise a considerable degree of care in the selection of the wood for the axe.

BOWDOIN COLLEGE.

THIS institution, seated at Brunswick, in the state of Maine, after some early preliminary efforts, received its charter from the Legislature of Massachusetts, to which the region was then attached, June 24, 1794. Five townships of land

Bowdoin College.

were granted from the unsettled districts of Maine, as a foundation for the College. A munificent grant of money and lands, of the estimated value of six thousand eight hundred dollars, made by the Hon. James Bowdoin, son of the governor from whom the college was named, was an additional means of support; though from the difficulty of bringing the lands into market, and the necessity of waiting for further funds, the institution did not go into operation till 1801, when the board of trustees and overseers elected the Rev. Joseph McKeen the first president. He was a man of marked character and usefulness, a native of Londonderry, N.H., born in 1757, who had been associated with the best interests of education and religion at the Academy of Andover, and in pastoral relations in Boston and Beverly, Mass., from the last of which he was called to the presidency.

The first college building was at the same time in progress on the site selected, on an elevated plain, about one mile south from the Androscoggin river. There, in September, 1802, the president and the professor of languages, John Abbot of Harvard, were installed: a platform erected in the open air, in the grove of pines on the land, serving the purpose of the as yet unfinished Massachusetts Hall. When this building was completed it was parlor, chapel, and hall for the college uses; the president living in one of the rooms with his family, and summoning his pupils to morning and evening prayers in the temporary chapel on the first floor, by striking with his cane on the staircase.* For two years the president, with Professor Abbot, sustained the college instruction alone, which commenced with the usual requisitions of the New England institutions.

At the first Commencement, in 1806, there were eight graduates. The following year the college met with a great loss in the death of President McKeen, whose character had imparted strength to the institution.

The Rev. Jesse Appleton, of Hampton, N. H., was chosen his successor. He had been a few years before a prominent candidate for the theological chair of Harvard University, and he now took an active part in his similar duties by the delivery of a course of more than fifty lectures on the most important subjects in theology, a portion of which has been since published. His system of instruction was accurate and thorough. He continued president of the college till his death, at the age of forty-seven, November 12, 1819. An edition of his works was published in two volumes at Andover, in 1837, embracing his course of Theological Lectures, his Academical Addresses, and a selection from his Sermons, with a Memoir of his Life and Character, by Professor Packard, who holds the chair of Ancient Languages and Classical Literature at Bowdoin.

The Rev. William Allen, who had been president of Dartmouth University, and to whom the public is indebted for the valuable Dictionary of American Biography, was chosen the new president, and continued in the office for twenty years, with the exception of a short interval in 1831, when he was removed by an act of the Legislature, which had taken to itself authority to control the affairs of the college, in consequence of a cession of the old charter from Massachusetts to the new state of Maine on its organization in 1820, and the procurement of a new charter, which placed the institution in a measure under the control of the state. The question was finally adjudicated before Mr. Justice Story, in the circuit court of the United States, when a decision was given sustaining the rights of the college, which had been violated, and President Allen was restored to his office.

On his retirement in 1839, he was succeeded by the Rev. Dr. Leonard Woods, son of the venerable Dr. Woods of Andover. As a philosophical writer and theologian, Dr. Woods has sustained a high reputation by his conduct of the early volumes of the *Literary and Theological Review*, published at New York in 1834, and subsequently. He has also published a translation, from the French, of De Maistre's *Essay on the Generative Principle of Political Constitutions*.

Of the college professors Dr. Parker Cleaveland, the eminent mineralogist, has held the chair

*Historical Sketch of Bowdoin College, in the Am. Quar. Reg. viii. 107, of which this notice is an abstract.

of Natural Philosophy since 1805. He is the author of a popular elementary treatise on Mineralogy and Geology, which has been long before the public in successive editions.

The Rev. Thomas C. Upham, the author of several works on mental and moral science, was appointed Professor of Mental Philosophy and Ethics in 1824. He still holds the office, and discharges also the duties of an instructor in the Hebrew language. He is the author of *The Elements of Mental Philosophy*; of a *Treatise on the Will*; of a volume of a practical character, entitled *Outlines of Imperfect and Disordered Mental Action*, published in 1843; and a series of works unfolding the law of Christianity from its spring in the inner life, which bear the titles *Principles of Interior or Hidden Life*, and the *Life of Faith*. In illustration of this development of purity and holiness, Professor Upham was led to a close study of the writings of Madame Guyon, which has resulted in the publication, in 1855, of two volumes from his pen, entitled, *Life and Religious Opinions and Experience of Madame de la Mothe Guyon: together with some account of the Personal History and Religious Opinions of Fenelon, Archbishop of Cambray*.

The poet Longfellow was chosen Professor of Modern Languages in 1829, and discharged the duties of the office till 1835, when he was called to a similar post at Harvard.

A medical school, founded in 1821, is attached to the college. By the catalogue of 1854 it appears that the number of students at that date was seventy, and of the four college classes one hundred and seventy-seven.

UNION COLLEGE.

UNION COLLEGE, Schenectady, New York, dates from the year 1795, when it received its charter from the Regents of the University, a body instituted in the state in 1784, to whom was intrusted the power of incorporating Colleges, which should be endowed by the citizens of a particular locality. Gen. Philip Schuyler took special interest in forwarding the subscription. There had, however, been an earlier effort to establish a College at Schenectady. In 1782, an earnest application had been made to the Legislature at Kingston for this object, which, it should be noticed, was pursued at a time when the interests of literature were generally suspended by the scenes of the Revolution. This was two years before the reopening of the College at New York.

The first President of the College was John Blair Smith, a brother of the better known President of the College of New Jersey, but himself a man of marked character and not without distinction in other portions of the country. He was born in 1756 at Pequea, in Pennsylvania, received his education at Princeton, pursued a course of theological study with his brother, then President of Hampden Sidney College in Virginia, and, in 1779, succeeded him in that position. His career as a preacher in the valley of Virginia became much celebrated. Dr. Alexander, who saw him in the midst of the revival scenes of the time, has left a vivid picture of the man: "In person he was about the middle size. His hair was uncommonly black, and was divided on the top and fell down on each side of the face. A large blue eye of open expression was so piercing, that it was common to say Dr. Smith looked you through. His speaking was impetuous; after going on deliberately for awhile, he would suddenly grow warm and be carried away with a violence of feeling, which was commonly communicated to his hearers."* In 1791, he was called to the Third Presbyterian Church in Philadelphia, and thence to the Presidency of Union, where he remained till 1799, returning to his former charge at Philadelphia, where he died within a few months of the epidemic then raging.

He was succeeded in the Presidency by Jonathan Edwards, a son of the metaphysician. His childhood had been passed at Stockbridge, Massachusetts, where communication with the Indians had taught him their language, and fitted him for the duties of a missionary among the aborigines, a career which the breaking out of the French war prevented his pursuing. He completed his studies at the College in New Jersey, was licensed as a preacher after a course of theology with the Rev. Dr. Bellamy, became Tutor at Princeton, and afterwards Pastor at Whiteham and at Colebrook in Connecticut. From this retired position he was called to the Presidency of Union, which he did not live long to occupy, dying two years after, August 1, 1801. He was the author of numerous productions, chiefly theological and controversial, following out his father's acute metaphysical turn. Besides *A Dissertation on Liberty and Necessity*, and a number of special Sermons, he published *Observations on the Language of the Stockbridge Indians*, communicated to the Connecticut Society of Arts and Sciences, and since edited for the Massachusetts Historical Society's Collections, by the philologist Pickering.

Jonathan Maxcy was the third President, a native of Attleborough, Massachusetts, where he was born in 1768.

The united terms of the three first Presidents were but nine years, during which the College had hardly given evidence of its present importance. At this time the Rev. Eliphalet Nott was called to its head. The present venerable octogenarian was then in his thirty-first year. He was born in 1773, of poor parents, in Ashford, Connecticut, and his youth had been passed in the frequent discipline of American scholars of that period, acquiring the means of properly educating himself by instructing others. He received the degree of Master of Arts from Brown University in 1795. He was soon licensed to preach, and established himself as clergyman and principal of an academy at Cherry Valley, in the state of New York, then a frontier settlement. From 1798 to his election to the College he was Pastor of the Presbyterian Church at Albany, where he delivered a discourse *On the Death of Hamilton*, which was published at the time, and which has been lately reprinted. It was an eloquent assertion of the high qualities of Hamilton, and a vigorous attack on the practice of duelling. The text, from the prophet Samuel, was a significant

* Life of Archibald Alexander, p. 54.

one for either branch of the discourse, "*How are the mighty fallen!*"

The college on Nott's accession had but few students, and was poorly endowed. It soon began to gain the former, and the state provided the latter by its act of 1814, which granted a sum of two hundred thousand dollars for its benefit, to be derived, however, from the proceeds of certain lotteries sanctioned for the purpose. Dr. Nott turned his financial and business skill to the matter, and secured a handsome endowment for the institution.

In 1854 the fiftieth anniversary of Dr. Nott's presidency was celebrated at Union, at the time of Commencement in July. A large number of the graduates assembled, and addresses were delivered by the Hon. Judge Campbell of New York, and by President Wayland of Brown University, who pronounced an academical discourse on the topic of The Education Demanded by the People of the United States. Dr. Nott himself spoke with his old eloquence, and various speeches were delivered at a special meeting of the alumni.

The particular influence of Dr. Nott in the administration of the college has been the practical turn which he has given to its discipline, in calling forth the earnest, manly qualities of his pupils, and repressing the opposite proclivities of youth. This is a personal influence for which he will be gratefully remembered.

Dr. Nott's publications have been chiefly in the periodicals and newspapers, and mostly anonymous. His *Addresses to Young Men*, *Temperance Addresses*, and a collection of Sermons, are his only published volumes. He has written largely on "Heat," and illustrated his theories by the practical achievement of the stove bearing his name. In the Digest of Patents, thirty appear granted to him for applications of heat to steam-engines, the economical use of fuel, &c. In 1851 the Rev. Laurens P. Hickok was appointed Vice-President.

Laurens P. Hickok was born in Danbury, Fairfield co., Ct., December 29, 1798. His father, Ebenezer, was a substantial farmer of strong mind and sound judgment, and of leading influence in the town, especially in ecclesiastical matters. Until sixteen, his son labored on the farm in summer and attended the district school in winter. He then was prepared for college by a noted teacher of the day, Captain Luther Harris, of Newtown; entering Union, and graduating in 1820. His mind was led to the study of theology, and he was licensed as a preacher by the Fairfield East Association in 1822. He preached at Newtown, and some years later was the successor to Dr. Lyman Beecher at Litchfield. In 1836 he became Professor of Theology in Western Reserve College, Ohio, and for eight years performed the influential duties of that post. In 1844 he removed to the Auburn Theological Seminary, and in 1852 accepted the Professorship of Mental and Moral Science, with the Vice-Presidency of Union College.

Desirous of placing mental philosophy on a firm basis to supersede partial and false systems tending to infidelity, he published in 1850 his *Rational Psychology*. He has also published a volume, *Empirical Psychology, or the Human Mind as given in Consciousness*. His *System of Moral Science* was published in 1853 as a college textbook. It is mainly divided into two parts, treating of pure morality and positive authority. Under the former are considered personal and relative duties to Mankind, and duties to Nature and to God; under the latter, Civil, Divine, and Family Government. Dr. Hickok has written articles in the Christian Spectator; the Biblical Repository, particularly on the *à priori* and *à posteriori* proofs of the being of God; and some contributions to the Bibliotheca Sacra. Various sermons on special occasions and college addresses have appeared from his pen.

In the list of Professors of Union appear two bishops of the Protestant Episcopal Church—Dr. Brownell of Connecticut, who, a graduate of the college, filled the chairs of Logic, Belles Lettres, and Chemistry, in different appointments from 1806 to 1819, and the Rt. Rev. Dr. Alonzo Potter,* of Pennsylvania, who was at different times Professor of Mathematics and Natural Philosophy, and of Rhetoric, from 1822 to 1845. Among the older Professors, the Rev. Andrew Yates, held the chair of the Latin and Greek Languages from 1797 to 1801, and of Moral Philosophy and Logic for a number of years subsequently to 1814. The Rev. Thomas Macauley, a graduate of the college of 1804, was at first tutor, and subsequently for two periods, from 1811 to 1814, and from 1814 to 1822, Professor of Mathematics and Natural Philosophy. The Rev. Robert Proudfit assumed the Professorship of Greek and Latin in 1812, and has now the rank of Emeritus Professor. In 1849 Mr. Tayler Lewis was appointed to the Professorship of Greek Language and

* Dr. Potter has extended the influence of his Episcopate by the sound Christian philosophy of his published Discourses, and by the course of Lectures on the Evidences of Christianity, in which he bore a leading part in Philadelphia, in the fall and winter of 1853-4. Before his election to his Bishopric, Dr. Potter had published an elementary work on "Science and the Arts of Industry," one on "Political Economy," and on "The School, its Uses, Objects, and Relations."

Literature, his devotion to which is sufficient to stamp the high scholarship of the college in this department.

Tayler Lewis

Tayler Lewis was born in Northumberland, in Saratoga county, New York, in 1802. His father was an officer in the Revolutionary war, and was an honored member of the Cincinnati Society at its close, when he had passed through its scenes and served with distinction in the battles of Monmouth and Germantown, at the siege of Fort Stanwix, and in the storming of the redoubts at the taking of Cornwallis at Yorktown. His mother was of a Dutch family in Albany, a niece of John Tayler, from whom our author derives his christian name, for many years Lieutenant-Governor of the state in the days of Tompkins and Clinton. Mr. Lewis graduated in 1820 at Union College, Schenectady, in the class of Judge Kent, Governor Seward, and Comptroller John C. Wright. He studied law in the office of Samuel A. Foot in Albany, in company with William Kent Though attracted by the study of such writers as Coke, Fearne, Blackstone, and Butler, and much interested in the logical questions of the law of evidence and real estate, he was not at ease with the practical conduct of the profession, touching which he had some conscientious scruples. He, however, rejecting offers of partnership at Albany, pursued the profession in the retired village of Fort Miller, Washington county, New York, where he had sufficient time for reflection, and where, at the suggestion of a clerical friend, he entered on the study of Hebrew to fill up the mental vacuum. The new occupation engrossed all his time and attention. He gave his days and nights to Hebrew. This led to a close and diligent study of the Bible in the language of the Old and New Testament. Homer and Plato followed with equal zest. Six years were devoted to biblical and classical studies, pursued with a scholar's unction and a pure love of literature, with no thought of using the stores thus accumulating in teaching or composition, or with any prospect of leaving the humble village. Nine years had now passed, when it became evident that law or literature must be relinquished. The former was the readiest sacrifice. In 1833 he married, abandoned the law, and took a classical school in the village of Waterford. In 1835 he went to Ogdensburg, St. Lawrence county, where he remained two years, then returned to Waterford, and shortly afterwards, through the influence of Mr. Foot and his old classmate Judge William Kent, was appointed Professor of Greek in the University of the City of New York. At this time he also became an active writer for the higher reviews, The *Literary and Theological*, the *Biblical Repository*, and others, to which he has continued a frequent contributor. His topics have been the relations of theology and philosophy, following generally the ideas of Calvin; the questions of the day in morals, politics, church and state government, and natural science regarded in their religious bearing.*

His special classical studies have been subordinate to those philosophical discussions. In 1845 he published a semi-classical, semi-theological work, *Plato contra Atheos*, and he has since prepared *A Translation of Plato's Theaetetus*, with notes and illustrations on its adaptedness to our own times. In 1844 he also published a volume on *The Nature and Ground of Punishment*.

The discoveries of geology and astronomy, in

* A list of these Miscellaneous Writings will be valuable to our readers. It offers many points of reference and special "aids to reflection."

Addresses.—Faith the Life of Science; delivered before the Phi Beta Phi Society, Union College, 1838. Natural Religion the Remains of Primitive Revelation; Delivered at Burlington, 1839. The Believing Spirit; Phi Beta Kappa Society, Dartmouth College, 1841. The True Idea of the State; Porter Rhetorical Society, Andover, 1843. The Revolutionary Spirit; Wesleyan University, Middletown, Connecticut, 1848. The Bible Everything or Nothing; New York Theological Seminary, 1847. Nature, Progress, Ideas; or, A Discourse on Naturalism; Phi Beta Kappa Society, Union College, 1849. *Lectures.*—Common School Education; Albany and Troy, January, 1848. Ancient Names for Soul; Albany and Rochester, 1849. Six Days of Creation, two Lectures; New York, January, 1853. *Articles in Reviews, &c.*—Economical Mode of Studying the Classics; Lit. and Theol. Review, Dec., 1838. Influence of the Classics; Lit. and Theol. Review, March, 1839. Natural and Moral Science; Lit. and Theol. Review, June, 1839. Review of Nordheimer's Hebrew Grammar; Bib. Rep., April, 1841. Review of Nordheimer's Hebrew Concordance; Bib. Rep. April, 1842. The Divine Attributes as Exhibited in the Grecian Poetry; Bib. Rep., July, 1842. Vestiges of Creation, Review of; Amer. Whig Review, May, 1845. Cases of Conscience; Amer. Whig Review, July, 1845. Human Rights, Art. 1; Amer. Whig Review, Oct., 1845. Human Rights, Art. 2; Amer. Whig Review, Nov., 1845. The Church Question? Amer. Bib. Rep. (60 pp.) Jan. 1846. Has the State a Religion; Amer. Review, March, 1846. The Nature of the Sufferings of Christ; Bib. Rep., July, 1846. Human Justice, or Government a Moral Power; Bib. Rep., Jan., 1847. Second article on the same subject; Bib. Rep., April, 1847. The Bible Everything or Nothing; Bib. Rep., January, 1848. Classical Criticism (Essay on); Knickerbocker, Sept., 1847. Association, or Fourierism; Methodist Quar. Review, Jan., 1848. Chalmers; Bib. Rep., April, 1848. Bible Ethics; Bib. Rep., July, 1848. Astronomical Views of the Ancients; Bib. Rep., April, 1849. Second Article on the same; Bib. Rep., July, 1849. The Spirit of the Old Testament; Bib. Rep., January, 1850. Spirituality of the Book of Job; Andover Bibliotheca, May, 1849. Second Article on the same; Andover Bibliotheca, Aug., 1849. Political Corruption; Whig Review, 1846. The Book of Proverbs; Bib. Rep., April, 1850. Names for Soul; Bib. Rep., Oct., 1850. Review of Hickok's Rational Psychology; Andover Bibliotheca, Jan., 1851. Second Article on the same; Andover Bibliotheca, April, 1851. Three Absurdities of Modern Theories of Education; Princeton Review, April, 1851. Numerous Articles in the Literary World. Theaetetus of Plato; Andover Bibliotheca, Jan., 1853. The Editor's Table; in Harper's New Monthly for three years, with one or two exceptions. Numerous Articles in the New York Observer.

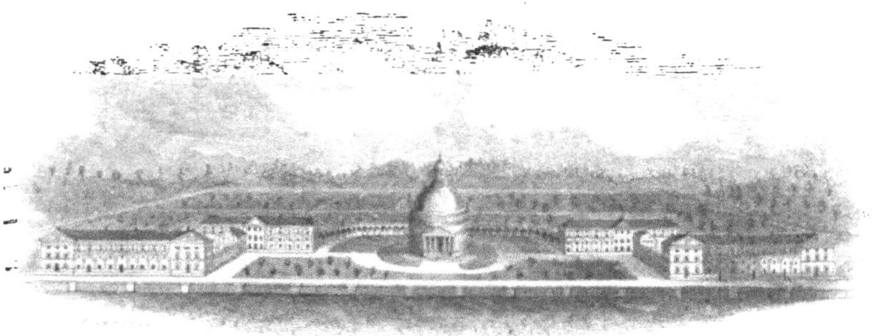

Union College.

their relation to the Biblical narrative, have employed much of his attention. His work published at Schenectady in 1855, entitled *The Six Days of Creation; or, Scriptural Cosmology, with the ancient idea of Time-Worlds in distinction from Worlds of Space*, is a novel and able view of the subject, displaying distinguished philological research and acumen.

Besides his illustration of these and kindred topics in the more scholastic journals, Professor Lewis has handled most of the great social, political, and philosophical topics of the times in the "Editor's Table" of *Harper's Magazine*, where his writings have exerted a healthful and widely extended influence.

Professor Isaac W. Jackson, a graduate of the college of 1826, and since 1831 Professor of Mathematics and Natural Philosophy, has illustrated his department by the production of text books on "Conic Sections," "Mechanics," and "Optics," in which these subjects are digested with ability, and presented with new researches by the author in a style of noticeable clearness and precision.

A Professorship of Civil Engineering has been held since 1845 by William Mitchell Gillespie, who has given to the public several works illustrating the subject of his instructions. His *Manual of Road-Making* has passed through a number of editions. In 1851 he published *The Philosophy of Mathematics*, a translation from the French of Auguste Comte; and in 1855 *The Principles and Practice of Land Surveying*. An early publication from his pen appeared in 1845, the sketch of a careful tourist, entitled *Rome; as seen by a New Yorker in* 1843-4. Mr. Gillespie was born in 1816, and is a graduate of Columbia College of 1834.

The College Programme of the "Civil Engineering Department" shows this subject to be pursued with a philosophical discrimination of its various parts, rendering it a general discipline of the faculties as well as a direct avenue to the large practical business in the country which must be based on the science. The course commences with the second term of the Sophomore year, and may be pursued separately from the classical and purely philosophical studies, the pupil receiving a special certificate of the progress which he may have made. This system of allowing a partial pursuit of the University Course was introduced as early as 1832, and more fully developed in 1849. The students may engage in various studies at choice, but must attend at least three recitations daily to entitle them to the privilege.

Mr. Elias Peissner, Instructor of Modern Languages, has published a grammar of the German language on a philosophical system, assisting the English student by first exhibiting to him the resemblances of the two tongues, an assistance which starts him far on the journey.

The view of the college buildings which we present includes the whole plan, though only one half is yet completed. The rest is expected to be soon accomplished.

In 1842, on the 22d July, the first semi-centennial anniversary of the college was celebrated by a variety of public exercises, including addresses by the Rev. Joseph Sweetman of the class of 1797, and by the Rev. Alonzo Potter of the class of 1818. There was also a dinner of the alumni presided over by John C. Spencer, who delivered an eloquent speech on the college, and the festivities were well sustained by speech and song from Bishop Doane, the Rev. J. W. Brown, Alfred B. Street, and other honored sons of the institution.

JOHN E. HOLBROOK.

Dr. John Edwards Holbrook, author of *North American Herpetology* and *Ichthyology of South Carolina*, was born at Beaufort, South Carolina, 1795. He became a graduate of Brown University, Providence, Rhode Island, and after taking a medical degree in Philadelphia, left home to pursue his professional studies at the schools of Edinburgh and London. Having passed nearly two years in Scotland and England, he proceeded to the continent, where he spent two more years, partly in Germany and Italy, but principally in Paris—always occupied in the study of his profession.

It was among the magnificent collections in the Museum of the Garden of Plants in Paris that Dr. Holbrook began the study of natural history, to which he has since devoted his life.

In 1822 he returned to the United States, and in 1824 was elected Professor of Anatomy in the Medical College of the State of South Carolina, a place which he still holds.

At the time Dr. Holbrook undertook the publication of his great work upon the *Reptiles of North America*, very little was known of the natural history of these animals in this part of the world, and the difficulties under which he labored from want of books and collections can hardly be appreciated now. In fact, he had to clear the whole field, upon which he has erected a monument which will remain the foundation of that branch of natural history in this country as long as science is cultivated. The work is particularly remarkable for the clearness and fulness of its descriptions, and the total absence of vagaries; the illustrations are natural and correct—not a single figure having been made from dead specimens, and all are colored from life. Of late Dr. Holbrook has been devoting his attention to a work on the fishes of the southern states, of which three numbers have been published, which will undoubtedly maintain the high rank of his previous scientific labors.*

* North American Herpetology, published in Philadelphia: J. Dobson, 1842. Ichthyology of South Carolina, published in Charleston: John Russell, 1854.

MARIA BROOKS.

Maria Brooks

MARIA DEL' OCCIDENTE, to adopt her poetical designation, was the descendant of a family of Welsh origin. Her grandfather had settled in Charlestown, Massachusetts, before the Revolutionary war. He was a man of wealth, and built there a fine house for his residence, from which he was driven when the town was burnt by the British. He retired to Medford, where his granddaughter, Maria Gowen, was born about 1795. Her father was a man of literary cultivation, and enjoyed the intimacy of the professors of Harvard, which doubtless lent its influence to the tastes of the young poetess who, before her ninth year, had committed to memory passages from Comus and Cato and the ancient classics. The loss of her father's property was followed by his death, and with these broken fortunes, at the age of fourteen she became engaged to a merchant of Boston, who provided for her education, and on its completion married her. Mercantile disaster succeeded a few years of prosperity, and a life of poverty and retirement followed. The wife turned her thoughts to poetry and wrote, at the age of twenty, an octosyllabic poem in seven cantos, which was never printed. In 1820 she published a small volume, *Judith, Esther, and other Poems; by a Lover of the Fine Arts;* in which she struck a new and peculiar view in American poetry. Concentrated and musical in expression, with equal force and delicacy of imagination, it was an echo of the refined graces of the noble old school of English poetry of the seventeenth century, in a new world in the nineteenth.

In 1823 the husband of Mrs. Brooks died, when she took up her residence with a relative in Cuba, where she speedily completed the first canto of *Zóphiël, or the Bride of Seven*, which was published at Boston in 1825. The five remaining cantos were written in Cuba. The death of her uncle, a planter of the island, who left her his property, gave her a settled income. She returned to the United States and lived in the neighborhood of Dartmouth College, where her son, now Captain Brooks of the United States Army, was pursuing his studies—the library of the institution supplying materials for the notes to her poem which she was then revising. In 1830 she accompanied her brother to Paris. In London she saw Washington Irving, then attached to the legation, who encouraged her in the production of the poem. With Southey, who warmly admired her poetical powers, and with whom she had held a correspondence from America, she passed the spring of 1831 at Keswick. Zóphiël was left in his hands for publication; and the proof sheets had been corrected by him when it appeared from the press of Kennett, a London publisher, in 1833.

Southey, in the Doctor, has pronounced Maria del' Occidente "the most impassioned and most imaginative of all poetesses."* If any one has since risen to divide the honor it is Mrs. Elizabeth Barrett Browning; otherwise Mrs. Brooks stands alone in one of the most refined and difficult provinces of creative art. Zóphiël, or the Bride of Seven, is an exquisite tale of an exiled Jewish maiden in Media, surrounded by the agencies of the spiritual world of demons, under the special influence of the fallen angel named in the title, and is evidently founded on the story, in the book of Tobit in the Apocrypha, of Sara the daughter of Raguel in Ecbatane, a city of Media, who "was reproached because she had been married to seven husbands, whom Asmodeus, the evil spirit had killed, before they had lien with her." Egla, the maiden, is all that exquisite beauty, grace, and tenderness can combine together in youthful womanhood—and though mostly passive in the story, her character and image are identified to the mind with distinctness. Zóphiël, who is in the place of Asmodeus, is the oriental representative of Apollo,

> a spirit sometimes ill; but ere
> He fell, a heavenly angel.

* The Doctor, chapter liv. First English Edition. Vol. ii. p. 178.

As this poem has been objected to, though without any sufficient reason, for obscurity in the narrative, we may cite for the reader's convenience a neat analysis of the plot which appeared in a contemporary review in Fraser's Magazine.

Zóphiël, a fallen angel, sees a Hebrew maid, and falls passionately in love with her, at the time that her parents wish her to marry a powerful and handsome Mede, by name Meles, who had won the old people's admiration by his skill in archery, exerted on the occasion of a victim-dove escaping from the altar as the Hebrew couple were about to perform a sacrifice. Meles just then happening to pass, let fly an arrow, and nailed the fugitive to a tree. He is accepted as the daughter's lover, in spite of her aversion. He enters the chamber where she is awaiting him:

But ere he yet, with haste, could draw aside
His broidered belt and sandals,—dread to tell,
Eager he sprang—he sought to clasp his bride:
He stopt—a groan was heard—he gasped and fell

Low by the couch of her who widowed lay,
Her ivory hands convulsive clasped in prayer,
But lacking power to move. And when 'twas day,
A cold black corse was all of Meles there.

Sardius, the king of Media, sends for Meles, who had been his ambassador to Babylon: search is made after him, and his corpse is found. The old Hebrew couple, and their daughter Egla, are brought prisoners to Sardius, and the latter describes the manner of Meles' death, and the circumstance of her being haunted by a spirit. This is taken for the raving of her unsettled brain, although she is detained in the palace, as the king has become enamoured of her. Idaspes, one of the nobles, fearful that Egla was in possession of some deadly art by which Meles fell, and which she might try upon Sardius, dissuades the king from approaching her; and Alcestes is destined to visit her during the night. He is killed by the same unseen hand. Sardius now offers a high reward to him who will unravel the mystery. Then steps forward another noble: he was bold, and descended from some god.

He came, and first explored with trusty blade;
But soon as he approached the fatal bride,
Opened the terrace-door, and half in shade
A form, as of a mortal, seemed to glide;

He flew to strike; but baffling still the blow,
And still receding from the chamber far,
It lured him on; and in the morning, low
And bloody lay the form.

All is dismay at the court. Rough old Philomars next claims permission to expose the trick. He enters the chamber, while his armed companions surround every avenue without, to prevent the escape of any fugitive. The precaution was vain, as Egla lay awaiting in bed the rough soldier. She heard Philomars' last struggle, and the suffocating noise of the lengthened death-pang. The next adventurer was Rosanes, who shared the same fate. Altheëtor, the favourite of Sardius, and his youthful musician, now falls ill with excessive love for Egla; his passion is discovered, and the king allows him to make the attempt which had proved fatal to so many.

Touching his golden harp to prelude sweet,
Entered the youth, so pensive, pale, and fair;
Advanced respectful to the virgin's feet,
And, lowly bending down, made tuneful parlance there.

Like perfume soft his gentle accents rose,
And sweetly thrilled the gilded roof along;
His warm devoted soul no terror knows,
And truth and love lead fervour to his song.

She hides her face upon her couch, that there
She may not see him die. No groan, she springs
Frantic between a hope-beam and despair,
And twines her long hair round him as he sings.

Then thus:—"Oh! Being who unseen but near
Art hovering now, behold and pity me!
For love, hope, beauty, music,—all that's dear,
Look,—look on me—and spare my agony!

"Spirit! in mercy, make me not the cause,
The hateful cause, of this kind being's death!
In pity kill me first!—He lives—he draws—
Thou wilt not blast?—he draws his harmless breath."

Still lives Altheëtor;—still unguarded strays
One hand o'er his fall'n lyre; but all his soul
Is lost—given up;—he fain would turn to gaze,
But cannot turn, so twined. Now, all that stole

Through every vein, and thrilled each separate nerve,
Himself could not have told,—all wound and clasped
In her white arms and hair. Ah! can they serve
To save him?—"What a sea of sweets!"—he gasped,

But 'twas delight:—sound, fragrance, all were breathing.
Still swelled the transport, "Let me look and thank:"
He sighed (celestial smiles his lip enwreathing),
"I die—but ask no more," he said and sank.

Still by her arms supported—lower—lower—
As by soft sleep oppressed; so calm, so fair—
He rested on the purple tap'stried floor,
It seemed an angel lay reposing there.

Zóphiël, in despair at not having obtained Egla's love, flies to the palace of Gnomes under the sea, following the guidance of Phraërion (Zephyrus), to obtain a draught which shall perpetuate life and youth in Egla. With difficulty they obtain it, but only on condition of taking back to the Gnome king in return a mortal bride. But as they are returning from their strange expedition, a tremendous storm occurs, in which Zóphiël lets fall the spar containing the drops of life. He and his companion reach the Libyan land, and the former is met by Satan himself, who demands of him the relinquishment of the hand of Egla, as he is enamoured of her; but Zóphiël refuses, and defies his power, when the superior fiend makes him feel it, and denounces destruction to his hopes.

The morning sun discovers Helon and Hariph, a young man and his aged guide, on the banks of the Tigris. The former is sorrowful, in consequence of a dream of the preceding evening, when Hariph gives him a box of *carneol*, as a preservative from evil; for in the hour of imminent danger he was to burn the contents. On proceeding, they come upon Zameïs and her guide, an aged man, overspent with fatigue, and in utter destitution. Zameïs had been married to one of the magnates of Babylon; but during the performance of the rights of Mylitta (the Assyrian Venus) she meets Meles, on an embassy at Babylon from Media, and falls desperately in love. During her husband's absence on another embassy she frequently sees Meles, and indulges her guilty passion; but the Mede, however, leaves her, and returns to his own country. The impassioned woman resolves to seek him through the world. Helon and Hariph relieve her. She finds her way to the bower of Egla, and is on the point of stabbing her to the heart, as the murderess of Meles, when Helon and his companion arrive to rescue her. This they effect. Zameïs dies from excess of passion; Helon is wedded to Egla, being the husband predestined for her; Hariph turns out to be the archangel Raphaël, who blesses the pair, and bids the lost spirit Zóphiël to indulge in hope.

The capabilities of this outline in a true poet's hands are manifest, but no one who has not read the poem with care—and whoever reads it once will be apt so to read it again and again—can do justice to the purity, sweetness, variety, and force of the versification, and the warm passionate nature which, without exaggeration or apparent effort, interpenetrates every portion of it. There is no vulgarity in the fate of the lovers. They seem to die worthily in the noble cause of honor and beauty. The pure maiden walks unscathed amidst these desperate fires. One charmed incident of Eastern romance succeeds another, with sentiment and description of nature blended with a certain cool spiritual breath of the peace which tempers the flames of passion burning through it. The imagery and ideas have been so thoroughly fused in the writer's mind, and come forth so naturally in the simple verses, that we would not suspect the deep study and costly elaboration of the work, which it is said was written over seven times, were we not reminded of these things by the learned quotations in the admirably written notes which carry us to Oriental, Classic, German, and French sources.*

Returning to America from England, Mrs. Brooks resided for a time at West Point, where her son, now an officer in the United States army, was stationed at the Military Academy as Assistant Professor, and afterwards at Governor's Island, New York.

In 1843 she had printed for private circulation a prose romance, *Idomen, or the Vale of Yumuri*, which, under a disguise of fiction, embodies the incidents of her career with much fine poetical description and philosophical reflection. At the close of the year she returned to her home in Cuba, a luxurious tropical residence, continuing to cultivate her poetic faculties in the production of some minor poems, and the planning and partial composition of an epic entitled, *Beatrix, the Beloved of Columbus*. It was her habit, says her correspondent, Dr. R. W. Griswold, "to finish her shorter pieces and entire cantos of longer poems, before committing a word of them to paper." Her *Ode to the Departed* was written in 1843. Her death occurred at Matanzas November 11, 1845.†

EGLA SLEEPING IN THE GROVE OF ACACIAS—FROM ZÓPHIËL.

Sèphora held her to her heart, the while
  Grief had its way; then saw her gently laid,
And bade her, kissing her blue eyes, beguile
  Slumbering, the fervid noon. Her leafy bed

Breathed forth o'erpowering sighs; increased the heat;
  Sleepless had been the night; her weary sense
Could now no more. Lone in the still retreat,
  Wounding the flowers to sweetness more intense

She sank. Thus kindly Nature lets our woe
  Swell till it bursts forth from the o'erfraught breast;
Then draws an opiate from the bitter flow,
  And lays her sorrowing child soft in the lap of rest.

Now all the mortal maid lies indolent;
  Save one sweet cheek, which the cool velvet turf

Had touched too rude, though all with blooms besprent,
  One soft arm pillowed. Whiter than the surf

That foams against the sea-rock looked her neck
  By the dark, glossy, odorous shrubs relieved,
That close inclining o'er her, seemed to reck
  What 'twas they canopied; and quickly heaved,

Beneath her robe's white folds and azure zone,
  Her heart yet incomposed; a fillet through
Peeped softly azure, while with tender moan,
  As if of bliss, Zephyr her ringlets blew

Sportive; about her neck their gold he twined;
  Kissed the soft violet on her temples warm,
And eyebrow just so dark might well define
  Its flexile arch; throne of expression's charm.

As the vexed Caspian, though its rage be past,
  And the blue smiling heavens swell o'er in peace,
Shook to the centre by the recent blast,
  Heaves on tumultuous still, and hath not power to cease;

So still each little pulse was seen to throb,
  Though passion and its pain were lulled to rest;
And ever and anon a piteous sob
  Shook the pure arch expansive o'er her breast.

Save that, a perfect peace was, sovereign, there
  O'er fragrance, sound, and beauty; all was mute;
Only a dove bemoaned her absent phere,
  Or fainting breezes swept the slumberer's lute.

EGLA AT THE BANQUET OF SARDIUS—FROM THE SAME.

But Egla this refused them; and forbore
  The folded turban twined with many a string
Of gems; and, as in tender memory, wore
  Her country's simpler garb, to meet the youthful king.

Day o'er, the task was done; the melting hues
  Of twilight gone, and reigned the evening gloom
Gently o'er fount and tower; she could refuse
  No more; and, led by slaves, sought the fair banquet-room.

With unassured yet graceful step advancing,
  The light vermillion of her cheek more warm
For doubtful modesty; while all were glancing
  Over the strange attire that well became such form.

To lend her space the admiring band gave way;
  The sandals on her silvery feet were blue;
Of saffron tint her robe, as when young day
  Spreads softly o'er the heavens, and tints the trembling dew.

Light was that robe, as mist; and not a gem
  Or ornament impedes its wavy fold,
Long and profuse; save that, above its hem,
  'Twas 'broidered with pomegranate-wreath, in gold.

And, by a silken cincture, broad and blue
  In shapely guise about the waist confined,
Blent with the curls that, of a lighter hue,
  Half floated, waving in their length behind;
The other half, in braided tresses twined,
  Was decked with rose of pearls, and sapphires azure too,

Arranged with curious skill to imitate
  The sweet acacia's blossoms; just as live
And droop those tender flowers in natural state;
  And so the trembling gems seemed sensitive;

And pendant, sometimes, touch her neck; and there
  Seem shrinking from its softness as alive.
O'er her arms flower-white, and round, and bare,
  Slight bandelets were twined of colours five;

* The notes of Zóphiël were written some in Cuba, some in Canada, some at Hanover, United States, some at Paris, and the last at Keswick, England, under the kind encouragement of Robert Southey, Esq.; and near a window which overlooks the beautiful lake Derwent, and the finest groups of those mountains which encircle completely that charming valley where the Greta winds over its bed of clean pebbles, looking as clear as dew.—*Author's Note.*

† A Biographical sketch of Mrs. Brooks, with an analysis of her poems, appeared in the Southern Literary Messenger for August, 1839. Griswold, to whom the public is indebted for the publication of several of her minor poems in *Graham's Magazine*, has added some interesting particulars in his Female Poets of America.

Like little rainbows seemly on those arms;
  None of that court had seen the like before;
Soft, fragrant, bright,—so much like heaven her charms,
  It scarce could seem idolatry t' adore.

He who beheld her hand forgot her face;
  Yet in that face was all beside forgot;
And he, who as she went, beheld her pace,
  And locks profuse, had said, "nay, turn thee not."

Placed on a banquet-couch beside the king,
  'Mid many a sparkling guest no eye forbore;
But, like their darts, the warrior-princes fling
  Such looks as seemed to pierce, and scan her o'er and o'er:

Nor met alone the glare of lip and eye—
  Charms, but not rare:—the gazer stern and cool,
Who sought but faults, nor fault or spot could spy;
  In every limb, joint, vein, the maid was beautiful.

Save that her lip, like some bud-bursting flower,
  Just scorned the bounds of symmetry, perchance,
But by its rashness gained an added power;
  Heightening perfection to luxuriance.

But that was only when she smiled, and when
  Dissolved th' intense expression of her eye;
And had her Spirit-love first seen her then
  He had not doubted her mortality.

MORNING SUNLIGHT—FROM THE SAME.

How beauteous art thou, O thou morning sun!—
  The old man, feebly tottering forth, admires
As much thy beauty, now life's dream is done,
  As when he moved exulting in his fires.

The infant strains his little arms to catch
  The rays that glance about his silken hair;
And Luxury hangs her amber lamps, to match
  Thy face, when turned away from bower and palace fair.

Sweet to the lip, the draught, the blushing fruit;
  Music and perfumes mingle with the soul;
How thrills the kiss, when feeling's voice is mute!
  And light and beauty's tints enhance the whole.

Yet each keen sense were dulness but for thee:
  Thy ray to joy, love, virtue, genius, warms;
Thou never weariest: no inconstancy
  But comes to pay new homage to thy charms.

How many lips have sung thy praise, how long!
  Yet, when his slumbering harp he feels thee woo,
The pleasured bard pours forth another song,
  And finds in thee, like love, a theme for ever new.

Thy dark-eyed daughters come in beauty forth
  In thy near realms; and, like their snow-wreaths fair,
The bright-haired youths and maidens of the North
  Smile in thy colours when thou art not there.

'Tis there thou bid'st a deeper ardour glow,*
  And higher, purer reveries completest;
As drops that farthest from the ocean flow,
  Refining all the way, from springs the sweetest.

Haply, sometimes, spent with the sleepless night,
  Some wretch impassioned, from sweet morning's breath,
Turns his hot brow and sickens at thy light;
  But Nature, ever kind, soon heals or gives him death.

SONG—FROM THE SAME.

Day, in melting purple dying,
Blossoms, all around me sighing,
Fragrance, from the lilies straying,
Zephyr, with my ringlets playing,
  Ye but waken my distress:
  I am sick of loneliness.

Thou, to whom I love to hearken,
Come, ere night around me darken;
Though thy softness but deceive me,
Say thou'rt true and I'll believe thee;
  Veil, if ill, thy soul's intent,
  Let me think it innocent!

Save thy toiling, spare thy treasure:
All I ask is friendship's pleasure:
Let the shining ore lie darkling,
Bring no gem in lustre sparkling;
  Gifts and gold are naught to me;
  I would only look on thee!

Tell to thee the high-wrought feeling,
Ecstasy but in revealing;
Paint to thee the deep sensation,
Rapture in participation,
  Yet but torture, if comprest
  In a lone unfriended breast.

Absent still! Ah! come and bless me!
Let these eyes again caress thee,
Once, in caution, I could fly thee:
Now, I nothing could deny thee;
  In a look if death there be,
  Come, and I will gaze on thee!

JOSEPH RODMAN DRAKE.

JOSEPH RODMAN DRAKE was born in the city of New York, August 7, 1795. His father died while he was quite young, and the family had to contend with adverse circumstances. There were four children, Joseph and three sisters—Louisa, Millicent, and Caroline, of whom the last shared in his poetic susceptibility. Drake obtained a good education, and studied medicine under Dr. Nicholas Romayne, who was strongly attached to his young pupil. He obtained his degree, and shortly after, in October, 1816, married Sarah, the daughter of Henry Eckford, a connexion which placed him in affluent circumstances. After his marriage he visited Europe with his wife, and his relative, Dr. De Kay, who had also married a daughter of Eckford, and who was subsequently known to the public as the author of a volume of

* It has been generally believed that "the cold in clime are cold in blood," but this on examination would, I am convinced, be found *physically untrue*; at least, in those climates near the equator. It is here that most cold-blooded animals, such as the tortoise, the serpent, and various tribes of beautiful insects, are found in the greatest perfection.

Fewer instances of delirium or suicide, occasioned by the passion of love, would, perhaps, be found within the tropics than in the other divisions of the earth. Nature, in the colder regions, appears to have given an innate warmth and energy proportionate to those efforts, which the severity of the elements and the numerous wants which they create, keep continually in demand.

Those who live, as it were, under the immediate protection of the sun, have little need of internal fires. Their blood is cool and thin; and living where everything is soft and flattering to the senses, it is not surprising that their thoughts seldom wander far beyond what their bright eyes can look upon.

Though sometimes subject to violent fits of jealousy, these generally pass off without leaving much regret or unhappiness behind, and any other object falling in their way (for they would not go far to seek it) would very soon become just as valuable to them as the one lost. Such of them as are constant are rather so from indolence, than from any depth of sentiment or conviction of excellence. "The man who reflects (says Rousseau) is a monster out of the order of nature." The natives of all tropical regions might be brought forward in proof of his assertion: they never look at remote results, or enter into refined speculations; and yet, are undoubtedly less unhappy than any other of the inhabitants of earth.—*Note by the Author.*

Travels in Turkey, and of the zoological portion of the Natural History of New York. His health failing at this time, he visited New Orleans in the winter of 1819, for its recovery. He returned to New York in the spring, fatally smitten with consumption, and died in the following autumn, on the 21st September, 1820, at the age of twenty-five. He is buried in a quiet, rural spot, at Hunt's Point, Westchester county, in the neighborhood of the island of New York, where he passed some of his boyish years with a relative, and where the memory of his gentle manners and winning ways still lingers. A monument contains a simple inscription of his name and age, with a couplet from the tributary lines of Halleck:—

> None knew him but to love him,
> Nor named him but to praise.

Drake was a poet in his boyhood. The anecdotes preserved of his early youth show the prompt

kindling of the imagination. His first rhymes were a conundrum, which he perpetrated when he was scarcely five. When he was but seven or eight years old, he was one day punished for some childish offence, by imprisonment in a portion of the garret shut off by some wooden bars, which had originally inclosed the place as a wine closet. His sisters stole up to witness his suffering condition, and found him pacing the room with something like a sword on his shoulder, watching an incongruous heap on the floor, in the character of Don Quixote at his vigils over the armor in the church. He called a boy of his acquaintance, named Oscar, "little Fingal;" his ideas from books thus early seeking living shapes before him in the world. In the same spirit, the child listened with great delight to the stories of an old lady about the Revolution. He would identify himself with the scene, and once, when he had given her a very energetic account of a ballad which he had read, upon her remarking it was a tough story, he quickly replied, with a deep sigh: "Ah! *we* had it tough enough that day, ma'am."

As a poet, "he lisped in numbers, for the numbers came." He wrote *The Mocking-Bird*, the earliest of his poems which has been preserved, when a mere boy. It shows not merely a happy facility, but an unusual consciousness of the imitative faculty in young poets. A portion of a poem, *The Past and the Present*, which furnished the concluding passage of Leon in the published volume, was communicated to a friend in MS. when the author was about fourteen. On his European tour in 1818, he addressed two long rhyming letters to his friend Halleck—one dated Dumfries, in May, in the measure of Death and Dr. Hornbook, and in English-Scotch; the other, dated Irvine, in the same month, mostly on Burns, in the eight-syllable iambic.

On his return home to New York, he wrote, in March, 1819, the first of the famous Croakers, the verses to *Ennui*, which he sent to the Evening Post, and which Coleman, the editor, announced to the public as "the production of genius and taste." The authorship was for a while kept secret. Drake communicated it to Halleck, who joined his friend in the series as Croaker, Jr., and they mostly signed the contributions, afterwards, Croaker & Co. Of the thirty or more poems of which the whole series was composed, Drake wrote nearly one half, including *The American Flag*, which appeared among them.

Though the poems have not been acknowledged by either author, and the public is of course somewhat in the dark as to these anonymous effusions, yet the mystery has been penetrated by various knowing persons of good memories and skilled in local and political gossip—of the result of whose labors the following is, we believe, a pretty accurate statement.

The Croakers, published in the Evening Post, appeared in rapid succession in one season, beginning with the lines by Drake, to Ennui, March 10, 1819, and ending July 24, with The Curtain Conversation by Halleck, that pleasant appeal of Mrs. Dash, since included among his poems under the title "Domestic Happiness." The following Croakers have been attributed to Drake: "On Presenting the Freedom of the City in a Gold Box to a Great General;" "The Secret Mine sprung at a late Supper," an obscure local political squib, of temporary interest; "To Mr. Potter, the Ventriloquist," who is supposed to be employed in the State Legislature, promoting a confusion of tongues among the members in *mal-à-propos* speeches; the first "Ode to Mr. Simpson, Manager and Purveyor of the Theatre,"—pleasant gossip about Woodworth, Coleman, Mrs. Barnes, Miss Leesugg who afterwards became Mrs. Hackett, and others: "The Battery War," a sketch of a forgotten debate in Tammany; "To John Minshull, Esq., Poet and Playwright, who formerly resided in Maiden-lane but now absent in England," a pleasant satire, light and effective, upon a melancholy poetaster of the times; the lines to John Lang, Esq.,

> In thee, immortal Lang! have all
> The sister graces met—
> Thou statesman! sage! and "editor"
> Of the New York Gazette;

the "Abstract of the Surgeon-General's Report," and, perhaps, the lines "Surgeon-General" himself—hitting off Dr. Mitchill's obvious peculiarities in the funniest manner; "To ——— ———, Esq.," a legal friend, who is invited from his law books to "the feast of reason and the flow of soul of the wits;" an "Ode to Impudence," which expresses the benefit and delight of paying debts in personal brass in preference to the usual gold and silver currency; an "Ode to Fortune," with a glimpse of the resources of an easy lounger about the city; the "Ode to Simon Dewitt, Esq., Surveyor-General," to whom it appears the public is indebted for those classic felicities in the naming of our rural towns Pompey, Ovid, Cicero, Manlius, and the like; "To Croaker, Jr.," in compliment to his associate Halleck,—with whom the honors of the whole, for wit and sentiment, are fairly divided.

The Culprit Fay arose out of a conversation in the summer of 1819, in which Drake, De Kay, Cooper the novelist, and Halleck were speaking of the Scottish streams and their adaptation to the uses of poetry by their numerous romantic associations. Cooper and Halleck maintained that our own rivers furnished no such capabilities, when Drake, as usual, took the opposite side of the argument; and, to make his position good, produced in three days The Culprit Fay. The scene is laid in the Highlands of the Hudson, but it is noticeable that the chief associations conjured up relate to the salt water; the poet drawing his inspiration from his familiar haunt on the Sound, at Hunt's Point.*

The Culprit Fay is a poem of exquisite fancy, filled with a vast assemblage of vitalized poetical images of earth, air and water, which come thronging upon the reader in a tumult of youthful creative ecstasy. We cannot suppose this poem to have been written otherwise than it was, in a sudden brilliant flash of the mind, under the auspices of the fairest associations of natural scenery and human loveliness. No churl could have worked so generously, prodigally bestowing poetical life upon the tiny neglected creatures which he brings within the range of the reader's unaccustomed sympathy. It is a Midsummer's Night's Dream after Shakespeare's Queen Mab; but the poet had watched this manifold existence of field and wave or he never would have described it, though a thousand Shakespeares had written. The story is pretty and sufficient for the purpose, which is not a very profound one—a mere junketing with a poet's fancy. The opening scenery is a beautiful moonlight view of the Highlands of the Hudson.

'Tis the middle watch of a summer's night—
The earth is dark, but the heavens are bright;
Nought is seen in the vault on high
But the moon, and the stars, and the cloudless sky,
And the flood which rolls its milky hue,
A river of light on the welkin blue.
The moon looks down on old Cronest,
She mellows the shades on his shaggy breast,
And seems his huge grey form to throw
In a silver cone on the wave below;
His sides are broken by spots of shade,
By the walnut bough and the cedar made,
And through their clustering branches dark
Glimmers and dies the fire-fly's spark—
Like starry twinkles that momently break
Through the rifts of the gathering tempest's rack.

The stars are on the moving stream,
 And fling, as its ripples gently flow,
A burnished length of wavy beam
 In an eel-like, spiral line below;
The winds are whist, and the owl is still,
 The bat in the shelvy rock is hid,
And nought is heard on the lonely hill
But the cricket's chirp, and the answer shrill
 Of the gauze-winged katy-did;
And the plaint of the wailing whip-poor-will,
 Who moans unseen, and ceaseless sings,
Ever a note of wail and wo,
 Till morning spreads her rosy wings,
And earth and sky in her glances glow.

The Culprit has been guilty of the enormity of falling in love with an earthly maid.

And left for her his woodland shade;
He has lain upon her lip of dew,
And sunned him in her eye of blue,
Fanned her cheek with his wing of air,
Played in the ringlets of her hair,
And, nestling on her snowy breast,
Forgot the lily-king's behest.

For this he is put on trial and sentenced at once. In consideration of the damage done to his wings he is to repair their wounded purity by seizing a drop from the glistening vapory arch in the moonlight of the leaping sturgeon, and since his flame-wood lamp has been extinguished he is to light it again from the last spark of a falling star. It was a pretty penance, but difficult of execution. The Fay, plunging into the wave in quest of the sturgeon, is met by an embattled host of those thorny, prickly, and exhaustive powers which lurk in the star-fish, the crab, and the leech.

Up sprung the spirits of the waves,
From sea-silk beds in their coral caves,
With snail-plate armour snatched in haste,
They speed their way through the liquid waste:
Some are rapidly borne along
On the mailed shrimp or the prickly prong,
Some on the blood-red leeches glide,
Some on the stony star-fish ride,
Some on the back of the lancing squab,
Some on the sideling soldier-crab;
And some on the jellied quarl that flings
At once a thousand streamy stings—
They cut the wave with the living oar
And hurry on to the moonlight shore,
To guard their realms and chase away
The footsteps of the invading Fay.

The activity of these foes is vigorously described.

Fearlessly he skims along,
His hope is high, and his limbs are strong,
He spreads his arms like the swallow's wing,
And throws his feet with a frog-like fling;
His locks of gold on the waters shine,
 At his breast the tiny foam-beads rise,
His back gleams bright above the brine,
 And the wake-line foam behind him lies.
But the water-sprites are gathering near
 To check his course along the tide;

* In a MS. copy of the Culprit Fay the author left a note, ingeniously removing the difficulty. "The reader will find some of the inhabitants of the salt water a little further up the Hudson than they usually travel; but not too far for the purposes of poetry."

Their warriors come in swift career
And hem him round on every side.
On his thigh the leech has fixed his hold,
The quarl's long arms are round him rolled,
The prickly prong has pierced his skin,
And the squab has thrown his javelin,
The gritty star has rubbed him raw,
And the crab has struck with his giant claw;
He howls with rage, and he shrieks with pain,
He strikes around, but his blows are vain;
Hopeless is the unequal fight,
Fairy! nought is left but flight.

He turned him round and fled amain
With hurry and dash to the beach again;
He twisted over from side to side,
And laid his cheek to the cleaving tide.
The strokes of his plunging arms are fleet,
And with all his might he flings his feet,
But the water-sprites are round him still,
To cross his path and work him ill.
They bade the wave before him rise;
They flung the sea-fire in his eyes,
And they stunned his ears with the scallop stroke,
With the porpoise heave and the drum-fish croak.
Oh! but a weary wight was he
When he reached the foot of the dog-wood tree.

Like wounded knight-errant, repairing his personal injuries with the simples at hand, he embarks this time in the shallow of a purple muscle-shell, meets the sturgeon, and catches the evanescent lustre. He has then the powers of the air to deal with in quest of the star; but they are less formidable, or he is better mounted on a fire-fly steed, which carries him safely through all opposition.

He put his acorn helmet on;
It was plumed of the silk of the thistle down:
The corslet plate that guarded his breast
Was once the wild bee's golden vest;
His cloak, of a thousand mingled dyes,
Was formed of the wings of butterflies;
His shield was the shell of a lady-bug queen,
Studs of gold on a ground of green;
And the quivering lance which he brandished bright,
Was the sting of a wasp he had slain in fight.
Swift he bestrode his fire-fly steed;
He bared his blade of the bent grass blue;
He drove his spurs of the cockle seed,
And away like a glance of thought he flew,
To skim the heavens and follow far
The fiery trail of the rocket-star.

With this armor he wins his way to the palace of the sylphid queen, who is for retaining him in that happy region. She is a kind damsel, for while he rejects her love, she speeds him on his errand with a charm. The star bursts, the flame is relighted, and there is a general jubilee on his return to the scenery of Crow Nest.

But hark! from tower on tree-top high,
The sentry elf his call has made,
A streak is in the eastern sky,
Shapes of moonlight! flit and fade!
The hill-tops gleam in morning's spring,
The skylark shakes his dappled wing,
The day-glimpse glimmers on the lawn,
The cock has crowed, and the Fays are gone.

The poems of Drake have not all been preserved. He wrote with great facility on the spur of the moment, and seldom cared for a piece after it was written, but would give it to the first friend who would ask him for it. Some of his best verses were written with his friends and family sitting round the winter hearth—a passing amusement of the hour. These impromptus, whether witty or sentimental, were equally felicitous. He always touched matters of feeling with delicacy, and the Croakers witness the pungency of his wit. The following epigram does not appear in the collection of his poems:—

IMPROMPTU.

Unveil her mind, but hide her face,
And love will need no fuel;
Alas! that such an ugly case,
Should hide so rich a jewel.

Of Drake's personal character and literary habits we are enabled to present several characteristic anecdotes, by the aid of Mr. James Lawson, who some time since prepared an elaborate notice of the poet for publication, and has kindly placed his manuscript notes at our disposal.

"Drake's reading," remarks Mr. Lawson, "commenced early, and included a wide range of books. His perception was rapid and his memory tenacious. He devoured all works of imagination. His favorite poets were Shakespeare, Burns, and Campbell. He was fond of discussion among his friends, and would talk by the hour, either side of an argument affording him equal opportunity. The spirit, force, and at the same time simplicity of expression, with his artless manner, gained him many friends. He had that native politeness which springs from benevolence, which would stop to pick up the hat or the crutch of an old servant, or walk by the side of the horse of a timid lady. When he was lost to his friends one of them remarked that it was not so much his social qualities which engaged the affections as a certain inner grace or dignity of mind, of which they were hardly conscious at the time.

"Free from vanity and affectation, he had no morbid seeking for popular applause. When he was on his death-bed, at his wife's request, Dr. De Kay collected and copied all his poems which could be found, and took them to him. 'See, Joe,' said he to him, 'what I have done.' 'Burn them,' he replied, 'they are valueless.'

"Halleck's acquaintance with Drake arose in a poetical incident on the Battery, one day, when in a retiring shower the heavens were spanned by a rainbow. De Kay and Drake were together, and Halleck was talking with them: the conversation taking the turn of some passing expression of the wishes of the moment, when Halleck whimsically remarked that it would be heaven for him, just then, to ride on that rainbow, and read Campbell. The idea arrested the attention of Drake. He seized Halleck by the hand, and from that moment they were friends.

"Drake's person was well formed and attractive: a fine head, with a peculiar blue eye, pale and cold in repose, but becoming dark and brilliant under excitement. His voice was full-toned and musical; he was a good reader, and sang with taste and feeling, though rarely."

A fastidious selection, including the Culprit Fay, was made from Drake's poems, and published in 1836 by the poet's only child, his daughter, married to the late Commodore De Kay, famed for his naval engagements in the La Plata while commanding the squadron of Buenos Ayres.

The Mocking-Bird, and several of the other poems among the following extracts, are not included in that volume, the only one of the author's writings which has appeared.

THE MOCKING-BIRD.

Early on a pleasant day,
In the poet's month of May,
Field and forest looked so fair,
So refreshing was the air,
That despite of morning dew
Forth I walked, where tangling grew,
Many a thorn and breezy bush;
Where the red-breast and the thrush,
Gaily raised their early lay,
Thankful for returning day.

Every thicket, bush, and tree,
Swelled the grateful harmony;
As it mildly swept along,
Echo seemed to catch the song;
But the plain was wide and clear,
Echo never whispered near!
From a neighboring mocking-bird,
Came the answering notes I heard.

Soft and low the song began,
I scarcely caught it as it ran,
Through the melancholy trill
Of the plaintive whip-per-will.
Through the ring-dove's gentle wail,
Chattering jay and whistling quail,
Sparrow's twitter, cat bird's cry,
Red bird's whistle, robin's sigh,
Black bird, blue bird, swallow, lark,
Each his native note might mark,
Oft he tried the lesson o'er,
Each time louder than before.
Burst at length the finished song,
Loud and clear it poured along;
All the choir in silence heard,
Hushed before this wonderous bird!

All transported and amazed,
Scarcely breathing—long I gazed:
Now it reached the loudest swell,
Lower, lower, now it fell,
Lower, lower, lower still,
Scarce it sounded o'er the rill.
Now the warbler ceased to sing,
Then he spread his downy wing.
And I saw him take his flight,
Other regions to delight.

Thus, in most poetic wise,
I began to moralize—

In fancy thus, the bird I trace,
An emblem of the rhyming race;
Ere with heaven's immortal fire,
Loud they strike the quivering lyre;
Ere in high, majestic song,
Thundering roars the verse along;
Soft they time each note they sing,
Soft they tune each varied string;
Till each power is tried and known,
Then the kindling spark is blown.

Thus, perchance, has Moore oft sung,
Thus his lyre hath Milton strung;
Thus immortal Harold's Childe,
Thus, O Scott, thy witch notes wild;
Thus has Pope's melodious lyre,
Beamed with Homer's martial fire;
Thus did Campbell's war blast roar,
Round the cliffs of Elsinore;
Thus he dug the soldier's grave,
Iser, by thy rolling wave.

SONNET.

Is thy heart weary of unfeeling men,
And chilled with the world's ice? Then come with me,
And I will bring thee to a pleasant glen
Lovely and lonely. There we'll sit, unviewed
By scoffing eye; and let our hearts beat free
With their own mutual throb. For wild and rude
The access is, and none will there intrude,
To poison our free thoughts, and mar our solitude!
Such scenes move not their feelings—for they hold
No fellowship with nature's loneliness;
The frozen wave reflects not back the gold
And crimson flushes of the sun-set hour;
The rock lies cold in sunshine—not the power
Of heaven's bright orb can clothe its barrenness.

TO THE DEFENDERS OF NEW ORLEANS.

Hail sons of generous valor,
Who now embattled stand,
To wield the brand of strife and blood,
For freedom and the land.
And hail to him your laurelled chief,
Around whose trophied name,
A nation's gratitude has twined,
The wreath of deathless fame.

Now round that gallant leader,
Your iron phalanx form,
And throw, like Ocean's barrier rocks,
Your bosoms to the storm.
Though wild as Ocean's wave it rolls,
Its fury shall be low,
For justice guides the warrior's steel,
And vengeance strikes the blow.

High o'er the gleaming columns,
The bannered star appears,
And proud amid its martial band,
His crest the eagle rears.
And long as patriot valor's arm
Shall win the battle's prize,
That star shall beam triumphantly,
That eagle seek the skies.

Then on, ye daring spirits,
To danger's tumults now,
The bowl is filled and wreathed the crown,
To grace the victor's brow;
And they who for their country die,
Shall fill an honored grave,
For glory lights the soldier's tomb,
And beauty weeps the brave.

BRONX.

I sat me down upon the green bank-side,
Skirting the smooth edge of a gentle river,
Whose waters seemed unwillingly to glide,
Like parting friends who linger while they sever;
Enforced to go, yet seeming still unready,
Backward they wind their way in many a wistful eddy.

Gray o'er my head the yellow-vested willow
Ruffled its hoary top in the fresh breezes,
Glancing in light, like spray on a green billow,
Or the fine frost-work which young winter freezes;
When first his power in infant pastime trying,
Congeals sad autumn's tears on the dead branches lying.

From rocks around hung the loose ivy dangling,
And in the clefts sumach of liveliest green,

Bright ising-stars the little beach was spangling,
The gold-cup sorrel from his gauzy screen
Shone like a fairy crown, enchased and beaded,
Left on some morn, when light flashed in their eyes unheeded.

The hum-bird shook his sun-touched wings around,
The bluefinch carolled in the still retreat;
The antic squirrel capered on the ground
Where lichens made a carpet for his feet:
Through the transparent waves, the ruddy minkle
Shot up in glimmering sparks his red fin's tiny twinkle.

There were dark cedars with loose mossy tresses,
White powdered dog-trees, and stiff hollies flaunting,
Gaudy as rustics in their May-day dresses,
Blue pelloret from purple leaves upslanting
A modest gaze, like eyes of a young maiden
Shining beneath dropt lids the evening of her wedding.

The breeze fresh springing from the lips of morn,
Kissing the leaves, and sighing so to lose 'em,
The winding of the merry locust's horn,
The glad spring gushing from the rock's bare bosom:
Sweet sights, sweet sounds, all sights, all sounds excelling,
Oh! 'twas a ravishing spot formed for a poet's dwelling.

And did I leave thy loveliness, to stand
Again in the dull world of earthly blindness?
Pained with the pressure of unfriendly hands,
Sick of smooth looks, agued with icy kindness?
Left I for this thy shades, where none intrude,
To prison wandering thought and mar sweet solitude?

Yet I will look upon thy face again,
My own romantic Bronx, and it will be
A face more pleasant than the face of men.
Thy waves are old companions, I shall see
A well-remembered form in each old tree,
And hear a voice long loved in thy wild minstrelsy.

TO ENNUI—FROM THE CROAKERS.

Avaunt! arch enemy of fun,
Grim nightmare of the mind;
Which way, great Momus! shall I run
A refuge safe to find?—
My puppy's dead—Miss Rumour's breath
Is stopt for lack of news,
And F*** is almost hyp'd to death
And L*** has got the blues.

I've read friend Noah's book quite through,
Appendix, notes, and all;
I've swallowed Lady Morgan's too,
I've blundered through De Staël,
The Edinburgh Review—I have seen 't
The last that has been shipt;
I've read, in short, all books in print,
And some in manuscript.

I'm sick of General Jackson's toast,
Canals are nought to me;
Nor do I care who rules the roast,
Clinton or John Targee:
No stock in any bank I own,
I fear no lottery shark:
And if the Battery were gone
I'd ramble in the Park.

Let gilded guardsmen shake their toes,
Let Altorf please the pit,
Let Mr. Hawkins "blow his nose"
And Spooner publish it.

Insolvent laws, let Marshall break,
Let dying Baldwin cavil;
And let tenth ward electors shake
Committees to the devil.

In vain, for like a cruel cat
That sucks a child to death,
Or like a Madagascar bat
Who poisons with his breath,
The fiend, the fiend is on me still;
Come, doctor!—here's your pay—
What lotion, potion, plaster, pill,
Will drive the beast away?

ODE TO FORTUNE—FROM THE CROAKERS.

Fair lady with the bandaged eye!
I'll pardon all thy scurvy tricks,
So thou wilt *cut* me and deny
Alike thy kisses and thy kicks:
I'm quite contented as I am—
Have cash to keep my duns at bay,
Can choose between beefsteaks and ham,
And drink Madeira every day.

My station is the middle rank,
My fortune just a competence—
Ten thousand in the Franklin Bank,
And twenty in the six per cents:
No amorous chains my heart enthrall,
I neither borrow, lend, nor sell;
Fearless I roam the City Hall,
And bite my thumb at Mr. Bell.*

The horse that twice a year I ride,
At Mother Dawson's eats his fill;
My books at Goodrich's abide,
My country-seat is Weehawk hill;
My morning lounge is Eastburn's shop
At Poppleton's I take my lunch;
Niblo prepares my mutton chop,
And Jennings makes my whiskey punch.

When merry, I the hours amuse
By squibbing bucktails, guards, and balls;
And when I'm troubled with the blues
Damn Clinton and abuse canals:
Then, Fortune! since I ask no prize,
At least preserve me from thy frown;
The man who don't attempt to rise
'Twere cruelty to tumble down.

TO CROAKER, JUNIOR—FROM THE CROAKERS.

Your hand, my dear Junior! we are all in a flame
To see a few more of your flashes;
The Croakers for ever! I'm proud of the name,
But brother, I fear, though our cause is the same,
We shall quarrel like Brutus and Cassius.

But why should we do so! 'tis false what they tell,
That poets can never be cronies:
Unbuckle your harness, in peace let us dwell,
Our goose quills will canter together as well
As a pair of Prime's mouse-colored ponies.

Once blended in spirit, we'll make our appeal,
And by law be incorporate too;
Apply for a charter in crackers to deal,
A fly-flapper rampant shall shine on our seal,
And the firm shall be "Croaker & Co."

Fun, prosper the union—smile, Fate, on its birth;
Miss Atropos shut up your scissors;
Together we'll range through the regions of mirth,
A pair of bright Gemini dropt on the earth,
The Castor and Pollux of quizzers.

* The sheriff.

THE AMERICAN FLAG—FROM THE CROAKERS.

When Freedom, from her mountain height,
  Unfurled her standard to the air,
She tore the azure robe of night,
  And set the stars of glory there!
She mingled with its gorgeous dyes
The milky baldric of the skies,
And striped its pure celestial white
With streakings of the morning light;
Then, from his mansion in the sun,
She called her eagle bearer down,
And gave into his mighty hand
The symbol of her chosen land!

Majestic monarch of the cloud!
  Who rear'st aloft thy regal form,
To hear the tempest trumpings loud,
And see the lightning-lances driven,
  When stride the warriors of the storm,
And rolls the thunder-drum of heaven!
Child of the sun! to thee 'tis given
To guard the banner of the free,
To hover in the sulphur smoke,
To ward away the battle stroke,
And bid its blendings shine afar,
Like rainbows on the cloud of war,
  The harbingers of victory.

Flag of the brave! thy folds shall fly,
The sign of hope and triumph high!
When speaks the signal trumpet tone
And the long line comes gleaming on,
(Ere yet the life-blood warm and wet
Has dimmed the glistening bayonet)
Each soldier eye shall brightly turn
To where thy skyborn glories burn,
And, as his springing steps advance,
Catch war and vengeance from the glance.
And when the cannon mouthings loud,
Heave in wild wreaths the battle shroud,
And gory sabres rise and fall,
Like shoots of flame on midnight's pall;
There shall thy meteor-glances glow,
  And cowering foes shall shrink beneath,
Each gallant arm that strikes below
  That lovely messenger of death.

Flag of the seas! on ocean wave
Thy stars shall glitter o'er the brave;
When death, careering on the gale,
Sweeps darkly round the bellied sail,
And frighted waves rush wildly back
Before the broadside's reeling rack,
Each dying wanderer of the sea
Shall look at once to heaven and thee,
And smile to see thy splendours fly
In triumph o'er his closing eye.

Flag of the free heart's hope and home,
  By angel hands to valour given;
Thy stars have lit the welkin dome
  And all thy hues were born in heaven!
For ever float that standard sheet!
Where breathes the foe but falls before us?
With freedom's soil beneath our feet,
And freedom's banner streaming o'er us?*

FITZ-GREENE HALLECK

WAS born at Guilford, in Connecticut, August, 1795. He early wrote verses. One of his effusions—it is said there were some earlier—was published in a New York paper, in 1809, when he was fourteen.* At the age of eighteen, in 1813, he came to New York, and entered the banking-house of Jacob Barker, with which he was associated for many years, subsequently performing the duties of a book-keeper in the private office of John Jacob Astor. Not long after the decease of that eminent millionaire, he retired to his birth-place, where he has since resided.

It is said that Halleck's first appearance in print was in the columns of *Holt's Columbian*, New York, where, in 1818, a poem appeared, with the signature of "A Connecticut Farmer's Boy," which the editor introduced with the remark, that he did not credit that authorship—"the verses were too good to be original!"† At this time too, Halleck belonged to "Swartwout's gallant corps, the Iron Grays," as he afterwards wrote in "Fanny," and stimulated their patriotism by a glowing Ode.

THE IRON GRAYS.

We twine the wreath of honor
  Around the warrior's brow,
Who, at his country's altar, breathes
  The life-devoting vow,
And shall we to the Iron Grays
  The meed of praise deny,
Who freely swore, in danger's day,
  For their native land to die.

For o'er our bleeding country
  Ne'er lowered a darker storm,
Than bade them round their gallant chief,
  The iron phalanx form.
When first their banner waved in air,
  Invasion's bands were nigh,
And the battle-drum beat long and loud,
  And the torch of war blazed high!

Though still bright gleam their bayonets,
  Unstained with hostile gore,
Far distant yet is England's host,
  Unheard her cannon's roar.
Yet not in vain they flew to arms;
  It made the foeman know
That many a gallant heart must bleed
  Ere freedom's star be low.

Guards of a nation's destiny!
  High is that nation's claim,
For not unknown your spirit proud,
  Nor your daring chieftain's name.
'Tis yours to shield the dearest ties
  That bind to life the heart,
That mingle with the earliest breath,
  And with our last depart.

The angel smile of beauty
  What heart but bounds to feel?
Her fingers buckled on the belt,
  That sheathes your gleaming steel;
And if the soldier's honoured death
  In battle be your doom,
Her tears shall bid the flowers be green
  That blossom round your tomb.

* The last four lines of The American Flag are by Halleck, in place of the following by Drake, which originally closed the poem:—

And fixed as yonder orb divine,
  That saw thy bannered blaze unfurled,
Shall thy proud stars resplendent shine,
  The guard and glory of the world.

* Notice in New York Mirror, Jan. 26, 1833.
† Biographical Art. on Halleck, by Mr. James Lawson, in South Lit. Mess., 1843.

Tread on the path of duty,
  Band of the patriot brave,
Prepared to rush, at honor's call,
  "To glory or the grave."
Nor bid your flag again be furled
  Till proud its eagles soar,
Till the battle-drum has ceased to beat,
  And the war-torch burns no more.

Halleck, however, gained his first celebrity in literature as a town wit, one of the producers, in connexion with his friend Drake, of the poetical squibs which appeared in the columns of the *Evening Post* in 1819, with the signature *Croaker & Co.*, when they quizzed Cobbett, Dr. Mitchill, the politicians of Tammany, the editors, aldermen, and small theatrical characters of the day, in poetical epistles to Edmund Simpson, Esq., manager of the theatre, and other vehicles of simple fun and well aimed satire. If these had nothing more to bring them into notice than their local allusion, they would have been forgotten, as hundreds of series of the kind have been; but their keen wit and finely moulded poetical phraseology have preserved them; and were it not for some delicacy in the avowed authorship and publication of verses filled with personalities, they would be an indispensable part of the volume which contains the collection of the poet's writings. As it is, several specimens of them are there, as of the simply poetical effusions—"The World is Bright before Thee," "There is an Evening Twilight of the Heart;" and of the lighter pieces, "Domestic Peace." The rest will undoubtedly be in request, and be some day accompanied by learned prose annotations from civic history.

As we have mentioned a number of these poems usually assigned to Drake as their author, we may add the titles of some of the others understood to be from the pen of Halleck. Among them are "The Forum," a picture of a literary debating society, to which the public were admitted, which had for its supporters some of the political celebrities of the city; "To Simon ——, a kick at a fashionable folly which reigns among the sons and daughters of the higher order, in the renowned city of Gotham, at this present writing;" Simon being a black caterer of fashionable entertainments—

    Prince of pastry cooks,
Oysters and ham, and cold neat's tongue,
  Pupil of Mitchill's cookery books,
And bosom friend of old and young;

several highly humorous epistles "To Edmund Simpson, Esq., Manager of the Theatre," in one of which he advises that stage director, if he would secure a profitable season, to disband his old company and employ the political actors at Albany, from the boards of the state legislature.

Halleck's lines "To Twilight," one of his earliest poems, appeared in the *Evening Post* of October, 1818. The next year, when the Croakers had made a reputation for themselves, the little poem was reprinted by the editor Coleman, with the following introduction:—"We republish the following beautiful lines from our own files of October last, for the three following reasons: first, because they deserve it for their intrinsic merit; they are the inspirations of poetry itself. Second, because they were injured in their first publication by a typographical error: and lastly, because they show that our correspondent Croaker (whose we have just discovered they are) no less resembles P. Pindar in his elegiac than in his humor and satiric vein."

Several of the Croakers appeared in the *National Advocate* published by Noah, and there are several longer pieces in the author's volume, as "The Recorder," and the lines "To Walter Bowne," which, though not numbered with the Croakers, have their general characteristics.

Fanny, which grew out of the success of the Croakers, was published in 1821. It is a satirical squib in Don Juan measure, at the fashionable literary and political enthusiasms of the day. The story which is the vehicle for this pleasantry, is simply the emergence of a belle from low birth and fortune to an elysium of fashionable prosperity, when the bubble bursts in bankruptcy. Like everything of the kind, which has the good fortune to be both personal and poetic, it made its hit. It owed its permanent success, of course, to its felicitous execution, in the happiest of musical verses. The edition was soon exhausted; it was not reprinted, and copies were circulated, fairly copied out in manuscript,—though a stray copy now and then, from a bookseller, who re-published the poem in Glasgow, helped to keep alive the tradition of its humor. The authorship was for a long while unacknowledged. In 1839 it was published by the Harpers, in a volume, with a few poems of similar character, collected by the author, and is now included in the standard edition of his writings.

In 1822 Halleck visited England and the Continent, of which tour we have a reminiscence in the poet's "Alnwick Castle."

In 1825, and subsequently, he was a contributor to Bryant's periodicals, the New York Review, and U. S. Review, where his *Marco Bozzaris* and *Burns* first appeared. A collection of these and other poems was published in a volume in 1827. They were reprinted, in other editions, by the Harpers; the Appletons, with illustrations by Weir, in 1847; and by Redfield, with additions to the poem "Connecticut," in 1852.

The characteristic of Halleck's poetry is its music; its perfection of versification, whether embalming a trifle of the hour or expressing a vigorous manly eloquence, a true lyric fire and healthy sentiment. Though of an old school of English literature, and fastidiously cultivated with a thorough knowledge of the author's predecessors, the poetry of Halleck is strictly original. In some of his poems he appears to have been led by dislike to even the suspicion of sentimentality to fasten a ludicrous termination to a serious emotion; but this is more dangerous to his imitators than injurious to his own powers. In Connecticut, which appears to be indebted to a happy idea struck out by Brainard, in his New Year's verse on the same theme, his subtle humor has happily blended the two qualities. For separate examples the reader may consult his "Field of the Grounded Arms," his "Burns," and his "Fanny."

TO ****.

The world is bright before thee,
  Its summer flowers are thine,
Its calm blue sky is o'er thee,
  Thy bosom pleasure's shrine;
And thine the sunbeam given
  To Nature's morning hour,
Pure, warm, as when from heaven
  It burst on Eden's bower.

There is a song of sorrow,
  The death-dirge of the gay,
That tells, ere dawn of morrow,
  These charms may melt away,
That sun's bright beam be shaded,
  That sky be blue no more,
The summer flowers be faded,
  And youth's warm promise o'er.

Believe it not—though lonely
  Thy evening home may be;
Though Beauty's bark can only
  Float on a summer sea;
Though Time thy bloom is stealing,
  There's still beyond his art
The wild-flower wreath of feeling,
  The sunbeam of the heart.

DOMESTIC HAPPINESS—FROM THE CROAKERS.

* * * * * The only bliss
Of Paradise that has survived the fall.
COWPER.

I.

"Beside the nuptial curtain bright,"
  The Bard of Eden sings,
"Young Love his constant lamp will light,
  And wave his purple wings."
But rain-drops from the clouds of care
  May bid that lamp be dim,
And the boy Love will pout and swear,
  'Tis then no place for him.

II.

So mused the lovely Mrs. Dash;
  'Tis wrong to mention names;
When for her surly husband's cash
  She urged in vain her claims.
"I want a little money, dear,
  For Vandervoort and Flandin,
Their bill, which now has run a year,
  To-morrow mean to hand in."

III.

"More?" cried the husband, half asleep,
  "You'll drive me to despair;"
The lady was too proud to weep,
  And too polite to swear.
She bit her lip for very spite,
  He felt a storm was brewing,
And dreamed of nothing else all night,
  But brokers, banks, and ruin.

IV.

He thought her pretty once, but dreams
  Have sure a wondrous power,
For to his eye the lady seems
  Quite altered since that hour;
And Love, who on their bridal eve,
  Had promised long to stay,
Forgot his promise, took French leave,
  And bore his lamp away.

SONG—FROM FANNY.

I.

Young thoughts have music in them, love
  And happiness their theme;
And music wanders in the wind
  That lulls a morning dream.
And there are angel voices heard,
  In childhood's frolic hours,
When life is but an April day
  Of sunshine and of showers.

II.

There's music in the forest leaves
  When summer winds are there,
And in the laugh of forest girls
  That braid their sunny hair.
The first wild bird that drinks the dew,
  From violets of the spring,
Has music in his song, and in
  The fluttering of his wing.

III.

There's music in the dash of waves
  When the swift bark cleaves their foam;
There's music heard upon her deck,
  The mariner's song of home,
When moon and star beams smiling meet
  At midnight on the sea—
And there is music—once a week
  In Scudder's balcony.

IV.

But the music of young thoughts too soon
  Is faint, and dies away,
And from our morning dreams we wake
  To curse the coming day.
And childhood's frolic hours are brief,
  And oft in after years
Their memory comes to chill the heart,
  And dim the eye with tears.

V.

To-day, the forest leaves are green,
  They'll wither on the morrow,
And the maiden's laugh be changed ere long
  To the widow's wail of sorrow.
Come with the winter snows, and ask
  Where are the forest birds?
The answer is a silent one,
  More eloquent than words.

VI.

The moonlight music of the waves
  In storms is heard no more,
When the living lightning mocks the wreck
  At midnight on the shore,
And the mariner's song of home has ceased,
  His corse is on the sea—
And music ceases when it rains
  In Scudder's balcony.

ON THE DEATH OF JOSEPH RODMAN DRAKE.

The good die first,
And they, whose hearts are dry as summer dust,
Burn to the socket.
WORDSWORTH.

Green be the turf above thee,
  Friend of my better days!
None knew thee but to love thee,
  Nor named thee but to praise.

Tears fell, when thou wert dying,
  From eyes unused to weep,
And long where thou art lying,
  Will tears the cold turf steep.

When hearts, whose truth was proven,
  Like thine, are laid in earth,
There should a wreath be woven
  To tell the world their worth;

And I, who woke each morrow
  To clasp thy hand in mine,
Who shared thy joy and sorrow,
  Whose weal and woe were thine:

It should be mine to braid it
  Around thy faded brow,
But I've in vain essayed it,
  And feel I cannot now.

While memory bids me weep thee,
  Nor thoughts nor words are free,
The grief is fixed too deeply
  That mourns a man like thee.

MARCO BOZZARIS.

At midnight, in his guarded tent,
  The Turk was dreaming of the hour
When Greece, her knee in suppliance bent,
  Should tremble at his power:
In dreams, through camp and court, he bore
The trophies of a conqueror;
  In dreams his song of triumph heard:
Then wore his monarch's signet ring:
Then pressed that monarch's throne—a king;
As wild his thoughts, and gay of wing,
  As Eden's garden bird.

At midnight, in the forest shades,
  Bozzaris ranged his Suliote band,
True as the steel of their tried blades,
  Heroes in heart and hand.
There had the Persian's thousands stood,
There had the glad earth drunk their blood
  On old Platæa's day;
And now there breathed that haunted air
The sons of sires who conquered there,
With arm to strike, and soul to dare,
  As quick, as far as they.

An hour passed on—the Turk awoke;
  That bright dream was his last;
He woke—to hear his sentries shriek,
"To arms! they come! the Greek! the Greek!"
He woke—to die 'midst flame, and smoke,
And shout, and groan, and sabre stroke,
  And death shots falling thick and fast
As lightnings from the mountain cloud;
And heard, with voice as trumpet loud,
  Bozzaris cheer his band:
"Strike—till the last armed foe expires;
Strike—for your altars and your fires;
Strike—for the green graves of your sires;
  God—and your native land!"

They fought—like brave men, long and well;
  They piled that ground with Moslem slain,
They conquered—but Bozzaris fell,
  Bleeding at every vein.
His few surviving comrades saw
His smile when rang their proud hurrah,
  And the red field was won;
Then saw in death his eyelids close
Calmly, as to a night's repose,
  Like flowers at set of sun.

Come to the bridal chamber, Death!
  Come to the mother's, when she feels,
For the first time, her first-born's breath;
  Come when the blessed seals
That close the pestilence are broke,
And crowded cities wail its stroke;
Come in consumption's ghastly form,
The earthquake shock, the ocean storm;
Come when the heart beats high and warm,
  With banquet song, and dance, and wine;
And thou art terrible—the tear,
The groan, the knell, the pall, the bier;
And all we know, or dream, or fear
  Of agony, are thine.

But to the hero, when his sword
  Has won the battle for the free,
Thy voice sounds like a prophet's word;
And in its hollow tones are heard
  The thanks of millions yet to be.
Come, when his task of fame is wrought—
Come, with her laurel-leaf, blood-bought—
  Come in her crowning hour—and then
Thy sunken eye's unearthly light
To him is welcome as the sight
  Of sky and stars to prisoned men:
Thy grasp is welcome as the hand
Of brother in a foreign land;
Thy summons welcome as the cry
That told the Indian isles were nigh
  To the world-seeking Genoese,
When the land wind, from woods of palm,
And orange groves, and fields of balm,
  Blew o'er the Haytian seas.

Bozzaris! with the storied brave
  Greece nurtured in her glory's time,
Rest thee—there is no prouder grave,
  Even in her own proud clime.
She wore no funeral weeds for thee,
  Nor bade the dark hearse wave its plume,
Like torn branch from death's leafless tree
In sorrow's pomp and pageantry,
  The heartless luxury of the tomb
But she remembers thee as one
Long loved, and for a season gone;
For thee her poet's lyre is wreathed,
Her marble wrought, her music breathed;
For thee she rings the birthday bells;
Of thee her babes' first lisping tells;
For thine her evening prayer is said
At palace couch and cottage bed;
Her soldier, closing with the foe,
Gives for thy sake a deadlier blow;
His plighted maiden, when she fears
For him, the joy of her young years,
Thinks of thy fate, and checks her tears:
  And she, the mother of thy boys,
Though in her eye and faded cheek

Is read the grief she will not speak,
The memory of her buried joys,
And even she who gave thee birth,
Will, by their pilgrim-circled hearth,
Talk of thy doom without a sigh:
For thou art Freedom's now, and Fame's;
One of the few, the immortal names,
That were not born to die.

A POET'S DAUGHTER.

*For the Album of Miss * * *, at the request of her Father.*

"A lady asks the Minstrel's rhyme."
A lady asks! There was a time
When, musical as play-bell's chime
To wearied boy,
That sound would summon dreams sublime
Of pride and joy.

But now the spell hath lost its sway,
Life's first-born fancies first decay,
Gone are the plumes and pennons gay
Of young romance;
There linger but her ruins gray,
And broken lance.

'Tis a new world—no more to maid,
Warrior, or bard, is homage paid;
The bay-tree's, laurel's, myrtle's shade,
Men's thoughts resign;
Heaven placed us here to vote and trade,
Twin tasks divine!

"'Tis youth, 'tis beauty asks; the green
And growing leaves of seventeen
Are round her; and, half hid, half seen,
A violet flower,
Nursed by the virtues she hath been
From childhood's hour."

Blind passion's picture—yet for this
We woo the life-long bridal kiss,
And blend our every hope of bliss
With her's we love;
Unmindful of the serpent's hiss
In Eden's grove.

Beauty—the fading rainbow's pride,
Youth—'twas the charm of her who died
At dawn, and by her coffin's side
A grandsire stands,
Age-strengthened, like the oak storm-tried
Of mountain lands.

Youth's coffin—hush the tale it tells!
Be silent, memory's funeral bells!
Lone in one heart, her home, it dwells
Untold till death,
And where the grave-mound greenly swells
O'er buried faith.

"But what if hers are rank and power,
Armies her train, a throne her bower,
A kingdom's gold her marriage dower,
Broad seas and lands!
What if from bannered hall and tower
A queen commands!"

A queen! Earth's regal moons have set.
Where perished Marie Antoinette!
Where's Bordeaux's mother! Where the jet-
Black Haytian dame!
And Lusitania's coronet!
And Angoulême!

Empires to-day are upside down,
The castle kneels before the town,
The monarch fears a printer's frown,
A brickbat's range;
Give me, in preference to a crown,
Five shillings change.

"But her who asks, though first among
The good, the beautiful, the young,
The birthright of a spell more strong
Than these hath brought her;
She is your kinswoman in song,
A Poet's daughter."

A Poet's daughter! Could I claim
The consanguinity of fame,
Veins of my intellectual frame!
Your blood would glow
Proudly to sing that gentlest name
Of aught below.

A Poet's daughter!—dearer word
Lip hath not spoke nor listener heard,
Fit theme for song of bee and bird
From morn till even,
And wind harp by the breathing stirred
Of star-lit heaven.

My spirit's wings are weak, the fire
Poetic comes but to expire,
Her name needs not my humble lyre
To bid it live;
She hath already from her sire
All bard can give.

CONNECTICUT.

From an Unpublished Poem.

The woods in which we had dwelt pleasantly rustled their green leaves in the song, and our streams were there with the sound of all their waters.

MONTROSE.

I.

—— still her gray rocks tower above the sea
That crouches at their feet, a conquered wave;
'Tis a rough land of earth, and stone, and tree,
Where breathes no castled lord or cabined slave;
Where thoughts, and tongues, and hands are bold and free,
And friends will find a welcome, foes a grave;
And where none kneel, save when to heaven they pray,
Nor even then, unless in their own way.

II.

Theirs is a pure republic, wild, yet strong,
A "fierce democracie," where all are true
To what themselves have voted—right or wrong—
And to their laws denominated blue;
(If red, they might to Draco's code belong;)
A vestal state, which power could not subdue,
Nor promise win—like her own eagle's nest,
Sacred—the San Marino of the West.

III.

A justice of the peace, for the time being,
They bow to, but may turn him out next year;
They reverence their priest, but disagreeing
In price or creed, dismiss him without fear;
They have a natural talent for foreseeing
And knowing all things; and should Park appear
From his long tour in Africa, to show
The Niger's source, they'd meet him with—we know.

IV.

They love their land, because it is their own,
And scorn to give aught other reason why;
Would shake hands with a king upon his throne,
And think it kindness to his majesty;
A stubborn race, fearing and flattering none.
Such are they nurtured, such they live and die;
All—but a few apostates, who are meddling
With merchandise, pounds, shillings, pence, and peddling;

V.

Or wandering through the southern countries, teaching
The A B C from Webster's spelling-book;
Gallant and godly, making love and preaching,
And gaining by what they call "hook and crook,"
And what the moralists call over-reaching,
A decent living. The Virginians look
Upon them with as favorable eyes
As Gabriel on the devil in paradise.

VI.

But these are but their outcasts. View them near
At home, where all their worth and pride is placed;
And there their hospitable fires burn clear,
And there the lowliest farm-house hearth is graced
With manly hearts, in piety sincere,
Faithful in love, in honor stern and chaste,
In friendship warm and true, in danger brave,
Beloved in life, and sainted in the grave.

VII.

And minds have there been nurtured, whose control
Is felt even in their nation's destiny;
Men who swayed senates with a statesman's soul,
And looked on armies with a leader's eye;
Names that adorn and dignify the scroll,
Whose leaves contain their country's history,
And tales of love and war—listen to one
Of the Green-Mountaineer—the Stark of Bennington.

VIII.

When on that field his band the Hessians fought,
Briefly he spoke before the fight began:
"Soldiers! those German gentlemen are bought
For four pounds eight and sevenpence per man,
By England's king; a bargain, as is thought.
Are we worth more? Let's prove it now we can;
For we must beat them, boys, ere set of sun,
OR MARY STARK'S A WIDOW." It was done.

IX.

Hers are not Tempe's nor Arcadia's spring,
Nor the long summer of Cathayan vales,
The vines, the flowers, the air, the skies, that fling
Such wild enchantment o'er Boccaccio's tales
Of Florence and the Arno; yet the wing
Of life's best angel, Health, is on her gales
Through sun and snow; and in the autumn time
Earth has no purer and no lovelier clime.

X.

Her clear, warm heaven at noon—the mist that shrouds
Her twilight hills—her cool and starry eves,
The glorious splendor of her sunset clouds,
The rainbow beauty of her forest leaves,
Come o'er the eye, in solitude and crowds,
Where'er his web of song her poet weaves;
And his mind's brightest vision but displays
The autumn scenery of his boyhood's days.

XI.

And when you dream of woman, and her love;
Her truth, her tenderness, her gentle power;
The maiden listening in the moonlight grove,
The mother smiling in her infant's bower;
Forms, features, worshipped while we breathe or move,
Be by some spirit of your dreaming hour
Borne, like Loretto's chapel, through the air
To the green land I sing, then wake, you'll find them there.

JAMES G. PERCIVAL.

JAMES GATES PERCIVAL was born in Kensington, Connecticut, a town of which his ancestors had been among the earliest inhabitants, on the 15th of September, 1795. He was the second son of Dr. James Percival, a physician of the place, who, dying in 1807, left his three sons to their mother's care.

An anecdote is related of his early childhood, indicative of strength of mind and purpose. He had just begun to spell, when a book, in compliance with the custom of the district school to which he belonged, was lent to him on Saturday, to be returned on the following Monday. He found, by spelling through its first sentences, that a portion of it related to astronomy. This so excited his interest, that he sat diligently to work, and, by dint of hard study, with the aid of the family, was able to read the portion he desired on the Monday morning with fluency. This achievement seemed to give him confidence in his powers, and he advanced so rapidly in his studies, that he soon compassed the limited resources of the school. At the age of sixteen he entered Yale College, and during his course frequently excited the commendation and interest of President Dwight. He was at the head of his class in 1815, and his tragedy of *Zamor*, afterwards published in his works, formed part of the Commencement exercises. He had previously begun his poetical career by the composition of a few fugitive verses during his college course, and yet earlier, it is said, had written a satire in his fourteenth year. In 1820 he published his first volume, containing the first part of *Prometheus*, a poem in the Spenserian stanza, and a few minor pieces. It was well received. In the same year, having been admitted to the practice of medicine,

he went to Charleston, S. C., with the intention of following his profession. There he engaged in literature, publishing the first number of *Clio* in that city in 1822. This publication, a neat pamphlet of about a hundred pages, was evidently induced by the similar form of the Sketch Book and the Idle Man. It was made up mostly of verse, to which a few essays were added. A second part followed, entirely of verse, and was succeeded, in 1822, by the first and second parts of *Clio*, a miscellany of prose and verse.

Dr. Percival was appointed, in 1824, an assistant-surgeon in the United States army, and Professor of Chemistry at the Military Academy at West Point. Finding a greater portion of his time occupied in the performance of its duties than he had anticipated, he resigned after a few months, and was appointed a surgeon in connexion with the recruiting service at Boston. In the same year a collected edition of his principal poems appeared in New York in two volumes, and was reprinted in London. In 1827 he published in New York the third part of *Clio*, and was closely engaged in the two following years in assisting in the preparation of the first quarto edition of Webster's Dictionary, a service for which he was well qualified by his philological acquirements. He next commenced the translation of Malte-Brun's Geography, and published the last part of his version in 1843.

While in college he was inferior to none of his classmates in the mathematics, yet his inclinations led him rather into the fields of classical literature. While engaged in the study of medicine, he also applied himself to botany with ardor, and made himself acquainted with natural history in general. Being necessarily much abroad and fond of exploring nature, he became a geologist, and as such has served privately and publicly. In 1835 he was appointed to make, in conjunction with Professor C. U. Shepard, a survey of the mineralogy and geology of Connecticut. In 1842 he published his *Report on the Geology of the State of Connecticut*. This work, of nearly five hundred pages, contains the results of a very minute survey of the rock formations of the state, and abounds with minute and carefully systematized details.

In the summer of 1854 he received from the governor a commission as State Geologist of Wisconsin, and he entered at once upon the work. His first annual report was published at Madison, Wisconsin, in 1855.* He is still engaged in this survey.

Dr. Percival is an eminent linguistic scholar, and has a critical knowledge of most of the languages of Modern Europe. As a specimen of his readiness, it may be mentioned that when Ole Bull was in New Haven in 1844 or 1845, he addressed to him a poem of four or five stanzas in the Danish language. This was printed in a New Haven paper of the day.†

The poems of Percival have spirit, freshness, and a certain youthful force of expression as the author harangues of love and liberty. The deliverance of oppressed nations; the yearnings and eloquence of the young heart ready to rejoice or mourn with a Byronic enthusiasm; the hour of exaltation in the triumph of love, and of gloom as some vision of the betrayal of innocence or the inroads of disease came before his mind: these were his prominent themes. There is the inner light of poetry in the idyllic sketch of ***Maria, the Village Girl***, where nature and the reality of life in the "long-drawn-out sweetness" of the imagery assume a visionary aspect.

In those days he struck the lyre with no hesitating hand. There is the first spring of life and passion in his verse. It would have been better, sometimes, if the author had waited for slow reflection and patient elaboration—since fancy is never so vigorous as to sustain a long journey alone. Percival, however, has much of the true heat. His productions have been widely popular, and perhaps better meet the generally received notion of a poet than the well filed compositions of many others who deserve more consideration at the hands of the judicious and critical.

THE SPIRIT OF POETRY—FROM CLIO.

The world is full of Poetry—the air
Is living with its spirit; and the waves
Dance to the music of its melodies,
And sparkle in its brightness—Earth is veiled,
And mantled with its beauty; and the walls,
That close the universe, with crystal, in,
Are eloquent with voices, that proclaim
The unseen glories of immensity,
In harmonies, too perfect, and too high
For aught, but beings of celestial mould,
And speak to man, in one eternal hymn,
Unfading beauty, and unyielding power.

The year leads round the seasons, in a choir
For ever charming, and for ever new,
Blending the grand, the beautiful, the gay,
The mournful, and the tender, in one strain,
Which steals into the heart, like sounds, that rise
Far off, in moonlight evenings, on the shore
Of the wide ocean resting after storms;
Or tones, that wind around the vaulted roof,
And pointed arches, and retiring aisles
Of some old, lonely minster, where the hand,
Skilful, and moved with passionate love of art,
Plays o'er the higher keys, and bears aloft
The peal of bursting thunder, and then calls,
By mellow touches, from the softer tubes,
Voices of melting tenderness, that blend
With pure and gentle musings, till the soul,
Commingling with the melody, is borne,
Rapt, and dissolved in ecstasy, to heaven.

'Tis not the chime and flow of words, that move
In measured file, and metrical array;
'Tis not the union of returning sounds,
Nor all the pleasing artifice of rhyme,
And quantity, and accent, that can give
This all-pervading spirit to the ear,
Or blend it with the movings of the soul.
'Tis a mysterious feeling, which combines
Man with the world around him, in a chain
Woven of flowers, and dipped in sweetness, till
He taste the high communion of his thoughts,
With all existences, in earth and heaven,
That meet him in the charm of grace and power.
'Tis not the noisy babbler, who displays,
In studied phrase, and ornate epithet,
And rounded period, poor and vapid thoughts,

* Pp. 101, 8vo.

† Extract from a poem of eight stanzas, composed by Dr. J. G. Percival, and addressed to Ole Bull, on the occasion of his first concert in New Haven, June 10, 1844:—

6th Stanza.

Norge, dit Sværd blev en Lire:
Himmelen gav hendes Toner,
Hiertet og Sielen at styre,
Fuld som af Kummerens Moner.

"Norway, thy sword has become a lyre—Heaven gave its tones, to lead heart and soul, filled as with grief's longings."

The poem, with an English version, may be found in the New Haven Daily Herald of June 11, 1844.

Which peep from out the cumbrous ornaments,
That overload their littleness.—Its words
Are few, but deep and solemn; and they break
Fresh from the fount of feeling, and are full
Of all that passion, which, on Carmel, fired
The holy prophet, when his lips were coals,
His language winged with terror, as when bolts
Leap from the brooding tempest, armed with wrath,
Commissioned to affright us, and destroy.

A PLATONIC BACCHANAL SONG.

Fill high the bowl of life for me—
Let roses mantle round its brim,
While heart is warm, and thought is free,
Ere beauty's light is waning dim—
Fill high with brightest draughts of soul,
And let it flow with feeling o'er,
And love, the sparkling cup, he stole
From Heaven, to give it briskness, pour.
O! fill the bowl of life for me,
And wreathe its dripping brim with flowers,
And I will drink, as lightly flee
Our early, unreturning hours.

Fill high the bowl of life with wine,
That swelled the grape of Eden's grove,
Ere human life, in its decline,
Had strowed with thorns the path of lov
Fill high from virtue's crystal fount,
That springs beneath the throne of Heaven,
And sparkles brightly o'er the mount,
From which our fallen souls were driven.
O! fill the bowl of life with wine,
The wine, that charmed the gods above,
And round its brim a garland twine,
That blossomed in the bower of love.

Fill high the bowl of life with spirit,
Drawn from the living sun of soul,
And let the wing of genius bear it,
Deep-glowing, like a kindled coal—
Fill high from that ethereal treasure,
And let me quaff the flowing fire,
And know awhile the boundless pleasure,
That Heaven-lit fancy can inspire.
O! fill the bowl of life with spirit,
And give it brimming o'er to me.
And as I quaff, I seem to inherit
The glow of immortality.

Fill high the bowl of life with thought
From that unfathomable well,
Which sages long and long have sought
To sound, but none its depths can tell—
Fill high from that dark stainless wave,
Which mounts and flows for ever on,
And rising proudly o'er the grave,
There finds its noblest course begun.
O! fill the bowl of life with thought,
And I will drink the bumper up,
And find, whate'er my wish had sought,
In that, the purest, sweetest cup.

THE SERENADE.

Softly the moonlight
Is shed on the lake,
Cool is the summer night—
Wake! O awake!
Faintly the curfew
Is heard from afar,
List ye! O list!
To the lively guitar.

Trees cast a mellow shade
Over the vale,
Sweetly the serenade
Breathes in the gale,
Softly and tenderly
Over the lake,
Gaily and cheerily—
Wake! O awake!

See the light pinnace
Draws nigh to the shore,
Swiftly it glides
At the heave of the oar,
Cheerily plays
On its buoyant car,
Nearer and nearer
The lively guitar.

Now the wind rises
And ruffles the pine,
Ripples foam-crested
Like diamonds shine,
They flash, where the waters
The white pebbles lave,
In the wake of the moon,
As it crosses the wave.

Bounding from billow
To billow, the boat
Like a wild swan is seen,
On the waters to float;
And the light dipping oars
Bear it smoothly along
In time to the air
Of the Gondolier's song.

And high on the stern
Stands the young and the brave,
As love-led he crosses
The star-spangled wave,
And blends with the murmur
Of water and grove
The tones of the night,
That are sacred to love.

His gold-hilted sword
At his bright belt is hung,
His mantle of silk
On his shoulder is flung,
And high waves the feather,
That dances and plays
On his cap where the buckle
And rosary blaze.

The maid from her lattice
Looks down on the lake,
To see the foam sparkle,
The bright billow break,
And to hear in his boat,
Where he shines like a star,
Her lover so tenderly
Touch his guitar.

She opens her lattice,
And sits in the glow
Of the moonlight and starlight,
A statue of snow;
And she sings in a voice,
That is broken with sighs,
And she darts on her lover
The light of her eyes.

His love-speaking pantomime
Tells her his soul—
How wild in that sunny clime
Hearts and eyes roll.
She waves with her white hand
Her white fazzolet,
And her burning thoughts flash
From her eyes' living jet.

The moonlight is hid
In a vapor of snow;
Her voice and his rebeck
Alternately flow;

Re-echoed they swell
From the rock on the hill;
They sing their farewell,
And the music is still.

TO SENECA LAKE.

On thy fair bosom, silver lake!
The wild swan spreads his snowy sail,
And round his breast the ripples break,
As down he bears before the gale.

On thy fair bosom, waveless stream!
The dipping paddle echoes far,
And flashes in the moonlight gleam,
And bright reflects the polar star.

The waves along thy pebbly shore,
As blows the north-wind, heave their foam;
And curl around the dashing oar,
As late the boatman hies him home.

How sweet, at set of sun, to view
Thy golden mirror spreading wide,
And see the mist of mantling blue
Float round the distant mountain's side.

At midnight hour, as shines the moon,
A sheet of silver spreads below,
And swift she cuts, at highest noon,
Light clouds, like wreaths of purest snow.

On thy fair bosom, silver lake!
O! I could ever sweep the oar,
When early birds at morning wake,
And evening tells us toil is o'er.

THE GRAVES OF THE PATRIOTS.

Here rest the great and good. Here they repose
After their generous toil. A sacred band,
They take their sleep together, while the year
Comes with its early flowers to deck their graves,
And gathers them again, as Winter frowns.
Theirs is no vulgar sepulchre—green sods
Are all their monument, and yet it tells
A nobler history than pillared piles,
Or the eternal pyramids. They need
No statue nor inscription to reveal
Their greatness. It is round them; and the joy
With which their children tread the hallowed ground
That holds their venerated bones, the peace
That smiles on all they fought for, and the wealth
That clothes the land they rescued,—these, though mute
As feeling ever is when deepest,—these
Are monuments more lasting than the fanes
Reared to the kings and demigods of old.
Touch not the ancient elms, that bend their shade
Over their lowly graves; beneath their boughs
There is a solemn darkness, even at noon,
Suited to such as visit at the shrine
Of serious liberty. No factious voice
Called them unto the field of generous fame,
But the pure consecrated love of home.
No deeper feeling sways us, when it wakes
In all its greatness. It has told itself
To the astonished gaze of awe-struck kings,
At Marathon, at Bannockburn, and here,
Where first our patriots sent the invader back
Broken and cowed. Let these green elms be all
To tell us where they fought, and where they lie.
Their feelings were all nature, and they need
No art to make them known. They live in us,
While we are like them, simple, hardy, bold,
Worshipping nothing but our own pure hearts,
And the one universal Lord. They need
No column pointing to the heaven they sought,
To tell us of their home. The heart itself,
Left to its own free purpose, hastens there,
And there alone reposes. Let these elms
Bend their protecting shadow o'er their graves,
And build with their green roof the only fane,
Where we may gather on the hallowed day
That rose to them in blood, and set in glory.
Here let us meet, and while our motionless lips
Give not a sound, and all around is mute
In the deep Sabbath of a heart too full
For words or tears—here let us strew the sod
With the first flowers of spring, and make to them
An offering of the plenty Nature gives,
And they have rendered ours—perpetually.

DANIEL PIERCE THOMPSON,

The historical novelist of Vermont, was born at Charlestown, Massachusetts, October 1, 1795. His grandfather, Daniel Thompson, of Woburn, a cousin of the well known Count Rumford, fell in the battle of Lexington. His mother was a descendant of the old primitive New England schoolmaster, Ezekiel Cheever. His father settled for awhile in business at Charlestown, but being unsuccessful withdrew to a wild farm of a few acres on Onion River in the town of Berlin, Vermont, which he had some time before purchased of one Lovel, a hunter, and son of the noted Indian fighter, the hero of Lovel's Pond in Fryburgh, Maine. Here the family lived a pioneer life in the wilderness, remote from schools and churches; if indeed the latter were not supplied in the Christian piety and devout religious exercises of the mother of the household, to the memory of whose virtues and instructions the heart of her son fondly turns. The youth was brought up in the labors of the farm, securing such elementary instruction as his home and a scanty winter attendance at the poor district school afforded. He was sighing for books to read when—he was then about sixteen—at the breaking up of the roads and ice in the spring, after an extraordinary freshet, which brought together the wrecks of bridges, mills, and trees, he found among the remains a thoroughly soaked volume. He dried the leaves, and with great zest read, for the first time, the verses of the English poets. The passages which he then admired he afterwards found to be the favorite passages of the world, "a fact," he has remarked, "which taught him a lesson of respect for the opinions of the uncultivated, by which he has often profited." He was now intent on procuring an education. It is difficult, in the matured state of society of the present day, with the appliances of education extended so freely on all sides, to estimate the natural strength of mind, and personal efforts and sacrifices, which led many a farmer's son half a century ago to the gates of the New England colleges. Daniel Webster rejoicing on his way to Dartmouth, and afterwards supporting his brother there by teaching, will recur to everyone.

The young Thompson, on looking around for resources, found that he was master of a small flock of sheep, which had come to be his under rather singular circumstances. When the family had set out for the wilderness his grandmother had put into his hand, in his childhood, a silver dollar which was to be invested in a ewe, the good lady calculating that the future growth of the flock, well tended, might in some way be of important service to him. He was now the owner, in consequence, of sixteen sheep. By a long process of inquiry he came to the knowledge that he could purchase, for their value in the market, a pair of two year old steers, which he might support in the summer in the woods free of cost, and by hiring raise to full grown oxen in a couple of years, when his sheep fund would be doubled. The money to be realized would help to support him in college. On this agricultural basis he began his preparations; diligently hunting mink and muskrat, the skins of which were saleable. He worked out with an old blacksmith the cost of a set of steel traps, and with the proceeds made the purchase of that rare book in Vermont at the time, Pike's large arithmetic, also a Latin grammar, lexicon, and Virgil. He was now in difficulty with the pronunciation of the latter, but he secured that from a graduate of Dartmouth, who had settled as a lawyer in a village growing up in his neighborhood, paying him, per contract, thirty-seven and a-half cents for three lessons in the language, which, with his own exertions, carried him through the grammar. Released by his father from his labor on the farm—an important consideration in that place and time—and having disposed of his cattle for seventy five dollars and a thick old-fashioned bull's-eye watch, which he thought might be of service to him in marking the hours in his contemplated school-keeping; and being fitted by his mother with an equipment of homespun wardrobe, he turned his steps one morning of September, 1815, to the house of a clergyman thirty miles off, who kept one or two pupils at a time in preparation for college. He here made such good use of his opportunities that in twelve weeks he had read the whole of Virgil; the winter he employed in studying human nature and adding to his means while boarding round as the schoolmaster of one of the wild districts of the country. A good preparation, he subsequently found it, for novel writing. A short time at a classical academy in the north-west of the state for his own studies, more school-keeping, with an interval of conscientious help rendered to his father in the severe toil of the farm, and he presented himself at Middlebury College. He passed the examination for the Sophomore class, studied hard and read extensively with close attention to English composition, and took his degree in the summer of 1820.

Through the friendship of Professor Keith of Alexandria, D. C., he now obtained an eligible private tutorship in a family in Virginia, in the vicinity of the mansions of the old Ex-Presidents, and so far profited by his opportunities as to procure an admission as attorney and counsellor of the inferior and superior courts of the state. After three or four years of this pleasant life he returned home and opened a law-office in Montpelier. He soon got the appointment of Register of Probate, was elected clerk of the legislature, which he held for three years, when he passed a year, on the appointment of the Governor, in compiling a volume of the statute laws. He has been since Judge of Probate of the county, County Clerk of the county and Supreme Court, and in 1853 he was elected Secretary of State.

Mr. Thompson's active pursuit of literature was somewhat accidental. He had from his college

D. P. Thompson

years contributed to periodicals tales and essays, but had written nothing of length till in 1835, upon noticing an offer for a prize tale by the New England Galaxy, published at Boston, he wrote his story of *May Martin, or the Money Diggers;* which, having gained the prize, proved so successful, that when he published it in a volume he was not able to hold the copyright from rival booksellers, who printed it with impunity, from the unprotected pages of the newspaper. This well told story was founded on incidents of actual occurrence in his neighborhood, with which he had become acquainted in the course of his professional business.

In 1840 Mr. Thompson published at Montpelier, *The Green Mountain Boys*, "intended to embody and illustrate a portion of the more romantic incidents which actually occurred in the early settlements of Vermont, with the use of but little more of fiction than was deemed sufficient to weave them together, and impart to the tissue a connected interest." *Locke Amsden, or the Schoolmaster*, followed in 1847. This work, the design of which is to illustrate the art of intellectual self-culture, and to serve the interests of popular education, involves no inconsiderable part of the author's autobiography, and is drawn largely from his personal observation. It is an interesting picture of a time already ancient—so rapidly has the cause of education developed itself in what was not many years since a scanty wild settlement.

The Rangers, or the Tory's Daughter, a counterpart to the Green Mountain Boys, was published in 1850. It is illustrative of the Revolutionary history of Vermont, and the northern campaigns of 1777; and is the result of a careful study of the time to which the author has made fiction subservient. The style in this, as in the preceding, is full and minute, the writer knowing the art of the story-teller, who must leave nothing for the mind of the listener outside of the narrative, but must engross the whole interest for himself and his tale.

This concludes the list of the author's works. They form a series which has attained high popularity in his state, and which has travelled far beyond it. The tales have been republished in England, where they have doubtless been read with interest as pictures of American history and society. The manly career of the author, resulting in his honorable success in life, and the interest of his books, have secured him a sterling popularity at home. He married in 1831 a daughter of E. K. Robinson of Chester, Vermont, and is surrounded by a family of children.

A SCHOOL COMMITTEE-MAN AND A LAWSUIT.

[Locke Amsden is in pursuit of a country engagement as a school teacher.]

The little knowledge *he* had gained,
Was all from simple nature drained.—GAY.

It was late in the season when our hero returned home; and having inadvertently omitted to apprise his friends of his intention to engage himself as a teacher of some of the winter schools in the vicinity of his father's residence, he found, on his arrival, every situation to which his undoubted qualifications should prompt him to aspire, already occupied by others. He was therefore compelled, unless he relinquished his purpose, to listen to the less eligible offers which came from such smaller and more backward districts or societies as had not engaged their instructors for the winter. One of these he was on the point of deciding to accept, when he received information of a district where the master, from some cause or other, had been dismissed during the first week of his engagement, and where the committee were now in search of another to supply his place. The district from which this information came, was situated in one of the mountain towns about a dozen miles distant, and the particular neighborhood of its location was known in the vicinity, to a considerable extent, by the name of the *Horn of the Moon;* an appellation generally understood to be derived from a peculiar curvature of a mountain that partially enclosed the place. Knowing nothing of the causes which had here led to the recent dismissal of the teacher, nor indeed of the particular character of the school, further than that it was a large one, and one, probably, which, though in rather a new part of the country, would yet furnish something like an adequate remuneration to a good instructor, Locke had no hesitation in deciding to make an immediate application for the situation. Accordingly, the next morning he mounted a horse, and set out for the place in question.

It was a mild December's day; the ground had not yet assumed its winter covering, and the route taken by our hero becoming soon bordered on either side by wild and picturesque mountain scenery, upon which he had ever delighted

To look from nature up to nature's God,

the excursion in going was a pleasant one. And occupied by the reflections thus occasioned, together with anticipations of happy results from his expected engagement, he arrived after a ride of a few hours, at the borders of the romantic looking place of which he was in quest.

At this point in his journey, he overtook a man on foot, of whom, after discovering him to belong somewhere in the neighborhood, he proceeded to make some inquiries relative to the situation of the school.

"Why," replied the man, "as I live out there in the tip of the Horn, which is, of course, at the outer edge of the district, I know but little about the school affairs; but one thing is certain, they have shipped the master, and want to get another, I suppose."

"For what cause was the master dismissed? For lack of qualifications?"

"Yes, lack of qualifications for our district. The fellow, however, had learning enough, as all agreed, but no spunk; and the young Bunkers, and some others of the big boys, mistrusting this, and being a little riled at some things he had said to them, took it into their heads to train him a little, which they did; when he, instead of showing any grit on the occasion, got frightened and cleared out."

"Why, sir, did his scholars offer him personal violence?"

"O no—not violence. They took him up quite carefully, bound him on to a plank, as I understood, and carried him on their shoulders, in a sort of procession, three times around the schoolhouse, and then, unloosing him, told him to go at his business again."

"And was all this suffered to take place without any interference from your committee?"

"Yes, our committee-man would not interfere in such a case. A master must fight his own way in our district."

"Who is your committee, sir?"

"Captain Bill Bunker is now. They had a meeting after the fracas, and chose a new one."

"Is he a man who is capable of ascertaining for himself the qualifications of a teacher?"

"O yes—at least I had as lief have Bill Bunker's judgment of a man who applied for the school as any other in the district; and yet he is the only man in the whole district but what can read and write, I believe."

"Your school committee not able to read and write?"

"Not a word, and still he does more business than any man in this neighborhood. Why, sir, he keeps a sort of store, sells to A, B, and C, and charges on book in a fashion of his own; and I would as soon trust to his book as that of any regular merchant in the country; though, to be sure, he has got into a jumble, I hear, about some charges against a man at t'other end of the Horn, and they are having a court about it to-day at Bunker's house, I understand."

"Where does he live?"

"Right on the road, about a mile ahead. You will see his name chalked on a sort of a shop-looking building, which he uses for a store."

The man here turned off from the road, leaving our hero so much surprised and staggered at what he had just heard, not only of the general character of the school of which he had come to propose himself as a teacher, but of the man who now had the control of it, that he drew up the reins, stopped his horse in the road, and sat hesitating some moments whether he would go back or forward. It occurring to him, however, that he could do as he liked about accepting any offer of the place which might be made him, and feeling, moreover, some curiosity to see how a man who could neither read nor write would manage in capacity of an examining school committee, he resolved to go forward, and present himself as a candidate for the school. Accordingly, he rode on, and soon reached a rough built, but substantial-looking farm-house, with sundry out-buildings, on one of which he read, as he had been told he might, the name of the singular occupant. In the last-named building, he at once perceived that there was a gathering of quite a number of individuals, the nature of which was explained to him by the hint he had received from his informant on the road. And tying his horse, he joined several who were going in, and soon found himself in the midst of the company assembled in the low, unfinished room which constituted the interior, as parties, witnesses, and spectators of a justice's court, the ceremonies of which were about to be commenced. There were no counters, counting-room, or desk; and a few broad shelves, clumsily put up on one side, afforded the only indication, observable in the interior arrangement of the room, of the use to which it was devoted. On these shelves were scattered, at intervals, small bunches of hoes, axes, bed-cords, and such articles as are generally purchased by those who purchase little; while casks of nails, grindstones, quintals of dried salt fish, and the like, arranged round the room on the floor, made up the rest of the owner's merchandise, an annual supply of which, it appeared, he obtained in the cities every winter in exchange for the products of his farm; ever careful, like a good political economist, that the balance of trade should not be against him. The only table and chair in the room were now occupied by the justice; the heads of casks, grindstones, or bunches of rakes, answering for seats for the rest of the company. On the left of the justice sat the defendant, whose composed look, and occasional knowing smile, seemed to indicate his confidence in the strength of his defence as well as a consciousness of possessing some secret advantage over his opponent. On the other hand sat Bunker, the plaintiff in the suit. Ascertaining from the remarks of the bystanders his identity with the committee-man he had become so curious to see, Locke fell to noting his appearance closely, and the result was, upon the whole, a highly favorable prepossession. He was a remarkably stout, hardy-looking man; and although his features were extremely rough and swarthy, they yet combined to give him an open, honest, and very intelligent countenance. Behind him, as backers, were standing in a group three or four of his sons, of ages varying from fifteen to twenty, and of bodily proportions promising anything but disparagement to the Herculean stock from which they originated. The parties were now called and sworn; when Bunker, there being no attorneys employed to make two-hour speeches on preliminary questions, proceeded at once to the merits of his case. He produced and spread open his account-book, and then went on to show his manner of charging, which was wholly by hieroglyphics, generally designating the debtor by picturing him out at the top of the page with some peculiarity of his person or calling. In the present case, the debtor, who was a cooper, was designated by the rude picture of a man in the act of hooping a barrel; and the article charged, there being but one item in the account, was placed immediately beneath, and represented by a shaded, circular figure, which the plaintiff said was intended for a cheese, that had been sold to the defendant some years before.

"Now, Mr. Justice," said Bunker, after explaining in a direct, off-hand manner, his peculiar method of book-keeping, "now, the article here charged the man had—I will, and do swear to it; for here it is in black and white. And I having demanded my pay, and he having not only refused it, but denied ever buying the article in question, I have brought this suit to recover my just due. And now I wish to see if he will get up here in court, and deny the charge under oath. If he will, let him; but may the Lord have mercy on his soul!"

"Well, sir," replied the defendant, promptly rising, "you shall not be kept from having your wish a minute; for I here, under oath, do swear, that I never bought or had a cheese of you in my life."

"Under the oath of God you declare it, do you?" sharply asked Bunker.

"I do, sir," firmly answered the other.

"Well, well!" exclaimed the former, with looks of utter astonishment, "I would not have believed that there was a man in all of the Horn of the Moon who would dare to do that."

After the parties had been indulged in the usual amount of sparring for such occasions, the justice interposed and suggested, that as the oaths of the parties were at complete issue, the evidence of the book itself, which he seemed to think was entitled to credit, would turn the scale in favor of the plaintiff, unless the defendant could produce some rebutting testimony. Upon this hint, the latter called up two of his neighbors, who testified in his behalf, that he himself always made a sufficient supply of cheese for his family; and they were further knowing, that, on the year of the alleged purchase, instead of buying, he actually sold a considerable quantity of the article.

This evidence seemed to settle the question in the mind of the justice; and he now soon announced, that he felt bound to give judgment to the defendant for his costs.

"Judged and sworn out of the whole of it, as I am a sinner!" cried the disconcerted Bunker, after sitting a moment working his rough features in indignant surprise; "yes, fairly sworn out of it, and saddled with a bill of costs to boot! But I can pay it; so reckon it up, Mr. Justice, and we will have it all squared on the spot. And, on the whole, I am not so sure but a dollar or two is well spent, at any time, in finding out a fellow to be a scoundrel who has been passing himself off among people for an honest man," he added, pulling out his purse, and angrily dashing the required amount down upon the table.

"Now, Bill Bunker," said the defendant, after very coolly pocketing his costs, "you have flung out a good deal of your stuff here, and I have bore it without getting riled a hair; for I saw, all the time, that you—correct as folks ginerally think you—that you didn't know what you was about. But now it's all fixed and settled, I am going jist to convince you that I am not quite the one that has sworn to a perjury in this 'ere business."

"Well, we will see," rejoined Bunker, eyeing his opponent with a look of mingled doubt and defiance.

"Yes, we *will* see," responded the other, determinedly; "we will see if we can't make you eat your own words. But I want first to tell you where you missed it. When you dunned me, Bunker, for the pay for a cheese, and I said I never had one of you, you went off a little too quick; you called me a liar, before giving me a chance to say another word. And then, I thought I would let you take your own course, till you took that name back. If you had held on a minute, without breaking out so upon me, I should have teld you all how it was, and you would have got your pay on the spot; but——"

"Pay!" fiercely interrupted Bunker, "then you admit you had the cheese, do you?"

"No, sir, I admit no such thing," quickly rejoined the former; "for I still say I never had a cheese of you in the world. But I *did* have a small grindstone of you at the time, and at just the price you have charged for your supposed cheese; and here is your money for it, sir. Now, Bunker, what do you say to that?"

"Grindstone—cheese—cheese—grindstone!" exclaimed the now evidently nonplussed and doubtful Bunker, taking a few rapid turns about the room, and occasionally stopping at the table to scrutinize anew his hieroglyphical charge; "I must think this matter over again. Grindstone—cheese—cheese—grindstone. Ah! I have it; but may God forgive me for what I have done! It *was* a grindstone, but I forgot to make a hole in the middle for the crank."

Upon this curious development, as will be readily imagined, the opposing parties were not long in effecting an amicable and satisfactory adjustment. And, in a short time, the company broke up and departed, all obviously as much gratified as amused at this singular but happy result of the lawsuit.

WILLIAM B. SPRAGUE.

THE Rev. Dr. Sprague was born in Andover, Connecticut, October 16, 1795. His father, Benjamin Sprague, a farmer, lived and died on the spot where he was born. The son was fitted for college at Colchester Academy under the venerable John Adams, and was much indebted in his education to the Rev. Dr. Abiel Abbot, now of Peterboro', N. H., then the Congregational Minister of Coventry, Connecticut. He was graduated at Yale in 1815, and then employed for nearly a year as a private tutor to a family in Virginia. He entered the Theological Seminary at Princeton in the autumn of 1816, and remained till the spring of 1819; was settled as colleague pastor with the Rev. Dr. Joseph Lathrop of the First Congregational Church in West Springfield, Massachusetts, in 1819; remained there ten years, and became settled as pastor of the Second Presbyterian Church in Albany in 1829, of which he is still (in 1854) the incumbent.

W B Sprague.

The long list of the writings of Dr. Sprague commences with an Installation Sermon in 1820, and several discourses on special occasions in the following year. In 1822 he published his *Letters to a Daughter*, a favorite didactic volume, republished in Scotland, and latterly printed in this country with the title *Daughter's Own Book*. His *Letters from Europe* appeared in 1828. In 1838 he published a life of Dr. E. D. Griffin, President of Williams College, and, in 1845, the life of Timothy Dwight, in "Sparks's American Biography." His other volumes are of a practical devotional character, as his *Lectures on Revivals of Religion* (1832); *Hints on Christian Intercourse* (1834); *Contrast between True and False Religion* (1837); *Aids to Early Religion* (1847); and *Words to a Young Man's Conscience* (1848). Besides these, he has written numerous introductions to biographical and other works, and is the author of more than one hundred published pamphlets. The latter are of a religious character, sermons in the direct line of his profession, and occasional discourses and addresses on educational, social, and other topics. Of these we may enumerate those of an historical and biographical character, as the Funeral Sermon of Dr. Joseph Lathrop, in 1821; a Thanksgiving Historical Discourse at West Springfield, in 1824; a Fourth of July Discourse at Northampton, in 1827; a sermon at Albany, in behalf of the Polish Exiles, in 1834; an oration commemorative of La Fayette, at Albany, in the same year; a Phi Beta Kappa address before the Society of Yale, in 1843; an address before the Philomathesian Society of Middlebury College, in 1844; an historical discourse in 1846, containing notices of the Second Presbyterian Church and Congregation at Albany, during thirty years from the period of their organization; other discourses commemorative of Dr. Chalmers, in 1847; of the Hon. Silas Wright, the same year; of the Hon. Ambrose Spencer, late Chief-justice of the State of New York, the following year; and, with many others, a discourse, in 1850, on the late Samuel Miller of Princeton. The fondness of Dr. Sprague for biographical study is well known, and is illustrated by his large collection of autographs. With Dr. Tefft of Savannah, he enjoys the reputation of possessing the largest collection of this kind in the country. The latest publication of Dr. Sprague is a book of sketches of the personalties of foreign travel, entitled, *Visits to European Celebrities*. It includes notices, among others, of Edward Irving, Rowland Hill, Robert Hall, Neander, Chalmers, Wilson, and Southey. He is understood to have prepared for publication a biographical work, an account of the Clergy of America of all denominations, from the earliest times.

JOHN P. KENNEDY.

JOHN PENDLETON KENNEDY, the eldest son of a Baltimore merchant, was born in that city on the twenty-fifth of October, 1795, and was graduated at the College of Baltimore in 1812.

In 1816 he was admitted to the bar, and was soon in successful practice. He was elected to the state House of Delegates in 1820, and in 1837 entered the House of Representatives. He was re-elected in 1841 and 1843, and in 1846 again became a member of the House of Delegates. He occupied a prominent position in Congress, as a leading member of the Whig party, and prepared the manifesto in which its representatives disclaimed any connexion with the administration of John Tyler. He was also the author of a volume entitled *A Defence of the Whigs*, published in 1844, and at an earlier period wrote with Warren Dutton of Massachusetts, and Charles Jared Ingersoll, of Pennsylvania, the address issued by the Protectionist Convention, held in New York in 1831.*

In 1818 he commenced his purely literary career, by the publication in numbers, at the intervals of a fortnight, of *The Red Book*. It contained lively gossiping satire of contemporary social matters, by Kennedy, with poetry by his associate in the work, Peter Hoffman Cruse, a native of Baltimore, who was afterwards the author of several able reviews and editor of the *Baltimore American*. Cruse died during the cholera summer of 1832, at the age of thirty-seven. The Red Book was continued during 1818 and 1819, until it formed two volumes.

A long interval elapsed before Kennedy's next appearance as an author, *Swallow Barn* not having been published until 1832. This is a collection of sketches of rural life in Virginia, at the commencement of the present century, linked into a connected whole by a slight story.

In 1835 *Horse-Shoe Robinson* appeared. The story was founded on the personal recollections of its hero, an old soldier of the Revolution, who derived his popular prænomen from the trade which he carried on before the war, of a blacksmith, and the practice of which he continued so far as hard blows were concerned, in the service of the country, in his native state of South Ca-

* Griswold's Prose Writers, p. 342.

J. P. Kennedy

Kennedy's Residence.

rolina. Mr. Kennedy, in the course of a journey in the western part of that region, fell in with this worthy, and afterwards turned to good account a long evening's conversation with him, by making it the groundwork of an excellent historical novel, its leading incidents being transcripts of the old man's veritable adventures.

In his next work, *Rob of the Bowl*, published in 1838, Mr. Kennedy went further back in American history than before, but with a similar adherence, in the main, to fact; the scene being laid in Maryland, in the days of her founder, Calvert. These three novels were reprinted in uniform volumes, with illustrations, in 1852, by G. P. Putnam.

In 1840 Mr. Kennedy published *The Annals of Quodlibet*, a political satire, suggested by the animated "log-cabin and hard cider" canvass preceding the election of Harrison and Tyler, in the same year.

In 1849 he published an elaborate life of his friend William Wirt, with extracts from his correspondence, forming two octavo volumes.

In addition to the works mentioned, Mr. Kennedy is the author of an *Address delivered before the Baltimore Society*, in 1833, an *Eulogy on Wirt*, in 1834, and *A Discourse at the Dedication of Green Mount Cemetery, in* 1839.

Mr. Kennedy writes with delightful ease and freshness. His works are evidently the natural product of his thought and observation, and are pervaded by the happy genial temperament which characterizes the man in his personal relations. We have a full reproduction in his volumes of the old Virginia life, with its old-time ideas of repose, content, and solid comfort; its hearty outdoor existence, and the "humors" which are apt, in a fixed state of society, to develop quaint features in master and dependants.

The author's books abound in delightful rural pictures and sketches of character, which, in easy style and quiet genial humor, recall the Sketch Book and Bracebridge Hall. The author has himself acknowledged the relationship in the graceful tribute to Irving which forms the dedication to the volume.

DESCRIPTION OF SWALLOW BARN.

Swallow Barn is an aristocratical old edifice, that squats, like a brooding hen, on the southern bank of the James River. It is quietly seated, with its vassal out-buildings, in a kind of shady pocket or nook, formed by a sweep of the stream, on a gentle acclivity thinly sprinkled with oaks, whose magnificent branches afford habitation and defence to an antique colony of owls.

This time-honored mansion was the residence of the family of Hazards; but in the present generation the spells of love and mortgage conspired to translate the possession to Frank Meriwether, who having married Lucretia, the eldest daughter of my late uncle, Walter Hazard, and lifted some gentlemanlike incumbrances that had been silently brooding upon the domain along with the owls, was thus inducted into the proprietary rights. The adjacency of his own estate gave a territorial feature to this alliance, of which the fruits were no less discernible in the multiplication of negroes, cattle, and poultry, than in a flourishing clan of Meriwethers.

The buildings illustrate three epochs in the history of the family. The main structure is upwards of a century old; one story high, with thick brick walls, and a double-faced roof, resembling a ship bottom upwards; this is perforated with small dormer windows, that have some such expression as belongs to a face without eye-brows. To this is added a more modern tenement of wood, which might have had its date about the time of the Revolution: it has shrunk a little at the joints, and left some crannies, through which the winds whisper all night long. The last member of the domicile is an upstart fabric of later times, that seems to be ill at ease in this antiquated society, and awkwardly overlooks the ancestral edifice, with the air of a grenadier recruit posted behind a testy little veteran corporal. The traditions of the house ascribe the existence of this erection to a certain family divan, where—say the chronicles—the salic law was set at nought, and some pungent matters of style were considered. It has an unfinished drawing-room, possessing an ambitious air of fashion, with a marble mantel, high ceilings, and large folding doors; but being yet unplastered, and without paint, it has somewhat of a melancholy aspect, and may be compared to an unlucky bark lifted by an extraordinary tide upon a sand-bank: it is useful as a memento to all aspiring householders against a premature zeal to make a show in the world, and the indiscretion of admitting females into cabinet councils.

These three masses compose an irregular pile, in which the two last described constituents are obsequiously stationed in the rear, like serving-men by the chair of a gouty old gentleman, supporting the squat and frowning little mansion which, but for the family pride, would have been long since given over to the accommodation of the guardian birds of the place.

The great hall door is an ancient piece of walnut work, that has grown too heavy for its hinges, and by its daily travel has furrowed the floor with a deep quadrant, over which it has a very uneasy journey. It is shaded by a narrow porch, with a carved pediment, upheld by massive columns of wood sadly split by the sun. A court-yard, in front of this, of a semicircular shape, bounded by a white paling, and having a gravel road leading from a large and variously latticed gateway around a grass plot, is embellished by a superannuated willow that stretches forth its arms, clothed with its pendant drapery, like a reverend priest pronouncing a benediction. A bridle-rack stands on the outer side of the gate, and near it a ragged, horse-eaten plum tree casts its skeleton shadow upon the dust.

Some Lombardy poplars, springing above a mass of shrubbery, partially screen various supernumerary buildings around the mansion. Amongst these is to be seen the gable end of a stable, with the date of its erection stiffly emblazoned in black bricks near the upper angle, in figures set in after the fashion of the work in a girl's sampler. In the same quarter a pigeon box, reared on a post, and resembling a huge tee-totum, is visible, and about its several doors and windows, a family of pragmatical pigeons are generally strutting, bridling and bragging at each other from sunrise until dark.

Appendant to this homestead is an extensive tract of land that stretches for some three or four miles along the river, presenting alternately abrupt promontories mantled with pine and dwarf oak, and small inlets terminating in swamps. Some sparse portions of forest vary the landscape, which, for the most part, exhibits a succession of fields clothed with a diminutive growth of Indian corn, patches of cotton or parched tobacco plants, and the occasional varieties of stubble and fallow grounds. These are surrounded with worm fences of shrunken chesnut, where lizards and ground squirrels are perpetually running races along the rails.

At a short distance from the mansion a brook glides at a snail's pace towards the river, holding its course through a wilderness of alder and laurel, and forming little islets covered with a damp moss. Across this stream is thrown a rough bridge, and not far below, an aged sycamore twists its complex roots about a spring, at the point of confluence of which and the brook, a squadron of ducks have a cruising ground, where they may be seen at any time of the day turning up their tails to the skies, like unfortunate gunboats driven by the head in a gale. Immediately on the margin, at this spot, the family linen is usually spread out by some sturdy negro women, who chant shrill ditties over their wash tubs, and keep up a spirited attack, both of tongue and hand, upon sundry little besmirched and bow-legged blacks, that are continually making somersets on the grass, or mischievously waddling across the clothes laid out to bleach.

Beyond the bridge, at some distance, stands a prominent object in this picture—the most time-worn and venerable appendage to the establishment:—a huge, crazy, and disjointed barn, with an immense roof hanging in penthouse fashion almost to the ground, and thatched a foot thick, with sun-burnt straw, that reaches below the eaves in ragged flakes, giving it an air of drowsy decrepitude. The rude enclosure surrounding this antiquated magazine is strewed knee-deep with litter, from the midst of which arises a long rack, resembling a chevaux de frise, which is ordinarily filled with fodder. This is the customary lounge of four or five gaunt oxen, who keep up a sort of imperturbable companionship with a sickly-looking wagon that protrudes its parched tongue, and droops its rusty swingle-trees in the hot sunshine, with the air of a dispirited and forlorn invalid awaiting the attack of a tertian ague: while, beneath the sheds, the long face of a plough horse may be seen, peering through the dark window of the stable, with a spectral melancholy: his glassy eye moving silently across the gloom, and the profound stillness of his habitation now and then interrupted only by his sepulchral and hoarse cough. There are also some sociable carts under the same sheds, with their shafts against the wall, which seem to have a free and easy air, like a set of roysterers taking their ease in a tavern porch.

Sometimes a clownish colt, with long fetlocks and dishevelled mane, and a thousand burrs on his tail, stalks about this region; but as it seems to be forbidden ground to all his tribe, he is likely very soon to encounter his natural enemy in some of the young negroes, upon which event he makes a rapid retreat, not without an uncouth display of his heels in passing; and bounds off towards the brook, where he stops and looks back with a saucy defiance, and, after affecting to drink for a moment, gallops away, with a hideous whinnying, to the fields.

PURSUITS OF A PHILOSOPHER.

From the house at Swallow Barn there is to be seen, at no great distance, a clump of trees, and in the midst of these an humble building is discernible, that seems to court the shade in which it is modestly embowered. It is an old structure built of logs. Its figure is a cube, with a roof rising from all sides to a point, and surmounted by a wooden weathercock, which somewhat resembles a fish, and somewhat a fowl.

This little edifice is a rustic shrine devoted to Cadmus, and here the sacred rites of the alphabet are daily solemnized by some dozen knotty-pated and freckled votaries not above three feet high, both in trowsers and petticoats. This is one of the many temples that stud the surface of our republican empire, where liberty receives her purest worship, and where, though in humble and lowly guise, she secretly breathes her strength into the heart and sinews of the nation. Here the germ is planted that fructifies through generations, and produces its hundredfold. At this altar the spark is kindled that propagates its fire from breast to breast, like the vast conflagrations that light up and purify the prairie of the west.

The school-house has been an appendage to Swallow Barn ever since the infancy of the last generation. Frank Meriwether has, in his time, extended its usefulness by opening it to the accommodation of his neighbors; so that it is now a theatre whereon a bevy of pigmy players are wont to enact the serio-comic interludes that belong to the first process of indoctrination. A troop of these little sprites are seen, every morning, wending their way across the fields, armed with tin kettles, in which are deposited their leather-coated apple-pies or other store for the day, and which same kettles are generally used, at the decline of the day, as drums or cymbals, to signalize their homeward march, or as receptacles of the spoil pilfered from blackberry bushes, against which these barefooted Scythians are prone to carry on a predatory war.

Throughout the day a continual buzz is heard from this quarter, even to the porch of the mansion-house. Hazard and myself occasionally make them a visit, and it is amusing to observe how, as we approach, the murmur becomes more distinct, until, reaching the door, we find the whole swarm running over their long, tough syllables, in a high concert pitch, with their elbows upon the desks, their hands covering their ears, and their naked heels beating time against the benches—as if every urchin believed that a polysyllable was a piece of music invented to torment all ears but his own. And, high above this din, the master's note is sounded in a lordly key, like the occasional touch of the horn in an orchestra.

This little empire is under the dominion of parson Chub. He is a plump, rosy old gentleman, rather short and thick set, with the blood-vessels meandering over his face like rivulets,—a pair of prominent blue eyes, and a head of silky hair, not unlike the covering of a white spaniel. He may be said to be a man of jolly dimensions, with an evident taste for good living; somewhat sloven in his attire, for his coat—which is not of the newest—is decorated with sundry spots that are scattered over it in constellations. Besides this, he wears an immense cravat, which, as it is wreathed around his short neck, forms a bowl beneath his chin, and—as Ned says—gives the parson's head the appearance of that of John the Baptist upon a charger, as it is sometimes represented in the children's picture books. His beard is grizzled with silver stubble, which the parson reaps about twice a week—if the weather be fair.

Mr. Chub is a philosopher after the order of Socrates. He was an emigrant from the Emerald Isle, where he suffered much tribulation in the disturbances, as they are mildly called, of his much-enduring country. But the old gentleman has weathered the storm without losing a jot of that broad, healthy benevolence with which nature has enveloped his heart, and whose ensign she has hoisted in his face. The early part of his life had been easy and prosperous, until the rebellion of 1798 stimulated his republicanism into a fever, and drove the full-blooded hero headlong into the quarrel, and put him, in spite of his peaceful profession, to standing by his pike in behalf of his principles. By this unhappy boiling over of the caldron of his valor he fell under the ban of the ministers, and tested his share of government mercy. His house was burnt over his head, his horses and hounds (for, by all accounts, he was a perfect Acteon) were "confiscate to the state," and he was forced to fly. This brought him to America in no very compromising mood with royalty.

Here his fortunes appear to have been various, and he was tossed to and fro by the battledoor of fate, until he found a snug harbour at Swallow Barn; where, some years ago, he sat down in that quiet repose which a worried and badgered patriot is best fitted to enjoy.

He is a good scholar, and having confined his reading entirely to the learning of the ancients, his republicanism is somewhat after the Grecian mould. He has never read any politics of later date than the time of the Emperor Constantine, not even a newspaper,—so that he may be said to have been contemporary with Æschines rather than Lord Castlereagh, until that eventful epoch of his life when his blazing roof-tree awakened him from his anachronistical dream. This notable interruption, however, gave him but a feeble insight into the moderns, and he soon relapsed to Thucydides and Livy, with some such glimmerings of the American Revolution upon his remembrance as most readers have of the exploits of the first Brutus.

The old gentleman has a learned passion for folios. He had been a long time urging Meriwether to make some additions to his collections of literature, and descanted upon the value of some of the ancient authors as foundations, both moral and physical, to the library. Frank gave way to the argument, partly to gratify the parson, and partly from the proposition itself having a smack that touched his fancy. The matter was therefore committed entirely to Mr. Chub, who forthwith set out on a voyage of exploration to the north. I believe he got as far as Boston. He certainly contrived to execute his commission with a curious felicity. Some famous Elzevirs were picked up, and many other antiques that nobody but Mr. Chub would ever think of opening.

The cargo arrived at Swallow Barn in the dead of winter. During the interval between the parson's return from his expedition and the coming of the books, the reverend little schoolmaster was in a remarkably unquiet state of body, which almost prevented him from sleeping: and it is said that the sight of the long expected treasures had the happiest effect upon him. There was ample accommodation for this new acquisition of ancient wisdom provided before its arrival, and Mr. Chub now spent a whole week in arranging the volumes on their proper shelves, having, as report affirms, altered the arrangement at least seven times during that period. Everybody wondered what the old gentleman was at all this time; but it was discovered afterwards, that he was endeavouring to effect a distribution of the works according to a minute division of human science, which entirely failed, owing to the unlucky accident of several of his departments being without any volumes.

After this matter was settled, he regularly spent his evenings in the library. Frank Meriwether was hardly behind the parson in this fancy, and took, for a short time, to abstruse reading. They both consequently deserted the little family circle every evening after tea, and might have continued to do so all the winter but for a discovery made by Hazard.

Ned had seldom joined the two votaries of science in their philosophical retirement, and it was whispered in the family that the parson was giving Frank a quiet course of lectures in the ancient philosophy, for Meriwether was known to talk a good deal, about that time, of the old and new Academicians. But it happened upon one dreary winter night, during a tremendous snow storm, which was banging the shutters and doors of the house so as to keep up a continual uproar, that Ned, having waited in the parlour for the philosophers until midnight, set out to invade their retreat—not doubting that he should find them deep in study. When he entered the library, both candles were burning in their sockets, with long, untrimmed wicks; the fire was reduced to its last embers, and, in an arm-chair on one side of the table, the parson was discovered in a sound sleep over Jeremy Taylor's Ductor Dubitantium, whilst Frank, in another chair on the opposite side, was snoring over a folio edition of Montaigne. And upon the table stood a small stone pitcher, containing a residuum of whiskey punch, now grown cold. Frank started up in great consternation upon hearing Ned's footstep beside him, and, from that time, almost entirely deserted the library. Mr. Chub, however, was not so easily drawn away from the career of his humour, and still shows his hankering after his leather-coated friends.

It is an amusing point in the old gentleman's character to observe his freedom in contracting engagements that depend upon his purse. He seems to think himself a rich man, and is continually becoming security for some of the neighbours. To hear him talk, it would be supposed that he meant to renovate the affairs of the whole county. As his intentions are so generous, Meriwether does not fail to back him when it comes to a pinch—by reason of which the good squire has more than once been obliged to pay the penalty.

Mr. Chub's character, as it will be seen from this description of him, possesses great simplicity. This has given rise to some practical jokes against him, which have caused him much annoyance. The tradition in the family goes, that, one evening, the worthy divine, by some strange accident, fell into an excess in his cups; and that a saucy chamber-maid found him dozing in his chair, with his pipe in his mouth, having the bowl turned downward, and the ashes sprinkled over his breast. He was always distinguished by a broad and superfluous ruffle to his shirt, and, on this occasion, the mischievous maid had the effrontery to set it on fire. It produced, as may be supposed, a great alarm to the parson, and, besides, brought him into some scandal; for he was roused up in a state of consternation, and began to strip himself of his clothes, not knowing what he was about. I don't know how far he exposed himself, but the negro woman who ran to his relief, made a fine story of it.

Hazard once reminded him of this adventure, in my presence, and it was diverting to see with what a comic and quiet sheepishness he bore the joke. He half closed his eyes and puckered up his mouth as Ned proceeded; and when the story came to the conclusion, he gave Ned a gentle blow on the breast with the back of his hand, crying out, as he did so, "Hoot toot, Mister Ned!"—then he walked to the front door, where he stood whistling.

JOHN GORHAM PALFREY,

THE son of a Boston merchant, and the grandson of a Revolutionary officer, William Palfrey, aide to Washington at Dorchester, was born in Boston, May 2, 1796. He was educated in his youth by William Payne, father of the celebrated tragedian, and afterwards at Exeter Academy; was graduated at Harvard in 1815, studied theology, and in 1818 took charge of the Brattle street congregation, till his appointment as Dexter professor of sacred literature in Harvard in 1831. In 1835 he became editor of the North American Review, and had charge of that periodical till 1843. From 1839 to '42 he delivered courses of lectures for the Lowell Institute on the *Evidences of Christianity*, which were subsequently published in two volumes octavo. He has also published four volumes of *Lectures on the Jewish Scriptures and Antiquities;* a supplementary volume on Quotations from the Old Testament in the New; and a volume of *Sermons on the Duties belonging to some of the Conditions and Relations of Private Life.*

He has published several historical discourses: a Fourth of July, Boston oration, in 1831; the discourse at the centennial celebration of Barnstable in 1839; the semi-centennial discourse before the Massachusetts Historical Society in 1844; two discourses on the History of the Brattle Street Church, and in Sparks's American Biography; the Life of William Palfrey, his ancestor, paymaster-general to the army of the Revolution.

Latterly, Mr. Palfrey has been much in public life, as a politician in his own state, and a representative to Congress in 1847 and since, where he has been a leader of the free-soil party. In 1846 he published in the *Boston Whig*, edited by Charles Francis Adams, a series of *Papers on the Slave Power*, which were collected into a pamphlet.*

In his work on the Evidences Dr. Palfrey pursues mainly the historical line of argument, with a consideration of the moral relations growing immediately from the doctrines of the Bible. In this method he belongs rather to the Norton than to the Channing school of Unitarians. Apart from the scholarship implied in the handling of his learned themes, his writings are peculiarly distinguished by the acumen of the legal mind. In the words of one of his friends, the Rev. Dr. Samuel Osgood, he is an example of the accomplished Christian lawyer.

His volume of Sermons on the Duties of Private Life shows him an experienced casuist, combining refinement and delicacy of perception with sound judgment.

RELIGIOUS OPPORTUNITIES OF AGE.

As we look for a pious spirit as the indispensable support and grace of age, so that period of life abounds with peculiar privileges for its culture. Before the view of the aged, life has been presented in a great diversity of aspects; and, in every new aspect, it has presented to their minds, with a new impression, the truth that the Providence of a wise and good being governs in the world, and that to do his will is the one great interest of man, his one sure way to genuine and lasting enjoyment. The retrospect, which they may take, is full of bright revelations to them of the perfections of his character; of the equity and benevolence of his government; of the excellence of his service. They reckon up precious and accumulated tokens of his parental goodness to themselves, kindling a deep, warm gratitude in their hearts. They have learned to number even their griefs among their blessings, explaining and vindicating to them, as the event of after years has often done, what had seemed for the time the darkest ways of Providence. And in such reflections, what was always matter of strong faith to them, has become rather matter of reality and knowledge,—that the Lord is indeed gracious and of tender mercy, and all his ways are righteousness and love.

That composed state of the mind, which it is reasonable to expect will be attained, to an increased extent, when the early ferment of the feelings has subsided, and the agitating cares of the world no longer press, greatly favors the growth of a pervading and vital piety. Age can look on all things with a cool, a just, and wise observation (and the view of true wisdom is always the view of religion); and as the chances of life have perforce inured it to disappointment and restraint in some forms, and the passions and impulses have, by a law of nature, lost much of their headlong force, the work of self-discipline has been made of easier execution, and a subdued and serene temper, akin to the temper of devotion, has

* Loring's Boston Orators, pp. 485-492.

been diffused over the soul. Age, again, has more ample leisure for those retired exercises, to which a devotional spirit prompts; and herein it has a privilege, which the pious mind will hold in peculiar estimation. In the more occupied period of earlier life, we could not praise a man, who should withdraw much time, day by day, from the duties of his worldly calling, to be given to the solitary exercises of religious study, meditation, and prayer. He must learn to turn his opportunities of this kind to the best account, because he cannot have them in such abundance as he would wish. The aged have the happiness of not being so restricted. They have more free access to enjoyments of the highest and purest character that can belong to man. They have leisure for investigations in that science of profoundest interest, of which God's word is the expositor. They have tranquil hours, in which they can look into the mysteries, and chide the wanderings, and nourish the good affections, of their own hearts. The world has no longer such demands on them, but that they may often go aside to solitary converse with their best friend; to communion with him, whose friendship has become continually more needful to them, on whose love they know they are soon to be thrown without even the vain appearance of any other resource, and to whose nearer society they have an humble hope then to be received. That age does afford such rich opportunities of this nature, is to be to them a leading occasion of gratitude that they have been brought to see that time; and to profit by those opportunities, to the full extent of their great worth, should be realized by them to be a chief part of the peculiar responsibility which age imposes.

Miss Sarah Palfrey, a daughter of the Hon. Mr. Palfrey, is the author of a recently published volume of poems (1855) bearing the title *Prémices, by E. Foxton*. It is chiefly made up of two ballad narratives: *Hilda*, a love song, and *The Princess's Bath*. These show originality and spirit, and a quick, lively temperament in the writer. We cite a picture of youthful studies from one of the shorter pieces, entitled *Manhood*:—

No more in swaddling-bands confined,
How from its cradle leaps the mind!
The viewless might of air to wield,
Bid the swollen clouds their lightnings yield,
Or from the surest holds of earth
To wring Time's rocky records forth,
Or from their lurking-places high
Hunt starting systems through the sky,
In haste the universe to explore,
While still its cry is, More! and More!
It raises, with a magic tome,
The demigods of Greece and Rome,
Till Servius' legions shake the plain,
And Homer's harp resounds again,
And, oftener, in communion sweet,
Sits on the Mount at Jesus' feet.
The longest day is all too brief
To bring the stripling's thirst relief;
By night, the good and great of old
In dreams to him their arms unfold;
The morning wakes to pleasing toil,
Cheered by the glad parental smile;
And generous friendship weaves the crown
That generous rivalry has won.
Thank God for life!

Still dance the years. Perfecting time
Has borne him on to early prime,
And paid, in golden hoard amassed,
The earnings of the thrifty past.
Each blessed earthly joy he knows;
The gleaming laurel wreathes his brows;
In wisdom, as in courage, great,
He firmly sways the helm of state;
While Virtue in his silver tone
Commands, with graces all his own,
Scarce less than his, his hearers feel
Their fervors for the common weal;
And, meek in beauty, by his side
A stately maiden blooms, a bride.
Thank God for life!

HORACE MANN

Is a native of Massachusetts, where he was born at Franklin, May 4, 1796. In his youth he fell in with an itinerant schoolmaster, Samuel Barrett, by whose proficiency in the languages he was animated in his studies. He was educated at Brown University, and pursued the study of the law in Litchfield, Conn., and Dedham, Mass., which he represented in the legislature. He took up his residence in Boston in 1836, and was elected to the state Senate. He was secretary of the Massachusetts Board of Education from 1837 to 1848, when he succeeded John Quincy Adams in Congress. He is chiefly known as a writer through his valuable series of Annual Education Reports, twelve in number, stored with ingenious and pertinent discussion of the various means and machinery to be employed in the work of popular education, both intellectual and physical. Through these he has identified himself with the progress of the public-school system of Massachusetts. He published in this connexion, as part of his seventh Annual Report to the legislature, a *Report of an Educational Tour in Germany, Britain*, &c., made in the year 1843.

Horace Mann

He has become eminent as a social reformer and philanthropist; taking under his charge the temperance question, among others. His lectures and addresses are vigorous and energetic, in a familiar colloquial manner—striking hard to produce an immediate impression.†

In 1853, he was elected President of Antioch College, where he also supports the duties of Professor of Political Economy, Intellectual and Moral Philosophy, Constitutional Law and Natural Theology.

This college was incorporated in 1852. It is situated at Yellow Springs, Green County, Ohio, at a healthy location convenient of access. From a prospectus of the institution we cite a few sentences declaratory of its plan, which has some peculiarities.

"The leading minds, under whose auspices and

* It was republished in London in 1846, with preface and notes, by W. B. Hodgson, Principal of the Mechanics' Institution, Liverpool.

† "A Few Thoughts for a Young Man," a Lecture before the Boston Mercantile Library Association. Ticknor. 8vo. 1850. Two Lectures on Intemperance: its effects on the poor and ignorant, and on the rich and educated. Syracuse: Hall, Mills, & Co., 1852. 18mo. pp. 127. A Few Thoughts on the Powers and Duties of Woman. Ib. 18mo. pp. 141.

by whose patronage Antioch College was founded, long ago called themselves 'Christians,' not invidiously but devoutly, and in honor of the author and finisher of their faith; and they have now selected a name by which to designate their Institution, at once scriptural and commemorative, because 'the Disciples were called Christians first in *Antioch*.'

"In some particulars of its aim and scope, this College differs from most of the higher literary institutions of the country. It recognises the claims of the female sex to equal opportunities of education with the male, and these opportunities it designs to confer. Its founders believe that labors and expenditures for the higher education of men will tend indirectly to elevate the character of women; but they are certain that all wise efforts for the improved education of women will speed the elevation of the whole human race.

"It is designed, in this College, not only to give marked attention to the study of the Laws of Human Health and Life, but to train up the pupils in a systematic obedience to them."

Opening its halls under the direction of its well known and efficient head, the college sprang at once into a state of prosperity. In the second year of its instruction in 1854, no less than four hundred students were in daily attendance; of these one third were females, who are admitted to equal privileges in all the advantages of the institution. In the list of the Faculty, we notice Miss R. M. Pennell, "Professor of Physical Geography, Drawing, Natural History, Civil History, and Didactics." The Greek and Latin languages are taught, and indeed all the usual branches of an American collegiate education.

Mr. Loring, in his "Hundred Boston Orators," gives us this sketch of the personal appearance of Mr. Mann. "He is tall, very erect, and remarkably slender, with silvery grey hair, animated and expressive features, light complexion, and rapid pace. As an orator, his smooth, flowing style, musical voice, and graceful manner, with fertility, amplitude, and energy of diction, often adorned with a graceful, rushing eloquence, that can be measured only by the celerity of his movements in the street, irresistibly captivate the breathless audience."

HEALTH AND TEMPERANCE—FROM THOUGHTS FOR A YOUNG MAN.

Were a young man to write down a list of his duties, Health should be among the first items in the catalogue. This is no exaggeration of its value; for health is indispensable to almost every form of human enjoyment; it is the grand auxiliary of usefulness; and should a man love the Lord his God with all his heart and soul and mind and strength, he would have ten times more heart and soul and mind and strength to love Him with, in the vigor of health, than under the palsy of disease. Not only the amount, but the quality of the labor which a man can perform, depends upon his health. The work savors of the workman. If the poet sickens, his verse sickens; if black, venous blood flows to an author's brain, it beclouds his pages; and the devotions of a consumptive man scent of his disease as Lord Byron's obscenities smell of gin. Not only "lying lips," but a dyspeptic stomach, is an abomination to the Lord. At least in this life, so dependent is mind upon material organization,—the functions and manifestations of the soul upon the condition of the body it inhabits,—that the materialist hardly states practical results too strongly, when he affirms that thought and passion, wit, imagination, and love, are only emanations from exquisitely organized matter, just as perfume is the effluence of flowers, or music the ethereal product of an Æolian harp.

In regard to the indulgence of appetite, and the management of the vital organs, society is still in a state of barbarism; and the young man who is true to his highest interests must create a civilization for himself. The brutish part of our nature governs the spiritual. Appetite is Nicholas the First, and the noble faculties of mind and heart are Hungarian captives. Were we to see a rich banker exchanging eagles for coppers by tale, or a rich merchant bartering silk for serge by the pound, we should deem them worthy of any epithet in the vocabulary of folly. Yet the same men buy pains whose prime cost is greater than the amplest fund of natural enjoyments. Their purveyor and market-man bring them home head-aches, and indigestion, and neuralgia, by hamper-fulls. Their butler bottles up stone, and gout, and the liver-complaint, falsely labelling them sherry, or madeira, or port, and the stultified masters have not wit enough to see through the cheat. The mass of society look with envy upon the epicure who, day by day, for four hours of luxurious eating suffers twenty hours of sharp aching; who pays a full price for a hot supper, and is so pleased with the bargain that he throws in a sleepless and tempestuous night as a gratuity. English factory children have received the commiseration of the world, because they were scourged to work eighteen hours out of the twenty-four; but there is many a theoretic republican who is a harsher Pharaoh to his stomach than this;—who allows it no more resting-time than he does his watch; who gives it no Sunday, no holiday, no *vacation* in any sense. Our pious ancestors enacted a law that suicides should be buried where four roads meet, and that a cart-load of stones should be thrown upon the body. Yet, when gentlemen or ladies commit suicide, not by cord or steel, but by turtle-soup or lobster-salad, they may be buried in consecrated ground, and under the auspices of the church, and the public are not ashamed to read an epitaph upon their tombstones false enough to make the marble blush. Were the barbarous old law now in force that punished the body of the suicide for the offence which his soul had committed, we should find many a Mount Auburn at the cross-roads. Is it not humiliating and amazing, that men, invited by the exalted pleasures of the intellect, and the sacred affections of the heart, to come to a banquet worthy of the gods, should stop by the wayside to feed on garbage, or to drink of the Circean cup that transforms them to swine!

If a young man, incited by selfish principles alone, inquires how he shall make his appetite yield him the largest amount of gratification, the answer is, *by Temperance*. The true epicurean art consists in the adaptation of our organs not only to the highest, but to the longest enjoyment. Vastly less depends upon the table to which we sit down, than upon the appetite which we carry to it. The palled epicure, who spends five dollars for his dinner, extracts less pleasure from his meal than many a hardy laborer who dines for a shilling. The desideratum is, not greater luxuries, but livelier *papillæ;* and if the devotee of appetite would propitiate his divinity aright, he would not send to the Yellow-stone for buffaloes' tongues, nor to France for *paté de fois gras*, but would climb a mountain, or swing an axe. With health, there is no end to the quantity or the variety from which the palate can extract its pleasures. Without health, no delicacy that nature or art produces can provoke a zest. Hence, when a man destroys his health, he destroys, so far as he is concerned, whatever of sweetness, of flavor and of savor, the teeming earth can produce. To him who has poisoned his appetite by excesses, the luscious pulp of grape or peach, the nectareous juices of orange or pine-apple, are but a loathing and a nausea. He has turned gardens and groves of delicious fruit into gardens and groves of ipecac and aloes. The same vicious indulgences that blasted his health, blasted all orchards and cane-fields also. Verily, the man who is physiologically "wicked" does not live out half his days; nor is this the worst of his punishment, for he is more than half dead while he appears to live.

GEORGE BUSH,

EMINENT as a theological writer, and for his advocacy of the doctrines of Swedenborg, was born at Norwich, Vermont, June 12, 1796. He was a graduate of Dartmouth, studied at Princeton Theological Seminary, took orders in the Presbyterian Church, and was for several years a missionary in Indiana. In 1831 he became Professor of Hebrew and Oriental Literature in the University of the city of New York, and at the same period Superintendent of the Press of the American Bible Society. In 1832 he published his *Life of Mahommed* in Harper's Family Library. In this work copious extracts from the false prophet's revelations are interwoven with his personal memoirs.

Geo. Bush

A Treatise on the Millennium appeared in 1832. The main object of this work was to show by a somewhat elaborate train of historical and critical induction, that the prophetical period technically termed the Millennium was past instead of future; that it was not a prosperous period of the church, but the reverse; and that the expected era to which the name Millennium is given, is really the New Jerusalem era developed in the closing chapters of the Apocalypse. An octavo volume of *Scripture Illustrations* published at this time by Dr. Bush, was a compilation from oriental tourists, archæologists, and commentators, with a view to cast light upon the sacred Scriptures in the departments of topography, manners, customs, costumes, arts, learning, usages of speech, &c. In 1835 his Hebrew Grammar for the use of schools, seminaries, and universities, appeared; and in 1840 the first of his series of Notes on the Books of the Old Testament, which have included Genesis, Exodus, Leviticus, Joshua, and Judges. These were marked as well by the ingenuity and boldness as by the learning of his speculations. He gave further attention to the sacred symbols and prophecy in the *Hierophant*, a monthly magazine, which he commenced in 1844. It contained a series of articles on Professor Stuart's canons of prophetical interpretation, which attracted considerable notice at the time, as rather unusual specimens of a kind but caustic criticism.

In the same year he published his *Anastasis; or the Doctrine of the Resurrection of the Body Rationally and Spiritually Considered*, in which he opposed the doctrine of the physical construction of the body in another world, with arguments from reason and revelation. The book met with much opposition from the pulpit and reviewers, and the author replied in his work, *The Resurrection of Christ, in answer to the Question whether He rose in a Spiritual and Celestial, or in a Material and Earthly Body*, and *The Soul, an Inquiry into Scriptural Psychology.*

After this Dr. Bush became connected with the Swedenborgian church, as one of its preachers, and devoted himself to the dissemination of the writings of that philosopher, by translation of his Diary and other works, and especially in his editorship of the *New Church Repository*. In 1847 he published a work on the connexion of the doctrines of Swedenborg and mesmerism. In his personal character Dr. Bush is remarkable for the kindness of his disposition. His love of mysticism harmonizes well with the pursuits of the gentle-minded scholar and ardent devotee of learning.

JOHN G. C. BRAINARD.

BRAINARD, the gentle poet of the Connecticut, the sylvan, placid stream which happily symbolizes his verse, was born in the state of that name at New London, October 21, 1796. His father had been a judge of the Superior Court, and the son for a while, after his education at Yale was completed, pursued the study of the law, but it was little adapted to his tastes and constitution, and after a brief trial of its practice at Middletown he abandoned it in February, 1822, for the editorship of a weekly paper at Hartford, the *Connecticut Mirror*. He is said to have neglected the politics of his paper, dismissing the tariff with a jest, while he displayed his ability in the literary and poetical department. His genius lay in the amiable walks of the *belles-lettres*, where the delicacy of his temperament, the correspondence of the sensitive mind to the weak physical frame, found its appropriate home and nourishment. His country needed results of this kind more than it did law or politics; and in his short life Brainard honored his native land. His genius is a flower plucked from the banks of the river which he loved, and preserved for posterity.

Before entering on the Mirror Brainard wrote a few pieces for a literary paper published by Cornelius Tuthill at New Haven, called The Microscope. His compositions in the Mirror were at once relished and appreciated. Though they were mostly on trite and occasional subjects, such as time out of mind had occupied with little notice the corner of the country newspaper, yet they had a freshness of spirit infused in them, a fine poetical instinct, which charmed the youths and maidens of Connecticut. This instinct of Brainard led him to the employment of the ballad, in which he gave rare promise, as he embodied the patriotism or the superstition of the country, in such poems as *Fort Griswold* and the *Black Fox of Salmon River*. The annual new year carrier's address of the newspaper, in place of the usual doggerel, became a poem in his hands. Even album verses assumed a hue of nature and originality. He writes

TO THE DAUGHTER OF A FRIEND.

I pray thee by thy mother's face,
And by her look and by her eye,
By every decent matron grace
That hovered round the resting-place
Where thy young head did lie;
And by the voice that soothed thine ear,
The hymn, the smile, the sigh, the tear,
That matched thy changeful mood;
By every prayer thy mother taught,
By every blessing that she sought,
I pray thee to be good.

The humor of Brainard was the natural accompaniment of his sensibility. It is deeply inwrought with his gentle nature.

In 1825 a first volume of *Poems* was published by Brainard at New York, mostly made up from the columns of his newspaper, which was favorably received. Not long after, in 1827, the poet was compelled by the inroad of consumption on his constitution to retire from his editorship. He went to the east end of Long Island for his health, and has left a touching memorial of his visit to the sea, in which the animation of his genius overcomes the despondency of his broken frame. He suffered and wrote verses till his death at his father's home, at New London, September 26, 1828.

After his death a second edition of Brainard's poems appeared in 1832, enlarged from the first, with the title *Literary Remains*, accompanied by a warmly written sketch of the poet's life by Whittier. This has been since followed by a third edition, with a portrait, an elegant and tasteful volume, published by Edward Hopkins, at Hartford, in 1842.

To the indications we have given of the poet's genius we have only to add a few personal traits. He was a small man, and sensitive on that score. His friends noticed the fine expression of his countenance when animated. He was negligent of his dress and somewhat abstracted. He wrote rapidly, and was ready in conversation, with playful repartee. His biographer, in the last edition of his poems, gives an instance of his wit. A preacher had come to New London, and labored heavily through a discourse, complaining all the time that *his mind was imprisoned*. When this difficulty was urged in defence of his dulness Brainard would not allow it, since "the preacher's mind might easily have sworn out." At another time he replied to a critic, who had pronounced the word "brine" in his verses on "The Deep," "to have no more business in sentimental poetry than a pig in a parlor," that the objector, "though his piece is dated Philadelphia, lives at a greater distance from the sea, and has got his ideas of the salt water from his father's pork barrel."*

ON CONNECTICUT RIVER.

From that lone lake, the sweetest of the chain
That links the mountain to the mighty main,
Fresh from the rock and swelling by the tree,
Rushing to meet and dare and breast the sea—
Fair, noble, glorious river! in thy wave
The sunniest slopes and sweetest pastures lave;
The mountain torrent, with its wintry roar,
Springs from its home and leaps upon thy shore:—
The promontories love thee—and for this
Turn their rough cheeks and stay thee for thy kiss.
Stern, at thy source, thy northern Guardians stand,
Rude rulers of the solitary land,
Wild dwellers by thy cold sequestered springs,
Of earth the feathers and of air the wings;
Their blasts have rocked thy cradle, and in storm
Covered thy couch and swathed in snow thy form—
Yet, blessed by all the elements that sweep
The clouds above, or the unfathomed deep,
The purest breezes scent thy blooming hills,
The gentlest dews drop on thy eddying rills,
By the mossed bank, and by the aged tree,
The silver streamlet smoothest glides to thee.

The young oak greets thee at the water's edge,
Wet by the wave, though anchored in the ledge.
—'Tis there the otter dives, the beaver feeds,
Where pensive oziers dip their willowy weeds,
And there the wild cat purs amid her brood,
And trains them, in the sylvan solitude,

* Memoir of Brainard, p. 33.

To watch the squirrel's leap, or mark the mink
Paddling the water by the quiet brink;—
Or to out-gaze the grey owl in the dark,
Or hear the young fox practising to bark.
Dark as the frost nip'd leaves that strewed the ground,
The Indian hunter here his shelter found;
Here cut his bow and shaped his arrows true,
Here built his wigwam and his bark canoe,
Speared the quick salmon leaping up the fall,
And slew the deer without the rifle ball.
Here his young squaw her cradling tree would choose,
Singing her chant to hush her swart pappoose,
Here stain her quills and string her trinkets rude,
And weave her warrior's wampum in the wood.
—No more shall they thy welcome waters bless,
No more their forms thy moonlit banks shall press,
No more be heard, from mountain or from grove,
His whoop of slaughter, or her song of love.

Thou didst not shake, thou didst not shrink when late
The mountain-top shut down its ponderous gate,
Tumbling its tree-grown ruins to thy side,
An avalanche of acres at a slide.
Nor dost thou stay, when winter's coldest breath
Howls through the woods and sweeps along the heath—
One mighty sigh relieves thy icy breast
And wakes thee from the calmness of thy rest.

Down sweeps the torrent ice—it may not stay
By rock or bridge, in narrow or in bay—
Swift, swifter to the heaving sea it goes
And leaves thee dimpling in thy sweet repose,
—Yet as the unharmed swallow skims his way,
And lightly drops his pinions in thy spray,
So the swift sail shall seek thy inland seas,
And swell and whiten in thy purer breeze,
New paddles dip thy waters, and strange oars
Feather thy waves and touch thy noble shores.
Thy *noble* shores! where the tall steeple shines,
At midday, higher than thy mountain pines,
Where the white schoolhouse with its daily drill
Of sunburnt children, smiles upon the hill,
Where the neat village grows upon the eye
Decked forth in nature's sweet simplicity—
Where hard-won competence, the farmer's wealth,
Gains merit, honor, and gives labor health,
Where Goldsmith's self might send his exiled band
To find a new "Sweet Auburn" in our land.

What Art can execute or Taste devise,
Decks thy fair course and gladdens in thine eyes—
As broader sweep the bendings of thy stream,
To meet the southern Sun's more constant beam.
Here cities rise, and sea-washed commerce hails
Thy shores and winds with all her flapping sails,
From Tropic isles, or from the torrid main—
Where grows the grape, or sprouts the sugar-cane—
Or from the haunts, where the striped haddock play,
By each cold northern bank and frozen bay.
Here safe returned from every stormy sea,
Waves the striped flag, the mantle of the free,
—That star-lit flag, by all the breezes curled
Of yon vast deep whose waters grasp the world.

In what Arcadian, what Utopian ground
Are warmer hearts or manlier feelings found,
More hospitable welcome, or more zeal
To make the curious "tarrying" stranger feel
That, next to home, here best may he abide,
To rest and cheer him by the chimney-side;
Drink the hale Farmer's cider, as he hears
From the grey dame the tales of other years.
Cracking his shagbarks, as the aged crone,
Mixing the true and doubtful into one,
Tells how the Indian scalped the helpless child
And bore its shrieking mother to the wild,
Butchered the father hastening to his home,
Seeking his cottage—finding but his tomb.
How drums and flags and troops were seen on high,
Wheeling and charging in the northern sky,
And that she knew what these wild tokens meant,
When to the Old French War her husband went.
How, by the thunder-blasted tree, was hid
The golden spoils of far famed Robert Kidd;
And then the chubby grand-child wants to know
About the ghosts and witches long ago,
That haunted the old swamp.
The clock strikes ten—
The prayer is said, nor unforgotten then
The stranger in their gates. A decent rule
Of Elders in thy puritanic school.

When the fresh morning wakes him from his dream,
And daylight smiles on rock, and slope, and stream,
Are there not glossy curls and sunny eyes,
As brightly lit and bluer than thy skies,
Voices as gentle as an echoed call,
And sweeter than the softened waterfall
That smiles and dimples in its whispering spray,
Leaping in sportive innocence away:—
And lovely forms, as graceful and as gay
As wild-brier, budding in an April day;
—How like the leaves—the fragrant leaves it bears,
Their sinless purposes and simple cares.

Stream of my sleeping Fathers! when the sound
Of coming war echoed thy hills around,
How did thy sons start forth from every glade,
Snatching the musket where they left the spade.
How did their mothers urge them to the fight,
Their sisters tell them to defend the right,—
How bravely did they stand, how nobly fall,
The earth their coffin and the turf their pall.
How did the aged pastor light his eye,
When to his flock he read the purpose high
And stern resolve, whate'er the toil may be,
To pledge life, name, fame, all—for Liberty.
—Cold is the hand that penned that glorious page—
Still in the grave the body of that sage
Whose lip of eloquence and heart of zeal,
Made Patriots act and listening Statesmen feel—
Brought thy Green Mountains down upon their foes,
And thy white summits melted of their snows,
While every vale to which his voice could come,
Rang with the fife and echoed to the drum.

Bold River! better suited are thy waves
To nurse the laurels clustering round their graves,
Than many a distant stream, that soaks the mud,
Where thy brave sons have shed their gallant blood,
And felt, beyond all other mortal pain,
They ne'er should see their happy home again.

Thou had'st a poet once,—and he could tell,
Most tunefully, whate'er to thee befell,
Could fill each pastoral reed upon thy shore—
—But we shall hear his classic lays no more
He loved thee, but he took his aged way,
By Erie's shore, and Perry's glorious day,
To where Detroit looks out amidst the wood,
Remote beside the dreary solitude.

Yet for his brow thy ivy leaf shall spread,
Thy freshest myrtle lift its berried head,
And our gnarled Charter oak put forth a bough,
Whose leaves shall grace thy TRUMBULL's honored brow

SALMON RIVER.

Hic viridis tenera prætexit arundine ripas
Mincius.—VIRGIL.

'Tis a sweet stream—and so, 'tis true, are all
That undisturbed, save by the harmless brawl
Of mimic rapid or slight waterfall,
Pursue their way
By mossy bank, and darkly waving wood,
By rock, that since the deluge fixed has stood,
Showing to sun and moon their crisping flood
By night and day.

But yet there's something in its humble rank,
Something in its pure wave and sloping bank,
Where the deer sported, and the young fawn drank
With unscared look:
There's much in its wild history, that teems
With all that's superstitious—and that seems
To match our fancy and eke out our dreams,
In that small brook.

Havoc has been upon its peaceful plain,
And blood has dropped there, like the drops of rain;
The corn grows o'er the still graves of the slain—
And many a quiver,
Filled from the reeds that grew on yonder hill,
Has spent itself in carnage. Now 'tis still,
And whistling ploughboys oft their runlets fill
From Salmon River.

Here, say old men, the Indian Magi made
Their spells by moonlight; or beneath the shade
That shrouds sequestered rock, or darkening glade,
Or tangled dell.
Here Philip came, and Miantonimo,
And asked about their fortunes long ago,
As Saul to Endor, that her witch might show
Old Samuel.

And here the black fox roved, and howled, and shook
His thick tail to the hunters, by the brook
Where they pursued their game, and him mistook
For earthly fox;
Thinking to shoot him like a shaggy bea.,
And his soft peltry, stript and dressed to wear,
Or lay a trap, and from his quiet lair
Transfer him to a box.

Such are the tales they tell. 'Tis hard to rhyme
About a little and unnoticed stream,
That few have heard of—but it is a theme
I chance to love;
And one day I may tune my rye-straw reed,
And whistle to the note of many a deed
Done on this river—which, if there be need,
I'll try to prove.

THE BLACK FOX OF SALMON RIVER.*

How cold, how beautiful, how bright,
The cloudless heaven above us shines;
But 'tis a howling winter's night—
'Twould freeze the very forest pines.

"The winds are up, while mortals sleep;
The stars look forth when eyes are shut;
The bolted snow lies drifted deep
Around our poor and lonely hut.

"With silent step and listening ear,
With bow and arrow, dog and gun,
We'll mark his track, for his prowl we hear,
Now is our time—come on, come on."

O'er many a fence, through many a wood,
Following the dog's bewildered scent,
In anxious haste and earnest mood,
The Indian and the white man went.

The gun is cocked, the bow is bent,
The dog stands with uplifted paw,
And ball and arrow swift are sent,
Aimed at the prowler's very jaw.

—The ball, to kill that fox, is run
Not in a mould by mortals made!
The arrow which that fox should shun,
Was never shaped from earthly reed!

The Indian Druids of the wood
Know where the fatal arrows grow—
They spring not by the summer flood,
They pierce not through the winter snow!

Why cowers the dog, whose snuffing nose
Was never once deceived till now?
And why, amid the chilling snows,
Does either hunter wipe his brow?

For once they see his fearful den,
'Tis a dark cloud that slowly moves
By night around the homes of men,
By day—along the stream it loves.

Again the dog is on his track,
The hunters chase o'er dale and hill,
They may not, though they would, look back,
They must go forward—forward still.

Onward they go, and never turn,
Spending a night that meets no day;
For them shall never morning sun
Light them upon their endless way.

The hut is desolate, and there
The famished dog alone returns;
On the cold steps he makes his lair,
By the shut door he lays his bones.

Now the tired sportsman leans his gun
Against the ruins of the site,
And ponders on the hunting done
By the lost wanderers of the night.

And there the little country girls
Will stop to whisper, and listen, and look,
And tell, while dressing their sunny curls,
Of the Black Fox of Salmon Brook.

THE SEA BIRD'S SONG.

On the deep is the mariner's danger,
On the deep is the mariner's death,
Who to fear of the tempest a stranger
Sees the last bubble burst of his breath?
'Tis the sea-bird, sea-bird, sea-bird,
Lone looker on despair,
The sea-bird, sea-bird, sea-bird,
The only witness there.

Who watches their course, who so mildly
Careen to the kiss of the breeze?
Who lists to their shrieks, who so wildly
Are clasped in the arms of the seas?
'Tis the sea-bird, &c.

Who hovers on high o'er the lover,
And her who has clung to his neck?
Whose wing is the wing that can cover,
With its shadow, the foundering wreck?
'Tis the sea-bird, &c.

My eye in the light of the billow,
My wing on the wake of the wave;
I shall take to my breast for a pillow,
The shroud of the fair and the brave.
I'm a sea-bird, &c.

* These lines are founded on a legend that is as well authenticated as any superstition of the kind; and as current in the place where it originated, as could be expected of one that possesses so little interest.—*Author's Note.*

My foot on the iceberg has lighted,
When hoarse the wild winds veer about;
My eye, when the bark is benighted,
Sees the lamp of the Light-House go out.
I'm the sea-bird, sea-bird, sea-bird,
Lone looker on despair;
The sea-bird, sea-bird, sea-bird,
The only witness there.

STANZAS.

The dead leaves strew the forest walk,
And withered are the pale wild flowers;
The frost hangs black'ning on the stalk,
The dew-drops fall in frozen showers.
Gone are the Spring's green sprouting bowers,
Gone Summer's rich and mantling vines,
And Autumn, with her yellow hours,
On hill and plain no longer shines.

I learned a clear and wild-toned note,
That rose and swelled from yonder tree—
A gay bird, with too sweet a throat,
There perched and raised her song for me.
The winter comes, and where is she?
Away—where summer wings will rove,
Where buds are fresh, and every tree
Is vocal with the notes of love.

Too mild the breath of Southern sky,
Too fresh the flower that blushes there,
The Northern breeze that rushes by,
Finds leaves too green, and buds too fair;
No forest tree stands stripped and bare,
No stream beneath the ice is dead,
No mountain top with sleety hair
Bends o'er the snows its reverend head.

Go there with all the birds—and seek
A happier clime, with livelier flight,
Kiss, with the sun, the evening's cheek,
And leave me lonely with the night.
—I'll gaze upon the cold north light,
And mark where all its glories shone—
See—that it all is fair and bright,
Feel—that it all is cold and gone.

GEORGE TICKNOR,

THE distinguished historian of Spanish literature, was born in the city of Boston, Mass., August 1, 1791. He was prepared for college at home, entered Dartmouth, and received his degree there at the early age of sixteen. He occupied himself the next three years in Boston with a diligent study of the ancient classics, when he engaged in the study of the law, and was admitted to the bar in 1813. The tastes of the scholar, however, prevailed over the practice of the profession, and in 1815 Mr. Ticknor sailed for Europe to accomplish himself in the thorough course of instruction of a German university. He passed two years at Gottingen in philological studies, which he continued during a residence of two years more in various capitals, as Paris, Madrid, Lisbon, Rome, and Edinburgh, making the acquaintance of eminent scholars on the continent and Great Britain, among others of Sir Walter Scott and Robert Southey, who admired his scholarship, and stock of curious Spanish lore. In 1819 he visited Abbotsford with Dr. J. G. Cogswell, "another well accomplished Yankee," as Scott makes mention of the young American scholars in a letter to Southey."* Mr. Ticknor had already at that time become a proficient in the romance dialects of the Provençal, and collected many of the curiosities of Castilian literature. It was probably these out-of-the-way acquisitions, which lay in the path of Scott's favorite studies, which led him, in the same letter, to note his visitor as "a wondrous fellow for romantic lore and antiquarian research." With Southey, Mr. Ticknor held and continued to hold till the death of the poet, the most intimate relations of friendly correspondence and association, in similar pursuits of learning and scholarship.

During this absence Mr. Ticknor was appointed in 1817 the first incumbent of a new professorship founded at Harvard, of the French and Spanish Languages and Literature, and of the Belles Lettres—in fact, a general Professorship of Modern Literature. Well qualified for the work he returned to America, and became actively engrossed in its duties, delivering lectures on French and Spanish Literature; on particular authors, as Dante and Goethe; on the English poets, and other kindred topics. "We well remember," says Mr. Prescott the historian, in an article in the North American Review,* "the sensation produced on the first delivery of these lectures, which served to break down the barrier which had so long confined the student to a converse with antiquity; they opened to him a free range among those great masters of modern literature, who had hitherto been veiled in the obscurity of a foreign idiom. The influence of this instruction was soon visible in the higher education as well as the literary ardor shown by the graduates. So decided was the impulse thus given to the popular sentiment, that considerable apprehension was felt lest modern literature was to receive a disproportionate share of attention in the scheme of collegiate education."

Geo: Ticknor.

After fifteen years passed in these liberal duties at Harvard, Mr. Ticknor, in 1835, resigned his professorship, and with his family paid a second visit to Europe. He passed three years there at

* Lockhart's Scott, ch. 44.

* January, 1850.

this time in England and the Continent; collecting books on Spanish literature, with the assistance of a scholar well known for his aid to American authors, Don Pascual de Gayangos, Professor of Arabic in the University of Madrid.

In 1840, after his return to America, completely armed by his studies in Europe, the mental experience of his previous course of lectures, and with the rich resources of an unexampled collection of Castilian literature in his library, Mr. Ticknor commenced his important work on Spanish literature. It had been his intention at first to prepare an edition of his lectures; but these he soon laid aside for his more comprehensive undertaking.

The History of Spanish Literature was published in three volumes in 1849, in London and New York; being stereotyped under the author's careful supervision at the Harvard University Press at Cambridge. The book at once took its position among scholars, and those best qualified to weigh its merits, on both sides of the Atlantic, as a standard contribution to the history of literature—a department which from some neglect, or from the inherent difficulties of such themes, has secured comparatively few classic productions. Though Spain had received more attention in this way than some other countries in the works of Bouterwek and Sismondi; yet from the partial attempts of these eminent writers, and from the hitherto unexplored fields of investigation now opened by Mr. Ticknor, the book of the latter was essentially a new production. The extent of its research was universally admired, and not less the extreme faithfulness with which the author had disclosed to the reader in the text and notes the exact means of information. There is certainly no work of the kind which surpasses this in diligent, conscientious research. The style was no less an indication of this faithful habit of mind. At once modest and dignified, and associated with a sound judgment, it followed the subject without prejudice, or those affectations which are the besetting and almost inevitable sins of writers on taste.

The History of Spanish Literature is divided by the author into three periods: from the first appearance of the present written language, to the early part of the reign of the Emperor Charles the Fifth, or from the end of the twelfth century to the beginning of the sixteenth; from the accession of the Austrian family to its extinction, to the end of the seventeenth century; and from the accession of the Bourbon family to the invasion of Bonaparte, or from the beginning of the eighteenth century to the early part of the nineteenth. To the first belong a valuable essay on the Origin of the Spanish Language; the early literature of the ballad, including the national poems of the Cid, the chronicle, the romance, and the drama, topics all of curious historical as well as literary interest, opening many points of learned and philosophical investigation. The second period introduces us to the glories of the Castilian, the theatre of Lope de Vega and Calderon, the novels of Cervantes, the historical and lyric schools—with the varied development of a rich, fertile, original literature. The third is the broken age of decline under historic influences which are skilfully traced.

In addition to the research and display of critical powers required in such a work, Mr. Ticknor had on his hands no inconsiderable care in translation both in prose and poetry. Here his labors are acknowledged to be exact and felicitous. He renders a dramatic sketch or a ballad poem with elegance and spirit.

In fine, to adopt the authority of a most competent judge of the whole matter, Mr. Prescott, "Mr. Ticknor's history is conducted in a truly philosophical spirit. Instead of presenting a barren record of books, which, like the catalogue of a gallery of paintings, is of comparatively little use to those who have not previously studied them, he illustrates the work by the personal history of their authors, and this, again, by the history of the times in which they lived; affording, by the reciprocal action of one and the other, a complete record of Spanish civilization, both social and intellectual. It would be difficult to find a work more thoroughly penetrated with the true Castilian spirit, or to which the general student, or the student of civil history, may refer to no less advantage than one who is simply interested in the progress of letters."* The History of Spanish Literature has been translated into Spanish and German.

The literary productions of Mr. Ticknor, besides this work, have been few. In 1837 he edited *The Remains of Nathaniel Appleton Haven, with a Memoir of his Life*; a tribute to the memory of an accomplished friend, of estimable character, who died the year previously at the early age of thirty-six, after he had given proofs of ability in several departments of literary effort.† Mr. Ticknor also published in 1825, in the North American Review, to which he was a contributor, a life of Lafayette, which, after being enlarged, passed through several editions in the United States and England, and was translated in France and Germany. Mr. Ticknor was also an early contributor to the Monthly Anthology.

In his character and pursuits, he is in the best sense of the word a liberal scholar, freely rendering his information to others, and assisting in the literary and benevolent or refined social movements of the day.‡

THE AUTHOR'S KEY-NOTE TO SPANISH LITERATURE.

There are two traits of the earliest Spanish literature which are so separate and peculiar, that they must be noticed from the outset,—religious faith and knightly loyalty,—traits which are hardly less apparent in the "Partidas" of Alfonso the Wise, in the stories of Don John Manuel, in the loose wit of the Archpriest of Hita, and in the worldly wisdom of the Chancellor Ayala, than in the professedly devout poems of Berceo, and in the professedly chival-

* North American Review, January, 1850. An admirable analysis of the whole work.

† N. A. Haven was born in Portsmouth, N. H., January 14, 1790, of an eminent family in the state. He was educated at Harvard, studied law, became versed in history and literature, and appeared as an orator on several public occasions. In 1814 he delivered a Fourth of July Oration at Portsmouth, the next year visited Europe, and settled on his return at Portsmouth. In 1816 he delivered a Phi Beta Kappa Address at Dartmouth. Between 1821 and 1825 he edited "The Portsmouth Journal." He delivered an oration at Portsmouth, May 21, 1823, on the second Centennial celebration of the landing of the first settlers. He wrote on several philanthropic topics, papers which are included in the Remains. He died at Portsmouth, June 3, 1826

‡ Men of the Time, 1852.

rous chronicles of the Cid and Fernan Gonzalez. They are, therefore, from the earliest period, to be marked among the prominent features in Spanish literature.

Nor should we be surprised at this. The Spanish national character, as it has existed from its first development down to our own days, was mainly formed in the earlier part of that solemn contest which began the moment the Moors landed beneath the rock of Gibraltar, and which cannot be said to have ended, until, in the time of Philip the Third, the last remnants of their unhappy race were cruelly driven from the shores which their fathers, nine centuries before, had so unjustifiably invaded. During this contest, and especially during the two or three dark centuries when the earliest Spanish poetry appeared, nothing but an invincible religious faith, and a no less invincible loyalty to their own princes, could have sustained the Christian Spaniards in their disheartening struggle against their infidel oppressors. It was, therefore, a stern necessity which made these two high qualities elements of the Spanish national character,—a character all whose energies were for ages devoted to the one grand object of their prayers as Christians and their hopes as patriots, the expulsion of their hated invaders.

But Castilian poetry was, from the first, to an extraordinary degree, an outpouring of the popular feeling and character. Tokens of religious submission and knightly fidelity, akin to each other in their birth, and often relying on each other for strength in their trials, are, therefore, among its earliest attributes. We must not, then, be surprised, if we hereafter find, that submission to the Church and loyalty to the king constantly break through the mass of Spanish literature, and breathe their spirit from nearly every portion of it,—not, indeed, without such changes in the mode of expression as the changed condition of the country in successive ages demanded, but still always so strong in their original attributes as to show that they survive every convulsion of the state, and never cease to move onward by their first impulse. In truth, while their very early development leaves no doubt that they are national, their nationality makes it all but inevitable that they should become permanent.

SPANISH LOVE BALLAD—FROM THE ROMANCERO OF PEDRO FLORES. 1594.

Her sister Miguela
Once chid little Jane,
And the words that she spoke
Gave a great deal of pain.

"You went yesterday playing,
A child like the rest;
And now you come out,
More than other girls dressed.

"You take pleasure in sighs,
In sad music delight;
With the dawning you rise,
Yet sit up half the night.

"When you take up your work,
You look vacant and stare,
And gaze on your sampler,
But miss the stitch there.

"You 're in love, people say,
Your actions all show it:—
New ways we shall have,
When mother shall know it.

"She 'll nail up the windows,
And lock up the door;
Leave to frolic and dance
She will give us no more.

"Old aunt will be sent
To take us to mass,
And stop all our talk
With the girls as we pass.

"And when we walk out,
She will bid our old shrew
Keep a faithful account
Of what our eyes do.

"And mark who goes by,
If I peep through the blind,
And be sure and detect us
In looking behind.

"Thus for your idle follies
Must I suffer too,
And, though nothing I've done,
Be punished like you."

"O, sister Miguela,
Your chiding pray spare;—
That I've troubles you guess,
But not what they are.

"Young Pedro it is,
Old Juan's fair youth;
But he's gone to the wars,
And where is his truth?

"I loved him sincerely,
I loved all he said;
But I fear he is fickle,
I fear he is fled!

"He is gone of free choice,
Without summons or call,
And 'tis foolish to love him,
Or like him at all."

"Nay, rather do thou
To God pray above,
Lest Pedro return,
And again you should love,"

Said Miguela in jest,
As she answered poor Jane;
"For when love has been bought
At cost of such pain,

"What hope is there, sister,
Unless the soul part,
That the passion you cherish
Should yield up your heart?

"Your years will increase,
But so will your pains,
And this you may learn
From the proverb's old strains:—

"'If, when but a child,
Love's power you own,
Pray, what will you do
When you older are grown?'"

HYMN ON THE ASCENSION—FROM THE SPANISH OF LUIS DE LEON.

And dost thou, holy Shepherd, leave,
Thine unprotected flock alone,
Here, in this darksome vale, to grieve,
While thou ascend'st thy glorious throne?

O, where can they their hopes now turn,
Who never lived but on thy love?
Where rest the hearts for thee that burn,
When thou art lost in light above?

How shall those eyes now find repose
That turn, in vain, thy smile to see?
What can they hear save mortal woes,
Who lose thy voice's melody?

And who shall lay his tranquil hand
  Upon the troubled ocean's might?
Who hush the winds by his command?
  Who guide us through this starless night?

For Thou art gone!—that cloud so bright,
  That bears thee from our love away,
Springs upward through the dazzling light,
  And leaves us here to weep and pray!

DON QUIXOTE.

This honor, if we may trust the uniform testimony of two centuries, belongs, beyond question, to his Don Quixote,—the work which, above all others, not merely of his own age, but of all modern times, bears most deeply the impression of the national character it represents, and has, therefore, in return, enjoyed a degree and extent of national favor never granted to any other. When Cervantes began to write it is wholly uncertain. For twenty years preceding the appearance of the First Part he printed nothing; and the little we know of him, during that long and dreary period of his life, shows only how he obtained a hard subsistence for himself and his family by common business agencies, which, we have reason to suppose, were generally of trifling importance, and which, we are sure, were sometimes distressing in their consequences. The tradition, therefore, of his persecutions in La Mancha, and his own averment that the Don Quixote was begun in a prison, are all the hints we have received concerning the circumstances under which it was first imagined; and that such circumstances should have tended to such a result is a striking fact in the history. not only of Cervantes, but of the human mind, and shows how different was his temperament from that commonly found in men of genius.

His purpose in writing Don Quixote has sometimes been enlarged by the ingenuity of a refined criticism, until it has been made to embrace the whole of the endless contrast between the poetical and the prosaic in our natures,—between heroism and generosity on one side, as if they were mere illusions, and a cold selfishness on the other, as if it were the truth and reality of life. But this is a metaphysical conclusion drawn from views of the work at once imperfect and exaggerated; a conclusion contrary to the spirit of the age, which was not given to a satire so philosophical and generalizing, and contrary to the character of Cervantes himself, as we follow it from the time when he first became a soldier, through all his trials in Algiers, and down to the moment when his warm and trusting heart dictated the Dedication of "Persiles and Sigismunda" to the Count de Lemos. His whole spirit, indeed, seems rather to have been filled with a cheerful confidence in human virtue, and his whole bearing in life seems to have been a contradiction to that discouraging and saddening scorn for whatever is elevated and generous, which such an interpretation of the Don Quixote necessarily implies.

Nor does he himself permit us to give to his romance any such secret meaning: for, at the very beginning of the work, he announces it to be his sole purpose to break down the vogue and authority of books of chivalry, and at the end of the whole, he declares anew, in his own person, that "he had no other desire than to render abhorred of men the false and absurd stories contained in books of chivalry;" exulting in his success, as an achievement of no small moment. And such, in fact, it was; for we have abundant proof that the fanaticism for these romances was so great in Spain, during the sixteenth century, as to have become matter of alarm to the more judicious. Many of the distinguished contemporary authors speak of its mischiefs, and among the rest the venerable Luis de Granada, and Malon de Chaide, who wrote the eloquent "Conversion of Mary Magdalen." Guevara, the learned and fortunate courtier of Charles the Fifth, declares that "men did read nothing in his time but such shameful books as 'Amadis de Gaula,' 'Tristan,' 'Primaleon,' and the like; the acute author of the "Dialogue on Languages," says that "the ten years he passed at court he wasted in studying 'Florisando,' 'Lisuarte,' 'The Knight of the Cross,' and other such books, more than he can name;" and from different sources we know, what, indeed, we may gather from Cervantes himself, that many who read these fictions took them for true histories. At last, they were deemed so noxious, that, in 1553, they were prohibited by law from being printed or sold in the American colonies, and in 1555 the same prohibition, and even the burning of all copies of them extant in Spain itself, was earnestly asked for by the Cortes. The evil, in fact, had become formidable, and the wise began to see it.

To destroy a passion that had struck its roots so deeply in the character of all classes of men, to break up the only reading which at that time could be considered widely popular and fashionable, was certainly a bold undertaking, and one that marks anything rather than a scornful or broken spirit, or a want of faith in what is most to be valued in our common nature. The great wonder is, that Cervantes succeeded. But that he did there is no question. No book of chivalry was written after the appearance of Don Quixote, in 1605; and from the same date, even those already enjoying the greatest favor ceased, with one or two unimportant exceptions, to be reprinted; so that, from that time to the present, they have been constantly disappearing, until they are now among the rarest of literary curiosities;—a solitary instance of the power of genius to destroy, by a single well-timed blow, an entire department, and that, too, a flourishing and favored one, in the literature of a great and proud nation.

The general plan Cervantes adopted to accomplish this object, without, perhaps, foreseeing its whole course, and still less all its results, was simple as well as original. In 1605, he published the First Part of Don Quixote, in which a country gentleman of La Mancha—full of genuine Castilian honor and enthusiasm, gentle and dignified in his character, trusted by his friends, and loved by his dependants—is represented as so completely crazed by long reading the most famous books of chivalry, that he believes them to be true, and feels himself called on to become the impossible knight-errant they describe,—nay, actually goes forth into the world to defend the oppressed and avenge the injured, like the heroes of his romances.

To complete his chivalrous equipment—which he had begun by fitting up for himself a suit of armor strange to his century—he took an esquire out of his neighborhood; a middle-aged peasant, ignorant and credulous to excess, but of great good-nature; a glutton and a liar; selfish and gross, yet attached to his master; shrewd enough occasionally to see the folly of their position, but always amusing, and sometimes mischievous, in his interpretations of it. These two sally forth from their native village in search of adventures, of which the excited imagination of the knight, turning windmills into giants, solitary inns into castles, and galley-slaves into oppressed gentlemen, finds abundance, wherever he goes; while the esquire translates them all into the plain prose of truth with an admirable simplicity, quite unconscious of its own humor, and rendered the more striking by its contrast with the lofty and courteous dignity and magnificent illusions of the superior personage. There could, of course, be but one consistent termination of adventures like these. The knight and his esquire suffer a series of ridiculous discomfitures, and are at last brought home like madmen, to their native village, where Cervantes leaves them, with an intimation that the story of their adventures is by no means ended. * * * This latter half of Don Quixote is a contradiction of the proverb Cervantes cites in it,—that second parts were never yet good for much. It is, in fact, better than the first. It shows more freedom and vigor; and if the caricature is sometimes pushed to the very verge of what is permitted, the invention, the style of thought, and, indeed, the materials throughout, are richer, and the finish is more exact. The character of Samson Carrasco, for instance, is a very happy, though somewhat bold, addition to the original persons of the drama; and the adventures at the castle of the duke and duchess, where Don Quixote is fooled to the top of his bent; the managements of Sancho as governor of his island; the visions and dreams of the cave of Montesinos; the scenes with Roque Guinart, the freebooter, and with Gines de Passamonte, the galley-slave and puppet-show man; together with the mock-heroic hospitalities of Don Antonio Moreno at Barcelona, and the final defeat of the knight there, are all admirable. In truth, every thing in this Second Part, especially its general outline and tone, show that time and a degree of success he had not before known, had ripened and perfected the strong manly sense and sure insight into human nature which are visible everywhere in the works of Cervantes, and which here become a part, as it were, of his peculiar genius, whose foundations had been laid, dark and deep, amidst the trials and sufferings of his various life.

But throughout both parts, Cervantes shows the impulses and instincts of an original power with most distinctness in his development of the characters of Don Quixote and Sancho; characters in whose contrast and opposition is hidden the full spirit of his peculiar humor, and no small part of what is most characteristic of the entire fiction. They are his prominent personages. He delights, therefore, to have them as much as possible in the front of his scene. They grow visibly upon his favor as he advances, and the fondness of his liking for them makes him constantly produce them in lights and relations as little foreseen by himself as they are by his readers. The knight, who seems to have been originally intended for a parody of the Amadis, becomes gradually a detached, separate, and wholly independent personage, into whom is infused so much of a generous and elevated nature, such gentleness and delicacy, such a pure sense of honor, and such a warm love for whatever is noble and good, that we feel almost the same attachment to him that the barber and the curate did, and are almost as ready as his family was to mourn over his death.

The case of Sancho is again very similar, and perhaps in some respects stronger. At first, he is introduced as the opposite of Don Quixote, and used merely to bring out his master's peculiarities in a more striking relief. It is not until we have gone through nearly half of the First Part that he utters one of those proverbs which form afterwards the staple of his conversation and humor; and it is not till the opening of the Second Part, and, indeed, not till he comes forth, in all his mingled shrewdness and credulity, as governor of Barataria, that his character is quite developed and completed to the full measure of its grotesque, yet congruous proportions.

Cervantes, in truth, came at last, to love these creations of his marvellous power, as if they were real, familiar personages, and to speak of them and treat them with an earnestness and interest that tend much to the illusion of his readers. Both Don Quixote and Sancho are thus brought before us, like such living realities, that at this moment, the figures of the crazed, gaunt, dignified knight, and of his round, selfish, and most amusing esquire, dwell bodied forth in the imaginations of more, among all conditions of men throughout Christendom, than any other of the creations of human talent. The greatest of the great poets—Homer, Dante, Shakespeare, Milton—have no doubt risen to loftier heights, and placed themselves in more imposing relations with the noblest attributes of our nature; but Cervantes—always writing under the unchecked impulse of his own genius, and instinctively concentrating in his fiction whatever was peculiar to the character of his nation—has shown himself of kindred to all times and all lands; to the humblest degrees of cultivation as well as to the highest; and has thus, beyond all other writers, received in return a tribute of sympathy and admiration from the universal spirit of humanity. * * * The romance, however, which he threw so carelessly from him, and which, I am persuaded, he regarded rather as a bold effort to break up the absurd taste of his time for the fancies of chivalry than as any thing of more serious import, has been established by an uninterrupted, and, it may be said, an unquestioned, success ever since, both as the oldest classical specimen of romantic fiction, and as one of the most remarkable monuments of modern genius. But though this may be enough to fill the measure of human fame and glory, it is not all to which Cervantes is entitled; for, if we would do him the justice that would have been dearest to his own spirit, and even if we would ourselves fully comprehend and enjoy the whole of his Don Quixote, we should, as we read it, bear in mind, that this delightful romance was not the result of a youthful exuberance of feeling and a happy external condition, nor composed in his best years, when the spirits of its author were light and his hopes high; but that—with all its unquenchable and irresistible humor, with its bright views of the world, and his cheerful trust in goodness and virtue—it was written in his old age, at the conclusion of a life nearly every step of which had been marked with disappointed expectations, disheartening struggles, and sore calamities; that he began it in a prison, and that it was finished when he felt the hand of death pressing heavy and cold upon his heart. If this be remembered as we read, we may feel, as we ought to feel, what admiration and reverence are due, not only to the living power of Don Quixote, but to the character and genius of Cervantes;—if it be forgotten or underrated, we shall fail in regard to both.

LA DAMA DUENDE OF CALDERON.

"The Fairy Lady," is another of Calderon's dramas that is full of life, spirit, and ingenuity. Its scene is laid on the day of the baptism of Prince Balthasar, heir-apparent of Philip the Fourth, which, as we know, occurred on the 4th of November, 1629; and the piece itself was, therefore, probably written and acted soon afterwards. If we may judge by the number of times Calderon complacently refers to it, we cannot doubt that it was a favorite with him; and if we judge by its intrinsic merits, we may be sure it was a favorite with the public.

Doña Angela, the heroine of the intrigue, a widow, young, beautiful, and rich, lives at Madrid, in the house of her two brothers; but, from circumstances connected with her affairs, her life there is so retired, that nothing is known of it abroad. Don Manuel, a friend, arrives in the city to visit one of these brothers; and, as he approaches the house, a lady strictly veiled stops him in the street, and conjures him, if he be a cavalier of honor, to prevent her from being further pursued by a gentleman already close behind. This lady is Doña Angela, and the gentleman is her brother, Don Luis, who is pursuing her only because he observes that she carefully conceals herself from him. The two cavaliers not being acquainted with each other,—for Don Manuel had come to visit the other brother,—a dispute is easily excited, and a duel follows, which is interrupted by the arrival of this other brother, and an explanation of his friendship for Don Manuel.

Don Manuel is now brought home, and established in the house of the two cavaliers, with all the courtesy due to a distinguished guest. His apartments, however, are connected with those of Doña Angela by a secret door, known only to herself and her confidential maid; and finding she is thus unexpectedly brought near a person who has risked his life to save her, she determines to put herself into a mysterious communication with him.

But Doña Angela is young and thoughtless. When she enters the stranger's apartment, she is tempted to be mischievous, and leaves behind marks of her wild humor that are not to be mistaken. The servant of Don Manuel thinks it is an evil spirit, or at best a fairy, that plays such fantastic tricks; disturbing the private papers of his master, leaving notes on his table, throwing the furniture of the room into confusion, and—from an accident—once jostling its occupants in the dark. At last, the master himself is confounded; and though he once catches a glimpse of the mischievous lady, as she escapes into her own part of the house, he knows not what to make of the apparition. He says:—

> She glided like a spirit, and her light
> Did all fantastic seem. But still her form
> Was human: I touched and felt its substance,
> And she had mortal fears, and, woman-like,
> Shrunk back again with dainty modesty.
> At last, like an illusion, all dissolved,
> And, like a phantasm, melted quite away
> If, then, to my conjectures I give rein,
> By heaven above, I neither know nor guess
> What I must doubt or what I may believe.

But the tricksy lady, who has fairly frolicked herself in love with the handsome young cavalier, is tempted too far by her brilliant successes, and, being at last detected in the presence of her astonished brothers, the intrigue, which is one of the most complicated and gay to be found on any theatre, ends with an explanation of her fairy humors and her marriage with Don Manuel.

WILLIAM H. PRESCOTT.

William Hickling Prescott, the historian, is the son of William Prescott, a distinguished jurist, who died at Boston in 1844, and the grandson of Colonel William Prescott, who commanded at Bunker Hill on the memorable 17th of June, 1775. The father of Mr. Prescott, who was one of the wisest and best as well as one of the ablest men that New England has produced, was a native of Pepperell in Massachusetts, but lived in Salem from 1789 to 1808; and there the Historian was born, May 4, 1796: his mother being the daughter of Thomas Hickling, who for nearly half a century held Washington's commission as Consul at St. Michael's. But Mr. Prescott's family having removed to Boston when he was hardly twelve years old, his literary training was chiefly in that city and in Cambridge, where he was graduated in 1814 with honors suited to the classical tastes he had cultivated with much more than common success, both during his University course and earlier.

His original intention was, to devote himself to the profession which his father's eminence had naturally made attractive to him. But, just as he was closing his academical career in Harvard College, an accident deprived him instantly of the use of one eye; and the other, after much suffering, became so enfeebled and impaired, that it was soon plain that he could devote himself to no course of life in which his occupations would not be controlled more or less by the results of this infirmity. He struggled against it, however, as well as he might. Two years he spent in travelling through England, France, and Italy, and in endeavors to procure alleviations for his misfortune from the great oculists of London and Paris; but it was all in vain. His general health, indeed, was strengthened and his character developed by it; but the infirmity from which he sought relief was beyond the reach of remedies, and had been so, no doubt, from the first.

Soon after his return home, therefore, he looked round to see what course was still open to him for that active period of life on whose threshold he then stood; and with a deliberation of purpose rare in one so young, he determined to become a historian. But first he went through a careful course of intellectual discipline in the classics of antiquity which had always been his favorite study, and in the literatures of France, Italy, and Spain, which followed them in natural sequence. To this task, he devoted, on a well considered plan, ten years; and, except that he often suffered severely from inflammations of the debilitated organ of sight, and that his reading and studies of all kinds were carried on to much disadvantage from the necessity of using the eyes of others rather than his own, they were years of great happiness to him. His industry never flagged; his courage never faltered; his spirits, buoyant by nature, never sank under the burdens imposed upon them. It was the period when he laid deep and sure the foundations of his coming success.

His next task was to choose a subject. In this, he was eminently fortunate. Sixty years had just elapsed since, in 1769, Dr. Robertson had succeeded in fastening the attention of the world on the reign of Charles V., when the power of Spain was greater than it ever was before or than it has ever been since, and when that wide European system was consolidated, which was first broken up by Buonaparte and which Buonaparte's conquerors have so imperfectly reconstructed. But Robertson did not go far enough back in the annals of Spain to make his work all that it should have been. The central point in the history of modern Spain is the capture of Grenada, and he should have embraced it in the plan of a work intended to present that country in its entrance upon the grand theatre of European affairs. All before that decisive epoch, for eight centuries, had been, as it were, preparation; all that has happened since, for four centuries, has been results and consequences. The power which had been created by the Moorish wars, and which had been exclusively concentrated upon them for so long a period, was then first let loose upon the rest of Europe, while, almost at the same moment, the discovery of America and its boundless wealth came in to give that power a life and efficiency which it never before possessed, and which, beyond the Pyrenees, had hardly been suspected or thought of; turning all the gentlemen of Spain into soldiers and sending them forth upon adventure to fight wherever the spirit of loyalty might call them, either for the glory of their monarchs or for the advancement of the Catholic faith. Robertson, indeed, in his elaborate and philosophical introduction to his history, has endeavored to supply this deficiency in his plan; but that Essay, a noble portico to his work, is rather an account of the state of things in the rest of Europe, out of which grew what is most distinctive in the character of more recent times, than an explanation of the previous condition of Spain itself, on which Charles V. established his vast power, and on whose basis Philip II. endeavored to build up an empire wider than the Roman, because it was to embrace the New World as well as the Old.

Mr. Prescott, no doubt, perceived this, and chose for the subject of his first work, *The Reign of Ferdinand and Isabella;* the grand consolidation of Spain into one compact monarchy; the final overthrow of Moslem power in Western Europe, and the discovery of America and its wealth. It was a noble subject, imposing in each of its greater divisions, and interesting alike to both hemispheres. With what ability he treated it, is known on the other side of the Atlantic no less than on this, for the original work, which after nearly ten years of faithful labor upon it first appeared in 1838, has not only been printed and reprinted in the United States, in England and France, but has been translated into Spanish, Italian, and German,

and is familiar, as one of the world's classics, wherever history is studied.

On looking again for a subject, Mr. Prescott may have been anew partly influenced by the imperfect success of Dr. Robertson, and partly or chiefly by the direction given already to his own inquiries in that portion of his Ferdinand and Isabella which relates to America. At any rate, Robertson's History of America, published in 1777, is entirely unequal to the claims it makes. Simancas was closed to him, and the admirable collection at the Lonja of Seville was not yet imagined, so that he had not the materials needful for his task; besides which his plan was not only too vast, but, in its separate parts, was ill proportioned and ill-adjusted. The great results, however, upon Spain, and indeed upon all Europe, of the conquests on the American continent made by Spanish adventurers, follow, by an almost inevitable succession, accounts such as Mr. Prescott had already given of its discovery. He therefore naturally turned his thoughts in this direction, and skilfully confining his labors to the two portions of the newly discovered countries that had the most influence on the fates and fortunes of Spain and of Europe, instead of extending them as Robertson had done over the whole of North and South America, he gave the world successively his *Conquest of Mexico* in 1843 and his *Conquest of Peru* in 1847. Both of these works are written largely from manuscript materials obtained in Spain. The first, from the very nature of its subject, is the most effective and popular, comprehending that marvellous series of military adventures, which read more like a cruel romance than the results of sober history; while the last, so full of philosophy in its accounts of the early traditions of Peru, and so full of wisdom in its explanation of the healing government of Gasca, is no less important for its teachings to the world. Both are written in Mr. Prescott's most attractive and brilliant style, and were followed by the amplest and most honorable success alike in Europe and America, and in their translations made on both sides of the Atlantic, and especially in Mexico, where two have appeared.

Mr. Prescott had now shown how the military power of Spain, which had been developed in a manner so extraordinary by the Moorish wars, had begun to spread its victories over Europe and America; and how the wealth found in its golden colonies was sustaining further and wider conquests that were soon destined to disturb all Christendom. We almost regret, therefore, that he had not continued the History of Spain and her foreign wars and conquests from the point where he left them at the end of the reign of Ferdinand and Isabella. Certainly, on one side, this is the view that immediately presents itself; for the work of Robertson on Charles V., important as it has been, cannot, we conceive, be regarded as the final record of the great and stirring period it embraces; so imperfect is his knowledge of the deep and complicated movements in Germany that belong to it, and so much is he wanting in a clear comprehension of Spain and of the Spanish character at the time they were becoming preponderant in Europe. Mr. Prescott, we are persuaded, would have treated this most attractive subject with the hand of a master, and so have rendered a new service to the History of the World at one of the turning points in its destinies. But it is understood that he has modestly decided otherwise, and that leaving Dr. Robertson in undisputed possession of the reign of Charles V., he is about to give the public the History of Philip II.

Here, no doubt, he has a field both ample and free; for, saving the slight history of Dr. Watson, which, since 1777, when it was published, has been good-naturedly received by the world as an account of the times of Philip II., Mr. Prescott will find no work on the subject worth naming, either in Spain or out of it. And yet such a subject might well have claimed, long since, the most earnest efforts of the highest talent. At home—in Spain we mean—its details are full of interest and of grave teachings. They begin with the solemn farce of the Cloister life of Charles V. by which all the elder historians have been duped, but which, thanks to Mr. Stirling, M. Mignet, and M. Gachard, can now be placed where it belongs and be exhibited as what it really was. Next, we have the dark death of the miserable and unworthy Don Carlos, of which his father may never be convicted, but from which he never can be absolved; and which after being turned into poetry by Schiller and so many others, among whom Lord John Russell should not have permitted himself to be placed, ought at last to be reduced to the plain prose of exact history. Later, we have the murder of Escovedo and the consequent shameful persecution of that brilliant adventurer, Antonio Perez, which Mignet again has set in its true light, as the heartless work of Philip, in order to conceal his own hand in a murder committed by his own orders. And above all and everywhere on the soil of Spain, or wherever Spanish power reached, we have the Inquisition and the Church stretching up like a black cloud between heaven and earth, and casting their blight over even the patriotism and loyalty of the Spanish people; allying their love of country to bigotry, and making their devotion to despotism, as it were, a part of their religious humility. All this, too, has never been explained as it ought to be, nor made the solemn warning to the world, which, in Mr. Prescott's hands, it will assuredly become.

Abroad, out of Spain, his subject is yet more striking. It embraces all Europe and its interests. The old wars against the Moors come up again; the siege of Malta; the cruel contest in the Alpuxarras; but, above all, Don John of Austria, the most romantic of military captains, and his victory at Lepanto, by which the hated Moslem was, for the second time, driven back from Western Europe by Spanish valor and enthusiasm;—how they rise before us, as if they belonged to the earlier period of Spanish history, and connect us with its heroic adventures. Then, to counterbalance them, come the conquest of Portugal, which, when Don Sebastian had mysteriously perished in Africa, fell an easy prey to his crafty cousin: the troubles with France in the days of the three last Henries, and during the struggles of French Protestantism, not forgetting the battle of St. Quentin, where a characteristic vow of Philip, breathed perhaps in personal fear, built the no less characteristic Escurial; the ruinous war of the Netherlands ending with their loss; and the strange relations with England, both when Philip reigned there with Mary, and when in the time of Elizabeth he undertook that bold conquest of the island which would have added the possession of North to that of South America—aye, and perhaps even that of all India beyond the Cape of Good Hope. Each of these subjects, we mean to say, is worthy of the highest historical talent, while all taken together and kept in their respective positions and proportions by the wary, inflexible, and unscrupulous genius of Philip himself—always in the foreground of his own affairs—always the master-spirit, whatever is done or proposed—and always carefully adjusting his projects into the vast framework of his own ambition to establish an Universal Monarchy, whose seat should be in the South of Europe, and whose foundations should be laid in the Faith of the Church of Rome;—these grand materials, thus grouped together, constitute a subject for history which the great masters of ancient or of modern times might well envy to Mr. Prescott. That it will—even more than anything he has yet done—insure him a place at their side, we do not doubt.

Since the appearance of Ferdinand and Isabella in 1838, literary bodies, at home and abroad, have showered on Mr. Prescott their higher honors; beginning with Columbia College in New York, which gave him the degree of Doctor of Laws in 1840, and ending, so far as we have observed, with a similar degree from the ancient University of Oxford in 1850; when, on a visit to England, he was received in a manner the most flattering by whatever is most distinguished in society and letters. In this interval, however (we think it was in 1845), he received the yet higher distinction of being elected a corresponding member of the class of Moral and Political Philosophy in the French Institute, as successor to Navarrete, the Spanish historian. The vacancy was certainly well and appropriately filled.

Except his great historical works, we believe that Mr. Prescott has published only a volume of Miscellanies, chiefly reviews from the North American, which appeared first in 1845, and has since been reprinted both in England and the United States.*

THE RETURN OF COLUMBUS AFTER HIS FIRST VOYAGE—FROM THE HISTORY OF FERDINAND AND ISABELLA.

In the spring of 1493, while the court was still at Barcelona, letters were received from Christopher Columbus, announcing his return to Spain, and the successful achievement of his great enterprise, by the discovery of land beyond the western ocean. The delight and astonishment, raised by this intelligence, were proportioned to the skepticism with which his project had been originally viewed. The sovereigns were now filled with a natural impatience to ascertain the extent and other particulars of the important discovery: and they transmitted instant instructions to the admiral to repair to Barcelona, as soon as he should have made the preliminary arrangements for the further prosecution of his enterprise.

The great navigator had succeeded, as is well known, after a voyage the natural difficulties of which had been much augmented by the distrust and mutinous spirit of his followers, in descrying

* We are indebted for this memoir to the pen of Mr. George Ticknor.

land on Friday, the 12th of October, 1492. After some months spent in exploring the delightful regions, now for the first time thrown open to the eyes of a European, he embarked in the month of January, 1493, for Spain. One of his vessels had previously foundered, and another had deserted him; so that he was left alone to retrace his course across the Atlantic. After a most tempestuous voyage, he was compelled to take shelter in the Tagus, sorely against his inclination. He experienced, however, the most honorable reception from the Portuguese monarch, John the Second, who did ample justice to the great qualities of Columbus, although he had failed to profit by them. After a brief delay, the admiral resumed his voyage, and crossing the bar of Saltes entered the harbor of Palos about noon, on the 15th of March, 1493, being exactly seven months and eleven days since his departure from that port.

Great was the agitation in the little community of Palos, as they beheld the well-known vessel of the admiral reëntering their harbor. Their desponding imaginations had long since consigned him to a watery grave; for, in addition to the preternatural horrors which hung over the voyage, they had experienced the most stormy and disastrous winter within the recollection of the oldest mariners. Most of them had relatives or friends on board. They thronged immediately to the shore, to assure themselves with their own eyes of the truth of their return. When they beheld their faces once more, and saw them accompanied by the numerous evidences which they brought back of the success of the expedition, they burst forth in acclamations of joy and gratulation. They awaited the landing of Columbus, when the whole population of the place accompanied him and his crew to the principal church, where solemn thanksgivings were offered up for their return; while every bell in the village sent forth a joyous peal in honor of the glorious event. The admiral was too desirous of presenting himself before the sovereigns, to protract his stay long at Palos. He took with him on his journey specimens of the multifarious products of the newly discovered regions. He was accompanied by several of the native islanders, arrayed in their simple barbaric costume, and decorated, as he passed through the principal cities, with collars, bracelets, and other ornaments of gold, rudely fashioned; he exhibited also considerable quantities of the same metal in dust, or in crude masses, numerous vegetable exotics, possessed of aromatic or medicinal virtue, and several kinds of quadrupeds unknown in Europe, and birds, whose varieties of gaudy plumage gave a brilliant effect to the pageant. The admiral's progress through the country was everywhere impeded by the multitudes thronging forth to gaze at the extraordinary spectacle, and the more extraordinary man, who, in the emphatic language of that time, which has now lost its force from its familiarity, first revealed the existence of a "New World." As he passed through the busy, populous city of Seville, every window, balcony, and housetop, which could afford a glimpse of him, is described to have been crowded with spectators. It was the middle of April before Columbus reached Barcelona. The nobility and cavaliers in attendance on the court, together with the authorities of the city, came to the gates to receive him, and escorted him to the royal presence. Ferdinand and Isabella were seated, with their son, Prince John, under a superb canopy of state, awaiting his arrival. On his approach, they rose from their seats, and extending their hands to him to salute, caused him to be seated before them. These were unprecedented marks of condescension to a person of Columbus's rank, in the haughty and ceremonious court of Castile. It was, indeed, the proudest moment in the life of Columbus. He had fully established the truth of his long-contested theory, in the face of argument, sophistry, sneer, skepticism, and contempt. He had achieved this, not by chance, but by calculation, supported through the most adverse circumstances by consummate conduct. The honors paid him, which had hitherto been reserved only for rank, or fortune, or military success, purchased by the blood and tears of thousands, were, in his case, a homage to intellectual power, successfully exerted in behalf of the noblest interests of humanity.

After a brief interval, the sovereigns requested from Columbus a recital of his adventures. His manner was sedate and dignified, but warmed by the glow of natural enthusiasm. He enumerated the several islands which he had visited, expatiated on the temperate character of the climate, and the capacity of the soil for every variety of agricultural production, appealing to the samples imported by him, as evidence of their natural fruitfulness. He dwelt more at large on the precious metals to be found in these islands, which he inferred, less from the specimens actually obtained, than from the uniform testimony of the natives to their abundance in the unexplored regions of the interior. Lastly, he pointed out the wide scope afforded to Christian zeal, in the illumination of a race of men, whose minds, far from being wedded to any system of idolatry, were prepared by their extreme simplicity for the reception of pure and uncorrupted doctrine. The last consideration touched Isabella's heart most sensibly; and the whole audience, kindled with various emotions by the speaker's eloquence, filled up the perspective with the gorgeous coloring of their own fancies, as ambition or avarice, or devotional feeling predominated in their bosoms. When Columbus ceased, the king and queen, together with all present, prostrated themselves on their knees in grateful thanksgivings, while the solemn strains of the Te Deum were poured forth by the choir of the royal chapel, as in commemoration of some glorious victory.

QUEEN ISABELLA—FROM THE SAME.

Her person was of the middle height, and well proportioned. She had a clear, fresh complexion, with light blue eyes and auburn hair,—a style of beauty exceedingly rare in Spain. Her features were regular, and universally allowed to be uncommonly handsome. The illusion which attaches to rank, more especially when united with engaging manners, might lead us to suspect some exaggeration in the encomiums so liberally lavished on her. But they would seem to be in a great measure justified by the portraits that remain of her, which combine a faultless symmetry of features with singular sweetness and intelligence of expression.

Her manners were most gracious and pleasing. They were marked by natural dignity and modest reserve, tempered by an affability which flowed from the kindliness of her disposition. She was the last person to be approached with undue familiarity; yet the respect which she imposed was mingled with the strongest feelings of devotion and love. She showed great tact in accommodating herself to the peculiar situation and character of those around her. She appeared in arms at the head of her troops, and shrunk from none of the hardships of war. During the reforms introduced into the religious houses, she visited the nunneries in person, taking her needle-work with her, and passing the day in the society of the inmates. When travelling in Galicia, she attired herself in the costume of the country, borrowing for that purpose the jewels and other ornaments of the ladies there, and returning them with liberal additions. By this condescending and captivating deportment, as well as by her higher qualities, she gained an ascendency over her turbulent subjects, which no king of Spain could ever boast.

She spoke the Castilian with much elegance and correctness. She had an easy fluency of discourse, which, though generally of a serious complexion, was occasionally seasoned with agreeable sallies, some of which have passed into proverbs. She was temperate even to abstemiousness in her diet, seldom or never tasting wine; and so frugal in her table, that the daily expenses for herself and family did not exceed the moderate sum of forty ducats. She was equally simple and economical in her apparel. On all public occasions, indeed, she displayed a royal magnificence; but she had no relish for it in private, and she freely gave away her clothes and jewels, as presents to her friends. Naturally of a sedate, though cheerful temper, she had little taste for the frivolous amusements which make up so much of a court life; and, if she encouraged the presence of minstrels and musicians in her palace, it was to wean her young nobility from the coarser and less intellectual pleasures to which they were addicted.

Among her moral qualities, the most conspicuous, perhaps, was her magnanimity. She betrayed nothing little or selfish, in thought or action. Her schemes were vast, and executed in the same noble spirit, in which they were conceived. She never employed doubtful agents or sinister measures, but the most direct and open policy. She scorned to avail herself of advantages offered by the perfidy of others. Where she had once given her confidence, she gave her hearty and steady support; and she was scrupulous to redeem any pledge she had made to those who ventured in her cause, however unpopular. She sustained Ximenes in all his obnoxious, but salutary reforms. She seconded Columbus in the prosecution of his arduous enterprise, and shielded him from the calumny of his enemies. She did the same good service to her favorite, Gonsalvo de Cordova; and the day of her death was felt, and, as it proved, truly felt by both, as the last of their good fortune. Artifice and duplicity were so abhorrent to her character, and so averse from her domestic policy, that when they appear in the foreign relations of Spain, it is certainly not imputable to her. She was incapable of harboring any petty distrust, or latent malice; and, although stern in the execution and exaction of public justice, she made the most generous allowance, and even sometimes advances, to those who had personally injured her.

But the principle, which gave a peculiar coloring to every feature of Isabella's mind, was piety. It shone forth from the very depths of her soul with a heavenly radiance, which illuminated her whole character. Fortunately, her earliest years had been passed in the rugged school of adversity, under the eye of a mother who implanted in her serious mind such strong principles of religion as nothing in after life had power to shake. At an early age, in the flower of youth and beauty, she was introduced to her brother's court; but its blandishments, so dazzling to a young imagination, had no power over hers; for she was surrounded by a moral atmosphere of purity,

Driving far off each thing of sin and guilt.

Such was the decorum of her manners, that, though encompassed by false friends and open enemies, not the slightest reproach was breathed on her fair name in this corrupt and calumnious court.

THE DEATH OF MONTEZUMA—FROM THE CONQUEST OF MEXICO.

The Indian monarch had rapidly declined, since he had received his injury, sinking, however, quite as much under the anguish of a wounded spirit, as under disease. He continued in the same moody state of insensibility as that already described; holding little communication with those around him, deaf to consolation, obstinately rejecting all medical remedies as well as nourishment. Perceiving his end approach, some of the cavaliers present in the fortress, whom the kindness of his manners had personally attached to him, were anxious to save the soul of the dying prince from the sad doom of those who perish in the darkness of unbelief. They accordingly waited on him, with father Olmedo at their head, and in the most earnest manner implored him to open his eyes to the error of his creed, and consent to be baptized. But Montezuma—whatever may have been suggested to the contrary—seems never to have faltered in his hereditary faith, or to have contemplated becoming an apostate; for surely he merits that name in its most odious application, who, whether Christian or Pagan, renounces his religion without conviction of its falsehood. Indeed, it was a too implicit reliance on its oracles, which had led him to give such easy confidence to the Spaniards. His intercourse with them had, doubtless, not sharpened his desire to embrace their communion; and the calamities of his country he might consider as sent by his gods to punish him for his hospitality to those who had desecrated and destroyed their shrines.

When father Olmedo, therefore, kneeling at his side, with the uplifted crucifix, affectionately besought him to embrace the sign of man's redemption, he coldly repulsed the priest, exclaiming, "I have but a few moments to live; and will not at this hour desert the faith of my fathers." One thing, however, seemed to press heavily on Montezuma's mind. This was the fate of his children, especially of three daughters, whom he had by his two wives; for there were certain rites of marriage, which distinguished the lawful wife from the concubine. Calling Cortés to his bedside, he earnestly commended these children to his care, as "the most precious jewels that he could leave him." He besought the general to interest his master, the emperor, in their behalf, and to see that they should not be left destitute, but be allowed some portion of their rightful inheritance. "Your lord will do this," he concluded, "if it were only for the friendly offices I have rendered the Spaniards, and for the love I have shown them,—though it has brought me to this condition! But for this I bear them no ill-will." Such, according to Cortés himself, were the words of the dying monarch. Not long after, on the 30th of June, 1520, he expired in the arms of some of his own nobles, who still remained faithful in their attendance on his person. "Thus," exclaims a native historian, one of his enemies, a Tlascalan, "thus died the unfortunate Montezuma, who had swayed the sceptre with such consummate policy and wisdom; and who was held in greater reverence and awe than any other prince of his lineage, or any, indeed, that ever sat on a throne in this Western World. With him may be said to have terminated the royal line of the Aztecs, and the glory to have passed away from the empire, which under him had reached the zenith of its prosperity." "The tidings of his death," says the old Castilian chronicler, Diaz, "were received with real grief by every cavalier and soldier in the army who had had access to his person; for we all loved him as a father,—and no wonder, seeing how good he was." This simple, but emphatic, testimony to his desert, at such a time, is in itself the best refutation of the suspicions occasionally entertained of his fidelity to the Christians.

It is not easy to depict the portrait of Montezuma in its true colors, since it has been exhibited to us under two aspects, of the most opposite and contradictory character. In the accounts gathered of him by the Spaniards, on coming into the country, he was uniformly represented as bold and warlike, unscrupulous as to the means of gratifying his ambition, hollow and perfidious, the terror of his foes, with a haughty bearing which made him feared even by his own people. They found him, on the contrary, not merely affable and gracious, but disposed to waive all the advantages of his own position, and to place them on a footing with himself; making their wishes his law; gentle even to effeminacy in his deportment, and constant in his friendship, while his whole nation was in arms against them. Yet these traits, so contradictory, were truly enough drawn. They are to be explained by the extraordinary circumstances of his position.

When Montezuma ascended the throne he was scarcely twenty-three years of age. Young, and ambitious of extending his empire, he was continually engaged in war, and is said to have been present himself in nine pitched battles. He was greatly renowned for his martial prowess, for he belonged to the *Quachictin*, the highest military order of his nation, and one into which but few even of its sovereigns had been admitted. In later life, he preferred intrigue to violence, as more consonant to his character and priestly education. In this he was as great an adept as any prince of his time, and, by arts not very honorable to himself, succeeded in filching away much of the territory of his royal kinsman of Tezcuco. Severe in the administration of justice, he made important reforms in the arrangement of the tribunals. He introduced other innovations in the royal household, creating new offices, introducing a lavish magnificence and forms of courtly etiquette unknown to his ruder predecessors. He was, in short, most attentive to all that concerned the exterior and pomp of royalty. Stately and decorous, he was careful of his own dignity, and might be said to be as great an "actor of majesty" among the barbarian potentates of the New World, as Louis the Fourteenth was among the polished princes of Europe.

He was deeply tinctured, moreover, with that spirit of bigotry, which threw such a shade over the latter days of the French monarch. He received the Spaniards as the beings predicted by his oracles. The anxious dread, with which he had evaded their proffered visit, was founded on the same feelings which led him so blindly to resign himself to them on their approach. He felt himself rebuked by their superior genius. He at once conceded all that they demanded,—his treasures, his power, even his person. For their sake, he forsook his wonted occupation, his pleasures, his most familiar habits. He might be said to forego his nature; and, as his subjects asserted, to change his sex and become a woman. If we cannot refuse our contempt for the pusillanimity of the Aztec monarch, it should be mitigated by the consideration, that his pusillanimity sprung from his superstition, and that superstition in the savage is the substitute for religious principle in the civilized man.

It is not easy to contemplate the fate of Montezuma without feelings of the strongest compassion;—to see him thus borne along the tide of events beyond his power to avert or control; to see him, like some stately tree, the pride of his own Indian forests, towering aloft in the pomp and majesty of its branches, by its very eminence a mark for the thunderbolt, the first victim of the tempest which was to sweep over its native hills! When the wise king of Tezcuco addressed his royal relative at his coronation, he exclaimed, "Happy the empire, which is now in the meridian of its prosperity, for the sceptre is given to one whom the Almighty has in his keeping; and the nations shall hold him in reverence!" Alas! the subject of this auspicious invocation lived to see his empire melt away like the winter's wreath; to see a strange race drop, as it were, from the clouds on his land; to find himself a prisoner in the palace of his fathers, the companion of those who were the enemies of his gods and his people; to be insulted, reviled, trodden in the dust, by the meanest of his subjects, by those who, a few months previous, had trembled at his glance; drawing his last breath in the halls of the stranger,—a lonely outcast in the heart of his own capital! He was the sad victim of destiny,—a destiny as dark and irresistible in its march, as that which broods over the mythic legends of Antiquity!

MONTEZUMA'S WAY OF LIFE—FROM THE CONQUEST OF MEXICO.

The domestic establishment of Montezuma was on the same scale of barbaric splendor as every thing else about him. He could boast as many wives as are found in the harem of an Eastern sultan. They were lodged in their own apartments, and provided with every accommodation, according to their ideas, for personal comfort and cleanliness. They passed their hours in the usual feminine employments of weaving and embroidery, especially in the graceful feather-work, for which such rich materials were furnished by the royal aviaries. They conducted themselves with strict decorum, under the supervision of certain aged females, who acted in the respectable capacity of duennas, in the same manner as in the religious houses attached to the *teocallis*. The palace was supplied with numerous baths, and Montezuma set the example, in his own person, of frequent ablutions. He bathed at least once, and changed his dress four times, it is said, every day. He never put on the same apparel a second time, but gave it away to his attendants. Queen Elizabeth, with a similar taste for costume, showed a less princely spirit in hoarding her discarded suits. Her wardrobe was, probably, somewhat more costly than that of the Indian emperor.

Besides his numerous female retinue, the halls and antechambers were filled with nobles in constant attendance on his person, who served also as a sort of body-guard. It had been usual for plebeians of merit to fill certain offices in the palace. But the haughty Montezuma refused to be waited upon by any but men of noble birth. They were not unfrequently the sons of the great chiefs, and remained as hostages in the absence of their fathers; thus serving the double purpose of security and state.

His meals the emperor took alone. The well-matted floor of a large saloon was covered with hundreds of dishes. Sometimes Montezuma himself, but more frequently his steward, indicated those which he preferred, and which were kept hot by means of chafing-dishes. The royal bill of fare comprehended, besides domestic animals, game from the distant forests, and fish which, the day before, was swimming in the Gulf of Mexico! They were dressed in manifold ways, for the Aztec *artistes*, as we have already had occasion to notice, had penetrated deep into the mysteries of culinary science.

The meats were served by the attendant nobles, who then resigned the office of waiting on the monarch to maidens selected for their personal grace and beauty. A screen of richly gilt and carved wood was drawn around him, so as to conceal him from vulgar eyes during the repast. He was seated on a cushion, and the dinner was served on a low table covered with a delicate cotton cloth. The dishes were of the finest ware of Cholula. He had a service of gold, which was reserved for religious celebrations. Indeed, it would scarcely have comported with even his princely revenues to have used it on ordinary occasions, when his table equipage was not allowed to appear a second time, but was given away to his attendants. The saloon was lighted by torches made of a resinous wood, which sent forth a sweet odor and, probably, not a little smoke, as they burned. At his meal, he was attended by five or six of his ancient counsellors, who stood at a respectful distance, answering his questions, and occasionally rejoiced by some of the viands with which he complimented them from his table.

This course of solid dishes was succeeded by another of sweetmeats and pastry, for which the Aztec cooks, provided with the important requisites of maize-flour, eggs, and the rich sugar of the aloe, were famous. Two girls were occupied at the further end of the apartment, during dinner, in preparing fine rolls and wafers, with which they garnished the board from time to time. The emperor took no other beverage than the *chocolatl*, a potation of chocolate, flavored with vanilla and other spices, and so prepared as to be reduced to a froth of the consistency of honey, which gradually dissolved in the mouth. This beverage, if so it could be called, was served in golden goblets, with spoons of the same metal or of tortoise-shell finely wrought. The emperor was exceedingly fond of it, to judge from the quantity,—no less than fifty jars or pitchers being prepared for his own daily consumption! Two thousand more were allowed for that of his household.

The general arrangement of the meal seems to have been not very unlike that of Europeans. But no prince in Europe could boast a dessert which could compare with that of the Aztec emperor. For it was gathered fresh from the most opposite climes; and his board displayed the products of his own temperate region, and the luscious fruits of the tropics, plucked, the day previous, from the green groves of the *tierra calliente*, and transmitted with the speed of steam, by means of couriers, to the capital. It was as if some kind fairy should crown our banquets with the spicy products that but yesterday were growing in a sunny isle of the far-off Indian seas!

After the royal appetite was appeased, water was handed to him by the female attendants in a silver basin, in the same manner as had been done before commencing his meal; for the Aztecs were as constant in their ablutions, at these times, as any nation of the East. Pipes were then brought, made of a varnished and richly gilt wood, from which he inhaled, sometimes through the nose, at others through the mouth, the fumes of an intoxicating weed, "called *tobacco*," mingled with liquid-amber. While this soothing process of fumigation was going on, the emperor enjoyed the exhibitions of his mountebanks and jugglers, of whom a regular corps was attached to the palace. No people, not even those of China or Hindostan, surpassed the Aztecs in feats of agility and legerdemain.

Sometimes he amused himself with his jester; for the Indian monarch had his jesters, as well as his more refined brethren of Europe, at that day. Indeed, he used to say, that more instruction was to be gathered from them than from wiser men, for they dared to tell the truth. At other times, he witnessed the graceful dances of his women, or took delight in listening to music,—if the rude minstrelsy of the Mexicans deserve that name,—accompanied by a chant, in a slow and solemn cadence, celebrating the heroic deeds of great Aztec warriors, or of his own princely line.

When he had sufficiently refreshed his spirits with these diversions, he composed himself to sleep, for in his *siesta* he was as regular as a Spaniard. On awaking, he gave audience to ambassadors from foreign states, or his own tributary cities, or to such caciques as had suits to prefer to him. They were introduced by the young nobles in attendance, and, whatever might be their rank, unless of the blood royal, they were obliged to submit to the humiliation of shrouding their rich dresses under the coarse mantle of *nequen*, and entering barefooted, with downcast eyes, into the presence. The emperor addressed few and brief remarks to the suitors, answering them generally by his secretaries; and the parties retired with the same reverential obeisance, taking care to keep their faces turned towards the monarch. Well might Cortés exclaim, that no court, whether of the Grand Seignior or any other infidel, ever displayed so pompous and elaborate a ceremonial!

Besides the crowd of retainers already noticed, the royal household was not complete without a host of artisans constantly employed in the erection or repair of buildings, besides a great number of jewellers and persons skilled in working metals, who found abundant demand for their trinkets among the dark-eyed beauties of the harem. The imperial mummers and jugglers were also very numerous, and the dancers belonging to the palace occupied a particular district of the city, appropriated exclusively to them.

The maintenance of this little host, amounting to some thousands of individuals, involved a heavy expenditure, requiring accounts of a complicated, and, to a simple people, it might well be, embarrassing nature. Every thing, however, was conducted with perfect order; and all the various receipts and disbursements were set down in the picture-writing of the country. The arithmetical characters were of a more refined and conventional sort than those for narrative purposes; and a separate apartment was filled with hieroglyphical ledgers, exhibiting a complete view of the economy of the palace. The care of all this was intrusted to a treasurer, who acted as a sort of major-domo in the household, having a general superintendence over all its concerns. This responsible office, on the arrival of the Spaniards, was in the hands of a trusty cacique named Tapia.

Such is the picture of Montezuma's domestic establishment and way of living, as delineated by the Conquerors and their immediate followers, who had the best means of information; too highly colored, it may be, by the proneness to exaggerate, which was natural to those who first witnessed a spectacle so striking to the imagination, so new and unexpected. I have thought it best to present the full details, trivial though they may seem to the reader, as affording a curious picture of manners, so superior in point of refinement to those of the other Aboriginal tribes on the North American continent. Nor are they, in fact, so trivial, when we reflect, that, in these details of private life, we possess a surer measure of civilization, than in those of a public nature.

In surveying them we are strongly reminded of the civilization of the East; not of that higher, intellectual kind which belonged to the more polished Arabs and the Persians, but that semi-civilization which has distinguished, for example, the Tartar races, among whom art, and even science, have made, indeed, some progress in their adaptation to material wants and sensual gratification, but little in reference to the higher and more ennobling interests of humanity. It is characteristic of such a people, to find a puerile pleasure in dazzling and ostentatious pageantry; to mistake show for substance; vain pomp for power; to hedge round the throne itself with a barren and burdensome ceremonial, the counterfeit of real majesty.

Even this, however, was an advance in refinement, compared with the rude manners of the earlier Aztecs. The change may, doubtless, be referred in some degree to the personal influence of Montezuma. In his younger days, he had tempered the fierce habits of the soldier with the milder profession of religion. In later life, he had withdrawn himself still more from the brutalizing occupations of war, and his manners acquired a refinement tinctured, it may be added, with an effeminacy, unknown to his martial predecessors.

CHARLES FOLLEN.

CHARLES THEODORE CHRISTIAN FOLLEN was born September 4th, 1796, at Romröd, in the Grand Duchy of Hesse Darmstadt. He lost his mother when he was three years old, but her place was supplied, so far as possible, by the tender care of his father's second wife. His intercourse with both these parents was always of the most affectionate nature, and maintained after his separation from them by frequent correspondence. He was educated at the college or *pedagogium*, and afterwards at the University of Giessen, and chose the law as his profession. While he was at the University the German War of Liberation broke out, and Charles Follen, with his brothers, enlisted, but was never in active service. On his return to the University he took a leading part in efforts for the improvement of the clubs of the students, endeavoring to impart to these associations a national in place of a sectional character. In March, 1818, he received his diploma as Doctor of Civil Law, and in the summer of the same year was employed in a case of national importance.

C. Follen

During the twenty years' continuance of the French wars the "communities" or municipal assemblies of the towns and villages of the province of Hesse, having to bear the brunt of the contest without assistance from the government of the Grand Dukedom, had, with the consent of the government, contracted large debts. The interest was regularly paid, and the creditors were satisfied, but advantage was taken of the circumstance after the peace, to deprive these corporations of the right of self-government on the plea that their expenditures had been extravagant. A law to this effect was published July 9. The communities applied to Follen to draw up a petition to the Grand Duke for its repeal. He did so; the document was presented, and at the same time made public through the press, and caused so strong an expression of public opinion that the law was soon repealed. He next drew up a petition asking for the fulfilment of the promise of a constitutional government made at the Congress of Vienna. These acts were so distasteful to those in authority that Follen was obliged to remove to Jena, where he delivered a course of lectures in the winter of 1818–19 on the Pandects of Justinian. In March the assassination of Kotzebue by Sand aroused the country. Follen was arrested in May as an accomplice, examined and discharged; but again arrested in October, confronted with Sand at Mannheim and acquitted, but forbidden to lecture at Jena. He retired to Giessen, but hearing that fresh persecutions were impending from the government, resolved to leave Germany. He escaped to Strasburg, where he passed some time in the study of architecture with his uncle Muller, who was employed by the government to make drawings of the Roman remains extant in the town.

He visited Paris and became acquainted with La Fayette, but in consequence of the decree which followed the assassination of the Duc de Berri, expelling foreigners not engaged in specified pursuits from the country, was obliged to remove to Switzerland. He received an invitation from the Countess of Benzel Sternau, who sympathized with his opinions, to visit her at her country-seat on the lake of Zurich; and accepting the proffered hospitality, remained in this beautiful place until he accepted an appointment as teacher in the cantonal school at Chur in the Grisons. He resigned this charge within a year, in consequence of the complaints which were made that his religious teachings did not accord with the prevailing Calvinism of the place. He immediately received the appointment of Professor of Civil and Ecclesiastical Law at Basle, and fulfilled his duties until, by the influence of the other European powers, the authorities were induced to order his arrest. He hurried through France to Havre, embarked in the *Cadmus*, which a few months before had brought La Fayette to America, and landed at New York December 19, 1824.

He wrote to La Fayette, then at Washington, on his arrival, and received from him introductions to Mr. Du Ponceau and Professor George Ticknor, by whose influence he was appointed teacher of German in Harvard University in the autumn of 1825. During the winter he accepted invitations to deliver a course of lectures on Civil Law, and in 1826 opened a school for gymnastics in Boston. In the winter of 1826 and '7 he was introduced, by the lady whom he afterwards married, to Dr. Channing, with whom he soon after commenced a preparation for the ministry. He commenced preaching in July, 1828, and shortly after was made teacher of Ecclesiastical History and Ethics in the

Theological School of Harvard, a temporary provision for five years having been made for the support of his German course. On the fifteenth of September of the same year he was married to Miss Eliza Lee Cabot of Boston.

His *German Grammar* was published about the same time. In 1830 he resigned his post in the divinity school, and gave a course of lectures on Moral Philosophy in Boston. In 1831 he was inaugurated Professor of German Literature at Harvard, on which occasion he pronounced an elaborate Inaugural Address. In the winter of 1832 he delivered a series of lectures on Schiller. In these, after a brief account of the life of the author, a critical analysis is given of each of his dramas, with numerous illustrative extracts translated by the lecturer in a happy manner. The course closes with a comparison between Schiller and his great contemporary Goethe. In 1834 the subscription for the German professorship expired, and was not renewed by the University in consequence, it is said, of Dr. Follen having identified himself prominently with the Abolition party. He was therefore obliged to withdraw. In 1836 he published a tract, *Religion and the Church*, designed to be the first of a series, but meeting with no support he abandoned the work. In the same year he accepted an invitation to take charge of a Unitarian congregation. He remained in this position until May, 1838, when he returned to Boston. In May, 1839, he received a call to a congregation at East Lexington, Massachusetts. In December of the same year he visited New York to deliver a course of lectures on German literature. He embarked on his return in the steamboat Lexington, January 13, 1840, and was one of the many who perished by the conflagration of that vessel in Long Island Sound.

Dr. Follen's works were collected and published in five volumes, in 1841. The first of these contains his life by his widow, with a selection from his poetical productions in the German language; the second, his sermons; the third, Lectures on Moral Philosophy, and an unfinished work on Psychology; the fourth, a portion, all that were written out, of his lectures on Schiller; the fifth, miscellaneous reviews and addresses.

SCHILLER'S LOVE OF LIBERTY—FROM THE LECTURES ON SCHILLER.

In what, now, I would ask, consists the individual literary character of Schiller as a dramatic poet? Goethe, in speaking of the individual tendency of Schiller's poetic nature and his own, said, "Schiller preached the gospel of freedom; I would not allow the rights of nature to be encroached upon." The word freedom is to be taken here in the sense of Kant's philosophy, as synonymous with the moral nature of man. His enthusiasm for freedom was manifested in his resistance against all kinds of unnatural and unreasonable restraint; freedom from oppression, from fear, from prejudice, and from sin. His love of liberty and hatred of oppression had taken root early in the unnatural discipline of the Charles Academy; it had grown by his experience of active life and the study of history. It appears as a wild, untamable impulse in Charles Moor. "The law has never formed a great man," he says, "but liberty hatches wonders and extremes." "Who is the greater tyrant," asks Fiesco, "he who shows the intention, or he who has the power, to become a tyrant?" "I hate the former, I fear the latter," answers Verrina; "let Andrea Doria die!" "Chains of iron or chains of silk,—they are chains," says Burgognino; "let Andrea Doria die!"

"Restore to man his lost nobility; let no duty bind him except the equally venerable rights of his fellow-men." These are the words of Posa to the tyrant king. To the queen, when he commits to her his last message to his friend Carlos, he says, "Tell him he shall realize the bold dream of a new state, the divine offspring of friendship!" It has been justly observed (by Menzel) that Schiller's Posa maintains the rights of mankind; his Maid of Orleans fights for the rights of nations; the rights of the individual are asserted by William Tell.

The second kind of freedom which I have mentioned, freedom from prejudice, appears in its healthiest, purest, and highest form, in the truly philosophic mind of Posa, while the same tendency appears in its perversion and state of insanity in the atheist, Francis Moor, who, by the chemical force of his wit, sublimates the whole substance of the moral world, respect and love, conscience and religion, into vapid prejudices, which he thinks he can blow away by the breath of his mouth.

Freedom from prejudice in a more confined sphere, and more practical form, appears in Ferdinand Walter and Louisa Miller, contending for the sacred rights of the heart, against the aristocracy of Ferdinand's father and Lady Milford.

The same principle appears in that scene of "William Tell," in which Rudenz, after his political conversion by Bertha, enters the house after his uncle's death, and, after being received by Walter Furst and others as their future feudal lord, aspires after the higher privilege of being considered by them as a friend of the friends of his country. When Melchthal refuses to give Rudenz his hand, Walter Furst says,

Give him your hand! his returning heart
Deserves confidence.
Melchthal. You have never respected
The husbandman; say, what shall we expect from you?
Rudenz. O do not remember the error of my youth!
Melchthal. Here is my hand!
The farmer's hand, my noble Sir, is also
A pledge of honor. What, without us, is
The knight? And our rank is older than yours.

Freedom from fear, is another element of Schiller's poetry. Courage, in its lower form, is the inspiring principle in "Wallenstein's Camp," while it appears as manly greatness in him who is the idol of the camp, who, when all his supports from without have dropped off, and left him a leafless trunk, feels and announces that now his time has come,—for,

It must be night for Friedland's stars to shine.

The same principle appears in William Tell, as a devoted trust in God, and in the goodness of his bow, his arm, and his conscience. It appears as elevated resignation in Mary Stuart, and as heroic inspiration in the Maid of Orleans.

The highest form of freedom, freedom from debasing immorality, purity of heart, is so characteristic of Schiller's poetry, that we may apply to it with peculiar truth the words of Klopstock, in describing German poetry. Schiller's poetry is a chaste virgin looking up to heaven. It is this which gives, to his great dramatic pictures, the highest ideal beauty, the beauty of holiness. It is the consciousness of holy innocence which gives to the simple daughter of the musician, Miller, a sense of rank which outshines all earthly distinctions, and will appear brightest where all these walls of partition must fall. "Then, mother," she says, "when every envelope of rank bursts, when men are nothing but men,—I shall bring with me nothing but my innocence. But my father says, ornaments and splendid titles will become cheap when God comes, and hearts rise in value. There, tears are accounted as triumphs, and beautiful thoughts as ancestors. Then I shall be a lady, my mother. And what advantage will he then have over his faithful girl?"

This is the brightest jewel in the diadem of the Spanish Queen, Elizabeth, as the Marquis of Posa describes her to his friend.

> Arrayed in nature's unassuming glory,
> With careless unconcern, all unacquainted
> With calculating, school-taught etiquette,
> Equally free from boldness and from fear.
> With calm, heroic step she moves along
> The narrow, middle path of modesty;
> Knows not that she exacted adoration,
> When she was far from dreaming of applause.

It is the consciousness of the purity of his purpose, which enables the single-hearted hunter of the Alps to bend his peaceful bow to works of blood. It was that purity which makes the simple wise, that enabled Bertha, of Bruneck, to open the eyes of her deluded lover to the deception of which he was the object, and to his own true destiny and duty.—The Maid of Orleans, the pure virgin, was intrusted with the standard of Heaven: it was the faith in her own purity which made the sword invincible in her hand.—But the power and beauty of this moral principle, the prophetic wisdom of childlike innocence, is most fully and gloriously displayed in Max and Thekla. When Max is wavering between the two ways, one of which leads to the possession of his Thekla, and is recommended to his heart by the filial gratitude he owes to her father,—while the other, pointed out by his conscience, is darkened by the treachery of his own father, and still more, by the certain loss of his highest hope in life,—it is in this moment of fearful doubt, that he says,

> Where is the voice of truth which I dare follow?
> It speaks no longer in my heart. We all
> But utter what our passionate wishes dictate:
> O that an angel would descend from heaven,
> And scoop for me the right, the uncorrupted,
> With a pure hand from the pure Fount of Light.
> (*His eyes glance on Thekla.*)
> What other angel seek I? To this heart,
> To this unerring heart will I submit it;
> Will ask thy love which has the power to bless
> The happy man alone, averted ever
> From the disquieted and guilty,—canst thou
> Still love me if I stay? Say that thou canst,
> And I am the Duke's * * * * * *
> * * * * * * * * * *
> ——— Speak and let thy heart decide it.
> *Thekla.* O thy own
> Hath long ago decided. Follow thou
> Thy heart's first feeling.
> * * * * * * * * ——— Being faithful
> To thine own self, thou art faithful too to me.
> If our fates part, our hearts remain united.
> A bloody hatred will divide for ever
> The houses Piccolomini and Friedland:
> But we belong not to our houses; ——— Go!

Thus, when conflicting passions, interests, and fears have darkened the way of duty before us, it is the inward light, it is purity of heart which reveals the narrow path. The pure in heart see the truth, because it is they alone that see God.

Schiller's enthusiasm for liberty was not a negative or destructive principle. He manifested in his poetry a striving after freedom from oppression, from fear, from prejudice, and sin, from all earthly and unreasonable restraints, that the spiritual principle of human nature might unfold itself purely and fully in the individual and in society. His love of freedom is only a manifestation of the spirit of love, of that pure delight in perfection, the love of nature, of man, and of God, which is the life of his poetry.

"Quiet kingdom of plants! in thy silent wonders I hear the steps of the Deity; thy meritless excellence carries my inquiring mind upward to the highest understanding; in thy still mirror I see his divine image reflected. Man troubles the silver stream; where man walks, the Creator disappears."

That Schiller loved in nature what excites most deeply those powers and passions which are peculiar to man, might be shown by many other passages. Who does not remember the sunset on the banks of the Danube, in "The Robbers"? "Thus is a hero's death adorable. When I was a boy, it was my favorite thought to live like the sun, to die like him. It was a boyish thought. There was a time when I could not sleep if I had forgotten my evening prayers. O my innocence! See, all have gone forth to sun themselves in the peaceful beam of spring;—why must I alone inhale infernal influences from the joys of heaven? All is so happy; all beings related to each other by the spirit of peace, the whole world one family, and one Father above! not my father;—I alone rejected, alone excluded from the ranks of the pure. Not to me the sweet name of child,—not to me the languishing look of the loved one,—never, never the embrace of a bosom friend."

Who does not remember the impression of the sunrise over Genoa upon the ambitious Fiesco, and that of the sunrise in the Alps upon the united Swiss? These are the words of Fiesco.

"This majestic city! mine! to rise upon it like the royal day, to brood over it with a monarch's power! One moment of royalty absorbs all the marrow of human existence. Split the thunder into its elementary syllables, and it becomes a lullaby for babes; join them together into one sudden peal, and the royal sound moves the eternal heavens."

In the Rütli, Rösselman, the priest, says, when he sees the morning place its glowing sentries on the mountain tops—

> By this pure light which greets us first of all
> The nations that are dwelling far below,
> Heavily breathing in the smoke of cities,
> Let us swear the oath of our new covenant.
> We will be one nation of brothers, never
> To separate in danger or distress.
> We will be free, free as our fathers were,
> And rather die than live in servitude.
> We 'll put our trust upon the highest God,
> And thus we will not fear the power of men.

The Swiss fisherman sees, in the fearful agitation of the lake, the power of the angel of divine vengeance, that has stirred up the deep waters against the tyrant that is floating upon them.

> Judgments of God! yes, it is he himself,
> The haughty Landvogt,—there he sails along,
> And with him, in his ship, he bears his crime.
> O swiftly the Avenger's arm has found him!
> Now o'er himself he knows a stronger master.
> The waves heed not his bidding;
> These rocks will not bow down their heads before
> His hat. Nay, do not pray, my boy, do not
> Attempt to stay the arm of the Avenger.

The restless, homesick spirit of the Queen of Scotland soars beyond her prison, and embarks in the clouds, flitting overhead.

> Hastening clouds! ye sailors on high!
> With you I would wander, with you I would fly.
> Greet for me sweetly the land of my youth!
> Doomed in this land of bondage to tarry,
> Ah! I have no one my message to carry.
> Free in the air is your lofty way,
> Far beyond this Queen's imperious sway.

In "The Misanthrope," the disappointed lover of man seeks consolation in nature.

"Man, noble, lofty phenomenon, most beautiful of all the thoughts of the Creator. How rich, how perfect did you proceed from his hands! What melodies slept in your breast before your passion destroyed the golden play! All beings around you seek and attain the beautiful stature of perfection; you alone stand unripe and misshapen in the faultless plan. Discerned by no eye, admired by no understanding, the pearl in the silent shell, the crystal in the depth of the mountain, strive after the most perfect form. Gratefully all the children of nature present the ripened fruits to the contented mother; wherever she has sowed, she finds a harvest; you alone, her dearest, her most favored son, are not among them; only what she gave to you she finds no more, she knows it no more in its disfigured beauty.

"Be perfect! Harmonies without number are slumbering in you, to awake at your bidding; call them forth by your excellence. To bless you is the coronal after which all beings are aspiring; your wild passion opposes this kind intention; you forcibly pervert the beneficent objects of nature. Fulness of life she has spread around you, and you extract death from it. Your hatred sharpened the peaceful iron into a sword; your avarice charges with crimes and curses the innocent gold; on your intemperate lip the life of the vine becomes poison. That which is perfect serves your crimes, but your crimes do not infect it. You can rob it of its destination, but of the obedience with which it serves you, you cannot deprive it. Be humane, or be a barbarian; with equally suitable pulsation the loyal heart will accompany your hatred or your gentleness."

The most vast and sublime illustration of the moral nature and destiny of man by the nature of God's creation, is to be found in the address of Posa to the Spanish King.

Look round
On God's beautiful world! Lo! it is founded
On freedom; and behold! how rich it is
Through freedom. He, the great Creator, throws
Into a drop of dew, an insect, and allows
That even in the dread realms of corruption
Desire should find delight. Your world, how narrow,
How poor! The rustling of a leaf affrights
The lord of Christendom. You, Sire, must tremble
At every virtue. He, rather than preclude
The beautiful phenomenon of freedom,
Even allows the dreadful host of evil
To rage in his creation. Him, the artist,
You see not; modestly he disappears
Behind eternal laws;—and the freethinker
Sees these, but sees not Him. Why does it need
A God? he says; the world is self-sufficient.
And never Christian's worship has extolled Him,
Better than that freethinker's blasphemy.

To these passages, selected from the dramatic compositions of Schiller, many others might be added from his various works, to show how his love of nature was characterized by the prevailing tendency of his mind. He loved nature for herself, in all her various shapes and moods; but he loved best those things in nature which call forth most effectually the energies, the strong and tender emotions and high aspirations of the soul, all that reminds man of his sublime destiny, and aids him in attaining it. He saw in her the true friend of man, exercising over him, according to the different states of his mind, an exhilarating or consoling, inspiriting or tranquillizing influence; again he saw in her a salutary enemy of man, rousing his active powers to constant watchfulness and brave resistance; finally, he found in her a prophet, that is sent to man to solve the dark enigmas of his own being and destiny.

Freedom and love, the two elements of our moral nature, of true humanity, are the living springs of Schiller's poetry. The history of his dramatic genius, which I have endeavored to set before you, shows how this spirit of freedom and love grew in him, to the end of his course. This spirit, which in "The Robbers," and other productions of his early life, which might well be called the heroic age of his genius, appears in the shape of Hercules, with the club and the lion-skin, going about to free the earth from tyrants and monsters; the same spirit appears in his "Carlos," and his later productions, in his "Maid of Orleans," his "Mary Stuart," his "William Tell." It is the instinct of liberty warring against the tyranny of circumstances and arbitrary institutions. In "The Conspiracy of Fiesco," it appears in the character of Fiesco himself, united with the ruling passion of ambition; while in that of Verrina it assumes the austere grandeur of a Roman and a Stoic. In "Intrigue and Love," all the imperfections of European governments are unsparingly exposed. The old Adam of the feudal world, with all his imperfections and deformities, is brought before the confessional of sound reason and enlightened philanthropy.

His poetry is, indeed, essentially a revelation of moral beauty; all his dramatic productions prove his faith, that while all other created beings are confined by necessary laws to a finite mode of existence, man alone possesses a creative power, being able to form his own character, and capable of infinite advancement. The freedom, the moral nature of man, is the native soil of his poetry; every good principle loves to grow in it, and, for this very reason, does not appear as the forced production of rigid self-control, but as springing up from the abundance of the heart with living grace and ideal beauty.

Mrs. Follen, after the death of her husband, undertook the entire charge of the education of their only son, a boy about ten years old. To facilitate this and other objects, she received into her house a few other pupils, all of whom she fitted for matriculation at Harvard. In addition to the Memoir of her husband, this lady is the author of *Sketches of Married Life; The Skeptic*, a tale; a volume of *Poems on Occasional Topics*, published in 1839, and a number of magazine tales and sketches.

The following is from her volume of poems.

ON THE DEATH OF A BEAUTIFUL GIRL.

The young, the lovely, pass away,
Ne'er to be seen again;
Earth's fairest flowers too soon decay
Its blasted trees remain.

Full oft, we see the brightest thing
That lifts its head on high,
Smile in the light, then droop its wing,
And fade away, and die.

And kindly is the lesson given;
Then dry the falling tear:
They came to raise our hearts to Heaven;
They go to call us there.

CALVIN COLTON.

Calvin Colton was born at Long Meadow, Massachusetts. He was graduated at Yale College in 1812; and after completing a course of divinity at Andover, was ordained a Presbyterian clergyman in 1815. He became a minister of a congregation at Batavia, New York, a position he retained until compelled in 1826, by the failure of his voice, to abandon preaching; after which, he employed himself by contributing to various religious and literary periodicals. In the summer of 1831, after having made a long tour through the states and territories of the American Union, he visited London as a correspondent of the New York Observer. During his residence in England he published in 1832, *A Manual for Emigrants to America*, and *The History and Character of American Revivals of Religion*, which passed through two or three editions: in 1833, incited by the constant attacks by the British press on everything connected with the people of this country, he published a spirited defence entitled *The Americans by an American in London*, and during the same year, *The American Cottager*, a popular religious story; *A Tour of the American Lakes and among the Indians of the North West Territory*, in two volumes, and *Church and State in America*, a defence of the voluntary system, in reply to some remarks of the Bishop of London.

C. Colton

Soon after his return to New York in 1835, he published *Four Years in Great Britain;* and in 1836, an anonymous work entitled *Protestant Jesuitism*, in which he reviewed the intriguing and intolerant course of many of the prominent religious and benevolent organizations of the country with openness and severity. His next work, *Thoughts on the Religious State of the Country, and Reasons for preferring Episcopacy*, presented the causes of his recent step in taking Episcopal orders.

Mr. Colton next devoted his attention to political topics. In 1838, he published, *Abolition a Sedition*, and *Abolition and Colonization Contrasted;* in 1839, *A Voice from America to England by an American Gentleman*, a work somewhat similar to his *Americans;* in 1840, *The Crisis of the Country, American Jacobinism*, and *One Presidential Term*, a series of tracts with the signature of "Junius" which were very widely circulated by the Whig party, and were supposed to have exerted a powerful influence on the election of General Harrison. In 1842, he edited a paper at Washington called the True Whig, and in 1843 and '4 published a new series, ten in number, of the *Junius Tracts*.

In November, 1844, he visited Henry Clay at Ashland, to collect materials for a Life of the great statesman; for whose elevation to the Presidency he had, in common with so great a multitude of his countrymen, labored long and arduously. Mr. Clay permitted free access to his papers, and the work was completed and published in the spring of 1844, in two octavo volumes.

In the same year he published *The Rights of Labor*, a work in defence of a protective tariff. It was followed by a second and more extensive work on political economy in 1848, entitled *Public Economy for the United States*, in which he advocates the protective system. His last work is a volume entitled *The Genius and Mission of the Protestant Episcopal Church in the United States*, in which his aim is to show the descent of that body from the Apostolic age, independent of the church of Rome; its purification from error at the Reformation and emancipation from state control at the American Revolution, with its subsequent rapid progress and consequent incumbent duties.

Mr. Colton was a few years since appointed professor of Political Economy in Trinity College, Hartford, a position which he still retains.

WALTER COLTON

Was born in Rutland, Vt., in 1797. He was graduated from Yale College in 1822, and after a three years' course at Andover, was ordained a Congregational clergyman. He became a teacher in an academy at Middletown, Conn.; and while thus occupied, wrote a prize essay on Duelling, and a number of articles in prose and verse, with the signature of "Bertram," for various journals.

W. Colton

In 1828, he became editor of the American Spectator, a weekly political paper at Washington, and an intimate friend of General Jackson, who in 1830, on a sea voyage being recommended for the benefit of Mr. Colton's health, offered him a consulship or a chaplaincy in the navy. He accepted the clerical post, and joined the West India squadron. A characteristic anecdote is related of his self-possession while on the station. He had occasion to comment with severity on the conduct of the police during an affray between several American sailors and a party of Spaniards, in which several of the former were killed. The mayor of the place, a Spaniard, rushed on the chaplain with a long knife, but being met by the other with a drawn pistol and a threat to shoot if he advanced a step, desisted.

On his return, he was appointed to the Constellation frigate, and made a three years' cruise in the Mediterranean, during which he derived the materials for his *Ship and Shore*, and *Visit to Constantinople and Athens*, volumes published in 1835 and 1836. He was next appointed Historiographer to the Exploring Expedition; but in consequence of the reduction of the force originally designed to be sent did not accompany it, but was stationed at Philadelphia as chaplain of the Navy Yard, and afterwards of the Naval Asylum. He also edited in 1841 and 1842, the Philadelphia North American, and wrote articles for other journals.

In 1844, he delivered a poem entitled *The Sailor* at the Commencement of the University of Vermont, which is still in manuscript. In 1846 he was married, and soon after ordered to the squadron for the Pacific. A short time after his arrival at Monterey he was appointed Alcalde of the city, an office which he discharged during the Mexican war with efficiency. He also established the *Californian*, the first newspaper printed in California, which was afterwards transferred to San Francisco, and entitled the Alta California. He was also the builder of the first school-house in the present state; and in a letter published in the Philadelphia North American, the first to make known the discovery of California gold to the residents of the Atlantic states. During his residence on the Pacific he wrote *Deck and Port* and *Three Years in California*.

He returned to Philadelphia in the summer of 1850, and was busily engaged in the preparation of additional volumes of his travels, when in consequence of exposure on a visit to Washington he took a violent cold, which led to a dropsy, of which he died on the 22d of January, 1851.

Two additional volumes from his pen, *Land and Lee* and *The Sea and the Sailor, Notes on France and Italy, and other Literary Remains*, appeared shortly after his decease; the last, accompanied by a Memoir of the author, from his friend the Rev. Henry T. Cheever.

The style of Mr. Colton's volumes is lively and entertaining. He has also his serious vein, is fond of sentiment, which often advances from prose into simple but harmonious verse. The long series of volumes to which his wanderings have extended, furnishes in this a proof of their popular acceptation.

HUGH SWINTON LEGARÉ.

Hugh Swinton Legaré, one of the ablest and most accomplished scholars the country has produced, was born in Charleston, South Carolina, January 2, 1797. As his name, in connexion with the place of his nativity, imports, he was of Huguenot ancestry. On his mother's side, from whom he derived the name of Swinton, he was of Scotch descent. His father dying left him entirely dependent, at an early age, upon his mother, a lady everyway qualified for the discharge of her duties. In his fourth year it was deemed necessary to inoculate the child with the small-pox. The virus acted with unusual power upon the system, and finally concentrated its force in large sores on the elbows and knees. He was thus compelled to lie on his back for some three months, and was reduced from a hearty state of health to a mere skeleton, being carried about on a pillow in his mother's arms. The tumors were finally healed, but produced a lasting effect on his growth, so that for eight or nine years he made scarcely any perceptible advance in stature. After that period he suddenly shot up, but the growth was almost entirely in the upper part of the body, leaving him with limbs of dwarfed proportions. The defects of his body, however, contributed in some measure to the development of his mind, by forcing him to seek employment and pleasure in intellectual rather than athletic exercises.

His education commenced at an early age, for he learnt to read while carried about, as we have related, in his mother's arms. He was sent to school before his sixth year, and passing through the hands of successive teachers—many of whom, themselves persons of distinguished abilities, expressed prognostications of his future eminence—entered the then recently established University of South Carolina at Columbia in his fourteenth year. His favorite studies during his collegiate career were the classics and philosophy. The other departments of the course were, however, not neglected, as he was graduated at the head of his class. He then commenced the study of the law under the charge of one of his former teachers, Mr. Mitchell King,* who had in the meantime become a leading practitioner of Charleston. After three years of diligent preparation he was, on arriving at the age of twenty-one, fully qualified for admission to the bar, but instead of presenting himself for examination he determined to pursue his legal studies at the European Universities.

In May, 1818, he sailed from Charleston to Bordeaux, and at once proceeded to Paris, where he remained several months. His previous study of many of the modern languages had qualified him to appear with advantage in continental society, but the chief portion of his time was devoted to the study of the law and of the languages, with which he had not as yet become thoroughly conversant.

From Paris he removed to Edinburgh instead of, as he originally proposed, Gottingen. On his arrival he entered the classes of civil law, natural philosophy, and mathematics, of the University, which were in the charge of Irving, Playfair, and Murray. He also attended the private class of the Professor of Chemistry, Dr. Murray. His chief attention was given to the law, but the testimony of his associate, Mr. Preston, proves him to have been a hard student in the other departments as well. "He gave three hours a day to Playfair, Leslie, and Murray, in the lecture-room. From eight to ten were devoted to Heineccius, Cujacius, and Terrasson; side by side with whom lay upon his table, Dante and Tasso, Guicciardini, Davila, and Machiavelli. To this mass of labor he addressed himself with a quiet diligence, sometimes animated into a sort of intellectual joy. On one occasion he found himself at breakfast, Sunday morning, on the same seat where he had breakfasted the day before—not having quitted it meantime."

At the conclusion of his course in Edinburgh he passed a year in travelling in Scotland, England, France, Belgium, the Rhine, and Switzerland, returning to Charleston by way of New York and Washington. His first attention on his return home was given to the affairs of his mother's plantation on John's Island near Charleston, which had suffered for want of efficiency in its management. He was elected from this district in the autumn after his arrival, a member of the Lower House of the General Assembly of the State for a term of two years, from 1820 to 1822. At the close of this period he became, in consequence of the requirements of his profession, a resident of Charleston, where the mother and son, being unwilling to be separated, the remainder of the family soon followed him.

His extensive erudition seems, as is sometimes the case, to have acted unfavorably to his success. Clients supposed him more at home in the study than the court-room. "Sir," said he, in answer to a query addressed to him at that time, "do you ask how I get along? Do you inquire what my trade brings me in? I will tell you. I have a variety of cases, and, by the bounty of Providence, sometimes get a fee; but in general, sir, I practise upon the old Roman plan; and, like Ci-

* Mr. King was a man of great benevolence as well as ability. At a subsequent period he accepted, at great loss and inconvenience, the office of Recorder and City Judge of Charleston, and performed its duties gratuitously, in order that the previous incumbent, Judge Axson, incapacitated by paralysis, might still continue in the receipt of his official emoluments. He continued these gratuitous services during the life of Judge Axson, and for a few months after his decease for the benefit of his surviving family.

H. S. Legaré

cero's, my clients pay me what they like—that is, often, nothing at all."

In 1824 he was again elected a member of the state legislature, where he remained until chosen by it Attorney-General of the state. During the stormy discussions of this period he was an advocate of the doctrine of states rights, but opposed to nullification.

On the organization of the Southern Review in 1827, he gave efficient aid in the plan and prosecution of the work, contributing on more than one occasion more than half the matter of a number. The increase of his professional practice, and his appointment finally as State Attorney, compelled him, after a few years, to cease his contributions, and the Review, deprived of his powerful aid, was soon after discontinued.

While State Attorney he was called to argue a case before the Supreme Court at Washington. The ability he displayed attracted universal admiration, and led to his intimate acquaintance with Mr. Livingston, then Secretary of State, whose eminence in the department of civil law rendered him competent to appreciate the talents and learning displayed by the pleader in the same field. The Secretary soon after tendered Legaré the appointment of Chargé d'Affaires at the Court of Brussels for the express purpose of enabling him to carry his study of the civil law still further with a view to qualify himself for the discussion of the question, as to what extent the incorporation of the system into that of the United States might be desirable. The appointment was accepted, and Legaré at once entered on its duties. These were slight, leaving him ample time for study, which he improved by a course of civil law under Savigny, and the acquisition of the Dutch, German, and Romaic languages. He remained in his mission for four years, returning in the summer of 1836 to New York, where he was met by the offer, earnestly pressed upon his acceptance, of a nomination for Congress. He was elected, and entered the House of Representatives at the commencement of the Van Buren administration. At the extra session in September he delivered a masterly speech in opposition to the policy of the sub-treasury. His opinions were those of the minority in his state, and at the next election he was defeated.

He returned with renewed ardor to his professional career, and distinguished himself greatly in the conduct of several important cases. He also entered warmly into the presidential contest of 1840, and delivered eloquent speeches at Richmond and New York. His article on Demosthenes, for the New York Review, was written about the same time.

In 1841 Legaré was appointed, by Mr. Tyler, Attorney-General of the United States. It was an office for which he was eminently qualified, and in which he eminently distinguished himself. After the withdrawal of Mr. Webster on the ratification of the Ashburton treaty, in the composition of which, especially in the portion regarding the right of search, Mr. Legaré had rendered important service, he discharged for some time the duties of the Department of State.

In January, 1843, he sustained a severe domestic affliction in the death of his mother, to whom he was devotedly attached. They were soon, however, to be united in death as they had been in life. In the following June the President and cabinet visited Boston to take part in the ceremonies attending the completion of the Bunker Hill Monument. Mr. Legaré was seized, on his arrival in Boston, with a disease of the bowels which had, during the previous autumn, produced such extreme suffering as to cause the declaration to his sister, that if it pleased God he would rather die than live in such torment. He was unable to take part in the celebration of the following day, Saturday, and on Sunday yielded to the solicitations of his friend, Professor George Ticknor, and was removed to his residence in Park street, where he died on the morning of the twentieth of the same month.

His writings were collected by his sister and published at Charleston in 1846, with a memoir.* They form two large octavo volumes, and contain his journals during his diplomatic residence abroad, filled with lively details of court gossip, his studies and observations, public and private correspondence, speeches and articles for the New York and Southern Reviews. These articles are for the most part on classical or legal subjects, the remainder being devoted, with few exceptions, to authors of the day. They display thorough erudition, and are admirable as models of hearty scholarship and finished composition.

CHARACTERISTICS OF LORD BYRON.†

Lord Byron's life was not a literary, or cloistered and scholastic life. He had lived generally in the

* Writings of Hugh Swinton Legaré, late Attorney-General, Acting Secretary of State of the United States; consisting of a Diary of Brussels, and Journal of the Rhine; extracts from his Private and Diplomatic Correspondence; Orations and Speeches, and Contributions to the New York and Southern Reviews; Prefaced by a Memoir of his Life. Edited by his Sister. Charleston, S. C.: Burges & James. 1846.

† From an article on Moore's Life of Byron in the Southern Review.

world, and always and entirely *for* the world. The *amat nemus et fugit urbes*, which has been predicated of the whole tuneful tribe, was only in a qualified sense a characteristic of his. If he sought seclusion, it was not for the retired leisure or the sweet and innocent tranquillity of a country life. His retreats were rather like that of Tiberius at Capreæ—the gloomy solitude of misanthropy and remorse, hiding its despair in darkness, or seeking to stupify and drown it in vice and debauchery. But, even when he fled from the sight of men, it was only that he might be sought after the more, and, in the depth of his hiding places, as was long ago remarked of Timon of Athens, he could not live without vomiting forth the gall of his bitterness, and sending abroad most elaborate curses in good verse to be admired of the very wretches whom he affected to despise. He lived in the world, and for the world—nor is it often that a career so brief affords to biography so much impressive incident, or that the folly of an undisciplined and reckless spirit has assumed such a motley wear, and played off, before God and man, so many extravagant and fantastical antics.

On the other hand, there was, amidst all its irregularities, something strangely interesting, something, occasionally, even grand and imposing in Lord Byron's character and mode of life. His whole being was, indeed, to a remarkable degree, extraordinary, fanciful, and fascinating. All that drew upon him the eyes of men, whether for good or evil—his passions and his genius, his enthusiasm and his woe, his triumphs and his downfall—sprang from the same source, a feverish temperament, a burning, distempered, insatiable imagination; and these, in their turn, acted most powerfully upon the imagination and the sensibility of others. We well remember a time—it is not more than two lustres ago—when we could never think of him ourselves but as an ideal being—a creature, to use his own words, "of loneliness and mystery"—moving about the earth like a troubled spirit, and even when in the midst of men, not *of* them. The enchanter's robe which he wore seemed to disguise his person, and like another famous sorcerer and sensualist—

> he hurled
> His dazzling spells into the spungy air,
> Of power to cheat the eye with blear illusion
> And give it false presentments.

It has often occurred to us, as we have seen Sir Walter Scott diligently hobbling up to his daily task in the Parliament House at Edinburgh, and still more when we have gazed upon him for hours seated down at his clerk's desk, with a countenance of most demure and business-like formality, to contrast him, in that situation, with the only man, who had not been, at the time, totally overshadowed and eclipsed by his genius. It was, indeed, a wonderful contrast! Never did two such men—competitors in the highest walks of creative imagination and deep pathos—present such a strange antithesis of moral character, and domestic habits and pursuits, as Walter Scott at home, and Lord Byron abroad. It was the difference between prose and poetry—between the dullest realities of existence and an incoherent, though powerful and agitating romance—between a falcon trained to the uses of a domestic bird, and, instead of "towering in her pride of place," brought to stoop at the smallest quarry, and to wait upon a rude sportsman's bidding like a menial servant—and some savage, untamed eagle, who, after struggling with the bars of his cage, until his breast was bare and bleeding with the agony, had flung himself forth, once more, upon the gale, and was again chasing before him the "whole herd of timorous and flocking birds," and making his native Alps, through all their solitudes, ring to his boding and wild scream. Lord Byron's pilgrimages to distant and famous lands—especially his first—heightened this effect of his genius and of his very peculiar mode of existence. Madame de Staël ascribes it to his good fortune or the deep policy of Napoleon, that he had succeeded in associating his name with some of those objects which have, through all time, most strongly impressed the imaginations of men, with the Pyramids, the Alps, the Holy Land, &c. Byron had the same advantage. His muse, like Horace's image of Care, mounted with him the steed and the gondola, the post-chaise, and the packet-ship. His poems are, in a manner, the journals and common-place books of the wandering Childe. Thus, it is stated or hinted that a horrible incident, like that upon which the Giaour turns, had nearly taken place within Byron's own observation while in the East. His sketches of the sublime and beautiful in nature seem to be mere images, or, so to express it, shadows thrown down upon his pages from the objects which he visited, only colored and illumined with such feelings, reflections, and associations, as they naturally awaken in contemplative and susceptible minds. His early visit to Greece, and the heartfelt enthusiasm with which he dwelt upon her loveliness even "in her age of woe"—upon the glory which once adorned, and that which might still await her—have identified him with her name, in a manner which subsequent events have made quite remarkable. His poetry, when we read it over again, seems to breathe of "the sanctified phrensy of prophecy and inspiration." He now appears to have been the herald of her resuscitation. The voice of lamentation, which he sent forth over Christendom, was as if it had issued from all her caves, fraught with the woe and the wrongs of ages, and the deep vengeance which at length awoke—and not in vain! In expressing ourselves as we have done upon this subject, it is to us a melancholy reflection that our language is far more suitable to what we *have* felt, than to what we now feel, in reference to the life and character of Lord Byron. The last years of that life—the wanton, gross, and often dull and feeble ribaldry of some of his latest productions, broke the spell which he had laid upon our souls; and we are by no means sure that we have not since yielded too much to the disgust and aversion which follow disenchantment like its shadow.

DAVID J. M'CORD

Was born near M'Cord's Ferry, South Carolina, January, 1797, and was educated at the College at Columbia, in that state; where, among his class-mates and intimates, were the late Hugh S. Legaré and Professor H. J. Nott.

In 1818 Mr. M'Cord was admitted to the bar, and soon acquired a large practice. Among his associates in the profession were the late Chancellor Harper, the Hon. W. C. Preston, Professor Nott, the Hon. W. F. De Saussure, Colonel Blanding, Colonel Gregg, and the Hon. A. P. Butler, since of the United States Senate. In connexion with Mr. Nott, he published two volumes of Law Reports of South Carolina, known as Nott and M'Cord's Reports, and afterwards, unassisted, four volumes of Law Reports and two of Chancery Reports. In connexion with Colonel Blanding, he published also one volume of the "South Carolina Law Journal."

In May, 1839, Mr. M'Cord was appointed by the Governor to publish the "Statutes at Large of South Carolina;" a work which had been commenced under the authority of the state, by his friend the late Dr. Thomas Cooper. Dr. Cooper's death occurring before the completion of the fourth volume of the work, it was transferred to Mr. M'Cord, by whom it was completed. The work is in ten volumes octavo, including a general index.

Mr. M'Cord, in addition to these literary labors of the law, was a frequent writer of various periodicals, chiefly on subjects of the science of government and political economy. He was a writer for both series of the Southern Review, under the editorship of Mr. Stephen Elliott and Mr. Simms.* In these articles he was an eloquent supporter of Southern institutions, and an earnest and able advocate of free trade.

Mr. M'Cord was for several years a representative of the district of Richland in the Legislature of South Carolina, and was Chairman of the Committee of Federal Relations, an important position at the time. To his exertions are principally due the abolition of the late Court of Appeals (composed of three judges), and the establishment of a system which, improved by subsequent suggestions of Mr. Pettigru, is now in force. Mr. M'Cord retired from the practice of the law in 1836, and after 1840 occupied himself almost entirely as a cotton planter.

He died after a brief illness, at his residence at Columbia, May 12, 1855.

The warm personal tribute to his memory in a notice of his merits at the bar and in society, appeared the following week in a newspaper at Columbia, from the pen of his friend and former law associate, the Hon. W. C. Preston. It is also a genial account of the higher social and literary society of Columbia—and, we may add, a happy reflection of the generous nature and accomplishments of the writer. We present it entire from the South Carolinian of May 17.

MESSRS. EDITORS: In the announcement of the death of Mr. M'Cord, in your paper of the 9th instant, you intimate an expectation that some one will furnish a notice of the life and character of that gentleman. Pending the performance of this pious office by some friend capable of executing it fitly, let me cast a glove into his grave, and place a sprig of cypress upon it. Such a work of tenderness I had fondly hoped to have received at his hand, instead of being called upon out of the ordinary course of nature to offer it at his tomb.

Many will bring tributes of sorrow, of kindness and affection, and relieve a heaving bosom by uttering words of praise and commendation; for in truth, during many years he has been the charm and delight of the society of Columbia, and of that society, too, when, in the estimation of all who knew it, it was the rarest aggregation of elegant, intellectual, and accomplished people that have ever been found assembled in our village. Thirty years since, amidst the cordial and unostentatious cordiality which characterised it, at a dinner party, for example, at Judge De Saussure's, eight or ten of his favorite associates wanted to do honor to some distinguished stranger—for such were never permitted to pass through the town without a tender of the hospitality of that venerable and elegant gentleman—whose prolonged life exhibited to another generation a pattern of old gentility, combined with a conscientious and effective performance of not only the smaller and more graceful duties of life, which he sweetened and adorned, but also of those graver and higher tasks which the confidence of his state imposed upon his talents and learning. To his elegant board naturally came the best and worthiest of the land. There was found, of equal age with the judge, that very remarkable man, Dr. Thomas Cooper, replete with all sorts of knowledge, a living encyclopædia—"*Multum ille et terris jactatus et alto*"—good-tempered, joyous, and of a kindly disposition. There was Judge Nott, who brought into the social circle the keen, shrewd, and flashing intellect which distinguished him on the bench. There was Abram Blanding, a man of affairs, very eminent in his profession of the law, and of most interesting conversation. There was Professor Robert Henry, with his elegant, accurate, and classical scholarship. There were Judges Johnston and Harper, whom we all remember, and lament, and admire.

These gentlemen and others were called, in the course of a morning walk of the Chancellor, to meet at dinner, it might be, Mr. Calhoun, or Captain Basil Hall, or Washington Irving, and amongst these was sure to be found David J. M'Cord, with his genial vivacity, his multifarious knowledge, and his inexhaustible store of amusing and apposite anecdotes. He was the life and pervading spirit of the circle—in short, a universal favorite. He was then in large practice at the bar, and publishing his Reports as State Reporter. His frank and fine manners were rendered the more attractive by an uncommonly beautiful physiognomy, which gave him the appearance of great youth.

M'Cord entered upon his profession in co-partnership with Henry Junius Nott; and when a year or two subsequently this gentleman, following the bent of his inclination for literature, quitted the profession, Mr. M'Cord formed a connexion with W. C. Preston—thus introducing this gentleman, who had then but just come to Columbia, into practice. The business of the office was extensive, and the connexion continued until their diverging paths of life led them away from the profession. The association was cordial and uninterrupted throughout, whether professional or social; and the latter did not cease until the grave closed upon M'Cord. While in the law, however, although assiduously addicted to the study of it, his heart acknowledged a divided allegiance with literature; which he seemed to compromise at length by addicting himself to cognate studies—of political economy, the *jural* sciences, and political ethics.

When he left the bar, and retired from the more strenuous pursuits of life, he found occupation and delight in these favorite studies—stimulated and enhanced by the vigorous co-operation and warm sympathy of his highly accomplished wife, who not only participated in the taste for, but shared in the labors of, these studies,—and amidst these congenial and participated pursuits the latter years of his life were passed.

Through life he had a passion for books. He loved them as friends—almost as children. He was always in the midst of them, and had one in his hand or in his pocket. The publication and editing of the Law Reports was a genial occupation for him.

When the compilation of our statutes was con-

* Among his contributions to the Review were—Political Economy, Manufactures, April, 1848; Memphis Convention, October, 1846; Lieber's Political Ethics, October, 1847; The Federal Constitution, November, 1848; Industrial Exchanges, July, 1849; Navigation Laws, January and April, 1850; California Gold, April, 1853; Life of a Negro Slave, Jan., 1853; Civil Liberty and Self Government, April, 1854; Africans at Home, July, 1854; Elements of Government, October, 1854.

For De Bow's Review at New Orleans, he wrote, How the South is affected by her Institutions, January, 1852; What is fair and equal Reciprocity, November, 1853; American Institutions, the Monroe Doctrine, &c., December, 1853.

fided by the state to Dr. Cooper, this gentleman, then feeling some touch of age, found a hearty co-laborer in M'Cord—who worked *con amore;* and, indeed, what with his love for the work and his friendship for Dr. Cooper, a large portion of the achievement was performed by him; and the last volume—the *Index*, I think—was exclusively *his;* thus furnishing at once a monument of his willingness to labor in a praiseworthy work, and the kindliness of his temper to do a favor to a friend.

He was conspicuous for spirit, candor, and friendship. He was faithful and true, fearless and warm-hearted; loved learning and philosophy—the learning which is consonant with the business and bosoms of men—the philosophy which is not "harsh and crabbed, as dull fools suppose," but genial and diffusive, running over into and permeating the affairs of life. As his early life was amidst struggle and bustle—the *fumum strepitumque* of the public arena—so his latter years were amidst the repose of an elegant and lettered retirement, in his well cultivated fields, and amongst his books. His last moments were solaced by the tender assiduities of his congenial help-mate, of his children, and of his old and long-familiar friends.

It was a somewhat curious coincidence, that the disease which terminated his existence, struck him in the Library of the College, whither his tastes and habits led him habitually.

To this we may here appropriately add an acknowledgment of the friendly services of the late Colonel M'Cord to the present work on American literature. We are indebted to his pen for much information of value relative to his literary associates at Columbia, the affairs of the college of which he was a trustee, and particularly for a sketch of his conversations with the late eminent Judge Cooper, with whom he was intimate—an interesting paper, which will be found in the appendix to the present volume.

LOUISA S. M'CORD, the widow of Colonel M'Cord, a lady of strong natural powers, who

Louisa S. McCord.

has cultivated with success both poetry and philosophy, is a resident of Columbia, South Carolina. She is the daughter of the eminent politician, the Hon. Langdon Cheves,* and was born in South Carolina, in December, 1810. In 1840 she was married to Colonel David J. M'Cord. Her winter residence is the plantation of Fort Mott, the scene of a heroic adventure in the revolutionary annals of the state, in which Mrs. Mott made herself famous by the voluntary sacrifice of her property.

The literary productions of Mrs. M'Cord are a volume of poems, *My Dreams*, published in Philadelphia in 1848; *Sophisms of the Protective Policy*, a translation from the French of Bastiat, issued by Putnam, New York, the same year; *Caius Gracchus*, printed at New York in 1851, and numerous contributions to the Southern Quarterly Review, De Bow's Review, and the Southern Literary Messenger, from 1849 to the present time.† These review papers, written with spirit and energy, are of a conservative character, with resources derived from the study of political economy, mainly treating the question of southern slavery in reference to the diversity of races, its comparison with the white laboring class, with a rather sharp handling of the novel of Mrs. Stowe.‡ Mrs. M'Cord has also discussed the woman's rights movements of the day with pungency and good sense. In one of these articles in reply to a proposition of the Westminster Review, that "a reason must be given why anything should be permitted to one person and interdicted to another," she exclaimed, "A reason! —a reason why man cannot drink fire and breathe

---

* The Hon. Langdon Cheves, the venerable contemporary of the Revolution, was born in Abbeville, S. C., September, 17, 1776. A lawyer by profession, he was elected to Congress in the winter of 1810-11, and became a member of the celebrated "war mess," as the coadjutors, Messrs. Cheves, Clay, Loundes, Calhoun, and Bibb, were termed, who carried the declaration of war in 1812. His speech on the "Merchants' Bonds" in December, 1811, was justly characterized by Mr. Clay, then Speaker of the House, as "a splendid exhibition of eloquence." His speeches on the Loan and Navy Bills in the beginning of 1812, gained him much distinction. Mr. Cheves was always opposed to the restrictive system. He succeeded Mr. Clay as Speaker of the House, and during his tenure of that office (which was till he left Congress, declining a re-election in March, 1815), not a single decision of his was ever reversed by that body. On leaving Congress, Mr. Cheves was chosen one of the Superior Judges of the Courts of Law of South Carolina, and in 1819 became President of the Bank of the United States at Philadelphia, the affairs of which he managed with great ability at an important crisis of its history. He held this arduous office for three years, and continued to reside for some time further in Pennsylvania, when he returned to South Carolina.

As a literary man, Mr. Cheves is known by his speeches in Congress, as well as by divers occasional papers; among others, his essays on the subject of the Bank, published with the signature of "Say," which attracted much attention. At a later period, his "occasional reviews," opposing nullification and advocating a Southern Confederacy, as a check upon the advancing movement of the non-slave-holding states; his letter on the same subject to the people of Columbia in 1830; his letter to the people of Pendleton; his letter to the "Charleston Mercury" on Southern Wrongs in 1844; his speech at the Nashville Convention, and other letters, show his accustomed qualities of power, vigor, and eloquence.

† The papers in the *Southern Quarterly Review*, are "Justice and Fraternity," July, 1849; "The Right to Labor," October, 1849; "Diversity of the Races, its bearing upon Negro Slavery," April, 1851; "Negro and White Slavery, wherein do they differ," July, 1851; Enfranchisement of Women," April, 1852; "Uncle Tom's Cabin," January, 1853; "Carey on the Slave Trade," January, 1854. In *De Bow's Review*, "Negro Mania," May, 1852; "Woman and her Needs," September, 1852; "British Philanthropy and American Slavery," March, 1853. *Southern Literary Messenger*, the paper, "Charity which does not begin at home," April, 1853.

‡ The "Uncle Tom" movement also called forth from Mrs. M'Cord, "A Letter to the Duchess of Sutherland from a Lady of South Carolina. July 30, 1853," published in the "Charleston Mercury," and reprinted in several northern papers.

water! A scientific answer about hydrogen and oxygen will not answer the purpose. These are facts, not reasons. Why? Why? Why is anything on God's earth what it is? Can Miss Martineau tell? We cannot. God has made it so, and reason, instinct, and experience, teach us its uses. Woman, Nature teaches you yours." Again she writes in reference to the demand for opportunities: "Even at her own fireside, may woman find duties enough, cares enough, troubles enough, thought enough, wisdom enough, to fit a martyr for the stake, a philosopher for life, or a saint for heaven."

Mrs. M'Cord herself illustrates her views of female life by her own daily example. She conducts the hospital on her own large plantation, attends to the personal wants of the negroes, and on one occasion perfectly set a fracture of a broken arm. Thoroughly accomplished in the modern languages of Europe, she employs her leisure in the education of her children.

The poetry of Mrs. M'Cord is simply and clearly uttered, and is the expression of a healthy nature. Her tragedy of Caius Gracchus, a dramatic poem for the closet, is balanced in its philosophy and argument, Cornelia wisely tempering the democratic fervor of her son. Many sound, pithy aphorisms of conduct may be extracted from this piece; all expressed with purity and precision. The character of Cornelia is well sustained.

THE VOICE OF YEARS.

It floated by, on the passing breeze,
The voice of years:
It breathed o'er ocean, it wandered through earth,
It spoke of the time when words had birth,
When the spirit of God moved over the sea,
When earth was only a thing—to be.
And it sighed, as it passed on that passing breeze,
The voice of years.

From ocean it came on a murmuring wave,
The voice of years:
And it spoke of the time ere the birth of light;
When earth was hushed, 'neath the ocean's might,
And the waters rolled, and the dashing roar,
Of the angered surge owned not yet the power,
Which whispers in that murmuring wave
The voice of years.

From earth it came, from her inmost deep,
The voice of years:
It murmured forth with the bubbling stream,
It came like the sound of a long-past dream—
And it spoke of the hour ere Time had birth,
When living thing moved not yet on earth,
And, solemnly sad, it rose from the deep,
The voice of years.

From heaven it came, on a beam of light,
The voice of years:
And it spoke of a God who reigned alone,
Who waked the stars, who lit the Sun.
As it glanced o'er mountain, and river, and wood,
It spoke of the good and the wonderful God;
And it whispered to praise that God of Light,
The voice of years.

It howled in the storm as it threatening passed,
The voice of years:
And it spoke of ruin, and fiercest might;
Of angry fiends, and of things of night;
But raging, as o'er the Earth it strode,
I knelt and I prayed to the merciful God,
And methought it less angrily howled as it passed,
The voice of years.

And it came from yon moss-grown ruin gray,
The voice of years:
And it spoke of myself, and the years which were gone,
Of hopes which were blighted, and joys which were flown;
Of the wreck of so much that was bright and was fair;
And it made me sad, and I wept to hear,
As it came from yon moss-grown ruin gray,
The voice of years.

And it rose from the grave, with the song of death,
The voice of years:
And I shuddered to hear the tale it told,
Of blighted youth, and hearts grown cold;
And anguish and sorrow which crept to the grave,
To hide from the spoiler the wound which he gave.
And sadly it rose from that home of death,
The voice of years.

But again it passed on the passing breeze,
The voice of years:
And it spoke of a God, who watched us here,
Who heard the sigh, and who saw the tear;
And it spoke of mercy, and not of wo;
There was love and hope in its whispering low;
And I listened to catch, on that passing breeze,
The voice of years.

And it spoke of a pain which might not last,
That voice of years:
And it taught me to think, that the God who gave
The breath of life, could wake from the grave;
And it taught me to see that this beautiful earth,
Was not only made to give sorrow birth;
And it whispered, that mercy must reign at last,
That voice of years.

And strangely methought, as it floated by,
That voice of years
Seemed fraught with a tone from some higher sphere,
It whispered around me, that God was near;
He spoke from the sunbeam; He spoke from the wave;
He spoke from the ruin; He spoke from the grave;
'Twas the voice of God, as it floated by,
That voice of years.

CORNELIA AND GRACCHUS.

[Act III. Scene 1.]

Gracchus.

Wolves breed not lambs, nor can the lioness
Rear fawns among her litter. You but chide
The spirit, mother, which is born from you.

Cornelia.

Curb it, my son; and watch against ambition!
Half demon and half god, she oft misleads
With the bold face of virtue. I know well
The breath of discontent is loud in Rome;
And a hoarse murmuring vengeance smoulders there
Against the tyrannous rule which, iron shod,
Doth trample out man's life. The crisis comes,
But oh! beware my son, how you shall force it!

Gracchus.

Nay, let it come, that dreaded day of doom,
When by the audit of his cruel wrongs
Heaped by the rich oppressor on the crowd
Of struggling victims, he must stand condemned
To vomit forth the ill-got gains which gorge
His luxury to repletion. Let it come!
The world can sleep no longer. Reason wakes
To know man's rights, and forward progress points.

Cornelia.

By reason led, and peaceful wisdom nursed,
All progress is for good. But the deep curse
Of bleeding nations follows in the track
Of mad ambition, which doth cheat itself
To find a glory in its lust of rule;
Which piling private ill on public wrong,
Beneath the garb of patriotism hides
Its large-mawed cravings; and would thoughtless plunge
To every change, however riot waits,
With feud intestine, by mad uproar driven,
And red-eyed murder, to reproach the deed.
Death in its direst forms doth wait on such.

Gracchus.

Man lives to die, and there's no better way
To let the shackled spirit find its freedom
Than in a glorious combat 'gainst oppression.
I would not grudge the breath lost in the struggle.

Cornelia.

Nor I, when duty calls. I am content,
May but my son prove worthy of the crisis;
Not shrinking from the trial, nor yet leaping
Beyond the marked outline of licensed right;
Curbing his passions to his duty's rule;
Giving his country all,—life, fortune, fame,
And only clutching back, with miser's care,
His all untainted honor. But take heed!
The world doth set itself on stilts, to wear
The countenance of some higher, better thing.
'Tis well to seek this wisely; but with haste
Grasping too high, like child beyond its reach
It trips in the aspiring, and thus falls
To lowlier condition. Rashness drags
Remorse and darkest evil in her train.
Pause, ere the cry of suffering pleads to Heaven
Against this fearful mockery of right;
This license wild, which smothers liberty
While feigning to embrace it.

Gracchus.

Thought fantastic
Doth drapery evil thus with unsketched ills.
No heart-sick maid nor dream-struck boy am I
To scare myself with these. There's that in man
Doth long to rise by nature. Ever he
Couching in lethargy, doth wrong himself.

Cornelia.

Most true and more. I reverence human mind;
And with a mingled love and pride I kneel
To nature's inborn majesty in man.
But as I reverence, therefore would I lend
My feeble aid, this mighty power to lead
To its true aim and end. Most often 'tis
When crowds do wander wide of right, and fall
To foul misuse of highest purposes,
The madness of their leaders drags them on.
I would not check aspiring, justly poised;
But rather bid you "on"—where light is clear
And your track plainly marked. I scorn the slang
Of "greedy populace," and "dirty crowd,"
Nor slander thus the nature which I bear.
Men in the aggregate not therefore cease
Still to be men; and where untaught they fall,
It is a noble duty, to awake
The heart of truth, that slumbers in them still.
It is a glorious sight to rouse the soul,
The reasoning heart that in a nation sleeps!
And Wisdom is a laggard at her task
When but in closet speculations toiling
She doth forget to share her thought abroad
And make mankind her heir.

HENRY JUNIUS NOTT

WAS the son of the Hon. Abram Nott (a distinguished judge of the South Carolina Bench), and was born on the borders of Pacolet river, Union District, South Carolina, November 4th, 1797. At a very early age he showed great fondness for poetry and old songs, reciting endless collections of verses, hymns, and corn-shucking catches. In 1806 his father removed to Columbia, where, at the "South Carolina College," young Nott was educated. While at college he was by no means distinguished for attention to the regular course of studies, yet few boys of his class had a higher reputation for talents or acquirements. He read much and never forgot anything. In 1818 he came to the Bar in Columbia, where he soon acquired a high standing and a good practice. This was in competition with a Bar distinguished for many years for its ability and learning. While engaged in the practice of the law Mr. Nott, in conjunction with his intimate friend D. J. M'Cord, published two volumes of Law Reports.

In 1821 preferring the pursuits of literature to the law, Mr. Nott abandoned his profession and took up his abode in France and Holland, the better to pursue his studies. Before his return, the professorship of Belles Lettres was established in the College of South Carolina, and he was elected, while still absent in Europe, to fill this position. On his return, about January, 1824, he commenced the fulfilment of its duties. His extensive reading, wonderful memory, and facility of quotation, united with a sprightly mind, ready wit, and amiable temper, rendered him an exceedingly popular lecturer.

A few years before his death Mr. Nott published in 1834 two volumes of tales called *Novellettes of a Traveller; or, Odds and Ends from the Knapsack of Thomas Singularity, Journeyman Printer.* These are taken from life (many of the incidents being at the time well known about Columbia), and exhibit in a style of much humor, the happy faculty possessed by Mr. Nott of catching every odd trait of character that presented itself. This peculiarity, with his various acquirements and accomplishments, rendered him a most agreeable companion.

Prof. Nott was a good Greek and Latin scholar, as well as master of several modern languages. While in Holland he met Prof. Gaisford of Oxford, for whom he contracted a high esteem, which was we presume mutual.

Mr. Nott wrote several articles for the "Southern Quarterly," of which we are enabled to mention the following:—Life of Wyttenbach, May, 1828; Life of Erasmus, February, 1829; Paul Louis Courier, February, 1830; Woolrych's Life of Judge Jeffrey, August, 1831; D'Aguesseau, February, 1832. These with a MS. novel (a pirate story founded upon historical events in the history of South Carolina) left at his death, and which has never been published, are all that we have of his literary productions.

Mr. Nott and his wife were lost in the wreck of the unfortunate steamer "The Home" off the coast of North Carolina 18th Oct. 1837, leaving an only daughter, now Mrs. W. McKenzie Parker of St. Andrews, S. C. We have been told by eye-witnesses of the fearful tragedy of the wreck in which he perished, that Mr. Nott might easily have saved himself, but, with generous devotion refusing to separate from his wife, he perished with her. No one in the community in which he dwelt was ever more beloved, and none could have been more deeply regretted.

As a specimen of his writing we extract the character of Mr. Hunt, from the story of Thomas Singularity.*

Though in all cases a prudent, gain-saving kind of a man, Mr. Hunt's bowels for once yearned with pity, and he pleaded with his spouse that, inasmuch as their marriage-bed was barren, they should at least give the little unfortunate a domicil till they could make due perquisition about it. This request was proposed in a singularly bland tone, but with that peculiar propriety and force of emphasis he was wont to use when he might not be gainsaid.

From day to day the foundling increased in the affection of his protector, to whom, strange as it may seem, he exhibited a prodigious likeness. This was enough, in the present generation, to excite the surmises and gibes of wicked fancies and slanderous tongues, although it was well known that Zephaniah came from the land of steady habits, and was then a burning and a shining light of orthodox faith. True it was, that "in life's merry morn" he had cut his gambols as wildly as an ass's colt, but he had long ago eschewed his youthful follies, and especially since entering the holy bands of wedlock, had been of staid, I had almost said of saintly, demeanor. He was regular every Sunday, or, as he always termed it, Sabbath, in attending morning and evening service, at the latter of which, of a verity, he generally took a comfortable snooze;—belonged to the Tract Society, Missionary Society, Peace Society, Temperance Society, Abolition Society, and the Society for the Promotion of Psalmody, whereof he led the bass. But as the bard of Avon has said or sung, "Be thou as chaste as ice, as pure as snow, thou shalt not escape calumny"—various young men that prowled about when honest people should be at home abed and asleep, intimated, in what might be called Irish hints, that they had espied the worthy Mr. Hunt at irregular places and at irregular hours. The censorious, too, had expressed their suspicions that as his helpmate was a good ten years older than himself, and had brought a substantial dowry, his match had proceeded more from a love of filthy lucre than from that etherial flame which warmed the bosom of chivalry or inspired the lay of the troubadour. The perfect "counterfeit presentment" that the foundling exhibited to the honest man, was a constant theme with those who wished to bring him to shame, and was eventually whispered by some kind friend into the ears of his spouse. Now although she had a "pretty considerable" belief in Zephaniah's marital faith and seraphic piety, still it must be confessed that she was but a woman, and the monster, whom poets portray as green-eyed, communicated a beryl tinge to the cat-like visual ray of Mrs. Hunt, that rapidly assumed the deepest hue of the emerald. She boldly upbraided her husband for contaminating the sanctuary of married life with the unholy fruits of his wayward propensities, and required that the bantling should forthwith be sent a-packing, as one roof could no longer cover both of them. Mr. Hunt, after expressing some astonishment at this outrageous and unmerited attack, replied with marvellous mildness and composure that, as for turning out of doors a helpless infant, cast, as it were, by Providence under his protection, he could not and would not do it; but that as for her staying under the same roof he, as a Christian, did not think himself authorized to employ any compulsion over one he had ever considered his equal, and that therefore she was at liberty to go, when and where to her seemed meet. Upon this she burst into a flood of tears, calling him a cruel, perjured man, with many other such endearing epithets, accompanied by loud screams and violent kicks. As I have before noticed, he was a man of wondrously composed temperament, and not liking scenes of this kind, he slipped off easily into the shop, where he drank a pint of Philadelphia beer, qualified with a gill of New England rum, then putting a quid of pigtail tobacco in his mouth, he bid his clerk to keep a tight eye on the shop, and walked off to attend a meeting of the Magdalen Society. Meanwhile the afflicted fair one, stealthily opening an eye, perceived that she was alone; and foreseeing that nothing was to be gained by a further contest, got up, wiped off her tears with the corner of her apron, and made up her mind to remain rather by her own cosy fireside, than to run the risk of going further and faring worse. Yet for a long tract of time she continued in the dumps, and poured forth her sorrows to the neighboring gossips, by all of whom her lord and master was vilipended as a barbarous husband and most salacious old heathen. He perhaps thinking, according to the proverb, that the least said is soonest mended, held "the noiseless tenor of his way," with as much composure as a veteran porker amid the impotent attacks of a nest of hornets, until, persuaded by his sober carriage, one half of his enemies began to doubt, and the other, turning fairly round, declared his wife a jealous, weak-minded body, and him an injured saint.

* Novellettes of a Traveller, i. 7.

STEPHEN OLIN,

The President of the Wesleyan University, was born in Leicester, Vermont, March 2, 1797, of a family which first settled in Rhode Island in 1678. His father, Henry Olin, who attained the dignity of judge of the Supreme Court in Vermont, was a man of force of character and of genuine humor. He directed his son's education, and inspired it with his own vigorous example. At seventeen Stephen taught a village school, then entered a lawyer's office at Middlebury, from which he transferred himself to the College at that place, where he completed his course in 1820. In his twenty-fourth year, while engaged as a teacher in a newly founded seminary in South Carolina, he became a Methodist preacher. In 1826 he be-

Stephen Olin

came Professor of Belles Lettres in Franklin College at Athens in Georgia, and in 1832 President of a Methodist institution, the Randolph Macon College in Virginia, in which he undertook the departments of Mental and Moral Science, Belles Lettres, and Political Philosophy. In 1837, driven thither by ill health, he visited Europe and the East, on a protracted journey of several years; and, on his return, published in 1843 his *Travels in Egypt, Arabia Petræa, and the Holy Land.* His last post of duty, varied by another visit to Europe, during which he was delegate to the Evangelical Alliance in London in 1846, was the Presidency of the Wesleyan University in Middletown, Connecticut. He died August 16, 1851, at the age of fifty-four.

Besides the book of travels alluded to, he published a series of Sermons and Lectures and Addresses, which were collected in a posthumous publication of his works by the Harpers in 1852. A large collection of his correspondence was also published in his *Life and Letters* in 1853, two volumes of Memoirs composed of the joint contributions of Dr. McClintock, the able editor of the Methodist Quarterly Review, Dr. Holdich, and other faithful friends.

The academic discourses of Dr. Olin disclose a well trained mind, seeking constantly for the principle to test the fact, and insisting upon the development of mental discipline before the mere accumulation of knowledge. He was a sound conservative in the cause of education, distrusting many of the pretentious expedients of the day. He appreciated the study of the classics in a course of instruction. His religious discourses were of a practical character, and maintain a high rank in Christian precept. His character and teachings gave him great influence with his students.

In person Dr. Olin was over six feet in height, of a large frame and broad shoulders, and a fine head. His voice was of great power and compass, while his gestures were stiff and constrained.

KATHARINE AUGUSTA WARE.

This lady, the daughter of Dr. Rhodes of Quincy, Mass., and wife of Charles A. Ware, of the Navy, is the author of a volume entitled *Power of the Passions, and other Poems*, published by Pickering in London in 1842. She was born in 1797, was married in 1819, wrote occasional poems for the papers, edited *The Bower of Taste* in Boston, and visiting Europe in 1839 died at Paris in 1843. She was a relative of Robert Treat Paine, and at the age of fifteen wrote some verses on his death.

VOICE OF THE SEASONS.

There is a voice in the western breeze,
As it floats o'er Spring's young roses,
Or sighs among the blossoming trees,
Where the spirit of love reposes.
It tells of the joys of the pure and young,
E'er they wander life's 'wildering paths among.

There is a voice in the Summer gale,
Which breathes among regions of bloom,
Or murmurs soft through the dewy vale,
In moonlight's tender gloom.
It tells of hopes unblighted yet,
And of hours the soul can ne'er forget.

There is a voice in the Autumn blast,
That wafts the falling leaf,
When the glowing scene is fading fast,
For the hour of bloom is brief;
It tells of life—of its sure decay,
And of earthly splendors that pass away

There is a voice in the wintry storm,
For the blasting spirit is there,
Sweeping o'er every vernal charm,
O'er all that was bright and fair;
It tells of death, as it moans around,
And the desolate hall returns the sound.

And there's a voice—a small, still voice,
That comes when the storm is past;
It bids the sufferer's heart rejoice,
In the haven of peace at last!
It tells of joys beyond the grave,
And of Him who died a world to save.

NATHANIEL GREENE.

Nathaniel Greene was born at Boscawen, N.H., May 20, 1797. By the death of his father, a lawyer of the town, he was thrown at the age of ten on his own exertions, and at first found occupation in a country store. The perusal of the autobiography of Franklin inspired him with the desire to become an editor, which led him, when Isaac Hill established the *New Hampshire Patriot* at Concord, to offer himself as an apprentice in the printing-office. This he did on the fourth of July of that year, and was accepted. He remained two years in this mechanical pursuit, when, at the early age of fifteen, he was placed in charge, as editor, of the *Concord Gazette*, of which he was the sole conductor till 1814, when he became engaged on the *New Hampshire Gazette*, at Portsmouth. In 1815 he removed to Haverhill, Mass., and edited the Gazette at that place. With this juvenile experience he started a new Democratic journal, *The Essex Patriot*, on his own account, in 1817, which he continued till he commenced *The Boston Statesman* in 1821, a paper which, as it grew from a semi-weekly to a tri-weekly and daily, vigorously supported the Democratic policy and the election of General Jackson. In 1829 he became postmaster of Boston, and disposed of his newspaper interest to his brother, the present able and witty editor of the *Boston Post*, Mr. Charles G. Greene.

Besides his writings as editor, Mr. Greene has employed the leisure of official life in the preparation of several works, chiefly versions from the German of popular tales. His tales and sketches translated from the Italian, German, and French, appeared in Boston in 1843.

ROBERT S. COFFIN,

The self-styled "Boston Bard," was a native of the state of Maine. He served his apprenticeship as a printer in Newburyport; worked on newspapers in Boston, New York, and Philadelphia, and illuminated their poet's corner with his verses. A number of these were collected in a volume entitled the *Oriental Harp, Poems of the Boston Bard*, with a stiff portrait of the author, in a Byronically disposed shirt collar. The contents are as varied as the productions of newspaper laureates are apt to be. Anything will inspire their ever-ready muse. The bard lying awake at night, hears "Yankee Doodle" in the street—

To arms, to arms! I waking, cried;
To arms! the foe is nigh.
A crutch! a hatchet! shovel! spade!
On; death or victory.

"Presenting a lady with a cake of soap," in itself a somewhat questionable liberty, seems to be made doubly so by the lecture which accompanies it, the moral as well as material alkali. The occasion is "improved" after the manner of Erskine's "Smoking spiritualized."

The sparkling gem of Indian mines
  Does not its VALUE lose,
Though on the robes of sluts it shines,
  Or decks the beggar's clothes.

* * * * * *

And lady, when this cake you press,
  Your snowy hands between,
And mark the bubble's varied dress
  Of azure, gold, and green;
Then, lady, think that bubble, brief,
  Of life an emblem true;
Man's but a bubble on the leaf,
  That breaks e'en at the view.

His muse is ready to greet all comers, from the "Mouse which took lodgings with the author in a public house, near the Park, New York,"

Fly not, poor trembler, from my bed,
  Beside me safely rest;
For here no murderous snare is spread,
  No foe may here molest,

up to General La Fayette. Christmas and the Fourth of July are of course celebrated, nor is the "First of May in New York" neglected, as a stanza or two of a comic song, "sung with applause at Chatham Garden," rattles off like the heterogeneous laden carts in active motion on that day.

First of May—clear the way!
  Baskets, barrows, trundles;
Take good care—mind the ware!
  Betty, where's the bundles?
    Pots and kettles, broken victuals,
    Feather beds, plaster heads,
    Looking-glasses, torn matrasses,
    Spoons and ladles, babies' cradles,
    Cups and saucers, salts and castors,
Hurry scurry—grave and gay,
All must trudge the first of May.

"A Large Nose and an Old Coat" show that the writer did not disdain familiar themes, while an "Ode to Genius, suggested by the present unhappy condition of the BOSTON BARD, an eminent poet of this country," stands in evidence that the bard held the poetaster's usual estimate of his powers.

Coffin was at one period of his life a sailor, or, to use his own expression, "a Marine Bachelor." He died at Rowley, Mass., in May, 1827, at the early age of thirty.

The following song would do honor to a poet of far higher pretensions.

SONG.

Love, the leaves are falling round thee;
  All the forest trees are bare;
Winter's snow will soon surround thee,
  Soon will frost thy raven hair:
    Then say with me,
    Love, wilt thou flee,
Nor wait to hear sad autumn's prayer;
    For winter rude
    Will soon intrude,
Nor aught of summer's blushing beauties spare.

Love, the rose lies withering by thee,
  And the lily blooms no more;
Nature's charms will quickly fly thee,
  Chilling rains around thee pour:
    Oh, then with me,
    Love, wilt thou flee,
Ere whirling tempests round thee roar,
    And winter dread
    Shall frost thy head,
And all thy raven ringlets silver o'er?

Love, the moon is shining for thee;
  All the lamps of heaven are bright;
Holy spirits glide before thee,
  Urging on thy tardy flight.
    Then say, with me,
    Love, wilt thou flee,
Nor wait the sun's returning light?
    Time's finger, rude,
    Will soon intrude
Relentless, all thy blushing beauties blight.

Love, the flowers no longer greet thee,
  All their lovely hues are fled;
No more the violet springs to meet thee,
  Lifting slow its modest head:
    Then say, with me,
    Love, wilt thou flee,
And leave this darkling desert dread,
    And seek a clime,
    Of joy sublime,
Where fadeless flowers a lasting fragrance shed!

N. L. FROTHINGHAM.

NATHANIEL LANGDON FROTHINGHAM was born at Boston July 23, 1793. After a preparation for college at the public schools of that city, he entered Harvard, where he completed his course in 1811. He next became an assistant teacher in the Boston Latin school, and afterwards a private tutor in the family of Mr. Lyman of Waltham. In 1812, when only nineteen, he was appointed instructor of Rhetoric and Oratory at Harvard, being the first incumbent of the office. He pursued theological studies at the same time, and on the 15th of March, 1815, was ordained pastor of the First Church in Boston; a charge which he retained until 1850, when he resigned in consequence of ill health.

Dr. Frothingham is the author of from forty to fifty sermons and addresses, published in separate forms,* and of a volume, *Sermons in the order of a Twelvemonth*, none of which had previously appeared. He has also contributed numerous prose articles to various religious periodicals. His poetical career was commenced by the delivery of a poem in the junior year of his col-

* The following list includes most of these productions:—On the Death of Dr. Joseph McKean: 1818. Artillery Election Sermon: 1825. On the Death of President John Adams: 1826. Plea against Religious Controversy: 1829. Terms of Acceptance with God: 1829. Centennial Sermon on Two Hundred Years Ago: 1830. Signs in the Sun; On the great Eclipse of February 12: 1831. Barabbas preferred: 1832. Centennial Sermon of the Thursday Lecture: 1833. On the Death of Lafayette: 1834. Twentieth Anniversary of my Ordination: 1835. On the Death of J. G. Stevenson, M.D.: 1835. At the Installation of Rev. Wm. P. Lunt, at Quincy: 1835. At the Ordination of Mr. Edgar Buckingham: 1836. The Ruffian Released: 1836. The Chamber of Imagery: 1836. Duties of Hard Times: 1837. On the Death of Joseph P. Bradlee: 1838. All Saints' Day: 1840. The New Idolatry: 1840. The Solemn Week: 1841. Death of Dr. T. M. Harris, and of Hon. Daniel Sargent: 1842. The Believer's Rest: 1843. On the Death of Rev. Dr. Greenwood: 1843. The Duty of the Citizen to the Law: 1844. Address to the Alumni of the Theological School: 1844. Deism or Christianity? Four Discourses: 1845. Ordination of O. Frothingham: 1847. Funeral of Rev. Dr. Thomas Gray: 1847. A Fast Sermon—National Sins: 1847. Paradoxes in the Lord's Supper: 1848. A Fast Sermon; God among the Nations: 1848. Water into the City of Boston: 1848. Salvation through the Jews: 1850. Death of Hon. P. C. Brooks: 1849. Gold: 1849. Sermon on resigning my Ministry: 1850. Great Men; Washington's Birth-Day: 1852. Days of Mourning must end: 1853.

lege course, at the inauguration of President Kirkland, which has never been published, but is still remembered with favor by its auditors. He has since contributed several occasional poems of great beauty to the magazines, written numerous hymns, which hold a place in the collections, and translated various specimens of the modern German poets. A collection of these, with the title *Metrical Pieces, Translated and Original*, is now in press.

HYMN.

O God, whose presence glows in all
Within, around us, and above!
Thy word we bless, thy name we call,
Whose word is Truth, whose name is Love.

That truth be with the heart believed
Of all who seek this sacred place;
With power proclaimed, in peace received,—
Our spirit's light, thy Spirit's grace.

That love its holy influence pour,
To keep us meek and make us free,
And throw its binding blessing more
Round each with all, and all with thee.

Send down its angel to our side,—
Send in its calm upon the breast;
For we would know no other guide,
And we can need no other rest.

THE MCLEAN ASYLUM, SOMERVILLE, MASS.

O House of Sorrows! How thy domes
Swell on the sight, but crowd the heart;
While pensive fancy walks thy rooms,
And shrinking Memory minds me what thou art!

A rich gay mansion once wert thou;
And he who built it chose its site
On that hill's proud but gentle brow,
For an abode of splendor and delight.

Years, pains, and cost have reared it high,
The stately pile we now survey;
Grander than ever to the eye;—
But all its fireside pleasures—where are they?

A stranger might suppose the spot
Some seat of learning, shrine of thought;—
Ah! here alone Mind ripens not,
And nothing reasons, nothing can be taught.

Or he might deem thee a retreat
For the poor body's need and ail;
When sudden injuries stab and beat,
Or in slow waste its inward forces fail.

Ah, heavier hurts and wastes are here!
The ruling brain distempered lies.
When Mind flies reeling from its sphere,
Life, health, aye, mirth itself, are mockeries

O House of Sorrows! Sorer shocks
Than can our frame or lot befall
Are hid behind thy jealous locks;
Man's Thought an infant, and his Will a thrall.

The mental, moral, bodily parts,
So nicely separate, strangely blent,
Fly on each other in mad starts,
Or sink together, wildered all and spent.

The sick—but with fantastic dreams!
The sick—but from their uncontrol!
Poor, poor humanity! What themes
Of grief and wonder for the musing soul!

Friends have I seen from free, bright life
Into thy drear confinement cast;
And some, through many a weeping strife,
Brought to that last resort,—the last, the last.

O House of Mercy! Refuge kind
For Nature's most unnatural state!
Place for the absent, wandering mind,
Its healing helper and its sheltering gate!

What woes did man's own cruel fear
Once add to his crazed brother's doom!
Neglect, aversion, tones severe,
The chain, the lash, the fetid, living tomb!

And now, behold what different hands
He lays on that crazed brother's head!
See how this builded bounty stands,
With scenes of beauty all around it spread.

Yes, Love has planned thee, Love endowed;—
And blessings on each pitying heart,
That from the first its gifts bestowed,
Or bears in thee each day its healthful part.

Was e'er the Christ diviner seen,
Than when the wretch no force could bind—
The roving, raving Gadarene—
Sat at his blessed feet, and in his perfect mind?

Mr. Richard Frothingham, Jun., the author of the thorough and valuable *History of the Siege of Boston*, is a relative of Dr. Frothingham.

ROBERT WALN.

Robert Waln was born in Philadelphia in 1797. He received a liberal education, but never engaged in professional pursuits. He published in 1819 *The Hermit in America on a visit to Philadelphia*, one of several imitations of an English work then popular, the Hermit in London. It contains a series of sketches on the fashionable pursuits and topics of city life, pleasantly written, but without any features of mark. In the following year he made a similar essay in verse by the publication of *American Bards, a Satire*. In this poem of nearly one thousand lines he reviews the leading aspirants of the day, praising Cliffton and Dwight and condemning Barlow and Humphreys. Lucius M. Sargent and Knight receive severe treatment, and the Backwoodsman is dealt with in like manner. In the course of the piece a number of minor writers of the ever renewed race of poetasters are mentioned, most of whom have long since been forgotten. A description of a newspaper with the approaches of a youthful bard is one of its best passages.

How oft, when seated in our elbow-chairs,
Resting at eve, from dull, diurnal cares,
We hold the daily chronicles of men,
And read their pages o'er and o'er again;
A varied charm creeps o'er the motley page,
Pleasing alike to infancy and age;
The Politician roams through every clime:
The Schoolboy dwells on Accidents,—and Rhyme:
The Merchant harps on Bank stock and Exchange,
As speculative notions widely range,
And humming all the advertisements o'er,
His searching thoughts, each inference explore;
A secret trust, from rich storehouses, grows;
A list of trifles, doubtful credit shows;
Still as he reads, the air-built castles rise,
While wealth and honours glisten in his eyes:
Old Ladies seek for Murders,—Fires—Escapes;
Old Maids for Births, and Recipes and Rapes.
Young Belles o'er Marriages and Fashions glance,
Or point, in raptures, to some new Romance;
Old age (with horror) reads of sudden death;
The fop, of perfumes for the hair or breath,

And as he lisps the Thespian Bill of Fare,
Twirls his gold-chain, and twists his whiskered hair:
All own the charms that deck the Daily News,
But none more warmly than the youthful Muse.

Nine times the midnight lamp has shed its rays
O'er that young laborer for poetic bays,
Who to the heights of Pindus fain would climb,
By seeking words that jingle into rhyme;
See how the varying passions flush his face!—
The hasty stamp!—the petulant grimace!—
His youthful brains are puzzled to afford
A rhyme to sound with some unlucky word,
'Till, by the Rhyming Dictionary's aid,
It finds a fellow, and the verse is made;
"For so the rhyme be at the verse's end,
No matter whither all the rest does tend."

Now, with a trembling step, he seeks the door,
So often visited in vain before,
Whose horizontal aperture invites
Communications from all scribbling wights,
He stops; and casts his timid eyes around;
Approaches;—footsteps on the pavement sound
With careless air, he wanders from the scene,
'Till no intruding passengers are seen;
Again returns;—fluttering with fears and hopes
He slides the precious scroll—and down it drops!
With hurried steps that would outstrip the wind,
And casting many a fearful glance behind,
He hastens home to seek the arms of sleep,
And dreams of quartos, bound in calf or sheep.

Gods! how his anxious bosom throbs and beats
To see the newsman creeping through the streets!
Thinks, as he loiters at each patron's door,
Whole ages passing in one short half-hour:
Now, from his tardy hand he grasps the news,
And, trembling for the honor of his muse,
Unfolds the paper; with what eager glance
His sparkling eyes embrace the vast expanse!
Now, more intent, he gazes on the print,
But not one single line of rhyme is in't!
The paper falls; he cries, with many a tear,
My God! my Ode to Cupid—is not here!
One hope remains; he claims it with a sigh,
And "Z to-morrow" meets his dazzled eye!

Waln published a second volume of verse in the same year entitled *Sisyphi Opus, or Touches at the Times, with other poems*, and in 1821 *The Hermit in Philadelphia*, a continuation of his previous work, but mostly occupied with a caveat against the introduction of foreign vices into the United States. He makes up a formidable list of wives sold at Smithfield, betting noblemen, and bruised prizefighters, as an offset to the stories by English travellers of society in our frontier settlements.

We next hear of our author as the supercargo of a vessel, in which capacity he made a voyage to China, turning his observations to account on his return by writing a history of that country, which was published in quarto numbers. He also undertook the editorship of the Lives of the Signers, after the publication of the third volume, and wrote several of the biographies which appeared in the subsequent portion of the series. In 1824 he published a *Life of Lafayette*. In addition to these works he was the author of numerous contributions to the periodicals of the day. He died in 1824.

HUNTING SONG.

'Tis the break of day, and cloudless weather,
The eager dogs are all roaming together,
The moor-cock is flitting across the heather,
Up, rouse from your slumbers,
Away!
No vapor encumbers the day;
Wind the echoing horn,
For the waking morn
Peeps forth in its mantle of grey.

The wild boar is shaking his dewy bristle,
The partridge is sounding his morning whistle,
The red-deer is bounding o'er the thistle
Up, rouse from your slumbers,
Away!
No vapor encumbers the day;
Wind the echoing horn,
For the waking morn
Peeps forth in its mantle of grey.

WILLIAM A. MUHLENBERG.

The Rev. Dr. Muhlenberg, a descendant from a family of revolutionary fame, was for many years the head of St. Paul's College, Flushing, Long Island, an institution which under his control attained a high measure of usefulness and reputation. He is now Rector of the Protestant Episcopal Church of the Holy Communion in the city of New York.

Dr. Muhlenberg published in 1828, *Church Poetry: Being portions of the Psalms in verse, and Hymns suited to the Festivals and Fasts and various occasions of the Church, selected and altered from various Authors.** He has since, in connexion with the Rev. Dr. Wainwright, published a work on Church Music, and has done much in the practical advancement of public taste in the same direction by the choral arrangements of his own church, while he has served church poetry as well as music by the production of several highly esteemed hymns. We give the best known of these in its original form, with a brief note from the Evangelical Catholic, a weekly paper conducted for about a year by Dr. Muhlenberg, descriptive of its introduction in the Episcopal collection (where it appears in an abridged form).

THE 187TH HYMN.

We have been so repeatedly urged by several of our readers to give them the whole of the original of "*I would not live alway*," that we at length comply, though somewhat reluctantly, as it has appeared at various times in print before—first in the Philadelphia *Episcopal Recorder*, somewhere about the year 1824. It was written without the remotest idea that any portion of it would ever be employed in the devotions of the Church. Whatever service it has done in that way is owing to the late Bishop of Pennsylvania, then the Rector of St. Ann's Church, Brooklyn, who made the selection of verses out of the whole, which constitutes the present hymn, and offered it to the Committee on Hymns, appointed by the General Convention of ——. The hymn was, at first, rejected by the committee, of which the unknown author was a member, who, upon a satirical criticism being made upon it, earnestly voted against its adoption. It was admitted on the importunate application of Dr. Onderdonk to the bishops on the committee. The following is a revised copy o the original:—

* Phila.; 12mo. pp. 268.

I WOULD NOT LIVE ALWAY.—*Job* vii. 16.

I would not live alway—live alway below!
Oh no, I'll not linger, when bidden to go.
The days of our pilgrimage granted us here,
Are enough for life's woes, full enough for its cheer.
Would I shrink from the path which the prophets of God,
Apostles and martyrs so joyfully trod?
While brethren and friends are all hastening home,
Like a spirit unblest, o'er the earth would I roam?

I would not live alway—I ask not to stay,
Where storm after storm rises dark o'er the way:
Where, seeking for peace, we but hover around,
Like the patriarch's bird, and no resting is found;
Where hope, when she paints her gay bow in the air,
Leaves its brilliance to fade in the night of despair,
And joy's fleeting angel ne'er sheds a glad ray,
Save the gloom of the plumage that bears him away.

I would not live alway—thus fettered by sin,
Temptation without, and corruption within;
In a moment of strength if I sever the chain,
Scarce the victory's mine ere I'm captive again.
E'en the rapture of pardon is mingled with fears,
And my cup of thanksgiving with penitent tears.
The festival trump calls for jubilant songs,
But my spirit her own *miserere* prolongs.

I would not live alway—no, welcome the tomb;
Since Jesus hath lain there I dread not its gloom:
Where He deigned to sleep, I'll too bow my head;
Oh! peaceful the slumbers on that hallowed bed.
And then the glad dawn soon to follow that night,
When the sunrise of glory shall beam on my sight,
When the full matin song, as the sleepers arise
To shout in the morning, shall peal through the skies.

Who, who would live alway—away from his God,
Away from yon heaven, that blissful abode,
Where the rivers of pleasure flow o'er the bright plains,
And the noontide of glory eternally reigns:
Where saints of all ages in harmony meet,
Their Saviour and brethren transported to greet;
While the songs of salvation exultingly roll,
And the smile of the Lord is the feast of the soul?

That heavenly music! what is it I hear?
The notes of the harpers ring sweet in the air;
And see, soft unfolding, those portals of gold!
The King, all arrayed in his beauty, behold!
Oh, give me, Oh, give me the wings of a dove!
Let me hasten my flight to those mansions above;
Aye, 'tis now that my soul on swift pinions would soar,
And in ecstasy bid earth adieu, evermore.

Dr. Muhlenberg is also the author of several pamphlets on topics connected with the church of which he is a prominent member, and the numerous charitable enterprises of the city with which his name is identified.

SAMUEL H. DICKSON

WAS born in Charleston, South Carolina, in 1798. His parents, from the north of Ireland, were both of unmixed Scottish blood. His father came to America before the Revolutionary war, and fought in the south under General Lincoln and others. He was in Charleston during the siege, but escaped in a canoe up Cooper river previous to the capitulation. He was long a resident in Charleston, where he taught the school of the South Carolina Society. He died in 1819. The maternal uncle of Dr. Dickson was Samuel Neilson, the editor of the Northern Star, the first paper published in Ireland advocating Catholic Emancipation, and was one of the first of the Protestants who became United Irishmen. He suffered a long imprisonment after the execution of Emmet, and, being at last released on condition of expatriating himself, came to this country and died at Poughkeepsie.

Saml Henry Dickson

The early education of Dr. Dickson was chiefly in Charleston College, a respectable high-school merely at that time, under Drs. Buist and Hedley and Judge King. He was sent to Yale College in 1811, joined the Sophomore class, and was graduated in due course. He commenced at once, in his seventeenth year, the study of medicine, entering the office of Dr. P. G. Prioleau, who had reached the highest point of professional eminence at the South, and whose practice was extended and lucrative in an almost unparalleled degree. In 1817, '18, and '19, he attended lectures in the University of Pennsylvania in its palmy days, when Chapman, Physick, and Wistar were among its faculty, and received the diploma in 1819. He returned to Charleston and became engaged in a large practice. In 1823 he delivered a course of lectures on Physiology and Pathology before the medical students of the city, the class consisting of about thirty. With Dr. Ramsay, who then read to the same class a course of lectures on Surgery, and Dr. Frost, he undertook the agitation of the subject of domestic medical instruction, and urged the institution of a Medical College in Charleston. He moved the Medical Society to petition to the Legislature for a charter, which was granted, and the school went into operation in 1824. He was elected without opposition to the professorship of the Institutes and Practice of Medicine, which chair he held until 1832, when he resigned it in consequence of a contest between the Medical Society and the College. The next year he was appointed to the same chair in the Medical College of the state of South Carolina, newly erected, with a liberal charter from the legislature. In 1847 he received the unanimous vote of the New York University to fill the chair rendered vacant by the death of Professor Revere, and removed to that city, where he lectured to large classes. In 1850, at the earnest request of his former colleagues, he resumed his connexion with the Medical School at Charleston.

His writings are varied and numerous. He has been a contributor to many of the periodicals of the day, and has delivered many occasional addresses, which have been published. His address before the Phi Beta Kappa of Yale in 1842, on the *Pursuit of Happiness*, is one of the most important of the latter. He has written many articles in the American Medical Journal of Philadelphia, the Medical Journal of New York, the Charleston Medical Journal and Review, and in some of the Western journals. He has published two large volumes on the Practice of Medicine, and, in 1852, a volume of *Essays on Life, Sleep, Pain, &c.*, embracing many important questions of philosophy and hygiene handled in an ingenious and popular manner; amply illustrated from copious stores of reading and extensive personal experience. This book is written in an ingenious and candid spirit; his Manual of Pathology and Therapeutics has gone through six or seven editions. A small volume of verses from his pen, printed but not published, has been noticed in the Southern Literary Messenger,* to which magazine he has sent several papers. In most of the Southern literary journals, the Rose-Bud, Magnolia, Literary Gazette, &c., will be found articles by him. To the Southern Quarterly Review he has been from its origin a frequent contributor. One of his recent articles was a review of Forsyth's Life of Sir Hudson Lowe. He has published a pamphlet on Slavery, originally printed in a Boston periodical, in which he maintains the essential inferiority of the negro, and the futility of the projects suggested for changing his condition at the South.

LINES.

I seek the quiet of the tomb,
There would I sleep;
I love its silence and its gloom
So dark and deep.

I would forget the anxious cares
That rend my breast;
Life's joys and sorrows, hopes and fears,
Here let me rest.

Weep not for me, nor breathe one sigh
Above my bier—
Depart and leave me tranquilly,
Repose is here.

Mock me not with the lofty mound
Of sculptured stone;
Lay me unmarked beneath the ground
All—all alone.

OLD AGE AND DEATH—FROM THE ESSAYS ON LIFE, SLEEP, PAIN, &c.

Death may be considered physiologically, pathologically, and psychologically. We are obliged to regard it and speak of it as the uniform correlative, and indeed the necessary consequence, or final result of life; the act of dying as the rounding off, or termination of the act of living. But it ought to be remarked that this conclusion is derived, not from any understanding or comprehension of the relevancy of the asserted connexion, nor from any *à priori* reasoning applicable to the inquiry, but merely *à posteriori* as the result of universal experience. All that has lived has died; and, therefore, all that lives must die.

The solid rock upon which we tread, and with which we rear our palaces and temples, what is it often, when microscopically examined, but a congeries of the fossil remains of innumerable animal tribes! The soil from which, by tillage, we derive our vegetable food, is scarcely anything more than a mere mixture of the decayed and decaying fragments of former organic being: the shells and exuviæ, the skeletons, and fibres, and exsiccated juices of extinct life.

* * * * * * * * *

I have stated that there is no reason known to us why Death should always "round the sum of life." Up to a certain point of their duration, varying in each separate set of instances, and in the comparison of extremes varying prodigiously, the vegetable and animal organisms not only sustain themselves, but expand and develop themselves, grow and increase, enjoying a better and better life, advancing and progressive. Wherefore is it that at this period all progress is completely arrested; that thenceforward they waste, deteriorate, and fail? Why should they thus decline and decay with unerring uniformity upon their attaining their highest perfection, their most intense activity? This ultimate law is equally mysterious and inexorable. It is true the Sacred Writings tell us of Enoch, "whom God took, and he was not;" and of Elijah, who was transported through the upper air in a chariot of fire; and of Melchisedek, the most extraordinary personage whose name is recorded, "without father, without mother, without descent: having neither beginning of days, nor end of life." We read the history without conceiving the faintest hope from these exceptions to the universal rule. Yet our fancy has always exulted in visionary evasions of it, by forging for ourselves creations of immortal maturity, youth, and beauty, residing in Elysian fields of unfading spring, amidst the fruition of perpetual vigor. We would drink, in imagination, of the sparkling fountain of rejuvenescence; nay, boldly dare the terror of Medea's caldron. We echo, in every despairing heart, the ejaculation of the expiring Wolcott, "Bring back my youth!"

Reflection, however, cannot fail to reconcile us to our ruthless destiny. There is another law of our being, not less unrelenting, whose yoke is even harsher and more intolerable, from whose pressure Death alone can relieve us, and in comparison with which the absolute certainty of dying becomes a glorious blessing. Of whatever else we may remain ignorant, each of us, for himself, comes to feel, realize, and know unequivocally that all his capacities, both of action and enjoyment, are transient, and tend to pass away; and when our thirst is satiated, we turn disgusted from the bitter lees of the once fragrant and sparkling cup. I am aware of Parnell's offered analogy—

The tree of deepest root is found
Unwilling still to leave the ground;

and of Rush's notion, who imputes to the aged such an augmenting love of life that he is at a loss to account for it, and suggests, quaintly enough, that it may depend upon custom, the great moulder of our desires and propensities; and that the infirm and decrepit "love to live on, because they have acquired a habit of living." His assumption is wrong in point of fact. He loses sight of the important principle that Old Age is a relative term, and that one man may be more superannuated, farther advanced in natural decay at sixty, than another at one hundred years. Parr might well rejoice at being alive, and exult in the prospect of continuing to live, at one hundred and thirty, being capable, as is affirmed, even of the enjoyment of sexual life at that age; but he who has had his "three sufficient warnings," who is deaf, lame, and blind; who, like the monk of the Escurial, has lost all his cotemporaries, and is condemned to hopeless solitude, and oppressed with the consciousness of dependence and imbecility, must look on Death not as a curse, but a refuge.

* * * * * * * * * * *

Strolling with my venerable and esteemed colleague, Prof. Stephen Elliott, one afternoon, through a field on the banks of the River Ashley, we came upon a negro basking in the sun, the most ancient looking personage I have ever seen. Our attempts, with his aid, to calculate his age, were of course conjectural; but we were satisfied that he was far

* S. Literary Messenger, July, 1844, vol. x. p. 424.

above one hundred. Bald, toothless, nearly blind, bent almost horizontally, and scarcely capable of locomotion, he was absolutely alone in the world, living by permission upon a place, from which the generation to which his master and fellow-servants belonged had long since disappeared. He expressed many an earnest wish for death, and declared, emphatically, that he "was afraid God Almighty had forgotten him."

* * * * * * * * *

Birds and fishes are said to be the longest lived of animals. For the longevity of the latter, ascertained in fish-ponds, Bacon gives the whimsical reason that, in the moist element which surrounds them, they are protected from exsiccation of the vital juices, and thus preserved. This idea corresponds very well with the stories told of the uncalculated ages of some of the inhabitants of the bayous of Louisiana, and of the happy ignorance of that region, where a traveller once found a withered and antique corpse—so goes the tale—sitting propped in an arm-chair among his posterity, who could not comprehend why he *slept* so long and so soundly.

But the Hollanders and Burmese do not live especially long; and the Arab, always lean and wiry, leads a protracted life amidst his arid sands. Nor can we thus account for the lengthened age of the crow, the raven, and the eagle, which are affirmed to hold out for two or three centuries.

There is the same difference among shrubs and trees, of which some are annual, some of still more brief existence, and some almost eternal. The venerable oak bids defiance to the storms of a thousand winters; and the Indian baobab is set down as a cotemporary at least of the Tower of Babel, having probably braved, like the more transient though long-enduring olive, the very waters of the great deluge.

It will be delightful to know—will Science ever discover for us?—what constitutes the difference thus impressed upon the long and short-lived races of the organized creation. Why must the fragrant shrub or gorgeous flower-plant die immediately after performing its functions of continuing the species, and the pretty ephemeron languish into non-existence just as it flutters through its genial hour of love and grace and enjoyment: while the banyan and the chestnut, the tortoise, the vulture, and the carp, formed of the same primary material elements, and subsisting upon the very same sources of nutrition and supply, outlast them so indefinitely?

Death from old age, from natural decay—usually spoken of as death without disease—is most improperly termed by writers an euthanasia. Alas! how far otherwise is the truth! Old age itself is, with the rarest exceptions, exceptions which I have never had the good fortune to meet with anywhere—old age itself is a protracted and terrible disease.

M'DONALD CLARKE,

THE MAD POET, as he was called in New York, where he figured as the author of numerous volumes, and as a well known eccentric in Broadway some twenty years since, was born in one of the New England states, we believe Connecticut. An inscription to the portrait of one of his books supplies the date of his birth, June 18, 1798. An allusion in the preface to another speaks of a scene with his mother at New London, when he was in his ninth year; and the same introduction records his first appearance, August 13, 1819, in Broadway, New York, thenceforward the main haunt and region of his erratic song.

M'Donald Clarke.

He was a poet of the order of Nat Lee, one of those wits in whose heads, according to Dryden, genius is divided from madness by a thin partition. He was amiable in his weaknesses, having no vices, always preserving a gentility of deportment, while he entertained his imagination with a constant glow of poetic reverie, investing the occasional topics of the town and the day with a gorgeous Byronic enthusiasm. He was constantly to be seen in Broadway, and was a regular attendant at the then, as now, fashionable Grace church. His blue cloak, cloth cap, and erect military air, enhanced by his marked profile, rendered him one of the lions of the pavement. With much purity and delicacy in his verses, it was his hobby to fall in love with, and celebrate in his rhymes, the belles of the city. This was sometimes annoying, however well meant on the part of the poet. Then, from the irregularity of his genius, his muse was constantly stooping from the highest heaven of invention to the lowest regions of the bathetic. The simple, honest nature of the man, however, prevailed; and though witlings occasionally made a butt of him, and entertained themselves with his brilliant flights and his frequent sharp wit, he was upon the whole regarded, by those who had any feeling for the matter, with a certain tenderness and respect.* His poems helped to support him. Judging from the number of editions and their present scarcity he probably succeeded, in some way or other, by subscription or the charity of publishers, in getting from them a revenue adequate to his humble wants.

We are not certain that the following are the titles of all his volumes. In 1820 appeared a slight brochure, a *Review of the Eve of Eternity and other Poems;* and in 1822, *The Elixir of Moonshine; being a collection of Prose and Po-*

* On one occasion Col. Stone of the Commercial, and John Lang of the Gazette, were engaged in a newspaper altercation, in the course of which Lang remarked that Stone's brains were like the poet's, a little zig-zag. McDonald stepped into the office of the Commercial, and seeing the Gazette, wrote this impromptu.

I'll tell Johnny Lang in the way of a laugh,
Since he has dragged my name in his petulant brawl,
That most people think it is better by half
To have brains that are zig-zag than no brains at all.

etry by the Mad Poet, a neat volume of one hundred and forty-eight small pages, published at the "Sentimental Epicure's Ordinary," and bearing the not very savory motto—

'Tis vain for present fame to wish,
 Our persons first must be forgotten,
For poets are like stinking fish,
 That never shine until they're rotten.

In 1825 Clarke published *The Gossip; or, a Laugh with the Ladies, a Grin with the Gentlemen, and Burlesque on Byron, a Sentimental Satire, with other Poems;* which gave Clason the opportunity of showing his cleverness by burlesquing burlesque. The next year he sent forth a mischievous volume of poetic *Sketches*, with some complaints of the "Dutch dignity" of the wealthy young belles who were insensible to his gallantries. Then there were two series of *Afara or the Belles of Broadway*, and a grand collection of the *Poems* in 1836. The last effusion of which we have met with the title is *A Cross and Coronet*, published in 1841. Disdaining to extract amusement from the wildest of these verses, we may cite a few of the others which do credit to the writer's feelings.

These are at the commencement of some stanzas on the death of the poet Brainard, who appears to have been his playfellow in their boyhood at New London.

So early to the grave, alas!—alas!
 Life is indeed a rushing dream:
His did on wings of lightning pass,
 Brightening a Nation with its beam.

Its happy dawn was spent with mine,
 And we were wont, in those young days,
Many a joyous hour to join
 In kindred tasks, and kindred plays.

Where now his shrouded form is laid,
 Our boyish footsteps used to go:
How oft, unthinkingly, we strayed
 In that sad place, long years ago!

Life was flushed with phantoms then,
 That tinged each object with their bloom;
We knew not years were coming, when
 They'd fade in the future's gloom:

We had not seen the frown of Hope—
 Knew not her eye had ever frowned—
That soon our hearts would have to grope
 For feelings—manhood never found.

Saddened as stormy moonlight, looks
 The memory of those half bright days,
When we have stolen away from books,
 And wasted hours in idle plays.

On Handy's Point—on Groton Height,
 We struck the ball, or threw the quoit,
Or calmly, in the cool twilight,
 From Hurlbut's wharf have flung the bait.

The following is in one of Clarke's frequent moods.

ON SEEING A YOUNG GIRL LOOK VERY WISHFULLY INTO THE STREET, FROM A WINDOW OF MISS ——'S BOARDING SCHOOL, IN BROADWAY.

Sequestered girl—and dost thou deem
 Thy lot is hard, because thou'rt hidden
From public life's bewildered stream,
 And public pleasure's fruit forbidden?

Thou little knowest how many cares
 Are scattered o'er the surge of fashion,
How soon its guilty scene impairs
 Each virtuous hope—each modest passion.

The world assumes a winning shape,
 That soils whate'er may dare to eye it,
And those young hearts alone escape,
 That have the fortitude to fly it.

It takes the mask of coaxing eyes,
 Of languid words, and bashful wooing,
Of tutored prayers, and treacherous sighs,
 To tempt the innocent to ruin.

Its look is warm—its heart is cold,
 Its accent sweet—its nature savage;
Its arms embrace with feeling's fold,
 Till they shall have the power to—ravage.

Those who have mingled in its clash,
 And outwardly would seem to prize it,
Its sweetest cup would gladly dash,
 And while they feel its smile—despise it.

The broken form—the ruffled cheek—
 The icy voice—the cheerless manner—
Disgusted hope and feeling speak,
 Worn out beneath a bandit's banner.

Maiden! in some yet shapeless years,
 Thou'lt find too true what I have spoken,
And read these lines perhaps with tears,
 That steal out from a heart that's broken.

There is the spirit of his New England home in these lines:—

SUNDAY IN SUMMER.

When the tumult and toil of the week have ceased,
How still is the morning that smiles in the east,
The sweet Sabbath morning that comes to refresh
Every soul that is faint in its prison of flesh.

The rich clouds are fringed with yellow and blue—
The lips of the flowers are silvered with dew—
The winds are reposed upon pillows of balm—
Enjoyment is throned on the clear azure calm.

The orchard trees bend their full arms to the earth,
In blessing the breast, where their beauty has birth,
And while bending in crimson luxuriance there,
Seem to have joined in the Sabbath's first prayer.

The little birds sing their gay hymns in the boughs—
The delicate winds from their cradles arouse—
The Sun gently lifts his broad forehead on high,
As Serenity presses her cheek to the sky.

And shall man, who *might* be an Angel in tears,
Would he weep out the stains of his sensual years,
While Nature is brim'd with affection and praise,
Be a stranger to God, on this dearest of days?

O no—the deep voice of the steeple is loud,
And City and Village in worship are bowed,
While the blue eyes of Summer look tenderly down,
And nothing but Sin has a fear or a frown.

M'Donald's mixture of crudities and sublimities attracted the public, we fear, more than his correcter pieces. He was the mad poet of the town, something like the fool in old plays, venting homilies in most melancholy jest, perhaps with a broken note of music, or a half caught felicity of genius grasped at in one of his quick random flights. Of his humorous efforts a single specimen may suffice, which he appears to have written on the completion of the

ASTOR HOUSE.

The winds of 1784,
 Beat on a young Dutchman's head,
Who on his brawny shoulders bore
 Beaver skins, he said

He'd sell, extremely cheap—
He sold a heap.

To the shaggy burden bent
 Firmly, for many a year,
From the copper seeds of a cent,
 Has reaped a golden harvest, here,
Till his name is smothered in bank stock,
And notched on the eternal rock.

His funeral monument is done—
 Crowned with its granite wreath—
Poverty, load the loudest gun,
 When he shall bequeath
His example—as Industry stares—
How to gild grey hairs.

A jovial tomb-stone,—whew!
 Such as but few on earth afford—
Many a Fellow will get blue,
 Many a mock-dirge be roared
From those gay corners, when New York
Hears other Centuries laugh, and talk.

Its front, to the flashing East,
 Let the broadside of the heaviest storm,
With wild, white lightnings creased,
 Thunder for Ages on its form,
'Twill stand through thick and thin,
Showers of—whiskey punch, within.

Benevolence, bid him build,
 A twin-tomb to that Alpine pile,
Have it with homeless orphans filled,
 Whose fond and grateful smile,
Shall memory's sweetest moonlight shed,
For ever, o'er his mouldering head.

Scorn and sentiment were the best winged arrows in Clarke's quiver. His indignation at fortune for her treatment of genius and beauty, and at the fopperies and impertinences of fashion, was unbounded; he would rant in these fits of indignation beyond the powers of the language; but he would always be brought back to human sensibility by the sight of a pretty face or an innocent look.

His verses are incongruous enough, grotesque and absurd to the full measure of those qualities, but a kind eye may be attracted by their very irregularity, and find some soul of goodness in them; and a lover of oddity—who would have subscribed for a copy when the poet was living—may innocently enough laugh at the crudities. At any rate we have thought some notice of the man worth presenting, if only as a curious reminiscence of city life in New York, and a gratification to the inquiring visitor at Greenwood Cemetery, who asks the meaning of the simple monument at "the Poet's Mound, Sylvan Water," upon which the death of M'Donald Clarke is recorded March 5, 1842.

ISAAC STARR CLASON,

A WRITER of fine talent but of a dissipated life, was born in New York in 1798. His father was a wealthy merchant of the city. The son had a good education and inherited a fortune. He wasted the latter in a course of prodigal living, and was driven to exhibit his literary accomplishments as a writer of poems, generally more remarkable for spirit than sobriety, as a teacher of elocution, and as an actor. He appeared on the boards of the Bowery and Park theatres in leading Shakespearian parts, but without much success. In 1825 he published *Don Juan, Cantos* XVII., XVIII., supplementary to the poem of Lord Byron, and in a kindred vein, not merely of the grossness but of the wit. It made a reputation for the author, and still remains probably the best of the numerous imitations of its brilliant original which have appeared. The scandal of the author's life faithfully reflected in it, added not a little to its piquancy.

This was followed, in 1826, by a collection of poems entitled *Horace in New York*. In this the author celebrates Malibran, then in the ascendant in opera, Dr. Mitchill, Halleck, and the Croakers, and other gossip of the town. In addition to these playful effusions, his capacity for serious verse is shown in some feeling lines to the memory of the orator and patriot Emmett.

In 1833 he wrote a poem founded on the "Beauchampe tragedy" of Kentucky; but the manuscript was never seen by any of his family, though he was heard to repeat passages from it. The poem is probably irrecoverably lost.

In 1834 Clason closed his life by a miserable tragedy in London, whither he had gone as a theatrical adventurer. Reduced to poverty, this man of naturally brilliant powers threw away the opportunities of life by suicide. In company with his mistress he carefully sealed the room in which they lodged in London against the admission of air, and lighted a fire of charcoal, from the fumes of which both were found suffocated.

NAPOLEON—FROM THE DON JUAN.

I love no land so well as that of France—
 Land of Napoleon and Charlemagne;
Renowned for valor, women, wit, and dance,
 For racy Burgundy, and bright Champagne—
Whose only word in battle was "advance,"
 While that "Grand Genius" who seemed born to reign—
Greater than Ammon's son, who boasted birth
From heaven, and spurned all sons of earth.

Greater than he, who wore his buskins high,
 A Venus armed, impressed upon his Seal—
Who smiled at poor Calphurnia's prophecy,
 Nor feared the stroke he soon was doomed to feel;
Who on the Ides of March breathed his last sigh,
 As Brutus plucked away his "cursed steel,"
Exclaiming as he expired, "Et tu Brute!"
 But Brutus thought he only did his duty.

Greater than he who at nine years of age,
 On Carthage' altar swore eternal hate,
Who with a rancor, time could ne'er assuage—
 With Feelings, no reverse could moderate—
With Talents, such as few would dare engage—
 With Hopes, that no misfortune could abate—
Died, like his rival, both with broken hearts:
Such was their fate, and such was Bonaparte's.

Napoleon Bonaparte! thy name shall live,
 Till Time's last echo shall have ceased to sound,
And if Eternity's confines can give
 To Space reverberation—round and round
The Spheres of Heaven, the long, deep cry of "Vive
 Napoleon!" in Thunders shall rebound—
The Lightning's flash shall blaze thy name on high,
Monarch of Earth, now Meteor of the Sky!

What! though on St. Helena's rocky shore,
 Thy head be pillowed, and thy form entombed,—
Perhaps that Son, the child thou didst adore,
 Fired with a father's fame, may yet be doomed

To crush the bigot Bourbon, and restore
 Thy mould'ring ashes, ere they be consumed;—
Perhaps, may run the course thyself didst run—
And light the World, as Comets light the sun;

'Tis better thou art gone; 'twere sad to see
 Beneath an "imbecile's" impotent reign,
Thy own unvanquished legions, doomed to be
 Cursed instruments of vengeance on poor Spain,—
That land so glorious once in chivalry,
 Now sunk in Slav'ry and in Shame again;
To see th' Imperial Guard, thy dauntless band,
Made tools for such a wretch as *Ferdinand.*

Farewell Napoleon! thine hour is past;
 No more earth trembles at thy dreaded name,
But France, unhappy France, shall long contrast
 Thy deeds with those of worthless *D'Angoulême.*
Ye Gods! how long shall slavery's thraldom last?
 Will France alone remain for ever tame?
Say! will no Wallace, will no Washington,
Scourge from thy soil the infamous Bourbon?

Is Freedom dead? Is Nero's reign restored?
 Frenchmen! remember Jena, Austerlitz!
The first, which made thy Emperor the Lord
 Of Prussia, and which almost threw in fits
Great Fred'rick William—he who at the board
 Took all the Prussian uniform to bits;
Fred'rick, the king of regimental tailors,
As *Hudson Lowe* the very prince of jailers.

Farewell Napoleon! hadst thou have died
 The coward scorpion's death—afraid, ashamed,
To meet Adversity's advancing tide,
 The weak had praised thee, but the wise had blamed:
But no! though torn from country, child, and bride,
 With Spirit unsubdued, with Soul untamed,
Great in Misfortune, as in Glory high,
Thou darest to live through life's worst agony.

Pity, for thee, shall weep her fountains dry!
 Mercy, for thee, shall bankrupt all her store!
Valor shall pluck a garland from on high!
 And Honor twine the wreath thy temples o'er!
Beauty shall beckon to thee from the Sky!
 And smiling Seraphs open wide Heaven's door!
Around thy head the brightest Stars shall meet,
And rolling Suns play sportive at thy feet!

Farewell Napoleon! a long farewell!
 A stranger's tongue, alas! must hymn thy worth;
No craven Gaul dare wake his Harp to tell
 Or sound in song the spot that gave thee birth.
No more thy Name, that with its magic spell
 Aroused the slumb'ring nations of the earth,
Echoes around thy land! 'tis past; at length,
France sinks beneath the sway of Charles the Tenth.

THOMAS ADDIS EMMET.

Son of a land, where Nature spreads her green,
But Tyranny secures the blossomed boughs;
Son of a race, long fed with Freedom's flame,
Yet trampled on when blazing in her cause:—
With reverence I greet thee, gifted man—
Youth's saucy blood subsides at thy grey hairs.

 Oh, what was the true working of thy soul—
What griefs—what thoughts played in thy pliant mind,
When, in the pride of manhood's steady glow,
Thy back was turned upon the fav'rite trees,
Which, to thy childhood, had bestowed a shade?
When every step, which bore thee to the shore,
Went from old paths, and hospitable roofs?—
Did not the heart's-tear tremble in thine eye,
A prayer for Erin quiver on thy lip,
As the ship proudly held her prow aloft,
And left the green isle in her creaming wake?

 And if a grief pressed on thy manly heart,
A prayer arose upon the ocean breeze,
At leaving each beloved face and scene:—
Did not the tear appear, and praise arise,
When stranger forms held out the friendly hand;
When shores, as strange, with smiles adopted thee?
Yes! yes! there was a tear:—a tear of joy;—
There was a prayer:—a prayer of gratitude.

 And well thou hast returned each kindness done,
A birth-right purchased by thy valued deeds;
And those who tendered thee a brother's grasp,
Bow, with respect, at thy intelligence,
And glory in the warmth their friendship showed.

 I love to see thee in the crowded court,
Filling the warm air with sonorous voice,
Which use hath polished, time left unimpaired—
Bold, from the knowledge of thy powers of mind;
Flowing in speech, from Nature's liberal gifts—
While thy strong figure and commanding arm,
Want but the toga's full and graceful fold,
To form a model worthy of old Rome.
I smile to see thy still unbending form
Dare winter's cold and summer's parching heat,
And buffet the wild crowd with gallant strength—
The slight bamboo poised graceful in thy hand,
And wielded with the air of Washington—
While thy light foot comes bravely from the earth,
As if the mind were working in the trunk.

 And yet, though I enjoy thy frosty strength,
There's something tells me in thy furrowed face,
A virtuous age cannot o'erstep the tomb!
A solemn something whispers to my soul,
The court will feel the silence at thy death,
More than it did thy bursts of eloquence.
While thy chair standing in thy now warm home,
Will have an awful void when thou art gone.
What is't to thee if thy long life should wane!
The immortal soul will unsubdued arise,
And glow upon the steps of God's own throne:
Like incense kindled on an altar's top.

 Cold as thy monument thy frame must be—
Warm as thy heart will be thy epitaph.
For thus the aching mind of valued friend,
Shall pay the last meed to the man he loved:
"Green as the grass around this quiet spot;
Pure as the Heavens above this cenotaph;
Warm as the sun that sinks o'er yonder hills;
And active as the rich, careering clouds;
Was he who lies in earth a thing of nought?
A thing of nought!—For what is man, great God?
A very worm; an insect of a day—
His body but the chrys'lis to his mind!
For, even here—here where the good man's laid,
And proud Columbia's genius grieves—
We can but murmur: Here an Emmet lies."

JOHN HUGHES.

This distinguished divine and controversialist was born in the north of Ireland, 1798. He came to America in his nineteenth year, and studied theology at the college of Mount St. Mary, Emmetsburg, Maryland. Soon after his ordination in 1825, he became the rector of a Roman Catholic church in Philadelphia, where he entered, in 1830, upon a newspaper discussion with the Rev. Dr. John Breckenridge, a leading divine of the Presbyterian church. The articles thus published were collected in a volume. An oral discussion between the same parties took place in

1834. In 1838, Dr. Hughes, having been appointed Bishop Administrator of New York, removed to that city. In 1840, he commenced an agitation of the School question, claiming either that no tax should be levied for educational purposes, or, if levied, its proceeds be distributed among the various religious denominations of the community, it being impossible, as he urged, to provide a system of education which could be tolerated by all. The reading of the ordinary Protestant version of the Bible he especially objected to. The long discussion of the subject which followed was maintained with great energy, perseverance, and ability by the prelate, who succeeded in obtaining a modification of the previously existing system. His claim that the church property of his denomination should be exclusively vested in the hands of the clergy, likewise urged at an early period of his episcopate, has also caused much discussion, and has been revived in the year 1855 in a controversy between Dr. Hughes and the Hon. Erastus Brooks, of the New York Senate, growing out of a statement by the latter that the Bishop was, in this manner, in possession of property to the value of five millions of dollars. The articles which have passed between the parties have been collected in two separate and rival publications. In 1850, Bishop Hughes and his diocese were promoted by Pius IX. to archiepiscopal rank. His energetic discharge of the duties of his elevated position has not interfered with his literary activity. He has constantly, as occasion has arisen, availed himself of the newspapers of the day to repel charges made against his denomination in relation to its action on contemporary questions, and has also frequently appeared as a lecturer. Several of his productions in the last named capacity have been published, and exhibit him, in common with his less elaborate efforts, as a vigorous, animated, and polished writer, decided in the expression of opinion, and quick in availing himself of every advantage of debate. The following are the titles of these addresses: *Christianity the only Source of Moral, Social, and Political Regeneration*, delivered in the hall of the House of Representatives of the United States in 1847, by request of the members of both houses of Congress; *The Church and the World; The Decline of Protestantism; Lecture on the Antecedent Cause of the Irish Famine in* 1847; *Lecture on Mixture of Civil and Ecclesiastical Power in the Middle Ages; Lectures on the Importance of a Christian Basis for the Science of Political Economy; Two Lectures on the Moral Causes that have produced the Evil Spirit of the Times; Debate before the Common Council of New York, on the Catholic Petition respecting the Common School Fund;* and *The Catholic Chapter in the History of the United States.*

Bishop Hughes is an impressive and agreeable speaker. In person he is tall and well proportioned, with a countenance expressive of benevolence and dignity.

FRANCIS L. HAWKS,

An eminent pulpit orator of the Protestant Episcopal Church, was born in North Carolina, at Newbern, June 10, 1798. His grandfather came with the colonial governor Tryon from England, and was employed as an architect in some of the prominent public works of the state, and was distinguished by his liberal opinions in the Revolution.

He was graduated at the University of North Carolina, and prosecuting the study of the law in the office of the Hon. William Gaston, was admitted to the bar at the age of twenty-one. He continued the practice of the law for several years in his native state, with distinguished success. A memorial of his career at this period is left to the public in his four volumes of *Reports of Decisions in the Supreme Court of North Carolina*, 1820–26, and his *Digest of all the Cases decided and reported in North Carolina.* In his twenty-third year he was elected to the Legislature of his state.

His youth had been marked by its high tone of character, and his personal qualities and inclinations led him to the church as his appropriate sphere. He was ordained by Bishop Ravenscroft in 1827. His earliest ministerial duties were in charge of a congregation in New Haven. In 1829 he became the assistant minister of St. James's Church, Philadelphia, in which Bishop White was rector. The next year he was called to St. Stephen's Church in New York, in which city his reputation for eloquence became at once permanently established. From St. Stephen's he passed to St. Thomas's Church in 1832, and continued his connexion with the parish till his removal to Mississippi in 1844. During the latter period of his brilliant career at St. Thomas's, he was relieved from a portion of his city parochial labors by an assistant, and devoted himself to a liberal plan of education, which he had matured with great ability, and the details of which were faithfully carried out. He established at Flushing, Long Island, a boarding school, to which he gave the name of St. Thomas's Hall. The grounds were prepared and the buildings erected by him; a liberal provision was made for the instruction and personal comforts of the students. He introduced order and method in all departments. Substantial comfort and prosperity pervaded the establishment on all sides. Unfortunately the experiment fell upon a period of great commer-

St. Thomas's Hall.

cial pressure, and the fruits of the hearty zeal, labor, and self-denial of its projector, were lost in its financial embarrassments. The failure of this institution was a serious loss to the cause of education. Its success would have greatly assisted to elevate the standard of the frequently mismanaged and even injurious country boarding schools. As a characteristic of Dr. Hawks's habitual consideration for the needy members of his profession, and of his own personal disinterestedness, it may be mentioned that it was his intention, when he had fairly established the institution, to leave it in the hands of appropriate trustees, with the simple provision that the sons of poor clergymen should receive from it, without charge, an education worthy the position due their parents.

Previous to his departure for the south-west, Dr. Hawks had, in 1836, passed a summer season in England, procuring, in accordance with a provision of the General Convention, copies of important papers relating to the early history of the Episcopal Church in America. In this he had the assistance of the eminent dignitaries of the English Church, and secured a large and valuable collection of MSS., which have been since frequently consulted on important topics of the ecclesiastical and civil history of the country. While at Flushing, after his return, he printed considerable portions of them in the Church Record, a weekly paper devoted to the cause of Christianity and education, which, commenced in November, 1840, was continued till October, 1842.* The Record was conducted by Dr. Hawks, and besides its support of Protestant theology in the agitations of the day induced by the publication of the "Oxford Tracts," in which Dr. Hawks maintained the old American churchmanship and respect for the rights of the laity, which he had learnt in the schools of White and Ravenscroft, the journal made also a liberal provision for the display of the sound old English literature, in a series of articles in which its wants were set forth from Sir Thomas More to De Foe. In 1837 Dr. Hawks established the *New York Review*, for a time continuing its active editor, and commencing its valuable series of articles on the leading statesmen of the country, with his papers on Jefferson and Burr.†

While in the south-west Dr. Hawks was elected Bishop of Mississippi, his confirmation in which office was met by opposition in the General Convention, where charges were proposed against him growing out of the financial difficulties of the St. Thomas's Hall education scheme. His vindication of his course in this matter occupied several hours at the Convention at Philadelphia, and is described by those who listened to it as a masterly and eloquent oration: clear and ample in statement, powerful and convincing in the noble appeal of the motives which had led him to the disastrous enterprise. A vote of acquittal was passed, and the matter referred to the Diocese of Mississippi, which expressed its entire confidence. The bishopric was, however, not accepted. He has since been tendered the bishopric of Rhode Island. In 1842 Dr. Hawks edited a volume of the Hamilton papers from MSS. confided to him by the venerable widow; but the undertaking was laid aside with a single volume, the work having been afterwards entered upon by Hamilton's son, with the assistance of Congress.* In 1844 he accepted the rectorship of Christ's Church in New Orleans, a position which he held for five years; during which time he also lent his assistance to the furtherance of the organization of the State University, of which he was made President. He returned to New York in 1849 at the request of his friends, with the understanding that provision was to be made for his St. Thomas's Hall obligations; the unabated admiration of his eloquence and personal qualities readily secured a sufficient fund for this object, and he has since filled the pulpit at Calvary Church.

Francis L. Hawks.

The literary publications of Dr. Hawks are two volumes of *Contributions to the Ecclesiastical History of the United States*, embracing the states of Virginia and Maryland; a volume of *The Constitutions and Canons of the Episcopal Church* with notes; a caustic essay on *Auricular Confession in the Protestant Episcopal Church*, published in 1850; an octavo, *Egypt and its Monuments*, in particular relation to biblical evidence; a translation of Rivero and Tschudi's *Antiquities of Peru*, in 1853; and several juvenile volumes of natural history and American annals published in the "Boy's and Girl's Library" by the Harpers, with the title "Uncle Philip's Conversations." Dr. Hawks is also the author of a few poems, mostly descriptive of incidents in his parochial relations, which have been recently

* Three volumes of this work were published by C. R. Lindon, an ingenious practical printer, and since the clever editor of the Flushing Gazette: two in quarto of the weekly, and a third in a monthly octavo.

† From the hands of Dr. Hawks the Review passed under the management of his associate in the enterprise, the Rev. Dr. C. S. Henry, the translator of Cousin, author of a History of Philosophy in Harpers' Family Library, and for many years Professor of Moral and Intellectual Philosophy in the New York University. When Dr. Henry retired from the Review, he was succeeded by that most accomplished man of letters, the organizer and first librarian of the Astor Library, Dr. J. G. Cogswell, by whom the work was conducted till its close in its tenth volume in 1841.

* The Official and other Papers of the late Major-General Alexander Hamilton, compiled chiefly from the originals in the possession of Mrs. Hamilton. 8vo. New York: Wiley and Putnam. 1842.

printed in the North Carolina collection of poetry entitled "Wood Notes." It is understood that he has in preparation a work on the *Antiquities of America*, a subject which has long employed his attention. In addition to these literary pursuits, which have been but episodes in his active professional career, Dr. Hawks has delivered several lectures and addresses, of which we may mention particularly a biographical sketch of Sir Walter Raleigh, and a vindication of the early position of North Carolina in the affairs of the Revolution. He has been also an active participant in the proceedings of the New York Ethnological, Historical, and Geographical Societies. Of the most important part of Dr. Hawks's intellectual labors, his addresses from the pulpit, it is enough to say that their merits in argument and rhetoric have deservedly maintained his high position as an orator, through a period and to an extent rare in the history of popular eloquence. A manly and unprejudiced conviction of Christian truth, a brilliant fancy, illuminating ample stores of reading, and a practical knowledge of the world; seldom seen physical powers; a deep-toned voice, expressive of sincere feeling and pathos, and easy and melodious in all its utterances; a warm Southern sensibility, and courageous conduct in action, are among the qualities of the man, which justify the strong personal influence which he has long exercised at will among his contemporaries.

APPEAL FOR UNION OF THE REVOLUTIONARY FATHERS AND STATESMEN;—FROM A THANKSGIVING SERMON AT CALVARY CHURCH, ON "THE DUTY OF CULTIVATING UNITY AND THE SPIRIT OF NATIONALITY."

We owe the cultivation of this spirit, the importance of which I have been endeavoring to establish, to the memory of our heroic old fathers. Theirs was the first great onward march in the work of making us a nation. Every step of that march was marked by their blood and sufferings. They did not know all that they were doing; but they did see, dimly rising up in the distance before them, freedom for themselves and their children, and freedom was the root of their planting, from which union and nationality sprung. What think you, could they come back from their graves and stand here among us to-day, to see the nation of which they planted the seed nearly eighty years ago; what think you they would say to us upon this subject? They would tell us of that dark, sad period, when without arms and without ammunition; with nothing but courage to supply the want of discipline, and with no leader but God Almighty, they looked in upon their brave hearts, and questioning them, received for response, "Be free, or die!" And then they solemnly swore, the Lord being their helper, that they would be free. They would tell us how they tore themselves away from weeping wives and children; and how the noble mothers from whom we sprung, chid the children for their tears, even while they wept themselves, and how, dashing the teardrops from their eyelids, they threw their arms around them for a parting embrace, and without a falter in the voice, rung out in clear, womanly tones, the words—often remembered afterwards in the battle strife—"Go, my brave husband! go, my daring boy! I give you to your bleeding country; I give you to the righteous cause of freedom; and if He so will it, I give you back to God." They would tell us how, through seven long years, they endured cold and hunger and nakedness; how they fought, how they bled, how some among them died; how God went with them and brought them through triumphant at last. They would tell us how they were more than compensated for all they had suffered, as they looked around, (as on this day,) and in this mighty nation of many millions, saw what God was working out in their seven long years of suffering. And who among us, as the story ceased, would dare to say to these venerable witnesses to the past, "Shall we throw away that which cost you so much; shall we break up our unity; shall we cease to be a nation?" Dare to say it? Why, a man's own conscience would rise up and call him accursed traitor, if he but dared to think it.

Is the spirit of our fathers dead within us? Has the blood of our noble old mothers ceased to flow in our veins? Who then are these white-haired old men that are sitting here around me? A remnant, a mere remnant! Remnant of what? Of those who, when our nation had attained just about half its present age, showed that the spirit of our Revolutionary fathers was not then dead. These are what remains of the veterans of the war of 1812. It is thirty years ago since they were in the vigor of life, and then they did just as their fathers had done before them. Their country wanted them, and they waited no second summons; they went forth and kept the field until their country gave them an honorable discharge. But in one thing they differed from their fathers. God permitted them to see, when they so promptly answered their country's call, and has permitted them, by prolonging their lives until now, more fully to see, what their fathers could only hope for: the immense advantages and blessings of a great, consolidated, united people. And how have they come up in a body to-day, requesting it as a privilege to do so, that they might unitedly thank God, among other national blessings, for the establishment and preservation of that nationality which the fathers of the Republic began, and to preserve the infant growth of which, they perilled their lives. "Honor to whom honor is due."

But there is yet another class to whom we owe it to cherish the spirit of a broad nationality. These, too, served their country, but not in the tented field. These were our patriot statesmen—the men who framed, expounded, and upheld the great principles of our political fabric. We may not, on an occasion like this, pass them by unmentioned. I cannot, of course, allude to all, but, since last we met, on an occasion like this, two have gone, whose lives were devoted to their country, with as pure a patriotism as ever animated an American heart; and each of whom gave, not merely commanding talents to the Republic, but by a sad coincidence gave also a *son*, and they wept alike, as they laid their dead soldier boys in honored graves. Need I name them? Not when I speak to Americans; for grief is yet too green in the nation's heart to call for names. These men knew the worth of unity and nationality. The one living among the new settlements of our magnificent lovely West, the other on the shores of old Massachusetts, near the very spot where one of the earliest colonies was planted; but what mattered it to them whether a State were on this side or the other of the mountains, whether it were planted by "pilgrim fathers" or "the hunters of Kentucky," so long as all was ONE. The one knew "no North, no South, no East, no West:" the other prayed that when he died, his eye might rest upon the gorgeous ensign of the Republic, and see every star in its place, while the rallying cry of his country should still be "Liberty and Union, now and for ever!" These men had studied the value of these *United* States; they could see but little value in them *disunited*. They saw the grand conception of a *continental*

Union in all its mighty consequences. They are dead; we shall hear their voices of wisdom no more. The one, in argument, smote like lightning, and shivered the rock into fragments; the other came with the ponderous force of the Alpine avalanche, and sweeping away rock, tree, hamlet, everything in its path, buried them out of sight for ever. I thank God for both, and pray that he may raise up others to fill their places. I thank Him for the wisdom He gave them, and pray that my country may treasure it up among her hallowed possessions. And when I think how universal and heartfelt was the individual grief of my countrymen at their loss, I cannot believe that their great principle of national unity will not survive them. They have gone down to the grave with the Christian's hope; peace be to their remains—honor to their memories.

TO AN AGED AND VERY CHEERFUL CHRISTIAN LADY.

Lady! I may not think that thou
Hast travelled o'er life's weary road,
And never felt thy spirit bow
Beneath affliction's heavy load.

I may not think those aged eyes
Have ne'er been wet with sorrow's tears;
Doubtless thy heart has told in sighs,
The tale of human hopes and fears.

And yet thy cheerful spirit breathes
The freshness of its golden prime,
Age decks thy brow with silver wreaths,
But thy young heart still laughs at Time.

Life's sympathies with thee are bright,
The current of thy love still flows,
And silvery clouds of living light,
Hang round thy sunset's golden close.

So have I seen in other lands,
Some ancient fane catch sweeter grace,
Of mellowed richness from the hands
Of Time, which yet could not deface.

Ah, thou hast sought 'mid sorrow's tears,
Thy solace from the lips of truth;
And thus it is that fourscore years
Crush not the cheerful heart of Youth.

So be it still!—for bright and fair,
His love I read on thy life's page;
And Time! thy hand lay gently there,
Spoil not this beautiful old age.

ALBERT BARNES,

THE author of the Series of Popular Biblical Commentaries, was born at Rome, New York, December 1, 1798. He was educated at Hamilton College, and entered the Theological Seminary at Princeton in 1820; was ordained and became pastor of a congregation at Morristown, N. J., and subsequently, in 1830, of the First Presbyterian Church in Philadelphia, where he has since remained. The series of *Notes* on the Scriptures, by which Dr. Barnes has obtained a wide-spread reputation as an author and commentator, was commenced during his residence at Morristown. His original design was to prepare a brief commentary on the Gospels for the use of Sunday Schools. After he had commenced, hearing that the Rev. James W. Alexander was engaged on a similar work for the American Sunday School Union, he wrote to him, proposing to abandon his project in favor of that of his friend. On Dr. Alexander's reply—that in consequence of his feeble health he was desirous to transfer his task to the able hand already occupied on the same project, Mr. Barnes determined to continue. The work appeared, and met with so favorable a reception that the author enlarged his design, and has since annotated most of the books of the Old and New Testament, with the same distinguished success. Besides these Commentaries, Dr. Barnes is the author of several volumes of Sermons *On Revivals* and *Practical Sermons for Vacant Congregations and Families;* some other devotional works, and an elaborate Introductory Essay to Bishop Butler's Analogy.

In his pastoral relations and personal character Dr. Barnes is highly esteemed, as well as for his eloquence in the pulpit.

By the adoption of the plan of writing at an early hour, he has been able to prepare the long series of volumes to which his commentaries extend, without any interference with the ordinary routine of his daily duties, all of the volumes to which we have referred, together with a work on Slavery, having been composed before nine o'clock in the morning.

WILLIAM TUDOR.

WILLIAM TUDOR, the son of a lawyer of the Revolution, from the office of John Adams, was born at Boston, January 28, 1799. He was educated at Phillips Academy, at Andover, and at Harvard, and afterwards became a clerk in the counting-room of John Codman. In the employ of the latter he visited Paris, where his literary inclinations were confirmed. He next sailed for Leghorn on a commercial venture; that failed, but he secured a European tour through Italy and the Continent. On his return to Boston he was an active member in founding the Anthology Club, publishing his European letters, with various entertaining miscellanies, in their monthly magazine.

This journal, which bore the name of *The Monthly Anthology*, was originally commenced in November, 1803, by Mr. Phineas Adams, a graduate of Harvard, and at the time teacher of a school in Boston. At the end of six months it fell into the hands of the Rev. William Emerson, who, joining a few friends with him, laid the foundation of the club. The magazine was then announced as edited "by a society of gentlemen." By the theory of the club every member was to write for the "Anthology," but the rule was modified, as usual, by the social necessities of the company, and the journal was greatly indebted to outsiders for its articles. The members, however, had the privilege of paying its expenses, which in those days could hardly have been expected to be met by the public. In giving an account of this work subsequently Mr. Tudor remarks, "whatever may have been the merit of the Anthology, its authors would have been sadly disappointed if they had looked for any other advantages to be derived from it than an occasional smile from the public, the amusement of their task, and the pleasure of their social meetings. The publication never gave enough to pay the moderate expense of their suppers, and through their whole career they wrote and paid for the pleasure of writing. Occasionally a promise was held out that the proceeds of the work would soon enable them to proceed without assessments, but the observance never came. The printers were changed several times, and whenever they paid anything it was an omen of ill luck to them."* Ten volumes of the Anthology were thus published from 1803 to 1811, supported by the best pens of Boston at the time: by Tudor, Buckminster, John Quincy Adams, George Ticknor, Dr. John Sylvester John Gardiner, and others.

In 1805 Mr. Tudor went to the West Indies to

establish for his brother agencies for a new branch of commerce, the exportation of ice. He was also engaged afterwards in some other commercial transactions in Europe requiring ability and address. In 1809 he had delivered the Fourth of July oration in Boston, and in 1810 prepared the Phi Beta Kappa address for Harvard. In December, 1814, he wrote the prospectus for the *North American Review*, the first number of which appeared in May, 1815, under his editorship. It originally was a combination of the magazine and review, admitting light articles, essays, and poems, while the staple was elaborate criticism, and appeared in this style every two months till December, 1818, when it was changed to a quarterly publication. Mr. Tudor wrote three fourths of the first four volumes.

In the year 1819 he published his volume of *Letters on the Eastern States*, a book which with some diffuseness handles topics of originality for the time with acuteness. In 1821 he published a volume of *Miscellanies*, collected from his contributions to the Monthly Anthology and the early volumes of the North American Review, which show the author's playful, learned humor, in a very agreeable light.† His spirited *Life of James Otis* appeared in 1823. It is a view of the times as well as of the man. The leading personages of the period are presented in its animated, picturesque pages.

It is to Tudor that Boston is indebted for the monument on Bunker Hill; he heard that the ground was to be sold, interested men of wealth in the purchase, and the work was commenced at his suggestion. At the close of the same year (1823) he received the appointment of consul for the United States at Lima, the duties of which he discharged till his transfer to the Atlantic coast in 1828 as *chargé d'affaires* at Rio Janeiro. He was successful in the negotiation of an indemnity for spoliations on American commerce. While at Rio he wrote a work, which was published anonymously at Boston in 1829, entitled *Gebel Teir*. It is in an ingenious vein of description and speculation touching the manners and politics of the most important nations of the world, whose affairs are discussed by a synod of birds who meet on a mountain in Africa, the book taking its name from a legendary conceit that Gebel Teir, in Egypt, was so called from an annual council of the birds of the universe on its summit. In this "politic congregation" the United States are represented for the Eastern portion by the wren; the pigeon for the West; the robin for the Middle; and the vulture and the mocking-bird for the South. The pheasant, the humming-bird, and the bat, are the members for Spain; the marten and thrush for England; the sparrow and cock for France; and the ibis for the Elysian Fields. In the speeches delivered at this parliament the reader may gather a very fair notion of the prevalent political ideas at home and abroad at the time of the publication of the book.

Mr. Tudor died suddenly at Rio, March 9, 1830. It is understood that he left many manuscripts relating to the countries which he visited nearly ready for the press, which with his official correspondence will probably be published.

As a member of the Anthology Club he was one of the founders of the munificent library and

Athenæum Library.

fine art association, the Boston Athenæum, a circumstance which brings him within the range of

* Notice of the Monthly Anthology in "Miscellanies," by W. Tudor.

† Among these papers are comic memoirs, after the fashion of learned societies, on Cranberry Sauce, Toast, the Purring of Cats; a Dissertation upon Things in General; the Miseries of Human Life, &c.

Mr. Quincy's recent memorial of that institution.* The society was incorporated in 1807. It received numerous important gifts, especially from the Perkins family. The collection of books exceeds fifty thousand volumes. Its American department is valuable, and its series of foreign reports of societies, etc., extensive. Among other specialities it has a large number of books and pamphlets which belonged to General Washington, that were purchased for the institution by a liberal subscription of gentlemen at Cambridge and Boston. After several changes of position the Library is now located in a sumptuous building in Beacon street, where the gallery of fine arts connected with it is also established. The price of a share is three hundred dollars; that of life membership, one hundred. The use of the library, without the privilege of taking out books, is extended to others on an annual payment of ten dollars.

Mr. Charles Folsom, an accomplished and efficient presiding officer, is the present librarian.

THE ELYSIAN FIELDS—FROM GEBEL TEIR.

The setting sun had now left the assembly in the shadow of the ancient rocks under which they met, and the approach of twilight was accompanied with the freshness of evening. The numerous assembly, true to nature, were preparing for repose, when the attention of the whole was irresistibly drawn to the form of a bird, which seemed an *Ibis*, that now occupied the perch, whose appearance was sudden, and whose coming was noiseless and unseen. The older members exhibited awe more than surprise, but those who were present for the first time felt a chilling dread. The mysterious delegate seemed unearthly and unsubstantial, a spectral hollowness marked his aspect, and the first sepulchral tones of his voice penetrated the whole audience, which sat in solemn, mute expectation.

"I come, Mr. President, to make my annual return from the shades below. Many of this assembly, whom I have seen before, know that after my death, three thousand years ago, my earthly remains were carefully embalmed by the priests of Memphis, and still repose in the catacombs of that ancient city. Nought created by God ever perishes, matter is transmuted into new combinations, but the essence of birds as well as of men, each in their kinds, is sublimated at once for an incorporeal, imperishable existence in the world of spirits. Many of the secrets of that world we are not allowed to disclose, and to gross corporeal minds they would be unintelligible. Such things as may be told I shall now relate to this assembly. Birds have instinct, and men have reason, to guide them in this world; the former seldom err, the latter often; could either race behold the terrific consequences of these errors, they would be less frequent; but sufficient warnings of them have been given, which it is not incumbent on me to repeat.

"My life having been adjudged blameless, my spirit winged its way to the fields of Elysium, while some of those who worshipped and embalmed my body were doomed to the banks of Phlegethon. Sad and harrowing would be the description of those dreary regions. I have dwelt upon and enforced it from time to time for twenty centuries, since I was first deputed to attend this assembly: I shall not now repeat it. But to instruct and incite the younger members here present, I will mention a few of the sights that gladden the eye in the Elysian Fields, where birds who have shown themselves faithful in their duties, vigilant sentinels when stationed on that service, valiant defenders of their nests, and careful providers for their young, enjoy the unceasing delights of Elysium, on a wing that never tires. They are there secure from attack and from suffering, in a blissful region, where peace for ever dwells, and violence or want can never enter.

"In these abodes of ever-during felicity a deep harmony and universal participation increase the charm of every delight. Among the varieties of ethereal enjoyment it is one to see the tenants of Elysium attended by the semblances of all those creations of their genius which ennobled their existence in this world. It is one of the rewards allotted to them that these embodied shadows shall there follow them; and the pleasure is mutual, as each purified from envy and all earthly passion enjoys the creations of others as well as his own. There the Grecian poets and artists are accompanied by the classic designs they invented. Homer is followed by Achilles, Nestor, Ulysses, Ajax, and a crowd of others. Sophocles and Euripides are attended by Clytemnestra, Iphigenia, Orestes, Jason, &c. The clouds and birds hover over Aristophanes. The sculptors have for companions their Apollo, Venus, and the Graces; and the painters their representations, even to the grapes that deceived the birds, and the curtain that deceived the artist. Virgil sees Æneas, Creusa, and Ascanius, Dido, Nisus, and Euryalus, and all his heroic and pastoral characters. Raphael is surrounded with the beautiful mothers and children he painted for Catholic worship, and Michael Angelo here compares that awful scene which he spread on the walls of the Sistine Chapel with the reality that exists around him.

"Petrarch sees his laurel covered with sonnets to Laura, who sits beneath its shade. Dante with Beatrice here realizes the scenes he tried to discover in this world; Ariosto has his wild, gay imaginations of ladies, magicians, and knights to recreate his fancy. Cervantes is accompanied by Don Quixote, Sancho, and all the characters of his brilliant genius. Rabelais has Panurge and his grotesque companions, and Fenelon is escorted by Mentor, Telemachus, Calypso, and Eulalia. Spenser has his allegoric visions. But of all who are thus gratified and contribute to the general delight, none is so distinguished as Shakespeare, around whom every creation of fancy, the gay, sad, heroic, terrific, fantastic, appears in a hundred forms. Falstaff and his buffoons, Autolycus and his clowns, Hamlet and Ophelia, Romeo and Juliet, Othello and Desdemona, Lear, Macbeth, Ariel, Miranda, Caliban, the Fairies of a Midsummer's Night, and the Witches of a Highland Heath, all attend his beck. Of late new groups have made their appearance as yet without their master. Some of these in all the various measures of poetry, others in the more serious steps of prose; and these were multiplied so fast, and exhibited so much invention, that it was at last thought they would realize the prodigies of any other imagination.

"The heroes and statesmen who are rewarded with a residence in these blissful fields, have yet one mark to designate their errors. They are at times partially or wholly enveloped in an appearance of mist, which impedes them from seeing or being seen by others. When this is examined, it is found to consist of an infinite number of minute, vapory pieces of paper, to represent their delusive statements, and their intrigues of ambition and rivalry; when this is dissipated, there appear over their heads in aerial letters of light, the great and useful measures they

* The History of the Boston Athenæum, with Biographical Notices of its deceased Founders. By Josiah Quincy. Cambridge: 1851.

prosecuted. The mist that encircles heroes is composed of an innumerable quantity of weapons of destruction, in miniature; as every man who fell in battle in a useless war, is here typified by a sword, ball, or spear, or if he perished of disease, by a small livid spot. Some are thus surrounded more than others. An illustrious chief, recently arrived, who extended his march to this spot where we assemble, is sometimes wholly enveloped: when the mist breaks away we see in the air inscriptions of 'religious toleration,' 'road over the Alps,' 'protection of the arts,' &c. But among all those who as a statesman or a warrior walks these blessed groves, there is but one combining both attributes, whose majestic form is for ever unshrouded; around whom there never flits the representation of a delusive statement, nor an effort of personal intrigue, nor a single minute resemblance of a destructive weapon to signify that a soldier perished in a battle fought with ambitious views; over his head appears in mild radiance an inscription: 'First in war, first in peace, and first in the hearts of his countrymen.'"

The form of the Ibis had now vanished as suddenly and silently as it first appeared; the influence of the hour replaced the feeling of awful attention by which it had been suspended. The nocturnal birds, the owls, whip-poor-wills, and bats began their career of nightly occupation and watching, while the rest of the immense assembly soon had their heads under their wings, and presented a more numerous collection than could be formed by the afternoon patients united of a thousand somniferous preachers.

ROBERT C. SANDS,

ONE of the most original of American humorists, a fine scholar, and a poet of ardent imagination, was born in the city of New York, May 11, 1799. His father, Comfort Sands, was a merchant of the city, who had borne a patriotic part in the early struggles of the Revolution. Sands early acquired a taste for the ancient classics, which his education at Columbia College confirmed, to which he afterwards added a knowledge of the modern tongues derived from the Latin. One of his college companions, two years his senior, was his friend and partner in his poetical scheme, James Wallis Eastburn. They projected while in college two literary periodicals, *The Moralist* and *Academic Recreations*. The first had but a single number; the other reached a volume;—Sands contributing prose and verse. Graduating with the class of 1815, he entered the law office of David B. Ogden, and contrary to the habit of young poets, studied with zeal and fidelity. His talent for writing, at this time, was a passion. He wrote with facility, and on a great variety of subjects; one of his compositions, a sermon, penned for a friend, finding its way into print, with the name of the clergyman who delivered it. In 1817 he published, in the measure which the works of Scott had made fashionable, *The Bridal of Vaumond*, founded, his biographer tells us, "on the same legend of the transformation of a decrepit and miserable wretch into a youthful hero, by compact with the infernal powers, which forms the groundwork of Byron's "Deformed Transformed."* This, though spoken of with respect, is not included in the author's writings. His literary history is at this time interwoven with that of his friend, Eastburn, with whom he was translating the Psalms of David into verse, and writing a poem, "Yamoyden," on the history of Philip, the Indian chieftain. This was planned by Eastburn, while he was pursuing his studies for the ministry, during a residence at Bristol, Rhode Island, in the vicinity of the Indian locality of the poem. It was based on a slight reading of Hubbard's Narrative of the Indian Wars. The two authors chose their parts, and communicated them when finished to each other; the whole poem being written in the winter of 1817 and following spring. While it was being revised, Eastburn, who in the meantime had taken orders in the Protestant Episcopal Church, died in his twenty-second year, December 2, 1819, on a voyage to Santa Cruz, undertaken to recover his health.

The poem was published the year following, in 1820, with an advertisement by Sands, who, on a further study of the subject, had made some additions to the matter. The proem, which celebrates the friendship of the two authors, and the poetical charm of their Indian subject, is justly considered one of the finest of Sands's literary achievements. The basis of the poem belongs to Eastburn.

The literary productions of the latter have never been collected. That they would form a worthy companion volume to the writings of his friend Sands, while exhibiting some characteristic differences of temperament, there is abundant proof in all that is known to the public to have proceeded from his pen. In the absence of further original material, we may here present the tribute paid to his genius by his brother, the Right Reverend Manton Eastburn, of the diocese of Massachusetts, in an oration pronounced in 1837, at the first semi-centennial anniversary of the incorporation of Columbia College by the legislature of New York.

"The remains," said Dr. Eastburn, "which Eastburn has left behind him are amazingly voluminous. I will venture to say that there are few, who, on arriving at the age of twenty-two, which was the limit of his mortal career, will be found to have accomplished so much literary composition. His prose writings, many of which appeared anonymously in a series of periodical essays, conducted by himself and some of his friends, take in an extensive range of moral and classical disquisition; and are models of the purest Addisonian English. The great charm, however, of all his writings, is the tone that breathes through them. Whatever be the subject, the reader is never allowed to forget, that the pages before him are indited with a pen dipped in the dew of heaven. An illustration of this peculiar feature of his productions will form the most appropriate ending of this brief offering to his memory. On one glorious night of June, 1819, during his residence as a parochial clergyman upon the eastern shore of Virginia, and a few months before his death, he sat up until the solemn hour of twelve to enjoy the scene. The moon was riding in her majesty; her light fell upon the waters of the Chesapeake; and all was hushed into stillness. Under the immediate inspiration of such a spectacle, he penned the following lines, which he has entitled 'The Summer Midnight.' After having given

* Memoir, by G. C. Verplanck, p. 7.

them to you, my fellow-collegians, I will leave you to decide whether the character I have just drawn be a true portrait, or has been dictated only by the natural enthusiasm of a brother's love.

" The breeze of night has sunk to rest,
Upon the river's tranquil breast;
And every bird has sought her nest,
Where silent is her minstrelsy;
The queen of heaven is sailing high,
A pale bark on the azure sky,
Where not a breath is heard to sigh—
So deep the soft tranquillity.

" Forgotten now the heat of day
That on the burning waters lay,
The noon of night her mantle grey
Spreads, for the sun's high blazonry;
But glittering in that gentle night
There gleams a line of silvery light,
As tremulous on the shores of white
It hovers sweet and playfully.

" At peace the distant shallop rides;
Not as when dashing o'er her sides
The roaring bay's unruly tides
Were beating round her gloriously;
But every sail is furled and still:
Silent the seaman's whistle shrill,
While dreamy slumbers seem to thrill
With parted hours of ecstasy.

" Stars of the many-spangled heaven!
Faintly this night your beams are given,
Tho' proudly where your hosts are driven
Ye rear your dazzling galaxy;
Since far and wide a softer hue
Is spread across the plains of blue,
Where in bright chorus, ever true,
For ever swells your harmony.

" O for some sadly dying note
Upon this silent hour to float,
Where from the bustling world remote
The lyre might wake its melody;
One feeble strain is all can swell
From mine almost deserted shell,
In mournful accents yet to tell
That slumbers not its minstrelsy.

" There is an hour of deep repose
That yet upon my heart shall close,
When all that nature dreads and knows
Shall burst upon me wondrously;
O may I then awake for ever
My harp to rapture's high endeavor,
And as from earth's vain scene I sever,
Be lost in Immortality!"

In 1822 and 1828, Sands was writing for the Literary Review, a monthly New York periodical, in conjunction with some friends, associated in a junto known as the Literary Confederacy. They were four in number, and had already contributed the series of papers, "The Neologist" to the Daily Advertiser, and "The Amphilogist" to the Commercial Advertiser; and in 1822 and 1828 he furnished, in conjunction with his friends, numerous articles to the Literary Review, a New York monthly periodical, and in the winter of 1823–4, the confederacy published the seven numbers of the *St. Tammany Magazine*.

In May, 1824, Sands commenced the *Atlantic Magazine*, which he edited, and for which he wrote many of the articles during its first volume;

Robert C. Sands

when it became the New York Review he again entered upon the editorship, which he continued, supplying many ingenious and eloquent papers till 1827. After this he became associated in the conduct of the Commercial Advertiser, a post which he occupied at his death.

In 1828, he wrote an *Historical Notice of Hernan Cortes*, to accompany a publication of the Cortes Letters for the South American market. For this purpose it was translated into Spanish by Manuel Dominguez, and was not published in the author's own language till the collection of his writings was made after his death. In this year *The Talisman* was projected. It turned out in the hands of its publisher, Elam Bliss, to be an annual, according to the fashion of the day, but it was originally undertaken by the poet Bryant, Verplanck, and Sands, as a joint collection of Miscellanies, after the manner of Pope, Swift, and their friends. The Talisman, under the editorship of the imaginary Francis Herbert, Esq., and written by the three authors, was continued to a third volume in 1880. It was afterwards re-issued according to the original plan, with the title of *Miscellanies*.

The "Dream of the Princess Papantzin," first published in the Talisman, founded on a legend recorded by the Abbé Clavigero, a poem of more than four hundred lines of blank verse, is considered by Mr. Verplanck "one of the most perfect specimens left by Mr. Sands of his poetic powers, whether we regard the varied music of the versification, the freedom and splendor of the diction, the nobleness and affluence of the imagery, or the beautiful and original use he has made of the Mexican mythology."

In 1831 Sands published the *Life and Correspondence of Paul Jones*. The next year he was again associated with Bryant in the brace of volumes entitled *Tales of the Glauber Spa*, to which Paulding, Leggett, and Miss Sedgwick were also contributors, and for which Sands wrote the humorous introduction, the tale of Mr. Green, and an imaginative version of the old Spanish fountain of youth story, entitled Boyuca. His last finished composition was a poem in the Commercial Advertiser, *The Dead of* 1832.

At the very instant of his death he was engaged upon an article of invention for the first number of the Knickerbocker Magazine upon *Esquimaux Literature*, for which he had filled his mind with the best reading on the country. It was while engaged on this article on the 17th December, 1832, that he was suddenly attacked by apoplexy. He had written with his pencil the line for one of the poems by which he was illustrating his topic,

Oh think not my spirit among you abides,

—— some uncertain marks followed from his stricken arm; he rose and fell on the threshold of his room, and lived but a few hours longer.

The residence of Sands for the latter part of his life was at Hoboken, then a rural village within sight of New York. In that quiet retreat, and in the neighborhood of the woods of Weehawken,

The Wood at Hoboken.

celebrated by his own pen as well as by the muse of Halleck, he drew his kindly inspirations of nature, which he hardly needed to temper his always charitable judgments of men. His character has been delicately touched by Bryant in the memoir in the Knickerbocker,* and drawn out with genial sympathy by Verplanck in the biography prefixed to his published writings.† Sands was a man of warm and tender feeling, a loving humorist whose laughter was the gay smile of profound sensibility; of a kindling and rapid imagination, which did not disdain the labor and acquisitions of mature scholarship. He died unmarried, having always lived at home in his father's house. It is related of him, in connexion with his love of nature, that he was so near-sighted that he had never seen the stars from his childhood to his sixteenth year, when he obtained appropriate glasses.

That American literature experienced a great loss in the early death of Sands, will be felt by the reader who makes acquaintance with his well cultivated, prompt, exuberant genius, which promised, had life been spared, a distinguished career of genial mental activity and productiveness.

* January, 1833.

† The Writings of Robert C. Sands, in Prose and Verse, with a Memoir of the Author. 2 vols. Harpers. 1834.

HOBOKEN.*

For what is nature? ring her changes round,
Her three flat notes are water, woods, and ground;
Prolong the peal—yet, spite of all her clatter,
The tedious chime is still—grounds, wood, and water.

Is it so, Master Satirist?—does the all-casing air, with the myriad hues which it lends to and borrows again from the planet it invests, make no change in the appearance of the *spectacula rerum*, the visible exhibitions of nature? Have association and contrast nothing to do with them? Nature can afford to be satirized. She defies burlesque. Look at her in her barrenness, or her terrific majesty—in her poverty, or in her glory—she is still the mighty mother, whom man may superficially trick out, but cannot substantially alter. Art can only succeed by following her; and its most magnificent triumphs are achieved by a religious observance of her rules. It is a proud and primitive prerogative of man, that the physical world has been left under his control, to a certain extent, not merely for the purpose of raising from it his sustenance, but of modifying its appearance to gratify the eye of taste, and, by beautifying the material creation, of improving the spiritual elements of his own being.

When the Duke of Bridgewater's engineer was examined by the House of Commons as to his views on the system of internal communication by water, he gave it as his opinion that rivers were made by the Lord to feed canals; and it is true that Providence has given us the raw material to make what we can out of it.

This may be thought too sublime a flourish for an introduction to the luxuriant and delightful landscape by Weir, an engraving from which embellishes the present number of the Mirror. But, though it may be crudely expressed, it is germain to the subject. Good taste and enterprise have done for Hoboken precisely what they ought to have done, without violating the propriety of nature. Those who loved its wild haunts before the metamorphosis, were, it is true, not a little shocked at what they could not but consider a desecration; and thought they heard the nymphs screaming—"We are off," when carts, bullocks, paddies, and rollers came to clear the forest sanctuary. They were ready to exclaim with the poet, Cardinal Bernis—

Quelle étonnante barbarie
D'asservir la varieté
Au cordeau de la symmetrie;
De polir la rusticité
D'un bois fait pour la reverie,
Et d'orner la simplicité
De cette riante prairie!†

But "*cette riante prairie*" is now one of the prettiest places you may see of a summer's day. It is appropriately called the Elysian Fields, and does, indeed, remind the spectator of

Yellow meads of asphodel,
And amaranthine bowers.

It is now clothed in vivid, transparent, emerald green; its grove is worthy of being painted by

* First published in the New York Mirror, to accompany a landscape by Weir, of which the wood engraving in this article is a copy.

† Oh, what a shocking thing to sacrifice
Variety to symmetry,
In such a wise!
To polish the rusticity
Of that old wood, designed for revery,
And ornament the simple grace,
Of that fair meadow's smiling face.—PRINTER'S DEVIL.

Claude Lorraine; and from it you may look, and cannot help looking, on one of the noblest rivers, and one of the finest cities in the universe.

Hoboken has been illustrated so often, in poetry and prose, and by the pencil of the limner, in late years, that it would be vain and superfluous to attempt a new description. A "sacred bard," one who will be held such in the appreciation of posterity, has spoken of the walk from this village to Weehawken as "one of the most beautiful in the world,"* and has given, in prose, a picture of its appearance. Another writer, whose modest genius (I beg your pardon, Messrs. Editors—he is one of your own gang) leavens the literary aliment of our town, and the best part of whom shall assuredly "escape libitina," has elegantly and graphically described the spot in illustrating another series of pictorial views.† Halleck's lines are as familiar as household words. Francis Herbert has made the vicinity the scene of one of his tough stories. At least half a dozen different views have been taken of it within the last two years. They embraced, generally, an extensive view of the river, bay, and city. Weir has selected a beautiful spot, in one of the new walks near the mansion of Colonel Stevens, with a glimpse of the splendid sheet of water through the embowering foliage. That gentleman, and lady with a parasol, in front of the prim, and who look a little prim themselves, seem to enjoy the loveliness of the scene, as well as the society of one another. Our country has reason to reckon with pride the name of Weir among those of her artists.

> The sunny Italy may boast
> The beauteous hues that flush her skies;

he has seen, admired, studied, and painted them; but he can find subjects for his pencil as fair, in his own land, and no one can do them more justice.

It is a fact not generally known, that there is, or was, an old town in Holland called Hoboken, from which, no doubt, this place was named. There was also a family of that name in Holland. A copy of an old work on medicine, by a Dutch physician of the name of Hoboken, is in the library of one of the eminent medical men of this city. The oldest remaining house *upon* it, for it is insulated, forms the rear of Mr. Thomas Swift's hotel upon the green, and was built sixty years ago, as may be seen by the iron memorandums practicated in the walls. There is at present a superb promenade along the margin of the river, under the high banks and magnesia rocks which overlook it, of more than a mile in length, on which it is intended to lay rails, for the edification of our domestic cockneys and others, who might not else have a chance of seeing a locomotive in operation, and who may be whisked to the Elysian fields before they will find time to comb their whiskers, or count the seconds.

In this genial season of the year, a more appropriate illustration could not be furnished for the Mirror than a view of this pleasant spot. We say, with Horace, let others cry up Thessalian Tempe, &c., our own citizens have a retreat from the dust and heat of the metropolis more agreeable—

> Quam domus Albuneæ resonantis,
> Et præceps Anio, et Tiburni lucus, et uda
> Mobilibus pomaria rivis.

But, as some of your readers may not undertand Latin, let us imitate, travesty, and doggrelize the ode of Flaccus bodily. There is an abrupt transition in the middle of it, which critics have differed about; but I suppose it is preserved as he wrote it; the whole of the old rascal's great argument being, that with good wine you may be comfortable in any place, even in Communipaw.

Laudabunt alii clarum Rhodon, &c.

> Let Willis tell, in glittering prose,
> Of Paris and its tempting shows;
> Let Irving while his fancy glows,
> Praise Spain, renowned—romantic!
> Let Cooper write, until it palls,
> Of Venice, and her marble walls,
> Her dungeons, bridges, and canals,
> Enough to make one frantic!
>
> Let *voyageurs* Macadamize,
> With books, the Alps that climb the skies,
> And ne'er forget, in anywise,
> Geneva's lake and city;
> And poor old Rome—the proud, the great,
> Fallen—fallen from her high estate,
> No cockney sees, but he must prate
> About her—what a pity!
>
> Of travellers there is no lack,
> God knows—each one of them a hack,
> Who ride to write, and then go back
> And publish a long story,
> Chiefly about themselves; but each
> Or in dispraise or praise, with breach
> Of truth on either side, will preach
> About some place's glory.
>
> For me—who never saw the sun
> His course o'er other regions run,
> Than those whose franchise well was won
> By blood of patriot martyrs—
> Fair fertile France may smile in vain;
> Nor will I seek thy ruins, Spain:
> Albion, thy freedom I disdain,
> With all thy monarch's charters.
>
> Better I love the river's side,
> Where Hudson's sounding waters glide,
> And with their full majestic tide
> To the great sea keep flowing:
> Weehawk, I loved thy frowning height,
> Since first I saw, with fond delight,
> The wave beneath the rushes bright,
> And the new Rome still growing.

[Here occurs the seeming hiatus above referred to. He proceeds as follows:]—

> Though lately we might truly say,
> "The rain it raineth every day,"
> The wind can sweep the clouds away,
> And open daylight's shutters:
> So, Colonel Morris, my fine man,
> Drink good champagne whene'er you can,
> Regardless of the temperance plan,
> Or what the parson utters.
>
> Whether in regimentals fine,
> Upon a spanking horse you shine,
> Or supervise the works divine
> Of scribblers like the present:
> Trust me, the good old stuff, the blood
> Of generous grapes, well understood
> On sea, on land, in town, in wood,
> Will make all places pleasant.
>
> For hear what Ajax Teucer said,*
> Whose brother foolishly went dead
> For spleen:—to Salamis he sped,
> *Sans* Telamon's dead body;
> His father kicked him off the stoop—
> Said he, "For this I will not droop;
> The world has realms wherein to *snoop*,
> And I am not a noddy.
>
> "Come, my brave boys, and let us go,
> As fortune calls, or winds may blow—
> Teucer your guide, the way will show—
> Fear no mishap nor sorrow:
> Another Salamis as fine,
> Is promised by the Delphic shrine:
> So stuff your skins to-night with wine,
> We'll go to sea to-morrow."

* American Landscape. Edited by W. C. Bryant, No. 1. This work was projected by the New York artists; but the project has been abandoned.

† Views of New York and its Environs. Published by Peabody & Co., and edited by T. S. Fay.

* The papa of the two Ajaces charged them, when they started for Troy, to bring one another home; or else he threatened not to receive the survivor. Ajax Telamon being miffed, because the armour of Achilles was awarded to Ulysses, went crazy, killed sheep, and made a holocaust of himself. When Teucer went home without him, the old gentleman shut the door in his face.—*Free translation of Mad. Dacier.*

PROEM TO YAMOYDEN.

Go forth, sad fragments of a broken strain,
The last that either bard shall e'er essay!
The hand can ne'er attempt the chords again,
That first awoke them, in a happier day:
Where sweeps the ocean breeze its desert way,
His requiem murmurs o'er the moaning wave;
And he who feebly now prolongs the lay,
Shall ne'er the minstrel's hallowed honours crave;
His harp lies buried deep, in that untimely grave!

Friend of my youth, with thee began the love
Of sacred song; the wont, in golden dreams,
'Mid classic realms of splendours past to rove,
O'er haunted steep, and by immortal streams;
Where the blue wave, with sparkling bosom gleams
Round shores, the mind's eternal heritage,
For ever lit by memory's twilight beams;
Where the proud dead that live in storied page,
Beckon, with awful port, to glory's earlier age.

There would we linger oft, entranced, to hear,
O'er battle fields, the epic thunders roll;
Or list, where tragic wail upon the ear,
Through Argive palaces shrill echoing, stole;
There would we mark, uncurbed by all control,
In central heaven, the Theban eagle's flight;
Or hold communion with the musing soul
Of sage or bard, who sought, 'mid pagan night,
In loved Athenian groves, for truth's eternal light.

Homeward we turned, to that fair land, but late
Redeemed from the strong spell that bound it fast,
Where mystery, brooding o'er the waters, sate
And kept the key, till three millenniums past;
When, as creation's noblest work was last,
Latest, to man it was vouchsafed, to see
Nature's great wonder, long by clouds o'ercast,
And veiled in sacred awe, that it might be
An empire and a home, most worthy for the free.

And here, forerunners strange and meet were found,
Of that blessed freedom, only dreamed before;—
Dark were the morning mists, that lingered round
Their birth and story, as the hue they bore.
"Earth was their mother;"—or they knew no more,
Or would not that their secret should be told;
For they were grave and silent; and such lore,
To stranger ears, they loved not to unfold,
The long-transmitted tales their sires were taught of old.

Kind nature's commoners, from her they drew
Their needful wants, and learned not how to hoard,
And him whom strength and wisdom crowned, they knew,
But with no servile reverence, as their lord.
And on their mountain summits they adored
One great, good Spirit, in his high abode,
And thence their incense and orisons poured
To his pervading presence, that abroad
They felt through all his works,—their Father, King, and God,

And in the mountain mist, the torrent's spray,
The quivering forest, or the glassy flood,
Soft falling showers, or hues of orient day,
They imaged spirits beautiful and good;
But when the tempest roared, with voices rude,
Or fierce, red lightning fired the forest pine,
Or withering heats untimely seared the wood,
The angry forms they saw of powers malign;
These they besought to spare, those blest for aid divine.

As the fresh sense of life, through every vein,
With the pure air they drank, inspiring came,
Comely they grew, patient of toil and pain,
And as the fleet deer's agile was their frame;
Of meaner vices scarce they knew the name;
These simple truths went down from sire to son,—
To reverence age,—the sluggish hunter's shame,
And craven warrior's infamy to shun,—
And still avenge each wrong, to friends or kindred done.

From forest shades they peered, with awful dread,
When, uttering flame and thunder from its side,
The ocean-monster, with broad wings outspread,
Came ploughing gallantly the virgin tide.
Few years have passed, and all their forests' pride
From shores and hills has vanished, with the race,
Their tenants erst, from memory who have died,
Like airy shapes, which eld was wont to trace,
In each green thicket's depth, and lone, sequestered place.

And many a gloomy tale, tradition yet
Saves from oblivion, of their struggles vain,
Their prowess and their wrongs, for rhymer meet,
To people scenes, where still their names remain;
And so began our young, delighted strain,
That would evoke the plumed chieftains brave,
And bid their martial hosts arise again,
Where Narraganset's tides roll by their grave,
And Haup's romantic steeps are piled above the wave.

Friend of my youth! with thee began my song,
And o'er thy bier its latest accents die;
Misled in phantom-peopled realms too long,—
Though not to me the muse averse deny,
Sometimes, perhaps, her visions to descry,
Such thriftless pastime should with youth be o'er;
And he who loved with thee his notes to try,
But for thy sake, such idlesse would deplore,
And swears to meditate the thankless muse no more.

But, no! the freshness of the past shall still
Sacred to memory's holiest musings be;
When through the ideal fields of song, at will,
He roved and gathered chaplets wild with thee;
When, reckless of the world, alone and free,
Like two proud barks, we kept our careless way,
That sail by moonlight o'er the tranquil sea;
Their white apparel and their streamers gay,
Bright gleaming o'er the main, beneath the ghostly ray;—

And downward, far, reflected in the clear
Blue depths, the eye their fairy tackling sees;
So buoyant, they do seem to float in air,
And silently obey the noiseless breeze;
Till, all too soon, as the rude winds may please,
They part for distant ports: the gales benign
Swift wafting, bore, by Heaven's all-wise decrees,
To its own harbour sure, where each divine
And joyous vision, seen before in dreams, is thine.

Muses of Helicon! melodious race
Of Jove and golden-haired Mnemosyné;
Whose art from memory blots each sadder trace,
And drives each scowling form of grief away!
Who, round the violet fount, your measures gay
Once trod, and round the altar of great Jove,
Whence, wrapt in silvery clouds, your nightly way
Ye held, and ravishing strains of music wove,
That soothed the Thunderer's soul, and filled his courts above.

Bright choir! with lips untempted, and with zone
Sparkling, and unapproached by touch profane;
Ye, to whose gladsome bosoms ne'er was known
The blight of sorrow, or the throb of pain;
Rightly invoked,—if right the elected swain,

On your own mountain's side ye taught of yore,
Whose honoured hand took not your gift in vain,
Worthy the budding laurel-bough it bore,—*
Farewell! a long farewell! I worship thee no more.

A MONODY MADE ON THE LATE MR. SAMUEL PATCH, BY AN ADMIRER OF THE BATHOS.

By waters shall he die, and take his end.—SHAKESPEARE.

Toll for Sam Patch! Sam Patch, who jumps no more,
This or the world to come. Sam Patch is dead!
The vulgar pathway to the unknown shore
Of dark futurity he would not tread.
No friends stood sorrowing round his dying bed;
Nor with decorous woe, sedately stepped
Behind his corpse, and tears by retail shed;—
The mighty river, as it onward swept,
In one great wholesale sob, his body drowned and kept.

Toll for Sam Patch! he scorned the common way
That leads to fame, up heights of rough ascent,
And having heard Pope and Longinus say,
That some great men had risen to falls, he went
And jumped, where wild Passaic's waves had rent
The antique rocks;—the air free passage gave,—
And graciously the liquid element
Upbore him, like some sea-god on its wave;
And all the people said that Sam was very brave.

Fame, the clear spirit that doth to heaven upraise,
Led Sam to dive into what Byron calls
The hell of waters. For the sake of praise,
He wooed the bathos down great water-falls;
The dizzy precipice, which the eye appals
Of travellers for pleasure, Samuel found
Pleasant, as are to women lighted halls,
Crammed full of fools and fiddles; to the sound
Of the eternal roar, he timed his desperate bound.

Sam was a fool. But the large world of such,
Has thousands—better taught, alike absurd,
And less sublime. Of fame he soon got much,
Where distant cataracts spout, of him men heard.
Alas for Sam! Had he aright preferred
The kindly element, to which he gave
Himself so fearlessly, we had not heard
That it was now his winding-sheet and grave,
Nor sung, 'twixt tears and smiles, our requiem for the brave.

He soon got drunk, with rum and with renown,
As many others in high places do;—
Whose fall is like Sam's last—for down and down,
By one mad impulse driven, they flounder through
The gulf that keeps the future from our view,
And then are found not. May they rest in peace!
We heave the sigh to human frailty due—
And shall not Sam have his? The muse shall cease
To keep the heroic roll, which she began in Greece—

With demigods, who went to the Black Sea
For wool (and if the best accounts be straight,
Came back, in negro phraseology,
With the same wool each upon his pate),
In which she chronicled the deathless fate
Of him who jumped into the perilous ditch
Left by Rome's street commissioners, in a state
Which made it dangerous, and by jumping which
He made himself renowned, and the contractors rich—

I say, the muse shall quite forget to sound
The chord whose music is undying, if
She do not strike it when Sam Patch is drowned.
Leander dived for love. Leucadia's cliff
The Lesbian Sappho leapt from in a miff,
To punish Phaon; Icarus went dead,
Because the wax did not continue stiff;
And, had he minded what his father said,
He had not given a name unto his watery bed.

And Helle's case was all an accident,
As everybody knows. Why sing of these?
Nor would I rank with Sam that man who went
Down into Ætna's womb—Empedocles,
I think he called himself. Themselves to please,
Or else unwillingly, they made their springs;
For glory in the abstract, Sam made his,
To prove to all men, commons, lords, and kings,
That "some things may be done, as well as other things."

I will not be fatigued, by citing more
Who jumped of old, by hazard or design,
Nor plague the weary ghosts of boyish lore,
Vulcan, Apollo, Phaeton—in fine
All Tooke's Pantheon. Yet they grew divine
By their long tumbles; and if we can match
Their hierarchy, shall we not entwine
One wreath? Who ever came "up to the scratch,"
And for so little, jumped so bravely as Sam Patch?

To long conclusions many men have jumped
In logic, and the safer course they took;
By any other, they would have been stumped,
Unable to argue, or to quote a book,
And quite dumb-founded, which they cannot brook;
They break no bones, and suffer no contusion,
Hiding their woful fall, by hook and crook,
In slang and gibberish, sputtering and confusion;
But that was not the way Sam came to *his* conclusion.

He jumped in person. Death or Victory
Was his device, "and there was no mistake,"
Except his last; and then he did but die,
A blunder which the wisest men will make.
Aloft, where mighty floods the mountains break,
To stand, the target of ten thousand eyes,
And down into the coil and water-quake,
To leap, like Maia's offspring, from the skies—
For this all vulgar flights he ventured to despise.

And while Niagara prolongs its thunder,
Though still the rock primeval disappears,
And nations change their bounds—the theme of wonder
Shall Sam go down the cataract of long years;
And if there be sublimity in tears,
Those shall be precious which the adventurer shed
When his frail star gave way, and waked his fears
Lest, by the ungenerous crowd it might be said.
That he was all a hoax, or that his pluck had fled.

Who would compare the maudlin Alexander,
Blubbering, because he had no job in hand,
Acting the hypocrite, or else the gander,
With Sam, whose grief we all can understand?
His crying was not womanish, nor planned
For exhibition; but his heart o'erswelled
With its own agony, when he the grand
Natural arrangements for a jump beheld,
And measuring the cascade, found not his courage quelled.

His last great failure set the final seal
Unto the record Time shall never tear,
While bravery has its honour,—while men feel
The holy natural sympathies which are
First, last, and mightiest in the bosom. Where
The tortured tides of Genesee descend,
He came—his only intimate a bear,—
(We know not that he had another friend),
The martyr of renown, his wayward course to end.

* Hesiod. Theog. l. 1. 60. 80.

The fiend that from the infernal rivers stole
  Hell-draughts for man, too much tormented him,
With nerves unstrung, but steadfast in his soul,
  He stood upon the salient current's brim;
  His head was giddy, and his sight was dim;
And then he knew this leap would be his last,—
  Saw air, and earth, and water wildly swim,
With eyes of many multitudes, dense and vast,
That stared in mockery; none a look of kindness cast.

Beat down, in the huge amphitheatre
  "I see before me the gladiator lie,"
And tier on tier, the myriads waiting there
  The bow of grace, without one pitying eye—
  He was a slave—a captive hired to die;—
Sam was born free as Cæsar; and he might
  The hopeless issue have refused to try;
No! with true leap, but soon with faltering flight,—
"Deep in the roaring gulf, he plunged to endless night."

But, ere he leapt, he begged of those who made
  Money by his dread venture, that if he
Should perish, such collection should be paid
  As might be picked up from the "company"
  To his Mother. This, his last request, shall be,—
Tho' she who bore him ne'er his fate should know,—
  An iris, glittering o'er his memory—
When all the streams have worn their barriers low,
And, by the sea drunk up, for ever cease to flow.

On him who chooses to jump down cataracts,
  Why should the sternest moralist be severe?
Judge not the dead by prejudice—but facts,
  Such as in strictest evidence appear.
  Else were the laurels of all ages sere.
Give to the brave, who have passed the final goal,—
  The gates that ope not back,—the generous tear;
And let the muse's clerk upon her scroll,
In coarse, but honest verse, make up the judgment roll.

Therefore it is considered, that Sam Patch
  Shall never be forgot in prose or rhyme;
His name shall be a portion in the batch
  Of the heroic dough, which baking Time
  Kneads for consuming ages—and the chime
Of Fame's old bells, long as they truly ring,
  Shall tell of him; he dived for the sublime,
And found it. Thou, who with the eagle's wing
Being a goose, would'st fly,—dream not of such a thing!

THE DEAD OF 1832.

Oh Time and Death! with certain pace,
  Though still unequal, hurrying on,
O'erturning in your awful race,
  The cot, the palace, and the throne!

Not always in the storm of war,
  Nor by the pestilence that sweeps
From the plague-smitten realms afar,
  Beyond the old and solemn deeps:

In crowds the good and mighty go,
  And to those vast dim chambers hie:—
Where mingled with the high and low,
  Dead Cæsars and dead Shakespeares lie!

Dread Ministers of God! sometimes
  Ye smite at once, to do His will,
In all earth's ocean-severed climes,
  Those—whose renown ye cannot kill!

When all the brightest stars that burn
  At once are banished from their spheres,
Men sadly ask, when shall return
  Such lustre to the coming years?

For where is he*—who lived so long—
  Who raised the modern Titan's ghost,
And showed his fate, in powerful song,
  Whose soul for learning's sake was lost!

Where he—who backwards to the birth
  Of Time itself, adventurous trod,
And in the mingled mass of earth
  Found out the handiwork of God!†

Where he—who in the mortal head,‡
  Ordained to gaze on heaven, could trace
The soul's vast features, that shall tread
  The stars, when earth is nothingness!

Where he—who struck old Albyn's lyre,§
  Till round the world its echoes roll,
And swept, with all a prophet's fire,
  The diapason of the soul!

Where he—who read the mystic lore,‖
  Buried, where buried Pharaohs sleep;
And dared presumptuous to explore
  Secrets four thousand years could keep!

Where he—who with a poet's eye¶
  Of truth, on lowly nature gazed,
And made even sordid Poverty
  Classic, when in HIS numbers glazed!

Where—that old sage so hale and staid,**
  The "greatest good" who sought to find;
Who in his garden mused, and made
  All forms of rule, for all mankind!

And thou—whom millions far removed††
  Revered—the hierarch meek and wise,
Thy ashes sleep, adored, beloved,
  Near where thy Wesley's coffin lies.

He too—the heir of glory—where
  Hath great Napoleon's scion fled?
Ah! glory goes not to an heir!
  Take him, ye noble, vulgar dead!

But hark! a nation sighs! for he,‡‡
  Last of the brave who perilled all
To make an infant empire free,
  Obeys the inevitable call!

They go, and with them is a crowd,
  For human rights who THOUGHT and DID,
We rear to them no temples proud,
  Each hath his mental pyramid.

All earth is now their sepulchre,
  The MIND, their monument sublime—
Young in eternal fame they are—
  Such are YOUR triumphs, Death and Time.

GRENVILLE MELLEN.

GRENVILLE MELLEN was born at Biddeford, Maine, June 19, 1799. He was the eldest son of the eminent Chief-justice Mellen, of the Supreme Court in that state. He was graduated at Harvard in 1818; studied law with his father, and settled at Portland, Maine. In 1823 he removed to North Yarmouth, in the same state, where he remained for five years. His poems at this period and subsequently to his death, appeared frequently in the periodicals, the magazines and annuals, of the time. In 1826 he pronounced before the Peace Society of Maine, at Portland, a poem, *The Rest of Empires*, and in 1828 an Anniversary Poem, before the Athenian

* Goethe and his Faust. † Cuvier. ‡ Spurzheim.
§ Scott. ‖ Champollion. ¶ Crabbe.
** Jeremy Bentham. †† Adam Clarke. ‡‡ Charles Carroll.

Society of Bowdoin College, *The Light of Letters.* He wrote for the United States Literary Gazette, a well sustained journal published at Boston. In 1827 he published *Our Chronicle of Twenty-Six*, a satire, and in 1829 *Glad Tales and Sad Tales*, a volume in prose, from his contributions to the periodicals. The chief collection of his poems appeared in Boston in 1833, *The Martyrs' Triumph, Buried Valley, and other Poems.*

G. Mellen

From Boston he came to reside in New York. His health, which was always delicate, was now much enfeebled; he was lingering with consumption when he made a voyage to Cuba, from which he returned without benefit, and died in New York September 5, 1841, at the residence of his friend, Mr. Samuel Colman, for whose family he felt the warmest affection, and whose house he had called his home for the latter years of his life. Before his death he was engaged upon a collection of his unpublished poems, which still remain in manuscript.

A glance at his poems shows a delicate susceptibility to poetical impression, tinged with an air of melancholy. He wrote with ease, often carelessly and pretentiously—often with eloquence. With a stronger constitution his verse would probably have assumed a more condensed, energetic expression. With a consciousness of poetic power he struggled with a feeble frame, and at times yielded to despondency. The memory of his tenderness and purity of character is much cherished by his friends.

THE BRIDAL.

Young Beauty at the altar! Oh! kneel down
All ye that come to gaze into her face,
And breathe low prayers for her. See at her side
Stand her pale parents in their latter days,
Pondering that bitter word—the last farewell!
The father, with a mild but tearless eye—
The mother, with both eye and heart in tears!
He, with his iron nature just put off,
Comes from the mart of noisy men awhile,
To witness holier vows than bind the world,
And taste, once more, the fount of sympathy!
She from the secret chamber of her sighs,
The home of woman! She has softly come
To stand beside her child—her only child—
And hear her pale-lipped promises. She comes
With hands laid meekly on her bosom—yet
With eye upraised, as tho' to catch one glance
Like that of childhood, from that pallid face
That hung for hours imploringly on hers,
In the long, watchful years of trial. Now,
She would endure those cruel years again,
To take her as an infant back to arms
That shielded and encircled her—ere she
Had blossomed into life. But lo! she stands
A plighted lovely creature at her side—
The child all lost in woman! The whole world
Contains for her no glory, now, like that
That centres in her full and thrilling heart.
Her eye roves not—is fixed not—but a deep
And lovely haze, as tho' she were in vision,
Has gathered on its dark transparency.
Her sight is on the future! Clouds and dreams!
Her head is bent—and on her varying cheek
The beautiful shame flits by—as hurrying thoughts
Press out the blood from th' o'erteeming citadel.
Roses and buds are struggling thro' her hair,
That hangs like night upon her brow—and see!
Dew still is on their bloom! Oh! emblem fair,
Of pure luxuriant youth—ere yet the sun
Of toiling, heated life hath withered it,
And scattered all its fragrance to the winds.

And doth she tremble—this long cherished flower!
As friends come closer round her, and the voice
Of adulation calls her from her dream!
Oh! wonder not that glowing youth like this,
To whom existence has been sunshine all,
A long, sweet dream of love—when on her ear
The tale of faith, of trial, and of death,
Sounds with a fearful music—should be dumb
And quake before the altar! Wonder not
That her heart shakes alarmingly—for now
She listens to the vow, that, like a voice
From out of heaven at night, when it comes down
Upon our fevered slumbers, steals on her
And calls to the recalless sacrifice!
Young maidens cluster round her; but she vows
Amid her bridal tears, and heeds them not.
Her thoughts are tossed and troubled—like lone barks
Upon a tempest sea, when stars have set
Under the heaving waters:—She hears not
The very prayers that float up round her; but
Veiling her eyes, she gives her heart away,
Deaf to all sounds but that low-voiced one
That love breathes through the temple of her soul!

Young Beauty at the altar! Ye may go
And rifle earth of all its loveliness,
And of all things created hither bring
The rosiest and richest—but, alas!
The world is all too poor to rival this!
Ye summon nothing from the place of dreams,
The orient realm of fancy, that can cope,
In all its passionate devotedness,
With this chaste, silent picture of the heart!
Youth, bud-encircled youth, and purity,
Yielding their bloom and fragrance up—in tears.

The promises have past. And welling now
Up from the lowly throng a faint far hymn
Breaks on the whispery silence—plaintively
Sweet voices mingling on the mellow notes,
Lift up the gathering melody, till all
Join in the lay to Jesus—all, save they
Whose hearts are echoing still to other sounds,
The music of their vows!

THE BUGLE.

> But still the dingle's hollow throat,
> Prolonged the swelling Bugle's note;
> The owlets started from their dream,
> The eagles answered with their scream.
> Round and around the sounds were cast,
> Till echo turned an answering blast.
> *Lady of the Lake.*

O, wild enchanting horn!
Whose music up the deep and dewy air,
Swells to the clouds, and calls on echo there,
Till a new melody is born.

Wake, wake again; the night
Is bending from her throne of Beauty down,
With still stars beaming on her azure crown,
Intense and eloquently bright!

Night, at its pulseless noon!
When the far voice of waters mourns in song,
And some tired watch-dog, lazily and long,
Barks at the melancholy moon!

Hark! how it sweeps away,
Soaring and dying on the silent sky,
As if some sprite of sound went wandering by,
With lone halloo and roundelay.

Swell, swell in glory out!
Thy tones come pouring on my leaping heart,
And my stirred spirit hears thee with a start,
As boyhood's old remembered shout.

Oh, have ye heard that peal,
From sleeping city's moon-bathed battlements,
Or from the guarded field and warrior tents,
Like some near breath around ye steal!

Or have ye, in the roar
Of sea, or storm, or battle, heard it rise,
Shriller than eagle's clamor to the skies,
Where wings and tempests never soar.

Go, go; no other sound,
No music, that of air or earth is born,
Can match the mighty music of that horn,
On midnight's fathomless profound!

PROSPER M. WETMORE.

PROSPER MONTGOMERY WETMORE was born at Stratford on the Housatonic, Connecticut, in 1799. At an early age he removed with his parents to New York. His father dying soon after, he was placed, when scarcely nine years of age, in a counting-room, where he continued as a clerk till he reached his majority. He has since that period been engaged in mercantile business in the city of New York.

With scant early opportunities for literary culture, Mr. Wetmore was not long in improving a natural tendency to the pursuits of authorship. He made his first appearance in print in 1816, at the age of seventeen, and soon became an important aid to the struggling literature, and, it may be added, writers of the times. He wrote for the magazines, the annuals, and the old Mirror; and as literature at that period was kept up rather as a social affair than from any reward promised by the trade, it became naturally associated with a taste for the green-room, and the patronage of the theatrical stars of the day. Mr. Wetmore was the companion of Price, Simpson, Brooks, Morris, and other members of a society which supported the wit and gaiety of the town.

P. M. Wetmore

In 1830 Mr. Wetmore published in an elegant octavo volume, *Lexington, with other Fugitive Poems*. This is the only collection of his writings which has been made. Lexington, a picture, in an ode, of the early revolutionary battle, is a spirited poem. It has fire and ease of versification. The Banner of Murat, The Russian Retreat, Greece, Painting, and several theatrical addresses possessing similar qualities, are among the contents of this volume.

In 1832 Mr. Wetmore delivered a poem in Spenserian stanza on Ambition, before one of the literary societies of Hamilton College, New York, which has not been printed.

In 1838 he edited a volume of the poems of James Nack, prefaced with a brief notice of the life of that remarkable person.

Mr. Wetmore, however, has been more generally known as a man of literary influence in society than as an author. He has been prominently connected with most of the liberal interests of the city, both utilitarian and refined—as Regent of the University, to which body he was appointed in 1833, promoting the public school system; as chairman of the committee on colleges and academies in the State Legislature, to which he was elected in 1834 and 1835; as member of the City Chamber of Commerce; as an efficient director of the Institution for the Deaf and Dumb; as President of the American Art-Union, which rapidly extended under his management to a national institution; and as a most active member and supporter of the New York Historical Society. These varied pursuits, the public indexes to more numerous private acts of liberality, have been sustained by a graceful personal manner, a sanguine temperament which preserves the freshness of youth, and a wide versatility of talent.

The military title of General Wetmore, by which he is widely known, is derived from his long and honorable service in the militia organization of the state, of which he was for many years Paymaster-General.

PAINTING.

Peopling, with art's creative power,
The lonely home, the silent hour.

'Tis to the pencil's magic skill
Life owes the power, almost divine,
To call back vanished forms at will,
And bid the grave its prey resign:
Affection's eye again may trace
The lineaments beloved so well;
The speaking look, the form of grace,
All on the living canvas dwell:
'Tis there the childless mother pays
Her sorrowing soul's idolatry;
There love can find, in after days,
A talisman to memory!
'Tis thine, o'er History's storied page,
To shed the halo light of truth;
And bid the scenes of by-gone age
Still flourish in immortal youth—
The long forgotten battle-field,
With mailed men to people forth;
In bannered pride, with spear and shield,
To show the mighty ones of earth—
To shadow, from the holy book,
The images of sacred lore;
On Calvary, the dying look
That told life's agony was o'er—
The joyous hearts, and glistening eyes,
When little ones were suffered near—
The lips that bade the dead arise,
To dry the widowed mother's tear:
These are the triumphs of the art,
Conceptions of the master-mind;
Time-shrouded forms to being start,
And wondering rapture fills mankind!

Led by the light of Genius on,
What visions open to the gaze!
'Tis nature all, and art is gone,
We breathe with them of other days:
Italia's victor leads the war,
And triumphs o'er the ensanguined plain:
Behold! the Peasant Conqueror
Piling Marengo with his slain:

That sun of glory beams once more,
  But clouds have dimmed its radiant hue.
The splendor of its race is o'er,
  It sets in blood on Waterloo!

What scene of thrilling awe is here!
  No look of joy, no eye for mirth;
With steeled hearts and brows austere,
  Their deeds proclaim a nation's birth.
Fame here inscribes for future age,
  A proud memorial of the free;
And stamps upon her deathless page,
  The noblest theme of history!

JAMES LAWSON,

A citizen of New York, and for many years connected with its literary interests, was born November 9, 1799, in Glasgow, Scotland. He was educated at the University of that city, and came early in life, at the close of the year 1815, to America, where he was received at New York in the counting-house of a maternal uncle. Mr. Lawson seems early to have taken an interest in American letters; for in 1821 we find him in correspondence with Mr. John Mennons, editor of the Greenock Advertiser, who was then engaged in publishing a miscellaneous collection of prose and verse, entitled the Literary Coronal. Mr. Mennons desired to introduce specimens of American authors, then a novelty to the British public, into his book, and Mr. Lawson supplied him with the materials. It was through this avenue and one or two kindred publications, that the merits of several of the best American authors first became known abroad. Halleck's "Fanny" was republished by Mr. Mennons in September, 1821, a fac-simile of the New York edition. In a second volume of the Literary Coronal of 1823, it was again re-published with poems by Bryant, Percival, James G. Brooks, and Miss Manley. An English edition of Salmagundi was published in the same year in the style of the Coronal, by Mr. Mennons, who was, perhaps, the first in the old world to seek after American poetry, and introduce abroad those felicitous short pieces of verse which have since become household words in England, through collections like his own. In this, he had a willing co-operator in Mr. Lawson, whose literary and personal friendship with the authors of the country has been a marked trait of his life.

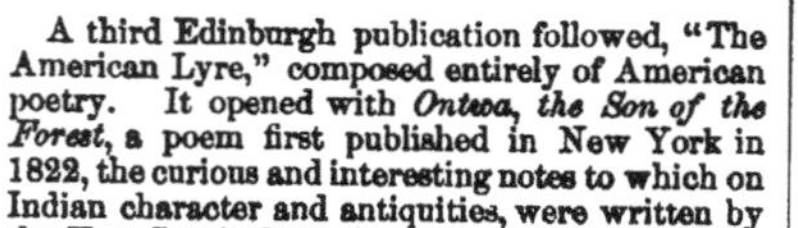

A third Edinburgh publication followed, "The American Lyre," composed entirely of American poetry. It opened with *Ontwa, the Son of the Forest*, a poem first published in New York in 1822, the curious and interesting notes to which on Indian character and antiquities, were written by the Hon. Lewis Cass, then Governor of Michigan. Ontwa is a spirited poem, an eloquent commemoration of the manners and extinction of the nation of the Eries.

Another volume of the Coronal, liberally supplied with American verse, appeared in 1826.

About this time the failure of the mercantile house in which Mr. Lawson was a partner, led him to turn his attention to literature. He had been already connected with the poet and editor, Mr. J. G. Brooks, in writing for the literary periodical of the latter, the *New York Literary Gazette, and American Athenæum*.*

In this, Mr. Lawson wrote the first criticism on Mr. Edwin Forrest, who had then just made his appearance in New York at the Bowery Theatre, under the management of Gilfert. This opening performance, in November, 1826, was Othello; and Mr. Lawson's criticism of several columns appeared in the next number of his friend's paper. It was shrewd, acute, freely pointing out defects, and confidently anticipating his subsequent triumphs.

The Literary Gazette, on its discontinuance, was immediately succeeded by an important newspaper enterprise, founded by Mr. J. G. Brooks, Mr. John B. Skilman, and Mr. James Lawson, as associates. This was the Morning Courier grown into the New York Courier and Enquirer. The first number of this journal was issued in 1827; and its first article was written by Mr. Lawson. The joint editorship of the paper continued till 1829, when new financial arrangements were made, and Noah's Enquirer was added to the Courier. Mr. Brooks and Mr. Lawson retired, when the latter immediately joined Mr. Amos Butler in the Mercantile Advertiser, with which he remained associated till 1833.

In 1830, a volume, *Tales and Sketches by a Cosmopolite*, from the pen of Mr. Lawson, was published by Elam Bliss, in New York. In these the writer finds his themes in the domestic life and romance of his native land, and in one instance ventures a dramatic sketch, a love scene, the precursor of the author's next publication, *Giordano*, a tragedy; an Italian state story of love and conspiracy, which was first performed at the Park Theatre, New York, in Nov. 1828. The prologue was written by the late William Leggett, and the epilogue, spoken by Mrs. Hilson, by Mr. Prosper M. Wetmore.

This is Mr. Lawson's only dramatic production, which has issued from the press. He has, however, in several instances, appeared before the public in connexion with the stage. He was associated with Mr. Bryant, Mr. Halleck, Mr. Wetmore, Mr. Brooks, and Mr. Leggett, on the committee which secured for Mr. Forrest the prize play of Metamora by the late J. A. Stone,† for which

* This weekly periodical was commenced by Mr. Brooks in the octavo form, Sept. 10, 1825, as the New York Literary Gazette and Phi Beta Kappa Repository; the latter portion of the title being taken from some dependence upon the support of members of that Society, which turned out to be nugatory. At the end of the volume, with the twenty-sixth number, the Phi Beta title was dropped, and an association effected with a similar publication. The American Athenæum, also weekly in quarto, conducted by George Bond, which had been commenced April 21, 1825, of which forty-four numbers had been issued. The joint publication bore the title "The New York Literary Gazette and American Athenæum," and as such was published in two quarto volumes, ending March 3, 1827.

† John Augustus Stone, the author of Metamora, was born in 1801, at Concord, Mass. He was an actor as well as dramatic writer, and made his first appearance in Boston as "Old Norval" in the play of Douglas. He acted in New York in 1826, and in Philadelphia afterwards at intervals. He received five hundred dollars from Mr. Forrest for Metamora. He wrote two other plays in which Mr. Forrest performed, *The Ancient Briton*, in which he took the part of Brigantius, and for which he paid the author a thousand dollars; and *Fauntleroy, The Banker of Rouen*, a version of the story of the English personage of that name. In the latter, the hero was executed on the stage by a machine bearing a close resemblance to an actual guillotine. The loaded knife descended; the private signal was imperfectly given, and the young American tragedian saved his head by a quick motion at the expense of his locks, which were closely

on its representation Mr. Wetmore wrote the prologue and Mr. Lawson the epilogue. Mr. L. was also one of the similar committee which selected Mr. J. K. Paulding's prize play of Nimrod Wildfire, or the Kentuckian in New York, for Mr. Hackett.

Mr. Lawson has also been a frequent contributor of criticism, essays, tales, and verse, to the periodicals of the day; among others, Herbert's American Monthly Magazine, the Knickerbocker, the Southern Literary Messenger, and Sargent's New Monthly.

These have, however, been but occasional employments, Mr. L., since his retirement from the active conduct of the press in 1833, having pursued the business of Marine Insurance, through which important interest he is well known in Wall street as an adjuster of averages, and in other relations.

THE APPROACH OF AGE.

Well, let the honest truth be told!
I feel that I am growing old,
And I have guessed for many a day,
My sable locks are turning grey—
At least, by furtive glances, I
Some very silvery hairs espy,
That thread-like on my temple shine,
And fain I would deny are mine:
While wrinkles creeping here and there,
Some score my years, a few my care.
The sports that yielded once delight,
Have lost all relish in my sight;
But, in their stead, more serious thought
A graver train of joys has brought,
And while gay fancy is refined,
Correct the taste, improve the mind.
I meet the friends of former years,
Whose smile approving, often cheers:
(How few are spared!) the poisonous draught
The reckless in wild frenzy quaffed,
In dissipation's giddy maze
O'erwhelmed them in their brightest days.
And one, my playmate when a boy,
I see in manhood's pride and joy;
He too has felt, through sun and shower,
Old Time, thy unrelenting power.
We talk of things which well we know
Had chanced some forty years ago;
Alas! like yesterday they seem,
The past is but a gorgeous dream!
But speak of forty coming years,
Ah, long indeed that time appears!
In nature's course, in forty more,
My earthly pilgrimage is o'er;
And the green turf on which I tread,
Will gaily spring above my head.

Beside me, on her rocking-chair,
My wife her needle plies with care,
And in her ever-cheerful smiles
A charm abides, that quite beguiles
The years that have so swiftly sped,
With their unfaltering, noiseless tread,
For we in mingled happiness,
Will not the approach of age confess.
But when our daughters we espy,
Bounding with laughing cheek and eye,
Our bosoms beat with conscious pride,
To see them blooming by our side.
God spare ye, girls, for many a day,
And all our anxious love repay!
In your fair growth we must confess
That time our footsteps closely press,
And every added year, indeed,
Seems to increase its rapid speed.

When o'er our vanished days we glance,
Far backward to our young romance,
And muse upon unnumbered things,
That crowding come on Memory's wings;
Then varied thoughts our bosoms gladden
And some intrude that deeply sadden:
—Fond hopes in their fruition crushed,
Beloved tones for ever hushed.—
We do not grieve that being's day
Is fleeting shadow-like away;
But thank thee, Heaven, our lengthened life
Has passed in love, unmarred by strife;
That sickness, sorrow, wo, and care,
Have fallen so lightly to our share.
We bless Thee for our daily bread,
In plenty on our table spread;
And Thy abundance helps to feed
The worthy poor who pine in need.
And thanks, that in our worldly way,
We have so rarely stepped astray.
But well we should in meekness speak,
And pardon for transgressions seek,
For oft, how strong soe'er the will
To follow good, we've chosen ill.

The youthful heart unwisely fears
The sure approach of coming years:
Though cumbered oft with weighty cares,
Yet age its burden lightly bears.
Though July's scorching heats are done,
Yet blandly smiles the slanting sun,
And sometimes, in our lovely clime,
Till dark December's frosty time.
Though day's delightful noon is past,
Yet mellow twilight comes, to cast
A sober joy, a sweet content,
Where virtue with repose is blent,
Till, calmly on the fading sight,
Mingles its latest ray with night.

SONNET—ANDREW JACKSON.

Come, stand the nearest to thy country's sire,
Thou fearless man, of uncorrupted heart;
Well worthy undivided praise thou art,
And 'twill be thine, when slumbers party ire,
Raised, by the voice of freemen, to a height
Sublimer far, than kings by birth may claim!
Thy stern, unselfish spirit dared the right,
And battled 'gainst the wrong. Thy holiest aim
Was freedom, in the largest sense, despite
Misconstrued motives, and unmeasured blame.
Above deceit, in purpose firm, and pure;
Just to opposers, and to friends sincere,
Thy worth shall with thy country's name endure,
And greener grow thy fame, through every coming year.

1837.

SONG.

When spring arrayed in flowers, Mary,
Danced with the leafy trees;
When larks sang to the sun, Mary,
And hummed the wandering bees;

…phaved. Stone also wrote *La Roque the Regicide*, *The Demoniac*, *Tancred*, and other pieces.

The circumstances of his death were melancholy. In a fit of derangement he threw himself into the Schuylkill and was drowned. The date of this event is recorded on a monument over his remains, which bears this inscription: "To the memory of John Augustus Stone, who departed this life June 1, 1834, aged thirty-three years," and on the reverse, "Erected to the Memory of the *Author* of Metamora, by his friend Edwin Forrest."

Then first we met and loved, Mary,
By Grieto's loupin' linn;
And blither was thy voice, Mary,
Than lintie's i' the whin.

Now autumn winds blaw cauld, Mary,
Amang the withered boughs;
And a' the bonny flowers, Mary,
Are faded frae the knowes;
But still thy love's unchanged, Mary,
Nae chilly autumn there,
And sweet thy smile as spring's, Mary,
Thy sunny face as fair.

Nae mair the early lark, Mary,
Trills on his soaring way;
Hushed is the lintie's sang, Mary,
Through a' the shortening day;
But still thy voice I hear, Mary,
Like melody divine;
Nae autumn in my heart, Mary,
And summer still in thine.

WILLIAM BOURNE OLIVER PEABODY—OLIVER WILLIAM BOURNE PEABODY.

The twin-brothers name together at the head of this article, the sons of Judge Oliver Peabody of Exeter, New Hampshire, were born at that place July 9, 1799. They were educated together at the celebrated academy under the charge of Dr. Abbot, entered Harvard College together at the early age of thirteen, and were graduated together in 1816.

This close union of birth and education was accompanied by a similarity of outward form and inward temperament. Both were men of eminent natural endowment, of ripe scholarship, of gentle and affectionate tempers, and both eventually dedicated their lives to the same path of professional duty, thus laboring in spirit though not in actual bodily presence, side by side, and separated in death by but a brief interval from one another.

At the outset of life, however, their courses were for a time separate, Oliver studying law, and William theology.

Oliver, after passing some time in his father's office, completed his legal education at Cambridge, and returned to practise in his native town, where he resided for eleven years, serving for a portion of the time in the state legislature, and being also occupied at different periods as editor of the Rockingham Gazette and Exeter News-Letter. In 1823, he delivered a poem before the Phi Beta Kappa Society at Harvard, and shortly after read a similar production at the celebration of the second centennial anniversary of the settlement of Portsmouth, New Hampshire.

In 1830, Mr. Peabody removed to Boston, where he became the assistant of his brother-in-law, the Hon. Alexander H. Everett, in the editorship of the North American Review. He was also for some years an assistant editor of the Boston Daily Advertiser. His connexion with the four periodicals we have named, was that of a contributor as well as a supervisor. The three journals contain many finished essays and choice poems from his pen, marked by a closeness of thought and elaborate execution, as well as a lively and humorous inspiration; while scarcely a number of the North American, during several years, was issued without one or more articles from his pen.

In 1836, Mr. Peabody was appointed Register of Probate in Suffolk county, a laborious office, which he resigned in 1842 in consequence of impaired health, and his acceptance of the professorship of English Literature in Jefferson College, an institution supported by the state of Louisiana. Finding a southern climate unsuited to his constitution, he returned in the following year to the North.

His views and tastes had been for some time turned in the direction of theology, and he now determined to enter the ministry. In 1845, he was licensed by the Boston Unitarian Association as a preacher, and in August of the same year became the minister of the Unitarian church of Burlington, Vermont, where the remainder of his life was passed in the di-charge (so far as his delicate health would permit) of his parochial duties. He died on the sixth of July, 1848.

William B. O. Peabody, immediately after receiving his degree, entered upon a preparation for the ministry in the Divinity school of Cambridge; and was, soon after his ordination, called to the charge of the Unitarian church at Springfield. He entered upon his duties in this place in 1820, when not quite twenty-one years of age; and it was here that the whole of his ministerial life was passed.

William B O Peabody

In addition to a conscientious discharge of the literary duties of his profession, Dr. Peabody of Springfield is said to have contributed a greater number of articles to the North American Review and Christian Examiner than any other person. He was also the author of several choice occasional poems published in the last named and other periodicals; and of the *Report of the Ornithology of Massachusetts*, prepared in fulfilment of his duties as one of the commission appointed for the scientific survey of the state.

Dr. Peabody's health, another of the many points of assimilation between himself and his brother, was feeble. He suffered a severe deprivation in 1843 by the loss of his wife, and in the following year by that of a daughter, who in some measure supplied the place of the head of his household. Neither bodily nor mental sufferings were, however, permitted to interpose more than a temporary pause in his constant course of useful labor. He died, after a confinement to his bed of but a few days, May 28, 1847.

A selection from Dr. Peabody's sermons was prepared for the press by his brother Oliver, who had nearly completed a memoir to accompany the volume, when his own life reached its termination. The work was completed by Everett Peabody, who, soon after its publication, prepared a selection from the contributions to the North American Review and poems of its author.

MONADNOCK.

Upon the far-off mountain's brow
The angry storm has ceased to beat,
And broken clouds are gathering now
In lowly reverence round his feet.
I saw their dark and crowded bands
On his firm head in wrath descending;

But there, once more redeemed, he stands,
And heaven's clear arch is o'er him bending.

I've seen him when the rising sun
Shone like a watch-fire on the height;
I've seen him when the day was done,
Bathed in the evening's crimson light;
I've seen him in the midnight hour,
When all the world beneath were sleeping,
Like some lone sentry in his tower
His patient watch in silence keeping.

And there, as ever steep and clear,
That pyramid of Nature springs!
He owns no rival turret near,
No sovereign but the King of kings:
While many a nation hath passed by,
And many an age unknown in story,
His walls and battlements on high
He rears in melancholy glory.

And let a world of human pride
With all its grandeur melt away,
And spread around his rocky side
The broken fragments of decay;
Serene his hoary head will tower,
Untroubled by one thought of sorrow:
He numbers not the weary hour;
He welcomes not nor fears to-morrow.

Farewell! I go my distant way:
Perhaps, not far in future years,
The eyes that glow with smiles to-day
May gaze upon thee dim with tears.
Then let me learn from thee to rise,
All time and chance and change defying,
Still pointing upward to the skies,
And on the inward strength relying.

If life before my weary eye
Grows fearful as the angry sea,
Thy memory shall suppress the sigh
For that which never more can be;
Inspiring all within the heart
With firm resolve and strong endeavor
To act a brave and faithful part,
Till life's short warfare ends for ever.

MAN GIVETH UP THE GHOST, AND WHERE IS HE?

Where is he? Hark! his lonely home
Is answering to the mournful call!
The setting sun with dazzling blaze
May fire the windows of his hall:
But evening shadows quench the light,
And all is cheerless, cold, and dim,
Save where one taper wakes at night,
Like weeping love remembering him.

Where is he? Hark! the friend replies:
"I watched beside his dying bed,
And heard the low and struggling sighs
That gave the living to the dead;
I saw his weary eyelids close,
And then—the ruin coldly cast,
Where all the loving and beloved,
Though sadly parted, meet at last."

Where is he? Hark! the marble says,
That "here the mourners laid his head;
And here sometimes, in after-days,
They came, and sorrowed for the dead:
But one by one they passed away,
And soon they left me here alone
To sink in unobserved decay,—
A nameless and neglected stone."

Where is he? Hark! 'tis Heaven replies:
"The star-beam of the purple sky,
That looks beneath the evening's brow,
Mild as some beaming angel's eye,
As calm and clear it gazes down,
Is shining from the place of rest,
The pearl of his immortal crown,
The heavenly radiance of the blest!"

LUCIUS M. SARGENT.

LUCIUS MANLIUS SARGENT was born at Boston June 25, 1786. He was the son of a leading merchant of that city, and in 1804 entered Harvard College. He was not graduated in course, but received an honorary degree of A.M. from the University in 1842. After leaving college he studied law in the office of Mr. Dexter. In 1813 he published *Hubert and Ellen, with other Poems*,* all of a pathetic and reflective character.

Mr. Sargent married a sister of Horace Binney of Philadelphia, one of the most accomplished scholars in the country, by whom he had three children, the eldest of whom, Horace Binney, was graduated with distinction at Harvard in 1843. Some time after the death of this lady he again married.

Mr. Sargent was an early advocate of the Temperance cause, and rendered important service to the movement by his public addresses and the composition of his *Temperance Tales*, a series of short popular stories, which have been extensively circulated in this country and reprinted in England, Scotland, Germany, and, it is to be hoped with good moral effect, in Botany Bay.

During the editorship of the Boston Transcript by his relative Mr. Epes Sargent, he contributed a series of satirical and antiquarian sketches to its columns under the title of *Dealings with the Dead by a Sexton of the Old School.* His other writings for the press have been numerous, but almost entirely anonymous.

Mr. Sargent makes a liberal use of a liberal fortune, possesses a fine library, and is a thorough scholar.

WINTHROP SARGENT, a kinsman of Lucius M. Sargent and son of George W. Sargent, was born in Philadelphia, September 23, 1825. He is the author of an "Introductory Memoir" prefixed to the Journals of officers engaged in Braddock's Expedition, printed by the Pennsylvania Historical Society in 1855 from the original manuscripts in the British Museum. Under the modest title we have cited Mr. Sargent has not only given the most thorough history of Braddock and his expedition that has ever appeared, but furnished one of the best written and most valuable historical volumes of the country. In the prosecution of his task he has used extensive research, and has grouped his large mass of varied and in many cases original material with admirable literary skill.

WILLIAM B. WALTER.

WILLIAM B. WALTER was born at Boston, April 19, 1796, and was graduated at Bowdoin College in 1818. He studied divinity at Cambridge, but did not follow the profession. He published, in 1821, a small volume of *Poems* at Boston, with a dedication to the Rev. John Pierpont, in which he says—"I cannot make the common, unprofit-

* Hubert and Ellen, with other poems, The Trial of the Harp, Billowy Water, The Plunderer's Grave, The Tear Drop, The Billow. By Lucius M. Sargent.

able, and to me exceedingly frivolous, apology—that these poems are the pleasant labors of idle or leisure hours. On the contrary, this volume, and I am proud to confess it, contains specimens of the precious and melancholy toil of years." The longest of these poems is entitled *Romance*. It opens with a picture of Palestine at the time of Our Saviour, from thence passes to the Crusades, and closes with reflections on nature, and on the vanity of human affairs. The remaining pieces, *The Death Chamber*, *Mourner of the Last Hope*, and others, are written in a strain of deep despondency.

Walter published in the same year a rambling narrative and descriptive poem, with the title of *Sukey*, the idea of which was evidently derived from the then recently published "Fanny." The story is little more than a thread connecting various passages of description and reflection. Sukey is introduced to us at the dame's school; grows up under the peaceful influences of country life; and has a lover who goes to sea while Sukey departs in a stage sleigh for a winter's visit to the city.

In due course of time Sukey becomes a belle, and figures at an evening party, which is minutely described, with its supper-table, jostling, and chit-chat about novels and poems, when suddenly "an Afric's form is seen," not one of the waiters, but a highly intelligent specimen of his race, who gives an animated and poetical description of a fight at sea with an Algerine pirate, whose vessel has just been brought into port by the victor, Sukey's lover.

The poem extends to one hundred and seventy-one six-line stanzas, and contains several melodious passages, many of which, however, are close imitations of Byron and Montgomery. The poem appeared in the same year with Fanny, and seems to have had a large circulation; the copy before us being printed at Baltimore, "from the second Boston edition," in a form similar to, and with the copyright notice of the original.

Walter died at Charleston, South Carolina, April 23, 1822.

MOURNER OF THE LAST HOPE.

Where grass o'ergrows each mouldering bone,
And stones themselves to ruins grown,
Like me, are death-like old.

I saw an Old Man kneel down by a grave,
All alone in the midnight stillness;
And his forehead bare,
Deep wrinkled with care,
Looked pale with a wintry chillness.

His hands were clasped o'er a grave newly dug,
And they shook with his soul-wrung sadness;
His blood slowly crept,
And he groaning wept,
As he thought of his visions of gladness.

The stars were along the wide depths of blue,
Shining down with a tremulous gleaming—
And the glorious moon,
At her highest noon,
Sat arrayed with the Spirits of Dreaming.

I asked the Old Man why he wept and prayed!
And his look was a look of sorrow!
Then he cried sad and wild—
Alas! for my child,
No waking hast thou for the morrow!

Years had wrought changes for him—as for all,
Now the last of his hopes slept beside him!
She was young and fair—
But now silent there!
No voice could I find to chide him.

Yea! a common tale, and a common lot,
From the breast to the charnel-house slumber!
Dark curses of fear
Wrap our being here—
Which time and thought cannot number.

She moved the fairest—the fairest among,
Like a young fairy shape of lightness;
And awakened the song
In the dance along,
Like a seraph of heaven in brightness.

None could gaze on her eye of lustrous blue,
And not feel his spirit heaving,
When it flashed in love,
Like a light from above,
The azure cloud brightly leaving.

And her cheek of snow was a cheek of health,
To those who knew not her weakness,
Till the hectic flush,
Like the day's faint blush,
Came o'er to disturb its meekness.

When she shrunk away from her pride of form,
Like a cloud in its loveliest shading,
Like the death-toned lute,
When winds are mute,
Or the rose in the summer's fading.

And the crowd did pass from the couch of woe;
All had finished each mournful duty;
And the garlands wove,
By the hands of love,
Hung around in a withering beauty.

Never sounded the death-bell in my ear,
With a knell so awful and weary,
As they buried her deep—
For a long, long sleep
In the lone place—so dark and dreary.

Oh, CHRIST! 'tis a strange and a fearful thought
That beauty like her's should have perished;
That the red lean worm
Should prey on a form,
Which a bosom of love might have cherished.

I loved her—Stranger! with soul of truth—
But God in his darkness hath smitten;
Who shall madly believe
That man may grieve
O'er the page of eternity written!

The Old Man rose, and he went his way,—
Oh, deep was his utterless mourning·
But the woes of the night—
No morrow's dear light
Will dispel with the ray of its dawning.

F. W. P. GREENWOOD.

FRANCIS WILLIAM PITT GREENWOOD was born in Boston, in 1797. After completing his college course at Harvard in 1814, he studied theology at the same university, and commenced his career as a preacher with great popularity, as the pastor of the New South Church, Boston, but was obliged at the expiration of a year to visit Europe for the benefit of his health. After passing a winter in Devonshire, England, he returned to this country, and settled in Baltimore, where he became the editor of the Unitarian Miscellany. In 1824 he returned to Boston, and became associate minister of King's Chapel. In 1827, he revised the liturgy used by the congregation, consisting of the Book of Common Prayer, with the passages relating to the Trinity and other articles of the faith of its authors, and the founders of King's Chapel, excised therefrom. In 1830, he also prepared a collection of hymns, which is in extensive use in the congregations of his denomination, and bears honorable testimony to the taste of its compiler. In 1838, Mr. Greenwood published a small volume of a popular character, *The Lives of the Apostles;* in 1833 a series of discourses on the *History of King's Chapel*, and about the same time a series of sermons delivered to the children of his congregation. During the years 1837 and 1838, he was an associate editor of the Christian Examiner, a journal to which he was throughout his life a frequent contributor of articles on literary topics, and on the tenets of the denomination of which he was a zealous advocate. In 1842 he published his *Sermons of Consolation*, a work of great beauty of thought and expression. Soon after this the author's health, which had never been completely restored, failed to such a degree, that he was unable to execute his purpose of preparing one or more additional series of his sermons for publication. He gradually sank under disease until his death, on the second of August, 1843.

A collection of *Miscellaneous Writings*, edited by his son, appeared in 1846. The volume contains his *Journal kept in England in* 1820–21, and a number of essays of a descriptive and reflective character, exhibiting the powers of the writer to the best advantage. We cite a passage from one of these on the

OPPORTUNITIES OF WINTER FOR INSTRUCTION.

In the warm portion of our year, when the sun reigns, and the fields are carpeted with herbs and flowers, and the forests are loaded with riches and magnificence, nature seems to insist on instructing us herself, and in her own easy, insensible way. In the mild and whispering air there is an invitation to go abroad which few can resist; and when abroad we are in a school where all may learn, without trouble or tasking, and where we may be sure to learn if we will simply open our hearts. But stern winter comes, and drives us back into our towns and houses, and there we must sit down, and learn and teach with serious application of the mind, and by the prompting of duty. As we are bidden to this exertion, so are we better able to make it than in the preceding season. The body, which was before unnerved, is now braced up to the extent of its capacity; and the mind which was before dissipated by the fair variety of external attractions, collects and concentrates its powers, as those attractions fade and disappear. The natural limits of day and night, also, conspire to the same end, and are in unison with the other intimations of the season. In summer, the days, glad to linger on the beautiful earth, almost exclude the quiet and contemplative nights, which are only long enough for sleep. But in the winter the latter gain the ascendency. Slowly and royally they sweep back with their broad shadows, and hushing the earth with the double spell of darkness and coldness, issue their silent mandates, and—while the still snow falls, and the waters are congealed—call to reflection, to study, to mental labor and acquisition.

The long winter nights! Dark, cold, and stern as they seem, they are the friends of wisdom, the patrons of literature, the nurses of vigorous, patient, inquisitive, and untiring intellect. To some, indeed, they come particularly associated, when not with gloom, with various gay scenes of amusement, with lighted halls, lively music, and a few (hundred) friends. To others, the dearest scene which they present is the cheerful fireside, instructive books, studious and industrious children, and those friends, whether many or few, whom the heart and experience acknowledge to be such. Society has claims; social intercourse is profitable as well as pleasant; amusements are naturally sought for by the young, and such as are innocent they may well partake of; but it may be asked, whether, when amusements run into excess, they do not leave their innocence behind them in the career; whether light social intercourse, when it takes up a great deal of time, has anything valuable to pay in return for that time; and whether the claims of society can in any way be better satisfied than by the intelligence, the sobriety, and the peaceableness of its members? Such qualities and habits must be acquired at home; and not by idleness even there, but by study. The winter evenings seem to be given to us, not exclusively, but chiefly, for instruction. They invite us to instruct ourselves, to instruct others, and to do our part in furnishing all proper means of instruction.

We must instruct ourselves. Whatever our age, condition, or occupation may be, this is a duty which we cannot safely neglect, and for the performance of which the season affords abundant opportunity. To know what other minds have done, is not the work of a moment; and it is only to be known from the records which they have left of themselves, or from what has been recorded of them. To instruct ourselves is necessarily our own work; but we cannot well instruct ourselves without learning from others. The stores of our own minds it is for ourselves to use for the best effects and to the greatest advantage; but if we do not acquire with diligence, from external sources, there would be very few of us who would have any stores to use. Let no one undervalue intellectual means, who wishes to effect intellectual ends. The best workman will generally want the best tools, and the best assortment of them.

We must instruct others. This duty belongs most especially to parents. All who have children, have pupils. The winter evening is the chosen time to instruct them, when they have past the tenderest years of their childhood. Those who have school-tasks to learn, should not be left to toil in solitude; but should be encouraged by the presence, and aided by the superior knowledge, of their parents, whose pleasure as well as duty it should be to lend them a helping hand along the road, not always easy, of learning. While the child is leaning over his book, the father and the mother should be nigh, that when he looks up in weariness or perplexity, he may find, at least, the assistance of sympathy. They need not be absolutely tied to the study-table, but they should not often hesitate between the calls of amusement abroad, and the demands for parental example, guidance, and companionship at home. They will lose no happiness by denying themselves many pleasures, and will find that the most brilliant of lustres are their own domestic lamp, and the cheerful and intelligent eyes of their children.

But all have not children; and the children of some are too young to be permitted to remain with their parents beyond the earliest hours of evening; and the children of others are old enough to accompany their parents abroad. For all those who think they could pleasantly and profitably receive instruction of a public nature, and for this purpose spend an hour or two away from their homes, there is, happily, a plenty of instruction provided. Winter is the very season for public instruction, and it must be said to their honor, that our citizens have excellently improved it as such. Opportunities for gaining useful knowledge have been provided, and they have not been neglected by those for whom the provision has been made. The fountains of waters have been opened, and the thirsty have been refreshed. Though home instruction is to be placed at the head of all instruction, yet there are numbers who have not instruction at home, and numbers who have none at home to whom they may communicate instruction; and there are numbers who find it convenient and useful to mingle public and domestic instruction together, or alternate the one with the other. And when it is considered that the public lectures referred to are charged with little expense to the hearers; that they are delivered by the best and ablest men among us; that hundreds of youth resort to them, many of whom are in all probability saved from idleness, and some from vice and crime; and that to all who may attend them they afford a rational employment of time, we may look to the continuance of such means of knowledge and virtue as one of the most inestimable of benefits.

RUFUS CHOATE,

The rapid and impetuous orator of New England, whose eloquence descends like the flood of a mountain river bearing along grand and minute objects in its course, was born at Ipswich, Essex County Massachusets, October 1, 1799. He was educated at Dartmouth, at the law school at Cambridge, and in the offices of Judge Cummings at Salem, and Attorney-General Wirt at Washington. He began the practice of the law at Danvers in 1824; passed some time at Salem, and removed to Boston in 1834, having previously occupied a seat in the state senate and in the house of representatives as a member of Congress. In 1842 he succeeded Daniel Webster in the United States Senate, resigning in 1845, and with these exceptions he has been exclusively engaged in his profession of the law.

His claims to literary notice rest upon his speeches in Congress and several addresses on public occasions. Of his speeches the most noted are those on the tariff, the Oregon question, and the annexation of Texas. Mr. Whipple, who has written an admirable analysis of their style,* in both its strength and weakness, celebrates their analogical power both of understanding and fancy, by which the most relevant and incongruous matters are alike made subservient to his argument; and gives some happy examples of the shrewd sense and humor which sometimes relieve his overburdened paragraphs. In one of these, in his speech on the Oregon question, he disposes of the old grudge against England:—

No, sir, we are above all this. Let the Highland clansman, half-naked, half-civilized, half-blinded by the peat-smoke of his cavern, have his hereditary enemy and his hereditary enmity, and keep the keen, deep, and precious hatred, set on fire of hell, alive if he can; let the North American Indian have his, and hand it down from father to son, by Heaven knows what symbols of alligators, and rattlesnakes, and war-clubs smeared with vermilion and entwined with scarlet; let such a country as Poland, cloven to the earth, the armed heel on the radiant forehead, her body dead, her soul incapable to die—let her remember the wrongs of days long past; let the lost and wandering tribes of Israel remember theirs—the manliness and the sympathy of the world may allow or pardon this to them: but shall America, young, free, and prosperous, just setting out on the highway of Heaven, "decorating and cheering the elevated sphere she just begins to move in, glittering like the morning star, full of life and joy"—shall she be supposed to be polluting and corroding her noble and happy heart, by moping over old stories of stamp-act, and the tax, and the firing of the Leopard on the Chesapeake in time of peace? No, sir; no, sir; a thousand times, No! We are born to happier feelings. We look on England as we look on France. We look on them from our new world, not unrenowned, yet a new world still; and the blood mounts to our cheeks, our eyes swim, our voices are stifled with the consciousness of so much glory; their trophies will not let us sleep, but there is no hatred at all—no hatred; all for honor, nothing for hate. We have, we can have, no barbarian memory of wrongs, for which brave men have made the last expiation to the brave.

Another passage, illustrating his humorous turn, may be placed alongside of this—his famous description of the New England climate, introduced as an illustration in a speech on the tariff:—

Take the New England climate in summer, you would think the world was coming to an end. Certain recent heresies on that subject may have had a natural origin there. Cold to-day; hot to-morrow; mercury at 80° in the morning, with wind at south-west; and in three hours more a sea turn, wind at east, a thick fog from the very bottom of the ocean, and a fall of forty degrees of Fahrenheit; now so dry as to kill all the beans in New Hampshire; then floods carrying off the bridges of the Penobscot and Connecticut; snow in Portsmouth in July; and the next day a man and a yoke of oxen killed by lightning in Rhode Island. You would think the world was twenty times coming to an end. But I do not know how it is: we go along; the early and the latter rain falls, each in its season; and seedtime and harvest do not fail; the sixty days of hot corn weather are pretty sure to be measured out to us. The Indian summer, with its bland south-west and mitigated sunshine, brings all up; and on the twenty-fifth of November, or thereabouts, being Thursday, three millions of grateful people, in meeting-houses, or around the family board, give thanks for a year of health, plenty, and happiness.

Rufus Choate

Of his *mots*, which pass current, one is this sentiment:—"What! banish the Bible from schools! Never, while there is a piece of Plymouth Rock left large enough to make a gun-flint of."*

* Article Hon. Rufus Choate. Whig Rev., Jan., 1847.

* The autograph of Mr. Choate is a celebrity. "It resembles," says Mr. Loring in his Boston Orators, "somewhat the map of Ohio, and looks like a piece of crayon sketching done in the dark with a three-pronged fork. His handwriting cannot be deciphered without the aid of a pair of compasses and a quadrant."

He possesses thought and feeling in the midst of his boldest extravagance. Mr. Loring relates an anecdote of his calm sensibility—of the impression made upon him by a great idea in simple language, which is very impressive:—

We will relate an instance of the excitable powers of our orator. In an argument on a case of impeachment, before a legislative committee, Mr. Choate remarked that he never read, without a thrill of sublimity, the concluding article in the Bill of Rights,—the language of which is borrowed directly from Harrington, who says he owes it to Livy,—that 'in the government of this commonwealth, the legislative department shall never exercise the executive and judicial powers, or either of them; the executive shall never exercise the legislative and judicial powers, or either of them; the judicial shall never exercise the legislative and executive powers, or either of them;—to the end that it may be a government of laws, and not of men;" thus providing that the three great departments shall be entirely independent of each other; and he remembered a story of a person who said that he could read Paradise Lost without affecting him at all, but that there was a passage at the end of Newton's Optics which made his flesh creep and his hair stand on end. I confess, said Mr. Choate, that I never read that article of the constitution without feeling the same,—" to the end that it may be a government of laws, and not of men."

April 21, 1841, Mr. Choate delivered a Eulogy in Boston on President Harrison, in which he characterized him as emphatically the Good President, in a noble passage in which his eloquence was tempered by the solemnity of the occasion.

In New York, on the Anniversary of the Landing of the Pilgrims in 1843, at the Tabernacle, he delivered the address in which he described a body of the Puritans flying from the Marian persecution to Geneva, where they found "a commonwealth without a king, and a church without a bishop." The sentiment was complimented at the dinner which followed at the Astor House, where Dr. Wainwright (since bishop) was present and replied. In 1852 he was one of the speakers at the meeting of the Circuit Court of Boston upon the decease of Webster, and afterwards, in July of the next year, delivered an elaborate eulogy on his illustrious friend at their common college at Dartmouth. It has been said that the art of constructing a long sentence has been lost by the feeble wits of the men of modern days; if so, the secret has been regained by Mr. Choate. One of the sentences in the Dartmouth oration on Webster, a summary of the statesman's career, occupied nearly five pages of printed matter in octavo.

THE STATESMANSHIP OF DANIEL WEBSTER.

It was while Mr. Webster was ascending through the long gradations of the legal profession to its highest rank, that by a parallel series of display on a stage, and in parts totally distinct, by other studies, thoughts, and actions, he rose also to be at his death the first of American Statesmen. The last of the mighty rivals was dead before, and he stood alone. Give this aspect also of his greatness a passing glance. His public life began in May, 1813, in the House of Representatives in Congress, to which this state had elected him. It ended when he died. If you except the interval between his removal from New Hampshire and his election in Massachusetts, it was a public life of forty years. By what political morality, and by what enlarged patriotism, embracing the whole country, that life was guided, I shall consider hereafter. Let me now fix your attention rather on the magnitude and variety and actual value of the service. Consider that from the day he went upon the Committee of Foreign Relations, in 1813, in time of war, and more and more, the longer he lived and the higher he rose, he was a man whose great talents and devotion to public duty placed and kept him in a position of associated or sole command; command in the political connexion to which he belonged, command in opposition, command in power; and appreciate the responsibilities which that implies, what care, what prudence, what mastery of the whole ground—exacting for the conduct of a party, as Gibbon says of Fox, abilities and civil discretion equal to the conduct of an empire. Consider the work he did in that life of forty years—the range of subjects investigated and discussed; composing the whole theory and practice of our organic and administrative politics, foreign and domestic: the vast body of instructive thought he procured and put in possession of the country; how much he achieved in Congress as well as at the bar; to fix the true interpretation, as well as to impress the transcendent value of the constitution itself, as much altogether as any jurist or statesman since its adoption; how much to establish in the general mind the great doctrine that the government of the United States is a government proper, established by the people of the States, not a compact between sovereign communities,—that within its limits it is supreme, and that whether it is within its limits or not, in any given exertion of itself, it is to be determined by the Supreme Court of the United States—the ultimate arbiter in the last resort—from which there is no appeal but to revolution; how much he did in the course of the discussions which grew out of the proposed mission to Panama, and, at a later day, out of the removal of the deposits, to place the executive department of the government on its true basis, and under its true limitations; to secure to that department all its just powers on the one hand, and on the other to vindicate to the legislative department, and especially to the senate, all that belonged to them; to arrest the tendencies which he thought at one time threatened to substitute the government of a single will, of a single person of great force of character and boundless popularity, and of a numerical majority of the people, told by the head, without intermediate institutions of any kind, judicial or senatorial, in place of the elaborate system of checks and balances, by which the constitution aimed at a government of laws, and not of men; how much, attracting less popular attention, but scarcely less important, to complete the great work which experience had shown to be left unfinished by the judiciary act of 1789, by providing for the punishment of all crimes against the United States; how much for securing a safe currency and a true financial system, not only by the promulgation of sound opinions, but by good specific measures adopted, or bad ones defeated; how much to develope the vast material resources of the country, and push forward the planting of the West—not troubled by any fear of exhausting old states—by a liberal policy of public lands, by vindicating the constitutional power of Congress to make or aid in making large classes of internal improvements, and by acting on that doctrine uniformly from 1813, whenever a road was to be built, or a rapid suppressed, or a canal to be opened, or a breakwater or a lighthouse set up above or below the flow of the tide, if so far beyond the ability of a single state, or of so wide utility to commerce or labor as to rise to the rank of a work general in its influences—another tie of union because another proof of the beneficence of union; how much to protect the vast mechanical and manufacturing interests of the country, a value of many hundreds of millions—after having been lured into existence against his counsels, against his science of political economy, by a policy of artificial encouragement—from being sacrificed, and the pursuits and plans of large regions and communities broken up, and the acquired skill of the country squandered by a sudden and capricious withdrawal of the promise of the government; how much for the right performance of the most delicate and difficult of all tasks, the ordering of the foreign affairs of a nation, free, sensitive, self-conscious, recognising, it is true, public law and a morality of the state, binding on the conscience of the state, yet aspiring to power, eminence, and command, its whole frame filled full and all on fire with American feeling, sympathetic with liberty everywhere—how much for the right ordering of the foreign affairs of such a state—aiming in all its policy, from his speech on the Greek question in 1823, to his letters to M. Hulsemann in 1850, to occupy the high, plain, yet dizzy ground which separates influence from intervention, to avow and promulgate warm good will to humanity, wherever striving to be free, to inquire authentically into the history of its struggles, to take official and avowed pains to ascertain the moment when its success may be recognised, consistently, ever, with the great code that keeps the peace of the world, abstaining from everything which shall give any nation a right under the law of nations to utter one word of complaint, still less to retaliate by war—the sympathy, but also the neutrality, of Washington—how much to compose with honor a concurrence of difficulties with the first power in the world, which anything less than the highest degree of discretion, firmness, ability, and means of commanding respect and confidence at home and abroad would inevitably have conducted to the last calamity—a disputed boundary line of many hundred miles, from St. Croix to the Rocky Mountains, which divided an exasperated and impracticable border population, enlisted the pride and affected the interests and controlled the politics of particular states, as well as pressed on the peace and honor of the nation, which the most popular administrations of the era of the quietest and best public feelings, the times of Monroe and of Jackson, could not adjust; which had grown so complicated with other topics of excitement that one false step, right or left, would have been a step down a precipice—this line settled for ever—the claim of England to search our ships for the suppression of the slave-trade silenced for ever, and a new engagement entered into by treaty, binding the national faith to contribute a specific naval force for putting an end to the great crime of man—the long practice of England to enter an American ship and impress from its crew, terminated for ever; the deck henceforth guarded sacredly and completely by the flag—how much, by profound discernment, by eloquent speech, by devoted life to strengthen the ties of Union, and breathe the fine and strong spirit of nationality through all our numbers—how much most of all, last of all, after the war with Mexico, needless if his counsels had governed, had ended in so vast an acquisition of territory, in presenting to the two great antagonist sections of our country so vast an area to enter on, so imperial a prize to contend for, and the accursed fraternal strife had begun—how much then, when rising to the measure of a true, and difficult, and rare greatness, remembering that he had a country to save as well as a local constituency to gratify, laying all the wealth, all the hopes, of an illustrious life on the altar of a hazardous patriotism, he sought and won the more exceeding glory which now attends—which in the next age shall more conspicuously attend—his name who composes an agitated and saves a sinking land—recall this series of conduct and influences, study them carefully in their facts and results—the reading of years—and you attain to a true appreciation of this aspect of his greatness—his public character and life.

THE CONSOLATIONS OF LITERATURE.*

I come to add the final reason why the *working man*—by whom I mean the whole *brotherhood of industry*—should set on mental culture and that knowledge which is wisdom, a value so high—only not supreme—subordinate alone to the exercises and hopes of religion itself. And that is, that therein he shall so surely find rest from labor; succor under its burdens; forgetfulness of its cares; composure in its annoyances. It is not always that the busy day is followed by the peaceful night. It is not always that fatigue wins sleep. Often some vexation outside of the toil that has exhausted the frame; some loss in a bargain; some loss by an insolvency; some unforeseen rise or fall of prices; some triumph of a mean or fraudulent competitor; "the law's delay, the proud man's contumely, the insolence of office, or some one of the spurns that patient merit from the unworthy takes"—some self-reproach, perhaps—follow you within the door; chill the fireside; sow the pillow with thorns; and the dark care is lost in the last waking thought, and haunts the vivid dream. Happy, then, is he who has laid up in youth, and has held fast in all fortune, a genuine and passionate love of reading. True balm of hurt minds; of surer and more healthful charm than "poppy or mandragora, or all the drowsy syrups of the world"—by that single taste, by that single capacity, he may bound in a moment into the still regions of delightful studies, and be at rest. He recalls the annoyance that pursues him; reflects that he has done all that might become a man to avoid or bear it; he indulges in one good long, human sigh, picks up the volume where the mark kept his place, and in about the same time that it takes the Mohammedan in the Spectator to put his head in the bucket of water and raise it out, he finds himself exploring the arrow-marked ruins of Nineveh with Layard; or worshipping at the spring-head of the stupendous Missouri with Clarke and Lewis; or watching with Columbus for the sublime moment of the rising of the curtain from before the great mystery of the sea; or looking reverentially on while Socrates—the discourse of immortality ended—refuses the offer of escape, and takes in his hand the poison, to die in obedience to the unrighteous sentence of the law; or, perhaps, it is in the contemplation of some vast spectacle or phenomenon of Nature that he has found his quick peace—the renewed exploration of one of her great laws—or some glimpse opened by the pencil of St. Pierre, or Humboldt, or Chateaubriand, or Wilson, of the "blessedness and glory of her own deep, calm, and mighty existence."

* From an address delivered at Danvers, Mass., September 29, 1854, at the dedication of the institute for purposes of literature, munificently founded by Mr. George Peabody, the eminent London banker, in his native town in Massachusetts.

Let the case of a busy lawyer testify to the priceless value of the love of reading. He comes home, his temples throbbing, his nerves shattered, from a trial of a week; surprised and alarmed by the charge of the judge, and pale with anxiety about the verdict of the next morning, not at all satisfied with what he has done himself, though he does not yet see how he could have improved it; recalling with dread and self-disparagement, if not with envy, the brilliant effort of his antagonist, and tormenting himself with the vain wish that he could have replied to it—and altogether a very miserable subject, and in as unfavorable a condition to accept comfort from wife and children as poor Christian in the first three pages of the Pilgrim's Progress. With a superhuman effort he opens his book, and in a twinkling of an eye he is looking into the full "orb of Homeric or Miltonic song," or he stands in the crowd breathless, yet swayed as forests or the sea by winds—hearing and to judge the Pleadings for the Crown; or the philosophy which soothed Cicero or Boethius in their afflictions, in exile, in prison, and the contemplation of death, breathes over his petty cares like the sweet south; or Pope or Horace laugh him into good humor, or he walks with Æneas and the Sybil in the mild light of the world of the laurelled dead—and the court-house is as completely forgotten as the dream of a preadamite life. Well may he prize that endeared charm, so effectual and safe, without which the brain had long ago been chilled by paralysis, or set on fire by insanity!

To these uses, and these enjoyments; to mental culture, and knowledge, and morality—the guide, the grace, the solace of labor on all its fields, we dedicate this charity! May it bless you in all your successions; and may the admirable giver survive to see that the debt which he recognises to the future is completely discharged; survive to enjoy in the gratitude, and love, and honor of this generation, the honor, and love, and gratitude, with which the latest will assuredly cherish his name, and partake and transmit his benefaction.

CONNECTICUT ACADEMY OF ARTS AND SCIENCES.

THE Connecticut Academy of Arts and Sciences was formed at New Haven, Conn., March 4, 1799, by an association of gentlemen. Its object was to concentrate the efforts of literary men in Connecticut in the promotion of useful knowledge.

Previous to this, the *Connecticut Society of Arts and Sciences* was established in the year 1786. This Society published, in 1788, at New Haven, a very valuable paper, by Jonathan Edwards, D.D., on the language of the Muhhekaneew Indians (8vo., pp. 17), but after a few years the Society gradually died out.

In October, 1799, the *Academy* was incorporated by the Legislature of Connecticut. At the first meeting, Dr. Timothy Dwight was elected the President, and he was annually re-elected to this office until his death in 1817. He had taken an active part in the establishment of the institution, and was one of its most efficient members.

In addition to the ordinary business of receiving communications on scientific subjects, the Academy, soon after its organization, engaged with great zeal in the enterprise of preparing a full statistical history of the cities, towns, and parishes, of the state of Connecticut. About the same time (Dec. 1799), they made an unsuccessful endeavor, with the concurrence of the American Academy and the American Philosophical Society, to procure an enlargement of the objects, and a greater particularity in the details of the National Census of 1800.

In the course of a few years, statistical and historical accounts of about thirty towns in Connecticut had been received.

The publication of these accounts was commenced in 1811 with that of the city of New Haven, by the Rev. Timothy Dwight (8vo. pp. 84). In 1815, the Academy published a *Statistical Account of several Towns in the County of Litchfield, Conn.* (8vo. pp. 40). In 1819 was published, under the patronage of the Academy, a *Statistical Account of the County of Middlesex*, by the Rev. D. D. Field (Middletown, 8vo. pp. 154).

These were only a small part of the town histories which had been received and arranged for the press. But so little interest was at that period generally felt in such matters, that it was not deemed desirable to continue the publication, and most of these communications still remain unprinted.

Several scientific papers having been from time to time read before the Academy, it was decided in 1809, to publish a selection from them. Accordingly, in 1810, there appeared at New Haven the first part of the *Memoirs of the Connecticut Academy of Arts and Sciences* (8vo. pp. 216). Part second followed in 1811, part third in 1813, and part fourth in 1816, completing a volume of 412 pages.

On the establishment of *The American Journal of Science and Arts* by Professor Silliman, the Academy discontinued the further issue of their Memoirs in a separate form, and adopted this work as their medium of publication. This important journal was commenced in July, 1818, and was sustained for many years at the private expense of Professor Silliman. In April, 1838, Benjamin Silliman, Jr., became associate editor, and has so continued. The first series of the Journal was completed in 1846, and comprises 50 volumes, the last one being a full Index to the forty-nine volumes preceding. A second series was commenced in 1846, under the editorship of Professors B. Silliman, B. Silliman, Jr., and James D. Dana, with whom other scientific gentlemen have since been associated, and it has now reached its twentieth volume. This journal is well known and appreciated throughout the learned world, and has become a very extensive repository of the scientific labors of our countrymen, and has done much to stimulate research and to diffuse knowledge.

Among many important papers communicated by members of the Academy, and presented to the public through the Journal of Science, may be named the elaborate *Essay on Musical Temperament*, by Prof. A. M. Fisher; also, several papers on *Meteorological Topics*, and especially on the *Rotative Character of Atlantic Gales and of Other Great Storms*, by Wm. C. Redfield; and most of the numerous papers on *Meteoric Showers*, and on the *Aurora Borealis*, by Professor Olmsted and others.*

GEORGE W. DOANE.

GEORGE WASHINGTON DOANE was born in Trenton, N. J., May 27, 1799. He was partly edu-

* See the Historical Sketch of the Conn. Acad. by E. C. Herrick, in Am. Quar. Reg., pp. 12-23. Aug., 1840.

cated in New York by the Rev. Edmund D. Barry, a classical instructor who taught three generations of pupils, and who died rector of the Episcopal church of St. Matthew in Jersey City, at the age of seventy-six, in 1852. Pursuing his studies at Geneva in Western New York, Mr. Doane entered Union College, where he was graduated in 1818. He was then for a short time a student of law in the city of New York, in the office of Richard Harrison. In 1821 he was ordained deacon in the Episcopal Church by Bishop Hobart, and was for four years an assistant minister in Trinity church, New York. In 1824 he was appointed Professor of Rhetoric and Belles Lettres in the new Washington, now Trinity, College, Hartford, Ct. In 1828 he went to Boston as assistant minister of Trinity church, of which he became rector in 1830. In 1829 he was married to Eliza Greene Perkins. On the 31st of October, 1832, he was consecrated Bishop of New Jersey, and the next year became rector of St. Mary's Church at Burlington.

At this beautiful town on the banks of the Delaware Bishop Doane, in addition to the more immediate duties of his diocese, has devoted himself to the cause of education, in connexion with two institutions known as St. Mary's Hall and Burlington College. The former, commenced in 1837, is a female seminary: the latter is an incorporated institution for the usual purposes of education, and was commenced in 1846.

In 1841 Bishop Doane visited England at the request of the Rev. Dr. Hook to preach the sermon at the consecration of the new parish church at Leeds,—the first instance of an American bishop preaching in an English pulpit under the new act authorizing the admission of the transatlantic clergy.

The literary productions of Dr. Doane have been numerous, though mostly confined to sermons and charges, and church periodical literature. He has edited the *Missionary*, a monthly religious newspaper and journal of his diocese. In 1842 a volume of his sermons was published by the Rivingtons in London.

He is the author of numerous short poems chiefly of a lyrical or simple devotional character, which have appeared from time to time in the journals. In 1824 he published a volume of his early poetical writings entitled *Songs by the Way, chiefly devotional; with Translations and Imitations.* Several of them have been included in the collection of hymns in use in the Protestant Episcopal Church. The translations are of Latin hymns, from the Italian of Metastasio, and from the odes of Horace. He has also edited Keble's Christian Year, introducing additions from Croswell and others, and a Selection from the Sermons and Poetical Remains of the Rev. Benjamin Davis Winslow, his assistant in St. Mary's Church.

In all these, and in the prose writings of Bishop Doane, there is an elegant taste, evidence of good English scholarship, and spirited expression. His pulpit style is marked by brevity and energy; witnessing to an activity of mind which has characterized his numerous labors in his diocese and in the cause of education. The latter have not been without financial difficulties, through which Bishop Doane has struggled, with success to the cause in which he has been engaged, though with no improvement to his pecuniary fortunes.

ON A VERY OLD WEDDING-RING.

The Device—Two hearts united.
The Motto—Dear love of mine, my heart is thine.

I like that ring—that ancient ring,
Of massive form, and virgin gold,
As firm, as free from base alloy,
As were the sterling hearts of old.

I like it—for it wafts me back,
Far, far along the stream of time,
To other men, and other days,
The men and days of deeds sublime.

But most I like it, as it tells
The tale of well-requited love;
How youthful fondness persevered,
And youthful faith disdained to rove—

How warmly *he* his suit preferred,
Though *she*, unpitying, long denied,
Till, softened and subdued, at last,
He won his fair and blooming bride.—
How, till the appointed day arrived,
They blamed the lazy-footed hours—
How then, the white-robed maiden train,
Strewed their glad way with freshest flowers—
And how, before the holy man,
They stood, in all their youthful pride,
And spoke those words, and vowed those vows,
Which bind the husband to his bride:
All this it tells;—the plighted troth—
The gift of every earthly thing—
The hand in hand—the heart in heart—
For this I like that ancient ring.

I like its old and quaint device;
"Two blended hearts"—though time may wear them,
No mortal change, no mortal chance,
"Till death," shall e'er in sunder tear them.
Year after year, 'neath sun and storm,
Their hopes in heav'n, their trust in God,
In changeless, heartfelt, holy love,
These two the world's rough pathways trod.
Age might impair their youthful fires,
Their strength might fail, 'mid life's bleak weather,
Still, hand in hand, they travelled on—
Kind souls! they slumber now together.

I like its simple poesy too:
"Mine own dear love, this heart is thine!"
Thine, when the dark storm howls along,
As when the cloudless sunbeams shine.
"This heart is thine, mine own dear love!"
Thine, and thine only, and for ever;
Thine, till the springs of life shall fail,
Thine, till the cords of life shall sever.

Remnant of days departed long,
Emblem of plighted troth unbroken,
Pledge of devoted faithfulness,
Of heartfelt, holy love, the token:
What varied feelings round it cling!—
For these I like that ancient ring.

EVENING.

"Let my prayer be——as the evening sacrifice."

Softly now the light of day
Fades upon my sight away;
Free from care, from labor free,
Lord, I would commune with Thee!
Thou, whose all-pervading eye
Naught escapes, without, within,
Pardon each infirmity,
Open fault, and secret sin.

Soon for me, the light of day
Shall for ever pass away;
Then, from sin and sorrow free,
Take me, LORD, to dwell with Thee!
Thou who sinless, yet hast known
All of man's infirmity;
Then, from Thy eternal throne,
JESUS, look with pitying eye.

CALEB CUSHING.

CALEB CUSHING, the son of Captain John N. Cushing, an eminent shipowner of Salisbury, Massachusetts, was born at that place January 7, 1800. He was fitted for College at the Public School, and graduated at Harvard with the honors of the salutatory oration, at the early age of seventeen. He delivered a poem before the Phi Beta Kappa Society in 1819, and an oration on the durability of the Federal Union, on taking his degree of Master of Arts. In 1819 he was appointed a tutor at Harvard, an office which he filled until July, 1821. In 1822 he commenced the practice of the law, in 1825 was elected to the House of Representatives, and the next year to the Senate of the State. In the same year he published a *History of Newburyport*, and a treatise on *The Practical Principles of Political Economy*. In 1824 he married a daughter of Judge Wilde of Boston. In 1826 he was an unsuccessful candidate for election to the Federal House of Representatives. He passed the years from 1829 to 1832 in foreign travel, and on his return published two small volumes of tales and sketches entitled *Reminiscences of Spain—the Country, its People, History, and Monuments*, and a *Review, Historical and Political, of the late Revolution in France, and the Consequent Events in Belgium, Poland, Great Britain, and other parts of Europe*—also in two volumes. In 1833 and 1834, Mr. Cushing was again elected by the town of Newburyport to the State Legislature, where his speech on the currency and public deposits attracted great favor.

C. Cushing

In 1835 he was elected to Congress, and remained a member of the House of Representatives until 1843. In 1836 he delivered an eloquent vindication of the New England character in reply to an onslaught by Benjamin Hardin, of Kentucky. He was an active member in the debates and business of the House. In 1840 he wrote a popular campaign *Life of General Harrison*. He afterwards supported the administration of President Tyler, by whom he was appointed, in 1843, Commissioner to China for the negotiation of a commercial treaty. He sailed in July in the steam-frigate Missouri. The vessel was burnt on the twenty-second of August, while off Gibraltar, and the minister proceeded by the overland route to his destination. A treaty was negotiated and signed July 3, 1844. He returned home by way of the Pacific and Mexico.

In 1846 Mr. Cushing was elected to the Legislature, and the next year was an unsuccessful candidate for the governorship of his State. He advocated an appropriation of twenty thousand dollars for the benefit of the Massachusetts volunteers in the Mexican war, but without success. He was elected colonel by these volunteers, and accompanied them to Mexico, where he was appointed a brigadier-general, and took part in the battle of Buena Vista. He was afterwards, at his request, transferred to the army of General Scott, under whom he served during the remainder of the war.

On his return, in 1849, he was again elected to the State Legislature. He was chosen in 1851 the first mayor of Newburyport, and in 1852 was appointed Attorney-General of the United States by President Pierce.

Mr. Cushing is the author of several addresses delivered on various anniversary occasions, and has contributed a number of articles to the North American Review.* Activity and energy have characterized his course whether in or out of office. An epigrammatic epitaph by Miss Hannah F. Gould, and the reply of Mr. Cushing, illustrate the character and the ready talent of the man:—

Lay aside all ye dead,
For in the next bed
Reposes the body of Cushing,
He has crowded his way
Through the world, they say,
And, even though dead, will be pushing.

Here lies one whose wit,
Without wounding, could hit,—
And green grows the grass that's above her;
Having sent every beau
To the regions below,
She has gone down herself for a lover.

CAROLINE, the wife of Mr. Cushing, is author of *Letters Descriptive of Public Monuments, Scenery, and Manners, in France and Spain*, two pleasant volumes of reminiscences of her tour in Europe with her husband.†

THEODORE SEDGWICK—CATHARINE M. SEDGWICK—THEODORE SEDGWICK.

THEODORE, the eldest son of Theodore Sedgwick, one of the judges of the Supreme Court of Massachusetts, was born in Sheffield, Berkshire, Mass., on the last day of the year 1781. He passed his boyhood at Stockbridge, where his father removed in 1788, completed his literary studies at Yale College in 1799, studied law in the office of Peter Van Schaack in Kinderhook, New York, and commenced practice in Albany in partnership with Harmanus Bleecker, afterwards the representative of the United States at the Hague. In 1808 he married Miss Susan Ridley, a granddaughter of Governor Livingston. He rapidly rose to eminence at the bar, but, finding his health failing, retired from practice in 1822 to the estate

* Oration at Newburyport, July 4, 1832.
Oration, July 4, 1833, for the American Colonization Society.
Address before the American Institute of Instruction, 1834.
Eulogy on Lafayette, delivered at Dover, N. H., 1834.
Popular Eloquence, an Address before the Literary Societies of Amherst College, Aug. 23, 1836.
Progress of America, an Oration delivered at Springfield, Mass., July 4, 1839.
Oration on the Errors of Popular Reformers, delivered before the Phi Beta Kappa Society at Cambridge, 1839.
Articles on Americus Vespuccius, Boccaccio, and Columbus, North Am. Review, xii. 418; xix. 68; xxi. 398.

† Loring's Boston Orators, pp. 518-524.

left by his father, who died in 1813, at Stockbridge.

In 1824 he was elected a member of the state house of representatives, and was again chosen in 1825 and 1827. He was twice nominated for Congress, but failed of his election owing to the minority of his party. He was an active politician though not a violent partisan, and expressed himself with clearness and decision on all the great questions and issues of the day. He took much interest in agriculture, and was twice president of the Berkshire Agricultural Society.

In 1836 Mr. Sedgwick published the first part of a work entitled *Public and Private Economy.* In this he traces the history of property and poverty, and the means to acquire the one and avoid the other, in a clear and interesting manner, showing the absolute necessity to a community of a spirit of thrift, economy, and industry—and of a safe system of currency and credit, based upon actual values, for the successful prosecution of its business relations. In 1838 and 1839 Mr. Sedgwick enlarged his work by the addition of a second and third part, principally devoted to an account of his observations in England and France during a tour in the summer of 1836. The condition of the masses in these countries, the extravagance of government, and the lack of provision for cheap conveniences or essentials of social life, are the chief topics discussed.

On the 6th of November, 1839, Mr. Sedgwick, who had just completed an address at a political meeting at Pittsfield prior to the state election, was seized by a fit of apoplexy which soon after caused his death.

C. M. Sedgwick

CATHARINE MARIA SEDGWICK, the daughter of the Hon. Theodore Sedgwick, was born at Stockbridge, Massachusetts. A member of a well trained family, she received an excellent education, and in 1822 published her first work, *A New England Tale.* This was commenced as a religious tract, but expanding in the writer's hands beyond the limits of such publications, she was induced by the solicitations of her friends to extend it to the size of a novel. Its success warranted their anticipations, and induced the writer to continue in the career so auspiciously commenced. In 1827 she published *Redwood*, a novel of the ordinary two-volume length. *Hope Leslie, or Early Times in America*, a novel of the same size, followed in the same year; *Clarence, a Tale of our Own Times*, in 1830; *Le Bossu*, in 1832; and the *Linwoods, or Sixty Years Since in America*, in 1835. A collection of shorter tales, published by her in various magazines, appeared in the same year.

In 1836 she published *The Poor Rich Man and the Rich Poor Man*, a popular tale, designed to show the superior advantages for happiness of a life of cheerful labor and domestic content in a comparatively humble sphere, over one of extravagance and makeshift in a more prominent position. The success of this soon led to the publication, in 1838, of a story of a similar character, *Live and Let Live;* and a delightful volume of juvenile tales, *A Love Token for Children*, which was followed by *Stories for Young Persons. Means and Ends, or Self-Training*, an attractive and sensible little volume of advice to young ladies on education and the formation of character, appeared about the same time.

In 1840 Miss Sedgwick published *Letters from Abroad to Kindred at Home*, in two volumes; a pleasant, sketchy account of some of the places she had seen, and the people she had met, during a recent tour in Europe.

Miss Sedgwick has contributed to the Lady's Book, *Milton Harvey*, *A Huguenot Family*, *Scenes from Life in Town*, *Fanny McDermot*, and other tales. She has also written for other periodicals.

Miss Sedgwick's life has been principally passed in the place of her birth, where she still resides. Stockbridge is one of the most beautiful villages of Berkshire, but its wide-spread celebrity is to be ascribed far more to the reputation which Miss Sedgwick's descriptions and works have given it, than to its great natural advantages.

The best trait of Miss Sedgwick's writings is the amiable home-sentiment which runs through them: her pen is always intent to improve life and cultivate its refinements; but besides this practical trait she has cultivated the imaginative element in American fiction with success. The Indian character in Hope Leslie is identified in the local feeling with the streams and mountain scenery of the region in which the author resides.

THEODORE SEDGWICK, a nephew of Miss Sedgwick, and a lawyer of the city of New York, is the author of a carefully prepared *Life of William Livingston* of New Jersey, published in 1833; of an elaborate work, *A Treatise on the Measure of Damages, or an Inquiry into the Principles which govern the Amount of Compensation recovered in Suits-at-Law;* and of numerous articles on social, literary, and political topics in the periodicals of the day. In 1840 he prepared a collection of the *Political Writings of William Leggett.*

Mr. Sedgwick was the first president of the New York Crystal Palace Company.

THE RESCUE OF EVERELL BY MAGAWISCA—FROM HOPE LESLIE.

Magawisca, in the urgency of a necessity that could brook no delay, had forgotten, or regarded as useless, the sleeping potion she had infused into the Mohawk's draught; she now saw the powerful agent was at work for her, and with that quickness of apprehension that made the operations of her mind as rapid as the impulses of instinct, she perceived that every emotion she excited but hindered the effect of the potion. Suddenly seeming to relinquish all purpose and hope of escape, she threw herself on a mat, and hid her face, burning with agonizing impatience, in her mantle. There we must leave her, and join that fearful company who were gathered together to witness what they believed to be the execution of exact and necessary justice.

Seated around their sacrifice-rock—their holy of holies—they listened to the sad story of the Pequod chief with dejected countenances and downcast eyes, save when an involuntary glance turned on Everell, who stood awaiting his fate, cruelly aggravated by every moment's delay, with a quiet dignity and calm resignation that would have become a hero or a saint. Surrounded by this dark cloud of savages, his fair countenance kindled by holy inspiration, he looked scarcely like a creature of earth.

There might have been among the spectators some who felt the silent appeal of the helpless, courageous boy; some whose hearts moved them to interpose to save the selected victim; but they were restrained by their interpretation of natural justice, as controlling to them as our artificial codes of laws to us.

Others, of a more cruel or more irritable disposition, when the Pequod described his wrongs and depicted his sufferings, brandished their tomahawks, and would have hurled them at the boy; but the chief said, "Nay, brothers, the work is mine; he dies by my hand—for my first-born—life for life; he dies by a single stroke, for thus was my boy cut off. The blood of sachems is in his veins. He has the skin, but not the soul of that mixed race, whose gratitude is like that vanishing mist," and he pointed to the vapor that was melting from the mountain tops into the transparent ether; "and their promises like this," and he snapped a dead branch from the pine beside which he stood, and broke it in fragments. "Boy as he is, he fought for his mother as the eagle fights for its young. I watched him in the mountain-path, when the blood gushed from his torn feet; not a word from his smooth lip betrayed his pain."

Mononotto embellished his victim with praises, as the ancients wreathed theirs with flowers. He brandished his hatchet over Everell's head, and cried exultingly, "See, he flinches not. Thus stood my boy when they flashed their sabres before his eyes and bade him betray his father. Brothers: My people have told me I bore a woman's heart towards the enemy. Ye shall see. I will pour out this English boy's blood to the last drop, and give his flesh and bones to the dogs and wolves."

He then motioned to Everell to prostrate himself on the rock, his face downward. In this position the boy would not see the descending stroke. Even at this moment of dire vengeance the instincts of a merciful nature asserted their rights.

Everell sank calmly on his knees, not to supplicate life, but to commend his soul to God. He clasped his hands together. He did not—he could not speak; his soul was

> Rapt in still communion, that transcends
> The imperfect offices of prayer.

At this moment a sunbeam penetrated the trees that inclosed the area, and fell athwart his brow and hair, kindling it with an almost supernatural brightness. To the savages, this was a token that the victim was accepted, and they sent forth a shout that rent the air. Everell bent forward and pressed his forehead to the rock. The chief raised the deadly weapon, when Magawisca, springing from the precipitous side of the rock, screamed "Forbear!" and interposed her arm. It was too late. The blow was levelled—force and direction given; the stroke, aimed at Everell's neck, severed his defender's arm, and left him unharmed. The lopped, quivering member dropped over the precipice. Mononotto staggered and fell senseless, and all the savages, uttering horrible yells, rushed towards the fatal spot.

"Stand back!" cried Magawisca. "I have bought his life with my own. Fly, Everell—nay, speak not, but fly—thither—to the east!" she cried, more vehemently.

Everell's faculties were paralysed by a rapid succession of violent emotions. He was conscious only of a feeling of mingled gratitude and admiration for his preserver. He stood motionless, gazing on her. "I die in vain, then," she cried, in an accent of such despair that he was roused. He threw his arms around her, and pressed her to his heart as he would a sister that had redeemed his life with her own, and then, tearing himself from her, he disappeared. No one offered to follow him. The voice of nature rose from every heart, and, responding to the justice of Magawisca's claim, bade him "God speed!" To all it seemed that his deliverance had been achieved by a miraculous aid. All—the dullest and coldest—paid involuntary homage to the heroic girl, as if she were a superior being, guided and upheld by supernatural power.

Everything short of a miracle she had achieved. The moment the opiate dulled the senses of her keeper, she escaped from the hut; and aware that, if she attempted to penetrate to her father through the semicircular line of spectators that enclosed him, she would be repulsed, and probably borne off the ground, she had taken the desperate resolution of mounting the rock where only her approach would be unperceived. She did not stop to ask herself if it were possible; but, impelled by a determined spirit, or rather, we would believe, by that inspiration that teaches the bird its unknown path, and leads the goat, with its young, safely over the mountain crags, she ascended the rock. There were crevices in it, but they seemed scarcely sufficient to support the eagle with his grappling talon; and twigs issuing from the fissures, but so slender that they waved like a blade of grass under the weight of the young birds that made a nest on them; and yet, such is the power of love, stronger than death, that with these inadequate helps Magawisca scaled the rock and achieved her generous purpose.

THE SHAKERS AT HANCOCK—FROM REDWOOD.

The Shaker society at Hancock, in Massachusetts, is one of the oldest establishments of this sect, which has extended its limits far beyond the anticipations of the "unbelieving world," and now boasts that its outposts have advanced to the frontiers of civilization—to Kentucky—Ohio—and Indiana; and rejoices in the verification of the prophecy, "a little one shall become a thousand, and a small one a strong nation."

The society is distributed into several families of a convenient size,* for domestic arrangements,

* No family, we believe, is permitted to exceed a hundred members. Hear and admire, ye housewives.

and the whole body is guided and governed by "elder brothers" and "elder sisters," whose "gifts" of superior wisdom, knowledge, or cunning, obtain for them these titles, and secure to them their rights and immunities. There are gradations of rank, or, as they choose to designate their distinctions, of "privilege" among them; but none are exempt from the equitable law of their religious community, which requires each individual to "labor with his hands according to his strength."

A village is divided into lots of various dimensions. Each inclosure contains a family, whose members are clothed from one storehouse, fed at the same board, and perform their domestic worship together. In the centre of the inclosure is a large building, which contains their eating-room and kitchen, their sleeping apartments, and two large rooms, connected by folding-doors, where they receive their visitors, and assemble for their evening religious service. All their mechanical and manual labors, distinct from the housewifery (a profane term in this application), are performed in offices at a convenient distance from the main dwelling, and within the inclosure. In these offices may be heard, from the rising to the setting of the sun, the cheerful sounds of voluntary industry—sounds as significant to the moral sense, as the smith's stroke upon his anvil to the musical ear. One edifice is erected over a cold perennial stream, and devoted to the various operations of the dairy—from another proceed the sounds of the heavy loom and the flying shuttle, and the buzz of the swift wheels. In one apartment is a group of sisters, selected chiefly from the old and feeble, but among whom were also some of the young and tasteful, weaving the delicate basket—another is devoted to the dress-makers (a class that obtains even among Shaking Quakers), who are employed in fashioning, after a uniform model, the striped cotton for summer wear, or the sad-colored winter russet; here is the patient teacher, and there the ingenious manufacturer; and wherever labor is performed, there are many valuable contrivances by which toil is lightened and success insured.

The villages of Lebanon* and Hancock have been visited by foreigners and strangers from all parts of our Union; if they are displeased or disgusted by some of the absurdities of the Shaker faith, and by their singular worship, none have withheld their admiration from the results of their industry, ingenuity, order, frugality, and temperance. The perfection of these virtues among them may, perhaps, be traced with propriety to the founder of their sect, who united practical wisdom with the wildest fanaticism, and who proved that she understood the intricate machine of the human mind, when she declared that temporal prosperity was the indication and would be the reward of spiritual fidelity.

The prosperity of the society's agriculture is a beautiful illustration of the philosophical remark, that "to temperance every day is bright, and every hour propitious to diligence." Their skilful cultivation preserves them from many of the disasters that fall like a curse upon the slovenly husbandry of the farmers in their vicinity. Their gardens always flourish in spite of late frosts and early frosts—blasts and mildew ravage their neighbors' fields without invading their territory—the mischievous daisy, that spreads its starry mantle over the rich meadows of the "world's people," does not presume to lift its yellow head in their green fields—and even the Canada thistle, that bristled little warrior, armed at all points, that comes in from the north, extirpating in its march, like the hordes of barbarous invaders, all the fair fruits of civilization, is not permitted to intrude upon their grounds.

It is sufficiently manifest that this felicity is the natural consequence and appropriate reward of their skill, vigilance, and unwearied toil; but they believe it to be a spiritual blessing—an assurance of peculiar favor, like that which exempted the Israelites from the seven Egyptian plagues—an accomplishment of the promise that every one that "hath forsaken houses, or brethren, or sisters, or father, or mother, or *wife*, or children, or lands, for my name's sake, shall *receive a hundred fold*."

The sisters, too, have their peculiar and appropriate blessings and exemptions. They are saved from those scourges of our land of liberty and equality, "poor help," and "no help." There are no scolding mistresses nor eye-servants among them.

It might be curious to ascertain by what magical process these felicitous sisters have expelled from their thrifty housewifery that busy, mischievous principle of all evil in the domestic economy of the "world's people," known in all its Protean shapes by the name of "bad luck;" the modern successor of Robin Goodfellow, with all the spite, but without the genius of that frolic-loving little spirit, he who

> Frights the maidens of the villagery,
> Skims milk, and sometimes labors in the quern,
> And bootless makes the breathless housewife churn,
> And sometimes makes the drink to bear no barm.

How much broken china, spoiled batches of bread, ruined tempers, and other common domestic disasters might be avoided by the discovery of this secret; what tribes of mice, ants, flies, and other household demons, might be driven from their strongholds! Perhaps those provoking solvers of mysteries, who are so fond of finding out the "reason of the thing," that they are daily circumscribing within most barren and inconvenient limits the dominion of the imagination, will pretend to have found the clue to this mystery in the exact order and elaborate neatness of the sisterhood.

The sisters themselves, certainly, hint at a sublime cause of their success, when in reply to a stranger's involuntary admiration of their stainless walls, polished floors, snow-white linen, and all the detail of their precise arrangement and ornamental neatness, they say, with the utmost gravity, "God is the God of order, not of confusion." The most signal triumph of the society is in the discipline of the children. Of these there are many among them; a few are received together with their "believing" parents; in some instances orphans, and even orphan families are adopted; and many are brought to the society by parents, who, either from the despair of poverty or the carelessness of vice, choose to commit their offspring to the guardianship of the Shakers. Now that the first fervors of enthusiasm are abated, and conversions have become rare, the adoption of children is a substantial aid to the continuance and preservation of the society. These little born rebels, natural enemies to the social compact, lose in their hands their prescriptive right to uproar and misrule, and soon become as silent, as formal, and as orderly as their elders.

We hope we shall not be suspected of speaking the language of panegyric rather than justice, if we add that the hospitalities of these people are never refused to the weary wayworn traveller, nor their alms to the needy; and that their faith (however absurd and indefensible its peculiarities) is tempered by some generous and enlightened principles, which those who had rather learn than scoff would do well to adopt. In short, those who know them well,

* The village at Lebanon is distinguished as the United Societies' centre of union.

and judge them equitably, will not withhold from them the praise of moral conduct which they claim, in professing themselves, as a community, a "harmless, just, and upright people."

HANNAH F. LEE.

MRS. HANNAH F. LEE, the author of numerous popular writings, is a native of Newburyport, Massachusetts, the daughter of an eminent physician of that place. She has been for many years a widow. Her residence is at Boston.

H. F. Lee.

In 1832, when the autobiography of Hannah Adams appeared, the "notices in continuation by a friend," forming half of the volume, were from her pen. Her first distinct publication was a novel, *Grace Seymour*, published at New York, the first edition of which was mostly burned in the great fire of 1835. In 1838, appeared anonymously, *The Three Experiments of Living*, a work which she wrote as a sketch of those times of commercial difficulty, without reference to publication. By the agency of the eminent philologist, John Pickering, it was brought before the public, and attained at once extraordinary success. This was followed immediately by a volume of romantic biography, *Historical Sketches of the Old Painters*, taking for the subjects the lives of Leonardo da Vinci, Michael Angelo, Correggio, and others. With a similar view of popularizing the lessons of history, Mrs. Lee wrote the works entitled *Luther, and his Times; Cranmer, and his Times;* and the *Huguenots in France and America;* books of careful reading and graphic description.

Mrs. Lee is also the author of a series of domestic tales, illustrating the minor morals of life and topics of education, as *Elinor Fulton; a sequel to Three Experiments of Living; Rich Enough*, the title of which indicates its purpose. *Rosanna, or Scenes in Boston*, written for the benefit of a charity school; *The Contrast, or Different Modes of Education; The World before you, or the Log Cabin;* and in 1849 a volume of *Stories from Life, for the Young*. Still regarding the tastes of youthful readers, with a style and subject calculated to gain the attention of all, she published, in 1852, a familiar *History of Sculpture and Sculptors*. A *Memoir of Pierre Toussaint*, a negro, born a slave in St. Domingo, who lived in New York to an advanced age, and who had been a devoted humble friend of her sister, Mrs. Philip Schuyler—a curious and interesting biography, published at Boston in 1858—completes the list of Mrs. Lee's useful and always interesting productions.*

GEORGE WOOD.

THE author of Peter Schlemihl in America, was born in Newburyport, Massachusetts, and was educated by the distinguished *littérateur* Samuel L. Knapp, then a young and talented lawyer, from whom his pupil imbibed his first love of literature. His mother removed with her family in 1816 to Alexandria, District of Columbia, and there he found employment as a clerk in a commission house. In December, 1819, he was appointed by Calhoun, then Secretary of War, a clerk in his

Geo. Wood

department. He was connected with the Treasury department from 1822 to 1845, for thirty-three years, when he came to New York to reside. In the latter city he wrote his *Peter Schlemihl in America*, which was published in Philadelphia in 1848. It is a sketchy satirical work of the school of Southey's "Doctor," adopting a slight outline of incident from the famous invention of Von Chamisso, and making it a vehicle for the humorous discussion of social manners, fashionable education and affectations, the morals of the stock exchange; and above all some of the religious and philosophical notions of the day, as Puseyism and Fourierism. The author's humorous hits are not equally successful, but his curious stores of reading are always entertaining; and with a better discipline in the art of literature his matter would appear to more advantage. After the publication of this book he returned to Washington, where he has since resided. A second work from his pen is announced at Boston with the title, *The Modern Pilgrims*.

THE CIRCLE OF FINANCIERS—FROM PETER SCHLEMIHL.

It is now some twenty years since I came to this city, merely to pass the winter and spring, and to return to Europe in June following. I had not been in the country for some years, and wishing to be as quiet as possible, I took private rooms at the "Star Hotel," and entered my name as Thomas Jones, and for a while was perfectly secure in my *incognito;* but accidentally meeting with some old friends, who had become conspicuous operators in Change Alley, I was drawn out from my retreat and almost compelled to accept their earnest and most hospitable invitations to their several houses. I assure you I was not at all prepared for the astonishing changes I found in their circumstances. Men whom I had left dealing in merchandise and stocks, in small sums, living in modest houses at a rent of four or five hundred dollars a year, now received me in splendid mansions, costing in themselves a fortune, and these were filled with the finest furniture, and adorned with mirrors of surpassing size and beauty. Their walls were covered with pictures, more remarkable for their antiquity than any beauty I could discern in them, but which they assured me were from the pencils of the "old masters." One of them even showed a "*Madonna in the Chair*," of which he had a smoky certificate pasted on the back, stating it to be a duplicate of that wonder of the art in the Pitti palace; and another had a "*Fornarini*," which he convinced me was genuine, though I was somewhat

* Mrs. Hale's Woman's Record.

skeptical at first, but of which I could no longer doubt when he showed me in the depth of the coloring of the shadow of her dress, the monogram of Raphael himself. There was one picture to which my especial attention was called, and upon which I was specially requested to pass my opinion. It seemed to me a mere mass of black paint, relieved by some few white spots; but what it was designed to represent was altogether beyond my skill to discover; and finding myself so perfectly at a loss, and not daring to venture a guess, I candidly confessed the embarrassment in which I was placed. My friends, for it was at a dinner party, all cried out, "it was capital," "a most admirable criticism," there was "nothing but black paint to be seen," etc.; but our host, not at all disconcerted, said that "the picture was a '*Salvator Rosa*,' and we should see it to be so, and we should enjoy our surprise." So he directed all the shutters to be closed save a single half window; and to be sure, there were discernible some armed men at the entrance of what we were told was a cave, in the act of throwing dice, and in the foreground some pieces of plate. "There," said he, "there's *the triumph of art!*"

He looked for applause, and it was given; for who could refuse to applaud the taste of a gentleman who gave good dinners, and whose wines were faultless? To be sure the merits of a picture so plastered with dark brown and black paint as to be undistinguishable, were not so much to my taste as his dinners and wines were; yet as he assured us it was a genuine "Salvator Rosa," having swallowed his wines, I must needs do the same with his pictures. I assure you, my dear madam, that this is no exaggeration of the "old masters" which I have had exhibited to me in this country. But whatever may have been my misgivings as to the genuineness of the particular "old masters," I had no doubt as to the sums paid for them, of which they showed me the receipted bills in order to make "assurance doubly sure." And though even then I might have had some lurking suspicions that in these matters my friends may have taken the copy for the original, I could not be mistaken as to the solidity and costliness of the rich plate with which their tables were literally covered. I have visited merchants of other countries, but none whose riches were more *apparent* than that of my friends in Babylon. It seemed as if the lamp of Aladdin had come into their possession, and that the wealth I saw in all their houses was created by some process purely magical.

Nor was my surprise limited by these exhibitions of taste and luxury. Their entertainments were varied and costly, their wines unsurpassed, except in the palaces of some of the princes of the German Empire. 'Tis true, they had no Johannisberg *in* their bottles, but the labels were in their proper places on the outside of them; and I was assured, and had no reason to doubt, that every bottle cost as much as the Johannisberg would have done had Prince Metternich brought his few hundred pipes into the wine market, instead of supplying only the tables of kings and emperors, as he is accustomed to do. The wine was indeed admirable, and was drunk with a gusto, and the glass was held up to the eye before drinking with that knowing air which few have any knowledge of, and which distinguishes men who know what they drink and how to drink.

Our conversation, I found, took a uniform turn to stocks; to grand systems of improvement of the country; digging canals, laying down railroads, and establishing new lines of packets, with some peculiarity of terms as to making a good "corner" on this stock, and "hammering down" another stock, and "bursting a bank" now and then; all of which, I was told, were "fair business transactions." They sometimes held a long talk as to getting up a "*leader*" for the organs of the party for a particular purpose; and on such occasions two or more would retire to a side-table to prepare the article, which was to be read and approved by the assembled party; or it might be to get up a set of patriotic resolves for congress, for their legislature, or for a ward committee. Indeed, there were few things these friends of mine did not take in hand; and so varied and multiform were their movements, that I was perfectly at a loss to conceive to what all these things tended. I was indeed charmed by the frankness with which they alluded to these matters before me, almost a stranger as I was to some of them; and seeing that they spoke of their moneyed affairs as being so prosperous, of which, indeed, I had the most marked and beautiful manifestations in everything that surrounded me, I ventured to mention, with no little diffidence, and as one hazarding a very great request, to a compliance with which I had no claims whatever, that I had some spare capital in foreign stocks which paid very low interest, and if they could point out a way of a better investment of this money, it would be conferring on me a very great favor to let me take some small amount of their stocks, which seemed so safe and lucrative. With a frankness and cordiality altogether irresistible, they at once told me it would gratify them all to make me a partner in their plans, all of which were sure to succeed. Nothing could have been more hearty than their several expressions of readiness to aid and serve me; and although I have had some acquaintance with men, I assure you I was for once perfectly disarmed of all suspicion of guile in these capitalists and financiers.

They asked me what amount of capital I had at command; when I told them that the amount of funds invested in stocks of the Bank of Amsterdam, which was then paying me but two and a half per cent., was some eight hundred thousand dollars, but that in the French funds I had some six millions of francs, besides other stocks in the English funds, all of which I would willingly transfer to stocks paying six and seven per cent. per annum. The looks of pleasure and surprise with which they received this announcement should have excited in me some suspicion and watchfulness; but I must confess, their expressions of pleasure at being able to serve me were so natural, and had so much of frank and noble bearing in them, and were seasoned with so many agreeable things complimentary to myself, that, I confess to you, my dear madam, I became the dupe of my own vanity.

The next week or two passed as the previous weeks had done; dinners almost every day; concerts, the opera, or the churches; soirées, evening parties, with glorious suppers, followed in unbroken succession. There were no more nor less attentions on the part of my friends, but somehow I found myself every day more and more in the society of two or three of these friends, who were either more assiduous in their attentions, or by a concert of action on the part of the others, these, more adroit, were appointed to manipulate me ready for the general use of the set. From these friends I first received the idea of settling in Babylon the Less for a few years, in which I was assured I could double my capital; and although at first the idea did not present itself to me in an attractive form, yet by degrees it was made to wear a very bright and cheerful aspect; so that at length I consented to entertain the idea as one which might possibly be adopted.

HENRY CARY.

This gentleman, whose meditative and humorous essays are known to the public by the signature of "John Waters," is a native of Boston, and a resident of New York. In the latter city, he has pursued the business of an East India merchant, and has become a man of wealth. He also fills the office of assistant president of the Phenix Fire Insurance Company in New York. His birth dates at the close of the last century.

His writings, which have been contributed to the New York American, under the editorship of Mr. Charles King, and the Knickerbocker Magazine, extending over a period of perhaps twenty years, consist of quaint poems in imitation of the old English ballad measures, or stanzas for music; sentimental, descriptive, critical, and humorous essays; generally what might be embraced under the words, practical æsthetics. Books, pictures, wines, gastronomy, love, marriage are his topics, to which he occasionally adds higher themes; for like a true humorist his mirth runs into gentle melancholy. His tastes may be described as Horatian. He pursues refined enjoyments, and elevates material things of the grosser kind, as the pleasures of the table, by the gusto corporeal and intellectual with which he invests them. He is eloquent on the cooking of a black-fish, capable of sublimity on oysters, which he can raise from their low oozy beds to the height of the constellations, and plays marvellously with the decanters. The home-feelings and old conservative associations have in his pen a defender, all the more effective by his habit of sapping a prejudice, and insinuating a moral, in a light, jesting way. When he treats of deeper sentiments, of the affections and religion, as he sometimes does, it is in a pure, fervent vein.

We present two of his papers from the Knickerbocker, which show his delicate handling in his different manners.

DO NOT STRAIN YOUR PUNCH.

One of my friends, whom I am proud to consider such; a Gentleman, blest with all the appliances of Fortune, and the heart to dispense and to enjoy them; of sound discretion coupled with an enlightened generosity; of decided taste and nice discernment in all other respects than the one to which I shall presently advert; successful beyond hope in his cellar; almost beyond example rich in his wine chamber; and last, not least, felicitous, to say no more, in his closet of Rums—this Gentleman, thus endowed, thus favored, thus distinguished, has fallen, can I write it? into the habit of—straining his Punch!

When I speak of Rums, my masters, I desire it to be distinctly understood that I make not the remotest allusion to that unhappy distillation from molasses which alone is manufactured at the present day throughout the West Indies since the emancipation of the Blacks; who desire nothing but to drink, as they brutally express it, "to make drunk come"—but to that etherial extract of the sugarcane, that Ariel of liquors, that astral spirit of the nerves, which, in the days when planters were born Gentlemen, received every year some share of their attention, every year some precious accession, and formed by degrees those stocks of Rum, the last reliques of which are now fast disappearing from the face of Earth.

And when I discourse on Punch, I would fain do so with becoming veneration both for the concoction itself, and, more especially, for the memory of the profound and original, but alas! *unknown* inventive Genius by whom this sublime compound was first imagined, and brewed—by whose Promethean talent and touch and Shakespearian inspiration, the discordant elements of Water, Fire, Acidity, and Sweetness were first combined and harmonized into a beverage of satisfying blessedness, or of overwhelming Joy!

My friend then—to revert to him—after having brewed his Punch according to the most approved method, passes the fragrant compound through a linen-cambric sieve, and it appears upon his hospitable board in a refined and clarified state, beautiful to the eye perhaps, but deprived and dispossessed by this process of those few lobes and cellular integuments, those little gushes of unexpected piquancy, furnished by the bosom of the lemon; and that, when pressed upon the palate and immediately dulcified by the other ingredients, so wonderfully heighten the zest, and go so far to give the nameless entertainment and exhilaration, the unimaginable pleasure, that belong to Punch!

Punch!—I cannot articulate the emphatic word without remarking, that it is a liquor that a man might "moralize into a thousand similes!" It is an epitome of human life! Water representing the physical existence and basis of the mixture; Sugar its sweetness; Acidity its animating trials; and Rum, the aspiring hope, the vaulting ambition, the gay and the beautiful of Spiritual Force!

Examine these ingredients separately. What is Water by itself in the way of Joy, except for bathing purposes? or Sugar, what is it, but to infants, when alone? or Lemon-juice, that, unless diluted, makes the very nerves revolt and shrink into themselves? or Rum, that in its abstract and proper state can hardly be received and entertained upon the palate of a Gentleman? and yet combine them all, and you have the full harmony, the heroism of existence, the diapason of human life!

Let us not then abridge our Water lest we diminish our animal being. Nor change the quantum of our Rum, lest wit and animation cease from among us. Nor our Sugar, lest we find by sad experience that "it is not good for man to live alone." And, when they occur, let us take those minor acids in the natural cells in which the Lemon nourished them for our use, and as they may have chanced to fall into the pitcher of our destiny. In short, let us not refine too much. My dear sirs, let us not strain our Punch!

When I look around me on the fashionable world, in which I occasionally mingle, with the experience and observation of an old man, it strikes me to be the prevailing characteristic of the age that people have departed from the simpler and I think the healthier pleasures of their Fathers. Parties, balls, soirées, dinners, morning calls, and recreations of all sorts are, by a forced and unnatural attempt at over-refinement, deprived of much of their enjoyment. Young men and maidens, old men and widows, either give up their pitchers in despair, or venturing upon the compound—strain their Punch.

Suppose yourself for the moment transported into a ball-room in a blaze of light, enlivened by the most animating music, and with not one square foot of space that is not occupied by the beauty and fashion of the day. The only individuals that have the power, except by the slowest imaginable side-long movement, of penetrating this tide of enchantment, are the Redown-Waltzers; before whom every person recedes for a few inches at each moment, then to resume his stand as wave after wave goes by.

You can catch only the half-length portraits of

the dancers; but these are quite near enough to enable you to gain by glimpses their full characteristic developements of countenance. Read them; for every conventional arrangement of the features has been jostled out of place by the inspiriting bob-a-bob movement of the dance.

Look before you—a woman's hand, exquisitely formed, exquisitely gloved in white and braceleted, with a wrist "round as the circle of Giotto," rests upon the black-cloth dress of her partner's shoulder; as light, as airy, and as pure, as a waif of driven snow upon a cleft of mountain rock, borne thither in some relenting lull or wandering of the tempest; and beautiful! too beautiful it seems for any lower region of the Earth.

She turns towards you in the revolving movement, and you behold a face that a celestial inhabitant of some superior star might descend to us to love and hope to be forgiven! Now listen, for this is the expression of that face:

"Upon my word this partner of mine is really a nice person! how charmingly exact his time is! what a sustaining arm he has, and how admirably, by his good management, he has protected my beautiful little feet against all the maladroit waltzers of the set! I have not had a single bruise notwithstanding the dense crowd; and my feet will slide out of bed to-morrow morning as white and spotless as the bleached and balmy linen between which I shall repose. Ah! if he could only steer us both through life as safely and as well! but, poor fellow! it would never do. They say he has no fortune, and for my part all that I could possibly expect from papa would be to furnish the house. How then should we be ever able to—strain our PUNCH!"

And he—the partner in this Waltz—instead of growing buoyant and elastic, at the thoughts that belong to his condition of youth and glowing health; —at the recollection of the ground over which he moves;—of the government of his own choice, the noblest because the freest in the world, that rules it; —of the fourteen hundred millions of unoccupied acres of fertile soil, wooing him to make his choice of climate, that belong to it;—of the deep blue sky of Joy and health that hangs above it;—of the GOD that watches over and protects us all;—and, lastly, of this precious being as the Wife that might make any destiny one of happiness by sharing it—what are the ideas that occupy *his* soul?

He muses over the approaching hour of supper, speculates upon his probable share of Steinberger Cabinet Wein, and doubts whether the Restaurateur who provides may or may not have had consideration enough to—strain the PUNCH.

Bear with me once more, gentle Reader, while I recite the title of this essay, "Do not strain your PUNCH."

ON PERCEPTION.

His are the mountains, and the valleys his,
And the resplendent rivers: his to enjoy
With a propriety that none can feel,
But who, with filial confidence inspired,
Can lift to Heaven an unpresumptuous eye,
And smiling say, "My Father made them all!"
Are they not his by a peculiar right,
And by an emphasis of interest his,
Whose eyes they fill with tears of holy joy,
Whose heart with praise, and whose exalted mind,
With worthy thoughts of that unwearied Love,
That planned, and built, and still upholds a world
So clothed with beauty?

COWPER.

Oh, Lady! we receive but what we give,
And in our life alone does nature live!

* * * * *

Ah! from the soul itself must issue forth
A light, a glory, a fair luminous cloud,
Enveloping the earth!
And from the soul itself must there be sent
A sweet and powerful Voice, of its own birth,
Of all sweet sounds the life and element!
O pure of heart! thou need'st not ask of me
What this strong music in the soul may be;
What and wherein it doth subsist,
This light, this glory, this fair luminous mist,
This beautiful, and beauty-making power;
Joy, O beloved, Joy, that ne'er was given
Save to the pure, and in their purest hour,
Life of our life, the parent and the birth,
Which wedding nature to us gives in dower,
A new Heaven and new Earth
Undreamt of by the sensual and the proud.
This is the strong Voice, this the luminous cloud!
Our inmost selves rejoice!
And thence flows all that glads or ear or sight,
All melodies the echoes of that Voice,
All colors a suffusion from that light.

COLERIDGE, FROM THE GREEK.

Joy, O my masters! joy to the young, the fair, the brave, the middle-aged, the old, and the decrepit! joy, true joy, to every Christian soul of mortal man! Joy, O beloved! that over the once sterile passages of earth, radiant spirits of song and beauty such as these should have passed for thine inexhaustible delight! scattering flowers that can never fade and breathing music incapable of death! revealing to thee treasures, by which thou art surrounded, richer than all "barbaric gold and pearl;" disclosing the latent glories of thine own nature; and proving that not to any future state of existence is deferred that highest of the beatitudes, "Blessed are the pure in heart, for they shall see GOD."

Yes!—where, to the sensual and the proud, there exist only darkness and dulness and vague chaotic masses of unformed nature, to thee, O pure in heart, there shall spring forth a new Heaven and a new Earth, wrought out in thy presence, and fashioned by the hand of HIM whose spirit breathes now upon thy spirit, as once HE breathed upon the dust of the ground and formed the father of thy race!

Thine are the mountains, and the valleys thine,
And the resplendent rivers!

I have placed at the head of this essay a fountain of golden light; and all that I can hope or can desire is, to behold some one young listener kneel with me at its brink, and fill his urn with Joy. So great a part of my own life has been wasted in quest of that which *is not bread*, nor light, nor joy, nor spiritual sustenance, that all its waning hours would be made comparatively rich by the consciousness of having pointed out to only one inquiring spirit the way that I have myself so lately found.

And therefore I venture to write these few unlearned words upon PERCEPTION, and upon the temper in which things should be perceived; with which they should be beheld, and studied, and welcomed to the heart. The experience that is requisite to acquire this temper is within the compass of the human life of every soul; and almost every moment of that life may be made a step towards the attainment of it. There is no position upon the surface of the earth so remote or desolate as not to yield full scope to the largest aspirations after such knowledge to the pure in heart. Indeed solitude, or the solitary communings of the soul within itself, are as indispensable to the acquisition of all spiritual knowledge, as the bustle and intercourse of ordinary life are to that which is merely worldly.

When that mysterious impersonation of the Evil principle was permitted to tempt the SAVIOUR of mankind towards the consequences of ill-regulated ambition, all the Kingdoms of the Earth were exposed in rotation to his view, and all the tumultuary glories of their dominion offered to his acceptance and enjoyment: and again, it was suggested to him that he should cast his body to the earth from a pinnacle of the temple, that thousands to do him honor might witness his miraculous escape from injury:—but it was in the lone stillness of the cloud-capt mountain, and from the narrow cleft of the overhanging rock, that the ALMIGHTY, yielding in part to the request of the august legislator of Israel, caused HIS goodness to pass in review before the Eyes of HIS astonished and enlightened servant; and when Moses descended from the mountain, it was necessary to veil his face from the people, because of the effulgence of spiritual life that beamed from it!

This should teach us that it is in retirement from what is called the world, that the soul mainly derives its spiritual good, while the crowd and occupations of society, not necessarily but more frequently, subject us to temptation and error. Joy then, O listener, in the mountain, and the valley, and the resplendent river! Let not an imagination of self-appropriation enter into thy thoughts, but enjoy because it is HIS gift, alike to thee and to all mankind.

Who owns Mont Blanc? whose is the Atlantic, or the Indian ocean? Thine, thou rich one! thine to sail over, thine to gaze upon, thine to raise thy hands from, upwards toward Heaven in thanks for the glories of thy King! Whose are the worlds on which thy sight shall then rest, and the boundless sea of blue in which thy soul is bathed with delight?

And, when thine eyes return again to earth in tears of holy joy, who formed the granitic peak, that oldest of HIS earthly creatures? or placed upon the ridges and summits of the Alleghany chain of mountains, the later wonder of those stupendous masses of limestone rock that rise in perpendicular structure to the clouds?

The traveller, emigrating to the west, descends from the covered wagon that contains his bed and his reposing children, and prepares his breakfast and his journey in the dawn of morning, before day has yet visited the vales below; and the smoke of his fire, guided by the vast wall of rock, mounts in an unbroken column to the skies. The small and delicately-pencilled flowers that are scattered at his feet or are trodden under by them, and that seem as if they could only abide in solitude, who planted them?

And the vine that creeps upward and finds for its tendrils jutting points and crevices that are inscrutable to the eye of man, how beautifully does its bright green foliage wave in contrast with the dark-grey of the towering mass of rock! And the azure, the purple, green, and golden birds and insects that play around and welcome the earliest sunbeams with a vivacity and joy that prove their lives to have been one long festival of native sport and pleasure! Everywhere, around, abroad, above, COLOR, COLOR, COLOR, the unspeakable language of GOD'S goodness and love, with which HE writes HIS promises in the Heavens and unnumbered comforts on the soul of man!

Now it is in this spirit that, when returning and mingling with the world, our powers of perception should be exercised and sustained. Teach thyself to enjoy the fortunes of thy friends, and enumerate the advantages of all mankind around thee as if they were all thine own. Do this without one envious, or repining, or selfish thought,

> And from thy soul itself shall issue forth
> A light, a glory, a fair luminous cloud
> Enveloping the earth!

Thou art childless perhaps, or poor, or embarrassed with debt, or old, and broken-hearted in thy hopes. But the hearth of one of thy friends is clustering with immortal gems of beauty and intelligence of every age and promise; go among them in this spirit; thou shalt be more welcome than ever, and every child shall be thine own!

And the one only daughter of another friend, in whom all his hopes are centred, and all to be realized—that opening bud of grace and beauty, of refinement, gentleness, and truth—let her be to thee a Treasury of Joy! There can need no word, no regard that might by possibility be deemed intrusive, no earnest expression even of thy trust in the happiness of all her womanly affections. But when thine eye sees her then let it give witness to her, and when thine ear hears her then let it bless her! Do this with a full heart and silent lips, and thou shalt share largely in the bright fortune of thy friend. Her image and her silvery voice shall come visit thee in thy walks or at thy lonely fire-side, and thou shalt count her among the jewels of thy soul.

The riches of another, thou shalt find unexpectedly to be thy wealth; and in his youth and vigor thou shalt become suddenly strong. Let another freely own the statuary or the painting, so that the sight of its magical beauties or its delicious hues be accorded to thee. And another the library; delight thou that the knowledge it contains is opened by the freshness of his heart to thy thankful and devout acquisition. Rejoice in his resources; share, at least in thought, in all his pleasures; his generosity; his acquisitions and his success in life so superior to thine own. Walk with him; build with him; delight in his garden; admire his fruits and flowers; love his dog; listen with him in rapture to his birds, thou shalt find cadences in their song sweeter than were ever known to thee before; and drink his wine with him in an honest and cheery companionship, with grateful reference to that BEING who planted the Vine to gladden the heart of man and warm it into social truth and tenderness.

Thus, that which many have esteemed the hardest requisition of Christianity, that we should love others, namely, as ourself, shall prove to thee a source of the richest and most refined and unfailing pleasure; and, without diminishing the abundance of those who surround thee, make thee a large and grateful sharer in it.

Thou shalt walk over the Earth like a Visitant from above, enjoying and promoting Virtue in every form; and unfolding, out of the beautiful and useful, the cheerful and the good. Thoughts for the happiness of others shall rise whispering from thy heart, in prayerful words, to the Spirit of Truth; and thou shalt know that they have all been heard. Thou shalt look upward for illumination, or for support, and no cloud intervene between thee and the Source of Light and Strength.

Young and old shall come forth to greet thee with open-handed Joy. And, if thou shouldest be WOMAN—flowers shall spring up to mark thy footsteps, the skies smile over thee, and the woods grow gay and musical at thine approach; for thou hast the happiness of others for their own sake at thine heart, thy pure heart, thy true heart, thy WOMAN'S heart—

> And thence, flows all that glads or ear or sight,
> All melodies the echoes of that voice,
> All colors, a suffusion from that light.

FRANCIS LIEBER.

FRANCIS LIEBER, professor of History and Political Philosophy and Economy in the State College of South Carolina at Columbia, a member of the French Institute, and author of numerous volumes which have for their range the most important topics of government and society, was born at Berlin, March 18, 1800. His boyhood fell upon the period of the Napoleonic "state and woe," and of the oppression of his native country. As a child his feelings were so impressed by the gloom of his family, that when the French entered Berlin in his sixth year, he was so moved by the spectacle as to be taken from the windows in a fit of loud sobbing. He himself relates another instance of sensibility in his life, when he first stood, in his youth, before the Madonna di San Sisto of Raphael, at Dresden. In a student's journey he walked there from Jena, living on bread and plums by the way. He was so overcome by his feelings before the picture, that his emotion attracted the attention of a lady, whom he afterwards discovered to be one of the daughters of the great Tieck. She spoke to him, and encouraged his sentiment.

The generous, sensitive nature of the boy was soon to be tried in a rugged school. At the age of fifteen, while he was studying medicine in the royal Pépinière, the war broke out anew against Napoleon. Lieber escaped the appointment of army-surgeon, which his youth revolted at, and entered as a volunteer with one of his brothers the regiment Colberg, which was stationed nearest the French frontier. He fought at Ligny and Waterloo, and received two severe wounds at the assault of Namur, on the 20th June. He was left for two days on the battle-field. On his return home he became a zealous follower of Dr. Jahn, while at the same time he prepared himself with ardor for the University of Berlin.

In 1819, soon after Sand's murder of Kotzebue had directed the attention of the government to the patriots, Lieber was arrested. After an imprisonment of four months he was dismissed, as it was stated "nothing could as yet be discovered against him," except general liberalism, while he was informed that he would not be permitted to study in a Prussian University, and that he could never expect "employment" in the state. He went to the University of Jena, where he took at once the degree of Doctor, to acquire the privileges of an "academic citizen" of that institution.

In 1820 the government informed him that he might pursue his studies in the University of Halle, but that he must never expect employment in "school or church." He passed his time here in the most retired way; yet the police interferences were so annoying that he resolved to live in Dresden. In the autumn of 1821 he travelled on foot through Switzerland to Marseilles with a view of embarking there as "Philhellene" for Greece. After a life of great privations in Greece for several months, during which he was reduced to the utmost want, he found himself obliged to reëmbark for Italy, where, in the house of the Prussian minister, Niebuhr, at Rome (which held at that time the distinguished Bunsen as Secretary of Legation), he found the kindest reception. In Niebuhr's house he wrote his German work, *Journal of my Sojourn in Greece in the year* 1822. (Leipsig, 1823.) This work was translated into Dutch, with the tempting title of the German Anacharsis, with a fancy portrait of the author. The Dutch publisher sent a box of very old Hock to the author, as an acknowledgment of the profit he had made out of the involuntary Anacharsis.

After about a year's residence in Rome, Lieber travelled with Niebuhr to Naples and back to Germany, where, in spite of the most positive assurances that henceforth he might live unmolested in Prussia, he was again imprisoned, in Köpnick, chiefly because he resolutely declined to give information concerning former associates. During this imprisonment, when he was allowed book and pen, he studied vigorously, reading Bayle's Dictionary and writing poems. When the investigation was over, he was offered a fellow-prisoner as a companion; but he preferred his books and verses. At length Niebuhr was called from Bonn to assist the Prussian Council of State, and did not rest till he saw his friend once more out of prison. When Lieber was released he selected some of his poems, and sent them to Jean Paul, with whom he had no acquaintance, asking the veteran philosopher for a frank opinion. Not hearing from him, Lieber set down the silence for disapproval. He was soon obliged to leave the country, and many years afterwards, when he was settled in South Carolina, Mrs. Lee, the American author of the Life of Jean Paul, wrote to ask him whether he was the famous Lieber to whom Richter had addressed the beautiful and encouraging letter on certain poems of his composition. Upon inquiry it was found that Jean Paul had written to Lieber, but the letter had never reached him. Jean Paul was now dead, and Lieber, in a distant country, no more wrote German poetry. He penned, however, a sonnet on the occasion, which was widely circulated in Germany.

The poems written in prison he published in Berlin, under the assumed name of Franz Arnold.

Having been informed that a third arrest was pending, he took refuge, in 1825, in England, where he lived a year in London, supporting himself by literary labors, and as a private teacher. While in London he wrote a pamphlet, in German, on the Lancastrian method of instruction, and also contributed to several German periodicals and journals.

F. Lieber.

In 1827 he came to the United States, where at first he delivered lectures on subjects of history and politics in several cities. He also founded a swimming school in Boston, according to the principles which General Pfuel, whose pupil he had been in Berlin, had introduced in the Prussian army. Dr. Lieber is a capital swimmer. He several times tried his skill with John Quincy Adams, when the latter was President of the United States.

In 1828 he commenced the publication, at Philadelphia, of the *Encyclopædia Americana*, which was completed in 1832. He took as his basis Brockhaus' Conversations-Lexicon. He then lived in Boston, where, not long after his arrival, he was visited by Justice Story, with whom a friendship sprang up, which continued during the life of the jurist. Story contributed many articles to the Encyclopædia, which are enumerated in his Life by his son, and feelingly acknowledged in Lieber's work on Civil Liberty and Self-Government.

While engaged in editing the cyclopædia he had occasion to address Joseph Buonaparte, then in this country, on some points respecting the life of Napoleon. This led to a considerable correspondence and a personal acquaintance, which Dr. Lieber has lately commemorated in an article in Putnam's Magazine on the publication of his deceased friend's correspondence.*

While in Boston he also published a translation of a French work on the July Revolution of 1830, and a translation of the Life of Caspar Hauser by Feuerbach, one of the foremost writers on criminal law in Germany. This translation passed through several editions.

In 1832 Dr. Lieber removed to New York, where he wrote a translation of the work of his friends De Beaumont and De Tocqueville on the Penitentiary System in the United States, with an introduction and numerous notes, which, in turn, were translated in Germany. While in New York he received the honorable charge of writing a plan of education and instruction for Girard College, which was published by the board of directors, and forms a thin octavo volume. In 1834 he settled in Philadelphia, where he began a Supplement to his Encyclopædia; but the times proved inauspicious, during the bank derangement, and the publishers deferred the work for a time.

In Philadelphia he published two works—*Letters to a Gentleman in Germany on a Trip to Niagara*, republished in London as "The Stranger in America," a change made by the London publisher, and *Reminiscences of an Intercourse with Niebuhr the Historian*, also republished in London. The latter has been translated into German by Mr. Hugo, son of the jurist of the name.

In 1838–9 he published his *Political Ethics* at Boston in two large octavo volumes, with the usual typographical luxury of the press of Messrs. Little and Brown. This work is divided into two parts. The first treats of Ethics, general and political; the second, which goes more into detail, of the morals of the state and of the citizen. The grand rules of right are laid down according to the exalted code of principle and honor, as the various questions are passed in review, in which private morality is in contact with the law; civil or social regulation. The work does not deal in abstractions, but discusses such topics as the liberty of the press, war and its manifold relations, voting, combinations for different purposes, the limitation of power, &c.

This was succeeded after a considerable interval in 1853 by a somewhat similar work on *Civil Liberty and Self-Government*, published at Philadelphia. It is a calm, ingenious, rational analysis of the essential principles and forms of freedom in ancient and modern states; exhibiting a much abused idea in its practical relation with the checks and counterchecks, and various machinery of political and legal institutions. As in his other works, the subject is everywhere illustrated by examples and deductions from history and biography, the author's wide reading and experience affording him, apparently, inexhaustible material for the purpose.

His *Legal Hermeneutics or Principles of Interpretation and Construction in Law and Politics*, is one of Dr. Lieber's chief works. The separation of interpretation from construction, and the ascertainment of principles peculiar to each, has been adopted by eminent American jurists, as Dr. Greenleaf in his work on Evidence.

His *Essays on Labor and Property* is one of his most important contributions to the science of political economy.

In 1844, Lieber visited Europe. While in Germany, he published two small works in German; one on *Extra Mural and Intra Mural Executions*, in which measures were proposed which the Prussian government has adopted avowedly on his suggestion; and *Fragments on Subjects of Penology*, a term which was first used by Lieber for the science of punishment, and which has since been adopted both in Europe and America. In 1848 he again visited Europe, and while at Frankfort, published in German *The Independence of the Law, The Judiciary*, and a *Letter on Two Houses of Legislature*.

Of the numerous remaining publications of Lieber, we may mention his *Translation of Ramshorn's Latin Synonymes*, in use as a school-book; his interesting compilation—*Great Events described by Great Historians or Eye-Witnesses; The Character of the Gentleman*, which takes a wide view of the quality, carrying it into provinces of public and social life where it has been too often forgotten. He thus seeks the gentleman in war, in politics, diplomacy, on the bench, at the bar, and on the plantation.

His *Essays on Subjects of Penal Law and the Penitentiary Systems*, published by the Philadelphia Prison Discipline Society; on the *Abuse of the Pardoning Power*, re-published as a document by the Legislature of New York; *Remarks on Mrs. Fry's Views of Solitary Confinement*, published in England; a *Letter on the Penitentiary System*, published by the Legislature of South Carolina, are so many appeals to practical philanthropy.

To these are to be added a pamphlet addressed to Senator Preston, urging international copyright law; a *Letter on Anglican and Gallican Liberty*, translated into German with many notes and additions by Mittermaier, the German Criminalist and Publicist; a paper on the *Vocal Sounds of Laura Bridgman, the Blind Deaf-Mute*, com-

* Putnam's Monthly, Jan., 1855.

pared with the Elements of Phonetic Language, published in the Smithsonian collections; a thin volume of English poetry, *The West and Other Poems*. If wanting in the ease and elegance of more polished productions, Dr. Lieber's occasional verses, like his other compositions, are marked by their force and meaning. Of one of them, an Ode on a proposed ship-canal between the Atlantic and Pacific, Prof. Longfellow remarked, "It is strong enough to make the canal itself if it could be brought to bear."

In this enumeration, we have not mentioned the review and minor articles of Lieber; nor do we pretend to have given all the pamphlets which have proceeded from his active pen. Dr. Lieber is at present engaged on an Encyclopædiac work of facts, to be entitled "The People's Dictionary of General Knowledge."

These various writings are severally characterized by the same qualities of ingenuity of thought, sound sense, and fertile illustration, drawn from books and intercourse with the world; and dependent to no inconsiderable degree, it may be added, upon a vigorous constitution and happy temperament.

In the just observation of Brockhaus' German Conversations-Lexicon "his works have a character wholly peculiar to themselves, since they are the result of German erudition and philosophical spirit, combined with English manliness and American liberty."

Since 1835, Dr. Lieber has been employed as Professor of History and Political Economy in South Carolina College at Columbia; to which has been added a professorship of Political Economy. In connexion with this duty, Dr. Lieber delivered an Inaugural on "History and Political Economy as necessary branches of superior education in Free States," abounding in ingenious and learned suggestion. As the most concise indication of the spirit which he infuses into the teaching of the liberal studies of his professorship, we may mention the furnishing and decorations of his lecture room. This is, in some respects, unique, though its peculiarity is one which might be followed to advantage in all seats of learning. In place of the usual bare walls and repulsive accessories of education, it is supplied with busts of the great men of ancient and modern times, set up on pedestals, and bracketed on the walls, which also bear Latin inscriptions; while the more immediate utilities are provided for in the large suspended maps and blackboards. A hand-writing on the wall exhibits the weighty and pithy aphorism—

NON SCHOLÆ SED VITÆ—VITÆ UTRIQUE.

Another on a panel saved by Dr. Lieber from the recent consumption by fire of the former College Chapel in which Preston, Legaré, and other distinguished men were graduated, records the favorite saying of Socrates in Greek characters—

ΧΑΛΕΠΑ ΤΑ ΚΑΛΑ

The busts, to which each class as it enters College makes an addition of a new one by a subscription, now number Cicero, Shakespeare, Socrates, Homer, Demosthenes, Milton, Luther, and the American statesmen, Washington, Hamilton, Calhoun, Clay, McDuffie, and Webster. One of the blackboards is assigned to the illustration of the doctor's historical lectures. It is called the "battle blackboard" and is permanently marked in columns headed,—name of the war; in what country or province the battle; when; who victorious, over whom; effects of the battle; peace.

OSCAR MONTGOMERY LIEBER, a son of Dr. Lieber, has published several works in connexion with his profession of Mining Engineer. His *Assayer's Guide*, which appeared at Philadelphia in 1852, has met with distinguished success.*

THE GENTLEMANLY CHARACTER IN POLITICS AND INSTITUTIONS—FROM THE ADDRESS ON THE CHARACTER OF THE GENTLEMAN.

The greater the liberty is which we enjoy in any sphere of life, the more binding, necessarily, becomes the obligation of self-restraint, and consequently the more important all the rules of action which flow from our reverence for the pure character of the gentleman—an importance which is enhanced in the present period of our country, because one of its striking features, if I mistake not, is an intense and general attention to rights, without a parallel and equally intense perception of corresponding obligations. But right and obligation are twins—they are each other's complements, and cannot be severed without undermining the ethical ground on which we stand—that ground on which alone civilization, justice, virtue, and real progress can build enduring monuments. Right and obligation are the warp and the woof of the tissue of man's moral, and therefore likewise of man's civil life. Take out the one, and the other is in worthless confusion. We must return to this momentous principle, the first of all moral government, and, as fairness and calmness are two prominent ingredients in the character of the gentleman, it is plain that this reform must be materially promoted by a general diffusion of a sincere regard for that character. Liberty, which is nothing else than the enjoyment of unfettered action, necessarily leads to licentiousness without an increased binding power within; for liberty affords to man indeed a free choice of action, but it cannot absolve him from the duty of choosing what is right, fair, liberal, urbane, and handsome.

Where there is freedom of action, no matter in what sphere or what class of men, there always have been, and must be, parties, whether they be called party, school, sect, or "faction." These will necessarily often act against each other; but, as a matter of course, they are not allowed to dispense with any of the principles of morality. The principle that everything is permitted in politics is so shameless and ruinous for all, that I need not dwell upon it here. But there are a great many acts which, though it may not be possible to prove them wrong according to the strict laws of ethics, nevertheless appear at once as unfair, not strictly honorable, or ungentlemanlike, and it is of the utmost importance to the essential prosperity of a free country, that these acts should not be resorted to; that in the minor or higher assemblies and in all party struggles, even the intensest, we ought never to abandon the standard of a gentleman. It is all important that parties keep in "good humour," as Lord Clarendon said of the whole country. One deviation from fairness, candor, decorum, and "fair play," begets another and worse in the opponent, and from the kindliest difference in opinion to the fiercest struggle of factions sword in hand, is but one unbroken gra-

* Brockhaus' Conversations-Lexicon.

dual descent, however great the distance may be, while few things are surer to forestall or arrest this degeneracy than a common and hearty esteem of the character of the gentleman. We have in our country a noble example of calmness, truthfulness, dignity, fairness, and urbanity—the constituents of the character which occupies our attention, in the father of our country; for Washington, the wise and steadfast patriot, was also the high-minded gentleman. When the dissatisfied officers of his army informed him that they would lend him their support, if he was willing to build himself a throne, he knew how to blend the dictates of his oath to the commonwealth, and of his patriotic heart, with those of a gentlemanly feeling towards the deluded and irritated. In the sense in which we take the term here, it is not the least of his honors that, through all the trying periods and scenes of his remarkable life, the historian and moralist can write him down, not only as Washington the Great, not only as Washington the Pure, but also as Washington the Gentleman. * * * I must not omit mentioning, at least, the importance of a gentlemanly spirit in all international transactions with sister nations of our race—and even with tribes which follow different standards of conduct and morality. Nothing seems to me to show more irresistibly the real progress which human society has made, than the general purity of judges, and the improvement of the whole administration of justice, with the leading nations, at least, on the one hand, and the vastly improved morals of modern international intercourse, holding diplomatic fraud and international trickery, bullying, and pettifogging, as no less unwise than immoral. History, and that of our own times, especially, teaches us that nowhere is the vaporing braggadocio more out of place, and the true gentleman more in his proper sphere, than in conducting international affairs. Fairness on the one hand, and collected self-respect on the other, will frequently make matters easy, where swaggering taunt, or reckless conceit and insulting folly, may lead to the serious misunderstanding of entire nations, and a sanguinary end. The firm and dignified carriage of our Senate, and the absence of petty passion or vain-gloriousness in the British Parliament, have brought the Oregon question to a fair and satisfactory end—an affair which, but a short time ago, was believed by many to be involved in difficulties which the sword alone was able to cut short. Even genuine personal urbanity in those to whom international affairs are intrusted, is very frequently of the last importance for a happy ultimate good understanding between the mightiest nations.

We may express a similar opinion with reference to war. Nothing mitigates so much its hardships, and few things, depending on individuals, aid more in preparing a welcome peace, than a gentlemanly spirit in the commanders, officers, and, indeed, in all the combatants towards their enemies, whenever an opportunity offers itself. I might give you many striking proofs, but I observe that my clepsydra is nearly run out. Let me merely add, as a fact worthy of notice, that political assassination, especially in times of war, was not looked upon in antiquity as inadmissible; that Sir Thomas More mentions the assassination of the hostile captain, as a wise measure resorted to by his Utopians; that the ambassadors of the British Parliament, and later, the Commonwealth-men in exile, were picked off by assassination; while Charles Fox, during the war with the French, arrested the man who offered to assassinate Napoleon, informed the French government of the fact, and sent the man out of the country; and Admiral Lord St. Vincent, the stern enemy of the French, directed his secretary to write the following answer to a similar offer made by a French emigrant: "Lord St. Vincent has not words to express the detestation in which he holds an assassin." Fox and Vincent acted like Christians and gentlemen.

I have mentioned two cheering characteristics of our period, showing an essential progress in our race. I ought to add a third, namely, the more gentlemanly spirit which pervades modern penal laws. I am well aware that the whole system of punition has greatly improved, because men have made penology a subject of serious reflection, and the utter fallacy of many of the principles, in which our forefathers seriously believed, has at length been exposed. But it is at the same time impossible to study the history of penal law without clearly perceiving that punishments were formerly dictated by a vindictive ferocity—an ungentlemanly spirit of oppression. All the accumulated atrocities heaped upon the criminal, and not unfrequently upon his innocent kin, merely because he was what now would gently be called "in the opposition," make us almost hear the enraged punisher vulgarly utter, "Now I have you, and you shall see how I'll manage you." Archbishop Laud, essentially not a gentleman, but a vindictive persecutor of every one who dared to differ from his coarse views of State and Church, presided in the Star-Chamber, and animated its members when Lord Keeper Coventry pronounced the following sentence on Dr. Alexander Leighton, a Scottish divine, for slandering Prelacy: "that the defendant should be imprisoned in the Fleet during life—should be fined ten thousand pounds—and, after being degraded from holy orders by the high commissioners, should be set in the pillory in Westminster—there be whipped—after being whipped, again be set in the pillory—have one of his ears cut off—have his nose slit—be branded in the face with a double S. S., for Sower of Sedition—afterwards be set in the pillory in Cheapside, and there be whipped, and after being whipped, again be set in the pillory and have his other ear cut off." The whole council agreed. There was no recommendation to pardon or mitigation. The sentence was inflicted. Could a gentleman have proposed, or voted for so brutal an accumulation of pain, insult, mutilation and ruin, no matter what the fundamental errors prevailing in penal law then were? Nor have I selected this, from other sentences, for its peculiar cruelty. Every student in history knows that they were common at the time, against all who offended authority, even unknowingly. Compare the spirit which could overwhelm a victim with such brutality, and all the branding, pillory, and whipping still existing in many countries, with the spirit of calmness, kindness, yet seriousness and dignity which pervades such a punitory scheme as the Pennsylvania eremitic penitentiary system, which for the very reason that it is gentlemanly, is the most impressive and penetrating, therefore the most forbidding of all.

Let me barely allude to the duties of the gentleman in those countries in which slavery still exists. Plato says, genuine humanity and real probity are brought to the test, by the behavior of a man to slaves, whom he may wrong with impunity. He speaks like a gentleman. Although his golden rule applies to all whom we may offend or grieve with impunity, and the fair and noble use of any power we may possess, is one of the truest tests of a gentleman, yet it is natural that Plato should have made the treatment of the slave the peculiar test, because slavery gives the greatest power. Cicero says we should use slaves no otherwise than we do our day laborers.

THE SHIP CANAL—FROM THE ATLANTIC TO THE PACIFIC.

An Ode to the American People and their Congress, on reading the Message of the United States President in December, 1847.

Rend America asunder
And unite the Binding Sea
That emboldens Man and tempers—
Make the ocean free.

Break the bolt that bars the passage,
That our River richly pours
Western wealth to western nations;
Let that sea be ours—

Ours by all the hardy whalers,
By the pointing Oregon,
By the west-impelled and working,
Unthralled Saxon son.

Long indeed they have been wooing,
The Pacific and his bride;
Now 'tis time for holy wedding—
Join them by the tide.

Have the snowy surfs not struggled
Many centuries in vain
That their lips might seal the union?
Lock then Main to Main.

When the mighty God of nature
Made this favored continent,
He allowed it yet unsevered,
That a race be sent,

Able, mindful of his purpose,
Prone to people, to subdue,
And to bind the land with iron,
Or to force it through.

What the prophet-navigator,
Seeking straits to his Catais,
But began, now consummate it—
Make the strait and pass.

Blessed the eyes that shall behold it,
When the pointing boom shall veer,
Leading through the parted Andes,
While the nations cheer!

There at Suez, Europe's mattock
Cuts the briny road with skill,
And must Darien bid defiance
To the pilot still?

Do we breathe this breath of knowledge
Purely to enjoy its zest?
Shall the iron arm of science
Like a sluggard rest?

Up then, at it! earnest people!
Bravely wrought thy scorning blade.
But there's fresher fame in store yet,
Glory for the spade.

What we want is naught in envy,
And for all we pioneer;
Let the keels of every nation
Through the isthmus steer.

Must the globe be always girdled
Ere we get to Bramah's priest?
Take the tissues of your Lowells
Westward to the East.

Ye, that vanquish pain and distance,
Ye, enmeshing Time with wire,
Court ye patiently for ever
Yon Antarctic ire?

Shall the mariner for ever
Double the impending capes,
While his longsome and retracing
Needless course he shapes?

What was daring for our fathers,
To defy those billows fierce,
Is but tame for their descendants;
We are bid to pierce.

Ye that fight with printing armies,
Settle sons on forlorn track,
As the Romans flung their eagles,
But to win them back.

Who, undoubting, worship boldness,
And, if baffled, bolder rise,
Shall we lag when grandeur beckons
To this good emprize?

Let the vastness not appal us;
Greatness is thy destiny.
Let the doubters not recall us;
Venture suits the free.

Like a seer, I see her throning,
WINLAND strong in freedom's health,
Warding peace on both the waters,
Widest Commonwealth.

Crowned with wreaths that still grow greener,
Guerdon for untiring pain,
For the wise, the stout, and steadfast:
Rend the land in twain.

Cleave America asunder,
This is worthy work for thee.
Hark! The seas roll up imploring
"Make the ocean free."

GEORGE BANCROFT.

GEORGE BANCROFT, the eminent American historian, was born at Worcester, Massachusetts, in the year 1800. His father, Aaron Bancroft, was the distinguished Congregationalist clergyman of that place.* He took particular care of his son's education, which was pursued at the academy of Dr. Abbot, at Exeter, New Hampshire. A contemporary letter, dated October 10, 1811, written by the eminent Dr. Nathan Parker, of Portsmouth, to Dr. Bancroft, records a visit to the school, with special mention of the promising George.

"I have this day," writes this friend of the family, "made a visit at Exeter, and spent an hour with George. I found him in good health, and perfectly satisfied with his situation. He appears to enter into the studies which he is pursuing with an ardor and laudable ambition which gives promise of distinction, and which must be peculiarly grateful to a parent. I conversed with him on his studies, and found him very ready to make discriminating remarks—and as much as I expected from him. I was surprised at the intelligence with which he conversed, and the maturity of mind which he discovered. * * * * * * I found that he had become acquainted with the distinctions which are conferred on those who excel, and was desirous of obtaining them. I was much pleased with the zeal which he discovered on this subject. He said there were prizes distributed every year, or every term (I forgot which), to those who excelled in particular studies. He expressed a great desire to obtain one, but said he was afraid he should not succeed, for he was the youngest but three in the academy, and he did not think he should gain a prize, but he would try. These, you may say, are trifling things, but they discover a disposition of

* *Ante*, vol. i. p. 407.

mind, with which I think you must be gratified. I made inquiries of Mr. Abbot concerning him. He observed that he was a very fine lad; that he appeared to have the stamina of a distinguished man; that he took his rank among the first scholars in the academy, and that he wished I would send him half a dozen such boys."

The word of promise thus spoken to the father's ear has not been broken to the world.

In 1817, before he had completed his seventeenth year, the youth received his degree of Bachelor of Arts at Cambridge. The next year he went to Europe, and studied at Gottingen and Berlin, where he availed himself of the best opportunities of literary culture presented by those eminent universities. Before his return to America, in 1822, he had made the tour of England, Switzerland, Germany, and Italy. His mind was now richly furnished with the treasures of ancient literature, with the superadded modern metaphysical culture of the German universities. The thoroughness of his studies is shown in the philosophical summaries of Roman history and policy, and of the literature of Germany, then rapidly gaining the ascendant, which he not long after published in America; while a thin volume of poems, published at Boston in 1823, witnesses to his poetical enthusiasm for the arts and nature, as he traversed the ruins of Italy and the sublime scenery of Switzerland. He also at this time, from his eighteenth to his twenty-fourth year, wrote a series of poetical translations of some of the chief minor poems of Schiller, Goethe, and other German authors, which appeared in the North American Review, and have been lately revived by the author, in his Collection of Miscellanies. He also wrote for the early volumes of Walsh's American Quarterly Review, a number of articles, marked by their academic and philosophic spirit; among others, a striking paper on the Doctrine of Temperaments; a kindred philosophical Essay on Ennui; and papers on Poland and Russia, of historical sagacity and penetration.

Immediately on his return to the United States, Mr. Bancroft had been appointed Tutor of Greek at Harvard, where he continued for a year; subsequently carrying out his plans of education, in connexion with his friend Dr. J. G. Cogswell, as principal of the Round Hill school, at Northampton, Massachusetts.

Mr. Bancroft early became a politician, attaching himself to the Democratic party. One of the fruits of his promotion of its interests was his appointment from President Van Buren, in 1838, to the collectorship of the port of Boston. He retained this office till 1841. In 1844 he was the candidate of the Democratic minority, in Massachusetts, for the office of Governor. He was invited by President Polk, in 1845, to a seat in the Cabinet as Secretary of the Navy, the duties of which he discharged with his customary energy and efficiency in the cause of improvement. The next year he was appointed Minister Plenipotentiary to Great Britain, and held this distinguished position till 1849. He then returned to the United States, and became a resident of the city of New York.

Here he has established his home, and here he is to be met with in the fashionable, literary, and political circles of the city. He has filled the office of President of the American Geographical Society; is a distinguished member of the American Ethnological and New York Historical Societies; and has on several occasions appeared as a public orator, in connexion with these and other liberal interests of the city. His summers are passed at his country-seat at Newport, Rhode Island.

Bancroft's Residence.

The most important work of Mr. Bancroft's literary career, his *History of the United States, from the Discovery of the American Continent*, appeared in a first volume, in 1834. It struck a new vein in American History, original in design and conception. Terse and pointed in style, in brief, ringing sentences, it took the subject out of the hands of mere annalists and commentators, and raised it to the dignity and interest of philosophical narration. The original preface stamped the character of the work, in its leading motives, the author's sense of its importance, and his reliance on the energetic industry which was to accomplish it. The picturesque account of the colonial period gave the public the first impression of the author's vivid narrative; while the tribute to Roger Williams was an indication of the allegiance to the principles of liberty which was to characterize the work. The second and third followed, frequently appearing in new editions.

The interval of Mr. Bancroft's absence in Europe was profitably employed in the prosecution of his historical studies, for which his rank of ambassador gave him new facilities of original research in the government archives of London and Paris. Approaching the revolutionary period he was at that stage of the narrative where this aid became of the utmost importance. It was freely rendered. The records of the State Paper Office of Great Britain, including a vast array of military and civil correspondence, and legal and commercial detail, were freely placed at his disposal by the Earl of Aberdeen, Viscount Palmerston, Earl Grey, and the Duke of Newcastle, who then held the office of Secretary of State. The records of the Treasury, with its series of Minutes and Letter Books, were, in like manner, opened by Lord John Russell: while in the British Museum and in the private collections of various noble families, the most interesting manuscripts were freely rendered to the historian. Among the latter were the papers of Chatham, the Earl of Shelburne, the Duke of Grafton, the Earl of Dartmouth, and several hundred notes which passed between George the Third and Lord North.

M. Guizot, the French minister, extended similar courtesies in Paris, where Mr. Bancroft was aided by M. Mignet, M. Lamartine, and De Tocqueville. The relations of America with other European states of the Continent were also examined.

In addition to these resources abroad, the progress of his work secured to Mr. Bancroft at home frequent valuable opportunities of the examination of original authorities in private and public collections in all parts of the country. Among these are the numerous manuscripts of the apostle of American liberty, Samuel Adams.

Thus armed, and, with the daily increasing resources of the already vast American historical library, fed by a thousand rills of publication, of biography, family memoirs, town and state histories, and the numerous modes of antiquarian development, Mr. Bancroft enters on each successive volume of his national work with an increased momentum. Resuming the record in 1852 with the publication of the fourth volume, which traces the period from 1748, the author advanced rapidly to the fifth and sixth, the last of which, bringing the narrative to the immediate commencement of the Revolution preceding the actual outbreak in Massachusetts, appeared in 1854. Here, on the threshold of the new era, the author pauses for a while; we may be sure to gather new strength for the approaching conflict.

The speciality of Mr. Bancroft's history is its prompt recognition and philosophical development of the elements of liberty existing in the country—from the settlement of the first colonists to the matured era of independence. He traces this spirit in the natural conditions of the land, in men and in events. History, in his view, is no accident or chance concurrence of incidents, but an organic growth which the actors control, and to which they are subservient. The nation became free, he maintains, from the necessity of the human constitution, and because it deliberately willed to be free. To this end, in his view, all thoughts, all passions, all delights ministered. To detect this prevailing influence, this hidden impulse to the march of events, in every variety of character, in every change of position, whether in the town meeting of New England or the parliament of England; whether in the yeoman or the governor; in the church or at the bar; in the habits of the sailor or of the pioneer; in the rugged independence of New England or the uneasy sufferance of Louisiana: this is our historian's ever present idea. The ardor of the pursuit may sometimes bend reluctant facts to its purpose, and the keener eye of retrospection may read with more certainty what lurked dimly in anticipation; but the main deduction is correct. The history of America is the history of liberty. The author never relaxes his grasp of this central law. Hence the manly vigor and epic grandeur of his story.

With this leading idea Mr. Bancroft associates the most minute attention to detail. His page is crowded with facts brought forward with the air of realities of the time. He does not disdain to cite in his text the very words of the old actors as they were uttered in the ballad, the sermon, the speech, or the newspaper of the day. This gives verisimilitude to his story. It is a history of the people as well as of the state.

George Bancroft

In 1855 Mr. Bancroft published a volume of *Literary and Historical Miscellanies*, containing a portion of his early Essays from the Reviews; his poetical translations from the German; several historical articles to which we have alluded, and a few occasional discourses, including an address in memory of Channing, in 1842; an oration commemorative of Andrew Jackson, spoken at Washington in 1845, and the eloquent discourse at the celebration of the fiftieth anniversary of the New York Historical Society, on "The Necessity, the Reality, and the Promise of the Progress of the Human Race"—topics which were handled by the light both of modern science and philosophy.

To this enumeration of Mr. Bancroft's writings we may add an Abridgment of his History of the Colonization of the United States; and among other speeches and addresses, a lecture on "The Culture, the Support, and the Object of Art in a Republic," in the course of the New York Historical Society in 1852; and another before the Mechanics' Institute of New York in 1853, on "The Office, Appropriate Culture, and Duty of the Mechanic."

COMPARISON OF JOHN LOCKE AND WILLIAM PENN.*

Every hope of reform from parliament vanished. Bigotry and tyranny prevailed more than ever, and Penn, despairing of relief in Europe, bent the whole energy of his mind to accomplish the establishment of a free government in the New World. For that

* From the Second Volume of the History

"heavenly end," he was prepared by the severe discipline of life, and the love, without dissimulation, which formed the basis of his character. The sentiment of cheerful humanity was irrepressibly strong in his bosom; as with John Eliot and Roger Williams, benevolence gushed prodigally from his ever-overflowing heart, and when, in his late old age, his intellect was impaired, and his reason prostrated by apoplexy, his sweetness of disposition rose serenely over the clouds of disease. Possessing an extraordinary greatness of mind, vast conceptions, remarkable for their universality and precision, and "surpassing in speculative endowments;" conversant with men, and books, and governments, with various languages, and the forms of political combinations, as they existed in England and France, in Holland, and the principalities and free cities of Germany, he yet sought the source of wisdom in his own soul. Humane by nature and by suffering; familiar with the royal family; intimate with Sunderland and Sydney; acquainted with Russell, Halifax, Shaftesbury, and Buckingham; as a member of the Royal Society, the peer of Newton and the great scholars of his age,—he valued the promptings of a free mind more than the awards of the learned, and reverenced the single-minded sincerity of the Nottingham shepherd more than the authority of colleges and the wisdom of philosophers. And now, being in the meridian of life, but a year older than was Locke, when, twelve years before, he had framed a constitution for Carolina, the Quaker legislator was come to the New World to lay the foundations of states. Would he imitate the vaunted system of the great philosopher? Locke, like William Penn, was tolerant; both loved freedom; both cherished truth in sincerity. But Locke kindled the torch of liberty at the fires of tradition; Penn at the living light in the soul. Locke sought truth through the senses and the outward world; Penn looked inward to the divine revelations in every mind. Locke compared the soul to a sheet of white paper, just as Hobbes had compared it to a slate, on which time and chance might scrawl their experience; to Penn, the soul was an organ which of itself instinctively breathes divine harmonies, like those musical instruments which are so curiously and perfectly framed, that, when once set in motion, they of themselves give forth all the melodies designed by the artist that made them. To Locke, "Conscience is nothing else than our own opinion of our own actions;" to Penn, it is the image of God, and his oracle in the soul. Locke, who was never a father, esteemed "the duty of parents to preserve their children not to be understood without reward and punishment;" Penn loved his children, with not a thought for the consequences. Locke, who was never married, declares marriage an affair of the senses; Penn reverenced woman as the object of fervent, inward affection, made, not for lust, but for love. In studying the understanding, Locke begins with the sources of knowledge; Penn with an inventory of our intellectual treasures. Locke deduces government from Noah and Adam, rests it upon contract, and announces its end to be the security of property; Penn, far from going back to Adam, or even to Noah, declares that "there must be a people before a government," and, deducing the right to institute government from man's moral nature, seeks its fundamental rules in the immutable dictates "of universal reason," its end in freedom and happiness. The system of Locke lends itself to contending factions of the most opposite interests and purposes; the doctrine of Fox and Penn, being but the common creed of humanity, forbids division, and insures the highest moral unity. To Locke, happiness is pleasure; things are good and evil only in reference to pleasure and pain; and to "inquire after the highest good is as absurd as to dispute whether the best relish be in apples, plums, or nuts;" Penn esteemed happiness to lie in the subjection of the baser instincts to the instinct of Deity in the breast, good and evil to be eternally and always as unlike as truth and falsehood, and the inquiry after the highest good to involve the purpose of existence. Locke says plainly, that, but for rewards and punishments beyond the grave, "it is *certainly right* to eat and drink, and enjoy what we delight in;" Penn, like Plato and Fenelon, maintained the doctrine so terrible to despots, that God is to be loved for his own sake, and virtue to be practised for its intrinsic loveliness. Locke derives the idea of infinity from the senses, describes it as purely negative, and attributes it to nothing but space, duration, and number; Penn derived the idea from the soul, and ascribed it to truth, and virtue, and God. Locke declares immortality a matter with which reason has nothing to do, and that revealed truth must be sustained by outward signs and visible acts of power; Penn saw truth by its own light, and summoned the soul to bear witness to its own glory. Locke believed "not so many men in wrong opinions as is commonly supposed, because the greatest part have no opinions at all, and do not know what they contend for;" Penn likewise vindicated the many, but it was because truth is the common inheritance of the race. Locke, in his love of tolerance, inveighed against the methods of persecution as "Popish practices;" Penn censured no sect, but condemned bigotry of all sorts as inhuman. Locke, as an American lawgiver, dreaded a too numerous democracy, and reserved all power to wealth and the feudal proprietaries; Penn believed that God is in every conscience, his light in every soul; and therefore, stretching out his arms, he built—such are his own words—"a free colony for all mankind." This is the praise of William Penn, that, in an age which had seen a popular revolution shipwreck popular liberty among selfish factions; which had seen Hugh Peters and Henry Vane perish by the hangman's cord and the axe; in an age when Sydney nourished the pride of patriotism rather than the sentiment of philanthropy, when Russell stood for the liberties of his order, and not for new enfranchisements, when Harrington, and Shaftesbury, and Locke, thought government should rest on property,—Penn did not despair of humanity, and, though all history and experience denied the sovereignty of the people, dared to cherish the noble idea of man's capacity for self-government. Conscious that there was no room for its exercise in England, the pure enthusiast, like Calvin and Descartes, a voluntary exile, was come to the banks of the Delaware to institute "THE HOLY EXPERIMENT."

BRADDOCK'S DEFEAT, 1755.

Early in the morning of the ninth of July, Braddock set his troops in motion. A little below the Youghiogeny they forded the Monongahela, and marched on the southern bank of that tranquil stream, displaying outwardly to the forests the perfection of military discipline, brilliant in their dazzling uniform, their burnished arms gleaming in the bright summer's sun, but sick at heart, and enfeebled by toil and unwholesome diet. At noon they forded the Monongahela again, and stood between the rivers that form the Ohio, only seven miles distant from their junction. A detachment of three hundred and fifty men, led by Lieutenant-Colonel Thomas Gage, and closely attended by a working party of two hundred and fifty, under St. Clair, advanced cautiously, with guides and flanking parties, along a path but twelve feet wide, towards the uneven woody country that was between them and Fort Duquesne. The general was following with the columns of artillery, baggage, and the main body of the army, when a very heavy and quick fire was heard in the front.

Aware of Braddock's progress by the fidelity of their scouts, the French had resolved on an ambuscade. Twice in council the Indians declined the enterprise. "I shall go," said De Beaujeu, "and will you suffer your father to go alone? I am sure we shall conquer;" and, sharing his confidence, they pledged themselves to be his companions. At an early hour, Contrecœur, the commandant at Fort Duquesne, detached De Beaujeu, Dumas, and De Lignery, with less than two hundred and thirty French and Canadians, and six hundred and thirty-seven savages, under orders to repair to a favorable spot selected the preceding evening. Before reaching it they found themselves in the presence of the English, who were advancing in the best possible order; and De Beaujeu instantly began an attack with the utmost vivacity. Gage should, on the moment, and without waiting for orders, have sent support to his flanking parties. His indecision lost the day. The onset was met courageously, but the flanking guards were driven in, and the advanced party, leaving their two six-pounders in the hands of the enemy, were thrown back upon the vanguard which the general had sent as a reinforcement, and which was attempting to form in face of a rising ground on the right. Thus the men of both regiments were heaped together in promiscuous confusion, among the dense forest trees and thickset underwood. The general himself hurried forward to share the danger and animate the troops; and his artillery, though it could do little harm, as it played against an enemy whom the forest concealed, yet terrified the savages and made them waver. At this time De Beaujeu fell, when the brave and humane Dumas, taking the command, gave new life to his party: sending the savages to attack the English in flank, while he with the French and Canadians, continued the combat in front. Already the British regulars were raising shouts of victory, when the battle was renewed, and the Indians, posting themselves most advantageously behind large trees "in the front of the troops and on the hills which overhung the right flank," invisible, yet making the woods re-echo their war-whoop, fired irregularly, but with deadly aim, at "the fair mark" offered by the "compact body of men beneath them." None of the English that were engaged would say they saw a hundred of the enemy, and "many of the officers, who were in the heat of the action the whole time, would not assert that they saw one."

The combat was obstinate, and continued for two hours with scarcely any change in the disposition of either side. Had the regulars shown courage, the issue would not have been doubtful: but terrified by the yells of the Indians, and dispirited by a manner of fighting such as they had never imagined, they would not long obey the voice of their officers, but fired in platoons almost as fast as they could load, aiming among the trees, or firing into the air. In the midst of the strange scene, nothing was so sublime as the persevering gallantry of the officers. They used the utmost art to encourage the men to move upon the enemy; they told them off into small parties of which they took the lead; they bravely formed the front; they advanced sometimes at the head of small bodies, sometimes separately, to recover the cannon, or to get possession of the hill; but were sacrificed by the soldiers, who declined to follow them, and even fired upon them from the rear. Of eighty-six officers, twenty-six were killed,—among them, Sir Peter Halket,—and thirty-seven were wounded, including Gage, and other field officers. Of the men, one half were killed or wounded. Braddock braved every danger. His secretary was shot dead; both his English aids were disabled early in the engagement, leaving the American alone to distribute his orders. "I expected every moment," said one whose eye was on Washington, "to see him fall. Nothing but the superintending care of Providence could have saved him." "An Indian chief—I suppose a Shawnee—singled him out with his rifle, and bade others of his warriors do the same. Two horses were killed under him; four balls penetrated his coat." "Some potent Manitou guards his life," exclaimed the savage. "Death," wrote Washington, "was levelling my companions on every side of me; but, by the all-powerful dispensations of Providence, I have been protected." "To the public," said Davies, a learned divine, in the following month, "I point out that heroic youth, Colonel Washington, whom I cannot but hope Providence has preserved in so signal a manner for some important service to his country." "Who is Mr. Washington?" asked Lord Halifax a few months later. "I know nothing of him," he added, "but that they say he behaved in Braddock's action as bravely as if he really loved the whistling of bullets." The Virginia troops showed great valor, and were nearly all massacred. Of three companies, scarcely thirty men were left alive. Captain Peyronney and all his officers, down to a corporal, were killed; of Polson's, whose bravery was honored by the Legislature of the Old Dominion, only one was left. But "those they call regulars, having wasted their ammunition, broke and ran, as sheep before hounds, leaving the artillery, provisions, baggage, and even the private papers of the general a prey to the enemy. The attempt to rally them was as vain as to attempt to stop the wild bears of the mountain." "Thus were the English most scandalously beaten." Of privates, seven hundred and fourteen were killed or wounded; while of the French and Indians, only three officers and thirty men fell, and but as many more wounded.

Braddock had five horses disabled under him; at last a bullet entered his right side, and he fell mortally wounded. He was with difficulty brought off the field, and borne in the train of the fugitives. All the first day he was silent; but at night he roused himself to say, "Who would have thought it?" The meeting at Dunbar's camp made a day of confusion. On the twelfth of July, Dunbar destroyed the remaining artillery, and burned the public stores and the heavy baggage, to the value of a hundred thousand pounds,—pleading in excuse that he had the orders of the dying general, and being himself resolved, in midsummer, to evacuate Fort Cumberland, and hurry to Philadelphia for winter quarters. Accordingly, the next day they all retreated. At night Braddock roused from his lethargy to say, "We shall better know how to deal with them another time," and died. His grave may still be seen, near the national road, about a mile west of Fort Necessity.

RURAL LIFE IN ENGLAND.*

But if aristocracy was not excluded from towns, still more did it pervade the rural life of England. The climate not only enjoyed the softer atmosphere that belongs to the western side of masses of land, but was further modified by the proximity of every part of it to the sea. It knew neither long continuing heat nor cold; and was more friendly to daily employment throughout the whole year, within

* From the Chapter, England as it was in 1763, in the Fifth Volume of the History.

doors or without, than any in Europe. The island was "a little world" of its own; with a "happy breed of men" for its inhabitants, in whom the hardihood of the Norman was intermixed with the gentler qualities of the Celt and the Saxon, just as nails are rubbed into steel to temper and harden the Damascus blade. They loved country life, of which the mildness of the clime increased the attractions; since every grass and flower and tree that had its home between the remote north and the neighborhood of the tropics would live abroad, and such only excepted as needed a hot sun to unfold their bloom, or concentrate their aroma, or ripen their fruit, would thrive in perfection: so that no region could show such a varied wood. The moisture of the sky favored a soil not naturally very rich: and so fructified the earth, that it was clad in perpetual verdure. Nature had its attractions even in winter. The ancient trees were stripped indeed of their foliage; but showed more clearly their fine proportions, and the undisturbed nests of the noisy rooks among their boughs; the air was so mild, that the flocks and herds still grazed on the freshly springing herbage; and the deer found shelter enough by crouching amongst the fern; the smoothly shaven grassy walk was soft and yielding under the foot; nor was there a month in the year in which the plough was idle. The large landed proprietors dwelt often in houses which had descended to them from the times when England was gemmed all over with the most delicate and most solid structures of Gothic art. The very lanes were memorials of early days, and ran as they had been laid out before the conquest; and in mills for grinding corn, water-wheels revolved at their work just where they had been doing so for at least eight hundred years. Hospitality also had its traditions; and for untold centuries Christmas had been the most joyous of the seasons.

The system was so completely the ruling element in English history and English life, especially in the country, that it seemed the most natural organization of society, and was even endeared to the dependent people. Hence the manners of the aristocracy, without haughtiness or arrogance, implied rather than expressed the consciousness of undisputed rank; and female beauty added to its loveliness the blended graces of dignity and humility—most winning, where acquaintance with sorrow had softened the feeling of superiority, and increased the sentiment of compassion.

Yet the privileged class defended its rural pleasures and its agricultural interests with impassioned vigilance. The game laws parcelling out among the large proprietors the exclusive right of hunting, which had been wrested from the king as too grievous a prerogative, were maintained with relentless severity; and to steal or even to hamstring a sheep was as much punished by death as murder or treason. During the reign of George the Second, sixty-three new capital offences had been added to the criminal laws, and five new ones, on the average, continued to be discovered annually; so that the criminal code of England, formed under the influence of the rural gentry, seemed written in blood, and owed its mitigation only to executive clemency.

But this cruelty, while it encouraged and hardened offenders, did not revolt the instinct of submission in the rural population. The tenantry, for the most part without permanent leases, holding lands at a moderate rent, transmitting the occupation of them from father to son through many generations,

> With calm desires that asked but little room,

clung to the lord of the manor as ivy to massive old walls. They loved to live in his light, to lean on his support, to gather round him with affectionate deference rather than base cowering; and, by their faithful attachment, to win his sympathy and care; happy when he was such an one as merited their love. They caught refinement of their superiors, so that their cottages were carefully neat, with roses and honeysuckles clambering to their roofs. They cultivated the soil in sight of the towers of the church, near which reposed the ashes of their ancestors for almost a thousand years. The whole island was mapped out into territorial parishes, as well as into counties, and the affairs of local interest, the assessment of rates, the care of the poor and of the roads, were settled by elected vestries or magistrates, with little interference from the central government. The resident magistrates were unpaid, being taken from among the landed gentry; and the local affairs of the county, and all criminal affairs of no uncommon importance, were settled by them in a body at their quarterly sessions, where a kind-hearted landlord often presided, to appal the convicted offender by the solemn earnestness of his rebuke, and then to show him mercy by a lenient sentence.

Thus the local institutions of England shared the common character; they were at once the evidence of aristocracy and the badges of liberty.

THE BOSTON MASSACRE, 1770.

On Friday the second day of March a soldier of the Twenty-ninth asked to be employed at Gray's Ropewalk, and was repulsed in the coarsest words. He then defied the ropemakers to a boxing match; and one of them accepting his challenge, he was beaten off. Returning with several of his companions, they too were driven away. A larger number came down to renew the fight with clubs and cutlasses, and in their turn encountered defeat. By this time Gray and others interposed, and for that day prevented further disturbance.

There was an end to the affair at the Ropewalk, but not at the barracks, where the soldiers inflamed each other's passions, as if the honor of the regiment were tarnished. On Saturday they prepared bludgeons, and being resolved to brave the citizens on Monday night, they forewarned their particular acquaintance not to be abroad. Without duly restraining his men, Carr, the Lieutenant-Colonel of the Twenty-ninth, made complaint to the Lieutenant-Governor of the insult they had received.

The council, deliberating on Monday, seemed of opinion, that the town would never be safe from quarrels between the people and the soldiers as long as soldiers should be quartered among them. In the present case the owner of the Ropewalk gave satisfaction by dismissing the workmen complained of.

The officers should, on their part, have kept their men within the barracks after night-fall. Instead of it they left them to roam the streets. Hutchinson should have insisted on measures of precaution, but he, too, much wished the favor of all who had influence at Westminster.

Evening came on. The young moon was shining brightly in a cloudless winter sky, and its light was increased by a new fallen snow. Parties of soldiers were driving about the streets, making a parade of valor, challenging resistance, and striking the inhabitants indiscriminately with sticks or sheathed cutlasses.

A band, which rushed out from Murray's Barracks in Brattle street, armed with clubs, cutlasses, and bayonets, provoked resistance, and an affray ensued. Ensign Maul, at the gate of the barrack-yard, cried to the soldiers, "Turn out and I will stand by you; kill them; stick them; knock them down; run your bayonets through them;" and one soldier after another levelled a firelock, and threatened to "make a lane" through the crowd. Just before nine, as an officer crossed King street, now State street, a barber's lad cried after him, "There goes a mean fellow who hath not paid my master for dressing his hair;" on which the sentinel stationed at the westerly end of the Custom-house, on the corner of King street and Exchange lane, left his post, and with his musket gave the boy a stroke on the head, which made him stagger, and cry for pain.

The street soon became clear, and nobody troubled the sentry, when a party of soldiers issued violently from the main guard, their arms glittering in the moonlight, and passed on hallooing, "Where are they? where are they? let them come." Presently twelve or fifteen more, uttering the same cries, rushed from the south into King street, and so by way of Cornhill, towards Murray's Barracks. "Pray, soldiers, spare my life," cried a boy of twelve, whom they met; "No, no; I'll kill you all," answered one of them, and knocked him down with his cutlass. They abused and insulted several persons at their doors, and others in the street, "running about like madmen in a fury," crying "Fire," which seemed their watchword, and "Where are they? knock them down." Their outrageous behavior occasioned the ringing of the bell at the head of King street.

The citizens, whom the alarm set in motion, came out with canes and clubs; and partly by the interference of well disposed officers, partly by the courage of Crispus Attucks, a mulatto, and some others, the fray at the barracks was soon over. Of the citizens, the prudent shouted "Home, Home;" others, it was said, called out, "Huzza for the main guard; there is the nest;" but the main guard was not molested the whole evening.

A body of soldiers came up Royal Exchange lane, crying "Where are the cowards?" and brandishing their arms, passed through King street. From ten to twenty boys came after them, asking, "Where are they, where are they?" "There is the soldier who knocked me down," said the barber's boy, and they began pushing one another towards the sentinel. He primed and loaded his musket. "The lobster is going to fire," cried a boy. Waving his piece about, the sentinel pulled the trigger. "If you fire you must die for it," said Henry Knox, who was passing by. "I don't care," replied the sentry; "damn them, if they touch me I'll fire." "Fire and be damned," shouted the boys, for they were persuaded he could not do it without leave from a civil officer; and a young fellow spoke out, "We will knock him down for snapping;" while they whistled through their fingers and huzzaed. "Stand off," said the sentry, and shouted aloud, "Turn out, main guard." "They are killing the sentinel," reported a servant from the Custom-house, running to the main guard. "Turn out; why don't you turn out?" cried Preston, who was Captain of the day, to the guard. "He appeared in a great flutter of spirits," and "spoke to them roughly." A party of six, two of whom, Kilroi and Montgomery, had been worsted at the Ropewalk, formed with a corporal in front, and Preston following. With bayonets fixed, they haughtily "rushed through the people," upon the trot, cursing them, and pushing them as they went along. They found about ten persons round the sentry, while about fifty or sixty came down with them. "For God's sake," said Knox, holding Preston by the coat, "take your men back again; if they fire, your life must answer for the consequences." "I know what I am about," said he, hastily, and much agitated. None pressed on them or provoked them, till they began loading, when a party of about twelve in number, with sticks in their hands, moved from the middle of the street, where they had been standing, gave three cheers, and passed along the front of the soldiers, whose muskets some of them struck as they went by. "You are cowardly rascals," said they, "for bringing arms against naked men;" "lay aside your guns, and we are ready for you." "Are the soldiers loaded?" inquired Palmes of Preston. "Yes," he answered, "with powder and ball." "Are they going to fire upon the inhabitants?" asked Theodore Bliss. "They cannot, without my orders," replied Preston; while the "town-born" called out, "Come on, you rascals, you bloody backs, you lobster scoundrels, fire if you dare; we know you dare not." Just then Montgomery received a blow from a stick thrown, which hit his musket; and the word "Fire" being given, he stepped a little on one side, and shot Attucks, who at the time was quietly leaning on a long stick. The people immediately began to move off. "Don't fire," said Langford, the watchman, to Kilroi, looking him full in the face, but yet he did so, and Samuel Gray, who was standing next Langford with his hands in his bosom, fell lifeless. The rest fired slowly and in succession on the people, who were dispersing. One aimed deliberately at a boy, who was running for safety. Montgomery then pushed at Palmes to stab him; on which the latter knocked his gun out of his hand, and levelling a blow at him, hit Preston. Three persons were killed, among them Attucks the mulatto; eight were wounded, two of them mortally. Of all the eleven, not more than one had had any share in the disturbance.

So infuriated were the soldiers, that, when the men returned to take up the dead, they prepared to fire again, but were checked by Preston, while the Twenty-ninth regiment appeared under arms in King street, as if bent on a further massacre. "This is our time," cried soldiers of the Fourteenth; and dogs were never seen more greedy for their prey.

The bells rung in all the churches; the town drums beat. "To arms, to arms," was the cry. And now was to be tested the true character of Boston. All its sons came forth, excited almost to madness: many were absolutely distracted by the sight of the dead bodies, and of the blood, which ran plentifully in the street, and was imprinted in all directions by the foot-tracks on the snow. "Our hearts," says Warren, "beat to arms; almost resolved by one stroke to avenge the death of our slaughtered brethren." But they stood self-possessed and irresistible, demanding justice, according to the law. "Did you not know that you should not have fired without the order of a civil magistrate?" asked Hutchinson, on meeting Preston. "I did it," answered Preston, "to save my men."

The people would not be pacified till the regiment was confined to the guard-room and the barracks; and Hutchinson himself gave assurances that instant inquiries should be made by the county magistrates. The body of them then retired, leaving about one hundred persons to keep watch on the examination, which lasted till three hours after midnight. A warrant was issued against Preston, who surrendered himself to the Sheriff; and the soldiers who composed the party were delivered up and committed to prison.

STUDY OF THE INFINITE—FROM THE NEW YORK HISTORICAL SOCIETY ADDRESS. 1854.

The moment we enter upon an enlarged consideration of existence, we may as well believe in beings that are higher than ourselves, as in those that are lower; nor is it absurd to inquire whether there is a plurality of worlds. Induction warrants the opinion, that the planets and the stars are tenanted, or are to be tenanted, by inhabitants endowed with reason; for though man is but a new comer upon earth, the lower animals had appeared through unnumbered ages, like a long twilight before the day. Some indeed tremulously inquire, how it may be in those distant spheres with regard to redemption? But the scruple is uncalled for. Since the Mediator is from the beginning, he exists for all intelligent creatures not less than for all time. It is very narrow and contradictory to confine his office to the planet on which we dwell. In other worlds the facts of history may be, or rather, by all the laws of induction, will be different; but the essential relations of the finite to the infinite are, and must be, invariable. It is not more certain that the power of gravity extends through the visible universe, than that throughout all time and all space, there is but one mediation between God and created reason.

But leaving aside the question, how far rational life extends, it is certain that on earth the capacity of coming into connexion with the infinite is the distinguishing mark of our kind, and proves it to be one. Here, too, is our solace for the indisputable fact, that humanity, in its upward course, passes through the shadows of death, and over the relics of decay. Its march is strown with the ruins of formative efforts, that were never crowned with success. How often does the just man suffer, and sometimes suffer most for his brightest virtues! How often do noblest sacrifices to regenerate a nation seem to have been offered in vain! How often is the champion of liberty struck down in the battle, and the symbol which he uplifted, trampled under foot! But what is the life of an individual to that of his country? Of a state, or a nation, at a given moment, to that of the race? The just man would cease to be just, if he were not willing to perish for his kind. The scoria that fly from the iron at the stroke of the artisan, show how busily he plies his task; the clay which is rejected from the potter's wheel, proves the progress of his work; the chips of marble that are thrown off by the chisel of the sculptor, leave the miracle of beauty to grow under his hand. Nothing is lost. I leave to others the questioning of Infinite power, why the parts are distributed as they are, and not otherwise. Humanity moves on, attended by its glorious company of martyrs. It is our consolation, that their sorrows and persecution and death are encountered in the common cause, and not in vain.

ROBERT GREENHOW.

ROBERT GREENHOW was born, in the year 1800, at Richmond, Virginia. He was the son of Robert Greenhow, one of the leading citizens of the place, who had at one time filled the office of mayor. Greenhow's mother perished in the conflagration of the Richmond theatre, and he himself narrowly escaped destruction in the same calamity. At the age of fifteen he removed to New York for the purpose of completing his education. He here became a student in the office of Drs. Hosack and Francis, and attended lectures at the College of Physicians and Surgeons, where he took his degree in 1821, having in the meantime mixed freely in the best society of the city, and gained universal respect by the extent of his acquirements and the activity of his mind. He early developed the powers of an unusually retentive memory, said to have been surpassed in the present generation only by that of the historian Niebuhr, a faculty that proved of the greatest service to him through life. After leaving college he visited Europe, where he became intimately acquainted with Lord Byron, and other distinguished men. After his return he delivered a course of lectures on chemistry before the Literary and Philosophical Society of New York.

In consequence of commercial disasters which at this period impaired his father's fortune, Greenhow was forced to rely on his own exertions for support. By the influence of his old friend, General Morgan Lewis, he obtained, in 1828, the appointment of translator to the Department of State at Washington.

In 1837 he prepared, by order of Congress, a Report upon the Discovery of the North-West coast of North America. The researches which he had previously made into the early history of Oregon and California were of essential service to himself and the country in this undertaking, as they contributed greatly to establish the claims of the United States secured by the Ashburton negotiations. The report was afterwards enlarged by the author, and published with the title of *History of Oregon and California*, which at once took the rank it has since maintained of a thoroughly reliable authority on the subject.

In December, 1848, Mr. Greenhow read a paper before the New York Historical Society, involving curious speculation and research, on the probabilities of the illustrious Archbishop Fenelon having passed some of the years of his youth as a missionary among the Iroquois or Five Nations in the western part of the state.* In a previous communication to the Society, dated Washington City, November 16, 1844, he recommends the preparation of a Memoir on the Discovery of the Atlantic Coasts of the United States, calling attention to the absence of popular information on the first discovery of Chesapeake Bay.

In 1850 Dr. Greenhow, on his way to California, passed four months in the City of Mexico, engaged in a minute examination of its monuments and archives. After his arrival in California he was appointed, in 1853, Associate Law Agent to the United States Land Commission for the determination of California claims, holding its sessions in San Francisco. His intimate acquaintance with the Spanish language and the technicalities of Mexican law, were of the greatest service in facilitating the public business. On the resignation of the land agent he made an application for the vacant office, which proved unsuccessful. After the appointment of the new incumbent, he resigned his post, to the great regret of all connected with the Commission.

He died in the spring of the following year, in consequence of the fracture of his thigh, occasioned by falling, during a dark night, into a deep excavation opened in one of the streets of San Francisco.

S. G. GOODRICH.

SAMUEL GRISWOLD GOODRICH, under his assumed name of Peter Parley, ranks among the best

* Supplement to Proceedings of N. Y. Hist. Soc., 1848, pp. 196-209.

known of our authors. He was born at Ridgefield, Connecticut, August 19, 1793, and commenced life as a publisher in Hartford. In 1824 he visited Europe, and on his return established himself as a publisher in Boston, where he commenced an original annual, *The Token*, which he edited for a number of years, the contributions and illustrations being the products of American authors and artists; Mr. Goodrich himself furnishing several poems, tales, and sketches to the successive volumes, and rendering a further service to the public by his encouragement of young and unknown authors, among whom is to be mentioned Nathaniel Hawthorne, the finest of whose "Twice-told Tales" were first told in The Token, and, strange to say, without attracting any considerable attention. The famous Peter Parley series was commenced about the same time; Mr. Goodrich turning to good account in his little square volumes his recent travels in Europe, and his tact in book arrangement and illustration. The Geography was an especial favorite, and it is probable that the primary fact of that science is settled in the minds of some millions of schoolboys past and present, in indissoluble connexion with the couplet by which it was first transmitted thereto,

> The world is round, and like a ball
> Seems swinging in the air.

Mr. Goodrich has, however, higher if not broader claims to poetic reputation, than are furnished by the little production we have cited. He has found time, amid his constant labor as a compiler, to assert his claims as an original author by the publication, in 1837, of *The Outcast, and Other Poems;* in 1841, of a selection from his contributions in prose and poetry to The Token and various magazines, with the title, *Sketches from a Student's Window;* and in 1851, by an elegantly illustrated edition of his *Poems*, including The Outcast. In 1838, Mr. Goodrich published *Fireside Education, by the author of Peter Parley's Tales*, a volume of judicious counsel to parents on that important topic, presented in a popular and attractive manner.

Mr. Goodrich is at present United States Consul at Paris, where he has made arrangements for the translation and introduction of his Peter Parley series into France, under his own supervision.

A simple enumeration of the various publications* of this gentleman under his own name, and that of his friend of the knee-breeches and stout cane, is the most significant comment which can be presented on a career of remarkable literary activity.

GOOD NIGHT.

The sun has sunk behind the hills,
  The shadows o'er the landscape creep;
A drowsy sound the woodland fills,
  And nature folds her arms to sleep:
    Good night—good night.

The chattering jay has ceased his din—
  The noisy robin sings no more—
The crow, his mountain haunt within,
  Dreams 'mid the forest's surly roar:
    Good night—good night.

The sunlit cloud floats dim and pale;
  The dew is falling soft and still;
The mist hangs trembling o'er the vale,
  And silence broods o'er yonder mill:
    Good night—good night.

The rose, so ruddy in the light,
  Bends on its stem all rayless now,
And by its side the lily white,
  A sister shadow, seems to bow:
    Good night—good night.

---

* We present the titles of these writings as we find them in Mr. Roorbach's carefully prepared Bibliotheca Americana.

Ancient History, 12mo.; Anecdotes of the Animal Kingdom, 16mo.; Book of Government and Laws; Book of Literature, Ancient and Modern; Enterprise, Industry, and Art of Man, 16mo.; Fireside Education, 12mo.; Glance at Philosophy, Mental, Moral, and Social, 16mo.; History of American Indians, 16mo.; History of All Nations on a New and Improved Plan, 1800 pp. small 4to.; Lights and Shadows of American History; Lights and Shadows of African History; Lights and Shadows of Asiatic History; Lights and Shadows of European History; Lives of Benefactors, including Patriots, Inventors, Discoverers, &c. 16mo.; Lives of Celebrated Women, 16mo.; Lives of Eccentric and Wonderful Persons; Lives of Famous Men of Modern Times; Lives of Famous Men of Ancient Times; Lives of Famous American Indians, 16mo.; Lives of Signers of Declaration of Independence; Manners and Customs of All Nations, 16mo.; Manners, Customs, and Antiquities of American Indians; Modern History, 12mo.; National Geography, 4to.; Pictorial History of England, France, Greece, Rome, and the United States, 12mo.; Pictorial Geography of the World, 8vo.; Pictorial Natural History, 12mo.; Poems, 12mo.; School Reader, First, 18mo.; School Reader, Second, 18mo.; School Reader, Third, 18mo.; School Reader, Fourth, 12mo.; School Reader, Fifth, 12mo.; South America and West Indies; Sow Well, Reap Well; Sketches from a Student's Window; Universal Geography; Wonders of Geology, 16mo.; The World and its Inhabitants.

Parley's Arithmetic; Africa; America; Anecdotes; Asia; Alexander Selkirk; Bible Dictionary; Bible Gazetteer; Bible Stories; Book of the United States; Book of Books, a Selection from Parley's Magazine; Consul's Daughter; Captive of Nootka; Columbus; Common School History; Dick Boldhero, 18mo.; Europe; Every-Day Book; Fables; Farewell; First Book of History, Western Hemisphere; First Book of Reading and Spelling, 18mo.; Fairy Tales; Flower Basket; Franklin; Gift, 16mo.; Geography for Beginners; Gardener; Greece; History of the World; History of North America; Humorist's Tales; Home in the Sea, 18mo.; Illustrations of Astronomy; Illustrations of Commerce; Illustrations of History and Geography; Illustrations of the Animal Kingdom; Illustrations of the Vegetable Kingdom; Islands; Mines of Different Countries; Moral Tales; Make the Best of It; Magazine; Miscellanies; New Geography for Beginners; New York; Picture Book; Picture Books, twelve kinds; Present; Rose Bud; Rome; Right is Might, 18mo.; Second Book of History, Eastern Hemisphere; Story of Captain Riley; Story of La Perouse; Ship; Sea; Sun, Moon, and Stars; Short Stories; Short Stories for Long Nights; Tales of Adventure; Tales for the Times; Tales of Sea and Land, 18mo.; Tale of the Revolution; Third Book of History, Ancient History; Three Months on the Sea; Truth-Finder, or Inquisitive Jack, 18mo.; Universal History; Wit Bought; What to Do, and How to Do It; Winter Evening Tales; Washington; Wonders of South America; Young America, or Book of Government.

The bat may wheel on silent wing—
The fox his guilty vigils keep—
The boding owl his dirges sing;
But love and innocence will sleep:
Good night—good night!

THE TEACHER'S LESSON.

I saw a child some four years old,
Along a meadow stray;
Alone she went—unchecked—untold—
Her home not far away.

She gazed around on earth and sky—
Now paused, and now proceeded;
Hill, valley, wood,—she passed them by
Unmarked, perchance unheeded.

And now gay groups of roses bright,
In circling thickets bound her—
Yet on she went with footsteps light,
Still gazing all around her.

And now she paused, and now she stooped,
And plucked a little flower—
A simple daisy 'twas, that drooped
Within a rosy bower.

The child did kiss the little gem,
And to her bosom pressed it;
And there she placed the fragile stem,
And with soft words caressed it.

I love to read a lesson true,
From nature's open book—
And oft I learn a lesson new,
From childhood's careless look.

Children are simple—loving—true;
'Tis Heaven that made them so;
And would you teach them—be so too—
And stoop to what they know.

Begin with simple lessons—things
On which they love to look:
Flowers, pebbles, insects, birds on wings—
These are God's spelling-book.

And children know His A, B, C,
As bees where flowers are set:
Would'st thou a skilful teacher be?—
Learn, then, this alphabet.

From leaf to leaf, from page to page,
Guide thou thy pupil's look,
And when he says, with aspect sage,
"Who made this wondrous book?"

Point thou with reverent gaze to heaven,
And kneel in earnest prayer,
That lessons thou hast humbly given,
May lead thy pupil there.

GEORGE HILL.

GEORGE HILL was born at Guilford, Connecticut, in 1796. He completed his collegiate studies with high honor at Yale in 1816; was then employed in one of the public offices at Washington, and entered the Navy in 1827 as a teacher of mathematics. In this capacity he made a cruise in the Mediterranean, where his *Ruins of Athens*, and several other poems suggested by its classic localities, were written. On his return, he was appointed librarian of the Department of State at Washington. After his resignation of this situation, he was appointed United States Consul for the southern portion of Asia Minor, a position he was also obliged to decline after a brief trial, in consequence of ill-health. Returning to Washington, he became a clerk in one of the Departments.*

Mr. Hill published, anonymously, The Ruins of Athens, with a few short poems, in 1831. These were reprinted, with a few others, in an edition bearing his name in 1839.*

The Ruins of Athens is a poem occupied with description and reflection, suggested to the author on a visit to the city, while yet under the sway of the Turks. It contains forty-one Spenserian stanzas, and is written in a subdued and careful manner. *Titania's Banquet* is a successful imitation of the Masques of the Elizabethan era, but the subject was, for obvious reasons, an injudicious choice for the author. The remainder of the volume is occupied by a few lyrical pieces, suggested by themes of domestic or national interest; several sonnets and imitations of the manner of Swift, Prior, Burns, Herrick, and others—a favorite exercise with the writers of the last century which we do not often meet with in the poets of the present day.

MEDITATION AT ATHENS—FROM THE RUINS OF ATHENS.

Approach! but not thou favored one, thou light
And sportive insect, basking in the ray
Of youth and pleasure, heedless of the night.
Dreamer! the shapes that in thy pathway play,
Thy morning pathway, elsewhere chase! away!
Come not, till like the fading weeds that twine
Yon time-worn capital, the thoughts, that prey
On hopes of high but baffled aim, decline,
And weary of the race the goal unwon resign.

Is thy hearth desolate, or trod by feet
Whose unfamiliar steps recall no sound
Of such, as, in thine early days, to greet
Thy coming, hastened? are the ties that bound
Thy heart's hopes severed? hast thou seen the ground
Close o'er her, thy young love? and felt, for thee
That earth contains no other? look around!
Here thou may'st find companions:—hither flee!
Where Ruin dwells, and men, nay, gods have ceased to be!

Wall, tower, and temple crushed and heaped in one
Wide tomb, that echoes to the Tartar's cry
And drum heard rolling from the Parthenon,
The wild winds sweeping through it, owl's grey eye
Gleaming among its ruins, and the sigh
Of the long grass that unmolested waves,
The race whose proud old monuments are by
To mock, but not to shame them, recreants, slaves,
The very stones should arm heaped on heroic graves!

Here let me pause, and blend me with the things
That were,—the shadowy world, that lives no more
But in the heart's cherished imaginings,—
The mighty and the beautiful of yore.
It may not be: the mount, the plain, the shore,
Whisper no living murmur, voice nor tread,
But the low rustling of the leaves and roar
Of the dull ceaseless surf, and the stars shed
Their light upon the flower whose beauty mocks the dead.

The Morn is up, with cold and dewy eye
Peeps, like a vestal from her cloister, forth.

* Everest's Poets of Connecticut, p. 277.
† The Ruins of Athens; Titania's Banquet, a Mask, other poems. By G. Hill. Boston: 1839. 8vo. pp. 160.

In blushing brightness; the grey peaks on high
Lift her old altars in the clear blue north;
The clouds ascend, on light winds borne, that come
Laden with fragrance; and from each high-place,
Where every god in turn has found a home,
Nature sends up her incense, and her face
Unveils to Him whose shrine and dwelling are all space.

Morn hushed as midnight! save perchance is heard
At times the hum of insect, or the grass
That sighs, or rustles by the lizard stirred:
And still we pause; and may, where empire was
And ruin is, no stone unheeded pass,—
No rude Memorial, that seems to wear
Vestige of that whose glory, as a glass
Shattered but still resplendent, lives,—and share
The spirit of the spot, the "dream of things that were."

Land of the free, of battle and the Muse!
It grieves me that my first farewell to thee
Should be my last: that, nurtured by the dews
Of thy pure fount, some blossoms from the tree,
Where many a lyre of ancient minstrelsy
Now silent hangs, I plucked, but failed to rear,
As 't is, a chance-borne pilgrim of the sea,
I lay them on thy broken altar here,
A passing worshipper, but humble and sincere.

LIBERTY.

There is a spirit working in the world,
Like to a silent subterranean fire;
Yet, ever and anon, some Monarch hurled
Aghast and pale attests its fearful ire.
The dungeoned Nations now once more respire
The keen and stirring air of Liberty.
The struggling Giant wakes, and feels he's free.
By Delphi's fountain-cave, that ancient Choir
Resume their song; the Greek astonished hears,
And the old altar of his worship rears.
Sound on! Fair sisters! sound your boldest lyre,—
Peal your old harmonies as from the spheres.
Unto strange Gods too long we've bent the knee,
The trembling mind, too long and patiently.

A. B. LONGSTREET,

The author of *Georgia Scenes*, and a native of that state, born at the close of the last century, has practised at intervals the somewhat diverse occupations of law and the ministry of the Methodist Church. He was for several years President of Emory College, at Oxford, Georgia. In his youth he was an intimate of George McDuffie and others, who became leading men of the South, and the adventures which he shared with these furnish some of the anecdotes of his capital book of humor, entitled, *Georgia Scenes, Characters, Incidents, &c., in the First Half Century of the Republic, by a Native Georgian*, which first appeared in a newspaper of the state, and subsequently in a volume from the press of the Harpers, in New York, in 1840. "They consist," the author tells us in his preface, "of nothing more than fanciful *combinations* of *real* incidents and characters; and throwing into those scenes, which would be otherwise dull and insipid, some personal incident or adventure of my own, real or imaginary, as it would best suit my purpose; usually *real*, but happening at different times and under different circumstances from those in which they are here represented. I have not always, however, taken this liberty. Some of the scenes are as literally true as the frailties of memory would allow them to be." In style and subject matter they are vivid, humorous descriptions, by a good story teller, who employs voice, manner, and a familiar knowledge of popular dialogue in their narration. They are quaint, hearty sketches of a rough life, and the manners of an unsettled country—such as are rapidly passing away in numerous districts where they have prevailed, and which may at some future and not very distant day, be found to exist only in such genial pages as Judge Longstreet's. Besides these collected Sketches, the author has been a contributor of similar papers, descriptive of local character, to the Magnolia, conducted by Mr. Simms, and the Orion, another magazine of South Carolina, edited by Mr. W. C. Richards.

GEORGIA THEATRICS—FROM THE GEORGIA SCENES.

If my memory fail me not, the 10th of June, 1809, found me, at about 11 o'clock in the forenoon, ascending a long and gentle slope in what was called "The Dark Corner" of Lincoln. I believe it took its name from the moral darkness which reigned over that portion of the county at the time of which I am speaking. If in this point of view it was but a shade darker than the rest of the county, it was inconceivably dark. If any man can name a trick or sin which had not been committed at the time of which I am speaking, in the very focus of all the county's illumination (Lincolnton), he must himself be the most inventive of the tricky, and the very Judas of sinners. Since that time, however (all humor aside), Lincoln has become a living proof "that light shineth in darkness." Could I venture to mingle the solemn with the ludicrous, even for the purposes of honorable contrast, I could adduce from this county instances of the most numerous and wonderful transitions from vice and folly to virtue and holiness, which have ever, perhaps, been witnessed since the days of the apostolic ministry. So much, lest it should be thought by some that what I am about to relate is characteristic of the county in which it occurred.

Whatever may be said of the *moral* condition of the Dark Corner at the time just mentioned, its *natural* condition was anything but dark. It smiled in all the charms of spring; and spring borrowed a new charm from its undulating grounds, its luxuriant woodlands, its sportive streams, its vocal birds, and its blushing flowers.

Rapt with the enchantment of the season and the scenery around me, I was slowly rising the slope, when I was startled by loud, profane, and boisterous voices, which seemed to proceed from a thick covert of undergrowth about two hundred yards in the advance of me, and about one hundred to the right of my road.

"You kin, kin you?"

"Yes, I kin, and am able to do it! Boo-oo-oo! Oh, wake snakes, and walk your chalks! Brimstone and —— fire! Don't hold me, Nick Stovall! The fight's made up, and let's go at it. —— my soul if I don't jump down his throat, and gallop every chitterling out of him before you can say 'quit!'"

"Now, Nick, don't hold him! Jist let the wild-cat come, and I'll tame him. Ned'll see me a fair fight, won't you, Ned?"

"Oh, yes; I'll see you a fair fight, blast my old shoes if I don't."

"That's sufficient, as Tom Haynes said when he saw the elephant. Now let him come."

Thus they went on, with countless oaths interspersed, which I dare not even hint at, and with much that I could not distinctly hear.

In Mercy's name! thought I, what band of ruffians has selected this holy season and this heavenly retreat for such Pandæmonian riots! I quickened my gait, and had come nearly opposite to the thick grove whence the noise proceeded, when my eye caught indistinctly, and at intervals, through the foliage of the dwarf-oaks and hickories which intervened, glimpses of a man or men, who seemed to be in a violent struggle; and I could occasionally catch those deep-drawn, emphatic oaths which men in conflict utter when they deal blows. I dismounted, and hurried to the spot with all speed. I had overcome about half the space which separated it from me, when I saw the combatants come to the ground, and, after a short struggle, I saw the uppermost one (for I could not see the other) make a heavy plunge with both his thumbs, and at the same instant I heard a cry in the accent of keenest torture, "Enough! My eye's out!"

I was so completely horrorstruck, that I stood transfixed for a moment to the spot where the cry met me. The accomplices in the hellish deed which had been perpetrated had all fled at my approach; at least I supposed so, for they were not to be seen.

"Now, blast your corn-shucking soul," said the victor (a youth about eighteen years old) as he rose from the ground, "come cutt'n your shines 'bout me agin, next time I come to the Courthouse, will you! Get your owl-eye in agin if you can!"

At this moment he saw me for the first time. He looked excessively embarrassed, and was moving off, when I called to him, in a tone emboldened by the sacredness of my office and the iniquity of his crime, "Come back, you brute! and assist me in relieving your fellow-mortal, whom you have ruined for ever!"

My rudeness subdued his embarrassment in an instant; and, with a taunting curl of the nose, he replied, "You needn't kick before you're spurr'd. There a'nt nobody there, nor ha'nt been nother. I was jist seein' how I could 'a' *fout*." So saying, he bounded to his plough, which stood in the corner of the fence about fifty yards beyond the battle ground.

And, would you believe it, gentle reader! his report was true. All that I had heard and seen was nothing more nor less than a Lincoln rehearsal; in which the youth who had just left me had played all the parts of all the characters of a Courthouse fight.

I went to the ground from which he had risen, and there were the prints of his two thumbs, plunged up to the balls in the mellow earth, about the distance of a man's eyes apart; and the ground around was broken up as if two stags had been engaged upon it.

BENJAMIN F. FRENCH.

Benjamin F. French was born in Virginia, June 8, 1799. After receiving a classical education he commenced the study of the law, a pursuit he was obliged to abandon in consequence of ill health. In 1825, having previously contributed a number of essays and poems to various periodicals, he published *Biographia Americana*, and shortly after *Memoirs of Eminent Female Writers*. In 1830 he removed to Louisiana, in order to enjoy a milder climate. Although actively engaged in planting and in commercial pursuits, he collected and translated many interesting documents in the French and Spanish languages relating to the early history of Louisiana. These he published, with selections from the narratives of Purchas and others in the English language, in a series of five volumes octavo, with the title, *Historical Collections of Louisiana, embracing many rare and valuable Documents relating to the Natural, Civil, and Political History of that State, compiled with Historical and Biographical Notes, and an Introduction, by B. F. French.* The successive volumes appeared in 1846, 1850, 1851, 1852, 1853; and two additional volumes, bringing the annals of the country down to the period of its cession to the United States, are nearly ready for publication. Mr. French has also in preparation two volumes of Historical Annals relating to the history of North America, from its discovery to the year 1850. He has of late been a resident of this city. Before leaving New Orleans he made a donation of a large portion of his extensive private library to the Fisk Free Library of that city.

FRANCIS PATRICK KENRICK,

Archbishop of Baltimore, and one of the first Latinists of the country, was born in Dublin, December 3, 1797. In 1815 he went to Rome, where he studied in the College of the Propaganda, and was ordained priest in 1821. In the same year he removed to Kentucky, and became professor in St. Joseph's College, Bardstown. In 1828 he wrote a series of letters, in an ironical vein, to the Rev. Dr. Blackburn, President of the Presbyterian College, Danville, who had opposed the doctrines of his church on the subject of the Eucharist, in a number of articles signed Omega, entitled *Letters of Omikron to Omega.* In 1829 he published four sermons preached in the cathedral at Bardstown. On the sixth of June, Trinity Sunday, 1830, he was consecrated bishop, and removed to Philadelphia, as the coadjutor of the Rt. Rev. Bishop Connell of that diocese, to whose office he succeeded in 1842.

In 1839 and 1840 he issued a work in the Latin language on dogmatic theology, in four volumes octavo, *Theologia Dogmatica*, which was followed in 1841, '2, and '3 by three volumes in the same language, entitled *Theologia Moralis.**

In 1837 he published a series of letters addressed to the Rt. Rev. John H. Hopkins, Protestant Episcopal Bishop of Vermont, *On the Primacy of the Holy See and the Authority of General Councils*, in reply to a work by that prelate. These were followed by a work on the Primacy, published in 1845, of which the letters we have just mentioned formed a large portion. A German translation of this work appeared in 1853. In 1841 Bishop Kenrick published a duodecimo volume on *Justification*, and in 1843 a treatise of similar size on *Baptism*. In 1849 he published a *Translation of the Four Gospels*, consisting of a revision of the Rhemish version, with critical notes, and in 1851 a similar translation of the remaining portion of the New Testament. He removed in the same year to Baltimore on his appointment as archbishop of that see.

Dr. Kenrick has recently published a series of letters with the title of *A Vindication of the Catholic Church*,† designed as a reply to Bishop

* 8vo. Phila. † 12mo. pp. 288.

Hopkins's "'End of Controversy' Controverted," or "Refutation of Milner's 'End of Controversy.'"

He has also prepared *Concilia Provincialia, Baltimori habita. Ab anno* 1829 *usque ad annum* 1849. *Baltimori:* 1851.

CHARLES PETTIT M'ILVAINE.

CHARLES PETTIT M'ILVAINE was born at Burlington, New Jersey, near the close of the last century. After being graduated at Princeton in 1816, he studied theology under the direction of the Rev. Dr. Charles Wharton, of Burlington. He was ordained and settled at Georgetown, D. C. While in this place he became acquainted with the Hon. John C. Calhoun, at whose instigation he received, and was induced to accept the chaplaincy at West Point, where he passed several years, until he received a call to the rectorship of St. John's Church, Brooklyn.

In the winter of 1831-32 Dr. M'Ilvaine delivered a series of lectures as a part of the course of instruction of the University of the City of New York, which had then just commenced operations. In these lectures, which were collected and published in 1832,* the writer confines himself to the historical branch of his subject, the chief topics dwelt upon being the authenticity of the New Testament, the credibility of the Gospel history, its divine authority as attested by miracles and prophecy, and the argument in favor of the truth of the Christian faith, to be drawn from its propagation and the fruits it has borne. In 1832 Dr. M'Ilvaine was consecrated Bishop of Ohio, where he has since remained, his residence, when not occupied in the visitation of his diocese, being at Cincinnati.

Bishop M'Ilvaine is the author of several addresses and other productions condemnatory of the doctrines commonly known as those of the "Oxford Tracts," and has recently, at the request of the Convention of his diocese, published a volume of sermons.†

STEPHEN H. TYNG.

STEPHEN HIGGINSON TYNG, one of the most energetic and popular preachers of the day, was born at Newburyport, Massachusetts, March 1, 1800. His father, the Hon. Dudley Atkins Tyng, an eminent lawyer of that state, married a daughter of the Hon. Stephen Higginson, of Boston, a member of the Convention which framed the Constitution of the United States. He was graduated at Harvard at the early age of seventeen. He at first engaged in mercantile pursuits, but after a short period commenced the study of theology, was ordained deacon in 1821 by Bishop Griswold, and took charge in the same year of St. George's Church, Georgetown, D. C. In 1823 he removed to Queen Ann's Parish, Prince George County, Maryland, and in 1829 became rector of St. Paul's Church, Philadelphia, a charge he resigned in 1833, when he was invited to the Church of the Epiphany in the same city. In 1845 he removed to New York, in acceptance of a call to the rectorship of St. George's Church, a position which he still retains. Since his incumbency the congregation have removed from the venerable edifice in Beekman street, long identified with the labors of the late highly respected Dr. James Milnor, which has again become one of the chapels of Trinity parish, to one of the largest and most costly edifices devoted to public worship in the city. The activity of the parish is in proportion to its wealth and numbers—a missionary whose field of action is among the poor of the neighborhood, and a Sunday school of over one thousand scholars, forming a portion of its parochial system. These results are due in a great measure to the activity of the rector, who is also a prominent member of many of the religious societies of the country, and an earnest advocate of the temperance and other social movements of the day.*

Dr. Tyng has long maintained a high reputation as a pulpit orator. His style of writing is energetic and direct. His readiness and felicity as an extempore speaker on anniversary and other occasions are also remarkable. His chief publications are his *Lectures on the Law and the Gospel; The Israel of God; Christ is All; Christian Titles*, an enumeration of the appellations applied to believers in the Scriptures, with appropriate comments. He has also published *Recollections in Europe*, drawn from personal observations during a brief tour abroad. Dr. Tyng has recently become associated in the editorship of the Protestant Churchman of this city.

ALEXANDER YOUNG,

ONE of the most useful and accomplished historical scholars of New England, was born in Boston, September 22, 1800. After a careful preliminary training at the Latin School, he entered Harvard College, where he completed his course in 1820. He next became an assistant teacher in the school in which his own education had been obtained, under the same principal, Benjamin A. Gould. After a short period of service he returned to Cambridge to devote himself to preparation for the ministry. Immediately after his ordination he became, in 1824, pastor of the New South Church, one of the leading Unitarian congregations of Boston, a position he filled with great success for the long period of twenty-nine years—the connexion closing only with life.

In 1839 he commenced his editorial labors by the preparation of a series, the Library of the Old English Prose Writers, in nine volumes. It was the first attempt in the United States to emulate the example of the best scholars of the day in England in the revival of the treasures of the Elizabethan literature, and did much to extend a knowledge of writers like Owen Felltham, Selden, Fuller, Izaak Walton, and Latimer, among general readers.

In 1841 Dr. Young published *The Chronicles of the Pilgrim Fathers of the Colony of Plymouth*,

---

* The Evidences of Christianity in their external division, exhibited in a course of lectures delivered in Clinton Hall, in the winter of 1831–32, under the appointment of the University of the City of New York. By C. P. M'Ilvaine, D.D. G. and C. and H. Carville. 1832.

† The Truth and the Life: Twenty-two Sermons by the Rt. Rev. C. P. M'Ilvaine. Carters. 1855. 8vo. pp. 508.

* In November, 1852, Dr. Tyng delivered an oration at the centennial anniversary of the initiation of Washington as a member of the Ancient and Honorable Fraternity of Free and Accepted Masons, in which, after passing several points of his character in review, he closed with a special tribute to his religious profession.

from 1602 to 1625; now first collected from Original Records and Contemporaneous Documents. This was succeeded, in 1846, by *The Chronicles of the First Planters of the Colony of Massachusetts Bay, from 1623 to 1636; now first collected from Original Records and Contemporaneous Manuscripts, and Illustrated with Notes.*

SAMUEL SEABURY.

Samuel Seabury, the son of the Rev. Charles Seabury, and grandson of Bishop Seabury, was born in the year 1801. He entered at an early age on the preparation for a mercantile career, but his taste for study, although little fostered by educational advantages, disinclined him for business pursuits. By great diligence and economy he fitted himself for the duties of a schoolmaster, and while thus occupied devoting his leisure hours to hard study, gradually, by his unaided efforts, made himself a learned man. In acknowledgment of these exertions, the complimentary degree of A.M. was conferred upon him by Columbia College.

Having completed a course of theological study, he was ordained Deacon by Bishop Hobart, April 12, 1826, and Priest, July 7, 1828. He commenced his ministerial labors as a missionary at Huntington and Oyster Bay, Long Island, and was afterwards transferred to Hallet's Cove, now Astoria. In 1830 he became Professor of Languages in the Flushing Institute, afterwards St. Paul's College, where he remained until he removed to New York in 1834, to take charge of the Churchman, a weekly religious newspaper. He conducted this journal with great energy and ability until 1849, when, in consequence of his engrossing parochial duties as rector of the Church of the Annunciation, a parish founded by him in 1838, he resigned his position as editor, and has since devoted himself entirely to ministerial labors.

Dr. Seabury is the author of *The Continuity of the Church of England in the Sixteenth Century*,* a work designed to show "that the Church of England, in renouncing the jurisdiction of the Bishop of Rome, and reforming itself from the errors and corruptions of Popery, underwent no organic change, but retained the ministry, faith, and sacraments of Christ, and fulfilled the conditions necessary to their transmission." The work consists of two discourses delivered by the author, to which he has added an appendix of far greater length, enforcing the positions of his connected argument. Dr. Seabury has published other discourses, and his articles, if collected from the Churchman and elsewhere, would occupy several volumes.

JOHN O. CHOULES.

The Rev. John Overton Choules, a clergyman of the Baptist denomination, was born in Bristol, England, Feb. 5, 1801. He came to the United States in 1824, and for three years was principal of an academy at Red Hook, on the Hudson, New York. He has since filled several parish relations at New York, in the neighborhood of Boston, at Jamaica Plains, and is at present pastor of the Second Baptist Church, at Newport, R. I.

J. O. Choules

His literary publications have been, apart from numerous contributions to the periodicals and newspapers, several successful compilations, editions of other authors, and a book of travels. In 1829 he edited J. Angell James's Church Member's Guide, published by Lincoln and Edmonds, at Boston, 1829; in 1830 The Christian Offering; and in 1831 The Beauties of Collyer, for the same publishers. A History of Missions, in two volumes, quarto, with plates, prepared by Dr. Choules, was published by Samuel Walker of Boston. In 1843 he edited for the Harpers an edition of Neal's History of the Puritans; and in 1846 furnished a preface and some notes to Mr. John Forster's Lives of the Statesmen of the Commonwealth. He has also edited Hinton's History of the United States, in quarto.

Young Americans Abroad, or Vacation in Europe, is the title of a volume in which Dr. Choules describes an excursion tour with several of his pupils. In 1853 he accompanied Capt. Vanderbilt, with a select party of friends, in his notable pleasure excursion to Europe in the North Star, a steamer of twenty-five hundred tons, which visited Southampton, the Baltic, and the waters of the Mediterranean to Constantinople. Of this unique voyage Dr. Choules published an account on his return, in his volume—*The Cruise of the Steam Yacht North Star; a Narrative of the Excursion of Mr. Vanderbilt's Party to England, Russia, Denmark, France, Spain, Italy, Malta, Turkey, Madeira, &c.*

One of the specialities of Dr. Choules is his acquaintance with the sterling old literature of the Puritans, of which he has an admirable collection in his library. His taste in books is generally excellent, and few men, it may be remarked, have mingled more with living celebrities, or have a better stock of the unwritten personal anecdote of the present day. It was Dr. Choules's good fortune to enjoy the personal friendship of the late Daniel Webster, of whom, in an obituary sermon delivered at Newport, November 21, 1852, he presented a number of interesting memorials.

GEORGE P. MARSH

Is a native of Vermont, born in Woodstock, in 1801. He was educated at Dartmouth, and shortly after settled in Burlington, in the practice of the law. In 1843 he was elected to Congress, and remained in the House of Representatives till 1849, when he was appointed by the administration of President Taylor Resident Minister at Constantinople, an office which he held till 1853.

Mr. Marsh's literary reputation rests upon his scholarship in an acquaintance with the Northern languages of Europe, in which he is a proficient; his *Compendious Grammar of the Old Northern or Icelandic Language, compiled and translated from the Grammars of Rask* (Burling-

* The Continuity of the Church of England in the Sixteenth Century. Two Discourses: with an Appendix and Notes. By Samuel Seabury, D.D. Second edition. New York: 1853. 8vo., pp. 174.

ton, 1838); several articles on *Icelandic Literature*, in the American Whig and Eclectic Review, and two Addresses, in which he has pursued the Gothic element in history. One of these discourses, entitled *The Goths in New England*, delivered in 1836 at Middlebury College, traced in a novel manner the presence of the race in the Puritans, who settled that portion of the country. In 1844 he delivered an address before the New England Society of the City of New York, in which he sketched, from his favorite point of view of the superiority of the Northern races, the influences at work in the formation and development of the Puritan character. The style of these addresses is animated, and their positions have been effective in securing public attention.

ANGLO-SAXON INFLUENCES OF HOME.*

In the sunny climes of Southern Europe, where a sultry and relaxing day is followed by a balmy and refreshing night, and but a brief period intervenes between the fruits of autumn and the renewed promises of spring, life, both social and industrial, is chiefly passed beneath the open canopy of heaven. The brightest hours of the livelong day are dragged in drowsy, listless toil, or indolent repose; but the evening breeze invigorates the fainting frame, rouses the flagging spirit, and calls to dance, and revelry, and song, beneath a brilliant moon or a starlit sky. No necessity exists for those household comforts, which are indispensable to the inhabitants of colder zones, and the charms of domestic life are scarcely known in their perfect growth. But in the frozen North, for a large portion of the year, the pale and feeble rays of a clouded sun but partially dispel, for a few short hours, the chills and shades of a lingering dawn, and an early and tedious night. Snows impede the closing labors of harvest, and stiffening frosts aggravate the fatigues of the wayfarer, and the toils of the forest. Repose, society, and occupation alike, must, therefore, be sought at the domestic hearth. Secure from the tempest that howls without, the father and the brother here rest from their weary tasks; here the family circle is gathered around the evening meal, and lighter labor, cheered, not interrupted, by social intercourse, is resumed, and often protracted, till, like the student's vigils, it almost "outwatch the Bear." Here the child grows up under the ever watchful eye of the parent, in the first and best of schools, where lisping infancy is taught the rudiments of sacred and profane knowledge, and the older pupil is encouraged to con over by the evening taper, the lessons of the day, and seek from the father or a more advanced brother, a solution of the problems which juvenile industry has found too hard to master. The members of the domestic circle are thus brought into closer contact; parental authority assumes the gentler form of persuasive influence, and filial submission is elevated to affectionate and respectful observance. The necessity of mutual aid and forbearance, and the perpetual interchange of good offices, generate the tenderest kindliness of feeling, and a lasting warmth of attachment to home and its inmates, throughout the patriarchal circle.

Among the most important fruits of this domesticity of life, are the better appreciation of the worth of the female character, woman's higher rank as an object, not of passion, but of reverence, and the reciprocal moral influence which the two sexes exercise over each other. They are brought into close communion, under circumstances most favorable to preserve the purity of woman, and the decorum of man, and the character of each is modified, and its excesses restrained, by the example of the other. Man's rude energies are softened into something of the ready sympathy and dexterous helpfulness of woman; and woman, as she learns to prize and to reverence the independence, the heroic firmness, the patriotism of man, acquires and appropriates some tinge of his peculiar virtues. Such were the influences which formed the heart of the brave, good daughter of apostolic JOHN KNOX, who bearded that truculent pedant, JAMES I., and told him she would rather receive her husband's head in her lap, as it fell from the headsman's axe, than to consent that he should purchase his life by apostasy from the religion he had preached, and the God he had worshipped. To the same noble school belonged that goodly company of the Mothers of New England, who shrank neither from the dangers of the tempestuous sea, nor the hardships and sorrows of that first awful winter, but were ever at man's side, encouraging, aiding, consoling, in every peril, every trial, every grief. Had that grand and heroic exodus, like the mere commercial enterprises to which most colonies owe their foundation, been unaccompanied by woman, at its first outgoing, it had, without a visible miracle, assuredly failed, and the world had wanted its fairest example of the Christian virtues, its most unequivocal tokens, that the Providence, which kindled the pillar of fire to lead the wandering steps of its people, yet has its chosen tribes, to whom it vouchsafes its wisest guidance and its choicest blessings. Other communities, nations, races, may glory in the exploits of their fathers; but it has been reserved to us of New England to know and to boast, that Providence has made the virtues of our mothers a yet more indispensable condition, and certain ground, both of our past prosperity and our future hope.

The strength of the domestic feeling engendered by the influences which I have described, and the truer and more intelligent mutual regard between the sexes, which is attributable to the same causes, are the principal reasons why those monastic institutions, which strike at the very root of the social fabric, and are eminently hostile to the practice of the noblest and loveliest public and private virtues, have met with less success, and numbered fewer votaries in Northern than in Southern Christendom. The celibacy of the clergy was last adopted, and first abandoned, in the North; the follies of the Stylites, the lonely hermitages of the Thebaid, the silence of La Trappe, the vows, which, seeming to renounce the pleasures of the world, do but abjure its better sympathies, and in fine, all the selfish austerities of that corrupted Christianity, which grossly seeks to compound by a mortified body for an unsubdued heart, originated in climates unfavorable to the growth and exercise of the household virtues.

* From the Address before the New England Society.

THOMAS COLE.

THOMAS COLE, the artist, with whom the use of the pen for both prose and verse was as favorite an employment as the handling of the pencil, though so thoroughly identified with American landscape, was a native of England. He was born at Bolton-le-Moor, Lancashire, February 1, 1801. His father was one of those men who seem to possess every virtue in life, and still to be separated by some "thin partition" from success. He was a manufacturer; and the son, in his very boyhood, became a kind of operative artist, engraving simple designs for calico. He had, as a youth, a natural vein of poetry about him which was encouraged by an old Scotchman, who repeated to him the national ballads of his country; while his imaginative love of nature was heightened by falling in with an enthusiastic description of the beauties of the North American states. In 1819, the family came to Philadelphia, where Cole worked on rude wood-engraving for a short time, with an episode of a visit to the island of St. Eustatia, till they left for the west, settling at Steubenville, Ohio, where the young artist passed a life of poverty and privation, travelling about the country as a portrait painter; groping his way slowly, but effectually, in the region of art. His love of nature and the amusements of his favorite flute alleviated the roughness of the track. Finding, in spite of prudence and economy, a near prospect of starvation before him in that country, at that time, he turned towards the great cities of the Atlantic. An anecdote of this period is curious, but perhaps not uncommon on such occasions. He was taking a solitary walk, unusually agitated by a recent conversation with his father. "Well," said he to himself, aloud, at the same moment picking up a couple of good-sized pebbles, "I will put one of these upon the top of a stick; if I can throw and knock it off with the other, I will be a painter; if I miss it, I will give up the thought for ever." Stepping back some ten or twelve paces he threw, and knocked it off. He turned and went home immediately, and made known his unalterable resolution.*

At Philadelphia he patiently struggled and suffered, selling a couple of pictures for eleven dollars, and ornamenting various articles, such as bellows, brushes, and japan-ware, with figures, views, birds, and flowers. In 1825, at New York, a better fortune awaited him. His first success identified him with his chosen scenery of the Catskills. He had visited that region, and painted on his return a view of the *Falls*. This was purchased by Colonel Trumbull, who made it a theme of liberal eulogy; and, with the friendship and appreciation of Dunlap and Durand, Cole made the acquaintance of the public. He was a prosperous painter at once.

His pictures, from that time, may be divided into three classes: his minute and literal presentations of wild American scenery; his Italian views of Florence and Sicily, the result of his two European visits; and his moral and allegorical series, as the Course of Empire and the Voyage of Life. In 1836, and subsequently, he resided on the Hudson, near the village of Catskill, where his death took place February 11, 1847, at the age of forty-six.

Though no separate publications of his numerous writings have appeared, they are well represented in the congenial life by his friend, the Rev. Mr. Noble. He wrote verses from his boyhood. Without ever possessing the highest inevitable tact of poetic invention, to fix the enthusiastic conception in permanent classic expression, and lacking the advantage of that early scholastic training which might greatly have helped him to supply this deficiency by condensation, his numerous poems are never wanting in feeling and delicacy. They were not offered to the public for judgment; and when they are withdrawn from

Thomas Cole.

the sanctity of his portfolio, they should be judged for what they were, private confessions and consolations to himself, to his love of nature and the devotion of the religious sentiment. The entire narrative of his life is studded, in his biography, with passages from these poems as they occur in his journals; fragments artless, simple, and sincere, always witnessing to the delights of nature, and expressing the fine spirituality which he sought in his ideal pictures, and which beamed from his eye and countenance.

In 1835 he composed a dramatic poem in twelve parts, called *The Spirits of the Wilderness*, the scene of which is laid in the White Mountains. It was further prepared for the press in 1837, but still remains unpublished. His biographer speaks of it as "a work of singular originality and much poetic power and beauty." He was also, at the period of his death, collecting a volume of miscellaneous poems for publication.

Cole was also a good writer of prose. He once, in early life, wrote for the Philadelphia *Saturday Evening Post* a tale called "Emma Moreton," which embraced incidents and descriptions drawn from his recent visit to the West Indies. He projected a work on Art. His letters are easy and natural. Several of his sketches of travel, *A Visit to Volterra and Vallombrosa* in 1831, and an *Excursion to South Peak* of the Catskills, in 1846, have been published in the *Literary World* from the pages of his autobiographical diary which he entitled *Thoughts and Reminiscences*.*

His Eulogy was pronounced by his friend Bryant, in an elaborate and thoughtful oration delivered before the National Academy of Design, at the church of the Messiah in New York, in May, 1848. During his life the poet had dedicated to him a fine sonnet on occasion of his first journey to Europe.

SONNET.

Thine eyes shall see the light of distant skies:
  Yet, Cole! thy heart shall bear to Europe's strand
  A living image of thy native land,
Such as on thy own glorious canvas lies.
Lone lakes—savannas where the bison roves—
  Rocks rich with summer garlands—solemn streams—
Skies, where the desert eagle wheels and screams—
Spring bloom and autumn blaze of boundless groves.
Fair scenes shall greet thee where thou goest—fair,

* Life by Noble, p. 42.

* Literary World for 1849. Nos. 102, 105, 114.

But different—everywhere the trace of men,
Paths, homes, graves, ruins, from the lowest glen
To where life shrinks from the fierce Alpine air.
Gaze on them, till the tears shall dim thy sight,
But keep that earlier, wilder image bright.
Bryant.

A SUNSET.

I saw a glory in the etherial deep;
A glory such as from the higher heaven
Must have descended. Earth does never keep
In its embrace such beauty. Clouds were driven
As by God's breath, into unearthly forms,
And then did glow, and burn with living flames,
And hues so bright, so wonderful and rare,
That human language cannot give them names;
And light and shadow strangely linked their arms
In loveliness: and all continual were
In change; and with each change there came new charms.
Nor orient pearls, nor flowers in glittering dew
Nor golden tinctures, nor the insect's wings,
Nor purple splendors for imperial view,
Nor all that art or earth to mortals brings,
Can e'er compare with what the skies unfurled.
These are the wings of angels, I exclaimed,
Spread in their mystic beauty o'er the world.
Be ceaseless thanks to God that, in his love,
He gives such glimpses of the life above,
That we, poor pilgrims, on this darkling sphere,
Beyond its shadows may our hopes uprear.

TWILIGHT.

The woods are dark; but yet the lingering light
Spreads its last beauty o'er the western sky.
How lovely are the portals of the night,
When stars come out to watch the daylight die.

The woods are dark; but yet yon little bird
Is warbling by her newly furnished nest.
No sound beside in all the vale is heard;
But she for rapture cannot, cannot rest.

THE TREAD OF TIME.

Hark! I hear the tread of time,
Marching o'er the fields sublime.
Through the portals of the past,
When the stars by God were cast
On the deep, the boundless vast.

Onward, onward still he strides,
Nations clinging to his sides:
Kingdoms crushed he tramples o'er:
Fame's shrill trumpet, battle's roar,
Storm-like rise, then speak no more.

Lo! he nears us—awful Time—
Bearing on his wings sublime
All our seasons, fruit and flower,
Joy and hope, and love and power:
Ah, he grasps the present hour.
* * * * * *

Underneath his mantle dark,
See, a spectre grim and stark,
At his girdle like a sheath,
Without passion, voice or breath,
Ruin dealing: Death—'tis Death!

Stop the ruffian, Time!—lay hold!—
Is there then no power so bold?—
None to thwart him in his way?—
Wrest from him his precious prey,
And the tyrant robber slay?

Struggle not, my foolish soul:
Let Time's garments round thee roll.
Time, God's servant—think no scorn—
Gathers up the sheaves of corn,
Which the spectre, Death, hath shorn.

Brightly through the orient far
Soon shall rise a glorious star:
Cumbered then by Death no more,
Time shall fold his pinions hoar,
And be named the Evermore.

SONG OF A SPIRIT.

An awful privilege it is to wear a spirit's form,
And solitary live for aye on this vast mountain peak;
To watch, afar beneath my feet, the darkly-heaving storm,
And see its cloudy billows over the craggy ramparts break;
To hear the hurrying blast
Torment the groaning woods,
O'er precipices cast
The desolating floods;
To mark in wreathed fire
The crackling pines expire;
To list the earthquake and the thunder's voice
Round and beneath my everlasting throne;
Meanwhile, unscathed, untouched, I still rejoice,
And sing my hymn of gladness, all alone.
* * * * * * * *

First to salute the sun, when he breaks through the night,
I gaze upon him still when earth has lost her light.
When silence is most death-like,
And darkness deepest cast;
The streamlet's music breath-like,
And dew is settling fast;
Far through the azure depth above is heard my clarion sound,
Like tones of winds, and waves, and woods, and voices of the ground.
I spread my shadeless pinions wide o'er this my calm domain:
A solitary realm it is; but here I love to reign.

ALEXANDER H. EVERETT.

Alexander Hill Everett was the second son of the Rev. Oliver Everett, and elder brother of the Hon. Edward Everett. He was prepared for college at the free-school of Dorchester, entered Harvard University the youngest member of his class, and was graduated at its head in 1806. He passed the succeeding year as an assistant teacher in the Phillips Academy at Exeter, N. H., and in 1807 commenced the study of the law in the office of John Quincy Adams at Boston, where he soon after began his literary career as a contributor to the Monthly Anthology.

In 1809, on the appointment of Mr. Adams as Minister to Russia, Mr. Everett accompanied him as *attaché* to the legation, and resided at St. Petersburg for two years. In 1811 he passed through Sweden to England, where he remained during the winter, and after a short visit to Paris returned home in 1812.

Soon after his arrival he was admitted to the bar and commenced practice. The stirring nature of the public events which then agitated the country soon, however, drew him into politics. He published a series of articles in the year 1813 in the Patriot, the leading democratic paper of

Boston, in favor of the war, which were collected into a pamphlet, with the title *Remarks on the Governor's Speech*. He also wrote in this journal a series of articles against the Hartford Convention. He was in the same year nominated for the state senate, but defeated by the predominance of the opposition party. He also about this time, as the orator for the year of the Phi Beta Kappa Society, delivered an address on Burke, in which he combated the views of that statesman on the French revolution. It is characteristic of the state of public feeling, that, although the usual resolution requesting a copy for publication was passed, the resolve was never put in execution.

Soon after the treaty of peace Mr. Everett was appointed secretary of legation to Governor Eustis of Massachusetts, Minister to the Netherlands. After remaining a year or two in Holland he returned to the United States, and was appointed by Mr. Monroe the successor of Mr. Eustis on the withdrawal of that gentleman, the post having been meanwhile changed to a *charg'ship*. He retained the office for six years, from 1818 to 1824, conducting the negotiations relative to the commercial intercourse of the two nations, and the claims of his country for spoliations suffered during the French ascendency, with great ability.

His official duties being insufficient to occupy more than a portion of his time, he devoted his leisure to the preparation of a work entitled *Europe, or a General Survey of the Political Situation of the Principal Powers, with Conjectures on their Future Prospects, by a Citizen of the United States*. It was published in Boston and London in 1821. A remark, characteristic of the tone of English criticism at that time on American books, appeared in a notice in the London Morning Chronicle, to the effect that the name of the author on the title-page must be a fiction, as the work was not only too purely English but too idiomatic to be the product of a foreign pen. *Europe* was favorably received, and translated into German, with a commentary by the celebrated Professor Jacobi of Halle, and also into French and Spanish.

In 1822 Mr. Everett published *New Ideas on Population, with Remarks on the Theories of Godwin and Malthus*. The latter writer, in his celebrated work on population, had taken the ground that the demand for subsistence is everywhere greater than the means of its supply, that the evil could not be met by any measures of governmental or private charity, and that the only means of remedy was to check the increase of the race by discountenancing marriage. Godwin denied that the power of increase in population was as great as Malthus affirmed, and asserted that the rapid growth of America was due to emigration. In answer to these and other theorists Mr. Everett showed that increase of population leads to division of labor and consequent increase of production; that the assertion of Malthus that every community had exhausted their means of comfortable support, was not borne out by the example of any people, the means of support having universally increased with the growth of population; and that Malthus's position that every community must subsist on the produce of its own territory was also untrue, commerce furnishing a means by which, even in case of a community exhausting the products of their territory, the products of their industry could readily be exchanged, in a more or less direct form, for the provisions of other portions of the globe, whose entire productiveness is as yet far from being developed, much less exhausted.

During this period Mr. Everett also contributed a number of articles to the North American Review, then under the editorship of his brother Edward, most of which are on topics connected with the leading French authors. They are finished in style and elaborate in treatment. The discussion of the authorship of *Gil Blas*, *Biography of St. Pierre*, the review of *Geoffroy on Dramatic Literature*, a sketch of the *Private Life of Voltaire*, a pleasant paper on the *Art of Happiness*, by Droz, are among them. In 1824 he returned home on leave of absence, and passed the winter in the United States. In 1825 he was appointed by Mr. Adams, soon after he became President of the United States, Minister to Spain. He devoted himself with great fidelity to the duties of this position, and was active in urging the recognition of the independence of the recently formed Spanish republics of the American continent on their mother country. He invited Washington Irving to Madrid, made him an *attaché* of the legation, and facilitated the researches which led to the production of the Life of Columbus. He also procured and transmitted to Mr. Prescott a large portion of the historical material of which that gentleman has made such admirable use, and in numerous other modes advanced the interests of his country and countrymen. Although laboriously occupied by his diplomatic duties he still continued his contributions to the North American, and prepared a work entitled *America, or a General Survey of the Political Situation of the Principal Powers of the Western Continent, with Conjectures on their future Prospects, by a Citizen of the United States*, a companion to his previous volume on Europe.

In 1829 he returned to the United States, and succeeded Mr. Jared Sparks as editor of the Review to which he had long contributed. He conducted the work for about five years, during which he wrote a number of important articles for its pages. In 1830 he was elected a member of the state senate.

As chairman of a committee of the tariff convention of 1833, he drew up the memorial in reply to that prepared by Mr. Gallatin, which emanated from the free-trade convention of the previous year. He was also the author of the address issued by the Convention of 1831, nominating Henry Clay for the presidency. After the defeat of that statesman, and the proclamation of General Jackson against Nullification, he became a supporter of the administration.

In 1840 Mr. Everett was despatched as a confidential commissioner to Cuba, to act during the absence of the consul, and investigate the charges which had been made against him of connivance in the use of the American flag by slavers. He was occupied for two months in this manner, and a short time after received a call to the presidency of Jefferson College, Louisiana, which he accepted, but was obliged, soon after commencing the duties of the office, to return to the North in consequence of ill health.

In 1842 Mr. Everett was a frequent contributor to the Boston Miscellany* of articles in prose and poetry. Among the latter were translations from the Latin and Italian, and a somewhat elaborate Eastern tale, *The Hermitage of Candoo*, founded on a Sanskrit fable of the Brahma-Purana.

In 1845 and 1846 Mr. Everett published two volumes of *Critical and Miscellaneous Essays, with Poems*, containing a selection from his writings for the North American and Democratic Reviews, to the last of which he furnished in 1844 an extended biographical sketch of the revolutionary refugee, *Harro Harring*, and other periodicals. In 1845 he received the appointment from President Polk of Commissioner to China, and set out for his post on the 4th of July in the same year, but on arriving at Rio de Janeiro became so unwell that he returned home. He sailed a second time in the summer of 1846 and arrived at Canton, but died a few months after establishing himself in that city, June 28, 1847.

THE YOUNG AMERICAN.

Scion of a mighty stock!
Hands of iron—hearts of oak—
Follow with unflinching tread
Where the noble fathers led!

Craft and subtle treachery,
Gallant youth! are not for thee:
Follow thou in word and deeds
Where the God within thee leads!

Honesty with steady eye,
Truth and pure simplicity,
Love that gently winneth hearts,—
These shall be thy only arts.

Prudent in the council train,
Dauntless on the battle plain,
Ready at the country's need
For her glorious cause to bleed.

Where the dews of night distil
Upon Vernon's holy hill;
Where above it gleaming far
Freedom lights her guiding star:

Thither turn the steady eye,
Flashing with a purpose high!
Thither with devotion meet,
Often turn the pilgrim feet!

Let the noble motto be
God,—the Country,—Liberty!
Planted on Religion's rock,
Thou shalt stand in every shock.

Laugh at danger far or near!
Spurn at baseness—spurn at fear!
Still with persevering might,
Speak the truth, and do the right!

So shall Peace, a charming guest,
Dove-like in thy bosom rest,
So shall Honor's steady blaze
Beam upon thy closing days.

Happy if celestial favor
Smile upon the high endeavor;
Happy if it be thy call
In the holy cause to fall.

* The Boston Miscellany of Literature and Fashion was edited by Nathan Hale, jr., and was published in two volumes, from January to December, 1842. It was a worthy attempt to infuse into the popular periodical literature a higher literary interest. Among its contributors were, besides Alexander Everett, J. R. Lowell, W. W. Story, Edward Everett, Nathaniel Hawthorne, T. W. Parsons, and others.

THE ART OF BEING HAPPY.*

According to our belief, the common sense of the world is therefore, as we have already remarked, against Mr. Droz on this point, and in favor of the diligent pursuit of some regular occupation, as a principal element of happiness. It is true that we hear at times from the Italians, of the *dolce far niente*, or the delight of having nothing to do; but even in the same quarter there are not wanting respectable authorities in favor of a different system. The Marquis of Spinola, an Italian general, celebrated for his military exploits in the war of the independence of the Netherlands, passed the latter part of his life in retirement, upon a handsome pension, and of course in the full fruition of the *dolce far niente;* but being one of those persons without occupation, who are also unoccupied, he found himself (as usually happens, even according to our author, with gentlemen of this description) rather ill at ease. While in this situation, he was informed of the death of one of his ancient comrades of inferior rank in the army, a captain perhaps, or possibly a colonel; and upon inquiring into the nature of his disease, was answered that he died of having nothing to do. *Mori della malattia di non tenere niente a fare. Basta*, replied the unhappy Marquis, with a strong feeling of sympathy in the fate of his departed brother of the war, *basta per un generale.* "'T is enough to have killed him, had he been a general."

Such, even on Italian authority, are the pleasures of the *dolce far niente.* They appear to be enjoyed in the same way in other ranks and walks of life. Read, for example, in Lafontaine, the story of the cheerful cobbler rendered miserable by a present of a hundred crowns, and finally returning in despair to lay them at the feet of his would-be benefactor, and recover his good humor and his last. Behold the luckless schoolboy (to recur again to one of the examples at which we have already hinted), torn from his natural occupation on some Thursday or Saturday afternoon, and perishing under the burden of a holiday. See him hanging at his mother's side, and begging her, with tears in his eyes, to give him something to do; while she, poor woman, aware that the evil is irremediable, can only console him, by holding out the prospect of a return to school the next day. Observe the tradesman who has made his fortune (as the phrase is), and retired from business, or the opulent proprietor enjoying his dignified leisure. How he toils at the task of doing nothing; as a ship without ballast at sea, when it falls calm after a heavy blow, labors more without stirring an inch, than in going ten knots an hour with a good breeze. "How he groans and sweats," as Shakespeare has it, under a happy life! How he cons over at night, for the third time, the newspaper which he read through twice, from beginning to end, immediately after breakfast! A wealthy capitalist, reduced by good fortune to this forlorn condition, has assured us, that he often begs the domestics, who are putting his room in order, to prolong the operation as much as possible, that he may enjoy again, for a little while, the lost delight of superintending and witnessing the performance of useful labor.

But this is not the worst. No sooner does he find himself in the state of unoccupied blessedness, than a host of unwished for visitants (doubtless the same with those who took possession of the swept and garnished lodgings of him in scripture) enter on his premises, and declare his body good prize. *Dyspep-*

* From an article in the North American Review for July, 1836, on an *Essai sur l'Art d'Etre Heureux*, par Joseph Droz, de l'Academie Française.

sia (a new name of horror) plucks from his lips the untasted morsel and the brimming bowl, bedims his eyes with unnatural blindness, and powders his locks with premature old age. *Hypochondria* (the accursed *blues* of the fathers) ploughs his cheeks with furrows, and heaps a perpetual cloud upon his brow. *Hepatitis* (like the vulture of Prometheus) gnaws at his liver. *Rheumatism* racks his joints; *Gout* grapples him by the great toe: so that what with "black spirits and white, blue spirits and grey," the poor man suffers martyrdom in every nerve and fibre, until *Palsy* or *Apoplexy*, after all the kindest of the tribe, gives him the *coup de grace*, and releases him from his misery. His elysium is much like that of the departed Grecian heroes in the Odyssey, who frankly avowed to Ulysses, that they would rather be the meanest day-laborers above ground, than reign supreme over all the shades below. * * * * * * * *

Has our author fully considered what he is saying, when he recommends to his disciples to take no interest in their employment, whatever it may be; to work at it carelessly and negligently, just long enough to obtain a bare living, and then hurry home to bed, or to the tavern to keep *Saint Monday?* Meeting him on his own ground, and taking our examples from the middling and lower walks of life, does Mr. Droz really mean to tell us, that a tailor, for instance, will best consult his happiness by working as little as possible at his trade, receiving as few orders as he can, executing those which he receives in a careless manner, disappointing his customers in the time of sending home their clothes, and instead of wielding incessantly the shears and needle, passing most of his precious hours in spinning street-yarn? Is that barber in a fair way to realize the *summum bonum*, who intentionally hacks the chins of the public with dull and wretched razors, or burns their ears with his curling tongs, on purpose to deter as many of them as he can from coming into his shop? Admitting for argument's sake (what no honorable man would allow for a moment), that the only object of exercising a profession is to obtain a bare subsistence; is it not perfectly clear, that an artist, who should follow the system of our author, would completely fail, even in this miserable purpose? If a tailor send home a coat awkwardly and unfashionably cut, or negligently made up, the indignant customer forthwith returns it on his hands, and transfers his orders to a more industrious and attentive workman. From making a few coats, and those badly, the recreant knight of the shears would very soon come to have none at all to make, and would inevitably starve by the side of his cold goose, upon a vacant shopboard. A barber, in like manner, who should adopt the ingenious practices alluded to above, for clearing his shop of the surplus number of long beards, would not probably find the ebbing tide stop exactly at the point necessary for supplying him with bread and bedclothes. He would soon find himself, like Ossian's aged heroes, lonely in his hall. From keeping his own shop, he would be compelled to enter as journeyman in that of another, and by continuing to pursue the same process, would sink in succession through the several gradations of house-servant, street porter, and vagabond, into the hospital, the port where all who sail by our author's chart and compass will naturally bring up. The only way, in fact, by which a man can expect to turn his labor to account, in any occupation, is by doing the best he can, and by putting his heart into his business, whatever it may be. He then takes the rank among his brothers of the trade, to which his talents entitle him; and if he cannot rise to the head of his art, he will at least be respectable, and will realize an honorable living. It is not every barber that can aspire to the fame of a Smallpeace, a Higgins, or a Williams; but any one who is diligent and assiduous in his shop, and who takes a just pride in seeing his customers leave it with glossy chins, well dressed hair, and neatly shaped *favorites*, should his natural aptitude be even something less than firstrate, will yet never want the comforts of life for himself and his family through the week, his five dollar bill to deposit in the savings bank on Saturday evening, and his extra joint to entertain a brother Strap on Sunday. And while he thus realizes an ample revenue, the zealous and attentive artist reaps, as he goes along through life, the best reward of his labor in the pleasure afforded him by the gratification of his honest pride, and the approbation of his fellow citizens.

JOHN, the brother of Edward and Alexander Everett, was born at Dorchester, Mass., February 22, 1801. He was educated in the Boston schools, where he was distinguished as a fine declaimer, and was graduated at Harvard in 1818. In the same year he accompanied the Rev. Horace Holley,* President of the Transylvania University, at Lexington, Kentucky, to that place, where he was employed for a short time as a tutor. On his return to Massachusetts he entered the law school at Cambridge, and soon after visited Europe as an *attaché* to the American legation at Brussels, during the *chargéship* of his brother Alexander. He next returned to Boston, studied law in the office of Daniel Webster, and contributed a few articles to the North American Review, then edited by his brother Edward. He was also the author of a few spirited odes sung at the celebrations of debating clubs, of which, from his readiness as an extempore speaker and warm interest in the political and other questions of the day, he was a prominent member. He was admitted to the bar in 1825, but the promise of an active career of honor and usefulness was soon after disappointed by his death, February 12, 1826.

JAMES G. AND MARY E. BROOKS.

JAMES GORDON BROOKS, the son of David Brooks, an officer of the Revolutionary army, was born at Claverack on the Hudson, September 3, 1801. He was graduated at Union College in 1819, and studied law at Poughkeepsie, but never engaged actively in the practice of the profession. It was in this place that he commenced his poetical career by the publication in the newspapers of the place of a few fugitive poems, with the signa-

* Horace Holley was born at Salisbury, Connecticut, February 13, 1781, graduated at Yale College in 1803, studied theology under the care of President Dwight, and was settled at Greenfield Hill. In 1809 he became a Unitarian, and the minister of the Hollis street church, Boston. He was a warm federalist, and often introduced his political opinions into the pulpit, where he was highly celebrated for his oratorical powers, graceful delivery, and fine personal appearance.

In 1818 Dr. Holley accepted the presidency of Transylvania University, where he remained nine years. He died of the yellow fever on his passage, after his resignation, from New Orleans to New York, July 31, 1827.

Dr. Holley was the author of addresses delivered in 1815 before the Washington Benevolent Society of Boston; in 1817 on the anniversary of the landing of the Pilgrims at Plymouth; of a funeral eulogy on Colonel James Morrison, a munificent benefactor of Transylvania University in 1823; of several published sermons, and articles in the Western Review and a few other periodicals. Several of these are reprinted in the graceful and touching memoir of the writer, by his wife.

ture of Florio, which attracted much attention. Various conjectures were made respecting their authorship, but the author succeeded in maintaining his incognito not only among his neighbors, but also in his own household.

James G Brooks

In 1823 Mr. Brooks removed to New York, where he became the literary editor of the Minerva, a belles-lettres journal which he conducted about two years. He then started the Literary Gazette, a weekly journal on the model of the English publication of the same name, which, after being continued for a few months, was united with the Athenæum, and conducted under the care of Mr. Brooks and Mr. James Lawson for two years. He then became an editor of the Morning Courier, with which he remained connected for about the same period. In these journals, and in the Commercial Advertiser, most of his poems were published, with the signature of Florio. They were great favorites, and placed the author in the popular estimate of his day in the same rank with Drake and Halleck as one of the poetical trio of the town.

In 1828 he married Miss Mary Elizabeth Akin, a young lady, a native of Poughkeepsie, who had been from an early age a writer of verse for periodicals under the signature of *Norna*. The year after a volume entitled *The Rivals of Este and other Poems, by James G. and Mary E. Brooks*, appeared.

In 1830 the pair removed to Winchester, Virginia, where Mr. Brooks edited a newspaper for a few years. In 1838 they again changed their residence to Rochester, and afterwards to Albany, in both of which places Mr. Brooks was connected with the press.

Mr. Brooks died at Albany in 1841. His widow has since that event resided, with their only child, a daughter, in the city of New York.

The productions of Mr. and Mrs. Brooks are separately arranged in the joint volume of their poems. The story from which the volume takes its name is by the lady, and is drawn from the ample storehouse of Italian family history. The Hebrew Melodies, versified renderings of passages from the Psalms and the Prophets, are also by her. The remainder of Mrs. Brooks's portion of the volume is occupied by other poems on topics of Italian romance, descriptions of natural scenery, and a few lyrical pieces. We select one of the Hebrew Melodies:—

JEREMIAH X. 17.

From the halls of our fathers in anguish we fled,
Nor again will its marble re-echo our tread;
For a breath like the Siroc has blasted our name,
And the frown of Jehovah has crushed us in shame.

His robe was the whirlwind, his voice was the thunder,
And earth at his footstep was riven asunder;
The mantle of midnight had shrouded the sky,
But we knew where He stood by the flash of his eye.

Oh, Judah! how long must thy weary ones weep,
Far, far from the land where their forefathers sleep;
How long ere the glory that brightened the mountain
Will welcome the exile to Siloa's fountain!

Passing to the latter half of the volume, we find at its commencement a poem on Genius, delivered originally before the Phi Beta Kappa Society at Yale. The briefer pieces which follow are, like the one which we have named, quiet in expression and of a pensive cast. A number devoted to the topic of death have a pathos and solemnity befitting the dirge. Others on the stirring theme of liberty, and the struggles in its behalf in Greece and elsewhere, are full of animation and spirit. All are smooth and harmonious in versification.

Mr. Brooks enjoyed a high social position in New York, where he was greatly esteemed for his ready wit and conversational powers, as well as generosity and amiability of character. He was a fluent and successful prose writer.

Mrs. Brooks, in addition to her literary abilities, possesses much skill as a designer. The plates in the Natural History of the State of New York, by her brother-in-law, Mr. James Hall, are from drawings made by her from nature.

Mrs. Hall, the sister of Mrs. Brooks, is the author of several pleasing poems which have appeared under the signature of Hinda.

FREEDOM.

When the world in throngs shall press
To the battle's glorious van;
When the oppressed shall seek redress,
And shall claim the rights of man;
Then shall freedom smile again
On the earth and on the main.

When the tide of war shall roll
Like imperious ocean's surge,
From the tropic to the pole,
And to earth's remotest verge
Then shall valor dash the gem
From each tyrant's diadem.

When the banner is unfurled,
Like a silver cloud in air,
And the champions of the world
In their might assemble there;
Man shall rend his iron chain,
And redeem his rights again.

Then the thunderbolts shall fall,
In their fury on each throne,
Where the despot holds in thrall
Spirits nobler than his own;
And the cry of all shall be,
Battle's shroud or liberty!

Then the trump shall echo loud,
Stirring nations from afar,
In the daring line to crowd,
And to draw the blade of war
While the tide of life shall rain,
And encrimson every plain.

Then the Saracen shall flee
From the city of the Lord;
Then, the light of victory
Shall illume Judea's sword:
And new liberty shall shine
On the Plains of Palestine.

Then the Turk shall madly view,
How his crescent waxes dim;
Like the waning moon whose hue
Fades away on ocean's brim;

Then the cross of Christ shall stand
On that consecrated land.

Yea, the light of freedom smiles
On the Grecian phalanx now,
Breaks upon Ionia's isles,
And on Ida's lofty brow;
And the shouts of battle swell,
Where the Spartan lion fell!

Where the Spartan lion fell,
Proud and dauntless in the strife:
How triumphant was his knell!
How sublime his close of life!
Glory shone upon his eye,
Glory which can never die!

Soon shall earth awake in might;
Retribution shall arise;
And all regions shall unite,
To obtain the glorious prize;
And oppression's iron crown,
To the dust be trodden down.

When the Almighty shall deform
Heaven in his hour of wrath;
When the angel of the storm,
Sweeps in fury on his path;
Then shall tyranny be hurled
From the bosom of the world.

Yet, O freedom! yet awhile,
All mankind shall own thy sway;
And the eye of God shall smile
On thy brightly dawning day;
And all nations shall adore
At thine altar evermore.

STANZAS.

Life hath its sunshine; but the ray
Which flashes on its stormy wave
Is but the beacon of decay,
A meteor gleaming o'er the grave;
And though its dawning hour is bright
With fancy's gayest colouring,
Yet o'er its cloud-encumbered night,
Dark ruin flaps his raven wing.

Life hath its flowers; and what are they?
The buds of early love and truth,
Which spring and wither in a day,
The gems of warm, confiding youth:
Alas! those buds decay and die,
Ere ripened and matured in bloom;
E'en in an hour, behold them lie
Upon the still and lonely tomb!

Life hath its pang of deepest thrill;
Thy sting, relentless memory!
Which wakes not, pierces not, until
The hour of joy hath ceased to be.
Then, when the heart is in its pall,
And cold afflictions gather o'er,
Thy mournful anthem doth recall
Bliss which hath died to bloom no more.

Life hath its blessings; but the storm
Sweeps like the desert wind in wrath,
To sear and blight the loveliest form
Which sports on earth's deceitful path.
O! soon the wild heart-broken wail,
So changed from youth's delightful tone,
Floats mournfully upon the gale,
When all is desolate and lone.

Life hath its hope; a matin dream,
A cankered flower, a setting sun,
Which casts a transitory gleam
Upon the even's cloud of dun
Pass but an hour, the dream hath fled,
The flowers on earth forsaken lie;
The sun hath set, whose lustre shed
A light upon the shaded sky.

JACOB B. MOORE.

JACOB BAILEY MOORE, the father of the subject of the present sketch, was born September 5, 1772, at Georgetown, on the Kennebeck, Maine. He was descended from a Scotch family, who emigrated to New England in the early part of the eighteenth century. Following the profession of his father, a physician, and during the Revolutionary war surgeon of a national vessel, he settled, after qualifying himself almost entirely by his own exertions, in the practice of medicine at Andover, in 1796, where he remained until he accepted, in 1812, the appointment of surgeon's mate in the Eleventh regiment of United States Infantry. He remained in the service until December of the same year, when he retired, much broken in health, and died on the 10th of January following.

Dr. Moore was an excellent musician, and composed several pieces, a few of which were published in Holyoke's Repository. He was also the author of numerous songs and epistles, which appeared in the newspapers of the day.

Jacob Bailey, the son of Dr. Moore, was born at Andover, October 31, 1797. He was apprenticed, while a boy, in the office of the New Hampshire Patriot, one of the leading journals of New England, and which is remarkable for the number of distinguished editors and politicians it has furnished, alike from its type-setting and editorial desks, to all parts of the country.

The Patriot was at this time owned by the celebrated Isaac Hill.* At the expiration of his indentures Mr. Moore became the partner of Mr. Hill, and afterwards, by marriage with Mr. Hill's sister, his brother-in-law. The two conducted the paper until January, 1823, when the partnership expired. Mr. Moore then devoted himself to the bookselling and publishing business.

He had previously, in April, 1822, commenced the publication of *Collections,—Topographical, Historical, and Biographical, relating principally to New Hampshire.* He was assisted

* Isaac Hill, one of the most influential political writers of the country, was born at Cambridge, Mass., April 6, 1788. He was taught the trade of a printer, and in 1809 removed to Concord, N. H., where he purchased the office of the American Patriot, a paper started about six months before, which he discontinued, and on the 18th of April, 1809, published the first number of the New Hampshire Patriot, a newspaper he continued to edit until 1829, filling at various times within the same period, the offices of senator and representative in the State Legislature. He was appointed Second Comptroller of the Treasury by General Jackson, but was rejected by the Senate, a rejection which led to his election by the Legislature of his state, as a member of the body which had refused to confirm his nomination. He remained in the Senate until 1836, when he was elected Governor of his State, an office which he filled during three successive terms. He afterwards established Hill's New Hampshire Patriot, a paper in which he opposed certain new measures of the Democratic party, of which he had long been the leader in the state, with such success, that he regained his impaired influence, and united his new paper with the Patriot, in which he had so long battled. He also, in January, 1839, commenced an agricultural periodical, The Farmer's Monthly Visitor, which is still continued.

The activity of his career was after this period much impaired by disease. He, however, still continued his interest in politics, and was an influential advocate of the Compromise Measures of 1850. He died at Washington, March 22, 1851.

in the editorship of this work by Dr. J. Farmer.* The publication comprised original articles of research, on topics embraced in its plan, and reprints of curious manuscripts, tracts, poems, and fugitive productions, illustrating the same topic. A portion of its pages was also devoted to reviews and other magazine matter, of a contemporary character. It was conducted with much ability until its close, in December, 1824. It forms, in its completed shape, a series of three octavo volumes.

The publication we have named was one of the first devoted to local history in the country. It did good service in calling attention to many important subjects, and fostering a spirit of close historical inquiry.

During the continuance of this work Mr. Moore also prepared and published with Dr. Farmer, *A Gazetteer of the State of New Hampshire*, in a duodecimo volume.

In 1824 Mr. Moore published *Annals of the Town of Concord, from its first Settlement in the year* 1726 *to the year* 1823, *with several Biographical Sketches; to which is added, A Memoir of the Penacook Indians*,† a work of much interest, research, and value.

In 1826 Mr. Moore commenced *The New Hampshire Journal*, a political paper, which he maintained with ability and influence until December, 1829, when it passed into other hands, and was soon after united with the New Hampshire Statesman. In 1828 he was elected a representative to the State Legislature, and in 1829 appointed sheriff of the county of Merrimack, an office which he retained for five years. After being connected for a short time with the *Concord Statesman*, he removed in 1839 to the city of New York, where he became the editor of *The Daily Whig*, an influential journal during the Harrison campaign. In 1840 he published *The Laws of Trade in the United States:* being an abstract of the statutes of the several States and Territories concerning Debtors and Creditors; a small volume, designed as a popular manual on the subject. After the election, he obtained an important clerkship in the Post-office department at Washington. On the accession of Mr. Polk, in 1845, he was removed, and returning to New York became librarian of the New York Historical Society.

In this position, congenial to his tastes as an historian, Mr. Moore remained, devoting himself earnestly to the preservation, arrangement, and enlargement of one of the most valuable collections of works illustrative of American History in existence, until by the changing fortunes of politics his friends were again placed in power in 1848, and he received the appointment of postmaster to San Francisco.

In this office Mr. Moore rendered an important service to the country by his indefatigable labors in systematizing the business of the department, under circumstances of unusual difficulty. He returned after the next change of administration, with a disease contracted in California, which closed his career a few months after, on the first of September, 1853.

In 1846 Mr. Moore published the first volume of the *Memoirs of American Governors*, embracing those of New Plymouth, from 1620 to 1692, and of Massachusetts Bay, from 1630 to 1689. It was his design to continue the series until it comprised Memoirs of the Colonial and Provincial Governors to the time of the Revolution. The portion relating to New England was left by him in MS., ready for the press, and much of the remainder of the work in a fragmentary form.

Mr. Moore was throughout his life an active collector of historical material. Even in California he found time to preserve the newspaper and fugitive literature of the eventful period of his sojourn.

Henry Eaton Moore, a brother of Jacob B. Moore, was born at Andover, N. H., 21st July, 1808. He served his time with his brother and Isaac Hill. He published the Grafton Journal at Plymouth, N. H., from the 1st January, 1825, till March, 1826, when it ceased. During the latter portion of his life he gave his whole attention to music; became a thorough proficient in the science, and distinguished as a teacher and composer. He was author of the *Musical Catechism; Merrimack Collection of Instrumental Music; New Hampshire Collection of Church Music; The Choir; a Collection of Anthems, Choruses, and Set Pieces; and the Northern Harp—a Collection of Sacred Harmony*. He died at East Cambridge, Mass., October 23, 1841.

John Weeks Moore, another brother of the same family, was born at Andover, N. H., April 11, 1807; was educated as a printer by his brother, Jacob B. Moore. He has been connected with several journals, and edited the Bellows Falls Gazette, Vt., for several years. His principal work is the *Complete Encyclopædia of Music,—Elementary, Technical, Historical, Biographical, Vocal, and Instrumental.**

WILLIAM H. SEWARD.

William Henry Seward, the son of Dr. Samuel S. Seward of Florida, Orange County, New York, was born in that village on the sixteenth of May, 1801. His early fondness for books induced his parents to give him a liberal education, and after a preparation at various schools in the neighbor-

* John Farmer was born at Chelmsford, Mass., June 12, 1789. He was a descendant of Edward Farmer, who emigrated from Warwickshire to Billerica, Mass., in 1760. He received the limited education afforded in his boyhood at the common schools, and at the age of sixteen became a clerk in a store at Amherst, New Hampshire. In 1810 he abandoned this occupation for that of school-keeping. He next studied medicine, and opened an apothecary's store at Concord, in 1821, with Dr. Samuel Morril, a circumstance to which he owes the title, popularly bestowed, of Doctor, having never completed a course of medical studies or applied for a degree.

It was in this position that he continued, in his leisure hours, to the close of his life, August 13, 1838, the laborious researches which he had already commenced, in the annals of New England.

Dr. Farmer's chief work is his *Genealogical Register of the First Settlers of New England, &c.; to which are added, various Biographical and Genealogical Notes*,* in which he traces the families of New England to their foundation in this country. He also prepared a new edition of Belknap's History of New Hampshire,† containing various corrections and illustrations of that work, and additional facts and notices of persons and events, therein mentioned.

Dr. Farmer was also the author of several tracts relating to local history, and a frequent contributor to the Collections of the Massachusetts and New Hampshire Historical Societies.

† pp. 112.

* Lancaster, Mass., 8vo. pp. 352. † Dover, N. H., 8vo. pp. 512.

* Roy. 8vo. pp. 1004. Boston: 1854.

hood of his residence, he entered Union College in 1816. After completing his course at that institution with distinguished honor, he studied law at New York with John Anthon, and afterwards with John Duer and Ogden Hoffman. Soon after his admission to the bar he commenced practice in Auburn, New York, where he married in 1824.

Mr. Seward rapidly rose to distinction in his profession. He took an active interest in favor of the re-election of John Quincy Adams to the Presidency, and presided at a convention of the young men of the state, held in furtherance of that object in Utica, August 12, 1828. In 1830 he was nominated and elected by the anti-masonic party a member of the State Senate, where he remained for four years. In 1833 he made a tour in Europe of a few months with his father, during which he wrote home a series of letters which were published in the Albany Evening Journal. He was nominated in 1834 as the candidate of the Whig party for the office of Governor of the State, and was defeated, but on his re-nomination in 1838 was elected. During his administration, his recommendation of the change in the school system, called for by the Roman Catholics, and which was finally adopted, caused much discussion and opposition.

His administration was one crowded with important events, and his course on many disputed questions was in opposition on some occasions to his party friends as well as political opponents, but was universally regarded as marked by personal ability. He was re-elected in 1840, but in 1842, declining a re-nomination, retired to the practice of his profession at Auburn. During the six following years he was principally engaged in this manner, appearing in the course of his duties as counsel in several important trials in the state and national tribunals with great success. He took an active part as a speaker in the presidential campaigns of 1844 and 1848, and in February, 1849, was chosen by a large majority United States Senator. On the expiration of his term in 1855, he was re-elected to the same body.

Mr. Seward has taken a prominent position in the Senate as an opponent of the compromise of 1850, and of the repeal of the Missouri compromise. In 1853 an edition of his works was published in New York in three octavo volumes, containing a complete collection of his speeches in the state and national senate, and before popular assemblies, with his messages as governor, his forensic arguments, a number of miscellaneous addresses, his letters from Europe, and selections from his public correspondence. One of the most valuable portions of these volumes, in a literary and historical point of view, is the *Notes on New York*, originally issued as the Introduction to the Natural History of New York, published by the legislature in 1842. It extends to 172 octavo pages, and contains a carefully prepared and highly interesting review of the intellectual progress of the state in science, literature, and art.

THE AMERICAN PEOPLE—THEIR MORAL AND INTELLECTUAL DEVELOPMENT.*

A kind of reverence is paid by all nations to antiquity. There is no one that does not trace its lineage from the gods, or from those who were especially favored by the gods. Every people has had its age of gold, or Augustan age, or heroic age—an age, alas! for ever passed. These prejudices are not altogether unwholesome. Although they produce a conviction of declining virtue, which is unfavorable to generous emulation, yet a people at once ignorant and irreverential would necessarily become licentious. Nevertheless, such prejudices ought to be modified. It is untrue, that in the period of a nation's rise from disorder to refinement, it is not able to continually surpass itself. We see the present, plainly, distinctly, with all its coarse outlines, its rough inequalities, its dark blots, and its glaring deformities. We hear all its tumultuous sounds and jarring discords. We see and hear the past, through a distance which reduces all its inequalities to a plane, mellows all its shades into a pleasing hue, and subdues even its hoarsest voices into harmony. In our own case, the prejudice is less erroneous than in most others. The revolutionary age was truly a heroic one. Its exigencies called forth the genius, and the talents, and the virtues of society, and they ripened amid the hardships of a long and severe trial. But there were selfishness, and vice, and factions, then, as now, although comparatively subdued and repressed. You have only to consult impartial history, to learn that neither public faith, nor public loyalty, nor private virtue, culminated at that period in our own country, while a mere glance at the literature, or at the stage, or at the politics of any European country, in any previous age, reveals the fact that it was marked, more distinctly than the present, by licentious morals and mean ambition.

Reasoning *à priori* again, as we did in another case, it is only just to infer in favor of the United States an improvement of morals from their established progress in knowledge and power; otherwise, the philosophy of society is misunderstood, and we must change all our courses, and henceforth seek safety in imbecility, and virtue in superstition and ignorance.

What shall be the test of the national morals? Shall it be the eccentricity of crimes? Certainly not; for then we must compare the criminal eccentricity of to-day with that of yesterday. The result of the comparison would be only this, that the crimes of society change with changing circumstances.

Loyalty to the state is a public virtue. Was it ever deeper-toned or more universal than it is now? I know there are ebullitions of passion and discontent, sometimes breaking out into disorder and violence; but was faction ever more effectually disarmed and harmless than it is now? There is a loyalty that springs from the affection that we bear to our native soil. This we have as strong as any people. But it is not the soil alone, nor yet the soil beneath our feet and the skies over our heads, that constitute our country. It is its freedom, equality, justice, greatness, and glory. Who among us is so low as to be insensible of an interest in them? Four hundred thousand natives of other lands every year voluntarily renounce their own sovereigns, and swear fealty to our own. Who has ever known an American to transfer his allegiance permanently to a foreign power?

The spirit of the laws, in any country, is a true index to the morals of a people, just in proportion to the power they exercise in making them. Who complains here or elsewhere, that crime or immorality blots our statute-books with licentious enactments?

The character of a country's magistrates, legislators, and captains, chosen by a people, reflects their own. It is true that in the earnest canvassing which

* From an Address at Yale College, 1854.

so frequently recurring elections require, suspicion often follows the magistrate, and scandal follows in the footsteps of the statesman. Yet, when his course has been finished, what magistrate has left a name tarnished by corruption, or what statesman has left an act or an opinion so erroneous that decent charity cannot excuse, though it may disapprove? What chieftain ever tempered military triumph with so much moderation as he who, when he had placed our standard on the battlements of the capital of Mexico, not only received an offer of supreme authority from the conquered nation, but declined it?

The manners of a nation are the outward form of its inner life. Where is woman held in so chivalrous respect, and where does she deserve that eminence better? Where is property more safe, commercial honor better sustained, or human life more sacred?

Moderation is a virtue in private and in public life. Has not the great increase of private wealth manifested itself chiefly in widening the circle of education and elevating the standard of popular intelligence? With forces which, if combined and directed by ambition, would subjugate this continent at once, we have made only two very short wars—the one confessedly a war of defence, and the other ended by paying for a peace and for a domain already fully conquered.

Where lies the secret of the increase of virtue which has thus been established? I think it will be found in the entire emancipation of the consciences of men from either direct or indirect control by established ecclesiastical or political systems. Religious classes, like political parties, have been left to compete in the great work of moral education, and to entitle themselves to the confidence and affection of society, by the purity of their faith and of their morals.

I am well aware that some, who may be willing to adopt the general conclusions of this argument, will object that it is not altogether sustained by the action of the government itself, however true it may be that it is sustained by the great action of society. I cannot enter a field where truth is to be sought among the disputations of passion and prejudice. I may say, however, in reply first, that the governments of the United States, although more perfect than any other, and although they embrace the great ideas of the age more fully than any other, are, nevertheless, like all other governments, founded on compromises of some abstract truths and of some natural rights.

As government is impressed by its constitution, so it must necessarily act. This may suffice to explain the phenomenon complained of. But it is true, also, that no government ever did altogether act out, purely and for a long period, all the virtues of its original constitution. Hence it is that we are so well told by Bolingbroke, that every nation must perpetually renew its constitution or perish. Hence, moreover, it is a great excellence of our system, that sovereignty resides, not in Congress and the president, nor yet in the governments of the states, but in the people of the United States. If the sovereign be just and firm and uncorrupted, the governments can always be brought back from any aberrations, and even the constitutions themselves, if in any degree imperfect, can be amended. This great idea of the sovereignty of the people over their government glimmers in the British system, while it fills our own with a broad and glowing light.

> Let not your king and parliament in one,
> Much less apart, mistake themselves for that
> Which is most worthy to be thought upon,
> Nor think they are essentially the STATE.
> Let them not fancy that the authority
> And privileges on them bestowed,
> Conferred, are to set up a majesty,
> Or a power or a glory of their own:
> But let them know it was for a deeper life
> Which they but represent;
> That there's on earth a yet auguster thing,
> Veiled though it be, than parliament or king.

Gentlemen, you are devoted to the pursuit of knowledge in order that you may impart it to the state. What Fenelon was to France, you may be to your country. Before you teach, let me enjoin upon you to study well the capacity and the disposition of the American people. I have tried to prove to you only that while they inherit the imperfections of humanity they are yet youthful, apt, vigorous, and virtuous, and therefore, that they are worthy, and will make noble uses of your best instructions.

WILLIAM H FURNESS.

WILLIAM HENRY FURNESS was graduated at Harvard College in 1820; studied theology, and soon after his ordination in 1823, became the minister of a Unitarian church in Philadelphia. He published in 1836 a volume on the *Four Gospels*, which he expanded into a large work in 1838, entitled *Jesus and His Biographers*. He is also the author of *A Life of Christ*; a manual of *Domestic Worship* and *Family Prayer Book*; and a number of published discourses, lectures, addresses, and contributions to reviews and other periodicals.

Dr. Furness has translated Schiller's "Song of the Bell," and a number of other German poems, with great beauty and fidelity. A portion of these have been collected in a small volume with the title, *Song of the Bell, and Other Poems*. He is also the author of several hymns included in the collection in use by his denomination.

His theological position is somewhat peculiar and quite conspicuous, even in a denomination so strongly marked by individualities as his own. He accepts for the most part the miraculous facts of the New Testament, yet accounts for them by the moral and spiritual forces resulting from the pre-eminent character of the Saviour, who, in his view, is an exalted form of humanity.

As a preacher, Dr. Furness has great power, and his sermons, of which he has a volume in press, are remarkable for the union of speculation and feeling.

HYMN.

What is this? and whither, whence,
This consuming secret sense,
Longing for its rest and food,
In some hidden, untried good?

Naught that charms the ear or eye
Can its hunger satisfy;
Active, restless, it would pierce
Through the outward universe.

'Tis the soul, mysterious name!
God it seeks, from God it came;
While I muse, I feel the fire,
Burning on, and mounting higher.

Onward, upward, to thy throne,
O thou Infinite, unknown,
Still it presseth, till it see
Thee in all, and all in thee.

HYMN.

I feel within a want
For ever burning there;

What I so thirst for, grant,
O Thou who hearest prayer!

This is the thing I crave,
A likeness to thy Son;
This would I rather have
Than call the world my own.

'Tis my most fervent prayer;
Be it more fervent still,
Be it my highest care,
Be it my settled will.

COLLEGE OF CHARLESTON, S. C.—SOUTH CAROLINA COLLEGE, COLUMBIA.

One of the first liberal institutions of learning founded in South Carolina was the College of Charleston. It was incorporated by an Act of the Legislature in 1786. Several legacies had been left by citizens of the state, endowing the first college which might be chartered, and these the College of Charleston shared in common with two others which were chartered on the same day.

The Rev. Dr. Robert Smith, afterwards Protestant Episcopal Bishop of the diocese, then the master of a grammar-school in Charleston, was appointed the Principal, and in 1794 the first class graduated with the degree of Bachelor of Arts. The old barracks of the city were employed as the college edifice; and here the studies were continued until 1825. The institution never having been separated from the grammar-school, did not acquire the rank of a college, and in a few years became merely a private school. In 1829 it was revived under the superintendence of Bishop Bowen, its oldest graduate, by the union of three of the principal private schools in the city; and by means of the liberality of the citizens the old barracks were removed and a more commodious building erected. Bishop Bowen, having reorganized the college, retired from its management, and was succeeded by the Rev. Jasper Adams, D.D. The grammar-school was still attached to the college; and financial difficulties having arisen, the exercises were suspended in 1835.

In 1837 the charter was amended, the college ceded its property to the city, which in return charged itself with its maintenance, and it was reorganized in 1838, the Rev. William Brantly being appointed president. Dr. Brantly died in 1845, and was succeeded by the present incumbent, W. Peronneau Finley. The faculty consists of a President, and Professors of Moral Sciences, Greek and Latin, Astronomy and Natural Philosophy, Mathematics, History and Belles Lettres, and of Zoology and Palæontology, with the Curatorship of the Museum or Cabinet of Natural History attached.

The late Elias Horry, Esq., by a donation of six thousand dollars, founded the Horry Professorship of Moral Philosophy, which is held ex officio by the President. In 1848 the citizens generally, by subscription, endowed a Professorship of History and Belles Lettres.

To the liberality of the citizens also, at the suggestion made in 1850, at the session in Charleston of the American Association for the Advancement of Science, the college is indebted for a very large and valuable Cabinet of Natural History. Among those who were most forward in contributing to this collection may be mentioned the names of Messrs. Tuomey, Holmes, Bachman, Audubon, and Agassiz. Dr. L. A. Frampton has presented his valuable library to the college, and the munificence of the legislature has supplied the means of building a suitable house for its reception. The late Ker Boyce, Esq., bequeathed by his will the sum of thirty thousand dollars, to be appropriated to the support of young men of the Baptist communion, while attending the course of instruction in the college. The average number of students is from fifty to sixty; and the curriculum does not differ materially from that of other colleges in the Union.

The Rev. J. W. Miles, eminent as a clergyman of the Protestant Episcopal Church in Charleston, for his scholarship and for his fine philosophical powers of mind, was connected with this institution as Professor of the History of Philosophy and of Greek Literature. His published addresses —a discourse before the graduating class in 1851; *The Ground of Morals*, a discourse on a similar occasion in 1852; and another, *The Student of Philology*, at the close of the same year before the Literary Societies of the South Carolina College —exhibit his scholarship, vigor, and originality of thought and enthusiasm. An elaborate work from his pen, published by John Russell in Charleston, *Philosophic Theology; or Ultimate Grounds of all Religious Belief based in Reason*, established his reputation as a theologian. The work is a metaphysical discussion of points of faith, "springing from the necessity which the mind of the writer has felt for rendering to itself a sufficient reason for its convictions respecting religious belief, upon grounds of certainty, beyond the ordinary sphere of controversy." Mr. Miles was the orator appointed by the joint committee of the city council and citizens of Charleston on occasion of the funeral of the Hon. John C. Calhoun. In his address he presented a philosophical view of the character and relations of the statesman. He has also been a contributor to the Southern Quarterly Review.

South Carolina College was founded by Act of Assembly in December, 1801, which declared that the proper education of youth should always be an object of legislative attention as contributing to the prosperity of society; and placed the institution in a central position "where all its youth may be educated for the good order and harmony of the whole." A board of trustees was established which secured to the college the services and influence of the first men of the state. The Governor, Lieutenant-Governor, the President of the Senate and Speaker of the House, and all the judges and chancellors are trustees ex officio, and twenty others are elected by the Legislature every four years. The Governor is President of the Board. Lately the Chairmen of the Committees of both houses on the College and Education, are made ex officio members. The full board is composed of thirty-six, generally of the most influential men in the state.

The accommodations for students are ample. A new hall for Commencement and other purposes has been lately added to the buildings, at an expense of about thirty-five thousand dollars. It is of the Corinthian order, of large dimensions, being one hundred and thirty feet in length, sixty-eight in breadth, and fifty-nine in height. The

South Carolina College.

library, though not large, is a very choice one. There are now upwards of 20,000 volumes; and it contains many rare and costly works. Gen. Charles Cotesworth Pinckney and Judge Johnson of the U. S. Court, were members of the committee who made the first purchase of books when the College went into operation. They were procured in London, from the well known bookseller, Lackington. Many of the finest volumes belonged to private libraries, and the names of some of the most distinguished men in England may be found in them, as former proprietors. The Legislature annually appropriates two thousand dollars for the purchase of books, and this, added to the tuition fund, would constitute a very liberal allowance; but for some years past the latter has been exhausted by repairs to which it is first applicable.

Persons not familiar with South Carolina have attributed to the influence of Mr. Calhoun that unanimity and conformity of opinion for which South Carolina has always been distinguished; but it is rather to be ascribed to early associations and influences, and most particularly of late to the influence which this favorite institution has had upon the rising generation.

For the later selections of books for the library it is much indebted to Dr. Cooper, Professors Henry, Nott, and Elliott, and President Thornwell, but most especially to the late Stephen Elliott, Professor Nott, and Professor now Bishop Elliott. A number of books were ordered by Mr. Stephen Elliott, and purchased by Mr. Henry Junius Nott, then in Europe, and afterwards Professor of Belles Lettres. Since 1836 the sum of $62,374 has been expended. The collection is rich in costly foreign works, illustrating the Fine Arts, Antiquities, Classical Literature, and the specialities of science.

Mr. F. W. M'Master is the present librarian.

The general welfare of the College is liberally provided for by its Endowment and the state appropriation. The President and seven professors are all furnished with comfortable residences. The salary of the President is three thousand dollars, payable quarterly in advance, and that of the Professors twenty-five hundred, payable in the same manner, from the public treasury. In 1845 the Comptroller-General reports the whole amount of expenditure by the state, on the College, up to that date, at $698,679 23. The annual appropriation amounts at present to $24,600. For many years the state has also appropriated $37,000 for free schools, and at the last meeting of the Legislature (Dec. 1854) it was increased to $74,600, besides some $8,000 for two military schools. No appropriation asked by the Board of Trustees has ever been refused. Of course great discretion and wisdom have been exercised in all cases where applications have been made.

The Presidents of the College have been—Jonathan Maxcy, 1804 to 1820; Stephen Elliott, 1820, declined to accept; Thomas Cooper, 1820, *pro tem.*; Thomas Cooper, 1821 to 1834; Robert Henry, 1834, *pro tem.*; Robert W. Barnwell, 1835 to 1843; Robert Henry, 1843 to 1845; Wm. C. Preston, 1845 to 1851; Jas. H. Thornwell, 1851 to 1855.

The first President, Dr. Maxcy, has the honor of having discharged that office with efficiency in three colleges. He was born in Attleborough, Mass., Sept. 2, 1768; was educated at Brown University, where in 1787, on taking his degree, he delivered a poem on the Prospects of America. He was then tutor in the College for four years. Having qualified himself for the ministry, in 1791 he was ordained pastor of the First Baptist Church at Providence, and the same day Professor of Divinity in the University. On the death of President Manning, in 1792, he was chosen his successor at the early age of twenty-four. He delivered at this time several discourses, which were published; a Sermon on the Death of Manning, Discourses on the Existence and Attributes of God and on the Doctrine of the Atonement. In 1802 he was called to succeed President Jonathan Edwards, at Union, where he remained till 1804. The rest of his life was passed as the head of the College at Columbia. He died June 4, 1820. His high personal qualities and virtues in his office were thus commemorated in 1854, in an oration by the Hon. James L. Pettigru, on the Semi-Centennial celebration of the College.

Jonathan Maxcy exerted no little influence on the character of the youth of his day; and his name is never to be mentioned by his disciples without reverence. He had many eminent qualifications for his office. His genius was æsthetic; persuasion flowed from his lips; and his eloquence diffused over every subject the bright hues of a warm imagination. He was deeply imbued with classical learning, and the philosophy of the human mind divided his heart with the love of polite literature. With profound piety, he was free from the slightest taint of bigotry or narrowness. Early in life he had entered into the ministry, under sectarian banners; but though he never resiled from the creed which he had adopted—so Catholic was his spirit—so genial his soul to the inspirations of faith, hope, and charity—that whether in the chair or the pulpit, he never seemed to us less than an Apostolic teacher. Never will the charm of his eloquence be erased from the memory on which its impression has once been made. His elocution was equally winning and peculiar. He spoke in the most deliberate manner; his voice was clear and gentle; his action composed and quiet; yet no man had such command over the noisy sallies of youth. His presence quelled every disorder. The most riotous offender shrank from the reproof of that pale brow and intellectual eye. The reverence that attended him stilled the progress of disaffection; and to him belonged the rare power—exercised in the face of wondering Europe by Lamartine—of quelling by persuasion, the spirit of revolt.

Thomas Cooper, one of the most active spirits sent over by the old world to establish themselves in the politics of the new, was born in London, October 22, 1759. Having been educated at Oxford, become a proficient in chemistry, and acquired a knowledge of the law and medicine, he brought these acquisitions to America, joining his friend, Dr. Priestley,* at Northumberland, having been driven from England by the part which he took in reference to French politics, in becoming the agent of an English democratic club to a revolutionary club in France, and issuing a pamphlet in reply to an attack on him by Burke, which was threatened with prosecution. In the United States he became a Jeffersonian politician, and attacking Adams in a newspaper communication, which he published in the Pennsylvania Reading Weekly Advertiser of October 26, 1799, was tried for a libel under the sedition law in 1800, and sentenced to six months' imprisonment and a fine of four hundred dollars.*

The Democratic party coming into power Governor M'Kean appointed Cooper, in 1806, President Judge of one of the Pennsylvania Common Pleas districts, an office which he filled with energy, but from which he was removed in 1811 by Governor Snyder at the request of the Legislature, on representations chiefly of an overbearing temper. He became Professor of Chemistry in Dickinson College at Carlisle, and subsequently, in 1816, held a professorship of Mineralogy and Chemistry in the University of Pennsylvania, and shortly after, in 1819, became at first Professor of Chemistry, then, in 1820, President of the South Carolina College. He also discharged the duties of Professor of Chemistry and Political Economy. Retiring from this post on account of age in 1834, he was employed by the Legislature of South Carolina in revising the statutes of the state. He died May 11, 1840.

Of his writings we may mention a volume of statistics entitled *Information respecting America*, published in London in 1794; a collection of Political Essays in 1800, contributed to the Northumberland Gazette in Pennsylvania, which he "conducted for a short time to enable the printer of that paper to proceed more expeditiously with a work of Dr. Priestley's then in the press;"† a translation of *The Institutes of Justinian*, which

* Priestley, the son of a cloth-dresser near Leeds, whose scientific discoveries in England had stamped him as one of the first chemists of the age, and whose religious and political principles, as a Unitarian and advocate of the French Revolution, had rendered him the object of popular persecution (his house and library in Birmingham were burnt by the mob in 1791), came to America, whither his sons had already emigrated in 1794. He arrived in New York on the fourth of June of that year, and was received with great attention by the citizens, who, not long after, proposed a subscription of a thousand dollars for a course of lectures on Experimental Philosophy, if he would deliver them. In July he went to Northumberland in Pennsylvania, where his son had an agricultural settlement. He soon established himself in his old habits, constructing a library, writing books as rapidly as usual, and resuming his chemical experiments. He was offered the Professorship of Chemistry in the University of Pennsylvania, with a good salary, and declined the appointment, preferring his own disposition of his time in retirement. He delivered two courses of public lectures, however, at Philadelphia in 1796 and 1797, on the *Evidences of Revelation*, which he published in two volumes, the first of which he dedicated to John Adams, who was then his hearer and admirer. His *Continuation of the History of the Christian Church, from the fall of the Western Empire to the present times*, was written in America and published at Northampton in four volumes in 1808. It was dedicated to Jefferson. He also wrote in this country, in reply to Volney's and Paine's attacks upon Revelation, and in addition to the Linn controversy, a number of miscellaneous theological productions, with a *Comparison of the Institutes of Moses with those of the Hindoos and other ancient nations*. On American politics Priestley found himself not altogether free from his old English difficulties, as his sympathy for France brought him in collision with the Federal party; though his latter days were soothed by the ascendency of his friend and correspondent Jefferson. In 1774, at Franklin's request, he had written an address to the people of England on the American disputes, calculated to show the injustice and impolicy of a war with the colonies. It was written by Priestley at Leeds, and Franklin corrected the proofs for him at London. His *Maxims of Political Arithmetic by a Quaker in Politics*, first published in the Aurora, February 26 and 27, 1798, contain in a very neat essay some admirable suggestions on free trade and national honor. He communicated his scientific papers to the Medical Repository of New York. The entire number of his publications reaches one hundred and forty-one. An edition of his works has been published in England in twenty-five volumes, edited by Towell Rutt. His *Memoirs* indicate the philosophical serenity of his character. They touch lightly upon his American period, as they close with the year 1795; but the continuation by his son Joseph Priestley contains many interesting notices of his residence at Northumberland, particularly a simple and affecting account of his death, which he met with great tranquillity at that place, February 6th, 1804, in his seventy-second year. A candid and discriminating account of his career has been written by Lord Brougham in his "Lives of Men of Letters and Science, who flourished in the time of George III." An anecdote given by Brougham is highly characteristic of Priestley's manners, and of his position in the religious world of America into which he was introduced. "He happened to visit a friend whose wife received him in her husband's absence, but feared to name him before a Calvinistic divine present. By accident his name was mentioned, and the lady then introduced him. But he of the Genevan school drew back, saying, 'Dr. Joseph Priestley?' and then added in the American tongue, (query, what does Lord Brougham mean by the American tongue? the Choctaw?) 'I cannot be cordial.' Whereupon the Doctor, with his usual placid demeanor, said that he and the lady might be allowed to converse until their host should return. By degrees the conversation became general; the repudiator was won over by curiosity first, then by gratification; he remained till a late hour hanging upon Priestley's lips; he took his departure at length, and told his host as he quitted the house, that never had he passed so delightful an evening; though he admitted that he had begun it 'by behaving like a fool and a brute.' One such anecdote (and there are many current) is of more force to describe its subject than a hundred labored panegyrics."

* Wharton's State Trials of the United States, pp. 659–681.

† Preface to Second Edition. Philadelphia. 1800.

appeared in Philadelphia in 1812; his *Medical Jurisprudence* in 1819. He was engaged in the publication of a magazine of scientific information, *The Emporium of Arts and Sciences*, five volumes of which appeared in Philadelphia from 1812 to 1814. Two of these were prepared by Dr. John Redman Coxe, the remainder by Dr. Cooper.

In 1826 he published at Columbia, South Carolina, his *Lectures on the Elements of Political Economy*. They were written as a class-book for his students, but are strongly impressed with his manly utterance of opinions for all readers. His advocacy of free trade at home and abroad, in foreign and domestic regulations, of trade and government, is urged in his bold, dogmatic style, with constant effect. His miscellaneous writings on law and medicine were numerous. In politics he always held a forcible pen. He was a vigorous pamphleteer in the nullification contest in South Carolina, taking the side of the ultra states rights doctrine.

Th. Cooper

Of his conversational powers, which were remarkable from the natural strength of his perception, his controversial taste, his knowledge of distinguished men, and his wide personal experience of memorable affairs, we are enabled to present something more than this general recognition in a few passages of his table-talk, copied for us by his friend and intimate, the late Colonel D. J. M'Cord, who entered them at the time in his note-book. Though the date is not given, the period is that of Dr. Cooper's last years at Columbia.

MEMORANDA OF TABLE-TALK OF JUDGE COOPER.

Sunday, 26. When I was going over to Paris with Watt during the French Revolution, being both members of the club at Manchester, we had letters from the club to Robespierre, Petion, and other members of the Jacobine clubs of Paris. I called on Petion and told him my business, and that I wished to be introduced to Robespierre. Petion was a clever fellow, and more like an Englishman than any Frenchman I have ever seen. Good, candid fellow, on whom you might rely. He took me to Robespierre's. We passed through a carpenter's shop, and went up a ladder to the place occupied by Robespierre. He was dressed up. A complete *petit maitre*, a dandy. A little pale man, with dark hair. He received me well. I told him that I had written an address to deliver to the club, and requested him to deliver it for me, as I spoke French badly. He said he would. I wrote the address, and Watt translated it into French. We went to the club (he mentioned which, but it has escaped me), and he with others sat under the canopy (I think he said) where the president sits. He mentioned who presided. After a while a loud noise was made, and a call for Citizen Cooper (*Citoyen Gouappè*) and Watt, and for the address of *Citoyen Gouappè* which had been formally announced. I requested Robespierre to take it and read it as he had promised. He declined, and I insisted, until he refused positively, when the noise increasing, I told him—"*Citoyen Robespierre, vous êtes un coquin!*" and with that I mounted and delivered my address, which was well received, and with considerable noise. After that (which was before Robespierre commenced his reign of blood), I kept company principally with the Brissotians. The day after the above affair took place at the club, several persons told me to take care of myself, for that Robespierre and his friends had their designs upon us. Spies were set upon us. We were informed of it, and their names furnished, which he mentioned. We invited them regularly to dinner, and the poor devils not being used to drinking wine, we always got them drunk after dinner. One evening, at the house of a person whose name I did not catch, where many Brissotians were present, Watt and I proposed that if they would gather as many friends as they could and go with us, to support us at the club, I would insult Robespierre before the whole assembly, and compel him to challenge us to fight. We should have broken him up that night. We did not care for responsibility there, it would have been all amusement. Such was our excitement, I would as leave have fought him as not. I would have liked it. We might have got him off, but d—n the bit these fellows would agree to join us. They would not risk it. At last we were denounced by Robespierre, and Watt went off to Germany, and I returned to England. Now those four months that I spent in Paris were the most happy and pleasant of my life. I laughed more than I ever did before or have since. I lived four years.

It is curious, but I believe the fact from what I saw, that during the most dreadful times of that Revolution, during its most bloody period, the people of Paris enjoyed more aggregate happiness than at any other period of their lives. Every moment was a century. When there every energy of my mind was called out, every moment engaged. Some important event unceasingly occurred, and incessantly occupied the mind. He laughed, and said that after he had left France he was set up as a candidate for convention, by some one, in opposition to the Duke of Orleans, but the duke beat him.

Speaking of the King of France, he was asked if he could have been saved. *Dr. C.* Aye! that he could. Very easily. The Brissotians were anxious to save him. Petion wrote to Pitt, or communicated through Marat, and some one else, with the English minister, and said that if he would furnish £100,000 he might be saved. Pitt refused it. H. could not believe that Pitt refused unless he considered it as a trick. P. thought he would have refused it, for the very reason that he wished the king killed, as his wish was that France would commit the greatest excesses, to deter England from following her detestable example. Mrs. Grant told him that she once dined in company with Pitt. She always spoke of it with great enthusiasm. It was an era in her life. Pitt came to dinner on an express promise that politics should not be introduced, as he was at that time in bad health. However, Pitt got in a good humor and seemed disposed to give them a talk on politics; and reclining back in his chair, with what she called the vacant stare of genius, gave them a talk of an hour's length.

Dr. C. speaking of the time he lived at Sunbury, Northumberland, Pa., he said it was a complete blank in his life. P. observed that he was then in hot water. Yes, but I have forgotten nearly everything in connexion with those matters. It got me in jail, where I stayed six months (in Philadelphia). But I there had good company every day and night. At night I had the best company in Philadelphia. They all called on me. Everything that was good was sent to me—wine—claret, Madeira, port, cider—everything came, God knows how or from where, and cost me nothing. However, I had to pay $400. Crafts the other day published my speech on that occasion. I had no counsel. I advocated my own cause. He was asked if the Constitutionality of the Alien and Sedition Law was questioned in the case? No, Chase would not suffer it. He then gave us some curious anecdotes concerning Chase.

Sunday, 16. Speaking of Dr. Johnson. P. called him a bigot in politics and religion. *Dr. C.* No! No! In a political conversation which I had with Dr. Johnson he said, "I believe in no such thing as the *jure divino* of kings. I have no such belief; but I believe that monarchy is the most conducive to the happiness and safety of the people of every nation, and therefore I am a monarchist, but as to its divine right, that is all stuff. I think every people have the right to establish such government as they may think most conducive to their interest and happiness."

Boswell, continued Dr. C., was the greatest fool I ever knew. He was a real idiot. I am sure I have a right to say so. He came to Lancaster assizes once when I was there. He took his seat at the bar, and Park (on insurance), Sir Samuel Romilly, myself, and perhaps some others, subscribed three guineas upon a brief, and docketed a feigned issue, and sent a fellow to employ him. He received the brief and the three guineas, and when the case was called, he rose at the bar, to the great amusement of the whole court, yet he proceeded to open the case, which the court soon understood, and on some pretence postponed the affair. He stayed in the same house with us, and I think he said he drank two or three bottles of port and got drunk.

Burke, he said, he knew very well. He was the most excessive talker he ever knew, and, at times, very tiresome. Speaking of the republican clubs in England during the French revolution, he said his party at Manchester made much more noise than any other in England. Burke denounced Dr. Priestley and himself (Dr. C.), one day in the House of Commons. Cooper replied to it in a pamphlet, which he had, and I have read. A young man, he said, must lay in a large stock of democracy, if he expects it to hold out to my age. We laughed, and told him that he had given up his democracy as to England, but not as to America. But he replied, that he was now a constitutional democrat. He was opposed to the many steps taken by the United States government, as well as the United States courts, towards a consolidated government. He thought none but freeholders were of *right* entitled to vote and to be represented. It might be policy in a nation to permit others, but all others are mere sojourners, and have no such *right*. It would be better if a compromise could be made between freeholders and numbers, but that could not be done.

He admitted that there was evil in general suffrage, and evil likewise in not suffering it, but it could not be claimed as a *right*. P. observed that Sir James Mackintosh had given up all his French politics. That he had heard him in a conversation of some hours, with his feet in the American fashion against the fire-place, give a character of Burke in the most elevated and eloquent strains. He said he had relinquished his notions on the French revolution, and that he had agreed perfectly with Mr. Burke, and that he had the most exalted ideas of his politics, literary taste, and eloquence.

Dr. C. expressed his surprise.

In 1792 he came to America, and he said in February, 1793, he returned to attend his friend Walker's trial for sedition, at Lancaster. Erskine and himself took seats at the bar as counsel for Walker. The case was tried, and they produced a witness who proved the perjury of a witness (Dunn), and subornation by the agents of the ministry. Walker was acquitted, and on motion of Erskine, Dunn was immediately committed. He, C., drew up a bill of indictment against him, and at the next assizes he was convicted, and imprisoned. He returned to America in September.

At Horne Tooke's, said the doctor, one day at dinner I met Thelwell, the Radical. Walker and he went up to Horne Tooke and told him that they were surprised to meet Thelwell there, that they were sure he was a spy from the violent and imprudent manner in which he spoke of government. Horne Tooke said that he had not invited him, and that Thelwell forced himself upon him. Tooke then turned to Thelwell and said, "You know that some time since, when it was expected that there would be a revolution in this country, that you had a list of gentlemen proscribed, who were first to be cut off, and that I was placed nearly at the top, and Mr. Cooper soon after." Thelwell never said a word. He could not deny it.—These radicals, he said, were great rascals.

February 22. Dr. C.: "Now M., I dine professor —— on Sunday, but will not have meat enough to feed you also. So come after dinner. Mind, I invite you to drink, not to eat." During the evening he said to me, when you become a member of the legislature take my advice, conciliate the fools; for they are always the majority. Be kind to them. Give them your ideas. Let them use them. Do their business for them. Write for them. Draw their bills and resolutions. Make one good speech during the session, and hold your peace. By that means you will gain them. Take my advice. Pursue it. It prescribes the course Legaré should have taken, but he chose the opposite. Sense, eloquence, speeches wont do. You must work into their favor.

March 2. Explained what he meant by saying that he had not taken in a sufficient stock of democracy. That it was running into excess in America, and that it had rendered the people too fond of change, and that these changes were too often effected by the ignorant and lower classes.

The Rev. Robert Henry, LL.D., the successor of Dr. Cooper in the College Presidency, was born in Charleston, S. C., on the 6th December, 1792, and received the first rudiments of education in that city. He commenced the study of the Latin language at the early age of six, and in 1803 was sent by his mother, then a widow, to the neighborhood of London, where for some time he remained under the private tuition of a highly respectable clergyman. In 1811 he entered the Edinburgh University, and was graduated there in 1814, and after a visit and short residence on the continent, returned to South Carolina in 1815. For two years he was minister to the French Hugnenot Church of Charleston, where once a month he preached in French. In November, 1818, at the suggestion of Judge King of Charleston, a highly competent judge of his merits, Mr. Henry was elected Professor of Logic and Moral Philosophy in the South Carolina College, and was afterwards made Professor of Metaphysics, Moral and Political Philosophy, and, perhaps, was the first person who gave lectures in the United States on Free Trade, and Political Economy generally. In 1834 he was made president of the College, which he resigned in 1835. At a subsequent period, in 1836, he was induced to accept the appointment of Professor of Metaphysics and Belles Lettres in the South Carolina College. In 1840 he was again appointed President, but in 1843, upon being relieved from certain duties in the government of the college, and allowed to reside without the precincts, accepted the Professorship of Greek, newly established, and expressly at his suggestion. He still continues to perform these learned duties.

Mr. Henry, to an intimate acquaintance with the ancient languages, unites a familiar knowledge of the modern. He speaks French, German, and Dutch fluently. His reading is encyclopædian, and his memory equal to his reading. His social qualities are eminent, and his conversation delightful and instructive. While Dr. Cooper was at his best, it was rare to meet such charming conversation as was exhibited at that time at the dinner tables, and other society at Columbia, in which Cooper, Preston, Henry, Legaré, Nott, Petigru, Harper, and others were conspicuous, and would not have appeared to disadvantage in the best London society, not even alongside of Rogers, or of Conversation Sharp, with both of whom Cooper had been specially intimate in his early European days.*

It is to be regretted that Mr. Henry's health has been very feeble for some years past. This may have rendered his works few in number, in proportion to his learning and abilities. He has published, in 1829, *Eulogy on Dr. E. D. Smith, late Professor of Chemistry in the South Carolina College.* In 1830, *Eulogy on Jonathan Maxcy, late President.* A Sermon on duelling, before the Legislature of South Carolina. In 1847, two Sermons at the Pinckney Lecture in Charleston. In 1850, *A Eulogy on John C. Calhoun.* For the Southern Review, he wrote articles on *Niebuhr's Roman History*, *La Motte Fouqué*, *Goethe's Wilhelm Meister*, and *Waterhouse's Junius.* Dr. Henry has always been a friend of free trade, and the constitutional rights of the states as opposed to a great central power.

The next President of the college, the Hon. William C. Preston, was the distinguished statesman, lawyer, and orator, of South Carolina. He was born December 27, 1794, at Philadelphia, while his father was at the National Congress at that place, as a member from Virginia. His maternal grandmother was the sister of Patrick Henry. He was educated at the University of North Carolina, and studied law in the office of William Wirt, at Richmond. From 1816 to 1819 he travelled in Europe, visiting England, France, and Switzerland, and residing for a while at Edinburgh, where he attended with Mr. Legaré the philosophical lectures at the university. In 1821 he was admitted to the practice of the law in Virginia. He removed the next year to Columbia, in South Carolina, and soon became engaged in political life. In 1824 he was elected to the House of Representatives, and in 1832 to the Senate of the United States. After ten years' service in the last position, where he maintained an eminent rank as an orator, he returned to the practice of the law in South Carolina. He held the Presidency of the College for six years, imparting to the institution the influence of his refined scholarship, elegant tastes, and winning manners. He retired in consequence of ill health, and has since resided at Columbia.

The Rev. Dr. James H. Thornwell, the successor to Mr. Preston, was born in Marlborough District, South Carolina, in 1811. He was educated at the South Carolina College, and was graduated, with the highest distinction in his class, in December, 1819. He afterwards commenced the study of the law, but soon abandoned it for the church. As a Presbyterian clergyman, he commenced preaching as minister of Waxsaw church. At the age of twenty-five he was elected Professor of Logic and Belles Lettres in the South Carolina College, the duties of which he performed with distinction for two years, but resigned, on being elected pastor of the Presbyterian church at Columbia, S. C. After two years' service there, where his reputation daily grew, he was induced to accept the Professorship of the Evidences of Christianity, and the position of chaplain, upon the resignation of those places by Mr. now Bishop Elliott. Here he remained until May, 1852, when he took charge of Glebe Street Church, Charleston. Previous to this removal, Mr. Thornwell had received very flattering invitations from various Northern cities, New York, Philadelphia, Baltimore, and St. Louis, but declined them all.

Upon the resignation of the Presidency by Mr. Preston, in December, 1852, Dr. Thornwell was elected to succeed him. He returned to Columbia, and has continued to fill the office with deserved distinction and popularity. The number of students is now about two hundred, and the college was never in a better condition either as to education, morals, or manners. To the great regret of the state generally, the Presbyterian synod have thought it advisable to demand the services of Dr. Thornwell for their theological seminary in Columbia, a call which he has felt it his duty, under his clerical obligations, to obey.*

* In this personal tribute, and in other parts of this article, we employ the words of the communication of the late D. J. M'Cord, whose sudden and lamented death occurred while this work was passing through the press. *Ante*, p. 249.

* The following is a list of Dr. Thornwell's publications :—1. A Sermon on the Vanity and Glory of Man, preached October 9, 1842, in the College Chapel. 2. A Sermon on the Necessity of the Atonement, preached December, 1842, in the College Chapel. 3. Arguments of Romanists Discussed and Refuted in relation to the Apocryphal Books of the Old Testament, published in New York, 1845. 4. Discourses on Truth, published in New York, 1855. 5. The following articles have been contributed to the Southern Presbyterian Review, printed in Columbia :—1. The Office of Reason in regard to Revelation. Vol. 1. Art. 1. No. 1. 2. The Christian Pastor. Vol. 1. No. 3.

Dr. Thornwell is familiar with Greek, Roman, French, German, and other languages and literature, and is as vigorous and unrelenting in the pursuit of new studies now, as when he left college. His popularity with the students, and his tact in the management of youth, connected with the high respect generally entertained for him in the state, must cause his withdrawal to be deeply felt.

ORESTES A. BROWNSON.

This eminent speculative inquirer, ingenious thinker, and exponent of various religious opinions in his writings, is a native of Vermont, where he was born about the beginning of the century. In his education he has been what is usually, though incorrectly, called a self-made man; and he must always have been an earnest one, for we find him early in life a diligent inquirer in the higher walks of religious philosophy. As the life of Mr. Brownson has been passed in the pursuits of the thinker and scholar, with little external incident beyond that involved in his several changes of opinion, which have carried him in succession through different associations and sets of companions, we may cite, as a portion of his biography, what he has himself chosen to say on the subject. "Much," he remarks in the preface to the collection of his Essays, in 1852, "has been said first and last in the newspapers as to the frequent changes I have undergone, and I am usually sneered at as a weathercock in religion and politics. This seldom disturbs me, for I happen to know that most of the changes alleged are purely imaginary. I was born in a Protestant community, of Protestant parents, and was brought up, so far as I was brought up at all, a Presbyterian. At the age of twenty-one I passed from Presbyterianism to what is sometimes called Liberal Christianity, to which I remained attached, at first under the form of Universalism, afterwards under that of Unitarianism, till the age of forty-one, when I had the happiness of being received into the Catholic Church. Here is the sum total of my religious changes. I no doubt experienced difficulties in defending the doctrines I professed, and I shifted my ground of defence more than once, but not the doctrines themselves.

"I was during many years, no doubt, a radical and a socialist, but both after a fashion of my own. I held two sets of principles, the one set the same that I hold now, the other the set I have rejected. I supposed the two sets could be held consistently together, that there must be some way, though I never pretended to be able to discover it, of reconciling them with each other. Fifteen years' trial and experience convinced me to the contrary, and that I must choose which set I would retain and which cast off. My natural tendency was always to conservatism, and democracy, in the sense I now reject it, I never held. In politics, I always advocated, as I advocate now, a limited government indeed, but a strong and efficient government. Here is the sum total of my political changes. I never acknowledged allegiance to any party. From 1838 to 1843, I acted with the Democratic party, because during those years it contended for the public policy I approved; since then I have adhered to no party. No party, as such, ever had any right to count on me, and most likely none ever will have. I do not believe in the infallibility of political parties, and I always did and probably always shall hold myself free to support the men and measures of any party, or to oppose them, according to my own independent convictions of what is or is not for the common good of my country." To this comprehensive outline and self-justification of an active career, we may supply some of the details as furnished by Mr. Brownson's publications.

His first work, published in 1836, entitled, *New Views of Christian Society and the Church*, was written while he was minister of an Independent congregation at Boston, which was called "The Society for Christian Union and Progress." It was marked by French and German opinions, which the writer put forward without particular reference to the religious body of Unitarians to which he was then attached. At this period Mr. Brownson was a contributor to the Christian Examiner. A novel which he published in 1840, *Charles Elwood, or the Infidel Converted*, is an autobiographic sketch, in which the writer shows minutely the mental struggle through which he had passed. The form of fiction is but a thin covering, and a slight impediment to, if it does not assist, a purely philosophical essay. It was about this time that Mr. Brownson commenced the course of independent periodical literature in which he has since been engaged. He published the *Boston Quarterly Review*, in five annual volumes, written from the commencement mostly by himself, from 1838 to 1842, when he merged the work in the Democratic Review at New York, to which he became a stated contributor. His articles "On the Origin and Ground of Government," "Democracy," and "Liberty," and similar topics, proved, however, to be of an unaccommodating character to the supporters of that journal, and Mr. Brownson withdrew from its pages to resume his independent Review, in which he could freely unfold his own sentiments and opinions without seeking to conciliate or being controlled by other interests. He then, in 1844, began at Boston the publication of the journal entitled *Brownson's Quarterly Review*, which has since been continued without interruption, having, in 1855, reached a twelfth annual volume, or a third of the third series. In this, Mr. Brownson having become a devoted member of the Papal Church, maintains his new views of Catholicism, in the same fluent, commanding style, once so well adapted to the energy of Democracy and the schemes of Socialism.

Art. 6. 3. The Elder Question. Vol. ii. No. 1. Art. 1. 4. Paul's Preaching at Athens. Vol. ii. No. 4. Art. 1. 5. Thoughts upon the Priesthood of Christ. Vol. iii. No. 4. Art. 2. 6. Philosophy of Religion (Review of Morell). Vol. iii. No. 2. Art. 5. 7. Philosophy of Religion (Review of Morell). Vol. iii. No. 3. Art. 6. 8. Slavery and the Religious Instruction of the Colored Population. Vol. iv. No. 1. Art. 6. The substance of this article was also published as a Sermon on the Rights and Duties of Masters. 9. Dissertation on Miracles (Matt. xxii. 9). Vol. iv. No. 4. Art. 2. 10. Validity of Popish Baptism; a series of articles commenced in Vol. v. No. 1, and continued in successive numbers. 11. Report on Slavery. Vol. v. No. 3. Art. 3. To these may be added a Sermon on the occasion of the Death of the Hon. J. C. Calhoun, preached in the College Chapel, April, 1850, a letter to Governor Manning, on Public Instruction in South Carolina, 1853, and a Sermon preached before the Legislature, December 1854, against demagogism, and on the duties of the legislator.

A novel, *The Spirit Rapper*, treating of the subject of demoniac agency, published in 1854, is the last of Mr. Brownson's separate publications. The style of Mr. Brownson is a remarkably felicitous one for the discussion of abstract topics; full, fluent, easily intelligible, meeting the philosophic requirements of the subject, at the same time preserving a popular interest, it was well adapted to enlist the popular ear. When employed in appeals to the laboring classes, and enforced by the living energy of the orator, its triumph was certain. As a vehicle for the speculations of the scholar it still preserves its attraction to those who delight in mental gladiatorial exercises, or are curious to note the reconciliation of the "chartered libertine" in doctrine to the authoritative voice of the Church.

NATHANAEL DEERING

Is a native of Portland, Maine, and the son of the late Mr. James Deering, an esteemed merchant of the city. He was educated at the Academy at Exeter and at Cambridge, where he was graduated at Harvard in 1810. He then studied law in the office of Chief-justice Whitman at Portland, and pursued the profession in the northern counties of his native state. He is now a resident of Portland.

Mr. Deering's literary productions are two five act tragedies—*Carabasset, or the Last of the Norridgewocks*, which was produced at the Portland Theatre in 1831, and *Bozzaris*. His miscellaneous writings, including numerous tales of humor of "Down East" life, have appeared from time to time in the journals of the day.

THE WRECK OF THE TWO POLLIES.

A Ballad.

'Twas a starless night, with drifting clouds,
  And angry heaved the seas;
Yet a pink-stern craft was under sail,
  Her name was the "Two Polleys."

And she was built at Mount Desert,
  And what might her cargo be?
She was for a long time on the Banks,
  And while there was very lucky.

But darker and darker grew the night,
  And loud did ocean roar;
So they two reefs in the mainsail took,
  And one reef in the fore.

The Skipper Bond was at the helm,
  Methinks I see him now—
The tobacco juice on his mouth and chin,
  And the salt spray on his brow.

The other hand was Isaac Small,
  And only one eye had he;
But that one eye kept a sharp look-out
  For breakers under the lee.

All unconcerned was Skipper Bond.
  For he was a seaman bold;
But he buttoned his fearnaught higher up,
  And, said he, "'Tis getting cold."

"Odd's bloods! I must the main brace splice,
  "So, Isaac, let us quaff—
"And as the wind's a snorter, mind
  "And mix it half and half."

The Skipper raised it to his lips,
  And soon the dipper drained:
A second and a third he took,
  Nor of its strength complained.

"Shake out the reefs! haul aft fore sheet!
  "I am not the man to flag,
"With a breeze like this, in the 'Two Polleys'—
  "So give her every rag."

Aghast poor Isaac heard the call,
  And tremblingly obeyed;
For he knew full well the Skipper was one
  Who would not be gainsayed.

"Isaac, my lad, now go below,
  "And speedily turn in;
"I'll call you when off Portland Light,
  "We now are off Seguin."

The Skipper was alone on deck—
  "Steady, my boys," he cried;
And hardly would the words escape,
  When "steady 'tis," he replied.

"A plague on all our Congress men!
  "Light-houses so thick I see—
"Odd's bloods! on such a darksome night
  "They bother exceedingly."

'Twas a sad mistake; he saw but one,
  And that was not Seguin;
But the Skipper's brain like the Light revolved
  So he lost his reckoning.

And what of her, the "Two Polleys?"
  She still did the helm obey;
Though her gunwales kissed the hissing surge,
  And her deck was washed with the spray.

She neared the rocks, and the waves ran high,
  But the Skipper heard not their roar;
His hand was clutched to the well-lashed helm,
  But his head was on the floor.

The sun shone out on Richmond's Isle—
  But what is that on the strand?
A broken mast and a tattered sail,
  Half buried in the sand.

And there were heaps of old dun fish,
  The fruits of many a haul,
But nothing was seen of the old Skipper,
  Nor of one-eyed Isaac Small.

Three days had gone when a "homeward bound"
  Was entering Casco Bay;
And Richmond's Isle bore Nor' Nor' West.
  And for that her course she lay.

Yet scarcely three knots did she make,
  For it was a cat's-paw breeze;
And the crew hung idly round her bows,
  Watching the porpoises.

But there leans one on the quarter rail,
  And a sudden sight he sees
Then floating past—'tis a smack's pink stern,
  And on it—the "Two Polleys."

ALBERT G. GREENE,

The author of the popular ballad of "Old Grimes," a poet of cultivation, and an ardent prosecutor of the historical literature of Rhode Island, is a native of that state, where he was born at Providence, February 10, 1802. He is a graduate of Brown University, a lawyer by profession, and has for a number of years filled the offices of Clerk of the Municipal Court of the city of Providence, and Clerk of the Common Council.

Mr. Greene's fugitive poems have never been collected, and a portion of them, of which the reputation has got abroad, are still in manuscript.

Among these is a quaint comic poem, entitled *The Militia Muster*, a remarkable thesaurus of the Yankee dialect, and of the vulgarisms of New England. One of the longest of Mr. Greene's serious poems, a ballad entitled *Canonchet*, is published in Updike's History of the Narraghansett Church.

Mr. Greene has been a curious collector of American poetry, of which he has a large library; and it is understood, contemplates a publication on the subject.

TO THE WEATHERCOCK ON OUR STEEPLE.

The dawn has broke, the morn is up,
  Another day begun;
And there thy poised and gilded spear
  Is flashing in the sun,
Upon that steep and lofty tower
  Where thou thy watch hast kept,
A true and faithful sentinel,
  While all around thee slept.

For years upon thee there has poured
  The summer's noon-day heat,
And through the long, dark, starless night,
  The winter storms have beat;
And yet thy duty has been done,
  By day and night the same,
Still thou hast met and faced the storm,
  Whichever way it came.

No chilling blast in wrath has swept
  Along the distant heaven,
But thou hast watched its onward course
  And instant warning given;
And when mid-summer's sultry beams
  Oppress all living things,
Thou dost foretell each breeze that comes
  With health upon its wings.

How oft I've seen, at early dawn,
  Or twilight's quiet hour,
The swallows, in their joyous glee,
  Come darting round thy tower,
As if, with thee, to hail the sun
  And catch its earliest light,
And offer ye the morn's salute,
  Or bid ye both—good night.

And when, around thee or above,
  No breath of air has stirred,
Thou seem'st to watch the circling flight
  Of each free, happy bird,
Till after twittering round thy head
  In many a mazy track,
The whole delighted company
  Have settled on thy back.

Then, if perchance amidst their mirth,
  A gentle breeze has sprung,
And prompt to mark its first approach,
  Thy eager form hath swung,
I've thought I almost heard thee say,
  As far aloft they flew—
"Now all away!—here ends our play,
  For I have work to do!"

Men slander thee, my honest friend,
  And call thee in their pride,
An emblem of their fickleness,
  Thou ever faithful guide.
Each weak, unstable human mind
  A "weathercock" they call;
And thus, unthinkingly, mankind
  Abuse thee, one and all.

They have no right to make thy name
  A by-word for their deeds:—

They change their friends, their principles,
  Their fashions, and their creeds;
Whilst thou hast ne'er, like them, been known
  Thus causelessly to range;
But when thou *changest sides*, canst give
  Good reason for the change.

Thou, like some lofty soul, whose course
  The thoughtless oft condemn,
Art touched by many airs from heaven
  Which never breathe on them,—
And moved by many impulses
  Which they do never know,
Who, 'round their earth-bound circles, plod
  The dusty paths below.

Through one more dark and cheerless night
  Thou well hast kept thy trust,
And now in glory o'er thy head
  The morning light has burst.
And unto Earth's true watcher, thus,
  When his dark hours have passed,
Will come "the day-spring from on high,"
  To cheer his path at last.

Bright symbol of *fidelity*,
  Still may I think of thee;
And may the lesson thou dost teach
  Be never lost on me;—
But still, in sun-shine or in storm,
  Whatever task is mine,
May I be faithful to *my* trust
  As thou hast been to *thine*.

THE BARON'S LAST BANQUET.

O'er a low couch the setting sun had thrown its latest ray,
Where in his last strong agony a dying warrior lay,
The stern old Baron Rudiger, whose frame had ne'er been bent
By wasting pain, till time and toil its iron strength had spent.

"They come around me here, and say my days of life are o'er,
That I shall mount my noble steed and lead my band no more;
They come, and to my beard they dare tell me now, that I,
Their own liege lord and master born,—that I, ha! ha! must die.

And what is death? I've dared him oft before the Paynim spear,—
Think ye he's entered at my gate, has come to seek me here?
I've met him, faced him, scorned him, when the fight was raging hot,—
I'll try his might—I'll brave his power; defy, and fear him not.

Ho! sound the tocsin from my tower, and fire the culverin,—
Bid each retainer arm with speed,—call every vassal in,
Up with my banner on the wall,—the banquet board prepare;
Throw wide the portal of my hall, and bring my armor there!"

An hundred hands were busy then—the banquet forth was spread—
And rung the heavy oaken floor with many a martial tread,
While from the rich, dark tracery along the vaulted wall,
Lights gleamed on harness, plume, and spear, o'er the proud old Gothic hall.

Fast hurrying through the outer gate the mailed retainers poured,
On through the portal's frowning arch, and thronged around the board.
While at its head, within his dark, carved oaken chair of state,
Armed cap-a-pie, stern Rudiger, with girded falchion, sate.

"Fill every beaker up, my men, pour forth the cheering wine,
There's life and strength in every drop,—thanksgiving to the vine!
Are ye all there, my vassals true?—mine eyes are waxing dim;
Fill round, my tried and fearless ones, each goblet to the brim.

"You're there, but yet I see ye not. Draw forth each trusty sword—
And let me hear your faithful steel clash once around my board:
I hear it faintly:—Louder yet!—What clogs my heavy breath?
Up all, and shout for Rudiger, 'Defiance unto Death!'"

Bowl rang to bowl—steel clang to steel—and rose a deafening cry
That made the torches flare around, and shook the flags on high:—
"Ho! cravens, do ye fear him?—Slaves, traitors! have ye flown?
Ho! cowards, have ye left me to meet him here alone!

But *I* defy him:—let him come!" Down rang the massy cup,
While from its sheath the ready blade came flashing half way up;
And with the black and heavy plumes scarce trembling on his head,
There in his dark, carved oaken chair, Old Rudiger sat, *dead*.

OLD GRIMES.

Old Grimes is dead; that good old man
We never shall see more:
He used to wear a long, black coat
All buttoned down before.

His heart was open as the day,
His feelings all were true;
His hair was some inclined to grey,
He wore it in a queue.

Whene'er he heard the voice of pain,
His breast with pity burned;
The large, round head upon his cane
From ivory was turned.

Kind words he ever had for all;
He knew no base design:
His eyes were dark and rather small,
His nose was aquiline.

He lived at peace with all mankind,
In friendship he was true:
His coat had pocket holes behind,
His pantaloons were blue.

Unharmed, the sin which earth pollutes
He passed securely o'er,
And never wore a pair of boots
For thirty years or more.

But good old Grimes is now at rest,
Nor fears misfortune's frown;
He wore a double-breasted vest;
The stripes ran up and down.

He modest merit sought to find,
And pay it its desert;
He had no malice in his mind,
No ruffles on his shirt.

His neighbors he did not abuse,
Was sociable and gay;
He wore large buckles on his shoes,
And changed them every day.

His knowledge, hid from public gaze,
He did not bring to view,—
Nor make a noise, town-meeting days,
As many people do.

His worldly goods he never threw
In trust to fortune's chances;
But lived (as all his brothers do)
In easy circumstances.

Thus undisturbed by anxious cares,
His peaceful moments ran;
And every body said he was
A fine old gentleman.

EDWARD COATE PINKNEY,

The lyric poet, was the son of the eminent lawyer and diplomatist of Maryland, William Pinkney, and was born in London, October, 1802, while his father was minister to the English Court. At the age of nine he was brought home with his parents to America, and was educated at the college at Baltimore. At fourteen he entered the navy as a midshipman, and remained nine years in the service, during which he became intimately acquainted with the classic scenes of the Mediterranean. After the death of his father in 1822, he resigned his appointment in the navy, married, and occupied himself with the law, which he pursued with some uncertainty.

The small volume of poems, sufficiently large to preserve his memory with all generous appreciators of true poetry as a writer of exquisite taste and susceptibility, appeared in Baltimore in 1825. It contained *Rodolph, a Fragment*, which had previously been printed anonymously for the author's friends. It is a powerful sketch of a broken life of passion and remorse, of a husband slain by the lover of his wife, of her early death in a convent, and of the paramour's wanderings and wild mental anticipations. Though a fragment, wanting in fulness of design and the last polish of execution, it is a poem of power and mark. There is an occasional inner music in the lines, demonstrative of the true poet. The imagery is happy and original, evidently derived from objects which the writer had seen in the impressible youth of his voyages in the navy. We follow the poem in a few of these similes. This is the striking opening.

The Summer's heir on land and sea
Had thrown his parting glance,
And Winter taken angrily
His waste inheritance.
The winds in stormy revelry
Sported beneath a frowning sky;
The chafing waves with hollow roar
Tumbled upon the shaken shore,
And sent their spray in upward shower
To Rodolph's proud ancestral tower,
Whose station from its mural crown
A regal look cast sternly down.

Here are the lady and her lover.

Like rarest porcelain were they,
Moulded of accidental clay:
She, loving, lovely, kind, and fair—
He, wise, and fortunate, and brave—
You'll easily suppose they were
A passionate and radiant pair,
Lighting the scenes else dark and cold,
As the sepulchral lamps of old,
A subterranean cave.
'Tis pity that their loves were vices,
And purchased at such painful prices;
'Tis pity, and Delight deplores
That grief allays her golden stores.
Yet if all chance brought rapture here,
Life would become a ceaseless fear
To leave a world then rightly dear.
Two kindred mysteries are bright,*
And cloud-like, in the southern sky;
A shadow and its sister-light,
Around the pole they float on high,
Linked in a strong though sightless chain,
The types of pleasure and of pain.

The sequel.

There was an age, they tell us, when
Eros and Anteros dwelt with men,
Ere selfishness had backward driven
The wrathful deities to heaven:
Then gods forsook their outshone skies,
For stars mistaking female eyes;
Woman was true, and man, though free,
Was faithful in idolatry.
No dial needed they to measure
Unsighing being—Time was pleasure,
And lustres, never dimmed by tears,
Were not misnamed from lustrous years.
Alas! that such a tale must seem
The fiction of a dreaming dream!—
Is it but fable?—has that age
Shone only on the poet's page,
Where earth, a luminous sphere portrayed,
Revolves not both in sun and shade?—
No!—happy love, too seldom known,
May make it for a while our own.

Yes, although fleeting rapidly,
It sometimes may be ours,
And he was gladsome as the bee,†
Which always sleeps in flowers.
Might this endure?—her husband came
At an untimely tide,
But ere his tongue pronounced her shame,
Slain suddenly, he died.
'Twas whispered by whose hand he fell,
And Rodolph's prosperous loves were gone.
The lady sought a convent-cell,
And lived in penitence alone;
Thrice blest, that she the waves among
Of ebbing pleasures staid not long,
To watch the sullen tide, and find
The hideous shapings left behind.
Such, sinking to its slimy bed,
Old Nile upon the antique land,
Where Time's inviolate temples stand,‡
Hath ne'er deposited.
Happy, the monster of that Nile,
The vast and vigorous crocodile;
Happy, because his dying day
Is unpreceded by decay:
We perish slowly—loss of breath
Only completes our piecemeal death.
She ceased to smile back on the sun,
Their task the Destinies had done;
And earth, which gave, resumed the charms,
Whose freshness withered in its arms:
But never walked upon its face,
Nor mouldered in its dull embrace,
A creature fitter to prepare
Sorrow, or social joy to share:
When her the latter life required,
A vital harmony expired;
And in that melancholy hour,
Nature displayed its saddest power,
Subtracting from man's darkened eye
Beauties that seemed unmeant to die,
And claiming deeper sympathy
Than even when the wise or brave
Descend into an early grave.
We grieve when morning puts to flight
The pleasant visions of the night;
And surely we shall have good leave,
When a fair woman dies, to grieve.
Whither have fled that shape and gleam
Of thought—the woman, and the dream?—
Whither have fled that inner light,
And benefactress of our sight?—

A second part describes the visions of Rodolph's distempered mind. In it occurs this fine passage on the prophetic sense of fear.

———Hearts are prophets still.
What though the fount of Castaly
Not now stains leaves with prophecy?
What though are of another age
Omens and Sybil's boding page?—
Augurs and oracles resign
Their voices—fear can still divine:
Dreams and hand-writings on the wall
Need not foretell our fortune's fall;
Domitian in his galleries,*
The soul all hostile advents sees,
As in the mirror-stone;
Like shadows by a brilliant day
Cast down from falcons on their prey;
Or watery demons, in strong light,
By haunted waves of fountains old,
Shown indistinctly to the sight
Of the inquisitive and bold.
The mind is capable to show
Thoughts of so dim a feature,
That consciousness can only know
Their presence, not their nature;
Things which, like fleeting insect-mothers
Supply recording life to others,
And forthwith lose their own.

The remaining poems were brief, consisting of a short poetical sketch, The Indian's Bride; a Reminiscence of Italy; an Occasional Prologue, delivered at the Greek Benefit in Baltimore in 1823, and a number of passionate, sensuous songs, dedicated to love and the fair.

The author did not long survive the publication of this volume. He died in Baltimore in 1828. An appreciative biographical notice of him appeared the year previously, from the pen of the late William Leggett, in the "Old Mirror," which speaks warmly of his shorter poems as "rich in beauties of a peculiar nature, and not surpassed by productions of a similar character in the English language." The poem "On Italy," Leggett especially admired. He particularly notes the power of the four lines beginning

* The Magellan clouds. † The Floriscomnia.
‡ The Pyramids.

* *Vide* Suetonius.

The winds are awed, nor dare to breathe aloud;

and the beauty of the portrait in "The Indian's Bride."

Exchanging lustre with the sun,
A part of day she strays—
A glancing, living, human smile,
On nature's face she plays.

The poems of Pinkney were published in a second edition at Baltimore in 1838, and in 1844 appeared, with a brief introduction by Mr. N. P. Willis, in the series of the Mirror Library entitled "The Rococo."

ITALY.

Know'st thou the land which lovers ought to choose?
Like blessings there descend the sparkling dews;
In gleaming streams the crystal rivers run,
The purple vintage clusters in the sun;
Odors of flowers haunt the balmy breeze,
Rich fruits hang high upon the vernant trees;
And vivid blossoms gem the shady groves,
Where bright-plumed birds discourse their careless loves.
Beloved!—speed we from this sullen strand
Until thy light feet press that green shore's yellow sand.

Look seaward thence, and naught shall meet thine eye
But fairy isles, like paintings on the sky;
And, flying fast and free before the gale,
The gaudy vessel with its glancing sail;
And waters glittering in the glare of noon,
Or touched with silver by the stars and moon,
Or flecked with broken lines of crimson light
When the far fisher's fire affronts the night.
Lovely as loved! towards that smiling shore
Bear we our household gods, to fix for evermore.

It looks a dimple on the face of earth,
The seal of beauty, and the shrine of mirth,
Nature is delicate and graceful there,
The place's genius, feminine and fair:
The winds are awed, nor dare to breathe aloud;
The air seems never to have borne a cloud,
Save where volcanoes send to heaven their curled
And solemn smokes, like altars of the world.
Thrice beautiful!—to that delightful spot
Carry our married hearts, and be all pain forgot.

There Art too shows, when Nature's beauty palls,
Her sculptured marbles, and her pictured walls;
And there are forms in which they both conspire
To whisper themes that know not how to tire:
The speaking ruins in that gentle clime
Have but been hallowed by the hand of Time,
And each can mutely prompt some thought of flame—
The meanest stone is not without a name.
Then come, beloved!—hasten o'er the sea
To build our happy hearth in blooming Italy.

THE INDIAN'S BRIDE.

Why is that graceful female here
With yon red hunter of the deer?
Of gentle mien and shape, she seems
For civil halls designed,
Yet with the stately savage walks
As she were of his kind.
Look on her leafy diadem,
Enriched with many a floral gem:
Those simple ornaments about
Her candid brow, disclose
The loitering Spring's last violet,
And Summer's earliest rose:
But not a flower lies breathing there,
Sweet as herself, or half so fair.
Exchanging lustre with the sun,
A part of day she strays—
A glancing, living, human smile,
On Nature's face she plays.
Can none instruct me what are these
Companions of the lofty trees?—

Intent to blend with his her lot,
Fate formed her all that he was not;
And, as by mere unlikeness thoughts
Associate we see,
Their hearts from very difference caught
A perfect sympathy.
The household goddess here to be
Of that one dusky votary,—
She left her pallid countrymen,
An earthling most divine,
And sought in this sequestered wood
A solitary shrine.
Behold them roaming hand in hand,
Like night and sleep, along the land;
Observe their movements:—he for her
Restrains his active stride,
While she assumes a bolder gait
To ramble at his side;
Thus, even as the steps they frame,
Their souls fast alter to the same.
The one forsakes ferocity,
And momently grows mild;
The other tempers more and more
The artful with the wild.
She humanizes him, and he
Educates her to liberty.

Oh, say not they must soon be old,
Their limbs prove faint, their breasts feel cold!
Yet envy I that sylvan pair,
More than my words express,
The singular beauty of their lot,
And seeming happiness.
They have not been reduced to share
The painful pleasures of despair:
Their sun declines not in the sky,
Nor are their wishes cast,
Like shadows of the afternoon,
Repining towards the past:
With naught to dread, or to repent,
The present yields them full content.
In solitude there is no crime;
Their actions are all free,
And passion lends their way of life
The only dignity;
And how should they have any cares?—
Whose interest contends with theirs?

The world, or all they know of it,
Is theirs:—for them the stars are lit;
For them the earth beneath is green,
The heavens above are bright;
For them the moon doth wax and wane,
And decorate the night;
For them the branches of those trees
Wave music in the vernal breeze;
For them upon that dancing spray
The free bird sits and sings,
And glittering insects flit about
Upon delighted wings;
For them that brook, the brakes among,
Murmurs its small and drowsy song;
For them the many-colored clouds
Their shapes diversify,
And change at once, like smiles and frowns,
The expression of the sky.

For them, and by them, all is gay,
And fresh and beautiful as they:
The images their minds receive,
Their minds assimilate,
To outward forms imparting thus
The glory of their state.
Could aught be painted otherwise
Than fair, seen through her star-bright eyes!
He too, because she fills his sight,
Each object falsely sees;
The pleasure that he has in her,
Makes all things seem to please,
And this is love;—and it is life
They lead,—that Indian and his wife.

A PICTURE-SONG.

How may this little tablet feign the features of a face,
Which o'er-informs with loveliness its proper share of space;
Or human hands on ivory enable us to see
The charms that all must wonder at, thou work of gods, in thee!

But yet, methinks, that sunny smile familiar stories tells,
And I should know those placid eyes, two shaded crystal wells;
Nor can my soul the limner's art attesting with a sigh,
Forget the blood that decked thy cheek, as rosy clouds the sky.

They could not semble what thou art, more excellent than fair,
As soft as sleep or pity is, and pure as mountain air;
But here are common, earthly hues, to such an aspect wrought,
That none, save thine, can seem so like the beautiful of thought.

The song I sing, thy likeness like, is painful mimicry
Of something better, which is now a memory to me,
Who have upon life's frozen sea arrived the icy spot,
Where men's magnetic feelings show their guiding task forgot.

The sportive hopes, that used to chase their shifting shadows on,
Like children playing in the sun, are gone—for ever gone;
And on a careless, sullen peace, my double-fronted mind,
Like Janus when his gates were shut, looks forward and behind.

Apollo placed his harp, of old, awhile upon a stone,
Which has resounded since, when struck, a breaking harp-string's tone;
And thus my heart, though wholly now from early softness free,
If touched, will yield the music yet, it first received of thee.

SONG.

I need not name thy thrilling name,
Though now I drink to thee, my dear,
Since all sounds shape that magic word,
That fall upon my ear,—Mary;
And silence, with a wakeful voice,
Speaks it in accents loudly free,
As darkness hath a light that shows
Thy gentle face to me,—Mary.

I pledge thee in the grape's pure soul,
With scarce one hope, and many fears,
Mixed, were I of a melting mood,
With many bitter tears,—Mary—
I pledge thee, and the empty cup
Emblems this hollow life of mine,
To which, a gone enchantment, thou
No more wilt be the wine,—Mary.

A HEALTH.

I fill this cup to one made up of loveliness alone,
A woman, of her gentle sex the seeming paragon;
To whom the better elements and kindly stars have given
A form so fair, that, like the air, 'tis less of earth than heaven.

Her every tone is music's own, like those of morning birds,
And something more than melody dwells ever in her words;
The coinage of her heart are they, and from her lips each flows
As one may see the burthened bee forth issue from the rose.

Affections are as thoughts to her, the measures of her hours;
Her feelings have the fragrancy, the freshness of young flowers;
And lovely passions, changing oft, so fill her, she appears
The image of themselves by turns,—the idol of past years.

Of her bright face one glance will trace a picture on the brain,
And of her voice in echoing hearts a sound must long remain;
But memory such as mine of her so very much endears,
When death is nigh my latest sigh will not be life's but hers.

I filled this cup to one made up of loveliness alone,
A woman, of her gentle sex, the seeming paragon—
Her health! and would on earth there stood some more of such a frame,
That life might be all poetry, and weariness a name.

BELA BATES EDWARDS.

THE successor, and previously the associate of Moses Stuart in his professorship at Andover, was the Rev. Bela B. Edwards, also prominently connected with the theological and educational literature of the country. He was born at Southampton, Massachusetts, July 4, 1802. His family was one of the oldest in the country, boasting "a long line of godly progenitors," originally springing from a Welsh stock, which contained among its descendants the two Jonathan Edwardses and President Dwight.* Mr. Edwards became a graduate of Amherst in 1824, and was subsequently for two years, from 1826 to 1828, a tutor in that college. He had previously, in 1825, entered the Andover Theological Seminary, where he continued his studies and was licensed as a preacher in 1830. Though with many fine qualities in the pulpit, which his biographer, Professor Parks, has fondly traced, he lacked the ordinary essentials of voice and manner for that vocation. The main energies of his life were to be devoted to the cause of instruction through the press and the professor's chair.

While tutor at Amherst he conducted in part a

* At least Mr. Edwards was disposed to maintain this view of his genealogy. Memoir by Edwards A. Park, p. 9.

weekly journal, the New England Inquirer, and was afterwards occasionally employed in superintending the Boston Recorder.

As Assistant Secretary of the American Education Society, he conducted, from 1828 to 1842, the valuable statistical and historical *American Quarterly Register*, a herculean work as he worked upon it, a journal of fidelity and laborious research in the biography of the pulpit and the annals of American seats of learning, and generally all the special educational interests of the country.*

In July, 1833, he established the *American Quarterly Observer*, a journal of the order of the higher reviews; which, after three volumes were published, was united in 1835 with the *Biblical Repository*, which had been conducted by Professor Robinson. Edwards edited the combined work known as the *American Biblical Repository*, until January, 1838.

In 1844 he became engaged in the publication of the *Bibliotheca Sacra and Theological Review* at Andover, which had been established the previous year at New York by Professor Robinson. He was employed in the care of this work till 1852. In January, 1851, the Biblical Repository was united with the Bibliotheca Sacra. "He was thus," adds Professor Parks, "employed for twenty-three years in superintending our periodical literature; and with the aid of several associates, left thirty-one octavo volumes as the monuments of his enterprise and industry in this onerous department." Dr. Edwards's own contributions to these periodicals were criticisms on the books of the day, the discussion of the science of education, and the cultivation of biblical literature.

Dr. Edwards's Professorship of Hebrew in the Andover Seminary dated from 1837. In 1848, on the retirement of Professor Stuart, he was elected to the chair of Biblical Literature. He had previously, in 1846–47, travelled in Europe, where he made the study of religious institutions, the universities, and other liberal objects, subservient to his professional labors. Professor Parks, with characteristic animation, has given, in his notice of this tour, the following pleasing picture of the inspirations which wait upon the serious American student visiting Europe.*

And when he made the tour of Europe for his health, he did not forget his one idea. He revelled amid the treasures of the Bodleian Library, and the Royal Library at Paris; he sat as a learner at the feet of Montgomery, Wordsworth, Chalmers, Mezzofanti, Neander, the Geological Society of London, and the Oriental Society of Germany, and he bore away from all these scenes new helps for his own comprehensive science. He had translated a Biography of Melancthon, for the sake, in part, of qualifying himself to look upon the towers of Wittemberg; and he could scarcely keep his seat in the rail-car, when he approached the city consecrated by the gentle Philip. He measured with his umbrella the cell of Luther at Erfurt, wrote his own name with ink from Luther's inkstand, read some of the notes which the monk had penned in the old Bible, gazed intently on the spot where the intrepid man had preached, and thus by the minutest observations he strove to imbue his mind with the hearty faith of the Reformer. So he might become the more profound and genial as a teacher. This was a ruling passion with him. He gleaned illustrations of divine truth, like Alpine flowers, along the borders of the Mer de Glace, and by the banks of "the troubled Arve," and at the foot of the Jungfrau. He drew pencil sketches of the battle-field at Waterloo, of Niebuhr's monument at Bonn, and of the cemetery where he surmised for a moment that perhaps he had found the burial-place of John Calvin. With the eye of a geologist, he investigated the phenomena of the Swiss glaciers, and with the spirit of a mental philosopher he analysed the causes of the impression made by the Valley of Chamouni. He wrote tasteful criticisms on the works of Salvator Rosa, Correggio, Titian, Murillo, Vandyke, Canova, Thorwaldsen; he trembled before the Transfiguration by Raphael, and the Last Judgment by Michael Angelo; he was refreshed with the Italian music, "unwinding the very soul of harmony;" he stood entranced before the colonnades and under the dome of St. Peter's, and on the walls of the Colosseum by moonlight, and amid the statues of the Vatican by torchlight, and on the roof of the St. John Lateran at sunset, "where," he says, "I beheld a prospect such as probably earth cannot elsewhere furnish;" he walked the Appian Way, exclaiming: "On this identical road,—the old pavements now existing in many places,—on these fields, over these hills, down these rivers and bays, Horace, Virgil, Cicero, Marius, and other distinguished Romans, walked, or wandered, or sailed; here, also, apostles and martyrs once journeyed, or were led to their scene of suffering; over a part of this very road there is no doubt that Paul travelled, when he went bound to Rome." He wrote sketches of all these scenes; and in such a style as proves his intention to regale his own mind with the remembrance of them, to adorn his lectures with descriptions of them, to enrich his commentaries with the images and the suggestions which his chaste fancy had drawn from them. But, alas! all these fragments of thought now sleep, like the broken statues of the Parthenon; and where is the power of genius that can restore the full meaning of these lines, and call back their lost charms! Where is that more than Promethean fire that can their light relume!

The remaining years of Edwards's life were spent in the duties of his Professorship at Andover, in which he taught both Greek and Hebrew. To perfect himself in German he took part in translating a volume of Selections from German Literature; and for a similar object engaged with President Barnes Sears, of the Newton Theological Institution, and Professor Felton of Harvard, in the preparation of the volume on classical studies entitled *Essays on Ancient Literature and Art, with the Biography and Correspondence of Eminent Philologists.** Professor Edwards's portions of this interesting and stimulating work were the Essays on the "Study of Greek Literature" and of "Classical Antiquity," and the chapter on "the School of Philology in Holland."

* This periodical was established in 1827 and called the Quarterly Journal of the American Education Society. In 1829 it took the name of the Quarterly Register and Journal of the American Education Society. In 1830 its title became the Quarterly Register of the American Education Society. From 1831 it was called the American Quarterly Register. The Rev. Elias Cornelius was associated with Mr. Edwards in editing the first and second volumes; the Rev. Dr. Cogswell in editing the tenth, eleventh, twelfth, and thirteenth; and the Rev. Samuel H. Riddell in editing the fourteenth volume.—Parks's Memoir, p. 76.

† Memoir, pp. 160–2.

* Published by Gould, Kendall, & Lincoln. 1843.

In 1844 Professor Edwards was associated with Mr. Samuel H. Taylor in translating the larger Greek Grammar of Dr. Kuhner, and in 1850 revising that work for a second edition.

While undergoing these toils and duties the health of the devoted student was broken and feeble. Symptoms of a pulmonary complaint had early appeared, and the overworked machine was now to yield before the labors imposed upon it. In the fall of 1845 Professor Edwards was compelled to visit Florida for his health, and the following spring, on his return to the north, sailed immediately for Europe, passing a year among the scholars and amidst the classic associations of England and the continent. He bestowed especial attention upon the colleges and libraries. In particular he visited the Red Cross Library in Cripplegate, London, founded by the Rev. Dr. Daniel Williams, an English Presbyterian Minister, who lived from 1644 to 1716. It is a collection of twenty thousand volumes, chiefly theological. The sight of this led Professor Edwards to propose a similar Puritan library to the Congregationalists of New England, which has been since, in part, carried out.*

He returned to Andover in May, 1847, resumed his studies, and while "yielding inch by inch to his insidious disease, with customary forethought, persisted in accumulating new materials for new commentaries." He prepared expositions of Habakkuk, Job, the Psalms, and the First Epistle to the Corinthians, and was engaged in other labors. In the autumn of 1851 he again visited the South fatally stricken, took up his residence in Athens, Georgia, and died at that place April 20, 1852, in the forty-ninth year of his age.

An honorable tribute to his memory was paid the following year in the publication, in Boston, of two volumes, *The Writings of Professor B. B. Edwards, with a Memoir by Edwards A. Park.* The selection contains sermons preached at Andover, and a series of essays, addresses, and lectures, not merely of scholastic but of general interest. The Memoir is a minute and thoughtful scholar's biography.

* Edwards's plan and arguments for the work are published in Professor Parks's Memoir.

WILLIAM LEGGETT.

William Leggett, an able and independent political writer, was born in the city of New York in the summer of 1802. He entered the college at Georgetown, in the district of Columbia, where he took a high scholastic rank, but in consequence of his father's failure in business, was withdrawn before the completion of his course, and in 1819 accompanied his father and family in their settlement on the then virgin soil of the Illinois prairies. The experience of western pioneer life thus acquired, was turned to good account in his subsequent literary career.

In 1822 he entered the navy, having obtained the appointment of midshipman. He resigned his commission in 1826, owing, it is said, to the harsh conduct of the commander under whom he sailed, and shortly after published a volume of verses, written at intervals during his naval career, entitled *Leisure Hours at Sea.** The poems show a ready command of language, a noticeable youthful facility in versification, and an intensity of feeling; beyond this they exhibit no peculiar merit, either of originality or scholarship. A single specimen will indicate their quality.

SONG.

Improbe amor, quid non mortalia pectora cogis!
ÆNEID, lib. 4.

The tear which thou upbraidest
  Thy falsehood taught to flow;
The misery which thou madest
  My cheek hath blighted so:
The charms, alas! that won me,
  I never can forget,
Although thou hast undone me,
  I own I love thee yet.

Go, seek the happier maiden
  Who lured thy love from me;
My heart with sorrow laden
  Is no more prized by thee:
Repeat the vows you made me,
  Say, swear thy love is true;
Thy faithless vows betrayed me,
  They may betray her too.

But no! may she ne'er languish
  Like me in shame and woe;
Ne'er feel the throbbing anguish
  That I am doomed to know!
The eye that once was beaming
  A tale of love for thee,
Is now with sorrow streaming,
  For thou art false to me.

He also wrote in the *Atlantic Souvenir*, one of the earliest of the American annuals, a prose tale,

The Rifle, in which he portrayed with spirit the scenes and incidents of western adventure. This

* Leisure Hours at Sea; being a few Miscellaneous Poems, by a Midshipman of the United States Navy—

Πως το οιγειως εργον αγαπω.
'T is pleasant, sure, to see one's *work* in print;
A book's a book, although there's nothing in't.
BYRON.

New York: George C. Morgan, and E. Bliss and E. White. 1825. 18mo. pp. 148.

met with such great success, from the novelty of its subject as well as its excellence of execution, that it was speedily followed by other tales of sea as well as land. The whole were subsequently collected under the title of *Tales by a Country Schoolmaster*.

In 1828 Mr. Leggett married Miss Elmira Leggett of New Rochelle, and in November of the same year commenced *The Critic*, a weekly literary periodical, in which the reviews, notices of the drama and the arts, the tales, essays, and entire contents, with the exception of a few poems, were from his own pen. Several of the last numbers were not only entirely written, but also set in type, and distributed to subscribers by himself. The editor displayed great ability as well as versatility, but the work was discontinued at the end of six months, for want of support, and united with the Mirror, to which its editor became a regular contributor.

In the summer of 1829 Leggett became, with Wm. C. Bryant, one of the editors of the Evening Post, a position which he retained until December, 1836. It is somewhat singular, that at the outset he stipulated that he should not be called upon for articles on political subjects, on which he had no settled opinions, and for which he had no taste. Before the year was out, however, adds his associate, Mr. Bryant, he found himself a zealous Democrat, and took decided ground in favor of free trade, against the United States Bank, and all connexion by the federal or state governments, with similar institutions, contending that banking, like other business operations, should be untrammelled by government aid or restriction. In 1835, during the riots, in which certain abolition meetings were attacked and dispersed with violence, he defended the right of liberty of speech with the same freedom with which he treated other questions. In October of this year he was attacked by a severe illness, that interrupted his editorial labors for a twelvemonth, which, in consequence of the absence in Europe of his associate, included the entire charge of the paper. Not long after his recovery he left the Post, which, it appeared after investigation on Mr. Bryant's return, had suffered in its finances, on account of his course on the abolition question, and the withdrawal of advertisers in consequence of the removal, by his order, from the notices of "houses for sale and to let," of the small pictorial representation of the article in question, for the sake of uniformity in the typographical appearance of the sheet.*

He then commenced a weekly paper, with the characteristic title of *The Plaindealer*. It was conducted with his usual ability, in its literary as well as political departments, and was widely circulated, but was involved in the failure of its publisher and discontinued at the expiration of ten months. Mr. Leggett did not afterwards engage in any new literary project, but passed the short remainder of his life, his health being greatly impaired, in retirement at his country place at New Rochelle, on Long Island Sound, which had been his home since his marriage.

In May, 1839, he was appointed by Mr. Van Buren Diplomatic Agent to the Republic of Guatemala, an event which gave pleasure to his friends, not only as a recognition of his public services, but from their hopes that a residence in a southern climate would be beneficial to his health. It was but a few days after, however, that the public were startled by the announcement of his death, in the midst of his preparations for departure, from a severe attack of bilious colic, on the evening of May 29, 1839.

* Bryant's History of the Evening Post.

Mr. Bryant has noted the peculiarities of Leggett in his published account of the *Evening Post*, and has dedicated a poetical tribute to his memory. In the first he speaks of him as "fond of study, and delighted to trace principles to their remotest consequences, whither he was always willing to follow them. The quality of courage existed in him almost to excess, and he took a sort of pleasure in bearding public opinion. He wrote with surprising fluency and often with eloquence, took broad views of the questions that came before him, and possessed the faculty of rapidly arranging the arguments which occurred to him in clear order, and stating them persuasively."

In the following the same pen expresses the sentiment inspired by these facts:—

IN MEMORY OF WILLIAM LEGGETT.

The earth may ring, from shore to shore,
With echoes of a glorious name,
But he, whose loss our tears deplore,
Has left behind him more than fame.

For when the death-frost came to lie
On Leggett's warm and mighty heart,
And quench his bold and friendly eye,
His spirit did not all depart.

The words of fire that from his pen
Were flung upon the fervid page,
Still move, still shake the hearts of men
Amid a cold and coward age.

His love of truth, too warm, too strong
For Hope or Fear to chain or chill,
His hate of tyranny and wrong,
Burn in the breasts he kindled still.

A collection of Leggett's political writings, in two volumes, edited by his friend Mr. Theodore Sedgwick, was published a few months after.

In person Mr. Leggett was of medium height, and compactly built, and possessed great powers of endurance.*

THE MAIN-TRUCK, OR A LEAP FOR LIFE.

Stand still! How fearful
And dizzy 'tis to cast one's eyes so low!

The murmuring surge,
That on th' unnumbered idle pebbles chafes,
Cannot be heard so high:—I'll look no more,
Lest my brain turn, and the deficient sight
Topple down headlong.—*Shakespeare.*

Among the many agreeable associates whom my different cruisings and wanderings have brought me acquainted with, I can scarcely call to mind a more pleasant and companionable one than Tom Scupper. Poor fellow! he is dead and gone now—a victim to that code of false honor which has robbed the navy of too many of its choicest officers. Tom and I were messmates during a short and delightful cruise, and, for a good part of the time, we belonged to the same

* Memoir by Theodore Sedgwick in Griswold's Biographical Annual.

watch. He was a great hand to spin yarns, which, to do him justice, he sometimes told tolerably well; and many a long mid-watch has his fund of anecdote and sea stories caused to slip pleasantly away. We were lying, in the little schooner to which we were attached, in the open roadstead of Laguyra, at single anchor, when Tom told me the story which I am about to relate, as nearly as I can remember, in his own words. A vessel from Baltimore had come into Laguyra that day, and by her I had received letters from home, in one of which there was a piece of intelligence that weighed very heavily on my spirits. For some minutes after our watch commenced, Tom and I walked the deck in silence, which was soon, however, interrupted by my talkative companion, who, perceiving my depression, and wishing to divert my thoughts, began as follows:—

The last cruise I made in the Mediterranean was in Old Ironsides, as we used to call our gallant frigate. We had been backing and filling for several months on the western coast of Africa, from the Canaries down to Mesurado, in search of slave-traders; and during that time we had some pretty heavy weather. When we reached the Straits, there was a spanking wind blowing from about west-south-west; so we squared away, and without coming to at the Rock, made a straight wake for old Mahon, the general rendezvous and place of refitting for our squadrons in the Mediterranean. Immediately on arriving there, we warped in alongside the Arsenal quay, where we stripped ship to a girtline, broke out the holds, tiers, and store-rooms, and gave her a regular-built overhauling from stem to stern. For a while, everybody was busy, and all seemed bustle and confusion. Orders and replies, in loud and dissimilar voices, the shrill pipings of the different boatswain's mates, each attending to separate duties, and the mingled clatter and noise of various kinds of work, all going on at the same time, gave something of the stir and animation of a dock-yard to the usually quiet arsenal of Mahon. The boatswain and his crew were engaged in fitting a new gang of rigging; the gunner in repairing his breechings and gun-tackles; the fo'castle-men in calking; the topmen in sending down the yards and upper spars; the holders and waisters in whitewashing and holystoning; and even the poor marines were kept busy, like beasts of burden, in carrying breakers of water on their backs. On the quay, near the ship, the smoke of the armorer's forge, which had been hoisted out and sent ashore, ascended in a thick black column through the clear blue sky; from one of the neighboring white stone warehouses the sound of saw and hammer told that the carpenters were at work: near by, a livelier rattling drew attention to the cooper, who in the open air was tightening the water-casks; and not far removed, under a temporary shed, formed of spare studding-sails and tarpaulins, sat the sailmaker and his assistants, repairing the sails, which had been rent by the many storms we had encountered.

Many hands, however, make light work, and in a very few days all was accomplished; the stays and shrouds were set up and new rattled down; the yards crossed, the running-rigging rove, and sails bent; and the old craft, fresh painted and all a-taunt-o, looked as fine as a midshipman on liberty. In place of the storm-stumps, which had been stowed away among the booms and other spare spars, amidships, we had sent up cap to'-gallant-masts and royal-poles, with a sheave for sky-sails, and hoist enough for sky-scrapers above them: so you may judge the old frigate looked pretty taunt. There was a Dutch line ship in the harbor; but though we only carried forty-four to her eighty, her main-truck would hardly have reached to our royal-mast head. The side-boys, whose duty it was to lay aloft and furl the skysails, looked no bigger on the yard than a good sized duff for a midshipman's mess, and the main-truck seemed not half as large as the Turk's-head knot on the manropes of the accommodation ladder.

When we had got everything ship-shape and man-of-war fashion, we hauled out again, and took our berth about half-way between the Arsenal and Hospital island; and a pleasant view it gave us of the town and harbor of old Mahon, one of the safest and most tranquil places of anchorage in the world. The water of this beautiful inlet—which, though it makes about four miles into the land, is not much over a quarter of a mile in width—is scarcely ever ruffled by a storm; and on the delightful afternoon to which I now refer, it lay as still and motionless as a polished mirror, except when broken into momentary ripples by the paddles of some passing waterman. What little wind we had in the fore part of the day, died away at noon; and, though the first dog-watch was almost out, and the sun was near the horizon, not a breath of air had risen to disturb the deep serenity of the scene. The Dutch liner, which lay not far from us, was so clearly reflected in the glassy surface of the water, that there was not a rope about her from her main-stay to her signal-halliards, which the eye could not distinctly trace in her shadowy and inverted image. The buoy of our best bower floated abreast our larboard bow; and that, too, was so strongly imaged, that its entire bulk seemed to lie above the water, just resting on it, as if upborne on a sea of molten lead; except when now and then, the wringing of a swab, or the dashing of a bucket overboard from the head, broke up the shadow for a moment, and showed the substance but half its former apparent size. A small polacca craft had got underway from Mahon in the course of the forenoon, intending to stand over to Barcelona; but it fell dead calm just before she reached the chops of the harbor; and there she lay as motionless upon the blue surface, as if she were only part of a mimic scene, from the pencil of some accomplished painter. Her broad cotton lateen sails, as they hung drooping from the slanting and taper yards, shone with a glistening whiteness that contrasted beautifully with the dark flood in which they were reflected; and the distant sound of the guitar, which one of the sailors was listlessly playing on her deck, came sweetly over the water, and harmonized well with the quiet appearance of everything around. The whitewashed walls of the lazaretto, on a verdant headland at the mouth of the bay, glittered like silver in the slant rays of the sun; and some of its windows were burnished so brightly by the level beams, that it seemed as if the whole interior of the edifice were in flames. On the opposite side, the romantic and picturesque ruins of fort St. Philip, faintly seen, acquired double beauty from being tipped with the declining light; and the clusters of ancient looking windmills, which dot the green eminences along the bank, added, by the motionless state of their wings, to the effect of the unbroken tranquillity of the scene.

Even on board our vessel, a degree of stillness unusual for a man-of-war prevailed among the crew. It was the hour of their evening meal; and the low hum that came from the gun-deck had an indistinct and buzzing sound, which, like the tiny song of bees of a warm summer noon, rather heightened than diminished the charm of the surrounding quiet. The spar-deck was almost deserted. The quarter-master of the watch, with his spy-glass in his hand, and dressed in a frock and trowsers of snowy whiteness, stood aft upon the tafferel, erect and motionless as a statue, keeping the usual lookout. A group of some half a dozen sailors had gathered together on the forecastle, where they were supinely lying under the shade of the bulwarks; and here and there, upon the gun-slides along the gangway, sat three or four others—one, with his clothes-bag beside him, overhauling his simple wardrobe; another working a set of clues for some favorite officer's hammock; and a third engaged, perhaps, in carving his name in rude letters upon the handle of a jack-knife, or in knotting a laniard by which to suspend it round his neck.

On the top of the boom-cover, and in the full glare of the level sun, lay black Jake, the jig-maker of the ship, and a striking specimen of African peculiarities, in whose single person they were all strongly developed. His flat nose was dilated to unusual width, and his ebony cheeks fairly glistened with delight, as he looked up at the gambols of a large monkey, which, clinging to the main-stay, just above Jake's woolly head, was chattering and grinning back at the negro, as if there existed some means of mutual intelligence between them. It was my watch on deck, and I had been standing several minutes leaning on the main fiferail, amusing myself by observing the antics of the black and his congenial playmate; but at length, tiring of the rude mirth, had turned towards the tafferel, to gaze on the more agreeable features of that scene which I have feebly attempted to describe. Just at that moment a shout and a merry laugh burst upon my ear, and looking quickly round, to ascertain the cause of the unusual sound on a frigate's deck, I saw little Bob Stay (as we called our commodore's son) standing half-way up the main-hatch ladder, clapping his hands, and looking aloft at some object that seemed to inspire him with a deal of glee. A single glance to the main-yard explained the occasion of his merriment. He had been coming up from the gun-deck, when Jacko, perceiving him on the ladder, dropped suddenly down from the main-stay, and running along the boom cover, leaped upon Bob's shoulder, seized his cap from his head, and immediately darted up the main-topsail sheet, and thence to the bunt of the main-yard, where he now sat, picking threads from the tassel of his prize, and occasionally scratching his side and chattering, as if with exultation for the success of his mischief. But Bob was a sprightly, active little fellow; and though he could not climb quite as nimbly as a monkey, yet he had no mind to lose his cap without an effort to regain it. Perhaps he was more strongly incited to make chase after Jacko from noticing me to smile at his plight, or by the loud laugh of Jake, who seemed inexpressibly delighted at the occurrence, and endeavored to evince, by tumbling about the boom-cloth, shaking his huge misshapen head, and sundry other grotesque actions, the pleasure for which he had no words.

"Ha, you d——d rascal, Jacko, hab you no more respec' for de young officer, den to steal his cab? We bring you to de gangway, you black nigger, and gib you a dozen on de bare back for a tief."

The monkey looked down from his perch as if he understood the threat of the negro, and chattered a sort of defiance in answer.

"Ha, ha! Massa Stay, he say you mus' ketch him 'fore you flog him; and it's no so easy for a midshipman in boots to ketch a monkey barefoot."

A red spot mounted to the cheek of little Bob, as he cast one glance of offended pride at Jake, and then sprang across the deck to the Jacob's ladder. In an instant he was half-way up the rigging, running over the ratlines as lightly as if they were an easy flight of stairs, whilst the shrouds scarcely quivered beneath his elastic motion. In a second more his hand was on the futtocks.

"Massa Stay!" cried Jake, who sometimes, from being a favorite, ventured to take liberties with the younger officers, "Massa Stay, you best crawl through de lubber's hole—it take a sailor to climb the futtock shroud."

But he had scarcely time to utter his pretended caution before Bob was in the top. The monkey, in the meanwhile, had awaited his approach, until he had got nearly up the rigging, when it suddenly put the cap on its own head, and running along the yard to the opposite side of the top, sprang up a rope, and thence to the topmast backstay, up which it ran to the topmast cross-trees, where it again quietly seated itself, and resumed its work of picking the tassel to pieces. For several minutes I stood watching my little messmate follow Jacko from one piece of rigging to another, the monkey, all the while, seeming to exert only as much agility as was necessary to elude the pursuer, and pausing whenever the latter appeared to be growing weary of the chase. At last, by this kind of manœuvring, the mischievous animal succeeded in enticing Bob as high as the royal-mast-head, when springing suddenly on the royal stay, it ran nimbly down to the foretop-gallant-mast-head, thence down the rigging to the foretop, when leaping on the foreyard, it ran out to the yard-arm, and hung the cap on the end of the studding-sail boom, where, taking its seat, it raised a loud and exulting chattering. Bob by this time was completely tired out, and, perhaps, unwilling to return to the deck to be laughed at for his fruitless chase, he sat down in the royal cross-trees; while those who had been attracted by the sport, returned to their usual avocations or amusements. The monkey, no longer the object of pursuit or attention, remained but a little while on the yard-arm; but soon taking up the cap, returned in towards the slings, and dropped it down upon deck.

Some little piece of duty occurred at this moment to engage me, as soon as which was performed, I walked aft, and leaning my elbow on the tafferel, was quickly lost in the recollection of scenes very different from the small pantomime I had just been witnessing. Soothed by the low hum of the crew, and by the quiet loveliness of everything around, my thoughts had travelled far away from the realities of my situation, when I was suddenly startled by a cry from black Jake, which brought me on the instant back to consciousness. "My God! Massa Scupper," cried he, "Massa Stay is on de main-truck!"

A cold shudder ran through my veins as the word reached my ear. I cast my eyes up—it was too true! The adventurous boy, after resting on the royal cross-trees, had been seized with a wish to go still higher, and, impelled by one of those impulses by which men are sometimes instigated to place themselves in situations of imminent peril, without a possibility of good resulting from the exposure, he had climbed the sky-sail pole, and, at the moment of my looking up, was actually standing on the main-truck! a small circular piece of wood on the very summit of the loftiest mast, and at a height so great from the deck that my brain turned dizzy as I looked up at him. The reverse of Virgil's line was true in this instance. It was comparatively easy to ascend—but to descend—my head swam round, and my stomach felt sick at thought of the perils comprised in that one word. There was nothing above him or around him but the empty air—and beneath him, nothing but a point, a mere point—a small, unstable wheel, that seemed no bigger from the deck than the button on the end of a foil, and the taper sky-sail pole itself scarcely larger than the blade. Dreadful temerity! If he should attempt to stoop, what could he take hold of to steady his descent? His feet quite covered up the small and fearful platform that he stood upon, and beneath that, a long, smooth, naked spar, which seemed to bend with his weight, was all that upheld him from destruction. An attempt to get down from "that bad eminence," would be almost certain death; he would inevitably lose his equilibrium, and be precipitated to the deck, a crushed and shapeless mass. Such was the nature of the thoughts that crowded through my mind as I first raised my eye, and saw the terrible truth of Jake's exclamation. What was to be done in the pressing and horrible exigency? To hail him, and inform him of his danger, would be but to insure his ruin. Indeed, I fancied that the rash boy already perceived the imminence of his peril; and I half thought that I could see his limbs begin to quiver, and his cheek turn deadly pale. Every moment I expected to see the dreadful catastrophe. I could not bear to look at him, and yet could not withdraw my gaze. A film came over my eyes, and a faintness over my heart. The atmosphere seemed to grow thick, and to tremble and waver like the heated air around a furnace; the mast appeared to totter, and the ship to pass from under my feet. I myself had the sensations of one about to fall from a great height, and making a strong effort to recover myself, like that of a dreamer who fancies he is shoved from a precipice, I staggered up against the bulwarks.

When my eyes were once turned from the dreadful object to which they had been riveted, my sense and consciousness came back. I looked around me—the deck was already crowded with people. The intelligence of poor Bob's temerity had spread through the ship like wild-fire—as such news always will—and the officers and crew were all crowding to the deck to behold the appalling—the heart-rending spectacle. Every one, as he looked up, turned pale, and his eye became fastened in silence on the truck—like that of a spectator of an execution on the gallows—with a steadfast, unblinking and intense, yet abhorrent gaze, as if momentarily expecting a fatal termination to the awful suspense. No one made a suggestion—no one spoke. Every feeling, every faculty seemed to be absorbed and swallowed up in one deep, intense emotion of agony. Once the first lieutenant seized the trumpet, as if to hail poor Bob, but he had scarce raised it to his lips, when his arm dropped again, and sank listlessly down beside him, as if from a sad consciousness of the utter inutility of what he had been going to say. Every soul in the ship was now on the spar-deck, and every eye was turned to the main-truck.

At this moment there was a stir among the crew about the gangway, and directly after another face was added to those on the quarter-deck—it was that of the commodore, Bob's father. He had come alongside in a shore boat, without having been noticed by a single eye, so intense and universal was the interest that had fastened every gaze upon the spot where poor Bob stood trembling on the awful verge of fate. The commodore asked not a question, uttered not a syllable. He was a dark-faced, austere man, and it was thought by some of the midshipmen that he entertained but little affection for his son. However that might have been, it was certain that he treated him with precisely the same strict discipline that he did the other young officers, or if there was any difference at all, it was not in favor of Bob. Some who pretended to have studied his character closely, affirmed that he loved his boy too well to spoil him, and that, intending him for the arduous profession in which he had himself risen to fame and eminence, he thought it would be of service to him to experience some of its privations and hardships at the outset.

The arrival of the commodore changed the direction of several eyes, which now turned on him to trace what emotions the danger of his son would occasion. But their scrutiny was foiled. By no outward sign did he show what was passing within. His eye still retained its severe expression, his brow the slight frown which it usually wore, and his lip its haughty curl. Immediately on reaching the deck, he had ordered a marine to hand him a musket, and with this stepping aft, and getting on the lookout-block, he raised it to his shoulder, and took a deliberate aim at his son, at the same time hailing him, without a trumpet, in his voice of thunder—

"Robert!" cried he, "jump! jump overboard! or I'll fire at you!"

The boy seemed to hesitate, and it was plain that he was tottering, for his arms were thrown out like those of one scarcely able to retain his balance. The commodore raised his voice again, and in a quicker and more energetic tone, cried,

"Jump! 'tis your only chance for life."

The words were scarcely out of his mouth, before the body was seen to leave the truck and spring out into the air. A sound, between a shriek and a groan, burst from many lips. The father spoke not—sighed not—indeed he did not seem to breathe. For a moment of intense agony a pin might have been heard to drop on deck. With a rush like that of a cannon ball, the body descended to the water, and before the waves closed over it, twenty stout fellows, among them several officers, had dived from the bulwarks. Another short period of bitter suspense ensued. It rose—he was alive! his arms were seen to move! he struck out towards the ship!—and despite the discipline of a man-of-war, three loud huzzas, an outburst of unfeigned and unrestrainable joy from the hearts of our crew of five hundred men, pealed through the air, and made the welkin ring. Till this moment the old commodore had stood unmoved. The eyes, that glistening with pleasure now sought his face, saw that it was ashy pale. He attempted to descend the horse-block, but his knees bent under him; he seemed to gasp for breath, and put up his hand, as if to tear open his vest; but before he accomplished his object, he staggered forward, and would have fallen on the deck, had he not been caught by old black Jake. He was borne into his cabin, where the surgeon attended him, whose utmost skill was required to restore his mind to its usual equability and self-command, in which he at last happily succeeded. As soon as he recovered from the dreadful shock, he sent for Bob, and had a long confidential conference with him; and it was noticed, when the little fellow left the cabin, that he was in tears. The next day we sent down our taunt and dashy poles, and replaced them with the stump-to'-gallant-masts; and on the third, we weighed anchor, and made sail for Gibraltar.

GEORGE P. MORRIS

WAS born in Philadelphia in 1802. He came early in life to New York, and formed an association with the late Samuel Woodworth, with whom he commenced the publication of the Mirror in 1823.

Mr. Morris conducted this journal with distinguished success till the completion of its twentieth volume in 1842, when its publication was interrupted by the universally spread financial disasters of the times. During this period it was the representative of the best literary, dramatic, and artistic interests of the day, having among its contributors, Bryant, Halleck, Paulding, Leggett, Hoffman, and numerous other writers of distinction, while Theodore S. Fay, Nathaniel P. Willis, William Cox, Epes Sargent, were more especially identified with its pages. It was, during the period for which it was published, one of the literary "institutions" of the country. In 1843 the periodical was revived, with the title *The New Mirror*, three volumes of which were published in the royal octavo form. Mr. Willis was again associated in the editorship with Mr. Morris, contributing some of his best sketches, while the earlier numbers were weekly illustrated by the pencil of the artist J. G. Chapman. The publication was successful, but an interpretation of the postage laws interfering with its circulation, Messrs. Morris and Willis projected a new enterprise in the *Evening Mirror*, a daily paper at New York, which was commenced in the autumn of 1844. The present editor of this journal, Mr. Hiram Fuller, soon became associated in this undertaking, which was conducted for more than two years by the three associates.

Geo. P. Morris.

At the close of 1845, Mr. Morris commenced alone a new weekly, *The National Press*. It was carried on by him for nearly a year, when his former literary partner, Mr. Willis, became associated in the paper, the title of which was then changed to the *Home Journal*. Under the joint editorship it soon became firmly established, and a general favorite as a popular newspaper of the fashionable and belles-lettres interests of the day.*

We have thus presented in an uninterrupted view Mr. Morris's series of newspaper enterprises, extending over a period of thirty years. The uniform success with which they have been attended is due to his editorial tact and judgment; his shrewd sense of the public requirements; and his provision for the more refined and permanently acceptable departments of literature. Good taste and delicacy have always presided over the journals conducted by Mr. Morris. The old Mirror was liberally connected with the arts of design, supplying a series of national portraits and views of scenery from originals by Leslie, Inman, Cole, Weir, engraved by Durand, Smillie, Casilear, and others, which have not since been surpassed in their department of illustration.

One of the earliest productions of Mr. Morris was his drama of *Brier Cliff*, which was produced at the Chatham Theatre, New York, in 1837, and acted for forty nights. It was constructed on incidents of the American Revolution. This remains unpublished. In 1842, he wrote the libretto of an opera, *The Maid of Saxony*, which was set to music by Mr. C. E. Horn, and performed for fourteen nights at the Park Theatre.

The songs of Mr. Morris have been produced at intervals during the whole term of his literary career. They have been successfully set to music, and popularly sung on both sides of the Atlantic. The themes include most varieties of situation, presenting the love ballad, the patriotic song, the expression of patriotism, of friendship, and numerous occasional topics.

Undercliff.

There have been several editions of the songs and ballads—from the press of Appleton, in 1840, with illustrations by Weir and Chapman; a miniature volume by Paine and Burgess, in 1846; and a costly illustrated octavo, *The Deserted Bride, and other productions*, from the press of Scribner, in 1853, accompanied by engravings from designs by Mr. Weir, who has also illustrated each stanza of the poem, *The Whip-poor-will*, in an earlier edition, printed from steel.

A collection of specimens of the *Song Writers of America*, of *National Melodies*, a joint composition with Mr. Willis of the *Prose and Poetry of Europe and America*, with a volume of prose sketches, *The Little Frenchman and his Water Lots*, in 1838, illustrated by the comic designer

* The first number of the New York Mirror and Ladies' Literary Gazette, was published in New York, Aug. 2, 1823; the last appeared Dec. 31, 1842. The "New Mirror" was published weekly, from April 8, 1843, to Sept. 28, 1844. The first number of the Evening Mirror appeared Oct 7, 1844. The National Press became the Home Journal, with its forty-first number, Nov. 21, 1846.

Johnston, complete the list of Mr. Morris's publications.

THE WHIP-POOR-WILL.

The plaint of the wailing Whip-poor-will,
Who mourns unseen and ceaseless sings
Ever a note of wail and woe,
Till morning spreads her rosy wings,
And earth and sky in her glances glow.
J. R. DRAKE.

Why dost thou come at set of sun,
Those pensive words to say?
Why whip poor Will?—What has he done—
And who is Will, I pray?

Why come from yon leaf-shaded hill,
A suppliant at my door?—
Why ask of me to whip poor Will?
And is Will really poor?

If poverty's his crime, let mirth
From out his heart be driven;
That is the deadliest sin on earth,
And never is forgiven?

Art Will himself?—It must be so—
I learn it from thy moan,
For none can feel another's woe
As deeply as his own.

Yet wherefore strain thy tiny throat,
While other birds repose?
What means thy melancholy note?—
The mystery disclose?

Still "Whip poor Will!"—Art thou a sprite,
From unknown regions sent,
To wander in the gloom of night,
And ask for punishment?

Is thine a conscience sore beset
With guilt?—or, what is worse,
Hast thou to meet writs, duns, and debt—
No money in thy purse?

If this be thy hard fate indeed,
Ah! well mayst thou repine;
The sympathy I give, I need—
The poet's doom is thine!

Art thou a lover, Will?—Hast proved
The fairest can deceive?
Thine is the lot of all who've loved
Since Adam wedded Eve!

Hast trusted in a friend, and seen
No friend was he in need!
A common error—men still lean
Upon as frail a reed.

Hast thou, in seeking wealth or fame,
A crown of brambles won?
O'er all the earth 'tis just the same
With every mother's son!

Hast found the world a Babel wide,
Where man to Mammon stoops?
Where flourish Arrogance and Pride,
While modest merit droops?

What, none of these?—Then, whence thy pain?
To guess it who's the skill?
Pray have the kindness to explain
Why I should whip poor Will?

Dost merely ask thy just desert?
What, not another word?—
Back to the woods again, unhurt—
I will not harm thee, bird!

But use thee kindly—for my nerves,
Like thine, have penance done,
"Use every man as he deserves
Who shall 'scape whipping?"—none!

Farewell, poor Will!—not valueless
This lesson by thee given;
"Keep thine own counsel, and confess
Thyself alone to Heaven!"

WOODMAN, SPARE THAT TREE.

Woodman, spare that tree!
Touch not a single bough!
In youth it sheltered me,
And I'll protect it now.
'Twas my forefather's hand
That placed it near his cot:
There, woodman, let it stand,
Thy axe shall harm it not!

That old familiar tree,
Whose glory and renown
Are spread o'er land and sea,
And wouldst thou hew it down?
Woodman, forbear thy stroke!
Cut not its earth-bound ties;
Oh, spare that aged oak,
Now towering to the skies!

When but an idle boy
I sought its grateful shade;
In all their gushing joy
Here too my sisters played.
My mother kissed me here;
My father pressed my hand—
Forgive this foolish tear,
But let that old oak stand!

My heart-strings round thee cling,
Close as thy bark, old friend!
Here shall the wild-bird sing,
And still thy branches bend.
Old tree! the storm still brave!
And, woodman, leave the spot:
While I've a hand to save,
Thy axe shall harm it not.

I'M WITH YOU ONCE AGAIN.

I'm with you once again, my friends,
No more my footsteps roam;
Where it began my journey ends,
Amid the scenes of home.
No other clime has skies so blue,
Or streams so broad and clear,
And where are hearts so warm and true
As those that meet me here?

Since last, with spirits wild and free,
I pressed my native strand,
I've wandered many miles at sea,
And many miles on land;
I've seen fair realms of the earth,
By rude commotion torn,
Which taught me how to prize the worth
Of that where I was born.

In other countries when I heard
The language of my own,
How fondly each familiar word
Awoke an answering tone!
But when our woodland songs were sung
Upon a foreign mart,
The vows that faltered on the tongue
With rapture thrilled the heart.

My native land! I turn to you,
With blessing and with prayer,
Where man is brave and woman true
And free as mountain air.
Long may our flag in triumph wave,
Against the world combined,
And friends a welcome—foes a grave,
Within our borders find.

A LEGEND OF THE MOHAWK.

In the days that are gone, by this sweet flowing water,
Two lovers reclined in the shade of a tree;
She was the mountain-king's rosy-lipped daughter,
The brave warrior-chief of the valley was he.
Then all things around them, below and above,
Were basking as now in the sunshine of love—
In the days that are gone, by this sweet flowing stream.

In the days that are gone, they were laid 'neath the willow,
The maid in her beauty, the youth in his pride;
Both slain by the foeman who crossed the dark billow,
And stole the broad lands where their children reside:
Whose fathers, when dying, in fear looked above,
And trembled to think of that chief and his love,
In the days that are gone, by this sweet flowing stream.

POETRY.

To me the world's an open book,
Of sweet and pleasant poetry;
I read it in the running brook
That sings its way towards the sea.
It whispers in the leaves of trees,
The swelling grain, the waving grass,
And in the cool, fresh evening breeze
That crisps the wavelets as they pass.

The flowers below, the stars above,
In all their bloom and brightness given,
Are, like the attributes of love,
The poetry of earth and heaven.
Thus Nature's volume, read aright,
Attunes the soul to minstrelsy,
Tinging life's clouds with rosy light
And all the world with poetry.

NEAR THE LAKE.

Near the lake where drooped the willow,
Long time ago!
Where the rock threw back the billow,
Brighter than snow;
Dwelt a maid, beloved and cherished
By high and low;
But with autumn's leaf she perished
Long time ago!

Rock, and tree, and flowing water,
Long time ago!
Bee, and bird, and blossom taught her
Love's spell to know!
While to my fond words she listened,
Murmuring low!
Tenderly her dove-eyes glistened,
Long time ago!

Mingled were our hearts for ever,
Long time ago!
Can I now forget her? Never!
No, lost one, no!
To her grave these tears are given,
Ever to flow;
She's the star I missed from heaven,
Long time ago!

THE CROTON ODE—WRITTEN AT THE REQUEST OF THE CORPORATION OF THE CITY OF NEW YORK.

Gushing from this living fountain,
Music pours a falling strain,
As the Goddess of the Mountain
Comes with all her sparkling train.
From her grotto-springs advancing,
Glittering in her feathery spray,
Woodland fays beside her dancing,
She pursues her winding way.

Gently o'er the rippling water,
In her coral-shallop bright,
Glides the rock-king's dove-eyed daughter,
Decked in robes of virgin white.
Nymphs and naiads, sweetly smiling,
Urge her bark with pearly hand.
Merrily the sylph beguiling
From the nooks of fairy-land.

Swimming on the snow-curled billow,
See the river spirits fair
Lay their cheeks, as on a pillow,
With the foam-beads in their hair.
Thus attended, hither wending,
Floats the lovely oread now,
Eden's arch of promise bending,
Over her translucent brow.

Hail the wanderer from a far land!
Bind her flowing tresses up!
Crown her with a fadeless garland,
And with crystal brim the cup,
From her haunts of deep seclusion,
Let Intemperance greet her too,
And the heat of his delusion
Sprinkle with this mountain-dew.

Water leaps as if delighted,
While her conquered foes retire!
Pale Contagion flies affrighted
With the baffled demon Fire!
Safety dwells in her dominions,
Health and Beauty with her move,
And entwine their circling pinions,
In a sisterhood of love!

Water shouts a glad hosanna!
Bubbles up the earth to bless!
Cheers it like the precious manna
In the barren wilderness.
Here we wondering gaze, assembled
Like the grateful Hebrew band,
When the hidden fountain trembled,
And obeyed the Prophet's wand.

Round the Aqueducts of story,
As the mists of Lethe throng,
Croton's waves in all their glory,
Troop in melody along.
Ever sparkling, bright and single,
Will this rock-ribbed stream appear
When Posterity shall mingle
Like the gathered waters here.

MY MOTHER'S BIBLE.

This book is all that's left me now:—
Tears will unbidden start—
With faltering lip and throbbing brow,
I press it to my heart.

For many generations past
  Here is our family tree:
My mother's hand this bible clasped;
  She, dying, gave it me.

Ah! well do I remember those
  Whose names these records bear;
Who round the hearth-stone used to close
  After the evening prayer,
And speak of what these pages said,
  In tones my heart would thrill!
Though they are with the silent dead,
  Here are they living still!

My father read this holy book,
  To brothers, sisters, dear;
How calm was my poor mother's look,
  Who leaned God's word to hear.
Her angel face—I see it yet!
  What thrilling memories come!
Again that little group is met
  Within the halls of home!

Thou truest friend man ever knew,
  Thy constancy I've tried,
When all were false I found thee true,
  My counsellor and guide.
The mines of earth no treasures give
  That could this volume buy;
In teaching me the way to live,
  It taught me how to die.

GEORGE W. BURNAP,

A CLERGYMAN of the Unitarian Church, and author of numerous publications, chiefly of a devotional character, was born in Merrimack, New Hampshire, in 1802. His father, the Rev. Jacob Burnap, was for a long time pastor of a Congregational church in that town. The son was a graduate of Harvard of 1824, and in 1827 succeeded the Rev. Jared Sparks, in the charge of the First Independent Church of Baltimore, Md.

In 1835 he commenced author by publishing a volume of *Lectures on the Doctrines of Controversy between Unitarians and other Denominations of Christians.* In 1840 he published a volume of *Lectures to Young Men on the Cultivation of the Mind, the Formation of Character, and the Conduct of Life;* in the same year, a volume of *Lectures on the Sphere and Duties of Women;* and in 1824, *Lectures on the History of Christianity.* In 1844 he contributed to Sparks's "American Biography," a memoir of Leonard Calvert, first governor of Maryland. In 1845 he published *Expository Lectures on the Principal Texts of the Bible which relate to the Doctrine of the Trinity:* a volume of *Miscellanies;* and a *Biography of Henry T. Ingalls.* In 1848 he published a small work entitled *Popular Objections to Unitarian Christianity Considered and Answered;* and in 1850, twenty discourses, *On the Rectitude of Human Nature.* He has been a contributor to the pages of The Christian Examiner since the year 1834.*

In 1855 he published a volume, entitled, *Christianity, its Essence and Evidence.* This work contains the results of his studies of the New Testament for twenty years, and may be looked upon probably as the most compendious statement of the biblical theology of the author's school of Unitarianism. He follows in the main the track of Andrews Norton; and with great boldness in animadverting upon some portions of the New Testament canon, he unites the most earnest defence of the supernatural origin of Christianity. He is a laborious student, a close reasoner, a terse and instructive writer. In richness of imagery and persuasive rhetoric he is less gifted than in clear statement and logical force.

ISOLATION OF THE AMERICAN COLONIES. A PROMOTION OF DEMOCRACY.*

This leads me to speak of the next cause of the Democracy of the North American Colonies, which I shall mention—*their isolation.* Three thousand miles of ocean intervened between them and the old world. This circumstance was not without the most decisive and important effects. The people had their own way, because they could not be controlled by their old masters at the distance of three thousand miles. *Nobility never emigrated.* There was nothing to tempt it to quit its ancient home. It was a plant of such a peculiar structure, that it would not bear translation to another soil. Here it would have withered and died, amidst the rugged forests and stern climate of America. A nobleman is the creation of a local conventionalism. He flourishes only in an artificial atmosphere. He must be seen by gas-light. He is at home only in courts and palaces.

The pomp of courts, and the splendor of palaces, are the contrivances, not more of human pride than of far-sighted policy. They are intended to impose on the imagination of the multitude; to lead them to associate with the condition of their superiors, the ideas of providential and unattainable superiority, to which it is their destiny and their duty to submit. Take them away from the stage on which they choose to exhibit themselves; strip them of their dramatic costume; take away the overhanging chandelier and the glare of the foot lights, and let them mingle in the common crowd, and they become as other men, and the crowd begin to wonder how they could ever have looked up to them with so much reverence.

They gained likewise advantages from associating together. An English nobleman had a hereditary right to a seat in the House of Lords. He made a part of the national legislature. This privilege was independent of the popular will. It was real power, a possession so flattering to the pride of man. There was no reason, therefore, why such a man should wish to leave his country. What could he find here congenial to his taste, or flattering to his pride, or tolerable to his habits of luxury and self-indulgence?

A rude village on the shore of the ocean, or on the banks of a stream, of a few log cabins, scattered here and there in the wilderness, was all the New World had to offer for many generations. Not many would emigrate to such a country, who had anything to leave behind. Much less was it to be expected, that those would come here, who had drawn the highest prizes in life at home. They could not seek a new organization of the social condition, in which they had nothing to gain and everything to lose. Here and there there might be an adventurer of condition, who came to this country to improve his broken fortunes; but then it was, as in all new countries, with a hope of returning to enjoy his gains in a country and a state of society, where refined enjoyment was possible.

* In this enumeration of Dr. Burnap's writings we are indebted to Mr. Redfield's publication, The Men of the Time, ed. 1852.

* From a Discourse, "Origin and Causes of Democracy in America," before the Maryland Society, Baltimore. 1853.

And after all, beyond a limited circle, America was, at that time, very little known and very little regarded by the people of England. And it is very much so to the present hour. The best informed people, strange as it may seem, know little more of the Geography of this country than they do of the interior of Africa; and thousands and thousands who move in respectable society, are ignorant whether we are white or copper-colored, speak the English language or Choctaw.

America, then, grew up in neglect and by stealth. Unattractive to the higher classes, she drew to herself the people. Here came the people, the hard-handed and stout-hearted, and carved out a New World for themselves. They adapted their institutions to their wants, and before the Old World was aware, there had sprung up on this broad continent a gigantic Republic, ready to take her position among the nations of the earth.

NICHOLAS MURRAY.

THIS writer, whose works have attracted a considerable share of attention from the Protestant community, was born in Ireland in 1802. There he was educated for the mercantile profession. He came to America in 1818, and was engaged for a short time in the printing-office of the Messrs. Harper, who were then laying the foundations for their large publishing establishment. This connexion has always been remembered with pleasure; and the Harpers have since published the numerous editions of the author's writings.

He entered Williams College, Mass., in 1822, and was graduated in due course in the front rank of his class. He then entered the Theological Seminary at Princeton in 1826, and left it in the spring of 1829, to take the pastorate of the church in Wilkesbarre, Pa., where he was ordained in November, 1829. In June, 1833, he was called as Pastor to the First Presbyterian Church of Elizabethtown, N. J. Here he has since remained, though frequently solicited to remove to New York, Brooklyn, Boston, Charleston, Cincinnati, St. Louis, Natchez, and to two theological professorships.

His first essay at writing for the public was, whilst in College. In Wilkesbarre, he wrote for the Christian Advocate, a monthly, edited by Dr. Ashbel Green, then ex-president of Princeton College. After his removal to Elizabethtown, he wrote for the papers, and a few articles for the *Literary and Theological Journal*, then edited by Dr. Woods. He also published a few occasional sermons. In 1844, he published a small volume, *Notes Historical and Biographical*, concerning Elizabethtown.

In 1847, appeared the first series of Controversial Letters to Bishop Hughes, by Kirwan, a *nom de plume* which soon became quite famous. In 1848, a second and third series of these Letters appeared. They have been translated into several languages.

In 1851, he published a pamphlet, *The Decline of Popery and its Causes*, in reply to one of Bishop Hughes. His *Romanism at Home*, which has passed through many editions, was published in 1852. In 1851, he made a tour in Europe, of which he published his observations in 1853, with the title *Men and Things as seen in Europe*. In 1854, appeared his *Parish Pencilling*, a sketch-book of clerical experiences.

CYNTHIA TAGGART.

THERE are few sadder stories in the whole range of literary biography than that of this lady, and on the other hand few which so happily exhibit the solace afforded in some instances by literary pursuits. Cynthia Taggart was the daughter of an old soldier of the Revolution. His father at the outset of the contest was possessed of a valuable farm at Middletown, six miles from Newport. During the British occupation of the neighborhood, he joined an expedition for the capture of the island. It was unsuccessful, and the British in revenge devastated his property. In the foray the son, afterwards the father of Cynthia, was taken prisoner and imprisoned at Newport jail. After a fortnight's incarceration, he made his escape through one of the cellar windows which were provided with wooden bars only, and getting clear of the town crossed to the mainland at Bristol ferry during the night on a rude raft formed of rails from the fences.

A like fate occurred to a small confiscated estate which was given to the father in consideration of his services and losses by the American authorities, so that the son, on the death of the father, succeeded to but a slender patrimony.

C. Taggart

His daughter, Cynthia Taggart, was born October 14, 1801. Owing to the humble, almost necessitous circumstances of the family, her educational advantages were confined to the instructions of the village school, and from these, owing to early ill health, she could only now and then profit. Although sickly from her birth, she enjoyed occasional intervals of health until her nineteenth year. The painful record of her subsequent career may be best left to her own simple recital.

Shortly after this period, I was seized with a more serious and alarming illness, than any with which I had hitherto been exercised, and in the progress of which my life was for many weeks despaired of. But after my being reduced to the brink of the grave, and enduring excruciating pain and excessive weakness for more than three months, it yielded to superior medical skill; and I so far recovered strength as to walk a few steps and frequently to ride abroad, though not without a great increase of pain an almost maddening agony of the brain, and a total deprivation of sleep for three or four nights and days successively.

From this time a complication of the most painful and debilitating chronic diseases ensued, and have continued to prey upon my frail system during the subsequent period of my life,—from which no permanent relief could be obtained, either through medicine or the most judicious regimen,—natural sleep having been withheld to an almost if not altogether unparalleled degree, from the first serious illness throughout the twelve subsequent years. This unnatural deprivation has caused the greatest debility, and an agonising painfulness and susceptibility of the whole system, which I think can neither be described nor conceived. After the expiration of a little more than three years from the above mentioned illness, the greater part of which period I was able to sit up two or three hours in a day, and frequently rode, supported in a carriage, a short distance, though, as before observed, not without great increase of pain, and a total watchfulness for many succeeding nights,—I was again attacked with a still more acutely painful and dangerous malady, from which recovery for several weeks seemed highly improbable, when this most alarming complaint again yielded to medical skill, and life continued, though strength has never more returned. And in what agony, in what excruciating tortures and restless languishing the greater part of the last nine years has been past, it is believed by my parents that language is inadequate to describe or the human mind to conceive. During both the former and latter period of these long-protracted and uncompromising diseases, every expedient that has been resorted to, with the blissful hope of recovery, has proved, not only ineffectual to produce the desired result, but has, invariably, greatly aggravated and increased my complicated complaints; from which it has been impossible to obtain the smallest degree of relief that could render life supportable, and preserve the scorching brain from phrensy, without the constant use of the most powerful anodynes.

Under these circumstances a number of poems were composed by her, and dictated to her father and sisters. One or two found their way to the Providence newspapers, others were read in manuscript by the physicians and clergyman who benevolently visited the poor invalid, and a small collection was finally published in 1833.

The pieces it contains are all of a melancholy cast. They are the meditations of the sick bed, unrelieved by any hope of recovery, the yearnings of a lover of nature for the liberty of woods and fields, of an active mind for food for thought. Considering the circumstances under which they were written they are noticeable productions.

The author lingered for several years after the publication of her volume, without any respite from illness until her death, on the twenty-third of March, 1849.

ON THE RETURN OF SPRING. 1825.

In vain, alas! are Nature's charms
  To those whom sorrows share,
In vain the budding flowers appear
  To misery's hopeless heir.

In vain, the glorious sun adorns
  And gladdens the lengthened day,
When grief must share the tedious hours
  That pass in long array;—

When stern disease with blighting power
  Has nipt life's transient bloom,
And long incessant agonies
  Unrespited consume.

How lost the glow that pleasure thrilled
  Once through the raptured breast,
When, bright in every blooming sweet,
  This beauteous earth was drest!

No joyous walk through flowery fields
  Shall e'er again delight;
For sorrow veils those pleasing scenes
  In deepest shades of night.

Now, worn with pain, oppressed with grief,
  To wretchedness a prey,
The night returns, and day succeeds,
  Without a cheering ray.

The room, with darkened windows sad,
  A dungeon's semblance bears,—
And all about the silent bed
  The face of misery wears:

Shut out from Nature's beauteous charms,
  And breath of balmy air,
Ah! what can chase the hopeless gloom,
  But Heaven,—but humble prayer!

ON A STORM. 1825.

The harsh, terrific, howling Storm,
With its wild, dreadful, dire alarm,
    Turns pale the cheek of mirth;
And low it bows the lofty trees,
And their tall branches bend with ease
    To kiss their parent earth.

The rain and hail in torrents pour;
The furious winds impetuous roar,—
    In hollow murmurs clash.
The shore adjacent joins the sound
And angry surges deep resound,
    And foaming billows dash.

Yet ocean doth no fear impart,
But soothes my anguish-swollen heart,
    And calms my feverish brain.
It seems a sympathizing friend,
That doth with mine its troubles blend,
    To mitigate my pain.

In all the varying shades of woe,
The night relief did ne'er bestow,
    Nor have I respite seen;
Then welcome, Storm, loud, wild, and rude,
To me thou art more kind and good,
    Than aught that is serene.

RUFUS DAWES.

THOMAS, the father of Rufus Dawes, and a Judge of the Supreme Court of Massachusetts, was born in Boston in 1757, and died in July, 1825. He was the author of a poem entitled *The Law given on Mount Sinai*, published in Boston, in 1777, in a pamphlet.

Rufus Dawes, the youngest but one of a large family of sixteen, was born at Boston, January 26, 1808. He entered Harvard in 1820, but was refused a degree, in consequence of his supposed participation in a disturbance of the discipline of the institution, a charge afterwards found to be unjust. The incident furnished the occasion of his first published poem, a satire on the Harvard faculty.* Mr. Dawes next studied law, was admitted, but never practised the profession. He contributed to the United States Literary Gazette, published at Cambridge, and conducted for a time at Baltimore, The Emerald, also a weekly paper. In 1830, he published *The Valley of the Nashaway and Other Poems*, and in 1839, *Geraldine, Athenia of Damascus, and Miscellaneous Poems.*

Mr. Dawes's chief poem, Geraldine, is a rambling composition of some three hundred and fifty stanzas, in the manner of Don Juan, and contains a series of episodical passages united by a somewhat extravagant plot. The tragedy is occupied with the siege of Damascus A.D. 634. Athenia, a noble lady, is beloved by Calous, the general in command of the city during the siege by the Turks. The latter, well nigh victorious, are about entering Damascus, when Calous re-

* Griswold's Poets of America, p. 268.

ceives private intelligence that succor will arrive on the morrow. To prevent the entrance of the Turks he feigns desertion, is thus received into the camp of the enemy, and promising to betray the city, gains a day's delay. At the expiration of that interval, he enters with the Turkish leader, and then cutting his way through the hostile troops, rejoins his own forces, and succeeds in arresting their flight. He next meets Athenia, and presses his suit, but she, believing him a traitor, stabs him fatally. Her father enters and undeceives her. Meanwhile the expected reinforcement having been defeated, the Turks succeed, and the piece concludes with the death of Athenia, who falls beside her lover's body on the entrance of the victors. The language of the drama is smooth and elegant.

The miscellaneous poems which follow in the volume comprise descriptions of natural scenery, passages of reflection, several songs, an ode on the death of Sir Walter Scott, and similar compositions sung at the celebration of laying the corner-stone of the Bunker Hill monument, and at a Printers' Celebration, at Baltimore. In 1840, Mr. Dawes published Nix's Mate, a spirited and successful historical romance.

Rufus Dawes

SUNRISE—FROM MOUNT WASHINGTON.

The laughing hours have chased away the night,
Plucking the stars out from her diadem:—
And now the blue-eyed Morn, with modest grace,
Looks through her half-drawn curtains in the east,
Blushing in smiles and glad as infancy.
And see, the foolish Moon, but now so vain
Of borrowed beauty, how she yields her charms,
And, pale with envy, steals herself away!
The clouds have put their gorgeous livery on,
Attendant on the day—the mountain tops
Have lit their beacons, and the vales below
Send up a welcoming;—no song of birds,
Warbling to charm the air with melody,
Floats on the frosty breeze; yet Nature hath
The very soul of music in her looks!
The sunshine and the shade of poetry.

I stand upon thy lofty pinnacle,
Temple of Nature! and look down with awe
On the wide world beneath us, dimly seen!
Around me crowd the giant sons of earth,
Fixed on their old foundations, unsubdued;
Firm as when first rebellion bade them rise
Unrifted to the Thunderer—now they seem
A family of mountains, clustering round
Their hoary patriarch, emulously watching
To meet the partial glances of the day.
Far in the glowing east the flickering light,
Mellowed by distance with the blue sky blending,
Questions the eye with ever-varying forms.

The sun comes up! away the shadows fling
From the broad hills—and, hurrying to the West,
Sport in the sunshine, till they die away.
The many beauteous mountain streams leap down
Out-welling from the clouds, and sparkling light
Dances along with their perennial flow.
And there is beauty in yon river's path,
The glad Connecticut! I know her well,
By the white veil she mantles o'er her charms:
At times, she loiters by a ridge of hills,
Sportfully hiding—then again with glee,
Out-rushes from her wild-wood lurking place,
Far as the eye can bound, the ocean-waves,
And hills and rivers, mountains, lakes and woods,
And all that hold the faculty entranced,
Bathed in a flood of glory, float in air,
And sleep in the deep quietude of joy.

There is an awful stillness in this place,
A Presence, that forbids to break the spell,
Till the heart pour its agony in tears.
But I must drink the vision while it lasts;
For even now the curling vapours rise,
Wreathing their cloudy coronals, to grace
These towering summits—bidding me away;—
But often shall my heart turn back again,
Thou glorious eminence! and when oppressed,
And aching with the coldness of the world,
Find a sweet resting-place and home with thee.

THE POET.

A poet's heart is always young,
  And flows with love's unceasing streams;
Oh, many are the lays unsung,
  Yet treasured with his dreams!

The spirits of a thousand flowers,—
  The loved,—the lost,—his heart enshrine;
The memory of blessed hours,
  And impulses divine.

Like water in a crystal urn,
  Sealed up for ever, as a gem,
That feels the sunbeams while they burn,
  But never yields to them;—

His heart may fire—his fevered brain
  May kindle with concentrate power,
But kind affections still remain
  To gild his darkest hour.

The world may chide—the heartless sneer,—
  And coldly pass the Poet by,
Who only sheds a sorrowing tear
  O'er man's humanity.

From broken hearts and silent grief
  From all unutterable scorn,
He draws the balm of sweet relief,
  For sufferers yet unborn.

His lyre is strung with shattered strings—
  The heart-strings of the silent dead—
Where memory hovers with her wings,
  Where grief is canopied.

And yet his heart is always young,
  And flows with love's unceasing streams;
Oh, many are the lays unsung,
  And treasured with his dreams!

JACOB ABBOTT—JOHN S. C. ABBOTT.

JACOB ABBOTT, who has acquired a high reputation as the author of a variety of works having for their object the moral and religious training, and the intellectual instruction of the young, is a native of Maine, where he was born at Hallowell in 1803. He was educated at Bowdoin, and at the Theological Seminary of Andover. He commenced

Jacob Abbott

his career as a writer with the books known as the "Young Christian" series, the first of which, bearing that title, appeared in Boston in 1825. It was followed in the series by three other volumes—*The Corner Stone; The Way to do Good; Hoaryhead and McDonner.* When these were completed, in 1830 Mr. Abbott commenced the Rollo series of juvenile writings, which reached twenty-four volumes, consisting of the *Rollo Books* in fourteen volumes, the *Lucy Books* in six, and the *Jonas Books* in four. The *Marco Paul* series followed in six volumes, and subsequently the *Franconia Stories*, published in New York, in ten volumes. A series of Illustrated Histories, to extend to some thirty volumes, was commenced with such ancient topics as Cyrus the Great, Xerxes, Romulus, Julius Cæsar, and including several from English history as Alfred the Great, William the Conqueror, Queen Elizabeth. These and others have appeared in rapid succession from the press of the Harpers, tastefully printed, and with the particular topic attractively set forth in a fluent, easy narrative. A new juvenile series of *Harper's Story Books* is still in progress, in monthly volumes. Mr. Abbott has great skill as a story-teller for the young. He avoids particularly all ambiguity and obscurity. His page is neither encumbered by superfluous matter, nor deficient in the necessary fulness of explanation.

John S. C. Abbott, brother of the preceding, a graduate of Bowdoin (of 1825), and a Congregational clergyman, is also a writer for the young. He is the author of the series of *Kings and Queens, or Life in the Palace*, published by the Harpers, which is to include Josephine, Maria Louisa, Louis Philippe, Nicholas, Victoria, and other popular personages. He has written in a similar form brief lives of Josephine, Maria Antoinette, and Madame Roland. He is best known, however, by his *History of Napoleon Bonaparte*, first published in Harpers' Magazine, 1852–1854, and reissued in two octavo volumes in 1855. This is written in a popularly attractive style, with much success as a narrative; while it has provoked considerable opposition by its highly eulogistic view of the character and deeds of its subject.

WILLIAM POST HAWES,

An essayist of an original sentiment and talent at description, was the son of Peter Hawes, a member of the bar in New York, and was born in that city February 4, 1803. He was educated at Columbia College, where he received his degree in 1821, when he became a student in the law-office of Mr. John Anthon,* and a practitioner after the usual course of three years' study. He thenceforth devoted himself with success to his profession till his early death.

The writings of Mr. Hawes consisted of several series of fugitive articles and essays, contributed to the newspapers, weekly periodicals, and magazines of the day. He wrote for the New York Mirror on *Quail*, and other matters; for the American Monthly Magazine, conducted by Mr. H. W. Herbert, and subsequently by Mr. Park Benjamin, the brilliant sporting sketches, full of dramatic life and rollicking fun, the *Fire Island Ana, or a Week at the Fire Islands;* several legends of Long Island wreckers and pirates; and the fine-hearted, humorous essay on some of the changes in the church-going associations of New York, a sketch worthy the genius of Charles Lamb, entitled *Hymn Tunes and Grave Yards.* To the Spirit of the Times and Turf Register, he contributed frequently, taking the signature of "Cypress, Jr.," a sure indication to the reader of a pleasant, ingenious vein of speculation on the favorite topics of the sportsman, mingled with personal humors of the writer's own. His *Classic Rhapsodies, Random Reminiscences* of his school-fellows, and other miscellanies, were all in mirth and good feeling. In his *Bank Melodies* he ventured a set of poetical parodies on the politicians of the day, somewhat in the style of the Croakers. His pen was often employed on political topics.

A collection of Hawes's writings was published in 1842, shortly after his death; two genial volumes, *Sporting Scenes*, and *Sundry Sketches, being the Miscellaneous Writings of J. Cypress, Jr.*, edited with a preliminary memoir by the author's friend, Mr. Henry William Herbert, a tribute warm, kindly, appreciative, such as one true disciple of Izaak Walton should render to another.

SOME OBSERVATIONS CONCERNING QUAIL.

October has arrived, and has entered into the kingdom prepared for him by his summery brethren departed. A kingdom, truly, within a republic, but mild, magnificent, *pro bono publico*, and full of good fruits; so that not a democrat, after strictest set of St. Tammany, but bows the knee. Hail! O king! His accomplished artists are preparing royal palaces among the woods and fields, and on the hill sides, painting the mountains and arching the streams with glories copied from the latest fashion of rainbows. His keen morning winds and cool evening moons, assiduous servants, are dropping diamonds upon the fading grass and tree-tops, and are driving in the feathery tenants of his marshes, bays, and brakes. Thrice happy land and water lord! See how they streak the early sky, piercing the heavy clouds with the accurate wedge of their marshalled cohorts, shouting *pæans* as they go—and how they plunge into well remembered waters, with an exulting sound, drinking in rest and hearty breakfasts! These be seges of herons, herds of cranes, droppings of sheldrakes, springs of teals, trips of wigeons, coverts of cootes, gaggles of geese, sutes of mallards, and badelynges of ducks; all of which the profane and uninitiated, miserable herd, call flocks of fowl, not knowing discrimination! Meadow and upland are made harmonious and beautiful with congregations of plovers, flights of doves, walks of snipes, exaltations of larks, coveys of partridges, and bevies of quail.* For all these vouchsafed comforts may we be duly grateful! but chiefly, thou sun-burned, frost-browed monarch, do we thank thee that thou especially bringest to vigorous maturity and swift strength, our own bird of our heart, our family chicken, *tetrao coturnix.*

The quail is peculiarly a domestic bird, and is attached to his birth-place and the home of his forefathers. The various members of the anatic families educate their children in the cool summer of the far north, and bathe their warm bosoms in July in the iced-

* Mr. Anthon is an eminent practitioner at the bar, a good scholar, and a man of general reading, sharing in the literary activities of his brothers, Professor Charles Anthon of Columbia College, and the Rev. Dr. Henry Anthon, the Rector of St. Mark's Church in New York. Mr. John Anthon is the author of a volume of "Reports of Cases determined at Nisi Prius in the Supreme Court of the State of New York, 1820," and of "An Analytical Abridgment of the Commentaries of Blackstone," with a prefatory "Essay on the Study of the Law."

* Stow. Stripe. Hakewell.

water of Hudson's Bay; but when Boreas scatters the rushes where they builded their bedchambers, they desert their fatherland, and fly to disport in the sunny waters of the south. They are cosmopolites entirely, seeking their fortunes with the sun. So, too, heavy-eyed, wise Master Scolopax fixes his place of abode, not among the hearths and altars where his infancy was nurtured, but he goeth a *skaaping* where best he may run his long bill into the mud, tracking the warm brookside of juxta-capricornical latitudes. The songsters of the woodland, when their customary crops of insects and berries are cut off in the fall, gather themselves together to renew their loves, and get married in more genial climates. Even black-gowned Mr. Corvus,—otherwise called Jim Crow,—in autumnal fasts contemplateth Australian carcases. Presently, the groves so vocal, and the sky so full, shall be silent and barren. The "melancholy days" will soon be here. Only thou, dear Bob White—not of the Manhattan—wilt remain. Thy cousin, *tetrao umbellus*, will be not far off, it is true; but he is mountainous and precipitous, and lives in solitary places, courting rocky glens and craggy gorges, misandronist. Where the secure deer crops the young mosses of the mountain stream, and the bear steals wild honey, there drums the ruffed strutter on his ancient hemlock log. Ice cools not his blood, nor the deep snow-drift, whence he, startled, whirrs impetuous to the solemn pines, and his hiding-places of laurel and tangled rhododendron, laughing at cheated dogs and wearied sportsmen. A bird to set traps for. Unfamiliar, rough, rugged hermit. Dry meat. I like him not.

The quail is the bird for me. He is no rover, no emigrant. He stays at home, and is identified with the soil. Where the farmer works, he lives, and loves, and whistles. In budding spring time, and in scorching summer—in bounteous autumn, and in barren winter, his voice is heard from the same bushy hedge fence, and from his customary cedars. Cupidity and cruelty may drive him to the woods, and to seek more quiet seats; but be merciful and kind to him, and he will visit your barn-yard, and sing for you upon the boughs of the apple-tree by your gateway. But when warm May first woos the young flowers to open and receive her breath, then begin the loves, and jealousies, and duels of the heroes of the bevy. Duels, too often, alas! bloody and fatal! for there liveth not an individual of the gallinaceous order, braver, bolder, more enduring than a cock quail, fighting for his ladye-love. Arms, too, he wieldeth, such as give no vain blows, rightly used. His mandible serves for other purposes than mere biting of grass-hoppers and picking up Indian corn. While the dire affray rages, Miss Quailina looketh on, from her safe perch on a limb, above the combatants, impartial spectatress, holding her love under her left wing, patiently; and when the vanquished craven finally bites the dust, descends and rewards the conquering hero with her heart and hand.

Now begin the cares and responsibilities of wedded life. Away fly the happy pair to seek some grassy tussock, where, safe from the eye of the hawk, and the nose of the fox, they may rear their expected brood in peace, provident, and not doubting that their *espousals* will be blessed with a numerous offspring. Oats harvest arrives, and the fields are waving with yellow grain. Now, be wary, oh kind-hearted cradler, and tread not into those pure white eggs ready to burst with life! Soon there is a peeping sound heard, and lo! a proud mother walketh magnificently in the midst of her children, scratching and picking, and teaching them how to swallow. Happy she, if she may be permitted to bring them up to maturity, and uncompelled to renew her joys in another nest.

The assiduities of a mother have a beauty and a sacredness about them that command respect and reverence in all animal nature, human or inhuman—what a lie does that word carry—except, perhaps, in monsters, insects, and fish. I never yet heard of the parental tenderness of a trout, eating up his little baby, nor of the filial gratitude of a spider, nipping the life out of his grey-headed father, and usurping his web. But if you would see the purest, the sincerest, the most affecting piety of a parent's love, startle a young family of quails, and watch the conduct of the mother. She will not leave you. No, not she. But she will fall at your feet, uttering a noise which none but a distressed mother can make, and she will run, and flutter, and seem to try to be caught, and cheat your outstretched hand, and affect to be wing-broken, and wounded, and yet have just strength to tumble along, until she has drawn you, fatigued, a safe distance from her threatened children, and the young hopes of her heart; and then will she mount, whirring with glad strength, and away through the maze of trees you have not seen before, like a close-shot bullet, fly to her skulking infants. Listen now. Do you hear those three half-plaintive notes, quickly and clearly poured out? She is calling the boys and girls together. She sings not now "Bob White!" nor "Ah! Bob White!" That is her husband's love-call, or his trumpet-blast of defiance. But she calls sweetly and softly for her lost children. Hear them "peep! peep! peep!" at the welcome voice of their mother's love! They are coming together. Soon the whole family will meet again. It is a foul sin to disturb them; but retread your devious way, and let her hear your coming footsteps, breaking down the briers, as you renew the danger. She is quiet. Not a word is passed between the fearful fugitives. Now, if you have the heart to do it, lie low, keep still, and imitate the call of the hen-quail. O, mother! mother! how your heart would die if you could witness the deception! The little ones raise up their trembling heads, and catch comfort and imagined safety from the sound. "Peep! peep!" they come to you, straining their little eyes, and clustering together, and answering, seem to say, "Where is she? Mother! mother! we are here!"

I knew an Ethiopian once—he lives *yet* in a hovel, on the brush plains of Matowacs—who called a whole bevy together in that way. He first shot the parent bird; and when the murderous villain had ranged them in close company, while they were looking over each other's necks, and mingling their doubts, and hopes, and distresses, in a little circle, he levelled his cursed musket at their unhappy breasts, and butchered——"What! all my pretty ones! Did you say all?" He did; and he lives yet! O, let me not meet that nigger six miles north of Patchogue, in a place where the scrub oaks cover with cavernous gloom a sudden precipice, at whose bottom lies a deep lake, unknown but to the Kwaack, and the lost deer hunter. For my soul's sake, let me not encounter him in the grim ravines of the Callicoon, in Sullivan, where the everlasting darkness of the hemlock forests would sanctify virtuous murder!

HYMN TUNES AND GRAVE-YARDS.

I went to church one night last week,

Ibam forte via sacra,—

as Horace has it; and into what shrine of shrines should my sinful feet be led, but into the freshly hallowed tabernacle of the new free chapel. It was

Carnival week among the Presbyterians, the season of Calvinistic Pentecost; and one of the missionary societies in the celebration of its blessed triumphs, *bulged out*, on that night, from the windows of the gigantic meeting-house, like the golden glories of thickly crowded wheat-sheafs from the granary of a heaven-prospered garnerer. Not, however, did the zeal of a Crusader against the Paynim, nor the expected rehearsal of the victories of the Christian soldier, draw me, unaccustomed, upon holy ground. Wherefore did I, just now, pricked by conscience, stop short in the middle of that line from Flaccus. I could not add

—sicut meus est mos.

"*Meus mos*" stuck in my throat. It was no good grace of mine. *Non nobis.* Reader, I confess to thee that I was charmed into the Tabernacle by a hymn tune.

Now, before I ask for absolution, let me declare, that my late unfrequent visitation of the church is to be attributed to no lack of disposition for faithful duty, but to the new-fangled notions and fashions of the elders and preachers, and to my dislike for the new church music.

It had been an unhappy day with me. My note lay over in the Manhattan; and I had ascertained that some "regulated" suburban "building lots," which I had bought a few days before, unsight unseen, upon the assurance of a "truly sincere friend," were lands covered with water, green mud, and blackberry bushes, in the bottom of a deep valley, untraversable and impenetrable as a Florida hammock. Abstracted, in uncomfortable meditation, I threaded my unconscious pathway homeward, the jargon of the confused noises of Broadway falling upon my tympanum utterly unheard. In this entranced condition, I came abreast of the steps of the covered entrance to the Tabernacle. Here was done a work of speedy disenchantment. A strain of music came floating down the avenue. It was an old and fondly remembered hymn. It was the favorite tune of my boyhood. It was the first tune I ever learned. It was what I loved to sing with my old nurse and little sisters, when I used to pray. It was the tune that even now always makes my heart swell, and brings tears into my eyes. It was Old Hundredth.

Fellow-sinner, peradventure, thou hast never sung Old Hundredth. Thou wert not blessed with pious parents. The star of the Reformation hath not shone upon thee. Thou hast not been moved and exalted by the solemn ecstasy of Martin Luther. Perhaps thou hast had eunuchs and opera-singers to do thy vicarious devotions, in recitative, and elaborate cantatas; scaling Heaven by appoggiaturas upon the rungs of a metrical ladder. Lay down this discourse. Such as thou cannot—yet I bethink me now how I shall teach thee to comprehend and feel. Thou hast seen and heard Der Freischutz? I know that thou hast. Be not ashamed to confess it before these good people. They play it at the play-house, it is true; but what of that; what else is it than a German camp-meeting sermon set to music? It is a solemn drama, showing, terribly, the certain and awful fate of the wicked. There is a single strain of an anthem in that operatic homily—worth all the rest of the piece;—dost thou not remember the harmony of the early matin hymn unexpectedly springing from the choir in the neighboring village church, which, faintly beginning, swells upon your ear, and upon poor Caspar's, too, pleading with his irresolute soul, just as the old head-ranger has almost persuaded the unhappy boy to renounce the devil, and to become good? Dost thou not remember, as the tune grows upon his ear, the strong resolution suddenly taken, the subdued joy, the meek rapture that illumine the face of the penitent; and how, with head bowed down and humble feet, he follows his old friend to the fountain of pardon and to the altar of reconciliation? I see that thou rememberest, and —thou art moved;—"Be these tears wet?"

Here I am happy to receive the congratulations of the reader, that the similarity of Caspar's case and my own is at an end. Poetical justice required that Von Weber's Zamiel should carry off repenting Caspar from the very entrance to the sanctuary;—the civil sexton of the Tabernacle asked me to walk in, and showed me to a seat.

The hymn went up like the fragrance of a magnificent sacrifice. Every voice in that crowded house was uplifted, and swelled the choral harmony. The various parts fell into each other like mingling water, and made one magnificent stream of music; but yet you could recognise the constituent melodies of which the harmonious whole was made up; you could distinguish the deep voice of manhood; the shrill pipe of boys, and the confident treble of the maiden communicant,—all singing with earnestness and strength, and just as God and religion taught them to sing, directly from the heart. To me, one of the best recommendations of Old Hundredth is, that every Protestant knows it, and can sing it. You cannot sing it wrong. There is no fugue, nor *da capo*, nor place to rest and place to begin, nor place to shake, nor any other meretricious affectation about it. The most ingenious chorister—and the church is cursed with some who are skilful to a wonder in dampening people's piety, by tearing God's praises to tatters—cannot find a place in Old Hundredth where he can introduce a flourish or a shake. *Deo gratias* for the comfortable triumph over vainglory. It would be as easy for a schoolmaster to introduce a new letter into the alphabet; and old Hundredth may be said, in some sense, once to have been the alphabet of Christian psalmody. I remember a time when it was a sort of A B C for Protestant children learning to sing. It was the universal psalm of family worship. But its day has gone by. It is not a fashionable tune. You seldom hear it except in the country churches, and in those not noted for high-priced pews and "good society."

There is much solemn effect in the accompaniment of vocal music by a discreetly played organ; but in my ears Old Hundredth suffers by the assistance. The hired organist and bellows-blower have each his quota of duty to perform, and they generally do it with so much zeal, that the more excellent music of the human voice is utterly drowned. And then there is a prelude, and a running up and down of keys, which takes off your attention, and makes you think of the flippancy of the player's fingers, and that your business is to listen and not to sing. No; if you would hear, and sing Old Hundredth aright, go into one of the Presbyterian meeting-houses that has retained somewhat of the simplicity and humility of the early church; or into the solemn aisles of the temples which the Creator hath builded in the woods for the Methodists to go out and worship in. There you may enjoy the tune in its original, incorrupt excellence, and join in a universal song of devotion from the whole assembled people.

To Martin Luther is ascribed the honor of writing Old Hundredth. But the tune was older than he. It took its birth with the Christian Church. It was born in the tone and inflection of voice with which the early Christians spoke their Saviour's praise. Martin Luther never did more than to catch the floating religion of the hymn, and write it in musical letters. It was such music that the poor of the world, out of whom the church was chosen, used to sing for their consolation amid the persecutions of their Pagan masters. It was such simple music that Paul and Silas sang, at midnight, in the prison-house. It was such that afterwards rang from crag to crag in the mountain fastnesses of Scotland, when the hunted Covenanters saluted the dawning Sabbath. Such simple music was heard at nightfall in the tents of the Christian soldiery, that prevailed, by the help of the God of battles, at Naseby and Marston Moor. Such sang our Puritan fathers, when, in distress for their forlorn condition, they gave themselves, first to God and then to one another. Such sang they on the shore of Holland, when, with prayers and tears, their holy community divided itself, and when the first American pilgrims trod, with fearful feet, the deck of the precious-freighted May-flower.

> Amidst the storm they sang,
> And the stars heard and the sea!
> And the sounding aisles of the dim woods rang
> To the anthem of the free!

* * * * * * * * *

Where are all the old hymn tunes that the churches used to sing? Where are "Majesty," and "Wells," and "Windham," and "Jordan," and "Devizes," and other tunes,—not all great compositions, but dear to us because our fathers sang them?

The old-fashioned church music has been pushed from its stool by two sets of innovators. First, from the rich, sleepy churches, it has been expelled by the choristers, who seem to prefer to set a tune which only themselves can warble, as if the better to show forth their clear *alto* voices and splendid power of execution. No objection is made to this monopoly of the musical part of the devotion of the congregations; for it is getting to be the fashion to believe that it is not polite to sing in church. Secondly, from the new-light conventicles, the expulsion has been effected by those reformers of the reformation, who have compelled Dr. Watts, not pious enough, forsooth, to stand aside for their own more spiritual performances. The old hymn tunes will not suit these precious compositions. But with genuine good taste in their adaptation of melodies to words, they have made a ludicrous enough collection of musical fancies, of all varieties, of tragedy and farce. Some of their ecstasies are intended to strike sinners down by wild whoopings copied from the incantations of Indian "medicine feasts," bringing present hell before the victim, and of which his frightened or crazed, but not converted nor convinced soul, has an antetaste in the howling of the discord. Of this sort of composition there is one which ought to be handed over to the Shaking Quakers to be sung with clapping of hands and dancing; I mean that abortion of some fanatic brain which is adapted to the horrid words of

> O! there will be wailing,
> Wailing, wailing, wailing,
> O! there will be wailing! &c.

Some preachers have thought it would be a good plan to circumvent the devil by stealing some of his song tunes; as though profane music could win souls to love piety better than the hymns of the saints; and accordingly they have introduced into their flocks such melodies as "Auld Lang Syne," and "Home, sweet Home!" O! could it be permitted to John Robinson, the pastor of the New England pilgrims; to John Cotton, he who, in the language of his biographer, was "one of those olive trees which afford a singular measure of oil for the illumination of the sanctuary"—to John Fisk, who for "twenty years did shine in the golden candlestick of Chelmsford"—to Brewster—to Mather—to any of those fathers of the American church, to revisit this world, what would they not lament of the descendants of the Pilgrims!

A SHARK STORY—FROM FIRE ISLAND ANA.

"Well, gentlemen," said Locus, in reply to a unanimous call for a story—the relics of supper having been removed, all to the big stone medicine jug,—"I'll go ahead, if you say so. Here's the story. It is true, upon my honor, from beginning to end—every word of it. I once crossed over to Faulkner's island, to fish for *tautaugs*, as the north side people call black fish, on the reefs hard by, in the Long Island Sound. Tim Titus,—who died of the dropsy down at Shinnecock point, last spring,—lived there then. Tim was a right good fellow, only he drank rather too much.

"It was during the latter part of July; the sharks and the dog-fish had just begun to spoil sport. When Tim told me about the sharks, I resolved to go prepared to entertain these aquatic savages with all becoming attention and regard, if there should chance to be any interloping about our fishing ground. So we rigged out a set of extra large hooks, and shipped some rope-yarn and steel chain, an axe, a couple of clubs, and an old harpoon, in addition to our ordinary equipments, and off we started. We threw out our anchor at half ebb tide, and took some thumping large fish;—two of them weighed thirteen pounds—so you may judge. The reef where we lay, was about half a mile from the island, and, perhaps, a mile from the Connecticut shore. We floated there very quietly, throwing out and hauling in, until the breaking of my line, with a sudden and severe jerk, informed us that the sea attorneys were in waiting, down stairs; and we accordingly prepared to give them a retainer. A salt pork cloak upon one of our magnum hooks, forthwith engaged one of the gentlemen in our service. We got him alongside, and by dint of piercing, and thrusting, and banging, we accomplished a most exciting and merry murder. We had business enough of the kind to keep us employed until near low water. By this time, the sharks had all cleared out, and the black fish were biting again; the rock began to make its appearance above the water, and in a little while its hard bald head was entirely dry. Tim now proposed to set me out upon the rock, while he rowed ashore to get the jug, which, strange to say, we had left at the house. I assented to this proposition; first, because I began to feel the effects of the sun upon my tongue, and needed something to take, by way of medicine; and secondly, because the rock was a favorite spot for a rod and reel, and famous for luck; so I took my *traps*, and a box of bait, and jumped upon my new station. Tim made for the island.

Not many men would willingly have been left upon a little barren reef, that was covered by every flow of the tide, in the midst of a waste of waters, at such a distance from the shore, even with an assurance from a companion more to be depended upon than mine, to return immediately, and lie by to take him off. But somehow or other, the excitement of my sport was so high, and the romance of the situation was so delightful, that I thought of nothing else but the prosecution of my fun, and the contemplation of the novelty and beauty of the scene. It was a mild pleasant afternoon in harvest time. The sky was clear and pure. The deep blue Sound, heaving all around me, was studded with craft of all descriptions and dimensions, from the dipping sail-boat to the rolling merchantman, sinking and rising like sea-birds sporting with their white wings in the surge. The grain and grass, on the neighboring farms, were gold and green, and gracefully they bent obeisance to a gentle breathing southwester. Farther off, the high upland and the distant coast gave a dim relief to the prominent features of the landscape, and seemed the rich but dusky frame of a brilliant fairy picture. Then, how still it was! not a sound could be heard, except the occasional rustling of my own motion, and the water beating against the sides, or gurgling in the fissures of the rock, or except now and then the cry of a solitary saucy gull, who would come out of his way in the firmament, to see what I was doing without a boat, all alone, in the middle of the Sound; and who would hover, and cry, and chatter, and make two or three circling swoops and dashes at me, and then, after having satisfied his curiosity, glide away in search of some other fool to scream at.

I soon became half indolent, and quite indifferent about fishing; so I stretched myself out, at full length, upon the rock, and gave myself up to the luxury of looking and thinking. The divine exercise soon put me fast asleep. I dreamed away a couple of hours, and longer might have dreamed, but for a tired fish-hawk, who chose to make my head his resting place, and who waked and started me to my feet.

"Where is Tim Titus!" I muttered to myself, as I strained my eyes over the now darkened water. But none was near me, to answer that interesting question, and nothing was to be seen of either Tim or his boat. "He should have been here long ere this," thought I, "and he promised faithfully not to stay long—could he have forgotten? or has he paid too much devotion to the jug?"

I began to feel uneasy, for the tide was rising fast, and soon would cover the top of the rock, and high water mark was at least a foot above my head. I buttoned up my coat, for either the coming coolness of the evening, or else my growing apprehensions, had set me trembling and chattering most painfully. I braced my nerves, and set my teeth, and tried to hum "begone dull care," keeping time with my fists upon my thighs. But what music! what melancholy merriment! I started and shuddered at the doleful sound of my own voice. I am not naturally a coward, but I should like to know the man who would not, in such a situation, be alarmed. It is a cruel death to die, to be merely drowned, and to go through the ordinary common-places of suffocation, but to see your death gradually rising to your eyes, to feel the water mounting, inch by inch, upon your shivering sides, and to anticipate the certainly coming, choking struggle for your last breath, when, with the gurgling sound of an overflowing brook taking a new direction, the cold brine pours into mouth, ears, and nostrils, usurping the seat and avenues of health and life, and, with gradual flow, stifling—smothering—suffocating!—It were better to die a thousand common deaths.

This is one of the instances, in which, it must be admitted, salt water is not a pleasant subject of contemplation. However, the rock was not yet covered, and hope, blessed hope, stuck faithfully by me. To beguile, if possible, the weary time, I put on a bait, and threw out for a fish. I was sooner successful than I could have wished to be, for hardly had my line struck the water, before the hook was swallowed, and my rod was bent with the dead hard pull of a twelve foot shark. I let it run about fifty yards, and then reeled up. He appeared not at all alarmed, and I could scarcely feel him bear upon my fine hair line. He followed the pull gently, and unresisting, came up to the rock, laid his nose upon its side, and looked up into my face, not as if utterly unconcerned, but with a sort of quizzical impudence, as though he perfectly understood the precarious nature of my situation. The conduct of my captive renewed and increased my alarm. And well it might; for the tide was now running over a corner of the rock behind me, and a small stream rushed through a cleft, or fissure, by my side, and formed a puddle at my very feet. I broke my hook out of the monster's mouth, and leaned upon my rod for support.

"Where is Tim Titus?"—I cried aloud—"Curse on the drunken vagabond! will he never come?"

My ejaculations did no good. No Timothy appeared. It became evident, that I must prepare for drowning, or for action. The reef was completely covered, and the water was above the soles of my feet. I was not much of a swimmer, and as to ever reaching the Island, I could not even hope for that. However, there was no alternative, and I tried to encourage myself, by reflecting that necessity was the mother of invention and that desperation will sometimes insure success. Besides, too, I considered and took comfort, from the thought that I could wait for Tim, so long as I had a foothold, and then commit myself to the uncertain strength of my arms and legs, for salvation. So I turned my bait box upside down, and mounting upon that, endeavored to comfort my spirits, and be courageous, but submissive to my fate. I thought of death, and what it might bring with it, and I tried to repent of the multiplied iniquities of my almost wasted life; but I found that that was no place for a sinner to settle his accounts. Wretched soul! pray, I could not.

The water had now got above my ankles, when, to my inexpressible joy, I saw a sloop bending down towards me, with the evident intention of picking me up. No man can imagine what were the sensations of gratitude which filled my bosom at that moment.

When she got within a hundred yards of the reef, I sung out to the man at the helm to luff up, and lie by, and lower the boat; but to my amazement, I could get no reply, nor no notice of my request. I entreated them for the love of heaven to take me off, and I promised, I know not what rewards, that were entirely beyond my power of bestowal. But the brutal wretch of a captain, muttering something to the effect of "that he hadn't time to stop," and giving me the kind and sensible advice to pull off my coat, and swim ashore, put the helm hard down, and away bore the sloop on the other tack.

"Heartless villain!"—I shrieked out in the torture of my disappointment; "may God reward your inhumanity." The crew answered my prayer with a coarse, loud laugh, and the cook asked me through a speaking trumpet, "If I wasn't afraid of catching cold,"—the black rascal!

It was now time to strip; for my knees felt the cold tide, and the wind, dying away, left a heavy swell, that swayed and shook the box upon which I was mounted, so that I had occasionally to stoop, and paddle with my hands, against the water, in order to preserve my perpendicular. The setting sun sent his almost horizontal streams of fire across the dark waters, making them gloomy and terrific, by the contrast of his amber and purple glories.

Something glided by me in the water, and then made a sudden halt. I looked upon the black mass, and, as my eye ran along its dark outline, I saw, with horror, it was a shark; the identical monster, out of whose mouth I had just broken my hook. He was fishing, now, for me, and was evidently only waiting for the tide to rise high enough above the rock, to glut at once his hunger and revenge. As the water continued to mount above my knees, he seemed to grow more hungry and familiar. At last, he made a desperate dash, and approached within an inch of my legs, turned upon his back, and opened his huge jaws for an attack. With desperate strength, I thrust the end of my rod violently at his mouth; and the brass head, ringing against his teeth, threw him back into the deep current, and I lost sight of him entirely. This, however, was but a momentary repulse; for in the next minute, he was close behind my back, and pulling at the skirts of my fustian coat, which hung dipping into the water. I leaned forward hastily, and endeavored to extricate myself from the dangerous grasp, but the monster's teeth were too firmly set, and his immense strength nearly drew me over. So, down flew my rod, and off went my jacket, devoted peace-offerings to my voracious visiter.

In an instant, the waves all around me were lashed into froth and foam. No sooner was my poor old sporting friend drawn under the surface, than it was fought for by at least a dozen enormous combatants! The battle raged upon every side. High, black fins rushed now here, now there, and long, strong tails scattered sleet and froth, and the brine was thrown up in jets, and eddied, and curled, and fell, and swelled, like a whirlpool in Hell-gate.

Of no long duration, however, was this fishy tourney. It seemed soon to be discovered that the prize contended for, contained nothing edible but cheese and crackers, and no flesh, and as its mutilated fragments rose to the surface, the waves subsided into their former smooth condition. Not till then did I experience the real terrors of my situation. As I looked around me to see what had become of the robbers, I counted one, two, three, yes, up to twelve, successively of the largest sharks I ever saw, floating in a circle around me, like divergent rays, all mathematically equidistant from the rock, and from each other; each perfectly motionless, and with his gloating, fiery eye fixed full and fierce upon me. Basilisks and rattle-snakes! how the fire of their steady eyes entered into my heart! I was the centre of a circle, whose radii were sharks! I was the unsprung, or rather *unchewed* game, at which a pack of hunting sea-dogs was making a dead point!

There was one old fellow, that kept within the circumference of the circle. He seemed to be a sort of captain, or leader of the band; or, rather, he acted as the coroner for the other twelve of the inquisition, that were summoned to sit on, and eat up my body. He glided around and about, and every now and then would stop, and touch his nose against some of his comrades, and seem to consult, or to give instructions as to the time and mode of operation. Occasionally, he would scull himself up towards me, and examine the condition of my flesh, and then again glide back, and rejoin the troupe, and flap his tail, and have another confabulation. The old rascal had, no doubt, been out into the highways and bye-ways, and collected this company of his friends and kin-fish, and invited them to supper. I must confess, that horribly as I felt, I could not help but think of a tea party of demure old maids, sitting in a solemn circle, with their skinny hands in their laps, licking their expecting lips, while their hostess bustles about in the important functions of her preparations. With what an eye have I seen such appurtenances of humanity survey the location and adjustment of some especial condiment, which is about to be submitted to criticism and consumption.

My sensations began to be, now, most exquisite indeed; but I will not attempt to describe them. I was neither hot nor cold, frightened nor composed; but I had a combination of all kinds of feelings and emotions. The present, past, future, heaven, earth, my father and mother, a little girl I knew once, and the sharks, were all confusedly mixed up together, and swelled my crazy brain almost to bursting. I cried, and laughed, and shouted, and screamed for Tim Titus. In a fit of most wise madness, I opened my broad-bladed fishing knife, and waved it around my head, with an air of defiance. As the tide continued to rise, my extravagance of madness mounted. At one time, I became persuaded that my tide-waiters were reasonable beings, who might be talked into mercy and humanity, if a body could only hit upon the right text. So, I bowed, and gesticulated, and threw out my hands, and talked to them, as friends and brothers, members of my family, cousins, uncles, aunts, people waiting to have their bills paid;—I scolded them as my servants; I abused them as duns; I implored them as jurymen sitting on the question of my life; I congratulated and flattered them as my comrades upon some glorious enterprise; I sung and ranted to them, now as an actor in a play-house, and now as an elder at a camp-meeting; in one moment, roaring

> On this cold flinty rock, I will lay down my head,

and in the next, giving out to my attentive hearers for singing, the hymn of Dr. Watts so admirably appropriate to the occasion,

> On slippery rocks I see them stand,
> While fiery billows roll below.

In the meantime, the water had got well up towards my shoulders, and while I was shaking and vibrating upon my uncertain foothold, I felt the cold nose of the captain of the band snubbing against my side. Desperately, and without a definite object, I struck my knife at one of his eyes, and by some singular fortune cut it clean out from the socket. The shark darted back, and halted. In an instant hope and reason came to my relief; and it occurred to me, that if I could only blind the monster, I might yet escape. Accordingly, I stood ready for the next attack. The loss of an eye did not seem to affect him much, for, after shaking his head once or twice, he came up to me again, and when he was about half an inch off, turned upon his back. This was the critical moment. With a most unaccountable presence of mind, I laid hold of his nose with my left hand, and with my right, I scooped out his remaining organ of vision. He opened his big mouth, and champed his long teeth at me, in despair. But it was all over with him. I raised my right foot and gave him a hard shove, and he glided off into deep water, and went to the bottom.

Well, gentlemen, I suppose you'll think it a hard story, but it is none the less a fact, that I served every remaining one of those nineteen sharks in the same fashion. They all came up to me, one by one, regularly, and in order; and I scooped their eyes out, and gave them a shove, and they went off into deep water, just like so many lambs. By the time I had scooped out and blinded a couple of dozen of them, they began to seem so scarce, that I thought I would swim for the island, and fight the rest for fun, on the way; but just then, Tim Titus hove in sight, and it had got to be almost dark, and I concluded to get aboard, and rest myself.

ALEXANDER SLIDELL MACKENZIE.

COMMANDER MACKENZIE, of the Navy, and the author of the *Year in Spain* and other popular works, was born in New York on the 6th of April, 1803. His father was John Slidell, a highly esteemed merchant of the city. His mother, Margery or May, as she was called, Mackenzie, was a native of the Highlands of Scotland, who came to America when she was quite a child. Mr. Slidell was a man of great intelligence and of a high moral and religious character. He was fond of books, and passed his evenings in reading aloud to his family, a trait which his son continued. There are no anecdotes of the early years of the latter preserved; but he has been heard to say that as a child he was no student and not at all precocious. He was at boarding-school until his early entrance into the Navy, January 1, 1815, at an age which precluded many opportunities of education; but the deficiency of which his indomitable habits of application in the study of literature and the sciences connected with his profession, and his strong natural powers of observation, fully supplied. His letters written at sixteen and seventeen, when he was on board of the Macedonian in the Pacific, exhibit thus early his settled habits of study, and his earnest sense of what was going on around him. At nineteen he took command of a merchant vessel to improve himself in his profession. In 1824 he was on duty in the brig Terrier on the West India station, seeking for pirates, when a second attack of yellow fever led to his return home; and in the autumn of 1825, the year of his appointment to a lieutenancy, he visited Europe, on leave of absence, for the benefit of his health. He spent a year in France, mostly in study, and then commenced the tour in Spain, the incidents of which he subsequently gave to the world in his publication, the *Year in Spain*, which first appeared in Boston in 1829 and about the same time in London. Washington Irving was in Spain at the time of Slidell's visit, engaged in writing his life of Columbus, and the two friends passed their time in intimacy. It is to Slidell that Irving alludes in a note to his work on Columbus where he says, "the author of this work is indebted for the able examination of the route of Columbus to an officer of the Navy of the United States, whose name he regrets not being at liberty to mention. He has been greatly benefited in various parts of this history by nautical information from the same intelligent source." The Year in Spain was received with great favor, and took its rank in England and America among the first productions of its class. It was reviewed in the Quarterly, the Monthly Review, and other influential publications in London, with many commendations on its spirit and interest, and the fund of information which the author had collected in familiar intercourse with the people; so that Washington Irving then in England, writing home, remarked, "It is quite the fashionable book of the day, and spoken of in the highest terms in the highest circles. If the Lieutenant were in London at present he would be quite a lion." It had the honor of a translation into the Swedish language.

In the years 1830–31–32, Mr. Slidell was on duty in the Mediterranean, in the Brandywine, Commodore Biddle. Upon his return home in 1833 he published a volume of *Popular Essays on Naval Subjects*, and projected a two years' course of travelling in Great Britain. He passed some time in England, made a short visit to Spain, and returned to finish his tour in England and Ireland, but was induced by the threatened conflict between the United States and France to return to America to resume, if necessary, the active duties of his profession. There being no probability of war he prepared at home his book, ***The American in England***, and shortly after the two volumes of ***Spain Revisited***. At this time, in 1836, he published a revised and enlarged edition of the Year in Spain, in New York. In 1837 he was ordered to the Independence as First Lieutenant, and filled the duties of executive officer to Commodore Nicholson. It was in the winter of this year that, in accordance with the request of a maternal uncle, he added, by an Act of the New York Legislature, his mother's name to his own. The Independence conveyed Mr. Dallas, the Minister to Russia, to St. Petersburg, which gave Lieutenant Slidell an opportunity to write home a description of the visit of the Emperor to the ship at Cronstadt. From Cronstadt the Independence proceeded to Brazil, where Lieutenant Slidell was placed in command of the Dolphin. His cruise in this vessel was of much interest. He was at Bahia during the siege of that place, and at its surrender, and was an eyewitness of many of the political events of the Rio de la Plata at that period, an account of some of which he published in a pamphlet at the time. General Rosas was his warm friend, and continued in correspondence with him for many years after. The American merchants of Rio Janeiro expressed their approval of his course. He returned from the Brazil station in 1839.

Alex. Slidell Mackenzie

Whilst in Boston, previously to the sailing of the Independence, he was requested by Mr. Sparks to contribute a life of Paul Jones to the series of American Biography. He anticipated writing this at sea, but his duties prevented. He commenced it on his return, and it was published in Boston in 1841.

He had a love of country life, not unusual with men who pass much of their lives upon the sea, and now established his home (he had married, in 1835, a daughter of the late Morris Robinson of New York) at a farm on the Hudson, midway between Sing Sing and Tarrytown. Here he afterwards passed his time when not occupied in his profession, to which, notwithstanding his success in literature, he always continued warmly attached as his first duty. In the summer of 1840, at the request of Dr. Grant Perry, he wrote the life of his father Commodore Oliver Perry. In 1841 he received his rank of Commander, and took charge of the Missouri Steamer till his command of the Brig Somers in May, 1842, then used as a school-ship and manned by apprentices. In this he was able to further his favorite plan of the improvement of the character of the service in the education of the sailor. He took with him on his first cruise to Porto Rico a young student of divinity to hold the services of the Episcopal church, a practice which he always observed in every vessel which he commanded. He sailed again with despatches for the squadron on the African coast in September of the same year. On the return voyage Midshipman Spencer was arrested, with a number of the crew, on a charge of mutiny. A council of officers decided that the execution of the three chief persons accused was a necessary measure, and the decision was carried into effect at the yard-arm. The Somers came into New York in December, when a Court of Enquiry of the three senior officers of the Navy, Commodores Stewart, Jacob Jones, and Dallas, justified the act. To remove any further grounds of complaint, at Commander Mackenzie's own request, a court-martial was held at New York in February, of which Commodore Downes was President, and eleven of his brother officers, his seniors or equals in rank, members. He was again acquitted, and the congratulations of large and influential bodies of his fellow citizens in New York, Philadelphia, and Boston, tendered to him. The citizens of Boston requested his bust, which was executed by Dexter and has been placed in the Athenæum. He remained at home till 1846, occupying himself in writing the *Life of Commodore Decatur*, which was published in the summer of that year. In May, 1846, he was sent by the President on a private mission to Cuba and thence sailed to Mexico. He was ordnance officer with Commodore Perry in the Mississippi at Vera Cruz, whence he returned in 1847. The next year he had command of the Mississippi. His health was now much impaired. He died at home September 13, 1848.

His literary characteristics are readily noted. Whatever he took in hand, whether the narrative of his own adventures, or the story of the lives of others, was pursued with diligence, a skill which he seems to have owed as much to nature as to art, and in a full equable style. His American lives of Paul Jones, Perry, and Decatur, are happy instances of biographical talent, and are productions which, no less by their treatment than their subject matter, will continue to be received with favor. His descriptions of travel are remarkable for their truthfulness and happy fidelity to nature, and the unaffected interest which they exhibit in whatever is going on about him. There is also a fertile vein of good humor which illustrates the old remark, that a book which it is a pleasure to read it has been also a pleasure to write. Greatly as Americans have excelled in this species of writing, the country has never probably had a better representative abroad describing the scenes which he visits. Spain, always a theme fruitful in the picturesque, loses nothing of its peculiar attractiveness in his hands. He travels as Irving, Inglis, Ford, and many others have done, with a constant eye to Gil Blas and Don Quixote. It is in a similar vein that he visits England, and doubtless his still unpublished *Tour in Ireland* presents the same attractive qualities. He appears always to have had this descriptive talent. A series of letters from his early years, written from different parts of the world, which we have seen, are graphic, minute, and faithful. He was always a conscientious student of life and nature as of books, and his pen was the ready chronicler of his observations. The style in this, as in most cases, marks the man. Though reserved in his manners, and somewhat silent, there was great gentleness and refinement in his disposition. His exactness in discipline and inflexible performance of duty as an officer, and his strict sense of religious no less than of patriotic obligations, while they gained him the respect, were not at the loss of the affection of his companions. The unforced humor and ease of his writings are easily read indications of his amiable character. In person Commander Mackenzie was well formed, graceful, with a fine observant eye, and animated expression of countenance.

ZARAGOZA—FROM SPAIN REVISITED.

On entering the gate of the Ebro I found myself within the famous old city of Zaragoza; renowned, in chronicles and ballads, for the achievements of its sons: the capital, moreover, of that glorious kingdom of Aragon, so illustrious for its ancient laws and liberties, for its conquests and extirpation of the Moors, and for the wisdom and prowess of its kings; but, above all, glorious now and for ever, for her resistance to a treacherous and powerful foe; a resistance undertaken in a frantic spirit of patriotism, pausing for no reflection and admitting of no reasoning, and which was continued in defiance of all the havoc occasioned in a place wholly indefensible, according to the arts of war, until, wasted by assaults, by conflagrations, by famine, by pestilence, and every horror, Zaragoza at length yielded only in ceasing to exist.

A few steps from the gate brought me to the great square. It was crowded with a vast concourse of people, consisting at once of the busy and the idle of a population of near sixty thousand souls: the busy brought there for the transaction of their affairs, and the idle in search of occupation, or for the retail and exchange of gossip. The arcades and the interior of the square were everywhere filled with such as sold bread, meat, vegetables, and all the necessaries of life, together with such rude fabrics as come within the compass of Spanish ingenuity. Beggars proclaimed their poverty and misfortune, and the compensation which Jesus and Mary would give, in another world, to such charitable souls as bestowed alms on the wretched in this; and blind men chanted a rude ballad which recounted the sad fate of a young woman forced to marry a man whom she did not love; or offered for sale verses, such as were suited for a gallant to sing beneath the balcony of his mistress. Trains of heavily-laden mules entered and disappeared again; and carts and wagons slowly lumbered through, creaking and groaning at every step. Here was every variety of dress peculiar to the different provinces of Spain. A few had wandered to this distant mart from the sunny land of Andalusia; but there were more from Catalonia, Valencia, and Biscay, Zaragoza being the great connecting thoroughfare between those industrious and commercial provinces. The scene was noisy, tumultuous, and full of vivacity and animation; and I felt that pleasure in contemplating it, which an arrival in a city of some importance never fails to afford, after the quiet and monotony of small villages.

Catching a distant view of the renowned Church of the Pillar on the left, and of the Aragonese Giralda, the new tower, on the opposite hand, I came into a street which seemed to be consecrated to learning. On either hand were bookshops, filled with antique tomes, bound in parchment, with clasps of copper, and having a monkish and conventual smell; while, seated upon the pavement at the sunny side, were scores of cloaked students, conning ragged volumes, and passing an apparent interval in the academic hours in preparation for rehearsal, and in storing up a stock of heat to carry them safely through the frigid atmosphere of some Gothic hall, in which the light of science was wooed with a pious exclusion of the assistance of the sun. Other students were more agreeably employed in gambling in the dirt for a few cuartos. One of them, who had been looking over the game, and had probably lost, followed me, holding out the greasy tatters of a broken cocked hat, and supplicating a little alms to pursue his studies. He had on a cloak which hung in tatters, a pair of black worsted stockings, foxy and faded, and possibly a pair of trousers, while a stock, streaked with violet, showed that he was a candidate for the church: a mass of uncombed and matted hair hung about his forehead; his teeth were stained, like his fingers, with the oil from the paper cigars; and his complexion and whole appearance indicated a person nourished from day to day on unwholesome food, irregularly and precariously procured. He followed me for some distance, whining forth his petition. At length I said to him, somewhat briefly—"*Perdon usted amigo! no hay nada!*"—and he happening to catch sight, at the same moment, of a half-smoked fragment of a cigar, stopped short, picked it up, and proceeded to prepare it for further fumigation.

Tracing our way through narrow, winding, and ill-paved alleys, we at length approached the southern portion of the city, and entered the spacious street called the Coso, which lies in the modern part of Zaragoza. It was on this side that the chief attack of the French was directed. They approached by a level plain, demolishing convents, churches, and dwellings; battering with their cannon, discharging bombs, and springing mines, until this whole district was reduced to a wide-extended heap of ruins. A few walls of convents, half demolished, arches yawning, and threatening to crush at each instant whoever may venture below, and a superb façade, standing in lonely grandeur, to attest the magnificence of the temple of which it originally formed part, still remain to testify to the heroic obstinacy with which Zaragoza resisted. Some modern houses have arisen in this neighborhood. They are of neat and tasteful construction, and form a singular contrast with the antiquated and crowded district through which I had just passed, not less than with the monastic ruins which frown upon and threaten to crush them, for their sacrilegious intrusion upon consecrated ground.

From the Coso a wide avenue extends to the gate of Madrid, and owes its opening and enlargement to the batteries of the French. Its origin is connected with a dreadful catastrophe, but its present uses are of the most peaceful kind. It is now a public walk, planted with trees, and enlivened by fountains; and the Zaragozana of our day now coquets and flourishes her fan, and plays off the whole battery of her charms, on the very spot where her father or her grandfather, or haply an ancestor of her own sex, poured forth their life's blood in defence of their country.

LODGINGS IN MADRID AND A LANDLADY—FROM THE SAME.

I was far too uncomfortable in my wretched inn to think of remaining there during the whole time I proposed to stay in Madrid. Florencia, who promised to find me a place, if possible, in her own neighborhood, said that there was no want of hired apartments about the Gate of the Sun; but there was some difficulty in finding such as were in all respects unexceptionable, since many establishments of this sort were kept by persons of somewhat equivocal character, who enticed young men into their houses with a view of fascinating and leading them astray. Nevertheless, at the end of a day or two, passed in diligent search, she sent me word to take possession of an apartment which she had retained for me in the street of Carmel, and which, though the entrance was in a different street, had its front just where I wanted it, on the street of Montera, and the balcony next to her own.

Immediately within the doorway, giving admission to a passage in itself sufficiently narrow, was a modest little moveable shop, which came and went, I knew not whither, morning and night, and which disappeared altogether on feast and bullfight days. It was kept by a thin, monastic-looking individual, who sold waxen tapers, arms, legs, eyes, ears, and babies, all religious objects connected with funeral ceremonies, or charms to offer at the shrine of some celebrated saint, for a happy delivery, or for the recovery of an afflicted member of the easily disordered tenement, in which our nobler part is shut up.

Having traversed this first passage opening on the street, I found myself on a crooked serpentine stairway, which turned to the right and to the left without reason or ceremony, and in almost utter darkness. Doors were scattered about on either hand, and I rang at half a dozen, saluted by the barking of dogs, the growling of Spaniards interrupted in the enjoyment of the siesta and torpid state which follow the repletion of a greasy dinner, or by the sharp and angry tones of scolding females, ere I at length found myself at the right one. Nor did I ever get used to the eccentricities of this most involved entrance. Coming home, night after night, at the dead hour of two or three, having patrolled the streets with a drawn dagger under my cloak, to defend myself against the robberies that were of constant occurrence, I used to get into the outer door by the aid of the double key which I carried, and reaching the end of the passage, I would commence ascending without any geometrical principle to guide me. When I should have turned to the left I would turn to the right, dislocating my foot against a wall, or else keep straight on until violently arrested, and in serious danger of damaging or distorting my nose. Sometimes I stepped up when I should have stepped down, and shook my whole frame to its centre. And thus I have more than once passed half an hour, moving about, like a troubled spirit, from the ground floor to the garret, fitting my key into strange doors, to the terror of the inmates, who, dreaming of robbery and murder, would begin to rattle sabres or bawl for assistance.

But to return to my new landlady. I must confess that I was not particularly disposed to be pleased either with her or her habitation, when I at length rang at the right door, and she admitted me. On entering the apartment designed for me, however, I found that it was far better than its approaches had foretold, being matted and furnished with more than usual neatness. The alcove, concealed by nice white curtains, contained a bed of inviting cleanliness, and the brasier and other articles of furniture, susceptible of receiving a polish, shone with the lustre of consummate house-wifery.

When I got before the broad light of the balcony, which enjoyed the sunny exposure so essential, where artificial heat of a wholesome kind is not to be procured, I had an opportunity of examining the person of my patrona; and I saw at a glance that Florencia had taken effectual means to protect me against every temptation of the devil. Doña Lucretia, whose present, rather than whose past history, doubtless rendered her name an appropriate one, was a hale, happy old lady, of five-and-fifty or more, still struggling to keep young. She was plump and well conditioned, with, however, a neat little foot, which she had somehow managed to keep within the dimensions of a small shoe, though her good keeping hastened to show itself above, in a fat and unconstrained ankle. Her eye, too, had some remains of lustre, and the long habit of leering and casting love-glances had left about it a certain lurking expression of roguery.

She was a native of Zamora, and had never married; not, by her account, for want of offers, for she had received many; but having seen that her father and mother had lived unhappily together, and her earliest recollections being of domestic disturbances, when the time arrived to think of this matter, and occasion called upon her to determine, for she told me, and I believed her, that she had been very handsome, she asked herself the question, "Shall I make the misery of my parents my own? or shall I not rather live singly blessed?" Having well weighed all these considerations, she, after mature deliberation, determined on philosophic principles for a life of liberty, since, though she admitted that men were a very good and useful race of animals, she said she never yet had seen one whom she was willing to erect into a permanent lord and master.

Her present pastimes were suited to her age; a little gossip each morning with a toothless old dame, who came to tell the parish news, of births, deaths, marriages, and murders, occupied the hour succeeding the domestic duties of the day, and went on without interruption, as the pipkin simmered with the daily puchero; on a feast-day, fan in hand, and mantilla duly adjusted, she would go in state to mass, taking the key of the door, and followed by the stout maid of all work, in the character of a dueña: at the bullfight she never fails to attend, for she was a zealous *aficionada;* and almost nightly she went off to a *teatro casero*, a reunion for private theatricals, held in the inelegant barrier of the Lavapies. The man who brushed my clothes and cleaned my boots, and between whom and the old lady there was a friendship of many years' standing, was one of the principal actors. I went for curiosity to see one performance, and was astonished, not only at the very tolerable style of the acting, but also at the singularity of the whole circumstance, of people in an humble sphere of life, instead of spending the little superfluity of their earnings in getting drunk, or congregating together in places from which the other sex was excluded, thus combining to fit up, and paint with the greatest taste, a little theatre, where they not only played farces and danced the bolero, but even commenced regularly, as at the great theatres, by going through a solemn didactic piece. On this occasion they played the Telos de Meneses, an old Spanish tragedy of the cloak and sword, filled with the most exaggerated and nobly extravagant sentiments.

A LONDON COFFEE-ROOM AT DINNER TIME—FROM THE AMERICAN IN ENGLAND.

The coffee-room, into which I now entered, was a spacious apartment of oblong form, having two chimneys with coal fires. The walls were of a dusky orange; the windows at either extremity were hung with red curtains, and the whole sufficiently well illuminated by means of several gas chandeliers. I hastened to appropriate to myself a vacant table by the side of the chimney, in order that I might have some company besides my own musing, and be able, for want of better, to commune with the fire. The waiter brought me the carte, the list of which did not present any very attractive variety. It struck me as very insulting to the pride of the Frenchman, whom I had caught a glimpse of on entering, not to say extremely cruel, to tear him from the joys and pastimes of his belle France, and conduct him to this land of fogs, of rain, and gloomy Sundays, only to roast sirloins and boil legs of mutton.

The waiter, who stood beside me in attendance, very respectfully suggested that the gravy-soup was exceedingly good; that there was some fresh sole, and a particularly nice piece of roast-beef. Being very indifferent as to what I ate, or whether I ate anything, and moreover quite willing to be relieved from the embarrassment of selecting from such an unattractive bill of fare, I laid aside the carte, not however before I had read, with some curiosity, the following singular though very sensible admonition, "Gentlemen are particularly requested not to miscarve the joints."

I amused myself with the soup, sipped a little wine, and trifled with the fish. At length I found myself face to face with the enormous sirloin. There was something at least in the rencounter which conveyed the idea of society; and society of any sort is better than absolute solitude.

I was not long in discovering that the different personages scattered about the room in such an unsocial and misanthropic manner, instead of being collected about the same board, as in France or my own country, and, in the spirit of good fellowship and of boon companions, relieving each other of their mutual ennuis, though they did not speak a word to each other, by which they might hereafter be compromised and socially ruined, by discovering that they had made the acquaintance of an individual several grades below them in the scale of rank, or haply as disagreeably undeceived by the abstraction of a pocket-book, still kept up a certain interchange of sentiment, by occasional glances and mutual observation. Man, after all, is by nature gregarious and social; and though the extreme limit to which civilization has attained in this highly artificial country may have instructed people how to meet together in public places of this description without intermixture of classes or mutual contamination, yet they cannot, for the life of them, be wholly indifferent to each other. Though there was no interchange of sentiments by words then, yet there was no want of mutual observation, sedulously concealed indeed, but still revealing itself in a range of the eye, as if to ask a question of the clock, and in furtive glances over a book or a newspaper.

In the new predicament in which I was now placed, the sirloin was then exceedingly useful. It formed a most excellent line of defence, an unassailable breastwork, behind which I lay most completely entrenched, and defended at all points from the sharp-shooting of the surrounding observers. The moment I found myself thus intrenched, I began to recover my equanimity, and presently took courage—bearing in mind always the injunction of the bill of fare, not to miscarve the joints—to open an embrasure through the tender-loin. Through this I sent my eyes sharp-shooting towards the guests at the other end of the room, and will, if the reader pleases, now furnish him with the result of my observations.

In the remote corner of the coffee-room sat a party of three. They had finished their dinner, and were sipping their wine. Their conversation was carried on in a loud tone, and ran upon lords and ladies, suits in chancery, crim. con. cases, and marriage settlements. I did not hear the word dollar once; but the grander and nobler expression of thousand pounds occurred perpetually. Moreover, they interlarded their discourse abundantly with foreign reminiscences and French words, coarsely pronounced, and awfully anglicised. I drew the conclusion from this, as well as from certain cant phrases and vulgarisms of expression in the use of their own tongue, such as "regularly done"—"completely floored"—"split the difference," that they were not the distinguished people of which they labored to convey the impression.

In the corner opposite this party of three, who were at the cost of all the conversation of the coffee-room, sat a long-faced, straight-featured individual, with thin hair and whiskers, and a bald head. There was a bluish tinge about his cheek-bones and nose, and he had, on the whole, a somewhat used look. He appeared to be reading a book which he held before him, and which he occasionally put aside to glance at a newspaper that lay on his lap, casting, from time to time, furtive glances over book or newspaper at the colloquial party before him, whose conversation, though he endeavored to conceal it, evidently occupied him more than his book.

Halfway down the room, on the same side, sat a very tall, rosy young man, of six-and-twenty or more; he was sleek, fair-faced, with auburn hair, and, on the whole, decidedly handsome, though his appearance could not be qualified as distinguished. He sat quietly and contentedly, with an air of the most thoroughly vacant bonhommie, never moving limb or muscle, except when, from time to time, he lifted to his mouth a fragment of thin biscuit, or replenished his glass from the decanter of black-looking wine beside him. I fancied, from his air of excellent health, that he must be a country gentleman, whose luxuriant growth had been nurtured at a distance from the gloom and condensation of cities. I could not determine whether his perfect air of quiescence and repose were the effect of consummate breeding, or simply a negative quality, and that he was not fidgety only because troubled by no thoughts, no ideas, and no sensations.

There was only one table between his and mine. It was occupied by a tall, thin, dignified-looking man, with a very grave and noble cast of countenance. I was more pleased with him than with any other in the room, from the quiet, musing, self-forgetfulness of his air, and the mild and civil manner in which he addressed the servants. These were only two in number, though a dozen or more tables were spread around, each capable of seating four persons. They were well-dressed, decent-looking men, who came and went quickly, yet quietly, and without confusion, at each call for George or Thomas. The patience of the guests seemed unbounded, and the object of each to destroy as much time as possible. The scene, dull as it was, furnished a most favourable contrast to that which is exhibited at the ordinaries of our great inns, or in the saloons of our magnificent steamers.

Having completed my observations under cover of the sirloin, I deposed my knife and fork, and the watchful waiter hastened to bear away the formidable bulwark by whose aid I had been enabled to reconnoitre the inmates of the coffee-room. A tart and some cheese followed, and then some dried fruits and thin wine biscuits completed my repast. Having endeavored ineffectually to rouse myself from the stupefaction into which I was falling, by a cup of indifferent coffee, I wheeled my capacious arm-chair round, and took refuge from surrounding objects by gazing in the fire.

The loquacious party had disappeared on their way to Drury Lane, having decided, after some discussion, that the hour for half price had arrived. The saving of money is an excellent thing; without economy, indeed, there can scarcely be any honesty. But, as a question of good taste, discussions about money matters should be carried on in a quiet and under tone in the presence of strangers. When they had departed, a deathlike stillness pervaded the scene. Occasionally, the newspaper of the thin gentleman might be heard to rumple as he laid it aside or resumed it; or the rosy gentleman from the country awoke the awful stillness by snapping a fragment of biscuit, or depositing his wine-glass upon the table. Then all was again silent, save when the crust of the seacoal fire fell in as it consumed, and the sleepy, simmering note in which the teakettle, placed by the grate in readiness either for tea or toddy, sang on perpetually.

RALPH WALDO EMERSON

WAS born in Boston some time about the year 1803. His father was a Unitarian clergyman, and the son was educated for the pulpit of the sect. After taking his degree at Harvard, in 1821 he studied divinity, and took charge of a congregation in Boston, as the colleague of Henry Ware, jun.; but soon becoming independent of the control of set regulations of religious worship, retired to Concord, where, in 1835, he purchased the house in which he has since resided. It has become identified as the seat of his solitary musings, with some of the most subtle, airy, eloquent, spiritual productions of American literature. Mr. Emerson first attracted public attention as a speaker, by his college orations. In 1837 he delivered a Phi-Beta-Kappa oration, *Man Thinking;* in 1838, his address to the senior class of the Divinity College, Cambridge, and *Literary Ethics, an Oration.* His volume, *Nature*, the key-note of his subsequent productions, appeared in 1839. It treated of freedom, beauty, culture in the life of the individual, to which outward natural objects were made subservient. *The Dial: a Magazine for Literature, Philosophy, and Religion*, of which Mr. Emerson was one of the original editors and chief supporters, was commenced in July, 1840. It was given to what was called transcendental literature, and many of its papers affecting a purely philosophical expression had the obscurity, if not the profundity, of abstract metaphysics. The orphic sayings of Mr. A. Bronson Alcott helped materially to support this character, and others wrote hardly less intelligibly, but it contained many acute and original papers of a critical character. In its religious views it had little respect for commonly received creeds.

The conduct of the work passed into the hands of Margaret Fuller, while Mr. Emerson remained a contributor through its four annual volumes. His chief articles were publications of the *Lec-*

tures on the Times, and similar compositions, which he had delivered. The duties of periodical literature were too restricted and exacting for his temperament, and his powers gained nothing by the demand for their display in this form. The style of composition which has proved to have the firmest hold upon him, in drawing out his thoughts for the public, is a peculiar species of lecture, in which he combines the ease and familiar turn of the essay with the philosophical dogmatism of the orator and modern oracle.

R. W. Emerson

The collections of his *Essays* and *Lectures* commenced with the publication in 1841 of a first series, followed by a second in 1844. His volume of *Poems* was issued in 1847. In 1848 he travelled in England, delivering a course of lectures in London on *The Mind and Manners of the Nineteenth Century*, including such topics as Relation of Intellect to Science; Duties of Men of Thought; Politics and Socialism; Poetry and Eloquence; Natural Aristocracy. He also lectured on the *Superlative in Manners and Literature*, and delivered lectures in other parts of England, in which country his writings have been received with great favor.

After his return he delivered a lecture on *English Character and Manners*, and has since visited the chief northern cities and literary institutions, delivering several courses of lectures on *Power*, *Wealth*, *the Conduct of Life*, and other topics, which, without obtruding his early metaphysics, tend more and more to the illustration of the practical advantages of life.

In 1850 appeared his volume *Representative Men:* including portraits of Plato, Swedenborg, Montaigne, Shakespeare, Napoleon, Goethe. His notices of Margaret Fuller form an independent portion of her Memoirs, published in 1852.

The characteristics of Emerson are, in the subject matter of his discourses, a reliance on individual consciousness and energy, independent of creeds, institutions, and tradition; an acute intellectual analysis of passions and principles, through which the results are calmly exhibited, with a species of philosophical indifferentism tending to license in practice, which in the conduct of life he would be the last to avail himself of. His style is brief, pithy, neglecting ordinary links of association, occasionally obscure from dealing with vague and unknown quantities, but always refined; while in his lectures it arrests attention in the deep, pure tone of the orator, and is not unfrequently, especially in his latter discourses, relieved by turns of practical sagacity and shrewd New England humor. It is a style, too, in which there is a considerable infusion of the poetical vision, bringing to light remote events and illustrations; but its prominent quality is wit, dazzling by brief and acute analysis and the juxtaposition of striking objects. In his poems, apart from their obscurity, Emerson is sometimes bare and didactic; at others, his musical utterance is sweet and powerful.

Mr. Emerson's pursuits being those of the author and philosopher, he has taken little part in the public affairs of the day, except in the matter of the slavery question, on which he has delivered several orations, in opposition to that institution.

The early death of a younger brother of Emerson, CHARLES CHAUNCY EMERSON, is remembered by those who knew him at Cambridge, with regret. He died May 9, 1836. A lecture which he delivered on Socrates is spoken of with admiration. Holmes, who was his companion in college, in his metrical essay on poetry, has given a few lines to his memory, at Harvard, where his name is on the catalogue of graduates for 1828.

Thou calm, chaste scholar! I can see thee now,
The first young laurels on thy pallid brow,
O'er thy slight figure floating lightly down,
In graceful folds the academic gown,
On thy curled lip the classic lines, that taught
How nice the mind that sculptured them with thought,
And triumph glistening in the clear blue eye,
Too bright to live,—but oh, too fair to die.

THE PROBLEM.

I like a church; I like a cowl:
I love a prophet of the soul;
And on my heart monastic aisles
Fall like sweet strains, or pensive smiles;
Yet not for all his faith can see
Would I that cowled churchman be.

Why should the vest on him allure,
Which I could not on me endure?

Not from a vain or shallow thought
His awful Jove young Phidias brought;
Never from lips of cunning fell
The thrilling Delphic oracle;
Out from the heart of nature rolled
The burdens of the Bible old;
The litanies of nations came,
Like the volcano's tongue of flame,
Up from the burning core below,—
The canticles of love and woe;
The hand that rounded Peter's dome,
And groined the aisles of Christian Rome,
Wrought in a sad sincerity;
Himself from God he could not free;

He builded better than he knew;—
The conscious stone to beauty grew.

Know'st thou what wove yon woodbird's nest
Of leaves, and feathers from her breast?
Or how the fish outbuilt her shell,
Painting with morn each annual cell?
Or how the sacred pine-tree adds
To her old leaves new myriads?
Such and so grew these holy piles,
Whilst love and terror laid the tiles.
Earth proudly wears the Parthenon,
As the best gem upon her zone;
And Morning opes with haste her lids,
To gaze upon the Pyramids;
O'er England's abbeys bends the sky,
As on its friends, with kindred eye;
For, out of Thought's interior sphere,
These wonders rose to upper air;
And Nature gladly gave them place,
Adopted them into her race,
And granted them an equal date
With Andes and with Ararat.

These temples grew as grows the grass;
Art might obey, but not surpass.
The passive Master lent his hand
To the vast soul that o'er him planned;
And the same power that reared the shrine,
Bestrode the tribes that knelt within.
Ever the fiery Pentecost
Girds with one flame the countless host,
Trances the heart through chanting choirs,
And through the priest the mind inspires.
The word unto the prophet spoken
Was writ on tables yet unbroken;
The word by seers or sibyls told,
In groves of oak, or fanes of gold,
Still floats upon the morning wind,
Still whispers to the willing mind.
One accent of the Holy Ghost
The heedless world hath never lost.
I know what say the fathers wise,—
The Book itself before me lies,
Old Chrysostom, best Augustine,
And he who blent both in his line,
The younger Golden Lips or mines,
Taylor, the Shakspeare of divines.
His words are music in my ear,
I see his cowled portrait dear;
And yet, for all his faith could see,
I would not the good bishop be.

TACT.

What boots it, thy virtue,
  What profit thy parts,
While one thing thou lackest,—
  The art of all arts?

The only credentials,
  Passport to success;
Opens castle and parlor,—
  Address, man, Address.

The maiden in danger
  Was saved by the swain;
His stout arm restored her
  To Broadway again.

The maid would reward him,—
  Gay company come;
They laugh, she laughs with them;
  He is moonstruck and dumb.

This clinches the bargain;
  Sails out of the bay;
Gets the vote in the senate,
  Spite of Webster and Clay;

Has for genius no mercy,
  For speeches no heed;
It lurks in the eyebeam,
  It leaps to its deed.

Church, market, and tavern,
  Bed and board, it will sway.
It has no to-morrow;
  It ends with to-day.

GOOD-BYE.

Good-bye, proud world! I'm going home:
Thou art not my friend, and I'm not thine.
Long through thy weary crowds I roam;
A river-ark on the ocean's brine,
Long I've been tossed like the driven foam;
But now, proud world! I'm going home.

Good-bye to Flattery's fawning face;
To Grandeur with his wise grimace;
To upstart Wealth's averted eye;
To supple Office, low and high;
To crowded halls, to court and street;
To frozen hearts and hasting feet;
To those who go, and those who come;
Good-bye, proud world! I'm going home.

I am going to my own hearth-stone,
Bosomed in yon green hills alone,—
A secret nook in a pleasant land,
Whose groves the frolic fairies planned;
Where arches green, the live-long day,
Echo the blackbird's roundelay,
And vulgar feet have never trod
A spot that is sacred to thought and God.

O, when I am safe in my sylvan home,
I tread on the pride of Greece and Rome;
And when I am stretched beneath the pines,
Where the evening star so holy shines,
I laugh at the lore and the pride of man,
At the sophist schools, and the learned clan;
For what are they all, in their high conceit,
When man in the bush with God may meet!

THE HUMBLE-BEE.

Burly, dozing, humble-bee,
Where thou art is clime for me.
Let them sail for Porto Rique,
Far-off heats through seas to seek;
I will follow thee alone,
Thou animated torrid zone!
Zigzag steerer, desert cheerer,
Let me chase thy waving lines;
Keep me nearer, me thy hearer,
Singing over shrubs and vines.

Insect lover of the sun,
Joy of thy dominion!
Sailor of the atmosphere;
Swimmer through the waves of air;
Voyager of light and noon;
Epicurean of June;
Wait, I prithee, till I come
Within earshot of thy hum,—
All without is martyrdom.

When the south wind, in May days,
With a net of shining haze
Silvers the horizon wall,
And, with softness touching all,
Tints the human countenance
With a color of romance,
And, infusing subtle heats,
Turns the sod to violets,
Thou, in sunny solitudes,
Rover of the underwoods,

The green silence dost displace
With thy mellow, breezy bass.

Hot midsummer's petted crone,
Sweet to me thy drowsy tone
Tells of countless sunny hours,
Long days, and solid banks of flowers;
Of gulfs of sweetness without bound
In Indian wildernesses found;
Of Syrian peace, immortal leisure,
Firmest cheer, and bird-like pleasure.

Aught unsavory or unclean
Hath my insect never seen;
But violets and bilberry bells,
Maple sap, and daffodels,
Grass with green flag half-mast high,
Succory to match the sky,
Columbine with horn of honey,
Scented fern, and agrimony,
Clover, catchfly, adder's tongue,
And brier roses, dwelt among;
All beside was unknown waste,
All was picture as he passed.

Wiser far than human seer,
Yellow-breeched philosopher!
Seeing only what is fair,
Sipping only what is sweet,
Thou dost mock at fate and care,
Leave the chaff, and take the wheat.
When the fierce north-western blast
Cools sea and land so far and fast,
Thou already slumberest deep;
Woe and want thou canst outsleep;
Want and woe, which torture us,
Thy sleep makes ridiculous.

THE APOLOGY.

Think me not unkind and rude
That I walk alone in grove and glen,
I go to the god of the wood,
To fetch his word to man.

Tax not my sloth that I
Fold my arms beside the brook;
Each cloud that floated in the sky,
Writes a letter in my book.

Chide me not, laborious band,
For the idle flowers I brought,
Every aster in my hand
Goes home loaded with a thought.

There was never mystery
But 'tis figured in the flowers;
Was never secret history
But birds tell it in the bowers.

One harvest from thy field
Homeward brought the oxen strong:
A second crop thine acres yield,
Whilst I gather in a song.

BEAUTY—FROM NATURE.

For better consideration, we may distribute the aspects of Beauty in a threefold manner.

1. First, the simple perception of natural forms is a delight. The influence of the forms and actions in nature is so needful to man, that, in its lowest functions, it seems to lie on the confines of commodity and beauty. To the body and mind which have been cramped by noxious work or company, nature is medicinal and restores their tone. The tradesman, the attorney comes out of the din and craft of the street, and sees the sky and the woods, and is a man again. In their eternal calm, he finds himself. The health of the eye seems to demand a horizon. We are never tired, so long as we can see far enough.

But in other hours, Nature satisfies by its loveliness, and without any mixture of corporeal benefit. I see the spectacle of morning from the hill-top over against my house, from day-break to sun-rise, with emotions which an angel might share. The long slender bars of cloud float like fishes in the sea of crimson light. From the earth, as a shore, I look out into that silent sea. I seem to partake its rapid transformations: the active enchantment reaches my dust, and I dilate and conspire with the morning wind. How does Nature deify us with a few and cheap elements! Give me health and a day, and I will make the pomp of emperors ridiculous. The dawn is my Assyria; the sun-set and moon-rise my Paphos, and unimaginable realms of faerie; broad noon shall be my England of the senses and the understanding; the night shall be my Germany of mystic philosophy and dreams.

Not less excellent, except for our less susceptibility in the afternoon, was the charm, last evening, of a January sunset. The western clouds divided and subdivided themselves into pink flakes modulated with tints of unspeakable softness; and the air had so much life and sweetness, that it was a pain to come within doors. What was it that nature would say? Was there no meaning in the live repose of the valley behind the mill, and which Homer or Shakspeare could not re-form for me in words? The leafless trees become spires of flame in the sunset, with the blue east for their background, and the stars of the dead calices of flowers, and every withered stem and stubble rimed with frost, contribute something to the mute music.

The inhabitants of cities suppose that the country landscape is pleasant only half the year. I please myself with the graces of the winter scenery, and believe that we are as much touched by it as by the genial influences of summer. To the attentive eye, each moment of the year has its own beauty, and in the same field, it beholds, every hour, a picture which was never seen before, and which shall never be seen again. The heavens change every moment, and reflect their glory or gloom on the plains beneath. The state of the crop in the surrounding farms alters the expression of the earth from week to week. The succession of native plants in the pastures and roadsides, which makes the silent clock by which time tells the summer hours, will make even the divisions of the day sensible to a keen observer. The tribes of birds and insects, like the plants punctual to their time, follow each other, and the year has room for all. By water-courses, the variety is greater. In July, the blue pontederia or pickerel-weed blooms in large beds in the shallow parts of our present river, and swarms with yellow butterflies in continual motion. Art cannot rival this pomp of purple and gold. Indeed the river is a perpetual gala, and boasts each month a new ornament.

But this beauty of Nature which is seen and felt as beauty, is the least part. The shows of day, the dewy morning, the rainbow, mountains, orchards in blossom, stars, moonlight, shadows in still water, and the like, if too eagerly hunted, become shows merely, and mock us with their unreality. Go out of the house to see the moon, and 't is mere tinsel; it will not please us when its light shines upon your necessary journey. The beauty that shimmers in the yellow afternoons of October, who ever could clutch it? Go forth to find it, and it is gone: 't is only a mirage as you look from the windows of a diligence.

2. The presence of a higher, namely, of the spiritual element is essential to its perfection. The high and divine beauty which can be loved without

effeminacy, is that which is found in combination with the human will. Beauty is the mark God sets upon virtue. Every natural action is graceful. Every heroic act is also decent, and causes the place and the bystanders to shine. We are taught by great actions that the universe is the property of every individual in it. Every rational creature has all nature for his dowry and estate. It is his, if he will. He may divest himself of it; he may creep into a corner, and abdicate his kingdom, as most men do, but he is entitled to the world by his constitution. In proportion to the energy of his thought and will, he takes up the world into himself. "All those things for which men plough, build, or sail, obey virtue;" said Sallust. "The winds and waves," said Gibbon, "are always on the side of the ablest navigators." So are the sun and moon and all the stars of heaven. When a noble act is done,—perchance in a scene of great natural beauty; when Leonidas and his three hundred martyrs consume one day in dying, and the sun and moon come each and look at them once in the steep defile of Thermopylæ; when Arnold Winkelried, in the high Alps, under the shadow of the avalanche, gathers in his side a sheaf of Austrian spears to break the line for his comrades; are not these heroes entitled to add the beauty of the scene to the beauty of the deed? When the bark of Columbus nears the shores of America;—before it, the beach lined with savages, fleeing out of all their huts of cane; the sea behind; and the purple mountains of the Indian Archipelago around, can we separate the man from the living picture? Does not the New World clothe his form with her palm groves and savannahs as fit drapery? Ever does natural beauty steal in like air, and envelope great actions. When Sir Harry Vane was dragged up the Tower-hill, sitting on a sled, to suffer death, as the champion of the English laws, one of the multitude cried out to him, "You never sate on so glorious a seat." Charles II., to intimidate the citizens of London, caused the patriot Lord Russell to be drawn in an open coach, through the principal streets of the city, on his way to the scaffold. "But," his biographer says, "the multitude imagined they saw liberty and virtue sitting by his side." In private places, among sordid objects, an act of truth or heroism seems at once to draw to itself the sky as its temple, the sun as its candle. Nature stretcheth out her arms to embrace man, only let his thoughts be of equal greatness. Willingly does she follow his steps with the rose and the violet, and bend her lines of grandeur and grace to the decoration of her darling child. Only let his thoughts be of equal scope, and the frame will suit the picture. A virtuous man is in unison with her works, and makes the central figure of the visible sphere. Homer, Pindar, Socrates, Phocian, associate themselves fitly in our memory with the geography and climate of Greece. The visible heavens and earth sympathize with Jesus. And in common life, whosoever has seen a person of powerful character and happy genius, will have remarked how easily he took all things along with him,—the persons, the opinions, and the day, and nature became ancillary to a man.

3. There is still another aspect under which the beauty of the world may be viewed, namely, as it becomes an object of the intellect. Beside the relation of things to virtue, they have a relation to thought. The intellect searches out the absolute order of things as they stand in the mind of God, and without the colors of affection. The intellectual and the active powers seem to succeed each other, and the exclusive activity of the one generates the exclusive activity of the other. There is something unfriendly in each to the other, but they are like the alternate periods of feeding and working in animals; each prepares and will be followed by the other. Therefore does beauty, which, in relation to actions, as we have seen, comes unsought, and comes because it is unsought, remain for the apprehension and pursuit of the intellect; and then again, in its turn, of the active power. Nothing divine dies. All good is eternally reproductive. The beauty of nature reforms itself in the mind, and not for barren contemplation, but for new creation.

All men are in some degree impressed by the face of the world; some men even to delight. This love of beauty is Taste. Others have the same love in such excess, that, not content with admiring, they seek to embody it in new forms. The creation of beauty is Art.

The production of a work of art throws a light upon the mystery of humanity. A work of art is an abstract or epitome of the world. It is the result or expression of nature, in miniature. For, although the works of nature are innumerable and all different, the result or the expression of them all is similar and single. Nature is a sea of forms radically alike and even unique. A leaf, a sunbeam, a landscape, the ocean, make an analogous impression on the mind. What is common to them all,—that perfectness and harmony, is beauty. The standard of beauty is the entire circuit of natural forms,—the totality of nature; which the Italians expressed by defining beauty "il piu nell' uno." Nothing is quite beautiful alone: nothing but is beautiful in the whole. A single object is only so far beautiful as it suggests this universal grace. The poet, the painter, the sculptor, the musician, the architect, seek each to concentrate this radiance of the world on one point, and each in his several work to satisfy the love of beauty which stimulates him to produce. Thus is Art, a nature passed through the alembic of man. Thus, in art, does nature work through the will of a man filled with the beauty of her first works.

The world thus exists to the soul to satisfy the desire of beauty. This element I call an ultimate end. No reason can be asked or given why the soul seeks beauty. Beauty, in its largest and profoundest sense, is one expression for the universe. God is the all-fair. Truth, and goodness, and beauty, are but different faces of the same All. But beauty in nature is not ultimate. It is the herald of inward and eternal beauty, and is not alone a solid and satisfactory good. It must stand as a part, and not as yet the last or highest expression of the final cause of Nature.

LOVE—FROM THE ESSAYS.

Every soul is a celestial Venus to every other soul. The heart has its Sabbaths and jubilees, in which the world appears as a hymeneal feast, and all natural sounds and the circle of the seasons are erotic odes and dances. Love is omnipresent in nature as motive and reward. Love is our highest word, and the synonym of God. Every promise of the soul has innumerable fulfilments: each of its joys ripens into a new want. Nature, uncontainable, flowing, forelooking, in the first sentiment of kindness anticipates already a benevolence which shall lose all particular regards in its general light. The introduction to this felicity is in private and tender relation of one to one, which is the enchantment of human life; which, like a certain divine rage and enthusiasm, seizes on man at one period, and works a revolution in his mind and body; unites him to his race, pledges him to the domestic and civic relations, carries him with new sympathy into nature, enhances the power of the senses, opens the imagination, adds to his character heroic and sacred attributes, establishes marriage, and gives permanence to human society.

The natural association of the sentiment of love with the heyday of the blood, seems to require that in order to portray it in vivid tints which every youth and maid should confess to be true to their throbbing experience, one must not be too old. The delicious fancies of youth reject the least savor of a mature philosophy, as chilling with age and pedantry their purple bloom. And, therefore, I know I incur the imputation of unnecessary hardness and stoicism from those who compose the Court and Parliament of Love. But from these formidable censors I shall appeal to my seniors. For, it is to be considered that this passion of which we speak, though it begin with the young, yet forsakes not the old, or rather suffers no one who is truly its servant to grow old, but makes the aged participators of it, not less than the tender maiden, though in a different and nobler sort. For, it is a fire that kindling its first embers in the narrow nook of a private bosom, caught from a wandering spark out of another private heart, glows and enlarges until it warms and beams upon multitudes of men and women, upon the universal heart of all, and so lights up the whole world and all nature with its generous flames. It matters not, therefore, whether we attempt to describe the passion at twenty, at thirty, or at eighty years. He who paints it at the first period, will lose some of its later; he who paints it at the last, some of its earlier traits. Only it is to be hoped that by patience and the muses' aid, we may attain to that inward view of the law, which shall describe a truth ever young, ever beautiful, so central that it shall commend itself to the eye at whatever angle beholden.

And the first condition is, that we must leave a too close and lingering adherence to the actual, to facts, and study the sentiment as it appeared in hope and not in history. For, each man sees his own life defaced and disfigured, as the life of man is not, to his imagination. Each man sees over his own experience a certain slime of error, whilst that of other men looks fair and ideal. Let any man go back to those delicious relations which make the beauty of his life, which have given him sincerest instruction and nourishment, he will shrink and shrink. Alas! I know not why, but infinite compunctions embitter in mature life all the remembrances of budding sentiment, and cover every beloved name. Everything is beautiful seen from the point of the intellect, or as truth. But all is sour, if seen as experience. Details are always melancholy; the plan is seemly and noble. It is strange how painful is the actual world,—the painful kingdom of time and place. There dwells care and canker and fear. With thought, with the ideal, is immortal hilarity, the rose of joy. Round it all the muses sing. But with names and persons and the partial interests of to-day and yesterday, is grief.

The strong bent of nature is seen in the proportion which this topic of personal relations usurps in the conversation of society. What do we wish to know of any worthy person so much as how he has sped in the history of this sentiment? What books in the circulating libraries circulate? How we glow over these novels of passion, when the story is told with any spark of truth and nature! And what fastens attention, in the intercourse of life, like any passage betraying affection between two parties? Perhaps we never saw them before, and never shall meet them again. But we see them exchange a glance, or betray a deep emotion, and we are no longer strangers. We understand them, and take the warmest interest in the development of the romance. All mankind love a lover. The earliest demonstrations of complacency and kindness are nature's most winning pictures. It is the dawn of civility and grace in the coarse and rustic. The rude village boy teazes the girls about the school-house door;—but to-day he comes running into the entry, and meets one fair child arranging her satchel; he holds her books to help her, and instantly it seems to him as if she removed herself from him infinitely, and was a sacred precinct. Among the throng of girls he runs rudely enough, but one alone distances him: and those two little neighbors that were so close just now, have learned to respect each other's personality. Or who can avert his eyes from the engaging, half-artful, half-artless ways of school girls who go into the country shops to buy a skein of silk or a sheet of paper, and talk half an hour about nothing, with the broad-faced, good-natured shop-boy. In the village, they are on a perfect equality, which love delights in, and without any coquetry the happy, affectionate nature of woman flows out in this pretty gossip. The girls may have little beauty, yet plainly do they establish between them and the good boy the most agreeable, confiding relations, what with their fun and their earnest, about Edgar, and Jonas, and Almira, and who was invited to the party, and who danced at the dancing-school, and when the singing-school would begin, and other nothings concerning which the parties cooed. By-and-by that boy wants a wife, and very truly and heartily will he know where to find a sincere and true mate, without any risk such as Milton deplores as incident to scholars and great men.

I have been told that my philosophy is unsocial, and that, in public discourses, my reverence for the intellect makes me unjustly cold to the personal relations. But now I almost shrink at the remembrance of such disparaging words. For persons are love's world, and the coldest philosopher cannot recount the debt of the young soul wandering here in nature to the power of love, without being tempted to unsay, as treasonable to nature, aught derogatory to the social instincts. For, though the celestial rapture falling out of heaven seizes only upon those of tender age, and although a beauty overpowering all analysis or comparison, and putting us quite beside ourselves, we can seldom see after thirty years, yet the remembrance of these visions outlasts all other remembrances, and is a wreath of flowers on the oldest brows. But here is a strange fact; it may seem to many men in revising their experience, that they have no fairer page in their life's book than the delicious memory of some passages wherein affection contrived to give a witchcraft surpassing the deep attraction of its own truth to a parcel of accidental and trivial circumstances. In looking backward, they may find that several things which were not the charm, have more reality to this groping memory than the charm itself which embalmed them. But be our experience in particulars what it may, no man ever forgot the visitations of that power to his heart and brain, which created all things new; which was the dawn in him of music, poetry, and art; which made the face of nature radiant with purple light, the morning and the night varied enchantments; when a single tone of one voice could make the heart beat, and the most trivial circumstance associated with one form is put in the amber of memory; when we became all eye when one was present, and all memory when one was gone; when the youth becomes a watcher of windows, and studious of a glove, a veil, a ribbon, or the wheels of a carriage; when no place is too solitary, and none too silent for him who has richer company and sweeter conversation in his new thoughts, than any old friends, though best and purest, can give him; for, the figures, the motions, the words of the beloved object are not like other images written in water, but, as Plutarch said, "enamelled in fire," and make the study of midnight.

Thou art not gone being gone, where'er thou art,
Thou leav'st in him thy watchful eyes, in him thy loving heart.

In the noon and the afternoon of life, we still throb at the recollection of days when happiness was not happy enough, but must be drugged with the relish of pain and fear; for he touched the secret of the matter, who said of love,

All other pleasures are not worth its pains,

and when the day was not long enough, but the night too must be consumed in keen recollections; when the head boiled all night on the pillow with the generous deed it resolved on: when the moonlight was a pleasing fever, and the stars were letters, and the flowers ciphers, and the air was coined into song; when all business seemed an impertinence, and all the men and women running to and fro in the streets, mere pictures.

The passion re-makes the world for the youth. It makes all things alive and significant. Nature grows conscious. Every bird on the boughs of the tree sings now to his heart and soul. Almost the notes are articulate. The clouds have faces, as he looks on them. The trees of the forest, the waving grass and the peeping flowers have grown intelligent; and almost he fears to trust them with the secret which they seem to invite. Yet nature soothes and sympathizes. In the green solitude he finds a dearer home than with men.

Fountain heads and pathless groves,
Places which pale passion loves,
Moonlight walks, when all the fowls
Are safely housed, save bats and owls,
A midnight bell, a passing groan,
These are the sounds we feed upon.

Behold there in the wood the fine madman! He is a palace of sweet sounds and sights; he dilates; he is twice a man; he walks with arms akimbo; he soliloquizes; he accosts the grass and the trees; he feels the blood of the violet, the clover, and the lily in his veins; and he talks with the brook that wets his foot.

The causes that have sharpened his perceptions of natural beauty, have made him love music and verse. It is a fact often observed, that men have written good verses under the inspiration of passion, who cannot write well under any other circumstances.

The like force has the passion over all his nature. It expands the sentiment; it makes the clown gentle, and gives the coward heart. Into the most pitiful and abject it will infuse a heart and courage to defy the world, so only it have the countenance of the beloved object. In giving him to another, it still more gives him to himself. He is a new man, with new perceptions, new and keener purposes, and a religious solemnity of character and aims. He does not longer appertain to his family and society. *He* is somewhat. *He* is a person. *He* is a soul.

MONTAIGNE—FROM REPRESENTATIVE MEN.

A single odd volume of Cotton's translation of the Essays remained to me from my father's library, when a boy. It lay long neglected, until, after many years, when I was newly escaped from college, I read the book, and procured the remaining volumes. I remember the delight and wonder in which I lived with it. It seemed to me as if I had myself written the book, in some former life, so sincerely it spoke to my thought and experience. It happened, when in Paris, in 1833, that in the cemetery of Père la Chaise, I came to a tomb of Auguste Collignon, who died in 1830, aged sixty-eight years, and who, said the monument, "lived to do right, and had formed himself to virtue on the Essays of Montaigne." Some years later, I became acquainted with an accomplished English poet, John Sterling; and, in prosecuting my correspondence, I found that, from a love of Montaigne, he had made a pilgrimage to his chateau, still standing near Castellan, in Perigord, and, after two hundred and fifty years, had copied from the walls of his library the inscriptions which Montaigne had written there. That Journal of Mr. Sterling's, published in the Westminster Review, Mr. Hazlitt has reprinted in the *Prolegomena* to his edition of the Essays. I heard with pleasure that one of the newly-discovered autographs of William Shakespeare was in a copy of Florio's translation of Montaigne. It is the only book which we certainly know to have been in the poet's library. And, oddly enough, the duplicate copy of Florio, which the British Museum purchased, with a view of protecting the Shakespeare autograph (as I was informed in the Museum), turned out to have the autograph of Ben Jonson in the fly-leaf. Leigh Hunt relates of Lord Byron, that Montaigne was the only great writer of past times whom he read with avowed satisfaction. Other coincidences, not needful to be mentioned here, concurred to make this old Gascon still new and immortal for me.

In 1571, on the death of his father, Montaigne, then thirty-eight years old, retired from the practice of law at Bordeaux, and settled himself on his estate. Though he had been a man of pleasure, and sometimes a courtier, his studious habits now grew on him, and he loved the compass, staidness, and independence of the country gentleman's life. He took up his economy in good earnest, and made his farms yield the most. Downright and plain-dealing, and abhorring to be deceived or to deceive, he was esteemed in the country for his sense and probity. In the civil wars of the League, which converted every house into a fort, Montaigne kept his gates open, and his house without defence. All parties freely came and went, his courage and honor being universally esteemed. The neighboring lords and gentry brought jewels and papers to him for safekeeping. Gibbon reckons, in these bigoted times, but two men of liberality in France,—Henry IV. and Montaigne.

Montaigne is the frankest and honestest of all writers. His French freedom runs into grossness; but he has anticipated all censure by the bounty of his own confessions. In his times, books were written to one sex only, and almost all were written in Latin; so that, in a humorist, a certain nakedness of statement was permitted, which our manners, of a literature addressed equally to both sexes, do not allow. But, though a biblical plainness, coupled with a most uncanonical levity, may shut his pages to many sensitive readers, yet the offence is superficial. He parades it: he makes the most of it: nobody can think or say worse of him than he does. He pretends to most of the vices; and, if there be any virtue in him, he says, it got in by stealth. There is no man, in his opinion, who has not deserved hanging five or six times; and he pretends no exception in his own behalf. "Five or six as ridiculous stories," too, he says, "can be told of me, as of any man living." But, with all this really superfluous frankness, the opinion of an invincible probity grows into every reader's mind.

"When I the most strictly and religiously confess myself, I find that the best virtue I have has in it some tincture of vice: and I am afraid that Plato, in his purest virtue (I, who am as sincere and perfect a lover of virtue of that stamp as any other whatever), if he had listened, and laid his ear close to himself, would have heard some jarring sound of human mixture; but faint and remote, and only to be perceived by himself."

Here is an impatience and fastidiousness at color or pretence of any kind. He has been in courts so long as to have conceived a furious disgust at appearances; he will indulge himself with a little cursing and swearing; he will talk with sailors and gipsies, use flash and street ballads: he has stayed in-doors till he is deadly sick; he will to the open air, though it rain bullets. He has seen too much of gentlemen of the long robe, until he wishes for cannibals; and is so nervous, by factitious life, that he thinks, the more barbarous man is, the better he is. He likes his saddle. You may read theology, and grammar, and metaphysics elsewhere. Whatever you get here, shall smack of the earth and of real life, sweet, or smart, or stinging. He makes no hesitation to entertain you with the records of his disease; and his journey to Italy is quite full of that matter. He took and kept this position of equilibrium. Over his name, he drew an emblematic pair of scales, and wrote *Que sçais je?* under it. As I look at his effigy opposite the title-page, I seem to hear him say, 'You may play old Poz, if you will; you may rail and exaggerate,—I stand here for truth, and will not, for all the states, and churches, and revenues, and personal reputations of Europe, overstate the dry fact,' as I see it; I will rather mumble and prose about what I certainly know,—my house and barns; my father, my wife, and my tenants; my old lean bald pate; my knives and forks; what meats I eat, and what drinks I prefer; and a hundred straws just as ridiculous,—than I will write, with a fine crow-quill, a fine romance. I like gray days, and autumn and winter weather. I am gray and autumnal myself, and think an undress, and old shoes that do not pinch my feet, and old friends who do not constrain me, and plain topics where I do not need to strain myself and pump my brains, the most suitable. Our condition as men is risky and ticklish enough. One cannot be sure of himself and his fortune an hour, but he may be whisked off into some pitiable or ridiculous plight. Why should I vapor and play the philosopher, instead of ballasting, the best I can, this dancing balloon? So, at least, I live within compass, keep myself ready for action, and can shoot the gulf, at last, with decency. If there be anything farcical in such a life, the blame is not mine: let it lie at fate's and nature's door."

The Essays, therefore, are an entertaining soliloquy on every random topic that comes into his head; treating everything without ceremony, yet with masculine sense. There have been men with deeper insight; but, one would say, never a man with such abundance of thoughts: he is never dull, never insincere, and has the genius to make the reader care for all that he cares for.

The sincerity and marrow of the man reaches to his sentences. I know not anywhere the book that seems less written. It is the language of conversation transferred to a book. Cut these words, and they would bleed; they are vascular and alive. One has the same pleasure in it that we have in listening to the necessary speech of men about their work, when any unusual circumstance gives momentary importance to the dialogue. For blacksmiths and teamsters do not trip in their speech; it is a shower of bullets. It is Cambridge men who correct themselves, and begin again at every half sentence, and, moreover, will pun, and refine too much, and swerve from the matter to the expression. Montaigne talks with shrewdness, knows the world, and books, and himself, and uses the positive degree: never shrieks, or protests, or prays: no weakness, no convulsion, no superlative: does not wish to jump out of his skin, or play any antics, or annihilate space or time; but is stout and solid; tastes every moment of the day; likes pain, because it makes him feel himself, and realize things; as we pinch ourselves to know that we are awake. He keeps the plain; he rarely mounts or sinks; likes to feel solid ground, and the stones underneath. His writing has no enthusiasms, no aspiration; contented, self-respecting, and keeping the middle of the road. There is but one exception,—in his love for Socrates. In speaking of him, for once his cheek flushes, and his style rises to passion.

Montaigne died of a quinsy, at the age of sixty, in 1592. When he came to die, he caused the mass to be celebrated in his chamber. At the age of thirty-three, he had been married. "But," he says, "might I have had my own will, I would not have married Wisdom herself, if she would have had me: but 'tis not to much purpose to evade it, the common custom and use of life will have it so. Most of my actions are guided by example, not choice." In the hour of death, he gave the same weight to custom. *Que sçais je?* What do I know?

This book of Montaigne the world has endorsed, by translating it into all tongues, and printing seventy-five editions of it in Europe: and that too, a circulation somewhat chosen, namely, among courtiers, soldiers, princes, men of the world, and men of wit and generosity.

Shall we say that Montaigne has spoken wisely, and given the right and permanent expression of the human mind, on the conduct of life?

GEORGE HENRY CALVERT

Was born at Baltimore, in Maryland, in 1803. His grandfather, Benedict Calvert of Mount Airy, Prince George's county, was a son of Lord Baltimore, and an intimate friend of General Washington. After the resignation of his commission at Annapolis, Washington passed the first night of his journey homeward at Mount Airy with the tory Benedict Calvert,—a circumstance severely commented on by the political enemies of the great Patriot.* The father of Calvert was George Calvert of Riverdale, an estate near Washington, now held and occupied by an eminent agriculturist, the brother of our author, Charles Calvert, and a favorite resort of Henry Clay, an intimate friend of the family. George Calvert, the parent, married Rosalie Eugenia Stier d'Artrelaer of Antwerp, a lineal descendant of Rubens, of a family of rank and antiquity. The chateau d'Artrelaer, a castellated mansion of the thirteenth or fourteenth century, is still in the possession of the family. Calvert's maternal grandfather came to America about the close of the last century, with his daughter, to escape the spoliations of the French emperor. Napoleonism is not one of his descendant's traits. Few writers have hit that assumption of power with more severity than our author in many of his philosophical reflections.

The birth of Calvert thus ascends in an honorable lineage in both the colonial and European

* In Sparks's Correspondence of Washington there is a letter to Benedict Calvert relative to a projected marriage between his daughter and a member of Washington's family.

field. He was educated at Harvard and at Gottingen, where he became thoroughly imbued with German literature. On his return to Maryland he was for several years the editor of the *Baltimore American*, at that time a neutral paper. While thus engaged he published in 1832 a volume, *Illustrations of Phrenology*, a collection of passages from the Edinburgh Phrenological Journal, with an introduction giving an analysis of the system. It is noticeable as the first book published in America on the subject. The same distinction belongs to his notice of the water cure, which he announced to his countrymen in a letter from Boppert, on the Rhine, August, 1848, which was published in the Baltimore American. His *Volume from the Life of Herbert Barclay* was published at Baltimore in 1833; a translation of Schiller's *Don Carlos*, in 1836; *Count Julian*, an original tragedy, in 1840; *Arnold and André*, a dramatic fragment; and two cantos of *Cabiro*, a poem in the Don Juan stanza, with a better earnestness, in the same year. In 1845 he published a translation in New York of a portion of the *Goethe and Schiller Correspondence;* in 1846, on his return from a tour abroad, a first series of *Scenes and Thoughts in Europe*, in which Hydropathy, the system of Fourier, and other favorite topics, were ably discussed; followed by a second in 1852.

With an episode of foreign travel in 1850, the fine spirit of which is chronicled in the last mentioned production, Mr. Calvert has been since 1843 a resident of Newport, Rhode Island, where, on the revival of its charter, he became the first mayor of the city in 1853. When the fortieth anniversary of the battle of Lake Erie was celebrated in that city the same year, he delivered the oration on the occasion—a graphic historical sketch of the battle. Mr. Calvert has also been a contributor to the *New York Review*, the *North American*, the *New York Quarterly*, and other publications.

The literary productions of Mr. Calvert are marked by their nice philosophical speculation, their sense of honor and of beauty, and their pure scholastic qualities. There is a certain fastidiousness and reserve of the retired thinker in the manner, with a fondness for the aphorism; though there is nothing of the selfish isolation of the scholar in the matter. The thought is original, strongly conceived, and uttered with firmness. The topics are frequently of every-day life, it being the author's motive to affect the public welfare by his practical suggestions from the laws of health, philosophy, and art. Of these he is at once a bold and delicate expounder, a subtle and philosophical critic.

WASHINGTON—FROM ARNOLD AND ANDRÉ.

. . . . Washington
Doth know no other language than the one
We speak: and never did an English tongue
Give voice unto a larger, wiser mind.
You'll task your judgment vainly to point out
Through all this desp'rate conflict, in his plans
A flaw, or fault in execution. He
In spirit is unconquerable, as
In genius perfect. Side by side I fought
With him in that disastrous enterprise,
Where rash young Braddock fell; and there I marked
The vet'ran's skill contend for mastery
With youthful courage in his wondrous deeds.
Well might the bloody Indian warrior pause,
Amid his massacre confounded, and
His baffled rifle's aim, till then unerring,
Turn from "that tall young man," and deem in awe
That the Great Spirit hovered over him;
For he, of all our mounted officers,
Alone came out unscathed from that dread carnage
To guard our shattered army's swift retreat.
For years did his majestic form hold place
Upon my mind, stampt in that perilous hour,
In th' image of a strong armed friend, until
I met him next, as a resistless foe.
'Twas at the fight near Princeton. In quick march,
Victorious o'er his van, onward we pressed;
When, moving with firm pace, led by the Chief
Himself, the central force encountered us.
One moment paused th' opposing hosts—and then
The rattling volley hid the death it bore:
Another—and the sudden cloud, uprolled,
Displayed, midway between the adverse lines,
His drawn sword gleaming high, the Chief—as though
That crash of deadly music, and the burst
Of sulphurous vapor, had from out the earth
Summoned the God of war. Doubly exposed
He stood unharmed. Like eagles tempest-borne
Rushed to his side his men; and had our souls
And arms with two-fold strength been braced, we yet
Had not withstood that onset. Thus does he
Keep ever with occasion even step,—
Now, warily before our eager speed
Retreating, tempting us with battle's promise,
Only to toil us with a vain pursuit—
Now, wheeling rapidly about our flanks,
Startling our ears with sudden peal of war,
And fronting in the thickest of the fight
The common soldier's death, stirring the blood
Of faintest hearts to deeds of bravery
By his great presence,—and his every act,
Of heady onslaught as of backward march,
From thoughtful judgment first inferred.

ALFIERI AND DANTE.

Alfieri tells, that he betook himself to writing, because in his miserable age and land he had no scope for action; and that he remained single because he would not be a breeder of slaves. He utters the despair, to passionate tears, which he felt, when young, and deeply moved by the traits of greatness related by Plutarch, to find himself in times and in a country where no great thing could be either said or acted. The feelings here implied are the breath of his dramas. In them, a clear nervous understanding gives rapid utterance to wrath, pride, and impetuous passion. Though great within his sphere, his nature was not ample and complex enough for the highest tragedy. In his composition there was too much of passion and too little of high emotion. Fully to feel and perceive the awful and pathetic in human conjunctions, a deep fund of sentiment is needed. A condensed tale of passion is not of itself a tragedy. To dark feelings, resolves, deeds, emotion must give breadth, and depth, and relief. Passion furnishes crimes, but cannot furnish the kind and degree of horror which should accompany their commission. To give Tragedy the grand compass and sublime significance whereof it is susceptible, it is not enough that through the storm is visible the majestic figure of Justice: the blackest clouds must be fringed with the light of Hope and Pity; while through them Religion gives vistas into the Infinite, Beauty keeping watch to repel what is partial or deformed. In Alfieri, these great gifts are not commensurate with his power of intellect and passion. Hence, like the French classic dramatists, he is obliged to bind his personages into too narrow a circle. They have not enough of moral liberty. They are not swayed merely, they are tyrannized over by the passions. Hence they want elasticity and color. They are like hard engravings.

Alfieri does not cut deep into character: he gives a clean outline, but broad flat surfaces without finish of parts. It is this throbbing movement in details, which imparts buoyancy and expression. Wanting it, Alfieri is mostly hard. The effect of the whole is imposing, but does not invite or bear close inspection. Hence, though he is clear and rapid, and tells a story vividly, his tragedies are not life-like. In Alfieri there is vigorous rhetoric, sustained vivacity, fervent passion; but no depth of sentiment, no play of a fleet rejoicing imagination, nothing "visionary," and none of the "golden cadence of poetry." But his heart was full of nobleness. He was a proud, lofty man, severe, but truth-loving and scornful of littleness. He delighted to depict characters that are manly and energetic. He makes them wrathful against tyranny, hardy, urgent for freedom, reclaiming with burning words the lost rights of man, protesting fiercely against oppression. There is in Alfieri a stern virility that contrasts strongly with Italian effeminateness. An indignant frown sits ever on his brow, as if rebuking the passivity of his countrymen. His verse is swollen with wrath. It has the clangor of a trumpet that would shame the soft piping of flutes.

Above Alfieri, far above him and all other Italian greatness, solitary in the earliness of his rise, ere the modern mind had worked itself open, and still as solitary amidst the after splendors of Italy's fruitfulness is Dante. Take away any other great poet or artist, and in the broad shining rampart wherewith genius has beautified and fortified Italy, there would be a mournful chasm. Take away Dante, and you level the Citadel itself, under whose shelter the whole compact cincture has grown into strength and beauty.

Three hundred years before Shakespeare, in 1265, was Dante born. His social position secured to him the best schooling. He was taught and eagerly learnt all the crude knowledge of his day. Through the precocious susceptibility of the poetic temperament, he was in love at the age of nine years. This love, as will be with such natures, was wrought into his heart, expanding his young being with beautiful visions and hopes, and making tuneful the poetry within him. It endured with his life, and spiritualized his latest inspirations. Soberly he afterwards married another, and was the father of a numerous family. In the stirring days of the Guelfs and Ghibellines, he became a public leader, made a campaign, was for a while one of the chief magistrates of Florence, her ambassador abroad more than once, and at the age of thirty-six closed his public career in the common Florentine way at that period, namely, by exile. Refusing to be recalled on condition of unmanly concessions, he never again saw his home. For twenty years he was an impoverished, wandering exile, and in his fifty-sixth year breathed his last at Ravenna.

But Dante's life is his poem. Therein is the spirit of the mighty man incarnated. The life after earthly death is his theme. What a mould for the thoughts and sympathies of a poet, and what a poet, to fill all the chambers of such a mould! Man's whole nature claims interpretation; his powers, wants, vices, aspirations, basenesses, grandeurs. The imagination of semi-Christian Italy had strained itself to bring before the sensuous mind of the South an image of the future home of the soul. The supermundane thoughts, fears, hopes of his time, Dante condensed into one vast picture—a picture cut as upon adamant with diamond. To enrich Hell, and Purgatory, and Paradise, he coined his own soul. His very body became transfigured, purged of its flesh, by the intensity of fiery thought. Gaunt, pale, stern, rapt, his "visionary" eyes glaring under his deep furrowed brow, as he walked the streets of Verona, he heard the people whisper, "That is he who has been down into Hell." Down into the depths of his fervent nature he had been, and kept himself lean by brooding over his passions, emotions, hopes, and transmuting the essence of them into everlasting song.

Conceive the statuesque grand imagination of Michael Angelo united to the vivid homely particularity of Defoe, making pictures out of materials drawn from a heart whose rapturous sympathies ranged with Orphean power through the whole gamut of human feeling, from the blackest hate up to the brightest love, and you will understand what is meant by the term *Dantesque*. In the epitaph for himself, written by Dante and inscribed on his tomb at Ravenna, he says:—"I have sung, while traversing them, the abode of God, Phlegethon and the foul pits." Traversing must be taken literally. Dante almost believed that he had traversed them, and so does his reader too, such is the control the poet gains over the reader through his burning intensity and graphic picturesqueness. Like the mark of the fierce jagged lightning upon the black night-cloud are some of his touches, as awful, as fearfully distinct, but not as momentary.

In the face of the contrary judgment of such critics as Shelley and Carlyle, I concur in the common opinion, which gives preference to the *Inferno* over the *Purgatorio* and *Paradiso*. Dante's rich nature included the highest and lowest in humanity. With the pure, the calm, the tender, the ethereal, his sympathy was as lively as with the turbulent, the passionate, the gross. But the hot contentions of the time, and especially their effect upon himself,—through them an outcast and proud mendicant,—

forced the latter upon his heart as his unavoidable familiars. All about and within him were plots, ambitions, wraths, chagrins, jealousies, miseries. The times and his own distresses darkened his mood to the lurid hue of Hell. Moreover, the happiness of Heaven, the rewards of the spirit, its empyreal joys, can be but faintly pictured by visual corporeal images, the only ones the earthly poet possesses. The thwarted imagination loses itself in a vague, dazzling, golden mist. On the contrary, the trials and agonies of the spirit in Purgatory and Hell, are by such images suitably, forcibly, definitely set forth. The sufferings of the wicked while in the flesh are thereby typified. And this suggests to me, that one bent, as many are, upon detecting Allegory in Dante, might regard the whole poem as one grand Allegory, wherein, under the guise of a picture of the future world, the poet has represented the effect of the feelings in this; the pangs, for example, of the murderer and glutton in Hell, being but a portraiture, poetically colored, of the actual torments on earth of those who commit murder and gluttony. Finally, in this there is evidence—and is it not conclusive?—of the superiority of the Book of Hell, that in that book occur the two most celebrated passages in the poem,—passages, in which with unsurpassed felicity of diction and versification, the pathetic and terrible are rounded by the spirit of poetry into pictures, where simplicity, expression, beauty, combine to produce effects unrivalled in this kind in the pages of literature. I refer of course to the stories of Francesca and Ugolino.

Dante's work is untranslatable. Not merely because the style, form, and rhythm of every great poem, being the incarnation of inspired thought, you cannot but lacerate the thought in disembodying it; but because, moreover, much of the elements of its body, the words namely in which the spirit made itself visible, have passed away. To get a faithful English transcript of the great Florentine, we should need a diction of the fourteenth century, moulded by a more fiery and potent genius than Chaucer. Not the thoughts solely, as in every true poem, are so often virgin thoughts; the words, too, many of them, are virgin words. Their freshness and unworn vigor are there alone in Dante's Italian. Of the modern intellectual movement, Dante was the majestic herald. In his poem are the mysterious shadows, the glow, the fragrance, the young life-promising splendors of the dawn. The broad day has its strength and its blessings; but it can give only a faint image of the glories of its birth.

The bitter woes of Dante, hard and bitter to the shortening of his life, cannot but give a pang to the reader whom his genius has exalted and delighted. He was a life-long sufferer. Early disappointed in love; not blest, it would seem, in his marriage; foiled as a statesman; misjudged and relentlessly proscribed by the Florentines, upon whom from the pits of Hell his wrath wreaked itself in a damning line, calling them, "Gente avara, invida, e superba;" a homeless wanderer; a dependant at courts where, though honored, he could not be valued; obliged to consort there with buffoons and parasites, he whose great heart was full of honor, and nobleness, and tenderness; and at last, all his political plans and hopes baffled, closing his mournful days far, far away from home and kin, wasted, sorrow-stricken, broken-hearted. Most sharp, most cruel were his woes. Yet to them perhaps we owe his poem. Had he not been discomfited and exiled, who can say that the mood or the leisure would have been found for such poetry? His vicissitudes and woes were the soil to feed and ripen his conceptions. They steeped him in dark experiences, intensified his passions, enriching the imagination that was tasked to people Hell and Purgatory; while from his own pains he turned with keener joy and lightened pen to the beatitudes of Heaven. But for his sorrows, in his soul would not have been kindled so fierce a fire. Out of the seething gloom of his sublime heart shot forth forked lightnings which still glow, a perennial illumination—to the eyes of men, a beauty, a marvel, a terror. Poor indeed he was in purse; but what wealth had he not in his bosom! True, he was a father parted from his children, a proud warm man, eating the bread of cold strangers; but had he not his genius and its bounding offspring for company, and would not a day of such heavenly labor as his outweigh a month, aye, a year of crushed pride? What though by the world he was misused, received from it little, his own even wrested from him; was he not the giver, the conscious giver, to the world of riches fineless? Not six men, since men were, have been blest with such a power of giving.

THE NUN.

From amidst the town flights of steps led me, on a Sunday morning, up a steep height, about two hundred feet, to the palace of the Grand Duke. Begilded and bedamasked rooms, empty of paintings or sculpture, were all that there was to see, so I soon passed from the palace to the terrace in front of it.

A landscape looks best on Sunday. With the repose of man Nature sympathizes, and in the inward stillness, imparted unconsciously to every spirit by the general calm, outward beauty is more faithfully imaged.

From the landscape my mind was soon withdrawn, to an object beneath me. Glancing over the terrace-railing almost into the chimneys of the houses below, my eyes fell on a female figure in black, pacing round a small garden inclosed by high walls. From the privileged spot where I stood, the walls were no defence, at least against masculine vision. The garden was that of a convent, and the figure walking in it was a nun, upon whose privacy I was thus involuntarily intruding. Never once raising her eyes from her book, she walked round and round the inclosure in the Sabbath stillness. But what to her was this weekly rest? She is herself an incessant sabbath, her existence is a continuous stillness. She has set herself apart from her fellows; she would no more know their work-day doings; she is a voluntary somnambulist, sleeping while awake; she walks on the earth a flesh-and-blood phantom. What a fountain of life and love is there dried up! To cease to be a woman! The warm currents that gush from a woman's heart, all turned back upon their source! What an agony!—And yet, could my eyes, that follow the quiet nun in her circumscribed walk, see through her prison into the street behind it, there they might, perchance at this very moment, fall on a sister going freely whither she listeth, and yet, inclosed within a circle more circumscribed a thousand fold than any that stones can build—the circle built by public reprobation. Not with downcast lids doth she walk, but with a bold stare that would out-look the scorn she awaits. No Sabbath stillness is for her—her life is a continuous orgie. No cold phantom is she—she has smothered her soul in its flesh. Not arrested and stagnant are the currents of her woman's heart—infected at their spring, they flow foul and fast. Not apart has she set herself from her fellows—she is thrust out from among them. Her mother knows her no more, nor her father, nor her brother, nor her sister. In exchange for the joys of daughter, wife, mother, woman, she has shame and lust. Great God! What a tragedy she is. To her agony all that the poor nun has suffered is beatitude.—Follow now, in your thought, the two back to their childhood, their sweet chirping innocence. Two dewy buds are they, exhaling from their folded hearts a richer perfume with each maturing month,—two beaming cherubs, that have left their wings behind them, eager to bless and to be blest, and with power to replume themselves from the joys and bounties of an earthly life. In a few short years what a distortion! The one is a withered, fruitless, branchless stem; the other, an unsexed monster, whose touch is poisonous. Can such things be, and men still smile and make merry? To many of its members, society is a Saturn that eats his children—a fiend, that scourges men out of their humanity, and then mocks at their fall.

A nun, like a suicide, is a reproach to Christianity—a harlot is a judgment on civilization.

BONAPARTE.

Bonaparte was behind his age; he was a man of the past. The value of the great modern instruments and the modern heart and growth he did not discern. He went groping in the mediæval times to find the lustreless sceptre of Charlemagne, and he saw not the paramount potency there now is in that of Faust. He was a great cannoneer, not a great builder. In the centre of Europe, from amidst the most advanced, scientific nation on earth, after nineteen centuries of Christianity, not to perceive that lead in the form of type is far more puissant than in the form of bullets; not to feel that for the head of the French nation to desire an imperial crown was as unmanly as it was disloyal, that a rivalry of rotten Austria and barbaric Russia was a despicable vanity; not to have yet learned how much stronger ideas are than blows, principles than edicts—to be blind to all this, was to want vision, insight, wisdom. Bonaparte was not the original genius he has been vaunted; he was a vulgar copyist, and Alexander of Macedon and Frederick of Prussia were his models. Force was his means, despotism his aim; war was his occupation, pomp his relaxation. For him the world was divided into two—his will, and those who opposed it. He acknowledged no duty, he respected no right, he flouted at integrity, he despiseth truth. He had no belief in man, no trust in God. In his wants he was ignoble, in his methods ignorant. He was possessed by the lust of isolated, irresponsible, boundless, heartless power, and he believed that he could found it with the sword and bind it with lies; and so, ere he began to grow old, what he had founded had already toppled, and what he had bound was loosed. He fell, and as if history would register his disgrace with a more instructive emphasis, he fell twice; and exhausted France, beleaguered by a million of armed foes, had to accept the restored imbecile Bourbons.

MOLIERE AND RACHEL.

At the *Théâtre Français*, I saw Molière and Rachel. It is no disparagement of Molière to call him a truncated Shakespeare. The naturalness, vigor, common sense, practical insight and scenic life of Shakespeare he has; without Shakespeare's purple glow, his reach of imagination and mighty intellectual grasp, which latter supreme qualities shoot light down into the former subordinate ones, and thus impart to Shakespeare's comic and lowest personages a poetic soul, which raises and refines them, the want whereof in Molière makes his low characters border on farce and his highest prosaic.

Rachel is wonderful. She is on the stage an embodied radiance. Her body seems inwardly illuminated. Conceive a Greek statue endued with speech and mobility, for the purpose of giving utterance to a profound soul stirred to its depths, and you have an image of the magic union in her personations of fervor and grace. Till I heard her, I never fully valued the might of elocution. She goes right to the heart by dint of intonation; just as, with his arm ever steady, the fencer deals or parries death by the mere motion of his wrist. Phrases, words, syllables, grow plastic, swell or contract, come pulsing with life, as they issue from her lips. Her head is superb; oval, full, large, compact, powerful. She cannot be said to have beauty of face or figure; yet the most beautiful woman were powerless to divert from her the eyes of the spectator. Her spiritual beauty is there more bewitching than can be the corporeal. When in the *Horaces* she utters the curse, it is as though the whole electricity of a tempest played through her arteries. It is not Corneille's *Camille*, or Racine's *Hermione*, solely that you behold, it is a dazzling incarnation of a human soul.

SUMNER LINCOLN FAIRFIELD.

SUMNER LINCOLN, the son of Dr. Abner Fairfield, a physician of Warwick, Massachusetts, was born in that town on the twenty-fifth of June, 1803. In 1806 his father, who had previously removed to Athens, a village on the Hudson, died, leaving a widow and two children in humble circumstances. The family retired to the home of the mother's father, a farm-house in Western Massachusetts, where Fairfield remained until his twelfth year. After a twelvemonth passed at school he entered Brown University. Here he studied so unremittingly, that, after a few months, he was attacked by a severe fit of sickness. On his recovery he endeavored to eke out his support by teaching, but failing in this was forced to leave college and seek a living as a tutor at the south. He passed two years in this occupation, and in preparation for the ministry, but in consequence of the death of his friend and instructor, the Rev. Mr. Cranston of Savannah, he changed his plan of life and returned to the north. He had during this period published "two pamphlets of rhymes," which, as we are informed in his biography by his widow "he ever after shrunk from reading," were probably of indifferent merit.

He returned to the north with the determination to pursue a literary life, and in December, 1825, sailed for London. He carried letters of introduction to the conductors of periodicals, and obtained engagements as a writer. His poem, *The Cities of the Plain*, a description of the destruction of Sodom and Gomorrah, appeared in the Oriental Herald, edited by J. S. Buckingham, the traveller and lecturer. He was received in France by La Fayette, and wrote his *Père la Chaise and Westminster Abbey*, at Versailles. He also wrote letters descriptive of his tour to the New York Literary Gazette, edited by James G. Brooks. He returned home in July, 1826, and soon after published a volume of poems, entitled *The Sisters of Saint Clara, a tale of Portugal*, which was followed in 1830 by *Abaddon, the*

Spirit of Destruction, and other Poems, another volume of poetry.

The next event in his life was his marriage to Miss Jane Frazee. He removed with his wife to Elizabethtown, with the intention of forming a classical school, but before the honeymoon was over the sheriff levied on their furniture and they were set adrift. They afterwards resided at Boston, Harper's Ferry, and Philadelphia, the husband gaining a precarious subsistence by writing for the press, and becoming somewhat soured by want of success. In 1828 he republished in a volume *The Cities of the Plain*, with a few miscellaneous pieces. A few months after, by the influence of his Philadelphia friends, he was placed at the head of Newtown Academy, about thirty miles from that city. The situation pleased him, and his affairs went on with unwonted serenity until one July afternoon a favorite pupil, while bathing with him in the river, was unfortunately drowned. The event caused a temporary disarrangement of the duties of the school, and threw such a gloom over the mind of the teacher that he insisted upon leaving his situation and removing to New York. By the exertions of his wife, in personally soliciting subscriptions, the means were secured, principally in Boston, whither the pair resorted in 1829, for the publication of a new poem, *The Last Night of Pompeii*, which appeared on their return to New York in 1832. It was maintained by Mr. Fairfield that he had anticipated in this poem the leading material of Bulwer's novel, bearing a similar title, published in London in 1834. His next enterprise was a monthly periodical. His wife was again his canvasser, and the North American Magazine was started in Philadelphia in 1833. He continued to edit it for five years, when, the enterprise proving unproductive, he disposed of the property to Mr. James C. Brooks of Baltimore.

The poet now became completely disheartened, fell into irregularities, and with a family of five children was often straitened in his finances. His health rapidly failed, and in the fall of 1843 he left Philadelphia with his mother for New Orleans. He arrived in the following spring, and was cheered by meeting with his old friend Mr. George D. Prentice. He died soon after, on the 6th of March, 1844.

His wife had for some time previously been engaged in obtaining subscriptions for a complete edition of his poems. The first of two contemplated volumes, but the only one published, appeared in 1841. In 1846 Mrs. Fairfield issued a small volume containing a life of her husband, from her pen, and a few of his poems.*

Mr. Fairfield possessed an ardent poetical temperament, with many of the qualities commonly assigned to the man of genius. He always maintained a certain heat of enthusiasm, but the flame burnt too rapidly for genuine inspiration. He was frequently common-place and turgid. His imagination was active but undisciplined, and led him to undertake comprehensive and powerful themes which required greater judgment than he had to bestow. He possessed various accomplishments, and particularly excelled as an instructor in his favorite historical and belles-lettres departments.

* In addition to the titles of Fairfield's separate publications, already given, we may add the Siege of Constantinople, Charleston, S. C., 1822; Lays of Melpomene, Portland, 1824; Mina, a Dramatic Sketch, with other Poems, Baltimore, 1825; The Heir of the World and Lesser Poems, Philadelphia, 1829.

PERE LA CHAISE.

Beautiful city of the dead! thou stand'st
Ever amid the bloom of sunny skies
And blush of odors, and the stars of heaven
Look, with a mild and holy eloquence,
Upon thee, realm of silence! Diamond dew
And vernal rain and sunlight and sweet airs
For ever visit thee; and morn and eve
Dawn first and linger longest on thy tombs
Crowned with their wreaths of love and rendering back
From their wrought columns all the glorious beams,
That herald morn or bathe in trembling light
The calm and holy brow of shadowy eve.
Empire of pallid shades! though thou art near
The noisy traffic and thronged intercourse
Of man, yet stillness sleeps, with drooping eyes
And meditative brow, for ever round
Thy bright and sunny borders; and the trees,
That shadow thy fair monuments, are green
Like hope that watches o'er the dead, or love
That crowns their memories; and lonely birds
Lift up their simple songs amid the boughs,
And with a gentle voice, wail o'er the lost,
The gifted and the beautiful, as they
Were parted spirits hovering o'er dead forms
Till judgment summons earth to its account.

Here 'tis a bliss to wander when the clouds
Paint the pale azure, scattering o'er the scene
Sunlight and shadow, mingled yet distinct,
And the broad olive leaves, like human sighs,
Answer the whispering zephyr, and soft buds
Unfold their hearts to the sweet west wind's kiss,
And Nature dwells in solitude, like all
Who sleep in silence here, their names and deeds
Living in sorrow's verdant memory.
Let me forsake the cold and crushing world
And hold communion with the dead! then thought,
The silent angel language heaven doth hear,
Pervades the universe of things and gives
To earth the deathless hues of happier climes.

All, who repose undreaming here, were laid
In their last rest with many prayers and tears,
The humblest as the proudest was bewailed,
Though few were near to give the burial pomp.
Lone watchings have been here, and sighs have risen
Oft o'er the grave of love, and many hearts
Gone forth to meet the world's smile desolate.

The saint, with scrip and staff, and scallop-shell
And crucifix, hath closed his wanderings here;
The subtle schoolman, weighing thistle-down
In the great balance of the universe,
Sleeps in the oblivion which his folios earned;
The sage, to whom the earth, the sea and sky
Revealed their sacred secrets, in the dust,
Unknown unto himself, lies cold and still;
The dark eyes and the rosy lips of love,
That basked in passion's blaze till madness came,
Have mouldered in the darkness of the ground;
The lover, and the soldier, and the bard—
The brightness, and the beauty, and the pride
Have vanished—and the grave's great heart is still!

Alas! that sculptured pyramid outlives
The name it should perpetuate! alas!
That obelisk and temple should but mock
With effigies the form that breathes no more.
The cypress, the acacia, and the yew
Mourn with a deep low sigh o'er buried power

And mouldered loveliness and soaring mind,
Yet whisper, "Faith surmounts the storm of death!"

Beautiful city of the dead! to sleep
Amid thy shadowed solitudes, thy flowers,
Thy greenness and thy beauty, where the voice,
Alone heard, whispers love—and greenwood choirs
Sing 'mid the stirring leaves—were very bliss
Unto the weary heart and wasted mind,
Broken in the world's warfare, yet still doomed
To bear a brow undaunted! Oh, it were
A tranquil and a holy dwelling-place
To those who deeply love but love in vain,
To disappointed hopes and baffled aims
And persecuted youth. How sweet the sleep
Of such as dream not—wake not—feel not here
Beneath the starlight skies and flowery earth,
'Mid the green solitudes of Père La Chaise!

ROBERT M. BIRD,

THE author of several successful plays and novels, was born at Newcastle, Delaware, in 1803. He was educated in Philadelphia, where he became a physician. His literary career commenced in 1828 by the publication, in the Philadelphia Monthly Magazine, of three tales entitled *The Ice Island*, *The Spirit of the Reeds*, and *The Phantom Players*, and a poem, *Saul's Last Day*. His tragedy of *The Gladiator* was soon after produced by Edwin Forrest, who enacted the principal character. The play still keeps possession of the stage as a favorite among his personations.

Spartacus was followed by *Oralloosa*, a tragedy whose scene is laid in Peru at the time of its conquest by the Spaniards. It was well received on its first presentation, but has since been laid aside.

The Broker of Bogota, the most finished of the author's dramatic compositions, was next produced, like its two predecessors, by Mr. Forrest, but has not obtained the permanent popularity of the Gladiator.*

* Mr. Rees, in his Dramatic Authors of America, mentions another dramatic production of Dr. Bird, hitherto unpublished, entitled Pelopidas.

In 1834 Dr. Bird published *Calavar, or the Knight of the Conquest, a Romance of Mexico*, in which he has presented a glowing and carefully prepared historical picture.

The Infidel, or the Fall of Mexico, a second historical novel on the same picturesque period, and introducing several of the personages of the previous tale, appeared in 1835.

In 1836 *Sheppard Lee*, a novel, was published anonymously, but has been generally attributed to the author of Calavar. It is a fanciful story of a farmer who, discontented with his position of moderate wealth and independence, falls into a swoon, and in that state undergoes a series of transmigrations into the bodies of several persons, whose circumstances in life he has heretofore deemed happier than his own. He finally returns with a thankful and contented heart to his pristine condition.

In 1837 the author's most successful work, *Nick of the Woods or the Jibbenainosay*, appeared. The scene of this spirited romance is laid in Kentucky soon after the close of the Revolutionary war. The characters are all the strongly individualized men of pioneer life, and the Indians are portrayed from the point of view of the settler as vindictive and merciless savages, unrelieved by any atmosphere of poetry or sentiment, and are probably more true to life than those of Cooper.

In 1838 Dr. Bird published *Peter Pilgrim, or a Rambler's Recollections*, a collection of magazine papers, including an account of the Mammoth Cave, of which he was one of the early explorers, and the first to describe with any degree of minuteness.

This work was followed in 1839 by *The Adventures of Robin Day*, a novel of romantic adventure, in which the hero, cast an unknown orphan on the shore of Barnegat, and brought up among the rude wreckers of the beach, works his way through many interesting and surprising adventures, in which marine risks and the Florida war contribute an exciting quota, to a fair degree of repose and prosperity. The interest of an involved plot in this, as in Dr. Bird's other fictions, is maintained with much skill, though with some sacrifice of the probabilities from the outset to the close.

After the publication of this work Dr. Bird devoted himself for several years almost exclusively to the cultivation of a farm. He returned to Philadelphia to edit the North American Gazette, of which he became one of the proprietors, and died in that city of a brain fever in January, 1854.

Dr. Bird's fictions possess great animation in the progress and development of the story. The conversational portions show the practised hand of the dramatist. The incidents of the story are also managed with a view to stage effect; and a proof of these dramatic qualities has been afforded in the success which has attended an adaptation of Nick of the Woods for the theatre, in every part of the country.

THE BEECH-TREE.

There's a hill by the Schuylkill, the river of hearts,
  And a beech-tree that grows on its side,
In a nook that is lovely when sunshine departs,
  And twilight creeps over the tide:

How sweet, at that moment, to steal through the grove,
 In the shade of that beech to recline,
And dream of the maiden who gave it her love,
 And left it thus hallowed in mine.

Here's the rock that she sat on, the spray that she held,
 When she bent round its grey trunk with me;
And smiled, as with soft, timid eyes, she beheld
 The name I had carved on the tree;—
So carved that the letters should look to the west,
 As well their dear magic became,
So that when the dim sunshine was sinking to rest
 The last ray should fall on her name.

The singing-thrush moans on that beech-tree at morn,
 The winds through the laurel-bush sigh,
And afar comes the sound of the waterman's horn,
 And the hum of the water-fall nigh.
No echoes there wake but are magical, each,
 Like words, on my spirit they fall;
They speak of the hours when we came to the beech,
 And listened together to all.

And oh, when the shadows creep out from the wood,
 When the breeze stirs no more on the spray,
And the sunbeam of autumn that plays on the flood,
 Is melting, each moment, away;
How dear, at that moment, to steal through the grove,
 In the shade of that beech to recline,
And dream of the maiden who gave it her love,
 And left it thus hallowed in mine.

A RESCUE—FROM NICK OF THE WOODS.

With these words, having first examined his own and Roland's arms, to see that all were in proper battle condition, and then directed little Peter to ensconce in a bush, wherein little Peter straightway bestowed himself, Bloody Nathan, with an alacrity of motion and ardor of look that indicated anything rather than distaste to the murderous work in hand, led the way along the ridge, until he had reached the place where it dipped down to the valley, covered with the bushes through which he expected to advance to a desirable position undiscovered.

But a better auxiliary even than the bushes was soon discovered by the two friends. A deep gully, washed in the side of the hill by the rains, was here found running obliquely from its top to the bottom affording a covered way, by which, as they saw at a glance, they could approach within twenty or thirty yards of the foe untirely unseen; and, to add to its advantages, it was the bed of a little water-course, whose murmurs, as it leaped from rock to rock, assured them they could as certainly approach unheard.

"Truly," muttered Nathan, with a grim chuckle, as he looked, first at the friendly ravine, and then at the savages below, "the Philistine rascals is in our hands, and we will smite them hip and thigh!"

With this inspiring assurance he crept into the ravine; and Roland following, they were soon in possession of a post commanding, not only the spot occupied by the enemy, but the whole valley.

Peeping through the fringe of shrubs that rose, a verdant parapet, on the brink of the gully, they looked down upon the savage party, now less than forty paces from the muzzles of their guns, and wholly unaware of the fate preparing for them. The scene of diversion and torment was over: the prisoner, a man of powerful frame but squalid appearance, whose hat,—a thing of shreds and patches,—adorned the shorn pate of one of the Indians, while his coat, equally rusty and tattered, hung from the shoulders of a second, lay bound under a tree, but so nigh that they could mark the laborious heavings of his chest. Two of the Indians sat near him on the grass, keeping watch, their hatchets in their hands, their guns resting within reach against the trunk of a tree overthrown by some hurricane of former years, and now mouldering away. A third was engaged with his tomahawk, lopping away the few dry boughs that remained on the trunk. Squatting at the fire, which the third was thus laboring to replenish with fuel, were the two remaining savages; who, holding their rifles in their hands, divided their attention betwixt a shoulder of venison roasting on a stick in the fire, and the captive, whom they seemed to regard as destined to be sooner or later disposed of in a similar manner.

The position of the parties precluded the hope Nathan had ventured to entertain of getting them in a cluster, and so doing double execution with each bullet; but the disappointment neither chilled his ardor nor embarrassed his plans. His scheme of attack had been framed to embrace all contingencies; and he wasted no further time in deliberation. A few whispered words conveyed his last instructions to the soldier; who, reflecting that he was fighting in the cause of humanity, remembering his own heavy wrongs, and marking the fiery eagerness that flamed from Nathan's visage, banished from his mind whatever disinclination he might have felt at beginning the fray in a mode so seemingly treacherous and ignoble. He laid his axe on the brink of the gully at his side, together with his foraging cap; and then, thrusting his rifle through the bushes, took aim at one of the savages at the fire, Nathan directing his piece against the other. Both of them presented the fairest marks, as they sat wholly unconscious of their danger, enjoying in imagination the tortures yet to be inflicted on the prisoner. But a noise in the gully,—the falling of a stone loosened by the soldier's foot, or a louder than usual plash of water—suddenly roused them from their dreams: they started up, and turned their eyes towards the hill.—"Now, friend!" whispered Nathan;—"if thee misses, thee loses thee maiden and thee life into the bargain.—Is thee ready?"

"Ready," was the reply.

"Right, then, through the dog's brain,—fire!"

The crash of the pieces, and the fall of the two victims, both marked by a fatal aim, and both pierced through the brain, were the first announcement of peril to their companions; who, springing up, with yells of fear and astonishment, and snatching at their arms, looked wildly around them for the unseen foe. The prisoner also, astounded out of his despair, raised his head from the grass, and glared around. The wreaths of smoke curling over the bushes on the hill-side, betrayed the lurking-place of the assailants; and savages and prisoner turning together, they all beheld at once the spectacle of two human heads,—or, to speak more correctly, two human caps, for the heads were far below them,—rising in the smoke, and peering over the bushes, as if to mark the result of the volley. Loud, furious, and exulting were the screams of the Indians, as with the speed of thought, seduced by a stratagem often practised among the wild heroes of the border, they raised and discharged their pieces against the imaginary foes so incautiously exposed to their vengeance. The caps fell, and with them the rifles that had been employed to raise them; and the voice of Nathan thundered through the glen, as he grasped his tomahawk and sprang from the ditch,—"Now, friend! up with thee axe, and do thee duty!"

With these words, the two assailants at once leaped into view, and with a bold hurrah, and bolder hearts, rushed towards the fire, where lay the undischarged rifles of their first victims. The savages yelled also in reply, and two of them bounded forward to dispute the prize. The third, staggered into momentary inaction by the suddenness and amazement of the attack, rushed forward but a step; but a whoop of exultation was on his lips, as he raised the rifle which *he* had not yet discharged, full against the breast of bloody Nathan. But his triumph was short-lived; so fatal as it must have proved to the life of Nathan, it was averted by an unexpected incident. The prisoner, near whom he stood, putting all his vigor into one tremendous effort, burst his bonds, and, with a yell ten times louder and fiercer than had yet been uttered, added himself to the combatants. With a furious cry of encouragement to his rescuers,—"Hurrah for Kentucky!—give it to 'em good!" he threw himself upon the savage, beat the gun from his hands, and grasping him in his brawny arms, hurled him to the earth, where, rolling over and over in mortal struggle, growling and whooping, and rending one another like wild beasts, the two, still locked in furious embrace, suddenly tumbled down the banks of the brook, there high and steep, and were immediately lost to sight.

Before this catastrophe occurred, the other Indians and the assailants met at the fire; and each singling out his opponent, and thinking no more of the rifles, they met as men whose only business was to kill or to die. With his axe flourished over his head, Nathan rushed against the tallest and foremost enemy, who, as he advanced, swung his tomahawk, in the act of throwing it. Their weapons parted from their hands at the same moment, and with perhaps equal accuracy of aim; but meeting with a crash in the air, they fell together to the earth, doing no harm to either. The Indian stooped to recover his weapon; but it was too late: the hand of Nathan was already upon his shoulder: a single effort of his vast strength sufficed to stretch the savage at his feet, and holding him down with knee and hand, Nathan snatched up the nearest axe. "If the life of thee tribe was in thee bosom," he cried with a look of unrelenting fury, of hatred deep and ineffaceable, "thee should die the dog's death, as thee does!" And with a blow furiously struck, and thrice repeated, he despatched the struggling savage as he lay.

He rose, brandishing the bloody hatchet, and looked for his companion. He found him upon the earth, lying upon the breast of his antagonist, whom it had been his good fortune to overmaster. Both had thrown their hatchets, and both without effect, Roland because skill was wanting, and the Shawnee because, in the act of throwing, he had stumbled over the body of one of his comrades, so as to disorder his aim, and even to deprive him of his footing. Before he could recover himself, Roland imitated Nathan's example, and threw himself upon the unlucky Indian—a youth, as it appeared, whose strength, perhaps at no moment equal to his own, had been reduced by recent wounds,—and found that he had him entirely at his mercy. This circumstance, and the knowledge that the other Indians were now overpowered, softened the soldier's wrath; and when Nathan, rushing to assist him, cried aloud to him to move aside, that he might 'knock the assassin knave's brains out,' Roland replied by begging Nathan to spare his life. "I have disarmed him," he cried,—"he resists no more—don't kill him."

"To the last man of his tribe!" cried Nathan with unexampled ferocity; and, without another word, drove the hatchet into the wretch's brain.

The victors now leaping to their feet, looked round for the fifth savage and the prisoner; and directed by a horrible din under the bank of the stream, which was resounding with curses, groans, heavy blows, and the plashing of water, ran to the spot, where the last incident of battle was revealed to them in a spectacle as novel as it was shocking. The Indian lay on his back suffocating in mire and water; while astride his body sat the late prisoner, covered from head to foot with mud and gore, furiously plying his fists, for he had no other weapons, about the head and face of his foe, his blows falling like sledge-hammers or battering-rams, with such strength and fury that it seemed impossible any one of them could fail to crush the skull to atoms; and all the while garnishing them with a running accompaniment of oaths and maledictions little less emphatic and overwhelming. "You switches gentlemen, do you, you exfluncticated, perditioned rascal? Ar'n't you got it, you niggur-in-law to old Sattan? you 'tarnal half-imp, you? H'yar's for you, you dog, and thar's for you, you dog's dog! H'yar's the way I pay you in a small-change of sogdologers!"

And thus he cried, until Roland and Nathan seizing him by the shoulders, dragged him by main force from the Indian, whom, as was found when they came to examine the body afterwards, he had actually pommelled to death, the skull having been beaten in as with bludgeons.—The victor sprang upon his feet, and roared his triumph aloud:—"Ar'n't I lick'd him handsome!—Hurrah for Kentucky and old Salt—Cock-a-doodle-doo!"

And with that, turning to his deliverers, he displayed to their astonished eyes, though disfigured by blood and mire, the never-to-be-forgotten features of the captain of horse-thieves, Roaring Ralph Stackpole.

WILLIAM BINGHAM TAPPAN,

The author of several volumes of pleasing occasional poems, was born in Beverly, Massachusetts, October 29, 1794. He published a volume of poems in Philadelphia in 1819, a portion of which he included in a larger collection in 1822. Another followed in 1834, and an additional volume, *The Poems of William B. Tappan, not contained in a former volume*, in 1836. A complete collection was formed in 1848, in four volumes, entitled, *Poetry of the Heart; Sacred and Miscellaneous Poems; Poetry of Life; The Sunday School, and other Poems.*

These productions are all brief, and on topics suggested in many instances by the clerical profession of their author. One of the longest is on the Sunday School, and amongst the most spirited, *A Sapphic for Thanksgiving.* We cite the opening stanzas—

When the old Fathers of New England sought to
Honor the Heavens with substance and with first fruits,
They, with their blessings—all uncounted—summed up
Their undeservings.

They praised Jehovah for the wheat sheaves gathered:
For corn and cattle, and the thrifty orchards;
Blessings of basket, storehouse, homestead, hamlet;
Of land and water.

They praised Jehovah for the Depth of Riches
Opened and lavished to a world of penury;
Mines—whose red ore, unpriced, unbought, is poured from
Veins unexhausted.

They made confession of their open errors;
Honestly told God of their secret follies;
Afresh their service as true vassals pledged him,
And then were merry.

Strong was their purpose; Nature made them nobles;
Religion made them kings, to reign for ever!
Hymns of Thanksgiving were their happy faces,
Beaming in music.

The author is a resolute advocate of total abstinence, and opponent of slavery. The picturesque incidents of the missionary career, the hazards of a sailor's life ashore as well as afloat, the joys and sorrows of the fireside, and the inspiriting themes of Christian faith, are also frequently and variously dwelt upon. The verses are uniformly smooth, musical, and in excellent taste.

THE SUNDAY SCHOOL.*

"Takes care of the Children!"—there's many
To sneer at a mission so small;
Thank God, in earth's famine, for any
Cheap crumbs of his mercy that fall!
For the crying-out wide desolations,
In Zion a table is spread;—
Coming up are the hungry by nations;
But where shall the Children be fed?

'T is noble—sublimity's in it,
When Charity maketh her proof,
And "speech," "resolution," and "minute,"
Stirs arches of Exeter-roof;
By gold, and a word, are at pleasure
The Cross and the Lion unfurled,
To take of Idolatry measure,
And vanquish for Jesus the world.

To contest, so brilliant and pleasant,
Let princes and emperors lead;—
Be lifeguards of noblemen present,
And prelates and baronets bleed;
We ask not, we wish not to battle
With them; but our disciplined band
Marshal onwards, and where the shots rattle
Behold us! the Infantry stand!

In the plebeian suburbs of Glos'ter,
More glory and royalty meet
Round him, who was eager to foster
The children that troubled the street;—
Aye, nobler, sublimer, and better
Her office and honors, we see,
Who, patiently, letter by letter,
Here teaches the child at the knee.

"Takes care of the Children!"—where growing
In August are vintage and corn,
Who gazes and thinks of the sowing
Of sweet little April with scorn?
"Small things" may be jeered by the scoffer,
Yet drops that in buttercups sleep,
Make showers;—and what would he offer
But sand, as a wall for the deep?

"Takes care of the Children!"—nor wasted
Is care on the weakest of these;
The culturer the product has tasted,
And found it the palate to please.
There are sheaves pushing higher and faster,
And Age has more branches and roots,—
But dearer are none to the Master
Than Childhood, in blossoms and fruits!

Our life is no "dream"—we began it
In tears, and on Time's narrow brink,
'Till farewells we wave to this planet,
We must wake up and labor and think,—
And effort concentrate, not scatter,
On objects all worthy of us;—
Where and how, we perceive is no matter,
Only blessing fix deep for the curse.

Yet, as choice in the vineyard's permitted,
Where labor is never in vain,
And patience and prayer, unremitted,
At last yield the harvest of grain—
In a world where the brambles oft sting us,
'T is well to choose pleasantest bowers;—
"Taking care of the Children" will bring us
The nearest to Heaven and Flowers!

* "A young German philanthropist, in seeking to carry out a favorite plan of benevolence towards the rising race, applied to the American Sunday School Union for help, because it is 'The Society that takes care of the Children.'"—*Twenty-third Annual Report.*

JOHN K. MITCHELL,

A PHYSICIAN of Philadelphia, and a contributor of professional literature to the American Medical and Physical Journal, is also the author of a volume, *Indecision, a Tale of the Far West, and other Poems*, published by Carey and Hart in 1839.

Dr. Mitchell was born at Shepardstown, Virginia, in 1798. His family was from Scotland; and on the death of his father, he was sent to be educated in Ayr and at Edinburgh. Returning to America, he studied medicine with Dr. Chapman at Philadelphia. In 1841, he was chosen professor of the Practice of Medicine in the Philadelphia Jefferson Medical College.

In addition to the writings alluded to, Dr. Mitchell published in 1821, a poem entitled *St. Helena, by a Yankee.*

Indecision, his longest production, is a didactic poem, "intended," says his friend, the late Joseph C. Neal, in a biographical notice in Graham's Magazine,* "to convey a moral of the most useful character, by proving—

That Indecision marks its path with tears;
That want of candor darkens future years;
That perfect truth is virtue's safest friend,
And that to shun the wrong is better than to mend.

And the poet has carried out the idea in a story of romantic incident, somewhat unequal and hasty at times, in its construction, but, on the whole, marked with power, and calculated deeply to interest the reader."

The following spirited lyric was written in 1820.

THE BRILLIANT NOR' WEST.

Let Araby boast of her soft spicy gale,
And Persia her breeze from the rose-scented vale;
Let orange-trees scatter in wildness their balm,
Where sweet summer islands lie fragrant and calm;
Give me the cold blast of my country again,
Careering o'er snow-covered mountain and plain,
And coming, though scentless, yet pure, to my breast,
With vigor and health from the cloudless Nor' West.

I languish where suns in the tropic sky glow,
And gem-studded waters on golden sands flow,
Where shrubs, blossom-laden, bright birds and sweet trees
With odors and music encumber the breeze;

* August, 1845, where will be found an enumeration of Dr. Mitchell's medical papers, and several Lectures before the Franklin Institute.

I languish to catch but a breathing of thee,
To hear thy wild winter-notes, brilliant and free,
To feel thy cool touch on my heart-strings opprest,
And gather a tone from the bracing Nor' West.

Mists melt at thy coming, clouds flee from thy wrath,
The marsh and its vapors are sealed on thy path,
For spotless and pure as the snow-covered North,
Their cold icy cradle, thy tempests come forth.
The blue robe is borrowed from clearest of skies,
Thy sandals were made where the driven snow lies,
And stars, seldom seen in this low world, are blest
To shine in thy coronet—brilliant Nor' West.

For ever, for ever, be thine, purest wind,
The lakes and the streams of my country to bind;
And oh! though afar I am fated to roam,
Still kindle the hearths and the hearts of my home!
While blows from the polar skies holy and pure
Thy trumpet of freedom, the land shall endure,
As snow in thy pathway, and stars on thy crest,
Unsullied and beautiful—glorious Nor' West.

THE NEW AND THE OLD SONG.

A new song should be sweetly sung,
It goes but to the ear;
A new song should be sweetly sung,
For it touches no one near:
But an old song may be roughly sung;
The ear forgets its art,
As comes upon the rudest tongue,
The tribute to the heart.

A new song should be sweetly sung,
For memory gilds it not;
It brings not back the strains that rung
Through childhood's sunny cot.
But an old song may be roughly sung,
It tells of days of glee,
When the boy to his mother clung,
Or danced on his father's knee.

On tented fields 'tis welcome still;
'Tis sweet in the stormy sea,
In forest wild, on rocky hill,
And away on the prairie lea:—
But dearer far the old song,
When friends we love are nigh,
And well known voices, clear and strong,
Unite in the chorus cry

Of the old song, the old song,
The song of the days of glee,
When the boy to his mother clung,
Or danced on his father's knee!
Oh, the old song—the old song!
The song of the days of glee,
The new song may be better sung,
But the good old song for me!

RICHARD PENN SMITH

WAS born in Philadelphia, and was educated as a lawyer. His father, William Moore Smith, who transmitted a taste for literature to his son, is spoken of as a poetical writer of reputation. The first appearance of Richard Penn Smith as an author was in the contribution of a series of Essays entitled "The Plagiary" to the Union. He was for five years, from 1822, the proprietor and editor of the Aurora, in which he succeeded Duane. He then returned to his profession of the law, still pursuing his literary tastes. In 1831 he published a novel of the American Revolution, *The Forsaken*. He is also the author of two volumes of short stories, *The Actress of Padua and other Tales*. He was a frequent writer of poetical pieces for the newspapers; but chiefly known as a ready writer of dramatic pieces for the stage. His tragedy of *Caius Marius*, written for Edwin Forrest, was brought out by the latter on the stage. He wrote numerous other successful plays, some of the titles of which are, *Quite Correct*, *The Eighth of January*, *The Sentinels*, *William Penn*, *the Water Witch*, *Is she a Brigand?* &c. Rees, in his Dramatic Authors, enumerates these, and tells an anecdote illustrating his equanimity while turning off these hasty productions for ready money. Leaving the theatre one night at the close of the performance of a piece of his composing, he met an old schoolfellow who, ignorant of his friend's share in it, saluted him. "Well, this is really the most insufferable trash that I have witnessed for some time." "True," replied Smith, "but as they give me a benefit to-morrow night as the author, I hope to have the pleasure of seeing you here again."

He died at his residence on the Schuylkill, August 12, 1854. He had ceased to write for some years before his death, having suffered from a dropsical affection.*

MRS. LOUISA J. HALL.

LOUISA JANE, the daughter of Dr. John Park, of Newburyport, was born in that place, February 7, 1802. Her father, in 1811, opened a school for young ladies in Boston, at which the daughter received a thorough education. She commenced writing at an early age, and a few of her poems appeared anonymously in the newspapers when she was about twenty.

In 1825, the first half of her dramatic poem of *Miriam* was read at a literary party in Boston; the author, unknown as such to the company, was present, and so much encouraged by the commendations the work received, that she completed it soon after. It was not published until 1837.

In 1831, she removed with her father to Worcester, where she was afflicted for four or five years with almost total blindness. Her deprivation was partially relieved by her father's kindness, who read to her for hours daily from his well stocked library, and assisted her in the preparation of two prose compositions, which she afterwards published, *Joanna of Naples*, a tale, and a life of Mrs. Elizabeth Carter, the learned friend of Dr. Johnson.

In 1840, Miss Park was married to the Rev. Edward B. Hall, a Unitarian clergyman of Providence, Rhode Island.

The scene of Miriam is laid in Rome, in the early ages of the Christian church. The characters of the piece are few, and the action confined entirely to the antagonism between the dominant idolatry and the yet persecuted Faith.

Miriam, a young Christian maiden, is summoned by her father and brother to attend the burial rites of one of their persecuted sect. Her refusal excites their surprise, but they depart on their errand. Paulus, the son of Piso, "a noble Roman, a persecutor of the Christians," enters. Unable to change his faith, she has remained behind for a farewell interview. While they are together, her brother Euphas returns, reproaches her for what

* Rees's Dramatic Authors of America.

he deems her immorality, and brings intelligence that the assembly had been surprised, and her father, with others, led to prison to be condemned to death. Euphas summons other Christians, who surround Paulus; and departs to propose to Piso, who is devotedly attached to his only son, an exchange of prisoners. The next scene introduces the merciless Roman ruler. Euphas is in despair, when Miriam enters. Her resemblance to her deceased mother powerfully affects Piso, who, years ago, a soldier in Syria, had wooed the latter when a maiden, and now discovers the rival who became her husband within his power. Finding he can save his son's life only by the release of all the captives, he promises that they shall return at the appointed time, the break of the following day. To this, and its first locality, the scene changes. The brother and sister return with the promise, and are soon followed by the mockery of its fulfilment. The Christian captives are introduced, bearing with them the aged Thraseno, stretched dead upon a bier, having been strangled in prison by order of his old rival. Miriam sinks under this accumulated misery. She rallies a moment as her lover proclaims that henceforth his part and lot are with those about him, and craves, as a sincere convert, the rite of baptism; but while the funeral dirge rises around the body of her father, her gentle spirit passes from earth.

We quote the concluding scene of the drama :—

Christians enter, and the group opening, displays the body of Thraseno on a bier.

Paulus. (*Springing forward.*) Oh foul and bloody deed!—and wretched son!
That knows too well whose treachery hath done this!
An aged Christian. Thus saith the man of blood, "My word is kept.
I send you him I promised. Have ye kept
Your faith with me? If so, there is naught more
Between us three. Bury your dead,—and fly!"
First Christian. A ruffian's strangling hand hath grasped this throat!
And on the purple lip convulsion still
Lingers with awful tale of violence.
Oh, fearful was the strife from which arose
Our brother's spirit to its peaceful home!
Let grief, let wrath, let each unquiet thought
Be still, and round the just man's dust ascend
The voice of pray'r.
Paulus. Not yet! oh! not *quite* yet!
Hear me, ye pale and horror-stricken throng!
Hear me, thou sobbing boy! My Miriam, turn—
Turn back thy face from the dim world of death,
And hear thy lover's voice!—What seest thou
In the blue heav'ns with fixed and eager gaze?
Miriam. Angels are gathering in the eastern sky—
The wind is playing 'mid their glittering plumes—
The sunbeams dance upon their golden harps—
Welcome is on their fair and glorious brows!
Hath not a holy spirit passed from earth,
Whom ye come forth to meet, seraphic forms?
Oh, fade not, fade not yet!—or take me too,
For earth grows dark beneath my dazzled eye!
Paulus. Miriam! in mercy spread not yet thy wings!
Spurn me not from the gate that opes for thee!
Miriam. In which world do I stand! A voice there was
Of prayer and woe. *That* must have rung on earth!
Say on.
Paulus. Christians! I must indeed say on
Or my full heart will break!—No heathen is't
On whom ye gaze with low'ring, angry eyes.
My father's blood—his name, his faith, his gods—
I here abjure; and only ask your prayers,
The purifying water on my brow,
And words of hope to soothe my penitence—
Ere I atone my father's crimes with blood.
[*Silence.*
And will none speak? Am I indeed cast off—
Rejected utterly? Will no one teach
The sinner how to frame the Christian's prayer,
Help me to know the Christian's God aright,
Wash from my brow the deep-red stains of guilt?
Must I then die in ignorance and sin?
Miriam. O earth! be not so busy with my soul!
Paulus! what wouldest thou?
Paulus. The rite that binds
New converts to your peaceful faith.
Miriam. Good brethren,
Hear ye his prayer! Search ye the penitent,
Bear him forth with you in your pilgrimage,
And when his soul in earnest hath drunk in
The spirit of Christ's law, seal him for Heaven——
And now—would that my chains were broke! Half-freed
My spirit struggles 'neath the dust that lies
So heavy on her wings!—Paulus, we part.
But oh, how different is the parting hour
From that which crushed my hopeless spirit erst!
Joy—joy and triumph now——
Paulus. Oh, name not joy.
Miriam. Why not? If but one ray of light from Heaven
Hath reached thy soul, I may indeed rejoice!
Ev'n thus, in coming days, from martyrs' blood
Shall earnest saints arise to do God's work.
And thus with slow, sure, silent step shall Truth
Tread the dark earth, and scatter Light abroad,
Till Peace and Righteousness awake, and lead
Triumphant, in the bright and joyous blaze,
Their happy myriads up to yonder skies!
Euphas. Sister! with such a calm and sunny brow
Stand'st thou beside our murdered father's bier?
Miriam. Euphas, thy hand!—Aye, clasp thy brother's hand!
Ye fair and young apostles! go ye forth—
Go side by side beneath the sun and storm,
A dying sister's blessing on your toils!
When ye have poured the oil of Christian peace
On passions rude and wild—when ye have won
Dark, sullen souls from wrath and sin to God—
Whene'er ye kneel to bear upon your prayers
Repentant sinners up to yonder heaven,
Be it in palace—dungeon—open air—
'Mid friends—'mid raging foes—in joy—in grief—
Deem not ye pray alone,—man never doth!
A sister spirit, ling'ring near, shall fill
The silent air around you with her prayers,
Waiting till ye too lay your fetters down,
And come to your reward!—Go fearless forth:
For glorious truth wars with you, and shall reign.
[*Seeing the bier.*
My father! sleepest thou?—Aye, a sound sleep.
Dreams *have* been there—oh, horrid dreams!—but now,
The silver beard heaves not upon thy breast,
The hand I press is deadly, deadly cold,
And thou wilt dream, wilt never suffer, more.
Why gaze I on this clay! It was not this—
Not this I reverenced and loved!——
My friends,
Raise ye the dirge; and though I hide my face
In my dead father's robe, think not I weep.

I would not have the sight of those I love
Too well,—ev'n at this solemn hour, too well,—
Disturb my soul's communion with the blest!
My brother,—sob not so!

DIRGE.

Shed not the wild and hopeless tear
Upon our parted brother's bier;
With heart subdued and steadfast eye,
Oh, raise each thought to yonder sky!

Aching brow and throbbing breast
In the silent grave shall rest;
But the clinging dust in vain
Weaves around the soul its chain.

Spirit, quit this land of tears,
Hear the song of rolli g spheres;
Shall our wild and selfish prayers
Call thee back to mortal cares?

Sainted spirit! fare thee well!
More than mortal tongue can tell
Is the joy that even now
Crowns our blessed martyr's brow!

Euphas. Paulus, arise!
We must away. Thy father's wrath——
Paulus. Oh, peace!
My Miriam,—speak to us!—she doth not stir!
Euphas. Methought I saw her ringlets move!
First Christian. Alas!
'Twas but the breeze that lifted those dark locks!
They never will wave more.
Euphas. It cannot be!
Let me but look upon her face!—Oh, God!
Death sits in that glazed eye!
First Christian. Aye, while we sung
Her father's dirge—across the young and fair
I saw death's shudder pass. Nay, turn not pale.
Borne on the solemn strain, her spirit soared
Most peacefully on high.——
Chastened ye are
And b nd by sorrow to your holy task.
Arise,—and in your youthful memories
Treasure the end of innocence.—Away,
Beneath far other skies, weep—if ye can—
The gain of those ye loved.
Euphas. Lift this fair dust.—
My brother! speechless, tearless grief for her
Who listeneth for thy pray'rs?
Paulus. My mind is dark.
The faith which she bequeathed must lighten it.
Come forth, and I will learn.—Oh, Miriam!
Can thy bright faith e'er comfort grief like mine?

MARIA J. McINTOSH.

Miss McIntosh, the author of a series of fictions, characterized by their truthfulness and happy style, is the descendant of a Scottish family, which came among the first settlers to Georgia. Her ancestors in Scotland were distinguished by the handling of the sword rather than the pen, though an uncle of her grandfather, Brigadier-General William McIntosh, who led the Highland troops in the rising of 1715, during a fifteen years' imprisonment in the Castle of Edinburgh, where he died, wrote a treatise on "Inclosing, Fallowing, and Planting in Scotland." With fortunes greatly diminished by the adherence of his family to the Stuarts, her great-grandfather, Capt. John More McIntosh, with one hundred adherents, sailed from Inverness, in 1735, for the colony of Georgia, and landing on the banks of the Alatamaha, named the place at which they settled New Inverness, now Darien, in the county which still retains the name of McIntosh. This John More McIntosh was the same who originated and was the first signer of the protest made by the colonists to the Board of Trustees in England, against the introduction of African slaves into Georgia. Of his sons and grandsons, seven bore commissions in the American Army of the Revolution. Of these, Major Lachlan McIntosh was the father of our author. He combined the dissimilar professions of the law and of arms. His standing as a lawyer was high in his native state, and after the war of the Revolution, political honors were often thrust upon him, and his pen was often employed in defence of the measures of his party. He was admired for his social qualities, and his warm heart and conversational talents are still remembered. He was married to an accomplished lady, who united great energy of character to purely feminine traits. Major McIntosh resided after the Revolution in the village of Sunbury, forty miles south of Savannah, on the seacoast of Georgia, where our author was born. In a reminiscence of this spot she thus records her impressions of its scenery. "Sunbury was beautifully situated about five miles from the ocean, on a bold frith or arm of the sea, stretching up between St. Catherine's Island on the one side and the main land on the other, forming, apparently, the horns of a crescent, at the base of which the town stood. It was a beautiful spot, carpeted with the short-leaved Bermuda grass, and shaded with oak, cedar, locust, and a flowering tree, the Pride of India. It was then the summer resort of all the neighboring gentry, who went thither for the sea air. Within the last twenty years it has lost its character for health, and is now a desolate ruin; yet the hearts of those who grew up in its shades still cling to the memory of its loveliness; a recollection which

M. J. McIntosh

exists as a bond of union between them, which no distance can wholly sever. Its sod, still green and beautiful as ever, is occasionally visited by a solitary pilgrim, who goes thither with something of the tender reverence with which he would visit the grave of a beloved friend."

In Sunbury, at an academy, which dispensed its favors to pupils of both sexes, Miss McIntosh received all of her education for which she was indebted to schools;* and there the first twenty years of her life were spent. After that time her home having been broken up by the death of her mother, she passed much of her time with a married sister, who resided in New York, and afterwards with her brother, Capt. James M. McIntosh of the U. S. navy, whose family had also removed to that city. In 1835, Miss McIntosh was induced to sell her property in Georgia, and invest the proceeds in New York. The investment proving injudicious, she was dependent on her friends or her pen. She characteristically chose the independence and intellectual development of the latter. Her first thought was to translate from the French. A friend advised her to attempt a juvenile series of publications, which should take the place in moral science which the popular "Peter Parley" books had taken in matters of fact, and suggested "Aunt Kitty" as a *nom de plume*. The story of *Blind Alice* was accordingly written in 1838, but did not find a publisher till 1841. Its success led to a second, *Jessie Grahame*, which was followed in quick succession by *Florence Arnott*, *Grace and Clara*, and *Ellen Leslie*. Each of these little works was designed for the inculcation and illustration of some moral sentiment. In Blind Alice it was the happiness springing from the exercise of benevolence; in Jessie Grahame, the love of truth; in Florence Arnott, the distinction between true generosity and its counterfeit; in Grace and Clara, the value of the homely quality of justice; and in Ellen Leslie, the influence of temper on domestic happiness. In 1844, *Conquest and Self-Conquest*, and *Woman an Enigma*, were published by the Harpers. In 1845, the same publishers brought out *Praise and Principle*, and a child's tale called *The Cousins*. Her next work, *To Seem and to Be*, was published in 1846 by the Appletons, who, in 1847, republished Aunt Kitty's Tales, collected from the previous editions into a single volume. In 1848, the same house published *Charms and Counter Charms*, and the next year, *Donaldson Manor*, a collection of articles written at various times for magazines, and strung together by a slight thread. In 1850, was brought out *Woman in America*, the only purely didactic work the author has published. In 1853, appeared *The Lofty and the Lowly*, a picture of the life of the slave and the master, in the southern portion of the United States.

In England, Miss McIntosh's books have enjoyed a good reputation, with a large popular sale. They were first introduced by the eminent tragedian, Mr. Macready, who, having obtained Aunt Kitty's Tales in this country to take home to his children, read them himself on the voyage, as he afterwards wrote to a friend in this city, with such pleasure, that soon after his arrival in London he placed them in the hands of a publisher, who reproduced them there. The author's other books have been published in England as they made their appearance in America, and in the competition for uncopyrighted foreign literature, by more than one London publisher; though with the liberty of occasionally changing the name.

THE BROTHERS; OR, IN THE FASHION AND ABOVE THE FASHION.*

"Some men are born to greatness—some achieve greatness—and some have greatness thrust upon them." Henry Manning belonged to the second of these three great classes. The son of a mercantile adventurer, who won and lost a fortune by speculation, he found himself at sixteen years of age called on to choose between the life of a Western farmer, with its vigorous action, stirring incident, and rough usage—and the life of a clerk in one of the most noted establishments in Broadway, the great source and centre of fashion in New York. Mr. Morgan, the brother of Mrs. Manning, who had been recalled from the distant West by the death of her husband, and the embarrassments into which that event had plunged her, had obtained the offer of the latter situation for one of his two nephews, and would take the other with him to his prairie-home.

"I do not ask you to go with me, Matilda," he said to his sister, "because our life is yet too wild and rough to suit a delicate woman, reared, as you have been, in the midst of luxurious refinements. The difficulties and privations of life in the West fall most heavily upon woman, while she has little of that sustaining power which man's more adventurous spirit finds in overcoming difficulty and coping with danger. But let me have one of your

* A few notes before us, from the pen of Miss McIntosh, contain a *souvenir* to the memory of this head master of Sunbury. "He was an *Irish Gentleman*—an epithet which he marked as quite distinct from that of a *Gentleman from Ireland*. He was a graduate of the University of Antrim;—a Presbyterian divine, yet not in early life after a very strict model. He would indeed, then, have answered Addison's demands well, being quite willing to avail himself of the eloquence of the classics of the pulpit, while he could take a hand readily, either in backgammon—Sir Roger de Coverley's special requisition—or in whist. In his latter years, however, for he has passed away from earth, he became an earnest and sincere Christian minister, and might have said to many of his order, 'I was in labors more abundant.' As a teacher he was unsurpassed. Taught in the niceties of his own language and of the dead languages, as few American scholars of that day were, he seemed especially gifted for the communication of knowledge to others. On his first arrival in this country he had resided in Alexandria, and had taught in the family of General Washington, as he was proud of remembering. When he came to Georgia he married;—there he continued to live, and there he died at a very advanced age, nearly, if not quite, a hundred. Even to the last year of his life he would have detected an imperfect concord or false prosody. When he was a teacher, the barbarous age of the rod and the ferule still continued, and the boys of his school sometimes complained that they were made to expiate by their application, not their own faults only, but also those of their fair companions, who were of course exempted from such punishments. To those who showed any interest in study, he was kind and indulgent. To myself he scarcely offered any constraint, permitting me often to choose my studies and prescribe my own lessons. The natural dislike of a vivacious girl to plod ever and ever in one beaten track, while boys, who were not always brighter than herself, were leaving her to penetrate into the higher mysteries of science, he stimulated rather than repressed, producing thus an emulation, which gave a healthy impulse to both parties. I remember often to have heard Dr. McWhir—for this was the name of the master—say, that this rivalry had done more for his school than a dozen rods, and I am quite sure that with it there mingled no bitterness, for some of those lads have been among the best friends of my life. The peculiar training of such a school must of course have exercised no small influence on the mental characteristics. It perhaps enabled me to exercise more readily the self-reliance necessary when thrown on my own resources,—yet it never inclined me for a moment to the vagaries of those who stand forth as the champions of women's rights. He who best understood the nature He had formed, assigned to woman a position of subjection and dependence, and I consider the noblest right to be, the right intelligently to obey His laws. In that obedience is found, doubtless, the highest honor of man or woman."

* From the Evenings at Donaldson Manor.

boys, and by the time he has arrived at manhood, he will be able, I doubt not, to offer you in his home all the comforts, if not all the elegances of your present abode."

Mrs. Manning consented; and now the question was, which of her sons should remain with her, and which should accompany Mr. Morgan. To Henry Manning, older by two years than his brother George, the choice of situations was submitted. He went with his uncle to the Broadway establishment, heard the duties which would be demanded from him, the salary which would be given, saw the grace with which the *élégants* behind the counter displayed their silks, and satins, and velvets, to the *élégantes* before the counter, and the decision with which they promulgated the decrees of fashion; and with that just sense of his own powers which is the accompaniment of true genius, he decided at once that there lay his vocation. George, who had not been without difficulty kept quiet while his brother was forming his decision, as soon as it was announced, sprang forward with a whoop that would have suited a Western forest better than a New York drawing-room, threw the Horace he was reading across the table, clasped first his mother and then his uncle in his arms, and exclaimed, "I am the boy for the West. I will help you to fell forests and build cities there, uncle. Why should not we build cities as well as Romulus and Remus?"

"I will supply your cities with all their silks, and satins, and velvets, and laces, and charge them nothing, George," said Henry Manning with that air of superiority with which the worldly-wise often look on the sallies of the enthusiast.

"You make my head ache, my son," complained Mrs. Manning, shrinking from his boisterous gratulation;—but Mr. Morgan returned his hearty embrace, and as he gazed into his bold, bright face, with an eye as bright as his own, replied to his burst of enthusiasm, "You *are* the very boy for the West, George. It is out of such brave stuff that pioneers and city-builders are always made."

Henry Manning soon bowed himself into the favor of the ladies who formed the principal customers of his employer. By his careful and really correct habits, and his elegant taste in the selection and arrangement of goods, he became also a favorite with his employers themselves. They needed an agent for the selection of goods abroad, and they sent him. He purchased cloths for them in England and silks in France, and came home with the reputation of a travelled man. Having persuaded his mother to advance a capital for him by selling out the bank stock in which Mr. Morgan had funded her little fortune, at twenty-four years of age he commenced business for himself as a French importer. Leaving a partner to attend to the sales at home, he went abroad for the selection of goods, and the further enhancement of his social reputation. He returned in two years with a fashionable figure, a most *recherché* style of dress, moustachios of the most approved cut, and whiskers of faultless curl—a finished gentleman in his own conceit. With such attractions, the *prestige* which he derived from his reported travels and long residence abroad, and the *savoir faire* of one who had made the conventional arrangements of society his study, he quickly rose to the summit of his wishes, to the point which it had been his life's ambition to attain. He became the umpire of taste, and his word was received as the fiat of fashion. He continued to reside with his mother, and paid great attention to her style of dress, and the arrangements of her house, for it was important that his mother should appear properly. Poor Mrs. Manning! she sometimes thought that proud title dearly purchased by listening to his daily criticisms on appearance, language, manners, which had been esteemed stylish enough in their day.

George Manning had visited his mother only once since he left her with all the bright imaginings and boundless confidence of fourteen, and then Henry was in Europe. It was during the first winter after his return, and when the brothers had been separated for nearly twelve years, that Mrs. Manning informed him she had received a letter from George, announcing his intention to be in New York in December, and to remain with them through most, if not all the winter. Henry Manning was evidently annoyed at the announcement.

"I wish," he said, "that George had chosen to make his visit in the summer, when most of the people to whom I should hesitate to introduce him would have been absent. I should be sorry to hurt his feelings, but really, to introduce a Western farmer into polished society——" Henry Manning shuddered and was silent. "And then to choose this winter of all winters for his visit, and to come in December, just at the very time that I heard yesterday Miss Harcourt was coming from Washington to spend a few weeks with her friend, Mrs. Duffield!"

"And what has Miss Harcourt's visit to Mrs. Duffield to do with George's visit to us?" asked Mrs. Manning.

"A great deal—at least it has a great deal to do with my regret that he should come just now. I told you how I became acquainted with Emma Harcourt in Europe, and what a splendid creature she is. Even in Paris she bore the palm for wit and beauty—and fashion too—that is in English and American society. But I did not tell you that she received me with such distinguished favor, and evinced so much pretty consciousness at my attentions, that had not her father, having been chosen one of the electors of President and Vice-President, hurried from Paris in order to be in this country in time for his vote, I should probably have been induced to marry her. Her father is in Congress this year, and you see, she no sooner learns that I am here, than she comes to spend part of the winter with a friend in New York."

Henry arose at this, walked to a glass, surveyed his elegant figure, and continuing to cast occasional glances at it as he walked backwards and forwards through the room, resumed the conversation, or rather his own communication.

"All this is very encouraging, doubtless; but Emma Harcourt is so perfectly elegant, so thoroughly refined, that I dread the effect upon her of any *outré* association—by the by, mother, if I obtain her permission to introduce you to her, you will not wear that brown hat in visiting her—a brown hat is my aversion—it is positively vulgar. But to return to George—how can I introduce him, with his rough, boisterous, Western manner, to this courtly lady?—the very thought chills me"—and Henry Manning shivered—"and yet how can I avoid it, if we should be engaged?"

With December came the beautiful Emma Harcourt, and Mrs. Duffield's house was thronged with her admirers. Her's was the form and movement of the Huntress Queen rather than of one trained in the halls of fashion. There was a joyous freedom in her air, her step, her glance, which, had she been less beautiful, less talented, less fortunate in social position or in wealth, would have placed her under the ban of fashion; but, as it was, she commanded fashion, and even Henry Manning, the very slave of conventionalism, had no criticism for her.

He had been among the first to call on her, and the blush that flitted across her cheek, the smile that played upon her lips, as he was announced, might well have flattered one even of less vanity.

The very next day, before Henry had had time to improve these symptoms of her favor, on returning home, at five o'clock to his dinner, he found a stranger in the parlor with his mother. The gentleman arose on his entrance, and he had scarcely time to glance at the tall, manly form, the lofty air, the commanding brow, ere he found himself clasped in his arms, with the exclamation, "Dear Henry! how rejoiced I am to see you again."

In George Manning the physical and intellectual man had been developed in rare harmony. He was taller and larger every way than his brother Henry, and the self-reliance which the latter had laboriously attained from the mastery of all conventional rules, was his by virtue of a courageous soul, which held itself above all rules but those prescribed by its own high sense of the right. There was a singular contrast, rendered yet more striking by some points of resemblance, between the pupil of society and the child of the forest—between the Parisian elegance of Henry, and the proud, free grace of George. His were the step and bearing which we have seen in an Indian chief; but thought had left its impress on his brow, and there was in his countenance that indescribable air of refinement which marks a polished mind. In a very few minutes Henry became reconciled to his brother's arrival, and satisfied with him in all respects but one—his dress. This was of the finest cloth, but made into large, loose trowsers, and a species of hunting-shirt, trimmed with fur, belted around the waist, and descending to the knee, instead of the tight pantaloons and closely fitting body coat prescribed by fashion. The little party lingered long over the table—it was seven o'clock before they arose from it.

"Dear mother," said George Manning, "I am sorry to leave you this evening, but I will make you rich amends to-morrow by introducing to you the friend I am going to visit, if you will permit me. Henry, it is so long since I was in New York that I need some direction in finding my way—must I turn up or down Broadway for Number —, in going from this street?"

"Number —," exclaimed Henry in surprise; "you must be mistaken—that is Mrs. Duffield's."

"Then I am quite right; for it is at Mrs. Duffield's that I expect to meet my friend this evening."

With some curiosity to know what friend of George could have so completely the *entrée* of the fashionable Mrs. Duffield's house as to make an appointment there, Henry proposed to go with him and show him the way. There was a momentary hesitation in George's manner before he replied; "Very well, I shall be obliged to you."

"But—excuse me, George—you are not surely going in that dress—this is one of Mrs. Duffield's reception evenings, and, early as it is, you will find company there."

George laughed as he replied; "They must take me as I am, Henry. We do not receive our fashions from Paris at the West."

Henry almost repented his offer to accompany his brother, but it was too late to withdraw; for George, unconscious of this feeling, had taken his cloak and cap, and was awaiting his escort. As they approached Mrs. Duffield's house, George, who had hitherto led the conversation, became silent, or answered his brother only in monosyllables, and then not always to the purpose. As they entered the hall, the hats and cloaks displayed there showed that, as Henry supposed, they were not the earliest visitors. George paused for a moment, and said, "You must go in without me, Henry. Show me to a room where there is no company," he continued, turning to a servant—"and take this card in to Mrs. Duffield—be sure to give it to Mrs. Duffield herself."

The servant bowed low to the commanding stranger; and Henry, almost mechanically, obeyed his direction, muttering to himself, "Free and easy, upon my honor." He had scarcely entered the usual reception-room, and made his bow to Mrs. Duffield, when the servant presented his brother's card. He watched her closely, and saw a smile playing over her lips as her eyes rested on it. She glanced anxiously at Miss Harcourt, and crossing the room to a group in which she stood, she drew her aside. After a few whispered words, Mrs. Duffield placed the card in Miss Harcourt's hand. A sudden flash of joy irradiated every feature of her beautiful face, and Henry Manning saw that, but for Mrs. Duffield's restraining hand, she would have rushed from the room. Recalled thus to a recollection of others, she looked around her, and her eyes met his. In an instant her face was covered with blushes, and she drew back with embarrassed consciousness—almost immediately, however, she raised her head with a proud, bright expression, and though she did not look at Henry Manning, he felt that she was conscious of his observation, as she passed with a composed yet joyous step from the room.

Henry Manning was awaking from a dream. It was not a very pleasant awakening; but as his vanity rather than his heart was touched, he was able to conceal his chagrin, and appear as interesting and agreeable as usual. He now expected, with some impatience, the *dénouement* of the comedy. An hour passed away, and Mrs. Duffield's eye began to consult the marble clock on her mantel-piece. The chime for another half hour rang out; and she left the room and returned in a few minutes, leaning on the arm of George Manning.

"Who is that?—What noble-looking man is that?" were questions Henry Manning heard from many—from a very few only the exclamation, "How oddly he is dressed!" Before the evening was over Henry began to feel that he was eclipsed on his own theatre—that George, if not *in the fashion*, was yet more *the fashion* than he.

Following the proud happy glance of his brother's eye, a quarter of an hour later, Henry saw Miss Harcourt entering the room in an opposite direction from that in which he had lately come. If this were a *ruse* on her part to veil the connexion between their movements, it was a fruitless caution. None who had seen her before could fail now to observe the softened character of her beauty, and those who saw

> A thousand blushing apparitions start
> Into her face—

whenever his eyes rested on her, could scarcely doubt his influence over her.

The next morning George Manning brought Miss Harcourt to visit his mother; and Mrs. Manning rose greatly in her son Henry's estimation when he saw the affectionate deference evinced towards her by the proud beauty.

"How strange my manner must have seemed to you sometimes!" said Miss Harcourt to Henry one day. "I was engaged to George long before I met you in Europe; and though I never had courage to mention him to you, I wondered a little that you never spoke of him. I never doubted for a moment that you were acquainted with our engagement."

"I do not even yet understand where and how you and George met."

"We met at home—my father was governor of the territory—State now—in which your uncle lives: our homes were very near each other's, and so we met almost daily while I was still a child. We have had all sorts of adventures together; for George was a great favorite with my father, and I was permitted to go with him anywhere. He has saved my life twice—once at the imminent peril of his own, when with the wilfulness of a spoiled child I would ride a horse which he told me I could not manage. Oh! you know not half his nobleness," and tears moistened the bright eyes of the happy girl.

Henry Manning was touched through all his conventionalism, yet the moment after he said, "George is a fine fellow, certainly; but I wish you could persuade him to dress a little more like other people."

"I would not if I could," exclaimed Emma Harcourt, while the blood rushed to her temples; "fashions and all such conventional regulations are made for those who have no innate perception of the right, the noble, the beautiful—not for such as he—he is above fashion."

What Emma would not ask, she yet did not fail to recognise as another proof of correct judgment, when George Manning laid aside his Western costume and assumed one less remarkable.

Henry Manning had received a new idea—that there are those who are above the fashion. Allied to this was another thought, which in time found entrance to his mind, that it would be at least as profitable to devote our energies to the acquisition of true nobility of soul, pure and high thought and refined taste, as to the study of those conventionalisms which are but their outer garment, and can at best only conceal, for a short time, their absence.

LYDIA MARIA CHILD.

THE maiden name of Mrs. Child was Francis. She was born in Massachusetts, but passed a portion of her earlier career in Maine, where her father removed shortly after her birth.

In the year 1824 she published her first work, *Hobomok*, a tale founded upon the early history of New England. The story told by Dr. Griswold in relation to this commencement of a long literary career is a curious one. While on a visit to her brother, the Rev. Convers Francis, minister in Watertown, Massachusetts, she accidentally met with the recent number of the North American Review and read an article on Yamoyden by Dr. Palfrey, in which the field offered by early New England history for the purposes of the novelist is dwelt upon. She took pen in hand and wrote off the first chapter of Hobomok. Her brother's commendation encouraged her to proceed, and in six weeks the story was completed. In the following year she published *The Rebels*, a tale of the Revolution. Like Hobomok it introduces the most prominent historical personages of its scene and time to the reader, and with such effect that a speech put in the mouth of James Otis is often quoted as having been actually pronounced by the statesman.

L. Maria Child,

In 1826 she married Mr. David L. Child, and in 1827 commenced *The Juvenile Miscellany*, a monthly magazine. She next issued *The Frugal Housewife*, a work on domestic economy and culinary matters, designed for families of limited means. In 1831 she published *The Mother's Book*, a volume of good counsel on the training of children, and in 1832 *The Girl's Book*, a work of somewhat similar nature. Her *Lives of Madame de Stael, Madame Roland, Lady Russell*, and *Madame Guyon*, were published about the same time in two volumes of the Ladies' Family Library, a series of books edited by her, for which she also prepared the *Biographies of Good Wives*, in one volume, and the *History of the Condition of Women in all Ages*, in two volumes.

In 1833 she published *The Coronal*, a collection of miscellanies in prose and verse, which she had previously contributed to various annuals, and in the same year *An Appeal for that Class of Americans called Africans*, a vigorous work which created a great sensation. Dr. Channing is said to have walked from Boston to Roxbury to see and thank the author, personally a stranger to him.

In 1835, *Philothea*, a classical romance of the days of Pericles and Aspasia, appeared. It is the most elaborate and successful of the author's productions, and is in close and artistic keeping with the classic age it portrays. Most of the statesmen and philosophers of the time are introduced in its pages with a generally close adherence to history, though in the character of Plato she has departed in a measure from this rule by dwelling on the mystical doctrines of the philosopher to the exclusion of his practical traits of character. The female characters, Philothea, Eudora, and the celebrated Aspasia, are portrayed with great beauty and delicacy.

In 1841 Mrs. Child and her husband, removing to New York, became the editors of the National Anti-Slavery Standard. In the same year she commenced a series of letters for the Boston Courier, which were afterwards republished in two volumes with the title of *Letters from New York*, a pleasant series of descriptions of the every-day life of the metropolis, abounding to the observant and appreciative eye in picturesque incident and suggestion for far-reaching thought. M'Donald Clarke forms the subject of one of these letters. Others are occupied by the humanitarian institutions of the city, others by flowers and markets. The peripatetic trades come in for their share of notice, nor are the pathetic narratives of want, temptation, and misery, the annals of the cellar and garret, omitted. Occasional excursions to the picturesque and historic villages of the Hudson, Staten Island, and other near at hand rural retreats, give an additional charm to these delightful volumes.

In 1846 Mrs. Child published a collection of her magazine stories under the title of *Fact and Fiction*. She has now in press a work in three volumes, one of the most elaborate which she has undertaken, entitled *The Progress of Religious Ideas*, embracing a view of every form of belief "from the most ancient Hindoo records to the complete establishment of the Catholic Church."

OLE BUL—FROM LETTERS FROM NEW YORK.

Welcome to thee, Ole Bul!
A welcome, warm and free!

For heart and memory are full
  Of thy rich minstrelsy.

'Tis music for the tuneful rills
To flow to from the verdant hills;
Music such as first on earth
Gave to the Aurora birth.

Music for the leaves to dance to;
Music such as sunbeams glance to;
Treble to the ocean's roar,
On some old resounding shore.

Silvery showers from the fountains;
Mists unrolling from the mountains;
Lightning flashing through a cloud,
When the winds are piping loud.

Music full of warbling graces,
Like to birds in forest places,
Gushing, trilling, whirring round,
Mid the pine trees' murm'ring sound.

The martin scolding at the wren,
Which sharply answers back again,
Till across the angry song
Strains of laughter run along.

Now leaps the bow, with airy bound,
Like dancer springing from the ground,
And now like autumn wind comes sighing,
Over leaves and blossoms dying.

The lark now singeth from afar,
Her carol to the morning star,
A clear soprano rising high,
Ascending to the inmost sky.

And now the scattered tones are flying,
Like sparks in midnight darkness dying,
Gems from rockets in the sky,
Falling—falling—gracefully.

Now wreathed and twined—but still evolving
Harmonious oneness is revolving;
Departing with the faintest sigh,
Like ghost of some sweet melody.

As on a harp with golden strings,
  All nature breathes through thee,
And with her thousand voices sings
  The infinite and free.

Of beauty she is lavish ever;
  Her urn is always full;
But to our earth she giveth never
  Another Ole Bul.

OLD AGE—FROM LETTERS FROM NEW YORK

Childhood itself is scarcely more lovely than a cheerful, kind, sunshiny old age.

How I love the mellow sage,
Smiling through the veil of age!
And whene'er this man of years
In the dance of joy appears,
Age is on his temples hung,
But his heart—*his heart is young!*

Here is the great secret of a bright and green old age. When Tithonus asked for an eternal life in the body, and found, to his sorrow, that immortal *youth* was not included in the bargain, it surely was because he forgot to ask the perpetual gift of loving and sympathizing.

Next to this, is an intense affection for nature, and for all simple things. A human heart can never grow old, if it takes a lively interest in the pairing of birds, the re-production of flowers, and the changing tints of autumn-ferns. Nature, unlike other friends, has an exhaustless meaning, which one sees and hears more distinctly, the more they are enamoured of her. Blessed are they who *hear* it; for through tones come the most inward perceptions of the spirit. Into the ear of the soul, which reverently *listens*, Nature whispers, speaks, or warbles, most heavenly arcana.

And even they who seek her only through science, receive a portion of her own tranquillity, and perpetual youth. The happiest old man I ever saw, was one who knew how the mason-bee builds his cell, and how every bird lines her nest; who found pleasure in a sea-shore pebble, as boys do in new marbles; and who placed every glittering mineral in a focus of light, under a kaleidoscope of his own construction. The effect was like the imagined riches of fairy land; and when an admiring group of happy young people gathered round it, the heart of the good old man leapt like the heart of a child. The laws of nature, as manifested in her infinitely various operations, were to him a perennial fountain of delight; and, like her, he offered the joy to all. Here was no admixture of the bad excitement attendant upon ambition or controversy; but all was serenely happy, as are an angel's thoughts, or an infant's dreams.

Age, in its outward senses, returns again to childhood; and thus should it do spiritually. The little child enters a rich man's house, and loves to play with the things that are new and pretty, but he thinks not of their market value, nor does he pride himself that another child cannot play with the same. The farmer's home will probably delight him more; for he will love living squirrels better than marble greyhounds, and the merry bob o'lincoln better than stuffed birds from Araby the blest; for *they* cannot sing into his heart. What *he* wants is life and love—the power of giving and receiving joy. To this estimate of things, wisdom returns, after the intuitions of childhood are lost. Virtue is but innocence on a higher plane, to be attained only through severe conflict. Thus life completes its circle; but it is a circle that *rises* while it revolves; for the path of spirit is ever spiral, containing *all* of truth and love in each revolution, yet ever tending upward. The virtue which brings us back to innocence, on a higher plane of wisdom, may be the childhood of another state of existence; and through successive conflicts, we may again complete the ascending circle, and find it holiness.

The ages, too, are rising spirally; each containing all, yet ever ascending. Hence, all our new things are old, and yet they are new. Some truth known to the ancients meets us on a higher plane, and we do not recognise it, because it is like a child of earth, which has passed upward and become an angel. Nothing of true beauty ever passes away. The youth of the world, which Greece embodied in immortal marble, will return in the circling Ages, as innocence comes back in virtue; but it shall return filled with a higher life; and that, too, shall point upward. Thus shall the Arts be glorified. Beethoven's music prophesies all this, and struggles after it continually; therefore, whosoever hears it, (with the *inward*, as well as the *outward* ear,) feels his soul spread its strong pinions, eager to pass "the flaming bounds of time and space," and circle all the infinite.

THE BROTHERS.

Three pure heavens opened, beaming in three pure hearts, and nothing was in them but God, love, and joy, and the little tear-drop of earth which hangs upon all our flowers.—*Richter*.

Few know how to estimate the precious gem of friendship at its real worth; few guard it with the tender care which its rarity and excellence deserve. Love, like the beautiful opal, is a clouded gem, which carries a spark of fire in its bosom; but true friendship, like a diamond, radiates steadily from its transparent heart.

This sentiment was never experienced in greater depth and purity than by David and Jonathan Trueman, brothers of nearly the same age. Their friendship was not indeed of that exciting and refreshing character, which is the result of a perfect accord of very different endowments. It was unison, not harmony. In person, habits, and manners, they were as much alike as two leaves of the same tree. They were both hereditary members of the Society of Friends, and remained so from choice. They were acquainted in the same circle, and engaged in similar pursuits. "Their souls wore exactly the same frockcoat and morning-dress of life; I mean two bodies with the same cuffs and collars, of the same color, button-holes, trimmings, and cut."

Jonathan was a little less sedate than his older brother; he indulged a little more in the quiet, elderly sort of humor of the "Cheeryble Brothers." But it was merely the difference between the same lake perfectly calm, or faintly rippled by the slightest breeze. They were so constantly seen together, that they were called the Siamese Twins. Unfortunately, this similarity extended to a sentiment which does not admit of partnership. They both loved the same maiden.

Deborah Winslow was the only daughter of one of those substantial Quakers, who a discriminating observer would know, at first sight, was "well to do in the world;" for the fine broadcloth coat and glossy hat spoke that fact with even less certainty than the perfectly comfortable expression of countenance. His petted child was like a blossom planted in sunny places, and shielded from every rude wind. All her little-lady-like whims were indulged. If the drab-colored silk was not exactly the right shade, or the Braithwaite muslin was not sufficiently fine and transparent, orders must be sent to London, that her daintiness might be satisfied. Her countenance was a true index of life passed without strong emotions. The mouth was like a babe's, the blue eyes were mild and innocent, and the oval face was unvarying in the delicate tint of the sweet pea blossom. Her hair never straggled into ringlets, or played with the breeze; its silky bands were always like molasses-candy, moulded to yellowish whiteness, and laid in glossy braids.

There is much to be said in favor of this unvarying serenity; for it saves a vast amount of suffering. But all natures cannot thus glide through an unruffled existence. Deborah's quiet temperament made no resistance to its uniform environment; but had I been trained in her exact sect, I should inevitably have boiled over and melted the moulds.

She had always been acquainted with the Trueman brothers. They all attended the same school, and they sat in sight of each other at the same meeting; though Quaker custom, ever careful to dam up human nature within safe limits, ordained that they should be seated on different sides of the house, and pass out by different doors. They visited the same neighbors, and walked home in company. She probably never knew, with positive certainty, which of the brothers she preferred; she had always been in the habit of loving them both; but Jonathan happened to ask first, whether she loved him.

It was during an evening walk, that he first mentioned the subject to David; and he could not see how his lips trembled, and his face flushed. The emotion, though strong and painful, was soon suppressed; and in a voice but slightly constrained, he inquired, "Does Deborah love thee, brother?"

The young man replied that he thought so, and he intended to ask her, as soon as the way opened.

David likewise thought, that Deborah was attached to him; and he had invited her to ride the next day, for the express purpose of ascertaining the point. Never had his peaceful soul been in such a tumult. Sometimes he thought it would be right and honorable to tell Deborah that they both loved her, and ask her to name her choice. "But then if she should prefer *me*," he said to himself, "it will make dear Jonathan very unhappy; and if she should choose *him*, it will be a damper on her happiness, to know that I am disappointed. If she accepts him, I will keep my secret to myself. It is a heavy cross to take up; but William Penn says, 'no cross, no crown.' In this case, I would be willing to give up the crown, if I could get rid of the cross. But then if I lay it down, poor Jonathan must bear it. I have always found that it brought great peace of mind to conquer selfishness, and I will strive to do so now. As my brother's wife, she will still be a near and dear friend; and their children will seem almost like my own."

A current of counter thoughts rushed through his mind. He rose quickly and walked the room, with a feverish agitation he had never before experienced. But through all the conflict, the idea of saving his brother from suffering remained paramount to his own pain.

The promised ride could not be avoided, but it proved a temptation almost too strong for the good unselfish man. Deborah's sweet face looked so pretty under the shadow of her plain bonnet; her soft hand remained in his so confidingly, when she was about to enter the chaise, and turned to speak to her mother; she smiled on him so affectionately, and called him Friend David, in such winning tones, that it required all his strength to avoid uttering the question, which for ever trembled on his lips: "Dost thou love me, Deborah?" But always there rose between them the image of that dear brother, who slept in his arms in childhood, and shared the same apartment now. "Let him have the first chance," he said to himself. "If he is accepted, I will be resigned, and will be to them both a true friend through life." A very slight pressure of the hand alone betrayed his agitation, when he opened the door of her house, and said, "Farewell, Deborah."

In a few days, Jonathan informed him that he was betrothed; and the magnanimous brother wished him joy with a sincere heart, concealing that it was a sad one. His first impulse was to go away, that he might not be daily reminded of what he had lost; but the fear of marring their happiness enabled him to choose the wiser part of making at once the effort that must be made. No one suspected the sacrifice he laid on the altar of friendship. When the young couple were married, he taxed his ingenuity to furnish whatever he thought would please the bride, by its peculiar neatness and elegance. At first, he found it very hard to leave them by their cozy pleasant fireside, and go to his own solitary apartment, where he never before had dwelt alone; and when the bride and bridegroom looked at each other tenderly, the glance went through his heart like an arrow of fire. But when Deborah, with gentle playfulness, apologized for having taken his brother away from him, he replied, with a quiet smile, "Nay, my friend, I have not lost a brother, I have only gained a sister." His self-denial seemed so easy, that the worldly might have thought it cost him little effort, and deserved no praise; but the angels loved him for it.

By degrees he resumed his wonted serenity, and

became the almost constant inmate of their house. A stranger might almost have doubted which was the husband; so completely were the three united in all their affections, habits, and pursuits. A little son and daughter came to strengthen the bond; and the affectionate uncle found his heart almost as much cheered by them, as if they had been his own. Many an agreeable young Friend would have willingly superintended a household for David; but there was a natural refinement in his character, which rendered it impossible to make a marriage of convenience. He felt more deeply than was apparent, that there was something wanting in his earthly lot; but he could not marry, unless he found a woman whom he loved as dearly as he had loved Deborah; and such a one never again came to him.

Their years flowed on with quiet regularity, disturbed with few of the ills humanity is heir to. In all the small daily affairs of life, each preferred the other's good, and thus secured the happiness of the whole. Abroad, their benevolence fell with the noiseless liberality of dew. The brothers both prospered in business, and Jonathan inherited a large portion of his father-in-law's handsome property. Never were a family so pillowed and cushioned on the carriage-road to heaven. But they were so simply and naturally virtuous, that the smooth path was less dangerous to them than to others.

Reverses came at last in Jonathan's affairs. The failure of others, less careful than himself, involved him in their disasters. But David was rich, and the idea of a separate purse was unknown between them; therefore the gentle Deborah knew no change in her household comforts and elegancies, and felt no necessity of diminishing their large liberality to the poor.

At sixty-three years old, the younger brother departed this life, in the arms of his constant friend. The widow, who had herself counted sixty winters, had been for some time gradually declining in health. When the estate was settled, the property was found insufficient to pay debts. But the kind friend, with the same delicate disinterestedness which had always characterized him, carefully concealed this fact. He settled a handsome fortune upon the widow, which she always supposed to be a portion of her husband's estate. Being executor, he managed affairs as he liked. He borrowed his own capital; and every quarter, he gravely paid her interest on his own money. In the refinement of his generosity, he was not satisfied to support her in the abundance to which she had been accustomed; he wished to have her totally unconscious of obligation, and perfectly free to dispose of the funds as she pleased.

His goodness was not limited to his own household. If a poor seamstress was declining in health, for want of exercise and variety of scene, David Trueman was sure to invite her to Niagara, or the Springs, as a particular favor to him, because he needed company. If there was a lone widow, peculiarly friendless, his carriage was always at her service. If there was a maiden lady uncommonly homely, his arm was always ready as an escort to public places. Without talking at all upon the subject, he practically devoted himself to the mission of attending upon the poor, the unattractive, and the neglected.

Thus the good old bachelor prevents his sympathies from congealing, and his heart from rusting out. The sunlight was taken away from his landscape of life; but little birds sleep in their nests, and sweet flowers breathe their fragrance lovingly through the bright moonlight of his tranquil existence.

EDMUND D. GRIFFIN.

Edmund D. Griffin, the second son of George Griffin, a leading member of the New York bar, and the author of a volume published in 1850, entitled *The Gospel its own Advocate*, was born at Wyoming, Pennsylvania, September 10, 1804. He was a grandson, on the mother's side, of Colonel Zebulon Butler, who defended the valley against the British attack which terminated in the memorable massacre of 1778. When two years old Edmund Griffin removed with his family to New York. He revisited Wyoming with his father in his thirteenth year, and attending religious service on the Sunday after their arrival, Mr. Griffin was requested in consequence of the absence of the clergyman to read a sermon. Not being very well he asked his son to read in his place, a request with which the boy, accustomed to obedience, after a moment's modest hesitation, complied.

After passing through various schools young Griffin was prepared for college by Mr. Nelson,* the celebrated blind teacher of New York. He entered Columbia in 1819, and maintained throughout his course a position at the head of his class. After a few months passed in a law office in 1823, he resolved to engage in the ministry of the Protestant Episcopal Church, soon after commenced his studies in the General Theological Seminary, and was ordained deacon by Bishop Hobart in August, 1826. The two following years were passed in the active discharge of professional duty as assistant minister of St. James's church, Hamilton Square, near New York, and of Christ church in the city, when he was compelled by a threatened affection of the lungs to abandon the labors of the church and the study. By this relaxation, combined with the invigorating effects of a three months' tour, his health was restored, but, by the advice of his friends, instead of recommencing preaching he sailed for Europe. After a tour through England and the Continent he returned to New York on the 17th of April, 1830. Within a week afterwards he was called upon to complete a course of lectures on the History of Literature, commenced by Professor McVickar at Columbia College, and necessarily abandoned at the time from illness. He complied with the request, and at once entered upon its execution, delivering within the months of May and June a course on Roman and Italian literature, with that of England to the time of Charles the Second. These lectures, though prepared almost contemporaneously with their delivery, were so acceptable by their warm appreciation of the subject and scholar's enthusiasm, not only to the students but also the trustees of the college, that the plan of an in-

* Mr. Nelson became totally blind in his twentieth year, when about completing his studies at college. He was poor, and had no one to look to for his own support, or that of his two sisters. With great resolution he determined to continue his studies and fit himself for the duties of a teacher. He taught his sisters to pronounce Latin and Greek, and from their reiterated repetition learnt by heart the text of the classics usually read in schools. A gentleman, out of sympathy with his endeavors, and confidence in his abilities, intrusted him with the education of his two sons. He succeeded so well with these, that, in a few months, he announced himself as the teacher of a New York school. He soon became widely known, and so successful that he gathered a handsome income from his exertions. He afterwards became a professor in Rutgers College.

dependent professorship of literature, for Mr. Griffin, was proposed.

The early part of the ensuing college vacation was spent in visits to his friends, and plans of study and future usefulness in his sacred profession. After a Saturday morning passed at the college with Professor Anthon in planning a course of study of the German language, to which he proposed to devote a portion of his remaining leisure, he employed the afternoon in a walk with his brother at Hoboken. He was taken ill on his return home with an attack of inflammation, sank rapidly, and died on the following Tuesday, August 31, 1830.

The news of his decease reached Bishop Hobart at Auburn, where he too was lying in a sickness which was to prove, within a few days afterwards, mortal. It is a fact of interest in the history of that eminent prelate, as well as in the present connexion, that the last letter written by him was one of condolence with the father of Mr. Griffin on their joint bereavement.

Mr. Griffin's Literary Remains were collected by his brother, and published with a memoir, written with characteristic feeling and taste, by his friend Professor McVickar, in two large octavo volumes. They include his poems, several of which are in the Latin language, and written at an early age; a tour through Italy and Switzerland in 1829, with extracts from a journal of a tour through France, England, and Scotland in the years 1828, '29, and '30; extracts from lectures on Roman, Italian, and English literature; and dissertations, written while the author was a student at the Theological Seminary. These were selected from manuscripts, which, if published in full, would have filled six octavo volumes. By far the greater portion of those printed, the journals and lectures, were necessarily written in great haste, and probably without any anticipation that they were to appear in print. The journals are the simple itinerary of a traveller, making no pretensions to any further literary merit; the lectures are more elaborate performances and possess much merit; the poems are few in number.

LINES ON LEAVING ITALY.

Deh! fossi tu men bella, o almen piu forte.—*Filicaia.*

Would that thou wert more strong, at least less fair,
 Land of the orange grove and myrtle bower!
To hail whose strand, to breathe whose genial air,
 Is bliss to all who feel of bliss the power.
To look upon whose mountains in the hour
 When thy sun sinks in glory, and a veil
Of purple flows around them, would restore
The sense of beauty when all else might fail.

Would that thou wert more strong, at least less fair,
 Parent of fruits, alas! no more of men!
Where springs the olive e'en from mountains bare,
 The yellow harvest loads the scarce tilled plain,
Spontaneous shoots the vine, in rich festoon
 From tree to tree depending, and the flowers
Wreathe with their chaplets, sweet though fading soon,
 E'en fallen columns and decaying towers.

Would that thou wert more strong, at least less fair,
 Home of the beautiful, but not the brave!
Where noble form, bold outline, princely air,
 Distinguished e'en the peasant and the slave:
Where, like the goddess sprung from ocean's wave,
 Her mortal sisters boast immortal grace,
Nor spoil those charms which partial nature gave,
 By art's weak aids or fashion's vain grimace.

Would that thou wert more strong, at least less fair,
 Thou nurse of every art, save one alone,
The art of self-defence! Thy fostering care
 Brings out a nobler life from senseless stone,
And bids e'en canvass speak; thy magic tone,
 Infused in music, now constrains the soul
With tears the power of melody to own,
 And now with passionate throbs that spurn control.

Would that thou wert less fair, at least more strong,
 Grave of the mighty dead, the living mean!
Can nothing rouse ye both? no tyrant's wrong,
 No memory of the brave, of what has been?
You broken arch once spoke of triumph, then
 That mouldering wall too spoke of brave defence—
Shades of departed heroes, rise again!
 Italians, rise, and thrust the oppressors hence!

Oh, Italy! my country, fare thee well!
 For art thou not my country, at whose breast
Were nurtured those whose thoughts within me dwell,
 The fathers of my mind? whose fame impress,
E'en on my infant fancy, bade it rest
 With patriot fondness on thy hills and streams,
E'er yet thou didst receive me as a guest,
 Lovelier than I had seen thee in my dreams?

Then fare thee well, my country, loved and lost:
 Too early lost, alas! when once so dear;
I turn in sorrow from thy glorious coast,
 And urge the feet forbid to linger here.
But must I rove by Arno's current clear,
 And hear the rush of Tiber's yellow flood,
And wander on the mount, now waste and drear,
 Where Cæsar's palace in its glory stood,
And see again Parthenope's loved bay,
 And Paestum's shrines, and Baiae's classic shore,
And mount the bark, and listen to the lay
 That floats by night through Venice—never more?
Far off I seem to hear the Atlantic roar—
 It washes not thy feet, that envious sea,
But waits, with outstretched arms, to waft me o'er
 To other lands, far, far, alas! from thee.

Fare, fare thee well once more. I love thee not
 As other things inanimate. Thou art
The cherished mistress of my youth; forgot
 Thou never canst be while I have a heart.
Lanched on those waters, wild with storm and wind,
 I know not, ask not, what may be my lot;
For, torn from thee, no fear can touch my mind,
 Brooding in gloom on that one bitter thought.

JOHN HENRY HOPKINS.

John Henry Hopkins, the son of a merchant of Dublin, was born in that city January 30, 1792. He was brought by his parents to this country in 1800. After receiving a classical education at school, he passed a twelvemonth in a counting-house in Philadelphia; assisted Wilson, the ornithologist, in the preparation of the plates to the first four volumes of his work; and was afterwards engaged for several years in the manufacture of iron. Mr. Hopkins married in 1816, and in 1817 was admitted to the bar at Pittsburg. He practised with great success until November, 1823, when he abandoned the profession to enter the ministry of the Protestant Episcopal Church. After his ordination as deacon, in December,

1823, by Bishop White, by whom he was also admitted to the priesthood in 1824, he became Rector of Trinity Church, Pittsburg, where he remained until 1831, when he removed to Boston as assistant minister of Trinity Church. In October, 1832, he was consecrated the first bishop of the diocese of Vermont, and has since that time resided at Burlington.

Bishop Hopkins is the author of several volumes on the evidences of Christianity, the primitive church, and the distinctive principles of Episcopacy,* all of which exhibit research, and are written in a forcible and animated style. He has also published a number of separate sermons and pamphlets.†

WILLIAM CROSWELL.

William, the third child of the Rev. Harry Croswell,* was born at Hudson, New York, November 7, 1804, and graduated from Yale College in 1822.

W. Croswell

The next four years were passed in desultory reading and study. His preference was early formed for a clerical career, but from a distrust of his fitness for the holy office, a distrust arising solely

---

* Christianity Vindicated, in seven Discourses on the External Evidences of the New Testament, with a Dissertation. Published by Ed. Smith, Burlington, Vt., 1833.

The Primitive Creed Examined and Explained, the first part containing sixteen discourses on the Apostles' Creed, for popular use—the second part containing a dissertation on the testimony of the early councils and the fathers, with observations on certain theological errors of the present day. Published by the same, 1834.

The Primitive Church, compared with the Protestant Episcopal Church of the present day, being an examination of the ordinary objections against the church in doctrine, worship, and government, designed for popular use, with a dissertation on sundry points of theology and practice. Published by V. Harrington at Burlington, Vt., 1835. A second edition, revised and improved, was printed the following year.

Essay on Gothic Architecture, with various plans and drawings for churches, designed chiefly for the use of the clergy. Royal quarto. Published by Smith & Harrington, Burlington, 1836.

The Church of Rome in her Primitive Purity, compared with the Church of Rome at the present day, addressed to the Roman Hierarchy. 12mo. Published by V. Harrington, Burlington, 1837. Republished, with an introduction by Rev. Henry Melvill, B.D., at London, in 1839.

The Novelties which Disturb our Peace. 12mo. Published by Herman Hooker, Philadelphia, 1844.

Sixteen Lectures on the Causes, Principles, and Results of the British Reformation. Phila., 1844.

The History of the Confessional. 12mo. Published by Harper & Brothers, New York, 1850.

The End of Controversy, Controverted: a Refutation of Milner's End of Controversy, in a series of letters addressed to the Roman Archbishop of Baltimore. 2 vols. 12mo. Published by Pudney & Russell, and Stanford & Swords, New York, in 1854.

† Sermon, preached by request before the Howard Benevolent Society, Boston, 1832.

Sermon, preached by request before the Church Scholarship Society at Hartford, Conn., 1832.

Sermon, preached by request, at Burlington, on the doctrine of Atonement, 1841.

Scripture and Tradition, Sermon preached at the Ordination of Deacons, New York, 1841.

Charge to the Clergy of Vermont, 1842.

Letter to the Right Rev. F. P. Kenrick, Roman Bishop of Philadelphia, 1842.

Second Letter to the Same, 1843, of which there were two editions.

Two Discourses on the Second Advent, of which there were four editions.

Humble but Earnest Address to the Bishops, Clergy, and Laity, on the Progress of Tractarianism. Published 1846.

Pastoral Letter and Correspondence with Rev. Wm. Henry Hoit.

Sermon before the General Convention of 1847.

Sermon on Episcopal Government, preached at the consecration of Bishop Potter, of Pennsylvania, 1845.

Letter to Rev. Dr. Seabury, on Tractarianism, 1847.

Two Discourses, preached by request in the Cathedral of Quebec, on the Religious Education of the Poor. Published 1835.

Lecture on the Defect of the Principle of Religious Authority in Modern Education, delivered by request before the American Institute of Instruction, at Montpelier, about the year 1846 or 1847.

Discourse on Fraternal Unity, delivered by appointment before the Missionary Board, at the General Convention of 1850, in Cincinnati.

Address, delivered by request of the Selectmen of St. Alban's, on the death of General Taylor, President of the United States, 1850.

Address, by request, before the Prot. Ep. Historical Society, New York, 1851.

Lecture on Slavery—its religious sanction, its political dangers, and the best method of doing it away, delivered before the Young Men's Associations of Buffalo and Lockport. Published by request, Phinney & Co., Buffalo, 1851.

Discourse, preached by request, in aid of the Fund for the Widows and Orphans of Deceased Clergymen. Boston, 1851.

The Case of the Rev. Mr. Gorham against the Bishop of Exeter considered, 1849.

Pastoral Letter on the Support of the Clergy, 1852.

Ditto, on the same subject, 1854.

Defence of the Constitution of the Diocese of Vermont, 1854.

Tract for the Church in Jerusalem, 1854.

The True Principles of Restoration to the Episcopal Office, in relation to the case of Right Rev. Henry U. Onderdonk, D.D., 1854.

Address, delivered by request before the House of Convocation of Trinity College, Hartford, Conn., 1854.

Discourse, by request, on the Historical Evidences of Christianity, at St. Andrew's Church, Philadelphia. Published 1854.

* Harry Croswell was in the early part of his life a prominent political editor of the Federal party. He commenced his career in The Balance, a paper published at Hudson, New York, which divided the honors with the Farmer's Museum at Walpole, as one of the first literary journals of the country. Mr. Croswell was associated in this enterprise with Ezra Sampson, a clergyman by education, who came to Hudson to officiate in the Presbyterian church of the village, but from lack of effectiveness as a public speaker retired from the pulpit. He subsequently gained a wide popular reputation as the author of a series of essays, with the title of The Brief Remarker, which were collected from the columns of the Hartford Courant, and printed in a volume. The collection was republished in 1855 by D. Appleton & Co. The essays it contains are briefly written compositions, and are in a vein of practical common sense. Mr. Sampson was also the author of *The Beauties of the Bible*, a selection of passages from the sacred volume, and of an *Historical Dictionary*.

Mr. Croswell wrote his editorials with vigor, and, in accordance with the prevailing spirit of the press at that time, spoke with great bitterness of his political opponents. An article published in the Wasp, a journal also under his direction, on Jefferson, led to a libel suit, and the celebrated trial in which Hamilton, in defence of the editor, made his last forensic effort.

Mr. Croswell afterwards removed to Albany, where he established a Federal paper. He was here prosecuted for a libel on Mr. Southwick, a leading democratic editor, who recovered damages. Mr. Croswell called on his political friends to enable him to meet the pecuniary requirements of their service, and on their refusal to do so retired from editorial life, and a few months after entered the ministry of the Episcopal Church.

from the modesty which characterized him through life, it was not until 1826 that he finally decided to enter the ministry. He commenced his preparatory studies at the General Theological Seminary in New York, where, owing to ill health, he remained but a short time. After passing a brief period at New Haven he went to Hartford, where he edited, with Mr. now Bishop Doane, a religious newspaper, The Episcopal Watchman. He commenced his poetical career in the columns of this journal with a number of sonnets and short poems, which were much admired and widely copied. At the end of the second year of their joint editorship Mr. Doane removed to Boston to become the rector of Trinity church, and Mr. Croswell retired to devote himself exclusively to his studies.

In 1828 he was ordained deacon by Bishop Brownell of Connecticut. He has described the emotions of this solemn event in one of the most beautiful of his compositions:—

THE ORDINAL.

Alas, for me, could I forget
  The memory of that day
Which fills my waking thoughts, nor yet
  E'en sleep can take away;
In dreams I still renew the rites
  Whose strong but mystic chain
The spirit to its God unites,
  And none can part again.

How oft the Bishop's form I see,
  And hear that thrilling tone
Demanding, with authority,
  The heart for God alone!
Again I kneel as then I knelt,
  While he above me stands,
And seem to feel as then I felt
  The pressure of his hands.

Again the priests, in meek array,
  As my weak spirit fails,
Beside me bend them down to pray
  Before the chancel rails;
As then, the sacramental host
  Of God's elect are by,
When many a voice its utterance lost,
  And tears dimmed many an eye.

As then they on my vision rose,
  The vaulted aisles I see,
And desk and cushioned book repose
  In solemn sanctity;
The mitre o'er the marble niche,
  The broken crook and key,
That from a Bishop's tomb shone rich
  With polished tracery;

The hangings, the baptismal font,—
  All, all, save me, unchanged,—
The holy table, as was wont,
  With decency arranged;
The linen cloth, the plate, the cup,
  Beneath their covering shine,
Ere priestly hands are lifted up
  To bless the bread and wine.

The solemn ceremonial past,
  And I am set apart
To serve the Lord, from first to last,
  With undivided heart.
And I have sworn, with pledges dire,
  Which God and man have heard,
To speak the holy truth entire
  In action and in word.

O Thou, who in Thy holy place
  Hast set Thine orders three,
Grant me, Thy meanest servant, grace
  To win a good degree;
That so, replenished from above,
  And in my office tried,
Thou mayst be honored, and in love
  Thy Church be edified.

In 1829 Mr. Croswell was admitted to the priesthood, and became rector of Christ church, an ancient edifice in the vicinity of Copp's Hill burial-ground, Boston. He continued his poetical contributions, which were almost exclusively on topics connected with church ordinances, or the duties and affections of Christian life. A portion of these were collected and appended by Bishop Doane to the first American edition of Keble's Christian Year.

In 1840 Mr. Croswell resigned the rectorship of Christ's, and accepted that of St. Peter's church, Auburn. He remained in this parish for four years, and during that period married, and became the father of a daughter.

In 1844 he returned to Boston to take the rectorship of a new parish, in process of formation by a number of Episcopalians and distinguished men of that city, among whom may be mentioned Mr. Richard H. Dana and his son, on the principle of a rigid adherence to the rubrics of the prayer-book in its worship, an enlarged system of parochial charity, and a provision by collections and subscriptions in the place of pew rents for the support of the rector, leaving the seats of the church free to all comers. An upper room was fitted up in an appropriate manner, and on the first Sunday in Advent, 1844, the new rector commenced the services of the parish, which, from this commencement, took the name of the Church of the Advent. Morning and evening prayer was henceforward continued every day of the year.

In conducting divine service, the rector, during the mutual acts of prayer and praise turned in the same direction with, instead of, as usual, facing the other worshippers, and preached in the surplice instead of changing it for a black gown. These practices gave great offence to the bishop of the diocese, Dr. Eastburn, who at the close of his first confirmation service in the church, expressed his disapprobation, coupled with a censure of a gilt cross placed over the communion table. This was followed in a few days by an official letter to the same effect addressed to the diocese by the bishop. Dr. Croswell, believing himself unjustly censured, responded in a letter, citing authorities from the primitive and subsequent ages of the church in defence of his plan. He also complained of the bishop for uncanonical conduct in publicly censuring a presbyter without giving the opportunity of defence by means of a trial. Both parties believing themselves in the right, no accommodation was made of the matter; the bishop refused to visit the church unless the practices he objected to were discontinued, and the parish held their course. In consequence of this, candidates for confirmation were obliged, accompanied by their rector, to resort to other churches to receive the rite. In spite of this unhappy difficulty the parish prospered. The rector was indefatigable in the discharge of the duties of charity, sallying forth at all hours and in all weathers to relieve the poor and needy, visit and comfort the sick and dying. During sea-ons of pestilence he remained in the city, continuing his church services as usual and redoubling his care of the sick, with the energy and devotion required by the crisis.

Such a career soon won its just meed of boundless honor and love from all who came within its sphere. It was, however, destined to be as brief as beautiful.

Seven years had thus passed from his arrival at Boston to become rector of the Church of the Advent, and the upper room had been exchanged for an edifice purchased from a congregation of another denomination, possessing no architectural beauty, but spacious and commodious, when in the delivery of a sermon to the children of the congregation at the afternoon service of Sunday, November 9, 1851, the rector's voice was observed to falter. He brought his discourse to an abrupt close, and gave out the first stanza of the hymn—

Soldiers of Christ, arise
  And put your armor on,
Strong in the strength which Christ supplies,
  Through his eternal Son.

This he announced instead of the lxxxviii., as the clxxxviii., which contains the following stanza:—

Determined are the days that fly
  Successive o'er thy head;
The numbered hour is on the wing
  That lays thee with the dead.

The choir, however, following directions previously given, sang the former. At its conclusion he knelt in his ordinary place at the chancel-rail, and said from memory, his book having dropped from his hand, a collect. He then, still kneeling, in place of as usual standing and facing the congregation, delivered, in a faltering voice, the closing benediction. A portion of the auditory went to his assistance, and bore him helpless to the vestry-room and in a carriage to his home. He was conscious, but unable to speak distinctly, and uttered but a few words. Apprised by his physicians of his imminent danger he closed his eyes as if in slumber. His friend, the Rev. Dr. Eaton, was soon by his bedside, and finding him unable to speak, and apparently unconscious, took his hand, and offered the "commendatory prayer for a sick person at the point of departure," provided by the Book of Common-Prayer. "As the word, amen, was pronounced by the venerable priest, the last breath was perceived to pass, gently, quietly, and without a struggle."

The beautiful harmony of the death with the life of Dr. Croswell, combined with the respect felt for his talents and example, called forth many expressions of sympathy with his bereaved family and congregation. At his funeral his body was carried from his house to the church by eight of his parishioners, and accompanied by a committee of wardens and vestrymen to the cemetery at New Haven, where it was buried, in conformity with the wishes of the deceased, "deep in the ground." The affecting scene of the ninth of November is commemorated regularly on the annual recurrence of the day by an appropriate sermon.

In 1853 a biography of Dr. Croswell, by his father, was published in one octavo volume. It contains, in addition to selections from his correspondence, a collection of his poems, scattered through the narrative in the order in which they were written, and in connexion with the events by which they were, in some cases, occasioned. These poems were never collected by their author, and have not appeared in a separate collective form since his death. Notwithstanding that their religious as well as poetic beauty demand their issue in a cheap, popular form, we should almost regret their severance from the connexion in which a wise and loving parental hand has placed them. As we meet them in turning over the pages of the biography they seem to us like the beautiful carvings, the string-courses, corbels, pendants, brackets, niches, and tabernacle work of a Christian cathedral, adorning and strengthening the solid fabric, while placing the ornamental in due subordination to the useful.

Although Dr. Croswell's poems were almost exclusively on topics suggested by the memorial seasons and observances of hallowed Christian usage or devoted to friendship, he occasionally wrote in a playful vein. His New Year's verses in the Argus for 1842, "From the Desk of Poor Richard, Jr.," are a clever reproduction with improvements of his own of that sage's maxims.

Poor Richard knows full well distress
  Is real, and no dream;
And yet life's bitterest ills have less
  Of bitter than they seem.
Meet like a man thy coward pains,
  And some, be sure, will flee;
Nor doubt the worst of what remains
  Will blessings prove to thee.

In 1848 he was called upon to deliver a Commencement poem at Trinity College. The poem may be said, in the language of his biographer, "to be a metrical essay on the reverence due to sacred places and holy things, and an exhortation to the cultivation of such reverence, especially in the church and its academical institutions." He reverts to his Alma Mater, Yale, with this allusion to its patron Berkeley.

There first we gazed on the serene expanse
Of Berkeley's bright and heavenly countenance,
And could not but contrast it, in our sport,
With thy pinched visage, prick-eared Davenport;
Nor queried, as we turned to either face,
Which were the real genius of the place.
Taught, in a brother's words, to love in thee
"Earth's every virtue, wit in poesy;"
O Berkeley, as I read, with moistened eyes,
Of thy sublime but blasted enterprise,
Refusing, in thy pure, unselfish aim,
To sell to vulgar wealth a founder's fame,
But in thy fervor sacrificing all
To objects worthy of the name of Paul,—
What joy to see in our official line
A faith revived, identical with thine;
Pledged to fulfil the spirit of thy scheme,
And prove thy college no ideal dream.
And when, on yonder walls, we now survey
The man "whose grace chalked his successor's way,"
And study, Samuel, thy majestic head,
By Berkeley's son to heaven's anointing led,
And see the ways of Providence combine
The gentle bishop with the masculine,
We pray this noblest offspring of thy see
May honor Berkeley, nor dishonor thee.

In his ideal picture of a university, he pays a tribute to several living authors.

Thus in the morning, far from Babel's dust,
These August days might yet be days august,
And words of power the place might glorify,
Which willingly the world would not let die.
There Dana might, in happiest mood, rehearse
Some last great effort of his deathless verse;
Or Irving, like Arcadian, might beguile
The golden hours with his melodious style;
Or he who takes no second living rank
Among the classics of the Church—Verplanck;
Or he whose course "right onward" here begun,
Now sheds its brightness over Burlington,
(Where our young sons like noble saplings grow,
And daughters like the polished pillars show,)
And with the elder worthies, join the throng
Of young adventurers for the prize of song.

TO MY FATHER.

My father, I recall the dream
Of childish joy and wonder,
When thou wast young as I now seem,
Say, thirty-three, or under;
When on thy temples, as on mine,
Time just began to sprinkle
His first grey hairs, and traced the sign
Of many a coming wrinkle.

I recognise thy voice's tone
As to myself I'm talking;
And this firm tread, how like thine own,
In thought, the study walking!
As, musing, to and fro I pass,
A glance across my shoulder
Would bring thine image in the glass,
Were it a trifle older.

My father, proud am I to bear
Thy face, thy form, thy stature,
But happier far might I but share
More of thy better nature;
Thy patient progress after good,
All obstacles disdaining,
Thy courage, faith, and fortitude,
And spirit uncomplaining.

Then for the day that I was born
Well might I joy, and borrow
No longer of the coming morn
Its trouble or its sorrow;
Content I'd be to take my chance
In either world, possessing
For my complete inheritance
Thy virtues and thy blessing!

NATURE AND REVELATION.

I wandered by the burying-place,
And sorely there I wept,
To think how many of my friends
Within its mansions slept;
And, wrung with bitter grief, I cried
Aloud in my despair,
"Where, dear companions, have ye fled?"
And Echo answered, "Where?"

While Nature's voice thus flouted me,
A voice from heaven replied,
"O, weep not for the happy dead
Who in the Lord have died;
Sweet is their rest who sleep in Christ,
Though lost a while to thee;
Tread in their steps, and sweeter still
Your meeting hour shall be!"

THIS ALSO SHALL PASS AWAY.

When morning sunbeams round me shed
Their light and influence blest,
When flowery paths before me spread,
And life in smiles is drest;
In darkling lines that dim each ray
I read, "This, too, shall pass away."

When murky clouds o'erhang the sky,
Far down the vale of years,
And vainly looks the tearful eye,
When not a hope appears,
Lo, characters of glory play
'Mid shades: "This, too, shall pass away."

Blest words, that temper pleasure's beam,
And lighten sorrow's gloom,
That early sadden youth's bright dream,
And cheer the old man's tomb.
Unto that world be ye my stay,
That world which shall not pass away.

PSALM CXXXVII.

By the waters of Babel we sat down and wept,
As we called our dear Zion to mind;
And our harps that in joy we so often had swept
Now sighed on the trees to the wind.

Then they that had carried us captive away,
In mockery challenged a song,
And ringing out mirth from our sadness, would say,
"Sing the strains that to Zion belong."

O, how shall we sing the ineffable song
In a godless and barbarous land!
If the minstrels of Salem could do her such wrong,
Be palsied each cunning right hand.

Let my tongue to the roof of my mouth ever cling,
If aught else should its praises employ,
Or if Salem's high glories it choose not to sing,
Above all terrestrial joy.

Remember the children of Edom, O Lord,
How they cried, in Jerusalem's woe,
Her ramparts and battlements raze with the sword,
Her temples and towers overthrow.

O daughter of Babel! thy ruin makes haste;
And blessed be he who devours
Thy children with famine and misery waste,
As thou, in thy rapine, served ours.

A SUNDAY-SCHOOL HYMN.

The sparrow finds a house,
The little bird a nest;
Deep in thy dwelling, Lord, they come,
And fold their young to rest.
And shall we be afraid
Our little ones to bring
Within thine ancient altar's shade,
And underneath thy wing?

There guard them as thine eye,
There keep them without spot,
That when the spoiler passeth by
Destruction touch them not.
There nerve their souls with might,
There nurse them with thy love,
There plume them for their final flight
To blessedness above.

HYMN FOR ADVENT.

While the darkness yet hovers,
The harbinger star
Peeps through and discovers
The dawn from afar;
To many an aching
And watch-wearied eye,

The dayspring is breaking
  Once more from on high.

With lamps trimmed and burning
  The Church on her way
To meet thy returning,
  O bright King of day!
Goes forth and rejoices,
  Exulting and free,
And sends from all voices
  Hosannas to thee.

She casts off her sorrows,
  To rise and to shine
With the lustre she borrows,
  O Saviour! from thine.
Look down, for thine honor,
  O Lord! and increase
In thy mercy upon her
  The blessing of peace.

Her children with trembling
  Await, but not fear,
Till the time of assembling
  Before thee draws near;
When, freed from all sadness,
  And sorrow, and pain,
They shall meet thee in gladness
  And glory again.

DE PROFUNDIS.

"There may be a cloud without a rainbow, but there cannot be a rainbow without a cloud."

My soul was dark
But for the golden light and rainbow hue,
That, sweeping heaven with their triumphal arc
Break on the view.

Enough to feel
That God indeed is good. Enough to know,
Without the gloomy cloud, he could reveal
No beauteous bow.

TRAVELLER'S HYMN.

"In journeyings often."

Lord! go with us, and we go
  Safely through the weariest length,
Travelling, if thou will'st it so,
  In the greatness of thy strength;
Through the day and through the dark,
  O'er the land, and o'er the sea,
Speed the wheel, and steer the bark,
  Bring us where we feign would be.

In the self-controlling car,
  'Mid the engine's iron din,
Waging elemental war,
  Flood without, and flood within,
Through the day, and through the dark,
  O'er the land, and o'er the sea,
Speed the wheel, and steer the bark,
  Bring us where we fain would be.

HORACE BUSHNELL.

THIS eminent thinker and divine is a native of Connecticut, born about the year 1804, in New Preston, in the town of Washington, Litchfield county. He was, as a boy, employed in a fulling-mill in his native village. He became a graduate of Yale in 1827. After this he was engaged for a while as a literary editor of the Journal of Commerce, at New York. He was, from 1829 to 1831, a tutor in Yale College; and, at this time, applied himself to the study of law, and afterwards of theology. In May, 1833, he was called to his present post of ministerial duty, as pastor of the North Congregational Church, in Hartford. He early became a contributor to the

Horace Bushnell

higher religious periodicals. In 1837, he delivered the Phi Beta Kappa oration at New Haven, *On the Principles of National Greatness.* His series of theological publications commenced in 1847, with his volume, *Views of Christian Nurture, and of Subjects adjacent thereto.* In this he presents his views of the spiritual economy of revivals, in which he marks out the philosophical limitations to a system which had been carried to excess. The "Organic Unity of the Family" is another chapter of this work, which shows the author's happy method of surrounding and penetrating a subject. This was followed, in 1849, by his book entitled *God in Christ—Three Discourses, delivered at New Haven, Cambridge, and Andover, with a Preliminary Dissertation on Language.* The view of the doctrine of the Trinity set forth in this book, met with discussion on all sides, and much opposition from some of the author's Congregational brethren, and was the means of bringing him before the Ministerial Association, with which he is connected. The argument was a metaphysical one, and pursued by Dr. Bushnell with his customary acumen. The main points of defence were presented to the public in 1851, in a new volume, *Christ in Theology; being the Answer of the Author before the Hartford Central Association of Ministers, October, 1849, for the Doctrines of the Book entitled God in Christ.* As an indication of the material with which Dr. Bushnell has to deal in these discourses, the enumeration of the elements of theological opinion may be cited from the Preface to this volume. "To see brought up," he writes, "in distinct array before us the multitudes of leaders and schools, and theologic wars of only the century past,—the Supralapsarians and Sublapsarians; the Arminianizers and the true Calvinists; the Pelagians and Augustinians; the Tasters and the Exercisers; Exercisers by Divine Efficiency and by Human Self-Efficiency; the love-to-being-in-general virtue, the willing-to-be-damned virtue, and the love-to-one's-greatest-happiness virtue; no ability, all ability, and moral and natural ability distinguished; disciples by the new-creating act of Omnipotence, and by change of the governing purpose; atonement by punishment and by expression; limited and general; by imputation and without imputation; Trinitarians of a three-fold distinction, of three psychologic persons, or of three sets of attributes; under a unity of oneness, or of necessary agreement, or of society and deliberative council;—nothing, I think, would more certainly disenchant us of our confidence in systematic orthodoxy and the possibility, in human language, of an exact theologic science, than an exposition so practical and serious, and withal so indisputably mournful, so mournfully indisputable." The remaining theological writings of Dr. Bushnell are included in his contributions to the Reviews.*

In another department of composition, that of the philosophical essay, mingling subtle and refined speculation with the affairs of every-day life, he has achieved distinguished success, in a manner peculiarly his own. With this class of his writings may be included a review of Brigham's Influence of Religion on Health in the Christian Spectator (viii. 51); an article on Taste and Fashion, in the New Englander, 1848; a Discourse before the Alumni of Yale College, 1843, on *The Moral Tendencies and Results of Human History*; an address before the Hartford County Agricultural Society, 1846; *Work and Play*, an oration before the Phi Beta Kappa, at Cambridge, 1848: and several special sermons, which have been printed, entitled *Unconscious Influence; the Day of Roads*—tracing the progress of civilization by the great national highways; a similar discourse, *The Northern Iron; Barbarism the First Danger*, in allusion to emigration; *Religious Music*; and *Politics under the Law of God*. In 1849, Dr. Bushnell pronounced an oration, *The Fathers of New England*, before the New England Society of New York; and, in 1851, *Speech for Connecticut, being an Historical Estimate of the State, delivered before, and printed by, the Legislature.*

PLAY, A LIFE OF FREEDOM.†

Thus it is that work prepares the state of play. Passing over now to this latter, observe the intense longing of the race for some such higher and freer state of being. They call it by no name. Probably most of them have but dimly conceived what they are after. The more evident will it be that they are after this, when we find them covering over the whole ground of life, and filling up the contents of history, with their counterfeits or misconceived attempts. If the hidden fire is seen bursting up on every side, to vent itself in flame, we may certainly know that the ground is full.

Let it not surprise you, if I name, as a first illustration here, the general devotion of our race to money. This passion for money is allowed to be a sordid passion,—one that is rankest in the least generous and most selfish of mankind; and yet a conviction has always been felt, that it must have its heat in the most central fires and divinest affinities of our nature. Thus, the poet calls it the *auri sacra fames*,—*sacra*, as being a curse, and that in the divine life of the race. Childhood being passed, and the play-fund of motion so far spent that running on foot no longer appears to be the joy it was, the older child, now called a man, fancies that it will make him happy to ride! Or he imagines, which is much the same, some loftier state of being, —call it rest, retirement, competence, independence, —no matter by what name, only be it a condition of use, ease, liberty, and pure enjoyment. And so we find the whole race at work to get rid of work; drudging themselves to-day, in the hope of play to-morrow. This is that *sacra fames*, which, misconceiving its own unutterable longings after spiritual play, proposes to itself the dull felicity of cessation, and drives the world to madness in pursuit of a counterfeit, which it is work to obtain, work also to keep, and yet harder work oftentimes to enjoy.

Here, too, is the secret of that profound passion for the drama, which has been so conspicuous in the cultivated nations. We love to see life in its feeling and activity, separated from its labors and historic results. Could we see all human changes transpire poetically or creatively, that is, in play, letting our soul play with them as they pass, then it were only poetry to live. Then to admire, love, laugh,—then to abhor, pity, weep,—all were alike grateful to us; for the view of suffering separated from all reality, save what it has to feeling, only yields a painful joy, which is the deeper joy because of the pain. Hence the written drama, offering to view in its impersonations a life one side of life, a life in which all the actings appear without the ends and simply as in play, becomes to the cultivated reader a spring of the intensest and most captivating spiritual incitement. He beholds the creative genius of a man playing out impersonated groups and societies of men, clothing each with life, passion, individuality, and character, by the fertile activity of his own inspired feeling. Meantime the writer himself is hidden, and cannot even suggest his existence. Hence egotism, which also is a form of work, the dullest, most insipid, least inspiring of all human demonstrations, is nowhere allowed to obtrude itself. As a reader, too, he has no ends to think of or to fear,—nothing to do, but to play the characters into his feeling as creatures existing for his sake. In this view, the drama, as a product of genius, is, within a certain narrow limit, the realization of play.

But far less effectively, or more faintly, when it is acted. Then the counterfeit, as it is more remote, is more feeble. In the reading we invent our own sceneries, clothe into form and expression each one of the characters, and play out our own liberty in them as freely, and sometimes as divinely, as they. Whatever reader, therefore, has a soul of true life and fire within him, finds all expectation balked, when he becomes an auditor and spectator. The scenery is tawdry and flat, the characters, definitely measured, have lost their infinity, so to speak, and thus their freedom, and what before was play descends to nothing better or more inspired than work. It is called going to the play, but it should rather be called going to the work, that is, to see a play worked, (yes, an *opera!* that is it!)—men and women inspired through their memory, and acting their inspirations by rote, panting into love, pumping at the fountains of grief, whipping out the passions into fury, and dying to fulfil the contract of the evening, by a forced holding of the breath. And yet this feeble counterfeit of play, which some of us would call only "very tragical mirth," has a power to the multitude. They are moved, thrilled it may be, with a strange delight. It is as if a something in their nature, higher than they themselves know, were quickened into power, —namely, that divine instinct of play, in which the summit of our nature is most clearly revealed.

In like manner, the passion of our race for war, and the eager admiration yielded to warlike exploits, are resolvable principally into the same fundamental cause. Mere ends and uses do not satisfy us. We must get above prudence and economy, into something that partakes of inspiration, be the cost what it may. Hence war, another and yet more magnificent counterfeit of play. Thus there is a great and lofty virtue that we call

* Articles: Review of "The Errors of the Times," a charge by the Rt. Rev. T. C. Brownell, Bishop of the Diocese of Connecticut: New Englander, vol. ii., 1844. Evangelical Alliance: Ib. v. 1847. Christian Comprehensiveness: Ib. vi. 1848. The Christian Trinity, a Practical Truth: Ib. xii. 1854.

In 1847, Dr. Bushnell addressed a "Letter to the Pope," which was printed in London.

† From the Phi Beta Kappa Oration, 1848.

courage (*cour-age*), taking our name from the heart. It is the greatness of a great heart, the repose and confidence of a man whose soul is rested in truth and principle. Such a man has no ends ulterior to his duty,—duty itself is his end. He is in it therefore as in play, lives it as an inspiration. Lifted thus out of mere prudence and contrivance, he is also lifted above fear. Life to him is the outgoing of his great heart (*heart-age*), action from the heart. And because he now can die, without being shaken or perturbed by any of the dastardly feelings that belong to self-seeking and work, because he partakes of the impassibility of his principles, we call him a hero, regarding him as a kind of god, a man who has gone up into the sphere of the divine.

Then, since courage is a joy so high, a virtue of so great majesty, what could happen but that many will covet both the internal exaltation and the outward repute of it? Thus comes bravery, which is the counterfeit, or mock virtue. Courage is of the heart, as we have said; bravery is of the will. One is the spontaneous joy and repose of a truly great soul; the other, bravery, is after an end ulterior to itself, and, in that view, is but a form of work,—about the hardest work, too, I fancy, that some men undertake. What can be harder, in fact, than to act a great heart, when one has nothing but a will wherewith to do it?

Thus you will see that courage is above danger, bravery in it, doing battle on a level with it. One is secure and tranquil, the other suppresses agitation or conceals it. A right mind fortifies one, shame stimulates the other. Faith is the nerve of one, risk the plague and tremor of the other. For if I may tell you just here a very important secret, there be many that are called heroes who are yet without courage. They brave danger by their will, when their heart trembles. They make up in violence what they want in tranquillity, and drown the tumult of their fears in the rage of their passions. Enter the heart and you shall find, too often, a dastard spirit lurking in your hero. Call him still a brave man, if you will, only remember that he lacks courage.

No, the true hero is the great, wise man of duty, —he whose soul is armed by truth and supported by the smile of God,—he who meets life's perils with a cautious but tranquil spirit, gathers strength by facing its storms, and dies, if he is called to die, as a Christian victor at the post of duty. And if we must have heroes, and wars wherein to make them, there is no so brilliant war as a war with wrong, no hero so fit to be sung as he who has gained the bloodless victory of truth and mercy.

But if bravery be not the same as courage, still it is a very imposing and plausible counterfeit. The man himself is told, after the occasion is past, how heroically he bore himself, and when once his nerves have become tranquillized, he begins even to believe it. And since we cannot stay content in the dull, uninspired world of economy and work, we are as ready to see a hero as he to be one. Nay, we must have our heroes, as I just said, and we are ready to harness ourselves, by the million, to any man who will let us fight him out the name. Thus we find out occasions for war,—wrongs to be redressed, revenges to be taken, such as we may feign inspiration and play the great heart under. We collect armies, and dress up leaders in gold and high colors, meaning, by the brave look, to inspire some notion of a hero beforehand. Then we set the men in phalanxes and squadrons, where the personality itself is taken away, and a vast impersonal person called an army, a magnanimous and brave monster, is all that remains. The masses of fierce color, the glitter of steel, the dancing plumes, the waving flags, the deep throb of the music lifting every foot,—under these the living acres of men, possessed by the one thought of playing brave today, are rolled on to battle. Thunder, fire, dust, blood, groans,—what of these?—nobody thinks of these, for nobody dares to think till the day is over, and then the world rejoices to behold a new batch of heroes!

And this is the devil's play, that we call war. We have had it going on ever since the old geologic era was finished. We are sick enough of the matter of it. We understand well enough that it is not good economy. But we cannot live on work. We must have courage, inspiration, greatness, play. Even the moral of our nature, that which is to weave us into social union with our kind before God, is itself thirsting after play; and if we cannot have it in good, why then let us have it in as good as we can. It is at least some comfort, that we do not mean quite as badly in these wars as some men say. We are not in love with murder, we are not simple tigers in feeling, and some of us come out of battle with kind and gentle qualities left. We only must have our play.

Note also this, that, since the metaphysics of fighting have been investigated, we have learned to make much of what we call the *moral* of the army; by which we mean the feeling that wants to play brave. Only it is a little sad to remember that this same moral, as it is called, is the true, eternal, moral nature of the man thus terribly perverted,—that which was designed to link him to his God and his kind, and ought to be the spring of his immortal inspirations.

There has been much of speculation among the learned concerning the origin of chivalry; nor has it always been clear to what human elements this singular institution is to be referred. But when we look on man, not as a creature of mere understanding and reason, but as a creature also of play, essentially a poet in that which constitutes his higher life, we seem to have a solution of the origin of chivalry, which is sufficient, whether it be true or not. In the forswearing of labor, in the brave adventures of a life in arms, in the intense ideal devotion to woman as her protector and avenger, in the self-renouncing and almost self-oblivious worship of honor,—what do we see in these but the mock moral doings of a creature who is to escape self-love and the service of ends in a free, spontaneous life of goodness,—in whom courage, delicacy, honor, disinterested deeds, are themselves to be the inspiration, as they are the end, of his being!

I might also show, passing into the sphere of religion, how legal obedience, which is work, always descends into superstition, and thus that religion must, in its very nature and life, be a form of play, —a worship offered, a devotion paid, not for some ulterior end, but as being its own end and joy. I might also show, in the same manner, that all the enthusiastic, fanatical, and properly quietistic modes of religion are as many distinct counterfeits, and, in that manner, illustrations of my subject. But this you will see at a glance, without illustration. Only observe how vast a field our illustrations cover. In the infatuated zeal of our race for the acquisition of money, in the drama, in war, in chivalry, in perverted religion,—in all these forms, covering almost the whole ground of humanity with counterfeits of play, that are themselves the deepest movements of the race, I show you the boundless sweep of this divine instinct, and how surely we may know that the perfected state of man is a state of beauty, truth, and love, where life is its own end and joy.

GEORGE DENISON PRENTICE,

The editor of the Louisville Journal, is a native of Connecticut, born at Preston, New London county, December 18, 1802. He was educated at Brown University, studied law but did not engage in the profession, preferring the pursuits of editorial life. In 1828 he commenced the *New England Weekly Review* at Hartford, a well conducted and well supported journal of a literary character, which he carried on for two years, when, resigning its management to Mr. Whittier, he removed to the West, established himself in Kentucky at Louisville, and shortly became editor of the "Journal," a daily paper in that city. In his hands it has become one of the most widely known and esteemed newspapers in the country; distinguished by its fidelity to Whig politics, and its earnest, able editorials, no less than by the lighter skirmishing of wit and satire. The "Prenticeiana" of the editor are famous. If collected and published with appropriate notes these *mots* would form an amusing and instructive commentary on the management of elections, newspaper literature, and political oratory, of permanent value as a memorial of the times.

The Louisville Journal has always been a supporter of the cause of education and of the literary interest in the West. It has hence become, in accordance with the known tastes of the editor, a favorite avenue of young poets to the public. Several of the most successful lady writers of the West have first become known through their contributions to the "Journal."

Mr. Prentice's own poetical writings are numerous. Many of them first appeared in the author's "Review" at Hartford. A number have been collected by Mr. Everest in the "Poets of Connecticut." They are in a serious vein, chiefly expressions of sentiment and the domestic affections. Our specimen is taken from Mr. Gallagher's "Selections from the Poetical Literature of the West."

THE FLIGHT OF YEARS.

Gone! gone for ever!—like a rushing wave
Another year has burst upon the shore
Of earthly being—and its last low tones,
Wandering in broken accents on the air,
Are dying to an echo.

The gay Spring,
With its young charms, has gone—gone with its leaves—
Its atmosphere of roses—its white clouds
Slumbering like seraphs in the air—its birds
Telling their loves in music—and its streams
Leaping and shouting from the up-piled rocks
To make earth echo with the joy of waves.
And Summer, with its dews and showers, has gone—
Its rainbows glowing on the distant cloud
Like Spirits of the Storm—its peaceful lakes
Smiling in their sweet sleep, as if their dreams
Were of the opening flowers and budding trees
And overhanging sky—and its bright mists
Resting upon the mountain-tops, as crowns
Upon the heads of giants. Autumn too
Has gone, with all its deeper glories—gone
With its green hills like altars of the world
Lifting their rich fruit-offerings to their God—
Its cool winds straying 'mid the forest aisles
To wake their thousand wind-harps—its serene
And holy sunsets hanging o'er the West
Like banners from the battlements of Heaven—
And its still evenings, when the moonlit sea
Was ever throbbing, like the living heart
Of the great Universe. Ay—these are now
But sounds and visions of the past—their deep,
Wild beauty has departed from the Earth,
And they are gathered to the embrace of Death,
Their solemn herald to Eternity.

Nor have they gone alone. High human hearts
Of Passion have gone with them. The fresh dust
Is chill on many a breast, that burned erewhile
With fires that seemed immortal. Joys, that leaped
Like angels from the heart, and wandered free
In life's young morn to look upon the flowers,
The poetry of nature, and to list
The woven sounds of breeze, and bird, and stream,
Upon the night-air, have been stricken down
In silence to the dust. Exultant Hope,
That roved for ever on the buoyant winds
Like the bright, starry bird of Paradise,
And chaunted to the ever-listening heart
In the wild music of a thousand tongues,
Or soared into the open sky, until
Night's burning gems seemed jewelled on her brow,
Has shut her drooping wing, and made her home
Within the voiceless sepulchre. And Love,
That knelt at Passion's holiest shrine, and gazed
On his heart's idol as on some sweet star,
Whose purity and distance make it dear,
And dreamed of ecstasies, until his soul
Seemed but a lyre, that wakened in the glance
Of the beloved one—he too has gone
To his eternal resting-place. And where
Is stern Ambition—he who madly grasped
At Glory's fleeting phantom—he who sought
His fame upon the battle-field, and longed
To make his throne a pyramid of bones
Amid a sea of blood? He too has gone!
His stormy voice is mute—his mighty arm
Is nerveless on its clod—his very name
Is but a meteor of the night of years
Whose gleams flashed out a moment o'er the Earth,
And faded into nothingness. The dream
Of high devotion—beauty's bright array—
And life's deep idol memories—all have passed
Like the cloud-shadows on a starlight stream,
Or a soft strain of music, when the winds
Are slumbering on the billow.

Yet, why muse
Upon the past with sorrow? Though the year
Has gone to blend with the mysterious tide
Of old Eternity, and borne along
Upon its heaving breast a thousand wrecks
Of glory and of beauty—yet, why mourn
That such is destiny? Another year
Succeedeth to the past—in their bright round
The seasons come and go—the same blue arch,
That hath hung o'er us, will hang o'er us yet—
The same pure stars that we have loved to watch,
Will blossom still at twilight's gentle hour
Like lilies on the tomb of Day—and still
Man will remain, to dream as he hath dreamed,
And mark the earth with passion. Love will spring
From the lone tomb of old Affections—Hope
And Joy and great Ambition, will rise up
As they have risen—and their deeds will be
Brighter than those engraven on the scroll
Of parted centuries. Even now the sea
Of coming years, beneath whose mighty waves
Life's great events are heaving into birth,
Is tossing to and fro, as if the winds
Of heaven were prisoned in its soundless depths
And struggling to be free.

Weep not, that Time
Is passing on—it will ere long reveal
A brighter era to the nations. Hark!
Along the vales and mountains of the earth
There is a deep, portentous murmuring,
Like the swift rush of subterranean streams,
Or like the mingled sounds of earth and air,
When the fierce Tempest, with sonorous wing,
Heaves his deep folds upon the rushing winds,
And hurries onward with his night of clouds
Against the eternal mountains. 'Tis the voice
Of infant FREEDOM—and her stirring call
Is heard and answered in a thousand tones
From every hill-top of her western home—
And lo—it breaks across old Ocean's flood—
And "FREEDOM! FREEDOM! is the answering shout
Of nations starting from the spell of years.
The day-spring!—see—'tis brightening in the heavens!
The watchmen of the night have caught the sign—
From tower to tower the signal-fires flash free—
And the deep watch-word, like the rush of seas
That heralds the volcano's bursting flame,
Is sounding o'er the earth. Bright years of hope
And life are on the wing!—Yon glorious bow
Of Freedom, bended by the hand of God,
Is spanning Time's dark surges. Its high Arch,
A type of Love and Mercy on the cloud,
Tells, that the many storms of human life
Will pass in silence, and the sinking waves,
Gathering the forms of glory and of peace,
Reflect the undimmed brightness of the Heavens.

CHARLES E. ARTHUR GAYARRE.

CHARLES E. ARTHUR GAYARRE was born in Louisiana on the 3d of January, 1805. He is of mixed descent, Spanish and French. His father, Charles Anastase Gayarré, and his mother, Marie Elizabeth Boré, were natives of Louisiana. His family is one of the most ancient in the state, and historic in all its branches and roots. Some of his ancestors were the contemporaries of Bienville and Iberville, the founders of the colony.

The subject of this notice was educated in New Orleans, at the college of the same name, where he pursued his studies with marked distinction. In 1825, when Mr. Edward Livingston laid before the Legislature of Louisiana the criminal code which he had prepared at the request of the state, Mr. Gayarré, then quite a youth, published a pamphlet, in which he opposed some of Mr. Livingston's views, and particularly the abolition of capital punishment, which Mr. Gayarré considered a premature innovation, and of dangerous application to the State of Louisiana, for certain reasons which he discussed at length. The pamphlet produced great sensation at the time, and the adoption of the code was indefinitely postponed by the legislature. In 1826 Mr. Gayarré went to Philadelphia, and studied law in the office of William Rawle. In 1829 he was admitted to the bar of that city; and in 1830 returned home, and published in French *An Historical Essay on Louisiana*, which obtained great success. That same year, only a few months after his return, he was elected, almost by a unanimous vote, one of the representatives of the city of New Orleans in the legislature, and was chosen by that body to write the "Address," which it sent to France, to compliment the French Chambers on the revolution of 1830. In 1831 he was appointed assistant or deputy attorney-general, in 1833 presiding judge of the city court of New Orleans; and in 1835, when he had just attained the constitutional age, was elected to the Senate of the United States for a term of six years. Ill health prevented Mr. Gayarré from taking his seat, and compelled him to go to Europe, where he remained until October, 1843. In 1844, shortly after his return, Mr. Gayarré was elected by the city of New Orleans to the legislature of the state, where he advocated and carried several important measures, among which was a bill to provide for the liabilities of the state, and which in a short time effected a reduction of two millions and a half of dollars. In 1846 he was re-elected at the expiration of his term; but on the very day the legislature met he was appointed secretary of state by Governor Johnson. That office was then one of the most important and laborious in the state, the secretary being at that time, besides his ordinary functions as such, superintendent of public education, and constituting with the treasurer the "Board of Currency," whose province it is to exercise supreme control and supervision over all the banks of the state. Mr. Gayarré discharged his multifarious duties in a manner which will long be remembered, particularly in connexion with the healthy condition in which he maintained the banks. At the expiration of his four years' term of office, he was re-appointed secretary of state by Governor Walker in 1850. Mr. Gayarré, during the seven years he was secretary of state, found time to publish in French a *History of Louisiana*, in two volumes, containing very curious documents, which he had collected from the archives of France. He also published in English, in one volume, the *Romance of the History of Louisiana*, and in English subsequently the *History of Louisiana*, in two volumes. This continuous work is not a translation of the one he wrote in French. It is cast in a different mould, and contains much matter not to be found in the French work. The *Romance of the History of Louisiana* is appended to it as an introduction. Mr. Redfield, of New York, has published Mr. Gayarré's history of the *Spanish Domination in Louisiana*, coming down to the 20th of December, 1803, when the United States took possession of the colony, in which work he makes some remarkable disclosures in relation to the Spanish intrigues in the West carried on with the co-operation of General Wilkinson and others, from 1786 to 1792, to dismember the Union, and gives a full account of the negotiations which led to the cession.

As secretary of state, Mr. Gayarré made so judicious a use of the sum of seven thousand dollars, which he had at his disposal for the purchase of books, that he may be said to be the father of the state library; and with the very limited sum of two thousand dollars, which, at his pressing request, was voted by the legislature for the purchase of historical documents, he succeeded, by dint of perseverance and after two years' negotiations, in obtaining very important documents from the archives of Spain, the substance of which he has embodied in his history of the *Spanish Domination in Louisiana*.

Mr. Gayarré has lately given to the public two lectures on *The Influence of the Mechanic Arts*, and a dramatic novel, called the *School for Politics*, a humorous and satirical exhibition of the party

Charles Gayarré

frauds and relaxed political sentiment of the day, which may be presumed to have grown out of the writer's experiences, some of which are detailed, in a more matter of fact form, in an *Address to the People of the State*, which he published on the "late frauds perpetrated at the election held on the 7th of November, 1853, in the city of New Orleans." Mr. Gayarré was on that occasion an independent candidate for Congress, refusing to be controlled by the party organization, and was defeated, though he polled a large and influential vote. His undisguised sentiments, in regard to the political manœuvres of the times, are freely expressed at the close of his pamphlet.

He has since taken part in the "Know-Nothing" organization of his native state; and was one of the delegates excluded from the general council of the party at Philadelphia in June, 1855, on the ground of their position as Roman Catholics. This drew from him a privately printed address, in which, with animation and vigor, he handles the question of religious proscription.

As a writer, the prose of Mr. Gayarré is marked by the French and Southern characteristics. It is warm, full, rhetorical, and constantly finds expression in poetical imagery. In his comedy, where the style is restrained by the conversational directness, there are many passages of firm, manly English. As an historian, though his narratives are highly colored, in a certain vein of poetical enthusiasm, they are based on the diligent study of original authorities, and are to be consulted with confidence; the subjects of his early volumes are in themselves romantic, and the story is always of the highest interest. His last volume brings him to the discussion of a most important era in our political history.

FATHER DAGOBERT.*

The conflict which had sprung up between the Jesuits and Capuchins, in 1755, as to the exercise of spiritual jurisdiction in Louisiana, may not have been forgotten. The Bishop of Quebec had appointed a Jesuit his Vicar-General in New Orleans, but the Capuchins pretended that they had, according to a contract passed with the India company, obtained exclusive jurisdiction in Lower Louisiana, and therefore had opposed therein the exercise of any pastoral functions by the Jesuits. The question remained undecided by the Superior Council, which felt considerable reluctance to settle the controversy by some final action, from fear perhaps of turning against itself the hostility of both parties, although it leaned in favor of the Capuchins. From sheer lassitude there had ensued a sort of tacit truce, when father Hilaire de Géneveaux, the Superior of the Capuchins, who, for one of a religious order proverbially famed for its ignorance, was a man of no mean scholarship and of singular activity, quickened by a haughty and ambitious temper, went to visit Europe, without intimating what he was about, and returned with the title of Apostolic Prothonotary, under which he claimed, it seems, the power to lord it over the Jesuit who was the Vicar-General of the Bishop of Quebec. Hence an increase of wrath on the part of the Jesuits and a renewal of the old quarrel, which ceased only when the Jesuits were expelled from all the French dominions. But the triumph of father Géneveaux was not of long duration; for, in 1766, the Superior Council, finding that he was opposed to their scheme of insurrection, had expelled him as a perturber of the public peace, and father Dagobert had become Superior of the Capuchins. They lived altogether in a very fine house of their own, and there never had been a more harmonious community than this one was, under the rule of good father Dagobert.

He had come very young in the colony, where he had christened and married almost everybody, so that he was looked upon as a sort of spiritual father and tutor to all. He was emphatically a man of peace, and if there was anything which father Dagobert hated in this world, if he could hate at all, it was trouble—trouble of any kind—but particularly of that sort which arises from intermeddling and contradiction. How could, indeed, father Dagobert not be popular with old and young, with both sexes, and with every class? Who could have complained of one whose breast harbored no ill feeling towards anybody, and whose lips never uttered a harsh word in reprimand or blame, of one who was satisfied with himself and the rest of mankind, provided he was allowed to look on with his arms folded, leaving angels and devils to follow the bent of their nature in their respective departments? Did not his ghostly subordinates do pretty much as they pleased? And if they erred at times—why—even holy men were known to be frail! And why should not their peccadilloes be overlooked or forgiven for the sake of the good they did? It was much better (we may fairly suppose him so to have thought, from the knowledge we have of his acts and character), for heaven and for the world, to let things run smooth and easy, than to make any noise. Was there not enough of unavoidable turmoil in this valley of tribulations and miseries? Besides, he knew that God was merciful, and that all would turn right in the end. Why should he not have been an indulgent shepherd for his flock, and have smiled on the prodigal son after repentance, and even before, in order not to frighten him away? If the extravagance of the sinning spendthrift could not be checked, why should not he, father Dagobert, be permitted, by sitting at the hospitable board, to give at least some dignity to the feast, and to exorcise away the ever lurking spirit of evil? Did not Jesus sit at meal with publicans and sinners? Why then should not

* From the History of the Spanish Domination in Louisiana.

father Dagobert, when he went out to christen, or to marry at some private dwelling, participate in convivialities, taste the juice of the grape, take a hand in some innocent game, regale his nostrils with a luxurious pinch of snuff, and look with approbation at the merry feats of the dancers? Where was the harm? Could not a father sanctify by his presence the rejoicings of his children? Such were perhaps some of the secret reasonings of the reverend capuchin.

By some pedantic minds father Dagobert might have been taxed with being illiterate, and with knowing very little beyond the litanies of the church. But is not ignorance bliss? Was it not to the want of knowledge, that was to be attributed the simplicity of heart, which was so edifying in one of his sacred mission, and that humility to which he was sworn? Is it not written; "Blessed are the poor in spirit; for theirs is the kingdom of heaven." Why should he understand Latin, or so many other musty inexplicable things? Was not the fruit of the tree of knowledge the cause of the perdition of man? Besides, who ever heard of a learned capuchin? Would it not have been a portentous anomaly? If his way of fasting, of keeping the holydays, of saying mass, of celebrating marriages, of christening, of singing prayers for the dead, and of hearing confessions, of inflicting penance, and of performing all his other sacerdotal functions, was contrary to the ritual and to the canons of the church—why—he knew no better. What soul had been thereby endangered? His parishioners were used to his ways? Was he, after fifty years of labor in the vineyard of the Lord, to change his manner of working, to admit that he had blundered all the time, to dig up what he had planted, and to undertake, when almost an octogenarian, the reform of himself and others? Thus, at least, argued many of his friends.

They were sure that none could deny, that all the duties of religion were strictly performed by his parishioners. Were not the women in the daily habit of confessing their sins? And if he was so very mild in his admonitions, and so very sparing in the infliction of harsh penance on them, why not suppose that it was because the Saviour himself had been very lenient towards the guiltiest of their sex? It was the belief of father Dagobert, that the faults of women proceeded from the head and not from the heart, because *that* was always kind. Why then hurl thunderbolts at beings so exquisitely delicate and so beautifully fragile—the porcelain work of the creator—when they could be reclaimed by the mere scratch of a rose's thorn, and brought back into the bosom of righteousness by the mere pulling of a silken string? As to the men, it is true that they never haunted the confessional; but perhaps they had no sins to confess, and if they had, and did not choose to acknowledge them, what could he do? Would it have been sound policy to have annoyed them with fruitless exhortations, and threatened them with excommunication, when they would have laughed at the *brutum fulmen*? Was it not better to humor them a little, so as to make good grow out of evil? Was not their aversion to confession redeemed by manly virtues, by their charity to the poor and their generosity to the church? Was not his course of action subservient to the interest both of church and state, within the borders of which it was calculated to maintain order and tranquillity, by avoiding to produce discontents, and those disturbances which are their natural results? Had he not a right, in his turn, to expect that his repose should never be interrupted, when he was so sedulously attentive to that of others, and so cheerfully complying with the exigencies of every flitting hour? When the colonists had thought proper to go into an insurrection, he, good easy soul, did not see why he should not make them happy, by chiming in with their mood at the time. Did they not, in all sincerity, think themselves oppressed, and were they not contending for what they believed to be their birthrights? On the other hand, when the Spaniards crushed the revolution, he was nothing loth, as vicar general, to present himself at the portal of the cathedral, to receive O'Reilly with the honors due to the representative of royalty, and to bless the Spanish flag. How could he do otherwise? Was it not said by the Master: "render unto Cæsar the things which are Cæsar's?" Why should the new lords of the land be irritated by a factious and bootless opposition? Why not mollify them, so as to obtain as much from them as possible, in favor of his church and of his dearly beloved flock? Why should he not be partial to the Spaniards? Had they not the reputation of being the strictest catholics in the world.

Such was the character of father Dagobert even in his youth. It had developed itself in more vigorous and co-ordinate proportions, as his experience extended, and it had suggested to him all his rules of action through life. With the same harmonious consistency in all its parts it had continued to grow, until more than threescore years had passed over father Dagobert's head. It was natural, therefore, notwithstanding what a few detractors might say, that he should be at a loss to discover the reasons why he should be blamed, for having logically come to the conclusions which made him an almost universal favorite, and which permitted him to enjoy "his ease in his own inn," whilst authorizing him to hope for his continuing in this happy state of existence, until he should be summoned to the "bourne whence no traveller returns." Certain it is that, whatever judgment a rigid moralist might, on a close analysis, pass on the character of father Dagobert, it can hardly be denied, that to much favor would be entitled the man, who, were he put to trial, could with confidence, like this poor priest, turn round to his subordinates and fellow-beings, and say unto them: "I have lived among you for better than half a century: which of you have I ever injured?" Therefore, father Dagobert thought himself possessed of an unquestionable right to what he loved so much: his ease, both in his convent and out of it, and his sweet uninterrupted dozing in his comfortable arm chair.

GEORGE W. BETHUNE.

Dr. Bethune, the popular divine, poet, and wit, was born March, 1805, in the city of New York. After receiving a liberal education, he was ordained in 1826 a Presbyterian minister, but in the following year joined the Dutch Reformed communion. His clerical career was commenced at Rhinebeck on the Hudson, from whence he removed to Utica; and in 1834, to Philadelphia. In 1849, he again removed to Brooklyn, where he still remains, at the head of a large and influential congregation.

Dr. Bethune is the author of *The Fruit of the Spirit*, *Early Lost, Early Saved*, *The History of a Penitent*; all popular works of a devotional character. In 1848, he published *Lays of Love and Faith, and other Poems*; and in 1850, a volume of *Orations, and Occasional Discourses*. He has also collected and published a portion of his Sermons.

In 1847, he edited the first American edition

of Walton's Angler, a work which he performed in a careful and agreeable manner, befitting his own reputation as an enthusiastic and highly celebrated follower of the "contemplative man's recreation," and as a literary scholar.

Geo. W. Bethune

Dr. Bethune traces his family descent from the Huguenots, and has frequently spoken on the claims of that devout, industrious, and enterprising class of the early settlers of our country, to the national gratitude and reverence. His efforts as an after-dinner and off-hand extempore speaker, are marked by genial humor and appreciation of the subject before him. At the convivial meetings of the National Academy of Design, and of the St. Nicholas Society, he is always called out; and his response is usually among the most noticeable features of the evening.

The volume of Dr. Bethune's orations comprises funeral discourses on the death of Stephen Van Rensselaer, the patroon, President Harrison and General Jackson; lectures and College addresses upon Genius, Leisure, its Uses and Abuses, the Age of Pericles, the Prospects of Art in the United States, the Eloquence of the Pulpit, the Duties of Educated Men, a Plea for Study, and the Claims of our Country upon its Literary Men.

SONG.

She's fresh as breath of summer morn,
She's fair as flowers in spring,
And her voice it has the warbling gush
Of a bird upon the wing;
For joy like dew shines in her eye,
Her heart is kind and free;
'Tis gladness but to look upon
The face of Alice Lee.

She knows not of her loveliness,
And little thinks the while,
How the very air grows beautiful
In the beauty of her smile;
As sings within the fragrant rose
The honey-gath'ring bee,
So murmureth laughter on the lips
Of gentle Alice Lee.

How welcome is the rustling breeze
When sultry day is o'er!
More welcome far the graceful step,
That brings her to the door;
'Tis sweet to gather violets:
But O! how blest is he,
Who wins a glance of modest love,
From lovely Alice Lee!

THE FOURTH OF JULY.

MAINE, from her farthest border, gives the first exulting shout,
And from NEW HAMPSHIRE'S granite heights, the echoing peal rings out;
The mountain farms of staunch VERMONT prolong the thundering call;
MASSACHUSETTS answers: "Bunker Hill!" a watchword for us all.
RHODE ISLAND shakes her sea-wet locks, acclaiming with the free,
And staid CONNECTICUT breaks forth in sacred harmony.
The giant joy of proud New York, loud as an earthquake's roar,
Is heard from Hudson's crowded banks to Erie's crowded shore,
NEW JERSEY, hallowed by their blood, who erst in battle fell,
At Monmouth's, Princeton's, Trenton's fight, joins in the rapturous swell.
Wide PENNSYLVANIA, strong as wide, and true as she is strong,
From every hill to valley, pours the torrent tide along.
Stand up, stout little DELAWARE, and bid thy volleys roll,
Though least among the old Thirteen, we judge thee by thy soul!
Hark to the voice of MARYLAND! over the broad Chesapeake
Her sons, as valiant as their sires, in cannonadings speak.
VIRGINIA, nurse of Washington, and guardian of his grave,
Now to thine ancient glories turn the faithful and the brave;
We need not hear the bursting cheer this holy day inspires,
To know that, in Columbia's cause, "Virginia never tires."
Fresh as the evergreen that waves above her sunny soil,
NORTH CAROLINA shares the bliss, as oft the patriot's toil;
And the land of Sumter, Marion, of Moultrie, Pinckney, must
Respond the cry, or it will rise e'en from their sleeping dust.
And GEORGIA, by the dead who lie along Savannah's bluff,
Full well we love thee, but we ne'er can love thee well enough;
From thy wild northern boundary, to thy green isles of the sea,
Where beat on earth more gallant hearts than now throb high in thee?
On, on, 'cross ALABAMA'S plains, the ever-flowery glades,
To where the Mississippi's flood the turbid Gulf invades;
There, borne from many a mighty stream upon her mightier tide,
Come down the swelling long huzzas from all that valley wide,
As wood-crowned Alleghany's call, from all her summits high,
Reverberates among the rocks that pierce the sunset sky,
While on the shores and through the swales 'round the vast inland seas,
The stars and stripes, 'midst freemen's songs, are flashing to the breeze.
The woodsman, from the mother, takes his boy upon his knee,
To tell him how their fathers fought and bled for liberty;
The lonely hunter sits him down the forest spring beside,
To think upon his country's worth, and feel his country's pride;
While many a foreign accent, which our God can understand,
Is blessing Him for home and bread in this free, fertile land.
Yes! when upon the eastern coast we sink to happy rest,
The Day of Independence rolls still onward to the west,
Till dies on the Pacific shore the shout of jubilee,

That woke the morning with its voice along the Atlantic sea.
—O God! look down upon the land which thou hast loved so well,
And grant that in unbroken truth her children still may dwell;
Nor, while the grass grows on the hill and streams flow through the vale,
May they forget their fathers' faith, or in their covenant fail!
God keep the fairest, noblest land that lies beneath the sun;
"Our country, our whole country, and our country ever one!"

NATIONAL CHARACTERISTICS.*

We are emphatically one people. The constant and expanding flood of emigrants from less favored lands gives in some sections a temporary, superficial diversity of customs, and even of language. Yet, as they come moved by an admiring wish to share our privileges, and a grateful respect for the nation which has made itself so prosperous, while it sets open its gates so hospitably wide, they readily adopt our usages, and soon become homogeneous with the mass through which they are distributed. Until they or their children are educated in free citizenship, they follow; but rarely, and then never successfully, attempt to lead. As the Anglo-Saxon tongue is the speech of the nation, so it is the Anglo-Saxon mind that rules. The sons of those who triumphed in the war of Independence have subdued the distant forest, making the wilderness to rejoice with the arts and virtues of their fathers. The patronymics borne by the most influential among them are most frequently such as are familiar and honorable among us. Summon together the dwellers in any town of our older, particularly of our more northern states, and you will find that there is scarcely a state of the Union where they have not relatives. The representative in Congress from the farthest west laughs over their school-boy frolics with the representative of the farthest east. The woodsman on the Aroostook talks of his brother on the Rio Grande; the tradesman in the seaport, of his son, a judge, in Missouri. The true-hearted girl, who has left her mountain birth-place to earn her modest *paraphernalia* amidst the ponderous din of a factory near the Atlantic coast, dreams sweetly on her toil-blest pillow of him who, for her dear sake, is clearing a home in the wilds of Iowa, or sifting the sands of some Californian Pactolus. We all claim a common history, and, whatever be our immediate parentage, are proud to own ourselves the grateful children of the mighty men who declared our country's independence, framed the bond of our Union, and bought with their sacred blood the liberties we enjoy. Nor is it an insincere compliment to assert, that, go where you will, New England is represented by the shrewdest, the most enlightened, the most successful, and the most religious of our young population. Nearly all our teachers, with the authors of our school-books, and a very large proportion of our preachers, as well as of our editors (the classes which have the greatest control over the growing character of our youth), come from or receive their education in New England. Wherever the New Englander goes, he carries New England with him. New England is his boast, his standard of perfection, and "So they do in New England!" his confident answer to all objectors. Great as is our reverence for those venerable men, he rather wearies us with his inexhaustible eulogy on the Pilgrim Fathers, who, he seems to think, have begotten the whole United States. Nay, enlarging upon the somewhat complacent notion of his ancestors, that God designed for them, "his chosen people," this Canaan of the aboriginal heathen, he looks upon the continent as his rightful heritage, and upon the rest of us as Hittites, Jebusites, or people of a like termination, whom he is commissioned to root out, acquiring our money, squatting on our wild lands, monopolizing our votes, and marrying our heiresses. Whence, or how justly, he derived his popular *sobriquet*, passes the guess of an antiquary; but certain it is, that if he meets with a David, the son of Jesse has often to take up the lament in a different sense from the original,—"I am distressed for thee, my Brother Jonathan!" Better still, his sisters, nieces, female cousins, flock on various honorable pretexts to visit him amidst his new possessions, where they own with no Sabine reluctance the constraining ardor of our unsophisticated chivalry; and happy is the household over which a New England wife presides! blessed the child whose cradle is rocked by the hand, whose slumber is hallowed by the prayers of a New England mother! The order of the Roman policy is reversed. He conquered, and then inhabited; the New Englander inhabits, then gains the mastery, not by force of arms, but by mother-wit, steadiness, and thrift. That there should be, among us of the other races, a little occasional petulance, is not to be wondered at; but it is only superficial. The New Englander goes forth not as a spy or an enemy, and the gifts which he carries excite gratitude, not fear. He soon becomes identified with his neighbors, their interests are soon his, and the benefits of his enterprising cleverness swell the advantage of the community where he has planted himself, thus tending to produce a moral homogeneousness throughout the confederacy. Yet let it be remembered that this New England influence, diffusing itself, like noiseless but transforming leaven, through the recent and future states, while it makes them precious as allies, would also make them formidable as rivals, terrible as enemies. The New Englander loses little of his main characteristics by migration. He is as shrewd, though not necessarily as economical, a calculator in the valley of the Mississippi, as his brethren in the east, and as brave as his fathers were at Lexington or Charlestown. It were the height of suicidal folly for the people of the maritime states to attempt holding as subjects or tributaries, directly or indirectly, the people between the Alleghanies and the Rocky Mountains; but those who have not travelled among our prairie and forest settlements can have only a faint idea of the filial reverence, the deferential respect, the yearning love, with which they turn to the land where their fathers sleep, and to you who guard their sepulchres. The soul knows nothing of distance; and, in their twilight musings, they can scarcely tell which is dearer to their hearts—the home of the kindred they have left behind them, or the home they have won for their offspring. Be it your anxious care, intelligent gentlemen of New England, that so strong a bond is never strained to rupture!

* * * * * * * * * *

To your Pilgrim Fathers the highest place may well be accorded; but forget not, that, about the time of their landing on the Rock, there came to the mouth of the Hudson men of kindred faith and descent—men equally loving freedom—men from the sea-washed cradle of modern constitutional freedom, whose union of free-burgher-cities taught us

* From the Harvard Address, "Claims of our Country on its Literary Men."

the lesson of confederate independent sovereignties, whose sires were as free, long centuries before *Magna Charta*, as the English are now, and from whose line of republican princes Britain received the boon of religious toleration, a privilege the states-general had recognised as a primary article of their government when first established; men of that stock, which, when offered their choice of favors from a grateful monarch, asked a University; men whose martyr-sires had baptized their land with their blood; men who had flooded it with ocean-waves rather than yield it to a bigot-tyrant; men, whose virtues were as sober as prose, but sublime as poetry;—the men of Holland! Mingled with these, and still further on, were heroic Huguenots, their fortunes broken, but their spirit unbending to prelate or prelate-ridden king. There were others (and a dash of cavalier blood told well in battle-field and council);—but those were the spirits whom God made the moral substratum of our national character. Here, like Israel in the wilderness, and thousands of miles off from the land of bondage, they were educated for their high calling, until, in the fulness of times, our confederacy with its Constitution was founded. Already there had been a salutary mixture of blood, but not enough to impair the Anglo-Saxon ascendency. The nation grew morally strong from its original elements. The great work was delayed only by a just preparation. Now God is bringing hither the most vigorous scions from all the European stocks, to "make of them all *one new* MAN!" not the Saxon, not the German, not the Gaul, not the Helvetian, but the AMERICAN. Here they will unite as one brotherhood, will have one law, will share one interest. Spread over the vast region from the frigid to the torrid, from Eastern to Western ocean, every variety of climate giving them choice of pursuit and modification of temperament, the ballot-box fusing together all rivalries, they shall have one national will. What is wanting in one race will be supplied by the characteristic energies of the others; and what is excessive in either, checked by the counter-action of the rest. Nay, though for a time the newly come may retain their foreign vernacular, our tongue, so rich in ennobling literature, will be the tongue of the nation, the language of its laws, and the accent of its majesty. ETERNAL GOD! who seest the end with the beginning, thou alone canst tell the ultimate grandeur of this people!

EDWARD SANFORD,

A POET, essayist, and political writer, is the son of the late Nathan Sanford, Chancellor of the State, and was born in the city of New York in 1805. He was educated at Union College, where he was graduated in 1824. He then engaged in the study of the law in the office of Mr. Benjamin F. Butler, but his tastes were opposed to the profession, and he did not pursue it.

He began an editorial career as editor of a newspaper in Brooklyn; was next associated with the New York Standard; and when that paper was compelled to yield to the commercial embarrassments of the day, he became one of the editors of the New York Times. The difficulties in politics which occurred after the second year of the establishment of that paper led him to undertake an engagement at Washington with Mr. Blair as associate editor of the Globe newspaper, then the organ of the Van Buren administration. In this relation his pen was employed in the advocacy and development of the sub-treasury system, then under discussion previous to its establishment as an integral portion of the financial policy of the country.

The illness of his father now withdrew him from Washington to the family residence at Flushing, Long Island. At this time he held the office, at New York, of Secretary to the Commission to return the duties on goods destroyed by the great fire of 1835. He was subsequently Assistant Naval Officer.

In 1843, he was elected to the Senate of the state of New York, and while there was an active and efficient, though quiet political manager and leader.

An anecdote of the Capitol exhibits his poetic talent. One day in the senate room he received a note from a correspondent on business; it was at the close of the session, and the whole house in the hurry and confusion which attend its last moments. He had a score or more measures to hurry through, and numerous others to aid in their passage, and thus pressed, answered the letter handed to him. A few days after he was surprised to learn that he had written this hasty reply in excellent verse.

Of the literary productions of Mr. Sanford, a few only have appeared with his name. Mr. Bryant included the quaint and poetical *Address to Black Hawk* in his collection of American poems, and Mr. Hoffman presented this and the author's *Address to a Mosquito*, written in a similar vein, in the "New York Book of Poetry."

To the New York Mirror, the Knickerbocker Magazine, and the Spirit of the Times, Mr. Sanford has been a frequent and genial contributor. His poem, *The Loves of the Shell Fishes*, has been justly admired for its fancy and sentiment, in delicate flowing verse, as he sings—

Not in the land where beauty loves to dwell,
  And bards to sing that beauty dwelleth there:
Not in the land where rules th' enchanter's spell
  And fashion's beings beautiful and rare;
Not in such land are laid the scenes I tell.
  No odors float upon its sunny air;
No ruddy vintage, and no tinted flowers
Gladden its fields or bloom within its bowers.

Mine is a lowlier lay—the unquiet deep—
  The world of waters; where man's puny skill
Has but along its surface dared to creep:
  The quaking vassal of its wayward will,
Exultant only when its calm waves sleep,
  And its rough voice is noiseless all and still,
And trembling when its crested hosts arise,
Roused from their slumbers by the wind's wild cries.

None but the dead have visited its caves;
  None but the dead pressed its untrampled floor.
Eyes, but all sightless, glare beneath its waves,
  And forms earth's worshippers might well adore,
Lie in their low and ever freshened graves,
  All cold and loveless far beneath its roar.
The bright-eyed maiden and the fair-haired bride,
And sire and son there slumber side by side.

* * * * * * * * * *

Smile not ye wise ones at my lowly lay,
  Nor deem it strange that underneath a shell
High thoughts exert their ever ruling sway
  And soft affections scorn not there to dwell.
That in an oyster's breast the living ray
  Of mind beams forth; or that its young thoughts
    swell

Less vauntingly in pride of place or birth
Than aught that breathes upon our upper earth.

Of blighted hopes and confidence betrayed—
Of princely dames and wights of low degree—
The story of a high-born oyster maid
And her calm lover, of low family:
And how they met beneath their oft sought shade,
The spreading branches of a coral tree,
Attended by a periwinkle page,
Selected chiefly for his tender age,

Sing scaly music. ————

The best of Mr. Sanford's poetical effusions are of this airy, delicate mood, facile and elegant.

His occasional political squibs were quite in the Croaker vein, as in this parody at the expense of the Whigs in the Harrison log-cabin campaign.

A HARD-CIDER MELODY.

Air—'Tis the last rose of summer.

'Tis the last of Whig loafers
Left singing alone,
All his pot-house companions
Are fuddled and gone.
No flower of his kindred,
No rum-blossom nigh,
With a song on his lips
And a drop in his eye.

I'll not leave thee, thou rose-bud,
To pine on the stem,
Since the others are snoring,
Go snore thou with them.
Thus kindly I lay
A soft plank 'neath thy head,
Where thy mates of the cabin
Lie, hard-cider dead.

So soon may I follow,
When the Whigs all decay,
And no cider is left us
To moisten our clay.
When the Whigs are all withered,
And hard-cider gone,
Oh! who would inhabit
This sad world alone?

As an essayist, Mr. Sanford holds a very happy pen. His articles of this class, in the newspapers of the day, touch lightly and pleasantly on cheerful topics. A humorous description of a city celebrity, *A Charcoal Sketch of Pot Pie Palmer*, first published in the old Mirror, is a highly felicitous specimen of his powers in this line, and is quite as worthy in its way as a satire as the celebrated Memoir of P. P., Clerk of the Parish.

ADDRESS TO BLACKHAWK.

There's beauty on thy brow, old chief! the high
And manly beauty of the Roman mould,
And the keen flashing of thy full dark eye
Speaks of a heart that years have not made cold,
Of passions scathed not by the blight of time,
Ambition, that survives the battle rout.
The man within thee scorns to play the mime
To gaping crowds that compass thee about.
Thou walkest, with thy warriors by thy side,
Wrapped in fierce hate, and high unconquered pride.

Chief of a hundred warriors! dost thou yet—
Vanquished and captive—dost thou deem that here—
The glowing day-star of thy glory set—
Dull night has closed upon thy bright career?

Old forest lion, caught and caged at last,
Dost pant to roam again thy native wild
To gloat upon the life-blood flowing fast
Of thy crushed victims; and to slay the child,
To dabble in the gore of wives and mothers,
And kill, old Turk! thy harmless pale-faced brothers.

For it was cruel, Black Hawk, thus to flutter
The dove-cotes of the peaceful pioneers,
To let thy pride commit such fierce and utter
Slaughter among the folks of the frontiers.
Though thine be old, hereditary hate,
Begot in wrongs, and nursed in blood, until
It had become a madness, 'tis too late
To crush the hordes who have the power, and will,
To rob thee of thy hunting grounds and fountains,
And drive thee back to the Rocky Mountains.

Spite of thy looks of cold indifference,
There's much thou'st seen that must excite thy wonder,
Wakes not upon thy quick and startled sense
The cannon's harsh and pealing voice of thunder?
Our big canoes, with white and wide-spread wings,
That sweep the waters, as birds sweep the sky;—
Our steamboats, with their iron lungs, like things
Of breathing life, that dash and hurry by?
Or if thou scorn'st the wonders of the ocean,
What think'st thou of our railroad locomotion?

Thou'st seen our Museums, beheld the dummies
That grin in darkness in their coffin cases;
What think'st thou of the art of making mummies,
So that the worms shrink from their dry embraces?
Thou'st seen the mimic tyrants of the stage
Strutting, in paint and feathers, for an hour;
Thou'st heard the bellowing of their tragic rage,
Seen their eyes glisten and their dark brows lower.
Anon, thou'st seen them, when their wrath cooled down,
Pass in a moment from a king—to clown.

Thou seest these things unmoved, say'st so, old fellow?
Then tell us, have the white man's glowing daughters
Set thy cold blood in motion? Hast been mellow
By a sly cup or so, of our fire waters?
They are thy people's deadliest poison. They
First make them cowards, and then white men's slaves.
And sloth, and penury, and passion's prey,
And lives of misery, and early graves.
For by their power, believe me, not a day goes,
But kills some Foxes, Sacs, and Winnebagoes.

Say, does thy wandering heart stray far away?
To the deep bosom of thy forest home,
The hillside, where thy young papooses play,
And ask, amid their sports, when wilt thou come?
Come not the wailings of thy gentle squaws,
For their lost warrior, loud upon thine ear,
Piercing athwart the thunder of huzzas,
That, yelled at every corner, meet thee here?
The wife that made that shell-decked wampum belt,
Thy rugged heart must think of her, and melt.

Chafes not thy heart, as chafes the panting breast
Of the caged bird against his prison bars,
That thou the crowned warrior of the west,
The victor of a hundred forest wars,
Should'st in thy age become a raree-show
Led like a walking bear about the town,
A new caught monster, who is all the go,
And stared at gratis, by the gaping clown?
Boils not thy blood, while thus thou'rt led about,
The sport and mockery of the rabble rout?

Whence came thy cold philosophy? whence came,
Thou tearless, stern, and uncomplaining one,
The power that taught thee thus to veil the flame
Of thy fierce passions? Thou despisest fun,
And thy proud spirit scorns the white men's glee,
Save thy fierce sport when at the funeral pile,
Of a bound warrior in his agony,
Who meets thy horrid laugh with dying smile,
Thy face, in length reminds one of a Quaker's,
Thy dances, too, are solemn as a Shaker's.

Proud scion of a noble stem! thy tree
Is blanched, and bare, and seared, and leafless now.
I'll not insult its fallen majesty,
Nor drive with careless hand the ruthless plough
Over its roots. Torn from its parent mould,
Rich, warm, and deep, its fresh, free, balmy air,
No second verdure quickens in our cold,
New, barren earth; no life sustains it there.
But even though prostrate, 'tis a noble thing,
Though crownless, powerless, "every inch a king."

Give us thy hand, old nobleman of nature,
Proud ruler of the forest aristocracy;
The best of blood glows in thy every feature.
And thy curled lip speaks scorn for our democracy,
Thou wear'st thy titles on that godlike brow;
Let him who doubts them, meet thine eagle eye,
He'll quail beneath its glance, and disavow
All questions of thy noble family;
For thou may'st here become, with strict propriety,
A leader in our city good society.

TO A MOSQUITO.

His voice was very soft, gentle, and low.—*King Lear.*
Thou of the soft low voice.—*Mrs. Hemans.*

Thou sweet musician that around my bed,
Dost nightly come and wind thy little horn,
By what unseen and secret influence led,
Feed'st thou my ear with music till 'tis morn?
The wind-harp's tones are not more soft than thine,
The hum of falling waters not more sweet,
I own, *indeed* I own thy song divine,
And when next year's warm summer night we meet,
(Till then farewell!) I promise thee to be
A patient listener to thy minstrelsy.

Thou tiny minstrel, who bid thee discourse
Such eloquent music? was't thy tuneful sire?
Some old musician? or did'st take a course
Of lessons from some master of the lyre?
Who bid thee twang so sweetly thy small trump?
Did Norton form thy notes so clear and full?
Art a phrenologist, and is thy bump
Of song developed on thy little skull?
At Niblo's hast thou been when crowds stood mute,
Drinking the bird-like tones of Cuddy's flute?

Tell me the burden of thy ceaseless song—
Is it thy evening hymn of grateful prayer?
Or lay of love, thou pipest through the long
Still night? With song dost drive away dull care?
Art thou a vieux garçon, a gay deceiver,
A wandering blade, roaming in search of sweets,
Pledging thy faith to every fond believer
Who thy advance with half-way shyness meets?
Or art o' the softer sex, and sing'st in glee
"In maiden meditation, fancy free."

Thou little Siren, when the nymphs of yore
Charmed with their songs till folks forgot to dine
And starved, though music fed, upon their shore,
Their voices breathed no softer lays than thine;
They sang but to entice, and thou dost sing
As if to lull our senses to repose,
That thou may'st use unharmed thy little sting
The very moment we begin to doze:
Thou worse than Syren, thirsty, fierce blood-sipper,
Thou living Vampire and thou Gallinipper.

Nature is full of music, sweetly sings
The bard (and thou sing'st sweetly too);
Through the wide circuit of created things,
Thou art the living proof the bard sings true.
Nature is full of thee: On every shore,
'Neath the hot sky of Congo's dusky child,
From warm Peru to icy Labrador,
The world's free citizen thou roamest wild.
Wherever "mountains rise or oceans roll,"
Thy voice is heard, from "Indus to the pole."

The incarnation of Queen Mab art thou,
And "Fancy's midwife,"—thou dost nightly sip
With amorous proboscis bending low,
The honey-dew from many a lady's lip—
(Though that they "straight on kisses dream" I doubt.)
On smiling faces and on eyes that weep,
Thou lightest, and oft with "sympathetic snout"
"Ticklest men's noses as they lie asleep;"
And sometimes dwellest, if I rightly scan,
"On the forefinger of an alderman."

Yet thou canst glory in a noble birth,
As rose the sea-born Venus from the wave,
So didst thou rise to life; the teeming earth,
The living water, and the fresh air gave
A portion of their elements to create
Thy little form, though beauty dwells not there.
So lean and gaunt that economic fate
Meant thee to feed on music or on air.
Our veins' pure juices were not made for thee,
Thou living, singing, stinging atomy.

The hues of dying sunset are most fair,
And twilight's tints just fading into night,
Most dusky soft; and so thy soft robes are
By far the sweetest when thou tak'st thy flight,
The swan's last note is sweetest, so is thine;
Sweet are the wind harp's tones at distance heard;
'Tis sweet in distance at the day's decline,
To hear the opening song of evening's bird.
But notes of harp or bird at distance float
Less sweetly on the ear than thy last note.

The autumn winds are wailing: 'tis thy dirge;
Its leaves are sear, prophetic of thy doom.
Soon the cold rain will whelm thee, as the surge
Whelms the tost mariner in its watery tomb.
Then soar and sing thy little life away;
Albeit thy voice is somewhat husky now.
'Tis well to end in music life's last day,
Of one so gleeful and so blithe as thou.
For thou wilt soon live through its joyous hours,
And pass away with autumn's dying flowers.

SONG—IMITATED FROM THE FRENCH.

If Jove, when he made this beautiful world,
Had only consulted me,
An ocean of wine should flow in the place
Of the brackish and bitter sea.
Red wine should pour from the fruitful clouds
In place of the tasteless rain,
And the fountains should bubble in ruby rills
To brim the sparkling main.

No fruit should grow but the round, full grape,
No bowers but the shady vine,
And of all earth's flowers, the queenly rose
Should alone in her beauty shine;
I'd have a few lakes for the choicest juice,
Where it might grow mellow and old,
And my lips should serve as a sluice to drain
Those seas of liquid gold.

CHARCOAL SKETCH OF POT PIE PALMER.

The poets have told us that it is of little use to be a great man, without possessing also a chronicler of one's greatness. Brave and wise men—perhaps the bravest and wisest that ever lived—have died and been forgotten, and all for the want of a poet or an historian to immortalize their valor or their wisdom. Immortality is not to be gained by the might of one man alone. Though its claimant be strong and terrible as an army with banners, he can never succeed without a trumpeter. He may embody a thousand minds; he may have the strength of a thousand arms—his enemies may quail before him as the degenerate Italians quailed before the ruthless sabaoth of the north; but without a chronicler of his deeds, he will pass by, like the rush of a whirlwind, with none to tell whence he cometh, or whither he goeth. A great man should always keep a literary friend in pay, for he may be assured that his greatness will never be so firmly established as to sustain itself without a prop. Achilles had his poet; and the anger of the nereid-born and Styx-dipped hero is as savage and bitter at this late day, as if he had just poured forth the vials of his wrath. The favorite son of the queen of love, albeit a pious and exemplary man, and free from most of the weaknesses of his erring but charming mother, might have travelled more than the wandering Jew, and, without the aid of a poet, the course of his voyage would now be as little known as the journal of a modern tourist, six months from the day of its publication. The fates decreed him a bard, and the world is not only intimate with every step of his wayfaring, but for hundreds of years it has been puzzling itself to discover his starting-place. There has lived but one man who has disdained the assistance of his fellow-mortals, and finished with his pen what he began with his sword. We refer to the author of Cæsar's Commentaries, the most accomplished gentleman, take him for all in all, that the world ever saw. Let us descend for a step or two in the scale of greatness, and see whence the lesser lights of immortality have derived their lustre. The Cretan Icarus took upon himself the office of a fowl, and was drowned for all his wings, yet floats in the flights of song, while the names of a thousand wiser and better men of his day passed away before their bodies had scarcely rotted. A poorer devil than the late Samuel Patch never cumbered this fair earth; but he is already embalmed in verse, and by one whose name cannot soon die. A cunning pen has engrossed the record of his deeds, and perfected his judgment roll of fame. He is a co-heir in glory with the boy of Crete—the one flew, and the other leaped, into immortality.

There is one name connected with the annals of our city, which should be snatched from oblivion. Would that a strong hand could be found to grasp it, for it is a feeble clutch that now seeks to drag it by the locks from the deep forgetfulness in which it is fast sinking. Scarcely ten years have passed, since the last bell of the last of the bellmen was rung, since the last joke of the joke-master general of our goodly metropolis was uttered, since the last song of our greatest street-minstrel was sung, and the last laugh of the very soul of laughter was pealed forth. Scarcely ten years have passed, and the public recollection of the man who made more noise in the world than any other of his time, is already dim and shadowy and unsubstantial. A brief notice of this extraordinary man has found admittance into the ephemeral columns of a newspaper. We will endeavor to enter his immortality of record in a place where future ages will be more likely to find it. As Dr. Johnson would have said, "of Pot Pie Palmer, let us indulge the pleasing reminiscence."

The character of Pot Pie Palmer was a kindly mingling of the elements of good-nature, gentleness of spirit, quickness and delicacy of perception, an intuitive knowledge of mankind, and an ambition, strange and peculiar in its aspirations, but boundless. There were sundry odd veins and streaks which ran through and wrinkled this goodly compound, in the shape of quips and quirks and quiddities, which crossed each other at such strange angles, and turned round such short corners, that few were able to analyse the moral anatomy of the man. It is not strange then, that his character should have been generally misunderstood. He was a jester by profession, but he was no mime. Unlike a clown at a country fair, who grins for half-pence, he asked no compensation for his services in the cause of public mirth. He was a volunteer in the business of making men merry, for it was no part of his calling to put the world in good humor, and it has never been hinted that he received a shilling from the corporation for his extra services in the cause of happiness and contentment. He might have been as serious as his own cart-horse, without the slightest risk of losing his place. If he had preserved a becoming gravity, he might have aspired to a higher office than that of the chief of the corporation scavengers; for a long face has ever been a passport to preferment. But he disdained to leave his humble calling as long as he was sure he could remain at its head. He knew full well that there were few who could chime with him, and he would play second to no man's music. He was mirthful, partly from a spirit of philanthropy, and partly because he was so filled with gleeful and fantastic associations, that they overflowed in spite of him. He was not merely a passive instrument that required the cunning touch of a master to awaken its music, or like a wind-harp that is voiceless till the wind sweeps over it. He was a piece of mechanism that played of its own accord, and was never mute, and his notes were as varied as those of a mock-bird. If there were those around him who could enjoy a joke, he offered them a fair share of it, and bade them partake of it and be thankful to the giver: and if there was no one at hand with whom to divide it, he swallowed it himself—and with an appetite that would make a dyspeptic forget that he had a stomach.

He was the incarnation of a jest. His face was a broad piece of laughter, done in flesh and blood. His nose had a whimsical twist, as the nose of a humorist should have. His mouth had become elongated by frequent cachinnations; for his laugh was of most extraordinary dimensions, and required a wide portal to admit it into the free air, and his eyes twinkled and danced about in his head as if they were determined to have a full share in the fun that was going on. Time had seamed his brow, but had also endued it with a soft and mellow beauty; for the spirit of mirth was at his side when he roughened the old man's visage, and had planted a smile in every furrow.

Pot Pie Palmer, like many other great men, was indifferent to the duties of the toilet; but it was not for want of a well appointed wardrobe, for he seldom made his appearance twice in the same dress; and it is not an insignificant circumstance in his biography, that he was the last distinguished personage that appeared in public in a cocked hat. In dress, manners, and appearance, he stuck to the old school, and there was nothing new about him but his jokes. He would sometimes, in a moment of odd fancy, exhibit himself in a crownless hat and bootless feet, probably in honor of his ancestors, the Palmers of yore, who wore their sandal shoon and scallop shell. It may be well to remark, while on the subject of his wardrobe, that there is not the slightest foundation for the rumor that Mr. Palmer wore red flannel next to his person. This mistake has probably arisen from the fact that he was seen dressed in scarlet at a fourth of July celebration. We are able to state, from the very best authority, that cotton and not wool was the raw material from which his dress on that occasion was fabricated, his outer garment having been a superb specimen of domestic calico; and that he assumed it for three especial reasons—firstly, in honor of the day—secondly, to encourage our infant manufactures, in the cause of which his exertions had always been active—and thirdly, because he had received a special invitation to dine with the common council.

Pot Pie Palmer was an autocrat within his own realms of humor. He had no peer in the joyous art. His whim-whams were his own, and he was the only professed wit that ever lived who was not addicted to plagiarism. He was a knight-errant in the cause of jollity. His worshipped ladye-love was an intellectual abstraction, the disembodied spirit of fun, and wo to the challenger who was bold enough to call her good qualities in question. It was rough tilting with the old but gallant knight. We have been witness to more than one tournament in which an essenced carpet knight cried craven, and left the ancient warrior in full possession of the field. But gentleness was the ordinary wont, as it was the nature of Pot Pie Palmer. He knew that to be the sad burden of his merry song, was a nine days' melancholy immortality even to the humblest, and it went to his heart to see a man laugh on the wrong side of his mouth. His humors were all in the spirit of kindness. He "carried no heart-stain away on his blade;" or if he incautiously inflicted a wound, he was ever ready to pour into it the oil and wine of a merry whim, so that its smart was scarcely felt before it was healed.

Pot Pie was a poet; for where humor is, poetry cannot be far off. They are akin to each other; and if their relationship be not sisterly, it is only so far removed as to make their union more thrillingly delightful. No one could tell where his songs came from, and it was a fair presumption that they were his own. He has been considered by many the only perfect specimen of an improvisatore that this country has ever produced. His lays were always an echo to the passing scenes around him. Like the last minstrel, he had songs for all ears. The sooty chimney-sweep who walked by, chanting his cheery song, was answered in notes that spoke gladness to his heart, and the poor fuliginous blackamoor passed on, piping away more merrily than ever. The anomalous biped who drove a clam-cart, would needs stop a moment for a word of kindness from Pot Pie and he would be sure to get it, for the Palmer was not a proud man. In the expansive character of his humor, he knew no distinctions. Even in his jokes with his brother bellmen, there was no assumption of superiority. He disdained to triumph over their dulness, and he rather sought to instil into their bosoms a portion of his own fire.

It was a part, nay the very essence of his calling, to receive from the tenants of the underground apartments of the houses where he had the honor to call, those superfluous vegetable particles which are discarded—especially in warm weather—from the alimentary preparations of well-regulated families. There was a smile resting on his cheek—a smile of benevolence—as the dusky lady of the lower cabinet transferred her odorous stores into his capacious cart; a graceful touch of his time-worn and dilapidated ram-beaver, and a loud compliment was roared forth in tones that made the passers-by prick up their ears, and the dingy female would rush in evident confusion down the cellar-steps, seemingly abashed at the warmth of his flattery, while at the next moment there would peal up from the depths, a ringing laugh that told how the joyous spirit of the negress had been gladdened, and that the bellman had uttered the very sentiment that was nearest her heart. He had his delicate allusions when the buxom grisette or simpering chambermaid presented herself at the door, half coy and half longing for a word of kindness, or perchance of flattery, and they were sure never to go away unsatisfied. For though there were tossings of pretty heads, and pert flings of well-rounded fo ms, and blushes which seemed to speak more of shame than of pleasure, you would be sure if you gave a glance the moment after at the upper casements, to see faces peering forth, glowing with laughter and delight.

Palmer's genius resembled that of Rabelais, for his humor was equally broad and equally uncontrollable. We have said that he was a poet, a street-minstrel of the very first rank. He threw a grace, beyond the reach of art, over the unwashed beauties of a scavenger's cart. It was to him a triumphal chariot, a car of honor: he needed no heralds to precede its march, no followers to swell its train; for he made music enough to trumpet the coming of a score of conquerors, and the boys followed him in crowds as closely as if they had been slaves chained to his chariot. He was to the lean and solemn beast that drew him on with the measured pace of an animal in authority, like the merry Sancho to his dappled ass. There never was a more practical antithesis than the horse and his master; and it must have been a dull beast that would not have caught a portion of the whim and spirit of such a companion. Unfortunately, the pedigree of Palmer's steed has been lost; and it will continue to be an unsettled point whether he came honestly by his dulness, or whether nature had made him dull in one of her pranksome moods. It is still more uncertain whether Palmer selected him out of compassion, or for the sake of making the stupidity of the animal a foil to his own merry humors.

Palmer carried us back to the latter part of the middle ages, when ladye love and minstrel rhyme were the ambition and the ruling passion of the bard-warriors of the time. The love of song was part of his nature; and he was enough of a modern to know that a song was worth little without a fitting accompaniment. With a boldness and originality that marked the character of the man, he selected an instrument devoted to any other purpose than that of music; and so great did his skill become, aided by an excellent ear and a perfect command of hand, that, had he possessed the advantages of admission into fashionable society, there is every reason to believe that the humble bell would soon have rivalled the ambitious violin. He was the Paganini of bellmen, the Apollo of street-music. He modulated the harmony of voice and hand with such peculiar skill, that the separate sounds flowed into each other as if they had been poured forth together from the same melodious fount. No harsh discord jarred upon the ear—no false note could be detected. His voice was naturally deficient in softness, and ill-adapted to express the tender emotions; but he had cultivated it so admirably, and managed its powers with such peculiar skill, that none could tell what might have been its original defects. He preferred the old and simple ballad style to the scientific quavering of more modern times. In his day, we had no Italian opera, and he was without a rival.

Palmer was a public man, and it is in his public character we speak of him. Little is known of his private life, or the secret motives and hidden springs which moved him to aspire to notoriety. There is a flying rumor that in his early years he was visited by a fortune-teller, who prophesied that he would make a noise in the world, and that the sybil's prediction was the cause of his aspiring to the office of corporation bellman. Our authority upon this point is apocryphal, and it must be strong evidence to convince us that superstition was a weakness that found admittance into Pot Pie's bosom. He was probably an obscure man previous to his taking upon himself the cares of public office; for we are assured by a highly respectable citizen, that it required the influence of strong political friends to secure him his situation. It is equally probable that he was not in affluent circumstances, as it is known that, on being inducted into office, he had not two shillings about him to pay the necessary fees: and that he made a compromise with the mayor, on that occasion, by advancing a number of first-rate jokes, which his honor was kind enough to receive as collateral security for the payment of his official demand. On taking possession of his office, he found that he was engaged in a calling which was in bad odor. Its ordinary duties were mechanical. He was brought in contact, in the transaction of his business, chiefly with the lower classes. His brothers in office were little better than patient drudges, who had no soul beyond receiving their stipulated salaries. Finding that his office could give him little reputation, he determined to give reputation to his office. He courted popularity, not by the arts of a demagogue, but by kindness and courtesy to all around him. He would occasionally throw a joke by the way-side; and, if it took root and produced good fruit, he would sow another in the same soil; and he thus continued his husbandry, until a blooming harvest of ripe humors and full-grown conceits had sprung up wherever he had passed. It is not improbable that Palmer's figure was in the mind's eye of our Bryant when he spoke of "a living blossom of the air." It is not strange that his popularity should soon have become general, but it is not a little singular that it should have experienced no ebb and flow. The fickle breath of popular favor was to him a breeze that always blew from the same point of the compass. During his long public career, there was no interval of diminished reputation, no brief period of questioned authority. He swayed the sceptre of his wit firmly to the last; and when it departed from his hand, there was none bold enough to claim it.

To form a correct estimate of the powers of one who, in one of the humblest pursuits of life—a pursuit calculated to beget and keep alive narrow and sordid views, to check all noble aspirations, all ambition for fame in the eyes of the world, and to lessen a man in his own eyes, had the spirit to soar above the common duties of his calling, to create himself a name, and to make himself the lion of his day, the wonder of his time, outrivalling all cotemporary lions and all imported wonders, and who had the ability to effect all this, we must place the bellman and his calling alongside of other men whose situations in life, in point of conventional respectability, are on a par with his. The collectors of anthracite coal-dust are as ambitious as he was to make a noise in the world, and they blow their trumpets as loudly as if they aspired to imitate the example of the conqueror of Jericho, and to make the walls of our city to crumble before their blast. But, like ranting actors, they only split the ears of the groundlings. There is nothing poetical in the shrill blast of their horns; and we have never seen one of them whom our imagination could body forth into any other shape than that of an everyday matter of fact, vulgar dustman. We are like the unpoetical clown—

> A cowslip by the river's brim
> A yellow cowslip was to him,
> But it was nothing more.

So in our eyes, a collector of ashes is simply a collector of ashes, and that is all we know or care about him. No Napoleon of his order has arisen among this class. No man of his time has sprung, phenix-like, from the ashes. Had the noisy tin-trumpet, instead of the clanging bell, been the emblem of Palmer's office, how would its base and common notes have been softened and melted into melody, till they spoke such eloquent music as even, in these latter days, visits not the ears of common mortals. Even the fame of poor Willis might have been dimmed; and the Kent-bugle, which he charmed into the utterance of such melting melody, might have been pronounced an inferior instrument to the mellow horn, when breathing the airs and variations of Pot Pie Palmer. The dull man of ashes, though possessing, as the emblem of his calling, a musical instrument, the very mention of which awakens a hundred stirring associations, has so far neglected the advantages of his situation, as to make himself the most unpoetical and unendurable of street-bores. Is there a milkman in the land who is distinguished for any thing beyond a peculiar art in mixing liquors, and for combining, with a greater or less degree of skill, lacteal and aqueous fluids? We have never seen the man. Descend in the scale. The sooty sweep, though he has a special license from the corporation to sing when and where he pleases, though the only street minstrel acknowledged and protected by our laws, is still regarded by the public eye as the poorest and humblest of all God's creatures; and there is no instance on record of his having, even in his most climbing ambition, aspired to any other elevation than the chimney-top. In brief, there is no humble public employment, no low dignity of office, with the single exception of that of the corporation bellmen, that can furnish an instance of its possessor having arrayed it in poetry and beauty; and to Pot Pie Palmer belongs the undivided and undisputed honor

> Green be the laurels on the Palmer's brow.

But, says some cynical critic, "where are the jests of your Yorick, where is the recorded or remembered proof of his wit, his music, or his poetry? Let us have some single specimen of those powers which you are applauding to the echo, or at least furnish us with some traits from which we can picture to ourselves the moral physiognomy of the man?" To this we have several answers. The fame of Pot Pie Palmer, to be secure, must rest chiefly on tradition. A dim legendary immortality will outlast all other kinds of fame, for no one can call its title in question. Its very dimness invests it with a soft poetic halo that lingers over and brightens it, giving it the enchantment of distance, and arraying it with mystic beauty. We abhor a downright matter of fact, palpable reputation, for sure as it is tangible, it is equally sure to be meddled with, and perhaps pulled to pieces. We wish to preserve, if possible, the fabric of Palmer's fame, from the touch of hands that would but discompose its delicate and fairy handiwork. Besides, we are fearful of marring a good joke by repeating it awkwardly. The spirit and soul of the Palmer are necessary to him who would repeat the Palmer's jokes. His was unwritten humor. We have sought diligently, but without success, for some account of his private life, but we have completely failed in our search. We are enabled to state, however, on the very best authority, that the Pot Pie papers, which have been preserved with religious care by his family, will in due time either be given to the public, or made use of as the basis of an article in the next edition of American Biography; and we think that Palmer's chance for fame is at least on a par with nine out of ten of those who figure in that department of the Dictionary of Universal Knowledge.

Poor old Pot Pie! The memory of the kind-hearted and joyous old man is sweet and savory. We think of him as one of those who were pleasant in their lives; while in his death he and his jests were not divided. They went down to the tomb together. Time, the beautifier, has already shed its soft lustre over the recollection of his humble cart and its odoriferous contents; and we think of it as sending forth to the pure air a perfume like the aroma breathed from a field of spices. We look in vain for a successor to fill the place left vacant by his departure; for a voice as blithe and cheery as his; for so cunning a hand; for a visage that beamed forth more mirth than Joe Miller ever wrote; for taste in vestimental architecture so arabesque and grotesque, and yet in such admirable unison with the humor of the man; for that intuitive perception of the character of human clay as never to throw away a jest upon a fruitless soil; and for so plentiful a garner of the seeds of mirth as to scatter them in daily profusion, while, like the oil of the widow's cruse, they never wasted. We do not think of him as of a hoary Silenus, mirthful from the effect of bacchanalian orgies, or as the Momus of this nether world, most witty when most ill-natured, or as of George Buchanan, or any other king's fool, for there is degradation connected with these jesters—but as the admirable Crichton of his time, the glass of fashion and the mould of form to the corporation scavengers, "the rose of the fair state," as one whose combination and whose form were such that, of all his class, we can select him alone and say, "here was a bellman." Glorious old Pot Pie!

> His name is now a portion in the batch
> Of the heroic dough which baking Time
> Kneads for consuming ages—and the chime
> Of Fame's old bells, long as they truly ring,
> Shall tell of him.

THEODORE S. FAY.

THEODORE S. FAY was born in the city of New York. After receiving a liberal education he studied law, and at an early age commenced a literary career as a contributor to the New York Mirror, of which he subsequently became one of the editors. In 1832 he published *Dreams and Reveries of a Quiet Man*, a collection in two volumes of his articles in the Mirror, including a series of papers on New York society entitled the Little Genius. The remaining portion is occupied with tales, essays, and editorial comments on the passing events of city life.

Mr. Fay sailed for Europe in 1833, and passed the three following years in travel. During his absence he wrote a record of his wanderings with the title of *The Minute Book*, and in 1835 published his first novel, *Norman Leslie*. The incidents of the plot are derived from those of a murder which occurred in New York at the commencement of the century, the public interest in which was greatly increased by the array of legal talent enlisted in the trial of the case; Burr, Hamilton, and Edward Livingston appearing for the prisoner, and Cadwallader D. Colden, the District Attorney, for the state. The novel is well managed and interesting. It met with a rapid sale, and a dramatized version by Miss Louisa H. Medina was played for several nights at the Bowery theatre.

Theo. S. Fay.

In 1837 Mr. Fay received the appointment of Secretary of Legation at Berlin, a post he retained, to the great gratification of all American travellers who visited that city, until 1853, when he was promoted to the post of Minister Resident at Berne, where he still remains. In 1840 he published a second novel, *The Countess Ida*, the scenes of which are laid in Europe. The plot involves the discouragement of the practice of duelling by exhibiting a hero who, possessed of undisputed personal bravery, displays a higher degree of courage in refusing to accept, or be led into offering a challenge. This was followed in 1843 by a novel of similar length and similar purpose, entitled *Hoboken, a Romance of New York*. The selection of this locality, which has obtained a celebrity in national annals as well as the records of the society of the adjoining city, in connexion with this miserable remnant of the barbarous uses of rude and lawless times, shows his earnestness in the denunciation of the evil.

Mr. Fay has since published *Robert Rueful* and *Sidney Clifton*, two short tales, and in 1851 a poetical romance entitled *Ulric, or The Voices*, the design of which is to show that the temptings of the evil one, the "voices" of the poem, may be driven back by resolute endeavor and Christian faith. The scene is laid in the early days of the Reformation, but has little to do with the historic events of the period. Ulric is a young noble of Germany, and the action of the poem occurs among the beautiful scenes and picturesque castles of the Rhine, advantages of which the author avails himself in many passages of effective description.

THE RHINE—FROM ULRIC.

> Oh come, gentle pilgrim,
> From far distant strand,

Come, gaze on the pride
  Of the old German land.
On that wonder of nature,
  That vision divine
Of the past and the present,
  The exquisite Rhine.
As soft as a smile,
  And as sweet as a song,
Its famous old billows
  Roll murm'ring along.
From its source on the mount
  Whence it flies in the sea,
It flashes with beauty
  As bright as can be.
With the azure of heaven,
  Its first waters flow,
And it leaps like an arrow
  Escaped from a bow;
While reflecting the glories
  Its hill-sides that crown,
It then sweeps in grandeur
  By castle and town.
And when, from the red
  Gleaming tow'rs of Mayence
Enchanted thou'rt borne
  In bewildering trance,
By death-breathing ruin,
  By life-giving wine—
By thy dark-frowning turrets,
  Old Ehrenbreitstein!
To where the half magic
  Cathedral looks down
On the crowds at its base,
  Of the ancient Cologne,
While in rapture thy dazzled
  And wondering eyes
Scarce follow the pictures,
  As bright, as they rise,
As the dreams of thy youth,
  Which thou vainly wouldst stay,
But they float, from thy longings,
  Like shadows away.
Thou wilt find on the banks
  Of the wonderful stream,
Full many a spot
  That an Eden doth seem.
And thy bosom will ache
  With a secret despair,
That thou canst not inhabit
  A landscape so fair,
And fain thou wouldst linger
  Eternity there.

AN OUTLINE SKETCH.

The young Lord D. yawned. Why did the young lord yawn? He had recently come into ten thousand a year. His home was a palace. His sisters were angels. His cousin was—in love with him. He, himself, was an Apollo. His horses might have drawn the chariot of Phœbus, but in their journey around the globe, would never have crossed above grounds more Eden-like than his. Around him were streams, lawns, groves, and fountains. He could hunt, fish, ride, read, flirt, sleep, swim, drink, muse, write, or lounge. All the appliances of affluence were at his command. The young Lord D. was the admiration and envy of all the country. The young Lord D.'s step sent a palpitating flutter through many a lovely bosom. His smile awakened many a dream of bliss and wealth. The Lady S.,—that queenly woman, with her majestic bearing, and her train of dying adorers, grew lovelier and livelier beneath the spell of his smile; and even Ellen B.,—the modest, beautiful creature, with her large, timid, tender blue eyes, and her pouting red lips—that rose-bud—sighed audibly, only the day before, when he left the room—and yet—and yet—the young Lord D. yawned.

It was a rich still hour. The afternoon sunlight overspread all nature. Earth, sky, lake, and air were full of its dying glory, as it streamed into the apartment where they were sitting, through the foliage of a magnificent oak, and the caressing tendrils of a profuse vine, that half buried the verandah beneath its heavy masses of foliage.

"I am tired to death," said the sleepy lord.

His cousin Rosalie sighed.

"The package of papers from London is full of news, and——" murmured her sweet voice timidly.

"I hate news."

"The poetry in the New Monthly is——"

"You set my teeth on edge. I have had a surfeit of poetry."

"Ellen B. is to spend the day with us to-morrow."

Rosalie lifted her hazel eyes full upon his face.

"Ellen B.!" drawled the youth, "she is a child, a pretty child. I shall ride over to Lord A.'s."

Rosalie's face betrayed that a mountain was off her heart.

"Lord A. starts for Italy in a few weeks," said Rosalie.

"Happy dog!"

"He will be delighted with Rome and Naples."

"Rome and Naples," echoed D., in a musing voice.

"Italy is a delightful, heavenly spot," continued his cousin, anxious to lead him into conversation.

"So I'm told," said Lord D., abstractedly.

"It is the garden of the world," rejoined Rosalie.

Lord D. opened his eyes. He evidently was just struck with an idea. Young lords with ten thousand a year are not often troubled with ideas. He sprang from his seat. He paced the apartment twice. His countenance glowed. His eyes sparkled.

"Rose—"

"Cousin—"

What a beautiful break. Rose trembled to the heart. Could it be possible that he was ——.

He took her hand. He kissed it, eagerly, earnestly, and enthusiastically.

She blushed and turned away her face in graceful confusion.

"Rose!"

"Dear, *dear* cousin!"—

"I have made up my mind."

"Charles!—"

"To-morrow!"

"Heavens!"

"I will start for Italy."

Ocean! Superb—endless—sublime, rolling, tumbling, dashing, heaving, foaming—*cœlum undique et undique pontus.* Lord D. gazed around. The white cliffs of Dover were fading in the distance. Farewell, England. It is a sweet melancholy, this bidding adieu to a mass—a speck in the horizon—a mere cloud, yet which contains in its airy and dim outline all that you ever knew of existence.

"Noble England!" ejaculated Lord D., "and dear mother—Ellen B.—pretty fawn—Rose too—sweet pretty dear Rose—what could mean those glittering drops that hung upon her lashes when I said adieu? Can it be that?—pshaw—I am a coxcomb. What! Rose? the little sunshiny Rose—the cheerful philosopher—the logical—the studious—the—the—the—!"

Alas! alas! What are logic, study, cheerfulness, philosophy, sunshine, to a warm-hearted girl of twenty—in love?

Lord D. went below.

Italy *is* a paradise. Surely Adam looked on such skies, such rivers, such woods, such mountains, such fields. How lavish, how bright, how rich is every thing around. Lord D. guided his horse up a mountain near Rome. The sun had just set; the warm heavens stretched above him perfectly unclouded; what a time to muse! what a place! The young nobleman fell into a reverie, which, the next moment, was broken by a shout of terror—the clashing of arms—a pistol shot, and a groan. He flew to the spot. A youth of twenty lay at the root of a tall tree, weltering in his blood. The assassin, terrified at the sight of a stranger, fled.

"I die," murmured the youth, with ashy lips.

"Can I aid you?" asked Lord D., thrilling with horror and compassion.

"Take this box. It contains jewels, and a *secret*, which I would not have revealed for the world. Carry it to England, to the Duke of R——. Open it not, no matter what happens. Swear never to reveal to any human being that you possess it—swear."

Lord D. hesitated.

"My life-blood ebbs away apace. Speak, oh speak, and bless a dying man—swear."

"I swear."

"Enough. I thank you—hide it in your bosom. God bless you—my—England—never see—home—again—never, nev—."

The full round moon, beautifully bright, went solemnly up the azure track of sky.

Lord D. dashed a tear from his eye, as he gazed on the pallid features of the youth, who stretched himself out in the last shuddering agony and convulsion of death. He placed his hand upon the stranger's bosom. The heart had ceased to beat. No longer the crimson gore flowed from the wound. The light foam stood on his pale lips.

"And he has a mother," said the chilled nobleman—"and a once happy home. For their sake, as well as his, his wishes shall be obeyed."

The tread of horses' feet came to his ear, and shouts and confused voices.

Lord D. thought the fugitive ruffian was returning with more of the gang.

"Shall I fly like a coward?" was his first thought; but again, he said, "why should I waste my life upon a set of banditti?"

He sprang to his saddle, in his hurry leaving behind him a kerchief—dashed the rowels into the flanks of the snorting steed, and was presently lost in the winding paths of the forest.

The midnight moon was shining silently into the apartment, as Lord D.'s eyes closed in sleep, after having lain for some time lost in thought upon his couch. His senses gradually melted into dreams.

"Ah Rosalie. Dear Rosalie."

The maiden suddenly grasped his throat with the ferocity of a fiend, when—ha! no Rosalie—but the iron gripe of a muscular arm dragged him from the bed, and shook his idle dreams to air.

"Bind the villain!" said a hoarse voice.

"Away, away to the duke's!"

Bewildered, indignant, alarmed, the astonished lord found himself bound, and borne to a carriage—the beautiful and soft fragments of Italian scenery flew by the coach windows.

If you would freeze the heart of an Englishman, and yet suffocate him with anger, thrust him into a dungeon. Lord D. never was so unceremoniously assisted to a change of location. A black-browed, dark-complexioned, mustachio-lipped soldier hurled him down a flight of broken steps, and threw after him a bundle of clothes.

"By St. George, my friend, if I had you on the side of a green English hill, I would make your brains and bones acquainted with an oaken cudgel. The uncivilized knave."

He lay for hours on a little straw. By-and-by some one came in with a lamp.

"Pray, friend, where am I?"

The stranger loosened his cord, and motioned him to put on his clothes. He did so—unable to repress the occasional explosion of an honest, heartfelt execration. When his toilet was completed, his guide took him by the arm, and led him through a long corridor, till, lo! a blaze of sunshiny daylight dazzled his eyes.

"You are accused of murder," said the duke, in French.

"Merciful Providence!" ejaculated D.

"Your victim was found weltering in his blood at your feet. You left this kerchief on his body. It bears your name. By your hand he fell. You have been traced to your lodgings. You must die."

A witness rushed forward to bear testimony in favor of the prisoner. Lord D. *could* not be the perpetrator of such a crime. He was a nobleman of honor and wealth.

"Where are his letters?"

He had brought none.

"What is the result of the search which I ordered to be made at his lodgings?"

"This box, my lord duke, and—"

The box was opened. It contained a set of superb jewels, the miniature of the murdered youth, and of a fair creature, probably his mistress.

Lord D. started.

"By heavens, it is Rosalie! I am thunderstruck."

"Enough," said the duke, "guilt is written in every feature. Wretch, murderer! To the block with him. To-morrow at daybreak let his doom be executed. Nay, sir, lower that high bearing, those fiery and flashing eyes, that haughty and commanding frown. Not thus should you meet your Creator."

Night, deep night. How silent! How sublime! The fated lord lay watching the sky, through the iron grating of his cell.

"Ah, flash on, myriads of overhanging worlds—ye suns, whose blaze is quenched by immeasurable distance. To-morrow just so with your calm, bright, everlasting faces, ye will look down upon my grave. Jupiter, brilliant orb! How lustrous! How wonderful! Ha! the north star—ever constant! Axis on which revolves this stupendous, heavenly globe. How often *at home* I have watched thy beams, with Rosalie on my arm. Rosalie, *dear* Rosalie—"

"I come to save you," said a soft, sweet voice.

"What! Boy—who art thou? Why dost—"

The young stranger took off his cap.

"No—yes! That forehead—those eyes—enchanting girl—angel—"

"Hush!" said Rosalie, laying her finger upon her lip.

Ocean—again—the deep, magnificent ocean—and life and freedom.

"Blow, grateful breeze—on, on, over the washing billows, light-winked bark. Ha! land ahead! England! Rosalie, my girl, see—"

Again on her lashes tears stood glittering.

How different from those that—

Onward, like the wind, revolve the rattling wheels. The setting sun reveals the tall groves, the great oak, the lawns, the meadows, the fountains.

"My mother!"

"My son!"

"Friends!"

A package from the duke.

"The murderer of ——— is discovered, and has paid the forfeit of his crimes. Will Lord D. again visit Italy?"

"Ay, with my *wife*—with Rosalie."

"And with *letters* and a *good character*," said Rosalie, archly.

WILLIAM COX.

THE author of two volumes, entitled *Crayon Sketches, by an Amateur*, published in New York in 1838, with a preface by Mr. Theodore S. Fay, was an Englishman by birth, who came to America early in life to practise his calling of a printer. He found employment in the *Mirror*, conducted by General Morris, and made a literary reputation by contributing a series of sketches to its columns. These were in a happy vein of humor and criticism, in a style of ease and simplicity, satirizing the literary infirmities of the times, hitting off popular actors—the writer being a genuine member of the old Park Pit—and discussing various pleasantries of the author's own. The essays pleased men of taste and good sense. One of them, in particular, a sketch of the old city constable Jacob Hays, "written during an awful prevalence of biographies," gained great celebrity at the time. Mr. Cox having reviewed the Miscellanies of Sands in the Mirror, Mr. Gulian C. Verplanck, in his life of that author, thus acknowledged the compliment:—"This was William Cox, who shortly after became a regular contributor to American periodical literature, and has since gained an enviable literary reputation by his *Crayon Sketches*, a series of essays full of originality, pleasantry, and wit, alternately reminding the reader of the poetical eloquence of Hazlitt, and the quaint humor and eccentric tastes of Charles Lamb."

Mr. Cox, after writing for a number of years for the Mirror, returned to England. His circumstances, we believe, were prosperous. He occasionally sent a genial letter in his old style to his friend Morris's Home Journal, where his acquaintances one day, we think in 1851, were pained to read his obituary.

BIOGRAPHY OF JACOB HAYS.

He is a man, take him for all in all
We shall not look upon his like again.
SHAKESPEARE.

Ladies and gentlemen, allow me to introduce to your acquaintance, Baron *Nabem*, a person who has a very *taking* way with him.—*Tom and Jerry.*

Perhaps there is no species of composition so generally interesting and truly delightful as minute and indiscriminate biography, and it is pleasant to perceive how this taste is gradually increasing. The time is apparently not far distant when every man will be found busy writing the life of his neighbor, and expect to have his own written in return, interspersed with original anecdotes, extracts from epistolary correspondence, the exact hours at which he was in the habit of going to bed at night and getting up in the morning, and other miscellaneous and useful information carefully selected and judiciously arranged. Indeed, it is whispered that the editors of this paper* intend to take Longworth's Directory for the groundwork, and give the private history of all the city alphabetically, without "fear or favor—love or affection." In Europe there exists an absolute biographical mania, and they are manufacturing lives of poets, painters, play-actors, peers, pugilists, pick-pockets, horse jockeys, and their horses, together with a great many people that are scarcely known to have existed at all. And the fashion now is not only to shadow forth the grand and striking outlines of a great man's character, and hold to view those qualities which elevated him above his species, but to go into the minutiæ of his private life, and note down all the trivial expressions and every-day occurrences in which, of course, he merely spoke and acted like any ordinary man. This not only affords employment for the exercise of the small curiosity and meddling propensities of his officious biographer, but is also highly gratifying to the general reader, inasmuch as it elevates him mightily in his own opinion to see it put on record that great men ate, drank, slept, walked, and sometimes talked just as he does. In giving the biography of the high constable of this city, I shall by all means avoid descending to undignified particulars; though I deem it important to state, before proceeding further, that there is not the slightest foundation for the report afloat that Mr. Hays has left off eating buckwheat cakes in a morning, in consequence of their lying too heavily on his stomach.

Where the subject of the present memoir was born, can be but of little consequence; who were his father and mother, of still less; and how he was bred and educated, of none at all. I shall therefore pass over this division of his existence in eloquent silence, and come at once to the period when he attained the acmé of constabulatory power and dignity by being created high constable of this city and its suburbs; and it may be remarked, in passing, that the honorable the corporation, during their long and unsatisfactory career, never made an appointment more creditable to themselves, more beneficial to the city, more honorable to the country at large, more imposing in the eye of foreign nations, more disagreeable to all rogues, nor more gratifying to honest men, than that of the gentleman whom we are biographizing, to the high office he now holds. His acuteness and vigilance have become proverbial; and there is not a misdeed committed by any member of this community, but he is speedily admonished that he will "have old Hays [as he is affectionately and familiarly termed] after him." Indeed, it is supposed by many that he is gifted with supernatural attributes, and can see things that are hid from mortal ken; or how, it is contended, is it possible that he should, as he does,

Bring forth the secret'st man of blood?

That he can discover "undivulged crime"—that when a store has been robbed, he, without step or hesitation, can march directly to the house where the goods are concealed, and say, "these are they"—or, when a gentleman's pocket has been picked, that, from a crowd of unsavory miscreants he can, with unerring judgment, lay his hand upon one and exclaim "you're wanted!"—or, how is it that he is gifted with that strange principle of ubiquity that makes him "here, and there, and everywhere"

---

* The New York Mirror.

at the same moment? No matter how, so long as the public reap the benefit; and well may that public apostrophize him in the words of the poet:—

> Long may he live! our city's pride!
> Where lives the rogue, but flies before him!
> With trusty crabstick by his side,
> And staff of office waving o'er him.

But it is principally as a literary man that we would speak of Mr. Hays. True, his poetry is "unwritten," as is also his prose; and he has invariably expressed a decided contempt for philosophy, music, rhetoric, the *belles lettres*, the fine arts, and in fact all species of composition excepting bailiffs' warrants and bills of indictment—but what of that? The constitution of his mind is, even unknown to himself, decidedly poetical. And here I may be allowed to avail myself of another peculiarity of modern biography, namely, that of describing a man by what he is not. Mr. Hays has not the graphic power or antiquarian lore of Sir Walter Scott—nor the glittering imagery or voluptuous tenderness of Moore—nor the delicacy and polish of Rogers—nor the spirit of Campbell—nor the sentimentalism of Miss Landon—nor the depth and purity of thought and intimate acquaintance with nature of Bryant—nor the brilliant style and playful humor of Halleck—no, he is more in the petit larceny manner of Crabbe, with a slight touch of Byronic power and gloom. He is familiarly acquainted with all those interesting scenes of vice and poverty so fondly dwelt upon by that reverend chronicler of little villany, and if ever he can be prevailed upon to publish, there will doubtless be found a remarkable similarity in their works. His height is about five feet seven inches, but who makes his clothes we have as yet been unable to ascertain. His countenance is strongly marked, and forcibly brings to mind the lines of Byron when describing his Corsair:—

> There was a laughing devil in his sneer
> That raised emotions both of hate and fear;
> And where his glance of "apprehension" fell,
> Hope withering fled, and mercy sighed, farewell!

Yet with all his great qualities, it is to be doubted whether he is much to be envied. His situation certainly has its disadvantages. Pure and blameless as his life is, his society is not courted—no man boasts of his friendship, and few indeed like even to own him for an intimate acquaintance. Wherever he goes his slightest action is watched and criticized; and if he happen carelessly to lay his hand upon a gentleman's shoulder and whisper something in his ear, even that man, as if there were contamination in his touch, is seldom or never seen afterwards in decent society. Such things cannot fail to prey upon his feelings. But when did ever greatness exist without some penalty attached to it?

The first time that ever Hays was pointed out to me, was one summer afternoon, when acting in his official capacity in the city hall. The room was crowded in every part, and as he entered with a luckless wretch in his gripe, a low suppressed murmur ran through the hall, as if some superior being had alighted in the midst of them. He placed the prisoner at the bar—a poor coatless individual, with scarcely any edging and no roof to his hat—to stand his trial for bigamy, and then, in a loud, authoritative tone, called out for "silence," and there was silence. Again he spoke—"hats off there!" and the multitude became uncovered; after which he took his handkerchief out of his left-hand coat pocket, wiped his face, put it back again, looked sternly around, and then sat down. The scene was awful and impressive; but the odor was disagreeable in consequence of the heat acting upon a large quantity of animal matter congregated together. My olfactory organs were always lamentably acute: I was obliged to retire, and from that time to this, I have seen nothing, though I have heard much of the subject of this brief and imperfect, but, I trust, honest and impartial memoir.

Health and happiness be with thee, thou prince of constables—thou guardian of innocence—thou terror of evil-doers and little boys! May thy years be many and thy sorrows few—may thy life be like a long and cloudless summer's day, and may thy salary be increased! And when at last the summons comes from which there is no escaping—when the warrant arrives upon which no bail can be put in—when thou thyself, that hast "wanted" so many, art in turn "wanted and must go,"

> Mayst thou fall
> Into the grave as softly as the leaves
> Of the sweet roses on an autumn eve,
> Beneath the small sighs of the western wind,
> Drop to the earth!

JOHN INMAN.

JOHN INMAN, for many years a prominent member of the New York press, as one of the editors of the Commercial Advertiser, was born at Utica, New York, in 1805. He was a brother of Henry Inman, the celebrated portrait painter.

Mr. Inman's progress in life was mainly due to his own exertions, his early advantages of education or influence having been slight. In 1823 he removed to North Carolina, where he remained for two years in charge of a school. The following twelve months were more agreeably occupied by a tour in Europe, earned by his previous toil. On his return he applied himself to the practice of the law, but in 1828 relinquished the profession and became an editor of the Standard, a New York newspaper. In 1830 he left this journal to connect himself with the Mirror.

In 1833 Mr. Inman married Miss Fisher, a sister of Miss Clara Fisher, Mrs. Vernon, and Mr. John Fisher, three of the best comedians of the "Old Park" stock company. In the same year he became an assistant to Colonel Stone in the editorship of the Commercial Advertiser. On the death of Colonel Stone in 1844, he succeeded to the chief charge of the journal, a position which he retained until incapacitated by his last illness from performing its duties.

Mr. Inman was also the editor for some years of the Columbian Magazine and of several volumes of selections, and a contributor to the New York Review, the Spirit of the Times, and several of the popular magazines, where his tales, and sketches, and occasional poems, were received with favor. His versatility as a writer may be estimated from the fact, that on one occasion he wrote an entire number of the Columbian Magazine when under his charge. He died on the 30th of March, 1850.

THOUGHTS AT THE GRAVE OF A DEPARTED FRIEND.

> Loved, lost one, fare thee well—too harsh the doom
> That called thee thus in opening life away;
> Tears fall for thee; and at thy early tomb,
> I come at each return of this blest day,
> When evening hovers near, with solemn gloom,
> The pious debt of sorrowing thought to pay,
> For thee, blest spirit, whose loved form alone
> Here mouldering sleeps, beneath this simple stone.

But memory claims thee still; and slumber brings
 Thy form before me as in life it came;
Affection conquers death, and fondly clings
 Unto the past, and thee, and thy loved name;
And hours glide swiftly by on noiseless wings,
 While sad discourses of thy loss I frame,
With her the friend of thy most tranquil years,
Who mourns for thee with grief too deep for tears.

Sunday Evening.

HORATIO GREENOUGH.

HORATIO GREENOUGH, the first of the eminent sculptors of the country, and a refined and vigorous prose writer, was born at Boston, September 6, 1805. Like most artists, he early manifested a taste for his future calling.

"Having," says his biographer, Mr. Tuckerman, "a decided sense of form, a love of imitating it, and a mechanical aptitude which kept his knife, pencil, and scissors continually active, he employed hours in carving, drawing, and moulding toys, faces, and weapons, by way of amusing himself and his comrades. I have seen a head evidently taken from an old Roman coin, executed upon a bit of compact plaster about the size of a penny, admirably cut by Greenough with a penknife and common nail, while a schoolboy, seated upon the door-step of one of his neighbors. The lady who observed this achievement, preserved the little medal with religious care; and was the first to give the young sculptor a commission. It was for her that he executed the beautiful ideal bust of the Genius of Love. This propensity soon took a higher range. It was encouraged by the mechanics and professional men around him, whose good-will his agreeable manners and obvious genius propitiated. One kind artisan taught him the use of fine tools; a stone-cutter, of more than ordinary taste, instructed him to wield a chisel; benevolent librarians allowed him the use of plates, casts, and manuals; a physician gave him access to anatomical designs and illustrations; and Binon, a French artist, known by his bust of John Adams in Faneuil Hall, Boston, encouraged him to model at his side. Thus, as a mere schoolboy, did Greenough glean the rudiments of an artistic education without formal initiation. With eclectic wisdom he sought and found the aid he required, while exploring the streets of his native town; one day he might be seen poring over a folio, or contemplating a plaster copy of a famous statue; and, on another, exercising his mechanical ingenuity at the office of Solomon Willard, whose family name yet stamps, with traditional value, many an old dial-plate in New England; now he eagerly watches Alpheus Cary as he puts the finishing touch to a cherub's head on a tombstone; and, again, he stands a respectful devotee before Shaw or Coggswell, waiting for some treasured volume on the process or the results of his favorite art, from the shelves of Harvard and the Athenæum. Some of his juvenile triumphs are still remembered by his playmates—especially a pistol ornamented with relievo flowers in lead, a series of carriages moulded in bee's-wax, scores of wooden daggers tastefully carved, a lion couchant, modelled with a spoon from a pound of butter, to astonish his mother's guests at tea, elaborate card-paper plans for estates, and, as a climax to these childish yet graceful experiments, a little figure of Penn cut in chalk from an engraving of his statue in the Port-Folio."

At the age of sixteen he entered Harvard College. During his course at this institution he enjoyed the society of Washington Allston, an association from which he derived advantages which he always acknowledged with enthusiasm. Years after, when his reputation had been long established, he replied to an application for biographical information respecting his career, "A note to Allston's life might tell all of me that is essential."

Towards the close of his senior year Greenough sailed for Marseilles, and from thence to Rome, where he devoted himself so unremittingly to the prosecution of his art that he became, under the influence of malaria, so prostrated as to be forced to return home. The sea voyage restored him to health, and after a few months he returned to Italy, and established himself in Florence. Here he remained for some time without obtaining any adequate recognition of his powers, until he received from the novelist Cooper an order for the "Chaunting Cherubs," a work suggested by a portion of a painting by Raphael. "Fenimore Cooper," the artist remarked several years after, "saved me from despair after my return to Italy. He employed me as I wished to be employed; and up to this moment has been as a father to me."

It was in part owing to Cooper's exertions that Greenough obtained the order from Congress for his colossal Washington. On the completion of this work he returned home to superintend its erection.

Horatio Greenough

In 1851 he again returned to the United States on a similar errand connected with his group of the Rescue, a work commemorative of the period of conflict with the Indian tribes in our history, and executed by order of Congress. Disgust with the change wrought in Florence by the reaction from the liberal triumphs of 1848, consigning the city to the despotism of military rule, and a desire to pursue his profession in his own country, furnished additional motives for the change. The transition from the quiet of an Italian studio to the activity of an American resident, desirous of taking his full share in the discussion of the agitated topics of the day, was one which excited as well as pleased him. He established himself at Newport, where he proposed to devote himself to his art; but this and other anticipations of usefulness and happiness were suddenly interrupted by an attack of brain fever, during the progress of which the patient was removed to the neighborhood of Boston, but without beneficial effect, his disease arriving at a speedy and fatal termination on the 18th of December, 1852.

A *Memorial of Horatio Greenough*, published in 1853, contains the only collection which has been made of his writings. These comprise a series of papers on the public works of the capitol city with the title of *Æsthetics at Washington*, essays on Social Theories, American Art and Architecture, on Beauty, a plan for the proposed Cooper monument, a scheme in which the writer took a deep interest, a defence of Trumbull's Declaration of Independence from the famous slur of Randolph, and a number of fragmentary remarks on various topics suggested by the study of nature and art. He also planned a course of lectures on Art, two of which were completed and delivered.

THE DESECRATION OF THE FLAG.

An American citizen, standing here upon the pavement of the principal avenue of the Metropolis, sees five ensigns of the United States flying within sight of each other. Two of these flags float over the halls of Congress, and announce a session of both branches of the legislature; a third adorns the roof of an omnibus as a gala decoration; a fourth appears on the roof-tree of a new hotel as a sign, or perhaps puff extraordinary; a fifth marks the site of an engine-house. I cannot but think that several of these flags are misplaced. Their use at the Capitol has always struck my eye as appropriate and beautiful. The other instances of their appearance which I have mentioned seem an abuse, a desecration of the national symbol of Union.

There is always a tendency in every community to seize upon and make use of that which is public, or of general influence and widely recognised significance. The same holy symbol which surmounts the cupola of all Roman Catholic cathedrals, is made in Italy to answer the end which in England is effected by a bit of board, bearing the words "commit no nuisance." When the position which it is desired to protect is particularly exposed, the cross is repeated ten, twenty, fifty times, and is even reinforced by verses in honor of saints, martyrs, and the Holy Virgin. A foreigner is much shocked by such a practice. The natives smile at his squeamishness—they are used to it; yet they all quote "*nec Deus intersit, etc.*," readily enough upon other occasions.

It is very clear that the national flag, however some persons may smile at the assertion, has a deep and noble significance, one which we should hold sacred and do nothing to impair. Were it a mere "bit of bunting," as the British Foreign Secretary thoughtlessly or artfully styled it, why should we see it universally paraded?

I believe no one will deny that the colors of the Union hoisted at the dockyards and arsenals assert the national possession—that they proclaim the nationality of our merchant ships in foreign parts, and sanction the display of our naval power. These and the like occasions call for them, and their appearance has a value and expression of a peculiar kind. Is it doubtful that the dragging them through the streets by whosoever chooses so to do, the parading them upon taverns, and raree-shows, and other like trivial occasions, tends to degrade and weaken their special meaning and value? I may be told that the abuse, if such it be, is rather within the region of taste than of legal observance. I regret that it is so, because the whole matter has assumed its present aspect, because it is "nobody's business" to interfere. It is merely as a question of taste that I speak of it, and as such, I believe that a little reflection will show, that accustomed as we are to see the flag hung out "*a-propos de bottes*," and sometimes hanging downwards too, so as almost to touch the heads of the horses as they pass, our indifference to the desecration is merely a measure of use and wont, and analogous, though not equal, to the obtuseness of the Catholic, who uses the cross of the Redeemer in lieu of a by-law or police regulation.

I have heard the right of each citizen to use the national flag stoutly maintained. I cannot see why the consular seal, or the gardens of the White House, are not equally at his mercy. There is another argument which may be called the *argumentum ad Buncombe*, and which might easily be resorted to to defend this and the like abuses, viz., That it is peculiarly American and democratic. The English long asserted a right to be coarse and uncourteous as a proof of sincerity and frankness. John Bull, they contended, was too honest to be civil. There is much nonsense of this sort in the old books. Excessive beer-drinking and other gluttonies were upheld as having some mysterious virtue in them. Sailors used to swear and blaspheme in a similar way. It was expected of them, and required no apology. When such notions yielded, as they must, to reflection and cultivation, it was seen at once that they had been only abuses or barbarisms ingeniously hitched on to other qualities, and identified with self-love.

JOHN R. BARTLETT.

John R. Bartlett was born at Providence, R. I., October 23, 1805, of an old Massachusetts family. He was educated at schools in Kingston and Montreal, in Canada, and at Lowville academy in the state of New York. On leaving school he was sent to Providence, his native place, and engaged as clerk in a mercantile house. Soon after coming of age he entered the banking house of the late Cyrus Butler at that place, as book-keeper, and, after being three years with him, was appointed cashier of the Globe Bank in Providence, which situation he held for six years. He took a liberal interest in the promotion of knowledge, being one of the original projectors of the Providence Athenæum, now one of the best public libraries, in proportion to the number of its volumes, in the country. He was also an active member of the Franklin Society of Rhode Island, an association for the cultivation of science, before which he occasionally lectured. The close confinement of the bank, and the occupation of several hours a day in study, wore upon his health, and he withdrew with his family to New York in 1837, to enter a large commission house in the city, engaged in the sale of American manufactures. The business, in the commercial difficulties of the times, was unsuccessful, and Mr. Bartlett turned to another pursuit adapted to his literary inclinations. He left Pine street for Broadway, where, in conjunction with Mr. Charles Welford, he established a book store for the importation and sale of choice English and foreign works. It soon became the daily resort of literary men of the city, and of scholars, on their visits to town, from all parts of the country. On all topics of research in American history, or the wide field of ethnology, or English classic literature, Mr. Bartlett, and his accomplished, well read partner, were unfailing authorities. Before the days of the Astor library, there was no better resort for literary information in the city than the well furnished book-store at No. 7 Astor House.

The literary associations of Mr. Bartlett at this time were much extended and enhanced by his active participation in the management of the New York Historical Society, of which he was for several years the corresponding secretary. He was also the projector, with Mr. Gallatin, of the American Ethnological Society, the first meeting of which was held at his house. Among its original members were the Rev. Drs. Hawks and Robinson, Mr. Catherwood, Mr. Schoolcraft, and the late John L. Stephens. The meetings of the society for several years were held at his residence, and at that of Mr. Gallatin. The doors were widely opened at Mr. Bartlett's, after the business of the evening had been disposed of, and his rooms saw a frequent gathering of the intelligence of the city, and of its numerous cultivated strangers and travellers from abroad. In 1848 Mr. Bartlett read before the New York Historical Society a series of *Reminiscences of Albert Gallatin*, with anecdotes of his conversations, which were published in the society's Proceedings for that year.

In 1849 he retired from the book business to Providence, and the next year was appointed by President Taylor commissioner to run the boundary line between the United States and Mexico, under the treaty of Guadalupe Hidalgo. The commission, which was the largest and most important ever sent out by the government for a similar purpose, was organized by him, and six weeks after his appointment he sailed from New York for the coast of Texas to enter upon his duties. He remained in the field until January, 1853, during which time he crossed the continent to California, and after various journeys there, recrossed by another route, making extensive surveys and explorations by the way. The whole of the extensive line of boundary was nearly completed by him when he was compelled to suspend operations and return to Washington. Certain gross errors existing in the map, which he was compelled by the treaty as well as his instructions to follow, led to the fixing of a boundary which gave dissatisfaction to the opponents of Mr. Fillmore's administration. Being in the majority in Congress, they appended a proviso to the appropriation for carrying on the survey, to the effect, that if the boundary was not fixed in a certain place, which in their opinion was the correct one, the money appropriated should not be used. Cut off from the means to carry on and complete the small portion which remained to be surveyed, Mr. Bartlett was driven to the necessity of suspending all operations when at Ringgold Barracks, near Camargo, on the Rio Grande, and of returning home. He was sustained by his old Whig friends, and removed by President Pierce.

The various surveys performed by his orders, while in the field, were not less than twenty-five hundred miles in extent; all of which were accompanied by elaborate astronomical, magnetic, and meteorological observations, executed by the officers of the expedition.

In 1854 Mr. Bartlett published his *Personal Narrative of Explorations and Incidents in Texas, New Mexico, California, Sonora, and Chihuahua, connected with the United States and Mexican Boundary Commission* during the years 1850-53. It is written with care and exactness, and derives its interest both from the simple, full, and accurate method of the narrator, and the novelty of the scenes which came under his view. In addition to these inherent qualities, the book appeared in a dress of unusual typographical excellence. The lithographic and woodcut illustrations from original designs by Mr. Henry C. Pratt, an artist who accompanied Mr. Bartlett, are numerous and well presented.*

In 1847 Mr. Bartlett published a small work on *The Progress of Ethnology*, and the next year in an octavo volume, *A Dictionary of Americanisms; A Glossary of Words and Phrases usually regarded as peculiar to the United States.* This work is now out of print, and Mr. Bartlett is preparing a new enlarged and revised edition. He has also the materials for a proposed work on *The Ethnology of the Indian Tribes in the States contiguous to the Mexican Boundary.*

JOHN LLOYD STEPHENS,

The original explorer of the Antiquities of Central America, was born at Shrewsbury, Monmouth County, New Jersey, Nov. 28, 1805. His father and mother were both natives of New Jersey. He was educated in New York, being prepared for Columbia College, which he entered at thirteen, by the celebrated blind teacher, Mr. Nelson. On the completion of his course he studied law with Daniel Lord, and subsequently entered the law school of Judge Gould at Litchfield, finally completing his studies with George W. Strong in New York. He early made a tour to a relative residing at Arkansas, then a journey of some adventure, and on his return descended the Mississippi to New Orleans in a flat-boat. He practised law for eight years, and became the associate of the literary men and politicians of the day, frequently speaking in defence of Democratic measures in Tammany. An affection of the throat led to a European tour for his recovery. In 1834 he embarked for Havre, landed on the coast of England, made his way to France, thence to Italy, Greece, Turkey, and Russia, returning by the way of Poland and Germany. From France he again set forth, through Marseilles to Egypt, and made the tour of the Nile as far as Thebes. He returned home in 1836. While abroad several of his letters from the Mediterranean had been published in his friend Hoffman's *American Monthly Magazine.* The success of these in their full, interesting personal narrative, encouraged the publication of his first book in 1837, the *Incidents of Travel in Egypt, Arabia Petraea, and the Holy Land*, followed the next year by *Incidents of Travel in Greece, Turkey, Russia, and Poland.* The success of these works, published by the Harpers, was remarkable. They were universally read and admired, and continue to be published in England and at home. The style was popular, rapid, easy, and energetic, communicating the zest and spirit of enjoyment of the traveller.

In 1839 a strong effort was made for his appointment, as agent of his state, New York, to Holland, for the Collection of the Colonial Records, but Whig opposition defeated his claims; when President Van Buren appointed him Special Ambassador to Central America to negotiate a treaty with that country. The story of his adventures was published on his return, in 1841, in his *Incidents of Travel in Central America, Chiapas, and Yucatan.* Like his other works, it was at once successful. It contained an account of the distracted politics of the country, and above

* We may refer for further papers of Mr. Bartlett on the subject, to the "Official Despatches and Correspondence connected with the United States and Mexican Boundary Commission" (Senate Doc. No. 119, 32d Congress, 1st Session), and "A Letter to the Hon. Alexander H. H. Stuart, Secretary of the Interior, in Defence of the Mexican Boundary Line" (Senate Doc. No. 6, Special Session, 1854).

all a revelation of the rich field of investigation in the antiquities of the region. In this work he was a pioneer, achieving his brilliant results of discovery by his accustomed personal energy. A second visit to Yucatan in 1842, chiefly to complete his antiquarian researches, resulted in the publication, in 1843, of his *Incidents of Travels in Yucatan.*

The exact, spirited delineations of the antiquities which appeared in the engravings of these volumes were from the pencil of Mr. Francis Catherwood, a fellow-traveller with Mr. Stephens, who subsequently prepared a costly folio work of plates of the same subject, which secured a deservedly high reputation. He was a man of science and an able railway surveyor, as well as an accomplished artist. His death with the passengers of the ill-fated steamer Arctic, in the autumn of 1854, was an event greatly regretted by those acquainted with his personal worth and scientific ability.

In 1846 Mr. Stephens was a delegate, being on both party tickets, to the State Convention of New York, to revise the Constitution, in which he took an active part.

In 1847 he engaged resolutely in the affairs of the Ocean Steam Navigation Company to connect New York and Bremen. The steam navigation of the Atlantic was then in its infancy, and the establishment of the company, with the building of the vessels, called forth all his resources. He sailed in the Washington on her first trip to Bremen. An account of his visit to Humboldt at the time was published in the Literary World in New York.

In 1849 he became an associate in the great enterprise to connect the two oceans of the Panama Railroad, and was elected Vice-President of the Company. He subsequently became President. He travelled over the Isthmus inspecting the route and making arrangements with the Government of New Granada for the work. On his mule-back journey to the capital he was thrown and injured in the spine; and in those circumstances of pain and distress carried on his communications with the government at Bogota. When the work was undertaken he visited the Isthmus to urge its prosecution, in the winters of 1850–1 and 1851–2. On his return, in the spring of 1852, he was attacked by a disease of the liver, which terminated his life October 12th of that year.

Stephens was a happy instance of the peculiar energies of the active American citizen. Prompt, acute, enterprising, he always sought advance posts of labor. The demand for activity of his nature required new fields of toil and exertion, hazardous and apparently romantic, though never separated from a practical design. The Panama Railroad is identified with his name, and its summit has been properly chosen as the site of a monument to his memory. Thus, too, his efforts in ocean steam navigation, and his zealous pursuit of American antiquities, not as a study in the closet, but as a practical achievement tasking powers of courage, resolution, and bodily prowess in new countries. His personal enthusiasm was the charm of his writings on the better known countries of the old world—where, to Americans at least, as at Petra and in Russia, he was something of an original adventurer.

THE BASTINADO AT CAIRO—FROM INCIDENTS OF TRAVEL IN EGYPT.

Having finished my purchases in the bazaars, I returned to my hotel ready to set out, and found the dromedaries, camels, and guides, and expected to find the letter for the governor of Akaba, which, at the suggestion of Mr. Linant, I had requested Mr. Gliddon to procure for me. I now learned, however, from that gentleman, that to avoid delay it would be better to go myself, first sending my caravan outside the gate, and representing to the minister that I was actually waiting for the letter, in which case he would probably give it to me immediately. I accordingly sent Paul with my little caravan to wait for me at the tombs of the califs, and, attended by the consul's janizary, rode up to the citadel, and stopped at the door of the governor's palace. The reader may remember that on my first visit to his excellency I saw a man whipped—this time I saw one bastinadoed. I had heard much of this, a punishment existing, I believe, only in the East, but I had never seen it inflicted before, and hope I never shall see it again. As on the former occasion, I found the little governor standing at one end of the large hall of entrance, munching, and trying causes. A crowd was gathered around, and before him was a poor Arab, pleading and beseeching most piteously, while the big tears were rolling down his cheeks; near him was a man whose resolute and somewhat angry expression marked him as the accuser, seeking vengeance rather than justice. Suddenly the governor made a gentle movement with his hand; all noise ceased; all stretched their necks and turned their eager eyes towards him; the accused cut short his crying, and stood with his mouth wide open, and his eyes fixed upon the governor. The latter spoke a few words in a very low voice, to me of course unintelligible, and, indeed, scarcely audible, but they seemed to fall upon the quick ears of the culprit like bolts of thunder; the agony of suspense was over, and, without a word or a look, he laid himself down on his face at the feet of the governor. A space was immediately cleared around; a man on each side took him by the hand, and stretching out his arms, kneeled upon and held them down, while another seated himself across his neck and shoulders. Thus nailed to the ground, the poor fellow, knowing that there was no chance of escape, threw up his feet from the knee-joint, so as to present the soles in a horizontal position. Two men came forward with a pair of long stout bars of wood, attached together by a cord, between which they placed the feet, drawing them together with the cord so as to fix them in their horizontal position, and leave the whole flat surface exposed to the full force of the blow. In the meantime two strong Turks were standing ready, one at each side, armed with long whips much resembling our common cowskin, but longer and thicker, and made of the tough hide of the hippopotamus. While the occupation of the judge was suspended by these preparations, the janizary had presented the consul's letter. My sensibilities are not particularly acute, but they yielded in this instance. I had watched all the preliminary arrangements, nerving myself for what was to come, but when I heard the scourge whizzing through the air, and, when the first blow fell upon the naked feet, saw the convulsive movements of the body, and heard the first loud, piercing shriek, I could stand it no longer; I broke through the crowd, forgetting the governor and everything else, except the agonizing sounds from which I was escaping; but the janizary followed close at my heels, and, laying his hand upon my arm, hauled me back to the governor. If I had consulted merely the impulse of feeling, I should have consigned him, and the governor, and the whole nation of Turks, to the lower regions; but it was all important not to offend this summary dispenser of justice, and I never made a greater sacrifice of feeling to expediency, than when I re-entered his presence. The shrieks of the unhappy criminal were ringing through the chamber, but the governor received me with as calm a smile as if he had been sitting on his own divan, listening only to the strains of some pleasant music, while I stood with my teeth clenched, and felt the hot breath of the victim, and heard the whizzing of the accursed whip, as it fell again and again upon his bleeding feet. I have heard men cry out in agony when the sea was raging, and the drowning man, rising for the last time upon the mountain waves, turned his imploring arms towards us, and with his dying breath called in vain for help; but I never heard such heart-rending sounds as those from the poor bastinadoed wretch before me. I thought the governor would never make an end of reading the letter, when the scribe handed it to him for his signature, although it contained but half a dozen lines; he fumbled in his pocket for his seal, and dipped it in the ink; the impression did not suit him, and he made another, and after a delay that seemed to me eternal, employed in folding it, handed it to me with a most gracious smile. I am sure I grinned horribly in return, and almost snatching the letter, just as the last blow fell, I turned to hasten from the scene. The poor scourged wretch was silent; he had found relief in happy insensibility; I cast one look upon the senseless body, and saw the feet laid open in gashes, and the blood streaming down the legs. At that moment the bars were taken away, and the mangled feet fell like lead upon the floor. I had to work my way through the crowd, and before I could escape I saw the poor fellow revive, and by the first natural impulse rise upon his feet, but fall again as if he had stepped upon red-hot irons. He crawled upon his hands and knees to the door of the hall, and here I rejoiced to see that, miserable, and poor, and degraded as he was, he had yet friends whose hearts yearned towards him; they took him in their arms and carried him away.

FREDERIC HENRY HEDGE.

FREDERIC H. HEDGE was born at Cambridge, Mass., December 12, 1805. His father, Levi Hedge, was from 1810 to 1827 Professor of Logic and Metaphysics in Harvard University, and in 1818 published a *System of Logic*, which has been much used as a text-book in colleges, has passed through several editions, and been translated into German. He was the son of a clergyman, and was born in Warwick, Mass., in 1767. He died in Cambridge the last day of 1843. He was a laborious student, and distinguished for his painstaking fidelity as an instructor.

His son Frederic was educated in Germany, where in 1818 he was sent under the care of the historian, George Bancroft. He was a pupil of a celebrated teacher, David Ilgen, at the Gymnasium of Schulpforte, where Klopstock, Fichte, and Ranke, were instructed in their youth. He returned to America in 1823, entered Harvard, and was graduated in 1825. He studied theology; was chosen pastor of a Church in Cambridge in 1829; afterwards, in 1835, removed to Bangor in Maine, where he had charge of a congregation, and in 1850 became pastor of the Westminster Church in Providence, R. I. His literary productions have been mostly in the department of speculative and spiritual philosophy. In this province he has been eminent, as an interpreter of the German mind. He has published orations, lectures, discourses, reviews of theology, philosophy, and literature.*

His poetical effusions are scattered through various periodicals and annuals. They are mostly translations from the German, of which he published several in the volume with Dr. Furness's version of the Song of the Bell at Philadelphia. One of these, which we print from a corrected copy, is

THE ANGELS' SONG—FROM GOETHE'S "FAUST."

Raphael.

The sun is still for ever sounding
 With brother spheres a rival song,
And on his destined journey bounding,
 With thunder-step he speeds along.
The sight gives angels strength, though greater
 Than angel's utmost thought sublime;
And all thy wondrous works, Creator,
 Are grand as in creation's prime.

---

* Of the public discourses we may mention a Fourth of July oration delivered to the citizens of Bangor; an Address at the opening of the Bangor Lyceum; Conservatism and Reform, a Phi Beta Kappa oration before the Societies of Harvard and Bowdoin.

Among Dr. Hedge's numerous articles to the Christian Examiner, we may refer to a review of Coleridge in March, 1833, noticeable as one of the earliest essays from an American pen on the transcendental philosophy of Germany; an Essay on Swedenborg, November, 1833; an Essay on Schiller, July, 1834; an Essay on Phrenology, November, 1834, which excited much attention, and called forth numerous replies; an Essay on the Genius and Writings of R. W. Emerson, January, 1845; an Essay on Natural Religion, January, 1853; an Ecclesiastical Christendom, July, 1851; Romanism in its worship, January, 1854.

The published sermons of Dr. Hedge include, with numerous others, a Discourse before the Ancient and Honorable Artillery Company, Boston, June, 1834; a Discourse on the Death of President Harrison, Bangor, 1841; on the Death of William Ellery Channing, Bangor, 1842; a Discourse before the Graduating Class of the Cambridge Divinity School, 1849.

Gabriel.

And fleetly, thought surpassing, fleetly
The earth's green pomp is spinning round,
And Paradise alternates sweetly
With night terrific and profound.
There foams the sea, its broad wave beating
Against the tall cliff's rocky base,
And rock and sea away are fleeting
In everlasting spheral chase.

Michael.

And storms with rival fury heaving,
From land to sea from sea to land,
Still as they rave, a chain are weaving
Of deepest efficacy grand.
There burning Desolation blazes,
Precursor of the Thunder's way;
But, Lord, thy servants own with praises
The milder movement of thy day.

The Three.

The sight gives angels strength, though greater
Than angel's utmost thought sublime,
And all thy wondrous works, Creator,
Are glorious as in Eden's prime.

His other translations from the German are chiefly included in the volume from his pen published by Carey and Hart in 1848, *The Prose Writers of Germany*, which contains biographical notices of the chief authors, with selections from their writings. In the winter of 1853-4 Dr. Hedge delivered a course of *Lectures on Mediæval History*, before the Lowell Institute at Boston.

CONSERVATISM AND REFORM.*

Authority is not only a guide to the blind, but a law to the seeing. It is not only a safe-conduct to those (and they constitute the larger portion of mankind) whose dormant sense has no intuitions of its own, but we have also to consider it, as affording the *awakened* but inconstant mind, a security against itself,—a centre of reference in the multitude of its own visions,—in the conflict of its own volitions, a centre of rest. Unbounded license is equally an evil, and equally incompatible with true liberty, in thought as in action. In the one as in the other, liberty must bound and bind itself for its own preservation and best effect. It must *legalize* and determine itself by self-imposed laws. Law and liberty are not adverse, but different sides of one fact. The deeper the law the greater the liberty: as organic life is at once more determinate and more free than unorganized matter, a plant than a stone, a bird than a plant, the intellectual life, like the physical, must bind itself, in order that it may become effective and free. It must organize itself by means of fixed principles which shall protect it equally, against encroachment without, and anarchy within. * * * The individual is the product of the Past. However he may renounce the connexion, he is always the child of his time. He can never entirely shake off that relation. All the efforts made to outstrip time, to anticipate the natural growth of man by a violent disruption of old ties and total separation from the Past, have hitherto proved useless, or useful, if at all, in the way of caution, rather than of fruit. The experiment has often been tried. Men of ardent temper and lively imagination, impatient of existing evils, from which no period is exempt, have renounced society, broke loose from all their moorings in the actual, and sought in the boundless sea of *dissent* the promised land of Reform. They found what they carried; they carried what they were; they were what we all are—the offspring of their time.

The aeronaut, who spurns the earth in his puffed balloon, is still indebted to it for his impetus and his wings: and still, with his utmost efforts, he cannot escape the sure attraction of the parent sphere. His floating island is a part of her main. He revolves with her orbit, he is sped by her wings. We who stand below and watch his motions, know that he is one of us. He may dally with the clouds awhile, but his home is not there. Earth he is, and to earth he must return.

The most air-blown reformer cannot overcome the moral gravitation which connects him with his time. He owes to existing institutions the whole philosophy of his dissent, and draws, from Church and State, the very ideas by which he would fight against them, or rise above them. The individual may withdraw from society, he may spurn at all the uses of civilized life, dash the golden cup of tradition from his lips, and flee to the wilderness "where the wild asses quench their thirst." He may find others who will accompany him in his flight; but let him not fancy that the course of reform will follow him there,—that any permanent organization can be based on dissent,—that society will relinquish the hard conquests of so many years and return again to original nature, wipe out the old civilization, and—with *rasa tabula*—begin the world anew. * * * There is no stand-point out of society, from which society can be reformed. "Give me where to stand," was the ancient postulate. "Find where to stand," says modern Dissent. "Stand where you are," says Goethe, "and move the world." * * * The scholar must not coquet, in imagination, with the dowered and titled institutions of the old world, and feel it a mischance which has matched him with a portionless Republic. Let him, rather, esteem it a privilege to be so connected, and glory in the popular character of his own government, as a genuine fruit of human progress, and the nearest approximation yet made to that divine right which all governments claim. Let him not think it a shame to be with and of the people, in every genuine impulse of the popular mind: not suffering the scholar to extinguish the citizen, but remembering that the citizen is before the scholar—the elder and higher category of the two. He shall find himself to have gained intellectually, as well as socially, by free and frequent intercourse with the people, whose instincts, in many things, anticipate his reflective wisdom, and in whose unconscious movements a fact is often forefelt before it is seen by reason; as the physical changes of our globe are felt by the lower animals before they appear to man. * * * Nothing is more natural, than that men, who have contributed something in their day to illustrate or extend the path of discovery in any direction, should cling with avidity to those conclusions which they have established for themselves, and which represent the natural boundaries of their own mind—"the butt and sea-mark of its utmost sail,"—nothing more natural than that they, for their part, should feel a disinclination to farther inquiry. But it ill becomes them to deny the possibility of farther discovery—to maintain that they have found the bottom of the well where truth lies hid, because they have reached the limits of their own specific gravity. One sees at once, that in some branches of inquiry this position is not only untenable, but the very enunciation of it absurd. It would require something more than the authority of Herschel to make us believe that creation stops with the limits of his forty feet reflector.

* From a Phi Beta Kappa Oration, 1843.

Nor would the assertion of Sir Humphrey Davy be sufficient to convince us that all the properties of matter have been catalogued in his report. By what statute of limitations are we forbidden to indulge the same hope of indefinite progress in every other direction, which remains to us in these!

MATTHEW F. MAURY.

MATTHEW FONTAINE MAURY, a descendant of the Rev. James Fontaine, an eminent Huguenot preacher (the founder of a large and influential American family, and author of an autobiography which has recently for the second time been republished in connexion with a highly interesting sketch of the worthy and his descendants, by one of their number, Miss Ann Maury of New York), was born in Spottsylvania county, Virginia, January 14, 1806. His parents removed to Tennessee in his fourth year. One of a family of nine children, in a newly settled country, he would have received few of the advantages of education had it not been for the care of the bishop of the diocese, the Rev. James H. Otey, who, forming a high opinion of his intellectual promise, did much to fit him for a life of future usefulness. In 1824 he obtained a midshipman's commission, was placed on board the Brandywine, and sailed with General Lafayette to France. On his return he accompanied the frigate to the Pacific, was transferred to the Vincennes, and in that vessel completed the circumnavigation of the globe. He again sailed, as passed-midshipman, to the Pacific, where he was transferred as lieutenant to the Potomac. While at sea he devoted his leisure time to the study of mathematics, a branch of knowledge in which he at first found himself unequal to the requirements of his profession. For the purpose of extending at the same time his knowledge of modern languages he made use of Spanish mathematical works. As he pursued his investigations he became greatly inconvenienced by the necessity of referring to a number of different volumes, and with a view to save others a like difficulty prepared, amid the annoyances and interruptions of life at sea, a work on navigation. It was commenced in the steerage of the Vincennes, concluded in the Potomac, and published about the year 1835, when it met with general acceptance. In the same year he was appointed astronomer to the South Sea Exploring Expedition, but, on the withdrawal of Commodore Jones from the chief command, declined the appointment.

In 1839 he contributed an article to the Southern Literary Messenger, entitled *A Scheme for rebuilding Southern Commerce*, containing observations on the Gulf Stream and Great Circle Sailing, which were afterwards more fully developed.

A few months later, in October, 1839, while on his way from Tennessee to join a surveying vessel in the harbor of New York, the stage-coach in which he was passing through Ohio was overturned, and the traveller broke a leg, dislocated a knee, and suffered other injuries, which, after several months' weary confinement, resulted in a permanent lameness, which disabled him for the active pursuit of his profession. He amused himself by writing, during the long period of imprisonment in a wretched wayside tavern to which his bandaged limb subjected him, a series of articles on various abuses in the Navy, which were

published in the Southern Literary Messenger, under the pleasant title of *Scraps from the Lucky Bag, by Harry Bluff*.

On his retirement from the Exploring Expedition, Lieutenant Maury was placed in charge of the collection of books and charts belonging to the government, which has since expanded into the National Observatory and Hydrographical office, now known as the Naval Observatory, the change of title having been made in 1855. Lieutenant Maury is at the head of both of these institutions, which owe their extent and efficiency mainly to his efforts. In 1842 he first proposed the plan for a system of uniform observations of winds and currents, which form the basis of his celebrated and valuable charts and sailing-directions.

In 1853 he attended a convention of maritime nations at Brussels to carry out his suggestions for a conference to determine upon a uniform system of observations at sea. Plans were adopted by which ships, under all the great flags of Christendom, are engaged in adding to the resources of science, mapping out roads on the ocean with the precision of engineers on terra firma, and striving to obtain with equal exactness the laws of the clouds above and the depths below.

In 1855 he published *The Physical Geography of the Sea*,* a work in which he has embodied the results of his varied investigations in a narrative of remarkable clearness and interest. His descriptions of natural phenomena, and of the voyages of rival vessels, sailing at the same dates to the same ports, along his sea lines, possess dramatic interest. A pleasant vein of humor shows itself now and then as he speaks of the rummaging of garrets and sea chests for old log-books which his investigations, naturally exciting the enthusiasm of others as well as himself, called forth. This quality of humor finds a wider scope in the magazine papers of the writer, and is a pleasant characteristic of his correspondence and conversation.

* 8vo. pp. 274. A second edition, revised and enlarged, immediately appeared.

In addition to this volume and the letter-press accompanying his various charts, Lieutenant Maury is the author of several addresses delivered in various parts of the country, among which we may mention those before the Geological and Mineralogical Society of Fredericksburg, May, 1836; before the Southern Scientific Convention at Memphis in 1849 on the Pacific railway, and at most of the other meetings of the same body; and at the first anniversary of the American Geographical and Statistical Society in the city of New York, 1854.

LAW OF COMPENSATION IN THE ATMOSPHERE.*

Whenever I turn to contemplate the works of nature, I am struck with the admirable system of compensation, with the beauty and nicety with which every department is poised by the others; things and principles are meted out in directions the most opposite, but in proportions so exactly balanced and nicely adjusted, that results the most harmonious are produced.

It is by the action of opposite and compensating forces that the earth is kept in its orbit, and the stars are held suspended in the azure vault of heaven; and these forces are so exquisitely adjusted, that, at the end of a thousand years, the earth, the sun, and moon, and every star in the firmament, is found to come to its proper place at the proper moment.

Nay, philosophy teaches us, when the little snowdrop, which in our garden walks we see raising its beautiful head to remind us that spring is at hand, was created, that the whole mass of the earth, from pole to pole, and from circumference to centre, must have been taken into account and weighed, in order that the proper degree of strength might be given to the fibres of even this little plant.

Botanists tell us that the constitution of this plant is such as to require that, at a certain stage of its growth, the stalk should bend, and the flower should bow its head, that an operation may take place which is necessary in order that the herb should produce seed after its kind; and that, after this, its vegetable health requires that it should lift its head again and stand erect. Now, if the mass of the earth had been greater or less, the force of gravity would have been different; in that case, the strength of fibre in the snow-drop, as it is, would have been too much or too little; the plant could not bow or raise its head at the right time, fecundation could not take place, and its family would have become extinct with the first individual that was planted, because its "seed" would not have been in "itself," and therefore it could not reproduce itself.

Now, if we see such perfect adaptation, such exquisite adjustment, in the case of one of the smallest flowers of the field, how much more may we not expect "compensation" in the atmosphere and the ocean, upon the right adjustment and due performance of which depends not only the life of that plant, but the well-being of every individual that is found in the entire vegetable and animal kingdoms of the world?

When the east winds blow along the Atlantic coast for a little while, they bring us air saturated with moisture from the Gulf Stream, and we complain of the sultry, oppressive, heavy atmosphere; the invalid grows worse, and the well man feels ill, because, when he takes this atmosphere into his lungs, it is already so charged with moisture that it cannot take up and carry off that which encumbers his lungs, and which nature has caused his blood to bring and leave there, that respiration may take up and carry off. At other times the air is dry and hot; he feels that it is conveying off matter from the lungs too fast; he realizes the idea that it is consuming him, and he calls the sensation parching.

Therefore, in considering the general laws which govern the physical agents of the universe, and regulate them in the due performance of their offices, I have felt myself constrained to set out with the assumption that, if the atmosphere had had a greater or less capacity for moisture, or if the proportion of land and water had been different—if the earth, air, and water had not been in exact counterpoise—the whole arrangement of the animal and vegetable kingdoms would have varied from their present state. But God chose to make those kingdoms what they are; for this purpose it was necessary, in his judgment, to establish the proportions between the land and water, and the desert, just as they are, and to make the capacity of the air to circulate heat and moisture just what it is, and to have it do all its work in obedience to law and in subservience to order. If it were not so, why was power given to the winds to lift up and transport moisture, or the property given to the sea by which its waters may become first vapor, and then fruitful showers or gentle dews? If the proportions and properties of land, sea, and air were not adjusted according to the reciprocal capacities of all to perform the functions required by each, why should we be told that he "measured the waters in the hollow of his hand, and comprehended the dust in a measure, and weighed the mountains in scales, and the hills in a balance?" Why did he span the heavens, but that he might mete out the atmosphere in exact proportion to all the rest, and impart to it those properties and powers which it was necessary for it to have, in order that it might perform all those offices and duties for which he designed it?

Harmonious in their action, the air and sea are obedient to law and subject to order in all their movements; when we consult them in the performance of their offices, they teach us lessons concerning the wonders of the deep, the mysteries of the sky, the greatness, and the wisdom, and goodness of the Creator. The investigations into the broad-spreading circle of phenomena connected with the winds of heaven and the waves of the sea are second to none for the good which they do and the lessons which they teach. The astronomer is said to see the hand of God in the sky; but does not the right-minded mariner, who looks aloft as he ponders over these things, hear his voice in every wave of the sea that "claps its hands," and feel his presence in every breeze that blows?

* From the Physical Geography of the Sea.

HERMAN HOOKER,

A BOOKSELLER of Philadelphia, who began life as a student of divinity at Princeton, and subsequently became a clergyman of the Protestant Episcopal Church, the active duties of which he was compelled to relinquish by ill health, was born at Poultney, Vermont, about the year 1806. He is the author of several works esteemed for their Christian philosophy; of these the chief are *The Portion of the Soul, or Thoughts on its Attributes and Tendencies as Indications of its Destiny*, published in 1835; *Popular Infidelity*, entitled in a late edition, *The Philosophy of Unbelief in Morals and Religion, as Discernible in the Faith and Character of Men; The Uses of Adversity and the Provisions of Consolation*; a volume of *Maxims;* and *The Christian Life, a Fight of Faith.*

As a characteristic specimen of Dr. Hooker's skilful evolution of his topic, we cite a passage of a practical character from the "Philosophy of Unbelief:"—

GRATITUDE TO GOD.

It requires no great insight into human nature, to discover the remnants of a now fallen, but once glorious structure; and, what is most remarkable, to see that the remains of this ancient greatness are more apt to be quickened and drawn out by their semblances and qualities, found in creatures, than by the bright and full perfection of them which is in the Creator;—that the heart puts on its most benign face, and sends forth prompt returns of gratitude and love to creatures who have bestowed on us favor and displayed other amiable qualities, while He, whose goodness is so great, so complete, so pervading, that there is none besides it, is unrequited, unheeded, unseen, though hanging out his glory from the heavens, and coming down to us in streams of compassion and love, which have made an ocean on earth that is to overflow and fill it. How strange it is, that all this love, so wonderful in itself, so undeserved, so diffused, that we see it in every beauty, and taste it in every enjoyment,—should be lost on creatures whose love for the gentler and worthier qualities of each other, runs so often into rapture and devotion? How strange that they should be so delighted with streams which have gathered such admixtures of earth, which cast up such "mire and dirt," and have such shallows and falls that we often wreck our hopes in them,—as not to be reminded by them of the great and unmixed fountain whence they have flowed, or of the great ocean, to whose dark and unbottomed depths they will at last settle, as too earthy to rise to its pure and glorious surface! There are many mysteries in human nature, but none greater than this: for while it shows man is so much a creature of sense and so devoid of faith, that objects, to gain his attention and affection, must not only be present to him, but have something of sense and self in them, we are still left to wonder how he could, with such manifestations of divine goodness in him, around him, and for him, have failed to see and adore them, and become so like a brute, as not to think of God, the original of all that is lovely, when thinking of those his qualities which so please and affect him in creatures; and this, though they be so soiled and defaced by sin, that his unmixed fondness for any the most agreeable of them, instead of being an accomplishment, is a sure indication of a mind sunk greatly below the standard allotted to it by the Creator.

Our wonder will be raised higher still, if we consider that our nature, when most corrupt and perverse, is not wholly lost to all sense of gratitude, but may be wrought upon by human kindness, when all the amazing compassion and love of God fail to affect it; if we consider that the very worst of men who set their faces against the heavens, affronting the mercy and defying the majesty thereof, are sometimes so softened with a sense of singular and undeserved favors, that their hearts swell with grateful sentiments towards their benefactors, and something akin to virtue is kindled up where nothing of the kind was seen before; we might think it incredible, if there was any doubting of what we see and know. When we see such men so ready to acknowledge their obligations to their fellows, and to return service for service; so impatient of being thought ungrateful, when they have any character or interest to promote by it, and sometimes when they have not; so strongly affected with the goodness of him who has interposed between them and temporal danger or death, and yet so little moved by the love of God in Christ, which has undertaken their rescue from eternal and deserved woes, and not merely their rescue, but their exaltation to fellowship with himself, and to the pleasures for evermore at his right hand,—a love compared with which the greatest love of creatures is as a ray of light to the sun, and that ray mixed and darkened, while this is so disinterested and free in the grounds and motives of it, that it is exercised towards those who have neither merit to invite, nor disposition to receive it; when we see this, and find that this love, so worthy in itself, so incomprehensible in its degree and in the benefits it would confer, is the only love to which they make no returns of thankfulness or regard, we may ascribe as much of it as we please to the hardness and corruption of their hearts, but that will not account for such conduct. Depravity, considered by itself, will not enable us fully to understand it. Depraved, sensual, and perverse as they are, they have something in them that is kindled by human kindness, and why should it not be kindled by the greater "kindness of God our Saviour?" It is not because it is a divine kindness; not that it is less needed—not that it is bestowed in less measure, or at less expense. And if it is because they do not apprehend this kindness, do not feel their need of it, do not see anything affecting in the measure and expense of it, this is infidelity; and it grows out of an entire misconception of their own character, and of the character and law of God. It is a total blindness to distant and invisible good and evil. It is a venturing of everything most important to themselves on an uncertainty, which they would not and could not do, if they had any understanding of the value of the interests at stake. They really see nothing important but the gratifications of sense and time: still they have the remains of a capacity for something higher. These may be contemplated with profit, if not with admiration. They resemble the motions in the limbs and heart of animals, when the head is severed from the body. They are symptoms of a life that of itself must come to nothing; a life that is solely pouring itself out on the ground. But as this is all the life they have, an image of life, and that only of life in death; and as the motions of it are only excited by the creature's kindness, we discover in their best virtues, or rather, in their only breathings and indications of virtue, the evidence of a faithless heart.

WILLIAM R. WILLIAMS.

A HIGHLY esteemed clergyman of the Baptist denomination, who has for many years past been minister of the Amity street congregation in New York. He is the son of a former clergyman, of Welsh origin, much respected in the city.

Though a quiet and retired student, fond of books and skilled in their various lore, and more given to discourse of his favorite topics at home than abroad, Dr. Williams has on several occasions afforded the public, beyond his attached congregation, proof of his ability.

His occasional addresses and lectures, chiefly in the direct course of his ministry, show a mind of fine order, exhibiting delicacy of taste, devotional earnestness, and the reading of the cultivated scholar. They are mostly included in a volume of *Miscellanies*, published in 1850, which contains *A Discourse on Ministerial Responsibility*, delivered before the Hudson River Baptist Association in 1835; An Address, *The Conservative Principle in our Literature*, delivered in 1843, before the literary societies of the Hamilton Literary and Theological Institution, Madison County, N. Y.; several eloquent occasional Sermons; and among other papers, one on *The Life and Times of Baxter*, which indicates the happy manner in which Dr. Williams employs the resources of his library. Another illustration of his copious stores of reading was afforded to the public in the hitherto unpublished Address pronounced in 1854 before the Alumni of Columbia College, New York, on occasion of the completion of a century in the career of that institution. It was a retrospective review of the literature and other liberal influences of the year of the college foundation, 1754.

Dr. Williams is also the author of two volumes of a practical devotional character, entitled *Religious Progress*, and *Lectures on the Lord's Prayer*.

Though the utterance of Dr. Williams is feeble, and his health apparently infirm, few clergymen of the day have a firmer hold upon their hearers. His delivery is in low measured tone; the main topic of the discourse flowing easily on, while occasional illustrations from history or biography fall like leaves from the trees, refreshing its banks, into the unconscious current of his style.

AN AGE OF PASSION.

Our age is eminently, in some of its leading minds, an age of *passion*. It is seen in the character of much of the most popular literature, and especially the poetry of our day. Much of this has been the poetry of intense passion, it mattered little how unprincipled that passion might be. An English scholar lately gone from this world (it is to Southey that we refer), branded this school of modern literature, in the person of its great and titled leader, as the Satanic school. It has talent and genius, high powers of imagination and language, and boiling energy; but it is, much of it, the energy of a fallen and revolted angel, with no regard for the right, no vision into eternity, and no hold on Heaven. We would not declaim against passion when employed in the service of literature. Informed by strong feelings, truth becomes more awful and more lovely; and some of the ages which unfettered the passions of a nation, have given birth to master-pieces of genius. But Passion divorced from Virtue is ultimately among the fellest enemies to literary excellence. When yoked to the car of duty, and reined in by principle, passion is in its appropriate place, and may accomplish a mighty service. But when, in domestic life, or political, or in the walks of literature, passion throws off these restraints and exults in its own uncontrolled power, it is as useless for purposes of good, and as formidable from its powers of evil, as a car whose fiery coursers have shaken off bit and rein, and trampled under foot their charioteer. The Maker of man made conscience to rule his other faculties, and when it is dethroned, the result is ruin. Far as the literature to which we have alluded spreads, it cherishes an insane admiration for mere talent or mental power. It substitutes as a guide in morals, sentiment for conscience; and makes blind feeling the irresistible fate, whose will none may dispute, and whose doings are beyond the jurisdiction of casuists or lawgivers. It has much of occasional tenderness, and can melt at times into floods of sympathy; but this softness is found strangely blended with a savage violence. Such things often co-exist. As in the case of the French hangman, who in the time of their great revolution was found, fresh from his gory work of the guillotine, sobbing over the sorrows of Werther, it contrives to ally the sanguinary to the sentimental. It seems, at first sight, much such an ill-assorted match as if the family of Mr. Wet-eyes in one of Bunyan's matchless allegories, were wedded to that of Giant Bloody-man in the other. But it is easily explained. It has been found so in all times when passion has been made to take the place of reason as the guide of a people, and conscience has been thrust from the throne to be succeeded by sentiment. The luxurious and the cruel, the fierce and the voluptuous, the licentious and the relentless readily coalesce; and we soon are made to perceive the fitness of the classic fable by which, in the old Greek mythology, Venus was seen knitting her hands with Mars, the goddess of sensuality allying herself with the god of slaughter. We say, much of the literature of the present and the last generation is thus the caterer of passion—lawless, fierce, and vindictive passion. And if a retired student may "through the loop-holes of retreat" read aright the world of fashion, passion seems at times acquiring an unwonted ascendency in the popular amusements of the age. The lewd pantomime and dance, from which the less refined fashion of other times would have turned her blushing and indignant face, the gorgeous spectacle and the shows of wild beasts, and even the sanguinary pugilistic combat, that sometimes recals the gladiatorial shows of old Rome, have become, in our day, the favorite recreations of some classes among the lovers of pleasure. These are, it should be remembered, nearly the same with the favorite entertainments of the later Greek empire, when, plethoric by its wealth, and enervated by its luxury, that power was about to be trodden down by the barbarian invasions of the north.

It is possible that the same dangerous ascendency of passion may be fostered, where we should have been slow to suspect it, by the ultraism of some good men among the social reformers of our time. Wilberforce was, in the judgment of Mackintosh, the very model of a reformer, because he united an earnestness that never flagged with a sweetness that never failed. There are good men that have nothing of this last trait. Amid the best intentions there is occasionally, in the benevolent projects even of this day, a species of Jack Cadeism, if we may be allowed the expression, enlisted in the service of reform. It seems the very opposite of the character of Wilberforce, nourishes an acridity and violence of temper that appears to delight in repelling, and seeks to enkindle feeling by wild exaggeration and personal denunciation; raves in behalf of good with the very spirit of evil, and where it cannot convince assent, would extort submission. Even truth itself, when administered at a scalding heat, cannot benefit the recipient; and the process is not safe for the hands of the administrator himself.

Far be it from us to decry earnestness when shown in the cause of truth and justice, or to forget how the passion awakened in some revolutionary crisis of a people's history, has often infused into the productions of genius an unwonted energy, and clothed them as with an immortal vigor. But it is passion yoked to the chariot of reason, and curbed by the strong hand of principle; laboring in the traces, but not grasping the reins. But set aside argument and truth, and give to passion its unchecked course, and the effect is fatal. It may at first seem to clothe a literature with new energy, but it is the mere energy of intoxication, soon spent, and for which there speedily comes a sure and bitter reckoning. The bonds of principle are loosened, the tastes and habits of society corrupted; and the effects are soon seen extending themselves to the very form and style of a literature as well as to the morality of its productions. The intense is substituted for the natural and true. What is effective is sought for rather than what is exact. Our literature therefore has little, in such portions of it, of the high finish and serene repose of the master-pieces of classic antiquity, where passion in its highest flights is seen wearing gracefully all the restraining rules of art: and power toils ever as under the severe eye of order.

WILLIAM GILMORE SIMMS,

One of the most consistent and accomplished authors by profession the country has produced, is a native of Charleston, South Carolina. He was born April 17, 1806. His father, who bore the same name, was of Scoto-Irish descent, and his mother, Harriet Ann Augusta Singleton, was of a Virginia family, which came early to the state, and was found in the Revolutionary times on the Whig side. William Gilmore Simms, the elder, having failed in Charleston as a merchant, removed to Tennessee, where he held a commission in Coffee's brigade of mounted men, under the command of Jackson, employed in the Indian war against the Creeks and Seminoles. His wife died while our author, the second son, was in his infancy, and he was left in the absence of his father to the care of his grandmother. Though his early education derived little aid from the pecuniary means of his family, which were limited, and though he had not the benefit of early classical training, yet the associations of this part of his life were neither unhappy nor unproductive, while his energy of character and richly endowed intellect were marking out an immediate path of mental activity and honor. Choosing the law for a profession, he was admitted to the bar at Charleston at the age of twenty-one. He did not long practise the profession, but turned its peculiar training to the uses of a literary life. His first active engagement was in the editorship of a daily newspaper, the *Charleston City Gazette*, in which he opposed the prevailing doctrines of nullification; he wrote with industry and spirit, but being interested in the paper as its proprietor, and the enterprise proving unsuccessful, he was stripped by its failure of the limited patrimony he had embarked in it.

The commencement of his career as an author had preceded this. He wrote verses at eight years of age, and first appeared before the public as a poet, in the publication, about 1825, of a *Monody on Gen. Charles Cotesworth Pinckney*. A volume, *Lyrical and other Poems*, appeared from his pen, in 1827, at Charleston, followed by *Early Lays* the same year. Another volume, *The Vision of Cortes, Cain, and other Poems*, appeared in 1829, and the next year a celebration, in verse, of the French Revolution of 1830, *The Tricolor, or Three Days of Blood in Paris*.

Shortly after this date, in 1832, Mr. Simms visited New York, where his imaginative poem, *Atalantis, a Story of the Sea*, published by the Harpers in that year, introduced him to the literary circles of the city, in which he was warmly welcomed. *Atalantis* was a successful poem with the publishers, a rarity at any time, and more noticeable in this case as the work of an unheralded, unknown author. It is written with easy elegance, in smooth blank verse, interspersed with frequent lyrics. Atalantis, a beautiful and virtuous princess of the Nereids, is alternately flattered and threatened by a monster into whose power she has fallen, by straying on the ocean beyond her domain, and becoming subject to his magical spells. She recovers her freedom by the aid of a shipwrecked Spanish knight, whose earthly nature enables him to penetrate the gross atmosphere of the island which the demon had extemporized for her habitation. The prison disappears, and the happy pair descend to the caves of ocean.

The next year the Harpers published Mr. Simms's first tale, *Martin Faber, the Story of a Criminal*, written in the intense passionate style. It secured at once public attention.

The author had now fairly entered upon the active literary life which he has since pursued without interruption; and so uniform has been his career, that a few words will sum up the incidents of his history. A second marriage to the daughter of Mr. Roach, a wealthy planter of the Barnwell district, his first wife having died soon after their union before his visit to New York; a seat in the state legislature, and the reception of the Doctorate of Laws from the University of Alabama: his summer residence at Charleston and his home winter life on the plantation Woodlands

Woodlands.

at Midway, with frequent visits to the northern cities; these are the few external incidents of a career, the events of which must be sought for in the achievements of the author. The latter are sufficiently numerous and important.

To proceed with their production in some classified order, the author's poems may be first enumerated. The publication, next to those already mentioned, was a volume in New York in 1839, *Southern Passages and Pictures*, lyrical, sentimental, and descriptive; *Donna Florida, a Tale*, in the Don Juan style with a Spanish heroine, published at Charleston in 1843; *Grouped Thoughts and Scattered Fancies*, a collection of sonnets; *Areytos, or Songs of the South*, 1846; *Lays of the*

Palmetto, a number of ballads illustrative of the progress of the South Carolina regiments in the Mexican war in 1848; a new edition of *Atalantis* the same year at Philadelphia, with a collection, *The Eye and the Wing; Poems Chiefly Imaginative; The Cassique of Accabee, a Tale of Ashley River, with other pieces*, New York, 1849; *The City of the Silent*, a poem delivered at the Consecration of Magnolia Cemetery, Charleston, in 1850.

In 1853, two volumes of poems were published by Redfield, comprising a selection, with revisions and additions, from the preceding. In dramatic literature, Mr. Simms has written *Norman Maurice, or the Man of the People*, in which the action is laid in the present day, and the author grapples resolutely in blank verse with the original every-day materials of familiar life. The scene opens in Philadelphia. Maurice is the suitor for the hand of Clarice, whom he marries, to the discomfiture of an intriguing aunt, Mrs. Jervas (whose name and character recall her prototype in Pamela), and a worthless Robert Warren, kinsman and enemy—who retains a forged paper which Maurice had playfully executed as a boyish freak of penmanship, which had been made negotiable, and which Maurice had "taken up," receiving from his cunning relative a copy of the paper in place of the original, the latter being kept to ruin him as time might serve. In the second act, we have Maurice pursuing his career in the west, in Missouri, as the Man of the People. In a lawsuit which he conducts for a widow, he confronts in her oppressor the fire-eating bully of the region, with whom he fights a duel, and is talked of for senator. The scoundrel Warren follows him, and seeks to gain control over his wife by threatening to produce the forged paper at a critical moment for his political reputation. She meets the villain to receive the paper, and stabs him. The widow's cause is gained; all plots, personal and political, discomfited; and Missouri, at the close, enjoys the very best prospect of securing an honest senator. Though this play is a bold attempt, with much new ground to be broken, it is managed with such skill, in poetical blank verse, and with so consistent, manly a sentiment, that we pay little attention to its difficulties. *Michael Bonham, or the Fall of the Alamo*, is a romantic drama founded upon an event in Texan history. Both of these have been acted with success. Mr. Simms has also adapted for stage purposes Shakespeare's play of Timon, with numerous additions of his own. This drama has been purchased by Mr. Forrest, and is in preparation for the stage.

Of Mr. Simms's Revolutionary Romances, *The Partisan*, published in 1835, was the earliest, the first of a trilogy completed by the publication of *Mellichampe* and *Katharine Walton, or the Rebel of Dorchester*, which contains a delineation of social life at Charleston in the Revolutionary period. The action of these pieces covers the whole period of active warfare of the Revolution in South Carolina, and presents every variety of military and patriotic movement of the regular and partisan encounter of the swamp and forest country. They include the career of Marion, Sumpter, Pickens, Moultrie, Hayne, and others, on the constant battle-field of the state, South Carolina being the scene of the most severe conflicts of the Revolution. These works have been succeeded at long intervals by *The Scout*, originally called *The Kinsmen, or the Black Riders of the Congaree*, and *Woodcraft, or Hawks about the Dovecot*, originally published as *The Sword and the Distaff*. *Eutaw*, which includes the great action known by this name, is the latest of the author's compositions in this field. *Guy Rivers, a Tale of Georgia*, the first regularly constructed novel of Mr. Simms, belongs to a class of border tales, with which may be classed *Richard Hurdis, or the Avenger of Blood, a Tale of Alabama; Border Beagles, a Tale of Mississippi; Beauchampe, a Tale of Kentucky*, founded upon a story of crime in the state, which has employed the pens of several American writers; *Helen Halsey, or the Swamp State of Conelachita; The Golden Christmas, a Chronicle of St. John's, Berkeley*.

The Historical Romances include *The Yemassee, a Romance of Carolina*, an Indian story, founded upon the general conspiracy of that Colony to massacre the whites in 1715—the portraiture of the Indian in this work, based by Mr. Simms upon personal knowledge of many of the tribes, correcting numerous popular misconceptions of the character; *Pelayo, a Story of the Goth*, and its sequel, *Count Julian*, both founded on the invasion of Spain by the Saracens, the fate of Roderick, and the apostasy of the traitor from whom the second work is named; *The Damsel of Darien*, the hero of which is the celebrated Vasco Nunez de Balboa, the discoverer of the Pacific; *The Lily and the Totem, or the Huguenots in Florida*, an historical romance, of one of the most finely marked and characteristic episodes in the colonial annals of the country, bringing into view the three rival nations of Spain, France, and the Red Men of the Continent, at the very opening of the great American drama before the appearance of the English; *Vasconcelos*, the scene of which includes the career of De Soto in Florida and the Havannah. In the last work Mr. Simms introduces the degradation of a knight by striking off his spurs, under the most imposing scenes of chivalry—one of the most delicate and elaborate of his many sketches. This was first published under the *nom de plume* of "Frank Cooper."

Another class of Mr. Simms's novels may be generally ranked as the moral and the imaginative, and are both of a domestic and romantic interest. This was the author's earliest vein, the series opening with *Martin Faber*, published in 1833, followed at intervals by *Carl Werner, Confession of the Blind Heart, The Wigwam and The Cabin*, a collection of tales, including several in which an interest of the imagination is sustained with striking effect; and *Castle Dismal, or the Bachelor's Christmas*, a domestic legend, in 1844, a South Carolina Ghost Story; *Marie de Berniere, a Tale of the Crescent City*, with other short romances.

In History, Mr. Simms has produced a *History of South Carolina*, and *South Carolina in the Revolution*, a critical and argumentative work, suggestive of certain clues overlooked by historians. A *Geography of South Carolina* may be ranked under this head, and reference should be made to the numerous elaborate review and magazine articles, of which a protracted discussion of the *Civil Warfare of the South* in the Southern Literary Messenger, the *American Loyalists of the Revolutionary Period* in the Southern Quarterly Review, and frequent papers illustrating the social and political history of the South, are the most noticeable. Mr. Simms's contributions to Biography embrace a *Life of Francis Marion*, embodying a minute and comprehensive view of the partisan warfare in which he was engaged; *The Life of John Smith*, which affords opportunity for the author's best narrative talent and display of the picturesque; a kindred subject, *The Life of the Chevalier Bayard*, handled *con amore*, and *The Life of General Greene*, of the Revolution. These are all works of considerable extent, and are elaborated with care.

In Criticism, Mr. Simms's pen has traversed the wide field of the literature of his day, both foreign and at home. He has edited the imputed plays of Shakespeare, with notes and preliminary essays.*

To Periodical literature he has always been a liberal contributor, and has himself founded and conducted several reviews and magazines. Among these may be mentioned *The Southern Literary Gazette*, a monthly magazine, which reached two volumes in 1825; *The Cosmopolitan, An Occasional; The Magnolia, or Southern Apalachian*, a literary magazine and monthly review, published at Charleston in 1842–3; *The Southern and Western Monthly Magazine and Review*, published in two volumes in 1845, which he edited; while he has frequently contributed to the Knickerbocker, Orion, Southern Literary Messenger, Graham's, Godey's, and other magazines. A review of Mrs. Trollope, in the American Quarterly for 1832, attracted considerable attention at the time. In 1849, Mr. Simms became editor of the Southern Quarterly Review, to which he had previously contributed, and which was revived by his writings and personal influence. Several Miscellaneous productions may be introduced in this connexion. *The Book of my Lady*, a melange, in 1833; *Views and Reviews of American History, Literature, and Art*, including several lectures, critical papers, and biographical sketches; *Father Abbot, or the Home Tourist, a Medley*, embracing sketches of scenery, life, manners, and customs of the South; *Egeria, or Voices of Thought and Counsel for the Woods and Wayside*, a collection of aphorisms, and brief essays in prose and verse; *Southward Ho!* a species of Decameron, in which a group of travellers interchanging opinion and criticism, discuss the scenery and circumstances of the South, with frequent introduction of song and story; *The Morals of Slavery*, first published in the Southern Literary Messenger, and since included in the volume entitled *The Pro-Slavery Argument*.

In addition to these numerous literary productions, Mr. Simms is the author of several orations on public occasions,—*The Social Principle, the True Secret of National Permanence*, delivered in 1842 before the literary societies of the University of Alabama; *The True Sources of American Independence*, in 1844, before the town council and citizens of Aiken, S. C.; *Self-Development*, in 1847, before the literary societies of Oglethorpe University, Georgia; *The Battle of Fort Moultrie*, an anniversary discourse on Sullivan's Island; two courses of lectures, of three each, *On Poetry and the Practical*, and *The Moral Character of Hamlet*.

W. Gilmore Simms

The numerous writings of Mr. Simms are characterized by their earnestness, sincerity, and thoroughness. Hard worker as he is in literature, he pursues each subject with new zeal and enthusiasm. They are a remarkable series of works, when it is considered how large a portion of them involve no inconsiderable thought and original research. But Mr. Simms is no ordinary worker. Much as he has accomplished, much lies before him,—and in the prime of life, with a physical constitution which answers every demand of the active intellect, he still pursues new game in the literary world.

As an author, he has pursued an honorable, manly career. His constant engagements in the press, as a critic and reviewer, have given him opportunities of extending favors to his brother writers, which he has freely employed. His generosity in this respect is noticeable. Nor has this kindness been limited by any local feeling; while his own state has found in him one of the chief, in a literary view the chief, supporter of her interests. As a novelist, Mr. Simms is vigorous in delineation, dramatic in action, poetic in his description of scenery, a master of plot, and skilled in the arts of the practised story teller. His own tastes lead him to the composition of poetry and the provinces of imaginative literature, and he is apt to introduce much of their spirit into his prose creations. His powers as an essayist, fond of discussing the philosophy

* A Supplement to the Plays of William Shakespeare, comprising the Seven Dramas which have been ascribed to his pen, but which are not included with his writings in modern editions, edited with notes, and an introduction to each play. 8vo. Cooledge & Brother: New York. 1848.

of his subject, are of a high order. He is ingenious in speculation and fertile in argument. Many as are his writings, there is not one of them which does not exhibit some ingenious, worthy, truthful quality.

THE BARD.

Where dwells the spirit of the Bard—what sky
Persuades his daring wing,—
Folded in soft carnation, or in snow
Still sleeping, far o'er summits of the cloud,
And, with a seeming, sweet unconsciousness,
Wooing his plume, through baffling storms to fly,
Assured of all that ever yet might bless
The spirit, by love and loftiest hope made proud,
Would he but struggle for the dear caress!—
Or would his giant spring,
Impelled by holiest ire,
Assail the sullen summits of the storm,
Bent with broad breast and still impatient form,
Where clouds unfold themselves in leaping fire!
What vision wins his soul,—
What passion wings his flight,—
What dream of conquest woos his eager eye!—
How glows he with the strife,—
How spurns he at control,—
With what unmeasured rage would he defy
The foes that rise around and threaten life!—
His upward flight is fair,
He goes through parting air,
He breaks the barrier cloud, he sees the eye that's there,
The centre of the realm of storm that mocked him but to dare!
And now he grasps the prize,
That on the summit lies,
And binds the burning jewel to his brow;
Transfigured by its bright,
He wears a mightier face,
Nor grovels more in likeness of the earth;—
His wing a bolder flight,
His step a wilder grace,
He glows, the creature of a holier birth;—
Suns sing, and stars glow glad around his light;
And thus he speeds afar,
'Mid gathering sun and star,
The sov'reign, he, of worlds, where these but subjects are;
And men that marked his wing with mocking sight,
Do watch and wonder now;—
Will watch and worship with delight, anon,
When far from hiss and hate, his upward form hath gone!

Oh! ere that van was won,
Whose flight hath braved the sun—
Whose daring strength and aim
Have scaled the heights of cloud and bared their breasts of flame;
What lowly toil was done,—
How slow the moments sped,—
How bitter were the pangs that vexed the heart and head!
The burden which he bore,
The thorns his feet that tore,
The cruel wounds he suffered with no moan,—
Alone,—and still alone!—
Denial, which could smile,
Beholding, all the while,
How salter than the sea were the salt tears he shed;
And over all, the curse,
Than all of these more worse.
Prostrate, before the common way, to bear
The feet of hissing things,
Whose toil it is to tear,
And cramp the glorious creature born to wings!
Ah! should he once despair!—

* * * * * * * * * *

Not lonely, with the sad nymph Solitude,
Deep in the cover of the ancient wood,
Where the sun leaves him, and the happy dawn,
Stealing with blushes over the gray lawn,
Stills finds him, all forgetful of the flight
Of hours, that passing still from dark to bright,
Know not to loiter,—all their progress naught:—
His eye, unconscious of the day, is bright
With inward vision; till, as sudden freed,
By the superior quest of a proud thought,
He darts away with an unmeasured speed;
His pinion purpling as he gains the height,
Where still, though all obscured from mortal sight,
He bathes him in the late smiles of the sun;—
And oh! the glory, as he guides his steed,
Flakes from his pinions falling, as they soar
To mounts where Eos binds her buskins on
And proud Artemis, watching by her well,
For one,—sole fortunate of all his race,—
With hand upon his mouth her beagle stays,
Lest he should baffle sounds too sweet to lose,
That even now are gliding with the dews.
How nobly he arrays
His robes for flight—his robes, the woven of songs,
Borrowed from starry spheres,—with each a muse
That, with her harmonies, maintains its dance
Celestial, and its circles bright prolongs.
Fair ever, but with warrior form and face,
He stands before the eye of each young grace
Beguiling the sweet passion from her cell,
And still subjecting beauty by the glance,
Which speaks his own subjection to a spell.
The eldest born of rapture, that makes Love,
At once submissive and the Conqueror.
He conquers but to bring deliverance,
And with deliverance light;—
To conquer, he has only to explore,—
And makes a permanent empire, but to spread,
Though speeding on with unobserving haste,—
A wing above the waste.
A single feather from his pinion shed,
A single beam of beauty from his eye,
Takes captive of the dim sleeping realm below,
Through eyes of truest worshippers, that straight
Bring shouts to welcome and bright flowers to wreathe
His altars; and, as those, to life from death,
Plucked sudden, in their gratitude and faith
Deem him a god who wrought the miracle,—
So do they take him to their shrines, and vow
Their annual incense of sweet song and smell,
For him to whom their happiness they owe.
Thus goes he still from desert shore to shore,
Where life in darkness droops, where beauty errs,
Having no worshippers,
And lacking sympathy for the light!—The eye
That is the spirit of his wing, no more,
This progress once begun, can cease to soar,
Suffers eclipse, or sleeps!—
No more be furled
The wing,—that, from the first decreed to fly,
Must speed to daily conquests, deep and high,
Till no domain of dark unlighted keeps,
And all the realm of strife beneath the sky
Grows one, in beauty and peace for evermore,—
Soothed to eternal office of delight,
By these that wing the soul on its first flight,
For these are the great spirits that shape the world!

BLESSINGS ON CHILDREN.

Blessings on the blessing children, sweetest gifts of Heaven to earth,
Filling all the heart with gladness, filling all the house with mirth;
Bringing with them native sweetness, pictures of the primal bloom,
Which the bliss for ever gladdens, of the region whence they come:
Bringing with them joyous impulse of a state withouten care,
And a buoyant faith in being, which makes all in nature fair;
Not a doubt to dim the distance, not a grief to vex thee, nigh,
And a hope that in existence finds each hour a luxury;
Going singing, bounding, brightening—never fearing as they go,
That the innocent shall tremble, and the loving find a foe;
In the daylight, in the starlight, still with thought that freely flies,
Prompt and joyous, with no question of the beauty in the skies;
Genial fancies winning raptures, as the bee still sucks her store,
All the present still a garden gleaned a thousand times before;
All the future, but a region, where the happy serving thought,
Still depicts a thousand blessings, by the winged hunter caught;
Life a chase where blushing pleasures only seem to strive in flight,
Lingering to be caught, and yielding gladly to the proud delight;
As the maiden, through the alleys, looking backward as she flies,
Woos the fond pursuer onward, with the love-light in her eyes.

Oh! the happy life in children, still restoring joy to ours,
Making for the forest music, planting for the wayside flowers;
Back recalling all the sweetness, in a pleasure pure as rare,
Back the past of hope and rapture bringing to the heart of care.
How, as swell the happy voices, bursting through the shady grove,
Memories take the place of sorrows, time restores the sway to love!
We are in the shouting comrades, shaking off the load of years,
Thought forgetting strifes and trials, doubts and agonies and tears;
We are in the bounding urchin, as o'er hill and plain he darts,
Share the struggle and the triumph, gladdening in his heart of hearts;
What an image of the vigor and the glorious grace we knew,
When to eager youth from boyhood, at a single bound we grew!
Even such our slender beauty, such upon our cheek the glow,
In our eyes the life and gladness—of our blood the overflow.
Bless the mother of the urchin! in his form we see her truth:
He is now the very picture of the memories in our youth;
Never can we doubt the forehead, nor the sunny flowing hair,
Nor the smiling in the dimple speaking chin and cheek so fair:
Bless the mother of the young one, he hath blended in his grace,
All the hope and joy and beauty, kindling once in either face.

Oh! the happy faith of children! that is glad in all it sees,
And with never need of thinking, pierces still its mysteries,
In simplicity profoundest, in their soul abundance blest,
Wise in value of the sportive, and in restlessness at rest,
Lacking every creed, yet having faith so large in all they see,
That to know is still to gladden, and 'tis rapture but to be.
What trim fancies bring them flowers; what rare spirits walk their wood,
What a wondrous world the moonlight harbors of the gay and good!
Unto them the very tempest walks in glories grateful still,
And the lightning gleams, a seraph, to persuade them to the hill:
'Tis a sweet and loving spirit, that throughout the midnight rains,
Broods beside the shuttered windows, and with gentle love complains;
And how wooing, how exalting, with the richness of her dyes,
Spans the painter of the rainbow, her bright arch along the skies,
With a dream like Jacob's ladder, showing to the fancy's sight,
How 'twere easy for the sad one to escape to worlds of light!
Ah! the wisdom of such fancies, and the truth in every dream,
That to faith confiding offers, cheering every gloom, a gleam!
Happy hearts, still cherish fondly each delusion of your youth,
Joy is born of well believing, and the fiction wraps the truth.

THE RATTLESNAKE—FROM THE YEMASSEE.

[The heroine, Bess Matthews, in the wood waits the coming of her lover.]

"He is not come," she murmured, half disappointed, as the old grove of oaks with all its religious solemnity of shadow lay before her. She took her seat at the foot of a tree, the growth of a century, whose thick and knotted roots, started from their sheltering earth, shot even above the long grass around them, and ran in irregular sweeps for a considerable distance upon the surface. Here she sat not long, for her mind grew impatient and confused with the various thoughts crowding upon it—sweet thoughts it may be, for she thought of him whom she loved,—of him almost only; and of the long hours of happy enjoyment which the future had in store. Then came the fears, following fast upon the hopes, as the shadows follow the sunlight. The doubts of existence—the brevity and the fluctuations of life; these are the contemplations even of happy love, and these beset and saddened her; till, starting up in that dreamy confusion which the scene not less than the subject of her musings had inspired, she glided among the old trees scarce conscious of her movement.

"He does not come—he does not come," she murmured, as she stood contemplating the thick copse spreading before her, and forming the barrier which terminated the beautiful range of oaks which constituted the grove. How beautiful was the green and garniture of that little copse of wood. The leaves were thick, and the grass around lay folded over and over in bunches, with here and there a wild flower, gleaming from its green, and making of it a beautiful carpet of the richest and most various texture. A small tree rose from the centre of a clump around which a wild grape gadded luxuriantly; and, with an incoherent sense of what she saw, she lingered before the little cluster, seeming to survey that which, though it seemed to fix her eye, yet failed to fill her thought. Her mind wandered —her soul was far away; and the objects in her vision were far other than those which occupied her imagination. Things grew indistinct beneath her eye. The eye rather slept than saw. The musing spirit had given holiday to the ordinary senses, and took no heed of the forms that rose, and floated, or glided away, before them. In this way, the leaf detached made no impression upon the sight that was yet bent upon it; she saw not the bird, though it whirled, untroubled by a fear, in wanton circles around her head—and the black snake, with the rapidity of an arrow, darted over her path without arousing a single terror in the form that otherwise would have shivered at its mere appearance. And yet, though thus indistinct were all things around her to the musing eye of the maiden, her eye was yet singularly fixed—fastened as it were, to a single spot—gathered and controlled by a single object, and glazed, apparently, beneath a curious fascination. Before the maiden rose a little clump of bushes,—bright tangled leaves flaunting wide in glossiest green, with vines trailing over them, thickly decked with blue and crimson flowers. Her eye communed vacantly with these; fastened by a starlike shining glance—a subtle ray, that shot out from the circle of green leaves—seeming to be their very eye—and sending out a lurid lustre that seemed to stream across the space between, and find its way into her own eyes. Very piercing and beautiful was that subtle brightness, of the sweetest, strangest power. And now the leaves quivered and seemed to float away, only to return, and the vines waved and swung around in fantastic mazes, unfolding ever-changing varieties of form and color to her gaze; but the star-like eye was ever steadfast, bright and gorgeous gleaming in their midst, and still fastened, with strange fondness, upon her own. How beautiful, with wondrous intensity, did it gleam, and dilate, growing larger and more lustrous with every ray which it sent forth. And her own glance became intense, fixed also; but with a dreaming sense that conjured up the wildest fancies, terribly beautiful, that took her soul away from her, and wrapt it about as with a spell. She would have fled, she would have flown; but she had not power to move. The will was wanting to her flight. She felt that she could have bent forward to pluck the gem-like thing from the bosom of the leaf in which it seemed to grow, and which it irradiated with its bright white gleam; but ever as she aimed to stretch forth her hand, and bend forward, she heard a rush of wings, and a shrill scream from the tree above her—such a scream as the mock-bird makes, when, angrily, it raises its dusky crest, and flaps its wings furiously against its slender sides. Such a scream seemed like a warning, and though yet unawakened to full consciousness, it startled her and forbade her effort. More than once in her survey of this strange object, had she heard that shrill note, and still had it carried to her ear the same note of warning, and to her mind the same vague consciousness of an evil presence. But the star-like eye was yet upon her own—a small, bright eye, quick like that of a bird, now steady in its place, and observant seemingly only of hers, now darting forward with all the clustering leaves about it, and shooting up towards her, as if wooing her to seize. At another moment, riveted to the vine which lay around it, it would whirl round and round, dazzlingly bright and beautiful, even as a torch, waving hurriedly by night in the hands of some playful boy;—but, in all this time, the glance was never taken from her own—there it grew, fixed—a very principle of light—and such a light—a subtle, burning, piercing, fascinating gleam, such as gathers in vapor above the old grave, and binds us as we look—shooting, darting directly into her eye, dazzling her gaze, defeating its sense of discrimination, and confusing strangely that of perception. She felt dizzy, for, as she looked, a cloud of colors, bright, gay, various colors, floated and hung like so much drapery around the single object that had so secured her attention and spell-bound her feet. Her limbs felt momently more and more insecure—her blood grew cold, and she seemed to feel the gradual freeze of vein by vein, throughout her person. At that moment a rustling was heard in the branches of the tree beside her, and the bird, which had repeatedly uttered a single cry above her, as it were of warning, flew away from his station with a scream more piercing than ever. This movement had the effect, for which it really seemed intended, of bringing back to her a portion of the consciousness she seemed so totally to have been deprived of before. She strove to move from before the beautiful but terrible presence, but for a while she strove in vain. The rich, star-like glance still riveted her own, and the subtle fascination kept her bound. The mental energies, however, with the moment of their greatest trial, now gathered suddenly to her aid; and, with a desperate effort, but with a feeling still of most annoying uncertainty and dread, she succeeded partially in the attempt, and threw her arms backwards, her hands grasping the neighboring tree, feeble, tottering, and depending upon it for that support which her own limbs almost entirely denied her. With her movement, however, came the full development of the powerful spell and dreadful mystery before her. As her feet receded, though but a single pace, to the tree against which she now rested, the audibly articulated ring, like that of a watch when wound up with the verge broken, announced the nature of that splendid yet dangerous presence, in the form of the monstrous rattlesnake, now but a few feet before her, lying coiled at the bottom of a beautiful shrub, with which, to her dreaming eye, many of its own glorious hues had become associated. She was, at length, conscious enough to perceive and to feel all her danger; but terror had denied her the strength necessary to fly from her dreadful enemy. There still the eye glared beautifully bright and piercing upon her own; and, seemingly in a spirit of sport, the insidious reptile slowly unwound himself from his coil, but only to gather himself up again into his muscular rings, his great flat head rising in the midst, and slowly nodding, as it were, towards her, the eye still peering deeply into her own;—the rattle still slightly ringing at intervals, and giving forth that paralysing sound, which, once heard, is remembered for ever. The reptile all this while appeared to be conscious of, and to sport with, while seeking to excite her terrors. Now, with his flat head, distended mouth, and curving neck, would it dart forward its long form towards her,—its fatal teeth, unfolding on either side of its upper jaws, seeming to threaten her with instantaneous death, whilst its powerful eye shot forth glances of that fatal power of fascination, malignantly bright, which, by paralysing, with a novel form of terror and of beauty, may readily account for the spell it possesses of binding the feet of the timid, and denying to fear even the privilege of flight. Could she have fled! She felt the necessity; but the power of her limbs was gone! and there still it lay, coiling and uncoiling, its arching neck glittering like a ring of brazed copper, bright and lurid; and the dreadful beauty of its eye still fastened, eagerly contemplating the victim, while the pendulous rattle still rang the death note, as if to prepare the conscious mind for the fate which is momently approaching to the blow. Meanwhile the stillness became death-like with all surrounding objects. The bird had gone with its scream and rush. The breeze was silent. The vines ceased to wave. The leaves faintly quivered on their stems. The serpent once more lay still; but the eye was never once turned away from the victim. Its corded muscles are all in coil. They have but to unclasp suddenly, and the dreadful folds will be upon her, its full length, and the fatal teeth will strike, and the deadly venom which they secrete will mingle with the life-blood in her veins.

The terrified damsel, her full consciousness restored, but not her strength, feels all the danger. She sees that the sport of the terrible reptile is at an end. She cannot now mistake the horrid expression of its eye. She strives to scream, but the voice dies away, a feeble gurgling in her throat. Her tongue is paralysed; her lips are sealed—once more she strives for flight, but her limbs refuse their office. She has nothing left of life but its fearful consciousness. It is in her despair, that, a last effort, she succeeds to scream, a single wild cry, forced from her by the accumulated agony; she sinks down upon the grass before her enemy—her eyes, however, still open, and still looking upon those which he directs for ever upon them. She sees him approach—now advancing, now receding—now swelling in every part with something of anger, while his neck is arched beautifully like that of a wild horse under the curb; until, at length, tired as it were of play, like the cat with its victim, she sees the neck growing larger and becoming completely bronzed as about to strike—the huge jaws unclosing almost directly above her, the long tubulated fang charged with venom, protruding from the cavernous mouth—and she sees no more. Insensibility came to her aid, and she lay almost lifeless under the very folds of the monster.

In that moment the copse parted—and an arrow, piercing the monster through and through the neck, bore his head forward to the ground, alongside the maiden, while his spiral extremities, now unfolding in his own agony, were actually, in part, writhing upon her person. The arrow came from the fugitive Occonestoga, who had fortunately reached the spot in season, on his way to the Block House. He rushed from the copse as the snake fell, and, with a stick, fearlessly approached him where he lay tossing in agony upon the grass. Seeing him advance the courageous reptile made an effort to regain his coil, shaking the fearful rattle violently at every evolution which he took for that purpose; but the arrow, completely passing through his neck, opposed an unyielding obstacle to the endeavor; and finding it hopeless, and seeing the new enemy about to assault him, with something of the spirit of the white man under like circumstances, he turned desperately round, and striking his charged fangs, so that they were riveted in the wound they made, into a susceptible part of his own body, he threw himself over with a single convulsion, and, a moment after, lay dead beside the utterly unconscious maiden.

JAMES H. HAMMOND.

James H. Hammond, Ex-Governor of the State of South Carolina, and a political writer of distinction, was born at Newberry district in that state, November 15, 1807. His father was a native of Massachusetts, a graduate of Dartmouth in 1802, who the next year emigrated to South Carolina and became Professor of Languages in the State College at Columbia. The son received his education at that institution, was admitted to the bar in 1828, and in 1830 became editor at Columbia of a very decided political paper of the nullification era and principles, called the *Southern Times*.

In 1831, on his marriage with Miss Fitzsimons, he retired from his profession, and settled at his plantation, Silver Bluff, on the eastern bank of the Savannah river, a site famous in the early history, being the point where De Soto found the Indian princess of Cofachiqui, where George Galphin subsequently established his trading post with the Indians, forming one of the frontier posts of the infant colony, distinguished in the Revolution by its leaguer, under Pickens and Lee. He did not, however, withdraw from politics; and as a member of the military family of Governor Hamilton and Governor Wayne, contributed his full quota to the nullification excitement, and recruiting for the nullification army of 1833. He was elected member of Congress, in which body he took his seat in 1835. His health, never vigorous, failed him so entirely in the following spring that he resigned his seat in Congress and travelled a year and a half in Europe, with no benefit to his constitution. For several years after he took no part in politics, though often invited to return to Congress, and generously tendered his seat there by his successor, Col. Elmore.

He was in 1841 elected General of his brigade of state militia, and in 1842 Governor of the state. In this capacity he paid particular attention to the state military organization, and under his auspices the several colleges were established on the West Point system. During his governorship he wrote a letter to the Free Church of Glasgow on Slavery, and two letters in reply to an anti-slavery circular of the English Clarkson, which have been since gathered and published in a Pro-Slavery volume, issued in Charleston. From the expiration of his term of service he has resided in retirement on his plantation.

His printed writings, besides a speech in Congress on Slavery, his Governor's Messages, and the letters we have mentioned, are a pamphlet on the Railroad System and the Bank of the State; a review of Mr. Elwood Fisher's "North and South" in the Southern Quarterly; an oration on the Manufacturing System of the State, delivered before the South Carolina Institute in 1849; an elaborate discourse on the Life, Character, and Services of Calhoun, at the request of the city council, in 1850; and an Oration before the Literary Societies of South Carolina College. These compositions severally display the statesman and the scholar of habits of intellectual energy. A passage from the conclusion of the college address exhibits their prevailing manner:—

INTELLECTUAL POWER.

Thus if we should pass in review all the pursuits of mankind, and all the ends they aim at under the instigation of their appetites and passions, or at the dictation of shallow utilitarian philosophy, we shall find that they pursue shadows and worship idols, or that whatever there is that is good and great and catholic in their deeds and purposes, depends for its accomplishment upon the intellect, and is accomplished just in proportion as that intellect is stored with knowledge. And whether we examine the present or the past, we shall find that knowledge alone is real power—"more powerful," says Bacon, "than the Will, commanding the reason, understanding, and belief," and "setting up a Throne in the spirits and souls of men." We shall find that the progress of knowledge is the only true and permanent progress of our race, and that however inventions, and discoveries, and events which change the face of human affairs, may appear to be the results of contemporary efforts or providential accidents, it is, in fact, the Men of Learning who lead with noiseless step the vanguard of civilization, that mark out the road over which—opened sooner or later—posterity marches; and from the abundance of their precious stores sow seed by the wayside, which spring up in due season, and produce an hundred fold; and cast bread upon the waters which is gathered after many days. The age which gives birth to the largest number of such men is always the most enlightened, and the age in which the highest reverence and most intelligent obedience is accorded to them, always advances most rapidly in the career of improvement.

And let not the ambitious aspirant to enrol himself with this illustrious band, to fill the throne which learning "setteth up in the spirits and souls of men," and wield its absolute power, be checked, however humble he may be, however unlikely to attain wealth or office, or secure homage as a practical man or man of action, by any fear that true knowledge can be stifled, overshadowed, or compelled to involuntary barrenness. Whenever or wherever men meet to deliberate or act, the trained intellect will always master. But for the most sensitive and modest, who seek retirement, there is another and a greater resource. The public press, accessible to all, will enable him, from the depths of solitude, to speak trumpet-tongued to the four corners of the earth. No matter how he may be situated—if he has facts that will bear scrutiny, if he has thoughts that burn, if he is sure he has a call to teach—the press is a tripod from which he may give utterance to his oracles; and if there be truth in them, the world and future ages will accept it. It is not Commerce that is King, nor Manufactures, nor Cotton, nor any single Art or Science, any more than those who wear the baubles-crowns. Knowledge is Sovereign, and the Press is the royal seat on which she sits, a sceptred Monarch. From this she rules public opinion, and finally gives laws alike to prince and people,—laws framed by men of letters; by the wandering bard; by the philosopher in his grove or portico, his tower or laboratory; by the pale student in his closet. We contemplate with awe the mighty movements of the last eighty years, and we held our breath while we gazed upon the heaving human mass so lately struggling like huge Leviathan, over the broad face of Europe. What has thus stirred the world? The press. The press, which has scattered far and wide the sparks of genius, kindling as they fly. Books, journals, pamphlets, these are the paixhan balls—moulded often by the obscure and humble, but loaded with fiery thoughts—which have burst in the sides of every structure, political, social, and religious, and shattered too often, alike the rotten and the sound. For in knowledge as in everything else, the two great principles of Good and Evil maintain their eternal warfare, "Ὁ ἀγὼν ἀντὶ πάντων ἀγώνων"—a war amid and above all other wars.

But in the strife of knowledge, unlike other contests—victory never fails to abide with truth. And the wise and virtuous who find and use this mighty weapon, are sure of their reward. It may not come soon. Years, ages, centuries may pass away, and the grave-stone may have crumbled above the head that should have worn the wreath. But to the eye of faith, the vision of the imperishable and inevitable halo that shall enshrine the memory is for ever present, cheering and sweetening toil, and compensating for privation. And it often happens that the great and heroic mind, unnoticed by the world, buried apparently in profoundest darkness, sustained by faith, works out the grandest problems of human progress: working under broad rays of brightest light; light furnished by that inward and immortal lamp, which, when its mission upon earth has closed, is trimmed anew by angels' hands, and placed among the stars of heaven.

M. C. M. Hammond, a younger brother of the preceding, was born in the Newberry district, December 12, 1814. He was educated at Augusta by a son of the Rev. Dr. Waddel, now a professor at Franklin College, Georgia. In 1832 he received a cadet's appointment at West Point, where in 1835 he delivered an oration to the corps, by the unanimous election of his class, on the Influence of Government on the Mind. He was a graduate of 1836. He served two years in the Seminole war, and also in the Cherokee difficulties in 1838; was then for three years stationed at Fort Gibson, Arkansas, returned again to Florida, and in 1842 resigned in ill health. He then married, and became a successful planter, while he occasionally wrote on topics of agriculture. He was then occupied, under Polk's administration, as paymaster in Louisiana and Texas, where he suffered a severe sun-stroke. Ill health again led to his resignation from the army in 1847. He had previously delivered a discourse before the Agricultural Society, which he had been mainly instrumental in forming, in Burke county, Georgia. In 1849 he began the publication of an elaborate series of military articles in the Southern Quarterly, on Fremont's Command and the Conquest of California; the Commercial and Political Position of California; the Mineral Resources of California; the Battles of the Rio Grande; of Buena Vista; Vera Cruz; Cerro Gordo; Contreras; Cherubusco; Molino del Rey; Chapultepec; the Secondary Combats of the War; an article on Amazonia; in all some six hundred pages, marked by their knowledge of military affairs, and ingenious, candid discrimination.

In 1852 he visited West Point as a member of the Board of Visitors, and was elected their president. He delivered an eloquent oration before the corps of cadets at their request, which was published. He is a resident of South Carolina, and, it is understood, is engaged in a translation of the great military authority Jomini on the art of war, and an original essay on the same subject in reference to the necessities of this country.

ROBERT M. CHARLTON.

This accomplished writer, to whom the engagements of literature were a relaxation from other duties, was born at Savannah, Ga., Jan. 19, 1807. His father was Judge Thomas U. P. Charlton, whose position and social virtues were renewed by the son. He was early admitted to the bar; on his arrival at age was in the state legislature; became United States District Attorney; and at twenty-seven was appointed Judge of the Supreme Court of the Eastern District of Georgia. In 1852 he was in the United States Senate. He was known for his polished oratory and his genial powers in society. His literary productions were in prose and verse: essays, sketches, lectures, and literary addresses. Many of these, including a series of sketches entitled *Leaves from the Portfolio of a Georgia Lawyer*, appeared in the Knickerbocker Magazine. They are all indicative of his cultivated talents and amiable temperament.

Robert M Charlton

In 1839 Mr. Charlton published a volume of poems, in which he included the poetical remains marked by a delicate sentiment, of his brother, Dr. Thomas J. Charlton, a young physician, who died in September, 1835, a victim to his professional zeal. This volume appeared in a second edition at Boston in 1842, with alterations and additions. It includes, besides the poems of the brothers, two prose compositions by R. M. Charlton, a eulogy on Doctor John Cumming, an esteemed citizen of Savannah, who was lost in the steamer Pulaski, and an historical lecture on Serjeant Jasper, the hero of Fort Moultrie and Savannah, delivered before the Georgia Historical Society in 1841.

The poems of Mr. R. M. Charlton are written in a facile style, expressive of a genial and pathetic susceptibility, rising frequently to eloquence.

He died at Savannah Jan. 8, 1854.

TO THE RIVER OGEECHEE.

O wave, that glidest swiftly
  On thy bright and happy way,
From the morning until evening,
  And from twilight until day,
Why leapest thou so joyously,
  Whilst coldly on thy shore,
Sleeps the noble and the gallant heart,
  For aye and evermore?

Or dost thou weep, O river,
  And is this bounding wave,
But the tear thy bosom sheddeth
  As a tribute o'er his grave?
And when, in midnight's darkness,
  The winds above thee moan,
Are they mourning for our sorrows,
  Do they sigh for him that's gone?

Keep back thy tears, then, river,
  Or, if they must be shed,
Let them flow but for the living:
  They are needless for the dead.
His soul shall dwell in glory,
  Where bounds a brighter wave,
But our pleasures, with his troubles,
  Are buried in the grave.

THEY ARE PASSING AWAY.

They are passing away, they are passing away—
The joy from our hearts, and the light from our day,
The hope that beguiled us when sorrow was near,
The loved one that dashed from our eye-lids the tear,
The friendships that held o'er our bosoms their sway;
They are passing away, they are passing away.

They are passing away, they are passing away—
The cares and the strifes of life's turbulent day,
The waves of despair that rolled over our soul,
The passions that bowed not to reason's control,
The dark clouds that shrouded religion's kind ray;
They are passing away, they are passing away.

Let them go, let them pass, both the sunshine and shower,
The joys that yet cheer us, the storms that yet lower:
When their gloom and their light have all faded and past,
There's a home that around us its blessing shall cast,
Where the heart-broken pilgrim no longer shall say,
"We are passing away, we are passing away."

THE DEATH OF JASPER—A HISTORICAL BALLAD.

'T was amidst a scene of blood,
  On a bright autumnal day,
When misfortune like a flood,
  Swept our fairest hopes away;
'T was on *Savannah's* plain,
  On the spot we love so well,
Amid heaps of gallant slain,
  That the daring Jasper fell!

He had borne him in the fight,
  Like a soldier in his prime,
Like a bold and stalwart knight,
  Of the glorious olden time;
And unharmed by sabre-blow,
  And untouched by leaden ball,
He had battled with the foe,
  'Till he heard the trumpet's call.

But he turned him at the sound,
  For he knew the strife was o'er,
That in vain on freedom's ground,
  Had her children shed their gore;
So he slowly turned away,
  With the remnant of the band,
Who, amid the bloody fray,
  Had escaped the foeman's hand.

But his banner caught his eye,
  As it trailed upon the dust,
And he saw his comrade die,
  Ere he yielded up his trust,
"To the rescue!" loud he cried,
  "To the rescue, gallant men!"
And he dashed into the tide
  Of the battle-stream again.

And then fierce the contest rose,
  O'er its field of broidered gold,
And the blood of friends and foes,
  Stained alike its silken fold;

But unheeding wound and blow,
He has snatched it midst the strife,
He has borne that flag away,
But its ransom is its life!

"To my father take my sword,"
Thus the dying hero said,
"Tell him that my latest word
Was a blessing on his head;
That when death had seized my frame,
And uplifted was his dart,
That I ne'er forgot the name,
That was dearest to my heart.

"And tell her whose favor gave
This fair banner to our band,
That I died its folds to save,
From the foe's polluting hand;
And let all my comrades hear,
When my form lies cold in death,
That their friend remained sincere,
To his last expiring breath."

It was thus that Jasper fell,
'Neath that bright autumnal sky;
Has a stone been reared to tell
Where he laid him down to die?
To the rescue, spirits bold!
To the rescue, gallant men!
Let the marble page unfold
All his daring deeds again!

WILLIAM A. CARRUTHERS,

The author of several novels written with spirit and ability, was a Virginian, and as we learn from a communication to the Knickerbocker Magazine,* in which he gives an account of a hazardous ascent of the Natural Bridge, of which he was a witness, was, in 1818, a student of Washington College, in the vicinity of that celebrated curiosity. We have no details of his life, beyond the facts of his publication of several books in New York about the year 1834, his retirement from Virginia to Savannah, Georgia, where he practised medicine, and wrote for the Magnolia and other Southern magazines, and where he died some years since.

His books which have come to our knowledge are, *The Cavaliers of Virginia, or the Recluse of Jamestown, an Historical Romance of the Old Dominion*, contrasting the manners of the conservative and revolutionary races, the followers of Charles and of Noll in the State; *The Kentuckian in New York, or the Adventures of Three Southerns*, a sketchy volume of romantic descriptive matter; and *The Knights of the Horse Shoe, a Traditionary Tale of the Cocked Hat Gentry in the Old Dominion*, published at Wetumpka, Alabama, in 1845. In the last book the author drew a pleasing and animated picture of the old colonial life in Virginia, in the days of Governor Spotswood. A passage from one of its early chapters will exhibit its genial spirit.

A KITCHEN FIRE-SIDE IN THE OLD DOMINION.

Imagine to yourself, reader, a fire-place large enough to roast an ox whole, and within which a common waggon load of wood might be absorbed in such a speedy manner as to horrify one of our city economical housewives—though now it was late in summer, and of course no such pile of combustibles enlivened the scene—besides, it was night, and the culinary operations of the day were over. A few blazing fagots of rich pine, however, still threw a lurid glare over the murky atmosphere, and here and there sat the several domestics of the establishment; some nodding until they almost tumbled into the fire, but speedily regaining the perpendicular without ever opening their eyes, or giving any evidence of discomposure, except a loud snort, perhaps, and then dozing away again as comfortably as ever. Others were conversing without exhibiting any symptoms of weariness or drowsiness.

In one corner of the fire-place sat old Sylvia, a Moor, who had accompanied the father of the Governor (a British naval officer) all the way from Africa, the birth-place of his Excellency. She had straight hair, which was now white as the driven snow, and hung in long matted locks about her shoulders, not unlike a bunch of candles. She was by the negroes called outlandish, and talked a sort of jargon entirely different from the broken lingo of that race. She was a general scape-goat for the whole plantation, and held in especial dread by the Ethiopian tribe. She was not asleep, nor dozing, but sat rocking her body back and forth, without moving the stool, and humming a most mournful and monotonous ditty, all the while throwing her large stealthy eyes around the room. In the opposite corner sat a regular hanger-on of the establishment, and one of those who kept a greedy eye always directed towards the fleshpots, whenever he kept them open at all. His name was June, and he wore an old cast-off coat of the Governor's, the waist buttons of which just touched his hips, while the skirts hung down to the ground in straight lines, or rather in the rear of the perpendicular, as if afraid of the constant kicking which his heels kept up against them when walking. His legs were bandied, and set so much in the middle of the foot as to render it rather a difficult matter to tell which end went foremost. His face was of the true African stamp: large mouth, flat nose, and a brow overhung with long, plaited queus, like so many whip-cords cut off short and even all round, and now quite grey. The expression of his countenance was full of mirthfulness and good humor, mixed with just enough of shrewdness to redeem it from utter vacuity. There was a slight degree of cunning twinkled from his small terrapin-looking eye, but wholly swallowed up by his large mouth, kept constantly on the stretch. He had the run of the kitchen; and, for these perquisites was expected and required to perform no other labor than running and riding errands to and from the capital; and it is because he will sometimes be thus employed that we have been so particular in describing him, and because he was the banjo player to all the small fry at Temple Farm. He had his instrument across his lap on the evening in question, his hands in the very attitude of playing, his eyes closed, and every now and then, as he rose up from a profound inclination to old Somnus, twang, twang, went the strings, accompanied by some negro doggrel just lazily let slip through his lips in half utterance, such as the following:—

Massa is a wealthy man, and all de nebors know it;
Keeps good liquors in his house, and always says—here goes it.

The last words were lost in another declination of the head, until catgut and voice became merged in a grunt or snort, when he would start up, perhaps, strain his eyes wide open, and go on again:

Sister Sally's mighty sick, oh what de debil ails her,
She used to eat good beef and beans, but now her stomach fails her.

The last words spun out again into a drawl to ac-

* July, 1838.

company a monotonous symphony, until all were lost together, by his head being brought in wonderful propinquity to his heels in the ashes.

While old June thus kept up a running accompaniment to Sylvia's Moorish monotony, on the opposite side of the fire, the front of the circle was occupied by more important characters.

Old Essex, the *major-domo* of the establishment, sat there in all the panoply of state. He was a tall, dignified old negro, with his hair queued up behind and powdered all over, and not a little of it sprinkled upon the red collar of his otherwise scrupulously clean livery. He wore small-clothes and knee-buckles, and was altogether a fine specimen of the gentlemanly old family servant. He felt himself just as much a part and parcel of the Governor's family as if he had been related to it by blood. The manners of Essex were very far above his mental culture; this no one could perceive by a slight and superficial observation, because he had acquired a most admirable tact (like some of his betters) by which he never travelled beyond his depth; added to this, whatever he did say was in the most appropriate manner, narrowly discerning nice shades of character, and suiting his replies to every one who addressed him. For instance, were a *gentleman* to alight at the hall door and meet old Essex, he would instantly receive the attentions due to a gentleman; whereas, were a gentlemanly dressed man to come, who feared that his whole importance might not be impressed upon this important functionary, Essex would instantly elevate his dignity in exact proportion to the fussiness of his visitor. Alas! the days of Essex's class are fast fading away. Many of them survived the Revolution, but the Mississippi fever has nearly made them extinct.

On the present occasion, though presumed to be not upon his dignity, the old major sat with folded arms and a benignant but yet contemptuous smile playing upon his features, illuminated as they were by the lurid fire-light, while Martin the carpenter told one of the most marvellous and wonder-stirring stories of the headless corpse ever heard within these walls, teeming, as they were, with the marvellous. Essex had often heard stories first told over the gentlemen's wine, and then the kitchen version, and of course knew how to estimate them exactly: now that before-mentioned incredulous smile began to spread until he was forced to laugh outright, as Martin capped the climax of his tale of horror, by some supernatural appearance of blue flames over the grave. Not so the other domestics, male and female, clustering around his chair; they were worked up to the highest pitch of the marvellous. Even old June ceased to twang his banjo, and at length got his eyes wide open as the carpenter came to the sage conclusion, that the place would be haunted.

It was really wonderful, with what rapidity this same point was arrived at by every negro upon the plantation, numbering more than a hundred; and these having wives and connexions on neighboring plantations, the news that Temple Farm was haunted became a settled matter for ten miles round in less than a week, and so it has remained from that day to this.

On the occasion alluded to, the story-teller for the night had worked his audience up to such a pitch of terror, that not one individual dared stir for his life, every one seeming to apprehend an instant apparition. This effect on their terrified imaginations was not a little heightened by the storm raging without. The distant thunder had been some time reverberating from the shores of the bay, mingling with the angry roar of the waves as they splashed and foamed against the beach, breaking, and then retreating for a fresh onset.

JAMES OTIS ROCKWELL.

JAMES O. ROCKWELL was, to a great extent, a self-made man. He was born at Lebanon, Conn., in 1807, and at an early age placed as an operative in a cotton factory at Paterson, New Jersey. When he was fourteen the family removed to Manlius, N. Y., and James was apprenticed to a printing establishment at Utica. He remained there about four years, writing for as well as working at the press, and then after a short sojourn in New York removed to Boston. After working a short time as a journeyman printer he obtained the situation of assistant editor of the Boston Statesman, from which he was soon promoted, in 1829, to the exclusive charge of a paper of his own, *The Providence Patriot*. "He continued," says his biographer Everest, "his editorial labors until the summer of 1831, when a 'card apologetic' announced to the readers of the *Patriot* that its editor had been 'accused of ill health—tried—found guilty—and condemned over to the physicians for punishment.' The following number was arrayed in tokens of mourning for his death."*

His poems are scattered through his own and other periodicals, having never been collected. They are all brief, and though bearing marks of an ill regulated imagination and imperfect literary execution, are animated by a true poetic flame.

SPRING.

Again upon the grateful earth,
  Thou mother of the flowers,
The singing birds, the singing streams,
  The rainbow and the showers:
And what a gift is thine!—thou mak'st
  A world to welcome thee;
And the mountains in their glory smile,
  And the wild and changeful sea.

Thou gentle Spring!—the brooding sky
  Looks welcome all around;
The moon looks down with a milder eye,
  And the stars with joy abound;
And the clouds come up with softer glow,
  Up to the zenith blown,
And float in pride o'er the earth below,
  Like banners o'er a throne.

Thou smiling Spring!—again thy praise
  Is on the lip of streams;
And the water-falls loud anthems raise,
  By day, and in their dreams;
The lakes that glitter on the plain,
  Sing with the stirring breeze;
And the voice of welcome sounds again
  From the surge upon the seas.

Adorning Spring! the earth to thee
  Spreads out its hidden love;
The ivy climbs the cedar tree,
  The tallest in the grove;
And on the moss-grown rock, the rose
  Is opening to the sun,
And the forest leaves are putting forth
  Their green leaves, one by one.

* Poets of Connecticut, p. 357. See also a further notice from the same pen, South Lit. Mess., July, 1838, in which a suspicion of suicide is hinted at.

As thou to earth, so to the soul
Shall after glories be,—
When the grave's winter yields control,
And the spirit's wings are free:
And then, as yonder opening flower
Smiles to the smiling sun,—
Be mine the fate to smile in heaven,
When my weary race is run.

GEORGE LUNT.

George Lunt was born at Newburyport, Massachusetts. He was graduated at Harvard in 1824; was admitted to the bar in 1831; practised for awhile at his native place, and since 1848 has pursued the profession in Boston.

In 1839, he published a volume of *Poems*, followed in 1843 by *The Age of Gold and other Poems*, and in 1854, by *Lyric Poems, Sonnets, and Miscellanies.* He is also the author of *Eastford, or Household Sketches, by Westley Brooke*, a novel of New England life, published in 1854.

We quote from Mr. Lunt's last published volume of poems, a characteristic specimen.

MEMORY AND HOPE.

Memory has a sister fair,
Blue-eyed, laughing, wild, and glad,
Oft she comes, with jocund air,
When her twin-born would be sad;
Hand-in-hand I love them best,
And to neither traitor prove,
Both can charm the aching breast,
Scarce I know which most to love.

Memory has a downcast face,
Yet 'tis winning, sweet, and mild,
Then comes Hope, with cheerful grace,
Like a bright enchanting child.
Now, I kiss this rosy cheek,
And the dimpling beam appears,
Then her pensive sister seek,
She too smiles, through pleasant tears.

Thus the heart a joy may take,
Else it were but hard to win,
And a quiet household make,
Where no jealousies come in.
If thy spirit be but true,
Love like this is sure to last,—
Happy he, who weds the two,
Hopeful Future,—lovely Past.

NATHANIEL PARKER WILLIS.

The family of Nathaniel Parker Willis trace back their descent to George Willis, who was born in England in 1602, and who, as a newly settled resident of Cambridge near Boston, was admitted "Freeman of Massachusetts," in 1638. By the maternal branch, dividing at the family of the grandfather of N. P. Willis, he is a descendant of the Rev. John Bailey, pastor of a church in Boston, in 1683. The portrait of the Rev. John Bailey was presented some years since to the Massachusetts Historical Society, by Nathaniel Willis, the father of N. P. Willis, to whom it had descended as the oldest of the sixth generation. Mr. Bailey was an exile for opinion's sake. He had begun his ministry at Chester, in England, at the age of 22, but was imprisoned for his non-conformist doctrines; and while waiting for his trial, had preached to crowds through the bars of Lancashire jail. He afterwards preached fourteen years in Limerick, Ireland, and was again imprisoned and tried for his opinions. He then fled from persecution to this country. The memoir of his ministry in Boston has been written by the Rev. Mr. Emerson. He died in 1697, and his funeral sermon was preached by the Rev. Cotton Mather.

The numerous descendants of these two names have been principally residents in New England, and are traceable mainly in the church records of their different locations. The majority have been farmers. Nathaniel Willis, the grandfather of N. P. Willis, was born in Boston in 1755. He was one of the proprietors and publishers of the Independent Chronicle, a leading political paper, from 1776 to 1784. He removed from Boston to Virginia, where he established the "Potomac Guardian," which he published several years at Martinsburgh. He thence removed to Ohio, and established the first newspaper ever published in that state, the "Scioto Gazette." He was for several years the Ohio State printer. It was among the memorabilia of his life that he had been an apprentice in the same printing-office with Benjamin Franklin; and that he was one of the adventurous "Tea-Party," who, in 1773, boarded the East India Company's ship in Boston harbor, and threw overboard her cargo of tea, to express their opinion of the tea-tax. He died at an advanced age on his farm near Chillicothe, to which he had retired, to pass his latter years in repose.

The poet's father, Nathaniel Willis, was for several years a political publisher and editor—the "Eastern Argus" having been established by him at Portland in 1803. With a change in his religious opinions and feelings, he returned to Boston, his native city, and there founded in 1816, the first religious newspaper in the world, the "Boston Recorder." This he conducted for twenty years, establishing, during the latter part of the same time, the first child's newspaper in the world, the "Youth's Companion." The latter he still conducts, having parted with the Recorder as too laborious a vocation for his advancing years, and its eminent success having realized for him a comfortable independence.

N. P. Willis

Nathaniel Parker Willis was born in Portland, Jan. 20, 1807. His father removed to Boston when he was six years of age. He was for a year or two a pupil of the Rev. Dr. McFarlane of Concord, N. H.; but at the Latin School of Boston and at the Phillips Academy at Andover, he received his principal education, previous to entering college. He was graduated at Yale in 1827. While in college he published several religious pieces of poetry under the signature of "Roy," and gained the prize of fifty dollars for the best poem, offered by "The Album," a gift book published by Lockwood. His mother, by whom he takes the name of Parker, was the daughter of Solomon Parker, a farmer of Massachusetts. She was a woman of uncommon talents, and of very exemplary piety and benevolence. Her husband's house being for many years the hospitable home of the clergy of their denomination, her friendship with some of the most eminent men of her time was intimate and constant; and her long and regular correspondence with the Rev. Dr. Payson, the Rev. Dr. Storrs, and others of the first minds of the period in which she lived, will, some day probably, be formed into a most interesting memoir. She died in 1844.

After his graduation, Mr. Willis first became the editor of "The Legendary," a series of volumes of tales published by S. G. Goodrich. He next established the "American Monthly Magazine," which he conducted for two years, then merging it in the "New York Mirror," conducted by Geo. P. Morris—that he might carry out a cherished purpose of a visit to Europe. His "Pencillings by the Way," contributed to the Mirror, give the history of his next four years of travel and adventure. During his first stay in Paris, Mr. Rives, the American Minister, attached him to his Legation, and it was with diplomatic passport and privilege that he made his leisurely visit to the different Courts and Capitals of Europe and the East. In 1835, after two years' residence in England, he married Mary Leighton Stace, daughter of the Commissary General William Stace, then in command of the arsenal at Woolwich, a distinguished officer, who was in the enjoyment of a large pension from government for his gallant conduct at Waterloo.

Immediately after his marriage, Mr. Willis returned to this country, and gratified his early passion for rural life, which had grown upon him with time and weariness of travel, by the purchase of a few acres in the valley of the Susquehannah, and the building of a small cottage in which he hoped to pass the remainder of his life. At this place, which he called "Glenmary," and from which he wrote the *Letters from Under a Bridge*, he passed four years. His one child by his first wife, Imogen his daughter, was born here.

By the failure of his publisher, the death of his father-in-law, and other simultaneous calamities, involving entirely his means of support, Mr. Willis was driven once more to active life; and returning to New York, he established, in connexion with Dr. Porter, *The Corsair*, a weekly journal. To arrange the foreign correspondence for this and visit his relatives, he made a short trip to England, engaging, among others, Mr. Thackeray, who was less known then than now to fame, and who wrote awhile for the Corsair. While abroad on this second tour, Mr. Willis published in London a miscellany of his magazine stories, poems, and European letters, with the title *Loiterings of Travel*. He also published in London his two plays "Bianca Visconti" and "Tortesa the Usurer," with the joint title *Two Ways of Dying for a Husband*. He also wrote about this time the letter-press for two serial publications by Virtue, on the Scenery of the United States and Ireland.

On his return to New York, he found that his partner Dr. Porter had suddenly abandoned their project in discouragement; and he soon after established, in connexion with his former partner Gen. Morris, the "Evening Mirror." The severe labor of this new and trying occupation made the first break in a constitution of great natural vigor, and the death of his wife occurring soon after, his health entirely gave way, and he was compelled once more to go abroad. A brain fever in England, and a tedious illness at the Baths of Germany, followed. On reaching Berlin, however, he met with his former literary partner, Theodore S. Fay; and Mr. Wheaton, the American minister, appointing him *attaché* to the Legation of which Mr. Fay was the Secretary, he determined to make this the home of his literary labors. Visiting England to place his daughter at school, however, he found himself too much prostrated in health to return to Germany, and soon after sailed once more with his daughter for home.

The change from the Evening Mirror to the Home Journal, which was made soon after by both partners, was a return to the more quiet paths of literature, which were better suited to both.

Upon this last enterprise, Mr. Willis is still actively employed, and its career has been, as is well known, eminently successful.

Since that time, the publications of Mr. Willis have of late consisted of editorial articles in the journal, and a series of special contributions written on his journeys in the western and southern states and among the West India islands, or from his new country residence of Idlewild on the plateau of the Highlands of the Hudson beyond West Point. A collection of his works in royal octavo

---

* Before he returned to America, his contributions to the Mirror giving an account of the society in which he moved and the places which he saw, had found their way to England, and falling into the hands of Lockhart, were reviewed by him with severity in the Quarterly for 1835. The chief points of the article were the correction of some technical errors touching the artificial distinctions of the aristocracy, and the charge that Willis had committed himself by printing his "unrestrained table-talk on delicate subjects, and capable of compromising individuals." This referred mainly to an account which Willis had published of the conversation of Moore at Lady Blessington's, in which the Irish poet commented with freedom on the career of O'Connell. It was an injudicious passage, which Willis regretted was published, not thinking at the time it was written that it would re-appear in England, though it contained, probably, nothing more than was generally known of the opinions of Moore on the Irish agitation. Moore, at any rate, was writing similar opinions himself in his Diary (since published), for the benefit of posterity. The immediate consequence of the agitation of the subject in the Quarterly was a public demand for the book, and a publisher's offer of three hundred pounds for the portion on hand in England,—about one half of what subsequently appeared in America, with the title of the collection thus made, *Pencillings by the Way*. Captain Marryatt, then editing the *Metropolitan Magazine*, made the volumes, on their publication, the subject of a personal article in that journal. Satisfaction was demanded by Willis, and shots were exchanged between the parties at Chatham.

Idlewild.

was published in 1846 by Redfield with the addition to the writings which we have enumerated up to that date of *Ephemera*, a gathering of brief newspaper miscellanies. His poems have been published in octavo, in a volume illustrated by Leutze.

A newly arranged edition of his writings, with new collections from his articles in his journal, is in course of publication by Scribner. The titles of these volumes are—

Rural Letters, and Other Records of Thoughts at Leisure; People I have Met, or Pictures of Society and People of Mark, drawn under a Thin Veil of Fiction; Life Here and There, or Sketches of Society and Adventures at Far-Apart Times and Places; Hurry-Graphs, or Sketches from Fresh Impressions of Scenery, Celebrities, and Society; Pencillings by the Way; A Summer Cruise in the Mediterranean on board an American Frigate; Fun Jottings, or Laughs I have taken a Pen To; A Health Trip to the Tropics, etc.; Letters from Idlewild; Famous Persons and Places; The Rag Bag.

In 1845, Mr. Willis married Cornelia, only daughter of the Hon. Joseph Grinnell, member of Congress from Massachusetts. The Home Journal, his "Health Trip to the Tropics," and his "Letters from Idlewild" give the outlines of his life for these latter years. By his second marriage he has three children, one son and two daughters.

The contributions of Mr. Willis to the various periodicals upon which he has been engaged, have been written with that invariable care and finish, which enable him now, in their collected form of nine volumes, to look upon them as the even and steady product of a career of literary industry, varying only in place and circumstances. They are severally characterized by their acute perception of affairs of life and the world; a delicate vein of sentiment, an increased ingenuity in the decoration and improvement of matters which in the hands of most writers would be impertinent and wearisome; in fine, their invention which makes new things out of old, whether among the palled commonplaces of the city, or the scant monotony of the country. In a series of some twenty years, Mr. Willis has ministered, with but few intervals of absence from his post, weekly through the journals with which he has been connected, to the entertainment and delight of the American public. That his pen is as fresh at the end of that time as at the beginning, is the best proof of his generously gifted nature. If, in the course of his "spiritings," he has occasionally provoked the more fastidious of his readers by far-fetched expressions or other conceptions, he has made his ground good, even on this debatable territory,—since the eccentricities have been offshoots of his originality, and maintained by a style, fresh, idiomatic, and in its construction really pure. As a gentleman may take many liberties not allowed to a clown, an author who writes English as well as Mr. Willis may be indulged with some familiarities with Priscian.

The poetry of Mr. Willis is musical and original. His Sacred Poems belong to a class of compositions which critics might object to, did not experience show them to be pleasurable and profitable interpreters to many minds. The versification of these poems is of remarkable smoothness. Indeed, they have gained the author reputation where his nicer powers would have failed to be appreciated. In another view, his novel in rhyme, of Lady Jane, is one of the very choicest of the numerous poems cast in the model of Don Juan; while his dramas are delicate creations of sentiment and passion, with a relish of the old poetic Elizabethan stage.

As a traveller, Mr. Willis has no superior in representing the humors and experiences of the world. He is sympathetic, witty, observant, and at the same time inventive. Looking at the world through a pair of eyes of his own, he finds material where others would see nothing: indeed, some of his greatest triumphs in this line have been in his rural sketches from Glenmary and Idlewild, continued with novelty and spirit, long after most clever writers would have cried out that straw and clay too for their bricks had been utterly exhausted. That this invention has been pursued through broken health, with unremitting diligence, is another claim to consideration, which the public should be prompt to acknowledge. Under the most favorable circumstances, a continuous career of newspaper literary toil is a painful drudgery. It weighs heavily on dull men of powerful constitution. The world then should be thankful, when the delicate fibres of the poet and man of genius are freely worked from day to day in its service.

THE BELFRY PIGEON.

On the cross-beam under the Old South bell
The nest of a pigeon is builded well.
In summer and winter that bird is there,
Out and in with the morning air:
I love to see him track the street,
With his wary eye and active feet;
And I often watch him as he springs,
Circling the steeple with easy wings,
'Till across the dial his shade has passed.
And the belfry edge is gained at last.
'Tis a bird I love, with its brooding note,
And the trembling throb in its mottled throat;
There's a human look in its swelling breast,
And the gentle curve of its lowly crest;
And I often stop with the fear I feel—
He runs so close to the rapid wheel.

Whatever is rung on that noisy bell—
Chime of the hour or funeral knell—

The dove in the belfry must hear it well.
When the tongue swings out to the midnight moon—
When the sexton cheerly rings for noon—
When the clock strikes clear at morning light—
When the child is waked with "nine at night"—
When the chimes play soft in the Sabbath air,
Filling the spirit with tones of prayer—
Whatever tale in the bell is heard,
He broods on his folded feet unstirred,
Or rising half in his rounded nest,
He takes the time to smoothe his breast,
Then drops again with filmed eyes,
And sleeps as the last vibration dies.
Sweet bird! I would that I could be
A hermit in the crowd like thee!
With wings to fly to wood and glen,
Thy lot, like mine, is cast with men;
And daily, with unwilling feet,
I tread, like thee, the crowded street;
But, unlike me, when day is o'er,
Thou canst dismiss the world and soar,
Or, at a half felt wish for rest,
Canst smoothe the feathers on thy breast,
And drop, forgetful, to thy nest.

I would that in such wings of gold
I could my weary heart upfold;
And while the world throngs on beneath,
Smoothe down my cares and calmly breathe;
And only sad with others' sadness,
And only glad with others' gladness,
Listen, unstirred, to knell or chime,
And, lapt in quiet, bide my time.

THE ANNOYER.

Common as light is love,
And its familiar voice wearies not ever.—SHELLEY.

Love knoweth every form of air,
And every shape of earth,
And comes, unbidden, everywhere,
Like thought's mysterious birth.
The moonlit sea and the sunset sky
Are written with Love's words,
And you hear his voice unceasingly,
Like song in the time of birds.

He peeps into the warrior's heart
From the tip of a stooping plume,
And the serried spears, and the many men,
May not deny him room.
He'll come to his tent in the weary night,
And be busy in his dream;
And he'll float to his eye in morning light
Like a fay on a silver beam.

He hears the sound of the hunter's gun,
And rides on the echo back,
And sighs in his ear, like a stirring leaf,
And flits in his woodland track.
The shade of the wood, and the sheen of the river,
The cloud and the open sky—
He will haunt them all with his subtle quiver,
Like the light of your very eye.

The fisher hangs over the leaning boat,
And ponders the silver sea,
For love is under the surface hid,
And a spell of thought has he;
He heaves the wave like a bosom sweet,
And speaks in the ripple low,
'Till the bait is gone from the crafty line,
And the hook hangs bare below.

He blurs the print of the scholar's book,
And intrudes in the maiden's prayer,
And profanes the cell of the holy man,
In the shape of a lady fair.
In the darkest night, and the bright daylight,
In earth, and sea, and sky,
In every home of human thought,
Will love be lurking nigh.

LOVE IN A COTTAGE.

They may talk of love in a cottage,
And bowers of trellised vine—
Of nature bewitchingly simple,
And milkmaids half divine;
They may talk of the pleasure of sleeping
In the shade of a spreading tree,
And a walk in the fields at morning,
By the side of a footstep free!

But give me a sly flirtation
By the light of a chandelier—
With music to play in the pauses,
And nobody very near:
Or a seat on a silken sofa,
With a glass of pure old wine,
And mamma too blind to discover
The small white hand in mine.

Your love in a cottage gets hungry,
Your vine is a nest for flies—
Your milkmaid shocks the Graces,
And simplicity talks of pies!
You lie down to your shady slumber
And wake with a bug in your ear,
And your damsel that walks in the morning
Is shod like a mountaineer.

True love is at home on a carpet,
And mightily likes his ease—
And true love has an eye for a dinner,
And starves beneath shady trees.
His wing is the fan of a lady,
His foot's an invisible thing,
And his arrow is tipped with a jewel,
And shot from a silver string.

UNSEEN SPIRITS.

The shadows lay along Broadway—
'Twas near the twilight-tide—
And slowly there a lady fair
Was walking in her pride.
Alone walked she; but, viewlessly,
Walked spirits at her side.

Peace charmed the street beneath her feet,
And Honor charmed the air;
And all astir looked kind on her,
And called her good as fair—
For all God ever gave to her
She kept with chary care.

She kept with care her beauties rare
From lovers warm and true—
For her heart was cold to all but gold,
And the rich came not to woo—
But honored well are charms to sell
If priests the selling do.

Now walking there was one more fair—
A slight girl, lily-pale;
And she had unseen company
To make the spirit quail—
'Twixt Want and Scorn she walked forlorn,
And nothing could avail.

No mercy now can clear her brow
For this world's peace to pray;
For, as love's wild prayer dissolved in air,

Her woman's heart gave way!—
But the sin forgiven by Christ in heaven
By man is curst alway!

LITTLE FLORENCE GRAY.

I was in Greece. It was the hour of noon,
And the Egean wind had dropped asleep
Upon Hymettus, and the thymy isles
Of Salamis and Egina lay hung
Like clouds upon the bright and breathless sea.
I had climbed up th' Acropolis at morn,
And hours had fled as time will in a dream
Amid its deathless ruins—for the air
Is full of spirits in these mighty fanes,
And they walk with you! As it sultrier grew,
I laid me down within a shadow deep
Of a tall column of the Parthenon,
And in an absent idleness of thought
I scrawled upon the smooth and marble base.
Tell me, O memory, what wrote I there?
The name of a sweet child I knew at Rome!

I was in Asia. 'Twas a peerless night
Upon the plains of Sardis, and the moon,
Touching my eyelids through the wind-stirred tent,
Had witched me from my slumber. I arose,
And silently stole forth, and by the brink
Of golden "Pactolus," where bathe his waters
The bases of Cybele's columns fair,
I paced away the hours. In wakeful mood
I mused upon the storied past awhile,
Watching the moon, that with the same mild eye
Had looked upon the mighty Lybian kings
Sleeping around me—Crœsus, who had heaped
Within the mouldering portico his gold,
And Gyges, buried with his viewless ring
Beneath yon swelling tumulus—and then
I loitered up the valley to a small
And humbler ruin, where the undefiled*
Of the Apocalypse their garments kept
Spotless; and crossing with a conscious awe
The broken threshold, to my spirit's eye
It seemed as if, amid the moonlight, stood
"The angel of the church of Sardis" still!
And I again passed onward, and as dawn
Paled the bright morning star, I lay me down
Weary and sad beside the river's brink,
And 'twixt the moonlight and the rosy morn,
Wrote with my fingers in the golden "sands."
Tell me, O memory! what wrote I there?
The name of the sweet child I knew at Rome!

The dust is old upon my "sandal-shoon,"
And still I am a pilgrim; I have roved
From wild America to spicy Ind,
And worshipped at innumerable shrines
Of beauty; and the painter's art, to me,
And sculpture, speak as with a living tongue,
And of dead kingdoms, I recall the soul,
Sitting amid their ruins. I have stored
My memory with thoughts that can allay
Fever and sadness; and when life gets dim,
And I am overladen in my years,
Minister to me. But when wearily
The mind gives over toiling, and, with eyes
Open but seeing not, and senses all
Lying awake within their chambers fine,
Thought settles like a fountain, clear and calm—
Far in its sleeping depths, as 'twere a gem,
Tell me, O memory what shines so fair?
The face of the sweet child I knew at Rome!

* "Thou hast a few names even in Sardis which have not defiled their garments; and they shall walk with me in white; for they are worthy." Revelation iii. 4.

LETTER TO THE UNKNOWN PURCHASER AND NEXT OCCUPANT OF GLENMARY.

SIR: In selling you the dew and sunshine ordained to fall hereafter on this bright spot of earth—the waters on their way to this sparkling brook—the tints mixed for the flowers of that enamelled meadow, and the songs bidden to be sung in coming summers by the feathery builders in Glenmary, I know not whether to wonder more at the omnipotence of money, or at my own impertinent audacity toward Nature. How you can *buy* the right to exclude at will every other creature made in God's image from sitting by this brook, treading on that carpet of flowers, or lying listening to the birds in the shade of these glorious trees—how I can *sell* it you—is a mystery not understood by the Indian, and dark, I must say, to me.

"Lord of the soil," is a title which conveys your privileges but poorly. You are master of waters flowing at this moment, perhaps, in a river of Judea, or floating in clouds over some spicy island of the tropics, bound hither after many changes. There are lilies and violets ordered for you in millions, acres of sunshine in daily instalments, and dew nightly in proportion. There are throats to be tuned with song, and wings to be painted with red and gold, blue and yellow; thousands of them, and all tributaries to you. Your corn is ordered to be sheathed in silk, and lifted high to the sun. Your grain is to be duly bearded and stemmed. There is perfume distilling for your clover, and juices for your grasses and fruits. Ice will be here for your wine, shade for your refreshment at noon, breezes and showers and snow-flakes; all in their season, and all "deeded to you for forty dollars the acre" Gods! what a copyhold of property for a fallen world!

Mine has been but a short lease of this lovely and well-endowed domain (the duration of a smile of fortune, five years, scarce longer than a five-act play); but as in a play we sometimes live through a life, it seems to me that I have lived a life at Glenmary. Allow me this, and then you must allow me the privilege of those who, at the close of life, leave something behind them: that of writing out my *will*. Though I depart *this* life, I would fain, like others, extend my ghostly hand into the future; and if wings are to be borrowed or stolen where I go, you may rely on my hovering around and haunting you, in visitations not restricted by cock-crowing.

Trying to look at Glenmary through your eyes, sir, I see too plainly that I have not shaped my ways as if expecting a successor in my lifetime. I did not, I am free to own. I thought to have shuffled off my mortal coil tranquilly here; flitting at last in company with some troop of my autumn leaves, or some bevy of spring blossoms, or with snow in the thaw; my tenants at my back, as a landlord may say. I have counted on a life-interest in the trees, trimming them accordingly; and in the squirrels and birds, encouraging them to chatter and build and fear nothing; no guns permitted on the premises. I have had my will of this beautiful stream. I have carved the woods into a shape of my liking. I have propagated the despised sumach and the persecuted hemlock and "pizen laurel." And "no end to the weeds dug up and set out again," as one of my neighbors delivers himself. I have built a bridge over Glenmary brook, which the town looks to have kept up by "the place," and we have plied free ferry over the river, I and my man Tom, till the neighbors, from the daily saving of the two miles round, have got the trick of it. And betwixt the aforesaid Glenmary brook and a certain muddy and plebeian gutter formerly permitted to join company with, and pollute it, I have procured a divorce at much trouble and pains, a guardian duty entailed of course on my successor.

First of all, sir, let me plead for the old trees of Glenmary! Ah! those friendly old trees! The cottage stands belted in with them, a thousand visible from the door, and of stems and branches worthy of the great valley of the Susquehannah. For how much music played without thanks am I indebted to those leaf-organs of changing tone? for how many whisperings of thought breathed like oracles into my ear? for how many new shapes of beauty moulded in the leaves by the wind? for how much companionship, solace, and welcome? Steadfast and constant is the countenance of such friends, God be praised for their staid welcome and sweet fidelity! If I love them better than some things human, it is no fault of ambitiousness in the trees. They stand where they did. But in recoiling from mankind, one may find them the next kindliest things, and be glad of dumb friendship. Spare those old trees, gentle sir!

In the smooth walk which encircles the meadow betwixt that solitary Olympian sugar-maple and the margin of the river, dwells a portly and venerable toad; who (if I may venture to bequeathe you, my friends) must be commended to your kindly consideration. Though a squatter, he was noticed in our first rambles along the stream, five years since, for his ready civility in yielding the way—not hurriedly, however, nor with an obsequiousness unbecoming a republican, but deliberately and just enough; sitting quietly on the grass till our passing by gave him room again on the warm and trodden ground. Punctually after the April cleansing of the walk, this jewelled *habitué*, from his indifferent lodgings hard by, emerges to take his pleasure in the sun; and there, at any hour when a gentleman is likely to be abroad, you may find him, patient on his *os coccygis*, or vaulting to his asylum of high grass. This year, he shows, I am grieved to remark, an ominous obesity, likely to render him obnoxious to the female eye, and, with the trimness of his shape, has departed much of that measured alacrity which first won our regard. He presumes a little on your allowance for old age; and with this pardonable weakness growing upon him, it seems but right that his position and standing should be tenderly made known to any new-comer on the premises. In the cutting of the next grass, slice me not up my fat friend, sir! nor set your cane down heedlessly in his modest domain. He is "mine ancient," and I would fain do him a good turn with you.

For my spoilt family of squirrels, sir, I crave nothing but immunity from powder and shot. They require coaxing to come on the same side of the tree with you, and though saucy to me, I observe that they commence acquaintance invariably with a safe mistrust. One or two of them have suffered, it is true, from too hasty a confidence in my greyhound Maida, but the beauty of that gay fellow was a trap against which nature had furnished them with no warning instinct! (A fact, sir, which would prettily point a moral!) The large hickory on the edge of the lawn, and the black walnut over the shoulder of the flower-garden, have been, through my dynasty, sanctuaries inviolate for squirrels. I pray you, sir, let them not be "reformed out," under your administration.

Of our feathered connexions and friends, we are most bound to a pair of Phebe-birds and a merry Bob-o'-Lincoln, the first occupying the top of the young maple near the door of the cottage, and the latter executing his bravuras upon the clump of alder-bushes in the meadow, though, in common with many a gay-plumaged gallant like himself, his whereabout after dark is a mystery. He comes every year from his rice-plantation in Florida to pass the summer at Glenmary. Pray keep him safe from percussion-caps, and let no urchin with a long pole poke down our trusting Phebes; annuals in that same tree for three summers. There are humming-birds, too, whom we have complimented and looked sweet upon, but they cannot be identified from morning to morning. And there is a golden oriole who sings through May on a dog-wood tree by the brook-side, but he has fought shy of our crumbs and coaxing, and let him go! We are mates for his betters, with all his gold livery! With these reservations, sir, I commend the birds to your friendship and kind keeping.

And now, sir, I have nothing else to ask, save only your watchfulness over the small nook reserved from this purchase of seclusion and loveliness. In the shady depths of the small glen above you, among the wild-flowers and music, the music of the brook babbling over rocky steps, is a spot sacred to love and memory. Keep it inviolate, and as much of the happiness of Glenmary as we can leave behind, stay with you for recompense!

HENRY WADSWORTH LONGFELLOW

Was born in Portland, Maine, February 27th, 1807, "in an old square wooden house, upon the edge of the sea." He entered Bowdoin College, where in due time he was graduated in the class with Hawthorne, in 1825. He wrote verses at this time for the *United States Literary Gazette*, printed at Boston.

For a short time after leaving college, he studied law in the office of his father, the Hon. Stephen Longfellow; but soon fell into the mode of life he has since pursued as a scholar, by the appointment to a Professorship of Modern Languages in his college, to accomplish himself for which he travelled abroad in 1826, making the usual tour of the continent, including Spain. He was absent three years; on his return, he lectured at Bowdoin College, as Professor of Modern Languages and Literature, and wrote articles for the North American Review, papers on Sir Philip Sidney, and other topics of polite literature. One of these, an Essay on the Moral and Devotional Poetry of Spain, included his noble translation of the Stanzas of the soldier poet Manrique on the death of his father.*

He also at this time penned the sketches of travel in *Outre Mer*, commencing the publication after the manner of Irving in his Sketch Book; but before the work was completed in this form, it was intrusted to the Harpers, who issued it entire in two volumes.

The elegance of the manner, the nice phrases and fanciful illustrations—a certain decorated poetical style—with the many suggestions of fastidious scholarship, marked this in the eye of the public as a book of dainty promise.

In 1835, Mr. Ticknor having resigned his Professorship of Modern Languages and Literature in Harvard, Mr. Longfellow was chosen his successor. He now made a second tour to Europe,

* This was published in a volume, by Allen & Ticknor, in 1833, with some translations of Sonnets by Lope de Vega and others.

preliminary to entering upon his new duties, visiting the northern kingdoms of Denmark, Sweden, Holland, and afterwards Switzerland.

Shortly after assuming his engagement at Harvard, he established himself, in 1837, as a lodger in the old Cragie House, the Washington Head Quarters, which has since become his own by purchase, and the past traditions and present hospitality of which have recently been celebrated by

Longfellow's Residence.

an appreciative pen.* It is from this genial residence, the outlook from which has furnished many a happy epithet and incident of the poet's verse, that *Hyperion, a Romance*, was dated in 1839, a dainty volume perfecting the happy promises of Outre Mer. Old European tradition, the quaint and picturesque of the past, are revived in its pages, by a modern sentiment and winning trick of the fancy, which will long secure the attractiveness of this pleasant volume. It has been always a scholar's instinct with Longfellow to ally his poetical style to some rare subject of fact or the imagination worthy of treatment; and those good services which he has rendered to history, old poets, and ancient art, will serve him with posterity, which asks for fruit, while the present is sometimes contented with leaves.

The first volume of original poetry published by Longfellow, was the *Voices of the Night* at Cambridge in 1839. It contained the "Psalm of Life," the "Midnight Mass for the Dying Year," the Manrique translation, and a number of the early poems of the Gazette. It at once became popular —many of its stanzas, eloquently expressive of moral courage or passive sentiment, veins since frequently worked in his poems, as Excelsior and Resignation, being fairly adopted as "household words." *Ballads and other Poems*, and a thin volume of *Poems on Slavery*, followed in 1842. The former has the translation in hexameters of "The Children of the Lord's Supper," from the Swedish of Bishop Tegner. Other delicate cream-colored volumes came on in due sequence. *The Spanish Student*, a play in three acts, in 1843; *The Belfry of Bruges* in 1846; *Evangeline, a Tale of Acadie*, a happy employment of the hexameter, the next year; *Kavanagh, a Tale*, an idyllic prose companion, in 1849; *The Seaside and the Fireside*, in 1850; and that quaint anecdotal poem of the middle ages in Europe, *The Golden Legend*, in 1851. These, with two volumes of minor poems from favorite sources, entitled *The Waif* and *The Estray*, prefaced each by a poetical introduction of his own, with a collection, *The Poets and Poetry of Europe*, in 1845, complete the list thus far of Longfellow's publications;* though some of his finest poems have since appeared in Putnam's Magazine, to which he is a frequent contributor. In 1854 he resigned his Professorship at Harvard.

Henry W. Longfellow

The same general characteristics run through all Mr. Longfellow's productions. They are the work of a scholar, of a man of taste, of a fertile fancy, and of a loving heart. He is "a picked man" of books, and sees the world and life by their light. To interest his imagination the facts around him must be invested with this charm of association. It is at once his aid and his merit that he can reproduce the choice pictures of the past and of other minds with new accessories of his own; so that the quaint old poets of Germany, the singers of the past centuries, the poetical vision and earnest teachings of Goethe, and the every-day humors of Jean Paul, as it were, come to live among us in American homes and landscape. This interpretation in its highest forms is one of the rarest benefits which the scholar can bestow upon his country. The genius of Longfellow has given us an American idyl, based on a touching episode of ante-revolutionary history, parallel with the Hermann and Dorothea of Goethe, in the exquisite story of Evangeline; has shown us how Richter might have surveyed the higher and inferior conditions, the

* G. W. Curtis, in the "Homes of American Authors."

* There have been other editions of several of these works; a collection made by the author in a cheap form published by the Harpers in 1846; the costly copy, illustrated by Huntington, published at Philadelphia in 1845; and the elegant editions of Evangeline, the Poems, the Golden Legend, and Hyperion, published by Bogue of London, with the wood-cut illustrations from original designs—for one series of which the artist made a tour on the continent—by Birket Foster.

schoolmaster, the clergyman, the lovers and the rustics of a New England village in his tale of Kavanagh; has reproduced the simple elegance of the lighter Spanish drama in his play of the Student; and in his Golden Legend has carried us, in his ingenious verse, to the heart of the Middle Ages, showing us the most poetic aspects of the lives of scholars, churchmen, and villagers,—how they sang, travelled, practised logic, medicine, and divinity, and with what miracle plays, jest, and grim literature they were entertained. His originality and peculiar merit consist in these felicitous transformations. If he were simply a scholar, he would be but an annalist or an annotator; but being a poet of taste and imagination, with an ardent sympathy for all good and refined traits in the world, and for all forms of the objective life of others, his writings being the very emanations of a kind generous nature, he has succeeded in reaching the heart of the public. All men relish art and literature when they are free from pedantry. We are all pleased with pictures, and like to be charmed into thinking nobly and acting well by the delights of fancy.

In his personal appearance, frank, graceful manner, fortune, and mode of life, Mr. Longfellow reflects or anticipates the elegance of his writings. In a home surrounded by every refinement of art and cultivated intercourse, in the midst of his family and friends, the genial humorist enjoys a retired leisure, from which many ripe fruits of literature may yet be looked for.

A PSALM OF LIFE—WHAT THE HEART OF THE YOUNG MAN SAID TO THE PSALMIST.

Tell me not, in mournful numbers,
  Life is but an empty dream!
For the soul is dead that slumbers,
  And things are not what they seem.

Life is real! Life is earnest!
  And the grave is not its goal;
Dust thou art, to dust returnest,
  Was not spoken of the soul.

Not enjoyment, and not sorrow,
  Is our destined end or way;
But to act, that each to-morrow
  Find us farther than to-day.

Art is long, and Time is fleeting,
  And our hearts, though stout and brave,
Still, like muffled drums, are beating
  Funeral marches to the grave.

In the world's broad field of battle,
  In the bivouac of Life,
Be not like dumb, driven cattle!
  Be a hero in the strife!

Trust no Future, howe'er pleasant!
  Let the dead Past bury its dead!
Act,—act in the living Present!
  Heart within, and God o'erhead!

Lives of great men all remind us
  We can make our lives sublime,
And, departing, leave behind us
  Footprints on the sands of time;

Footprints, that perhaps another,
  Sailing o'er life's solemn main,
A forlorn and shipwrecked brother,
  Seeing, shall take heart again.

Let us, then, be up and doing,
  With a heart for any fate;
Still achieving, still pursuing,
  Learn to labor and to wait.

FOOTSTEPS OF ANGELS.

When the hours of Day are numbered,
  And the voices of the Night
Wake the better soul, that slumbered,
  To a holy, calm delight;

Ere the evening lamps are lighted,
  And, like phantoms grim and tall,
Shadows from the fitful fire-light
  Dance upon the parlour-wall;

Then the forms of the departed
  Enter at the open door;
The beloved, the true-hearted,
  Come to visit me once more;

He, the young and strong, who cherished
  Noble longings for the strife,
By the road-side fell and perished,
  Weary with the march of life!

They, the holy ones and weakly,
  Who the cross of suffering bore,
Folded their pale hands so meekly,
  Spake with us on earth no more!

And with them the Being Beauteous,
  Who unto my youth was given,
More than all things else to love me,
  And is now a saint in heaven.

With a slow and noiseless footstep
  Comes that messenger divine,
Takes the vacant chair beside me,
  Lays her gentle hand in mine.

And she sits and gazes at me
  With those deep and tender eyes,
Like the stars, so still and saint-like,
  Looking downward from the skies.

Uttered not, yet comprehended,
  Is the spirit's voiceless prayer,
Soft rebukes, in blessings ended,
  Breathing from her lips of air.

O, though oft depressed and lonely,
  All my fears are laid aside,
If I but remember only
  Such as these have lived and died!

GOD'S-ACRE.

I like that ancient Saxon phrase, which calls
  The burial-ground God's-Acre! It is just;
It consecrates each grave within its walls,
  And breathes a benison o'er the sleeping dust.

God's-Acre! Yes, that blessed name imparts
  Comfort to those who in the grave have sown
The seed that they had garnered in their hearts
  Their bread of life, alas! no more their own.

Into its furrows shall we all be cast,
  In the sure faith that we shall rise again
At the great harvest, when the archangel's blast
  Shall winnow, like a fan, the chaff and grain.

Then shall the good stand in immortal bloom,
  In the fair gardens of that second birth;
And each bright blossom mingle its perfume
  With that of flowers which never bloomed on earth.

With thy rude ploughshare, Death, turn up the sod,
  And spread the furrow for the seed we sow;
This is the field and Acre of our God.
  This is the place where human harvests grow!

EXCELSIOR.

The shades of night were falling fast,
As through an Alpine village passed
A youth, who bore, 'mid snow and ice,
A banner with the strange device,
Excelsior!

His brow was sad; his eye beneath
Flashed like a falchion from its sheath,
And like a silver clarion rung
The accents of that unknown tongue,
Excelsior!

In happy homes he saw the light
Of household fires gleam warm and bright;
Above, the spectral glaciers shone,
And from his lips escaped a groan,
Excelsior!

"Try not the pass!" the old man said;
"Dark lowers the tempest overhead,
The roaring torrent is deep and wide!"
And loud that clarion voice replied,
Excelsior!

"O, stay," the maiden said, "and rest
Thy weary head upon this breast!"
A tear stood in his bright blue eye,
But still he answered, with a sigh,
Excelsior!

"Beware the pine-tree's withered branch!
Beware the awful avalanche!"
This was the peasant's last good-night;
A voice replied, far up the height,
Excelsior!

At break of day, as heavenward
The pious monks of Saint Bernard
Uttered the oft-repeated prayer,
A voice cried through the startled air,
Excelsior!

A traveller, by the faithful hound,
Half-buried in the snow was found,
Still grasping in his hand of ice
That banner with the strange device,
Excelsior!

There, in the twilight cold and gray,
Lifeless, but beautiful, he lay,
And from the sky, serene and far,
A voice fell, like a falling star,
Excelsior!

RAIN IN SUMMER.

How beautiful is the rain!
After the dust and heat,
In the broad and fiery street,
In the narrow lane,
How beautiful is the rain!

How it clatters along the roofs,
Like the tramp of hoofs!
How it gushes and struggles out
From the throat of the overflowing spout!
Across the window-pane
It pours and pours;
And swift and wide,
With a muddy tide,
Like a river down the gutter roars
The rain, the welcome rain!
The sick man from his chamber looks
At the twisted brooks;
He can feel the cool
Breath of each little pool;
His fevered brain
Grows calm again,
And he breathes a blessing on the rain.
From the neighbouring school
Come the boys,
With more than their wonted noise
And commotion;

And down the wet streets
Sail their mimic fleets,
Till the treacherous pool
Engulfs them in its whirling
And turbulent ocean.

In the country, on every side,
Where far and wide,
Like a leopard's tawny and spotted hide,
Stretches the plain,
To the dry grass and the drier grain
How welcome is the rain!

In the furrowed land
The toilsome and patient oxen stand;
Lifting the yoke-encumbered head,
With their dilated nostrils spread,
They silently inhale
The clover-scented gale,
And the vapors that arise
From the well watered and smoking soil.
For this rest in the furrow after toil
Their large and lustrous eyes
Seem to thank the Lord,
More than man's spoken word.

Near at hand,
From under the sheltering trees,
The farmer sees
His pastures, and his fields of grain,
As they bend their tops
To the numberless beating drops
Of the incessant rain.
He counts it as no sin
That he sees therein
Only his own thrift and gain.

These, and far more than these,
The Poet sees!
He can behold
Aquarius old
Walking the fenceless fields of air;
And from each ample fold
Of the clouds about him rolled
Scattering everywhere
The showery rain,
As the farmer scatters his grain.

He can behold
Things manifold
That have not yet been wholly told,—
Have not been wholly sung nor said.
For his thought, that never stops,
Follows the water-drops
Down to the graves of the dead,
Down through chasms and gulfs profound,
To the dreary fountain-head
Of lakes and rivers under ground;
And sees them, when the rain is done,
On the bridge of colors seven
Climbing up once more to heaven,
Opposite the setting sun.

Thus the seer,
With vision clear,
Sees forms appear and disappear,
In the perpetual round of strange,
Mysterious change
From birth to death, from death to birth,
From earth to heaven, from heaven to earth;
Till glimpses more sublime
Of things, unseen before,
Unto his wondering eyes reveal
The Universe, as an immeasurable wheel
Turning for evermore
In the rapid and rushing river of Time.

RESIGNATION.

There is no flock, however watched and tended,
But one dead lamb is there!
There is no fireside, howsoe'er defended,
But has one vacant chair!

The air is full of farewells to the dying,
And mournings for the dead;
The heart of Rachel for her children crying
Will not be comforted!

Let us be patient! these severe afflictions
Not from the ground arise,
But oftentimes celestial benedictions
Assume this dark disguise.

We see but dimly through the mists and vapors;
Amid these earthly damps
What seem to us but dim funereal tapers
May be Heaven's distant lamps.

There is no Death! what seems so is transition;
This life of Mortal breath
Is but a suburb of the life elysian,
Whose portal we call Death.

She is not dead—the child of our affection—
But gone unto that school
Where she no longer needs our poor protection,
And Christ himself doth rule.

In that great cloister's stillness and seclusion
By guardian angels led,
Safe from temptation, safe from sin's pollution,
She lives, whom we call dead.

Day after day we think what she is doing,
In those bright realms of air;
Year after year, her tender steps pursuing,
Behold her grown more fair.

Thus do we walk with her, and keep unbroken
The bond which nature gives,
Thinking that our remembrance, though unspoken,
May reach her where she lives.

Not as a child shall we again behold her;
For when with raptures wild
In our embraces we again enfold her,
She will not be a child;

But a fair maiden, in her Father's mansion,
Clothed with celestial grace;
And beautiful with all the soul's expansion
Shall we behold her face.

And though at times, impetuous with emotion
And anguish long suppressed,
The swelling heart heaves moaning like the ocean
That cannot be at rest;

We will be patient! and assuage the feeling
We cannot wholly stay;
By silence sanctifying, not concealing,
The grief that must have way.

THE OLD CLOCK ON THE STAIRS.

L'éternité est une pendule, dont le balancier dit et redit sans cesse ces deux mots seulement, dans le silence des tombeaux: "Toujours! jamais! Jamais! toujours!"
JACQUES BRIDAINE.

Somewhat back from the village street
Stands the old-fashioned country-seat,
Across its antique portico
Tall poplar-trees their shadows throw;
And from its station in the hall
An ancient timepiece says to all,—
"For ever—never!
Never—for ever!"

Halfway up the stairs it stands,
And points and beckons with its hands
From its case of massive oak,
Like a monk, who, under his cloak,
Crosses himself, and sighs, alas!
With sorrowful voice to all who pass,—
"For ever—never!
Never—for ever!"

By day its voice is low and light;
But in the silent dead of night,
Distinct as a passing footstep's fall,
It echoes along the vacant hall,
Along the ceiling, along the floor,
And seems to say at each chamber door,—
"For ever—never!
Never—for ever!"

Through days of sorrow and of mirth,
Through days of death and days of birth,
Through every swift vicissitude
Of changeful time, unchanged it has stood,
And as if, like God, it all things saw,
It calmly repeats those words of awe,—
"For ever—never!
Never—for ever!"

In that mansion used to be
Free-hearted Hospitality;
His great fires up the chimney roared;
The stranger feasted at his board;
But, like the skeleton at the feast,
That warning timepiece never ceased,—
"For ever—never!
Never—for ever!"

There groups of merry children played,
There youths and maidens dreaming strayed;
O precious hours! O golden prime,
And affluence of love and time!
Even as a miser counts his gold,
Those hours the ancient timepiece told,—
"For ever—never!
Never—for ever!"

From that chamber, clothed in white,
The bride came forth on her wedding night;
There, in that silent room below,
The dead lay in his shroud of snow,
And in the hush that followed the prayer,
Was heard the old clock on the stair,—
"For ever—never!
Never—for ever!"

All are scattered now and fled,
Some are married, some are dead;
And when I ask with throbs of pain,
"Ah! when shall they all meet again!"
As in the days long since gone by,
The ancient timepiece makes reply,—
"For ever—never!
Never—for ever!"

Never here, for ever there,
Where all parting, pain, and care,
And death, and time shall disappear,—
For ever there, but never here!
The horologe of Eternity
Sayeth this incessantly,—
"For ever—never!
Never—for ever!"

THE JEWISH CEMETERY AT NEWPORT.

How strange it seems! These Hebrews in their graves,
Close by the street of this fair sea-port town;
Silent beside the never-silent waves,
At rest in all this moving up and down!

The trees are white with dust, that o'er their sleep
Wave their broad curtains in the south-wind's breath,

While underneath such leafy tents they keep
 The long, mysterious Exodus of Death.

And these sepulchral stones, so old and brown,
 That pave with level flags their burial-place,
Are like the tablets of the Law, thrown down
 And broken by Moses at the mountain's base.

The very names recorded here are strange,
 Of foreign accent, and of different climes;
Alvares and Rivera interchange
 With Abraham and Jacob of old times.

"Blessed be God! for he created Death!"
 The mourners said: "and Death is rest and peace."
Then added, in the certainty of faith:
 "And giveth Life, that never more shall cease."

Closed are the portals of their Synagogue,
 No Psalms of David now the silence break,
No Rabbi reads the ancient Decalogue
 In the grand dialect the Prophets spake.

Gone are the living but the dead remain,
 And not neglected, for a hand unseen,
Scattering its bounty, like a summer rain,
 Still keeps their graves and their remembrance green.

How came they here? What burst of Christian hate,
 What persecution, merciless and blind,
Drove o'er the sea,—that desert, desolate—
 These Ishmaels and Hagars of mankind?

They lived in narrow streets and lanes obscure,
 Ghetto or Judenstrass', in mirk and mire:
Taught in the school of patience to endure
 The life of anguish and the death of fire.

All their lives long, with the unleavened bread
 And bitter herbs of exile and its fears,
The wasting famine of the heart they fed,
 And slaked its thirst with marsh of their tears.

Anathema maranatha! was the cry
 That rang from town to town, from street to street;
At every gate the accursed Mordecai
 Was mocked and jeered, and spurned by Christian feet.

Pride and humiliation hand in hand
 Walked with them through the world where'er they went;
Trampled and beaten were they as the sand,
 And yet unshaken as the continent.

For in the background figures vague and vast,
 Of patriarchs and of prophets rose sublime,
And all the great traditions of the Past
 They saw reflected in the coming time.

And thus for ever with reverted look
 The mystic volume of the world they read,
Spelling it backward like a Hebrew book,
 Till life became a legend of the Dead.

But ah! what once has been shall be no more!
 The groaning earth in travail and in pain
Brings forth its races, but does not restore,
 And the dead nations never rise again.

SCENERY OF THE MISSISSIPPI—FROM EVANGELINE.

Onward o'er sunken sands, through a wilderness sombre with forests,
Day after day they glided adown the turbulent river;
Night after night, by their blazing fires, encamped on its borders.
Now through rushing chutes, among green islands, where plumelike
Cotton-trees nodded their shadowy crests, they swept with the current,
Then emerged into broad lagoons, where silvery sand-bars
Lay in the stream, and along the wimpling waves of their margin,
Shining with snow-white plumes, large flocks of pelicans waded.
Level the landscape grew, and along the shores of the river,
Shaded by China trees, in the midst of luxuriant gardens,
Stood the houses of planters, with negro-cabins and dove-cots.
They were approaching the region where reigns perpetual summer,
Where through the Golden Coast, and groves of orange and citron,
Sweeps with majestic curve the river away to the eastward.
They, too, swerved from their course; and, entering the Bayou of Plaquemine,
Soon were lost in a maze of sluggish and devious waters,
Which, like a net-work of steel, extended in every direction.
Over their heads the towering and tenebrous boughs of the cypress
Met in a dusky arch, and trailing mosses in mid air
Waved like banners that hang on the walls of ancient cathedrals.
Death-like the silence seemed, and unbroken, save by the herons
Home to their roosts in the cedar-trees returning at sunset,
Or by the owl, as he greeted the moon with demoniac laughter.
Lovely the moonlight was as it glanced and gleamed on the water,
Gleamed on the columns of cypress and cedar sustaining the arches,
Down through whose broken vaults it fell as through chinks in a ruin.
Dream-like, and indistinct, and strange were all things around them;
And o'er their spirits there came a feeling of wonder and sadness,—
Strange forebodings of ill, unseen and that cannot be compassed.

* * * * * * * *

Softly the evening came. The sun from the western horizon
Like a magician extended his golden wand o'er the landscape;
Twinkling vapors arose; and sky and water and forest,
Seemed all on fire at the touch, and melted and mingled together.
Hanging between two skies, a cloud with edges of silver,
Floated the boat, with its dripping oars, on the motionless water.
Filled was Evangeline's heart with inexpressible sweetness.
Touched by the magic spell, the sacred fountains of feeling
Glowed with the light of love, as the skies and waters around her.
Then from a neighboring thicket the mocking-bird, wildest of singers,
Swinging aloft on a willow spray that hung o'er the water,
Shook from his little throat such floods of delirious music,
That the whole air and the woods and the waves seemed silent to listen.

Plaintive at first were the tones and sad; then soaring to madness
Seemed they to follow or guide the revel of frenzied Bacchantes.
Then single notes were heard, in sorrowful, low lamentation;
Till, having gathered them all, he flung them abroad in derision,
As when, after a storm, a gust of wind through the tree-tops
Shakes down the rattling rain in a crystal shower on the branches.
With such a prelude as this, and hearts that throbbed with emotion,
Slowly they entered the Têche, where it flows through the green Opelousas,
And through the amber air, above the crest of the woodland,
Saw the column of smoke that rose from a neighboring dwelling;—
Sounds of a horn they heard, and the distant lowing of cattle.

PIC-NIC AT ROARING BROOK—FROM KAVANAGH.

Every state, and almost every county, of New England, has its Roaring Brook,—a mountain streamlet, overhung by woods, impeded by a mill, encumbered by fallen trees, but ever racing, rushing, roaring down through gurgling gullies, and filling the forest with its delicious sound and freshness; the drinking-place of home-returning herds: the mysterious haunt of squirrels and blue-jays, the sylvan retreat of school-girls, who frequent it on summer holidays, and mingle their restless thoughts, their overflowing fancies, their fair imaginings, with its restless, exuberant, and rejoicing stream.

Fairmeadow had no Roaring Brook. As its name indicates, it was too level a land for that. But the neighbouring town of Westwood, lying more inland, and among the hills, had one of the fairest and fullest of all the brooks that roar. It was the boast of the neighbourhood. Not to have seen it, was to have seen no brook, no waterfall, no mountain ravine. And, consequently, to behold it and admire, was Kavanagh taken by Mr. Churchill as soon as the summer vacation gave leisure and opportunity. The party consisted of Mr. and Mrs. Churchill, and Alfred, in a one-horse chaise, and Cecilia, Alice, and Kavanagh, in a carryall—the fourth seat in which was occupied by a large basket, containing what the Squire of the Grove, in Don Quixote, called his "fiambreras,"—that magniloquent Castilian word for cold collation. Over warm uplands, smelling of clover and mint; through cool glades, still wet with the rain of yesterday; along the river; across the rattling and tilting planks of wooden bridges; by orchards, by the gates of fields, with the tall mullen growing at the bars; by stone walls overrun with privet and barberries; in sun and heat, in shadow and coolness,—forward drove the happy party on that pleasant summer morning.

At length they reached the Roaring Brook. From a gorge in the mountains, through a long, winding gallery of birch, and beech, and pine, leaped the bright, brown waters of the jubilant streamlet; out of the woods, across the plain, under the rude bridge of logs, into the woods again,—a day between two nights. With it went a song that made the heart sing likewise, a song of joy, and exultation, and freedom, a continuous and unbroken song of life, and pleasure, and perpetual youth. Like the old Icelandic Scald, the streamlet seemed to say,—

"I am possessed of songs such as neither the spouse of a king, nor any son of man, can repeat: one of them is called the Helper; it will help thee at thy need, in sickness, grief, and all adversity."

The little party left their carriages at a farmhouse by the bridge, and followed the rough road on foot along the brook: now close upon it, now shut out by intervening trees. Mr. Churchill, bearing the basket on his arm, walked in front with his wife and Alfred. Kavanagh came behind with Cecilia and Alice. The music of the brook silenced all conversation; only occasional exclamations of delight were uttered,—the irrepressible applause of fresh and sensitive natures, in a scene so lovely. Presently, turning off from the road, which led directly to the mill, and was rough with the tracks of heavy wheels, they went down to the margin of the brook.

"How indescribably beautiful this brown water is!" exclaimed Kavanagh. "It is like wine, or the nectar of the gods of Olympus; as if the falling Hebe had poured it from the goblet."

"More like the mead or metheglin of the northern gods," said Mr. Churchill, "spilled from the drinking-horns of Valhalla."

But all the ladies thought Kavanagh's comparison the better of the two, and in fact the best that could be made; and Mr. Churchill was obliged to retract, and apologize for his allusion to the celestial ale-house of Odin.

Ere long they were forced to cross the brook, stepping from stone to stone, over the little rapids and cascades. All crossed lightly, easily, safely; even "the sumpter mule," as Mr. Churchill called himself, on account of the pannier. Only Cecilia lingered behind, as if afraid to cross. Cecilia, who had crossed at that same place a hundred times before,—Cecilia, who had the surest foot, and the firmest nerves, of all the village maidens,—she now stood irresolute, seized with a sudden tremor; blushing and laughing at her own timidity, and yet unable to advance. Kavanagh saw her embarrassment, and hastened back to help her. Her hand trembled in his; she thanked him with a gentle look and word. His whole soul was softened within him. His attitude, his countenance, his voice were alike submissive and subdued. He was as one penetrated with the tenderest emotions.

It is difficult to know at what moment love begins; it is less difficult to know that it has begun. A thousand heralds proclaim it to the listening air; a thousand ministers and messengers betray it to the eye. Tone, act, attitude and look,—the signals upon the countenance,—the electric telegraph of touch; all these betray the yielding citadel before the word itself is uttered, which, like the key surrendered, opens every avenue and gate of entrance, and makes retreat impossible.

The day passed delightfully with all. They sat upon the stones and the roots of trees. Cecilia read, from a volume she had brought with her, poems that rhymed with the running water. The others listened and commented. Little Alfred waded in the stream, with his bare white feet, and launched boats over the falls. Noon had been fixed upon for dining; but they anticipated it by at least an hour. The great basket was opened, endless sandwiches were drawn forth, and a cold pastry, as large as that of the Squire of the Grove. During the repast, Mr. Churchill slipped into the brook, while in the act of handing a sandwich to his wife, which caused unbounded mirth; and Kavanagh sat down on a mossy trunk, that gave way beneath him, and crumbled into powder. This, also, was received with great merriment.

After dinner, they ascended the brook still farther—indeed, quite to the mill, which was not going. It had been stopped in the midst of its work. The saw still held its hungry teeth fixed in the heart of a pine. Mr. Churchill took occasion to make known to the company his long cherished purpose of writing a poem called "The Song of the Saw-Mill," and enlarged on the beautiful associations of flood and forest connected with the theme. He delighted himself and his audience with the fine fancies he meant to weave into his poem, and wondered that nobody had thought of the subject before. Kavanagh said that it had been thought of before; and cited Kerner's little poem, so charmingly translated by Bryant. Mr. Churchill had not seen it. Kavanagh looked into his pocket-book for it, but it was not to be found; still he was sure that there was such a poem. Mr. Churchill abandoned his design. He had spoken,—and the treasure, just as he touched it with his hand, was gone for ever.

The party returned home as it came, all tired and happy, excepting little Alfred, who was tired and cross, and sat sleepy and sagging on his father's knee, with his hat cocked rather fiercely over his eyes.

Mr. Samuel Longfellow, a brother of the preceding, an accomplished Unitarian divine, is the minister of a congregation at Brooklyn, N. Y. He was a graduate of Harvard of the class of 1839. He has written several hymns which are included in the collection of Higginson and Johnston. In 1853 he prepared a tasteful collection of poetry, published by Ticknor and Co., entitled, *Thalatta: a Book for the Sea Side.* Among its numerous articles we notice this single contribution of his own.

EVENING WALK BY THE BAY.

The evening hour had brought its peace,
  Brought end of toil to weary day;
From wearying thoughts to find release,
  I sought the sands that skirt the bay.
Dark rain-clouds southward hovering nigh,
  Gave to the sea their leaden hue,
But in the west the open sky,
  Its rose-light on the waters threw.

I stood, with heart more quiet grown,
  And watched the pulses of the tide,
The huge black rocks, the sea weeds brown,
  The grey beach stretched on either side,
The boat that dropped its one white sail,
  Where the steep yellow bank ran down,
And o'er the clump of willows pale,
  The white towers of the neighboring town.

A cool light brooded o'er the land,
  A changing lustre lit the bay;
The tide just plashed along the sand,
  And voices sounded far away.
The Past came up to Memory's eye,
  Dark with some clouds of leaden hue,
But many a space of open sky
  Its rose-light on those waters threw.

Then came to me the dearest friend,
  Whose beauteous soul doth, like the sea,
To all things fair new beauty lend,
  Transfiguring the earth to me.
The thoughts that lips could never tell,
  Through subtler senses were made known;
I raised my eyes,—the darkness fell,—
  I stood upon the sands, alone.

HENRY WILLIAM HERBERT.

Mr. Herbert presents the somewhat rare combination in this country, where too little attention is given to physical in connexion with intellectual training, of the scholar, the sportsman, and the novelist. He is the eldest son of the Hon. and Rev. William Herbert, Dean of Manchester, author of the poem of Attila, and a second son of the Earl of Carnarvon. He was born in London, April 7, 1807, was educated at home under a private tutor until twelve years of age, and then, after a year passed at a private school, sent to Eton, April, 1820. In October, 1825, he entered Caius College, Cambridge, and was graduated with distinction in January, 1829. At the close of the following year he removed to the United States, and has since resided in the city of New York and at his country seat, the Cedars, in its vicinity at Newark. During the eight years after his arrival he was employed as principal Greek teacher in the classical school of the Rev. R. Townsend Huddart in the City of New York. In 1833, in company with Mr. A. D. Patterson, he commenced the American Monthly Magazine, which he conducted, after the conclusion of the second year, in connexion with Mr. C. F. Hoffman until 1836, when the periodical passed into the charge of Mr. Park Benjamin. Nearly one half the matter of several numbers was written by Mr. Herbert, who kept up a fine spirit of scholarship in its pages. In 1834 an historical novel, which he had commenced in the magazine, *The Brothers, a Tale of the Fronde*, was published by the Harpers. It was followed in 1837 by *Cromwell*, in 1843 by *Marmaduke Wyvil*, and in 1848 by *The Roman Traitor*, a classical romance founded on the Conspiracy of Catiline.

During the period of the publication of these works Mr. Herbert was also a constant contributor to the New York Spirit of the Times. His sporting articles in that periodical have been collected under the titles of *My Shooting Box*, *The Warwick Woodlands*, and *Field Sports of the United States.* The last of these extends to two volumes octavo, and contains, in addition to the matters

Henry Wm. Herbert

especially pertaining to *Venator* and *Piscator*, a full account of the characteristics of the fish, flesh, and fowl treated of.

Mr. Herbert, in his division of his time, must nearly realize that of Izaak Walton's Scholar, "all summer in the field and all winter in the study," as in addition to the productions we have mentioned he has written a fine metrical translation of the Agamemnon, published in a small volume, with a number of briefer versions from the classics, in the "Literary World" and other periodicals. He has also been a constant contributor of tales and sketches, mostly drawn from romantic incidents in European history, to the monthly magazine. Several of these have been collected into volumes under the titles of *The Cavaliers of England, or the Times of the Revolutions of* 1642 *and* 1688; *The Knights of England, France, and Scotland;* and *the Chevaliers of France from the Crusaders to the Marechals of Louis XIV.* He has also collected two volumes on the classical period, *The Captains of the Old World, their Campaigns, Character, and Conduct, as Compared with the Great Modern Strategists*, an account of the great military leaders who flourished from the time of the Persian Wars to the Roman Republic; and a work, *The Captains of the Roman Republic.*

Mr. Herbert's style is ample and flowing, with a certain finished elegance marking the true man of letters. Though only occasionally putting his pen to verse, a poetical spirit of enthusiasm runs through his writings.

THE LAST BEAR ON THE HILLS OF WARWICK.

It was a hot and breathless afternoon, toward the last days of July—one of those days of fiery, scorching heat, that drive the care-worn citizens from their great red-hot oven, into those calm and peaceful shades of the sweet unsophisticated country, which, to them, savour far more of purgatory than they do of paradise,—"for quiet, to quick bosoms, is a hell," —and theirs are quick enough, heaven knows, in Wall-street. It was a hot and breathless afternoon —the sun, which had been scourging the faint earth all day long with a degree of heat endurable by those alone who can laugh at one hundred degrees of Fahrenheit, was stooping toward the western verge of heaven; but no drop of diamond dew had as yet fallen to refresh the innocent flowers, that hung their heads like maidens smitten by passionate and ill-requited love; no indication of the evening breeze had sent its welcome whisper among the motionless and silent tree-tops. Such was the season and the hour when, having started, long before Dan Phœbus had arisen from his bed, to beat the mountain swales about the greenwood lake, and having bagged, by dint of infinite exertion and vast *sudor*, present alike to dogs and men, our thirty couple of good summer Woodcock, Archer and I paused on the bald scalp of Round Mountain.

Crossing a little ridge, we came suddenly upon the loveliest and most fairy-looking *ghyll*—for I must have recourse to a north-country word to denote that which lacks a name in any other dialect of the Anglo-Norman tongue—I ever looked upon. Not, at the most, about twenty yards wide at the brink, nor above twelve in depth, it was clothed with a dense rich growth of hazel, birch, and juniper; the small rill brawling and sparkling in a thousand mimic cataracts over the tiny limestone ledges which opposed its progress—a beautiful profusion of wild flowers—the tall and vivid spikes of the bright scarlet habenaria—the gorgeous yellow cups of the low-growing enothera—and many gaily-colored creepers decked the green marges of the water, or curled, in clustering beauty, over the neighbouring coppice. We followed for a few paces this fantastic cleft, until it widened into a circular recess or cove—the summit-level of its waters—whence it dashed headlong, some twenty-five or thirty feet, into the chasm below. The floor of this small basin was paved with the bare rock, through the very midst of which the little stream had worn a channel scarcely a foot in depth, its clear cold waters glancing like crystal over its pebbly bed. On three sides it was hemmed in by steep banks, so densely set with the evergreen junipers, interlaced and matted with cat-briars and other creeping plants, that a small dog could not, without a struggle, have forced its way through the close thicket. On the fourth side, fronting the opening of the rift by which the waters found their egress, there stood a tall, flat face of granite rock, completely blocking up the glen, perfectly smooth and slippery, until it reached the height of forty feet, when it became uneven, and broke into many craggy steps and seams, from one of which shot out the broad stem and gnarled branches of an aged oak, overshadowing, with its grateful umbrage, the sequestered source of that wild mountain spring. The small cascade, gushing from an aperture midway the height of the tall cliff, leaped, in a single glittering thread, scarcely a foot broad, and but an inch or two in volume, into the little pool which it had worn out for its own reception in the hard stone at the bottom. Immediately behind this natural fountain, which, in its free leap, formed an arch of several feet in diameter, might be seen a small and craggy aperture, but little larger than the entrance of a common well, situate close to the rock's base, descending in a direction nearly perpendicular for several feet, as might be easily discovered from without.

"There, Frank," cried Harry, as he pointed to the cave—"*there* is the scene of my Bear story; and *here*, as I told you, is the sweetest nook, and freshest spring, you ever saw or tasted!"

"For the sight," replied I, "I confess. As to the taste, I will speak more presently." While I replied, I was engaged in producing from my pocket our slight stores of pilot biscuit, salt, and hard-boiled eggs, whereunto Harry contributed his quota in the shape of a small piece of cold salt pork, and—tell it not in Gath—two or three young, green-topped, summer onions. Two modest-sized dram bottles, duly supplied with old Farintosh, and a dozen or two of right Manilla cheroots, arranged in tempting order, beside the brimming basin of the nymph-like cascade, completed our arrangement; and, after having laved our heated brows and hands, begrimed with gunpowder, and stained with the red witness of volucrine slaughter, stretched on the cool granite floor, and sheltered from the fierce rays of the summer sun by the dark foliage of the oak—we feasted, happier and more content with our frugal fare, than the most lordly epicure that ever strove to stimulate his appetite to the appreciation of fresh luxuries.

"Well, Harry," exclaimed I, when I was satiate with food, and while, having already quaffed two moderate horns, I was engaged in emptying, alas! the last remaining drops of whiskey into the silver cup, sparkling with pure cold water—"Well, Harry, the spring *is* fresh, and cold, and tasteless, as any water I ever *did* taste! Pity it were not situate in some Faun-haunted glen of green Arcadia, or some sweet flower-enamelled dell of merry England, that it might have a meeter legend for romantic ears than your Bear story—some minstrel dream of Dryad, or Oread, or of Dian's train, mortal-wooed!—some frolic tale of Oberon and his blithe Titania!—or, stranger yet, some thrilling and disastrous lay, after the German school, of woman wailing for her demon lover! But, sith it may not be, let's have the Bear."

"Well, then," replied that worthy, "first, as you must know, the hero of my tale is—alas! that I must say *was*, rather—a brother of Tom Draw, than whom no braver nor more honest man, no warmer friend, no keener sportsman, ever departed to his long last home, dewed by the tears of all who knew him. He *was*—but it boots not to weave long reminiscences—you know the brother who still survives; and, knowing him, you have the veritable picture of the defunct, as regards soul, I mean, and spirit—for he was not a mountain in the flesh, but a man only—and a stout and good one—as, even more than my assertion, my now forthcoming tale will testify. It was the very first winter I had passed in the United States, that I was staying up here for the first time likewise. I had, of course, become speedily intimate with Tom, with whom, indeed, it needs no longer space so to become; and scarcely less familiar with his brother, who, at that time, held a farm in the valley just below our feet. I had been resident at Tom's above six weeks; and, during that spell, as he would call it, we had achieved much highly pleasant and exciting slaughter of Quail, Woodcock, and Partridge; not overlooking sundry Foxes, red, black, and grey, and four or five right Stags of ten, whose blood had dyed the limpid waters of the Greenwood Lake. It was late in the autumn; the leaves had fallen; and lo! one morning we awoke and found the earth carpeted far and near with smooth white snow. Enough had fallen in the night to cover the whole surface of the fields, hill, vale, and cultivated level, with one wide vest of virgin purity—but that was all! for it had cleared off early in the morning, and frozen somewhat crisply; and then a brisk breeze rising, had swept it from the trees, before the sun had gained sufficient power to thaw the burthen of the loaded branches.

"Tom and I, therefore, set forth, after breakfast, with dog and gun, to beat up a large bevy of Quail which we had found on the preceding evening, when it was quite too late to profit by the find, in a great buckwheat stubble, a quarter of a mile hence on the southern slope. After a merry tramp, we flushed them in a hedgerow, drove them up into this swale, and used them up considerable, as Tom said. The last three birds pitched into that bank just above you; and, as we followed them, we came across what Tom pronounced, upon the instant, to be the fresh track of a Bear. Leaving the meaner game, we set ourselves to work immediately to trail old bruin to his lair, if possible;—the rather that, from the loss of a toe, Tom confidently, and with many oaths, asserted that this was no other than 'the damndest etarnal biggest Bar that ever had been knowed in Warwick,'—one that had been acquainted with the sheep and calves of all the farmers round, for many a year of riot and impunity. In less than ten minutes we had traced him to this cave, whereunto the track led visibly, and whence no track returned. The moment we had housed him, Tom left me with directions to sit down close to the den's mouth, and there to smoke my cigar, and talk to myself aloud, until his return from reconnoitring the *locale*, and learning whether our friend had any second exit to his snug *hiemalia*. 'You needn't be scar't now, I tell you, Archer,' he concluded; 'for he's a deal too 'cute to come out, or even show his nose, while he smells 'bacca and hears woices. I'll be back to-rights!'

"After some twenty-five or thirty minutes, back he came, blown and tired, but in extraordinary glee!

"'There's no help for it, Archer; he's got to smell hell anyways!—there's not a hole in the hull hill side, but this!'

"'But can we bolt him?' inquired I, somewhat dubiously.

"'Sartain!' replied he, scornfully,—'sartain; what is there now to hinder us! I'll bide here quietly, while you cuts down into the village, and brings all hands as you can raise—and bid them bring lots of blankets, and an axe or two, and all there is in the house to eat and drink, both: and a heap of straw. Now don't be stoppin' to ask me no questions—shin it, I say, and jest call in and tell my brother what we've done, and start him up here right away—leave me your gun, and all o' them cigars. Now, strick it.'

"Well, away I went, and, in less than an hour, we had a dozen able-bodied men, with axes, arms, provisions—edible and potable—enough for a week's consumption, on the ground, where we found Tom and his brother, both keeping good watch and ward. The first step was to prepare a shanty, as it was evident there was small chance of bolting him ere nightfall. This was soon done, and our party was immediately divided into gangs, so that we might be on the alert both day and night. A mighty fire was next kindled over the cavern's mouth—the rill having been turned aside—in hopes that we might smoke him out. After this method had been tried all that day, and all night, it was found wholly useless—the cavern having many rifts and rents, as we could see by the fumes which arose from the earth at several points, whereby the smoke escaped without becoming dense enough to force our friend to bolt. We then tried dogs; four of the best the country could produce were sent in, and a most demoniacal affray and hubbub followed within the bowels of the earthfast rock; but, in a little while, three of our canine friends were glad enough to make their exit, mangled, and maimed, and bleeding; more fortunate than their companion, whose greater pluck had only earned for him a harder and more mournful fate. We sent for fire-works; and kept up, for some three hours, such a din, and such a stench, as might have scared the devil from his lair; but bruin bore it all with truly stoical endurance. Miners were summoned next; and we essayed to blast the granite, but it was all in vain, the hardness of the stone defied our labors. Three days had passed away, and we were now no nearer than at first—every means had been tried, and every means found futile. Blank disappointment sat on every face, when Michael Draw, Tom's brother, not merely volunteered, but could not be by any means deterred from going down into the den, and shooting the brute in its very hold. Dissuasion and remonstrance were in vain—he was bent on it!—and, at length Tom, who had been the most resolved in opposition, exclaimed, 'If he will go, let him!' so that decided the whole matter.

"The cave, it seemed, had been explored already, and its localities were known to several of the party, but more particularly to the bold volunteer who had insisted on this perilous enterprise. The well-like aperture, which could alone be seen from without, descended, widening gradually as it got farther from the surface, for somewhat more than eight feet. At that depth the fissure turned off at right angles, running nearly horizontally, an arch of about three feet in height, and some two yards in length, into a small and circular chamber, beyond which there was no passage whether for man or beast, and in which it was certain that the well-known and much-detested Bear had taken up his winter quarters. The plan, then, on which Michael had resolved, was to descend into this cavity, with a rope securely fastened under his arm-pits, provided with a sufficient quantity of lights, and his good musket—to worm himself feet forward, on his back, along the horizontal tunnel, and to shoot at the eyes of the fierce monster, which would be clearly visible in the dark den by the reflection of the torches; trusting to the alertness of his comrades from without, who were instructed, instantly on hearing the report of his musket-shot, to haul him out hand over hand. This mode decided on, it needed no long space to put it into execution. Two narrow laths of pine wood were procured, and half a dozen auger holes drilled into each—as many candles were inserted into these temporary candelabra, and duly lighted. The rope was next made fast about his chest—his musket carefully loaded with two good ounce bullets, well wadded in greased buckskin—his butcher-knife disposed in readiness to meet his grasp—and in he went, without one shade of fear or doubt on his bold, sun-burnt visage. As he descended, I confess that my heart fairly sank, and a faint sickness came across me, when I thought of the dread risk he ran in courting the encounter of so fell a foe, wounded and furious, in that small narrow hole, where valor, nor activity, nor the high heart of manhood, could be expected to avail anything against the close hug of the shaggy monster.

"Tom's ruddy face grew pale, and his huge body quivered with emotion, as, bidding him 'God speed,' he griped his brother's fist, gave him the trusty piece which his own hand had loaded, and saw him gradually disappear, thrusting the lights before him with his feet, and holding the long queen's arm cocked and ready in a hand that trembled not—the *only* hand that trembled not of all our party! Inch by inch his stout frame vanished into the narrow fissure; and now his head disappeared, and still he drew the yielding rope along! Now he has stopped, there is no strain upon the cord!—there is a pause! —a long and fearful pause! The men without stood by to haul, their arms stretched forward to their full extent, their sinewy frames bent to the task, and their rough lineaments expressive of strange agitation! Tom, and myself, and some half dozen others, stood on the watch with ready rifles, lest, wounded and infuriate, the brute should follow hard on the invader of its perilous lair. Hark to that dull and stifled growl! The watchers positively shivered, and their teeth chattered with excitement. There! there! that loud and bellowing roar, reverberated by the ten thousand echoes of the confined cavern, till it might have been taken for a burst of subterraneous thunder!—that wild and fearful howl—half roar of fury—half yell of mortal anguish!

With headlong violence they hauled upon the creaking rope, and dragged, with terrible impetuosity, out of the fearful cavern—his head striking the granite rocks, and his limbs fairly clattering against the rude projections, yet still with gallant hardihood retaining his good weapon—the sturdy woodman was whirled out into the open air unwounded; while the fierce brute within rushed after him to the very cavern's mouth, raving and roaring till the solid mountain seemed to shake and quiver.

"As soon as he had entered the small chamber, he had perceived the glaring eyeballs of the monster; had taken his aim steadily between them, by the strong light of the flaring candles; and, as he said, had lodged his bullets fairly—a statement which was verified by the long-drawn and painful moanings of the beast within. After a while, these dread sounds died away, and all was still as death. Then once again, undaunted by his previous peril, the bold man—though, as he averred, he felt the hot breath of the monster on his face, so nearly had it followed him in his precipitate retreat—prepared to beard the savage in his hold. Again he vanished from our sight.—again his musket-shot roared like the voice of a volcano from the vitals of the rock!—again, at mighty peril to his bones, he was dragged into daylight!—but this time, maddened with wrath and agony, yelling with rage and pain, streaming with gore, and white with foam, which flew on every side, churned from his gnashing tusks, the Bear rushed after him. One mighty bound brought it clear out of the deep chasm—the bruised trunk of the daring hunter, and the confused group of men who had been stationed at the rope, and who were now, between anxiety and terror, floundering to and fro, hindering one another—lay within three or, at most, four paces of the frantic monster; while, to increase the peril, a wild and ill-directed volley, fired in haste and fear, was poured in by the watchers, the bullets whistling on every side, but with far greater peril to our friends than to the object of their aim. Tom drew his gun up coolly—pulled—but no spark replied to the unlucky flint. With a loud curse he dashed the useless musket to the ground, unsheathed his butcher-knife, and rushed on to attack the wild beast, single-handed. At the same point of time, I saw my sight, as I fetched up my rifle, in clear relief against the dark fur of the head, close to the root of the left ear!—my finger was upon the trigger, when, mortally wounded long before, exhausted by his dying effort—the huge brute pitched headlong, without waiting for my shot, and, within ten feet of his destined victims, 'in one wild roar expired.' He had received all four of Michael's bullets!—the first shot had planted one ball in his lower jaw, which it had shattered fearfully, and another in his neck!—the second had driven one through the right eye into the very brain, and cut a long deep furrow on the crown with the other! Six hundred and odd pounds did he weigh! He was the largest, and the last! None of his shaggy brethren have visited, since his decease, the woods of Warwick!—nor shall I ever more, I trust, witness so dread a peril so needlessly encountered."

GEORGE B. CHEEVER

WAS born April 17, 1807, at Hallowell, Maine. He was educated at Bowdoin and at Andover, and ordained pastor of the Howard Street Church, Salem, in 1832. In the same year he visited Europe, where he remained two years and a half. In 1839 he became pastor of the Allen Street Church, New York, and in 1846 of the Church of the Puritans, a beautiful edifice erected by a congregation formed of his friends, a position which he still retains. In 1844 he again visited Europe for a twelvemonth.

Dr. Cheever's first publications were the *American Common-Place-Book of Prose*, in 1828, and a similar volume of *Poetry* in 1829. These were followed by *Studies in Poetry, with Biographical Sketches of the Poets*, in 1830, and in 1832 by *Selections from Archbishop Leighton*, with an introductory essay. In 1835 he acquired a wide reputation as an original writer by the publication of *Deacon Giles's Distillery*, a temperance tract, describing a dream in which the demoniacal effects of the spirits therein concocted were embodied in an inferno, which was forcibly described. It was published on a broadside, with rude cuts, by no means behind the text in energy. Deacon Giles was a veritable person, and not relishing the satire as well as his neighbors, brought an action, the result of which confined the author to the Salem jail for thirty days of the month of December.

In 1837 Mr. Cheever gave some of the results of his European experiences to the public in the columns of the *New York Observer*. In 1841 he published *God's Hand in America*, and the year following *The Argument for Punishment by Death*, in maintenance of the penalty. In 1843, *The Lectures on Pilgrim's Progress*, which had been previously delivered with great success in his own church, were published. Whether owing to the writer's sympathy with Bunyan, from his own somewhat similar labors, dangers, and sufferings in the temperance cause, this volume is one of the ablest of his productions. On his return from his second visit to Europe he published *The Wanderings of a Pilgrim in the Shadow of Mont Blanc and the Jungfrau Alp*, a work which was favorably received. It was followed by *The Journal of the Pilgrims at Plymouth, in New England, reprinted from the original volume, with Historical and Local Illustrations of Providences, Principles, and Persons*. This volume consists of a reprint of the work usually known as "Mourt's Relation;" the remaining half of the volume being occupied with original remarks on the topics indicated in the title.

In 1849 he issued *The Hill Difficulty, and other Allegories*, illustrative of the Christian career, which was followed by a somewhat similar work, *The Windings of the River of the Water of Life*.

In addition to these volumes Dr. Cheever has written a number of articles for the United States Literary Gazette, Quarterly Register, New Monthly Magazine, North American Review, Quarterly Observer, and Biblical Repository. He edited during the years 1845 and 1846 the New York Evangelist, a Presbyterian weekly journal.

PEDESTRIANISM IN SWITZERLAND.

A man should always travel in Switzerland as a pedestrian, if possible. There is no telling how much more perfectly he thus communes with nature, how much more deeply and without effort he drinks in the spirit of the meadows, the woods, the running streams and the mountains, going by them and among them, as a friend with a friend. He seems to hear the very breath of Nature in her stillness, and sometimes when the whole world is hushed, there are murmurs come to him on the air, almost like the distant evening song of angels. Indeed the world of Nature is filled with quiet soul-like sounds, which, when one's attention is gained to them, make a man feel as if he must take his shoes from his feet and walk barefooted, in order not to disturb them. There is a language in Nature that requires not so much a fine ear as a listening spirit; just as there is a mystery and a song in religion, that requires not so much a clear understanding as a *believing* spirit. To such a listener and believer there comes

> A light in sound, a sound-like power in light,
> Rhythm in all thought, and joyaunce everywhere—
> Methinks it should have been impossible
> Not to love all things in a world so filled,
> Where the breeze warbles, and the mute still air
> Is music slumbering on her instrument.

The music of the brooks and waterfalls, and of the wind among the leaves, and of the birds in the air, and of the children at play, and of the distant villages, and of the tinkling pleasant bells of flocks upon the mountain sides, is all lost to a traveller in a carriage, or rumbling vehicle of any kind; whereas a pedestrian enjoys it, and enjoys it much more perfectly than a man upon a mule. Moreover, the pedestrian at every step is gaining health of body and elasticity of spirits. If he be troubled with weak lungs, let him carry his own knapsack, well strapped upon his shoulders; it opens and throws back the chest, and strengthens the weakest parts of the bodily system. Besides this, the air braces him better than any tonic. By day and by night it is an exhilarating cordial to him, a *nepenthe* to his frame.

The pedestrian is a laboring man, and his sleep is sweet. He rises with the sun, or earlier, with the morning stars, so as to watch the breaking of the dawn. He lives upon simple food with an unsuspicious appetite. He hums his favorite tunes, peoples the air with castles, cons a passage in the gospels, thinks of the dear ones at home, cuts a cane, wanders in Bypath meadow, where there is no Giant Despair, sits down and jots in his note-book, thinks of what he will do, or whistles as he goes for want of thought. All day long, almost every faculty of mind and body may be called into healthful, cheerful exercise. He can make out-of-the-way excursions, go into the cottages, chat with the people, sketch pictures at leisure. He can pray and praise God when and where he pleases, whether he comes to a cross and sepulchre, or a church, or a cathedral, or a green knoll under a clump of trees, without cross, or saint, or angel; and if he have a Christian companion, they two may go together as pleasantly and profitably as Christian and Hopeful in the Pilgrim's Progress.

ELEMENTS OF THE SWISS LANDSCAPE.

Passing out through a forest of larches, whose dark verdure is peculiarly appropriate to it, and going up towards the baths of Leuk, the interest of the landscape does not at all diminish. What a concentration and congregation of all elements of sublimity and beauty are before you! what surprising contrasts of light and shade, of form and color, of softness and ruggedness! Here are vast heights above you, and vast depths below, villages hanging to the mountain sides, green pasturages and winding paths, chalets dotting the mountains, lovely meadow slopes enamelled with flowers, deep immeasurable ravines, torrents thundering down them; colossal, overhanging, castellated reefs of granite; snowy peaks with the setting sun upon them. You command a view far down over the valley of the Rhone, with its villages and castles, and its mixture of rich farms and vast beds and heaps of mountain fragments, deposited by furious torrents. What affects the mind very powerfully on first entering upon these scenes is the deep dark blue, so intensely deep and overshadowing, of the gorge at its upper end, and at the magnificent proud sweep of the granite barrier, which there shuts it in, apparently without a passage. The mountains rise like vast supernatural intelligences taking a material shape, and drawing around themselves a drapery of awful grandeur; there is a forehead of power and majesty, and the likeness of a kingly crown above it.

Amidst all the grandeur of this scenery I remember to have been in no place more delighted with the profuse richness, delicacy, and beauty of the Alpine flowers. The grass of the meadow slopes in the gorge of the Dala had a depth and power of verdure, a clear, delicious greenness, that in its effect upon the mind was like that of the atmosphere in the brightest autumnal morning of the year, or rather, perhaps, like the colors of the sky at sunset. There is no such grass-color in the world as that of these mountain meadows. It is just the same at the verge of the ice oceans of Mont Blanc. It makes you think of one of the points chosen by the Sacred Poet to illustrate the divine benevolence (and I had almost said, no man can truly understand why it was chosen, who has not travelled in Switzerland). "*Who maketh the grass to grow upon the mountains.*"

And then the flowers, so modest, so lovely, yet of such deep exquisite hue, enamelled in the grass, sparkling amidst it, "a starry multitude," underneath such awful brooding mountain forms and icy precipices, how beautiful! All that the Poets have ever said or sung of Daisies, Violets, Snow-drops, King-cups, Primroses, and all modest flowers, is here out-done by the mute poetry of the denizens of these wild pastures. Such a meadow slope as this, watered with pure rills from the glaciers, would have set the mind of Edwards at work in contemplation on the beauty of holiness. He has connected these meek and lowly flowers with an image, which none of the Poets of this world have ever thought of. To him the divine beauty of holiness "made the soul like a field or garden of God, with all manner of pleasant flowers; all pleasant, delightful, and undisturbed; enjoying a sweet calm, and the gentle, vivifying beams of the Sun. The soul of a true Christian appears like such a little white flower as we see in the spring of the year; low and humble on the ground; opening its bosom to receive the pleasant beams of the Sun's glory; rejoicing, as it were, in a calm rapture; diffusing around a sweet fragrancy; standing peacefully and lovingly in the midst of other flowers round about; all in like manner opening their bosoms to drink in the light of the Sun."

Very likely such a passage as this, coming from the soul of the great theologian (for this is the poetry of the soul, and not of the artificial sentiment, nor of the mere worship of nature), will seem to many persons like violets in the bosom of a glacier. But no poet ever described the meek, modest flowers so beautifully, *rejoicing in a calm rapture*. Jonathan Edwards himself, with his grand views of sacred theology and history, his living piety, and his great experience in the deep things of God, was like a mountain glacier, in one respect, as the "parent of perpetual streams," that are then the deepest, when all the fountains of the world are the driest; like, also, in another respect, that in climbing his theology you get very near to heaven, and are in a very pure and bracing atmosphere; like, again, in this, that it requires much spiritual labor and discipline to surmount his heights, and some care not to fall into the *crevasses*; and like, once more, in this, that when you get to the top, you have a vast, wide, glorious view of God's great plan, and see things in their chains and connections, which before you only saw separate and piecemeal.

THE REV. HENRY T. CHEEVER, a brother of Dr. Cheever, has written several volumes, derived in part from his experiences as a sailor. The first of these, *A Reel in a Bottle: being the Adventures of a Voyage to the Celestial Country*, is a nautical version of the Pilgrim's Progress, in which pilgrims Peter and Paul put to sea in a well appointed craft, and after various storms and conflicts anchor at the Celestial City. The plan is carried out in an ingenious and fanciful manner. Mr. Cheever's other publications are—*The Island World of the Pacific: Life in the Sandwich Islands;* and *The Whale and his Captors.*

THOMAS WARD,

THE son of an esteemed citizen of Newark, N. J., was born in that city June 8, 1807. He was educated at Princeton, and received his degree as a physician at the Rutgers Medical College in New York. He pursued the profession, however, but a short time; foreign travel and the engagements of the man of wealth, with the literary amusements of the amateur author, fully occupying his attention. After some skirmishing with the muse, and a number of more labored contributions to the New York American, he published a volume in 1842—*Passaic, a Group of Poems touching that river: with other Musings: by Flaccus*, the signature he had employed in the newspaper. The Passaic poems celebrate the ambition of Sam Patch, the modern hero of the stream; the sentimental story of a lover, who makes a confidant of the river; a melancholy incident of the death of a young lady who perished at the falls; and "The Retreat of Seventy-six," an incident of the Revolution.

The "Musings in Various Moods," which occupy the second portion of the volume, are descriptive, sentimental, and satirical; if so kindly a man can be said to indulge in the last mode of writing. His taste leads him rather to picture the domestic virtues and social amenities of life.

TO PASSAIC.

Bless thee! bright river of my heart—
The blue, the clear, the wild, the sweet:
Though faint my lyre, and rude my art,
Love broke discretion's bands apart,
And bade me offer at thy feet
My murmuring praise, howe'er unmeet:
Aware, discourse to lovers dear
Insipid strikes the listener's ear,
Yet have I rashly sung to prove
The strength, the fervor of a love
That none, to whom thy charms are known,
Would seek to hide, or blush to own.

Yes! oft have I indulged my dream
By many a fair and foreign stream;
But vain my wandering search to see
A rival in far lands to thee.
Rhine, Tiber, Thames, a queenly throng—
The world's idolatry and song—
Have roved, have slumbered, sung, and sighed,
To win my worship to their tide:
Have wound their forms with graceful wiles,
And curled their cheeks with rippling smiles;
Have leaped in waves, with frolic dance,
And winking tossed me many a glance:
Still, still my heart, though moved, was free,
For love, dear native stream, of thee!
For Rhine, though proudly sweeps her tide
Through hills deep-parted, gaping wide—
Whereon grey topping castles sprout,
As though the living rock shot out—
Too rudely woos me, who despise
The charms wherein no softness lies;
While Thames, who boasts a velvet brim,
And meadows beautifully trim,
Too broadly shows the trace of art,
To win the wishes of the heart;
And Tiber's muddy waves must own
Their glory is the past's alone.

No water-nymphs these eyes can see,
Mine Indian beauty, match with thee!—
For all, whate'er their fame, or place,
Lack the wild freshness of thy face—
That touch of Nature's antique skill
By modern art unrivalled still.

I've traced thee from thy place of birth
Till, finding sea, thou quittest earth—
From that far spot in mountain land
Where heaving soft the yellow sand,
Thy infant waters, clear and rife,
Gush sudden into joyous life;
To yon broad bay of vivid light,
Where pausing rivers all unite,
As singly fearing to be first
To quench devouring Ocean's thirst—
I've followed, with a lover's truth,
The gambols of thy torrent youth;
Have chased, with childish search, and vain,
Thy doublings on the marshy plain;
Have idled many a summer's day
Where flower-fields cheered thy prosperous way;
Nor have I faithless turned aside
When rocky troubles barred thy tide,
Tossing thee rudely from thy path
Till thou wert wrought to foaming wrath.
Nor when the iron hand of fate
Dethroned thee from thy lofty state,
And hurled thee, with a giant's throw,
Down to the vale—where far below,
Thy tides, by such rude ordeal tried,
With purer, heavenlier softness glide.
Through every change of good or ill,
My doting heart pursued thee still,
And ne'er did rival waters shine
With traits so varying rich as thine:
What separate charms in each I see,
Rare stream, seem clustered all in thee!
Now brightly wild, now coyly chaste,
Now calm, now mad with passionate haste—
Grandeur and softness, power and grace,
All beam from thy bewitching face.
Nor are the notes thy voice can range,
Less striking for their endless change—
Hark!—what alarming clamors ring,
Where far thy desperate currents spring
Into yon chasm, so deep and black,
The arrested soul turns shuddering back;
Nor dares pursue thee, through the rent
Down to the stony bottom, sent
Loud thundering—that the beaten rock
Trembles beneath the ponderous shock,
And thy commanding voice profound
Bids silence to all meaner sound!—
And when in peace thy evening song
In silver warblings floats along,
No whispering waters far or near,
Murmur such music to mine ear.

JOSEPH C. NEAL,

An original humorist, was a native of New Hampshire, where he was born at Greenland, February 3d, 1807. His father had been a principal of a school in Philadelphia, and had retired in ill-health to the country, where he discharged the duties of a Congregational clergyman. He died while his son was in infancy, and the family returned to Philadelphia. Mr. Neal was early attracted to editorial life, and was, for a number of years, from 1831, engaged in conducting the *Pennsylvanian* newspaper. The labor proved too severe for a delicate constitution, and he was compelled to travel abroad to regain lost health, and finally, in 1844, to relinquish his daily journal, when he established a popular weekly newspaper, *Neal's Saturday Gazette.* This he continued with success to the time of his death, in the year 1847.

Joseph C. Neal

The forte of Mr. Neal was a certain genial humor, devoted to the exhibition of a peculiar class of citizens falling under the social history description of the genus "loafer." Every metropolis breeds a race of such people, the laggards in the rear of civilization, who lack energy or ability to make an honorable position in the world, and who fall quietly into decay, complaining of their hard fate in the world, and eking out their deficient courage by a resort to the bar-room. The whole race of small spendthrifts, inferior pretenders to fashion, bores, half-developed inebriates, and generally gentlemen enjoying the minor miseries and social difficulties of life, met with a rare delineator in Mr. Neal, who interpreted their ailments, repeated their slang, and showed them an image which they might enjoy, without too great a wound to their self-love. A quaint vein of speculation wrapped up this humorous dialogue. The sketches made a great hit a few years since, when they appeared, and for their preservation of curious specimens of character, as well as for their other merits, will be looked after by posterity.

There were several series of these papers, contributed by Mr. Neal to the Pennsylvanian, the author's Weekly Gazette, the Democratic Review, and other journals, which were collected in several volumes, illustrated by David C. Johnston, entitled *Charcoal Sketches; or Scenes in a Metropolis.* The alliterative and extravagant titles of the sketches take off something from the reality, which is a relief to the picture; since it would be painful to be called to laugh at real misery, while we may be amused with comic exaggeration.

UNDEVELOPED GENIUS—A PASSAGE IN THE LIFE OF P. PILGARLICK PIGWIGGEN, ESQ.

The world has heard much of unwritten music, and more of unpaid debts; a brace of unsubstantialities, in which very little faith is reposed. The minor poets have twangled their lyres about the one, until the sound has grown wearisome, and until, for the sake of peace and quietness, we heartily wish that unwritten music were fairly written down, and published in Willig's or Blake's best style, even at the risk of hearing it reverberate from every piano in the city: while iron-visaged creditors—all creditors are of course hard, both in face and in heart, or they would not ask for their money—have chattered of unpaid debts, ever since the flood, with a wet finger, was uncivil enough to wipe out pre-existing scores, and extend to each skulking debtor the "benefit of the act." But *undeveloped genius*, which is, in fact, itself unwritten music, and is very closely allied to unpaid debts, has, as yet, neither poet, trumpeter, nor biographer. Gray, indeed, hinted at it in speaking of "village Hampdens," "mute inglorious Miltons," and "Cromwells guiltless," which showed him to be a man of some discernment, and possessed of inklings of the truth. But the general science of mental geology, and through that, the equally important details of mineralogy and mental metallurgy, to ascertain the unseen substratum of intellect, and to determine its innate wealth, are as yet unborn; or, if phrenology be admitted as a branch of these sciences, are still in uncertain infancy. Undeveloped genius, therefore, is still undeveloped, and is likely to remain so, unless this treatise should awaken some capable and intrepid spirit to prosecute an investigation at once so momentous and so interesting. If not, much of it will pass through the world undiscovered and unsuspected; while the small remainder can manifest itself in no other way than by the aid of a convulsion, turning its possessor inside out like a glove; a method, which the earth itself was ultimately compelled to adopt, that stupid man might be made to see what treasures are to be had for the digging.

There are many reasons why genius so often remains invisible. The owner is frequently unconscious of the jewel in his possession, and is indebted to chance for the discovery. Of this, Patrick Henry was a striking instance. After he had failed as a shopkeeper, and was compelled to "hoe corn and dig potatoes," alone on his little farm, to obtain a meagre subsistence for his family, he little dreamed that he had that within, which would enable him to shake the throne of a distant tyrant, and nerve the arm of struggling patriots. Sometimes, however, the possessor is conscious of his gift, but it is to him as the celebrated anchor was to the Dutchman; he can neither use nor exhibit it. The illustrious Thomas Erskine, in his first attempt at the bar, made so signal a failure as to elicit the pity of the good-natured, and the scorn and contempt of the less feeling part of the auditory. Nothing daunted, however, for he felt undeveloped genius strong within him, he left the court; muttering with more profanity than was proper, but with much truth, "By ——! it is in me, and it shall come out!" He was right; it was in him; he did get it out, and rose to be Lord Chancellor of England.

But there are men less fortunate; as gifted as Erskine, though perhaps in a different way, they swear frequently, as he did, but they cannot get their genius out. They feel it, like a rat in a cage, beating against their barring ribs, in a vain struggle to escape; and thus, with the materials for building a reputation, and standing high among the sons of song and eloquence, they pass their lives in obscurity, regarded by the few who are aware of their existence, as simpletons—fellows sent upon the stage solely to fill up the grouping, to applaud their superiors, to eat, sleep, and die.

P. Pilgarlick Pigwiggen, Esq., as he loves to be styled, is one of these unfortunate undeveloped gentlemen about town. The arrangement of his name shows him to be no common man. Peter P. Pigwiggen would be nothing, except a hailing title to call him to dinner, or to insure the safe arrival of dunning letters and tailors' bills. There is as little character about it as about the word towser, the individuality of which has been lost by indiscriminate application. To all intents and purposes, he might just as well be addressed as "You Pete Pigwiggen," after the tender materual fashion, in which, in his youthful days, he was required to quit dabbling in the gutter, to come home and be spanked. But

P. PILGARLICK PIGWIGGEN, ESQ.

—the aristocracy of birth and genius is all about it. The very letters seem tasselled and fringed with the cobwebs of antiquity. The flesh creeps with awe at the sound, and the atmosphere undergoes a sensible change, as at the rarefying approach of a supernatural being. It penetrates the hearer at each perspiratory pore. The dropping of the antepenultimate in a man's name, and the substitution of an initial therefor, has an influence which cannot be defined—an influence peculiarly strong in the case of P. Pilgarlick Pigwiggen—the influence of undeveloped genius—analogous to that which bent the hazel rod, in the hand of Dousterswivel, in the ruins of St. Ruth, and told of undeveloped water.

But to avoid digression, or rather to return from a ramble in the fields of nomenclature, P. Pilgarlick Pigwiggen is an undeveloped genius—a wasted man; his talents are like money in a strong box, returning no interest. He is, in truth, a species of Byron in the egg; but unable to chip the shell, his genius remains unhatched. The chicken moves and faintly chirps within, but no one sees it, no one heeds it. Peter feels the high aspirations and the mysterious imaginings of poesy circling about the interior of his cranium; but there they stay. When he attempts to give them utterance, he finds that nature forgot to bore out the passage which carries thought to the tongue and to the finger ends; and as art has not yet found out the method of tunnelling or of driving a drift into the brain, to remedy such defects, and act as a general jail delivery to the prisoners of the mind, his divine conceptions continue pent in their osseous cell. In vain does Pigwiggen sigh for a *splitting* headache—one that shall ope the sutures, and set his fancies free. In vain does he shave his forehead and turn down his shirt collar, in hope of finding the poetic vomitory, and of leaving it clear of impediment; in vain does he drink vast quantities of gin to raise the steam so high that it may burst imagination's boiler, and suffer a few drops of it to escape; in vain does he sit up late o' nights, using all the cigars he can lay his hands on, to smoke out the secret. 'Tis useless all. No sooner has he spread the paper, and seized the pen to give bodily shape to airy dreams, than a dull dead blank succeeds. As if a flourish of the quill were the crowing of a "rooster," the dainty Ariels of his imagination vanish. The feather drops from his checked fingers, the paper remains unstained, and P. Pilgarlick Pigwiggen is still an undeveloped genius.

Originally a grocer's boy, Peter early felt that he had a soul above soap and candles, and he so diligently nursed it with his master's sugar, figs, and brandy, that early one morning he was unceremoniously dismissed with something more substantial than a flea in his ear. His subsequent life was passed in various callings; but call as loudly as they would, our hero paid little attention to their voice. He had an eagle's longings, and with an inclination to stare the sun out of countenance, it was not to be expected that he would stoop to be a barn-yard fowl. Working when he could not help it; at times pursuing check speculations at the theatre doors, by way of turning an honest penny, and now and then gaining entrance by crooked means, to feed his faculties with a view of the performances, he likewise pursued his studies through all the ballads in the market, until qualified to read the pages of Moore and Byron. Glowing with ambition, he sometimes pined to see the poet's corner of our weekly periodicals graced with his effusions. But though murder may out, his undeveloped genius would not. Execution fell so far short of conception, that his lyrics were invariably rejected.

Deep, but unsatisfactory, were the reflections which thence arose in the breast of Pigwiggen.

"How is it," said he—"How is it I can't level down my expressions to the comprehension of the vulgar, or level up the vulgar to a comprehension of my expressions? How is it I can't get the spigot out, so my verses will run clear? I know what I mean myself, but nobody else does, and the impudent editors say it's wasting room to print what nobody understands. I've plenty of genius—lots of it, for I often want to cut my throat, and would have done it long ago, only it hurts. I'm chock full of genius and running over; for I hate all sorts of work myself, and all sorts of people mean enough to do it. I hate going to bed, and I hate getting up. My conduct is very eccentric and singular. I have the miserable melancholics all the time, and I'm pretty nearly always as cross as thunder, which is a sure sign. Genius is as tender as a skinned cat, and flies into a passion whenever you touch it. When I condescend to unbuzzum myself, for a little sympathy, to folks of ornery intellect—and caparisoned to me, I know very few people that ar'n't ornery as to brains—and pour forth the feelings indigginus to a poetic soul, which is always biling, they ludicrate my sitiation, and say they don't know what the deuse I'm driving at. Isn't genius always served o' this fashion in the earth, as Hamlet, the boy after my own heart, says? And when the slights of the world, and of the printers, set me in a fine frenzy, and my soul swells and swells, till it almost tears the shirt off my buzzum, and even fractures my dickey—when it expansuates and elevates me above the common herd, they laugh again, and tell me not to be pompious. The poor plebinians and worse than Russian serfs!—It is the fate of genius—it is his'n, or rather I should say, her'n—to go through life with little sympathization and less cash. Life's a field of blackberry and raspberry bushes. Mean people squat down and pick the fruit, no matter how they black their fingers; while genius, proud and perpendicular, strides fiercely on, and gets nothing but scratches and holes torn in its trousers. These things are the fate of genius, and when you see 'em, there is genius too, although the editors won't publish its articles. These things are its premonitories, its janisaries, its cohorts, and its consorts.

"But yet, though in flames in my interiors, I can't get it out. If I catch a subject, while I am looking at it, I can't find words to put it in; and when I let go, to hunt for words, the subject is off like a shot. Sometimes I have plenty of words, but then there is either no ideas, or else there is such a water-works and cataract of them, that when I catch one, the others knock it out of my fingers. My genius is good, but my mind is not sufficiently manured by 'ears."

Pigwiggen, waiting it may be till sufficiently "manured" to note his thoughts, was seen one fine morning, not long since, at the corner of the street, with a melancholy, abstracted air, the general character of his appearance. His garments were of a rusty black, much the worse for wear. His coat was buttoned up to the throat, probably for a reason more cogent than that of showing the moulding of his chest, and a black handkerchief enveloped his neck. Not a particle of white was to be seen about him; not that we mean to infer that his "sark" would not have answered to its name, if the muster roll of his attire had been called, for we scorn to speak of a citizen's domestic relations, and, until the contrary is proved, we hold it but charity to believe that every man has as many shirts as backs. Peter's cheeks were pale and hollow; his eyes sunken, and neither soap nor razor had kissed his lips for a week. His hands were in his pockets—they had the accommodation all to themselves—nothing else was there.

"Is your name Peter P. Pigwiggen?" inquired a man with a stick, which he grasped in the middle.

"My name is P. Pilgarlick Pigwiggen, if you please, my good friend," replied our hero, with a flush of indignation at being miscalled.

"You'll do," was the nonchalant response; and "the man with a stick" drew forth a parallelogram of paper, curiously inscribed with characters, partly written and partly printed, of which the words, "The commonwealth greeting," were strikingly visible; you'll do, Mr. P. Pilgarlick Pigwiggen Peter. That's a *capias ad respondendum*, the English of which is, you're cotched because you can't pay; only they put it in Greek, so as not to hurt a gentleman's feelings, and make him feel flat afore the company. I can't say much for the manners of the big courts, but the way the law's polite and a squire's office is genteel, when the thing is under a hundred dollars, is cautionary."

There was little to be said. Peter yielded at once. His landlady, with little respect for the incipient Byron, had turned him out that morning, and had likewise sent "the man with a stick," to arrest the course of undeveloped genius. Peter walked before, and he of the "taking way" strolled leisurely behind.

* * * * * * * * * *

"It's the fate of genius, squire. The money is owed."

"But how can I help it? I can't live without eating and sleeping. If I wasn't to do those functionaries, it would be suicide, severe beyond circumflexion."

"Well, you know, you must either pay or go to jail."

"Now, squire, as a friend—I can't pay, and I don't admire jail—as a friend, now."

"Got any bail?—No!—what's your trade—what name is it?"

"Poesy," was the laconic, but dignified reply.

"Pusey?—Yes, I remember Pusey. You're in the shoe-cleaning line, somewhere in Fourth street. Pusey, boots and shoes cleaned here. Getting whiter, ar'n't you? I thought Pusey was a little darker in the countenance."

"P-o-e-s-y!" roared Peter, spelling the word at the top of his voice; "I'm a poet."

"Well, Posy, I suppose you don't write for nothing. Why didn't you pay your landlady out of what you received for your books, Posy?"

"My genius ain't developed. I haven't written any thing yet. Only wait till my mind is manured, so I can catch the idea, and I'll pay off all old scores."

"'Twont do, Posy. I don't understand it at all. You must go and find a little undeveloped bail, or I must send you to prison. The officer will go with you. But stay; there's Mr. Grubson in the corner—perhaps he will bail you."

Grubson looked unpromising. He had fallen asleep, and the flies hummed about his sulky copper-colored visage, laughing at his unconscious drowsy efforts to drive them away. He was aroused by Pilgarlick, who insinuatingly preferred the request.

"I'll see you hanged first," replied Mr. Grubson; "I goes bail for nobody. I'm undeveloped myself on that subject,—not but that I have the greatest respect for you in the world, but the most of people's cheats."

"You see, Posy, the development won't answer. You must try out of doors. The officer will go with you."

"Squire, as a friend, excuse me," said Pilgarlick. "But the truth of the matter is this. I'm delicate about being seen in the street with a constable. I'm principled against it. The reputation which I'm going to get might be injured by it. Wouldn't it be pretty much the same thing, if Mr. Grubson was to go with the officer, and get me a little bail!"

"I'm delicate myself," growled Grubson; "I'm principled agin that too. Every man walk about on his own 'sponsibility; every man bail his own boat, You might jist as well ask me to swallow your physic, or take your thrashings."

Alas! Pilgarlick knew that his boat was past bailing. Few are the friends of genius in any of its stages—very few are they when it is undeveloped. He, therefore, consented to sojourn in "Arch west of Broad," until the whitewashing process could be performed, on condition he were taken there by the "alley way;" for he still looks ahead to the day, when a hot-pressed volume shall be published by the leading booksellers, entitled Poems, by P. Pilgarlick Pigwiggen, Esq.

RICHARD HILDRETH.

Richard Hildreth was born June 28, 1807, in the old town of Deerfield, Massachusetts. His father was the Rev. Hosea Hildreth, a prominent congregational clergyman, who was the last old-school divine of latitudinarian views to join the Unitarian from the Calvinistic church of New England. In his profession he always stood in high esteem for ability, public spirit, and active benevolence. During Richard's fourth year his father removed with his family to Exeter, New Hampshire, the seat of Exeter Academy, where the son was fitted for college.

Hildreth was graduated at Harvard College in 1826. Here he proved himself a successful student of the prescribed course, without, however, entirely confining himself to it. Besides his extensive readings in history, political economy, and ethics, he became familiar with the whole body of Greek and Latin authors in their original languages. Embracing the pursuit of law he next entered the office at Newburyport, Massachusetts, of L. W. Marston, where his remarkable power of close and long-continued application excited the astonishment of all who knew him.

In 1827, during Mr. Hildreth's residence at Newburyport, his literary life took its commencement in a series of articles contributed to a magazine then lately started in Boston by Mrs. Sarah Jane Hale. Not long after he became a contributor to Willis's Boston Magazine (the first editorial experiment of that popular writer), and subsequently to Joseph T. Buckingham's New England Magazine. Many of these miscellaneous compositions are worthy of republication in a collected form.

In July, 1832, while practising the legal profession in Boston, he was induced to accept the post of editor of the Boston *Atlas*. For several years Mr. Hildreth's connexion with the new paper gave it a decided pre-eminence among the political journals of New England. A series of ably written articles from his pen, published in 1837, relative to the design of certain influential men in the southwest of procuring the separation of Texas from the Mexican government, prior to any general suspicion of the affair, powerfully contributed to excite the strenuous opposition which was afterwards manifested in different parts of the Union to the annexation of Texas.

Ill health in the autumn of 1834 compelled Mr. Hildreth to seek a residence on a plantation at the South, where he lived for about a year and a half. While thus sojourning, his story of *Archy Moore*, the forerunner of anti-slavery novels, was written. This work, which appeared in 1837, was republished in England, where it received an elaborate review in the Spectator, as well as in other literary periodicals. In 1852 it was given to the public in an enlarged form, under the title of *The White Slave*. It purports to be the autobiography of a Virginia slave, the son of his owner, whose Anglo-Saxon superiority of intellect and spirit is inherited by him. The period of the story is during the war of 1812 with Great Britain. After passing through the vicissitudes of his servile lot in the household, on the plantation, and on the auction block, Archy, the hero, with others of his condition, is taken on board a vessel for a more southern port. But in the passage the ship is captured by the enemy, who at once liberate them. He then becomes a British sailor, in which capacity he rises to distinction and settles in England, where he finally attains the position of an opulent merchant. The narrative, as continued subsequently to the first publication, proceeds to represent Archy returning about the year 1835 to his native land, where, after a complicated series of adventures, his slave-wife and two children, whom he had left in slavery, are restored to him, and are thence carried to his foreign home.

During the summer of 1836 Mr. Hildreth employed his pen in translating from the French of Dumont a work, published at Boston in two 16mo. volumes, in 1840, under the title of *Bentham's Theory of Legislation.* He also at the same time wrote a *History of Banks*, advocating the system of free-banking, with security to bill-holders,—a plan since introduced successfully into New York and other states. Passing the winter of 1837–8 in Washington, as correspondent of the Boston Atlas, he returned to the editorial chair a warm supporter of the election to the presidency of General Harrison, of whom he wrote an electioneering biography, which appeared in pamphlet form.

Abandoning journalism, Mr. Hildreth next published, in 1840, *Despotism in America*, an ably-prepared discussion of the political, economical, and social results of the slaveholding system in the United States. To this work in 1854 was added a chapter on *The Legal Basis of Slavery*, embracing the substance of two articles written by him for Theodore Parker's short-lived Massachusetts Review. A letter to Andrews Norton, the Unitarian theologian of Cambridge, on *Miracles* followed, together with other controversial pamphlets on various speculative topics. These works were marked by keen and vigorous argument, but at times by an unsparing severity of language that materially interfered with their popularity.

In 1840 Mr. Hildreth, for the benefit of his health, again had resort to a warmer climate. But a three years' residence at Demerara, in British Guiana, did not diminish his activity. Acting successively as editor of two newspapers published at Georgetown, the capital of the country, he vigorously discussed the adoption of the new system of free labor, and the best policy to be pursued in the circumstances in which the colony was placed. There can be no doubt as to the side which he would join in regard to the former subject. While in British Guiana he also found time to write his *Theory of Morals*, published in 1844, as well as the *Theory of Politics*, which was given to the world from the press of the Messrs. Harper in 1853.

In the preface to the first mentioned work the author announces his purpose of giving to the world six treatises, bearing the collective title of Rudiments of the Science of Man, and designed to appear in the following order: Theory of Morals, Theory of Politics, Theory of Wealth, Theory of Taste, Theory of Knowledge, Theory of Education. The peculiarity of these treatises, according to Mr. Hildreth's intention, was the attempt to apply rigorously to the subjects discussed the inductive method of investigation, which, he supposed, might be employed as successfully in ethical and kindred science as it has been in the domain of physical discoveries.

This may, perhaps, be the case, but such an experiment often involves a disregard of established doctrines and assumptions, which is much less palatable to the mass of men than any similar contemptuous treatment of their notions of physical science, in consequence of the more decided enlistment of the feelings in matters pertaining to moral, political, and social questions, than in any other.

If Mr. Hildreth entertained any doubts on this point, he must, by this time, have been convinced of the fact here stated, by the outcry raised by the North American Review and Brownson's Quarterly against the former of his two volumes—the Theory of Morals and the Theory of Politics. Yet, in spite of what has been said to the contrary, we cannot help looking upon them as among the most original contributions which this country has furnished on the topics of which they treat.

In saying this no assent is given to all the doctrines broached in them. The author, like Bentham, of whom he appears to be a strong admirer, is an independent, dispassionate, and patient thinker, but, like him, is too much governed by the test of utility, and too much enamored of his rigid method of investigation, to reach conclusions which shall be entirely satisfactory, in sciences so proverbially inexact and uncertain as those of ethics or politics.

Of the two treatises already submitted to the public the Theory of Politics is altogether the most philosophical and best matured. It is divided into three parts, the first part treating of the Elements of Political Power, under which head are discussed the various forms which the political equilibrium, called government, has taken, the forces which produce it, and the means whereby it is sustained or overturned. The second contains a philosophical and historical review of the Forms of Government and Political Revolutions, in which the forms assumed by government during the world's history are specified chronologically, and the causes traced which have led to their commencement and overthrow. In part third are considered Governments in their Influence upon the Progress of Civilization and upon Human Happiness in general; and here, in a section entitled Of Democracies, may be found a theoretical vindication of the democratic system of government which will amply repay perusal. The survey is taken from the American stand-point, and the results are developed with a conclusiveness of reasoning little short of mathematical.

Finding the public too little interested in his speculative inquiries Mr. Hildreth turned his attention to completing his *History of the United States*, a work which he had projected as far back as his life in college. This afforded him constant occupation for seven years, during which he wrote little else, with the exception of a few articles in the Massachusetts Quarterly Review. The first volume was issued by the Harpers in 1849, and the entire work, in six volumes, in the course of the three succeeding years. In regard to this elaborate history, which covers the period beginning with the settlement of the country and concluding with the end of President Monroe's first term, we may safely remark that it has secured its author a prominent and permanent place among American historians. He has here embodied the matured results of long-continued and exhausting labor, carried on by a mind not ill-adapted to historical inquiry, acute, comprehensive, endowed with an inflexible honesty of purpose, and never avoiding the sober duties of the historian for the sake of rhetorical display. In the last three volumes may be found the only thorough and complete account of the federal government for the time of which it treats. There is hardly any question of domestic or foreign policy which can interest an American citizen that is not elucidated in its pages, such matters having been so fully discussed in the early period of our government that there has been but little advance or modification in regard to the views then taken concerning them. Mr. Hildreth has terminated his history with Monroe's first term, at which time began that fusion of parties which prepared the way for the state of political affairs now existing. To this point refer the concluding remarks of the sixth volume:—

With the re-annexation of Florida to the Anglo-American dominion, the recognised extension of our western limit to the shores of the Pacific, and the partition of those new acquisitions between slavery and freedom, closed Monroe's first term of office; and with it a marked era in our history. All the old landmarks of party, uprooted as they had been, first by the embargo and the war with England, and then by peace in Europe, had since, by the bank question, the internal improvement question, and the tariff question, been completely superseded and almost wholly swept away.. At the Ithuriel touch of the Missouri discussion, the slave interest, hitherto hardly recognised as a distinct element in our system, had started up, portentous and dilated, disavowing the very fundamental principles of modern democracy, and again threatening, as in the Federal Convention, the dissolution of the Union. It is from this point, already beginning indeed to fade away in the distance, that our politics of to-day take their departure.

In his portraitures of political men, Mr. Hildreth perhaps too often "wears the cap of the executioner." Of this peculiarity his austere comments upon the characters and lives of Jefferson, Madison, John Adams, and J. Q. Adams, are an example. No statute of limitations, no popular canonization of the offender avails against the impartial severity of his criticism. But to the memories of Washington and Hamilton he pays a uniform and deserved homage, as may be seen by the passage subjoined:—

In Hamilton's death the Federalists and the country experienced a loss second only to that of Washington. Hamilton possessed the same rare and lofty qualities, the same just balance of soul, with less, indeed, of Washington's severe simplicity and awe-inspiring presence, but with more of warmth, variety, ornament, and grace. If the Doric in architecture be taken as the symbol of Washington's character, Hamilton's belonged to the same grand style as developed in the Corinthian—if less impressive, more winning. If we add Jay for the Ionic, we have a trio not to be matched, in fact not to be approached in our history, if, indeed, in any other. Of earth-born Titans, as terrible as great, now angels, and now toads and serpents, there are everywhere enough. Of the serene and benign sons of the celestial gods, how few at any time have walked the earth!

As an example of the more animated descriptive style of the historian we select a portion of his account of the duel of Hamilton and Burr:—

It was not at all in the spirit of a professed duellist, it was not upon any paltry point of honor, that Hamilton had accepted this extraordinary challenge, by which it was attempted to hold him answerable for the numerous imputations on Burr's character bandied about in conversation and the newspapers for two or three years past. The practice of duelling he utterly condemned; indeed, he had himself already been a victim to it in the loss of his eldest son, a boy of twenty, in a political duel some two years previously. As a private citizen, as a man under the influence of moral and religious sentiments, as a husband, loving and loved, and the father of a numerous and dependent family, as a debtor honorably disposed, whose creditors might suffer by his death, he had every motive for avoiding the meeting. So he stated in a paper which, under a premonition of his fate, he took care to leave behind him. It was in the character of a public man. It was in that lofty spirit of patriotism, of which examples are so rare, rising high above all personal and private considerations—a spirit magnanimous and self-sacrificing to the last, however in this instance uncalled for and mistaken—that he accepted the fatal challenge. "The ability to be in future useful," such was his own statement of his motives, "whether in resisting mischief or effecting good in those crises of our public affairs which seem likely to happen, would probably be inseparable from a conformity with prejudice in this particular."

With that candor towards his opponents by which Hamilton was ever so nobly distinguished, but of which so very seldom, indeed, did he ever experience any return, he disavowed in this paper, the last he ever wrote, any disposition to affix odium to Burr's conduct in this particular case. He denied feeling towards Burr any personal ill-will, while he admitted that Burr might naturally be influenced against him by hearing of strong animadversions in which he had indulged, and which, as usually happens, might probably have been aggravated in the report. Those animadversions, in some cases, might have been occasioned by misconstruction or misinformation; yet his censures had not proceeded on light grounds nor from unworthy motives. From the possibility, however, that he might have injured Burr, as well as from his general principles and temper in relation to such affairs, he had come to the resolution which he left on record, and communicated also to his second, to withhold and throw away his first fire, and perhaps even his second; thus giving to Burr a double opportunity to pause and reflect.

The grounds of Weehawk, on the Jersey shore, opposite New York, were at that time the usual field of these single combats, then, chiefly by reason of the inflamed state of political feeling, of frequent occurrence, and very seldom ending without bloodshed. The day having been fixed, and the hour appointed at seven o'clock in the morning, the parties met, accompanied only by their seconds. The bargemen, as well as Dr. Hosack, the surgeon, mutually agreed upon, remained as usual at a distance, in order, if any fatal result should occur, not to be witnesses.

The parties having exchanged salutations, the seconds measured the distance of ten paces; loaded the pistols; made the other preliminary arrangements, and placed the combatants. At the appointed signal, Burr took deliberate aim, and fired. The ball entered Hamilton's side, and as he fell his pistol too was unconsciously discharged. Burr approached him apparently somewhat moved; but on the suggestion of his second, the surgeon and barge-men already approaching, he turned and hastened away, Van Ness coolly covering him from their sight by opening an umbrella.

The surgeon found Hamilton half-lying, half-sitting on the ground, supported in the arms of his second. The pallor of death was on his face. "Doctor," he said, "this is a mortal wound;" and, as if overcome by the effort of speaking, he immediately fainted. As he was carried across the river the fresh breeze revived him. His own house being in the country, he was conveyed at once to the house of a friend, where he lingered for twenty-four hours in great agony, but preserving his composure and self-command to the last.

Mr. Hildreth has throughout his life been much engaged in newspaper discussions of topics interesting to the community, and at the present time is an effective contributor to the New York Tribune, and other influential political journals. The amount of literary drudgery, such as editing geographical cyclopædias and works of a similar character, which he has performed, attests his singular mental vigor and activity, as well as the inadequate remuneration of more congenial literary labor. He is now busied in the composition of a work on *Japan as it Was and as it Is*.*

* We are indebted for this notice of Mr. Hildreth to the pen of Mr. W. S. Thayer, himself an accomplished litterateur, as his critical articles contributed to his friend Mr. Charles Hale's excellent Boston periodical "To-Day," and his occasional poems, correspondence, and other articles latterly published in the New York *Evening Post*, with which he has been connected, sufficiently witness.

W. S. W. RUSCHENBERGER.

William S. W. Ruschenberger was born in Cumberland county, New Jersey, September 4, 1807. His father, Peter Ruschenberger, a German, died a short time before the birth of his only son.

While an infant, Ruschenberger was removed to Philadelphia, where his mother supported herself and her child by keeping a school for several years. He was educated at New York and Philadelphia, and prepared for college, when he commenced, in 1824, the study of medicine in the office of Prof. Chapman. In June, 1826, he obtained the appointment of surgeon's-mate in the navy, and made a cruise to the Pacific in the frigate Brandywine. After an absence of thirty-eight months, he returned to his studies, and obtained his medical diploma in March, 1830. Having passed an examination as surgeon in the navy in March, 1831, he made a second cruise to the Pacific, which occupied about three years. The results of his observations were given to the public in 1835, in an octavo volume entitled *Three Years in the Pacific, by an Officer of the United States Navy*.

In March, 1835, he sailed in the sloop-of-war Peacock as surgeon of the fleet for the East India squadron. After an absence of over two years, he landed at Norfolk in November, 1837. In the following spring, Lea & Blanchard published his *Voyage Round the World, including an Embassy to Siam and Muscat*. The work was reprinted by Bentley in London, with the omission of various passages commenting upon the English government.

In 1843 Dr. Ruschenberger was ordered to the United States Naval Hospital, New York, where he remained until 1847, during which period he laid the foundation of the naval laboratory, designed to furnish the service with unadulterated drugs. He next sailed to the East Indies, but returned under orders in the following year. After being stationed at New York and Philadelphia, he sailed as surgeon of the Pacific squadron October 9, 1854.

In addition to the works already noticed, Dr. Ruschenberger is the author of a series of manuals—*Elements of Anatomy and Physiology, Mammalogy, Ornithology, Herpetology and Ichthyology, Conchology, Entomology, Botany, and Geology*, and of several pamphlets* and numerous articles on subjects connected with the navy in the Southern Literary Messenger and Democratic Review. He has also written much on medical and scientific topics in the American Journal of the Medical Sciences, Silliman's Journal, Medical and Surgical Journal, Journal of Pharmacy, Medical Examiner, Boston Medical and Surgical Journal, and the National Intelligencer. He has also edited American reprints of Marshall on the Enlisting, Discharging, and Pensioning of Soldiers, 1840; and Mrs. Somerville's Physical Geography, 1850-53.

* The Navy. Hints on the Reorganization of the Navy, including an Examination of the Claims of its civil officers to an Equality of Rights. 8vo. pp. 71. Wiley & Putnam, New York. 1845.
Examination of a Reply to Hints on the Reorganization of the Navy. Idem.
Assimilated Rank in the Civil Branch of the Navy. Jan., 1848. Phila.
An Examination of the Legality of the General Orders which confer assimilated rank on officers of the Civil Branch of the United States Navy. By a Surgeon. Phila., Feb., 1848.
A Brief History of an Existing Controversy on the subject of Assimilated Rank in the Navy of the United States. By W. S. W. R. 8vo. pp. 108. Sept., 1850. Phil'a.

JONATHAN LAWRENCE, JR.

Jonathan Lawrence, Jr., was born in New York November 19, 1807. He was graduated from Columbia College at the early age of fifteen, and studied law with Mr. W. Sloeson, whose partner he became on his admission to the bar. He devoted himself earnestly to his profession, his essays and poems being the fruit of hours of relaxation; but in the midst of high promise of future excellence he was removed by death on the 26th of April, 1833.

A selection from his writings was prepared and privately printed by his brother soon after. The volume contains essays on Algernon Sidney, Burns, English comedy, the Mission to Panama (on the affairs of the South American republics), two Dialogues of the Dead (imaginary conversations between Milton and Shakespeare, and Charles II. and Cowper, in the style of Walter Savage Landor), and a number of poems, miscellaneous in subject, grave and reflective in tone.

TO ——

Oh, the spring has come again, love,
  With beauty in her train,
And her own sweet buds are springing
  To her merry feet again.
They welcome her onward footsteps,
  With a fragrance full of song,

And they bid her sip from each dewy lip
Of the rosy-tinted throng.

Oh, the spring has come again, love,
And her eye is bright and blue,
With a misty passionate light that veils
The earth in its joyous hue;
And a single violet in her hair,
And a light flush in her cheek,
Tell of the blossoms maids should wear,
And the love tales they should speak.

The spring has come again, love,
And her home is everywhere;
She grows in the green and teeming earth,
And she fills the balmy air;
But she dearly loves, by some talking rill,
Where the early daisy springs,
To nurse its leaves and to drink her fill
Of the sweet stream's murmurings.

The spring has come again, love,
On the mountain's side she throws
Her earliest morning glance, to find
The root of the first wild rose;
And at noon she warbles through airy throats,
Or sounds in the whirring wing
Of the minstrel throng, whose untaught notes
Are the joyous hymns of spring.

Oh, the spring has come again, love,
With her skylark's cloudy song;
Hark! how his echoing note rings clear
His fleecy bowers among.
Her morning laughs its joyous way,
In a flood of rosy light,
And her evening clouds melt gloriously,
In the starry blue of night.

Oh, the spring has come again, love,
And again the spring shall go;
And withered her sweetest flowers, and dead
Her soft brooks' silvery flow;
And her leaves of green shall fade and die
When their autumn bloom is past,
Beautiful as her cheek whose tint
Looks loveliest at the last.

Oh, life's spring can come but once, love,
And its summer will soon depart,
And its autumn flowers will soon be nipped,
By the winter of the heart;
But yet we can fondly dream, love,
That a fadeless spring shall bloom,
When the sun of a new existence dawns
On the darkness of the tomb.

CORNELIUS CONWAY FELTON,

Eliot Professor of Greek Literature in Harvard University, Cambridge, Massachusetts, was born Nov. 6, 1807, at Newbury, now West Newbury, Mass., on the Merrimack, about six miles from Newburyport. The family of Felton dates from an early period—the first of the name having established himself in the town of Danvers at or about the year 1636. Mr. Felton was prepared for College chiefly at the Franklin Academy, Andover, under the late Simeon Putnam, an eminent classical scholar and teacher. On his entrance at Harvard University in 1823 in his sixteenth year, the Greek examiners were the Hon. Edward Everett, then Eliot Professor of Greek Literature, George Bancroft the Historian, then Greek tutor, and Dr. Popkin afterwards Eliot Professor. Like many other New England students, being obliged to earn money for the payment of College bills, he taught winter schools in the sophomore and junior years, besides teaching the mathematics the last six months of the junior year in the Round Hill School, Northampton, under the charge of J. G. Cogswell (now of the Astor Library), and George Bancroft. He was graduated in 1827.

For the next two years, in conjunction with two classmates, the late Henry Russell Cleveland and Seth Sweetser, now the Rev. Seth Sweetser, D.D., Pastor of one of the principal religious societies in Worcester, Mass., Mr. Felton had charge of the Livingston County High School in Genesee, New York. In 1829 he was appointed Latin tutor in Harvard University; in 1830 Greek tutor; and in 1832 College Professor of the Greek language. In 1834 he received his appointment of Eliot Professor of Greek literature, (the third Professor on that foundation; Mr. Everett and John Snelling Popkin having preceded him), the duties of which he has since discharged* with the exception only of the time passed in a foreign tour from April, 1853, to May, 1854. In this journey he visited England, Scotland and Wales, France, Germany, Switzerland, Italy, travelling thence to Malta and Constantinople. On his return stopping at Smyrna, and several of the Greek islands, he arrived in Athens in Oct. 1853, and remained in Greece, the principal object of his tour, till the following February. In Europe, previous to visiting Greece, he was occupied chiefly with the collections of art and antiquities in London, Paris, Berlin, Munich, Dresden, Venice, Florence, Rome, Naples. In Greece he was engaged, partly in travelling through the country, in visiting the most celebrated places for the purpose of illustrating Ancient Greek History and Poetry, and in studying at Athens the remains of ancient art, the present language and literature of Greece, the constitution and laws of the Hellenic kingdom, attending courses of lectures at the University, and in visiting the common schools and gymnasia. Returning from Greece to Italy, he revisited the principal cities, especially Naples, Rome, and Florence, studying anew the splendid collections of art and antiquities. Having pursued a similar course in France and England, he returned to the United States in May, 1854, and immediately resumed the duties of the Greek Professorship at Cambridge.

The professional occupation of Dr. Felton being that of a public teacher, his studies have embraced the principal languages and literatures of modern Europe as well as the ancient, and something of Oriental literature. His literary occupations have been various. While in college he was one of the editors and writers of a students' periodical called the Harvard Register. Of numerous addresses on public occasions, he has published an address at the close of the first year of the Livingston County High School, 1828; a discourse delivered at the author's inauguration as professor of Greek literature; an address delivered at the dedication of the Bristol County Academy in Taunton, Mass.; an address at a meeting of the

* There is not one now connected with college who was connected with it when he was appointed Tutor. In term of service, though not in years, he is the oldest member of any department of the University.

American Academy of Arts and Sciences, on moving resolutions on the death of Daniel Webster; and an oration delivered before the Alumni of Harvard University.

Mr. Felton's contributions to periodical literature embrace numerous articles in the North American Review, and critical notices commencing with the year 1830; various articles and notices published in the Christian Examiner from the same date; numerous reviews and notices published in Willard's Monthly Review, between June, 1832, and December, 1833, afterwards in Buckingham's New England Magazine; and occasional contributions to other periodical publications, such as the Bibliotheca Sacra, the Methodist Quarterly Review, the Knickerbrocker Magazine, the Whig Review, with articles in various newspapers, among others the Boston Daily Advertiser, Boston Courier, the Evening Traveller.

The separate volumes of Dr. Felton, his editions of the classics, and contributions to general literature, are hardly less numerous. For the first series of Sparks's American Biography he wrote the life of Gen. Eaton. In 1833 he edited the Iliad of Homer with Flaxman's Illustrations and English notes, since revised and extended, having passed through numerous editions. In 1840, he translated Menzel's work on German literature, published in three volumes in Ripley's Specimens of Foreign Literature. In 1840, he published a Greek reader, selections from the Greek authors in prose and poetry, with English notes and a vocabulary—which has been since revised and passed through six or seven editions. In 1841, he edited the Clouds of Aristophanes, with an introduction and notes in English, since revised and republished in England. In 1843, in conjunction with Professors Sears and Edwards, he prepared a volume entitled Classical Studies, partly original and partly translated. The greater part of the biographical notices, some of the analyses, as those of the Heldenbuch, and the more elaborate one of the Niebelungenlied, together with several poetical translations in Longfellow's Poets and Poetry of Europe, published in 1845, were from his pen. In 1847, he edited the Panegyricus of Isocrates and the Agamemnon of Æschylus, with introductions and notes in English. A second edition of the former, revised, appeared in 1854.

In 1849, he prepared a volume entitled, *Earth and Man, being a translation of a course of lectures on Comparative Physical Geography, in its relation to the History of Mankind, delivered in French in Boston, by Professor Arnold Guyot.* This work has gone through numerous editions in this country, has been reprinted in at least four independent editions in England, and has been widely circulated on the Continent, having been translated into German.

In 1849, he edited the Birds of Aristophanes, with introduction and notes in English, republished in England; in 1852, a Memorial of Professor Popkin, consisting of a selection of his lectures and sermons, to which is prefixed a biographical sketch of eighty-eight pages. In 1852, he published selections from the Greek historians, arranged in the order of events. In 1855, a revised edition of Smith's History of Greece, with preface, notes, additional illustrations, and a continuation from the Roman conquest to the present time; the latter embracing a concise view of the present political condition, the language, literature, and education in the kingdom of Hellas, together with metrical translations of the popular poetry of modern Greece. His latest work has been the preparation of an edition of Lord Carlisle's Diary in Turkish and Greek waters, with a Preface, notes, and illustrations. He has also published selections from modern Greek authors in prose and poetry, including History, Oratory, Historical Romance, Klephtic Ballads, Popular Poems and Anacreontics.

As Professor, besides teaching classes in the Text books, he has delivered many courses of lectures on Comparative Philology and History of the Greek language and literature through the classical periods, the middle ages, and to the present day.

Outside of the University, besides numerous lectures delivered before Lyceums, Teachers' Institutes, and other popular bodies, Dr. Felton has delivered three courses before the Lowell Institute in Boston. The first (in the winter of 1851–2), of thirteen lectures on the History and Criticism of Greek Poetry; the second (in 1853), of twelve lectures on the Life of Greece; the third, in the Autumn of 1854, on the Downfall and Resurrection of Greece.

To these extended literary labors, Dr. Felton has brought a scholar's enthusiasm. He has not confined his attention to the technicalities of his profession, but illustrated its learned topics in a liberal as well as in an acute literal manner, while he has found time to entertain in his writings the current scientific and popular literature of the day. As an orator he is skilful and eloquent in the disposition and treatment of his subjects. We have already alluded* to his elevated composition on the approaching death of Webster, and as a further indication of his manner, we may cite a passage from his address before the Association of the Alumni of Harvard in 1854.

ROME AND GREECE IN AMERICA.

An ancient orator, claiming for his beloved Athens the leadership among the states of Greece, rests his argument chiefly on her pre-eminence in those intellectual graces which embellish the present life of man, and her inculcation of those doctrines which gave to the initiated a sweeter hope of a life beyond the present. Virgil, in stately hexameters, by the shadowy lips of father Anchises in Elysium, calls on the Roman to leave these things to others:—

> Excudent alii spirantia mollius æra;
> Credo equidem; vivos ducent de marmore vultus;
> Orabunt causas melius, cœlique meatus
> Describent radio et surgentia sidera dicent.
> Tu regere imperio populos, Romane, memento,
> Hæ tibi erunt artes; pacisque imponere morem,
> Parcere subjectis, et debellare superbos.

These lines strike the key-notes to Greek and Roman character,—Greek and Roman history. During the long existence of the Athenian Republic, amidst the interruptions of foreign and domestic wars,—her territory overrun by Hellenic and Barbarian armies, her forests burned, her fields laid waste, her temples

* *Ante*, p. 31.

levelled in the dust,—in those tumultuous ages of her democratic existence, the fire of her creative genius never smouldered. She matured and perfected the art of historical composition, of political and forensic eloquence, of popular legislation, of lyric and dramatic poetry, of music, painting, architecture, and sculpture; she unfolded the mathematics, theoretically and practically, and clothed the moral and metaphysical sciences in the brief sententious wisdom of the myriad-minded Aristotle, and the honeyed eloquence of Plato. Rome overran the world with her arms, and though she did not always spare the subject, she beat down the proud, and laid her laws upon the prostrate nations. Greece fell before the universal victor, but she still asserted her intellectual supremacy, and, as even the Roman poet confessed, the conquered became the teacher and guide of the conqueror. At the present moment, the intellectual dominion of Greece—or rather of Athens, the school of Greece—is more absolute than ever. Her Plato is still the unsurpassed teacher of moral wisdom; her Aristotle has not been excelled as a philosophic observer; her Æschylus and Sophocles have been equalled only by Shakespeare. On the field of Marathon, we call up the shock of battle and the defeat of the Barbarian host; but with deeper interest still we remember that the great dramatic poet fought for his country's freedom in that brave muster. As we gaze over the blue waters of Salamis, we think not only of the clash of triremes, the shout of the onset, the pæan of victory; but of the magnificent lyrical drama in which the martial poet worthily commemorated the naval triumph which he had worthily helped to achieve.

All these things suggest lessons for us, even now. We have the Roman passion for universal empire, under the names of Manifest Destiny and Annexation. I do not deny the good there is in this, nor the greatness inherent in extended empire, bravely and fairly won. But the empire of science, letters, and art, is honorable and enviable, because it is gained by no unjust aggression on neighboring countries; by no subjection of weaker nations to the rights of the stronger; by no stricken fields, reddened with the blood of slaughtered myriads. No crimes of violence or fraud sow the seed of disease, which must in time lay it prostrate in the dust; its foundations are as immovable as virtue, and its structure as imperishable as the heavens. If we must add province to province, let us add realm to realm in our intellectual march. If we must enlarge our territory till the continent can no longer contain us, let us not forget to enlarge with equal step the boundaries of science and the triumphs of art. I confess I would rather, for human progress, that the poet of America gave a new charm to the incantations of the Muse; that the orator of America spoke in new and loftier tones of civic and philosophic eloquence; that the artist of America overmatched the godlike forms, whose placid beauty looks out upon us from the great past,—than annex to a country, already overgrown, every acre of desert land, from ocean to ocean and from pole to pole. If we combine the Roman character with the Greek, the Roman has had its sway long enough, and it is time the Greek should take its turn. Vast extent is something, but not everything. The magnificent civilization of England, and her imperial sway over the minds of men, are the trophies of a realm, geographically considered, but a satellite to the continent of Europe, which you can traverse in a single day. An American in London pithily expressed the feeling naturally excited in one familiar with our magnificent spaces and distances, when he told an English friend he dared not go to bed at night, for fear of falling overboard before morning. The states of Greece were of insignificant extent. On the map of the world they fill a scarcely visible space, and Attica is a microscopic dot. From the heights of Parnassus, from the Acrocorinthos, the eye ranges over the whole land, which has filled the universe with the renown of its mighty names. From the Acropolis of Athens we trace the scenes where Socrates conversed, and taught, and died; where Demosthenes breathed deliberate valor into the despairing hearts of his countrymen; where the dramatists exhibited their matchless tragedy and comedy; where Plato charmed the hearers of the Academy with the divinest teaching of Philosophy, while the Cephissus murmured by under the shadow of immemorial olive groves; where St. Paul taught the wondering but respectful sages of the Agora, and the Hill of Mars, the knowledge of the living God, and the resurrection to life eternal. There stand the ruins of the Parthenon, saluted and transfigured by the rising and the setting sun, or the unspeakable loveliness of the Grecian night,—beautiful, solemn, pathetic. In that focus of an hour's easy walk, the lights of ancient culture condensed their burning rays; and from this centre they have lighted all time and the whole world.

ELIZABETH MARGARET CHANDLER.

Elizabeth Margaret, the daughter of Thomas Chandler, a Quaker farmer in easy circumstances, was born at Centre, near Wilmington, Delaware, December 24, 1807. She was educated at the Friends' schools in Philadelphia, and at an early age commenced writing verses. At eighteen she wrote a poem, *The Slave Ship*, which gained a prize offered by the Casket, a monthly magazine. She next became a contributor to the Genius of Universal Emancipation, an anti-slavery periodical of Philadelphia, in which most of her subsequent productions appeared.

In 1830, Miss Chandler removed with her aunt and brother (she had been left an orphan at an early age) to the territory of Michigan. The family settled near the village of Tecumseh, Lenawee county, on the river Raisin; the name of Hazlebank being given to their farm by the poetess. She continued her contributions from this place in prose and verse on the topic of Slavery until she was attacked in the spring of 1834 by a remittent fever; under the influence of which she gradually sank until her death on the twenty-second of November of the same year.

In 1836, a collection of *The Poetical Works of Elizabeth Margaret Chandler, with a Memoir of her Life and Character, by Benjamin Lundy*, the editor of the journal with which she was connected, appeared at Philadelphia. The volume also contains a number of *Essays, Philanthropical and Moral*, from the author's pen.

Miss Chandler's poems are on a variety of subjects; but whatever the theme, it is in almost every instance brought to bear on the topic of Slavery. Her compositions are marked by spirit, fluency, and feeling.

JOHN WOOLMAN.

Meek, humble, sinless as a very child,
  Such wert thou,—and, though unbeheld, I seem
Oft-times to gaze upon thy features mild,
  Thy grave, yet gentle lip, and the soft beam
Of that kind eye, that knew not how to shed
  A glance of aught save love, on any human head.

Servant of Jesus! Christian! not alone
  In name and creed, with practice differing wide,
Thou didst not in thy conduct fear to own
  His self-denying precepts for thy guide.
Stern only to thyself, all others felt
Thy strong rebuke was love, not meant to crush, but
  melt.

Thou, who didst pour o'er all the human kind
  The gushing fervor of thy sympathy!
E'en the unreasoning brute failed not to find
  A pleader for his happiness in thee.
Thy heart was moved for every breathing thing,
By careless man exposed to needless suffering.

But most the wrongs and sufferings of the slave,
  Stirred the deep fountain of thy pitying heart;
And still thy hand was stretched to aid and save,
  Until it seemed that thou hadst taken a part
In their existence, and couldst hold no more
A separate life from them, as thou hadst done before.

How the sweet pathos of thy eloquence,
  Beautiful in its simplicity, went forth
Entreating for them! that this vile offence,
  So unbeseeming of our country's worth,
Might be removed before the threatening cloud,
Thou saw'st o'erhanging it, should burst in storm and
  blood.

So may thy name be reverenced,—thou wert one
  Of those whose virtues link us to our kind,
By our best sympathies; thy day is done,
  But its twilight lingers still behind,
In thy pure memory; and we bless thee yet,
For the example fair thou hast before us set.

LAUGHTON OSBORNE.

The only account which we have met with of this gentleman, a member of a New York family, is in the late Mr. Poe's "Sketches of the Literati," and that furnishes little more than a recognition of the genius of the author, which is in some respects akin to that of his critic. Mr. Osborne has published anonymously, and all of his books have been of a character to excite attention. They are bold, discursive, play some tricks with good taste and propriety; and upon the whole are not less remarkable for their keenness of perception than for their want of judgment in its display. With more skill and a just proportion, the writer's powers would have made a deeper impression on the public. As it is, he has rather added to the curiosities of literature than to the familiar companions of the library. Mr. Osborne was a graduate of Columbia College, of the class of 1827.

Laughton Osborn

His first book, *Sixty Years of the Life of Jeremy Levis*, was published in New York in 1831, in two stout duodecimo volumes. It is a rambling Shandean autobiography; grotesque, humorous, sentimental, and satirical, though too crude and unfinished to hold a high rank for any of those qualities.

Mr. Poe mentions its successor, *The Dream of Alla-ad-Deen, from the Romance of Anastasia*, by Charles Erskine White, D.D., a pamphlet of thirty-two small pages, the design of which he states to be, "to reconcile us to death and evil on the somewhat unphilosophical ground that comparatively we are of little importance in the scale of creation."

The Confessions of a Poet appeared in Philadelphia in 1835. Its prefatory chapter, announcing the immediate suicide of the Nero, prepares the reader for the passionate romance of the intense school which follows.

In 1838 a curious anomalous satire was published at Boston, in a full-sized octavo volume, of noticeable typographical excellence, *The Vision of Rubeta, an Epic Story of the Island of Manhattan, with Illustrations done on Stone*. In the relation of text and notes, and a certain air of learning, it bore a general resemblance to Mathias's "Pursuits of Literature." The labor was out of all proportion to the material. The particular game appeared to be the late Col. Stone, and his paper the *Commercial Advertiser*. The contributors to the New York American, the New York Review, and other periodicals of the time, also came in for notice; but the jest was a dull one, and the book failed to be read, notwithstanding its personalities. Among its other humors was a rabid attack on Wordsworth, the question of whose genius had by that time been settled for the rest of the world; and something of this was resumed in the author's subsequent volume, in 1841, published by the Appletons, entitled *Arthur Carryl, a Novel by the Author of the Vision of Rubeta, Cantos first and second. Odes; Epistles to Milton, Pope, Juvenal, and the Devil; Epigrams; Parodies of Horace; England as she is; and other minor Poems, by the same.* This is, upon the whole, the author's best volume. The critical prefaces exhibit his scholarship to advantage; the Odes, martial and amatory, are ardent and novel in expression; the Epistles to Milton, Pope, Juvenal—severally imitations of the blank verse, the couplet, and the hexameters of the originals—are skilful exercises; while the chief piece, Arthur Carryl, a poem of the Don Juan class, has many felicitous passages of personal description, particularly of female beauty.

The next production of Mr. Osborne, indicative of the author's study and accomplishments as an artist, was of a somewhat different character, being an elaborate didactic *Treatise on Oil Painting*, which was published by Wiley and Putnam. It was remarkable for its care and exactness, and was received as a useful manual to the profession.

The author's notes and illustrations exhibit his acquaintance with art, and show him to be a traveller, "a picked man of countries." From a poetic fragment, entitled "England as she is," he appears to have been a resident of that country in 1833. His permanent home is, we believe, New York.

SONNET—THE REPROACH OF VENUS.

The Queen of Rapture hovered o'er my bed,
Borne on the wings of Silence and the Night:
She touched with hers my glowing lips and said,
While my blood tingled with the keen delight,
"And is the spirit of thy youth then fled,
That made thee joy in other themes more bright!

For satire only must thine ink be shed,
And none but boys and fools my praises write?"
"O, by these swimming eyes," I said, and sighed,
"And by this pulse, which feels and fears thine art,
Thou know'st, enchantress, and thou seest with pride,
Thou of my being art the dearest part?
Let those sing love to whom love is denied;
But I, O queen, I chant thee in my heart."

TO JUVENAL.

Lord of the iron harp! thou master of diction satiric,
Who, with the scourge of song, lashed vices in monarch and people,
And to the scoff of the age, and the scorn of all ages succeeding,
Bared the rank ulcers of sin in the loins of the Mistress of Nations!
I, who have touched the same chords, but with an indifferent finger,
Claim to belong to the quire, at whose head thou art seated supernal.
More, I have read thee all through, from the first to the ultimate spondee,—
Therefore am somewhat acquaint with thy spirit and manner of thinking.
Knowing thee, then, I presume to address without more introduction
Part of this packet to thee, and, out of respect to thy manes,—
Owing not less unto thine than I rendered to Pope's and to Milton's,—
Whirl my brisk thoughts o'er the leaf, on the wheels of thy spondees and dactyls.
Doubtless, by this time at least, thou art fully conversant with English;
But, shouldst thou stumble at all, lo! Pope close at hand to assist thee.

Last of the poets of Rome! thou never wouldst dream from what region
Cometh this greeting to thee; no bard of thy kind hath yet mounted
Up to the stars of the wise, from the bounds of the Ocean Atlantic.
Green yet the world of the West, how should it yield matter for satire?
Hither no doubt, from thy Latium, the stone-eating husband of Rhea
Fled from the vices of men, as thou in thy turn, rather later,
Went to Pentapolis. Here, the Saturnian age is restored:
Witness Astræa's own form on the dome of the palace of justice!
Here, in his snug little cot, lives each one content with his neighbor,
Envy, nor Hatred, nor Lust, nor any bad passion, triumphant;
Avarice known not in name,—for devil a soul hath a stiver.

How then, you ask, do we live? O, nothing on earth is more simple!
A. has no coat to his back; or B. is deficient in breeches;
C. makes them both without charge, and comes upon A. for his slippers,
While for his shelterless head B. gratefully shapes him a beaver,
'T is the perfection of peace! social union most fully accomplished!
Man is a brother to man, not a rival, or slave, or oppressor.
Nay, in the compact of love, all creatures are joyful partakers.

THE DEATH OF GENERAL PIKE.

'Twas on the glorious day
When our valiant triple band*
Drove the British troops away
From their strong and chosen stand;
When the city York was taken,
And the Bloody Cross hauled down
From the walls of the town
Its defenders had forsaken.

The gallant Pike had moved
A hurt foe to a spot
A little more removed
From the death-shower of the shot;
And he himself was seated
On the fragment of an oak,
And to a captive spoke,
Of the troops he had defeated.

He was seated in a place,
Not to shun the leaden rain
He had been the first to face,
And now burned to brave again,
But had chosen that position
Till the officer's return
The truth who 'd gone to learn
Of the garrison's condition.

When suddenly the ground
With a dread convulsion shook,
And arose a frightful sound,
And the sun was hid in smoke;
And huge stones and rafters, driven
Athwart the heavy rack.
Fell, fatal on their track
As the thunderbolt of Heaven.

Then two hundred men and more,
Of our bravest and our best,
Lay all ghastly in their gore,
And the hero with the rest.
On their folded arms they laid him;
But he raised his dying breath:
"On, men, avenge the death
Of your general!" They obeyed him.

They obeyed. Three cheers they gave,
Closed their scattered ranks, and on.
Though their leader found a grave,
Yet the hostile town was won.
To a vessel straight they bore him
Of the gallant Chauncey's fleet,
And, the conquest complete,
Spread the British flag before him.

O'er his eyes the long, last night
Was already falling fast;
But came back again the light
For a moment; 't was the last.
With a victor's joy they fired,
'Neath his head by signs he bade
The trophy should be laid;
And, thus pillowed, Pike expired.

EDWARD S. GOULD.

Edward S. Gould, a merchant of New York, whose occasional literary publications belong to several departments of literature, is a son of the late Judge Gould† of Connecticut, and was born at

* The troops that landed to the attack were in three divisions.

† James Gould (1770–1888) was the descendant of an English family which early settled in America. He was educated at Yale; studied with Judge Reeve at the law school at Litchfield; and on his admission to the bar, became associated with him in the conduct of that institution. The school became highly distinguished by the acumen and ability of its chief instructors and the many distinguished pupils who went forth

Litchfield in that state May 11, 1808. As a writer of Tales and Sketches, he was one of the early contributors to the Knickerbocker Magazine, and has since frequently employed his pen in the newspaper and periodical literature of the times; in Mr. Charles King's American in its latter days, where his signature of "Cassio" was well known; in the New World, the Mirror, the Literary World, and other journals. In 1836, he delivered a lecture before the Mercantile Library Association of New York, "American Criticism on American Literature," in which he opposed the prevalent spirit of ultra-laudation as injurious to the interests of the country. In 1839, he published a translation of Dumas's travels in Egypt and Arabia Petræa; in 1841, the Progress of Democracy by the same author; and in 1842-3, he published through the enterprising New World press, Translations of Dumas's Impressions of Travel in Switzerland; Balzac's Eugenie Grandet and Father Goriot; Victor Hugo's Handsome Pecopin and A. Royer's Charles de Bourbon.

In 1843, he also published *The Sleep Rider, or the Old Boy in the Omnibus, by the Man in the Claret-Colored Coat;* a designation which grew out of an incident at the City Arsenal during the exciting election times of 1834. A riot occurred in the sixth ward, which the police failed to suppress, and certain citizens volunteered to put it down. They took forcible possession of the Arsenal and supplied themselves with arms against the opposition of Gen. Arcularius, the keeper. Gen. A. made a notable report of the assault to the legislature, in which an unknown individual in a claret-colored coat was the hero: and the term, the man in the claret-colored coat, immediately became a by-word. Mr. Gould wrote for the Mirror a parody on the report, purporting to come from the celebrated "Man in Claret," which made a great hit in literary circles. The Sleep Rider is a clever book of Sketches, a series of dramatic and colloquial Essays, presented after the runaway fashion of Sterne.

As a specimen of its peculiar manner, we may cite a brief chapter, which has a glance at the novelist.

. . . . *fiction.*
MUNCHAUSEN.

I have ever sympathized deeply with the writer of fiction; the novelist, that is, et id genus omne.

He sustains a heavier load of responsibility——

I beg pardon, my dear sir. I know you are nice in the matter of language; and that word was not English when the noblest works in English literature were written. But sir, though I dread the principle of innovation, I do feel that "responsibility" is indispensable at the present day: it saves a circumlocution, in expressing a common thought, and there is no other word that performs its exact duty. Besides, did not the immortal Jackson use it and *take* it?

I say, then, He sustains a heavier load of responsibility than any other man. First of all, he must invent his plot—a task which, at this time of the world, and after the libraries that have been written, is no trifle. Then, he must create a certain number of characters for whose principles, conduct, and fate, he becomes answerable. He must employ them judiciously; he must make them all—from a cabin-boy to a King—speak French and utter profound wisdom on every imaginable and unimaginable subject—taking special care that no one of them, by any chance, shall feel, think, act, or speak as any human being, in real life, ever did or would or could feel, think, act, or speak; and in the meantime, and during all time, he must, by a process at once natural, dexterous, and superhuman, relieve these people from all embarrassments and quandaries into which, in his moments of fervid inspiration, he has inadvertently thrown them.

Now, my dear sir, when you come to reflect on it this is a serious business.

The historian, on the other hand, has a simple task to perform. His duty is light. He has merely to tell the truth. His wisdom, his invention, his dexterity, all go for nothing. I grant you, some historians have gained a sort of reputation—but how can they deserve it when all that is true in their books is borrowed; and all that is original, is probably false?

I was led into this train of reflection—which, in good sooth, is not very profound, though perhaps not the less useful on that account—while mending my pen: and I felicitated myself that I was no dealer in fiction. For, said I, had I invented this narrative and rashly put nine people into a magnetic slumber in an omnibus, how should I ever get them out again?

Fortunately, I stand on smooth ground here. I am telling the truth. I am relating events as they occurred. I am telling you, my dear sir, what actually took place in this omnibus, and I hope to inform you, ere long, what took place out of it. In short, I am a historian, whose simple duty is to proceed in a direct line.

And now, having mended my pen, I will get on as fast as the weather and the state of the roads permit.

The same year Mr. Gould published an *Abridgment of Alison's History of Europe* in a single octavo volume,* which from the labor and care bestowed upon it has claims of its own to consideration. The entire work of Alison was condensed from the author's ten volumes, and entirely re written, every material fact being preserved while errors were corrected; a work the more desirable in consequence of the diffuse style and occasional negligence of the original author. The numerous editions which the book has since passed through, afford best proof of its utility and faithful execution.

In 1850, Mr. Gould published *The Very Age*,† a comedy written for the stage. The plot turns on distinctions of fashionable life, and the as-

---

from it, including John C. Calhoun, John M. Clayton, John Y. Mason, Levi Woodbury, Francis L. Hawks, Judge Theron Metcalf, James G. King, Daniel Lord, William C. Wetmore, and George Griffin, of the bar of New York. In 1816, Mr. Gould was appointed Judge of the Superior Court and Supreme Court of Errors of Connecticut. His legal reputation survives in his well known law book, *Treatise on the Principles of Pleading in Civil Actions.*

There is a memoir of Judge Gould in the second volume of Mr. G. H. Hollister's History of Connecticut, 1855.

* History of Europe, from the Commencement of the French Revolution in 1789 to the restoration of the Bourbons in 1815, by Archibald Alison, F.R.S.E., Advocate, abridged from the last London edition, for the use of general readers, colleges, academies, and other seminaries of learning, by Edward S. Gould. 4th ed. New York. A. S. Barnes & Co. 1845. 8vo. pp. 583.

† "The Very Age," a comedy in five acts—"to hold as 'twere the mirror up to nature; to show virtue her own feature, scorn her own image, and *the very age* and body of the time his form and pressure."—Hamlet. By Edward S. Gould. New York. D. Appleton & Co. 1850. 18mo. pp. 158.

sumption by one of the characters of the favorable position in the intrigue of a foreign Count; while a serious element is introduced in the female revenge of a West Indian, who had been betrayed in her youth by the millionaire of the piece.

JOHN W. GOULD, a brother of the preceding, was born at Litchfield, Conn., Nov. 14, 1814. He was a very successful writer of tales and sketches of the sea; his fine talents having been directed to that department of literature by one or more long voyages undertaken for the benefit of his health. He died of consumption, at sea, in the twenty-fourth year of his age, Oct. 1, 1838.

His writings were originally published in detached numbers of the New York Mirror and the Knickerbocker Magazine in the years 1834–5; and after his death, in 1838, were collected in a handsome volume, containing also a biographical sketch and his private journal of the voyage on which he died. This volume was issued by his brothers for private circulation only.* The tales and sketches of the volume, under the title of *Forecastle Yarns*, were published by the New World press in 1843, and in a new edition by Stringer & Townsend, New York, 1854.

An unfinished story found among his papers after his death, will convey a correct impression of Mr. Gould's descriptive powers. The fragment is entitled

MAN OVERBOARD.

"Meet her, quartermaster!" hailed the officer of the deck; "hold on, everybody!"

Torn from my grasp upon the capstan by a mountain-wave which swept us in its power, I was borne over the lee-bulwarks; and a rope which I grasped in my passage, not being belayed, unrove in my hands, and I was buried in the sea.

"Man overboard!" rang along the decks. "Cut away the life-buoy!"

Stunned and strangling, I rose to the surface, and instinctively struck out for the ship; while, clear above the roar of the storm and the dash of the cold, terrible sea, the loud thunder of the trumpet came full on my ear:

"Man the weather main and maintop-sail braces; slack the lee ones; round in; stand by to lower away the lee-quarter boat!"

My first plunge for the ship, whose dim outline I could scarcely perceive in the almost pitchy darkness of the night, most fortunately brought me within reach of the life-buoy grating. Climbing upon this, I used the faithless rope, still in my hand, to lash myself fast; and, thus freed from the fear of immediate drowning, I could more quietly watch and wait for rescue.

The ship was now hidden from my sight; but, being to leeward, I could with considerable distinctness make out her whereabout, and judge of the motions on board. Directly, a signal-lantern glanced at her peak; and oh! how brightly shone that solitary beam on my straining eye!—for, though rescued from immediate peril, what other succor could I look for, during that fearful swell, on which no boat could live a moment? What could I expect save a lingering, horrid death?

Within a cable's length, lay my floating home, where, ten minutes before, not a lighter heart than mine was inclosed by her frowning bulwarks; and, though so near that I could hear the rattling of her cordage and the rustling thunder of her canvas, I could also hear those orders from her trumpet which extinguished hope.

"Belay all with that boat!" said a voice that I knew right well; "she can't live a minute!"

My heart died within me, and I closed my eyes in despair. Next fell upon my ear the rapid notes of the drum beating to quarters, with all the clash, and tramp, and roar of a night alarm; while I could also faintly hear the mustering of the divisions, which was done to ascertain *who* was missing. Then came the hissing of a rocket, which, bright and clear, soared to heaven; and again falling, its momentary glare was quenched in the waves.

Drifting from the ship, the hum died away: but see—that sheet of flame!—the thunder of a gun boomed over the stormy sea. Now the blaze of a blue-light illumines the darkness, revealing the tall spars and white canvass of the ship, *still* near me!

"Maintop there!" came the hail again, "do you see him to leeward?"

"No, sir!" was the chill reply.

The ship now remained stationary, with her light aloft; but I could perceive nothing more for some minutes; they have given me up for lost.

That I could see the ship, those on board well knew, provided I had gained the buoy: but their object was to discover me, and now several blue-lights were burned at once on various parts of the rigging. How plainly could I see her rolling in the swell!—at one moment engulfed, and in the next rising clear above the wave, her bright masts and white sails glancing, the mirror of hope, in this fearful illumination; while I, covered with the breaking surge, was tossed wildly about, now on the crest, now in the trough of the sea.

"There he is, Sir! right abeam!" shouted twenty voices, as I rose upon a wave.

"Man the braces!" was the quick, clear, and joyous reply of the trumpet: while, to cheer the forlorn heart of the drowning seaman, the martial tones of the bugle rung out, "*Boarders, away!*" and the shrill call of the boatswain piped, "Haul taut and belay!" and the noble ship, blazing with light, fell off before the wind.

A new danger now awaited me; for the immense hull of the sloop-of-war came plunging around, bearing directly down upon me; while her increased proximity enabled me to discern all the minutiæ of the ship, and even to recognise the face of the first lieutenant, as, trumpet in hand, he stood on the forecastle.

Nearer yet she came, while I could move only as the wave tossed me; and now, the end of her flying-jib-boom is almost over my head!

"Hard a-port!" hailed the trumpet at this critical moment; "round in weather main-braces; right the helm!"

The spray from the bows of the ship, as she came up, dashed over me, and the increased swell buried me for an instant under a mountain-wave; emerging from which, there lay my ship, hove-to, not her length to windward!

"Garnet," hailed the lieutenant from the lee-gangway, "are you there, my lad?"

"Ay, ay, Sir!" I shouted in reply; though I doubted whether, in the storm, the response could reach him; but the thunder-toned cheering which, despite the discipline of a man-of-war, now rung from the decks and rigging, put *that* fear at rest,

* John W. Gould's Private Journal of a Voyage from New York to Rio Janeiro; together with a brief sketch of his life, and his Occasional Writings, edited by his brothers. Printed for private circulation only. New York. 1839. 8vo. pp. 207.

and my heart bounded with rapture in the joyous hope of a speedy rescue.

"All ready!" hailed the lieutenant again: "heave!" and four ropes, with small floats attached, were thrown from the ship and fell around me. None, however, actually touched me; and for this reason the experiment failed; for I could not move my unwieldy grating, and dared not leave it; as by so doing, I might in that fearful swell miss the rope, be unable to regain my present position, and drown between the two chances of escape.

I was so near to the ship that I could recognise the faces of the crew on her illuminated deck, and hear the officers as they told me where the ropes lay; but the fearful alternative I have mentioned, caused me to hesitate, until I, being so much lighter than the vessel, found myself fast drifting to leeward. I *then* resolved to make the attempt, but as I measured the distance of the nearest float with my eye, my resolution again faltered, and the precious and final opportunity was lost! Now, too, the storm which, as if in compassion, had temporarily lulled, roared again in full fury; and the safety of the ship required that she should be put upon her course.

* * * * * * * * *

ASA GREENE.

Asa Greene was a physician of New England, who came to New York about 1830, and finally established himself as a bookseller in Beekman street. He was the author of *The Travels of Ex-Barber Fribbleton*, a satire on Fidler and other scribbling English tourists; *The Life and Adventures of Dr. Dodimus Duckworth, A.N.Q., to which is added the History of a Steam Doctor*, a semi-mock-heroic biography of a spoiled child, who grows up to be an awkward clown, but is gradually rounded off into a country practitioner of repute. The incidents of the story are slight, and the whole is in the style of the broadest farce, but possesses genuine humor. This appeared in 1833. In 1834 he published *The Perils of Pearl Street, including a Taste of the Dangers of Wall Street, by a Late Merchant*, a narrative of the fortunes or misfortunes of a country lad, who comes to New York in search of wealth, obtains a clerkship, next becomes a dealer on his own account, fails, and after a few desperate shifts, settles down as a professor of book-keeping, and, by the venture of the volume before us, of book-making.

The Perils of Pearl street is in a quieter tone than Dodimus Duckworth, but shares in its humor. Peter Funks and drumming, shinning and speculations, with the skin-flint operations of boarding-house keepers, are its chief topics. Greene was also the author of another volume, *A Glance at New York*, which bears his imprint as publisher in 1837, and was for some time editor of the Evening Transcript, a pleasant daily paper of New York. He was found dead in his store one morning in the year 1837.

PETER FUNK.

The firm of Smirk, Quirk & Co. affected a great parade and bustle in the way of business. They employed a large number of clerks, whom they boarded at the different hotels, for the convenience of drumming; besides each member of the firm boarding in like manner, and for a similar purpose. They had an immense pile of large boxes, such as are used for packing dry-goods, constantly before their door, blocking up the side-walk so that it was nearly impossible to pass. They advertised largely in several of the daily papers, and made many persons believe, what they boasted themselves, that they sold more dry-goods than any house in the city.

But those who were behind the curtain, knew better. They knew there was a great deal of vain boast and empty show. They knew that Peter Funk was much employed about the premises, and putting the best possible face upon every thing.

By the by, speaking of Peter Funk, I must give a short history of that distinguished personage. When, or where, he was born, I cannot pretend to say. Neither do I know who were his parents, or what was his bringing up. He might have been the child of thirty-six fathers for aught I know; and instead of being brought up, have, as the vulgar saying is, come up himself.

One thing is certain, he has been known among merchants time out of mind; and though he is despised and hated by some, he is much employed and cherished by others. He is a little, bustling, active, smiling, bowing, scraping, quizzical fellow, in a powdered wig, London-brown coat, drab kerseymere breeches, and black silk stockings.

This is the standing portrait of Peter Funk,—if a being, who changes his figure every day, every hour, and perhaps every minute, may be said to have any sort of fixed or regular form. The truth is, Peter Funk is a very Proteus; and those who behold him in one shape to-day, may, if they will watch his transformations, behold him in a hundred different forms on the morrow. Indeed there is no calculating, from his present appearance, in what shape he will be likely to figure next. He changes at will, to suit the wishes of his employers.

His mind is as flexible as his person. He has no scruples of conscience. He is ready to be employed in all manner of deceit and deviltry; and he cares not who his employers are, if they only give him plenty of business. In short, he is the most active, industrious, accommodating, dishonest, unprincipled, convenient little varlet that ever lived.

Besides all the various qualities I have mentioned, Peter Funk seems to be endowed with ubiquity—or at least with the faculty of being present in more places than one at the same time. If it were not so, how could he serve so many masters at once? How could he be seen in one part of Pearl street buying goods at auction; in another part, standing at the door with a quill behind each ear; and in a third, figuring in the shape of a box of goods, or cooped up on the shelf, making a show of merchandise where all was emptiness behind?

With this account of Peter Funk, my readers have perhaps, by this time, gathered some idea of his character. If not, I must inform them that he is the very imp of deception; that his sole occupation is to deceive; and that he is only employed for that purpose. Indeed, such being his known character in the mercantile community, his name is sometimes used figuratively to signify any thing which is employed for the purpose of deception—or as the sharp ones say, to gull the flats.

Such being the various and accommodating character of Peter Funk, it is not at all surprising that his services should be in great demand. Accordingly he is very much employed in Pearl street, sometimes under one name, and sometimes under another—for I should have mentioned, as a part of his character, that he is exceedingly apt to change names, and has as many *aliases* as the most expert rogue in Bridewell or the Court of Sessions. Sometimes he takes the name of John Smith, sometimes James Smith, and sometimes simply Mr. Smith. At other times he is called Roger Brown, Simon White, Bob Johnson, or Tommy Thompson. In short, he has an endless variety of names, under which he passes before the world for so many different persons. The initiated only know, and every body else is gulled.

Peter Funk is a great hand at auctions. He is constantly present, bidding up the goods as though he was determined to buy everything before him. He is well known for bidding higher than any body else; or at all events running up an article to the very highest notch, though he finally lets the opposing bidder take it, merely, as he says, to accommodate him—or, not particularly wanting the article himself, he professes to have bid upon it solely because he thought it a great pity so fine a piece of goods should go so very far beneath its value.

It is no uncommon thing to see the little fellow attending an auction in his powdered wig, his brown coat, his drab kerseys, as fat as a pig, as sleek as a mole, and smiling with the most happy countenance, as if he were about to make his fortune. It is no uncommon thing, to see him standing near the auctioneer, and exclaiming, as he keeps bobbing his head in token of bidding—"A superb piece of goods! a fine piece of goods! great pity it should go so cheap—I don't want it, but I'll give another twenty-five cents, rather than it should go for nothing." The opposite bidder is probably some novice from the country—some honest Johnny Raw, who is shrewd enough in what he understands, but has never in his life heard of Peter Funk. Seeing so very knowing and respectable a looking man, bidding upon the piece of goods and praising it up at every nod, he naturally thinks it must be a great bargain, and he is determined to have it, let it cost what it will. The result is, that he gives fifty per cent. more for the article than it is worth; and the auctioneer and Peter Funk are ready to burst with laughter at the prodigious gull they have made of the poor countryman.

By thus running up goods, Peter is of great service to the auctioneers, though he never pays them a cent of money. Indeed it is not his intention to purchase, nor is it that of the auctioneer that he should. Goods nevertheless are frequently struck off to him; and then the salesman cries out the name of Mr. Smith, Mr. Johnson, or some other among the hundred aliases of Peter Funk, as the purchaser. But the goods, on such occasions, are always taken back by the auctioneer, agreeably to a secret understanding between him and Peter.

In a word, Peter Funk is the great *under-bidder* at all the auctions, and might with no little propriety be styled the under-bidder general. But this sort of characters are both unlawful and unpopular—not to say odious—and hence it becomes necessary for Peter Funk, *alias* the under-bidder, to have so many aliases to his name, in order that he may not be detected in the underhanded practice of under-bidding.

To avoid detection, however, he sometimes resorts to other tricks, among which one is, to act the part of a ventriloquist, and appear to be several different persons, bidding in different places. He has the knack of changing his voice at will, and counterfeiting that of sundry well-known persons; so that goods are sometimes knocked off to gentlemen who have never opened their mouths.

But a very common trick of Peter's, is, to conceal himself in the cellar, from whence, through a convenient hole near the auctioneer, his voice is heard bidding for goods; and nobody, but those in the secret, know from whence the sound proceeds. This is acting the part of Peter Funk in the cellar.

But Peter, for the most part, is fond of being seen in some shape or other; and it matters little what, so that he can aid his employers in carrying on a system of deception. He will figure in the shape of a box, bale, or package of goods; he will appear in twenty different places, at the same time, on the shelf of a jobber—sometimes representing a specimen of English, French, or other goods—but being a mere shadow, and nothing else—a phantasma—a show without the substance. In this manner it was, that he often figured in the service of Smirk, Quirk & Co.; and while people were astonished at the prodigious quantity of goods they had in their store, two thirds at least of the show was owing to Peter Funk.

WILLIAM D. GALLAGHER.

WILLIAM D. GALLAGHER, one of the leading writers of the West, was born at Philadelphia in 1808. His father was a native of Ireland, who emigrated to this country after the failure of the Rebellion of 1798, in which he had taken a prominent part on the popular side.

After his death his widow, removed in 1816 to Ohio, and settled at Cincinnati, where the son became a printer. As with many others of the same craft, the setting of type was after a while exchanged for the production of "copy." Mr. Gallagher became editor of a literary periodical, the Cincinnati Mirror, which he continued for some time, contributing to its pages from his own pen a number of prose tales and poems, which attracted much attention. The enterprise, as is usually the case with pioneer literary efforts, was pecuniarily unsuccessful. During a portion of its career, Mr. Gallagher also edited the Western Literary Journal, published at Cincinnati, a work which closed a brief existence in 1836. He has since been connected with the Hesperian, a publication of a similar character, and of a similarly brief duration.

The first production of Mr. Gallagher which attracted general public attention was a poem published anonymously in one of the periodicals, entitled *The Wreck of the Hornet*. This was reprinted in the first collection of his poems, published in a thin volume in 1835, entitled *Errato*. The chief poem of this collection is the *Penitent, a Metrical Tale*.

A second part of Errato appeared in the fall of 1835. It opens with *The Conqueror*, a poem of six hundred and sixty lines on Napoleon. The third and concluding number of the series appeared in 1837, and contained a narrative poem entitled *Cadwallen*, the incidents of which are drawn from the Indian conflicts of our frontier history.

The chief portions of Errato are occupied by a number of poems of description and reflection, with a few lyrical pieces interspersed, all of which possess melody, and have won a favorable reception throughout the country.

In 1841 Mr. Gallagher edited a volume entitled *Selections from the Poetical Literature of the West*, a work peculiarly appropriate for one who had done so much by his labors in behalf of literature, as well as his own contributions to the common stock, to foster and honor the necessarily arduous pursuit of literature in a new country.

AUGUST.

Dust on thy mantle! dust,
Bright Summer, on thy livery of green!
A tarnish, as of rust,
Dims thy late brilliant sheen:
And thy young glories—leaf, and bud, and flower—
Change cometh over them with every hour.

Thee hath the August sun
Looked on with hot, and fierce, and brassy face:
And still and lazily run,
Scarce whispering in their pace,
The half-dried rivulets, that lately sent
A shout of gladness up, as on they went.

Flame-like, the long mid-day—
With not so much of sweet air as hath stirred
The down upon the spray,
Where rests the panting bird,
Dozing away the hot and tedious noon,
With fitful twitter, sadly out of tune.

Seeds in the sultry air,
And gossamer web-work on the sleeping trees!
E'en the tall pines, that rear
Their plumes to catch the breeze,
The slightest breeze from the unfreshening west,
Partake the general languor, and deep rest.

Happy, as man may be,
Stretched on his back, in homely bean-vine bower,
While the voluptuous bee
Robs each surrounding flower,
And prattling childhood clambers o'er his breast,
The husbandman enjoys his noon-day rest.

Against the hazy sky,
The thin and fleecy clouds, unmoving, rest.
Beneath them far, yet high
In the dim, distant west,
The vulture, scenting thence its carrion-fare,
Sails, slowly circling in the sunny air.

Soberly, in the shade,
Repose the patient cow, and toil-worn ox;
Or in the shoal stream wade,
Sheltered by jutting rocks:
The fleecy flock, fly-scourged and restless, rush
Madly from fence to fence, from bush to bush.

Tediously pass the hours,
And vegetation wilts, with blistered root—
And droop the thirsting flowers,
Where the slant sunbeams shoot;
But of each tall old tree, the lengthening line,
Slow-creeping eastward, marks the day's decline.

Faster, along the plain,
Moves now the shade, and on the meadow's edge:
The kine are forth again,
The bird flits in the hedge.
Now in the molten west sinks the hot sun.
Welcome, mild eve!—the sultry day is done.

Pleasantly comest thou,
Dew of the evening, to the crisped-up grass;
And the curled corn-blades bow,
As the light breezes pass,
That their parched lips may feel thee, and expand,
Thou sweet reviver of the fevered land.

So, to the thirsting soul,
Cometh the dew of the Almighty's love;
And the scathed heart, made whole,
Turneth in joy above,
To where the spirit freely may expand,
And rove, untrammelled, in that "better land."

THE LABORER.

Stand up erect! Thou hast the form
And likeness of thy God!—who more?
A soul as dauntless 'mid the storm
Of daily life, a heart as warm
And pure as breast e'er wore.

What then?—Thou art as true a MAN
As moves the human mass among;
As much a part of the Great Plan
That with Creation's dawn began,
As any of the throng.

Who is thine enemy?—the high
In station, or in wealth the chief?
The great, who coldly pass thee by,
With proud step, and averted eye?
Nay! nurse not such belief.

If true unto thyself thou wast,
What were the proud one's scorn to thee?
A feather, which thou mightest cast
Aside, as idly as the blast
The light leaf from the tree.

No:—uncurbed passions—low desires—
Absence of noble self-respect—
Death, in the breast's consuming fires,
To that high nature which aspires
For ever, till thus checked:

These are thine enemies—thy worst:
They chain thee to thy lowly lot—
Thy labor and thy life accurst.
Oh, stand erect! and from them burst!
And longer suffer not!

Thou art thyself thine enemy!
The great!—what better they than thou?
As theirs, is not thy will as free?
Has God with equal favors thee
Neglected to endow?

True, wealth thou hast not: it is but dust!
Nor place: uncertain as the wind!
But that thou hast, which, with thy crust
And water, may despise the lust
Of both—a noble mind.

With this, and passions under ban,
True faith, and holy trust in God,
Thou art the peer of any man.
Look up, then—that thy little span
Of life may be well trod!

JOHN GREENLEAF WHITTIER

Is of a Quaker family, established, in spite of old Puritan persecutions, on the banks of the Merrimack, where, at the homestead in the neighborhood of Haverhill, Massachusetts, the poet was born in 1808. Until his eighteenth year he lived at home, working on the farm, writing occasional verses for the Haverhill Gazette, and turning his hand to a little shoemaking, one of the industrial resources with which the New England farmer sometimes ekes out the family subsistence.* Then came two years of town academy learning, when

* In a genial article on Mr. Whittier from the pen of Mr. W. S. Thayer in the North American Review for July, 1854, to which we are under obligations for several facts in the present notice, there is this explanation of the shoemaking incident:—"Indeed, upon the strength of this, 'the gentle craft of leather' have laid an especial claim to him as one of their own poets: but we are afraid that mankind would go barefooted if St. Crispin had never had a more devoted disciple. It is characteristic of the thrift of New England farmers to provide extra occupation for a rainy day, and during the winter season, or when the weather is too inclement for out-of-door work, the farmer and his sons turn an honest penny by giving their attention to some employment equally remunerative. For this purpose they have near the farm-house a small shed stocked with the appropriate implements of labor. But from what we know of Whittier's life, it could not have been long before he violated the Horatian precept which forbids the shoemaker to go beyond his last."

he became editor, in 1829, at Boston, of the American Manufacture, a newspaper in the tariff interest. In 1830 he became editor of the paper which had been conducted by Brainard at Hartford, and when the "Remains" of that poet were published in 1832, he wrote the prefatory memoir. In 1831 appeared, in a small octavo volume, at Hartford, his *Legends of New England*, which represents a taste early formed by him of the quaint Indian and colonial superstitions of the country, and which his friend Brainard had delicately touched in several of his best poems. *The Supernaturalism of New England*, which he published in 1847, may be considered a sequel to this volume. There was an early poem published by Whittier, *Moll Pitcher*, a tale of a witch of Nahant, which may be classed with these productions, rather poetical essays in prose and verse on a favorite subject than, strictly speaking, poetical creations.

Kindred in growth to these, was his Indian story, *Mogg Megone*, which appeared in 1836, and has its name from a leader among the Saco Indians in the war of 1677. It is a spirited version, mostly in the octosyllabic measure, of Indian affairs and character from the old narratives, with a lady's story of wrong and penitence, which introduces the rites of the Roman Church in connexion with the Indians. *The Bridal of Pennacook* is another Indian poem, with the skeleton of a story out of Morton's New England's Canaan, which is made the vehicle for some of the author's finest ballad writings and descriptions of nature. Another reproduction of this old period is the *Leaves from Margaret Smith's Journal*, written in the antique style brought into vogue by the clever Lady Willoughby's Diary. The fair journalist, with a taste for nature, poetry, and character, and fully sensitive to the religious influences of the spot, visits New England in 1678, and writes her account of the manners and influences of the time to her cousin in England, a gentleman to

whom she is to be married. In point of delicacy and happy description, this work is full of beauties; though the unnecessary tediousness of its form will remain a permanent objection to it.

Returning to the order of our narrative, from these exhibitions of Whittier's early tastes, we find him, after a few years spent at home in farming, and representing his town in the state legislature, engaged in the proceedings of the American Anti-Slavery Society, of which he was elected a secretary in 1836, and in defence of its principles editing the Pennsylvania Freeman in Philadelphia. *The Voices of Freedom*, which form a section of his poems in the octavo edition of his writings, afford the best specimens of these numerous effusions.* The importance attached to them by the abolition party has probably thrown into the shade some of the finer qualities of his mind.

In 1840 Mr. Whittier took up his residence in Amesbury, Massachusetts, where his late productions have been written, and whence he forwards his contributions to the National Era at Washington; collecting from time to time his articles in books.

In 1850 appeared his volume, *Old Portraits and Modern Sketches*, a series of prose essays on Bunyan, Baxter, Ellwood, Nayler, Andrew Marvell, the Quaker John Roberts, for the ancients; and the Americans, Leggett, the abolition writer Rogers, and the poet Dinsmore for the moderns. In the same year he published *Songs of Labor and other Poems*, in which he seeks to dignify and render interesting the mechanic arts by the associations of history and fancy. *The Chapel of the Hermits, and other Poems*, was published in 1853. The chief poem commemorates an incident in the lives of Rousseau and St. Pierre, when they were visiting a hermitage, and while waiting for the monks, Rousseau—as the anecdote is recorded in the "Studies of Nature,"—proposed some devotional exercises. Whittier illustrates by this his Quaker argument for the spiritual independence of the soul, which will find its own nutriment for itself.

Mr. Whittier has written too frequently on occasional topics of local or passing interest, to claim for all his verses the higher qualities of poetry. Many of them are purely didactic, and serve the purposes of forcible newspaper leaders. In others he has risen readily to genuine eloquence, or tempered his poetic fire by the simplicity of true pathos. Like most masters of energetic expression, he relies upon the strong Saxon elements of the language, the use of which is noticeable in his poems.

THE NEW WIFE AND THE OLD.†

Dark the halls, and cold the feast—
Gone the bridemaids, gone the priest!
All is over—all is done,
Twain of yesterday are one!
Blooming girl and manhood grey,
Autumn in the arms of May!

Hushed within and hushed without,
Dancing feet and wrestlers' shout;

* Boston: Mussey and Co., 1850, with illustrations by Billings.

† This Ballad is founded upon one of the marvellous legends connected with the famous Gen. M., of Hampton, N.H., who was regarded by his neighbors as a Yankee Faust, in league with the adversary. I give the story as I heard it when a child from a venerable family visitant.

Dies the bonfire on the hill;
All is dark and all is still,
Save the starlight, save the breeze
Moaning through the grave-yard trees;
And the great sea-waves below,
Like the night's pulse, beating slow.

From the brief dream of a bride
She hath wakened, at his side.
With half uttered shriek and start—
Feels she not his beating heart?
And the pressure of his arm,
And his breathing near and warm?

Lightly from the bridal bed
Springs that fair dishevelled head,
And a feeling, new, intense,
Half of shame, half innocence,
Maiden fear and wonder speaks
Through her lips and changing cheeks.

From the oaken mantel glowing
Faintest light the lamp is throwing
On the mirror's antique mould,
High-backed chair, and wainscot old,
And, through faded curtains stealing,
His dark sleeping face revealing.

Listless lies the strong man there,
Silver-streaked his careless hair;
Lips of love have left no trace
On that hard and haughty face;
And that forehead's knitted thought
Love's soft hand hath not unwrought.

"Yet," she sighs, "he loves me well,
More than these calm lips will tell.
Stooping to my lowly state,
He hath made me rich and great,
And I bless him, though he be
Hard and stern to all save me!"

While she speaketh, falls the light
O'er her fingers small and white;
Gold and gem, and costly ring
Back the timid lustre fling—
Love's selectest gifts, and rare,
His proud hand had fastened there.

Gratefully she marks the glow
From those tapering lines of snow;
Fondly o'er the sleeper bending
His black hair with golden blending,
In her soft and light caress,
Cheek and lip together press.

Ha!—that start of horror!—Why
That wild stare and wilder cry,
Full of terror, full of pain?
Is there madness in her brain?
Hark! that gasping, hoarse and low:
"Spare me—spare me—let me go!"

God have mercy!—Icy cold
Spectral hands her own enfold,
Drawing silently from them
Love's fair gifts of gold and gem,
"Waken! save me!" still as death
At her side he slumbereth.

Ring and bracelet all are gone,
And that ice-cold hand withdrawn;
But she hears a murmur low,
Full of sweetness, full of woe,
Half a sigh and half a moan:
"Fear not! give the dead her own!"

Ah!—the dead wife's voice she knows!
That cold hand whose pressure froze,
Once in warmest life had borne
Gem and band her own hath worn

"Wake thee! wake thee!" Lo, his eyes
Open with a dull surprise.

In his arms the strong man folds her,
Closer to his breast he holds her;
Trembling limbs his own are meeting,
And he feels her heart's quick beating:
"Nay, my dearest, why this fear?"
"Hush!" she saith, "the dead is here!"

"Nay, a dream—an idle dream."
But before the lamp's pale gleam
Tremblingly her hand she raises,—
There no more the diamond blazes,
Clasp of pearl, or ring of gold,—
"Ah!" she sighs, "her hand was cold!"

Broken words of cheer he saith,
But his dark lip quivereth,
And as o'er the past he thinketh,
From his young wife's arms he shrinketh;
Can those soft arms round him lie,
Underneath his dead wife's eye?

She her fair young head can rest
Soothed and child-like on his breast,
And in trustful innocence
Draw new strength and courage thence;
He, the proud man, feels within
But the cowardice of sin!

She can murmur in her thought
Simple prayers her mother taught,
And His blessed angels call,
Whose great love is over all;
He, alone, in prayerless pride,
Meets the dark Past at her side.

One, who living shrank with dread
From his look, or word, or tread,
Unto whom her early grave
Was as freedom to the slave,
Moves him at this midnight hour,
With the dead's unconscious power!

Ah, the dead, the unforgot!
From their solemn homes of thought,
Where the cypress shadows blend
Darkly over foe and friend,
Or in love or sad rebuke,
Back upon the living look.

And the tenderest ones and weakest,
Who their wrongs have borne the meekest,
Lifting from those dark, still places,
Sweet and sad-remembered faces,
O'er the guilty hearts behind
An unwitting triumph find.

A DREAM OF SUMMER.

Bland as the morning breath of June
The southwest breezes play;
And, through its haze, the winter noon
Seems warm as summer's day.
The snow-plumed Angel of the North
Has dropped his icy spear;
Again the mossy earth looks forth,
Again the streams gush clear.

The fox his hill-side cell forsakes,
The muskrat leaves his nook,
The bluebird in the meadow brakes
Is singing with the brook.
"Bear up, oh mother Nature!" cry
Bird, breeze, and streamlet free;
"Our winter voices prophesy
Of summer days to thee!"

So, in those winters of the soul,
By bitter blasts and drear

O'erswept from Memory's frozen pole,
Will sunny days appear.
Reviving Hope and Faith, they show
The soul its living powers,
And how beneath the winter's snow
Lie germs of summer flowers!

The Night is mother of the Day,
The Winter of the Spring,
And ever upon old Decay
The greenest mosses cling.
Behind the cloud the star-light lurks,
Through showers the sunbeams fall;
For God, who loveth all His works,
Has left His Hope with all!

PALESTINE.

Blest land of Judea! thrice hallowed of song,
Where the holiest of memories pilgrim-like throng;
In the shade of thy palms, by the shores of thy sea,
On the hills of thy beauty, my heart is with thee.

With the eye of a spirit I look on that shore,
Where pilgrim and prophet have lingered before;
With the glide of a spirit I traverse the sod
Made bright by the steps of the angels of God.

Blue sea of the hills!—in my spirit I hear
Thy waters, Genesaret, chime on my ear;
Where the Lowly and Just with the people sat down,
And thy spray on the dust of His sandals was thrown.

Beyond are Bethulia's mountains of green,
And the desolate hills of the wild Gadarene;
And I pause on the goat-crags of Tabor to see
The gleam of thy waters, O dark Galilee!

Hark, a sound in the valley! where swollen and strong,
Thy river, O Kishon, is sweeping along;
Where the Canaanite strove with Jehovah in vain,
And thy torrent grew dark with the blood of the slain.

There down from his mountains stern Zebulon came,
And Napthali's stag, with his eye-balls of flame,
And the chariots of Jabin rolled harmlessly on,
For the arm of the Lord was Abinoam's son!

There sleep the still rocks and the caverns which rang
To the song which the beautiful prophetess sang,
When the princes of Issachar stood by her side,
And the shout of a host in its triumph replied.

Lo, Bethlehem's hill-site before me is seen,
With the mountains around, and the valleys between;
There rested the shepherds of Judah, and there
The songs of the angels rose sweet on the air.

And Bethany's palm trees in beauty still threw
Their shadows at noon on the ruins below;
But where are the sisters who hastened to greet
The lowly Redeemer, and sit at His feet?

I tread where the TWELVE in their way-faring trod;
I stand where they stood with the chosen of God—
Where His blessing was heard and His lessons were taught,
Where the blind were restored and the healing was wrought.

Oh, here with His flock the sad Wanderer came—
These hills He toiled over in grief, are the same—
The founts where He drank by the wayside still flow,
And the same airs are blowing which breathed on His brow!

And throned on her hills sits Jerusalem yet,
But with dust on her forehead, and chains on her feet;
For the crown of her pride to the mocker hath gone,
And the holy Shechinah is dark where it shone.

But wherefore this dream of the earthly abode
Of Humanity clothed in the brightness of God?
Where my spirit but turned from the outward and dim,
It could gaze, even now, on the presence of Him!

Not in clouds and in terrors, but gentle as when,
In love and in meekness, He moved among men;
And the voice which breathed peace to the waves of the sea,
In the hush of my spirit would whisper to me!

And what if my feet may not tread where He stood,
Nor my ears hear the dashing of Galilee's flood,
Nor my eyes see the cross which He bowed him to bear,
Nor my knees press Gethsemane's garden of prayer.

Yet loved of the Father, Thy Spirit is near
To the meek, and the lowly, and penitent here;
And the voice of Thy love is the same even now,
As at Bethany's tomb, or on Olivet's brow.

Oh, the outward hath gone!—but in glory and power,
The SPIRIT surviveth the things of an hour;
Unchanged, undecaying, its Pentecost flame
On the heart's sacred altar is burning the same!

GONE.

Another hand is beckoning us,
Another call is given;
And glows once more with Angel-steps
The path which reaches Heaven.

Our young and gentle friend whose smile
Made brighter summer hours,
Amid the frosts of autumn time
Has left us, with the flowers.

No paling of the cheek of bloom
Forewarned us of decay;
No shadow from the Silent Land
Fell around our sister's way.

The light of her young life went down,
As sinks behind the hill
The glory of a setting star—
Clear, suddenly, and still.

As pure and sweet, her fair brow seemed—
Eternal as the sky;
And like the brook's low song, her voice—
A sound which could not die.

And half we deemed she needed not
The changing of her sphere,
To give to Heaven a Shining One,
Who walked an Angel here.

The blessing of her quiet life
Fell on us like the dew;
And good thoughts, where her footsteps pressed,
Like fairy blossoms grew.

Sweet promptings unto kindest deeds
Were in her very look;
We read her face, as one who reads
A true and holy book:

The measure of a blessed hymn,
To which our hearts could move;
The breathing of an inward psalm;
A canticle of love.

We miss her in the place of prayer,
And by the hearth-fire's light;
We pause beside her door to hear
Once more her sweet "Good night!"

There seems a shadow on the day,
Her smile no longer cheers;
A dimness on the stars of night,
Like eyes that look through tears.

Alone unto our Father's will
One thought hath reconciled;
That He whose love exceedeth ours
Hath taken home His child.

Fold her, oh Father! in thine arms,
And let her henceforth be
A messenger of love between
Our human hearts and Thee.

Still let her mild rebuking stand
Between us and the wrong,
And her dear memory serve to make
Our faith in Goodness strong.

And, grant that she who, trembling, here
Distrusted all her powers,
May welcome to her holier home
The well beloved of ours.

CHARLES FENNO HOFFMAN.

Charles Fenno Hoffman is the descendant of a family which established itself in the State of New York during its possession by the Dutch. His maternal grandfather, from whom he derived the name of Fenno, was an active politician and writer of the federal party during the administration of Washington. His father, Judge Hoffman, was an eminent member of the bar of the United States. He pleaded and won his first cause at the age of seventeen, and at twenty-one filled the place previously occupied by his father in the New York Legislature. One of his sons is Ogden Hoffman, who has long maintained a high position as an eloquent pleader.

C. F. Hoffman

Charles Fenno Hoffman, the son of Judge Hoffman by a second marriage, was born in the city of New York in 1806. At the age of six years he was placed at a Latin Grammar School in the city, and three years after was sent to the Poughkeepsie Academy, a celebrated boarding-school on the Hudson. Owing, it is said, to harsh treatment, he ran away. His father not wishing to coerce him unduly, instead of sending him back, placed him in the charge of a Scottish gentleman in a village of New Jersey. While on a visit home in 1817 an accident occurred, an account of which is given in a paragraph quoted from the New York Gazette in the Evening Post of October 25, from which it appears that "he was sitting on Courtlandt-street Dock, with his legs hanging over the wharf, as the steamboat was coming in, which caught one of his legs and crushed it in a dreadful manner." It was found necessary to amputate the injured limb above the knee. Its place was supplied by a cork substitute, which seemed to form no impediment to the continuance of the out-door life and athletic exercises in which its wearer was a proficient. At the age of fifteen he entered Columbia College, where he was more distinguished in the debating society than in the class. He left College during his junior year, but afterwards received the honorary degree of Master of Arts from the institution. He next studied law with the late Harmanus Bleecker, at Albany, at the age of twenty-one was admitted to the bar, and practised for three years in New York. He then abandoned a professional for a literary life, having already tried his pen in anonymous contributions while a clerk to the Albany newspapers, and while an attorney to the New York American, in the editorship of which he became associated with Mr. Charles King. A series of articles by him, designated by a star, added to the literary reputation of the journal.

In 1833 Mr. Hoffman made a tour to the Prairies for the benefit of his health. He contributed a series of letters, descriptive of its incidents, to the American, which were collected and published in 1834, in a couple of volumes bearing the title *A Winter in the West*, which obtained a wide popularity in this country and England. His second work, *Wild Scenes in the Forest and the Prairie*, appeared in 1837. It was followed by the romance of Greyslaer, founded on the celebrated Beauchamp murder case in Kentucky.

The Knickerbocker Magazine was commenced in 1833 under the editorship of Mr. Hoffman. It was conducted by him with spirit, but after the issue of a few numbers passed into the hands of Timothy Flint. He was subsequently connected with the American Monthly Magazine, and was for a while engaged in the editorship of the New York Mirror. His continuous novel of Vanderlyn was published in the former in 1837. His poetical writings, which had long before become widely and favorably known, were first collected in a volume entitled *The Vigil of Faith and Other Poems*, in 1842. The main story which gave the book a title is an Indian legend of the Adirondach, which we take to be a pure invention of the author,—a poetic conception of a bride slain by the rival of her husband, who watches and guards the life of his foe lest so hated an object should intrude upon the presence of his mistress in the spirit world. It is in the octosyllabic measure, and in a pathetic, eloquent strain.

In 1844 a second poetical volume, including numerous additions, appeared with the title, *Borrowed Notes for Home Circulation*—suggested by an article which had recently been published in the Foreign Quarterly Review on the Poets and

Poetry of America, which was then attracting considerable attention. A more complete collection of his poems than is contained in either of these volumes appeared in 1845.

During 1846 and 1847 Mr. Hoffman edited for about eighteen months the Literary World. After his retirement he contributed to that journal a series of essays and tales entitled *Sketches of Society*, which are among his happiest prose efforts. One of these, *The Man in the Reservoir*, detailing the experiences of an individual who is supposed to have passed a night in that uncomfortable lodging-place of water and granite, became, like the author's somewhat similar narrative of The Man in the Boiler, a favorite with the public. This series was closed in December, 1848. During the following year the author was attacked by a mental disorder, which unhappily has permanently interrupted a brilliant and useful literary career.

The author's fine social qualities are reflected in his writings. A man of taste and scholarship, ingenious in speculation, with a healthy love of out-of-door life and objects, he unites the sentiment of the poet and the refinements of the thinker to a keen perception of the humors of the world in action. His conversational powers of a high order; his devoted pursuit of literature; his ardent love of Americanism in art and letters; his acquaintance with authors and artists; a certain personal chivalry of character;—are so many elements of the regard in which he is held by his friends, and they may all be found perceptibly imparting vitality to his writings. These, whether in the department of the essay, the critique, the song, the poem, the tale, or novel, are uniformly stamped by a generous nature.

SPARKLING AND BRIGHT.

Sparkling and bright in liquid light,
Does the wine our goblets gleam in,
With hue as red as the rosy bed
Which a bee would choose to dream in.
Then fill to-night with hearts as light,
To loves as gay and fleeting
As bubbles that swim on the beaker's brim,
And break on the lips while meeting.

Oh! if Mirth might arrest the flight
Of Time through Life's dominions,
We here awhile would now beguile
The grey-beard of his pinions
To drink to-night with hearts as light,
To loves as gay and fleeting
As bubbles that swim on the beaker's brim,
And break on the lips while meeting.

But since delight can't tempt the wight,
Nor fond regret delay him,
Nor Love himself can hold the elf,
Nor sober Friendship stay him,
We'll drink to-night with hearts as light,
To loves as gay and fleeting
As bubbles that swim on the beaker's brim,
And break on the lips while meeting.

THE MINT JULEP.

'Tis said that the gods, on Olympus of old
(And who the bright legend profanes with a doubt),
One night, 'mid their revels, by Bacchus were told
That his last butt of nectar had somehow run out!
But determined to send round the goblet once more,
They sued to the fairer immortals for aid
In composing a draught, which till drinking were o'er,
Should cast every wine ever drank in the shade.

Grave Ceres herself blithely yielded her corn,
And the spirit that lives in each amber-hued grain,
And which first had its birth from the dew of the morn,
Was taught to steal out in bright dewdrops again.

Pomona, whose choicest of fruits on the board
Were scattered profusely in every one's reach,
When called on a tribute to cull from the hoard,
Expressed the mild juice of the delicate peach.

The liquids were mingled while Venus looked on
With glances so fraught with sweet magical power,
That the honey of Hybla, e'en when they were gone,
Has never been missed in the draught from that hour.

Flora then, from her bosom of fragrancy, shook
And with roseate fingers pressed down in the bowl,
All dripping and fresh as it came from the brook,
The herb whose aroma should flavor the whole.

The draft was delicious, and loud the acclaim,
Though something seemed wanting for all to bewail;
But Juleps the drink of immortals became,
When Jove himself added a handful of hail.

ROOM, BOYS, ROOM.

There was an old hunter camped down by the rill,
Who fished in this water, and shot on that hill.
The forest for him had no danger nor gloom,
For all that he wanted was plenty of room!
Says he, "The world's wide, there is room for us all;
Room enough in the greenwood, if not in the hall.
Room, boys, room, by the light of the moon,
For why shouldn't every man enjoy his own room?"

He wove his own nets, and his shanty was spread
With the skins he had dressed and stretched out overhead;
Fresh branches of hemlock made fragrant the floor,
For his bed, as he sung when the daylight was o'er,
"The world's wide enough, there is room for us all;
Room enough in the greenwood, if not in the hall.
Room, boys, room, by the light of the moon,
For why shouldn't every man enjoy his own room?"

That spring now half choked by the dust of the road,
Under boughs of old maples once limpidly flowed;
By the rock whence it bubbles his kettle was hung,
Which their sap often filled while the hunter he sung,
"The world's wide enough, there is room for us all;
Room enough in the greenwood, if not in the hall.
Room, boys, room, by the light of the moon,
For why shouldn't every man enjoy his own room?"

And still sung the hunter—when one gloomy day,
He saw in the forest what saddened his lay,—
A heavy wheeled wagon its black rut had made,
Where fair grew the greensward in broad forest glade—
"The world's wide enough, there is room for us all;
Room enough in the greenwood, if not in the hall.
Room, boys, room, by the light of the moon,
For why shouldn't every man enjoy his own room?"

He whistled to his dog, and says he, "We can't stay;
I must shoulder my rifle, up traps, and away;"
Next day, 'mid those maples the settler's axe rung,
While slowly the hunter trudged off as he sung,

"The world's wide enough, there is room for us all;
Room enough in the greenwood, if not in the hall.
Room, boys, room, by the light of the moon,
For why shouldn't every man enjoy his own room?"

RIO BRAVO—A MEXICAN LAMENT.*

Rio Bravo! Rio Bravo,
Saw men ever such a sight?
Since the field of Roncesvalles
Sealed the fate of many a knight.

Dark is Palo Alto's story,
Sad Resaca Palma's rout,
On those fatal fields so gory,
Many a gallant life went out.

There our best and bravest lances,
Shivered 'gainst the Northern steel,
Left the valiant hearts that couched them
'Neath the Northern charger's heel.

Rio Bravo! Rio Bravo!
Minstrel ne'er knew such a fight,
Since the field of Roncesvalles
Sealed the fate of many a knight.

Rio Bravo, fatal river,
Saw ye not while red with gore,
Torrejon all headless quiver,
A ghastly trunk upon thy shore!

Heard you not the wounded coursers,
Shrieking on your trampled banks,
As the Northern winged artillery
Thundered on our shattered ranks!

There Arista, best and bravest,
There Raguena tried and true,
On the fatal field thou lavest,
Nobly did all men could do.

Vainly there those heroes rally,
Castile on Montezuma's shore,
"Rio Bravo"—"Roncesvalles,"
Ye are names blent evermore.

Weepest thou, lorn lady Inez,
For thy lover mid the slain,
Brave La Vega's trenchant falchion,
Cleft his slayer to the brain.

Brave La Vega who all lonely,
By a host of foes beset,
Yielded up his sabre only,
When his equal there he met.

Other champions not less noted,
Sleep beneath that sullen wave,
Rio Bravo, thou hast floated
An army to an ocean grave.

On they came, those Northern horsemen,
On like eagles toward the sun,
Followed then the Northern bayonet,
And the field was lost and won.

Oh! for Orlando's horn to rally,
His Paladins on that sad shore,
"Rio Bravo"—"Roncesvalles,"
Ye are names blent evermore.

THE MAN IN THE RESERVOIR—A FANTASIE PIECE.

You may see some of the best society in New York on the top of the Distributing Reservoir, any of these fine October mornings. There were two or three carriages in waiting, and half a dozen senatorial-looking mothers with young children, pacing the parapet, as we basked there the other day in the sunshine—now watching the pickerel that glide along the lucid edges of the black pool within, and now looking off upon the scene of rich and wondrous variety that spreads along the two rivers on either side.

"They may talk of Alpheus and Arethusa," murmured an idling sophomore, who had found his way thither during recitation hours, "but the Croton in passing over an arm of the sea at Spuyten-duyvil, and bursting to sight again in this truncated pyramid, beats it all hollow. By George, too, the bay yonder looks as blue as ever the Ægean Sea to Byron's eye, gazing from the Acropolis! But the painted foliage on these crags!—the Greeks must have dreamed of such a vegetable phenomenon in the midst of their greyish olive groves, or they never would have supplied the want of it in their landscape by embroidering their marble temples with gay colors. "Did you see that pike break, Sir?"

"I did not."

"Zounds! his silver fin flashed upon the black Acheron, like a restless soul that hoped yet to mount from the pool."

"The place seems suggestive of fancies to you?" we observed in reply to the rattlepate.

"It is, indeed, for I have done up a good deal of anxious thinking within a circle of a few yards where that fish broke just now."

"A singular place for meditation—the middle of the reservoir!"

"You look incredulous, Sir—but it's a fact. A fellow can never tell, until he is tried, in what situation his most earnest meditations may be concentrated. I am boring you, though?"

"Not at all. But you seem so familiar with the spot, I wish you could tell me why that ladder leading down to the water is lashed against the stonework in yonder corner?"

"That ladder," said the young man, brightening at the question, "why the position, perhaps the very existence of that ladder, resulted from my meditations in the reservoir, at which you smiled just now. Shall I tell you all about them?"

"Pray do."

Well, you have seen the notice forbidding any one to fish in the reservoir. Now when I read that warning, the spirit of the thing struck me at once, as inferring nothing more than that one should not sully the temperance potations of our citizens by steeping bait in it, of any kind; but you probably know the common way of taking pike with a slipnoose of delicate wire. I was determined to have a touch at the fellows with this kind of tackle.

I chose a moonlight night; and an hour before the edifice was closed to visitors, I secreted myself within the walls, determined to pass the night on the top. All went as I could wish it. The night proved cloudy, but it was only a variable drift of broken clouds which obscured the moon. I had a walking cane-rod with me which would reach to the margin of the water, and several feet beyond if necessary. To this was attached the wire about fifteen inches in length.

I prowled along the parapet for a considerable time, but not a single fish could I see. The clouds made a flickering light and shade, that wholly foiled my steadfast gaze. I was convinced that should they come up thicker, my whole night's adventure would be thrown away. "Why should I not descend the sloping wall and get nearer on a level with the fish, for thus alone can I hope to see one?" The question had hardly shaped itself in my mind before I had one leg over the iron railing.

* This originally appeared in the Columbian Magazine, with the following lines of introduction. "Such of the readers of the Columbian as have seen the Vera Cruz Journal containing the original of the Rio Bravo Lament, by the popular Mexican poet, Don Jose Maria Joacquin du Ho Axoe de Saltillo, will perhaps not find the following hasty translation unacceptable."

If you look around you will see now that there are some half dozen weeds growing here and there, amid the fissures of the solid masonry. In one of the fissures from whence these spring, I planted a foot, and began my descent. The reservoir was fuller than it is now, and a few strides would have carried me to the margin of the water. Holding on to the cleft above, I felt round with one foot for a place to plant it below me.

In that moment the flap of a pound pike made me look round, and the roots of the weed upon which I partially depended, gave way as I was in the act of turning. Sir, one's senses are sharpened in deadly peril; as I live now, I distinctly heard the bells of Trinity chiming midnight, as I rose to the surface the next instant, immersed in the stone cauldron, where I must swim for my life heaven only could tell how long!

I am a capital swimmer; and this naturally gave me a degree of self-possession. Falling as I had, I of course had pitched out some distance from the sloping parapet. A few strokes brought me to the edge. I really was not yet certain but that I could clamber up the face of the wall anywhere. I hoped that I could. I felt certain at least there was some spot where I might get hold with my hands, even if I did not ultimately ascend it.

I tried the nearest spot. The inclination of the wall was so vertical that it did not even rest me to lean against it. I felt with my hands and with my feet. Surely, I thought, there must be some fissure like those in which that ill-omened weed had found a place for its root!

There was none. My fingers became sore in busying themselves with the harsh and inhospitable stones. My feet slipped from the smooth and slimy masonry beneath the water; and several times my face came in rude contact with the wall, when my foothold gave way on the instant that I seemed to have found some diminutive rocky cleet upon which I could stay myself.

Sir, did you ever see a rat drowned in a half-filled hogshead? how he swims round, and round, and round; and after vainly trying the sides again and again with his paws, fixes his eyes upon the upper rim as if he would *look himself* out of his watery prison.

I thought of the miserable vermin, thought of him as I had often watched thus his dying agonies, when a cruel urchin of eight or ten. Boys are horribly cruel, sir; boys, women, and savages. All child-like things are cruel; cruel from a want of thought and from perverse ingenuity, although by instinct each of these is so tender. You may not have observed it, but a savage is as tender to its own young as a boy is to a favorite puppy—the same boy that will torture a kitten out of existence. I thought, then, I say, of the rat drowning in a half-filled cask of water, and lifting his gaze out of the vessel as he grew more and more desperate, and I flung myself on my back, and floating thus, fixed my eyes upon the face of the moon.

The moon is well enough, in her way, however you may look at her; but her appearance is, to say the least of it, peculiar to a man floating on his back in the centre of a stone tank, with a dead wall of some fifteen or twenty feet rising squarely on every side of him (the young man smiled bitterly as he said this, and shuddered once or twice before he went on musingly)! The last time I had noted the planet with any emotion she was on the wane. Mary was with me, I had brought her out here one morning to look at the view from the top of the Reservoir. She said little of the scene, but as we talked of our old childish loves, I saw that its fresh features were incorporating themselves with tender memories of the past, and I was content.

There was a rich golden haze upon the landscape, and as my own spirits rose amid the voluptuous atmosphere, she pointed to the waning planet, discernible like a faint gash in the welkin, and wondered how long it would be before the leaves would fall! Strange girl, did she mean to rebuke my joyous mood, as if we had no right to be happy while nature withering in her pomp, and the sickly moon wasting in the blaze of noontide, were there to remind us of "the-gone-for-ever?" "They will all renew themselves, dear Mary," said I, encouragingly, "and there is one that will ever keep tryste alike with thee and Nature through all seasons, if thou wilt but be true to one of us, and remain as now a child of nature."

A tear sprang to her eye, and then searching her pocket for her card-case, she remembered an engagement to be present at Miss Lawson's opening of fall bonnets, at two o'clock!

And yet, dear, wild, wayward Mary, I thought of her now. You have probably outlived this sort of thing, sir; but I, looking at the moon, as I floated there upturned to her yellow light, thought of the loved being whose tears I knew would flow when she heard of my singular fate, at once so grotesque, yet melancholy to awfulness.

And how often we have talked, too, of that Carian shepherd who spent his damp nights upon the hills, gazing as I do on the lustrous planet! who will revel with her amid those old superstitions? Who, from our own unlegended woods, will evoke their yet undetected, haunting spirits? Who peer with her in prying scrutiny into nature's laws, and challenge the whispers of poetry from the voiceless throat of matter? Who laugh merrily over the stupid guesswork of pedants, that never mingled with the infinitude of nature, through love exhaustless and all-embracing, as we have? Poor girl, she will be companionless.

Alas! companionless for ever—save in the exciting stages of some brisk flirtation. She will live hereafter by feeding other hearts with love's lore she has learned from me, and then, Pygmalion-like, grow fond of the images she has herself endowed with semblance of divinity, until they seem to breathe back the mystery the soul can truly catch from only one.

How anxious she will be lest the coroner shall have discovered any of her notes in my pocket!

I felt chilly as this last reflection crossed my mind. Partly at thought of the coroner, partly at the idea of Mary being unwillingly compelled to wear mourning for me, in case of such a disclosure of our engagement. It is a provoking thing for a girl of nineteen to have to go into mourning for a deceased lover, at the beginning of her second winter in the metropolis.

The water, though, with my motionless position, must have had something to do with my chilliness. I see, sir, you think that I tell my story with great levity; but indeed, indeed I should grow delirious did I venture to hold steadily to the awfulness of my feelings the greater part of that night. I think indeed, I must have been most of the time hysterical with horror, for the vibrating emotions I have recapitulated did pass through my brain even as I have detailed them.

But as I now became calm in thought, I summoned up again some resolution of action.

I will begin at that corner (said I), and swim around the whole enclosure. I will swim slowly and again feel the sides of the tank with my feet. If die I must, let me perish at least from well directed though exhausting effort, not sink from mere bootless weariness in sustaining myself till the morning shall bring relief.

The sides of the place seemed to grow higher as I now kept my watery course beneath them. It was not altogether a dead pull. I had some variety of emotion in making my circuit. When I swam in the shadow it looked to me more cheerful beyond in the moonlight. When I swam in the moonlight I had the hope of making some discovery when I should again reach the shadow. I turned several times on my back to rest just where those wavy lines would meet. The stars looked viciously bright to me from the bottom of that well; there was such a company of them; they were so glad in their lustrous revelry; and they had such space to move in? I was alone, sad to despair, in a strange element, prisoned, and a solitary gazer upon their mocking chorus. And yet there was nothing else with which I could hold communion?

I turned upon my breast and struck out almost frantically, once more. The stars were forgotten, the moon, the very world of which I as yet formed a part, my poor Mary herself was forgotten. I thought only of the strong man there perishing; of me in my lusty manhood, in the sharp vigor of my dawning prime, with faculties illimitable, with senses all alert, battling there with physical obstacles which men like myself had brought together for my undoing. The Eternal could never have willed this thing! I could not and I would not perish thus. And I grew strong in insolence of self-trust; and I laughed aloud as I dashed the sluggish water from side to side.

Then came an emotion of pity for myself—of wild, wild regret; of sorrow, oh, infinite for a fate so desolate, a doom so dreary, so heart-sickening. You may laugh at the contradiction if you will, sir, but I felt that I could sacrifice my own life on the instant, to redeem another fellow creature from such a place of horror, from an end so piteous. My soul and my vital spirit seemed in that desperate moment to be separating; while one in parting grieved over the deplorable fate of the other.

And then I prayed!

I prayed, why or wherefore I know not. It was not from fear. It could not have been in hope. The days of miracles are passed, and there was no natural law by whose providential interposition I could be saved. *I* did not pray; it prayed of itself, my soul within me.

Was the calmness that I now felt, torpidity? the torpidity that precedes dissolution, to the strong swimmer who, sinking from exhaustion, must at last add a bubble to the wave as he suffocates beneath the element which now denied his mastery? If it were so, how fortunate was it that my floating rod at that moment attracted my attention as it dashed through the water by me. I saw on the instant that a fish had entangled himself in the wire noose. The rod quivered, plunged, came again to the surface, and rippled the water as it shot in arrowy flight from side to side of the tank. At last driven towards the southeast corner of the Reservoir, the small end seemed to have got foul somewhere. The brazen butt, which, every time the fish sounded, was thrown up to the moon, now sank by its own weight, showing that the other end must be fast. But the cornered fish, evidently anchored somewhere by that short wire, floundered several times to the surface, before I thought of striking out to the spot.

The water is low now and tolerably clear. You may see the very ledge there, sir, in yonder corner, on which the small end of my rod rested when I secured that pike with my hands. I did not take him from the slip-noose, however; but standing upon the ledge, handled the rod in a workmanlike manner, as I flung that pound pickerel over the iron-railing upon the top of the parapet. The rod, as I have told you, barely reached from the railing to the water. It was a heavy, strong bass rod which I had borrowed in "the Spirit of the Times" office; and when I discovered that the fish at the end of the wire made a strong enough knot to prevent me from drawing my tackle away from the railing around which it twined itself as I threw, why, as you can at once see, I had but little difficulty in making my way up the face of the wall with such assistance. The ladder which attracted your notice is, as you see, lashed to the iron railing in the identical spot where I thus made my escape; and for fear of similar accidents they have placed another one in the corresponding corner of the other compartment of the tank ever since my remarkable night's adventure in the Reservoir.

We give the above singular relation verbatim as heard from the lips of our chance acquaintance; and although strongly tempted to "work it up" after the fantastic style of a famous German namesake, prefer that the reader should have it in its American simplicity.

LUCRETIA MARIA AND MARGARET MILLER DAVIDSON.

THE sisters Lucretia Maria and Margaret Miller, were the daughters of Dr. Oliver Davidson, and Margaret Miller his wife. The parents were persons of education and refinement; and the mother, herself a poetess, had enjoyed the instructions of the celebrated Isabella Graham at New York. She was sensitive in body as well as mind, and subject to frequent attacks of sickness. Her daughter Lucretia was born at Plattsburgh, on the shore of Lake Champlain, September 27, 1808. Her infancy was sickly, and in her second year an attack of typhus fever threatened her life. She recovered from this, however, and with it the lesser disorders with which she had been also troubled, disappeared. At the age of four she was sent to school and soon learned to read and form letters in sand. She was an unwearied student of the little story books given her, neglecting for these all the ordinary plays of her age. We soon hear of her making books of her own. Her mother one day, when preparing to write a letter, missed a quire of paper; expressing her wonder, the little girl came forward and said, "Mamma, I have used it." Her mother, surprised, asked her how? Lucretia burst out crying and said, "she did not like to tell." She was not pressed to do so, and paper continued to disappear. Lucretia was often found busy with pen and ink, and in making little blank books; but would only cry and run away if questioned.

When she was six years old, these little books came to light on the removal of a pile of linen on a closet shelf, behind which they were hidden. "At first," says her biographer Miss Sedgwick, "the hieroglyphics seemed to baffle investigation. On one side of the leaf was an artfully sketched picture; on the other, Roman letters, some placed upright, others horizontally, obliquely, or backwards, not formed into words, nor spaced in any mode. Both parents pored over them till they ascertained the letters were poetical explanations in metre and rhyme of the picture in the reverse.

The little books were carefully put away as literary curiosities. Not long after this, Lucretia came running to her mother, painfully agitated, her face covered with her hands, and tears trickling down between her slender fingers—'Oh, Mama! mama!' she cried, sobbing, 'how could you treat me so? You have not used me well! My little books! you have shown them to papa, —Anne—Eliza, I know you have. Oh, what shall I do?' Her mother pleaded guilty, and tried to soothe the child by promising not to do so again; Lucretia's face brightened, a sunny smile played through her tears as she replied, 'Oh, mama, I am not afraid you will do so again, for I have burned them all;' and so she had! This reserve proceeded from nothing cold or exclusive in her character; never was there a more loving or sympathetic creature. It would be difficult to say which was most rare, her modesty, or the genius it sanctified."

She soon after learned to write in more legible fashion, and in her ninth year produced the following lines, the earliest of her compositions which has been preserved:—

ON THE DEATH OF MY ROBIN.

Underneath this turf doth lie
A little bird which ne'er could fly,
Twelve large angle worms did fill
This little bird, whom they did kill.
Puss! if you should chance to smell
My little bird from his dark cell,
Oh! do be merciful, my cat,
And not serve him as you did my rat.

She studied hard at school, and when needlework was given her as a preventive against this undue intellectual effort, dashed through the task assigned her with great rapidity, and studied harder than before. Her mother very properly took her away from school, and the child's health improved in consequence. She now frequently brought short poems to her mother, who always received them gladly, and encouraged her intellectual efforts. The kind parent has given us a glimpse of her daughter, engaged in her eleventh year in composition. "Immediately after breakfast she went to walk, and not returning to dinner, nor even when the evening approached, Mr. Townsend set forth in search of her. He met her, and as her eye encountered his, she smiled and blushed, as if she felt conscious of having been a little ridiculous. She said she had called on a friend, and, having found her absent, had gone to her library, where she had been examining some volumes of an Encyclopædia to aid her, we believe, in the oriental story she was employed upon. She forgot her dinner and her tea, and had remained reading, standing, and with her hat on, till the disappearance of daylight brought her to her senses.

A characteristic anecdote is related of her "cramming" for her long poem, *Amir Khan.* "I entered her room—she was sitting with scarcely light enough to discern the characters she was tracing; her harp was in the window, touched by a breeze just sufficient to rouse the spirit of harmony; her comb had fallen on the floor, and her long dark ringlets hung in rich profusion over her neck and shoulders, her cheek glowed with animation, her lips were half unclosed, her full dark eye was radiant with the light of genius, and beaming with sensibility, her head rested on her left hand, while she held her pen in her right—she looked like the inhabitant of another sphere; she was so wholly absorbed that she did not observe my entrance. I looked over her shoulder and read the following lines:—

What heavenly music strikes my ravished ear,
So soft, so melancholy, and so clear?
And do the tuneful nine then touch the lyre,
To fill each bosom with poetic fire?
Or does some angel strike the sounding strings
Who caught from echo the wild note he sings?
But ah! another strain, how sweet! how wild!
Now rushing low, 'tis soothing, soft, and mild.

"The noise I made in leaving the room roused her, and she soon after brought me her 'Lines to an Æolian Harp.'"

In 1824, an old friend of her mother and a frequent visitor, the Hon. Moss Kent, happened to take up some of Lucretia's MS. poems which had been given to his sister. Struck with their merit he went to the mother to see more, and on his way met the poetess, then a beautiful girl of sixteen; much pleased with her conversation, he proposed to her parents, after a further examination of her poems, to adopt her as his own daughter. They acquiesced in his wishes so far as to consent to his sending her to Mrs. Willard's seminary at Troy* to complete her education.

She was delighted with the opportunity afforded her of an improved literary culture, and on the 24th of November, 1824, left home in good health, which was soon impaired by her severe study. The chief mischief, however, appears to have been done by her exertions in preparing for the public examination of the school. Miss Davidson fell sick, Mrs. Willard sent for Dr. Robbins, who bled, administered an emetic, and allowed his patient, after making her still weaker, to resume her preparation for examination, for which she "must study morning, noon, and night, and rise between two and four every morning." The great event came off, "in a room crowded almost to suffocation," on the 12th of February.

* Emma, the daughter of Samuel Hart, and a descendant from Thomas Hooker, the founder of Hartford, was born at New Berlin, Conn., in February, 1787. At the age of sixteen, she commenced the career to which her life has been devoted as the teacher of the district school of her native town.

After filling in succession the post of principal of several academies, she took charge of an institution of the kind at Middlebury, Vermont, where in 1809 she married Dr. John Willard of that state.

In 1819, Mrs. Willard, at the invitation of Governor Clinton, and other distinguished men of the state of New York, removed to Waterford to take charge of an institution for female education, incorporated, and in part supported, by the legislature.

In consequence of being unable to secure an appropriate building at Waterford, Mrs. Willard accepted an invitation to establish a school at Troy, and in 1821 commenced the institution which has long been celebrated as the Troy Female Seminary, and with which she remained connected until 1838.

In 1830, Mrs. Willard made a tour in Europe, and on her return published her Travels, devoting her share of the proceeds of the sale to the support of a school in Greece, founded mainly by her exertions, for the education of female teachers.

Mrs. Willard has, since her retirement from Troy, resided at Hartford, where she has written and published several addresses on the subject of Female Education, especially as connected with the common-school system. She is also the author of a *Manual of American History*, *A Treatise on Ancient Geography*, and other works which have had an extensive school circulation. In 1830 she published a small volume of poems, and in 1846 *A Treatise on the Motive Powers which produce the Circulation of the Blood*, a work which attracted much attention on its appearance; and in 1849, *Last Leaves of American History*, a continuation of her "Manual."

In the spring vacation she returned home. Her mother was alarmed at the state of her health, but the physician called by her father to aid him in the treatment of her case recommending a change of scene and air, she was allowed to follow her wishes and return to school, the establishment of Miss Gibson at Albany being at this time selected. She had been there but a few weeks when her disease, consumption, assumed its worst features. Her mother hurried to her, and removed her home in July. It is a touching picture that of her last journey. "She shrunk painfully from the gaze her beauty inevitably attracted, heightened as it was by that disease which seems to delight to deck the victim for its triumph." She reached home. "To the last she manifested her love of books. A trunk filled with them had not been unpacked. She requested her mother to open it at her bed-side, and as each book was given to her, she turned over the leaves, kissed it, and desired to have it placed on a table at the foot of her bed. There they remained to the last day, her eye often fondly resting on them." She wrote while confined to her bed her last poem:—

There is a something which I dread,
It is a dark and fearful thing;
It steals along with withering tread,
Or sweeps on wild destruction's wing.

That thought comes o'er me in the hour
Of grief, of sickness, or of sadness:
'Tis not the dread of death; 'tis more—
It is the dread of madness.

Oh! may these throbbing pulses pause,
Forgetful of their feverish course;
May this hot brain, which, burning glows
With all a fiery whirlpool's force,

Be cold and motionless, and still
A tenant of its lowly bed;
But let not dark delirium steal—
[Unfinished.]

The fear was a groundless one, for her mind was calm, collected, and tranquil during the short period that intervened before her death, on the 27th of August, 1825, one month before her seventeenth birthday.

THE WIDE WORLD IS DREAR.

(Written in her sixteenth year.)

Oh say not the wide world is lonely and dreary!
Oh say not that life is a wilderness waste!
There's ever some comfort in store for the weary,
And there's ever some hope for the sorrowful breast.

There are often sweet dreams which will steal o'er the soul,
Beguiling the mourner to smile through a tear,
That when waking the dew-drops of mem'ry may fall,
And blot out for ever, the wide world is drear.

There is hope for the lost, for the lone one's relief,
Which will beam o'er his pathway of danger and fear;
There is pleasure's wild throb, and the calm "joy of grief,"
Oh then say not the wide world is lonely and drear!

There are fears that are anxious, yet sweet to the breast,
Some feelings, which language ne'er told to the ear,
Which return on the heart, and there lingering rest,
Soft whispering, this world is not lonely and drear.

'Tis true, that the dreams of the evening will fade,
When reason's broad sunbeam shines calmly and clear;
Still fancy, sweet fancy, will smile o'er the shade,
And say that the world is not lonely and drear.

Oh, then mourn not that life is a wilderness waste!
That each hope is illusive, each prospect is drear,
But remember that man, undeserving, is blest,
And rewarded with smiles for the fall of a tear.

HINDOO BURIAL SERVICE—VERSIFIED.

We commend our brother to thee, oh earth!
To thee he returns, from thee was his birth!
Of thee was he formed, he was nourished by thee;
Take the body, oh earth! the spirit is free.

Oh air! he once breathed thee, thro' thee he survived,
And in thee, and with thee, his pure spirit lived:
That spirit hath fled, and we yield him to thee;
His ashes be spread, like his soul, far and free.

Oh fire! we commit his dear reliques to thee,
Thou emblem of purity, spotless and free;
May his soul, like thy flames, bright and burning arise,
To its mansion of bliss, in the star-spangled skies.

Oh water! receive him; without thy kind aid
He had parched 'neath the sunbeams or mourned in the shade;
Then take of his body the share which is thine,
For the spirit hath fled from its mouldering shrine.

MARGARET MILLER DAVIDSON, at the time of her sister's death, was in her third year, having been born March 26, 1823. Her life seems in almost every respect a repetition of that of her departed sister. The same precocity was early developed. When she was six years old she read the English poets with "enthusiastic delight." While standing at the window with her mother she exclaimed—

See those lofty, those grand trees;
Their high tops waving in the breeze;
They cast their shadows on the ground,
And spread their fragrance all around.

At her mother's request she wrote down the little impromptu, but committed it to paper in a consecutive sentence, as so much prose. The act was, however, the commencement of her literary career, and she every day, for some time after, brought some little scrap of rhyme to her parent. She was at the same time delighting the children of the neighborhood by her improvised stories, which she would sometimes extend through a whole evening.

Her education was conducted at home, under her mother's charge. She advanced so rapidly in her studies that it was necessary to check her ardor, that over exertion might not injure her health. When about seven years old, an English gentleman who had been much interested in the poems of Lucretia Davidson, visited her mother, in order to learn more concerning an author he so much admired. While the two were conversing, Margaret entered with a copy of Thomson's Seasons in her hand, in which she had marked the passages which pleased her. The gentleman, overcoming the child's timidity by his gentleness, soon became as much interested in the younger as in the elder sister, and the little incident led to a friendship which lasted through life.

During the summer she passed a few weeks at Saratoga Springs and New York. She enjoyed her visit to the city greatly, and returned home with improved health. In the winter she removed with her mother to the residence of a married sister in Canada. The tour was undertaken for the health of her parent, but with ill success, as an illness followed, which confined her for eighteen months to her bed, during which her life was often despaired of. The mother recovered, but in January, 1833, the daughter was attacked by scarlet fever, from which she did not become free until April. In May the two convalescents proceeded to New York. Margaret remained here several months, and was the life and soul of the household of which she was the guest. It was proposed by her little associates to act a play, provided she would write one. This she agreed to do, and in two days "produced her drama, *The Tragedy of Alethia*. It was not very voluminous," observes Mr. Irving, "but it contained within it sufficient of high character and astounding and bloody incident to furnish out a drama of five times its size. A king and queen of England resolutely bent upon marrying their daughter, the Princess Alethia, to the Duke of Ormond. The Princess most perversely and dolorously in love with a mysterious cavalier, who figures at her father's court under the name of Sir Percy Lennox, but who, in private truth, is the Spanish king, Rodrigo, thus obliged to maintain an incognito on account of certain hostilities between Spain and England. The odious nuptials of the princess with the Duke of Ormond proceed: she is led, a submissive victim, to the altar; is on the point of pledging her irrevocable word; when the priest throws off his sacred robe, discovers himself to be Rodrigo, and plunges a dagger into the bosom of the king. Alethia instantly plucks the dagger from her father's bosom, throws herself into Rodrigo's arms, and kills herself. Rodrigo flies to a cavern, renounces England, Spain, and his royal throne, and devotes himself to eternal remorse. The queen ends the play by a passionate apostrophe to the spirit of her daughter, and sinks dead on the floor.

"The little drama lies before us, a curious specimen of the prompt talent of this most ingenious child, and by no means more incongruous in its incidents than many current dramas by veteran and experienced playwrights.

"The parts were now distributed and soon learnt; Margaret drew out a play-bill in theatrical style, containing a list of the dramatis personæ, and issued regular tickets of admission. The piece went off with universal applause; Margaret figuring, in a long train, as the princess, and killing herself in a style that would not have disgraced an experienced stage heroine."

In October she returned home to Ballston, the family residence having been changed from Plattsburgh, as the climate on the lake had been pronounced too trying for her constitution. She amused the family, old and young, during the winter, by writing a weekly paper called *The Juvenile Aspirant*. Her education was still conducted by her mother, who was fully competent to the task, and unwilling to trust her at a boarding-school. She studied Latin with her brother, under a private tutor. When she was eleven her delicate frame, rendered still more sensitive by a two months' illness, received a severe shock from the intelligence of the death of her sister, resident in Canada. A change of scene being thought desirable, she paid another visit to New York, where she remained until June. In December she was attacked by a liver complaint, which confined her to her room until Spring. "During this fit of illness her mind had remained in an unusual state of inactivity; but with the opening of spring and the faint return of health, it broke forth with a brilliancy and a restless excitability that astonished and alarmed. 'In conversation,' says her mother, 'her sallies of wit were dazzling. She composed and wrote incessantly, or rather would have done so, had I not interposed my authority to prevent this unceasing tax upon both her mental and physical strength. Fugitive pieces were produced every day, such as *The Shunamite*, *Belshazzar's Feast*, *The Nature of Mind*, *Boabdil el Chico*, &c. She seemed to exist only in the regions of poetry.' We cannot help thinking that these moments of intense poetical exaltation sometimes approached to delirium, for we are told by her mother that 'the image of her departed sister Lucretia mingled in all her aspirations; the holy elevation of Lucretia's character had taken deep hold of her imagination, and in her moments of enthusiasm she felt that she had close and intimate communion with her beautiful spirit.'"

In the autumn of 1835 the family removed to a pleasant residence, "Ruremont," near the Shot Tower, on Long Island Sound, below Hell Gate.

Here Mrs. Davidson received a letter from her English visitor, inviting Margaret and herself to pass the winter with him and the wife he had recently married at Havana.

Margaret M. Davidson

The first winter at the new home was a mournful one, for it was marked by the death of her little brother Kent. Margaret's own health was also rapidly failing—the fatal symptoms of consumption having already appeared. The accumulated grief was too much for the mother's feeble frame. "For three weeks," she says, "I hovered upon the borders of the grave, and when I arose from this bed of pain—so feeble that I could not sustain my own weight, it was to witness the rupture of a blood-vessel in her lung, caused by exertions to suppress a cough."

"Long and anxious were the days and nights spent in watching over her. Every sudden movement or emotion excited the hemorrhage. 'Not a murmur escaped her lips,' says her mother, 'during her protracted sufferings. "How are you, my love? how have you rested during the night?" "Well, dear mamma; I have slept sweetly." I have been night after night beside her restless couch, wiped the cold dew from her brow, and kissed her faded cheek in all the agony of grief, while she unconsciously slept on; or if she did awake, her calm sweet smile, which seemed to emanate from heaven, has, spite of my reason, lighted my heart with hope. Except when very ill, she was ever a bright dreamer. Her visions were usually of an unearthly cast: about heaven and angels. She was wandering among the stars; her sainted sisters were her pioneers; her cherub brother walked hand in hand with her through the gardens of paradise! I was always an early riser, but after Margaret began to decline I never disturbed her until time to rise for breakfast, a season of social intercourse in which she delighted to unite, and from which she was never willing to be absent. Often when I have spoken to her she would exclaim, "Mother, you have disturbed the brightest visions that ever mortal was blessed with! I was in the midst of such scenes of delight! Cannot I have time to finish my dream?" And when I told her how long it was until breakfast, "it will do," she would say, and again lose herself in her bright imaginings; for I considered these as moments of inspiration rather than sleep. She told me it was not sleep. I never knew but one except Margaret, who enjoyed this delightful and mysterious source of happiness—that one was her departed sister Lucretia. When awaking from these reveries, an almost ethereal light played about her eye, which seemed to irradiate her whole face. A holy calm pervaded her manner, and in truth she looked more like an angel who had been communing with kindred spirits in the world of light, than anything of a grosser nature.'"

It was during this illness that Margaret became acquainted with Miss Sedgwick. The disease unexpectedly yielding to care and skill, the invalid was enabled during the summer to make a tour to the western part of New York. Soon after her return, in September, the air of the river having been pronounced unfavorable for her health, the family removed to New York. Margaret persevered in the restrictions imposed by her physicians against composition and study for six months; but was so unhappy in her inactive state, that with her mother's consent she resumed her usual habits. In May, 1837, the family returned to Ballston. In the fall an attack of bleeding at the lungs necessitated an order from her physicians that she should pass the winter within doors. The quiet was of service to her health. We have a pleasant and touching picture of her Christmas, in one of her poems written at the time.

* TO MY MOTHER AT CHRISTMAS.

Wake, mother, wake to hope and glee,
  The golden sun is dawning!
Wake, mother, wake, and hail with me
  This happy Christmas morning!

Each eye is bright with pleasure's glow,
  Each lip is laughing merrily;
A smile hath passed o'er winter's brow,
  And the very snow looks cheerily.

Hark to the voice of the awakened day,
  To the sleigh-bells gaily ringing,
While a thousand, thousand happy hearts
  Their Christmas lays are singing.

'Tis a joyous hour of mirth and love,
  And my heart is overflowing!
Come, let us raise our thoughts above,
  While pure, and fresh, and glowing.

'Tis the happiest day of the rolling year,
  But it comes in a robe of mourning,
Nor light, nor life, nor bloom is here
  Its icy shroud adorning.

It comes when all around is dark,
  'Tis meet it so should be,
For its joy is the joy of the happy heart,
  The spirit's jubilee.

It does not need the bloom of spring,
  Or summer's light and gladness,
For love has spread her beaming wing,
  O'er winter's brow of sadness.

'Twas thus he came, beneath a cloud
  His spirit's light concealing,
No crown of earth, no kingly robe
  His heavenly power revealing.

His soul was pure, his mission love,
  His aim a world's redeeming;
To raise the darkened soul above
  Its wild and sinful dreaming.

With all his Father's power and love,
  The cords of guilt to sever;
To ope a sacred fount of light,
  Which flows, shall flow for ever.

Then we shall hail the glorious day,
  The spirit's new creation,
And pour our grateful feelings forth,
  A pure and warm libation.

Wake, mother, wake to chastened joy,
  The golden sun is dawning!
Wake, mother, wake, and hail with me
  This happy Christmas morning.

The winter was occupied by a course of reading in history, and by occasional composition. In May the family removed to Saratoga. Margaret fancied herself, under the balmy influences of the season, much better—but all others had abandoned hope. It is a needless and painful task to trace step by step the progress of disease. The closing scene came on the 25th of the following November.

The poetical writings of Lucretia Davidson, which have been collected, amount in all to two hundred and seventy-eight pieces, among which are five of several cantos each. A portion of these were published, with a memoir by Professor S. B. F. Morse, in 1829. The volume was well received, and noticed in a highly sympathetic and laudatory manner by Southey, in the Quarterly Review.* The poems were reprinted, with a life by Miss Sedgwick, which had previously appeared in Sparks's American Biography.

Margaret's poems were introduced to the world under the kind auspices of Washington Irving. Revised editions of both were published in 1850 in one volume, a happy companionship which will doubtless be permanent.

A volume of *Selections from the Writings of Mrs. Margaret M. Davidson, the Mother of Lucretia Maria and Margaret M. Davidson, with a preface by Miss C. M. Sedgwick*, appeared in 1844. It contains a prose tale, *A Few Eventful Days in* 1814; a poetical version of Ruth and of Ossian's McFingal, with a few Miscellaneous Poems.

Lieutenant L. P. Davidson, of the U. S. army, the brother of Margaret and Lucretia, who also died young, wrote verses with elegance and ease.†

EMMA C EMBURY.

Mrs. Embury, the wife of Mr. Daniel Embury, a gentleman of wealth and distinguished by his intellectual and social qualities, a resident of Brooklyn, New York, is the daughter of James R. Manly, for a long while an eminent New York physician. She early became known to the public as a writer of verses in the columns of the New York Mirror and other journals under the signature of "Ianthe." In the year 1828 a volume from her pen was published, *Guido, and Other Poems, by Ianthe.* This was followed by a volume on *Female Education*, and a long series of tales and sketches in the magazines of the day, which were received with favor for their felicitous sentiment and ease in composition. Constance Latimer is one of these, which has given title to a collection of the stories, *The Blind Girl and Other Tales.* Her *Pictures of Early Life, Glimpses of Home Life or Causes and Consequences*, are similar volumes. In 1845 she contributed the letter-press, both prose and verse, to an illustrated volume in quarto, *Nature's Gems, or American Wild Flowers.* She has also written a volume of poems, *Love's Token-Flowers*, in which these symbols of sentiment are gracefully interpreted. In 1848 appeared her volume, *The Waldorf Family, or Grandfather's Legends*, in which the romantic lore of Brittany is presented to the young.

Emma C. Embury

These writings, which exhibit good sense and healthy natural feeling, though numerous, are to be taken rather as illustrations of domestic life and retired sentiment than as the occupation of a professed literary career.

Of her poetry, her songs breathe an air of nature, with much sweetness.

BALLAD.

The maiden sat at her busy wheel,
  Her heart was light and free,
And ever in cheerful song broke forth
  Her bosom's harmless glee:
Her song was in mockery of love,
  And oft I heard her say,
"The gathered rose and the stolen heart
  Can charm but for a day."

I looked on the maiden's rosy cheek,
  And her lip so full and bright,
And I sighed to think that the traitor love
  Should conquer a heart so light:
But she thought not of future days of woe,
  While she carolled in tones so gay—
"The gathered rose and the stolen heart
  Can charm but for a day."

A year passed on, and again I stood
  By the humble cottage door;
The maid sat at her busy wheel,
  But her look was blithe no more;
The big tear stood in her downcast eye,
  And with sighs I heard her say,
"The gathered rose and the stolen heart
  Can charm but for a day."

Oh, well I knew what had dimmed her eye,
  And made her cheek so pale:
The maid had forgotten her early song,
  While she listened to love's soft tale;
She had tasted the sweets of his poisoned cup,
  It had wasted her life away—
And the stolen heart, like the gathered rose,
  Had charmed but for a day.

---

* The following lines were addressed from Greta Hall, in 1842, by Caroline Southey, "To the Mother of Lucretia and Margaret Davidson."

Oh, lady! greatly favored! greatly tried!
  Was ever glory, ever grief like thine,
  Since her's,—the mother of the Man divine—
The perfect one—the crowned, the crucified?
Wonder and joy, high hopes and chastened pride
  Thrilled thee; intently watching, hour by hour,
  The fast unfolding of each human flower,
In hues of more than earthly brilliance dyed—
And then, the blight—the fading—the first fear—
  The sickening hope—the doom—the end of all;
Heart-withering, if indeed all ended here.
  But from the dust, the coffin, and the pall,
Mother bereaved! thy tearful eyes upraise—
Mother of angels! join their songs of praise.

† Some lines from his pen, entitled *Longings for the West*, are printed in the South. Lit. Mess. for Feb. 1843.

LINES SUGGESTED BY THE MORAVIAN BURIAL-GROUND AT BETHLEHEM.

When in the shadow of the tomb
  This heart shall rest,
Oh! lay me where spring flow'rets bloom
  On earth's bright breast.

Oh! ne'er in vaulted chambers lay
  My lifeless form;
Seek not of such mean, worthless prey
  To cheat the worm.

In this sweet city of the dead
  I fain would sleep,
Where flowers may deck my narrow bed,
  And night dews weep.

But raise not the sepulchral stone
  To mark the spot;
Enough, if by thy heart alone
  'Tis ne'er forgot.

ABSENCE.

Come to me, love; forget each sordid duty
  That chains thy footsteps to the crowded mart,
Come, look with me upon earth's summer beauty,
  And let its influence cheer thy weary heart.
    Come to me, love!

Come to me, love; the voice of song is swelling
  From nature's harp in every varied tone,
And many a voice of bird and bee is telling
  A tale of joy amid the forests lone.
    Come to me, love!

Come to me, love; my heart can never doubt thee,
  Yet for thy sweet companionship I pine;
Oh, never more can joy be joy without thee,
  My pleasures, even as my life, are thine.
    Come to me, love!

OH! TELL ME NOT OF LOFTY FATE.

Oh! tell me not of lofty fate,
  Of glory's deathless name;
The bosom love leaves desolate,
  Has naught to do with fame.

Vainly philosophy would soar—
  Love's height it may not reach;
The heart soon learns a sweeter lore
  Than ever sage could teach.

The cup may bear a poisoned draught,
  The altar may be cold,
But yet the chalice will be quaffed—
  The shrine sought as of old.

Man's sterner nature turns away
  To seek ambition's goal!
Wealth's glittering gifts, and pleasure's ray,
  May charm his weary soul;

But woman knows one only dream—
  That broken, all is o'er;
For on life's dark and sluggish stream
  Hope's sunbeam rests no more.

CAROLINE LEE HENTZ.

Mrs. Hentz is a daughter of General John Whiting, and a native of Lancaster, Massachusetts. She married, in 1825, Mr. N. M. Hentz, a French gentleman, at that time associated with Mr. Bancroft in the Round Hill School at Northampton. Mr. Hentz was soon after appointed Professor in the college at Chapel Hill, North Carolina, where he remained for several years. They then removed to Covington, Kentucky, and afterwards to Cincinnati and Florence, Alabama. Here they conducted for nine years a prosperous female Academy, which in 1843 was removed to Tuscaloosa, in 1845 to Tuskegee, and in 1848 to Columbus, Georgia.

While at Covington, Mrs. Hentz wrote the tragedy of *De Lara, or the Moorish Bride*, for the prize of $500, offered by the Arch Street Theatre, of Philadelphia. She was the successful competitor, and the play was produced, and performed for several nights with applause. It was afterwards published.

In 1843 she wrote a poem, *Human and Divine Philosophy*, for the Erosophic Society of the University of Alabama, before whom it was delivered by Mr. A. W. Richardson.

In 1846 Mrs. Hentz published *Aunt Patty's Scrap Bag*, a collection of short stories which she had previously contributed to the magazines. This was followed by *The Mob Cap*, 1848; *Linda, or the Young Pilot of the Belle Creole*, 1850; *Rena, or the Snow Bird*, 1851; *Marcus Warland, or the Long Moss Spring; Eoline, or Magnolia Vale*, 1852; *Wild Jack; Helen and Arthur, or Miss Thusa's Spinning Wheel*, 1853; *The Planter's Northern Bride*, two volumes, the longest of her novels, in 1854.

Mrs. Hentz has also written a number of fugitive poems which have appeared in various periodicals. Her second tragedy, *Lamorah, or the Western Wilds*, an Indian play, was performed, and published in a newspaper at Columbus. The scenes and incidents of her stories are for the most part drawn from the Southern states, and are said to be written in the midst of her social circle, and in the intervals of the ordinary avocations of a busy life.

THE SNOW FLAKES.

Ye're welcome, ye white and feathery flakes,
That fall like the blossoms the summer wind shakes
From the bending spray—Oh! say do ye come,
With tidings to me, from my far distant home?

"Our home is above in the depths of the sky—
In the hollow of God's own hand we lie—
We are fair, we are pure, *our* birth is divine—
Say, what can we know of thee, or of thine?"

I know that ye dwell in the kingdoms of air—
I know ye are heavenly, pure, and fair;
But oft have I seen ye, far travellers roam,
By the cold blast driven, round my northern home.

"We roam over mountain, and valley, and sea,
We hang our pale wreaths on the leafless tree:
The herald of wisdom and mercy we go,
And perchance the far home of thy childhood we know.

"We roam, and our fairy track we leave,
While for nature a winding sheet we weave—
A cold, white shroud that shall mantle the gloom,
Till her Maker recalls her to glory and bloom."

Oh! foam of the shoreless ocean above!
I know thou descendest in mercy and love:
All chill as thou art, yet benign is thy birth,
As the dew that impearls the green bosom of Earth.

And I've thought as I've seen thy tremulous spray,
Soft curling like mist on the branches lay,
In bright relief on the dark blue sky,
That thou meltest in grief when the sun came nigh.

"Say, whose is the harp whose echoing song
Breathes wild on the gale that wafts us along?

The moon, the flowers, the blossoming tree,
Wake the minstrel's lyre, they are brighter than
we."

The flowers shed their fragrance, the moonbeams
their light,
Over scenes never veiled by your drap'ry of white;
But the clime where I first saw your downy flakes
fall,
My own native clime is far dearer than all.

Oh! fair, when ye clothed in their wintry mail,
The elms that o'ershadow my home in the vale,
Like warriors they looked, as they bowed in the
storm,
With the tossing plume and the towering form.

Ye fade, ye melt—I feel the warm breath
Of the redolent South o'er the desolate heath—
But tell me, ye vanishing pearls, where ye dwell,
When the dew-drops of Summer bespangle the
dell?

"We fade,—we melt into crystalline spheres—
We weep, for we pass through a valley of tears;
But onward to glory—away to the sky—
In the hollow of God's own hand we lie."

SARAH HELEN WHITMAN.

Mrs. Whitman is a daughter of Mr. Nicholas Power, of Providence, a direct descendant of a follower of Roger Williams in his banishment. She was married at an early age to Mr. John Winslow Whitman, a descendant of Governor Winslow, with whom she removed to Boston, where her husband practised law with eminent success. He was soon after attacked by a disease which in a brief period closed his life. His widow returned to her native city of Providence, where she has since resided.

Sarah Helen Whitman

Mrs. Whitman published in 1853 *Hours of Life and Other Poems*, a few of which are translations from the German. She is also the author of three ballads founded on the fairy stories of the Golden Ball, the Sleeping Beauty, and Cinderella, portions of which are from the pen of her sister, Miss Anna Marsh Power; and of several elaborate critical articles on German and other authors of modern Europe, in the chief languages of which she is a proficient.

Mrs. Whitman's volume of poems is a book of a rare passionate beauty, marked by fine mental characteristics. The chief poem, "Hours of Life," is a picture of the soul in its progress through time, and its search out of disappointment and experience for peace and security. Its learned philosophical spirit is not less remarkable than its tenderness and spiritual melody.

The volume also contains numerous descriptions of scenery and poems of sentiment, in which passion is intimately blended with nature. Several of these are devoted to the memory of the late Edgar A. Poe, whose wild poetic creations and melancholy career have awakened in the author's mind a peculiar sympathy and imaginative interest.

QUEST OF THE SOUL—FROM THE HOURS OF LIFE.

* * * * * * * * * *

O'erwearied with life's restless change
From extacy to agony,
Its fleeting pleasures born to die,
The mirage of its phantasie,
Its worn and melancholy range
Of hopes that could no more estrange
The married heart of memory,
Doomed, while we drain life's perfumed wine,
For the dull Lethean wave to pine,
And, for each thrill of joy, to know
Despair's slow pulse or sorrow's throe—
I sought some central truth to span
These wide extremes of good and ill—
I longed with one bold glance to scan
Life's perfect sphere,—to rend at will
The gloom of Erebus,—dread zone—
Coiled like a serpent round the throne
Of heaven,—the realm where Justice veils
Her heart and holds her even scales,—
Where awful Nemesis awaits
The doomed, by Pluto's iron gates.

In the long noon-tide of my sorrow,
I questioned of the eternal morrow;
I gazed in sullen awe
Far through the illimitable gloom
Down-deepening like the swift mælstroom,
The doubting soul to draw
Into eternal solitudes,
Where unrelenting silence broods
Around the throne of Law.

I questioned the dim chronicle
Of ages gone before—
I listened for the triumph songs
That rang from shore to shore,
Where the heroes and the conquerors wrought
The mighty deeds of yore—
Where the foot-prints of the martyrs
Had bathed the earth in gore,
And the war-horns of the warriors
Were heard from shore to shore.

Their blood on desert plains was shed—
Their voices on the wind had fled—
They were the drear and shadowy Dead!

Still, through the storied past, I sought
An answer to my sleepless thought;
In the cloisters old and hoary
Of the mediæval time—
In the rude ancestral story
Of the ancient Runic rhyme.

I paused on Grecian plains, to trace
Some remnant of a mightier race,
Serene in sorrow and in strife,
Calm conquerors of Death and Life,
Types of the god-like forms that shone
Upon the sculptured Parthenon.

But still, as when Prometheus bare
From heaven the fiery dart,
I saw the "vulture passions" tear
The proud Caucasian heart—
The war of destiny with will
Still conquered, yet conflicting still.

I heard loud Hallelujas
From Israel's golden lyre,
And I sought their great Jehovah
In the cloud and in the fire.
I lingered by the stream that flowed
"Fast by the oracle of God"—
I bowed, its sacred wave to sip—

Its waters fled my thirsting lip.
The serpent trail was over all
Its borders,—and its palms that threw
Aloft their waving coronal,
Were blistered by a poison dew.

Serener elements I sought,
Sublimer altitudes of thought,
The truth Saint John and Plato saw,
The mystic light, the inward law;
The Logos ever found and lost,
The aureola of the Ghost.

I hailed its faint auroral beam
In many a Poet's delphic dream,
On many a shrine where faith's pure flame
Through fable's gorgeous oriel came.
Around the altars of the god,
In holy passion hushed, I trod,
Where once the mighty voice of Jove
Rang through Dodona's haunted grove.
No more the dove with sable plumes*
Swept through the forest's gorgeous glooms;
The shrines were desolate and cold,
Their pæans hushed, their story told,
In long, inglorious silence lost,
Like fiery tongues of Pentecost.

No more did music's golden surge
The mortal in immortal merge:
High canticles of joy and praise
Died with the dream of other days;
I only heard the Mænad's wail,
That shriek that made the orient pale:
Evohe!—ah evohe!
The mystic burden of a woe
Whose dark enigma none may know; †
The primal curse—the primal throe.
Evohe!—ah—evohe!
Nature shuddered at the cry
Of that ancient agony.

Still the fabled Python bound me—
Still the serpent coil enwound me—
Still I heard the Mænad's cry,
Evohe!—ah—evohe!

* * * * * * * * * *

Wearied with man's discordant creed,
I sought on Nature's page to read
Life's history, ere yet she shrined
Her essence in the incarnate mind;
Intent her secret laws to trace
In primal solitudes of space,
From her first, faint atomic throes,
To where her orbéd splendor glows
In the vast, silent spheres that roll
For ever towards their unknown goal.

I turned from dull alchemic lore
With starry Chaldeans to soar,
And sought, on fancy's wing, to roam
That glorious galaxy of light
Where mingling stars, like drifting foam,
Melt on the solemn shores of night;
But still the surging glory chased
The dark through night's chaotic waste,
And still, within its deepening voids,
Crumbled the burning asteroids.

Long gloating on that hollow gloom,
Methought that in some vast maelstroom,
The stars were hurrying to their doom,—
Bubbles upon life's boundless sea,
Swift meteors of eternity,
Pale sparks of mystic fire, that fall
From God's unwaning coronal.

Is there, I asked, a living woe
In all those burning orbs that glow
Through the blue ether!—do they share
Our dim world's anguish and despair—
In their vast orbits do they fly
From some avenging destiny—
And shall their wild eyes pale beneath
The dread anathema of Death!

Our own fair earth—shall she too drift,
For ever shrouded in a weft
Of stormy clouds, that surge and swirl
Around her in her dizzy whirl:—
For ever shall a shadow fall
Backward from her golden wall,
Its dark cone stretching, ghast and grey,
Into outer glooms away!—

From the sad, unsated quest
Of knowledge, how I longed to rest
On her green and silent breast!

I languished for the dews of death
My fevered heart to steep,
The heavy, honey-dews of death,
The calm and dreamless sleep.

I left my fruitless lore apart,
And leaned my ear on Nature's heart,
To hear, far from life's busy throng,
The chime of her sweet undersong.
She pressed her balmy lips to mine,
She bathed me in her sylvan springs;
And still, by many a rural shrine,
She taught me sweet and holy things.
I felt her breath my temples fan,
I learned her temperate laws to scan,
My soul, of hers, became a conscious part;
Her beauty melted through my inmost heart.

Still I languished for the word
Her sweet lips had never spoken,
Still, from the pale shadow-land,
There came nor voice nor token;
No accent of the Holy Ghost
Whispered of the loved and lost;
No bright wanderer came to tell
If, in worlds beyond the grave,
Life, love, and beauty, dwell.

* * * * * * * * * * *

A holy light began to stream
Athwart the cloud-rifts, like a dream
Of heaven; and lo! a pale, sweet face,
Of mournful grandeur and imperial grace—
A face whose mystic sadness seemed to borrow
Immortal beauty from that mortal sorrow—
Looked on me; and a voice of solemn cheer
Uttered its sweet evangels on my ear;
The open secrets of that eldest lore
That seems less to reveal than to restore.

"Pluck thou the Life-tree's golden fruit,
Nor seek to bare its sacred root;
Live, and in life's perennial faith
Renounce the heresy of death:

* "The priestesses of Dodona assert that two black pigeons flew from Thebes in Egypt; one of which settled in Lybia, the other among themselves: which latter, resting on a beech-tree, declared with a human voice that here was to be the oracle of Jove."—*Herodotus. Book II. ch. 52.*

† "The Mænads, in their wild incantations, carried serpents in their hands, and with frantic gestures, cried out Eva! Eva! Epiphanius thinks that this invocation related to the mother of mankind; but I am inclined to believe that it was the word Epha or Opha, rendered by the Greeks, Ophis, *a serpent.* I take Abaddon to have been the name of the same ophite God whose worship has so long infected the world. The learned Heinsius makes Abaddon the same as the serpent Python."—*Jacob Bryant's Analysis of Ancient Mythology.*

While Mænads cry aloud Evoe, Evoe!
That voice that is contagion to the world.
Shelley's Prometheus.

Believe, and every sweet accord
Of being, to thine ear restored,
Shall sound articulate and clear;
Perfected love shall banish fear,
Knowledge and wisdom shall approve
The divine synthesis of love."

"Royally the lilies grow
On the grassy leas,
Basking in the sun and dew,
Swinging in the breeze.
Doth the wild-fowl need a chart
Through the illimitable air?
Heaven lies folded in my heart;
Seek the truth that slumbers there;
Thou art Truth's eternal heir."

"Let the shadows come and go;
Let the stormy north wind blow:
Death's dark valley cannot bind thee
In its dread abode;
There the Morning Star shall find thee,
There the living God.
Sin and sorrow cannot hide thee—
Death and hell cannot divide thee
From the love of God."

In the mystic agony
On the Mount of Calvary,
The Saviour with his dying eyes
Beheld the groves of Paradise.

"Then weep not by the charnel stone
Nor veil thine eyelids from the sun.
Upward, through the death-dark glides,
The spirit on resurgent tides
Of light and glory on its way:
Wilt thou by the cerements stay?—
Thou the risen Christ shalt see
In redeemed Humanity.
Though mourners at the portal wept,
And angels lingered where it slept,
The soul but tarried for a night,
Then plumed its wings for loftier flight."

"Is thy heart so lonely?—Lo,
Ready to share thy joy and woe,
Poor wanderers tarry at thy gate,
The way-worn and the desolate,
And angels at thy threshold wait:
Would'st thou love's holiest guerdon win—
Arise, and let the stranger in."

"The friend whom not thy fickle will,
But the deep heart within thee, still
Yearneth to fold to its embrace,
Shall seek thee through the realms of space.
Keep the image Nature sealed
On thy heart, by love annealed,
Keep thy faith serene and pure;
Her royal promises are sure,
Her sweet betrothals shall endure."

"Hope thou all things and believe;
And, in child-like trust, achieve
The simplest mandates of the soul,
The simplest good, the nearest goal;
Move but the waters and their pulse
The broad ocean shall convulse."

"When love shall reconcile the will
Love's mystic sorrow to fulfil,
Its fiery baptism to share,—
The burden of its cross to bear,—
Earth shall to equilibrium tend,
Ellipses shall to circles bend,
And life's long agony shall end."

"Then pluck the Life-tree's golden fruit,
No blight can reach its sacred root.
E'en though every blossom fell
Into Hades, one by one,
Love is deeper far than Hell—
Shadows cannot quench the sun."

"Can the child-heart promise more
Than the father hath in store?—
The blind shall see—the dead shall live;
Can the man-child forfeit more
Than the father can forgive?
The Dragon, from his empire driven,
No more shall find his place in Heaven,
'Till e'en the Serpent power approve
The divine potency of love."

"Guard thy faith with holy care,—
Mystic virtues slumber there;
'Tis the lamp within the soul
Holding genii in control:
Faith shall walk the stormy water—
In the unequal strife prevail—
Nor, when comes the dread avatar
From its fiery splendors quail.
Faith shall triumph o'er the grave,
Love shall bless the life it gave."

THE TRAILING ARBUTUS.

There's a flower that grows by the greenwood tree,
In its desolate beauty more dear to me,
Than all that bask in the noontide beam
Through the long, bright summer by fount and stream.
Like a pure hope, nursed beneath sorrow's wing,
Its timid buds from the cold moss spring,
Their delicate hues like the pink sea-shell,
Or the shaded blush of the hyacinth's bell,
Their breath more sweet than the faint perfume
That breathes from the bridal orange-bloom.

It is not found by the garden wall,
It wreathes no brow in the festal hall,
But it dwells in the depths of the shadowy wood,
And shines, like a star, in the solitude.
Never did numbers its name prolong,
Ne'er hath it floated on wings of song,
Bard and minstrel have passed it by,
And left it, in silence and shade, to die.
But with joy to its cradle the wild-bees come,
And praise its beauty with drony hum,
And children love, in the season of spring,
To watch for its earliest blossoming.

In the dewy morn of an April day,
When the traveller lingers along the way,
When the sod is sprinkled with tender green
Where rivulets water the earth, unseen,
When the floating fringe on the maple's crest
Rivals the tulip's crimson vest,
And the budding leaves of the birch-trees throw
A trembling shade on the turf below,
When my flower awakes from its dreamy rest
And yields its lips to the sweet south-west,
Then, in those beautiful days of spring,
With hearts as light as the wild-bird's wing,
Flinging their tasks and their toys aside,
Gay little groups through the wood-paths glide,
Peeping and peering among the trees
As they scent its breath on the passing breeze,
Hunting about, among lichens grey,
And the tangled mosses beside the way,
Till they catch the glance of its quiet eye,
Like light that breaks through a cloudy sky.

For me, sweet blossom, thy tendrils cling
Round my heart of hearts, as in childhood's spring,
And thy breath, as it floats on the wandering air,
Wakes all the music of memory there.
Thou recallest the time when, a fearless child

I roved all day through the wood-walks wild,
Seeking thy blossoms by bank and brae
Wherever the snow-drifts had melted away.

Now as I linger, 'mid crowds alone,
Haunted by echoes of music flown,
When the shadows deepen around my way
And the light of reason but leads astray,
When affections, nurtured with fondest care
In the trusting heart, become traitors there,
When, weary of all that the world bestows,
I turn to nature for calm repose,
How fain my spirit, in some far glen,
Would fold her wings, 'mid thy flowers again!

A STILL DAY IN AUTUMN.

I love to wander through the woodlands hoary,
In the soft gloom of an autumnal day,
When Summer gathers up her robes of glory
And, like a dream of beauty, glides away.

How through each loved, familiar path she lingers,
Serenely smiling through the golden mist,
Tinting the wild grape with her dewy fingers,
Till the cool emerald turns to amethyst,—

Kindling the faint stars of the hazel, shining
To light the gloom of Autumn's mouldering halls,
With hoary plumes the clematis entwining,
Where, o'er the rock, her withered garland falls.

Warm lights are on the sleepy uplands waning
Beneath dark clouds along the horizon rolled,
Till the slant sunbeams through their fringes raining,
Bathe all the hills in melancholy gold.

The moist winds breathe of crispèd leaves and flowers,
In the damp hollows of the woodland sown,
Mingling the freshness of autumnal showers
With spicy airs from cedarn alleys blown.

Beside the brook and on the umbered meadow,
Where yellow fern-tufts fleck the faded ground,
With folded lids beneath their palmy shadow,
The gentian nods, in dewy slumbers bound.

Upon those soft, fringed lids the bee sits brooding
Like a fond lover loth to say farewell;
Or, with shut wings, through silken folds intruding,
Creeps near her heart his drowsy tale to tell.

The little birds upon the hillside lonely,
Flit noiselessly along from spray to spray,
Silent as a sweet, wandering thought, that only
Shows its bright wings and softly glides away.

The scentless flowers, in the warm sunlight dreaming,
Forget to breathe their fulness of delight,—
And through the trancèd woods soft airs are streaming,
Still as the dew-fall of the summer night.

So, in my heart, a sweet, unwonted feeling
Stirs, like the wind in ocean's hollow shell,
Through all its secret chambers sadly stealing,
Yet finds no words its mystic charm to tell.

BLOOMS NO MORE.

Oh primavera, gioventù dell' anno,
Bella madre di fiori,
Tu torni ben, ma teco
Non tornano i sereni
E fortunati di delle mie gioie.
GUARINI.

I dread to see the summer sun
Come glowing up the sky,
And early pansies, one by one,
Opening the violet eye.

Again the fair azalia bows
Beneath her snowy crest;
In yonder hedge the hawthorn blows,
The robin builds her nest;

The tulips lift their proud tiàrs,
The lilac waves her plumes;
And, peeping through my lattice bars,
The rose-acacia blooms.

But she can bloom on earth no more,
Whose early doom I mourn;
Nor Spring nor Summer can restore
Our flower, untimely shorn.

She was our morning glory,
Our primrose, pure and pale,
Our little mountain daisy,
Our lily of the vale.

Now dim as folded violets,
Her eyes of dewy light;
And her rosy lips have mournfully
Breathed out their last good-night.

'Tis therefore that I dread to see
The glowing Summer sun;
And the balmy blossoms on the tree,
Unfolding one by one.

HENRY REED.

HENRY REED, the late Professor of Literature and Moral Philosophy in the University of Pennsylvania, whose sudden death among the passengers of the steamer Arctic cast a shade over the intelligent circle in which he moved, belonged to an old and honored family in the state. His grandfather was Joseph Reed, the President of Pennsylvania, the secretary and confidant of Washington, and the incorruptible patriot, whose memorable answer to a munificent proposal of bribery and corruption from the British commissioners in 1778, is among the oft-repeated anecdotes of the Revolution:—"I am not worth purchasing, but, such as I am, the king of Great Britain is not rich enough to do it."

The wife of this honored lawyer and civilian also holds a place in the memoirs of the Revolution. Esther de Berdt, as she appears from the correspondence and numerous anecdotes in the biography prepared by her grandson, the subject of this notice,* was a lady of marked strength of character and refined disposition. She was the daughter of Dennis de Berdt, a London merchant much connected with American affairs, and the predecessor of Dr. Franklin as agent for the Province of Massachusetts. Having become acquainted with Mr. Reed in the society of Americans in which her father moved, she became his wife under circumstances of mournful interest, after the death of her parent, when removing to America she encountered the struggle of the Revolution, sustaining her family with great fortitude during the necessary absence of her husband on public duties. After acting well her part of a mother in America in those troublous times, and receiving the congratulations of Washington, she died in Philadelphia before the contest was closed, in 1780. The memoir by her grandson is a touching and delicate tribute to her memory,

* The Life of Esther De Berdt, afterwards Esther Reed, of Pennsylvania. Privately printed. Philadelphia: C. Sherman, Printer, 1853.

and a valuable contribution to the historical literature of the country.

Henry Reed

Henry Reed was born in Philadelphia, July 11, 1808. He received his early education in the classical school of James Ross, a highly esteemed teacher of his day in Philadelphia. Passing to the University of Pennsylvania, he attained his degree of Bachelor of Arts in 1825. He then pursued the study of the law in the office of John Sargent, and was admitted to the bar in 1829. After a short interval, he was, in the year 1831, elected Assistant Professor of English Literature in his University, and shortly after Assistant Professor of Moral Philosophy. In 1835 he was elected Professor of Rhetoric and English Literature. It was on a leave of absence from these college duties, that, in the spring of 1854, he left America for a summer visit to Europe, a pilgrimage which he had long meditated; and it was on his return in the ill-fated Arctic that he perished in the wreck of that vessel, September 27 of the same year. He had thus passed one-half of his entire period of life in the literary duties of his college, as professor.

When we add to these few dates, Professor Reed's marriage in 1834 to Elizabeth White Bronson, a grand-daughter of Bishop White, we have completed the external record of his life, save in the few publications which he gave to the world. A diligent scholar, and of a thoroughbred cultivation in the best schools of English literature and criticism, of unwearied habits of industry, he would probably, as life advanced, have further served his country by new offerings of the fruits of his mental discipline and studies.

The chief compositions of Professor Reed were several courses of lectures which he delivered to the public at the University of Pennsylvania, and of which a collection has been published since his death, by his brother, Mr. William B. Reed, with the title, *Lectures on English Literature, from Chaucer to Tennyson.* The tastes, mental habits, and associations of the writer, are fully exhibited in these productions, which cover many topics of moral and social philosophy, besides the criticism of particular authors. As a scholar and thinker, Mr. Reed belonged to a school of English writers who received their first impulses from the genius of Wordsworth and Coleridge. It is characterized by its sound conservatism, reverential spirit, and patient philosophical investigation. He was early brought into communication with Wordsworth, whom he assisted by the supervision and arrangement of an American edition of his poems. The preface to this work, and an elaborate article in the New York Review, of January, 1839, which appeared from his pen, show his devotion to this master of modern poetry. After the death of the poet, he superintended the publication of the American edition of the memoirs by Dr. Christopher Wordsworth.

With the Coleridge family, he maintained a similar correspondence and intimate relation. A memoir which he prepared of Sara Coleridge for the Literary World,* though brief, was so carefully and characteristically executed, that it appeared not long after reprinted entire among the obituaries of the Gentleman's Magazine.

A passage, referring to his foreign tour, from the personal introductory notice prefixed to the Lectures, will exhibit this relation to his English friends.

No American, visiting the Old World as a private citizen, ever received a kinder or more discriminating welcome. The last months of his life were pure sunshine. Before he landed in England, his friends, the family of Dr. Arnold, whom he had only known by correspondence, came on board the ship to receive him; and his earliest and latest hours of European sojourn were passed under the roof of the great poet whose memory he most revered, and whose writings had interwoven themselves with his intellectual and moral being. "I do not know," he said in one of his letters to his family, "what I have ever done to deserve all this kindness." And so it was throughout. In England he was at home in every sense; and scenes, which to the eye were strange, seemed familiar by association and study. His letters to America were expressions of grateful delight at what he saw and heard in the land of his forefathers, and at the respectful kindness with which he was everywhere greeted: and yet of earnest and loyal yearning to the land of his birth—his home, his family, and friends. It is no violation of good taste here to enumerate some of the friends for whose kind welcome Mr. Reed was so much indebted; I may mention the Wordsworths, Southeys, Coleridges, and Arnolds, Lord Mahon, Mr. Baring, Mr. Aubrey De Vere, Mr. Babbage, Mr. Henry Taylor, and Mr. Thackeray—names, one and all, associated with the highest literary or political distinction.

He visited the Continent, and went, by the ordinary route, through France and Switzerland, as far south as Milan and Venice, returning by the Tyrol to Inspruck and Munich, and thence down the Rhine to Holland. But his last associations were with the cloisters of Canterbury (that spot, to my eye, of matchless beauty), the garden vales of Devonshire, the valley of the Wye, and the glades of Rydal. His latest memory of this earth was of beautiful England in her summer garb of verdure. The last words he ever wrote were in a letter of the 20th September to his venerable friend, Mrs. Wordsworth, thanking her and his English friends generally for all she and they had done for him.

Professor Reed edited several books in con-

* No. 290, Aug. 21, 1852.

nexion with his courses of instruction. In 1845 he prepared an edition of Alexander Reid's Dictionary of the English Language, and in 1847 edited "with an introduction and illustrative authorities," G. F. Graham's English Synonymes —the series of poetical citations added by him, being confined to Shakespeare, Milton, and Wordsworth. He also edited American reprints of Thomas Arnold's Lectures on Modern History, and Lord Mahon's History of England from the Peace of Utrecht to the Peace of Paris.

In 1851 he edited the Poetical Works of Thomas Gray, for which he prepared a new memoir, written with his accustomed judgment and precision. An Oration on a True Education was delivered by him before the Zelosophic Society of the University of Pennsylvania in 1848. To this enumeration is to be added a life of his grandfather, Joseph Reed, published in Mr. Sparks's series of American biography.*

The life and correspondence of Joseph Reed have been given to the public at length by Mr. William B. Reed, who is also the author of several published addresses and pamphlets, chiefly on historical subjects. Among them are *A Letter on American History* in 1847, originally written for circulation among a few friends interested in the organization of a department of that study in Girard College; an Address before the Historical Society in Pennsylvania in 1848; an Address before the Alumni of the University of Pennsylvania in 1849; and a Reprint of the original Letters from Washington to Joseph Reed, in connexion with the Sparks and Lord Mahon controversy.†

POETICAL AND PROSE READING.‡

It is a good practical rule to keep one's reading well proportioned in the two great divisions, prose and poetry. This is very apt to be neglected, and the consequence is a great loss of power, moral and intellectual, and a loss of some of the highest enjoyments of literature. It sometimes happens that some readers devote themselves too much to poetry; this is a great mistake, and betrays an ignorance of the true use of poetical studies. When this happens, it is generally with those whose reading lies chiefly in the lower and merely sentimental region of poetry, for it is hardly possible for the imagination to enter truly into the spirit of the great poets, without having the various faculties of the mind so awakened and invigorated, as to make a knowledge of the great prose writers also a necessity of one's nature.

The disproportion lies usually in the other direction—prose reading to the exclusion of poetry. This is owing chiefly to the want of proper culture, for although there is certainly a great disparity of imaginative endowment, still the imagination is part of the universal mind of man, and it is a work of education to bring it into action in minds even the least imaginative. It is chiefly to the wilfully unimaginative mind that poetry, with all its wisdom and all its glory, is a sealed book. It sometimes happens, however, that a mind, well gifted with imaginative power, loses the capacity to relish poetry simply by the neglect of reading metrical literature. This is a sad mistake, inasmuch as the mere reader of prose cuts himself off from the very highest literary enjoyments; for if the giving of power to the mind be a characteristic, the most essential literature is to be found in poetry, especially if it be such as English poetry is, the embodiment of the very highest wisdom and the deepest feeling of our English race. I hope to show in my next lecture, in treating the subject of our language, how rich a source of enjoyment the study of English verse, considered simply as an organ of expression and harmony, may be made; but to readers who confine themselves to prose, the metrical form becomes repulsive instead of attractive. It has been well observed by a living writer, who has exercised his powers alike in prose and verse, that there are readers "to whom the poetical form merely and of itself acts as a sort of veil to every meaning, which is not habitually met with under that form, and who are puzzled by a passage occurring in a poem, which would be at once plain to them if divested of its cadence and rhythm; not because it is thereby put into language in any degree more perspicuous, but because prose is the vehicle they are accustomed to for this particular kind of matter, and they will apply their minds to it in prose, and they will refuse their minds to it in verse."

The neglect of poetical reading is increased by the very mistaken notion that poetry is a mere luxury of the mind, alien from the demands of practical life—a light and effortless amusement. This is the prejudice and error of ignorance. For look at many of the strong and largely cultivated minds, which we know by biography and their own works, and note how large and precious an element of strength is their studious love of poetry. Where could we find a man of more earnest, energetic, practical cast of character than Arnold!—eminent as an historian, and in other the gravest departments of thought and learning, active in the cause of education, zealous in matters of ecclesiastical, political, or social reform; right or wrong, always intensely practical and single-hearted in his honest zeal; a champion for truth, whether in the history of ancient politics or present questions of modern society; and, with all, never suffering the love of poetry to be extinguished in his heart, or to be crowded out of it, but turning it perpetually to wise uses, bringing the poetic truths of Shakespeare and of Wordsworth to the help of the cause of truth; his enthusiasm for the poets breaking forth, when he exclaims, "What a treat it would be to teach Shakspeare to a good class of young Greeks in regenerate Athens; to dwell upon him line by line and word by word, and so to get all his pictures and thoughts leisurely into one's mind, till I verily think one would, after a time, almost give out light in the dark, after having been steeped, as it were, in such an atmosphere of brilliance!"

This was the constitution not of one man alone, but of the greatest minds of the race; for if our Anglo-Saxon character could be analysed, a leading characteristic would be found to be the admirable combination of the practical and the poetical in it. This is reflected in all the best English literature, blending the ideal and the actual, never severing its highest spirituality from a steady basis of sober good sense—philosophy and poetry for ever disclosing affinities with each other. It was no false boast when it was said that "Our great poets have been our best political philosophers;" nor would it be to add, that they have been our best moralists. The reader, then, who, on the one hand, gives himself wholly to visionary poetic dreamings, is false to his Saxon blood; and equally false is he who divor-

* Life and Correspondence of Joseph Reed, Military Secretary of General Washington at Cambridge, President of the Executive Council of Pennsylvania, &c. 2 vols. 8vo. Phila. 1847.

† *Ante*, vol. i. p. 180.

‡ From Professor Reed's Lectures on English Literature.

ces himself from communion with the poets. There is no great philosopher in our language in whose genius imagination is not an active element; there is no great poet in whose character the philosophic element does not largely enter. This should teach us a lesson in our studies of English literature.

For the combination of prose and poetic reading, a higher authority is to be found than the predominant characteristic of the Saxon intellect as displayed in our literature. In the One Book, which, given for the good of all mankind, is supernaturally fitted for all phases of humanity and all conditions of civilization, observe that the large components of it are history and poetry. How little else is there in the Bible! In the Old Testament all is chronicle and song, and the high-wrought poetry of prophecy. In the New Testament are the same elements, with this difference, that the actual and the imaginative are more interpenetrated—narrative and parable, fact and poetry blended in matchless harmony; and even in the most argumentative portion of holy Writ, the poetic element is still present, to be followed by the vision and imagery of the Apocalypse.

Such is the unquestioned combination of poetry and prose in sacred Writ—the best means, we must believe, for the universal and perpetual good of man; and if literature have, as I have endeavored to prove, a kindred character, of an agency to build up our incorporeal being, then does it follow that we should take this silent warning from the pages of Revelation, and combine in our literary culture the same elements of the actual and the ideal or imaginative.

COMPANIONSHIP OF THE SEXES IN THE STUDY OF LITERATURE.

All that is essential literature belongs alike to mind of woman and of man; it demands the same kind of culture from each, and most salutary may the companionship of mind be found, giving reciprocal help by the diversity of their power. Let us see how this will be. In the first place, a good habit of reading, whether in man or woman, may be described as the combination of passive recipiency from the book and the mind's reaction upon it; this equipoise is true culture. But, in a great deal of reading, the passiveness of impression is well nigh all, for it is luxurious indolence, and the reactive process is neglected. With the habitual novel-reader, for instance, the luxury of reading becomes a perpetual stimulant, with no demand on the mind's own energy, and slowly wearing it away. The true enjoyment of books is when there is a co-operating power in the reader's mind—an active sympathy with the book; and those are the best books which demand that of you. And here let me notice how unfortunate and, indeed, mischievous a term is the word "taste" as applied in intercourse with literature or art; a metaphor taken from a passive sense, it fosters that lamentable error, that literature, which requires the strenuous exertion of action and sympathy, may be left to mere passive impressions. The temptation to receive an author's mind unreflectingly and passively is common to us all, but greater, I believe, for women, who gain, however, the advantages of a readier sympathy and a more unquestioning faith. The man's mind reacts more on the book, sets himself more in judgment upon it, and trusts less to his feelings; but, in all this, he is in more danger of bringing his faculties separately into action; he is more apt to be misled by our imperfect systems of metaphysics, which give us none but the most meagre theories of the human mind, and which are destined, I believe, to be swept away, if ever a great philosopher should devote himself to the work of analysing the processes of thought. That pervading error of drawing a broad line of demarcation between our moral and intellectual nature, instead of recognising the intimate interdependence of thought and feeling, is a fallacy that scarce affects the workings of a woman's spirit. If a gifted and cultivated woman take a thoughtful interest in a book, she brings her whole being to bear on it, and hence there will often be a better assurance of truth in her conclusions than in man's more logical deductions, just as, by a similar process, she often shows finer and quicker tact in the discrimination of character. It has been justly remarked, that, with regard "to women of the highest intellectual endowments, we feel that we do them the utmost injustice in designating them by such terms as 'clever,' 'able,' 'learned,' 'intellectual;' they never present themselves to our minds as such. There is a sweetness, or a truth, or a kindness—some grace, some charm, some distinguishing moral characteristic which keeps the intellect in due subordination, and brings them to our thoughts, temper, mind, affections, one harmonious whole."

A woman's mind receiving true culture and preserving its fidelity to all womanly instincts, makes her, in our intercourse with literature, not only a companion, but a counsellor and a helpmate, fulfilling in this sphere the purposes of her creation. It is in letters as in life, and there (as has been well said) the woman "who praises and blames, persuades and resists, warns or exhorts upon occasion given, and carries her love through all with a strong heart, and not a weak fondness—she is the true helpmate."

Cowper, speaking of one of his female friends, writes, "She is a critic by nature and not by rule, and has a perception of what is good or bad in composition, that I never knew deceive her; insomuch that when two sorts of expressions have pleaded equally for the precedence in my own esteem, and I have referred, as in such cases I always did, the decision of the point to her, I never knew her at a loss for a just one."

His best biographer, Southey, alluding to himself, and to the influence exerted on Wordsworth's mind by the genius of the poet's sister, adds the comment, "Were I to say that a poet finds his best advisers among his female friends, it would be speaking from my own experience, and the greatest poet of the age would confirm it by his. But never was any poet more indebted to such friends than Cowper. Had it not been for Mrs. Unwin, he would probably never have appeared in his own person as an author; had it not been for Lady Austin, he never would have been a popular one."

The same principles which cause the influences thus salutary to authorship, will carry it into reading and study, so that by virtue of this companionship the logical processes in the man's mind shall be tempered with more of affection, subdued to less of wilfulness, and to a truer power of sympathy; and the woman's spirit shall lose none of its earnest, confiding apprehensiveness in gaining more of reasoning and reflection; and so, by reciprocal influences, that vicious divorcement of our moral and intellectual natures shall be done away with, and the powers of thought and the powers of affection be brought into that harmony which is wisdom. The woman's mind must rise to a wiser activity, the man's to a wiser passiveness; each true to its nature, they may consort in such just companionship that strength of mind shall pass from each to each; and thus chastened and invigorated, the common humanity of the sexes rises higher than it could be carried by either the powers peculiar to man or the powers peculiar to woman.

Now in proof of this, if we were to analyse the philosophy which Coleridge employed in his judgment on books, and by which he may be said to have made criticism a precious department of literature—raising it into a higher and purer region than was ever approached by the contracted and shallow dogmatism of the earlier schools of critics—it would, I think, be proved that he differed from them in nothing more than this, that he cast aside the wilfulness and self-assurance of the more reasoning faculties; his marvellous powers were wedded to a child-like humility and a womanly confidingness, and thus his spirit found an avenue, closed to feeble and less docile intellects, into the deep places of the souls of mighty poets; his genius as a critic rose to its majestic height, not only by its inborn manly strength, but because, with woman-like faith, it first bowed beneath the law of obedience and love.

It is a beautiful example of the companionship of the manly and womanly mind, that this great critic of whom I have been speaking proclaimed, by both principle and practice, that the sophistications which are apt to gather round the intellects of men, clouding their vision, are best cleared away by that spiritual condition more congenial to the souls of women, the interpenetrating the reasoning powers with the affections.

Coleridge taught his daughter that there is a spirit of love to which the truth is not obscured; that there are natural partialities, moral sympathies, which clear rather than cloud the vision of the mind; that in our communion with books, as with mankind, it is not true that "love is blind." The daughter has preserved the lesson in lines worthy of herself, her sire, and the precious truth embodied in them:

Passion is blind, not love; her wondrous might
Informs with three-fold power man's inward sight;
To her deep glance the soul, at large displayed,
Shows all its mingled mass of light and shade:
Men call her blind, when she but turns her head,
Nor scan the fault for which her tears are shed.
Can dull Indifference or Hate's troubled gaze
See through the secret heart's mysterious maze?
Can Scorn and Envy pierce that "dread abode"
Where true faults rest beneath the eye of God?
Not theirs, 'mid inward darkness, to discern
The spiritual splendours, how they shine and burn.
All bright endowments of a noble mind
They, who with joy behold them, soonest find;
And better none its stains of frailty know
Than they who fain would see it white as snow.

GEORGE STILLMAN HILLARD

Was born at Machias, Maine, September 22, 1808. He was educated at the Boston Latin school, of which he afterwards published some curious reminiscences. He entered Harvard, where his name appears in the catalogue of graduates in 1828, and where, in the senior year of his course, he was one of the editors of the college periodical, The Harvard Register. He next passed to the law school of the college and the office of Charles P. Curtis, where he pursued his legal studies, and soon became an accomplished member of the Suffolk bar. In 1833 or 1834 Mr. Hillard was, with Mr. George Ripley, a conductor of the weekly

Geo. S. Hillard

Unitarian newspaper, the Christian Register. In 1835 he delivered the anniversary address on the Fourth of July before the city authorities. He has been a member of the city council and an influential representative in both branches of the State Legislature.

The literary occupations with which Mr. Hillard has varied an active professional life are numerous. He edited in 1839 a Boston edition of the Poetical Works of Spenser, to which he wrote a critical introduction. In 1843 he was the Phi Beta Kappa orator at Cambridge.

In 1847 he delivered twelve lectures, in the course of the Lowell Institute, on the genius and writings of John Milton, which remain unpublished. Having made a tour to Europe in the years 1846 and 1847, he published in 1853, some time after his return, a record of a portion of his journey, entitled *Six Months in Italy*. It is a book of thoughts, impressions, and careful description of objects of history, art, and of social characteristics of a permanent interest; and has acquired a position with the public seldom accorded to the mere record of personal adventure.

In 1852 Mr. Hillard was chosen by the city council of Boston to deliver the public eulogy, in connexion with the procession and funeral services of the thirtieth of November, in memory of Daniel Webster. His address on this occasion was marked by its ease, dignity, and eloquence.

Besides these writings, Mr. Hillard is the author of a memoir of Captain John Smith, in Mr. Sparks's series of American Biography.

As a contributor to the best journals of his time articles from his pen have frequently appeared on select topics. He was one of the body of excellent writers attached to Mr. Buckingham's New England Magazine, where he wrote a series of Literary Portraits, the articles Selections from the Papers of an Idler, etc. To the North American Review and Christian Examiner he has occasionally furnished critical articles.* In addition to the addresses already enumerated we may mention discourses on Geography and History, read before the American Institute of Instruction, Boston, 1846; on the Dangers and Duties of the Mercantile Profession, before the Mercantile Library Association of Boston, in 1850; and an oration before the New England Society of the Pilgrims of New York, in 1851.

RUINS IN ROME—FROM SIX MONTHS IN ITALY.

The traveller who visits Rome with a mind at all inhabited by images from books, especially if he come from a country like ours, where all is new, enters it with certain vague and magnificent expectations on the subject of ruins, which are pretty sure to end in disappointment. The very name of a ruin paints a picture upon the fancy. We construct at once an airy fabric which shall satisfy all the claims of the imaginative eye. We build it of such material that every fragment shall have a beauty of its own. We shatter it with such graceful desolation that all the lines shall be picturesque, and every broken outline traced upon the sky shall at once charm and sadden the eye. We wreathe it with a becoming drapery of ivy, and crown its battlements with long grass, which gives a voice to the wind

* We may refer to his articles in the North American Review on Sebastian Cabot, vol. xxxiv.; Chief-Justice Marshall, vol. xliii.; Prescott's Mexico, vol. lviii. In the Christian Examiner he has reviewed Ticknor's Spanish Literature, vol. xlviii.; and Everett's Orations and Speeches, vol. xlix.

that waves it to and fro. We set it in a becoming position, relieve it with some appropriate background, and touch it with soft melancholy light—with the mellow hues of a deepening twilight, or, better still, with the moon's idealizing rays.

In Rome, such visions, if they exist in the mind, are rudely dispelled by the touch of reality. Many of the ruins in Rome are not happily placed for effect upon the eye and mind. They do not stand apart in solitary grandeur, forming a shrine for memory and thought, and evolving an atmosphere of their own. They are often in unfavorable positions, and bear the shadow of disenchanting proximities. The tide of population flows now in different channels from those of antiquity, and in far less volume; but Rome still continues a large capital, and we can nowhere escape from the debasing associations of actual life. The trail of the present is everywhere over the past. The forum is a cattle-market strewn with wisps of hay, and animated with bucolical figures that never played upon the pipe of Tityrus, or taught the woods to repeat the name of Amaryllis. The pert villa of an English gentleman has intruded itself into the palace of the Cæsars—as discordant an object to a sensitive Idealist as the pink parasol of a lady's-maid, which put to flight the reveries of some romantic traveller under the shadow of the great pyramid. The Temple of Antoninus Pius is turned into the custom-house. The mausoleum of Augustus is encrusted with paltry houses, like an antique coin embedded in lava, and cannot even be discovered without the help of a guide. The beautiful columns of the Theatre of Marcellus—Virgil's Marcellus—are stuck upon the walls of the Orsini Palace, and defaced by dirty shops at the base. Ancient grandeur is degraded to sordid modern uses. "Mummy is become merchandise; Mizraim cures wounds, and Pharaoh is sold for balsams."

To most men, ruins are merely phenomena, or, at most, the moral of a tale; but to the antiquary they are texts. They have a secondary interest, founded upon the employment they have given to the mind, and the learning they have called forth. We value everything in proportion as it awakens our faculties, and supplies us with an end and aim. The scholar, who finds in a bath or a temple a nucleus for his vague and divergent reading to gather around, feels for it something like gratitude as well as attachment; for though it was merely a point of departure, yet, without it, the glow and ardor of the chase would not have quickened his languid energies into life. Scott, in his introduction to the "Monastery," has described with much truth as well as humor the manner in which Captain Clutterbuck became interested in the ruins of Kennaqhair—how they supplied him with an object in life, and how his health of body and mind improved the moment he had something to read about, think about, and talk about. Every ruin in Rome has had such devoted and admiring students, and many of these shapeless and mouldering fabrics have been the battle-grounds of antiquarian controversy, in which the real points at issue have been lost in the learned dust which the combatants have raised. The books which have been written upon the antiquities of Rome would make a large library; but when we walk down, on a sunny morning, to look at the Basilica of Constantine or the Temple of Nerva, we do not think of the folios which are slumbering in the archives, but only of the objects before us.

THE PICTURESQUE IN ROME—FROM SIX MONTHS IN ITALY.

Every young artist dreams of Rome as the spot where all his visions may be realized; and it would indeed seem that there, in a greater degree than anywhere else, were gathered those influences which expand the blossoms, and ripen the fruit of genius. Nothing can be more delicious than the first experiences of a dreamy and imaginative young man who comes from a busy and prosaic city, to pursue the study of art in Rome. He finds himself transported into a new world, where everything is touched with finer lights and softer shadows. The hurry and bustle to which he has been accustomed are no longer perceived. No sounds of active life break the silence of his studies, but the stillness of a Sabbath morning rests over the whole city. The figures whom he meets in the streets move leisurely, and no one has the air of being due at a certain place at a certain time. All his experiences, from his first waking moment till the close of the day, are calculated to quicken the imagination and train the eye. The first sound which he hears in the morning, mingling with his latest dreams, is the dash of a fountain in a neighboring square. When he opens his window, he sees the sun resting upon some dome or tower, grey with time, and heavily freighted with traditions. He takes his breakfast in the ground-floor of an old palazzo, still bearing the stamp of faded splendor, and looks out upon a sheltered garden, in which orange and lemon trees grow side by side with oleanders and roses. While he is sipping his coffee, a little girl glides in, and lays a bunch of violets by the side of his plate, with an expression in her serious black eyes which would make his fortune if he could transfer it to canvas. During the day, his only difficulty is how to employ his boundless wealth of opportunity. There are the Vatican and the Capitol, with treasures of art enough to occupy a patriarchal life of observation and study. There are the palaces of the nobility, with their stately architecture, and their rich collections of painting and sculpture. Of the three hundred and sixty churches in Rome, there is not one which does not contain some picture, statue, mosaic, or monumental structure, either of positive excellence or historical interest. And when the full mind can receive no more impressions, and he comes into the open air for repose, he finds himself surrounded with objects which quicken and feed the sense of art. The dreary monotony of uniform brick walls, out of which doors and windows are cut at regular intervals, no longer disheartens the eye, but the view is everywhere varied by churches, palaces, public buildings, and monuments, not always of positive architectural merit, but each with a distinctive character of its own. The very fronts of the houses have as individual an expression as human faces in a crowd. His walks are full of exhilarating surprises. He comes unawares upon a fountain, a column, or an obelisk—a pine or a cypress—a ruin or a statue. The living forms which he meets are such as he would gladly pause and transfer to his sketch-book—ecclesiastics with garments of flowing black, and shovel-hats upon their heads—capuchins in robes of brown—peasant girls from Albano, in their holiday boddices, with black hair lying in massive braids, large brown eyes, and broad, low foreheads—beggars with white beards, whose rags flutter picturesquely in the breeze, and who ask alms with the dignity of Roman senators. Beyond the walls are the villas, with their grounds and gardens, like landscapes sitting for their pictures; and then the infinite, inexhaustible Campagna, set in its splendid frame of mountains, with its tombs and aqueducts, its skeleton cities and nameless ruins, its clouds and cloud-shadows, its memories and traditions. He sees the sun go down behind the dome of St. Peter's, and light up the windows of the drum with his red blaze, and the dusky veil of twilight gradually extend over the whole horizon. In the moonlight evenings he walks to the Colosseum, or to the piazza of St. Peter's, or to the ruins of the Forum, and under a light which conceals all that is unsightly, and idealizes all that is impressive, may call up the spirit of the past, and bid the buried majesty of old Rome start from its tomb.

To these incidental influences which train the hand and eye of an artist, indirectly, and through the mind, are to be added many substantial and direct advantages,—such as the abundance of models to draw from, the facility of obtaining assistance and instruction, the presence of an atmosphere of art, and the quickening impulse communicated by constant contact with others engaged in the same pursuits, and animated with the same hopes. If, besides all these external influences, the mind of the young artist be at peace,—if he be exempt from the corrosion of anxious thoughts, and live in the light of hope, there would seem to be nothing wanting to develope every germ of power, and to secure the amplest harvest of beauty.

HUGH MOORE,

A self-educated man, and practical printer, was born in Amherst, N. H., Nov. 19, 1808. He served his time as an apprentice with his brother-in-law, Elijah Mansur, at Amherst; published *Time's Mirror*, a weekly newspaper, at Concord for a short time, in the autumn of 1828; commenced the Democratic Spy at Sanbornton, October, 1829, which was removed to Gilford in 1830, and discontinued in June, the same year. He was afterwards editor of the Burlington Centinel, and at one time connected with the Custom House in Boston. He died at Amherst, February 13, 1837.

The New Hampshire Book, which gives two specimens of his poetical pieces, which were written when he was quite young, speaks of his death as occurring when he was "about entering upon a station of increased honor and responsibility."

OLD WINTER IS COMING.

Old Winter is coming again—alack!
How icy and cold is he!
He cares not a pin for a shivering back—
He's a saucy old chap to white and black—
He whistles his chills with a wonderful knack,
For he comes from a cold countree!

A witty old fellow this Winter is—
A mighty old fellow for glee!
He cracks his jokes on the pretty, sweet miss,
The wrinkled old maiden, unfit to kiss,
And freezes the dew of their lips: for this
Is the way with old fellows like he!

Old Winter's a frolicsome blade I wot—
He is wild in his humor, and free!
He'll whistle along, for "the want of thought,"
And set all the warmth of our furs at naught,
And ruffle the laces by pretty girls bought—
A frolicsome fellow is he!

Old winter is blowing his gusts along,
And merrily shaking the tree!
From morning 'till night he will sing his song—
Now moaning, and short—now howling, and long,
His voice is loud—for his lungs are strong—
A merry old fellow is he!

Old Winter's a tough old fellow for blows,
As tough as ever you see!
He will trip up our *trotters*, and rend our clothes,
And stiffen our limbs from our fingers to toes—
He minds not the cries of his friends or his foes—
A tough old fellow is he!

A cunning old fellow is Winter, they say,
A cunning old fellow is he!
He peeps in the crevices day by day,
To see how we're passing our time away—
And marks all our doings from grave to gay
I'm afraid he is peeping at me!

SPRING IS COMING.

Every breeze that passes o'er us,
Every stream that leaps before us,
Every tree in silvan brightness
Bending to the soft winds' lightness;
Every bird and insect humming
Whispers sweetly, "Spring is coming!"

Rouse thee, boy! the sun is beaming
Brightly in thy chamber now;
Rouse thee, boy! nor slumber, dreaming
Of sweet maiden's eye and brow.
See! o'er Nature's wide dominions,
Beauty revels as a bride;
All the plumage of her pinions
In the rainbow's hues is dyed!

Gentle maiden, vainly weeping
O'er some loved and faithless one;
Rouse thee! give thy tears in keeping
To the glorious morning sun!
Roam thou where the flowers are springing,
Where the whirling stream goes by;
Where the birds are sweetly singing
Underneath a blushing sky!

Rouse thee, hoary man of sorrow!
Let thy grief no more subdue;
God will cheer thee on the morrow,
With a prospect ever new.
Though you now weep tears of sadness,
Like a withered flower bedewed;
Soon thy heart shall smile in gladness
With the holy, just, and good!

Frosty Winter, cold and dreary,
Totters to the arms of Spring,
Like the spirit, sad and weary,
Taking an immortal wing.
Cold the grave to every bosom,
As the Winter's keenest breath;
Yet the buds of joy will blossom
Even in the vale of Death!

B. B. THATCHER.

Benjamin B. Thatcher was born in the state of Maine in the year 1809. His father was a distinguished lawyer, and for many years a representative in Congress. The son, on the completion of his course at Bowdoin College in 1826, commenced the study of law, and was admitted to practice at Boston, where he resided during the remainder of his life. He was a constant contributor to the leading literary periodicals of the day, and in 1832 published a work entitled *Indian Biography*, which forms two volumes of Harpers' Family Library. He afterwards prepared two volumes on *Indian Traits*, for a juvenile series, "The Boys' and Girls' Library," issued by the same house. He also wrote a brief memoir of Phillis Wheatley. In 1838 he visited Europe for the benefit of his health, but returned after passing nearly two years in England, in a worse state than that in which he left home.

He died on the fourteenth of July, 1840. His poems are numerous, and mostly of a meditative and descriptive character. They are all brief, and like most of his prose productions, are scattered over a number of annuals and magazines.

THE LAST REQUEST.

Bury me by the ocean's side—
Oh! give me a grave on the verge of the deep,
Where the noble tide
When the sea-gales blow, my marble may sweep—
And the glistering turf
Shall burst o'er the surf,
And bathe my cold bosom in death as I sleep!

Bury me by the sea—
That the vesper at eve-fall may ring o'er my grave,
Like the hymn of the bee,
Or the hum of the shell, in the silent wave!
Or an anthem roar
Shall be rolled on the shore
By the storm, like a mighty march of the brave!

Bury me by the deep—
Where a living footstep never may tread;
And come not to weep—
Oh! wake not with sorrow the dream of the dead,
But leave me the dirge
Of the breaking surge,
And the silent tears of the sea on my head!

And grave no Parian praise;
Gather no bloom for the heartless tomb,—
And burn no holy blaze
To flatter the awe of its solemn gloom!
For the holier light
Of the star-eyed night,
And the violet morning, my rest will illume:—

And honors more dear
Than of sorrow and love, shall be strown on my clay
By the young green year,
With the fragrant dews and crimson array.—
Oh! leave me to sleep
On the verge of the deep,
Till the skies and the seas shall have passed away!

HANNAH F. GOULD.

HANNAH FLAGG GOULD is the daughter of a soldier of the Revolution, who fought in the battle of Lexington, and served in the army throughout the war. She was born at Lancaster, Vermont, but removed soon after to Newburyport, Mass. While yet a child she lost her mother. Her father survived for several years, his declining age being tenderly cared for and cheered by his constant companion, his daughter, whose subsequent poems contain many touching traces of their intercourse.

Hannah Flagg Gould

Miss Gould's poems, after a favorable reception in several periodicals, were collected in a volume in 1832. By 1835, a second had accumulated, and a third appeared in 1841. In 1846, she collected a volume of her prose contributions, entitled *Gathered Leaves.*

Miss Gould's poems are all short, and simple in subject, form, and expression. They are natural, harmonious, and sprightly. She treats of the patriotic themes of the Revolution, and the scenes of nature and incidents of society about the ordinary path of woman; and her household themes have gained her a widely extended audience.

Some of her prettiest poems were written for children, with whom they are favorites. In 1850, she published *The Youth's Coronal,* a little collection of verses of this class.

THE FROST.

The Frost looked forth one still, clear night,
And whispered, "Now I shall be out of sight,
So through the valley and over the height,
In silence I'll take my way.
I will not go on like that blustering train,
The wind and the snow, the hail and the rain,
Who make so much bustle and noise in vain,
But I'll be as busy as they!"

Then he flew to the mountain, and powdered its crest;
He lit on the trees, and their boughs he drest
In diamond beads—and over the breast
Of the quivering lake, he spread
A coat of mail, that it need not fear
The downward point of many a spear,
That he hung on its margin, far and near,
Where a rock could rear its head.

He went to the windows of those who slept,
And over each pane, like a fairy, crept;
Wherever he breathed, wherever he stepped,
By the light of the morn were seen
Most beautiful things; there were flowers and trees,
There were bevies of birds and swarms of bees;
There were cities with temples and towers; and these
All pictured in silver sheen!

But he did one thing that was hardly fair—
He peeped in the cupboard, and finding there
That all had forgotten for him to prepare,
"Now, just to set them a-thinking,
I'll bite this basket of fruit," said he,
"This costly pitcher I'll burst in three;
And the glass of water they've left for me
Shall 'tchick!' to tell them I'm drinking!"

MARY DOW.

"Come in, little stranger," I said,
As she tapped at my half-open door,
While the blanket pinned over her head,
Just reached to the basket she bore.

A look full of innocence fell
From her modest and pretty blue eye,
As she said, "I have matches to sell,
And hope you are willing to buy.

"A penny a bunch is the price;
I think you'll not find it too much;
They're tied up so even and nice,
And ready to light with a touch."

I asked, "what's your name, little girl?"
"'T is Mary," said she, "Mary Dow."
And carelessly tossed off a curl,
That played o'er her delicate brow.

"My father was lost in the deep,
The ship never got to the shore;
And mother is sad, and will weep,
When she hears the wind blow and sea roar.

"She sits there at home without food,
Beside our poor sick Willie's bed;
She paid all her money for wood,
And so I sell matches for bread.

"For every time that she tries,
Some things she'd be paid for, to make,
And lays down the baby, it cries,
And that makes my sick brother wake.

"I'd go to the yard and get chips,
But then it would make me too sad;
To see men there building the ships,
And think they had made one so bad.

"I've one other gown, and with care,
We think it may decently pass,
With my bonnet that's put by to wear
To meeting and Sunday-school class.

"I love to go there, where I'm taught
Of One, who 's so wise and so good,
He knows every action and thought,
And gives e'en the raven his food.

"For He, I am sure, who can take
Such fatherly care of a bird,
Will never forget or forsake
The children who trust to his word.

"And now, if I only can sell
The matches I brought out to-day,
I think I shall do very well,
And mother 'll rejoice at the pay."

"Fly home, little bird," then I thought,
"Fly home full of joy to your nest!"
For I took all the matches she brought,
And Mary may tell you the rest.

IT SNOWS.

It snows! it snows! from out the sky
The feathered flakes, how fast they fly,
Like little birds, that don't know why
They 're on the chase, from place to place,
While neither can the other trace.
It snows! it snows! a merry play
Is o'er us, on this heavy day!

As dancers in an airy hall,
That hasn't room to hold them all,
While some keep up, and others fall,
The atoms shift, then, thick and swift,
They drive along to form the drift,
That weaving up, so dazzling white,
Is rising like a wall of light

But now the wind comes whistling loud,
To snatch and waft it, as a cloud,
Or giant phantom in a shroud;
It spreads! it curls! it mounts and whirls,
At length a mighty wing unfurls;
And then, away! but, where, none knows,
Or ever will.—It snows! it snows!

To-morrow will the storm be done;
Then, out will come the golden sun:
And we shall see, upon the run
Before his beams, in sparkling streams,
What now a curtain o'er him seems.
And thus, with life, it ever goes;
'Tis shade and shine!—It snows! it snows!

THE VETERAN AND THE CHILD.

"Come, grandfather, show how you carried your gun
To the field, where America's freedom was won,
Or bore your old sword, which you say was new then,
When you rose to command, and led forward your men;
And tell how you felt with the balls whizzing by,
Where the wounded fell round you, to bleed and to die!"

The prattler had stirred, in the veteran's breast,
The embers of fires that had long been at rest.
The blood of his youth rushed anew through his veins;
The soldier returned to his weary campaigns;
His perilous battles at once fighting o'er,
While the soul of nineteen lit the eye of four-score.

"I carried my musket, as one that must be
But loosed from the hold of the dead, or the free!
And fearless I lifted my good, trusty sword,
In the hand of a mortal, the strength of the Lord!
In battle, my vital flame freely I felt
Should go, but the chains of my country to melt!

"I sprinkled my blood upon Lexington's sod,
And Charlestown's green height to the war-drum I trod.
From the fort, on the Hudson, our guns I depressed,
The proud coming sail of the foe to arrest.
I stood at Stillwater, the Lakes and White Plains,
And offered for freedom to empty my veins!

"Dost now ask me, child, since thou hear'st where I've been,
Why my brow is so furrowed, my locks white and thin—
Why this faded eye cannot go by the line,
Trace out little beauties, and sparkle like thine;
Or why so unstable this tremulous knee,
Who bore 'sixty years since,' such perils for thee?

"What! sobbing so quick? are the tears going to start?
Come! lean thy young head on thy grandfather's heart!
It has not much longer to glow with the joy
I feel thus to clasp thee, so noble a boy!
But when in earth's bosom it long has been cold,
A man, thou 'lt recall, what, a babe, thou art told."

HYMN OF THE REAPERS.

Our Father, to fields that are white,
Rejoicing, the sickle we bear,
In praises our voices unite
To thee, who hast made them thy care.

The seed, that was dropped in the soil,
We left, with a holy belief
In One, who, beholding the toil,
Would crown it at length with the sheaf.

And ever our faith shall be firm
In thee, who hast nourished the root;
Whose finger has led up the germ,
And finished the blade and the fruit!

The heads, that are heavy with grain,
Are bowing and asking to fall:
Thy hand is on mountain and plain,
Thou maker and giver of all!

Thy blessings shine bright from the hills,
The valleys thy goodness repeat;
And, Lord, 't is thy bounty that fills
The arms of the reaper with wheat!

Oh! when with the sickle in hand,
The angel thy mandate receives,
To come to the field with his band
To bind up, and bear off thy sheaves,

May we be as free from the blight,
As ripe to be taken away,
As full in the year, to thy sight,
As that which we gather to-day!

Our Father, the heart and the voice
Flow out our fresh off'rings to yield.
The Reapers! the Reapers rejoice,
And send up their song from the field!

PARK BENJAMIN.

Park Benjamin is descended from a New England family, which came originally from Wales. His father resided as a merchant in Demerara, in British Guiana. The son in his infancy suffered from an illness, the improper treatment of which left him with a permanent lameness. He was brought to America, was educated in New England, studied law at Cambridge, and was admitted to practice in Connecticut. He soon, however, withdrew from the law to the pursuits of literature, embarking in the editorship of the New England Magazine in March, 1835, shortly after the retirement of its projector, Mr. Buckingham. In less than a year he brought the work to New York, continuing it with the publishing house of Dearborn and Co., with which he became connected, as the American Monthly Magazine, five volumes of which were published from January, 1836, to June, 1838. He next published the New Yorker, a weekly journal, in association with Horace Greeley; and in January, 1840, established the New World, a weekly newspaper of large size, which met the wants of the day by its cheap, wholesale republication of the English magazine literature. It was also well sustained by a *corps* of spirited writers which the editor drew round him in its original departments. Of those more immediately connected with the conduct of the paper were Epes Sargent, James Aldrich, H. C. Deming, and Rufus W. Griswold; while among the frequent contributors were Judge W. A. Duer, Judge J. D. Hammond, author of the Life and Times of Silas Wright, H. W. Herbert, Charles Lanman, W. M. Evarts, John O. Sargent, John Jay, E. S. Gould, and many others.

Mr. Aldrich was a merchant of New York, and the writer of a number of poems which find a place in the collections, though never brought together by the author into a volume. One of the most popular of these is entitled

A DEATH-BED.

Her suff'ring ended with the day,
  Yet lived she at its close,
And breathed the long, long night away
  In statue-like repose.

But when the sun in all his state,
  Illumed the eastern skies,
She passed through glory's morning-gate,
  And walked in Paradise!

The success of the New World led to the cheap publishing enterprises of Winchester, which were conducted with boldness, and had for the time a marked effect on the book trade.* Mr. Benjamin conducted the New World for nearly five years, when it passed into the hands of Mr. Charles Eames, a writer of marked ability, by whom it was edited for a short time in 1845, when it was finally discontinued. In 1846 Mr. Benjamin projected, at Baltimore, The Western Continent, a weekly newspaper on the plan of the New World. It was published only for a short time. The next year he published another weekly paper on a similar plan, involving a liberal outlay of expenditure, The American Mail, of which twelve numbers were issued from June 5 to August 21.

Since the discontinuance of these newspaper enterprises Mr. Benjamin has frequently appeared before the public with favor and success, in different parts of the country, as a lecturer on popular topics and literature.

Park Benjamin

Mr. Benjamin's poems, lyrics, and occasional effusions are numerous, but have not been collected. They are to be found scattered over the entire periodical literature of the country for the last twenty years. His only distinct publications have been several college poems of a descriptive and satirical character. A poem on *The Meditation of Nature* was delivered before the alumni of Washington College, at Hartford, in 1832; *Poetry, a Satire*, before the Mercantile Library Association of New York, the same year; *Infatuation*, before the Mercantile Library of Boston, in 1844.

THE DEPARTED.

The departed! the departed!
  They visit us in dreams,
And they glide above our memories
  Like shadows over streams,
But where the cheerful lights of home
  In constant lustre burn,
The departed, the departed,
  Can never more return.

The good, the brave, the beautiful,
  How dreamless is their sleep,
Where rolls the dirge-like music
  Of the ever-tossing deep!
Or where the hurrying night winds
  Pale winter's robes have spread
Above their narrow palaces,
  In the cities of the dead!

I look around and feel the awe
  Of one who walks alone
Among the wrecks of former days,
  In mournful ruin strown
I start to hear the stirring sounds
  Among the cypress trees,
For the voice of the departed
  Is borne upon the breeze.

That solemn voice! it mingles with
  Each free and careless strain;
I scarce can think earth's minstrelsy
  Will cheer my heart again.
The melody of summer waves,
  The thrilling notes of birds,
Can never be so dear to me
  As their remembered words.

I sometimes dream their pleasant smiles
  Still on me sweetly fall,
Their tones of love I faintly hear
  My name in sadness call.
I know that they are happy,
  With their angel-plumage on,

* One of the most extensive of the Winchester publications was an entire reprint in numbers of Johns' translation of Froissart's Chronicles. The success of this work, in popular form, at a low price, was a decided triumph for his system. He also made a hit with the early translation of Sue's Mysteries of Paris, which was executed by Mr. Deming.

But my heart is very desolate
 To think that they are gone.

INDOLENCE.

Time! thou destroy'st the relics of the past,
 And hidest all the footprints of thy march
 On shattered column and on crumbled arch,
By moss and ivy growing green and fast.
Hurled into fragments by the tempest-blast,
 The Rhodian monster lies: the obelisk,
 That with sharp line divided the broad disc
Of Egypt's sun, down to the sands was cast:
And where these stood, no remnant-trophy stands,
 And even the art is lost by which they rose:
Thus, with the monuments of other lands,
 The place that knew them now no longer knows.
Yet triumph not, oh, Time; strong towers decay,
But a great name shall never pass away!

SPORT.

To see a fellow of a summer's morning,
 With a large foxhound of a slumberous eye
 And a slim gun, go slowly lounging by,
About to give the feathered bipeds warning,
That probably they may be shot hereafter,
Excites in me a quiet kind of laughter;
For, though I am no lover of the sport
 Of harmless murder, yet it is to me
 Almost the funniest thing on earth to see
A corpulent person, breathing with a snort,
 Go on a shooting frolic all alone;
For well I know that when he's out of town,
He and his dog and gun will all lie down,
 And undestructive sleep till game and light are flown.

STEPHEN GREENLEAF BULFINCH,

A UNITARIAN CLERGYMAN, and contributor to the collection of hymns in use in that denomination, was born in Boston, June 18th, 1809. At nine years of age he was taken to Washington, in the District of Columbia, where his father, Charles Bulfinch, had been appointed architect of the Capitol. He was graduated at the Columbian College, D. C., in 1826, and entered the Divinity School at Cambridge the following year. From 1830 to 1837, with some interruptions, he ministered as a Unitarian clergyman at Augusta, Georgia. After this he preached and kept school at Pittsburgh, Pa., for a short time, and was then engaged in similar relations for six years at Washington, D. C. In 1845 he became settled at Nashua, N. H., and in 1852 removed to Boston, where he has been since established.

His writings are a volume, *Contemplations of the Saviour*, published at Boston in 1832; a volume of *Poems* published at Charleston, South Carolina, in 1834; *The Holy Land*, issued in Ware's Sunday Library in 1834; *Lays of the Gospel*, 1845; a devotional volume, *Communion Thoughts*, 1852; with several sermons and contributions to the Magazines.

LINES ON VISITING TALLULAH FALLS, GEORGIA.

 The forest, Lord! is thine;
Thy quickening voice calls forth its buds to light;
 Its thousand leaflets shine,
Bathed in thy dews, and in thy sunbeams bright.

 Thy voice is on the air,
Where breezes murmur through the pathless shades;
 Thy universal care
These awful deserts, as a spell pervades.

 Father! these rocks are thine,
Of Thee the everlasting monument,
 Since at thy glance divine,
Earth trembled and her solid hills were rent.

 Thine is this flashing wave,
Poured forth by thee from its rude mountain urn,
 And thine yon secret cave,
Where haply, gems of orient lustre burn.

 I hear the eagle scream;
And not in vain his cry! Amid the wild
 Thou hearest! Can I deem
Thou wilt not listen to thy human child?

 God of the rock and flood!
In this deep solitude I feel thee nigh.
 Almighty, wise and good,
Turn on thy suppliant child a parent's eye.

 Guide through life's vale of fear
My placid current, from defilement free,
 Till, seen no longer here,
It finds the ocean of its rest in Thee!

ROBERT CHARLES WINTHROP.

MR. WINTHROP is justly and honorably considered a representative man of Massachusetts. Tracing his descent through six generations of a family always eminent in the state, he arrives at the first emigrant of the name, John Winthrop, who became the first Governor of the colony, and who bore not only the truncheon of office but the pen of the chronicler.*

His son John, the Governor of Connecticut, was also a man of liberal tastes, was one of the founders of the Royal Society, and contributed to its proceedings and collections. His second wife was a step-daughter of Hugh Peters. Of his two sons, one of them, Fitz John, was Governor of Connecticut, and the younger, Wait Still (a family and not a fanciful Puritanical designation), became Chief Justice of the Superior Court of Massachusetts. The latter left a son John, who renewed the connexion with the Royal Society and removed to England. His son John married in New England and was a gentleman of wealth and leisure, passing his time in New London, Conn. His son, Thomas Lindall Winthrop, in the fifth generation of the American founder of the family, filled the position of Lieutenant Governor of Massachusetts. He married a daughter of Sir John Temple, the associate of Franklin in England, and a grand-daughter of Governor James Bowdoin.

Thus honorably connected, in the direct and collateral branches of the family tree, Robert Charles Winthrop was born in Boston, May 12, 1809. He was educated at the Boston Latin school, and once, as "a medal boy," received a set of books from the city authorities. He was graduated at Harvard in 1828. For the next three years he studied law with Daniel Webster. Being a man of fortune, with an inherited taste for public life, he chose employment in affairs of the state in preference to the more private pursuit of the law. He took a prominent part in military affairs as captain of the Boston Light Infantry and other civic stations of the kind. In 1834 he became a member of the Massachusetts State Legislature, and was speaker of its House of Representatives from 1838 till his election to Congress in 1840.

* *Ante*, vol. i. pp. 25-85.

Robt. C. Winthrop.

After seven years' service in the national House of Representatives he was chosen its speaker for the sessions of 1848–9. In 1850 he was appointed by the executive of Massachusetts to succeed Webster in the Senate, when the latter withdrew to the office of Secretary of State under President Fillmore. In 1851 he was a candidate for the office of Governor of Massachusetts, and received 65,000 votes, the two other candidates receiving about 40,000 and 30,000 respectively; but an absolute majority being required for an election by the people, he was defeated by a coalition of the minority parties in the legislature.

Besides his political relations Mr. Winthrop is President of the Massachusetts Historical Society, of which his father was also President, and which he lately represented in 1854, delivering a speech of much ability at the semi-centennial anniversary of the New York Historical Society; a member of the American Antiquarian Society, and of other kindred institutions.

The claims to literary distinction of Mr. Winthrop are through his Addresses and Orations. A series of these is strung along the whole course of his public life; all marked by their careful execution, literary propriety, and marked utility. They are easy, natural, finished performances, whether addressed to the State Legislature or the larger audience of national Representatives; whether in the popular political meeting, at an Agricultural, Scientific, or Historical Anniversary, or at the brilliant Public Dinner The prominent trait of the orator and rhetorician, as he shows himself on these occasions, is self-command; command of himself and of his subject. In person at once lithe and full-formed, tall and erect, he speaks with plenary, distinct tone, without the least effort. Each thought takes its appropriate place in his skilful method, which seems rather the result of a healthy physique of the mind than of art. In temper he is moderate, as his counsels in affairs of state have shown. This disposition is reflected in his discourses. The style has a tendency to expansion which might degenerate into weakness were it not relieved by the frequent points of a poetical or fanciful nature, at times of great ingenuity.

The Congressional speeches of Mr. Winthrop, with others of a special character, are included in a volume of *Addresses and Speeches on Various Occasions*, published in 1852. It includes, besides his political efforts, his address on the laying the corner-stone of the national monument to Washington at the Seat of Government, July 4, 1848; his Maine Historical Society address on the life of James Bowdoin, and several educational and other themes. Since that volume was issued he has published his address before the association of the alumni of Harvard in 1852; a Lecture on Algernon Sidney before the Boston Mercantile Library Association in 1853; and in the same season his Lecture on Archimedes and Franklin, which gave the suggestion and impulse to the erection of a statue of Franklin in Boston.*

PEACE BETWEEN ENGLAND AND AMERICA.†

If it be a fit subject for reproach, to entertain the most anxious and ardent desire for the peace of this country, its peace with England, its peace with all the world, I submit myself willingly to the fullest measure of that reproach. War between the United States and Great Britain for Oregon! Sir, there is something in this idea too monstrous to be entertained for a moment. The two greatest nations on the globe, with more territorial possessions than they know what to do with already, and bound together by so many ties of kindred, and language, and commercial interest, going to war for a piece of barren earth! Why, it would put back the cause of civilization a whole century, and would be enough not merely to call down the rebuke of men, but the curse of God. I do not yield to the honorable gentleman in a just concern for the national honor. I am ready to maintain that honor, whenever it is really at stake, against Great Britain as readily as against any other nation. Indeed, if war is to come upon us, I am quite willing that it should be war with a first-rate power—with a foeman worthy of our steel.

Oh! the blood more stirs,
To rouse a lion, than to start a hare.

If the young Queen of England were the veritable Victoria whom the ancient poets have sometimes described as descending from the right hand of Jupiter to crown the banner of predestined Triumph, I would still not shrink from the attempt to vindicate the rights of my country on every proper occasion. To her forces, however, as well as to ours, may come the "*cita mors*," as well as the "*Victoria læta.*" We have nothing to fear from a protracted war with any nation, though our want of preparation might give us the worst of it in the first encounter. We are all and always ready for war, when there is no other alternative for maintaining our country's honor. We are all and always ready for any war into which a Christian man, in a civilized land, and in this age of the world, can have the face to enter. But I thank God that there are very few such cases. War and honor are fast getting to have less and less to do with each other. The highest honor of any

* "Life and Public Services of R. C. Winthrop," American Review, March, 1848. Loring's Hundred Boston Orators. Wheeler's Biog. and Polit. Hist. of Congress, 1848, vol. i.

† From a Speech in Congress, 1844.

country is to preserve peace, even under provocations which might justify war. The deepest disgrace to any country is to plunge into war under circumstances which leave the honorable alternative of peace. I heartily hope and trust, Sir, that in deference to the sense of the civilized world, in deference to that spirit of Christianity which is now spreading its benign and healing influences over both hemispheres with such signal rapidity, we shall explore the whole field of diplomacy, and exhaust every art of negotiation, before we give loose to that passion for conflict which the honorable gentleman from Pennsylvania seems to regard as so grand and glorious an element of the American character.

OBJECTS AND LIMITS OF SCIENCE.*

There are fields enough for the wildest and most extravagant theorizings, within his own appropriate domain, without overleaping the barriers which separate things human and divine. Indeed, I have often thought that modern science had afforded a most opportune and providential safety-valve for the intellectual curiosity and ambition of man, at a moment when the progress of education, invention, and liberty, had roused and stimulated them to a pitch of such unprecedented eagerness and ardor. Astronomy, Chemistry, and more than all, Geology, with their incidental branches of study, have opened an inexhaustible field for investigation and speculation. Here, by the aid of modern instruments and modern modes of analysis, the most ardent and earnest spirits may find ample room and verge enough for their insatiate activity and audacious enterprise, and may pursue their course not only without the slightest danger of doing mischief to others, but with the certainty of promoting the great e[illegible] of scientific truth.

Let them lift their vast reflectors or refractors to the skies, and detect new planets in their hiding-places. Let them waylay the fugitive comets in their flight, and compel them to disclose the precise period of their orbits, and to give bonds for their punctual return. Let them drag out reluctant satellites from "their habitual concealments." Let them resolve the unresolvable nebulæ of Orion or Andromeda. They need not fear. The sky will not fall, nor a single star be shaken from its sphere.

Let them perfect and elaborate their marvellous processes for making the light and the lightning their ministers, for putting "a pencil of rays" into the hand of art, and providing tongues of fire for the communication of intelligence. Let them foretell the path of the whirlwind and calculate the orbit of the storm. Let them hang out their gigantic pendulums, and make the earth do the work of describing and measuring her own motions. Let them annihilate human pain, and literally "charm ache with air, and agony with *ether*." The blessing of God will attend all their toils, and the gratitude of man will await all their triumphs.

Let them dig down into the bowels of the earth. Let them rive asunder the massive rocks, and unfold the history of creation as it lies written on the pages of their piled up strata. Let them gather up the fossil fragments of a lost Fauna, reproducing the ancient forms which inhabited the land or the seas, bringing them together, bone to his bone, till Leviathan and Behemoth stand before us in bodily presence and in their full proportions, and we almost tremble lest these dry bones should live again! Let them put nature to the rack, and torture her, in all her forms, to the betrayal of her inmost secrets and confidences. They need not forbear. The foundations of the round world have been laid so strong that they cannot be moved.

But let them not think by searching to find out God. Let them not dream of understanding the Almighty to perfection. Let them not dare to apply their tests and solvents, their modes of analysis or their terms of definition, to the secrets of the spiritual kingdom. Let them spare the foundations of faith. Let them be satisfied with what is revealed of the mysteries of the Divine Nature. Let them not break through the bounds to gaze after the Invisible,—lest the day come when they shall be ready to cry to the mountains, Fall on us, and to the hills, Cover us!

* From an Address to the Alumni of Harvard University, 1852.

VISIT OF CICERO TO THE GRAVE OF ARCHIMEDES.*

While Cicero was quæstor in Sicily,—the first public office which he ever held, and the only one to which he was then eligible, being but just thirty years old, (for the Roman laws required for one of the humblest of the great offices of state the very same age which our American Constitution requires for one of the highest,)—he paid a visit to Syracuse, then among the greatest cities of the world.

The magistrates of the city, of course, waited on him at once, to offer their services in showing him the lions of the place, and requested him to specify anything which he would like particularly to see. Doubtless, they supposed that he would ask immediately to be conducted to some one of their magnificent temples, that he might behold and admire those splendid works of art with which,—notwithstanding that Marcellus had made it his glory to carry not a few of them away with him for the decoration of the Imperial City,—Syracuse still abounded, and which soon after tempted the cupidity, and fell a prey to the rapacity, of the infamous Verres.

Or, haply, they may have thought that he would be curious to see and examine the ear of Dionysius, as it was called,—a huge cavern, cut out of the solid rock in the shape of a human ear, two hundred and fifty feet long and eighty feet high, in which that execrable tyrant confined all persons who came within the range of his suspicion,—and which was so ingeniously contrived and constructed, that Dionysius, by applying his own ear to a small hole, where the sounds were collected as upon a tympanum, could catch every syllable that was uttered in the cavern below, and could deal out his proscription and his vengeance accordingly, upon all who might dare to dispute his authority, or to complain of his cruelty.

Or they may have imagined perhaps, that he would be impatient to visit at once the sacred fountain of Arethusa, and the seat of those Sicilian Muses whom Virgil so soon after invoked in commencing that most inspired of all uninspired compositions, which Pope has so nobly paraphrased in his glowing and glorious Eclogue—the Messiah.

To their great astonishment, however, Cicero's first request was, that they would take him to see the tomb of *Archimedes*. To his own still greater astonishment, as we may well believe, they told him in reply, that they knew nothing about the tomb of Archimedes, and had no idea where it was to be found, and they even positively denied that any such tomb was still remaining among them.

But Cicero understood perfectly well what he was talking about. He remembered the exact description of the tomb. He remembered the very verses which had been inscribed on it. He remembered

* From the Lecture, "Archimedes and Franklin," November 29, 1858.

the sphere and the cylinder which Archimedes had himself requested to have wrought upon it, as the chosen emblems of his eventful life. And the great orator forthwith resolved to make search for it himself.

Accordingly, he rambled out into the place of their ancient sepulchres, and, after a careful investigation, he came at last to a spot overgrown with shrubs and bushes, where presently he descried the top of a small column just rising above the branches. Upon this little column the sphere and the cylinder were at length found carved, the inscription was painfully decyphered, and the tomb of Archimedes stood revealed to the reverent homage of the illustrious Roman quæstor.

This was in the year 76 before the birth of our Saviour. Archimedes died about the year 212 before Christ. One hundred and thirty-six years, only, had thus elapsed since the death of this celebrated person, before his tombstone was buried up beneath briers and brambles, and before the place and even the existence of it were forgotten, by the magistrates of the very city, of which he was so long the proudest ornament in peace, and the most effective defender in war.

What a lesson to human pride, what a commentary on human gratitude, was here! It is an incident almost precisely like that which the admirable and venerable Dr. Watts imagined or imitated, as the topic of one of his most striking and familiar Lyrics:—

> Theron, amongst his travels, found
> A broken statue on the ground;
> And searching onward as he went,
> He traced a ruined monument.
> Mould, moss, and shades had overgrown
> The sculpture of the crumbling stone,
> Yet ere he pass'd, with much ado,
> He guessed, and spelled out, Sci-pi-o.
> "Enough," he cried; "I'll drudge no more
> In turning the dull stoics o'er;
> * * * * * * *
> For when I feel my virtue fail,
> And my ambitious thoughts prevail,
> I'll take a turn among the tombs,
> And see whereto all glory comes."

I do not learn, however, that Cicero was cured of his eager vanity and his insatiate love of fame by this "turn" among the Syracusan tombs. He was then only just at the threshold of his proud career, and he went back to pursue it to its bloody end, with unabated zeal, and with an ambition only extinguishable with his life.

And after all, how richly, how surpassingly, was this local ingratitude and neglect made up to the memory of Archimedes himself, by the opportunity which it afforded to the greatest orator of the greatest Empire of antiquity, to signalize his appreciation and his admiration of that wonderful genius, by going out personally into the ancient graveyards of Syracuse, and with the robes of office in their newest gloss around him, to search for his tomb and to do honor to his ashes! The greatest orator of Imperial Rome anticipating the part of Old Mortality upon the gravestone of the great mathematician and mechanic of antiquity! This, surely, is a picture for mechanics in all ages to contemplate with a proud satisfaction and delight.

NATHANIEL HAWTHORNE

Was born at Salem, Massachusetts, of a family of whom we have some glimpses in one of his late prefaces. His earliest American ancestor came from England, in the early part of the seventeenth century, "a soldier, legislator, judge, a ruler in the church;" like the venerable Dudley "no libertine," in his opinions, since he persecuted the Quakers with the best of them. His son was a man of respectability in his day, for he took part in the burning of the witches. The race established by these founders of the family, "from father to son, for above a hundred years followed the sea; a grey-headed shipmaster in each generation retiring from the quarter-deck to the homestead, while a boy of fourteen took the hereditary place before the mast, confronting the salt spray, and the gale which had blustered against his sire and grandsire." From this old home at Salem, bleached and weatherbeaten, like most of the old houses there, Nathaniel Hawthorne went forth one day to College. He was a fellow student with Longfellow at Bowdoin, Maine, where he was graduated in 1825. His earliest acknowledged publications were his series of papers in the *Token*, from year to year; the popular annual conducted by Mr. S. G. Goodrich, who early appreciated the fine sensitive genius which adorned his pages —though the public, which seldom has any profound understanding of literature in a book of amusement, scarcely recognised the new author. A portion of these stories and essays were collected in a volume, with the title *Twice Told Tales*, in 1837. Longfellow reviewed the book with enthusiasm, in the *North American;* but the publication languished, and a second edition was rather urged by his friends than called for by the public, when it appeared with a second series of the *Tales* in 1842.

It was about this time that Hawthorne became connected for a while with the occupants of the Brook Farm at Roxbury; a community of literati and philosophers, who supported the freedom of a rural life by the independent labor of their hands. Hawthorne took part in the affair, dropped his pen for the hoe, and looked over the horns and bristles of the brutes it was his lot to provide for, to the humanities gathered around him. Though he spiritualized the affair quite beyond any recognition of its actual condition, Brook Farm was the seed, in his mind, of the Blithedale Romance.

His next publication was *The Journal of an African Cruiser*, which he re-wrote from the MS. of his friend and college companion, Mr. Horatio Bridge, of the United States Navy. It is a carefully prepared volume of judicious observation of the Canaries, the Cape de Verd, Liberia, Madeira, Sierra Leone, and other places of interest on the West Coast of Africa.

Hawthorne had now changed his residence to Concord, carrying with him his newly married wife, Miss Peabody, where he occupied the Old Manse, which he has described with quaint and touching fidelity in the introduction to the further collection of his papers from the magazines, the New England, the American Monthly, and a new gleaning of the fruitful old Token—to which he gave the title, *Mosses from an Old Manse*. He lived in close retirement in this old spot, concentrating his mind upon his habitual fancies for three years, during which time, if we are to take literally, and it is probably not far from the truth, the pleasant sketch of his residences by his friend, Mr. G. W. Curtis, he was not seen by more than a dozen of the villagers.

In 1846 Mr. Polk was President, and Mr. Bancroft the historian Secretary of the Navy, when

The Old Manse.

Hawthorne's friends secured his appointment as Surveyor in the Custom-House at Salem. He held this post for a year, discharging its duties with unfailing regularity, and meditating the characters of his associates, as the event proved, when he was dismissed on a change of the political powers at Washington, and wrote *The Scarlet Letter*, in the preface to which he gives an account of his Custom-House Experiences, with a literary photograph of that honored building and its occupants.

The *Scarlet Letter* was at last a palpable hit, It was published by Ticknor & Co., and had been wisely enlarged at the suggestion of the author's friend, Mr. J. T. Fields, a member of the firm, from a sketch containing the germ of the story, to an entire volume.

The Scarlet Letter is a pyschological romance. The hardiest Mrs. Malaprop would never venture to call it a novel. It is a tale of remorse, a study of character, in which the human heart is anatomized, carefully, elaborately, and with striking poetic and dramatic power. Its incidents are simply these: A woman, in the early days of Boston, becomes the subject of the discipline of the court of those times, and is condemned to stand in the pillory and wear henceforth, in token of her shame, the scarlet letter A attached to her bosom. She carries her child with her to the pillory. Its other parent is unknown. At this opening scene her husband, from whom she had been separated in Europe, preceding him by ship across the Atlantic, reappears from the forest, whither he has been thrown by shipwreck on his arrival. He was a man of a cold intellectual temperament, and devotes his life thereafter to search for his wife's guilty partner, and a fiendish revenge. The young clergyman of the town, a man of a devout sensibility and warmth of heart, is the victim, as the Mephistophilean old physician fixes himself by his side, to watch over him and protect his health, an object of great solicitude to his parishioners, and, in reality, to detect his suspected secret, and gloat over his tortures. This slow, cool, devilish purpose, like the concoction of some sublimated hell broth, is perfected gradually and inevitably. The wayward, elfish child, a concentration of guilt and passion, binds the interests of the parties together, but throws little sunshine over the scene. These are all the characters, with some casual introductions of the grim personages and manners of the period, unless we add the scarlet letter, which, in Hawthorne's hands, skilled to these allegorical, typical semblances, becomes vitalized as the rest. It is the hero of the volume. The denouement is the death of the clergyman on a day of public festivity, after a public confession, in the arms of the pilloried, branded woman. But few as are these main incidents thus briefly told, the action of the story, or its passion, is "long, obscure, and infinite." It is a drama in which thoughts are acts. The material has been thoroughly fused in the writer's mind, and springs forth an entire perfect creation.

The public, on the appearance of the Scarlet Letter, was for once apprehensive, and the whole retinue of literary reputation-makers fastened upon the genius of Hawthorne. He had retired from Salem to Berkshire, Massachusetts, where he occupied a small, charmingly situated farmer's house at Lenox, on the Lake called the Stockbridge Bowl. There he wrote the *House of the Seven Gables*, published in 1851, one of the most elaborate and powerfully drawn of his later volumes.

In the preface to this work Mr. Hawthorne establishes a separation between the demands of the novel and the romance, and under the privilege of the latter, sets up his claim to a certain degree of license in the treatment of the characters and incidents of his coming story. This license is in the direction of the spiritualities of the piece, in favor of a process semi-allegorical, by which an acute analysis may be wrought out, and the truth of feeling be minutely elaborated; an apology, in fact, for the preference of character to action, and of character for that which is allied to the darker elements of life—the dread blossoming of evil in the soul, and its fearful retributions. The House of the Seven Gables, one for each deadly sin, may be no unmeet adumbration of the corrupted soul of man. It is a ghostly, mouldy abode, built in some eclipse of the sun, and raftered with curses dark; founded on a grave, and sending its turrets heavenward, as the lightning rod transcends its summit, to invite the wrath supernal. Every darker shadow of human life lingers in and about its melancholy shelter. There all the passions allied to crime,—pride in its intensity, avarice with its steely gripe, and unrelenting conscience, are to be expiated in the house built on injustice. Wealth there withers, and the human heart grows cold: and thither are brought as accessories the chill glance of speculative philosophy, the descending hopes of the aged laborer, whose vision closes on the workhouse, the poor necessities of the humblest means of livelihood, the bodily and mental dilapidation of a wasted life.

> A residence for woman, child and man,
> A dwelling-place,—and yet no habitation
> A Home,—but under some prodigious ban
> Of excommunication.
>
> O'er all there hung a shadow and a fear;
> A sense of mystery the spirit daunted,
> And said as plain as whisper in the ear,
> The place is haunted!

Yet the sunshine casts its rays into the old building, as it must, were it only to show us the darkness.

The story of the House of the Seven Gables is a tale of retribution, of expiation, extending over a period of two hundred years, it taking all that while to lay the ghost of the earliest victim, in the time of the Salem witchcraft; for, it is to Salem that this blackened old dwelling, mildewed with easterly scud, belongs. The yeoman who originally struck his spade into the spot, by the side of a crystal spring, was hanged for a wizard, under the afflictive dispensation of Cotton Mather. His land passed by force of law under cover of an old sweeping grant from the State, though not without hard words and thoughts and litigations, to the possession of the Ahab of the Vineyard, Colonel Pyncheon, the founder of the house, whose statuesque death-scene was the first incident of the strongly ribbed tenement built on the ground thus suspiciously acquired. It was a prophecy of the old wizard on his execution at Gallows' Hill, looking steadfastly at his rival, the Colonel, who was there, watching the scene on horseback, that "God would give him blood to drink." The sudden death of apoplexy was thereafter ministered to the magnates of the Pyncheon family. After an introductory chapter detailing this early history of the house, we are introduced to its broken fortunes of the present day, in its decline. An old maid is its one tenant, left there with a life interest in the premises by the late owner, whose vast wealth passed into the hands of a cousin, who immediately, touched by this talisman of property, was transformed from a youth of dissipation into a high, cold, and worldly state of respectability. His portrait is drawn in the volume with the repeated limnings and labor of a Titian, who, it is known, would expend several years upon a human head. We see him in every light, walk leisurely round the vast circle of that magical outline, his social position, till we close in upon the man, narrowing slowly to his centre of falsity and selfishness. For a thorough witch laugh over fallen hollow-heartedness and pretence, there is a terrible sardonic greeting in the roll-call of his uncompleted day's performances as he sits in the fatal chamber, death-cold, having drunk the blood of the ancient curse. Other inmates gather round old maid Hepzibah. A remote gable is rented to a young artist, a daguerreotypist, and then comes upon the scene the brother of the old maid, Clifford Pyncheon, one day let out from life incarceration for —what circumstantial evidence had brought home to him—the murder of the late family head. Thirty years had obliterated most of this man's moral and intellectual nature, save in a certain blending of the two with his physical instinct for the sensuous and beautiful. A rare character that for our spiritual limner to work upon! The agent he has provided, nature's ministrant to this feebleness and disease, to aid in the rebuilding of the man, is a sprig of unconscious spontaneous girlhood—who enters the thick shades of the dwelling of disaster as a sunbeam, to purify and nourish its stagnant life. Very beautiful is this conception, and subtly wrought the chapters in which the relation is developed. Then we have the sacrifice of pride and solitary misanthropy in the petty retail shop Hepzibah opens for the increasing needs of the rusty mansion.

The scene passes on, while Hepzibah, her existence bound up in the resuscitation of Clifford, supported by the salient life of the youthful womanhood of Phœbe, fulfils her destiny at the Old House —where, for a little sprinkling of pleasantry to this sombre tale, comes a voracious boy to devour the gingerbread Jim Crows, elephants, and other seductive fry of the quaintly arranged window. His stuffed hide is a relief to the empty-waistcoated ghosts moving within. There is a humble fellow too, one Uncle Venner, a good-natured servitor at small chores—a poor devil in the eye of the world—of whom Hawthorne, with kindly eye, makes something by digging down under his tattered habiliments to his better-preserved human heart. He comes to the shop, and is a kind of out-of-door appendant to the fortunes of the house.

The Nemesis of the House is pressing for a new victim. Judge Pyncheon's thoughts are intent on an old hobby of the establishment, the procurement of a deed which was missing, and which was the evidence wanting to complete the title to a certain vast New Hampshire grant—a portentous and arch-deceiving ignis fatuus of the family. Clifford is supposed to know something of this matter; but, knowledge or not, the Judge is the one man in the world whom he will not meet. Every instinct of his nature rises within him, in self-protection of his weak, sensitive life, against the stern magnetic power of the coarse, granite judge. More than that lies underneath. Clifford had been unjustly convicted by those suspicious death-marks of his suddenly deceased relative—and the Judge had suffered it, holding all the time the key which would have unlocked the mystery,—besides some other shades of criminality. To escape an interview with this man, Clifford and Hepzibah leave the house in flight, while Judge Pyncheon sits in the apartment of his old ancestor, waiting for him. He is dead in his chair of apoplexy.

The fortunes of the House, after this tremendous purgation, look more brightly for the future. The diverted patrimony of his ex-respectability—the Governor in posse of Massachusetts—returns to its true channel to irrigate the dry heart of the Old Maid, and furnish Clifford the luxuries of the beautiful. The daguerreotypist, who turns out to be the descendant of the wizard,—the inventor of the curse—marries Phœbe, of course, and the parties have left the Old House, mouldering away in its by-street, for the sunny realm of a country summer retreat.

A Wonder Book for Boys and Girls, a series of delicately modernized versions of old classical myths and legends, followed, in a vein of fancy, pleasantry, and earnest sympathy, with the fresh simple mind of childhood.

Several small earlier volumes of a similar adaptation for the young, entitled *Grandfather's Chair*, in which biographical events of the old Puritan history were arranged about that family heirloom, with another volume of *Biographical Stories*, were also about this time collected and published together.

Then came in answer to the increasing demand, a new collection from the bountiful stock of the magazines and annuals, *The Snow Image and other Twice Told Tales*, at least as quaint, poetical, and reflective as its predecessors.

Hawthorne had now attained those unexpected desiderata, a public and a purse, and with the contents of the latter he purchased a house in Concord—not the Old Manse, for that had passed into the hands of a son of the old clergyman; but a cottage once occupied by Alcott, the philosopher of the Orphic Sayings. His latest book, the *Blithedale Romance*, dates from this new home, the "Wayside."

It has been generally understood that the character of Zenobia in this work was drawn, in some of its traits, from the late Margaret Fuller, who was an occasional visitor to the actual Brook Farm. The work, however, is anything but a literal description. In philosophical delineation of character, and its exhibition of the needs and shortcomings of certain attempts at improvement of the social state, set in a framework of imaginative romance, it is one of the most original and inventive of the author's productions.

In 1852, when his old friend and college companion, Franklin Pierce, was nominated for the Presidency, Mr. Hawthorne came forward as his biographer—a work which he executed in moderate space and with literary decorum. When the President was duly installed the following year, Hawthorne was not forgotten. One of the most lucrative offices of the government was bestowed upon him—the consulship at Liverpool—which, at the present time, he is still in the enjoyment of.

Nathaniel Hawthorne

The neglect of Hawthorne's early writings compared with the subsequent acknowledgment of their merits, is a noticeable fact in the history of American literature. He has himself spoken of it. In a preface to a new edition of the *Tales*, in 1851, he says: "The author of 'Twice Told Tales' has a claim to one distinction, which, as none of his literary brethren will care about disputing it with him, he need not be afraid to mention. He was, for a good many years, the obscurest man of letters in America. These stories were published in magazines and annuals, extending over a period of ten or twelve years, and comprising the whole of the writer's young manhood, without making (so far as he has ever been aware) the slightest impression on the public. One or two among them, the 'Rill from the Town Pump,' in perhaps a greater degree than any other, had a pretty wide newspaper circulation; as for the rest, he has no ground for supposing that, on their first appearance, they met with the good or evil fortune to be read by anybody." And he goes on to say how the most "effervescent" period of his productive faculties was chilled by this neglect. He burnt at this period many of his writings quite as good as what the public have since eagerly called for.

This early neglect is the more remarkable, as there is scarcely a trait of his later writings which did not exist in perfection in the first told tales. Without undervaluing the dramatic unity, the constructive ability, and the philosophical development of the Scarlet Letter, the House with the Seven Gables, and the Blithedale Romance, this neglect was the more extraordinary looking at the maturity and finished execution of the early writings, which contained something more than the germ of the author's later and more successful volumes. Though in the longer works, dramatic unity of plot, sustained description, and acute analysis, are supported beyond the opportunities of a short tale, it would be easy to enumerate sketches of ordinary length in the early writings which exhibit these qualities to advantage. The genius of Mr. Hawthorne, from the outset, has been marked by its thorough mastery of means and ends. Even his style is of that nature of simplicity,—a pure, colorless medium of his thought—that it seems to have attained its perfection at once, without undergoing those changes which mark the improvements of writers of composite qualities. The whole matter which he works in is subdued to his hand; so that the plain current of his language, without any foreign aid of ornament, is equal to all his necessities, whether he is in company with the laughter of playful children, the dignified ancestral associations of family or history, or the subtle terrors and dismays of the spiritual world. The calm, equable, full, unvarying style is everywhere sufficient.

In the mastery of the supernatural, or rather spiritual, working in the darker passages of life, the emotions of guilt and pain, the shadows which cross the happiest existence, Hawthorne has a peculiar vein of his own. For these effects he relies upon the subtle analogies or moralities which he traces with exquisite skill, finding constantly in nature, art, and the commonest experiences of life, the ready material of his weird and gentle homilies. This fondness for allegory and the parable reacts upon his every-day topics, giving to his description fulness and circumstantiality of detail, to which he is invited by his warm sympathy with what is passing on about him. However barren the world may appear to many minds, it is full of significance to him. In his solitude and retirement, for into whatever public positions he may be oddly cast he will always be in retirement, the genius of the author will create pictures to delight, solace, and instruct the players of the busy world, who see less of the game than this keen-sighted, sympathetic looker-on.

THE GRAY CHAMPION.

There was once a time when New England groaned under the actual pressure of heavier wrongs than those threatened ones which brought on the Revotion. James II., the bigoted successor of Charles the Voluptuous, had annulled the charters of all the colonies, and sent a harsh and unprincipled soldier to take away our liberties and endanger our religion. The administration of Sir Edmund Andros lacked scarcely a single characteristic of tyranny: a Governor and Council, holding office from the King, and wholly independent of the country; laws made and taxes levied without concurrence of the people, immediate or by their representatives; the rights of private citizens violated, and the titles of all landed property declared void; the voice of complaint stifled by restrictions on the press; and finally, disaffection overawed by the first band of mercenary troops that ever marched on our free soil. For two years our ancestors were kept in sullen submission, by that filial love which had invariably secured their allegiance to the mother country, whether its head chanced to be a Parliament, Protector, or popish Monarch. Till these evil times, however, such allegiance had been merely nominal, and the colonists had ruled themselves, enjoying far more freedom than is even yet the privilege of the native subjects of Great Britain.

At length, a rumor reached our shores, that the Prince of Orange had ventured on an enterprise, the success of which would be the triumph of civil and religious rights and the salvation of New England. It was but a doubtful whisper; it might be false, or the attempt might fail; and, in either case, the man that stirred against King James would lose his head. Still the intelligence produced a marked effect. The people smiled mysteriously in the streets, and threw bold glances at their oppressors; while far and wide there was a subdued and silent agitation, as if the slightest signal would rouse the whole land from its sluggish despondency. Aware of their danger, the rulers resolved to avert it by an imposing display of strength, and perhaps to confirm their despotism by yet harsher measures. One afternoon in April, 1689, Sir Edmund Andros and his favorite councillors, being warm with wine, assembled the red-coats of the Governor's Guard, and made their appearance in the streets of Boston. The sun was near setting when the march commenced.

The roll of the drum, at that unquiet crisis, seemed to go through the streets less as the martial music of the soldiers, than as a muster-call to the inhabitants themselves. A multitude, by various avenues, assembled in King street, which was destined to be the scene, nearly a century afterwards, of another encounter between the troops of Britain and a people struggling against her tyranny. Though more than sixty years had elapsed since the Pilgrims came, this crowd of their descendants still showed the strong and sombre features of their character, perhaps more strikingly in such a stern emergency than on happier occasions. There was the sober garb, the general severity of mien, the gloomy but undismayed expression, the scriptural forms of speech, and the confidence in Heaven's blessing on a righteous cause, which would have marked a band of the original Puritans, when threatened by some peril of the wilderness. Indeed, it was not yet time for the old spirit to be extinct; since there were men in the street, that day, who had worshipped there beneath the trees, before a house was reared to the God for whom they had become exiles. Old soldiers of the Parliament were here too, smiling grimly at the thought that their aged arms might strike another blow against the house of Stuart. Here, also, were the veterans of King Philip's war, who had burned villages and slaughtered young and old with pious fierceness, while the godly souls throughout the land were helping them with prayer. Several ministers were scattered among the crowd, which, unlike all other mobs, regarded them with such reverence, as if there were sanctity in their very garments. These holy men exerted their influence to quiet the people, but not to disperse them. Meantime, the purpose of the Governor in disturbing the peace of the town, at a period when the slightest commotion might throw the country into a ferment, was almost the universal subject of inquiry, and variously explained.

"Satan will strike his master-stroke presently," cried some, "because he knoweth that his time is short. All our godly pastors are to be dragged to prison. We shall see them at a Smithfield fire in King street!"

Hereupon, the people of each parish gathered closer round their minister, who looked calmly upwards and assumed a more apostolic dignity, as well befitted a candidate for the highest honor of his profession, the crown of martyrdom. It was actually fancied, at that period, that New England might have a John Rogers of her own, to take the place of that worthy in the Primer.

"The Pope of Rome has given orders for a new St. Bartholomew!" cried others. "We are to be massacred, man and male child!"

Neither was this rumor wholly discredited, although the wiser class believed the Governor's object somewhat less atrocious. His predecessor under the old charter, Bradstreet, a venerable companion of the first settlers, was known to be in town. There were grounds for conjecturing, that Sir Edmund Andros intended at once to strike terror by a parade of military force, and to confound the opposite faction by possessing himself of their chief.

"Stand firm for the old charter, Governor!" shouted the crowd, seizing upon the idea. "The good old Governor Bradstreet!"

While this cry was at the loudest, the people were surprised by the well-known figure of Governor Bradstreet himself, a patriarch of nearly ninety, who appeared on the elevated steps of a door, and, with characteristic mildness, besought them to submit to the constituted authorities.

"My children," concluded this venerable person, "do nothing rashly. Cry not aloud, but pray for the welfare of New England, and expect patiently what the Lord will do in this manner!"

The event was soon to be decided. All this time the roll of the drum had been approaching through Cornhill, louder and deeper, till, with reverberations from house to house, and the regular tramp of martial footsteps, it burst into the street. A double rank of soldiers made their appearance, occupying the whole breadth of the passage, with shouldered matchlocks, and matches burning, so as to present a row of fires in the dusk. Their steady march was like the progress of a machine, that would roll irresistibly over everything in its way. Next, moving slowly, with a confused clatter of hoofs on the pavement, rode a party of mounted gentlemen, the central figure being Sir Edmund Andros, elderly, but erect and soldier-like. Those around him were his favorite councillors, and the bitterest foes of New England. At his right hand rode Edward Randolph, our arch enemy, that "blasted wretch," as Cotton Mather calls him, who achieved the downfall of our ancient government, and was followed with a sensible curse through life and to his grave. On the other side was Bullivant, scattering jests and mockery as he rode along. Dudley came behind, with a downcast look, dreading, as well he might, to meet the indignant gaze of the people, who beheld him, their only countryman by birth, among the oppressors of his native land. The captain of a frigate in the harbor, and two or three civil officers under the Crown, were also there. But the figure which most attracted the public eye, and stirred up the deepest feeling, was the Episcopal clergyman of King's Chapel, riding haughtily among the magistrates in his priestly vestments, the fitting representative of prelacy and persecution, the union of church and state, and all those abominations which had driven the Puritans to the wilderness. Another guard of soldiers, in double rank, brought up the rear.

The whole scene was a picture of the condition of New England, and its moral, the deformity of any government that does not grow out of the nature of things and the character of the people. On one side the religious multitude, with their sad visages and dark attire, and on the other, the group of despotic rulers, with the high churchman in the midst, and here and there a crucifix at their bosoms, all magnificently clad, flushed with wine, proud of unjust authority, and scoffing at the universal groan. And the mercenary soldiers, waiting but the word to deluge the street with blood, showed the only means by which obedience could be secured.

"Oh! Lord of Hosts!" cried a voice among the crowd, "provide a Champion for thy people!"

This ejaculation was loudly uttered, and served as a herald's cry to introduce a remarkable personage. The crowd had rolled back, and were now huddled together nearly at the extremity of the street, while the soldiers had advanced no more than a third of its length. The intervening space was empty—a paved solitude, between lofty edifices, which threw almost a twilight shadow over it. Suddenly, there was seen the figure of an ancient man, who seemed to have emerged from among the people, and was walking by himself along the centre of the street, to confront the armed band. He wore the old Puritan dress, a dark cloak and a steeple-crowned hat, in the fashion of at least fifty years before, with a heavy sword upon his thigh, but a staff in his hand, to assist the tremulous gait of age.

When at some distance from the multitude, the old man turned slowly round, displaying a face of antique majesty, rendered doubly venerable by the hoary beard that descended on his breast. He made a gesture at once of encouragement and warning, then turned again and resumed his way.

"Who is this gray patriarch?" asked the young men of their sires.

"Who is this venerable brother?" asked the old men among themselves.

But none could make reply. The fathers of the people, those of fourscore years and upwards, were disturbed, deeming it strange that they should forget one of such evident authority, whom they must have known in their early days, the associate of Winthrop and all the old Councillors, giving laws, and making prayers, and leading them against the savage. The elderly men ought to have remembered him, too, with locks as gray in their youth, as their own were now. And the young! How could he have passed so utterly from their memories—that hoary sire, the relic of long departed times, whose awful benediction had surely been bestowed on their uncovered heads in childhood.

"Whence did he come? What is his purpose? Who can this old man be?" whispered the wondering crowd.

Meanwhile, the venerable stranger, staff in hand, was pursuing his solitary walk along the centre of the street. As he drew near the advancing soldiers, and as the roll of their drum came full upon his ear, the old man raised himself to a loftier mien, while the decrepitude of age seemed to fall from his shoulders, leaving him in gray but unbroken dignity. Now, he marched onwards with a warrior's step, keeping time to the military music. Thus the aged form advanced on one side, and the whole parade of soldiers and magistrates on the other, till, when scarcely twenty yards remained between, the old man grasped his staff by the middle, and held it before him like a leader's truncheon.

"Stand!" cried he.

The eye, the face, and attitude of command; the solemn yet warlike peal of that voice, fit either to rule a host in the battle-field or be raised to God in prayer, were irresistible. At the old man's word and outstretched arm, the roll of the drum was hushed at once, and the advancing line stood still. A tremulous enthusiasm seized upon the multitude. That stately form, combining the leader and the saint, so gray, so dimly seen, in such an ancient garb, could only belong to some old champion of the righteous cause, whom the oppressor's drum had summoned from his grave. They raised a shout of awe and exultation, and looked for the deliverance of New England.

The Governor, and the gentlemen of his party, perceiving themselves brought to an unexpected stand, rode hastily forward, as if they would have pressed their snorting and affrighted horses right against the hoary apparition. He, however, blenched not a step, but glancing his severe eye round the group which half encompassed him, at last bent it sternly on Sir Edmund Andros. One would have thought that the dark old man was chief ruler there, and that the Governor and Council, with soldiers at their back, representing the whole power and authority of the Crown, had no alternative but obedience.

"What does this old fellow here?" cried Edward Randolph, fiercely. "On, Sir Edmund! Bid the soldiers forward, and give the dotard the same choice that you give all his countrymen—to stand aside or be trampled on!"

"Nay, nay, let us show respect to the good grandsire," said Bullivant, laughing. "See you not he is some old round-headed dignitary, who hath lain asleep these thirty years, and knows nothing of the change of times? Doubtless, he thinks to put us down with a proclamation in Old Noll's name!"

"Are you mad, old man?" demanded Sir Edmund Andros, in loud and harsh tones. "How dare you stay the march of King James's Governor?"

"I have staid the march of a King himself, ere now," replied the gray figure, with stern composure. "I am here, Sir Governor, because the cry of an oppressed people hath disturbed me in my secret place; and beseeching this favor earnestly of the Lord, it was vouchsafed me to appear once again on earth in the good old cause of his saints. And what speak ye of James? There is no longer a popish tyrant on the throne of England, and by to-morrow noon his name shall be a by-word in this very street, where ye would make it a word of terror. Back, thou that wast a Governor, back! With this night thy power is ended—to-morrow, the prison!—back, lest I foretell the scaffold!"

The people had been drawing nearer and nearer, and drinking in the words of their champion, who spoke in accents long disused, like one unaccustomed to converse, except with the dead of many years ago. But his voice stirred their souls. They confronted the soldiers, not wholly without arms, and ready to convert the very stones of the street into deadly weapons. Sir Edmund Andros looked at the old man; then he cast his hard and cruel eye over the multitude, and beheld them burning with that lurid wrath, so difficult to kindle or to quench; and again he fixed his gaze on the aged form, which stood obscurely in an open space, where neither friend nor foe had thrust himself. What were his thoughts, he uttered no word which might discover. But whether the oppressor was overawed by the Gray Champion's look, or perceived his peril in the threatening attitude of the people, it is certain that he gave back, and ordered his soldiers to commence a slow and guarded retreat. Before another sunset, the Governor, and all that rode so proudly with him, were prisoners, and long ere it was known that James had abdicated King William was proclaimed throughout New England.

But where was the Gray Champion? Some reported that when the troops had gone from King street, and the people were thronging tumultuously in their rear, Bradstreet, the aged Governor, was seen to embrace a form more aged than his own. Others soberly affirmed, that while they marvelled at the venerable grandeur of his aspect, the old man had faded from their eyes, melting slowly into the hues of twilight, till where he stood there was an empty space. But all agreed that the hoary shape was gone. The men of that generation watched for his reappearance, in sunshine and in twilight, but never saw him more, nor knew when his funeral passed, nor where his gravestone was.

And who was the Gray Champion? Perhaps his name might be found in the records of that stern Court of Justice which passed a sentence too mighty for the age, but glorious in all after times for its humbling lesson to the monarch and its high example to the subject. I have heard, that whenever the descendants of the Puritans are to show the spirit of their sires the old man appears again. When eighty years had passed he walked once more in King street. Five years later, in the twilight of an April morning, he stood on the green, beside the meeting-house, at Lexington, where now the obelisk of granite, with a slab of slate inlaid, commemorates the first fallen of the Revolution. And when our fathers were toiling at the breastwork on Bunker's Hill, all through that night the old warrior walked his rounds. Long, long may it be ere it comes again! His hour is one of darkness, and adversity, and peril. But should domestic tyranny oppress us, or the invader's step pollute our soil, still may the Gray Champion come; for he is the type of New England's hereditary spirit; and his shadowy march on the eve of danger must ever be the pledge that New England's sons will vindicate their ancestry.

SIGHTS FROM A STEEPLE.

So! I have climbed high, and my reward is small. Here I stand, with wearied knees, earth, indeed, at a dizzy depth below, but heaven far, far beyond me still. O that I could soar up into the very zenith, where man never breathed, nor eagle ever flew, and where the ethereal azure melts away from the eye, and appears only a deepened shade of nothingness! And yet I shiver at that cold and solitary thought. What clouds are gathering in the golden west, with direful intent against the brightness and the warmth of this summer afternoon! They are ponderous air-ships, black as death, and freighted with the tempest; and at intervals their thunder, the signal-guns of that unearthly squadron, rolls distant along the deep of heaven. These nearer heaps of fleecy vapor—methinks I could roll and toss upon them the whole day long!—seem scattered here and there, for the repose of tired pilgrims through the sky. Perhaps—for who can tell?—beautiful spirits are disporting themselves there, and will bless my mortal eye with the brief appearance of their curly locks of golden light, and laughing faces, fair and faint as the people of a rosy dream. Or, where the floating mass so imperfectly obstructs the color of the firmament, a slender foot and fairy limb, resting too heavily upon the frail support, may be thrust through, and suddenly withdrawn, while longing fancy follows them in vain. Yonder again is an airy archipelago, where the sunbeams love to linger in their journeyings through space. Every one of those little clouds has been dipped and steeped in radiance, which the slightest pressure might disengage in silvery profusion, like water wrung from a sea-maid's hair. Bright they are as a young man's visions, and, like them, would be realized in chillness, obscurity, and tears. I will look on them no more.

In three parts of the visible circle, whose centre is this spire, I discern cultivated fields, villages, white country-seats, the waving lines of rivulets, little placid lakes, and here and there a rising ground, that would fain be termed a hill. On the fourth side is the sea, stretching away towards a viewless boundary, blue and calm, except where the passing anger of a shadow flits across its surface, and is gone. Hitherward, a broad inlet penetrates far into the land; on the verge of the harbor, formed by its extremity, is a town; and over it am I, a watchman, all-heeding and unheeding. Oh! that the multitude of chimneys could speak, like those of Madrid, and betray, in smoky whispers, the secrets of all who, since their first foundation, have assembled at the hearths within! Oh, that the Limping Devil of Le Sage would perch beside me here, extend his wand over this contiguity of roofs, uncover every chamber, and make me familiar with their inhabitants! The most desirable mode of existence might be that of a spiritualized Paul Pry, hovering invisible round man and woman, witnessing their deeds, searching into their hearts, borrowing brightness from their felicity, and shade from their sorrow, and retaining no emotion peculiar to himself. But none of these things are possible; and if I would know the interior of brick walls, or the mystery of human bosoms, I can but guess.

Yonder is a fair street, extending north and south. The stately mansions are placed each on its carpet of verdant grass, and a long flight of steps descends from every door to the pavement. Ornamental trees, the broad-leafed horse chestnut, the elm so lofty and bending, the graceful but infrequent willow, and others whereof I know not the names, grow thrivingly among brick and stone. The oblique rays of the sun are intercepted by these green citizens, and by the houses, so that one side of the street is a shaded and pleasant walk. On its whole extent there is now but a single passenger, advancing from the upper end; and he, unless distance, and the medium of a pocket-spyglass do him more than justice, is a fine young man of twenty. He saunters slowly forward, slapping his left hand with his folded gloves, bending his eyes upon the pavement, and sometimes raising them to throw a glance before him. Certainly, he has a pensive air. Is he in doubt, or in debt? Is he, if the question be allowable, in love? Does he strive to be melancholy and gentlemanlike? Or, is he merely overcome by the heat? But I bid him farewell, for the present. The door of one of the houses, an aristocratic edifice, with curtains of purple and gold waving from the windows, is now opened, and down the steps come two ladies, swinging their parasols, and lightly arrayed for a summer ramble. Both are young, both are pretty; but methinks the left hand lass is the fairer of the twain; and though she be so serious at this moment, I could swear that there is a treasure of gentle fun within her. They stand talking a little while upon the steps, and finally proceed up the street. Meantime, as their faces are now turned from me, I may look elsewhere.

Upon that wharf, and down the corresponding street, is a busy contrast to the quiet scene which I have just noticed. Business evidently has its centre there, and many a man is wasting the summer afternoon in labor and anxiety, in losing riches, or in gaining them, when he would be wiser to flee away to some pleasant country village, or shaded lake in the forest, or wild and cool sea-beach. I see vessels unlading at the wharf, and precious merchandise strown upon the ground, abundantly as at the bottom of the sea, that market whence no goods return, and where there is no captain nor supercargo to render an account of sales. Here, the clerks are diligent with their paper and pencils, and sailors ply the block and tackle that hang over the hold, accompanying their toil with cries, long drawn and roughly melodious, till the bales and puncheons ascend to upper air. At a little distance, a group of gentlemen are assembled round the door of a warehouse. Grave seniors be they, and I would wager—if it were safe, in these times, to be responsible for any one—that the least eminent among them, might vie with old Vincentio, that incomparable trafficker of Pisa. I can even select the wealthiest of the company. It is the elderly personage, in somewhat rusty black, with powdered hair, the superfluous whiteness of which is visible upon the cape of his coat. His twenty ships are wafted on some of their many courses by every breeze that blows, and his name—I will venture to say, though I know it not—is a familiar sound among the far separated merchants of Europe and the Indies.

But I bestow too much of my attention in this quarter. On looking again to the long and shady walk, I perceive that the two fair girls have encountered the young man. After a sort of shyness in the recognition, he turns back with them. Moreover, he has sanctioned my taste in regard to his companions by placing himself on the inner side of the pavement, nearest the Venus to whom I—enacting, on a steeple-top, the part of Paris on the top of Ida—adjudged the golden apple.

In two streets, converging at right angles towards my watchtower, I distinguish three different processions. One is a proud array of voluntary soldiers in bright uniform, resembling from the height whence I look down, the painted veterans that garrison the windows of a toyshop. And yet, it stirs my heart; their regular advance, their nodding plumes, the sun-flash on their bayonets and musket-barrels, the roll of their drums ascending past me, and the fife ever and anon piercing through—these things have wakened a warlike fire, peaceful though I be. Close to their rear marches a battalion of schoolboys, ranged in crooked and irregular platoons, shouldering sticks, thumping a harsh and unripe clatter from an instrument of tin, and ridiculously aping the intricate manœuvres of the foremost band. Nevertheless, as slight differences are scarcely perceptible from a church spire, one might be tempted to ask, 'Which are the boys?'—or rather, 'Which the men?' But, leaving these, let us turn to the third procession, which, though sadder in outward show, may excite identical reflections in the thoughtful mind. It is a funeral. A hearse, drawn by a black and bony steed, and covered by a dusty pall; two or three coaches rumbling over the stones, their drivers half asleep; a dozen couple of careless mourners in their every-day attire; such was not the fashion of our fathers, when they carried a friend to his grave. There is now no doleful clang of the bell, to proclaim sorrow to the town. Was the King of Terrors more awful in those days than in our own, that wisdom and philosophy have been able to produce this change? Not so. Here is a proof that he retains his proper majesty. The military men, and the military boys, are wheeling round the corner, and meet the funeral full in the face. Immediately, the drum is silent, all but the tap that regulates each simultaneous footfall. The soldiers yield the path to the dusty hearse and unpretending train, and the children quit their ranks, and cluster on the sidewalks, with timorous and instinctive curiosity. The mourners enter the church-yard at the base of the steeple, and pause by an open grave among the burial-stones; the lightning glimmers on them as they lower down the coffin, and the thunder rattles heavily while they throw the earth upon its lid. Verily, the shower is near, and I tremble for the young man and the girls, who have now disappeared from the long and shady street.

How various are the situations of the people covered by the roofs beneath me, and how diversified are the events at this moment befalling them! The new-born, the aged, the dying, the strong in life, and the recent dead, are in the chambers of these many mansions. The full of hope, the happy, the miserable, and the desperate, dwell together within the circle of my glance. In some of the houses over which my eyes roam so coldly, guilt is entering into hearts that are still tenanted by a debased and trodden virtue—guilt is on the very edge of commission, and the impending deed might be averted; guilt is done, and the criminal wonders if it be irrevocable. There are broad thoughts struggling in my mind, and, were I able to give them distinctness, they would make their way in eloquence. Lo! the rain-drops are descending.

The clouds, within a little time, have gathered over all the sky, hanging heavily, as if about to drop in one unbroken mass upon the earth. At intervals, the lightning flashes from their brooding hearts, quivers, disappears, and then comes the thunder, travelling slowly after its twin-born flame. A strong wind has sprung up, howls through the darkened streets, and raises the dust in dense bodies, to rebel against the approaching storm. The disbanded soldiers fly, the funeral has already vanished like its dead, and all people hurry homeward—all that have a home; while a few lounge by the corners, or trudge on desperately, at their leisure. In a narrow lane, which communicates with the shady street, I discern the rich old merchant, putting himself to the top of his speed, lest the rain should convert his hair-powder to a paste. Unhappy gentleman! By the slow vehemence, and painful moderation wherewith he journeys, it is but too evident that Podagra has left its thrilling tenderness in his great toe. But yonder, at a far more rapid pace, come three other of my acquaintance, the two pretty girls and the young man, unseasonably interrupted in their walk. Their footsteps are supported by the risen dust, the wind lends them its velocity, they fly like three seabirds driven landward by the tempestuous breeze. The ladies would not thus rival Atalanta, if they but knew that any one were at leisure to observe them. Ah! as they hasten onward, laughing in the angry face of nature, a sudden catastrophe has chanced. At the corner where the narrow lane enters into the street, they come plump against the old merchant, whose tortoise motion has just brought him to that point. He likes not the sweet encounter; the darkness of the whole air gathers speedily upon his visage, and there is a pause on both sides. Finally, he thrusts aside the youth with little courtesy, seizes an arm of each of the two girls, and plods onward, like a magician with a prize of captive fairies. All this is easy to be understood. How disconsolate the poor lover stands! regardless of the rain that threatens an exceeding damage to his well fashioned habiliments, till he catches a backward glance of mirth from a bright eye, and turns away with whatever comfort it conveys.

The old man and his daughters are safely housed, and now the storm lets loose its fury. In every dwelling I perceive the faces of the chambermaids as they shut down the windows, excluding the impetuous shower, and shrinking away from the quick fiery glare. The large drops descend with force upon the slated roofs, and rise again in smoke. There is a rush and roar, as of a river through the air, and muddy streams bubble majestically along the pavement, whirl their dusky foam into the kennel, and disappear beneath iron grates. Thus did Arethusa sink. I love not my station here aloft, in the midst of the tumult which I am powerless to direct or quell, with the blue lightning wrinkling on my brow, and the thunder muttering its first awful syllables in my ear. I will descend. Yet let me give another glance to the sea, where the foam breaks out in long white lines upon a broad expanse of blackness, or boils up in far distant points, like snowy mountain-tops in the eddies of a flood; and let me look once more at the green plain, and little hills of the country, over which the giant of the storm is riding in robes of mist, and at the town, whose obscured and desolate streets might beseem a city of the dead; and turning a single moment to the sky, now gloomy as an author's prospects, I prepare to resume my station on lower earth. But stay! A little speck of azure has widened in the western heavens; the sunbeams find a passage, and go rejoicing through the tempest; and on yonder darkest cloud, born, like hallowed hopes, of the glory of another world, and the trouble and tears of this, brightens forth the Rainbow!

OLIVER WENDELL HOLMES,

Whose polished verses and playful satiric wit are the delight of his contemporaries, as they will be cherished bequests of our own day to posterity, is a son of the author of the Annals, the Doctor of Divinity at Cambridge. At that learned town of Massachusetts, he was born August 29, 1809. He was educated at the Phillips Academy at Exeter, and graduated at Harvard in 1829. He then gave a year to the law, during which time he was entertaining the good people of Cambridge with various anonymous effusions of a waggish poetical character, in the *Collegian*,* a periodical published by a number of undergraduates of Harvard University in 1830, in which John O. Sargent wrote the versatile papers in prose and verse, signed Charles Sherry; and the accomplished William H. Simmons, a brilliant rhetorician, and one of the purest readers we have ever listened to, was "Lockfast," translating Schiller, enthusiastic on Ossian, and snapping up college jokes and trifles; and Robert Habersham, under the guise of "Mr. Airy," and Theodore Wm. Snow as "Geoffrey la Touche," brought their quotas to the literary pic-nic. Holmes struck out a new vein among them, just as Praed had done in the Etonian and Knight's Quarterly Magazine. Of the twenty-five pieces published by him, some half dozen have been collected in his "Poems." The "Meeting of the Dryads," on occasion of a Presidential thinning of the college trees; "The Spectre Pig" and "Evening by a Tailor," are among them.

As a lawyer, Holmes, like most of the American literati who have generally begun with that profession, was evidently falling under the poets' censure, "penning a stanza when he should engross;" when he turned his attention to medicine, and forswore for a time the Muses. He was, however, guilty of some very clever anonymous contributions to a volume, the *Harbinger*, mainly written by himself, Park Benjamin, and Epes Sargent, and which was published for the benefit of a charitable institution.* In 1833, the year of this production, he visited Europe, residing chiefly at Paris, in the prosecution of his medical studies.

After nearly three years' residence abroad, he returned to take his medical degree at Cambridge, in 1836, when he delivered *Poetry, a Metrical Essay*, before the Harvard Phi Beta Kappa; which he published the same year, in the first acknowledged volume of his Poems.† In "Poetry," he describes four stages of the art, the Pastoral, Martial, Epic, and Dramatic; successfully illustrating the two former by his lines on "The Cambridge Churchyard" and "Old Ironsides," which last has become a national lyric, having first been printed in the *Boston Daily Advertiser* when the frigate Constitution lay at the Navy Yard in Charlestown, and the department had resolved upon breaking her up—a fate from which she was preserved by the verses, which ran through the newspapers with universal applause, and were circulated in the city of Washington in handbills.‡

In this poem he introduced a descriptive passage on Spring, at once literal and poetical, in a vein which he has since followed out with brilliant effect. The volume also contained "The Last Leaf," and "My Aunt," which established Holmes's reputation for humorous quaintness. In his preface he offers a vindication of the extravagant in literature; but it is only a dull or unthinking mind which would quarrel with such extravagances as his humor sometimes takes on, or deny the force of his explanation that, "as material objects in different lights repeat themselves in shadows variously elongated, contracted, or exaggerated, so our solid and sober thoughts caricature themselves in fantastic shapes, inseparable from their originals, and having a unity in their

* The Collegian. In six numbers. Cambridge: Hilliard & Brown.

* The Harbinger; a May Gift, dedicated to the ladies who have so kindly aided the New England Institution for the Education of the Blind. Boston: Carter, Hendee & Co., 1833. 12mo. pp. 96.

† Poems by Oliver Wendell Holmes. Boston: Otis, Broaders & Co., 1836. 12mo. pp. 163.

‡ Benjamin's American Monthly Magazine, January, 1837.

extravagance, which proves them to have retained their proportions in certain respects, however differing in outline from their prototypes."

In 1838 Dr. Holmes became Professor of Anatomy and Physiology at Dartmouth. On his marriage in 1840, he established himself in Boston, where he acquired the position of a fashionable and successful practitioner of medicine. In 1847 he was made Parkman Professor of Anatomy and Physiology, in the Medical School at Harvard.

His chief professional publications are his Boylston Prize Dissertations for 1836–7, on *Indigenous Intermittent Fever in New England, Nature and Treatment of Neuralgia, and Utility and Importance of Direct Exploration in Medical Practice; Lectures on Homœopathy and other Delusions* in 1841; Report on Medical Literature to the American Association, 1848; and occasional articles in the journals, of which the most important is "the Contagiousness of Puerperal Fever," in the New England Journal of Medicine and Surgery, April, 1843.

Dr. Holmes is celebrated for his *vers d'occasion*, cleverly introduced with impromptu graces (of course, entirely unpremeditated) at medical feasts and Phi Beta Kappa Festivals, and other social gatherings, which are pretty sure to have some fanciful descriptions of nature, and laugh loudly at the quackeries, both the properly professional, and the literary and social of the day. His *Terpsichore* was pronounced on one of these opportunities, in 1843. His *Stethoscope Song* was one of these effusions; his *Modest Request* at Everett's inauguration at Harvard another, and many more will be remembered.

Urania, a Rhymed Lesson, with some shrewd hits at the absurd, and suggestions of the practical in the social economy of the day, was delivered before the Boston Mercantile Library Association, in 1846. *Astrea* is a Phi Beta Kappa poem, pronounced by the author at Yale College in 1850.

In 1852 Dr. Holmes delivered a course of lectures on the *English Poets of the Nineteenth Century*, a portion of which he subsequently repeated in New York. The style was precise and animated; the illustrations, sharp and cleanly cut. In the criticism, there was a leaning rather to the bold and dashing bravura of Scott and Byron, than the calm philosophical mood of Wordsworth. Where there was any game on the wing, when the "servile herd" of imitators and the poetasters came in view, they were dropped at once by a felicitous shot. Each lecture closed with a copy of verses humorous or sentimental, growing out of the prevalent mood of the hour's discussion.

In look and manners, Dr. Holmes is the vivacious sparkling personage his poems would indicate. His smile is easily invoked; he is fond of pun and inevitable at repartee, and his conversation runs on copiously, supplied with choice discriminating words laden with the best stores of picked fact from the whole range of science and society; and of ingenious reflection in a certain vein of optimism. As a medical lecturer, his style must be admirable, at once clear and subtle, popular and refined.

In the winter season he resides at Boston; latterly amusing himself with the profitable variety of visiting the towns and cities of the Northern and Middle States in the delivery of lectures, of which he has a good working stock on hand. The anatomy of the popular lecture he understands perfectly—how large a proportion of wit he may safely associate with the least quantity of dulness; and thus he carries pleasure and refinement from the charmed salons of Beacon street to towns and villages in the back districts, suddenly opened to light and civilization by the straight cut of the railroad. In summer, or rather in spring, summer, and autumn, the Doctor is at his home on the Housatonic, at Pittsfield, with acres around him, inherited from his maternal ancestors, the Wendells, in whom the whole township was once vested. In 1735, the Hon. Jacob Wendell bought the township of Pontoosuc, and his grandson now resides on the remnant of twenty-four thousand ancestral acres.*

Oliver Wendell Holmes

In remembrance of one of the ancient Indian deeds he calls his residence Canoe Place. He has described the river scenery of the vicinity in a poem which has been lately printed.†

The muse of Holmes is a foe to humbug. There is among his poems "A professional ballad—the Stethoscope Song," descriptive of the practices of a young physician from Paris, who went about knocking the wind out of old ladies, and terrifying young ones, mistaking, all the while, a buzzing fly in the instrument for a frightful array of diseases expressed in a variety of terrible French appellations. The exposure of this young man is a hint of the author's process with the social grievances and absurdities of the day. He clears the moral atmosphere of the morbid literary and other pretences afloat. People breathe freer for his verses. They shake the cobwebs out of the system, and keep up in the world that brisk healthy current of common sense, which is to the mind what circulation is to the body. A tincture of the Epicurean Philosophy is not a bad corrective of ultraism, Fourierism, transcendentalism, and

* O. W. Holmes's remarks at the Berkshire Jubilee, August, 1844.

† The Knickerbocker Gallery.

other morbidities. Dr. Holmes sees a thing objectively in the open air, and understands what is due to nature, and to the inevitable conventionalisms of society. He is a lover of the fields, trees, and streams, and out-of-door life; but we question whether his muse is ever clearer in its metaphysics than when on some convivial occasion it ranges a row of happy faces, reflected in the wax-illuminated plateau of the dining table.

OUR YANKEE GIRLS.

Let greener lands and bluer skies,
  If such the wide earth shows,
With fairer cheeks and brighter eyes,
  Match us the star and rose;
The winds that lift the Georgian's veil
  Or wave Circassia's curls,
Waft to their shores the sultan's sail,—
  Who buys our Yankee girls?

The gay grisette, whose fingers touch
  Love's thousand chords so well;
The dark Italian, loving much,
  But more than *one* can tell;
And England's fair-haired, blue-eyed dame,
  Who binds her brow with pearls;—
Ye who have seen them, can they shame
  Our own sweet Yankee girls?

And what if court and castle vaunt
  Its children loftier born?—
Who heeds the silken tassel's flaunt
  Beside the golden corn?
They ask not for the dainty toil
  Of ribboned knights and earls,
The daughters of the virgin soil,
  Our freeborn Yankee girls!

By every hill whose stately pines
  Wave their dark arms above
The home where some fair being shines,
  To warm the wilds with love,
From barest rock to bleakest shore
  Where farthest sail unfurls,
That stars and stripes are streaming o'er,—
  God bless our Yankee girls!

OLD IRONSIDES.

Ay, tear her tattered ensign down!
  Long has it waved on high,
And many an eye has danced to see
  That banner in the sky;
Beneath it rung the battle shout,
  And burst the cannon's roar;—
The meteor of the ocean air
  Shall sweep the clouds no more!

Her deck, once red with heroes' blood
  Where knelt the vanquished foe,
When winds were hurrying o'er the flood
  And waves were white below,
No more shall feel the victor's tread,
  Or know the conquered knee;—
The harpies of the shore shall pluck
  The eagle of the sea!

O better that her shattered hulk
  Should sink beneath the wave;
Her thunders shook the mighty deep,
  And there should be her grave;
Nail to the mast her holy flag,
  Set every threadbare sail,
And give her to the god of storms,—
  The lightning and the gale!

THE CHURCH-YARD AT CAMBRIDGE.

Our ancient church! its lowly tower,
  Beneath the loftier spire,
Is shadowed when the sunset hour
  Clothes the tall shaft in fire;
It sinks beyond the distant eye,
  Long ere the glittering vane,
High wheeling in the western sky,
  Has faded o'er the plain.

Like Sentinel and Nun, they keep
  Their vigil on the green;
One seems to guard, and one to weep,
  The dead that lie between;
And both roll out, so full and near,
  Their music's mingling waves,
They shake the grass, whose pennoned spear
  Leans on the narrow graves.

The stranger parts the flaunting weeds,
  Whose seeds the winds have strown
So thick beneath the line he reads,
  They shade the sculptured stone;
The child unveils his clustered brow,
  And ponders for a while
The graven willow's pendent bough,
  Or rudest cherub's smile.

But what to them the dirge, the knell?
  These were the mourner's share;—
The sullen clang, whose heavy swell
  Throbbed through the beating air;—
The rattling cord,—the rolling stone,—
  The shelving sand that slid,
And, far beneath, with hollow tone
  Rung on the coffin's lid.

The slumberer's mound grows fresh and green,
  Then slowly disappears;
The mosses creep, the gray stones lean
  Earth hides his date and years;
But long before the once-loved name
  Is sunk or worn away,
No lip the silent dust may claim,
  That pressed the breathing clay.

Go where the ancient pathway guides,
  See where our sires laid down
Their smiling babes, their cherished brides,
  The patriarchs of the town;
Hast thou a tear for buried love?
  A sigh for transient power?
All that a century left above,
  Go, read it in an hour!

The Indian's shaft, the Briton's ball,
  The sabre's thirsting edge,
The hot shell shattering in its fall,
  The bayonet's rending wedge,—
Here scattered death; yet seek the spot,
  No trace thine eye can see,
No altar,—and they need it not
  Who leave their children free!

Look where the turbid rain-drops stand
  In many a chiselled square,
The knightly crest, the shield, the brand
  Of honored names were there;—
Alas! for every tear is dried
  Those blazoned tablets knew,
Save when the icy marble's side
  Drips with the evening dew.

Or gaze upon yon pillared stone,
  The empty urn of pride;
There stand the Goblet and the Sun,—
  What need of more beside?
Where lives the memory of the dead,
  Who made their tomb a toy?

Whose ashes press that nameless bed?
Go, ask the village boy!

Lean o'er the slender western wall,
Ye ever-roaming girls;
The breath that bids the blossom fall
May lift your floating curls,
To sweep the simple lines that tell
An exile's date and doom;
And sigh, for where his daughters dwell,
They wreathe the stranger's tomb.

And one amid these shades was born,
Beneath this turf who lies,
Once beaming as the summer's morn,
That closed her gentle eyes;—
If sinless angels love as we,
Who stood thy grave beside,
Three seraph welcomes waited thee,
The daughter, sister, bride!

I wandered to thy buried mound
When earth was hid below
The level of the glaring ground,
Choked to its gates with snow,
And when with summer's flowery waves
The lake of verdure rolled,
As if a Sultan's white-robed slaves
Had scattered pearls and gold.

Nay, the soft pinions of the air,
That lift this trembling tone,
Its breath of love may almost bear,
To kiss thy funeral stone;—
And, now thy smiles have past away,
For all the joy they gave,
May sweetest dews and warmest ray
Lie on thine early grave!

When damps beneath, and storms above,
Have bowed these fragile towers,
Still o'er the graves yon locust-grove
Shall swing its Orient flowers;—
And I would ask no mouldering bust,
If e'er this humble line,
Which breathed a sigh o'er others' dust,
Might call a tear on mine.

L'INCONNUE.

Is thy name Mary, maiden fair?
Such should, methinks, its music be
The sweetest name that mortals bear,
Were best befitting thee;
And she, to whom it once was given,
Was half of earth and half of heaven.

I hear thy voice, I see thy smile,
I look upon thy folded hair;
Ah! while we dream not they beguile,
Our hearts are in the snare;
And she, who chains a wild bird's wing,
Must start not if her captive sing.

So, lady, take the leaf that falls,
To all but thee unseen, unknown;
When evening shades thy silent walls,
Then read it all alone;
In stillness read, in darkness seal,
Forget, despise, but not reveal!

THE LAST LEAF.

I saw him once before,
As he passed by the door,
And again
The pavement stones resound
As he totters o'er the ground
With his cane.

They say that in his prime,
Ere the pruning-knife of Time
Cut him down,
Not a better man was found
By the Crier on his round
Through the town.

But now he walks the streets,
And he looks at all he meets
Sad and wan,
And he shakes his feeble head,
That it seems as if he said,
"They are gone."

The mossy marbles rest
On the lips that he has prest
In their bloom,
And the names he loved to hear
Have been carved for many a year
On the tomb.

My grandmamma has said,—
Poor old lady, she is dead
Long ago,—
That he had a Roman nose,
And his cheek was like a rose
In the snow.

But now his nose is thin,
And it rests upon his chin
Like a staff,
And a crook is in his back,
And a melancholy crack
In his laugh.

I know it is a sin
For me to sit and grin
At him here;
But the old three-cornered hat,
And the breeches, and all that,
Are so queer!

And if I should live to be
The last leaf upon the tree
In the spring,—
Let them smile, as I do now,
At the old forsaken bough
Where I cling.

MY AUNT.

My aunt! my dear unmarried aunt!
Long years have o'er her flown;
Yet still she strains the aching clasp
That binds her virgin zone;
I know it hurts her,—though she looks
As cheerful as she can;
Her waist is ampler than her life,
For life is but a span.

My aunt, my poor deluded aunt!
Her hair is almost gray;
Why will she train that winter curl
In such a spring-like way?
How can she lay her glasses down,
And say she reads as well
When, through a double convex lens,
She just makes out to spell?

Her father,—grandpapa! forgive
This erring lip its smiles,—
Vowed she should make the finest girl
Within a hundred miles.
He sent her to a stylish school;
'Twas in her thirteenth June;
And with her, as the rules required,
"Two towels and a spoon."

They braced my aunt against a board,
To make her straight and tall;
They laced her up, they starved her down,
To make her light and small;

They pinched her feet, they singed her hair,
They screwed it up with pins;—
O never mortal suffered more
In penance for her sins.

So, when my precious aunt was done,
My grandsire brought her back;
(By daylight, lest some rabid youth
Might follow on the track;)
"Ah!" said my grandsire, as he shook
Some powder in his pan,
"What could this lovely creature do
Against a desperate man!"

Alas! nor chariot, nor barouche,
Nor bandit cavalcade
Tore from the trembling father's arms
His all-accomplished maid.
For her how happy had it been!
And Heaven had spared to me
To see one sad, ungathered rose
On my ancestral tree.

EVENING—BY A TAILOR.

Day hath put on his jacket, and around
His burning bosom buttoned it with stars.
Here will I lay me on the velvet grass,
That is like padding to earth's meagre ribs.
And hold communion with the things about me.
Ah me! how lovely is the golden braid,
That binds the skirt of night's descending robe!
The thin leaves, quivering on their silken threads,
Do make a music like to rustling satin,
As the light breezes smoothe their downy nap.

Ha! what is this that rises to my touch
So like a cushion? Can it be a cabbage?
It is, it is that deeply injured flower,
Which boys do flout us with;—but yet I love thee,
Thou giant rose, wrapped in a green surtout.
Doubtless in Eden thou didst blush as bright
As these, thy puny brethren; and thy breath
Sweetened the fragrance of her spicy air;
But now thou seemest like a bankrupt beau,
Stripped of his gaudy hues and essences,
And growing portly in his sober garments.

Is that a swan that rides upon the water?
O no, it is that other gentle bird,
Which is the patron of our noble calling.
I well remember, in my early years,
When these young hands first closed upon a goose;
I have a scar upon my thimble finger,
Which chronicles the hour of young ambition.
My father was a tailor, and his father,
And my sire's grandsire, all of them were tailors;
They had an ancient goose,—it was an heir-loom
From some remoter tailor of our race.
It happened I did see it on a time
When none was near, and I did deal with it,
And it did burn me,—oh, most fearfully!

It is a joy to straighten out one's limbs,
And leap elastic from the level counter,
Leaving the petty grievances of earth,
The breaking thread, the din of clashing shears,
And all the needles that do wound the spirit,
For such a pensive hour of soothing silence.
Kind Nature, shuffling in her loose undress,
Lays bare her shady bosom; I can feel
With all around me;—I can hail the flowers
That sprig earth's mantle,—and yon quiet bird,
That rides the stream, is to me as a brother.
The vulgar know not all the hidden pockets,
Where Nature stows away her loveliness.
But this unnatural posture of the legs
Cramps my extended calves, and I must go
Where I can coil them in their wonted fashion.

ON LENDING A PUNCH-BOWL.

This ancient silver bowl of mine—it tells of good old times,
Of joyous days, and jolly nights, and merry Christmas chimes;
They were a free and jovial race, but honest, brave, and true,
That dipped their ladle in the punch when this old bowl was new.

A Spanish galleon brought the bar,—so runs the ancient tale;
'Twas hammered by an Antwerp smith, whose arm was like a flail;
And now and then between the strokes, for fear his strength should fail,
He wiped his brow, and quaffed a cup of good old Flemish ale.

'Twas purchased by an English squire to please his loving dame,
Who saw the cherubs, and conceived a longing for the same;
And oft, as on the ancient stock another twig was found,
'Twas filled with caudle spiced and hot, and handed smoking round.

But, changing hands, it reached at length a Puritan divine,
Who used to follow Timothy, and take a little wine,
But hated punch and prelacy; and so it was, perhaps,
He went to Leyden, where he found conventicles and schnaps.

And then, of course, you know what's next,—it left the Dutchman's shore
With those that in the Mayflower came,—a hundred souls and more,—
Along with all the furniture, to fill their new abodes,—
To judge by what is still on hand, at least a hundred loads.

'Twas on a dreary winter's eve, the night was closing dim,
When old Miles Standish took the bowl, and filled it to the brim;
The little Captain stood and stirred the posset with his sword,
And all his sturdy men at arms were ranged about the board.

He poured the fiery Hollands in,—the man that never feared,—
He took a long and solemn draught, and wiped his yellow beard;
And one by one the musketeers,—the men that fought and prayed,—
All drank as 't were their mother's milk, and not a man afraid.

That night, affrighted from his nest, the screaming eagle flew,
He heard the Pequot's ringing whoop, the soldier's wild halloo;
And there the sachem learned the rule he taught to kith and kin;
"Run from the white man when you find he smells of Hollands gin!"

A hundred years, and fifty more, had spread their leaves and snows,
A thousand rubs had flattened down each little cherub's nose;
When once again the bowl was filled, but not in mirth or joy,
'Twas mingled by a mother's hand to cheer her parting boy.

Drink, John, she said, 'twill do you good,—poor child you 'll never bear
This working in the dismal trench, out in the midnight air;
And if,—God bless me,—you were hurt, 't would keep away the chill;
So John *did* drink,—and well he wrought that night at Bunker's Hill!

I tell you, there was generous warmth in good old English cheer;
I tell you, 't was a pleasant thought to bring its symbol here.
'T is but the fool that loves excess;—hast thou a drunken soul?
Thy bane is in thy shallow skull, not in my silver bowl!

I love the memory of the past,—its pressed yet fragrant flowers,—
The moss that clothes its broken walls,—the ivy on its towers,—
Nay, this poor bauble it bequeathed,—my eyes grow moist and dim,
To think of all the vanished joys that danced around its brim.

Then fill a fair and honest cup, and bear it straight to me;
The goblet hallows all it holds, whate'er the liquid be;
And may the cherubs on its face protect me from the sin,
That dooms one to those dreadful words,—"My dear, where *have* you been?"

THE PILGRIM'S VISION.

In the hour of twilight shadows
The Puritan looked out;
He thought of the "bloody Salvages"
That lurked all round about,
Of Wituwamet's pictured knife
And Pecksuot's whooping shout;
For the baby's limbs were feeble,
Though his father's arms were stout.

His home was a freezing cabin
Too bare for the hungry rat,
Its roof was thatched with ragged grass
And bald enough of that;
The hole that served for casement
Was glazed with an ancient hat;
And the ice was gently thawing
From the log whereon he sat.

Along the dreary landscape
His eyes went to and fro,
The trees all clad in icicles,
The streams that did not flow;
A sudden thought flashed o'er him,—
A dream of long ago,—
He smote his leathern jerkin
And murmured "Even so!"

"Come hither, God-be-Glorified,
And sit upon my knee,
Behold the dream unfolding,
Whereof I spake to thee
By the winter's hearth in Leyden
And on the stormy sea;
True is the dream's beginning,—
So may its ending be!

"I saw in the naked forest
Our scattered remnant cast
A screen of shivering branches
Between them and the blast;
The snow was falling round them,
The dying fell as fast;
I looked to see them perish,
When lo, the vision passed.

"Again mine eyes were opened;—
The feeble had waxed strong,
The babes had grown to sturdy men,
The remnant was a throng;
By shadowed lake and winding stream
And all the shores along,
The howling demons quaked to hear
The Christian's godly song.

"They slept,—the village fathers,—
By river, lake, and shore,
When far adown the steep of Time
The vision rose once more;
I saw along the winter snow
A spectral column pour,
And high above their broken ranks
A tattered flag they bore.

"Their Leader rode before them,
Of bearing calm and high,
The light of Heaven's own kindling
Throned in his awful eye;
These were a Nation's champions
Her dread appeal to try;
God for the right! I faltered,
And lo, the train passed by.

"Once more;—the strife is ended,
The solemn issue tried,
The Lord of Hosts, his mighty arm
Has helped our Israel's side;
Grey stone and grassy hillock
Tell where our martyrs died,
But peaceful smiles the harvest,
And stainless flows the tide.

"A crash,—as when some swollen cloud
Cracks o'er the tangled trees!
With side to side, and spar to spar,
Whose smoking decks are these?
I know Saint George's blood-red cross,
Thou Mistress of the Seas,—
But what is she, whose streaming bars
Roll out before the breeze?

"Ah, well her iron ribs are knit,
Whose thunders strive to quell
The bellowing throats, the blazing lips,
That pealed the Armada's knell!
The mist was cleared,—a wreath of stars
Rose o'er the crimsoned swell,
And, wavering from its haughty peak,
The cross of England fell!

"O trembling Faith! though dark the morn,
A heavenly torch is thine;
While feebler races melt away,
And paler orbs decline,
Still shall the fiery pillar's ray
Along the pathway shine,
To light the chosen tribe that sought
This Western Palestine!

"I see the living tide roll on;
It crowns with flaming towers
The icy capes of Labrador,
The Spaniard's 'land of flowers!'
It streams beyond the splintered ridge
That parts the Northern showers;
From eastern rock to sunset wave
The Continent is ours!"

He ceased,—the grim old Puritan,—
Then softly bent to cheer
The pilgrim-child whose wasting face
Was meekly turned to hear;
And drew his toil-worn sleeve across,
To brush the manly tear

From cheeks that never changed in woe,
  And never blanched in fear.

The weary pilgrim slumbers,
  His resting-place unknown;
His hands were crossed, his lids were closed,
  The dust was o'er him strown;
The drifting soil, the mouldering leaf,
  Along the sod were blown;
His mound has melted into earth,
  His memory lives alone.

So let it live unfading,
  The memory of the dead,
Long as the pale anemone
  Springs where their tears were shed,
Or, raining in the summer's wind
  In flakes of burning red,
The wild rose sprinkles with its leaves
  The turf where once they bled!

Yea, when the frowning bulwarks
  That guard this holy strand
Have sunk beneath the trampling surge
  In beds of sparkling sand,
While in the waste of ocean
  One hoary rock shall stand,
Be this its latest legend,—
  HERE WAS THE PILGRIM'S LAND!

BRANTZ MAYER

WAS born in Baltimore, Maryland, September 27, 1809. His father, Christian Mayer, was a native of Ulm, in Würtemburg; his mother was a lady of Pennsylvania. He was educated at St. Mary's College, and privately by the late Michael Powers. He then went to India, visiting Java, Sumatra, and China; returned in 1828; studied law, travelled throughout Europe, and practised his profession in America, taking a part in politics till 1841, when he received the appointment of Secretary of Legation at Mexico. There he resided till 1843, when he resigned. Since that time, he has practised law at his native city, edited the *Baltimore American* for a portion of the time, written numerous articles for the press, daily, monthly, and quarterly, all of which have appeared anonymously. His acknowledged publications are observations and speculations on Mexico, deduced from his residence there, and historical memoirs. His *Mexico as it was and as it is*, was published in 1844, and his *Mexico—Aztec, Spanish, and Republican*, in two volumes in 1851.

In 1844, he also published *A Memoir, and the Journal of Charles Carroll of Carrollton during his Mission to Canada with Chase and Franklin in* 1776, in 8vo.

In 1851, he delivered the Anniversary Discourse before the Maryland Historical Society, which he published with the title, *Tah-gah-jute; or Logan and Captain Michael Cresap.* It is a vindication of a worthy backwoodsman and captain of the Revolution from the imputation of cruelty in the alleged "speech" of Logan, handed down by Jefferson. Logan is made out a passionate drunken savage, passing through various scenes of personal revenge, and ending his career in a melée induced by himself, under the idea that in a fit of intoxication he had murdered his wife. Colonel Cresap, on the other hand, appears not only entirely disconnected with the attack on Logan's family, but becomes of interest as a well tried, courageous pioneer of the western civilization—a type of his class, and well worthy a chapter in the historical narrative of America. The history of the speech is somewhat of a curiosity. It was not spoken at all, but was a simple message, communicated in an interview with a single person, an emissary from the British camp, by whom it was reported on his return.

In 1854, Mr. Mayer published *Captain Canot, or Twenty Years of an African Slaver*, a book which, from its variety of adventure, and a certain story-telling faculty in its pages, may easily be mistaken, as it has been, for a work of pure invention. But such is not the case. Captain Canot, whose name is slightly altered, is an actual personage, who supplied the author with the facts which he has woven into his exciting narrative. The force of the book consists in its cool, matter-of-fact account of the wild life of the Slave Trader on the western coast of Africa; the rationale of whose iniquitous proceedings is unblushingly avowed, and given with a fond and picturesque detail usually reserved for topics for which the civilized world has greater respect and sympathy. As a picture of a peculiar state of life it has a verisimilitude, united with a romantic interest worthy the pages of De Foe.

The Maryland Historical Society, with which several of the literary labors of Mr. Mayer have been identified, of which he is an active superintendent, and to which he has been a liberal benefactor, was founded on the 27th February, 1844, at a meeting called by him. It became possessed of a valuable building, the Athenæum, the following year, in conjunction with the Baltimore Library Company, by a voluntary subscription of citizens; and recently in 1854, the Library Company having ceded its collection of books and rights in the property to the Historical Society, the latter is now in the enjoyment of one of the most valuable endowments of the kind in the country.

This building was erected under the direction of the architect Robert Cary Long, a gentleman of taste and energy in his profession, and a cultivator of literature. He came to New York in 1848, where he was fast establishing himself in general estimation, when he was suddenly cut off at the outset of what promised to be an active career, by the cholera in July, 1849. He was about publishing a work on architecture, had delivered an ingenious paper before the New York Historical Society on *Aztec Architecture*, and written a series of Essays on topics growing out of his profession, entitled *Architectonics*, in the *Literary World*. He was a man of active mind, intent on the practical employment of his talents, while his amiable qualities endeared him to his friends in society.

On the completion of the Athenæum, the Inaugural Discourse was delivered by Mr. Mayer, who took for his subject *Commerce, Literature, and Art.*

The joint library now (1854) numbers about

fourteen thousand volumes. The collection of MSS., of which a catalogue has been issued, is peculiarly valuable and well arranged. The Maryland State MSS. are numerous, including the "Gilmor Papers," presented to the Society by Robert Gilmor, embracing the Early and Revolutionary Period. The "Peabody Index," prepared by Henry Stevens at the expense of George Peabody, the banker in London, is a catalogue in eleven costly volumes of 1729 documents, in the State Paper office in London, of the Colonial Period. The Library has also a collection of Coins and Medals, and a Gallery of Art, which is a nucleus for the exhibitions in the city, and which has an excellent feature in a series of good copies of the works of the Old Masters.

LITERARY INFLUENCES IN AMERICA.*

It was remarked by Mr. Legaré,—one of the purest scholars given by America to the world—in advising a young friend, at the outset of his life, that, "nothing is more perilous in America than to be too long learning, or to get the name of bookish." Great, indeed, is the experience contained in this short paragraph! It is a sentence which nearly banishes a man from the fields of wealth, for it seems to deny the possibility of the concurrent lives of thought and action. The "bookish" man cannot be the "business" man! And such, indeed, has been the prevailing tone of public sentiment for the last thirty or forty years, since it became the parental habit to cast our children into the stream of trade to buffet their way to fortune, as soon as they were able either to make their labor pay, or to relieve their parents from a part of the expense of maintenance. Early taught that the duty of life is incompatible with the pursuits of a student, the young man whose school years gave promise of renown, speedily finds himself engaged in the mechanical pursuit of a business upon which his bread depends, and either quits for ever the book he loved, or steals to it in night and secrecy, as Numa did to the tangled crypt when he wooed Egeria!

In the old world there are two classes to which Literature can always directly appeal,—government, and the aristocracy. That which is elegant, entertaining, tasteful, remotely useful, or merely designed for embellishment, may call successfully on men who enjoy money and leisure, and are ever eager in the pursuit of new pleasures. This is particularly the case with individuals whose revenues are the mere alluvium of wealth,—the deposit of the golden tide flowing in with regularity,—but not with those whose fortunes are won from the world in a struggle of enterprise. Such men do not enjoy the refreshing occupation of necessary labor, and consequently, they crave the excitement of the intellect and the senses. Out of this want, in Europe, has sprung the Opera,—that magnificent and refined luxury of extreme wealth—that sublime assemblage of all that is exquisite in dress, decoration, declamation, melody, picture, motion, art,—that marriage of music and harmonious thought, which depends, for its perfect success, on the rarest organ of the human frame. The patrons of the Opera have the time and the money to bestow as rewards for their gratification; and yet, I am still captious enough to be discontented with a patronage, springing, in a majority of cases, from a desire for sensual relaxation, and not offered as a fair recompense in the barter that continually occurs in this world between talent and money. I would level the mind of the mass *up* to such an appreciative position, that, at last, it would regard Literature and Art as wants, not as pastimes,—as the substantial food, and not the frail confectionery of life.

And what is the result, in our country, of this unprotective sentiment towards Literature? The answer is found in the fact that nearly all our young men whose literary tastes and abilities force them to use the pen, are driven to the daily press, where they sell their minds, by retail, in paragraphs;—where they print their crudities without sufficient thought or correction;—where the iron tongue of the engine is for ever bellowing for novelty;—where the daily morsel of opinion must be coined into phrases for daily bread,—and where the idea, which an intelligent editor should expand into a volume, must be condensed into an aphoristic sentence.

Public speaking and talk, are also the speediest mediums of plausible conveyance of opinion in a Republic. The value of talk from the pulpit, the bar, the senate, and the street corner, is inappreciable in America. There is no need of its cultivation among us, for fluency seems to be a national gift. From the slow dropping chat of the provoking button-holder, to the prolonged and rotund tumidities of the stump orator—everything can be achieved by a harangue. It is a fearful facility of speech! Men of genius talk the results of their own experience and reflection. Men of talent talk the results of other men's minds: and thus, in a country where there are few habitual students,—where there are few professed authors,—where all are mere *writers*, where there is, in fact, scarcely the seedling germ of a national literature, we are in danger of becoming mere telegraphs of opinion, as ignorant of the full meaning of the truths we convey as are the senseless wires of the electric words which thrill and sparkle through their iron veins.

It is not surprising, then, that the mass of American reading consists of newspapers and novels;—that nearly all our good books are imported and reprinted;—that, with a capacity for research and composition quite equal to that of England, our men become editors instead of authors. No man but a well paid parson, or a millionaire, can indulge in the expensive delights of amateur authorship. Thus it is that Sue is more read than Scott. Thus it is that the *intense* literature of the weekly newspapers is so prosperous, and that the laborer, who longs to mingle cheaply the luxuries of wealth, health, and knowledge, purchases, on his way homeward, with his pay in his pocket, on Saturday night, a lottery ticket, a Sunday newspaper, and a dose of quack physic, so that he has the chance of winning a fortune by Monday, whilst he is purifying his body and amusing his mind, without losing a day from his customary toil!

In this way we trace downward from the merchant and the literary man to the mechanic, the prevailing notion in our country of necessary devotion to labor as to a dreary task, without respite or relaxation. This is the expansive illustration of Mr. Legaré's idea, that no man must get, in America, the repute of being "bookish." And yet, what would become of the world without these derided "bookish" men?—these recorders of history—these developers of science—these philosophers—these writers of fiction—these thousand scholars who are continually adding by almost imperceptible contributions to the knowledge and wealth of the world! Some there are, who, in their day and generation, indeed *appear* to be utterly useless;—men who *seem* to be literary idlers, and yet, whose works tell upon the world in the course of ages. Such was the charac-

* From the Discourse, "Commerce, Literature, and Art."

ter of the occupations of Atticus, in Rome, and of Horace Walpole, in England. Without Atticus,—the elegant scholar, who stood aloof from the noisy contests of politics and cultivated letters,—we should never have had the delicious correspondence addressed to him by Cicero. Without the vanity, selfishness, avarice, and dilettantism of Walpole, we should never have enjoyed that exquisite mosaic-work of history, wit, anecdote, character and incident, which he has left us in the letters addressed to his various friends. Too idle for a sustained work, too gossiping for the serious strain that would have excluded the malice, scandal, and small talk of his compositions,—he adopted the easy chat of familiar epistles, and converted his correspondence into an intellectual curiosity shop whose relics are now becoming of inestimable value to a posterity which is greedy for details.

No character is to be found in history that unites in itself so many various and interesting objects as that of the friend of Atticus. Cicero was a student, a scholar, a devoted friend of art, and, withal, an eminent "man of business." He was at home in the Tusculum and the Senate. It was supposed, in his day, that a statesman should be an accomplished man. It was the prevailing sentiment, that polish did not impair strength. It was believed that the highest graces of oratory—the most effective wisdom of speech,—the conscientious advice of patriotic oratory,—could only be expected from a zealous student who had exhausted the experience of the world without the dread of being "bookish." It was the opinion that cultivation and business moved hand in hand,—and that Cicero could criticise the texture of a papyrus, the grain and chiselling of a statue, or the art of a picture, as well as the foreign and domestic relations of Rome. Taste, architecture, morals, poetry, oratory, gems, rare manuscripts, curious collections, government, popular favor, all, in turn, engaged his attention, and, for all, he displayed a remarkable aptitude. No man thought he was less a "business man" because he filled his dwelling with groups of eloquent marble; because he bought and read the rarest books; because he chose to mingle only with the best and most intellectual society; because he shunned the demagogue and never used his arts even to suppress crime! Cicero would have been Cicero had he never been consul. Place gave nothing to him but the chance to save his country. It can bestow no fame; for fame is won by the qualities that should win place; whilst place is too often won by the tricks that should condemn the practicer. It were well, both on the score of accomplishment and of personal biography, that our own statesmen would recollect the history of a man whose books and orations will endear him to a posterity which will scarcely know that he was a ruler in Rome!

SAMUEL TYLER.

SAMUEL TYLER was born 22d October, 1809, in Prince George's County, Maryland. His father, Grafton Tyler, is a tobacco planter and farmer, and resides on the plantation where Samuel was born, and where his ancestors have dwelt for several generations. Samuel received his early education at a school in the neighborhood, and subsequently at the seminary of Dr. Carnahan at George Town, in the District of Columbia. The Doctor, soon afterwards, was elected President of Princeton College in New Jersey, and the Rev. James M'Vean became his successor. The Latin and Greek languages and their literatures were the studies which were at once the pleasure and the business of this instructor's life. Inspired with his teacher's enthusiasm, the young Tyler became a pupil worthy of his master. So fascinated was he with Greek literature, that for the last year he remained at this school he devoted fourteen hours out of every twenty-four to the study, until the Greek forms of expression became as familiar as those of his native tongue.

In 1827 Mr. Tyler passed a short time at Middlebury College, Vermont. Returning to Maryland, he entered himself as a student of law in the office in Frederick City of John Nelson, since Attorney-General of the United States, and now a distinguished member of the Baltimore bar. The Frederick bar had, for many years, been distinguished for its learning and ability; and therefore Frederick City was considered the best law school in Maryland. Cases were tried in the Frederick Court after the most technical rules of practice, as much so as at any time in Westminster Hall. The present Chief-Justice of the United States, Mr. Taney, built up his professional character at the Frederick bar, and stepped from it to the first place at the bar of Baltimore city.

Mr. Tyler was admitted to the bar in 1831, and has continued to reside, in the prosecution of his profession, in Frederick city, as affording more leisure for the indulgence of his literary pursuits than a large city, where the practice of his profession would be likely to engross his whole time.

An article on "Balfour's Inquiry into the Doctrine of Universal Salvation," in the Princeton Review for July, 1836, was the beginning of Mr. Tyler's authorship. In the Princeton Review for July, 1840, he published an article on the Baconian Philosophy; and in the same journal for July, 1841, an article on Leuhart the mathematician. In the Princeton Review for April, 1843, Mr. Tyler published an article on Psychology, followed by other papers; in July of the same year, on the Influence of the Baconian Philosophy; in October, 1844, on Agricultural Chemistry, in review of Liebig; July, 1845, on the Connexion between Philosophy and Revelation; July, 1846, on Bush on the Soul; and in the number for July, 1852, an article on Humboldt's Cosmos. Mr. Tyler is the author of the article on Whately's Logic in the number of the American Quarterly Review published immediately before that journal was merged in the New York Review. He also wrote the article on Brougham's Natural Theology and that on Rauch's Psychology in the Baltimore Literary and Religious Magazine, edited by Dr. R. J. Breckinridge.

In 1844 Mr. Tyler published the first, and in 1846 the second edition of his *Discourse of the Baconian Philosophy*. This work has received the approbation of eminent thinkers and men of science in America, and has been signalized by the approbation of Sir William Hamilton.

In 1848 Mr. Tyler published in New York *Burns as a Poet and as a Man*, of which one or more editions have appeared in Great Britain.

A convention of delegates elected by the people of Maryland, assembled in 1850 to frame a new Constitution for the state. The subject of reforming the laws was a matter that engaged much of the consideration of the body. Amongst other things, it was proposed to incorporate in the new constitution a provision abolishing what is called special pleading in actions at law. This induced Mr. Tyler to address to the convention, of which he was not a member, a written defence of the importance of retaining special pleading in law procedure; and also showing that all law procedure should be simplified. This view of the subject of law reform finally prevailed, and a provision was incorporated in the new constitution requiring the Legislature to elect three commissioners to simplify the pleadings and practice in all the Courts of the State. Mr. Tyler was elected one of these commissioners. In the division of the work amongst himself and his colleagues it was assigned to him to prepare the first report, which should embrace a general discussion of the subject of law reform, and also present a simplified system of special pleading for all the courts of law in the state. When the report was published, its profound discussion on the relative merits of the Common Law and the Civil Law won the approbation of many of the first lawyers of the county, while the propriety of the simplifications in the system proposed has been generally acknowledged.

GEORGE BURGESS.

The author of a new poetical version of the Book of Psalms, and Bishop of the Diocese of Maine, was born at Providence, Rhode Island, October 31, 1809. Upon being graduated at Brown University in 1826, he became a tutor in that institution, and subsequently continued his studies at the Universities of Bonn, Gottingen, and Berlin. After entering the ministry, he was rector of Christ Church, Hartford, from 1834 to 1847, when he was consecrated to his present office.

In 1840, he published *The Book of Psalms, translated into English Verse*, an animated and successful version. He is also the author of *Pages from the Ecclesiastical History of New England; The Last Enemy, Conquering and Conquered*, two academic poems, and several published Sermons.

PSALM XLVII.*

O, all ye nations, clap your hands,
And let your shouts of victory ring,
To praise the Lord of all your lands,
The broad creation's awful King.

He treads the realms beneath our feet,
He breaks the hostile armies down,
And gives and guards his chosen seat,
The home of Jacob's old renown.

God is gone up with shouting throngs;
Before him pealed the trumpet's call!
Oh, sing to God with lofty songs;
Sing praises to the Lord of all!

Oh, sing to God a royal strain,
To earth's high King a raptured cry!
God o'er the nations spreads his reign,
God lifts his holy seat on high.

The heirs of many a Gentile throne,
With God's and Abraham's seed adore.
The shields of earth are all his own,
As high as heaven his glorious soar.

* "For the chief musician, a Psalm of the Sons of Korah." Whether it was composed for the dedication of the temple, or on any other festival, it is impossible to decide; but it can hardly be read without being referred, in its highest allusion, to the ascension of the Saviour.

God is gone up with shouting throngs. The Son of God, returning to his heavenly throne, with all the pomp of a conqueror, is welcomed by the songs and harps of heaven, and shall soon receive the praises of all the earth.

ALBERT PIKE.

Albert Pike was born at Boston on the 29th of December, 1809. When he was four years old his family removed to Newburyport, where his boyhood was passed, until his matriculation at Harvard in his sixteenth year. Not having the requisite means of support he soon left college, and became an assistant teacher and afterwards principal of the Newburyport Academy. After a few years passed in teaching in this and other towns, during which he continued his classical studies in private, he started in the spring of 1831 for the West. Arriving at St. Louis, having travelled over much of the intervening distance on foot, he joined a band of forty in an expedition to Santa Fe. He arrived at that place on the 25th of the following November, and passed about a year as a clerk in a store, and in travelling about with merchandise in the country. In September, 1832, he left Taos with a company of trappers, visited the head-waters of the Red river and the Brazos, and with four others, separating from the main party, directed his course to Arkansas, and arrived at Fort Smith in November, well nigh naked and penniless. He passed the winter in teaching near the fort, and after attempting to establish a school at a place in the settlements, which was broken up in consequence of his falling ill of a fever, accepting the invitation of the editor of the Arkansas Advocate, at Little Rock, who had been greatly pleased by some poetical communications he had furnished to the paper, became his partner. In 1834 he succeeded to the entire proprietorship of the journal. In 1836 he sold out his newspaper property and commenced the practice of the law, having studied and been admitted to the profession during his editorial career. He also published at Boston a volume containing an account in prose of his adventurous journeyings, and a number of poems suggested by the noble scenery through which he had passed.

Albert Pike

He has since published *Hymns to the Gods*, written in his earlier days of school-keeping. A number of other poems by him have also appeared in several periodicals.

Mr. Pike served with distinction as a volunteer in the Mexican war. He occupies a prominent position as a public man in the Southwest. He published in 1854, *Nugæ, by Albert Pike, printed for private distribution*, a collection of his poems, including the Hymns to the Gods.*

HYMN TO CERES.

Goddess of bounty! at whose spring-time call,
When on the dewy earth thy first tones fall,
Pierces the ground each young and tender blade,
And wonders at the sun; each dull, grey glade
Is shining with new grass; from each chill hole,
Where they had lain enchained and dull of soul,
The birds come forth, and sing for joy to thee,
Among the springing leaves; and fast and free,

* Griswold's Poets of America.

The rivers toss their chains up to the sun,
And through their grassy banks leapingly run,
When thou hast touched them;—thou who ever art
The goddess of all beauty;—thou whose heart
Is ever in the sunny meads and fields;
To whom the laughing earth looks up and yields
Her waving treasures;—thou that in thy car
With winged dragons, when the morning star
Sheds his cold light, touchest the morning trees
Until they spread their blossoms to the breeze;—
O, pour thy light
Of truth and joy upon our souls this night,
And grant to us all plenty and good ease!

O thou, the goddess of the rustling corn!
Thou to whom reapers sing, and on the lawn
Pile up their baskets with the full eared wheat;
While maidens come, with little dancing feet,
And bring thee poppies, weaving thee a crown
Of simple beauty, bending their heads down
To garland thy full baskets; at whose side,
Among the sheaves of wheat, doth Bacchus ride
With bright and sparkling eyes, and feet and mouth
All wine-stained from the warm and sunny south;
Perhaps one arm about thy neck he twines,
While in his car ye ride among the vines,
And with the other hand he gathers up
The rich, full grapes, and holds the glowing cup
Unto thy lips—and then he throws it by,
And crowns thee with bright leaves to shade thine eye,
So it may gaze with richer love and light
Upon his beaming brow: If thy swift flight
Be on some hill
Of vine-hung Thrace—O, come, while night is still,
And greet with heaping arms our gladdened sight!

Lo! the small stars, above the silver wave,
Come wandering up the sky, and kindly lave
The thin clouds with their light, like floating sparks
Of diamonds in the air; or spirit barks,
With unseen riders, wheeling in the sky.
Lo! a soft mist of light is rising high,
Like silver shining through a tint of red,
And soon the queenéd moon her love will shed,
Like pearl mist, on the earth and on the sea,
Where thou shalt cross to view our mystery.
Lo! we have torches here for thee, and urns,
Where incense with a floating odor burns,
And altars piled with various fruits and flowers,
And ears of corn, gathered at early hours,
And odors fresh from India, with a heap
Of many-colored poppies:—Lo! we keep
Our silent watch for thee, sitting before
Thy ready altars, till to our lone shore
Thy chariot wheels
Shall come, while ocean to the burden reels,
And utters to the sky a stifled roar.

FAREWELL TO NEW ENGLAND.

Farewell to thee, New England!
Farewell to thee and thine!
Good-bye to leafy Newbury,
And Rowley's hills of pine!

Farewell to thee, brave Merrimac!
Good-bye old heart of blue!
May I but find, returning,
That all, like thee, are true!

Farewell to thee, old Ocean!
Grey father of mad waves!
Whose surge, with constant motion,
Against the granite raves.

Farewell to thee, old Ocean!
I shall see thy face once more,
And watch thy mighty waves again,
Along my own bright shore.

Farewell the White Hill's summer-snow,
Ascutney's cone of green!
Farewell Monadnock's regal glow,
Old Holyoke's emerald sheen!

Farewell grey hills, broad lakes, sweet dells,
Green fields, trout-peopled brooks!
Farewell the old familiar bells!
Good-bye to home and books!

Good-bye to all! to friend and foe!
Few foes I leave behind:
I bid to all, before I go,
A long farewell, and kind.

Proud of thee am I, noble land!
Home of the fair and brave!
Thy motto evermore should stand,
"Honor, or honor's grave!"

Whether I am on ocean tossed,
Or hunt where the wild deer run,
Still shall it be my proudest boast,
That I'm New England's son.

So, a health to thee, New England,
In a parting cup of wine!
Farewell to leafy Newbury,
And Rowley's woods of pine!

ADRIAN ROUQUETTE.

The Abbé Adrian Rouquette, an ecclesiastic of the Roman Catholic Church, a native of Louisiana, is of mingled European and American parentage; his father, Dominique Rouquette, being a

A. Rouquette

Frenchman, and his mother, Louise Cousin, a native of Louisiana. He was born in New Orleans, and received his education in France, at the Royal College of Nantes; studied for the bar but relinquished it for the church, becoming attached to the Catholic seminary at New Orleans, where he officiates on stated occasions during the week, passing the rest of his time in retirement and study at his residence at Mandeville, in the parish of St. Tammany, in that state. He has cultivated poetic writing in both French and

English, with ease and elegance, and is also the author of some eloquent prose compositions. His chief volume of poems, *Les Savanes, Poésies Américaines*, was published at Paris and New Orleans in 1841. It contains numerous expressions of sentiment and emotion of the school of Chateaubriand, in his American writings, several of whose themes he pursues. There are also poems of personal feeling exhibiting warmth and tenderness. Of the American descriptive passages we may present a *Souvenir of Kentucky*, written in 1838:—

SOUVENIR DE KENTUCKY.

Kentucky, the bloody land!

* * * * * *

Le Seigneur dit à Osée: "Après cela, néanmoins, je l'attirerai doucement à moi, je l'amènerai dans la solitude, et je lui parlerai au cœur."

(*La Bible* OSEE.)

Enfant, je dis un soir: Adieu, ma bonne mère!
Et je quittai gaîment sa maison et sa terre.
Enfant, dans mon exil, une lettre, un matin,
(O Louise!) m'apprit que j'étais orphelin!
Enfant, je vis les bois du Kentucky sauvage,
Et l'homme se souvient des bois de son jeune âge!
Ah! dans le Kentucky les arbres sont bien beaux:
C'est la *terre de sang*, aux indiens tombeaux,
Terre aux belles forêts, aux séculaires chênes,
Aux bois suivis de bois, aux magnifiques scènes;
Imposant cimetière, où dorment en repos
Tant de *rouges-tribus* et tant de *blanches-peaux;*
Où l'ombre du vieux Boon, immobile génie,
Semble écouter, la nuit, l'éternelle harmonie,
Le murmure éternel des immenses déserts,
Ces mille bruits confus, ces mille bruits divers,
Cet orgue des forêts, cet orchestre sublime,
O Dieu! que seul tu fis, que seul ton souffle anime!
Quand au vaste clavier pèse un seul de tes doigts,
Soudain, roulent dans l'air mille flots à la fois:
Soudain, au fond des bois, sonores basiliques,
Bourdonne un océan de sauvages musiques;
Et l'homme, à tous ces sons de l'orgue universel,
L'homme tombe à genoux, en regardant le ciel!
Il tombe, il croit, il prie; et, chrétien sans étude,
Il retrouve, étonné, Dieu dans la solitude!

A portion of this has been vigorously rendered by a writer in the *Southern Quarterly Review*.*

"Here, with its Indian tombs, the Bloody Land
Spreads out:—majestic forests, secular oaks,
Woods stretching into woods; a witching realm,
Yet haunted with dread shadows;—a vast grave,
Where, laid together in the sleep of death,
Rest myriads of the red men and the pale.
Here, the stern forest genius, veteran Boon,
Still harbors: still he hearkens, as of yore,
To never ceasing harmonies, that blend,
At night, the murmurs of a thousand sounds,
That rise and swell capricious, change yet rise,
Borne from far wastes immense, whose mingling strains—
The forest organ's tones, the sylvan choir—
Thy breath alone, O God! can'st animate.
Making it fruitful in the matchless space!
Thy mighty fingers pressing on its keys,
How suddenly the billowy tones roll up
From the great temples of the solemn depths,
Resounding through the immensity of wood
To the grand gushing harmonies, that speak
For thee, alone, O Father. As we hear
The unanimous concert of this mighty chaunt,
We bow before thee; eyes uplift to Heaven,
We pray thee, and believe. A Christian sense
Informs us, though untaught in Christian books
Awed into worship, as we learn to know
That thou, O God, art in the solitude!"

* July, 1854.

In 1846 the Abbé Rouquette pronounced an animated Discourse at the Cathedral of St. Louis, on occasion of the anniversary of the Battle of New Orleans. In 1848 he published *Wild Flowers*, a volume of sacred poetry, written in English, in which his style is restrained. It falls in the rank of occasional verses, within the range of topics growing out of the peculiar views of his church, and shows a delicate sensibility in its choice of subjects.

In 1852 a prose work appeared from his pen, entitled *La Thébaïde en Amérique, ou Apologie de la Vie Solitaire et Contemplative;* a species of tract in which the religious retreats from the world supported by the Roman Catholic church, are defended by various philosophical and other considerations, colored by the writer's sentimental poetic view.

THE NOOK.

L'humble coin qu'il me faut pour prier et chanter.
The humble nook where I may sing and pray.

Victor Laprade.

The nook! O lovely spot of land,
Where I have built my cell;
Where, with my Muse, my only friend,
In peacefulness I dwell.

The nook! O verdant seat of bliss,
My shelter from the blast
Midst deserts, smiling *oasis*,
Where I may rest at last.

The nook! O home of birds and flowers,
Where I may sing and pray;
Where I may dream, in shady bowers,
So happy night and day.

The nook! O sacred, deep retreat,
Where crowds may ne'er intrude;
Where men with God and angels meet
In peaceful solitude;

O paradise, where I have flown;
O woody, lovely spot,
Where I may live and die alone,
Forgetful and forgot!

TO NATURE, MY MOTHER.

Dear Nature is the kindest mother still.—*Byron.*

O nature, powerful, smiling, calm,
To my unquiet heart,
Thy peace, distilling as a balm,
Thy mighty life impart.

O nature, mother still the same,
So lovely mild with me,
To live in peace, unsung by fame—
Unchanged, I come to thee;

I come to live as saints have lived
I fly where they have fled,
By men unholy never grieved,
In prayer my tears to shed.

Alone with thee, from cities far,
Dissolved each earthly tie,
By some divine, magnetic star,
Attracted still on high.

Oh! that my heart, inhaling love
And life with ecstasy,
From this low world to worlds above,
Could rise exultingly!

FRANCOIS DOMINIQUE ROUQUETTE, the brother of the preceding, is also an author. He was born January 2, 1810, at New Orleans, educated there under Prof. Rochefort at the Orleans college, and pursued his classical studies at Nantes, in France. In 1828 he returned to the United States; studied law with Rawle, the author of the work on the Constitution of the United States, at Philadelphia; but preferring the profession of literature, returned to France, where he published a volume of poetry, *Les Meschacébennes*, and was encouraged by Beranger, Victor Hugo, Barthelemy, and others. M. Rouquette has led the life of a traveller or of retirement, and has prepared a work on the Choctaw Nation, which he proposes to publish in French and English, as he writes with ease in both languages.

JONES VERY

Is the author of a volume of *Essays and Poems* published in Boston in 1839. It contains three articles in prose on Epic Poetry, Shakespeare, and Hamlet, and a collection of Poems, chiefly sonnets, which are felicitous in their union of thought and emotion. They are expressions of the spiritual life of the author, and in a certain metaphysical vein and simplicity, their love of nature, and sincerity of utterance, remind us of the meditations of the philosophical and pious writers in the old English poetry of the seventeenth century. The subtle essay on Shakespeare illustrates the universality of his genius by a condition of the higher Christian life.

Jones Very

The author of these productions is a native and resident of Salem, Massachusetts. His father was a sea captain, with whom he made several voyages to Europe. Upon the death of this parent he prepared himself for college, and was a graduate of Harvard of 1836, where he became for awhile a tutor of Greek. "While he held this office," says Griswold, "a religious enthusiasm took possession of his mind, which gradually produced so great a change in him, that his friends withdrew him from Cambridge, and he returned to Salem, where he wrote most of the poems in the collection of his writings."*

TO THE PAINTED COLUMBINE.

Bright image of the early years
When glowed my cheek as red as thou,
And life's dark throng of cares and fears
Were swift-winged shadows o'er my sunny brow!

Thou blushest from the painter's page,
Robed in the mimic tints of art;
But Nature's hand in youth's green age
With fairer hues first traced thee on my heart.

The morning's blush, she made it thine,
The morn's sweet breath, she gave it thee,
And in thy look, my Columbine!
Each fond-remembered spot she bade me see.

I see the hill's far-gazing head,
Where gay thou noddest in the gale;
I hear light-bounding footsteps tread
The grassy path that winds along the vale.

I hear the voice of woodland song
Break from each bush and well-known tree,
And on light pinions borne along,
Comes back the laugh from childhood's heart of glee.

O'er the dark rock the dashing brook,
With look of anger, leaps again,
And, hastening to each flowery nook,
Its distant voice is heard far down the glen.

Fair child of art! thy charms decay,
Touched by the withered hand of Time;
And hushed the music of that day,
When my voice mingled with the streamlet's chime;

But in my heart thy cheek of bloom
Shall live when Nature's smile has fled;
And, rich with memory's sweet perfume,
Shall o'er her grave thy tribute incense shed.

There shalt thou live and wake the glee
That echoed on thy native hill;
And when, loved flower! I think of thee,
My infant feet will seem to seek thee still.

THE WIND-FLOWER.

Thou lookest up with meek confiding eye
Upon the clouded smile of April's face,
Unharmed though Winter stands uncertain by
Eyeing with jealous glance each opening grace.
Thou trustest wisely! in thy faith arrayed
More glorious thou than Israel's wisest King;
Such faith was his whom men to death betrayed
As thine who hear'st the timid voice of Spring,
While other flowers still hide them from her call
Along the river's brink and meadow bare.
These will I seek beside the stony wall,
And in thy trust with childlike heart would share,
O'erjoyed that in thy early leaves I find
A lesson taught by him who loved all human kind.

THE NEW BIRTH.

'Tis a new life;—thoughts move not as they did
With slow uncertain steps across my mind,
In thronging haste fast pressing on they bid
The portals open to the viewless wind
That comes not save when in the dust is laid
The crown of pride that gilds each mortal brow,
And from before man's vision melting fade
The heavens and earth;—their walls are falling now,—
Fast crowding on, each thought asks utterance strong;
Storm-lifted waves swift rushing to the shore,
On from the sea they send their shouts along,
Back through the cave-worn rocks their thunders roar;
And I a child of God by Christ made free
Start from death's slumbers to Eternity.

DAY.

Day! I lament that none can hymn thy praise
In fitting strains, of all thy riches bless;
Though thousands sport them in thy golden rays,
Yet none like thee their Maker's name confess.
Great fellow of my being! woke with me
Thou dost put on thy dazzling robes of light,
And onward from the east go forth to free
Thy children from the bondage of the night;
I hail thee, pilgrim! on thy lonely way,
Whose looks on all alike benignant shine;
A child of light, like thee, I cannot stay,
But on the world I bless must soon decline,
New rising still, though setting to mankind,
And ever in the eternal West my dayspring find.

* Poets and Poetry of America.

NIGHT.

I thank thee, Father, that the night is near
When I this conscious being may resign;
Whose only task thy words of love to hear,
And in thy acts to find each act of mine;
A task too great to give a child like me,
The myriad-handed labors of the day,
Too many for my closing eyes to see,
Thy words too frequent for my tongue to say;
Yet when thou see'st me burthened by thy love,
Each other gift more lovely then appears,
For dark-robed night comes hovering from above,
And all thine other gifts to me endears;
And while within her darkened couch I sleep,
Thine eyes untired above will constant vigils keep.

THE LATTER RAIN.

The latter rain,—it falls in anxious haste
Upon the sun-dried fields and branches bare,
Loosening with searching drops the rigid waste,
As if it would each root's lost strength repair;
But not a blade grows green as in the Spring,
No swelling twig puts forth its thickening leaves;
The robins only 'mid the harvests sing
Pecking the grain that scatters from the sheaves;
The rain falls still,—the fruit all ripened drops,
It pierces chestnut burr and walnut shell,
The furrowed fields disclose the yellow crops,
Each bursting pod of talents used can tell,
And all that once received the early rain
Declare to man it was not sent in vain.

NATURE.

The bubbling brook doth leap when I come by,
Because my feet find measure with its call,
The birds know when the friend they love is nigh,
For I am known to them both great and small;
The flower that on the lovely hill-side grows
Expects me there when Spring its bloom has given;
And many a tree and bush my wanderings knows,
And e'en the clouds and silent stars of heaven;
For he who with his Maker walks aright,
Shall be their lord as Adam was before;
His ear shall catch each sound with new delight,
Each object wear the dress that then it wore;
And he, as when erect in soul he stood,
Hear from his Father's lips that all is good.

THE PRAYER.

Wilt thou not visit me?
The plant beside me feels thy gentle dew;
And every blade of grass I see,
From thy deep earth its moisture drew.

Wilt thou not visit me?
Thy morning calls on me with cheering tone;
And every hill and tree
Lend but one voice, the voice of Thee alone.

Come, for I need thy love,
More than the flower the dew, or grass the rain
Come gentle as thy holy dove,
And let me in thy sight rejoice to live again.

I will not hide from them,
When thy storms come, though fierce may be their wrath;
But bow with leafy stem,
And strengthened follow on thy chosen path.

Yes, Thou wilt visit me;
Nor plant nor tree thy eye delight so well,
As when from sin set free
My spirit loves with thine in peace to dwell.

MARGARET FULLER OSSOLI.

Margaret Fuller, whose native disposition, studies, association with her contemporaries, and remarkable fate, will secure her a permanent place among the biographies of literary women, was born in Cambridgeport, Mass., the 23d of May, 1810. In a chapter of autobiography which was found among her papers, she speaks of her father as a working lawyer (he was also a politician and member of Congress), with the ordinary activities of men of his class; but of her mother as of a delicate, sensitive, spontaneous nature. During her early years the whole attention of Margaret was confined to books. She was taught the Latin and English grammar at the same time, and began to read the former language at six years of age. Her father set her this task-work of study, which soon grew into a necessity. At fifteen she describes her day's performances to a friend. She was studying Greek, French, and Italian literature, Scottish metaphysics—we may be sure a full share of English reading—and writing a critical journal of the whole at night. The result of this was a forced product of the parental discipline; but it would have been no product at all without a vigorous, generous nature. This the pupil possessed. Her temperament, bold and confident, assimilated this compulsory education; and she extracted a passionate admiration for Rome out of her Latin studies. The passage in which she records this is noticeable as an illustration of her character:—

In accordance with this discipline in heroic common sense, was the influence of those great Romans, whose thoughts and lives were my daily food during those plastic years. The genius of Rome displayed itself in Character, and scarcely needed an occasional wave of the torch of thought to show its lineaments, so marble strong they gleamed in every light. Who, that has lived with those men, but admires the plain force of fact, of thought passed into action? They take up things with their naked hands. There is just the man, and the block he casts before you,—no divinity, no demon, no unfulfilled aim, but just the man and Rome, and what he did for Rome. Everything turns your attention to what a man can become, not by yielding himself freely to impressions, not by letting nature play freely through him, but by a single thought, an earnest purpose, an indomitable will, by hardihood, self-command, and force of expression. Architecture was the art in which Rome excelled, and this corresponds with the feeling these men of Rome excite. They did not grow,—they built themselves up, or were built up by the fate of Rome, as a temple for Jupiter Stator. The ruined Roman sits among the ruins; he flies to no green garden; he does not look to heaven; if his intent is defeated, if he is less than he meant to be, he lives no more. The names which end in "*us*," seem to speak with lyric cadence. That measured cadence,—that tramp and march,—which are not stilted, because they indicate real force, yet which seem so when compared with any other language,—make Latin a study in itself of mighty influence. The language alone, without the literature, would give one the *thought* of Rome. Man present in nature, commanding nature too sternly to be inspired by it, standing like the rock amid the sea, or moving like the fire over the land, either impassive or irresistible; knowing not the soft mediums or fine flights of life, but by the force which he expresses, piercing to the centre.

We are never better understood than when we speak of a "Roman virtue," a "Roman outline." There is somewhat indefinite, somewhat yet unfulfilled in the thought of Greece, of Spain, of modern Italy; but ROME! it stands by itself, a clear Word. The power of will, the dignity of a fixed purpose is what it utters. Every Roman was an Emperor. It is well that the infallible church should have been founded on this rock; that the presumptuous Peter should hold the keys, as the conquering Jove did before his thunderbolts, to be seen of all the world. The Apollo tends flocks with Admetus; Christ teaches by the lonely lake, or plucks wheat as he wanders through the fields some Sabbath morning. They never come to this stronghold; they could not have breathed freely where all became stone as soon as spoken, where divine youth found no horizon for its all-promising glance, but every thought put on before it dared issue to the day in action, its *toga virilis*.

Suckled by this wolf, man gains a different complexion from that which is fed by the Greek honey. He takes a noble bronze in camps and battle-fields; the wrinkles of councils well beseem his brow, and the eye cuts its way like the sword. The Eagle should never have been used as a symbol by any other nation: it belonged to Rome.

The history of Rome abides in mind, of course, more than the literature. It was degeneracy for a Roman to use the pen; his life was in the day. The "vaunting" of Rome, like that of the North American Indians, is her proper literature. A man rises; he tells who he is, and what he has done; he speaks of his country and her brave men; he knows that a conquering god is there, whose agent is his own right hand; and he should end like the Indian, "I have no more to say."

It never shocks us that the Roman is self-conscious. One wants no universal truths from him, no philosophy, no creation, but only his life, his Roman life felt in every pulse, realized in every gesture. The universal heaven takes in the Roman only to make us feel his individuality the more. The Will, the Resolve of Man!—it has been expressed,—fully expressed!

I steadily loved this ideal in my childhood, and this is the cause, probably, why I have always felt that man must know how to stand firm on the ground, before he can fly. In vain for me are men more, if they are less, than Romans. Dante was far greater than any Roman, yet I feel he was right to take the Mantuan as his guide through hell, and to heaven.

This education acting upon a sensitive nature made excitement a necessity. Her school life, described by herself in the sketch of Mariana in her book the Summer on the Lakes, appears a constant effort to secure activity for herself and the notice of others by fantastic conduct. One of her companions at Cambridge, the Rev. F. H. Hedge, then a student of Harvard, describes her at thirteen: "A child in years, but so precocious in her mental and physical developments, that she passed for eighteen or twenty. Agreeably to this estimate, she had her place in society as a lady full-grown." At twenty-two, led by the review articles of Carlyle, she entered upon the study of German literature, reading the works of Goethe, Schiller, Tieck, Novalis, and Richter, within the year. She was at this time fond of society, as she always was. Her admiration of the personal qualities of others was strong and undisguised. In possession of power and authority and self-will, in the world of books, nature was not to be defeated: she was dependent to a proportionate degree upon the sympathy of others. In this way she became a kind of female confessor, listening to the confidences and experiences of her young friends.

In 1833 she removed with her father to Groton. His death occurred there shortly after, in 1835, and the following year Margaret Fuller became a teacher in Boston of Latin and French in Mr. Alcot's school, and had her own æsthetic classes of young ladies in French, German, and Italian, with whom she read portions of Schiller, Goethe, Lessing, Tasso, Ariosto, and Dante.

In 1837 she became principal teacher in the Greene-street school at Providence, "to teach the elder girls her favorite branches."

These literary engagements are of less consequence in her biography than her friendships—of the story of which the memoirs published after her death are mostly composed. She became acquainted with Miss Martineau on her visit to this country in 1835. Her intimacy with Emerson grew up in visits to Concord about the same time. His notices of her conversation and spiritual refinements are graphic. Her conversational powers, in the familiarity of the congenial society at Concord, were freely exercised. Emerson says, "the day was never long enough to exhaust her opulent memory; and I, who knew her intimately for ten years—from July, 1836, till August, 1846, when she sailed for Europe—never saw her without surprise at her new powers." Nor was this charm confined to her philosophical friends: she had the art of drawing out her humblest companions. Her mind, with all its fine culture, was essentially manly, giving a common-sense, dogmatic tone to her remarks. It is noticeable how large a space criticism occupies in her writings. It is her chief province; and criticism as exhibited by her pen or words, whether antagonistic or otherwise, is but another name for sympathy.

The Providence arrangement does not appear to have lasted long. She soon took up her residence in Boston or its vicinity, employing herself in 1839 in a species of lectureship or class of ladies—they were called Conversations—in which German philosophy, æsthetic culture of the Fine Arts, etc., were made the topics of instruction. These exercises are thus described "by a very competent witness," in Mr. Emerson's portion of the Memoirs, in a few sentences, which show the spirit in which they were received by her admirers:—"Margaret used to come to the conversations very well dressed, and altogether looked sumptuously. She began them with an exordium, in which she gave her leading views; and those exordiums were excellent, from the elevation of the tone, the ease and flow of discourse, and from the tact with which they were kept aloof from any excess, and from the gracefulness with which they were brought down, at last, to a possible level for others to follow. She made a pause, and invited the others to come in. Of course, it was not easy for every one to venture her remark, after an eloquent discourse, and in the presence of twenty superior women, who were all inspired. But whatever was said, Margaret knew how to seize the good meaning of it with hospitality, and to make the speaker feel glad, and not sorry, that she had spoken."

She also employed herself at this time, as afterwards, in composition. She published in 1839 a translation of Eckermann's Conversations with Goethe, and in 1841 the Letters of Gunderode and Bettine. The two first volumes of the Dial were edited by her in 1840-41. For this quarterly publication, supported by the writings of Emerson and his friends, she wrote papers on Goethe, Beethoven, the Rhine and Romaic ballads, and the poems of Sterling. The Dial made a reputation for itself and its conductors; but they might have starved on its products. Emerson tells us that "as editor she received a compensation which was intended to be two hundred dollars per annum, but which, I fear, never reached even that amount."

In 1843 she travelled to the West, to Lake Superior and Michigan, and published an account of the journey, full of subtle reflection, and with some studies of the Indian character, in the book entitled *Summer on the Lakes.*

In 1844 Margaret Fuller came to New York, induced by an offer of well paid, regular employment upon the Tribune newspaper. She resided in the family of Mr. Greeley, in a picturesquely situated house on the East river, one of the last footholds of the old rural beauties of the island falling before the rapid mercantile encroachments of the city. Here she wrote a series of somewhat sketchy but always forcible criticisms on the higher literature of the day, a complete collection of which would add to her reputation. A portion of them were included in the volume from her pen, *Papers on Literature and Art,* published in New York in 1846. Her work entitled *Woman in the Nineteenth Century* was published at this time from the Tribune office.

In the spring of 1846 she accompanied her friends, Mr. Marcus Spring of Brooklyn, New York, and his wife to Europe. Her contributions to the Tribune were continued in letters from England and the Continent. She saw the chief literary celebrities, Wordsworth, De Quincey, Chalmers, and Carlyle. At Paris she became intimate with George Sand. At Rome she took part in the hopes and revolutionary movements of Mazzini, and when the revolution broke out was appointed by the Roman commissioner for the service of the wounded, during the siege by the French troops, to the charge of the hospital of the Fate-Bene Fratelli. In a letter to Emerson dated June, 1849, she describes her visits to the sick and wounded, and her walks with the convalescents in the beautiful gardens of the Pope's palace on the Quirinal:—"The gardener plays off all his water-works for the defenders of the country, and gathers flowers for me, their friend." At this time she acquainted her mother with her marriage.

Shortly after her arrival at Rome, in 1847, she had been separated on the evening of Holy Thursday from her companions at vespers in St. Peter's. A stranger, an Italian, seeing her perplexity, offered his assistance. This was the son of the Marquis Ossoli. The acquaintance was continued, and Ossoli offered his hand. He was at first refused, but afterwards they were married in December, after the death of his father. The marriage was for a while kept secret, on the ground that the avowal of his union with a person well known as a liberal would render him liable to exile by the government, while he might, by secrecy, be ready to avail himself of employment under the new administration then looked forward to. September 5, 1848, their child, Angelo, was born at Rieti among the mountains.

The fortunes of the revolution being now broken by the occupation of the French, Ossoli with his wife and child left Rome on their way to America. They passed some time in Florence, and on the 17th May, 1850, embarked from Leghorn in the ship *Elizabeth,* bound for New York. The captain fell ill of small-pox, and died the 3d of June, off Gibraltar. On the 9th they set sail again; the child sickened of the disease and recovered; on the 15th of July the vessel was off the Jersey coast, and the passengers made their preparations for arriving in port the next day. That night the wind increased to a gale of great violence. The ship was driven past Rockaway to the beach of Fire Island, where, early on the morning of the 16th, she struck upon the sand. The bow was elevated and the passengers took refuge in the forecastle, the sea sweeping over the vessel. Some of the passengers were saved by floating ashore on a plank. One of them, Horace Sumner of Boston, perished in the attempt. It was proposed to Margaret to make the trial. She would not be separated from her husband and child, but would wait for the life-boat. It never came. The forecastle became filled with water. The small party left went on the deck by the foremast. A sea struck the quarter. The vessel was entirely broken up. The dead body of the child floated to the shore; the husband and wife were lost in the sea. This happened at nine o'clock in the morning, in mid-summer of the year, and at a place the usual resort at that time of pleasure-loving citizens. As if to enhance the sudden contrast of life and death the disaster took place within full sight of the people on the shore. The simple expedient of passing a rope to the land, attached to a barrel, at the proper time, might, one of the most experienced of those present told us, have saved every life: but the captain was not there.

It was known that Madame Ossoli had with her the manuscript of a History of the Revolution in Italy, which her study of the people, her knowledge of the leaders, her love of freedom, and participation in the struggle, well qualified her to write. Diligent search was made for it among the property which came ashore from the wreck, but it could not be found. The waves had closed over that too—which might long have survived the longest term of life.

So perished this intellectual, sympathetic, kind, generous, noble-hearted woman.

The materials for the study of her life are ample in the jointly prepared Memoirs by her friends, the Rev. James Freeman Clarke, the Rev. F. H. Hedge, the Rev. W. H. Channing, and Ralph Waldo Emerson. These able writers have taken separate portions of her career, with which they have been particularly acquainted, for illustration, and the result is a biography preservative of far more than is usually kept for posterity of the peculiar moods and humors of so individual a life.

A DIALOGUE.

POET. Approach me not, man of cold, steadfast eye and compressed lips. At thy coming nature shrouds herself in dull mist; fain would she hide her sighs and smiles, her buds and fruits even in a veil of snow. For thy unkindly breath, as it pierces her mystery, destroys its creative power. The birds draw back into their nests, the sunset hues into their clouds, when you are seen in the distance with your tablets all ready to write them into prose.

CRITIC. O my brother, my benefactor, do not thus repel me. Interpret me rather to our common mother; let her not avert her eyes from a younger child. I know I can never be dear to her as thou art, yet I am her child, nor would the fated revolutions of existence be fulfilled without my aid.

POET. How meanest thou? What have thy measurements, thy artificial divisions and classifications, to do with the natural revolutions? In all real growths there is a "give and take" of unerring accuracy; in all the acts of thy life there is falsity, for all are negative. Why do you not receive and produce in your kind, like the sunbeam and the rose? Then new light would be brought out, were it but the life of a weed, to bear witness to the healthful beatings of the divine heart. But this perpetual analysis, comparison, and classification, never add one atom to the sum of existence.

CRITIC. I understand you.

POET. Yes, that is always the way. You understand me, who never have the arrogance to pretend that I understand myself.

CRITIC. Why should you?—that is my province. I am the rock which gives you back the echo. I am the tuning-key, which harmonizes your instrument, the regulator to your watch. Who would speak, if no ear heard? nay, if no mind knew what the ear heard?

POET. I do not wish to be heard in thought but in love, to be recognised in judgment but in life. I would pour forth my melodies to the rejoicing winds. I would scatter my seed to the tender earth. I do not wish to hear in prose the meaning of my melody. I do not wish to see my seed neatly put away beneath a paper label. Answer in new pæans to the soul of our souls. Wake me to sweeter childhood by a fresher growth. At present you are but an excrescence produced by my life; depart, self-conscious Egotist, I know you not.

CRITIC. Dost thou so adore Nature, and yet deny me? Is not Art the child of Nature, Civilization of Man? As Religion into Philosophy, Poetry into Criticism, Life into Science, Love into Law, so did thy lyric in natural order transmute itself into my review.

POET. Review! Science! the very etymology speaks. What is gained by looking again at what has already been seen? What by giving a technical classification to what is already assimilated with the mental life?

CRITIC. What is gained by living at all?

POET. Beauty loving itself,—Happiness!

CRITIC. Does not this involve consciousness?

POET. Yes! consciousness of Truth manifested in the individual form.

CRITIC. Since consciousness is tolerated, how will you limit it?

POET. By the instincts of my nature, which rejects yours as arrogant and superfluous.

CRITIC. And the dictate of my nature compels me to the processes which you despise, as essential to my peace. My brother (for I will not be rejected), I claim my place in the order of nature. The Word descended and became flesh for two purposes, to organize itself, and to take cognizance of its organization. When the first Poet worked alone, he paused between the cantos to proclaim, "It is very good." Dividing himself among men, he made some to create, and others to proclaim the merits of what is created.

POET. Well! if you were content with saying, "it is very good;" but you are always crying, "it is very bad," or ignorantly prescribing how it might be better. What do you know of it? Whatever is good could not be otherwise than it is. Why will you not take what suits you, and leave the rest? True communion of thought is worship, not criticism. Spirit will not flow through the sluices nor endure the locks of canals.

CRITIC. There is perpetual need of protestantism in every church. If the church be catholic, yet the priest is not infallible. Like yourself, I sigh for a perfectly natural state, in which the only criticism shall be tacit rejection, even as Venus glides not into the orbit of Jupiter, nor do the fishes seek to dwell in fire. But as you soar towards this as a Maker, so do I toil towards the same aim as a Seeker. Your pinions will not upbear you towards it in steady flight. I must often stop to cut away the brambles from my path. The law of my being is on me, and the ideal standard seeking to be realized in my mind bids me demand perfection from all I see. To say how far each object answers this demand is my criticism.

POET. If one object does not satisfy you, pass on to another, and say nothing.

CRITIC. It is not so that it would be well with me. I must penetrate the secret of my wishes, verify the justice of my reasonings. I must examine, compare, sift, and winnow; what can bear this ordeal remains to me as pure gold. I cannot pass on till I know what I feel and why. An object that defies my utmost rigor of scrutiny is a new step on the stair I am making to the Olympian tables.

POET. I think you will not know the gods when you get there, if I may judge from the cold presumption I feel in your version of the great facts of literature.

CRITIC. Statement of a part always looks like ignorance, when compared with the whole, yet may promise the whole. Consider that a part implies the whole, as the everlasting No the everlasting

Yes, and permit to exist the shadow of your light, the register of your inspiration.

As he spake the word he paused, for with it his companion vanished, and left floating on the cloud a starry banner with the inscription "Afflatur Numine." The Critic unfolded one on whose flag-staff he had been leaning. Its heavy folds of pearly gray satin slowly unfolding, gave to view the word NOTITIA, and *Causarum* would have followed, when a sudden breeze from the west caught it, those heavy folds fell back round the poor man, and stifled him probably,—at least he has never since been heard of.

JAMES H. PERKINS.

JAMES HANDASYD PERKINS, a writer of an acute mind and versatile powers, was born in Boston July 31, 1810. His parents were Samuel G. Perkins and Barbara Higginson. He was educated by Mr. S. P. Miles, afterwards a tutor of mathematics at Harvard, and at the Phillips Academy at Exeter, and the Round Hill school at Northampton. He wrote clever tales and verses at this period, humorous and sentimental.

At the age of eighteen he entered the counting-house of his uncle, Mr. Thomas H. Perkins, who was engaged in the Canton trade. He remained faithful to the discharge of the routine duties of this occupation for more than two years. The necessities of a poetic and naturally despondent nature, however, grew upon him, and demanded other employment for his faculties. In the winter of 1830 he found relief in a business tour to England and thence to the West Indies, of which his faithful friend and biographer, Mr. William Henry Channing, has preserved some interesting memorials. His letters on the journey are spirited and abounding with character; thoughtful on serious points and amusing in the lighter.

Returning home in the summer of 1831, he abandoned mercantile life and sought a home in the West. He took up his residence at Cincinnati, and devoted his attention to the study of the law with his friend the Hon. Timothy Walker. He studied laboriously and conscientiously; but the toil was too severe in the practice of the profession for an infirm constitution, and a scrupulous conscience was still more in the way. His pen offered the next field, and he laid on the sh.fting foundation of the magazines and newspapers some of the corner-stones of the "Literature of the West." He conducted the Western Monthly Magazine, and edited the Evening Chronicle, a weekly paper which he purchased in the winter of 1835, and united with the Cincinnati Mirror then published by Mr. William D. Gallagher and Mr. Thomas H. Shreve, who has been since prominently associated with the Louisville Gazette. The last mentioned gentleman remarks of his friend's powers, "Had Mr. Perkins devoted himself to humorous literature he would have stood at the head of American writers in that line."* His fancy was fresh and original; and his descriptive talent, as exhibited in Mr. Channing's collection of his writings, a pleasurable and ready faculty.

Literature, however meritorious, was hardly, under the circumstances, a sufficient reliance. Mr. Perkins was now a married man in need of a settled support, when the failure of his publisher induced him to engage in rural life. Failing in the scheme of a plantation on the Ohio he took a few acres near Cincinnati with the view of raising a nursery of fruit trees. To acquire information in this new line, and make arrangements for the publication of two books which he meditated on the "Constitutional Opinions of Judge Marshall," and "Reminiscences of the St. Domingo Insurrection," of which his father had been an eye-witness, he paid a visit to New England. Neither of his plans was carried out; but a new and honorable career was found for him on his return to Cincinnati in the performance of the duty of Minister at Large, a mission of benevolence to which he devoted the remainder of his life. He brought his characteristic fervor to the work, and gave a practical direction to the charities of the city; alms-giving, in his view, being but subordinate to the elevation of the poor in the self-respect and rewards of labor. He also identified himself with the cause of prison discipline and reform, and gave much attention to education. He was a generous supporter of the Mercantile Library Association of Cincinnati. He was the first President of the Cincinnati Historical Society in 1844, and was afterwards Vice-President of the Ohio Historical Society; his fondness for the latter pursuits being liberally witnessed by his publication, *The Annals of the West*, and his subsequent series of historical sketches of that region in the North American Review from 1839 to 1847, characterized by their research and excellent descriptive style.*

In the latter part of his life, Mr. Perkins interested himself in a plan of Christian Union, to which he was led by his quick sensitive mind.

His death, December 14, 1849, was under melancholy circumstances. He had been thrown, during the day, into a state of nervous agitation by the supposed loss of his children, who had failed to return home at a time appointed, and in the evening he proposed a walk to recover his spirits. He took his course to a ferry-boat on the river, and in a st.te of depression threw himself into the stream and was drowned.

Thus closed the career of a man of subtle powers, keen and delicate perceptions, of honorable attainments in literature, and of philanthropic usefulness in the business affairs of society.

From the few verses preserved in the interesting memoirs by Mr. Channing, who has traced his career with an unaffected admiration of his virtues, and with the warmth of personal friendship, we select two passages which exhibit something of the nature of the man.

POVERTY AND KNOWLEDGE.

Ah, dearest, we are young and strong,
With ready heart and ready will
To tread the world's bright paths along;
But poverty is stronger still.

* Channing's Memoir and Writings of Perkins, i. 91.

* The articles are, Fifty Years of Ohio, July, 1838; Early French Travellers in the West, January, 1839; English Discoveries in the Ohio Valley, July, 1839; The Border War of the Revolution, October, 1839; The Pioneers of Kentucky, January, 1846; Settlement of the North-Western Territory, October, 1847. He also wrote for the North American Review of January, 1850, an article on Australia; and for the New York Review, July, 1839, an article on The French Revolution.

Yet, my dear wife, there is a might
That may bid poverty defiance,—
The might of knowledge; from this night
Let us on her put our reliance.

Armed with her sceptre, to an hour
We may condense whole years and ages;
Bid the departed, by her power,
Arise, and talk with seers and sages.

Her word, to teach us, may bid stop
The noonday sun; yea, she is able
To make an ocean of a drop,
Or spread a kingdom on our table.

In her great name we need but call
Scott, Schiller, Shakspeare, and, behold!
The suffering Mary smiles on all,
And Falstaff riots as of old.

Then, wherefore should we leave this hearth,
Our books, and all our pleasant labors,
If we can have the whole round earth,
And still retain our home and neighbours?

Why wish to roam in other lands?
Or mourn that poverty hath bound us?
We have our hearts, our heads, our hands,
Enough to live on,—friends around us,—

And, more than all, have hope and love.
Ah, dearest, while those last, be sure
That, if there be a God above,
We are not and cannot be poor!

ON THE DEATH OF A YOUNG CHILD.

Stand back, uncovered stand, for lo!
The parents who have lost their child
Bow to the majesty of woe!

He came, a herald from above,—
Pure from his God he came to them,
Teaching new duties, deeper love;
And, like the boy of Bethlehem,
He grew in stature and in grace.
From the sweet spirit of his face
They learned a new, more heavenly joy,
And were the better for their boy.
But God hath taken whom he gave,
Recalled the messenger he sent!
And now beside the infant's grave
The spirit of the strong is bent.

But though the tears must flow, the heart
Ache with a vacant, strange distress,—
Ye did not from your infant part
When his clear eye grew meaningless,
That eye is beaming still, and still
Upon his Father's errand he,
Your own dear, bright, unearthly boy,
Worketh the kind, mysterious will,
And from this fount of bitter grief
Will bring a stream of joy;—
O, may this be your faith and your relief!

Then will the world be full of him; the sky,
With all its placid myriads, to your eye
Will tell of him; the wind will breathe his tone;
And slumbering in the midnight, they alone,
Your father and your child, will hover nigh.
Believe in him, behold him everywhere,
And sin will die within you,—earthly care
Fall to its earth,—and heavenward. side by side,
Ye shall go up beyond this realm of storms,
Quick and more quick, till, welcomed there above,
His voice shall bid you, in the might of love,
Lay down these weeds of earth, and wear your native forms.

BENSON J. LOSSING.

Benson J. Lossing, the son of a farmer, was born in the town of Beekman, Dutchess County, N. Y. His paternal ancestors came from Holland in 1670, and were the first settlers in the county. His maternal ancestors were among the early English settlers on Long Island, who came from Massachusetts Bay and intermarried with the Dutch at New Amsterdam, now New York.

At a common district school Mr. Lossing received a meagre portion of the elementary branches of an English education. After the death of his mother, young Lossing, after passing a short time on a farm, in the autumn of 1826, was apprenticed to a watchmaker in Poughkeepsie, the county town of his native place. So satisfactory had his conduct been during this period, that before the expiration of his apprenticeship his employer made him an offer of partnership in his business, which was accepted.

Meantime, he devoted every moment of leisure to study, although opportunities as yet for obtaining books were extremely limited. His business connexion proving unsuccessful he relinquished it, after an experiment of upwards of two years; and in the autumn of 1835, he became joint owner and editor of the *Poughkeepsie Telegraph*, the leading weekly paper of the county. The co-partnership of Killey and Lossing continued for six years.

In January, 1836, was commenced the publication of a small semi-monthly paper entirely devoted to literature, entitled *The Poughkeepsie Casket*, which was solely edited by Mr. Lossing. The Casket was a great favorite throughout Dutchess and the neighboring counties, and gave evident token of the correct taste and sound judgment of its youthful editor. Having, moreover, a taste for art, and being desirous of illustrating his little periodical, Mr. Lossing placed himself under the tuition of J. A. Adams, the eminent wood-engraver in the city of New York, pleased with the practical application of engraving to his editorial business. The same autumn he went to New York to seek improvement in the use of the pencil by drawing in the Academy of Design.

About this time, Mr. Lossing was called upon to undertake the editorship of the Family Magazine, which work he also illustrated in a superior manner. He now became permanently settled in New York as an engraver, but continued his business connexion in Poughkeepsie until the autumn of 1841. While engaged throughout the day in his increasing engraving business, he performed his editorial labors at night and early in the morning, and at the same period, during the winter of 1840–41, wrote a valuable little volume entitled *An Outline History of the Fine Arts*, which was published as No. 108 of Harpers' Family Library. In the autumn of 1846, he wrote a book entitled *Seventeen Hundred and Seventy-Six*, consisting of upwards of five hundred pages royal octavo, and illustrated by seventy engravings; and shortly after, produced three biographical and historical pamphlets of upwards of one hundred pages each; together with the *Lives of the Signers of the Declaration of Independence*, a duodecimo volume of over four hundred pages. This, and the subsequent year, he also edited a small paper entitled *The Young People's Mirror*, published by Edward Walker, which met with a ready reception from that class of the community.

In June, 1848, Mr. Lossing conceived the idea and plan of the Pictorial Field Book of the Revolution. He defined the size of the proposed pages; drew some rough sketches in sepia as indications of the manner in which he intended to introduce the illustrations, and with a general description of the plan of his work, submitted it to the consideration of the Messrs. Harper and Brothers. Four days afterwards they had concluded a bargain with him, involving an expenditure of much labor and many thousands of dollars; and something within a month afterwards Mr. Lossing was on his way to the battle-fields and other localities of interest connected with the war for Independence. In the collection of his materials, he travelled upwards of nine thousand miles, not in a continuous journey from place to place, but a series of journeys, undertaken whenever he could leave his regular business, the supervision of which he never omitted. Although the Field Book was upwards of four years in hand, yet the aggregate time occupied in travelling, making sketches and notes, drawing a large portion of the pictures on the blocks for engraving, and writing the work, was only about twenty months. The work was published in thirty numbers, the first issued on the first of June, 1850; the last in December, 1852. It was just beginning to be widely and generally known, and was enjoying a rapidly increasing sale, when the great conflagration of the Harpers' establishment in 1853 destroyed the whole remainder of the edition. It was out of print for a year, but a new and revised edition was put to press in March, 1855.

During portions of 1853–54, Mr. Lossing devoted much time to the preparation of an Illustrated History of the United States for schools and families; and early in 1855 completed a work of four hundred pages which he entitled *Our Countrymen*, containing numerous brief sketches with portraits on wood of remarkable persons eminent by their connexion with the history of the United States.

During the last three years, Mr. Lossing has been engaged in collecting materials for an elaborate illustrated history of the war of 1812, and also a history of the French Empire in America; each to be uniform in size of page and style with his Field Book. He has also formed an association with Mr. Lyman C. Draper, well known throughout the west as an indefatigable collector of traditions, manuscripts, journals, letters, &c., relating to the history and biography of the settlements and settlers beyond the Alleganies, for the purpose of producing a series of volumes commencing with the life of Daniel Boone.

Mr. Lossing has also contributed many valuable papers to various publications of the day, especially to Harpers' Magazine, in a series of American biographical articles in which his pen and pencil are equally employed.

ANN S. STEPHENS.

Mrs. Stephens is a native of Connecticut. She married at an early age and removed to Portland, Maine, where she commenced and continued for some time, the Portland Magazine. In 1836 she edited the Portland Sketch Book, a collection of Miscellanies by the writers of the state. She afterwards removed with her husband to New York, where she has since resided.

Ann S Stephens

A tale from her pen, *Mary Derwent*, won a prize of four hundred dollars offered by one of the periodicals, and its publication brought the author prominently forward as a popular writer for the magazines, to which she has contributed a large number of tales, sketches, and poems. Her last and most elaborate work is the novel of *Fashion and Famine*, a story of the contrasts of city life. It is of the intense school, and contains many scenes of questionable taste and probability, with much that is excellent in description and the delineation of character. One of the best drawn personages of the book is a well to do and kindly huckster woman of Fulton Market. The scenes about her stall, and at the farm whose abundance constantly replenishes her stock, are in a pleasant vein. The chief interest of the plot centres on a trial for murder, and the scenes connected with it are written with energy and effect. We present the introduction of the Strawberry Girl to the market-woman in the opening scene of the book.

THE STRAWBERRY GIRL.

Like wild flowers on the mountain side,
Goodness may be of any soil;
Yet intellect, in all its pride,
And energy, with pain and toil,
Hath never wrought a holier thing
Than Charity in humble birth.
God's brightest angel stoops his wing,
To meet so much of Heaven on earth.

The morning had not fully dawned on New York, yet its approach was visible everywhere amid the fine scenery around the city. The dim shadows piled above Weehawken were warming up with purple, streaked here and there with threads of rosy gold. The waters of the Hudson heaved and rippled to the glow of yellow and crimson light, that came and went in flashes on each idle curl of the waves. Long Island lay in the near distance like a thick, purplish cloud, through which the dim outline of house, tree, mast and spire loomed mistily, like half-formed objects on a camera obscura.

Silence—that strange, dead silence that broods over a scene crowded with slumbering life—lay upon the city, broken only by the rumble of vegetable carts and the jar of milk-cans, as they rolled up from the different ferries; or the half-smothered roar of some steamboat putting into its dock, freighted with sleeping passengers.

After a little, symptoms of aroused life became visible about the wharves. Grocers, carmen, and huckster-women began to swarm around the provision boats. The markets nearest the water were opened, and soon became theatres of active bustle.

The first market opened that day was in Fulton

street. As the morning deepened, piles of vegetables, loads of beef, hampers of fruit, heaps of luscious butter, cages of poultry, canary birds swarming in their wiry prisons, forests of green-house plants, horse-radish grinders with their reeking machines, venders of hot coffee, root beer and dough nuts, all with men, women, and childrens swarming in, over, and among them, like so many ants, hard at work, filled the spacious arena, but late a range of silent, naked, and gloomy looking stalls. Then carts, laden and groaning beneath a weight of food, came rolling up to this great mart, crowding each avenue with fresh supplies. All was life and eagerness. Stout men and bright-faced women moved through the verdant chaos, arranging, working, chatting, all full of life and enterprise, while the rattling of carts outside, and the gradual accumulation of sounds everywhere, bespoke a great city aroused, like a giant refreshed, from slumber.

Slowly there arose out of this cheerful confusion, forms of homely beauty, that an artist or a thinking man might have loved to look upon. The butchers' stalls, but late a desolate range of gloomy beams, were reddening with fresh joints, many of them festooned with fragrant branches and gorgeous garden flowers. The butchers standing, each by his stall, with snow-white apron, and an eager, joyous look of traffic on his face, formed a display of comfort and plenty, both picturesque and pleasant to contemplate.

The fruit and vegetable stands were now loaded with damp, green vegetables, each humble root having its own peculiar tint, often arranged with a singular taste for color, unconsciously possessed by the woman who exercised no little skill in setting off her stand to advantage.

There was one vegetable stand to which we would draw the reader's particular attention; not exactly as a type of the others, for there was something so unlike all the rest, both in this stall and its occupant, that it would have drawn the attention of any person possessed of the slightest artistical taste. It was like the arrangement of a picture, that long table heaped with fruit, the freshest vegetables, and the brightest flowers, ready for the day's traffic. Rich scarlet radishes glowing up through their foliage of tender green, were contrasted with young onions swelling out from their long emerald stalks, snowy and transparent as so many great pearls. Turnips, scarcely larger than a hen's egg, and nearly as white, just taken fresh and fragrant from the soil, lay against heads of lettuce, tinged with crisp and greenish gold, piled against the deep blackish green of spinach and water-cresses, all moist with dew, or wet with bright water-drops that had supplied its place, and taking a deeper tint from the golden contrast. These with the red glow of strawberries in their luscious prime, piled together in masses, and shaded with fresh grape leaves; bouquets of roses, hyacinths, violets, and other fragrant blossoms, lent their perfume and the glow of their rich colors to the coarser children of the soil, and would have been an object pleasant to look upon, independent of the fine old woman who sat complacently on her little stool, at one end of the table, in tranquil expectation of customers that were sure to drop in as the morning deepened.

And now the traffic of the day commenced in earnest. Servants, housekeepers, and grocers, swarmed into the market. The clink of money—the sound of sharp, eager banter—the dull noise of the butcher's cleaver, were heard on every hand. It was a pleasant scene, for every face looked smiling and happy. The soft morning air seemed to have brightened all things into cheerfulness.

With the earliest group that entered Fulton market that morning was a girl, perhaps thirteen or fourteen years old, but tiny in her form, and appearing far more juvenile than that. A pretty quilted hood, of rose-colored calico, was turned back from her face, which seemed naturally delicate and pale; but the fresh air, and perhaps a shadowy reflection from her hood, gave the glow of a rose-bud to her cheeks. Still there was anxiety upon her young face. Her eyes of a dark violet blue, drooped heavily beneath their black and curling lashes, if any one from the numerous stalls addressed her; for a small splint basket on her arm, new and perfectly empty, was a sure indication that the child had been sent to make purchase; while her timid air—the blush that came and went on her face—bespoke as plainly that she was altogether unaccustomed to the scene, and had no regular place at which to make her humble bargains. The child seemed a waif cast upon the market; and she was so beautiful, notwithstanding her humble dress of faded and darned calico, that at almost every stand she was challenged pleasantly to pause and fill her basket. But she only cast down her eyes and blushed more deeply, as with her little bare feet she hurried on through the labyrinth of stalls, toward that portion of the market occupied by the huckster-women. Here she began to slacken her pace, and to look about her with no inconsiderable anxiety.

"What do you want, little girl; anything in my way?" was repeated to her once or twice as she moved forward. At each of these challenges she would pause, look earnestly into the face of the speaker, and then pass on with a faint wave of the head, that expressed something of sad and timid disappointment.

At length the child—for she seemed scarcely more than that—was growing pale, and her eyes turned with a sort of sharp anxiety from one face to another, when suddenly they fell upon the buxom old huckster-woman, whose stall we have described. There was something in the good dame's appearance that brought an eager and satisfied look to that pale face. She drew close to the stand, and stood for some seconds, gazing timidly on the old woman. It was a pleasant face, and a comfortable, portly form enough, that the timid girl gazed upon. Smooth and comely were the full and rounded cheeks, with their rich autumn color, dimpled like an over-ripe apple. Fat and good-humored enough to defy wrinkles, the face looked far too rosy for the thick, grey hair that was shaded, not concealed, by a cap of clear white muslin, with a broad, deep border, and tabs that met like a snowy girth to support the firm, double chin. Never did your eyes dwell upon a chin so full of health and good humor as that. It sloped with a sleek, smiling grace down from the plump mouth, and rolled with a soft, white wave into the neck, scarcely leaving an outline, or the want of one, before it was lost in the white of that muslin kerchief, folded so neatly beneath the ample bosom of her gown. Then the broad linen apron of blue and white check, girding her waist, and flowing over the smooth rotundity of person, was a living proof of the ripeness and wholesome state of her merchandise.—I tell you, reader, that woman, take her for all in all, was one to draw the attention, aye, and the love of a child, who had come forth barefooted and alone in search of kindness.

RALPH HOYT.

Mr. Hoyt, the author of a number of poems which have become popular favorites through their spirit and sincerity, is a clergyman of the

Protestant Episcopal Church in New York. He is a native of the city. His early years were passed in the country on Long Island. He had the benefit of a good education, and after some practice at various mechanical pursuits, became himself a teacher in turn, wrote occasionally for the newspapers, and in 1842 took orders in the church. In 1846 the church of the Good Shepherd was organized as the result of the missionary labors of Mr. Hoyt, who has since continued its minister, supporting its feeble fortunes through many privations. He has latterly resided at a cottage pleasantly situated on the high ground in the rear of the Palisades, at the village of Fort Lee, New Jersey, opposite New York; and he has there shown his accustomed spirit and activity, his humble home being partly the work of his own hands, while a simple but convenient church, of small but sufficient dimensions, on the main street of the village, has been built by his own labor and ingenuity, with moderate aid from his friends. He holds religious services there a part of each Sunday.

Ralph Hoyt

Mr. Hoyt's poems are simple in expression, and of a delicate moral or devout sentiment. They touch tenderly upon the disappointments of life, with a sorrowful refrain. In another mood his verse is hopeful and animated. The title of his longest poem, *The Chaunt of Life*, which is but a fragmentary composition, indicates the burden of his song; which is of the common feelings, longings, and experiences of the world. A cheerful love of nature, an eye for the picturesque, a quaint originality of expression, are exhibited in many of his poems, which have already found their way into the popular collections of the school-books.

SNOW; A WINTER SKETCH.

The blessed morn has come again;
  The early gray
Taps at the slumberer's window pane,
  And seems to say
Break, break from the enchanter's chain,
  Away, away!

'Tis winter, yet there is no sound
  Along the air,
Of winds upon their battle-ground,
  But gently there,
The snow is falling,—all around
  How fair—how fair!

The jocund fields would masquerade;
  Fantastic scene!
Tree, shrub, and lawn, and lonely glade
  Have cast their green,
And joined the revel, all arrayed
  So white and clean.

E'en the old posts, that hold the bars
  And the old gate,
Forgetful of their wintry wars,
  And age sedate,
High capped, and plumed, like white hussars,
  Stand there in state.

The drifts are hanging by the sill,
  The eaves, the door;
The hay-stack has become a hill;
  All covered o'er
The wagon, loaded for the mill
  The eve before.

Maria brings the water-pail,
  But where's the well?
Like magic of a fairy tale,
  Most strange to tell,
All vanished, curb, and crank, and rail!
  How deep it fell!

The wood-pile too is playing hide;
  The axe, the log,
The kennel of that friend so tried,
  (The old watch-dog,)
The grindstone standing by its side,
  Are all now *incog.*

The bustling cock looks out aghast
  From his high shed;
No spot to scratch him a repast
  Up curves his head,
Starts the dull hamlet with a blast,
  And back to bed.

Old drowsy dobbin, at the call,
  Amazed, awakes;
Out from the window of his stall
  A view he takes;
While thick and faster seem to fall
  The silent flakes.

The barn-yard gentry, musing, chime
  Their morning moan;
Like Memnon's music of old time
  That voice of stone!
So marbled they—and so sublime
  Their solemn tone.

Good Ruth has called the younker folk
  To dress below;
Full welcome was the word she spoke,
  Down, down they go,
The cottage quietude is broke,—
  The snow!—the snow!

Now rises from around the fire
  A pleasant strain;
Ye giddy sons of mirth, retire!
  And ye profane!
A hymn to the Eternal Sire
  Goes up again.

The patriarchal Book divine,
  Upon the knee,

Opes where the gems of Judah shine,
(Sweet minstrelsie!)
How soars each heart with each fair line,
Oh God, to Thee!

Around the altar low they bend,
Devout in prayer;
As snows upon the roof descend,
So angels there
Come down that household to defend
With gentle care.

Now sings the kettle o'er the blaze;
The buckwheat heaps;
Rare Mocha, worth an Arab's praise,
Sweet Susan steeps;
The old round stand her nod obeys,
And out it leaps.

Unerring presages declare
The banquet near;
Soon busy appetites are there;
And disappear
The glories of the ample fare,
With thanks sincere.

Now tiny snow-birds venture nigh
From copse and spray,
(Sweet strangers! with the winter's sky
To pass away;)
And gather crumbs in full supply,
For all the day.

Let now the busy hours begin:
Out rolls the churn;
Forth hastes the farm-boy, and brings in
The brush to burn;
Sweep, shovel, scour, sew, knit, and spin,
'Till night's return.

To delve his threshing John must hie;
His sturdy shoe
Can all the subtle damp defy;
How wades he through!
While dainty milkmaids slow and shy,
His track pursue.

Each to the hour's allotted care;
To shell the corn;
The broken harness to repair;
The sleigh t' adorn;
As cheerful, tranquil, frosty, fair,
Speeds on the morn.

While mounts the eddying smoke amain
From many a hearth,
And all the landscape rings again
With rustic mirth;
So gladsome seems to every swain
The snowy earth.

THE WORLD-SALE.

There wandered from some mystic sphere,
A youth, celestial, down to earth;
So strangely fair seemed all things here,
He e'en would crave a mortal birth;
And soon, a rosy boy, he woke,
A dweller in some stately dome;
Soft sunbeams on his vision broke,
And this low world became his home.

Ah, cheated child! Could he but know
Sad soul of mine, what thou and I!
The bud would never wish to blow,
The nestling never long to fly;
Perfuming the regardless air,
High soaring into empty space;
A blossom ripening to despair,
A flight—without a resting place!

How bright to him life's opening morn!
No cloud to intercept a ray;
The rose had then no hidden thorn,
The tree of life knew no decay.
How greeted oft his wondering soul
The fairy shapes of childish joy,
As gaily on the moments stole
And still grew up the blooming boy.

How gently played the odorous air
Among his wavy locks of gold,
His eye how bright, his cheek how fair,
As still youth's summer days were told.
Seemed each succeeding hour to tell
Of some more rare unfolding grace;
Some swifter breeze his sail to swell,
And press the voyager apace!

He roved a swain of some sweet vale,
Or climbed, a daring mountaineer;
And oft, upon the passing gale,
His merry song we used to hear;
Might none e'er mount a fleeter steed,
His glittering chariot none outvie,
Or village mart, or rural mead,
The hero he of heart and eye.

Anon a wishful glance he cast
Where storied thrones their empire hold,
And soon beyond the billowy Vast
He leaped upon the shores of old!
He sojourned long in classic halls,
At learning's feast a favored guest,
And oft within imperial walls,
He tasted all delights, save—rest!

It was a restless soul he bore,
And all unquenchable its fire;
Nor banquet, pomp, nor golden store,
Could e'er appease its high desire.
And yet would he the phantom band
So oft deceiving still pursue,
Delicious sweets in every land,
But ah, not lasting, pure, or true!

He knelt at many a gorgeous shrine;
Reclined in love's voluptuous bowers;
Yet did his weary soul repine,
Were listless still the lingering hours.
Then sped an argosie to bear
The sated truant to his home,
But sorrow's sombre cloud was there,
'Twas dark in all that stately dome.

Was rent at last life's fair disguise,
And that Immortal taught to know
He had been wandering from the skies,
Alas, how long—alas, how low.
Deluded,—but the dream was done;
A conqueror,—but his banner furled;
The race was over,—he had won,—
But found his prize—a worthless World!

Oh Earth, he sighed, and gazed afar,
How thou encumberest my wing!
My home is yonder radiant star,
But thither thee I cannot bring.
How have I tried thee long and well,
But never found thy joys sincere,
Now, now my soul resolves to sell
Thy treasures strewn around me here!

The flatteries I so long have stored
In memory's casket one by one,
Must now be stricken from the hoard;
The day of tinselled joy is done!
Here go the useless jewels! see
The golden lustre they impart!
But vain the smiles of earth for me,
They cannot gild a broken heart!

THE WORLD FOR SALE!—Hang out the sign;
 Call every traveller here to me;
Who'll buy this brave estate of mine,
 And set me from earth's bondage free!
'Tis going!—yes, I mean to fling
 The bauble from my soul away;
I'll sell it, whatsoe'er it bring;—
 The World at Auction here to-day!

It is a glorious thing to see;
 Ah, it has cheated me so sore!
It is not what it seems to be:
 For sale! It shall be mine no more:
Come, turn it o'er and view it well;
 I would not have you purchase dear;
'Tis going—going! I must sell!
 Who bids! Who'll buy the Splendid Tear!

Here's Wealth in glittering heaps of gold,
 Who bids! but let me tell you fair,
A baser lot was never sold;
 Who'll buy the heavy heaps of care!
And here, spread out in broad domain,
 A goodly landscape all may trace;
Hall, cottage, tree, field, hill and plain;
 Who'll buy himself a Burial Place!

Here's Love, the dreamy potent spell
 That beauty flings around the heart!
I know its power, alas, too well!
 'Tis going! Love and I must part!
Must part! What can I more with Love!
 All over the enchanter's reign!
Who'll buy the plumeless, dying dove,
 An hour of bliss,—an age of Pain!

And Friendship,—rarest gem of earth,
 (Who e'er hath found the jewel his?)
Frail, fickle, false and little worth,
 Who bids for Friendship—as it is!
'Tis going—going!—Hear the call;
 Once, twice, and thrice!—'Tis very low!
'Twas once my hope, my stay, my all,
 But now the broken staff must go!

Fame! hold the brilliant meteor high;
 How dazzling every gilded name!
Ye millions, now's the time to buy!
 How much for Fame! How much for Fame!
Hear how it thunders! would you stand
 On high Olympus, far renowned,
Now purchase, and a world command!—
 And be with a world's curses crowned!

Sweet star of Hope! with ray to shine
 In every sad foreboding breast,
Save this desponding one of mine,
 Who bids for man's last friend and best!
Ah, were not mine a bankrupt life,
 This treasure should my soul sustain;
But Hope and I are now at strife,
 Nor ever may unite again.

And Song!—For sale my tuneless lute;
 Sweet solace, mine no more to hold;
The chords that charmed my soul are mute,
 I cannot wake the notes of old!
Or e'en were mine a wizard shell,
 Could chain a world in raptures high;
Yet now a sad farewell!—farewell!
 Must on its last faint echoes die.

Ambition, fashion, show, and pride,
 I part from all for ever now;
Grief is an overwhelming tide,
 Has taught my haughty heart to bow.
Poor heart! distracted, ah, so long,
 And still its aching throb to bear;
How broken, that was once so strong;
 How heavy, once so free from care.

Ah, cheating earth!—could man but know,
 Sad soul of mine, what thou and I,—
The bud would never wish to blow,
 The nestling never long to fly!
Perfuming the regardless air;
 High soaring into empty space;
A blossom ripening to despair,
 A flight—without a resting place!

No more for me life's fitful dream;
 Bright vision, vanishing away!
My bark requires a deeper stream;
 My sinking soul a surer stay.
By death, stern sheriff! all bereft,
 I weep, yet humbly kiss the rod;
The best of all I still have left,—
 My Faith, my Bible, and my God.

STRIKE!

I've a liking for this "striking,"
 If we only do it well;
Firm, defiant, like a giant,
 Strike!—and make the effort tell!

One another, working brother,
 Let us freely now advise:
For reflection and correction
 Help to make us great and wise.

Work and wages, say the sages,
 Go for ever hand in hand;
As the motion of an ocean,
 The supply and the demand.

My advice is, strike for prices
 Nobler far than sordid coin;
Strike with terror, sin and error,
 And let man and master join.

Every failing, now prevailing,
 In the heart or in the head,—
Make no clamor—take the hammer—
 Drive it down,—and strike it dead!

Much the chopping, lopping, propping,
 Carpenter, we have to do,
Ere the plummet, from the summit,
 Mark our moral fabric true.

Take the measure of false pleasure;
 Try each action by the square;
Strike a chalk-line for your walk-line:
 Strike, to keep your footsteps there!

The foundation of creation
 Lies in Truth's unerring laws;
Man of mortar, there's no shorter
 Way to base a righteous cause.

Every builder, painter, gilder,
 Man of leather, man of clothes,
Each mechanic in a panic
 With the way his labor goes.

Let him reason thus in season;
 Strike the root of all his wrong,
Cease his quarrels, mend his morals,
 And be happy, rich, and strong.

WILLIS GAYLORD CLARK.—LEWIS GAYLORD CLARK.

THE twin brothers Clark were born at Otisco, Onondaga county, New York, in the year 1810. Their father had served in the Revolutionary war, and was a man of reading and observation. Willis, on the completion of his education, under the care of this parent and the Rev. George Colton, a relative on his mother's side, went to Philadelphia, where he commenced a weekly periodical similar in plan to the New York Mirror. It was unsuccessful and soon discontinued. He next became an assistant of the Rev. Dr. Brantley, a Baptist clergyman (afterwards President of the College of South Carolina), in the editorship of the Columbian Star, a religious newspaper. He retired from this position to take charge of the Philadelphia Gazette, the oldest daily journal of that city. He became its proprietor, and continued his connexion with it until his death.

One of the most successful of Clark's literary productions was the *Ollapodiana*, a series of brief essays, anecdotes, and observations, continued from month to month in the Knickerbocker Magazine, of which his brother Lewis had become the editor.

Mr. Clark was married in 1836 to Anne P. Caldcleugh, the daughter of a gentleman of Philadelphia. She was attacked by consumption, and died not long after her marriage. Her husband soon followed her, falling a victim to a lingering disease in June, 1841.

Clark's poems, with the exception of *The Spirit of Life*—pronounced before the Franklin Society of Brown University in 1833—are brief, and were written for and published in his own journals and the magazines and annuals of the day. A portion were collected in a volume during his lifetime, and a complete edition appeared in New York in 1847. His *Ollapodiana* have also been collected, with a number of other prose sketches and his poems, in a volume of his *Literary Remains*, published in 1844.

The humors and sensibility of the essayist and poet, alike witness to his warm, amiable sympathies. His mirth was rollicking, exuberant in animal spirits, but always innocent, while his muse dwelt fondly on the various moods of nature, and portrayed domestic tenderness in the consolations of its darker hours of suffering and death.

Mr. Lewis Gaylord Clark is the editor of the Knickerbocker Magazine, having conducted that periodical since its third volume in 1834. He has become widely known by his monthly *Editor's Table* and *Gossip with Readers and Correspondents*, embracing a collection of the jests and *on dits* of the day, connected by a light running comment. A selection from the *Gossip* was published in one volume in 1852, with the title *Knick-Knacks from an Editor's Table*,* and a compliment has recently been paid to its author in the shape of a volume containing original contributions by many of the leading writers of the day, accompanied by their portraits, entitled *The Knickerbocker Memorial*.

A SONG OF MAY.

The spring scented buds all around me are swelling,
 There are songs in the stream, there is health in the gale;
A sense of delight in each bosom is dwelling,
 As float the pure day-beams o'er mountain and vale;
The desolate reign of Old Winter is broken,
 The verdure is fresh upon every tree;
Of Nature's revival the charm—and a token
 Of love, oh thou Spirit of Beauty! to thee.

The sun looketh forth from the halls of the morning,
 And flushes the clouds that begirt his career;
He welcomes the gladness and glory, returning
 To rest on the promise and hope of the year.
He fills with rich light all the balm-breathing flowers,
 He mounts to the zenith, and laughs on the wave;
He wakes into music the green forest-bowers,
 And gilds the gay plains which the broad rivers lave.

The young bird is out on his delicate pinion—
 He timidly sails in the infinite sky;
A greeting to May, and her fairy dominion,
 He pours, on the west wind's fragrant sigh:
Around, above, there are peace and pleasure,
 The woodlands are singing, the heaven is bright;
The fields are unfolding their emerald treasure,
 And man's genial spirit is soaring in light.

Alas! for my weary and care-haunted bosom!
 The spells of the spring-time arouse it no more;
The song in the wild-wood, the sheen of the blossom,
 The fresh-welling fountain, their magic is o'er!
When I list to the streams, when I look on the flowers,
 They tell of the Past with so mournful a tone,
That I call up the throngs of my long-vanished hours,
 And sigh that their transports are over and gone.

From the wide-spreading earth, from the limitless heaven,
 There have vanished an eloquent glory and gleam;
To my veiled mind no more is the influence given,
 Which coloreth life with the hues of a dream:
The bloom-purpled landscape its loveliness keepeth—
 I deem that a light as of old gilds the wave;
But the eye of my spirit in heaviness sleepeth,
 Or sees but my youth, and the visions it gave.

Yet it is not that age on my years hath descended,
 'Tis not that its snow-wreaths encircle my brow;
But the *newness* and sweetness of Being are ended,
 I feel not their love-kindling witchery now:
The shadows of death o'er my path have been sweeping;
 There are those who have loved me debarred from the day;
The green turf is bright where in peace they are sleeping,
 And on wings of remembrance my soul is away.

It is shut to the glow of this present existence,
 It hears, from the Past, a funeral strain;
And it eagerly turns to the high-seeming distance,
 Where the last blooms of earth will be gurnered again;
Where no mildew the soft damask-rose cheek shall nourish,
 Where Grief bears no longer the poisonous sting;
Where pitiless Death no dark sceptre can flourish,
 Or stain with his blight the luxuriant spring.

It is thus that the hopes which to others are given,
 Fall cold on my heart in this rich month of May;
I hear the clear anthems that ring through the heaven,
 I drink the bland airs that enliven the day;
And if gentle Nature, her festival keeping,
 Delights not my bosom, ah! do not condemn;

* Mr. Clark had previously published a volume of articles from the Knickerbocker, by Washington Irving, Mr. Cary, Mr. Shelton, and others, entitled *The Knickerbocker Sketch-Book*.

O'er the lost and the lovely my spirit is weeping,
  For my heart's fondest raptures are buried with them.

TO MY BOY.

Thou hast a fair unsullied cheek,
    A clear and dreaming eye,
Whose bright and winning glances speak
    Of life's first revelry;
And on thy brow no look of care
Comes like a cloud, to cast a shadow there.

In feeling's early freshness blest,
    Thy wants and wishes few:
Rich hopes are garnered in thy breast,
    As summer's morning dew
Is found, like diamonds, in the rose,
Nestling, 'mid folded leaves, in sweet repose.

Keep thus, in love, the heritage
    Of thy ephemeral spring;
Keep its pure thoughts, till after-age
    Weigh down thy spirit's wing;
Keep the warm heart, the hate of sin,
And heavenly peace will on thy soul break in.

And when the even-song of years
    Brings in its shadowy train
The record of life's hopes and fears,
    Let it not be in vain,
That backward on existence thou canst look,
As on a pictured page or pleasant book.

LINES

Written at Laurel Hill Cemetery, near Philadelphia.

Here the lamented dead in dust shall lie,
  Life's lingering languors o'er—its labors done;
Where waving boughs, betwixt the earth and sky,
  Admit the farewell radiance of the sun.

Here the long concourse from the murmuring town,
  With funeral pace and slow, shall enter in;
To lay the loved in tranquil silence down,
  No more to suffer, and no more to sin.

And here the impressive stone, engraved with words
  Which Grief sententious gives to marble pale,
Shall teach the heart, while waters, leaves, and birds
  Make cheerful music in the passing gale.

Say, wherefore should we weep, and wherefore pour
  On scented airs the unavailing sigh—
While sun-bright waves are quivering to the shore,
  And landscapes blooming—that the loved should die?

There is an emblem in this peaceful scene:
  Soon, rainbow colors on the woods will fall;
And autumn gusts bereave the hills of green,
  As sinks the year to meet its cloudy pall.

Then, cold and pale, in distant vistas round,
  Disrobed and tuneless, all the woods will stand!
While the chained streams are silent as the ground,
  As Death had numbed them with his icy hand.

Yet, when the warm soft winds shall rise in spring,
  Like struggling day-beams o'er a blasted heath,
The bird returned shall poise her golden wing,
  And liberal Nature break the spell of Death.

So, when the tomb's dull silence finds an end,
  The blessed Dead to endless youth shall rise;
And hear the archangel's thrilling summons blend
  Its tones with anthems from the upper skies.

There shall the good of earth be found at last,
  Where dazzling streams and vernal fields expand;
Where Love her crown attains—her trials past—
  And, filled with rapture, hails the better land!

OLD SONGS.

Give me the songs I loved to hear,
  In sweet and sunny days of yore;
Which came in gushes to my ear
  From lips that breathe them now no more;
From lips, alas! on which the worm,
  In coiled and dusty silence lies,
Where many a loved, lamented form
  Is hid from Sorrow's filling eyes!

Yes! when those unforgotten lays
  Come trembling with a spirit-voice,
I mind me of those early days,
  When to respire was to rejoice:
When gladsome flowers and fruitage shone
  Where'er my willing footsteps fell;
When Hope's bright realm was all mine own,
  And Fancy whispered, "All is well."

Give me old songs! They stir my heart
  As with some glorious trumpet-tone:
Beyond the reach of modern art,
  They rule its thrilling cords alone,
Till, on the wings of thought, I fly
  Back to that boundary of bliss,
Which once beneath my childhood's sky
  Embraced a scene of loveliness!

Thus, when the portals of mine ear
  Those long-remembered lays receive,
They seem like guests, whose voices cheer
  My breast, and bid it not to grieve:
They ring in cadences of love,
  They tell of dreams now vanished all:
Dreams, that descended from above—
  Visions, 'tis rapture to recall!

Give me old songs! I know not why,
  But every tone they breathe to me
Is fraught with pleasures pure and high,
  With honest love or honest glee:
They move me, when by chance I hear,
  They rouse each slumbering pulse anew;
Till every scene to memory dear
  Is pictured brightly to my view.

I do not ask those sickly lays
  O'er which affected maidens bend;
Which scented fops are bound to praise,
  To which dull crowds their homage lend
Give me some simple Scottish song,
  Or lays from Erin's distant isle:
Lays that to love and truth belong,
  And cause the saddest lip to smile!

EDGAR A. POE.

THE family of Edgar A. Poe was of ancient respectability in Maryland. His grandfather, David Poe, served in the Revolution, and was the personal friend of Lafayette. His father, David Poe, Jr., was a law student at Baltimore, when, in his youth, he fell in love with an English actress on the stage, Elizabeth Arnold, married her, and took to the boards himself. Their son Edgar was born in Baltimore in January, 18[illegible]. After a career of several years of theatrical life, passed in the chief cities of the Union, the parents both died within a short period at Richmond, leaving three orphan children.

Edgar was a boy of beauty and vivacity, and attracted the attention of a friend of his parents, John Allan, a wealthy merchant of Virginia, by whom he was adopted, and his education liberally provided for. In 1816 he was taken by Mr. and Mrs. Allan to England, and deposited for a stay of four or five years at a school near London; a passage of his youth which he has recurred to in almost the only instance in his writings in which he has any personal allusion to his own affairs. It was a trait, too, in his conversation that he seldom spoke of his own history. In his tale of William Wilson he has touched these early school-days with a poetical hand, as he recalls the awe of their formal discipline, and the admiration with which he saw the dingy head-master of the week ascend the village pulpit in clerical silk and dignity on Sunday. He returned home in his eleventh year, passed a short time at a Richmond academy, and entered the University at Charlottesville, where he might have attained the highest honors from the celerity of his wit as a student, had he not thrown himself upon a reckless course of dissipation which led to his expulsion from the college. His biographer, Griswold, tells us that he was at this time celebrated for his feats of personal hardihood: "On one occasion, in a hot day of June, swimming from Richmond to Warwick, seven miles and a half, against a tide running probably from two to three miles an hour." He left Charlottesville in debt, though he had been generously provided for by his friend Allan, whose benevolence, however, could not sustain the drafts freely drawn upon him for obligations incurred in gambling. Poe quarrelled with his benefactor, and abandoned his home with the Byronic motive, it is said, of assisting the Greeks in their struggle for liberty. He went abroad and passed a year in Europe, the history of which would be a matter of singular curiosity, if it could be recovered. It is known that he did not reach Greece, and that he was one day involved in some difficulty at St. Petersburgh, from which he was relieved by the American Minister, Mr. Henry Middleton, who provided him with the means of returning home.* He was afterwards received into favor by Mr. Allan, who procured him an entrance as a cadet at West Point, an institution with which his wayward and reckless habits, and impracticable mind, were so much at war, that he was compelled to retire from it within the year. Mr. Allan having lost his first wife, married again, and Poe, still received with favor at the house, was soon compelled to leave it for ever, doubtless from gross misconduct on his part, for Mr. Allan had proved himself a much-enduring benefactor.

Poe was now thrown upon his own resources. He had already written a number of verses, said to have been produced between his sixteenth and nineteenth years, which were published in Baltimore in 1829, with the title *Al Aaraaf, Tamerlane, and Minor Poems*.† Taking the standards of the country, and the life of the young author in Virginia into consideration, they were singular productions. A certain vague poetic luxury and sensuousness of mere sound, distinct from definite meaning, peculiarities which the author refined upon in his latest and best poems, characterize these juvenile effusions. Al Aaraaf is an oriental poetic mystification, with some fine chanting in

* Griswold's Memoirs, x.

† Baltimore: Hatch & Dunning, 1829. 8vo. pp. 71.

Edgar A. Poe

it, particularly a melodious dithyrambic on one of the poet's airy maidens, Ligeia.

A certain longing of passion, without hearty animality, marked thus early the ill-regulated disposition of a man of genius uncontrolled by the restraint of sound principle and profound literary motives. Other young writers have copied this strain, and have written verses quite as nonsensical without any corruption of heart; but with Poe the vein was original. His whole life was cast in that mould; his sensitive, spiritual organization, deriving no support from healthy moral powers, became ghostly and unreal.* His rude contact with the world, which might have set up a novelist for life with materials of adventure, seems scarcely to have impinged upon his perceptions. His mind, walking in a vain show, was taught nothing by experience or suffering. Altogether wanting in the higher faculty of humor, he could extract nothing from the rough usages of the world but a cold, frivolous mockery of its plans and pursuits. His intellectual enjoyment was in the power of his mind over literature as an art; his skill, in forcing the mere letters of the alphabet, the dry elements of the dictionary, to take forms of beauty and apparent life which would command the admiration of the world. This may account for his sensitiveness as to the recep-

* A lady of this city wittily mentioned her first impressions of his unhappy, distant air, in the opening lines of Goldsmith's Traveller:

> Remote, unfriended, melancholy, slow,
> Or by the lazy Scheldt, or wandering *Po*.

A gentleman, who was a fellow-cadet with him at West Point, has described to us his utter inefficiency and state of abstractedness at that place. He could not or would not follow its mathematical requirements. His mind was off from the matter-of-fact routine of the drill, which in such a case as his seemed practical joking, on some etherial, visionary expedition. He was marked, says our informant, for an early death, if only from the incompatibility of soul and body. They had not the usual relations to each other, and were on such distant terms of acquaintance that a separation seemed inevitable!

tion of his writings. He could afford to trust nothing to the things themselves, since they had no root in realities. Hence his delight in the exercise of his powers as a destructive critic, and his favorite proposition that literature was all a trick, and that he could construct another Paradise Lost, or something equivalent to it, to order, if desirable.

With this fine, sensitive organization of the intellect, and a moderate share of scholarship, Poe went forth upon the world as an author. It is a little singular, that, with intellectual powers sometimes reminding us, in a partial degree, of those of Coleridge,—poetic exercises, take Kubla Khan for instance, being after Poe's ideal,—the two should have had a similar adventure in the common ranks of the army. Coleridge, it will be remembered, was for a short time a dragoon in London, under the assumed name of Comberbatch; Poe enlisted in the ranks and deserted.*

About this time, in 1833, a sum was offered by the Baltimore Saturday Visitor for a prize poem and tale. Mr. Kennedy, the novelist, was on the committee. Poe sent in several tales which he had composed for a volume, and readily secured the prize for his *MS. found in a Bottle*,—incidentally assisted, it is said, by the beauty of his handwriting. Mr. Kennedy became acquainted with the author, then, as almost inevitable with a man of genius depending upon such scanty resources as the sale of a few subtle productions, in a state of want and suffering, and introduced him to Mr. T. W. White, the conductor of the Southern Literary Messenger, who gave him employment upon his publication. Poe in 1835 removed to Richmond, and wrote chiefly in the critical department of the magazine. He was rapidly making a high reputation for the work in this particular, by his ingenuity, when the connexion was first interrupted and soon finally severed, in 1837, by his irregularities. At Richmond he married his cousin Virginia Clemm, a delicate and amiable lady, who after a union of some ten years fell a victim of consumption.

In 1838 a book from Poe's pen, growing out of some sketches which he had commenced in the Messenger, *The Narrative of Arthur Gordon Pym of Nantucket*, was published by the Harpers.† It is a fiction of considerable ingenuity, but the author, who was generally anything but indifferent to the reception of his writings, did not appear in his conversation to pride himself much upon it. This book was written in New York at the close of the year. Poe settled in Philadelphia, and was employed by Burton, the comedian, upon his Gentleman's Magazine, with a salary of ten dollars a week. His *Tales of the Grotesque and Arabesque*, a collection of his scattered magazine stories, were published in two volumes by Lea and Blanchard, Philadelphia, in 1840.

The arrangement with Burton lasted more than a year, when it was broken up, it is said, by Poe's wanton depreciation of the American poets who came under review, and by a final fit of intoxication. He then projected a new magazine, to be called after William Penn, but it was a project only. When Graham established his magazine in 1840 he engaged Poe as its editor, and the weird, spiritual tales, and ingenious, slashing criticisms were again resumed, till the old difficulties led to a termination of the arrangement at the end of a year and a half. Several of his most striking tales, *The Gold Bug*, *The Murders of the Rue Morgue*, were written at this period. A development of the plot of Barnaby Rudge, in Graham's Magazine, before the completion of that novel in England, secured the admiration of Dickens.

In 1844 Poe took up his residence in New York, projecting a magazine to be called The Stylus, and anticipating the subscriptions to the work, which never appeared. When Morris and Willis commenced this year the publication of the Evening Mirror, Poe was for a while engaged upon it, though his sympathies with the actual world were far too feeble for a daily journalist.

The poem of the *Raven*, the great hit of Poe's literary career, was published in the second number of Colton's Whig Review, in February, 1845. The same year he commenced the Broadway Journal, in conjunction with Mr. Charles F. Briggs, and had actually perseverance enough to continue it to its close in a second volume, after it had been abandoned by his associate, in consequence of difficulties growing out of a joint editorship. It was during this period that Poe accepted an invitation to deliver a poem before the Boston Lyceum. When the time for its delivery came Poe was unprepared with anything for the occasion, and read, with more gravity than sobriety in the emergency, his juvenile publication Al Aaraaf. The ludicrous affair was severely commented upon by the Bostonians, and Poe made it still more ridiculous by stating in his Broadway Journal that it was an intentional insult to the genius of the Frog Pond! Poe next wrote a series of random sketches of *The New York Literati** for Godey's Lady's Book. In one of them he chose to caricature an old Philadelphia friend, Dr. Thomas Dunn English, who retaliated in a personal newspaper article. The communication was reprinted in the Evening Mirror in New York, whereupon Poe instituted a libel suit against that journal, and recovered several hundred dollars, with which he refitted a small cottage he now occupied on a hill-side at Fordham, in Westchester county, where he lived with his wife and his mother-in-law, Mrs. Maria Clemm, by whose unwearied guardianship he was protected in his frequently recurring fits of illness, and by whose prudent and skilful management he was provided for at other times.

* Griswold's Memoirs, xi.

† The Narrative of Arthur Gordon Pym of Nantucket, comprising the details of a Mutiny and atrocious Butchery on board the American brig Grampus, on her way to the South Seas, in the month of June, 1827, with an Account of the Recapture of the Vessel by the Survivors; their Shipwreck and subsequent horrible Sufferings from Famine; their Deliverance by means of the British schooner Jane Gray; the brief Cruise of this latter Vessel in the Antarctic Ocean; her Capture, and the Massacre of her Crew among a Group of Islands in the Eighty-fourth parallel of Southern Latitude: together with the incredible Adventures and Discoveries still farther South to which that distressing Calamity gave rise. Harper & Brothers, 1838. 12mo. pp. 201.

* They are now included in a thick volume of the author's works, published by Redfield, which contains the memoir by Dr. Griswold. It is entitled, The Literati: Some Honest Opinions about Autorial Merits and Demerits, with occasional Words of Personality; together with Marginalia, Suggestions, and Essays. With here and there a nice observation, the sketches of the Literati are careless papers, sometimes to be taken for nothing more than mere jest. Some of the longer critical papers are admirable.

In 1848 he delivered a lecture at the Society Library in New York, entitled Eureka, an Essay on the Material and Spiritual Universe; the ingenious obscurities of which are hardly worth the trouble of unravelling, if they are at all intelligible.

His wife was now dead, and he was preparing for marriage with a highly-cultivated lady of New England, when the union was broken off. After this, in 1849, he made a tour to Maryland and Virginia, delivering lectures by the way, and having concluded a new engagement of marriage was on his way to New York to make some arrangements, when he fell into one of his now frequently recurring fits of intoxication at Baltimore, was carried in a fit of insanity from the street to the hospital, and there died on Sunday morning, October 7, 1849, at the age of thirty-eight.

At the close of this melancholy narrative a feeling of deep sorrow will be entertained by those familiar with the author's undoubted genius. It will be difficult to harmonize this wild and reckless life with the neatness and precision of his writings. The same discrepancy was apparent in his personal conduct. Neat to fastidiousness in his dress, and, as we have noticed, in his handwriting; ingenious in the subtle employment of his faculties, with the nice sense of the gentleman in his conduct and intercourse with others while personally before them—there were influences constantly reversing the pure, healthy life these qualities should have represented. Had he been really in earnest, with what a solid brilliancy his writings might have shone forth to the world. With the moral proportioned to the intellectual faculty he would have been in the first rank of critics. In that large part of the critic's perceptions, a knowledge of the mechanism of composition, he has been unsurpassed by any writer in America; but lacking sincerity, his forced and contradictory critical opinions are of little value as authorities, though much may be gathered from them by any one willing to study the peculiar mood in which they were written. In ingenuity of invention, musical effects, and artificial terrors for the imagination, his poems as well as his prose sketches are remarkable. His intricate police story, The Murders of the Rue Morgue, secured admiration when it was translated in Paris, where such details are of frequent occurrence. The mesmeric revelation of *The Facts in the Case of M. Valdemar*, published in the Whig Review, imposed upon some innocent philosophic people in England as a report of actual phenomena. As a good specimen of his peculiar literary logic we may refer to his article *The Philosophy of Composition*, in which he gives the rationale of his creation of the poem The Raven. Having first determined to write a popular poem, he determines the allowable extent: it must be brief enough to be read at a single sitting, and the brevity "must be in the direct ratio of the intensity of the intended effect;" one hundred lines are the maximum, and the poem turns out, "in fact, one hundred and eight." The length being settled, the "effect" was to be universally appreciable, and "beauty" came to be the object of the poem, as he holds it to be the especial object of all true poetry; then the "tone" must be sad, "beauty in its supreme development invariably exciting the sensitive soul to tears." As "an artistic piquancy" he brings in "the refrain" as an old approved resource, and as its most effective form, a single word. The sound of that word was important, and the long ŏ being "the most sonorous vowel," and *r* "the most producible consonant," *nevermore* came to hand, "in fact it was the very first which presented itself." To get the word in often enough, stanzas were to be employed, and as a rational creature would be out of his senses uttering the spell, "a non-reasoning creature capable of speech" was called for, hence the Raven. Death is the theme, as universal and the saddest, and most powerful in alliance with beauty: so the death of a beautiful woman is invoked. The rest is accounted for *à priori* in the same explicit manner in this extraordinary criticism.

Though in any high sense of the word, as in the development of character, Poe would hardly be said to possess much humor, yet with his skill in language, and knowledge of effects, he was a master of ridicule, and could turn the merest nonsense to a very laughable purpose. Instances of this will occur to the reader of his writings, especially in his criticisms and satiric sketches; but they will hardly bear to be detached for quotation, as they must be approached along his gradual course of rigmarole. With more practical knowledge of the world, and more stamina generally, he might have been a very powerful satirist. As it was, too frequently he wasted his efforts on paltry literary puerilities.

His inventions, both in prose and verse, take a sombre, morbid hue. They have a moral aspect, though it is not on the surface. Apparently they are but variations of the forms of the terrible, in its quaint, melodramatic character: in reality they are the expressions of the disappointment and despair of the soul, alienated from happy human relations; misused faculties:

Sweet bells jangled, out of tune, and harsh.

While we admire their powerful eccentricity, and resort to them for a novel sensation to our jaded mental appetites, let us remember at what cost of pain, suffering, and disappointment they were produced; and at what prodigal expense of human nature, of broken hopes, and bitter experiences, the rare exotics of literature are sometimes grown.

THE HAUNTED PALACE.

In the greenest of our valleys
  By good angels tenanted,
Once a fair and stately palace—
  Radiant palace—reared its head.
In the monarch Thought's dominion—
  It stood there!
Never seraph spread a pinion
  Over fabric half so fair!

Banners yellow, glorious, golden,
  On its roof did float and flow,
(This—all this—was in the olden
  Time long ago,)
And every gentle air that dallied,
  In that sweet day,
Along the ramparts plumed and pallid,
  A winged odour went away.

Wanderers in that happy valley,
  Through two luminous windows, saw

Spirits moving musically,
To a lute's well-tuned law,
Round about a throne where, sitting
(Porphyrogene!)
In state his glory well befitting,
The ruler of the realm was seen.

And all with pearl and ruby glowing
Was the fair palace door,
Through which came flowing, flowing, flowing,
And sparkling evermore,
A troop of Echoes, whose sweet duty
Was but to sing,
In voices of surpassing beauty,
The wit and wisdom of their king.

But evil things, in robes of sorrow,
Assailed the monarch's high estate.
(Ah, let us mourn!—for never sorrow
Shall dawn upon him desolate!)
And round about his home the glory
That blushed and bloomed,
Is but a dim-remembered story
Of the old time entombed.

And travellers, now, within that valley,
Through the red-litten windows see
Vast forms, that move fantastically
To a discordant melody,
While, like a ghastly rapid river,
Through the pale door
A hideous throng rush out for ever
And laugh—but smile no more.

LENORE.

Ah! broken is the golden bowl! the spirit flown forever!
Let the bell toll!—a saintly soul floats on the Stygian river;
And, Guy De Vere, hast *thou* no tear!—weep now or never more!
See! on yon drear and rigid bier low lies thy love, Lenore!
Come! let the burial rite be read—the funeral song be sung!—
An anthem for the queenliest dead that ever died so young—
A dirge for her the doubly dead in that she died so young.

"Wretches! ye loved her for her wealth and hated her for her pride,
And when she fell in feeble health, ye blessed her—that she died!
How *shall* the ritual, then, be read!—the requiem how be sung
By you—by yours, the evil eye,—by yours the slanderous tongue
That did to death the innocence that died, and died so young?"

Peccavimus; but rave not thus! and let a Sabbath song
Go up to God so solemnly the dead may feel no wrong!
The sweet Lenore hath "gone before," with Hope, that flew beside,
Leaving thee wild for the dear child that should have been thy bride—
For her, the fair and *debonair*, that now so lowly lies,
The life upon her yellow hair but not within her eyes—
The life still there, upon her hair—the death upon her eyes.

"Avaunt! to-night my heart is light. No dirge will I upraise,
But waft the angel on her flight with a Pæan of old days!
Let *no* bell toll;—lest her sweet soul, amid its hallowed mirth,
Should catch the note, as it doth float—up from the damnéd Earth.
To friends above, from fiends below, the indignant ghost is riven—
From Hell unto a high estate far up within the Heaven—
From grief and groan, to a golden throne, beside the King of Heaven."

THE RAVEN.

Once upon a midnight dreary, while I pondered, weak and weary,
Over many a quaint and curious volume of forgotten lore,
While I nodded, nearly napping, suddenly there came a tapping,
As of some one gently rapping, rapping at my chamber door.
"'Tis some visiter," I muttered, "tapping at my chamber door—
Only this, and nothing more."

Ah, distinctly I remember it was in the bleak December,
And each separate dying ember wrought its ghost upon the floor.
Eagerly I wished the morrow;—vainly I had sought to borrow
From my books surcease of sorrow—sorrow for the lost Lenore—
For the rare and radiant maiden whom the angels name Lenore—
Nameless here for evermore.

And the silken sad uncertain rustling of each purple curtain
Thrilled me—filled me with fantastic terrors never felt before;
So that now, to still the beating of my heart, I stood repeating
"'Tis some visiter entreating entrance at my chamber door—
Some late visiter entreating entrance at my chamber door;—
This it is, and nothing more."

Presently my soul grew stronger; hesitating then no longer,
"Sir," said I, "or Madam, truly your forgiveness I implore;
But the fact is I was napping, and so gently you came rapping,
And so faintly you came tapping, tapping at my chamber door,
That I scarce was sure I heard you"—here I opened wide the door;—
Darkness there, and nothing more.

Deep into that darkness peering, long I stood there wondering, fearing,
Doubting, dreaming dreams no mortal ever dared to dream before;
But the silence was unbroken, and the darkness gave no token,
And the only word there spoken was the whispered word, "Lenore!"
This I whispered, and an echo murmured back the word, "Lenore!"
Merely this, and nothing more.

Back into the chamber turning, all my soul within me burning,
Soon I heard again a tapping somewhat louder than before.
"Surely," said I, "surely that is something at my window lattice;
Let me see, then, what thereat is, and this mystery explore—
Let my heart be still a moment and this mystery explore;—
'Tis the wind and nothing more!"

Open here I flung the shutter, when, with many a flirt and flutter,
In there stepped a stately raven of the saintly days of yore;
Not the least obeisance made he; not an instant stopped or stayed he;
But, with mien of lord or lady, perched above my chamber door—
Perched upon a bust of Pallas just above my chamber door—
Perched, and sat, and nothing more.

Then this ebony bird beguiling my sad fancy into smiling,
By the grave and stern decorum of the countenance it wore,
"Though thy crest be shorn and shaven, thou," I said, "art sure no craven,
Ghastly grim and ancient raven wandering from the Nightly shore—
Tell me what thy lordly name is on the Night's Plutonian shore!"
Quoth the raven, "Nevermore."

Much I marvelled this ungainly fowl to hear discourse so plainly,
Though its answer little meaning—little relevancy bore;
For we cannot help agreeing that no living human being
Ever yet was blessed with seeing bird above his chamber door—
Bird or beast upon the sculptured bust above his chamber door,
With such a name as "Nevermore."

But the raven, sitting lonely on the placid bust, spoke only
That one word, as if his soul in that one word he did outpour.
Nothing farther then he uttered—not a feather then he fluttered—
Till I scarcely more than muttered, "Other friends have flown before—
On the morrow *he* will leave me, as my hopes have flown before."
Then the bird said "Nevermore."

Startled at the stillness broken by reply so aptly spoken,
"Doubtless," said I, "what it utters is its only stock and store
Caught from some unhappy master whom unmerciful Disaster
Followed fast and followed faster till his songs one burden bore—
Till the dirges of his Hope that melancholy burden bore
Of 'Never—nevermore.'"

But the raven still beguiling all my sad soul into smiling,
Straight I wheeled a cushioned seat in front of bird, and bust, and door;
Then, upon the velvet sinking, I betook myself to linking
Fancy unto fancy, thinking what this ominous bird of yore—
What this grim, ungainly, ghastly, gaunt, and ominous bird of yore
Meant in croaking "Nevermore."

This I sat engaged in guessing, but no syllable expressing
To the fowl whose fiery eyes now burned into my bosom's core;
This and more I sat divining, with my head at ease reclining
On the cushion's velvet lining that the lamplight gloated o'er,
But whose velvet violet lining with the lamplight gloating o'er,
She shall press, ah, nevermore!

Then, methought, the air grew denser, perfumed from an unseen censer
Swung by angels whose faint foot-falls tinkled on the tufted floor.
"Wretch," I cried, "thy God hath lent thee—by these angels he hath sent thee
Respite—respite and nepenthe from thy memories of Lenore!
Quaff, oh, quaff, this kind nepenthe and forget this lost Lenore!"
Quoth the raven, "Nevermore."

"Prophet!" said I, "thing of evil!—prophet still, if bird or devil!—
Whether Tempter sent, or whether tempest tossed thee here ashore,
Desolate, yet all undaunted, on this desert land enchanted—
On this home by Horror haunted—tell me truly, I implore—
Is there—*is* there balm in Gilead?—tell me—tell me, I implore!"
Quoth the raven, "Nevermore."

"Prophet!" said I, "thing of evil—prophet still, if bird or devil!
By that Heaven that bends above us—by that God we both adore—
Tell this soul with sorrow laden if, within the distant Aidenn,
It shall clasp a sainted maiden whom the angels name Lenore—
Clasp a rare and radiant maiden whom the angels name Lenore."
Quoth the raven, "Nevermore."

"Be that word our sign of parting, bird or fiend!" I shrieked, upstarting—
"Get thee back into the tempest and the Night's Plutonian shore!
Leave no black plume as a token of that lie thy soul hath spoken!
Leave my loneliness unbroken!—quit the bust above my door!
Take thy beak from out my heart, and take thy form from off my door!"
Quoth the raven, "Nevermore."

And the raven, never flitting, still is sitting, still is sitting
On the pallid bust of Pallas just above my chamber door;
And his eyes have all the seeming of a demon's that is dreaming,
And the lamplight o'er him streaming throws his shadow on the floor;
And my soul from out that shadow that lies floating on the floor
Shall be lifted—nevermore!

A DESCENT INTO THE MAELSTROM.

The ways of God in Nature, as in Providence, are not as our ways; nor are the models that we frame any way commensurate to the vastness, profundity, and unsearchableness of His works, *which have a depth in them greater than the well of Democritus.—Joseph Glanville.*

We had now reached the summit of the loftiest crag. For some minutes the old man seemed too much exhausted to speak.

"Not long ago," said he at length, "and I could have guided you on this route as well as the youngest of my sons; but, about three years past, there happened to me an event such as never happened before to mortal man—or at least such as no man ever survived to tell of—and the six hours of deadly terror which I then endured have broken me up body and soul. You suppose me a *very* old man—but I am not. It took less than a single day to change these hairs from a jetty black to white, to weaken my limbs, and to unstring my nerves, so that I tremble at the least exertion, and am frightened at a shadow. Do you know I can scarcely look over this little cliff without getting giddy?"

The "little cliff," upon whose edge he had so carelessly thrown himself down to rest that the weightier portion of his body hung over it, while he was only kept from falling by the tenure of his elbow on its extreme and slippery edge—this "little cliff" arose, a sheer unobstructed precipice of black shining rock, some fifteen or sixteen hundred feet from the world of crags beneath us. Nothing would have tempted me to within half a dozen yards of its brink. In truth so deeply was I excited by the perilous position of my companion, that I fell at full length upon the ground, clung to the shrubs around me, and dared not even glance upward at the sky—while I struggled in vain to divest myself of the idea that the very foundations of the mountain were in danger from the fury of the winds. It was long before I could reason myself into sufficient courage to sit up and look out into the distance.

"You must get over these fancies," said the guide, "for I have brought you here that you might have the best possible view of the scene of that event I mentioned—and to tell you the whole story with the spot just under your eye."

* * * * * * * * *

"You have had a good look at the whirl now," said the old man, "and if you will creep round this crag, so as to get in its lee, and deaden the roar of the water, I will tell you a story that will convince you I ought to know something of the Moskoe-ström."

I placed myself as desired, and he proceeded.

"Myself and my two brothers once owned a schooner-rigged smack of about seventy tons burthen, with which we were in the habit of fishing among the islands beyond Moskoe, nearly to Vurrgh. In all violent eddies at sea there is good fishing, at proper opportunities, if one has only the courage to attempt it; but among the whole of the Lofoden coastmen, we three were the only ones who made a regular business of going out to the islands, as I tell you. The usual grounds are a great way lower down to the southward. There fish can be got at all hours, without much risk, and therefore these places are preferred. The choice spots over here among the rocks, however, not only yield the finest variety, but in far greater abundance; so that we often got in a single day, what the more timid of the craft could not scrape together in a week. In fact, we made it a matter of desperate speculation—the risk of life standing instead of labor, and courage answering for capital.

"We kept the smack in a cove about five miles higher up the coast than this; and it was our practice, in fine weather, to take advantage of the fifteen minutes' slack to push across the main channel of the Moskoe-ström, far above the pool, and then drop down upon anchorage somewhere near Otterholm, or Sandflesen, where the eddies are not so violent as elsewhere. Here we used to remain until nearly time for slack-water again, when we weighed and made for home. We never set out upon this expedition without a steady side-wind for going and coming—one that we felt sure would not fail us before our return—and we seldom made a miscalculation upon this point. Twice, during six years, we were forced to stay all night at anchor on account of a dead calm, which is a rare thing indeed just about here; and once we had to remain on the grounds nearly a week, starving to death, owing to a gale which blew up shortly after our arrival, and made the channel too boisterous to be thought of. Upon this occasion we should have been driven out to sea in spite of everything (for the whirlpools threw us round and round so violently, that, at length, we fouled our anchor and dragged it), if it had not been that we drifted into one of the innumerable cross currents—here to-day and gone to-morrow—which drove us under the lee of Flimen, where, by good luck, we brought up.

"I could not tell you the twentieth part of the difficulties we encountered 'on the grounds'—it is a bad spot to be in, even in good weather—but we made shift always to run the gauntlet of the Moskoe-ström itself without accident; although at times my heart has been in my mouth when we happened to be a minute or so behind or before the slack. The wind sometimes was not as strong as we thought it at starting, and then we made rather less way than we could wish, while the current rendered the smack unmanageable. My eldest brother had a son eighteen years old, and I had two stout boys of my own. These would have been of great assistance at such times, in using the sweeps, as well as afterward in fishing—but, somehow, although we ran the risk ourselves, we had not the heart to let the young ones get into the danger—for, after all is said and done, it *was* a horrible danger, and that is the truth.

"It is now within a few days of three years since what I am going to tell you occurred. It was on the tenth day of July, 18—, a day which the people of this part of the world will never forget—for it was one in which blew the most terrible hurricane that ever came out of the heavens. And yet all the morning, and indeed until late in the afternoon, there was a gentle and steady breeze from the south-west, while the sun shone brightly, so that the oldest seaman amongst us could not have foreseen what was to follow.

"The three of us—my two brothers and myself—had crossed over to the islands about two o'clock, P.M., and had soon nearly loaded the smack with fine fish, which, we all remarked, were more plenty that day than we had ever known them. It was just seven, *by my watch*, when we weighed and started for home, so as to make the worst of the Strom at slack water, which we knew would be at eight.

"We set out with a fresh wind on our starboard quarter, and for some time spanked along at a great rate, never dreaming of danger, for indeed we saw not the slightest reason to apprehend it. All at once we were taken aback by a breeze from over Helseggen. This was most unusual—something that had never happened to us before—and I began to feel a little uneasy, without exactly knowing why. We put the boat on the wind, but could make no headway at all for the eddies, and I was upon the point of proposing to return to the anchorage, when.

looking astern, I saw the whole horizon covered with a singular copper-colored cloud that rose with the most amazing velocity.

"In the meantime the breeze that had headed us off fell away, and we were dead becalmed, drifting about in every direction. This state of things, however, did not last long enough to give us time to think about it. In less than a minute the storm was upon us—in less than two the sky was entirely overcast—and what with this and the driving spray, it became suddenly so dark that we could not see each other in the smack.

"Such a hurricane as then blew it is folly to attempt describing. The oldest seaman in Norway never experienced any thing like it. We had let our sails go by the run before it cleverly took us; but, at the first puff, both our masts went by the board as if they had been sawed off—the mainmast taking with it my youngest brother, who had lashed himself to it for safety.

"Our boat was the lightest feather of a thing that ever sat upon water. It had a complete flush deck, with only a small hatch near the bow, and this hatch it had always been our custom to batten down when about to cross the Ström, by way of precaution against the chopping seas. But for this circumstance we should have foundered at once—for we lay entirely buried for some moments. How my elder brother escaped destruction I cannot say, for I never had an opportunity of ascertaining. For my part, as soon as I had let the foresail run, I threw myself flat on deck, with my feet against the narrow gunwale of the bow, and with my hands grasping a ring-bolt near the foot of the foremast. It was mere instinct that prompted me to do this—which was undoubtedly the very best thing I could have done—for I was too much flurried to think.

"For some moments we were completely deluged, as I say, and all this time I held my breath, and clung to the bolt. When I could stand it no longer I raised myself upon my knees, still keeping hold with my hands, and thus got my head clear. Presently our little boat gave herself a shake, just as a dog does in coming out of the water, and thus rid herself, in some measure, of the seas. I was now trying to get the better of the stupor that had come over me, and to collect my senses so as to see what was to be done, when I felt somebody grasp my arm. It was my elder brother, and my heart leaped for joy, for I had made sure that he was overboard—but the next moment all this joy was turned into horror—for he put his mouth close to my ear, and screamed out the word '*Moskoe-ström!*'

"No one ever will know what my feelings were at that moment. I shook from head to foot as if I had had the most violent fit of the ague. I knew what he meant by that one word well enough—I knew what he wished to make me understand. With the wind that now drove us on, we were bound for the whirl of the Ström, and nothing could save us!

"You perceive that in crossing the Ström *channel*, we always went a long way up above the whirl, even in the calmest weather, and then had to wait and watch carefully for the slack—but now we were driving right upon the pool itself, and in such a hurricane as this! 'To be sure,' I thought, 'we shall get there just about the slack—there is some little hope in that'—but in the next moment I cursed myself for being so great a fool as to dream of hope at all. I knew very well that we were doomed, had we been ten times a ninety-gun ship.

"By this time the first fury of the tempest had spent itself, or perhaps we did not feel it so much, as we scudded before it, but at all events the seas, which at first had been kept down by the wind, and lay flat and frothing, now got up into absolute mountains. A singular change, too, had come over the heavens. Around in every direction it was still as black as pitch, but nearly overhead there burst out, all at once, a circular rift of clear sky—as clear as I ever saw—and of a deep bright blue—and through it there blazed forth the full moon with a lustre that I never before knew her to wear. She lit up everything about us with the greatest distinctness—but, O God, what a scene it was to light up!

"I now made one or two attempts to speak to my brother—but, in some manner which I could not understand, the din had so increased that I could not make him hear a single word, although I screamed at the top of my voice in his ear. Presently he shook his head, looking as pale as death, and held up one of his fingers, as if to say '*listen!*'

"At first I could not make out what he meant—but soon a hideous thought flashed upon me. I dragged my watch from its fob. It was not going. I glanced at its face by the moonlight, and then burst into tears as I flung it far away into the ocean. *It had run down at seven o'clock! We were behind the time of the slack, and the whirl of the Ström was in full fury!*

"When a boat is well built, properly trimmed, and not deep laden, the waves in a strong gale, when she is going large, seem always to slip from beneath her—which appears very strange to a landsman—and this is what is called *riding* in sea phrase. Well, so far we had ridden the swells very cleverly; but presently a gigantic sea happened to take us right under the counter, and bore us with it as it rose—up—up—as if into the sky. I would not have believed that any wave could rise so high. And then down we came with a sweep, a slide, and a plunge, that made me feel sick and dizzy, as if I was falling from some lofty mountain-top in a dream. But while we were up I had thrown a quick glance around—and that one glance was all-sufficient. I saw our exact position in an instant. The Moskoe-ström whirlpool was about a quarter of a mile dead ahead—but no more like the every-day Moskoe-ström, than the whirl as you now see it is like a mill-race. If I had not known where we were, and what we had to expect, I should not have recognised the place at all. As it was, I involuntarily closed my eyes in horror. The lids clenched themselves together as if in a spasm.

"It could not have been more than two minutes afterward until we suddenly felt the waves subside, and were enveloped in foam. The boat made a sharp half turn to larboard, and then shot off in its new direction like a thunderbolt. At the same moment the roaring noise of the water was completely drowned in a kind of shrill shriek—such a sound as you might imagine given out by the waste pipes of many thousand steam-vessels, letting off their steam all together. We were now in the belt of surf that always surrounds the whirl; and I thought, of course, that another moment would plunge us into the abyss—down which we could only see indistinctly on account of the amazing velocity with which we were borne along. The boat did not seem to sink into the water at all, but to skim like an air-bubble upon the surface of the surge. Her starboard side was next the whirl, and on the larboard arose the world of ocean we had left. It stood like a huge writhing wall between us and the horizon.

"It may appear strange, but now, when we were in the very jaws of the gulf, I felt more composed than when we were only approaching it. Having made up my mind to hope no more, I got rid of a great deal of that terror which unmanned me at first. I suppose it was despair that strung my nerves.

"It may look like boasting—but what I tell you is truth—I began to reflect how magnificent a thing it was to die in such a manner, and how foolish it was in me to think of so paltry a consideration as my own individual life, in view of so wonderful a manifestation of God's power. I do believe that I blushed with shame when this idea crossed my mind. After a little while I became possessed with the keenest curiosity about the whirl itself. I positively felt a *wish* to explore its depths, even at the sacrifice I was going to make; and my principal grief was that I should never be able to tell my old companions on shore about the mysteries I should see. These, no doubt, were singular fancies to occupy a man's mind in such extremity—and I have often thought since, that the revolutions of the boat around the pool might have rendered me a little light-headed.

"There was another circumstance which tended to restore my self-possession; and this was the cessation of the wind, which could not reach us in our present situation—for, as you saw yourself, the belt of surf is considerably lower than the general bed of the ocean, and this latter now towered above us, a high, black, mountainous ridge. If you have never been at sea in a heavy gale, you can form no idea of the confusion of mind occasioned by the wind and spray together. They blind, deafen, and strangle you, and take away all power of action or reflection. But we were now, in a great measure, rid of these annoyances—just as death-condemned felons in prison are allowed petty indulgences, forbidden them while their doom is yet uncertain.

"How often we made the circuit of the belt it is impossible to say. We careered round and round for perhaps an hour, flying rather than floating, getting gradually more and more into the middle of the surge, and then nearer and nearer to its horrible inner edge. All this time I had never let go of the ring-bolt. My brother was at the stern, holding on to a small empty water-cask which had been securely lashed under the coop of the counter, and was the only thing on deck that had not been swept overboard when the gale first took us. As we approached the brink of the pit he let go his hold upon this, and made for the ring, from which, in the agony of his terror, he endeavored to force my hands, as it was not large enough to afford us both a secure grasp. I never felt deeper grief than when I saw him attempt this act—although I knew he was a madman when he did it—a raving maniac through sheer fright. I did not care, however, to contest the point with him. I knew it could make no difference whether either of us held on at all; so I let him have the bolt, and went astern to the cask. This there was no great difficulty in doing; for the smack flew round steadily enough, and upon an even keel—only swaying to and fro, with the immense sweeps and swelters of the whirl. Scarcely had I secured myself in my new position, when we gave a wild lurch to starboard, and rushed headlong into the abyss. I muttered a hurried prayer to God, and thought all was over.

"As I felt the sickening sweep of the descent, I had instinctively tightened my hold upon the barrel, and closed my eyes. For some seconds I dared not open them—while I expected instant destruction, and wondered that I was not already in my death-struggles with the water. But moment after moment elapsed. I still lived. The sense of falling had ceased; and the motion of the vessel seemed much as it had been before while in the belt of foam, with the exception that she now lay more along. I took courage, and looked once again upon the scene.

"Never shall I forget the sensations of awe, horror, and admiration with which I gazed about me. The boat appeared to be hanging, as if by magic, midway down, upon the interior surface of a funnel vast in circumference, prodigious in depth, and whose perfectly smooth sides might have been mistaken for ebony, but for the bewildering rapidity with which they spun around, and for the gleaming and ghastly radiance they shot forth, as the rays of the full moon, from that circular rift amid the clouds which I have already described, streamed in a flood of golden glory along the black walls, and far away down into the inmost recesses of the abyss.

"At first I was too much confused to observe anything accurately. The general burst of terrific grandeur was all that I beheld. When I recovered myself a little, however, my gaze fell instinctively downward. In this direction I was able to obtain an unobstructed view, from the manner in which the smack hung on the inclined surface of the pool. She was quite upon an even keel—that is to say, her deck lay in a plane parallel with that of the water—but this latter sloped at an angle of more than forty-five degrees, so that we seemed to be lying upon our beam-ends. I could not help observing, nevertheless, that I had scarcely more difficulty in maintaining my hold and footing in this situation, than if we had been upon a dead level; and this, I suppose, was owing to the speed at which we revolved.

"The rays of the moon seemed to search the very bottom of the profound gulf; but still I could make out nothing distinctly, on account of a thick mist in which everything there was enveloped, and over which there hung a magnificent rainbow, like that narrow and tottering bridge which Mussulmen say is the only pathway between Time and Eternity. This mist, or spray, was no doubt occasioned by the clashing of the great walls of the funnel, as they all met together at the bottom—but the yell that went up to the Heavens from out of that mist, I dare not attempt to describe.

"Our first slide into the abyss itself, from the belt of foam above, had carried us a great distance down the slope; but our farther descent was by no means proportionate. Round and round we swept—not with any uniform movement—but in dizzying swings and jerks, that sent us sometimes only a few hundred yards—sometimes nearly the complete circuit of the whirl. Our progress downward, at each revolution, was slow, but very perceptible.

"Looking about me upon the wide waste of liquid ebony on which we were thus borne, I perceived that our boat was not the only object in the embrace of the whirl. Both above and below us were visible fragments of vessels, large masses of building timber and trunks of trees, with many smaller articles, such as pieces of house furniture, broken boxes, barrels and staves. I have already described the unnatural curiosity which had taken the place of my original terrors. It appeared to grow upon me as I drew nearer and nearer to my dreadful doom. I now began to watch, with a strange interest, the numerous things that floated in our company. I *must* have been delirious—for I even sought *amusement* in speculating upon the relative velocities of their several descents toward the foam below. 'This fir tree,' I found myself at one time saying, 'will certainly be the next thing that takes the awful plunge and disappears,'—and then I was disappointed to find that the wreck of a Dutch merchant ship overtook it and went down before. At length, after making several guesses of this nature, and being deceived in all—this fact—the fact of my invariable miscalculation—set me upon a train of reflection that made my limbs again tremble, and my heart beat heavily once more.

"It was not a new terror that thus affected me, but the dawn of a more exciting *hope*. This hope arose partly from memory, and partly from present observation. I called to mind the great variety of buoyant matter that strewed the coast of Lofoden, having been absorbed and then thrown forth by the Moskoe-ström. By far the greater number of the articles were shattered in the most extraordinary way—so chafed and roughened as to have the appearance of being stuck full of splinters—but then I distinctly recollected that there were *some* of them which were not disfigured at all. Now I could not account for this difference except by supposing that the roughened fragments were the only ones which had been *completely absorbed*—that the others had entered the whirl at so late a period of the tide, or, for some reason, had descended so slowly after entering, that they did not reach the bottom before the turn of the flood came, or of the ebb, as the case might be. I conceived it possible, in either instance, that they might thus be whirled up again to the level of the ocean, without undergoing the fate of those which had been drawn in more early, or absorbed more rapidly. I made, also, three important observations. The first was, that, as a general rule, the larger the bodies were, the more rapid their descent—the second, that, between two masses of equal extent, the one spherical, and the other *of any other shape*, the superiority in speed of descent was with the sphere—the third, that, between two masses of equal size, the one cylindrical, and the other of any other shape, the cylinder was absorbed the more slowly. Since my escape, I have had several conversations on this subject with an old school-master of the district; and it was from him that I learned the use of the words 'cylinder' and 'sphere.' He explained to me—although I have forgotten the explanation—how what I observed was, in fact, the natural consequence of the forms of the floating fragments—and showed me how it happened that a cylinder, swimming in a vortex, offered more resistance to its suction, and was drawn in with greater difficulty than an equally bulky body, of any form whatever.

"There was one startling circumstance which went a great way in enforcing these observations, and rendering me anxious to turn them to account, and this was that, at every revolution, we passed something like a barrel, or else the yard or the mast of a vessel, while many of these things, which had been on our level when I first opened my eyes upon the wonders of the whirlpool, were now high up above us, and seemed to have moved but little from their original station.

"I no longer hesitated what to do. I resolved to lash myself securely to the water cask upon which I now held, to cut it loose from the counter, and to throw myself with it into the water. I attracted my brother's attention by signs, pointed to the floating barrels that came near us, and did everything in my power to make him understand what I was about to do. I thought at length that he comprehended my design—but, whether this was the case or not, he shook his head despairingly, and refused to move from his station by the ring-bolt. It was impossible to reach him; the emergency admitted of no delay; and so, with a bitter struggle, I resigned him to his fate, fastened myself to the cask by means of the lashings which secured it to the counter, and precipitated myself with it into the sea, without another moment's hesitation.

"The result was precisely what I had hoped it might be. As it is myself who now tell you this tale—as you see that I *did* escape—and as you are already in possession of the mode in which this escape was effected, and must therefore anticipate all that I have farther to say—I will bring my story quickly to conclusion. It might have been an hour, or thereabout, after my quitting the smack, when, having descended to a vast distance beneath me, it made three or four wild gyrations in rapid succession, and, bearing my loved brother with it, plunged headlong, at once and for ever, into the chaos of foam below. The barrel to which I was attached sunk very little farther than half the distance between the bottom of the gulf and the spot at which I leaped overboard, before a great change took place in the character of the whirlpool. The slope of the sides of the vast funnel became momently less and less steep. The gyrations of the whirl grew, gradually, less and less violent. By degrees, the froth and the rainbow disappeared, and the bottom of the gulf seemed slowly to uprise. The sky was clear, the winds had gone down, and the full moon was setting radiantly in the west, when I found myself on the surface of the ocean, in full view of the shores of Lofoden, and above the spot where the pool of the Moskoe-ström *had been*. It was the hour of the slack—but the sea still heaved in mountainous waves from the effects of the hurricane. I was borne violently into the channel of the Ström, and in a few minutes was hurried down the coast into the 'grounds' of the fishermen. A boat picked me up—exhausted from fatigue—and (now that the danger was removed) speechless from the memory of its horror. Those who drew me on board were my old mates and daily companions—but they knew me no more than they would have known a traveller from the spirit-land. My hair, which had been raven-black the day, before, was as white as you see it now. They say too that the whole expression of my countenance had changed. I told them my story—they did not believe it. I now tell it to *you*—and I can scarcely expect you to put more faith in it than did the merry fishermen of Lofoden."

CHARLES SUMNER.*

CHARLES SUMNER was born at Boston, January 6, 1811. His father, Charles Pinckney Sumner, was high sheriff of Suffolk county, Massachusetts. Mr. Sumner was prepared for college at the Latin school, Boston, and graduated at Harvard in 1830. In 1831 he entered the law school of the same university, and while pursuing his studies, wrote several articles for the American Jurist, and soon after became editor of hat periodical. He commenced the practice of his profession in Boston in 1834, was soon after appointed reporter to the Circuit Court, and published three volumes of reports. He also lectured during three successive winters at the Cambridge Law School, at the request of the Faculty, during the absence of Professors Greenleaf and Story.

C. Sumner

In 1836 he edited "A Treatise on the Practice of the Courts of Admiralty in Civil Causes of Maritime Jurisdiction, by Andrew Dunlap," adding an appendix equal in extent to the original work. In 1837 he sailed for Europe, where he remained three years, enjoying unusual advantages of social intercourse with the most distinguished men of the day.

While in Paris, at the request of the Minister,

* Loring's Hundred Boston Orators.

General Cass, he wrote a defence of the American claim to the north-eastern boundary, which was republished from Galignani's Messenger, where it originally appeared, in the leading American journals, and universally regarded as an able presentation of the argument. It was during the same visit to Paris that he suggested to Mr. Wheaton the project of writing a History of the Law of Nations. The impression made by Mr. Sumner in England may be judged of from the complimentary remark made by Baron Parke, on the citation in the Court of Exchequer, of Sumner's Reports, in a case under consideration, to the effect that the weight of the authority was not "entitled to the less attention because reported by a gentleman whom we all knew and respected."

After his return, he again, in 1848, lectured in Cambridge, and in 1844–6 edited an edition of Vesey's Reports in twenty volumes, to which he contributed a number of valuable notes, many of which are concise treatises on the points in question. He also introduced a number of biographical notices of the eminent persons whose names occur in the text.

After the death of Judge Story, in 1845, Mr. Sumner was universally spoken of as his appropriate successor in the Law School, an opinion in accordance with the openly expressed wish of the deceased. He, however, expressed a disinclination to accept the post, and the appointment was not tendered.

Mr. Sumner took an active part as a public speaker in opposition to the annexation of Texas, and in support of Mr. Van Buren for the Presidency in the canvass of 1848. In 1851 he was elected the successor of Mr. Webster in the United States Senate.

Mr. Sumner's name is prominently identified with the Peace party—some of his finest oratorical efforts having been made in favor of the project of a Congress of Nations as the supreme arbiter of international disputes.

Mr. Sumner's *Orations and Speeches* were collected and published in Boston in two stout duodecimo volumes in 1850. The collection opens with an oration delivered before the authorities of the city of Boston, July 4, 1845, entitled *The True Grandeur of Nations*, in which the speaker enforced his peace doctrines by arguments drawn not only from the havoc and desolation attendant on and following the conflict, but by an enumeration of the cost of the state of preparation, maintained, not in view of impending danger, but as an every-day condition of military defence. In the next oration, *The Scholar, the Jurist, the Artist, the Philanthropist*, delivered before the Phi Beta Kappa Society at Harvard, in 1846, we have a feeling and eloquent memorial of John Pickering, Joseph Story, Washington Allston, and William Ellery Channing.

This is followed by a *Lecture on White Slavery in the Barbary States*, a curious and picturesquely presented chapter of history. We have next an *Oration on Fame and Glory*, occupied in a great measure by an argument on the superior honors of peace.

The Law of Human Progress, a Phi Beta Kappa Society Oration at Union College in 1848, follows, in which a history is given of the gradual recognition of the doctrine of the progress of the human race, and a brilliant series of sketches of Leibnitz, Herder, Descartes, Pascal, Turgot, Condorcet, and others of its early advocates, presented. The address exhibits to advantage the speaker's varied learning, and his happy art in the disposal of his acquirements.

The second volume opens with an address before the American Peace Society, entitled *The War System of the Commonwealth of Nations*, in a portion of which the author has followed the plan of his last mentioned discourse by tracing through the record of history the progress of the cause, and the advocates to whom that progress was in great measure due.

The remainder of the work is occupied by a number of speeches delivered on various political occasions, touching on the Mexican war, the Free Soil party, the Fugitive Slave Law and other matters growing out of the slavery question, maintaining decided views with an energy and ability which have been followed by rapid political elevation.

In addition to the works we have mentioned, Mr. Sumner is the author of a small volume on *White Slavery in the Barbary States.*

Mr. George Sumner, the brother of Charles Sumner, is the author of *An Address on the Progress of Reform in France*, delivered in 1853, and of other similar productions. He has passed several years in Europe, and has acquired a thorough knowledge of the politics, social condition, and intellectual products of its leading states. He possesses a taste for statistics and unwearied industry in research, combined with the ability to place the results of investigation before the public in a pleasing and attractive form.

WAR.

I need not dwell now on the waste and cruelty of war. These stare us wildly in the face, like lurid meteor-lights, as we travel the page of history. We see the desolation and death that pursue its demoniac footsteps. We look upon sacked towns, upon ravaged territories, upon violated homes; we behold all the sweet charities of life changed to wormwood and gall. Our soul is penetrated by the sharp moan of mothers, sisters, and daughters—of fathers, brothers, and sons, who, in the bitterness of their bereavement, refuse to be comforted. Our eyes rest at last upon one of those fair fields, where nature, in her abundance, spreads her cloth of gold, spacious and apt for the entertainment of mighty multitudes—or, perhaps, from the curious subtlety of its position, like the carpet in the Arabian tale, seeming to contract so as to be covered by a few only, or to dilate so as to receive an innumerable host. Here, under a bright sun, such as shone at Austerlitz or Buena Vista—amidst the peaceful harmonies of nature—on the Sabbath of peace—we behold bands of brothers, children of a common Father, heirs to a common happiness, struggling together in the deadly fight, with the madness of fallen spirits, seeking with murderous weapons the lives of brothers who have never injured them or their kindred. The havoc rages. The ground is soaked with their commingling blood. The air is rent by their commingling cries. Horse and rider are stretched together on the earth. More revolting than the mangled victims, than the gashed limbs, than the lifeless trunks, than the spattering brains, are the lawless passions which sweep, tempest-like, through the fiendish tumult.

Nearer comes the storm and nearer, rolling fast and frightful on.
Speak, Ximena, speak and tell us, who has lost and who has won?
"Alas! alas! I know not; friend and foe together fall,
O'er the dying rush the living; pray, my sister, for them all!"

Horror-struck, we ask, wherefore this hateful contest? The melancholy, but truthful answer comes, that this is the *established* method of determining justice between nations!

The scene changes. Far away on the distant pathway of the ocean two ships approach each other, with white canvas broadly spread to receive the flying gales. They are proudly built. All of human art has been lavished in their graceful proportions, and in their well compacted sides, while they look in dimensions like floating happy islands of the sea. A numerous crew, with costly appliances of comfort, hives in their secure shelter. Surely these two travellers shall meet in joy and friendship; the flag at the mast-head shall give the signal of fellowship; the happy sailors shall cluster in the rigging, and even on the yard-arms, to look each other in the face, while the exhilarating voices of both crews shall mingle in accents of gladness uncontrollable. It is not so. Not as brothers, not as friends, not as wayfarers of the common ocean, do they come together; but as enemies. The gentle vessels now bristle fiercely with death-dealing instruments. On their spacious decks, aloft on all their masts, flashes the deadly musketry. From their sides spout cataracts of flame, amidst the pealing thunders of a fatal artillery. They, who had escaped "the dreadful touch of merchant-marring rocks"—who had sped on their long and solitary way unharmed by wind or wave—whom the hurricane had spared—in whose favor storms and seas had intermitted their immitigable war—now at last fall by the hand of each other. The same spectacle of horror greets us from both ships. On their decks, reddened with blood, the murders of St. Bartholomew and of the Sicilian Vespers, with the fires of Smithfield, seem to break forth anew, and to concentrate their rage. Each has now become a swimming Golgotha. At length these vessels—such pageants of the sea—once so stately—so proudly built—but now rudely shattered by cannon-balls—with shivered masts and ragged sails—exist only as unmanageable wrecks, weltering on the uncertain waves, whose temporary lull of peace is now their only safety. In amazement at this strange, unnatural contest—away from country and home—where there is no country or home to defend—we ask again, wherefore this dismal duel? Again the melancholy but truthful answer promptly comes, that this is the *established* method of determining justice between nations.

ROBERT T. CONRAD.

ROBERT T. CONRAD, the author of the highly successful tragedy of Aylmere, was born in Philadelphia about the year 1810. After completing his preliminary education, he studied law with his uncle, Mr. Thomas Kittera; but in place of the practice of the profession, devoted himself to an editorial career, by the publication of the Daily Commercial Intelligencer, a periodical he subsequently merged in the Philadelphia Gazette.

In consequence of ill health he was forced to abandon the toil of daily editorship. He returned to the practice of the law, and was immediately appointed Recorder of the Recorder's Court, Philadelphia. After holding this office for two years, he became a judge of the Court of Criminal Sessions; and on the abolition of that tribunal, was appointed to the bench of the General Sessions established in its place.

R. T. Conrad

Mr. Conrad occupies a prominent place in, and is now Mayor of Philadelphia, having been elected to that office by the Native American party.

Mr. Conrad wrote his first tragedy before his twenty-first year. It was entitled *Conradin*, and performed with success.

Aylmere was written some years after. It is the property of Mr. Edwin Forrest, and has proved one of his most successful plays. The hero, Jack Cade, assumes the name of Aylmere during his concealment in Italy, to escape the consequences of a daring act of resistance to tyranny in his youth. He returns to England, and heads the insurrection which bears his name in history. The democratic hero is presented with energy, and the entire production abounds in spirited scenes and animated language. The tragedy was published by the author in 1852 in a volume entitled *Aylmere, or the Bondman of Kent; and Other Poems.* The leading article of the latter portion of the collection, The Sons of the Wilderness—Reflections beside an Indian Mound, extending to three hundred and seventy lines, is a meditative poem on the Indians, reciting their wrongs and sympathizing with their fate in a mournful strain. The remaining pieces are for the most part of a reflective character.

FREEDOM.

* * * * * * *

Whence but from God can spring the burning love
Of nature's liberty? Why does the eye
Watch, raised and raptured, the bright racks that rove,
Heaven's free-born, frolic in the harvest sky?

The wind which bloweth where it listeth, why
Hath it a charm? Why love we thus the sea,
Lordless and limitless? Or the cataract cry,
With which Niagara tells eternity
That she is chainless now, and will for ever be!

Or why, in breathing nature, is the slave
That ministers to man, in lowly wise,
Or beast or bird, a thing of scorn? Where wave
The prairie's purple seas, the free horse flies,
With mane wide floating, and wild-flashing eyes,
A wonder and a glory; o'er his way,
The ne'er-tamed eagle soars and fans the skies.
Floating, a speck upon the brow of day,
He scans the unbourned wild—and who shall say him nay?

If Freedom thus o'er earth, sea, air, hath cast
Her spell, and is Thought's idol, man may well,
To star-crowned Sparta in the glimmering past,
Turn from the gilded agonies which swell
Wrong's annals. For the kindling mind will dwell
Upon Leonidas and Washington,
And those who for God's truth or fought or fell,
When kings whose tombs are pyramids, are gone.
Justice and Time are wed: the eternal truth lives on.

Ponder it, freemen! It will teach that Time
Is not the foe of Right! and man may be
All that he pants for. Every thought sublime
That lifts us to the right where truth makes free,
Is from on high. Pale virtue! Yet with thee
Will gentle freedom dwell, nor dread a foe!
Self-governed, calm and truthful, why should she
Shrink from the future? 'Neath the last sun's glow,
Above expiring Time, her starry flag shall flow!

For, even with shrinking woman, is the Right
A cherished thought. The hardy hordes which threw
Rome from the crushed world's empire, caught the light
That led them from soft eyes, and never knew
Shame, fear, nor fetter. The stern Spartan drew,
From matrons weeping o'er each recreant son,
His spirit; and our Indian thus will woo
The stake—his forest Portia by—smile on,
Till the death-rattle ring and the death-song is done.

Fame is *man's* vassal; and the Maid of France,
The shepherd heroine, and Padilla's dame,
Whose life and love and suffering mock romance,
Are half forgotten. Corday—doth her name
Thrill you? Why, Brutus won eternal fame:
Was his, a Roman man's, a bolder blow
Than that weak woman's? For the cause the same—
Marat a worse than Cæsar. Blood may flow
In seas for Right, and ne'er a holier offering know!

* * * * * * * * *

The desert rock may yield a liberty—
The eagle's; but in cities, guarded Right
Finds her first home. Amid the many, she
Gives union, strength, and courage. In the night
Of time, from leaguered walls, her beacon light
Flashed o'er the world. And Commerce, whose white wing
Makes the wide desert of the ocean bright,
Is Freedom's foster nurse; and though she fling
Her wealth on many a shore, on none where fetters ring!

And weath diffused is Freedom's child and aid.
Give me—such is her prayer—nor poverty,
Nor riches! For while penury will degrade,
A heaped-up wealth corrupts. But to the free
The angel hope is Knowledge. It may be,
Has been, a despot; for, with unspread glow,
Truth is a rayless sun, whose radiance we,
However bright it burn, nor feel, nor know.
'Tis power; and power unshared is curst, and works but woe!

Make it an atmosphere that all may breathe,
And all are free. Each struggle in the past
That Right smiles o'er, was truthful. Laurels wreathe
All who,—as when our country rose—have cast
Oppression down; that act all time will last,
The Ararat of History, on whose brow
The sacred ark of Liberty stood fast,
Sunned in the truth; while the tame, turbid flow
Of Slavery's deluge spread o'er all the world below.

* * * * * * * *

Labor on Freedom waits (what hope to cheer
The slave to toil?), the labor blithe, whose day
Knows not a want, whose night knows not a tear;
And wealth; and high-browed science; and the play
Of truth-enamoured mind, that mocks the sway
Of court or custom; beauty-loving art;
And all that scatters flowers on life's drear way.
Hope, courage, pride, joy, conscious mirth upstart,
Beneath her smile, to raise the mind and glad the heart.

* * * * * * * * *

Twin-born with Time was Freedom, when the soul,
Shoreless and shining, met the earliest day:
But o'er Time's tomb—when passes by the scroll
Of the scorched sky—she'll wing her radiant way,
Freed from the traitor's taint, the tyrant's sway;
Chastened and bright, to other spheres will flee;
Sun her unruffled joys in Heaven's own ray,—
Where all the crushed are raised, the just are free—
Her light the living God—her mate eternity!

FREDERICK WILLIAM THOMAS.

F. W. THOMAS was born in Baltimore about the year 1810. In 1830 he removed to Cincinnati, and on his descent of the Ohio composed a poem of some six or eight stanzas, which appeared in the Commercial Daily Advertiser on his arrival at his destination. This he subsequently enlarged and recited in public, and in 1833 published with the title—*The Emigrant, or Reflections when descending the Ohio.*

In 1835 Mr. Thomas published the novel of *Clinton Bradshaw.* The hero of this story is a young lawyer, who is brought in the course of his professional pursuits in contact with criminals, while his desire to advance himself in politics introduces him to the low class of hangers-on and wire-pullers of party.

The publication made a sensation by the spirit and animation with which it was written and the bold delineations of character it contained. It was followed in 1836 by *East and West*, a story which introduces us in its progress to the two great geographical divisions of our country, and possesses animation and interest. An account of a race between two Mississippi steamboats, terminating in the usual explosion, is deservedly celebrated as a passage of vigorous description.

In 1840 Mr. Thomas published *Howard Pinckney*, a novel of contemporary American life. He is also the author of *The Beechen Tree, a Tale told in Rhyme*, published by the Harpers, and of several fugitive poems of merit. The song which we quote has attained a wide popularity.

'TIS SAID THAT ABSENCE CONQUERS LOVE.

'Tis said that absence conquers love!
  But, oh! believe it not;
I've tried, alas! its power to prove,
  But thou art not forgot.
Lady, though fate has bid us part,
  Yet still thou art as dear—
As fixed in this devoted heart,
  As when I clasped thee here.

I plunge into the busy crowd,
  And smile to hear thy name;
And yet, as if I thought aloud,
  They know me still the same;
And when the wine-cup passes round,
  I toast some other fair;—
But when I ask my heart the sound,
  Thy name is echoed there.

And when some other name I learn,
  And try to whisper love,
Still will my heart to thee return,
  Like the returning dove.
In vain! I never can forget,
  And would not be forgot;
For I must bear the same regret,
  Whate'er may be my lot.

E'en as the wounded bird will seek
  Its favorite bower to die,
So, lady! I would hear thee speak,
  And yield my parting sigh.
'T is said that absence conquers love!
  But, oh! believe it not;
I've tried, alas! its power to prove
  But thou art not forgot.

HORACE GREELEY.

Horace Greeley, a prominent journalist, was born at Amherst, New Hampshire, February 3, 1811. He received a limited common school education, the deficiencies of which he, however, in some measure supplied by unwearied activity from his earliest years in the pursuit of knowledge. At the age of fourteen, his parents having

Horace Greeley

in the meantime removed to Vermont, he obtained employment as an apprentice in the office of the Northern Spectator, Pultney, Vermont. In 1830, the paper was discontinued and he returned home; but soon after made a second engagement to work as an apprentice in Erie, Pa., for fifty dollars a year, out of which he saved enough in a few months to expend twenty-five or thirty dollars for his father, then a farmer on the line between Chautauque county, New York, and Pennsylvania, and pay his travelling expenses to New York, where he arrived in August, 1831, "with a suit of blue cotton jean, two brown shirts, and five dollars in cash." He obtained work as a journeyman printer, and continued thus employed for eighteen months. In 1834, he commenced with Jonas Winchester, afterwards the publisher of the New World, a weekly paper of sixteen pages quarto, called the New Yorker. It was conducted with much ability as a political and literary journal, but was not successful. Its conductors gave it a long and fair trial of several years, and were finally compelled to abandon the enterprise. While editing this journal Mr. Greeley also conducted, in 1838, the Jeffersonian, published by the Whig Central Committee of the State, and the Log Cabin, a "campaign" paper, published for six months preceding the presidential election of 1840.

Mr. Greeley's next enterprise was the publication of the New York Tribune, the first number of which appeared on Saturday, April 10, 1841. It soon took the stand which it has since maintained of a thoroughly appointed, independent, and spirited journal. In the July after its commencement, its editor formed a partnership with Mr. Thomas McElrath, in conjunction with whom the paper has been since conducted.

In 1848 Mr. Greeley was elected a member of the House of Representatives. In 1851 he visited Europe, and was chosen chairman of one of the jurias of the World's Fair at London. His letters written during his journey to the Tribune, were collected on his return in a volume, with the title *Glances at Europe*. In 1853 he edited a volume of papers from the Tribune, *Art and Industry as Represented in the Exhibition at the Crystal Palace, New York.* A number of addresses delivered by him on various occasions have been also collected in a volume, with the title of *Hints towards Reforms.*

Mr. Greeley has been fortunate in securing, during an early stage of his career, a biographer who combines in an unusual degree the essential characteristics of enthusiasm, research, and good sense. Mr. J. Parton has presented to the public in *The Life of Horace Greeley*, a volume well balanced in its proportions, and attractive in style.

ANDREW PRESTON PEABODY,

The present editor of the North American Review, was born in Beverley, Mass., March 19, 1811. He was graduated at Harvard in 1826; studied at the Cambridge Divinity School; remained a year at the college as mathematical tutor in 1832 and 1833; and was ordained in the latter year pastor of the South Congregational Church in Portsmouth, N. H., to which he is still attached.

In the course of his ministerial life he has published in 1844, *Lectures on Christian Doctrine*, and in 1847, *Sermons of Consolation*. He has written memoirs, and edited the writings of the Rev. Jason Whitman, James Kinnard, Jr., J. W. Foster, and Charles A. Cheever, M. D. His published sermons and pamphlets are numerous. It is chiefly as a periodical writer that Mr. Peabody has become generally known. He was for several years one of the editors of the Christian Register, and has been for a long time a prominent contributor to the Christian Examiner and North American Review, of which he became the editor on the retirement of Mr. Francis Bowen, at the commencement of 1854.*

* To recapitulate the different editorships of the North American, from a passage to our hand in the recently published "Memoirs of Youth and Manhood," by Prof. Sidney Willard, of Harvard. Mr. William Tudor commenced the work in

Mr. Peabody's review articles cover most of the social and educational questions of the day, with the discussion of many topics of miscellaneous literature. He handles a ready and vigorous pen, is clear and animated in style, and well skilled in the arts of the reviewer. His address before the united literary societies of Dartmouth College on "the Uses of Classical Literature," is a suggestive analysis of this important question.

Mr. Peabody is at present engaged in editing and preparing for the press, a Memoir of the late Gov. William Plumer of New Hampshire, from a manuscript life, left by his son the late Hon. William Plumer.

FIRST VIVID IMPRESSIONS IN THE ANCIENT CLASSICS.*

The Greek and Roman authors lived in a newer, younger world than ours. They were in the process of learning many things now well known. They were taking first glances, with earnestness and wonder, at many things now old and trite,—no less worthy of admiration than they were then, but dropped from notice and neglected. They give us first impressions of many forms of nature and of life,—impressions, which we can get nowhere else. They show us ideas, sentiments, and opinions in the process of formation,—exhibit to us their initial elements,—reveal their history. They make known to us essential steps in human culture, which, in these days of more rapid progress, we stride over unmarked. They are thus invaluable aids in the study of the human mind, and of the intellectual history of the race,—in the analysis of ideas and opinions,—in ascertaining, apart from our artificial theories, the ultimate, essential facts in every department of nature and of human life. For these uses, the classics have only increased in value with the lapse of time, and must still grow more precious with every stage of human progress and refinement, so that classical literature must ever be a favorite handmaid of sound philosophy.

On subjects of definite knowledge, what we call the progress of knowledge is, in one aspect, the growth of ignorance. As philosophy becomes more comprehensive, it becomes less minute. As it takes in broader fields of view, it takes less accurate cognizance of parts and details. Even language participates in this process. Names become more general. Definitions enumerate fewer particulars. What are called axioms, embrace no longer self-evident propositions alone, but those also, which have been so established by the long and general consent of mankind, that the proofs on which they rest, and the truths which they include, are not recurred to. A schoolboy now takes on trust, and never verifies, principles, which it cost ages of research to discover and mature. What styles itself analysis goes not back to the "primordia rerum." Now, the more rigid and minute our analysis, the more accurate of course our conceptions. Indeed, we do not fully understand general laws or comprehensive truths, until we have traced them out in detail, and seen them mirrored back from the particulars which they include. A whole can be faithfully studied only in its parts; and every part obeys the law, and bears the type of the system, to which it belongs, so that, the more numerous the parts with which we are conversant, the more profound, intimate, vivid, experimental, is our knowledge of the whole. This minute, exhausting analysis we may advantageously prosecute by the aid of ancient philosophy and science. Laugh as we may at the puerile theories in natural history, broached or endorsed by Aristotle and by Pliny, they often, by their detailed sketches of facts and phenomena, which we have left unexamined because we have thought them well known, invest common things with absorbing interest, as the exponents of far reaching truths and fundamental laws. In like manner, in Plato's theories of the universe and of the human soul, or in the ethical treatises of Cicero, though we detect in them much loose and vague speculation, and many notions which shun the better light of modern times, we often find the constituent elements of our own ideas,—the parent thoughts of our truest thoughts,—those ultimate facts in the outward and the spiritual universe, which suggest inquiry and precede theory.

A similar train of remark applies emphatically to the departments of rhetoric and eloquence. I know of no modern analysis of the elements and laws of written or uttered discourse, which can bear a moment's comparison with those of Cicero or Quintilian. We may, indeed, have higher moral conceptions of the art of writing and of oratory than they had. We may perhaps hold forth a loftier aim. We may see more clearly than they did, the intrinsic dignity of the author's or the orator's vocation; and may feel, as none but a Christian can, of what incalculable moment for time and for eternity his influence may be. But these eighteen centuries have only generalized, without augmenting, the catalogue of instruments by which mind is to act on mind, and heart on heart,—of the sources of argument and modes of appeal, which those master-rhetoricians defined in detail. Nor is it possible that, eighteen centuries hence, the "De Oratore" of Cicero should seem less perfect, or be less fruitful, or constitute a less essential part, than now, of the training of him, who would write what shall live, or utter what is worthy to be heard. Modern rhetoricians furnish us with weapons of forensic attack and defence, ready cast and shaped, and give us technical rules for their use. Cicero takes us to the mine and to the forge,—exhibits every stage of elaboration through which the weapons pass,—proves their temper, tries their edge for us. By his minute subdivision of the whole subject of oratory, by his detailed description of its kinds, its modes, and its instruments, by his thorough analysis of arguments, and of the sources whence they are drawn, he wrote in anticipation a perfect commentary on the precepts of succeeding rhetoricians; and we must look to him to test the principles and to authenticate the laws, which they lay down. And this preëminence belongs not to his transcendent genius alone; but is, to a great degree, to be traced to the fact, that he wrote when oratory as an art was young in Rome, and had perished before it grew old in Greece,—when it had no established rules, no authoritative canons, no prescriptive forms, departure from which was high treason to the art, when therefore it was incumbent on the orator to prove, illustrate, and defend whatever rules or forms he might propose.

The view of ancient literature now under consideration obviously extends itself to the whole field of poetry. In our habitual straining after the vast and grand, we pass by the poetry of common and little things, and are hardly aware how much there is worthy of song in daily and unnoticed scenes and events,—in

May, 1815, and edited it for two years. Then, from May, 1817, to March, 1818, inclusive, it was edited by Jared Sparks; from May, 1818, to Oct. 1819, inclusive, by Edward T. Channing; from Jan. 1820, to Oct. 1823, inclusive, by Edward Everett; from Jan. 1824, to April, 1830, inclusive, by Jared Sparks; from July, 1830, to Oct. 1835, by Alexander H. Everett; from Jan. 1836, to Jan. 1843, by John G. Palfrey; from 1843 to 1853, by Francis Bowen; and since, by Andrew P. Peabody.

* From the address on the "Uses of Classical Literature."

> the unenduring clouds,
> In flower and tree, in every pebbly stone
> That paves the brooks, the stationary rocks,
> The moving waters, the invisible air.

The region of the partly known and dimly seen, the confines of the unexplored, constitute in all ages the poet's chosen field. But that field has been continually diminishing before the resistless progress of truth and fact. Science has measured the stars, sounded the sea, and made the ancient hills tell the story of their birth. Fancy now finds no hiding-place in grove or cavern,—no shrine so secluded, so full of religious awe, as to have been left unmeasured and uncatalogued. Poetry, impatient of the line and compass of exact science, is thus driven from almost every earthly covert; and dreary, prosaic fact, is fast establishing its undivided empire over land, and sea, and sky. It is therefore refreshing and kindling to go back in ancient song to

> The power, the beauty, and the majesty
> That had their haunts in dale, or piny mountain,
> Or forest by slow stream, or pebbly spring,
> Or chasms and watery depths.

Then the world was young, and infant science had not learned to roam. Mystery brooded over the whole expanse of nature. Darkness was upon the face of the deep. The veil was unremoved from grotto and from forest.

We often talk of the poetry of common life. What now styles itself thus, is, for the most part, stupid prose on stilts. The real poetry of common life was written when what is our common life was poetic,—heroic,—when our merest common-places of existence were rare and grand. The themes of ancient song are almost all of this class; and the great poems of antiquity derive an absorbing, undying interest and charm from the fact, that they bring out the wayside poetry of ordinary life, which gunpowder, steam, the loadstone, and the march of mind have banished from the present age, and which can never be written again unless the world strides back to barbarism. The expedition of the Argonauts,—so vast that they paused two years on their way to gather strength and courage,—a tourist of the *cockney* class, darting through the Hellespont on the fire-wings of modern navigation, would hardly enter on his journal. The shipmaster, who could not shun Charybdis without falling into Scylla, would be remanded without a dissenting voice to the forecastle. The Odyssey was founded on a mere coasting voyage; its chief adventures turn upon nautical blunders, which would cast shame on the most awkward skipper of a modern fishing smack. The siege of Troy would now be finished in a fortnight; and the Latian war would hardly fill a newspaper paragraph. The ex-Governor of New Hampshire publishes *fifty-two* Georgics a year, each containing more of agricultural science than Virgil could have gleaned through the whole Roman empire; while Virgil's beautiful fictions about the bees have been supplanted by Huber's stranger facts.

Such are the themes of classic song,—thus trite, unromantic, prosaic, as now regarded and handled. But they are in fact what they were in the glowing verse of antiquity. Abridged and materialized though they be in our mechanical age, they are full of the richest materials for poetry, of grand and beautiful forms, of the types of an infinite presence, and of skill and power beyond thought,—full too of thrilling human experience, of man's vast aims and wild darings, of his wrath and his tenderness, his agony and his triumph. What though the loiterer on the steamboat deck heeds not the "monstra natantia," which made the hair of the ancient helmsman erect with fear? They are none the less there—fearful, marvellous, and mighty. What though we have analysed the thunder-bolt, and know how to turn it harmless from our homes? Still, when we hear at midnight the voice that breaks the cedars, we feel that not a trait of majesty or beauty has faded from that ineffably sublime passage of Virgil,—

> Ipse pater, media nimborum in nocte, corusca
> Fulmina molitur dextra; quo maxima motu
> Terra tremit, fugere feræ, et mortalia corda
> Per gentes humilis stravit pavor.

What though any farmer's boy would laugh to scorn the river-goddess's recipe for replenishing the wasted beehive? Time has taken nothing from the truth to nature and to actual life, from the deep pathos and intense beauty of her son's lamentation, and of her own quick maternal sympathy, and anxious, persevering love. Yes; this ancient poetry, wide as it often is of fact, is full of truth. It beats throughout with the throbbings of the universal human heart,—of that heart, which, under the present reign of iron and steam, dares not full and free utterance; but which, in those simple days, spoke as it felt, and has left us, in verse that cannot die, its early communings with itself, with nature, with life's experience, and with the infinite Unknown.

WILLIAM INGRAHAM KIP.

The first member of the old New York family of Kip, who appears in history, was Ruloff de Kype, a partisan of the Duke of Guise in the French civil wars connected with the Reformation. He was a native of Brittany, and on the defeat of his party took refuge in Holland. He afterwards joined the army of the Duke of Anjou, and was killed in battle near Jarnac. His son Ruloff became a Protestant, and remained in Holland, where the next in descent, Henry, was born in 1576. On arriving at manhood, he took an active part in "The Company of Foreign Countries," an association formed for the purpose of obtaining access to the Indies, by a different route from that possessed by Spain and Portugal. They first attempted to sail round the northern seas of Europe and Asia, but their expedition, despatched in 1594, was obliged to return on account of the ice in the same year. In 1609, they employed Henry Hudson to sail to the westward, in the little Half Moon, with happier results.

Henry Kype came to New Amsterdam in 1635. He returned to Holland, but his sons remained, and rose to important positions as citizens and landed proprietors. One, Hendrick, became in 1647 and 1649 one of the council chosen by the people, to assist Governor Stuyvesant in the administration. Another, Jacobus, was Secretary of the city council, and received a grant of land on Kip's Bay, East River, where he built a house in 1641, which remained standing until 1850, when it was demolished on the opening of Thirty-fifth street. A third, Jacob, owned the ground now occupied by the Park. Five generations of the family were born at the house at Kip's Bay, a portion of whom settled at Rhinebeck. The mansion was occupied for a brief period by General Washington, and after the capture of the city as the head-quarters of the British officers. The proprietor, Jacobus Kip, was a Whig, and his son served in the American army. Other members of the family were officers in the British service.

W. Ingraham Kip

William Ingraham Kip is the eldest son of Leonard Kip, for many years President of the North River Bank, and is connected through his mother's family with Captain Ingraham, the spirited liberator of Martin Kozsta. He was born in New York, October 3, 1811, and prepared for college at schools in that city. After passing a twelvemonth at Rutgers College, he completed the remaining three years of his college course at Yale, in 1831. He commenced and continued for some time the study of law, which he then changed for that of Divinity, and was graduated from the General Theological Seminary of the Protestant Episcopal Church, and ordained Deacon in 1835. His first parochial charge was at St. Peter's Church, Morristown, New Jersey, where he remained a year. He was next Assistant Minister of Grace Church, New York, and in 1838 called to the Rectorship of St. Peter's Church, Albany, where he remained, with the exception of a portion of the years 1844 and 1845, passed in Europe, until his consecration as Missionary Bishop of California, in October, 1853. He soon after removed to San Francisco, where he now resides, actively engaged in the arduous duties of his important position.

In 1843 he published *The Lenten Fast*, a volume in which the origin, propriety, and advantages of the observance of the season are pointed out. It has passed through six editions. In 1844, *The Double Witness of the Church*, an exposition of the *Via Media* between Roman Catholic and unepiscopal Protestant doctrines, appeared. It is regarded as one of the most valuable of the many works on the subject, and has passed through several editions. The *Christmas Holidays in Rome*, a volume derived from the author's observations in 1844, appeared in the following year. In 1846 he prepared *The Early Jesuit Missions in North America*, an interesting and valuable volume, drawn from the *Lettres Edifiantes et Curieuses ecrites des Missions Etrangères*, the original narratives of the Jesuit missionaries and other contemporary records.

In 1851 he issued in London, and afterwards in this country, a work on *The Early Conflicts of Christianity*—the conflicts including those of heresies within as well as opponents without the Early Church. The volume gives an animated picture of the varied scenes of the period.

Bishop Kip's latest publication is a volume on *The Catacombs of Rome*, published in 1854. It contains a description, drawn from personal inspection, of these venerated resting-places of the fathers and confessors of the church of the first three centuries; and an account of the inscriptions and symbols which they contain, accompanied with pictorial representations and fac-similes, from Arringhi's folio and other early and rare works.

These volumes are all written for popular circulation in a popular style, and are of moderate size. They, however, indicate ample and thorough research, and have given their author, in connexion with his highly successful pulpit compositions, and numerous articles in the New York Review, Church Review, Evergreen, American Monthly Magazine, Churchman, and other periodicals, a high position as a theologian and scholar, as well as author.

ELIHU BURRITT.

Elihu Burritt, "the learned Blacksmith," was born at New Britain, Connecticut, December 8, 1811, of an old New England family. His father was a shoemaker, a man of ready apprehension and charitable sympathies and action. He had ten children, and of his five sons the eldest and the youngest have both attained literary distinction. The former, Elijah, early developed a fondness for the mathematics. His friends sent him to college. The fruits of his studies have been a work entitled *Log Arithmetic*, published before he was twenty-one, and his *Geography of the Heavens*, which is in general use as a schoolbook.

Elihu Burritt

The youngest of the sons was Elihu. He had received only a limited district school education, when, on his father's death, he was apprenticed at the age of seventeen to a blacksmith. He had acquired, however, a taste for the observations written in books from the narratives of the old revolutionary soldiers who came to his father's house. He wished to know more, and life thus taught him the use of books. When his apprenticeship was ended he studied with his brother, who, driven from his career as a schoolmaster at the South, had returned to establish himself in this capacity in his native town, learning something of Latin, French, and Mathematics. At the end of six months he returned to the forge, watching the castings in the furnace with a copy of the Greek grammar in his hand. He took some intervals from his trade for the study of his favorite grammars, gradually adding to his stock of languages till he attacked the Hebrew. To procure oriental books he determined to embark from Boston as a sailor, and spend his wages at the first European port in books, but was diverted from this by the inducements of the library of the Antiquarian Society at Worcester, the happily endowed institution of Isaiah Thomas, in a thrifty manufacturing town which offered employment for his arm as well as his brain. Here, in 1837, he forged and studied, recording in his diary such entries as these. "*Monday*, June 18, headache; forty pages Cuvier's Theory of the Earth, sixty-four pages French, eleven hours forging. *Tuesday*, sixty-five lines of Hebrew, thirty pages of French, ten pages Cuvier's Theory, eight lines Syriac, ten ditto Danish, ten ditto Bohemian, nine ditto Polish, fifteen names of stars, ten hours forging." When the overwearied brain was arrested by a headache he worked that off by a few hours' extra forging.

> Thus on his sounding anvil shaped
> Each burning deed and thought.

A letter to a friend inquiring for employment as a translator of German, and telling his story, reached Edward Everett, then Governor of Massachusetts, who read the account at a public meeting, and Burritt became at once installed among the curiosities of literature. He was invited to pursue his studies at Harvard, but he preferred the forge at Worcester, airing his grammatical knowledge by the publication of a monthly periodical to teach French entitled *The Literary Gemini*. This was published in 1839 and continued for a year. In 1840 he commenced as a lecturer, one of the few profitable avenues of literary occupation open in the country, which he has since pursued with distinguished success. He translated Icelandic sagas and papers from the Samaritan, Arabic, and Hebrew, for the *Eclectic Review*, still adding to his stock of languages. In 1844 he commenced at Worcester a paper called *The Christian Citizen*, in which he was diverted from philology to philanthropy, advocating peace and fraternity. He published his *Olive Leaves* at this time from the same office. He became engaged in circulating a mutual system of addresses in behalf of peace between England and America, and in 1846 was the proprietor and editor of *The Peace Advocate*. His *Bond of Brotherhood* was a periodical tract which he circulated among travellers. In the same year he went to England, where he enjoyed a cordial reception and full employment among the philanthropists, writing for Douglas Jerrold's weekly newspaper, and forming peace associations. One of his latest employments of this kind was the distribution, in 1852, of a series of "friendly addresses" from Englishmen through the different departments of France.

Burritt's latest publication (1854) is entitled *Thoughts and Things at Home and Abroad*, a collection of various contributions to the press, written with a certain enthusiasm, without exactness of thought and expression, in the form of sketches, and covering the favorite topics of the writer in war, temperance, and kindred subjects.

WHY I LEFT THE ANVIL.

I see it, you would ask me what I have to say for myself for dropping the hammer and taking up the quill, as a member of your profession. I will be honest now, and tell you the whole story. I was transposed from the anvil to the editor's chair by the genius of machinery. Don't smile, friends, it was even so. I had stood and looked for hours on those thoughtless, iron intellects, those iron-fingered, sober, supple automatons, as they caught up a bale of cotton, and twirled it in the twinkling of an eye, into a whirlwind of whizzing shreds, and laid it at my feet in folds of snow-white cloth, ready for the use of our most voluptuous antipodes. They were wonderful things, those looms and spindles; but they could not spin thoughts; there was no attribute of Divinity in them, and I admired them, nothing more. They were excessively curious, but I could estimate the whole compass of their doings and destiny in finger power; so I am away and left them spinning—cotton.

One day I was tuning my anvil beneath a hot iron, and busy with the thought, that there was as much intellectual philosophy in my hammer as in any of the enginery agoing in modern times, when a most unearthly screaming pierced my ears: I stepped to the door, and there it was, the great Iron Horse! Yes, he had come looking for all the world like the great Dragon we read of in Scripture, harnessed to half a living world and just landed on the earth, where he stood braying in surprise and indignation at the "base use" to which he had been turned. I saw the gigantic hexiped move with a power that made the earth tremble for miles. I saw the army of human beings gliding with the velocity of the wind over the iron track, and droves of cattle travelling in their stables at the rate of twenty miles an hour towards their city-slaughter-house. It was wonderful. The little busy bee-winged machinery of the cotton factory dwindled into insignificance before it. Monstrous beast of passage and burden! it devoured the intervening distance, and welded the cities together! But for its furnace heart and iron sinews, it was nothing but a beast, an enormous aggregation of—horse power. And I went back to the forge with unimpaired reverence for the intellectual philosophy of my hammer. Passing along the street one afternoon I heard a noise in an old building, as of some one puffing a pair of bellows. So without more ado, I stepped in, and there, in a corner of a room, I saw the chef d'œuvre of all the machinery that has ever been invented since the birth of Tubal Cain. In its construction it was as simple and unassuming as a cheese press. It went with a lever—with a lever, longer, stronger, than that, with which Archimedes promised to lift the world.

"It is a printing press," said a boy standing by the ink trough with a queueless turban of brown paper on his head. "A printing press!" I queried musingly to myself. "A printing press! what do you print?" I asked. "Print!" said the boy, staring at me doubtfully, "why we print thoughts." "Print thoughts!" I slowly repeated after him; and we stood looking for a moment at each other in mutual admiration, he in the absence of an idea, and I in pursuit of one. But I looked at him the hardest, and he left another ink mark on his forehead from a pathetic motion of his left hand to quicken his apprehension of my meaning. "Why, yes," he reiterated, in a tone of forced confidence, as if passing an idea, which, though having been current a hundred years, might still be counterfeit, for all he could show on the spot, "we print thoughts, to be sure." "But, my boy," I asked in honest soberness, "what are thoughts, and how can you get hold of them to print them?" "Thoughts are what come out of the people's minds," he replied. "Get hold of them, indeed? Why minds arn't nothing you can get hold of, nor thoughts either. All the minds that ever thought, and all the thoughts that minds ever made, wouldn't make a ball as big as your fist. Minds, they say, are just like air; you can't see them; they don't make any noise, nor have any color; they don't weigh anything. Bill Deepcut, the sexton, says, that a man weighs just as much when his mind has gone out of him as he did before.—No, sir, all the minds that ever lived wouldn't weigh an ounce troy."

"Then how do you print thoughts?" I asked. "If minds are thin as air, and thoughts thinner still, and make no noise, and have no substance, shade, or color, and are like the winds, and more than the winds, are anywhere in a moment; sometimes in heaven, and sometimes on earth and in the waters under the earth; how can you get hold of them? how can you see them when caught, or show them to others?"

Ezekiel's eyes grew luminous with a new idea, and pushing his ink-roller proudly across the metallic page of the newspaper, replied, "Thoughts work and walk in things what make tracks; and we take them tracks, and stamp them on paper, or iron, wood, stone, or what not. This is the way we print thoughts. Don't you understand?"

The pressman let go the lever, and looked interrogatively at Ezekiel, beginning at the patch on his stringless brogans, and following up with his eye to the top of the boy's brown paper buff cap. Ezekiel comprehended the felicity of his illustration, and wiping his hands on his tow apron, gradually assumed an attitude of earnest exposition. I gave him an encouraging wink, and so he went on.

"Thoughts make tracks," he continued impressively, as if evolving a new phase of the idea by repeating it slowly. Seeing we assented to this proposition inquiringly, he stepped to the type-case, with his eye fixed admonishingly upon us. "Thoughts make tracks," he repeated, arranging in his left hand a score or two of metal slips, "and with these here letters we can take the exact impression of every thought that ever went out of the heart of a human man; and we can print it too," giving the inked form a blow of triumph with his fist, "we can print it too, give us paper and ink enough, till the great round earth is blanketed around with a coverlid of thoughts, as much like the pattern as two peas." Ezekiel seemed to grow an inch at every word, and the brawny pressman looked first at him, and then at the press, with evident astonishment. "Talk about the mind's living for ever!" exclaimed the boy, pointing patronizingly at the ground, as if mind were lying there incapable of immortality until the printer reached it a helping hand, "why the world is brimful of live, bright, industrious thoughts, which would have been dead, as dead as a stone, if it hadn't been for boys like me who have run the ink rollers. Immortality, indeed! why, people's minds," he continued, with his imagination climbing into the profanely sublime, "people's minds wouldn't be immortal if 'twasn't for the printers—at any rate, in this here planetary burying-ground. We are the chaps what manufacture immortality for dead men," he subjoined, slapping the pressman graciously on the shoulder. The latter took it as if dubbed a knight of the legion of honor, for the boy had put the mysteries of his profession in sublime apocalypse. "Give us one good healthy mind," resumed Ezekiel, "to think for us, and we will furnish a dozen worlds as big as this with thoughts to order. Give us such a man, and we will insure his life; we will keep him alive for ever among the living. He can't die, no way you can fix it, when once we have touched him with these here bits of inky pewter. He shan't die nor sleep. We will keep his mind at work on all the minds that live on the earth, and all the minds that shall come to live here as long as the world stands."

"Ezekiel," I asked, in a subdued tone of reverence, "will you print my thoughts too?"

"Yes, that I will," he replied, "if you will think some of the right kind." "Yes, that we will," echoed the pressman.

And I went home and thought, and Ezekiel has printed my "thought-tracks" ever since.

ALFRED B. STREET.

The early associations of Mr. Street were of a kind favorable to the development of the tastes which mark his literary productions. The son of the Hon. Randall S. Street, he was born at Poughkeepsie, on the Hudson, and at an early age removed with his father to Monticello in Sullivan county, then almost a wilderness. The scenery of these beautiful regions is reproduced in his poems, and the faithfulness and minuteness of the picture show the firmness of the impression upon the youthful mind.

Alfred B. Street.

Mr. Street studied law as well as nature, at Monticello, and on his admission to the bar removed to Albany, where he has since resided. He married a daughter of Mr. Smith Weed, of that place, and has for several years held the appointment of state librarian.

Mr. Street commenced his literary career at an early age as a poetical writer for the magazines. His first volume, *The Burning of Schenectady, and other Poems*, was published in 1842. The leading poem is a narration of a well known incident of the colonial history of New York; the remaining pieces are of a descriptive character. A second collection, *Drawings and Tintings*, appeared in 1844. It includes a poem on Nature, of decided merit in its descriptions of the phenomena of the seasons, which was pronounced by the author in 1840 before the Euglossian Society of Geneva College.

In 1849 Mr. Street published in London, and in the same year in this country, *Frontenac, or the Atotarho of the Iroquois, a Metrical Romance*, a poem of some seven thousand lines in the octosyllabic measure, founded on the expedition of Count Frontenac, governor-general of Canada, against the powerful Indian tribe of the Iroquois. The story introduces many picturesque scenes of Indian life, and abounds in passages of description of natural scenery, in the author's best vein of careful elaboration.

In 1842, a collection of the poems of Mr. Street, embracing, with the exception of a few juvenile pieces and the romance of Frontenac, all that he had written to that period, was published in New York. He has since contributed to various magazines a number of pieces sufficient to form a volume of similar size. He has also written a narrative poem, of which La Salle is the hero, extending to some three thousand lines, which still remains in manuscript. He is besides the author of a number of prose tale sketches, which have appeared with success in the magazines of the day.

Mr. Street's poems are chiefly occupied with descriptions of the varied phases of American scenery. He has won a well merited reputation by the fidelity of his observation. As a descriptive writer he is a patient and accurate observer of Nature,—daguerreotyping the effects of earth and air, and the phenomena of vegetable and animal life in their various relation to the landscape. He has been frequently described by critics by comparison with the minute style of the painters of the Dutch school. Mr. Tuckerman, in an article in the Democratic Review, has thus alluded to this analogy, and to the home atmosphere of the author's descriptions of American nature:—"Street is a true Flemish painter, seizing upon objects in all their verisimilitude. As we read him, wild flowers peer up from among brown leaves; the drum of the partridge, the ripple of waters, the flickering of autumn light, the sting of sleety snow, the cry of the panther, the roar of the winds, the melody of birds, and the odor of crushed pine-boughs are present to our senses. In a foreign land his poems would transport us at once to home. He is no second-hand limner, content to furnish insipid copies but draws from reality. His pictures have the freshness of originals. They are graphic, detailed, never untrue, and often vigorous; he is essentially an American poet."

THE SETTLER.

His echoing axe the settler swung
  Amid the sea-like solitude,
And rushing, thundering, down were flung
  The Titans of the wood;
Loud shrieked the eagle as he dashed
From out his mossy nest, which crashed
  With its supporting bough,
And the first sunlight, leaping, flashed
  On the wolf's haunt below.

Rude was the garb, and strong the frame
  Of him who plied his ceaseless toil:
To form that garb, the wild-wood game
  Contributed their spoil;
The soul that warmed that frame, disdained
The tinsel, gaud, and glare, that reigned
  Where men their crowds collect;
The simple fur, untrimmed, unstained,
  This forest tamer decked.

The paths which wound 'mid gorgeous trees,
  The streams whose bright lips kissed their flowers,
The winds that swelled their harmonies
  Through those sun-hiding bowers,
The temple vast—the green arcade,
The nestling vale, the grassy glade,
  Dark cave and swampy lair;
These scenes and sounds majestic, made
  His world, his pleasures, there.

His roof adorned, a pleasant spot,
  'Mid the black logs green glowed the grain,
And herbs and plants the woods knew not,
  Throve in the sun and rain.
The smoke-wreath curling o'er the dell,
The low—the bleat—the tinkling bell,
  All made a landscape strange,
Which was the living chronicle
  Of deeds that wrought the change.

The violet sprung at Spring's first tinge,
  The rose of Summer spread its glow,
The maize hung on its Autumn fringe,
  Rude Winter brought his snow;
And still the settler labored there,
His shout and whistle woke the air,
  As cheerily he plied
His garden spade, or drove his share
  Along the hillock's side.

He marked the fire-storm's blazing flood
  Roaring and crackling on its path,
And scorching earth, and melting wood,
  Beneath its greedy wrath;
He marked the rapid whirlwind shoot,
Trampling the pine tree with its foot,
  And darkening thick the day
With streaming bough and severed root,
  Hurled whizzing on its way.

His gaunt hound yelled, his rifle flashed,
  The grim bear hushed its savage growl,
In blood and foam the panther gnashed
  Its fangs with dying howl;
The fleet deer ceased its flying bound,
Its snarling wolf foe bit the ground,
  And with its moaning cry,
The beaver sank beneath the wound
  Its pond-built Venice by.

Humble the lot, yet his the race!
  When liberty sent forth her cry,
Who thronged in Conflict's deadliest place,
  To fight—to bleed—to die.
Who cumbered Bunker's height of red,
By hope, through weary years were led,
  And witnessed Yorktown's sun

Blaze on a Nation's banner spread,
A Nation's freedom won.

AN AUTUMN LANDSCAPE.

A knoll of upland, shorn by nibbling sheep
To a rich carpet, woven of short grass
And tiny clover, upward leads my steps
By the seamed pathway, and my roving eye
Drinks in the vassal landscape. Far and wide
Nature is smiling in her loveliness,
Masses of woods, green strips of fields, ravines,
Shown by their outlines drawn against the hills,
Chimneys and roofs, trees, single and in groups,
Bright curves of brooks, and vanishing mountain tops
Expand upon my sight. October's brush
The scene has colored; not with those broad hues
Mixed in his later palette by the frost,
And dashed upon the picture, till the eye
Aches with the varied splendor, but in tints
Left by light scattered touches. Overhead
There is a blending of cloud, haze and sky;
A silvery sheet with spaces of soft hue;
A trembling veil of gauze is stretched athwart
The shadowy hill-sides and dark forest-flanks;
A soothing quiet broods upon the air,
And the faint sunshine winks with drowsiness.
Far sounds melt mellow on the ear: the bark—
The bleat—the tinkle—whistle—blast of horn—
The rattle of the wagon-wheel—the low—
The fowler's shot—the twitter of the bird,
And e'en the hue of converse from the road.
The grass, with its low insect-tones, appears
As murmuring in its sleep. This butterfly
Seems as if loth to stir, so lazily
It flutters by. In fitful starts and stops
The locust sings. The grasshopper breaks out
In brief harsh strains; amidst its pausing chirps
The beetle glistening in its sable mail,
Slow climbs the clover-tops, and e'en the ant
Darts round less eagerly.
What difference marks
The scene from yester-noontide. Then the sky
Showed such rich, tender blue, it seemed as if
'Twould melt before the sight. The glittering clouds
Floated above, the trees danced glad below
To the fresh wind. The sunshine flashed on streams,
Sparkled on leaves, and laughed on fields and woods.
All, all was life and motion, as all now
Is sleep and quiet. Nature in her change
Varies each day, as in the world of man
She moulds the differing features. Yea, each leaf
Is variant from its fellow. Yet her works
Are blended in a glorious harmony,
For thus God made His earth. Perchance His breath
Was music when he spake it into life,
Adding thereby another instrument
To the innumerable choral orbs
Sending the tribute of their grateful praise
In ceaseless anthems toward His sacred throne.

THEODORE PARKER

Is a native of Massachusetts, born in or about the year 1812, at Lexington, the son of a farmer, and grandson of a Revolutionary soldier. He studied theology among the Unitarians at Cambridge; became a graduate of its theological school in 1836, and was afterwards settled as minister of the Second Church in Roxbury. From 1840 to 1842 he was a contributor to the Dial and Christian Examiner, of papers chiefly on theological topics, which he collected in a volume of *Critical and Miscellaneous Writings* in 1843. In 1842 he published a treatise, *A Discourse of Matters relating to Religion*, in an octavo volume. It was the substance of a series of lectures delivered the previous season in Boston, and constituted a manifesto of the growing changes of the author in his doctrinal opinions, which had widely departed from points of church authority, the inspiration of the scriptures and the divine character of the Saviour. He had previously in May, 1841, startled his associates by his *Discourse on the Transient and Permanent in Christianity*, preached at the ordination of Mr. Charles C. Shackford, in Harris Place Church in Boston. Both these publications were met and opposed in the Christian Examiner.

Theodore Parker.

Proscribed by the Unitarian Societies of Boston on account of the promulgation of his new views, Mr. Parker organized, by the aid of his friends, a congregation, which met in the old Melodeon in the city, and has since transferred itself to the ample accommodations of the new Music Hall. He has published a memorial of this change, in *Two Sermons, on leaving an old and entering a new place of worship*. His title, as appears from his printed discourses, is Minister of the Twenty-Eighth Congregational Society in Boston. In his new quarters he holds an independent service, delivering a weekly discourse on Sunday morning, frequently taking for his theme some topic of the times or point of morality. The questions of slavery, war, social and moral reforms of various kinds, are discussed with much acute analysis, occasional effective satire, and a rather unprofitable reliance on the powers of the individual. As a practical teacher, he is in the unfortunate position of a priest without a church, and a politician without a state. Though he interweaves some elegance of fancy in his discourses, yet it is of a dry quality, a flower of a forced growth, and his manner and matter seem equally unaffected by tender poetic imagination. He has nothing of the air of hearty impulse of a democratic leader of revolutionary opinion, as might be supposed, from the drift of his printed discourses. As a speaker he is slow, didactic, positive, and self-sufficient.

Mr. Parker has published several series of discourses, entitled *Sermons of Theism, Atheism, and the Popular Theology*, and *Ten Sermons of Religion*, from which his moral views may be gathered.

He has borne a prominent part in the agitation of the Fugitive Slave Law, of which he is a vigorous denouncer. A number of his discourses on this and other social topics are included in his two volumes, *Speeches, Addresses, and Occasional Sermons*, published in 1852. He also delivered an elaborate critical essay on the character of John Quincy Adams, immediately after the death of that statesman, and a similar discourse, remarkable for its severity, on Daniel Webster.

As a specimen of Mr. Parker's manner on a topic of more general agreement than most of his writings afford, we may cite a few passages from a sermon published by him in 1854 on

OLD AGE.

I cannot tell where childhood ends, and manhood begins; nor where manhood ends, and old age begins. It is a wavering and uncertain line, not straight and definite, which borders betwixt the two. But the outward characteristics of old age are obvious enough. The weight diminishes. Man is commonly heaviest at forty, woman at fifty. After that, the body shrinks a little; the height shortens as the cartilages become thin and dry. The hair whitens and falls away. The frame stoops, the bones become smaller, feebler, have less animal and more mere earthy matter. The senses decay, slowly and handsomely. The eye is not so sharp, and while it penetrates further into space, it has less power clearly to define the outline of what it sees. The ear is dull; the appetite less. Bodily heat is lower; the breath produces less carbonic acid than before. The old man consumes less food, water, air. The hands grasp less strongly; the feet less firmly tread. The lungs suck the breast of heaven with less powerful collapse. The eye and ear take not so strong a hold upon the world:—

And the big manly voice,
Turning again to childish treble, pipes
And whistles in his sound.

The animal life is making ready to go out. The very old man loves the sunshine and the fire, the arm-chair and the shady nook. A rude wind would jostle the full-grown apple from its bough, full-ripe, full-colored, too. The internal characteristics correspond. General activity is less. Salient love of new things and of new persons, which bit the young man's heart, fades away. He thinks the old is better. He is not venturesome; he keeps at home. Passion once stung him into quickened life; now that gad-fly is no more buzzing in his ears. Madame de Staël finds compensation in Science for the decay of the passion that once fired her blood; but Heathen Socrates, seventy years old, thanks the gods that he is now free from that "ravenous beast," which had disturbed his philosophic meditations for many a year. Romance is the child of Passion and Imagination;—the sudden father that, the long protracting mother this. Old age has little romance. Only some rare man, like Wilhelm Von Humboldt, keeps it still fresh in his bosom.

In intellectual matters, the venerable man loves to recall the old times, to revive his favorite old men,—no new ones half so fair. So in Homer, Nestor, who is the oldest of the Greeks, is always talking of the old times, before the grandfathers of men then living had come into being; "not such as live in these degenerate days." Verse-loving John Quincy Adams turns off from Byron and Shelley and Wieland and Goethe, and returns to Pope,

Who pleased his childhood and informed his youth.

The pleasure of hope is smaller; that of memory greater. It is exceeding beautiful that it is so. The venerable man loves to set recollection to beat the roll-call, and summon up from the grave the old time, "the good old time,"—the old places, old friends, old games, old talk, nay, to his ear the old familiar tunes are sweeter than anything that Mendelssohn, or Strauss, or Rossini can bring to pass. Elder Brewster expects to hear St. Martins and Old Hundred chanted in Heaven. Why not? To him Heaven comes in the long-used musical tradition, not in the neologies of sound.

* * * * * * * * * * *

Then the scholar becomes an antiquary; he likes not young men unless he knew their grandfathers before. The young woman looks in the newspaper for the marriages, the old man for the deaths. The young man's eye looks forward; the world is "all before him where to choose." It is a hard world; he does not know it: he works a little, and hopes much. The middle-aged man looks around at the present; he has found out that it is a hard world; he hopes less and works more. The old man looks back on the fields he has trod; "this is the tree I planted; this is my footstep," and he loves his old house, his old carriage, cat, dog, staff, and friend. In lands where the vine grows, I have seen an old man sit all day long, a sunny autumn day, before his cottage door, in a great arm-chair, his old dog couched at his feet, in the genial sun. The autumn wind played with the old man's venerable hairs; above him on the wall, purpling in the sunlight, hung the full clusters of the grape, ripening and maturing yet more. The two were just alike; the wind stirred the vine leaves, and they fell; stirred the old man's hair and it whitened yet more. Both were waiting for the spirit in them to be fully ripe. The young man looks forward; the old man looks back. How long the shadows lie in the setting-sun; the steeple a mile long reaching across the plain, as the sun stretches out the hills in grotesque dimensions. So are the events of life in the old man's consciousness.

WILLIAM HAYNE SIMMONS—JAMES WRIGHT SIMMONS.

DR. W. H. SIMMONS is a native of South Carolina, and at present a resident of East Florida. He is a graduate of the medical school of Philadelphia, but has never practised the profession. He published anonymously some years since at Charleston, an Indian poem, with the title, *Onea*, which contains descriptive passages of merit. Mr. Simmons is also the author of a *History of the Seminoles*. The following is from his pen:—

THE BELL BIRD.*

Here Nature, clad in vestments rich and gay,
Sits like a bride in gorgeous palace lone;

* "It is generally supposed," says the Rev. R. Walsh, in his Notices of Brazil, "that the woods abound with birds whose flight and note continually enliven the forest, but nothing can be more still and solitary than everything around. The silence is appalling, and the desolation awful; neither are disturbed by the sight or voice of any living thing, save one—which only adds to the impression. Among the highest trees, and in the deepest glens, a sound is sometimes heard so singular, that the noise seems quite unnatural. It is like the clinking of metals, as if two lumps of brass were struck together; and resembles sometimes the distant and solemn tolling of a church bell, struck at long intervals. This extraordinary sound proceeds from a bird called Araponga, or Quiraponga. It is about the

And sees naught move, and hears no sound all day,
Save from its cloudy source the torrent tumbling,
And to the mountain's foot its glories humbling,
Or wild woods to the desert gale that moan!
Or, far, the Araponga's note deep toiling
From the tall pine's glossy spine, where the breeze,
Disporting o'er the green and shoreless seas,
Impels the leafy billows, ever rolling.
It comes again! sad as the passing bell,
That solitary note!—unseen whence swell
The tones so drear—so secret is the shade
Where that coy dweller of the gloom has made
His perch. On high, behind his verdant screen,
He nestles; or, like transient snow-flake's flash,
Or flying foam that winds from torrent's dash,
Plunges to stiller haunts, where hangs sublime
The trav'lling water vine, its pitcher green
Filled from the cloud, where ne'er the bear may climb,
Or thirsting savage, when the summer ray
Has dried each fount, and parched the desert way.
Here safe he dips refreshed his pearly bill
In lymph more pure than from a spring or rill;
No longer by the wand'ring Indian shared,
The dewy draught he there may quaff unscared,—
For vacant now glooms ev'ry glen or grove
Where erst he saw the quivered Red Man rove;
Saw, like the otter's brood upon the stream,
His wild-eyed offspring sport, or, 'neath the tree,
Share with the birds kind nature's bounty free.
Changed is the woodland scene like morning dream!
The race has vanished, to return no more,
Gone from the forest's side, the river's shore.
Is it for this, thou lone and hermit bird!
That thus thy knell-like note so sad is heard!
Sounding from ev'ry desert shade and dell
Where once they dwelt, where last they wept farewell!
They fled—till, wearied by the bloody chase;
Or stopped by the rich spoil, their brethren pale,
Sated, the dire pursuit surceased a space.
While Memory's eye o'er the sad picture fills,
They fade! nor leave behind or wreck or trace;
The valiant tribes forgotten on their hills,
And seen no more in wilderness or vale.

James Wright Simmons, a younger brother of the preceding, was born in South Carolina. He studied at Harvard, wrote verses, afterwards travelled in Europe, and returned to America to reside in the West. In 1852 he published at Boston a poem, *The Greek Girl;* a sketch in the desultory style made fashionable by Don Juan, and so well adapted to the expression of emotion. It breathes a poetic spirit, and bears traces of the author's acquaintance with books and the world. Mr. Simmons has written several other poems of an occasional or satirical character, and is also the author of a series of metrical tales, *Woodnotes from the West*, which are still in manuscript. The following, from the volume containing the "Greek Girl," are in a striking vein of reflection.

size of a small pigeon; white, with a red circle round the eyes. It sits on the tops of the highest trees, and in the deepest forests; and though constantly heard in the most desert places, is very rarely seen. It is impossible to conceive anything of a more solitary character than the profound silence of the woods, broken only by the metallic and almost preternatural sound of this invisible bird, wherever you go. I have watched with great perseverance when the sound seemed quite near to me, and never once caught a glimpse of the cause. It passed suddenly over the tops of very high trees, like a large flake of snow, and immediately disappeared."

TO HIM WHO CAN ALONE SIT FOR THE PICTURE.

If to be free from aught of guile,
Neither to do nor suffer wrong;
Yet in thy judgments gentle still,
Serene—inflexible in will,
Only where some great duty lies;
Prone to forgive, or, with a smile,
Reprove the errors that belong
To natures that fall far below
The height of thy empyreal brow:
Of self to make a sacrifice,
Rather than view another's woe;
And guided by the same fixed law
Supreme, to yield, in argument,
The bootless triumph that might draw
Down pain upon thy opponent:
By fate oppressed, "in each hard instance tried,"
Still seen with Honor walking by thy side;
E'en in those hours when all unbend,
And by some thoughtless word offend,
Thy conscious spirit, great and good,
Neither upborne, nor yet subdued,
Impressed by sense of human ill,
Preserv'st its even tenor still;
While 'neath that calm, clear surface lie
Thoughts worthy of Eternity!
And passions—shall I call them so!
Celestial attributes! that glow
Radiant as wing of Seraphim,
Lighting thy path, in all else dim.
Placed on their lofty eminence,
Thou see'st the guerdons that to thee belong,
Passed to the low-browed temple, burn intense—
Standing between thee and the throng
Of noble minds, thy great compeers!
And still the same serenity appears,
Like stars in its own solitude—
Setting its seal on thy majestic blood!
If elements like these could give
The record that might bid them live,
The mighty dead—Saint, Sophist, Sage,
Achilles in his tent—
Might claim in vain a brighter page,
A haughtier monument.

TWILIGHT THOUGHTS.

Ye're fading in the distance dim,
Illusions of the heart!
Yes, one by one, recalled by Him—
I see ye all depart.

The swelling pride, the rising glow,
The spirit that would mount!
The mind that sought all things to know—
And drank at that dread fount.

Over whose waters, dark and deep,
Their sleepless vigils still
Those melancholy Daughters keep,
Or by thy sacred Hill!

Deep Passion's concentrated fire,
The soul's volcanic light!
A Phœnix on her fun'ral pyre,
The Eden of a night!

The wish to be all things—to soar,
And comprehend the universe;
Yet doomed to linger on the shore,
And feel our fettered wings a curse!

To drink in Beauty at a glance,
Its graces and its bloom;
Yet weave the garlands of Romance
To decorate the tomb!

To sigh for some dear Paradise,
Exempt from age or death;

To live for ever in those eyes,
  And breathe but with that breath!

To be awakened from such dream,
  With the remembrance clinging still!
Like flowers reflected in a stream,
  When all is changed and chill.

To feel that life can never bring
  Its Rainbow back to our lost sky!
Plucks from the hand of death its sting,
  The grave its victory!

FRANCES SARGENT OSGOOD.

Mrs. Osgood was a member of a family distinguished by literary ability. Mrs. Wells,* the author of a graceful volume of Poems, was the daughter of Frances's mother by a previous marriage, and her youngest sister, Mrs. E. D. Harrington, and her brother, A. A. Locke, are known as successful magazine writers. Their father, Mr. Joseph Locke, was a well educated merchant of Boston, where his daughter Frances was born about the year 1812.

The chief portion of her childhood was passed in the village of Hingham, a locality peculiarly adapted by its beautiful situation for a poetic culture, which soon developed itself in her youthful mind. She was encouraged in writing verses by her parents, and some of her productions being seen by Mrs. Lydia Maria Child, were so highly approved, as to be inserted by her in a juvenile Miscellany which she at that time conducted. They were rapidly followed by others from the same facile pen, which soon gave their signature, "Florence," a wide reputation.

In 1834, Miss Locke formed the acquaintance of Mr. S. S. Osgood, a young painter already favorably known in his profession. She sat to him for her portrait, and the artist won the heart of the sitter. Soon after their marriage they went to London, where they remained four years, during which Mr. Osgood pursued his art of portrait-painting with success; and his wife's poetical compositions to various periodicals met with equal favor. In 1839, a collection of her poems was issued by a London publisher, with the title of *A Wreath of Wild Flowers from New England*. A dramatic poem, Elfrida, in the volume, impressed her friend James Sheridan Knowles the dramatist, so favorably, that he urged her to write a piece for the stage. In compliance with the suggestion, she wrote *The Happy Release or the Triumphs of Love*, a play in three acts. It was accepted by one of the theatres, and would have been produced had not the author, while engaged in the reconstruction of a scene, been suddenly summoned home by the melancholy news of the death of her father. She returned with Mr. Osgood to Boston in 1840. They soon afterwards removed to New York, where, with a few intervals of absence, the remainder of her life was passed. Her poetical contributions appeared at brief intervals in the magazines, for which she also wrote a few prose tales and sketches. In 1841 she edited *The Poetry of Flowers and Flowers of Poetry*, and in 1847, *The Floral Offering*, two illustrated gift books.

Frances S. Osgood.

Mrs. Osgood's physical frame was as delicate as her mental organization. She suffered frequently from ill health, and was an invalid during the whole of the winter of 1847–8. During the succeeding winter she rallied, and her husband, whose own health required the reinvigorating influence of travel, with a view to this object, and to a share in the profitable adventure which at that time was tempting so many from their homes, sailed for California in February, 1849. He returned after an absence of a year, with restored health and ample means, to find his wife fast sinking in consumption. The husband carried the wife in his arms to a new residence, where, with the happy hopefulness characteristic of her disorder, she selected articles for its furniture and decoration, from patterns brought to her bedside. The rapidly approaching termination of her disorder was soon gently made known to her, and received, after a few tears at the thought of leaving her husband and two young children, with resignation. The evening but one after she wrote for a young girl at her side, who was making and teaching her to make paper flowers, the following lines:—

You've woven roses round my way,
  And gladdened all my being;
How much I thank you, none can say,
  Save only the All-seeing.

I'm going through the eternal gates,
  Ere June's sweet roses blow;
Death's lovely angel leads me there,
  And it is sweet to go.

The touching prophecy was fulfilled, by her calm death, five days after, on Sunday afternoon, May 12, 1850. Her remains were removed to Boston, and laid beside those of her mother and daughter, at Mount Auburn, on Wednesday of the same week.

---

* Anna Maria Foster was born about 1794 in Gloucester, a sea-port town of Massachusetts. Her father died during her infancy, and her mother marrying some years after Mr. Joseph Locke, became the mother of Mrs. Osgood. Miss Foster married in 1899 Mr. Thomas Wells, an officer of the United States revenue service, and the author of a few prize poems. In 1881 she published *Poems and Juvenile Sketches* in a small volume, and has since occasionally contributed to periodicals, her chief attention having been given to a young ladies' school.

Mrs. Osgood's poems were collected and published in New York, in 1846, and in one of the series of illustrated volumes of the works of American poets, by A. Hart of Philadelphia, in 1849.

In 1851 a volume containing contributions by her many literary friends, entitled the *Memorial*, was published by G. P. Putnam of New York. It contained a memoir from the pen of Mr. Griswold. It was an illustrated gift-book, and the profits of its sale were intended for the erection of a monument to the gifted writer, in whose honor it was issued.

Of a rare gracefulness and delicacy, Mrs. Osgood lived a truly poetic life. Her unaffected and lively manners, with her ready tact in conversation, combined with an unusual facility in writing verses, charmed a large circle of friends, as her winning lines in the periodicals of the day engaged the attention of the public. As an instance of her playfulness of mind, she wrote a collection of ludicrous and humorous verses for a child's book, to set off some rude engravings of *The Cries of New York*. The fanciful and the delicate in sentiment, supplied the usual themes of her verses, touched at times with passionate expression, and a darker shade, as the evils of life closed around her.

TO THE SPIRIT OF POETRY.

Leave me not yet! Leave me not cold and lonely,
Thou dear Ideal of my pining heart!
Thou art the friend—the beautiful—the only,
Whom I would keep, tho' all the world depart!
Thou, that dost veil the frailest flower with glory,
Spirit of light and loveliness and truth!
Thou that didst tell me a sweet, fairy story,
Of the dim future, in my wistful youth!
Thou, who canst weave a halo round the spirit,
Thro' which naught mean or evil dare intrude,
Resume not yet the gift, which I inherit
From Heaven and thee, that dearest, holiest good!
Leave me not now! Leave me not cold and lonely,
Thou starry prophet of my pining heart!
Thou art the friend—the tenderest—the only,
With whom, of all, 'twould be despair to part.
Thou that cam'st to me in my dreaming childhood,
Shaping the changeful clouds to pageants rare,
Peopling the smiling vale, and shaded wildwood,
With airy beings, faint yet strangely fair;
Telling me all the sea-born breeze was saying,
While it went whispering thro' the willing leaves,
Bidding me listen to the light rain playing
Its pleasant tune, about the household eaves;
Tuning the low, sweet ripple of the river,
Till its melodious murmur seemed a song,
A tender and sad chant, repeated ever,
A sweet, impassioned plaint of love and wrong!
Leave me not yet! Leave me not cold and lonely,
Thou star of promise o'er my clouded path!
Leave not the life, that borrows from thee only
All of delight and beauty that it hath!

Thou, that when others knew not how to love me,
Nor cared to fathom half my yearning soul,
Didst wreathe thy flowers of light, around, above me,
To woo and win me from my grief's control.
By all my dreams, the passionate, the holy,
When thou hast sung love's lullaby to me,
By all the childlike worship, fond and lowly,
Which I have lavished upon thine and thee.
By all the lays my simple lute was learning,
To echo from thy voice, stay with me still!
Once flown—alas! for thee there's no returning!
The charm will die o'er valley, wood, and hill.
Tell me not Time, whose wing my brow has shaded,
Has withered spring's sweet bloom within my heart,
Ah, no! the rose of love is yet unfaded,
Tho' hope and joy, its sister flowers, depart.

Well do I know that I have wronged thine altar,
With the light offerings of an idler's mind,
And thus, with shame, my pleading prayer I falter,
Leave me not, spirit! deaf, and dumb, and blind!
Deaf to the mystic harmony of nature,
Blind to the beauty of her stars and flowers.
Leave me not, heavenly yet human teacher,
Lonely and lost in this cold world of ours!
Heaven knows I need thy music and thy beauty
Still to beguile me on my weary way,
To lighten to my soul the cares of duty,
And bless with radiant dreams the darkened day:
To charm my wild heart in the worldly revel,
Lest I, too, join the aimless, false, and vain;
Let me not lower to the soulless level
Of those whom now I pity and disdain!
Leave me not yet!—leave me not cold and pining,
Thou bird of paradise, whose plumes of light,
Where'er they rested, left a glory shining;
Fly not to heaven, or let me share thy flight!

LABOR.

Labor is rest—from the sorrows that greet us;
Rest from all petty vexations that meet us,
Rest from sin-promptings that ever entreat us,
Rest from world-syrens that lure us to ill.
Work—and pure slumbers shall wait on the pillow,
Work—thou shalt ride over Care's coming billow;
Lie not down wearied 'neath Woe's weeping willow!
Work with a stout heart and resolute will!

Labor is health! Lo the husbandman reaping,
How through his veins goes the life current leaping;
How his strong arm, in its stalwart pride sweeping,
Free as a sunbeam the swift sickle guides.
Labor is wealth—in the sea the pearl groweth,
Rich the queen's robe from the frail cocoon floweth,
From the fine acorn the strong forest bloweth,
Temple and statue the marble block hides.

Droop not, tho' shame, sin, and anguish are round thee!
Bravely fling off the cold chain that hath bound thee;
Look to yon pure heaven smiling beyond thee,
Rest not content in thy darkness—a clod!
Work—for some good be it ever so slowly;
Cherish some flower be it ever so lowly;
Labor!—all labor is noble and holy;
Let thy great deeds be thy prayer to thy God.

Pause not to dream of the future before us;
Pause not to weep the wild cares that come o'er us:
Hark how Creation's deep, musical chorus,
Unintermitting, goes up into Heaven!
Never the ocean-wave falters in flowing;
Never the little seed stops in its growing;
More and more richly the Rose-heart keeps glowing,
Till from its nourishing stem it is riven.

"Labor is worship!"—the robin is singing,
"Labor is worship!"—the wild bee is ringing,
Listen! that eloquent whisper upspringing,
Speaks to thy soul from out nature's great heart.
From the dark cloud flows the life-giving shower;
From the rough sod blows the soft breathing flower,
From the small insect—the rich coral bower,
Only man in the plan shrinks from his part.

Labor is life!—'tis the still water faileth;
Idleness ever despaireth, bewaileth:
Keep the watch wound for the dark rust assaileth!
Flowers droop and die in the stillness of noon.
Labor is glory!—the flying cloud lightens;
Only the waving wing changes and brightens;
Idle hearts only the dark future frightens;
Play the sweet keys wouldst thou keep them in tune!

SONG—SHE LOVES HIM YET.

She loves him yet!
I know by the blush that rises
Beneath the curls,
That shadow her soul-lit cheek;
She loves him yet!
Through all love's sweet disguises
In timid girls,
A blush will be sure to speak.

But deeper signs
Than the radiant blush of beauty,
The maiden finds,
Whenever his name is heard;
Her young heart thrills,
Forgetting herself—her duty—
Her dark eye fills,
And her pulse with hope is stirred.

She loves him yet!—
The flower the false one gave her
When last he came,
Is still with her wild tears wet.
She'll ne'er forget,
Howe'er his faith may waver,
Through grief and shame,
Believe it—she loves him yet.

His favorite songs
She will sing—she heeds no other;
With all her wrongs,
Her life on his love is set.
Oh! doubt no more!
She never can wed another;
Till life be o'er,
She loves—she will love him yet.

TO A DEAR LITTLE TRUANT.

When are you coming? The flowers have come!
Bees in the balmy air happily hum:
Tenderly, timidly, down in the dell
Sighs the sweet violet, droops the Harebell:
Soft in the wavy grass glistens the dew—
Spring keeps her promises—why do not you?

Up in the air, love, the clouds are at play;
You are more graceful and lovely than they.!
Birds in the woods carol all the day long;
When are you coming to join in the song?
Fairer than flowers and purer than dew!
Other sweet things are here—why are not you?

When are you coming? We've welcomed the Rose!
Every light zephyr, as gaily it goes,
Whispers of other flowers met on its way;
Why has it nothing of you, love, to say?
Why does it tell us of music and dew?
Rose of the South! we are waiting for you!

Do, darling, come to us!—'mid the dark trees,
Like a lute murmurs the musical breeze;
Sometimes the Brook, as it trips by the flowers,
Hushes its warble to listen for yours!
Pure as the Violet, lovely and true!
Spring should have waited till she could bring *you!*

SEBA SMITH—ELIZABETH OAKES SMITH.

THE maiden name of this lady was Prince. She is descended on both her father's and mother's side from distinguished Puritan ancestry, and was born in the vicinity of Portland, Maine.

Miss Prince, at an early age, was married to Mr. Seba Smith, then editing a newspaper in Portland, who has since, under the "nom de plume" of Jack Downing, obtained a national reputation. In addition to the original series of the famous letters bearing the signature we have named, collected in a volume in 1833, and which are among the most successful adaptations of the Yankee dialect to the purposes of humorous writing, Mr. Smith is the author of *Powhatan, a Metrical Romance*, in seven cantos, published in New York in 1841, and of several shorter poems which have appeared in the periodicals of the day. He is also a successful writer of tales and essays for the magazines, a portion of which were collected in 1855, with the title *Down East*. In 1850 he published an elaborate scientific work entitled *New Elements of Geometry*.

Mrs. Smith's earliest poems were contributed to various periodicals anonymously, but in consequence of business disasters in which her husband became involved, she commenced the open profession of authorship as a means of support for her family. She has since been a constant contributor in prose and verse to the magazines.

E. Oakes Smith

An early collection of Mrs. Smith's poems published in New York, was followed in 1843 by *The Sinless Child and Other Poems*. The leading production of this volume originally appeared in the Southern Literary Messenger. It is a romance, with several episodes, written in the ballad style. As an indication of its measure and frequent felicities of expression we quote a few stanzas.

MIDSUMMER.

'Tis the summer prime, when the noiseless air
In perfumed chalice lies,
And the bee goes by with a lazy hum,
Beneath the sleeping skies:
When the brook is low, and the ripples bright,
As down the stream they go,
The pebbles are dry on the upper side,
And dark and wet below.

The tree that stood where the soil's athirst,
  And the mulleins first appear,
Hath a dry and rusty-colored bark,
  And its leaves are curled and sere;
But the dogwood and the hazel-bush
  Have clustered round the brook—
Their roots have stricken deep beneath,
  And they have a verdant look.

To the juicy leaf the grasshopper clings,
  And he gnaws it like a file;
The naked stalks are withering by,
  Where he has been erewhile.
The cricket hops on the glistering rock,
  Or pipes in the faded grass;
The beetle's wing is folded mute,
  Where the steps of the idler pass.

Mrs. Smith is also the author of *The Roman Tribute*, a tragedy in five acts, founded on the exemption of the city of Constantinople from destruction, by the tribute paid by Theodosius to the conquering Attila, and *Jacob Leisler*, a tragedy founded upon a well known dramatic incident in the colonial history of New York.

She has also written *The Western Captive*, a novel, which appeared in 1842, and a fanciful prose tale, *The Salamander; a Legend for Christmas*. In 1851 she published *Woman and her Needs*, a volume on the Woman's Rights question, of which Mrs. Smith has been a prominent advocate by her pen, and occasionally as a public lecturer. Her last publication, *Bertha and Lily, or the Parsonage of Beech Glen, a Romance*, is a story of American country life. It contains some good sketches of character, and is in part devoted to the development of the author's social views.

STRENGTH FROM THE HILLS.

Come up unto the hills—thy strength is there.
  Oh, thou hast tarried long,
Too long amid the bowers and blossoms fair,
  With notes of summer song.
Why dost thou tarry there? What though the bird
  Pipes matin in the vale—
The plough-boy whistles to the loitering herd,
  As the red daylight fails.

Yet come unto the hills, the old strong hills,
  And leave the stagnant plain;
Come to the gushing of the newborn rills,
  As sing they to the main;
And thou with denizens of power shalt dwell
  Beyond demeaning care;
Composed upon his rock, 'mid storm and fell,
  The eagle shall be there.

Come up unto the hills—the shattered tree
  Still clings unto the rock,
And flingeth out his branches wild and free,
  To dare again the shock.
Come where no fear is known: the seabird's nest
  On the old hemlock swings,
And thou shalt taste the gladness of unrest,
  And mount upon thy wings.

Come up unto the hills. The men of old—
  They of undaunted wills—
Grew jubilant of heart, and strong, and bold,
  On the enduring hills—
Where came the soundings of the sea afar,
  Borne upward to the ear,
And nearer grew the morn and midnight star,
  And God himself more near.

THE POET.

Non vox sed votum.

  Sing, sing—Poet, sing!
With the thorn beneath thy breast,
Robbing thee of all thy rest;
Hidden thorn for ever thine,
Therefore dost thou sit and twine
  Lays of sorrowing—
Lays that wake a mighty gladness,
Spite of all their sorrowing sadness.

  Sing, sing—Poet, sing!
It doth ease thee of thy sorrow—
"Darkling" singing till the morrow;
Never weary of thy trust,
Hoping, loving, as thou must,
  Let thy music ring;
Noble cheer it doth impart,
Strength of will and strength of heart.

  Sing, sing—Poet, sing!
Thou art made a human voice;
Wherefore shouldst thou not rejoice
That the tears of thy mute brother
Bearing pangs he may not smother,
  Through thee are flowing—
For his dim, unuttered grief,
Through thy song hath found relief!

  Sing, sing—Poet, sing!
Join the music of the stars,
Wheeling on their sounding cars;
Each responsive in its place
To the choral hymn of space—
  Lift, oh lift thy wing—
And the thorn beneath thy breast,
Though it pain, shall give thee rest.

CAROLINE M. KIRKLAND.

CAROLINE M. STANSBURY was born in the city of New York. Her grandfather was the author of several popular humorous verses on the events of the Revolution, which were published in Rivington's Gazette and other newspapers of the time. Her father was a bookseller and publisher of New York. After his death, the family removed to the western part of the state, where Miss Stansbury married Mr. William Kirkland.* After a residence of several years at Geneva, Mr. and Mrs. Kirkland removed to Michigan, where they resided for two years at Detroit, and for six months in the interior, sixty miles west of the city. In 1843 they removed to the city of New York.

Mrs. Kirkland's letters from the West were so highly relished by the friends to whom they were addressed, that the writer was induced to prepare a volume from their contents. *A New Home—Who'll Follow? by Mrs. Mary Clavers*, appeared

* Mr. Kirkland was a cultivated scholar, and at one time a member of the Faculty of Hamilton College. He was the author of a series of *Letters from Abroad*, written after a residence in Europe, and of numerous contributions to the periodical press, among which may be mentioned, an article on the London Foreign Quarterly Review, in the Columbian, "English and American Monthlies" in Godey's Magazine, "Our English Visitors" in the Columbian, "The Tyranny of Public Opinion in the United States" in the Columbian, "The West, the Paradise of the Poor" in the Democratic Review, and "The United States Census for 1880" in Hunt's Merchants' Magazine.

In 1846 Mr. Kirkland, not long before his death, commenced with the Rev. H. W. Bellows, the Christian Inquirer, a weekly journal of the Unitarian denomination.

in 1839. Its delightful humor, keen observation, and fresh topic, made an immediate impression. *Forest Life*, and *Western Clearings*, gleanings from the same field, appeared in 1842 and 1846.

In 1846 Mrs. Kirkland published *An Essay on the Life and Writings of Spenser*, accompanied by a reprint of the first book of the Fairy Queen. In July, 1847, she commenced the editorship of the Union Magazine,—a charge she continued for eighteen months, until the removal of the periodical to Philadelphia, where it was published with the title of Sartain's Magazine, when Prof. John S. Hart, an accomplished literary gentleman of that city, was associated with Mrs. Kirkland in the editorship.

C. M. Kirkland

In 1848 Mrs. Kirkland visited Europe, and on her return published two pleasant volumes of her letters contributed to the magazine during her journey, with the title *Holidays Abroad, or Europe from the West*.

In 1852 Mrs. Kirkland published *The Evening Book, or Fireside Talk on Morals and Manners, with Sketches of Western Life*, and in 1853, a companion volume, *A Book for the Home Circle, or Familiar Thoughts on Various Topics, Literary, Moral, and Social*, containing a number of pleasantly written and sensible essays on topics of interest in every-day society, with a few brief stories. In 1852 she wrote the letterpress for *The Book of Home Beauty*, a holiday volume, containing the portraits of twelve American ladies. Mrs. Kirkland's text has no reference to these illustrations, but consists of a slight story of American society, interspersed with poetical quotations.

Mrs. Kirkland's writings are all marked by clear common sense, purity of style, and animated thought. Her keen perception of character is brought to bear on the grave as well as humorous side of human nature, on its good points as well as its foibles. Ever in favor of a graceful cultivation of the mind, her satire is directed against the false refinements of artificial life as well as the rude angularities of the back-woods. She writes always with heartiness, and it is not her fault if the laugh which her humorous sketches of character excites is not a good-natured one, in which the originals she has portrayed would do well to join with the rest of the world.

MEETING OF THE "FEMALE BENEFICENT SOCIETY."

At length came the much desired Tuesday, whose destined event was the first meeting of the society. I had made preparations for such plain and simple cheer as is usual at such feminine gatherings, and began to think of arranging my dress with the decorum required by the occasion, when, about one hour before the appointed time, came Mrs. Nippers and Miss Clinch, and ere they were unshawled and unhooded, Mrs. Flyter and her three children—the eldest four years, and the youngest six months. Then Mrs. Muggles and her crimson baby, four weeks old. Close on her heels, Mrs. Briggs and her little boy of about three years' standing, in a long tailed coat, with vest and decencies of scarlet circassian. And there I stood in my gingham wrapper and kitchen apron; much to my discomfiture and the undisguised surprise of the Female Beneficent Society.

"I always calculate to be ready to begin at the time appointed," remarked the gristle-lipped widow.

"So do I," responded Mrs. Flyter and Mrs. Muggles, both of whom sat the whole afternoon with baby on knee, and did not sew a stitch.

"What! isn't there any work ready?" continued Mrs. Nippers, with an astonished aspect; "well, I *did* suppose that such smart officers as *we* have would have prepared all beforehand. We always used to at the East."

Mrs. Skinner, who is really quite a pattern-woman in all that makes woman indispensable, viz., cookery and sewing, took up the matter quite warmly, just as I slipped away in disgrace to make the requisite reform in my costume.

When I returned, the work was distributed, and the company broken up into little knots or coteries; every head bowed, and every tongue in full play. I took my seat at as great a distance from the sharp widow as might be,—though it is vain to think of eluding a person of her ubiquity,—and reconnoitred the company who were "done off" (indigenous) "in first-rate style," for this important occasion. There were nineteen women with thirteen babies—or at least "young 'uns," (indigenous,) who were not above gingerbread. Of these thirteen, nine held large chunks of gingerbread, or dough-nuts, in trust, for the benefit of the gowns of the society; the remaining four were supplied with bunches of maple-sugar, tied in bits of rag, and pinned to their shoulders, or held dripping in the fingers of their mammas.

Mrs. Flyter was "slicked up" for the occasion in the snuff-colored silk she was married in, curiously enlarged in the back, and not as voluminous in the floating part as is the wasteful custom of the present day. Her three immense children, white-haired and blubber-lipped like their amiable parent, were in pink ginghams and blue-glass beads. Mrs. Nippers wore her unfailing brown merino and black apron; Miss Clinch her inevitable scarlet calico; Mrs. Skinner her red merino, with baby of the same; Mrs Daker shone out in her very choicest city finery, (where else could she show it, poor thing!) and a dozen other Mistresses shone in their "'t other gowns," and their tamboured collars. Mrs. Doubleday's pretty black-eyed Dolly was neatly stowed in a small willow basket, where it lay looking about with eyes full of sweet wonder, behaving itself with marvellous quietness and discretion, as did most of the other little torments, to do them justice.

Much consultation, deep and solemn, was held as to the most profitable kinds of work to be undertaken by the Society. Many were in favor of making up linen, cotton linen of course, but Mrs. Nippers assured the company that shirts never used to sell well at the East, and therefore she was perfectly certain that they would not do here. Pincushions and such like feminilities were then proposed; but at these Mrs. Nippers held up both hands, and showed a double share of blue-white around her eyes. Nobody about her needed pincushions, and besides, where should we get materials! Aprons, capes, caps, collars, were all proposed with the same ill success. At length Mrs. Doubleday, with an air of great deference, inquired what Mrs. Nippers would recommend.

The good lady hesitated a little at this. It was more her forte to object to other people's plans, than to suggest better; but, after a moment's consideration, she said she should think fancy-boxes, watch-cases, and alum-baskets, would be very pretty.

A dead silence fell on the assembly, but of course it did not last long. Mrs. Skinner went on quietly cutting out shirts, and in a very short time furnished each member with a good supply of work, stating that any lady might take work home to finish if she liked.

Mrs. Nippers took her work, and edged herself into a coterie of which Mrs. Flyter had seemed till then the magnet. Very soon I heard, "I declare it's a shame!" "I don't know what 'll be done about it!" "She told me so with her own mouth!" "O, but I was there myself!" etc., etc., in many different voices; the interstices well filled with undistinguishable whispers "not loud but deep."

It was not long before the active widow transferred her seat to another corner; Miss Clinch plying her tongue, not her needle, in a third. The whispers and the exclamations seemed to be gaining ground. The few silent members were inquiring for more work.

"Mrs. Nippers has the sleeve! Mrs. Nippers, have you finished that sleeve?"

Mrs. Nippers colored, said "No," and sewed four stitches. At length the "storm grew loud apace." "It will break up the society——"

"What *is* that?" asked Mrs. Doubleday, in her sharp treble. "What is it, Mrs. Nippers? *You* know all about it."

Mrs. Nippers replied that she only knew what she had heard, etc., etc., but, after a little urging, consented to inform the company in general, that there was great dissatisfaction in the neighborhood; that those who lived in *log-houses* at a little distance from the village, had not been invited to join the society; and also that many people thought twenty-five cents quite too high for a yearly subscription.

Many looked aghast at this. Public opinion is nowhere so strongly felt as in this country, among new settlers. And as many of the present company still lived in log-houses, a tender string was touched.

At length, an old lady, who had sat quietly in a corner all the afternoon, looked up from behind the great woollen sock she was knitting—

"Well, now! that's queer!" said she, addressing Mrs. Nippers with an air of simplicity simplified. "Miss Turner told me you went round her neighborhood last Friday, and told that Miss Clavers and Miss Skinner despised every body that lived in log-houses; and you know you told Miss Briggs that you thought twenty-five cents was too much; didn't she, Miss Briggs?" Mrs. Briggs nodded.

The widow blushed to the very centre of her pale eyes, but "e'en though vanquished," she lost not her assurance. "Why, I'm sure I only said that we only paid twelve-and-a-half cents at the East; and as to log-houses, I don't know, I can't just recollect, but I didn't say more than others did."

But human nature could not bear up against the mortification; and it had, after all, the scarce credible effect of making Mrs. Nippers sew in silence for some time, and carry her colors at half-mast the remainder of the afternoon.

At tea each lady took one or more of her babies in her lap and much grabbing ensued. Those who wore calicoes seemed in good spirits and appetite, for green tea at least, but those who had unwarily sported silks and other unwashables, looked acid and uncomfortable. Cake flew about at a great rate, and the milk and water, which ought to have quietly gone down sundry juvenile throats, was spirted without mercy into various wry faces. But we got through. The astringent refreshment produced its usual crisping effect upon the vivacity of the company. Talk ran high upon almost all Montacutian themes.

"Do you have any butter now?" "When are you going to raise your barn?" "Is your man a going to kill this week?" "I ha'n't seen a bit of meat these six weeks." "Was you to meetin' last Sabbath?" "Has Miss White got any wool to sell?" "Do tell if you've been to Detroit?" "Are you out of candles?" "Well, I *should* think Sarah Teals wanted a new gown!" "I hope we shall have milk in a week or two," and so on; for, be it known, that, in a state of society like ours, the bare necessaries of life are subjects of sufficient interest for a good deal of conversation. More than one truly respectable woman of our neighborhood has told me, that it is not very many years since a moderate allowance of Indian meal and potatoes was literally all that fell to their share of this rich world for weeks together.

"Is your daughter Isabella well?" asked Mrs. Nippers of me solemnly, pointing to little Bell who sat munching her bread and butter, half asleep, at the fragmentious table.

"Yes, I believe so, look at her cheeks."

"Ah, yes! it was her cheeks I was looking at. They are so *very* rosy. I have a little niece who is the very image of her. I never see Isabella without thinking of Jerushy; and Jerushy is most dreadfully scrofulous."

Satisfied at having made me uncomfortable, Mrs. Nippers turned to Mrs. Doubleday, who was trotting her pretty babe with her usual proud fondness.

"Don't you think your baby breathes rather strangely?" said the tormenter.

"Breathes! how!" said the poor thing, off her guard in an instant.

"Why, rather croupish, I think, if *I* am any judge. I have never had any children of my own to be sure, but I was with Mrs. Green's baby when it died, and——"

"Come, we'll be off!" said Mr. Doubleday, who had come for his spouse. "Don't mind the envious vixen"—aside to his Polly.

Just then, somebody on the opposite side of the room happened to say, speaking of some cloth affair, "Mrs. Nippers says it ought to be sponged."

"Well, sponge it then by all means," said Mr. Doubleday, "nobody else knows half as much about sponging:" and, with wife and baby in tow, off walked the laughing Philo, leaving the widow absolutely transfixed.

"What *could* Mr. Doubleday mean by that?" was at length her indignant exclamation.

Nobody spoke.

"I am sure," continued the crest-fallen Mrs. Campaspe, with an attempt at a scornful giggle, "I am sure if any body understood him, I would be glad to know what he *did* mean."

"Well now, I can tell you," said the same simple old lady in the corner, who had let out the secret of Mrs. Nippers's morning walks. "Some folks call that *sponging* when you go about getting your dinner here and your tea there, and sich like; as you know you and Meesy there does. That was what he meant, I guess." And the old lady quietly put up her knitting and prepared to go home.

There have been times when I have thought that almost any degree of courtly duplicity would be preferable to the *brusquerie* of some of my neighbors: but on this occasion I gave all due credit to a simple and downright way of stating the plain truth. The scrofulous hint probably brightened my mental and moral vision somewhat.

Mrs. Nippers's claret cloak and green bonnet, and Miss Clinch's ditto ditto, were in earnest requisition, and I do not think that either of them spent a day out that week.

HOSPITALITY.

Like many other virtues, hospitality is practised in its perfection by the poor. If the rich *did their share*, how would the woes of this world be lightened! how would the diffusive blessing irradiate a wider and a wider circle, until the vast confines of society would bask in the reviving ray! If every forlorn widow whose heart bleeds over the recollection of past happiness made bitter by contrast with present poverty and sorrow, found a comfortable home in the ample establishment of her rich kinsman; if every young man struggling for a foothold on the slippery soil of life, were cheered and aided by the countenance of some neighbor whom fortune had endowed with the power to confer happiness; if the lovely girls, shrinking and delicate, whom we see every day toiling timidly for a mere pittance to sustain frail life and guard the sacred remnant of gentility, were taken by the hand, invited and encouraged, by ladies who pass them by with a cold nod—but where shall we stop in enumerating the cases in which true, genial hospitality, practised by the rich ungrudgingly, without a selfish drawback—in short, practised as the poor practise it—would prove a fountain of blessedness, almost an antidote to half the keener miseries under which society groans!

Yes: the poor—and children—understand hospitality after the pure model of Christ and his apostles. We can cite two instances, both *true*.

In the western woods, a few years since, lived a very indigent Irish family. Their log-cabin scarcely protected them from the weather, and the potato field made but poor provision for the numerous rosy cheeks that shone through the unstopped chinks when a stranger was passing by. Yet when another Irish family poorer still, and way-worn, and travel-soiled, stopped at their door—children, household goods and all—they not only received and entertained them for the night, but kept them many days, sharing with this family, as numerous as their own, the *one* room and loft which made up their poor dwelling, and treating them in all respects as if they had been invited guests. And the mother of the same family, on hearing of the death of a widowed sister who had lived in New York, immediately set on foot an inquiry as to the residence of the children, with a view to coming all the way to the city to take the orphans home to her own house and bring them up with her own children. We never heard whether the search was successful, for the circumstance occurred about the time that we were leaving that part of the country; but that the intention was sincere, and would be carried into effect if possible, there was no shadow of doubt.

As to the children and their sincere, generous little hearts, we were going to say, that one asked his mother, in all seriousness, "Mamma, why don't you ask the *poor people* when you have a party? Doesn't it say so in the Bible?" A keen reproof, and unanswerable.

The nearest we recollect to have observed to this construction of the sacred injunction, among those who may be called the rich—in contradistinction to those whom we usually call the poor, though our kind friends were far from being what the world considers rich—was in the case of a city family, who lived well, and who always on a Christmas day, Thanksgiving, or other festival time, when a dinner more generous than ordinary smoked upon the board, took care to invite their homeless friends who lived somewhat poorly, or uncomfortably—the widow from her low-priced boarding house; the young clerk, perhaps, far from his father's comfortable fireside; the daily teacher, whose only deficiency lay in the purse—these were the guests cheered at this truly hospitable board; and cheered heartily—not with cold, half-reluctant civility, but with the warmest welcome, and the pleasant appendix of the long, merry evening with music and games, and the frolic dance after the piano. We would not be understood to give this as a solitary instance, but we wish we knew of many such.

The forms of society are in a high degree inimical to true hospitality. Pride has crushed genuine social feeling out of too many hearts, and the consequence is a cold sterility of intercourse, a soul-stifling ceremoniousness, a sleepless vigilance for self, totally incompatible with that free, flowing, genial intercourse with humanity, so nourishing to all the better feelings. The sacred love of home—that panacea for many of life's ills—suffers with the rest. Few people have homes nowadays. The fine, cheerful, every-day parlor, with its table covered with the implements of real occupation and real amusement; mamma on the sofa, with her needle; grandmamma in her great chair, knitting; pussy winking at the fire between them, is gone. In its place we have two gorgeous rooms, arranged for company but empty of human life; tables covered with gaudy, ostentatious, and useless articles—a very mockery of anything like rational pastime—the light of heaven as cautiously excluded as the delicious music of free, childish voices; every member of the family wandering in forlorn loneliness, or huddled in some "back room" or "basement," in which are collected the only means of comfort left them under this miserable arrangement. This is the substitute which hundreds of people accept in place of home! Shall we look in such places for hospitality? As soon expect figs from thistles. Invitations there will be occasionally, doubtless, for "society" expects it; but let a country cousin present himself, and see whether he will be put into the state apartments. Let no infirm and indigent relative expect a place under such a roof. Let not even the humble individual who placed the stepping-stone which led to that fortune, ask a share in the abundance which would never have had a beginning but for his timely aid. "We have changed all that!"

But setting aside the hospitality which has any reference to duty or obligation, it is to be feared that the other kind—that which is exercised for the sake of the pleasure it brings—is becoming more and more rare among us. The deadly strife of emulation, the mad pursuit of wealth, the suspicion engendered by rivalry, leave little chance for the spontaneity, the *abandon*, the hearty sympathy which give the charm to social meetings and make the exercise of hospitality one of the highest pleasures. We have attempted to dignify our simple republicanism by far-away melancholy imitations of the Old World; but the incongruity between these forms and the true spirit of our institutions is such, that all we gain is a bald emptiness, gilded over with vulgar show. Real dignity, such as that of John Adams when he lived among his country neighbors as if he had never seen a court, we are learning to despise. We persist in making ourselves the laughing-stock of really refined people, by forsaking our true ground and attempting to stand upon that which shows our deficiencies to the greatest disadvantage. When shall we learn that the "spare feast—a radish and an egg," if partaken by the good and the cultivated, has a charm which no expense can purchase? When shall we look at the spirit rather than the semblance of things—when give up the shadow for the substance?

P. HAMILTON MYERS

Is the author of a series of well written, popular American historical romances, commencing with *The First of the Knickerbockers, a tale of* 1673, published by Putnam in 1848, and speedily followed by *The Young Patroon, or Christmas in* 1690, and *The King of the Hurons*. Mr. Myers is also the author of four prize tales, for two of which *Bell Brandon or the Great Kentrip Estate*, and *The Miser's Heir or the Young Millionaire*, he received two hundred dollars each, from the Philadelphia *Dollar Newspaper*. The others were entitled *The Gold Crushers*, and *Ellen Welles, or the Siege of Fort Stanwix.*

P. Hamilton Myers

These stories are of a pleasing sentiment, and neat in description. The author is a native of New York, born in Herkimer village, Herkimer county, in August, 1812. He is a lawyer by profession, and now a resident of Brooklyn, New York. In addition to his story-telling faculty, Mr. Myers is an agreeable essayist. In 1841 he delivered a poem, *Science*, before the Euglossian Society of Geneva College.

THOMAS MACKELLAR

Was born in the city of New York, August 12, 1812. His father came from Scotland to New York, and married into the Brasher family, once possessed of a considerable portion of the city lands. Young Mackellar was provided with a good education by his father, whose failing fortunes soon required his son's aid. Compelled early in life to seek a living, he learnt the business of a printer, and among other engagements in the calling became proof-reader in the office of Messrs. Harper & Brothers, doubtless qualified for the post by a diligent application to books which had become habitual to him. At this time in his seventeenth year, he constantly penned verses.

In 1833 he left New York for Philadelphia, entered the stereotype foundry of Mr. L. Johnson as proof-reader, became foreman, and finally a partner in this important establishment, to which he is now attached.

Mr. Mackellar's volumes of poetry, *Droppings from the Heart, or Occasional Poems*, published in 1844, and *Lines for the Gentle and Loving* in 1853, are written with earnestness and fluency, inspired by a devotional spirit and a tender feeling to the claims of family and friendship, expressive of the author's hopeful and hearty struggle with the world. They indicate a courage which meets with success in life, and a sympathy which finds a ready response from the good and intelligent.

True to his Scottish lineage, Mr. Mackellar has a turn for humor as well as sentiment in his verses. His volume, *Tam's Fortnight's Ramble and other Poems*, puts his notions and opinions vented in the course of a holiday excursion on the Hudson River in a highly agreeable light, as the record of a manly personal experience.

A POET AND HIS SONG.

He was a man endowed like other men
  With strange varieties of thought and feeling:
His bread was earned by daily toil; yet when
  A pleasing fancy o'er his mind came stealing,
He set a trap and snared it by his art,
And hid it in the bosom of his heart.
  He nurtured it and loved it as his own,
And it became obedient to his beck;
He fixed his name on its submissive neck,
  And graced it with all graces to him known,
And then he bade it lift its wing and fly
  Over the earth, and sing in every ear
  Some soothing sound the sighful soul to cheer,
Some lay of love to lure it to the sky.

SINGING ON THE WAY.

Far distant from my father's house
  I would no longer stay;
But gird my soul and hasten on,
  And sing upon my way!
    And sing! and sing!
  And sing upon the way!

The skies are dark, the thunders roll,
  And lightnings round me play;
Let me but feel my SAVIOUR near,
  I'll sing upon the way!
    And sing! and sing!
  And sing upon my way!

The night is long and drear, I cry;
  O when will come the day?
I see the morning-star arise,
  And sing upon the way!
    And sing! and sing!
  And sing upon my way!

When care and sickness bow my frame,
  And all my powers decay,
I'll ask Him for his promised grace,
  And sing upon the way!
    And sing! and sing!
  And sing upon my way!

He'll not forsake me when I'm old,
  And weak, and blind, and grey;
I'll lean upon his faithfulness,
  And sing upon the way!
    And sing! and sing!
  And sing upon my way!

When grace shall bear me home to GOD—
  Disrobed of mortal clay,

I'll enter in the pearly gates,
And sing upon the way!
And sing! and sing!
An everlasting day!

WILLIAM STARBUCK MAYO.

Dr. Mayo is a descendant from the Rev. John Mayo, a clergyman of an ancient English family, who came to New England in 1630, and was the first pastor of the South Church at Boston. On his mother's side he traces his descent through the Starbuck family to the earliest settlers of Nantucket. He was born at Ogdensburg, on the northern frontier of New York, whither the family had removed in 1812, and was educated at the school of the Rev. Josiah Perry, a teacher of high local reputation. At the age of twelve years he entered the academy of Potsdam, where he received a good classical education; and at seventeen commenced the study of medicine at the College of Physicians and Surgeons in the city of New York. After receiving his diploma, in 1833, he devoted himself for several years to the practice of his profession. He then, urged in part by the pursuit of health and in part by the love of adventure, determined to make a tour of exploration to the interior of Africa. He was prevented, however, from penetrating further than the Barbary States. After an excursion in Spain he returned home.

W S Mayo

In 1849 Dr. Mayo published *Kaloolah, or Journeyings to the Djébel Kumri*, a work which he had written some time before. It purports to be the Autobiography of Jonathan Romer, a youth who, after various romantic and marvellous adventures in his native American woods, goes to Africa, where he rivals Munchausen in his traveller's experiences. He finally penetrates to a purely fictitious Utopia, where he indulges in some quiet satire at the usages of civilization, and in his description of the great city of the region furnishes some valuable hints on municipal sanitary reform. He marries Kaloolah, a beautiful princess—"not too dark for a brunette"—whom he has rescued from a slave barracoon and protected through many subsequent scenes of danger, and settles down to domestic felicity in the city of Killoam.

The story is crowded with exciting and varied incident, and the interest is maintained throughout with dramatic skill.

Kaloolah was favorably received by the public, and was followed in 1850 by *The Berber, or the Mountaineer of the Atlas*, a story the scene of which is laid in Africa at the close of the seventeenth century. It is of more regular construction than Kaloolah, and equally felicitous in dramatic interest. Both abound in descriptions of the natural scenery and savage animals of the tropics and other regions, minutely accurate in scientific detail.

Dr. Mayo's next volume was a collection of short tales, which he had previously published anonymously in magazines, with the title suggested by the prevalent California excitement of the day—*Romance Dust from the Historic Plācer*. He soon after married and spent a year or two in Europe. Since his return he has resided in New York.

A LION IN THE PATH.

It was early on the morning of the sixth, that, accompanied by Kaloolah and the lively Clefenha, I ascended the bank for a final reconnoissance of the country on the other bank of the river. It was not my intention to wander far, but, allured by the beauty of the scene, and the promise of a still better view from a higher crag, we moved along the edge of the bank until we had got nearly two miles from our camp. At this point the line of the bank curved towards the river so as to make a beetling promontory of a hundred feet perpendicular descent. The gigantic trees grew quite on the brink, many of them throwing their long arms far over the shore below. The trees generally grew wide apart, and there was little or no underwood, but many of the trunks were wreathed with the verdure of parasites and creepers, so as to shut up, mostly, the forest vistas with immense columns of green leaves and flowers. The stems of some of these creepers were truly wonderful: one, from which depended large bunches of scarlet berries, had, not unfrequently, stems as large as a man's body. In some cases, one huge plant of this kind, ascending with an incalculable prodigality of lignin, by innumerable convolutions, would stretch itself out, and, embracing several trees in its folds, mat them together in one dense mass of vegetation.

Suddenly we noticed that the usual sounds of the forest had almost ceased around us. Deep in the woods we could still hear the chattering of monkeys and the screeching of parrots. Never before had our presence created any alarm among the denizens of the tree-tops; or, if it had, it had merely excited to fresh clamour, without putting them to flight. We looked around for the cause of this sudden retreat.

"Perhaps," I replied to Kaloolah's inquiry, "there is a storm gathering, and they are gone to seek a shelter deeper in the wood."

We advanced close to the edge of the bank, and looked out into the broad daylight that poured down from above on flood and field. There was the same bright smile on the distant fields and hills; the same clear sheen in the deep water; the same lustrous stillness in the perfumed air; not a single prognostic of any commotion among the elements.

I placed my gun against a tree, and took a seat upon an exposed portion of one of its roots. Countless herds of animals, composed of quaggas, zebras, gnus, antelopes, hart-beests, roeboks, springboks, buffalos, wild-boars, and a dozen other kinds, for which my recollection of African travels furnished no names, were roaming over the fields on the other side of the river, or quietly reposing in the shade of the scattered mimosas, or beneath the groups of lofty palms. A herd of thirty or forty tall ungainly figures came in sight, and took their way, with awkward but rapid pace, across the plain. I knew them at once to be giraffes, although they were the first that we had seen. I was straining my eyes to discover the animal that pursued them, when Kaloolah called to me to come to her. She was about fifty yards farther down the stream than where I was sitting. With an unaccountable degree of carelessness, I arose and went towards her, leaving my gun leaning against the tree. As I advanced, she ran out to the extreme point of the little promontory I have mentioned, where her maid was standing, and pointed to something over the edge of the cliff.

"Oh, Jon'than!" she exclaimed, "what a curious and beautiful flower! Come, and try if you can get it for me!"

Advancing to the crest of the cliff, we stood looking down its precipitous sides to a point some twenty feet below, where grew a bunch of wild honeysuckles. Suddenly a startling noise, like the roar of thunder, or like the boom of a thirty-two pounder, rolled through the wood, fairly shaking the sturdy trees, and literally making the ground quiver beneath our feet. Again it came, that appalling and indescribably awful sound! and so close as to completely stun us. Roar upon roar, in quick succession, now announced the coming of the king of beasts. "The lion! the lion!—Oh, God of mercy, where is my gun?" I started forward, but it was too late. Alighting, with a magnificent bound, into the open space in front of us, the monster stopped, as if somewhat taken aback by the novel appearance of his quarry, and crouching his huge carcass close to the ground, uttered a few deep snuffling sounds, not unlike the preliminary crankings and growlings of a heavy steam-engine, when it first feels the pressure of the steam.

He was, indeed, a monster!—fully twice as large as the largest specimen of his kind that was ever condemned, by gaping curiosity, to the confinement of the cage. His body was hardly less in size than that of a dray-horse; his paw as large as the foot of an elephant; while his head!—what can be said of such a head? Concentrate the fury, the power, the capacity and the disposition for evil of a dozen thunder-storms into a round globe, about two feet in diameter, and one would then be able to get an idea of the terrible expression of that head and face, enveloped and set off as it was by the dark frame-work of bristling mane.

The lower jaw rested upon the ground; the mouth was slightly open, showing the rows of white teeth and the blood-red gums, from which the lips were retracted in a majestic and right kingly grin. The brows and the skin around the eyes were corrugated into a splendid glory of radiant wrinkles, in the centre of which glowed two small globes, like opals, but with a dusky lustrousness that no opal ever yet attained.

For a few moments he remained motionless, and then, as if satisfied with the result of his close scrutiny, he began to slide along the ground towards us; slowly one monstrous paw was protruded after the other; slowly the huge tufted tail waved to and fro, sometimes striking his hollow flanks, and occasionally coming down upon the ground with a sound like the falling of heavy clods upon a coffin. There could be no doubt of his intention to charge us, when near enough for a spring.

And was there no hope? Not the slightest, at least for myself. It was barely possible that one victim would satisfy him, or that, in the contest that was about to take place, I might, if he did not kill me at the first blow, so wound him as to indispose him for any further exercise of his power, and that thus Kaloolah would escape. As for me, I felt that my time had come. With no weapon but my long knife, what chance was there against such a monster? I cast one look at the gun that was leaning so carelessly against the tree beyond him, and thought how easy it would be to send a bullet through one of those glowing eyes into the depths of that savage brain. Never was there a fairer mark! But, alas! it was impossible to reach the gun! Truly, "there was a lion in the path."

I turned to Kaloolah, who was a little behind me. Her face expressed a variety of emotions; she could not speak or move, but she stretched out her hand, as if to pull me back. Behind her crouched the black, whose features were contracted into the awful grin of intense terror; she was too much frightened to scream, but in her face a thousand yells of agony and fear were incarnated.

I remember not precisely what I said, but, in the fewest words, I intimated to Kaloolah that the lion would, probably, be satisfied with attacking me; that she must run by us as soon as he sprang upon me, and, returning to the camp, waste no time, but set out at once under the charge of Hugh and Jack. She made no reply, and I waited for none, but, facing the monster, advanced slowly towards him—the knife was firmly grasped in my right hand, my left side a little turned towards him, and my left arm raised, to guard as much as possible against the first crushing blow of his paw. Further than this I had formed no plan of battle. In such a contest the mind has but little to do—all depends upon the instinct of the muscles; and well for a man if good training has developed that instinct to the highest. I felt that I could trust mine, and that my brain need not bother itself as to the manner my muscles were going to act.

Within thirty feet of my huge foe I stopped—cool, calm as a statue; not an emotion agitated me. No hope, no fear: death was too certain to permit either passion. There is something in the conviction of the immediate inevitableness of death that represses fear; we are then compelled to take a better look at the king of terrors, and we find that he is not so formidable as we imagined. Look at him with averted glances and half-closed eyes, and he has a most imposing, overawing presence; but face him, eye to eye; grasp his proffered hand manfully, and he sinks from a right royal personage into a contemptible old gate-keeper on the turnpike of life.

I had time to think of many things, although it must not be supposed from the leisurely way in which I here tell the story that the whole affair occupied much time. Like lightning, flashing from link to link along a chain conductor, did memory illuminate, almost simultaneously, the chain of incidents that measured my path in life, and that connected the present with the past. I could see the whole of my back track "blazed" as clearly as ever was a forest path by a woodman's axe; and ahead! ah, there was not much to see ahead! 'Twas but a short view; death hedged in the scene. In a few minutes my eyes would be opened to the pleasant sights beyond; but, for the present, death commanded all attention. And such a death! But why such a death! What better death, except on the battle-field, in defence of one's country! To be killed by a lion! Surely there is a spice of dignity about it, maugre the being eaten afterwards. Suddenly the monster stopped, and erected his tail, stiff and motionless, in the air. Strange as it may seem, the conceit occurred to me that the motion of his tail had acted as a safety-valve to the pent up muscular energy within: "He has shut the steam off from the 'scape-pipe, and now he turns it on to his locomotive machinery. God have mercy upon me! —He comes!"

But he did not come! At the instant, the light figure of Kaloolah rushed past me: "Fly, fly, Jon-'than!" she wildly exclaimed, as she dashed forward directly towards the lion. Quick as thought, I divined her purpose, and sprang after her, grasping her dress and pulling her forcibly back almost from within those formidable jaws. The astonished animal gave several jumps sideways and backwards, and stopped, crouching to the ground and growling and lashing his sides with renewed fury. He was clearly taken aback by our unexpected charge upon him, but it was evident that he was not to be frightened into abandoning his prey. His mouth was made up for us, and there could be no doubt, if his motions were a little slow, that he considered us as good as gorged.

"Fly, fly, Jon'than!" exclaimed Kaloolah, as she struggled to break from my grasp. "Leave me! Leave me to die alone, but oh! save yourself, quick! along the bank. You can escape—fly!"

"Never, Kaloolah," I replied, fairly forcing her with quite an exertion of strength behind me. "Back, back! Free my arm! Quick, quick! He comes!" 'Twas no time for gentleness. Roughly shaking her relaxing grasp from my arm she sunk powerless, yet not insensible, to the ground, while I had just time to face the monster and plant one foot forward to receive him.

He was in the very act of springing! His huge carcass was even rising under the impulsion of his contracting muscles, when his action was arrested in a way so unexpected, so wonderful, and so startling, that my senses were for the moment thrown into perfect confusion. Could I trust my sight, or was the whole affair the illusion of a horrid dream? It seemed as if one of the gigantic creepers I have mentioned had suddenly quitted the canopy above, and, endowed with life and a huge pair of widely distended jaws, had darted with the rapidity of lightning upon the crouching beast. There was a tremendous shaking of the tree tops, and a confused wrestling, and jumping, and whirling over and about, amid a cloud of upturned roots, and earth, and leaves, accompanied with the most terrific roars and groans. As I looked again, vision grew more distinct. An immense body, gleaming with purple, green, and gold, appeared convoluted around the majestic branches overhead, and stretching down, was turned two or three times around the struggling lion, whose head and neck were almost concealed from sight within the cavity of a pair of jaws still more capacious than his own.

Thus, then, was revealed the cause of the sudden silence throughout the woods. It was the presence of the boa that had frightened the monkey and feathered tribes into silence. How opportunely was his presence manifested to us! A moment more and it would have been too late.

Gallantly did the lion struggle in the folds of his terrible enemy, whose grasp each instant grew more firm and secure, and most astounding were those frightful yells of rage and fear. The huge body of the snake, fully two feet in diameter where it depended from the trees, presented the most curious appearances, and in such quick succession that the eye could scarcely follow them. At one moment smooth and flexile, at the next rough and stiffened, or contracted into great knots—at one moment overspread with a thousand tints of reflected color, the next distended so as to transmit through the skin the golden gleams of the animal lightning that coursed up and down within.

Over and over rolled the struggling beast, but in vain all his strength, in vain all his efforts to free himself. Gradually his muscles relaxed in their exertions, his roar subsided to a deep moan, his tongue protruded from his mouth, and his fetid breath, mingled with a strong, sickly odor from the serpent, diffused itself through the air, producing a sense of oppression, and a feeling of weakness like that from breathing some deleterious gas.

I looked around. Kaloolah was on her knees, and the negress insensible upon the ground a few paces behind her. A sensation of giddiness warned me that it was time to retreat. Without a word I raised Kaloolah in my arms, ran towards the now almost motionless animals, and, turning along the bank, reached the tree against which my gun was leaning.

Darting back I seized the prostrate negress and bore her off in the same way. By this time both females had recovered their voices, Clefenha exercising hers in a succession of shrieks, that compelled me to shake her somewhat rudely, while Kaloolah eagerly besought me to hurry back to the camp. There was now, however, no occasion for hurry. The recovery of my gun altered the state of the case, and my curiosity was excited to witness the process of deglutition on a large scale which the boa was probably about to exhibit. It was impossible, however, to resist Kaloolah's entreaties, and, after stepping up closer to the animals for one good look, I reluctantly consented to turn back.

The lion was quite dead, and with a slow motion the snake was uncoiling himself from his prey and from the tree above. As well as I could judge, without seeing him straightened out, he was between ninety and one hundred feet in length—not quite so long as the serpent with which the army of Regulus had its famous battle, or as many of the same animals that I have since seen, but, as the reader will allow, a very respectable sized snake. I have often regretted that we did not stop until at least he had commenced his meal. Had I been alone I should have done so. As it was, curiosity had to yield to my own sense of prudence, and to Kaloolah's fears.

We returned to our camp, where we found our raft all ready. The river was fully half a mile wide, and it was necessary to make two trips; the first with the women and baggage, and the last with the horses. It is unnecessary to dwell in detail upon all the difficulties we encountered from the rapid currents and whirling eddies of the stream; suffice it that we got across in time for supper and a good night's sleep, and early in the morning resumed our march through the most enchanting country in the world.

WILLIAM HENRY CHANNING,

A GRADUATE of Harvard in 1829, and of the Cambridge divinity school in 1833, is a nephew of the late Dr. William Ellery Channing, and the son of the late Francis Dana Channing. He is the author of several valuable biographical publications, including the *Memoirs of the Rev. James H. Per-*

kins of Cincinnati, an important contribution to the *Margaret Fuller Memoirs*, and in 1848 a comprehensive *Memoir of William Ellery Channing, with Extracts from his Correspondence and Manuscripts*. In the arrangement of these works Mr. Channing, in addition to his own sympathetic comments, has preserved to the extent of his original materials an autobiographic narrative of the lives of the subjects, and has drawn together ample illustrations from various other sources. In 1840 he translated for Mr. Ripley's series of Specimens of Foreign Literature, *Jouffroy's Introduction to Ethics, including a Critical Survey of Moral Systems.*

A few years since he had charge of an independent congregation in New York, and edited a weekly reform journal, *The Present*, in the interests of transcendental socialism, which lasted not beyond two years. He is now minister of the Unitarian church in Liverpool, lately under the care of the Rev. John Hamilton Thom, the biographer of Blanco White.

Mr. Channing is not of the Strauss or Parker school of rationalists, but more devotional and affirmative, at times approaching Swedenborgianism in his disposition to unite a bold spiritual philosophy with church life and social reorganization. He has rare talents as an extempore speaker and preacher.

William Ellery Channing, also a nephew of the late Dr. Channing, from whom his name is derived, and the son of Dr. Walter Channing, the medical writer and professor at Harvard, is the author of two series of *Poems*, published in Boston in 1843 and 1847; of a series of psychological essays in The Dial of 1844, entitled *Youth of the Poet and Painter;* a volume of thoughtful observations, *Conversations in Rome: between an Artist, a Catholic, and a Critic*, published in 1847; and *The Woodman and other Poems*, 1849.

There is much originality and a fine vein of reflection in both this author's prose and verse,—touching on the themes of the scholar, the love of nature, and the poetic visionary.

THE POET.

Each day, new Treasure brings him for his share,
So rich he is he never shall be poor,
His lessons nature reads him o'er and o'er,
As on each sunny day the Lake its shore.

Though others pine for piles of glittering gold
A cloudless Sunset furnishes him enough,
His garments never can grow thin or old,
His way is always smooth though seeming rough.

Even in the winter's depth the Pine-tree stands,
With a perpetual Summer in its leaves,
So stands the Poet with his open hands,
Nor care nor sorrow him of Life bereaves.

For though his sorrows fall like icy rain,
Straightway the clouds do open where he goes,
And e'en his tears become a precious gain;
'Tis thus the heart of Mortals that he knows.

The figures of his Landscape may appear
Sordid or poor, their colors he can paint,
And listening to the hooting he can hear,
Such harmonies as never sung the saint.

And of his gain he maketh no account,
He's rich enough to scatter on the way;
His springs are fed by an unfailing fount,
As great Apollo trims the lamp of day.

'Tis in his heart, where dwells his pure Desire
Let other outward lot be dark or fair;
In coldest weather there is inward fire,
In fogs he breathes a clear celestial air.

So sacred is his Calling, that no thing
Of disrepute can follow in his path,
His Destiny too high for sorrowing,
The mildness of his lot is kept from wrath.

Some shady wood in Summer is his room,
Behind a rock in Winter he can sit,
The wind shall sweep his chamber, and his loom
The birds and insects, weave content at it.

Above his head the broad Skies' beauties are,
Beneath, the ancient carpet of the earth;
A glance at that, unveileth every star,
The other, joyfully it feels his birth.

So let him stand, resigned to his Estate,
Kings cannot compass it, or Nobles have,
They are the children of some handsome fate,
He, of Himself, is beautiful and brave.

WILLIAM HAGUE.

The Rev. William Hague, a prominent clergyman of the Baptist denomination, is a native of the state of New York. He was graduated at Hamilton College, N. Y., in 1826, and has since filled important stations in the pulpit of his denomination at Providence, in Boston, at Newark, N. J., and at his present station of Albany, New York. He is the author of numerous occasional addresses and orations, including Discourses on the Life and Character of John Quincy Adams, and the missionary Adoniram Judson. He has lately, in 1855, published two volumes, *Christianity and Statesmanship, with Kindred Topics*, and *Home Life*, a series of lectures. In the former he has treated of the various relations of government and religion in matters of home regulation, and especially the condition of Eastern Europe, now rapidly rising into new importance: in the latter he pursues the most prominent circumstances of domestic and social life. In both cases he shows the man of reading and of sound moderate opinions.

Margaret Fuller, who met Mr. Hague at Providence in 1837, has happily characterized his force as a preacher and lecturer in a passage of her diary:—"He has a very active intellect, sagacity, and elevated sentiment; and, feeling strongly that God is love, can never preach without earnestness. His power comes first from his glowing vitality of temperament. His moral attraction is his individuality. I am much interested in this truly animated being."*

THE CULTIVATION OF TASTE.

"Nothing is beautiful but what is true," say the Rhetoricians. This is a universal maxim. Conformity to truth is beauty, real and permanent. Study nature. Seek truth. The laws of nature are distinguished by simplicity, and simplicity has an abiding charm whether it appear in literature or art, in character or manners. Thence affectation always displeases when it is discovered. Though affectation be the fashion, yet it appears contemptible as soon as it loses the delusive charm of novelty or a name. In France, fashion once declared for an affected ne-

* Memoirs of Margaret Fuller Ossoli, i. 184.

gligence of dress. Thence we hear Montaigne saying, "I have never yet been apt to imitate the negligent garb, observable among the young men of our time, to wear my cloak on one shoulder, my bonnet on one side, and one stocking in somewhat more disorder than the other, meant to express a manly disdain of such exotic ornaments, and a contempt of art." There is no beauty in the *cultivated* negligence even of trifles. It is only that which is occasional, appropriate, and which indicates a mind engaged and absorbed in something worthy of it which truly pleases. Scott saw it in his Lady of the Lake, when he said,

> With head upraised, and look intent,
> And eye and ear attentive bent,
> And locks flung back, and lips apart,
> Like monument of Grecian art,
> In listening mood she seemed to stand,
> The guardian Naiad of the strand.

No kindred grace adorns her of whom it may be said—

> Coquet and coy, at once her air,
> Both studied, tho' both seem neglected;
> Careless she is with artful care,
> Affecting to seem unaffected.

Truth to nature, then, is beauty, and to study the laws of nature is to chasten and develope the taste for beauty.

Another means of cultivating good taste, is to study the *expression of character or design* in which the beauty of objects consists. In the material world, every thing beautiful is a manifestation of certain qualities which are by nature agreeable to the mind; and to ascertain what these are, to point them out distinctly, to classify them, is a pleasing mode of refining and quickening the taste for beauty. "The longer I live," said one, "the more familiar I become with the world around me. Oh! that I could feel the keen zest of which I was susceptible when a boy, and all was new and fair!" "The longer I live," says another, "the more charmed I become with the beauties of a picture or a landscape." The first of these had a natural taste for beauty which he had never developed by studying the expressions of character, which constitute the loveliness of creation. The other, regarding the outward universe as a splendid system of signs, directed his attention to the thing signified; loved to contemplate the moral qualities which were beaming forth from all the surrounding objects, and thus saw open before him a boundless field, ever glowing with new colors and fresh attractions. The first, as he heard a piece of music, might from the mechanism of his nature feel some pleasure arising from novelty, or a regular succession of sounds, which familiarity would soon dispel. The other, as he studied the expression of character, which those tones gave forth, as for instance, with the loud sound he associated the ideas of power or peril, with the low, those of delicacy and gentleness, with the acute, those of fear and surprise, with the grave, solemnity and dignity; he would become more and more deeply touched and enraptured, while listening to the music of nature in the voice of singing winds or in the plaint of an Æolian harp, in the crash of thunder or in the roar of the cataract, in the murmur of the brook or in the moan of the ocean, in the sigh of the zephyr or in the breath of the whirlwind, or while listening to the music of art breaking forth from the loud-sounding trumpet, the muffled drum, or Zion's lyre which hangs upon religion's shrine.

SAMUEL OSGOOD.

The Rev. Samuel Osgood, of the Unitarian Church, of New York, is a member of a family of honorable lineage in the old world and the new. The family is of English ancestry, and seems to have belonged to the solid yeomanry of the old Saxon times. The American progenitor was John Osgood, who was born July 23, 1595, and who emigrated from Andover, England, previous to the year 1639, and who, with Governor Bradstreet, founded the town of Andover, Mass., where his large farm is still held by his descendants. He had four sons, John, Stephen, Christopher, and Thomas.

From the first son John, in the sixth generation from the father, was descended the Hon. Samuel Osgood, of Revolutionary memory and of Revolutionary virtue, who has a claim of his own upon attention here as the author of several productions. He was born February 14, 1748, at Andover, Mass., was a graduate of Harvard of 1770, and applied himself for a while to the study of theology, when the War of Independence breaking out, he took part in its affairs; was in the skirmish at Lexington; became aide to General Ward; then an important member of the provincial congress of Massachusetts; a delegate to the congress of the confederation at Philadelphia in 1781, and in 1785 First Commissioner of the National Treasury. He was succeeded in this latter office, on the new adjustment of the Constitution, by Alexander Hamilton. This duty, and his appointment by Washington as Postmaster General, kept him at New York, of which city he was a resident in the latter portion of his prolonged life, holding various positions of trust and confidence. His mansion in Franklin square has an historical name, as the head-quarters of Washington. His publications were chiefly of a religious character, "Remarks on Daniel and Revelations," "A Letter on Episcopacy," a volume on "Theology and Metaphysics," another of "Chronology." He was an elder of the Brick Presbyterian Church in Beekman street, where he was interred at his death, August 12, 1813.*

The Rev. David Osgood, one of the most noted of the New England divines, of the Federalist stamp in politics, and of the Arminian school in theology, was descended from the second son Stephen, in the fifth generation from the progenitor, John Osgood. He died at the age of seventy-four, in 1822, having led a distinguished career as the minister of Medford. His publications were numerous occasional discourses.

The Rev. Samuel Osgood is descended from the third son, Christopher Osgood, of Andover, in the seventh generation from John, the founder of the family in America. He was born in Charlestown, Mass., August 30, 1812; became a graduate of Harvard in 1832, and completed his theological education at Cambridge in 1835. After two years of travel he was appointed pastor of the Unitarian Congregational Church in Nashua, N. H., in 1837; and at the close of the year 1841, took charge of the Westminster Congregational Church in Providence, R. I. In October, 1849, he succeeded the Rev. Dr. Dewey

* There is a notice of Samuel Osgood, prefatory to a genealogical account of the family, in J. B. Holgate's American Genealogy.

as pastor of the Church of the Messiah, in Broadway, New York.

Mr. Osgood has published translations from the German of *Olshausen on the Passion of Christ*, in Boston, 1839, and *De Wette's Practical Ethics*, with an original introduction, Boston, 1842, in two volumes. His original works are several volumes of a devotional character, and numerous articles of research, scholarship, and philosophical acumen, in the higher periodical literature. He has published *Studies in Christian Biography, or Hours with Theologians and Reformers*, including several of the Church fathers, Calvin, Grotius, George Fox, Swedenborg, Jonathan Edwards, and others; *God with Man, or Footprints of Providential Leaders*, devoted to biblical characters of the Old and New Testament; *The Hearth Stone; Thoughts upon Home Life in our Cities*, and *Mile-Stones in our Life Journey*, the latter peculiarly exhibiting the kindly, earnest, affectionate tone of the author's pastoral ministrations.

Mr. Osgood has been a frequent contributor to the Christian Examiner, as well as to other literary and theological journals; while as one of the editors of the Christian Inquirer, the weekly newspaper organ of the Unitarians in New York, he has diligently completed the round of periodical literature in all its relations. Whilst a temporary resident of the West in 1836 and 1837, he was co-editor of the Western Messenger, a religious monthly, published in Kentucky. His associate in this enterprise was the Rev. James Freeman Clarke, a graduate of Harvard of 1829; formerly a Unitarian minister at Louisville, Kentucky, and afterwards at Boston. The Western Messenger was a monthly magazine, published chiefly at Louisville, and for a time at Cincinnati. Mr. Clarke is the author of numerous short poems, of a portion of the Memoirs of Margaret Fuller, and of two religious works, "The Doctrine of Forgiveness," and "On Prayer."

Mr. Osgood's published orations, speeches, and sermons, have also been numerous, and include the prominent topics of the day connected with education and literary institutions.* Among his personal connexions with the latter, is his prominent participation in the management of the New York Historical Society.

As a speaker, Mr. Osgood is clear, full, and emphatic, a well toned voice seconding a ready command of appropriate language. He is well read as a scholar, fertile in analysis, and happy in the use of illustrations from history, biography, or morals. In his pulpit relations he is ranked among the more evangelical class of Unitarian clergymen; and although a fond student of German literature, and an independent thinker, has never yielded to the rationalism characteristic of German theology. He usually preaches without notes, and his sermons and pastoral care are more strongly marked by love for the associations, festivals, literature, and men of the ancient church, than is common with ministers of the extreme Protestant school to which he belongs by position. He was brought up under the ministry of the Rev. James Walker, the President of Harvard, took his religious views and philosophical principles from that eminent moralist and theologian, and has continued to sustain towards him a close personal and professional relation.

* The following are the principal miscellaneous publications of Mr. Osgood in pamphlets and periodicals. In the Western Messenger:—Physical Theory of Another Life, 1836; Dewey's Old World and New, 1836; Love of the Tragic, 1837; Robespierre, 1837; D'Holbach's System of Nature, 1838; Prescott, Bancroft, and Carlyle, 1838. In the Christian Examiner:—Education in the West, 1837; Debates on Catholicism, 1837; De Wette's System of Religion, 1838; De Wette's Theological Position, 1838; American Education, 1839; Satanic School in Literature, 1839; Education of Mothers, 1840; Jouffroy's Ethics, 1840; Christian Ethics before the Reformation, 1840 Christian Ethics since the Reformation, 1841; Isaac Taylor on Spiritual Christianity, 1842; St. Paul's Epistles, 1842; Isaac Williams, the Poet of Puseyism, 1843; Theodore Parker's De Wette on the Old Testament, 1844; Preaching Extempore, 1844; Conventions and Conferences, 1845; Relation between Old and New Testaments, 1845; St. Augustine and his Times, 1846; St. Augustine and his Works, 1846; Memoir of Charles J. Fox, Esq., of Nashua, 1846; Hugo Grotius and his Times, 1847; John Wesley, 1847; Jonathan Edwards, 1848; Christianity and Socialism, 1848; St. Theresa and the Devotees of Spain, 1849; Modern Ecclesiastical History, 1850; The German in America, 1851; Recent Aspects of Judaism, 1853; The Church of the First Three Centuries, 1853; Milton in our Day, 1854; Americans and Men of the Old World, 1855; in the North American Review, Chrysostom and his Eloquence, 1846; in the Bibliotheca Sacra, St. Jerome and his Times, 1848; Socialism in the United States, Christian Review, 1852; The Blouse in both Hemispheres, New York Quarterly, 1854; Modern Prophets, Putnam's Monthly, 1854; Loyola, and the Jesuit Reaction, 1854. He has published the following sermons:—The Star of Bethlehem, 1840; Manifestation of God, 1841; Farewell at Nashua, 1841; Memory and Hope; Two Sermons on leaving Providence, 1849; Death of President Taylor, 1850; Quarter Century of the Church of the Messiah, 1851; The Scholar's Death: a Tribute to Andrews Norton, 1853; Devotion and Trade: Sermon at Louisville, Ky., 1854; Loss of the Arctic, 1854; Lessons of the Year of Calamities, 1854; Fifteen Sermons in the volume already named, and entitled "God with Men," 1853. Speeches and Addresses published:—American Principles—an Oration, 1839; The State of Education in New Hampshire—an Address, 1841; William Penn and Roger Williams—Speech at Philadelphia, 1846; The Schools of New England—Speech at New England Dinner, 1849; Speech before the Massachusetts Bible Society, 1851; The Services of Fenimore Cooper, 1852; Remarks on the Death of Daniel Webster, 1852; Speech in Baltimore on Church Principles, 1853; The Founders of Maryland—Remarks at Baltimore, 1853; The Principle of Mutual Insurance—a Mercantile Address, 1853; The Plymouth Celebration, 1853; Semi-Centennial of the New York Historical Society, 1854; The Oriental Races—Address at the Inauguration of the Jewish Institute, 1854; American Eloquence—Speech on the Birth-day of Henry Clay, 1855.

REMINISCENCES OF BOYHOOD—FROM MILE-STONES IN OUR LIFE-JOURNEY.

From the old battle hill, I can see the site of the school-house where two or three hundred boys were gathered together to be whipped and taught as their fathers were before them. A new edifice, indeed, has taken the place of our school, yet upon its statelier front I can see, as if drawn in the air by a strange pencil, the outline of that ancient building, with its round belfry, whose iron tongue held such imperial command of our hours. It costs no great effort to summon back one of those famous Examination Days that absorbed the anticipation of months, and made the week almost breathless with anxiety. There shines the nicely sanded floor, which the cunning sweeper had marked in waving figures, to redeem it from association with any vulgar dust. There sit the School Committee, chief among them the trim chairman, upon whose lips, when he pronounces the final opinion of the board, the very fates seem to rest their judgment. There, too, is the throng of parents, kindred, and friends, who have come to note the performances of the boys, to look pity upon their mistakes, and to smile sympathy upon their successes. Should the presidential chair fall to his lot, no prouder and more radiant day can come to the school-boy, than when, with new clothes and shining shoes, he stands forth to speak his well-conned piece, and wears away among the admiring crowd the ribboned medal that marks his triumph.

Our schoolmasters were great characters in our eyes, and the two who held successively the charge of the grammar department, made a prominent figure in our wayside chat, and to this day we can find some trace of their influence in our very speech and manner. They were men of very different stamp and destiny. The first of them was a tall fair-faced man, with an almost perpetual smile. I always felt kindly towards him, though it was not easy to decide whether his smile was the expression of his good-nature, or the mask of his severity. He wore it very much the same when he flogged an offender, as when he praised a good recitation. He seemed to delight in making a joke of punishment, and it was a favorite habit of his, to fasten upon the end of his rattan the pitch and gum taken from the mouths of masticating urchins, and then, coming upon their idleness unawares, he would insert the glutinous implement in their hair not to be withdrawn without an adroit jerk and the loss of some scalp locks. Poor fellow! his easy nature probably ruined him, and he left the school, not long to follow any industrious calling. When, a few years afterwards, I met him in Boston, with the marks of broken health and fortune in his face and dress, the sight was shocking to all old associations, as if a dignity quite sacerdotal had fallen into the dust. His earthly troubles have long been ended, and I take some pleasure in recording a kind and somewhat grateful feeling towards one whose name I have not heard spoken these many years. His successor was a man of different mould, a stern, resolute man, his face full of an expression that seemed to say that circumstances are but accidents, and it is the will that makes or mars the man. He was not in robust health, and it seemed to some of us, who were thoughtful of his feelings, that were it not for this, he would have been likely to pursue a more ambitious career, and give to the bar the excellent gifts that he devoted to teaching. He was a most faithful teacher, and his frown, like the rain cloud, had a richer blessing for many a wayward idler, than his predecessor's perennial smile. He has borne the burden and the heat of the day for many a long year, with ample success, and when he falls at his post, it will be with the consciousness of having done a good work for his race, in a calling far more honored by Heaven than any of the more ambitious spheres that perhaps won his youthful enthusiasm. Well says the noble Jean Paul Richter:—"Honor to those who labor in school-rooms! Although they may fall from notice like the spring blossoms, like the spring blossoms they fall that the fruit may be born."

There are two other personages that have much to do with every youth's education, and whose names are household words in every New England home. The doctor and the minister figure largely in every boy's meditations, and in our day, the loyalty that we felt towards their professions had not been troubled by a homœopathic doubt or a radical scruple. In our case, it needed no especial docility to appreciate these functionaries.* Our doctor was a most emphatic character, a man of decided mark in the eyes alike of friends and enemies. He was very impatient of questions, and very brief yet pithy in his advice, which was of marvellous point and sagacity. He lost his brevity, however, the moment that other subjects were broached, and he could tell a good story with a dramatic power that would have made him famous upon the stage. He was renowned as a surgeon, and could guide the knife within a hair's breadth of a vital nerve or artery with his left hand quite as firmly as with his right. This ambi-dexterity extended to other faculties, and he was quite as keen at a negotiation as at an amputation. He was no paragon of conciliation, and many of the magnates of the profession appeared to have little liking for him, and sometimes called him a poor scholar, rude in learning and taste, but lucky in his mechanical tact. But he beat them out of this notion, as of many others, by giving an anniversary discourse before the State Medical Association, which won plaudits from his severest rivals, for its classical elegance, as well as its professional learning and sagacity. It was said that the wrong side of him was very wrong and very rough. But those of us who knew him as a friend, tender and true, never believed that he had any wrong side. Certain it is, that they who grew up under his practice have been little inclined to exchange the regular school of medicine, with its scientific method and gradual progress, for any new nostrums of magical pretensions.

Our minister had the name of being the wise man of the town, and I do not remember to have heard a word in disparagement of his mind or motives, even among those who questioned the soundness of his creed. His voice has always been as no other man's to many of us, whether heard as for the first time at a father's funeral, as by me when a child five years old, or in the pulpit from year to year. He came to our parish when quite young, and when theological controversy was at its full height. A polemic style of preaching was then common, and undoubtedly in his later years of calm study, and more broad and spiritual philosophising, he would have read with some good-natured shakes of the head, the more fiery discourses of his novitiate, whilst he might recognise, throughout, the same spirit of manly independence, republican humanity, and profound reverence that have marked his whole career. There was always something peculiarly impressive in his preaching. Each sermon had one or more pithy sayings that a boy could not forget; and when the thoughts were too profound or ab-

* Dr. William J. Walker, of Charlestown, Mass., and the Rev. James Walker, now President of Harvard.

stract for our comprehension, there was an earnestness and reality in the manner which held the attention, like a brave ship under full sail that fixes the gaze of the spectator, though he may not know whither she is bound or what is her cargo, sure enough that she is loaded with something, and is going right smartly somewhere. It was evident that our minister was a faithful student and indefatigable thinker. When the best books afterwards came in our way, we found that the guiding lines of moral and spiritual wisdom had already been set before us, and we had been made familiar with the well winnowed wheat from the great fields of humanity. Every thought, whether original or from books, bore the stamp of the preacher's own individuality; and may well endorse the saying, that upon topics of philosophic analysis and of practical morals he was without a superior, if not without a rival in our pulpits. It is a great thing for young people to grow up under happy religious auspices, and religion itself has a new charm and power when dispensed by a man who is always named in the family with reverence and tenderness. The world would be far better, and Christian service would be much more truly valued, if there were more just and emphatic tribute paid to efficient pastoral labor. Our well known minister has now a more conspicuous station; but he cannot easily have deeper influence than when pastor for a score of years over a united parish, and one of the leaders of public opinion upon all topics of high importance. It is well that the new post is in such harmony with the previous career; for the head of a college, according to our old-fashioned ideas, should be a minister, and he should always abide in due manner by the pastoral office.

THE AGE OF ST. AUGUSTINE—FROM STUDIES IN CHRISTIAN BIOGRAPHY.

As we close our sketch with this vivid picture before us, we cannot but glance at the changes that have come over Christendom since Augustine's time. Could the legend preserved by Gibbon, and told of seven young men of that age, who were said to have come forth alive from a cave at Ephesus, where they had been immured for death by the Pagan Emperor Decius, and whence they were said to have emerged, awakened from nearly two centuries of slumber, to revisit the scenes of their youth and to behold with astonishment the cross displayed triumphant, where once the Ephesian Diana reigned supreme;—could this legend be virtually fulfilled in Augustine, dating the slumber from the period of his decease; could the great Latin father have been saved from dissolution and have sunk into a deep sleep in the tomb where Possidius and his clerical companions laid him with solemn hymns and eucharistic sacrifice, while Genseric and his Vandals were storming the city gates; and could he but come forth in our day, and look upon our Christendom, would he not be more startled than were the seven sleepers of Ephesus? There indeed roll the waves of the same great sea; there gleam the waters of the river on which so many times he had gazed, musing upon its varied path from the Atlas mountains to the Mediterranean, full of lessons in human life; there stretches the landscape in its beauty, rich with the olive and the fig-tree, the citron and the jujube. But how changed are all else. The ancient Numidia is ruled by the French, the countrymen of Martin and Hilary; it is the modern Algiers. Hippo is only a ruin, and near its site is the bustliug manufacturing town of Bona. At Constantine, near by, still lingers a solitary church of the age of Constantine, and the only building to remind Augustine of the churches of his own day. In other places, as at Bona, the mosque has been converted into the Christian temple, and its mingled emblems might tell the astonished saint how the Cross had struggled with the Crescent, and how it had conquered. Go to whatever church he would on the 28th of August, he would hear a mass in commemoration of his death, and might learn that similar services were offered in every country under the sun, and in the imperial language which he so loved to speak. Let him go westward to the sea coast, and he finds the new city, Algiers, and if he arrived at a favorable time, he might hear the cannon announcing the approach of the Marseilles steamer, see the people throng the shore for the last French news, and thus contemplate at once the mighty agencies of the modern world, powder, print, and steam. Although full of amazement, it would not be all admiration. He would find little in the motley population of Jews, Berbers, Moors, and French, to console him for the absence of the loved people of his charge, whose graves not a stone would appear to mark.

Should he desire to know how modern men philosophised in reference to the topics that once distracted his Manichean period, he would find enough to interest and astonish him in the pages of Spinoza and Leibnitz, Swedenborg and Schelling; and would be no indifferent student of the metaphysical creeds of Descartes, and Lock, and Kant. Much of novelty would undoubtedly appear to him united with much familiar and ancient. Should he inquire into the state of theology through Christendom, in order to trace the influence of his favorite doctrines of original sin and elective grace, he would learn that they had never in their decided forms been favorites with the Catholic Church, that the imperial mother had canonised his name and proscribed his peculiar creed, and that the principles that fell with the walls of the hallowed Port Royal, had found their warmest advocates in Switzerland, in Scotland, and far America, beyond the Roman communion. He would recognise his mantle on the shoulders of Calvin of Geneva, and his followers, Knox of Scotland, and those mighty Puritans who trusting in God and his decreeing will, colonised our own New England, and brought with them a faith and virtue that have continued, while their stern dogmas have been considerably mitigated in the creed of their children. The Institutes of Calvin would assure him that the modern age possessed thinkers clear and strong as he, and the work of Edwards on the Will would probably move him to bow his head as before a dialectician of a logic more adamantine than his own, and make him yearn to visit the land of a divine, who united an intellect so mighty with a spirit so humble and devoted. Should he come among us, he would find multitudes to respect his name, and to accept his essential principles, though few, if any, to agree with him in his views of the doom of infants, or of the limited offer of redemption. He would think much of our orthodoxy quite Pelagian, even when tested by the opinion of present champions of the ancient faith. In the pages of Channing he would think of his old antagonist, Pelagius, revived with renewed vigor, enlarged philosophy, and added eloquence. He might call this perhaps too fond champion of the dignity of man by the name, Pelagius, —like him in doctrine, like him, as the name denotes, a dweller by the sea. Who shall say how much the influences of position helped to form the two champions of human nature, the ancient Briton and the modern New Englander, both in part at least of the same British race, both nursed by the sea-side, the one by the shores of Wales or Brittany, the other by the beach of Rhode Island. "No spot on earth," says

Channing, "has helped to form me so much as that beach. There I lifted up my voice in praise amidst the tempest. There, softened by beauty, I poured out my thanksgiving and contrite confessions. There, in reverential sympathy with the mighty power around me, I became conscious of power within."

How long before the human soul shall reach so full a development, that faith and works, reason and authority, human ability and divine grace shall be deemed harmonious, and men cease to be divided by an Augustine and Pelagius, or an Edwards and Channing? Although this consummation may not soon, if ever, be, and opinions may still differ, charity has gained somewhat in the lapse of centuries. Those who are usually considered the followers of Pelagius have been first to print a complete work of Augustine in America—his Confessions. The Roman Church, backed by imperial power and not checked by Augustine, drove the intrepid Briton into exile and an unknown grave. He who more than any other man wore his mantle of moral freedom in our age died, honored throughout Christendom, and the bell of a Roman cathedral joined in the requiem as his remains were borne through the thronged streets of the city of his home.

THE ACADEMY OF NATURAL SCIENCES OF PHILADELPHIA.

This association originated in the social gatherings of a few friends of natural science in the city of Philadelphia. Its founders were John Speakman, a member of the Society of Friends, engaged in business as an apothecary, and Jacob Gilliams, a dentist. These gentlemen were in the habit of meeting Thomas Say and William Bartram at the residence of the latter at Kingsessing, near Philadelphia, and the pleasure and profit resulting from these interviews led to the desire of forming a plan by which reunions of these and other friends of science could be secured at stated intervals.

A meeting was called for this purpose by Messrs. Speakman and Gilliams at the residence of the first named on the evening of January 25, 1812, at which the following persons were present by invitation—Dr. Gerard Troost, Dr. Camillus McMahon Man, Messrs. John Shinn, Jr., Nicholas S. Parmentier. Steps were taken to form an organization, which was perfected on the 21st of March following, and the name of Thomas Say was by general consent added to the number of original members. An upper room was rented, and the collection of books and specimens commenced. Thomas Say was appointed the first Curator.

Thomas Say was born in the city of Philadelphia, July 27, 1787. He was the son of Dr. Benjamin Say, a druggist, who introduced him into the same business. He subsequently became associated in business with his friend Speakman. By injudicious endorsements the partnership became involved, and the business brought to a close. Mr. Say afterwards became curator of the Academy. His simple habits of life, while thus occupied, are pleasantly described by Dr. Ruschenberger:

"He resided in the Hall of the Academy, where he made his bed beneath a skeleton of a horse, and fed himself on bread and milk; occasionally he cooked a chop or boiled an egg; but he was wont to regard eating as an inconvenient interruption to scientific pursuits, and often expressed a wish that he had been made with a hole in his side, in which he might deposit, from time to time, the quantity of food requisite for his nourishment. He lived in this manner several years, during which time his food did not cost, on an average, more than twelve cents a day."

In 1818 Mr. Say joined Messrs. Maclure, Ord, and Peale, in a scientific exploration of the islands and coast of Georgia. They visited East Florida for the same purpose; but their progress to the interior was arrested by the hostilities between the people of the United States and the Indians. In 1819–20 he accompanied as chief geologist the expedition headed by Major Long to the Rocky Mountains, and in 1823 to the sources of the St. Peter's river and adjoining country. In 1825 he removed with Maclure and Owen to the New Harmony settlement. He remained after the separation of his two associates as agent of the property, and died of a fever, October 10, 1834.

His chief work is his *American Entomology*, published at Philadelphia in three beautifully illustrated octavo volumes, by S. A. Mitchell, in 1824–5. He also commenced a work on *American Conchology*, six numbers of which were published before his death. He was also a frequent contributor to the journal of the Academy and other similar periodicals. A list of his articles by Mr. E. C. Herrick is published in the twenty-seventh volume of the Am. Journal of Science.*

Gerard Troost, the first President of the Academy, was born at Bois le Duc, Holland, March 15, 1776. He was educated in his native country, received the degree of Doctor of Medicine at the University of Leyden, and practised for a short time at Amsterdam and the Hague. He then entered the army, where he served at first as a private soldier and afterwards as an officer of the first rank in the medical department. In 1807 he was sent by Louis Buonaparte, then King of Holland, to Paris to pursue his favorite studies in natural science. He there translated into the Dutch language Humboldt's Aspects of Nature.

In 1809 he was sent by the King of Holland to Java, on a tour of scientific observation. He took passage from a northern port in an American vessel to escape the British cruisers, proposing to sail to New York and thence to his destination. The vessel was, however, captured by a French privateer, and carried into Dunkirk, where the naturalist was imprisoned until the French government was informed of his position. On his release, he proceeded to Paris, where he obtained a passport for America. He embarked at Rochelle, and arrived at Philadelphia in 1810.

After the abdication of Louis Buonaparte, he determined to make the United States his permanent residence, and turned his chemical knowledge to good account by establishing a manufactory of alum in Maryland.

Dr. Troost resigned the presidency of the Academy in 1817, and was succeeded by Mr. Maclure. He was afterwards, about 1821, appointed the first Professor of Chemistry in the College of Pharmacy at Philadelphia, but resigned in the following year.

* Encyclopædia Americana, xiv. 588.

In 1825 he joined Owen's community at New Harmony, where he remained until 1827, when he removed to Nashville. In the following year he became professor of Chemistry, Geology, and Mineralogy in the University of that city, and in 1831 Geologist of the state of Tennessee, an office he retained until its abolition in 1849.

Dr. Troost died at Nashville on the 14th of August, 1850. During his presidency the Academy removed, in 1815, to a hall built for its accommodation by Mr. Gilliams, in Gilliams court, Arch street, and placed at its disposal at an annual rent of two hundred dollars.

WILLIAM MACLURE, the successor of Dr. Troost, was born in Scotland in 1763. After acquiring a large fortune by his commercial exertions in London, he established himself about the close of the century in the United States. In 1803 he returned to England as one of a commission appointed to settle claims of American merchants for spoliations committed by France during her revolution.

On his return, he made a geological survey of the United States. "He went forth," says a writer in the Encyclopædia Americana,* "with his hammer in his hand, and his wallet on his shoulder, pursuing his researches in every direction, often amid pathless tracts and dreary solitudes, until he had crossed and recrossed the Alleghany mountains no less than fifty times. He encountered all the privations of hunger, thirst, fatigue, and exposure, month after month, and year after year, until his indomitable spirit had conquered every difficulty and crowned his enterprise with success."

Mr. Maclure published an account of his researches, with a map and other illustrations, in the Transactions of the American Philosophical Society, in 1817. It bears date January 20, 1809, and was the first work of the kind undertaken in the United States. Mr. Maclure became a member of the Academy on the sixth of June, 1812, and its president on the thirtieth of December, 1817. He was a munificent benefactor as well as valuable member of the association, his gifts amounting in the aggregate to $25,000.

One of his favorite plans of public usefulness was the establishment of an University for the study of the natural sciences. Selecting Owen's settlement at New Harmony as the field of his operations, he persuaded Dr. Troost and Messrs. Say and Lesueur to accompany him in 1825 to that place. After the failure of the scheme Mr. Maclure visited Mexico, in the hope of restoring his impaired health, and died at the capital of that country during a second visit, on the 23d of March, 1840.

Mr. Maclure presented over five thousand volumes to the library of the academy, and purchased in Paris the copperplates of several important and costly works on botany and ornithology, with a view to their reproduction in a cheap form in the United States. It is to his liberality thus exerted, that we owe the American edition of Michaux's Sylva by Thomas Nuttall.

On the death of Mr. Maclure, Mr. William Hembel became president of the Academy. Mr. Hembel was born at Philadelphia, September 24, 1764. He studied medicine, and served as a volunteer in the medical department of the army in Virginia during a portion of the Revolution, but owing to a deafness which he believed would incapacitate him for duty as a practitioner, refused to apply for the diploma which he was fully qualified to receive. He, however, practised for many years gratuitously among the poor of the city, and was in other respects conspicuous for benevolence. His favorite branch of study was chemistry.

Mr. Hembel resigned his presidency in consequence of advancing infirmity, in December, 1849, and died on the 12th of June, 1851. He was succeeded by Dr. Morton.

SAMUEL GEORGE MORTON was born at Philadelphia in 1799. His father died when he was quite young, and he was placed at a Quaker school by his mother, a member of that society. From this he was removed to a counting-house, but manifesting a distaste for business was allowed to follow the bent of his inclination and study for a profession. That of medicine was the one selected—Quaker tenets tolerating neither priest nor lawyer. After passing through the usual course of preliminary study under the able guidance of the celebrated Dr. Joseph Parrish, he received a diploma, and soon after sailed for Europe, on a visit to his uncle. He passed two winters in attendance on the medical lectures of the Edinburgh school, and one in a similar manner at Paris, travelling on the Continent during the summer. He returned in 1824, and commenced practice. He had before his departure been made a member of the Academy, and now took an active part in its proceedings. Geology was his favorite pursuit. In 1827 he published an *Analysis of Tabular Spar from Bucks County*; in 1834 *A Synopsis of the Organic Remains of the Cretaceous Group of the United States*; in the same year a medical work, *Illustrations of Pulmonary Consumption, its Anatomical Characters, Causes, Symptoms, and Treatment*, with twelve colored plates; and in 1849, *An Illustrated System of Human Anatomy, Special, General, and Microscopic*. During this period he was actively engaged in the duties of his profession, having, in addition to a large private practice, filled the professorship of Anatomy in Pennsylvania College, from 1839 to 1843, and served for several years as one of the physicians and clinical teachers of the Alms-House Hospital.

He commenced in 1830 his celebrated collection of skulls, one of the most important labors of his life. He thus relates its origin:—

"Having had occasion, in the summer of 1830, to deliver an introductory lecture to a course of Anatomy, I chose for my subject *The different Forms of the Skull, as exhibited in the five Races of Men*. Strange to say, I could neither buy nor borrow a cranium of each of these races, and I finished my discourse without showing either the Mongolian or the Malay. Forcibly impressed with this great deficiency in a most important branch of science, I at once resolved to make a collection for myself."

His friends warmly seconded his endeavors, and the collection, increased by the exertions of over one hundred contributors in all parts of the world, soon became large and valuable. At the

* xiv. 407.

time of his death it numbered 918 human specimens. It has been purchased by subscription for, and is now deposited in, the Academy, and is by far the finest collection of its kind in existence.

The first use made of the collection by Morton was the preparation of the *Crania Americana*, published in 1839, with finely executed lithographic illustrations. It was during the progress of this work that he became acquainted with George R. Gliddon, of Cairo, in consequence of an application to him for Egyptian skulls. It was followed after the arrival of Mr. Gliddon, in 1842, by an intimate acquaintance, and the publication in 1844 of a large and valuable work, the *Crania Ægyptiaca*.

Morton finally adopted the theory of a diverse origin of the human race, and maintained a controversy on the subject with the Rev. Dr. John Bachman of Charleston.

Dr. Morton died at Philadelphia, after an illness of five days, on the 15th of May, 1851. A selection of his inedited papers was published, with additional contributions from Dr. J. C. Nott and George R. Gliddon, under the title of *Types of Mankind: or Ethnological Researches, based upon the Ancient Monuments, Paintings, Sculptures, and Crania of Races, and upon their Natural, Geographical, Philological, and Biblical History*. It is prefaced by a memoir of Dr. Morton, to which we are indebted for the materials of this notice.

JOSIAH C. NOTT, the son of the Hon. Abraham Nott, was born in Union District, South Carolina, March 31, 1804. His father removed with his family in the following year to Columbia. After his graduation at the college of South Carolina in 1824, Mr. Nott commenced the study of medicine in Philadelphia, where he received his diploma in 1828. After officiating as demonstrator of Anatomy to Drs. Physick and Hosack for two years, he returned to Columbia, where he remained, engaged in practice, until 1835. A portion of the two succeeding years was passed in professional study abroad. In 1836 he removed to Mobile, Alabama, where he has since resided. In 1848 he published his chief work—*The Biblical and Physical History of Man*. He has also written much on Medical Science, the Natural History of Man, Life Insurance, and kindred topics, for the American Journal of Medical Science, the Charleston Medical Journal, New Orleans Medical Journal, De Bow's Commercial Review, the Southern Quarterly Review, and other periodicals.

MR. GEORGE ORD, the friend, assistant, and biographer of Wilson, himself a distinguished ornithologist, succeeded Dr. Morton.

In 1826 the Academy purchased a building, originally erected as a Swedenborgian place of worship, to which its collections were removed. Their increase, after a few years, rendered enlarged accommodations necessary, and on the 25th of May, 1839, the corner-stone of the building in Broad street, now occupied by the institution, was laid. The first meeting was held in the new hall on the 7th of February, 1840. In 1847 an enlargement became necessary, and was effected.

In 1817 the Society commenced the publication of *The Journal of the Academy of Natural Sciences*. It was published at first monthly, and afterwards continued at irregular intervals until 1842.

In March, 1841, the publication of the *Proceedings of the Academy* was commenced. It is still continued; the numbers appearing once in every two months. A second series of the *Journal* was commenced in December, 1847.

These periodicals are supported by subscriptions, and by the interest on a legacy of two thousand dollars, bequeathed by Mrs. Elizabeth Stott.*

JOHN C. FREMONT.

JOHN CHARLES FREMONT is the son of a French emigrant gentleman, who married a Virginia lady. He was born in South Carolina, January, 1813. His father dying when he was four years old, the care of his education devolved upon his mother. He advanced so rapidly in his studies that he was graduated at the Charleston College at the age of seventeen. After passing a short time in teaching mathematics, by which he was enabled to contribute to the support of his mother and family, he devoted himself to civil engineering with such success that he obtained an appointment in the government expedition for the survey of the head waters of the Mississippi, and was afterwards employed at Washington in drawing maps of the country visited. He next proposed to the Secretary of War to make an exploration across the Rocky Mountains to the Pacific. The plan was approved, and in 1842, with a small company of men, he explored and opened to commerce and emigration the great South Pass. In his Report, published by government on his return, he portrayed the natural features, climate, and productions of the region through which he had passed, with great fulness and clearness. His adventures were also described in a graphic and animated style; and the book, though a government report, was very widely circulated, and has since been reprinted by publishers in this country and England, and translated into various foreign languages. Stimulated by his success and love of adventure, he soon after planned an expedition to Oregon. Not satisfied with his discoveries in approaching the mountains by a new route, crossing their summits below the South Pass, visiting the Great Salt Lake and effecting a junction with the surveying party of the Exploring Expedition, he determined to change his course on his return. With but twenty-five companions, without a guide, and in the face of approaching winter, he entered a vast unknown region. The exploration was one of peril, and was carried through with great hardship and suffering, and some loss of life. No tidings were received from the party for nine months, while, travelling thirty-five hundred miles in view of, or over perpetual snows, they made known the region of Alta California, including the Sierra Nevada, the valleys of San Joaquin and Sacramento, the gold region, and almost the whole surface of the country. Fremont returned to Washington in August, 1844. He wrote a Report of his second

* Notice of the Origin, Progress, and Present Condition of the Academy of Natural Sciences of Philadelphia. By W. S. W. Ruschenberger, M. D., Phila. 1852.

expedition, which he left as soon as completed in the printer's hands, to depart on a third, the object of which was, the examination in detail of the Pacific coast, and the result, the acquisition of California by the United States. He took part in some of the events of the Mexican war, and at its close, owing to a difficulty with two American commanders, was deprived of his commission by a court-martial, and sent home a prisoner. His commission was restored on his arrival at Washington, by the President, and he soon after again started for California on a private exploration, to determine the best route to the Pacific. On the Sierra San Juan one third of his force of thirty-three men, with a number of mules, was frozen to death; and their brave leader, after great hardships, arrived at Santa Fé on foot, and destitute of everything. The expedition was refitted and reinforced, and Fremont started again, and in a hundred days, after penetrating through and sustaining conflicts with Indian tribes, reached the Sacramento. The judgment of the military court was reversed, the valuable property acquired during his former residence secured, and the State of California returned her pioneer explorer to Washington as her first senator in 1850.

Colonel Fremont married a daughter of the Hon. Thomas H. Benton. He has, during the recesses of Congress, continued his explorations at his private cost and toil, in search of the best railway route to the Pacific.

The Reports to Government of his expeditions have been the only publications of Col. Fremont; but these, from the exciting nature, public interest, and national importance of their contents, combined with the clear and animated mode of their presentation, have sufficed to give him a place as author as well as traveller.

JAMES NACK.

JAMES NACK holds a well nigh solitary position in literature, as one, who deprived from childhood of the faculties of hearing and speech, has yet been able not only to acquire by education a full enjoyment of the intellectual riches of the race, but to add his own contribution to the vast treasury. He was born in the city of New York, the son of a merchant, who by the loss of his fortune in business was unable to afford him many educational advantages. The want was, however, supplied by the care of a sister, who taught the child to read before he was four years old. The activity of his mind and ardent thirst for knowledge carried him rapidly forward from this point, until in his ninth year an accident entailed upon him a life-long misfortune.

As he was carrying a little playfellow in his arms down a flight of steps his foot slipped; to recover himself he caught hold of a heavy piece of furniture, which falling upon him injured his head so severely, that he lay for several hours without sign of life, and for several weeks mentally unconscious. When he recovered it was found that the organs of sound were irrevocably destroyed. The loss of hearing was gradually followed by that of speech. He was placed as soon as possible in the Institution for the Deaf and Dumb, where the interrupted course of his mental training was soon resumed. He showed great aptitude for the acquirement of knowledge, and an especial facility in the mastery of foreign languages. After leaving the institution he continued, with the aid of the few books he possessed, a private course of study.

He had for some time before this written occasional poems, of one of which, *The Blue Eyed Maid*, he had given a copy to a friend, who handed it to his father, Mr. Abraham Asten. That gentleman was so much struck by its promise, that he sought other specimens of the author's skill. These confirming his favorable impressions, he introduced the young poet to several literary gentlemen of New York, under whose auspices a volume of his poems, written between his fourteenth and seventeenth years, was published. It was received with favor by critics and the public. Mr. Nack soon after became an assistant in the office of Mr. Asten, then clerk of the city and county. In 1838 he married, and in 1839 published his second volume, *Earl Rupert and other Tales and Poems*, with a memoir of the author, by Mr. Prosper M. Wetmore.

THE OLD CLOCK.

Two Yankee wags, one summer day,
Stopped at a tavern on their way,
Supped, frolicked, late retired to rest,
And woke to breakfast on the best.

The breakfast over, Tom and Will
Sent for the landlord and the bill;
Will looked it over; "Very right—
But hold! what wonder meets my sight!
Tom! the surprise is quite a shock!"—
"What wonder? where?"—"The clock! the clock!"

Tom and the landlord in amaze
Stared at the clock with stupid gaze,
And for a moment neither spoke;
At last the landlord silence broke—

"You mean the clock that's ticking there?
I see no wonder I declare;
Though may be, if the truth were told,
'Tis rather ugly—somewhat old;
Yet time it keeps to half a minute;
But, if you please, what wonder's in it?"

"Tom; don't you recollect," said Will,
"The clock at Jersey near the mill,
The very image of this present,
With which I won the wager pleasant?"
Will ended with a knowing wink—
Tom scratched his head and tried to think.
"Sir, begging pardon for inquiring,"
The landlord said, with grin admiring,
"What wager was it?"

"You remember
It happened, Tom, in last December,
In sport I bet a Jersey Blue
That it was more than he could do,
To make his finger go and come
In keeping with the pendulum,
Repeating, till one hour should close,
Still, '*Here she goes—and there she goes*'—
He lost the bet in half a minute."

"Well, if *I* would, the deuse is in it!"
Exclaimed the landlord; "try me yet,
And fifty dollars be the bet."
"Agreed, but we will play some trick

To make you of the bargain sick!"
"I'm up to that!"
"Don't make us wait,
Begin. The clock is striking eight."
He seats himself, and left and right
His finger wags with all its might,
And hoarse his voice, and hoarser grows,
With—"*here she goes—and there she goes!*"

"Hold!" said the Yankee, "plank the ready!"
The landlord wagged his finger steady,
While his left hand, as well as able,
Conveyed a purse upon the table.
"Tom, with the money let's be off!"
This made the landlord only scoff;
He heard them running down the stair,
But was not tempted from his chair;
Thought he, "the fools! I'll bite them yet!
So poor a trick shan't win the bet."
And loud and loud the chorus rose
Of, "*here she goes—and there she goes!*"
While right and left his finger swung,
In keeping to his clock and tongue.

His mother happened in, to see
Her daughter; "where is *Mrs. B——?*
When will she come, as you suppose?
Son!"
"*Here she goes—and there she goes!*"

"Here?—where?"—the lady in surprise
His finger followed with her eyes;
"Son, why that steady gaze and sad?
Those words—that motion—are you mad?
But here's your wife—perhaps she knows
And"
"*Here she goes—and there she goes!*"

His wife surveyed him with alarm,
And rushed to him and seized his arm;
He shook her off, and to and fro
His fingers persevered to go,
While curled his very nose with ire,
That *she* against him should conspire,
And with more furious tone arose
The, "*here she goes—and there she goes!*"

"Lawks!" screamed the wife, "I'm in a whirl!"
Run down and bring the little girl;
She is his darling, and who knows
But"——
"*Here she goes—and there she goes!*"

"Lawks! he is mad! what made him thus?
Good Lord! what will become of us?
Run for a doctor—run—run—run—
For Doctor Brown and Doctor Dun,
And Doctor Black, and Doctor White,
And Doctor Grey, with all your might."

The doctors came and looked and wondered,
And shook their heads, and paused and pondered,
'Till one proposed he should be bled,
"No—leeched you mean"—the other said—
"Clap on a blister," roared another,
"No—cup him"—"no—trepan him, brother!"
A sixth would recommend a purge,
The next would an emetic urge,
The eighth, just come from a dissection,
His verdict gave for an injection;
The last produced a box of pills,
A certain cure for earthly ills;
"I had a patient yesternight,"
Quoth he, "and wretched was her plight,
And as the only means to save her,
Three dozen patent pills I gave her,
And by to-morrow I suppose
That"——
"*Here she goes—and there she goes!*"

"You all are fools," the lady said,
"The way is, just to shave his head.
Run, bid the barber come anon"—
"Thanks, mother," thought her clever son,
"*You* help the knaves that would have bit me,
But all creation shan't outwit me!"
Thus to himself, while to and fro
His finger perseveres to go,
And from his lip no accent flows
But "*here she goes—and there she goes!*"

The barber came—"Lord help him! what
A queerish customer I've got;
But we must do our best to save him—
So hold him, gemmen, while I shave him!"
But here the doctors interpose—
"A woman never"——
"*There she goes!*"

"A woman is no judge of physic,
Not even when her baby *is* sick.
He must be bled"—"no—no—a blister"—
"A purge you mean"—"I say a clyster"—
"No—cup him—" "leech him—" "pills! pills! pills!"
And all the house the uproar fills.

What means that smile? what means that shiver?
The landlord's limbs with rapture quiver,
And triumph brightens up his face—
His finger yet shall win the race!
The clock is on the stroke of nine—
And up he starts——"'Tis mine! 'tis mine!"
"What do you mean?"
"I mean the fifty!
I never spent an hour so thrifty;
But you, who tried to make me lose,
Go, burst with envy, if you choose!
But how is this? where are they?"
"Who?"
"The gentlemen—I mean the two
Came yesterday—are they below?"
"They galloped off an hour ago."
"Oh, purge me! blister! shave and bleed!
For, hang the knaves, I'm mad indeed!"

FRANCIS BOWEN,

Professor of Moral Philosophy in Harvard College, and late editor of the North American Review, was born in Charlestown, Massachusetts. He became a graduate at Cambridge in 1833, and from 1835 to 1839 was tutor in the institution in the department which he now occupies, of Philosophy and Political Economy. He subsequently occupied himself exclusively with literary pursuits, while he continued his residence at Cambridge. In 1842 he published *Critical Essays on the History and Present Condition of Speculative Philosophy;* and in the same year an edition of Virgil, for the use of schools and colleges. In January, 1843, he became editor of the North American Review, and discharged the duties of this position till the close of 1853, when the work passed into the hands of its present editor, Mr. A. P. Peabody. During the latter portion of his editorship of the Review, Mr. Bowen's articles on the Hungarian question attracted considerable attention by their opposition to the popular mode of looking upon the subject under the influences of the Kossuth agitation.

In the winter of 1848 and 1849 Mr. Bowen delivered before the Lowell Institute in Boston a series of *Lectures on the Application of Meta-*

physical and Ethical Science to the Evidences of Religion.

Mr. Bowen is also the author of several volumes of American Biography in Mr. Sparks's series, including Lives of Sir William Phipps, Baron Steuben, James Otis, and General Benjamin Lincoln.

In 1853 Mr. Bowen accepted the chair at Harvard, of Natural Theology, Moral Philosophy, and Political Economy.

JOHN MILTON MACKIE,

The author of a life of Leibnitz and other works, was born in 1813, in Wareham, Plymouth county, Massachusetts. He was educated at Brown University, where he was graduated in 1832, and where he was subsequently a tutor from 1834 to 1838.

His writings, in their scholarship, variety, and spirit, exhibit the accomplished man of letters. In 1845 he published a *Life of Godfrey William Von Leibnitz*, on the basis of the German work of Dr. G. E. Guhrauer. This was followed in 1848 by a contribution to American history in a volume of Mr. Sparks's series of biography, a *Life of Samuel Gorton, one of the first settlers in Warwick, Rhode Island.*

J. Milton Mackie

In 1855 Mr. Mackie published a volume of clever sketches, the result of a portion of a European tour, entitled *Cosas de España; or, Going to Madrid via Barcelona.* It was a successful work in a field where several American travellers, as Irving, Mackenzie, Cushing, Wallis, and others, have gathered distinguished laurels. Mr. Mackie treats the objects of his tour with graphic, descriptive talent, and a happy vein of individual humor.

A number of select review articles indicate the author's line of studies, which, however, include a wider field of research. To the North American he has contributed papers on the Autobiography of Heinrich Steffens (vol. 57); Gervinus's History of German Literature (vol. 58); Professor Gammell's Life of Roger Williams (vol. 61). To the American Whig Review, The Life and Writings of Job Durfee (vol. 7); The Revolution in Germany in 1848 (vol. 8); and The Principles of the Administration of Washington (vol. 10). To vol. 8 of the Christian Review, an article on M. Guizot on European Civilization.

Mr. Mackie has been a contributor to Putnam's Magazine, where, in December, 1854, he published a noticeable article entitled "Forty Days in a Western Hotel."

HOLIDAYS AT BARCELONA—FROM COSAS DE ESPAÑA.

Spanish life is pretty well filled up with holidays. The country is under the protection of a better-filled calendar of saints than any in Christendom, Italy, perhaps, excepted. But these guardians do not keep watch and ward for naught: they have each their "solid day" annually set apart for them, or, at least, their afternoon, wherein to receive adoration and tribute money. The poor Spaniard is kept nearly half the year on his knees. His prayers cost him his *pesetas*, too; for, neither the saints will intercede nor the priests will absolve, except for cash. But his time spent in ceremonies, the Spaniard counts as nothing. The fewer days the laborer has to work, the happier is he. These are the dull prose of an existence essentially poetic. On holidays, on the contrary, the life of the lowest classes runs as smoothly as verses. If the poor man's *porron* only be well filled with wine, he can trust to luck and the saints for a roll of bread and a few onions. Free from care, he likes, three days in the week, to put on his best—more likely, his only bib-and-tucker—and go to mass, instead of field or wharf duty. He is well pleased at the gorgeous ceremonies of his venerable mother-church: at the sight of street processions, with crucifix and sacramental canopy, and priests in cloth of purple and of gold. The spectacle also of the gay promenading, the music, the parade and mimic show of war, the free theatres, the bull-fights, the streets hung with tapestry, and the town hall's front adorned with a flaming full length of Isabella the Second—these constitute the brilliant passages in the epic of his life. Taking no thought for the morrow after the holiday, he is wiser than a philosopher, and enjoys the golden hours as they fly. Indeed, he can well afford to do so; for, in his sunny land of corn and wine, the common necessaries of life are procured with almost as little toil as in the bread-fruit islands of the Pacific.

All the Spaniard's holidays are religious festivals. There is no Fourth of July in his year. His mirth, accordingly, is not independent and profane, like the Yankee's. Being more accustomed also to playtime, he is less tempted to fill it up with excesses. It is in the order of his holiday to go, first of all, to church; and a certain air of religious decorum is carried along into all the succeeding amusements. Neither is his the restless, capering enjoyment of the Frenchman, who begins and ends his holidays with dancing; nor the chattering hilarity of the Italian, who goes beside himself over a few roasted chestnuts and a monkey. The Spaniard wears a somewhat graver face. His happiness requires less muscular movement. To stand wrapped in his cloak, statue-like, in the public square; to sit on sunny bank, or beneath shady bower, is about as much activity as suits his dignity. Only the sound of castanets can draw him from his propriety; and the steps of the *fandango* work his brain up to intoxication. Spanish festal-time, accordingly, is like the hazy, dreamy, voluptuous days of the Indian summer, when the air is as full of calm as it is of splendor, and when the pulses of Nature beat full, but feverless.

The holiday is easily filled up with pleasures. The peasant has no more to do than to throw back his head upon the turf, and tantalize his dissolving mouth by holding over it the purple clusters, torn from overhanging branches. The beggar lies down against a wall, and counts into the hand of his companion the pennies they have to spend together during the day—unconscious the while that the sand of half its hours has already run out. The village-beauty twines roses in her hair, and looks out of the window, happy to see the gay-jacketed youngsters go smirking and ogling by. The belles of the town lean over their flower balconies, chatting with neighbors, and raining glances on the throng of admirers who promenade below. Town and country wear their holiday attire with graceful, tranquil joy. Only from the cafés of the one, and the *ventorillos* of the other, may perchance be heard the sounds of revelry; where the guitar is thrummed with a gaiety not heard in serenades; where the violin leads youthful feet a round of pleasures, too fast for sureness of footing; and where the claque of the castanets rings out merrily above laugh and song, firing the heart with passions which comport not well with Castilian gravity.

CHARLES F. BRIGGS.

Mr. Briggs is a native of Nantucket. He has been for many years a resident of the city of New York, and has been during the greater part of the period connected with the periodical press.

In 1845 he commenced the Broadway Journal with the late Edgar A. Poe, by whom it was continued after Mr. Briggs's retirement.

Mr. Briggs has also been connected with the Evening Mirror. He published in this journal a series of letters, chiefly on the literary affectations of the day, written in a vein of humorous extravaganza, and purporting to be from the pen of Fernando Mendez Pinto.

In 1839 he published a novel, *The Adventures of Harry Franco, a Tale of the Great Panic*. This was followed by *The Haunted Merchant*, 1843, and *The Trippings of Tom Pepper, or the Results of Romancing*, 1847. The scene of these novels is laid in the city of New York at the present day. They present a humorous picture of various phases of city life, and frequently display the satirical vein of the writer.

Mr. Briggs is the author of a number of felicitous humorous tales and sketches, contributed to the Knickerbocker and other magazines. He has also written a few poetical pieces, several of which have appeared in Putnam's Monthly Magazine, with which he has been connected as editor. Others are published in a choice volume of selections, *Seaweeds from the Shores of Nantucket*.

One of his most successful productions is a little story, published in pamphlet form, with the title, *Working a Passage; or, Life in a Liner*. It gives an account of a voyage to Liverpool in the literal vein of a description from the forecastle.

AN INTERRUPTED BANQUET—FROM LIFE IN A LINER.

Among the luxuries which the captain had provided for himself and passengers was a fine green turtle, which was not likely to suffer from exposure to salt water, so it was reserved, until all the pigs, and sheep, and poultry had been eaten. A few days before we arrived, it was determined to kill the turtle and have a feast the next day. Our cabin gentlemen had been long enough deprived of fresh meats to make them cast liquorish glances towards their hard-skinned friend, and there was a great smacking of lips the day before he was killed. As I walked aft occasionally I heard them congratulating themselves on their prospective turtle-soup and force-meat balls; and one of them, to heighten the luxury of the feast, ate nothing but a dry biscuit for twenty-four hours, that he might be able to devour his full share of the unctuous compound. It was to be a gala day with them; and though it was not champagne day, that falling on Saturday and this on Friday, they agreed to have champagne a day in advance, that nothing should be wanting to give a finish to their turtle. It happened to be a rougher day than usual when the turtle was cooked, but they had become too well used to the motion of the ship to mind that. It happened to be my turn at the wheel the hour before dinner, and I had the tantalizing misery of hearing them laughing and talking about their turtle, while I was hungry from want of dry bread and salt meat. I had resolutely kept my thoughts from the cabin during all the passage but once, and now I found my ideas clustering round a tureen of turtle in spite of all my philosophy. Confound them, if they had gone out of my hearing with their exulting smacks, I would not have envied their soup, but their hungry glee so excited my imagination that I could see nothing through the glazing of the binnacle but a white plate with a slice of lemon on the rim, a loaf of delicate bread, a silver spoon, a napkin, two or three wine glasses of different hues and shapes, and a water goblet clustering around it, and a stream of black, thick, and fragrant turtle pouring into the plate. By and by it was four bells; they dined at three. And all the gentlemen, with the captain at their head, darted below into the cabin, where their mirth increased when they caught sight of the soup plates. "Hurry with the soup, steward," roared the captain. "Coming, sir," replied the steward. The cook opened the door of his galley, and out came the delicious steam of the turtle, such as people often inhale, and step across the street of a hot afternoon to avoid, as they pass by Delmonico's in South William Street. Then came the steward with a large covered tureen in his hand, towards the cabin gangway. I forgot the ship for a moment in looking at this precious cargo, the wheel slipped from my hands, the ship broached to with a sudden jerk, the steward had got only one foot upon the stairs, when this unexpected motion threw him off his balance and down he went by the run, the tureen slipped from his hands, and part of its contents flew into the lee scuppers, and the balance followed him in his fall.

I laughed outright. I enjoyed the turtle a thousand times more than I should have done if I had eaten the whole of it. But I was forced to restrain my mirth, for the next moment the steward ran upon deck, followed by the captain in a furious rage, threatening if he caught him to throw him overboard. Not a spoonful of the soup had been left in the coppers, for the steward had taken it all away at once to keep it warm. In about an hour afterwards the passengers came upon deck, looking more sober than I had seen them since we left Liverpool. They had dined upon cold ham.

WITHOUT AND WITHIN.

My coachman in the moonlight, there,
  Looks through the side-light of the door;
I hear him with his brethren swear,
  As I could do—but only more.

Flattening his nose against the pane,
  He envies me my brilliant lot,
And blows his aching fists in vain,
  And wishes me a place more hot.

He sees me to the supper go,
  A silken wonder by my side,
Bare arms, bare shoulders, and a row
  Of flounces, for the door too wide.

He thinks how happy is my arm
  'Neath its white-gloved and jewelled load,
And wishes me some dreadful harm,
  Hearing the merry corks explode.

Meanwhile I inly curse the bore
  Of hunting still the same old coon,
And envy him, outside the door,
  In golden quiets of the moon.

The winter wind is not so cold
  As the bright smiles he sees me win,
Nor our host's oldest wine so old
  As our poor gabble—watery—thin.

I envy him the ungyved prance
  By which his freezing feet he warms,
And drag my lady's chains and dance
  The galley slave of dreary forms.

O! could he have my share of din
  And I his quiet!—past a doubt
'Twould still be one man bored within,
  And just another bored without.

CHRISTOPHER PEASE CRANCH.

C. P. Cranch, a son of Chief Justice Cranch, was born at Alexandria, in the District of Columbia, March 8, 1813. After being graduated at the Columbian College, Washington, in 1831, he studied divinity at Cambridge University, and was ordained. In 1844 he published a volume of *Poems* at Philadelphia. It is marked by a quiet, thoughtful vein of spiritual meditation, and an artist's sense of beauty.

Mr. Cranch has for a number of years past devoted himself to landscape painting, and has secured a prominent position in that branch of art.

THE BOUQUET.

She has brought me flowers to deck my room,
  Of sweetest sense and brilliancy;
She knew not that she was the while
  The fairest flower of all to me.

Since her soft eyes have looked on them,
  What tenderer beauties in them dwell!
Since her fair hands have placed them there,
  O how much sweeter do they smell!

Beside my inkstand and my books
  They bloom in perfume and in light.
A voice amid my lonesomeness,
  A shining star amid my night.

The storm beats down upon the roof,
  But in this room glide summer hours,
Since she, the fairest flower of all,
  Has garlanded my heart with flowers.

HENRY THEODORE TUCKERMAN.

The Tuckerman family is of English origin, and has existed more than four centuries in the county of Devon, as appears from the parish registers and monumental inscriptions.* By the mother's side, Mr. Tuckerman is of Irish descent. The name of the family is Keating. In Macaulay's recent history he thus speaks of one of her ancestors as opposing a military deputy of James II., in his persecution of the Protestant English in Ireland in 1686:—"On all questions which arose in the Privy Council, Tyrconnel showed similar violence and partiality. John Keating, Chief-Justice of the Common Pleas, a man distinguished for ability, integrity, and loyalty, represented with great mildness, that perfect equality was all that the general could ask for his own church." The subject of this notice is a nephew of the late Rev. Dr. Joseph Tuckerman—a memoir of whom appeared in England within a few years, and who is known and honored as the originator of the ministry at large, in Boston, one of the most efficient of modern Protestant charities. His mother was also related to and partly educated with another distinguished Unitarian clergyman, Joseph Stevens Buckminster.

* It is still represented there—the name belonging to several of the gentry. In the seventeenth century the Tuckermans intermarried with the Fortescue family, that of Sir Edward Harris, and that (now extinct) of "Giles of Bowden;" the former is now represented by the present Earl of Fortescue. Previous to this a branch of the Tuckermans emigrated to Germany. In a history of the county of Braunselweig, by William Hanemann, published in Luneberg in 1827, allusion is made to one of this branch—Peter Tuckerman, who is mentioned as the last abbot of the monastery of Riddaghausen; he was chosen to the chapter in 1631, and, at the same time, held the appointment of court preacher at Wolfenbuttell. Some of his writings are extant, and his monument is an imposing and curious architectural relic.

Henry T. Tuckerman.

Henry Theodore Tuckerman was born in Boston, Massachusetts, April 20, 1813. His early education was begun and completed in the excellent schools of that city and vicinity. In 1833, after preparing for college, the state of his health rendered it necessary for him to seek a milder climate. In September he sailed from New York for Havre, and after a brief sojourn in Paris, proceeded to Italy, where he remained until the ensuing summer, and then returned to the United States. He resumed his studies, and in the fall of 1837, embarked at Boston for Gibraltar, visited that fortress and afterwards Malta, then proceeded to Sicily, passed the winter in Palermo, and made the tour of the island; in the following summer driven from Sicily by the cholera, of the ravages of which he has given a minute account, he embarked at Messina for Leghorn, passed the ensuing winter (1838) chiefly at Florence, and early the next summer returned home; in 1845 he removed from Boston to New York, where he has since resided, except in the summer months, which he has passed chiefly at Newport, R. I. In 1850 he received from Harvard College the honorary degree of Master of Arts. In the winter of 1852 he visited London and Paris for a few weeks.

The writings of Mr. Tuckerman include poems, travels, biography, essay, and criticism. A characteristic of his books is that each represents some phase or era of experience or study. Though mainly composed of facts, or chapters which have in the first instance appeared in the periodical literature of the country,* they have none of them an occasional or unfinished air. They are the studies of a scholar; of a man true to his convictions and the laws of art. His mind is essentially philosophical and historical; he per-

* Mr. Tuckerman has been a contributor to all the best magazine literature of the day: in Walsh's Review, the North American Review, the Democratic, Graham's Magazine, the Literary World, the Southern Literary Messenger, Christian Examiner, &c. As his chief contributions have been collected, or are in process of collection, in his books, we need not refer to particular articles.

ceives truth in its relation to individual character, and he takes little pleasure in the view of facts unless in their connexion with a permanent whole. Hence what his writings sometimes lose in immediate effect, they gain on an after perusal. His productions pass readily from the review or magazine to the book.

Taking his writings in the order of publication, they commenced with a collection of essays, tales, and sketches in 1835, entitled *The Italian Sketch Book*, which has since been enlarged in a second and third edition. With many of the author's subsequent productions, it took a favorable view of the Italian character, when it was the fashion to undervalue it. Among other novelties in its sketches, it contained an account of the little Republic of San Marino. The prominent topics of the country, as they occur to a man of education, were presented in a picturesque manner. After the author's return from a second Italian tour, he published in 1839 *Isabel, or Sicily a Pilgrimage*, in which with a thin disguise of fiction, allowing the introduction of sentiment, discussion, and story, the peculiar features of the island, in its natural beauties and its remains of art, are exhibited. After a considerable interval, another volume of travel appeared, the result of a visit to England in 1853. It is entitled *A Month in England*. Mr. Tuckerman has also published in the magazines a few chapters of a similar memorial of France on the same tour. Like the former works, they are books of association rather than of mere daily observation. The author while abroad studies character as it is expressed in men and institutions; making what he sees subordinate to what he thinks. In the volume on England, there is a graphic and humorous description of the universal reception of Mrs. Stowe's book during the Uncle Tom mania, which shows a capability his readers might wish to have had oftener exercised, of presenting the exciting events of the day.

In 1846 a volume, the first of his collections from the magazines, *Thoughts on the Poets*, was published in New York. It contained articles on some of the masters of the Italian school, and the chief English poets of the nineteenth century, with two American subjects in Drake and Bryant. The critical treatment is acute and kindly, reaching its end by an ingenious track of speculation. This was followed by a series of home studies, *Artist Life, or Sketches of American Painters;* the materials of which were drawn in several instances from facts communicated by the artists themselves. They are studies of character, in which the artist and his work illustrate each other. The selection of subjects ranges from West to Leutze. The sketches are written *con amore*, with a keen appreciation of the unworldly, romantic, ideal life of the artist. Picturesque points are eagerly embraced. There is a delicate affection to the theme which adapts itself to each artist and his art. The paper on Huntington, in particular, has this sympathetic feeling. With these sketches of "Artist Life," may be appropriately connected, *A Memorial of Horatio Greenough*, prefixed to a selection from the sculptor's writings, and published in 1853. It brings into view the writer's Italian experiences, his personal friendship, and is a tasteful record of the man and of his art.

In 1849 and '51 Mr. Tuckerman published two series of papers, which he entitled, *Characteristics of Literature illustrated by the Genius of Distinguished Men*. The types of character which he selected, and the favorites of his reading and study whom he took for their living portraiture, show the extent and refinement of his tastes. In choosing Sir Thomas Browne and Horne Tooke for his philosophers, he was guided by love for the poetical and curious. He delicately discriminated between the Humorist and the Dilettante in Charles Lamb and Shenstone. Hazlitt was his Critic; Beckford, with his refined writing, love of art, and poetical adventure, was "picked man" of Travel; Steele his good-natured Censor; Burke his Rhetorician; Akenside his Scholar; Swift his Wit; Humboldt his Naturalist; Talfourd his Dramatist; Channing his Moralist; and Edward Everett his Orator. In all this we may perceive a leaning to the quiet and amiable, the order of finished excellence of thoroughbred men. Widely scattered as these twenty-two papers were in the periodical literature of the country when they first appeared, they indicate the careful and tasteful literary labor with which Mr. Tuckerman has served the public in the culture of its thought and affections. The tempting power of the critic has never led him aside to wound a contemporary interest, or thwart a rival author. He has written in the large and liberal spirit of a genuine scholar. While mentioning these claims as a literary critic, we may refer to a genial and comprehensive *Sketch of American Literature*, in a series of chapters appended to Shaw's "English Literature," reprinted as a text-book for academies.

In a similar classification of a more general nature, out of the range of literature, Mr. Tuckerman has published a series of *Mental Portraits, or Studies of Character*, in which Boone represents the Pioneer; Lafitte, the Financier; Korner, the Youthful Hero; Giacomo Leopardi, the Sceptical Genius; and Gouverneur Morris, the Civilian.

In this choice of topics, Mr. Tuckerman has latterly been frequently directed to American subjects of an historical interest. Besides his elaborate papers on the artists and authors of the country, he has written, among other sketches of the kind, *A Life of Commodore Silas Talbot*, of the American navy,* and an appreciative article in a recent number of the North American Review,† on the personal character and public services of De Witt Clinton.

The Optimist, a Collection of Essays, published in 1850, exhibits the author in a highly agreeable light. In an easy Horatian spirit, he runs over the usual means and ends of the world, throwing a keen glance at popular notions of living, which destroy life itself; and gathering up eagerly, with the art of a man whose experience has taught him to economize the legitimate sources of pleasure within his reach, every help to cheerfulness and refinement. Some of these essays are picturesque, and show considerable ingenuity; all exhibit a thoughtful study of the times.

From a still more individual private view of life, are *The Leaves from the Diary of a Dreamer*, delicately published in 1853 by Pickering in London,

* Published by J. C. Riker, New York, 1850.
† Oct., 1854.

in quaint old type of the English Augustan period of literature. Under the guise of the posthumous journal of an invalid traveller in Italy, the sensitive emotions of a passionate lover, with a keen susceptibility to the art and nature around him, are described. There are frequent personal anecdotes in this volume of such personages of the times, as Byron, Sismondi, and Hawthorne.

The chief of Mr. Tuckerman's poems, collected and published in Boston in 1851, is *The Spirit of Poetry*, an elaborate essay in heroic verse of some seven hundred lines. It traces the objects of fancy and sentiment in life and nature with an observant eye. The miscellaneous poems are tributes to the outer world, passages of sentiment or memorials of historical events, expressing the more subtle spirit of the author's life of travel and study.

MARY.

What though the name is old and oft repeated,
  What though a thousand beings bear it now;
And true hearts oft the gentle word have greeted,—
  What though 'tis hallowed by a poet's vow?
We ever love the rose, and yet its blooming
  Is a familiar rapture to the eye,
And yon bright star we hail, although its looming
  Age after age has lit the northern sky.

As starry beams o'er troubled billows stealing,
  As garden odors to the desert blown,
In bosoms faint a gladsome hope revealing,
  Like patriot music or affection's tone—
Thus, thus for aye, the name of Mary spoken
  By lips or text, with magic-like control,
The course of present thought has quickly broken,
  And stirred the fountains of my inmost soul.

The sweetest tales of human weal and sorrow,
  The fairest trophies of the limner's fame,
To my fond fancy, Mary, seem to borrow
  Celestial halos from thy gentle name:
The Grecian artist gleaned from many faces,
  And in a perfect whole the parts combined,
So have I counted o'er dear woman's graces
  To form the Mary of my ardent mind.

And marvel not I thus call my ideal,
  We inly paint as we would have things be,
The fanciful springs ever from the real,
  As Aphrodite rose from out the sea;
Who smiled upon me kindly day by day,
  In a far land where I was sad and lone?
Whose presence now is my delight alway?
  Both angels must the same blessed title own.

What spirits round my weary way are flying,
  What fortunes on my future life await,
Like the mysterious hymns the winds are sighing,
  Are all unknown,—in trust I bide my fate;
But if one blessing I might crave from Heaven,
  'T would be that Mary should my being cheer,
Hang o'er me when the chord of life is riven,
  Be my dear household word, and my last accent here.

ROME.

Roma! Roma! Roma!
Non è più come era prima.

A terrace lifts above the People's square,
    Its colonnade;
About it lies the warm and crystal air,
    And fir-tree's shade.

Thence a wide scene attracts the patient gaze,
    Saint Peter's dome
Looms through the far horizon's purple haze,
    Religion's home!

Columns that peer between huge palace walls,
    A garden's bloom,
The mount where crumble Cæsar's ivied halls,
    The Castle-Tomb;

Egypt's red shaft and Travertine's brown hue,
    The moss-grown tiles,
Or the broad firmament of cloudless blue
    Our sight beguiles.

Once the awed warrior from yon streamlet's banks,
    Cast looks benign,
When pointing to his onward-moving ranks,
    The holy sign.

Fair women from these casements roses flung
    To strew his way,
Who Laura's graces so divinely sung
    They live to-day.

In those dim cloisters Palestine's worn bard
    His wreath laid by,
Yielding the triumph that his sorrows marred,
    Content to die.

From yonder court-yard Beatrice was led,
    Whose pictured face
Soft beauty unto sternest anguish wed
    In deathless grace.

Here stood Lorraine to watch on many an eve
    The sun go down;
There paused Corinne from Oswald to receive
    Her fallen crown.

By such a light would Raphael fondly seek
    Expression rare,
Or make the Fornarina's olive cheek
    Love's blushes wear.

A shattered bridge here juts its weedy curve
    O'er Tiber's bed,
And there a shape whose name thrills every nerve,
    Arrests the tread.

O'er convent gates the stately cypress rears
    Its verdant lines,
And fountains gaily throw their constant tears
    On broken shrines.

Fields where dank vapors steadily consume
    The life of man,
And lizards rustle through the stunted broom,—
    Tall arches span.

There the wan herdsman in the noontide sleeps,
    The gray kine doze,
And goats climb up to where on ruined heaps
    Acanthus grows.

From one imperial trophy turn with pain
    The Jews aside,
For on it emblems of their conquered fane
    Are still descried.

The mendicant, whose low plea fills thine ear
    At every pass,
Before an altar kings have decked, may hear
    The chanted mass.

On lofty ceilings vivid frescoes glow,
    Auroras beam;
The steeds of Neptune through the water go,
    Or Sybils dream.

As in the flickering torchlight shadows weaved
    Illusions wild,
Methought Apollo's bosom slightly heaved,
    And Juno smiled!

Aerial Mercuries in bronze upspring,
Dianas fly,
And marble Cupids to their Psyches cling,
Without a sigh.

In grottoes, see the hair of Venus creep
Round dripping stones,
Or thread the endless catacombs where sleep
Old martyrs' bones.

Upon this esplanade is basking now
A son of toil,
But not a thought rests on his swarthy brow
Of Time's vast spoil.

His massive limbs with noblest sculptures vie,
Devoid of care
Behold him on the sunny terrace lie,
And drink the air!

With gestures free and looks of eager life,
Tones deep and mild,
Intent he plies the finger's harmless strife
A gleesome child!

The shaggy Calabrese, who lingers near,
At Christmas comes to play
His reeds before Madonna every year,
Then hastes away.

Now mark the rustic pair who dance apart:
What gay surprise!
Her clipsome bodice holds the Roman heart
That lights her eyes:

His rapid steps are timed by native zeal;
The manly chest
Swells with such candid joy that we can feel
Each motion's zest.

What artless pleasure her calm smile betrays,
Whose glances keen
Follow the pastime as she lightly plays
The tambourine!

They know when chestnut groves repast will yield,
Where vineyards spread;
Before their saint at morn they trustful kneeled,
Why doubt or dread?

A bearded Capuchin his cowl throws back,
Demurely nigh;
A Saxon boy with nurse upon his track,
Bounds laughing by.

Still o'er the relics of the Past around
The Day-beams pour,
And winds awake the same continuous sound
They woke of yore.

Thus Nature takes to her embrace serene
What Age has clad,
And all who on her gentle bosom lean
She maketh glad.

TRUE ENTHUSIASM—FROM A COLLOQUIAL LECTURE ON NEW ENGLAND PHILOSOPHY.

Let us recognise the beauty and power of true enthusiasm; and whatever we may do to enlighten ourselves and others, guard against checking or chilling a single earnest sentiment. For what is the human mind, however enriched with acquisitions or strengthened by exercise, unaccompanied by an ardent and sensitive heart? Its light may illumine, but it cannot inspire. It may shed a cold and moonlight radiance upon the path of life, but it warms no flower into bloom; it sets free no ice-bound fountains. Dr. Johnson used to say, that an obstinate rationality prevented him from being a Papist. Does not the same cause prevent many of us from unburdening our hearts and breathing our devotions at the shrines of nature? There are influences which environ humanity too subtle for the dissecting knife of reason. In our better moments we are clearly conscious of their presence, and if there is any barrier to their blessed agency, it is a formalized intellect. Enthusiasm, too, is the very life of gifted spirits. Ponder the lives of the glorious in art or literature through all ages. What are they but records of toils and sacrifices supported by the earnest hearts of their votaries? Dante composed his immortal poem amid exile and suffering, prompted by the noble ambition of vindicating himself to posterity; and the sweetest angel of his paradise is the object of his early love. The best countenances the old painters have bequeathed to us are those of cherished objects intimately associated with their fame. The face of Raphael's mother blends with the angelic beauty of all his Madonnas. Titian's daughter and the wife of Corregio again and again meet in their works. Well does Foscolo call the fine arts *the children of Love*. The deep interest with which the Italians hail gifted men, inspires them to the mightiest efforts. National enthusiasm is the great nursery of genius. When Cellini's statue of Perseus was first exhibited on the Piazza at Florence, it was surrounded for days by an admiring throng, and hundreds of tributary sonnets were placed upon its pedestal. Petrarch was crowned with laurel at Rome for his poetical labors, and crowds of the unlettered may still be seen on the Mole at Naples, listening to a reader of Tasso. Reason is not the only interpreter of life. The fountain of action is in the feelings. Religion itself is but a state of the affections. I once met a beautiful peasant woman in the valley of the Arno, and asked the number of her children. "I have three here and two in paradise," she calmly replied, with a tone and manner of touching and grave simplicity. Her faith was of the heart. Constituted as human nature is, it is in the highest degree natural that rare powers should be excited by voluntary and spontaneous appreciation. Who would not feel urged to high achievement, if he knew that every beauty his canvas displayed, or every perfect note he breathed, or every true inspiration of his lyre, would find an instant response in a thousand breasts? Lord Brougham calls the word "impossible" the mother-tongue of little souls. What, I ask, can counteract self-distrust, and sustain the higher efforts of our nature, but enthusiasm? More of this element would call forth the genius, and gladden the life of New England. While the mere intellectual man speculates, and the mere man of acquisition cites authority, the man of feeling acts, realizes, puts forth his complete energies. His earnest and strong heart will not let his mind rest; he is urged by an inward impulse to embody his thought; he must have sympathy, he must have results. And nature yields to the magician, acknowledging him as her child. The noble statue comes forth from the marble, the speaking figure stands out from the canvas, the electric chain is struck in the bosoms of his fellows. They receive his ideas, respond to his appeal, and reciprocate his love.

THE HOME OF THE POET ROGERS—FROM A MONTH IN ENGLAND.

The aquatic birds in St. James's Park, with their variegated plumage, may well detain loiterers of maturer years than the chuckling infants who feed them with crumbs, oblivious of the policeman's eye, and the nurse's expostulations; to see an American wild duck swim to the edge of the lake, and open its glossy bill with the familiar airs of a pet canary, is doubtless a most agreeable surprise; nor can an artistic eye fail to note the diverse and picturesque forms of the many noble trees, that even when leafless, yield a rural charm to this glorious promenade (the elms are praised by Evelyn); but these woodland amenities, if they cause one often to linger on his way to the Duke of Sunderland's and Buckingham palace; and if the thought, that it was here, while taking his usual daily walk, that Charles received the first intimation of the Popish plot, lure him into an historical reverie, neither will long withdraw the attention of the literary enthusiast from the bit of green sward before the window of Rogers, which, every spring morning, until the venerable poet's health sent him into suburban exile, was covered with sparrows expectant of their banquet from his aged yet kindly hand. The view of the park from this drawing-room bow-window instantly disenchants the sight of all town associations. The room where this vista of nature in her genuine English aspect opens, is the same so memorable for the breakfasts, for many years, enjoyed by the hospitable bard and his fortunate guests. An air of sadness pervaded the apartment in the absence of him, whose taste and urbanity were yet apparent in every object around. The wintry sun threw a gleam mellow as the light of the fond reminiscence he so gracefully sung, upon the Turkey carpet, and veined mahogany. It fell, as if in pensive greeting, on the famous Titian, lit up the cool tints of Watteau, and made the bust found in the sea near Pozzuoli wear a creamy hue. When the old housekeeper left the room, and I glanced from the priceless canvas or classic urn, to the twinkling turf, all warmed by the casual sunshine, the sensation of comfort never so completely realized as in a genuine London breakfast-room, was touched to finer issues by the atmosphere of beauty and the memory of genius. The groups of poets, artists, and wits, whose commune had filled this room with the electric glow of intellectual life, with gems of art, glimpses of nature, and the charm of intelligent hospitality, to evoke all that was most gifted and cordial, reassembled once more. I could not but appreciate the suggestive character of every ornament. There was a Murillo to inspire the Spanish traveller with half-forgotten anecdotes, a fine Reynolds to whisper of the literary dinner where Garrick and Burke discussed the theatre and the senate; Milton's agreement for the sale of "Paradise Lost," emphatic symbol of the uncertainty of fame; a sketch of Stonehenge by Turner, provocative of endless discussion to artist and antiquary; bronzes, medals, and choice volumes, whose very names would inspire an affluent talker in this most charming imaginable nook, for a morning colloquy and a social breakfast. I noticed in a glass vase over the fireplace, numerous sprigs of orange blossoms in every grade of decay, some crumbling to dust, and others but partially faded. These, it appeared, were all plucked from bridal wreaths, the gift of their fair wearers, on the wedding-day, to the good old poet-friend; and he, in his bacheloric fantasy, thus preserved the withered trophies. They spoke at once of sentiment and of solitude.

CHARLES T. BROOKS.

Charles T. Brooks was born at Salem, Mass., June 20, 1813. At Harvard, which he entered in 1828, a sensitive and studious youth, he obtained his introduction, through Dr. Follen, to the world of German poetry and prose, with which his literary labors have been since so prominently identified. Schiller's song of Mary Stuart on a temporary release from captivity, was one of the earliest, as it has been one of the latest poems which he has attempted.

The subject of his valedictory at Cambridge was, "The Love of Truth, a Practical Principle." Three years afterwards, on completing his studies at the Theological school, he read a dissertation on "the old Syriac version of the New Testament," and shortly after, on taking his second degree at the University, delivered an oration on "Decision of character, as demanded in our day and country." He began his career as a preacher at Nahant, in the summer of 1835. After officiating in different parts of New England, chiefly in Bangor, Augusta, and Windsor, Vt., he was settled in Newport, Rhode Island, in January, 1837, where he has since continued in charge of the congregation worshipping in the church in which Channing held the dedication service in 1836. Channing also preached the sermon at his ordination in June, 1837, the one published in his works, as afterwards repeated to Mr. Dwight at Northampton. In October of the same year, Mr. Brooks was married to Harriet, second daughter of the late Benjamin Hazard, lawyer and legislator of Rhode Island.

Charles T. Brooks

His course as an author began in the year 1838 with a translation of Schiller's *William Tell*, which was published anonymously at Providence. The year or two following, he translated from the same author, the dramas of *Mary Stuart* and the *Maid of Orleans*, which yet (1855) remain unpublished. In 1840 he translated the *Titan* of Jean Paul Richter, a work of great labor and rare delicacy, which is also unpublished. In 1842 a volume of his miscellaneous specimens of German song was published as one of Mr. Ripley's* series of Foreign Literature, by

* Mr. George Ripley, to whom scholars are under obligations for this series of "Specimens of Foreign Standard Literature," published in fifteen volumes, between the years 1838 and 1845, is the present accomplished literary editor and critic of the New York Tribune, a work to which he brings rare tact and philosophical acumen. He was the chief manager of the Brook Farm Association, with which his friend and associate in the Tribune, Mr. Charles A. Dana, a good scholar, a forcible writer and effective speaker, was also connected. Mr. Ripley's services to literature are important in numerous journals. In 1840 he published in Boston an essay "On the Latest Form of Infidelity."

Munroe & Co., of Boston. In 1845 he published an article on *Poetry* in the Christian Examiner, The same year he delivered the Phi Beta Kappa poem at Cambridge. In 1847, Munroe & Co. published his translation of Schiller's *Homage of the Arts, with Miscellaneous Pieces from Ruckert, Freiligrath, and other German Poets.* In this year, too, he recited a poem entitled *Aquidneck*, upon the hundredth anniversary of the Redwood Library at Newport. This was published next year by Burnet at Providence, in a little volume containing several other commemorative pieces. In 1851, Mr. Brooks published at Newport a pamphlet, *The Controversy touching the Old Stone Mill, in the town of Newport, Rhode Island, with Remarks Introductory and Conclusive:* a pleasant dissection of the subject, calculated to set entirely at rest any pretensions of the Northman to an antiquarian property in that curious though sufficiently simple structure.

In June, 1853, Ticknor & Co. published his *German Lyrics*, containing specimens of Anastasius Grun, and others of the living poets of Germany, selected from a mass of translations in part previously printed in the Literary World, and in part in manuscript. He has since published a little collection named *Songs of Field and Flood*, printed by John Wilson at Boston.

In 1853, Mr. Brooks made a voyage to India for his health, the incidents and sensations of which he has embodied in a narrative entitled, *Eight Months on the Ocean, and Eight Weeks in India*, which is still in MS. Among other unpublished writings by Mr. Brooks, is a choice translation of the humorous poem of the German University students, *The Life, Opinions, Actions, and Fate of Hieronimus Jobs the Candidate*, of which he has printed several chapters in the Literary World,* and which has been further made familiar to the public, by the exhibition in Mr. Boker's Gallery of German Painting in New York, of the exquisite paintings by Hasenclever, of scenes from its pages.

Mr. Brooks is also, besides his quaint and felicitous translations from the minor German poets, the author of numerous occasional verses—a series of Festival, New Year, and Anniversary addresses, all ready and genial, with a frequent infusion of a humorous spirit.

NEWPORT—FROM AQUIDNECK.

Hail, island-home of Peace and Liberty!
Hail, breezy cliff, grey rock, majestic sea!
Here man should walk with heavenward lifted eye,
Free as the winds, and open as the sky!
O thou who here hast had thy childhood's home,
And ye who one brief hour of summer roam
These winding shores to breathe the bracing breeze,
And feel the freedom of the skies and seas,
Think what exalted, sainted minds once found
The sod, the sand ye tread on, holy ground!
Think how an Allston's soul-enkindled eye
Drank in the glories of our sunset-sky!
Think how a Berkeley's genius haunts the air,
And makes our crags and waters doubly fair!
Think how a Channing, "musing by the sea,"
Burned with the quenchless love of liberty!
What work God witnessed, and that lonely shore,
Wrought in him 'midst the elemental roar!
How did that spot his youthful heart inform,
Dear in the sunshine,—dearer in the storm.
"The Father reigneth, let the Earth rejoice
And tremble!"—there he lifted up his voice
In praise amid the tempest—softened there
By nature's beauty rose the lowly prayer.
There as, in reverential sympathy,
He watched the heavings of the giant sea,
Stirred by the Power that ruled that glorious din,
Woke the dread consciousness of power within!

They are gone hence—the large and lofty souls;
And still the rock abides—the ocean rolls;
And still where Reason rears its beacon-rock,
The Powers of Darkness dash with angry shock.
In many an anxious vigil, pondering o'er
Man's destiny on this our western shore,
Genius of Berkeley! to thy morning-height
We lift the piercing prayer—"What of the night?"
And this thy Muse, responsive, seems to say:
"*Not yet* is closed the Drama or the Day:
Act well thy part, how small soe'er it be,
Look not to Heaven alone—Heaven looks to thee!"
Spirit of Channing! to thy calm abode,
We, doubtful plodders of this lowly road,
Call: "From thy watch-tower say, for thou canst see,
How fares the wavering strife of liberty?"
And the still air replies, and the green sod,
By thee beneath these shades, in musing, trod,—
And these then lonely wal's, where oft was caught
The electric spark of high, heroic thought,—
And yonder page that keeps for ever bright,
Of that great thought the burning shining light,—
All these, with voice of power—of God,—to-day
Come to the soul, and calmly, strongly say:
"Be faithful unto death in Freedom's strife,
And on thy head shall rest the crown of life."

LINES ON HEARING MENDELSSOHN'S MIDSUMMER NIGHT'S DREAM PERFORMED BY THE GERMANIANS AT NEWPORT.

It haunts me still—I hear, I see, once more
That moonlight dance of fairies on the shore.
I hear the skipping of those airy feet;
I see the mazy twinkling, light and fleet.
The sly sharp banter of the violin
Wakes in the elfin folk a merry din;
And now it dies away, and all is still;
The silver moon-beam sleeps upon the hill;
The flute's sweet wail, a heavenly music, floats,
And like bright dew-drops fall the oboe's notes.
And hark; again that light and graceful beat
Steals on the ear, of trooping, tiny feet,—
While, heard by fits across the watery floor,
The muffled surf-drum booms from some far shore
And now the fairy world is lost once more
In the grand swell of ocean's organ-roar,—
And all is still again;—again the dance
Of sparkling feet reflects the moon-beam's glance;
Puck plays his antics in the o'erhanging trees,—
Music like Ariel's floats on every breeze.—
Thus is the Midsummer Night's Dream to me,
Pictured by music and by memory,
A long midsummer day's reality.

THE SABBATH—FROM THE GERMAN OF KRUMMACHER.

The Sabbath is here!
Like a dove out of heaven descending,
Toil and turmoil suspending,
Comes in the glad morn!
It smiles on the highway,
And down the green by-way,
'Mong fields of ripe corn.

* Nos. 245, 203.

The Sabbath is here!
Behold! the full sheaves own the blessing,
So plainly confessing
A Father's mild care.
In Sabbath-noon stillness,
The crops in their fulness
How graceful and fair!

The Sabbath is here!
No clank of the plough-chain we hear, now,—
No lash, far or near, now,—
No creaking of wheels.
With million low voices
The harvest rejoices
All over the fields.

The Sabbath is here!
The seed we in faith and hope planted;
God's blessing was granted;
It sprang to the light,
We gaze now, and listen
Where fields wave and glisten,
With grateful delight.

The Sabbath is here!
Give praise to the Father, whose blessing
The fields are confessing!
Soon the reapers will come,
With rustling and ringing
Of sickles, and bringing
The yellow sheaves home.

The Sabbath is here!
The seed we in fond hope are sowing
Will one day rise, glowing
In the smile of God's love.
In dust though we leave it,
We trust to receive it
In glory above!

SYLVESTER JUDD,

The author of *Margaret*, and a clergyman of the Unitarian Church, of a marked individuality of opinion and an earnest spiritual and moral life, was born at Westhampton, Hampshire county, Mass., July 23, 1813. His grandfather, Sylvester Judd, a man of character and influence in his day, was one of the first settlers of the place and the son of the Rev. Jonathan Judd, the first clergyman of Southampton, and for sixty years pastor of that flock. The father of our author, also Sylvester Judd, though engaged in trade in the country at Westhampton, applied himself so vigorously to study that he attained a considerable knowledge of Greek, Latin, and French; worked his way through a course of the higher mathematics, and became generally conversant with polite literature. He married a daughter of Aaron Hall, of Norwich, a man of good repute in the Revolutionary era.

The young Sylvester Judd, the third of the name in the direct line, passed his early years at Westhampton, under the usual earnest influences of the old New England Puritan homes. At the age of nine years, his father having become unfortunate in business, and his habits of study having got the better of his pursuit of trade, he removed to Northampton, to become proprietor and editor of the Hampshire Gazette, with which a younger brother, then recently deceased, had been connected. At this spot the boyhood and youth of Sylvester were passed; a period of religious influence which was marked by his conversion during a revival. Then came a struggle between devotion to trade, to which the slender fortunes of his father invited him, and a natural tendency to an educated life. It ended in his entry at Yale College, where he received his degree in 1836. The picture of his college life, as published by Miss Arethusa Hall, shows an earnest, devotional spirit. After leaving Yale, he took charge of a private school at Templeton, Mass. "There, for the first time," says his biographer, "he began to have intercourse with that denomination of Christians termed Unitarians, and came to understand more fully their distinguishing views. Previously, he had been very little acquainted with Unitarian works or Unitarian preaching; but he now perceived that the deductions of his own unbiassed mind, and the conclusions towards which he found it verging, were much in harmony with those received by this body of Christians." As his old opinions changed, a social struggle occurred with his family, friends, and supporters. He felt that he was out of place with these former associations, and declined the offer of a professorship in Miami College, Ohio. "Feeling and thinking thus," he writes to his brother, "you see I could not become connected with an Old School Presbyterian College." A record of his conflict is preserved in a manuscript which he prepared for the private use of his father's family, entitled "Cardiagraphy," an exposition of his theological difficulties and conclusions, which is published in his biography. It was now evident to his family that they must resign all hope of the Calvinistic minister. The issue had been made in all conscientiousness, and Mr. Judd choosing another path, entered the Divinity School at Harvard in 1837. At the completion of his course, in 1840, he became engaged to supply the pulpit of the Unitarian church in Augusta, Maine, and was

Sylvester Judd

soon formally installed as pastor. He married the next year a daughter of the Hon. Revel Williams, of Augusta.

In 1843 he seems first to have turned his attention to authorship. His *Margaret, a Tale of the Real and Ideal; including Sketches of a Place not before described, called Mons Christi*, was commenced at that time and reached the public in 1845. A second revised and improved edition appeared in two volumes in 1851.

As the best account of the scope of this work, we may cite the remarks of its author on the subject from a letter to a brother clergyman:—

"The book designs to promote the cause of liberal Christianity, or, in other words, of a pure Christianity: it would give body and soul to the divine elements of the gospel. It aims to subject bigotry, cant, pharisaism, and all intolerance. Its basis is Christ: him it would restore to the church, him it would develop in the soul, him it would enthrone in the world. It designs also, in judicious and healthful ways, to aid the cause of peace, temperance, and universal freedom. In its retrospective aspect, it seeks to preserve some reminiscences of the age of our immediate fathers, thereby describing a period of which we have no enduring monuments, and one the traces of which are fast evanescing. The book makes a large account of nature, the birds and flowers, for the sake of giving greater individuality to, and bringing into stronger relief, that which the religious mind passes over too loosely and vaguely. It is a New England book, and is designed to embody the features and improve the character of our own favored region.

"But more particularly, let me say, the book seems fitted partially to fill up a gap long left open in Unitarian literature,—that of imaginative writings. The Orthodox enjoy the works of Bunyan, Hannah More, Charlotte Elizabeth, the Abbotts, &c., &c. But what have we in their place? The original design of the book was almost solely to occupy this niche; although, I fancy, you may think it has somewhat passed these limits. It seems to me, that this book is fitted for a pretty general Unitarian circulation; that it might be of some use in the hands of the clergy, in our families, Sunday-school libraries, &c. My own personal education in, and acquaintance with, 'Orthodoxy,' as well as my idea of the prevalent errors of the age, lead me to think such a book is needed."

The above will sufficiently explain its theological bearings. As a novel or romance, in the ordinary sense, it is crudely expressed and inartistic; as a vigorous sketch of old New England life and character, of fresh, vivid portraiture and detail, and particularly in its descriptive passages of nature, for the minute study of which in plants, birds, and other accessories, the author had an especial fondness, it is a production of marked merit. Of the several criticisms passed upon it, the most complimentary must be considered the admirable series of drawings made from its pages by the artist Mr. F. O. C. Darley, whose pencil has brought out with extraordinary beauty and effect the varieties of character of the book, and its occasional dramatic and picturesque scenes. These sketches are now being prepared for publication, and when issued, by their delicacy and vigor of expression, will form ready interpreters no less of the genius of the artist than the author to the public.

In 1850 Mr. Judd published *Philo, an Evangeliad*, a didactic poem in blank verse. It was rude and imperfect in execution. Again resorting to the author for an elucidation of its design, we find the following expression in a characteristic letter to a friend:—

TO THE REV. E. E. H.

Augusta, Dec. 21, 1849.

My dear Sir, —Will you accept a copy of "Philo," and a brief claviary?

First, the book is an "attempt."

Second, it is an epical or heroic attempt.

Third, it would see if in liberal and rational Christianity, and there is no other, and that is Unitarianism, are epic and heroic elements.

Fourth, it remembers that Calvinism has its "Course of Time;" and it asks if Unitarianism, that is, the innermost of reason and divinity, will have any thing; or rather, approaching, humbly, of course, the altar of Great Thought and Feeling, it would like to know if it would be agreeable to that altar to receive a little gift, a turtle-dove and a small pigeon, of Unitarian faith and hope.

Fifth, and correlatively, it asks if, in this very sensible and sound age of ours, imagination must needs be inactive, and awed by philosophy, utility, steam.

Sixth, and more especially, if any of the foregoing points are admitted, the book seeks through the medium of poetry to interpret prophecy. It is conceived that prophecy, the Apocalypse for example, was once poetry; and moreover that we shall fail to understand prophecy until it is recast in its original form.

This observation applies particularly to that most interesting, yet most enigmatical matter, the second coming of Christ, &c., &c.

What may be the fortune of "Philo," I am neither prophet nor poet enough to tell.

I am not a beggar of applause, as I would not be the pensioner of dulness.

With sincere regards, I am yours, &c.

SYLVESTER JUDD.

In the same year with the publication of Philo appeared *Richard Edney and the Governor's Family, a Rus-Urban Tale, simple and popular, yet cultured and noble, of Morals, Sentiment, and Life, practically treated and pleasantly illustrated; containing also Hints on Being Good and Doing Good.* It was intended by the author as a modern companion to Margaret, introducing the career of a young man among the rural and town incidents of New England life. The incidents at a sawmill, and other descriptions, point out the local studies of the author in Maine. Like the author's previous books, as a purely literary production, it was "caviare to the general;" as an expression of the writer's peculiar mood and opinions in a certain unfettered, individual essay style, its perusal will well reward curiosity. A description of a snow-storm was one of the felicities of Margaret; Richard Edney opens with another in the same vivid, minutely truthful manner.

In addition to these published writings of Mr. Judd, he completed a dramatic production in five acts—*The White Hills, an American Tragedy*, which remains in manuscript. An analysis of it, with several passages, is given in the biography of the author, where it is stated to be chiefly moral in its aim—"its object being to mirror the consequences of a man's devoting himself to an all-absorbing love of gain,—to the supreme worship of Mammon," the idea being suggested by the general rage for California gold, at the time of the composition of the play prevalent in the community. The location of the plot in the White Mountains was an improvement of the same Indian legend mentioned in Sullivan's History of Maine, upon which Mr. Hawthorne founded his tale of the Great Carbuncle.

Mr. Judd, in addition to his services in the pulpit, found frequent opportunities as a lyceum lecturer on topics growing out of the religious ideas which were the mainspring of his life. He took a prominent part in the social reforms of the day, opposed war, slavery, and advocated the cause of temperance. He was fond of children and of country life; one of the favorite recreations of his ministry at Augusta being an annual rural festival, in June, with his young parishioners. He felt the beauty of the old observance of Christmas, and was accustomed on the eve of that day to open his church, decorated for the occasion with the time-honored evergreens. His kindly disposition and genial activity, his study of language and habits of composition, have been described by a fond and appreciative pen in the admirably prepared volume, Life and Character of the Rev. Sylvester Judd, published in 1854, and "tenderly and most lovingly" dedicated by its author, Arethusa Hall, "to the three little children whose father was translated from their home before they were old enough to know and comprehend him."

The Rev. Sylvester Judd died after a short illness at his home in Augusta, Jan. 20, 1853.

A posthumous work from his pen—*The Church in a Series of Discourses*—was published in 1854.

A NEW ENGLAND SNOW-STORM AND A HOME SCENE—FROM MARGARET.

An event common in New England is at its height. It is snowing, and has been for a whole day and night, with a strong north-east wind. Let us take a moment when the storm intermits, and look in at Margaret's and see how they do. But we cannot approach the place by any of the ordinary methods of travel; the roads, lanes, and by-paths are blocked up: no horse or ox could make his way through those deep drifts, immense mounds and broad plateaus of snow. If we are disposed to adopt the means of conveyance formerly so much in vogue, whether snow-shoes or magic, we may possibly get there. The house or hut is half sunk in a snow bank; the waters of the Pond are covered with a solid enamel as of ivory; the oxen and the cow in the barn-yard, look like great horned sheep in their fleeces of snow. All is silence, and lifelessness, and if you please to say, desolation. Hens there are none, nor turkeys, nor ducks, nor birds, nor Bull, nor Margaret. If you see any signs of a human being, it is the dark form of Hash, mounted on snow-shoes, going from the house to the barn. Yet there are the green hemlocks and pines, and firs, green as in summer, some growing along the flank of the hill that runs north from the Indian's Head, looking like the real snow-balls, blossoming in mid-winter, and nodding with large white flowers. But there is one token of life, the smoke coming from the low grey chimney, which, if you regard it as one, resembles a large, elongated, transparent balloon; or if you look at it by piece-meal, it is a beautiful current of bluish-white vapor, flowing upward unendingly; and prettily is it striped and particolored as it passes successively the green trees, the bare rocks, and white crown of the hill behind, nor does its interest cease even when it disappears among the clouds. Some would dwell a good while on that smoke, and see in it manifold out-shows and denotements of spiritualities; others would say, the house is buried so deep, it must come up from the hot mischief-hatching heart of the earth; others still would fancy the whole Pond lay in its winding-sheet, and that if they looked in, they would behold the dead faces of their friends. Our own sentiment is, that that smoke comes from a great fire in the great fire-place, and that if we should go into the house, we should find the family as usual there; a fact which, as the storm begins to renew itself, we shall do well to take the opportunity to verify.

Flourishing in the centre of these high-rising and broad-spreading snows, unmoved amid the fiercest onsets of the storm, comfortable in the extremity of winter, the family are all gathered in the kitchen, and occupied as may be. In the cavernous fire-place burns a great fire, composed of a huge green back-log, a large green fore-stick, and a high cob-work of crooked and knotty refuse-wood, ivy, hornbeam, and beech. Through this the yellow flame leaps and forks, and the bluish-grey smoke flows up the ample sluice-way of the chimney. From the ends of the wood the sap fries and drips on the sizzling coals below, and flies off in angry steam. Under the forestick great red coals roll out, sparkle a semibrief, lose their grosser substance, indicate a more ethereal essence in prototypal forms of white, down-like cinders, and then fall away into brown ashes. To a stranger the room has a sombre aspect, rather heightened than relieved by the light of the fire burning so brightly at mid-day. The only connexion with the external air is by the south window-shutter being left entirely open, forming an aperture through the logs of about two feet square; yet when the outer light is so obscured by a storm, the bright fire within must anywhere be pleasant. In one corner of the room sits Pluck, in a red flannel shirt and leather apron, at work on his kit mending a shoe; with long and patient vibration and equipoise he draws the threads, and interludes the strokes with snatches of songs, banter, and laughter. The apartment seems converted into a workshop; for next the shoemaker stands the shingle-maker, Hash, who with froe in one hand and mallet in the other, by dint of smart percussion, is endeavoring to rive a three-cornered billet of hemlock on a block. In the centre of the room sits Brown Moll, with still bristling and grizzly hair, pipe in her mouth, in a yellow woollen long-short and black petticoat, winding a ball of yarn from a windle. Nearer the fire are Chilion and Margaret, the latter also dressed in woollen, with the Orbis Pictus, or world displayed, a book of Latin and English, adorned with cuts, which the Master lent her; the former with his violin, endeavoring to describe the notes in Dr. Byles's Collection of Sacred Music, also a loan of the Master's, and at intervals trailing on the lead of his father in some popular air. We shall also see that one of Chilion's feet is raised on a stool, bandaged, and apparently disabled. Bull, the dog, lies rounded on the hearth, his nose between his paws, fast asleep. Dick, the grey squirrel, sits swinging listlessly in his wire wheel, like a duck on a wave. Robin, the bird, in its cage, perched on its roost, shrugs and folds itself into its feathers as if it were night. Over the fire-place, on the rough stones that compose the chimney, which day and night through all the long winter are ever warm, where Chilion has fixed some shelves, are Margaret's flowers; a blood-root in the marble pot Rufus Palmer gave her, and in wooden moss-covered boxes, pinks, violets, and buttercups, green and flowering. Here also, as a sort of mantel-tree ornament, sits the marble kitten which Rufus made under a cedar twig. At one end of the crane in the vacant side of the fire-place hang rings of pumpkin rinds drying for beer. On the walls are suspended strings of dried apples, bunches of yarn, and the customary fixtures of coats, hats, knapsacks, &c. On the sleepers above is a chain-work of cobwebs, loaded and knapped with dust, quivering and gleaming in the wind that courses with little or no obstruction through all parts of the house. Near Hash stands the draw-horse, on which he smoothes and squares his shingles; underneath it and about lies a pile of fresh, sweet-scented, white shavings and splinters. Through the yawns of the back door, and sundry rents in the logs of the house, filter in unweariedly fine particles of snow, and thus along the sides of the room rise little cone-shaped, marble-like pilasters. Between Hash and his father, elevated on blocks, is the cider barrel. These are some of the appendages, inmates, and circumstances of the room. Within doors is a mixed noise of lapstone, mallets, swifts, fiddle, fire; without is the rushing of the storm.

* * * * * * * * * *

"You *shall* fetch some wood, Meg, or I'll warm your back with a shingle," said her mother, flinging out a threat which she had no intention of executing. "Hash is good for something, that he is."

* * * * * * * * * *

Hash, spurred on by this double shot, plied his mallet the harder, and declared with an oath that *he* would not get the wood, that they might freeze first; adding that he hauled and cut it, and that was his part.

Chilion whispered his sister, and she went out for the purpose in question. It was not excessively cold, since the weather moderated as the storm increased, and she might have taken some interest in that tempestuous outer world. Her hens, turkeys, and ducks, who were all packed together, the former on their roost under the shed, the latter in one corner, also required feeding; and she went in and got boiled potatoes, which they seemed glad to make a meal of. The wind blazed and racketed through the narrow space between the house and the hill. Above, the flakes shaded and mottled the sky, and fell twirling, pitching, skimble-scamble, and anon, slowly and more regularly, as in a minuet; and as they came nearer the ground, they were caught up by the current, and borne in a horizontal line, like long, quick spun, silver threads, afar over the white fields. There was but little snow in the shed, although entirely open on the south side; the storm seeming to devote itself to building up a drift in front. This drift had now reached a height of seven or eight feet. It sloped up like the roof of a pyramid, and on the top was an appendage like a horn, or a plume, or a marble jet d'eau, or a frozen flame of fire; and the elements in all their violence, the eddies that veered about the corner of the house, the occasional side-blasts, still dallied, and stopped to mould it, and finish it; and it became thinner, and more tapering, and spiral; each singular flake adjusting itself to the very tip, with instinctive nicety; till at last it broke off by its own weight—then a new one went on to be formed.

* * * * * * * * * *

That day and all that night the snow continued to fall, and the wind raged. When Margaret went to her loft, she found her bed covered with a pile of snow that had trickled through the roof. She shook the coverlid, undressed, laid herself on her thistle-down pallet—such a one had she been able to collect and make—to her sleep. The wind surged, swelled, puffed, hissed, whistled, shrieked, thundered, sighed, howled, by turns. The house jarred and creaked; her bed rocked under her; loose boards on the roof clappered and rattled; the snow pelted her window-shutter. In such a din and tustle of the elements lay the child. She had no sister to nestle with her, and snug her up; no gentle mother to fold the sheets about her neck, and tuck in the bed; no watchful father to come with a light, and see that she slept safe. Alone and in darkness she climbed into her chamber, alone and in darkness she wrapt herself in the bed. In the fearfulness of that night she sung or said to herself some words of the Master's, which he, however, must have given her for a different purpose—for of needs must a stark child's nature in such a crisis appeal to something above and superior to itself, and she had taken a floating impression that the Higher Agencies, whatever they might be, existed in Latin:—

O sanctissima, O purissima,
Dulcis Virgo Maria,
Mater amata, intemerata!
Ora, ora pro nobis!

As she slept amid the passion of the storm, softly did the snow from the roof distil upon her feet, and sweetly did dreams from heaven descend into her soul.

HENRY B. HIRST.

Mr. Hirst is a native of Philadelphia, where he was born August 23, 1813. In 1830 he commenced the study of the law, but was not admitted to practice, owing to interruptions in his plans, until 1843.

Mr. Hirst's poetical career was also commenced at a comparatively late period, his first published poems having appeared in Graham's Magazine, when he was about thirty. In 1845 he published at Boston *The Coming of the Mammoth; the Funeral of Time, and other Poems.* The chief production of the volume describes the terror and desolation caused by a herd of Mammoth, all of whom are destroyed by lightning, with the exception of one survivor, who, pursued by warriors, takes his course across the Mississippi, the prairies, traverses the rocky mountains, and plunges unscathed into the Pacific. The remaining poems display vigor and feeling, and include a number of well written sonnets.

Mr. Hirst's next work, *Endymion, a Tale of Greece,* in four cantos, appeared in 1848. It is an eloquent classic story, varied from the old Greek legend, and was written, the author tells us, before he had perused the poem of Keats.

In 1849 he published *The Penance of Roland, a Romance of the Peine Forte et Dure, and other Poems.* The story of the romance is that of a knight, who, having slain his wife in a fit of jealousy, is arrested, and refusing to plead, is subjected to the ingenious old penalty of pressure by weight. He persists in his determination, that his estates, which would otherwise be escheated to the crown, may pass to his heir. In his agony he is visited by his nephew, who confesses to have slandered the murdered lady. The knight's last moments are cheered by a vision of his wife, and he dies repentant and happy. This striking narrative is wrought into a poem of much spirit and beauty. The volume also contains a ballad, *Florence*, an interesting story, poetically narrated. The remaining poems are descriptive and reflective, and are eloquent in tone, with occasional traces of imitation.

THE ROBIN.

The woods are almost bare; the mossy trees
Moan as their mottled leaves are hurried by,
Like sand before the Simoom, over the leas,
Yellowing in Autumn's eye:

And very cold the bleak November wind
Shrills from the black Nor'-West, as fitfully blow
The gusts, like fancies through a maniac mind,
Eddying to and fro.

Borne, like those leaves, with piercing cries, on high
The Robins come, their wild, autumnal wail,
From where they pass, dotting the angry sky,
Sounding above the gale.

Down, scattered by the blast, along the glen,
Over the browning plains, the flocks alight,
Crowding the gum in highland or in fen,
Tired with their southward flight.

Away, away, flocking they pass, with snow
And hail and sleet behind them, where the South
Shakes its green locks, and delicate odors flow
As from some fairy mouth.

Silently pass the wintry hours: no song,
No note, save a shrill querulous cry
When the boy sportsman, cat-like, creeps along
The fence, and then—then fly.

Companioned by the cautious lark, from field
To field they journey, till the winter wanes,
When to some wondrous instinct each one yields,
And seeks our northern plains.

March and its storms: no matter how the gale
May whistle round them, on, through snow, and sleet,
And driving hail, they pass, nor ever quail,
With tireless wings and feet.

Perched here and there on some tall tree—as breaks
The misty dawn, loud, clarionet-like, rings
Their matin hymn, while Nature also wakes
From her long sleep, and sings.

Gradually the flocks grow less, for, two by two,
The Robins pass away,—each with his mate;
And from the orchard, moist with April dew,
We hear their pretty prate;

And from the apple's snowy blossoms come
Gushes of song, while round and round them crowd
The busy, buzzing bees, and, over them, hum
The humming-birds aloud.

The sparrow from the fence; the oriole
From the now budding sycamore; the wren
From the old hat; the blue bird from his hole
Hard by the haunts of men;

The red-start from the wood-side; from the meadow,
The black-cheek, and the martin in the air;
The mournful wood-thrush from the forest shadow
With all of fair and rare

Among those blossoms of the atmosphere,—
The birds,—our only Sylphids,—with one voice,
From mountain side and meadow, far and near,
Like them at spring rejoice.

May, and in happy pairs the Robins sit
Hatching their young,—the female glancing down
From her brown nest. No one will trouble it,
Lest heaven itself should frown

On the rude act, for from the smouldering embers
On memory's hearth flashes the fire of thought,
And each one by its flickering light remembers
How flocks of Robins brought,

In the old time, leaves, and sang, the while they covered
The innocent babes forsaken. So they rear
Their fledglings undisturbed. Often has hovered
While I have stood anear

A Robin's nest, o'er me that simple story,
Gently and dove-like, and I passed away
Proudly, and feeling it as much a glory
As 'twas in Cæsar's day

To win a triumph, to have left that nest
Untouched; and many and many a schoolboy time,
When my sure gun was to my shoulder prest,
The thought of that old rhyme

Came o'er me, and I let the Robin go.
—At last the young are out, and to the woods
All have departed: Summer's sultry glow
Finds them beside the floods.

Then Autumn comes, and fearful of its rage
They flit again. So runs the Robin's life;
Spring, Summer, Autumn, Winter sees its page
Unstained with care or strife.

J. L. H. McCRACKEN

WAS the son of a New York merchant, and pursued his father's business. He was engaged in the trade with western Africa, and it was on a business visit to Sierra Leone that his death occurred from a fever of the climate, March 25, 1853. It was about his fortieth year. Mr. McCracken bore a distinguished part in New York society by his fortune, his amateur pursuit of literature, and his fine conversational powers. He wrote for the magazines and journals—in particular for the Knickerbocker, under the editorship of Hoffman, and Mr. Benjamin's "American Monthly" where one of his papers was entitled *The Education of the Blood*. A very clever sketch, *The Art of Making Poetry by an Emeritus Professor*, appeared in the second number of the Knickerbocker. He wrote a few trifles for Yankee Doodle. In 1849, he published in the Democratic Review a comedy in five acts, of New York life, entitled *Earning a Living*. He had also a hand in a Democratic free-trade paper, which had a short career.

THE ART OF MAKING POETRY.

I'll rhyme you so eight years together, dinners, suppers, and sleeping hours excepted—it is the right butter women rate to market.—*As You Like It.*

Cardinal Richelieu is reported to have said once that he would make so many dukes that it should be a shame to be one, and a shame not to be one. It appears, however, that he changed his mind afterwards, inasmuch as, down to St. Simon's time, there were only twelve or thirteen dukes in France, besides the blood-royal. At present they are more plenty, though it is even yet some distinction to be a duke, out of Italy; and in Poland there is an express law against the title being borne by any man who has not a clear income of three hundred dollars a year to support its dignity. In Bavaria, you may be made a baron for 7000 rix-dollars (or $5250)—or a count for 30,000 rix-dollars, but in this last case you must not follow any trade or profession; bankers, accordingly, content themselves with baronies, usually, like sensible men, preferring substance to sound; as, in fact, when it is perfectly well known you are able to buy a dozen counts and their titles, the world gives you credit as for the possession—perhaps more. But what Cardinal Richelieu threatened with regard to dukedoms has, in fact, been effected by the progress of the world with regard to another title as honorable, perhaps, as that of duke, though few of its possessors could retain it if the Polish regulation mentioned above were to be applied to it and enforced. I mean the title of poet. To be a poet, or, rather—for there is still some reverence left for that name—to be a versifier, is in these days a shame, and not to be one is a shame. That is, it is a shame for any man to take airs or pique himself on a talent now so common, so much reduced to rule and grown absolutely mechanical, and to be learned like arithmetic: and, on the other hand, for these same reasons, it is a shame not in some degree to possess it, or have it for occasions at command. It is convenient sometimes to turn some trifle from a foreign language, to hit off a scrap for a corner of a newspaper, to write a squib or an epigram, or play a game at crambo, and for all these emergencies the practised versifier is prepared. He has, very likely, the frames of a few verses always ready in his mind, constructed for the purpose, into which he can put any given idea at a moment's warning, with as much certainty as he could put a squirrel or a bird into a cage he had ready for it. These frames may consist merely of the rhymes, or *bouts rimés*, being common-place words, such as would be easily lugged in *a-propos* to anything; or they may be very common-place verses ready made, upon which an appropriate travestie could easily be superinduced; or, finally, their places may be supplied by the actual verses of some author, who should, however, be, if possible, but little known, which may be travestied impromptu. This will be better understood by an instance, and as I am now making no secret of the matter, I will take those well-known lines of Moore:—

Vain was that man—and false as vain,
  Who said, were he ordained to run
His long career of life again,
  He would do all that he had done.
It is not thus the voice that dwells
  In coming birth-days, speaks to me;
Far otherwise, of time it tells,
  Wasted unwisely—carelessly.

Now, suppose I wish to make love in poetry. I am a despairing lover—or will suppose myself one for the present, and my griefs may be poured out in this same measure, and with so many of these same words, as to leave no ground for any claim to authorship for me in the following stanza:—

Vain are the hopes, ah! false as vain,
  That tempt me weary thus to run
My long career of love again,
  And only do what I have done.
Ah! not of hope the light that dwells
  In yonder glances speaks to me;
Of an obdurate heart it tells,
  Trifling with hearts all carelessly.

And now take the same stanza, only change the circumstance to something as different as possible. I am a flaming patriot, the enemy is at our gates, and I am to excite my fellow citizens to arms. It will go to the self-same tune and words:—

Our country calls, and not in vain,
  Her children are prepared to run
Their fathers' high career again;
  And may we do as they have done.
In every trumpet voice there dwells
  An echo of their fame for me;
Oh, who can hear the tale it tells,
  And pause supinely—carelessly.

Again, which is a more possible case in our country, I am disgusted with an unprincipled mob orator, some indescribably low, but gifted scion of perdition, one whom no prose can reach; why, have at him with the same arms,—they are always ready:—

Thou bad vain man, thou false as vain,
  If Satan were ordained to run
A free career on earth again,
  He would do all that thou hast done.
It is of him the voice that dwells
  In thy gay rhetoric speaks to me,
Of horrors scoffingly it tells,
  Of crime and suffering carelessly.

Or, lastly—for one may get too much of this—I am enraged with a bad singer or musician, and want to gibbet him. Lo! is not Tom Moore my executioner:—

I stop my ears, but all in vain—
  In vain to distant corners run:
He imitates the owls again,
  And will do all that they have done.
Of roasting cats the voice that dwells
  In such discordance, speaks to me;
Of Tophet up in arms it tells,
  With doors left open carelessly.

* * * * * * * *

I quit here for a moment the subject of rhyme, to say a word or two upon blank verse, that mortal humbug which "prose poets" are so fond of, and, certainly, the world would soon be full of it, if any body were fond of them. There is no more difficulty or skill in cutting up a given quantity of prose into blank verse, than there is in sawing up a log into planks. Both operations certainly reflect credit on their original inventors, and would immortalize them if we knew their names; but Fame would have her hands full, and her mouth too, if she should occupy herself in these days with all the handicraftsmen in both or either. The best way, perhaps, of setting this in a clear point of view, is to exemplify it; and, for this purpose, it would not be difficult to pitch upon authors whose whole writings, or nearly so, would bear being written as blank verse, though they were given out as prose. For instance, there is John Bunyan, the whole of whose works it would be easier to set up into verse than to restore some works, now held to be such, to their metrical shape, if, by any accident, the ends of their lines should get confused. Let the reader try his skill in reconstructing, with the visible signs of poetry, the following extract from Samson Agonistes, from line 118, omitting the next three, and going on to line 130:—

See how he lies at random, carelessly diffused * * * in slavish habit, ill-fitted weeds, o'er-worn and soiled, or do my eyes misrepresent; can this be he, that heroic, that renowned, irresistible Samson, whom, unarmed, no strength of man or fiercest wild beast could withstand; who tore the lion as the lion tears the kid, ran on embattled armies clad in iron, and weaponless himself, made arms ridiculous, &c.

But to return to Bunyan; take the following extract, which is *verbatim* from his "World to Come." It is more correct metre than much that we find written as verse in the old dramatists, though it is always printed as prose:—

Now, said my guardian angel, you are on
The verge of hell, but do not fear the power
Of the destroyer;
For my commission from the imperial throne
Secures you from all dangers.
Here you may hear from devils and damned souls
The cursed causes of their endless ruin;
And what you have a mind to ask, inquire;
The devils cannot hurt you, though they would,
For they are bound
By him that has commissioned me, of which
Themselves are sensible, which makes them rage,
And fret, and roar, and bite their hated chains.
But all in vain.

And so on, *ad infinitum*, or throughout the "World to Come."

But not to seek eccentric writers and farfetched examples, let us take a popular and noted one, even Dr. Johnson himself; everybody will recognise the opening sentence of Rasselas:—

Ye who listen with credulity to the whispers of fancy, and pursue with eagerness the phantoms of hope, who expect that age will perform the promises of youth, and that the deficiencies of the present day will be supplied by the morrow, attend to the history of Rasselas, prince of Abyssinia.

This is prose incontrovertibly. In two minutes it shall be as incontrovertibly blank verse:—

Oh, ye, who listen with credulity
To fancy's whispers, or with eagerness
Phantoms of hope pursue, or who expect
Age will perform the promises of youth,
Or that the present day's deficiencies
Shall by the morrow be supplied, attend
To Rasselas, the Abyssinian Prince,
His history. Rasselas was fourth son, &c.

I do not suspect any reader of this Magazine of stupidity enough to find a difficulty here, or of wit enough to imagine one. The process speaks for itself, and so far requires no comment; but in carrying it a step or two farther, we shall see by what alchemy gold may be transmuted into baser metals and into tinsel, and how the rogue who steals, or the poor devil who borrows it, may so thoroughly disguise it as to run no risk at last in passing it openly for his own. I take the first six lines only of the above, and tipping them with rhymes, they suffer a little violence, and read thus:—

Oh, ye who listen,—a believing race—
To fancy's whispers, or with eager chase
Phantoms of hope pursue, expecting still
Age will the promises of youth fulfil,
Or that the morrow will indeed amend
The present day's deficiencies, attend—

Now, in this shape they might do pretty well, had they not been taken purposely from a notorious part of a notorious work; for one might borrow even from Rasselas, in the middle or anywhere less in sight, and few indeed are the critics who would detect and expose the cheat. But the next stage of our progress would distance the major part even of these. That a scrap from Rasselas should be set to Yankee Doodle is an idea which seems to have been reserved from all time to be first broached in the present article. But if not the same, there are similar things done hourly; and if the written monuments of genius, like the temples and palaces of antiquity, were themselves diminished by all the materials they supply to new constructions, how much would there be remaining of them now. Imagine a chasm in Moore or Byron for every verse any lover has scrawled in an album, or any Cora or Matilda in a newspaper; or reverse the case, and imagine the masters of the lyre and of the pen reclaiming, throughout the world, whatever is their own, in whatever hands, and in whatever shape it might be now existing. The Scotch freebooter was warned upon his death-bed—rather late, but it was the first time the parson had had a chance at him—that in another world all the people he had robbed, and all the valuables he had robbed them of, sheep, horses, and cattle, would rise up to bear witness against him. "Why then," said he, in a praiseworthy vein of restitution, "if the horses, and kye, and a' will be there, let ilka shentleman tak her ain, and Donald will be an honest man again." Now, I should like to be by, at a literary judgment, when "ilka shentleman should tak her ain," to have righteousness rigidly laid to the line, and see who would in fact turn out to be "a shentleman" and have a balance left that was "her ain," and who would be a Donald, left with nothing, a destitute "*bipes implumis.*" Then, and not till then, will I give back the following piece of morality to Rasselas, and indeed, in the shape into which I am now going to put it, I think it will not be till then that he, or anybody for him, will lay claim to it.

Air—*Yankee Doodle.*

Listen ye, who trust as true
All the dreams of fancy,
Who with eager chace pursue
Each vain hope you can see,
Who expect that age will pay
All that youth may borrow,
And that all you want to day
Will be supplied to-morrow.

JOHN ROMEYN BRODHEAD,

Author of a "History of the State of New York," &c., is descended from an old New York family, the ancestor of which, Captain Daniel Brodhead, of Yorkshire, England, was an officer in the expedition under Colonel Nicolls against New Netherland in 1664, and settled in Esopus, or Kingston, Ulster county, in 1665. His grandfather, Charles W. Brodhead, of Marbletown, Ulster county, was a captain of grenadiers in the Revolutionary Army, and was present at the surrender of General Burgoyne at Saratoga. His father was the late Rev. Jacob Brodhead, D.D., a distinguished clergyman of the Reformed Dutch church, and formerly one of the ministers of the Collegiate churches in the city of New York. His mother was a daughter of the late John N. Bleecker of Albany. His father having removed to Philadelphia in 1813, to take charge of the First Reformed Dutch church there, Mr. Brodhead was born in that city on the second day of January, 1814, and was named after his uncle, the late Rev. John B. Romeyn, D.D. He was thoroughly drilled at grammar-schools in Philadelphia and New Brunswick, and at the Albany Academy. In 1826 his father returned to New York, where Mr. Brodhead was prepared for Rutgers College, of which he entered the junior class, and from which he was graduated in 1831 with the degree of Bachelor of Arts. Immediately afterwards he began the study of the law in the office of Hugh Maxwell, Esq., and in 1835 was licensed to practise his profession. This he did for two years in the city of New York in partnership with Mr. Maxwell. His tastes, however, inclining him to literary pursuits, Mr. Brodhead went, in 1837, to reside with his parents, who were then living at Saugerties in Ulster county, where he occupied himself chiefly in the study of American history. In 1839 he went to Holland, where his kinsman, the late Mr. Harmanus Bleecker, was *Chargé d' Affaires*, and was attached to the United States Legation at the Hague. While there he projected the work of writing the history of New York. In the mean time the Legislature, at the suggestion of the New York Historical Society, had passed an act on the 2d of May, 1839, to appoint an agent to procure and transcribe documents in Europe relative to the Colonial History of this State.

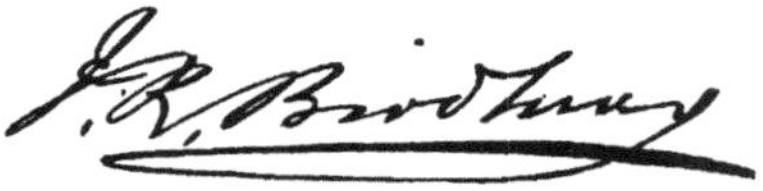

Under this act, Governor Seward, who had always manifested a warm interest in the success of the measure, commissioned Mr. Brodhead as agent in the spring of 1841. The particular objects of this agency were to procure such additional historical records as should render the archives of New York as complete and comprehensive as possible; and the agent was accordingly required to procure all papers in the public offices of European governments, in his judgment "relating to or in any way affecting the colonial or other history of this state."

During the three following years Mr. Brodhead devoted his whole time to the execution of this delicate and responsible duty, and was laboriously occupied in searching the archives of Holland, England, and France, for such papers as he thought would illustrate the history of New York, and serve to fill up the gaps in the existing state records at Albany. In this work he received the friendly aid and advice of Mr. Bleecker, Mr. Stevenson, Mr. Everett, and General Cass, who then represented the United States at the Hague, London, and Paris, and by whose intervention the various public offices in those cities were liberally opened to the researches of the agent.

The result of this enterprise was the procurement of a vast collection of historical documents, consisting of more than five thousand separate papers, and comprising a large part of the official correspondence of the colonial authorities of New York with the governments at home. Many of these documents had never before been known to the historian, though they are of acknowledged importance. From the Hague and Amsterdam Mr. Brodhead obtained a collection of Holland records which fill sixteen large volumes, and relate to the period during which New Netherland was under the Dutch dominion. From London forty-seven volumes were procured, containing copies of the instructions of the English government to its officers in New York, and the reports of those officers to the home authorities, with other interesting papers. From the archives of the Marine and War departments at Paris seventeen volumes were collected, which contain, besides many other documents relating to Canada in connexion with New York, most of the correspondence of the French Generals Dieskau, Montcalm, and Vaudreuil.

With this rich harvest Mr. Brodhead came back to New York in the summer of 1844; and Mr. Bancroft, after carefully examining the collection, pronounced that "the ship in which he returned was more richly freighted with new materials for American history than any that ever crossed the Atlantic." Mr. Brodhead was immediately invited to deliver the address before the New York Historical Society at its fortieth anniversary, which took place on the 20th November, 1844. This address, which embodied a statement of some of the results of Mr. Brodhead's researches in Europe, was published by the society, together with an account of the festival which followed, on which occasion John Quincy Adams and Albert Gallatin met in public for the last time.

In February, 1845, Mr. Brodhead, having deposited his transcripts in the secretary's office, submitted his final report as historical agent, which was laid before the Legislature by a message from Governor Wright, and was printed by order of the Senate as document No. 47 of that session. This report contains a detailed statement of the researches of the agent, and also a full analytical catalogue of the several documents comprised in the eighty volumes of Mr. Brodhead's collection. It may here be added that all these documents are now in course of publication in ten large quarto volumes, under an act of the Legislature passed on the 30th of March, 1849.

Upon the appointment of Mr. Bancroft as Minister to Great Britain in 1846, President Polk, at his request, commissioned Mr. Brodhead to be Secretary of the United States Legation at London. There he remained, until both minister and secretary were recalled by President Taylor in 1849. On his return to New York, Mr. Brodhead applied himself diligently to the execution of the work he had so long meditated, the *History of the State of New York*, the first volume of which, embracing the period under the Dutch, from 1609 to 1664, was published by the Harpers early in 1853. This book was well received by the public.

The extensive stores of original material collected by the author enabled him to present many curious and important facts of picturesque and local interest for the first time, while the main progress of the work unfolded the peculiar commercial restrictive system of trading monopoly, the regulations of the West India Company, and the domestic institution of the patroonships, which, at first the protection, soon became an impediment to the fortunes of the colony. The various political and social influences of the New Netherlands presenting the earnest, liberal, and popular elements of the home country, are exhibited with care and fidelity to the manuscript and other authorities which are constantly referred to, and passages of which are frequently embroidered in the text. The remaining distribution of the subject by the author, embraces the three periods from 1664 to the cession of Canada in 1763, from that date to the inauguration of Washington in 1789, and thence to the present day.

In the autumn of 1853 Mr. Brodhead was appointed by President Pierce Naval Officer of the Port and District of New York. While his official duties engross the most of his time, he does not neglect the prosecution of his history, nor withdraw his attention from literary labors. Among other things of this nature he prepared and delivered, by special request, an address on the Commercial History of New York, before the Mercantile Library Association, at the opening of the new Clinton Hall in Astor Place on the 8th of June, 1854. This address was published by the association.

In the spring of 1855 Mr. Brodhead received from the President the appointment of Consul-General of the United States at Japan. This office, however, he did not accept; and he still holds the post of Naval Officer of the Port of New York.

LOUIS LEGRAND NOBLE

WAS born in the vale of the Butternut Creek in Otsego county, New York, in 1812. He passed his early years in rural life and its associations at this place and in western New York, when he removed with his parents, in his twelfth year, to Michigan

Territory, then considered in the region of the Far West. The family settlement was on the Huron river, in the midst of the primitive and unfettered influences of a world of natural beauty, well adapted to graft on the heart of an ingenuous, susceptible youth, a lifelong love of nature. This vigorous existence, combining the toils of a frontier residence with the sports of the field, supplied the stock of poetical associations since liberally interwoven with the author's prose and poetical compositions. In the midst of the labors of the field, inspired by the books which had fallen in his way, he penned verses and planned various comprehensive poetical schemes. From this at once toilsome and visionary life he was called by the death of his father to a survey of the actual world. He applied himself resolutely to study, and having pursued the course of instruction in the General Theological Seminary of the Protestant Episcopal Church in New York, was in 1840 admitted to orders. He about this time published a few poems, *Pewatem* in the New World, and *Nimahmin* in Graham's Magazine, both Indian romances, and pure inventions of the author, together with a number of miscellaneous descriptive poems.

Louis L. Noble

After his ordination, Mr. Noble was settled for a time in North Carolina, in a parish on the Albemarle river. Still devoted to nature, he passed his summers in extensive tours in the Alleghanies. In 1844 he became rector of a church at Catskill, on the Hudson, where he enjoyed an intimate acquaintance with the artist Cole; the two friends being drawn to each other by a common love of nature and poetical sympathies. An ample record of this intercourse is preserved in Mr. Noble's eloquent memorial of his companion, modestly bearing its title from the artist's chief pictures, *The Course of Empire, Voyage of Life, and other Pictures of Thomas Cole, N.A., with Selections from his Letters and Miscellaneous Writings: illustrative of his Life, Character and Genius.* Mr. Cole died in 1848, and this work was undertaken, with full possession of his numerous manuscripts, shortly after. It did not, however, appear from the press till 1853. Its best characteristic is its sympathy with the genius of its subject. It may pass for an autobiography of the artist, so faithfully is his spirit represented by a kindred mind.

Mr. Noble, in 1854, removed to Chicago, Illinois, where he is at present rector of a parish.

His poems are numerous, existing, we believe, more largely in manuscript than in print. They are marked by their faithful description of nature, and a dreamy, poetical spirit, in harmony with the landscape.

TO A SWAN, FLYING BY NIGHT ON THE BANKS OF THE HURON.

Oh, what a still, bright night!—the dropping dew
Wakes startling echoes in the sleeping wood:
The round-topped groves across yon polished lake
Beneath a moon-light glory seem to bend.
But, hark!—what sound—out of the dewy deep,
How like a far-off bugle's shrillest note
It sinks into the listening wilderness.
A Swan—I know her by the trumpet-tone:
Winging her airy way in the cool heaven,
Piping her midnight melody, she comes.
Beautiful bird!—at this mysterious hour
Why on the wing, with chant so wild and shrill?—
The loon, most wakeful of the water-fowl,
Sung out her last good-night an hour ago;
Midway, she sits upon the glassy cove,
Whist as the floating lily at her side,
The purple-pinioned hern, that loves to fan,
At evening late, as thin and chill an air,
With the wild-duck is nodding in the reeds.
Frightened, perchance, from solitary haunt,
At grassy isle, or silver-sanded bank,
By barking fox, now, heedless of alarm,
With thy own music and its echo pleased,
Thou sail'st, at random, on the aërial tide.
Lone minstrel of the night, if such thou roamest,
His own who would not wish thy strong white wings?—
Whether thou wheel'st into a thinner air,
Or sink'st aslant to regions of the dew,
How spirit-like thy bugle-tones must seem,
In whispers dying in the upper deep—
How sweet the mellow echoes, coming up,
Like answering calls, to tempt thee down to rest!
And hither, haply, thou wilt bend thy neck
To shake thy quills and bathe thy snowy breast.
Till morn, if thy down-glancing eye catch not
Thy startling image rising in the lake.
Lone wanderer, that see'st, from thy far height,
The dark land set with many a star-bright pond,
Alight:—thou wilt not find a lovelier rest.
Lilies, like thy own feathery bosom fair,
Lie thick as stars around its sheltering isles.
Fearless, among them, as their guardian queen,
'Neath over-bending branches shalt thou glide,
Till early birds shake down the heavy dew,
And whistling pinions warn thee to the wing.
Now clearer sounds thy voice, and thou art nigh:—
From central sky thy clarion music falls,
Oh, what a mystic power hath one wild throat,
Vocal, at midnight, in the depths of heaven?—
What soothing harmonies the trembling air
Through the etherial halls may breathe, that ear
Which asks no echo—the internal ear,
Alone can list. But, hark, how hill and dell
Catch up the falling melody! They come,
The dulcet echoes from the hollow woods,
Like music of their own: while lingering in

From misty isles, steal softest symphonies.
It hath strange might to thrill each living heart.
The weary hunter, listening with hushed breath,
As the sweet tones with his sensations play,
A gentle tingling feels in every vein,
And all forgets his home and toilsome hunt.
River, that linkest in one sparkling chain
The crescent lakes and ponds of Washtenug,
For ever be thy darkening oaks uncut;
Thy plains unfurrowed and thy meads unmown!
That thy wild singing-birds, unscared, may blend,
Daily, with thine, their own free minstrelsy,
And nightly, wake thy silent solitudes.

Bird of the tireless wing, thou wilt not stoop;
Thine eye is on the border of the sky,
Skirted, perchance, by Huron or St. Clair.
The chasing moonbeams, glancing on thy plumes,
Reveal thee now a thing of life and light,
Lessening and sinking in the mistless blue.
There, thou art lost—thy bugle-tones are hushed!—
Tinkle the wood-vaults with far-dropping dew:
Yet, in mine ear thy last notes linger still;
And, like the close of distant music mild,
Die, with a pleasing sadness, on my heart.

HENRY NORMAN HUDSON.

H. N. Hudson

Mr. Hudson was born January 28, 1814, in the town of Cornwall, Addison County, Vermont. The first eighteen years of his life were mainly spent on the farm and in the common school. For his early religious instruction he was indebted to the Rev. Jedediah Bushnell, whom he speaks of as "a minister of the old New England school, a venerable and excellent man, a somewhat stiff and rigid Calvinist, indeed, but well fraught with the best qualities of a Christian pastor and gentleman." At the age of eighteen, Mr. Hudson removed to Middlebury, a town adjoining Cornwall, where he became apprenticed to Mr. Ira Allen, for the purpose of learning the trade of coach-making. Here he continued as apprentice and journeyman about four years, when he resolved to secure the benefit of a college education. He began the work of preparation in the fall of 1835, entered the Freshman class of Middlebury College the following August, and was graduated in 1840. His next three years were spent in teaching at the South, one year at Kentucky, and two years in Huntsville, Alabama. Having early acquired a taste for reading, and especially occupied himself with the study of Shakespeare, he found time to write out a course of lectures on his favorite author, which he first delivered at Huntsville, and shortly after at Mobile, in the winter of 1843–4. The next spring he repeated the course at Cincinnati. Induced by his success in these places he visited Boston the following winter, where the lectures were listened to by large and intelligent audiences, bringing the author both fame and profit. The first result was to enable him to discharge his pecuniary obligations to the friends by whose aid he had been assisted while in college. The lectures were repeated in New York, Philadelphia, and other cities with varying success, and finally appeared from the press of Baker and Scribner, in New York, in 1848.

Mr. Hudson's early religious views had undergone considerable change from the Congregationalism in which he was brought up, when in 1844 he became acquainted in Boston with the late Dr. William Croswell, who had then just entered on his ministerial work in the parish of the Advent. Earnestly attached to the man and his doctrines, Mr. Hudson became a member of the congregation, and not long after a candidate for orders in the diocese of New York. He was ordained by Bishop Whittingham, in Trinity Church, in 1849.

The following year, at the solicitation of Messrs. Munroe and Co., of Boston, he engaged to edit the works of Shakespeare in eleven volumes, on the plan and in the style of the Chiswick edition published in 1826. This work is now in course of completion, having reached its eighth volume, the publication having been somewhat delayed by the elaborate care bestowed upon it by the editor, and the necessity he has been under of associating with it more remunerating pursuits. The chief points in the edition are a thorough revision and restoration of the text according to the ancient copies, notes carefully selected and compactly written, and an introduction, historical, bibliographical, and critical, to each play.

In November, 1852, Mr. Hudson became party to an arrangement to edit the Churchman newspaper in New York. He entered upon the work, which he discharged with eminent ability, on the first of January, 1853, and continued in it till September 9, 1854, when he withdrew in consequence of what seemed to him unreasonable encroachments of the proprietor upon his province.

In addition to these editorial and other labors, Mr. Hudson has written a number of elaborate articles in the monthly and quarterly periodicals, including *Thoughts on Education*, in the Democratic Review,* a paper which contains the substance of a well digested volume; *On Lord Mahon's and Macaulay's Histories*, an essay on *The Right Sources of Moral and Political Knowledge*, in the Church Review; and a masterly review of Bailey's Festus in the American Whig Review. In 1850 Mr. Hudson published a sermon, *Old Wine in Old Bottles*, originally preached at the Church of the Advent, in Boston.

The style of Mr. Hudson is marked by a certain rugged strength and quaintness; occasionally reminding the reader, in its construction and the analytical subtleties of which it is the vehicle,

* May and July, 1845.

of the old school of English theological writing. His composition is labored, sinewy, and profound. As a moralist, his views are liberal and enlarged, while opposed as far as possible to maudlin philanthropy and sentimentality. As a critic of Shakespeare he is acute, philosophical, reverential; following the school of Coleridge, and reproducing from the heart of the subject the elements of the author's characters, which are drawn out in a fine amplification.

THE WEIRD SISTERS—FROM THE LECTURES ON SHAKESPEARE.

The Weird Sisters are the creatures not of any pre-existing superstition, but purely of Shakespeare's own mind. They are altogether unlike any thing else that art or superstition ever invented. The old witches of northern mythology would not have answered the poet's purpose; those could only act upon men,—these act within them; those opposed themselves against human will,—these identify themselves with it; those could inflict injury,—these inflict guilt; those could work men's physical ruin,—these win men to work their own spiritual ruin. Macbeth cannot resist them, because they take from him the very will and spirit of resistance. Their power takes hold of him like a fascination of hell: it seems as terrible and as inevitable as that of original sin; insuring the commission of crime, not as a matter of necessity, for then it would be no crime, but simply as a matter of fact. In using them, Shakespeare but borrowed the drapery of pre-existing superstition to secure faith in an entirely new creation. Without doing violence to the laws of human belief he was thus enabled to enlist the services of old credulity in favor of agents or instruments suited to his peculiar purpose.

The Weird Sisters are a combination of the terrible and the grotesque, and hold the mind in suspense between laughter and fear. Resembling old women save that they have long beards, they bubble up into human shape, but are free from all human relations; without age, or sex, or kin; without birth, or death; passionless and motionless; anomalous alike in looks, in action, and in speech; nameless themselves, and doing nameless deeds. Coleridge describes them as the imaginative divorced from the good; and this description, to one who understands it, expresses their nature better than any thing else I have seen. Gifted with the powers of prescience and prophecy, their predictions seem replete with an indescribable charm which works their own fulfilment, so as almost to leave us in doubt whether they predestinate or produce, or only foresee and foretell the subsequent events.

Such as they are,—

> So withered and so wild in their attire;
> That look not like the inhabitants o' the earth,
> And yet are on't,—

such is the language in which they mutter their horrid incantations. It is, if such a thing be possible or imaginable, the poetry of hell, and seems dripping with the very dews of the pit. A wondrous potency, like the fumes of their charmed pot, seems stealing over our minds as they compound the ingredients of their hell-broth. In the materials which make up the contents of their cauldron, such as

> Toad, that under coldest stone,
> Days and nights hast thirty-one
> Sweltered venom, sleeping got;
> Witch's mummy; maw and gulf
> Of the ravined salt-sea shark;
> Root of hemlock, digg'd i' the dark;
> Liver of blaspheming Jew;
> Gall of goat; and slips of yew,
> Slivered in the moon's eclipse;
> Nose of Turk, and Tartar's lips;
> Finger of birth-strangled babe,
> Ditch-delivered by a drab;
> ——sow's blood, that hath eaten
> Her nine farrow; grease that's sweaten
> From the murderer's gibbet;—

there is a strange confusion of the natural and supernatural, which serves to enchant and bewilder the mind into passiveness. Our very ignorance of any physical efficacy or tendency in the substances and conditions here specified, only enhances to our imagination their moral potency; so that they seem more powerful over the soul inasmuch as they are powerless over the body.—The Weird Sisters, indeed, and all that belong to them, are but poetical impersonations of evil influences: they are the imaginative, irresponsible agents or instruments of the devil; capable of inspiring guilt, but not of incurring it; in and through whom all the powers of their chief seem bent up to the accomplishment of a given purpose. But with all their essential wickedness there is nothing gross, or vulgar, or sensual about them. They are the very purity of sin incarnate; the vestal virgins, so to speak, of hell; radiant with a sort of inverted holiness; fearful anomalies in body and soul, in whom every thing seems reversed; whose elevation is downwards; whose duty is sin; whose religion is wickedness; and the law of whose being is violation of law! Unlike the Furies of Eschylus, they are petrific, not to the senses, but to the thoughts. At first, indeed, on merely looking at them, we can hardly keep from laughing, so uncouth and grotesque is their appearance: but afterwards, on looking into them, we find them terrible beyond description; and the more we look into them, the more terrible do they become; the blood almost curdling in our veins as, dancing and singing their infernal glees over embryo murders, they unfold to our thoughts the cold, passionless, inexhaustible malignity and deformity of their nature.

In beings thus made and thus mannered; in their fantastical and unearthly aspect, awakening mixed emotions of terror and mirth; in their ominous reserve and oracular brevity of speech, so fitted at once to overcome scepticism, to sharpen curiosity, and to feed ambitious hopes; in the circumstances of their prophetic greeting, a blasted heath, as a spot deserted by nature and sacred to infernal orgies,—the influences of the place thus falling in with the supernatural style and matter of their discourses; in all this we recognise a peculiar adaptedness to generate even in the strongest minds a belief in their predictions.

What effect, then, do the Weird Sisters have on the action of the play? Are their discourses necessary to the enacting of the subsequent crimes? and, if so, are they necessary as the cause, or only as the condition of those crimes? Do they operate to deprave, or only to develope the characters brought under their influence? In a word, do they create the evil heart, or only untie the evil hands? These questions have been variously answered by critics. Not to dwell on these various answers, it seems to me tolerably clear, that the agency of the Weird Sisters extends only to the inspiring of confidence in what they predict. This confidence they awaken in Banquo equally as in Macbeth; yet the only effect of their proceedings on Banquo is to try and prove his virtue. The fair inference, then, is, that they furnish the motives, not the principles of action; and these motives are of course to good or to bad, according to the several preformations and predispositions of character whereon they operate. But what relation does motive bear to action? On this point, too, it seems to me there has been much of needless confusion. Now moral action, like vision, presupposes two things, a condition and a cause. Light and visual power are both indispensable to sight; there can be no vision without light; yet the cause of vision, as every body knows, is the visual power pre-existing in the eye. Neither can we walk without an area to walk upon; yet nobody, I suppose, would pronounce that area the cause of our walking. On the contrary, that cause is obviously within ourselves; it lies in our own innate mobility; and the area is necessary only as the condition of our walking. In like manner both will and motive are indispensable to moral action. We cannot act without motives, any more than we can breathe without air; yet the cause of our acting lies in certain powers and principles within us. As, therefore, vision springs from the meeting of visual power with light, so action springs from the meeting of will with motive. Surely, then, those who persist in holding motives responsible for our actions, would do well to remember, that motives can avail but little after all without something to be moved.

One of the necessary conditions of our acting, in all cases, is a belief in the possibility and even the practicability of what we undertake. However ardent and lawless may be our desire of a given object, still a conviction of the impossibility of reaching it necessarily precludes all efforts to reach it. So fully are we persuaded that we cannot jump over the moon, that we do not even wish, much less attempt to do it. Generally, indeed, apprehensions and assurances more or less strong of failure and punishment in criminal attempts operate to throw us back upon better principles of action; we make a virtue of necessity; and from the danger and difficulty of indulging evil and unlawful desires, fall back upon such as are lawful and good; wherein, to our surprise, nature often rewards us with far greater pleasures than we had anticipated from the opposite course. He who removes those apprehensions and assurances from any wicked enterprise, and convinces us of its safety and practicability, may be justly said to furnish us motives to engage in it; that is, he gives us the conditions upon which, but not the principles from which, our actions proceed; and therefore does not, properly speaking, deprave, but only developes our character. For example, in ambition itself, unchecked and unrestrained by any higher principles, are contained the elements of all the crimes necessary to the successful prosecution of its objects. I say successful prosecution; for such ambition is, from its nature, regardless of every thing but the chances of defeat: so that nothing less than the conviction or the apprehension that crimes will not succeed, can prevent such ambition from employing them.

E. H. CHAPIN

WAS born in Union Village, Washington County, New York, December 29, 1814. His first studies were given to the law, but he soon became engaged in the ministry. He was settled first over a congregation at Richmond, Va., in 1838, and subsequently from 1840 to 1848 was stationed at Charlestown and Boston. In 1848 he became a resident of New York, and is now pastor of the Fourth Universalist Society in the city, occupying the edifice in Broadway, re-erected for the congregation of the Rev. H. W. Bellows.

Mr. Chapin's chief reputation is as a pulpit orator and lecturer, his lyceum engagements extending through the country. His style is marked by its poetical fervor and frequent happy illustrations, and an ingenious vein of thought. His delivery is calm and winning.

E. H. Chapin.

His chief publications are of a practical devotional character, bearing the titles, *Hours of Communion; Crown of Thorns; A Token for the Sorrowing; Discourses on the Lord's Prayer and the Beatitudes; Characters in the Gospels, illustrating Phases of Character at the Present Day.* In 1853 and in 1854 he published *Moral Aspects of City Life*, and *Humanity in the City*—two series of his courses on topics of social life; fashions, amusements, and vices; the relation of machinery and labor, wealth and poverty; the temptations to crime, and other themes of a similar character, which are exhibited in a philosophical, devotional spirit, with equal earnestness and kindliness.

VOICES OF THE DEAD—FROM THE CROWN OF THORNS.

"He being dead yet speaketh." The departed have voices for us. In order to illustrate this, I remark, in the first place, that the dead speak to us, and commune with us, *through the works which they have left behind them.* As the islands of the sea are the built up casements of myriads of departed lives; as the earth itself is a great catacomb; so we, who live and move upon its surface, inherit the productions and enjoy the fruits of the dead. They have bequeathed to us by far the larger portion of all that influences our thoughts, or mingles with the circumstances of our daily life. We walk through the streets they laid out. We inhabit the houses they built. We practise the customs they established. We gather wisdom from the books they wrote. We pluck the ripe clusters of their experience. We boast in their achievements. And by these they speak to us. Every device and influence they have left behind tells their story, and is a voice of the dead. We feel this more impressively when we enter the customary place of one recently departed, and look around upon his work. The half-finished labor, the utensils hastily thrown aside, the material that exercised his care and received his last touch, all express him and seem alive with his presence. By them, though dead, he speaketh to us with a freshness and tone like his words of yesterday. How touching are those sketched forms, those unfilled outlines, in that picture which employed so fully the time and genius of the great artist—Belshazzar's Feast! In the incomplete process, the transition-state of an idea from its conception to its realization, we are brought closer to the mind of the artist; we detect its springs and hidden workings, and therefore feel its *reality* more than in the finished effort. And this is one reason why we are more impressed at beholding the work just left than in gazing upon one that has been for a long time abandoned. Having had actual communion with the contriving mind, we recognise its presence more readily in its production; or else the recency of the departure heightens the expressiveness with which everything speaks of the departed. The dead child's cast-off garment, the toy just tossed aside, startles us as though with his renewed presence. A year hence they will suggest him to us, but with a different effect.

But though not with such an impressive tone, yet just as much, in fact, do the productions of those long gone speak to us. Their *minds* are expressed there, and living voice can do little more. Nay, we are admitted to a more intimate knowledge of them than was possessed by their contemporaries. The work they leave behind them is the *sum-total* of their lives—expresses their ruling passion—reveals, perhaps, their real sentiment. To the eyes of those placed on the stage with them, they walked as in a show, and each life was a narrative gradually unfolding itself. We discover the moral. We see the results of that completed history. We judge the quality and value of that life by the residuum. As "a prophet has no honor in his own country," so one may be misconceived in his own time, both to his undue disparagement and his undue exaltation; therefore, can another age better write his biography than his own. His work, his permanent result, speaks for him better, at least truer, than he spoke for himself. The rich man's wealth, the sumptuous property, the golden pile that he has left behind him—by it, being dead, does he not yet speak to us? Have we not, in that gorgeous result of toiling days and anxious nights, of brain-sweat and soul-rack, the man himself, the cardinal purpose, the very life of his soul? which we might have surmised while he lived and wrought, but which, now that it remains the whole sum and substance of his mortal being, speaks far more emphatically than could any other voice he might have used. The expressive lineaments of the marble, the pictured canvass, the immortal poem—by it, *genius*, being dead, yet speaketh. To us, and not to its own time, is unhoarded the wealth of its thought and the glory of its inspiration. When it is gone—when its lips are silent, and its heart still—then is revealed the cherished secret over which it toiled, which was elaborated from the living alembic of the soul, through gainful days and weary nights—the sentiment which could not find expression to contemporaries—the gift, the greatness, the lyric power, which was disguised and unknown so long. Who, that has communed with the work of such a spirit, has not felt in every line that thrilled his soul, in every wondrous lineament that stamped itself upon his memory for ever, that the dead can speak, yea, that they have voices which speak most truly, most emphatically, when they *are* dead? So does *Industry* speak, in its noble monuments, its precious fruits! So does *Maternal Affection* speak, in a chord that vibrates in the hardest heart, in the pure and better sentiment of after-years. So does *Patriotism* speak, in the soil liberated and enriched by its sufferings. So does the *Martyr* speak, in the truth which triumphs by his sacrifice. So does the *great man* speak, in his life and deeds, glowing on the storied page. So does the *good man* speak, in the character and influence which he leaves behind him. The voices of the dead come to us from their works, from their results, and these are all around us.

But I remark, in the *second* place, that the dead speak to us in *memory* and *association*. If their voices may be constantly heard in their works, we do not always heed them; neither have we that care and attachment for the great congregation of the departed, which will at any time call them up vividly before us. But in that congregation there are those whom we have known intimately and fondly, whom we cherished with our best love, who lay close to our bosoms. And these speak to us in a more private and peculiar manner,—in mementos that flash upon us the whole person of the departed, every physical and spiritual lineament—in consecrated hours of recollection that open up all the train of the past, and re-twine its broken ties around our hearts, and make its endearments present still. Then, then, though dead, they speak to us. It needs not the vocal utterance, nor the living presence, but the mood that transforms the scene and the hour supplies these. That face that has slept so long in the grave, now bending upon us, pale and silent, but affectionate still—that more vivid recollection of every feature, tone, and movement, that brings before us the departed, just as we knew them in the full flush of life and health—that soft and consecrating spell which falls upon us, drawing in all our thoughts from the present, arresting, as it were, the current of our being, and turning it back and holding it still as the flood of actual life, rushes by us—while in that trance of soul the beings of the past are shadowed—old friends, old days, old scenes recur, familiar looks beam close upon us, familiar words reëcho in our ears, and we are closed up and absorbed with the by-gone, until tears dissolve the film from our eyes, and some shock of the actual wakes us from our reverie;—all these, I say, make the dead to commune with us really as though in bodily form they should come out from the chambers of their mysterious silence, and speak to us. And if life consists in *experiences*, and not mere physical contacts—and if love and communion belong to that experience, though they take place in meditation, or dreams, or by actual contact—then, in that hour of remembrance, have we really lived with the departed, and the departed have come back and lived with us. Though dead, they have spoken to us. And though memory sometimes induces the spi... of heaviness—though it is often the agent of conscience and wakens us to chastise—yet, it is wonderful how, from events that were deeply mingled with pain, it will extract an element of sweetness. A writer, in relating one of the experiences of her sick-room, has illustrated this. In an hour of suffering, when no one was near her, she went from her bed and her room to another apartment, and looked out upon a glorious landscape of sunrise and spring-time. "I was suffering too much to enjoy this picture at the moment," she says, "but how was it at the end of the year? The pains of all those hours were annihilated, as completely vanished as if they had never been; while the momentary peep behind the window-curtain made me possessor of this radiant picture for evermore." "Whence this wide difference," she asks, "between the good and the evil? Because the good is indissolubly connected with ideas—with the unseen realities which are indestructible." And though the illustration which she thus gives bear the impression of an individual peculiarity, instead of an universal truth, still, in the instance to which I apply it, I believe it will very generally hold true, that memory leaves a pleasant rather than a painful impression.

At least, there is so much that is pleasant mingled with it, that we would not willingly lose the faculty of memory—the consciousness that we can thus call back the dead and hear their voices—that we have the power of softening the rugged realities which only suggest our loss and disappointment, by transferring the scene and the hour to the past and the departed. And, as our conceptions become more and more spiritual, we shall find the *real* to be less dependent upon the outward and the visible—we shall learn how much life there is in a thought—how veritable are the communions of spirit with spirit; and the hour in which memory gives us the voices of the dead will be prized by us as an hour of actual experience, and such opportunities will grow more precious to us. No, we would not willingly lose this power of memory. * * * * * * *

Well, then, is it for us at times to listen to the voices of the dead. By so doing we are better fitted for life and for death. From that audience we go purified and strengthened into the varied discipline of our mortal state. We are willing to *stay*, knowing that the dead are so near us, and that our communion with them may be so intimate. We are willing to *go*, seeing that we shall not be wholly separated from those we leave behind. We will toil in our lot while God pleases, and when He summons us we will calmly depart. When the silver cord becomes untwined, and the golden bowl broken—when the wheel of action stands still in the exhausted cistern of our life, may we lie down in the light of that faith which makes so beautiful the face of the dying Christian, and has converted death's ghastly silence to a peaceful sleep. May we rise to a holier and more visible communion, in the land without a sin and without a tear. Where the dead shall be closer to us than in this life. Where not the partition of a shadow or a doubt shall come between.

T. S. ARTHUR

WAS born in 1809, near Newburgh, Orange county, New York. In 1817, his parents removed to

Baltimore, where he lived till 1841, when he removed to Philadelphia, where he has since resided.

His boyhood, as we learn from a brief autobiography prefixed to one of his books, was passed with but few advantages of instruction in Maryland. He left school to be apprenticed, when he entered upon a course of self-education. His sight failing him when he became his own master, he abandoned the trade which he had learnt, and was for three years a clerk. In 1833, he went to the West as agent for a Banking Company; the institution failed and he returned to Baltimore. He then associated himself with a friend as editor of a newspaper, and soon became engaged in the active career of authorship, which he has since pursued with popular favor. His writings embrace numerous series of works of fiction of a domestic moral character; pictures of American life subordinated to a moral sentiment. He has published more than fifty volumes, besides numerous tales in cheap form.*

GENTLE HAND.

When and where, it matters not now to relate—but once upon a time, as I was passing through a thinly peopled district of country, night came down upon me, almost unawares. Being on foot, I could not hope to gain the village toward which my steps were directed, until a late hour; and I therefore preferred seeking the shelter and a night's lodging at the first humble dwelling that presented itself.

Dusky twilight was giving place to deeper shadows, when I found myself in the vicinity of a dwelling, from the small uncurtained windows of which the light shone with a pleasant promise of good cheer and comfort. The house stood within an enclosure, and a short distance from the road along which I was moving with wearied feet. Turning aside, and passing through the ill-hung gate, I approached the dwelling. Slowly the gate swung on its wooden hinges, and the rattle of its latch, in closing, did not disturb the air until I had nearly reached the little porch in front of the house, in which a slender girl, who had noticed my entrance, stood awaiting my arrival.

A deep, quick bark answered, almost like an echo, the sound of the shutting gate, and, sudden as an apparition, the form of an immense dog loomed in the doorway. At the instant when he was about to spring, a light hand was laid upon his shaggy neck and a low word spoken.

"Go in, Tiger," said the girl, not in a voice of authority, yet in her gentle tones was the consciousness that she would be obeyed; and, as she spoke, she lightly bore upon the animal with her hand, and he turned away, and disappeared within the dwelling.

"Who's that?" A rough voice asked the question; and now a heavy-looking man took the dog's place in the door.

"How far is it to G——?" I asked, not deeming it best to say, in the beginning, that I sought a resting-place for the night.

"To G——!" growled the man, but not so harshly as at first. "It's good six miles from here."

"A long distance; and I'm a stranger, and on foot,"

---

* We give a list of most of these writings, though not in the order of their production:—Sketches of Life and Character, 8vo., pp. 420; Lights and Shadows of Real Life, 8vo., pp. 500; Leaves from Book of Human Life, 12mo.; Golden Grains from Life's Harvest Field, 12mo.; the Loftons and the Pinkertons, 12mo.; Heart Histories and Life Pictures; Tales for Rich and Poor, 6 vols. 18mo.; Library for the Household 12 vols. 18mo.; Arthur's Juvenile Library, 12 vols. 16mo.; Cottage Library, 6 vols. 18mo.; Ten Nights in a Bar-Room, 12mo.; Six Nights with Washingtonians, 18mo.; Advice to Young Men, 18mo.; Advice to Young Ladies, 18mo.; Maiden, Wife, and Mother, 3 vols. 18mo.; Tales of Married Life, 3 vols. 18mo.; Stories of Domestic Life, 3 vols. 18mo.; Tales from Real Life, 3 vols. 18mo.; Tired of House-keeping, 18mo.; Novels in Cheap Form, 20 vols.

said I. "If you can make room for me until morning, I will be very thankful."

I saw the girl's hand move quickly up his arm, until it rested on his shoulder, and now she leaned to him still closer.

"Come in. We'll try what can be done for you."

There was a change in the man's voice that made me wonder.

I entered a large room, in which blazed a brisk fire. Before the fire sat two stout lads, who turned upon me their heavy eyes, with no very welcome greeting. A middle-aged woman was standing at a table, and two children were amusing themselves with a kitten on the floor.

"A stranger, mother," said the man who had given me so rude a greeting at the door; "and he wants us to let him stay all night."

The woman looked at me doubtingly for a few moments, and then replied coldly—

"We don't keep a public house."

"I am aware of that, ma'am," said I; "but night has overtaken me, and it's a long way yet to———."

"Too far for a tired man to go on foot," said the master of the house, kindly, "so it's no use talking about it, mother; we must give him a bed."

So unobtrusively, that I scarcely noticed the movement, the girl had drawn to the woman's side. What she said to her I did not hear, for the brief words were uttered in a low voice; but I noticed, as she spoke, one small, fair hand rested on the woman's hand. Was there magic in that gentle touch? The woman's repulsive aspect changed into one of kindly welcome, and she said:

"Yes, it's a long way to G———. I guess we can find a place for him."

Many times more, during that evening, did I observe the magic power of that hand and voice—the one gentle yet potent as the other.

On the next morning, breakfast being over, I was preparing to take my departure, when my host informed me that if I would wait for half an hour he would give me a ride in his wagon to G———, as business required him to go there. I was very well pleased to accept of the invitation. In due time, the farmer's wagon was driven into the road before the house, and I was invited to get in. I noticed the horse as a rough-looking Canadian pony, with a certain air of stubborn endurance. As the farmer took his seat by my side, the family came to the door to see us off.

"Dick!" said the farmer in a peremptory voice, giving the rein a quick jerk as he spoke.

But Dick moved not a step.

"Dick! you vagabond! get up." And the farmer's whip cracked sharply by the pony's ear.

It availed not, however, this second appeal. Dick stood firmly disobedient. Next the whip was brought down upon him, with an impatient hand; but the pony only reared up a little. Fast and sharp the strokes were next dealt to the number of half-a-dozen. The man might as well have beaten his wagon, for all his end was gained.

A stout lad now came out into the road, and catching Dick by the bridle, jerked him forward, using, at the same time, the customary language on such occasions, but Dick met this new ally with increased stubbornness, planting his forefeet more firmly, and at a sharper angle with the ground. The impatient boy now struck the pony on the side of his head with his clinched hand, and jerked cruelly at his bridle. It availed nothing, however; Dick was not to be wrought upon by any such arguments.

"Don't do so, John!" I turned my head as the maiden's sweet voice reached my ear. She was passing through the gate into the road, and, in the next moment, had taken hold of the lad and drawn him away from the animal. No strength was exerted in this; she took hold of his arm, and he obeyed her wish as readily as if he had no thought beyond her gratification.

And now that soft hand was laid gently on the pony's neck, and a single low word spoken. How instantly were the tense muscles relaxed—how quickly the stubborn air vanished.

"Poor Dick!" said the maiden, as she stroked his neck lightly, or softly patted it with a child-like hand.

"Now, go along, you provoking fellow!" she added, in a half-chiding, yet affectionate voice, as she drew up the bridle. The pony turned toward her, and rubbed his head against her arm for an instant or two; then, pricking up his ears, he started off at a light, cheerful trot, and went on his way as freely as if no silly crotchet had ever entered his stubborn brain.

"What a wonderful power that hand possesses!" said I, speaking to my companion, as we rode away.

He looked at me for a moment as if my remark had occasioned surprise. Then a light came into his countenance, and he said, briefly—

"She's good! Everybody and everything loves her."

Was that, indeed, the secret of her power? Was the quality of her soul perceived in the impression of her hand, even by brute beasts! The father's explanation was, doubtless, the true one. Yet have I ever since wondered, and still do wonder, at the potency which lay in that maiden's magic touch. I have seen something of the same power, showing itself in the loving and the good, but never to the extent as instanced in her, whom, for want of a better name, I must still call "Gentle Hand."

WILLIAM H. C. HOSMER.

Mr. Hosmer was born at Avon, in the valley of the Genesee, New York, May 25, 1814. He was graduated at Geneva College, and soon after commenced the study of the law with his father, the Hon. George Hosmer, one of the oldest members of the bar of Western New York. Mr. Hosmer was in due course licensed, and has practised his profession with success.

His parents having settled in the Genesee valley while it was yet occupied by the Seneca Indians, Mr. Hosmer's attention was early directed to the history and legends of the race whose home, possessions, and stronghold, had been for a succession of ages in that valley, and whose footprints were yet fresh upon its soil. His mother conversed fluently in the dialect of the tribe, and was familiar with its legends. These circumstances naturally directed Mr. Hosmer in the choice of a theme for his first poem, *Yonnondio*, an Indian tale in seven cantos, published in 1844.

In 1854 Mr. Hosmer published a complete collection of his *Poetical Works* in two volumes duodecimo. The first contains the Indian romance of Yonnondio, followed by legends of the Senecas, Indian traditions and songs, Bird Notes, a series of pleasantly versified descriptions of a few American birds, and the Months, a poetical calendar of nature. The second contains Occasional Poems,

Historic scenes drawn from European history, Martial Lyrics, several of which are in honor of the Mexican war, Songs and Ballads, Funeral Echoes, Sonnets, and Miscellaneous Poems. The enumeration displays the variety of the writer's productions. He maintains throughout a spirited and animated strain.

OCTOBER.

What is there saddening in the autumn leaves?
Have they that "green and yellow melancholy"
That the sweet poet spake of?
BRAINERD.

The tenth one of a royal line
Breathes on the wind his mandate loud,
And fitful gleams of sunlight shine
Around his throne of cloud:
The Genii of the forest dim
A many-colored robe for him
Of fallen leaves have wrought;
And softened is his visage grim
By melancholy thought.

No joyous birds his coming hail,
For Summer's full-voiced choir is gone,
And over Nature's face a veil
Of dull, gray mist is drawn:
The crow, with heavy pinion-strokes,
Beats the chill air in flight, and croaks
A dreary song of dole:
Beneath my feet the puff-ball smokes,
As through the fields I stroll.

An awning broad of many dyes
Above me bends, as on I stray,
More splendid than Italian skies
Bright with the death of day;
As in the sun-bow's radiant braid
Shade melts like magic into shade,
And purple, green, and gold,
With carmine blent, have gorgeous made
October's flag unrolled.

The partridge, closely ambushed, hears
The crackling leaf—poor, timid thing!
And to a thicker covert steers
On swift, resounding wing:
The woodland wears a look forlorn,
Hushed is the wild bee's tiny horn,
The cricket's bugle shrill—
Sadly is Autumn's mantle torn,
But fair to vision still.

Black walnuts, in low, meadow ground,
Are dropping now their dark, green balls,
And on the ridge, with rattling sound,
The deep brown chestnut falls.
When comes a day of sunshine mild,
From childhood, nutting in the wild,
Outbursts a shout of glee;
And high the pointed shells are piled
Under the hickory tree.

Bright flowers yet linger:—from the morn
Yon Cardinal hath caught its blush,
And yellow, star-shaped gems adorn
The wild witch-hazel bush;
Rocked by the frosty breath of Night,
That brings to frailer blossoms blight,
The germs of fruit they bear,
That, living on through Winter white,
Ripens in Summer air.

The varied aster tribes unclose
Bright eyes in Autumn's smoky bower,
And azure cup the gentian shows,
A modest little flower:
Their garden sisters pale have turned,
Though late the dahlia I discerned
Right royally arrayed:
And phlox, whose leaf with crimson burned
Like cheek of bashful maid.

In piles around the cider-mill
The parti-colored apples shine,
And busy hands the hopper fill,
While foams the pumice fine—
The cheese, with yellow straw between
Full, juicy layers, may be seen,
And rills of amber hue
Feed a vast tub, made tight and clean,
While turns the groaning screw.

From wheat-fields, washed by recent rains,
In flocks the whistling plover rise
When night draws near, and leaden stains
Obscure the western skies:
The geese, so orderly of late,
Fly over fence and farm-yard gate,
As if the welkin black
The habits of a wilder state
To memory brought back.

Yon streamlet to the woods around,
Sings, flowing on, a mournful tune,
Oh! how unlike the joyous sound
Wherewith it welcomed June!
Wasting away with grief, it seems,
For flowers that flaunted in the beams
Of many a sun-bright day—
Fair flowers!—more beautiful than dreams
When life hath reached its May.

Though wild, mischievous sprites of air,
In cruel mockery of a crown,
Drop on October's brow of care
Dead wreaths and foliage brown,
Abroad the sun will look again,
Rejoicing in his blue domain,
And prodigal of gold,
Ere dark November's sullen reign
Gild stream and forest old.

Called by the west wind from her grave,
Once more will summer re-appear,
And gladden with a merry stave
The wan, departing year;
Her swiftest messenger will stay
The wild bird winging south its way,
And night, no longer sad,
Will emulate the blaze of day,
In cloudless moonshine clad.

The scene will smoky vestments wear,
As if glad Earth—one altar made—
By clouding the delicious air
With fragrant fumes, displayed
A sense of gratitude for warm,
Enchanting weather after storm,
And raindrops falling fast,
On dead September's mouldering form,
From skies with gloom o'ercast.

JOEL TYLER HEADLEY

WAS born at Walton, Delaware county, New York, December 8, 1814. He was graduated at Union College in 1839, and studied for the ministry at the Auburn Theological Seminary. Compelled by ill-health to relinquish this calling, he travelled in Europe in 1842 and 1843, passing a considerable portion of his time in Italy. On his return to America in 1844, he prepared a volume descriptive of his foreign tour, *Letters from Italy*, followed by *The Alps and the Rhine*. They

were published in the popular series of Wiley and Putnam's Library of American Books, and were received with unusual favor by the public. In 1846 Mr. Headley achieved a still more decided success in the publication of his spirited biographical sketches, *Napoleon and his Marshals*, to which *Washington and his Generals* in the next year was an American companion. *A Life of Oliver Cromwell*, based mainly upon Carlyle's researches, in 1848; *The Imperial Guard of Napoleon*, based upon a popular French history by Emile Marco de St. Hilaire, in 1851; *Lives of Scott and Jackson* in 1852; *A History of the War of* 1812, in 1853, and a *Life of Washington*, first published in Graham's Magazine in 1854, followed in sequence the author's first successes in popular biography and history.

Headley's Residence.

A spirited volume of travelling sketches, the result of a summer excursion in northern New York, *The Adirondack, or Life in the Woods*, appeared from Mr. Headley's pen in 1849, which, with two volumes of biblical sketches, *Sacred Mountains* and *Sacred Scenes and Characters*, and a volume of *Miscellanies, Sketches, and Rambles*, completes the list, thus far, of his publications.

His books, impressed by the keen, active temperament of the author, are generally noticeable for the qualities of energy and movement, which are at the secret of their popular success.

Mr. Headley resides at a country seat in the neighborhood of Newburgh on the Hudson. In 1854 he was chosen to represent his District in the State Legislature.

WASHINGTON AND NAPOLEON.

No one, in tracing the history of our struggle, can deny that Providence watched over our interests, and gave us the only man who could have conducted the car of the Revolution to the goal it finally reached. Our revolution brought to a speedy crisis the one that must sooner or later have convulsed France. One was as much needed as the other, and has been productive of equal good. But in tracing the progress of each, how striking is the contrast between the instruments employed—Napoleon and Washington. Heaven and earth are not wider apart than were their moral characters, yet both were sent of Heaven to perform a great work. God acts on more enlarged plans than the bigoted and ignorant have any conception of, and adapts his instruments to the work he wishes to accomplish. To effect the regeneration of a comparatively religious, virtuous, and intelligent people, no better man could have been selected than Washington. To rend asunder the feudal system of Europe, which stretched like an iron frame-work over the people, and had rusted so long in its place, that no slow corrosion or steadily wasting power could affect its firmness, there could have been found no better than Bonaparte. Their missions were as different as their characters. Had Bonaparte been put in the place of Washington, he would have overthrown the Congress, as he did the Directory, and taking supreme power into his hands, developed the resources, and kindled the enthusiasm of this country with such astonishing rapidity, that the war would scarcely have begun ere it was ended. But a vast and powerful monarchy, instead of a republic, would have occupied this continent. Had Washington been put in the place of Bonaparte, his transcendent virtues and unswerving integrity would not have prevailed against the tyranny of faction, and a prison would have received him, as it did Lafayette. Both were children of a revolution, both rose to the chief command of the army, and eventually to the head of the nation. One led his country step by step to freedom and prosperity, the other arrested at once, and with a strong hand, the earthquake that was rocking France asunder, and sent it rolling under the thrones of Europe. The office of one was to defend and build up Liberty, that of the other to break down the prison walls in which it lay a captive, and rend asunder its century-bound fetters. To suppose that France could have been managed as America was, by any human hand, shows an ignorance as blind as it is culpable. That, and every other country of Europe, will have to pass through successive stages before they can reach the point at which our revolution commenced. Here Liberty needed virtue and patriotism, as well as strength—on the continent it needed simple *power*, concentrated and terrible power. Europe at this day trembles over that volcano Napoleon kindled, and the next eruption will finish what he begun. Thus does Heaven, selecting its own instruments, break up the systems of oppression men deemed eternal, and out of the power and ambition, as well as out of the virtues of men, work the welfare of our race.

LAFAYETTE.

He did not possess what is commonly termed genius, nor was he a man of remarkable intellectual powers. In youth, ardent and adventurous, he soon learned under Washington to curb his impulses, and act more from his judgment. Left to himself, he probably never would have reached any great eminence—but there could have been no better school for the fiery young republican, than the family of Washington. His affection and reverence for the latter gradually changed his entire character. Washington was his model, and imitating his self-control and noble patriotism, he became like him in patriotism and virtue. The difference between them was the same as that between an original and a copy. Washington was a man of immense strength of character—not only strong in virtue, but in intellect and will. Everything bent before him, and the entire nation took its impress from his mind. Lafayette was strong in integrity, and nothing could shake his unalterable devotion to the welfare of man. Enthusiastically wedded to republican institutions, no temptation could induce him to seize on, or aid power which threatened to overthrow them. Although somewhat vain and conceited, he was generous, self-sacrificing, and benevolent. Few men have passed through so many and so fearful scenes as he. From a young courtier, he passed into the self-denying, toilsome life of a general in the ill-clothed, ill-fed, and ill-disciplined American army—thence into the vortex of the French Revolution and all its horrors—thence into the gloomy prison of Olmutz. After a few years of retirement, he appeared on our shores to receive the welcome of a grateful people, and hear a nation shout his praise, and bear him from one limit of the land to another in its arms. A few years pass by, and with his gray hairs falling about his aged countenance, he stands amid the students of Paris, and sends his feeble shout of defiance to the throne of the Bourbon, and it falls. Rising more by his virtue than his intellect, he holds a prominent place in the history of France, and linked with Washington, goes down to a greater immortality than awaits any emperor or mere warrior of the human race.

His love for this country was deep and abiding. To the last his heart turned hither, and well it might:—his career of glory began on our shores—on our cause he staked his reputation, fortune, and life, and in our success received the benediction of the good the world over. That love was returned with interest, and never was a nobler exhibition of a nation's gratitude, than our reception of him at his last visit. We love him for what he did for us—we revere him for his consistency to our principles amid all the chaos and revolutions of Europe; and when we cease to speak of him with affection and gratitude, we shall show ourselves unworthy of the blessings we have received at his hands. "HONOR TO LAFAYETTE!" will ever stand inscribed on our temple of liberty until its ruins shall cover all it now contains.

HARRIET BEECHER STOWE,

THE daughter of the Rev. Dr. Lyman Beecher, was born in Litchfield, Connecticut, about the year 1812. Her elder sister, Esther Catherine Beecher, born in 1800 at East Hampton, Long Island, had established in 1822 a successful female seminary at Hartford, Connecticut. With this establish-

H B Stowe

ment Harriet was associated from her fifteenth year till her marriage in her twenty-first with the Rev. Calvin E. Stowe, at that time Professor of Languages and Biblical Literature in the Divinity school at Cincinnati, whither Mrs. Stowe accompanied him, and where, during a long residence, she became interested in the question of slavery, which has furnished the topic of her chief literary production. Mrs. Stowe was well known at home as a writer before her famous publication, which gave her a world-wide reputation. She had written a number of animated moral tales, which showed a quick perception and much earnestness in expression, a collection of which was published by the Harpers in 1849 entitled *The May Flower; or, Sketches of the Descendants of the Pilgrims.* A new edition, much enlarged, appeared in 1855. Her great work, *Uncle Tom's Cabin; or, Life among the Lowly*, appeared as a book from the press of Jewett & Co. in Boston in 1852. It had been previously published week by week in chapters in the National Era, an anti-slavery paper at Washington.

Uncle Tom, the hero of the story, is a negro slave, noted for a faithful discharge of his duties, a circumstance which does not exempt him from the changes in condition incident to his position. His master, a humane man, becomes embarrassed in his finances and sells the slave to a dealer. After passing through various hands he dies at the south-west. The fortunes of two runaway slaves contribute to the interest of the book. The escape on the floating ice of the Ohio from the slave to the free state forms one of its most dramatic incidents. Masters as well as slaves furnish the dramatis personæ, and due justice is rendered to the amiable and strong points of southern character. The story of little Eva, a beautiful child, dying at an early age, is narrated with literary skill and feeling.

Many of the scenes of Uncle Tom's Cabin having been objected to as improbable, the author, in justification of the assailed portions, published

A Key to Uncle Tom's Cabin, a collection of facts on the subject of slavery drawn from southern authorities. These, however, still leave the question of the probability of Uncle Tom's adventures an open one, the opponents of the book asserting that the pecuniary value of his virtues would have secured a permanent home and kind treatment to so exemplary a character, without regard to the confessedly strong feeling of attachment existing in the old settled portions of the south towards trustworthy family servants.

Uncle Tom was originally published in book form in two duodecimo volumes. A handsomely illustrated edition subsequently appeared. The sale of these editions had, by the close of 1852, reached to two hundred thousand copies. In England twenty editions in various forms, ranging in price from ten shillings to sixpence a copy, have been published. The aggregate sale of these up to the period we have mentioned, is stated by a late authority* to have been more than a million of copies. "In France," the Review adds, "Uncle Tom still covers the shop windows of the Boulevards; and one publisher alone, Eustace Barba, has sent out five different editions in different forms. Before the end of 1852 it had been translated into Italian, Spanish, Danish, Swedish, Dutch, Flemish, German, Polish, and Magyar. There are two different Dutch translations, and twelve different German ones; and the Italian translation enjoys the honor of the Pope's prohibition. It has been dramatized in twenty different forms and acted in every capital in Europe and in the free states of America."

Soon after the publication of Uncle Tom's Cabin Mrs. Stowe, in company with her husband and the Rev. Charles Beecher, her brother, visited Great Britain. Her observations were communicated to the public some time after her return by the issue, in conjunction with her husband, of two volumes of travels, *Sunny Memories of Foreign Lands*.

The great reputation of her novel, and the sympathy of all classes of the English people with the views it contained, had secured to the author an universally favorable reception, and we have consequently much in her volumes of lords and ladies, but these fortunately do not "all her praise engross," for she has an eye for art, literature, and humanitarian effort. She expresses her opinion on art with warmth and freedom, without, however, always securing the respect of the critical reader for her judgment.

The Rev. Charles Beecher contributes his journal of a tour on the Continent to his sister's volumes.

UNCLE TOM IN HIS CABIN.

The cabin of Uncle Tom was a small log building, close adjoining to "the house," as the negro *par excellence* designates his master's dwelling. In front it had a neat garden-patch, where, every summer, strawberries, raspberries, and a variety of fruits and vegetables, flourished under careful tending. The whole front of it was covered by a large scarlet bignonia and a native multiflora rose, which, entwisting and interlacing, left scarce a vestige of the rough logs to be seen. Here, also, in summer, various brilliant annuals, such as marigolds, petunias, four-o'clocks, found an indulgent corner in which to unfold their splendors, and were the delight and pride of Aunt Chloe's heart.

Let us enter the dwelling. The evening meal at the house is over, and Aunt Chloe, who presided over its preparation as head cook, has left to inferior officers in the kitchen the business of clearing away and washing dishes, and come out into her own snug territories, to "get her ole man's supper;" therefore, doubt not that it is her you see by the fire, presiding with anxious interest over certain frizzling items in a stewpan, and anon with grave consideration lifting the cover of a bake-kettle, from whence steam forth indubitable intimations of "something good." A round, black, shining face is hers, so glossy as to suggest the idea that she might have been washed over with white of eggs, like one of her own tea rusks. Her whole plump countenance beams with satisfaction and contentment from under her well-starched checked turban, bearing on it, however, if we must confess it, a little of that tinge of self-consciousness which becomes the first cook of the neighborhood, as Aunt Chloe was universally held and acknowledged to be.

A cook she certainly was, in the very bone and centre of her soul. Not a chicken, or turkey, or duck in the barn-yard but looked grave when they saw her approaching, and seemed evidently to be reflecting on their latter end; and certain it was that she was always meditating on trussing, stuffing, and roasting, to a degree that was calculated to inspire terror in any reflecting fowl living. Her corn-cake, in all its varieties of hoe-cake, dodgers, muffins, and other species too numerous to mention, was a sublime mystery to all less practised compounders; and she would shake her fat sides with honest pride and merriment, as she would narrate the fruitless efforts that one and another of her compeers had made to attain to her elevation.

The arrival of company at the house, the arranging of dinners and suppers "in style," awoke all the energies of her soul; and no sight was more welcome to her than a pile of travelling trunks launched on the verandah, for then she foresaw fresh efforts and fresh triumphs.

Just at present, however, Aunt Chloe is looking into the bake-pan; in which congenial operation we shall leave her till we finish our picture of the cottage.

In one corner of it stood a bed, covered neatly with a snowy spread; and by the side of it was a piece of carpeting of some considerable size. On this piece of carpeting Aunt Chloe took her stand, as being decidedly in the upper walks of life; and it and the bed by which it lay, and the whole corner, in fact, were treated with distinguished consideration, and made, as far as possible, sacred from the marauding inroads and desecrations of little folks. In fact, that corner was the *drawing-room* of the establishment. In the other corner was a bed of much humbler pretensions, and evidently designed for *use*. The wall over the fireplace was adorned with some very brilliant scriptural prints, and a portrait of General Washington, drawn and colored in a manner which would certainly have astonished that hero, if ever he had happened to meet with its like.

On a rough bench in the corner, a couple of woolly-headed boys, with glistening black eyes and fat shining cheeks, were busy in superintending the first walking operations of the baby, which, as is usually the case, consisted in getting up on its feet, balancing a moment, and then tumbling down,—each successive failure being violently cheered, as something decidedly clever.

A table, somewhat rheumatic in its limbs, was

* Edinburgh Review, April, 1855, p. 293.

drawn out in front of the fire, and covered with a cloth, displaying cups and saucers of a decidedly brilliant pattern, with other symptoms of an approaching meal. At this table was seated Uncle Tom, Mr. Shelby's best hand, who, as he is to be the hero of our story, we must daguerreotype for our readers. He was a large, broad-chested, powerfully-made man, of a full glossy black, and a face whose truly African features were characterized by an expression of grave and steady good sense, united with much kindliness and benevolence. There was something about his whole air self-respecting and dignified, yet united with a confiding and humble simplicity.

He was very busily intent at this moment on a slate lying before him, on which he was carefully and slowly endeavoring to accomplish a copy of some letters, in which operation he was overlooked by young Master George, a smart, bright boy of thirteen, who appeared fully to realize the dignity of his position as instructor.

"Not that way, Uncle Tom,—not that way," said he, briskly, as Uncle Tom laboriously brought up the tail of his g the wrong side out; "that makes a *q*, you see."

"La sakes, now, does it?" said Uncle Tom, looking with a respectful, admiring air, as his young teacher flourishingly scrawled *q*'s and *g*'s innumerable for his edification; and then, taking the pencil in his big, heavy fingers, he patiently re-commenced.

"How easy white folks al'us does things!" said Aunt Chloe, pausing while she was greasing a griddle with a scrap of bacon on her fork, and regarding young Master George with pride. "The way he can write, now! and read, too! and then to come out here evenings and read his lessons to us,—it's mighty interestin'!"

"But, Aunt Chloe, I'm getting mighty hungry," said George. "Isn't that cake in the skillet almost done?"

"Mose done, Mas'r George," said Aunt Chloe, lifting the lid and peeping in,—"browning beautiful—a real lovely brown. Ah! let me alone for dat. Missis let Sally try to make some cake, t'other day; jes to *larn* her, she said. 'O, go way, Missis,' says I; 'it really hurts my feelin's, now, to see good vittles spiled dat ar way! Cake ris all to one side—no shape at all; no more than my shoe;—go way!'"

And with this final expression of contempt for Sally's greenness, Aunt Chloe whipped the cover off the bake-kettle, and disclosed to view a neatly-baked pound-cake, of which no city confectioner need to have been ashamed. This being evidently the central point of the entertainment, Aunt Chloe began now to bustle about earnestly in the supper department.

"Here you, Mose and Pete! get out de way, you niggers! Get away, Polly honey,—mammy 'll give her baby somefin by and by. Now, Mas'r George, you jest take off dem books, and set down now with my old man, and I'll take up the sausages, and have de first griddle full of cakes on your plates in less dan no time."

"They wanted me to come to supper in the house," said George; "but I knew what was what too well for that, Aunt Chloe."

"So you did—so you did, honey," said Aunt Chloe, heaping the smoking batter-cakes on his plate; "you know'd your old aunty'd keep the best for you. O, let you alone for dat! Go way!" And, with that, aunty gave George a nudge with her finger, designed to be immensely facetious, and turned again to her griddle with great briskness.

"Now for the cake," said Master George, when the activity of the griddle department had somewhat subsided; and, with that, the youngster flourished a large knife over the article in question.

"La bless you, Mas'r George!" said Aunt Chloe, with earnestness, catching his arm, "you wouldn't be for cuttin' it wid dat ar great heavy knife! Smash all down—spile all de pretty rise of it. Here, I've got a thin old knife, I keeps sharp a purpose. Dar now, see! comes apart light as a feather! Now eat away—you won't get anything to beat dat ar."

"Tom Lincon says," said George, speaking with his mouth full, "that their Jinny is a better cook than you."

"Dem Lincons an't much count, no way!" said Aunt Chloe, contemptuously; "I mean, set along side *our* folks. They's 'spectable folks enough in a kinder plain way; but, as to gettin' up anything in style, they don't begin to have a notion on't. Set Mas'r Lincon, now, alongside Mas'r Shelby! Good Lor! and Missis Lincon,—can she kinder sweep it into a room like my missis,—so kinder splendid, yer know! O, go way! don't tell me nothin' of dem Lincons!"—and Aunt Chloe tossed her head as one who hoped she did know something of the world.

"Well, though, I've heard you say," said George, "that Jinny was a pretty fair cook."

"So I did," said Aunt Chloe,—"I may say dat. Good, plain, common cookin', Jinny'll do;—make a good pone o' bread,—bile her taters *far*,—her corn cakes isn't extra, not extra now, Jinny's corn cakes isn't, but then they's far,—but, Lor, come to de higher branches, and what *can* she do? Why, she makes pies—sartin she does; but what kinder crust? Can she make your real flecky paste, as melts in your mouth, and lies all up like a puff? Now, I went over thar when Miss Mary was gwine to be married, and Jinny she jest showed me de weddin' pies. Jinny and I is good friends, ye know. I never said nothin'; but go long, Mas'r George! Why, I shouldn't sleep a wink for a week, if I had a batch of pies like dem ar. Why, dey wan't no 'count 'tall."

"I suppose Jinny thought they were ever so nice," said George.

"Thought so!—didn't she? Thar she was, showing 'em, as innocent—ye see, it's jest here, Jinny *don't know*. Lor, the family an't nothing! She can't be spected to know! 'Tan't no fault o' hern. Ah, Mas'r George, you doesn't know half your privileges in yer family and bringin' up!" Here Aunt Chloe sighed, and rolled up her eyes with emotion.

"I'm sure, Aunt Chloe, I understand all my pie and pudding privileges," said George. "Ask Tom Lincon if I don't crow over him every time I meet him."

* * * * * * * * * *

By this time Master George had arrived at that pass to which even a boy can come (under uncommon circumstances), when he really could not eat another morsel, and, therefore, he was at leisure to notice the pile of woolly heads and glistening eyes which were regarding their operations hungrily from the opposite corner.

"Here, you Mose, Pete," he said, breaking off liberal bits, and throwing it at them; "you want some, don't you? Come, Aunt Chloe, bake them some cakes."

And George and Tom moved to a comfortable seat in the chimney-corner, while Aunt Chloe, after baking a goodly pile of cakes, took her baby on her lap, and began alternately filling its mouth and her own, and distributing to Mose and Pete, who seemed rather to prefer eating theirs as they rolled about on the floor under the table, tickling each other, and occasionally pulling the baby's toes.

"O! go long, will ye?" said the mother, giving now and then a kick, in a kind of general way, under the table, when the movement became too obstreperous. "Can't ye be decent when white folks comes to see ye? Stop dat ar, now, will ye? Better mind yourselves, or I'll take ye down a button-hole lower, when Mas'r George is gone!"

What meaning was couched under this terrible threat, it is difficult to say; but certain it is that its awful indistinctness seemed to produce very little impression on the young sinners addressed.

* * * * * * * *

"Well, now, I hopes you're done," said Aunt Chloe, who had been busy in pulling out a rude box of a trundle-bed; "and now, you Mose and you Pete, get into thar; for we's goin' to have the meetin'."

"O mother, we don't wanter. We wants to sit up to meetin',—meetin's is so curis. We likes 'em."

"La, Aunt Chloe, shove it under, and let 'em sit up," said Master George, decisively, giving a push to the rude machine.

Aunt Chloe, having thus saved appearances, seemed highly delighted to push the thing under, saying, as she did so, "Well, mebbe 'twill do 'em some good."

The house now resolved itself into a committee of the whole to consider the accommodations and arrangements for the meeting.

"What we's to do for cheers now, *I* declare I don't know," said Aunt Chloe. As the meeting had been held at Uncle Tom's weekly, for an indefinite length of time, without any more "cheers," there seemed some encouragement to hope that a way would be discovered at present.

"Old Uncle Peter sung both the legs out of dat oldest cheer, last week," suggested Mose.

"You go long! I'll boun' you pulled 'em out; some o' your shines," said Aunt Chloe.

"Well, it'll stand, if it only keeps jam up agin de wall!" said Mose.

"Den Uncle Peter mus'n't sit in it, cause he al'ays hitches when he gets a singing. He hitched pretty nigh across de room t'other night," said Pete.

"Good Lor! get him in it then," said Mose, "and den he'd begin, 'Come saints and sinners, hear me tell,' and den down he'd go,"—and Mose imitated precisely the nasal tones of the old man, tumbling on the floor, to illustrate the supposed catastrophe.

"Come now, be decent, can't ye?" said Aunt Chloe; "an't yer shamed?"

Master George, however, joined the offender in the laugh, and declared decidedly that Mose was a "buster." So the maternal admonition seemed rather to fail of effect.

"Well, ole man," said Aunt Chloe, "you'll have to tote in them ar bar'ls."

"Mother's bar'ls is like dat ar widder's, Mas'r George was reading 'bout in de good book,—dey never fails," said Mose, aside to Pete.

"I'm sure one on 'em caved in last week," said Pete, "and let 'em all down in de middle of de singin'; dat ar was failin', warnt it?"

During this aside between Mose and Pete, two empty casks had been rolled into the cabin, and being secured from rolling by stones on each side boards were laid across them, which arrangement, together with the turning down of certain tubs and pails, and the disposing of the rickety chairs, at last completed the preparation.

"Mas'r George is such a beautiful reader, now, I know he'll stay to read for us," said Aunt Chloe; "'pears like 'twill be so much more interestin'."

George very readily consented, for your boy is always ready for anything that makes him of importance.

The room was soon filled with a motley assemblage, from the old gray-headed patriarch of eighty to the young girl and lad of fifteen. A little harmless gossip ensued on various themes, such as where old Aunt Sally got her new red head-kerchief, and how "Missis was a going to give Lizzy that spotted muslin gown, when she'd got her new berage made up;" and how Mas'r Shelby was thinking of buying a new sorrel colt, that was going to prove an addition to the glories of the place. A few of the worshippers belonged to families hard by, who had got permission to attend, and who brought in various choice scraps of information, about the sayings and doings at the house and on the place, which circulated as freely as the same sort of small change does in higher circles.

After a while the singing commenced to the evident delight of all present. Not even all the disadvantage of nasal intonation could prevent the effect of the naturally fine voices, in airs at once wild and spirited. The words were sometimes the well-known and common hymns sung in the churches about, and sometimes of a wilder, more indefinite character, picked up at camp-meetings.

The chorus of one of them, which ran as follows, was sung with great energy and unction:—

Die on the field of battle,
Die on the field of battle,
Glory in my soul.

Another special favorite had oft repeated the words—

O, I'm going to glory,—wont you come along with me?
Don't you see the angels beck'ning, and a calling me away?
Don't you see the golden city and the everlasting day?

There were others, which made incessant mention of "Jordan's banks," and "Canaan's fields," and the "New Jerusalem;" for the negro mind, impassioned and imaginative, always attaches itself to hymns and expressions of a vivid and pictorial nature; and, as they sung, some laughed, and some cried, and some clapped hands, or shook hands rejoicingly with each other, as if they had fairly gained the other side of the river.

Various exhortations or relations of experience followed, and intermingled with the singing. One old gray-headed woman, long past work, but much revered as a sort of chronicle of the past, rose, and leaning on her staff, said—

"Well, chil'en! Well, I'm mighty glad to hear ye all and see ye all once more, 'cause I don't know when I'll be gone to glory; but I've done got ready, chil'en; 'pears like I'd got my little bundle all tied up, and my bonnet on, jest a waitin' for the stage to come along and take me home; sometimes, in the night, I think I hear the wheels a rattlin', and I'm lookin' out all the time; now, you jest be ready too, for I tell ye all, chil'en," she said, striking her staff hard on the floor, "dat ar *glory* is a mighty thing! It's a mighty thing, chil'en,—you don'no nothing about it,—it's *wonderful*." And the old creature sat down, with streaming tears, as wholly overcome, while the whole circle struck up

O Canaan, bright Canaan,
I'm bound for the land of Canaan.

Master George, by request, read the last chapters of Revelation, often interrupted by such exclamations as "The *sakes* now!" "Only hear that!" "Jest think on't!" "Is all that a comin' sure enough?"

George, who was a bright boy, and well trained in religious things by his mother, finding himself an object of general admiration, threw in expositions of his own, from time to time, with a commendable seriousness and gravity, for which he was admired by the young and blessed by the old; and it was agreed, on all hands, that "a minister couldn't lay it off better than he did;" that "'twas reely 'mazin'!"

Uncle Tom was a sort of patriarch in religious matters in the neighborhood. Having naturally an organization in which the *morale* was strongly predominant, together with a greater breadth and cultivation of mind than obtained among his companions, he was looked up to with great respect, as a sort of minister among them; and the simple, hearty, sincere style of his exhortations might have edified even better educated persons. But it was in prayer that he especially excelled. Nothing could exceed the touching simplicity, the child-like earnestness of his prayer, enriched with the language of Scripture, which seemed so entirely to have wrought itself into his being, as to have become a part of himself, and to drop from his lips unconsciously; in the language of a pious old negro, he "prayed right up." And so much did his prayer always work on the devotional feelings of his audiences, that there seemed often a danger that it would be lost altogether in the abundance of the responses which broke out everywhere around him.

HARRIET FARLEY.

THE editor of "The Lowell or New England Offering," in an autobiographic sketch published in Mrs. Hale's "Woman's Record," gives the following characteristic account of her career:—

"My father is a Congregational clergyman, and at the time of my birth was settled in the beautiful town of Claremont, in the state of New Hampshire. Though I left this place when six years of age, I still remember its natural beauties, which even then impressed me deeply. The Ashcutney Mountain, Sugar River, with its foaming falls, the distant hills of Vermont, all are in my memory. My mother was descended from the Moodys, somewhat famous in New England history. One of them was the eccentric and influential Father Moody. Another was Handkerchief Moody, the one who wore, so many years, 'the minister's veil.' One was the well known Trustee Moody, of Dumwell Academy, who educated my grandmother. She was a very talented and estimable lady.

"My father was of the genuine New Hampshire stock—from a family of pious, industrious, agricultural people; his brothers being deacons, and some of his sisters married to deacons. I have not learned that any of them ever committed a disgraceful act. His grandmother was eminent for her medical knowledge and skill, and had as much practice as is usually given to a country doctor. His mother was a woman of fine character, who exerted herself, and sacrificed much, to secure his liberal education. His sisters were energetic in their coöperation with their husbands, to secure and improve homes among the White and the Green Mountains, and Wisconsin. So much for progenitors.

"I was the sixth of ten children, and, until fourteen, had not that health which promises continued life. I was asthmatic, and often thought to be in a consumption. I am fortunate now in the possession of excellent health, which may be attributed to a country rearing, and an obedience to physical laws, so far as I understand them. At fourteen years of age I commenced exertions to assist in my own maintenance, and have at different times followed the different avocations of New England girls. I have plaited palm-leaf and straw, bound shoes, taught school, and worked at tailoring; besides my labors as a weaver in the factory, which suited me better than any other.

"After my father's removal to the little town of Atkinson, New Hampshire, he combined the labors of preceptor of one of the two oldest Academies in the state, with his parochial duties; and here, among a simple but intelligent people, I spent those years which give the tone to female character. At times there was a preceptress to the Academy; but it was in the summer, when I was debilitated, and my lessons were often studied on my bed. I learned something of French, drawing, ornamental needlework, and the usual accomplishments—for it was the design of my friends to make me a teacher—a profession for which I had an instinctive dislike. But my own feelings were not consulted. Indeed, perhaps it was not thought how much these were outraged; but their efforts were to suppress the imaginative and cultivate the practical. This was, undoubtedly, wholesome discipline; but it was carried to a degree that was painful, and drove me from my home. I came to Lowell, determined that if I had my own living to obtain, I would get it in my own way; that I would read, think, and *write, when I could*, without restraint; that if I did well I would have the credit of it; if ill, my friends should be relieved from the blame, if not from the stigma. I endeavored to reconcile them to my lot, by a devotion of all my spare earnings to them and their interests. I made good wages; I dressed economically; I assisted in the liberal education of one brother, and endeavored to be the guardian angel of a lovely sister, who, after many years of feebleness, is now perhaps a guardian angel to me in heaven. Twice before this had I left 'the mill,' to watch around the death-beds of loved ones—my elder sister, and a beautiful and promising brother. Two others had previously died; two have left their native state for a Texan home. So you will see that my feelings must have been severely tried. But all this has, doubtless, been beneficial to me.

"It was something so new to me to be praised and encouraged to write, that I was at first overwhelmed by it, and withdrew as far as possible from the attentions that some of my first contributions to the 'Offering' directed towards me. It was with great reluctance that I consented to edit, and was quite as unwilling at first to assist in publishing. But circumstances seem to have compelled me forward as a business woman, and I have endeavored to *do my duty*.

"I am now the proprietor of 'The New England Offering.' I do all the publishing, editing, canvassing, and, as it is bound in my office, I can in a hurry help fold, cut covers, stitch, &c. I have a little girl to assist me in the folding, stitching, &c.; the rest, after it comes from the printer's hand, is all my own work. I employ no agents, and depend upon no one for assistance. My edition is four thousand."

The Lowell Offering was commenced in 1841.

In 1848 Miss Farley published a volume chiefly made up of her contributions to that periodical, entitled *Shells from the Strand of the Sea of Genius*. Another volume from the various writers in the same publication was collected by Charles Knight, in London, and published in one of his popular libraries in 1849—*Mind among the Spindles*.

ELIZABETH F. ELLET.

MRS. ELIZABETH FRIES ELLET was born at Sodus Point, on Lake Ontario, New York, in October, 1818. Her maiden name was Lummis. Her father was a physician, Dr. William Nixon Lummis, the pupil and the friend of Rush, whom he strongly resembled in person. He was of a New

Jersey family, and became one of the pioneers of Western New York, expending a fortune in improvements in the country adjoining Sodus bay, of which others reaped the advantage. He was a man of talent and religious character, and admired for his social qualities. His second wife, the mother of our author, was Sarah, the daughter of Captain John Maxwell, an officer in the American army during the Revolutionary war, and the niece of General William Maxwell in the same service.

Mrs. Ellet was educated in English and French at the female seminary, under the care of Susan Marriott, an accomplished English Quaker lady, at Aurora, Cayuga county, New York. She was early married to Dr. William H. Ellet, who has occupied the professorship of chemistry at Columbia College, New York, and in the South Carolina College at Columbia. In 1849 they came to reside permanently in New York.

E. F. Ellet.

The poetical talent was marked in Mrs. Ellet at a very early age. She wrote good verses at fifteen, and in 1835 published a volume of poems. At the same period appeared a tragedy from her pen entitled *Teresa Contarini*, founded on a Venetian historic incident, which was performed on the stage. In 1841 a volume in prose appeared from her pen, *The Characters of Schiller*, a critical essay on the genius of that author, and analysis of his characters. *Scenes in the Life of Joanna of Sicily*, partly historical and partly fanciful; and a small volume for children, *Rambles about the Country*, appeared about the same time. Mrs. Ellet also, at this period, contributed articles to the American Quarterly Review, the North American and the New York Reviews, on Italian and French dramatic and lyric poetry, and wrote tales and poems for monthly magazines in New York, Philadelphia, and Charleston. In 1848 she published her work, *The Women of the American Revolution*, in two volumes, to which a third was subsequently added. It was an undertaking requiring not only a special sympathy (which Mrs. Ellet possessed through her family associations) and literary skill, but much labor and research. These memoirs, which shed so important a light on the history of the Revolution, were chiefly compiled from original materials, manuscripts of the times, or personal recollections of the surviving friends of the heroines. A companion volume, *The Domestic History of the Revolution*, is a connected narrative exhibiting the life of the period.

Another collection of memoirs is *The Pioneer Women of the West*, written from original materials. *Summer Rambles in the West* describes a tour through several of the western states, with a full description of parts of Minnesota Territory.

She is also the author of a pleasant volume, *Evenings at Woodlawn*, a collection of European legends and traditions; of *Novellettes of the Musicians*, a series of tales, original and selected from the German, founded on incidents in the personal history of artists, and illustrative of their character and the style of their works. Her *Watching Spirits*, an illustrated volume, is an essay on the presence and agency of spirits in this world, as described in the Holy Scriptures.

LINES TO ——.

Thou in faithfulness hast afflicted me.—Ps. cxix. 75.

Smitten of Heaven—and murmuring 'neath the rod—
Whose days are heavy with their freight of gloom:
  Drooping and faint, with eyes
  Not yet by Faith unclosed—

Art thou repining that thou stand'st apart,
Like the tree lightning-blasted? wrung with pain,
  No sympathy can heal—
  No time can e'er assuage.

This life to thee is but a sea of woe,
Whose deep unto its deep of sorrow calls:
  While others walk a maze
  Of flowers, and smiles, and joys!

Look up—thou lone and sorely stricken one!
Look up—thou darling of the Eternal Sire!
  More blest a thousand-fold
  Than they—the proudly gay!

For them earth yields her all of bliss;—for *thee*
Kind Heaven doth violence to its heart of love;
  And Mercy holds thee fast,
  Fast in her iron bonds—

And wounds thee lest thou 'scape her jealous care,
And her *best* gifts—the cross and thorn—bestows,
  They dwell within the vale,
  Where fruits and flowers abound.

Thou on affliction's high and barren place;
But round about the mount chariots of fire—
  Horses of fire—encamp
  To keep thee safe for heaven.

JEDIDIAH V. HUNTINGTON.

MR. HUNTINGTON was born in 1814, and educated as a physician. After practising his profession for several years, he became, in December, 1839, a candidate for orders in the Protestant Episcopal Church, and a professor in St. Paul's College, Flushing. After his ordination he was for a short time rector of a church in Middlebury, Vermont. He then visited Europe, and remained for several years in Italy. On his return he became a Roman Catholic, but did not enter the priesthood of that communion. After a residence of a few years in New York, he removed to Baltimore, where he edited a monthly magazine. In

1855 he again removed to St. Louis, and edited a weekly journal, "The Leader," a literary, political, and family newspaper.

In 1843 he published a volume of *Poems*, mostly of a religious and reflective character, including several translations from the hymns of the Breviary. His next publication, *Alice, or the New Una*, appeared in London, in 1849, during his residence abroad. It is a singular compound of the art, the religious and the fashionable novel, and contained many scenes whose warmth of description laid the work open to censure. Its beauty of language, and picturesque descriptions of natural scenery, attracted much attention. It was reprinted during the same year in the United States, and, in 1852, appeared in a revised edition with many judicious alterations. Mr. Huntington's second novel, *The Forest*, was published in 1852. It is a continuation of Lady Alice, the leading characters being transferred from Europe to the Adirondack Mountains. The fine scenery of the region is depicted with beauty, but the fiction is, like its predecessor, deficient in the vigorous delineation of character.

THE SONG OF THE OLD YEAR.
December 31st, 1838.

Of brethren we six thousand be,
  Nor one e'er saw another;
By birth-law dire must each expire
  To make way for a brother;
Old Father Time our common sire,
  Eternity our mother.

When we have spent the life she lent,
  Her breast we do not spurn;
The very womb from which we loom,
  To it we still return;
Its boundless gloom becomes a tomb
  Our shadows to inurn.

In the hour of my birth, there was joy and mirth;
  And shouts of gladness filled my ear;
But directly after each burst of laugh
  Came sounds of pain and fear;
—The groans of the dying, the bitter crying
  Of those who held them dear.

The regular beat of dancing feet
  Ushered my advent in;
But on the air the voice of prayer
  Arose above the din;
Its accents sweet did still entreat
  Pardon for human sin.

As thus began my twelve-months' span
  Through the infinite extended;
So ever hath run on my path,
  'Twixt joy and grief suspended;
But chiefly measured by things most treasured,
  In death with burdens blended.

The bell aye tolls for departing souls
  Of those whom I have slain;
The ceaseless knell to me doth tell
  Each minute of my reign.
Their bodies left of life bereft,
  Would cumber hill and plain.

But I have made, with my restless spade,
  Their thirty-million graves;
With constant toil upturning the soil,
  Or parting the salt-sea waves,
To find a bed for my countless dead
  In the secret ocean-caves.

By fond hopes blighted, of true vows plighted
  Showing the little worth;
By affections wasted: by joys scarce tasted,
  Or poisoned ere their birth;
I have proved to many, there is not any
  Pure happiness on earth.

And prophetic power upon the hour
  Of my expiring waits;
What I have been not enters in
  With me the silent gates:
The fruit within its grace, or sin,
  For endless harvest waits.

And lo, as I pass with that running glass
  That counts my last moments of sorrow,
The tale I tell, if pondered well,
  The soul of young hope must harrow;
For mirrored in me, ye behold what shall be
  In the New-Year born to-morrow.

RUFUS WILMOT GRISWOLD

Was born in Rutland county, Vermont, Feb. 15, 1815, of an old New England family which contributed some of the earliest settlers to the country. Much of his early life, as we learn from a biographical article which originally appeared in the Knickerbocker Magazine, "was spent in voyaging about the world; before he was twenty years of age, he had seen the most interesting portions of his own country, and of southern and central Europe." He afterwards studied divinity and became a preacher of the Baptist denomination. He is chiefly known to the public, however, through his literary productions. He became early connected with the press; was associated in the editorship of the New Yorker, the Brother Jonathan, and New World newspapers, and other journals in Boston and Philadelphia. In 1842, he was the editor of Graham's Magazine, which he conducted with eminent success, drawing to the work the contributions of some of the best authors of the country who found liberal remuneration, then a novelty in American literature, from the generous policy of the publisher.

R. W. Griswold

In 1850, Mr. Griswold projected *The International Monthly Magazine*, five volumes of which were published by Messrs. Stringer and Townsend of New York. Like all of his undertakings of this character, it was liberally devoted to the notice and support of American authors, with whom Mr. Griswold has constantly maintained an extensive personal acquaintance.

His most prominent relations of this kind, however, have been through his series of books, *The Poets and Poetry of America*, the first edition of which appeared in 1842; *The Prose Writers of America*, which was first published in 1846; and the *Female Poets of America*, in 1849. They were the first comprehensive illustrations of the literature of the country, and have exerted an important influence through their criticisms, and on the reputation of the numerous authors included, in their reception at home and abroad.

Mr. Griswold is also the author of a volume, *The Poets and Poetry of England in the Nineteenth Century*, in similar style with the American series, and has edited an octavo volume, *The Sacred Poets of England and America*.

In 1847, he was engaged in Philadelphia in the preparation of two series of biographies, *Washington and the Generals of the American Revolution*, and *Napoleon and the Marshals of the Empire.*

Mr. Griswold, among other illustrations of American history and society, is the author of an interesting appendix to an edition of D'Israeli's Curiosities of Literature, entitled *The Curiosities of American Literature*. In 1842, he published in New York a volume on an excellent plan, worthy of having been continued, entitled *The Biographical Annual.*

Among other productions of his pen should be mentioned an early volume of Poems in 1841; a volume of Sermons, and a Discourse in 1844, on *The Present Condition of Philosophy.*

His latest publication is, *The Republican Court, or American Society in the Days of Washington*, a costly printed volume from the press of the Appletons, in 1854. On the thread of the domestic life of Washington, Mr. Griswold hangs a social history of the period, which he is thus enabled to sketch in its leading characteristics in the northern, middle, and southern states; the career of the great founder of the Republic, fortunately for the common sympathy of the whole, having been associated with all these elements of national life. The book is full of interesting matter from the numerous memoirs and biographies, is illustrated by a number of portraits of the more eminent ladies of the time, and has been well received by the public.

Dr. Griswold is at present engaged on a revision of his larger works on American literature, which have passed through numerous editions with successive improvements.

BENJAMIN DAVIS WINSLOW

Was born in Boston, February 13, 1815. His early years were passed at home, at the residence of Gen. William Hall, at Boston, and with the Rev. Samuel Ripley at Waltham, where he received his first instructions in Latin. He was prepared for Harvard under the tuition of Mr. D. G. Ingraham, of Boston, received his degree at this college in 1835, entered the General Theological Seminary of the Protestant Episcopal Church at New York, pursued the usual term of study, and was ordained Deacon in 1838, by his friend Bishop Doane of New Jersey, to whom he became assistant minister of St. Mary's Church, Burlington. The brief remaining portion of his life was passed in this service. He died November 21, 1839.

A genial memorial of his Sermons and Poetical Remains, in an octavo volume, was prepared by Bishop Doane, entitled *The True Catholic Churchman, in his Life and in his Death.* The sermons are earnest doctrinal compositions, written with ease and elegance. The poems, many of which are devoted to sacred church associations, are all in a truthful and fervent vein, with a happy facility of execution, and on the score both of taste and piety are well worthy to be associated with the kindred compositions of the author's friends, Croswell and Doane.

THOUGHTS FOR THE CITY.

Out on the city's hum!
My spirit would flee from the haunts of men
To where the woodland and leafy glen
Are eloquently dumb.

These dull brick walls which span
My daily walks, and which shut me in;
These crowded streets, with their busy din—
They tell too much of man.

Oh! for those dear wild flowers,
Which in their meadows so brightly grew,
Where the honey-bee and blithe bird flew
That gladdened boyhood's hours.

Out on these chains of flesh!
Binding the pilgrim who fain would roam,
To where kind nature hath made her home,
In bowers so green and fresh.

But is not nature here?
From these troubled scenes look up and view
The orb of day, through the firmament blue,
Pursue his bright career.

Or, when the night-dews fall,
Go watch the moon with her gentle glance
Flitting over the clear expanse—
Her own broad star-lit hall.

Mortal the earth may mar,
And blot out its beauties one by one;
But he cannot dim the fadeless sun,
Or quench a single star.

And o'er the dusky town,
The greater light that ruleth the day,
And the heav'nly host, in their bright array
Look gloriously down.

So, 'mid the hollow mirth,
The din and strife of the crowded mart;
We may ever lift up the eye and heart
To scenes above the earth.

Blest thought, so kindly given!
That though he toils with his boasted might,
Man cannot shut from his brother's sight
The things and thoughts of Heaven!

T. B. THORPE.

T. B. Thorpe was born at Westfield, Mass., March 1, 1815. His father Thomas Thorpe, a man of literary genius, was a clergyman, who died in New York city at the early age of twenty-six. His son lived in New York till his transfer to the Wesleyan University at Middletown, Connecticut, where he passed three years; but his health failing him, in 1836 he left Connecticut for the south, where he resided in Louisiana to the year 1853. In early life he displayed a taste for painting. His picture of "the Bold Dragoon," illustrative of Irving's story, was executed in his seventeenth year, and exhibited at the old American Academy of Fine Arts. Like Irving himself, he left the pencil for the pen, and turned his talent for grouping and sketching to the kindred province of descriptive writing. He soon became known as the author of a series of western tales, adopting the name of Tom Owen, the Bee-Hunter, the title of one of his first stories, the subject of which was an eccentric personage—to whom the author has given a wild flavor of poetry—a "bee-hunter" by profession, with whom he fell in shortly after his removal to the south.

T. B. Thorpe.

For many years Mr. Thorpe was an editor of one of the leading political newspapers in New Orleans, devoted to the interests of Henry Clay. In this enterprise, notwithstanding his fine literary tact, political knowledge, and untiring energy, he was compelled, for lack of pecuniary resources, to leave the field to others. On the announcement of the war with Mexico, he distinguished himself by his zeal in raising volunteers; and as bearer of dispatches to General Taylor he was not only early in the field, but had a most excellent position to witness the scenes of war. His letters, published in a New Orleans paper, were the first that reached the United States. The descriptions of the American camp, the country, and the Mexican people, were extensively published. Immediately after General Taylor took possession of Metamoras, he prepared, in 1846, a volume entitled *Our Army on the Rio Grande*, succeeded by *Our Army at Monterey*. These two volumes, according to their extent, have furnished most of the materials that have been wrought into the subsequent histories relating to the events which they describe.

Mr. Thorpe bore an active part in the election of General Taylor to the Presidency. He took the field as a speaker, and became one of the most popular and efficient orators of the South-West. His speeches were marked by their good sense, brilliancy of expression, and graphic humorous illustration.

In 1853, Mr. Thorpe removed to New York with his family, and among other literary enterprises prepared a new collection of his sketches, which were published by the Appletons, with the title, *The Hive of the "Bee-Hunter."* This miscellany of sketches of peculiar American character, scenery, and rural sports, is marked by the simplicity and delicacy with which its rough humors are handled. The style is easy and natural, the sentiment fresh and unforced, showing a fine sensibility. In "the Bee-Hunter," there is a vein of poetry, which has been happily caught by Darley in the illustration which accompanies the sketch in the volume. In proof of the fidelity of Mr. Thorpe's hunting scenes, there is an anecdote connected with some of his writings. His taste for life in the back-woods, the hunter's camp fire, and the military bivouac, shown in his published sketches, had attracted the attention in England of Sir William Drummond Stewart, an eccentric Scotch nobleman, who projected and accomplished a tour in the Rocky Mountains. On his arrival at New Orleans, he endeavored to secure Mr. Thorpe as a member of his party; an offer which could not be conveniently accepted. While Sir William was absent, however, Mr. Thorpe wrote a series of letters, purporting to give an account of the "Doings of the Expedition," which were published in this country and England as genuine, Sir William himself pronouncing them the most truthful of all that were written, all the while supposing they were from some member of his party.

Mr. Thorpe is a contributor to Harpers' Magazine, where he has published several descriptive articles on southern life and products, and a sketch, "The Case of Lady Macbeth Medically Considered."

TOM OWEN, THE BEE-HUNTER.

As a country becomes cleared up and settled, bee-hunters disappear, consequently they are seldom or never noticed beyond the immediate vicinity of their homes. Among this backwoods fraternity, have flourished men of genius in their way, who have died unwept and unnoticed, while the heroes of the turf, and of the chase, have been lauded to the skies for every trivial superiority they may have displayed in their respective pursuits.

To chronicle the exploits of sportsmen is commendable—the custom began as early as the days of the antediluvians, for we read, that "Nimrod was a mighty hunter before the Lord." Familiar, however, as Nimrod's name may be—or even Davy Crockett's—how unsatisfactory their records, when we reflect that Tom Owen, the bee-hunter, is comparatively unknown!

Yes, the mighty Tom Owen has "hunted," from the time that he could stand alone until the present time, and not a pen has inked paper to record his exploits. "Solitary and alone" has he traced his game through the mazy labyrinth of air; marked, I hunted;—I found;—I conquered;—upon the carcasses of his victims, and then marched homeward with his spoils; quietly and satisfiedly, sweetening his path through life; and, by its very obscurity, adding the principal element of the sublime.

It was on a beautiful southern October morning, at the hospitable mansion of a friend, where I was staying to drown dull care, that I first had the pleasure of seeing Tom Owen.

He was, on this occasion, straggling up the rising ground that led to the hospitable mansion of mine host, and the difference between him and ordinary men was visible at a glance; perhaps it showed itself as much in the perfect contempt of fashion that he displayed in the adornment of his outward man, as it did in the more elevated qualities of his mind, which were visible in his face. His head was adorned with an outlandish pattern of a hat—his nether limbs were encased by a pair of inexpressibles, beautifully fringed by the brier-bushes through which they were often drawn; coats and vests, he considered as superfluities; hanging upon his back were a couple of pails, and an axe in his right hand, formed the varieties that represented the corpus of Tom Owen.

As is usual with great men, he had his followers, who, with a courtier-like humility, depended upon the expression of his face for all their hopes of success.

The usual salutations of meeting were sufficient to draw me within the circle of his influence, and I at once became one of his most ready followers.

"See yonder!" said Tom, stretching his long arm into infinite space, "see yonder—there's a bee."

We all looked in the direction he pointed, but that was the extent of our observations.

"It was a fine bee," continued Tom, "black body, yellow legs, and went into that tree,"—pointing to a towering oak blue in the distance. "In a clear day I can see a bee over a mile, easy!"

When did Coleridge "talk" like that? And yet Tom Owen uttered such a saying with perfect ease.

After a variety of meanderings through the thick woods, and clambering over fences, we came to our place of destination, as pointed out by Tom, who selected a mighty tree containing sweets, the possession of which the poets have likened to other sweets that leave a sting behind.

The felling of a mighty tree is a sight that calls up a variety of emotions; and Tom's game was lodged in one of the finest in the forest. But "the axe was laid at the root of the tree," which in Tom's mind was made expressly for bees to build their nests in, that he might cut them down, and obtain possession of their honeyed treasure. The sharp axe, as it played in the hands of Tom, was replied to by a stout negro from the opposite side of the tree, and their united strokes fast gained upon the heart of their lordly victim.

There was little poetry in the thought, that long before this mighty empire of States was formed, Tom Owen's "bee-hive" had stretched its brawny arms to the winter's blast, and grown green in the summer's sun.

Yet such was the case, and how long I might have moralized I know not, had not the enraged buzzing about my ears satisfied me that the occupants of the tree were not going to give up their home and treasure, without showing considerable practical fight. No sooner had the little insects satisfied themselves that they were about to be invaded, than they began, one after another, to descend from their airy abode, and fiercely pitch into our faces; anon a small company, headed by an old veteran, would charge with its entire force upon all parts of our body at once.

It need not be said that the better part of valor was displayed by a precipitate retreat from such attacks.

In the midst of this warfare, the tree began to tremble with the fast repeated strokes of the axe, and then might have been seen a "bee-line" of stingers precipitating themselves from above, on the unfortunate hunter beneath.

Now it was that Tom shone forth in his glory, for his partisans—like many hangers-on about great men, began to desert him on the first symptoms of danger; and when the trouble thickened, they, one and all, took to their heels, and left only our hero and Sambo to fight the adversaries. Sambo, however, soon dropped his axe, and fell into all kinds of contortions; first he would seize the back of his neck with his hands, then his legs, and yell with pain. "Never holler till you get out of the woods," said the sublime Tom, consolingly; but writhe the negro did, until he broke, and left Tom "alone in his glory."

Cut,—thwack! sounded through the confused hum at the foot of the tree, marvellously reminding me of the interruptions that occasionally broke in upon the otherwise monotonous hours of my school-boy days.

A sharp cracking finally told me the chopping was done, and, looking aloft, I saw the mighty tree balancing in the air. Slowly, and majestically, it bowed for the first time towards its mother earth,—gaining velocity as it descended, it shivered the trees that interrupted its downward course, and falling with thundering sounds, splintered its mighty limbs, and buried them deeply in the ground.

The sun for the first time in at least two centuries, broke uninterruptedly through the chasm made in the forest and shone with splendor upon the magnificent Tom, standing a conqueror among his spoils.

As might be expected, the bees were very much astonished and confused, and by their united voices proclaimed death, had it been in their power, to all their foes, not, of course, excepting Tom Owen himself. But the wary hunter was up to the tricks of his trade, and, like a politician, he knew how easily an enraged mob could be quelled with smoke; and smoke he tried, until his enemies were completely destroyed.

We, Tom's hangers-on, now approached his treasure. It was a rich one, and, as he observed, "contained a rich chance of plunder." Nine feet, by measurement, of the hollow of the tree were full, and this afforded many pails of pure honey.

Tom was liberal, and supplied us all with more than we wanted, and "toted," by the assistance of Sambo, his share to his own home, soon to be devoured, and soon to be replaced by the destruction of another tree, and another nation of bees.

Thus Tom exhibited within himself, an unconquerable genius which would have immortalized him, had he directed it in following the sports of Long Island or New Market.

We have seen the great men of the southern turf glorying around the victories of their favorite sport—we have heard the great western hunters detail the soul-stirring adventures of a bear-hunt—we have listened with almost suffocating interest, to the tale of a Nantucket seaman, while he portrayed the death of a mighty whale—and we have also seen Tom Owen triumphantly engaged in a bee-hunt—we beheld and wondered at the sports of the turf—the field—and the sea—because the objects acted on by man were terrible, indeed, when their instincts were aroused.

But, in the bee-hunt of Tom Owen, and its consummation,—the grandeur *visible* was imparted by the mighty mind of Tom Owen himself.

GEORGE EDWARD ELLIS

WAS born in Boston in 1815. He became a graduate of Harvard in 1833; studied at the Divinity school at Cambridge, and was ordained in Charlestown in 1838 as successor to the Rev. (now President) James Walker, in the ministry of the Harvard church.

He has been one of the editors of the Christian Register, the religious paper of the Massachusetts Unitarians, and is now associated with the brilliant pulpit orator, the Rev. Dr. George Putnam, in the editorship of the Christian Examiner His reading, scholarship, literary readiness, vivacity, and good English style, admirably qualify him for the work of periodical literature.*

Mr. Ellis is the author of three volumes of biography in Mr. Sparks's American series: the lives of John Mason—the author of the history of the Pequot war—Anne Hutchinson, and William Penn.

His contributions to periodical literature are numerous, embracing many articles in the New York Review, the North American, and the Christian Examiner. He has frequently delivered occasional discourses and orations, and his published addresses of this kind would make a large volume. Mr. Ellis is an active member of the Massachusetts Historical Society, of the practical working of which body he lately gave a pleasant account in a communication to the fellow New York society, of which he is a corresponding member. In his religious views, Mr. Ellis belongs to the class of Unitarians who earnestly advocate the supernatural authority of the gospel, and resist the assaults of the new school of rationalists; while in respect to practical reforms, he has sometimes taken quite bold ground with the progressive party.

ORGAN MELODIES.†

There is a sort of instinctive feeling within us that an organ should be reserved for only sacred uses. The bray of the martial trumpet seems akin to the din and clangor of a military movement. The piano is the appropriate ornament and instrument of the household room of comfort and domestic delight. Lesser instruments, with their gay tones, and their lighter lessons for the heart, adapt themselves to the unstable emotions of the hour—in revelry, excitement, or gratification. To each of them there is a season, and from our youth to our age these varied instruments may minister to us, according to their uses and our sensibilities. The harp which the monarch of Israel swept as the accompaniment to his divine lyrics; the timbrel which Miriam, the sister of Aaron, took in her hand when she raised the glad pæan—"Sing ye to the Lord, for he hath triumphed gloriously;" the silver trumpets which the priests blew to proclaim the great Jewish festivals; the horn and the psaltery, the sackbut and the dulcimer, which lifted up the anthems of the Tabernacle or the Temple-worship, were not without a sacred influence, helping with their strings or pipes the effect of holy song. But the religious sentiment is the largest that fills the heart of man; its sweep and compass are the widest, and in the course of our own short lives that religious sentiment will range like "a song of degrees" over all the varying emotions of the soul, engaging every tone to give it utterance.

"Praise the Lord with gladness," is the key-note of one Psalm. "Out of the depths have I cried to Thee, O Lord," is the plaintive moan of another. "Sing unto the Lord, all the earth," is the quickening call to a general anthem. "Keep silence before Me, O Islands!" stills the trembling spirit into a low whisper of its fear. "The Lord is my Shepherd," is the beautiful pastoral lyric for the serene life of still waters. "He bowed the heavens and came down, he did fly upon the wings of the wind; the Lord also thundered in the heavens, and he shot out lightnings from the sky"—this is the Psalm for the stormy elements or a troubled heart. "O Lord, rebuke me not in thine anger!" is now our imploring cry; "Though he slay me, yet will I trust in Him," is now the boast of the resigned spirit. "The lines are fallen to me in pleasant places," is the bright lyric of the heart that finds its joy on earth. "O, that I had wings like a dove, for then would I flee away and be at rest!" is the burden of the heart when it sighs and moans over the wreck of mortal delights. "Thou hast made man but a little lower than the angels!" is the tone which befits the feeling of our human dignity. "Lord, thou hast been our dwelling-place in all generations: thou carriest us away as with a flood," is the mingled note of melancholy and faith with which we contemplate our failing years, and yield up one after another from our earthly fellowship to the summons of the everliving God—the everlasting Refuge.

Thus, through the whole range of emotions and sensibilities of the heart, in its thrills and wails, in its elation and its gloom, in penitence, remorse, submission and hope, in gratitude, aspiration, or high desire—that heart varies its note, but sincerity will make music of all its utterances in psalm or dirge. Precious, precious beyond all our terms of praise, are those religious songs and hymns which come to us from the prophetic lips once touched with the fire of God. If they are dear to us, how dear must they have been to those who sung them in their majestic and solemn Hebrew tones, beneath the cedars that bowed, and the hills that melted, and in the corn-fields that laughed when the song of praise arose to God. How many glad harvests with their laden vintages and garners, how many rejoicing scenes of happiness, and how many ancient sorrows born of our inevitable lot on the earth, stand for ever painted and rehearsed in the Psalms of David. Over no single scene or incident in Jewish history are we so completely engaged in sympathy with their sad fortunes as in one in which the tender melodies of sacred song, and the holy uses of music, bring them touchingly before us. When they were

* We may here glance at the history of the Examiner. It grew out of the Christian Disciple, a monthly publication commenced by the Rev. Noah Worcester, under the auspices of Dr. Channing and others, in 1813. At the completion of its sixth volume, in 1818, Dr. Worcester surrendered it to the Rev. Henry Ware, Jr., who published the work every two months for five years. In 1824, passing into the hands of the Rev. J. G. Palfrey, its title was changed to the Christian Examiner. He was its editor for two years, when it was conducted from 1826 to 1831 by Mr. Francis Jenks. In the latter year it was transferred to the Rev. James Walker and the Rev. Francis William Pitt Greenwood. It was edited by the former six years, Mr. Greenwood's health not allowing him to labor upon it, when Dr. Walker was succeeded by the Rev. William Ware, and the latter in turn, after a few years, by the Rev. Messrs. Lamson and Gannett, from whose hands it passed to the care of Messrs. Putnam and Ellis.—*Sidney Willard's Memories*, ii. 281–2.

† From a discourse at Charlestown—The Consecration of an Organ. 1853.

weary captives in pagan Babylon, their tearful hearts turned back to their beloved Jerusalem: "By the rivers of Babylon there we sat down: yea, we wept when we remembered Zion. We hanged our harps upon the willows in the midst thereof. For there they that carried us away captive required of us a song; and they that wasted us required of us mirth, saying, 'Sing us one of the songs of Zion.' How shall we sing the Lord's song in a strange land?" That burst of sadness is of itself a fond and precious song.

CYRUS A. BARTOL,

A colleague of Dr. Lowell in the ministry of the West church, Boston, is a graduate of Bowdoin of 1832, and of the Harvard divinity school in 1835. He has published numerous occasional sermons, and is the author of two volumes, *The Christian Spirit and Life* and *The Christian Body and Form*. He brings in these discourses a somewhat elaborate literary style, uniting metaphysical insight to poetical sentiment, to the usual exhortations of the pulpit. He has in preparation a volume of meditative essays suggested by a recent European tour. A miniature book of selections from his writings has been made, entitled *Grains of Gold*.

ALLSTON'S BELSHAZZAR'S FEAST—FROM A DISCOURSE ON PERFECTION.

In yonder village, a painter paces, in quiet meditation, his little room. Beautiful pictures has he sent forth to charm every beholder; but he alone is not satisfied. He draws some grand theme from the mighty chronicle of the Bible. He would turn the words of the rapt prophet into colors. He would hold up to the eyes of men a scene of the divine judgments, that should awe down every form of sin, and exalt every resolve of holiness in their hearts. The finished result of his labors is shortly expected. But the idea of perfection has seized with an overmastering grasp upon him, and it must give him pause. How shall that awful writing of doom be pencilled on the plastered wall? How shall that finger, as it were of a man's hand, and yet the finger of God, be revealed? How shall those voluptuous forms below, that have been all relaxed with the wine and the feast and the dalliance of the hour, be represented in their transition so swift to conscience-stricken alarm, prostrate terror, ineffectual rage, and palsied suspense, as they are confronted by those flaming characters of celestial indignation, which the soothsayers, with magic scrolls, and strange garb, and juggling arts, can but mutter and mumble over, and only the servant of Almighty God calmly explain? How shall it be done according to the perfect pattern shown in the Mount of Revelation of God's word? The artist thinks and labors, month by month, and year after year. The figures of Babylonish king and consort, of Hebrew seer and maiden, and of Chaldee magician, grow into expressive portraits under his hand. The visible grandeur of God the Judge, over against the presumptuous sins of man, approaches its completeness. The spectator would now be entranced with the wondrous delineation. But the swiftly conceiving mind which shapes out its imaginations of that dread tribunal, so suddenly set up in the hall of revelry, is not yet content. The idea of perfection, that smote it, smites it again. The aspiration after a new and higher beauty, that carried it to one point, lifts it to another, and bears it far aloft, in successive flights, ever above its own work. Yet still, on those few feet of canvas, the earnest laborer breathes out, for the best of a lifetime, the patient and exhaustless enthusiasm of his soul. He hides the object, dear as a living child to its mother, from every eye, and presses on to the mark. If he walks, he catches a new trait of expression, some new line of lustrous illumination, to transfer to this painted scripture which he is composing. If he sleeps, some suggestion of an improvement will steal even into his dreams. In weariness and in sickness, he still climbs slowly, painfully, to his task. In absence, his soul turns back, and makes all nature tributary to his art. And on his expiring day he seizes his pencil to strive, by another stroke still, after the perfection which flies before him, and leaves his work as with the last breath of his mouth, and movement of his hand, upon it, to show, amid unfinished groups, and the measured lines for a new trial, that, if absolute perfection cannot be reached here on earth, yet heights of splendor and excellence can be attained, beyond all the thoughts of him whom the glorious idea has never stirred. What a lesson for us in our moral and religious struggles! What a rebuke for our idle loiterings in the heavenward way! What a shame to our doubtings about that perfection to which God and Christ and apostles call!

GEORGE WASHINGTON GREENE.

George Washington Greene, the son of N. R. Greene, and grandson of Major-General Greene of the Revolutionary army, was born at East Greenwich, Kent county, Rhode Island, April 8, 1811. He entered Brown University in 1824, but was obliged to leave the institution in his junior year in consequence of ill-health. He next visited Europe, where, with the exception of a few short visits home, he remained until 1847. In 1837 he received the appointment of United States consul at Rome, an office which he retained until his recall by President Polk in 1845. On his return he became professor of modern languages in Brown University. In 1852 he removed to the city of New York, where he has since resided.

During Mr. Greene's residence in Italy he devoted much attention to the collection of materials for a history of that country from the fall of the Western Empire in 476 to the present time, and was about preparing the first volume of his proposed work for the press when he was compelled to lay aside the undertaking in consequence of the failure of his eyesight.

In 1835 he published an article in the North American Review, the first of a long series of contributions to that and other critical journals of the country. A portion of these papers have been collected in a volume with the title *Historical Studies*, published by G. P. Putnam in 1850. The titles of these are Petrarch, Machiavelli, The Reformation in Italy, Italian Literature in the first half of the Nineteenth Century, Manzoni, The Hopes of Italy, Historical Romance in Italy, Libraries, Verazzano, and Charles Edward. It will be seen from the enumeration that the subjects treated of are, with two exceptions, drawn from Italian history or literature. The exceptions are such but in part, for in all discourse of libraries the ancient home of learning must be prominent, and the Italian burial-place of the exiled Stuarts has probably contributed much to the perpetuity of their reputation.

During the last year of his residence in Rome

Mr. Greene prepared a life of his grandfather, General Greene, for Sparks's American Biography. Since his return to the United States he has been engaged in arranging the papers of General Greene for publication, and in the preparation of a more extended biography to accompany the work. The first volume of this important contribution to American history will appear during the winter of 1855–6, and will contain a new and elaborate life of the General. The remaining six will be occupied with his official papers, public and private letters, etc. On the completion of this work it is Mr. Greene's intention to resume his History of Italy. In 1854 he edited an edition of the Works of Addison, in five volumes.

BOTTA, THE HISTORIAN.

The same causes which concurred in giving him so decided a taste for the best writers of his native tongue, led him to view with particular fondness the school in which they had been formed. His profound knowledge of Latin favored the cultivation of this partiality, and enabled him to study at the very sources of classic eloquence. Hence, when he took up his pen for the composition of history, it was with a mind warm from the meditation of Livy, of Tacitus, and of those who, by treading closely in their footsteps, have formed the most durable school of modern history. Thus the form of his works, naturally,—we had almost said, necessarily,—became classic. His narrative is arranged and conducted with consummate art. Sketches, portraits, and full descriptions are disposed at proper intervals, according to the nature and importance of the incident or of the person. If there be an important question to weigh, he puts it in the form of a debate, and makes you a listener to the discussions of the actual heroes of the scene. It is thus that he brings you to the grave deliberations of the Venetian senate, or placing you, as it were, in some hidden recess, discloses to you the midnight counsels of a band of conspirators. And often, so powerful is the charm of his eloquence, you feel excited, chilled, terror-struck,—moved, in short, by turns, with all the feelings that such a scene is calculated to awaken.

His narrations, if compared with those of the great historians of antiquity, will be found to possess two of the highest qualities of which this kind of writing is susceptible; clearness and animation. He never wrote until he had completed his study of the event; and then, by the assistance of a most exact and retentive memory, he wrote it out just in the order in which it arranged itself in his head. He was thus enabled to give his narrative that appearance of unity of conception, which it is impossible to communicate, unless where the mind has, from the very first, embraced the subject in its full extent. The glow of composition, moreover, was never interrupted, and he was free to enter with the full force of his feelings into the spirit of the scenes he was describing. Hence many who deny him others of the higher qualities of an historian, allow him to be one of the most fascinating of narrators.

His descriptions have more of the warmth of poetry in them than those of any other modern historian with whose works we are acquainted. Here, indeed, he seems to be upon his own ground; and, whether he describe a battle-field, a midnight assault, a sack, the siege or the storming of a city or of a fortress,—the convulsions, in short, of man or of nature herself,—he is everywhere equally master of his subject. His eye seems to take in the whole at a glance, and seize instinctively upon those points which are best calculated to characterize the scene. If he leaves less to the reader than Tacitus or Sallust, the incidents that he introduces are so well chosen, that they seize forcibly upon the imagination, and never fail to produce their full effect. His description of the flight of the French exiles from Savoy, of the passages of the Alps by Bonaparte and by Macdonald, of the sack of Pavia, of the siege of Famagosta, and of the earthquake in Calabria, may be cited as equal to anything that ever was written. Read the taking of Siena by Cosimo the First. You are moved as if you were on the spot, and were witnessing with your own eyes that scene of horror. You can see the band of exiles worn down, emaciated, by watching and by want. The whole story of the past is graven upon their deathlike countenances. As the melancholy train moves slowly onward, sighs, tears, ill suppressed groans force their way. They touch even the hearts of the victors. Every hand is stretched out to succor and to console. But grief and hardship have done their work. Their files were thin, when they passed for the last time the gate of their beloved home; but, ere they reach the banks of the Arbia, many a form has sunk exhausted and death-struck by the way. And, to complete the picture, he adds one little touch, which we give in the original, for the force of the transposition would be lost in English. "Sapevano bene di aver perduto una patria, ma se un' altra ne avrebbero trovata, nol sapevano."

The portraits of Botta are not equal to the other parts of his writings. No writer ever described character by action better than he; but, in the uniting of those separate traits which constitute individual character, and those slight and delicate shades which diversify it, he often fails. The same may be said of his views of the general progress of civilization. He never, indeed, loses sight of this capital point; and some of his sketches, such for example as the whole first book of his "History of Italy from 1789," are admirable; but the development of the individual and of society, and their mutual and reciprocal action, are not kept so constantly in view, and made to march on with the body of the narrative, with all that distinctness and precision, which we have a right to expect from so great a writer.

The moral bearing of every event, and of every character, is, on the contrary, always placed in full relief. Here his judgment is never at fault; and the high and the low, the distant and the near, are alike brought with stern impartiality to answer for their deeds at the tribunal of historical morality. "O si," he cries, addressing himself, after the relation of one of the most horrid acts ever perpetrated, to those who flatter themselves with the hope that their greatness will always prove a sufficient screen from the infamy that they deserve, "infamativi pure co' fatti, che la storia vi infamerà co' detti." And nowhere is the goodness of his own heart more apparent than in the delight with which he dwells upon those few happy days which sometimes break in like an unexpected gleam of sunshine upon the monotonous gloom of history; entering into all the minuter details, and setting off the event and its hero, by some well-chosen anecdote or apposite reflection.

Of his style we have, perhaps, already said enough. Purity of diction, richness, variety, and an almost intuitive adaptation of construction and of language to the changes of the subject, are its leading characteristics. The variety of his terms is wonderful; and no one, who has not read him with attention, can form a correct idea of the power and inexhaustible resources of the Italian. A simple narrator, an exciting orator, soft, winning, stern, satirical at will, consummate master of all the secrets of art, he seems to us to have carried many parts of historical composition to a very high pitch of perfection; and, if in some he appear less satisfactory, it is because he falls below the standard that we have formed from his own writings, rather than any that we have derived from those of others.

ANDREW JACKSON DOWNING

WAS born at Newburgh, in the Hudson Highlands, October 30, 1815. His father was a

A. J. Downing

nurseryman at that place, and died in the year 1822. The family were in humble circumstances, and Downing's education was confined to the teaching of the academy at Montgomery, near his native town. At the age of sixteen he joined his brother in the management of his nursery. He formed soon after the acquaintance of the Baron de Liderer, the Austrian Consul-General, and other gentlemen possessed of the fine country estates in the neighborhood, and began to write descriptions of the beautiful scenery about him, in the New York Mirror and other journals. In June, 1838, he married the daughter of J. P. De Wint, Esq., his neighbor on the opposite side of the Hudson. His first architectural work was the construction of his own house, an elegant Elizabethan cottage. In 1841, he published his Treatise on the *Theory and Practice of Landscape Gardening, adapted to North America, with a view to the Improvement of Country Residences, with Remarks on Rural Architecture.* It was highly successful, and orders for the construction of houses and decoration of grounds followed orders for copies to his publishers. He next published in 1845, *The Fruits and Fruit Trees of America.* In 1846 he was invited to become the editor of the Horticulturist, a small monthly magazine published in Albany. He accepted the charge, and wrote an essay a month for it, until the close of his life.

In 1849 he added *Additional Notes and Hints to Persons about Building in this country*, to an American reprint of Wightwick's "Hints to Young Architects."

In 1850 he visited England for the purpose of obtaining a competent assistant in the large architectural business which was pressing upon him. He remained only during the summer, visiting with great delight those perfect examples of his art, the great country seats of England. In the same year appeared his *Architecture of Country Houses; including Designs for Cottages, Farm-houses, and Villas.* In 1851 he was commissioned by President Fillmore to lay out and plant, in pursuance of an act of Congress, the public grounds in the city of Washington, lying near the White House, Capitol, and Smithsonian Institution. He was actively employed in this and other professional labors of a more private character, when on the 27th of July he embarked with his wife on board the steamboat Henry Clay for the city, on his way to Newport. As they proceeded down the river it was soon found that the boat was racing with its rival the "Armenia." It was too common a nuisance to excite alarm, until the boats were near Yonkers, when the Henry Clay was discovered to be on fire. In passing from the lower to the upper deck Mrs. Downing was separated by the crowd from her husband, and saw him no more, until his dead body was brought to their home the next day. He was seen by one of the passengers throwing chairs from the upper deck of the boat, to support those who had leaped overboard, and a little after struggling in the water, with others clinging to him. He was heard to utter a prayer, and seen no more. His *Rural Essays* were collected and published in 1853, with a well written and sympathetic memoir by George W. Curtis, and "A Letter to his Friends," by Miss Bremer, who was Mr. Downing's guest during a portion of her visit to this country, and a most enthusiastic admirer of the man and his works.

Downing's employments have undoubtedly exercised a great and salutary influence on the taste of the community. His works, in which he has freely availed himself of those of previous writers on the same topic, have been extensively read, and their suggestions have been realized on many an acre of the banks of his native Hudson, and other favorite localities. His style as an essayist was, like that of the man, pleasant, easy, and gentlemanly.

EDMUND FLAGG.

EDMUND FLAGG is descended from an old New England family, and the only son of the late Edmund Flagg, of Chester, N. H. He was born in the town of Wiscasset, Maine, on the twenty-fourth day of November, 1815. He was graduated at Bowdoin in 1835, and immediately after went to the West with his mother and sister, passing the winter at Louisville, where he taught the classics to a few boys, and was a frequent contributor to Prentice's "Louisville Journal." He passed the summer of 1836 in wandering over the prairies of Illinois and Missouri, writing *Sketches of a Traveller* for the "Louisville Journal," which were afterwards published in a work entitled *The Far West.*

During the succeeding fall and winter, Mr. Flagg read law with the Hon. Hamilton R. Gamble, now Judge of the Supreme Court of Missouri, and commenced practice in the courts. In 1838, he edited the "St. Louis Daily Commercial Bulletin," and during that fall published *The Far West* in two volumes, from the press of the Harpers. In December, he became connected with George D. Prentice, Esq., in the editorship of "The Louisville Literary News-Letter." In the spring of 1840, in consequence of ill health, he accepted an invitation to practise law with the Hon. Sargent S. Prentiss, of Vicksburg, Miss., a resident of that place.

In 1842, Mr. Flagg conducted the "Gazette" published at Marietta, Ohio, and at the same time wrote two novels—*Carrero, or The Prime Minister*, and *Francis of Valois*, which were published in New York. In 1844–5, he conducted the "St. Louis Evening Gazette;" and, for several years succeeding, was "Reporter of the Courts" of St. Louis County. In the meantime, he published several prize novels, among which were *The Howard Queen, Blanche of Artois*, and also several dramas, successfully produced in the theatres of St. Louis, Louisville, Cincinnati, and New York.

In the spring of 1848, Mr. Flagg went out as Secretary to the Hon. Edward A. Hannegan, American Minister to Berlin. The appointment afforded him an opportunity to travel over England, Germany, and France. On his return, he resumed his residence and the practice of the law at St. Louis. In 1850, he received the appointment of consul for the Port of Venice, under the administration of President Taylor. He visited England and Wales, travelled through central Europe to Venice, and entered upon the duties of his consulate, corresponding in the meantime with several of the New York Journals. In the fall of 1851, he visited Florence, Rome, Naples, and the other Italian cities, and in November embarked at Marseilles for New Orleans. On his arrival, he proceeded to St. Louis, and took charge of a democratic newspaper at that place.

In the following year, his last work was published in New York, in two volumes, entitled *Venice, The City of the Sea.* It comprises the history of that capital from the invasion by Napoleon, in 1797, to its capitulation to Radetzky, after its revolution, and the terrible siege of 1848 and '49. A third volume, to be entitled *North Italy since* 1849, is, we understand, nearly ready for publication.

In 1853 and 1854, Mr. Flagg contributed a number of articles illustrating the cities and scenery of the West to the United States Illustrated, published by Mr. Meyer of New York. Mr. Flagg has also written occasional poetical pieces for various magazines.*

RICHARD H. DANA, Jr.,

The author of "Two Years before the Mast," was born at Cambridge in 1815. He is the son of Richard H. Dana the poet. In his boyhood, he had a strong passion for the sea, and had he consulted his inclination only, would have entered the Navy. Influenced by the advice of his father, he chose a student's life at home, and entered Harvard. Here he was exposed to one of those difficulties which college faculties sometimes put in the way of the students by their mismanagement. There was some misconduct, and an effort was made to compel one of the class to witness against his companion. Dana, as one of the prominent rebels, was rusticated. As it was on a point of honor, it was no great misfortune to him, the less as he passed into the family, and under the tutorship of the Rev. Leonard Woods, at Andover, now the president of Bowdoin—with whom he enjoyed the intimacy of a friend of rare mental powers and scholarship. On returning to Cambridge, an attack of measles in one of the college vacations injured his eye-sight so materially, that he had to resign his books. For a remedy, he thought of his love of the sea, and resolved to rough it on a Pacific voyage as a sailor, though he had every facility for ordinary travel and adventure.

On the 14th of August, 1834, he set sail accordingly in the brig Pilgrim from Boston, for a voyage round Cape Horn to the western coast of North America; performed his duty throughout with spirit, while the object of the voyage was accomplished in the traffic for hides, little thinking while toiling on the cliffs and in the unsteady anchorages of California of the speedy familiarity which his countrymen would have with the region, and returned in the ship in September, 1836, to the harbor of Boston.

Richd H. Dana Jr

In the year 1840, he published an account of this adventure in the volume *Two Years before the Mast, a Personal Narrative of Life at Sea.** For this, he received for the entire copyright but two hundred and fifty dollars, a fact which shows the very recent low standard of American literary property. A publisher now could hardly expect so lucky a windfall. It was immediately successful, passing through numerous editions, being reprinted in London, where the British Admiralty adopted it for distribution in the Navy, and translated into several of the languages of the Continent, including even the Italian. It has been quoted, too, with respect for its authority on naval matters, by Lords Brougham and Carlisle in the House of Lords.

The work, written out from his journal and notes of the voyage, was undertaken with the idea of presenting the plain reality of a sailor's life at sea. In this, its main object, it has been eminently successful. It has not only secured the admiration of gentle readers on shore, but, a much rarer fortune, has been accepted as a true picture by Jack himself. A copy of the book is no unusual portion of the scant equipment of his chest in the forecastle. Its popularity is further witnessed by the returns of the cheap lending libraries in England, where it appears high on the list of the books in demand. The cause is obvious. The author is a master of narrative, and the story is told with a thorough reality. It is probably the most truthful account of a sailor's

* The Native Poets of Maine.

* Harpers' Family Library, New York.

life at sea ever written. Its material is actual experience, and its style the simple straight-forward language of a disciplined mind, which turns neither to the right nor to the left from its object. It is noticeable, that in this universally read book, the writer uses the technical language of the ship; so that the account is to that extent sometimes unintelligible. On this, he makes a profound remark. "I have found," says he, "from my own experience, and from what I have heard from others, that plain matters of fact in relation to customs and habits of life new to us, and descriptions of life under new aspects, act upon the inexperienced through the imagination, so that we are hardly aware of our want of technical knowledge." It has, too, this advantage. A technical term can be explained by easy reference to a dictionary; a confused substitute for it may admit of no explanation. Good sense and good humor sum up the enduring merits of this book. It is life itself, —a passage of intense unexaggerated reality.

Mr. Dana had, after his return from abroad, entered the senior class at Harvard, from which institution he was graduated in 1837, when he pursued his studies at the Law-School under Judge Story and Professor Greenleaf. His proficiency in these preparatory studies in moot courts and the exercises of his pen, showed his acute legal mind, and when he began to practise law his success was rapid. He was aided in maritime cases by the reputation of his book; while he employed his influence to elevate a much abused branch of practice, though in Boston it takes a higher rank from being pursued in the United States Courts. His practice is also extensive in the State Courts.*

In 1850, Mr. Dana edited, with a preliminary preface, *Lectures on Art and Poems, by Washington Allston.*†

His *Seaman's Manual* is a technical dictionary of sea terms, and an epitome of the laws affecting the mutual position of master and sailor. It is reprinted in England, and in use in both countries as a standard work.

Of late, Mr. Dana has been prominently before the public as a member of the Free-Soil party of Massachusetts, and in his vigorous opposition to the Fugitive Slave Law. His speech in the case of the negro Anthony Burns, in 1854, is noticeable, not only for its acute analysis of the evidence offered, but for its clear picturesque statement. The life-like character of some of its descriptions—though no personal remarks were made on any individual—inspired a cowardly, brutal street attack, in a blow struck at his head by a slung shot, which, had it varied a little, would have proved fatal.

In a later case, an argument before the Supreme Court of Maine, at Bangor, July 22, 1854, in an action brought by a naturalized citizen of the Roman Catholic faith, for injuries in the removal of his child from the public school, in consequence of the parents' rejection of the ordinary version of the Bible read there, and consequent interference with the school regulations, Mr. Dana has pronounced not merely an eloquent, but an able, legal, and philosophical argument in defence of the superintending school committee, and of the accepted translation of the Scriptures. His argument was sustained by the judgment of the court.

In 1853, Mr. Dana was prominently engaged in the State Convention of Massachusetts. His course there, in the discussion of topics of enlarged interest, determined his rank in the higher walk of his profession.

We are enabled on this point to present adequate authority in a letter on the subject from a leader in the Convention, the Hon. Rufus Choate.

Boston, Sept. 29, 1854.

Charles Scribner, Esq.

Sir—I received some time since an inquiry respecting the position occupied by Mr. Dana in the Convention for revising the constitution of Massachusetts; to which I would have made an immediate reply, but for an urgent engagement. When I was relieved from that, I unfortunately had overlooked your letter, which I have only just now recovered.

The published debates of that body indicate quite well, though not adequately, the space he filled in the convention. He took a deep interest in its proceedings; attended its sessions with great punctuality, and by personal effort and influence, and occasional very effective speech, had a large share in doing good and resisting evil. He was classed with the majority in the body, consisting in a general way of those friendly to its convocation, and friendly to pretty extended and enterprising schemes of change; but on some fundamental questions he differed decidedly from them, and upon one of these—that concerning the tenure of judicial office—he displayed conspicuous ability and great zeal, and enforced with persuasive and important effect the soundest and most conservative opinions. In general, there, as in all things, and in all places, he was independent, prompt, and firm; and was universally esteemed not more for his talent, culture, and good sense, than for his sincerity and honor. I differed often from him, but always with pain, if not self-distrust, with no interruption of the friendship of many years.

I am very truly,
Your serv't,
Rufus Choate.

An article by Mr. Dana, on the Memoir of the Rev. Dr. William Croswell, whom he had defended in an able and eloquent speech on an Ecclesiastical trial in the North American Review for April, 1854, may be mentioned for its feeling and judicious estimate of a man to whom the Reviewer stood in the relations of friend and parishioner.

Mr. Dana is married to a grand-daughter of the Rev. James Marsh. His residence is at Cambridge, in the vicinity of the College.

HOMEWARD BOUND—FROM TWO YEARS BEFORE THE MAST.

It is usual, in voyages round the Cape from the Pacific, to keep to the eastward of the Falkland Islands; but as it had now set in a strong, steady, and clear south-wester, with every prospect of its lasting, and we had had enough of high latitudes, the captain determined to stand immediately to the northward, running inside of the Falkland Islands. Accordingly, when the wheel was relieved at eight o'clock, the order was given to keep her due north, and all hands were turned up to square away the yards and make sail. In a moment the news ran

* The account of Dana in "Livingston's American Lawyers," Part iv. June 1852, contains references to his important cases up to the time when it was written.

† New York, Baker and Scribner, 1850.

through the ship that the captain was keeping her off, with her nose straight for Boston, and Cape Horn over her taffrail. It was a moment of enthusiasm. Every one was on the alert, and even the two sick men turned out to lend a hand at the halyards. The wind was now due south-west, and blowing a gale to which a vessel close-hauled could have shown no more than a single close-reefed sail; but as we were going before it, we could carry on. Accordingly, hands were sent aloft, and a reef shaken out of the top-sails, and the reefed fore-sail set. When we came to mast-head the top-sail yards, with all hands at the halyards, we struck up "Cheerily, men," with a chorus which might have been heard half way to Staten Land. Under her increased sail, the ship drove on through the water. Yet she could bear it well; and the Captain sang out from the quarter-deck—"Another reef out of that fore top-sail, and give it to her!" Two hands sprang aloft; the frozen reef-points and earings were cast adrift, the halyards manned, and the sail gave out her increased canvass to the gale. All hands were kept on deck to watch the effect of the change. It was as much as she could well carry, and with a heavy sea astern, it took two men at the wheel to steer her. She flung the foam from her bows; the spray breaking aft as far as the gangway. She was going at a prodigious rate. Still, everything held. Preventer braces were reeved and hauled taut: tackles got upon the backstays; and each thing done to keep all snug and strong. The captain walked the deck at a rapid stride, looked aloft at the sails, and then to windward; the mate stood in the gangway, rubbing his hands, and talking aloud to the ship—"Hurrah, old bucket! the Boston girls have got hold of the tow-rope!" and the like; and we were on the forecastle, looking to see how the spars stood it, and guessing the rate at which she was going,—when the captain called out —"Mr. Brown, get up the top-mast studding-sail! What she can't carry she may drag!" The mate looked a moment; but he would let no one be before him in daring. He sprang forward,—"Hurrah, men! rig out the top-mast studding-sail boom! Lay aloft, and I'll send the rigging up to you!"—We sprang aloft into the top; lowered a girt-line down, by which we hauled up the rigging; rove the tacks and halyards; ran out the boom and lashed it fast, and sent down the lower halyards, as a preventer. It was a clear starlight night, cold and blowing; but everybody worked with a will. Some, indeed, looked as though they thought the 'old man' was mad, but no one said a word. We had had a new top-mast studding-sail made with a reef in it,—a thing hardly ever heard of, and which the sailors had ridiculed a good deal, saying that when it was time to reef a studding-sail, it was time to take it in. But we found a use for it now; for, there being a reef in the top-sail, the studding-sail could not be set without one in it also. To be sure, a studding-sail with reefed top-sails was rather a new thing; yet there was some reason in it, for if we carried that away, we should lose only a sail and a boom; but a whole top-sail might have carried away the mast and all.

While we were aloft, the sail had been got out, bent to the yard, reefed, and ready for hoisting. Waiting for a good opportunity, the halyards were manned and the yard hoisted fairly up to the blocks, but when the mate came to shake the catspaw out of the downhaul, and we began to boom-end the sail, it shook the ship to her centre. The boom buckled up and bent like a whip-stick, and we looked every moment to see something go; but, being of the short, tough upland spruce, it bent like whalebone, and nothing could break it. The carpenter said it was the best stick he had ever seen. The strength of all hands soon brought the tack to the boom-end, and the sheet was trimmed down, and the preventer and the weather brace hauled taut to take off the strain. Every rope-yarn seemed stretched to the utmost, and every thread of canvass; and with this sail added to her, the ship sprang through the water like a thing possessed. The sail being nearly all forward, it lifted her out of the water, and she seemed actually to jump from sea to sea. From the time her keel was laid, she had never been so driven; and had it been life or death with every one of us, she could not have borne another stitch of canvass.

Finding that she would bear the sail, the hands were sent below, and our watch remained on deck. Two men at the wheel had as much as they could do to keep her within three points of her course, for she steered as wild as a young colt. The mate walked the deck, looking at the sails, and then over the side to see the foam fly by her,—slapping his hands upon his thighs and talking to the ship—"Hurrah, you jade, you 've got the scent!—you know where you're going!" And when she leaped over the seas, and almost out of the water, and trembled to her very keel, the spars and masts snapping and creaking—"There she goes!—There she goes—handsomely!—As long as she cracks she holds!"—while we stood with the rigging laid down fair for letting go, and ready to take in sail and clear away if anything went. At four bells we hove the log, and she was going eleven knots fairly; and had it not been for the sea from aft which sent the chip home, and threw her continually off her course, the log would have shown her to have been going much faster. I went to the wheel with a young fellow from the Kennebec, who was a good helmsman: and for two hours we had our hands full. A few minutes showed us that our monkey-jackets must come off; and cold as it was, we stood in our shirt-sleeves in a perspiration; and were glad enough to have it eight bells and the wheel relieved. We turned in and slept as well as we could, though the sea made a constant roar under her bows, and washed over the forecastle like a small cataract.

At four o'clock we were called again. The same sail was still on the vessel, and the gale, if there was any change, had increased a little. No attempt was made to take the studding-sail in: and, indeed, it was too late now. If we had started anything toward taking it in, either tack or halyards, it would have blown to pieces, and carried something away with it. The only way now was to let everything stand, and if the gale went down, well and good; if not, something must go—the weakest stick or rope first—and then we could get it in. For more than an hour she was driven on at such a rate that she seemed actually to crowd the sea into a heap before her, and the water poured over the sprit-sail yard as it would over a dam. Towards daybreak the gale abated a little, and she was just beginning to go more easily along, relieved of the pressure, when Mr. Brown, determined to give her no respite, and depending upon the wind's subsiding as the sun rose, told us to get along the lower studding-sail. This was an immense sail, and held wind enough to last a Dutchman a week,—hove-to. It was soon ready, the boom topped up, preventer guys rove, and the idlers called up to man the halyards; yet such was still the force of the gale, that we were nearly an hour setting the sail; carried away the outhaul in doing it, and came very near snapping off the swinging boom. No sooner was it set than the ship tore on again like one that was mad, and began to steer as wild as a hawk. The men at the wheel were puffing and blowing at their work, and the helm was going hard up and hard down, constantly. Add to this, the gale did not lessen as the day come on, but the sun rose in clouds. A sudden lurch threw the man from the weather wheel across the deck and against the side. The mate sprang to the wheel, and the man, regaining his feet, seized the spokes, and they hove the wheel up just in time to save her from broaching to, though nearly half the studding-sail went under water; and as she came to the boom stood up at an angle of forty-five degrees. She had evidently more on her than she could bear; yet it was in vain to try to take it in—the clewline was not strong enough; and they were thinking of cutting away, when another wide yaw and a come-to snapped the guys, and the swinging boom came in with a crash against the lower rigging. The outhaul block gave way, and the top-mast studding-sail boom bent in a manner which I never before supposed a stick could bend. I had my eye on it when the guys parted, and it made one spring and buckled up so as to form nearly a half circle, and sprang out again to its shape. The clewline gave way at the first pull; the cleat to which the halyards were belayed was wrenched off, and the sail blew round the sprit-sail yard and head guys, which gave us a bad job to get it in. A half hour served to clear all away, and she was suffered to drive on with her top-mast studding-sail set, it being as much as she could stagger under.

During all this day and the next night we went on under the same sail, the gale blowing with undiminished force; two men at the wheel all the time; watch and watch, and nothing to do but to steer and look out for the ship, and be blown along;—until the noon of the next day—

Sunday, July 24th, when we were in latitude 50° 27′ S., longitude 62° 13′ W., having made four degrees of latitude in the last twenty-four hours. Being now to the northward of the Falkland Islands, the ship was kept off, north-east, for the equator; and with her head for the equator, and Cape Horn over her taffrail, she went gloriously on; every heave of the sea leaving the Cape astern, and every hour bringing us nearer to home, and to warm weather.

THE ENGLISH BIBLE.*

* * * * * * * * *

This is the common English Bible, which has always been used. It is not a "*Protestant* Bible." Great portions of the translation were made by men in the bosom of the General Church, before the Reformation, by Wickliffe, Tyndale, Coverdale, and Matthew. Testimony to its accuracy has been borne by learned men of the Roman Church. Leddes calls it "of all versions the most excellent for accuracy, fidelity, and the strictest attention to the letter of the text;" and Selden calls it "the best version in the world." As a well of pure English undefiled, as a fountain of pure idiomatic English, it has not its equal in the world. It was fortunately—may we not without presumption say providentially—translated at a time when the English language was in its purest state. It has done more to *anchor* the English language in the state it then was than all other books together. The fact that so many millions of each succeeding generation, in all parts of the world where the English language is used, read the same great lessons in the same words, not only keeps the language anchored where it was in its best state, but it preserves its universality, and frees it from all material provincialisms and *patois*, so that the same words, phrases, and idioms are used in London, New York, San Francisco, Australia, China, and India. To preserve this unity and steadfastness, the Book of Common Prayer has done much; Shakespeare, Milton, and Bunyan have done much; but the English Bible has done ten-fold more than they all.

From the common English Bible, too, we derive our household words, or phrases and illustrations, the familiar speech of the people. Our associations are with its narratives, its parables, its histories, and its biographies. If a man knew the Bible in its original Greek and Hebrew by heart, and did not know the common English version, he would be ignorant of the speech of the people. In sermons, in public speeches, from the pulpit, the bar, and the platform, would come allusions, references, quotations—that exquisite electrifying by conductors, by which the heart of a whole people is touched by a word, a phrase, in itself nothing, but everything in its power of conducting—and all this would be to him an unknown world. No greater wrong, intellectually, could be inflicted on the children of a school, aye, even on the Roman Catholic children, than to bring them up in ignorance of the English Bible. As well might a master instruct his pupil in Latin, and send him to spend his days among scholars, and keep him in ignorance of the words of Virgil and Horace, and Cicero and Terence and Tacitus. As a preparation for life, an acquaintance with the common English Bible is indispensable.

* * * * * * * * *

If the Bible is not read, where so well can the principles of morality and all the virtues be taught? "How infinitely superior," says Maurice, "is a gospel of facts to a gospel of notions!" How infinitely superior to abstract ethics are the teachings of the narratives and parables of the Bible! What has ever taken such a hold on the human heart, and so influenced human action? The story of Jacob and Esau, the unequalled narrative of Joseph and his brethren, Abraham and Isaac, Absalom, Naaman the Syrian, the old prophet, the wild, dramatic poetical histories of Elijah and Elisha, the captivities of the Jews, the episode of Ruth, unsurpassed for simple beauty and pathos, and time would fail me to tell of Daniel, Isaiah, Samuel, Eli, and the glorious company of the apostles, the goodly fellowship of the prophets, and the noble army of martyrs. Where can a lesson of fraternity and equality be struck so deeply into the heart of a child as by the parable of Lazarus and Dives? How can the true nature and distinctions of charity be better expounded than by the parables of the widow who cast her mite into the treasury, and the woman with the alabaster box of precious ointment? Can the prodigal son, the unjust steward, the lost sheep, ever be forgotten? Has not the narrative of the humble birth, the painful life, the ignominious death of our Lord, wrought an effect on the world greater than any and all lives ever wrought before? even on those who doubt the miracles, and do not believe in the mystery of the Holy Incarnation, and the glorious Resurrection and Ascension.

Remember, too, we beseech you, that it is at the school alone that many of these children can read or hear these noble teachings. If the book is closed to them there, it is open to them nowhere else.

Nor would I omit to refer to the reading of the Bible as a part of the education of the fancy and imagination. Whatever slight may be thrown upon

* From the argument in the school case before the Supreme Court of Maine.

these faculties by men calling themselves practical men, they are powerful agents in the human system which no man can neglect or abuse with impunity. Preoccupy, preoccupy the minds of the young with the tender, the beautiful, the rhythmical, the magnificent, the sublime, which God in his bounty, and wisdom too, has poured out so profusely into the minds of his evangelists and prophets! Nowhere can be found such varieties of the beautiful and sublime, the magnificent and simple, the tender and terrific. And all this is brought to our doors and offered to our daily eye. If the mind of the youth, girl, and boy is not preoccupied by what is moral, virtuous, and religious, the world is ready to attack the fancy and imagination with all the splendor and seductions of sense and sin. Their minds will have the food for imagination and fancy, and if they are not led to the Psalms, and Isaiah, and Job, and the Apocalypse, and the narratives and parables, they will find it in Shelley, Byron, Rousseau, and George Sand, and the feebler and more debased novels of the modern press of France.

ANNA CORA MOWATT.

Anna Cora, the daughter of Samuel G. Ogden, a New York merchant, was born in Bordeaux, France, during her father's residence in that city. Her early years were passed in a fine old chateau in its neighborhood, called La Castagne. One of its apartments was fitted up as a theatre, in which the numerous children of the family, of which the future Mrs. Mowatt was the tenth, amused themselves with dramatic entertainments, for which several of them evinced decided talent. The family removed a few years after to New York.

While yet a school girl, Anna, in her fifteenth year, became the wife of Mr. James Mowatt, a lawyer of New York. The story of her first acquaintance with her lover, who soon began to escort her to and from school, gallantly bearing her satchel, and the courtship and run-away match which speedily followed, are very pleasantly told in the lady's autobiography. The only reason for the elopement being the unwillingness of the couple to wait until the lady had passed seventeen summers, they soon received the paternal pardon, and retired to a country residence at Flatbush, Long Island. Here the education of the "child-wife," as she was prettily styled, was continued by the husband, several years the senior. Some pleasant years were passed in Sunday-school teaching, fortune-telling at fancy fairs, "shooting swallows on the wing," in sportsman tramps through the woods, private theatricals, and the composition of an epic poem, *Pelayo, or the Cavern of Covadonga*, in five cantos, which was published by the Harpers, and followed by a satire entitled *Reviewers Reviewed*, directed against the critics who had taken the liberty to cut up the poem. Both appeared as the work of "Isabel."

Mrs. Mowatt's health failing, she accompanied a newly married sister and brother in a tour to Europe. She wrote a play, *Gulzara, or the Persian Slave*, during her absence, had appropriate scenes and dresses made in Paris for its representation, and soon after her return produced the piece with great applause at a party at her residence, in honor of her father's birthday.

Meanwhile Mr. Mowatt had taken part in the speculations of the day, and a commercial revulsion occurring, was "utterly ruined"—a weakness in the eyes preventing him from resuming his old profession of the law.

Anna Cora Mowatt

The elder Vandenhoff had just before met with great success in a course of dramatic readings, and the wife, casting about for ways and means of support, determined to bring her dramatic talents into account in this manner. She gained her husband's consent with some difficulty, and, preferring the verdict of a stranger audience, gave her first reading at Boston, and with decided success. She soon after appeared in New York, where she read to large audiences, but the tacit disapproval of friends and the exertions required brought on a fit of sickness, from which she suffered for the two following years.

She next, her husband having become a publisher, turned her attention to literature, and wrote a number of stories for the magazines with the signature of "Helen Berkley." These were followed by a longer story, *The Fortune Hunter*, and by the five act comedy of *Fashion*, which was written for the stage, and produced at the Park Theatre, March, 1845. It met with success there and at theatres in other cities, and emboldened its author, forced by the failure of her husband in the publishing business, to contribute to their joint support, to try her fortune as an actress. She made her first appearance on the classic boards of the Park Theatre, June, 1845, as Pauline in the Lady of Lyons, and played a number of nights with such approval that engagements followed in other cities, and she became one of the most successful of "stars." She appeared in her own play of Fashion, and in 1847 wrote and performed a new five act drama, *Armand*.

In 1847 Mrs. Mowatt visited England with her husband, and made her first bow to an English audience in the month of December, at Manchester. She was successful, and remained in England several years.

In February, 1851, Mr. Mowatt died. After a temporary retirement, his widow went through a round of farewell performances, and returned in July to her native land. In August she appeared at Niblo's Garden, and after a highly successful engagement, made a brilliant farewell tour through the Union prior to her retirement from the stage at New York, in 1854. A few days afterwards she was married to Mr. William F. Ritchie, a gentleman of Richmond, Va.

In 1854 Mrs. Mowatt published the *Autobiography of an Actress, or Eight Years on the Stage*, a record of her private and professional life to that date.

TIME.

Nay, rail not at Time, though a tyrant he be,
And say not he cometh, colossal in might,
Our beauty to ravish, put pleasure to flight,
  And pluck away friends, e'en as leaves from the tree;
And say not Love's torch, which like Vesta's should burn,
The cold breath of Time soon to ashes will turn.

  You call Time a robber? Nay, he is not so,—
While Beauty's fair temple he rudely despoils,
The mind to enrich with its plunder he toils;
  And, sowed in his furrows, doth wisdom not grow?
The magnet 'mid stars points the north still to view;
So Time 'mong our friends e'er discloses the true.

  Though cares then should gather, as pleasures flee by,
Though Time from thy features the charm steal away,
He'll dim too mine eye, lest it see them decay;
  And sorrows we've shared, will knit closer love's tie:
Then I'll laugh at old Time, and at all he can do,
For he'll rob me in vain, if he leave me but *you!*

MARY E. HEWITT.

Mary E. Moore was born in Malden, Massachusetts. After her father's death her mother removed to Boston, where the daughter remained until her marriage with the late Mr. James L. Hewitt. She has since resided in the city of New York. In 1845 Mrs. Hewitt published *Songs of our Land and Other Poems*, a selection from her contributions to various periodicals. In 1850 she edited *The Gem of the Western World*, a holiday volume, and *The Memorial*, a volume of contributions by the authors of the day, designed as a mark of respect to the memory of Mrs. Osgood. Mrs. Hewitt was lately married to Mr. Stebbins, of New York.

Her poems are marked by their good sense, hearty expression, and natural feeling.

GOD BLESS THE MARINER.

God's blessing on the Mariner!
  A venturous life leads he—
What reck the landsmen of their toil,
  Who dwell upon the sea?

The landsman sits within his home,
  His fireside bright and warm;
Nor asks how fares the mariner
  All night amid the storm.

God bless the hardy Mariner!
  A homely garb wears he,
And he goeth with a rolling gait,
  Like a ship upon the sea.

He hath piped the loud "ay, ay, sir!"
  O'er the voices of the main,
Till his deep tones have the hoarseness
  Of the rising hurricane.

His seamed and honest visage
  The sun and wind have tanned,
And hard as iron gauntlet
  Is his broad and sinewy hand.

But oh! a spirit looketh
  From out his clear, blue eye,
With a truthful, childlike earnestness,
  Like an angel from the sky.

A venturous life the sailor leads
  Between the sky and sea—
But when the hour of dread is past,
  A merrier who, than he?

He knows that by the rudder bands
  Stands one well skilled to save;
For a strong hand is the Steersman's
  That directs him o'er the wave.

TO MARY.

Thine eye is like the violet,
  Thou hast the lily's grace;
And the pure thoughts of a maiden's heart
  Are writ upon thy face.
And like a pleasant melody
  That to memory hath clung,
Falls thy voice, in the loved accent
  Of mine own New England tongue.

New England—dear New England!—
  All numberless they lie,
The green graves of my people,
  Beneath her fair, blue sky.
And the same bright sun that shineth
  On thy home at early morn,
Lights the dwellings of my kindred,
  And the house where I was born.

Oh, fairest of her daughters!
  That bids me so rejoice
'Neath the starlight of thy beauty,
  And the music of thy voice—
While memory hath power
  In my heart her joys to wake,
I love thee, Mary, for thine own,
  And for New England's sake.

EMMA D. E. N. SOUTHWORTH.

Mrs. Southworth is descended, both on the father's and mother's side, from families of high rank, who emigrated to America in 1632, and settled at St. Mary's, where they have continued to reside for two centuries. She was born in the city of Washington, in the house and room once occupied by General Washington, on the 26th of December, 1818. Her father, who had married in 1816 a young lady of fifteen, died in 1822, leaving his family straitened in resources, in consequence of losses previously incurred by the French spoliations on American commerce. Her mother afterwards married Mr. Joshua L. Henshaw, of Boston, by whom Miss Nevitte was educated.

Emma D.E.N. Southworth

In 1841 she became Mrs. Southworth. Thrown upon her own resources in 1843, with two infants to support, a dreary interval in her life succeeded, which was broken by the successful publication of her first novel, *Retribution*, in 1849. She had previously published, in 1846, an anonymous sketch in the National Era, with which the editor, Dr. Bailey, was so well pleased, that he sought out the writer, and induced her to write other sketches and tales of a similar kind. *Retribution* was commenced as one of these, and was intended to be concluded in two numbers, but the subject grew under the author's hand. Every week she supplied a portion to the paper, "until weeks grew into months, and months into quarters, before it was finished." During its composition she was supporting herself as a teacher in a public school, and in addition to the entire charge of eighty boys and girls thus imposed upon her, and of one of her children who was extremely ill, was forced by the meagreness of her pecuniary resources to give close attention to her household affairs. Her health broke down under the pressure of these complicated labors and sorrows. Meanwhile her novel reached its termination, and was published complete by Harper and Brothers. The author, to use her own words, "found herself born, as it were, into a new life; found independence, sympathy, friendship, and honor, and an occupation in which she could delight. All this came very suddenly, as after a terrible storm a sunburst." Her child recovered, and her own malady disappeared.

The successful novel was rapidly followed by others. *The Deserted Wife* was published in 1850; *Shannondale* and *The Mother-in-Law* in 1851; *Children of the Isle* and *The Foster Sisters* in 1852; *The Curse of Clifton; Old Neighborhoods and New Settlements*, and *Mark Sutherland* in 1853, *The Lost Heiress* in 1854, and *Hickory Hall*, in 1855. These novels display strong dramatic power, and contain many excellent descriptive passages of the Southern life and scenery to which they are chiefly devoted.

SUSAN WARNER—ANNA B. WARNER.

Miss Warner is the daughter of Mr. Henry Warner, a member of the bar of the city of New York. She has for some years resided with the remainder of her father's family on Constitution Island, near West Point, in the finest portion of the Hudson highlands.

Susan Warner

Miss Warner made a sudden step into eminence as a writer, by the publication in 1849 of *The Wide, Wide World*, a novel, in two volumes. It is a story of American domestic life, written in an easy and somewhat diffuse style.

Her second novel, *Queechy*, appeared in 1852. It is similar in size and general plan to *The Wide, Wide World*, and contains a number of agreeable passages descriptive of rural life. The heroine, Fleda, is introduced to us as a little girl. Her sprightly, natural manner, and shrewd American common sense, contribute greatly to the attractions of the book. The "help" at the farm, male and female, are pleasantly hit off, and give a seasoning of humor to the volumes.

Miss Warner is also the author of *The Law and the Testimony*, a theological work of research and merit, and of a prize essay on the Duties of American Women.

Miss Anna B. Warner, a younger sister of Miss Susan Warner, is the author of *Dollars and Cents*, a novel, as its title indicates, of practical American life, published in 1853, and of a series of juvenile tales, *Anna Montgomery's Book Shelf*, three volumes of which, *Mr. Rutherford's Children* and *Carl Krinken*, have appeared.

CHESTNUT GATHERING—FROM QUEECHY.

In a hollow, rather a deep hollow, behind the crest of the hill, as Fleda had said, they came at last to a noble group of large hickory trees, with one or two chestnuts, standing in attendance on the outskirts. And also as Fleda had said, or hoped, the place was so far from convenient access that nobody had visited them; they were thick hung with fruit. If the spirit of the game had been wanting or failing in Mr. Carleton, it must have roused again into full life at the joyous heartiness of Fleda's exclamations. At any rate no boy could have taken to the business better. He cut, with her permission, a stout long pole in the woods; and swinging himself lightly into one of the trees showed that he was a master in the art of whipping them. Fleda was delighted but not surprised; for from the first moment of Mr. Carleton's proposing to go with her she had been privately sure that he would not prove an inactive or inefficient ally. By whatever slight tokens she might read this, in whatsoever fine characters of the eye, or speech, or manner, she knew it; and knew it just as well before they reached the hickory trees as she did afterwards.

When one of the trees was well stripped the young gentleman mounted into another, while Fleda set herself to hull and gather up the nuts under the one first beaten. She could make but little headway, however, compared with her companion; the nuts fell a great deal faster than she could put them in her basket. The trees were heavy laden, and Mr. Carleton seemed determined to have the whole crop; from the second tree he went to the third. Fleda was bewildered with her happiness; this was doing business in style. She tried to calculate what the whole quantity would be, but it went beyond her; one basketful would not take it, nor two, nor three,—it wouldn't *begin to*, Fleda said to herself. She went on hulling and gathering with all possible industry.

After the third tree was finished Mr. Carleton threw down his pole, and resting himself upon the ground at the foot, told Fleda he would wait a few moments before he began again. Fleda thereupon left off her work too, and going for her little tin pail presently offered it to him temptingly, stocked with pieces of apple-pie. When he had smilingly taken one, she next brought him a sheet of white paper with slices of young cheese.

"No, thank you," said he.

"Cheese is very good with apple-pie," said Fleda, competently.

"Is it?" said he, laughing. "Well—upon that—I think you would teach me a good many things, Miss Fleda, if I were to stay here long enough."

"I wish you would stay and try, sir," said Fleda, who did not know exactly what to make of the shade of seriousness which crossed his face. It was gone almost instantly.

"I think anything is better eaten out in the woods than it is at home," said Fleda.

"Well, I don't know," said her friend. "I have no doubt that is the case with cheese and apple-pie, and especially under hickory trees which one has been contending with pretty sharply. If a touch of your wand, Fairy, could transform one of these shells into a goblet of Lafitte or Amontillado we should have nothing to wish for."

'Amontillado' was Hebrew to Fleda, but 'goblet' was intelligible.

"I am sorry," she said, "I don't know where there is any spring up here,—but we shall come to one going down the mountain."

"Do you know where all the springs are?"

"No, not all, I suppose," said Fleda, "but I know a good many. I have gone about through the woods so much, and I always look for the springs."

* * * * * * * *

They descended the mountain now with hasty step, for the day was wearing well on. At the spot where he had stood so long when they went up, Mr. Carleton paused again for a minute. In mountain scenery every hour makes a change. The sun was lower now, the lights and shadows more strongly contrasted, the sky of a yet calmer blue, cool and clear towards the horizon. The scene said still the same that it had said a few hours before, with a touch more of sadness; it seemed to whisper "All things have an end—thy time may not be for ever —do what thou wouldest do—'while ye have light believe in the light that ye may be children of the light.'"

Whether Mr. Carleton read it so or not, he stood for a minute motionless, and went down the mountain looking so grave that Fleda did not venture to speak to him, till they reached the neighborhood of the spring.

"What are you searching for, Miss Fleda?" said her friend.

She was making a busy quest here and there by the side of the little stream.

"I was looking to see if I could find a mullein leaf," said Fleda.

"A mullein leaf? what do you want it for?"

"I want it—to make a drinking cup of," said Fleda; her intent bright eyes peering keenly about in every direction.

"A mullein leaf! that is too rough; one of these golden leaves—what are they?—will do better; won't it?"

"That is hickory," said Fleda. "No; the mullein leaf is the best, because it holds the water so nicely.—Here it is!—"

And folding up one of the largest leaves into a most artist-like cup, she presented it to Mr. Carleton.

"For me was all that trouble?" said he. "I don't deserve it."

"You wanted something, sir," said Fleda. "The water is very cold and nice."

He stooped to the bright little stream, and filled his rural goblet several times.

"I never knew what it was to have a fairy for my cup-bearer before," said he. "That was better than anything Bordeaux or Xeres ever sent forth."

He seemed to have swallowed his seriousness, or thrown it away with the mullein leaf. It was quite gone.

"This is the best spring in all grandpa's ground," said Fleda. "The water is as good as can be."

"How come you to be such a wood and water spirit? you must live out of doors. Do the trees ever talk to you? I sometimes think they do to me."

"I don't know—I think *I* talk to *them*," said Fleda.

"It's the same thing," said her companion, smiling. "Such beautiful woods!"

"Were you never in the country before in the fall, sir?"

"Not here—in my own country often enough—but the woods in England do not put on such a gay face, Miss Fleda, when they are going to be stripped of their summer dress—they look sober upon it—the leaves wither and grow brown, and the woods have a dull russet color. Your trees are true Yankees—they 'never say die!'"

EMILY C. JUDSON.

Miss Emily Chubbuck was born at Morrisville, a town of Central New York. Soon after ceasing to be a school girl, with a view of adding to the limited means of her family and increasing her own knowledge, she became a teacher in a female seminary at Utica. It was with similar views that she commenced her literary career by writing a few poems for the Knickerbocker Magazine, and some little books for children, of a religious character, for the American Baptist Publication Society. In 1844 she sent a communication to the New York Weekly Mirror, with the signature of "Fanny Forester." Mr. Willis, the editor, wrote warmly in favor of the writer, who soon became a frequent contributor to his paper.

Fanny Forester

While passing the winter at Philadelphia with a clerical friend, the Rev. Mr. Gillette, Miss Chubbuck became acquainted with Dr. Judson, the celebrated Baptist missionary. He had recently lost his second wife, and applied to the young author to write her biography. Intimacy in the preparation of the work led to such mutual liking that the pair were married not long after, in July, 1846, and sailed immediately for India. They arrived at the missionaries' residence at Maulmain, where they resided until Dr. Judson fell sick, and was ordered home by his physicians.

His wife was unable to accompany him, and he embarked in a very weak state in the early part of 1850 for America. He died at sea on the twelfth of April of the same year. His widow returned not long after, her own health impaired by an Eastern climate, and after lingering a few months, died on the first of June, 1854.

Mrs. Judson was the author of *Alderbrook, a Collection of Fanny Forester's Village Sketches and Poems*, in two volumes, published in 1843. *A Biographical Sketch of Mrs. Sarah B. Judson*, 1849. *An Olio of Domestic Verses*, 1852, a collection of her poems; *How to be Great, Good, and Happy*, a volume designed for children; a small prose volume, *My Two Sisters, a Sketch from Memory*, and a number of other poems and prose sketches for various periodicals. The sprightliness and tenderness of Mrs. Judson's early sketches gained her a reputation which was rapidly extended by her subsequent publications, especially by those embodying, in a simple and unostentatious manner, her wider experiences of life as the wife of a missionary. The modest title of her collection of poems is an indication of her character, but should not be suffered to overshadow the merits of the choice contents of the book.

One of the latest productions of Mrs. Judson's pen was an admirable letter in defence of her children's property in her deceased husband's literary remains. His papers had been placed in the hands of President Wayland, and incorporated by him in a life of their author, when a rival and unauthorized work from the same materials was announced, and finally published. The letter of Mrs. Judson was addressed to the publisher of the last named volume, and came before the public in the evidence produced on the trial of the alleged invasion of copyright. It deserves to be remembered not only from the interest connected with the circumstances which called it forth, but as a spirited and well reasoned assertion of the rights of literary property.

WATCHING.

Sleep, love, sleep!
The dusty day is done.
Lo! from afar the freshening breezes sweep,
Wild over groves of balm,
Down from the towering palm,
In at the open casement cooling run,
And round thy lowly bed,
Thy bed of pain,
Bathing thy patient head,
Like grateful showers of rain,
They come;
While the white curtains, waving to and fro,
Fan the sick air;
And pityingly the shadows come and go,
With gentle human care,
Compassionate and dumb.

The dusty day is done,
The night begun;
While prayerful watch I keep.
Sleep, love, sleep!
Is there no magic in the touch
Of fingers thou dost love so much?
Fain would they scatter poppies o'er thee now,
Or, with a soft caress,
The tremulous lip its own nepenthe press
Upon the weary lid and aching brow,
While prayerful watch I keep—
Sleep, love, sleep!

On the pagoda spire
The bells are swinging,
Their little golden circles in a flutter
With tales the wooing winds have dared to utter,
Till all are singing
As if a choir
Of golden-nested birds in heaven were singing;
And with a lulling sound
The music floats around,
And drops like balm into the drowsy ear;
Commingling with the hum
Of the Sepoy's distant drum,
And lazy beetle ever droning near,
Sounds these of deepest silence born,
Like night made visible by morn;
So silent, that I sometimes start
To hear the throbbings of my heart,
And watch, with shivering sense of pain,
To see thy pale lids lift again.

The lizard with his mouse-like eyes,
Peeps from the mortise in surprise
At such strange quiet after day's harsh din;
Then ventures boldly out,
And looks about,
And with his hollow feet,
Treads his small evening beat,
Darting upon his prey
In such a tricksy, winsome sort of way,
His delicate marauding seems no sin.
And still the curtains swing,
But noiselessly;
The bells a melancholy murmur ring,
As tears were in the sky;
More heavily the shadows fall,
Like the black foldings of a pall,
Where juts the rough beam from the wall;
The candles flare
With fresher gusts of air;
The beetle's drone
Turns to a dirge-like solitary moan;
Night deepens, and I sit, in cheerless doubt, alone.

ANNE CHARLOTTE BOTTA.

Anne C. Lynch was born at Bennington, Vermont. Her father, at the age of sixteen, joined the United Irishmen of his native country, and was an active participant in the rebellion of 1798. He was offered pardon and a commission in the English army on the condition of swearing allegiance to the British government. On his refusal, he was imprisoned for four years, and then banished. He came to America, married, and died in Cuba during a journey undertaken for the benefit of his health, a few years after the birth of his daughter.

After receiving an excellent education at a ladies' seminary in Albany, Miss Lynch removed to Providence, where she edited, in 1841, the Rhode Island Book, a tasteful selection from the writings of the authors of that state. She soon after came to the city of New York, where she has since resided.

A collection of Miss Lynch's poems has been published in an elegant volume, illustrated by Durand, Huntington, Darley, and other leading American artists. Miss Lynch is also favorably known as a prose writer by her contributions of essays and tales to the magazines of the day.

In 1855, Miss Lynch was married to Mr. Vin-

cenzo Botta, formerly Professor of Philosophy in the College of Sardinia, and member of the National Parliament.

THOUGHTS IN A LIBRARY.

Speak low!—tread softly through these halls;
 Here Genius lives enshrined;
Here reign, in silent majesty,
 The monarchs of the mind.

A mighty spirit host they come,
 From every age and clime;
Above the buried wrecks of years,
 They breast the tide of Time.

And in their presence chamber here
 They hold their regal state,
And round them throng a noble train,
 The gifted and the great.

Oh, child of Earth! when round thy path
 The storms of life arise,
And when thy brothers pass thee by
 With stern unloving eyes;

Here shall the poets chant for thee
 Their sweetest, loftiest lays;
And prophets wait to guide thy steps
 In wisdom's pleasant ways.

Come, with these God-anointed kings
 Be thou companion here;
And in the mighty realm of mind,
 Thou shalt go forth a peer!

TO —— WITH FLOWERS.

Go, ye sweet messengers,
 To that dim-lighted room
Where lettered wisdom from the walls
 Sheds a delightful gloom.

Where sits in thought profound
 One in the noon of life,
Whose flashing eye and fevered brow
 Tell of the inward strife;

Who in those wells of lore
 Seeks for the pearl of truth,
And to Ambition's fever dream
 Gives his repose and youth.

To him, sweet ministers,
 Ye shall a lesson teach;
Go in your fleeting loveliness,
 More eloquent than speech.

Tell him in laurel wreaths
 No perfume e'er is found,
And that upon a crown of thorns
 Those leaves are ever bound.

Thoughts fresh as your own hues
 Bear ye to that abode—
Speak of the sunshine and the sky
 Of Nature and of God.

PARKE GODWIN.

Parke Godwin was born at Paterson, New Jersey, February 25, 1816. His father was an officer of the war of 1812, and his grandfather a soldier of the Revolution. He was educated at Kinderhook, and entered Princeton College in 1831, where he was graduated in 1834. He then studied law at Paterson, N. J., and having removed to the West, was admitted to practice in Kentucky, but did not pursue the profession. In 1837, he became assistant editor of the Evening Post, in which position he remained, with a single year excepted, to the close of 1853—thirteen years of active editorial life. In February, 1843, Mr. Godwin commenced the publication of a weekly, political, and literary Journal, somewhat on the plan of Mr. Leggett's Plaindealer, entitled "The Pathfinder." Mr. John Bigelow, at present associated with Mr. Bryant in the proprietorship and editorship of the Post, and the author of a volume of travels, *Jamaica in* 1850, contributed a number of articles to this journal. Though well conducted in all its departments, it was continued but about three months, when it was dropped with the fifteenth number. During the period of Mr. Godwin's connexion with the Post, besides his constant articles in the journal, he was a frequent contributor to the Democratic Review, where numerous papers on free trade, political economy, democracy, course of civilization, the poetry of Shelley, and the series on law reformers, Bentham, Edward Livingston, and others; and the discussion of the subject of Law Reform, in which the measures taken in the state of New York were anticipated, are from his pen. He has since written a similar series of papers on the public questions of the day, in Putnam's Monthly Magazine, with which he is prominently connected. In 1850, he published a fanciful illustrated tale, entitled *Vala*, in which he turned his acquaintance with the quaint mythologies of the north, and the poetic arts connecting the world of imagination with the world of reality, to the illustration of incidents in the life of Jenny Lind. It is a succession of pleasant pictures constructed with much ingenuity. The volume was published in quarto with illustrations, by the author's friends, Hicks, Rossiter, Wolcott, and Whitley.

Another proof of Mr. Godwin's acquaintance with German literature, is his translation of

Goethe's Autobiography, published by Wiley in New York, and adopted by Bohn in London; and of a series of the tales of Zschokke. He has written besides a popular account of Fourier's writings, and a small volume on *Constructive Democracy*.

It is understood that he has been for some time engaged on a book to be entitled *The History and Organization of Labor*, and the preparation of another, *The Nineteenth Century, with its Leading Men and Movements*. He has also promised the public a book of travels, *A Winter Harvest*, the result of a visit to Europe a few years since, during which he had personal interviews with the leading French and English political reformers.

JOHN G. SAXE.

John G. Saxe was born at Highgate, Franklin County, Vermont, June 2, 1816. He was graduated at Middlebury College in 1839, studied law, was admitted to the bar, and has since been engaged in the practice of the profession in his native State.

In 1849 Mr. Saxe published a volume of *Poems* including *Progress, a Satire*, originally delivered at a college commencement, and a number of shorter pieces, many of which had previously appeared in the Knickerbocker Magazine.

In the same year Mr. Saxe delivered a poem on *The Times* before the Boston Mercantile Library Association. This production is included in the enlarged edition of his volume, in 1852. He has since frequently appeared before the public on college and other anniversaries, as the poet of the occasion, well armed with the light artillery of jest and epigram. In the summer of 1855 he pronounced a brilliant poem on Literature and the Times, at the Second Anniversary of the Associate Alumni of the Free Academy in New York.

RHYME OF THE RAIL.

Singing through the forests,
Rattling over ridges,
Shooting under arches,
Rumbling over bridges,
Whizzing through the mountains,
Buzzing o'er the vale,—
Bless me! this is pleasant,
Riding on the rail!

Men of different "stations"
In the eye of Fame,
Here are very quickly
Coming to the same.
High and lowly people,
Birds of every feather,
On a common level
Travelling together!

Gentleman in shorts,
Looming very tall;
Gentleman at large;
Talking very small;
Gentleman in tights,
With a loose-ish mien;
Gentleman in gray,
Looking rather green.

Gentleman quite old,
Asking for the news;
Gentleman in black,
In a fit of blues;
Gentleman in claret,
Sober as a vicar;
Gentleman in Tweed,
Dreadfully in liquor!

Stranger on the right,
Looking very sunny,
Obviously reading
Something rather funny.
Now the smiles are thicker,
Wonder what they mean?
Faith, he's got the Knicker-
Bocker Magazine!

Stranger on the left,
Closing up his peepers,
Now he snores amain,
Like the Seven Sleepers;
At his feet a volume
Gives the explanation,
How the man grew stupid
From "Association!"

Ancient maiden lady
Anxiously remarks,
That there must be peril
'Mong so many sparks;
Roguish looking fellow,
Turning to the stranger,
Says it's his opinion
She is out of danger!

Woman with her baby,
Sitting vis-a-vis;
Baby keeps a squalling,
Woman looks at me;
Asks about the distance,
Says it's tiresome talking,
Noises of the cars
Are so very shocking!

Market woman careful
Of the precious casket,
Knowing eggs are eggs,
Tightly holds her basket;

Feeling that a smash,
 If it came, would surely
Send her eggs to pot
 Rather prematurely!

Singing through the forests,
 Rattling over ridges,
Shooting under arches,
 Rumbling over bridges,
Whizzing through the mountains,
 Buzzing o'er the vale;
Bless me! this is pleasant,
 Riding on the rail!

SONNET TO A CLAM.

Dum tacent clamant.

Inglorious friend! most confident I am
 Thy life is one of very little ease;
 Albeit men mock thee with thy similes
And prate of being "happy as a clam!"
What though thy shell protects thy fragile head
 From the sharp bailiffs of the briny sea?
 Thy valves are, sure, no safety-valves to thee,
While rakes are free to desecrate thy bed,
And bear thee off,—as foemen take their spoil,
 Far from thy friends and family to roam:
 Forced, like a Hessian, from thy native home,
To meet destruction in a foreign broil!
 Though thou art tender, yet thy humble bard
 Declares, O clam! thy case is shocking hard!

MY BOYHOOD.

Ah me! those joyous days are gone!
I little dreamt, till they were flown,
 How fleeting were the hours!
For, lest he break the pleasing spell,
Time bears for youth a muffled bell,
And hides his face in flowers!

Ah! well I mind me of the days,
Still bright in memory's flattering rays
 When all was fair and new;
When knaves were only found in books,
And friends were known by friendly looks,
 And love was always true!

While yet of sin I scarcely dreamed,
And everything was what it seemed,
 And all too bright for choice;
When fays were wont to guard my sleep
And *Crusoe* still could make me weep,
 And *Santaclaus*, rejoice!

When heaven was pictured to my thought,
(In spite of all my mother taught
 Of happiness serene)
A theatre of boyish plays—
One glorious round of holidays,
 Without a school between!

Ah me! these joyous days are gone;
I little dreamt till they were flown,
 How fleeting were the hours!
For, lest he break the pleasing spell,
Time bears for youth a muffled bell,
 And hides his face in flowers!

JESSE AMES SPENCER

WAS born June 17, 1816, at Hyde Park, Dutchess county, New York. His father's family, originally from England, came over with the colony which founded Saybrook, Connecticut. On his mother's side (her name was Ames) he claims distant connexion with Fisher Ames, the orator and patriot. Having removed to New York city in the year 1825, he received a good English education, and for several years was an assistant to his father as city surveyor. He chose at first to learn a trade, and acquired a competent knowledge of the printing business with Sleight & Robinson at the age of 17. He then determined to engage in preparation for the sacred ministry. He entered Columbia College in 1834, and was graduated with high classical honors in 1837. He then pursued the course at the General Theological Seminary of the Protestant Episcopal Church, and was ordained deacon July, 1840. He accepted the rectorship of St. James's church, Goshen, New York, directly after. Health having failed him in 1842, by advice of his physicians, he spent the winter of 1842–3 at Nice, Sardinia. Returning to New York in 1843, he devoted himself to teaching, in schools and privately, to editing a juvenile magazine, *The Young Churchman's Miscellany*, and other literary labors. Early in the year 1848 he had a severe illness; was again sent abroad; travelled through England, Scotland, etc., during the summer in company with Mr. George W. Pratt. With the same gentleman he arrived in Alexandria in December, 1848; ascended the Nile, spent some months in Egypt, crossed the desert in March, 1849, travelled through the Holy Land, and in May of the same year left for Europe. He reached New York in August, 1849. The following year he accepted the professorship of Latin and Oriental languages in Burlington College, New Jersey. He was afterwards nominated for professor of ecclesiastical history in the General Theological Seminary, and failed of the appointment by only one vote. He was chosen editor and secretary of the General Protestant Episcopal Sunday School Union and Church Book Society, November, 1851, which office he still holds.

Dr. Spencer's writings are, a volume of *Discourses*, in 1843; a *History of the English Reformation*, 18mo., 1846; an edition of the *New Testament in Greek, with Notes on the Historical Books*, 12mo., 1847; *Cæsar's Commentaries, with copious Notes, Lexicon*, etc., 12mo., 1848; and a volume of foreign travel, *Egypt and the Holy Land*, the first edition of which appeared in 1849.

Dr. Spencer has edited a valuable series of classical books by the late T. K. Arnold, and has contributed largely to the current literature of the time.

FREDERICK WILLIAM SHELTON

WAS born at Jamaica, Queens County, Long Island, where his father, Dr. Nathan Shelton, a graduate of Yale, lived, much respected as a physician. The son was graduated at the College of New Jersey in 1834. He subsequently employed much of his time in literature at his home on Long Island, writing frequently for the Knickerbocker Magazine, to which he contributed a series of local humorous sketches, commencing with The Kushow Property, a tale of Crowhill in 1848, and followed by *The Tinnecum Papers*, and other miscellaneous articles, including several refined criticisms of Vincent Bourne, Charles Lamb, and other select authors.

In 1837, Mr. Shelton published anonymously his first volume, *The Trollopiad; or Travelling Gentlemen in America*, a satire, by Nil Admirari, Esq., dedicated to Mrs. Trollope. It is in rhyming pentameter, shrewdly sarcastic, and liberally garnished with notes preservative of the memory of the series of gentlemen, whose hurried tours in America and flippant descriptions were formerly so provocative of the ire of native writers. As a clever squib, and a curious record of a past state of literature, the *Trollopiad* is worthy a place in the libraries of the curious.

In 1847, Mr. Shelton was ordained a minister of the Protestant Episcopal Church; and in the discharge of the duties of this vocation, has occupied country parishes at Huntington, Long Island, and the old village of Fishkill, Dutchess county, New York. In 1854 he became rector of a church at Montpelier, Vermont, where he is at present established.

Several of his writings have grown out of his experiences as a rural clergyman, and are among the happiest sketches of the fertile topic afforded in that field under the voluntary system in America which have yet appeared. He is a genial, kindly humorist, and his pictures of this class in *The Rector of St. Bardolph's, or Superannuated*, published in 1852, and *Peeps from a Belfry, or the Parish Sketch Book*, in 1855, while truthfully presenting all that is due to satire, are so tempered by pathos and simplicity that they would have won the heart of the Vicar of Wakefield himself.

In another more purely moral vein Mr. Shelton has published two apologues, marked by poetical refinement, and a delicate, fanciful invention: *Salander and the Dragon* (in 1850), and *Crystalline, or the Heiress of Fall Downe Castle*. These are fairy tales designed to exhibit the evils in the world of suspicion and detraction.

In yet another line Mr. Shelton has published a volume, *Up the River*, composed of a series of rural sketches, dating from his parish in Dutchess county, on the Hudson. It is an exceedingly pleasant book in its tasteful, truthful observations of nature and animal life, and the incidents of the country, interspersed with occasional criticism of favorite books, and invigorated throughout by the individual humors of the narrator.

Mr. Shelton has also published two lectures on *The Gold Mania*, and *The Use and Abuse of Reason*, delivered before the Huntington (Long Island) Library Association in 1850.

A BURIAL AMONG THE MOUNTAINS—FROM PEEPS FROM A BELFRY.

Several times has the summer come and gone—several times have the sear and crisped leaves of autumn fallen to the ground, since it was my privilege to administer for a single winter to a small parish in the wilderness. I call it the wilderness only in contradistinction to the gay and splendid metropolis from which I went. For how great the contrast from the din of commerce, from noisy streets, attractive sights, and people of all nations, to a village among the mountains, where the attention is even arrested by a falling leaf. It was among the most magnificent scenes of nature, whose massive outlines have imprinted themselves on my recollection with a distinctness which can never be effaced.

I account it a privilege to have spent a winter in Vermont. The gorgeous character of the scenery, the intelligence and education of its inhabitants, the excellence yet simplicity of living, its health and hospitality, rendered the stay both profitable and agreeable. Well do I remember those Sunday mornings, when, with the little Winooski river on the right hand, wriggling through the ice, and with a snow-clad spur of the mountains on the left, I wended my solitary way through the cutting wind to the somewhat remote and somewhat thinly-attended little church. But the warmth, intelligence, refinement, and respectful attention of that small band of worshippers fully compensated for the atmosphere without, which often ranged below zero. It is true that a majority of the inhabitants had been educated to attend the Congregational (usually denominated the Brick Church), where a young man of fine talents, who was my friend, administered to the large flock committed to his charge.

How oft with him I've ranged the snow-clad hill,
  Where grew the pine-tree and the towering oak!
And as the white fogs all the valley fill,
  And axe re-echoed to the woodman's stroke,
While frozen flakes were squeaking under foot,
  And distant tinklings from the vale arise,
Upward and upward still the way we took,
  As souls congenial tower toward the skies.

We talked of things which did beseem the place,
  Matters of moment to the Church and State,
The upward, downward progress of the race,
  Predestination, Destiny, and Fate.
He tracked the thoughts of Calvin or of Kant,
  Such lore as from his learned sire he drew;
I searched the tomes of D'Oyley and of Mant,
  Or sipped the sweetness of Castalian dew.
So when the mountain path grew dim to view,
  And woollen tippets were congealed or damp,
Swift to the vale our journey we renew,
  Relight the fire, and trim the student's lamp.

Ordinary occurrences impress themselves more deeply, associated with scenes whose features are so grand. A conversation with a friend will be remembered with greater accuracy if it be made upon the mountain or in the storm; and not with less devotion does the heart respond to the worship of God if his holy temple be builded among scenes of beauty, if it have no pillars but the uncarved rocks, no rafters but the sunbeams, and no dome but the skies. Thus, while residing on the mountains, I kept on the tablets of memory an unwritten diary, from which it is pleasant to draw forth an occasional leaf.

It was in the month of January, when the boreal breath is so keen, after such a walk with my friend to the summit of the mountain, that I returned at nightfall to my chamber, with my camlet cloak and hat completely covered with snow. The flakes were large, starry, and disposed themselves in the shape of crystals. After much stamping of the feet, shaking the cloak, and thumping with a drum-like sound upon the hat, I began to stuff into the box-stove (for nothing but Russian stoves will keep you warm in Vermont) a plenty of maple-wood which abounds in those regions, and which, after hickory, makes the most delightful fire in the world. Then, having dried my damp feet, looked reflectingly into the coals, answered the tea-bell, and, as a mere matter of course, drank a cup of the weed called tea, I returned to my solitary apartment, snuffed the candles, laid out a due quantity of ruled "Sermon paper," wiped the rusty steel pens, and began to reflect, What theme will be most appropriate for the season? Let me examine the Lessons—let me see if I can find some sentiment in the Epistle or Gospel for the day, on which it will be proper to enlarge. Such search in the Prayer Book is never in vain. The course is marked out—the path clear. For not more equally is the natural year distinguished by day and night, cold and heat, storm and sunlight, winter and spring, summer and autumn, than is the "Year of our Lord" by times and seasons, which are the events in His lifetime, and which are the very periods by which to direct our course. If in this work-day world the daily service of the sanctuary cannot be attended, let the devout Christian, let the earnest Churchman, at least read, mark, learn, and inwardly digest, those daily lessons which the Church, through Holy Writ, teaches.

Scarce had I disposed myself for an evening's work, when I was called on with a request to perform funeral services on the next day, over the body of a poor Irish laborer, killed suddenly on the line of the railroad by the blasting of rocks.

The priest was absent; for although there was a numerous body, perhaps several hundred Irish Catholics in that vicinity, he came only once in six weeks. During the interval those poor people were left without shepherd; and as they had a regard for the decencies of Christian burial, they sometimes, as on this occasion, requested the church clergyman to be at hand. I willingly consented to do what appeared a necessary charity, although I apprehended, and afterwards learned, that the more rigid and disciplined of the faith were indignant, and kept away from the funeral rites, which they almost considered profane. Nor could I disrespect their scruples, considering the principles whence they grew.

The snow fell all night to the depth of several feet, and when the morrow dawned, the wind blew a hurricane, filling the air with fine particles of snow, and making the cold intense. Muffling myself as well as possible, I proceeded two miles to the Irish shanty where the deceased lay, which was filled to its utmost capacity with a company of respectful friends and sincere mourners. It was, indeed, a comfortless abode; but for the poor man who reposed there in his pine coffin, it was as good a tenement as the most sumptuous palace ever reared. When I see the dead going from an abode like this, the thought comes up that perhaps they have lost little, and are gaining much; that the grave over which the grass grows, and the trees wave, and the winds murmur, is, after all, a peaceful haven and a place of rest. But when they go from marble halls and splendid mansions, the last trappings appear a mockery, and I think only of what they have left behind.

Standing in one corner of that small cabin among the sobbing relatives, while the winds of winter howled without their requiem of the departed year, I began to read the Church's solemn office for the dead:—

"I am the Resurrection and the life, saith the Lord: he that believeth in Me, though he were dead, yet shall he live; and whosoever liveth and believeth in Me shall never die."

Having completed the reading of those choral words, which form the opening part of the order for burial, and the magnificent and inspiring words of St. Paul, the procession was formed at the door of the hovel and we proceeded on foot.

The wind-storm raged violently, so that you could scarce see, by reason of the snowy pillar, while the drifts were sometimes up to your knees. The walk was most dreary. On either hand the mountains lifted their heads loftily, covered to the summit with snows; the pine trees and evergreens which skirted the highway, presented the spectacle of small pyramids; every weed which the foot struck was glazed over; and the bushes, in the faint beams of the struggling light, sparkled with gems. In a wild, Titanic defile, gigantic icicles hung from the oozing rocks; and as we passed a mill stream, we had the sight of a frozen water-fall, arrested in its descent, and with all its volume, spray, and mist, as if by the hand of some enchanter changed suddenly into stone.

All these objects, in my walks through the mountains, had impressed their lessons of the magnificence and glory of God. But what new ideas did the same scenes suggest, associated as they were with this wintry funeral.

At last we arrived at the place of graves. It was an acclivity of the mountain; a small field surrounded by a rude fence, in one corner of which were erected many wooden crosses; and a pile of sand, or rather of sandy frozen clods, dug out with a pickaxe, and cast upon the surrounding snows, indicated the spot of this new sepulture. There was not a single marble erected, not a monument of brown stone, or epitaph; but the emblem of the cross alone denoted that it was the resting-place of the lowliest of the lowly—of the poor sons of Erin, the hewers of wood and drawers of water, who had from time to time, in these distant regions, given up their lives to toil, to suffering, or to crime. But the mountain in which they were buried was itself a monument which, without any distinction, in a spot where all were equal, was erected equally for all. There is no memorial, even of the greatest, so good as the place in which they repose; and when I looked at the Sinai-like peak which rose before us, I thought that these poor people had, in their depth of poverty, resorted to the very God of nature to memorize their dead.

But I must not forget to notice, by way of memorial, the history of that poor man. He was one of those who lived by the sweat of the brow. By digging and delving in the earth; by bearing heavy burdens, and performing dangerous work, he obtained a living by hard labor, "betwixt the daylight and dark;" and while the famine was raging in his own land, like many of his race who exhibit the same noble generosity and devotion (what an example to those of loftier rank!) he had carefully saved his earnings and transmitted them to his relatives. They arrived too late. His father and mother had already died of starvation; but his only sister had scarce reached the doors of this poor man's hovel, after so long a journey, when, as she awaited anxiously his return that evening, from his daily work, the litter which contained his body arrived at the door!

I reflected upon this little history, as we approached the grave upon the mountain side, and, melancholy as the scene was, with the snows drifting upon our uncovered heads, I would not have exchanged the good which it did my soul, for the warmest and best-lighted chamber where revelry abounds; and as I repeated those most touching words, "O Lord, God most holy, O Lord, most mighty, O holy and most merciful Saviour, deliver us not into the bitter pains of eternal death," I thought that the surrounding gloom was itself suggestive of hope to the Christian soul. In a few months more, the mountains would again be clothed with verdure, and the little hills would rejoice on every side. As the winds died away into vernal gales, as the icicles fell from the rocks, as the snows vanished, they would be succeeded by the voice of the blooming and beautiful earth, with all its forest choirs, prolonging the chant of thanksgiving. How much more should the body of him, which now lay cold in its grave, with the clods and the snows of the mountains piled upon it, awake to a sure, and, it was to be hoped, a joyous resurrection. With such cheering thoughts we hurried away from the spot, when the service was ended, humbly praying that a portion of consolation might be conveyed to the heart of her, who, in a strange land, mourned the loss of an only brother. *In pace requiescat.*

JOHN O. SARGENT—EPES SARGENT.

John Osborne Sargent was born in Gloucester, Massachusetts, and passed his childhood there and in the town of Hingham. He was sent to the Latin school in Boston, the prize annals of which, and the record of a Latin ode, and a translation from the Elegy of Tyrtæus, of his compositions, show his early proficiency in classical education. He passed to Harvard and was graduated in 1830. While there he established the clever periodical of which we have already spoken in the notice of one of its contributors, Dr. O. W. Holmes,* The Collegian. He was further assisted in it by the late William H. Simmons, the accomplished elocutionist and essayist; Robert Habersham, jr., of Boston, Frederick W. Brune of Baltimore, and by his brother, Epes Sargent.

On leaving college Mr. Sargent studied law in the office of the Hon. William Sullivan of Boston, and commenced its practice in that city. This was at the period of political agitation attending the financial measures of President Jackson. Mr. Sargent became a political writer and speaker in the Whig cause, and was elected to the lower house of the Legislature of Massachusetts. For some three years he was almost a daily writer for the editorial columns of the Boston Atlas, and added largely by his articles to the reputation which the paper at that time enjoyed as an efficient, vigorous party journal.

In 1838 Mr. Sargent removed to the city of New York, and was well known by his pen and oratory during the active political career which resulted in the election of General Harrison to the presidency. The Courier and Enquirer, for three or four years at this time, was enriched by leading political articles from his hand. At the close of the contest he re-engaged in the active pursuit of his profession. To this he devoted himself, with rigid seclusion from politics for eight years, with success.

He was drawn, however, again into politics in the canvass which resulted in the election of General Taylor, upon whose elevation to the presidency he became associated with Mr. Alexander C. Bullitt of Kentucky, in the establishment of the Republic newspaper at Washington. Its success was immediate and unprecedented. In about six months it numbered more than thirty thousand staunch Whigs on its subscription list. Its course, however, was not acceptable to the members of the cabinet. A rupture was finally brought about in consequence of the attempt of Messrs. Bullitt and Sargent to separate General Taylor from the cabinet in the matter of the Galphin claim, and their determination to support Mr. Clay's measures of compromise against the known wishes of the administration. A withdrawal from the editorship of the paper was the result. After Mr. Fillmore's accession to the presidency by the death of Taylor, a change in the policy of the administration ensued, which enabled Mr. Sargent to return to the Republic, which he conducted with spirit and efficiency to the close of the presidential term. Mr. Sargent enjoyed the entire confidence of President Fillmore, and was tendered by him the mission to China.

Since the advent of the Pierce cabinet Mr. Sargent has occupied himself exclusively with professional pursuits in the city of Washington, where he is engaged in an extensive legal practice.

Mr. Sargent has published several anonymous pamphlets on political and legal subjects which have been largely circulated. His *Lecture on the late Improvements in Steam Navigation and the Arts of Naval Warfare*, which contains a biographical sketch of John Ericsson, has been several times republished in England, and translated into several of the continental languages. He is an accomplished scholar in the modern languages. Some of his poetical translations from the German enjoy a high reputation.

Epes Sargent, a brother of the preceding, was born at Gloucester, Massachusetts, but at a very early age removed with his family to Boston. He was subsequently at school at Hingham. At nine years of age he was placed at the public Latin school in Boston, where he continued five years, with the exception of a period of six months, during which he made a visit with his father to Russia. While in St. Petersburgh he was often at the palace, examining the fine collection of paintings at the "Hermitage," or wandering through the splendid apartments. While here also he was much noticed by Baron Stieglitz, the celebrated banker and millionaire, who offered to educate him with his son, and take him into his counting-room, under very favorable conditions. The proposition, however, was declined. Returning to school in Boston, young Sargent was one of half a dozen boys who started a small weekly paper called the Literary Journal. In it he published some account of his Russian experiences.

Mr. Sargent was admitted a member of the freshman class of Harvard University, but did not remain at Cambridge. Some years afterwards he was called upon to deliver the poem before the Phi Beta Kappa Society of that institution.

Epes Sargent

At an early age Mr. Sargent engaged in editorial life. He first became connected with the Boston Daily Advertiser, but some change occurring in the management of that journal he associated

* *Ante*, p. 511.

himself with Mr. S. G. Goodrich in the preparation of the "Peter Parley" books. His labors in book-making were various and numerous for a series of years.

In 1836 he wrote for Miss Josephine Clifton a five-act play, entitled *The Bride of Genoa*, which was brought out at the Tremont Theatre with much success, and often repeated. It was subsequently acted by Miss Cushman at the Park Theatre on the occasion of her sister's début. It was published in the New World newspaper under the title of The Genoese, but the author has never thought it worthy of a permanent adoption.

On the 20th of November, 1837, the tragedy of *Velasco*, written for Miss Ellen Tree, was produced at the Tremont Theatre, Boston, with marked success. It was afterwards brought out at the Park Theatre, New York, and the principal theatres in the country. The play was published and dedicated to the author's personal friend, the Hon. William C. Preston of South Carolina, under whose auspices it was produced at Washington.

Velasco was brought out in London in 1850–51, and played at the Marylebone Theatre for a number of nights. It was decidedly successful, though severely criticised by most of the papers.

In 1837 Mr. Sargent became editorially connected with the Boston Atlas, and passed much of his time at Washington writing letters to that journal. About the year 1839–40 he removed to New York on the invitation of General Morris, and took charge for a short time of the Mirror. He now wrote a number of juvenile works for the Harpers, of which two, *Wealth and Worth*, and *What's to be Done?* had a large sale. He also wrote a comedy, *Change makes Change*, first produced at Niblo's, and afterwards by Burton in Philadelphia. Recently Mr. Burton applied to the author for a copy to produce at the Chambers street establishment, and it was found that none was in existence. In 1846 he commenced and edited for some time the Modern Standard Drama, an enterprise which he afterwards sold out, and which is now a lucrative property.

A matrimonial alliance now drew him eastward again. He established himself at Roxbury within a short distance of Boston, and after editing the Transcript for a few years, withdrew from newspaper life, and engaged exclusively in literary pursuits. In 1852 he produced the *Standard Speaker*—a work of rare completeness in its department, which has already passed through thirteen large editions. A life of Benjamin Franklin, with a collection of his writings, followed: then lives of Campbell, Collins, Goldsmith, Gray, Hood, and Rogers, attached to fine editions of their poetical works, published by Phillips, Sampson & Co., Boston. Recently Mr. Sargent has put forth a series of five Readers for schools, the success of which is justly due to the minute care and elaboration bestowed upon them, and the good taste with which they are executed.

In March, 1855, Mr. Sargent produced at the new Boston theatre, under the auspices of his old friend Mr. Barry, who had ushered into the world his two early dramatic productions, the five-act tragedy of *The Priestess*, which was played with decided success, Mrs. Hayne (born Julia Dean) performing the part of Norma, the heroine. The play is partially, in the latter acts, founded on the operatic story of Norma.

In 1849 an edition of Mr. Sargent's poems, under the title of *Songs of the Sea and other Poems*, was published by Ticknor & Fields. It is composed chiefly of a number of spirited lyrics, several of which have been set to music. A series of sonnets is included: Shells and Sea-weeds, Records of a Summer Voyage to Cuba. The expression in these, as in all the poetical writings of the author, is clear and animated.

In addition to these numerous engagements of a career of great literary activity, Mr. Sargent has been connected as a contributor and editor with various magazines and periodicals.

As a lecturer he has been widely known before the Mercantile Library Association in Boston and similar associations in the Eastern and middle states.

He was on terms of intimacy with Mr. Clay, and wrote a life of that distinguished statesman. In a preface to a recent edition of this life, Mr. Horace Greeley says: "I have reason to believe that Mr. Clay himself gave the preference, among all the narratives of his life which had fallen under his notice, to that of Epes Sargent, first issued in 1842, and republished with its author's revisions and additions in the summer of 1848."

A LIFE ON THE OCEAN WAVE.

A life on the ocean wave,
  A home on the rolling deep;
Where the scattered waters rave,
  And the winds their revels keep!
Like an eagle caged, I pine
  On this dull, unchanging shore:
O! give me the flashing brine,
  The spray and the tempest's roar!

Once more on the deck I stand,
  Of my own swift-gliding craft:
Set sail! farewell to the land!
  The gale follows fair abaft.
We shoot through the sparkling foam
  Like an ocean-bird set free;—
Like the ocean-bird, our home
  We'll find far out on the sea.

The land is no longer in view,
  The clouds have begun to frown;
But with a stout vessel and crew,
  We'll say, Let the storm come down!
And the song of our hearts shall be,
  While the winds and the waters rave,
A home on the rolling sea!
  A life on the ocean wave!

THE DEATH OF WARREN.

When the war-cry of Liberty rang through the land,
To arms sprang our fathers the foe to withstand;
On old Bunker Hill their entrenchments they rear,
When the army is joined by a young volunteer.
"Tempt not death!" cried his friends; but he bade
  them good-by,
Saying, "O! it is sweet for our country to die!"

The tempest of battle now rages and swells,
'Mid the thunder of cannon, the pealing of bells;
And a light, not of battle, illumes yonder spire—
Scene of woe and destruction;—'tis Charlestown on
  fire!

The young volunteer heedeth not the sad cry,
But murmurs, "'Tis sweet for our country to die!"
With trumpets and banners the foe draweth near:
A volley of musketry checks their career!
With the dead and the dying the hill-side is strown,
And the shout through our lines is, "The day is our own!"
"Not yet," cries the young volunteer, "do they fly!
Stand firm!—it is sweet for our country to die!"

Now our powder is spent, and they rally again;—
"Retreat!" says our chief, "since unarmed we remain!"
But the young volunteer lingers yet on the field,
Reluctant to fly, and disdaining to yield.
A shot! Ah! he falls! but his life's latest sigh
Is, "'Tis sweet, O, 'tis sweet for our country to die!"

And thus Warren fell! Happy death! noble fall!
To perish for country at Liberty's call!
Should the flag of invasion profane evermore
The blue of our seas or the green of our shore,
May the hearts of our people re-echo that cry,—
"'Tis sweet, O, 'tis sweet for our country to die!"

O YE KEEN BREEZES.

O ye keen breezes from the salt Atlantic,
Which to the beach, where memory loves to wander,
On your strong pinions waft reviving coolness,
Bend your course hither!

For, in the surf ye scattered to the sunshine,
Did we not sport together in my boyhood,
Screaming for joy amid the flashing breakers,
O rude companions?

Then to the meadows beautiful and fragrant,
Where the coy Spring beholds her earliest verdure
Brighten with smiles that rugged sea-side hamlet,
How would we hasten?

There under elm-trees affluent in foliage,
High o'er whose summit hovered the sea-eagle,
Through the hot, glaring noontide have we rested
After our gambols.

Vainly the sailor called you from your slumber:
Like a glazed pavement shone the level ocean;
While, with their snow-white canvass idly drooping,
Stood the tall vessels.

And when, at length, exulting ye awakened,
Rushed to the beach, and ploughed the liquid acres,
How have I chased you through the shivered billows,
In my frail shallop!

Playmates, old playmates, hear my invocation!
In the close town I waste this golden summer,
Where piercing cries and sounds of wheels in motion
Ceaselessly mingle.

When shall I feel your breath upon my forehead?
When shall I hear you in the elm-trees' branches?
When shall we wrestle in the briny surges,
Friends of my boyhood?

PHILIP PENDLETON COOKE—JOHN ESTEN COOKE.

Philip Pendleton Cooke, the son of the late John R. Cooke, an eminent member of the Virginia bar, was born in Martinsburg, Berkeley Co., Va., October 26, 1816. He entered Princeton College at the early age of fifteen; and after completing his course, studied law with his father at Winchester. He wrote a few sketches in prose and verse for the Virginian, and the early numbers of the Southern Literary Messenger. Before he was of age, he was engaged in professional practice and also a married man. An ardent lover of field sports, and surrounded at his home on the Shenandoah near the Blue Ridge, with every temptation for these pursuits, he became a thorough sportsman. At this time, he penned a romance of about three hundred lines, entitled *Emily*, which was published in Graham's Magazine. This was followed by the *Froissart Ballads*, which appeared in a volume in 1847. This was his only separate publication. He afterwards wrote part of a novel, *The Chevalier Merlin*, which appeared, so far as completed, in the Southern Literary Messenger. He also wrote for the same periodical, the tales entitled *John Carpe*, *The Two Country Houses*, *The Gregories of Hackwood*, *The Crime of Andrew Blair*, *Erysicthon*, *Dante*, and a number of reviews.

P. P. Cooke

Mr. Cooke died suddenly, January 20, 1850, at the early age of thirty-three.

With the exception of the Froissart Ballads, which he wrote with great rapidity, at the rate of one a day, Mr. Cooke composed slowly; and his published productions, felicitous as they are, do not, in the judgment of those who knew him, present a full exhibition of the powers of his mind. He shone in conversation, and was highly prized by all about him for his intellectual and social qualities. His manner was stately and impressive.

The poems of Mr. Cooke are in a bright animated mood, vigorous without effort, preserving the freedom of nature with the discipline of art. The ballads, versifications of old Froissart's chivalric stories, run off trippingly with their sparkling objective life. In its rare and peculiar excellence, in delicately touched sentiment, Florence Vane has the merit of an antique song.

FLORENCE VANE.

I loved thee long and dearly,
Florence Vane;
My life's bright dream, and early
Hath come again;
I renew in my fond vision,
My heart's dear pain,
My hope, and thy derision,
Florence Vane.

The ruin lone and hoary,
The ruin old,
Where thou didst mark my story,
At even told,—
That spot—the hues Elysian
Of sky and plain—
I treasure in my vision,
Florence Vane.

Thou wast lovelier than the roses
In their prime;
Thy voice excelled the closes
Of sweetest rhyme;
Thy heart was as a river
Without a main.
Would I had loved thee never,
Florence Vane!

But, fairest, coldest wonder!
Thy glorious clay
Lieth the green sod under—
Alas the day!
And it boots not to remember
Thy disdain—
To quicken love's pale ember,
Florence Vane.

The lilies of the valley
By young graves weep,
The pansies love to dally
Where maidens sleep;
May their bloom, in beauty vying,
Never wane
Where thine earthly part is lying,
Florence Vane!

YOUNG ROSALIE LEE.

I love to forget ambition,
And hope, in the mingled thought
Of valley, and wood, and meadow,
Where, whilome, my spirit caught
Affection's holiest breathings—
Where under the skies, with me
Young Rosalie roved, aye drinking
From joy's bright Castaly.

I think of the valley and river,
Of the old wood bright with blossoms;
Of the pure and chastened gladness
Upspringing in our bosoms.
I think of the lonely turtle
So tongued with melancholy;
Of the hue of the drooping moonlight,
And the starlight pure and holy.

Of the beat of a heart most tender,
The sigh of a shell-tinct lip
As soft as the land-tones wandering
Far leagues over ocean deep;
Of a step as light in its falling
On the breast of the beaded lea
As the fall of the faery moonlight
On the leaf of yon tulip tree.

I think of these—and the murmur
Of bird, and katydid,
Whose home is the grave-yard cypress
Whose goblet the honey-reed.
And then I weep! for Rosalie
Has gone to her early rest;
And the green-lipped reed and the daisy
Suck sweets from her maiden breast.

JOHN ESTEN COOKE, a younger brother of the preceding, is the author of a series of fictions, produced with rapidity, which have in a brief pe-

Jno Esten Cooke.

riod gained him the attention of the public. He was born in Winchester, Frederick county, Virginia, November 3, 1830. When a year or more old, his father took up his residence on his estate of Glengary, near Winchester, whence, on the burning of the house in 1839, the family removed to Richmond. Mr. Cooke's first publication, if we except a few tales and sketches contributed to Harpers' and Putnam's Magazines, the Literary World, and perhaps other journals, was entitled, *Leather Stocking and Silk, or Hunter John Myers and his Times, a Story of the Valley of Virginia*, from the press of the Harpers in 1854. The chief character, the hunter, is drawn from life, and is a specimen of manly, healthy, mountain nature, effectively introduced in the gay domestic group around him. This was immediately followed by the *Youth of Jefferson, or a Chronicle of College Scrapes, at Williamsburgh, in Viginia, A.D.* 1764. The second title somewhat qualifies the serious purport of the first, which might lead the reader to look for a work of biography; but in fact, the book, with perhaps a meagre hint or two of tradition, is a fanciful view of a gayer period than the present, with the full latitude of the writer of fiction. Love is, of course, a prominent subject of the story, and is tenderly and chivalrously handled. Scarcely had these books made their appearance, almost simultaneously, when a longer work from the same, as yet anonymous, source, was announced in *The Virginia Comedians, or Old Days in the Old Dominion, edited from the MSS. of C. Effingham, Esq.* It is much the largest, and by far the best of the author's works thus far. The scene has the advantage of one of the most capable regions of romance in the country, the life and manners of Virginia in the period just preceding the Revolution, combining the adventure of woodland and frontier life with the wealth and luxury of the sea-board. We are introduced to one of the old manorial homesteads on James river, where the dramatis personæ have little else to do than to develope their traits and idiosyncrasies with a freedom fettered only by the rules of art and the will of the writer. The privilege is not suffered to pass unimproved. The whole book is redolent of youth and poetic susceptibility to the beauties of nature, the charms of woman, and the quick movement of life. Some liberties are taken with historical personages—there is a flitting study of Patrick Henry in a certain shrewd man in an old red cloak; Parson Tag has doubtless had his parallel among the high living clergy and stage manager Hallam we know existed, though we trust with very different attributes from those to which the necessity of the plot here subjects him. These are all, however, but shadowy hints; the author's active fancy speedily carrying him beyond literal realities. In its purely romantic spirit, and the variety and delicacy of its portraitures of the sex, the Virginia Comedians is a work of high merit and promise. The success of this work induced Mr. Cooke to avow his authorship, and take the benefit in literature of his growing reputation, though still devoted to his profession of the law.

A subsequent publication from his pen,—still another, we believe, is announced,—is entitled *Ellie, or the Human Comedy*, a picture of life in the old sense of the word, a representation of manners. It is a novel of the sentimental school of the day, contrasting high and low life in the city—the scene is laid at Richmond—a young girl, who gives name to the book, furnishing the sunbeam to the social life in which she is cast. In this portrait of girlish life, the writer, as he tells us, "has tried to show how a pure spirit, even though it be in the bosom of a child, will run through the variegated woof of that life which surrounds it, like a thread of pure gold, and that all who come in contact with it, will carry away something to elevate and purify them, and make them better." The character is in a mood in which the author has been most successful.

The most noticeable characteristic of Mr. Cooke's style is its gay, happy facility—the proof of a generous nature. It carries the reader, in these early works, lightly over any defects of art, and provides for the author an easy entrance to the best audience of the novelist, youth and womanhood.

PROLOGUE TO THE VIRGINIA COMEDIANS.

The memories of men are full of old romances; but they will not speak—our skalds. King Arthur lies still wounded grievously, in the far island valley of Avilyon: Lord Odin in the misty death realm: Balder the Beautiful, sought long by great Hermoder, lives beyond Hela's portals, and will bless his people some day when he comes. But when? King Arthur *ever is to* come: Odin will one day wind his horn and clash his wild barbaric cymbals through the Nordland pines as he returns, but not in our generation: Balder will rise from sleep and shine again the white sun god on his world. But always these things will be: Arthur and the rest are meanwhile sleeping.

Romance is history: the illustration may be lame—the truth is melancholy. Because the men whose memories hold this history will not speak, it dies away with them! the great past goes deeper and deeper into mist: becomes finally a dying strain of music, and is no more remembered for ever.

Thinking these thoughts I have thought it well to set down here some incidents which took place on Virginia soil, and in which an ancestor of my family had no small part: to write my family romance in a single word, and also, though following a connecting thread, a leading idea, to speak briefly of the period to which these memories, as I may call them, do attach.

That period was very picturesque: illustrated and adorned, as it surely was, by such figures as one seldom sees now on the earth. Often in my evening reveries, assisted by the partial gloom resulting from the struggles of the darkness and the dying firelight, I endeavor, and not wholly without success, to summon from their sleep these stalwart cavaliers, and tender graceful dames of the far past. They rise before me and glide onward—manly faces, with clear eyes and lofty brows, and firm lips covered with the knightly fringe: soft, tender faces, with bright eyes and gracious smiles and winning gestures; all the life and splendor of the past again becomes incarnate! How plain the embroidered doublet, and the sword-belt, and the powdered hair, and hat adorned with its wide floating feather! How real are the ruffled breasts and hands, the long-flapped waistcoats, and the buckled shoes! And then the fairer forms: they come as plainly with their looped-back gowns all glittering with gold and silver flowers, and on their heads great masses of curls with pearls interwoven! See the gracious smiles and musical movement—all the graces which made those dead dames so attractive to the outward eye—as their pure faithful natures made them priceless to the eyes of the heart.

If fancy needed assistance, more than one portrait hanging on my walls might afford it. Old family portraits which I often gaze on with a pensive pleasure. What a tender maiden grace beams on me from the eyes of Kate Effingham yonder; smiling from the antique frame and blooming like a radiant summer—she was but seventeen when it was taken—under the winter of her snow-like powder, and bright diamond pendants, glittering like icicles! The canvas is discolored, and even cracked in places, but the little place laughs merrily still—the eyes fixed peradventure upon another portrait hanging opposite. This is a picture of Mr. William Effingham, the brave soldier of the Revolution, taken in his younger days, when he had just returned from college. He is most preposterously dressed in flowing periwig and enormous ruffles; and his coat is heavy with embroidery in gold thread: he is a handsome young fellow, and excepting some pomposity in his air, a simple-looking, excellent, honest face.

Over my fireplace, however, hangs the picture which I value most—a portrait of my ancestor, Champ Effingham, Esq. The form is lordly and erect; the face clear and pale; the eyes full of wondrous thought in their far depths. The lips are chiselled with extraordinary beauty, the brow noble and imaginative—the whole face plainly giving indication of fiery passion, and no less of tender softness. Often this face looks at me from the canvas, and I fancy sometimes that the white hand, covered as in Vandyke's pictures with its snowy lace, moves from the book it holds and raises slowly the forefinger and points toward its owner's breast. The lips then seem to say, "Speak of me as I was: nothing extenuate: set down nought in malice!"—then the fire-light leaping up shows plainly that this all was but a dream, and the fine pale face is again only canvas, the white hand rests upon its book:—my dream ends with a smile.

EPILOGUE.

It was one of those pure days which, born of spring, seem almost to rejoice like living things in the bright flowers and tender buds:—and she was failing.

All the mountain winds were faintly blowing on the smiling trees, and on the white calm brow of one who breathed the pure delightful airs of opening spring, before she went away to breathe the airs of that other land, so far away, where no snows come, or frost, or hail, or rain; but spring reigns ever, sublimated by the light which shines on figures in white garments round the central throne.

She heard those figures calling, calling, calling, with their low soft voices full of love and hope; calling ever to her in the purple twilight dying o'er the world; rejoicing every one that she was coming.

She looked upon the faces seen through mist around her, and besought them smiling, not to weep for her, but look to the bright land where she was going—for her faith was strong. She begged them to take tender care of the flower which lay but now upon her bosom, and not think of her. A voice had told her in the night that she was waited for: and now the sun was fading in the west, and she must go.

Alcestis-like she kissed them on their brows and pointed to the skies: the time had almost come.

She looked with dim faint eyes, as in a dream, upon that past which now had flowed from her and left her pure:—she saw the sunset wane away and die above the rosy headlands, glooming fast:—she murmured that her hope was steadfast ever; that she heard the angels; that they called to her, and bade her say farewell to all that was around her on this earth, for now the expected time had come.

The tender sunset faded far away, and over the great mountains drooped the spangled veil, with myriads of worlds all singing as her heart was singing now. She saw the rosy flush go far away, and die away, and leave the earth: and then the voice said Come!

She saw a cross rise from the far bright distance, and a bleeding form: she saw the heavenly vision slowly move, and ever nearer, nearer, brighter with the light of heaven. She saw it now before her, and her arms were opened. The grand eternal stars came out above—the sunset died upon her brow—she clasped the cross close to her bosom—and so fell asleep.

THE DEATH OF A MOUNTAIN HUNTER—FROM LEATHER STOCKING AND SILK.

His thoughts then seemed to wander to times more deeply sunken in the past than that of the event his words touched on. Waking he dreamed; and the large eyes melted or fired with a thousand memories which came flocking to him, bright and joyous, or mournful and sombre, but all now transmuted by his almost ecstasy to one glowing mass of purest gold. He saw now plainly much that had been dark to him before; the hand of God was in all, the providence of that great almighty being in every autumn leaf which whirled away!

Again, with a last lingering look his mental eyes surveyed that eventful border past, so full of glorious splendor, of battle shocks, and rude delights; so full of beloved eyes, now dim, and so radiant with those faces and those hearts now cold; again leaving the present and all around him, he lived for a moment in that grand and beauteous past, instinct for him with so much splendor and regret.

But his dim eyes returned suddenly to those much loved faces round him; and those tender hearts were overcome by the dim, shadowy look.

The sunset slowly waned away, and falling in red splendor on the old gray head and storm-beaten brow, lingered there lovingly and cheerfully. The old hunter feebly smiled.

"You'll be good girls," he murmured wistfully, drawing his feeble arm more closely round the children's necks, "remember the old man, darlin's!"

Caroline pressed her lips to the cold hand, sobbing. Alice did not move her head, which, buried in the counterpane, was shaken with passionate sobs.

* * * * * * * *

The Doctor felt his pulse and turned with a mournful look to his brother. Then came those grand religious consolations which so smoothe the pathway to the grave; he was ready—always—God be thanked, the old man said; he trusted in the Lord.

And so the sunset waned away, and with it the life and strength of the old storm-beaten mountaineer—so grand yet powerless, so near to death yet so very cheerful.

"I'm goin'," he murmured, as the red orb touched the mountain, "I'm goin', my darlin's; I always loved you all, my children. Darlin', don't cry," he murmured feebly to Alice, whose heart was near breaking, "don't any of you cry for me."

The old dim eyes again dwelt tenderly on the loving faces, wet with tears, and on those poor trembling lips. There came now to the aged face of the rude mountaineer, an expression of grandeur and majesty, which illumined the broad brow and eyes like a heavenly light. Then those eyes seemed to have found what they were seeking; and were abased. Their grandeur changed to humility, their light to shadow, their fire to softness and unspeakable love. The thin feeble hands, stretched out upon the cover, were agitated slightly, the eyes moved slowly to the window and thence returned to the dear faces weeping round the bed; then whispering:

"The Lord is good to me! he told me he was comin' 'fore the night was here; come! come—Lord Jesus—come!" the old mountaineer fell back with a low sigh—so low that the old sleeping hound dreamed on.

The life strings parted without sound; and hunter John, that so long loved and cherished soul, that old strong form which had been hardened in so many storms, that tender loving heart—ah, more than all, that grand and tender heart—had passed as calmly as a little babe from the cold shadowy world to that other world; the world, we trust, of light, and love, and joy.

HORACE BINNEY WALLACE.

Horace Binney Wallace, the son of John B. Wallace, an eminent lawyer of Philadelphia, was born in that city, February 26, 1817. The first two years of his collegiate course were passed at the University of Pennsylvania, and the remaining portion at Princeton College, where he was graduated in 1835. He studied with great thoroughness the science of the law, and at the age of twenty-seven contributed notes to Smith's Selections of Leading Cases in various branches of the Law, White and Tudor's Selection of Leading Cases in Equity, and Decisions of American Courts in several departments of the Law, which have been adopted with commendation by the highest legal authorities.

His attention was, however, by no means confined to professional study. He devoted much time to scientific study, and projected several theories on subjects connected therewith, while in literature he produced an anonymous novel, *Stanley*, which, with many faults of construction, contains passages of admirably expressed thought.

Mr. Wallace published a number of articles anonymously in various periodicals. He was much interested in philosophical speculation, and bestowed much attention on the theory of Comte, by whom he was highly prized.

In April, 1849, Mr. Wallace sailed for Europe, and passed a year in England, Germany, France, and Italy. On his return he devoted himself with renewed energy to literary pursuits. He projected a series of works on commercial law, in the preparation of which he proposed to devote a year or two at a foreign university to the exclusive study of the civil law. In the spring of 1852 his eyesight became impaired, owing, as was afterwards discovered, to the incipient stages of congestion of the brain, produced by undue mental exertion. By advice of his physicians he embarked on the thirteenth of November for Liverpool. Finding no improvement in his condition on his arrival, he at once proceeded to Paris in quest of medical advice. His cerebral disease increased, and led to his death by suicide at Paris, on the sixteenth of December following.

In 1855 a volume was published in Philadelphia entitled, ***Art, Scenery, and Philosophy in Europe; Being Fragments from the Portfolio of the late Horace Binney Wallace, Esquire, of Philadelphia.*** It contains a series of essays on the principles of art, detailed criticisms on the principal European cathedrals, a few travelling sketches, papers on Michael Angelo, Leonardo da Vinci, Fra Bartolomeo, Perugino, and Raphael, and an article on Comte.

These writings, though not designed for publication, and in many instances in an unfinished state, display great depth of thought, command of language, knowledge of the history as well as æsthetic principles of art, and a finely cultivated taste. Occasional passages are full of poetic imagery, growing naturally out of enthusiastic admiration of the subject in hand. Some of the finest of these passages occur in the remarks on the Cathedral of Milan, a paper which, although endorsed by the writer "very unfinished," and no doubt capable of finer elaboration, is one of the best in the series of which it forms a portion.

THE INTERIOR OF ST. PETER'S.

What a world within Life's open world is the interior of St. Peter's!—a world of softness, brightness, and richness!—fusing the sentiments in a refined rapture of tranquillity—gratifying the imagination with splendors more various, expansive, and exhaustless than the natural universe from which we pass,—typical of that sphere of spiritual consciousness, which, before the inward-working energies of faith, arches itself out within man's mortal being. When you push aside the heavy curtain that veils the sanctuary from the world without, what a shower of high and solemn pleasure is thrown upon your spirit! A glory of beauty fills all the Tabernacle! The majesty of a Perfection, that seems fragrant of delightfulness, fills it like a Presence. Grandeur, strength, solidity,—suggestive of the fixed Infinite,—float unsphered within those vaulted spaces, like clouds of lustre. The immensity of the size,—the unlimitable richness of the treasures that have been lavished upon its decoration by the enthusiastic prodigality of the Catholic world through successive centuries,—dwarfs Man and the Present, and leaves the soul open to sentiments of God and Eternity. The eye, as it glances along column and archway, meets nothing but variegated marbles and gold. Among the ornaments of the obscure parts of the walls and piers, are a multitude of pictures, vast in magnitude, transcendent in merit,—the master-pieces of the world,—the communion of St. Jerome,—the Burial of St. Petronilla,—the Transfiguration of the Saviour,—not of perishable canvass and oils, but wrought in mosaic, and fit to endure till Time itself shall perish.

It is the sanctuary of Space and Silence. No throng can crowd these aisles; no sound of voices or of organs can displace the venerable quiet that broods here. The Pope, who fills the world with all his pompous retinue, fills not St. Peter's; and the roar of his quired singers, mingling with the sonorous chant of a host of priests and bishops, struggles for an instant against this ocean of stillness, and then is absorbed into it like a faint echo. The mightiest ceremonies of human worship,—celebrated by the earth's chief Pontiff, sweeping along in the magnificence of the most imposing array that the existing world can exhibit,—seem dwindled into insignificance within this structure. They do not explain to our feelings the uses of the building. As you stand within the gorgeous, celestial dwelling—framed not for man's abode—the holy silence, the mysterious fragrance, the light of ever-burning lamps, suggest to you that it is the home of invisible spirits,—an outer-court of Heaven,—visited, perchance, in the deeper hours of a night that is never dark within its walls, by the all-sacred Awe itself.

When you enter St. Peter's, Religion, as a local reality and a separate life, seems revealed to you. Far up the wide nave, the enormous baldachino of jetty bronze, with twisted columns and tint-like canopy, and a hundred brazen lamps, whose unextinguished flame keeps the watch of Light around the entrance to the crypt where lie the martyred remains of the Apostle, the rock of the church, give an oriental aspect to the central altar, which seems to typify the origin of the Faith which reared this Fane. Holiest of the holy is that altar. No step less sacred than a Pope's may ascend to minister before it; only on days the most august in the calendar, may even the hand which is consecrated by the Ring of the Fisherman be stretched forth to touch the vessels which rest on it. At every hour, over some part of the floor, worshippers may be seen kneeling, wrapt each in solitary penitence or adoration. The persons mystically habited, who journey noiselessly across the marble, bow and cross themselves, as they pass before this or that spot, betoken the recognition of something mysterious, that is unseen, invisible. By day illuminated by rays only from above, by night always luminous within—filled by an atmosphere of its own, which changes not with the changing cold and heat of the seasons without,—exhaling always a faint, delightful perfume,—it is the realm of piety,—the clime of devotion—a spiritual globe in the midst of a material universe.

ELIHU G. HOLLAND

Was born of New England parentage at Solon, Cortlandt county, New York, April 14, 1817. His first published work was a volume entitled *The Being of God and the Immortal Life*, in 1846. His aim was to assert the doctrines of the divine existence and the immortality of man by arguments derived from the elements of human nature. In 1849 he published, at Boston, a volume, *Reviews and Essays*. It embraces an elaborate paper on the character and philosophy of Confucius, an analysis of the genius of Channing, an article on Natural Theology, and Essays on Genius, Beauty, the Infinite, Harmony, &c. This was followed in 1852 by another volume entitled *Essays: and a Drama in Five Acts*. The essays were in a similar range with those of its predecessor. The drama is entitled *The Highland Treason*, and is a version of the affair of Arnold and André. In 1853 he published a *Memoir of the Rev. Joseph Badger*, the revival preacher of the Christian connexion.* Though luxuriant and prolix in expression, with a tendency to over statement in the transcendental style, the writings of Mr. Holland show him to be a student and thinker.

We present a pleasing passage from an Essay on "American Scenery."

THE SUSQUEHANNAH.

It is difficult to imagine a more continuous line of beauty than the course of the Susquehannah, a river whose mild grace and gentleness combined with power render it a message of nature to the affections and to the tranquil consciousness. This trait of mildness, even in its proudest flow, seems to hover upon its banks and waters as the genius of the scene. No thunder of cataracts anywhere announces its fame. It is mostly the contemplative river, dear to fancy, dear to the soul's calm feeling of unruffled peace. This river of noble sources and many tributaries, traverses the vale of Wyoming, where, in other years, we have been delighted with its various scenery. Its mountain ramparts, which rise somewhat majestically to hail her onward progress, are crowned with a vegetation of northern fir, whilst the verdant and fertile valley is graced with the foliage of the oak, chestnut, and sycamore. At Northumberland, where the east and the west branch unite, the river rolls along with a noble expanse of surface; opposite the town rises, several hundred feet, a dark perpendicular precipice of rock, from which the whole prospect is exceedingly picturesque. The Alleghany Mountains, which somehow seem to bear a paternal relation to this river, lend it the shadow of their presence through great distances. These mountains, though they never rise so high as to give the impression of power and sublimity, are never monotonous. Though they are not generally gothic, but of rounded aspect, the northern part has those that are steep and abrupt, sharp-crested and of notched and jagged outline. The Susquehannah is wealthy also in aboriginal legend, and in abundant foliage. Its rude raft likewise aids the picture. It has many beautiful sources, particularly that in the lovely lake of Cooperstown; and no thought concerning its destiny can be so eloquent as the one expressed by our first American novelist whose name is alike honored by his countrymen and by foreign nations. He spoke of it as "the mighty Susquehannah, a river to which the Atlantic herself has extended her right arm to welcome into her bosom." Other scenery in Pennsylvania we have met, which, though less renowned than Wyoming and the Juniata, is not less romantic and beautiful. A noble river is indeed the image of unity, a representative of human tendencies, wherein many separate strivings unite in one main current of happiness and success. Man concentrates himself like a river in plans and purposes, and seek his unity in some chief end as the river seeks it in the sea.

* An analysis of this work will be found in the Christian Examiner for July, 1854.

WILLIAM A. JONES

Is a member of a family long distinguished for the eminent men it has furnished to the bar and the bench, in the state of New York, including the ante-revolutionary period. He was born in New York June 26, 1817. In 1836 he was graduated at Columbia College, and is now attached to that institution as librarian. His contributions to the press have been numerous, chiefly articles in the department of criticism. To Dr. Hawks's *Church Record* he furnished an extended series of articles on Old English Prose Writers; to *Arcturus* numerous literary papers, and afterwards wrote for the Whig and Democratic Reviews. He has published two volumes of these and other Essays and Criticisms: *The Analyst, a Collection of Miscellaneous Papers*, in 1840, and *Essays upon Authors and Books* in 1849. In the last year he also published a Memorial of his father, the late Hon. David S. Jones, with an Appendix, containing notices of the Jones Family of Queens County.

A passage from an article in the Democratic Review exhibits his style, in a eulogy of a favorite author.

HAZLITT.

William Hazlitt we regard, all things considered, as the first of the regular critics in this nineteenth century, surpassed by several in some one particular quality or acquisition, but superior to them all in general force, originality, and independence. With less scholarship considerably than Hunt or Southey, he has more substance than either; with less of Lamb's fineness and nothing of his subtle humor, he has a wider grasp and altogether a more manly cast of intellect. He has less liveliness and more smartness than Jeffrey, but a far profounder insight into the mysteries of poesy, and apparently a more genial sympathy with common life. Then, too, what freshness in all his writings, "wild wit, invention ever new:" for although he disclaims having any imagination, he certainly possessed creative talent and fine ingenuity. Most of his essays are, as has been well remarked, "original creations," not mere homilies or didactic theses, so much as a new illustration from experience and observation of great truths colored and set off by all the brilliant aids of eloquence, fancy, and the choicest stores of accumulation.

As a literary critic he may be placed rather among the independent judges of original power than among the trained critics of education and acquirements. He relies almost entirely on individual impressions and personal feeling, thus giving a charm to his writings, quite apart from, and independent of, their purely critical excellencies. Though he has never published an autobiography,* yet all of his works are, in a certain sense, confessions. He pours out his feelings on a theme of interest to him, and treats the impulses of his heart and the movements of his mind as historical and philosophical data. Though he almost invariably trusts himself, he is almost as invariably in the right. For, as some are born poets, so he too was born a critic, with no small infusion of the poetic character. Analytic judgment (of the very finest and rarest kind), and poetic fancy, naturally rich, and rendered still more copious and brilliant by the golden associations of his life, early intercourse with honorable poets, and a most appreciative sympathy with the master-pieces of poesy. Admirable as a genial critic on books and men, of manners and character, of philosophical systems and theories of taste and art, yet he is more especially the genuine critic in his favorite walks of art and poesy; politics and the true literature of real life—the domestic novels, the drama, and the belles-lettres.

As a descriptive writer, in his best passages, he ranks with Burke and Rousseau; in delineation of sentiment, and in a rich rhetorical vein, he has whole pages worthy of Taylor or Lord Bacon. There is nothing in Macaulay for profound gorgeous declamation, superior to the character of Coleridge, or of Milton, or of Burke, or of a score of men of genius whose portraits he has painted with love and with power. In pure criticism who has done so much for the novelists, the essayists, writers of comedy; for the old dramatists and elder poets? Lamb's fine notes are mere notes—Coleridge's improvised criticisms are merely fragmentary, while if Hazlitt has borrowed their opinions in some cases, he has made much more of them than they could have done themselves. Coleridge was a poet—Lamb a humorist. To neither of these characters had Hazlitt any fair pretensions, for with all his fancy he had a metaphysical understanding (a bad ground for the tender plant of poesy to flourish in), and to wit and humor he laid no claim, being too much in earnest to indulge in pleasantry and jesting—though he has satiric wit at will and the very keenest sarcasm. Many of his papers are prose satires, while in others there are to be found exquisite *jeux d'esprit*, delicate banter, and the purest intellectual refinements upon works of wit and humor. In all, however, the critical quality predominates, be the form that of essay, criticism, sketch, biography, or even travels.

THOMAS WILLIAM PARSONS,

THE author of a translation of *The First Ten Cantos of the Inferno of Dante*, published in 1848, and of a volume of original *Poems* in 1854, is a native of, and resident at, Boston. His writings bear witness to his sound classical education, as well as to the fruits of foreign travel. The translation of Dante, in the stanza of the original, has been much admired by scholars. The Poems exhibit variety in playful satire, epistle, ballad, the tale, description of nature, of European antiquities, and the occasional record of personal emotion. In all, the subject is controlled and elevated by the language of art. It is the author's humor in the Epistles which open the volume to address several foreign celebrities in the character of an English traveller in America, writing to Charles Kemble on the drama; to Edward Moxon, the London publisher, on the state of letters; and to Rogers and Landor on poetry and art generally. In the Epistle to Landor, the comparatively barren objects of American antiquities are placed by the side of the storied associations of Italy. The land is pictured as existing "in Saturn's reign before the stranger came," like the waste Missouri; when the view is changed to the Roman era:—

* * * * * * * * * * *

Soon as they rose—the Capitolian lords—
  The land grew sacred and beloved of GOD;
Where'er they carried their triumphant swords
  Glory sprang forth and sanctified the sod.

Nay, whether wandering by Provincial Rome,
  Or British Tyne, we note the Cæsar's tracks,
Wondering how far from their Tarpeian flown,
  The ambitious eagles bore the prætor's axe.

Those toga'd fathers, those equestrian kings,
  Are still our masters—still within us reign,
Born though we may have been beyond the springs
  Of Britain's floods—beyond the outer main.

For, while the music of their language lasts,
  They shall not perish like the painted men—
Brief-lived in memory as the winter's blasts!—
  Who here once held the mountain and the glen.

From them and theirs with cold regard we turn,
  The wreck of polished nations to survey,
Nor care the savage attributes to learn
  Of souls that struggled with barbarian clay.

With what emotion on a coin we trace
  Vespasian's brow, or Trajan's chastened smile,
But view with heedless eye the murderous mace
  And checkered lance of Zealand's warrior-isle.

Here, by the ploughman, as with daily tread
  He tracks the furrows of his fertile ground,
Dark locks of hair, and thigh-bones of the dead,
  Spear-heads, and skulls, and arrows, oft are found.

On such memorials unconcerned we gaze;
  No trace returning of the glow divine,
Wherewith, dear WALTER! in our Eton days
  We eyed a fragment from the Palatine.

It fired us then to trace upon the map
  The forum's line—proud empire's church-yard paths—
Ay, or to finger but a marble scrap
  Or stucco piece from Diocletian's baths.

Cellini's workmanship could nothing add,
  Nor any casket, rich with gems and gold,
To the strange value every pebble had
  O'er which perhaps the Tiber's wave had rolled.

One of the longer poems—*Ghetto di Roma*, a story of the Jewish proscription—is admirably told; picturesque in detail, simple in movement, and the pathos effectively maintained without apparent effort. The lines *On the Death of Daniel Webster* are among the ablest which that occasion produced. The chaste and expressive lines, *Steuart's Burial*, are the record of a real incident. The friend of the author whose funeral is literally described, was Mr. David Steuart Robertson, a gentleman well known by his elegant rural hospitality at his residence at Lancaster to the wits and good society of Boston.

The healthy objective life of the poems, and their finished expression, will secure them a reputation long after many of the feeble literary affectations of the day are forgotten.

* The Liber Amoris can hardly be called an exception.

ON A BUST OF DANTE.

See, from this counterfeit of him
Whom Arno shall remember long,
How stern of lineament, how grim,
The father was of Tuscan song.
There but the burning sense of wrong,
Perpetual care and scorn, abide;
Small friendship for the lordly throng;
Distrust of all the world beside.

Faithful if this wan image be,
No dream his life was—but a fight;
Could any Beatrice see
A lover in that anchorite?
To that cold Ghibeline's gloomy sight
Who could have guessed the visions came
Of Beauty, veiled with heavenly light,
In circles of eternal flame?

The lips as Cumæ's cavern close,
The cheeks with fast and sorrow thin,
The rigid front, almost morose,
But for the patient's hope within,
Declare a life whose course hath been
Unsullied still, though still severe,
Which, through the wavering days of sin,
Kept itself icy-chaste and clear.

Not wholly such his haggard look
When wandering once, forlorn, he strayed,
With no companion save his book,
To Corvo's hushed monastic shade;
Where, as the Benedictine laid
His palm upon the pilgrim guest,
The single boon for which he prayed
The convent's charity was rest.*

Peace dwells not here—this rugged face
Betrays no spirit of repose;
The sullen warrior sole we trace,
The marble man of many woes.
Such was his mien when first arose
The thought of that strange tale divine,
When hell he peopled with his foes,
The scourge of many a guilty line.

War to the last he waged with all
The tyrant canker-worms of earth;
Baron and duke, in hold and hall,
Cursed the dark hour that gave him birth;
He used Rome's harlot for his mirth;
Plucked bare hypocrisy and crime;
But valiant souls of knightly worth
Transmitted to the rolls of Time.

O, Time! whose verdicts mock our own,
The only righteous judge art thou;
That poor, old exile, sad and lone,
Is Latium's other VIRGIL now:
Before his name the nations bow;
His words are parcel of mankind,
Deep in whose hearts, as on his brow,
The marks have sunk of DANTE's mind.

STEUART'S BURIAL.

The bier is ready and the mourners wait,
The funeral car stands open at the gate.
Bring down our brother; bear him gently, too;
So, friends, he always bore himself with you.
Down the sad staircase, from the darkened room,
For the first time, he comes in silent gloom:
Who ever left this hospitable door
Without his smile and warm "good-bye," before?
Now we for him the parting word must say
To the mute threshold whence we bear his clay.

The slow procession lags upon the road,—
'T is heavy hearts that make the heavy load;
And all too brightly glares the burning noon
On the dark pageant—be it ended soon!
The quail is piping and the locust sings,—
O grief, thy contrast with these joyful things!
What pain to see, amid our task of woe,
The laughing river keep its wonted flow!
His hawthorns there—his proudly-waving corn—
And all so flourishing—and so forlorn!
His new-built cottage, too, so fairly planned,
Whose chimney ne'er shall smoke at his command.

Two sounds were heard, that on the spirit fell
With sternest moral—one the passing bell!
The other told the history of the hour,
Life's fleeting triumph, mortal pride and power.
Two trains there met—the iron-sinewed horse
And the black hearse—the engine and the corse!
Haste on your track, you fiery-winged steed!
I hate your presence and approve your speed;
Fly! with your eager freight of breathing men,
And leave these mourners to their march again!
Swift as my wish, they broke their slight delay,
And life and death pursued their separate way.

The solemn service in the church was held,
Bringing strange comfort as the anthem swelled,
And back we bore him to his long repose,
Where his great elm its evening shadow throws—
A sacred spot! There often he hath stood,
Showed us his harvests and pronounced them good.
And we may stand, with eyes no longer dim,
To watch new harvests and remember him.

Peace to thee, STEUART!—and to us! the All-wise
Would ne'er have found thee readier for the skies
In his large love He kindly waits the best,
The fittest mood, to summon every guest;
So, in his prime, our dear companion went,
When the young soul is easy to repent:
No long purgation shall he now require
In black remorse—in penitential fire;
From what few frailties might have stained his morn
Our tears may wash him pure as he was born.

* It is told of DANTE that, when he was roaming over Italy, he came to a certain monastery, where he was met by one of the friars, who blessed him, and asked what was his desire; to which the weary stranger simply answered, "*Pace.*"

JOHN W. BROWN.

JOHN W. BROWN was born in Schenectady, New York, August 21, 1814, and was graduated at Union College in 1832. He entered the General Theological Seminary in 1833, and on the completion of his course of study was ordained Deacon, July 3, 1836, and took charge of a parish at Astoria, Long Island, with which he was connected during the remainder of his life. In 1838 he established a school, the Astoria Female Institute, which he conducted for seven years. In 1845 he became editor of the Protestant Churchman, a weekly periodical. In the fall of 1848 Mr. Brown visited Europe for the benefit of his health. He died at Malta on Easter Monday, April 9, 1849.

In 1842 Mr. Brown published *The Christmas Bells: a Tale of Holy Tide: and other Poems*, a volume of pleasing verses suggested by the seasons and services of his church.

In the Christmas Bells he has described with beauty and feeling the effect of the holy services of the season upon the old and young. The poem has been set to music.

Mr. Brown was also the author of *Constance*, *Virginia*, *Julia of Baiæ*, and a few other prose tales of a religious character for young readers.

THE CHRISTMAS BELLS.

The bells—the bells—the Christmas bells
How merrily they ring!
As if they felt the joy they tell
To every human thing.
The silvery tones, o'er vale and hill,
Are swelling soft and clear,
As, wave on wave, the tide of sound
Fills the bright atmosphere.

The bells—the merry Christmas bells,
They're ringing in the morn!
They ring when in the eastern sky
The golden light is born;
They ring, as sunshine tips the hills,
And gilds the village spire—
When, through the sky, the sovereign sun
Rolls his full orb of fire.

The Christmas bells—the Christmas bells,
How merrily they ring!
To weary hearts a pulse of joy,
A kindlier life they bring.
The poor man on his couch of straw,
The rich, on downy bed,
Hail the glad sounds, as voices sweet
Of angels overhead.

The bells—the silvery Christmas bells,
O'er many a mile they sound!
And household tones are answering them
In thousand homes around.
Voices of childhood, blithe and shrill,
With youth's strong accents blend,
And manhood's deep and earnest tones
With woman's praise ascend.

The bells—the solemn Christmas bells,
They're calling us to prayer;
And hark, the voice of worshippers
Floats on the morning air.
Anthems of noblest praise there'll be.
And glorious hymns to-day,
TE DEUMS loud—and GLORIAS:
Come, to the church—away.

JOHN LOTHROP MOTLEY,

A MEMBER of a Boston family, and graduate of Harvard of 1831, is the author of two novels of merit, *Morton's Hope, or The Memoirs of a Provincial*, and *Merry Mount, a Romance of the Massachusetts Colony*.

The first of these fictions appeared in 1839. The scene of the opening portion is laid at Morton's Hope, a quiet provincial country-seat in the neighborhood of Boston. In consequence of disappointment in a love affair, the hero leaves his country and passes some time among the German University towns, the manners of which are introduced with effect. Towards the middle of the second volume, he is summoned home by the news of the death of his uncle, and a hint from a relative that the fortune which this event places in his hands can be better employed in the service of his country, now engaged in the struggle of the Revolution, than in an aimless foreign residence. He returns home, becomes an officer in the Continental army, distinguishes himself, and regains his lost mistress.

In *Merry Mount* the author has availed himself of the picturesque episode of New England history presented in the old narrative of Thomas Morton, of which we have previously given an account.* Both of these fictions are written with spirit; the descriptions, which are frequent, are carefully elaborated; and the narrative is enlivened with frequent flashes of genuine humor.

Mr. Motley is at present residing at Dresden, where he has been some time engaged in writing a History of Holland, which will no doubt prove a work of high merit, as an animated and vigorous portraiture of the Dutch struggle of independence.

GOTTINGEN—FROM MORTON'S HOPE.

Gottingen is rather a well-built and handsome looking town, with a decided look of the Middle Ages about it. Although the college is new, the town is ancient, and like the rest of the German University towns, has nothing external, with the exception of a plain-looking building in brick for the library and one or two others for natural collections, to remind you that you are at the seat of an institution for education. The professors lecture, each on his own account, at his own house, of which the basement floor is generally made use of as an auditorium. The town is walled in, like most of the continental cities of that date, although the ramparts, planted with linden-trees, have since been converted into a pleasant promenade, which reaches quite round the town, and is furnished with a gate and guard at the end of each principal avenue. It is this careful fortification, combined with the nine-story houses, and the narrow streets, which imparts the compact, secure look peculiar to all the German towns. The effect is forcibly to remind you of the days when the inhabitants were huddled snugly together, like sheep in a sheep-cote, and locked up safe from the wolfish attacks of the gentlemen highwaymen, the ruins of whose castles frown down from the neighbouring hills.

The houses are generally tall and gaunt, consisting of a skeleton of frame-work, filled in with brick, with the original rafters, embrowned by time, projecting like ribs through the yellowish stucco which covers the surface. They are full of little windows, which are filled with little panes, and as they are built to save room, one upon another, and consequently rise generally to eight or nine stories, the inhabitants invariably live as it were in layers. Hence it is not uncommon to find a professor occupying the two lower stories or strata, a tailor above the professor, a student upon the tailor, a beer-seller conveniently upon the student, a washerwoman upon the beer-merchant, and perhaps a poet upon the top; a pyramid with a poet for its apex, and a professor for the base.

The solid and permanent look of all these edifices, in which, from the composite and varying style of architecture, you might read the history of half a dozen centuries in a single house, and which looked as if built before the memory of man, and like to last for ever, reminded me, by the association of contrast, of the straggling towns and villages of America, where the houses are wooden boxes, worn out and renewed every fifty years; where the cities seem only temporary encampments, and where, till people learn to build for the future as well as the present, there will be no history, except in pen and ink, of the changing centuries in the country.

As I passed up the street, I saw on the lower story of a sombre-looking house, the whole legend of Samson and Delilah rudely carved in the brown freestone, which formed the abutments of the house op-

* *Ante*, vol. i. p. 26.

posite; a fantastic sign over a portentous shop with an awning ostentatiously extended over the side-walk, announced the café and ice-shop: overhead, from the gutters of each of the red-tiled roofs, were thrust into mid-air the grim heads of dragons with long twisted necks, portentous teeth, and goggle eyes, serving, as I learned the first rainy day, the peaceful purpose of a water spout; while on the side-walks, and at every turn, I saw enough to convince me I was in an university town, although there were none of the usual architectural indications. As we passed the old gothic church of St. Nicholas, I observed through the open windows of the next house, a party of students smoking and playing billiards, and I recognised some of the faces of my Leipzig acquaintance. In the street were plenty of others of all varieties. Some, with plain caps and clothes, and a meek demeanour, sneaked quietly through the streets, with portfolios under their arms. I observed the care with which they turned out to the left, and avoided collision with every one they met. These were camels or "studious students" returning from lecture—others swaggered along the side-walk, turning out for no one, with clubs in their hands, and bull-dogs at their heels—these were dressed in marvellously fine caps and polonaise coats, covered with cords and tassels, and invariably had pipes in their mouths, and were fitted out with the proper allowance of spurs and moustachios. These were "Renomists," who were always ready for a row.

At almost every corner of the street was to be seen a solitary individual of this latter class, in a ferocious fencing attitude, brandishing his club in the air, and cutting carto and tierce in the most alarming manner, till you were reminded of the truculent Gregory's advice to his companion: "Remember thy swashing blow."

All along the street, I saw, on looking up, the heads and shoulders of students projecting from every window. They were arrayed in tawdry smoking caps and heterogeneous-looking dressing gowns, with the long pipes and flash tassels depending from their mouths. At his master's side, and looking out of the same window, I observed, in many instances, a grave and philosophical-looking poodle, with equally grim moustachios, his head reposing contemplatively on his fore-paws, and engaged apparently, like his master, in ogling the ponderous housemaids who were drawing water from the street pumps.

We passed through the market square, with its antique fountain in the midst, and filled with an admirable collection of old women, some washing clothes, and some selling cherries, and turned at last into the Nagler Strasse. This was a narrow street, with tall rickety houses of various shapes and sizes, arranged on each side, in irregular rows; while the gaunt gable-ended edifices, sidling up to each other in one place till the opposite side nearly touched, and at another retreating awkwardly back as if ashamed to show their faces, gave to the whole much the appearance of a country dance by unskilful performers. Suddenly the postillion drove into a dark, yawning doorway, which gaped into the street like a dragon's mouth, and drew up at the door-step of the "King of Prussia." The house bell jingled—the dogs barked—two waiters let down the steps, a third seized us by the legs, and nearly pulled us out of the carriage in the excess of their officiousness; while the landlord made his appearance cap in hand on the threshold, and after saluting us in Latin, Polish, French, and English, at last informed us in plain German, which was the only language he really knew, that he was very glad to have the honour of "recommending himself to us."

We paid our "brother-in-law," as you must always call the postillion in Germany, a magnificent drink-geld, and then ordered dinner.

SAMUEL A. HAMMETT.

Mr. Hammett was born in 1816 at Jewett City, Connecticut. After being graduated at the University of the City of New York, he passed some ten or twelve years in the South-west, engaged in mercantile pursuits, and for a portion of the time as Clerk of the District Court of Montgomery county, Texas. In 1848 he removed to New York, where he has since resided.

Mr. Hammett has drawn largely on his frontier experiences in his contributions to the Spirit of the Times, Knickerbocker, Democratic and Whig Reviews, and Literary World. He has published two volumes—*A Stray Yankee in Texas*, and *The Wonderful Adventures of Captain Priest*, with the scene Down East. They are sketchy, humorous, and inventive.

HOW I CAUGHT A CAT, AND WHAT I DID WITH IT—FROM A STRAY YANKEE IN TEXAS.

At last behold us fairly located upon the banks of the river, where Joe had selected a fine, hard shingle beach upon which to pitch our camp. This same camp was an extemporaneous affair, a kind of *al fresco* home, formed by setting up a few crotches to sustain a rude roof of undressed shingles, manufactured impromptu,—there known as "boards,"—supported upon diminutive rafters of cane.

This done, a cypress suitable for a canoe, or "dug out," was selected, and in two days shaped, hollowed out, and launched. Fairly embarked now in the business, I found but little difficulty in obtaining a supply of green trout and other kinds of river fish, but the huge "Cats"—where were they? I fished at early morn and dewy eve, ere the light had faded out from the stars of morning, and after dame Nature had donned her *robe de nuit*,—all was in vain.

Joe counselled patience, and hinted that the larger species of "Cats" never ran but during a rise or fall in the river, and must then be fished for at night.

One morning, heavy clouds in the north, and the sound of distant thunder, informed us that a storm was in progress near the head waters of our stream. My rude tackle was looked after, and bait prepared in anticipation of the promised fish, which the perturbed waters of the river were to incite to motion.

Night came, and I left for a spot where I knew the Cats must frequent; a deep dark hole, immediately above a sedgy flat. My patience and perseverance at length met with their reward. I felt something very carefully examining the bait, and at last tired of waiting for the bite, struck with force.

I had him, a huge fellow, too; backwards and forwards he dashed, up and down, in and out. No fancy tackle was mine, but plain and trustworthy, at least so I fondly imagined.

At last I trailed the gentleman upon the sedge, and was upon the eve of wading in and securing him, when a splash in the water which threw it in every direction, announced that something new had turned up, and away went I, hook, and line, into the black hole below. At this moment my tackle parted, the robber—whether alligator or gar I knew not—disappeared with my half captured prey, and I crawled out upon the bank in a blessed humor.

My fishing was finished for the evening; but

repairing the tackle as best I could, casting the line again into the pool, and fixing the pole firmly in the knot-hole of a fallen tree, I abandoned it, to fish upon its own hook.

When I arose in the morning, a cold "norther" was blowing fiercely, and the river had risen in the world during the night. The log to which my pole had formed a temporary attachment, had taken its departure for parts unknown, and was in all human probability at that moment engaged in making an experimental voyage on account of "whom it may concern."

The keen eyes of Joe, who had been peering up and down the river, however, discovered something upon the opposite side that bore a strong resemblance to the missing pole, and when the sun had fairly risen, we found that there it surely was, and moreover its bowing to the water's edge, and subsequent straightening up, gave proof that a fish was fast to the line.

The northern blast blew shrill and cold, and the ordinarily gentle current of the river was now a mad torrent, lashing the banks in its fury, and foaming over the rocks and trees that obstructed its increased volume.

Joe and I looked despairingly at each other, and shook our heads in silence and in sorrow.

Yet there was the pole waving to and fro, at times when the fish would repeat his efforts to escape—it was worse than the Cup of Tantalus, and after bearing it as long as I could, I prepared for a plunge into the maddened stream. One plunge, however, quite satisfied me; I was thrown back upon the shore, cold and dispirited.

During the entire day there stood, or swung to and fro, the wretched pole, now upright as an orderly sergeant, now bending down and kissing the waters at its feet.

The sight I bore until flesh and blood could no more endure. The sun had sunk to rest, the twilight was fading away, and the stars were beginning to peep out from their sheltering places inquiringly, as if to know why the night came not on, when I, stung to the soul, determined at any hazard to dare the venture.

Wringing the hand of Joe, who shook his head dubiously, up the stream I bent my course until I reached a point some distance above, from which the current passing dashed with violence against the bank, and shot directly over to the very spot where waved and wagged my wretched rod, cribbed by the waters, and cabined and confined among the logs.

I plunged in, and swift as an arrow from the bow, the water hurried me on, a companion to its mad career. The point was almost gained, when a shout from Joe called my attention to the pole: alas, the fish was gone, and the line was streaming out in the fierce wind.

That night was I avenged; a huge cat was borne home in triumph. How I took it, or where, it matters not; for so much time having been occupied in narrating how I did not, I can spare no more to tell how I did.

The next point was to decide as to the cooking of him. Joe advised a barbacue; "a fine fellow like that," he said, "with two inches of clear fat upon his back-bone, would make a noble feast." Let not the two inches of clear fat startle the incredulous reader; for in that country of lean swine, I have often heard that the catfish are used to fry bacon in.

But to the cooking.

We cooked him that night, and we cooked him next day,
And we cooked him in vain until both passed away.

He would *not* be cooked, and was in fact much worse; and not half so honest as a worthy old gander—once purchased by a very innocent friend of mine—that was found to contain in its maw a paper embracing both his genealogy and directions with reference to the advisable mode of preparing him for the table; of which all that I remember is, that parboiling for sixteen days was warmly recommended as an initial step.

Sixteen days' parboiling I am convinced would but have rendered our friend the tougher. We tried him over a hot fire, and a slow one,—we smoked him, singed him, and in fine tried all known methods in vain, and finally consigned him again, uneaten, to the waters.

CORNELIUS MATHEWS.

Cornelius Mathews was born October 28, 1817, in the village of Port Chester, in Westchester county, State of New York. It is a spot situated on the Sound, on the borders of Connecticut, and was, until recently, before modern taste had altered the name, designated Saw-pitts, from the branch of industry originally pursued there. The early country life of Mr. Mathews in Westchester, on the banks of Byram river, or by the rolling uplands of Rye and its picturesque lake, is traceable through many a page of his writings, in fanciful descriptions of nature based upon genuine experience, and in frequent traits of the rural personages who filled the scene. Mr. Mathews was among the early graduates of the New York University, an association which he revived some years afterwards, by an address on *Americanism*, before one of the societies. His literary career began early. For the American Monthly Magazine of 1836, he wrote both in verse and prose. A series of poetical commemorations of incidents of the Revolution entitled, *Our Forefathers*, in this journal, are from his pen, with the animated critical sketches of Jeremy Taylor and Owen Felltham, among some revivals of the old English prose writers. In the New York Review for 1837 he wrote a paper, *The Ethics of Eating*, a satiric sketch of the ultra efforts at dietetic reform then introduced to the public. He was also a contributor to the Knickerbocker Magazine of humorous sketches. In the Motley Book in 1838, a collection of tales and sketches, he gave further evidence of his capacity for pathos and humor in description. It was followed the next year by *Behemoth, a Legend of the Moundbuilders*, an imaginative romance, in which the physical sublime was embodied in the great mastodon, the action of the story consisting in the efforts of a supposed ante-Indian race to overcome the huge monster. This "fossil romance" was a purely original invention, with very slender materials in the books of Priest, Atwater, and others; but such hints as the author procured from these and similar sources, were more than repaid in the genial notes which accompanied the first edition.

In 1840 his sketch of New York city electioneering life, *The Politicians*, a comedy, appeared; the subject matter of which was followed up in *The Career of Puffer Hopkins* in 1841, a novel which embodies many phases of civic political life, which have rapidly passed away. Both the play and the tale were the precursors of many similar attempts in local fiction and description.

Cornelius Mathews.

At this time, from December, 1840, to May, 1842, Mr. Mathews was engaged in the editorship of Arcturus, a Journal of Books and Opinion, a monthly magazine, of which three volumes appeared; and in which he wrote numerous papers, fanciful and critical, including the novel just mentioned.

In 1843 he published *Poems on Man in the Republic*, in which, with much vigor of thought, he passes in review the chief family, social, and political relations of the citizen. His *Big Abel and the Little Manhattan*, a "fantasy piece," is a picture of New York, sketched in a poetical spirit, with the contrast of the native original Indian element with the present developments of civilization; personated respectively by an Indian, and a representative of the first Dutch settlers.

In 1846 Mr. Murdoch brought upon the stage at Philadelphia Mr. Mathews's tragedy of *Witchcraft*, a story of the old Salem delusion, true to the weird and quaint influences of the time. The suspected mother in the piece, Ambla Bodish, is an original character well sustained. The play was successful on the stage. Mr. Murdoch also performed in it at Cincinnati, where it was received with enthusiasm. A second play, *Jacob Leisler*, founded on a passage of New York colonial history, was also first performed at Philadelphia in 1848, and subsequently with success in New York and elsewhere.

One of the difficulties Witchcraft had to contend with on the representation, was the age of the heroine. An actress could scarcely be found who would sacrifice the personal admiration of the hour to the interest of the powerful and truthful dramatic delineation in the mother, grey with sorrow and time. As a contemporary testimony to the merits of the play in poetic conception and character, we may quote the remarks by the late Margaret Fuller, published in her Papers on Literature and Art. "Witchcraft is a work of strong and majestic lineaments; a fine originality is shown in the conception, by which the love of a son for a mother is made a sufficient *motiv* (as the Germans call the ruling impulse of a work) in the production of tragic interest; no less original is the attempt, and delightful the success, in making an aged woman a satisfactory heroine to the piece through the greatness of her soul, and the magnetic influence it exerts on all around her, till the ignorant and superstitious fancy that the sky darkens and the winds wait upon her as she walks on the lonely hill-side near her hut to commune with the Past, and seek instruction from Heaven. The working of her character on the other agents of the piece is depicted with force and nobleness. The deep love of her son for her, the little tender, simple ways in which he shows it, having preserved the purity and poetic spirit of childhood by never having been weaned from his first love, a mother's love, the anguish of his soul when he too becomes infected with distrust, and cannot discriminate the natural magnetism of a strong nature from the spells and lures of sorcery, the final triumph of his faith, all offered the highest scope to genius and the power of moral perception in the actor. There are highly poetic intimations of those lowering days with their veiled skies, brassy light, and sadly whispering winds, very common in Massachusetts, so ominous and brooding seen from any point, but from the idea of witchcraft invested with an awful significance. We do not know, however, that this could bring it beyond what it has appeared to our own sane mind, as if the air was thick with spirits, in an equivocal and surely sad condition, whether of purgatory or downfall; and the air was vocal with all manner of dark intimations. We are glad to see this mood of nature so fitly characterized. The sweetness and *naiveté* with which the young girl is made to describe the effects of love upon her, as supposing them to proceed from a spell, are also original, and there is no other way in which this revelation could have been induced that would not have injured the beauty of the character and position. Her visionary sense of her lover, as an ideal figure, is of a high order of poetry, and these facts have very seldom been brought out from the cloisters of the mind into the light of open day."

Moneypenny, or the Heart of the World, a Romance of the Present Times, a novel of contrasted country and city life, was published in 1850, and in the same year *Chanticleer, a Thanksgiving Story of the Peabody Family*, an idyllic tale of a purely American character. *A Pen and Ink Panorama of New York City*, is a little volume in which the author has gathered up his contributions to the journals of the day, a series of fanciful and picturesque sketches, chiefly illustrative of a favorite topic in his writings.

Besides these works, Mr. Mathews has been a constant writer in the journalism of the day, frequently in the Literary World of critical articles and sketches, and on social and other topics in the daily press of New York. He is also prominently identified with the discussion of the International Copyright Question, a subject which he has illustrated in his *Address of the Copyright Club to the American People*, and other writings, with ingenuity and felicity.

A characteristic of Mr. Mathews's writings is their originality. He has chosen new subjects, and treated them in a way of his own, never without energy and spirit.

A collected edition of Mr. Mathews's writings has been published from the press of the Harpers. A second edition of the Poems on Man was published in 1846. An edition of Chanticleer has been published by Redfield.

THE JOURNALIST.

As shakes the canvass of a thousand ships,
Struck by a heavy land breeze, far at sea—
Ruffle the thousand broad-sheets of the land,
Filled with the people's breath of potency.

A thousand images the hour will take,
From him who strikes, who rules, who speaks, who sings;
Many within the hour their grave to make—
Many to live, far in the heart of things.

A dark-dyed spirit he who coins the time,
To virtue's wrong, in base disloyal lies—
Who makes the morning's breath, the evening's tide,
The utterer of his blighting forgeries.

How beautiful who scatters, wide and free,
The gold-bright seeds of loved and loving truth!
By whose perpetual hand, each day, supplied—
Leaps to new life the empire's heart of youth.

To know the instant and to speak it true,
Its passing lights of joy, its dark, sad cloud,
To fix upon the unnumbered gazers' view,
Is to thy ready hand's broad strength allowed.

There is an in-wrought life in every hour,
Fit to be chronicled at large and told—
'Tis thine to pluck to light its secret power,
And on the air its many-colored heart unfold.

The angel that in sand-dropped minutes lives,
Demands a message cautious as the ages—
Who stuns, with dusk-red words of hate, his ear,
That mighty power to boundless wrath enrages.

Hell not the quiet of a Chosen Land,
Thou grimy man over thine engine bending;
The spirit pent that breathes the life into its limbs,
Docile for love is tyrannous in rending.

Obey, Rhinoceros! an infant's hand,
Leviathan! obey the fisher mild and young,
Vexed Ocean! smile, for on thy broad-beat sand
The little curlew pipes his shrilly song.

THE POOR MAN.

Free paths and open tracts about us lie,
'Gainst Fortune's spite, though deadliest to undo:
On him who droops beneath the saddest sky,
Hopes of a better time must flicker through.

No yoke that evil hours would on him lay,
Can bow to earth his unreturning look;
The ample fields through which he plods his way
Are but his better Fortune's open book.

Though the dark smithy's stains becloud his brow,
His limbs the dank and sallow dungeon claim;
The forge's light may take the halo's glow,
An angel knock the fetters from his frame.

In deepest needs he never should forget
The patient Triumph that beside him walks
Waiting the hour, to earnest labor set,
When, face to face, his merrier Fortune talks.

Plant in thy breast a measureless content,
Thou poor man, cramped with want or racked with pain,
Good Providence, on no harsh purpose bent,
Has brought thee there, to lead thee back again.

No other bondage is upon thee cast
Save that wrought out by thine own erring hand;
By thine own act, alone, thine image placed—
Poorest or President, choose thou to stand.

A man—a man through all thy trials show!
Thy feet against a soil that never yielded
Other than life, to him that struck a rightful blow
In shop or street, warring or peaceful fielded!

DIETETIC CHARLATANRY.

We think one of the rarest spectacles in the world must be (what is called) a *Graham* boarding-house at about the dinner-hour. Along a table, from which, perhaps, the too elegant and gorgeous luxury of a cloth is discarded, (for we have never enjoyed the felicity of an actual vision of this kind,) seated some thirty lean-visaged, cadaverous disciples, eyeing each other askance—their looks lit up with a certain cannibal spirit, which, if there were any chance of making a full meal off each other's bones, might perhaps break into dangerous practice. The gentlemen resemble busts cut in chalk or white flint; the lady-boarders (they will pardon the allusion) mummies preserved in saffron. At the left hand of each stands a small tankard or pint tumbler of cold water, or, perchance, a decoction of hot water with a little milk and sugar—"a harmless and salutary beverage;"—at the right, a thin segment of bran-bread. Stretched on a plate in the centre lie, melancholy twins! a pair of starveling mackerel, flanked on either side by three or four straggling radishes, and kept in countenance by a sorry bunch of asparagus served up without sauce. The van of the table is led by a hollow dish with a dozen potatoes, rather corpses of potatoes, in a row, lying at the bottom.

At those tables look for no conversation, or for conversation of the driest and dullest sort. Small wit is begotten off spare viands. They, however, think otherwise. "*Vegetable food tends to preserve a delicacy of feeling, a liveliness of imagination, and acuteness of judgment seldom enjoyed by those who live principally on meat.*" Green peas, cabbage, and spinach are enrolled in a new catalogue. They are no longer culinary and botanical. They take rank above that. They are become metaphysical, and have a rare operation that way; they "tend to preserve a delicacy of feeling," &c. Cauliflower is a power of the mind; and asparagus, done tenderly, is nothing less than a mental faculty of the first order. "Buttered parsnips" are, no doubt, a great help in education; and a course of vegetables, we presume, is to be substituted at college in the place of the old routine of Greek and Latin classics. The student will be henceforth pushed forward through his academic studies by rapid stages of Lima beans, parsley, and tomato.

* * * * * * * * * * * *

There is a class of sciolists, who believe that all kinds of experiments are to be ventured upon the human constitution: that it is to be hoisted by pulleys and depressed by weights: pushed forward by rotary principles, and pulled back by stop-springs and regulators. They have finally succeeded in looking upon the human frame, much as a neighboring alliance of stronger powers regard a petty state which is doing well in the world and is ambitious of rising in it. It must be kept under. It must be fettered by treaties and protocols without number. This river it must not cross: at the foot of that mountain it must pause. An attempt to include yonder forest in its territories, would awaken the wrath of its powerful superiors, and they would crush it instantly. Or the body is treated somewhat as a small-spirited carter treats his horse; it must be kept on a handful of oats and made to do a full day's work. Famine has become custodian of the key which unlocks the gate of health to knowledge, to religious improvement and the millennium.

LITTLE TRAPPAN.

Tenderly let us deal with the memory of the dead—though they may have been the humblest of the living! Let us never forget that though they are parted from us, with a recollection of many frailties clinging about their mortal career, they have passed into a purer and a better light, where these very frailties may prove to have been virtues in disguise—a grotesque tongue to be translated into the clear speech of angels when our ears come to be purged of the jargon-sounds of worldly trade and selfish fashion. While we would not draw from household concealments into the glare of general notice any being whose life was strictly private, we may, with unblamed pen, linger for a moment, in a hasty but not irrespective sketch, over the departure of one whose peculiarities—from the open station he held for many years—were so widely known, that no publicity can affront his memory. Thousands will be pleased sorrowfully to dwell with a quaint regret over his little traits and turns of character, set forth in their true light by one who wished him well while living, and who would entomb him gently now that he is gone.

Whoever has had occasion any time, for the last ten years, to consult a file of newspapers at the rooms of the New York Society Library, must remember a singular little figure which presented itself skipping about those precincts with a jerky and angular motion. He must recollect in the first half-minute after entering, when newly introduced, having been rapidly approached by a man of slender build, in a frock coat, low shoes, a large female head in a cameo in his bosom, an eye-glass dangling to and fro; and presently thrusting into his very face a wrinkled countenance, twitchy and peculiarly distorted, in (we think it was) the left eye. This was little Trappan himself, the superintendent of the rooms, and arch-custodian of the filed newspapers: who no doubt asked you sharply on your first appearance, rising on one leg, as he spoke:

"Well, sir, what do you want?"

This question was always put to a debutant with a sternness of demeanor and severity of tone, absolutely appalling. But wait a little, and you will see the really kind old gentleman softening down, and meek as a lamb, leading you about to crop of the sweetest bunches his garden of preserves could furnish. It was his way only: and, while surprised into admiration of his new suavity, you were lingering over an open paper which he had spread before you with alacrity, you were startled into fresh and greater wonder, at the uprising of a voice in a distant quarter, shouting, roaring almost in a furious key, and demanding with clamorous passion—

"Why the devil gentlemen couldn't conduct themselves *as* gentlemen, and keep their legs off the tables!"

Looking hastily about, you discover the little old man, planted square in the middle of the floor, firing hot shot and rapid speech, in broadsides, upon a doubled-up man, half on a chair, and half on the reading-table—with a perfect chorus of eyes rolling about the room from the assembled readers, centring upon the little figure in its spasm. Silence again for three minutes, and all the gentlemen present are busy with the afternoon papers (just come in), when suddenly a second crash is heard, and some desperate unknown mutilator of a file—from which an oblong, three inches by an inch and a half, is gone—is held up to the scorn, contumely, and measureless detestation of the civilized world. The peal of thunder dies away, and with it the spare figure has disappeared at a side door, out of the Reading Room into the Library; but it is not more than a couple of minutes after, that the Reading Room tables are alive with placards, bulletins, and announcements in pen and ink, variously requiring, imploring, and warning frequenters of the room against touching said files with unholy hands. These are no sooner set and displayed, than the irrepressible Superintendent is bending over some confidential friend at one of the tables, and making him privately and fully acquainted with the unheard of outrages which require these violent demonstrations.

And yet a kind old man was he! We drop a tear much more promptly—from much nearer the heart—over his lonely grave, than upon the tomb of even men as great and distinguished as the City Aldermen, who once welcomed Father Mathew among us with such enthusiasm. Little Trappan had his ways, and they were not bad ways—take them altogether. He cherished his ambition as well as other men. It was an idea of his own—suggested from no foreign source, prompted by the movement of no learned society—to make a full, comprehensive, and complete collection of all animated creatures of the bug kind taken within the walls and in the immediate purlieus of the building (for such he held the edifice of the New York Society to be *par excellence*). This led him into a somewhat more active way of life than he had been used to, and involved him in climbings, reachings-forth of the arms, rapid scurries through apartments, in pursuit of flies, darning needles, bugs, and beetles, which, we sometimes thought, were exhausting too rapidly the scant vitality of the old file-keeper. He however achieved his object in one of the rarest museums of winged and footed creatures to be found anywhere. We believe he reckoned at the time of his demise, twenty-three of the beetle kind, fourteen bugs, and one mouse, in his depository. In one direction he was foiled. There was a great bug, of the roach species, often to be seen about the place—a hideously ill-favored and ill-mannered monster—which, with a preternatural activity, seemed to possess the library in every direction—sometimes on desk, sometimes on ladder, tumbling and rolling about the floor—and perpetually, with a sort of brutish instinct of spite, throwing himself in the old man's way, and continually thwarting his plans. And he was never, with all his activity and intensity of purpose, able to capture the great bug *and stick a pin through him*, as he desired. This, we think, wore upon the old man and finally shortened his days. It is not long since that the little superintendent yielded up the ghost. We hope some friend to his memory will succeed in mastering the bug, and in carrying out the (known) wishes of the deceased.

This curious and rare collection was, however, but a subordinate ambition of the late excellent superintendent. It was a desire of his—the burning and longing hope of his life—to found a library which should be in some measure worthy of the great city of New York. With this object in view, he made it a point to frequent all the great night auctions of Chatham street, the Bowery, and Park Row: and he scarcely ever returned of a night without bringing home some rare old volume or pamphlet not to be had elsewhere for love or money—which nobody had ever heard of before—and which never cost him more than twice its value.

He seemed to have acquired his peculiar taste in the selection and purchase of books from that learned and renowned body, the trustees of the Society Library, with which he had been so long associated. It has been supposed by some that he was prompted in his course by a spirit of rivalry with the parent institution. There is some plausibility in this conjecture, for at the time of his death he was pushing it hard—having accumulated in the course of ten years' diligent devotion of the odd sums he could spare from meat and drink and refreshment, no less than three hundred volumes, pamphlets, and odd numbers of old magazines. We suppose, that in acknowledgment of a generous emulation, it is the intention of the Trustees to place a tablet to his memory on the walls of the Parent Institution.

There is a single other circumstance connected with the career of the deceased superintendent scarcely worth mentioning. It is perhaps too absurd and frivolous to refer to at all: and to save ourselves from being held in light esteem by every intelligent reader, and impelling him to laugh in our very face, we shall be obliged to disclose it tenderly, and under a generality.

A character so marked and peculiar as Little Trappan (Old Trap, as he was familiarly called) could have scarcely failed to attract more or less, the attention of the observers of human nature. They would have spied the richness of the land, and dwelt with lingering pleasantry on his little traits of character and disposition from day to day. And it would have so happened that among these he could not have escaped the regard of men who made it a business to study, and to describe human nature in its varieties. For instance, if Little Trappan had been, under like circumstances, a denizen of Paris, he might probably, long before this, have figured in the quaint notices of Jules Janin; Hans Christian Andersen would have taken him for a god-send in Stockholm: Thackeray must have developed him, we can readily suppose, with some little change in one of his brilliant sketches or stories.

Then what a time we should have had of it! Such merry enjoyment, such peals of honest laughter, over the eccentricities of little old Trap; such pilgrimages to the library to get a glimpse of him; such paintings by painters of his person; such sketches by sketchers; such a to-do all round the world! But it was his great and astounding misfortune to belong to this miserable, wo-begone, and fun-forsaken city of New York, and to have fallen, as we are told (though we know nothing about it), into the hands of nobody but a wretched American humorist, who, it is vaguely reported, has made him the hero of a book of some three hundred and fifty pages—as in a word—New York is New York—Little Trappan, Little Trappan—and the author a poor devil native scribbler—why, the less said about the matter the better! We trust, however, his friendly rivals, the trustees of the library, will be good enough to erect the tablet; if not, they will oblige us by passing a resolution on the subject.

GEORGE W PECK

WAS born in Rehoboth, Bristol county, Massachusetts, December 4, 1817. His ancestor, Joseph Peck, who came from Hingham in Norfolk, England, was one of the small company who settled the town in 1641.* The Plymouth court appointed him to "administer" marriage there in 1650. His descendants, for six generations, have lived at or near the spot where he built his cabin. In the war of the Revolution three members of the family, uncles of our author, served in the continental army; one fell at Crown Point, another at Trenton, and the third became crippled and a pensioner. The father of Mr. Peck was a farmer, and added to this the business of sawing plank for ships. Until his death, in 1827, his son was bred to work upon the farm, with, however, good schooling at the district school and at home.

G. W. Peck

After various pupilage and preparation for college under teachers of ability, and the interval of a year passed at Boston in the bookstore of the Massachusetts Sunday School Society, Mr. Peck entered Brown University in 1833. After receiving his degree in 1837 he went to Cincinnati and thence to Louisville. Opposite the latter city in Jeffersonville, Indiana, he taught school three months; and afterwards, on a plantation near Louisville. He then taught music at Madison, Indiana, and at Cincinnati. At the close of the year he started in the latter city a penny paper, The Daily Sun, which attained considerable prosperity. It was merged, the following year, in The Republican, Mr. Peck still continuing to take part in its editorship. After its early extinction he found employment for some months as clerk of a steamboat.

He left the West the next spring and returned to Bristol, Rhode Island, whither his mother had removed, and entered the office of Governor Bullock as a law student. The following year he continued his studies at Boston with Mr. R. H. Dana, Jr., until he was admitted to the bar in 1843. He continued in the office of Mr. Dana for about two years. During this time he delivered lectures on many occasions in the city and country towns. Finding himself ill adapted for the extemporaneous speaking of the bar he turned from the profession to literature, and wrote several communications for the Boston Post, which were so well received that he was engaged as musical and dramatic critic for that paper in the winter of 1843–4, and continued to write for it for some time after. Among his novelties in prose and verse were a series of *Sonnets of the Sidewalk.*

In the spring of 1845, through the aid of the Hon. S. A. Eliot, and a few other known patrons of music, Mr. Peck started and conducted *The Boston Musical Review*, four numbers of which were published. In the winter of the same year he was engaged as a violin player in the orchestra of the Howard Athenæum, continuing to write and report for various journals. In June, 1846, he convoyed a party of Cornish miners to the copper region of Lake Superior.

In the fall of that year he went to New York, and through an acquaintance with Mr. H. J. Raymond, then associated in the conduct of the paper, was engaged as a night editor on the Courier and

* Rehoboth is celebrated as the theatre of "King Philip's War." Its first minister, the Rev. Samuel Newman, wrote there, partly, as tradition says, by the light of pine knots, a folio Concordance to the Bible, afterwards published in London. The first English Mayor of New York City, Captain Thomas Willet, was a native of Rehoboth.—History of Rehoboth, by Leonard Bliss.

Enquirer. He shortly after became a regular contributor to Mr. Colton's American Review, and was its associate editor from July, 1848, to January, 1849. He next published a species of apologue entitled *Aurifodina; or, Adventures in the Gold Region.* From that time he was variously employed as writer and correspondent of the reviews and newspapers, the American and Methodist Quarterly Reviews, the Literary World, Courier and Enquirer, the Art-Union Bulletin, &c., till February, 1853, when he sailed from Boston for Australia. After nine weeks at Melbourne, where he witnessed the first developments of the gold excitement, and wrote the first Fourth of July address ever spoken on that continent, he crossed the Pacific, visited Lima and the Chincha Islands, and returned to New York after a year's absence. As a result of this journey he published in New York, in 1854, a volume, *Melbourne and the Chincha Islands; with Sketches of Lima, and a Voyage Round the World*, a book of noticeable original observation and reflection; in which the author brings a fine critical vein to the study of character under unusual aspects, and such as seldom engage the attention of a cultivated scholar.

Mr. Peck has, since the production of this book, resided at Cape Ann and Boston, writing a series of *Summer Sketches*, and other correspondence descriptive and critical, for the New York Courier and Enquirer. Mr. Peck is a well read literary critic of insight and acumen, and a writer of freshness and originality.

THE GOVERNOR OF THE CHINCHAS.

I did not go ashore till the next morning after my arrival, when ——, whom I mentioned having met at Callao, took me with him to the Middle island. The landing is under the precipice, on a ledge that makes out in front of a great cave, extending quite through the point, over which, a hundred feet above, project shears for hoisting up water and provision. On the ledge, a staircase, or rather several staircases, go up in a zigzag to close by the foot of the shears; the lowest staircase, about twenty feet long, hangs from shears at the side of the ledge at right angles with the rest in front of the cave, and is rigged to be hoisted or lowered according to the tide, and to be drawn up every evening, or whenever the Governor of the Island chooses to enjoy his dignity alone.

A few rods from the edge of the cliff, directly over the cave, is the palace of the said governor, who styles himself in all his State papers,

"KOSSUTH."

The palace is a large flat-roofed shanty, constructed of rough boards, and the canes and coarse rush matting which answers generally for the commonest sort of dwellings in Peru. It has, if I remember correctly, two apartments, with a sort of portico, two or three benches, a table, and grass hammock in front surrounded by a low paling, forming a little yard, where a big dog usually mounts guard. One of the apartments is probably the storeroom; there is a kitchen shanty adjoining the piazza on the side most exposed to the sun. The other is the bed-chamber and dining-room of Governor Kossuth and his aids. It contains three or four cot beds, an old table, and writing desk, and is decorated with a few newspapers, colored lithographs, and old German plans of the battles of Frederick the Great. Over Kossuth's couch are some cheap single barrel pistols; the floor is guano. The situation overlooks nearly all the shipping between the Middle and North islands. Directly under it, but far beneath, the cavern from before which the stairs go up, runs through and opens into a narrow bight or cove, whose precipices reach up to within a few yards of the shanty. The noise of the surf comes up here in a softened monotone; below are a hundred tall vessels—the North island with its strange rocks and dark arches fringed with foam—in the distance, north and east, the hazy bay of Pisco lying in the sunshine, and if it be afternoon, the snowy Andes.

We found Kossuth at home. He is a Hungarian, or at least looks like one, and has selected a Hungarian name. He is a middle sized, half soldier-like, youngish individual, with quick gray eyes, and an overgrown red moustache. He wears his hair trimmed close at the back of his head, which goes up in a straight wall, broadening as it goes, and causing his ears to stand out almost at right angles. From this peculiarity, as well as his general cast of countenance, he looks combative and hard. But his forehead, gathering down in a line with his nose, and his speech and actions show so much energy of character, that he does not look like a very bad fellow after all. He is full of life, and display, and shrewdness, and swearing, and broken English. I rather liked him.* His favorite exclamation is "Hellanfire!" and he loves to show his authority. He was polite enough to me, though the captains often complained of being annoyed by his caprices.

He invited me to come ashore and see him, and offered to tell me "all the secrets of the island." He told me that he was one of the party of Hungarians who came to New York on the representations of Ujhazy, who had obtained for them a grant of land. But he said, that land was of no use to them, they were soldiers—they could not work. Ujhazy, who had been a landowner at home, and not a military man, had made a blunder in obtaining land—they wanted employment in the army, or as engineers and the like. That he, (Kossuth,) finding how matters stood, left New York for New Orleans, where he joined the Lopez expedition. From this he escaped, he did not tell me how, into Mexico, thence reached San Francisco, where he joined Flores, and so came to South America. Here, when that expedition failed, he took service in Peru, and finally had obtained the place he held on this island, where he said he meant to make money enough to buy land, and tell other people to work, but not to work himself. He pitied the poor Chinese slaves here, but what could he do? He could only make them work—and so on.

He talked and exclaimed "Hellanfire!" and gesticulated, altogether with so much rapidity that it was an effort to follow him; treated us to some of the wine of the country, (very much like the new wine of Sicily,) and other good things; cold ham, sardines, and preserved meats, which he says the captains present him with, more than he wants, and he never knows where they come from. According to him they all expect cargoes at once, and as he cannot accommodate them, they try to influence him by arguments and long talks and flattery, and in every sort of way, and he gets wearied to death in his efforts to please them—poor man! He told all this with a lamentable voice and face, and every now and then a roguish twinkle of the eye, that made it a great trial of the nerves to listen to him without laughing—knowing as I did the exact sum which

* He appreciates Shakespeare. I gave the Spanish doctor an old copy, and Kossuth bought it of him. I told him it showed he must have some claim to his name.

had been paid him by some captains, to get loaded before the expiration of their lay days!

After finishing our call upon him, we walked over the height of the island; that is, over the rounded hill of guano which covers it, and of which but a small portion comparatively has been cut away on one side for shipment. The average height of the rock which is the substratum of the island, is from an hundred and fifty to two and three hundred feet. Kossuth's place stands on the surface of this at about the lowest of those elevations. On this the guano lies as upon a scaffolding or raised platform rising out of the sea. It lies on a smooth rounded mound, and is on this island about a hundred and sixty feet in the central part, supposing the rock to maintain the average level of the height when it is exposed. Perhaps twenty acres or more have been cut away from the side of the hill towards the north or lee side the island, next the shipping.

J. ROSS BROWNE.

MR. BROWNE commenced his career as a traveller in his eighteenth year by the descent of the Ohio and Mississippi from Louisville to New Orleans. His subsequent adventures are so well and concisely narrated in his last published volume, *Yusef*, that the story cannot be better presented than in his own words:—

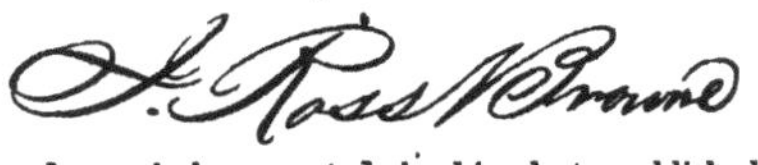

Ten years ago, after having rambled all over the United States—sixteen hundred miles of the distance on foot, and sixteen hundred in a flat-boat—I set out from Washington with fifteen dollars, to make a tour of the East. I got as far east as New York, when the last dollar and the prospect of reaching Jerusalem came to a conclusion at the same time. Sooner than return home, after having made so good a beginning, I shipped before the mast in a whaler, and did some service, during a voyage to the Indian Ocean, in the way of scrubbing decks and catching whales. A mutiny occurred at the island of Zanzibar, where I sold myself out of the vessel for thirty dollars and a chest of old clothes; and spent three months very pleasantly at the consular residence, in the vicinity of his Highness the Imaum of Muscat. On my return to Washington, I labored hard for four years on Bank statistics and Treasury reports, by which time, in order to take the new administration by the fore-lock, I determined to start for the East again. The only chance I had of getting there was, to accept of an appointment as third lieutenant in the Revenue service, and go to California, and thence to Oregon, where I was to report for duty. On the voyage to Rio, a difficulty occurred between the captain and the passengers of the vessel, and we were detained there nearly a month. I took part with the rebels, because I believed them to be right. The captain was deposed by the American consul, and the command of the vessel was offered to me; but, having taken an active part against the late captain, I could not with propriety accept the offer. A whaling captain, who had lost his vessel near Buenos Ayres, was placed in the command, and we proceeded on our voyage round Cape Horn. After a long and dreary passage we made the island of Juan Fernandez. In company with ten of the passengers, I left the ship seventy miles out at sea, and went ashore in a small boat, or the purpose of gathering up some tidings in regard to my old friend Robinson Crusoe. What befell us on that memorable expedition is fully set forth in a narrative published in Harpers' Magazine. Subsequently we spent some time in Lima, "the City of the Kings." It was my fortune to arrive penniless in California, and to find, by way of consolation, that a reduction had been made by Congress in the number of revenue vessels, and that my services in that branch of public business were no longer required. While thinking seriously of taking in washing at six dollars a dozen, or devoting the remainder of my days to mule-driving as a profession, I was unexpectedly elevated to the position of post-office agent; and went about the country for the purpose of making post-masters. I only made one—the post-master of San Jose. After that, the Convention called by General Riley met at Monterey, and I was appointed to report the debates on the formation of the State Constitution. For this I received a sum that enabled me to return to Washington, and to start for the East again. There was luck in the third attempt, for, as it may be seen, I got there at last, having thus visited the four continents, and travelled by sea and land a distance of a hundred thousand miles, or more than four times round the world, on the scanty earnings of my own head and hands.

In 1846 Mr. Browne published *Etchings of a Whaling Cruise, with Notes of a Sojourn on the Island of Zanzibar. To which is appended a brief History of the Whale Fishery, its Past and Present Condition.* It contains a spirited and faithful description of an interesting portion of the author's experience as a whaler, which does not appear to have favorably impressed him with the ordinary conduct of the service. He writes warmly in condemnation of the harsh treatment to which sailors are in his judgment exposed. The work is valuable as an accurate presentation of an important branch of our commercial marine, and as a graphic and humorous volume of personal adventure.

On his return from Europe, Mr. Browne published *Yusef, or the Journey of the Frangi; A Crusade in the East.* It is a narrative of the usual circuit of European travellers in the East, the dragoman of the expedition standing godfather to the book. His humorous peculiarities, with those of the author's occasional fellow travellers, are happily hit off. The pages of the volume are also enlivened by excellent comic sketches from the author's designs.

JOHN TABOR'S RIDE—A YARN FROM THE ETCHINGS OF A WHALING CRUISE.

"I was cruising some years ago," he began, "on the southern coast of Africa. The vessel in which I was at the time had been out for a long time, and many of the crew were on the sick-list. I had smuggled on board a large quantity of liquor, which I had made use of pretty freely while it lasted. Finding the crew in so helpless a condition, the captain put into Algoa Bay, where we had a temporary hospital erected for the benefit of the sick. I saw that they led a very easy life, and soon managed to get on the sick-list myself. As soon as I got ashore I procured a fresh supply of liquor from some of the English settlers there, and in about a week I was laid up with a fever in consequence of my deep potations. One night, while I lay in the hospital burning with this dreadful disease, I felt an unusual sensation steal over me. My blood danced through my veins. I sprang up from my catanda as strong as a lion. I thought I never was better in my life, and I wondered how it was I had so long been deceived as to my disease. A thrilling desire to exert myself came over me. I would have given worlds to contend with some giant. It seemed to me I could tear him to pieces, as a wolf would tear a lamb. Elated with the idea of my infinite power, I rushed out and ran toward the beach, hoping to meet a stray elephant or hippopotamus on the way that I might pitch him into the sea; but very fortunately, I saw none. It was a calm, still night. There was scarcely a ripple on the bay. I put my ear to the sand to listen; for I thought I heard the breaches of a whale. I waited for a repetition of the sounds, scarcely daring to breathe, lest I should miss them. Not a murmur, except the low heaving of the swell upon the beach, broke the stillness of the night. I was suddenly startled by a voice close behind me, shouting, 'There she breaches!' and jumping up, I saw, standing within a few yards of me, such a figure as I shall never forget, even if not occasionally reminded of his existence, as I was to-night. The first thing I could discern was a beard, hanging down from the chin of the owner in strings like rope yarns. It had probably once been white, but now it was discolored with whale-gurry and tar. The old fellow was not more than five feet high. He carried a hump on his shoulders of prodigious dimensions; but notwithstanding his apparent great age, which must have been over a hundred years, he seemed as spry and active as a mokak. His dress consisted of a tremendous sou-wester, a greasy duck jacket, and a pair of well-tarred trowsers, something the worse for the wear. In one hand he carried a harpoon; in the other a coil of short warp. I felt very odd, I assure you, at the sudden apparition of such a venerable whaleman. As I gazed upon him, he raised his finger in a mysterious and solemn manner, and pointed toward the offing. I looked, and saw a large whale sporting on the surface of the water. The boats were lying upon the beach. He turned his eyes meaningly toward the nearest. I trembled all over; for I never experienced such strange sensations as I did then.

"'Shall we go?' said he.

"'As you say,' I replied.

"'You are a good whaleman, I suppose? Have you ever killed your whale at a fifteen fathom dart?'

"I replied in the affirmative.

"'Very well,' said he, 'you'll do.'

"And without more delay, we launched the boat and pushed off. It was a wild whale-chase, that! We pulled and tugged for upwards of an hour. At last we came upon the whale, just as he rose for the second time. I sprang to the bow, for I wanted to have the first iron into him.

"'Back from that!' said the old whaleman, sternly.

"'It's my chance,' I replied.

"'Back, I tell you! I'll strike that whale!'

"There was something in his voice that inspired me with awe, and I gave way to him. The whale was four good darts off; but the old man's strength was supernatural, and his aim unerring. The harpoon struck exactly where it was pointed, just back of the head.

"'Now for a ride!' cried the old man; and his features brightened up, and his eyes glared strangely. 'Jump on, John Tabor, jump on!' said he.

"'How do you mean?' said I; for although I had killed whales, and eat of them too, such an idea as that of riding a whale-back never before entered my mind.

"'Jump on, I say, jump on, John Tabor!' he repeated, sternly.

"'Damme if I do!' said I, and my hair began to stand on end.

"'You must,' shouted the old whaleman.

"'But I won't!' said I, resolutely.

"'Won't you?' and with that he seized me in his arms, and, making a desperate spring, reached the whale's back and drove the boat adrift. He then set me down, and bade me hold on to the seat of his ducks, while he made sure his own fastening by a good grip of the iron pole. With the other hand he drew from his pocket a quid of tobacco and rammed it into his mouth; after which he began to hum an old song. Feeling something rather uncommon on his back, the whale set off with the speed of lightning, whizzing along as if all the whalers in the Pacific were after him.

"'Go it!' said the old man, and his eyes flashed with a supernatural brilliancy. 'Hold fast, John Tabor! stick on like grim Death!'

"'What the devil kind of a wild-goose chase is this?' said I, shivering with fear and cold; for the spray came dashing over us in oceans.

"'Patience!' rejoined the old man; 'you'll see presently.' Away we went, leaving a wake behind us for miles. The land became more and more indistinct. We lost sight of it entirely. We were on the broad ocean.

"'On! on! Stick to me, John Tabor!' shouted the old man, with a grin of infernal ecstacy.

"'But where are you bound?' said I. 'Damme if this don't beat all the crafts I ever shipped in!' and my teeth chattered as if I had an ague.

"'Belay your jaw-tackle, John Tabor! Keep your main hatch closed, and hold on. Go it! go it, old sperm!'

"Away we dashed, bounding from wave to wave like a streak of pigtail lightning. Whizz! whizz! we flew through the sea. I never saw the like. At this rate we travelled till daylight, when the old man sang out, 'Land oh!'

"'Where away?' said I, for I had no more idea of our latitude and longitude than if I had been dropped down out of the clouds. 'Off our weather eye?'

"'That's the Cape of Good Hope!'

"Ne'er went John Gilpin faster than we rounded the cape.

"'Hard down your flukes!' shouted my companion, and in five minutes Table Mountain looked blue in the distance. The sun had just risen above the horizon, when an island appeared ahead.

"'Land oh!' cried the old man.

"'Why, you bloody old popinjay,' said I, peeping through the clouds of spray that rose up before us, 'where are you steering?'

"'That's St. Helena!'

"'The devil you say!' and before the words were well out of my mouth we shot past the island and left it galloping astern.

"Stick on! stick on, John Tabor!' cried old greasy-beard; and I tightened my grasp on the seat of his ducks. The sea was growing rough. We flew onward like wildfire.

"'Land oh!' shouted the old man again.

"'Where's that?' said I, holding on with all my might.

"'That's Cape Hatteras!'

"Our speed now increased to such a degree that my hat flew off, and the wind whistled through my hair, for it stood bolt upright the whole time, so fearful was I of losing my passage. I had travelled in steam-boats, stages, and locomotives, but I had never experienced or imagined anything like this. I couldn't contain myself any longer; so I made bold to tell the old chap with the beard what I thought about it.

"'Shiver me!' said I, 'if this isn't the most outlandish, hell-bent voyage I ever went. If you don't come to pretty soon, you and I'll part company.'

"'Land ho!' roared the old man.

"'In the devil's name,' said I, 'what d'ye call that?'

"'Nantucket,' replied my comrade.

"We passed it in the winking of an eye, and away we went up Buzzard's Bay. The coast was lined with old whaling skippers, spying us with glasses; for certainly so strange a sight was never seen before or since.

"'There she breaches!' cried some.

"'There she blows!' cried others; but it was all one to them. We were out of sight in a jiffy.

"The coast of Massachusetts was right ahead. On, on we flew. Taborstown, the general receptacle for Tabors, stood before us. High and dry we landed on the beach. Still onward went the whale, blowing and pitching, and tearing up the sand with his flukes.

"'My eyes!' said I, scarcely able to see a dart ahead, 'look out, or you'll be foul of the town pump!'

"'Go it! Never say die! Hold fast, John Tabor!' shouted the old chap; and helter-skelter we flew down Main-street, scattering children, and women, and horses, and all manner of live stock and domestic animals, on each side. The old Cape Horn and plum-pudding captains rushed to their doors at a sight so rare.

"'There she breaches! There she breaches!' resounded through the town fore and aft; and with the ruling passion strong even in old age, they came hobbling after us, armed with lances, harpoons, and a variety of old rusty whale-gear, the hindmost singing out,

"'Don't you strike that whale, Captain Tabor!' and the foremost shouting to those behind, 'this is my chance, Captain Tabor!' while the old man with the long beard, just ahead of me, kept roaring,

"'Stick fast, John Tabor! hang on like grim Death, John Tabor!'

"And I did hang on. As I had predicted, we fetched up against the town pump; and so great was the shock, that the old fellow flew head-foremost over it, leaving in my firm grasp the entire seat of his ducks. I fell myself; but being further aft, I didn't go quite so far as my comrade. However, I held on to the stern-sheets. As the old man righted up, he presented a comical spectacle to the good citizens of Taborstown. The youngsters seeing such an odd fish floundering about, got their miniature lances and harpoons to bear upon him, in a manner that didn't tickle his fancy much.

"The whale at length got under weigh again, and onward we went, with about twenty irons dangling at each side. I grasped the old man by the collar of his jacket this time. A shout of laughter followed us.

"'You've lost your whale, Captain Tabor!' cried one.

"'The devil's in the whale, Captain Tabor!' cried another.

"'As long as I've been Captain Tabor,' said a third, 'I never saw such a whale.'

"'As sure as I'm Captain Tabor, he's bewitched,' observed a fourth.

"'Captain Tabor, Captain Tabor! I've lost my irons!' shouted a fifth.

"'Who's that aboard, Captain Tabor?' asked a sixth.

"'That's John Tabor!' replied the seventh.

"'John Tabor, John Tabor, hold fast!' roared the old man, and away we went as if possessed of the devil, sure enough. Over hills and dales, and through towns and villages flew we, till the Alleghanies hove in sight. We cleared them in no time, and came down with a glorious breach right into the Alleghany River. Down the river we dashed through steam-boats, flat-boats, and all manner of small craft, till we entered the Ohio. Right ahead went we, upsetting every thing in our way, and astonishing the natives, who never saw any thing in such a shape go at this rate before. We entered the Mississippi, dashed across all the bends, through swamp and canebrake, and at last found ourselves in the Gulf of Mexico, going like wildfire through a fleet of whalers. Nothing daunted, the whale dashed ahead; the coast of South America hove in sight. Over the Andes went we—into the Pacific—past the Sandwich Islands—on to China—past Borneo—up the Straits of Malacca—through the Seychelles Islands—down the Mozambique Channel, and at last we fetched up in Algoa Bay. We ran ashore with such headway that I was pitched head-foremost into the sand, and there I fastened as firm as the stump of a tree. You may be sure, out of breath as I was, I soon began to smother. This feeling of suffocation became so intolerable, that I struggled with the desperation of a man determined not to give up the ghost. A confusion of ideas came upon me all at once, and I found myself sitting upright in my catanda in the old hospital——"

Here Tabor paused.

"Then it was all a dream?" said I, somewhat disappointed. He shook his head, and was mysteriously silent for a while.

HENRY DAVID THOREAU.

Two of the most noticeable books in American literature on the score of a certain quaint study of natural history and scenery, are Mr. Thoreau's volumes on the Concord and Merrimack rivers, and Life in the Woods. The author is a humorist in the old English sense of the word, a man of humors, of Concord, Mass., where, in the neighborhood of Emerson and Hawthorne, and in the enjoyment of their society, he leads, if we may take his books as the interpreter of his career, a meditative philosophic life.

Henry D. Thoreau.

We find his name on the Harvard list of graduates of 1837. In 1849, having previously been a contributor to the Dial, and occupied himself in school-keeping and trade in an experimental way, he published *A Week on the Concord and Merrimack Rivers*. It is a book of mingled essay and description, occasionally rash and conceited, in a certain transcendental affectation of expression on religious subjects; but in many other passages remarkable for its nicety of observation, and acute literary and moral perceptions. It is divided into seven chapters, of the days of the week. A journey is accomplished in the month of August, 1839, descending the Concord river, from the town of that name, to the Merrimac; then ascending the latter river to its source: thence backward to the starting point. This voyage is performed by the author in company with his brother, in a boat of their own construction, which is variously rowed, pulled, dragged, or propelled by the wind along the flats or through the canal; the travellers resting at night under a tent which they carry with them. The record is of the small boating adventures, and largely of the reflections, real or supposed, suggested by the moods or incidents of the way. There are a variety of illustrations of physical geography, the history of the interesting settlements along the way; in the botanical excursions, philosophical speculations and literary studies.

The author, it will be seen from the date of his publication, preserved the Horatian maxim, of brooding over his reflections, if not keeping his copy, the approved period of gestation of nine years.

His next book was published with equal deliberation. It is the story of a humor of the author, which occupied him a term of two years and two months, commencing in March, 1845. *Walden, or Life in the Woods*, was published in Boston in 1854. The oddity of its record attracted universal attention. A gentleman and scholar retires one morning from the world, strips himself of all superfluities, and with a borrowed axe and minimum of pecuniary capital, settles himself as a squatter in the wood, on the edge of a New England pond near Concord. He did not own the land, but was permitted to enjoy it. He felled a few pines, hewed timbers, and for boards bought out the shanty of James Collins, an Irish laborer on the adjacent Fitchburg railroad, for the sum of four dollars twenty-five cents. He was assisted in the raising by Emerson, George W. Curtis, and other celebrities of Concord, whose presence gave the rafters an artistic flavor. Starting early in the spring, he secured long before winter by the labor of his hands "a tight shingled and plastered house, ten feet wide by fifteen long, and eight feet posts, with a garret and a closet, a large window on each side, two trap-doors, one door at the end, and a brick fire-place opposite." The exact cost of the house is given:—

Thoreau's House.

Boards,	$8 03½,	mostly shanty boards.
Refuse shingles for roof and sides,	4 00	
Laths,	1 25	
Two second-hand windows with glass,	2 43	
One thousand old brick,	4 00	
Two casks of lime,	2 40	That was high.
Hair,	0 31	More than I needed.
Mantle-tree iron,	0 15	
Nails,	3 90	
Hinges and screws,	0 14	
Latch,	0 10	
Chalk,	0 01	
Transportation,	1 40	I carried a good part on my back.
In all,	$28 12½	

These are all the materials excepting the timber, stones, and sand, which I claimed by squatter's right. I have also a small wood-shed adjoining, made chiefly of the stuff which was left after building the house.

The rest of the account from Mr. Thoreau's ledger is curious, and will show "upon what meats this same Cæsar fed," that he came to interest the public so greatly in his housekeeping:—

By surveying, carpentry, and day-labor of various other kinds in the village in the mean while, for I have as many trades as fingers, I had earned $13 34. The expense of food for eight months, namely, from July 4th to March 1st, the time when these estimates were made, though I lived there more than two years,—not counting potatoes, a little green corn, and some peas, which I had raised, nor considering the value of what was on hand at the last date, was

Rice,	$1 73½		
Molasses,	1 73	Cheapest form of the saccharine.	
Rye meal,	1 04¾		
Indian meal,	0 99¾	Cheaper than rye.	
Pork,	0 22		
Flour,	0 88	Cost more than Indian meal, both money and trouble.	All experiments which failed.
Sugar,	0 80		All experiments which failed.
Lard,	0 65		All experiments which failed.
Apples,	0 25		All experiments which failed.
Dried apple,	0 22		All experiments which failed.
Sweet potatoes,	0 10		All experiments which failed.
One pumpkin,	0 06		All experiments which failed.
One watermelon,	2		All experiments which failed.
Salt,	3		All experiments which failed.

Yes, I did eat $8 74, all told; but I should not thus unblushingly publish my guilt, if I did not know that most of my readers were equally guilty with myself, and that their deeds would look no better in print. The next year I sometimes caught a mess of fish for my dinner, and once I went so far as to slaughter a woodchuck which ravaged my bean-field,—effect his transmigration, as a Tartar would say,—and devour him, partly for experiment's sake; but though it afforded me a momentary enjoyment, notwithstanding a musky flavor, I saw that the longest use would not make that a good practice, however it might seem to have your woodchucks ready dressed by the village butcher.

Clothing and some incidental expenses within the same dates, though little can be inferred from this item, amounted to

	$8 40¾
Oil and some household utensils,	2 00

So that all the pecuniary outgoes, excepting for washing and mending, which for the most part were done out of the house, and their bills have not yet been received,—and these are all and more than all the ways by which money necessarily goes out in this part of the world,—were

House,	$28 12½
Farm one year,	14 72½
Food eight months,	8 74
Clothing, &c. eight months,	8 40¾
Oil, &c., eight months,	2 00
In all,	$61 99¾

I address myself now to those of my readers who have a living to get. And to meet this I have for farm produce sold

	$23 44
Earned by day-labor,	13 34
In all,	$36 78

which subtracted from the sum of the outgoes leaves a balance of $25 21¾ on the one side,—this being very nearly the means with which I started, and the measure of expenses to be incurred,—and on the other, beside the leisure and independence and health thus secured, a comfortable house for me as long as I chose to occupy it.

He had nothing further to do after his "family baking," which, the family consisting of a unit, could not have been large or have come round very often, than to read, think, and observe. Homer appears to have been his favorite book. The thinking was unlimited, and the observation that of a man with an instinctive tact for the wonders of natural history. He sees and describes insects, birds, such "small deer" as approached him, with a felicity which would have gained him the heart of Izaak Walton and Alexander Wilson. A topographical and hydrographical survey of Walden Pond, is as faithful, exact, and labored, as if it had employed a government or admiralty commission.

As in the author's previous work, the immediate incident is frequently only the introduction to higher themes. The realities around him are occasionally veiled by a hazy atmosphere of transcendental speculation, through which the essayist sometimes stumbles into abysmal depths of the bathetic. We have more pleasure, however, in dwelling upon the shrewd humors of this modern contemplative Jacques of the forest, and his fresh, nice observation of books and men, which has occasionally something of a poetic vein. He who would acquire a new sensation of the world about him, would do well to retire from cities to the banks of Walden pond; and he who would open his eyes to the opportunities of country life, in its associations of fields and men, may loiter with profit along the author's journey on the Merrimack, where natural history, local antiquities, records, and tradition, are exhausted in vitalizing the scene.

A CHARACTER—FROM WALDEN.

Who should come to my lodge this morning but a true Homeric or Paphlagonian man,—he had so suitable and poetic a name that I am sorry I cannot print it here,—a Canadian, a wood-chopper and post maker, who can hole fifty posts in a day, who made his last supper on a woodchuck which his dog caught. He, too, has heard of Homer, and, "if it were not for books," would "not know what to do rainy days," though perhaps he has not read one wholly through for many rainy seasons. Some priest who could pronounce the Greek itself, taught him to read his verse in the Testament in his native parish far away; and now I must translate to him, while he holds the book, Achilles' reproof to Patroclus, for his sad countenance.—"Why are you in tears, Patroclus, like a young girl?"

Or have you alone heard some news from Phthia?
They say that Menœtius lives yet, son of Actor,
And Peleus lives, son of Æacus, among the Myrmidons.
Either of whom having died, we should greatly grieve.

He says, "That's good." He has a great bundle of white-oak bark under his arm for a sick man, gathered this Sunday morning. "I suppose there's no harm in going after such a thing to-day," says he. To him Homer was a great writer, though what his writing was about he did not know. A more simple and natural man it would be hard to find. Vice and disease, which cast such a sombre moral hue over the world, seemed to have hardly any existence for him. He was about twenty-eight years old, and had left Canada and his father's house a dozen years before to work in the States, and earn money to buy a farm with at last, perhaps in his native country. He was cast in the coarsest mould; a stout but sluggish body, yet gracefully carried, with a thick sunburnt neck, dark bushy hair, and dull sleepy blue eyes, which were occasionally lit up with expression. He wore a flat gray cloth cap, a dingy wool-colored greatcoat, and cowhide boots. He was a great consumer of meat, usually carrying his dinner to his work a couple of miles past my house,—for he chopped all summer,—in a tin pail; cold meats, often cold woodchucks, and coffee in a stone bottle which dangled by a string from his belt; and sometimes he offered me a drink. He came along early, crossing my beanfield, though without anxiety or haste to get to his work, such as Yankees exhibit. He wasn't a-going to hurt himself. He didn't care if he only earned his board. Frequently he would leave his dinner in the bushes, when his dog had caught a woodchuck by the way, and go back a mile and a half to dress it and leave it in the cellar of the house where he boarded, after deliberating first for half an hour whether he could not sink it in the pond safely till nightfall,—loving to dwell long upon these themes. He would say, as he went by in the morning, "How thick the pigeons are! If working every day were not my trade, I could get all the meat I should want by hunting pigeons, woodchucks, rabbits, partridges,—by gosh! I could get all I should want for a week and one day."

A BATTLE OF ANTS—FROM WALDEN.

One day when I went out to my wood-pile, or rather my pile of stumps, I observed two large ants, the one red, the other much larger, nearly half an inch long, and black, fiercely contending with one another. Having once got hold they never let go, but struggled and wrestled and rolled on the chips incessantly. Looking farther, I was surprised to find that the chips were covered with such combatants, that it was not a *duellum*, but a *bellum*, a war between two races of ants, the red always pitted against the black, and frequently two red ones to one black. The legions of these Myrmidons covered all the hills and vales in my wood-yard, and the ground was already strewn with the dead and dying, both red and black. It was the only battle which I have ever witnessed, the only battle-field I ever trod while the battle was raging; internecine war; the red republicans on the one hand, and the black imperialists on the other. On every side they were engaged in deadly combat, yet without any noise I could hear, and human soldiers never fought so resolutely. I watched a couple that were fast locked in each other's embraces, in a little sunny valley amid the chips, now at noon-day prepared to fight till the sun went down, or life went out. The smaller red champion had fastened himself like a vice to his adversary's front, and through all the tumblings on that field never for an instant ceased to gnaw at one of his feelers near the root, having already caused the other to go by the board; while the stronger black one dashed him from side to side, and, as I saw on looking nearer, had already divested him of several of his members. They fought with more pertinacity than bull-dogs. Neither manifested the least disposition to retreat. It was evident that their battle-cry was—Conquer or die. In the mean while there came along a single red ant on the hill-side of this valley, evidently full of excitement, who either had despatched his foe, or had not yet taken part in the battle; probably the latter, for he had lost none of his limbs; whose mother had charged him to return with his shield or upon it. Or perchance he was some Achilles, who had nourished his wrath apart, and had now come to avenge or rescue his Patroclus. He saw this unequal combat from afar —for the blacks were nearly twice the size of the red,—he drew near with rapid pace till he stood on his guard within half an inch of the combatants; then, watching his opportunity, he sprang upon the black warrior, and commenced his operations near the root of his right fore-leg, leaving the foe to select among his own members; and so there were three united for life, as if a new kind of attraction had been invented which put all other locks and cements to shame. I should not have wondered by this time to find that they had their respective musical bands stationed on some eminent chip, and playing their national airs the while, to excite the slow and cheer the dying combatants. I was myself excited somewhat even as if they had been men. The more you think of it, the less the difference. And certainly there is not the fight recorded in Concord history, at least, if in the history of America, that will bear a moment's comparison with this, whether for the numbers engaged in it, or for the patriotism and heroism displayed. For numbers and for carnage it was an Austerlitz or Dresden. Concord Fight! Two killed on the patriots' side, and Luther Blanchard wounded! Why here every ant was a Buttrick,— "Fire! for God's sake fire!"—and thousands shared the fate of Davis and Hosmer. There was not one hireling there. I have no doubt that it was a principle they fought for, as much as our ancestors, and not to avoid a three-penny tax on their tea; and the results of this battle will be as important and memorable to those whom it concerns as those of the battle of Bunker Hill, at least.

I took up the chip on which the three I have particularly described were struggling, carried it into my house, and placed it under a tumbler on my window-sill, in order to see the issue. Holding a microscope to the first-mentioned red ant, I saw that, though he was assiduously gnawing at the near foreleg of his enemy, having severed his remaining feeler, his own breast was all torn away, exposing what vitals he had there to the jaws of the black warrior, whose breast-plate was apparently too thick for him to pierce; and the dark carbuncles of the sufferer's eyes shone with ferocity, such as war only could excite. They struggled half an hour longer under the tumbler, and when I looked again the black soldier had severed the heads of his foes from their bodies, and the still living heads were hanging on either side of him like ghastly trophies at his saddle-bow, still apparently as firmly fastened as ever, and he was endeavoring with feeble struggles, being without feelers and with only the remnant of a leg, and I know not how many other wounds, to divest himself of them; which at length, after half an hour more, he accomplished. I raised the glass, and he went off over the window-sill in that crippled state. Whether he finally survived that combat, and spent the remainder of his days in some Hotel des Invalides, I do not know; but I thought that his industry would not be worth much thereafter. I never learned which party was victorious, nor the cause of the war; but I felt for the rest of that day as if I had had my feelings excited and harrowed by witnessing the struggle, the ferocity and carnage, of a human battle before my door.

Kirby and Spence tell us that the battles of ants have long been celebrated and the date of them recorded, though they say that Huber is the only modern author who appears to have witnessed them. "Æneas Sylvius," say they, "after giving a very circumstantial account of one contested with great obstinacy by a great and small species on the trunk of a pear tree," adds that "'This action was fought in the pontificate of Eugenius the Fourth, in the presence of Nicholas Pistoriensis an eminent lawyer, who related the whole history of the battle with the greatest fidelity. A similar engagement between great and small ants is recorded by Olaus Magnus, in which the small ones, being victorious, are said to have buried the bodies of their own soldiers, but left those of their giant enemies a prey to the birds. This event happened previous to the expulsion of the tyrant Christiern the Second from Sweden." The battle which I witnessed took place in the Presidency of Polk, five years before the passage of Webster's Fugitive-Slave Bill.

ARTHUR CLEVELAND COXE.

ARTHUR CLEVELAND COXE is the son of the Rev. Samuel H. Coxe, of Brooklyn, the author of *Quakerism, not Christianity; Interviews, Memorable and Useful, from Diary and Memory, reproduced;* and other publications. He was born at Mendham, New Jersey, May 10, 1818. On his mother's side he is a grandson of the Rev. Aaron Cleveland, an early poet of Connecticut.

Mr. Cleveland was born at Haddam, February 8, 1744. His father, a missionary of the Society for the Propagation of the Gospel, dying when the son was but thirteen years of age, the latter received few educational advantages. He, however, at the age of nineteen, produced a descriptive poem, *The Philosopher and Boy*, of some merit. He soon after became a Congregational minister. In 1775 he published a poem on *Slavery*, in blank verse. He was also the author of several satirical poems directed against the Jeffersonians. He died on the twenty-first of September, 1815.*

Mr. Coxe was prepared for college under the private tuition of Professor George Bush. He entered the University of the City of New York, and was graduated in 1838. During his freshman year he wrote a poem, *The Progress of Ambition*, and in 1837 published *Advent, a Mystery*, a poem after the manner of the religious dramas of the Middle Ages. In 1838 appeared *Athwold, a Romaunt*, and *Saint Jonathan, the Lay of the Scald*, designed as the commencement of a semi-humorous poem, in the Don Juan style.

Mr. Coxe soon after became a student in the General Theological Seminary, New York. While at this institution he delivered a poem, *Athanasion*, before the Alumni of Washington College, Hartford, at the Commencement in 1840. In the same year he published *Christian Ballads*, a collection of poems, suggested for the most part by the holy seasons and services of his church. Five editions of this popular volume have since appeared.

Mr. Coxe was ordained deacon in July, 1841, and in the August following became rector of St. Anne's church, Morrisania, where he wrote his poem *Halloween*, privately printed in 1842. He was next called to St. John's church, at Hartford. During his residence at that place he published, in 1845, *Saul, a Mystery*, a dramatic poem of much greater length than his Advent, but, like that production, modelled on the early religious

* Everest's Poets of Connecticut.

plays. He is at present rector of Grace church, Baltimore.

In addition to his poetical volumes Mr. Coxe has published Sermons on Doctrine and Duty, preached to the parishioners of St. John's church, Hartford, and numerous articles in the Church Review and other periodicals. He has also translated a work of the Abbé Laborde, on the *Impossibility of the Immaculate Conception as an Article of Faith*, with notes.

OLD TRINITY.

Easter Even, 1840.

Thy servants think upon her stones, and it pitieth them to see her in the dust.—*Psalter*.

The Paschal moon is ripe to-night
On fair Manhada's bay,
And soft it falls on Hoboken,
As where the Saviour lay;
And beams beneath whose paly shine
Nile's troubling angel flew,
Show many a blood-besprinkled door
Of our passover too.

But here, where many an holy year
It shone on arch and aisle,
What means its cold and silver ray
On dust and ruined pile?
Oh, where's the consecrated porch,
The sacred lintel where,
And where's that antique steeple's height
To bless the moonlight air?

I seem to miss a mother's face
In this her wonted home;
And linger in the green churchyard
As round that mother's tomb.
Old Trinity! thou too art gone!
And in thine own blest bound,
They've laid thee low, dear mother church,
To rest in holy ground!

The vaulted roof that trembled oft
Above the chaunted psalm;
The quaint old altar where we owned
Our very Paschal Lamb;
The chimes that ever in the tower
Like seraph-music sung,
And held me spell-bound in the way
When I was very young;—

The marble monuments within;
The 'scutcheons, old and rich;
And one bold bishop's effigy
Above the chancel-niche;
The mitre and the legend there
Beneath the colored pane;
All these—thou knewest, Paschal moon,
But ne'er shalt know again!

And thou wast shining on this spot
That hour the Saviour rose!
But oh, its look that Easter morn,
The Saviour only knows.
A thousand years—and 'twas the same,
And half a thousand more;
Old moon, what mystic chronicles,
Thou keepest, of this shore!

And so, till good Queen Anna reigned,
It was a heathen sward:
But when they made its virgin turf,
An altar to the Lord,
With holy roof they covered it;
And when Apostles came,
They claimed, for Christ, its battlements,
And took it in God's name.

Then, Paschal moon, this sacred spot
No more thy magic felt,
Till flames brought down the holy place,
Where our forefathers knelt:
Again, 'tis down—the grave old pile;
That mother church sublime!
Look on its roofless floor, old moon,
For 'tis thy last—last time!

Ay, look with smiles, for never there
Shines Paschal moon agen,
Till breaks the Earth's great Easter-day
O'er all the graves of men!
So wane away, old Paschal moon,
And come next year as bright;
Eternal rock shall welcome thee,
Our faith's devoutest light!

They rear old Trinity once more:
And, if ye weep to see,
The glory of this latter house
Thrice glorious shall be!
Oh lay its deep foundations strong,
And, yet a little while,
Our Paschal Lamb himself shall come
To light its hallowed aisle.

HE STANDETH AT THE DOOR AND KNOCKETH.

In the silent midnight watches,
List,—thy bosom door!
How it knocketh—knocketh—knocketh,
Knocketh evermore!
Say not 't is thy pulse is beating:
'Tis thy heart of sin;
'Tis thy Saviour knocks, and crieth—
"Rise, and let me in."

Death comes on with reckless footsteps,
To the hall and hut:
Think you, Death will tarry, knocking,
Where the door is shut?
Jesus waiteth, waiteth, waiteth—
But the door is fast;
Grieved away thy Saviour goeth;
Death breaks in at last!

Then, 'tis time to stand entreating
Christ to let thee in;
At the gate of heaven beating,
Wailing for thy sin.
Nay,—alas, thou guilty creature!
Hast thou then forgot?
Jesus waited long to know thee,
Now he knows thee not.

THE VOLUNTEER'S MARCH.

March—march—march!
Making sounds as they tread,
Ho-ho! how they step,
Going down to the dead!
Every stride, every tramp,
Every footfall is nearer,
And dimmer each lamp,
As darkness grows drearer:
But ho! how they march,
Making sounds as they tread
Ho-ho! how they step,
Going down to the dead!

March—march—march!
Making sounds as they tread,
Ho-ho! how they laugh,
Going down to the dead!
How they whirl, how they trip,
How they smile, how they dally,
How blithesome they skip,
Going down to the valley!

Oh ho! how they march,
  Making sounds as they tread;
Ho-ho! how they skip,
  Going down to the dead!

March—march—march!
  Earth groans as they tread;
Each carries a skull,
  Going down to the dead!
Every stride—every stamp,
  Every footfall is bolder;
'Tis a skeleton's tramp,
  With a skull on his shoulder.
But ho! how he steps
  With a high tossing head,
That clay-covered bone,
  Going down to the dead!

JOHN STEINFORT KIDNEY

Is the author of a volume, *Catawba River, and Other Poems*, published in 1847. He is a clergyman of the Protestant Episcopal Church, settled at Saratoga Springs, New York. He was born in 1819, in Essex County, N. J., where his ancestors had lived for a hundred and fifty years, was educated partly at Union College, and gave some attention to the law before entering the church through the course of instruction of the General Theological Seminary. After his ordination he was for a time rector of a parish in North Carolina, and afterwards in Salem, N. J.

His verses show an individual temperament, and the tastes of a scholar and thinker.

COME IN THE MOONLIGHT.

Come in the moonlight—come in the cold,
Snow-covered the earth,
Yet O, how inviting!
Come—O come!

Come, ye sad lovers, friends who have parted,
Lonely and desolate,
All heavy-hearted ones,
Come—O come!

Come to the beauty of frost in the silence,
Cares may be loosened,
Loves be forgotten,—
Come—O come!

Deep is the sky;—pearl of the morning,
Rose of the twilight,
Lost in its blueness,
Come—O come!

Look up and shudder; see the lone moon
Like a sad cherub
Passing the clouds,
Come—O come!

Lo! she is weeping;—tears in the heaven
Twinkle and tremble.
Tenderest sister!
Come—O come!

Keen is the air;—keener the sparkles
Sprinkling the snow-drift,
Glancing and glittering,
Come—O come!

Look to the earth—from earth to her sister,
See which is brightest!
Both white as the angels!
Come—O come!

Robed in the purity heaven hath sent her,
Gone are the guilt-stains—
Drowned in the holiness.
Come—O come!

Grief hath no wailing:—Rapture is silent.
Colder and purer
Freezes the spirit!
Come—O come!

GEORGE H. COLTON.

George Hooker Colton, the son of the Rev. George Colton, was born at Westford, Otsego County, New York, on the 27th of October, 1818. He was graduated, with a high rank in his class, at Yale College, in 1840. In the fall of the same year, while engaged as a teacher in Hartford, he determined to write a poem on the Indian Wars, in which the newly elected President, General Harrison, had been engaged. It was to have appeared at the time of the Inauguration, but, the plan expanding as the author proceeded, was not published until the spring of 1842.

The poem, *Tecumseh, or the West Thirty Years Since*, is in nine cantos, in the octosyllabic measure and style of Sir Walter Scott, with the usual ordinary felicities of illustration bestowed upon this class of compositions in America, of which many have been produced with little success.

In 1842 Mr. Colton also prepared, from the materials which he had accumulated during the progress of his poem, a course of lectures on the Indians, which were delivered in various places during 1842 and 1843.

In the summer of 1844 he delivered a poem before the Phi Beta Kappa Society at Yale College.

In January, 1845, he published the first number of the American Whig Review, a monthly magazine of politics and literature, under his editorship. Mr. Colton entered upon this important enterprise with great energy, securing a large number of the leading politicians and authors of the country as its friends and contributors. He edited the work with judgment, wrote constantly for its pages, and had succeeded in gaining a fair measure of success, when he was seized in November, 1847, by a violent attack of typhus fever, which put an end to his life on the first of December following.*

PHILIP SCHAFF.

Dr. Philip Schaff, Professor of Theology in the Seminary of the German Reformed Church at Mercersburg, Pa., the author of a History of the Apostolic Church and of other theological works, which have received considerable attention in America, is a native of Switzerland. He was born at Coire (Chur), Canton Graubundten, January 1, 1819. He was educated at the college of his native city, afterwards at the Gymnasium of Stuttgart, and in the Universities of Tubingen, Halle, and Berlin. He received his degree in 1841, as Doctor of Philosophy and Bachelor of Divinity, at the University of Berlin, which subsequently (1854) presented him the Diploma of D.D. honoris causâ. At the conclusion of his early college life, he travelled for nearly two years through Germany, Switzerland, France, and Italy, as tutor of a young Prussian nobleman. In 1842 he became a lecturer on theology in the University of Berlin, after having gone through the examination of public academic teachers. In 1843, he received a unanimous call as professor of Church History and Exegesis to the Theologi-

* New Englander, vii. 239.

cal Seminary at Mercersburg, Pennsylvania, from the Synod of the German Reformed Church of the United States, on the recommendations of Drs. Neander, Hengstenberg, Tholuck, Muller, Krummacher, and others, who had been consulted about a suitable representative of German Evangelical Theology for America. In the spring of 1844 he left Berlin, and after some months' travel in Southern Germany, Switzerland, Belgium, and England, he crossed the Atlantic and soon identified himself with American interests.

He has since been engaged in teaching the various branches of exegetical and historical theology at Mercersburg, both in the German and English languages, with the exception of the year 1854, which he spent on a visit to his friends in Europe.

The Church History of Dr. Schaff is remarkable for its thorough and apparently exhaustive learning, for its clear style and somewhat artistic groupings, for its union of doctrinal persistency with philosophical enlargement. His position is that of strong supernaturalism, with great emphasis upon the church organism, and the high Lutheran doctrine of divine grace, which is saved from Calvinism by the decided high church view of the sacraments.

His life of Augustine is a scholarlike and philosophical development of the great saint's doctrinal positions from his experience and life.*

Marshall College, with which, under the presidency of the Rev. Dr. John W. Nevin, Dr. Schaff held the Professorship of Æsthetics and German Literature, was first situated at Mercersburg, Franklin Co. Pa., and was founded under a charter from the Legislature of Pennsylvania in 1835. It sprang originally out of the high school attached to the Theological Seminary of the German Reformed Church, and is in intimate union with that institution. By an act of the state in 1850, it was united with Franklin College at Lancaster, and in 1853 was removed to that place, the new institution bearing the title Franklin and Marshall College.

Adolphus L. Koeppen, author of a series of lectures on Geography and History, and a valuable publication on the subject, is Professor of German Literature, Æsthetics, and History, in this institution.

Dr. Nevin, the associate of Professor Schaff, is also the author of a work on *The Mystical Presence, a Vindication of the Reformed or Calvinistic Doctrine of the Holy Eucharist*, and other theological writings of the school of divinity to which he is attached, and of which the Mercersburg Review, commenced in January, 1849, has been the organ.

JAMES RUSSELL LOWELL

Is the descendant of an old New England family, which has long held important stations in Massachusetts. His ancestor, Percival Lowell, settled in the town of Newbury in 1639. His grandfather, John Lowell, was an eminent lawyer, a member of Congress and of the convention which formed the first constitution of Massachusetts. His father is Charles Lowell, the venerable pastor of the West Church in Boston; his mother was a native of New Hampshire, a sister of the late Capt. Robert T. Spence of the U. S. Navy, and is spoken of as of remarkable powers of mind and possessing in an eminent degree the faculty of acquiring languages.*

J. R. Lowell.

James Russell Lowell, who is named after his father's maternal grandfather, Judge James Russell, of Charlestown, was born at the country-seat of Elmwood, the present residence of the family, at Cambridge, Mass., February 22, 1819. He was educated in the town, and in 1838 received

* The following is a list of the publications of Dr. Schaff:—

1. The Sin against the Holy Ghost, and the Dogmatical and Ethical Inferences derived from it. With an Appendix on the Life and Death of Francis Spiera. Halle, 1841. (German.)

2. James, the Brother of the Lord, and James the Less. An exegetical and historical essay. Berlin, 1842. (German.)

3. The Principle of Protestantism, as related to the present state of the Church. Chambersburg, Pa., 1845. (German and English Translation, with an Introduction by Dr. Nevin.)

4. What is Church History? A Vindication of the Idea of Historical Development. Philadelphia, 1846. (English.)

5. History of the Apostolic Church, with a General Introduction to Church History. First German edition, Mercersburg, Pa., 1851. Second German edition, Leipzic, 1854. (English translation by the Rev. E. Yeomans, New York, 1858. Reprinted in Edinburgh, 1854.)

6. Life and Labors of St. Augustine (English edition, New York, 1858, and another, London, 1854. German edition, Berlin, 1854.)

7. America. The Political, Social, and Religious Condition of the United States of N. A. Berlin, 1854. (German. An English translation will appear before the end of 1855.)

8. Der Deutsche Kirchenfreund ("The German Church Friend, or Monthly Organ for the General Interests of the German Churches in America," commenced in 1848, and edited and published by Dr. Schaff till the close of the 6th volume in 1858; now continued by the Rev. William J. Mann, Philadelphia, Pa.)

9. Several Tracts and Orations on Anglo-Germanism, Dante, Systematic Benevolence, etc. etc., and Articles in the Bibliotheca Sacra, Methodist Quarterly, Mercersburg Review, and other journals of America and Germany.

* This faculty is inherited by her daughter, Mrs. Putnam, whose controversy with Mr. Bowen, editor of the North American Review, respecting the late war in Hungary, brought her name prominently before the public. Mrs. Putnam converses readily in French, Italian, German, Polish, Swedish, and Hungarian, and is familiar with twenty modern dialects, besides the Greek, Latin, Hebrew, Persic, and Arabic. Mrs. Putnam made the first translation into English of Frederica Bremer's novel of the Neighbors, from the Swedish. The translation by Mary Howitt was made from the German.—*Homes of American Authors*—Art. Lowell.

his degree at Harvard. His first production in print, a class poem, appeared at this time. This was succeeded, in 1841, by a collection of poems—*A Year's Life*. It was marked by a youthful delicacy and sensibility, with a leaning to transcendental expression, but teeming with proofs of the poetic nature, particularly in a certain vein of tenderness. In January, 1843, he commenced, in conjunction with his friend Mr. Robert Carter, the publication of *The Pioneer, a Literary and Critical Magazine*, which, though published in the form of a fashionable illustrated magazine, was of too fine a cast to be successful. But three monthly numbers were issued: they contained choice articles from Poe, Neal, Hawthorne, Parsons, Dwight, and others, including the editors. This unsuccessful speculation was an episode in a brief career at the bar, which Mr. Lowell soon relinquished for a literary life. The reception of Mr. Lowell's first poetic volume had been favorable, and encouraged the author's next adventure, a volume containing the *Legend of Brittany, Miscellaneous Poems and Sonnets*, in 1844. There was a rapid advance in art in these pages, and a profounder study of passion. The leading poem is such a story as would have engaged the heart of Shelley or Keats. A country maiden is betrayed and murdered by a knightly lover. Her corpse is concealed behind the church altar, and the guilty presence made known on a festival day by a voice demanding baptism for the unborn babe in its embrace. The murderer is struck with remorse, and ends his days in repentance. The story thus outlined is delicately told, and its repulsiveness overcome by the graces of poetry and feeling with which it is invested in the character of the heroine Margaret. The poem in blank verse entitled *Prometheus*, which followed the legend in the volume, afforded new proof of the author's ability. It is mature in thought and expression, and instinct with a lofty imagination. The prophecy of the triumph of love, humanity, and civilization, over the brute and sensual power of Jove, is a fine modern improvement of the old fable. The apologue of *Rhœcus* is also in a delicate, classical spirit.

The next year Mr. Lowell gave the public a volume of prose essays—a series of critical and æsthetic *Conversations on some of the Old Poets*, Chaucer and the dramatists Chapman and Ford being the vehicles for introducing a liberal stock of reflections on life and literature generally. It is a book of essays, displaying a subtle knowledge of English literature, to which the form of dialogue is rather an incumbrance.

Another series of *Poems*, containing the spirit of the author's previous volume, followed in 1848. About the same time appeared *The Vision of Sir Launfal*, founded on a legend of a search for the San Greal. The knight in his dream discovers charity to the suffering to be the holy cup.

As a diversion to the pursuit of sentimental poetry, Mr. Lowell at the close of the year sent forth a rhyming estimate of contemporaries in a *Fable for Critics*, which, though not without some puerilities, contains a series of sharply drawn portraits in felicitous verse.

The Biglow Papers, edited with an Introduction, Notes, Glossary, and Copious Index, complete the record of this busy year. The book purports to be written by Homer Wilbur, A.M., Pastor of the First Church in Jaalam and (prospective) Member of many Literary, Learned, and Scientific Societies. It is cast in the Yankee dialect, and is quite an artistic product in that peculiar lingo. The subject is an exposure of the political pretences and shifts which accompanied the war with Mexico, the satire being directed against war and slavery. It is original in style and pungent in effect.

This is Mr. Lowell's last published volume, his time having been since occupied in a residence abroad, though he has occasionally written for the North American Review, Putnam's Magazine, and other journals, and was for a time a stated contributor to the Anti-slavery Standard.

He was married in December, 1844, to Miss Maria White, of Watertown, a lady whose literary genius, as exhibited in a posthumous volume privately printed by her husband in 1855, deserves a record in these pages. She was born July 8, 1821, and died October 27, 1853. We quote from the memorial volume alluded to, which is occupied with a few delicately simple poems of her composition, chiefly divided between records of foreign travel and domestic pathos, this touching expression of resignation:—

THE ALPINE SHEEP—ADDRESSED TO A FRIEND AFTER THE LOSS OF A CHILD.

When on my ear your loss was knelled,
And tender sympathy upburst,
A little spring from memory welled,
Which once had quenched my bitter thirst,

And I was fain to bear to you
A portion of its mild relief,
That it might be a healing dew,
To steal some fever from your grief.

After our child's untroubled breath
Up to the Father took its way,
And on our home the shade of Death,
Like a long twilight haunting lay,

And friends came round, with us to weep
Her little spirit's swift remove,
The story of the Alpine sheep
Was told to us by one we love.

They, in the valley's sheltering care,
Soon crop the meadows' tender prime,
And when the sod grows brown and bare,
The Shepherd strives to make them climb

To airy shelves of pasture green,
That hang along the mountain's side,
Where grass and flowers together lean,
And down through mist the sunbeams slide.

But naught can tempt the timid things
The steep and rugged path to try,
Though sweet the shepherd calls and sings,
And seared below the pastures lie,

Till in his arms his lambs he takes,
Along the dizzy verge to go,
Then, heedless of the rifts and breaks,
They follow on o'er rock and snow.

And in those pastures, lifted fair,
More dewy-soft than lowland mead,
The shepherd drops his tender care,
And sheep and lambs together feed.

This parable, by Nature breathed,
Blew on me as the south-wind free

O'er frozen brooks, that flow unsheathed
From icy thraldom to the sea.

A blissful vision, through the night
Would all my happy senses sway
Of the Good Shepherd on the height,
Or climbing up the starry way,

Holding our little lamb asleep,
While, like the murmur of the sea,
Sounded that voice along the deep,
Saying, "Arise and follow me."

It is to the death of Maria Lowell, at Cambridge, that Mr. Longfellow alludes in his poem published in Putnam's Magazine in April, 1854, entitled

THE TWO ANGELS.

Two angels, one of Life, and one of Death,
Passed o'er the village as the morning broke;
The dawn was on their faces, and beneath,
The sombre houses hearsed with plumes of smoke.

Their attitude and aspect were the same,
Alike their features and their robes of white;
But one was crowned with amaranth, as with flame,
And one with asphodels, like flakes of light.

I saw them pause on their celestial way,
Then said I, with deep fear and doubt oppressed,
"Beat not so loud, my heart, lest thou betray
The place where thy beloved are at rest!"

And he who wore the crown of asphodels,
Descending, at my door began to knock,
And my soul sank within me, as in wells
The waters sink before an earthquake's shock.

I recognised the nameless agony,
The terror and the tremor and the pain,
That oft before had filled and haunted me,
And now returned with threefold strength again.

The door I opened to my heavenly guest,
And listened, for I thought I heard God's voice,
And knowing whatsoe'er he sent was best,
Dared neither to lament nor to rejoice.

Then with a smile that filled the house with light,
"My errand is not Death, but Life," he said,
And ere I answered, passing out of sight
On his celestial embassy he sped.

'Twas at thy door, O friend! and not at mine,
The angel with the amaranthine wreath,
Pausing, descended, and with voice divine,
Whispered a word that had a sound like Death.

Then fell upon the house a sudden gloom,
A shadow on those features fair and thin,
And softly, from that hushed and darkened room,
Two angels issued, where but one went in.

All is of God! If he but wave his hand,
The mists collect, the rain falls thick and loud,
Till with a smile of light on sea and land,
Lo! he looks back from the departing cloud.

Angels of Life and Death alike are His;
Without his leave they pass no threshold o'er;
Who then would wish or dare, believing this,
Against his messengers to shut the door?

In 1854 Mr. Lowell delivered a course of lectures before the Lowell Institute on English Poetry, including the old ballad writers Chaucer, Pope, and others, to Wordsworth and Tennyson. They were marked by an acute critical spirit and enlivened by wit and fancy.

Mr. Lowell has edited the poems of Andrew Marvell and Donne in the series of Messrs. Little & Brown's standard edition of the English poets.

Early in 1855 he was appointed to the Belles Lettres professorship lately held by Mr. Longfellow in Harvard College, with the privilege of passing a preliminary year in Europe before entering on its duties.

MARGARET—FROM THE LEGEND OF BRITTANY.

Fair as a summer dream was Margaret,—
Such dream as in a poet's soul might start
Musing of old loves while the moon doth set:
Her hair was not more sunny than her heart,
Though like a natural golden coronet
It circled her dear head with careless art,
Mocking the sunshine, that would fain have lent
To its frank grace a richer ornament.

His loved-one's eyes could poet ever speak,
So kind, so dewy, and so deep were hers,—
But, while he strives, the choicest phrase too weak,
Their glad reflection in his spirit blurs;
As one may see a dream dissolve and break
Out of his grasp when he to tell it stirs,
Like that sad Dryad doomed no more to bless
The mortal who revealed her loveliness.

She dwelt for ever in a region bright,
Peopled with living fancies of her own,
Where nought could come but visions of delight,
Far, far aloof from earth's eternal moan;
A summer cloud thrilled through with rosy light,
Floating beneath the blue sky all alone,
Her spirit wandered by itself, and won
A golden edge from some unsetting sun.

The heart grows richer that its lot is poor,—
God blesses want with larger sympathies,—
Love enters gladliest at the humble door,
And makes the cot a palace with his eyes;—
So Margaret's heart a softer beauty wore,
And grew in gentleness and patience wise,
For she was but a simple herdsman's child,
A lily chance-sown in the rugged wild.

There was no beauty of the wood or field
But she its fragrant bosom-secret knew,
Nor any but to her would freely yield
Some grace that in her soul took root and grew;
Nature to her glowed ever new-revealed,
All rosy-fresh with innocent morning dew,
And looked into her heart with dim, sweet eyes
That left it full of sylvan memories.

O, what a face was hers to brighten light,
And give back sunshine with an added glow,
To wile each moment with a fresh delight,
And part of memory's best contentment grow!
O, how her voice, as with an inmate's right,
Into the strangest heart would welcome go,
And make it sweet, and ready to become
Of white and gracious thoughts the chosen home!

None looked upon her but he straightway thought
Of all the greenest depths of country cheer,
And into each one's heart was freshly brought
What was to him the sweetest time of year
So was her every look and motion fraught
With out-of-door delights and forest lere;
Not the first violet on a woodland lea
Seemed a more visible gift of spring than she.

AN INCIDENT IN A RAILROAD CAR.

He spoke of Burns: men rude and rough
Pressed round to hear the praise of one
Whose heart was made of manly, simple stuff
As homespun as their own.

And, when he read, they forward leaned,
Drinking, with thirsty hearts and ears,
His brook-like songs whom glory never weaned
From humble smiles and tears.

Slowly there grew a tender awe,
Sun-like, o'er faces brown and hard,
As if in him who read they felt and saw
Some presence of the bard.

It was a sight for sin and wrong
And slavish tyranny to see,
A sight to make our faith more pure and strong
In high humanity.

I thought, these men will carry hence
Promptings their former life above,
And something of a finer reverence
For beauty, truth, and love.

God scatters love on every side,
Freely among his children all,
And always hearts are lying open wide,
Wherein some grains may fall.

There is no wind but soweth seeds
Of a more true and open life,
Which burst, unlooked-for, into high-souled deeds,
With wayside beauty rife.

We find within these souls of ours
Some wild germs of a higher birth,
Which in the poet's tropic heart bear flowers
Whose fragrance fills the earth.

Within the hearts of all men lie
These promises of wider bliss.
Which blossom into hopes that cannot die,
In sunny hours like this.

All that hath been majestical
In life or death, since time began,
Is native in the simple heart of all,
The angel heart of man.

And thus, among the untaught poor,
Great deeds and feelings find a home,
That cast in shadow all the golden lore
Of classic Greece and Rome.

O, mighty brother-soul of man,
Where'er thou art, in low or high,
Thy skyey arches with exulting span
O'er-roof infinity!

All thoughts that mould the age begin
Deep down within the primitive soul,
And from the many slowly upward win
To one who grasps the whole:

In his broad breast the feeling deep
That struggled on the many's tongue,
Swells to a tide of thought, whose surges leap
O'er the weak thrones of wrong.

All thought begins in feeling,—wide
In the great mass its base is hid,
And, narrowing up to thought, stands glorified
A moveless pyramid.

Nor is he far astray who deems
That every hope, which rises and grows broad
In the world's heart, by ordered impulse streams
From the great heart of God.

God wills, man hopes: in common souls
Hope is but vague and undefined,
Till from the poet's tongue the message rolls
A blessing to his kind.

Never did Poesy appear
So full of heaven to me, as when
I saw how it would pierce through pride and fear
To the lives of coarsest men.

It may be glorious to write
Thoughts that shall glad the two or three
High souls, like those far stars that come in sight
Once in a century;—

But better far it is to speak
One simple word, which now and then
Shall waken their free nature in the weak
And friendless sons of men;

To write some earnest verse or line,
Which, seeking not the praise of art,
Shall make a clearer faith and manhood shine
In the untutored heart.

He who doth this, in verse or prose,
May be forgotten in his day,
But surely shall be crowned at last with those
Who live and speak for aye.

THE FIRST SNOW FALL.

The snow had begun in the gloaming,
And busily all the night
Had been heaping field and highway
With a silence deep and white.

Every pine and fir and hemlock
Wore ermine too dear for an earl,
And the poorest twig on the elm-tree
Was ridged inch-deep with pearl.

From sheds, new-roofed with Carrara,
Came chanticleer's muffled crow,
The stiff rails were softened to swan's-down,
And still fluttered down the snow.

I stood and watched by the window
The noiseless work of the sky,
And the sudden flurries of snow-birds
Like brown leaves whirling by.

I thought of a mound in sweet Auburn
Where a little headstone stood,
How the flakes were folding it gently,
As did robins the babes in the wood.

Up spoke our own little Mabel,
Saying, "Father, who makes it snow?"
And I told of the good Allfather
Who cares for us all below.

Again I looked at the snowfall,
And thought of the leaden sky
That arched o'er our first great sorrow,
When that mound was heaped so high.

I remembered the gradual patience
That fell from that cloud like snow,
Flake by flake, healing and hiding
The scar of that deep-stabbed woe.

And again to the child I whispered.
"The snow that husheth all,
Darling, the merciful Father
Alone can make it fall!"

Then, with eyes that saw not, I kissed her,
And she, kissing back, could not know
That *my* kiss was given to her sister
Folded close under deepening snow.

THE COURTIN'.

Zekle crep' up, quite unbeknown,
An' peeked in thru the winder.
An' there sot Huldy all alone,
'ith no one nigh to hender.

Agin' the chimbly crooknecks hung,
An' in amongst 'em rusted
The old queen's arm thet gran'ther Young
Fetched back from Concord busted.

The wannut logs shot sparkles out
Towards the pootiest, bless her!
An' leetle fires danced all about
The chiny on the dresser.

The very room, coz she was in,
Looked warm from floor to ceilin',
An' she looked full as rosy agin
Es th' apples she was peelin'.

She heerd a foot an' knowed it, tu,
Araspin' on the scraper,—
All ways to once her feelins flew
Like sparks in burnt-up paper.

He kin' o' l'itered on the mat,
Some doubtfle o' the seekle;
His heart kep' goin' pitypat,
But hern went pity Zekle.

WILLIAM W. STORY,

The poet and artist, is the son of the late Judge Story. He was born in Salem, February 19, 1819. He became a graduate of Harvard in 1838, and applied himself diligently, under his father's auspices, to the study of the law. He was a frequent contributor, in prose and verse, to the Boston Miscellany, edited by Mr. Nathan Hale, in 1842. In his legal career he published *Reports of Cases argued and determined in the Circuit Court of the United States for the First Circuit*, 2 vols. Boston, 1842–5, and *A Treatise on the Law of Contracts not under Seal*, Boston, 1844.

In the last year he delivered the Phi Beta Kappa poem at Harvard, *Nature and Art*, an indication of the tastes which were to govern his future life.

His single volume of *Poems* was published by Messrs. Little and Brown in 1847. They are the productions of a man of cultivated taste, and of a quick susceptibility to impressions of the ideal.

In 1851 Mr. Story discharged an honorable debt to the memory of his father, in the publication of the two diligently prepared volumes of *The Life and Letters of Joseph Story*, a full, genial biography, written with enthusiasm and fidelity.

It was at this period, or earlier, that Mr. Story turned his attention particularly to art, in which he has achieved much distinction as a sculptor. He has resided for some time in Italy. Among his works, as an artist, are an admired statue of his father, and various busts in marble, including one of his friend Mr. J. R. Lowell. He has modelled a "Shepherd Boy," "Little Red Riding Hood," and other works. Besides achieving success in these varied pursuits of law, letters, and art, Mr. Story is an accomplished musician.

CHILDHOOD.

Along my wall in golden splendor stream
The morning rays,
As when they woke me from the happy dream
Of childish days.

Then every morning brought a sweet surprise,—
When I was young—
Even as a lark, that carols to the skies,
My spirit sung.

To lie with early-wakened eyes, and hear
The busy clock,
While through our laughter, sounded shrilly clear
The crowing cock—
To count the yellow bars of light, that fell
Through the closed blind,
Was joy enough—O, strange and magic spell!
A guileless mind.

The cares of day have thickened round me since—
The morning brings
Work, duties—and that wondering innocence
Hath taken wings.

Dear were those thoughtless hours, whose sunny change
Had gleams of heaven!
But dearer Duty's ever-widening range,
Which Thought hath given!

MIDNIGHT.

Midnight in the sleeping city! Clanking hammers beat no more;
For a space the hum and tumult of the busy day are o'er.

Streets are lonely and deserted, where the sickly lamplights glare,—
And the steps of some late passer only break the silence there.

Round the grim and dusky houses, gloomy shadows nestling cower,
Night hath stifled life's deep humming into slumber for an hour.

Sullen furnace fires are glowing over in the suburbs far,
And the lamp in many a homestead shineth like an earthly star.

O'er the hushed and sleeping city, in the cloudless sky above,
Never-fading stars hang watching in eternal peace and love.

Years and centuries have vanished, change hath come to bury change,
But the starry constellations on their silent pathway range.

Great Orion's starry girdle—Berenice's golden hair—
Ariadne's crown of splendor—Cassiopeia's shining chair;

Sagittarius and Delphinus, and the clustering Pleiad train,
Aquila and Ophiucus, Pegasus and Charles's Wain;

Red Antares and Capella, Aldebaran's mystic light,
Alruccabah and Arcturus, Sirius and Vega white;

They are circling calm as ever on their sure but hidden path,
As when mystic watchers saw them with the reverent eye of Faith.

So unto the soul benighted, lofty stars there are, that shine
Far above the mists of error, with a changeless light divine.

Lofty souls of old beheld them, burning in life's shadowy night,
And they still are undecaying 'mid a thousand centuries' flight.

Love and Truth, whose light and blessing, every reverent heart may know,
Mercy, Justice, which are pillars that support this life below;

These in sorrow and in darkness, in the inmost soul we feel,
As the sure, undying impress of the Almighty's burning seal.

Though unsolved the mighty secret, which shall thread the perfect whole,
And unite the finite number unto the eternal soul,
We shall one day clearly see it—for the soul a time shall come,
When unfranchised and unburdened, thought shall be its only home;—
And Truth's fitful intimations, glancing on our fearful sight,
Shall be gathered to the circle of one mighty disk of light.

EDWIN PERCY WHIPPLE

Was born at Gloucester, Massachusetts, March 8, 1819. His father, Matthew Whipple, who died while the son was in his infancy, is described as possessing "strong sense, and fine social powers." One of his ancestors was a signer of the Declaration of Independence. His mother, Lydia Gardiner, was of a family in Maine noted for its mental powers. She early removed to Salem, Massachusetts, where her son was educated at the English High School. At fourteen he published articles in a Salem newspaper; and at fifteen, on leaving school, became a clerk in the Bank of General Interest in that city. He was next employed, in 1837, in the office of a large broker's firm of Boston, and shortly was appointed Superintendent of the News Room of the Merchants' Exchange in State street. He had been a prominent member of the Mercantile Library Association, and one of a club of six which grew out of it, which held its sessions known as "The Attic Nights," for literary exercises and debate. There Whipple was a leader in the display of his quick intellectual fence and repartee, extensive stores of reading, and subtle and copious critical faculty. In 1840 he was introduced to the public by the delivery of a poem before the Mercantile Association, sketching the manners and satirizing the absurdities of the day, according to the standard manner of these productions, which will be hereafter sought for as valuable illustrations of the times. A critical article from his pen, on Macaulay, in the Boston Miscellany for February, 1843, attracted considerable attention. In October of that year, his lecture on the Lives of Authors was delivered before the Mercantile Library Association, and from that time he has been prominently before the public as a critic and lecturer, in the leading journals, and at the chief lyceums in the country. He has written in the *North American Review*, *The American Review*, *Christian Examiner*, *Graham's Magazine*, and other journals, extensive series of articles on the classical English authors and historical, biographical, and social topics, marked by their acute characterization and fertility of illustration. His lectures, embracing a similar range of subjects, are philosophical in their texture, marked by nice discrimination, occasionally pushing a favorite theory to the verge of paradox; and when the reasoning faculties of his audience are exhausted, relieving the discussion by frequent picked anecdote, and pointed thrusts of wit and satire.

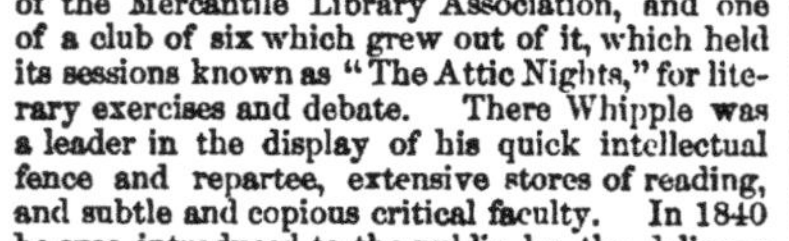

He is greatly in request as a lecturer, has probably lectured a thousand times in the cities and towns of the middle and northern states, from St. Louis to Bangor, has on numerous occasions addressed the literary societies of various Colleges, as Brown, Dartmouth, Amherst, the New York University; and in 1850 was the Fourth of July orator before the city authorities of Boston. Two collections of his writings have been published by Messrs. Ticknor & Fields,—*Essays and Reviews*, in two volumes, and *Lectures on Subjects Connected with Literature and Life*.

THE GENIUS OF WASHINGTON.*

This illustrious man, at once the world's admiration and enigma, we are taught by a fine instinct to venerate, and by a wrong opinion to misjudge. The might of his character has taken strong hold upon the feelings of great masses of men, but in translating this universal sentiment into an intelligent form, the intellectual element of his wonderful nature is as much depressed as the moral element is exalted, and consequently we are apt to misunderstand both. Mediocrity has a bad trick of idealizing itself in eulogising him, and drags him down to its own low level while assuming to lift him to the skies. How many times have we been told that he was not a man of genius, but a person of "excellent common sense," of "admirable judgment," of "rare virtues;" and by a constant repetition of this odious cant, we have nearly succeeded in divorcing comprehension from his sense, insight from his judgment, force from his virtues, and life from the man. Accordingly, in the panegyric of cold spirits, Washington disappears in a cloud of commonplaces; in the rhodomontade of boiling patriots he expires in the agonies of rant. Now the sooner this bundle of mediocre talents and moral qualities, which its contrivers have the audacity to call George Washington, is hissed out of existence, the better it will be for the cause of talent and the cause of morals; contempt of that is the beginning of wisdom. He had no genius, it seems. O no! genius, we must suppose, is the peculiar and shining attribute of some orator, whose tongue can spout patriotic speeches, or some versifier, whose muse can "Hail Columbia," but not of the man who supported states on his arm, and carried America in his brain. The madcap Charles Townsend, the motion of whose pyrotechnic mind was like the whizz of a hundred rockets, is a man of genius; but George Washington, raised up above the level of even eminent statesmen, and with a nature moving with the still and orderly celerity of a planet round its sun,—he dwindles, in comparison, into a kind of angelic dunce? What is genius? Is it worth anything? Is splendid folly the measure of its inspiration? Is wisdom its base and summit,—that which it recedes from, or tends towards? And by what definition do you award the name to the creator of an epic, and deny it to the creator of a country? On what principle is it to be lavished on him who sculptures in perishing marble, the image of possible excellence, and withheld from him who built up in himself a transcendant character, indestructible as the obligations of Duty, and beautiful as her rewards?

Indeed, if by the genius of action you mean will enlightened by intelligence, and intelligence ener-

* From an oration, "Washington and the Principles of the Revolution."

gised by will,—if force and insight be its characteristics, and influence its test,—and, especially, if great effects suppose a cause proportionably great, that is, a vital, causative mind,—then is Washington most assuredly a man of genius, and one whom no other American has equalled in the power of working morally and mentally on other minds. His genius, it is true, was of a peculiar kind, the genius of character, of thought and the objects of thought, solidified and concentrated into active faculty. He belongs to that rare class of men,—rare as Homers and Miltons, rare as Platos and Newtons,—who have impressed their characters upon nations without pampering national vices. Such men have natures broad enough to include all the facts of a people's practical life, and deep enough to discern the spiritual laws which underlie, animate, and govern those facts. Washington, in short, had that greatness of character which is the highest expression and last result of greatness of mind, for there is no method of building up character except through mind. Indeed, character like his is not *built* up, stone upon stone, precept upon precept, but *grows* up, through an actual contact of thought with things,—the assimilative mind transmuting the impalpable but potent spirit of public sentiment, and the life of visible facts, and the power of spiritual laws, into individual life and power, so that their mighty energies put on personality, as it were, and act through one centralizing human will. This process may not, if you please, make the great philosopher, or the great poet, but it does make the great *man*,—the man in whom thought and judgment seem identical with volition,—the man whose vital expression is not in words but deeds,—the man whose sublime ideas issue necessarily in sublime acts, not in sublime art. It was because Washington's character was thus composed of the inmost substance and power of facts and principles, that men instinctively felt the perfect reality of his comprehensive manhood. This reality enforced universal respect, married strength to repose, and threw into his face that commanding majesty, which made men of the speculative audacity of Jefferson, and the lucid genius of Hamilton, recognise, with unwonted meekness, his awful superiority.

CHARLES WILKINS WEBBER

WAS born on the 29th May, 1819, at Russelville, Kentucky. His mother, Agnes Maria Webber, was the daughter of General John Tannehill, and niece of the Hon. William Wilkins, both of Pittsburg. General Tannehill had served with distinction as an officer of the Revolution. His eldest son, Wilkins Tannehill, is known as the author of a book entitled *Sketches of the History of Literature from the Earliest Period to the Revival of Letters in the Fifteenth Century*,* remarkable for its various reading and the spirit which animates it, and the singularity of its production at an early date west of the Alleghanies. The Preface modestly states the author's design, "Prepared during intervals of occasional leisure from the duties of an employment little congenial with literary pursuits, and without any opportunity for consulting extensive libraries, it aspires only to the character of sketches, without pretending to be a complete history. It is an attempt by a 'backwoodsman,' to condense and comprise within a narrow compass, the most prominent and interesting events, connected with the progress of literary and scientific improvement, from the earliest period through a long succession of ages, and amidst a great variety of circumstances." As such it is an exceedingly creditable production. Its author was also for many years editor of the Nashville Herald, the first Clay-Whig paper ever published in Tennessee. This learned, modest, and useful man, having spent the greater portion of his life in close and unremitting literary labors, is now (in 1854) blind and rapidly declining in years. It is understood that his most valuable researches have been in the field of American antiquities.

* Sketches of the History of Literature. from the Earliest Period to the Revival of Letters in the Fifteenth Century. Indocti discant, ament meminisse periti. By Wilkins Tannehill. 8vo. pp. 344. Nashville: John S. Simpson, 1827.

The grandfather, General Tannehill, having met with heavy reverses of fortune, died leaving his family comparatively helpless. In this strait they found a home in the house of a brother of his wife, Charles Wilkins of Lexington, a wealthy and generous gentleman, whose memory is warmly cherished by the older families of that portion of Kentucky. The children were educated with great care, and the daughters grew up to be accomplished women. After the death of their uncle they removed with their mother to Nashville, to reside with her eldest son, Wilkins Tannehill. Here the eldest daughter married, and on her removing to the new town of Hopkinsville, Ky., was accompanied by her young sister Agnes, who became the wife of a physician from North Kentucky, Doctor Augustine Webber.

Of this marriage C. W. Webber was the second child, and first son. For forty years past Dr. Webber has stood prominent in his profession in South Kentucky, and has been noted as an intelligent, liberal, and devoted churchman and Whig.

It is, however, to his mother, a lady of great beauty of character, that C. W. Webber is most indebted for his early tastes. The education which her son received as the companion of her artistic excursions, for she possessed a natural genius for art, into the natural world, determined in a great measure the character of his future pursuits.

His early life, to his nineteenth year, was spent in miscellaneous study and the sports of the field, when, after the death of his mother, we find him wandering upon the troubled frontier of Texas. He soon became associated with the celebrated Colonel Jack Hays, Major Chevalier, Fitzgerald, &c., whose names are noted as forming the nucleus around which the famous Ranger Organization was constituted. After several years spent here, in singular adventures—many of which have been given to the world in his earlier books, *Old Hicks the Guide*, *Shot in the Eye*, and *Gold Mines of the Gila*—he returned to his family in Kentucky. He now further prosecuted his study of medicine, upon which he had originally entered with the design of making it his profession.

Becoming, however, deeply interested in controversial matters during a period of strong religious excitement which prevailed throughout the whole country, he entered the Princeton Theological Seminary as a candidate for the ministry. He, however, remained there but a short time.

From this time, his pen was to be his sole dependence. He had already tried its point in an article which appeared in the Nassau Monthly, which was edited by a committee of students. This paper was called "Imagination, and the Soul," and had attracted considerable attention both in the College and in the Seminary.

Arrived in New York, his first night was spent at "Minnie's Land," the residence of Audubon, whose acquaintance he had previously formed during the last Rocky Mountain tour of the old Naturalist, for whose character, from a similarity of tastes, he had nourished a most enthusiastic admiration. He listened to the counsel of the venerable sage with affectionate respect. Among other things, Audubon urged upon him to dedicate the best years of his life to the study of the natural history of South America, which he only regretted the want of years to grapple with.

Finding himself at New York utterly without acquaintances who could aid him, he resolved upon introducing himself, and a manuscript which he had prepared, to Mr. Bryant the poet, for whom he had conceived from his writings a high personal admiration, which was fully confirmed by his interview. He found Mr. Bryant at the office of the Evening Post; the poet smiled upon his eager enthusiasm, a self-confidence which had in it a touch of despair, and kept his manuscript for perusal. The result, the next day, was a letter of introduction to Winchester the publisher, who immediately engaged from the young writer a series of papers on "Texan Adventure" to be published in his flourishing newspaper, the New World.

On the failure of Winchester in his bold but rash conflict with the Harpers, Mr. Webber was again thrown out of employment, but was soon engaged in writing a number of sketches and other papers for the Democratic Review. The most important of these was called *Instinct, Reason, and Imagination*, and published under the sobriquet of C. Wilkens Eimi. About this time, the story of the *Shot in the Eye*, one of the best known of his productions, was written.

The manuscript was delivered to Mr. O'Sullivan, and after being in his possession for several months, was misplaced and lost sight of by him, and, after a long search, supposed to be irrecoverably lost. The story was then re-written for the Whig Review, and appeared in its second number. But having been unexpectedly found by Mr. O'Sullivan, it was published simultaneously in the Democratic Review, without the knowledge of Mr. Webber.

His connexion with the Whig Review as associate editor and joint proprietor, continued for over two years, in which time the magazine ran up to an unprecedented circulation for one of its class.

The Shot in the Eye, Charles Winterfield Papers, Adventures upon the Frontiers of Texas and Mexico, with a long paper on Hawthorne, are the principal articles by him which will be remembered by the earlier readers of the Review, although a great amount of critical and other miscellaneous matter was comprised within the sum of his editorial labors.

About this time, Mr. Webber was a contributor to the early numbers of the Literary World of papers on Western Life and Natural History.

He contracted also with the Sunday Despatch, which was just then commencing, for the story of *Old Hicks the Guide*, which for more than three months occupied the columns of that paper. The copyright of this story was finally sold to the Harpers for two hundred dollars.

C. W. Webber

Mr. Webber's next enterprise was one on a mammoth scale, projected by him in connexion with the two sons of John J. Audubon, the ornithologist. The design was to issue a magnificent monthly of large size, to be illustrated in each number by a splendid copperplate colored engraving, taken from a series of unpublished pictures by the elder Audubon, and to be edited by Mr. Webber. Only the first number was ever completed, and it was never published, owing to the many discouragements growing out of the protracted illness of John Woodhouse Audubon, and his immediate departure, while convalescing, with a view to the permanent restoration of his health, by overland travel to California. The immense expense which it was found would attend the prosecution of the work had also its effect in deterring its issue. Among the contributors to this first number were Hawthorne, Whipple, Headley, Street, Constable, Wallace, &c. The leading paper, *Eagles and Art*, was by Mr. Webber.

In the meantime he continued to write occasionally for the Democratic Review, Graham's Magazine, &c. In March, 1849, simultaneously with the discovery of gold in California, appeared the *Gold Mines of the Gila*, all but a few concluding chapters of which he had written several years previously. This work was considered by the author rather as a voluminous prospectus of an enterprise of exploration to the gold region, once attempted during his Texan experiences, and now again projected in the Centralia Exploring Expedition, than as a formal book. To the chivalrous appeal, dedicated to the ladies of America, and addressed to its young men for their coöperation in the dangerous effort to resolve by examination the mystery of the unknown region lying between the river Gila and the Colorado of the West, there was a ready response. The required number of young men from all parts of the country had expressed their readiness to participate in the enterprise, under the leadership of Mr. Webber. Preparations were very far advanced, and the journey to New Orleans commenced, when, on arriving at Washington, he was met by the news of the loss of all the horses of the expedition, which had been collected at Corpus Christi to await their arrival. The Camanches carried off every animal, and, as they had been collected from the mountains at great trouble and as peculiarly adapted for this service, the loss proved irretrievable. The news of the ravages of the cholera along the whole line of the South-western border completed the defeat of the projected rendezvous.

Mr. Webber instantly commenced a new movement, by which he hoped to effect this purpose. The experiences of this year of the utter insufficiency of the means of transportation across the great desert to the gold regions, as limited to the horse, ox, and mule, of the country, offered an opening for urging upon the government the project of employing the African and Asiatic camel for such purposes. The vast endurance, capacity for burden, and speed, together with the singular frugality of this animal, seemed to him to indicate its introduction as the great desideratum of service in the South-west. This object has been assiduously pursued by Mr. Webber since 1849, and it may be mentioned as an instance of his perseverance, that he succeeded in obtaining from the last legislature of New York a charter for the organization of a camel company, and that the Secretary of War has warmly recommended the project to Congress in an official report.

In the meantime, the literary labors of Mr. Webber have by no means been suspended. His marriage, which occurred in Boston in 1849, had furnished him with an artistic collaborator in his wife. With her assistance, as the artist of many of its abundant illustrations, the first volume of *The Hunter Naturalist* was completed, and published in the fall of 1851 by Lippincott, Grambo & Co.

The prosecution of this work, to be continued through a series of volumes, was impeded by the author's serious illness, in spite of which, however, he succeeded in getting out, during the year 1852, two new books—*Spiritual Vampirism*, in which the heretical *isms* of the day are made the subject of dramatic and withering exposure, and *Tales of the Southern Border*, both of which were published by Lippincott & Co.

In the fall of 1853 the second volume of the Hunter Naturalist—*Wild Scenes and Song Birds*—appeared from the press of G. P. Putnam & Co. Of this Mrs. Webber was also the Natural History illustrator.

Mr. Webber's style is full, rapid, and impulsive, combining a healthy sense of animal life and out-of-door sensation, with inner poetical reflection. His narrative is borne along no less by his mental enthusiasm than by the lively action of its stirring Western themes. As a critic, many of his papers have shown a subtle perception with a glowing reproduction of the genius of his author.

A NIGHT HUNT IN KENTUCKY—FROM WILD SCENES AND WILD HUNTERS.

Now the scene has burst upon us through an opening of the trees!—There they are! Negroes of all degrees, size, and age, and of dogs—

> Mastiff, greyhound, mongrel grim,
> Hound or spaniel, brack or lym,
> Or bobtail tike, or trundle tail.

All are there, in one conglomerate of active, noisy confusion. When indications of the hurried approach of our company are perceived, a great accession to the hubbub is consequential.

Old Sambo sounds a shriller note upon his horn, the dogs rise from independent howls to a simultaneous yell, and along with all the young half-naked darkies rush to meet us. The women come to the doors with their blazing lamps lifted above their heads, that they may get a look at the "young masters," and we, shouting with excitement, and blinded by the light, plunge stumbling through the meeting current of dogs and young negroes, into the midst of the gathering party. Here we are suddenly arrested by a sort of awe as we find ourselves in the presence of old Sambo. The young dogs leap upon us with their dirty fore-paws, but we merely push aside their caresses, for old Sambo and his old dog Bose are the two centres of our admiration and interest.

Old Sambo is the "Mighty Hunter before"—*the moon!* of all that region. He is seamed and scarred with the pitiless siege of sixty winters! Upon all matters appertaining to such hunts, his word is "*law*," while the "tongue" of his favorite and ancient friend Bose is recognised as "*gospel*." In our young imaginations, the two are respectfully identified.

Old Sambo, with his blanket "roundabout"—his cow's-horn trumpet slung about his shoulders by a tow string—his bare head, with its greyish fleece of wool—the broad grin of complacency, showing his yet sound white teeth—and rolling the whites of his eyes benignantly over the turmoil of the scene—was to us the higher prototype of Bose. He, with the proper slowness of dignity, accepts the greet of our patting caresses, with a formal wagging of the tail, which seems to say—"O, I am used to this!" while, when the young dogs leap upon him with obstreperous fawnings, he will correct them into propriety with stately snarling. They knew him for their leader!—they should be more respectful!

Now old Sambo becomes patronizing to *us*, as is necessary and proper in our new relations! From his official position of commander-in-chief, he soon reduces the chaos around us into something like subjection, and then in a little time comes forth the form of our night's march. A few stout young men who have obeyed his summons have gathered around him from the different huts of the Quarter—some with axes, and others with torches of pine and bark. The dogs become more restless, and we more excited, as these indices of immediate action appear.

Now, with a long blast from the cow's horn of Sambo, and a deafening clamor of all sizes, high and low—from men, women, children, and dogs, we take up the line of march for the woods. Sambo leads, of course. We are soon trailing after him in single file, led by the glimmer of the torches far ahead.

Now the open ground of the plantation has been passed, and as we approach the deep gloom of the bordering forest—

> Those perplexed woods,
> The nodding horror of whose shady brows
> Threats the forlorn and wandering passenger—

even the yelpings of the excited dogs cease to be heard, and they dash on into the darkness as if they were going to work—while we with our joyous chattering subsided into silence, enter these "long-drawn aisles" with a sort of shiver; the torches showing, as we pass in a dim light, the trees—their huge trunks vaulting over head into the night, with here and there a star shining like a gem set into their tall branching capitals—while on either side we look into depths of blackness as unutterably dreary to us as thoughts of death and nothingness. Oh, it was in half trembling wonder then, we crowded, trampling on the heels of those before, and, when after awhile the rude young negroes would begin to laugh aloud, we felt that in some sort it was profane.

But such impressions never lasted long in those days. Every other mood and thought gives way to the novelty and contagious excitement of adventure. We are soon using our lungs as merrily as the rest. The older dogs seem to know perfectly, from the direction taken, what was the game to be pursued for the night. Had we gone up by the old Field where the Persimmon trees grow, they would have understood that "possums" were to be had; but as old Sambo led off through the deep woods towards the swamps, it said "coons" to them as plain as if they had been Whigs of 1840.

The flush of blood begins to subside as we penetrate deeper into the wood, and as we hear old Sambo shout to his staff officers and immediate rear guard, "Hush dat 'ar jawing, you niggers, dar," we take it for granted that it is a hint, meant not to be disrespected by *us*, that silence is necessary, lest we should startle the game too soon and confuse the dogs.

All is silence now, except the rustle of our tramp over the dried autumn leaves, and occasional patter of the feet of a dog who ranges near to our path. Occasionally a white dog comes suddenly out of the darkness into view and disappears as soon, leaving our imagination startled as if some curious sprite had come "momently" from out its silent haunts to peep at us. Then we will hear the rustling of some rapid thing behind us, and looking round, see nothing; then spring aside with a nervous bound and fluttering pulse, as some black object brushes by our legs—"Nothin' but dat dog, Nigger Trimbush," chuckles a darkie, who observed us—but the couplet,—

> And the kelpie must flit from the black bog pit,
> And the brownie must not tarry,

flashes across our memory from the romance of superstition, with the half shudder that is the accompaniment of such dreamy images.

Hark, a dog opens—another, then another! We are still in a moment, listening—all eyes are turned upon old Sambo, the oracle. He only pauses for a minute.

"Dem's de pups—ole dogs aint dar!" A pause. "Pshaw, nothin but a ole har!"—and a long, loud blast of the horn sounds the recall.

We move on—and now the frosty night air has become chilly, and we begin to feel that we have something to do before us. Our legs are plied too lustily on the go-ahead principle for us to have time to talk. The young dogs have ceased to give tongue; for like unruly children they have dashed off in chase of what came first, and as the American hare ("*Lepus Americanus*") is found nearly everywhere, it was the earliest object.

Just when the darkness is most deep, and the sounds about our way most hushed, up wheels the silver moon, and with a mellowed glory overcomes the night. The weight of darkness has been lifted from us, and we trudge along more cheerily! The dogs are making wider ranges, and we hear nothing of them. The silence weighs upon us, and old Sambo gives an occasional whoop of encouragement. We would like, too, to relieve our lungs, but *he* says, "nobody mus holler now but dem dat de dog knows: make 'em bother!" We must perforce be quiet; for "*de dog*" means Bose, and we must be deferential to his humors!

Tramp, tramp, tramp, it has been for miles, and not a note from the dogs. We are beginning to be fatigued; our spirits sink, and we have visions of the warm room and bed we have deserted at home. The torches are burning down, and the cold, pale moon-light is stronger than that they give. One after another the young dogs come panting back to us, and fall lazily into our wake. "Hang coon hunts in general!—this is no joke; all cry and no wool!"

Hark! a deep-mouthed, distant bay! The sound is electrical; our impatience and fatigue are gone! All ears and eyes, we crowd around old Sambo. The oracle attitudinizes. He leans forward with one ear turned towards the earth in the direction of the sound. Breathlessly we gaze upon him. Hark! another bay; another; then several join in. The old man has been unconsciously soliloquizing from the first sound.

"Golly, dat's nigger Trim!" in an under tone; "he know de coon!" Next sound. "Dat's a pup; shaw!" Pause. "Dat's a pup, agin! Oh, niggers, no coon dar!"

Lifting his outspread hand, which he brings down with a loud slap upon his thigh; "Yah! yah! dat's ole Music; look out, niggers!" Then, as a hoarse, low bay comes booming to us through a pause, he bounds into the air with the caperish agility of a colt, and breaks out in ecstasy, "Whoop! whoop! dat's de ole dog; go my Bose!" Then striking hurriedly through the brush in the direction of the sounds, we only hear from him again,

"Yah! yah! yah! dat's a coon, niggers! Bose dar!" And away we rush as fast as we can scramble through the underbrush of the thick wood. The loud burst of the whole pack opening together, drowns even the noise of our progress.

The cry of a full pack is maddening music to the hunter. Fatigue is forgotten, and obstacles are nothing. On we go; yelling in chorus with the dogs. Our direction is towards the swamp, and they are fast hurrying to its fastnesses. But what do we care! Briars and logs; the brush of dead trees; plunges half leg deep into the watery mire of boggy places are alike disregarded. The game is up! Hurrah! hurrah! we must be in at the death! So we scurry, led by the maddening chorus—

> —while the babbling echo mocks the hounds.

Suddenly the reverberations die away. Old Sambo halts. When we get into ear-shot the only word we hear is "Tree'd!" This from the oracle is sufficient. We have another long scramble, in which we are led by the monotonous baying of a single dog.

We have reached the place at last all breathless. Our torches have been nearly extinguished. One of the young dogs is seated at the foot of a tree, and looking up, it bays incessantly. Old Sambo pauses for awhile to survey the scene. The old dogs are circling round and round, jumping up against the side of every tree, smelling as high as they can reach. They are not satisfied, and Sambo waits for *his* tried oracles to solve the mystery. He regards them steadily and patiently for awhile; then steps forward quickly, and beats off the young dog who had "lied" at the "tree."

The veterans now have a quiet field to themselves, and after some further delay in jumping up the sides of the surrounding trees, to find the scent, they finally open in full burst upon the trail. Old Sambo exclaims curtly, as we set off in the new chase,

"Dat looks like coon! *but cats is about!*"

Now the whole pack opens again, and we are off after it. We all understand the allusion to the *cats*, for we know that, like the raccoon, this animal endeavors to baffle the dogs by running some distance up a tree, and then springing off upon another, and so on until it can safely descend. The young dogs take it for granted that he is in the first tree, while the older ones sweep circling round and round until they are convinced that the animal has not escaped. They thus baffle the common trick which they have learned through long experience, and recovering the trail of escape, renew the chase.

Under ordinary circumstances we would already have been sufficiently exhausted, but the magnetism of the scene lifts our feet as if they had been shod with wings. Another weary scramble over every provoking obstacle, and the solitary baying of a dog is heard again winding up the "cry."

When we reached the "tree" this time, and find it is another "feint," we are entirely disheartened, and all this excitement and fatigue of the night reacting upon us leaves us utterly exhausted, and disinclined to budge one foot further. Old Sambo comes up—he has watched with an astute phiz the movements of the dogs for some time.

"Thought dat ware a *ole* coon from de fust! Dat's a mighty ole coon!" with a dubious shake of his head. "*Ole* coon nebber run dat long!" Another shake of the head, and addressing himself to his "staff:" "Ole coon nebber run'ed dis fur, niggers!" Then turning to us—"Massas, dat a cat!—'taint no coon!"

The dogs break out again, at the same moment, and with peculiar fierceness, in full cry. "Come 'long, niggers!—maby dat's a coon—maby 'taint!" and off he starts again.

We are electrified by the scenes and sounds once more, and "follow, still follow," forgetting everything in the renewed hubbub and excitement. Wearily now we go again over marsh and quagmire, bog and pond, rushing through vines, and thickets, and dead limbs. Ah, what glimpses have we of our cozy home during this wild chase! Now our strength is gone—we are chilled, and our teeth chatter—the moon seems to be the centre of cold as the sun is of heat, and its beams strike us like arrows of ice. Yet the cry of the dogs is onward, and old Sambo and his staff yell *on!*

Suddenly there is a pause! the dogs are silent, and we hold up! "Is it all lost?" we exclaim, as we stagger, with our bruised and exhausted limbs, to a seat upon an old log. The stillness is as deep as midnight—the owl strikes the watch with his too-whoo! Hah! that same hoarse, deep bay which first electrified us comes booming again through the stillness.

"Yah! yah! dat ole coon am done for! Bose got he, niggers—Gemmen, come on!"

The inspiring announcement, that *Bose* had tree'd at last, is balm to all our wounds, and we follow in the hurry-scurry rush to the tree. Arrived there, we find old Bose on end barking up a great old oak, while the other dogs lie panting around. "Dare he am," says old Sambo. "Make a fire, niggers!" There is but a single stump of a torch left; but in a little while they have collected dried wood enough to kindle a great blaze.

"Which nigger's gwine to climb dat tree?" says old Sambo, looking round inquiringly. Nobody answers. The insinuations he had thrown out, that it *might* be a cat, have had their effect upon the younger darkies. Sambo waits, in dignified silence, for an answer, and throwing off his horn, with an indignant gesture, he says,—

"You d—n pack of chicken-gizzards, niggers!—climb de tree myself!" and straightway the wiry old man, with the activity of a boy, springs against the huge trunk, and commences to ascend the tree.

Bose gives an occasional low yelp as he looks after his master. The other dogs sit with upturned noses, and on restless haunches, as they watch his ascent.

Nothing is heard for some time, but the fall of dead branches and bark which he throws down. The fire blazes high, and the darkness about us, beyond its light, is unpenetrated even by the moon. We stand in eager groups watching his ascent. He is soon lost to our view amongst the limbs; yet we watch on until our necks ache, while the eager dogs fidget on their haunches, and emit short yelps of impatience. We see him, against the moon, far up amongst the uppermost forks, creeping like a beetle, up, still up! We are all on fire—the whole fatigue and all the bruises of the chase forgotten! our fire crackles and blazes fiercely as our impatience, and sends quick tongues of light, piercing the black throng of forest sentinels about us.

Suddenly the topmost branches of the great oak begin to shake, and seem to be lashing the face of the moon.

"De cat! de cat! look out down dar!" The dogs burst into an eager howl! He is shaking him off! A dark object comes thumping down into our midst, and shakes the ground with its fall. The eager dogs rush upon it! but we saw the spotted thing with the electric flashing of its eyes. Yells and sputtering screams—the howls of pain—the gnashing growls of assault—the dark, tumbling struggle that is rolled, with its fierce clamors, out from our fire-light into the dark shadows of the wood, are all enough to madden us.

We all rush after the fray, and strike wildly into its midst with the clubs and dead limbs we have snatched, when one of *the* body-guards happens to think of his axe, and with a single blow settles it!

All is over! We get home as we may, and about the time

> —— the dapple grey coursers of the morn
> Beat up the light with their bright silver hoofs,
> And chase it through the sky,

we creep cautiously into our back window, and sleep not the less profoundly for our fatigue, that we have to charge our late hour of rising, next day, upon Bacon or the Iliad, instead of the "Night Hunt."

HENRY AUGUSTUS WISE.

Henry A. Wise, the son of George Stuart Wise, an officer of the United States Navy, was born at Brooklyn, New York, in May, 1819. He is descended on his father's side from an old English royalist family, several of whom were taken prisoners after the "Penruddock rebellion," and sent to Virginia about the year 1665.

At the age of fourteen, young Wise, through the influence of his cousin the present governor of Virginia, was appointed a midshipman, and received his first baptism in salt water under the auspices of Captain John Percival, the Jack Percy of his "Tales for the Marines," with whom he served for five years. Many of the scenes portrayed in his recent sketches were no doubt derived from his early experiences.

After passing his examination, he served in the

naval squadron on the coasts of Florida during the Seminole war; and later on his promotion to a lieutenantcy, in the Pacific, in California and Mexico during the war. On his return to the United States he married the daughter of the Hon. Edward Everett. He has recently completed a cruise in the Mediterranean, where he filled the part of flag-lieutenant to the squadron.

H. A. Wise

In 1849 Lieut. Wise published *Los Gringos.** The title of the book is taken from the epithet used in California and Mexico to describe the descendants of the Anglo-Saxon race, and is nearly equivalent to that of *Greenhorn* in our own language. As far as concerns the author, however, never was the epithet more misapplied; for in the varied scenes and adventures he describes, he is entirely *au fait;* and whether on ship or ashore, "chasing the wild deer" or being chased by the grizzly bear, shooting brigands or dancing fandangoes, swimming with the Sandwich Island girls or "doctoring" interesting young ladies in fits, he is equally at home. "Style," says Buffon, "is the man himself," and we could not have a truer picture of the gay and gallant young officer than he has given in his book.

Los Gringos was followed in 1855 by *Tales for the Marines*, a lively, spirited volume of adventure, humorous, sentimental, and melodramatic, on shipboard, off the coast of Africa, and in Rio Janeiro. Sailors, pirates, slavers, smugglers, senoritas, caymans, boa constrictors, all bear a part in the conduct of an amusing series of adventures, some of which are sufficiently marvellous to try the faith of the proverbially easy of belief class of the service to whom they are especially addressed.

Lieut. Wise possesses a keen eye for the humorous and the picturesque, and writes in an off-hand and spirited style. We present one of the scenes of his sketches. A party of desperadoes, with whom bloody encounters have previously taken place, are surprised by a detachment from the U. S. corvette Juniata.

AN ATTACK—FROM TALES FOR THE MARINES.

Mr. Spuke at this epoch was busy on a little tour of inspection, around the cargoes of the lighters, punching his steel-like knuckles into the sacks of sugar, dipping his claws of fingers into the bung holes of the *pipas* of rum to test the strength by sucking his digits afterwards, then smelling pinches and handfuls of coffee berries, in all which business pursuits he appeared quite at home. Upon his own boat coming on shore again with his copper treasure, he joined the Maltese, and with the assistance of the boy and the black oarsman, the bags were carried up about fifty yards on the beach, midway between the water and the cane huts.

This was no sooner effected than a signal was given to the cornet, and down from their concealment in the bushes ran the squad of sojers, while the fat officer, rushing up, laid his hand on the blue coat with bright brass buttons, which hung over the back of Mr. Spuke. This was the first intimation that individual had of the ambuscade; but, jerking himself free, he exclaimed,—

"By spikes! what on airth air yu abeout?" The suddenness and violence of the movement nearly twitched the officer off his legs.

When Mr. Spuke glanced round, and beheld the militia, with their bayonets at a charge, he seemed to recover himself at once; and striding over the sacks of metal, with his legs wide apart, he said,—

"Wal, ye darn'd Portingees, what air ye up tu? This here is my property, and ther custom-house permits is right and reg'lar—ask them dons theer—all honist folks—no idee on gittin quit of payin the fees."

Here he beckoned to the factors, who, with Mag, came to the spot; and there they stood, in a lump, just as the cutter of the Flirt was dashed alongside of the schooner.

I could not have stood it any longer; but just then Hazy exclaimed, "Now, my friends, it is our turn!" while the padron roared out in Portuguese, "Seize, or shoot down those villains, if they stir an inch. I arrest them for smuggling counterfeit coin." And I screamed to Mag, "Yes, you hag, and I've an account to settle with you for the affair in that den in Rio."

The Maltese was the first who made a bolt; but he had not moved a yard before Hazy's cockswain, Harry Greenfield, fetched him a tap with the gig's brass tiller, which laid him out, as meek as milk, on the strand.

When the combination burst with its real force upon Spuke and his female companion, the latter squinted furtively around, to see, perhaps, if a chance for escape presented itself; but observing all retreat cut off, her ugly mug began to assume a pale-blue, ashes-of-roses hue; and she put her hand in her bosom and partially exposed her tapering knife.

"Drop that, you piratical she-devil, or I'll ——" She must have looked full into the muzzle of the big-mouthed ship's pistol I pointed at her, before she removed her hand from the weapon; and then only to carry the gin jug to her hideous mouth; but she did not utter a word. Not so, however, with Mr. Spuke; he saw the game was up, and that not only his vessel was seized, and his liberty about to be cramped for an indefinite period, but, worse than all, he was to lose all his hard-earned gains.

Taking up the words as they were uttered by the padron, and losing all his drawly, nasal twang, he said, in a cold, deliberate tone,—

"O, ho! there's been spyin' goin' on, and I'm to be robbed, eh? Now, I'm an Ameriken, clear grit! and you, dam yer, my countryman," shaking his hand aloft at Hazy, "air standin' by to see me imposed upon by these cussed merlatters, when it's your dooty to pertect me. But, by spikes! let me see the first feller as 'll ris his finger jint to seize Elnathan Spuke."

With this, he bared his great slabs of arms to the shoulders; and there he stood, a powerful, towering giant,—glaring with the wrinkled, compressed lips, open nostril, and fierce, cunning eye of a tiger, ready for a spring.

"Arrest him, soldiers!" shouted the now excited padron; and the cornet drew his sword. Before, however, the blade was well out of its sheath, the fellow at bay gave him a tremendous kick in the stomach, which sent him fairly spinning up off the sand; and then he fell with a groan, completely *hors de combat*. At the moment the soldiers, who, as I told you, seemed by no means veterans in war, advanced, with fixed bayonets, upon the smuggler. Evading the first two men, he gave a sudden bound,

* Los Gringos; or, An Inside View of Mexico and California, with Wanderings in Peru, Chili, and Polynesia. Baker and Scribner. 12mo. pp. 453.

grasped the musket by the muzzle from the weak arms of one of the puny troop, and, with a deep-muttered imprecation of, "By the Eternal, let her rip," gave the weapon a half sweep over his head; and bringing it round, the foremost men went down like grain before a sickle. Recovering himself again, he made the heavy piece whirl on high, and brought it, for the second time, upon the backs of the panic-stricken soldiers; but the flint-lock catching some part of their equipments, the cock snapped, the piece flashed, held fire an instant, and then exploded full in the face of the Yankee. The charge traversed his upper jaw, nose, and one eye, leaving him blinded, and the blackened blood and powder clinging to his mutilated features. He spun round nearly a turn, by the force of the explosion, yet never relaxed his gripe on the muzzle of the musket, until, with a confused lurch, the breech of the gun touched the sand, and he fell forward with all his weight. The point of the bayonet entered nearly at his breast bone, and transfixed him to the pipe. He fell over sideways, and lay a dead man, deluging in blood the sacks of money he had made such desperate efforts to defend.

By this time the dismayed soldiers, who had turned tail from the one man, began to fire an irregular *feu de joie* right in amongst the crowd of us. They were too wild, however, to do much damage; only grazing the ear of one of the factors, and putting a ball into the foot of the Maltese—and a very severe and painful wound he found it.

During this skrimmage my attention was for a moment diverted from my own especial game; and when I looked again, I saw the hag running like a rat towards the thicket. Makeen fired his pistol at her, but the ball only cut off a twig, and scattered some leaves without touching her. I reserved my shot, and, with a cry that brought the whole assembly, with the exception of the soldiers, we plunged after Mag. She took the main road, a well-beaten track for mules and beasts, which led from the mouth of the river to the city; and though it wound about here and there, we could still keep her in sight, as she parted the bushes right and left in her flight. Presently, the thick undergrowth gave place to loftier vegetation; and between the trunks of the palms and cocoas we caught glimpses of narrow lagoons beyond, patched with light-green and white water lilies. On the opposite side, the land rose higher, and the forest was composed of heavy timber.

The woman still held on with great speed, and must have known she was running with a noose round her neck, for she never looked behind, or gave heed in the slightest degree to our yells to stop or be shot. There were a number of paths made by cattle, which crossed the road at intervals, and, all at once, Mag turned to the left into one of them. A pair of huge vampire bats rose from a branch with a boding croak; and as the woman leaped over the grass and leaves, one of the factors gave a shout of warning, and tried to stop me from going farther. Shaking off his grasp, however, I jumped on, with Mak and Hazy at my heels, into the thicket. In a minute we had entirely passed the dense foliage, and before us lay the long, narrow lagoon, cradled in its black, slimy, muddy banks, while directly through the centre, leading to the opposite shore, was apparently a clear, open bridge, matted and bound with roots, grasses, and rank vegetation of all sorts, with a little clump of bushes and parasitical plants at every few paces, but still showing a green, even road over the water. Mag was about a hundred yards in advance of us, and splashing a short distance into the mud and water, she sprang upon the bending mangrove roots, and, finding that they bore her weight, continued on her course.

"Hold!" roared the padron; "gentlemen, for God's sake don't go an inch farther!"

"*O! cuidado!*" screamed the factor. "Beware! it is certain death!" cried they, both out of breath. "That witch can't escape; the mire will prevent her on the other side."

At this moment, Mag, perceiving she was no longer pursued, turned about, and shaking her knife in one hand, and applying the gin jug to her lips with the other, she took a long pull, and then yelled derisively,—

"O, you hounds! you thought to hang me, eh? the hemp isn't planted yet for my throat; and you, ye devil's asp, let me once lay hold upon you, I'll take an oath to find your heart the next time. *Adios*," she said, as she again applied the jug to her mouth, and hurling it upon the slimy surface of the pool, wheeled to resume her flight.

I am glad to say that this was the last swig of gin and the last intelligible remarks which Miss Margaret, as Spuke respectfully styled her, ever uttered in this world.

No sooner had the water been disturbed by the splash of the empty bottle, than we noticed a little succession of rolling, unbroken billows along by the vegetable bridge. The flat, sickly leaves and flowers began to undulate, and as Mag stepped from the green laced, living fabric to a projecting root, we saw the huge, triangular-shaped snout of a red spectacled alligator, and the dull, protruding eyes, with the fringed, scaly crest between, slowly pushed above the water; and then a sharp, rattling snap upon the hard-baked clay of the gin jug.

"The cayman!" exclaimed the padron; and as the monster rolled his jaws more out of water, the irregular, reddish, marbled yellow and green spots were visible underneath, before he sank with his prize.

The factor ejaculated, "*O! vermelho cayman!*"

The noise of the breaking gin vessel did not, however, distract the attention of Mag, but as she trod on the elastic mass of the bridge, it yielded, and agitated the pool with a loud splash. The next moment, as if the impulse had been felt in every direction, the same unbroken undulations as before swelled up under the greenish, stagnant lagoon, and in less time than it takes to wink, the water broke with a rush upwards, within a few feet of the woman. The enormous mail-clad hide of the cayman appeared; the tail rose with a diagonal motion; and the head, with the distended, serrated jaws, the reddish tongue and yellow mouth inside them, gleamed hot and dry in the beams of the morning sun; the whole monster forming a curving bend of full twenty feet before and behind the now terrified hag. At the same instant the hard, flexible tail made a side sweep, quick as thought, which, striking Mag a crushing blow about her waist, doubled her up with a broken back, and she was swept into the frightful jaws, open to full stretch, and inclined sideways to receive the prey. Simultaneously with our groans of horror, the heretofore quiet pool was all alive with the projecting, ridgy bodies of the monsters, and for a few minutes we heard nothing but the violent snapping of their huge jaws, and the blows of their powerful tails. At last the water once more began to settle down into peace; the broad, flat leaves and stems of the pure white lilies, which had been torn and crushed by the commotion amongst the denizens below, gradually resumed their beds; and, save a few bubbles, and an occasional undulation, with a strong odor of musk, there was nothing left to show where the hag had met her horrid death.

"Come, let's crawl out of this swamp," said the padron, "or some of those hungry caymans will be after having a taste of us."

SAGACITY OF LOBSTERS—FROM THE SAME.

"Very sagacious creeters," chimed in an old salt, who was carefully laying up nettles for his hammock clews: "I know'd a dog once as would tell the time o' day by the skipper's nose, and would drink grog too like a Christian."

"Bless ye," again broke out the gaunt, bony fisherman, "dogs isn't a circumstance to lobsters for sagaciousness! Why, mateys, I was on the pint of tellin' you, that after my trip to Greenland and the coast of Labrador, the old people thought I had 'bout sowed my wild oats." "I thought you said grass," twanged in the young mountaineer; but the whaler, without deigning a glance at the cub, went on. "And I settled down stiddy at the lobster business. Nat Pochick and me was 'prentices in a smack for better nor five years, in war times too, until our time was out, when we bought the old smack at a bargain, and drove a lively trade in the same business. We used to take the lobsters, where the best on 'em comes from, along the moniment shore, down about Plymouth, and we ran 'em through the Vineyard Sound to York, by way of Montauk. Well, one day, when we had the well of the schooner as full as ever it could stick with claws and feelers, like darned fools we tried to shorten the distance by runnin' outside of Nantucket; but jest as we got off Skonset, what should we see but the old Ramillies seventy-four, the admiral's ship, a-hidin' under Tom Nevers' Head; and in less than a minute an eighteen pound shot come spinnin' across our bows, and two big double-banked boats was making the water white as they pulled towards us. We know'd, as well as could be, that them Britishers didn't want the old smack, nor care a snap for the lobsters; but we did believe sartin' that they wouldn't mind clappin' hold on two sich likely chaps as my partner and me, to sarve under the king's flag. So we up helm and ran the smack and the cargo slap on to the Old Man's Shoal; but jest afore she struck we jumped into the yawl, and paddled to the beach, where we saved being captured. Well, the smack was knocked into splinters by the breakers in less than an hour. Now, my hearties," said the whaler, as he paused and gazed around the group of listeners, "every blessid one of them lobsters went back to the ground where they was took, as much as a hundred miles from the reef where the old craft was wracked! and there's great Black Dan, of Marsfield, will tell ye the same; for ye must bear in mind, that every fisherman has his partiklar shaped pegs to chock the claws of the lobsters with, and every one of our lobsters was kitched agin with our 'dentical pegs in 'em! This, boys, was the last trip as ever we made in that trade, though Nat Pochick, out of fondness for the things, established himself on the old Boston bridge, where he is to this day, a-bilin', may be, five or six thousand lobsters of a mornin', which he sells off like hot cakes in the arternoons."

HERMAN MELVILLE.

HERMAN MELVILLE was born in the city of New York, August 1, 1819. On his father's side he is of Scotch extraction, and is descended in the fourth degree from Thomas Melville, a clergyman of the Scotch Kirk, who, from the year 1718 and for almost half a century, was minister of Scoonie parish, Leven, Fifeshire.* The minister of Scoonie had two sons—John Melville, who became a member of his majesty's council in Grenada, and Allan Melville, who came to America in 1748, and settled in Boston as a merchant. Dying young, the latter left an only son, Thomas Melville, our author's grandfather, who was born in Boston, and, as appears by the probate records on the appointment of his guardian in 1761, inherited a handsome fortune from his father. He was graduated at Princeton College, New Jersey in 1769, and in 1772 visited his relatives in Scotland. During this visit he was presented with the freedom of the city of St. Andrews and of Renfrew. He returned to Boston in 1773, where he became a merchant, and in December of that year was one of the Boston Tea Party. He took an active part in the Revolutionary war, and, as major in Craft's regiment of Massachusetts artillery, was in the actions in Rhode Island in 1776. Commissioned by Washington in 1789 as naval officer of the port of Boston, he was continued by all the presidents down to Jackson's time in 1829.† To the time of his death Major Melville continued to wear the antiquated three-cornered hat, and from this habit was familiarly known in Boston as the last of the cocked-hats. There is still preserved a small parcel of the veritable tea in the attack upon which he took an active part. Being found in his shoes on returning from the vessel it was sealed up in a vial, although it was intended that not a particle should escape destruction! The vial and contents are now in possession of Chief-Justice Shaw of Massachusetts.

Our author's father, Allan Melville, was an importing merchant in New York, and made frequent visits to Europe in connexion with his business. He was a well educated and polished man, and spoke French like a native.

On his mother's side Mr. Melville is the grandson of General Peter Gansevoort of Albany, New York, the "hero of Fort Stanwix," having successfully defended that fort in 1777 against a large force of British and Indians, commanded by General St. Leger.

The boyhood of Herman Melville was passed at Albany and Lansingburgh, New York, and in the country, at Berkshire, Massachusetts. He had early shown a taste for literature and composition.

In his eighteenth year he shipped as a sailor in a New York vessel for Liverpool, made a hurried

* Article Scoonie, Sinclair's Statistical Account of Scotland, vol. v. p. 115. Dr. George Brewster, minister of Scoonie, who died June 20, 1855, succeeded the Rev. David Swan, who was the successor of our author's ancestor. It is worthy of remark that the united years of these three clergymen, in the same desk, was one hundred and thirty-six years.—Obituary notice in Scotsman, June 23, 1855.

† Major Melville was the nearest surviving male relative of General Robert Melville, who was descended from a brother of the minister of Scoonie, the first and only Captain-General and Governor-in-chief of the Islands ceded to England by France in 1763, and at the time of his death, which occurred in 1809, was with one exception the oldest General in the British army.—County Annual Register, Scotland, 1809 and '10, vol. i. part 6. In the genealogy of General Melville, contained in Douglass's Baronage of Scotland, published in 1798, the Boston family are stated to be descended from the same branch of the Melville family as General Melville.

visit to London when he arrrived in port, and returned home "before the mast." His next adventure was embarking, Jan. 1, 1841, on a whaling vessel for the Pacific for the sperm fishery. After eighteen months of the cruise, the vessel, in the summer of 1842, put into the Marquesas, at Nukuheva. Melville, who was weary of the service, took the opportunity to abandon the ship, and with a fellow sailor hid himself in the forest, with the intention of resorting to a neighboring peaceful tribe of the natives. They mistook their course, and after three days' wandering, in which they had traversed one of the formidable mountain ridges of the island, found themselves in the barbarous Typee valley. Here Melville was detained "in an indulgent captivity" for four months. He was separated from his companion, and began to despair of a return to civilization, when he was rescued one day on the shore by a boat's crew of a Sidney whaler. He shipped on board this vessel, and was landed at Tahiti the day when the French took possession of the Society Islands, establishing their "Protectorate" at the cannon's mouth. From Tahiti, Melville passed to the Sandwich Islands, spent a few months in observation of the people and the country, and in the autumn of 1843 shipped at Honolulu as "ordinary seaman" on board the frigate United States, then on its return voyage, which was safely accomplished, stopping at Callao, and reaching Boston in October, 1844. This voyaging in the merchant, whaling, and naval service rounded Melville's triple experience of nautical life. It was not long after that he made his appearance as an author. His first book, *Typee*, a narrative of his Marquesas adventure, was published in 1846, simultaneously by Murray in London* and Wiley and Putnam in New York. The spirit and vigorous fancy of the style, and the freshness and novelty of the incidents, were at once appreciated. There was, too, at the time, that undefined sentiment of the approaching practical importance of the Pacific in the public mind, which was admirably calculated for the reception of this glowing, picturesque narrative. It was received everywhere with enthusiasm, and made a reputation for its author in a day. The London Times reviewed it with a full pen, and even the staid Gentleman's Magazine was loud in its praises.

Mr. Melville followed up this success the next year with *Omoo, a Narrative of Adventures in the South Seas*, which takes up the story with the escape from the Typees, and gives a humorous account of the adventures of the author and some of his ship companions in Tahiti. For pleasant, easy narrative, it is the most natural and agreeable of his books. In his next book, in 1849—*Mardi, and a Voyage Thither*—the author ventured out of the range of personal observation and matter-of-fact description to which he had kept more closely than was generally supposed,† and projected a philosophical romance, in which human nature and European civilization were to be typified under the aspects of the poetical mythological notions and romantic customs and traditions of the aggregate races of Polynesia. In the first half of the book there are some of the author's best descriptions, wrought up with fanciful associations from the quaint philosophic and other reading in the volumes of Sir Thomas Browne, and such worthies, upon whose pages, after his long sea fast from books and literature, the author had thrown himself with eager avidity. In the latter portions, embarrassed by his spiritual allegories, he wanders without chart or compass in the wildest regions of doubt and scepticism. Though, as a work of fiction, lacking clearness, and maimed as a book of thought and speculation by its want of sobriety, it has many delicate traits and fine bursts of fancy and invention. Critics could find many beauties in Mardi which the novel-reading public who long for amusement have not the time or philosophy to discover. Mr. Melville, who throughout his literary career has had the good sense never to argue with the public, whatever opportunities he might afford them for the exercise of their disputative faculties, lost no time in recovering his position by a return to the agreeable narrative which had first gained him his laurels. In the same year he published *Redburn; his First Voyage, being the Sailor-boy Confessions and Reminiscences of the Son of a Gentleman, in the Merchant Service*. In the simplicity of the young sailor, of which the pleasant adventure of leaving the forecastle one day and paying his respects to the captain in the cabin, is an instance, this book is a witty reproduction of natural incidents. The lurid London episode, in the melo-dramatic style, is not so fortunate. Another course of Melville's nautical career, the United States naval service, furnished the subject of the next book—*White Jacket, or the World in a Man-of-war*, published in 1850. It is a vivid daguerreotype of the whole life of the ship. The description is everywhere elevated from commonplace and familiarity by the poetical associations which run through it. There is many a good word spoken in this book, as in the author's other writings, for the honor and welfare of Poor Jack. Punishment by flogging is unsparingly condemned.

In 1851 *Moby-Dick, or the Whale*, appeared, the most dramatic and imaginative of Melville's books. In the character of Captain Ahab and his contest with the whale, he has opposed the metaphysical energy of despair to the physical sublime of the ocean. In this encounter the whale becomes a representative of moral evil in the world. In the purely descriptive passages, the details of the fishery, and the natural history of the animal, are narrated with constant brilliancy of illustration from the fertile mind of the author.*

* It was brought to the notice of Mr. Murray in London by Mr. Gansevoort Melville, then Secretary of Legation to the Minister, Mr. Louis McLane. Mr. Gansevoort Melville was a political speaker of talent. He died suddenly in London of an attack of fever in May, 1846.

† Lt. Wise, in his lively, dashing book of travels—An Inside View of Mexico and California, with Wanderings in Peru, Chili, and Polynesia—pays a compliment to Melville's fidelity: "Apart from the innate beauty and charming tone of his narratives, the delineations of island life and scenery, from my own personal observation, are most correctly and faithfully drawn."

* Just at the time of publication of this book its catastrophe, the attack of the ship by the whale, which had already good historic warrant in the fate of the Essex of Nantucket, was still further supported by the newspaper narrative of the Ann Alexander of New Bedford, in which the infuriated animal demonstrated a spirit of revenge almost human, in

Pierre, or the Ambiguities, was published in 1852. Its conception and execution were both literary mistakes. The author was off the track of his true genius. The passion which he sought to evolve was morbid or unreal, in the worst school of the mixed French and German melodramatic.

Since the publication of this volume, Mr. Melville has written chiefly for the magazines of Harper and Putnam. In the former, a sketch, entitled *Cock-a-doodle doo!* is one of the most lively and animated productions of his pen; in the latter, his *Bartleby the Scrivener*, a quaint, fanciful portrait, and his reproduction, with various inventions and additions, of the adventures of *Israel Potter*,* an actual character of the Revolution, have met with deserved success.

Melville's Residence.

Mr. Melville having been married in 1847 to a daughter of Chief Justice Shaw of Boston, resided for a while at New York, when he took up his residence in Berkshire, on a finely situated farm, adjacent to the old Melville House, in which some members of the family formerly lived; where, in the immediate vicinity of the residence of the poet Holmes, he overlooks the town of Pittsfield and the intermediate territory, flanked by the Taconic range, to the huge height of Saddle-back.

Gray-lock, cloud girdled, from his purple throne,
 A voice of welcome sends,
And from green sunny fields, a warbling tone
 The Housatonic blends.†

In the fields and in his study, looking out upon the mountains, and in the hearty society of his family and friends, he finds congenial nourishment for his faculties, without looking much to cities, or troubling himself with the exactions of artificial life. In this comparative retirement will be found the secret of much of the speculative character engrafted upon his writings.

REDBURN CONTEMPLATES MAKING A SOCIAL CALL ON THE CAPTAIN IN HIS CABIN.

What reminded me most forcibly of my ignominious condition was the widely altered manner of the captain toward me. I had thought him a fine, funny gentleman, full of mirth and good humor, and good will to seamen, and one who could not fail to appreciate the difference between me and the rude sailors among whom I was thrown. Indeed I had made no doubt that he would in some special manner take me under his protection, and prove a kind friend and benefactor to me; as I had heard that some sea-captains are fathers to their crew; and so they are; but such fathers as Solomon's precepts tend to make—severe and chastising fathers; fathers whose sense of duty overcomes the sense of love, and who every day, in some sort, play the part of Brutus, who ordered his son away to execution, as I have read in our old family Plutarch.

Yes, I thought that Captain Riga, for Riga was his name, would be attentive and considerate to me, and strive to cheer me up, and comfort me in my lonesomeness. I did not even deem it at all impossible that he would invite me down to the cabin of a pleasant night, to ask me questions concerning my parents, and prospects in life; besides obtaining from me some anecdotes touching my great-uncle, the illustrious senator; or give me a slate and pencil, and teach me problems in navigation; or perhaps engage me at a game of chess. I even thought he might invite me to dinner on a sunny Sunday, and help me plentifully to the nice cabin fare, as knowing how distasteful the salt beef and pork, and hard biscuit of the forecastle must at first be to a boy like me, who had always lived ashore, and at home.

And I could not help regarding him with peculiar emotions, almost of tenderness and love, as the last visible link in the chain of associations which bound me to my home. For, while yet in port, I had seen him and Mr. Jones, my brother's friend, standing together and conversing; so that from the captain to my brother there was but one intermediate step; and my brother and mother and sisters were one.

And this reminds me how often I used to pass by the places on deck, where I remembered Mr. Jones had stood when he first visited the ship lying at the wharf; and how I tried to convince myself that it was indeed true, that he had stood there, though now the ship was so far away on the wide Atlantic Ocean, and he, perhaps, was walking down Wall-street, or sitting reading the newspaper in his counting-room, while poor I was so differently employed.

When two or three days had passed without the captain's speaking to me in any way, or sending word into the forecastle that he wished me to drop into the cabin to pay my respects, I began to think whether I should not make the first advances, and whether indeed he did not expect it of me, since I was but a boy, and he a man; and perhaps that might have been the reason why he had not spoken to me yet, deeming it more proper and respectful for me to address him first. I thought he might be offended, too, especially if he were a proud man, with tender feelings. So one evening, a little before sundown, in the second dog-watch, when there was no more work to be done, I concluded to call and see him.

After drawing a bucket of water, and having a good washing, to get off some of the chicken-coop stains, I went down into the forecastle to dress myself as neatly as I could. I put on a white shirt in place of my red one, and got into a pair of cloth trowsers instead of my duck ones, and put on my new pumps, and then carefully brushing my shooting-jacket, I put that on over all, so that upon the whole I made quite a genteel figure, at least for a

turning upon, pursuing, and destroying the vessel from which he had been attacked.

* "The Life and Adventures of Israel R. Potter (a native of Cranston, Rhode Island), who was a soldier in the American Revolution," were published in a small volume at Providence, in 1824. The story in this book was written from the narrative of Potter, by Mr. Henry Trumbull, of Hartford, Ct.

† Ode for the Berkshire Jubilee, by Fanny Kemble Butler.

forecastle, though I would not have looked so well in a drawing-room.

When the sailors saw me thus employed, they did not know what to make of it, and wanted to know whether I was dressing to go ashore; I told them no, for we were then out of sight of land; but that I was going to pay my respects to the captain. Upon which they all laughed and shouted, as if I were a simpleton; though there seemed nothing so very simple in going to make an evening call upon a friend. Then some of them tried to dissuade me, saying I was green and raw; but Jackson, who sat looking on, cried out, with a hideous grin, "Let him go, let him go, men—he's a nice boy. Let him go; the captain has some nuts and raisins for him." And so he was going on when one of his violent fits of coughing seized him, and he almost choked.

As I was about leaving the forecastle, I happened to look at my hands, and seeing them stained all over of a deep yellow, for that morning the mate had set me to tarring some strips of canvas for the rigging, I thought it would never do to present myself before a gentleman that way; so for want of kids I slipped on a pair of woollen mittens, which my mother had knit for me to carry to sea. As I was putting them on, Jackson asked me whether he shouldn't call a carriage; and another bade me not to forget to present his best respects to the skipper. I left them all tittering, and coming on deck was passing the cook-house, when the old cook called after me, saying, I had forgot my cane.

But I did not heed their impudence, and was walking straight toward the cabin-door, on the quarter-deck, when the chief mate met me. I touched my hat, and was passing him, when, after staring at me till I thought his eyes would burst out, he all at once caught me by the collar, and with a voice of thunder wanted to know what I meant by playing such tricks aboard a ship that he was mate of? I told him to let go of me, or I would complain to my friend the captain, whom I intended to visit that evening. Upon this he gave me such a whirl round, that I thought the Gulf Stream was in my head, and then shoved me forward, roaring out I know not what. Meanwhile the sailors were all standing round the windlass looking aft, mightily tickled.

Seeing I could not effect my object that night, I thought it best to defer it for the present; and returning among the sailors, Jackson asked me how I had found the captain, and whether the next time I went I would not take a friend along and introduce him.

The upshot of this business was, that before I went to sleep that night, I felt well satisfied that it was not customary for sailors to call on the captain in the cabin; and I began to have an inkling of the fact, that I had acted like a fool; but it all arose from my ignorance of sea usages.

And here I may as well state, that I never saw the inside of the cabin during the whole interval that elapsed from our sailing till our return to New York; though I often used to get a peep at it through a little pane of glass, set in the house on deck, just before the helm, where a watch was kept hanging for the helmsman to strike the half hours by, with his little bell in the binnacle, where the compass was. And it used to be the great amusement of the sailors to look in through the pane of glass, when they stood at the wheel, and watch the proceedings in the cabin; especially when the steward was setting the table for dinner, or the captain was lounging over a decanter of wine on a little mahogany stand, or playing the game called *solitaire*, at cards, of an evening; for at times he was all alone with his dignity; though, as will ere long be shown, he generally had one pleasant companion, whose society he did not dislike.

The day following my attempt to drop in at the cabin, I happened to be making fast a rope on the quarter-deck, when the captain suddenly made his appearance, promenading up and down, and smoking a cigar. He looked very good-humored and amiable, and it being just after his dinner, I thought that this, to be sure, was just the chance I wanted.

I waited a little while, thinking he would speak to me himself; but as he did not, I went up to him and began by saying it was a very pleasant day, and hoped he was very well. I never saw a man fly into such a rage; I thought he was going to knock me down; but after standing speechless awhile, he all at once plucked his cap from his head and threw it at me. I don't know what impelled me, but I ran to the lee scuppers where it fell, picked it up, and gave it to him with a bow; when the mate came running up, and thrust me forward again; and after he had got me as far as the windlass, he wanted to know whether I was crazy or not; for if I was, he would put me in irons right off, and have done with it.

But I assured him I was in my right mind, and knew perfectly well that I had been treated in the most rude and ungentlemanly manner both by him and Captain Riga. Upon this, he rapped out a great oath, and told me if ever I repeated what I had done that evening, or ever again presumed so much as to lift my hat to the captain, he would tie me into the rigging, and keep me there until I learned better manners. "You are very green," said he, "but I'll ripen you." Indeed this chief mate seemed to have the keeping of the dignity of the captain, who in some sort seemed too dignified personally to protect his own dignity.

I thought this strange enough, to be reprimanded, and charged with rudeness for an act of common civility. However, seeing how matters stood, I resolved to let the captain alone for the future, particularly as he had shown himself so deficient in the ordinary breeding of a gentleman. And I could hardly credit it, that this was the same man who had been so very civil, and polite, and witty, when Mr. Jones and I called upon him in port.

But this astonishment of mine was much increased, when some days after, a storm came upon us, and the captain rushed out of the cabin in his night-cap, and nothing else but his shirt on; and leaping up on the poop, began to jump up and down, and curse and swear, and call the men aloft all manner of hard names, just like a common loafer in the street.

Besides all this, too, I noticed that while we were at sea, he wore nothing but old shabby clothes, very different from the glossy suit I had seen him in at our first interview, and after that on the steps of the City Hotel, where he always boarded when in New York. Now, he wore nothing but old-fashioned snuff-colored coats, with high collars and short waists; and faded, short-legged pantaloons, very tight about the knees; and vests that did not conceal his waistbands, owing to their being so short, just like a little boy's. And his hats were all caved in, and battered, as if they had been knocked about in a cellar; and his boots were sadly patched. Indeed, I began to think that he was but a shabby fellow after all, particularly as his whiskers lost their gloss, and he went days together without shaving; and his hair, by a sort of miracle, began to grow of a pepper and salt color, which might have been owing, though, to his discontinuing the use of some kind of dye while at sea. I put him down as a sort of impostor! and while ashore, a gentleman on false pretences, for no gentleman would have treated another gentleman as he did me.

Yes, Captain Riga, thought I, you are no gentleman, and you know it.

CAROLINE M. SAWYER.

Caroline M. Fisher was born in the latter part of the year 1812, in the village of Newton, Massachusetts. She was carefully educated at home by an invalid uncle, who was thoroughly conversant with foreign literature, and succeeded in imparting his fine taste as well as varied accomplishments to his pupil. She commenced writing at an early age, but did not make her appearance in the magazines until after her marriage with the Rev. T. J. Sawyer, an eminent Universalist divine, in 1832, when she removed to New York. In 1847 her husband accepted the presidency of the Universalist Seminary at Clinton, New York, where they have since resided.

Mrs. Sawyer has written a number of poems and prose tales for the periodicals of the day, which have not been collected. She has also translated in prose and verse from the German.

THE BLIND GIRL.

Crown her with garlands! 'mid her sunny hair
Twine the rich blossoms of the laughing May,
The lily, snowdrop, and the violet fair,
And queenly rose, that blossoms for a day.
Haste, maidens, haste! the hour brooks no delay—
The bridal veil of soft transparence bring;
And as ye wreathe the gleaming locks away,
O'er their rich wealth its folds of beauty fling—
She *seeth* now!

Bring forth the lyre of sweet and solemn sound,
Let its rich music be no longer still;
Wake its full chords, till, sweetly floating round,
Its thrilling echoes all our spirits fill.
Joy for the lovely! that her lips no more
To notes of sorrow tune their trembling breath;
Joy for the young, whose starless course is o'er;
Iö! sing Pæans for the bride of Death!
She seeth now!

She has been dark; through all the weary years,
Since first her spirit into being woke,
Through those dim orbs that ever swam in tears,
No ray of sunlight ever yet hath broke.
Silent and dark! herself the sweetest flower
That ever blossomed in an earthly home,
Unuttered yearnings ever were her dower,
And voiceless prayers that light at length might come.
She seeth now!

A lonely lot! yet oftentimes a sad
And mournful pleasure filled her heart and brain,
And beamed in smiles—e'er sweet, but never glad,
As sorrow smiles when mourning winds complain.
Nature's great voice had ever for her soul
A thrilling power the sightless only know;
While deeper yearnings through her being stole,
For light to gild that being's darkened flow.
She seeth *now!*

Strike the soft harp, then! for the cloud hath past,
With all its darkness, from her sight away;
Beauty hath met her waiting eyes at last,
And light is hers within the land of day.
'Neath the cool shadows of the tree of life,
Where bright the fount of youth immortal springs,
Far from this earth, with all its weary strife,
Her pale brow fanned by shining seraphs' wings,
She seeth now!

Ah, yes, she seeth! through yon misty veil,
Methinks e'en now her angel-eyes look down,
While round me falls a light all soft and pale—
The moonlight lustre of her starry crown;
And to my heart as earthly sounds retire,
Come the low echoes of celestial words,
Like sudden music from some haunted lyre,
That strangely swells when none awake its chords.
But, hush! 'tis past; the light, the sound, are o'er:
Joy for the maiden! she is dark no more!
She seeth now!

LOUISA C. TUTHILL.

Louisa C. Higgins, a member of an old New England family, was born at New Haven, and at an early age, in 1817, married Mr. Cornelius Tuthill of that city. Mr. Tuthill was a gentleman of literary tastes, and edited, for two years, a periodical called The Microscope, in which the poet Percival was first introduced to the public.

After the death of Mr. Tuthill, in 1825, Mrs. Tuthill became an anonymous contributor to the magazines. Her first appearance *in propriâ personâ* as an author was on the title-page of *The Young Ladies' Reader*, a volume of selections published in 1839. This volume was followed by *The Young Ladies' Home*, a collection of tales and essays illustrating domestic pursuits and duties. Her next production consisted of a series of tales for young persons. They are entitled *I will be a Gentleman; I will be a Lady; Onward, right Onward; Boarding School Girl; Anything for Sport; A Strike for Freedom, or Law and Order;* each occupying a volume of about one hundred and fifty pages of moderate size, published between 1844 and 1850.

In 1852 Mrs. Tuthill commenced a new series with a tale entitled *Braggadocio. Queer Bonnets, Tip Top,* and *Beautiful Bertha,* followed in 1853 and 1854. She has now in progress another series entitled *Success in Life,* including six volumes, with the titles *The Merchant, The Lawyer, The Mechanic, The Artist, The Farmer,* and *The Physician.*

Mrs. Tuthill is also the author of a novel for mature readers published in 1846 with the title *My Wife,* and of a tasteful volume, *The History of Architecture,* published in 1848. In 1849 she prepared *The Nursery Book,* a volume of counsel to mothers on the care of their young offspring.

The writings of Mrs. Tuthill are admirably adapted for the class to whom they are addressed, and have met with success. They are sensible and practical in their aims, and written in an agreeable style. Mrs. Tuthill is at present a resident of Princeton, New Jersey.

PLINY MILES.

Pliny Miles, whose name is pleasantly suggestive of his principal pursuit, that of a traveller and observer of nature, is a son of Captain Jonathan E. Miles, one of the early settlers of Watertown, New York. He was educated on the farm, but on coming of age engaged in merchandise, and afterwards studied law. He next passed five years in travelling through the United States, supporting himself by lecturing and writing letters in the newspapers. At the expiration of this period he passed a second term of five years in a similar manner in the Old World.

Pliny Miles.

Mr. Miles's newspaper correspondence, under the staid signature, on the *lucus a non lucendo* principle, of *Communipaw*, would fill several volumes. But a single episode of his journeyings, *Rambles in Iceland*, has yet appeared in book form. It is a pleasant record of a tour, involving some adventure and exposure in an unfrequented part of the world. In place of a citation from its pages we however present a more comprehensive, and at the same time concise account of Mr. Miles's "voyages and travels," which we find in the New York Illustrated News of October 29, 1853. The statement was elicited by some exception being taken at one of Mr. Miles's letters on Western railroads,—his accuracy being called in question on the plea that he was "the stationary correspondent of the Post."

In the name of buffaloes and sea breezes what would you have, my dear fellow? I've been in every sea-port on the Atlantic, from Newfoundland to Key West; danced over the sparkling waves of the Moro Castle; "schoonered" it through the Gulf of Mexico; travelled every foot of the Mississippi, from the Belize to the Falls of St. Anthony, 2,300 miles, and the most of it several times over; wandered five hundred miles into the Indian territory, beyond the white settlements; steamed up the Illinois; stayed a while at Peoria, got caught there in an awful snow storm, and then went through the great lakes and the St. Lawrence to the Falls of the Montmorency. I have visited every great curiosity, nearly every state capital, and every State in the Union except California and Texas. Across the "herring pond" I travelled through almost every kingdom, and saw nearly every crowned head in Europe; wandered over the highlands of Scotland; stoned the cormorants in Fingal's cave; shot sea-gulls in Shetland; eat plovers and other wild birds in Iceland; cooked my dinner in the geysers; cooled my punch with the snows of Mount Hecla, and toasted my shins at the burning crater on its summit. I trod the rough mountains of Norway; celebrated "Independence Day" off its coast; fished in the Maelstrom, or near it; ate sour crout with the Dutch, frogs with the Frenchmen, and macaroni with the Italians; walked over the top of Vesuvius in one day, from Pompeii to Naples; lay all night near Ætna's summit, seeing an eruption with red hot rocks shooting a thousand feet in the air; sailed by Stromboli at midnight; landed where St. Paul did at Rhegium, saw the Coliseum by moonlight, visited Corsica's rocky isle, Sardinia and Elba, and steamed close to Monte Christo's home; admired the Chateau d'If at Marseilles, and spent months among the vine-clad hills of la belle France. Why, yes, man, I've been up in a balloon and down in a diving bell; shot alligators in the Mississippi and sparrows in Northumberland; eaten "corn dodgers" in Tennessee, black bread in Denmark, white bread in London, and been where I found it precious hard work to get any bread at all. I've rode in a Jersey wagon in Florida, a go-cart in Illinois, and on an English express train at fifty miles an hour, and gone a-foot and carried a knapsack when I found travelling dear and wanted to save money. I've been sixty-five voyages at sea; rode over nearly every railroad in Europe and more than one-half in this country, and travelled over a hundred thousand miles, and scarcely slept six nights in a place for more than ten years.

RICHARD B. KIMBALL,

A DESCENDANT from an old and influential family, was born in Lebanon, New Hampshire. After completing his collegiate course at Dartmouth in 1834, and devoting the year following to the study of the law, he went to Europe, where he continued his legal studies in Paris, and made an extensive and thorough tour in Great Britain and on the Continent. On his return he commenced the practice of his profession at Waterford, New York, but soon after removed to the City of New York, where, with the exception of the time occupied in a second European tour in 1842, he has since resided.

Mr. Kimball has for several years been a constant contributor to the Knickerbocker Magazine.

In 1849 his novel *St. Leger or the Threads of Life* was reprinted from the pages of that periodical. It is the story of a mind in pursuit of truth, and the mental repose consequent on a decided faith. In connexion with this main thread we have many scenes of active life, romantic adventure, and picturesque description.

In the same year Mr. Kimball published *Cuba and the Cubans*, and in 1853 a pleasant volume of tales and sketches, entitled, *Romance of Student Life Abroad.*

AMELIA B. WELBY,

THE author of *Poems by Amelia*, first published in the Louisville Journal, and afterwards in Boston and New York, was born at St. Michael's, in Mary-

Amelia B Welby.

land, in 1821. She removed with her father early to the West, and resided in Kentucky at Lexington and Louisville, where she was married to Mr. George Welby. She died in 1852.

The chief edition of Mrs. Welby's poems was published by Messrs. Appleton in 1850, with a series of tasteful illustrations by R. C. Weir. The frequent elegiac topics of the verses of this author may have assisted their popularity. They are mostly upon themes of domestic life and natural emotion; and, without profound poetical culture, are written with ease and animation.

THE OLD MAID.

Why sits she thus in solitude? her heart
  Seems melting in her eyes' delicious blue;
And as it heaves, her ripe lips lie apart,
  As if to let its heavy throbbings through;
In her dark eye a depth of softness swells,
  Deeper than that her careless girlhood wore;
And her cheek crimsons with the hue that tells
  The rich, fair fruit is ripened to the core.

It is her thirtieth birthday! With a sigh
  Her soul hath turned from youth's luxuriant bowers,
And her heart taken up the last sweet tie
  That measured out its links of golden hours!
She feels her inmost soul within her stir
  With thoughts too wild and passionate to speak;
Yet her full heart—its own interpreter—
  Translates itself in silence on her cheek.

Joy's opening buds, affection's glowing flowers,
  Once highly sprang within her beaming track;
Oh, life was beautiful in those lost hours!
  And yet she does not wish to wander back!
No! she but loves in loneliness to think
  On pleasures past, though never more to be;
Hope links her to the future, but the link
  That binds her to the past is memory!

From her lone path she never turns aside,
  Though passionate worshippers before her fall,
Like some pure planet in her lonely pride,
  She seems to soar and beam above them all!
Not that her heart is cold! emotions new
  And fresh as flowers are with her heart-strings knit;
And sweetly mournful pleasures wander through
  Her virgin soul, and softly ruffle it.

For she hath lived with heart and soul alive
  To all that makes life beautiful and fair;
Sweet thoughts, like honey-bees, have made their hive
  Of her soft bosom-cell, and cluster there;
Yet life is not to her what it hath been;
  Her soul hath learned to look beyond its gloss,
And now she hovers, like a star, between
  Her deeds of love, her Saviour on the cross!

Beneath the cares of earth she does not bow,
  Though she hath ofttimes drained its bitter cup,
But ever wanders on with heavenward brow,
  And eyes whose lovely lids are lifted up!
She feels that in that lovelier, happier sphere,
  Her bosom yet will, bird-like, find its mate,
And all the joys it found so blissful here
  Within that spirit-realm perpetuate.

Yet sometimes o'er her trembling heart-strings thrill
  Soft sighs, for raptures it hath ne'er enjoyed;
And then she dreams of love, and strives to fill
  With wild and passionate thoughts the craving void.

And thus she wanders on,—half sad, half blest,—
  Without a mate for the pure, lonely heart,
That, yearning, throbs within her virgin breast,
  Never to find its lovely counterpart!

JANE T. WORTHINGTON.

This lady, the wife of Dr. F. A. Worthington, a physician of Ohio, whose maiden name was Jane Tayloe Lomax, was a native of Virginia. Her writings in prose and verse appeared frequently in the Southern Literary Messenger. Her compositions were in a vein of excellent sense and refinement.

MOONLIGHT ON THE GRAVE.

It shineth on the quiet graves
  Where weary ones have gone,
It watcheth with angelic gaze
  Where the dead are left alone;
And not a sound of busy life
  To the still graveyard comes,
But peacefully the sleepers lie
  Down in their silent homes.

All silently and solemnly
  It throweth shadows round,
And every gravestone hath a trace
  In darkness on the ground:
It looketh on the tiny mound
  Where a little child is laid,
And it lighteth up the marble pile
  Which human pride hath made.

It falleth with unaltered ray
  On the simple and the stern,
And it showeth with a solemn light
  The sorrows we must learn;
It telleth of divided ties
  On which its beam hath shone,
It whispereth of heavy hearts
  Which "brokenly live on."

It gleameth where devoted ones
  Are sleeping side by side,
It looketh where a maiden rests
  Who in her beauty died.
There is no grave in all the earth
  That moonlight hath not seen;
It gazeth cold and passionless
  Where agony hath been.

Yet it is well: that changeless ray
  A deeper thought should throw,
When mortal love pours forth the tide
  Of unavailing woe;
It teacheth us no shade of grief
  Can touch the starry sky,
That all our sorrow liveth here—
  The glory is on high.

LUCY HOOPER.

Miss Hooper was born in Newburyport, Massachusetts, February 4, 1816. She was carefully trained by her father, and was wont in after life to attribute her facility in composition to the exertions of this parent. At the age of fifteen she removed with her family to Brooklyn, where the remaining ten years of her life were passed.

Most of Miss Hooper's poems were contributed to the Long Island Star, a daily paper, where they appeared signed with her initials. She was also the author of a few prose sketches, collected in a volume in 1840, with the title *Scenes from Real Life*, and a prize essay on *Domestic Happiness*.

Lucy Hooper died on Sunday, August 1, 1841.

The estimation in which she was held, was touchingly shown in the numerous testimonies to her gentle excellences published after her decease, prefixed to the volume of her *Complete Poetical Works*, published in 1848.* Among these we find verses by Whittier and Tuckerman.

Lucy Hooper was a devout member of the Episcopal Church, and many of her poems are naturally drawn from the incidents of its ritual. Others are of a descriptive or reflective character.

THE DAUGHTER OF HERODIAS.

Written after seeing, among a collection of beautiful paintings, (copies from the old masters, recently sent to New York from Italy,) one representing the daughter of Herodias, bearing the head of John the Baptist on a charger, and wearing upon her countenance an expression, not of triumph, as one might suppose, but rather of soft and sorrowful remorse, as she looks upon the calm and beautiful features of her victim.

Mother! I bring thy gift,
Take from my hand the dreaded boon—I pray
Take it, the still pale sorrow of the face
Hath left upon my soul its living trace,
Never to pass away;
Since from these lips one word of idle breath
Blanched that calm face—oh! mother, this is death.

What is it that I see
From all the pure and settled features gleaming?
Reproach! reproach! My dreams are strange and wild;
Mother! had'st thou no pity on thy child?
Lo! a celestial smile seems softly beaming
On the hushed lips—my mother, can'st thou brook
Longer upon thy victim's face to look?

Alas! at yestermorn
My heart was light, and to the viol's sound
I gaily danced, while crowned with summer flowers,
And swiftly by me sped the flying hours,
And all was joy around:
Not *death!* Oh! mother, could I say thee nay?
Take from thy daughter's hand thy boon away!

Take it! my heart is sad,
And the pure forehead hath an icy chill—
I dare not touch it, for avenging Heaven
Hath shuddering visions to my fancy given,
And the pale face appals me, cold and still,
With the closed lips—oh! tell me, could I know
That the pale features of the dead were so?

I may not turn away
From the charmed brow, and I have heard his name
Even as a prophet by his people spoken—
And that high brow, in death, bears seal and token
Of one whose words were flame:
Oh! Holy Teacher! could'st thou rise and live,
Would not these hushed lips whisper, "I forgive?"

Away with lute and harp,
With the glad heart for ever, and the dance,
Never again shall tabret sound for me;
Oh! fearful mother! I have brought to thee
The silent dead, with his rebuking glance,
And the crushed heart of one, to whom are given
Wild dreams of judgment and offended Heaven!

CATHARINE LUDERS.

A NUMBER of brief poems of a delicate and simple turn of expression and of a domestic pathetic interest have appeared from time to time in the magazines and the Literary World, by "Emily Hermann." The author is Mrs. Catharine Luders, lately a resident of the West, in Indiana.

THE BUILDING AND BIRDS.

We are building a pleasant dwelling,
And the orchard trees are set;
Yellow violets soon will open,
With tiny streaks of jet.

The wild-cherry buds are swelling,
And the brook runs full below;
Dim harebells in the garden,
And crocuses are in blow.

In the tops of the tulip-giants,
In the red-bud and the oak,
The spring-birds are all beginning
The pleasures of home to invoke.

They've built in our little parlour,
Where the floor was lately laid,
And it pleased us to give them shelter
In the nice new nest they made.

Those merry grey forest-rangers
To the green West now have come,
Wayfarers, like us, and strangers,
To build them a pleasant home.

They've reared a domestic altar
To send up their hymns at even;
Their songs and our own may mingle
Sometimes at the gates of heaven!

PLANTING IN RAIN.

We planted them in the rain,
When the skeleton building rose,
And here we sit, in the sultry day,
Where grateful shadows close.

We read in our pleasant books,
Or help the children play,
And weave long wreaths of dandelions
When the down is blown away.

The murmuring bell we hear,
For lowing herds are nigh,
With softened twilight in our heart,
And memories gone by.

Wild doves and orioles
Build in the orchard trees,
And where, on earth, are people poor
Who greet such friends as these!

They at our porch peep in
And sing their roundelay,
While bright-eyed rabbits near the steps,
In their nimble, fearless way.

In autumn, with apron in hand,
Cornelia waits near yon tree,
To catch the fruit from the grateful root,
Here set by our brothers and me.

Thus, where dense thickets rose,
And mouldering trees have lain,
Much happiness dwells for human hearts,
Under vines that were planted in rain.

THE LITTLE FROCK.

A common light blue muslin frock
Is hanging on the wall,
But no one in the household now
Can wear a dress so small.

The sleeves are both turned inside out,
And tell of summer wear;
They seem to wait the owner's hands
Which last year hung them there.

* 8vo. pp. 404.

'Twas at the children's festival
  Her Sunday dress was soiled—
You need not turn it from the light—
  To me it is not spoiled!

A sad and yet a pleasant thought
  Is to the spirit told
By this dear little rumpled thing,
  With dust in every fold.

Why should men weep that to their home
  An angel's love is given—
Or that before them she is gone
  To blessedness in heaven!

ESTELLE ANNA LEWIS.

MRS. LEWIS was born near Baltimore, Maryland, at the country-seat of her father, Mr. J. N. Robinson, who died while his daughter was in her infancy. He was a gentleman of large fortune, and of strongly marked qualities of character. His wife was a daughter of an officer of the Revolutionary war.

Our author was educated at the Female Seminary of Mrs Willard at Troy, where she added to the usual accomplishments of a polite education, a knowledge of Latin and even the study of law. During these school days, she published a series of stories in the Family Magazine, edited by Solomon Southwick at Albany. Leaving the seminary in 1841, she was married to Mr. S. D. Lewis, a lawyer of Brooklyn, N. Y., in which city she has since resided.

Estelle Anna Lewis.

Her first volume of poems, chiefly lyrical, *The Records of the Heart*, was published by the Appletons in 1844.

In 1846, Mrs. Lewis published a poem, *The Broken Heart, a Tale of Hispaniola*, in the Democratic Review. *The Child of the Sea, and Other Poems*, appeared from the press of Mr. George P. Putnam, in 1848.

In 1849, *The Angel's Visit*, *The Orphan's Hymn*, *The Prisoner of Perote*, etc., were printed in Graham's Magazine. In 1851, appeared in the same magazine, *The Cruise of Aureana*, *Melodiana's Dream*, *Adelina to Adhemer*, a series of sonnets from the Italian, and during the same year, a series of sonnets entitled, *My Study*, in the Literary World. In 1852, the Appletons issued the *Myths of the Minstrel*. In 1854, Mrs. Lewis published in Graham's Magazine, *Art and Artists in America*, a series of critical and biographical essays.

The poems of Mrs. Lewis are marked by a certain passionate expression, united with the study of poetic art. Her chief production, *The Child of the Sea*, exhibits ability in the construction of the story—a tale of sea adventure, of love and revenge,—and has force of imagination as a whole, and in its separate illustrations.

MY STUDY.

This is my world—my angel-guarded shrine,
Which I have made to suit my heart's great need,
When sorrow dooms it overmuch to bleed:
Or, when aweary and athirst I pine
For genial showers and sustenance divine;
When Love, or Hope, or Joy my heart deceive,
And I would sit me down alone to grieve—
My mind to sad or studious mood resign.
Here oft, upon the stream of thought I lie,
Floating whichever way the waves are flowing—
Sometimes along the banks of childhood going,
Where all is bud, and bloom, and melody,
Or, wafted by some stronger current, glide,
Where darker frown the steeps and deeper flows the tide.

Yes, 'tis my Cáabá—a shrine below,
Where my Soul sits within its house of clay,
Listing the steps of angels come and go—
Sweet missioned Heralds from the realms of day.
One brings me rays from Regions of the sun,
One comes to warn me of some pending dart,
One brings a laurel leaf for work well done,
Another, whispers from a kindred Heart.—
Oh! this I would not change for all the gold
That lies beneath the Sacramento's waves,
For all the Jewels Indian coffers hold,
For all the Pearls in Oman's starry caves—
The lessons of all Pedagogues are naught
To those I learn within this holy Fane of thought.

Here blind old Homer teaches lofty song;
The Lesbian sings of Cupid's pinions furled,
And how the heart is withered up by wrong;
Dante depictures an infernal world,
Wide opening many a purgatorial aisle;
Torquato rings the woes of Palestine,
Alphonso's rage and Leonora's smile—
Love, Beauty, Genius, Glory all divine;
Milton depaints the bliss of Paradise,
Then flings apart the ponderous gates of Hell,
Where Satan on the fiery billow lies,
"With head uplift," above his army fell,—
And Avon's Bard, surpassing all in art,
Unlocks the portals of the human heart.

GREECE—FROM THE CHILD OF THE SEA.

Shrine of the Gods! mine own eternal Greece!
When shall thy weeds be doffed—thy mourning cease?
The gyves that bind thy beauty rent in twain,
And thou be living, breathing Greece again!
Grave of the mighty! Hero—Poet—Sage—
Whose deeds are guiding stars to every age!
Land unsurpassed in glory and despair,
Still in thy desolation thou art fair!

Low in sepulchral dust lies Pallas' shrine—
Low in sepulchral dust thy Fanes divine—
And all thy visible self; yet o'er thy clay,
Soul, beauty, lingers, hallowing decay.

Not all the ills that war entailed on thee,
Not all the blood that stained Thermopylæ—
Not all the desolation traitors wrought—
Not all the woe and want invaders brought—
Not all the tears that slavery could wring
From out thy heart of patient suffering—
Not all that drapes thy loveliness in night,
Can quench thy spirit's never-dying light;
But hovering o'er the lust of gods enshrined,
It beams, a beacon to the march of mind—
An oasis to sage and bard forlorn—
A guiding star to centuries unborn.

For thee I mourn—thy blood is in my veins—
To thee by consanguinity's strong chains
I'm bound and fain would die to make thee free;
But oh! there is no Liberty for thee!
Not all the wisdom of thy greatest One—*
Not all the bravery of Thetis' Son—
Not all the weight of mighty Phœbus' ire—
Not all the magic of the Athenian's Lyre—
Can ever bid thy tears or mourning cease
Or rend one gyve that binds thee, lovely Greece.
Where Corinth weeps beside Lepanto's deep,
Her palaces in desolation sleep.
Seated till dawn on moonlit column, I
Have sought to probe eternal Destiny;
I've roamed, fair Hellas, o'er thy battle-plains.
And stood within Apollo's ruined fanes,
Invoked the spirits of the past to wake,
Assist with swords of fire thy chains to break;
But only from the hollow sepulchres,
Murmured, "Eternal slavery is hers!"
And on thy bosom I have laid my head
And poured my soul out—tears of lava shed;
Before thy desecrated altars knelt,
To calmer feelings felt my sorrows melt,
And gladly with thee would have made my home,
But pride and hate impelled me o'er the foam,
To distant lands and seas unknown to roam.

THE FORSAKEN.

It hath been said, for all who die
There is a tear;
Some pining, bleeding heart to sigh
O'er every bier:
But in that hour of pain and dread
Who will draw near
Around my humble couch, and shed
One farewell tear?

Who watch life's last, departing ray
In deep despair,
And soothe my spirit on its way
With holy prayer?
What mourner round my bier will come
"In weeds of woe,"
And follow me to my long home—
Solemn and slow?

When lying on my clayey bed,
In icy sleep,
Who there by pure affection led
Will come and weep—
By the pale moon implant the rose
Upon my breast,
And bid it cheer my dark repose,
My lowly rest?

Could I but know when I am sleeping
Low in the ground,
One faithful heart would there be keeping
Watch all night round,
As if some gem lay shrined beneath
The sod's cold gloom,
'Twould mitigate the pangs of death,
And light the tomb.

Yes, in that hour if I could feel
From halls of glee
And Beauty's presence *one* would steal
In secrecy,
And come and sit and weep by me
In night's deep noon—
Oh! I would ask of Memory
No other boon.

But ah! a lonelier fate is mine—
A deeper woe:
From all I love in youth's sweet time
I soon must go—
Draw round me my cold robes of white,
In a dark spot
To sleep through Death's long, dreamless night,
Lone and forgot.

* Lycurgus.

JULIA WARD HOWE.

The father of Mrs. Howe, Samuel Ward, the New York banker, whose liberality was freely expended on public-spirited and educational objects, as the Historical Society, the University, and Stuyvesant Institute of New York, was born in Rhode Island, a descendant of an old soldier of Cromwell, who settled in Newport after the

Julia Ward Howe

accession of Charles II., and who married a granddaughter of Roger Williams. Their son Richard became Governor of the State, and one of his sons, Samuel, was from 1774 to 1776 a member of the Old Continental Congress. This Samuel left a son Samuel, who served in the war of the Revolution, and was with Arnold in his expedition to Quebec. He was the grandfather of our author.

Her mother, a daughter of the late Mr. B. C. Cutler, of Boston, was a lady of poetic culture, a specimen of whose occasional verses is given in Griswold's Female Poets of America.

Miss Ward, after having received an education of unusual care and extent from the most accomplished teachers, was married in 1843 to the distinguished Philhellene and philanthropist of Boston, Dr. Samuel G. Howe, with whom she has resided in Europe, under peculiarly favorable opportunities for the study of foreign art and life. A volume of poems from her pen, *Passion Flowers*, published in 1854, is a striking expression of her culture, and of thoughts and experience covering a wide range of emotion, from sympathies with the "nationalities" of Europe, to "the fee griefs due to a single breast."

An appreciative critic in the Southern Quarterly Review* has thus characterized the varying features of the book.

"The art is subordinate to the feeling; the thought more prominent than the rhyme; there is far more earnestness of feeling than fastidiousness of taste:—instead of being the result of a dalliance with fancy, these effusions are instinct with the struggle of life; they are the offspring of experience more than of imagination. They are written by a woman who knows how to think as well as to feel; one who has made herself familiar with the higher walks of literature; who has deeply pondered Hegel, Comte, Swedenborg, Goethe, Dante, and all the masters of song, of philosophy, and of faith. Thus accomplished, she has travelled, enjoyed cultivated society, and gone through the usual phases of womanly development and duty. Her muse, therefore, is no casual impulse of juvenile emotion, no artificial expression, no spasmodic sentiment; but a creature born of wide and deep reflection; of study, of sorrow, yearning, love, care, delight, and all the elements of real, and thoughtful, and earnest life."

THE CITY OF MY LOVE.

She sits among the eternal hills,
Their crown, thrice glorious and dear,
Her voice is as a thousand tongues
Of silver fountains, gurgling clear.

Her breath is prayer, her life is love,
And worship of all lovely things;
Her children have a gracious port,
Her beggars show the blood of kings.

By old Tradition guarded close,
None doubt the grandeur she has seen;
Upon her venerable front
Is written: "I was born a Queen!"

She rules the age by Beauty's power,
As once she ruled by armèd might;
The Southern sun doth treasure her
Deep in his golden heart of light.

Awe strikes the traveller when he sees
The vision of her distant dome,
And a strange spasm wrings his heart
As the guide whispers, "There is Rome!"

Rome of the Romans! where the Gods
Of Greek Olympus long held sway;
Rome of the Christians, Peter's tomb,
The Zion of our later day.

Rome, the mailed Virgin of the world,
Defiance on her brows and breast;

* July, 1854.

Rome, to voluptuous pleasure won,
Debauched, and locked in drunken rest.

Rome, in her intellectual day,
Europe's intriguing step-dame grown;
Rome, bowed to weakness and decay,
A canting, mass-frequenting crone.

Then th' unlettered man plods on,
Half chiding at the spell he feels,
The artist pauses at the gate,
And on the wonderous threshold kneels.

The sick man lifts his languid head
For those soft skies and balmy airs;
The pilgrim tries a quicker pace,
And hugs remorse, and patters prayers.

For ev'n the grass that feeds the herds
Methinks some unknown virtue yields
The very hinds in reverence tread
The precincts of the ancient fields.

But wrapt in gloom of night and death,
I crept to thee, dear mother Rome;
And in thy hospitable heart,
Found rest and comfort, health and home.

And friendships, warm and living still,
Although their dearest joys are fled;
True sympathies that bring to life
The better self, so often dead.

For all the wonder that thou wert,
For all the dear delight thou art,
Accept an homage from my lips,
That warms again a wasted heart.

And, though it seem a childish prayer,
I've breathed it oft, that when I die,
As thy remembrance dear in it,
That heart in thee might buried lie.

ALICE B. HAVEN,

The author of numerous poems and tales, and of several volumes published under the name of "Cousin Alice," was born at Hudson, New York.

Alice B. Neal.

Her maiden name was Bradley. She early became a contributor to the periodicals of the day. In 1846 she was married to the late Joseph C.

Neal, the author of the Charcoal Sketches. Upon his death, a few months afterwards, she took charge of the literary department of Neal's Gazette, of which her husband had been a proprietor, and conducted it for several years with ability. Her articles, poems, tales, and sketches, appeared frequently during this time in the leading monthly magazines. A volume from her pen, *The Gossips of Rivertown, with Sketches in Prose and Verse*, was published in 1850. The main story is an illustration of the old village propensity of scandal, along with which the traits and manners of country life are exhibited in a genial, humorous way. Mrs. Haven is also the author of a series of juvenile works, published under the name of "Cousin Alice." They are stories written to illustrate various proverbial moralities, and are in a happy vein of dialogue and description, pervaded by an unobtrusive religious feeling. They are entitled, *Helen Morton's Trial; No Such Word as Fail; Contentment better than Wealth; Patient Waiting No Loss; All's not Gold that Glitters, or the Young Californian*, etc.

In 1853 Mrs. Neal was married to Mr. Samuel L. Haven, and has since resided at Mamaroneck, Westchester county, New York.

TREES IN THE CITY.

'Tis beautiful to see a forest stand,
  Brave with its moss-grown monarchs and the pride
Of foliage dense, to which the south wind bland
  Comes with a kiss, as lover to his bride;
To watch the light grow fainter, as it streams
  Through arching aisles, where branches interlace,
Where sombre pines rise o'er the shadowy gleams
  Of silver birch, trembling with modest grace.

But they who dwell beside the stream and hill,
  Prize little treasures there so kindly given;
The song of birds, the babbling of the rill,
  The pure unclouded light and air of heaven.
They walk as those who seeing cannot see,
  Blind to this beauty even from their birth,
We value little blessings ever free,
  We covet most the rarest things of earth.

But rising from the dust of busy streets,
  These forest children gladden many hearts;
As some old friend their welcome presence greets
  The toil-worn soul, and fresher life imparts.
Their shade is doubly grateful when it lies
  Above the glare which stifling walls throw back,
Through quivering leaves we see the soft blue skies,
  Then happier tread the dull, unvaried track.

And when the first fresh foliage, emerald-hued,
  Is opening slowly to the sun's glad beams,
How it recalleth scenes we once have viewed,
  And childhood's fair but long-forgotten dreams!
The gushing spring, with violets clustering round—
  The dell where twin flowers trembled in the breeze—
The fairy visions wakened by the sound
  Of evening winds that sighed among the trees.

There is a language given to the flowers—
  To me, the trees "dumb oracles" have been;
As waving softly, fresh from summer showers,
  Their whisper to the heart will entrance win.
Do they not teach us purity may live
  Amid the crowded haunts of sin and shame,
And over all a soothing influence give—
  Sad hearts from fear and sorrow oft reclaim!

And though transferred to uncongenial soil,
  Perchance to breathe alone the dusty air,
Burdened with sounds of never-ceasing toil—
  They rise as in the forest free and fair;
They do not droop and pine at adverse fate,
  Or wonder why their lot should lonely prove,
But give fresh life to hearts left desolate,
  Fit emblems of a pure, unselfish love.

THE CHURCH.

I will show thee the bride, the Lamb's wife.—Rev. xxi. 9.

Clad in a robe of pure and spotless white,
  The youthful bride with timid step comes forth
  To greet the hand to which she plights her troth,
Her soft eyes radiant with a strange delight.
The snowy veil which circles her around
  Shades the sweet face from every gazer's eye,
  And thus enwrapt, she passes calmly by—
Nor casts a look but on the unconscious ground.
So should the Church, the bride elect of Heaven,—
  Remembering Whom she goeth forth to meet,
  And with a truth that cannot brook deceit
Holding the faith, which unto her is given—
  Pass through this world, which claims her for a while,
  Nor cast about her longing look, nor smile.

CATHERINE WARFIELD—ELEANOR LEE,

"Two Sisters of the West," as they appeared on the title-page of a joint volume, *The Wife of Leon and Other Poems*, published in New York in 1843, are the daughters of the Hon. Nathaniel Ware, of Mississippi, and were born near the city of Natchez. Miss Catherine Ware was married to Mr. Warfield of Lexington, Kentucky; Miss Eleanor to Mr. Lee of Vicksburg. A second volume of their joint contribution, *The Indian Chamber and Other Poems*, appeared in 1846. The part taken by either author in the volumes is not distinguished. The poems in ballad, narrative, and reflection, exhibit a ready command of poetic language, and a prompt susceptibility to poetic impressions. They have had a wide popularity.

I WALK IN DREAMS OF POETRY.

I walk in dreams of poetry;
  They compass me around;
I hear a low and startling voice
  In every passing sound;
I meet in every gleaming star,
  On which at eve I gaze,
A deep and glorious eye, to fill
  My soul with burning rays.

I walk in dreams of poetry;
  The very air I breathe
Is filled with visions wild and free,
  That round my spirit wreathe;
A shade, a sigh, a floating cloud,
  A low and whispered tone—
These have a language to my brain,
  A language deep and lone.

I walk in dreams of poetry,
  And in my spirit bow
Unto a lone and distant shrine,
  That none around me know,
From every heath and hill I bring
  A garland rich and rare,
Of flowery thought and murmuring sigh,
  To wreathe mine altar fair.

I walk in dreams of poetry:
  Strange spells are on me shed;
I have a world within my soul
  Where no one else may tread—

A deep and wide-spread universe,
  Where spirit-sound and sight
Mine inward vision ever greet
  With fair and radiant light.

My footsteps tread the earth below,
  While soars my soul to heaven:
Small is my portion here—yet there
  Bright realms to me are given.
I clasp my kindred's greeting hands,
  Walk calmly by their side,
And yet I feel between us stands
  A barrier deep and wide.

I watch their deep and household joy
  Around the evening hearth,
When the children stand beside each knee
  With laugh and shout of mirth.
But oh! I feel unto my soul
  A deeper joy is brought—
To rush with eagle wings and strong,
  Up in a heaven of thought.

I watch them in their sorrowing hours,
  When, with their spirits tossed,
I hear them wail with bitter cries
  Their earthly prospects crossed;
I feel that I have sorrows wild
  In my heart buried deep—
Immortal griefs that none may share
  With me—nor eyes can weep.

And strange it is: I cannot say
  If it is wo or weal,
That thus unto my heart can flow
  Fountains so few may feel;
The gift that can my spirit raise
  The cold, dark earth above,
Has flung a bar between my soul
  And many a heart I love.

Yet I walk in dreams of poetry,
  And would not change that path,
Though on it from a darkened sky
  Were poured a tempest's wrath.
Its flowers are mine, its deathless blooms,
  I know not yet the thorn;
I dream not of the evening glooms
  In this my radiant morn.

Oh! still in dreams of poetry,
  Let me for ever tread,
With earth a temple, where divine,
  Bright oracles are shed:
They soften down the earthly ills
  From which they cannot save;
They make a romance of our life;
  They glorify the grave.

SHE COMES TO ME.

She comes to me in robes of snow,
  The friend of all my sinless years—
Even as I saw her long ago,
  Before she left this vale of tears.

She comes to me in robes of snow—
  She walks the chambers of my rest,
With soundless footsteps sad and slow,
  That wake no echo in my breast.

I see her in my visions yet,
  I see her in my waking hours;
Upon her pale, pure brow is set
  A crown of azure hyacinth flowers.

Her golden hair waves round her face,
  And o'er her shoulders gently falls:
Each ringlet hath the nameless grace
  My spirit yet on earth recalls.

And, bending o'er my lowly bed,
  She murmurs—"Oh, fear not to die!—
For thee an angel's tears are shed,
  An angel's feast is spread on high.

"Come, then, and meet the joy divine
  That features of the spirits wear:
A fleeting pleasure here is thine—
  An angel's crown awaits thee there.

"Listen! it is a choral hymn"—
  And, gliding softly from my couch,
Her spirit-face waxed faint and dim,
  Her white robes vanished at my touch.

She leaves me with her robes of snow—
  Hushed is the voice that used to thrill
Around the couch of pain and wo—
  She leaves me to my darkness still.

SARAH S. JACOBS,

A lady of Rhode Island, the daughter of a Baptist clergyman, the late Rev. Bela Jacobs, is remarkable for her learning and cultivation. She has of late resided at Cambridgeport, Mass. There has been no collection of her writings, except the few poems which have been brought together in Dr. Griswold's Female Poets of America.

BENEDETTA.

By an old fountain once at day's decline
  We stood. The wingèd breezes made
Short flights melodious through the lowering vine,
  The lindens flung a golden, glimmering shade,
And the old fountain played.
I a stern stranger—a sweet maiden she,
And beautiful as her own Italy.
At length she smiled; her smile the silence broke,
And my heart finding language thus it spoke:
  "Whenever Benedetta moves,
    Motion then all Nature loves;
  When Benedetta is at rest,
    Quietness appeareth best.
  She makes me dream of pleasant things,
    Of the young corn growing;
  Of butterflies' transparent wings
    In the sunbeams rowing;
  Of the summer dawn
    Into daylight sliding;
  Of Dian's favorite fawn
    Among laurels hiding;
  Of a movement in the tops
    Of the most impulsive trees;
  Of cool, glittering drops
    God's gracious rainbow sees;
  Of pale moons; of saints
    Chanting anthems holy;
  Of a cloud that faints
    In evening slowly;
  Of a bird's song in a grove,
    Of a rosebud's love;
  Of a lily's stem and leaf,
    Of dew-silvered meadows;
  Of a child's first grief;
    Of soft-floating shadows;
  Of the violet's breath
    To the moist wind given;
  Of early death
    And heaven."

I ceased: the maiden did not stir,
  Nor speak, nor raise her bended head;
And the green vines enfoliaged her,
  And the old fountain played.
Then from the church beyond the trees

Chimed the bells to evening prayer:
Fervent the devotions were
Of Benedetta on her knees;
And when her prayer was over,
A most spiritual air
Her whole form invested,
As if God did love her,
And his smile still rested
On her white robe and flesh,
So innocent and fresh—
Touching where'er it fell
With a glory visible.

She smiled, and crossed herself, and smiled again
Upon the heretic's sincere "Amen!"
"Buona notte," soft she said or sung—
It was the same on that sweet southern tongue—
And passed. I blessed the faultless face,
All in composed gentleness arrayed;
Then took farewell of the secluded place;
And the tall lindens flung a glimmering shade
And the old fountain played.

And this was spring. In the autumnal weather,
One golden afternoon I wandered thither;
And to the vineyards, as I passed along,
Murmured this fragment of a broken song:

"I know a peasant girl serene—
What though her home doth lowly lie!
The woods do homage to their queen,
The streams flow reverently nigh
Benedetta, Benedetta!

"Her eyes, the deep, delicious blue
The stars and I love to look through;
Her voice the low, bewildering tone,
Soft winds and she have made their own
Benedetta, Benedetta!"

She was not by the fountain—but a band
Of the fair daughters of that sunny land
Weeping they were, and as they wept they threw
Flowers on a grave. Then suddenly I knew
Of Benedetta dead:
And weeping too,
O'er beauty perished,
Awhile with her companions there I stood,
Then turned and went back to my solitude;
And the tall lindens flung a glimmering shade,
And the old fountain played.

ELIZABETH C. KINNEY.

Mrs. Elizabeth C. Kinney is a native of New York, the daughter of Mr. David L. Dodge, a merchant of the city. She is married to Mr. William B. Kinney, editor of the Newark Daily Advertiser, where, as well as in the magazines and literary journals of the day, many of her poetic compositions have appeared. In 1850, she accompanied her husband on his mission as Chargé d'Affaires to Sardinia. A fruit of her residence abroad has been a narrative poem entitled *Felicita, a Metrical Romance;* the story of a lady sold into Moorish captivity by her father, who is rescued by a slave; and after having passed through a sorrowful love adventure, dies in a convent. The numerous occasional poems of Mrs. Kinney have not been collected.

THE SPIRIT OF SONG.

Eternal Fame! thy great rewards,
Throughout all time, shall be
The right of those old master bards
Of Greece and Italy;
And of fair Albion's favored isle,
Where Poesy's celestial smile
Hath shone for ages, gilding bright
Her rocky cliffs and ancient towers,
And cheering this New World of ours
With a reflected light.

Yet, though there be no path untrod
By that immortal race—
Who walked with Nature as with God,
And saw her face to face—
No living truth by them unsung,
No thought that hath not found a tongue
In some strong lyre of olden time—
Must every tuneful lute be still
That may not give the world a thrill
Of their great harp sublime?

Oh, not while beating hearts rejoice
In music's simplest tone,
And hear in Nature's every voice
An echo to their own!
Not till these scorn the little rill
That runs rejoicing from the hill,
Or the soft, melancholy glide
Of some deep stream through glen and glade,
Because 'tis not the thunder made
By ocean's heaving tide!

The hallowed lilies of the field
In glory are arrayed,
And timid, blue-eyed violets yield
Their fragrance to the shade;
Nor do the wayside flowers conceal
Those modest charms that sometimes steal
Upon the weary traveller's eyes
Like angels, spreading for his feet
A carpet, filled with odors sweet,
And decked with heavenly dyes.

Thus let the affluent soul of Song—
That all with flowers adorns—
Strew life's uneven path along,
And hide its thousand thorns:
Oh, many a sad and weary heart,
That treads a noiseless way apart,
Has blessed the humble poet's name
For fellowship, refined and free,
In meek wild-flowers of poesy,
That asked no higher fame!

And pleasant as the waterfall
To one by deserts bound,
Making the air all musical
With cool, inviting sound—
Is oft some unpretending strain
Of rural song, to him whose brain
Is fevered in the sordid strife
That Avarice breeds 'twixt man and man,
While moving on, in caravan,
Across the sands of Life.

Yet not for these alone he sings:
The poet's breast is stirred
As by the spirit that takes wings
And carols in the bird!
He thinks not of a future name,
Nor whence his inspiration came,
Nor whither goes his warbled song:
As Joy itself delights in joy,
His soul finds life in its employ,
And grows by utterance strong.

SARA JANE LIPPINCOTT.

This lady, whose productions in prose and verse are known to the public under her *nom de plume* "Grace Greenwood," was born at Onondaga, in the State of New York, of New England parentage. Her early years were passed at Rochester, New York. Her father afterwards removed to New Brighton, a picturesquely situated village in Beaver Co., Western Pennsylvania, where she has since chiefly resided. In 1853 she was married to Mr. Lippincott, of Philadelphia.

Grace Greenwood

Two series of *Greenwood Leaves*, portions of which were originally contributed as letters to the New Mirror of Messrs. Morris and Willis, have been published in Boston by Messrs. Ticknor and Co., who also issued a volume of the author's *Poetical Works* in 1851. Mrs. Lippincott has also published *Haps and Mishaps of a Tour in Europe*, including an enthusiastic account of numerous European friends of the author, and several juvenile books, *History of My Pets*, *Recollections of My Childhood and Merrie England*.

The prose writings of "Grace Greenwood" are animated by a hearty spirit of out-of-door life and enjoyment, and a healthy, sprightly view of society. Her poems are the expressions of a prompt, generous nature.

ARIADNE.

[The demi-god, Theseus, having won the love of Ariadne, daughter of the king of Crete, deserted her on the isle of Naxos. In Miss Bremer's "H—— Family," the blind girl is described as singing, "*Ariadne à Naxos*," in which Ariadne is represented as following Theseus, climbing a high rock to watch his departing vessel, and calling on him in her despairing anguish.]

Daughter of Crete, how one brief hour,
 Ere in thy young love's early morn,
Sends storm and darkness o'er thy bower—
 Oh doomed, oh desolate, oh lorn!
The breast which pillowed thy fair head
 Rejects its burden—and the eye
Which looked its love so earnestly,
Its last cold glance hath on thee shed—
The arms which were thy living zone,
Around thee closely, warmly thrown,
Shall others clasp, deserted one!

Yet, Ariadne, worthy thou
Of the dark fate which meets thee now,
For thou art grovelling in thy woe—
Arouse thee! joy to bid him go.
For god above, or man below,
Whose love's warm and impetuous tide
Cold interest or selfish pride
Can chill, or stay, or turn aside,
Is all too poor and mean a thing
One shade o'er woman's brow to fling
 Of grief, regret, or fear.
To cloud one morning's rosy light,
Disturb the sweet dreams of one night,
To cause the soft lash of her eye
To droop one moment mournfully,
 Or tremble with one tear!

'Tis thou should'st triumph—thou art free
 From chains that bound thee for awhile—
This, this the farewell meet for thee,
 Proud princess, on that lonely isle!

"Go, to thine Athens bear thy faithless name!
 Go, base betrayer of a holy trust!
Oh, I could bow me in my utter shame,
 And lay my crimson forehead in the dust,
If I had ever loved thee as thou art,
Folding mean falsehood to my high, true heart!

"But thus I loved thee not. Before me bowed
 A being glorious in majestic pride
And breathed his love, and passionately vowed
 To worship only me, his peerless bride;
And this was thou, but crowned, enrobed, entwined
With treasures borrowed from my own rich mind.

"I knew thee not a creature of my dreams,
 And my rapt soul went floating into thine;
My love around thee poured such halo beams
 Had'st thou been true had made thee all divine
And I, too, seemed immortal in my bliss,
When my glad lip thrilled to thy burning kiss.

"Shrunken and shrivelled into Theseus now
 Thou stand'st—the gods have blown away
The airy crown which glittered on thy brow,
 The gorgeous robes which wrapt thee for a day.
Around thee scarce one fluttering fragment clings,
A poor, lean beggar in all glorious things!

"Nor will I deign to cast on thee my hate—
 It were a ray to tinge with splendour still
The dull, dim twilight of thy after fate—
 Thou shalt pass from me like a dream of ill,
Thy name be but a thing that crouching stole,
Like a poor thief, all noiseless from my soul!

"Though thou hast dared to steal the sacred flame
 From out that soul's high heaven, she sets thee free,
Or only chains thee with thy sounding shame—
 Her memory is no Caucasus for thee!
And even her hovering hate would o'er thee fling
Too much of glory from its shadowy wing!

"Thou think'st to leave my life a lonely night—
 Ha, it is night all glorious with its stars!
Hopes yet unclouded beaming forth their light,
 And free thoughts welling in their silver cars,
And queenly pride, serene, and cold, and high,
Moves the Diana of its calm, clear sky.

"If poor and humble thou believest me,
 Mole of a demi-god, how blind art thou!
For I am rich in scorn to pour on thee,
 And gods shall bend from high Olympus' brow,
And gaze in wonder on my lofty pride—
Naxos be hallowed, I be deified!"

On the tall cliff, where cold and pale,
Thou watchest his receding sail,

Where thou, the daughter of a king,
Wail'st like a breaking wind-harp's string—
Bend'st like a weak and wilted flower,
Before a summer evening's shower;
There should'st rear thy royal form
Like a young oak amid the storm
Uncrushed, unbowed, unriven!
Let thy last glance burn through the air,
And fall far down upon him there,
Like lightning stroke from heaven!

There should'st thou mark o'er billowy crest,
His white sail flutter and depart;
No wild fears surging at thy breast,
No vain hopes quivering round thy heart!
And this brief, burning prayer alone,
Leap from thy lips to Jove's high throne:

"Just Jove, thy wrathful vengeance stay,
And speed the traitor on his way!
Make vain the siren's silver song,
Let nereids smile the wave along!
O'er the wild waters send his barque,
Like a swift arrow to its mark!
Let whirlwinds gather at his back,
And drive him on his dastard track!
Let thy red bolts behind him burn,
And blast him should he dare to turn!"

ALICE CAREY—PHEBE CAREY.

Alice Carey was born in Mount Healthy, near Cincinnati, in 1822. She first attracted notice as a writer by a series of sketches of rural life in the National Era, with the signature of Patty Lee. In 1850 she published, with her younger sister Phebe, a volume of *Poems* at Philadelphia.

A volume of prose sketches—*Clovernook, or Recollections of Our Neighborhood in the West*—followed in 1851. A second series of these pleasant papers appeared in 1853. A third gleaning from the same field, for the benefit of more youthful readers, was made in 1855 in *Clovernook Children*. *Lyra, and Other Poems*, was published in 1852; followed by *Hagar, a Story of To-day*, in 1853. She has since published two other stories—*Married, not Mated*, and *Hollywood*—and a new collection of *Poems* in 1855.

Miss Alice Carey has rapidly attained a deservedly high position. Her poems are thoughtful, forcible, and melodiously expressed. In common with her prose writings, they are drawn from her own observation of life and nature.

PICTURES OF MEMORY.

Among the beautiful pictures
That hang on Memory's wall,
Is one of a dim old forest,
That seemeth best of all:
Not for its gnarled oaks olden,
Dark with the mistletoe;
Not for the violets golden
That sprinkle the vale below;
Not for the milk-white lilies
That lean from the fragrant hedge,
Coquetting all day with the sunbeams,
And stealing their golden edge;
Not for the vines on the upland
Where the bright red berries rest,
Nor the pinks, nor the pale, sweet cowslip,
It seemeth to me the best.

I once had a little brother,
With eyes that were dark and deep—
In the lap of that old dim forest
He lieth in peace asleep:
Light as the down of the thistle,
Free as the winds that blow,
We roved there the beautiful summers
The summers of long ago;
But his feet on the hills grew weary,
And, one of the autumn eves,
I made for my little brother
A bed of the yellow leaves.

Sweetly his pale arms folded
My neck in a meek embrace,
As the light of immortal beauty
Silently covered his face:
And when the arrows of sunset
Lodged in the tree-tops bright,
He fell, in his saint-like beauty,
Asleep by the gates of light.
Therefore, of all the pictures
That hang on Memory's wall,
The one of the dim old forest
Seemeth the best of all.

MULBERRY HILL.

Oh, sweet was the eve when I came from the mill,
Adown the green windings of Mulberry Hill:
My heart like a bird with its throat all in tune,
That sings in the beautiful bosom of June.

For there, at her spinning, beneath a broad tree,
By a rivulet shining and blue as the sea,
I first saw my Mary—her tiny feet bare,
And the buds of the sumach among her black hair.

They called me a bold enough youth, and I would
Have kept the name honestly earned, if I could;
But, somehow, the song I had whistled was hushed,
And, spite of my manhood, I felt that I blushed.

I would tell you, but words cannot paint my delight,
When she gave the red buds for a garland of white,
When her cheek with soft blushes—but no, 'tis in vain!
Enough that I loved, and she loved me again.

Three summers have come and gone by with their charms,
And a cherub of purity smiles in my arms,
With lips like the rosebud and locks softly light
As the flax which my Mary was spinning that night.

And in the dark shadows of Mulberry Hill,
By the grass-covered road where I came from the mill,
And the rivulet shining and blue as the sea,
My Mary lies sleeping beneath the broad tree.

NOBILITY.

Hilda is a lofty lady,
Very proud is she—
I am but a simple herdsman
Dwelling by the sea.
Hilda hath a spacious palace,
Broad, and white, and high;
Twenty good dogs guard the portal—
Never house had I.

Hilda hath a thousand meadows—
Boundless forest lands:
She hath men and maids for service—
I have but my hands.
The sweet summer's ripest roses
Hilda's cheeks outvie—
Queens have paled to see her beauty—
But my beard have I.

Hilda from her palace windows
Looketh down on me,
Keeping with my dove-brown oxen
By the silver sea.

When her dulcet harp she playeth,
  Wild birds singing nigh,
Cluster, listening, by her white hands—
  But my reed have I.

I am but a simple herdsman,
  With nor house nor lands;
She hath men and maids for service—
  I have but my hands.
And yet what are all her crimsons
  To my sunset sky—
With my free hands and my manhood
  Hilda's peer am I.

MISS PHEBE CAREY has, like her sister, been a frequent contributor to the periodicals of the day. She published in 1854 a volume of *Poems and Parodies.*

COMING HOME.

How long it seems since first we heard
  The cry of "land in sight!"
Our vessel surely never sailed
  So slowly till to-night.
When we discerned the distant hills,
  The sun was scarcely set,
And, now the noon of night is passed,
  They seem no nearer yet.

Where the blue Rhine reflected back
  Each frowning castle wall,
Where, in the forest of the Hartz,
  Eternal shadows fall—
Or where the yellow Tiber flowed
  By the old hills of Rome—
I never felt such restlessness,
  Such longing for our home.

Dost thou remember, oh, my friend,
  When we beheld it last,
How shadows from the setting sun
  Upon our cot were cast?
Three summer-times upon its walls
  Have shone for us in vain;
But oh, we're hastening homeward now,
  To leave it not again.

There, as the last star dropped away
  From Night's imperial brow,
Did not our vessel "round the point?"
  The land looks nearer now!
Yes, as the first faint beams of day
  Fell on our native shore,
They're dropping anchor in the bay,
  We're home, we're home once more!

ELISE JUSTINE BAYARD.

MISS E. J. BAYARD, the daughter of Mr. Robert Bayard of Glenwood, near Fishkill, N. Y., is the author of a number of poems, several of which have appeared in the Knickerbocker Magazine and Literary World. The following is noticeable for its thought and feeling, and no less for its happy literary execution.

FUNERAL CHANT FOR THE OLD YEAR.

'Tis the death-night of the solemn Old Year!
  And it calleth from its shroud
  With a hollow voice and loud,
    But serene:
And it saith—"What have I given
That hath brought thee nearer heaven?
Dost thou weep, as one forsaken,
For the treasures I have taken?
Standest thou beside my hearse
With a blessing or a curse?
Is it well with thee, or worse
    That I have been?

'Tis the death-night of the solemn Old Year!
  The midnight shades that fall,—
  They will serve it for a pall,
    In their gloom;—
And the misty vapours crowding
Are the withered corse enshrouding;
And the black clouds looming off in
The far sky, have plumed the coffin,
But the vaults of human souls,
Where the memory unrolls
All her tear-besprinkled scrolls,
    Are its tomb!

'Tis the death-night of the solemn Old Year!
  The moon hath gone to weep
  With a mourning still and deep
    For her loss:—
The stars dare not assemble
Through the murky night to tremble—
The naked trees are groaning
With an awful, mystic moaning—
  Wings sweep upon the air,
  Which a solemn message bear,
  And hosts, whose banners wear
    A crowned cross!

'Tis the death-night of the solemn Old Year!
  Who make the funeral train
  When the queen hath ceased to reign?
    Who are here
With the golden crowns that follow
All invested with a halo?
With a splendour transitory
Shines the midnight from their glory,
  And the pæan of their song
  Rolls the aisles of space along,
  But the left hearts are less strong,
    For they were dear!

'Tis the death-night of the solemn Old Year!
  With a dull and heavy tread
  Tramping forward with the dead
    Who come last?
Ling'ring with their faces groundward,
Though their feet are marching onward,
They are shrieking,—they are calling
On the rocks in tones appalling,
  But Earth waves them from her view,—
  And the God-light dazzles through,
  And they shiver, as spars do,
    Before the blast!

'Tis the death-night of the solemn Old Year!
  We are parted from our place
  In her motherly embrace,
    And are lone!
For the infant and the stranger
It is sorrowful to change her—
She hath cheered the night of mourning
With a promise of the dawning;
  She hath shared in our delight
  With a gladness true and bright:
  Oh! we need her joy to-night—
    But she is gone!

CAROLINE MAY.

THIS lady is the daughter of a clergyman of the Dutch Reformed Church of the City of New York. The chief collection of her poems is included in a few pages of Mr. Griswold's Female Poets of America. She is the editor of a Collection of the Female Poets of America, which appeared at Philadelphia in 1848, and of a volume, *Treasured Thoughts from Favorite Authors.*

THE SABBATH OF THE YEAR.

It is the sabbath of the year;
And if ye'll walk abroad,
A holy sermon ye shall hear,
Full worthy of record.
Autumn the preacher is; and look—
As other preachers do,
He takes a text from the one Great Book,
A text both sad and true.

With a deep, earnest voice, he saith—
A voice of gentle grief,
Fitting the minister of Death—
"Ye all fade as a leaf;
And your iniquities, like the wind,
Have taken you away;
Ye fading flutterers, weak and blind,
Repent, return, and pray."

And then the Wind ariseth slow,
And giveth out a psalm—
And the organ-pipes begin to blow,
Within the forest calm;
Then all the Trees lift up their hands,
And lift their voices higher,
And sing the notes of spirit bands
In full and glorious choir.

Yes! 'tis the sabbath of the year!
And it doth surely seem,
(But words of reverence and fear
Should speak of such a theme.)
That the corn is gathered for the bread,
And the berries for the wine,
And a sacramental feast is spread,
Like the Christian's pardon sign.

And the Year, with sighs of penitence,
The holy feast bends o'er;
For she must die, and go out hence—
Die, and be seen no more.
Then are the choir and organ still,
The psalm melts in the air,
The Wind bows down beside the hill,
And all are hushed in prayer.

Then comes the Sunset in the West,
Like a patriarch of old,
Or like a saint who hath won his rest,
His robes, and his crown of gold;
And forth his arms he stretcheth wide,
And with solemn tone and clear
He blesseth, in the eventide,
The sabbath of the year.

HARRIET WINSLOW LIST.

The following poem was brought into notice a few years since by Mr. Longfellow, who included it in the choice collection of minor poems, *The Waif.* It was printed there anonymously with the omission of a few of its stanzas. The author was Miss Harriet Winslow, since married to Mr. Charles List of Pennsylvania.

TO THE UNSATISFIED.

Why thus longing, thus for ever sighing
For the far-off, unattained and dim;
While the beautiful all around thee lying,
Offers up its low, perpetual hymn?

Wouldst thou listen to its gentle teaching,
All thy restless yearning it would still,
Leaf and flower and laden bee are preaching
Thine own sphere, though humble, first to fill.

Poor indeed thou must be, if around thee
Thou no ray of light and joy canst throw;
If no silken cord of love hath bound thee
To some little world through weal or woe;

If no dear eyes thy fond love can brighten,—
No fond voices answer to thine own;
If no brother's sorrow thou canst lighten
By daily sympathy and gentle tone.

Not by deeds that win the crowd's applauses,
Not by works that give thee world-renown,
Not by martyrdom, or vaunted crosses,
Canst thou win and wear the immortal crown:

Daily struggling, though unloved and lonely,
Every day a rich reward will give;
Thou wilt find, by hearty striding only,
And truly loving, thou canst truly live.

Dost thou revel in the rosy morning,
When all nature hails the lord of light;
And his smile, the mountain-tops adorning,
Robes yon fragrant field in radiance bright.

Other hands may grasp the field and forest;
Proud proprietors in pomp may shine:
But with fervent love if thou adorest,
Thou art wealthier;—all the world is thine.

Yet, if through earth's wide domains thou rovest,
Sighing that they are not thine alone,
Not those fair fields, but thyself thou lovest,
And their beauty, and thy wealth are gone.

Nature wears the colours of the spirit;
Sweetly to her worshipper she sings;
All the glory, grace, she doth inherit
Round her trusting child she fondly flings.

ELIZABETH LLOYD.

Miss Elizabeth Lloyd, a lady of Philadelphia, is the author of the following poem, which recently attracted attention in "going the rounds of the press." It was stated in the newspapers to have been taken from an Oxford edition of Milton's Works.

MILTON ON HIS BLINDNESS.

I am old and blind!
Men point at me as smitten by God's frown:
Afflicted and deserted of my kind,
Yet am I not cast down.

I am weak, yet strong:
I murmur not, that I no longer see;
Poor, old, and helpless, I the more belong,
Father Supreme! to Thee.

O merciful One!
When men are farthest, then art Thou most near;
When friends pass by, my weakness to shun,
Thy chariot I hear.

Thy glorious face
Is leaning toward me, and its holy light
Shines in upon my lonely dwelling-place—
And there is no more night.

On my bended knee,
I recognise Thy purpose, clearly shown;
My vision Thou hast dimmed, that I may see
Thyself, Thyself alone.

I have naught to fear;
This darkness is the shadow of Thy wing;
Beneath it I am almost sacred—here
Can come no evil thing.

Oh! I seem to stand
Trembling, where foot of mortal ne'er hath been,
Wrapped in the radiance from Thy sinless land,
Which eye hath never seen.

Visions come and go;
Shapes of resplendent beauty round me throng;
From angel lips I seem to hear the flow
Of soft and holy song.

It is nothing now,
When heaven is opening on my sightless eyes,
When airs from Paradise refresh my brow,
The earth in darkness lies.

In a purer clime,
My being fills with rapture—waves of thought
Roll in upon my spirit—strains sublime
Break over me unsought.

Give me now my lyre!
I feel the stirrings of a gift divine:
Within my bosom glows unearthly fire
Lit by no skill of mine.

CAROLINE CHESEBRO'.

Miss Chesebro' was born at Canandaigua, where she has always resided with her family. Her first literary articles, a series of tales and sketches, were written for Graham's Magazine and Holden's Dollar Magazine in 1848. Since that time contributions have appeared from her pen in The Knickerbocker, Putnam's, Harpers', and other magazines, and in the newspapers, to which on two occasions, in Philadelphia and New York, she contributed prize tales. In 1851 she published a collection of tales and sketches, *Dream-Land by Daylight, a Panorama of Romance*. The title is suggestive of the fanciful, reflective, and occasionally sombre character of the work, qualities which also mark Miss Chesebro's later and more elaborate productions, *Isa, a Pilgrimage*, and *The Children of Light, a Theme for the Times*, tales, each occupying a separate volume, and written with energy and thoughtfulness. The scene of these writings is laid in America at the present day. They are grave in tone, and aim rather at the exhibition of mental emotion than the outward, salient points of character.

THE BLACK FROST.

Methinks
This word of love is fit for all the world,
And that for gentle hearts another name
Would speak of gentler thoughts than the world owns.

It was a clear, calm night. Brightly shone the innumerable stars: the fixed orbs of giant magnitude, the little twinkling points of light, the glorious constellations—in their imperial beauty stood they, gazing upon the mysterious face of darkness—a clear, calm, terribly cold night.

Winter had not as yet fairly set in. There had been no snow, but it was very late in the autumn, and the grass, and the flowering shrubs and trees, looked as though they had each and all felt the cruel breath of the Destroyer, as he pronounced the doom upon them.

People rubbed their hands, and talked with quivering lips of the hard winter coming, as they hastened, in the increasing shadows of the night, to their homes. The children, warmed and gladdened by the bright fires that were kindled on the hearth-stones, romped, and frolicked, and prophesied, with knowing looks, about snow-balling, sleigh-rides, skating, and all manner of fun. The young girls met together, and talked merrily of coming gaieties; the old man wondered whether he should see another spring-time; and the poor crept to their beds at nightfall, glad to forget everything—cold, hunger, and misery—in sleep.

Midnight came. More and more brightly shone the stars—they glowed, they trembled, and smiled on one another. The cold became intense—in the deep silence how strangely looked the branches of the leafless trees! how desolate the gardens and the forest—how *very still* the night did seem!

Close beside an humble cottage, under a huge bush of flowering-currant, had flourished all the autumn a tiny violet-root. And still, during the increasing cold of the latter days, the leaves had continued green and vigorous, and the flowers opened.

There had been an arrival at the cottage that day. Late in the afternoon, a father and mother, with their child, had returned from long wandering in foreign lands.

A student had watched their coming. In the morning, he had gathered a flower from that little root in their garden, and now, as he sat in the long hours of night, poring over his books, he kept the violet still beside him, in a vase which held the treasures of a green-house, and his eyes rested often on the pale blue modest flower.

At nightfall, a youthful form had stood for a moment at the cottage-door, and the young invalid's eyes, which so eagerly sought all familiar things, at last rested on those still living flowers—flowers, where she had thought to find all dead, even as were those buds which once gave fair promise of glorious opening in her girl-heart! Unmindful of the cold and dampness, she stepped from the house, and passed to the violet-root, and, gathering all the flowers but one, she placed them in her hair, and then hastened with a shiver back to the cottage.

In the fast-increasing cold, the leaves that were left bowed down close to the earth, and the delicate flowers crowning the pale, slender stem, trembled under the influence of the frost.

The little chamber where Mary lay down to rest, was that which, from her childhood, had been set apart for her occupation; a pleasant room, endeared to her by a thousand joyful dreams dreamed within its shade—solemnized to her also by that terrible wakening to sorrow which she had known.

She reclined now on her bed in the silentness, the darkness; but she rested not, she slept not. The young girl's eyes, fixed on the far-off stars, on the glorious heavens, her thoughts wandered wild and free, but her body was circled by the arm of Death.

She had not yet slept at all that night; she had not slept for many nights. Winter was reigning in Mary's heart—it had long reigned there. She was remembering now, while others nestled in the arms of forgetfulness, those days that were gone, when she had looked with such trust and joy upon the years to be—how that she had longed for the slowly-unfolding future to develop itself fully, completely! how she had wholly given herself to the fancies and the hopes of the untried. Alas! she had reached, she had passed, too soon, that crisis of life which unfolds next to the expectant the season of winter—she had seen the gay flowers fading, the leaves withering, the glory of summer pass. And yet how young, how very young she was!

They who saw the shadow brooding over her, out of which she could not move, they who loved, who almost worshipped her, the father and the mother, had in every manner sought, how vainly! to stop the course of that disease which fastened upon her—they could not dispel the sorrow which had blighted her life. She also, for a moment, desperately as they, had striven with her grief, but now, in the cheerless autumn time, she was come back to her home, feeling that it would be easier there to die.

Gazing from her couch out upon the "steadfast skies"—thinking on the past, and the to-come—the to-come of the dying! Yet the thought of death and judgment terrified her not. Surely she would find mercy and heart's ease in the Heaven over which the merciful is king!

But suddenly, in the night's stillness, in the coldness and the darkness, she arose; and steadfastly gazed, for an instant, upward, far upward, where a star shot from the zenith, down, down, to the very horizon. She fell back at the sight, her spirit sped away with that swift glory flash—*Mary was dead!*

In that moment the student also stood beside his window. The fire in the grate had died away, the lamp was nearly exhausted; wearied with his long-continued work, he had risen, and now, for an instant, stood looking upon the heavens. There was sadness and weariness in his heart. The little violet, and the travellers' return, had strangely affected him: for once he found not in his books the satisfaction which he sought: he felt that another life than that of a plodding book-worm might be led by him. His dreams in the morning hour were not pleasant as he slept. They were solely of one whose love he had set at naught for the smiles of a sterner love; of one whom he now thought of, as in the spring-time of his life, when she was all the world to him. And now that she was come again, and he should see her once more! ah, he would bow before her as he once had, and she, who was ever so gentle, so loving, so good, would not spurn him: she would forget his forgetfulness, she would yet give to him that peace, that joy which he had never quaffed at the fountains of learning!

Up rose the sun, and people saw how the Black Frost was over the earth, binding all things in its hard, close, cold embrace. Later in the morning, a little child, passing by the cottage, paused and peeped through the bars upon the violet-root. Yesternight, when she went home from school, she saw the flowers blooming there, the pale, blue, faint-hearted looking flowers—and now she remembered to look if they were there still. But though she looked long and steadfastly where the sunlight fell beneath the currant-bush, she could not see that she sought for; so passing quietly through the gate, she stooped down where the violets had been, and felt the leaves, and knew that they were frozen; and it was only by an effort that she kept back the fast-gathering tears, when she looked on the one flower Mary had left, and saw how it was drooped and dead.

But a sadder sight, and one more full of meaning, was presented in the pleasant chamber, whose window opened on the yard where the blossoming bushes grew. For there a woman bent over the bed whereon another frost-killed flower lay, moaning in the bitterness of grief, the death of her one treasure!

Still later in the day another mourner stood in that silent place, thinking of the meteor and the violet. It was the student, he who in remorse and anguish came, bemoaning the frost-blighted. Too late, too late, he came to tell his love—too late to crave forgiveness, too late to soothe the broken-hearted! Now stood he himself in the valley of the shadow of woe.

And the snow and the storms abounded. Winter was come!

EDWARD MATURIN,

The author of several historical novels, and of a volume of poems of merit, is the son of the celebrated Irish novelist and dramatist, the Rev. Charles Robert Maturin. He has for a number of years been a resident of New York, and has married an American lady.

Mr. Maturin has published *Montezuma, The Last of the Aztecs*, a spirited prose romance, drawn from the brilliant and pathetic history of the Mexican chieftain, followed by *Benjamin, the Jew of Granada*, a story the scene of which is laid in the romantic era of the fall of the Moslem empire in Spain, and in 1848, *Eva, or the Isles of Life and Death;* a historical romance of the twelfth century in England, in which Dermod M'Murrough acts a leading part.

In 1850 he published *Lyrics of Spain and Erin*, a volume of genuine enthusiasm, and refined though irregular poetic expression. The author, who shows much of the poet in his prose writings, finds in the stirring historical ballad of Spain and the pathetic legend of Ireland his appropriate themes.

The latest production of Mr. Maturin was *Bianca*, a passionate story of Italian and Irish incident, published by the Harpers in 1853.

THE SEASONS—FROM A POEM "THE WOODS."

What spirit moves within your holy shrine?
'Tis Spring—the year's young bride, that gladly pours
Above—around—an effluence Divine
Of light and life, falling in golden showers—
And with her come the sportive nymphs in dance
Like waves that gambol in the Summer's glance,
Untwining bowers from their Winter's sleep,
Unlocking rivers from their fountains deep,
Tinting the leaf with verdure, that had lain
Long-hid, like gold within the torpid grain,
Chaunting her choral song, as Nature's eyes
First greet the bridal of the earth and skies.

The Spring is past;—and blushing summer comes,
Music and sunshine throng her scented way;
The birds send gladly from their bowered homes,
Their pæan at the birth of flowery May!
From close to shut of Day; yes, far and near
The spell of mystic music chains the ear;
All Nature, from her bosom pouring forth
Sounds such as make a Temple of the earth
Returns in one full stream of harmony
The angel-echoes that she hears on high—
Beautiful Summer! fling thy crown of flowers
O'er this dull earth through winter's weary hours;
Let them not fade—oh! let not sere and blight
Darken thy prism'd couch with shade of Night;
Let not thy music ever break its spell,
Like heaven-bound pilgrim bidding earth "Farewell!"
Oh! silence not thy music—let thy flowers
Be earth's bright stars responding to the skies;
Wreathing her graves with those immortal bowers
Thy rosy hand 'twined 'round the Dead in Paradise!

Oh! not a vision here but it must pass
Like our own image from Life's spectre-glass;
Summer is faded, and the Autumn sere
Gathers the fallen leaves upon her bier,
And, like the venomed breath of the Simoom
That turns Zahara's desert to a tomb,
Breathes on the buried Summer's shrined abode,
And leaves a spectre what she found—a God!
'Tis thus, ye woods! your melancholy tale
Hath more of truth than rose and lily pale,
When the bright glories of the summer vie
To make the earth a mirror of the sky.
In Autumn's time-worn volume do we read
The sacred moral—All things earthly fade;
And trace upon the page of every leaf
That first and latest human lesson—grief!

But hark! that dreary blast that rolls
Like heart-wrung wailings of unburied souls,
'Tis winter's breath
That comes from the land of Death
Where the Arctic fetters the main;
Like the lightning it darts
When its meteor parts
And dissolves, like the cloud in rain;
And now pale Winter cometh frore
From the dark North's drear and lifeless shore;
And round his form, trembling and old,
Hangs his snow-robe in drifting fold,
As that ye see on the mountain-height,
Like Death asleep in the calm moonlight—
His diadem gleams with the icicle bright,
And his sceptre of ice to destroy and to smite;
Like a monarch he sweeps from the mount to the vale,
In his chariot that glistens with hoar-frost and hail:
His palace the iceberg adorned with spars,
Like a wandering heaven all fretted with stars.

WILLIAM ROSS WALLACE

Is a native of Lexington, Kentucky. He received his education in that state, studied law and came to New York, where he has been since a resident. In 1848, he published *Alban, a Poetical Composition*, "a romance of New York, intended to illustrate the influence of certain prejudices of society and principles of law upon individual character and destiny.* In 1851, he published *Meditations in America, and other Poems.* They are mostly marked by a certain grandeur of thought and eloquence of expression.

OF THINE OWN COUNTRY SING.

I met the wild-eyed Genius of our Land
In Huron's forest vast and dim;
I saw her sweep a harp with stately hand;
I heard her solemn hymn.

She sang of Nations that had passed away
From her own broad imperial clime;
Of Nations new to whom she gave the sway:
She sang of God and Time.

I saw the PAST with all its rhythmic lore:
I saw the PRESENT clearly glow;
Shapes with veiled faces paced a far dim shore
And whispered "Joy" and "Wo!"

Her large verse pictured mountain, vale, and bay,
Our wide, calm rivers rolled along,
And many a mighty Lake and Prairie lay
In the shadow of her Song.

As in Missouri's mountain range, the vast
Wild Wind majestically flies
From crag to crag till on the top at last
The wild Wind proudly dies.

So died the Hymn.—"O Genius! how can I
Crown me with Song as thou art crowned?"
She, smiling, pointed to the spotless sky
And the forest-tops around—

Then sang—"Not to the far-off Lands of Eld
Must thou for inspiration go:
There Milton's large imperial organ swelled,
There Avon's waters flow.

"No Alien-Bard where TASSO's troubled lyre
Made sorrow fair, unchallenged dwells—
Where deep-eyed Danté with the wreath of fire
Came chanting from his Hells.

"Yet sometimes sing the old majestic themes
Of Europe in her song enshrined:
These going wind-like o'er thy Sea of Dreams,
May liberalize the mind.

"Or learn from mournful ASIA, as she lies
Musing at noon beneath her stately palms,
Her angel-lore, her wide-browed prophecies,
Her solemn-sounding psalms:

"Or sit with ARABIC when her eyes of flame
Smoulder in dreams, beneath their swarthy lids,
Of youthful Sphynx, and Kings at loud acclaim
On new-built Pyramids.

"But know thy Highest dwells at Home: there Art
And choral Inspirations spring;
If thou would'st touch the Universal Heart,
OF THINE OWN COUNTRY SING.

* Griswold's Poets of America, Art. Wallace.

CHARLES ASTOR BRISTED,

THE only son of the late Rev. John Bristed and Magdalen Bentzon, eldest daughter of the late John Jacob Astor, was born in New York in 1820. He entered Yale College, where he took the first Berkeleian prize for Latin composition *solus* in the freshman and sophomore years, and divided the Berkeleian classical prize of the senior year with A. R. Macdonough, a son of Commodore Macdonough. He was a frequent contributor at this time to the Yale Literary Magazine. Having completed his studies at Yale, he went to England, and passed five years at the University of Cambridge, taking his B.A. degree at Trinity College in 1845. At Trinity he gained a classical prize the first year, the under-graduate and bachelor prizes for English essays, and the first prize-cup for an English oration. He was also elected foundation-scholar of the college in 1844. In the university he gained the under-graduate's Latin essay prize in 1843, and was placed eighth in the Classical Tripos of his year.

Having returned to America, he was married in 1847 to the daughter of the late Henry Brevoort, one of the earliest friends and collaborators of Washington Irving.

C. A. Bristed

Mr. Bristed was at this time and afterwards a frequent contributor of articles, poetical translations, critical papers on the classics, and sketches of society, to the Literary World, Knickerbocker, the Whig Review, and other journals. Mr. Bristed edited in 1849 *Selections from Catullus*, a school edition, by G. G. Cookesley, one of the assistant-masters of Eton, which he revised, with additional notes.

In 1850 he published *A Letter to the Hon. Horace Mann*, in reply to some reflections of the latter on Stephen Girard and John Jacob Astor, in a tract entitled "Thoughts for a Young Man."

In 1852 appeared *The Upper Ten Thousand*, a collection of sketches of New York society, contributed to Fraser's Magazine; which being written for an English periodical, were minute in description of matters familiar at home, but this particularity gave interest to the life-like narration in America as well. A certain personal piquancy added to the attraction.

At the same time Mr. Bristed published two volumes of a graver character, *Five Years in an English University*, in which he described with spirit, in a knowing, collegiate style, the manners, customs, studies, and ideas of a complex organization and mode of life but little understood in America. In a rather extensive appendix to the first edition of this work the author added a series of his college orations and prize essays, and of the examination papers of the university. The work was an acceptable one to scholars, and those interested in the educational discipline on this side of the Atlantic, as well as to the general reader.

Of late years Mr. Bristed has passed much of his time in Paris, and in the summer at Baden-Baden. In a frequent correspondence with the New York Spirit of the Times he has recorded the life of Europe passing under his eye, in matters of art, literature, the drama, and the social aspect of the times. He has also resumed his contributions to Fraser's Magazine on American topics. An article in the number for July, 1855, from his pen, treats of the relation of the English press to the United States.

The writings of Mr. Bristed exhibit the union of the man of the world and of books. His pictures of society are somewhat remarkable for a vein of freedom and candor of statement. As a critic of Greek and Latin classical topics he is diligent and acute, displaying some of the best qualities of the trained English university man. He has also published numerous occasional clever poetical translations of classical niceties from Theocritus, Ovid, and such moderns as Walter de Mapes.

HENRY R. JACKSON

Was born at Athens, Georgia, in 1820. He is the son of Dr. Henry Jackson, formerly professor of natural philosophy in Franklin college in that state. He was educated to the bar, and early held the office of United States district attorney for Georgia. At the commencement of the war with Mexico he raised at Savannah a company of one hundred men, called the Jasper Greens; marched to Columbus to form a regiment; was elected colonel, proceeded to Mexico, and served with distinction. On his return he was appointed Judge of the Superior Court of the Eastern District of Georgia. He is at present Resident Minister at Vienna, to which he was appointed in 1853.

In 1850 Mr. Jackson published a volume, a collection of fugitive verses, *Tallulah and other Poems*. Its themes are chiefly local, and of a patriotic interest, or occupied with the fireside affections. The expression is spirited and manly. His Georgia lyrics, and his descriptions of the scenery of the state, are animated and truthful productions.

THE LIVE-OAK.

With his gnarled old arms, and his iron form,
 Majestic in the wood,
From age to age, in the sun and storm,
 The live-oak long hath stood;
With his stately air, that grave old tree,
 He stands like a hooded monk,
With the grey moss waving solemnly
 From his shaggy limbs and trunk.

And the generations come and go,
 And still he stands upright,
And he sternly looks on the wood below,
 As conscious of his might.
But a mourner sad is the hoary tree,
 A mourner sad and lone,
And is clothed in funeral drapery
 For the long since dead and gone.

For the Indian hunter beneath his shade
 Has rested from the chase;
And he here has woo'd his dusky maid—
 The dark-eyed of her race;
And the tree is red with the gushing gore
 As the wild deer panting dies:
But the maid is gone, and the chase is o'er,
 And the old oak hoarsely sighs.

In former days, when the battle's din
 Was loud amid the land,
In his friendly shadow, few and thin,
 Have gathered Freedom's band,
And the stern old oak, how proud was he
 To shelter hearts so brave!
But they all are gone—the bold and free—
 And he moans above their grave.

And the aged oak, with his locks of grey,
 Is ripe for the sacrifice;
For the worm and decay, no lingering prey,
 Shall he tower towards the skies!
He falls, he falls, to become our guard,
 The bulwark of the free,
And his bosom of steel is proudly bared
 To brave the raging sea!

When the battle comes, and the cannon's roar
 Booms o'er the shuddering deep,
Then nobly he'll bear the bold hearts o'er
 The waves, with bounding leap.
Oh! may those hearts be as firm and true,
 When the war-clouds gather dun,
As the glorious oak that proudly grew
 Beneath our southern sun.

HENRY W. PARKER.

The Rev. Henry W. Parker, of Brooklyn, New York, is the author of a volume of poems published at Auburn, New York, in 1850. It is a delicate book, with many proofs of refinement and scholarship, while a certain philosophical texture runs through it. An appendix contains several ingenious and fine-thoughted prose papers.

In 1851 Mr. Parker recited a poem, *The Story of a Soul*, before the Psi Upsilon Convention at Hamilton College.

THE CITY OF THE DEAD.

Go forth and breathe the purer air with me,
 And leave the city's sounding streets;
There is another city, sweet to see,
 Whose heart with no delirium beats;
The solid earth beneath it never feels
 The dance of joy, the rush of care,
The jar of toil, the mingled roll of wheels;
 But all is peace and beauty there.

No spacious mansions stand in stately rows
 Along that city's silent ways;
No lofty wall, nor level pavement, glows,
 Unshaded from the summer rays;

No costly merchandise is heaped around,
No pictures stay the passer-by,
Nor plumed soldiers march to music's sound,
Nor toys and trifles tire the eye.

The narrow streets are fringed with living green,
And weave about in mazes there;
The many hills bewilder all the scene,
And shadows veil the noonday glare.
No clanging bells ring out the fleeting hours,
But sunlight glimmers softly thro',
And marks the voiceless time in golden showers
On velvet turf and lakelets blue.

The palaces are sculptured shafts of stone
That gleam in beauty thro' the trees;
The cottages are mounds with flowers o'ergrown;
No princely church the stranger sees,
But all the grove its pointed arches rears,
And tinted lights shine thro' the leaves,
And prayers are rained in every mourner's tears
Who for the dead in silence grieves.

And when dark night descends upon the tombs,
No reveller's song nor watchman's voice
Is here! no music comes from lighted rooms
Where swift feet fly and hearts rejoice;
'Tis darkness, silence all; no sound is heard
Except the wind that sinks and swells,
The lonely whistle of the midnight bird,
And brooks that ring their crystal bells.

A city strange and still!—its habitants
Are warmly housed, yet they are poor—
Are poor, yet have no wish, nor woes and wants;
The broken heart is crushed no more,
No love is interchanged, nor bought and sold,
Ambition sleeps, the innocent
Are safe, the miser counts no more his gold,
But rests at last and is content.

A city strange and sweet!—its dwellers sleep
At dawn, and in meridian light,—
At sunset still they dream in slumber deep,
Nor wake they in the weary night;
And none of them shall feel the hero's kiss
On Sleeping Beauty's lip that fell,
And woke a palace from a trance of bliss
That long had bound it by a spell.

A city strange and sad!—we walk the grounds,
Or seek some mount, and see afar
The living cities shine, and list the sounds
Of throbbing boat and thundering car.
And *we* may go; but all the dwellers here,
In autumn's blush, in winter's snow,
In spring and summer's bloom, from year to year,
They ever come, and never go!

CHARLES G. EASTMAN,

Of Vermont, for some time editor of the Vermont Patriot at Montpelier, is the author of a volume of *Poems* published in 1848. They are marked by facility in the use of lyric and ballad measures, and many are in a familiar sportive vein.

A PICTURE.

The farmer sat in his easy chair
Smoking his pipe of clay,
While his hale old wife with busy care
Was clearing the dinner away;
A sweet little girl with fine blue eyes
On her grandfather's knee was catching flies.

The old man laid his hand on her head,
With a tear on his wrinkled face,
He thought how often her mother, dead,
Had sat in the self-same place;
As the tear stole down from his half-shut eye,
"Don't smoke!" said the child, "how it makes you cry!"

The house-dog lay, stretched out on the floor
Where the shade after noon used to steal,
The busy old wife by the open door
Was turning the spinning wheel,
And the old brass clock on the mantel-tree
Had plodded along to almost three,—

Still the farmer sat in his easy chair,
While close to his heaving breast,
The moistened brow and the cheek so fair
Of his sweet grandchild were pressed;
His head, bent down, on her soft hair lay—
Fast asleep were they both, that summer day!

JOHN ORVILLE TERRY,

Of Orient, a village of Suffolk county, Long Island, published in New York in 1850 a volume of characteristic rural life, entitled *The Poems of J. O. T., consisting of Song, Satire, and Pastoral Descriptions, chiefly depicting the Scenery, and illustrating the Manners and Customs of the Ancient and Present Inhabitants of Long Island.* The book answers to its title. The verses are written with ease and fervor, though sometimes carelessly, and have a genuine flavor of reality in the portraits of individuals, the various characteristics of nature and the seasons, the sea, and landscape. In his patriotic and satirical effusions, the author has something of the spirit of Freneau.

AUNT DINAH.

Embowered in shade, by the side of a wood,
The cot of aunt Dinah delightfully stood,
A rural retreat, in simplicity drest,
Sequestered it sat like a bird in its nest:
Festooned with the brier, and scented with rose,
Its windows looked out on a scene of repose,
Its wood all in green, and its grass all in bloom,
Like the dwelling of peace in a grove of perfume.

Tho' the skin of aunt Dinah was black as a coal,
The beams of affection enlightened her soul;
Like gems in a cavern, that sparkle and blaze,
The darkness but adds to the strength of their rays;
Or the moon looking out from her evening shroud,
Or the sun riding forth from the edge of a cloud,
So benevolence shone in her actions alway,
And the darkness of life became radiant with day.

What tho' she were poor, aunt Dinah's estate
The world was unable to give or create,
Her wealth was her virtues, and brightly they shone,
With a lustre unborrowed, and beauty their own;
Her nature was goodness, her heart was a mine
Of jewels, more precious than words can define,
And she gave them with such a profusion and grace,
Their light gave complexion and hue to her face.

Aunt Dinah has gone to the land of the good,
And her ashes repose by her favorite wood,
But her lonely old cottage looks out o'er the plain,
As if it would welcome its mistress again;
And long may it stand in that rural retreat,
To mind us of her we no longer may meet,
When we go after blackberries, joyful and gay,
And forget the kind hostess who welcomed us aye.

CHARLES OSCAR DUGUÉ,

The author of several volumes of poetry in the French language, is a native of Louisiana, born at New Orleans, May 1, 1821. His parents were both Americans by birth, of French descent. He was early sent to France, where he was educated at Clermont Ferrand in Auvergne, and at the College of St. Louis in Paris. While a student, he wrote verses, which Chateaubriand commended for their noble and natural expression, without affectation or extravagance. Thus encouraged, on his return to New Orleans, he published in 1847 his *Essais Poétiques*, the topics of which are descriptions of Southern scenery, sentimental and occasional poems. In 1852 he published two dramatic works, on subjects drawn from the romantic legends of Louisiana;—*Mila ou La Mort de La Salle*, and *Le Cygne, ou Mingo*, an Indian plot, in which Tecumseh is one of the characters. In the same year he took the field as editor of a daily paper in New Orleans, *l'Orléanais*, in which he advocated the Compromise Resolutions. Mr. Dugué is now a member of the bar at New Orleans. He has written a manuscript work, entitled *Philosophie Morale*, which is to be published in French and English.

XAVIER DONALD MACLEOD.

MR. MCLEOD is the son of the Rev. Alexander McLeod, a Presbyterian clergyman of eminence, who emigrated to this country in 1794, and the grandson of Niel McLeod, the entertainer of Dr. Johnson at Mull in the Hebrides. Mr. McLeod was born in the city of New York, November 17, 1821, and took orders in the Episcopal Church in 1845. After being settled for a short time in a country parish, he in 1848 visited Europe, where he became a Roman Catholic. Since his return in 1852, Mr. McLeod has devoted himself to authorship, a career which he commenced at an early age, having contributed tales and poems to the New Yorker in 1841. He has published *Pynnshurst, his Wanderings and his Ways of Thinking*, a romance of European travel, *The Blood-Stone*, a story of talismanic influence, *Lescure, or the Last Marquis*, and the Life of Sir Walter Scott, prepared from the Life by Lockhart. His last work is a biography of the present efficient mayor of the city of New York, Fernando Wood. Mr. McLeod has been a frequent contributor in prose and verse to the magazines of the day.

E. G. SQUIER.

EPHRAIM GEORGE SQUIER was born in the town of Bethlehem, Albany County, New York, June 17, 1821. He is a lineal descendant of Cornet Auditor Samuel Squier, one of Oliver Cromwell's lieutenants, who figures in the Correspondence, the "Thirty-Five Unpublished Letters of Cromwell," communicated to the historian Carlyle, and published by him in Fraser's Magazine.

The younger sons of this Samuel Squier emigrated to America, and their descendants took an active part in the colonial events which followed the Restoration. The great-grandfather of our author, Philip Squier, served under Wolcott in the capture of Louisburg; and his grandfather, Ephraim Squier, fought side by side with Col. Knowlton at Bunker Hill. He was also with Arnold in the terrible winter journey through the wilderness of the Kennebec, in the expedition against Canada. He lived to be one of the veterans of the war, dying in 1842 at the venerable age of ninety-seven. The father of the subject of our present sketch is a devoted Methodist minister in the northern part of New York and of Vermont. In his youth, Squier obtained his education according to the New England fashion, by working on the farm in summer, and teaching a common school in winter. At eighteen, we find him attempting literature in the publication of a little paper in the village of Charlton, Saratoga County, while more seriously qualifying himself for the profession of a Civil Engineer. The disastrous period of 1837–39, which put a stop for a time to all works of public improvement, necessarily diverted Mr. Squier from the career which he had marked out for himself. His knowledge of engineering, however, has since been of the most effectual service to him, in his investigations both at home and abroad, and has contributed much to their success. Diverted in this manner from his profession, Mr. Squier next made his appearance in print, in 1840, as the editor of a monthly periodical in Albany, entitled *Parlor Magazine*, which lasted a year, and which was succeeded by the *Poet's Magazine*, based upon the idea of making a contemporaneous collection of American poetry, a sort of National Anthology. But two numbers were issued.

His next effort was of more pith and importance, in his contributions to and virtual editorship of the *New York State Mechanic* (1841–2), published at Albany, and occupied with the interests of the mechanics, and a change in the prison system of the state, injurious to their callings. At this time he prepared a volume of information on the Chinese.*

In 1843 he went to Hartford, Connecticut, and for two years edited the *Hartford Daily Journal*, an ardent advocate of Henry Clay, as a type of American character; and to his duties as editor added the part of an efficient organizer of the Whig party in Connecticut.

Early in 1845, Mr. Squier accepted the editorship of the *Scioto Gazette* published at Chillicothe, Ohio, with which he retained his connexion for nearly three years, interrupted only by his election as Clerk of the Legislative Assembly of the State during the winter of 1847–8. Immediately upon his arrival in Ohio, in conjunction with Dr. Davis, he commenced a systematic investigation of the Aboriginal Monuments of the Mississippi Valley, the results of which he embodied in a voluminous Memoir, which was published by the Smithsonian Institution, and constitutes the first volume of its *Contributions to Knowledge*.†

Previously to this, the researches of Mr. Squier had attracted the attention of the venerable Albert Gallatin, at whose request he prepared a Memoir on the Ancient Monuments of the West, which was published in the *Transactions of the American Ethnological Society*, and also in a separate form.‡

---

* The Chinese as they are, &c., by G. T. Lay; with Illustrative and Corroborative Notes, Additional Chapters on the Ancient and Modern History, Ancient and Modern Intercourse, &c. By E. G. Squier. 8vo. Albany. 1843.

† Ancient Monuments of the Mississippi Valley, comprising the Results of Extensive Original Surveys and Explorations. By E. G. Squier, A.M., and E. H. Davis, M.D. 4to. pp. 400.

‡ Observations on the Aboriginal Monuments of the Mis-

E. Geo. Squier

The work published by the Smithsonian Institution, in the number, variety, and value of the facts which it embodies, is undoubtedly entitled to a front rank in all that relates to American Archæology. The memoir of Mr. Caleb Atwater published in 1820, in the Transactions of the American Antiquarian Society, was, previously to the appearance of this work, the only authority on the subject. In the language of Mr. Gallatin, "it is very incomplete, has many mistakes, and is in no degree comparable to the work published by the Smithsonian Institution," which has been accepted as a standard in the department to which it relates. The results of Mr. Squier's inquiries into our Western antiquities are briefly;

1st. That the earthworks of the West are of a high but indeterminate antiquity; one, nevertheless, sufficiently great to admit of physical and natural changes, which, in historic regions, it has required thousands of years to bring about.

2d. That the ancient population of the Mississippi Valley was numerous and widely spread, as evinced from the number and magnitude of the ancient monuments, and the extensive range of their occurrence.

3d. That this population was essentially homogeneous in blood, customs, and habits; that it was stationary and agricultural; and although not having a high degree of civilization, was nevertheless possessed of systematic forms of religion and government.

4th. That the facts of which we are in possession, suggest a probable ancient connexion between the race of the mounds, and the semi-civilized aboriginal families of Central America and Mexico, but that there exists no direct evidence of such relationship.

Upon the question, What became of the race of the Mounds? Mr. Squier has not, we believe, expressed an opinion. His writings, however, imply a total disregard of all hypotheses which would ascribe the ancient monuments of the Mississippi Valley to others than a purely aboriginal origin, as idle puerile fancies.*

The "Ancient Monuments" was followed by another publication from Mr. Squier's pen by the Smithsonian Institution in 1849;—*Aboriginal Monuments of the State of New York, from Original Surveys and Explorations*, under the auspices of the New York Historical Society, a work which was afterwards enlarged in a volume entitled, *Antiquities of the State of New York, with a Supplement on the Antiquities of the West.* This work established that the small and irregular earthworks, and other aboriginal remains, north-east of the great lakes, were to be ascribed to a comparatively recent period, and were probably due to the Indian tribes found in occupation of the country at the time of the discovery.

When General Taylor became President in 1848, Mr. Squier received the appointment of Chargé d'Affaires of the United States to the republics of Central America, in the discharge of which he negotiated three treaties with Nicaragua, Honduras, and San Salvador respectively. As an ardent advocate of American rights and interests, as well as of the political independence of the Central American States, he secured a personal influence on the Isthmus which has been directed to several objects of political and general interest, amongst which the opening, on most advantageous terms, of two new inter-oceanic routes, is not the least. His dispatches, published under order of Congress, fill two considerable volumes. He nevertheless found time, in the short period of his official duties, which were brought to a termination on the death of General Taylor, to make various explorations into the antiquities of the country, an account of which, as well as of his general political and social observations, etc., is included in his two valuable volumes entitled *Nicaragua; its People, Scenery, and Monuments*, published in 1852, which in original investigation, spirit of adventure, and picturesque narrative, is a companion to Stephens's Incidents of Travel in Central America and Yucatan.

Mr. Squier had previously, in 1851, published his volume, *The Serpent Symbol, or the Worship of the Reciprocal Principles of Nature in America*, the object of which seems to have been to show that the many resemblances, amounting in some instances to identities, between the manners, customs, institutions, and especially religions, of the great families of men in the old and new world, were not necessarily derivative, or the results of connexions or relationship, recent or remote. On the contrary, that these resemblances are due to like organizations, influenced by common natural suggestions, and the moulding force of circumstances.

On the publication of the work on Nicaragua,

---

sissippi Valley, the Character of the Ancient Earthworks, Structure and Purposes of the Mounds, etc., etc. By E. G. Squier.

* Monumental Evidences of the Discovery of America by the Northmen, Critically Examined.—London Ethnological Journal, December, 1849. Review of "A Memoir on the European Colonization of America in Ante-Historic Times." By Dr. Zestermann. London. 1852.

Mr. Squier visited Europe, where he was introduced to the chief geographical and ethnological societies of England, Germany, and France; made the personal acquaintance of Humboldt, Ritter (who has introduced a translation of his work on Nicaragua to the German public), Lepsius, Jomard, Maury, and the remaining leaders of archæological and geographical science. The first diploma of the Geographical Society of France, for 1852, was awarded to Mr. Squier, who was at the same time elected associate of the National Society of Antiquarians of France, an honor which has been conferred upon only one other American, the Hon. Edward Everett.

While in Europe Mr. Squier kept up his taste for antiquarian investigations by an examination of the remains at Stonehenge, the results of which were communicated in a paper to the American Ethnological Society.* He also, in conjunction with Lord Londesborough, made some interesting explorations amongst the early British barrows of the north of England, near Scarborough.

In 1853 Mr. Squier again visited Central America for the purpose of investigating the line of an inter-oceanic railway, which his deductions on his previous visit had led him to consider possible, between some convenient harbor on the Gulf of Mexico and the Bay of Fonseca on the Pacific. The result of this special point of investigation has been communicated to the public in Mr. Squier's preliminary report of the Honduras Inter-Oceanic Railway Company, of which he is Secretary. His further observations and adventures, at this time, are included in the two works which he has prepared, entitled *Honduras and San Salvador, Geographical, Historical, and Statistical*, with original maps and illustrative sketches, and a more personal volume, *Hunting a Pass*, comprising adventures, observations, and impressions during a year of active explorations in the States of Nicaragua, Honduras, and San Salvador, Central America. The numerous illustrations to these works are remarkable for their merit. They are from the pencil of the artist, Mr. D. C. Hitchcock, who accompanied Mr. Squier on his journeys as draftsman. The various vocabularies, plans, drawings of monuments, and other archæological materials collected during this last expedition, it is presumed will be embodied in a separate form.

Besides the writings which we have enumerated, Mr. Squier has been an industrious contributor to the periodical, newspaper, and scientific literature of the day, on topics of politics affecting the foreign relations of the country with the States of Central America; the antiquities and ethnology of the aboriginal tribes of the country, in various journals, and in the Transactions of the American Ethnological Society, of which he has been a prominent member.

ELISHA KENT KANE,

The eminent Arctic explorer, was born in Philadelphia, Feb. 3, 1822. He took his degree at the Medical University of Pennsylvania in 1843; entered the United States Navy as assistant surgeon, and was attached as a physician to the first American embassy to China. Availing himself of the facilities of his position, he visited parts of China, the Philippines, Ceylon, and the interior of India. He is said to have been the second, if not the first person, having been certainly the first white person, to descend the crater of the Tael of Luzon, suspended by a bamboo rope around his body, from a projecting crag, two hundred and three feet above the scoriæ and debris. Upon this expedition, or one which followed it to the Indian Archipelago, he narrowly escaped with his life from the Ladrones who assailed him, sustained successfully an attack of an entire tribe of savages of the Negrito race, and was exposed to hardships under which his travelling companion, Baron Loe of Prussia, sank and died at Java. After this he ascended the Nile to the confines of Nubia, and passed a season in Egypt. He travelled through Greece on foot, and returned in 1846 through Europe to the United States. He was at once ordered to the coast of Africa, and when there, in 1847, made an effort to visit the slave marts of Whydah. He took the African fever, and was sent home in a very precarious state of health, from which, however, he recovered sufficiently to visit Mexico during the war as a volunteer. He made his way through the enemy's country with despatches for the American Commander-in-Chief from the President, with the notorious spy company of the brigand Dominguez as his escort; and, after a successful engagement with a party of the enemy whom they encountered at Nopaluca, he was forced to combat his companions single-handed to save the lives of his prisoners, Major-General Torrejon, General Gaona, and others, from their fury. He had his horse killed under him, and was badly wounded; but was restored to health by the hospitality and kind nursing of the grateful Mexicans, particularly the Gaona family of Puebla, by whom he was thus enabled to remain on service in Mexico till the cessation of hostilities.*

When the first Grinnell Expedition for the recovery of Sir John Franklin was projected in 1850, Dr. Kane was appointed senior surgeon and naturalist of the squadron, composed of the Advance and the Rescue, which set sail from New York May 22 of that year, under the command of Lieut. De Haven. After traversing the waters of Baffin's Bay to Melville Bay the expedition crossed to Lancaster Sound and Barrow Straits, and ascended Wellington Channel, where the notable discoveries were made which have given to the map of the world the names of Maury Channel, Grinnell Land, and Mount Franklin. The winter was passed by the expedition imbedded in the ice floe. From the thirteenth of January, 1851, to the fifth of June, the vessels drifted a distance of six hundred miles, when the ice pack immediately surrounding them was broken up in Baffin's Bay. At this time Dr. Kane met Lieut. Bellot, the young French officer whose melancholy fate in the Arctic Regions in August, 1853, was so greatly enhanced to the public mind by the successful results of the efforts at discovery which were announced at the same moment with his death.

* Literary World, January 17 and 24, 1852.

* We find the preceding statement of facts in that excellent contribution to contemporary biography, "The Men of the Time," published by Redfield.

He was then attached to the Prince Albert of the English expedition. After visiting the Greenland settlements of Pröven and Uppernavik, with an unsuccessful attempt, against floes and icebergs, to resume the search through Wellington Channel, the expedition returned to New York in September. The duties and scientific employments of Dr. Kane during the voyage were arduous and constant. After his return he employed himself upon the preparation of his journal for publication, and bringing before the public in lectures at Washington and the chief Atlantic cities, his views in reference to another attempt at Arctic discovery. His account of his voyage, *The U. S. Grinnell Expedition in Search of Sir John Franklin; A Personal Narrative*, was written and left for publication in the hands of the Harpers, when he sailed on his second Arctic expedition from New York, on the 31st May, 1853, in command of the Advance, fitted out by the liberality of Mr. Grinnell of New York, and Mr. Peabody, the wealthy broker of London. His design on this voyage was to advance to the head of Baffin's Bay, and in the winter and spring of 1854 traverse with dogs and sledges the upper portions of the peninsula or island of Greenland, in an endeavor to reach the supposed open Polar sea.

The publication of the book which Dr. Kane had left behind him was delayed by the burning of the edition, just then completed, at the great fire of the Messrs. Harper's establishment in Cliff and Pearl streets in December, 1853. The stereotype plates were saved, and the work was published in the spring of 1854. It is written with great fidelity and spirit, in a style highly characteristic of the life and energy of the man. Its descriptions are vivid, and its felicity of expression remarkable, illuminating to the unscientific reader the array of professional and technical terms with which the subject is appropriately invested. There is a frosty crystallization, as it were, about the style, in keeping with the theme. The scientific merits of the work are important, particularly in the careful study of the ice formations, on which subject Dr. Kane has mentioned his intention to prepare an elaborate essay for the Smithsonian publications. Not the least attraction of the book are the numerous careful drawings and spirited illustrations from the pencil of Dr. Kane himself.

Dr. Kane has also been a contributor to the scientific journals of Europe and America. In 1848 he published a paper on Kyestine, which was well received by the medical profession.

ARCTIC INCIDENTS.

I employed the dreary intervals of leisure that heralded our Christmas in tracing some Flemish portraitures of things about me. The scenes themselves had interest at the time for the parties who figured in them; and I believe that is reason enough, according to the practice of modern academics, for submitting them to the public eye. I copy them from my scrap-book, expurgating only a little.

"We have almost reached the solstice; and things are so quiet that I may as well, before I forget it, tell you something about the cold in its sensible effects, and the way in which as sensible people we met it.

"You will see, by turning to the early part of my journal, that the season we now look back upon as the perfection of summer contrast to this outrageous winter was in fact no summer at all. We had the young ice forming round us in Baffin's Bay, and were measuring snow-falls, while you were sweating under your grass-cloth. Yet I remember it as a time of sunny recreation, when we shot bears upon the floes, and were scrambling merrily over glaciers and murdering rotges in the bright glare of our day-midnight. Like a complaining brute, I thought it cold then—I, who am blistered if I touch a brass button or a ramrod without a woollen mit.

"The cold came upon us gradually. The first thing that really struck me was the freezing up of our water-casks, the drip-candle appearance of the bung-holes, and our inability to lay the tin cup down for a five-minutes' pause without having its contents made solid. Next came the complete inability to obtain drink without manufacturing it. For a long time we had collected our water from the beautiful fresh pools of the icebergs and floes; now we had to quarry out the blocks in flinty, glassy lumps, and then melt it in tins for our daily drink. This was in Wellington Channel.

"By-and-by the sludge which we passed through as we travelled became pancakes and snow-balls. We were glued up. Yet, even as late as the 11th of September, I collected a flowering Potentilla from Barlow's Inlet. But now anything moist or wet began to strike me as something to be looked at—a curious, out-of-the-way production, like the bits of broken ice round a can of mint-julep. Our decks became dry, and studded with botryoidal lumps of dirty foot-trodden ice. The rigging had nightly accumulations of rime, and we learned to be careful about coiled ropes and iron work. On the 4th of October we had a mean temperature below zero.

"By this time our little entering hatchway had become so complete a mass of icicles, that we had to give it up, and resort to our winter door-way. The opening of a door was now the signal for a gush of smoke-like vapor: every stove-pipe sent out clouds of purple steam; and a man's breath looked like the firing of a pistol on a small scale.

"All our eatables became laughably consolidated, and after different fashions, requiring no small experience before we learned to manage the peculiarities of their changed condition. Thus, dried apples became one solid breccial mass of impacted angularities, a conglomerate of sliced chalcedony. Dried peaches the same. To get these out of the barrel, or the barrel out of them, was a matter impossible. We found, after many trials, that the shortest and best plan was to cut up both fruit and barrel by repeated blows with a heavy axe, taking the lumps below to thaw. Saur-kraut resembled mica, or rather talcose slate. A crow-bar with chiseled edge extracted the *laminæ* badly; but it was perhaps the best thing we could resort to.

"Sugar formed a very funny compound. Take *q. s.* of cork raspings, and incorporate therewith another *q. s.* of liquid gutta percha caoutchouc, and allow to harden: this extemporaneous formula will give you the brown sugar of our winter cruise. Extract with the saw; nothing but the saw will suit. Butter and lard, less changed, require a heavy cold chisel and mallet. Their fracture is conchoidal, with hæmatitic (iron-ore pimpled) surface. Flour undergoes little change, and molasses can at —28° be half scooped, half cut by a stiff iron ladle.

"Pork and beef are rare specimens of Florentine mosaic, emulating the lost art of petrified visceral monstrosities seen at the medical schools of Bologna and Milan: crow-bar and handspike! for at —30° the axe can hardly chip it. A barrel sawed in half, and kept for two days in the caboose house at +76°, was still as refractory as flint a few inches below the surface. A similar bulk of lamp oil, denuded of the staves, stood like a yellow sandstone roller for a gravel walk.

"Ices for the dessert come of course unbidden, in all imaginable and unimaginable variety. I have tried my inventive powers on some of them. A Roman punch, a good deal stronger than the noblest Roman ever tasted, forms readily at —20°. Some sugared cranberries, with a little butter and scalding water, and you have an impromptu strawberry ice. Many a time at those funny little jams, that we call in Philadelphia 'parties,' where the lady-hostess glides with such nicely-regulated indifference through the complex machinery she has brought together, I have thought I noticed her stolen glance of anxiety at the cooing doves, whose icy bosoms were melting into one upon the supper-table before their time. We order these things better in the Arctic. Such is the 'composition and fierce quality' of our ices, that they are brought in served on the shaft of a hickory broom; a transfixing rod, which we use as a stirrer first and a fork afterward. So hard is this terminating cylinder of ice, that it might serve as a truncheon to knock down an ox. The only difficulty is in the processes that follow. It is the work of time and energy to impress it with the carving-knife, and you must handle your spoon deftly, or it fastens to your tongue. One of our mess was tempted the other day by the crystal transparency of an icicle to break it in his mouth; one piece froze to his tongue, and two others to his lips, and each carried off the skin: the thermometer was at —28°."

SAMUEL ELIOT,

The author of a *History of Liberty*, was born at Boston, the son of William H. Eliot, December 22, 1821. He was educated in Boston and at Harvard, where he was graduated in 1839. He continued his studies in Europe. He formed the idea of writing a *History of Liberty* in Rome, where he spent the winter of 1844–5, and has since been engaged upon the work.

In 1847, he published in Boston, *Passages from the History of Liberty*, in which he traced the career of the early Italian reformers, Arnaldo da Brescia, Giovanni di Vicenza, and others; of Savonarola; of Wycliffe in England, and the War of the Communities in Castile.

Sam l Eliot

The first series of his more elaborate history in two volumes, appeared in 1849 with the title, *The Liberty of Rome*. In 1853, this work was reprinted in a revised form as *The History of Liberty: Part I. The Ancient Romans*, and in the same year appeared two similar volumes relating to *The Early Christians*. These constituted two parts of an extensive work, of which three others are projected, devoted successively to the Papal Ages, the Monarchical Ages, and the American Nation.

The speciality of Mr. Eliot's historic labors is fully indicated in their title. It is to read the past, not for the purpose of curiosity, entertainment, or controversy, for the chronicle of kings and emperors, or the story of war and conquest, unless for their subordination to the progress of Liberty. His work is therefore a critical analysis rather than a narrative. As such it possesses much philosophical acumen, and bears evidences of a diligent study of the original and later authorities. The conception of the work is a noble one, and it may without vanity be said to be appropriately undertaken by an American.

As a specimen of the author's manner, we present a passage at the close of the history of Roman liberty with the establishment of the Emperors, and at the dawn of the new divine dispensation for all true freedom and progress of humanity in Christianity.

CLOSE OF ANTIQUITY.

Thus is our Era to be named of Hope.
CARLYLE, *French Revolution*, Book III. ch. 8.

The course of the olden time was run. Its generations had wrought the work appointed them to do. Their powers were exhausted. Their liberty, in other words, their ability to exercise their powers, was itself overthrown.

From the outset there had been no union amongst men. The opposite system of centralization, by which the many were bound to the few, had prevailed at the beginning. Weakened, indeed, but more than ever developed, it prevailed also at the end. To renew and to extend this system had been the appointed work of the ancient Romans. Not to unite, not to liberate the human race, had they been intrusted with dominion. It was to reduce mankind, themselves included, to dissension and to submission, that the Romans were allowed their liberty.

To such an end their liberty, like that of the elder nations, was providentially adapted. As a possession, it was in the hands not of the best, but of the strongest. As a right, it was not the right to improve one's self, but that to restrain others. It was the claim to be served by others. It was not the privilege of serving others. Much less was it the privilege of serving God. Struggling amidst the laws of man, instead of resting upon those of God, it was the liberty of men destined to contention until they fell in servitude.

There were exceptions. Not every one lost himself in the dust and the agony of strife. Not every generation spent itself in conflicts. The physical powers were not always the only ones in exercise. At times the intellectual powers obtained development. At rarer seasons, the spiritual powers evinced themselves. A generation might thus attain to a liberty far wider than that of its predecessors. An individual might thus rise to a liberty far higher than that of his contemporaries. Yet these were but exceptions. The rule, confirmed by them, was the tendency of men to a lower, rather than a higher state. Indirectly, they were led towards the higher state, for which the lower was the necessary preparation. But the passage was to be made through the lower. Every bad work that succeeded, every good work that failed, brought mankind nearer to the end of the prevailing evil. The advent of the approaching good was hastened by every downward step towards prostration.

From the masses of the clouds the light first fades away. It presently vanishes from the patches in the skies originally undimmed. Then darkness overspreads the heavens. Men fall supine upon the earth. The night of universal humiliation sets in. But the gloom is not unbroken. Overshadowed as is the scene, it is not overwhelmed. There still remain the vales where truth has descended. There still exist the peaks to which love in its longing has climbed. Desires too earnest to have been wasted, principles too honest to have been unproductive, still linger in promise of the coming day. Men were to be humbled. They needed to feel the insecurity of their liberty, of the powers which made it their right, of the laws which made it their possession. But they did not need to be bereft of the good which their laws and their powers, however imperfect, comprehended.

The day of redemption followed. It was not too late. It was not too soon. The human race had been tried. It had not been annihilated. Then the angels sang their song of glory to God and peace amongst His creatures. We may believe that when the morning came, the oppression and the servitude of old had left their darkest forms amidst the midnight clouds. Before the death of Augustus, the Business of THE FATHER had already been begun in the Temple at Jerusalem; and near by, THE SON was increasing in wisdom and in stature and in favor with God and man.

The sea, as it were, whereon wave has pursued wave through day and night, through years and centuries, before our eyes, is thus illumined with the advancing light which we have been waiting to behold. And as we stand upon the shore, conscious of the Spirit that has moved upon the face of the waters, we may lift our eyes with more confiding faith to the over-watching Heaven.

JAMES T. FIELDS

WAS born in Portsmouth, New Hampshire, in 1820. His partnership in the publishing house of Ticknor and Co. of Boston, whose liberal literary dealings with eminent authors at home and abroad he has always warmly seconded, has identified him with the best interests of literature.

James T. Fields

He is the poets' publisher of America, as Moxon has been of England, and like his brother of the craft in London, writes good verses himself. On two occasions, in 1838 and '48, Mr. Fields has delivered a poem before the Boston Mercantile Association. Sentiment and point, in good set iambics and clashing rhymes, are the approved necessities of these affairs. Mr. Fields's poems on "Commerce" and "the Post of Honor" are wanting in neither. An elegantly printed little volume, in the highest luxury of the press, contains his miscellaneous poems. They are truthful and unaffected in sentiment, finished and delicate in expression.

WORDSWORTH.

The grass hung wet on Rydal banks,
  The golden day with pearls adorning,
When side by side with him we walked
  To meet midway the summer morning.

The west wind took a softer breath,
  The sun himself seemed brighter shining,
As through the porch the minstrel stept—
  His eye sweet Nature's look enshrining.

He passed along the dewy sward,
  The blue-bird sang aloft "good-morrow!"
He plucked a bud, the flower awoke,
  And smiled without one pang of sorrow.

He spoke of all that graced the scene
  In tones that fell like music round us,
We felt the charm descend, nor strove
  To break the rapturous spell that bound us.

We listened with mysterious awe,
  Strange feelings mingling with our pleasure;
We heard that day prophetic words,
  High thoughts the heart must always treasure.

Great Nature's Priest! thy calm career,
  With that sweet morn, on earth has ended—
But who shall say thy mission died
  When, winged for Heaven, thy soul ascended!

DIRGE FOR A YOUNG GIRL.

Underneath the sod, low lying,
    Dark and drear,
Sleepeth one who left, in dying,
    Sorrow here.

Yes, they're ever bending o'er her,
    Eyes that weep;
Forms that to the cold grave bore her
    Vigils keep.

When the summer moon is shining
    Soft and fair,
Friends she loved in tears are twining
    Chaplets there.

Rest in peace, thou gentle spirit,
    Throned above;
Souls like thine with God inherit
    Life and love!

EVENTIDE.

This cottage door, this gentle gale,
Hay-scented, whispering round,
Yon path-side rose, that down the vale
Breathes incense from the ground,
    Methinks should from the dullest clod
    Invite a thankful heart to God.

But, Lord, the violet, bending low,
Seems better moved to praise;
From us, what scanty blessings flow,
How voiceless close our days:—
    Father, forgive us, and the flowers
    Shall lead in prayer the vesper hours.

DONALD G. MITCHELL.

Mr. Mitchell was born in Norwich, Connecticut, April, 1822. His father was the pastor of the Congregational church of that place, and his grandfather a member of the first Congress at Philadelphia, and for many years Chief Justice of the Supreme Court of Connecticut.

After being prepared for college at a boarding-school, young Mitchell entered Yale, and was graduated in due course in 1841. His health being feeble, he passed the three following years on his grandfather's estate in the country. He became much interested in agriculture, wrote a number of letters for the Cultivator at Albany, and gained a silver cup from the New York Agricultural Society, as a prize for a plan of farm buildings.

He next crossed the ocean, and spent half a winter in the island of Jersey, and the other half in rambling over England on foot, visiting in this manner every county, and writing letters to the Albany Cultivator. After passing eighteen months on the continent he returned home, and commenced the study of the law in New York city. He soon after published, *Fresh Gleanings; or, A New Sheaf from the Old Fields of Continental Europe; by Ik. Marvel*, a pleasant volume of leisurely observation over a tour through some of the choice places of Central Europe. Mr. Mitchell's health suffering from confinement in a city office, he again visited Europe, and passed some of the eventful months of 1848 in the capital and among the vineyards of France.

On his return, Mr. Mitchell published in 1850, *The Battle Summer, being Transcriptions from Personal Observations in Paris during the year 1848; by Ik. Marvel*, a volume in which he carried the quaint brevity of style, somewhat apparent in the Fresh Gleanings, to an injudicious extent, coupling with this an unfortunate imitation of Carlyle's treatment of similar scenes in the History of the French Revolution. His next production was *The Lorgnette*, a periodical in size and style resembling Salmagundi. It appeared anonymously, and although attracting much attention in fashionable circles, the author's incognito was for some time preserved. It was written in a quiet, pure style, and contains some of the best passages in the author's writings.

During the progress of the Lorgnette, Mr. Mitchell published the *Reveries of a Bachelor*, a contemplative view of life from the slippered ease of the chimney corner. A slight story runs through the volume, containing some pathetic scenes tenderly narrated.

A volume of a similar character, *Dream Life*, appeared in the following year. In 1853 Mr. Mitchell received the appointment of United States Consul at Venice. He retained the office but a short time, and after passing several months in Europe, engaged in the collection of materials for a proposed history of Venice, returned home the summer of 1855. He is at present residing on a country-seat which he has purchased in the neighborhood of New Haven.

Mr. Mitchell's last publication, *Fudge Doings*, was originally published in the Knickerbocker Magazine. It consists of a series of sketches, in a connected form, of city fashionable life, in the vein of the Lorgnette.

LETTERS—FROM THE REVERIES OF A BACHELOR.

Blessed be letters!—they are the monitors, they are also the comforters, and they are the only true heart-talkers. Your speech, and their speeches, are conventional; they are moulded by circumstances; they are suggested by the observation, remark, and influence of the parties to whom the speaking is addressed, or by whom it may be overheard.

Your truest thought is modified half through its utterance by a look, a sign, a smile, or a sneer. It is not individual; it is not integral: it is social and mixed,—half of you, and half of others. It bends, it sways, it multiplies, it retires, and it advances, as the talk of others presses, relaxes, or quickens.

But it is not so with Letters:—there you are, with only the soulless pen, and the snow-white, virgin paper. Your soul is measuring itself by itself, and saying its own sayings: there are no sneers to modify its utterance,—no scowl to scare,—nothing is present, but you and your thought.

Utter it then freely—write it down—stamp it—burn it in the ink!—There it is, a true soul-print!

Oh, the glory, the freedom, the passion of a letter! It is worth all the lip-talk of the world. Do you say, it is studied, made up, acted, rehearsed, contrived, artistic?

Let me see it then; let me run it over; tell me age, sex, circumstances, and I will tell you if it be studied or real; if it be the merest lip-slang put into words, or heart-talk blazing on the paper.

I have a little pacquet, not very large, tied up with narrow crimson ribbon, now soiled with frequent handling, which far into some winter's night I take down from its nook upon my shelf, and untie, and open, and run over, with such sorrow, and such joy,—such tears and such smiles, as I am sure make me for weeks after, a kinder and holier man.

There are in this little pacquet, letters in the familiar hand of a mother—what gentle admonition—what tender affection!—God have mercy on him who outlives the tears that such admonitions, and such affection call up to the eye! There are others in the budget, in the delicate, and unformed hand of a loved, and lost sister;—written when she and you were full of glee, and the best mirth of youthfulness; does it harm you to recall that mirthfulness? or to trace again, for the hundredth time, that scrawling postscript at the bottom, with its *i's* so carefully dotted, and its gigantic *t's* so carefully crossed, by the childish hand of a little brother?

I have added latterly to that pacquet of letters; I almost need a new and longer ribbon; the old one is getting too short. Not a few of these new and cherished letters, a former Reverie has brought to me; not letters of cold praise, saying it was well done, artfully executed, prettily imagined—no such thing: but letters of sympathy—of sympathy which means sympathy—the παθήμι and the συν.

It would be cold and dastardly work to copy them; I am too selfish for that. It is enough to say that they, the kind writers, have seen a heart in the Reverie—have felt that it was real, true. They know it; a secret influence has told it. What matters it, pray, if literally there was no wife, and no dead child, and no coffin, in the house? Is not feeling, feeling and heart, heart? Are not these fancies thronging on my brain, bringing tears to my eyes, bringing joy to my soul, as living, as anything human can be living? What if they have no material type—no objective form? All that is crude, —a mere reduction of ideality to sense,—a transformation of the spiritual to the earthy,—a levelling of soul to matter.

Are we not creatures of thought and passion? Is anything about us more earnest than that same thought and passion? Is there anything more real, —more characteristic of that great and dim destiny to which we are born, and which may be written down in that terrible word—Forever?

Let those who will then, sneer at what in their wisdom they call untruth—at what is false, because it has no material presence: this does not create falsity; would to Heaven that it did!

And yet, if there was actual, material truth, superadded to Reverie, would such objectors sympathize the more? No!—a thousand times, no; the heart that has no sympathy with thoughts and feelings that scorch the soul, is dead also—whatever its mocking tears and gestures may say—to a coffin or a grave!

Let them pass, and we will come back to these cherished letters.

A mother who has lost a child, has, she says, shed a tear—not one, but many—over the dead boy's coldness. And another, who has not, but who trembles lest she lose, has found the words failing as she reads, and a dim, sorrow-borne mist, spreading over the page.

Another, yet rejoicing in all those family ties that make life a charm, has listened nervously to careful reading, until the husband is called home, and the coffin is in the house—"Stop!" she says; and a gush of tears tells the rest.

Yet the cold critic will say—"it was artfully done." A curse on him!—it was not art: it was nature.

Another, a young, fresh, healthful girl-mind, has seen something in the love-picture—albeit so weak —of truth; and has kindly believed that it must be earnest. Aye, indeed is it, fair, and generous one, —earnest as life and hope! Who indeed with a heart at all, that has not yet slipped away irreparably and for ever from the shores of youth—from that fairy land which young enthusiasm creates, and over which bright dreams hover—but knows it to be real? And so such things will be real, till hopes are dashed, and Death is come.

Another, a father, has laid down the book in tears. —God bless them all! How far better this, than the cold praise of newspaper paragraphs, or the critically contrived approval of colder friends!

Let me gather up these letters carefully,—to be read when the heart is faint, and sick of all that there is unreal and selfish in the world. Let me tie them together, with a new, and longer bit of ribbon—not by a love knot, that is too hard—but by an easy slipping knot, that so I may get at them the better. And now they are all together, a snug pacquet, and we will label them not sentimentally (I pity the one who thinks it), but earnestly, and in the best meaning of the term—SOUVENIRS DU CŒUR.

Thanks to my first Reverie, which has added to such a treasure!

THOMAS BUCHANAN READ

WAS born in Chester county, Pennsylvania, March 12, 1822. His boyhood was passed among the scenes of country life until the age of seventeen, when, after the death of his father, he moved to Cincinnati, and obtained a situation in the studio of Clevinger the sculptor. Devoting himself to the fine arts, he soon obtained some local reputation as a portrait painter, and in 1841 removed to New York, with the intention of devoting himself to the art as a profession. He went within a year to Boston, where, in 1843–4 he published in the "Courier" a number of lyrics, and in 1847 his first volume of *Poems*. It was followed by a second of *Lays and Ballads* in 1848, published at Philadelphia, whither he had removed in 1846. In 1848 he made a collection of specimens of the Female Poets of America, and has published an edition of his own verses, elegantly illustrated. He has passed some time in Europe with a view to the study of painting, and is now pursuing that object with success in Rome.

T. Buchanan Read

A choice edition of Mr. Read's poems, delicately illustrated by Kenny Meadows, was published by Delf and Trübner, in London, in 1852. In 1853 a new and enlarged edition appeared at Philadelphia.

The latest production of Mr. Read, published in Philadelphia in 1855, during the author's residence in Italy, *The New Pastoral*, is the most elaborate of his compositions. It is a series of thirty-seven sketches, forming a volume of two hundred and fifty pages, mostly in blank verse. The thread which connects the chapters together is the emigration of a family group of Middle Pennsylvania to the Mississippi. The description of their early residence; the rural manners and pursuits; the natural scenery of their home; the phenomena of the seasons; the exhibitions of religious, political, and social life; the school; the camp meeting; the election; Independence Day, with an elevating love theme in the engagement of a village maiden to a poetic lover in Europe; the incidents of the voyage on the Ohio, with frequent episodes and patriotic aspirations, are all handled with an artist's eye for natural and moral beauty. The book presents a constant succession of truthful, pleasing images, in the healthy vein of the Goldsmiths and Bloomfields.

The characteristics we have noted describe Mr. Read's poems in his several volumes, which have exhibited a steady progress and development, in the confidence of the writer, in plain and simple objects, in strength of fancy and poetic culture.

THE CLOSING SCENE.

Within this sober realm of leafless trees,
The russet year inhaled the dreamy air,
Like some tanned reaper in his hour of ease,
When all the fields are lying brown and bare.

The gray barns, looking from their hazy hills
O'er the dim waters widening in the vales,
Sent down the air a greeting to the mills,
On the dull thunder of alternate flails.

All sights were mellowed, and all sounds subdued,
The hills seemed farther, and the streams sang low;
As in a dream, the distant woodman hewed
His winter log with many a muffled blow.

Th' embattled forests, erewhile armed in gold,
Their banners bright with every martial hue,
Now stood, like some sad beaten host of old,
Withdrawn afar in Time's remotest blue.

On slumb'rous wings the vulture tried his flight;
The dove scarce heard his sighing mate's complaint;
And like a star slow drowning in the light,
The village church-vane seemed to pale and faint.

The sentinel cock upon the hill-side crew;
Crew thrice, and all was stiller than before—
Silent till some replying wanderer blew
His alien horn, and then was heard no more.

Where erst the jay within the elm's tall crest
Made garrulous trouble round the unfledged young;
And where the oriole hung her swaying nest
By every light wind like a censer swung;

Where sang the noisy masons of the eves,
The busy swallows circling ever near,
Foreboding, as the rustic mind believes,
An early harvest and a plenteous year;

Where every bird which charmed the vernal feast
Shook the sweet slumber from its wings at morn,
To warn the reapers of the rosy east,
All now was songless, empty, and forlorn.

Alone, from out the stubble piped the quail,
And croaked the crow through all the dreary gloom;
Alone the pheasant, drumming in the vale,
Made echo to the distant cottage loom.

There was no bud, no bloom upon the bowers;
The spiders wove their thin shrouds night by night;
The thistle-down, the only ghost of flowers,
Sailed slowly by—passed noiseless out of sight.

Amid all this—in this most cheerless air,
And where the woodbine sheds upon the porch
Its crimson leaves, as if the year stood there,
Firing the floor with his inverted torch—

Amid all this, the centre of the scene,
The white-haired matron, with monotonous tread
Plied her swift wheel, and with her joyless mien
Sat like a Fate, and watched the flying thread.

She had known sorrow. He had walked with her,
Oft supped, and broke with her the ashen crust,
And in the dead leaves still she heard the stir
Of his black mantle trailing in the dust.

While yet her cheek was bright with summer bloom,
Her country summoned, and she gave her all,
And twice war bowed to her his sable plume;
He gave the swords to rest upon the wall.

Re-gave the swords—but not the hand that drew,
And struck for liberty the dying blow;
Nor him, who to his sire and country true
Fell 'mid the ranks of the invading foe.

Long, but not loud, the droning wheel went on,
Like the low murmurs of a hive at noon;
Long, but not loud, the memory of the gone
Breathed through her lips a sad and tremulous tune.

At last the thread was snapped, her head was bowed:
Life drooped the distaff through his hands serene;
And loving neighbors smoothed her careful shroud,
While Death and Winter closed the autumn scene.

PENNSYLVANIA—FROM THE NEW PASTORAL.

Fair Pennsylvania! than thy midland vales,
Lying 'twixt hills of green, and bound afar
By billowy mountains rolling in the blue,
No lovelier landscape meets the traveller's eye.
There Labour sows and reaps his sure reward,
And Peace and Plenty walk amid the glow
And perfume of full garners. I have seen
In lands less free, less fair, but far more known,
The streams which flow through history and wash
The legendary shores—and cleave in twain
Old capitols and towns, dividing oft
Great empires and estates of petty kings
And princes, whose domains full many a field,
Rustling with maize along our native West,
Out-measures and might put to shame! and yet
Nor Rhine, like Bacchus crowned, and reeling through
His hills—nor Danube, marred with tyranny,
His dull waves moaning on Hungarian shores—
Nor rapid Po, his opaque waters pouring
Athwart the fairest, fruitfulest, and worst
Enslaved of European lands—nor Seine,
Winding uncertain through inconstant France—
Are half so fair as thy broad stream whose breast
Is gemmed with many isles, and whose proud name
Shall yet become among the names of rivers
A synonym of beauty—Susquehanna!

THE VILLAGE CHURCH—FROM THE NEW PASTORAL.

About the chapel door, in easy groups,
The rustic people wait. Some trim the switch,
While some prognosticate of harvests full,
Or shake the dubious head with arguments
Based on the winter's frequent snow and thaw,
The heavy rains, and sudden frosts severe.
Some, happily but few, deal scandal out,
With look askance pointing their victim. These
Are the rank tares in every field of grain—
These are the nettles stinging unaware—
The briars which wound and trip unheeding feet—
The noxious vines, growing in every grove!
Their touch is deadly, and their passing breath
Poison most venomous! Such have I known—
As who has not?—and suffered by the contact.
Of these the husbandman takes certain note,
And in the proper season disinters
Their baneful roots; and to the sun exposed,
The killing light of truth, leaves them to pine
And perish in the noonday! 'Gainst a tree,
With strong arms folded o'er a giant chest,
Stands Barton, to the neighbourhood chief smith;
His coat, unused to aught save Sunday wear,
Grown too oppressive by the morning walk,
Hangs on the drooping branch: so stands he oft
Beside the open door, what time the share
Is whitening at the roaring bellows' mouth.
There, too, the wheelwright—he, the magistrate—
In small communities a man of mark—
Stands with the smith, and holds such argument
As the unlettered but observing can;
Their theme some knot of scripture hard to solve.
And 'gainst the neighbouring bars two others fan,
Less fit the sacred hour, discussion hot
Of politics; a topic, which inflamed,
Knows no propriety of time or place.
There Oakes, the cooper, with rough brawny hand,
Descants at large, and, with a noisy ardour,
Rattles around his theme as round a cask;
While Hanson, heavy-browed, with shoulders bent,
Bent with great lifting of huge stones—for he
A mason and famed builder is—replies
With tongue as sharp and dexterous as his trowel,
And sentences which like his hammer fall,
Bringing the flinty fire at every blow!
  But soon the approaching parson ends in peace
The wordy combat, and all turn within.
Awhile rough shoes, some with discordant creak,
And voices clearing for the psalm, disturb
The sacred quiet, till, at last, the veil
Of silence wavers, settles, falls; and then
The hymn is given, and all arise and sing.
Then follows prayer, which from the pastor's heart
Flows unpretending, with few words devout
Of humble thanks and askings; not, with lungs
Stentorian, assaulting heaven's high wall,
Compelling grace by virtue of a siege!
This done, with loving care he scans his flock,
And opes the sacred volume at the text.
Wide is his brow, and full of honest thought—
Love his vocation, truth is all his stock.
With these he strives to guide, and not perplex
With words sublime and empty, ringing oft
Most musically hollow. All his facts
Are simple, broad, sufficient for a world!
He knows them well, teaching but what he knows.
He never strides through metaphysic mists,
Or takes false greatness because seen through fogs;
Nor leads 'mid brambles of thick argument
Till all admire the wit which brings them through:
Nor e'er essays, in sermon or in prayer,
To share the hearer's thought; nor strives to make
The smallest of his congregation lose
One glimpse of heaven, to cast it on the priest.
Such simple course, in these ambitious times,
Were worthy imitation; in these days,
When brazen tinsel bears the palm from worth,
And trick and pertness take the sacred desk;
Or some coarse thunderer, armed with doctrines new,
Aims at our faith a blow to fell an ox—
Swinging his sledge, regardless where it strikes,
Or what demolishes—well pleased to win
By either blows or noise!—A modern seer,
Crying destruction! and, to prove it true,
Walking abroad, for demolition armed,
And boldly levelling where he cannot build!
  The service done, the congregation rise,
And with a freshness glowing in their hearts,
And quiet strength, the benison of prayer,
And wholesome admonition, hence depart.
Some, loath to go, within the graveyard loiter,
Walking among the mounds, or on the tombs,
Hanging, like pictured grief beneath a willow,
Bathing the inscriptions with their tears; or here,
Finding the earliest violet, like a drop
Of heaven's anointing blue upon the dead,
Bless it with mournful pleasure; or, perchance,
With careful hands, recall the wandering vine,
And teach it where to creep, and where to bear
Its future epitaph of flowers. And there,
Each with a separate grief, and some with tears,
Ponder the sculptured lines of consolation.

"The chrysalis is here—the soul is flown,
And waits thee in the gardens of the blest!"
"The nest is cold and empty, but the bird
Sings with its loving mates in Paradise!"
"Our hope was planted here—it blooms in heaven!"
"She walks the azure field, 'mid dews of bliss,
While 'mong the thorns our feet still bleed in this!"
"This was the fountain, but the sands are dry—
The waters have exhaled into the sky!"
"The listening Shepherd heard a voice forlorn,
And found the lamb, by thorns and brambles torn,
And placed it in his breast! Then wherefore mourn?"

Such are the various lines; and, while they read,
Methinks I hear sweet voices in the air,
And winnowing of soft, invisible wings,
The whisperings of angels breathing peace!

FREDERICK L. COZZENS,

The author of numerous popular sketches in the Knickerbocker and Putnam's Magazines, is a native of New York City. He early became engaged in mercantile life, and is at present a leading wine-merchant.

In 1853 he published a volume of sketches in prose and verse entitled *Prismatics, by Richard Haywarde.* It was tastefully illustrated from designs by Elliott, Darley, Kensett, Hicks, and Rossiter. He has since written a series of sketches for Putnam's Monthly, humorously descriptive of a cockney residence in the country, under the title of *The Sparrowgrass Papers*, which are announced for publication in a volume by Derby.

Fred^c. S. Cozzens

Mr. Cozzens is also the author of a very pleasant miscellany published in connexion with his business, entitled *The Wine Press.* In addition to much information on the important topic of the native culture of the grape, it is enlivened by many clever essays and sketches in the range of practical æsthetics.

BUNKER HILL; AN OLD-TIME BALLAD.

It was a starry night in June; the air was soft and still,
When the "minute-men" from Cambridge came, and gathered on the hill:
Beneath us lay the sleeping town, around us frowned the fleet,
But the pulse of freemen, not of slaves, within our bosoms beat;
And every heart rose high with hope, as fearlessly we said,
"We will be numbered with the free, or numbered with the dead!"
"Bring out the line to mark the trench, and stretch it on the sward!"
The trench is marked—the tools are brought—we utter not a word,
But stack our guns, then fall to work, with mattock and with spade,
A thousand men with sinewy arms, and not a sound is made:
So still were we, the stars beneath, that scarce a whisper fell;
We heard the red-coat's musket click, and heard him cry, "All's well!"
And here and there a twinkling port, reflected on the deep,
In many a wavy shadow showed their sullen guns asleep.
Sleep on, thou bloody hireling crew! in careless slumber lie;
The trench is growing broad and deep, the breast-work broad and high:
No striplings we, but bear the arms that held the French in check,
The drum that beat at Louisburg, and thundered in Quebec!
And thou, whose promise is deceit, no more thy word we'll trust,
Thou butcher GAGE! thy power and thee we'll humble in the dust;
Thou and thy tory minister have boasted to thy brood,
"The lintels of the faithful shall be sprinkled with our blood!"
But though these walls those lintels be, thy zeal is all in vain:
A thousand freemen shall rise up for every freeman slain;
And when o'er trampled crowns and thrones they raise the mighty shout,
This soil their Palestine shall be; their altar this redoubt:
See how the morn is breaking! the red is in the sky;
The mist is creeping from the stream that floats in silence by;
The Lively's hull looms through the fog, and they our works have spied,
For the ruddy flash and roundshot part in thunder from her side;
And the Falcon and the Cerberus make every bosom thrill,
With gun and shell, and drum and bell, and boatswain's whistle shrill;
But deep and wider grows the trench, as spade and mattock ply,
For we have to cope with fearful odds, and the time is drawing nigh!

Up with the pine tree banner! Our gallant PRESCOTT stands
Amid the plunging shells and shot, and plants it with his hands;
Up with the shout! for PUTNAM comes upon his reeking bay,
With bloody spur and foamy bit, in haste to join the fray;
And POMEROY, with his snow-white hairs, and face all flush and sweat,
Unscathed by French and Indian, wears a youthful glory yet.
But thou, whose soul is glowing in the summer of thy years,
Unvanquishable WARREN, thou (the youngest of thy peers)
Wert born, and bred, and shaped, and made to act a patriot's part,
And dear to us thy presence is as heart's blood to the heart!
Well may ye bark, ye British wolves! with leaders such as they,
Not one will fail to follow where they choose to lead the way—
As once before, scarce two months since, we followed on your track,
And with our rifles marked the road ye took in going back.
Ye slew a sick man in his bed; ye slew with hands accursed,
A mother nursing, and her blood fell on the babe she nursed;
By their own doors our kinsmen fell and perished in the strife;
But as we hold a hireling's cheap, and dear a freeman's life,
By Tanner brook, and Lincoln bridge, before the shut of sun,
We took the recompense we claimed—a score for every one!
Hark! from the town a trumpet! The barges at the wharf
Are crowded with the living freight—and now they're pushing off;
With clash and glitter, trump and drum, in all its bright array,
Behold the splendid sacrifice move slowly o'er the bay!
And still and still the barges fill, and still across the deep,
Like thunder-clouds along the sky, the hostile transports sweep;
And now they're forming at the Point—and now the lines advance:
We see beneath the sultry sun their polished bayonets glance;
We hear a-near the throbbing drum, the bugle challenge ring;
Quick bursts, and loud, the flashing cloud, and rolls from wing to wing;
But on the height our bulwark stands, tremendous in its gloom,
As sullen as a tropic sky, and silent as a tomb.
And so we waited till we saw, at scarce ten rifles' length,
The old vindictive Saxon spite, in all its stubborn strength;
When sudden, flash on flash, around the jagged rampart burst
From every gun the livid light upon the foe accurst:
Then quailed a monarch's might before a free-born people's ire;
Then drank the sward the veteran's life, where swept the yeoman's fire;

Then, staggered by the shot, we saw their serried columns reel,
And fall, as falls the bearded rye beneath the reaper's steel:
And then arose a mighty shout that might have waked the dead,
"Hurrah! they run! the field is won!" "Hurrah! the foe is fled!"
And every man hath dropped his gun to clutch a neighbor's hand,
As his heart kept praying all the while for Home and Native Land.
Thrice on that day we stood the shock of thrice a thousand foes,
And thrice that day within our lines the shout of victory rose!
And though our swift fire slackened then, and reddening in the skies,
We saw, from Charlestown's roofs and walls, the flamy columns rise;
Yet while we had a cartridge left, we still maintained the fight,
Nor gained the foe one foot of ground upon that blood-stained height.
What though for us no laurels bloom, nor o'er the nameless brave
No sculptured trophy, scroll, nor hatch, records a warrior-grave!
What though the day to us was lost! Upon that deathless page
The everlasting charter stands, for every land and age!
For man hath broke his felon bonds, and cast them in the dust,
And claimed his heritage divine, and justified the trust;
While through his rifted prison-bars the hues of freedom pour
O'er every nation, race, and clime, on every sea and shore,
Such glories as the patriarch viewed, when 'mid the darkest skies,
He saw above a ruined world the Bow of Promise rise.

GEORGE WILLIAM CURTIS.

GEORGE WILLIAM CURTIS is a native of Providence, R. I., where he was born in 1824. His grandfather, on the mother's side, was James Barrill, remembered as an eminent Rhode Islander, and for his Senator's speech in Congress on the Missouri Compromise Bill. He died at Washington, and is buried there in the Congressional cemetery.

At six years of age young Curtis was placed at school near Boston, and there remained until he was eleven. He returned to Providence, pursuing his studies till he was fifteen, when his father, George Curtis, removed with his family to New York. In a pleasant article in Putnam's Magazine, with the title *Sea from Shore*, our author has given an imaginative reminiscence of his early impressions of Providence, then in the decay of its large India trade.* Of late years manufactories and machine shops have supplanted the quaint old stores upon many of the docks; but the town, at the head of the Narraghansett bay, is fortunate in its situation, upon a hill at the confluence of two rivers, sloping to the east, west, and south; and the stately houses of its earlier merchants upon the ascent towards the south, form as fine a cluster of residences as are seen in any of our cities.

* Putnam's Magazine, July, 1851. The passage is in the author's best fanciful vein.

In New York our author was smitten with the love of trade, and deserted his books for a year to serve in a large foreign importing house. Though not without its advantages, the pursuit was abandoned at the end of that time, and the clerk became again a student, continuing with tutors until he was eighteen, when, in a spirit of idyllic enthusiasm, he took part in the Brook Farm Association in West Roxbury, Mass. He remained there a year and a half, enjoying the novel experiences of nature and the friendship of his cultivated associates, and still looks back upon the period as a pleasurable pastoral episode of his life.*

From Brook Farm and its agricultural occupations, after a winter in New York, being still enamored of the country, he went to Concord, in Massachusetts, and lived in a farmer's family, working hard upon the farm and taking his share of the usual fortunes of farmers' boys—with a very unusual private accompaniment of his own, in the sense of poetic enjoyment, unless the poet Bloomfield's Farmer's Boy be taken as the standard. At Concord he saw something of Emerson, much of Hawthorne, who had taken up his residence there after the Brook Farm adventure, and a little of Henry Thoreau, and of the poet William Ellery Channing. It was at this time that Emerson tried the formation of a club out of the individual "unclubable" elements of the philosophic personages in the neighborhood, which Mr. Curtis has pleasantly described in the Homes of American Authors.†

During these years, Mr. Curtis was constantly studying and perfecting himself in the various accomplishments of literature, and after two summers and a winter passed in Concord, he sailed for Europe in August, 1846. He landed at Marseilles, and proceeding along the coast to Genoa, Leghorn, and Florence, passed the winter in Rome in the society of the American artists then resident there, Crawford, Hicks, Kensett, Cranch, Terry, and Freeman. In the spring he travelled through southern Italy and reached Venice in August. At Milan he met Mr. George S. Hillard and the Rev. Frederic H. Hedge, and crossed the Stelvio with them in the autumn into Germany. There he matriculated at the University of Berlin, and spent a portion of his time in travel, visiting every part of Germany and making the tour of the Danube into Hungary as far as Pesth. He was in Berlin during the revolutionary scenes of March, 1848. The next winter he passed in Paris, was in Switzerland in the summer, and in the following autumn crossed into Italy, and went to Sicily from Naples. He made the tour of the island, and visited Malta and the East, returning to America in the summer of 1850.

* Some further mention of this peculiar affair will be found in the notice of Hawthorne. In the preface to the Blithedale Romance, Hawthorne calls upon Curtis to become the historian of the settlement—"Even the brilliant Howadji might find as rich a theme in his youthful reminiscences of Brook Farm, and a more novel one,—close at hand as it lies,—than those which he has since made so distant a pilgrimage to seek, in Syria and along the current of the Nile."

† The papers of Mr. Curtis in this volume, published by Putnam in 1858 are the sketches of Emerson, Longfellow. Hawthorne and Bancroft.

In the autumn of that year he prepared the *Nile Notes of an Howadji*, much of which was written, as it stands, upon the Nile. During the winter he was connected with the Tribune newspaper, and the following season the *Notes* were published by the Harpers and by Bentley in London. In the summer of 1851 a travelling tour furnished letters from the fashionable watering-places to the Tribune, and the autumn and winter were spent in Providence, where a second series of Eastern reminiscences and sketches—*The Howadji in Syria*—was written, which was published by the Harpers the next spring, and the same publishing season the Tribune letters were rewritten and printed, with illustrations by Kensett, in the volume entitled *Lotus Eating*.

Returning to New York in the autumn of 1852, he became one of the original editors of Putnam's Monthly, and wrote the series of satiric sketches of society, the *Potiphar Papers*, which were collected in a volume in 1853. Besides the Potiphar Papers, he has written numerous articles for Putnam's Magazine, including several poetical essays, in the character of a simple-minded merchant's clerk, with his amiable, common-sense wife Prue for a heroine. *Dinner Time*, *My Chateaux*, and *Sea from Shore*, belong to this series.

He has also written for Harpers' Magazine a picturesque historical paper on Newport,* some tales of fashionable society by Smythe, Jr., and other papers.

In the winter of 1853 he took the field as a popular lecturer with success in different parts of the country.

In 1854 he delivered a poem before a literary society at Brown University, at Providence.

It is understood that Mr. Curtis is at present (1855) engaged upon a life of Mehemet Ali: a topic which will test his diligence and powers in a new department of composition.

* In the number for August, 1854.

UNDER THE PALMS—FROM THE NILE NOTES.

A motion from the river won,
Ridged the smooth level, bearing on
My shallop through the star-strown calm,
Until another night in night
I entered, from the clearer light,
Imbowered vaults of pillar'd Palm.

Humboldt, the only cosmopolitan and a poet, divides the earth by beauties, and celebrates as dearest to him, and first fascinating him to travel, the climate of palms. The palm is the type of the tropics, and when the great Alexander marched triumphing through India, some Hindoo, suspecting the sweetest secret of Brama, distilled a wine from the palm, the glorious phantasy of whose intoxication no poet records.

I knew a palm-tree upon Capri. It stood in select society of shining fig-leaves and lustrous oleanders; it overhung the balcony, and so looked, far over-leaning, down upon the blue Mediterranean. Through the dream-mists of southern Italian noons, it looked up the broad bay of Naples and saw vague Vesuvius melting away; or at sunset the isles of the Syrens, whereon they singing sat, and wooed Ulysses as he went; or in the full May moonlight the oranges of Sorrento shone across it, great and golden, permanent planets of that delicious dark. And from the Sorrento where Tasso was born, it looked across to pleasant Posylippo, where Virgil is buried, and to stately Ischia. The palm of Capri saw all that was fairest and most famous in the bay of Naples.

A wandering poet, whom I knew—sang a sweet song to the palm, as he dreamed in the moonlight upon that balcony. But it was only the free-masonry of sympathy. It was only syllabled moonshine. For the palm was a poet too, and all palms are poets.

Yet when I asked the bard what the palm-tree sang in its melancholy measures of waving, he told me that not Vesuvius, nor the Syrens, nor Sorrento, nor Tasso, nor Virgil, nor stately Ischia, nor all the broad blue beauty of Naples bay, was the theme of that singing. But partly it sang of a river for ever flowing, and of cloudless skies, and green fields that never faded, and the mournful music of water-wheels, and the wild monotony of a tropical life—and partly of the yellow silence of the Desert, and of drear solitudes inaccessible, and of wandering caravans, and lonely men. Then of gardens overhanging rivers, that roll gorgeous-shored through Western fancies—of gardens in Bagdad watered by the Euphrates and the Tigris, whereof it was the fringe and darling ornament—of oases in those sere sad deserts where it overfountained fountains, and every leaf was blessed. More than all, of the great Orient universally, where no tree was so abundant, so loved, and so beautiful.

When I lay under that palm-tree in Capri in the May moonlight, my ears were opened, and I heard all that the poet had told me of its song.

Perhaps it was because I came from Rome, where the holy week comes into the year as Christ entered Jerusalem, over palms. For in the magnificence of St. Peter's, all the pomp of the most pompous of human institutions is on one day charactered by the palm. The Pope borne upon his throne, as is no other monarch,—with wide-waving Flabella attendant, moves, blessing the crowd through the great nave. All the red-legged cardinals follow, each of whose dresses would build a chapel, so costly are they, and the crimson-crowned Greek patriarch with long silken black beard, and the crew of motley which the Roman clergy is, crowded after in shining splendor.

No ceremony of imperial Rome had been more imposing, and never witnessed in a temple more imperial. But pope, patriarch, cardinals, bishops, ambassadors, and all the lesser glories, bore palm branches in their hands. Not veritable palm branches, but their imitation in turned yellow wood; and all through Rome that day, the palm branch was waving and hanging. Who could not see its beauty, even in the turned yellow wood? Who did not feel it was a sacred tree as well as romantic?

For palm branches were strewn before Jesus as he rode into Jerusalem, and for ever, since, the palm symbolizes peace. Wherever a grove of palms waves in the low moonlight or starlight wind, it is the celestial choir chanting peace on earth, good-will to men. Therefore is it the foliage of the old religious pictures. Mary sits under a palm, and the saints converse under palms, and the prophets prophesy in their shade, and cherubs float with palms over the Martyr's agony. Nor among pictures is there any more beautiful than Correggio's Flight into Egypt, wherein the golden-haired angels put aside the palm branches, and smile sunnily through, upon the lovely Mother and the lovely child.

The palm is the chief tree in religious remembrance and religious art. It is the chief tree in romance and poetry. But its sentiment is always Eastern, and it always yearns for the East. In the West it is an exile, and pines in the most sheltered gardens. Among Western growths in the Western air, it is as unsphered as Hafiz in a temperance society. Yet of all Western shores it is happiest in Sicily; for Sicily is only a bit of Africa drifted westward. There is a soft Southern strain in the Sicilian skies, and the palms drink its sunshine like dew. Upon the tropical plain behind Palermo, among the sun-sucking aloes, and the thick, shapeless cactuses, like elephants and rhinoceroses enchanted into foliage, it grows ever gladly. For the aloe is of the East, and the prickly pear, and upon that plain the Saracens have been, and the palm sees the Arabian arch, and the oriental sign-manual stamped upon the land.

In the Villa Serra di Falco, within sound of the vespers of Palermo, there is a palm beautiful to behold. It is like a Georgian slave in a pacha's hareem. Softly shielded from eager winds, gently throned upon a slope of richest green, fringed with brilliant and fragrant flowers, it stands separate and peculiar in the odorous garden air. Yet it droops and saddens, and bears no fruit. Vain is the exquisite environment of foreign fancies. The poor slave has no choice but life. Care too tender will not suffer it to die. Pride and admiration surround it with the best beauties, and feed it upon the warmest sun. But I heard it sigh as I passed. A wind blew warm from the East, and it lifted its arms hopelessly, and when the wind, love-laden with the most subtile sweetness, lingered, loth to fly, the palm stood motionless upon its little green mound, and the flowers were so fresh and fair—and the leaves of the trees so deeply hued, and the native fruit so golden and glad upon the boughs—that the still warm garden air seemed only the silent, voluptuous sadness of the tree; and had I been a poet my heart would have melted in song for the proud, pining palm.

But the palms are not only poets in the West, they are prophets as well. They are like heralds sent forth upon the farthest points to celebrate to the traveller the glories they foreshow. Like spring birds they sing a summer unfading, and climes where Time wears the year as a queen a rosary of diamonds. The mariner, eastward-sailing, hears tidings from the chance palms that hang along the southern Italian shore. They call out to him across the gleaming calm of a Mediterranean noon, "Thou happy mariner, our souls sail with thee."

The first palm undoes the West. The Queen of Sheba and the Princess Shemselnihar look then upon the most Solomon of Howadji's. So far the Orient has come—not in great glory, not handsomely, but as Rome came to Britain in Roman soldiers. The crown of imperial glory glittered yet and only upon the seven hills, but a single ray had penetrated the northern night—and what the golden house of Nero was to a Briton contemplating a Roman soldier, is the East to the Howadji first beholding a palm.

At Alexandria you are among them. Do not decry Alexandria as all Howadji do. To my eyes it was the illuminated initial of the oriental chapter. Certainly it reads like its heading—camels, mosques, bazaars, turbans, baths, and chibouques: and the whole East rows out to you, in the turbaned and fluttering-robed rascal who officiates as your pilot and moors you in the shadow of palms under the pacha's garden. Malign Alexandria no more, although you do have your choice of camels or omnibuses to go to your hotel, for when you are there and trying to dine, the wild-eyed Bedoueen who serves you, will send you deep into the desert by masquerading costume and his eager, restless eye, looking as if he would momently spring through the window, and plunge into the desert depths. These Bedoueen or Arab servants are like steeds of the sun for carriage horses. They fly, girt with wild fascination, for what will they do next?

As you donkey out of Alexandria to Pompey's Pillar, you will pass a beautiful garden of palms, and by sunset nothing is so natural as to see only those trees. Yet the fascination is lasting. The poetry of the first exiles you saw, does not perish in the presence of the nation, for those exiles stood beckoning like angels at the gate of Paradise, sorrowfully ushering you into the glory whence themselves were outcasts for ever:—and as you curiously looked in passing, you could not believe that their song was truth, and that the many would be as beautiful as the one.

Thenceforward, in the land of Egypt, palms are perpetual. They are the only foliage of the Nile, for we will not harm the modesty of a few Mimosas and Sycamores by foolish claims. They are the shade of the mud villages, marking their site in the landscape, so that the groups of palms are the number of villages. They fringe the shore and the horizon. The sun sets golden behind them, and birds sit swinging upon their boughs and float glorious among their trunks; on the ground beneath are flowers; the sugar-cane is not harmed by the ghostly shade nor the tobacco, and the yellow flowers of the cotton-plant star its dusk at evening. The children play under them, and the old men crone and smoke, the donkeys graze, the surly bison and the conceited camels repose. The old Bible pictures are ceaselessly painted, but with softer, clearer colors than in the venerable book.

The palm-grove is always enchanted. If it stretch inland too alluringly, and you run ashore to stand under the bending boughs to share the peace of the doves swinging in the golden twilight, and to make yourself feel more scripturally, at least to surround yourself with sacred emblems, having small other hope of a share in the beauty of holiness—yet you will never reach the grove. You will gain the trees, but it is not the grove you fancied—that golden gloom will never be gained—it is an endless El Dorado gleaming along these shores. The separate columnar trunks ray out in foliage above, but there is no shade of a grove, no privacy of a wood, except, indeed, at sunset,

A privacy of glorious light.

Each single tree has a little shade that the mass standing at wide ease can never create the shady solitude, without which there is no grove.

But the eye never wearies of palms more than the ear of singing birds. Solitary they stand upon the sand, or upon the level, fertile land in groups, with a grace and dignity that no tree surpasses. Very soon the eye beholds in their forms the original type of the columns which it will afterward admire in the temples. Almost the first palm is architecturally suggestive, even in those Western gardens—but to artists living among them and seeing only them! Men's hands are not delicate in the early ages, and the fountain fairness of the palms is not very flowingly fashioned in the capitals, but in the flowery perfection of the Parthenon the palm triumphs. The forms of those columns came from Egypt, and that which was the suspicion of the earlier workers, was the success of more delicate designing. So is the palm inwound with our art and poetry and religion, and of all trees would the Howadji be a palm, wide-waving peace and plenty, and feeling is kin to the Parthenon and Raphael's pictures.

FRANCIS PARKMAN.

Francis Parkman, the son of an esteemed clergyman of the same name, was born in Boston on the sixteenth of September, 1823. After completing his collegiate course at Harvard in 1844, he made a tour across the Prairies, the results of which were given to the public in a series of papers, *The Oregon Trail*, published in the Knickerbocker Magazine, and afterwards collected in a volume with the title, *Sketches of Prairie and Rocky Mountain Life*.

F. Parkman. Jr.

Mr. Parkman next occupied himself with historical composition. Familiar with actual Indian life on and beyond the frontier, he naturally turned his attention to the many picturesque scenes of a similar character in our annals. He selected a subject of limited scope, and on comparatively virgin ground.

The History of the Conspiracy of Pontiac, and the War of the North American Tribes against the English Colonies after the Conquest of Canada, appeared in an octavo volume in 1851. The work attracted attention by its individuality of subject, respect by its evidences of thorough investigation, and popularity by its literary merits. Mr. Parkman at once attained a foremost rank as a historian. His volume is written in a clear, animated tone, giving in its pages due prominence to the picturesque scenery as well as the dramatic action of its topic.

Mr. Parkman is at present occupied in the preparation of a History of French Discovery and Colonization in North America, a subject well adapted to his powers.

THE ILLINOIS.

We turn to a region of which, as yet, we have caught but transient glimpses; a region which to our forefathers seemed remote and strange, as to us the mountain strongholds of the Apaches, or the wastes of farthest Oregon. The country of the Illinois was chiefly embraced within the boundaries of the state which now retains the name. Thitherward, from the east, the west, and the north, three mighty rivers rolled their tributary waters; while countless smaller streams—smaller only in comparison—traversed the land with a watery network, impregnating the warm soil with exuberant fecundity. From the eastward, the Ohio—La Belle Rivière—pursued its windings for more than a thousand miles. The Mississippi descended from the distant north; while from its fountains in the west, three thousand miles away, the Missouri poured its torrent towards the same common centre. Born among mountains, trackless even now, except by the adventurous footstep of the trapper,—nurtured amid the howling of beasts and the war-cries of savages, never silent in that wilderness,—it holds its angry course through sun-scorched deserts, among towers and palaces, the architecture of no human hand, among lodges of barbarian hordes, and herds of bison blackening the prairie to the horizon. Fierce, reckless, headstrong, exulting in its tumultuous force, it plays a thousand freaks of wanton power; bearing away forests from its shores, and planting them, with roots uppermost, in its quicksands; sweeping off islands, and rebuilding them; frothing and raging in foam and whirlpool, and, again, gliding with dwindled current along its sandy channel. At length, dark with uncurbed fury, it pours its muddy tide into the reluctant Mississippi. That majestic river, drawing life from the pure fountains of the north, wandering among emerald prairies and wood-crowned bluffs, loses all its earlier charm with this unhallowed union. At first, it shrinks, as with repugnance, and along the same channel the two streams flow side by side, with unmingled waters. But the disturbing power prevails at length; and the united torrent bears onward in its might, boiling up from the bottom, whirling in many a vortex, flooding its shores with a malign deluge fraught with pestilence and fever, and burying forests in its depths to insnare the heedless voyager. Mightiest among rivers, it is the connecting link of adverse climates and contrasted races; and while at its northern source the fur-clad Indian shivers in the cold,—where it mingles with the ocean, the growth of the tropics springs along its banks, and the panting negro cools his limbs in its refreshing waters.

To these great rivers and their tributary streams the country of the Illinois owed its wealth, its grassy prairies, and the stately woods that flourished on its deep, rich soil. This prolific land teemed with life.

It was a hunter's paradise. Deer grazed on its meadows. The elk trooped in herds, like squadrons of cavalry. In the still morning, one might hear the clatter of their antlers for half a mile over the dewy prairie. Countless bison roamed the plains, filing in grave procession to drink at the rivers, plunging and snorting among the rapids and quicksands, rolling their huge bulk on the grass, or rushing upon each other in hot encounter, like champions under shield. The wildcat glared from the thicket; the raccoon thrust his furry countenance from the hollow tree, and the opossum swung, head downwards, from the overhanging bough.

With the opening spring, when the forests are budding into leaf, and the prairies gemmed with flowers; when a warm, faint haze rests upon the landscape—then heart and senses are inthralled with luxurious beauty. The shrubs and wild fruit-trees, flushed with pale red blossoms, and the small clustering flowers of grape-vines, which choke the gigantic trees with Laocoon writhings, fill the forest with their rich perfume. A few days later, and a cloud of verdure overshadows the land, while birds innumerable sing beneath its canopy, and brighten its shades with their glancing hues.

Yet this western paradise is not free from the curse of Adam. The beneficent sun, which kindles into life so many forms of loveliness and beauty, fails not to engender venom and death from the rank slime of pestilential swamp and marsh. In some stagnant pool, buried in the jungle-like depths of the forest, where the hot and lifeless water reeks with exhalations, the water-snake basks by the margin, or winds his checkered length of loathsome beauty across the sleepy surface. From beneath the rotten carcass of some fallen tree, the moccason thrusts out his broad flat head, ready to dart on the intruder. On the dry, sun-scorched prairie, the rattlesnake, a more generous enemy, reposes in his spiral coil. He scorns to shun the eye of day, as if conscious of the honor accorded to his name by the warlike race, who, jointly with him, claim lordship over the land. But some intrusive footstep awakes him from his slumbers. His neck is arched; the white fangs gleam in his distended jaws; his small eyes dart rays of unutterable fierceness; and his rattles, invisible with their quick vibration, ring the sharp warning which no man will rashly contemn.

The land thus prodigal of good and evil, so remote from the sea, so primitive in its aspect, might well be deemed an undiscovered region, ignorant of European arts; yet it may boast a colonization as old as that of many a spot to which are accorded the scanty honors of an American antiquity. The earliest settlement of Pennsylvania was made in 1681; the first occupation of the Illinois took place in the previous year. La Salle may be called the father of the colony. That remarkable man entered the country with a handful of followers, bent on his grand scheme of Mississippi discovery. A legion of enemies rose in his path; but neither delay, disappointment, sickness, famine, open force, nor secret conspiracy, could bend his soul of iron. Disasters accumulated upon him. He flung them off, and still pressed forward to his object. His victorious energy bore all before it, but the success on which he had staked his life served only to entail fresh calamity, and an untimely death; and his best reward is, that his name stands forth in history an imperishable monument of heroic constancy. When on his way to the Mississippi in the year 1680, La Salle built a fort in the country of the Illinois, and, on his return from the mouth of the great river, some of his followers remained, and established themselves near the spot. Heroes of another stamp took up the work which the daring Norman had begun. Jesuit missionaries, among the best and purest of their order, burning with zeal for the salvation of souls, and the gaining of an immortal crown, here toiled and suffered, with a self-sacrificing devotion which extorts a tribute of admiration even from sectarian bigotry. While the colder apostles of Protestantism labored upon the outskirts of heathendom, these champions of the cross, the forlorn hope of the army of Rome, pierced to the heart of its dark and dreary domain, confronting death at every step, and well repaid for all, could they but sprinkle a few drops of water on the forehead of a dying child, or hang a gilded crucifix round the neck of some warrior, pleased with the glittering trinket. With the beginning of the eighteenth century, the black robe of the Jesuit was known in every village of the Illinois. Defying the wiles of Satan and the malice of his emissaries, the Indian sorcerers, exposed to the rage of the elements, and every casualty of forest life, they followed their wandering proselytes to war and to the chase; now wading through morasses, now dragging canoes over rapids and sand-bars; now scorched with heat of the sweltering prairie, and now shivering houseless in the blasts of January. At Kaskaskia and Cahokia they established missions, and built frail churches from the bark of trees, fit emblems of their own transient and futile labors. Morning and evening, the savage worshippers sang praises to the Virgin, and knelt in supplication before the shrine of St. Joseph.

Soldiers and fur-traders followed where these pioneers of the church had led the way. Forts were built here and there throughout the country, and the cabins of settlers clustered about the mission-houses. The new colonists, emigrants from Canada or disbanded soldiers of French regiments, bore a close resemblance to the settlers of Detroit, or the primitive people of Acadia, whose simple life poetry has chosen as an appropriate theme. The Creole of the Illinois, contented, light-hearted, and thriftless, by no means fulfilled the injunction to increase and multiply, and the colony languished in spite of the fertile soil. The people labored long enough to gain a bare subsistence for each passing day, and spent the rest of their time in dancing and merry-making, smoking, gossiping, and hunting. Their native gayety was irrepressible, and they found means to stimulate it with wine made from the fruit of the wild grape-vines. Thus they passed their days, at peace with themselves, hand and glove with their Indian neighbors, and ignorant of all the world beside. Money was scarcely known among them. Skins and furs were the prevailing currency, and in every village a great portion of the land was held in common. The military commandant, whose station was at Fort Chartres, on the Mississippi, ruled the colony with a sway absolute as that of the Pacha of Egypt, and judged civil and criminal cases without right of appeal. Yet his power was exercised in a patriarchal spirit, and he usually commanded the respect and confidence of the people. Many years later, when, after the War of the Revolution, the Illinois came under the jurisdiction of the United States, the perplexed inhabitants, totally at a loss to understand the complicated machinery of republicanism, begged to be delivered from the intolerable burden of self-government, and to be once more subjected to a military commandant.

ERASTUS W. ELLSWORTH

WAS born November, 1823, in East Windsor, Conn., where he is at present a resident. He was educated at Amherst College, studied law, but was diverted from the profession by a taste for mechanical ingenuities, and has mainly occupied himself as an inventor or machinist. A spirited poem from his pen, *The Railroad Lyric*, is an eloquent expression of these tastes.

Erastus W. Ellsworth

Having contributed various poems to Sartain's Magazine, the International, and Putnam's Monthly, in 1855 he published a collection from them at Hartford. The longest of these is devoted to that old favorite theme of the Muse, the desertion of Ariadne by Theseus. Others are patriotic, celebrating General Putnam, Nathan Hale, and Mount Vernon. Still another class is on familiar topics, in a light sportive style. The following, in a quaint vein of morality, is among the most successful.

WHAT IS THE USE?

I saw a man, by some accounted wise,
For some things said and done before their eyes,
Quite overcast, and in a restless muse,
Pacing a path about,
And often giving out:
"What is the use?"

Then I, with true respect: What meanest thou
By those strange words, and that unsettled brow?
Health, wealth, the fair esteem of ample views,
To these things thou art born.
But he as one forlorn:
"What is the use?

"I have surveyed the sages and their books,
Man, and the natural world of woods and brooks,
Seeking that perfect good that I would choose;
But find no perfect good,
Settled and understood.
What is the use?

"Life, in a poise, hangs trembling on the beam,
Even in a breath bounding to each extreme
Of joy and sorrow; therefore I refuse
All beaten ways of bliss,
And only answer this:
What is the use?

"The hoodwinked world is seeking happiness.
'Which way?' they cry, 'here?' 'no!' 'there?' 'who can guess?'
And so they grope, and grope, and grope, and cruise
On, on, till life is lost,
At blindman's with a ghost.
What is the use?

"Love first, with most, then wealth, distinction, fame,
Quicken the blood and spirit on the game.
Some try them all, and all alike accuse—
'I have been all,' said one,
'And find that all is none.'
What is the use?

"In woman's love we sweetly are undone;
Willing to attract, but harder to be won,
Harder to keep, is she whose love we choose.
Loves are like flowers that grow
In soils on fire below.
What is the use?

"Some pray for wealth, and seem to pray aright:
They heap until themselves are out of sight;
Yet stand, in charities, not over shoes,
And ask of their old age,
As an old ledger page,
What is the use?

"Some covet honors, and they have their choice,
Are dogged with dinners and the popular voice;
They ride a wind—it drops them—and they bruise;
Or, if sustained, they sigh:
'That other is more high.'
What is the use?

'Some try for fame—the merest chance of things
That mortal hope can wreak towards the wings
Of soaring Time—they win, perhaps, or lose—
Who knows? Not he, who, dead,
Laurels a marble head.
What is the use?

"The strife for fame and the high praise of power,
Is as a man, who, panting up a tower,
Bears a great stone, then, straining all his thews,
Heaves it, and sees it make
A splashing in a lake.
What is the use?

"Fame is the spur that the clear spirit doth raise
To scorn delights, and live laborious days.
Thus the great lords of spiritual fame amuse
Their souls, and think it good
To eat of angels' food.
What is the use?

"They eat their fill, and they are filled with wind.
They do the noble works of noble mind.
Repute, and often bread, the world refuse.
They go unto their place,
The greatest of the race.
What is the use?

"Should some new star, in the fair evening sky
Kindle a blaze, startling so keen an eye
Of flamings eminent, athwart the dews,
Our thoughts would say: No doubt
That star will soon burn out.
What is the use?

"Who'll care for me, when I am dead and gone?
Not many now, and surely, soon, not one;
And should I sing like an immortal Muse,
Men, if they read the line,
Read for their good, not mine;
What is the use?

"And song, if passable, is doomed to pass—
Common, though sweet as the new-scythed grass.
Of human deeds and thoughts Time bears no news,
That, flying, he can lack,
Else they would break his back.
What is the use?

"Spirit of Beauty! Breath of golden lyres!
Perpetual tremble of immortal wires!
Divinely torturing rapture of the Muse!
Conspicuous wretchedness!
Thou starry, sole success!—
What is the use!

"Doth not all struggle tell, upon its brow,
That he who makes it is not easy now,
But hopes to be? Vain hope that dost abuse!
Coquetting with thine eyes,
And fooling him who sighs.
What is the use?

"Go pry the lintels of the pyramids;
Lift the old king's mysterious coffin lids—
This dust was theirs whose names these stones confuse,
These mighty monuments
Of mighty discontents.
What is the use?

"Did not he sum it all, whose Gate of Pearls
Blazed royal Ophir, Tyre, and Syrian girls—
The great, wise, famous monarch of the Jews?
Though rolled in grandeur vast,
He said of all, at last:
What is the use?

"O! but to take, of life, the natural good,
Even as a hermit caverned in a wood,
More sweetly fills my sober-suited views,
Than sweating to attain
Any luxurious pain.
What is the use?

"Give me a hermit's life, without his beads—
His lantern-jawed and moral-mouthing creeds;
Systems and creeds the natural heart abuse.
What need of any Book,
Or spiritual crook?
What is the use?

"I love, and God is love; and I behold
Man, Nature, God, one triple chain of gold—
Nature in all sole Oracle and Muse.
What should I seek, at all,
More than is natural?
What is the use?"

Seeing this man so heathenly inclined—
So wilted in the mood of a good mind,
I felt a kind of heat of earnest thought;
And studying in reply,
Answered him, eye to eye:—

Thou dost amaze me that thou dost mistake
The wandering rivers for the fountain lake.
What is the end of living?—happiness?—
An end that none attain,
Argues a purpose vain.

Plainly, this world is not a scope for bliss,
But duty. Yet we see not all that is,
Or may be, some day, if we love the light.
What man is, in desires,
Whispers where man aspires.

But what and where are we?—what now—to-day?
Souls on a globe that spin our lives away—
A multitudinous world, where Heaven and Hell,
Strangely in battle met,
Their gonfalons have set.

Dust though we are, and shall return to dust,
Yet being born to battles, fight we must;
Under which ensign is our only choice.
We know to wage our best,
God only knows the rest.

Then since we see about us sin and dole,
And some things good, why not, with hand and soul
Wrestle and succor out of wrong and sorrow—
Grasping the swords of strife,
Making the most of life?

Yea, all that we can wield is worth the end,
If sought as God's and man's most loyal friend.
Naked we come into the world, and take
Weapons of various skill—
Let us not use them ill.

As for the creeds, Nature is dark at best;
And darker still is the deep human breast.
Therefore consider well of creeds and Books,
Lest thou mayst somewhat fail
Of things beyond the veil.

Nature was dark to the dim starry age
Of wistful Job; and that Athenian sage,
Pensive in piteous thought of Faith's distress;
For still she cried with tears:
"More light, ye crystal spheres!"

But rouse thee, man! Shake off this hideous death!
Be man! Stand up! Draw in a mighty breath!
This world has quite enough emasculate hands,
Dallying with doubt and sin.
Come—here is work—begin!

Come, here is work—and a rank field—begin.
Put thou thine edge to the great weeds of sin;
So shalt thou find the use of life, and see
Thy Lord, at set of sun,
Approach and say: "Well done!"

This at the last: They clutch the sapless fruit.
Ashes and dust of the Dead Sea, who suit
Their course of life to compass happiness;
But be it understood
That, to be greatly good,
All is the use.

WILLIAM W. CALDWELL

Was born at Newburyport, Massachusetts, in 1823. He was educated at Bowdoin college, where he received his degree in 1843, and has since resided in his native place, engaged in the buisness of a druggist. A man of taste and refinement, he has pursued poetry and literature as the ornaments of life. His occasional verses, on simple heartfelt themes, are truthful in expression and sentiment, and happy in poetic execution. He has published also translations from the German poets.

ROBIN'S COME!

From the elm-tree's topmost bough,
Hark! the Robin's early song!
Telling one and all that now
Merry spring-time hastes along;
Welcome tidings thou dost bring,
Little harbinger of spring,
Robin's come!

Of the winter we are weary,
Weary of its frost and snow,
Longing for the sunshine cheery,
And the brooklet's gurgling flow;
Gladly then we hear thee sing
The reveillé of the spring.
Robin's come!

Ring it out o'er hill and plain,
Through the garden's lonely bowers,
Till the green leaves dance again,
Till the air is sweet with flowers!
Wake the cowslip by the rill,
Wake the yellow daffodil!
Robin's come!

Then as thou wert wont of yore,
Build thy nest and rear thy young,
Close beside our cottage door,
In the woodbine leaves among;
Hurt or harm thou need'st not fear,
Nothing rude shall venture near.
Robin's come!

Swinging still o'er yonder lane,
Robin answers merrily;
Ravished by the sweet refrain,
Alice claps her hands in glee,
Calling from the open door,
With her soft voice, o'er and o'er,
Robin's come!

WHAT SAITH THE FOUNTAIN?

What saith the Fountain,
Hid in the glade,
Where the tall mountain
Throweth its shade?

"Deep in my waters, reflected serene,
All the soft beauty of heaven is seen;
Thus let thy bosom from wild passions free
Ever the mirror of purity be!"

What saith the Streamlet,
Flowing so bright,
Clear as a beamlet
Of silvery light?
"Morning and evening still floating along,
Upward for ever ascendeth my song;
Be thou contented, whate'er may befal,
Cheerful in knowing that God is o'er all."

What saith the River,
Majestic in flow,
Moving for ever
Calmly and slow?
"Over my surface the great vessels glide,
Ocean-ward borne by my strong heaving tide;
Work thou too, brother, life vanisheth fast,
Labor unceasing, rest cometh at last."

What saith the Ocean,
Boundless as night;
Tumultuous in motion,
Resistless in might?
"Fountain to streamlet, streamlet to river,
All in my bosom commingle for ever;
Morning to noontide and noontide to night,
Soon will Eternity veil thee from sight."

JOHN R. THOMPSON

WAS born in Richmond, Va., October 23, 1823. He was educated at a school at East Haven in Connecticut, and at the University of Virginia, where he received the degree of Bachelor of Arts in 1845, having passed an interval of two years in the study of the law. In 1847, he became editor of the Southern Literary Magazine, which he has since conducted.

Jno. R. Thompson

Mr. Thompson, besides the articles in his own journal, has contributed numerous poems to the Knickerbocker, Literary World, and International Magazine.

His editorship of the Messenger, the longest lived periodical of the South, and always an important medium of communication of the best Southern authors with the public, has been marked by its liberality and courtesy towards authors of all portions of the country. His poetical writings are finished with care, and display a delicate sentiment.

THE WINDOW PANES AT BRANDON.*

As within the old mansion the holiday throng
re-assembles in beauty and grace,
And some eye looking out of the window, by chance,
these memorial records may trace—
How the past, like a swift-coming haze from the sea,
in an instant, surrounds us once more,
While the shadowy figures of those we have loved,
all distinctly are seen on the shore!

Through the vista of years, stretching dimly away,
we but look, and a vision behold—
Like some magical picture the sunset reveals with
its colors of crimson and gold—
All suffused with the glow of the hearth's ruddy
blaze, from beneath the gay "mistletoe bough,"
There are faces that break into smiles as divinely as
any that beam on us now.

While the Old Year departing strides ghost-like
along o'er the hills that are dark with the
storm,
To the New the brave beaker is filled to the brim,
and the play of affection is warm:
Look once more—as the garlanded Spring re-appears,
in her footsteps we welcome a train
Of fair women, whose eyes are as bright as the gem
that has cut their dear names on the pane.

From the canvas of Vandyke and Kneller that hangs
on the old-fashioned wainscoted wall,
Stately ladies, the favored of poets, look down on
the guests and the revel and all;
But their beauty, though wedded to eloquent verse,
and though rendered immortal by Art,
Yet outshines not the beauty that breathing below,
in a moment takes captive the heart.

Many winters have since frosted over these panes
with the tracery-work of the rime,
Many Aprils have brought back the birds to the
lawn from some far-away tropical clime—
But the guests of the season, alas! where are they?
some the shores of the stranger have trod,
And some names have been long ago carved on the
stone, where they sweetly rest under the sod.

How uncertain the record! the hand of a child, in
its innocent sport, unawares,
May, at any time, lucklessly shatter the pane, and
thus cancel the story it bears:
Still a portion, at least, shall uninjured remain—
unto trustier tablets consigned—
The fond names that survive in the memory of friends
who yet linger a season behind.

Recollect, oh young soul, with ambition inspired!—
let the moral be read as we pass—
Recollect the illusory tablets of fame have been ever
as brittle as glass:
Oh then be not content with the name there inscribed,—for as well may you trace it in dust,—
But resolve to record it where long it shall stand, in
the hearts of the good and the just!

A PICTURE.

Across the narrow dusty street
I see at early dawn,
A little girl with glancing feet,
As agile as the fawn.

An hour or so and forth she goes,
The school she brightly seeks,
She carries in her hand a rose
And two upon her cheeks.

The sun mounts up the torrid sky—
The bell for dinner rings—
My little friend, with laughing eye,
Comes gaily back and sings.

The week wears off and Saturday,
A welcome day, I ween,
Gives time for girlish romp and play;
How glad my pet is seen!

But Sunday—in what satins great
Does she not then appear!
King Solomon in all his state
Wore no such pretty gear.

* Upon the window panes at Brandon, on James River, are inscribed the names, cut with a diamond ring, of many of those who have composed the Christmas and May parties of that hospitable mansion in years gone by.

I fling her every day a kiss,
And one she flings to me:
I know not truly when it is
She prettiest may be.

BENEDICITE.

I saw her move along the aisle—
The chancel lustres burned the while—
With bridal roses in her hair,
Oh! never seemed she half so fair.

A manly form stood by her side,
We knew him worthy such a bride;
And prayers went up to God above
To bless them with immortal love.

The vow was said. I know not yet
But some were filled with fond regret:
So much a part of us she seemed
To lose her quite we had not dreamed.

Like the "fair Inez," loved, caressed,
She went into the distant west,
And while one heart with joy flowed o'er,
Like her she saddened many more.

Lady, though far from childhood's things
Thy gentle spirit folds its wing,
We offer now for him and thee
A tearful Benedicite!

GEORGE H. BOKER.

George Henry Boker is a native of Philadelphia, where he was born in the year 1824. In 1841 he was graduated at Nassau Hall, Princeton, and after a tour in Europe returned to Philadelphia, where he has since resided.

In 1847 he published *The Lesson of Life and other Poems;* and in 1848, *Calaynos*, a tragedy. This was received with favor, and in April, of the following year, acted with success at Sadlers' Wells Theatre, London. The scene is laid in Spain, the interest turns upon the hostile feeling between the Spanish and Moorish races.

Geo: H. Boker

Mr. Boker's second tragedy, *Anne Boleyn*, was soon after published and produced upon the stage.

He has since written *The Betrothal*, *Leonor de Guzman*, and a comedy, *All the World a Mask*, all of which have been produced with success.

He has also contributed several poetical compositions of merit to the periodicals of the day.

Mr. Boker has wisely avoided, in his dramatic composition, the stilted periods of the classic, and the vagueness of the "unacted" drama. His plays have the action befitting the stage, and the finish requisite for the closet. His blank verse is smooth, and his dialogue spirited and colloquial.

THE DEATH OF DOÑA ALDA—FROM CALAYNOS.

Calaynos. What would'st thou, Alda?—Cheer thee, love, bear up!
Doña Alda. Thy face is dim, I cannot see thine eyes:
Nay, hide them not; they are my guiding stars—
Have sorrow's drops thus blotted out their light?
Thou dost forgive me, love—thou'lt think of me?
Thou'lt not speak harshly, when I'm 'neath the earth?
Thou'lt love my memory, for what once I was?
Calaynos. Yes, though I live till doom.
Doña Alda. O happiness!
Come closer—this thy hand? Have mercy, heaven!
Yes, press me closer—close—I do not feel.—
Calaynos. O God of mercy, spare!
Doña Alda. A sunny day—
Oh!—(*She faints.*)
Calaynos. Bear her in—I am as calm as ice.
Come when she wakes—I cannot see her thus.
[*Exeunt* Oliver *and servants, bearing* Doña Alda.
'Tis better so;—but then the thoughts come back
Of the young bride I welcomed at the gate.—
I kissed her, yes, I kissed her—was it there?
Yes, yes, I kissed her there, and in the chapel—
The dimly lighted chapel.—I see it all!
Here was old Hubert, there stood Oliver—
The priest, the bridesmaids, groomsmen—every face;
All the retainers that around us thronged,
Smiling for joy, with ribands in their caps.—
And shall they all, all follow her black pall,
With weeping eyes and doleful, sullen weeds?
For they all love her:—Oh, she was so kind,
So kind and gentle, when they stood in need;
And never checked them, if they murmured at her,
But found excuses for their discontent.—
They'll miss her: for her path was like an angel's,
And every place seemed holier where she came,
Ah me, ah me! I would this life were past!
Stay, love, watch o'er me; I will join thee soon.
[*A cry within.*
So quickly gone! And ere I said farewell!
[*Rushes to the door.*
(*Re-enter* Oliver.)
Oliver. My lord—
Calaynos. Yes, yes, she's dead—I will go in.
[*Exit.*
Oliver. O, dreadful ending to a fearful night!
This shock has shattered to the very root
The strength of his great spirit. Mournful night!
And what will day bring forth?—but wo on wo.
Ah, death may rest awhile, and hold his hand,
Having destroyed this wondrous paragon,
And sapped a mind, whose lightest thought was worth
The concentrated being of a herd.
Yet shall the villain live who wrought this wo?—
By heaven I swear, if my lord kill him not,
I, though a scholar and unused to arms,
Will hunt him down—ay, should he course the earth,
And slay him like a felon!

If this is sin, let fiends snap at my soul,
But I will do it! Lo, where comes my lord,
Bent down and withered, like a broken tree,
Prostrate with too much bearing.
(*Re-enter* CALAYNOS.)
Calaynos. Oliver,
I stole to see her; not a soul was there,
Save an old crone that hummed a doleful tune,
And winked her purblind eyes, o'errun with tears.
O, boy, I never knew I loved her so!
I held my breath, and gazed into her face—
Ah, she was wondrous fair. She seemed to me,
Just as I've often seen her, fast asleep.
When from my studies cautiously I've stole,
And bent above her, and drank up her breath,
Sweet as a sleeping infant's,—Then perchance,
Yet in her sleep, her starry eyes would ope,
To close again behind their fringy clouds,
Ere I caught half their glory. There's no breath,
There's not a perfume on her withered lips,
Her eyes ope not, nor ever will again.—
But tell me how she died.—She suffered not?
Oliver. She scarcely woke from her first fainting here;
Or if she did, she gave no sign nor word.
Awhile she muttered, as if lost in prayer;
Some who stood close thought once they caught thy name;
But grief had dulled my sense, I could not hear.
Then she slid gently to a lethargy;
And so she died—we knew not when she went.
Calaynos. Here is the paper which contains her story:
I fain would clear her name, fain think her wronged.
[*Reads.*
O, double-dealing villain!—Moor—bought her!
Impious monster—false beyond belief!
But she is guiltless—hear'st thou, Oliver?
Nay, read; I cannot move thee as she can.
[OLIVER *reads.*
He called me Moor.—True, true, I did her wrong:
The sin is mine; I should have told her that.
I only kept it back to save her pain;
I feared to lose respect by telling her.
I see how he could heighten that grave wrong,
And spur her nigh to madness with his taunts.
She fell, was senseless, without life or reason—
Why tigers spare inanimated forms—
So bore her off. Then lie on lie—O base!
The guilt all mine. Why did I hide my birth?
Ah, who can tell how soon one seed of sin,
Which we short-sighted mortals think destroyed,
May sprout and bear, and shake its noxious fruit
Upon our heads, when we ne'er dream of ill;
For nought that is can ever pass away!
Oliver. And shall this villain live?
Calaynos. No, no, by heaven!
Those fellows on the wall would haunt me then.—
I hear your voices, men of crime and blood,
Ring in mine ears, and I obey the call.
[*Snatches a sword from the wall.*
How precious is the blade which justice wields,
To chasten wrong, or set a wrong to right!
[*Draws.*
Come forth, thou minister of bloody deeds,
That blazed a comet in the van of war,
Presaging death to man, and tears to earth.—
Pale, gleaming tempter, when I clutch thee thus,
Thou, of thyself, dost plead that murder's right,
And mak'st me half believe it luxury.
Thy horrid edge is thirsting for man's gore,
And thou shalt drink it from the point to hilt.—
To horse, to horse! the warrior blood is up;
The tiger spirit of my warlike race
Burns in my heart, and floods my kindling veins.—
Mount, Oliver, ere pity's hand can hide
The bloody mist that floats before mine eyes—
To horse, to horse! the Moor rides forth to slay!
[*Exeunt.*

BAYARD TAYLOR.

BAYARD TAYLOR is the son of a Pennsylvania farmer, a descendant of the first emigration with Penn, and was born January 11, 1825, in the village of Kennett Square, Chester county, in that state. He received a country education, and at the age of seventeen became an apprentice in a printing-office in Westchester. He employed his limited leisure in learning Latin and French, and writing verses, which were cordially received by Willis and Griswold, then conducting the New York Mirror and Graham's Magazine. The success of these led him to collect the poems in a volume in 1844, entitled *Ximena*, with the object of gaining reputation enough to secure employment as a contributor to some of the leading newspapers, while he was making a tour in Europe which he projected. He succeeded in his object, procuring from Mr. Chandler of the Philadelphia United States Gazette, and from Mr. Patterson of the Saturday Evening Post, an advance of a hundred dollars for letters to be written abroad, and with this, in addition to forty dollars for some poems in Graham's Magazine, he started on his European tour. With some further remittances from home he was enabled to make the tour of England, Scotland, Germany, Switzerland, Italy, and France, during a journey of two years, his expenses for the time being but five hundred dollars. How this was accomplished by the frugal pedestrian was told in his account of the tour on his return in 1846, when he published his *Views-a-Foot.* He next engaged in the editing and publication of a newspaper at Phœnixville, Pa., to which he gave his labors for a year with an unprofitable pecuniary result. At the close of 1847 he came to New York to prosecute his career of authorship, wrote for the Literary World, and in February, 1848, secured a position as a permanent writer for the Tribune, shortly after publishing his volume of poems, *Rhymes of Travel.* The next year he became proprietor of a share of the paper and one of its associate editors. His literary labors have been since connected with that journal. He visited California in 1849, and returned by way of Mexico in 1850, writing letters for the Tribune, which he revised and collected in the volumes, *El Dorado, or Adventures in the Path of Empire.* In the summer of 1851 he set out on a protracted tour in the East, leaving a third volume of poems with his publisher, *A Book of Romances, Lyrics, and Songs.*

In this new journey he proceeded to Egypt by way of England, the Rhine, Vienna, and Trieste, reaching Cairo early in November. He immediately proceeded to Central Africa, and after passing through Egypt, Nubia, Ethiopia, and Soudân, to the kingdom of the Shillook negroes on the White Nile, reached Cairo again in April, 1852, having made a journey of about four thousand miles in the interior of Africa. He then made the tour of Palestine and Syria, extending his journey northwards to Antioch and Aleppo, and thence by way of Tarsus, the defiles of the Taurus, Konieh (Iconium), the forests of Phrygia, and the Bithynian Olympus to Constantinople, where he arrived

Bayard Taylor

about the middle of July. After a month's stay he sailed for Malta and Sicily, reaching the foot of Mount Ætna in time to witness the first outbreak of the eruption of 1852. Thence he passed to Italy, the Tyrol, Germany, and England. In October he took a new departure from England for Gibraltar, spent a month in the south of Spain, and proceeded by the overland route to Bombay. He set out on the 4th of January, 1853, and after a tour of twenty-two hundred miles in the interior of India, reached Calcutta on the 22d of February. He there embarked for Hong Kong, by way of Penang and Singapore. Soon after his arrival in China he was attached to the American legation, and accompanied the minister, Colonel Marshall, to Shanghai, where he remained two months. On the arrival of Commodore Perry's squadron he entered the naval service for the purpose of accompanying it to Japan. He left on the 17th of May, and after visiting and exploring the Loo Choo and Bonin Islands, arrived in the bay of Yedo on the 8th of July. The expedition to which he was attached, remained there nine days, engaged with the ceremonials of delivering the President's letter, and then returned to Loo Choo and China. Taylor then spent a month in Macao and Canton, and sailed for New York on the 9th of September. After a voyage of one hundred and one days, during which the vessel touched at Angier in Java, and St. Helena, he reached New York on the 20th of December, 1853, after an absence of two years and four months, having accomplished upwards of fifty thousand miles of travel. His letters, describing the journey, were all this while published in the Tribune. In their enlarged and improved form they furnish material for several series of volumes.

The characteristics of Mr. Taylor's writings are, in his poems, ease of expression, with a careful selection of poetic capabilities, a full, animated style, with a growing attention to art and condensation. His prose is equable and clear, in the flowing style; the narrative of a genial, healthy observer of the many manners of the world which he has seen in the most remarkable portions of its four quarters.

In person he is above the ordinary height, manly and robust, with a quick, resolute way of carrying out his plans with courage and independence; and with great energy and perseverance, he combines a happy natural temperament and benevolence.

BEDOUIN SONG.

From the Desert I come to thee
On a stallion shod with fire;
And the winds are left behind
In the speed of my desire.
Under thy window I stand,
And the midnight hears my cry:
I love thee, I love but thee,
With a love that shall not die
Till the sun grows cold,
And the stars are old,
And the leaves of the Judgment
Book unfold!

Look from thy window and see
My passion and my pain;
I lie on the sands below,
And I faint in thy disdain.
Let the night-winds touch thy brow
With the heat of my burning sigh,
And melt thee to hear the vow
Of a love that shall not die
Till the sun grows cold,
And the stars are old,
And the leaves of the Judgment
Book unfold!

My steps are nightly driven,
By the fever in my breast,
To hear from thy lattice breathed
The word that shall give me rest.
Open the door of thy heart,
And open thy chamber door,
And my kisses shall teach thy lips
The love that shall fade no more
Till the sun grows cold,
And the stars are old,
And the leaves of the Judgment
Book unfold!

KILIMANDJARO.

Hail to thee, monarch of African mountains,
Remote, inaccessible, silent, and lone—
Who, from the heart of the tropical fervors,
Liftest to heaven thine alien snows,
Feeding for ever the fountains that make thee
Father of Nile and Creator of Egypt!

The years of the world are engraved on thy forehead;
Time's morning blushed red on thy first-fallen snows;
Yet lost in the wilderness, nameless, unnoted,
Of man unbeholden, thou wert not till now.
Knowledge alone is the being of Nature,
Giving a soul to her manifold features,
Lighting through paths of the primitive darkness
The footsteps of Truth and the vision of Song.
Knowledge has born thee anew to Creation,
And long-baffled Time at thy baptism rejoices.
Take, then, a name, and be filled with existence,
Yea, be exultant in sovereign glory,
While from the hand of the wandering poet
Drops the first garland of song at thy feet.

Floating alone, on the flood of thy making,
Through Africa's mystery, silence, and fire,
Lo! in my palm, like the Eastern enchanter,
I dip from the waters a magical mirror,

And thou art revealed to my purified vision.
I see thee, supreme in the midst of thy co-mates,
Standing alone 'twixt the Earth and the Heavens,
Heir of the Sunset and Herald of Morn.
Zone above zone, to thy shoulders of granite,
The climates of Earth are displayed, as an index,
Giving the scope of the Book of Creation.
There, in the gorges that widen, descending
From cloud and from cold into summer eternal,
Gather the threads of the ice-gendered fountains—
Gather to riotous torrents of crystal,
And, giving each shelvy recess where they dally
The blooms of the North and its evergreen turfage,
Leap to the land of the lion and lotus!
There, in the wondering airs of the Tropics
Shivers the Aspen, still dreaming of cold:
There stretches the Oak, from the loftiest ledges,
His arms to the far-away lands of his brothers,
And the Pine-tree looks down on his rival, the Palm.

Bathed in the tenderest purple of distance,
Tinted and shadowed by pencils of air,
Thy battlements hang o'er the slopes and the forests,
Seats of the Gods in the limitless ether,
Looming sublimely aloft and afar.
Above them, like folds of imperial ermine,
Sparkle the snow-fields that furrow thy forehead—
Desolate realms, inaccessible, silent,
Chasms and caverns where Day is a stranger,
Garners where storeth his treasures the Thunder,
The Lightning his falchion, his arrows the Hail!

Sovereign Mountain, thy brothers give welcome:
They, the baptized and the crownéd of ages,
Watch-towers of Continents, altars of Earth,
Welcome thee now to their mighty assembly.
Mont Blanc, in the roar of his mad avalanches,
Hails thy accession; superb Orizaba,
Belted with beech and ensandalled with palm;
Chimborazo, the lord of the regions of noonday;—
Mingle their sounds in magnificent chorus
With greeting august from the Pillars of Heaven
Who, in the urns of the Indian Ganges
Filters the snows of their sacred dominions,
Unmarked with a footprint, unseen but of God.

Lo, unto each is the seal of his lordship,
Nor questioned the right that his majesty giveth:
Each in his awful supremacy forces
Worship and reverence, wonder and joy.
Absolute all, yet in dignity varied,
None has a claim to the honors of story,
Or the superior splendors of song,
Greater than thou, in thy mystery mantled—
Thou, the sole monarch of African mountains,
Father of Nile and Creator of Egypt!

RICHARD HENRY STODDARD

Was born at Hingham, Massachusetts. He has latterly resided in New York, where, having previously been a contributor to the Knickerbocker and other magazines, he published in 1849 a first collection of poems, entitled *Foot Prints.* In 1852 a collection of the author's maturer *Poems* appeared from the press of Ticknor and Co. The verses of Mr. Stoddard are composed with skill in a poetic school of which Keats may be placed at the head. He has a fondness for poetic luxuries, and his reader frequently participates in his enjoyment. He has achieved some success in the difficult province of the Ode, and has—an equally rare accomplishment—touched several delicate themes in song with graceful simplicity.

R. H. Stoddard.

AUTUMN.

Divinest Autumn! who may sketch thee best,
  For ever changeful o'er the changeful globe?
Who guess thy certain crown, thy favorite crest,
  The fashion of thy many-colored robe?
Sometimes we see thee stretched upon the ground,
  In fading woods where acorns patter fast.
Dropping to feed thy tusky boars around,
  Crunching among the leaves the ripened mast;
Sometimes at work where ancient granary-floors
  Are open wide, a thresher stout and hale,
  Whitened with chaff upwafted from thy flail,
While south winds sweep along the dusty floors;
And sometimes fast asleep at noontide hours,
  Pillowed on sheaves, and shaded from the heat,
    With Plenty at thy feet,
Braiding a coronet of oaten straw and flowers!
What time, emerging from a low hung cloud,
  The shining chariot of the Sun was driven
Slope to its goal, and Day in reverence bowed
  His burning forehead at the gate of Heaven;—
Then I beheld thy presence full revealed,
Slow trudging homeward o'er a stubble-field;
Around thy brow, to shade it from the west,
  A wisp of straw entwisted in a crown;
  A golden wheat-sheaf, slipping slowly down,
Hugged tight against thy waist, and on thy breast,
Linked to a belt, an earthen flagon swung;
    And o'er thy shoulder flung,
Tied by their stems, a bundle of great pears,
  Bell shaped and streaky, some rich orchard's pride;
  A heavy bunch of grapes on either side,
    Across each arm, tugged downward by the load,
Their glossy leaves blown off by wandering airs;
  A yellow-rinded lemon in thy right,
  In thy left hand a sickle caught the light,
    Keen as the moon which glowed
      Along the fields of night:
One moment seen, the shadowy masque was flown,
And I was left, as now, to meditate alone.

Hark! hark!—I hear the reapers in a row,
  Shouting their harvest carols blithe and loud,
  Cutting the rustled maize whose crests are bowed
With ears o'ertasselled, soon to be laid low;

Crooked earthward now, the orchards droop their boughs
With red-cheek fruits, while far along the wall,
Full in the south, ripe plums and peaches fall
In tufted grass where laughing lads carouse;
And down the pastures, where the horse goes round
His ring of tan, beneath the mossy shed,
Old cider-presses work with creaky din,
Oozing in vats, and apples heap the ground;
And hour by hour, a basket on his head,
Up-clambering to the spout, the ploughman pours them in!

Sweet-scented winds from meadows newly mown
Blow eastward now; and now for many a day
The fields will be alive with wains of hay
And stacks not all unmeet for Autumn's throne!
The granges will be crowded, and the men
Half-smothered, as they tread it from the top;
And then the wains will go, and come again,
And go and come until they end the crop.
And where the melons stud the garden vine,
Crook-necked or globy, smaller carts will wait,
Soon to be urged o'erloaded to the gate
Where apples drying on the stages shine;
And children soon will go at eve and morn
And set their snares for quails with baits of corn;
And when the house-dog snuffs a distant hare,
O'errun the gorgeous woods with noisy glee;
And when the walnuts ripen, climb a tree,
And shake the branches bare!
And by and by, when northern winds are out,
Great fires will roar in chimneys huge at night,
While chairs draw round, and pleasant tales are told:
And nuts and apples will be passed about,
Until the household, drowsy with delight,
Creep off to bed a-cold!

Sovereign of Seasons! Monarch of the Earth!
Steward of bounteous Nature, whose rich alms
Are showered upon us from thy liberal palms,
Until our spirits overflow with mirth!
Divinest Autumn! while our garners burst
With plenteous harvesting, and heaped increase,
We lift our eyes to thee through grateful tears.
World-wide in boons, vouchsafe to visit first,
And linger last long o'er our realm of Peace,
Where freedom calmly sits, and beckons on the Years!

THE TWO BRIDES.

I saw two maidens at the kirk,
And both were fair and sweet:
One in her wedding robe,
And one in her winding sheet.

The choristers sang the hymn,
The sacred rites were read,
And one for life to Life,
And one to Death was wed.

They were borne to their bridal beds,
In loveliness and bloom;
One in a merry castle,
The other a solemn tomb.

One on the morrow woke
In a world of sin and pain;
But the other was happier far,
And never woke again!

WILLIAM ALLEN BUTLER

Is the son of the eminent lawyer and politician Benjamin F. Butler, a member of the cabinet of Jackson and Van Buren, to whom, in 1824, in connexion with John Duer and the late John C. Spencer, was intrusted the important work of revising the statutes of the state of New York, and author of several addresses and a few poetical contributions to the Democratic Review, and other periodicals.

William Allen Butler was born in Albany in 1825. After completing his course at the University of the City of New York, and his law studies in the office of his father, he passed a year and a half abroad. Since his return he has been actively engaged in the practice of his profession.

Mr. Butler is the author of a number of poems, and is also a spirited prose writer. He has contributed to the Democratic Review several translations from Uhland; to the Art-Union Bulletin, *The Cities of Art and the Early Artists*, a series of biographical and critical sketches of the Old Masters; and to the Literary World a few pleasant sketches of travel, with the title *Out-of-the-Way Places in Europe*, and several humorous papers in prose and verse, entitled *The Colonel's Club.*

In 1850 he was the author of *Barnum's Parnassus: being Confidential Disclosures of the Prize Committee on the Jenny Lind Song, with Specimens of leading American Poets in the happiest effulgence of their genius;* a poetical squib, which passed rapidly through several editions.

UHLAND.

It is the Poet Uhland from whose wreathings
Of rarest harmony, I here have drawn,
To lower tones and less melodious breathings,
Some simple strains of truth and passion born.

His is the poetry of sweet expression,
Of clear unfaltering tune, serene and strong;
Where gentlest thoughts and words in soft procession,
Move to the even measures of his song.

Delighting ever in his own calm fancies,
He sees much beauty where most men see naught,
Looking at Nature with familiar glances,
And weaving garlands in the groves of Thought.

He sings of Youth, and Hope, and high Endeavor,
He sings of Love, (oh, crown of Poesie!)
Of Fate, and Sorrow, and the Grave, forever
The end of strife, the goal of Destiny.

He sings of Fatherland, the minstrel's glory,
High theme of memory and hope divine,
Twining its fame with gems of antique story,
In Suabian songs and legends of the Rhine;

In Ballads breathing many a dim tradition,
Nourished in long belief or Minstrel rhymes,
Fruit of the old Romance, whose gentle mission
Passed from the earth before our wiser times.

Well do they know his name amongst the mountains,
And plains and valleys of his native Land;
Part of their nature are the sparkling fountains
Of his clear thought, with rainbow fancies spanned.

His simple lays oft sings the mother cheerful
Beside the cradle in the dim twilight;
His plaintive notes low breathes the maiden tearful
With tender murmurs in the ear of Night.

The hill-side swain, the reaper in the meadows,
Carol his ditties through the toilsome day;
And the lone hunter in the Alpine shadows,
Recalls his ballads by some ruin gray.

Oh precious gift! oh wondrous inspiration!
Of all high deeds, of all harmonious things,
To be the Oracle, while a whole Nation
Catches the echo from the sounding strings.

Out of the depths of feeling and emotion
Rises the orb of Song, serenely bright,
As who beholds across the tracts of ocean,
The golden sunrise bursting into light.

Wide is its magic World—divided neither
By continent, nor sea, nor narrow zone;
Who would not wish sometimes to travel thither,
In fancied fortunes to forget his own!

JOHN L. McCONNEL.

Mr. McConnel was born in Illinois, November 11, 1826. After studying law with his father, Murray McConnel, a distinguished lawyer and politician of the West, he entered and was graduated at the Transylvania Law School, Lexington, Ky.

On the sixth of June, 1846, he entered the regiment of Col. Harding, as a volunteer in the ranks. Before leaving the rendezvous at Alton, he was made first lieutenant of his company, and promoted to a captaincy at the battle of Buena Vista, where he was twice wounded. After serving out his term he returned home, and commenced the practice of the law at Jacksonville, Illinois, where he has since resided.

In the spring of 1850 Mr. McConnel published *Talbot and Vernon;* in the autumn of the same year *Graham, or Youth and Manhood;* and in 1851 *The Glenns.* The scene of these novels is laid in the West; and the author has drawn on his experiences of the Mexican War and his skill as a lawyer in the construction of his plots.

These were followed in 1853 by *Western Characters*, a collection of sketches of the prominent classes in the formative period of western society. It is one of the author's most successful volumes.

Mr. McConnel is at present engaged upon a continuation of this work, and also upon a *History of Early Explorations in America*, having especial reference to the labors of the early Roman Catholic missionaries.

A WESTERN POLITICIAN OF THE FIRST GROWTH.

A description of his personal appearance, like that of any other man, will convey no indistinct impression of his internal character.

Such a description probably combined more characteristic adjectives than that of any other personage of his time—adjectives, some of which were applicable to many of his neighbors, respectively, but *all* of which might be bestowed upon him *only.* He was tall, gaunt, angular, swarthy, active, and athletic. His hair was, invariably, black as the wing of the raven; even in that small portion which the cap of racoon-skin left exposed to the action of sun and rain, the gray was but thinly scattered; imparting to the monotonous darkness only a more iron character. As late as the present day, though we have changed in many things, light-haired men seldom attain eminence among the western people: many of our legislators are *young* enough, but none of them are *beardless.* They have a bilious look, as if, in case of illness, their only hope would lie in calomel and jalap. One might understand, at the first glance, that they are men of *talent*, not of *genius;* and that physical energy, the enduring vitality of the body, has no inconsiderable share in the power of the mind.

Corresponding to the sable of the hair, the politician's eye was usually small, and intensely black—not the dead, inexpressive jet, which gives the idea of a hole through white paper, or of a cavernous socket in a death's head; but the keen, midnight darkness, in whose depths you can see a twinkle of starlight—where you feel that there is meaning as well as color. There might be an expression of cunning along with that of penetration—but, in a much higher degree, the blaze of irascibility. There could be no doubt, from its glance, that its possessor was an excellent hater; you might be assured that he would never forget an injury or betray a friend.

A stoop in the shoulders indicated that, in times past, he had been in the habit of carrying a heavy rifle, and of closely examining the ground over which he walked; but what the chest thus lost in depth it gained in breadth. His lungs had ample space in which to play—there was nothing pulmonary even in the drooping shoulders. Few of his class have ever lived to a very advanced age, but it was not for want of iron constitutions, that they went early to the grave. The same services to his country, which gave the politician his prominence, also shortened his life.

From shoulders thus bowed, hung long, muscular arms—sometimes, perhaps, dangling a little ungracefully, but always under the command of their owner, and ready for any effort, however violent. These were terminated by broad, bony hands, which looked like grapnels—their grasp, indeed, bore no faint resemblance to the hold of those symmetrical instruments. Large feet, whose toes were usually turned in, like those of the Indian, were wielded by limbs whose vigor and activity were in keeping with the figure they supported. Imagine, with these peculiarities, a free, bold, rather swaggering gait, a swarthy complexion, and conformable features and tones of voice: and—excepting his costume—you have before your fancy a complete picture of the early western politician.

ICHABOD CRANE BEYOND THE ALLEGHANIES.

A genuine specimen of the class to which most of the early schoolmasters belonged, never felt any misgivings about his own success, and never hesitated to assume any position in life. Neither pride nor modesty was ever suffered to interfere with his action. He would take charge of a numerous school, when he could do little more than write his own name, just as he would have undertaken to run a steamboat, or command an army, when he had never studied engineering or heard of strategy. Nor would he have failed in either capacity: a week's application would make him master of a steam-engine, or a proficient (after the *present manner* of proficiency) in tactics; and as for his school, he could himself learn at night what he was to teach others on the following day! Nor was this mere "conceit"—though, in some other respects, that word, in its limited sense, was not inapplicable—neither was it altogether ignorant presumption; for one of these men was seldom known to fail in anything he undertook: or, if he did fail, he was never found to be cast down by defeat, and the resiliency of his nature justified his confidence.

* * * * * * * * *

Properly to represent his lineage, therefore, the schoolmaster could be neither dandy nor dancing-master; and, as if to hold him to his integrity, nature had omitted to give him any temptation, in his own person, to assume either of these respectable characters. The tailor that could shape a coat to fit *his* shoulders, never yet handled shears; and he would have been as ill at ease in a pair of fashionable pantaloons, as if they had been lined with chestnut-burrs. He was generally above the medium height, with a very decided stoop, as if in the habit of carrying burthens: and a long, high nose, with light blue eyes, and coarse, uneven hair, of a faded weather-stain color, gave his face the expression answering to this lathy outline. Though never very slender, he was always thin: as if he had been flattened out in a rolling-mill; and rotundity of corporation was a mode of development not at all characteristic. His complexion was seldom florid, and not often decidedly pale; a sort of sallow discoloration was its prevailing hue, like that which marks the countenance of a consumer of "coarse" whiskey and strong tobacco. But these failings were not the cause of his cadaverous look—for a faithful representative of the class held them both in commendable abhorrence—*they were not the vices of his nature.*

There was a subdivision of the class, a secondary type, not so often observed, but common enough to entitle it to a brief notice. *He* was, generally, short, squat, and thick—the latitude bearing a better proportion to the longitude than in his lank brother—but never approaching anything like roundness. With this attractive figure he had a complexion of decidedly bilious darkness, and what is commonly called a "dish-face." His nose was depressed between the eyes, an arrangement which dragged the point upward in the most cruel manner, but gave it an expression equally ludicrous and impertinent. A pair of small, round, black eyes, encompassed—like two little feudal fortresses, each by its moat—with a circle of yellowish white, peered out from under brows like battlements. Coarse, black hair, always cut short, and standing erect, so as to present something the appearance of a *chevaux de frise*, protected a hard, round head—a shape most appropriate to his lineage—while, with equal propriety, ears of corresponding magnitude stood boldly forth to assert their claim to notice.

Both these types were distinguished for large feet, which no boot could enclose, and hands broad beyond the compass of any glove. Neither was ever known to get drunk, to grow fat, to engage in a game of chance, or to lose his appetite: it became the teacher of "ingenuous youth" to preserve an exemplary bearing before those whom he was endeavoring to benefit; while respectable "appearances," and proper appreciation of the good things of life, were the *alpha* and *omega* of his system of morality.

J. M. LEGARÉ,

A POET of South Carolina, and a resident, we believe, of Charleston, and a relative of the late Hugh S. Legaré, is the author of a volume, *Orta-Undis and Other Poems*, published in 1848. They are marked by their delicacy of sentiment and a certain scholastic refinement.

AMY.

This is the pathway where she walked,
The tender grass pressed by her feet.
The laurel boughs laced overhead,
Shut out the noonday heat.

The sunshine gladly stole between
The softly undulating limbs.
From every blade and leaf arose
The myriad insect hymns.

A brook ran murmuring beneath
The grateful twilight of the trees,
Where from the dripping pebbles swelled
A beech's mossy knees.

And there her robe of spotless white,
(Pure white such purity beseemed!)
Her angel face and tresses bright
Within the basin gleamed.

The coy sweetbriers half detained
Her light hem as we moved along!
To hear the music of her voice
The mockbird hushed his song.

But now her little feet are still,
Her lips the EVERLASTING seal;
The hideous secrets of the grave
The weeping eyes reveal.

The path still winds, the brook descends,
The skies are bright as then they were.
My Amy is the only leaf
In all that forest sear.

AUGUSTUS JULIAN REQUIER

WAS born at Charleston, South Carolina, May 27, 1825. He was educated in that city, and having selected the law as his profession, was called to the bar in 1844. From a very early age Mr. Requier was a regular contributor to the newspapers and periodicals, and in his seventeenth year published *The Spanish Exile*, a play in blank verse, which was acted with success. A year or two after he published *The Old Sanctuary*, a romance, the scene of which is laid in Carolina before the Revolution. He soon after removed to Marion, South Carolina, where, during the leisure intervals which occur in the life of a country barrister, many of his more mature and elaborate pieces in prose and verse were composed. These have never been collected in book form. The most prominent of them are "The Phantasmagoria," "Marco Bozzaris," a tragedy; "The Dial Plate," "Treasure Trove," "To Mary on Earth," "The Thornless Rose," "The Charm," "The Image," "The Blackbeard," "The three Misses Grimball," a sketch; the Farewell Address to the Palmetto Regiment, delivered at the Charleston Theatre by Mrs. Mowatt, and mentioned in her "Autobiography;" the "Welcome" to the same regiment on its return from Mexico, and an "Ode to Shakespeare."

Mr. Requier subsequently removed to Mobile, Alabama, where he now resides. Since 1850 he has ceased to write, being altogether engrossed by his professional pursuits, to which he is entirely devoted, and in which he has attained distinction. He is at present Attorney of the United States for the southern district of Alabama, having been appointed to that office by Mr. Pierce in 1853.

ODE TO SHAKESPEARE.

He went forth into Nature and he sung,
Her first-born of imperial sway—the lord

Of sea and continent and clime and tongue;
Striking the Harp with whose sublime accord
The whole creation rung!

He went forth into Nature and he sung,
Her grandest terrors and her simplest themes,
The torrent by the beetling crag o'erhung,
And the wild-daisy on its brink that gleams
Unharmed, and lifts a dew-drop to the sun!
The muttering of the tempest in its halls
Of darkness turreted; beheld alone
By an o'erwhelming brilliance which appals—
The turbulence of Ocean—the soft calm
Of the sequestered vale—the bride-like day,
Or sainted eve, dispensing holy balm
From her lone lamp of silver thro' the grey
That leads the star-crowned Night adown the mountain way:

These were his themes and more—no little bird
Lit in the April forest but he drew
From its wild notes a meditative word—
A gospel that no other mortal knew:
Bard, priest, evangelist! from nature's cells
Of riches inexhaustible he took
The potent ring of her profoundest spells,
And wrote great Nature's Book!

They people earth and sea and air,
The dim, tumultuous band,
Called into being everywhere
By his creative wand;
In kingly court and savage lair,
Prince, Peasant, Priest, and Sage and Peer,
And midnight hag and ladye fair,
Pure as the white rose in her hair,
And warriors that, on barbéd steed,
Burn to do the crested deed,
And lovers that delighted rove
When moonlight marries with the grove,
Glide forth—appear!
To breathe or love or hate or fear;
And with most unexampled wile,
To win a soul-enraptured smile,
Or blot it in a tear.

Hark! a horn,
That with repeated winding shakes,
O'er hill and glen and far responsive lakes,
The mantle of the morn!
Now, on the mimic scene,
The simplest of all simple pairs
That ever drew from laughter tears,
Touchstone and Audrey, hand in hand,
Come hobbling o'er the green;
While Rosalind, in strange disguise,
With manly dress but maiden eyes,
Which, spite herself, will look sidewise,
E'en in this savage land;
And her companion like the flower,
That beaten by the morning shower
Still in resplendent beauty stoops,
Looking loveliest whilst it droops,
Step faintly forth from weariness,
All snowy in their maidenhood;
Twin-lilies of the wilderness—
A shepherd and his shepherdess,
In Arden's gloomy wood!

But comes anon, with halting step and pause,
A miserable man!
Revolving in each lengthened breath he draws,
The deep, dark problem of material laws,
That life is but a span.
Secluded, silent, solitary, still,
Lone in the vale and last upon the hill,
Companionless beside the haunted stream,
Walking the stars in the meridian beam,
Himself the shade of an o'ershadowing dream;
Blighting the rose
With his imaginary woes,
And weaving bird and tree and fruit and flower
Into a charm of such mysterious power,
Such plaintive tale
The beauteous skies grow pale,
And the rejoicing earth looks wan,
Like Jacques—her lonely, melancholy man!

Ring silver-sprinkling, gushing bells—
Blow clamorous pipes replying,
In tipsy merriment that swells
For ever multiplying!
He comes! with great sunshiny face
And chuckle deep and glances warm,
Sly nods and strange attempts at grace,
A matron on each arm;
He comes! of wit the soul and pith,
Custodian and lessor.
Room for him! Sir John Falstaff with
The merry Wives of Windsor.

Lo! on a blasted heath,
Lit by a flashing storm,
The threatening darkness underneath,
Three of the weird form!
Chanting, dancing all together,
For a charm upon the heather,
Filthy hags in the foul weather!

The spell works, and behold;
A castle in the midnight hour,
Muffled 'mid battlement and tower,
Whereon the crystal moon doth lower
Antarctically cold!
A blackbird's note hath drilled the air
And left the stillness still more drear;
Twice hath the hornéd owl around
The Chapel flown, nor uttered sound;
The night-breeze now doth scarcely blow.
And now, 'tis past and gone;
But the pale moon that like the snow
Erewhile descending shone.
Encrimsoned as the torch of Mars,
While cloud on cloud obscure the stars
And rolls above the trees,
Cleaves the dark billows of the Night
Like a shot-smitten sail on flight
Over the howling seas—
God! what a piercing shriek was there,
So deep and loud and wild and drear
It bristles up the moistened hair
And bids the blood to freeze!
Again—again—
Athwart the brain,
That lengthened shriek of life-extorted pain!
And now, 'tis given o'er:
But from that pile despairingly doth soar
A voice which cries like the uplifted main,
"Glamis hath murdered sleep—Macbeth shall sleep no more!"

Thick and faster now they come,
In procession moving on,
Neath the world-embracing dome
Of the unexhausted one;
Mark them, while the cauldron bubbles,
Throwing spells upon the sight,
And the wizard flame redoubles
In intensity of light:
Here is one—a rustic maiden
Of the witching age;
Cheeks with beauty overladen,
Blushing like a sunset Aidenn,
Mistress Anne Page!
Here another that doth follow,

Full of starch decorum:
A wise man this Cousin Shallow,
Justice of the Quorum;
A third is timid, slight, and tender,
Showing harmless Master Slender;
A fourth, doth frowningly reveal,
His princely mantle jewelled o'er,
By knightly spurs upon his heel
And clanging sound of martial steel,
The dark, Venetian Moor!
The fifth advances with a start,
His eye transfixing like a dart,
Black Richard of the lion-heart!
And now they rush along the scene,
In crowds with scarce a pause between,
Prelates high, in church and state,
Speakers dexterous in debate,
Courtiers gay in satin hose,
Clowns fantastic and jocose,
Soldiers brave and virgins fair,
Nymphs with golden flowing hair,
And spirits of the azure air,
Pass, with solemn step and slow,
Pass, but linger as they go,
Like images that haunt the shade,
Or visions of the white cascade,
Or sunset on the snow.
Then, then, at length, the crowning glory comes,
Loud trumpets speak unto the sky, and drums
Unroll the military chain!
From pole to pole,
Greet wide the wonder of the poet's soul:
With raven plume,
And posture rapt in high, prophetic gloom,—
Hamlet, the Dane!

Bright shall thine altars be,
First of the holy minstrel band,
Green as the vine-encircled land
And vocal as the sea!
Thy name is writ
Where stars are lit,
And thine immortal shade,
'Mid archangelic clouds displayed
On Fame's imperial seat,
Sees the inseparable Nine
In its reflected glory shine,
And Nature at its feet.

PAUL H. HAYNE

Is a son of Lieut. Hayne of the United States Navy, and nephew of Robert G. Hayne of senatorial celebrity. He was born in Charleston, South Carolina, in 1831, and has been a frequent contributor to many of the southern magazines, more particularly the Southern Literary Messenger. He was editor of the Charleston Literary Gazette, and is now connected with the editorial department of the Evening News, a daily journal also published in Charleston. His poems, collected in a volume in 1855, are spirited, and he has cultivated the music of verse with effect. His longest poem is entitled *The Temptation of Venus, a Monkish Legend.*

SONNET.

The passionate Summer's dead; the sky's aglow
With roseate flushes of matured desire,
The winds at eve are musical and low,
As sweeping chords of a lamenting lyre,
Far up among the pillared clouds of fire,
Whose pomp of grand procession upward rolls
With gorgeous blazonry of pictured folds,
To celebrate the Summer's past renown;
Ah me! how regally the heavens look down,
O'ershadowing beautiful, autumnal woods,
And harvest-fields with hoarded increase brown,
And deep-toned majesty of golden floods,
That lift their solemn dirges to the sky,
To swell the purple pomp that floateth by.

A PORTRAIT.

I.

The laughing Hours before her feet,
Are strewing vernal roses,
And the voices in her soul are sweet,
As music's mellowed closes,
All hopes and passions heavenly-born,
In her have met together,
And Joy diffuses round her morn
A mist of golden weather.

II.

As o'er her cheek of delicate dyes,
The blooms of childhood hover,
So do the tranced and sinless eyes,
All childhood's heart discover,
Full of a dreamy happiness,
With rainbow fancies laden,
Whose arch of promise glows to bless
Her spirit's beauteous Adenn.

III.

She is a being born to raise
Those undefiled emotions,
That link us with our sunniest days,
And most sincere devotions;
In her, we see renewed, and bright,
That phase of earthly story,
Which glimmers in the morning light
Of God's exceeding glory.

IV.

Why in a life of mortal cares,
Appear these heavenly faces,
Why on the verge of darkened years,
These amaranthine graces!
'Tis but to cheer the soul that faints,
With pure and blest evangels,
To prove if Heaven is rich with Saints,
That earth may have her Angels.

V.

Enough! 'tis not for me to pray
That on her life's sweet river,
The calmness of a virgin day,
May rest, and rest for ever;
I know a guardian Genius stands,
Beside those waters lowly,
And labors with immortal hands,
To keep them pure and holy.

HAMILTON COLLEGE, NEW YORK.

The founding of Hamilton College is due to the far-seeing generosity of the Rev. Samuel Kirkland, who labored more than forty years as a missionary among the Oneida Indians. Mr. Kirkland was born in Norwich, Connecticut, December 1, 1744, and was graduated from Nassau Hall in 1765. He was the father of three sons and three daughters. The eldest daughter, who was married to John H. Lothrop, Esq., of Utica, is the mother of the Rev. Samuel Kirkland Lothrop, D.D., of Boston, whose recently published life of his grandfather is embraced in Sparks's Library of American Biography. The youngest daughter, Eliza, was married in 1818 to the Rev. Edward Robinson, D.D., now a professor in the Union Theological Seminary of New York. One of his sons, Dr. John Thornton Kirkland, was elected in 1810 to the Presidency of Harvard College. He and his brother, George Whitfield, were twins, and were born at General Herkimer's, on the Mohawk, while their mother was journeying on horseback from Oneida to Connecticut. Her return to Oneida was greeted by the Indians with great rejoicing. They adopted the boys into their tribe, calling George La-go-ne-osta, and John Ali-gan-o-wis-ka, which means fair-face.

Mr. Kirkland died of pleurisy, February 28, 1808. He was buried in Clinton, in a private inclosure, near his house. Here on one side rest the remains of his second wife and youngest daughter; on the other side, those of the celebrated Skenandoa. The ownership of the Kirkland mansion has passed out of the family. At the last Annual Meeting of the trustees of the institution which he founded, they voted to remove the coffins from these grounds to the College Cemetery, and to erect over them an appropriate monument.

It was through the influence of Mr. Kirkland that the "Hamilton Oneida Academy" was incorporated in 1793. In the same year he conveyed to its trustees several hundred acres of land. In the preamble to the title-deed, he states that the gift is made "for the support of an Academy in the town of Whitestown, county of Herkimer, contiguous to the Oneida Nation of Indians, for the mutual benefit of the young and flourishing settlements in said county, and the various tribes of confederated Indians, earnestly wishing that the institution may grow and flourish; that the advantages of it may be extensive and lasting; and that, under the smiles of the Lord of wisdom and goodness, it may prove an eminent means of diffusing useful knowledge, enlarging the bounds of human happiness, aiding the reign of virtue, and the kingdom of the blessed Redeemer."

Among the teachers of the academy was Dr. James Murdock, now a resident of New Haven, and translator of Mosheim's "Historical Commentaries on the State of Christianity."

The academy lived eighteen years, and was largely patronized. At length its guardians were pressed with a demand from the surrounding community for a higher institution. The charter for Hamilton College was obtained in 1812, and Dr. Azel Backus of Bethlem, Connecticut, was elected its first President. He was born near Norwich, Connecticut, October 13, 1765. In early life his companions were rude, if not dissolute; and his youth was marked with great looseness of opinion on matters of religion. He was graduated from Yale College in 1787. After leaving college he was associated for a time with his class-mate, John H. Lothrop, Esq., in the management of a grammar-school at Weathersfield, Connecticut. He was licensed to preach in 1789, and soon after succeeded Dr. Bellamy as pastor of the church in Bethlem, Connecticut. Dr. Backus died December 9, 1816, of typhus fever. One of his children, Mary Ann, was the first wife of the Hon. Gerrit Smith of Peterton; another, the Hon. F. F. Backus, is a distinguished physician in Rochester, New York.

A volume of Dr. Backus's sermons was published after his death, with a brief sketch of his life. His biography yet remains to be written in a manner worthy of the part which he sustained in caring for the first wants of a college which has since identified itself with the educational interests of Central New York. A careful memoir, written somewhat after the manner of Xenophon's Memorabilia or Boswell's Johnson, would be welcomed by many readers. In his intercourse with students, Dr. Backus combined affectionate severity with a seasoning of manly eccentricity. The proverb, "who makes a jest makes an enemy," was reversed in his experience. He was out-spoken and fond of a joke. When speaking of that which he disapproved, his thoughts naturally clothed themselves in the language of ridicule. He was quick and pungent at repartee, as is shown by the following anecdote, which is only one out of many which might be given.

During the administration of Jefferson, Dr. Backus preached a Thanksgiving Sermon at Bethlem, in which his abhorrence of the political views of the day was expressed with characteristic freedom and severity. For thus daring to speak the truth, he incurred a civil prosecution, and was summoned by the sheriff to go with him to Hartford, there to await his trial. As a matter of grace, the reverend prisoner was allowed to ride in his own conveyance, while the officer followed behind. The parson's horse happened to be one of the fastest. He picked over the miles with a rapidity that astonished the sheriff, while it kept him at a respectable distance in the rear. At length, with much ado, the latter managed to bring himself within tongue-shot; and leaning forward, exclaimed, "Why, Doctor Backus, you ride as if the very devil were after you!"

"And so he is!" replied the doctor, without turning his head.

The second President of Hamilton College was Dr. Henry Davis, an alumnus of Yale College, who had been a tutor at Williams and Yale, a Professor of Greek at Union, and President of Middlebury. His administration covered a period of sixteen years, during which the College fluctuated between the extremes of prosperity and depression.

In the years 1829 and 1830, no students were graduated. This was owing to a long and bitter quarrel between Dr. Davis and a portion of the trustees, growing out of a case of discipline. After his resignation of the presidency in 1833, Dr. Davis published a thick pamphlet entitled, "A Narrative of the Embarrassments and Decline of Hamilton College." This, with one or two occasional discourses, is all that went from his hand to the printer's. Dr. Davis was distinguished for his strength of humor, his gravity of manners, unyielding integrity, and strong attachment to the pupils whom he had instructed. He died March 7, 1852, at the age of eighty-two.

The third President was Dr. Sereno Edwards Dwight, a son of Timothy Dwight. He was elected in 1833 and resigned in 1835. The great historical fact of his presidency was a successful effort to raise by subscription fifty thousand dollars, for increasing the productive funds of the college. Dr. Dwight was fitted by nature and

Hamilton College.

acquired gifts for the triumphs of pulpit oratory. The failure of his health at first made him fitful in the happy use of his talents, and finally forced him to give up addressing public bodies or discharging public duties. He died recently, November 30, 1850. The last fifteen years of his life were saddened by his infirmity, and passed in close retirement.

The fourth president was Dr. JOSEPH PENNEY, a native of Ireland, and educated at one of its higher institutions. The reputation for learning, piety, and executive talent which he had won by his labors in the ministry at Rochester, New York, and Northampton, Massachusetts, led the friends of Hamilton to think that he was the man to preside successfully over its affairs. The fact that he was unacquainted with the internal peculiarities of an American College caused him to make some mistakes, disquieting to himself and the institution. He chose to resign in 1839. Dr. Penney still lives; broken in health, yet enjoying the unabated esteem of his friends. His publications are somewhat numerous, yet mostly of a transient form and character.

The fifth President, Dr. SIMEON NORTH, is a native of Berlin, Connecticut, and a graduate of Yale College, of the class of 1825. He served his Alma Mater two years as a tutor, and in 1829 was elected to the chair of Ancient Languages in Hamilton College. When he went to Clinton, the embarrassments of the institution were such as to threaten its life. The war between Dr. Davis and the trustees was raging fiercely. There were but nine students in all the classes. The treasury was empty. Debt and dissension covered the future with gloomy clouds. The Faculty now consisted of the President, Prof. James Hadley, Prof. John H. Lothrop, Prof. North, and Tutor E. D. Maltbie. They engaged zealously and unitedly in efforts to revive the institution, and to regain for it the public confidence. They were successful.

In 1833, when Dr. Davis resigned, the graduating class numbered twenty.

In 1839, Dr. North was elected to the Presidency, as the successor of Dr. Penney, an office which he still holds. The friends and pupils of President North have frequently expressed their appreciation of his public efforts, by requesting permission to publish them. If his published discourses and addresses were collected, they would form a large volume. The most important of these are a series of Baccalaureate Sermons; discourses preached at the funerals of Professor Catlin, Treasurer Dwight, and President Davis; an Inaugural Discourse, a sermon before the Oneida County Bible Society, and an oration before the Phi Beta Kappa of Yale College.

To Hamilton College is conceded a high rank in the culture of natural and effective elocution. Much credit is due, in this respect, to the teachings of the Rev. Dr. Mandeville, who filled the chair of Rhetoric and Oratory eight years, commencing in 1841. His class-book entitled "The Elements of Reading and Oratory," first published in 1845, is now widely used in colleges, academies, and high-schools. Dr. Mandeville's system of speaking is still taught at Hamilton, with some decided improvements by Professor A. J. Upson.

Hamilton College has not been forgotten by men of liberality and large means. The Hon. Wm. Hale Maynard, a graduate of Williams College, and a gifted lawyer, who died of the cholera in 1832, bequeathed to the college the bulk of his estate, amounting to twenty thousand dollars, for the founding of a Law Department.

Prof. John H. Lothrop, now Chancellor of the University of Wisconsin, was the first occupant of this chair. It is now worthily filled by Prof. Theodore W. Dwight, whose able instructions in legal science attract students from remote sections of the country. The college confers the degree of LL.B. upon those who complete the regular course of legal studies.

Another of the benefactors of the college, the Hon. S. Newton Dexter, resides at Whitesboro, and enjoys the satisfaction of seeing a centre of learning made more thrifty and efficient through his liberality. What Mr. Maynard did by testament, Mr. Dexter chose to do by an immediate donation. In 1836, when the college was severely crippled by debt, he came forward with a gift of fifteen thousand dollars for endowing the chair of Classical Literature. This department is supposed to have been chosen as the object of his munificence, not more from its acknowledged importance in a collegiate institution, than on account of his esteem for the character and scholarly attainments of its then incumbent, the Rev. Dr. North, who was afterwards promoted to the Presidency.

The department of Classical Literature is now occupied by Professor Edward North, a highly accomplished scholar and man of letters, to whom we are indebted for this spirited notice of his college. He succeeded Professor John Finley Smith in 1844. Professor Smith was a musical artist of rare gifts and attainments.

The grounds about the college have been recently enlarged and improved. They now embrace twenty acres, which have been thoroughly drained, hedged, planted with trees and flowering shrubs, and put into lawn, with winding drives and gravelled walks. These improvements have been made under the conviction that no seat of generous culture can be called complete, unless it provides facilities for the study of vegetable growths. Plato's College was a grove of platans and olives,—philosophy and trees have always been fond of each other's company. The location of the college, on the brow of a hill that slopes to the West, and commands a wide view of the Oriskany Valley, is healthful and inviting. In this valley lies the village of Clinton, with a population of twelve hundred. In the distance, to the left, the city of Utica, the valley of the Mohawk, and the Trenton hills are distinctly visible.

The rural quiet of the place, its elevation, and extended, unbroken horizon, render it most favorable for astronomical observations. An Observatory has been erected, and furnished with a telescope, the longest in this country next to the one at Cambridge. It was made by Messrs. Spencer and Eaton of Canastota, who are alumni of the institution. A large Laboratory has been built, with the new apparatus which the French and German chemists have recently invented. A stone building, originally used as a boarding-hall, has been fitted up for a Cabinet, and now contains ten thousand specimens in Geology, Mineralogy, and Natural History. A Gymnasium has also been built and attractively furnished.

THE UNIVERSITY OF VIRGINIA.*

The University of Virginia is situated in the County of Albemarle, Virginia, about one mile and a half west of the village of Charlottesville, and four miles in nearly the same direction from Monticello, which was the residence, and contains the tomb of Thomas Jefferson. It is built on moderately elevated ground, and forms a striking feature in a beautiful landscape. On the south-west it is shut in by little mountains, beyond which, a few miles distant, rise the broken and occasionally steep and rugged, but not elevated ridges, the characteristic feature of which is expressed by their name of Ragged Mountains. To the north-west the Blue Ridge, some twenty miles off, presents its deep-colored outline, stretching to the north-east, and looking down upon the mountain-like hills that here and there rise from the plain without its eastern base. To the east the eye rests upon the low range of mountains that bounds the view as far as the vision can extend north-eastward and south-westward along its slopes, except where it is interrupted directly to the east by a hilly but fertile plain through which the Rivanna, with its discolored stream, flows by the base of Monticello. To the south the view reaches far away until the horizon meets the plain, embracing a region lying between mountains on either hand, and covered with forests interspersed with spots of cultivated land.

This University is a State institution, endowed, and built, and under the control of the state. It owes its origin, its organization, and the plan of its buildings to Mr. Jefferson, who made it the care of his last years to bring it into being, and counted it among his chief claims to the memory of posterity that he was its founder.*

The Act of Assembly establishing the University of Virginia and incorporating the Rector and Board of Visitors, is dated January 25, 1819; and the University was opened for the admission of students March 25, 1825.

It is under the government of the Rector and Board of Visitors, by whom are enacted its laws, and to whom is committed the control of its finances, the appointment and removal of its officers, and the general supervision of its interests. The Visitors, seven in number at first, but afterwards increased to nine, are appointed every fourth year by the governor of the state, and the Rector is chosen by the Visitors from among their own number. The first Rector was Mr. Jefferson, followed in succession by Mr. Madison, Chapman Johnson, Esq., and Joseph C. Cabell, Esq.

The University of Virginia comprises nine schools, viz. I. Ancient Languages, in which are taught the Latin, Greek, and Hebrew languages, with ancient history and literature. II. Modern Languages, in which are taught the French, Italian, Spanish, and German languages, and the Anglo-Saxon form of the English language, with modern history and literature. III. Mathematics, comprising pure and mixed Mathematics. IV. Natural Philosophy, comprising, besides the usual subjects, Mineralogy and Geology. V. Chemistry and Pharmacy. VI. Medicine, comprising Medi-

* We have pleasure in presenting this view, from the competent pen of the former chairman of the Faculty, Dr. Gessner Harrison, of an institution the peculiar organization of which has been little understood.

* Among Mr. Jefferson's papers was found, after his death, the following epitaph :—

HERE LIES BURIED
THOMAS JEFFERSON.
AUTHOR OF THE DECLARATION OF AMERICAN INDEPENDENCE,
OF THE STATUTE OF VIRGINIA FOR RELIGIOUS FREEDOM,
AND FATHER OF THE UNIVERSITY OF VIRGINIA.

See Tucker's Life of Jefferson, ii. 497.

The University of Virginia.

cal Jurisprudence, Obstetrics, and the Principles and Practice of Medicine. VII. Comparative Anatomy, Physiology, and Surgery. VIII. Moral Philosophy, comprising Rhetoric and Belles Lettres, Ethics, Mental Philosophy, and Political Economy. IX. Law, comprising also Government and International Law.

To each school is assigned one professor, except the school of Law, which has two. In the school of Ancient Languages, the professor is aided by two assistant instructors, and in Modern Languages and Mathematics by one each. In the Medical department there is a lecturer on Anatomy and Materia Medica, and a demonstrator of Anatomy.

The administration of the laws of the University, and their interpretation, is committed to the Faculty, consisting of the professors of the several schools and the chairman of the Faculty. The professors are appointed by the Board of Visitors. The chairman, who has little power beyond the general supervision of the execution of the laws, none over the schools, is chosen annually by the Board of Visitors from among the members of the Faculty, and receives as such a salary of five hundred dollars. The professors are responsible to the Board of Visitors alone for the proper discharge of their duties, and have intrusted to them, each in his own school, the conduct of its studies, subject only to the laws prescribing the subjects to be taught, the hours of lecture, and the method of instruction generally by lectures, examinations, and exercises, according to the nature of the subject.

The income of the University is derived chiefly from an annuity from the state of fifteen thousand dollars, subject of late years to a charge of about four thousand five hundred dollars for the benefit of thirty-two state students, who receive gratuitous instruction, together with board and room rent free; from rents of dormitories and hotels; from matriculation fees; and from surplus fees of tuition in the several schools, accruing to the University after the professor shall have received a maximum of two thousand dollars.

Each professor is paid a fixed salary of one thousand dollars a year, and receives the tuition fees paid by students for attending his lectures up to the maximum of two thousand dollars. Any excess of fees above this sum is paid into the treasury of the University. The fee paid by students for tuition is ordinarily twenty-five dollars to each professor attended. This mode of compensation, making the income of the professor to depend so largely upon tuition fees, was designed to act as an incentive to activity and faithfulness on the part of the professor, his own and the prosperity of the school being identified in the matter of emolument as well as of reputation. The maximum limit of income from fees received by the professor is a thing of late adoption, introduced since the number of students attending some of the schools has become very large. It remains to be seen whether this invasion of the principle is the wisest mode of disposing of the question of excessive fees; especially when no provision is made for a minimum income, and none, for the most part, for excess of labor from large numbers frequenting a school.

The method of instruction is by lectures and examinations, with the use of text-books selected by the professor. The professor is expected, so far as the nature of the subject allows it, to deliver lectures on the subjects of instruction, setting forth and explaining the doctrines to be taught, so that by the help of the lectures and of the text-book, the student may not only have the opportunity of understanding these doctrines but of having them more vividly impressed on his attention and memory. The examination of the class at each meeting upon the preceding lecture, embraces both the text and the teaching of the professor, and is aimed at once to secure the student's attention to both, and to afford the advantage of a review, and, when needed, of a further clearing up of the subject.

For the purpose of accommodating the lectures to the wants and previous attainments of the students, and of giving a larger course of instruction, most of the schools are divided into classes called junior and senior. In the school of Mathematics there is also an intermediate class, and a class of mixed Mathematics. In the school of Law also there is an intermediate class. The lectures to each class occupy an entire session of nine months. A student is generally allowed, except in law, to attend, without additional fee, all the classes in a school the same session, so as to receive instruction, if he choose and be able, in the whole course in one year.

Two public examinations of all the members of each school are held every session, one about its middle, the other at its close. These examinations are conducted chiefly in writing. A set of questions, with numerical values attached, is proposed to the whole class, and its members are distributed into four divisions, according to the value of their answers. To insure fairness at these examinations, every student is required to attach to his answers a declaration in writing, that he has neither given nor received aid during the examination. This same certificate is attached also to all examination papers written for degrees.

Students are admitted at and above the age of sixteen, and are free to attend the schools of their choice; but they are ordinarily required to attend three schools.

The session is of nine months' duration continuously, and without any holidays except Christmas-day. Lectures are delivered during six days of the week, and a weekly report is made to the chairman of the Faculty by each professor of the subjects of the lectures and examinations in his school, and of the time occupied in each.

Degrees are conferred in each of the schools of the University upon those students who give evidence of having a competent knowledge of the subjects taught in the school. Certificates of proficiency also are bestowed for like knowledge of certain subjects that may be attended separately, as Medical Jurisprudence, Mineralogy, Geology, &c. Examinations are held with a view to these honors towards the end of each session, and are conducted mostly in writing. The extent and difficulty of these examinations, and the strictness used in judging of the value of the answers, secure a standard of attainment much higher than usual, and render the degrees in individual schools objects of ambition to all, and strong incentives to diligence and accuracy in study. A register of each student's answers at the daily examinations, and of his written exercises, is kept by the professor; and, in deciding on his fitness to receive a degree, regard is had to his average standing in his class. The time of his residence as a student is not counted among his qualifications for this distinction. He may obtain a degree, whenever he shall have proved that he is worthy of it by standing satisfactorily the examinations proposed as a test equally for all.

Besides the degrees conferred in individual schools, and certificates of proficiency in certain subjects, the degree of Bachelor of Arts is bestowed on such students as have obtained degrees in any two of the literary schools (viz. Ancient Languages, Modern Languages, and Moral Philosophy), and in any two of the scientific schools (viz. Mathematics, Natural Philosophy, and Chemistry); besides giving evidence of a certain proficiency in the remaining two academical schools, and furnishing an essay or oration to be approved by the Faculty.

The degree of Master of Arts is conferred upon such students as have obtained degrees in all the six academical schools, besides furnishing an essay or oration to be approved by the Faculty, and standing a satisfactory examination in review on all the studies of the course, except those in which he has been admitted to degrees in the current session.

No honorary degrees are conferred by this University.

The University of Virginia has been in operation thirty years, and although it has had to contend with some prejudices, has had a good degree of success, as well in regard to the numbers frequenting it as to the character for scholarship accorded to its alumni. The number of matriculates entered for the session of 1854–5 was five hundred and fourteen; of these three hundred and twenty were exclusively academical, one hundred and fifty-six exclusively professional, and thirty-eight partly academical and partly professional.

The University of Virginia has introduced into its constitution and into its practical working some marked peculiarities; and as its apparent success has called attention to these, it may be well to notice some of them briefly, and to state summarily the chief grounds upon which they are approved and justified.

1. The first and most striking peculiarity is the allowing every student to attend the schools or studies of his choice, only requiring ordinarily that he shall attend three; the conferring degrees in individual schools; the suffering candidates to stand the examinations held for degrees without regard to the time of residence; and the bestowing no degrees as honorary distinctions, but only upon adequate proof made by strict examination, that they are deserved.

This at once sets aside the usual college curriculum, with the attendant division into Freshmen, Sophomore, &c., classes, and, in the opinion of some, is followed as a necessary consequence by the loss to the student of a regular and complete course of study and of mental discipline, which they assume to be given by the usual plan of our colleges. It is taken for granted by such that the student, being free to choose, will attend such studies alone as may suit his spirit of self-indulgence, avoiding those which are difficult; and that the voluntary system does not admit of a regular course. It is said in answer, that the records of the University of Virginia show that the fact contradicts the assumption that the more difficult studies will be avoided, the schools of Ancient Languages and of Mathematics, for example, having always had a fair proportion of students. And that, although no student is compelled by law to follow a certain defined course, yet in practice, and by the influences of causes easily seen, a very large proportion do pursue a regular course; and that the University of Virginia holds out inducements to accomplish a complete course by establishing for its higher degrees a standard which makes them objects of very great desire. Further, as to the matter of a complete course of study and of mental discipline, it is said that it is too much to assume that the best way of securing there is by the usual college curriculum and the division into freshmen, &c., classes, this being the very question in issue, and the system of independent schools and free choice of studies having been adopted with the very view of giving what the common plan does not; that the alleged evil effects of the voluntary system do not and ought not to follow; and that, on the contrary, it has decided advantages.

It is not pretended that every one entering the University of Virginia obtains a complete education. For some it is not necessary, however desirable, that they should become conversant with all the branches of a liberal education. And yet it is of great advantage to them and to society if they can be well trained in even a few departments of knowledge—those most suited to their wants or to their tastes. They should not be excluded from partial benefits of education because they cannot derive the highest.

And then, if an examination be made of the names of those who, in our Colleges and Universities generally, enter the Freshman or Sophomore classes, and of those who graduate, or pass through the senior class, it will be found that but few of the former are found among the latter, not more than about a fourth. And this, though it results inevitably from the very practice of admitting to degrees by classes, that of those who obtain the degree, much too large a proportion have really very moderate attainments, and could not possibly stand a strict examination on the whole or any considerable part of the course. So in the University of Virginia, a very small proportion obtain the highest degree, or fully accomplish the regular academic course, and beyond comparison a smaller proportion than on the usually adopted plan; and this because the standard is purposely made high. Admitting that this very small number is properly educated, the question to be answered is, Whether it be true, as alleged by some, that all those who come short of this complete course fail of obtaining an amount of knowledge, and especially a mental discipline, equal to that supplied by the common course?

To reach a satisfactory answer to this question it is to be observed, say the advocates of the voluntary system, first, that for the practical purposes of life, and for a right mental discipline, a small field of knowledge, thoroughly cultivated with a hearty energy, and by methods which set the student to thinking and inquiring for himself, is of incomparably more value than a large field cultivated in a negligent and superficial way. A man may study many things and have little sound knowledge and less vigorous training of the mind. A man may so learn a few things as to be able to direct his faculties with their utmost power to the accomplishment of any task.

Secondly, That to secure this energetic, self-propelling activity of the student, which is indispensably necessary to the best discipline of mind, and to the acquisition of habits of thorough and accurate investigation, two things mainly contribute. First, the waking up to an earnest spirit of inquiry and of thoroughness of investigation on the part of the student, by exciting and keeping erect his attention, and variously subjecting his powers to the proof by the lectures and by searching oral examinations; and, secondly, a high standard of examinations for honors, these being bestowed only upon satisfactory evidence of good attainments and capacity. Without the former condition the latter would be impossible; without the latter the former would be insufficient.

Thirdly, That the voluntary system offers peculiar advantages for fulfilling these conditions, which, however able the professors, the common system does not. The several schools being wholly independent, the standard of examinations for degrees may be placed as high as the means and mode of instruction, and what is fairly demanded by the true interest of the student, may allow. A person standing his examination for a degree in Latin and Greek will not be passed, though undeserving, for fear he may not secure his degree in the Mathematics, and so on. The honor being conferred upon reaching a comparatively high standard, and without the question of giving or refusing it being complicated by a regard to the regular progression of classes, it is comparatively easy to maintain the standard. It is one thing for a student to fail and be rejected upon the studies of a single school, the effect ceasing here, and quite another to be cast down in all his classes for failure on one study, with the result of postponing the period of his graduation for a whole year. But the common system allows no good alternative. No College, upon this system, can refuse to pass men who ought to be rejected; for then it consents, under multiplied difficulties, to reduce the ranks of the senior class to something like the proportion of those who obtain the Master's degree under the system adopted at the University of Virginia.

To answer, then, the question above proposed, it is alleged by its friends, that in the system adopted at the University of Virginia, the conditions for obtaining a good mental discipline and accurate knowledge are in some good degree, although imperfectly, fulfilled by the means of lectures, rigid examinations conducted chiefly in writing where degrees are concerned, and a comparatively high standard in conferring degrees. That, putting out of view the idle and those wanting capacity, and those who attend a single course of lectures, there remains a class of students, considerable in number, and respectable for talent and industry, who from lack of time and means, or for other cause, succeed in accomplishing only a partial course, obtaining degrees in some two or three schools, and attending lectures profitably in some one or two more in which they do not stand for degrees. And thus the number that go through such a course of study as, with the mode of instruction employed, involves a useful extent of knowledge and a sound discipline of mind, would seem to be in fair proportion to those who succeed in completing the usual College curriculum.

Again, there is a considerable class of students who aim at completing the entire course of literary and scientific studies, according to the scheme of the University of Virginia, but fail of entire success. But it does not follow, because they fail of obtaining the highest degree under a system with a higher standard for degrees, that they do not obtain as much of knowledge and of sound mental discipline as the same persons would have done if they had succeeded under a system with a lower standard. Under the one system they fail because the standard is high, under the other they would succeed because the standard is low. This on the supposition that the grade of instruction is the same. But it may be assumed that where the standard of examinations for degrees is higher, the grade of instruction also will be higher, and the training more vigorous. There must be some just relation between the teaching and the requirements for degrees. And so it may very well occur that a man shall be a better trained scholar failing under the one system than succeeding under the other.

The advocates of the system introduced at the University of Virginia not only deny that it is followed by the evil effects alleged, but urge, on the other hand, that it avoids, as it was designed to avoid, the obvious and acknowledged evils inherent in the usual course adopted of conferring degrees upon those who complete the curriculum, well nigh as a matter of course, and with but slight examination. They allege that when the standard is reasonably high, and maintained by rigid examinations, without regard to the time of residence, only a few, and those the most diligent and capable, can measure up to it. That to accommodate the standard to the measure of the whole, or nearly the whole of a class, it must be made much too low. That by admitting to the higher degrees those alone who can stand rigid examinations, and show good ability and accurate attainments, real value is given to the degrees, and the best exertions secured of those who seek them. That the use of lectures and oral examinations, in the ordinary course of instruction, affords a better means of disciplining the mind, of begetting habits of active and sustained attention, as well as of thorough investigation. That, as a result, there is obtained, under this system, a better training and a more thorough knowledge on the part of many who fail of success, than the other system ordinarily secures to those who succeed. And that the fact that only a very few obtain the Master's degree at the University of Virginia—some seven in the session of 1854–5 out of 350 exclusively academical students—only shows the extent and rigor of the examinations for this degree, there required by law and enforced in practice.

2. A second peculiarity of the University of Virginia is found in its method of instruction, more especially in the freer use of lectures, followed by oral examinations. Text-books are by no means discarded; but the professor is expected to go before and set in order the truths to be taught, marking their relations, stating their grounds, enlarging upon, explaining, confirming, correcting, and supplementing the text, as the case may require. Every lecture is preceded by an oral examination of the class on the preceding lecture and the corresponding text. And this examination is on the subject itself, whether discussed in the lecture or the text-book, and is conducted with reference to what ought to be held in regard to it, and not simply to what may have been said about it either in the lecture or in the text-book. This method, it is affirmed, is attended by two most beneficial results. First, it stimulates the professor to greater efforts to make himself wholly master of his subject, and to be qualified to view it on every side. It can hardly do less, seeing he is conscious that it is expected of him to exhibit himself as capable of presenting the doctrines belonging to his subject with clearness and force, and not merely of propounding questions on a text-book. He must needs give himself to his work with zeal and assiduity if he would meet the responsibility which his position imposes, or gain the reputation which it places within his reach. Secondly, it excites and maintains the interest and attention of the student a hundred fold. He not only shares the interest of the lecturer, which is one advantage of oral discourse, but finds it a necessity from which he cannot escape, if he would acquit himself well at the examination to follow, as his own self-respect and a regard for the good opinion of his teacher and fellows oblige him to wish to do, that he should give earnest heed to the words of the professor. Above all he learns to enter, with the professor for his guide, upon the serious and earnest investigation of the subject in hand in all its relations, if not from the simple love of truth, yet still because he knows that he may be required to render answers not furnished by the text, nor yet perhaps directly by the lecture, but involved in the principles set forth in either. Thus he is aroused to a spirit of active and manly inquiry, is kept awake to all that he hears and reads, and is led to consider the proper knowledge of a subject to be bounded, not by the partial, perhaps false teachings of a text-book, but by the limits of the true and real. Under the strong impulse of such a spirit, and of the ambition to meet the demands of a standard of examinations for degrees which more fail than succeed in reaching, it is no wonder that he works, and works with an energy, with a sharpness of attention, and with a perseverance of industry, which bring a double reward in stores of solid knowledge and in invaluable habits of mind.

3. A third peculiarity of the University of Virginia is the system of written examinations for honors. This is claimed to have the advantage of securing greater accuracy and fairness, and is regarded as indispensable for maintaining a high standard for degrees. It was introduced by the first professors from the practice of Cambridge University, England; and when supplemented by some oral examination, as the subject may demand, seems liable only to the objection of its great laboriousness to both student and professor.

In a word, whatever success the University of Virginia has had in giving intellectual culture, whether in the academical or professional departments, is mainly referred by its friends to the laborious industry and zeal in the immediate work of the lecture-room, displayed by professors and students alike. These, again, are very largely owing to the use of lectures, and of strict oral and written examinations, both having reference to a reasonably high standard for degrees. And for the introduction of these, the independent position of the several schools, and the free choice of studies, if not absolutely necessary, as they can hardly be said to be, are at least most favorable.

4. A fourth peculiarity is the absence of sectarian influence and control in the University. Much prejudice did arise on this point. Al-

though the importance of man's religious duties was acknowledged in a report of the Rector and Board of Visitors, written by Mr. Jefferson, and although the invitation was given by the Board to the various religious denominations in the state, to establish schools of theology on the grounds of the University, yet because, in the anxiety to shut out the control of any particular sect, no provision was made for religious instruction by the University itself, very many believed that it was designed altogether to exclude religious influence from the institution. A plan, however, was adopted early in the history of the University, whereby the services of religion are regularly performed in a chapel furnished by the Board of Visitors, yet without invading the principle of religious equality. By this plan it was provided that a Chaplain should be appointed by the Faculty every year, from the prevailing religious denominations of the state, taken in rotation. Subsequently the appointment was made for two years. The salary of the Chaplain is provided by the voluntary contributions of the professors, students, and other residents. He holds divine service twice every Sabbath, and daily morning prayers in the chapel. These services all the students are invited to attend; but they are not compelled to be present. As many as attend deport themselves with invariable order and reverence. Besides these services, the students have their own public prayer-meeting, and a society for missionary inquiry, and conduct the Sunday school connected with the chapel, and others in the neighborhood. Nowhere, it is said, is more respect paid to the solemn services of the Christian religion, and in no community is more effectually extinguished the spirit of sectarian bigotry.

5. A fifth peculiarity relates to the discipline. Only one point can be noticed, namely the permitting of students to answer or not, as they may choose, in their own case; the not compelling them to testify against themselves or against each other; and, generally, the assuming that they are incapable of falsehood, and treating them accordingly. The result is, that, as a rule, hardly admitting an exception, no student can venture to speak falsely. He may decline to answer, when charged with an offence against the laws, although he very rarely does; but if he answer, the public sentiment, if not his own sense of moral obligation, will oblige him to speak truly.

For carrying into execution the plan of a University which he had projected, Mr. Jefferson considered it wisest to rely upon men as little as possible wedded to the prevalent system, and not likely to be cramped by its routine. A reform in regard to the extent as well as the mode of instruction, could be had only by seeking men of marked ability in their several departments, and who had either enjoyed the advantages of the foreign universities of most repute, or won distinction by their talent and attainments. To this view was owing the selection from abroad of a majority of the original corps of professors. This policy, naturally enough, excited some prejudice; and although justified by the necessities of the case, as far at least as a reform in the course of instruction was concerned, was attended by its own difficulties touching the important point of discipline. It was not intended to be continued beyond the present exigency, and has not, in fact, been followed in the subsequent appointments to chairs in the University, although it is admitted to be consistent with the interests of the institution to employ the best talents and attainments, wherever found conjoined with the other necessary qualifications. Of the eight original professors, five were from abroad, one from New York, and two from Virginia. Of the present fifteen professors and other instructors, ten are Virginians and alumni of the University of Virginia, and only two from abroad.

The first professor of the school of Ancient Languages was Mr. George Long, of England, a Master of Arts and Fellow of Trinity College, Cambridge. A man of marked ability and attainments, thoroughly trained in the system of his college, having a mind far more than most men's scrupulously demanding accuracy in the results of inquiry, and scouting mere pretension, he aimed and was fitted to introduce something better than what then passed current as classical learning. Although he had as yet little knowledge of comparative philology, and could hardly be said to have cultivated the science of language with the enlarged spirit of philosophy which pervades his writings; his uncompromising exactness, and his masterly knowledge of his subject, inspired his pupils with the highest conceptions of a true scholarship. After three years' service he resigned, in order to accept the professorship of Greek in the London University. His contributions to philology, Roman law, criticism, biography, &c., have been large and valuable, and have obtained for him a place among the most eminent scholars of his country.

He was succeeded by the present incumbent of the chair, Gessner Harrison, M.D., one of his pupils, who has published an "Exposition of some of the Laws of the Latin Language."

The first professor of the School of Modern Languages was George Blaettermann, LL.D., a German, at the time of his appointment residing in London, and who came recommended for his extensive knowledge of modern languages, and for his ability. He occupied the chair until 1840, and gave proof of extensive acquirements, and of a mind of uncommon natural vigor and penetration. In connexion more especially with the lessons on German and Anglo-Saxon, he gave to his students much that was interesting and valuable in comparative philology also, a subject in which he found peculiar pleasure. His successors have been Charles Kraitsir, M.D., who has published some curious and learned works on philology, and M. Schele de Vere, LL.D., the author of a work on Comparative Philology, and of a Spanish Grammar and Exercises.

The first professor of Mathematics was Mr. Thomas Hewett Key, of England, a Master of Arts of Trinity College, Cambridge. Besides his ability as a mathematician, he had the advantage of good classical and general attainments; and by his earnest manner, his clearness of illustration, and his rare power of anticipating and removing the learner's difficulties, succeeded to a remarkable degree in gaining the attention and exciting the interest of his hearers. He resigned at the same time with Mr. Long, in order to accept the professorship of Latin in the London University, and has since gained distinction by his labors as a philologist.

He was succeeded by Mr. Charles Bonnycastle, of England, who, upon Mr. Key's resignation, was transferred from the chair of Natural Philosophy to that of Mathematics, which he continued to fill until his death in 1841. He was educated at the Royal Military Academy at Woolwich, of which his father was a professor, and was distinguished by the force and originality of his mind, no less than by his profound knowledge of mathematics. His fine taste, cultivated by much reading, his general knowledge, and his abundant store of anecdote, made him a most agreeable and instructive companion to all; and this, though his really kind feelings were partly hidden by a cold exterior. His only published work bore the title of *Inductive Geometry*, and this did not meet with success. Among his pupils, he left behind him a reputation for ability as high as it was universal.

His successor, Mr. Sylvester, of England also, who remained only part of one year, was followed by Mr. Edward H. Courtenay, LL.D., a native of Maryland, a graduate at West Point, and who had held a professorship in West Point Military Academy, and again in the University of Pennsylvania. He discharged the duties of the chair with eminent ability and faithfulness until his death in 1853. He left behind him a work on the *Differential and Integral Calculus*, which has lately been published, and been adopted as a text-book in the University of Virginia. Mr. Courtenay's clear and sagacious mind, his large and thorough knowledge of his subject, and clearness in communicating it, his laborious devotion to his duties, and not less his unswerving integrity, his retiring modesty, and his amiable condescension, won for him the unbounded confidence and regard of his colleagues and of his pupils.

The chair is now filled by Albert T. Bledsoe, LL.D., a graduate of West Point, formerly a professor in the University of Mississippi, and the author of a work on the *Will*, and of one entitled *A Theodicy*.

Upon the transfer of Mr. Charles Bonnycastle from the chair of Natural Philosophy to that of Mathematics, he was succeeded by Robert M. Patterson, M.D., of Philadelphia, formerly a professor in the University of Pennsylvania, and subsequently director of the U. S. Mint. He filled the chair of Natural Philosophy for several years, and had the reputation of a clear, elegant, and able lecturer, while his refined manners, cultivated tastes, and amiable disposition, won for him the warm regard of all that had the pleasure of knowing him.

He was succeeded by Mr. William B. Rogers, LL.D., who filled the chair until 1853; a gentleman deservedly eminent for his ability, varied learning and science, for his eloquence as a lecturer, and for his contributions to his favorite science of Geology. He resigned in 1853; and was succeeded by the present incumbent, Mr. Francis H. Smith, A.M., a Virginian, and an alumnus of the University.

The first professor of Chemistry was John P. Emmet, M.D., who was educated at the West Point Military Academy, and took his degree in medicine in the College of Physicians and Surgeons, New York city. He was born in Dublin, Ireland, and was the son of Thomas Addis Emmet, Esq. His striking native genius, his varied science, his brilliant wit, his eloquence, his cultivated and refined taste for art, his modesty, his warm-hearted and cheerful social virtues, won for him the admiration and lasting regard of his colleagues and of his pupils. He occupied the chair of Chemistry and Materia Medica until sickness and death closed prematurely, in 1842, a career not less useful than honorable.

He was succeeded by Robert E. Rogers, M.D., of Philadelphia, now professor of chemistry in the University of Pennsylvania, and by J. Lawrence Smith, M.D., of South Carolina, now professor in the Medical School at Louisville, Kentucky. The present incumbent of the chair is Socrates Maupin, M.D., of Virginia, formerly a professor in Hampden Sydney College, Virginia, and in Richmond Medical College, and an alumnus of the University of Virginia.

The first professor of Medicine was Robley Dunglison, M.D., of England, who as a writer, and by his learning in his profession and generally, as well as by his ability, was pointed out as well fitted to take charge of this school, when it was designed rather to afford the opportunity of cultivation in medical science to the general student than to give a preparation for the practice of the profession. After eight years he resigned, and has gained a wide celebrity by his distinguished ability as a lecturer, and by his varied and valuable contributions to medical literature.

His successors have been A. T. Magill, M.D., of Virginia, Robert E. Griffith, M.D., of Philadelphia, and the present incumbent, Henry Howard, M.D., of Maryland, formerly a professor in the medical department of the University of Maryland, all men of learning and ability in their profession.

The chair of Anatomy, Physiology, and Surgery (now of Comparative Anatomy, etc.) has been added to the original schools of the university, and is now filled by James L. Cabell, M.D., a Virginian, and an alumnus of the university. He was preceded by Augustus L. Warner, M.D., of Maryland, afterwards a professor in the Richmond Medical College.

Special Anatomy and Materia Medica are taught by John S. Davis, M.D., an alumnus of the University.

The chair of Moral Philosophy was first filled by Mr. George Tucker, a native of Bermuda, but educated at William and Mary College, Virginia. He was for many years a member of the legal profession, and for some time a member of Congress from Virginia. Before receiving his appointment to the chair by Mr. Jefferson, he had published, among other writings, a volume of essays, characterized by the purity and elegance of style, and by the force and clearness of thought, which have marked all his writings. During his residence at the university he published the *Life of Jefferson*, an essay on *Money and Banks*, one on *Rents, Wages, and Profits*, and another on the *Progress of the United States in Population and Wealth during a Period of Fifty Years, as Exhibited by the Decennial Census*, besides contributing to the periodicals of the day, as he has done since his retirement, important articles on questions of political economy, etc. To moral philosophy and the other subjects originally assigned to the chair, he caused rhetoric, belles-lettres, and political economy to be added, and gave them their proper value in the course of study in the school. Bringing to the discharge of his duties a mind remarkable for clearness and accuracy, great industry and thoroughness of research, and an extensive knowledge of men, and of books in almost every department of learning, he allowed no topic to pass under review without investing it with the interest of original and searching investigation. Hence his pupils derived not only profit directly from his instructions, but an impulse in the direction of self-culture of the utmost value.

He was succeeded, upon his resignation in 1845, after a service of twenty years, by the present incumbent, the Rev. William H. McGuffey, D.D., LL.D., a native of Pennsylvania, but for many years a popular professor in different colleges of Ohio.

The first professor of Law, that entered upon the duties of the chair, was John Tayloe Lomax, Esq., of Virginia, who, after some five years, resigned the chair to accept the office of judge of the Circuit Court of Virginia. He is the author of works of much labor and value, entitled a *Digest of the Law of Real Property* and the *Law of Executors and Administrators.*

He was succeeded by John A. G. Davis, Esq., of Virginia, who met an untimely end by the hands of a murderer, in the person of a student, in the year 1840. He was the author of a work on the criminal law, and was distinguished alike by his legal attainments and ability as a lecturer and by his virtues as a man.

The chair of Law was next filled by Judge Henry St. George Tucker of Virginia, who had long occupied with distinguished ability the place of president of the Court of Appeals of the state, and was as remarkable for the elegant graces of his well stored mind as for his learning and acumen in his peculiar province of the law, and for the polish and charm of his life and manners. He was the author of two volumes of *Commentaries on Blackstone*, etc.

The present incumbents of the two chairs of Law, into which the original school has been divided, are John B. Minor, LL.D., and J. P. Holcombe, Esq., both of Virginia, and both alumni of the university. The latter is the author of a work on Equity.

TRINITY COLLEGE.

The charter of Washington (now Trinity) College, in Connecticut, was obtained in 1823. It was given at the request of members of the Protestant Episcopal Church. At several intervals in the earlier history of the state, application had been made to the Legislature for a charter without success. It was requisite that thirty thousand dollars should be subscribed as an endowment. Fifty thousand were readily obtained, "by offering to the larger towns the privilege of fair and laudable competition for its location, when Hartford, never wanting in public spirit and generous outlays, gained the victory over her sister cities." The college buildings were commenced at Hartford in June, 1824, and recitations were held in the autumn of the same year. The first president of the institution was the Bishop of the Protestant Episcopal Church in Connecticut, Dr. Thomas C. Brownell, who held the station for seven years, till 1831. On his retirement he was succeeded by the Rev. Dr. N. S. Wheaton, who presided over its fortunes for five years, till 1837. The Hobart Professorship of Belles-Lettres and Oratory was endowed at this time in the sum of twenty thousand dollars, subscribed by members of the Episcopal Church in New York. In 1835 more than one hundred thousand dollars had been raised for this institution, ninety thousand of which had been given by individuals. The state made a grant of eleven thousand dollars. The next incumbent of the presidency was the Rev. Dr. Silas Totten (now professor of William and Mary), who at the time of his choice was professor of Mathematics and Natural Philosophy in the college. His administration lasted twelve years, during which the endowment of the Seabury Professorship of Mathematics and Natural Philosophy was completed and Brownell Hall erected. In 1845 the title of the college was changed, by an act of the legislature, to Trinity College. In this period statutes were enacted by the trustees, modelled after a feature in the English universities, "committing the superintendence of the course of study and discipline to a Board of Fellows, and empowering specified members of the *Senatus Academicus*, as the House of Convocation, to assemble under their own rules, and to consult and advise for the interests and benefit of the college."* The object of this general external organization was to secure the co-operation and counsel of the alumni of the institution, all of whom are members of the House of Convocation, which includes the president, fellows, and professors. The Board of Fellows is composed of leading men in the church specially interested in the welfare of the college. They are the official examiners, report on degrees, and propose amendments of the statutes to the trustees. There are also a chancellor and visiter, who superintend the religious interests: an office which has been thus far filled by the bishop of the diocese.

Dr. Totten, on his retirement, was succeeded in 1849 by the Rev. John Williams, a descendant of the family which gave the Rev. Elisha Williams as a president to Yale. Two years after Dr. Williams was elected assistant bishop of the diocese of Connecticut.

In 1854 the Rev. Dr. Daniel Rogers Goodwin, formerly professor of modern languages at Bowdoin, succeeded to the presidency.

Many eminent men have been connected with the institution as professors and lecturers. The Rev. Dr. S. F. Jarvis held a professorship of Oriental Literature; Horatio Potter, now bishop of the diocese of New York, of Mathematics and Natural Philosophy—a professorship held also by Mr. Charles Davies, author of the extensive series of mathematical text-books generally in use throughout the country. The Rev. Dr. Thomas W. Coit, the learned author of *Puritanism, or a*

* Beardsley's Historical Address, p. 17.

Churchman's Defence against its Aspersions by an Appeal to its Own History, has been professor of Ecclesiastical History; and the Hon. W. W. Ellsworth, professor of Law.*

THE UNIVERSITY OF THE CITY OF NEW YORK.

This institution owes its origin to the exertions of a few gentlemen of the city of New York, among whom were the Rev. J. M. Mathews, afterwards Chancellor of the University, and the Rev. Jonathan M. Wainwright, of whom we have already spoken. A pamphlet was prepared after several conversational discussions of the plan, which was printed with the title, "Considerations upon the Expediency and the Means of Establishing a University in the City of New York." This was read at a meeting of the friends of education, held on the sixth of January, 1830, in the building since known as the New City Hall, and adopted as an expression of the views of the assembly. A charter of incorporation was obtained in 1831, by which the government of the University was confided to a Council of thirty-two members, chosen by the stockholders of the institution, with the addition of the Mayor and four members of the Common Council of the city. The University commenced its instructions in October, 1832, with seven professors and forty-two students, in rooms hired for the purpose in Clinton Hall. The first class, consisting of three students, was graduated in 1833, and the first public commencement held in 1834 in the Middle Dutch Church in Nassau street.

Steps were immediately taken for the erection of a suitable edifice, and the edifice was commenced in July, 1833, and so far completed as to be occupied in 1836. It was formally dedicated "to the purposes of Science, Literature, and Religion," on the twentieth of May, 1837. The building occupies the front of an entire block of ground, facing the Washington Parade Ground, and was the first introduction, on any considerable scale, of the English collegiate style of architecture. It contains, in addition to a large and elaborately decorated chapel, and spacious lecture halls, a number of apartments not at present required for the purposes of education, a portion of which are now occupied by the valuable library of the New York Historical Society and the American Geographical Society. The erection of this building, and the period of commercial depression which followed its commencement, weighed heavily on the fortunes of the young institution. By the devotion of its professors, however, who continued to occupy their respective chairs at reduced salaries, its instructions have been steadily maintained. Various appeals to the public for pecuniary aid have been liberally responded to, and by a vigorous effort on the part of the present Chancellor, the Rev. Isaac Ferris, the long pressing incubus of debt has been entirely removed.

The University of the City of New York.

The foundations of the institution were laid on a broad and liberal basis, contemplating instruction in every department of learning, with the exception of a school of theology, this omission being made to avoid any charge of sectarianism. A large number of professors were appointed, among whom the institution has the honor of numbering S. F. B. Morse, whose early experiments in the departments of science which have since given him a fame as enduring and extended as the elements he has subjected to the service of his fellow men, were made during his connexion with the University. The course of instruction has, however, thus far, with the exception of a Medical School, been confined to the usual undergraduate collegiate course.

The first Chancellor of the University was the Rev. James M. Mathews, D.D., who, for many years preceding his appointment, had occupied a prominent position among the clergy of the Dutch Reformed Church in the city of New York. He rendered good service to the institution by his unwearying labors in the presentation of its claims to public attention, and bore his full share of the difficulties attending its early years. He was succeeded by the Hon. Theodore Frelinghuysen, now president of Rutgers College, in which connexion he has already been spoken of in these pages. After his removal from the University to Rutgers in 1850, the office he had filled remained vacant until 1853, when the present efficient and respected incumbent, the Rev. Isaac Ferris, a clergyman of the Dutch Reformed Church, and at the head of the Rutgers Female Institute, was appointed.

In the list of the first professors we meet the names of the Rev. Charles P. McIlvaine, at present Bishop of the Protestant Episcopal Church of Ohio, Henry Vethake, and the Rev. Henry P. Tappan, both of whom are now at the head of important seats of learning, and the Rev. George Bush, all of whom have received notices at an earlier period of our work. With these were associated for a short time, the distinguished mathematician, David B. Douglas, LL.D., and Dr. John Torrey, one of the most eminent botanists of the country, and a leading member of the Lyceum of Natural History of New York, the American Association of Science, and other similar Institutions.

* We are indebted for the materials of this notice of Trinity College to the excellent Historical Address pronounced before the House of Convocation of Trinity College, in Christ Church, Hartford, in 1851, by the Rev. E. E. Beardsley, rector of St. Thomas's Church, New Haven, and from time to time in the Churchman's Almanac.

Lorenzo L. Da Ponte was at the same time appointed Professor of the Italian Language and Literature, and retained the office until his death in 1840. He was the son of Lorenzo Da Ponte, an Italian scholar, forced from his native country on account of his liberal political opinions, and author of an agreeable autobiography, *Memorie di Lorenzo Da Ponte Da Ceneda*, published in New York in three small volumes in 1823. Professor Da Ponte was a man of liberal culture and great amiability of character, and author of a history of Florence and of several elementary works of instruction on the Italian language.

In 1836, Isaac Nordheimer was appointed Professor of the Hebrew and German languages. He was a man of great learning, and author of a History of Florence and of a Hebrew Grammar, in use as a text-book in our theological Seminaries. He continued his connexion with the institution until his death in 1842.

The Rev. Cyrus Mason was appointed Professor of the Evidences of Christianity in 1836, and occupied a prominent position in the Faculty and business relations of the Institution until his retirement in 1850.

In 1838 Tayler Lewis was appointed Professor of the Greek Language and Literature, and the Rev. C. S. Henry of Moral Philosophy. The first of these gentlemen has already been noticed in relation to his present sphere of labor at Union College.

Caleb Sprague Henry was born at Rutland, Massachusetts, and graduated at Dartmouth College, in 1825. After a course of theological study at Andover, he was settled as a Congregational minister at Greenfield, Mass., and subsequently at Hartford, Conn., until 1835, when he took orders in the Protestant Episcopal Church. He was appointed in the same year Professor of Intellectual and Moral Philosophy in Bristol College, Pa., and remained in that Institution until 1837, when he removed to New York, and established the New York Review, the first number of which appeared in March, 1837. He conducted this periodical until 1840, when it passed into the hands of Dr. J. G. Cogswell, who had been associated in its conduct during the previous twelvemonth.

Professor Henry remained at the University until 1852. During this period, in addition to the active discharge of the duties of his chair, he published in 1845 an *Epitome of the History of Philosophy, being the work adopted by the University of France for instruction in the colleges and high schools. Translated from the French, with additions, and a continuation of the history from the time of Reid to the present day.**

The original portion of this work is equal in extent to one fourth of the whole, and consists, on the plan of the previous portions, of concise biographies of the leading philosophical writers of modern Europe, with a brief exposition of their doctrines. Professor Henry has executed this difficult task with research and exactness. His work is a standard autherity on the subject, and has received the commendation of Sir William Hamilton and other leading philosophers.

Professor Henry is also the author of *The Elements of Psychology*, a translation of Cousin's examination of Locke's Essay on the Understanding, with an introduction, notes, and appendix, published at Hartford in 1834, and New York in 1839; of a *Compendium of Christian Antiquities;** and of a volume of *Moral and Philosophical Essays.*† He has also published a number of college addresses,‡ mostly devoted to the discussion of his favorite subject of university education. The style of these writings, like that of his instructions, is distinguished by energy, directness, and familiar illustration.

During the years 1847–1850 Dr. Henry officiated as rector of St. Clement's Church, New York. Since his retirement from the University, he has resided in the vicinity of the city, and has been a frequent contributor to the Church Review and other periodicals of the day.

Benjamin F. Joslin, M.D., was appointed in 1838 Professor of Mathematics and Natural Philosophy. He resigned his appointment in 1844. He is the author of several valuable papers on philosophical subjects, which have appeared in Silliman's Journal. He has also written frequently on medical topics, and is a prominent advocate of the system of Hahnemann.

In 1839 Dr. John W. Draper was appointed Professor of Chemistry. Dr. Draper is a native of England. He came to the United States in early life, and was graduated as a physician at the University of Pennsylvania in 1836. His inaugural thesis on that occasion was published by the Faculty of the institution, a distinction conferred in very few cases. Dr. Draper soon after became Professor in Hampden Sidney College, Virginia. He still remains connected with the University, and has contributed in an eminent degree to its honor and usefulness, by his distinguished scientific position, and the thoroughness of his instructions. Dr. Draper has devoted much attention to the study of the action of light, and was the inventor of the application of the daguerreotype process to the taking of portraits. He is the author of text-books on Chemistry and Natural Philosophy, of a large quarto work on the Influence of Light on the Growth and Development of Plants; of a large number of addresses delivered in the course of his academic career, and of numerous articles on physiological, medical, optical, and chemical subjects, which have appeared in the medical journals of this country and in the London and Edinburgh Philosophical Magazine. These papers, it is estimated, would, if collected, fill an octavo volume of one thousand pages. Several have been trans-

---

* 2 vols. 12mo.

* Phila. 1837. † New York, 1839.

‡ Principles and Prospects of the Friends of Peace, a discourse delivered in Hartford in 1834.

The Advocate of Peace. A Quarterly Journal, vol. i., 1834-5.

Importance of Exalting the Intellectual Spirit of the Nation; and the Need of a Learned Class. 2d Edition. New York: 1787. Delivered before the Phi Sigma Nu Society of the University of Vermont, August, 1836.

Position and Duties of the Educated Men of the Country. New York: 1840.

The Gospel a Formal and Sacramental Religion. A Sermon. 2d Edition. New York: 1844.

The True Idea of the University, and its Relation to a Complete System of Public Instruction. New York: 1853.

lated in France, Germany, and Italy. He is entitled from these productions to high literary as well as scientific rank, from the purity of style which characterizes their composition, and the frequent passages of eloquence and of genuine humor to be found at no long intervals in their pages.

Dr. Draper has been a member of the Medical Faculty of the University since its formation, and was appointed by the unanimous voice of his associates president of that body in 1851.

Mr. Elias Loomis, the author of several important scientific text-books, was in 1844 appointed Professor of Mathematics.

Professor Loomis is a graduate of Yale College, and was appointed Professor of Mathematics and Natural Philosophy in the University in 1844, having previously filled the same professorship in Western Reserve College, Ohio. He is the author of several volumes and papers on mathematics and astronomy.*

In 1846 Mr. George J. Adler was appointed Professor of the German language. Professor Adler was born in Germany in 1821, came to the United States in 1833, and was graduated at the University in 1844. He is the author of a German Grammar published in 1846, a German Reader in 1847, and a German and English Dictionary, in a volume of large size, in 1848. He has since, in 1851, published an abridgment of this work, and in 1853, a *Manual of German Literature*, with elaborate critical prefaces on the authors from whom the specimens contained in the volume have been taken.

In 1850 Professor Adler published an able metrical translation of the Iphigenia of Goethe. He is also the author of several articles on German and classical literature in the Literary World. He resigned his professorship in 1854, and has since been occupied in private tuition and literary pursuits.

In 1852 Mr. Howard Crosby was appointed Professor of Greek. Mr. Crosby was born in the city of New York and was graduated at the University in 1844. Visiting Europe a few years after, he made an extensive tour in the Levant, the results of which were given to the public in a pleasant and scholarly volume, in 1851.† In the following year he published an edition of the Œdipus Tyrannus of Sophocles.

The alumni of the literary departments of the University now number over five hundred.

THE UNIVERSITY OF MICHIGAN.

THE UNIVERSITY OF MICHIGAN owes its foundation to an act of Congress of 1826, which appropriated two entire townships, including more than forty-six thousand acres of land, within what was then a territory, "for the use and support of a university, and for no other use or purpose whatever." When Michigan became a state the subject engaged the earnest attention of its legislators. An organization was recommended in 1837 in the report of the Rev. J. D. Pierce, the first superintendent of public instruction, and the first law under the state legislation establishing "The University of Michigan" was approved March 18th of that year. In this act the objects were stated to be "to provide the inhabitants of the state with the means of acquiring a thorough knowledge of the various branches of literature, science, and the arts." A body of regents was to be appointed by the governor of the state, with the advice and consent of the Senate. The governor, lieutenant-governor, judges of the Supreme Court, and chancellor of the state, were ex-officio members. Three departments were provided: of literature, science, and the arts; of law, and of medicine. Fifteen professorships were liberally mapped out in the first of these; three in the second, and six in the third. The institution was to be presided over by a chancellor. An additional act located the University in or near the village of Ann Arbor, on a site to be conveyed to the regents free of cost, and to include not less than forty acres.

An important question soon arose with the legislature in determining the policy of granting charters for private colleges in the state. Opinions on the subject were obtained from Dr. Wayland, Edward Everett, and others, who agreed in stating the advantage of forming one well endowed institution, in preference to the division of means and influence among many. The legislature did not adopt any exclusive system, though the obvious policy of concentrating the state support upon the University has been virtually embraced.

A system of branches or subsidiary schools in the state, intermediate between the primary school and the college, was early organized. They were to supply pupils to the University.

The first professor chosen, in 1838, was Dr. Asa Gray, now of Cambridge, in the department of botany and zoology. Five thousand dollars were placed at his disposal for the purchase of books in Europe as the commencement of the University library. This secured a collection of nearly four thousand volumes.

Dr. Houghton was also appointed professor of geology and mineralogy. The mineralogical collection of Baron Lederer of Austria was purchased, and added to the collections in geology, mineralogy, botany, and zoology, made within the geographical area of Michigan by the state geologist and his corps.

The income of the University, partaking of the embarrassments of the times, scanty and uncertain, and mainly absorbed in the erection of the buildings and the support of the branches, was not in 1840 sufficient for the full organization of the main institution. There were two hundred and forty-seven students in that year in the branches. In 1842 a portion of the money expended on these schools was withdrawn, and devoted to the faculty of the still unformed univer-

---

* Elements of Algebra, 12mo., pp. 260. A Treatise on Algebra, 8vo., pp. 884. Elements of Geometry and Conic Sections, 8vo., pp. 226. Trigonometry and Tables, 8vo., pp. 344. Elements of Analytical Geometry, and of the Differential and Integral Calculus, 8vo., pp. 278. An Introduction to Practical Astronomy, with a Collection of Astronomical Tables, 8vo., pp. 497. Recent Progress of Astronomy, especially in the United States.—He has contributed to the Transactions of the American Philosophical Society, nine memoirs relating to Astronomy, Magnetism, and Meteorology; and to the American Journal of Science and Arts from twenty to thirty papers on various questions of science. The Proceedings of the American Association for the Advancement of Science also contain a number of his papers, and several have appeared in other periodicals.

† Land of the Moslem, a Narrative of Oriental Travel, by El Mukattem.

sity. Professors of Mathematics and of Latin and Greek were appointed.

In the report of the regents of 1849 it appears that there were thirty-eight students in the department of literature and sciences, under the charge of seven professors. No chancellor had been as yet appointed. Each of the professors presided, on a system of rotation, as president of the faculty.

It was not till December, 1852, that Dr. Henry P. Tappan, eminent as a writer on metaphysical subjects, the author of two treatises on the *Will* and a work on the *Elements of Logic*, and formerly professor of intellectual and moral philosophy in the University of the City of New York, was inaugurated the first chancellor. The subject of university education had long employed his attention, and he studied its practical working in England and Prussia during a foreign tour, of which he gave to the public a record in his volumes entitled *A Step from the New World to the Old*. His inaugural address contained an able programme of the objects to be pursued in a true university course. He has since again visited Europe, further studied the workings of education in Prussia, and secured valuable acquisitions for the literary and scientific resources of the University. Among these were the instruments for a first class observatory, now established at the university by the liberality of the citizens of Detroit, over which an eminent foreign astronomer, Dr. Francis Brunnow, the associate of Encke at the Royal Observatory at Berlin, is now presiding.

The revision of the course of studies engaged Dr. Tappan's attention. It is now symmetrically arranged to include every object of a liberal education, with provision for expansion as the growing needs and resources of the institution may demand. The liberally endowed primary schools of the state, a system of associated or union schools in districts, the introduction of normal schools lead to the ordinary under-graduate course of the university, which it is proposed to extend by the introduction of lectures for those students who may wish to proceed further. A scientific course may be pursued separately, and the plan embraces instruction on agricultural subjects.

The following passages from Chancellor Tappan's Report to the Board of Regents at the close of 1853 will exhibit the liberal spirit of the scholar which he brings to his work :—

The ideal character of the Prussian system must belong to every genuine system of education. We must always begin with assuming that man is to be educated because he is man, and that the development of his powers is the great end of education, and one which really embraces every other end. Especially is it important to hold this forth among a people like that of the United States, where the industrial arts and commerce are such general and commanding objects. In the immense reach of our material prosperity, we are in danger of forgetting our higher spiritual nature, or, at least, of preserving only a dim and feeble consciousness of it. We are in danger of becoming mere creatures of the earth—earthy, and of reducing all values to the standard of material utility. And yet man is good and happy only as his moral and intellectual nature is developed. He does not fill up the measure of his being by merely building houses for his comfortable accommodation, and by providing for himself abundance of wholesome food. He has capacities for knowledge, truth, beauty, and virtue also: and these, too, must be satisfied.

Besides philosophy, science, poetry, and the fine arts, in general, are no less essential to national existence and character than agriculture, manufactures, and commerce. In the first place, the latter could never exist in a perfect form without the former, since all improvement must be dependent upon knowledge and taste: and, in the second place, great principles widely diffused, and great men for the offices of the state and of society at large, and great deeds to signalize a nation's existence, and works of literature and art to convey the spirit of a people to other nations, and to the following generations, all depend upon the spiritual cultivation of the human being. Nay, farther, there is no country in which national existence and character will so depend upon this higher cultivation as in ours. Here are vast multitudes collected from other nations, as well as of native growth, thrown together in a breadth of territory whose resources dazzle the imagination, and, for the present, defy calculation. And these multitudes constantly increasing, and with so wide a field to act in, are in a state of freedom such as no people has ever before possessed. We are in a state approximating to absolute self-government. It is not the mere force of laws, and the executive authority of the officers of government, which can control and regulate such a people. We ourselves make and alter our constitution and laws. And laws when made become, in effect, null and void unless sustained by popular opinion.

It is the noblest form of government when a people are prepared for it, and a form which implies that they are prepared for it. It is a form which shows less of the outward form of government, because it supposes a people so enlightened and moral that they do not require it. Rational thought, the principles of truth and virtue, and an incorruptible patriotism, supersede a police, standing armies, and courts of justice. In such a state, it is at least demanded that the enlightened and the good shall predominate. As all this is implied in our constitution and laws, so, as wise men and true patriots, we must try to make it good. And to this end we require a higher education of the people than obtains in any other country. And on the same principle, we ought to have more philosophers, men of science, artists, and authors, and eminent statesmen—in fine, more great men than any other people. We want the highest forms of culture multiplied not merely for embellishment, but to preserve our very existence as a nation.

If we ever fall to pieces it will be through a people ignorant and besotted by material prosperity, and because cunning demagogues and boastful sciolists shall abound more than men of high intelligence and real worth.

The University is supported by the sale of the lands appropriated by the general government and by grants from the state. Students are admitted from all portions of the country on paying an initiation fee of only ten dollars for permanent membership. Room rent and the services of a janitor are secured by paying annually a sum varying from five to seven dollars and fifty cents—so that the instruction is virtually free.

A medical department is in successful operation.*

* Full information on the entire school system of the state will be found in an octavo volume, entitled System of Public

The number of under-graduate students in 1855 was two hundred and eighty-eight, including fourteen in the partial course, and one hundred and thirty-three in the medical department. Of these one hundred and forty-two were from Michigan; sixteen other states of the Union were represented; there were five students from Canada West, one from England, and one from the Sandwich Islands.

THE NATIONAL INSTITUTE.

The National Institute, at the seat of government at Washington, was organized in May, 1840, for the promotion of science and the useful arts, and to establish a National Museum of Natural History. The first directors were the late Joel R. Poinsett, then Secretary of War, the Hon. James K. Paulding, Secretary of the Navy, with whom were associated, as "Councillors," the Hon. John Q. Adams, Col. J. J. Abert, Col. Joseph G. Totten, Dr. Alexander McWilliams, and A. O. Dayton. Francis Markoe, Jr., was the early and efficient Corresponding Secretary. Sections were planned of geology and mineralogy, of chemistry, of the application of science to the arts, of literature and the fine arts, of natural history, of agriculture, of astronomy, of American history and antiquities, of geography and natural philosophy, of natural and political sciences.

Ex-President John Quincy Adams and Peter S. Duponceau, among others, took an active interest in its proceedings. An address was delivered by Mr. Poinsett in 1841, on its object and importance. The Association was incorporated in 1842 by the name of "The National Institute for the Promotion of Science."

Mr. Levi Woodbury, then a member of the Senate, was chosen to succeed Mr. Poinsett as President in 1845.

The first Vice-President of the Society was Mr. Peter Force, whose valuable services to the country, in the preparation of the Documentary History of the Origin and Progress of the United States, will secure him the gratitude of future ages. He now holds the office of President. The present Corresponding Secretary is Mr. Joseph C. G. Kennedy. Mr. William W. Turner, formerly instructor in Hebrew in the Union Theological Seminary, New York, the associate of Dr. E. A. Andrews in the American adaptation of Freund's Latin-German Lexicon, and at present Librarian of the Patent Office at Washington, is the Recording Secretary of the Institute.

One of the objects of the Society, as the nucleus of a National Museum, was soon attained. The Secretary of War deposited a valuable collection of Indian portraits and curiosities. The Society fell heir to the effects, books, and papers, of a local "Columbian Institute for the Promotion of Arts and Sciences," the charter of which had run out. The collections were placed in the Patent Office, together with the objects of science sent home by the United States Exploring Expedition under Capt. Wilkes. The Institute also received many valuable additions to its library and Museum from France, through the agency of M. Vattemare; and numerous choice contributions from various distant parts of the world. Donations from all sides were numerous.

A special meeting or congress was held in April, 1844, to which scientific men were generally invited. An address was delivered by the Hon. R. J. Walker of Mississippi. Ten daily meetings were held, at which papers were read by men distinguished in science.

In 1845, an annual address was delivered before the Institute by the Hon. Levi Woodbury.

The publications of the Institute have been limited, for the want of pecuniary endowment. It has depended on the precarious subscriptions of members, and has languished with funds inadequate for its ordinary business purposes. Four Bulletins have been issued in 1841, 1842, 1845, and 1846. These contain many interesting notices of the growing activity of the country in the departments of science. The meetings of the Society, however, called forth many elaborate papers, which were read in public from time to time, and printed in the National Intelligencer.

The activity of the Institute has lately revived, chiefly through the exertions of a few of its members. The publication of a new series of Proceedings was commenced in 1855, and valuable papers have been recently read at the meetings, which are held once a fortnight, from October to May, in the Agricultural Room of the Patent Office. The Library, which contains between three and four thousand volumes, with a considerable collection of maps, charts, and engravings, occupies a room in the same building. To these have been added a large and valuable collection of the crude and manufactured products of British Guiana, embracing all the woods of that country, in specimens of longitudinal and cross sections, numbering several hundred; all the fruits, seeds, medicinal roots, barks, models of houses, boats, furniture, manufactures of every kind, Indian curiosities, and implements, fibrous and textile fabrics, the birds (beautifully preserved), and a few of the quadrupeds. This collection was prepared, at very great expense, by a large number of the British residents of the colony, chiefly, it is believed, through the exertions of the late Consul of the United States, Mr. W. E. Dennison, and were designed first for exhibition at the New York Crystal Palace and afterwards to be deposited in the Federal Capitol.

Besides this, there has been added a large and valuable collection of British crude and manufactured products made by order of Her Majesty's Government, being a full duplicate of that exhibited at the London Crystal Palace in 1851, and subsequently at the New York Crystal Palace.

THE SMITHSONIAN INSTITUTION.

The liberal founder of this institution was James Smithson, whose will making the bequest for its support, dated October 23, 1826, commences with the following paragraph:—"I, James Smithson, son of Hugh, first Duke of Northumberland, and Elizabeth, heiress of the Hungerfords of Audley, and niece of Charles the Proud, Duke of Somer-

Instruction and Primary School Law of Michigan, with Explanatory Notes, Forms, Regulations, and Instructions; a Digest of Decisions; a Detailed History of Public Instruction, etc. Prepared by Francis W. Shearman. Published by the state in 1852.

set, now residing in Bentinck street, Cavendish square, do, &c." Mr. Smithson was the illegitimate son of a Duke of Northumberland. His mother was a Mrs. Macie, of an old family in Wiltshire, of the name of Hungerford. He was educated at Oxford, where he bore his mother's name. He distinguished himself by his proficiency in chemistry, and received an honorary degree at the university in 1786. He subsequently contributed a number of papers to the Philosophical Transactions of the Royal Society, of which he was a member, and to the Annals of Philosophy.* Provided with a liberal fortune by his father, he passed life as a bachelor, living in lodgings in London, and in the chief cities of the Continent. He was of feeble health and reserved manners.† At the time of his death in 1829 he resided at Genoa. His will provided that the bulk of his estate, in case of a failure of heirs to a nephew, should be given "to the United States of America, to found at Washington, under the name of the Smithsonian Institution, an establishment for the increase and diffusion of knowledge among men."

By the death of the nephew without heirs in 1835, the property devolved upon the United States. The testator's executors communicated the fact to the United States Chargé d'Affaires at London, by whom it was brought to the knowledge of the State Department at Washington. A message on the subject was sent to Congress by President Jackson, December 17, 1835. A Committee of the House of Representatives, of which John Quincy Adams was chairman, was appointed to examine the subject. In accordance with their report, Congress passed an act, July 1, 1836, authorizing the President to assert and prosecute with effect the right of the United States to the legacy, making provision for the reception of the fund by the Treasury, and pledging the national credit for its faithful application, "in such manner as Congress may hereafter direct." Mr. Richard Rush, the American Minister to Great Britain from 1817 to 1825, of which service he published a narrative, "A Residence at the Court of London," often referred to for its faithful and animated contemporary picture of the Court and Parliament, was appointed the agent to procure the fund. He discharged his duties with such ability that by the close of the year 1838, the American Secretary of the Treasury was in possession of a sum resulting from the bequest, of five hundred and fifteen thousand, one hundred and sixty-nine dollars.

For seven years the fund was suffered to accumulate without the object of the bequest having been fairly undertaken. In August, 1846, after considerable agitation of the subject in various forms, an act was passed by Congress constituting the President, Vice-President, the Secretaries of State, the Treasury, War, and the Navy; the Postmaster-General; the Attorney-General; the Chief Justice of the Supreme Court, the Commissioner of the Patent Office, and Mayor of Washington, and such persons as they might elect honorary members, an "establishment" under the name of "the Smithsonian Institution for the increase and diffusion of knowledge among men." The members and honorary members hold stated and special meetings for the supervision of the affairs of the Institution, and for advice and instruction of the actual managers, a Board of Regents, to whom the financial and other affairs are intrusted. The Board of Regents consists of three members *ex officio* of the establishment, namely, the Vice-President of the United States, the Chief Justice of the Supreme Court, and the Mayor of Washington, together with twelve other members, three of whom are appointed by the Senate from its own body, three by the House of Representatives from its members, and six citizens appointed by a joint resolution of both houses, of whom two are to be members of the National Institute, and resident in Washington; the remainder from the states, but not more than one from a single state. The terms of service of the members vary with the periods of office which give them the position. The citizens are chosen for six years. The Regents elect one of their number as Chancellor, and an Executive Committee of three.* This board elects a Secretary and other officers for conducting the active operations of the Institution.

The Act of Congress directs the formation of a library, a museum (for which it grants the collections belonging to the United States), and a gallery of art, together with provisions for physical research and popular lectures, while it leaves to the Regents the power of adopting such other parts of an organization as they may deem best suited to promote the objects of the bequest. The Regents, at a meeting in December, 1847, resolved to divide the annual income, which had become thirty thousand nine hundred and fifty dollars, into two equal parts, to be apportioned one part to the increase and diffusion of knowledge, by means of original research and publications; the other to be applied in accordance with the requirements of the Act of Congress, to the gradual formation of a Library, a Museum, and a Gallery of Art. In the details of the first, it was proposed "to stimulate research, by offering rewards, consisting of money, medals, &c., for original memoirs on all subjects of investigation;" the memoirs to be published in quarto, under the title of "Smithsonian Contributions to Knowledge," after having been approved of by a commission of persons of reputation in the particular branch of knowledge. No memoir on a subject of physical science is to be published, "which does not furnish a positive addition to human knowledge resting on original research;" and all unverified speculations to be rejected. It was also proposed "to appropriate a portion of the income annually to special objects of research, under the direction of suitable persons." Observations and experiments in the natural sciences, investigations in statistics, history, and ethnology, were to come under this head. The results

* An anecdote of Smithson's chemical pursuits has been preserved by Mr. Davies Gilbert, President of the Royal Society, in an address to that body in 1830.—"Mr. Smithson declared, that happening to observe a tear gliding down a lady's cheek he endeavored to catch it on a crystal vessel, that one-half of the drop escaped, but having preserved the other half, he submitted it to re-agents, and detected what was then called microcosmic salt, with muriate of soda, and, I think, three or four more saline substances, held in solution."

† Letter from the Hon. Richard Rush to the Hon. John Forsyth, London, May 12, 1838. Eighth Annual Report, Smithsonian Institution, p. 128.

* The body is thus arranged in 1855.

The Smithsonian Institution.

were to be published in quarto. For the diffusion of knowledge, it was proposed "to publish a series of reports, giving an account of the new discoveries in science, and of the changes made from year to year in all branches of knowledge not strictly professional," and also to publish occasionally separate treatises on subjects of general interest.

For the library it was proposed first, to form a complete collection of the transactions and proceedings of all the learned societies of the world, the more important current periodical publications, and a stock of all important works in bibliography.

The first of the series of original memoirs was the quarto volume of Messrs. Squier and Davis, on "The Ancient Monuments of the Mississippi Valley," published in 1848. This has since been followed by six others, composed of papers from various eminent scholars of the country, on special topics of astronomy, paleontology, physical geography, botany, philology, and other branches of science. Among the contributors are Mr. Sears C. Walker, astronomical assistant of the United States Coast Survey, of Researches relative to the Planet Neptune; Dr. Robert W. Gibbes, of South Carolina, of a paper on the Mososaurus; Dr. Robert Hare, on the Explosiveness of Nitre; several papers on Paleontology, by Dr. Joseph Leidy, Professor of Anatomy in the University of Pennsylvania; botanical articles, by Drs. Torrey and Gray; a Grammar and Dictionary of the Dakota language, collected by the members of the Dakota Mission, and edited by the Rev. S. R. Riggs of the American Board; and a paper by Mr. S. F. Haven, Librarian of the Antiquarian Society, Worcester, reviewing, for bibliographical and historical purposes, the literature and deductions respecting the subject of American antiquities. It should be mentioned, that though from their form the books are in the first instance expensive, yet as no copyright is taken, they may be freely reprinted, and disseminated in various ways.

Fifteen hundred copies of each of the "Memoirs" forming the Contributions are printed, which are distributed to learned societies and public libraries abroad and at home; states and territories, colleges, and other institutions of the United States. The publications of these several bodies are received in return. A system of the distribution of scientific works published by the government has become an important part of the useful agency of the institution in "diffusing knowledge among men" throughout the world.

An extensive system of meteorological observations, embracing the whole country, has been carried out by the institution. Several reports of the results have been published in a series of Temperature Tables, Tables of Precipitation, and Charts of Temperature, and a manual of directions and observations prepared by Mr. Arnold Guyot, author of a volume of lectures on comparative physical geography, entitled "Earth and Man," and Professor of Geology and Physical Geography in the College of New Jersey. The reduction of the observations collected by the Smithsonian system was performed from 1851 to 1854, by Mr. Lorin Blodget. Since his retirement from the duty, the materials have been sent for reduction to Professor James H. Coffin, of Lafayette College, Easton, Pa. Public lectures, of a popular character, are delivered in a room for the purpose in the Smithsonian building, during the winter. A small sum is paid to the lecturers, who have been among the chief professional and literary men of the country.

An extensive system of scientific correspondence is carried on by the officers of the society, who receive and communicate much valuable information in this way. The annual reports of the Regents, in their interest and variety, exhibit fully this development of the Institution.*

The building occupied by the Institution was completed in the spring of 1855. It is four hundred and twenty-six feet in length, and of irregular width and height. It was erected from the designs of Mr. James Renwick, of New York, and is in the Lombard style of architecture. Its cost, including furniture, is estimated at about three hundred thousand dollars.

The chief acting officer of the Institution is the Secretary, who has the general superintendence of its literary and scientific operations. He is aided by "an Assistant Secretary, acting as Librarian." The former office has been held from the commencement by Joseph Henry, late Professor of Natural Philosophy at the College of New Jersey, and author of a valuable series of Contributions to Electricity and Magnetism, published in the American Philosophical Transactions, Silliman's Journal, the Journal of the Franklin Institute, and other similar publications. He was the first to apply the principle of magnetism as a motor, and has made many other valuable contributions to science.

The first Assistant Secretary was Mr. Charles C. Jewett, former Professor of Modern Languages and Literature at Brown University. In his capacity of librarian, he prepared a valuable report on the Public Libraries of the United States of America, which was printed by order of Congress in 1850, as an appendix to the fourth annual report of the Board of Regents of the Institution. He also perfected a system of cataloguing public or other important libraries, by stereotyping separately the title of each work, so that in printing or reprinting, these plates may be used as type, securing both accuracy and economy.

Professor Spencer F. Baird, editor of the Iconographic Encyclopædia, is now Assistant Secretary, and has been actively engaged in the adjustment of the museum. The exchange of publications and specimens with foreign and domestic institutions, a work involving an immense amount of correspondence and other labor, are also under his care; besides which, he has aided in fitting out the natural history department of nearly all the government exploring expeditions for several years. A report from his pen, "On the Fishes observed on the coasts of New Jersey and Long Island during the summer of 1854," is appended to the Ninth Annual Report of the Institution.

Considerable agitation has arisen in the councils of the Institution and before the public, with respect to the disposition of the funds in the matter of the formation of a large public library. Congress, by the act of 1846, led by the eloquent speech of Rufus Choate the previous year on the subject in the Senate, and the advocacy of George P. Marsh in the House of Representatives, allowed an annual sum for this purpose of twenty-five thousand dollars.† The arrangement of the fund, however, and the views of the managers which have leaned rather to scientific than literary purposes, and promoted expensive schemes of publication, have thus far defeated this object. A struggle in the body of the Regents on the library question, and the exercise of discretion in the interpretation of the original act of Congress, has ended in the resignation of the Hon. Rufus Choate, member as citizen of Massachusetts, and the withdrawal of Mr. Charles C. Jewett, the assistant secretary, acting as librarian.*

The whole question is one of much intricacy of detail, involving the method of appropriation of the fund for building and the practical available resources on hand, as well as the theoretical adjustment of the respective claims of literature and science; and the relative advantages of a grand national library, and a system of learned publications.†

THE ASTOR LIBRARY, NEW YORK.

This institution was founded by the late John Jacob Astor of the city of New York, by a bequest which is thus introduced in a portion of his will, dated August 22, 1839: "Desiring to render a public benefit to the city of New York, and to contribute to the advancement of useful knowledge, and the general good of society, I do, by this codicil, appropriate four hundred thousand dollars out of my residuary estate, to the establishment of a public library in the city of New York." To carry out his intentions, he named as trustees the Mayor of the City and Chancellor of the State *ex officio;* Washington Irving, William B. Astor, Daniel Lord, jr., James G. King, Joseph G. Cogswell, Fitz Greene Halleck, Henry Brevoort, jr., Samuel B. Ruggles, Samuel Ward, jr., and Charles A. Bristed.

The trustees were incorporated by the state legislature in January, 1849. Mr. Washington Irving was immediately after elected President, and Mr. Joseph G. Cogswell, who had been long engaged in the work, having entered upon it previously to the death of Mr. Astor, was confirmed as superintendent. In the words of the Annual Report to the Legislature for 1858, signed by Mr. Washington Irving: "Mr Astor himself, during his life, had virtually selected Mr. Cogswell for that important post; and it is but due alike to both to add, that the success of the library must be mainly attributed to the wisdom of that selection."

---

* We would particularly refer to the Ninth Annual Report for the year 1854, for a highly interesting exhibition of the practical working of the Institution.

† When the Institution was set in motion in 1846, an additional sum of two hundred and forty-two thousand dollars had accrued from interest, which was allowed in the act of Congress for building purposes, leaving the income of the original sum, about thirty thousand dollars a year, for the support of the establishment. To increase this fund, a portion of the accumulated interest has been added to the principal, and gradual appropriations made for the buildings. Under this plan the objects of the Institution are somewhat delayed, but its income will hereafter be increased, it is calculated, by some ten thousand dollars per annum.

* Since the retirement of Mr. Jewett, the library has been placed temporarily under the charge of Mr. Charles Girard, a former pupil of Professor Agassiz, who is engaged on a catalogue of the publications of learned societies and periodicals in the library, the first part of which is published in Vol. vii. of the Contributions.

† We may refer for the arguments on this subject to the majority and minority reports in 1854, of the Hon. James A. Pearce and the Hon. James Meacham of the Special Committee of the Board of Regents on the Distribution of the Income. An article in the North American Review for October, 1854, by Mr. Charles Hale, gives the views of the "library" party.

The Astor Library.

By the terms of the bequest, seventy-five thousand dollars were allowed for the erection of the library building; one hundred and twenty thousand for purchasing books and furniture; while the remaining two hundred and five thousand dollars were to be invested "as a fund for paying the value of the site of the building, and for maintaining and gradually increasing the said library, and to defray the necessary expenses of taking care of the same, and of the accommodation of persons consulting the library." A site for the building was to be chosen from property of the testator on Astor or Lafayette Place. The selection was made from the latter, a plot of ground, sixty-five feet in front and rear, and one hundred and twenty feet in depth. Twenty-five thousand dollars were paid for this ground. The corner-stone of the building was laid in March, 1850; the whole was completed for the prescribed sum in the summer of 1853. The following extract from the Report for that year exhibits some interesting details of the excellent financial management which has attended this undertaking.

An additional expenditure of $1590, for groined arches, which became desirable to render the building more secure from fire, was liberally borne by Mr. William B. Astor. It was not practicable to include in this $75,000, sundry items of expense for equipping the building, including apparatus for warming, ventilating, and lighting, and the shelves needed for the books. The running length of the shelves is between twelve and thirteen thousand feet, and they have cost $11,000. The aggregate of these various items of equipment is $17,141.99. It has been paid mainly by surplus interest accruing from the funds while the building was in progress, amounting to 16,000.53, and the residue by a premium of $3672.87, which was realized from the advance in value of U. S. stocks, in which a part of the funds was temporarily invested; so that, after paying in full for the building and its equipments, the fund of $180,000 not only remains undiminished, but has been increased $2530.88. It is wholly invested in mortgages, except $3500 in U. S. stock, charged at par, but with 122 per cent. in market. There is no interest in arrear on any of the mortgages.

The statement with regard to the library fund is equally satisfactory.

Of the fund of $120,000, especially devoted to the purchase of books, the trustees cannot state with entire precision the amount expended up to December 31, 1853, for the reason given in the treasurer's report, that several of the bills and accounts yet remain unliquidated. He states, however, the amount actually advanced by him to be $91,513.83, and he estimates the unsettled bills at $4500, making $96,113.83 in all. This will leave an unexpended balance of $23,886.17 applicable to the further purchases of books, in addition to that part of the income of the $180,000 to be annually devoted to the gradual increase of the library. The number of volumes now purchased and on the shelves is about 80,000. The superintendent states that the expenditure of the remaining $23,886.17 will probably increase the number to one hundred thousand.

It is seldom that the collection of books of a public library is made with equal opportunities, and with equal ability and fidelity. From the outset the work has been systematically undertaken. The superintendent began his labors with the collection of an extensive series of bibliographical works provided at his own cost, and which he has generously presented to the library. While the building was in progress, Mr. Cogswell was employed in making the best purchases at home and abroad, visiting the chief book marts of Europe personally for this object. When the building, admirably adapted for its purpose, by its light, convenience, elegance, and stability, was ready, a symmetrical collection of books had been prepared for its shelves. The arrangement follows the classification of Brunet, in his "Manuel du Libraire." Theology, Jurisprudence, the Sciences and Arts (including Medicine, the Natural Sciences, Chemistry and Physics, Metaphysics and Ethics, the Mathematics, and the Fine Arts, separately arranged); Literature, embracing a valuable linguistic collection, and a distinct grouping of the books of the ancient and modern tongues; History, with its various accessories of Biography, Memoirs, its Civil and Ecclesiastical divisions and relations to various countries—follow each other in sequence.

To these divisions is to be added "a special technological department, to embrace every branch of practical industry and the mechanic arts," generously provided for at an expense of more than twelve thousand dollars, by a gift from Mr. William B. Astor.

With respect to the extent of the use of the library, we find the following interesting statement in the Annual Report of the Superintendent, dated Jan. 1855.

One hundred volumes a day is a low average of the daily use, making the whole number which have been in the hands of readers since it was opened about 30,000, and as these were often single volumes of a set of from two to fifty volumes, it may be considered certain that more than half of our whole collection has been wanted during the first year. But this is a matter in which numerical statistics do not afford much satisfaction; nothing short of a specification of the books read or consulted would show the importance which the library is to the public, as a source of information and knowledge, and as this cannot be given, a more general account must serve as a substitute. On observing the classes and kinds of books which have been called for, I have been particularly struck with the evidence thus afforded of the wide range which the American mind is now taking in thought and research; scholastic theology, transcendental metaphysics, abstruse mathematics, and oriental philology have found many more readers than Addison and Johnson; while on the other hand, I am happy to be able to say, that works of practical science and of knowledge for every-day use, have been in great demand. Very few have come to the library without some manifestly distinct aim; that is, it has been little used for mere desultory reading, but for the most part with a specific view. It would not be easy to say which department is most consulted, but there is naturally less dependence upon the library for books of theology, law, and medicine, than in the others, the three faculties being better provided for in the libraries of the institutions especially intended for them. Still, in each of these departments, the library has many works not elsewhere to be found. It is now no longer merely a matter of opinion; it is shown by experience that the collection is not too learned for the wants of the public. No one fact will better illustrate this position than the following: in the linguistic department it possesses dictionaries and grammars, and other means of instruction in more than a hundred languages and dialects, four-fifths of which have been called for during the first year of its operation. Our mathematical, mechanical and engineering departments are used by great numbers, and they are generally known to be so well furnished, that students from a distance have found it a sufficient object to induce them to spend several weeks in New York to have the use of them. The same remark applies to natural history, all branches of which are studied here. In entomology we are said to have the best and fullest collection in this country to which naturalists have free access. Passing to the historical side of the library we come to a department in which a very general interest has been taken—far more general than could have been anticipated in our country—it is that of heraldry and genealogy. Among the early purchases for the library there were but few books of this class, as it was supposed but few would be wanted; a year or two's experience proved the contrary, and the collection has been greatly enlarged; it is now sufficiently ample to enable any one to establish his armorial bearings, and trace his pedigree at least as far back as the downfall of the Western empire. From this rapid glance at the library, it has been seen that there are students and readers in all departments of it, and that no one greatly preponderates over the rest; still I think it may be stated, that on the whole that of the fine arts, taken collectively, is the one which has been most extensively used; practical architects and other artists have had free access to it, many of whom have often had occasion to consult it.

The arrangements of the library afford every requisite facility for the consultation of these books. It is open to visitors from all parts of the country or the world, without fee or special introduction. All may receive the benefit of its liberal endowment. It is simply to open the door, ascend the cheerful stairway to the main room, and write on a printed form provided the title of a desired volume. As every day finds the library richer in books, and a system of special catalogues by departments is in preparation, creating new facilities in the use of them, the visitor will soon, if he may not already, realize the prediction of Mr. George Bancroft, "of what should and must become the great library of the Western Continent." We could, at the close of our long journey in these volumes, wish for no more cheerful omen of the bountiful literary future.

THE END

INDEX.

[The capitals indicate the longer biographical articles, which may be consulted for the detailed account of the persons referred to. The names in italics indicate the selections.]

Milton Keynes UK
Ingram Content Group UK Ltd.
UKHW040632170124
436182UK00004B/134

CW00516996

Australian PRIME MINISTERS

Edited by Michelle Grattan

Delegates to the discussions in 1900 in London with the British Government on Australian Federation: Alfred Deakin and Edmund Barton, both future Australian prime ministers, Sir James Dickson, Sir Philip Fysh, and Charles Kingston.

A group of past Australian prime ministers gather in July 2000 at Buckingham Palace, London, to commemorate the centenary of Federation: Malcolm Fraser (1975–83), Bob Hawke (1983–91), incumbent prime minister John Howard, Queen Elizabeth II, Sir John Gorton (1968–71) and Gough Whitlam (1972–75).

Preface

to the revised edition

This book was originally prepared to coincide with the Centenary of Australia's Federation. Since then, the prime ministership of John Howard has ended and that of Kevin Rudd begun. When the book was written, Howard had already laid down important markers for his time as the nation's leader, but had not yet reached what would be the halfway mark of his term as PM. Kevin Rudd was a relative newcomer to the federal Parliament. In this edition the original introduction has been left virtually unchanged; it should be read as an essay on the first 100 years. The Howard chapter has been rewritten and extended as we can now make judgements about his full political career. A chapter about Rudd has been added. Rudd's term has become the prime-ministership-in progress, sharing much with those who have gone before but, as always when the political wheel turns, full of the promise and excitement of its infancy.

MICHELLE GRATTAN, March 2008

Acknowledgements

Many people contributed to this book. My first thanks are to the writers, not just for their pieces, but also for their patience in dealing with many editorial queries. Some kindly also read and commented on the introduction. Gia Metherell has been the backbone of the project: besides selecting and gathering a fine range of pictures, she prepared the table of prime ministerial backgrounds and helped me with research for the introduction and the Howard chapter. Judith Ion, Pera Wells, Gabrielle Hooton and Karen Ingram have also assisted with research and checking. Paul Kelly and the late Ron Younger read drafts, spotted errors, made invaluable suggestions and gave general encouragement. Kate Merrifield, project coordinator, coped with innumerable faxes, often handwritten, corrections, and third and fourth thoughts with extraordinary equanimity. Deborah Nixon, publisher, was supportive at difficult times and perceptive; Jacqueline Kent contributed ideas as well as copy editing a text made more difficult by the number of authors. Thanks also to Michael McGrath for his help and patience with the revision.

Published in Australia by
New Holland Publishers (Australia) Pty Ltd
Sydney • Auckland • London • Cape Town

1/66 Gibbes Street Chatswood NSW 2067 Australia
218 Lake Road Northcote Auckland New Zealand
86 Edgware Road London W2 2EA United Kingdom
80 McKenzie Street Cape Town 8001 South Africa

First published in 2000 and reprinted in 2000, 2001, 2003, 2006
Revised edition 2008, reprinted in 2009

National Library of Australia Cataloguing-in-Publication Data:
Australian prime ministers.
Includes bibliographical references and index.
ISBN 978 1 74110 7272 (hbk)

1. Prime ministers – Australia – Biography. 2. Australia – Politics and government. I. Grattan, Michelle. II. Title.

994.040922

Publisher: Fiona Schultz
Editor: Michelle Grattan
Project Editor: Michael McGrath
Proofreader: Maria Sutera
Designer: Tania Gomes
Cover Design: Gomes/McGrath
Production Manager: Olga Dementiev
Printer: Mcpherson's Printing Group, Maryborough, Victoria

Contents

Introduction

Australians are largely ignorant about their early prime ministers, and frequently cynical about their more contemporary national leaders. Our history studies have been light on personalities; our media defines politics in terms of them. As the nation prepared to celebrate its hundredth birthday, the National Council for the Centenary of Federation commissioned research that found Edmund Barton, the founding prime minister, was a forgotten figure by the end of the century that he ushered in – 64 per cent had not heard of him. The council ran advertisements asking, 'What kind of country would forget the name of its first prime minister?'

The first hundred years of nationhood saw 25 prime ministers, a rich cast of characters, diverse in personality, background, ability and achievement but sharing (even the more unlikely of them) a common drive for power. We get the leaders we deserve, the cliche says. In a century of leaders, however, Australians have got all sorts of deserts. As sociologist Sol Encel wrote, '[t]here is no such thing as an identikit for a prime minister'.[1]

Imagine, if you will, this select band gathered in the vast Members' Hall of Parliament House. Only three (Bob Hawke, Paul Keating and John Howard) are familiar with this imposing and impersonal space, flanked by the Cabinet suite, the Senate and the House of Representatives, and with a covered reflecting pool in the middle. For the others, 'Parliament House' was the white wedding-cake building down the road, suited to intimacy and intrigue, or, in the case of those serving before 1927, the stately Victorian Parliament at the top of Melbourne's Bourke Street. Picture the cultivated Alfred Deakin reminiscing with Barton about their shared struggle to Federation: the town meetings, the referenda, the setbacks, the ultimate triumph. Perhaps they're chuckling over that day in London negotiating a crucial detail of the Constitution, when in a moment of exultation they and Charles Kingston, 'three middle-aged and solidly built statesmen', 'seized each other's hands and danced, in a ring, round the room'.[2] As they talk, Deakin, whom Joseph Cook likened to a 'beautiful, stately but timid giraffe',[3] casts a journalistic eye over his surroundings. Even as PM, Deakin wrote regular despatches to the London *Morning Post* as its anonymous 'Australian Correspondent'. These frequently commented on the doings of Mr Deakin – an arrangement, as he said, 'fit for fiction rather than real life'.[4]

Look again and here is the indefatigable Billy Hughes, a man with a 'wardrobe of masks'[5] and unquenchable ambition, who coveted the attorney-generalship (again, and in vain) in his eighties. He might be exchanging a word with Joe Lyons, whom the prime ministership killed: they share the tag of Labor 'rats' who split their parties and crossed over to lead the conservative forces. Over there are the heroes of 'old Labor', John Curtin, who conquered alcoholism but never his brooding depression, and Ben Chifley, always ready with support, off to the Lodge in response to a note in which the wartime PM pleaded for company when he felt 'spiritually bankrupt'. Chris Watson might glance at them with a touch of envy: they're celebrated, but the man who led the world's first national Labor government is only an historical footnote. Watson's another in the club of 'rats', but he left Labor's ranks after, not before or during, his prime ministership; the party forgave him enough to mourn him when he died.

Bob Hawke is smiling as he mingles, but suddenly his face darkens: he's remembering that summer day when caucus 'ratted' on him to elect Keating, although Hawke had delivered more elections than any other Labor PM. A little apart is Gough Whitlam, who made himself and his party the voices of 'suburbia', where the working class of the 1920s, 1930s, and 1940s transformed into the mortgaged middle class of the 1950s, 1960s and 1970s. Keating stands alone, popular with 1990s Labor 'true believers', but his place in history forged as treasurer in the 1980s rather than as prime minister. Now we spy Stanley Melbourne Bruce, the very name conjuring up the Cambridge-educated conservative gentleman politician who could have stepped out of a Scott Fitzgerald novel that celebrated his era, albeit in another country.

Whitlam might soon wander over, recalling a visit to Parliament as a twelve-year-old when the only occupant of the government front bench was Bruce, 'sprawling on it and wearing spats'. And there is Labor's Jim Scullin, who never had a hope against the Depression, an 'unlucky Prime Minister' for whom '[e]vents were too much'.[6] Could he be talking to Malcolm Fraser, blown away by a relatively mild economic chill in the 1980s? And look at Howard giving the briefest nod to Fraser, his one-time leader, but falling into deep conversation with John Gorton: straitlace meets larrikin. As we overhear the Country Party's Earle Page snarling about Hughes and Robert Menzies and witness 'Black Jack' John McEwen's hostile glare at Bill McMahon, watch how the imperial Menzies is slipping 'Chif' a recent whodunnit, in the spirit of friendship that sometimes exists alongside the conflict. Visualise many of these men eyeing each other, reliving the bitter enmities among allies as well as between opponents, fights over elections and successions. Then something strange happens. They fall to comparing how much they have in common as members of the nation's most exclusive club.

When Whitlam won the 1972 'It's Time' election, Menzies sent him a message. 'You have been emphatically called to an office of great power and great responsibility', Menzies wrote. 'Nobody knows better than I do what demands will be made upon your mental vigour and physical health. I hope you will be able to maintain both …' Whitlam responded:

> I was profoundly moved by your magnanimous message on my election to this great office. No Australian is more conscious than I how much the lustre, honour and authority of that office owe to the manner in which you held it with such distinction for so long. No Australian understands better than you the private feelings of one now facing the change from the years of leading the Opposition to the burdens and rewards of leading the nation. You would, I think, be surprised to know how much I feel indebted to your example, despite the great differences in our philosophies. In particular, your remarkable achievement in rebuilding your own party and bringing it so triumphantly to power within six years has been an abiding inspiration to me.[7]

Of course, sometimes the hatreds endure to the grave. Possibly one or two invitations to our function might be returned on the grounds of unacceptable company. But despite the passions and angers of the political divides, there's a certain fellow feeling among those who have been prime minister. They have experienced the burdens and responsibilities of a job rewarded more modestly than a pop star and almost always ending in tears. A handful of staff and senior public servants (and the families) observe the relentless pressure at one remove. But only other occupants of the office can completely understand. This can lead to some unexpected bonds. The nation's constitutional system was strained frighteningly by the

1975 crisis – or so it seemed at the time – when Fraser's Opposition blocked the Whitlam government's budget and Governor-General Sir John Kerr stepped in to break the deadlock by sacking Whitlam and installing Fraser as caretaker PM. A quarter of a century later, Fraser and Whitlam appeared side by side in a pro-republic television advertisement. They agreed 'it's time' to change the system. By now they thought a republic could have prevented the crisis they had created.

In longevity and mythology, positive and negative, Menzies stands out in the ranks of Australian prime ministers, the stayer, serving a total of more than eighteen years, in two spells.[8] The first began at the end of the 1930s, as Australia, still in Britain's shadow, headed towards World War II. The second ended in the mid 1960s; Australia still wore some of its insular garb but it was changing and diversifying, economically and socially. It was also deeply embroiled in the Vietnam conflict, driven by Cold War fears, American connections and a recurring dread of a threat from the north. Menzies has been a reference point for successors. Howard pays homage. Labor critics deride him for doing so little in so long. But even Keating, telling staff after the 1993 election that he needed to get above the ruck, is reported to have said: 'For want of a better word, I should be more Menzian.'[9]

At the other end of the time line from Menzies' generational reign, three caretaker PMs, Labor's Frank Forde and the Country Party's Earle Page and John McEwen, were in office eight days, 20 days and 23 days respectively.[10] The latter two made brutal use of their seat-warming power. McEwen exercised a veto to drive McMahon out of the Liberal contest for the prime minister's job. In 1939 Page unsuccessfully tried to stymie Menzies' prime ministerial chances (as CP leader, Page had caused the fall of Hughes nearly two decades earlier). The only other CP prime minister, Artie Fadden, was a stopgap who fell in 40 days. Fadden was one of the several post-1927 PMs not to move into the Lodge (the others were Scullin, Chifley and Howard).[11] A Country Party colleague presciently advised Fadden: 'Artie, you'll scarcely have enough time to wear a track from the back door to the shithouse before you'll be out.' The shortest-serving of the other PMs was Watson, in office in 1904 for less than four months.[12]

In the opening decade of Federation, five men held the prime ministership in seven changes of office;[13] in contrast, one held the job through the whole of the 1950s and half the 1960s and another for most of the 1980s. In the fluid early days of the Commonwealth, with the party system yet to polarise, the Protectionist liberal Deakin had three separate periods in the job.[14] So did Labor's Andrew Fisher.[15] Apart from these two and Menzies, no one has had broken periods in office.

Three PMs have died in power (Lyons, Curtin and Harold Holt, who drowned). Of the rest, leaving aside the caretakers, almost all went out involuntarily, through defeat in elections or by parliamentary vote, party coups or pressure, or ill health. It's a job of high insecurity: indeed not even success, as measured by election victories, is a surefire guarantee of survival. Of the postwar prime ministers Chifley, McMahon, Fraser, Keating and Howard [in 2007] were defeated at the ballot box; Whitlam, after being dismissed by the governor-general when he failed to have his Budget ratified by an intransigent Senate, lost the subsequent election. John Gorton was torpedoed by his party, quitting the leadership when the party room was tied on a vote of confidence. After leading Labor to a record four election wins, Hawke then lost a caucus ballot to challenger Keating. Those PMs who exited of their own choosing were Menzies, Barton and Fisher, although debates could be had about the latter two.

Tossed or forced out of the job, some have left Parliament at once (including Fraser, Hawke and Keating); others have fought on in opposition or government to serve others or resurrect themselves. Cook was prime minister for only fifteen months in 1913–14, but then acting PM from April to September 1921 when Hughes was overseas. Some look back, from inside or outside Parliament, with feelings of anger, regret, or relevance deprivation. Hughes plotted for literally decades; in Donald Horne's description, 'a little bag of bones done up in gent's natty suiting',[16] he died still a parliamentarian, aged ninety. Bruce, ensconced in London, toyed with the idea of a deal with conservative powerbrokers to return him to Parliament and the prime ministership, but he only wanted to be a 'non-party' leader. George Reid sat in the House of Commons in retirement. Forde sat in the Queensland Parliament. Several early PMs parachuted into the high commissionership in London. Two recent departees, Hawke and Keating, set themselves up as consultants and facilitators for international business.

It is hard to imagine a former PM these days battling on like a Hughes or an early Menzies. Yet after being routed in 1975 Whitlam stayed to lead Labor in 1977 (only to suffer a second humiliation). For all its exhilaration, there's mostly a certain sense of inevitable denouement about the prime ministerial career: the high hopes and ambitious programs followed by the inevitable falling short, and souring of public opinion, which grows ever more fickle. Few modern ex-prime ministers seem to build an entirely satisfying post-prime ministerial life. Arguably, we do not deal well with our former leaders. Or perhaps the aura and power of the office make its occupant seem larger than life, including to himself; when that goes, he feels like a fallen giant.

Non-Labor governments held office for just over two-thirds of the century following Federation – 67-plus years compared with 32-plus years. After World War II, the non-Labor parties occupied the Treasury benches for some 35 years to Labor's more than 20 years. Of the 25 prime ministers in the century, 15 were non-Labor, nine Labor, while Hughes served for just over a year as Labor prime minister before defecting and forming the National Labor Party, which quickly merged with the Liberal Party to become the Nationalist Government.

Five of Australia's first seven leaders were foreign born – Watson, Reid, Fisher, Cook and Hughes.[17] All came from the British Isles except Watson, who was born in Chile.[18] No prime minister since Hughes has been born overseas. The nation's leaders have come predominantly from the eastern seaboard mainland states. Only Curtin and Hawke were from Western Australia[19] (and Curtin had gone there, from Victoria, while Hawke, born in South Australia, had left WA for Victoria). Lyons was the only Tasmanian. Leaving aside its possible claim to Hawke, South Australia has not had a prime minister.

Many of the nation's leaders have come from modest origins, even on the conservative side. No fewer than eleven have had legal qualifications: in Hughes' case, acquired while in Parliament – and he served as attorney-general. Their pre-parliamentary employment included a wide range of jobs. Tough starts were the norm rather than the exception – especially in the early days and among Labor – but wealthy parents have not been a prerequisite for top office in the conservative ranks. Watson left school at ten to work on the railways before becoming an apprentice in the printing trade at thirteen. Fisher quit school early to work in the coalmines of Scotland. Cook at the age of nine began as a pitboy in England. Hughes' early career included unskilled work, union organising, shopkeeping and much else. Scullin was a farmhand, woodchopper, miner and shopkeeper.

Lyons was a messenger when he was nine, and a scrub cutter at twelve. At fifteen, Fadden was a canecutter; later he qualified as an accountant and set up his own business. The ill-health of his father saw Curtin working from age thirteen to help support his family. Chifley drove trains; later he romanticised 'the eyes of 14 carriages looking at you round the bends'; the whistles of engines were 'music to me still'.[20] The majority of the non-Labor prime ministers had fathers who were in business, large or small. None of the last half dozen incumbents of the century, three Liberal, three Labor, experienced the struggletown upbringing of many of their predecessors. McMahon was from a wealthy Sydney family; Whitlam's father was crown solicitor; Fraser came from a grazing family; Hawke was son of a clergyman;[21] Keating's working-class father later had a successful small business; the Howards operated a suburban garage.

Half the Labor PMs were from Irish Catholic backgrounds, with Watson, Fisher, Whitlam and Hawke notable exceptions. Lyons has been the only Catholic conservative prime minister – and he came from Labor ranks. About half the prime ministers were educated at state primary schools; about five attended state secondary schools. Around ten attended private secondary schools, some (like Menzies) on scholarships. Five went to both state and Catholic schools. Several did not finish secondary school, leaving at the age of thirteen or younger. More than one-third had no tertiary qualifications. Four, one of them Labor, studied at Oxbridge: Bruce at Cambridge, and Fraser, Gorton and Hawke (a Rhodes Scholar) at Oxford.

Looking at their stories one is struck by how many had hard young lives. Often they battled with personal deprivation and trauma. Fisher's father was forced to stop mining after contracting pneumoconiosis. Cook's father was killed in a mining accident when Joseph was twelve, leaving him 'as eldest son, ... head of the family and its principal breadwinner'.[22] Hughes' mother died when he was seven. Lyons' father, after losing all his money on the Melbourne Cup, suffered a breakdown. The financial crash of the 1890s saw Page's father ruined. Chifley was sent to live with his grandfather when he was five; he said later, 'I went for a holiday and came back nine years later'.[23] McEwen lost his mother when he was an infant and his father when he was seven. Gorton's mother, who was his father's de facto wife, died when he was seven. McMahon's mother died when he was four and his father when he was sixteen. Howard's father died when Howard was sixteen.[24] It could be said that many of them were forced to become adults before their time, assuming responsibilities and making decisions. Many too, were early self-improvers – voracious readers and, among the earlier, more impoverished ones, diligent attenders at night school.

A few have had dream runs to power. Bruce entered Parliament in 1918, became treasurer in 1921 and prime minister in early 1923. Hawke was elected in 1980, Opposition leader the day the 1983 election was called and PM within weeks. Howard, in contrast, defied big odds to get the job long after he was written off. The office in Australia has been an exclusively male world. In the nation's first 100 years, there was never a prospect of a woman holding the top job.

The century of PMs can be placed into four very broad time groupings. The early national leaders – between 1901 and World War I – were creating the framework and architecture of the fledgling nation that was starting out in a mood of optimism and a time of economic prosperity. Barton, Deakin and Reid had major parts of their careers already behind them in the struggle to nationhood. Barton and Deakin had been the most enthusiastic federationists; Reid had been the voice of caution, pressing amendments to the proposed Constitution.

The new nation also saw the Labor Party consolidating as a major political force of the future: Watson and Fisher helped shape it. The early governments put in place national institutions, including the High Court and the arbitration system. Although the protection-versus-free trade argument that had been the big divide in colonial politics continued for several years, the new federation enshrined the high tariff policy that would be accepted for most of the century. There was all-round agreement on the White Australia Policy, which was quickly translated into legislation and then upheld by every prime minister until Holt. The Fisher Labor government introduced social legislation but set a pattern for the future when its several referenda to extend Commonwealth powers failed. Meanwhile the shifting, fractured party system, cause of much manoeuvring and time-wasting in the early Federation years, had moved to the broad Labor versus non-Labor model that would endure – despite schisms on the Labor side and new starts by the conservatives – for the rest of the century.

The next clutch of leaders, those in office between World War I and the end of World War II, had to confront national crises on a scale not experienced by any of their successors. World War I took a huge toll of young Australian manhood, while forging the Anzac tradition. Conscription split the country in 1916–17, with Hughes the dividing force, and fractured the Labor Party. World War II – only time Australia has faced the threat of invasion – saw an often traumatised Curtin agonising over decisions with life and death implications for thousands of Australian fighting men, but this time Labor was able to manage the conscription debate. In between, Scullin's prime ministership was destroyed, in bitterness and desperation, by a depression that brought misery and economic wrangling, a time when '[h]uman impatience was aroused to fever pitch by unemployment, poverty, and suffering' and '[a]lmost hourly, for months, Canberra dreaded tidings of a major uprising'.[25] Some had the easier years of this gruelling generation: Bruce oversaw the 1920s but lost office and his seat (something that happened to no other PM until Howard in 2007) just as the Depression hit. Lyons' 1930s period saw the nation climb out of the economic pit, but his leadership was under threat when he died.

Those who governed between the end of World War II and the early 1970s were confronted with the challenge of strengthening and managing a diversifying economy and changing the social face of a country that continued to place a high value on being one people. Chifley started the giant Snowy Mountains scheme, a symbol of postwar Australia, and Menzies and his successors completed it. When the scheme celebrated its fiftieth anniversary in 1999 it was said that it could never be built now: people had become too cautious, rules and regulations too prohibitive. The Chifley government, and later Menzies, oversaw the transformation of Australia under mass migration. It changed the face of the country and attitudes changed with it – although slowly. In the 1950s migrants were 'New Australians', a term that summed up the assimilationist approach. It would take until the late 1970s and 1980s for multiculturalism to come into full play, but by then, with the era of 'full employment' a thing of the past, immigration had become a subject of sharp political dispute.

In the last quarter of the century the issue facing prime ministers and their governments was the internationalising of the economy. The oil shock of the early 1970s sent the warning signals and delivered a body blow to the Whitlam government. Hawke was the first of the modern 'economic rationalist' prime ministers, despite Fraser's 'smaller government' rhetoric. The opening and reforming of the Australian economy cut across party lines; it was a unifying policy theme of the 1980s–1990s Labor governments and the Coalition government of the later 1990s as they responded to globalising pressures.

Through the century of Federation, Australia's place in the world was a preoccupation of its prime ministers. But the content of that place has changed dramatically. The young nation saw itself both under Britain's wing and automatically her ally. Still, the mother country had to be watched or the far-flung parts of the Empire could find their interests overlooked. PMs made frequent trips 'home'. Nearing mid century loyalties, based on pragmatism, became divided: Curtin, despite his earlier anti-imperial stance and his famous 1941 appeal to the United States, in 1943 was casting Australia's future place firmly in the setting of the British Empire, which he described as 'an instinctive association, which has been sanctified by blood'.[26] The Empire link was in part protection against the 'teeming millions of coloured races' to Australia's north.[27]

Menzies was an Empire man, but geopolitical and security realities of the cold war era were pushing Australia towards America. Increasingly from the 1960s the region became the focal point, militarily, in trade and diplomatically, partly as a consequence of the US alliance, which saw the politically divisive commitment to the Vietnam War, but also as Australia sought to forge a middle power role and come to terms with its neighbourhood. All PMs have to deal with foreign policy but some come to it with more enthusiasm and ambition than others. Fraser stretched into issues – Rhodesian independence, the 'north-south' dialogue between developed and developing countries – far beyond Australia's sphere of immediate influence. Hawke and Keating were strong regional players, the former being a creator of the Asia Pacific Economic Co-operation forum and the latter concluding a security agreement with Indonesia (which the Indonesians repudiated in 1999 during the East Timor crisis). The attraction of foreign policy for a prime minister is great, even when he has taken little interest previously. At one point in Keating's treasurership Japanese diplomats asked the writer why he was so reluctant to visit their country; as PM, he was an Asia enthusiast.

During the century, the job of prime minister changed hugely, while also retaining its essence. That essence is power. The prime minister has more formal and direct political power than any other single figure in our system. The qualifications 'formal' and 'direct' are important, because the limits on the PM's power are also strong and come from several sources, including Cabinet, Parliament, party, media and – most obviously – the electorate. Looking at the power of the prime minister is like the old conundrum of whether the glass is half full or half empty. The power is great, but so are the restraints. Professor Pat Weller says:

> The power is institutional, not personal. Prime ministers are at the centre of a swirling torrent of political forces. They cannot exercise authority in all directions at once; the resources of an individual are limited. Judgements have to be made about which initiative will be pursued, which will be delayed and what the costs of decisions will be. Prime ministers must constantly negotiate and usually compromise. They are not the only actors in the political game; other ministers, business and union leaders, backbenchers, the media, all have to be taken into account. Political support must be gained and then painstakingly retained; it cannot just be demanded and then taken for granted. Governing is for prime ministers a continuous estimation of how others will react to the use of power, and how much effort is needed to achieve a desired end. Prime Ministers' power and time are not infinite.[28]

On the other hand a senior prime ministerial adviser is struck by just 'how powerful they can be – a prime minister has more votes than his Cabinet colleagues put together. I thought the process was a tad more democratic [than this] but even in a country like Australia, one man can wield a hell of a lot of authority. It's only when people lose confidence in the person making the decisions that that authority is dissipated.'[29]

Non-Labor PMs have been able to choose their ministries – within the practical limits of accommodating states, internal party groupings and coalition partners. Labor's first and last prime ministers of the century had that freedom: Watson had it before the caucus-choice system came to prevail: Keating in effect insisted on it and his wish was granted after he clinched the unwinnable election in 1993. Like their non-Labor counterparts, Labor PMs have always been able to allocate the portfolios. [Kevin Rudd chose his own ministers and moved to ensure that future Labor leaders have that right in the new century.]

In the years since Federation the prime ministership has gone from the age of horse and buggy and primitive motor car to the jet era. Distance has been one defining factor in Australian politics. In earlier days, politicians travelled the country by train, working and socialising on the long trips to and from parliamentary sittings first in Melbourne and then Canberra. Those from the West had to spend many weekends in the 'bush capital' before fast flights made a dash back to electorate and family the practice between back-to-back sittings. Modern transport has made prime ministerial domestic travel easier. But it has also led to the occupants of the office feeling the need to do more of it. Technology and the imperatives of politics have shrunk overseas trips from months – in Hughes's case well over a year, with war diplomacy stretching into the Versailles Peace Conference – to days. By Whitlam's time a trip of more than a month invited strong political attack. No new century PM would consider spending more than about a fortnight out of the country at any one time.

Has the prime minister's job become more difficult? The knee-jerk answer must be 'of course'. But what is 'difficult'? It certainly has become more complicated; not only is modern policy often highly complex, but the federal government is involved in a vastly more extensive range of policy than initially. Did Howard have tougher responsibilities than Curtin had in the depths of wartime, or Scullin as he grappled with a depression the likes of which the country has not seen since? The circumstances of the time determine how grave are the decisions to be made. But the quantity of demands on the prime minister has grown exponentially, and so has his daily exposure and accountability. Today's PM has to be personally familiar with nearly every aspect of government. Those who want to lobby government, whether interest groups or companies, have the resources to do so, and the PM must personally see many of them. Modern transport, modern communications and modern life means there's nowhere to hide (apart from occasionally in a dressing room, of which more later).

No modern PM takes on a specific portfolio. Yet for half a century it was commonplace for the PM to also have a major ministry. Barton, Deakin and Reid held the position of minister for external affairs. (Indeed for the first decade of Federation, the PM did not have his own department; bureaucratically, he sat within the Department of External Affairs.[30]) Watson was treasurer; so was Fisher, in each of his three terms; Chifley, treasurer under Curtin, kept that job when he became PM and even stayed in his old parliamentary office. As recently as the 1970s, Whitlam was minister for foreign affairs for part of his prime ministership.

The paraphernalia underpinning the prime ministership has expanded enormously. Today's PM has an all-up staff of around forty, a proliferation that began in the 1970s. But even at the start the need for some 'political' staff help was recognised. Barton appointed Thomas Bavin (later NSW premier) as his secretary, telling Parliament 'if I did not have the services of a private secretary allowed me, I should be so seriously hampered that I should have to consider whether I could do the work'.[31] While early private secretaries served several prime ministers, the need for compatibility was recognised. In 1916 Percy Deane was brought in from outside the public service; his rapid rise, it was reported, was due to his 'genius' for getting on with Hughes: 'When the great man was ruffled Deane alone could unruffle him.'[32] Generations of personal minders have been 'unruffling' their PMs ever since.

From Whitlam on, prime ministers have increasingly wanted their own firepower to second-guess the bureaucracy. They also came to trust that bureaucracy less and less. When Menzies took over from Chifley, he left in place Chifley's top bureaucrats. When Howard defeated Keating, he sacked one-third of the departmental heads immediately. Through the years the Prime Minister's Department has adapted to the needs and priorities of its political master. From 1950 to 1966 it had responsibility for education, reflecting in part Menzies' personal interest in the area. In Fraser's time the department built a quick-fix capability, with its experts being alternative sources of advice in major policy areas. Ministers could easily find themselves sidelined; for example, during controversy over health policy, the PM's Department produced a reworked scheme for Fraser.

The modern PM has moved towards, but not to, the presidential style. Since the Liberals in 1968 chose Gorton over the intellectual but introverted Hasluck, largely because they thought Gorton a better television performer, media skills have been a paramount requirement for the job. Clem Lloyd has argued elsewhere that more than any other factor 'the conduct of the contemporary Australian prime ministership has been shaped by the impact of television'.[33] Radio is nearly as vital to the modern prime ministership, the medium of an extended conversation with the electorate. The television news cycle has transformed electioneering; the hall meeting giving way to the staged 'pic fac', the outdoor oratory to the studio interview skill. Modern PMs are exceptionally media alert. Howard listened to early morning radio while taking his daily walk, then rang his media staff to put the reaction into action. Blanket and instant media coverage has also brought more minute scrutiny, and increased the risks of the job, both because the PM receives more exposure and because errors are more obvious and instantly spotted and reported. When Howard, talking on radio about the petrol pricing aspect of his tax package made a tiny slip in the amount involved, the news that night picked up on it as the PM not knowing the details of his own policy.

For all the change, the driving force behind prime ministers' communications strategies, styles and methods is the same: getting the message across. In an era when media numbers were fewer, television not on the scene and relations between politicians and the Canberra press gallery more personal, Curtin briefed journalists twice a day, often with highly confidential information that was meant more for passing on to proprietors than for immediate publication. It was an effective pitch. At times the media/prime ministerial relationship is close; not infrequently it is raw, though usually leaders check their tongues more than Gorton when he referred to some journalists as 'slimy white things that crawl out of sewers'.[34]

Apart from selling themselves and their governments to the public, PMs through the century and across parties have other central aspects of work in common: presiding over Cabinet, answering to Parliament, massaging their party. But the quantity and range of work has changed during the century [and beyond] and methods of handling the load vary between incumbents, down to whether they are 'morning' or 'night' people. John Bunting, Cabinet secretary, contrasted Menzies' preference for not arriving at the office before 9.45am with that of his successor Holt, 'whose day began at seven, or even six with the first newspaper deliveries ... But his was a day that mainly wound down, whereas the Menzies day wound upwards.'[35]

Whatever the individual habits, 'the work and the pressure are unremitting. There is no escape. There is no opportunity for any prime minister to be at other than full pitch virtually all the time, whatever his inclinations to the contrary. The only true respite is sleep, and there is little enough of that.'[36] Some have been neat managers of Cabinet; under others, it's been a shambles. Bruce as treasurer under Hughes concluded 'it was impossible to have any well regulated procedures for the Cabinet. As a result I ceased putting items on the Cabinet Agenda with regard to Treasury matters and simply went ahead and did whatever I thought was necessary.'[37] As PM, Bruce, reflecting his business background, sought a methodical approach to administration. The official history of the Prime

Minister's Department records that Bruce 'insisted that ministers prepare briefs on their agenda items, and discuss these privately with the Prime Minister before Cabinet met. In this way Bruce could personally arrange and control agenda items.'[38] But the Scullin government reverted to 'the earlier haphazard system, with no organised agenda nor record of decisions'[39] despite attempts at being more organised. Menzies' 'conduct of Cabinet meetings was altogether a *tour de force*. He achieved orderliness and purpose and result, and all in an atmosphere of informality.'[40]

Whitlam's Cabinet agenda was 'too crowded to allow opportunity for the appropriate consideration of every measure, bills were often ill-considered and poorly drafted, and under sheer pressure of business, items were let through that in other circumstances might have been questioned more closely.'[41] Reportedly, 'Whitlam on occasion did literally grind his teeth at an obstructive minister, in Cabinet.'[42] Fraser, who was heavily interventionist over a wide gamut of policy, would have endless Cabinet meetings, often running late into the night, that left ministers exhausted and privately cranky. Keating's biographer, John Edwards, notes that Keating was often late for Cabinet and frequently changed meeting times: Keating may well have believed that 'he was putting substance before procedure' but '[i]n the minds of his ministers he was simply disorganised'.[43] Keating was also impatient with the textbook 'open door' approach for ministers and when they bothered him too much he sometimes 'hid in his dressing room and told the staff to say he was out'.[44]

Despite the oft-talked about decline of Parliament, it has always been and remains an important showcase for the PM, as well as, given the Senate's power, an arbiter of the fate of his government's legislation. No government has fallen on the floor of the House since Fadden's in 1941. But the Senate's threatened blocking of supply in 1974 prompted Whitlam to call an election, and its actual blocking of the 1975 Budget caused a constitutional crisis and led to Whitlam's dismissal and defeat. More obviously, with an enlarged Senate combining with proportional representation voting, government control of the Upper House will be a rarity.

Part of the prime minister's job is to negotiate with the minor 'balance of power' Senate players. If Howard had failed to reach a deal with the Democrats over the GST in 1999, he would have been forced to either abandon his tax package or later take it to a double dissolution, which very likely he would have lost. Parliamentary oratory and cut and thrust no longer have the place they did in the days of Deakin, who was cheered from both sides of Parliament when in 1902 (as attorney-general) he held the House's attention for more than three hours expounding the detail of the Judiciary Bill.[45] Parliament remains, however, a potent and sometimes brutal testing ground for the PM and his ministerial team. Whitlam constantly bested McMahon in the House. Frequent bad performances at the despatch box will quickly undermine a leader's authority, and a PM declines to give Parliament its due at his peril. Keating's decision not to appear in Question Time every day rebounded, and will not be tried by a PM again in a hurry.

In a 1997–98 series of addresses by five of the six living occupants of the prime ministerial office, John Gorton outlined the qualities of 'a good prime minister'. Apart from the givens of 'intelligence and integrity', Gorton said:

> He needs a good constitution for long, hard and stressful work. He needs stamina to keep going. He must have a deep love of this country – its institutions, its values, its idiosyncrasies. He must understand that being prime minister is only a temporary job, because he can get into trouble very quickly. Politics is a demanding business. Political leaders come under the kinds of pressure that few people experience in their professional lives. So the tendency is to avoid conflict, not to stir up anything, to govern in a low risk political environment. A good prime minister could not accept this easy option. So to make a difference, a difference to people's lives in a positive way, Prime Ministers need to grab opportunities when they arise. I would nominate this last point – the need to recognise and grasp opportunities – as the most important quality a Prime Minister needs.[46]

Intelligence, imagination, nous, stamina, guts – these are what it takes to handle this unique job successfully – and, usually, a dash of luck. In practice, no leader can bring or sustain all those qualities, and that gives a ring of sadness to many of the profiles that follow. More positively, each prime minister reflects in some significant way the Australia of his times; through their stories we read our history, and it has its share of heroes.

MICHELLE GRATTAN

Sir Edmund Barton

I JANUARY 1901 – 24 SEPTEMBER 1903

Without Barton … Australia would not have federated on 1 January 1901.

BY GEOFFREY BOLTON

Few Australians knew the name of the first commonwealth prime minister until the recent spate of propaganda for the centenary of Federation – and those who could identify Edmund Barton often knew little more of him that the nick-name 'Tosspot Toby', coined by the malicious John Norton, publisher of the newspaper *Truth*, because of Barton's reputed over-fondness for drink. A middle-class male, overweight, conformist and comfortable with his British inheritance, Barton could be seen as lacking the qualities of ethnicity, gender, class and glamour that might appeal to Australians at the end of the twentieth century. Faithfully married for over forty years, he generated no picturesque yarns of excessive virility, as Parkes did. A pragmatic politician whose strength lay in his skill at negotiating workable compromises, he failed to impress future generations by creating an ideology such as Deakinite liberalism or the faith of the early labour movement. Unlike Deakin, he wrote no memoirs of Federation, so future historians took their source material from accounts that pushed Deakin into the foreground.

Barton has been too much neglected. Without Barton, often in tandem with his lifelong friend and political antagonist George Reid, Australia would not have federated on 1 January 1901. Without Barton as first prime minister, a Cabinet of strong-willed leaders accustomed to wielding power in their own colonies would not have held together unchanged for two and a half years. Instead of laying the foundations of the Commonwealth of Australia, the first federal parliament would have lost credit in a welter of party manoeuvring. The solutions that emerged were not always heroic, but they were workable arrangements on which the future could build. Old men looking back on the Federation period agreed with Sir Robert Garran that Barton had been 'the one man for the job'.

Born on 18 January 1849 in the Sydney suburb of Glebe, Edmund Barton was the youngest of eleven surviving children of William and Mary Louisa Barton. William was a Micawberish businessman and investor remembered as Sydney's first stockbroker. His remarkably energetic and intelligent wife managed and taught at several girls' schools as well as managing the family. Theirs was long remembered as 'one of the most literary households in Sydney'. Edmund's elder brother and mentor, George Burdett Barton, was one of the earliest champions of Australian literature. From this background Edmund went to a brilliant career at school and at the University of Sydney, majoring in classics and taking many prizes. He graduated Master of Arts in 1870. In the same year he met Jeanie Ross from Newcastle. He qualified as a barrister and solicitor in 1872, but it was another five years before he and Jeanie could afford to marry.

His main recreations were rowing and cricket. Although only a poor fieldsman and a moderate bat, he graduated to wicketkeeper and proved a hardworking committeeman for the University of Sydney club. This experience, combined with attendance at the School of Arts Debating Society, to which his fishing mate George Reid introduced him, cured him of diffidence as a public speaker. An interest in politics followed. In 1876 he unsuccessfully contested the University of Sydney seat in the New South Wales Legislative Assembly. Having come into the public eye early in 1879 when, as umpire at a cricket match between New South Wales and the English eleven he defused a potential riot, he won the seat of University at a second attempt later that year. When the seat was abolished in 1880 he became member for Wellington, and later for East Sydney.

In January 1883 George Reid engineered Barton's election as Speaker, the youngest ever to hold that office. Perhaps schooled by his experience of umpiring, Barton presided efficiently over the turbulent 'bear garden of Macquarie Street'. Some spoke of him as a potential premier but in 1887 he resigned, accepting nomination to the Legislative Council. In these years the factional politics of New South Wales were stabilising into a two-party system, with the Free Traders led by Sir Henry Parkes opposed by Protectionists seeking to encourage local industries by the use of tariffs. Barton became a leading Protectionist, serving as attorney-general in the short-lived Dibbs ministry of 1889, but he seemed too interested in his family and in the sociability of the Athenaeum Club to put great effort into politics. His full enthusiasm was kindled only when Parkes in October 1889 made his Tenterfield speech urging the Australian colonies to form a Federation.

Barton's interest in Federation probably dated back to 1883, when an intercolonial conference in Sydney led to the creation of a federal council. It was a toothless body, since New South Wales and (except briefly) South Australia did not participate. Parkes favoured the model of the United States, with a House of Representatives elected on a population basis and a Senate representing the states, a model that appealed to Barton. At a Lithgow speech in November 1889 he signalled support for the federal cause, thus ensuring that it would be seen as bipartisan. After the other Australian colonies and New Zealand agreed to send delegates to the Federal Convention at Sydney in March 1891 it was not surprising that the New South Wales Parliament chose Barton among its seven nominees.

He made a strong impression at the convention, partly through his constructive interventions in debate (especially in defusing disagreement about the powers of the Senate) and partly through good luck. Queensland's Sir Samuel Griffith, in charge of convention business, intended to finalise the text of the draft Constitution with a small working party on the government steamer *Lucinda* during the Easter weekend. At the last moment one of the party, Tasmania's Inglis Clark, fell ill, and Barton came in his place. With Griffith and South Australia's Charles Kingston, Barton produced the document that is essentially the Australian Constitution of today. It was accepted by the convention and was then intended for presentation to the parliaments of the various participating colonies. As New South Wales had taken the initiative, the others waited for that colony to take the lead.

Delays followed. Except for Western Australia, the colonies were sliding into the worst financial depression in fifty years, and were preoccupied with their economies. Parkes lost office in October 1891 and, although the Protectionist government that replaced him included Barton as attorney-general, it was November 1892 before Barton could introduce enabling legislation into the New South Wales Parliament. In the interval he served for five months as acting premier and had to deal with a prolonged Broken Hill strike. Although he behaved with studious moderation, the jailing of five union leaders left him in bad odour with the Labor Party for some time.

Realising that Federation was unlikely to win public support unless it was seen as a genuinely grassroots movement, Barton went to the Riverina in December 1892 and in that sympathetic environment launched the first Federal Leagues at Corowa and Albury, with a dozen others following in the next few months. It was planned that a central Federation League should be set up at a meeting in Sydney in July 1893, but the meeting was almost taken over by republicans, and Parkes, Reid, and other Free Trade politicians stood aloof, doubting the success of the league. At the same time overwork and perhaps overeating and drinking caused a temporary breakdown in Barton's health. When the Federation League sponsored the Corowa conference of July–August 1893 he was unable to attend. In December 1893, having mishandled criticism for accepting a retainer from a contractor who was suing the railway commissioners, Barton was obliged to resign office, and at the elections of mid 1894, when he stood for the new seat of Randwick, he was defeated. Meanwhile, he had fallen deeply into debt during the financial crisis of 1892–93. It was the lowest point of his career, and few could have imagined that within three years he would recover to assume leadership of a buoyant federal movement.

Preoccupied with providing for a wife and six children, Barton could do little more for the federal movement than continue addressing meetings in suburban halls promoting the Federation League. Many were poorly attended, and it might have seemed that the public was apathetic and the federal cause in eclipse, together with Barton's political fortunes. But George Reid was premier of New South Wales from 1894 to 1899, and, although politically opposed to Barton, he was coming to see merit in the idea of Australian Federation. The Corowa conference had endorsed a proposal that the Constitution should be ratified by a second National Convention, whose delegates should be chosen by the voters of each colony and not, as previously, by the parliaments. In 1895 Reid persuaded a premiers' conference to back this scheme. The election of delegates took place in the late summer of 1897 and did much to stimulate public interest in Federation. In New South Wales Barton headed the list of ten successful delegates. With nearly two-thirds of all votes cast, he was well ahead of Reid.

It was an astonishing comeback, revealing how much Barton was identified as 'Mr Federation' in the eyes of the public, as a result of his single-minded advocacy of the cause. Parkes, the only possible alternative, had died the previous year. It probably helped that Barton had been out of Parliament since 1894. He could appeal to Australians who mistrusted professional politicians as a private citizen above politics, wholeheartedly preaching the Federation gospel. In later campaigning he made a good deal of this status; this was of course shrewd politics, but it partly explains his success. He made a handsome public figure, clean-shaven, with iron-grey hair and a stately presence (in his prime he weighed more than one hundred kilograms). His oratory was improving. When underprepared he was verbose, bewildering his audience with long and involved, though never ungrammatical, trains of thought. With repetition and experience his presentation improved and he developed a skill in repartee very useful in an era of open-air mass meetings whose all-male audiences regarded politics as a form of street theatre.

Barton was unanimously chosen leader of the second Federal Convention. At its three sessions between March 1897 and March 1898 in Adelaide, Sydney, and Melbourne he steered its agenda with conspicuous success. His great skill lay in his capacity to broker workable compromises and win their acceptance by a majority of delegates. This quality revealed itself early in the Adelaide session when a major showdown seemed likely because the smaller colonies wanted the Senate, as states' House, to possess equal or even slightly greater powers than the House of Representatives. The delegates from New South Wales and Victoria, representing two-thirds of Australia's population, objected; they could not sell such an undemocratic arrangement to their voters. Barton's tactics, aided by some adroit lobbying, ensured that a narrow majority endorsed the compromise that prevented the Senate from amending financial bills; not enough to satisfy the democrats of the labour movement or to guard against a future crisis such as arose in 1975, but sufficient to win acceptance at the time. The draft Constitution, which emerged in March 1898, bore the stamp of Barton's pragmatic moderation. During its framing Barton himself shifted from earlier conservative views, coming to accept the granting of the vote to women and federal involvement in industrial arbitration.

The Constitution Bill was now to be submitted to the voters of the six Australian colonies. Very few proposed constitutional changes in Australian history have cleared that hurdle, and none as important as the decision to federate. Barton was the main architect of a Constitution that might not have been the most democratic imaginable or the most likely to resolve all the potential areas of conflict between Commonwealth and states, but it met one critical test: the approval of a majority of voters everywhere in Australia.

In 1898 this was by no means a sure thing. Hit by the depression of the early 1890s, Victoria, Tasmania and South Australia might be expected to vote 'yes' to an Australian common market. Queensland and

Western Australia were lagging, but the four south-eastern colonies could go ahead without them. New South Wales was pivotal. Reid, dependent for his majority on Labor support, could not appear too enthusiastic and was lampooned as the fence-sitting 'Yes-No' Reid. This left Barton as chief spokesman for the 'Yes' cause. During April and May 1898 he campaigned throughout New South Wales, coining the phrase: 'A continent for a nation, and a nation for a continent'. But the New South Wales Parliament insisted that the 'Yes' vote must muster not just a simple majority, but a minimum of 80,000 supporters. The referendum on 3 June 1898 produced 71,595 'Yes' voters against 66,228 'No'. A second poll would be necessary.

Disappointment fed Barton's mistrust of Reid. At the general election of July 1898 he opposed the premier in his own constituency but was narrowly beaten. An obliging backbencher resigned the seat of Hastings and Macleay. Barton was opposed, but won the seat comfortably. During this campaign a supporter dubbed him 'Australia's noblest son' and the term stuck, although Barton found it embarrassing. The Protectionist leader of the Opposition, William Lyne, stepped down in favour of Barton in September 1898. He was not enough of a partisan to be a very effective Opposition leader. After Reid succeeded in extracting a number of changes to the Constitution from his fellow premiers, he and Barton co-operated in pushing the Federation legislation through the New South Wales Parliament against the opposition of Labor democrats and conservatives of the 'if-it-ain't-broke-don't-fix-it' school. Together they led the case for a 'Yes' vote at a second referendum in June 1899. This time success came by a margin of 107,420 votes to 82,741.

In August 1899 Barton handed the leadership of the Protectionist Opposition back to Lyne. Lyne had opposed Federation as insufficiently democratic, but he was much more likely than Barton to win the backing of the Labor Party, and he was a canny tactician. It was commonly expected that the prime ministership of the Australian Commonwealth would be offered to the premier of New South Wales as representing the senior Australian colony. It was understood that if Lyne were premier he would not want the post for himself, but would recommend Barton. Barton went off to Queensland to participate in the last stages of the referendum there. He encountered a rough campaign but Queensland voted 'Yes', leaving Western Australia as the only straggler. Meanwhile

Lyne persuaded the Labor Party to desert Reid and became premier. Barton's case for appointment as first prime minister would rest not on his role in New South Wales politics but on his standing as national federal leader.

That standing was further enhanced in 1900. The British government invited an Australian delegation to visit London while the Australian Commonwealth legislation was shepherded through the British Parliament. Barton was the New South Wales nominee, and although he was the only member of the party who had not previously visited Britain, he was regarded as its leader. Strongly supported by Alfred Deakin from Victoria and Charles Kingston from South Australia, Barton confronted British demands that the Australians should drop Section 74 of the Constitution. This provided that the last court of appeal for constitutional cases should no longer be the judicial committee of the Privy Council in London, but should lie with the Australian High Court when that was set up. The British government was concerned that an Australian court might not be sufficiently respectful of British interests, especially those involving trade or investment. Barton and his colleagues were also white-anted by a curious combination of interests within Australia – mostly conservatives in the legal profession and businessmen dependent on British investment, but also sections of the labour movement – who argued that Australian judges could not possibly display the wisdom and impartiality of the British judiciary.

Barton's stubbornness on this issue resulted partly from some unhappy experiences of his own with the Privy Council, but was fed mainly by a belief that if Australians were capable of framing their own Constitution, they were capable of interpreting it. Eventually a compromise was reached, under which the Privy Council might hear appeals from Australia if the High Court approved. The episode won Barton the respect of the British authorities, and in the later part of 1900 officials of the Colonial Office communicated with him in a manner that suggested that they expected him to become Australia's first prime minister.

Barton himself shared that expectation, and in the last weeks of 1900 was discussing the possible makeup of the first federal Cabinet with his close friends O'Connor and Deakin. When the Earl of Hopetoun arrived late in December to take up appointment as governor-general, he still felt bound to invite the premier of New South Wales, and instead of declining,

Lyne (now Sir William) accepted. As Lyne had been an opponent of Federation, many were surprised. Barton refused to serve in his Cabinet and maintained a discreet silence while Deakin and other friends lobbied to discourage potential Cabinet ministers from joining a Lyne ministry. On Christmas Eve Lyne threw in his hand and Barton was sent for. It was he who on New Year's Day at Centennial Park was filmed, in one of the world's first newsreels, taking the oath of allegiance from the hands of Hopetoun.

Barton formed a strong Cabinet. Six members were ex-premiers, including Lyne. His two closest allies were his oldest friends R.E. O'Connor, who was to lead the Senate, and Deakin. They were not an easy team to manage, ranging as they did from the radical Kingston of South Australia to the conservative Forrest of Western Australia – both strong-willed characters accustomed to getting their own way – but under Barton's leadership they held together unchanged for two and a half years. Once again Barton's capacity for achieving consensus as the first among equals proved an essential ingredient for stability. His policy speech, made at Maitland West in his constituency of Hunter on 18 January 1901, called for a policy of tariff protection to encourage Australian industries, the adoption of a 'white Australia' policy and the development of national policies in defence, especially in the Pacific, industrial arbitration, and the construction of transcontinental railways. Reid, leading a Free Trade Opposition, found himself caught by the point that in order to raise revenue the new Commonwealth would need to impose tariffs, since at that time income and land taxes were still confined to the states. At the elections on 29–30 March Barton's Protectionists won 32 seats in the House of Representatives, as against 27 for Reid's Free Traders and 16 Labor men who held the balance of power. Because of the promise of the White Australia Policy they pledged support to the Barton ministry.

The new Commonwealth Parliament was opened by the Duke of York and Cornwall (later King George V) on 9 May 1901 in what were intended to be temporary quarters in Parliament House, Melbourne. The management of that Parliament confronted Barton and his colleagues with ongoing problems. In the Senate 11 Protectionists and 8 Labor senators faced 17 Free Traders; too close a margin for comfort in an era of loose party discipline. Even in the Lower House it was necessary for the government to negotiate a fresh majority for almost every major piece of legislation. Barton's personal circumstances were not ideal, since he could not afford for his wife and younger children to join him in Melbourne. A small self-contained flat was improvised for him in an attic of Parliament House. Here he would conduct business with Atlee Hunt, the efficient permanent secretary of his department, or sit up late at night yarning with his closest associates, Deakin, Kingston and Forrest, boiling a billy in the fireplace.

The first parliamentary session was a marathon, lasting from May 1901 to mid 1902 with only a four-week break over Christmas. It did not take long to set up the infrastructure for the new Commonwealth, although in its early weeks Barton claimed that he could carry its entire paperwork in his gladstone bag. In order to consolidate Labor support, the Barton government moved early to implement the White Australia Policy. Despite protests from Queensland, it proved easy to pass legislation ending the practice of indenturing Pacific Islanders on contract to work in the canefields, compensating the sugar industry with bounties on sugar grown by 'white' labour and tariff protection against foreign imports.

It was less easy to secure agreement on immigration policy. Many members, including most of the Labor Party, favoured a simple ban on non-European immigration. The British government, with an empire in India and a potential ally in Japan, could not agree to this, and the Australians proposed that any immigrant might be required to take a fifty-word dictation test in any European language. Barton himself would have preferred the test to be in English, thus placing all immigrants on an equal footing, but he did not have the numbers. It took much patient negotiation to get the legislation through Parliament, and more to persuade Governor-General Hopetoun to assent to it without reference to London, but by the end of 1901 it was in place.

It took even longer to legislate for tariff policy, since different interest groups objected to almost every item scheduled for customs duty, and the proposals were fought through item by item. The Commonwealth emerged with less revenue than at first planned, and since there was an obligation to pay three-quarters of any surplus to the states until 1911, there was insufficient for increased defence spending, the introduction of old-age pensions and other planks in the Barton government's policy.

During the early months of 1902 Barton succumbed to a form of depression that had overtaken him once before, at the time of his financial trouble in 1893. At such times he had a tendency to seek consolation in food and drink. This gave rise to the legend of 'Tosspot Toby', a name publicised by John Norton of *Truth*, who had once been an erratic supporter of Barton's but had grown bitterly resentful of his success. Barton was never an alcoholic, but his bulimic tendency in depressive phases led to gossip. However, supported by Deakin, O'Connor and Atlee Hunt he recovered his equipoise in time to participate in a conference of British Empire prime ministers held in London in July 1902 at the time of Edward VII's coronation. His appointment as Knight Grand Cross of the Order of St Michael and St George, the highest honour then open to a colonial, probably assisted his recovery. He had refused several previous offers of a knighthood.

In London Barton achieved his objective of keeping Australia's outlay in support of the Royal Navy to the lowest decent figure, fending off British demands for the commitment of Australians for service overseas and Australian advocates of an independent navy – for which there were not as yet the funds. He inadvertently stirred up trouble by visiting the aged Pope Leo XIII in Rome. They conversed in Latin, and the Pope presented Barton with a medallion, thus stirring up Protestants in Australia to clamour that Barton was too friendly with the Vatican. Barton was certainly aware of the value of the Catholic vote – he attended St Patrick's Day functions hosted by Cardinal Moran at a time when the state government was unwilling to be represented because of sectarian pressure – but although the protests continued for several months after his return to Australia they eventually fizzled out.

During 1903 the Commonwealth Parliament's main business was the creation of a High Court and the passage of legislation for a federal arbitration system. By this time the Australian economy was suffering from the effects of a prolonged drought, and many thought the High Court a needless extravagance, but eventually the creation of a three-member judiciary was approved. In the process Barton firmly denied that he meant to appoint himself as first chief justice.

The arbitration legislation gave even more trouble. Kingston, the minister in charge, resigned in July 1903 when Cabinet would not approve his proposal to extend the Bill's coverage to merchant seamen. Of all the ministry he was the best regarded by the Labor Party, and his departure weakened the government. An election was due in late 1903 or early 1904 and survival seemed increasingly to depend on Barton's leadership. *The Bulletin*, not always a friendly critic, reported that the 'thinner and more abstemious' prime minister was back on his best form. In reality his health was no longer equal to the pressures of office. When it proved impossible for the government to frame arbitration legislation acceptable to Labor, it was time for Barton to resign. Honouring his pledge not to make himself chief justice he offered the post to Sir Samuel Griffith; but he and O'Connor would fill the other places on the High Court.

The decision to quit politics prolonged his life. As a justice of the High Court he was notable mainly for his readiness to side with Griffith in adhering to the strict terms of the agreement between the Commonwealth and states, resisting attempts by colleagues such as Isaacs and Higgins to extend the Commonwealth's power, especially in areas such as industrial arbitration. Remembering that it had taken great effort to secure agreement to any form of Federation, Barton was reluctant to disturb the balance even in the face of social and economic changes and the impact of the 1914–18 war. When Griffith retired in 1919 Barton cherished hopes of serving a few years as chief justice in a valedictory lap of honour. Although all his brother judges favoured him, the Hughes government decided to appoint an outsider, (Sir) Adrian Knox. They thought Barton's health too uncertain. Only a few months later, on 7 January 1920, he died of a heart attack while holidaying at Medlow Bath in the Blue Mountains.

Barton's term as prime minister resulted in three major achievements, none of which possesses obvious appeal a hundred years later. By establishing the infrastructure of the Commonwealth government and providing a stable ministry for its first thirty months, he ensured firm foundations for the new federal government; but this was the kind of success that later generations would take for granted. His White Australia Policy no longer finds favour in a multicultural Australia, though it is understandable that a generation who could remember the American Civil War was anxious to avoid the racial tensions that might come of economic conflict. And the use of the tariff as a means of protecting Australian industries no longer commends itself in a globalising economy. For these reasons it is easy to underrate his contribution. Nevertheless, without his skills as a mediator it is unlikely that the Commonwealth of Australia would have come into being on 1 January 1901 or that it would have won early credibility. And he remains, with the exception of Sir Robert Menzies and possibly Andrew Fisher, the only one of Australia's twenty-five prime ministers to retire at a time of his own choosing.

Alfred Deakin

24 SEPTEMBER 1903 – 27 APRIL 1904
5 JULY 1905 – 13 NOVEMBER 1908
2 JUNE 1909 – 29 APRIL 1910

In his vices as well as his virtues he was touched with greatness.

BY STUART MACINTYRE

'What truth can there be in history when a leader is a puzzle to his contemporaries?'[1] The question was asked by a man who had worked alongside Alfred Deakin in the Federal Conventions during the 1890s and in the national Parliament from its establishment in 1901. He declared his puzzlement in 1909 when he was about to become a minister in the government that Alfred Deakin formed in that year.

This would be the third time Deakin served as the country's prime minister. In 1903 he succeeded Edmund Barton, leading a Protectionist ministry that held office with the support of the Labor Party until the following year. From 1905 to 1908 he governed again on the same basis. But in 1909 he joined with his former opponents, the Free Traders, to form the Liberal Party and eject the Labor Party from the government benches. 'Judas! Judas! Judas!' roared an enraged former ally.[2]

If Deakin was a mystery to his colleagues, his public career was an object of wonder even to himself. As a young man he was a spiritualist who claimed to receive messages from the dead. He then entered into an intense and solitary religious introspection that provided him with what he called 'clues' as to his conduct. And so in 1909 he prayed for guidance: 'Infinite Spirit of Love in whom we live and move and have our higher being grant that the interminable complexities of my public life may be resolved for the best, and that I may accept whatever part and lot makes the best service possible to me.'[3]

The conclusion he drew was that he should set aside his partisan loyalties and resume office, yet he was adamant that he did so without any personal ambition and only as sacred duty: 'Not for myself O God, not for myself – for myself least and last – but for Thy purpose, for Thy will, for my country and kin first and always be my retention of official place …'[4] He had long ceased to find pleasure in public life and after electoral defeat in 1910 he emerged from what he called 'the nightmare (and daymare) of responsibility' as if waking from a dream. Two years later, when he laid down the leadership of his party, he recorded in his diary, 'Last Day, thank God … Thoroughly exhausted, but oh such an immense release and relief.'[5]

A man who believes his political destiny to be divinely ordained is likely to incur the bafflement of others who operate according to more worldly motives, especially when these higher promptings bring him personal advantage. Deakin's fastidious honour only aggravated the anger of those who were sacrificed to his impeccable rectitude. In 1904 he put out a minority Labor government less than four months after he had undertaken to give it a fair trial. In 1905 he did the same to a coalition government he had also encouraged. The abandonment of his own party stalwarts in 1909 completed the circle, and out of these manoeuvres he ensured that he was the central and dominant figure in the early years of Commonwealth government. Small wonder that he confessed to himself, 'I act alone, live alone, and think alone.'[6]

Deakin's parliamentary career extended continuously over more than three decades. He had entered the Victorian Parliament in 1879 while still in his early twenties. He represented his colony and later his country at Imperial Conferences in London, where as early as 1887 his singular talent was recognised, and he inspired a generation of younger Australians with his own idealism. Yet he was surely the only prime minister in Australian history to have received inner messages from spiritual sources – and he was certainly the only one to have secretly doubled as a journalist who wrote regular accounts of Australian politics in which he reported his own conduct as if describing the actions of an inscrutable stranger.

Yet his celebrity was assured. By the time he retired from Parliament, he had placed a distinctive imprint on the country's institutions: its immigration policy and defence forces, the system of economic protection and wage regulation, social services, federal–state relations and much else besides. More than anyone else, he turned the idea of the Commonwealth into a functioning reality. Yet he regarded all this as failure, and looked on the business of politics as a hollow sham, allowing or even encouraging base behaviour.

The devices he created to secure the country for the white race, to use its material plenty for the common benefit, and to reconcile divisions in a unified purpose – all of these had lasting force well into the century. So axiomatic were the institutional arrangements he had made in the formative years of the Commonwealth that even in the 1980s they could be described by journalist Paul Kelly as the 'Australian Settlement'.[7] Yet by then the core elements of that settlement were being dismantled. With their removal Deakin's legacy became unrecognisable. Disjointed fragments of it – the White Australia Policy, British race patriotism, protectionism, state control, the damming of rivers and channelling of desires – are held up for condemnation. The moral purpose that animated him and that he sought to realise in national life is so far removed from our own values as to be unintelligible.

Alfred Deakin was born in August 1856 in Melbourne, the second child and only son of improving English immigrants. His father became a partner in a coaching business and later a manager of Cobb and Co. While Alfred was young the family moved from the inner suburb of Fitzroy to the more salubrious South Yarra, so that from the age of eight he attended the nearby Melbourne Grammar School, where he was a gifted, dreamy pupil. At the University of Melbourne he studied law, though there were also spells as a schoolteacher and private tutor, for the family finances were still precarious and both father and son had a talent for making bad investments and unwise loans.

Deakin was already forming friendships based on shared intellectual interests in speculative thought, already searching for spiritual guidance and committing his discoveries to paper – a habit he continued for the rest of his life. He was admitted to the Melbourne bar in 1877, took chambers and filled in the time left by his infrequent briefs in writing outside the law. He was taken up by David Syme, the owner of the *Age*, who had built the circulation of that newspaper far beyond that of any competitor and used it to impose his own idiosyncratic brand of interventionist liberalism on Victorian politics. Syme was a notoriously shy, suspicious, misanthropic and grim tyrant, yet he was somehow drawn to the loquacious young man. In his own words, Deakin became 'the pet of the proprietor'.[8] As such, he was nominated as the Liberal candidate in the by-election for a constituency on the outskirts of Melbourne in 1879. He won the contest but astonished the members of the Victorian Parliament by combining his maiden speech with an announcement that he was resigning the seat because of doubts about the poll. A further by-election went against him, so he finally entered the Parliament in 1880, after standing for the seat a third time.

Deakin embarked on his political career during an acute constitutional crisis. The Liberal ministry, with a large majority in the democratic

Lower House, had sought to extend a temporary arrangement for the payment of members by attaching it to legislation that authorised expenditure. The conservatives, with a permanent majority in the unrepresentative Upper House, had rejected that legislation. The government retaliated by dismissing senior public servants. Behind this particular confrontation lay twenty years of conflict between the two Houses and two parties, the Liberals championing the interests of manufacturers, workers and farmers with protection of local industry and land reform, the Conservatives defending a social hierarchy in which the wealthy pastoralists and professional elite withstood the levelling masses.

Deakin was a cuckoo in the nest of the plebeians. Tall, dark and carefully groomed, he seemed too fastidious for the rough-and-tumble of popular politics. He differed from the older liberal champions, also, in having been born and raised in the colonies. David Syme's harsh Scottish speech mingled with the Cockney accents of Graham Berry, the premier when Deakin entered politics, and the precise Anglo-Irish diction of George Higinbotham, the great champion of democratic reform who had retired to the Supreme Court and was revered by Deakin's generation. His former headmaster noted that Deakin was the first of 'my Grammar School pupils' to have entered the Victorian Parliament. 'Would that it had been in a better cause!'[9]

His entry into politics coincided with his marriage in 1882 to Pattie Browne, whom he met through a shared interest in spiritualism. She was the nineteen-year-old daughter of a wealthy businessman who did not encourage the marriage. It was dogged also by the close relationship between Alfred and his elder sister Catherine, to whom he entrusted his own daughters' education. At first the young couple lived with Alfred's parents; several years later they built their own home, 'Llanarth', close by in South Yarra. The marriage was a cornerstone of Deakin's domestic life, and he would describe it as a 'sacred circle' within which he 'rested and recuperated' and was 'reinforced, encouraged, solaced and soothed to sweet content'.[10] That he was for so long unaware of the tension between the two women who were dearest to him suggests remarkable preoccupation.

The constitutional crisis ended in a compromise that Deakin helped arrange. It was an augury of his instinctive preference for the middle way, establishing him as a mender and a conciliator. He was never the partisan, always the practical idealist, and he understood compromise as a necessary and indeed honourable political skill.

Deakin served in all the coalition ministries of the 1880s. He took office in 1883 as minister for public works and water supply. In 1884 he chaired a Royal Commission on Irrigation, led a tour of inspection to the United States and introduced pioneering legislation that placed the ownership of natural waters in the public hands. Irrigation was one of his enthusiasms; he thought of it as redeeming the country, bringing plenty out of wilderness.

He was also responsible for the first Australian legislation to regulate working conditions. Though weakened by the Legislative Council, the Factories and Shops Act of 1885 provided for the inspection of factories, set limits on the hours of work for women and juveniles and introduced compensation for work injuries.

In 1885 Deakin became the leader of the Victorian Liberals, who remained in coalition with the Conservatives until 1890. As chief secretary he represented his colony at the 1887 Imperial Conference in London, where he affronted the British representatives by pressing local interests in the Pacific region. He did so, however, not out of any desire for greater independence, but rather because he wished to strengthen the cohesion and capacity of the Empire. It was at this conference that he was offered and refused a knighthood. Aged just thirty, he was the assertive young colonial statesman, a native-born colonial nationalist and an independent Australian Briton.

There was another side to this nurturing of the British race in the colonies. In 1886 Deakin introduced legislation that tightened the administration of the colony's Aboriginal reserves. These small vestiges of land had been set aside for the protection of the indigenous people on the assumption that they were incapable of surviving outside them, but the signs of successful adaptation confounded those expectations of imminent demise. The new law provided for the removal of those of mixed descent, who were to be absorbed into white society and expunged of their aboriginality.

Through these and other measures Deakin fostered the development of the colony. Then came the crash, in which, as chairman of several land companies, he lost both his and his father's capital. He was complicit in the special bankruptcy laws passed by the members of the Victorian legislature, allowing debtors to make private deals with their creditors and to protect themselves from ruin and disgrace. He did not use the special laws himself but made good his fortune at the bar, appearing on behalf of the chief villains. He also filled his pockets by appearing for his former patron David Syme in a long-running and expensive libel case brought by the dodgy commissioner of railways against whom the *Age* conducted a long vendetta. The ***Bulletin*** delighted in the spectacle of Alfred Deakin, lawyer, accusing Richard Speight, commissioner, of being importuned by various politicians, including the Hon. Alfred Deakin MLA!

There was another period during this economic depression when Chief Secretary Deakin was not at his best – the maritime strike of 1890. This was the great confrontation between the employers and the newly formed union movement, triggered by the shipowners' dismissal of the maritime officers for affiliating to the Trades Hall Council, and it brought the ports to a standstill. Deakin proclaimed his sympathies with the workers for, if a choice had to be made between 'a little flesh and blood with much capital' and 'a great deal of flesh and blood with little capital', then surely 'the living and thinking weight must carry our sympathies'. But once the strikers picketed the landing of supplies, and especially when they stopped the gas supply on which public lighting depended, his sympathy evaporated. A city without light! What opportunities would that give 'the worthless and ill-disposed persons in any city' to pillage innocent citizens? He therefore called out troops to break the strike. As he saw it, 'The question was whether the city was to be handed over to mob law and the tender mercy of roughs and rascals, or whether it was to be governed, as it had always been governed, under law in peace and order.'[11]

Late in October the coalition government was defeated and Deakin moved to the backbenches. He stayed there throughout the 1890s in order to concentrate his efforts on the cause of Federation. There had been talk of bringing the separate colonies together for decades, and a weak Federal Council was established in 1885 to co-ordinate their common interests, but the endeavour to create a new national government was only just beginning. Henry Parkes, the premier of New South Wales, had called late in 1889 for a convention to prepare the Constitution for such a federal government. Representatives of the colonial governments of Australia and New Zealand had met in a sweltering Melbourne early in

1890 to discuss this proposal, and Deakin was one of the two Victorian representatives at that conference. He was again a Victorian delegate when the Convention met in Sydney in 1891, and from then until the final passage of the Commonwealth of Australia Act in 1900 he was involved at every significant turn on the tortuous path to nationhood.

Deakin regarded the creation of the Commonwealth of Australia as nothing less than a sacred mission. From the very beginning he was the champion of the federal cause in his own colony of Victoria, which in turn was its principal stronghold. He did not seek national leadership of the movement, for he appreciated that this role had to be performed by a statesman from New South Wales, which was the other most populous colony and far more divided over the merits of the federal scheme. Accordingly Deakin deferred to Parkes at the first Federal Convention of 1891; and when a second Convention met in Adelaide in 1897 he allowed Parkes' successor, George Reid, to take the limelight – despite his private disgust at the childish vanity of the first and his deep mistrust of the second. In the account he wrote of 'The Inner History of the Federal Cause', he describes his own role thus: 'Of Deakin it is unnecessary to say anything except that ... he devoted himself from the first to the task of smoothing away resentments and overcoming difficulties ... and in every way subordinating his votes and speeches and silences as he believed would most contribute to the attainment of Union.'[12]

So his life of devotion to Federation required 'self-suppression in public coupled with continuous activity in private'. Apart from deferring to the premiers of New South Wales, he also threw his weight behind the national leadership of Edmund Barton. It was above all necessary that the federal cause be championed by a leading figure in New South Wales, and Barton enjoyed Deakin's constant support and friendship. When at last the Commonwealth was realised and the new governor-general commissioned a rival to form the first government, it was Deakin who rallied the waverers to ensure that the blunder was amended, and that Barton became Australia's first prime minister.

Deakin's liberalism channelled his aspiration for a democratic Commonwealth that would unite the Australian people in a fully representative national government. At the same time he was conscious that the less populous colonies required safeguards, and behind the scenes he facilitated the necessary compromise between the majoritarian principle embodied in the House of Representatives with the claims for equal representation of states in the Senate. As a federalist he accepted that there must be a division of powers between the Commonwealth and the states, but sought to ensure that the national government had adequate powers.

Once these arrangements had been hammered out by the Second Convention in a draft Constitution, Deakin defended it with everything in his power. He personally persuaded David Syme to accept the accommodation and end the criticism by the *Age* newspaper that imperilled its acceptance. His passionate speech at a dinner of the Australian Natives' Association in Bendigo in 1898 rallied support against those more advanced democratic nationalists who thought it gave too much away to the conservative localists. Equally, he stood up to the British government in London in 1900 when it sought to amend the Constitution, chiefly to ensure that British courts would serve as courts of appeal from the Australian High Court. On the eve of the proclamation of the Commonwealth, he described it as 'the birthday of a whole people'.[13]

An early exercise in Australian cinematography captured the public events of Commonwealth Inauguration Day on 1 January 1901 – the procession through the city of Sydney to the pavilion at Centennial Park where the governor-general read the Queen's proclamation. One after another the new ministers appear on the flickering screen to be sworn into office, Barton in marmoreal solemnity, Lyne in evening dress, Forrest and Kingston in diplomatic uniform. Deakin alone regards the camera, enigmatic in his moment of triumph.

The first federal election in March 1901 was fought between the Protectionists and the Free Traders. The Protectionists under Barton were by no means emphatic in advocating trade protection except as a source of revenue, but undertook to carry through the measures needed to give effect to the new national government. The Free Traders under Reid warned against interference with the market and generally derided Barton's grandiloquence. In Victoria, however, the Protectionists took a more advanced form, as the self-styled National Liberal Organisation, and offered a progressive platform of state regulation and national development. These Deakinite Protectionists did best in Victoria, where they won two-thirds of the vote, but nationally the two parties were roughly equal in strength. The balance of power was held by the fledgling Labor Party.

The ministry formed by Barton therefore governed with Labor support. Deakin took the office of attorney-general and played a crucial role in piloting the legislation to establish the public service, create a High Court and determine the franchise. As leader of the House of Representatives he piloted the Immigration Restriction Act, which used the dictation test to exclude aliens. Similarly, the legislation that admitted women to vote in Commonwealth elections simultaneously excluded Aborigines. The principle of White Australia was asserted both absolutely, as an expression of innate Anglo-Saxon superiority, and on the basis of what we would now call cultural relativism. Deakin was no insular colonial; he had a keen awareness and appreciation of other civilisations. Yet the goals of the Commonwealth, the realisation of its social ideals, required an homogeneous people joined in a monoculture. 'One people, one flag, one destiny', was the federal motto.

Deakin was already a national figure when the politicians from the far-flung local Parliaments assembled in Melbourne's Parliament House as federal representatives. He quickly demonstrated his celebrated qualities of eloquence, acuity and affability. His oratory was legendary: he had a rich voice, a remarkable range of expression and rapid but exact articulation that threaded complex syntax in a virtuoso performance. While he could soar on rhetorical flights, in formulating and executing policy he combined a command of detail with sharpness of purpose. Still only forty-five years of age, he set strangers at ease with his warmth and courtesy. Younger men were captivated by his interest in them. The Labor leaders Chris Watson and later Andrew Fisher were among those who responded to his charm. When others lost their tempers Deakin refused provocation – yet beneath the exterior of 'Affable Alfred', the bright eyes and smiling face, some sensed the withholding of genuine engagement. He was humble in his habits, journeyed to office by bicycle or tram, but the gates of his home in South Yarra remained shut to visitors.

During this period he also began writing weekly reports on Australian politics for the London *Morning Post*. These anonymous commentaries allowed Deakin to bring Australian developments to the attention of British readers, and their anonymity permitted him the freedom to comment publicly on the events in which he was involved in ways that would have been impossible had their authorship been known. As such, they complement the solitary introspection he maintained in notebooks as he scrutinised his conduct. A selection of the *Morning Post* articles gathered for publication by John La Nauze provides a lively and instructive perspective on national politics in the early years of the Commonwealth.

Deakin was acting prime minister when Barton attended an Imperial Conference in 1902, and he succeeded his friend when Barton retired to the High Court in 1903. Three months later the government was returned at the general election, with its numbers reduced to parity with the Labor Party. It would be impossible, Deakin concluded, to carry on government except in coalition, but the Labor Party rejected all overtures for such an arrangement. Deakin could thus expect greater uncertainty at a time when he was beginning to feel the strain on his health of long parliamentary sittings, onerous administrative duties and frequent travel. He slept poorly, suffered gastric disturbance and was susceptible to colds. Still, at the end of the year, he went down to the family holiday house at Point Lonsdale and turned once more to his notebooks. On Christmas Eve he prayed: 'Let me march straight to the goal whatever it may be in the superficial sphere in which I live and upon which I seek to work. As my opportunities are great, grant me strength, guidance, consistency, confidence, sincerity, patience and absolute personal abnegation.'[14]

In the new year of 1904 Deakin was in Adelaide and spent a day reading and writing in Government House while his host attended the cricket match where the Ashes were in balance. A fortnight later, in a speech back in Melbourne, he suggested that the present arrangement of three parties of equal strength made stable government impossible. What kind of cricket could be played, he asked, with three elevens instead of two, where one played sometimes with one side, sometimes with the other and sometimes for itself? Following his analogy, Deakin resigned office in April and put in one of the other elevens, the Labor Party. This was the first national labour government to take government anywhere in the world, but it was scarcely a genuine one, and it lasted less than four months. Deakin had resigned because Labor insisted on amendments to his Conciliation and Arbitration Bill, and the Protectionists in turn defeated the Labor government by voting with the Free Traders to amend Labor's Bill.

Deakin appreciated that the rise of the labour movement threatened both his party and the very basis of his liberalism. The Labor Party's appeal to workers was not merely eroding his own electoral base but was outflanking his own form of state intervention. Whereas he appealed to a common citizenry, Labor fostered a class loyalty of almost tribal intensity. As Deakin had put it in 1901, 'they constitute a caste in politics' and 'they help to demoralise politics by bartering their tally of votes for concessions to their class, and by their indifference to all other issues'.[15] By putting Labor into government he aimed at driving home the realisation of their minority status and at the same time fostering their appreciation of national responsibilities. After a brief interlude he turned them out and was clearly nettled by their angry recriminations. In an uncharacteristic lapse, he likened the most vitriolic of the Labor members, Billy Hughes, to an 'ill-bred urchin whom one sees dragged from a tart-shop kicking and screaming as he goes'.[16]

After Labor had been taught a lesson, it was the turn of George Reid and his Free Traders. In response to the growing strength of the Labor Party, Reid was embarking on a campaign to combat the 'Socialist tiger'. This anti-socialist mobilisation in turn threatened to polarise opinion and further isolate Deakin's Liberals, so he authorised the formation of a coalition government comprising the Free Traders and a section of the Protectionists. Led by Reid, that ministry struggled through the final parliamentary session of 1904 and was turned out when the Parliament reassembled in 1905. Deakin's role in first allowing and then destroying the government brought a new round of recrimination but achieved its purpose: Labor was committed to supporting him in office.

Deakin's second government lasted from 1905 until 1908, despite a reduction of its numbers in the 1906 election. During this period he was able to carry out a large part of his program and to give effect to the liberal conception of freedom in both its negative and positive senses. The new nation state was to offer freedom from coercion and external threat, and freedom for its citizens to work out their own destiny as independent Australian Britons. The positive meaning of freedom yielded a particular kind of protection – by state regulation and limited public provision – from exploitation, hunger and insecurity. Crucial here was Deakin's doctrine of the New Protection, linking tariff protection for local industry to the maintenance of Australian living standards.

Deakinite liberalism set limits on the operation of the market to nurture a particular kind of nation-building social solidarity that would promote both equity and efficiency – he thus regarded as a sham the Free Trade gestures towards laissez-faire capitalism of his adversary George Reid.

The search for national security from external threat assumed new urgency at this time. The arms race of the major European powers was intensifying as they scrambled for overseas territories and Britain's naval supremacy came under threat. Australians were alarmed at the presence of France and Germany in the south-west Pacific. Deakin took a keen interest in the administration of Papua, which the Commonwealth had assumed from Britain. He pressed the British to annex the New Hebrides and was angered by its inept and secretive agreement with France for joint control. Meanwhile, the Japanese destruction of a Russian fleet signalled a new danger to Australia's north. Deakin went to the 1907 Imperial Conference in London with a proposal for an imperial secretariat that would give self-governing dominions such as Australia a voice in foreign policy, and was rebuffed. He wanted to renegotiate the agreement whereby Australia contributed to the cost of the Royal Navy yet was denied consultation in its disposition, and was again rebuffed. He responded by inviting the American 'Great White Fleet' to visit Australian ports in 1908, and began preparations for the creation of an Australian navy. He also introduced legislation to set up compulsory military training.

At home Deakin consolidated economic protection as a settled feature of national policy with his delineation of the 'New Protection'. The first tariff duties were principally designed to raise revenue, but the government now extended the protection of local industry with an additional twist: henceforth it was available only to employers who provided 'fair and reasonable' wages. The determination of a fair and reasonable wage was the task of the Commonwealth Arbitration Court, which was an additional component of the national program.

Thus in 1907 it fell to Deakin's old friend Henry Bournes Higgins, as the president of the Arbitration Court, to ascertain the meaning of a fair and reasonable wage in a case concerning Harvester, a large manufacturer of agricultural machinery. Higgins determined that such a wage should be sufficient to maintain a man as a 'human being in a civilized community'; furthermore, since 'marriage is the usual fate of adults', it must provide for the needs of a family. There was a successful High Court challenge to the decision and some years elapsed before the standard it set was extended (the so-called sufficient wage became known as the 'basic wage' and was regularly adjusted for changes in the cost of living) across the Australian workforce, but the principles of Higgins' Harvester judgment became a fundamental feature of national life. Wages were to be determined not by bargaining but by an independent arbitrator. They were to be based not on profits or productivity but on human need. They were premised on the male breadwinner, with men's wages sufficient to support a family and women restricted to certain occupations and paid only enough to support a single person. They constituted a national standard.

Around these arrangements a residual system of social welfare was created. The great majority of Australians were expected to meet their needs through protected employment and a legally prescribed wage. To this logic of the male breadwinner were allowed special cases where the state offered direct assistance: Deakin's government introduced an old age pension in 1908 and in 1912 a Labor government added a maternity benefit to assist mothers with the expense of childbirth. The government continued to promote immigration and economic development through state assistance and public enterprise. A transcontinental railway to link the continent from east to west, the most ambitious of the public works programs begun at this time, symbolised the nation-building role of the Commonwealth.

Such were the components of a system meant to insulate the domestic economy from external shocks in order to protect the national standard of living. Contemporaries took great pride in its generous and innovative character. Social investigators came from Britain, France, Germany and the United States to examine the workings of this 'social laboratory' that had apparently solved the problems of national insecurity and unrest. Seen from a late-twentieth-century vantage point, as its institutional forms were dismantled, it was judged more harshly. An economic historian suggests that a system of 'domestic defence' meant to provide protection from risk lost the capacity for 'flexible adjustment' and innovation. One political commentator sees the 'Australian Settlement' as a premature lapse into an illusory certainty that left 'a young nation with geriatric arteries'.[17]

These judgments give priority to the economic aspects of the national reconstruction. They consider that national reconstruction sacrificed efficiency to equity, and in truth Deakin had only limited interest in economic policy. They make insufficient recognition of the fundamental inequities of race and gender it institutionalised and they exaggerate its amelioration of class divisions, for the Australian Settlement did not settle conflict between capital and labour, which continued to generate major disputes in defiance of industrial arbitration. But the principal object of the national reconstruction was not the economy, nor social justice, but the nation. Deakin sought to modify the market to create national mastery of material circumstances, to weld a thinly peopled continent with distant centres and regional differences into a secure whole and to regulate its divergent interests to serve national goals. That was not simply a defensive or protective project; it was an affirmative and dynamic one.

The second Deakin ministry fell at the end of 1908 when Labor withdrew support. Apart from the fact that the Labor Party now had 27 members to the Protectionists' 16 (in a House of Representatives of 75), there was a growing feeling that it had exhausted the utility of the liberal program. During the summer recess Deakin negotiated the Fusion of the Free Traders with all but four of his own Protectionists into a new Liberal Party. The Liberals took office when the 1909 session began and lost it at the general election of April 1910. There were some important measures – the decision to build the Australian navy, a financial agreement to provide payments to the states – but this was hardly a liberal administration in anything but name, and Deakin himself was struggling as his physical and mental powers waned. Loss of memory was a particular torment. The loss of respect from advanced liberals who refused to join the Fusion brought a new note of rancour into his parliamentary proceedings. He stayed on as party leader for three years after the electoral defeat, but was a mere shadow of his former self.

He himself was wrestling with the terminal crisis of his political ideals. There was always a note of pessimism in Deakin. During the depression and turmoil of the early 1890s he had confided to his notebook that 'the Liberalism of the old days, of the old colonists is a spent force; we play with its name and glorify its shadow; it is dead, it has passed. The new generation care far less for politics and are far less trained to cope with their difficulties.' The object of colonial progress had been a shared plenitude, yet it depressed him to note how little love of literature, art or ideas there was among the leisured artisans and businessmen. 'Selfishness and shams, cant and materialism rule us, up and down and through and through.'[18]

He had revived his faith in the people through the goal of national citizenship. No one did more than Deakin to establish the Commonwealth and to give it meaning, but here again he registered a growing disappointment. As he prepared for the general election of 1910 that would result in his final loss of office, he set down a reckoning of what he had achieved:

> I am saddened not with these prospects but with the sense of opportunities missed or ignored ... saddened because I can achieve so little more and have accomplished so little in the past – also because everything in Australia (and in the world) is so obviously imperfect, inchoate, confused, stained and wickedly filled with false antagonisms, coarseness and incapacity, that the promised land of humanity still lies far out of sight ... Such is the public end of A.D.[19]

He retired from public life in 1913. His final years were a torment of sleeplessness, declining health, aphasia and loss of memory. His last public meeting was a conscription rally at the Melbourne Cricket Ground in 1917, an inauspicious place for one who had recoiled from crowds at sporting events with their base passions. Those passions found violent expression on this occasion as anti-conscriptionists hurled stones and bottles at the bellicose little prime minister, Billy Hughes, on the platform. Deakin wanted to speak but was unable to do so, and his message was published:

> Fellow Countrymen – I have lived and worked to help you keep Australia white and free. The supreme Choice is given to you on December 20th. On that day you can say the word that shall keep her name white and for ever free.
>
> God in his wisdom has decreed that at this great crisis in our history my tongue must be silent owing to my failing powers. He alone knows how I yearn, my fellow Australians, to help you say that magic word ...[20]

They did not. He lived in a twilight until death provided merciful release in 1919. His achievements remain, and he is rightly one of the few names of that era who is remembered today, for in his vices as well as his virtues he was touched with greatness.

John Christian Watson

27 APRIL 1904 – 18 AUGUST 1904

No Labor leader was more skilled at relating harmoniously with all elements in the party.

BY ROSS MCMULLIN

In 1904 J.C. Watson led the first national Labor government not just in Australia, but in the world. He was widely respected within and beyond his party for his ability, integrity and, above all, his unflagging affability, an attribute of special significance during the time he was Labor's leader. In that era of intractable parliamentary unwieldiness his party had to pursue its objectives in concert with non-Labor MPs, and Watson's amiable personality was an important factor in Labor's capacity to negotiate desirable outcomes. However, having 'never been the same' since his difficult four months as prime minister without a majority in either chamber 'knocked his nerves to tatters',[1] he dreaded the prospect of returning to office in similar circumstances and went out of his way to avoid it. After he left Parliament the conscription eruption led to his departure from the party, but bitterness in his case was minimal; Labor, unrelentingly resentful of defectors as a rule, retained a soft spot for its first prime minister.

Australian Labor's initial national leader was born on 9 April 1867 at Valparaiso, Chile. The son of Johan Cristian and Martha Tanck, his name apparently was initially Johan Cristian Tanck, like his father's. Within two years Martha married George Watson; growing up with them in New Zealand, her son acquired her second husband's surname and became known as John Christian Watson.

School ended for young Chris at the age of ten, when he began work as an assistant to railway construction workers. For a time he helped out on his stepfather's farm, then he became an apprentice compositor. Losing his job in 1886 he decided to migrate to Sydney, where he found work as a stablehand at Government House. One day the governor, Lord Carrington, initiated a brief chat and gave him sixpence for a beer; Watson spent it on a book.

Reverting to employment as a compositor, Watson became prominent in trade union affairs. In January 1890, having just married thirty-year-old dressmaker Ada Jane Low, he was elected as a delegate to the NSW Trades and Labour Council (TLC), and involved himself in the labour movement's endeavours to get its own representatives into Parliament and discussions about how they should operate once they were there.

In April 1891 he became inaugural secretary of the West Sydney branch of the new Labor party, and at the New South Wales election two months later was chief campaign organiser in that multi-member electorate: Labor won all four seats. The following year he became both TLC president and chairman of the Labor party shortly after turning twenty-five, and led a deputation – on horseback – to Parliament House to persuade Labor's fractious MPs they should support a motion denouncing the government's repressive intervention in a bitter mining dispute at Broken Hill.

Watson's prominence at such a remarkably young age resulted from his temperament as well as his ability. Genuine and humane, patient and reliable in his dealings with people, he radiated the calm wisdom of an old head on young shoulders while retaining an attractively handsome and athletic appearance; not quite six feet tall (1.8 metres), he had blue eyes and dark brown hair, moustache and beard. While passionate oratory was not his forte, he was intelligent, tactful and articulate; his influential contribution as Labor refined its structures and procedures through difficult controversies during the 1890s ensured that his leadership capacity was increasingly acknowledged.

Entering the NSW Parliament himself in 1894, Watson soon became recognised as one of Labor's leading MPs during the party's 'support in return for concessions' phase, when it maintained a policy of backing non-Labor governments on condition that Labor objectives were implemented.

There were pronounced Labor misgivings about the draft Constitution that was the proposed basis for Federation; Watson shared them and campaigned against it. Once it was endorsed by majority verdict of the people, however, he accepted that Labor had to accept it. Watson was prominent at the intercolonial Labor conference in January 1900 that established the party on a federal basis with a national platform of policy objectives to take to the inaugural national election. He stood, successfully, as Labor's candidate for the lower house seat of Bland.

At the first meeting of the Federal Parliamentary Labor Party (FPLP) in May 1901 Watson was elected leader. Having New South Wales, the oldest and most populated colony, as his state of origin was a big help; Labor had advanced further there than in any other colony, and no state had provided more Labor members to the House of Representatives. Watson's elevation was also assisted by the absence from that meeting of Jim McGowen, the NSW Labor leader who had been defeated in the federal seat he contested, and Billy Hughes. However, Watson was widely esteemed and had conspicuous leadership qualities.

The parliamentary situation presented particular problems. For the first decade of Federal Parliament Labor was one of three parties of sufficiently similar strength that none could attain a parliamentary majority on its own. The challenge for Watson was to maintain caucus cohesion in testing parliamentary circumstances while continuing Labor's progress and achieving policy objectives along the way. Avoiding the artful traps that had ensnared NSW Labor and ruptured its MPs' solidarity during the 1890s was a paramount goal.

Support in return for concessions was the FPLP's tactical approach under Watson. He was familiar with its implementation in New South Wales and it suited his leadership style as well as the parliamentary situation. Staying on the crossbenches, providing flexible support on a case by case basis to the Protectionists who formed Australia's first ministry under Edmund Barton, was a congenial role for Watson; a protectionist himself, he admired the most significant individual in the Protectionist party, Alfred Deakin, who became prime minister after Barton resigned to become a High Court judge. Moreover, the Protectionists had more progressive instincts and were more likely to be responsive to Labor's reform priorities than the Free Traders led by George Reid.

The FPLP's tactical approach proceeded satisfactorily enough until a dramatic railway strike in Victoria. The conservative Victorian government's repressive response to the dispute reinforced Labor's commitment to a key objective, compulsory arbitration. The federal government was disinclined to bring state public servants (including railway workers) within the ambit of its Conciliation and Arbitration Bill, but the FPLP was adamant and the Bill was shelved. At the 1903 federal election, held when this issue was prominent, Labor achieved significant gains. Soon afterwards Deakin fatalistically reintroduced the controversial Bill, and an FPLP amendment extending its coverage was again carried; Deakin resigned, advising the governor-general to send for Watson.

On 23 April 1904 the former compositor who had earned a crust shovelling manure at Government House was invited to form the first national Labor government anywhere in the world. His party gave him a free hand to choose his ministers. Besides Hughes, an obvious inclusion, the six FPLP colleagues Watson chose included Scottish-born miner Andrew Fisher and Hugh Mahon, a prickly Western Australian loner whose commitment to the cause of Irish nationalism had resulted in a jail term in Dublin. Since Hughes was the only lawyer in caucus and a most inexperienced one, Watson included as his Attorney-General a radical Deakinite Protectionist, H.B. Higgins.

Many conservatives regarded a national Labor government as unthinkable. They found it hard to adjust to having a compositor-trade unionist as prime minister with miners, a labourer and an ardent Irish nationalist in his Cabinet. 'It will exist entirely on sufferance', declared the *Argus*, and 'has no claim to an extended life.'[2] The sight of Labor ministers occupying the Treasury benches reduced some of their predecessors to apoplexy. Deakin gave assurances of 'the utmost fair play',[3] but those outraged by the advent of a Labor government lost no time in plotting to remove it. The Watson government soon looked very vulnerable. Watson raised the prospect of an alliance with the more progressive Protectionists and obtained the FPLP's endorsement; but when he floated the proposal with Deakin the Protectionists were too divided on the issue for it to proceed.

So the Watson government struggled on alone. There were no conspicuous mistakes, but without a majority in either parliamentary chamber it was tough going, for Watson most of all. As he toiled to find a way to enshrine Labor objectives in legislation, even the ultra-patient prime minister became exasperated: 'I despair of seeing any good come out of this government', he told Higgins.[4] In fact Australians were becoming increasingly accustomed to the concept of a national Labor government, an important achievement. The Conciliation and Arbitration Bill lurched along, with Watson making unwilling concessions rather than abandoning it altogether, but when an amendment dealing with preference to unionists was carried against the government Watson resigned with honour and relief on 17 August.

Reid became prime minister and Watson reopened negotiations with the Protectionists. After Reid began a cynical anti-Labor propaganda offensive, denouncing the 'Socialist tiger' at every opportunity, Watson encouraged Deakin to move against Reid. He assured Deakin that 'you can rely on our active support ... We, and especially myself, don't want office, but I have the utmost anxiety to stop the retrogressive movement which Reid is heading'.[5] Shortly afterwards, in July 1905, Deakin replaced Reid as prime minister.

That same month Watson was disturbed by the outcome of several debates at his party's first interstate Conference since 1902. Federal Conference was the supreme body in the party's structure, and Watson felt aggrieved about several decisions at the 1905 Conference. After a debate about Labor's links with other parties, it was decided that no alliance could apply 'beyond the then existing Parliament'[6] and there would be no immunity for coalition allies at elections. Watson told the 1905 Conference delegates that the alliance with the Protectionists 'had more than justified itself';[7] the organisations had undisputed charge of policy, platform and preselections, he conceded, but they had no business dictating parliamentary tactics to the politicians. However, while pursuing Labor objectives in unworkable parliamentary circumstances was undeniably difficult for Watson and the FPLP, within the wider movement the longer view tended to prevail; Labor enthusiasts savouring their party's progress regarded pacts of electoral immunity as ill-judged, especially as the seats held by the progressive Protectionists were precisely those most vulnerable to Labor capture.

Watson was also perturbed when Charlie Frazer, a young FPLP backbencher, spearheaded a radical departure from the traditional method of selecting ministers. This had conventionally been the prerogative of the government leader, but at the 1905 Conference Frazer advocated that caucus should choose, a change consistent with fundamental Labor principles of equality and decision-making by the majority. His motion was softened by an amendment that ministers should be recommended rather than selected by caucus, but Watson regarded this notion as a repugnant reflection on his leadership. During the 1890s he had been instrumental himself in the establishment of Labor's unique organisational features embodying its commitment to equality, democracy and solidarity, but these 1905 innovations he abhorred.

Later in July Watson stunned colleagues by offering his resignation. If 'given no greater voice' in selecting ministers 'than the rawest recruit in the Party', he wrote, clearly tilting at Frazer, 'I most decidedly could not continue to lead.' That Conference decision was 'a censure upon myself ... and it was particularly hard to find it supported by several' FPLP members.[8] The gruelling pressures arising from the unwieldy parliamentary situation were increasingly telling, his health had deteriorated and there was minimal administrative assistance. Placated by heartfelt expressions of admiration from startled colleagues and the appointment of a deputy leader (Fisher) to lighten his load, he agreed to continue.

But the writing was on the wall. Watson remained as leader for two further years while the FPLP maintained its support for the Deakin government, but in October 1907 he resigned. This time, though only forty, he was unequivocal and unshiftable. Ill-health, the relentless demands of the leadership, the 1905 Conference decisions, the time away from home (especially the grindingly repetitive travel to Melbourne for parliamentary sittings), his wife's dissatisfaction with his frequent absence – all played their part. There were many pleas for him to reconsider. A Labor women's delegation approached Ada Watson, but met with a disarming response: 'I only want what you women all want – my husband at home with me'.[9]

Watson's detractors in the party sometimes wished he had more fire, but no Labor leader was more skilled at relating harmoniously with all elements in the party and with other MPs. His qualities were most suited to Labor's earliest years, before the realignment of federal politics into what basically amounted to Labor versus the rest, a time when the FPLP pursued its goals in concert with some non-Labor politicians and was intent on reassuring the electorate that it was not, as its enemies alleged, a bunch of wild-eyed extremists.

Caucus elected Fisher as his successor. Watson stayed in Parliament until the 1910 election. Amid growing FPLP restlessness about Labor's subsidiary role supporting the Protectionists, negotiations with Deakin were handled on the FPLP's behalf by Watson, with Fisher's blessing. When this dissatisfaction culminated in the withdrawal of that support and the advent of a Fisher Labor government, Watson contended that Fisher should be able to choose his ministers himself, but the FPLP upheld the 1905 Conference ruling that the composition of Cabinet was a matter for caucus; Watson then played a crucial lobbying role to ensure Fisher was given the ministry he wanted.

After leaving Parliament Watson remained influential in the ALP, serving on party executives and campaigning for the cause. When Labor split during the Great War he sided with the conscriptionists and left the ALP, but without the rancour and lasting ill-will associated with the departure of Hughes and others. Active in business, he retained public prominence through his involvement in soldier settlement administration and at the National Roads and Motorists' Association (NRMA), which became, thanks to his accomplished presidential contribution spanning two decades, Australia's leading motoring organisation. Friendly with Labor luminaries past and present, Watson was seventy-four when he died in November 1941. Prime Minister Curtin contravened the ALP tradition of enduring hostility to defectors by honouring him with a warm obituary tribute in both the caucus room and the House of Representatives.

Sir George Houstoun Reid

18 AUGUST 1904 – 5 JULY 1905

Since the 1980s Reid has undergone something of a 'resurrection'.

BY HELEN IRVING

George Houstoun Reid, Australia's fourth prime minister, is one of Australia's least-remembered. He rose to the office in August 1904 from the floor of Parliament without the drama or surprise of an election. His period at the head of government was brief. He was, furthermore, not the 'first' of anything still thought worthy of celebration. He does hold the record as the first, indeed the only, Free Trade prime minister, but he cannot be counted as the leader of the first Free Trade government, for his was an uneasy coalition with old opponents, the Protectionists. The significance of such an arrangement is now virtually lost to Australian political memory. For all this there is considerable irony in Reid's obscurity, for he was one of the most colourful, remarkable and loved politicians ever thrown up in Australian life. His impact was, furthermore, lasting and profound.

Reid, the seventh child of a Presbyterian minister, came from his birthplace in Scotland to Australia as a child and was educated in Melbourne and Sydney. For fifteen years he worked in the civil service, studying law after work and learning the speaking skills he would later put to such brilliant effect, in young men's debating societies. In 1879 he was admitted to the New South Wales bar. One year later he stood successfully for the seat of East Sydney and entered the colonial Parliament. There he remained almost continuously for thirty years. In 1894 Reid took the once-hallowed place of Sir Henry Parkes as Free Trade premier of New South Wales. It was a critical time in the life of the colonies: the grip of depression was still tight and the Labor Party had made sudden and irreversible inroads into the Parliaments. After the failure of the first Federal Convention in 1891, calls for Federation were growing louder.

It was Reid who carried out policies of economic reconstruction that rescued his colony earlier than its rival, Victoria. And it was Reid who in early 1895 brought the other premiers to the table to embrace a new, popular process for achieving Federation. It was Reid who, after the second Federal Convention had completed its work in 1898, stood before the Town Hall in Sydney and confessed his ambivalence about the newly drafted Constitution Bill. He had been an elected delegate to the Convention where the Bill was written and felt he must remain loyal to its work. But its provisions, he said, were unfair to his colony, and the people of New South Wales should remember this at the forthcoming referendum on the Bill. When the 1898 referendum failed, as he had hoped it would, Reid again engineered negotiations with the other premiers and achieved an amended Constitution, its provisions more favourable to the voters of New South Wales. The outcome was success in the second referendum, in 1899, and the certain accomplishment of Federation. For his initial equivocation on the Constitution, however, even as prime minister, he was ever after known as 'Yes–No' Reid.

It was not a wounding epithet; indeed Reid seems to have enjoyed it, just as he did the regular press caricatures of his great unwieldy body, his baby face and his absurd monocle. He was a consummate performer – 'perhaps the best platform speaker in the Empire'[1] – at once amusing and informative to his audiences, who 'flocked to his election meetings as to popular entertainment'.[2] The record of his speeches can still make the modern reader laugh aloud. At one meeting a heckler called out to him, pointing at his stomach: 'What are you going to call it, George?' Reid replied, 'If it's a boy, I'll call it after myself. If it's a girl I'll call it Victoria. But if, as I strongly suspect, it's nothing but piss and wind, I'll name it after you.' But that was not all. Reid was a skilled political operator, 'an astute politician often mistaken for a clown'.[3] By 1901, some thought him 'probably the biggest political force in Australia'.[4] He was reported to be the only politician in the Commonwealth inauguration procession in Sydney on 1 January 1901 to receive an ovation from the crowd. Most of his fellow politicians, even opponents, shared their approval.

Two powerful politicians, however, did not. Henry Parkes regarded Reid with contempt and thought him a 'babbling lunatic'. But Parkes died in 1896, less than two years after Reid became premier and eight before he became prime minister; the two men were in any case reconciled at Parkes's deathbed. The second politician harboured a hatred that was to prove enduring and powerful. Alfred Deakin, Victoria's leading federationist of the 1890s, first attorney-general and Protectionist deputy in the Commonwealth government, loathed George Reid. In Deakin's writings lie one of the most scathing and compelling sketches ever drawn of a politician: physically monstrous, personally repulsive, morally questionable, ambitious, 'inordinately vain and resolutely selfish', cunning, vituperative and shallow.[5]

For many years Deakin's words shaped perceptions of Reid. Some historians portrayed him as personally responsible for setting back Federation;[6] others depicted him as a man with few friends, an 'unwholesome' player in games of 'political chicanery'.[7] Over the years, however, such impressions have come under challenge as the political complexities of Reid's era are better understood and a wider range of sources employed. Since the 1980s Reid has undergone something of a 'resurrection', and is now acknowledged as a progressive, liberal politician of his time, and a colourful, lovable man who did not take himself too seriously. Reid's great 'sin', in the eyes of one historian, was simply to enjoy public life: 'the unforgivable sin of this rambunctious, shambling mountain who was apt to disarm an opponent with the invitation to "have a lolly", a supply of which he habitually carried in his copious pockets'.[8]

Deakin's sketch of Reid was written in secret in 1900 and it remained unpublished for more than four decades. But it was a portent of things immediately to come. Reid was too good-natured to hold grudges, but Deakin's hatred had a major impact upon the development of Australian politics in the first decade of the Commonwealth.

In March 1901, along with almost all leading colonial politicians, both Reid and Deakin stood for election to the new federal Parliament. It was Edmund Barton, already the appointed first prime minister, who led his Protectionist Party to victory and retained office. Reid, heading the Free Trade Party, took the consolation prize as first Commonwealth leader of the Opposition. It was not an office that satisfied his hopes, and it heralded a career in federal politics which was 'to be something of an anticlimax'.[9] In the early stages of the Commonwealth, however, when constitutional powers were being exercised for the first time, the Opposition leader's role was scarcely insignificant.

A free trade regime within the Commonwealth had been ordained by the Constitution, and the Commonwealth Parliament had exclusive powers to levy customs and excise duties. There would, therefore, be free trade within and tariffs at Australia's borders. But the Commonwealth was also required to return three-quarters of all its customs and excise revenue to the states for ten years, and this meant a higher tariff than Free Traders would have wished. Their battle, then, was to maintain a workable revenue tariff without slipping into Protectionist levels.

Consultation and compromise between Free Traders and Protectionists was unavoidable, and the attitude of their respective leaders was critical. In addition, Labor's presence in Parliament was substantial from the start, growing at each election, until in 1903 the 'Three Elevens' stood virtually shoulder to shoulder and fiscal policy, which for more than a decade had been the great party differentiator, became merely one issue among others. The search for a 'fiscal truce' began, and Reid was enthusiastic. Barton and Reid were old friends, but in 1903 Deakin took over as Protectionist leader and prime minister. The chances of a lasting truce, even a provisional one, were now slim.

Other issues filled the Commonwealth Parliament's early agenda: immigration policy, defence, the federal judiciary, industrial arbitration. The Opposition forced a reduction in the inaugural numbers of High Court judges from five to three and obstructed the Conciliation and Arbitration Bill in whatever form it was presented, although Reid himself stood apart from this. In other arenas, as an old-style liberal, he was vigilant against what he considered excessive official discretion and overregulation. His anti-socialism was hardening.

In April 1904 Labor withdrew its support from Deakin and his government fell, to be replaced by Labor under Watson. Deakin, now leader of the Opposition, 'rushed into my arms', said Reid, 'and suddenly developed a very pointed spirit of antagonism to his former allies'.[10] A shaky agreement was reached; the fiscal question would be allowed to sleep until the next election. But when the Watson Labor government itself collapsed only four months later and Reid became prime minister, Deakin refused to join the Reid ministry. Another Victorian protectionist, Allan McLean, agreed to a truce of sorts, sharing the entitlements of the prime minister's office and taking the Trade and Customs portfolio. Reid's ministry had a good mix of talented Protectionists and Free Traders, and a good cross-section of state representatives. McLean was, furthermore, a Catholic, while Reid, championed by the militant Protestants of New South Wales, had been embroiled in sectarian strife for some years.

At the start things looked promising, but Reid's majority was in truth too small to be workable. In the wings to one side stood the liberal Protectionists, hostile to the very idea of a fiscal truce. On the other side waited the Labor Party, unshakable in its distrust of Reid. Only two weeks after Parliament began sitting Watson moved a vote of no confidence, which occupied fifteen days of debate and gained the support of the disgruntled Protectionists. Reid survived by a majority of two and limped through with the passage of supply and only a handful of Bills before the long summer recess began.

Six Acts alone were passed during Reid's brief government: one, the Life Assurance Companies Act, was already waiting from the prorogation of the previous Parliament. The Sea Carriage of Goods Act provided some protection for exporters against unfair provisions in bills of lading. There was a new Defence Act and a new version of the 1901 Acts Interpretation Act, and the long-awaited Seat of Government Act was passed. Five years earlier Reid had brought the colonial premiers to concede the federal capital to New South Wales as the price of Federation. Now Parliament, after many alternative bids, chose Dalgety, New South Wales, 'that salubrious mountain resort'.[11] But, like so much of the era, even this plan did not survive and within three years the search for a federal site began again. Ten other Bills were submitted without issue and there were several lengthy debates over parliamentary resolutions on imperial matters, including Chinese labour in the Transvaal and Home Rule for Ireland.

Reid's big success was the passage of the Conciliation and Arbitration Act. Many have noted the great irony that 'the one historical achievement' of the Reid–McLean ministry was the passage of this Bill, 'which had already brought down both its earlier sponsors', the Deakin and Watson governments.[12] Where the previous regimes had stumbled on union membership and the proposal to bring state employees under the Act, Reid managed to see these through, although remaining cynically doubtful of their constitutional validity. The Court of Conciliation and Arbitration established by the Act survived and evolved into one of the key institutions of Australian political life in the twentieth century. To Reid's credit goes its establishment, if neither its promotion nor its conception.

Overall, however, the government achieved little. During the six months' parliamentary recess, a Royal Commission on the tariff began its work and Reid conducted a speaking tour of the states, waving the anti-socialist and anti-Labor banner as he went. Neither initiative would be productive. Parliament resumed in June 1905; Reid's ministry had only one month to live.

Deakin, who had begun to renegotiate Labor support, was breathing down Reid's neck. Only days earlier he had given what was understood as a 'notice to quit' speech, directed at the government. Back in Parliament Watson denounced Reid, and Deakin immediately followed with an amendment to the address-in-reply. He disavowed any alliance with the Free Traders, reaffirmed his commitment to protectionism and criticised Reid's anti-socialist stance. The amendment was handsomely carried. Reid was refused a dissolution. He resigned and, with Labor support, Deakin stepped back into office.

Reid's days in politics were effectively over. Although he resumed the leadership of the Opposition and campaigned vigorously in the 1906 general election on an anti-socialist platform, his personal style was no longer a dependable asset. It belonged to 'the raffish inner Sydney electorates in the late-nineteenth-century days of gaslight and torchlight rallies addressed from public-house balconies'.[13] He hung on for two more years before resigning. In 1910 he left Australia to take up, very successfully, the post of first high commissioner to Britain, then a seat in the House of Commons, where he remained until his death in 1918.

Reid had scarcely left the Commonwealth Parliament when Deakin and the new Free Trade leader Joseph Cook engineered the anti-Labor 'Fusion' that Reid had sought for years. Reid had been among the first of the old practitioners to see that lines of party demarcation in the twentieth century would no longer be drawn around fiscal policy. The new lines divided opponents from proponents of government intervention, advocates of 'caucus' politics from individualists, regulators by government from believers in regulation by the market. Once in Commonwealth politics Reid, unlike Deakin, saw these lines as absolute. His politics were increasingly shaped by anti-Labor ideology, not only in Parliament but through the establishment of anti-socialist leagues and later the Australian Democratic Union. But he lost the chance of carrying the new, dogmatic liberalism through into Commonwealth politics. It is Deakin who is remembered for the Free-Trade–Protectionist 'Fusion' and often held up by the modern Liberal Party of Australia as their progenitor. In this they are mistaken. That paternity belongs to George Reid.

For Deakin's period in office 5 July 1905 – 13 November 1908, see pages 36–53.

Andrew Fisher

13 NOVEMBER 1908 – 2 JUNE 1909

29 APRIL 1910 – 24 JUNE 1913

17 SEPTEMBER 1914 – 27 OCTOBER 1915

Unquestionably, Fisher was one of Australia's finest prime ministers.

BY CLEM LLOYD

(*Enter Fisher. po-faced with a knife in his back.*)
FISHER: Good morning Mr Attorney-General. What is it you have to say to me?
HUGHES: Congratulations Mr Prime Minister on your appointment to London as High Commissioner. I shall endeavour to fill your exalted office with the necessary sweetness and light.
(*Fisher bewildered blinks once and turns to go. Gaily Hughes sticks another knife in his back.*)

Michael Boddy and Bob Ellis, *The Legend of King O'Malley*[1]

The dim, dour Scotsman of Boddy and Ellis' fine political farce, complete with kilt, sporran, bonnet and bagpipes, ever peeping over his shoulder for Billy Hughes' dirk in his back is, alas, all too often Australia's perception of Andrew Fisher, its fifth prime minister. Yet the reality was much more substantial. Unquestionably, Fisher was one of Australia's finer prime ministers: a legislator who, with Alfred Deakin, directed the writing of much of the early Commonwealth statute book; an administrator who established great Commonwealth institutions such as the defence forces, the Commonwealth Bank and the Prime Minister's Department; a political leader largely responsible for guiding the Australian Labor Party to predominance in national politics. He was a friend, even a patron, of William Morris Hughes, capable of keeping the mercurial little Welshman in line, not the complaisant victim of popular myth. He deserves to be much more warmly remembered by his fellow Australians.

According to family tradition, Andrew Fisher might have descended from the great Scottish chieftain Sir William Wallace, the legendary Braveheart of cinematic fame. The legend attributes to Wallace an exceptionally long arm, presumably an advantage in combat and often a characteristic of his descendants. When Andrew Fisher was born at Crosshouse, in Central Ayrshire, Scotland on 29 August 1862 he did not have the 'Wallace arm'. His daughter Margaret, perhaps fancifully, recorded that some of her brothers had it. A pity! Links with Braveheart might have given resonance, colour and dimension to Fisher's drab, lugubrious stereotype.[2]

Part of the reason for this sad neglect of Fisher may be that he lived less than half of his life in the country of which he became prime minister. He spent his youth and early manhood in Scotland, emigrating to central Queensland when he was twenty-three. His last dozen years were lived in London, where he died in 1928 at the age of sixty-six. His radical labour principles were moulded not in colonial Australia but in the collieries of Ayrshire. One of Fisher's mentors was the great labour leader James Keir Hardie, another Ayrshire miner who rose from child labour in the pits to political eminence. Both rode the path to political glory in the van of ascendant labour parties, Keir Hardie in Victorian Britain, Fisher in a federated Australia.

The historian Arthur W. Jose described Fisher's career as a 'triumph of character'.[3] The wellsprings of Fisher's character are unexceptionable and easily sourced. His family tree included weavers, rural workers, blacksmiths and small farmers, and by the 1850s mostly coalminers. According to family tradition his grandfather, John Fisher, was blacklisted by mine owners and walked the streets with his wife and five children, one crippled and another a babe in arms. One of his sons was Robert (or 'Rab') Fisher, also a miner with radical principles forced out of colliery work by a combination of blacklisting and miner's catarrh. He married Jane Garvin, a blacksmith's daughter. Andrew Fisher was the second of their six sons and two daughters. (One daughter died in early adolescence, the other devoted her life to caring for her family.)

'Rab' Fisher's neighbours found him a difficult personality, but to his children he was very stern but fair. He enjoyed their company, took them for long walks to make them physically fit, and counselled them with sensitivity. The Fishers were adherents of a Presbyterian sect known colloquially as the 'Wee Frees'. Throughout his life Andrew Fisher was staunchly Presbyterian, a Sunday school superintendent in his earlier years, observing sabbatarian disciplines as far as politics permitted. He was strictly teetotal, taking liquor only when seriously ill. The Scottish model of community co-operation was an important part of the Fisher inheritance. The family savings were invested in the Crosshouse Co-operative, which Robert Fisher helped found. Young Andrew Fisher used its reading room from childhood.[4]

Fisher attended the village school but left early to work in the coalpits. One account holds that he was 'dedicated' to mining not long after the age of nine. More likely he was nearer twelve, the legal age for boys to work in the pits. With his elder brother John, he probably started mining early to boost family income reduced by a disabled father able to do only light work. Their sacrifices gave educational opportunities to their younger brothers, who were able to obtain professional qualifications. The terrible privations of Scottish mining, including virtual slave labour of women and children as young as five, had been ameliorated by the British Parliament in the 1840s. Young male recruits worked mainly on filling and moving the coal wagons before they cut coal, but their work was still arduous and dangerous.[5]

To further his education, Andrew took some tutoring from the local minister, went to evening classes in nearby Kilmarnock and read extensively in politics and English poetry. He was elected secretary of the Crosshouse branch of the Ayrshire Miners' Union in 1879, when he was seventeen. In 1881, he was a leader of a bold strike lasting for ten weeks but ending in total defeat. Fisher was blacklisted but eventually obtained work because of his skills with machinery. However, it was plain by the mid 1880s that his incipient militancy jeopardised his future in the Ayrshire mines.

The great Scottish diaspora extending from the Highland Clearances of the eighteenth century to the late Victorian era brought Fisher to the central Queensland mines in the mid 1880s. Strongly influenced by their mother, Fisher and his younger brother James joined a small group of Crosshouse emigrants for Australia, arriving in August 1885 at Brisbane. Not finding work at the nearby Ipswich mines, the brothers went to those of central Queensland, where many Ayrshire miners and families had settled. Andrew Fisher worked in the Burrum mines north-west of Maryborough, mainly at Torbanlea, where he helped sink a new shaft and briefly held a management position. His radicalism again brought him into conflict with the mine ownership. His support for a Saturday half-holiday for miners led to his ostracism by management, and might have cost him a senior post at another mine. Embittered by this rejection, and dissatisfied with the limited cultural and social opportunities of Burrum, he moved in the late 1880s to the flourishing goldmines at Gympie, south of Maryborough.

At Gympie, Fisher found the cleaner quartz mining and greater diversity of a large provincial centre greatly to his taste. He thrived on the ferment of labour politics sparked by the shearers' strike of 1891, and led a spirited but non-violent demonstration outside the home of a conservative Cabinet minister. After the savage repression of the shearers' strike and the introduction of punitive industrial legislation, Fisher emerged as a leader of the Amalgamated Miners' Union in Gympie, then of the Workers' Political Organisation, the precursor of the Queensland Labor Party. In the 1893 state elections Fisher was elected one of two members for Gympie in the state Parliament. Parliamentary politics sharpened his skills and he read copiously in the well-stocked parliamentary library. In public policy, Fisher showed specific interest in state banking, the sugar industry, workers' compensation, public works and industrial conciliation and arbitration.

As a parliamentary tactician, Fisher advocated Labor Party co-operation with non-Labor factions, where possible without compromising Labor's industrial principles and autonomy. His defeat at state elections in 1896 convinced him that the Labor Party needed its own press to win and maintain government. Drawing on his own resources, he helped establish the *Gympie Truth* as a foil to the *Gympie Times*, owned by political rivals. Unable to go back to mining, Fisher worked as a bookbinder and council auditor. He survived a serious attack of typhoid, then was re-elected to Parliament in 1899. He quickly reasserted his seniority as one of four ministers in the Dawson Labor government of December 1899 – the first labour government in Australia and probably the first in the world. It lasted seven days, one journalist comparing its political life cycle with that of a butterfly.[6] Fisher had supported the Federation movement through the 1890s, but strongly opposed the participation of Queensland colonial troops in the South African (or Boer) war of 1899-1901.

By 1901 Fisher had excellent prospects of state Labor leadership and, ultimately, the premiership. Instead he chose the new polity of federal Australia, a milieu of boundless opportunity, but also of extreme hazards. At the first federal election in May 1901 he won the federal seat of Wide Bay, based on Maryborough and Gympie, and held it continuously until his retirement in 1915. Completing a memorable political and personal year, on 31 December 1901, the Scottish festival of Hogmanay, he married Margaret Jane Irvine, his landlady's daughter. He was thirty-nine, his wife twenty-seven. In a pungent reprise of Fisher's mining days, his bride's sister fetched from a nearby mine the water to cook the chicken for the wedding breakfast. The bride's youngest sister, aged eleven, accompanied the pair on the early days of their honeymoon because the family thought she needed 'a little holiday'.[7]

Fisher's entry to the Commonwealth Parliament at its inception was superbly timed. The large contingent of Labor members had no natural leaders because Labor politics had been largely indifferent to the debates and processes of the 1890s. It had to find leaders among its parliamentary ranks. The House of Representatives blended into the so-called 'Three Elevens' with broad groupings of Labor, Liberal Protectionists (or Deakinites), and mainly conservative Free Traders. It was virtually impossible for any single group to govern in its own right. Thus office was dependent either on a coalition of two 'elevens', or a minority 'eleven' governing with the support of one other 'eleven'. This cast a pall over initiative and innovation in public policy, protracting the adoption of an effective tariff framework.

Tactically, the 'Three Elevens' configuration was a godsend for Labor, which was organised on the lines of a conventional political party from the beginning. Thus it could throw guaranteed numbers behind one or other of the two non-Labor groups. This allowed Labor to support policies consistent with its platform except on industrial issues. In practice, this meant that Labor mostly supported Deakin and the 'Deakinites'. The main beneficiaries of this unwieldy dispensation were Alfred Deakin and the three dominant Labor leaders: Chris Watson, Andrew Fisher and Billy Hughes.

Among Fisher's greatest political assets were his superb presence, robust physique, elegantly chiselled visage and graceful bearing. At thirty-nine, in the prime of life when he entered Parliament, Fisher was unquestionably the most physically distinguished of all Australia's prime ministers, generally an unprepossessing lot. He had filled out a little, but largely retained the hard body and pliant muscularity of the young miner. Although not a dandy, he dressed fashionably and well, 'always well groomed in a sober way, very neat, always the owner of a good hat and clean boots. His wispy moustache had flourished like the native shrubs of his electorate ...'[8] Fisher spoke with an Ayrshire accent; Hansard reporters found his words difficult to transcribe when he became excited and lapsed into a Scottish buzz.

In his early years in the federal Parliament Fisher moved cautiously, content to watch and wait. His signal advantages, perhaps, were his reputation for steadiness and his unequivocal party loyalty. He did not lack ego, and he had a brimming confidence in his own ideas. While his formal speeches were often uninspiring, he excelled at reproducing the thoughts of others. As the historian and journalist Malcolm Ellis said: 'He was a good sorter out and groomer of other people's ideas. He could thresh the acceptable ones out of the wildly visionary. He was not an originator. Nobody knew till the end of his days where his plans and phrases came from unless they were obvious in origin. But he was a worker, he was sincere.'[9] Some journalists thought he deliberately cultivated simplicity and a low estimate of his perspicacity: 'It suited him to think that his opponents should think his bowling was unorthodox on the wicket. The "wrong-un" was there all the same.'[10]

By 1904, his political stature within caucus earned him the post of minister for trade and customs, and fifth ranking in Chris Watson's foundation Labor government that survived for four months. Back in Opposition, the Labor caucus in August 1905 elected Fisher to a new post as assistant leader in the House of Representatives. He beat the scintillating, thrusting Billy Hughes for the job, reputedly by one vote. When Watson stood down in 1907, Fisher was the logical choice as his successor, again defeating Hughes.

As Labor leader he had consistently supported the economic, social and defence policies of his close friend and mentor Alfred Deakin. He had assured Deakin, who was a minority prime minister, that he would never see him humiliated by withdrawal of Labor Party support. However, with his party colleagues constantly urging another independent Labor government, and critical of Deakin's tariff and and pensions proposals, Fisher reluctantly abandoned the Deakinites.

He became prime minister on 13 November 1908, his first brief prime ministership lasting just over six months, until 2 June 1909. He also took the Treasury portfolio, as he did in his two subsequent prime ministerships. His first government was essentially a pawn in the great realignment of federal politics in 1908–09, with the gradual resolution of the tariff (or fiscal) question, and consequent coalescing of the non-Labor elements. This strained and ultimately destroyed Fisher's close political friendship with Alfred Deakin.

Although it lacked the numbers to pass major legislation, the first Fisher government affirmed Labor's credentials to provide stable, competent and responsible national government. Most importantly, it enabled Fisher to embark on what historian Malcolm Ellis described as 'defence planning on a grand scale'.[11] Over three administrations, one during wartime, he carved out an enduring framework for defence administration and was instrumental in building the Commonwealth armed services. Using the executive power, he built on policies initiated by Deakin, ordering three destroyers and making plans for compulsory military training.

Labor was summarily ejected from government in May 1909, when the Fusion Party was formed, uniting the Labor Party's traditional political enemies. The Fusion outnumbering Labor by two to one, Deakin became prime minister and leader of what became known as the Liberal Party. The advent of the Fusion sparked an extraordinary sequence of virulent ructions and eruptions. At the height of one violent, vilifying debate, the Speaker, Sir Frederick Holder, was heard to mutter, 'Terrible! Terrible!' before slumping dead in his chair. Fisher was in front of a real firing line for the first time, and the vindictive parliamentary sittings sapped his strength. Malcolm Shepherd, his secretary, recorded that Fisher's hair, tinged with grey when he became a minister in 1904, was silver white after this 'season of ceaseless excitement'.[12]

The turmoil sparked by the Fusion cost Fisher the prime ministership and hastened his physical and mental decline. It also enhanced his reputation and presented him with his greatest political opportunity. During the election campaign of 1910, Fisher skilfully exploited Deakin's opportunism in destroying the previous Labor government. 'Now what can you do with a man like that?' was his consistent refrain on the hustings.[13] The electorate decided that what it could do with Deakin was throw him out and return Fisher with a convincing majority. Labor became the first Australian federal party to win government in its own right. Fisher took his triumph quietly enough 'but it was the quietness of exaltation. For the first time a Government of the Commonwealth had a chance to unfold its wings without some other party perched on its aching neck.'[14]

In these favourable circumstances, with majorities in both Houses, Fisher embarked on an exhilarating wave of public policy inception, innovation and embellishment, seismic in its dimensions and impact. In three years of unimpeded government he transformed a skimpy

Commonwealth statute book by adding twenty-three pieces of new legislation, almost all significant. True, this did not comprise a logical, tightly co-ordinated program; there were gaps and inconsistencies and much depended much on Fisher's whims and perceptions of opportunities. Nor was it wholly attributable to Fisher. The caucus and its committees contributed a great deal as, in legal and judicial areas, did Billy Hughes. By any criterion, though, it was an exciting and overwhelmingly constructive exercise. Apart from parliamentary legislation, Fisher used the executive power freely. A breathless listing of heads of approved legislation and executive action prepared by Deakin's enthusiastic secretary gives some notion of the amplitude, significance and enduring richness of what can be justly called the Fisher canon.

> *Northern Territory Acceptance Act*, providing for the transfer to the Commonwealth of the Northern territory ...
> *Naval Defence act*, which brought the royal Australian Navy into being ... [act], by which the Commonwealth took over all state debts ...
> *State of Government* administration act, providing for the transfer of the federal Government, and Parliament to Canberra in federal Capital territory ... *Commonwealth Bank act*, by which was established the great Commonwealth Bank ... *Invalid and old age pensions act* ... *Maternity Allowance Act* ... *Workmen's compensation act* ... *Land Tax Act* ... *Postal Rates Act* ...[15]

The list streams on. There were amendments bringing conciliation and arbitration into the 'modern era', as well as the Commonwealth Land Tax Act and the Commonwealth Notes Act, which allowed the Commonwealth to take over the business of issuing paper currency, previously done by private banks. Billy Hughes as attorney-general brought down the Judiciary Bill, defining the powers of the High Court and the Commonwealth. Compulsory military training was introduced, Duntroon Military College was founded.

Indeed, the pulse of change might have perplexed and ultimately exhausted an electorate accustomed to sluggish public policy and torpid administration. Three years of Labor was enough for the country, or so it seemed. It is difficult to explain otherwise why Fisher's government was rejected at the general elections of May 1913, although only by a one-seat margin. This was the only significant blemish on Fisher's political leadership. It might have been due in part to the distracting impact of six referendum proposals held conjointly with the election and also lost narrowly. (Fisher and the Labor caucus had bravely opted to extend Commonwealth powers by referendum.) Joseph Cook, who replaced Deakin as Liberal leader, became prime minister; Fisher easily beat challenges from Billy Hughes and William Higgs to retain Opposition leadership.

Because the Cook government lacked a Senate majority, Labor could block its legislation. Thus both sides could joust for a double dissolution of the Parliament at a time of political advantage. This was the kernel of Fisher's strategy for Labor revival. In early 1914 he sensed that the electoral mood was swinging back to Labor. With its policymaking hamstrung through lack of a Senate majority, Cook's government also favoured a double dissolution at this time. The crucial deadlock emerged in May over legislation to restrict preference to trade unionists. Fisher's keen political instincts were vindicated in the rout of Cook's Liberal government at the September 1914 double dissolution election, the first in the Australian Federation.

As prime minister, Fisher inherited the Great War, then thirty-one days old. Although Fisher had rejected Australian involvement in the Boer War, his imperial patriotism was fundamentally strong. During the election campaign he issued a stirring patriotic invocation that remains his principal claim on the Australian memory. At a campaign meeting at Colac, Victoria on 31 July 1914 he brandished imperial patriotism and the Union Jack in unequivocal terms: 'All, I am sure, will regret the critical position existing at the present time and pray that a disastrous war might be averted. But should the worst happen after everything has been done that honour will permit, Australians will stand beside our own to help and defend her to our last man and our last shilling.'[16]

A few days later, at Benalla, Fisher elevated the war above party and campaign politics, proclaiming that in time of emergency, 'there are no parties at all. We stand united against the common foe'. Again he said that 'our last man and our last shilling will be offered and supplied to the mother country'. Fisher repeated the pledge for a third time as prime minister: 'We shall pledge our last man and our last shilling to see this war brought to a successful issue.'[17]

Fisher deserves much credit for preserving harmony between the parties and within the Parliament during what was a new and tremendous experience for all Australians. Nor was there much to cavil about in his conduct of the war's first year. He had a fine team of experienced ministers, most notably the bellicose Hughes and Senator George Pearce, his capable defence minister. The first division of the AIF was recruited, trained and got away to the Middle East in good time. Although Fisher was not informed of the Gallipoli landing until after it had happened, the Australian performance gave lustre to his policies. He appeared to be at the peak of his political career, primed for a long run in office. Instead he resigned abruptly as prime minister in October 1915 to become Australian high commissioner in London.

Some historians, notably Malcolm Ellis, have presented Fisher's departure as a fall from office, most likely caused by gathering dissension within the ALP and what Ellis described vividly as his proximity to the 'consuming fires' of Billy Hughes.[18] Certainly, Hughes coveted the prime ministership which he felt had been his by merit since 1901. Australian political tradition has represented Fisher in some degree as a victim of Hughes' leaping ambition. Fisher respected, perhaps envied, Hughes' volcanic energy, brilliance, biting eloquence and tactical skills on the parliamentary floor. But he had always had the measure of Hughes in caucus, defeating him in leadership ballots and curbing his excesses. Indisputably, Fisher quit the prime ministership at a time of his own choosing for a job that, in the eyes of many Australians, was of comparable stature.

Very likely he also retired because of ill-health, evidenced in a gradual onset of premature senile decay and nervous exhaustion triggered by the cruel demands of war. Fisher's private secretary, Malcolm Shepherd, recorded that in 1914–15 Fisher was afflicted by extreme listlessness and mental fatigue, confined often to his bed while fulfilling all formal duties.[19] His energies were further attenuated by a series of draining parliamentary debates on wartime regulations, restrictions of civil liberties and the war census. In many ways these confrontations taxed caucus solidarity, serving as grim harbingers of what conscription for overseas service would eventually bring. In early 1915 Fisher retreated to New Zealand, ostensibly for war talks but actually to recuperate from what seems to have been a nervous collapse. He was also frustrated by lack of consultation by the Imperial government over war policy and by the High Command over the control and disposition of Australian troops. Fisher might have felt that his presence in London might improve Australian involvement in imperial decisionmaking and access to war intelligence. Perhaps, also, he hankered for home after thirty years in Australia.

As high commissioner Fisher chose to observe the public service protocol of impartiality, declining public comment on the two conscription referenda and their implications. Much has been written about whether or not Fisher would have supported conscription as prime minister. Despite his patriotic rhetoric he would probably have stuck to lifelong principles and opposed it. Whatever aspirations he might have had for influence in London were rudely dashed by Hughes' assumption, as prime minister, of an overriding role. Hughes spent long periods in London and effectively thrust his high commissioner aside. Very likely Hughes resented Fisher's even-handedness on conscription, despite his 'last man, last shilling' pledge. After the war ended in November 1918 Hughes was churlish in his treatment of his predecessor, declining initially to support even a short extension of Fisher's high commissionership. Although highly sensitive to Hughes' slights, Fisher made no complaint.

Although sidelined by Hughes, Fisher performed useful service as high commissioner. He represented Australia on the Dardanelles Commission which investigated the Gallipoli fiasco, visited the Australian troops in France and solicitously guarded their entitlements, and built a warm, trusting relationship with the AIF commander General Birdwood. Increasingly, however, Fisher's diplomacy and public life were constrained by cumulative debility. In 1921 he returned to Australia, mainly to sort out his business affairs and personal papers. He was warmly welcomed, with old colleagues urging him to return to Labor politics, even the leadership of a party devastated by Hughes' desertion and the great schism over conscription. But he returned to the United Kingdom, where he made an unsuccessful attempt to obtain preselection for a Scottish seat in the House of Commons.

Fisher spent his last few years living a sequestered life, mostly in London. Like his great compatriot Alfred Deakin, his final years were blighted by what historian Herbert Campbell Jones vividly described as a 'horrible sinking into senility'. In some respects Fisher's dwindling away was the more prolonged and pathetic. He was sixty-six when he died, his death certificate describing the cause as premature senile decay, heart disease and influenza. His daughter Margaret Fisher recorded in her memoir: 'On the day before he died, my father, Andrew Fisher, could not write his own name.'[20] He died on 22 October 1928 and was buried, after a state funeral, in Hampstead cemetery, London.

Fisher's most incisive critic was Malcolm Shepherd, his private secretary through his three prime ministerships. Shepherd was often critical of his boss, who could be cantankerous and inclined to procrastination, even indolence, about political basics such as preparing for speeches and press briefings. Fisher was also extremely touchy about any perceived slight to his official position, although this edginess was probably due as much to perceived affront to the Labor Party as to himself. Despite defects, some substantial, Shepherd concluded that Fisher's earnestness, decency, intelligence and sincerity far outweighed the blemishes.

Fisher and Alfred Deakin have been the only Australian prime ministers (to date) to hold the post for three separate terms. (Robert Menzies was prime minister twice for two separate terms.) And apart from Edmund Barton and Robert Menzies, Fisher has been the only Australian prime minister voluntarily to choose the time and manner of his leaving the job. His departure was not dictated by political failure, death or ill-health. Altogether, Fisher was prime minister for almost five years, a remarkable achievement given that in the first decade of Federation the party lines were still fluid and minority governments were the rule.

As federal leader Fisher did much to build the ethos, organisation and platform of the Australian Labor Party, drawing on rich experience in the labour politics of Britain and colonial Queensland. He was unreservedly dedicated to the tenets of social democracy as achieved through constitutional government, with little sympathy for class warfare, and relied on progressive public policy to reduce social divisiveness and inequalities. Rather oddly, he concluded that Labor's entry to parliamentary politics meant that 'we are all socialists now'.[21]

In Queensland he had been a pacifier among the wild spirits of early labour politics. As Malcolm Ellis said, 'Andrew Fisher went amongst hot-blooded men keyed up to violence and turned their energies into lawful channels.'[22] In a muted way, a similar civilising influence was evident in his firm yet flexible handling of a federal party reflecting complex historical, regional and ideological elements, often restive and querulous of leadership. Fisher accepted and guided his party's evolution, exercising a substantial influence but not seeking to dictate or dominate. Although responsive to evolving party machinery outside Parliament, he kept the federal caucus free of any suggestion of external interference. In all, Fisher was leader of the Federal Parliamentary Labor Party for five years in government and three in Opposition. No one has led the federal Labor Party better. Probably only Curtin has led it as well.

In a budding Commonwealth administration, where virtually everything remained to be done, and much of the statute book was blank, Fisher's problems in defining and scheduling his policies into a practical program were largely irrelevant. He was content to take his chances as they came. His objectives were expressed in blunt imperatives: 'We'll have a worker's compensation bill now.'[23] Not even the most obdurate or tentative of public servants could prevaricate or temporise in the face of such an injunction. For the legislative draftsmen, a world of opportunity opened for explanation, embellishment and implementation. It was Fisher's good fortune to establish at bedrock federal public policy, institutions and laws largely unfettered by the institutional constraints and rigidities of later years.

Sir Joseph Cook

24 JUNE 1913 – 17 SEPTEMBER 1914

He seemed to regard his journey from trade unionist and labour radical to conservative imperialist as an entirely natural and unremarkable progression.

BY JOHN RICKARD

History – and historians – can be ruthless in marginalising leaders and dignitaries who, in their own time, were prominent figures in the political and social landscape. Sir Joseph Cook, it is true, was prime minister for a mere fifteen months in 1913 and 1914, but he had a long and, some would say, distinguished career over three decades in New South Wales and Commonwealth politics. Moreover, his is a classic colonial success story of the English working-class migrant who makes the journey, not only from Britain to one of its most distant colonies, but from pitboy in a coalmine to prime minister of the new dominion of Australia. Cook is also notable as an early defector from the Labor Party, which had made its NSW parliamentary debut in 1891 – the first in a line of Labor 'rats' (the ugly term was already in use in Cook's day) which includes two subsequent prime ministers, Billy Hughes and Joe Lyons. Yet Cook has no place in Australian popular memory today, except perhaps in the former coalmining community of Lithgow from where he launched his political career.

Historians have not been helpful to Sir Joseph's reputation. J. A. La Nauze, the biographer of Deakin, dismisses Cook as an 'irascible, untiring, humourless little man'; Fitzhardinge, the biographer of Hughes, characterises him as 'loyal, but plodding and unimaginative'. Cook's own biographer, John Murdoch, is also less than flattering, depicting his subject as an opportunist who 'seldom would be able to give inspiration, and never a great vision', but who was, significantly, 'a spectacular political survivor'. F. K. Crowley, in the *Australian Dictionary of Biography*, gives a more balanced view, weighing the charge of opportunism against Cook's undoubted sense of duty, 'as he understood it'. But he, too, concludes that Cook was 'an eminently successful politician', carefully withholding the accolade of 'statesman'.[1]

There can, however, be no disputing Cook's importance in the early development of Australian politics. Between 1909, when he succeeded George Reid as leader of the Free Trade Party, and his retirement from politics in 1921, he played a major role in shaping the party system as we know it today. Members of the modern Liberal Party sometimes look to Deakin as a founding father, but there is a case for saying that Cook is equally important, if not more so, as a founder of the anti-Labor tradition in Australia.

He was born Joseph Cooke – he was later to discard the 'e' – in Vale Pleasant, Silverdale, in the county of Staffordshire, on 7 December 1860. The village of Silverdale took its name from the silver birch trees that distinguished the valley, but by 1860 the pastoral landscape had been disfigured by coalmines. Joseph's father, William Cooke, was a butty miner, leasing a coal face and hiring labour as a sub-contractor: it was a system that did not make for mine safety. He was killed in a mining accident when Joseph was twelve years old.

Joseph, the eldest son of the family, received some education at St Luke's Church of England school, where there was a sympathetic headmaster, but at the age of nine he was working in a local colliery as a pitboy. However, as a result of the passing of the 1870 Elementary Education Act, he briefly returned to school. With the death in 1873 of his father, aged only thirty-nine, the family was threatened with poverty, and Joseph, now the male head of the family, went back down the mine.

In spite of – or perhaps because of – the family's frugal circumstances, Joseph developed an appetite for education and self-improvement. The Cookes were drawn to the Primitive Methodist sect, which was strong in small mining communities such as Silverdale. Primitive Methodism emphasised both self-improvement and lay participation, and young Joseph was a voracious reader, known to have a book with him down the mine to read during lunch breaks. By sixteen he had given his first sermon as a lay preacher; at eighteen he had joined the Liberal Club, where he began to develop his skills as a debater.

Given the strong links between the Methodist sects and trade unionism, it is no surprise that the articulate young Joseph became involved in the local union. The 1880s were hard times, with prolonged strikes in the Silverdale collieries in 1883 and 1884. Finding himself unemployed, Joseph got a job with a railway company cleaning engines, work he disliked. In 1884 tragedy struck the family again when his younger brother, Albert, was killed in a mining accident.

These circumstances were an understandable cause for restlessness, reinforced by his marriage in 1885 to Mary Turner, a schoolteacher who encouraged and supported Joseph in his educational endeavours; she also had a brother who had emigrated to Australia, settling in Lithgow, New South Wales. His optimistic letters home helped the young couple make their own decision to migrate. On Christmas Day 1885 Joseph sailed for Australia to prepare the way; Mary, already pregnant, was to follow with the baby.

Joseph would appear to have been a model migrant, with the advantage that he found in Lithgow a community and culture that were familiar to him. He immediately got work as a skilled miner in the Vale of Clwydd colliery. Soon he was active as a lay preacher with the Primitive Methodists, and by the end of 1886 was the trade union lodge president at the colliery. By the time Mary and their child arrived in 1887 he had not only built their simple four-room home, but was beginning to establish himself as a figure in a predominantly working-class community.

With the help of Mary he also sought occupation beyond the coalmine. He worked hard at shorthand, gaining a Pitman's certificate for 150 words a minute, and acquired some knowledge of accountancy. For a short time he was manager of a local weekly newspaper and also did some work as an auditor. He became general secretary of the local trade union in 1889.

Joseph had brought republican and protectionist sympathies with him from England: both were to be discarded as he sorted out his political priorities. He was greatly influenced by the single-tax dogma preached by the American prophet Henry George, according to which the land would in effect be nationalised and thrown open for closer settlement. The single-tax theory was gaining popularity in the colonies where the land still seemed to be in the grip of the squatters. However, the theory was predicated on free trade, to which Joseph now also committed himself.

But Joseph's real induction to colonial politics came with the national maritime strike of 1890, in the course of which shearers and coalminers were drawn into the fray in support of maritime workers. Joseph became involved with the Labour Defence Committee, which was attempting, with difficulty, to co-ordinate the strike. The miners went back to work, but the strike and its failure helped turn the trade unions to political action, and when the infant Labor Party mobilised for the 1891 NSW election, Joseph Cook was the new party's candidate for Hartley, the electorate that covered Lithgow. So it was that, little more than five years after his arrival in the colony, Cook entered the NSW Parliament, one of thirty-five Labor members whose election marked the beginning of a new era in Australian politics.

The young member for Hartley was personable – 5'9" tall (1.75 metres) and certainly not 'little' as described by La Nauze, with receding hair compensated for by a neat, dark beard, good features and a confident manner. His democratic platform included the eight-hour day, the regulation of coalmines, a land tax, female suffrage and local option – the right given to a district, usually exercised by referendum, to prohibit the sale of alcohol within its boundaries (as a dedicated Methodist Cook was a teetotaller). But if this program seemed radical it was soon clear that Cook himself, like most of the Labor members, was respectable, hard-working and committed to the values of parliamentary democracy.

Political parties were still in the process of formation, and Labor was innovative in developing grassroots organisation in the electorates. In the Legislative Assembly the inexperienced Labor members held the balance of power between Free Traders and Protectionists, but were not agreed as to how they should exercise it. Cook was elected leader of the parliamentary party in 1893, but when in 1894 a party conference insisted on the pledge of caucus solidarity, Cook and a number of Free Traders withdrew. Cook still regarded himself as a representative of labour, though one committed to the Free Trade cause, now under the leadership of George Reid. When Reid won the 1894 election and wanted to emphasise his government's democratic credentials, he offered Cook the position of postmaster-general in his Cabinet. Cook was remarkably lucky to be in the right place at the right time, but he had in a short time established a reputation as a parliamentary debater and a leader with a command of the issues.

Cook proved himself a capable administrator as postmaster-general and later secretary for mines. Reid had a reformist agenda, dominated by the introduction of land taxation, and Cook became his loyal disciple. The success of the Reid government, which survived until 1899, provided the foundation for Cook's subsequent career. He was much influenced by Reid during the debate on Federation. As premier and a leading member of the Federal Convention, Reid felt bound to support the Constitution put to the voters in 1898, though he made clear his lack of enthusiasm for it; Cook took the hint and opposed it outright. But when Reid, having won concessions at the Premiers' Conference that liberalised the Constitution, advocated its adoption at the 1899 referendum, Cook followed suit.

However, Cook had no intention of following Reid into federal politics in 1901: his ambitions remained focused on NSW politics. But when approached to accept nomination as the Free Trade candidate for the new federal seat of Parramatta, which included Lithgow, he allowed himself to be persuaded. As a member of the first Federal Parliament he continued his support for Reid, but was still capable of expressing radical views, if more at a level of pious hope than practical politics. So for example, in 1902, while opposing the granting of bonuses to encourage manufacturers, he expressed a preference for 'the Commonwealth undertaking the work of manufacturing pig iron, and supplying it to the people of Australia'.[2] But as Reid forsook the radicalism of his NSW past and hoisted the flag of anti-socialism, Cook moved with him. In a revealing speech in 1904 he spoke of 'the working classes' and 'their economic theories', implicitly distancing himself from his origins, and went on to embrace anti-socialism.[3]

Cook was not included in the Cabinet of Reid's short-lived government of 1904–05, but in 1905 his loyalty was rewarded when he was elected deputy leader of the Free Trade Party. Any doubts conservative Free Traders had about Cook's radical past had now been largely overcome: he was a party man through and through, and once he had adopted a cause he was tenacious and combative in advancing it.

In 1908 Labor withdrew its support from the Deakin Protectionist government and took office itself. There was immediate speculation about a possible anti-Labor 'fusion' of the Free Traders and Protectionists. Reid, however, was not held in high esteem by Deakin, and in any case had been increasingly perfunctory in his parliamentary leadership. He cheerfully took his cue and resigned, bestowing his blessing on Cook as his successor, and after some hesitation Cook was empowered to commence negotiations with the Protectionists. In doing so he had to reach agreement not only with Deakin, who initially resisted his approaches, but also with Sir John Forrest and the conservative Protectionists. Cook was patient throughout these complex negotiations, and although in the end he conceded Deakin most of his policy stipulations, not to mention the leadership of the Fusion, it was in the knowledge that the new party would inevitably have a conservative stamp.

Cook became deputy leader and minister for defence in the Fusion government that took office in May 1909. He bore much of the responsibility for managing the government's busy legislative program in Parliament, having to deal with an angry Labor Opposition that felt it had been cheated of office. Cook's own main legislative achievement was the Defence Act which, in laying the basis for Australia's military program and providing for compulsory military training for boys and young men, enjoyed bipartisan support. In 1910 he was host to Lord Kitchener, who visited Australia to advise the Commonwealth on defence.

Deakin came to value Cook's loyalty, much as Reid had, but both were taken aback by the 1910 election which saw the Fusion government swept from office by a buoyant Labor Party. With Deakin's health deteriorating, Cook's responsibilities in Opposition increased. When Deakin resigned the leadership in 1913, the old division between Protectionists and Free Traders reasserted itself, the former looking to Sir John Forrest, the latter to Cook. Forrest was distressed when Deakin cast his vote for Cook, who won the leadership ballot by 20 votes to 19. Although Deakin privately noted that Cook had 'some unhappy deficiencies of temper and an anti-protectionist record', he recognised that Cook's services as deputy leader had been 'unfaltering, honourable, untiring and capable'.[4]

Given the fragile nature of the Liberal Party's unity, Cook's policy for the 1913 election was unadventurous; the Liberals gained a majority of one in the House of Representatives but were decisively outnumbered in the Senate. Having won the leadership by the narrowest of margins, Cook had attained office in similar fashion. There was little hope of passing significant legislation, so from the outset he went on the attack and sought to bring on a double dissolution. He deliberately provoked the Opposition by introducing legislation to abolish preference to trade unionists in government employment and to restore postal voting at federal elections, which Labor had always seen as disadvantaging it.

When the Senate had, for the second time, rejected the Government Preference Prohibition Bill, Cook wanted to immediately put the case for a double dissolution to the governor-general, Sir Ronald Munro-Ferguson. A meeting of Liberal members preferred to wait until the second Bill had also been rejected by the Senate but Cook, supported by his attorney-general, W.H. Irvine, went ahead regardless. At a time when the powers of the governor-general were by no means clear, Cook submitted to Munro-Ferguson that the governor-general's discretion to grant or refuse a double dissolution under Section 57 of the Constitution was 'a discretion which can only be exercised by him in accordance with the advice of his Ministers'.[5] Munro-Ferguson asked whether he might consult the leader of the Opposition, Andrew Fisher, but Cook demurred. Munro-Ferguson then sought and obtained Cook's agreement to his consulting the chief justice, Sir Samuel Griffith, who, while upholding the governor-general's independent discretionary power, nevertheless supported Cook's right to a double dissolution. Thus Cook achieved the first double dissolution in Commonwealth history, in the face of protests from the Labor Opposition which, ironically, supported the maintenance of the governor-general's independence.

No sooner was the election campaign under way than the growing crisis in Europe escalated into war. Cook interrupted his campaigning to organise Australia's military preparations, hardly leaving his office for several weeks. When the army proposed an expeditionary force of 12,000 soldiers to be ready for embarkation within six weeks, Cook insisted that the number be raised to 20,000. The government also called a meeting of state premiers with a view to placing Australia's economy on a war footing.

Cook assumed that the circumstances of war would favour the incumbent government. Labor, however, appeared just as fervent in its support for the empire in its hour of need, and could point proudly to its own advocacy of Australian defence. The election on 5 September saw Labor elected, with decisive majorities in both Houses: Cook's double dissolution strategy had backfired.

If Cook was despondent about the electors' rejection of him, he did not show it. Within two years, however, the political scene had been transformed, with the Labor Party divided over the introduction of conscription and the departure of Prime Minister Hughes and his supporters from the party. In this new and volatile situation the Liberals were divided as to tactics, some arguing that they should join with Labor in Parliament to defeat the new minority Hughes government and force an election, which they were confident of winning. But Cook feared that a three-cornered contest might actually favour Labor, and preferred negotiating a coalition with Hughes.

Cook disliked Hughes, considering him 'sly' and 'a man of many thoughts but no ideas'.[6] Yet he must have appreciated the irony of the two of them, both Labor pioneers, negotiating another fusion of anti-Labor forces. After much hesitation on both sides the deal was done: Hughes continued as prime minister with Cook once again relegated to the role of loyal deputy. In the complex allotment of portfolios he did not even get defence, having to make do with the navy ministry. The government triumphed at the 1917 election, after which the two groups formally merged to create the National Party. Cook never warmed to the impetuous and arrogant Hughes, who at times showed impatience with his deputy and circumvented him. Nevertheless he remained an important figure in the government and served as treasurer during 1920–21.

The prime minister and his deputy travelled to England in April 1918 to represent Australia at the Imperial War Conference. Cook had not made the journey 'home' since his emigration thirty-two years earlier and, surprisingly, was not keen to go. Nevertheless he was much moved when Silverdale gave him a hero's welcome. At the end of the war Hughes and Cook stayed on to represent Australia as part of the British delegation to the Versailles Conference. Cook was appointed chief British representative on the commission that determined the borders of Czechoslovakia. Although he had been vigorously anti-German during the war, he privately thought the treaty had been done 'in hot blood' and was unnecessarily vindictive.[7]

Cook retired from politics to become high commissioner to Britain in 1921. He greatly enjoyed his London years, relishing life at the imperial centre. He had been made a privy councillor in 1914 and a Knight Grand Cross of the Order of St Michael and St George in 1918: the young labour leader who had flirted with republicanism had long been a devotee of empire. He returned to Australia in 1927 and retired to the salubrious Sydney suburb of Bellevue Hill, where he died in 1947.

A Labor member once taunted Cook that 'the ghost of his former principles' would 'haunt him night by night'.[8] Cook refused to oblige: he seemed to regard his journey from trade unionist and labour radical to conservative imperialist as an entirely natural and unremarkable progression. Although he was sometimes slow to make decisions, he was never troubled by personal doubt. Nor did he question the orthodoxies of his time: he took White Australia for granted and, in spite of his religious temperament, had no interest in the Aborigines and their fate. His commitment to Methodism was the one continuity in his life, though he appeared to give up being a teetotaller.

His term as prime minister was unproductive, but in the circumstances could hardly have been otherwise. His distinguishing characteristics as a political leader were his combative style and his commitment to party, the latter perhaps owing something to inherited values of trade union solidarity. His real importance lies in his contribution to the shaping and reshaping of anti-Labor sentiment as a political force. At a time when party politics was still in its infancy in Australia, Cook proved adept at reconciling conflicting interest groups and, in his readiness to sacrifice personal ambition to the cause of party unity, did much to guide anti-Labor through the difficult transformations of its early years. On Cook's death Hughes, that great survivor, paid tribute to his loyalty, and described him as 'a great debater, a dour fighter, and underneath all that a most lovable personality'.[9] His opponents might not have seen him as lovable, but there could be no doubting that the pitboy from Silverdale had made his mark in Australia.

For Fisher's period in office 17 September 1914–27 October1915, see pages 72–86.

William Morris Hughes

27 OCTOBER 1915 – 9 FEBRUARY 1923

To the returning servicemen Hughes was 'the Little Digger', a symbol of Australian self-confidence.

BY GEOFFREY BOLTON

When a committee advising the Australian Bicentennial Authority tried to decide on the names of two hundred Australians who contributed significantly to the nation's history, few caused greater controversy than Billy Hughes. Undeniably he was a memorable character, but was there anything constructive about a career whose major landmark was the conscription controversy of the 1914–18 war, which split the Australian Labor Party, revived sectarianism and divided the Australian public as possibly no other issue has before or since? A wrecker of governments from the Reid ministry in New South Wales in 1899 to the Bruce–Page coalition of 1929, could he be redeemed by his legislative record or the strident nationalism that some found increasingly old-fashioned? When the first round of names was selected, Hughes was set aside. Then it was pointed out that the selection contained too few Catholics and Archbishop Daniel Mannix, who had similarly been set aside as too contentious, was admitted to the list. 'Well,' said a seasoned old public servant, 'if we include Mannix we've got to take Hughes.' So Hughes entered the pantheon on the archbishop's coattails. The repercussions in the next world must have been formidable.

Several authors, notably Farmer Whyte, L. F. Fitzhardinge and Donald Horne, have endeavoured to analyse his performance, but Hughes continues to defy definition. Colourfully outspoken though he was, he had a strong streak of deviousness, which extended even to the basic data of his life. Though he trumpeted his Welsh origins, he was born of Welsh parents in the inner London suburb of Pimlico, and although he gave his year of birth as 1864, it was 1862. Brought up in respectable lower-middle-class circumstances, partly in London and partly in the Welsh border country, he was remembered as 'a speedy runner and a notable marbles player'. As a teenager he became a pupil–teacher and caught the eye of the inspector, Matthew Arnold, the noted poet and essayist, who gave him the works of Shakespeare and left him with a love of good literature. Having worked as a pupil–teacher, he sought opportunity elsewhere, however, and late in 1884 he took ship for Australia.

Hughes spent the next eighteen months of his life travelling the outback in Queensland and New South Wales. In later life he was prone to yarn romantically about his adventures, but the reality was a good deal harsher. A scrawny new chum without bush skills, he lived rough and earned little, aggravating his deafness and dyspepsia, and – so he admitted in old age – fearful of homosexual rape. These experiences fostered in him a bleakly Hobbesian view of life as a remorselessly competitive struggle in which an individual such as Hughes could compensate for his lack of brute strength only by the agile use of his wits. Keeping his own counsel, he would never become a good team player, although his individualism was tempered by a belief in strong government as a means of securing co-operation and buttressing national efficiency.

By mid 1886 he was in Sydney where he soon married – whether formally or de facto has never been determined – Elizabeth Cutts, by whom he was to have six children. In 1890 they set up a mixed shop in Balmain, where Hughes made a living by mending umbrellas and doing other odd jobs while his wife took in washing. The sale or exchange of books soon became a staple of the Hughes' shop, hence the scene of an unofficial discussion group on political questions of the day. These were the years after the maritime strike of 1890, when Australian working-class involvement in politics has seldom been greater. A Labor Electoral League formed to bring working-class members into Parliament found itself wielding the balance of power between the older Free Trade and Protectionist parties in New South Wales for much of the decade following the 1891 elections. The movement was still in the process of developing its tactics and philosophy. In a movement dominated by veteran trade unionists, Hughes was not at first a prominent figure, but his ideas developed rapidly in those years and he soon came to the fore.

Having begun as a supporter of Henry George, who advocated social reform through a single tax on the unimproved rental value of all land, Hughes progressed by 1892 to membership of the Socialist League. The League was regarded as the advance guard of the labour movement, but many of its members, Hughes among them, already saw socialism as a goal to be achieved by persuasion rather than revolutionary compulsion. The productive forces of society, he wrote, would increase in efficiency under 'one authority, wielding its powers intelligently and constantly'. Throughout his long life he never lost his vision of centralised control as essential for national and economic efficiency, and many businessmen would never bring themselves to trust his judgment.

Rapidly gaining in experience and confidence, Hughes took an increasingly prominent part in Labor Conferences, founded and largely wrote a short-lived radical weekly, the *New Order*, and in the summer of 1893–94 served as political organiser for an area of New South Wales extending from Yass to Parkes. Increasingly regarded as a potential parliamentary candidate, he was expected to contest a seat in this region, but refused nomination for anywhere beyond 'a penny tram section' of his Balmain home, and was endorsed for the Lang division based on Pyrmont and Ultimo. He won the seat in July 1894 and easily retained it until his entry into federal politics in 1901.

His success revealed his mastery of politics as theatre. At that time political campaigning involved addressing audiences of several hundred – leaders such as Reid and Barton drew thousands – at open-air rallies or in crowded halls. In this brawling masculine atmosphere an inept or unpopular speaker ran the risk of being pelted with rotten eggs or bags of flour. Lang, a waterfront constituency, was particularly unruly. Quick-witted and picturesque in his invective, Hughes learned that he could confront and often face down hostile audiences. The voters responded to his 'straightforward attitude and intelligent reasoning' as well as to his oratory. He also showed himself a shrewd operator in the party room. From 1894 Labor supported the Free Trade government of George Reid, extracting a number of reforms in working conditions and a land and income tax. After the 1898 election Reid was more than ever dependent on Labor support, but his preoccupation with Federation alienated many Labor men who, like Hughes, opposed the proposed Constitution as insufficiently democratic and saw it as diverting Reid from social reform. When in 1899 Reid refused to legislate for the early closing of shops, Hughes persuaded Lyne, the leader of the Protectionist Opposition, to support this and other measures in the Labor program. He then argued a somewhat reluctant caucus into switching Labor's support from Reid to Lyne, who became premier. The episode showed a mastery of the techniques for extracting concessions in return for support, as well as a readiness to win over constituencies, such as the largely 'white-collar' shop assistants not previously regarded as natural Labor material.

Hughes also consolidated his standing in the trade unions. Since the 1890 maritime strike the waterside unions had been weak and ineffectual. Hughes, as member for Lang, supported attempts at reorganisation, but it took his direct intervention late in 1899 to bring success. Using his status as an MP to secure access to the wharves, Hughes built up a network of organisers and paid-up members before launching the renewed Wharf Labourers' Union in the last week of 1899, with himself as secretary. His powers were wide and he used them to steer the union towards securing its goals by negotiation and arbitration, using the strike only as a last resource. This did not please some of the more militant members, and Hughes needed all his platform skills to keep control. A *Sydney Morning Herald* reporter recalled one meeting: 'He stood at bay, a sallow, emaciated figure ... He reasoned and pleaded with them; he ridiculed them; he swore at them and assailed them as a host of misguided idiots. The meeting ended in wild cheers for him, and there was no strike.' But his methods worked; by 1902 the union boasted 2600 members, more than three-quarters of those eligible, and had gained very substantial improvements in wages and hours, with preference for unionists. Hughes also became president of the Trolley, Draymen and Carters' Union. He was undoubtedly Australia's most successful union leader. As Fitzhardinge wrote: 'This position had been won entirely by energetic organisation and shrewd and fearless bargaining, without a strike and virtually without expense to the unions concerned.'[1]

Despite his opposition to Federation, Hughes not surprisingly decided to stand for the new Commonwealth Parliament. Its powers included defence, industrial arbitration and responsibility for establishing the White Australia Policy, all issues dear to Hughes. He stood for West Sydney, the electorate that included the Lang division and most of the waterfront, and won easily. Once again Labor found itself in a position to offer support in return for concessions, and although it backed Edmund Barton's Protectionist ministry in essentials, the party used its numbers to modify government policies. Thus Hughes was well to the fore among the Labor members who cut items from the tariff on which the Commonwealth depended for its revenue. On the other hand, he passionately advocated that Australia should raise its own defence force. In the light of the tariff cuts and a major drought, the Barton government preferred to renew the existing arrangements, under which Australia made a financial contribution to the upkeep of the Royal Navy and took advice from British officers about the conduct of its volunteer forces. Hughes foresaw that British and Australian interests might not always overlap. He was already convinced that a technologically advanced Japan menaced Australian security, whereas Britain was forming a strategic alliance with Japan. To his way of thinking the only responsible solution was the formation of a national militia. Every adult male between the ages of eighteen and sixty should be obliged to undergo regular part-time training, although conscientious objectors might be exempted on payment of a special capitation tax. This would promote national spirit and send a message to the rest of the world without encouraging militarism or disrupting business.

Few other members had thought through defence questions so thoroughly. The Labor Party was divided between some who were attracted by Hughes' concept of a citizen army, others who were pacifists, and still others like Andrew Fisher who objected to compulsion – though Hughes argued that the state used compulsion in health and education, so why not have national defence? In 1903 he moved for the introduction of compulsory national service, but withdrew the proposal before it could be voted on. He continued a campaign of propaganda in favour of the idea, joined the all-party National Defence League to educate public opinion and was vindicated in 1908–09 when the policy was adopted with the support of all major political parties. This was not the end of the story.

As a leading frontbencher, Hughes was naturally included when J. C. Watson formed the first Labor government in April 1904. Amid all his other occupations, Hughes had recently found time to qualify for the Bar, largely to assist his work in the arbitration courts. He waived his right to become attorney-general in favour of the non-Labor sympathiser H. B. Higgins, instead serving as minister for external affairs. Of more significance during the Watson government's four-month tenure was Hughes' appointment as chairman of a strong Royal Commission on the Navigation Bill. After two years the Royal Commission produced a report exposing the harsh conditions under which merchant seamen worked, and recommending reforms. Meanwhile the British government became interested and proposed a conference between the United Kingdom, Australia and New Zealand to secure unified action. When this took place in 1907 Hughes was chosen as one of the four Australian delegates, and made a much stronger impression than the nominal leader, Lyne. It was his first visit to Britain since he had left in 1884. The natty ex-Cabinet minister with a fashionably slim and drooping moustache presented a marked contrast to the youthful emigrant.

This was not the only respect in which he was leaving his past behind him. Obsessively busy with politics, he had less and less in common with his wife Elizabeth and their six children, and spent little time with them. When his wife died in 1906 he experimented briefly with using his eldest daughter Ethel as official hostess, but in 1911 married for the second time. His second wife was Mary Campbell, a pastoralist's daughter, and while she provided a good-tempered and caring ambience for her wayward husband's comfort, she might also have cut him off from his old associates and first family. He now owned a motor car and wrecked it on his honeymoon – and ran a thirty-hectare hobby farm at Wilberforce on the Hawkesbury River. He was drifting too far from the hungry radicals on the left wing of the labour movement, who were not satisfied with the workings of the arbitration system and who might be enticed by the direct action methods advocated by the International Workers of the World.

Yet he was still the unparalleled 'Mr Fixit' of the industrial arena, intervening at the eleventh hour to avert damaging strikes and to patch up acceptable compromises with a skill that would not be matched in the labour movement until the heyday of Bob Hawke at the ACTU. In 1908 his dexterous conduct of a strike on the Sydney waterfront ended with the surrender of the coastal shipping companies and their acceptance of the principle of preference for unionists. He was less successful when called on to manage a strike called by the Newcastle coalminers late in 1909, partly because the miners' leader, Peter Bowling, repudiated Hughes' Fabian tactics – and then became a hero when the state government ordered his arrest and had him clapped in leg-irons.

Some of Hughes' most useful work for his party was undertaken between 1907 and 1911 when the conservative *Daily Telegraph* invited him to contribute a weekly column presenting 'The Case of Labor'. In lively, vigorous and combative prose he argued week after week in defence of the moderate Labor position. 'Under socialism the State would own and control the means of production, distribution and exchange,' he wrote, 'Private property in all other forms of wealth would remain, and other institutions, social and political, would not be affected by the change.' He pointed out that even anti-socialist state governments operated a number of industries. Hughes argued that Labor governments would be more effective in imposing quality control on manufacturers and retailers. He was at his most telling in his attacks on the anti-labour forces.

In 1907 the leadership of the Labor Party passed to Andrew Fisher with Hughes as his deputy, a combination of opposites that lasted for eight years. Tired of supporting the minority Deakin government, Labor ousted it in November 1908 and formed a ministry, this time with Hughes as attorney-general. In May 1909 Deakin led the two anti-labour parties into a combined 'Fusion Party', with whose support he became prime minister for the third time. On two successive days Hughes denounced the manoeuvre in speeches that rank high in the Commonwealth Parliament's treasury of abuse and invective. 'What a career his has been!' said Hughes of Deakin. 'In his hands, at various times, have rested the banners of every party in the country. He has proclaimed them all, he has held them all, and he has betrayed them all ... Last night the honourable member abandoned the finer resources of political assassination and resorted to the bludgeon of the cannibal ... I hear from this side of the House some mention of Judas. I do not agree with that; it is not fair – to Judas, for whom there is this to be said, that he did not gag the man whom he betrayed, nor did he fail to hang himself afterwards ...' Deakin's credibility as a statesman took a battering. In April 1910 the voters turned him out in favour of a Fisher Labor government with substantial majorities in both Houses, and Hughes was once more attorney-general and deputy leader.

During the next three years Hughes was closely associated with the Fisher government's reform program, serving twice as acting prime minister during Fisher's absence overseas. His most distinctive contribution lay in the field of attempted constitutional reform. Australia's economic and industrial growth already involved the Commonwealth in areas of responsibility not envisaged during the Convention debates of the 1890s. Under the leadership of Sir Samuel Griffith the High Court often took a narrow view of federal powers, partly through conservatism and partly through a wish to uphold the original agreement between states and the Commonwealth. Hughes accordingly sought the extension of Commonwealth powers at a referendum. Four questions were proposed, extending federal power over trade, commerce, labour and employment and granting authority over combinations and monopolies.

Unfortunately the state governments resisted any encroachment by the Commonwealth, none more vehemently than William Holman, once Hughes' ally in the Socialist League but now attorney-general in the first Labor government in New South Wales. The public was also discouraged by having to vote for all four questions en bloc; 'like a chain-gang', in Deakin's phrase. At the referendum of 26 April 1911 the 'No' vote won in all states except Western Australia.

Wishing to demonstrate the limits of the Commonwealth's powers to move against monopolies, Hughes then took on the Coal Vend, a cartel of coalmine owners and shippers who controlled prices. Unfortunately by launching a prosecution under legislation of 1906 requiring proof that a monopoly operated to the public detriment, and not by tougher 1910 laws removing this condition, Hughes ran into a rebuff from the High Court. In a majority ruling the Court held that no public detriment had been proved. Again, a Royal Commission on the sugar industry seeking to expose the monopoly exercised by the Colonial Sugar Refining Company ran into an impasse when the company refused to testify. The High Court ruled that the Royal Commission had no power to compel the company to give evidence. Hughes might not have been too sorry at these outcomes, since they proved his point that the Commonwealth's powers were inadequate and gave him grounds for submitting the four referendum questions to a second poll, to be conducted on the same day as the general election on 31 May 1913. This time the four questions were submitted separately, but although three states voted 'Yes', all were defeated by a narrow margin. Hughes never had any luck with his referenda.

The election resulted in the return of the Liberals under Joseph Cook, with a majority of one in the House of Representatives and a massive Labor majority in the Senate. This was a recipe for deadlock, and in June 1914 Cook obtained the approval of a new governor-general, Sir Ronald Munro-Ferguson, for a double dissolution of Parliament. During the election campaign the international situation darkened, and on 4 August 1914 Australia, as part of the British Empire, went to war against Germany and its allies. Hughes at once urged that the elections should be cancelled. The politicians must set an example of national unity. There was also calculation: if Cook refused the truce – which he did – he would bear the discredit in the eyes of the public of playing politics at a moment of crisis. This might have influenced the outcome of the election on

5 September, when Labor won comfortably and Hughes became attorney-general for the third time.

The war completed a major change in his economic thinking. Once a Free Trader, he was now convinced that the security of the British Empire, and of Australia in particular, lay in the development and control of its own industries and in the orderly marketing, under government influence, of its major export commodities. He was especially perturbed at the penetration of German-controlled companies into Australia's base metal industries, and by the end of 1915 had engineered the creation of the Australian Metals Exchange, controlling the export of all base metals. He also took the main role in negotiating mixed forms of control, involving Commonwealth and state governments and producer interests, for the marketing of sugar and wheat. Working neither on overseas precedents nor on a predetermined plan, Hughes sought remedies that might prove efficient enough to carry on into peacetime. In a world where competition could be expected in peace or war, Hughes was steering Australia neither to a free market economy nor to socialism, but to pragmatic methods designed for Australian conditions.

Fisher was uncomfortable in the role of wartime prime minister. During the first year of hostilities he delegated an increasing amount of responsibility to Hughes who, despite continuing health problems, especially with his digestion and hearing, seemed inexhaustibly energetic. In October 1915, when Fisher resigned to become high commissioner in London, Hughes was his unopposed successor. His authority was not yet absolute. He was increasingly criticised by elements on the left wing of the party who did not share Hughes' subordination of all other policies to the war effort. Hughes also jettisoned plans to conduct a third referendum to secure for the Commonwealth increased powers over the economy, preferring to rely on the state governments to delegate the necessary powers to the federal government for the duration of the war. When the states reneged on the deal, his critics claimed that Hughes had never been sincere about forcing the issue. But he still seemed secure enough to plan a journey to Britain early in 1916 as one of his first priorities as prime minister.

Hughes had several motives for making this journey. The British government had not consulted Australia nearly often enough about the deployment of troops at Gallipoli during 1915, and Hughes wanted a more effective voice in the future. Australia's export trade was badly hampered by shipping problems, and Hughes hoped to press for improvements. He also wanted to voice deep Australian concerns about the future of the Pacific. At the outbreak of the war Australian and New Zealand forces occupied the German colonies in New Guinea and the South Pacific but Japan, entering the war as Britain's ally, seized the islands north of the equator. Hughes feared that the Japanese would use their position to force changes in Australia's trade and immigration policies, and he did not trust Britain to defend the White Australia policy.

When he reached London in March 1916 he made an immediate impact with a speech to the Empire Parliamentary Association urging that the British Empire must abandon free trade to function as a tariff bloc excluding Germany and other competitors. Coming at a time when war weariness was translating itself into disenchantment with the British coalition government under H. H. Asquith, Hughes' new and distinctive approach seemed a breath of fresh air, and he found himself invited from one end of Britain to the other as a widely reported public speaker. His energetic commitment to winning the war masked a disregard of the complexities of policymaking, but won him widespread acclaim in the media, honorary degrees from leading universities and a speedy reputation as an Empire statesman. David Low's cartoons captured the image of the fiery Hughes prancing on the table of the British Cabinet while a nervous Asquith asked his colleague Lloyd George: 'Speak to him in Welsh, David, and pacify him!' Of all the British Cabinet, Lloyd George was the one with whom Hughes struck up the closest rapport. They might have been distantly related. Both were outsiders mistrusted by the conservatives for their radical past but revelling in the challenges of wartime administration. However, when Lloyd George displaced Asquith as prime minister at the end of 1916, he and Hughes would not always see eye to eye.

While in the United Kingdom Hughes lobbied hard on behalf of Australia's interests in shipping, trade, and the Pacific, without much result beyond establishing his mark as a stubborn and slippery negotiator. He went to an Allied economic conference in Paris, thus setting a precedent for distinctive Australian representation when the time came for peacemaking. There is no evidence that Hughes had this long-term objective in mind, but it was an example of his talent for constructive improvisation. Most of all he spent time with the troops behind the front line in France, and came away with an enormous admiration for them. Their performance seemed to vindicate all his hopes for an Australian citizen army, but the casualty rate was high. Hughes began to doubt whether recruitment could continue in sufficient numbers unless Australia followed the example of the British government and introduced conscription.

He returned to Australia at the beginning of August 1916 to find the Liberal opposition, most of the media and many leading public figures clamouring for conscription. But the working class and the trade unions were far less enthusiastic, and many farmers feared the loss of workers. The numbers coming forward as volunteers were falling off significantly, and after the heavy losses on the Somme in mid 1916 it was open to doubt whether Australia could maintain its existing forces in the field. Hughes would have preferred to introduce conscription by Act of Parliament, following the precedents of Britain and New Zealand. He soon realised that his party would split over the question and he might not have the numbers in the Senate. His only chance of success lay in the possibility that the voters would support conscription through a referendum. With great difficulty he persuaded the caucus to approve a referendum by the narrowest of margins, though it was clear that the majority included a number of anti-conscriptionists who expected the poll to support their stand. It was also agreed that if voluntary recruiting failed to supply the numbers required by the Army Council the deficit might be made up by applying compulsion to single men.

In staking the outcome on a referendum Hughes was probably unaware of a crucial shift in public opinion. Many Irish-Australians, hitherto supportive of the war effort, were shaken when the British authorities suppressed the Easter uprising in Dublin with what many saw as unnecessary harshness. Perhaps as damaging to the chances of a 'Yes' vote was the belief that cheap foreign labour would be brought into Australia to fill the jobs left behind by the conscripts. This furphy was given wings by the fortuitous arrival of two shiploads of Maltese immigrants. Within the trade union movement hostility to conscription went further. Hughes was expelled from the Wharf Labourers' Union and the Trolley, Draymen and Carters' Union, which he had done so much to create. As yet, however, with one exception, the Hughes Cabinet remained solid.

As polling day on 28 October drew closer, Hughes' impatience and desperation betrayed him into roughshod tactics that probably lost him support. He began to associate the opponents of conscription with extremist groups such as the Industrial Workers of the World (then facing charges of treason and arson). The day before the election he authorised a regulation that would have empowered returning officers to set aside the votes of men aged between twenty-one and thirty-five who might have evaded the call-up. Three of his Cabinet colleagues resigned in protest and the regulation was cancelled. The damage was done: by a narrow margin the 'No' vote triumphed. Hughes' prestige was in tatters. His opponents within the ALP called for a special meeting of caucus on 14 November. Although several of the anti-conscriptionists urged mediation, the militants could not be pacified. After a stormy meeting Hughes said, 'Enough of this. Let those who think with me follow me', and led twenty-four members out of the party room. It was a decisive moment. To some it seemed that 'the Labor Party had blown its brains out'.[2]

Hughes formed a new ministry from what was called the National Labor Party. His followers tended to come from the older members of the original Labor Party, the bush workers and small shopkeepers recruited in the 1890s. Those who remained with the Labor Party included many who had come fairly recently into Parliament. As the smallest among three parliamentary parties the National Labor government could survive only with the support of the Liberal Opposition. Then and later some argued that, with conscription out of the way, it might have been possible to knit together the two fragments of the Labor Party. It was too late. Hughes was too unpopular with the left wing of the party and his tirades against the Irish would have the effect of alienating many otherwise moderate Catholics. By February 1917 a merger was negotiated between the National Labor Party and the Liberals, forming a new Nationalist Party. Hughes became prime minister of a Cabinet including four of his own team and six former Liberals. It was uncannily like Deakin's predicament of 1909; a prime minister surviving with the help of his former enemies. But Hughes had greater stamina and wiliness than Deakin, and it would take six years to displace him.

None of the ex-Liberals could challenge him. Cook was too loyal and mediocre, Forrest too old, the former Victorian premier W. A. Watt too temperamental. All the same, Hughes was now an isolated figure, his closest ally in Cabinet the reliable but stolid Senator George Pearce. His mastery of the new party was incomplete, as he found when he attempted to invite Parliament to prolong its life until six months after the end of the war. To do so he needed to detach two or three of the Labor majority in the Senate, but his manoeuvres were so slippery that two Tasmanian Liberals refused to support the proposal, and Hughes desisted. Instead he called a general election in May 1917. He ran a lively campaign and scored a landslide victory. He himself quit West Sydney for a safer seat in Bendigo, reinforcing his Victorian credentials with a small farm at Sassafras in the Dandenongs.

During the election Hughes committed himself not to propose conscription unless the war situation deteriorated, in which event a second referendum would be held. As 1917 wore on the war continued to go badly. Losses on the western front were grievous, Italy was reeling and the Bolshevik revolution knocked Russia out of the war. At home industrial strife was at its worst for many years, and many, including Hughes, blamed foreign subversion. In November the Hughes government decided to conduct a second referendum on conscription. The prime minister unwisely staked the government's survival on the success of this poll, and pledged that he and his party would not attempt to govern if refused their wish.

The campaign was much more bitter than in 1916. Archbishop Mannix of Melbourne, earlier a restrained advocate of the 'No' vote, now became the symbol of Irish-Australian resistance to conscription and a special focus of Hughes' vituperation. The sole remaining Labor government in Australia, led by T.J. Ryan in Queensland, also stood high among the ranks of Hughes' enemies. There was a good deal of knockabout farce as the Queensland government tried to override Hughes' ban on anti-conscriptionist propaganda. When speeches by Ryan and his deputy, E.G. Theodore, were censored, the two ministers read the offending passages to the Queensland Legislative Assembly and Theodore had the banned bits emphasised in bold type in Hansard. Hughes ordered the seizure of all copies of the relevant Hansard, oversaw a raid on the Government Printing Office and embarked on a welter of lawsuits against Ryan without satisfaction. Eventually the offending Hansard was released.

While preaching the 'Yes' cause in Queensland, Hughes behaved like a man embattled. At Warwick railway station he completely lost control of himself when an egg was thrown in his direction, and for his own safety had to be restrained by a police sergeant. He responded by setting up the Commonwealth police force as a body that would do his bidding if state governments proved recalcitrant. Cooler counsel ensured that during the rest of the war the Commonwealth Police Force was not used provocatively.

The second conscription referendum was beaten by a wider margin than the first. Perhaps because of Mannix, Victoria joined the states with a 'No' majority. Hughes was now stuck with his promise to resign in the event of a 'No' victory. After tortuous manoeuvres designed to ensure that no alternative would be likely to offer, Hughes duly handed in his ministry's resignation on 8 January 1918, but was sworn in again on the same evening. The governor-general took the opportunity of urging him to improve the government's administrative methods, but it was no use. Hughes, wrote Munro-Ferguson, 'never had the elements of a business training', and his secretive nature made it 'difficult for him to let any single thing go out of his own hand'.

The governor-general, with Hughes' consent, made one more attempt to find a common policy for securing reinforcements without conscription. He convened a conference of delegates from across the political spectrum in April 1918. The conference sat for seven days without much result. Hughes was in turns provocative and conciliatory; each side doubted the good faith of the other. As it happened, from that time on until the end of the war, voluntary recruiting improved; but Hughes was no longer in Australia to monitor the situation.

The Imperial War Cabinet in London, which Dominion prime ministers were entitled to attend, was to meet at intervals during six weeks from mid June 1918. Hughes travelled by way of the United States, where he tried to impress an unresponsive President Woodrow Wilson and other leading public figures with Australia's fears about postwar security in the Pacific. In London he preached the same message, gaining some sympathy from other Dominion prime ministers. However, it was as yet far from certain that Australia's interests would be adequately safeguarded after the war.

The other prime ministers departed in August, but Hughes remained, partly to argue Australia's case for better access to British markets –

Fisher as high commissioner was not aggressive or effective enough – and partly to spread his gospel of the British Empire as a trading bloc. In this he was less successful than in 1916. The message was not new, the need for charismatic leadership was met by British Prime Minister Lloyd George, and Hughes' health at the time was not good. His greatest triumph came when he visited the Australian troops in France. In August 1918 the months of retreat ended, and Australians were prominent among the counter-attacking forces that within three months would bring Germany to sue for an armistice. Hughes was popular with the AIF, and some of the glory of victory was shed on 'the Little Digger'.

With the approach of peace his Cabinet colleagues readily agreed that Hughes should remain overseas to safeguard Australian interests during the peacemaking process. Perhaps they were in no hurry to have him back; acting Prime Minister W.A. Watt, having been a state premier himself, was not over-tolerant of interference and ran the day-to-day business of Cabinet more smoothly than Hughes. The decision meant that Hughes would have his moment on the international stage as an Australian speaking for distinctively Australian interests.

With the end of hostilities in November 1918 Hughes played his cards aggressively. He needed to because Lloyd George, whose deviousness fully matched Hughes' own, was not taking the Dominion prime ministers into his confidence while drawing up the terms for peace, and it seemed probable that these would be based on a memorandum of Fourteen Points drawn up by President Wilson. Wilson's Fourteen Points included the removal of tariffs and other economic barriers and a right of intervention on colonial issues. Neither was welcomed by the Australian Cabinet.

Hughes' first concern was to ensure that Australia would be independently represented in the peacemaking process, as well as forming part of the British delegation. Canada, South Africa and New Zealand would have been satisfied with lesser status, but by the end of the year all were ready to accept a formula that saw the Dominion representatives as delegates in their own right as well as alternate members of the British delegation.

The Versailles Peace Conference opened in Paris on 18 January 1919. Within three weeks Hughes was notorious for his persistence in defying

President Wilson, and when necessary Lloyd George, in upholding what he perceived as Australia's paramount interests. Wilson proposed that the former German and Turkish colonies should be administered by one or other of the Allied powers under a mandate or trust until they were ready for independence. Hughes, resigned to the Japanese occupation of the former German colonies north of the Pacific, was adamant that New Guinea and the adjacent islands should become Australian possessions. Anything less might allow at least Japanese commercial penetration and threaten Australian security.

A compromise was proposed under which underdeveloped colonies such as New Guinea and Samoa might be mandated for 999 years, but it was not certain whether this would be accepted. The memorable clash between Wilson and Hughes has been variously reported, but when Wilson asked if Australia was prepared to defy the opinion of the whole civilised world, and Hughes replied, 'That's about the size of it, Mr President', nobody has ever been quite sure whether Hughes was deliberately standing up to Wilson or whether, because of trouble with his hearing aid, he had not really heard the question. It seems certain that when Wilson again asked Hughes whether he would set his five million Australians against the 1200 million represented by the Allies, Hughes simply replied: 'I represent sixty thousand dead.' No Australian spokesman previously had spoken so forcefully in an international forum.

Hughes won the 999-year mandate over New Guinea and the adjacent islands and successfully insisted that the phosphate-rich island of Nauru, instead of being mandated to Britain alone, should be jointly controlled by Britain, Australia and New Zealand, with Australia providing the administration. He also managed to block Japanese attempts to secure a clause affirming racial equality in the covenant of the League of Nations. To senior statesmen in Britain and the United States he was a nuisance, but to most Australians he was, in the terms of David Low's cartoon, Horatius defending the bridge of White Australia – or the larrikin defying the professorial Wilson.

Having gained his point on the issues of racial equality and New Guinea, he made no further effort to develop a distinctive Australian foreign policy. He was content to serve as part of the British team on the issue of the reparations to be expected from Germany, favouring tough terms. He appointed an Australian trade commissioner to the United

States but made no attempt to foster the development of a distinctive Australian foreign service. It would be Canada that, a few years later, asserted its right to negotiate directly with the United States over trade issues, just as it would be South Africa and (after 1922) the Irish Free State that pushed boundaries of constitutional autonomy. Despite his spectacular performance in Paris, Hughes was not systematically interested in enlarging Australian self-rule.

To the returning servicemen Hughes was 'the Little Digger', a symbol of Australian self-confidence to cherish. When he returned from the Peace Conference to London's Victoria station a crowd of about five hundred Australian soldiers hoisted him on their shoulders, crammed a slouch hat on his head and paraded him down the street. He cut short his time in London in order to return home on a troopship. He returned to similar scenes in Australia. It was, wrote one observer, like the triumph of a Roman victor.

Such acclaim did not translate itself into political power. Australia in 1919 was a jaded nation. The war had been followed by the lethal Spanish influenza epidemic, industrial strife was still rampant and returning ex-servicemen clashed with left-wingers and others whose ideas they disliked. Even the ex-servicemen's organisations complained when Hughes would not grant them privileges such as five years' exemption from income tax, though he forged a lasting alliance between conservative governments and the Returned Soldiers' and Sailors' Imperial League of Australia (later the Returned Services League).

The Hughes government went to the polls in December 1919, at the same time submitting yet another referendum for enlarging the powers of the Commonwealth. Once again the voters said 'No'. They also cut the government's majority to the point that it depended on the support of a reliable independent. Not that Labor improved its showing greatly. A new element arrived, in the shape of an eleven-member Country Party, profiting by the recent introduction of preferential voting and vowing to play the old game of 'support in return for concessions'. In particular, they objected to the Hughes government's policy of high tariffs.

Now Hughes' tendency to play a lone hand began to work against him. He was seen as too dictatorial and too unpredictable to manage the Country Party, and he was still distrusted by many in his own Nationalist Party. He was still full of ideas for developing the authority of the

Commonwealth government, but he had neither the support systems nor the patience to sell them to Parliament. His next three years in office were to see a series of bold and often brilliantly imaginative initiatives. A few bore good fruit, but most were rebuffed or dropped when it was evident that support would not come quickly.

Among his senior ministers, only the reliable Pearce would last the distance. Watt resigned in a huff in 1920. Cook was the most experienced in a Cabinet of mostly second-raters. Two very able businessmen were coming forward, Walter Massy-Greene, an authority on tariff matters but unacceptable to the Country Party, and the young Stanley Melbourne Bruce, a returned officer with an incisive mind for finance, but neither was as yet senior or experienced enough.

At the 1919 elections Hughes promised to legislate for a Constitutional Convention. This might have given him a convincing mandate for change, but he was oddly hesitant and clumsy about carrying the promise into effect. It proved difficult to arrive at a formula for selecting delegates. Late in 1921 Hughes eventually came up with a proposal that half should be directly elected and half nominated in equal numbers by the state parliaments. This pleased neither democrats who wanted a fully elected Convention nor states-righters, and the proposal was withdrawn. However, in 1922 the Northern Territory, previously without parliamentary representation, was allowed a member of the House of Representatives with limited rights.

During 1920 and 1921, much parliamentary time was taken up by tariff reform. The result confirmed the Hughes government's intention of increasing protection for Australian industries. The Country Party and other rural members fought for compensatory measures, but on the whole were left dissatisfied. With much difficulty a tariff board was set up to monitor the effects of tariff changes and to discourage monopolies and exploitation. Although originally authorised for only two years, it survived to become the ancestor of the modern Productivity Commission.

It was a strength in Hughes that he was alert to technological change and the need to adapt the machinery of government accordingly, especially in the light of wartime experience. In 1920 an Institute of Science and Industry was created, which Bruce was to expand six years later into the Council for Scientific and Industrial Research (now the Commonwealth Scientific and Industrial Research Organisation).

Hughes described himself as a 'fanatic' about aviation, and in 1920 the Department of Civil Aviation was set up to control routing and safety regulations, though he failed to follow through on a Premiers' Conference agreement to transfer power over aviation to the Commonwealth. He also negotiated an agreement with the Anglo-Persian Oil Company to set up the Commonwealth Oil Refineries, with the company controlling the technical and business arrangements and a power of veto to the Commonwealth. This had the immediate effect of almost halving the price of motor fuel in Australia and gave a great impetus to the use of rural motor transport, tractors and private cars. Hughes was also aware of the defence implications: 'The last war,' he told the House, 'was a petrol war', and he encouraged the search for payable oil deposits in Australia.

This awareness of modern technology brought about his most productive interventions when he visited London for the last time as minister attending an Imperial Conference in 1921. He tried to interest the British in promoting a regular service of airships or conventional commercial aircraft between Britain and Australia, but it would be more than a decade before this came to pass. He also secured permission for Australia, unlike other parts of the British Commonwealth, to set up its own direct overseas wireless links. This led to the creation of a partnership with Amalgamated Wireless similar to the Commonwealth Oil Refineries arrangement. Australia in the 1920s was consequently well advanced in its use of wireless. Hughes became a director of Amalgamated Wireless for the rest of his life.

While he was in London, his main concern in foreign policy was to encourage the renewal of the Anglo-Japanese alliance, which he now saw as insurance for Japan's good behaviour in the Pacific. In December 1921 the British Empire, the United States, Japan and France put their names to a treaty. This seemed to justify Hughes' belief that Australian interests could be served by working within the consultative processes of the British Empire.

He returned home to an unsatisfactory political situation. The Country Party was unwilling to co-operate regularly with the Nationals while Hughes remained in control. Labor was still seething at his roughshod tactics late in 1920 in using the government's majority to expel Hugh Mahon from Parliament when the emotional Irishman used fiery language in denouncing British measures against the Sinn Fein rebels. Even when the Irish Free State was granted self-government at the end of 1921 the rancour against Hughes continued.

Hughes took advantage of Cook's resignation to promote Bruce to treasurer and Massy-Greene (who was seen as his potential successor) as minister for defence. His Cabinet looked stronger, but Hughes was still too much of an individualist to make the most of the businesslike methods they would have brought to the ministry.

Even in the field of industrial relations Hughes' old skill and luck were deserting him. An erratic economy and industrial conflict marked postwar Australia. A Royal Commission on the basic wage reported late in 1920 that the wage in New South Wales should be 40 per cent higher to provide workers with a satisfactory living standard. This was an impossible target and it simply increased Hughes' discredit with workers and employers alike.

In 1920 Hughes also sought to augment the Commonwealth arbitration machinery by legislating for a system of special tribunals for specific industries or industrial disputes. In the process he managed to antagonise the respected Mr Justice Higgins, who quit the arbitration court, and the tribunals never became a serious option.

He made his last throw early in 1922, calling a round-table conference of unions and employers in Sydney, which he chaired. The delegates orated at each other for a fortnight without any meeting of minds. Hughes was yesterday's man. His standing, in the eyes of many, was further compromised by the knowledge that he had accepted £25,000 as a testimonial from admirers of his defence of Australia's interests at the peace conference. He approached the elections due at the end of 1922 sufficiently dubious of his chances to abandon his seat at Bendigo in favour of the blue-ribbon conservative constituency of North Sydney.

The election results were ominous. Labor gained only three seats in the House of Representatives and a few more in the Senate, but the balance of power now rested with the fourteen members of the Country Party, and there were five so-called Liberals, of whom W. A. Watt and J. G. Latham were unfriendly. Massy-Greene lost his seat. This left Bruce as the new man with whom the Country Party was prepared to form a coalition, after two months of Byzantine manoeuvring. On 2 February 1923 Hughes announced his resignation to the National Party.

Hughes might have hoped that the new coalition would not last. 'I'm more fit to attend a woman in her hour of need than Dr Page is to be Treasurer of his country,' he said. But as the months passed it became evident that Hughes would not be summoned for an early comeback. For the next six years he would remain a disgruntled backbencher muttering criticisms of the 'lesser men' who had replaced him, and living comfortably from shrewd investments and occasional journalism.

Out of office his status as a legendary character increased. Without the responsibility of policymaking he could be accepted as a national icon, 'the Little Digger', always at his place on Anzac Day in Sydney as the veterans marched past. He played up to the picturesque image. His witticisms became more outrageous, his shows of temper more colourful, his inability to keep his private secretaries a national joke. Nevertheless, he had not lost his appetite for power.

By 1928 several other backbenchers had scores to settle with the Bruce–Page government and Hughes gained a kind of informal leadership among them. Several times he and some of the others voted with Labor against the government. The climax came in September 1929 when Bruce's legislation for dismantling much of the federal arbitration system and returning it to the states gave Hughes an issue on which he could figure as an authority. Hughes moved an amendment that the new legislation should not come into operation until the public was consulted either through a general election or a referendum. The amendment was carried by one vote. Bruce would have to seek an immediate election. Hughes was observed in the King's Hall of the new Parliament House, lighting a cigarette 'with a Sphinx-like smile'.[3]

There was more to Hughes' action than vengeance. He genuinely believed that the Bruce–Page government had been too kind to big business and too negligent of the workers. Perhaps, as one commentator suggests, he 'was himself a victim of the popular semi-mystical conception of "Billy Hughes" as … the only man to lead and save Australia in times of trouble'.[4]

He was to be disappointed. He stood in North Sydney as an Independent Nationalist and had no trouble in trouncing the endorsed candidate. Labor was returned with a big enough majority in the House of Representatives not to require help from independents. Hughes attempted to form an Australian Party with the dissident Nationalists as a nucleus for a party who might seize the middle ground from the extremes of capital and labour. During 1930–31 the new party struggled for survival. Hughes did not consult his colleagues and financial support was slow in coming as the Great Depression gripped Australia. Eventually, when Lyons left Labor to form the United Australia Party, Hughes was glad to come in under the new umbrella.

Lyons, having shared the experience of moving from Labor to a new party, was more sympathetic to Hughes than Bruce had proven. Reconstituting his ministry in October 1934 he made Hughes minister for health and repatriation, perhaps as a balance to Page and his Country Party colleagues who re-entered Cabinet shortly afterwards. A British friend compared Hughes to 'a rogue elephant … meekly piling teak'. He was still an unpredictable element, however, and in November 1935 was obliged to resign from Cabinet because of his book *Australia and War To-Day*, in which he challenged the Lyons government's trust in economic sanctions as a means of restraining dictators such as Mussolini, who was invading Ethiopia at the time. Public opinion was inclined to side with Hughes, and within three months Lyons invited him back into Cabinet.

For the next five years he served in non-Labor Cabinets, as minister for external affairs until Lyons' death in April 1939, then as attorney-general and from September 1940 minister for the navy. The approach of World War II stimulated the old warhorse, and in the summer of 1938–39 he successfully conducted a recruiting campaign to double the strength of the volunteer militia. On Lyons' death he ran for the leadership of the party, losing to R. G. Menzies by a fairly narrow majority and becoming deputy leader. In the intrigues against Menzies during the early part of the war he seems mainly to have been a spectator. When the coalition government was defeated in October 1941 he at last succeeded Menzies as leader of the United Australia Party, agreeing to serve under Arthur Fadden as deputy leader of the Opposition.

There was no real chance of a second coming. The Curtin government succeeded in providing a sense of national unity during the crisis years of 1942–43. Hughes, as a member of the all-party Advisory War Council, was sufficiently impressed not to resign when the Opposition pulled out of the Council in 1944. Once again he was expelled from his party. He was not in the wilderness for long, for when Menzies formed the Liberal Party he moved to reinstate Hughes as an elder statesman in 1945.

Hughes was now out of touch with the labour movement, and like many of his generation tended to see communism as the main enemy. He was fairly comfortable in the Liberal Party.

But not too comfortable. They continued to give him endorsement, and at the elections of 1949 and 1951 he held the new electorate of Bradfield for the Liberals. In 1952, when the Menzies government decided to dispose of its holding in the Commonwealth Oil Refineries, the old back-bencher once again defied the party whip. 'The old ring and fire ... had gone,' remembered the leader of the Opposition, Dr Evatt, 'but the nervous energy, the vitality, and the deep conviction of the man were all still apparent.' His colleagues were tolerant of the mutineer. On his ninetieth birthday (which they thought his eighty-eighth) they gave him a testimonial dinner. Menzies, in an elegant speech, remarked that he had been a member of every party. 'Never the Country Party,' interjected Fadden. 'No,' rasped Hughes, 'had to draw the line somewhere, didn't I?'

A month later, on 28 October 1952, he was dead, victim to pneumonia, the 'old man's friend'. Crowds lined the streets at his funeral procession, and many leading Australians attended the burial at Sydney's Northern Suburbs cemetery. It was a humid afternoon, and as the coffin was lowered into the ground the reverent silence was broken by a crack of thunder, followed by the voice of Sir Arthur Fadden: 'He's arrived.'

Stanley Melbourne Bruce

9 FEBRUARY 1923 – 22 OCTOBER 1929

Bruce approached the tasks of prime minister as if they were those of the managing director of the national economy.

BY JUDITH BRETT

'Gentleman' was the word most often used to refer to Stanley Melbourne Bruce, Prime Minister of Australia from 1923–29. Hair smoothly brushed back, with the fashionable good looks of a silent movie star, he stares gravely from his photos or leans nonchalantly against his latest motor car in spats and plus fours. The contrast with his predecessor could not be greater. Where Billy Hughes was short and uncouth, Bruce was tall, handsome and always impeccably dressed; where Hughes was spontaneous and excitable, with the orator's gift for both stirring language and cutting insult, Bruce was always polite and unruffled and spoke in measured, ponderous prose.

Above all else, Bruce was predictable; he could be relied on to spring no surprises and to 'do the right thing' according to the conservative social and political conventions of the day. Bruce's conservatism offered reassurance to a country riven with divisions in the aftermath of the conscription battles and grieving its 60,000 war dead, but as the 1920s progressed and the divisions failed to heal, its limitations became obvious. He worked hard and was committed to good government, but he lacked both the political flexibility and the understanding of ordinary Australians to provide either unifying or inspiring leadership.

Although Bruce was Australian born, there hung about him a nostalgic aura of Edwardian England, when men in boaters and women in elegant long dresses watched the rowing at Henley or motored through the countryside. Bruce had panache, and a reassuring connection with British values and experience. He was born in 1883, the son of an Ulster Protestant immigrant who had made good in the golden age of Australian economic growth after 1860 as a partner in a soft goods importing business. After attending Melbourne Grammar, where he was captain of the school, as well as of football, cricket and rowing, Bruce went up to Cambridge in 1902 to study law and to continue his rowing. On graduating he established himself as a successful rowing coach and lawyer and became chairman of the London board of the family company. By the time he was twenty-eight he had the very substantial income of £5000 per year and in 1913 he married Ethel Dunlop, a wealthy Australian girl on a visit 'home'. When war broke out he was in Australia attending to family business, but he returned to Britain to enlist. He was wounded in the Gallipoli campaign and again in France, and in 1917 was repatriated from the army and awarded the Military Cross.

Captain Bruce returned to Australia in 1917 to take over the management of the family firm and was soon being asked to speak at recruiting rallies urgently seeking volunteers after the rejection of the first conscription referendum. His participation drew the handsome wounded soldier–businessman to the attention of the Nationalist Party, and he was persuaded to contest a by-election in the federal seat of Flinders. The Nationalist Party had been formed in the wake of the Labor government's split after the failure of the 1916 referendum on conscription. The labour movement had opposed conscription and when the federal parliamentary caucus met after the referendum, Billy Hughes came under strong personal attack, to which he responded by calling on those who thought as he did to follow him from the room. Twenty-three did, and they joined the opposition Liberal Party to form a 'Nationalist' government; a party organisation soon followed.

Although Hughes remained leader and prime minister, the Nationalist Party was unstable, formed in the heat of passionate wartime loyalties but bound to falter when peace brought cooler economic issues back into the centre of government concerns. The Nationalists' business supporters felt the government needed men of sound business and financial experience to counter the Labor element, and particularly Hughes' propensity for extravagance and support for government enterprise. Not only did Bruce have proven business experience, but also a distinguished war record, an important electoral asset in a country still at war and during the years that followed; throughout the 1920s Nationalist Party candidates regularly cited war service as their pre-eminent qualification for a political career and its absence could prove a liability, as Robert Menzies later discovered.

Bruce won the seat of Flinders at the by-election and held it at the 1919 election. He did not draw his backbencher salary and spent a good deal of time attending to his business interests. He was often abroad, and on one such trip in 1921 he interrupted a golfing holiday at Le Touquet to represent Australia at the League of Nations when a delegate was needed at short notice. On his return he was offered the position of treasurer by Hughes, who was coming under increasing pressure from the old Liberal sections of the Nationalist Party to accommodate business demands for a reduction in government expenditure.

Bruce accepted, and for the rest of the decade the affairs of his firm took second place to those of the nation.

Bruce became prime minister in 1923 essentially because he was in the right place at the right time and was the opposite of Hughes in almost every way. Although the non-labour wing of the Nationalists was increasingly uneasy with Hughes' leadership and there were calls to dissolve a wartime alliance that had outlived its usefulness, it is doubtful whether pressure from within the party would have been sufficient to topple so wily and experienced a politician, and Bruce himself was certainly not interested in moving against Hughes. But with the introduction of preferential voting at the 1919 election, a new player had entered federal politics: the Country Party, which represented the small farmers who had long felt their interests neglected by the city-based non-labour parties of big business, finance and the urban middle classes. At the 1922 election the Country Party won 14 seats, robbing the Nationalists of their absolute majority and gaining the balance of power. Their starting price for entering a coalition government was Hughes' head. Hughes was seen as the cause of the government's extravagance, and besides, he had ridiculed the new party mercilessly. Country Party leader Earle Page was firm: he was not prepared to be a member of any government led by Hughes. Bruce, however, was an acceptable alternative. With his sound business background he had performed well as treasurer, and his calm, considered demeanour offered the promise of a co-operative working relationship. After futile attempts to stave off the inevitable, a humiliated Hughes resigned and Bruce formed a coalition Nationalist–Country Party government.

Bruce's longest-lasting contribution to Australian politics was the alliance he and Earle Page forged between the country's major non-labour party and the Country Party. The new party was nervous of being swallowed up by the larger and more experienced Nationalists, and Bruce agreed to generous coalition terms. The government was to be called the Bruce–Page government, with the Country Party leader second in the ministry and the Country Party having five of the eleven Cabinet positions, including treasurer and postmaster-general. It is puzzling why Bruce conceded so much to the newcomer; it had after all polled only a little over one-tenth of the national vote while the Nationalists had polled more than one-third, yet had been given almost half the ministries.

Perhaps Bruce's relative political inexperience was the reason, or perhaps his genuine belief in a national interest overrode considerations of sectional political advantage. Whatever the reason, the terms set for the coalition were difficult to wind back, tying the Country Party firmly to the Nationalists and their successors at the federal level. Bruce and Page also negotiated an electoral pact in which the parties could not, with some exceptions, stand candidates against each other's sitting members, and which provided for joint Senate tickets. However, in one respect the Country Party was disappointed with the alliance. It soon became clear that the protective tariffs on manufacturing would not be dismantled, and that the only option was to join the manufacturers behind the stockade and go for protection all round.

Bruce was successful in bringing the new Country Party and the disgruntled rural interests it represented into the centre of government. He was not, however, so successful with other interests. Australia had emerged from the war a divided country, with the Labor Party's claims to legitimacy badly shaken. In the eyes of many, its opposition to conscription had revealed its alliance with the forces of disloyalty, an alliance confirmed by the 1917 Russian Revolution, which gave new confidence to the radicals in the party and therefore new plausibility to attacks on Labor's legitimacy. The wartime revival of sectarianism had also increased Catholic identification with the Labor Party.

When Bruce first put himself forward for election in 1918 he did so not as a politician but 'as a plain businessman and as a plain soldier'. This is the key to understanding his approach to both the Nationalist Party and the responsibilities of the prime ministership. He had served the nation as a soldier and would now do so in another way. He was firmly committed to the idea that the Nationalist Party was the vehicle for a unified national interest, and he resisted moves from influential non-labour politicians such as John Latham to revive the government's Liberal identity. He was also committed to preserving something of the Nationalists' ex-Labor element, insisting on the inclusion in his government of George Pearce, a former Labor minister and erstwhile close associate of Hughes. Bruce entered politics to serve the nation, not the party, and his suspicion of party allegiances, politicians and sectional politics was in keeping with a current that ran throughout the politics of the 1920s to manifest itself spectacularly in the citizens' movements of 1930–31.

In the face of the obvious conflicts and divisions within Australian society, Bruce insisted on the existence of a unified national interest, which he defined almost entirely in materialist terms. He believed that increased wealth, prosperity and happiness depended on increased production, and that the nation could be made more productive only through the application of good, sound business principles. Who, after all, could argue with the goal of development? He increased incentives to producers, whom he regarded as the real engines of economic growth, established various marketing schemes and attempted to improve the efficiency of the national economy. In a statement that was to be echoed many times in the 1980s, Bruce insisted, 'We were guided not by ideological motives, but by strict business principles', and he supported the selling of government-owned enterprises with the claim that it was not the function of the government to compete in the open market, but to govern.

In the early 1920s there was much talk among men of affairs of the need for 'clean' government, a modernist image of a streamlined, efficient government, shorn of the irrationalities of special pleading, political deals and inefficient traditional practices. For Bruce, 'strict business principles' were not the bearers of any class or partisan values, but simple and transparent agents of a practical and impersonal rationality that could be directed toward the common good of national development. Bruce supplemented this with a modern faith in experts who, in providing relevant scientific and economic information, would similarly guide government policy down rational paths. He set up a host of fact-finding commissions to report on ways of improving the efficiency of government practices and established the Council for Scientific and Industrial Research to provide expert advice to producers. At heart he was a centralist, concerned with administrative and economic efficiency and clear lines of accountability, and he tried to reform aspects of Commonwealth-state relations, even tackling the notoriously inefficient lack of a uniform rail gauge. He failed in this, but had more success in reforming financial relations, replacing federal per capita grants to the states with federal government responsibility for state debts, and establishing the Loan Council to eliminate the confusion in government borrowings. He was also the first prime minister to use Section 96 of the Constitution to make earmarked grants to the states, which he did for road building, and he oversaw the transfer of the federal Parliament to its new home in Canberra.

Bruce approached the tasks of prime minister as if they were those of the managing director of the national economy, or perhaps of a military commander. As the chief officer he had the final responsibility, so he felt he also needed full authority between elections. He was thus impatient with the checks and balances of parliamentary democracy and had little sympathy for states' rights. Rejecting the inevitability of conflicts of interest, he had little time for the processes of consultation and compromise in the formation of policy and was generally remote and inaccessible to lobbyists and interest groups. He demanded total obedience and loyalty from his Cabinet and attempted to bypass Parliament whenever he could. During his term as prime minister, Parliament sat on average for only fifty-nine days a year, the smallest number of sitting days of any federal government up to that time. Bruce's ideal was the strong leader. As he told his biographer, Cecil Edwards:

> If in a democracy, you have the good fortune to get a Prime Minister of the capacity to be the kind of leader that almost approaches the point of being a dictator, it's incomparably the best form of government ... He can be sacked at the next General Election.

The Bruce–Page government picked up the prewar agenda of nation-building, but without the same optimism and consensus with which Australians had embarked on the new century, and with an even greater sense of the importance of Great Britain to the country's future prosperity. Australia needed 'Men, Money and Markets', and it was Bruce's hope that Great Britain would provide all three: migrants to expand the population and fill the empty land; capital investment to help settle the new migrants and develop infrastructure; and markets for Australian rural exports through an expanded system of preferential imperial trade, all within a secure and strong imperial framework in which Australia was a proud white British dominion.

When he attended the Imperial Conferences of 1923 and 1926, at which Britain's relationship with her white dominions was renegotiated, Bruce was more interested in strengthening imperial economic and defence ties than in loosening diplomatic and constitutional ones. The pressure for the latter was coming from Canada and South Africa, where sizable non-British minorities bridled under the British connection, not from Australia, where the overwhelming majority of the population still identified themselves as British. Australia still saw its defence as relying on continued British presence in the Far East and gave little serious thought to the contradictions already apparent between Britain's national and imperial interests. Bruce did, however, think that Australia needed to be better informed about British foreign policy, and in 1924 appointed Richard Casey as a liaison officer with the Foreign Office.

Bruce's strategy for developing Australia was only partially successful. The assisted migration schemes were costly, as were the associated schemes to settle the 'empty' land with the expanded population. As well, during the 1920s the expanding urban population was demanding that governments provide them with a modern standard of living – electricity, telephones, improved housing standards, better roads and bridges to accommodate the new motor cars, sewerage and better water. Australian governments borrowed heavily to meet these demands; about 70 per cent of capital inflow during the period came from their borrowings. When added to the still unpaid loans used to finance World War I, this debt greatly expanded governments' international interest commitments. Nor did Britain see the role of trade in the maintenance of imperial family ties in quite the same way as Australia; the British government's first obligation was to British consumers, not high-waged Australian producers, and imperial preferences were not expanded as Bruce had hoped. The result of this, combined with the high levels of borrowing by state and federal governments, was that Australia headed into the late 1920s with a rising level of foreign debt, mainly to British financial institutions, and stagnating export income from primary industries hobbled with high costs by protection.

Signs of trouble with Bruce's unifying vision of national development were apparent by 1925 as the economy began to stall. Bruce was convinced that high wages were a major cause of Australia's economic difficulties and that agitators in the union movement stood in the way of the industrial relations reform necessary to enable the downward adjustment of the cost of labour. As the decade progressed he became increasingly focused on industrial relations and on the influence of 'alien' agitators in fomenting industrial unrest for their own sinister political purposes. With Attorney-General John Latham he made various legislative attempts to control what he saw as unlawful industrial action.

In 1926 the government amended the Crimes Act to increase its powers against revolutionary associations and to make it illegal to strike in disputes, which were proclaimed to be 'a serious industrial offence'. This was a direct blow against the unionists' right to strike, which even moderate unionists valued as a last resort measure to redress the balance of the employees' inherently weaker bargaining position. Although such efforts were largely unsuccessful in stopping industrial action, they created a climate of conflict and distrust around the government which ensured its place as a ruling-class government in the demonology of Labor history.

Bruce's perception of strikes as the work of an alien few was the result of his inability to admit to the existence of genuine differences of interest within Australian society, as well as his own remoteness from ordinary Australians' experience. He showed no understanding of the necessity of rank and file support for successful strike action, nor of the bonds of solidarity and common experience that linked men engaged in poorly paid, demeaning and dangerous work. Nor did he show any sympathy with the hardships of many Australians' lives. He was also largely indifferent to social welfare issues, in the main seeing pensions as a burdensome cost to government and a likely disincentive to hard work and effort.

The limitations of Bruce's social experience were here starkly apparent. Bruce was a stolidly unimaginative, wealthy man who inhabited an extraordinarily narrow and privileged social world. His major leisure activities were golf, horse riding and motoring, and his social life centred on the leather armchairs and well-furnished tables of the Melbourne Club. Out of Australia during his youth and early adulthood, serving in the British not the Australian army, he had few old friends and associates to give him access to other experiences. When he was urging Australians to tighten their belts, he built himself a sixteen-room Spanish mansion in Frankston, and he regarded Labor's criticisms as an impertinent intrusion into his private affairs.

Bruce made the reform of industrial relations the central issue of the 1925 election, campaigning for the introduction of secret ballots into union elections and for the strengthening of the powers of the Commonwealth Court of Conciliation and Arbitration. This was the first federal election in which voting was compulsory, and simple slogans were needed to explain the choices to the 40 per cent of electors who had not bothered to turn out in 1922. It was also the first of the full 'Red scare' federal election campaigns, and Bruce's press officer, Cecil Edwards, describes his campaigning:

> ... his serious and rather grand manner impressed the voters; when he spoke of 'law and order' it really sounded as if they were threatened by hordes of lawless and orderless agitators; when he said he would deport trade unionists who disagreed with him, it sounded almost democratic.

In contrast to the heated language Bruce used to describe the dangers of Bolshevism, he presented the Australian voters with a view of themselves as simple folk needing guidance and reassurance: 'Amidst all this turmoil, the ordinary citizen, whose life is far removed from political controversy, finds himself utterly confused and knows not where to turn for guidance ... And when I speak of the ordinary citizen I speak of those who constitute the overwhelming majority of our people ... It is to these men and women of moderate and sane views that I would address myself tonight.' Sanity, Safety, Stability – these were the Nationalists' key symbols for the moderate, sensible middle way that would reconcile competing groups in the national interest and resolve political conflicts within the orderly processes of parliamentary democracy. In 1925 these principles delivered an easy victory.

The 1928 election re-ran the Red scare campaign, but not quite so floridly nor as successfully as in 1925, and the government's majority was reduced. It appealed again to Australians to vote for 'sane and safe Government, combined with sound progressive policies [to] carry us along the road to great prosperity', and it again blamed the lack of progress on continuing industrial trouble. But by 1928 it was becoming clear that more than industrial trouble was blocking the road to prosperity. Unemployment was 11 per cent, and the 1927–28 budget had a deficit of nearly five and a half million pounds. Bruce had no new ideas as to how to tackle the downturn. He hoped it would be temporary, but when it failed to pass he became increasingly bewildered and frustrated. The old solutions of providing bounties as industries fell into difficulties, keeping taxes low, maintaining loans and keeping a close watch on welfare expenditure were not working; in fact, many of the experts on whose advice he depended were arguing that they were making matters worse. A team of economic experts invited from Britain attacked not only the high tariffs but the expensive rural settlement schemes, the practices of loan financing, the arbitration system and the bounties to encourage production: the very core policies on which Bruce had built his vision of expanding national productivity. And if the national cake was not going to expand but to contract, difficult political decisions about the distribution of pain would have to be made. When the government dropped prosecution proceedings against the wealthy coalmine owner John Brown for an illegal lockout, the contrast with its pursuit of unions for breaches of the industrial relations law was glaring, confirming the government's class bias in the eyes of many of its working-class opponents.

In 1926 Bruce had attempted to rationalise Commonwealth and state responsibilities for industrial relations in a referendum. The proposals were complex, including giving the Commonwealth an ill-defined power over essential services, and the government was defeated. The non-labour interests opposed the increase in the power of the Commonwealth at the expense of the states, while many Labor supporters suspected that the government's immediate aim was to give the Commonwealth the power to override legislation of Labor state governments seen as too favourable to workers' interests.

In 1929 Bruce made another attempt at rationalisation, this time in the opposite direction, by proposing to hand all industrial relations powers back to the states, except in the maritime industries and for federal public servants. This was a bombshell. Nothing about these plans had been mentioned during the election; in fact the Nationalists' platform had proposed that the Commonwealth should have wider powers over industrial relations, in keeping with the intent of the defeated referendum proposal. The legislation was defeated during its passage through Parliament when Billy Hughes, finally taking his revenge on Bruce for what he saw as his betrayal in 1922, led an assorted group of opponents across the floor. A frustrated Bruce called another election less than twelve months after the last, in which he campaigned almost exclusively on the necessity of restoring power over industrial relations to the states. It is unlikely that Bruce believed that this was the magic solution to the country's mounting economic woes, and certainly no one else did. In a landslide victory for Labor the government was defeated, and Bruce suffered the humiliation of losing his own seat of Flinders. The severe and fiercely independent John Latham replaced him as Nationalist leader and Labor leader James Scullin replaced him as prime minister.

Stanley Melbourne Bruce was an unimaginative man, with few points of identification with ordinary Australians. In good times he would have been a steady-as-she-goes prime minister, providing the good government that he saw as the obligation of his class. He was, however, incapable of seeing his own class interests as part of the broad national picture. This is not unusual among the wealthy, but it is a great liability for the leader of a political party claiming to represent the interests of the nation as a whole, particularly once the going gets tough. Not only was Bruce widely seen as too close to the interests of the employers in his handling of industrial relations conflicts, but his wealth and limited social experience rendered him unable to identify with the economic insecurities of thousands of Australians; nor could they identify with him. As the Great Depression developed, this would have been a major liability. Even had he not lost the largely unnecessary election in 1929, Bruce was unlikely to have survived long as prime minister in the inevitably heightened class conflicts of the Depression.

James Henry Scullin

22 OCTOBER 1929 – 6 JANUARY 1932

A simple man of inflexible integrity ... He was failed by circumstances, as well as by friend and foe alike.

BY JOHN MOLONY

Australia's ninth prime minister had a brief tenure of office. James Henry Scullin assumed the leadership of his country on 22 October 1929. He was the first native-born Labor prime minister and the first Catholic leader of the Labor Party. A few days after he took office Wall Street collapsed and the Great Depression began. That event defined the fate of his government during the next two years. Scullin lost office on 19 December 1931. Forty years later one writer described him as 'a prophet destroyed' and another claimed he was 'the man who failed even at failure'. The truth lay in between. To his sorrow, the Depression fulfilled his prophecies. No failure marked the integrity of his personality. He was failed by circumstances, as well as by friend and foe alike.

Scullin was born on 18 September 1876 at his parents' home near the railway siding of Trawalla about forty-two kilometres from Ballarat. The home was a modest dwelling belonging to the Victorian railways, for which his Irish-born father, John, worked as a fettler and gatekeeper. Both his father and mother, Ann Logan, came to Australia from County Derry, Ireland, where the Catholic population kept alive memories of the plantation of Protestant settlers and the ravages of Cromwell. James, the fourth of eight children, grew up in a home where Ireland and its miseries were ever present.

Passing his early life on the edge of the western district of Victoria, where vast areas of land were still held by owners whose fathers had been squatters, also made a mark on him. The modest social life enjoyed by the Scullins mostly centred on their friendship with Catholic selectors who struggled, often in vain, to eke out an existence on small blocks of land. The young Scullin grew into an adult with a determination to do all he could for the poor. He saw a tax on land, especially on land held by those he continued to call 'squatters', as one means of achieving that result. His standing up to the majesty and power of the British monarch when the day came for him to propose a native-born Australian as governor-general stemmed also from the mental and spiritual ambience of the fettler's home at Trawalla.

Catholic education in the bush was not available, so Scullin went to the Trawalla state school until 1887. The family then moved to Mt Rowan, near Ballarat, where he continued his schooling. At the age of twelve he looked for a job. Unskilled, he worked variously as a farmhand, wood-chopper and miner. The collapse of Melbourne's land boom, subsequent bank crashes and depression, as well as a drought of previously unknown length, combined to give the young worker an experience of tough times. Lacking a federal government until 1901, Australians witnessed the helplessness of colonial governments as they tried to confront the problems of the depression. Scullin was always a strong upholder of Federation, and he wanted to see it strengthened with more power than the original Constitution had stipulated.

From 1900 to 1910 Scullin ran a grocer's shop in Ballarat. He gave much of his leisure to reading, especially the English classics, and to his membership of the Catholic Young Men's Society, where he learnt oratorical and debating skills. He used these successfully in debating competitions held by the Ballarat South Street Society, and they were later to stand him in good stead. Perhaps impressed by the British labour leader Tom Mann, who visited Ballarat frequently, Scullin joined the local branch of the Political Labor Council in 1903. Turning to politics almost as if it was his natural arena, in 1906 he stood for the federal seat of Ballarat held by Prime Minister Alfred Deakin. Ramsay MacDonald, who became prime minister in the first British Labour government in 1924, was then visiting Australia and generously helped in the campaign, but to no avail; Scullin was roundly defeated by Australia's elder statesman. His candidature, however, enhanced his reputation.

While campaigning, Scullin had explained the Labor Party's objective as a form of socialism that rejected syndicalism and revolution. To him that kind of socialism would secure 'to all citizens the full fruits of their labour'. Although Leo XIII's encyclical *Rerum Novarum* (1891) had condemned socialism, Scullin's knowledge of Catholic social teaching was minimal and had no appreciable effect on his consciousness. In later life, when asked for his attitude towards state aid for Catholic schools, he replied that it was not a federal matter. Firmly committed to state intervention in other ways, he wrote, 'Justice and humanity demand interference whenever the weak are being crushed by the strong.' While never exhibiting sectarian bias, he remained committed to his faith and its practice throughout his life. His words on justice and humanity were inscribed on his tombstone.

From 1906 to 1910 Scullin travelled throughout western and northern Victoria as an organiser for the Australian Workers' Union. His absence from the grocer's shop meant its virtual neglect, but he found time to court Sarah Maria, the Ballarat-born daughter of Michael McNamara, from County Clare, Ireland. Sarah was a woman of quiet disposition, a dressmaker of some skill and a 'painter of pictures, in no small way'. They were married in St Patrick's Cathedral, Ballarat, on 11 November 1907. Their union of almost fifty years was cemented by intense loyalty to each other and, although they remained childless, the marriage was happy. Scullin, described as a 'short wiry figure with an eager, intelligent face', expressed a forthright love of his country as well as for his wife, but in all else he was reserved in his manner. His main forms of recreation were playing the violin in a duet with Sarah at the piano, and walking. He neither drank nor smoked.

In 1910, having built an electoral base, Scullin won the south-west Victorian seat of Corangamite in federal Parliament, where Labor had become the first party to have a majority in both Houses. He lost the seat in 1913 by a narrow margin but, having retained his Ballarat residence, he became editor of the local Labor daily, the *Evening Echo*, in which he supported and urged a firm anti-conscription line in World War I. Increasingly alarmed at the excesses of that 'accursed thing', capitalism, he led the push for the Labor Party to adopt a socialisation objective in 1921. Emotional rather than intellectual, idealistic more than practical, his commitment to socialism gradually diminished and was virtually extinct by 1929, prompted by his increasing concern at the developments in Soviet Russia.

In 1922 Scullin won the safe Labor seat of Yarra in Melbourne, which he held until 1949. For fifteen of those years he lived in the industrial suburb of Richmond, the heart of his electorate. By walking its streets he was able to meet his voters and understand their problems. The party, decimated by the split over conscription, was out of power, but by 1922 it was making ground and Scullin, by then an experienced parliamentarian, began to play a significant role on the Opposition benches. To the satisfaction of some former Labor colleagues who regarded him as a traitor, William Morris Hughes was deposed from the prime ministership by the Country Party and was succeeded by Stanley Melbourne Bruce in 1923. A patrician in manner and dress, decent, courteous and honest, Bruce was

1. The opening of the Commonwealth Parliament in the Exhibition Building, Melbourne, on 9 May 1901, by the Duke of Cornwall and York, later King George V. The ceremony was held there to accommodate the large number of guests, instead of at the Victorian Parliament House in Spring Street, Melbourne, home of the Federal Parliament from 1901 to 1927.

2. The first federal ministry, 1901–03. Australia's first prime minister, Edmund Barton, is seated second left, between his rival for the prime ministership, Sir William Lyne, far left, and the Governor-General, the Earl of Hopetoun. Barton's successor, Alfred Deakin, sits second from right, next to Sir George Turner. Standing, from left, are James George Drake, Richard Edward O'Connor, Sir Philip Fysh, Charles Kingston and Sir John Forrest.

3. Charles Kingston, standing, introduces the first tariff bill in the House of Representatives, Melbourne, in 1901. Seated to his right, Prime Minister Edmund Barton faces his lifelong friend and political antagonist, George Reid, top Speaker's end, across the table. Reid was later to become prime minister, as were Alfred Deakin, on the government's front bench, fifth from the Speaker's end; Joseph Cook, second from the Speaker's end on the Opposition front bench, and in the foreground third from right, Chris Watson. Others in this first parliament, later to become prime ministers, were Andrew Fisher and Billy Hughes.

4. Edmund Barton with his close friend and political ally, Alfred Deakin, who succeeded him as prime minister when Barton retired to the High Court in 1903.

5. In 1904 Chris Watson (centre) formed the first national Labor government in the world. His ministry included two future prime ministers, Andrew Fisher (bottom right) and Billy Hughes (top).

6. Australia's fourth prime minister, leader of the Free Trade Party George Reid, was dubbed 'Mr Yes-No Reid' after his equivocation over the Constitution. (See opposite.) With his portly figure, baby face and absurd monocle, Reid, was a favourite with cartoonists who invariably showed him with his Dry Dog (free trade). Livingston Hopkins's Bulletin *cartoon before the 1903 elections has Reid telling his Dry Dog: 'Stand back, you beast. If he sees you I shall not be able to catch him.'*

7. In 1907, during his second term as prime minister, Deakin attended the Imperial Conference in London where he pressed unsuccessfully for self-governing dominions, such as Australia to have a voice in foreign policy. During an exhausting round of social engagements, the tall, distinguished Deakin impressed the British with his legendary powers of oratory. The Illustrated London News *devoted a double-page spread, above, to portraying his 'magnificent speech' at the Pilgrim's Club dinner for 'the Premiers of his Majesty's Dominions beyond the Seas' at Claridge's Hotel on 19 April 1907.*

YES
NO
BOW
WOW
Here you have Mr Reid (& Co) coming at last to a definite understanding on the Protection Question
A. Vincent

8. In November 1908, Andrew Fisher became Australia's second Labor prime minister. The radical labour principles of the Scottish-born former miner were moulded in the collieries of Ayrshire as were those of his mentor, the great British labour leader and MP, James Keir Hardie, who also rose from child labour in the pits to political eminence.

9. Alfred Deakin, right, at Ballara, his holiday house at Point Lonsdale in 1909 with the leader of the Free Trade Party, Joseph Cook. The Protectionist Deakin became prime minister for the third and last time in mid-1909 after talks with Cook led to the formation of the Fusion Party uniting traditionally opposed Free Traders and Protectionists against Labor and subsequently evolving into the Liberal Party with Deakin as its leader and Cook as deputy leader.

10. By 1910 Andrew Fisher was back as prime minister and spearheading an ambitious plan of legislative innovation which included the establishment of the Commonwealth Bank and of Canberra as the federal capital. Here, Fisher, second from left, stands with Governor-General Lord Denman, Lady Denman and the flamboyant maverick MP, King O'Malley, at a ceremony on 12 March 1913, to name Canberra.

11. Joseph Cook, third from left hands folded, was, like Fisher, a pit boy and working-class migrant. However, the one-time trade unionist and labour radical chose a different path to Fisher, becoming a conservative imperialist and playing a major role in the formation of the Liberal Party. Here, in November 1913, Cook, as prime minister, with his wife, Mary, far right, attends the commemoration of the 125th anniversary of the first Government House in Parramatta.

12. After Andrew Fisher's retirement in 1915, his ambitious and fiery deputy, William Morris 'Billy' Hughes, became prime minister. He was popular with Australian troops abroad in World War I, but at home his push for conscription led to a bitter split in the Labor Party and the formation of the National Party. He lobbied energetically in Britain for Australian interests during the war and defied United States President Woodrow Wilson at the Versailles Peace Conference. In 1919, after his homecoming, returning servicemen carried Hughes along George St, Sydney. To them he was 'the Little Digger', a symbol of Australian self-confidence.

13. Debonair and wealthy, Stanley Melbourne Bruce could not have been more different from his predecessor, Billy Hughes. Pictured with his Rolls-Royce in 1923, the year in which he took office, Bruce took a businessman's approach to government.

14. The first Bruce–Page ministry, 1923. Bruce, remarkable in spats and bow-tie, second from left, forged a long-lasting alliance between his Nationalist Party and the Country Party, led by Earle Page, seated second right.

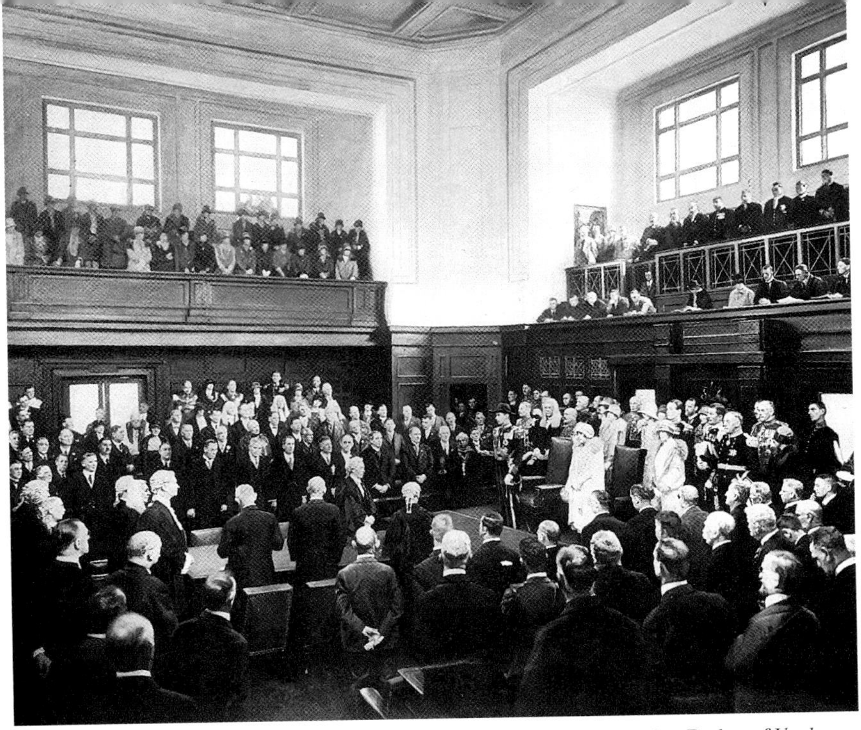

15. On 9 May 1927, during Bruce's term as prime minister, the Duke of York opened the provisional Parliament House in Canberra.

16. Backbencher Billy Hughes records a talk to the nation during the 1929 elections which followed a Hughes-led revolt by disgruntled MPs against the Bruce–Page government, and which culminated in Bruce's crushing defeat by Labor's James Scullin.

17. James Scullin, a one-time Ballarat grocer, came to power in a sweeping Labor victory in 1929. He was a noted orator: here at a Labor Day picnic at Long Gully near Adelaide, he urges workers to 'eternal vigilance' of the reforms that had been gained.

18. Prime Minister Scullin sparked outrage with his insistence on an Australian as governor-general instead of the usual British appointee. A shocked George V was finally forced to assent when Scullin remained resolute, threatening to go to the polls. In a significant moment in Australian nationalism, former Chief Justice Sir Isaac Isaacs (centre on the dais) with Scullin by his side (immediate left), was sworn in with full fanfare as the first Australian-born governor-general on 22 January 1931 in Melbourne.

19. *Jubilant supporters in Latrobe, Tasmania, hoist up a victorious Joe Lyons on election day in December 1931 when his United Australia Party toppled Scullin's Labor government.*

20. *Lyons talks to workers on the wharves in Brisbane. The ex-Tasmanian premier, one of Australia's most popular prime ministers, appealed to ordinary voters with his down-to-earth style.*

21. The largest family to occupy the Lodge, Lyons and his wife, Enid – later a political figure in her own right – and their eleven children, were a comforting symbol during the Depression years even though in reality the family was often separated because of the demands of schooling and frequent travel.

22. On 5 April 1939 after suffering a heart attack – at first thought to be 'a severe chill' – Prime Minister Lyons was admitted to Sydney's St Vincent's Hospital for observation but was soon fighting for his life. His family and government ministers, including his coalition partner, Sir Earle Page, right, and Treasurer Richard Casey, left, rushed to his death-bed, remaining at the hospital throughout the following night. Lyons died on the morning of Good Friday, 7 April, the first Australian prime minister to die in office. That afternoon at Admiralty House, Page was sworn in as prime minister.

23. R. G. Menzies succeeded Joe Lyons as leader of the United Australia Party. After a vitriolic speech attacking Menzies, caretaker Prime Minister Sir Earle Page resigned, and on 26 April 1939 Menzies took office. Here, on 3 September 1939, a sombre prime minister broadcasts to the nation the news that Australia is at war with Germany.

24. Prime Minister Menzies chairs the first meeting in November 1940 of the all-Party Advisory War Council which included six past, present and future prime ministers among its members. From left: Opposition members Jack Beasley, Norman Makin, Frank Forde, and John Curtin; and the Government's Robert Menzies, Billy Hughes, Percy Spender, Arthur Fadden and Harold Holt.

25. In August 1941, after dissatisfaction with his leadership, Menzies resigned, declaring: 'I have been done ... I'll lie down and bleed awhile'. Here, Arthur Fadden, who replaced him as prime minister, at the table, with his deputy, Billy Hughes, left, listens as Opposition leader John Curtin addresses the Parliament. An aloof Menzies, far right, watches proceedings.

PIX

Vol 9, No. 3
Saturday, January 17, 1942

JOHN CURTIN—THE NATION'S LEADER

THIS unconventional study of Prime Minister John Curtin was taken by PIX at Canberra on a day when the temperature was as hot as the Pacific situation. It has fallen to the lot of Mr. Curtin to shoulder greater responsibilities than any other Prime Minister in the history of Australia. He has done so with an appreciation of the difficulties which confront us. He sounded a warning and an inspiration when he broadcast to the nation: "This is our darkest hour. Let that be fully realised. Our efforts in the past two years must be as nothing compared with the efforts we must now put forward." John Curtin was born at Creswick, Victoria, 56 years ago. He took a keen interest in Labor politics from youthful days. He was secretary of Victorian Timber Workers' Union; editor of "Westralian Worker" (1917-1928)); represented Fremantle in Commonwealth Parliament 1928-1931, then since 1934. Curtin is typic ally Australian in his love of sport. He played first grade football and cricket for Brunswick, Victoria. In politics he is noted for his moderate views, wide know ledge of political economy and for his capacity as a trenchant debater. John Curtin found romance in politics. He met his wife as a result of travelling to Hobart to help in an election campaign. His work was to support Mr. Abraham Needham. Visiting the Need ham home, he met candidate's daughter, Elsie, who, at 17, was member of Labor Party. For once, young Cur tin's capacity as a polished speaker was used for more intimate affairs than politics. He married Miss Needham. For years, she has been her husband's greatest helpmate.

PIX——Page Three

See Next Pages

26. In October 1941, Labor leader John Curtin moved a no-confidence vote, bringing down the Fadden government, and reluctantly assuming the mantle of Australia's wartime leader. He was soon feeling the heat, as Pix *magazine reported in January 1942. Australia, Curtin warned, was facing its 'darkest hour'.*

the most unlikely of Australia's leaders. Despite his relationship to only one small segment of the people represented by wealth and social standing, Bruce remained prime minister for six years.

The tinsel years of the 1920s were marked by false prosperity, and Scullin rapidly became a prophet of doom. He feared the continuation of a negative trade balance, increasing external debt, a stagnating economy that produced an unemployment rate of 8 per cent and the neglect of local manufacturing industry because of the refusal to apply high tariffs to imported goods. He was especially incensed when Bruce, whom he compared with Mussolini, privatised the Commonwealth Woollen Mills at Geelong in 1923 and removed the Commonwealth Bank from ministerial oversight, virtually handing it over to private control.

When Scullin took his seat at the first sitting of the federal Parliament in Canberra on 9 May 1927 he did so as deputy leader of his party. One year later he became leader. Previously an opponent of the choice of Canberra as the seat of the national Parliament, he was now proud to write, 'it is the capital'. Turning quickly to more pressing matters, he complained about the continuous floating of overseas loans as well as the amount of capital brought in from overseas, which he called 'financial imperialism run mad'. He was opposed to selling the Commonwealth Shipping Line and claimed there was 'an anti-Australian government in office' that squandered the assets of the people and favoured the rich. The number of immigrants being assisted to enter the country when unemployment was running at 11 per cent also caused him concern. Looking back to the depression of the 1890s, Scullin hoped that Australia would not see again the 'deflation and distress' of those days. He was heard with listless lack of interest and rendered helpless by the fact that the disaster he had foreseen was about to strike. At the time, Australian democracy was still a healthy plant and debate in the House had not become a sterile formality. As a result, Scullin, by the force of his arguments and oratory, was sometimes able to persuade the government to modify its proposed legislation, especially on fiscal matters.

The crisis that arose in Parliament was not financial but industrial. The government was determined to curb the power and influence of the trade unions and the wages and living conditions of the workers by discriminatory legislation. Throughout 1928 and 1929, when there were regular strikes, accompanied at times by violence, especially among waterside workers, timberworkers and coalminers, Scullin unflinchingly stood by the strikers. The response of Bruce was very different. Thwarted in his attempt to gain further control over the workers, he decided to hand over effective determination of industrial disputes to the states. Such a step would have dismantled the Commonwealth arbitration system.

Probably unwittingly, Bruce gave a hostage to fortune in that the electorate was not prepared to countenance a step that would have grave industrial, social and economic repercussions. Bruce lost both government and his own seat in the federal election in October 1929, and said that the result was 'ghastly'. He advised Scullin to emulate his example and play regular golf in order to maintain his strength. Not being a golfer and anticipating little leisure, an elated Scullin summarily rejected his proposal and began his prime ministership with undisguised enthusiasm.

Bruce was fortunate in not having to pick up the burden that he and his government had helped create. The Australian electorate turned to Labor because Bruce was seen as the betrayer of those who needed the intervention of the government to maintain their way of life and retain their dignity. They saw Scullin as a moderate, sensible and decent leader and Labor as the upholder of their rights but, in asking a prophet to assume the mantle of leader, they and he were unaware that the times were against them all. Nothing could reverse the trends determined by the international financial situation and the past profligacy that left Australia singularly vulnerable to it. The most that could be expected of the new government was that by carrying out prudent policies, the worst effects of what became known as the Great Depression would be mitigated.

As a small fund-saving gesture Scullin continued to live in a modest suite at the Hotel Canberra rather than at the Lodge. His health had already been impaired by constant overwork, but he faced the future with unfounded buoyancy and optimism. Labor had not occupied the Treasury benches for thirteen years, many members of caucus were inexperienced, and none of Scullin's Cabinet – himself included – had held ministerial responsibility at the federal level, though 'Red Ted' Theodore and Joseph Lyons had been premiers of Queensland and Tasmania respectively. Many of the senior public servants had become comfortable under conservative governments and change was irksome to them. Within Parliament Scullin faced a hostile Senate, where 29 Opposition members overwhelmingly outnumbered 7 Labor men. They used their numbers to thwart the initiatives of his government, although they stopped short of taking the ultimate step of refusing supply.

The reasons behind the downfall of Scullin's government are numerous and complex. But basically, no government can govern unless it has the power to do so, and Scullin's lacked that power. His only solution was to go quickly for a double dissolution in the hope of removing the dead hand of the Senate. He rejected that option, but not because he was afraid of failure at the polls. Perhaps he unwisely hoped that the gravity of the crisis would evoke its own response and the conservatives would put the national interest before political gain. Men who regard themselves as born to rule, a common characteristic of conservative governments, relinquish power with chagrin and fight relentlessly to regain it. Scullin's opponents were of that ilk and granted him not an inch, especially in the Senate.

The compelling fact was that in Australia, as elsewhere, grave economic problems demanded new solutions but few experts, including John Maynard Keynes, were certain of how they ought to react. Little money was available to implement Labor's policies on matters such as child endowment, old age pensions, unemployment insurance and the like. Nonetheless, in the remaining weeks of 1929, Scullin did manage to increase social service payments, raise tariffs, take Australia off the gold standard and cut back assisted immigration. The economy worsened sharply in 1930 with a marked drop in production, falls in business activity and unemployment rising to 20 per cent and beyond. Scullin's treasurer, Theodore, resigned in July when doubts were cast on his probity, and on 25 August the prime minister left to attend an Imperial Conference in London.

Scullin achieved practically nothing of any real economic value for Australia and the visit is memorable for only one incident. Native born but reared within a home in which concepts of Irish nationality were strong, Scullin had long concentrated his attention and conviction on the genuine worth of Australian nationality. As a symbol of that nationality he was determined that an Australian, Isaac Isaacs, would be appointed the next governor-general. The alarm among conservative circles in Australia was expressed by John Latham, leader of the federal Opposition, who saw Scullin's step as anti-British and an expression of 'strident and narrow Australian jingoism'. A profoundly shocked George V considered Isaac's nomination entirely unacceptable and felt that the Australian Prime

Minister had no right to suggest it. Called to an audience with the King, Scullin quickly realised that the only obstacle to the appointment of the native-born chief justice of the High Court was his Australian nationality. The King was aware that Scullin had told his private secretary, Lord Stamfordham, that he was prepared to fight both a referendum and an election in Australia on the issue 'whether an Australian is to be barred from the office of governor-general because he is an Australian'. When Scullin remained steadfast the King assented. It was one of the most significant steps taken in the name of Australian nationality.

Scullin's six-month absence from Australia was the most telling mistake of his short prime ministership. When he returned in January 1931 he realised that the Depression was a clear but undiagnosed malady demanding action, but the favoured cures were provisional and hesitant. Looking for decisive measures he imprudently reappointed Theodore as treasurer and thereby caused two leading ministers, Lyons and Fenton, to resign and help create the United Australia Party. Undaunted, the clever and long-sighted Theodore suggested solutions based on the creation of bank credit. Such proposals were anathema to the Senate and financial circles. Those who questioned Theodore's integrity easily cast them into doubt.

In the circumstances Scullin was forced to rely on outsiders whose expertise seemed impeccable. The Commonwealth Bank was already beyond direct government control, but to reappoint Robert Gibson as its chairman was a grave mistake. Gibson refused to implement government policy on credit expansion unless Scullin reduced pensions, which he refused to do, but it meant any financial supply line from the bank was cut. Another setback came when Scullin invited Sir Otto Niemeyer of the Bank of England to advise how Australia should confront its crisis. Niemeyer, by conviction and training, was incapable of advising anything but wage cuts, belt tightening, no more loans and debt payment. These were all remedies that gave comfort to the Opposition, where men who had played a role in creating the very problems the nation confronted now cried shamefully for the implementation of measures that would result in savage wage cuts, reduced spending and lost jobs. Unemployment continued to rise while once-proud men lined up in thousands for the dole or 'jumped the rattler' in a futile search for work.

A little respite followed the implementation of the 'Premiers' Plan' which cut expenditure. Keynes said that the plan 'saved the economic structure of Australia'. Wheat and wool prices, the backbone of the economy, rose, and things began to look a little better, although on economic policies the Labor Party was deeply divided and eventually split into three factions. Scullin's enemies decided the time had come to topple him. The party was riddled with opposing factions and it was inevitable that political regroupings would occur. In the end Scullin and his government were brought down by the supporters of Jack Lang, the preposterous and self-appointed saviour of the people. Lang was the Labor premier of New South Wales and his response to state debt was to renege on payments to London. Scullin's former minister, J. A. 'Stabber Jack' Beasley, led a group of Labor members allied with Lang to form an 'unholy alliance' with Lyons and the United Australia Party. They voted Scullin out of office and Labor polled miserably in the election of 19 December 1931, winning only 14 seats. Two future Labor prime ministers, John Curtin and Ben Chifley, lost their seats. Bruce was returned for Flinders. Joseph Aloysius Lyons, reared and nurtured in the ideals and policies of the Labor Party, became prime minister as leader of his United Australia Party, a ragbag assortment of ambitious conservatives and disgruntled Laborites.

The episode was the ultimate betrayal in Labor Party history. Scullin's downfall was largely due to his attempt to remain true to the ideals and policies of the party he led. If it is argued that the powerful economic forces at work in Australia and elsewhere were too much for him, it is reasonable to ask whether the Bruce government would have shown greater skill and foresight in the crisis of the Depression than they did in the years leading up to it. When the next national crisis came, in 1939, the conservative forces fell into disarray and demoralisation and the country turned to Labor. A few years after losing office Scullin said that many experts in the financial world had described his government as one that 'courageously saved Australia' from falling into economic and social chaos. He then asked, 'Have we to wait for 100 years for historians to give us the credit that we should be given now?'

To the last Scullin remained a Labor man devoted to the welfare of Australia, saying: 'We shall serve our country in the interests of democracy and justice.' Eschewing any temptation to pass his days in the pursuit of wealth or personal gratification, he spent the remainder of his active life in Parliament as the member for Yarra and as Labor's elder statesman. The party remained bitterly divided, especially in New South Wales, and the federal election of 1934 resulted in the gain of only four seats. Scullin spoke little in the ensuing Parliament but protested strongly against the attempt to use the Immigration Act to exclude the communist agitator Egon Kisch from entering Australia. He also remained firmly committed to the abolition of the death penalty. His health had deteriorated and his resignation from the leadership in September 1935 came as no surprise. John Curtin was elected in his place and Scullin went happily to the backbench.

In 1938 he spoke tellingly of the need for a national legislature with the power and will to represent the people. He said, 'We hardly know where we are in respect of a constitution', and, 'We are ruled in a large number of cases, not by a majority of the people, but by a majority of the justices of the High Court or members of the Privy Council.' Scullin wanted a special session of Parliament to develop constitutional reforms, to be followed by a referendum, but his proposal came to nothing. Perhaps surprisingly to those who judged his interests as narrow, he did plead successfully for greater support for writers through the Commonwealth Literary Fund. Deploring the inferiority complex that led Australians to conclude that culture only existed elsewhere, he sounded a high note of nationality, stating, 'We must appraise and cultivate our own heritage, and, because of our youth and virility, encourage to the maximum the cultural possibilities of our own native land.' In some slight recognition of Aboriginal rights to their own land his government, in 1931, had declared the first Aboriginal reserve, made up of the 49,920 square kilometres of Arnhem Land in the Northern Territory. The step was taken in recognition that, to preserve their own culture, the Aborigines needed a place where they could live their traditional lifestyle without interference from whites.

During the years of World War II Scullin occupied an office between those of Curtin and Chifley and was called by some 'His Grey Eminence'. Although he wanted no Cabinet role, both Labor prime ministers regularly sought his advice and drew on his experience. In 1918, after vigorously opposing conscription for foreign service, he had said he would not hesitate to introduce it were an enemy to threaten the 'hearths and homes of this young democracy'. In 1943 he supported Curtin's decision, partly motivated by American pressure, to extend the area where conscripts could serve to Timor, Ambon and Dutch New Guinea. He also helped to introduce a uniform federal tax and formulate a 'pay as you earn' system, and virtually accused Menzies of dishonesty in opposing it.

On 8 May 1947 Scullin stood to speak for the last time in Parliament. Earle Page had sat down after attacking the Commonwealth Literary Fund for providing a grant to James Normington Rawling to write a biography of the colonial poet, patriot and ardent republican Charles Harpur. Page's grounds were that Normington Rawling was a communist sympathiser. It was a distasteful episode but Scullin, who had long served as an active member of the granting body, ennobled the debate by stating that he judged cases only on their merits and that he would never have dreamed of delving into the political convictions of anyone who applied for a grant. It was the same thirst for a just and decent society that had moved him in 1931 to introduce a Bill for the formation of the Australian Broadcasting Commission. The Bill lapsed on the day Scullin lost office but, when Lyons reintroduced it on 9 March 1932, Scullin spoke for it and hoped that the new ABC would never become 'an instrument of suppression or misrepresentation'.

Living with his wife in a new and somewhat more substantial home in Hawthorn, across the Yarra from Richmond, Scullin spent the last years of his life in increasing bouts of ill-health. He retired from Parliament before the 1949 elections in which Chifley lost office largely because of his attempt to nationalise the private banks – a measure to which Scullin was not opposed. No one saw it as ironic when a group of manufacturers, mindful of Scullin's assistance to them with his tariff wall in 1929–31, raised £4,400 on his behalf. That sum, invested mostly in Australian shares, doubled his assets.

Scullin died on 28 January 1953. After a solemn requiem mass celebrated by Archbishop Daniel Mannix in St Patrick's Cathedral, his remains were laid to rest in the Melbourne general cemetery alongside some of his old mates from the Australian Workers' Union. The inventory of his personal estate, including shares worth £4937 5s 10d which he left to Sarah Maria, who died nine years later, revealed that he had no land or property other than his home and he possessed no 'Watches, Trinkets, Jewellery, etc'. He did have a 'Cabinet Gramophone (Out of Order)', valued at £1 and a 'Worn Carpet Square' worth £2. In life and in death, James Henry Scullin of Trawalla was a simple man of inflexible integrity.

Joseph Aloysius Lyons

6 JANUARY 1932 – 7 APRIL 1939

It needed no spin doctors to craft Joe and Enid Lyons into salt-of-the-earth Australian family folk ... The Lyons family in the Lodge was a unifying and comforting symbol for the many seeking security in these years.

BY ANNE HENDERSON

For entertaining high was not his height
Nor even was when raised there by fate
No! a simple fire lit his mind
A generous charity was stamped upon his speech
A homely grace lent liking to his wit
And ageless verity did guide his seeking feet.[1]

In these words Rosemary Lyons recalled the strong but humble character of her father, long after his death on 7 April 1939 while prime minister of Australia. Yet Joe Lyons has suffered in historical memory for those very qualities of self-effacing good humour, qualities endearing in a personal sense but unfamiliar in most who achieve high office.

New South Wales Premier Bob Carr is fond of retelling his experiences in asking school children to name Australian prime ministers. He is surprised that even primary students can sometimes name Edmund Barton, Robert Menzies, even Ben Chifley. But ask a class of Australian schoolchildren who was Joe Lyons and the answer will be, 'Joe who?'

Yet Joe Lyons, prime minister of Australia 1932–39, was in his time the most popular prime minister Australia has ever had. His caricature as a cuddly koala derived from his bush of wavy hair and genuinely friendly demeanour. In the first century of Federation, he served as long as Malcolm Fraser (discounting Fraser's period as caretaker prime minister) and was arguably more popular than Bob Hawke. Only Prime Ministers Hughes, Menzies and Hawke served longer.

Popularity doesn't always survive in history – especially with no cheer squad to write that history – or if the prime minister concerned does not live on to be interviewed or to write memoirs. Joe Lyons PM became a victim of his life's choices and his fate. In 1931 he resigned from the Scullin Labor Cabinet at a time of division within Labor ranks between those who followed Scullin and a small breakaway group called the Lang Laborites, aligned with the populist NSW Premier J. T. Lang. For a time Lyons sat on the Opposition benches, joined by a small group of Labor defectors – James Fenton, John Price, Joel Gabb and David McGrath. Later Lyons and his group linked up with the conservatives to form a new party.

A former Labor premier of Tasmania and acting Labor treasurer in the Depression days of December 1930, when he pulled off a successful loan conversion, Lyons would become the spearhead for the formation of the United Australia Party. Elected leader of the UAP Opposition replacing Nationalist leader John Latham (7 May 1931), Lyons announced the news to Parliament amid recriminations and denunciations from his former Labor colleagues sitting opposite. Lyons led the UAP to three successive election victories, an historic first for any party. When the UAP toppled the Scullin government in December 1931 it won an absolute majority, governing without the Country Party until 1934. Lyons' fate, however, was to die in office on Good Friday 1939 of coronary occlusion.

In the historical records, Lyons has suffered because he lacked a faction. He had deserted Labor; its historians would not claim him. Conversely, as the UAP fell away (the party that never wrote a political platform) and the Liberal Party emerged in the mid 1940s, the conservative side of politics celebrated its development in the glow of the Menzies era – devoid of Labor defectors such as Joe Lyons. Lyons' brief as prime minister was to tackle weighty matters of monetary planning and the tricky behind-the-scenes politics of smoothing and uniting an abnormal collection of Cabinet egos and conflicting personalities: not so colourful for the historical records. Moreover, Lyons took a self-effacing approach, playing the role of one among equals.

Early Lyons budgets were conservative, holding firm against any temptation to spend heavily as a way of solving the problem of unemployment. After all, Lyons had begun his defection from Labor by crossing the floor of the House over Treasurer Theodore's proposed £18 million fiduciary note issue. Lyons fiercely opposed debt as a way of easing the jobs crisis. Depression notwithstanding, the conservative governments of Lyons made financial responsibility the order of the day, promising to relieve taxpayers only if Australia's economy improved quickly. Farmers affected by falling prices were given some relief and costs were trimmed by lowering pensions and public service salaries. The problem of rebellious NSW Labor Premier J. T. Lang was solved when State Governor Sir Philip Game dismissed him on 13 May 1932, calling on UAP leader Bertram Stevens to form a ministry. The UAP easily won the state election that followed in June.

By mid 1934 there were signs of economic recovery, allowing the Commonwealth to make a grant of £2 million to the states. But the most significant tussle of the Lyons years was with Earle Page, leader of the Country Party, over the question of tariffs. At the Ottawa Imperial Economic Conference of July–August 1932 there was criticism of Australia's tariff regime and a recommendation of a return to pre-Scullin tariffs, in effect a lowering of tariffs in some areas. But Lyons largely retained the Scullin tariffs. Country Party leader Earle Page objected strongly; in his view the government was 'protecting industries with no sound prospects for success'.[2]

After the 1934 federal election, Lyons was forced to govern in coalition with the Country Party. There were further divisions in Cabinet and government seemed to drift timidly. The *Age* editorial on 30 July 1935, typical of criticism of the later Lyons years, opined that 'few governments have derived so much self-satisfaction from doing so little'. As UAP leader, Lyons compromised reformist instincts from his Labor years. Little of his government's legislation had lasting effect; the creation of the Commonwealth Grants Commission in 1933 was an exception, as was the increased emphasis on defence in his last term. In 1938 Lyons opposed the introduction of conscription only to launch a successful recruitment drive headed by Billy 'Little Digger' Hughes.

Recollections of Lyons have not always been fair. They include many opinions from colleagues who were at times also his political rivals. Former prime minister Stanley Melbourne Bruce opined to Enid Lyons that a prime minister needed a hide like a rhinoceros, an overpowering ambition and a 'mighty conceit of himself. And your poor husband has none of them.'[3] Bruce believed a prime minister should be a 'dictator'. In her autobiography *So We Take Comfort*, Enid Lyons acknowledged Bruce's view of her husband's deficiencies, but later she recorded how former Nationalist leaders John Latham and Stanley Bruce tended, in private, to reduce Joe Lyons to a nice chap dependent on guidance, with a contest between them as to who was chief 'nursemaid'. Joe, she said, was grateful to both men for 'their valuable and deeply acknowledged help' as he settled into his role as prime minister. After all, he was making his way in a newly formed party of political strangers. But, as Enid Lyons pointed out, Joe Lyons' 'previous political experience extended over a period that equalled the record of both of them together'.

In an ironic observation of Bruce, Enid Lyons recalled:

> Everything he did, he did with panache. It distinguished even the way he lost an election. ... He lost the prime ministership, he lost his seat, and he lost face. In his own electorate he converted a majority of nearly 11,000 into a minority, and in the parliament converted a coalition government party of 42 into an opposition of 24, ten of whom were members of the Country Party. ... What he failed to appreciate is that winning elections is not just a gift from God, nor the result of three weeks on the hustings. Some of the qualities of leadership are involved at least, and a presentable record of achievement is not without its value.[4]

Unlike Bruce and Latham, Robert Menzies was generous, writing that Lyons, setting out to restore 'a revived confidence in the future, a steady increase in the volume of employment, an improved business investment induced by optimism which had been so disastrously shaken ... succeeded in his task. In his own undemonstrative way, he illustrated the moral force of leadership.' To Menzies, Lyons was a 'brilliant parliamentarian ... no secondary person' and had 'a real command in the House'.[5]

A man for the times was Lyons. However, he has often been described as some sort of caretaker until a real political hero could take over. His early death and Dame Enid's later success as a federal parliamentarian have also meant that his own record was overshadowed. Joe Lyons was politically astute, his abilities understated; Robert Menzies attested to these qualities in his autobiography *Afternoon Light*. He appealed to ordinary voters with down-to-earth honesty and abroad he met world figures, whether British royalty, the Roosevelts or Mussolini's son-in-law, with ease.

Then there was the continuing furphy of the 'ambitious wife', a woman seventeen years his junior, active in politics, just thirty-three and the mother of ten when he became prime minister. Joe's pet name for her was 'girl'. Enid Lyons, ambitious wife, is a cliché trotted out by many able commentators and historians. From a present-day perspective, Enid Lyons was a talented woman discovering the liberation of public life and enjoying the partnership her liberal-minded husband offered. Their son Brendan Lyons recalls his mother being 'very crabby' about the label: 'She lived for 30 or 40 years longer and became a popular figure in her own right. She was tremendous. But if you analysed their achievements in government, Dad was a mile ahead.'[6]

Regardless, Menzies' biographer, Allan Martin, writes that Enid's ambitions for Lyons 'exceeded those of the prime minister himself'.[7] And Mungo MacCallum, in a *Sydney Morning Herald* piece of 31 July 1999 likening Prime Minister John Howard to Joe Lyons, referred to Enid Lyons as 'a fiercely ambitious driving force' – MacCallum concluding that Enid Lyons was another Janette Howard.

So who was Joe Lyons?

Loose comparisons are often made across the historical canvas to help understand personality and character. Joe Lyons and John Howard are compared as the plain men of politics, lacking the style of great men but playing a canny game behind the scenes. They find their moment. There is truth in this, although not because of their respective partners. Enid Lyons and Janette Howard could not be more different. But there are other differences.

Unlike John Howard, who would appear as the plain man but who was middle-class from the cradle, Joe Lyons knew what poverty meant. His empathy with the plight of so many in the years he was prime minister was keenly felt. As he resigned from the Labor Party at the time of the fiduciary note debate, Lyons made a passionate speech in which he empathised with the unemployed and expressed guilt at the irresponsibility of comfortable politicians: 'All over this country ... good, honest fellows are tramping the country looking for work that they cannot obtain, yet we sit here, talking nonsense.'[8]

Joe Lyons was born in Stanley, Tasmania, in 1879. His father, a descendent of Irish settlers, prospered in business until he ventured all his savings on the 1887 Melbourne Cup and lost the lot. Aged nine, young Joe, the fourth child in the family, was sent to work for three shillings a week as a messenger in a draper's store. Later, as a 'printer's devil' he set type, proofread and distributed handbills in a newspaper office, where he protested about the conditions and finally left. By twelve he was cutting scrub. His maiden aunts Etty and Mary Carroll eventually sent him back to school – in Stanley. At seventeen, after a stint as a monitor (trainee teacher), he took on a teaching career.

Joe Lyons began humbly. But his protest against work conditions as a printer's devil showed he had grit and fight in him. Thrust into a profession that gave responsibility and little status, he quickly surmised his lot. In *A Political Love Story* Kate White records how Lyons' appointments to remote schools in Tasmania encouraged his 'many disagreements with the Education Department'. At Tullah in 1905, he delayed opening his school because desks had not arrived. He also found there were no blackboards or rulers for the forty pupils ready for learning. His director of education objected to his complaints. But Lyons was on a mission. He would work where he was appreciated, or leave – a somewhat Irish (and Australian) working-class ethic. A simple dignity of spirit: what else is there to fight with but withdrawal of services?

Transferred that year to Smithton and appointed head teacher, he became active in politics, joining the Duck River branch of the Workers' Political League, the early name for the Tasmanian Labor Party. His teaching record deteriorated further. Enid Lyons recollected that his political activities were regarded with 'scant approval'. He was demoted and transferred to the north-east tin mining town of Pioneer. The place was enough to raise hackles in this potential rebel, with its small barn-like schoolhouse for local children while the managers and their families had comfortable houses and did not mix with the miners. Here, as in other towns, Lyons organised a debating club. In Pioneer he was popular with the parents, who presented him with an award. Within a year, to better his qualifications, Lyons had enrolled in the new teachers' college opening in Hobart; and he continued his association with the Workers' Political League.

By the time Lyons had received an enhanced posting to Launceston, following his highly successful graduation from Hobart teachers' college, he was openly politically active and militant. In October 1908 he wrote to the director of education advising that he would possibly be a Labor candidate in the forthcoming state election. Many of Lyons' complaints about the teaching profession were subsequently upheld by a Royal Commission report of March 1909. Lyons resigned his teaching career, throwing in his lot with winning a seat in Tasmania's Parliament for the electorate of Wilmot. It was a gambler's move, but if it failed not quite as devastating as his father's bet on the Melbourne Cup.

The 1909 state election was the first in Tasmania under the Hare–Clarke (proportional) system – an attempt by the conservatives to weaken the solidarity of Labor candidates. It divided the state into five six-member electorates. Such a system advantages personally popular candidates. Parties must select a list of candidates who compete against each other for seats. Joe Lyons was placed second on the Labor ticket. He took to his bicycle, riding across the electorate, joining up Labor Party members. Lyons won and Labor increased to 12 of the 30 parliamentary seats. Lyons' newfound appeal with voters helped him. He would represent Wilmot, state and federally, for thirty years. From 1914–16 he was a minister in the Earle Labor government, as treasurer, minister for education and minister for railways. His strong opposition to conscription advanced his profile among his parliamentary colleagues and by 1919 Lyons was Tasmania's Opposition leader. He was Tasmania's premier from 1923–28, a period believed by many to be his happiest and most fruitful years in politics.[9]

Prior to becoming Opposition leader Lyons married Enid Burrell in 1915. It was no ordinary match. Joe Lyons – after whom the Lyons Group of Christian-oriented conservative parliamentarians was named in the 1990s – became infatuated in 1913, while Minister for Education, with a fifteen-year-old teacher trainee. He married her when she was just seventeen. It was enough to worry both Joe and his party for a time – that this would break as an open scandal. Kate White in *A Political Love Story* wrote:

> He was in love, hopelessly in love, even dangerously in love with a woman half his age. She was a teacher at Burnie; he was her employer, the Minister of Education. It was a situation that could produce a major, and unwanted, scandal for the Labor government.[10]

Joe Lyons was a complex character, never more than in his courtship of Enid. Years later Enid wrote in her memoirs that their letters and contact, before Joe proposed, had been strictly formal. But their correspondence suggests, as recorded by Kate White, a chemistry was being played out long before Joe proposed. With precocious chat, teasing playfulness, flirtatious cheek, they engaged at a distance over months. It was harmless enough, since they married at the first opportunity, but no harmless affair had it become public property. Even among those who knew the couple personally, Joe was accused of 'cradle snatching'. Enid was very young. Her wedding photo, reproduced in *So We Take Comfort,* shows a very pretty girl, pricelessly innocent in her high-necked wedding frock, her veil more in keeping with a first communion or confirmation candidate than one about to be married.

But the match was a true one. Enid impressed Joe with her intellectual capabilities – matriculating at fifteen at a time when girls rarely stayed at secondary school. She had qualified as a teacher at sixteen. Lyons' belief in Enid persisted, justifiably, through all their time together. She would become his pupil. He instilled in her an understanding of political nuances and encouraged her politically. Enid's mother had brought them together from her own belated involvement in Labor politics. She had taken Enid as a student to watch the Tasmanian Parliament – where Enid and Joe had met. As they became engaged, Enid was overwhelmed by the outcome. Joe was her mother's associate and closer in age to her mother. And when their differences of religion threatened to destroy the match, Enid, a Methodist, chose instruction in the Catholic religion and converted.

Joe Lyons was as ambitious as any politician set on a path to the top. In December 1919, seeking a more successful career in politics, he tried to win a federal seat (Darwin, later Braddon). It was a time of low fortunes for Tasmanian Labor. Enid was twenty-one and very ill, as well as pregnant and caring for two toddlers. Later she confessed to being divided over the outcome: if he won and had to travel to Canberra, their separation worried her.

Lyons encouraged Enid to take part in politics. She did his paperwork in campaigns and in 1922 stood in when one of his speakers was ill. Driving home Joe gave Enid a helpful hint on delivering speeches: 'Don't be too conversational.' In the June 1925 state election, while premier, Joe asked Enid to stand as a Labor candidate for Denison. She was listed too far down the ticket to win, and Joe's strategy was to deflect votes from Edith Waterworth, a women's non-party candidate. In that election, Joe Lyons not only had his wife standing as a candidate, but also his mother-in-law. The children caught measles and passed it on to their parents. Joe was accused of having 'a childish complaint' and cancelled campaigning while his face cleared up. Then the children caught whooping cough, dangerous in those days. Still, both Joe and Enid Lyons tramped the election trail, Joe out of Hobart, Enid coming and going, sharing the care of the children with Ada, her home help, and a nurse. But Enid discovered a talent, and a love, for public speaking, and the family survived. This was to be their political strategy thereafter – a somewhat chaotic family life amid political success.

On returning to Opposition in 1929, Lyons again became restless. At Scullin's request he stood for the federal seat of Wilmot and won, on a promise he would be in a Labor Cabinet after the election.

The 1920s in Australia was a volatile period of right and left. Accusations such as 'Bolshevik' and 'Red' were flung at Catholic Laborites like Jack Lang. The extremely Protestant, anti-Catholic NSW government of George Fuller after 1923 and the rise of right-wing militants gave voice to Empire loyalists. Masons and Orange Lodge groups were counteracted by the formation of the Catholic Knights of the Southern Cross. Catholics increased in numbers among Labor's elected representatives to around one-third; business elites were solidly Protestant. Even at a personal level divisions persisted. Following Joe Lyons' funeral in 1939, Treasurer Richard Casey persuaded Enid 'to let him put aside residual anti-papist scruples and pay for the education of one of her sons as a boarder with the Jesuits in Melbourne'.[11] Historian Michael Hogan has written: 'One of the myths of Australian history is that the nation came of age during the First World War, that the experience of Gallipoli cemented a new unity ... Perhaps there is something in the myth. But it needs to be balanced by an assessment of that period as one of great social division between Australians, especially on the bases of class, ethnicity and religion.'[12]

The emergence in 1931 of Catholic Joe Lyons with his Irish and Labor background leading a revamped conservative group called the United Australia Party was both a wily and a breathtaking development. He was one of the few conservative leaders before 1972 who was not a Mason. For middle-class and nominally Protestant voters it was natural to vote conservative when, in their view, the alternative was Labor dominated by 'either papist Rome or godless Moscow'.[13]

Enter the Group of Six – a pragmatic business group brought together by Stanliforth Ricketson, a stockbroker and partner with J. B. Were and Son, who knew Lyons from Devonport. It also included the young Robert Menzies, by then member for Kooyong. They believed Lyons alone could lead a conservative party capable of toppling Labor. It was a plot hatched possibly, as Allan Martin coyly suggests, 'between the spears and the cooking pots of the Savage Club' in the heart of elitist Protestant Melbourne.[14] With the Lang Laborites in Canberra determined to split the party, and with the obvious tension between Lyons and Theodore, they had seen an opportunity. They made initial contact with Lyons while he was acting treasurer when Scullin left for overseas in August 1930. Theodore had stood down as treasurer in July while being investigated over a mines scandal. Scullin had assumed responsibilty for Treasury. Through Menzies, Lyons became close to Nationalist parliamentarians. In December 1930, when Latham called for national unity to fight the Depression, Lyons supported him. The Group also gave Lyons invaluable contact with networks in business.

The visit of Sir Otto Niemeyer from the Bank of England in August 1930 had forced Scullin into the so-called Melbourne Agreement, requiring all governments to cut spending to reduce the price of exports and encourage trade. There was an outcry from the unions. Lyons, as acting treasurer, was opposed in caucus by (Red) Ted Theodore, with a more expansionary program. Caucus adopted Theodore's plan. In October, caucus forced Lyons to seek extensive credit from the Commonwealth Bank for public works; the bank refused. In November, caucus voted for John Curtin's proposal to postpone for a year redemption of £28 million of Commonwealth bonds. Lyons, furious, determined he would raise the £28 million. Deferral was Lang-style repudiation.[15]

Lyons raised the money for the loan conversion (eventually oversubscribed) in a nationwide appeal that drew funds from small and large investors; a surge to support the nation. In Melbourne he addressed a huge rally alongside the Nationalist W. A. Watt in a show of unity, what Allan Martin describes as a 'juxtaposition [that] symbolised the need to put aside party differences for a patriotic end'.[16] During the campaign to raise the money Lyons became even closer to the Group, which watched his performance with admiration.

When Scullin returned from overseas, Lyons had every right to expect he would be given the Treasury portfolio; Scullin had supported him in his loan conversion strategy and he had triumphed. But Theodore was given Treasury, to appease the unions. Lyons was horrified. In a move echoing his resignation from the Education Department, Lyons resigned from Cabinet, along with James Fenton, on 29 January 1931. In March he went to Melbourne for discussions with the Group; on the 13th Lyons voted against Scullin in a no-confidence motion in Parliament; a small band of four Labor defectors formed around Lyons in the Parliament, and by the end of March there was tacit agreement that Latham would step down for Lyons as Nationalist Party leader. Lyons still held back. A United Australia movement was formed, supported by the powerful citizens' groups that had sprung up around patriotic and anti-socialist feeling. The UAM also incorporated the Nationalists, but was not a political party. The movement, like the citizens' groups, looked to Lyons as a 'non-party' leader, a non-politician's politician in an era of alienation with political power plays. Joe Lyons inspired electors to feel he belonged to them, not the party.

Invited to speak in Adelaide to a Citizens' Leagues conference on 9 April 1931, Joe and Enid Lyons attracted an audience of 3000. Arriving at Adelaide station for the conference they had been mobbed, with Lyons shouting from the train: 'We shall strike a match tonight that will start a blaze throughout Australia.'[17] On their return to Melbourne by train Joe and Enid Lyons addressed large crowds at stops along the way, as if in election mode. The Murdoch newspapers in Adelaide and Melbourne supported them, with Keith Murdoch proclaiming Lyons as the leader 'Australia is seeking'. According to Desmond Zwar, Murdoch threw his support behind Lyons against Scullin 'using every weapon of pen and printer's ink'.[18]

The United Australia Party was soon formed – an amalgamation in Federal Parliament of Lyons and his band of defectors with the Nationalists. Lyons was elected leader. Premier Lang, meanwhile, had defaulted on interest due to the Commonwealth. Theodore's policy was in tatters. It was full steam ahead to an election victory for the new political network a handful of businessmen had crafted. But Lyons was no pawn. He was Opposition leader, and he would be prime Minister of Australia before the end of the year.

In December 1931 two Catholic leaders, Scullin and Lyons, contested an historic election battle. Catholics worried by the excesses of Lang and Labor's shift to the left could now choose their preferred Catholic leader in an age when religious affiliation held more sway than political party groupings. The foundling political groupings had been barely decades in the making. The fluidity of politics recognised this. Within a year the UAP had won the state elections of New South Wales and Victoria. Lyons was to govern for seven years in apparent tranquillity. Historian Michael Hogan comments: 'Not surprisingly the total ALP vote fell to an almost catastrophic 27 per cent, compared with the 49 per cent of the first preference vote that had elected Scullin in 1929. Middle-class Catholic voters would return to support Labor in strength in the 1940s, but the safety net of Catholic middle class votes could no longer be relied on.'[19]

However, behind the scenes the UAP was a nest of impatient egos. Writing to Bruce, following the 1932 Premiers' Conference, Lyons observed: 'We are now back in Canberra after having had a most unpleasant week in Melbourne at the Premiers' Conference. We have got rid of Lang but unfortunately we now have a Stevens to contend with. At least one could go out and attack Lang in the open. In the case of Stevens, one is continually sabotaged from behind.'[20]

In time the ambitious UAP premier of New South Wales, Bertram Stevens, would harbour hopes of a move to Canberra politics. By early 1939 Sir Sydney Snow, UAP head in Sydney and a wealthy businessman, was promoting Stevens as Lyons' successor. As his biographer Philip Hart would write in a PhD thesis (sadly never published), Lyons was severely underestimated.

Mid term, conservatives like Country Party leader Earle Page offered arrangements for a 'true conservative' to return to lead the UAP. In March 1934, Page informed his party that he was willing to resign his seat to enable Stanley Bruce (then high commissioner in London) to re-enter Australian politics.[21] The idea was that Bruce would depose Lyons: some delusion. Nevertheless, for some years, Bruce would seriously toy with the idea of returning to Australian politics as a 'non-party' person ready to assume the role of prime minister. There were also the ambitions of Richard Casey and Robert Menzies who were serious contenders, as well as Archdale Parkhill, member for Warringah from 1927 but defeated in 1937, who by 1934 had hopes of toppling Lyons. According to Allan Martin, Parkhill, 'while a staunch admirer of Lyons, saw himself as the natural successor to the leadership'.[22] By October 1938 the able Charles Hawker, member for Wakefield 1929–38, was preparing to challenge Lyons – but he was killed in an air crash.

The stability of the Lyons governments was helped by the improving economic landscape. Lyons' policy of reducing debt and government spending has proved to be economic wisdom. The other stabilising factor was undoubtedly Lyons' pull of votes at election time, along with his honest empathy for ordinary people. He took advantage of the availability of air travel (by July 1938 he had travelled 480,000 kilometres on the hustings, meeting Australians) and he used the new medium of radio to great effect. Lyons spoke, as Robert Menzies has written, 'easily and with a rare combination of dignity and simplicity'.[23] And it needed no spin doctors to craft Joe and Enid Lyons into salt-of-the-earth Australian family folk. But it tested the marriage and their health – Joe travelling endlessly between Tasmania and the mainland, Enid juggling life in Melbourne, Devonport and Canberra. As early as 1933 Frederick Stewart, member for Parramatta, privately offered to stand aside from his seat for Joe so the Lyons family could live closer to Canberra. [24]

Promotional shots of the Lyons family, complete with ten or eleven children at the Lodge, belied the fact that the very much split up Lyons family – between primary schools and boarding schools and term holidays – meant that the longest stint Enid ever spent at the Lodge was five weeks. She also managed to traverse the country (as Pattie Menzies would do later for her husband's governments), speaking at endless public functions. The Lyons family in the Lodge was a unifying and comforting symbol for the many seeking security in these years. Enid Lyons was a great communicator of homespun wisdom – another plus.

Philip Hart has written of Joe Lyons:

> If he was as incompetent, vacillating, dependent on his ministers, and intellectually ill-equipped to comprehend basic government policy as critics alleged, why did his ministers tolerate his leadership, and make not even one attempt in seven years to displace him? How can the allegation that he was a weakling that did not know his own mind be reconciled with his firm, principled stands against inflation in 1930 and 1931? … How did he manage to keep a Cabinet generally united and efficient that contained men like Page, Menzies, Gullett, Hughes, Thorby, and Cameron, strongly opinionated men who personally disliked one another? How could a government with so little to show for its existence after 1934 win an election in 1937?[25]

The simple answer is that Lyons was underestimated by his colleagues and critics.

By 1938, however, the triumph at the 1937 polls, due largely to Lyons' marathon efforts at campaigning (9600 kilometres and 43 meetings in 43 days), was forgotten. The nagging question by now was who would succeed Joe Lyons and when? Government was aimlessly drifting, Lyons appeared strained by the job day to day, and contenders were flexing their muscles in the backroom. But no one contender – Casey, Menzies, Bruce, Stevens or anyone else – stood above the rest. Keith Murdoch now recommended Menzies, but feared his unpopularity. Menzies, echoing Paul Keating years later, believed Lyons had promised him the succession and he was being denied it.[26] Numbers games were played out privately, Lyons often consulted as to who should take over. Just weeks before he died, he asked Stanley Bruce to consider succeeding him.[27]

It is hard to know just what Lyons felt at all this, except the extreme stress. He was ready to go. Anticipating this, he and Enid had sent the younger children to school in Devonport [28] but there was no obvious successor. Lyons' son Barry believes many in Cabinet feared losing their jobs under Menzies.[29] There was pressure to stay, and he had eleven children, with bills and private education costs and so on. The stage was set for tragedy. While many of his colleagues were appeasers, Lyons was both appeaser and at heart a pacifist. Europe was readying for war. The Depression was no longer a priority. Labor was starting to regroup.

By early 1939 Cabinet pressures often overwhelmed Lyons, as his boyhood friend Frank Green, then clerk of the House of Representatives, recalled.

Menzies resigned from Cabinet on 14 March over delaying legislation to introduce national insurance, legislation eventually passed but which Menzies never proclaimed. Many saw his resignation as an excuse to undermine Lyons. Menzies by then had lost Lyons' support. After Menzies' October 1938 speech on the need for leadership (widely reported and interpreted by many as criticising Lyons), Lyons had increasingly believed Menzies was undermining him. Of the tensions in Cabinet, Green wrote:

> Lyons walked out of Cabinet and came to my room, as he explained, 'to get out of the way' ... he wanted to resign and end the torture, but was being urged to wait for something to take place. I gathered that he had been offered an appointment by the British Government and was awaiting details of the terms and conditions before he resigned as prime minister. ... [the day before Good Friday] he spoke of his worries saying: 'I should never have left Tasmania ... this situation is killing me.' A few minutes later he was on his way to Sydney by car, but along the road he had a heart attack and died in a Sydney hospital a day later.[30]

That feeling of being cut off from Tasmanian roots has been shared by Barry and Peter Lyons, who felt they would have been better off at school in Devonport, although Barry has spoken well of his Jesuit education at Melbourne's Xavier College.[31] Joe and Enid Lyons retained their family home in Devonport, 'Home Hill' (now a museum), where they returned for holidays. Enid was there for Easter 1939 when Joe collapsed. He was admitted to Sydney's St Vincent's hospital, where he suffered further heart attacks. Travel between Tasmania and the mainland was then difficult. Without BHP's plane, for the leg to Melbourne, Enid would not have reached Sydney before Joe died on Good Friday.

Joe Lyons was remembered by huge crowds at services in Sydney and Canberra before his body was taken by navy vessel to Devonport where another large crowd saw him buried. Dame Enid had sharply turned down Cabinet's suggestion that her Joe should be buried in Canberra, saying he 'would go home'. Her husband's death left her bedridden for months.

In a letter to Dame Enid Lyons after Joe's death, Dame Mary Gilmore wrote: 'I would still feel I voted Labor if I voted for him ... his heart was with the people, and it neither changed with position nor wavered with circumstance.'[32]

Sir Earle Page

7 APRIL 1939 – 26 APRIL 1939

Page had an intense dislike of Nationalist Prime Minister Billy Hughes, whom he distrusted as a 'fig leaf socialist' ,and an increasingly obsessive hatred of Menzies, whom he regarded as arrogant, duplicitous and anti-Country Party.

BY BRIAN COSTAR & PETER VLAHOS

Serving as briefly as he did, Earle Page made little impact on the office of Australian Prime Minister. Similarly, his policy contributions were undistinguished. Yet Page remains an important historical figure in Australian federal party politics. He took over the leadership of the Country Party from the inconsistent Tasmanian Bill McWilliams in 1921 and held the post until 1939. This was a time in which the Country Party wove itself in the fabric of Australian politics and it was Page, against the opposition of the separatist Victorian branch, who crafted the strategy of non-Labor coalition government that persists into the present.

Earle Page was born on 8 August 1880 in the northern New South Wales town of Grafton. His father suffered financial ruin in the 1890s depression but aided by scholarships Page graduated from the University of Sydney medical school in 1902. He worked first in Sydney but later returned to Grafton, where his career as a doctor flourished to the extent that he established a small private hospital. He soon became active in the Northern New South Wales Separation (New State) League, and the Farmers' and Settlers' Association, and it was this involvement that gradually drew him from medicine to politics. Following a family tradition, he was elected to the South Grafton shire council in 1913 and became part owner of a local newspaper.

He enlisted in the AIF in January 1916 and served briefly overseas in the army medical corps, but was back in Grafton in June 1917. Ignoring a request to present in Sydney for military duties, he won the federal seat of Cowper as an independent in 1919, but joined the federal Country Party in 1920. Page had a meteoric rise in the new party and was elected its leader in April 1921. He soon developed an intense dislike of Nationalist Prime Minister Billy Hughes, whom he distrusted as a 'fig leaf socialist'.

The Country Party had been founded by the Farmers' and Settlers' Association of Western Australia in 1913 as a protest against alleged metropolitan exploitation of regional and rural Australia. By the 1920s the party, under various titles, was represented in the federal Parliament and in those of all the states. It is, under its current National Party name, Australia's second-oldest political party and one of the few continuous agrarian parties remaining in the world.

At the 1922 federal elections the Nationalist Party lost its majority on the floor of the House of Representatives and was required to negotiate with the Country Party to remain in government. Page drove a hard bargain, demanding the replacement of Hughes as prime minister – he was supplanted by Stanley Melbourne Bruce – and the appointment of five Country Party members in a Cabinet of eleven. His success in securing both objectives represented the pinnacle of his political influence.

The Bruce-Page coalition remained in power from 1923 to 1929, with Page as deputy prime minister and treasurer. The government was undistinguished, gaining a reputation for inconsistent economic policies and for political repression of trade unions and other left-wing elements. Billy Hughes avenged his 1923 humiliation by engineering the government's defeat on the floor of the House on 10 September 1929.

The Scullin Labor government elected on 22 October was overwhelmed by the Great Depression. In May 1931 Joseph Lyons led the new United Australia Party, consisting of six Labor defectors plus the Nationalist members – and supported by some decidedly unsavoury non-parliamentary elements. As early as April 1931 the then Nationalist leader John Latham had written to Page suggesting the 'formation of a single Opposition Party' – a suggestion that did not find favour with Page.[1] The UAP won the December 1931 election, but its majority was uncertain, which encouraged Lyons to continue discussions with Page. The new leader received much advice urging him not to bring the Country Party, and specifically Page, into the Cabinet; for his part, Page was counselled by his adviser, Ulrich Ellis, to have nothing to do with the UAP – 'a spare parts party' – because it would be both unstable and hostile to country interests.[2] Nevertheless Page remained open to temptation, but made it a condition of the Country Party entering a coalition that it be allocated the Customs portfolio – something the manufacturing industry backers of the UAP would not countenance.

Page, acting on a resolution of a meeting of Country Party parliamentarians, telegrammed Lyons in late December 1931 offering himself as a minister without pay or portfolio as a link between the Country Party and the government; Lyons replied in the negative two months after the UAP Cabinet was sworn. One year later Lyons offered three Cabinet vacancies to the CP on condition that he chose the ministers. Page replied that as leader he must be involved in any Cabinet selection and that the Country Party required consultations on policy matters, which Lyons rejected.[3] Page offered his resignation as leader if this would pave the way for Country Party entry into the Cabinet, but his deputy Tom Paterson declared that he too would resign if Page stepped down, and this effectively ended the matter.[4]

Lyons required Country Party assistance to form government after the 1934 election, but on this occasion Page was unable to secure the favourable terms of 1923. The Lyons/Page coalition was inherently unstable, united only by the personal skills of the prime minister. When Lyons died on 7 April 1939 the UAP had no deputy leader and the governor-general commissioned Page as prime minister. In accepting the commission Page declared that he would relinquish the post once the UAP chose a leader, but in the event that leader was Robert Menzies, neither Page nor the Country Party would serve in his government.

Page's major activity during his nineteen days in office was to go to extraordinary lengths to induce former prime minister Stanley Bruce to return to Australia to lead the non-Labor parties. Page was motivated by his desire to see the formation of a 'national government' to prosecute the war that everybody knew was coming, and his increasingly obsessive hatred of Menzies whom he regarded as arrogant, duplicitous and anti-Country Party. Bruce imposed conditions that could not be met, and when Menzies was duly elected leader of the UAP on 18 April 1939, Page made good his threat and refused all offers of a coalition.

At the next sitting of the House of Representatives, on 20 April 1939 Page, while still prime minister and contrary to the advice of colleagues, made a vicious attack on Menzies. The attack centred on Menzies' alleged disloyalty to Lyons in a speech he had made in Sydney on the subject of leadership in 1939 and on Menzies' resignation of his officer's commission in 1915, an action that ensured he did not serve overseas during the Great War.

The speech split the Country Party: Arthur Fadden and three others left it to sit on the crossbenches for a time. With war declared and the two parties ill-prepared and bickering over the coalition agreement, Page was forced to resign as Country Party leader because of the conflict with Menzies, whom Page described as being 'unable to lead a flock of homing pigeons'. He took no part in the new ministry, although he returned to Cabinet as minister for commerce after the September 1940 election, when several Country Party ministers lost their seats.

Page's vitriolic denunciation of Menzies harmed him rather than his target. It was 'the nadir of his political career'.[5] In the aftermath of the 1940 election the leadership of the Country Party was declared vacant, prompting a three-cornered contest among the incumbent Archie Cameron, Page and

John McEwen. After a dispute over Page's candidature, Cameron withdrew. When the vote was deadlocked and no compromise seemed possible, the powerbrokers of the party suggested Arthur Fadden be placed in charge as interim leader. The seriousness of the war situation led to Fadden's confirmation as leader on 12 March 1941 – a post he held for the next seventeen years.

During Fadden's own brief prime ministership Page was appointed special envoy to the British War Cabinet in September 1941. Before Page could reach London the Fadden government lost office, but the incoming Labor government maintained his appointment. Despite being repudiated by Prime Minister Curtin for appearing to collude with Churchill to divert the 7th Australian Division to Burma, he remained in the United Kingdom until the end of the war.

When the Menzies/Fadden coalition won the 1949 election, Page was appointed minister for health. While described by a sympathetic biographer as 'a crowning achievement',[6] Page's 1953 National Health Act was a seriously flawed piece of policy. Motivated by individualistic ideology and heavily influenced by the medical profession, Page saw it as a 'bulwark against the socialisation of medicine'. A more acute observer identified the failings of the policy which were to bedevil Australia for twenty years until the introduction of Medibank in 1974: '... the main beneficiaries were not the lowest income groups in the community. Those who gained most were middle and high income groups and the producers of private health services: doctors, private hospitals and private health insurance agencies. As well as being of least benefit to the worst off, the Page system established a medical system rather than a health system. It entrenched private medical practice and reduced the capacity of the states to provide a comprehensive range of health services.'[7]

As one of Australia's four 'caretaker' prime ministers, Page's nineteen-day interregnum left no indelible imprint on the course of Australian political history. Yet he remains a significant political figure, having served as the member for Cowper from 1919 to 1961, leader of the Country Party from 1921–39, deputy prime minister and treasurer 1923–29, minister for commerce 1934–39 and minister for health 1937–39 and minister for health 1937–39 and 1949–56. Page died on 20 December 1961 while awaiting the outcome of the vote in Cowper: had he lived, he would have been defeated.

Sir Robert Gordon Menzies

26 APRIL 1939 – 29 AUGUST 1941

19 DECEMBER 1949 – 26 JANUARY 1966

He was an Empire man ... yet it would be unfair to consider him some sort of reactionary fossil.

BY ALLAN MARTIN

Robert Menzies, dubbed 'Ming' in his later years by some friends and most enemies, was twice prime minister of Australia: from 1939 to 1941 and from 1949 to 1966. 'Ming' was a contraction of 'Minghies', one Scottish pronunciation of his name that Menzies himself always repudiated. The name also recalled Ming the Merciless, the fabled oriental tyrant in the contemporary comic strip *Flash Gordon*. How far Menzies was a despot, whether 'democratic', as some obituarists put it when he died in 1978, or 'oriental'-like, as enemies generally believed, will long be a subject of controversy among historians. But incontestable at the time of writing is that he has been federal Australia's longest-serving prime minister. Few believe that his record can ever be beaten.

Born in December 1894 at Jeparit, a tiny township in the Wimmera district of Victoria, Menzies quickly became a highly achieving young man. Schooling in Ballarat and then at Melbourne's Wesley College, supported by scholarships, took him to the University of Melbourne, where he studied law, graduating in 1916 with first-class honours. A voluble talker, often with a cutting wit, he was a big fish in a little university pond, especially one depleted of males by the war. In 1916 he was president of the Students' Representative Council and of the Students' Christian Union, and he edited the *Melbourne University Magazine* (*MUM*). His editorials and articles in this journal stressed the virtues of hard work and service to others. He had little time for students who cultivated 'the friendship of the billiard room' and, forgetting the real purpose of university life, 'freely squander their parents' money'. *MUM* was also, in his hands, a highly patriotic if not jingoistic publication, thus fitting well with majority opinion in the university where, as the war dragged on, elements in both staff and student communities found harsh ways of persecuting so-called 'shirkers'. Menzies himself did not enlist, a fact of which he was cruelly reminded throughout his life. In *MUM* he wrote his apologia: 'I do not think I am either sublimely ignorant, sublimely conceited or sublimely selfish when I say that the path of duty does not always lead to the recruiting depot – duty has to many in this respect been a hard taskmaster.' There is no reason to disbelieve the story that an internal family conference decided that with two brothers in the AIF, Menzies' duty was to stay at home to look after and partly support his parents. His only sister, having eloped with a soldier of whom her parents disapproved, could not be relied on for ordinary familial duties. At the same time, Menzies' enthusiastic public and private support for conscription had to encompass the virtual certainty that if conscription were brought in, he himself would have been one of the first drafted. This could have overridden (possibly to his relief?) whatever other loyalties or scruples kept him out of the AIF.

Family conferences remained important in Menzies' scheme of things. That their conclusions were influential, sometimes binding, must be partly attributed to the firm disciplinary tradition in which the Menzies children were brought up. Bob's father, James, was general storekeeper in Jeparit. A peppery man of sturdy Scots descent, he was remembered by his four children as too kindly to be a good businessman, giving generous credit to the poor farmers who were his main customers while struggling to meet the demands of his own suppliers. But he could also be, as Bob once put it, 'dogmatic and intolerant ... His temper was quick. We, his sons, got to know that "whom the Lord loveth, he chasteneth".' Being a reasonable speaker and a self-trained man of some experience, James Menzies soon emerged as a leader in the little community he served. He was a member and twice president of the local shire council, a founder of the Jeparit branch of the Australian Natives' Association, and was prominent in establishing organisations ranging from the local Progress Association to the Caledonian Society. The Church was a special focus for his energy: he became a dedicated and highly emotional Methodist lay preacher. Elected in 1911 to the Victorian Parliament as member for Lowan, James did not shine as a conventional politician. A mass of nervous energy, he collapsed when making his maiden speech; this and other incidents taught his son to distrust the public expression of emotion. 'In effect,' he was to write in his memoirs, 'in my own later public and political life ... I aimed at a cold, and as I hoped, logical exposition. It was years before I ever exhibited emotion either in the House or on the platform.'

By contrast, Menzies' mother Kate appears to have been 'calm, human and understanding and in the end, with patience, would secure a victory for sweet reasonableness ... She was always the first port of call for those who needed comfort. She had what I came to recognise and admire, the judicial temperament.' Her father, John Sampson, a Cornishman who had emigrated to become a goldminer in Creswick, had been associated with W. G. Spence in the pioneer Australian Miners' Union, and as an old man saw much of Bob Menzies while the latter was a schoolboy in Ballarat.

Menzies cherished memories of the political education he had gained from long friendly arguments with this grandfather and an uncle, Sydney Sampson, who sat for thirteen years in the federal Parliament as member for Wimmera.

Suspicion of public displays of emotion and admiration of the judicial temperament – key elements in Bob Menzies' early experience – fitted well with career prospects foreshadowed by his university work in the law and the extraordinary drive and intelligence he showed in all his studies from the beginning. Few denied that he was something of a prodigy, though friends who knew him well also detected a streak of ruthlessness. Fellow student Percy Joske, for example, looking back from 1978, wrote:

> Menzies' strength at the Bar and subsequently in politics lay in his personality. He had an incredible degree of charm and good looks. His personality was forceful and determined and like many another Scot he would ride roughshod over his opponents. He employed his cutting tongue without hesitation. As he always spoke with great authority and was readily quoted, his talk could and did cause harm to the unfortunate at whom it was aimed ... [He had] a fierce determination to succeed, which made him cause offence to others, often thereby doing himself harm.

As a newly called barrister Menzies had the good fortune in 1918 to read with the leading Victorian junior Owen Dixon. Though by this time Dixon had built up an extensive practice, Menzies was the first of the few pupils he accepted. Menzies and Dixon took some cases together but by the end of 1919 individual briefs for cases were combining with opinion work to keep Menzies busy and to lay the basis for a sound income. Then in 1920 he won in the High Court a judgment that suddenly made him famous. In the so-called 'Engineers' case, the young barrister, arguing alone and with daring creativity for six days against what he himself called 'a thickly populated ... and hostile Bar table', persuaded a majority of judges that, contrary to current assumptions, members of a union – in this case the Amalgamated Society of Engineers – who worked in state-owned enterprises (a West Australian government-owned sawmill and a machine-shop) could come within the scope of the Commonwealth's arbitration power. States' rights were partly at issue (hence the galaxy of talent facing Menzies at the Bar table: all the states except Queensland had briefed counsel against him). The judgment had various implications: the major constitutional one was to expand greatly the potential scope of Commonwealth power over that of the states.

As well as being a constitutional landmark, the Engineers victory was a personal victory for Menzies. 'I was very young, twenty-five years old, and a success meant a great deal to me. In fact, I got married on the strength of it,' he wrote. He married in 1920 and his bride was Pattie May Leckie. She was five years younger than he, had lost her mother when she was only seven, and had been educated at two of Melbourne's more exclusive girls' schools, Presbyterian Ladies' College, East Melbourne, and Fintona in Camberwell. Her father, for a time a storekeeper in the central eastern Victorian town of Alexandra, had been educated at Scotch College, established a firm of lithographic printers and canister makers in Melbourne and was elected to the Victorian Legislative Assembly in 1913 and to the Commonwealth House of Representatives in 1917. Defeated in 1919, he gave up his political career until 1934, when he was elected to the Senate. Pattie and her father established a particularly close relationship. She shared his political interests and travelled with him on most election tours – fitting preparation for a woman who became a political wife.

In the 1920s, his principal years as an advocate, Menzies worked – in his wife's words – 'fantastically hard'. He estimated that at this time his weekly hours of work averaged about eighty. Given that he liked to keep part of the weekend sacrosanct for his family, this was probably not an exaggeration. (Bob and Pattie Menzies had three children: Ken in 1922, Ian in 1923 and Heather in 1928.) Fortunately, courts were not normally convened before late morning, so a great deal of preparation could be done late at night, as was Menzies' habit. Nevertheless, his capacity to strike to the heart of an issue meant that he used his working time with outstanding efficiency. This also helps explain how in the 1920s he managed to become involved in more than his professional work. He joined the Savage, a semi-literary club whose location in Melbourne's law district made it a convenient focus for him and his fellow professionals. Besides lawyers, he became acquainted with an ever-widening circle of friends: young businessmen, shopkeepers and clerks. Before long he began making small forays into the local politics that were coming to interest some of these men.

Menzies remembered almost jocularly the reasoning that led him to become more fully involved in politics: 'Well, here you are, you are practising your profession; you are earning a lot of money – as money was thought of in those days – and you've got an enormous amount of work to do. But isn't it a rather narrow sort of existence? Isn't it about time that you cut out of this and did a certain amount of public work?'

The words carry a strong echo of the ambitious self-confidence so far evident in the young Menzies' career, though equally they reflect the family tradition of public service he had always known, bolstered by the dynamics of the Melbourne of his day. In the 1920s Melbourne and its suburbs grew considerably, both in numbers of people and in geographical spread. Industrial and transport development swelled the ranks of traditional blue-collar workers and their organisations, though socially the greatest growth was perhaps in the middle-class suburbs such as Caulfield and Camberwell, Hawthorn and Kew. Professional and business people mostly belonged to the social groups who occupied these suburbs; Menzies and his family lived in Kew. The new middle classes were strongly attracted to such values as stability, patriotism and responsibility. Reformism was in the air. One of the most formidable organisations established in the middle 1920s was the Constitutional Club, which drew its strength from middle-class elements and set up rooms, speaking classes and a library in the city next to the law courts. Its members, who were interested in providing a counterpoise to the socialist objectives of some Country Party members, pledged loyalty to King and Empire and the maintenance of constitutional government.

Many thought state politics were urgently in need of repair. The instability and unproductiveness of Victoria's governments were something of a scandal: between 1923 and 1929 there were eight separate ministries. Office had come to depend on shifting coalitions in which a faction-ridden Country Party usually held the balance of power between the Nationalists (the more conservative party resulting from the Labor split over conscription during World War I) and the Labor Party. Most reformers were not adept at diagnosing what was happening, but many agreed that more than anything the state needed to attract into politics a new breed of men equipped to raise its tone. This, it was thought, would be the prime task of the Constitutional Club.

Menzies' wish for 'a little bit of public work' took the form of standing successfully at a Legislative Council by-election for East Yarra in 1928. Then in the general election of 1929 he captured the Assembly (Lower House) seat of Nunawading. Almost immediately after his election to the Legislative Council he was made minister without portfolio, then after the election of 1929 he became attorney-general and minister for railways in the government of Sir Stanley Argyle. That Menzies so quickly made his mark was a tribute to his energy, acumen and natural speaking ability. On all sides he was greeted as a new ornament to political life. Frederic Eggleston, then the most respected commentator on the Victorian scene, considered him 'one of the most brilliant of the young men who have entered politics for many years'.

His work for the Constitution Club and his public speaking quickly earned him the admiration of such activists as Wilfrid Kent Hughes, war hero and ex-Rhodes scholar, who drew him into the orbit of the Nationalist Party. In an early move after his election Menzies joined Kent Hughes and others from the Constitution Club to establish within that party a new ginger group, the 'Young Nationalists', whose aim was to train young speakers and generally raise morale along Constitutional Club lines. By September 1931 the Young Nationalist influence in the party apparatus, the Nationalist Federation, was sufficient to win Menzies its presidency. In an acceptance speech, he made no bones about where he stood on the political spectrum: 'We have suffered too much from people who have no political convictions beyond a more or less genteel adherence to our side of politics. That kind of adherence is worthless. We must have people who believe in things, and who are prepared to go out and struggle to make their beliefs universal.'

On the hustings and in his first parliamentary speeches Menzies denounced the way in which, as he saw it, 'predatory' political parties were prone to rob the state. All parties were responsible to some extent, though the various forms of the Country and Labor parties Victoria had known were the worst, both joining in a constant scramble for concessions for the sectional interests they represented. These opinions were prejudices that would remain with Menzies for most of his life. While Menzies betrayed many signs of ambition, the overwhelming fact was that he had entered politics because, in the best sense of the word, he felt he was 'called' to it.

Just as he arrived on the parliamentary scene, the dreadful trial of the Great Depression began. Menzies thought deeply about the role of the state and public policy. Certain sections of the federal Labor Party wished to repudiate loans owing abroad and, in some cases, to allow debt-ridden farmers and others to avoid repayment of loans from banks or private individuals. The solutions advocated to deal with the distressed state of many borrowers ranged from repudiation to a moratorium on debt. Who would make the greater sacrifice to restore financial equilibrium: the bondholder and lender of capital or the recipient of pensions and other social services on which the welfare of the less fortunate in society depended? The issues were complex and the debate fierce, but Menzies, as guardian of the status quo, knew exactly where he stood. Whatever the circumstances, he was the implacable defender of the sanctity of contracts initially entered into freely. To him, these were the basis on which any viable democratic society had to rest: they symbolised the crucial elements of stability: regularity, predictability, reliability. In the long and depressing controversies over the various 'plans' that economists and politicians put forward in their attempts to solve Australia's social and fiscal problems, he remained the steely advocate of orthodoxy.

The sanctity of contracts was one fundamental aspect of Menzies' constitutionalism: his respect for British institutions was another. This basic assumption was confirmed when in 1935 Menzies made his first trip to England, at the age of forty-one. But long before that his education, particularly in the law, had taught him and most constitutional lawyers of his generation that Australia had not only inherited these institutions but was an integral part of the imperial polity they constituted and served. As they had evolved over centuries from English needs, experience and ideals, these institutions had an authority that no theoretically contrived system could match. Menzies' Britishness was never a garment he consciously put on; his education and environment had made it part of his very fibre.

Menzies and those who agreed with his views were not mere theorists: they were also men of action. A federal Labor government, elected in 1929 under James Scullin, had to work out the way debt and debt repayments would be handled. But within a year caucus had voted to defer for a year the conversion of a £24 million internal loan falling due in December 1930. The acting treasurer Joseph Lyons decided on the apparently quixotic course of disobeying, redeeming the loan and preserving

Australia's credit reputation abroad. Setting aside conventional political loyalties, Menzies and a group of Melbourne notables rallied to his support and helped organise the successful refloat of the loan. The whole episode generated extraordinarily emotional and patriotic sentiments. Newspapers as far afield as Hobart and Perth carried impassioned appeals for subscriptions and offered prizes for slogans that would encourage people to invest. 'Lend or end!', 'invest or see', 'lend your cash and stop the crash' – these and other slogans indicated the enthusiastic participation of 'ordinary' people. Their enthusiasm was also reflected in what can only be called a social pandemic: the headlong growth during 1930–31 in South Australia, Victoria and New South Wales of Citizens' Leagues dedicated to maintaining law and order and preserving the credit reputation of the country.

Lyons' rejection of caucus' directions virtually put him out of the Labor Party. He was successfully wooed for the leadership of a new non-Labor party that quickly developed from the Citizens' Leagues and smaller, more powerful groups concerned to avoid the abandonment of the financial system proposed by some within the Labor Party. This new organisation was the United Australia Party (UAP), and it at once replaced the Nationalists. When the Nationalist chief John Latham stepped down in his favour, Lyons accepted the leadership. As Menzies' friend Wilfrid Kent Hughes put it, when writing to congratulate Latham, 'The public won't have the Natls as their rallying point, therefore we have got to find some other course … I trust [your] sacrifice will not be in vain.'

The Scullin government lost a vote in the House of Representatives in November 1931; the subsequent election gave Lyons, the new UAP (Opposition) leader, the opportunity to form a government. Latham became his attorney-general, then resigned in 1934 to become chief justice of the High Court. Menzies was persuaded to enter federal politics by standing at a by-election for Latham's blue-ribbon seat of Kooyong. He won easily, holding the constituency at all subsequent elections until his voluntary retirement in 1966. In the immediate future, Lyons' first government was confirmed in office by a further electoral victory in 1934.

Menzies joined the federal Cabinet as attorney-general on the understanding that before the 1937 election he should step into the prime ministership. Though a gentle man, popular as an election winner, Lyons was tired and often ill. Sir Maurice Hankey, the powerful secretary of the

British Cabinet, visiting Australia in 1934, found Lyons 'a frightfully decent old boy'. He thought Menzies, 'according to British standards, rather a rough diamond; very contemptuous of soft and soppy policies, but a good fellow at bottom and quite fearless of responsibilities'. According to Hankey, procedure in Lyons' Cabinet was 'loose and rambling': 'There is a nominal agenda paper but they don't stick to it and wander all over the place ...' Menzies, entering the Commonwealth Cabinet for the first time, was appalled, and contrasted the procedure unfavourably with that of the Victorian Cabinet.

From the beginning Menzies showed signs of abrasiveness and, though he and Lyons were good friends, he did not always get on well with all his other colleagues. It was not to his taste always to play second fiddle to men, like Lyons, whom he regarded as his intellectual inferiors. Moreover, he did not suffer fools gladly, especially if they were people whose political stock-in-trade he did not care for, such as some contemporary leaders of the Country Party.

Lyons was hardly a dynamic leader. Considering the speed and emotion of the UAP's initial growth, it can easily be seen as a kind of populist body, demonstrating Menzies' original belief that those who had the instinct for politics had a responsibility to undertake work for what they saw as the common good. The party had been founded to cope with an emergency, but what would its future be once that emergency was over? The UAP had caused a major reshaping of the Australian party system, but from 1934 onwards, when the worst of the Depression was beginning to ease, there were few indications of any significant internal discussion about the party's direction. Lyons gave no guidance and senior ministers, especially Menzies and Earle Page, the Country Party leader and deputy prime minister, were abroad for long stretches in the middle to late 1930s attending to imperial matters, watching a threatening international situation and conducting trade negotiations, particularly with Britain. In something of a scandal, Parliament was kept in long recess before and after the election of 1937, during which the promise that Menzies should become leader was simply set aside. Keeping Lyons in the saddle paid off electorally: the government held office, but as the international situation deteriorated, the prime minister's weakness convinced more and more people of affairs that, as the newspaper proprietor Keith Murdoch put it, Lyons had 'lost his usefulness'.

But who should replace him? The Melbourne *Argus* was pushing Menzies, but others disagreed, and were inclined to express regret at his foibles. Menzies' relations with others were not ideal; it was surprising, some thought, to find a man who had made so many enemies in politics and so few real friends. Menzies still needed to develop the capacity for self-criticism necessary to curb his damaging wit or allow him to build up a following of real disciples. Keith Murdoch considered that 'Bob has a curiously disconcerting way of discouraging adherence, whilst in fact eagerly seeking it. He is a most difficult man to work for ... Certainly he is confiding when one is alongside him, but he never invites confidence. The public is beginning to actually dislike him, which is a great pity. Each week now he is becoming less likely as prime minister.'

Lyons, ill and exhausted, died in April 1939, and Page, as leader of the minor coalition party, became acting prime minister. He announced that he would step down in favour of whoever was elected UAP leader and who would naturally replace Lyons as prime minister – but if that man were Menzies, the coalition with the Country Party would end. In the House Page then made an attack on Menzies that the *Sydney Morning Herald* described as 'a violation of the decencies of debate without parallel in the annals of Federal Parliament'. With war threatening, Page asked, who could think of Menzies as an effectual leader of the nation? Few knew the immediate background to the attack. The journalist Roy Curthoys described it breathlessly in a confidential letter to J. R. Darling, headmaster of Geelong Grammar. and a prominent member of the Melbourne Club. 'In some ways,' he wrote, 'Menzies deserved it, for I have heard him talk among comparative strangers in terms so contemptuous of Page that I have gasped, and of course these strictures have got back to Page, and he has brooded over them so long that when his resentment did find expression it, too, was something that took one's breath away.'

Not to be browbeaten, UAP members overcame fears of Menzies' foibles, recognised his superior qualities and elected him their leader. On 26 April 1939 he became prime minister with an all-UAP Cabinet. But respite from further worry was short-lived. In September Hitler's attack on Poland was the finale of a series of expansionist moves in Europe. Britain, which had guaranteed Poland's integrity, declared war on Germany. Without dissent, Parliament accepted Menzies' assumption that Britain's declaration of war involved an identical declaration by Australia. A new and testing phase of Menzies' career had begun: could he rise to the occasion and provide the sagacious and practical leadership required for success in the office that fate had thrust upon him at such a crucial time?

A common answer to this question is 'No': 'As prime minister from 1939 to 1941,' one historian recently wrote baldly, 'he was a failure.' This extreme judgment swoops on Menzies' partial inability to secure and hold the confidence of all his parliamentary supporters, sets aside the tempo of the war itself and accepts the myth that Menzies' pro-British orientation made him subservient to British policy and unimaginative about issues of Australian security. In so doing it pays little regard to much recent research. A major theme with many contemporary Labor apologists – of whom in this respect Curtin himself was not one – was that Menzies and those who worked with him failed properly to mobilise the resources of the nation and left it to their successors to 'save' Australia from the Japanese. Curtin's attitude was in tune with that of F. G. Shedden, head of the defence department and the man who had worked most closely with Menzies after the outbreak of war. Shedden wrote to Menzies in December 1941 that it had been 'a great experience to be associated with you in the transition to a war footing and the first two years of the war administration. Credit has still to be given to your Government for the planning and preparation that rendered the transition so smooth. Tribute has yet to be paid to the great foundations laid by you at a time when you lacked the advantage of effect on national psychology and morale of a war in the Pacific.'

The timing of early wartime exigencies was all-important, and in this respect an Australian government of any colour would have been at a great disadvantage. The war began technically in September 1939 with Germany's invasion of Poland. But it was May 1940 before the Germans mounted their spring offensive against Belgium and France, bringing to a close the so-called 'phoney war' of almost nine months. The British Prime Minister Neville Chamberlain resigned and Winston Churchill formed an all-party 'National' government. In June France surrendered, Italy entered the war and the Battle of Britain loomed. Though primarily European in its thrust, the war had entered a new and serious phase.

Before June 1940, however, the government did a great deal to set up Australia's war effort, though some thought too little had been done while others argued that too much had been attempted. Service recruitment and manufacturing expansion (munitions, even aircraft) soaked up surviving unemployment, taxation was still not prohibitively heavy and the distant war could not be said to have brought a significant decline in living standards. Paul Hasluck has nevertheless argued that in the first two years of the war, 'precious' work had already been done: 'One of the greatest advantages enjoyed by Australia when war spread to the Far East was that many of the initial difficulties and most of the routine tasks organising a nation for war had already been mastered.'

Under the Menzies government's National Security Act, militiamen (who could not be sent on overseas service) were called up and the recruitment of a second AIF began. Menzies resisted what he called 'minds which are heavily indoctrinated by the "old soldiers'" ... point of view' that the AIF should be sent to Britain's aid forthwith. Australia's circumstances, he said, were completely different from those of 1914. Then Japan had been an ally. Now, upon the Japanese relationship and prospects (as he told Dominion Affairs Secretary Anthony Eden) 'must depend absolutely the part other than defensive which Australia will be able to take in the war'. But the British government unilaterally arranged scarce shipping for transporting troops, the New Zealand government, without consulting Australia, announced that it was sending an expeditionary force, and R. G. Casey pushed Menzies to despatch a matching AIF division. The die was thus cast, but Menzies furiously noted that the British had shown 'a quite perceptible disposition to treat Australia as a colony and to make insufficient allowance for the fact that it is for the Government to determine whether and when Australian forces shall go out of Australia'. On 10 January the first contingents of this 6th Division sailed for final training in the Middle East. British military planners had their eye on them for an expected French offensive in the coming summer.

The Menzies government, strengthened in March 1940 when Page was replaced as Country Party leader by Archie Cameron, thus allowing the Coalition to resume, still held power after a general election in September. But they held it only by a hair's breadth – it was a hung Parliament and they were supported by two independents. Before the election Menzies had tried in vain to persuade the Labor Party to form, with the UAP, a national administration like Churchill's. Curtin was adamantly opposed to entering an all-party arrangement, believing that a government united by one set of political principles, with a common outlook on the problems of the country, would do far better service to the nation than a combined government. He could also see that in a national government a de facto Opposition in the form of communists would arise, attracting all those dissatisfied with the government generally.

Deeply concerned at Churchill's cavalier attitude to the defence of Singapore (among other things, the British prime minister pooh-poohed the idea of this 'bastion' ever succumbing to a land-based attack), Menzies decided to visit England to break through intransigence and insist, face to face, on Australian claims for help in the Pacific. The trip, which lasted from February until May 1941, was, however, a failure. France had fallen some months before his arrival, the German air blitz against Britain was well under way and the German invasion of the British Isles was expected at any moment. Neither troops nor substantial naval units could be spared.

Already Commonwealth soldiers, chiefly Australians and New Zealanders, had fought victoriously against Italians in north Africa. These men were considered the one available British force when (after complex negotiations) it was decided to undertake a risky campaign to assist Greece against German invasion. By this time Menzies was in London, where, admitted by courtesy to the deliberations of the British Cabinet, he fumed at what he saw as Churchill's dictatorial ways and fought with only limited success to have the troops for Greece properly equipped. He quarrelled with Churchill on various matters and came home in a mood of general disillusionment. But his lasting memory was admiration of the courage of British people under the blitz and horror at the effect of something he saw for the first time: the destruction total war could bring. He saw Bristol after midnight on 21 March 1941 and wrote:

> A frightful scene. Street after street afire, furniture litters the footpaths; poor old people shocked & dazed are led along to shelter. The Guild Hall is a beacon of fire. Buildings blaze and throw out sparks like a bushfire … Picture Melbourne blazing from Flinders to Lonsdale, from Swanston or Russell to Elizabeth streets; with hundreds of back street houses burning as well. Every now & then a delayed action bomb explodes or a building collapses. Millions of pounds go west in an hour. I am in a grim sense glad to have seen it.

How deeply this sight was etched on his memory is reflected by his translation of it to his peaceful Melbourne. Perhaps this was a crucial experience for the horror with which he was later to contemplate some of the implications of the Cold War.

The unhappy result of Menzies' wartime trip to England is well known. While he was away certain UAP members, including ministers, were plotting against him. They resented his sometimes overbearing manner and sharp wit; some thought he lacked leadership skills; others maintained that he was unpopular in the electorate and the government could not carry its wartime responsibilities with him as the head. After complex manoeuvres and Labor's refusal to agree to the formation of a British-style national government, Menzies had the galling experience of appearing to lose majority support at a special Cabinet meeting at which all ministers agreed to declare their positions. Menzies, his wife and his father-in-law concluded that, as his political leadership appeared to rest upon 'nothing better than quicksands' he should resign. He rang his father James in Melbourne and, as he said: 'I left him at the other end of the telephone breathing threatenings and slaughter. He, in fact, at once convened one of our famous family conferences, which reached conclusions similar to my own.' Later, after calling a party meeting at which he announced his resignation, Menzies stumbled away with his secretary Cecil Looker, who in later recollection observed that, with tears in his eyes, Menzies had blurted out: 'I have been done ... I'll lie down and bleed awhile.' Menzies resigned both the prime ministership and later the leadership of the party. It was the most humiliating personal collapse in the history of federal politics in Australia. His deputy, Country Party leader Arthur Fadden, was commissioned to form a new ministry, but instability continued. When two Victoria-based independents, Coles and Wilson, voted against Fadden's Budget, the way was open for Curtin to become prime minister.

'Bleeding' did not last long. From the Opposition benches Menzies warmly supported Curtin's prosecution of the war, especially after Japan's attack on Pearl Harbor at the end of 1941 heralded perils Australia had never faced before. At the same time Menzies indignantly repudiated the charge of Labor extremists that his own administration had failed to put the country on a proper war footing. He carried out part of this debate in weekly radio broadcasts modelled on the 'fireside chats' with which Roosevelt had encouraged the American people during the Depression. By July 1943 he had made eighty such broadcasts, in which, as he said, 'I have tried to put in simple language the difficulties that face us today and for the future.' They effectively demonstrated Menzies' refusal to be neutralised.

After Menzies' resignation the UAP elected the seventy-nine-year-old Billy Hughes its leader; under his faltering lead the Coalition was trounced in the 1943 election. Though the war in the Pacific was still far from over, the immediate danger for Australia had receded, thanks chiefly to American naval victories in the Coral Sea and at Midway and the success of principally Australian troops in decisive battles in the Owen Stanley Ranges of New Guinea. Labor's unity and morale were high, but the UAP, as Paul Hasluck once put it, was 'rattling at every joint'. Hughes resigned and Menzies was again elected leader. In the face of disaster, he and others carried out studies of the state of the party, all of which concluded that a new start had to be made to unify the very disparate anti-Labor Party forces. They also needed to take advantage of the ALP's creation of the Ministry for Postwar Reconstruction and the concerted moves by the Labor government towards social planning in employment, welfare, national health and economic policy. This centrally controlled use of resources was seen by the business sector and by non-Labor voters as a frightening step towards socialism and away from the Australian way of life, and Menzies became an eloquent opponent of Labor's planning concepts. He and his supporters also sought ways of releasing these anti-Labor groups from the control of powerful behind-the-scenes organisations that controlled their finance, notably the businessmen-dominated Institutes of Public Affairs in Victoria, New South Wales, South Australia and Queensland.

In October 1944 Menzies convened a conference in Canberra, bringing together a wide range of organisations and individuals 'for an effort to secure unity of action and organisation among those political groups which stand for a liberal, progressive policy and are opposed to Socialism with its bureaucratic administration and restriction of personal freedom'. On the eve of the conference, Menzies had read a seventy-page pamphlet by the Victorian IPA economic adviser C.D. Kemp. Called 'Looking Forward', it was a businessman's argument about the virtues of free enterprise. Menzies adopted the recommendations and promoted the paper as 'the finest statement of basic political and academic problems made in Australia for many years ... [which should] ... be conveyed to the people as widely as possible'. After the meeting delegates placed orders for 21,000 copies. The conference agreed that a 'Federal body representing liberal thought' should be established. A second convention was held in December 1944 in Albury at which the Liberal Party's constitution was finalised, based on a draft Menzies had himself drawn up. The stated purpose of the new party was to create a nation 'looking primarily to the encouragement of individual initiative and enterprise as the dynamic course of reconstruction and progress'. Reflecting the importance attached to the new party raising and controlling its own funds, a membership fee was fixed at 2s 6d for adults and 1s for juniors. The Canberra correspondent of the *Argus* recognised that the newly born Liberal Party was Menzies' party: 'His initiative, leadership, hard work and persuasiveness have brought it to its present stage. Physically he stood head and shoulders above most of the delegates, and intellectually he undoubtedly did ... His draftsmanship runs through all the documents, and the more they are studied, the more the new party is seen to be the Menzies party.'

Whatever the claims of others, there can be no doubt that Menzies was the chief organiser and most effective orator. It was a far cry from the collapse of a few years before.

When Parliament resumed, Menzies announced that the small ex-UAP group he led were henceforth to be known as the Liberals, the official Opposition. Menzies accepted the fact that the government had come back with an overwhelming mandate and assured the governing party that he and his followers would not raise issues that were dead. But matters were likely to arise on which there were differing points of view and on such matters the Opposition would express its opinions 'with such vigour and skill as we possess ... because it is of the first importance for Australia that the people should get to understand that this Parliament not only makes the laws – which are determined by a majority – but is also the supreme debating society of the country. The function of an Opposition in this country, as the Prime Minister said many times when he was in my present position, is to see that the opinions of all sections of the people are put clearly and resolutely. We propose to put them clearly and resolutely.'

Menzies was giving notice of what became for the next few years one of his chief political objectives: to develop in a new, disciplined way the office of the leader of the Opposition.

We are fortunate that a few of the letters Menzies wrote during this period to his son Ken, then serving as a soldier in the islands to the north, have survived, and in almost throwaway asides tell much about his private thinking in these formative days. By contrast with former times, he was well received in meetings he held in New South Wales, he was pleased with the parliamentary performances of most of his followers, and 'you will be delighted to know that the personal attitude of the fellows towards myself is excellent and that old criticisms appear to be forgotten'. It was, however, not long before he felt less happy about the performance of some Liberals in Parliament: 'There is just a slight disposition to feel unduly optimistic about the next election. There is not a sufficient disposition to study bills closely. There is a sad falling-off in manners, much to my regret, because I feel that whatever comes or goes people of my Party ought to set a good example in courtesy and dignity of debate.'

Here is a good example of the elevated, almost aristocratic, conception of politics and political debate that Menzies frequently expressed, almost as if he believed that debating superiority, together with an elevated conception of public service, gave a party a kind of moral authority. He was, as Gough Whitlam once said, a great parliamentarian, a stickler for the rules of decorum in the House. He had in him a touch of the old eighteenth-century pre-party belief that the duty of a member of Parliament was to listen to the debate and decide an attitude to the question at issue which depended on the arguments he had heard. And he was capable of still finding meaning in the notion of 'a little bit of public work' that had at the beginning drawn him into politics: 'If you were to ask me what I thought the most deep-seated fault in Australia I would unhesitatingly reply that the old notion of disinterested public service has almost disappeared and that politics has come to be merely regarded as a war of interests in which much loot is to be won from the defeated.'

By the end of the war Menzies felt that Labor's insistence on prolonging wartime controls and its attempts to engineer a planned economy could lead to its rejection by farmers and small businessmen. As the industrial disturbances accompanying Chifley's efforts to keep inflation in check brought shortages and distress to the general public Menzies joined those convinced that a change of government would occur, and withdrew from all his professional commitments to concentrate on preparation for the next, the 1946, election. But in the election Labor won a decisive victory, losing some seats in the House of Representatives, but still scoring 43 as against the Liberals' 18 and the Country Party's 11, with 1 Lang Labor and 1 independent. The result no doubt broadly reflected a continuation of the prestige won by the wartime ALP leadership and widespread support for the idealistic postwar plans it sought to effect.

Menzies was devastated. His leadership was again called into question and he told Owen Dixon that, as the Liberal Party could never win with him at its head, he would leave politics altogether and go back to the Bar. He meant that: it was a real crisis, the closest he ever came in his long career to bringing his work as a politician to a precipitate close.

In the end Menzies stayed on, though he faced recurring party criticisms and moves in various quarters to unseat him. However, as C. B. Shedvin has perceptively written, in 1947 Prime Minister Ben Chifley himself opened the way for the Liberals to take 'the high moral ground for the first time since the outbreak of war'. Banking legislation carried by the Chifley government in 1945 had in various ways achieved Labor's major goal that in such a crisis as the Great Depression the government of the day, rather than a quite independent board of the Commonwealth Bank, should have a major say on the extension of public credit. After a minor clause in this body of legislation had been challenged in the High Court, Chifley baldly announced the nationalisation of the banks and Menzies replied that he would take the leadership in 'this great new struggle for civic freedom'. Not only that: by resigning and challenging the party to replace him, he seized the chance to settle the leadership question for good. With a general election due at the end of 1949, he observed that any decision made now 'must be adhered to for years to come'.

The move worked: in 1947 Menzies was unanimously re-elected leader of the Liberal Party. Anecdotal evidence suggests that, having already been surprised and pleased at the improved attitude some of his key colleagues were taking towards him, he was now able to take a more benign, relaxed attitude to them while retaining his authority as leader of the party. Although he spent some months out of the country in 1948, he was still firmly in control when the run-up to the 1949 election campaign came. Menzies had a decisive victory – the Liberals won 54 seats, the Country Party 20 and Labor 47. The average age of the new Liberal members (there were thirty-nine of them) was forty-three; twelve were under thirty. A high proportion of them were ex-servicemen. That this group was eager for change and could be assumed to appeal to the swinging voter, especially in middle Australia, must have been an important factor in the Liberal–Country Party victory.

Winning that campaign and becoming prime minister clinched Menzies' hold on the leadership. In the sixteen years of his prime ministership there were occasional rumblings about him and a few members qualified to be called, in the memory of one senior public servant, 'burrs under Menzies' saddle'. But these were minor aberrations: the plain fact was that by this time Menzies had no rival and there was no one in the party with the necessary gifts to take his place. In the years after 1949 he would also demonstrate what his sometime deputy Arthur Fadden called 'a maturity in leadership which was lacking during his previous term of office'.

There is something about Menzies that is not often remarked upon but that, almost paradoxically, seems crucial to his rise in popular favour. The late Don Rawson put it this way, when writing of the confident prime minister who won the 1958 election:

> Menzies was, and is, unmistakably an Australian type, something which is often not appreciated by those who find his popularity difficult to understand, and who think of Australians in terms of some of the simpler national stereotypes. Urbane but tough-minded, with a powerful but not a wide-ranging intellect, and an ample share of what may be described as either moral courage or arrogance, he exemplifies many of the qualities of the Australian managerial and professional classes. His voice, with its well-articulated consonants and full vowels, could nevertheless be the product of no other country than his own. He is never seen in a more characteristic setting than at an election meeting, when his superb lucidity and powerful but restrained irony will suddenly be interrupted while the Prime Minister crudely and bitterly taunts some luckless interjector. It is a combination of qualities which many Australians find attractive.

Despite the great care he took always to separate Liberal Party policies from those of Chifley and Labor, Menzies appreciated and assumed that in the normal course of events he would be using the skills of the outstanding group of public servants whom the Chifley government had assembled, most notably in the Department of Postwar Reconstruction. As was later made clear by Dr H. C. Coombs, members of the department were for the most part excited converts to the ideas of J. M. Keynes in his *General Theory of Employment, Interest and Money*. Though there were differences in detail, they were broadly sympathetic to the thrust of the theory that, with the sufferings of the Depression and World War II still all too recent, lay behind Labor's plans for full employment, for demobilisation and training schemes for ex-servicemen, and for commissions of inquiry to study particular aspects of the postwar scene, such as agricultural policy, housing and social security.

After the election of 1949 a few of Menzies' colleagues, particularly in the Country Party, wanted him to 'cleanse' the public service by getting rid of those, like Coombs, who were known to have favoured the 'socialistic' ideas of the previous government. Menzies refused, on the grounds that under the Westminster system a permanent public service that served every administration, whatever its colour, was the one guarantee of probity in government. From high office to low, he was not let down.

During Menzies' first three to four years of office, the Cold War and his vendetta against communism were his chief preoccupations, both locally and in his overseas travels. He visited England in 1948, just after his own Liberal Party – horrified by the communist coup in Czechoslovakia – decided to make the banning of the local Communist Party one of its formal aims. What had happened in Europe, it was reasoned, could happen in Australia. The Berlin blockade, whose immediate results Menzies was in England to sense at close quarters, brought the first high point of Cold War fears. Menzies accepted the widely held fear that Soviet rulers were co-ordinating plans to defeat the West. He came back from extensive travels in 1950–51 convinced of the possibility that Australia might have only three years to prepare for a third world war.

In his first three to four years in office, Menzies made concerted efforts to destroy the Communist Party of Australia. His first attempt to ban it failed; the second time he tried he managed to pass legislation against the party, only to have it disallowed by the High Court. When he took the issue to the people in a 1951 referendum, asking for the government to have the banning powers denied it by the court, it was narrowly defeated. The issues aroused by these legislative efforts, especially certain illiberal aspects of the proposed banning process, made this a period of high political emotion. Leader of the Opposition Dr H. V. Evatt led the attack from the Labor side, claiming that in defeating the 1951 referendum, the Australian people had 'rejected the Menzies campaign of unscrupulous propaganda and hysteria' and saved themselves and their children from the 'insidious aggressions of a police state'. Menzies, while urbanely accepting defeat ('as a democrat I respect and recognise the popular voting') expressed his belief that the electors had been misled by a 'wicked and unscrupulous "No" campaign'. Such emotionally charged exchanges intensified when in 1954 fears of Soviet activities in Australia were dramatically raised by the defection from the Soviet embassy of secret service officers Vladimir Petrov and his wife Evdokia, who claimed to have important information about espionage activities in Australia. This 'spy scare' played into Menzies' hands: anti-communism and the threat of Australian society being undermined by a fifth column remained central to his propaganda armoury, and he used it very effectively against Evatt. From late 1955 it was briefly muted by the temporary easing of world tensions when Khruschev came to power in Moscow.

There was an important reorientation of defence priorities at the 1951 Commonwealth Prime Ministers' Conference. Menzies and leading New Zealand delegates agreed that in case of global war their chief responsibility should not be to send troops to defend the Middle East, as previously envisaged, but to assist in the defence of Malaya and, by means of defensive agreements such as that which set up the South East Asia Treaty Organisation (SEATO), to lure the United States into the area. Australian defence policy, then, was changing focus decisively, making a switch that would lead to greater responsibilities in South-East Asia.

At the end of 1950 Menzies established the National Security Resources Board (NSRB), which he himself chaired, comprising businessmen and top civil servants to supervise stockpiling and economic planning for development generally and defence in particular. In July 1951 he introduced legislation to give the NSRB bite by reimposing, with a few exceptions, the powers enjoyed by the Commonwealth government during the war. This emergency measure greatly alarmed some government supporters, who feared a return to the wartime controls against which they had fought so vigorously in 1949. But it underlined the fact that the strategies of combining development for prosperity and for national security were not always compatible. In this case, when the 1951 Budget was brought down public servants in the Treasury and the NSRB decreed a sharp increase in taxation to halt inflation. The government offered some relief from this 'Horror Budget' in the following year.

By July 1955, the London *Economist* noted that 'stability characterises Australia in the sixth year of the Menzies regime; but it is a vulnerable stability'. Australia had had a number of years of substantial prosperity, with good seasons, high earnings and employment levels, and rapidly increasing production in many industries. But there were serious clouds on the economic horizon: the danger of inflation and the development of a substantial trade deficit.

Menzies himself recognised that the problems facing Australia were those of prosperity, not of depression. The government was attempting to build up a many-sided economy, to enlarge the population and to carry through extensive preparations for defence. In a major statement in Parliament in September 1955 Menzies highlighted the extent of current prosperity, but indicated that four trends gave cause for concern. The community's purchasing power was high, giving an unprecedented level of demand for goods and services and as a result, thanks to the limits of local resources, a 'vast' demand was being created for imported goods; expansion of export earnings was made difficult by increasing levels of wages and costs; the terms of trade – thanks chiefly to unfavourable prices for Australian produce in the world's markets – were moving against the country.

What was to be done? The government's policy was to call on the community generally to exercise voluntary self-restraint. But the government would also act coercively. Import restrictions would be stepped up and trade missions would be sent abroad in search of new markets. And there would be a new effort at open communication. Routinely, in the autumn session of Parliament the prime minister would himself present an economic report on the state of the nation.

From the mid 1950s Menzies scored three achievements of which he was always proud: the reform of the Cabinet system, the development of Canberra and the expansion of universities. Following the 1955 election Menzies divided his ministry into two parts: an inner Cabinet of twelve senior ministers and an outer ministry consisting of ten junior members. Menzies also announced a reshuffle of departmental duties that became very significant in the days that lay ahead. The old departments of trade and agriculture were abolished, their functions being split between two new ones, trade and primary industry. The first was headed by the forceful John McEwen, designated as a member of Cabinet, whose increased power was intended to help in the drive he soon announced for greater exports.

Menzies gave priority to constructing the foundations that were to make a rejuvenated Canberra a fitting capital for a new nation. In August 1957, the government enacted a National Capital Development Commission Bill to concentrate in one body the responsibility of planning and developing Canberra. The main challenge behind the Bill was the government's decision to move the defence department from Melbourne to Canberra by 1959. Menzies declared: 'We believe that for complete efficiency the headquarters of the Cabinet, of the Prime Minister's Department, of the Treasury, of the Department of External Affairs and of Defence should all be within immediate reach of each other in the federal capital.' Together with their families, 1100 public servants would initially be moved. Canberra would undergo unprecedented expansion to provide schools, homes and services to meet the needs of newcomers and the backlog of shortages that those already there suffered.

In 1956 Menzies appointed Sir Keith Murray, chairman of the British University Grants Committee, to report on the state of Australian universities. The Murray Committee assessed that between 1945 and 1956 student enrolments had almost doubled, from 16,500 to 31,000 and predicted an increase of 120 per cent from 1957 to 1967. Better accommodation and equipment were urgently needed. Based on the recommendations of the Murray Committee, the government set up a University Grants Committee to advise the states and the Commonwealth about university finance and developmental policy. In the interim the government provided an emergency three-year injection of Commonwealth funds into the system for capital expenditure, increasing academic salaries and an emergency grant.

In 1958 Menzies rejoiced in the greatest federal electoral victory since the establishment of the Commonwealth Parliament. The Australian economy gained in buoyancy; so much so that in February 1960 Cabinet decided that import licensing could at last be abolished. However, alternative control measures were not included in the Budget brought down in August and an adverse drift in the balance of payments soon became evident. Before long severe action seemed necessary, and on 15 November Treasurer Harold Holt announced a package of drastic deflationary measures, ranging from steeply increased sales tax on motor vehicles to tough restrictions on bank loans. This was the notorious 'credit squeeze' of 1960, destined to pass into legend as the archetypal example of the 'stop' phase in the 'stop-go' management sometimes thought of as characteristic of economic policy in the Menzies era.

The measures imposed understandably caused a great outcry from business and unionists. There were some bankruptcies and early signs of unemployment. Evident recovery from the recession did not come quickly and dissatisfaction grew when in August 1961 Holt brought down a 'stand-still' Budget. Although Menzies approached the December election confident that he would win by a clear margin, the government escaped defeat by a hairsbreadth: the ALP won 60 seats, the Coalition 62. This meant that after providing a Speaker, the government would have a majority of 1 in the House of Representatives. It was an almost unbelievable change from the majority of 32 in the previous Parliament.

In foreign affairs, Menzies seems to have believed that at the leadership level diplomacy primarily involved not necessarily detailed agreements – that could be left to subordinates – but the good-humoured 'meeting of minds' on generalities. This concept made him at times acceptable to European leaders from (Adenauer to de Gaulle) and almost always to British and American notables.

Menzies went to England almost every year for regular meetings of British Commonwealth prime ministers but was progressively more disillusioned as previous colonies gained their independence and new 'native' states multiplied, quickly outnumbering the old 'white' nucleus and altering the thrust of many of the discussions. Not that he failed to make some good friends among the new rulers (the Tunku of Malaya was a special case in point), but it was a while before he stopped bemoaning the breakdown or absence of freedoms in the new systems of government.

In hindsight we might conclude that the persistence of some old imperial ideas disabled Menzies as a policymaker to some extent when he came to office after World War II. 'Civilised' in the best sense of the word, he was usually circumspect about what he said and to whom. But, in common with some British Tory friends, he found it difficult to set aside in private the notion that the white man, mentally and by culture, was naturally superior to the 'coloured'. He assumed, particularly in the Pacific, that after the war 'old' possessions would be restored to their prewar rulers: decolonisation was a process he could not understand or for a time accept.

Menzies had progressively to come to terms with the common press and political criticism that his orientation was overwhelmingly European, that he thought of Asia as an area to fly over or otherwise bypass on his way to Europe, particularly to England. In due course, diplomacy and geography made that notion less and less tenable. His first external affairs ministers, Sir Percy Spender and Richard Casey, focused attention on the Pacific, and chiefly because of their initiatives Menzies began to accept that Australia's insecurity as a European country in the region meant that her defence had to be defence in depth.

Menzies, it must be said, went some way to meeting the expectations of Australia's neighbours in diplomatic terms, but at the level of direct contact this took some time and was marked by some unfortunate hiccups. In 1956 the Department of External Affairs planned a prime ministerial state visit to Japan; appropriate when trade department officers in both governments were negotiating what turned out to be an epoch-making agreement. But Menzies became embroiled in the Suez crisis, the unhappy sequence of events that followed the Egyptian leader Nasser's abrupt nationalisation of the Suez Canal. Menzies led an international mission to Cairo to try and persuade Nasser that the canal should be controlled by an international body established by treaty and associated with the United Nations. His talks with Nasser broke down when US President Eisenhower unexpectedly declared that the United States would not countenance the use of force against Egypt. When the British and French later bombed Egyptian installations, Menzies declared Australia's support and maintained this untenable position at the United Nations in opposing a resolution censuring Britain and France for their action. From any point of view, it was one of the more inglorious passages of his career.

An extensive trip to Asia became inevitable in 1957. But though a visit to Japan forged personal links between Menzies and Prime Minister Kishi, there were few other results. Menzies and Dame Pattie went on to Thailand and Manila, then to New Guinea and the Northern Territory. A chest infection laid the sixty-two-year-old Menzies low after his return to Australia and the whole experience made him permanently reluctant to show the flag in territories too far north of Australia. Late in 1959, he nevertheless agreed to a six-day goodwill visit to Indonesia, highly necessary at a time when the West Irian issue was still undecided. The *Sydney Morning Herald* correspondent Bruce Grant thought the visit went 'well enough', but that Asia was 'not Mr Menzies' field'. He added, 'It will probably take another generation before Australia produces a leader who can approach some of the new nations of Asia with any certainty of understanding.'

Successive Menzies governments committed themselves to continuing, even expanding, Australia's population through migration: projects like the Snowy Mountains hydro-electric scheme and the general economic growth of the 1950s and 1960s demanded no less. But where were the new people to come from? Menzies' commitment to White Australia can only be interpreted as a stand against Asian migrants in the flesh. By 1965 the growing difficulty of recruiting migrants meant accepting those from Turkey and the Middle East, people who were hardly 'White', or European. It can safely be said that Menzies never contemplated accepting migrants from Asia. While in Australia itself public opinion in the 1960s came more and more to disapprove of continuing the White Australia Policy, Menzies refused point-blank to endorse a suggestion by his Immigration minister Hubert Opperman that it be dropped.

At the 1961 meeting of Commonwealth prime ministers, the crucial issue was South Africa: now that it had at referendum voted to become a republic, was its application to stay in the Commonwealth acceptable? Being a republic was not the main issue; everyone knew that South Africa's racial policy was the real problem. Menzies and British Prime Minister Harold Macmillan 'worked like horses' over a series of drafts to find words that would be acceptable to all and would therefore keep the Commonwealth intact. The final statement expressed 'deep concern' about the impact of South Africa's racist policies on 'the relations between member countries of the Commonwealth, which is itself a multi-racial association of peoples'. Under mounting pressure, South Africa withdrew its application to re-enter the Commonwealth. Menzies made no bones about his belief that South Africa had been 'pushed out'. He began to feel that the balance of power had changed so much that his own views had become relatively unimportant.

In December 1961, almost a year after this meeting of Commonwealth prime ministers, Menzies received an invitation from R. A. Butler, representing Tories opposed to Macmillan's growing hopes of taking Britain into the European Common Market, to come to London to put the Commonwealth case against that 'as only you can do it'. But Menzies declined and later reverted to his earlier conviction that Britain must herself decide what policy to follow and accepted that the Commonwealth had become a much looser association. 'The old hopes of concerting common policies have gone.'

By this time Menzies had already responded positively to the 1962 United States request for allies to help in supporting the government of South Vietnam against communist subversion. However, virtual full employment meant that recruitment for the army had been dangerously disappointing. In October 1964, as a result of Sukarno's 'confrontation' policy against the foundation of Malaysia, Australian troops were for the first time in history in combat with Indonesian troops, following the landing of a party of sixty Indonesian raiders on the Malayan coast, south of Malacca.

Cabinet made the decision, announced by Menzies in November 1964, that the key measure in a reformed defence strategy was compulsory national service for the army, based at the beginning on a ballot of men turning twenty in 1965. Those called up would be liable for two years' full-time service, including overseas services as required, followed by three years in the reserve. The Opposition attacked conscription as an admission of past failures in preparing the defences of Australia. The point struck to the heart of an issue that brooded over many years of the Menzies ascendancy: how, in a relatively small economy, the chronically conflicting elements of postwar recovery, migration, development and defence were to be balanced.

On 7 April 1965, the Foreign Affairs and Defence (FAD) Committee of Cabinet decided that Australia should offer a battalion to support the American defence of South Vietnam. Menzies believed that 'the security of Australia would be at stake if South Vietnam fell'. The offer was conveyed to the Americans through the Australian ambassador in Washington, but was leaked to the press on 28 April and published the following day. Word came through to the government on that day that South Vietnam had agreed to ask for Australian troops, and in the evening session of the House of Representatives Menzies announced that it had been agreed 'weeks and weeks ago' that an Australian battalion would go to Vietnam. As one of his last major acts as prime minister Menzies committed Australian troops to fight a war that would progressively divide the nation and eventually threaten the survival of the Coalition government.

Outsiders occasionally registered doubts about the government's 'general appearance of unexciting competence' being a source of continuing strength, and complained, as did British High Commissioner Carrington in 1957 before he knew the Australian scene well, that the 'government is far too much a one-man show'. Though Carrington thought Menzies' position as leader was 'unchallenged and unchallengeable', he believed that Menzies had 'more to thank his colleagues for than he himself would perhaps readily acknowledge'.

Menzies' record at the polls after 1949 was however scarcely that of a prime minister on sufferance. Including the last election he called in 1963 he won seven in a row, the possible outcomes of only three of them (1951, 1954 and 1961) being at all doubtful. Though after the mid 1950s he benefited from the splitting of the Labor vote caused by the creation of the Democratic Labor Party, his real, uncanny strength was the feel his long years of experience in the upper echelons of politics had given him of when and how to strike by calling an election and fighting it vigorously, good-humouredly and supremely relevantly.

Throughout the alarums and excursions of Menzies' long period in office, there is little to contradict the notion that he saw the chief purpose of a properly constituted administration to be that of providing stable and honest government as he saw it. It was in the 1950s and 1960s that Menzies profited most from the economic boom that, though he might not claim to have been its creator, gained much from his positive economic policies and the stability and probity of the governments he headed.

In 1966 the Liberal Party had been in power federally for sixteen uninterrupted years, and was governing five of the six states; Labor, particularly under Arthur Calwell, had been neutralised as an electoral threat all over the country. Menzies must have felt a sense of satisfaction: a generation of able Liberal parliamentarians, many the so-called 'forty-niners', were ready to follow the principles of the party he had founded. Moreover, in his treasurer, Harold Holt, he had a successor with a great deal of experience, though a man of very different stamp.

On Australia Day 1966 – perhaps a day chosen for its symbolic value? – Robert Menzies, aged seventy-two, stepped down as Australia's longest-serving prime minister. He therefore became, with Barton and Fisher, one of this country's few prime ministers to leave of his own accord, at a time of his choosing.

Though for most Australians his second prime ministership is equated with the steady prosperity of Australia in the 1950s, an era that for some still holds the rosy glow of nostalgia, it is worth remembering that Menzies' thirty-eight years of active parliamentary life saw for Australia the major traumas of the middle to late twentieth century: the Great Depression, World War II, postwar reconstruction and the Cold War. He experienced the political fallout of each, though they served to confirm his views, which were, nominally at least, opposed to those of Labor thinkers.

Future generations seeking to place and describe Menzies in his country's history will need to see him encompassing a long period of time and change. In this perspective, those who consider him as less than a man for all seasons have strong arguments on their side. He was born in the late nineteenth century, educated in the early twentieth, escaping the worst traumas of World War I and specialising in constitutional law which, more than any other professional study, emphasised the Englishness of Australian institutions. He was an Empire man, British to the bootstraps, not just admiring turn-of-the-century imperial ideas, but imbibing and making them permanently his own. Yet it would be unfair to consider him some sort of reactionary fossil; above all, for many years, he had the ability to express and guide the beliefs and aspirations of his people in a magisterial, good-humoured style. Even his opponents generally recognised him as a gentlemanly opponent and a man of principle.

Menzies' earlier years out of politics were active and fulfilling. He did not have the frustrations of being in mid life searching desperately for a life after politics. Menzies was in his seventies when he left politics – well beyond normal community retirement age. He was installed as Lord Warden of the Cinque Ports, an honorary office previously held by Churchill. The office carried entitlement to an antique uniform and a stake in a castle built by Henry VIII. As always when he went to Britain, Menzies enjoyed the pomp and the history. Though he always felt British in Britain, English journalists persisted in seeing him as an archetypal Australian. There were also, in these years, writing, travelling, lectures. As the years passed, however, failing health and the inevitable isolation of old age blighted him. When his old opponent Arthur Calwell died in 1973 Menzies, too ill to attend the funeral service, sat in a car outside, weeping. Liberals made their pilgrimages to see the grand old man of their party but he still felt a certain loneliness. One new friendship that developed was with

B. A. Santamaria, the Catholic activist who had been a central player in the Labor turbulence which contributed to the Menzies government's longevity. On his retirement, Menzies had made it clear he was bowing out completely from politics. Inevitably, he did not follow this intention to the letter, although he resisted the temptation to become a public commentator. After Holt's drowning Menzies encouraged Paul Hasluck's bid for Liberal leadership, but the party chose Gorton. He approved of Governor-General Kerr's dismissal of Whitlam. Menzies died at his Melbourne home on 15 May 1978, aged eighty-three. While the nation by then had moved well beyond the Menzies era, he still embodied for his party the golden age of successful Liberal politics. As historian Janet McCalman says, Menzies in his day 'penetrated and comprehended the soul of the middle class in a way no other Australian politician has then or since … it was not what he did that lives in the memory, but what he was'.[1]

Sir Arthur William Fadden

29 AUGUST 1941 – 7 OCTOBER 1941

Fadden lacked the opportunity and political authority to make a major impact on history. His most important contribution was to hold together the two conservative sides of politics and to preserve the federal coalition as an effective political entity.

BY BRIAN COSTAR & PETER VLAHOS

The forty days from 29 August to 7 October 1941 during which 'Artie' Fadden was Prime Minister of Australia can be described as a transition period that saw the expected demise of a fractured and demoralised coalition government and its replacement by a determined and purposeful Labor administration. In a period of political instability at home and world war abroad, Fadden lacked the opportunity and political authority to make a major impact on history. His most important contribution was to hold together the two conservative sides of politics and to preserve the federal coalition as an effective political entity.

Fadden was born in the sugar-producing town of Ingham, north Queensland, on 13 April 1895. His parents were Irish immigrants, his father a member of the Queensland police force. Educated at a government school in Mackay, he went to work at an early age as a canecutter, working on sugar plantations in Queensland's tropical north. But he was determined to achieve a better lot in life. He was given work in the office of a sugar mill, then became an assistant town clerk of the city of Mackay; three years later he was promoted to town clerk after exposing the incumbent's fraudulent behaviour. It was no surprise that the conservative politics of local government would divert the young Fadden from the Labor Party to the Country Party.

Fadden embarked on his formal political career as a member of the Townsville City Council in 1930. He narrowly won the Legislative Assembly seat of Kennedy for the Country Progressive National Party in 1932, the year the Labor Party was returned to office in Queensland. While serving only one term, Fadden impressed by using his accountancy training (gained at night school in Mackay) to criticise the financial policies of the Forgan Smith government. So successful was he that it was alleged that the ALP influenced the 1935 electoral redistribution to render Kennedy unwinnable for him. Fadden transferred to the Mackay-based seat of Mirani but was defeated in the Labor landslide of 1935. The sudden death of the sitting member Sir Littleton Groom in 1936 paved the way for his entry into federal Parliament as member for the seat of Darling Downs.[1]

During his first four years in Canberra he was to witness the demise of the United Australia Party (UAP), a situation exacerbated by the sudden death of Prime Minister Joseph Lyons in April 1939. Following Lyons' death, Fadden fell out with leader of the Country Party, Earle Page, because of the personal and political attacks he launched on Robert Menzies, Lyons' heir apparent. Fadden strongly objected to Page's actions and chose to withdraw from the parliamentary wing of the Country Party, as did his colleagues B.H. Corser, T.J. Collins and A.O. Badman.[2] Soon after World War II began the Country Party offered to end its differences with Menzies if a new ministry could be selected by arrangement between himself and Page. When Menzies rejected this offer because it would appear to involve Page's own entry into the Cabinet, Page offered to place himself in the hands of his party. He resigned as party leader on 13 September 1939 and John McEwen and Archie Cameron contested the position.

The wrong candidate won. Cameron renewed the Country Party's demand for an equal say in the choice of ministers, Menzies again refused and the prospect of coalition lapsed. Within days of assuming the leadership, the irascible Cameron also managed to prolong the estrangement of Fadden and the three other dissidents from the Country Party. On 21 September he angrily attacked the good faith of those, including some members of his own party, who had voted for Curtin's Bill allowing for conscientious objection to military service. Fadden took the opportunity to declare that he, Corser, Collins and Badman did not consider Cameron their leader.[3]

In November 1939 Fadden and his group of supporters returned to the Country Party, and Menzies (now prime minister) included Country Party members in his March 1940 Cabinet. Fadden was appointed minister without portfolio assisting the treasurer, as well as minister for supply and development.[4] On the sudden deaths of three UAP ministers in August 1940 (Sir Henry Gullett, J.V. Fairbairn and G.A. Street) in a plane crash, Fadden was appointed minister for air and civil aviation, while retaining his assisting roles.[5]

Following the conservative parties' near-defeat at the federal election of 1940, the Country Party, having lost two ministers, resolved to remove Cameron from the leadership in October 1940. The leadership contest became a three-cornered one, among Cameron, Page and McEwen. After Cameron withdrew from the contest Page and McEwen tied, with eight votes each. To break the deadlock, Fadden was appointed acting leader until the deadlock was resolved. The Country Party members chose to formally accept him as their leader on 12 March 1941.

Having been promoted to treasurer on 28 October 1940, Fadden joined the all-party Advisory War Council. In November he brought down the first of his record eleven Budgets, the first full-scale war Budget, estimating war expenditure of £186 million for 1940-41.

Fadden's relationship with Menzies was complex but cordial. It was said that they became friends as politicians, never as men; it was always politics that dictated their relationship. Fadden's lack of a university education kept him in awe of Menzies. Nevertheless, it was Fadden who became the chief architect of their combined success as a coalition in later years. For the affable Fadden, it was difficult to comprehend how Menzies took for granted the loyalty of friends and colleagues. When Menzies left for a four-month visit to London on 24 January 1941, Fadden became acting prime minister. However, Menzies' political position was neither stable nor secure. While in London his authority completely disappeared, due to the continuing efforts by some members of the United Australia Party to remove him from office. In this politically charged atmosphere, even Fadden could not escape the accusations that he was involved in clandestine efforts against Menzies. These were without substance, and Fadden remained loyal. When Menzies returned in May 1941 and announced that he would prefer to become Australia's representative in London for the duration of the war, Fadden kept his own counsel. Menzies seemed oblivious to the concerns of his colleagues, and while rebuffed by both the Opposition and his own party, he chose to remain as prime minister, but his arrogance isolated him politically.

In September 1941 Menzies lost a UAP vote of confidence and resigned. The party infighting and divisions that had led to his downfall intensified because no viable leadership alternative existed. The Country Party chose to exploit this dissent in its coalition partner's ranks by making plain its belief that the only person capable of holding the government together was Fadden. A desperately divided UAP had no alternative but to agree, and handed the office of prime minister to its junior partner.

Fadden retained the Treasury; Menzies, who remained UAP leader, was appointed minister for defence co-ordination and the minister chosen to represent Australia in the British War Cabinet was Earle Page. Fadden's administration was destined to collapse. The Labor Party

Opposition sensibly resolved to attack the government's legitimacy to hold office and the opportunity was presented by Fadden's 1941 Budget. On 30 September 1941 the Labor Party caucus resolved that the proposed budgetary methods were 'contrary to true equality and sacrifice'[6] and should be 'recast to ensure a more equitable distribution of the national burden'.[7] Labor Party leader John Curtin used this resolution when, in the parliamentary Committee of Supply on 7 October 1941, he moved that the first item in the estimates be reduced by one pound, a standard way of expressing no confidence in a ministry. With Labor gaining the support of the two independents Wilson and Coles, Fadden's fate was sealed. He called on Governor-General Lord Gowrie and advised him to appoint Labor leader John Curtin as prime minister.

Fadden's sudden demise also revealed his strength of character and his affability even in the most difficult of situations. On the day the House was expected to vote on Curtin's amendment, Curtin called at Fadden's office on his way to lunch. 'Well, boy,' Curtin asked, 'have you got the numbers? I hope so, but I don't think you have!' Fadden calmly replied, 'No, John, I haven't got them. I have heard that Wilson spent the weekend at Evatt's home, and I can't rely on Coles.' 'Well there it is,' said Curtin, 'Politics is a funny game.'[8] Fadden simply smiled.

Surprisingly, the UAP then chose Billy Hughes as its leader, and the joint parties elected Fadden as leader of the Opposition. Both the UAP and the Country Party were heavily defeated in the 1943 federal elections and Fadden was replaced by Menzies, although Fadden remained the leader of the Country Party for the remainder of his parliamentary career.

As Labor introduced successive measures to expand the role of government in the economy, Fadden campaigned against what he saw as the advance of socialism. He urged the electorate to vote 'No' in the 'Fourteen Powers' referendum of 1944, which aimed at increasing the authority of the Commonwealth. During the 1946 election campaign he condemned the Chifley government for its plans to nationalise the banks and for its alleged soft line on communism.[9]

When Menzies took what was left of the UAP and established the Liberal Party, he and Fadden worked towards a coalition government. Reinvigorated, the Country Party formed a cohesive force behind Fadden and by 1949 was prepared to make an electoral agreement with the Liberal Party. Convinced he had an election winner, Fadden helped persuade Menzies to promise to abolish petrol rationing. At the polls of 10 December 1949 the Liberal/Country Party coalition was returned to power with Fadden as deputy prime minister and treasurer.

The immediate issue confronting the new government was inflation, caused by an increased consumer demand and exacerbated after June 1950 by the outbreak of the Korean war. The price of wool increased dramatically in 1950–51. Menzies and his supporters argued for an appreciation of the Australian pound; Fadden and the Country Party opposed such a policy shift. Cabinet was so divided on the issue that had not three Liberals sided with Fadden, the coalition might have dissolved. Nor could Cabinet agree to alternative proposals for an export tax on wool or for a special wool tax, both potentially disastrous for the support base of the Country Party. A compromise solution, embodied in the Wool Sales Deduction Scheme of 1950, provided for 20 per cent of the value of wool sold or exported to be paid to the Treasury as a credit against woolgrowers' income tax obligations. This scheme was repealed in 1951 when wool prices began to decrease, but growers were furious; even a decade later Fadden's actions generated anger.

Further concerns were to surface with primary producers and with the Country Party's rank and file when Fadden brought down his 1951–52 'horror Budget', which entailed a large counter-inflationary surplus. After this budget Fadden was so unpopular that he remarked: 'I could have had a meeting of all my friends and supporters in a one-man telephone booth …'[10] Farmers were particularly angered by the changes to the long-standing law permitting primary producers to average their incomes over five years for taxation purposes. Due to the wool boom, woolgrowers gained benefits not available to others – the portion of their income above £4000 was removed from the averaging scheme. The government's fiscal and economic policies continued to alarm primary producers throughout Fadden's term as treasurer, but he achieved much on their behalf. Notwithstanding the provisional tax, many supportive taxation measures were introduced, including increased depreciation rates and the abolition of the federal land tax in 1952.

In January 1952 Fadden went on his first official visit overseas, to attend a Commonwealth Finance Ministers' conference in London. The meeting had been called in response to a balance of payments crisis in the countries whose economies were tied to the pound sterling.

Asserting the Australian government's desire to accelerate economic development, Fadden opposed British proposals that sterling area countries should restrict imports from the dollar area and Europe; Fadden 'took the line that the sterling area could no longer continue as a closed and discriminatory system'.[11] While in London, he was invested with a knighthood (KCMG, 1951) by King George VI and was sworn in as a member of the Privy Council, an honour sponsored by Curtin in 1942. Fadden was elevated to the honour of GCMG in 1958.

Throughout the 1950s the private banks pressured the government to eliminate what they claimed to be unfair competition from the Commonwealth Bank of Australia. For all his willingness to be supportive of the private banks, Fadden had no intention of reducing the commercial activities of the publicly owned system. In 1957 he introduced legislation to revise the banking system. These reforms established the Reserve Bank of Australia, which was given the task of carrying out central banking activities and controlling the issue of notes. Fadden's reforms also saw the establishment of the Commonwealth Banking Corporation, with authority over the Commonwealth Savings and Trading banks and over the newly established Commonwealth Development Bank of Australia. Fadden regarded the Development Bank as his 'own brainchild ... designed to overcome the lack of adequate long term borrowing finance for farm development and small industries requirements.'[12]

Indeed, as treasurer, Fadden was fortunate that his period in office was one of national prosperity, during which there were generally good seasons and high prices for rural products. He relied heavily on the advice of Sir Roland Wilson, the head of the treasury, but he also knew how to exercise independent judgment. As H.C. Coombs observed, Fadden 'read all official papers and listened attentively' to advice but he also was able to deliver an assessment of a particular issue confronting him, with 'judgment that was intuitive'.[13] Fadden was also a shrewd assessor who knew the quality of advice when it was given and could quickly determine its political implications.

His habit of cultivating the confidence, and indeed affection, of his colleagues won him co-operation and loyalty. Indeed, his relationship with H.C. Coombs is an example of this. With the defeat of the Chifley government in 1949, Coombs' future as governor of the Commonwealth

Bank was in doubt, due to both Fadden's and Menzies' pronouncements during the election campaign. His dismissal from the office of governor was considered a *fait accompli*. But it was not to be. Fadden, now deputy prime minister and treasurer, rang Coombs to tell him 'to ignore all the gossip and to be assured of Fadden's confidence in him'. This action alone, according to Coombs, fortified the widely held view that Fadden was an essentially generous person who inspired confidence in those he worked with.[14]

While treasurer, Fadden chaired twenty meetings of the Australian Loan Council and attended many conferences of the International Monetary Fund and the International Bank for Reconstruction and Development.

After twenty-two years in Parliament and more Budgets than any other treasurer, Sir Arthur Fadden announced his retirement from federal politics in March 1958. His deputy, John McEwen, was elected to the leadership unopposed, but Menzies made it clear that, past custom notwithstanding, the Country Party had no exclusive claim to the Treasury. This was a further indication of the Country Party's weaker standing in the coalition, but there was nothing weak about the new leader himself, as time would reveal.

One of Fadden's last life ambitions was be appointed chairman of the new Commonwealth Banking Corporation board, but he was to be bitterly disappointed when a committee headed by John McEwen appointed (Sir) Warren McDonald to the post. Fadden subsequently refused the government's offer to chair the Australian National Airlines Commission. While living in Brisbane, he accepted directorships of a wide range of companies and worked on his memoirs *They Called Me Artie,* which was published in 1969.

Fadden's interest in politics and in the future of the Country Party never waned, even long after his retirement from active political life. He became concerned with moves within the Country Party to change its name and to contest urban seats as well as those in its traditional heartland. Although he acknowledged the steady decline in Country Party representation at federal and state levels, he saw no political advantage in such changes. He always maintained his belief that the interests of primary producers and the inhabitants of country towns could be given proper attention only by a sectional party that understood their needs and desires. For the Country Party to increase its numerical strength, Fadden argued that it needed to win country seats held by its opponents. This issue remains vital for the Country Party – now the National Party – even in today's politics. Sir Arthur Fadden died in Brisbane on 21 April 1973.

John Joseph Curtin

7 OCTOBER 1941 – 5 JULY 1945

Curtin's honesty of purpose, strength of character, power of oratory and political acumen all marked him out as a great leader.

BY DAVID DAY

John Curtin continues to be regarded with admiration and affection across the political divide. Country Party leader Arthur Fadden considered him the greatest Australian prime minister, a judgment with which many Australians would concur. Curtin's honesty of purpose, strength of character, power of oratory and political acumen all marked him out as a great leader. During the stressful months of early 1942 he found the fortitude to assert Australian interests in the face of threats from Churchill and pressure from Roosevelt. He did not 'save' Australia, since an invasion was never attempted, but he did ensure that the nation produced a creditable war effort and that it emerged united and unburdened with war debt. His government also laid the groundwork for many of the enlightened features that came to characterise postwar Australia. The nation was fortunate to have had the benefit of his defiantly Australian leadership during its most desperate time. In his 1942 Christmas message, Curtin had called on Australians to make selflessness 'the guiding factor in everything that comes to pass'. It had been the watchword of his life.

John Curtin was born in Creswick, Victoria on 8 January 1885, the eldest son of Irish immigrants. Curtin's devoutly Catholic mother Kate Bourke had left Ireland with her parents in 1875 for Melbourne, where her father established himself as a publican in inner-suburban Fitzroy. Curtin's father was a police constable who had been disciplined for forcibly fondling a woman while on his beat in Port Melbourne and had subsequently sought a transfer to the gold mining town of Creswick in the mountains north-west of Melbourne. He was not only burdened with the shame of his impulsive behaviour but also laid low and made irascible by rheumatoid arthritis. It was to Creswick that he took the twenty-four-year-old Kate after their marriage in Melbourne's St Patrick's Cathedral in June 1883.

At the time of Curtin's birth, his father might also have been suffering from the syphilis that would kill him many years later. The chronic ill-health of Curtin's father forced him to resign from the police force when Curtin was just five years old, and to leave Creswick and seek employment as a publican, presumably because of his wife's experience in that trade. For several years the Curtins ran the Letterkenny Hotel in Melbourne's Little Lonsdale Street, close by St Francis' church. Attached to the church was a two-room school run by the Christian Brothers, where young Curtin received his earliest education.

Curtin's parents had become publicans just as the 1890s depression was forcing many people out of work. In 1894, the Curtins followed many of their customers to the countryside, taking over a small hotel in the wheat-growing town of Charlton about 270 kilometres from Melbourne, where Curtin attended the local state school and was an altar boy at the Catholic church. It seems that for a time he even planned to become a priest. Although he attended seven or eight different schools during his childhood, his education was not as poor as is commonly claimed. His peripatetic schooling left him with a lifelong interest in learning.

Unfortunately, a prolonged drought made the Mallee farmers just as unable as the people of Melbourne to patronise the Curtins' pub. The family had left Charlton by May 1896, with his parents managing pubs in a succession of country towns around Melbourne. By 1898 the now impoverished family had returned to Melbourne, where John's ailing father seems never to have worked again. The burden of supporting the family, now comprising four children, fell upon Curtin's mother, who took in sewing at piecework rates, and upon young John. Curtin's first job was as a messenger with the short-lived bohemian magazine *The Rambler*, edited by the promising artist Norman Lindsay, who also came from Creswick and whose doctor father had delivered Curtin into the world. Other jobs followed, from copyboy at the *The Age* to messenger boy at a city club.

From 1898 to 1917 Curtin lived in the working-class suburb of Brunswick, where his family shifted frequently from one rented house to another, all within a tight square of houses known disparagingly as Paddy's Town. It was an Irish Catholic enclave close by several brickworks and potteries. As a boy, Curtin had a job in one of the brickworks and later played football and cricket with local teams. During this time he left the Catholic Church, first joining the Salvation Army before becoming a convinced rationalist. In 1902, at the age of seventeen, he became involved in politics, with Frank Anstey, a newly elected state MP and the president of the Brunswick Football Club, being his guide and mentor in leading him towards socialism. The English-born Anstey, who had run away to sea as a young boy before landing in Australia, was a messianic figure whose political language was studded with religious allusions.

Despite having spurned the Catholicism of his childhood and embraced rationalism, Curtin seems to have been partly attracted to socialism by the religiosity of its discourse and the churchlike manner of some of its organisations, particularly the Victorian Socialist Party. He came to socialism just as the labour movement was experiencing dramatic growth in its size and political importance. There had been a short-lived Labor government in Queensland in 1899, making it the first such government in the world, while five years later the thirty-seven-year-old John Christian Watson became Australia's first Labor prime minister, leading a minority Labor government of the newly federated nation. These were exciting times to be alive, with Labor's future dominance of the political arena apparently unstoppable. The party promised to usher in policies that would restrain the unbridled rapacity of capitalism and do away with the poverty that had blighted Curtin's late childhood years.

Curtin's interest in politics coincided with his first long-term job as an estimates clerk at the Titan Manufacturing Company in South Melbourne, where he worked from 1903 to 1911, helping to produce hardware for the building industry. With the security of his employment, Curtin's family no longer had to fear the knock of the rent collector and were able to move to a larger and more comfortable home. Curtin became an active member of the Tinsmiths' Union and marched behind its banner in the annual Eight Hour Day procession through Melbourne's streets. Away from work, he spent many evenings avidly reading at the public library, not just the latest socialist tracts from Britain and the United States, but also poetry and history and popular novels. He was a young man trying to make sense of his fast-changing world.

Although he would become an active member of the Brunswick branch of the Labor Party and an ardent supporter of Anstey's radical labourism, Curtin devoted most of his early political energy to the even more radical Victorian Socialist Party, established in 1906 by the British trade union activist Tom Mann. Like Anstey, Mann came from a troubled background, having lost his mother at the age of three, and he spent part of his childhood working in an English coalmine. Mann made his international reputation as one of the leaders of the historic London dock strike in 1889, when supportive action by workers around the world, and particularly in Australia, demonstrated the potential of working-class solidarity. He arrived in Melbourne in late 1902 as part of a lecture tour of the

Australasian colonies, and was quickly recruited into the local labour movement as an organiser.

Curtin later recalled how Mann 'infected masses of men the world over with divine enthusiasm for action'. He was 'a MAN, a truly dynamic man'. In 1905, Mann began organising a new party to stiffen the resolve of the labour movement for the 'prolonged warfare' that would have to be borne before the expected collapse of capitalism occurred. The Socialist Party had about 1500 members by 1907 and Curtin immersed himself in its multifarious activities, beginning with a survey of Melbourne's poor. He later recalled visiting homes 'that were without furniture; in many cases rags and bags served as bedding; food was lacking; and invariably the hearth was fireless for want of fuel. The experience was sorrowful and maddening.'

The Socialist Party did not aim at competing with the parliamentary aspirations of the Labor Party but at spreading the message of socialism through political evangelism. It had a weekly newspaper, the *Socialist*, regular street corner meetings, classes in public speaking, literature and economics, a Sunday night lecture in a Melbourne theatre and even a socialist Sunday school. It had an orchestra, afternoon teas in the Socialist Hall, camps in the bush and picnics by the Yarra or at the seaside. Curtin honed his speaking skills in its classes and lectured on economics to his fellow adherents. These activities would have helped to overcome his natural shyness, exacerbated by the muscular distortion of one eye, which had the disconcerting effect of making him appear to be looking in two directions at once. It marred the otherwise handsome appearance of his tall and athletic frame.

The social side of the VSP was important for Curtin, providing warm friendships and welcoming family circles that could compensate for his own stressful family circumstances. For a time, Curtin was part of a close foursome with fellow activist Frank Hyett and two sisters, Ethel and Nancy Gunn. Curtin's fondness for young Nancy Gunn was said to have been so intense that they talked of marriage. But it was not to be. In late July 1906 Nancy caught a cold that developed into pneumonia. In just over a week she was dead, at the age of sixteen. Curtin was devastated. Nancy's untimely death is said to have been the reason he turned to alcohol during the bouts of depression that would dog him for the rest of his life. It also saw him commit himself even more forcefully to the socialist cause.

Political struggles within the Socialist Party in late 1908 saw Curtin side with Mann and Hyett in trying to keep the party as a broad church of believers rather than a party of purists standing in open opposition to the Labor Party. At the same time, as the Labor Party continued to disappoint the hopes of socialists by rejecting a commitment to socialism, Mann increasingly looked to industrial organisation to provide the surest path to their goal.

As the Socialist Party became increasingly riven with factions, Mann sought other outlets for his restless energy. In early 1909 he was arrested in Broken Hill for trying to organise the miners there. Acquitted of a charge of sedition, he returned to Melbourne triumphant, telling a May Day crowd that the 'revolution is upon us'. But it was not to be. Seven months later, with the Socialist Party continuing to unravel, Mann was off, ending his Australian sojourn and steaming back to England, where he became a leading light in the British Communist Party.

Mann's departure did not stop the disputes within the Socialist Party, nor did it stop disgruntled members leaving it. Curtin did what he could to reignite the old fervour, taking over as honorary secretary in August 1910 and trying unsuccessfully to revive the program of street corner meetings. He resigned as secretary in February 1911, and also from his job at Titan, to take up an appointment as secretary of the Victorian Timber Workers' Union. It would allow him to put into practice the political ideas of the departed Mann.

The union had about 2500 members awkwardly split between workers in urban timberyards and timbercutters in distant forests. Curtin toured the bush camps by train and on foot, enrolling new members and pressuring those who had allowed their membership to lapse. He established and edited a monthly newspaper, the *Timber Worker*, which combined union news with political propaganda. While he increased the membership of the union by about 50 per cent, the hoped-for revolution seemed no closer.

It was Curtin's union role that introduced him to the woman who would later become his wife. It happened in Hobart in April 1912, after Curtin had gone to meet Tasmanian officials of the union. Elsie Needham was the twenty-two-year-old daughter of Abraham Needham, a radical activist and former Methodist preacher. A painter by trade, Needham took his family to South Africa in the late 1890s to escape the depressed Australian conditions. While in Capetown, he helped establish the Social Democratic

Federation and edited its newspaper. In 1906 he was arrested and briefly jailed for inciting a riot. Now he was in the calmer political clime of Hobart, where Curtin quickly warmed to his rousing language and the attractions of his comely daughter. Theirs would be a prolonged courtship, carried out mainly by correspondence and lasting almost five years.

Curtin left Tasmania imbued with confidence about the imminence of revolution. But other forces were also at work in the world, with a rising tide of militarism sweeping across Europe. Like many others, Curtin was appalled by the prospect of war and worked desperately to avert it. In his writings and speeches he opposed Australian participation in future European wars and attacked the Labor Party for supporting conscription for home defence. Curtin suggested that Australia's defence would be best secured by an air force that could be moved about the continent to meet threats wherever they appeared. Given the rudimentary development of air power prior to World War I, it was a farcical suggestion that was, at best, ahead of its time.

Curtin had more success in convincing the labour movement to adopt measures designed to prevent war. In early 1914 the Victorian Trades Hall Council agreed to commit itself to a resolution of international socialists requiring workers to strike in the event of war. But war came regardless in August 1914, with such resolutions being swept aside by the press of patriotic workers eager to join the European fray. With a federal election being held in Australia, the labour movement was keen to downplay its former anti-war stance for fear of an electoral backlash. As it happened, Curtin was standing for Parliament himself, having been convinced by Anstey to stand in the conservative seat of Balaclava against the former Victorian premier, W. A. Watt. Curtin was lauded in the newspaper *Labor Call* as being 'one of those rare men who carry the impress of greatness'. In modern parlance, he had charisma.

The election campaign, against the background of the distant war, placed a terrific strain on Curtin, who was often the worse for drink. It was made worse by Elsie having gone to South Africa for an extended stay with friends. Before her departure, Curtin had declared his love for her and proposed that they marry, to which she immediately agreed. Although later claiming that she 'would have given anything to have been able to grab my baggage from the hold and run down the gang-plank again', she went ahead with her voyage.

While Curtin was unsuccessful in the election, the Labor Party under Andrew Fisher won government, only to be confronted with the task of organising the nation's contribution for the distant war. Anstey was one of the few MPs who spoke against the war, claiming it was due to the 'greed of wealth'. For his part, Curtin described war as the 'assassin's trade', blaming it on the 'competition for overseas markets'. Curtin, however, was not a pacifist, arguing that pacifism was 'inherently fallacious', since force would always 'rule the world'.

Although it was feared that the war would destroy the chances of the labour movement achieving the overthrow of capitalism, Curtin argued optimistically that the war would allow socialism to have its day. This early optimism gradually waned as it became clear that the war would last much longer than most people had anticipated. The landing of Australian troops at Gallipoli in April 1915 put added pressure on Curtin's anti-war stance. In mid November 1915 he suddenly resigned as union secretary. His anti-war views were increasingly out of step with those of other officials and he had suffered the embarrassment of his assistant defrauding the union of its funds. Most importantly, he had devoted nearly five years of his life to the union without there being any sign of it advancing the wider struggle for socialism. As he explained to Elsie, there was no 'real working-class advantage' to be had in staying on.

Out of work for the first time in more than a decade, Curtin looked forward to having a 'loaf'. But the Australian Workers' Union soon sent him off to the Riverina district to advise on the organisation of its fast-growing membership. Bigger issues were also pressing, as Billy Hughes took over as prime minister and held out the prospect of introducing conscription for overseas service. Curtin was appointed secretary of the Trades Union Anti-Conscription committee, with *Labor Call* predicting that he was 'likely to do great things for the anti-conscription movement – the one movement nowadays that matters'. Although the paper also described him as 'operating with the energy of a tornado', he was still drinking too heavily and was hospitalised for a time in mid 1916 to try and effect a cure. While in hospital, Anstey counselled him to be 'proud of the conquest that you are going to achieve and the good that you yet will do'. He was hardly out of hospital before Billy Hughes returned from London announcing that conscription was unavoidable if the numbers of Australian troops in the trenches of France were to be maintained.

Curtin travelled the country to galvanise the labour movement in opposition to Hughes. Braving taunts and tossed eggs from hostile crowds and defying a call-up to military camp, Curtin set out the anti-conscription case plainly and logically. When the people went to the polls in November 1916, the anti-conscriptionists found they had narrowly won, although Curtin was jailed in December for defying the call-up. He was released after three days when appeals were made to the Labor government, which soon after split in two, with Hughes and his proconscriptionist colleagues joining with the conservatives to form a Nationalist Party government.

Curtin was exhausted by the struggle and his reputation was tarnished by his penchant for the bottle. His personal salvation came in early 1917, when he was offered the editorship of the weekly *Westralian Worker* in Perth. At his rushed farewell from Melbourne, Curtin looked forward optimistically to the day when Australia would become 'a republic of the discontented peoples of the earth'.

Curtin now had a chance to vindicate the faith that his closest friends and associates continued to place in him. As he told one of his supporters, he had a 'chance of being useful to the world and to myself'. He also had the opportunity to marry Elsie if only she would agree to follow him to Perth, which she did. They were married in a registry office on 21 April 1917 and set up house in rented accommodation in the working-class suburb of Subiaco. With his position as editor and his credentials as a propagandist and speaker, Curtin was soon accorded a leading position in the labour movement. When Hughes announced a new plebiscite on conscription, scheduled for December 1917, Curtin became one of its leading opponents in the west. After one meeting he was fined for allegedly making a statement 'likely to cause disaffection to His Majesty'. Once again, Hughes failed to win over conscription.

Curtin had been convinced that the end of the war would see the overthrow of capitalism. Instead, he found that the Armistice ushered in a climate of reaction that marginalised the labour movement. The 1919 federal election, at which Curtin stood for the conservative seat of Perth, saw the Labor Party rejected in favour of the flag-waving Nationalists under Hughes. Curtin was laid low by the effort of electioneering and seems to have suffered a serious depressive episode. Fortunately, his parents-in-law now lived with the young couple, with his father-in-law helping with Curtin's editorial duties while his mother-in-law helped with their two young children, a daughter born in December 1917 and a son in January 1921.

Curtin continued to call for the overthrow of capitalism in the pages of the *Westralian Worker*, but his experience in Perth was causing him to moderate his views. The labour movement in Western Australia was unique in combining its parliamentary and industrial wings in one organisation. Curtin's involvement with the industrial wing inevitably led him to be involved with the parliamentary wing and to espouse its reformist agenda. The *Westralian Worker* was also increasingly controlled by the relatively conservative officials of the Australian Workers' Union. As editor, Curtin was forced to reflect their views. He was also involved with the non-aligned Australian Journalists' Association, being elected president of the West Australian branch in June 1920.

By 1923 the family had shifted to Jarrad Street, Cottesloe, a beachside suburb between Perth and Fremantle, after living in nearby Napier Street. The modest bungalow was designed by Curtin with a book-lined lounge and a wraparound verandah on three sides in which to sleep during the heat of Perth's summers and on which to walk on wet days as he planned his speeches.

In 1924 the federal government appointed Curtin as the labour representative at a conference of the International Labor Organisation in Geneva. Curtin's experience there, and his subsequent visits to Paris and London, where the first Labour government had just been formed, were important in convincing him that the labour movement should concentrate its energies on achieving incremental reform through parliamentary means. As he told journalists upon his return to Perth, the 'era of opportunity' for overthrowing capitalism had passed and Labor governments were now 'the hope of the world'.

Back in Western Australia, Curtin became a stalwart supporter of the new Labor government led by his close friend Phillip Collier. His support for Collier saw Curtin caught offside in a dispute between the government and the communist-led Seamen's Union, which led to his being blacklisted for some months by the union. The following year he made his first serious attempt to enter federal Parliament, standing for the seat of Fremantle in the 1925 election. Anstey was anxious to have Curtin alongside him in Parliament to 'make sure that the principles for which this party is supposed to stand shall also be triumphant and not be submerged by undertakers, vacillators and quitters'. But the conservative government of Stanley Melbourne Bruce used law and order issues to keep Labor out. Curtin returned to his editing, his lectures for journalists at the university and his cricket games with the local Cottesloe club.

In 1928 the Bruce government appointed Curtin as a Labor representative to a Royal Commission into child endowment. The prolonged absences from home, as the Commission held hearings around Australia, saw Curtin once again hitting the bottle hard. His mood was not helped by being in the minority on a Commission that was determined to maintain the status quo. Fortunately for Curtin, the federal election of November 1928 allowed him to stand successfully for Parliament in the seat of Fremantle, although the Labor Party still fell short of a majority. On leaving for Canberra, Curtin assured well-wishers that he would not betray their trust, declaring that the urge to do his best in the workers' movement would keep him wholesome. A year later, Bruce's government was once more forced to the polls.

The election of James Scullin's Labor government in October 1929 convinced Curtin that his time had come. But he found himself excluded from the ministry as Labor took charge of an economy staggering towards the precipice created by the Wall Street crash. The government was forced by the banks to cut back the entitlements of workers and social welfare recipients. As Anstey observed, without control of the Senate, Labor was 'in office but not in power'. He and Curtin urged the government to call another election to obtain a mandate for radical measures, including nationalisation of the banks. Rebuffed, Curtin and Anstey were often found together, drunk and disheartened.

The Depression caused Labor to split into three parts. Some MPs, under the Tasmanian Joe Lyons, joined with the conservatives in the newly formed United Australia Party, while a group of Labor MPs from New South Wales split from the federal ALP to pay allegiance to Jack Lang, the former Labor premier. Curtin was instrumental in having the Langites expelled from the party and establishing a federal branch in New South Wales to compete with Lang and his supporters.

When Labor was forced back to the polls in 1931, its disappointed supporters threw it out of office. Losing heavily in Fremantle, Curtin faced an uncertain future. Depressed by his rejection, he initially sought a position in the eastern states, but nothing was forthcoming. Instead, he worked as a freelance sports journalist for his old paper and was paid by the Labor Party as a publicity officer, contributing political articles to local and interstate newspapers. More lucrative employment came when Collier was returned as premier in 1933 and employed Curtin to draw up a submission for the Commonwealth Grants Commission.

In 1934, Curtin was urged by Anstey to take over his safe Labor seat in Melbourne. But Curtin refused, trying instead to pressure Anstey to stay on. In a revealing comment, he told Anstey that while he also had his 'days of dark clouds', they were both 'standard bearers in a holy war and we must go on and not yield while life is left to us'. Curtin stood once more for Fremantle at the September 1934 election, winning narrowly in a poll that saw Labor gain only four extra seats in the House of Representatives while the Langites added five MPs to their number.

It was a very different world from that of Curtin's first term in Canberra. Economic issues were giving way to issues of security. The conservative government of Joe Lyons was committed to the system of imperial defence, locking Australia into the defence of Britain and its Empire rather than defending the Australian continent. Curtin called for Australia to secure its own defence before contributing to that of the Empire.

Curtin's sure grasp of these and other issues helped attract the attention of his fellow MPs. When it came time in September 1935 to replace the ailing and ineffectual Scullin, Curtin was urged to stand as party leader. Although Scullin's deputy Frank Forde was the favoured candidate, Curtin won the position by one vote after promising his supporters to abstain from drinking. While worried about being too old for the job, having just turned fifty, Curtin set to the task with as much vigour as he could muster, declaring confidently that there was 'a great destiny for the Labor Party in the life of the Nation'.

It was not just the party that needed to be inspired. The nation too had been dismayed by the Depression. After the bright-eyed optimism of the 1920s, the country was losing population as disappointed immigrants returned to their homelands and the birthrate declined. Curtin tried to encourage the doubters and the hand-wringers, declaring to a welcoming crowd in Perth in December 1935 that Australia could still develop 'a standard of civilisation greater than the world has yet known'.

However, events elsewhere soon threw a deepening shadow over such expressions of confidence. The Italian invasion of Abyssinia in 1935 and the civil war in Spain were potentially divisive issues for the Labor Party, with its strong Catholic element being sympathetic to the Spanish rebels and the Italians. Anxious to avoid splits in Labor's ranks, Curtin refused to support sanctions against Italy or to support the republican government in Spain against the rebels. Instead, by concentrating on the glaring deficiencies in the Australian defence position, he achieved a unified position on the question of local defence that distinguished it from the government's support for imperial defence. He drew on advice from worried army officers to back his arguments. Curtin's political strategy was tested at the 1937 federal election. Accused by Lyons of being isolationist, Labor was largely rejected at the polls.

Undeterred, Curtin continued with his arguments against Australian involvement in European wars, even as Hitler made such a war more likely. Equally anxious to avoid war, Lyons and his ministers supported the appeasement policies of British Prime Minister Neville Chamberlain. Both sides were relieved by the Munich agreement of 1938, although few had any illusions that peace would last. Six months later Hitler marched into Czechoslovakia. The invasion coincided with political turmoil in Australia as Robert Menzies resigned from the government in frustration at Lyons not stepping aside and making him prime minister. Lyons tried to shore up his position by inviting Curtin to join a national government but Curtin declined, conscious of the divisions it would create in Labor's ranks. In the event, Lyons died from a heart attack in April 1939 and the ambitious Menzies was installed in his place.

When war finally came in September 1939, Curtin agreed that Hitler had to be stopped but opposed any suggestion that conscription for overseas service should be introduced to do it. He also opposed any expeditionary force being sent overseas, arguing that Australia's 'primary responsibility' was one of 'safeguarding our own people'. But an expeditionary force was soon committed after Britain gave assurances to Menzies about Japan and about its own ability to protect Australia from invasion. Although Curtin continued to warn that committing forces to Europe would expose Australia to danger, his words were not heeded. The first of four divisions was dispatched overseas, naval units were sent to Singapore and later to the Mediterranean, and the air force was converted into a training organisation to supply air crew for Britain.

The war failed to boost Menzies' electoral stocks. During the first eight months, when little fighting occurred, Menzies proved unable to provide inspirational war leadership. He had not helped his cause by announcing on the outbreak of war that Australians should maintain an attitude of 'business as usual'. In March 1940 Labor won a by-election in the formerly conservative seat of Corio. However, the swing towards Labor was imperilled when the NSW branch of the party, after being patched together by Curtin, once more began to self-destruct, eventually splitting into three warring factions. The split came after the NSW Annual Conference passed a motion condemning the possibility of Australia declaring war against Russia. Denounced by the press, the motion linked Labor in the minds of the electorate with the Communist Party. Lang seized the opportunity to establish what he called the Non-Communist Australian Labor Party.

More than ever anxious to avoid accusations of disloyalty, Curtin became fulsome in his praise of Menzies' war leadership, assuring Australians that the country was now better prepared to meet the possibility of an attack. While Curtin was criticised by some Labor MPs for being too co-operative with the Menzies government, his steady leadership of the party and his moderate policies brought it big political gains at the federal election of September 1940, forcing Menzies to rely on the support of two independent MPs, Arthur Coles and Alex Wilson.

Ironically, this election almost saw Curtin lose his own seat of Fremantle. With his defeat being widely predicted Curtin submitted his resignation as leader, apparently content to return to his family and his books in Cottesloe. His expected absence from Parliament was widely regretted. Two Labor MPs offered to resign their seats in his favour while Billy Hughes paid tribute to Curtin's 'sincerity, his ability and the fact that he had the confidence of the Labor Movement'. When the belated news of his victory was announced, Curtin resumed the burdens of leadership.

The Labor ranks were now much augmented, with the former High Court judge, Dr H. V. Evatt, the Victorian Labor activist Arthur Calwell and the former train driver Ben Chifley falling in behind Curtin. While Evatt and Calwell were anxious for Labor to attain power and became critical of Curtin for not exploiting the government's weakness, Chifley was to provide a rock of friendship that would help to get Curtin through the darker moments of the war.

The close election result, combined with the worsening war situation, saw renewed pressure on Curtin to co-operate with the minority Menzies government to form a national government, But Labor would only agree to a multi-party Advisory War Council that gave Curtin and his colleagues valuable experience in making war decisions. Their concern about Australia's defence preparedness was heightened by a report that exposed the parlous state of Singapore's defences. Since the Singapore naval base acted as the linchpin of Australia's defence, this was worrying news indeed. It caused Curtin and his colleagues to press for Britain to base a fleet at Singapore while Menzies set off for London in January 1941 to pressure the British government in person.

Menzies' four-month absence from Australia left the minority government in charge of the Country Party leader Arthur Fadden, who developed a warm and co-operative relationship with Curtin. Despite criticism from his Labor colleagues, Curtin acknowledged the government's mandate and refused to challenge it during Menzies' absence. As he informed Parliament after the election, the Australian people wanted 'complete co-operation by those who are charged with the responsibility to ensure the safety of our country'. Curtin issued a joint statement with Fadden in February 1941 warning of the deteriorating security position in the Pacific and calling upon all Australians to make 'the maximum effort to carry us through the vital months ahead'. He also agreed to Australian troops being sent to Singapore after Australia received an assurance from Churchill that Britain would send a fleet there if Australia were threatened.

Menzies returned to Australia in May 1941 after achieving little in the way of boosting the defences of either Singapore or Australia. Instead, he had agreed to Australian forces being used in the ill-fated defence of Greece against a German invasion. By June 1941 this had led to about 8000 Australian casualties and the whole British position in the Mediterranean being imperilled. As a result, the possibility of securing British naval forces for the Pacific was much reduced.

Despite this military disaster and its implications for Australia, Menzies might have remained as prime minister had he been less eager to transfer his undoubted talents to the British Parliament. Curtin was keen to allow Menzies' minority government to remain in office, even to the extent of accommodating the Prime Minister's wish to revisit London. A frustrated H. V. Evatt sought to undercut Curtin by suggesting to Menzies the establishment of a national government with Evatt as one of its leading lights. When Menzies rebuffed such advances, the spurned Evatt sought Menzies' downfall. A growing number of conservative MPs also had Menzies in their sights, eventually forcing his resignation on 28 August 1941.

Instead of Curtin taking over, Fadden governed until the two independent MPs, Wilson and Coles, withdrew their support from the government on 3 October 1941. Curtin now had a chance to prove his mettle in the unwelcome role of war leader. He told his secretary, 'I will need all your prayers, Gladys, taking this job.' Political observers in Canberra had wondered whether Curtin was up to the task of governing, given his reluctance to harass Menzies and his succession of stress-related illnesses. However, the burdens of office saw him justify the faith of his supporters. The journalist Allan Fraser claimed that 'within weeks, he had the job completely at his fingertips'.

Supporting Curtin in office was the stalwart figure of Ben Chifley, appointed as treasurer, and the experienced figure of James Scullin, adviser and confidant without portfolio. Evatt's restless energy and ambition were kept in check by his appointment as both attorney-general and minister for external affairs. Curtin's deputy, Frank Forde, was made army minister, while Curtin retained for himself the overall responsibility for defence. Heading the Defence Department and also acting as secretary for the War Cabinet was Frederick Shedden, a public servant who now became Curtin's closest adviser. Watching the prime minister's political back was the Labor journalist Don Rodgers, whose work as press officer was important in augmenting Curtin's public image.

Curtin and his colleagues did not have long to meet the defence challenge from Japan. On 8 December 1941, Curtin was woken in his room at Melbourne's Victoria Coffee Palace with news of the Japanese attack on Pearl Harbor. 'Well, it has come,' responded Curtin resignedly. A War Cabinet meeting that morning at Victoria Barracks saw the chiefs of staff advise the government of the nation's desperate defence situation. As Shedden explained, there was not one army division in Australia that could be deployed 'as a good fighting force' against a possible invasion. The government continued to place its hopes in Singapore's ability to withstand attack and in the largely symbolic presence there of the British warships, *Prince of Wales* and *Repulse*. According to Curtin, they 'altered the whole position'. The government also took great comfort from the United States' entry into the war.

Anxious that the Pacific should not become a strategic backwater, Curtin called for a strong Allied response. Specifically, he wanted Britain to make good its promises to defend Australia. In a broadcast to the 'men and women of Australia', Curtin warned that it was their 'darkest hour' and called for their 'inflexible determination that we as a nation of free people shall survive'. In a sign of his government's more independent outlook Curtin explicitly declared war against Japan, rather than saying that Australia was at war simply as a consequence of Britain being at war, as Menzies had done with Germany.

Curtin's earlier doubts about Britain's ability or willingness to spring to Australia's defence were now confirmed. After the *Prince of Wales* and *Repulse* were swiftly sunk, token British reinforcements were sent as the Japanese landed on Malaya and began advancing towards Singapore. Blasting the reinforcements as 'utterly inadequate', Curtin foresaw the Australian troops in Malaya facing a disaster similar to that suffered in Greece. He looked to Washington to provide the forces that Britain was unwilling to send.

This dramatic switch in the Australian outlook was encapsulated in Curtin's New Year message to the Australian people published in the Melbourne *Herald* on 27 December 1941. He declared: 'Without any inhibitions of any kind, I make it quite clear that Australia looks to America, free of any pangs as to our traditional links or kinship with the United Kingdom.' His words caused an outraged reaction from conservative Australians, while Churchill denounced its sentiments as 'insulting' and threatened to broadcast over Curtin's head to the Australian people. Curtin moved to still the criticism by claiming that the message did not signify any break with Britain.

Despite this, Curtin's disputes with Churchill worsened as the defence situation grew bleaker during January 1942. While Churchill was resigned to the loss of Singapore and was concentrating instead on holding Burma, the Australian government denounced its possible evacuation as 'an inexcusable betrayal'. The stress of these disputes wore away at Curtin's health, forcing him to take a fortnight's break in Perth from 21 January.

Curtin returned to Canberra early in February 1942, in time for the fall of Singapore on 15 February. Warning that 'the battle for Australia' was beginning, he was in hospital with gastritis when Japanese aircraft launched the first of many raids on Darwin just four days later. Despite the attacks on Australia, Churchill was keen to retain control of the two divisions of Australian troops then returning from the Middle East. He wanted at least one to be diverted to Burma and, supported by Roosevelt, pressed Curtin to send troops there. While awaiting a reply, Churchill unilaterally directed the ships towards Burma. Curtin was furious, insisting that they be returned to Australia, although later agreeing to allow a large part of the next division to stop off in Ceylon as a temporary garrison. Curtin identified so closely with the troops on these convoys that he was unable to sleep for days at a time as the ships crossed the Indian Ocean. According to Allan Fraser, when they finally arrived in Australia Curtin reacted like 'a man released from great darkness and unhappiness'.

The burden of war leadership was almost more than Curtin could bear, and he sought to shift that part of it relating to strategic decisions onto his military commanders. He recalled General Blamey from the Middle East to take charge of the Australian army. However, Blamey's return in late March was overshadowed by the arrival just days earlier of the American general, Douglas MacArthur, appointed by Roosevelt with Curtin's agreement as Supreme Commander of the South-West Pacific Area. On his arrival, MacArthur told Curtin: 'You take care of the rear and I will handle the front.' This was what Curtin wanted to hear. As he assured Blamey when welcoming him back to Australia, the government would not interfere with their military decisions since 'military matters are for military men'. MacArthur not only removed much of the responsibility for strategic decisionmaking from Curtin's shoulders, but his very presence seemed to be reassuring proof that Australia would not be abandoned by the Allies, with MacArthur pledging 'all the mighty power of my country and all the blood of my countrymen'.

The country needed not just troops and aeroplanes to defend the continent but landing grounds, roads and docks, particularly across the sparsely populated north. Curtin appointed his old Labor colleague E. G. Theodore to head an Allied Works Council and gave him draconian powers to ensure that labour and resources were provided for the council's urgent construction work. He also sent Evatt off to Washington and London to seek military supplies. In a radio broadcast to the American people, Curtin claimed that Australia was 'fighting mad' and its people 'will trade punches' with the Japanese 'until we rock the enemy back on his heels'.

Evatt's trip proved largely fruitless, although it did finally confirm for Curtin the secret Anglo-American agreement to fight a holding war in the Pacific while concentrating the weight of Allied strength on the defeat of Germany. While this agreement left Australia dangerously exposed to invasion during the first half of 1942, the American naval victories of the Coral Sea and Midway Island in May and June 1942 effectively removed that threat. Fortunately, the Japanese had decided of their own accord that the capture of Australia would be too heavy a burden for their overstretched army. They decided instead to isolate Australia.

Curtin's stirring speeches during the first six months of the Pacific war had done much to unify and inspire the nation to a greater war effort. He expected that all Australians would be as willing as he was to devote their every waking hour, and even their lives if necessary, to the war effort. He had used the Battle of the Coral Sea to call on all Australians to match the devotion to duty being shown by the service personnel fighting to secure their safety. The speech, made in Parliament, was delivered with all the sincerity and emotion that Curtin was capable of mustering. Don Rodgers claimed that it brought tears to the eyes of half the journalists in the press gallery. Ross Gollan reported in the *Sydney Morning Herald* that everyone in the audience emerged that afternoon 'a better Australian'.

While Australia was secure from invasion, Curtin's task as prime minister became even harder as he called for a total war effort in the face of growing public complacency. For a time, he continued to argue, despite the naval victories, that Australians still 'face invasion, and the horrors that accompany it'. The Japanese landings in New Guinea in July 1942 and the subsequent landward attack on Port Moresby seemed to bear out his warnings. Against the background of these desperate battles, Curtin called for a 'season of austerity' as his government introduced rationing on all manner of civilian goods, from tea and sugar to clothes. By October 1942, the American minister in Canberra, Nelson Johnson, was able to assure Roosevelt of the tremendous transformation in the Australian outlook that Curtin had been able to achieve. The 'black blanket of despair' had been lifted, thanks largely to Curtin's 'honesty of purpose' and 'innate integrity'.

Curtin's hold over the party and the people was seen in his introduction of conscription for overseas service. The issue had been raised by the conservatives ever since Curtin's accession to power, and particularly after Pearl Harbor. Although Curtin had argued that it was unnecessary and needlessly divisive, the fighting in New Guinea gave it an added political edge, since the conscripted militia there were not allowed to pursue the Japanese across the border into Dutch New Guinea, nor could they accompany MacArthur forward to the Philippines. The whole question was highlighted by the American press, and the Opposition planned to emphasise it during the 1943 election campaign.

Curtin raised the issue of conscription at a Labor Conference in November 1942 and, after bitter protests from Arthur Calwell and others, allowed it to be referred to the various state executives of the party. At a subsequent special Conference in January 1943, his proposal in favour was approved. Curtin partly appeased the consequent bitterness in Labor ranks by severely restricting the area to which conscripts could be sent. This effectively defused conscription as a political issue for Labor at the forthcoming election but opened up divisions within the Opposition as Menzies formed a dissident group pushing for one Australian army, combining conscripts and volunteers and able to be sent anywhere.

Curtin's handling of the conscription issue showed the canny political footwork that allowed him to remain Labor leader for ten years. Despite having to rely for nearly two years on the support of two independent MPs for his survival, he was able to provide strong and inspirational leadership during the nation's most difficult time. His leadership contrasted sharply with the previous two years under Menzies, and ensured the ALP's overwhelming election victory in August 1943. Instead of Labor being caught out over conscription, the conservatives under the seventy-nine-year-old Billy Hughes were wrong-footed by allegations, first raised by the feisty Labor MP Eddie Ward, that they had been willing to abandon to the Japanese all of Australia north of the so-called 'Brisbane Line', from Brisbane to Adelaide. Labor was also favoured for offering a hopeful vision of the postwar world.

The 1943 election was a triumphant vindication of Curtin's war leadership, giving Labor control of both Houses of Parliament. In its wake, Billy Hughes was deposed for the last time and Robert Menzies given another chance as conservative leader. It was perhaps in response to Menzies' return that Curtin marked the last two years of his prime ministership with protestations of loyalty to Britain. He had become disenchanted with the American 'saviours' and worried about their designs on the South Pacific. At least with Britain Australia could assert an increasing amount of independence within the waning imperial system. This was the thinking that lay behind the Anzac Agreement of January 1944, which saw Australia and New Zealand join together in a declaration seeking to limit the spread of American influence to north of the equator.

In the face of American hostility, Curtin quietly shelved the Anzac Agreement when he travelled to Washington and London in April 1944. His primary purpose during this trip was to obtain Anglo-American approval for Australia to shift the balance of its war effort to producing food and other supplies, rather than providing personnel for the services. With MacArthur having no intention of taking Australian troops forward with him towards Tokyo, Curtin found ready agreement for his plans. He was not successful, though, in obtaining agreement from other Dominion leaders for a proposed Imperial Secretariat that would co-ordinate the foreign policy of the Empire. However, his attempt to do so successfully neutralised any conservative attack on Labor for being disloyal to the Empire. He was determined, so he said privately, to end the conservatives' 'monopoly of the Union Jack'. To this end, he had secured the appointment of the king's brother, the Duke of Gloucester, as governor-general, despite its being Labor policy that an Australian be appointed. This helped smooth Curtin's way in London, as did his comment that Australians were 'seven million Britishers'.

Curtin returned to Australia exhausted by the stress of travelling. Part of the trip was by air, which he feared, and part by sea across the Pacific Ocean, where Japanese submarines were still exacting a toll from Allied shipping. His heart was giving out and he seemed to know it. He returned to face a referendum that sought to give the government greater powers over the peacetime economy, but he took little part in the campaign and the referendum was roundly defeated. Although Elsie had accompanied him to America, she returned to Perth while he remained in Canberra alone, as he had done for most of the war. The manageress of the Kurrajong Hotel, where Curtin usually stayed in preference to the Lodge, together with her two farming brothers, provided him with close friendships in Canberra and helped keep him away from alcohol when Elsie was not there.

The stressful toll of Curtin's position, combined with a heavy cigarette habit, his past alcohol abuse and a diet rich in animal fats, wore away at his health. After a brief visit home to Perth in October 1944 Curtin suffered a serious heart attack in Melbourne on 3 November. Hospitalised for nearly two months, he did not resume his duties until late January 1945. Despite his poor health, his commitment to the party and the nation would not allow him to retire. Back in Parliament he faced an energetic Opposition, newly formed into the Liberal Party under Menzies and anxious to derail the measures Labor was planning for postwar Australia. Curtin was unable to cope and was back in hospital in April with congestion of the lungs. Released to the Lodge, he never recovered sufficiently to resume his duties. On 5 July 1945, with victory in the Pacific just six weeks away, he died, to almost universal dismay.

Francis Michael Forde

6 JULY 1945 – 13 JULY 1945

... an ideal deputy, the 'wind beneath the wings' of three men who flew high. There was no question about his devotion to his party and its leaders, so Prime Ministers Scullin, Curtin and Chifley could always count on his staunch support.

BY ELAINE BROWN

Frank Forde, deputy to John Curtin, stepped into the prime ministership when Curtin died and lost it to Ben Chifley a week later. Because of this and various contests in his long, eventful career, Forde has often been portrayed as one of Australia's political losers. This judgment, however, is unfair to the man and underrates his contribution to Australian public life. He was essentially a team player, and the story of his service to party and Parliament raises critical questions about the nature of leadership and the ways in which a political career can be influenced by perceptions, changing circumstances – and just plain luck.

As a mature politician, Forde enjoyed considerable support within the Federal Parliamentary Labor Party, and for fourteen years his peers readily elected him deputy leader to more charismatic men. Although he was never elected prime minister in his own right, it can be said that Forde – personable, hard-working, astute and respected – was an ideal deputy, the 'wind beneath the wings' of three men who flew high. There was no question about his devotion to his party and its leaders, so Prime Ministers Scullin, Curtin and Chifley could always count on his staunch support.

Forde was born on 18 July 1890 at Mitchell, a small town on the newly laid western railway line in south-west Queensland. His Irish Catholic immigrant parents – John Forde, a railway foreman, and Ellen, née Quirk – named him Francis Michael. He was the second son and second child in a close family of four sons and two daughters.

At the local primary school Forde was such a bright pupil that his parents made sacrifices to send him to a school conducted by the Christian Brothers in Toowoomba, where he stayed until the age of twenty, completing his secondary education while training and working as a teacher. This experience encouraged a lifelong interest in reading and learning, and his spare-time activity of debating gave him the skills from which he developed his formal style of public speaking.

Although his background and upbringing were typical of a man who might engage in Labor politics, the young Forde did not consider a political career. His ambition to better himself and please his parents led him to follow a number of occupations that required study, and he became in turn a railway clerk, a telegraphist at the Brisbane GPO and a telephone technician. In 1914 he was transferred to the Rockhampton post office as assistant to the district engineer.

As president of the Rockhampton branch of a patriotic friendly society known as the Australian Natives' Association, Forde became drawn into the public debates of the period. He was soon noticed by James Larcombe, MLA for the seat of Keppel, who in 1915 invited him to join the Australian Labor Party and became his mentor. This was a heady time for the ALP in Queensland. T. J. Ryan had just become premier in a run of power that was to last, with only one break, for forty years. It was also the time of World War I, and the issue of conscription split the nation. Although he had a brother in the army, Forde opposed conscription and spoke against it at public rallies. In 1916, when John Adamson, the member for Rockhampton in the Queensland Parliament, resigned from the ALP over conscription, twenty-six-year-old Forde vigorously contested the subsequent by-election. With campaign support from Premier Ryan, the blue-eyed 'boy with pearly teeth and rosy cheeks' won the seat by 657 votes.[1]

Forde's maiden speech in the Queensland Parliament in July 1917 revealed unusual confidence, practised oratory, thorough preparation and a good grasp of issues.[2] He worked hard in his electorate, advocated the popular 'new states' policy of the Central Queensland Separation Movement and was returned for Rockhampton in the elections of 1918 and 1920. Since membership of a trade union was a distinct advantage in Labor politics, he belatedly joined the Electrical Trades Union in 1919.

In 1921 the Theodore Labor government passed the controversial Legislative Assembly Act Amendment Act, designed to permit a state member who stood unsuccessfully for the federal Parliament to return to his state seat without having to face an election.[3] Because Frank Forde was seen to be the first potential beneficiary of this legislation, it became known derisively as the 'Forde Enabling Bill'. Federal Parliament countered the Queensland move by amending the Commonwealth Act of 1902, and in October 1922 Forde resigned Rockhampton to contest the huge federal seat of Capricornia, which had become vacant because the sitting member, William Guy Higgs, had been expelled from the ALP and had joined the Nationalists. Forde won Capricornia and held it for twenty-four years. When he arrived at the Parliament in Melbourne, he was, as he had been in Queensland, the youngest member.

On 25 February 1925, at the age of thirty-five, Forde married Veronica (Vera) Catherine O'Reilly of Wagga Wagga, New South Wales. After his marriage, which produced a son and three daughters, he faced the difficulties of combining family life and electorate responsibilities at Rockhampton in the north of the country with parliamentary duties in the distant south.

Forde began his apprenticeship for ministerial office in 1927, when he served on the Royal Commission on the Moving Picture Industry, for which the commissioners travelled 27,000 kilometres, interviewed 250 witnesses and produced a comprehensive report.[4] On the election of the Scullin Labor government in 1929, he was appointed to the public accounts committee and made assistant to James Fenton, the minister for trade and customs. When Fenton resigned in 1930, Forde became minister for trade and customs, and in 1931 he was also acting minister for markets and transport. In these portfolios he showed a capacity for conscientious and efficient administration, but the protectionist tariff policies he pursued did little to solve the problems of the Great Depression.

In an atmosphere of deep division, Forde supported Prime Minister Scullin's acceptance of the deflationary Premiers' Plan, by which the state premiers sought to counter the Depression by increasing taxation and reducing interest rates and government expenditure. Then the Labor government cracked and, perceived to have abandoned its principles on wages and welfare, was soundly defeated in the 1931 elections. Forde, surviving in Capricornia, was elected deputy leader of a greatly reduced Federal Parliamentary Labor Party and performed so well that when Scullin resigned through ill-health in 1935, Forde was expected to become leader. However, supporters of John Curtin, who had opposed the Premiers' Plan, urged him to stand and lobbied on his behalf. Curtin was elected by 11 votes to 10. Forde, stunned but gracious in defeat, remained deputy leader.[5]

Under Curtin's outstanding leadership, the Labor Party was reunited. In 1940, after the outbreak of World War II, Forde was elected as one of three ALP representatives on the all-party Advisory War Council. From 1941, when Curtin became wartime prime minister, Forde served in the War Cabinet and managed the thankless army portfolio, dealing, not always harmoniously, with the forceful General Sir Thomas Blamey.[6]

For four years, while continuing to carry out his administrative and parliamentary duties, Forde shared the exhausting and unwelcome burden of conducting the war. Acutely aware of the problems of raising resources and manpower to defend Australia, he supported Curtin through painful though necessary policy changes: on conscription, for example, which went against long-held beliefs, on the withdrawal of Australian troops from the Middle East for the defence of the Pacific, and on the need for Australia to turn for assistance from Britain to the United States. However, when it was proposed that Australian defence forces might withdraw strategically from the northern third of the continent if the Japanese invaded, Forde stood firm. He opposed the 'Brisbane Line' plan, which would have seen his Capricornia electorate abandoned, and was instrumental in ensuring that the whole of Australia would be defended. [7] He served twice as acting prime minister and minister for defence – from April to July 1944, when Curtin was overseas, and from October 1944 to January 1945, when Curtin was ill.

In 1944 Forde led an Australian ministerial delegation to New Zealand and was made a Privy Councillor. In 1945 Curtin chose both Forde and the minister for external affairs, Dr Herbert Vere Evatt, to lead an Australian delegation, first to the Commonwealth Ministers' Conference in London and then to the San Francisco Conference for International Co-operation. Forde's presence as a senior minister irritated the brilliant Evatt, who nevertheless managed to shine during the negotiations, which led to the signing of the United Nations Charter.[8]

While Forde was overseas, Ben Chifley served as acting prime minister during John Curtin's final illness and was favoured by Curtin to succeed him. Forde arrived home three days before Curtin's death on 5 July, and the next day was sworn in as caretaker prime minister. A week later a ballot of the Federal Parliamentary Labor Party made Ben Chifley prime minister, and Forde resumed the role of loyal, long-serving deputy.

As minister for defence in the Chifley government, Forde supervised the demobilisation of the armed forces, becoming unpopular when he refused appeals to release some servicemen early, and even more unpopular when his public statements on the rate of demobilisation proved to be too optimistic. His wartime devotion to duty went unrewarded. He was accused of having lost touch with his electorate, which was experiencing severe drought, and he was also criticised for moving his family to Sydney during the war. In the postwar election of September 1946, he lost Capricornia to a war hero, Lt-Col Charles W. Davidson.

Forde's defeat, however, was followed by one of the happiest periods of his life. In 1947 he moved with his family to Ottawa, Canada, where for seven years he served as Australian high commissioner. All the attributes and skills that had made him popular as a young politician came into play as he travelled and entertained, promoting and interpreting his country so successfully that the Menzies Liberal government extended his original appointment by one year.

Returning to Queensland in 1954, Forde did not consider retirement. Instead he worked as an organiser for the Queensland ALP, stood unsuccessfully in the seat of Wide Bay, and then won a by-election for the northern seat of Flinders. Returning to the Queensland Parliament as a backbencher was not easy for a man who had held high office, but the reliable Forde, although a Catholic, was considered a potential leader of mainstream Labor when the ALP was shattered by the bitter sectarian battle known as the Split. In 1957, after expelling Premier Vince Gair, the Queensland ALP was decimated at the polls. Forde lost Flinders, first by one vote, and then, after an appeal to the electoral commission which resulted in a fresh election, by a larger margin. Present near the strong beginning of the ALP's forty-year run in Queensland, Forde was also caught up in its ignominious end.

Bowing out of active politics at the age of sixty-nine, Forde appeared twice more in public. In 1964 Prime Minister Robert Menzies sent him to represent Australia at the funeral of the American general, Douglas MacArthur, with whom he had worked closely during the war; and in 1972 Prime Minister Gough Whitlam invited him to lunch in Canberra, to celebrate with other surviving stalwarts the return to power of a federal Labor government.

Forde lived in independent and healthy retirement in Brisbane until his death on 28 January 1983 at the age of ninety-two. The deaths of his only son Gerard in 1966 and his wife Vera in 1967 were great personal blows, but he was sustained by the company of old friends and enjoyment of his family, including his daughter-in-law, Canadian-born Leneen Forde, who was to serve as Queensland's first woman governor from 1992 to 1997.

Forde's biographer, David Gibson, has suggested that during times of dissension and division within the ALP, Forde's propensity to put the party first sometimes conflicted with his own beliefs and judgment, and that he often felt misunderstood. In the long term, however, his faithfulness to principle rather than to personal ambition enabled him to ride out political storms with his integrity intact. Realistic in the face of disappointment, he carried into extreme old age a lack of bitterness and a continuing engagement with life that won the admiration of people who knew him.

Forde was given a state funeral in Brisbane. After the interment, Senator John Button and federal Labor leader Bill Hayden had a heart-to-heart talk which resulted in Hayden's standing aside to allow Bob Hawke to become leader of the ALP and subsequently prime minister.[9] With his capacity for appreciating the twists and turns of fate and politics, Forde would almost certainly have been amused.

Joseph Benedict Chifley

13 JULY 1945 – 19 DECEMBER 1949

What made Chifley special as a leader ... was that in his everyday dealings with people he genuinely and effortlessly symbolised the ideals of the labour movement.

BY ROSS MCMULLIN

Ben Chifley was one of his nation's most impressive prime ministers. Australia's Treasurer for four years, he continued in that position after his elevation to the prime ministership in 1945. For the next four years he retained that dual role, widely seen at the time as a daunting workload and regarded ever since as a barely conceivable combination; no one during the half century since the Chifley government has attempted to be prime minister and treasurer concurrently.[1] Partly as a result of holding both those positions, Chifley dominated his government more than most Australian prime ministers.

Chifley has a hallowed place in his party's history. He remains one of Labor's most revered leaders. In any selection of a notional all-time ALP ministry he would probably be shaded by Curtin for the top job, but his loyalty and solidarity as well as his capacity and popularity would make him a certainty for the position of deputy leader, and he would have very strong claims to be treasurer. His evocative labelling of Labor's objective as 'the light on the hill' has enjoyed enduring prominence and appeal. With Curtin, he confirmed through his prime ministership that the labour movement could provide Australia with more capable leadership than any pre-1941 government had managed.

Joseph Benedict Chifley was born on 22 September 1885 at Bathurst, New South Wales. Eldest son of a local native-born blacksmith and his Irish-born wife, young Ben was separated from his parents and younger brothers at the age of five. For the next nine years he rarely saw them while he lived at his grandfather's farm about twenty kilometres north-east of Bathurst at Limekilns, where he slept on chaffbags in a humble wattle-and-daub shack with an earthen floor and helped out with farm chores. Schooling was part-time and very basic; long afterwards Chifley admitted he would rather have had the educational opportunities of his political opponent R.G. Menzies than a million pounds.

It was an upbringing dominated by solitude; any company he had usually consisted of appreciably older adults. As a result Chifley developed a youthful resourcefulness and responsibility, a maturity beyond his years. He also became a voracious reader, which helped overcome the deficiencies of his education as well as being a typical response to childhood loneliness. Another probable consequence was the strong emphasis that became evident in his adult personality on being and staying in a group, a sense of belonging and a reluctance to sever associations, which inclined him towards the labour movement and remained a feature of his influential involvement in both its industrial and political wings.

In adulthood he did not focus on the impact of this separation from his family as a youngster. What he did single out as influential was the misery he observed in the 1890s depression. There were signs of what was to come even before he returned to live with his parents and brothers in Bathurst after his grandfather's death in 1899. Asked one evening at Limekilns what he wanted to do in later life, he lifted his nose from a book momentarily: 'Member of parliament,' he replied.[2]

Attending a Bathurst high school briefly, he found he was behind most of his contemporaries because of his part-time schooling at Limekilns, despite the diverse reading that continued to be his main recreation (he also enjoyed playing and following sport). He entered the workforce as a junior employee in a local store and hated it; the wealthy proprietor, a pillar of his local church, exploited the staff, so young Ben joined the NSW Railways instead. Attending classes four nights a week and studying assiduously for over a decade, he progressed so rapidly that he became fully qualified as a first-class engine driver, the youngest in the state.

Chifley liked engine-driving immensely. The power of the engines, the sound of the whistle that was like 'music to me',[3] even the long evening trips through difficult mountain country – he enjoyed it all. Chugging along 'at night with fourteen carriages behind' gave him 'a lot of pleasure', he enthused. 'There was always something fascinating about the eyes of fourteen carriages looking at you round the bends.'[4] He also developed a reputation among railwaymen – and, in due course, beyond – as an informed, loyal and effective activist in the trade union movement.

In June 1914 he married Elizabeth McKenzie, daughter of a fellow train driver. 'During our courtship days', she later recalled, 'Ben talked to me mainly about politics and economics'.[5] She was as devoutly Presbyterian as he was Roman Catholic. It was a time of pronounced sectarianism, and prevailing Catholic doctrine outlawed 'mixed marriage'. The consequences of getting married in a Protestant church by a Protestant minister made it a momentous step for a committed

Catholic like Chifley, but he was also committed to Elizabeth. 'One of us has to take the knock', he said. 'It'd better be me.'[6]

The labour movement was engulfed by traumatic upheaval during the Great War. Chifley opposed conscription for overseas military service, the issue at the heart of Labor's devastating schism, and in 1917, when a tumultuous transport dispute erupted in Sydney and Bathurst railwaymen came out in support, he became prominently involved as one of the strike leaders. The authorities recruited 'loyalists' (scabs) to maintain a limited transport service, and eventually the strikers in Sydney gave up although their Bathurst comrades wanted to fight on. The strikers were vindictively punished in contravention of the settlement terms, losing seniority and accrued entitlements, in contrast to the preferential treatment enjoyed by loyalists. Chifley himself was dismissed, although his leadership throughout the strike had been constructive and measured.

Though belatedly reinstated, he was unable to resume as a driver. He had to put up with working under men he had either trained himself or knew to have scabbed during the strike. It was humiliating, and financially obnoxious as well. The 'instructor has been fireman to his pupil',[7] he observed; the strike had left an enduring 'legacy of bitterness and a trail of hate'.[8] Chifley's persistent endeavours to have these injustices corrected were at last rewarded by one of the first actions of incoming premier Jack Lang after his victory in the 1925 NSW election, when Lang restored the 1917 strikers' seniority and entitlements.

By then Chifley had decided to pursue a parliamentary career himself. Winning ALP preselection for the federal electorate of Macquarie (which included his beloved Bathurst), he was unsuccessful at the 1925 election but, re-endorsed three years later, was this time victorious, as Labor captured eight seats from the coalition government. Macquarie was extensive and dauntingly diverse – the Blue Mountains and the western plains, affluent resorts and mixed farming, coalminers and fruitgrowers. Essentially a country electorate, Macquarie was not easy for Labor to capture or keep.

Within a year, however, Chifley retained it with a substantially increased majority at the election that removed the discredited coalition from office. The forty-four-year-old new member for Macquarie joined jubilant caucus colleagues in Canberra to celebrate the advent of the first national ALP government since the conscription split. Ahead of them, however, was a demoralising sequence of events. The Great Depression, coming on top of the difficult financial situation the Scullin government inherited, once again triggered explosive tensions within the ALP. Bitter breakaway groups on both the left and right of official Labor perpetuated the rupture of party cohesion. As the government disintegrated Chifley remained characteristically loyal, and had a brief stint in Cabinet. While he was to regret his support of the notorious Premiers' Plan reductions, at the time he was motivated by the Labor principle of displaying solidarity in upholding an unpopular majority decision made by the party entity (in this case Cabinet) authorised to make it. As Defence minister he was quietly impressive, enhancing his reputation and gaining valuable experience in administration and the ways of the bureaucracy. But there was an anti-Labor landslide at the 1931 federal election that swept away no fewer than seven of Scullin's ministers; among them was Chifley, swamped in Macquarie by the irresistible tide.

Internal problems had plagued the New South Wales ALP for much of the 1920s, but became even worse in the 1930s when Lang and his followers hijacked the state branch in defiance of the party's federal authorities. Chifley had been relatively uninvolved in the chaotic 1920s ructions, but he was a prominent crusader in the fierce fight against the Langites during the 1930s. From 1934 he was president of the 'official' federal ALP in New South Wales, and he challenged Lang directly at the 1935 state election, standing as the federal ALP candidate in his powerful adversary's stronghold of Auburn. In this fierce contest the odds were stacked against Chifley, but he persevered; he lost, predictably and convincingly, and permanently damaged his vocal cords in the process, but helped pave the way for the eventual revival of the federal ALP in his state, which was crucial to its prospects of national resurgence. (A reminder long afterwards that he had once been described in the early 1920s as 'the silver-tongued orator of the West' produced a chuckle, then a quip in that familiar gravelly rasp: 'There's no silver there now, boy, just a lot of rusty old chains knocking together.'[9])

Even in the hostile environment of Auburn, Chifley's electioneering dexterity was grudgingly acknowledged. At his initial meeting, with Langites out in force to give him a hot reception, Chifley's anti-Lang ally Bill Colbourne became increasingly anxious:

> At eight o'clock Ben Chifley wasn't there, and I was running around trying to find him, all excited. About ten past eight Ben strolled in. I said, 'Quick! Hurry up. This meeting'll be in an uproar in a minute if you don't get up on that stage.' And Ben said, 'Aw, they know I'm coming. They'll wait, they'll wait. They've got their minds made up, Bill, they'll wait.' Well, he went out on to the stage, and there *was* uproar, but when it subsided he said, 'I owe this meeting an apology. I'm very sorry to be late, but there's a reason for it. I arrived in Auburn early enough this evening, but I've been up to my knees in paspalum, trying to get here, I've been slipping on unmade footpaths and in gutters, I've been crossing roads with potholes in them, and we wouldn't tolerate this class of stuff even in the outskirts of Bathurst where I'm an alderman. But here in this district I understand that Mr Lang has been the mayor for a long time, and I think I'm entitled to blame *him*.'

Even the 'most rabid Langite realised the humour of it', Colbourne affirmed, admiring Chifley's skill in taking the sting out of his audience's antagonism.[10]

It was also in 1935 that a special opportunity came Chifley's way. The Lyons government invited him to become a Labor representative on its Royal Commission into banking and finance. Lyons was a former caucus colleague and admirer: when he had removed himself from the Scullin government to lead Labor's opponents, he tried to persuade Chifley to become his treasurer. Chifley's loyalty and solidarity made any such notion inconceivable, but this Royal Commission he regarded as a superb opportunity to familiarise himself with the whole financial system and government's role in it. He treated his eighteen months on the commission as a kind of higher education qualification. The commission's final report included criticism of the way the banking system had operated during the Great Depression and Chifley's firm minority advocacy of bank nationalisation.

By 1940, with World War II under way, Lang no longer in control in New South Wales and federal Labor on the way back under John Curtin, Chifley was ready to have another crack at Macquarie, which had been retained by Labor's opponents since 1931. Having won preselection and endured further Langite disruption, he had the misfortune to be hospitalised with double pneumonia throughout the election campaign.

Friends and comrades rallied to his aid in telling testimony to the support and loyalty he gave and inspired in others. Macquarie went to preferences, but Chifley prevailed.

The outcome in the overall election was even closer. Eventually it became clear that the 36 seats won by the government parties in the House of Representatives were matched by 32 Labor MPs and four Langite breakaways, with the balance of power to be held by two Victorian independents. In these circumstances some ALP luminaries hungry for office, notably the party's new glamour frontbencher Dr H. V. Evatt, wanted Curtin to seize the initiative decisively and push the fragile coalition over the brink. They felt frustrated and furious when Curtin refused. Chifley supported Curtin's more measured, patient approach. Like Scullin, another influential Curtin adviser, and Curtin himself, Chifley had firsthand experience of the difficulties a Labor government would face if it could not be certain of getting the numbers in Parliament. To survive without a majority in either chamber an ALP ministry would need every ounce of moral legitimacy it could muster; it was crucial to avoid being tainted by obnoxious opportunism.

Chifley's support of Curtin's approach was vindicated as the coalition sank into disarray and Labor took office with the independents' backing. The caucus ministerial ballot elevated Chifley into Cabinet, as expected – he had been a member of the caucus executive since the 1940 election – but his appointment as Treasurer, with only Curtin and Deputy Prime Minister Frank Forde above him in seniority, was a surprise. No lime-lighter, Chifley had been unobtrusive since returning to Parliament, staying out of the headlines (unlike Evatt and other colleagues) and making few speeches in the House. But his qualifications were compelling. His purposeful endeavours had endowed him with a sound grasp of public finance – Curtin (and Scullin) knew Chifley knew his stuff – and in a highly inexperienced Cabinet he was one of the few who had been a minister before.

Also influential was Curtin's personal reliance on Chifley. They had much in common. Both had stood unsuccessfully in 1925, won in 1928, experienced the turmoil and humiliation of the Scullin government and lost their seats in 1931. While Curtin had returned to Parliament before Chifley, they had also been firm allies in the prolonged internal struggle against the Langites. The support and solidarity Chifley provided were invaluable to the new prime minister, who felt daunted and occasionally overwhelmed by the relentless pressures of leading Australia in a global conflict that seemed to be threatening its very existence. Arriving in Canberra one evening after a long car journey from Bathurst, Chifley was given a message from Curtin summoning him to the Lodge: 'Come over whenever you arrive, I'm spiritually bankrupt tonight.'[11]

A feature of their close friendship was their complementary blend of attributes. Despite Chifley's heavy workload (in 1942 he became Minister for Postwar Reconstruction as well as Treasurer) he was always approachable and never seemed flustered or hurried. His natural aptitude for dealing with people enabled him to shield Curtin from some of the tasks the new prime minister found so draining. Chifley's capable management of the national economy and the financing of the war effort not only left Curtin free to concentrate on defence and war strategy; the Treasurer also received deputations and skilfully managed parliamentary business on Curtin's behalf, bringing more efficiency and flair to that important organisational role than had ever been seen in the House of Representatives. Curtin was often withdrawn and preoccupied with war problems, was uncomfortably distant from his backbenchers, and had intermittently testy relations with assertive ministers such as Evatt and Eddie Ward; Chifley, in contrast, was very popular in caucus, and Evatt and Ward were both fond of him. 'I would not like to think how I could carry on this job without what I get from old Ben', Curtin said.[12]

Only ten days after the Curtin government was sworn in, Chifley placed his Budget proposals before Cabinet. He lifted taxation on the wealthy and increased company, sales and land tax. In 1942, wary of inflation, he introduced controls on wages, prices and profits; he also initiated a national income tax scheme, which survived a High Court challenge by recalcitrant states and proved an enduringly significant reform. His administration was outstanding – Australia, numerous observers concluded, had known no finer treasurer – and, while no orator, he could defend his priorities in spirited fashion:

> For years the working class, which is now expected to assist in the conduct of the war, either on the battlefield or in the munitions factories, was treated worse than farm horses or pit ponies in the mines. They were thrown into the streets, where they were left to starve. Despite that treat-

> ment they are now expected suddenly to develop intense feelings of patriotism. To their eternal credit they have done so, although they have suffered the greatest privations because of the insistence of ... coalition governments upon the observance of an antiquated banking policy.[13]

And there were no special favours. Notorious ALP powerbroker John Wren telephoned Curtin to protest about one of Chifley's taxation measures – 'This bill hits Mr Theodore and myself very severely, and I want you to do something about it' – but Chifley's reply, relayed by Curtin, was that the legislation would proceed, and Wren should 'let Mr Theodore know that the Senate rejected a similar provision introduced by him in the days of the Scullin government'.[14]

Proper planning for the adjustment to peace was a high ALP priority, affirmed and reaffirmed at wartime party conferences. Curtin's appointment of Chifley as Postwar Reconstruction (PWR) minister clearly showed the importance the government attached to it. The new department attracted a variety of talented visionaries preoccupied with creating a better social climate than Australians had previously known. They wanted to avoid the dislocation of the previous transition from world war to peace and to help create international financial structures that would prevent the devastating economic crashes of the past. Above all they wanted to ensure full employment, despite the massive problems generated as thousands of Australians in the armed forces and other war work returned to peacetime activities. They were confident the doctrines of Keynesian economics would be the key. Under the benevolent eye of Chifley, a wholehearted Keynesian, the idealists flourished at PWR, plunging into exciting research and formulating optimistic plans for the future. Particularly notable was the White Paper entitled 'Full Employment in Australia', a detailed blueprint of the government's primary PWR goal and the foundation of Labor's aspirations for 'a new social order' in peacetime Australia.

The PWR Director-General, H. C. Coombs, was impressed by Chifley's blend of reformist idealism and realistic pragmatism. He was 'an exciting man to work for, because you could always submit an idea to him. If ... you thought there was an answer to a problem, you could put it up and you'd know he would listen. He could be excited by it, just as you could be excited by it yourself, but before it got through to the final stages Chif would expose it to the other aspect of his character by being exceedingly tough and critical both from the political and administrative point of view'.[15]

Chifley's administration was also shaped by 'his warm human outlook on people and their doings', according to another senior PWR official, Harold Breen; he was 'not concerned merely, like so many reformers, with a collective abstraction, but deeply interested in persons and in the realities of their daily lives'.[16] Journalist Oliver Hogue agreed:

> Chifley ... had a logical mind, but he humanized all his thinking, even on politics ... He understood the human heart, the ideals, the ambitions, the follies and the passions of men and women. Chifley put tolerance amongst the highest virtues, and he had it in large measure himself ... [He] was easy, courteous and considerate with great and small alike ... He took his great defeats as he took his great victories, with modesty and humility.[17]

Late in the war Curtin's health deteriorated alarmingly. It was a difficult time for those close to him, Chifley especially. As Curtin struggled on in office he became more tired, more temperamental and more tormented than ever; his absences in hospital added to Chifley's already onerous responsibilities. When Curtin was readmitted to hospital while Forde was overseas, Chifley was quietly impressive as acting prime minister for two months. Curtin died on 5 July 1945. Forde, now back home, was sworn in as prime minister pending the caucus election of Curtin's successor. Chifley was ambivalent about standing, but Scullin and others convinced him he should. He won the ballot easily.

Soon after being sworn in as Australia's sixteenth prime minister he was able to announce officially that Japan had surrendered. If anyone needed a break at the end of 1945 it was Chifley – as medical warnings he received from his doctor confirmed – but he decided to make a surprise trip to New Guinea to spend Christmas with Australian soldiers awaiting discharge there. He directed his press secretary Don Rodgers and private secretary Murray Tyrrell to organise it with the utmost secrecy. The top military brass were distinctly peeved when they arrived unexpectedly, but Chifley brushed this coolness aside and headed straight for the ordinary soldiers he had come to visit. Joining a group of privates without any formality, he sat down, introduced himself ('I'm

Chifley') and asked them how they were going. 'When we got back to Canberra,' Tyrrell later recalled, 'we spent days … making sure that Mum, wife or sweetheart got the message that Bill, John or Joe was well and fit.'[18] Before they returned, however, they encountered a severe storm that threatened to be too much for the plane conveying them. Chifley's calmness in adversity was memorable. He was somehow asleep despite the racket of the engines and the storm, but Tyrrell decided to wake him to pass on the pilot's warning that the plane and its occupants might soon find themselves in the ocean. 'Look, when we're in Canberra, in Parliament House and in my office, I'm the captain', Chifley proclaimed. 'Up here [the pilot's] the captain, there's nothing I can do about it and I'm going back to sleep'.[19] So he did; the pilot managed to keep their heads above water.

Chifley's integrity was undisputed. His word was his bond; once he committed himself he could not be shifted. You have to be 'scrupulously honest', he advised Fred Daly, 'but there's nothing to stop you being a bit bloody foxy'.[20] Daly, like many others, revered Chifley; he was not the only newcomer to appreciate the fatherly interest Chifley took in inexperienced MPs. As prime minister, Chifley continued to be remarkably accessible. Ministers or backbenchers with a problem or issue to raise would be tensely intent on minimising inroads into his time, aware of his immense workload as treasurer as well as prime minister, but Chifley would sit them down for a chat, ask about their family, and in due course unhurriedly direct the conversation back to the point at issue. He was very adept at maintaining contact with a wide range of friends and associates, sometimes ringing up for a meandering yarn that helped him stay informed and in touch with public sentiment.

There has surely never been a more down-to-earth, unpretentious Australian prime minister than Ben Chifley. 'Listen, son, never get your feet off the ground',[21] he would regularly counsel colleagues who might be developing swollen egos. Chifley practised what he preached. He preferred to stay on in his small room at the humble Kurrajong Hotel rather than move into the customary prime minister's residence, the Lodge, which he used only for distinguished guests. (Elizabeth Chifley remained at Bathurst; he joined her there whenever he could.) Shunning pomp and glamour, Chifley never owned a dinner suit and politely avoided engagements where he was expected to wear one. During a trip to England he was visited by a fussy stickler for protocol in connection with his imminent swearing-in as a member of the Privy Council; at the ceremony, Chifley was informed, he would have to wear kneebreeches. He predictably gave that idea short shrift, leaving the official nonplussed – 'I don't know, Mr Prime Minister, *what* we're going to do' – but Chifley amiably tapped him on the knee: 'I'll bet you two bob I'm still sworn in'.[22] The official trips Chifley made as prime minister were short, businesslike and economical; he was careful with taxpayers' money.

Six feet tall and ruggedly handsome, Chifley complemented his attractive appearance with an appealing personality that combined charm and humility with dignity and integrity. There was also a determined commitment to improving the lot of those most in need, and an insatiable appetite for the gruelling administrative grind that was part and parcel of accomplishing this objective. Chifley (according to his biographer L. F. Crisp) had 'a remorseless rather than a darting or an original intelligence. His power lay in his capacities for tenacious pursuit of problems as they presented themselves, for tireless sifting of the issues in terms of his Labor objectives, for realistic grasp of essentials, for patient mastering of practical detail and for simple, forceful exposition of his findings and solutions. To sum up, the basis of his strength was a remarkably keen, if largely self-tutored, intellect, matched with a zest for administration and a first class political temperament'.[23]

Nelson Lemmon, a talented member of Chifley's Cabinet, was particularly impressed by his chief's 'terrific capacity' for penetrating documentary analysis; Lemmon could take hours to dissect a lengthy detailed proposal, but 'you'd take it to him, and he'd simply read through it and he'd pick out the faults in a couple of minutes that you might have taken half a day to get. He just seemed to have that gift of going through a great document, a great submission, and being able to tell you, virtually within the twinkle of an eye, whether it was right or wrong, where its failures were. The work he did was prodigious'.[24]

Chifley would typically be in his office by around 8.30am, and it would not be until midnight, or later still, that he sauntered back to the Kurrajong in his distinctive slouching gait. Meals he begrudged as an unnecessary interruption, but he routinely shut his office door at lunchtime while he consumed his regular tea and toast and, as in his engine-driving days, curled up for a brief snooze. His pipe was never far away and became an entrenched accessory in his public image, though some observers sensed he used more matches than tobacco.

Under Chifley the government maintained its reform momentum. Returned soldiers were provided with a war gratuity and entitlement to vocational training, loans, special unemployment allowances and preference in employment for seven years. Every effort was made to avoid the mistakes made in arrangements for soldiers returning from the Great War. Soldier settlement schemes were organised much better this time. Returned soldiers benefited, along with other Australians, from the creation of the Commonwealth Employment Service. Australia's national government involved itself more extensively in education than ever before, acknowledging its responsibility to returned soldiers as well as introducing a scheme of university scholarships. Lengthy discussions and negotiations about a planned revival of peacetime construction culminated in a housing agreement binding all state governments and complementing priorities for major construction activity outside the housing sector. Australia's vital export industries, wool and wheat, were given firm postwar foundations. Plans were advanced for the establishment of an Australian motor vehicle industry. An imaginative immigration scheme was launched (and proved outstandingly successful, benefiting Australia in a variety of ways). Life insurance was comprehensively regulated. Understandable ALP concerns about hostile media coverage prompted the government to legislate that the Australian Broadcasting Commission had to establish its own news service and broadcast proceedings of the national Parliament. The Hospital Benefits Act established free public ward treatment by introducing hospital subsidies to the states.

Chifley was spearheading the heyday of 1940s Labor. With the war over, his government could focus wholeheartedly on reforming Australia. Immensely influential was the calamitous Great Depression and the paramount necessity to avoid a repetition. No member of the government was more committed to this priority than the prime minister himself. The hardships and miseries of the 1930s and his assessment of their causes were abiding preoccupations; he was determined to provide security for Australians who most needed it. 'I have been unable to hate anybody', he observed. 'The only things I hate are the want, misery and insecurity of any people in any country.'[25] He maintained a tight rein on the economy, retaining wartime controls to keep a lid on the postwar inflationary pressure he dreaded as the potential instigator of a replay of the 1930s. Prices, imports, rents and the states continued to be curbed, rationing was retained and consumer demand contained; the financing of Australia's immense war effort did not (unlike what happened in the Great War) result in an escalation of overseas debt, which was in fact substantially reduced, an especially creditable achievement. The impact of the Depression was of course acutely familiar not just to Chifley, but to millions of Australians as well; there was considerable support for the wide-ranging initiatives his government implemented with firm centralised control (although by the end of the 1940s it was increasingly apparent that many Australians wanted the restrictions removed). Chifley's accomplished stewardship contributed significantly to the relatively smooth economic sailing of the 1950s and 1960s.

'Leave it to the Doc', Chifley would often say when a policy issue arose concerning Evatt's portfolio responsibilities as Attorney-General and Foreign Affairs Minister. This was understandable in view of Evatt's awesome intellect and mercurial brilliance as draftsman and international statesman, but his inept handling of appointments to the High Court confirmed that leaving it to the Doc was not always a good idea because his political judgment was unreliable; Chifley, in fact, did sometimes overrule him. Support for Britain, weakened by years of desperate struggle against Hitler's Germany, was a foreign policy priority for Chifley. Suspicious of American initiatives designed, he felt, to supplant Britain as Australia's closest powerful ally, he arranged for his government to assist Britain financially in a number of ways.

Chifley and his government received a heartening re-endorsement from the people at the 1946 election. Although Labor lost seven seats, the ALP primary vote had hardly altered since the remarkable triumph of 1943, which had been a stunning landslide and the most comprehensive victory Chifley's party had ever achieved in federal politics; moreover, Labor had never before won successive federal elections. So the overall outcome in 1946, despite the defeat of Forde and another minister, was undeniably satisfying. Labor also increased its majority in the Senate, but had mixed success with three constitutional referenda submitted to the electorate concurrently with the election. The proposed enlargement of the national government's power over social security was approved by the voters, but two other extensions, concerning employment and marketing, failed very narrowly.

A feature of Chifley's leadership was his skilful handling of caucus. In fiery party meetings he was adept at soothing tensions. When a press controversy arose over substandard conditions aboard the *Yoizuki*, a former Japanese destroyer conveying prisoners of war back to Japan, backbencher Allan Fraser became animated about it although most Australians were desensitised to such concerns at that time because of the terrible experiences endured in Japanese captivity. Nevertheless Fraser was very steamed up, and passionately insisted in caucus that action was essential. 'Don't get your blood pressure up, Allan', Chifley responded, adding that a Labor MP 'was in Orange at the weekend and he thought he would test out public feeling about this matter, so he asked a person in the street what he thought of the *Yoizuki* case and the chap replied, "It's a scandal – the trainer, jockey and horse should get life".'[26] The tension dissolved into unrestrained mirth.

Fraser and others noticed that Chifley frequently managed to steer caucus skilfully in the direction he wanted on particular issues involving the perennial conflict between principle and pragmatism. Summing up after a lengthy debate when everyone who wanted a say had been given one, Chifley would often say it was all very well to be practical, but the ALP was committed to principles and there were times when they had to be upheld irrespective of the cost. Alternatively, he would sometimes emphasise how much he admired Labor members with ideals, but there were times when commonsense should prevail. It was rare for him not to get the result he wanted.

This adroitness was displayed in his handling of the long-running Bretton Woods controversy. Chifley was convinced that it was desirable to establish the sort of international economic co-operation exemplified in the Bretton Woods agreement, which established an International Monetary Fund to supervise exchange rates and assist nations battling balance of payments problems; a World Bank would also provide loan capital in appropriate circumstances. However, traditional ALP hostility to the practitioners of high finance guaranteed that Chifley would have a difficult task persuading his party that Australia should ratify the agreement. He decided to shelve the issue temporarily, hoping opposition would subside as Labor's PWR reforms proceeded.

When debate resumed, however, he found hostility had abated minimally. Ward and other non-ratifiers revived memories of the Great Depression and the role of influential financiers in the demise of the Scullin government. But international economic co-operation was the best way of avoiding such crises, countered Scullin and other Bretton Woods advocates, and the agreement should be ratified even if its provisions were not ideally suited to Australia's particular requirements. When the ALP federal executive met in November 1946 half the delegates had been instructed (by the state branches they were representing) to oppose ratification, but after Chifley addressed the meeting he succeeded in achieving endorsement of ratification by a majority of 7 to 5. With caucus about to determine its position on the issue, this was a pleasing outcome for Chifley: under ALP rules the federal executive's decision was binding on caucus members and could only be overturned by Federal Conference, the supreme decision-making body in the party structure. Caucus grappled with the issue for three meetings. After spirited debate, a caucus motion to refer the issue to Federal Conference was upheld by 29 votes to 26.

Chifley accepted this setback with good grace and considered his options. A special Federal Conference could only occur if requested by at least four states. So if three state executives did not want one, no special Conference would take place and the federal executive's previous determination would therefore bind party members. While Ward and other activists were debating Bretton Woods publicly, Chifley concentrated on trying to persuade the state executives to see things his way. He was very pleased when three eventually announced their opposition to a special Conference on the question. With that option now ruled out, the prime minister reintroduced the issue to caucus in a shrewdly timed move, straight after informing Labor MPs that taxes would be reduced and pensions raised. On this occasion the caucus vote went his way, 33 votes to 24. This was a triumph for Chifley. He had to work long and hard to get there, but his tact, patience and acute grasp of the nuances and sometimes unwieldy processes of his party enabled him to obtain the result he wanted with the least possible disturbance to ALP cohesion. It was the equivalent for Chifley of Curtin's difficult struggle to amend party policy on conscription.

On banking policy, the most controversial issue of his prime ministership, Chifley stunned his colleagues. He had come to conclude that the changes required to prevent a repetition of the Scullin government's disastrous experience during the Great Depression could be achieved in legislation; Labor's 1945 Banking Act, he felt, had made nationalisation unnecessary. In August 1947, however, the High Court ruled an aspect of this legislation unconstitutional (in one of a series of decisions that frustrated the Curtin and Chifley governments and reinforced the impression gained by ALP supporters that the bench was reserving its most restrictive interpretations of the national government's constitutional powers for the times when Labor was politically ascendant). On the following Saturday morning Chifley and his Cabinet colleagues met to consider the government's response. Chifley himself had not wanted to include in the 1945 Banking Act the particular clause the court had just invalidated, but it was clear, he told his ministers, that the private banks planned to challenge other more vital aspects of the legislation. The government could either wait and react to these challenges as they arose or deal with them pre-emptively, in accordance with party policy, by nationalising banking. His ministers gradually realised he was recommending nationalisation. They were amazed, then jubilant. Chifley asked each minister in turn for his views. All supported nationalisation. 'Well, that's the decision then', Chifley concluded. 'Wait a minute', interjected Commerce and Agriculture minister Reg Pollard, 'what about you, Chif – where do you stand?' The reply was vintage Chifley: 'With you and the boys, Reggie, to the last ditch'.[27]

Chifley's reversion to his prewar advocacy of nationalisation was the crucial factor in this bombshell. As well as being a warmly admired leader, his expertise and experience on financial questions were profoundly respected. After what happened to the Scullin government, there was a keen resolve among Labor activists to ensure no subsequent ALP government would be so powerless to control the banks and the national economy. Once Chifley indicated he had lost his belief that Labor's banking objectives could be achieved without nationalisation, it was no surprise his ministers followed him so readily. Whether the banks would have proceeded to challenge other more vital provisions of the 1945 Banking Act, as Chifley concluded, remains unclear. Analysts sceptical that the banks were so minded have condemned the nationalisation decision as unnecessary as well as politically perilous. Its riskiness was crystal clear. Fervent opposition was inevitable.

The banks retaliated with a massive political and legal counter-offensive. No ALP reform in the entire history of the party has generated greater hostility. Bank nationalisation was condemned as the prelude to a host of dire calamities, including a communist takeover. Funds for this campaign were unlimited. Activists doorknocked assiduously, distributed countless leaflets and warned pensioners and other needy Australians that nasty Mr Chifley was plotting to steal their savings. ALP backbenchers in marginal seats, swamped by this anti-nationalisation torrent, needed colleagues' help just to open their mail; it was, Fred Daly affirmed, a 'frightening' propaganda deluge.[28] After a lengthy and celebrated legal contest the High Court ruled the nationalisation legislation unconstitutional; the government appealed to the Privy Council, unsuccessfully. So, after two years of hysteria and headlines, the Chifley government had sustained a severe reverse from the perspective of public perception. In fact a concession by the banks that they were now prepared to accept Labor's 1945 banking reforms enabled ALP enthusiasts to claim victory on the merits of the issue, but it was decidedly Pyrrhic in view of the damage inflicted on the government.

Another challenging issue for Prime Minister Chifley was the 1949 coal strike. Industrial upheaval was widespread in the immediate post-war era, but Chifley felt he had been instrumental in fixing the coal industry problems that had troubled both the Scullin and Curtin governments; he had been a prime mover in the establishment of a Coal Industry Tribunal to deal with industrial disputes and a Joint Coal Board to supervise and regulate the industry, its workforce and communities. The miners had already achieved significant gains under these arrangements, and further benefits were on the way.

Chifley readily acknowledged the hardships of a miner's life, but concluded that such a strike at such a time was unjustified. He felt it smacked of ingratitude after what his government had done for the miners, and also of calculated communist-inspired disruption designed to sabotage Labor's carefully planned economic achievements. (The strike occurred because miners not at all linked or sympathetic to communism had genuine industrial grievances, but the Communist Party did involve itself in this strike more fully than it had in any previous large Australian dispute.) The Chifley government, despite the misgivings of some senior ministers, acted firmly. Special legislation was introduced, which led to jail sentences for miners' union leaders and other prominent communist unionists. Many Labor enthusiasts were appalled, but by consulting widely Chifley kept ALP dissent within acceptable limits, even after the decision to send in the army to revive coal production. This highly controversial decision – the use of the armed forces in industrial disputes was specifically forbidden in the ALP platform, as it had been by Chifley himself as Defence minister in 1931 – was justified as unique action in unique circumstances to counter a political strike engineered by enemies of Labor. Soon afterwards the strike collapsed. It was a major setback for the Communist Party, but the public had endured substantial inconvenience during a harsh winter.

Two months later Chifley called an election. During the campaign he concentrated on Labor's proud record in government. Its accomplished management of the massive transition to peace without the widely feared adverse effects on employment and the economy was a magnificent feat; no individual was more responsible than Chifley. Since 1946 his government had passed more Acts and more significant legislation than had been enacted in any other national Parliament. As well as maintaining economic growth and full employment, it had played a visionary role in the successful establishment of the immigration program, the Australian National University, the Snowy Mountains Scheme and the Australian manufacture of the Holden car. Since 1941 pension levels had doubled and Labor had done more for farmers than the Country Party had managed since its genesis.

For some years Chifley had been using an original metaphor to describe Labor's overall objective. In mid-1949 he put it this way:

> I try to think of the labour movement, not as putting an extra sixpence into somebody's pocket, or making somebody prime minister or premier, but as a movement bringing something better to the people, better standards of living, greater happiness to the mass of the people. We have a great objective – the light on the hill – which we aim to reach by working for the betterment of mankind not only here but anywhere we may give a helping hand.[29]

He also used this phrase in his 1949 policy speech:

> It is the duty and the responsibility of the community, and particularly those more fortunately placed, to see that our less fortunate fellow citizens

> are protected from those shafts of fate which leave them helpless and without hope ... That is the objective for which we are striving. It is ... the beacon, the light on the hill, to which our eyes are always turned and to which our efforts are always directed.[30]

In contrast to Chifley's emphasis on Labor's 1940s record, his opponents were more inclined to focus on fresh initiatives (child endowment for the first child, abolition of the petrol rationing Chifley reintroduced shortly before the election) designed to capitalise on irritation with Labor's maintenance of 'controls'. Attempts were made to persuade Chifley to feature some new forward-looking initiatives during the campaign, but he was sceptical about pre-election sweeteners and doubtful about even the effectiveness of campaigning, believing voters had by and large decided months earlier. He was also determined not to relax his tight grip on the economy, and very hard to shift once he had made up his mind. Also, after eight demanding years at the apex of government, Chifley was jaded and in poor health. The upshot was that Labor's campaign was complacent and lacklustre. Its deficiencies were magnified by the disparity in campaign expenditure: the ALP's opponents had at their disposal an election budget probably more than ten times Labor's.

The result was a devastating defeat for Chifley and his government. Shattered Labor activists knew it was an election that should never have been lost. In fact there has probably never been – neither during the half century that followed, nor in the preceding half century since Federation – an ALP federal election defeat more avoidable, more undeserved and therefore more sickening for party supporters. Subsequent events, which consigned Labor to the wilderness of opposition for twenty-three years, sharpened the pain of this perception. Talented ministers lost their seats, including Nelson Lemmon and John Dedman, a potential future leader who never returned to Parliament. The 1949 election result is the biggest blot on Chifley's generally admirable record as a Labor leader and prime minister. His government had fallen, he observed, because people who could not afford a bus ticket when Labor came to office were now up in arms about petrol rationing.

Characteristically, though, he did not dodge responsibility for the defeat. Chifley's biggest defect as prime minister – the low priority he gave to the presentational, public relations side – had contributed substantially to the outcome. It was particularly evident in his handling of the bank nationalisation controversy, a crucial factor in his government's downfall. The announcement of the sensational Cabinet decision was confined to a brief, matter-of-fact statement Rodgers handed to journalists. Chifley evidently sensed a storm of outrage was inevitable whatever form the announcement took, and the government simply had to batten down the hatches and sail through it; but the abruptness of his terse statement, unsupplemented for weeks, squandered a valuable opportunity to publicise a reasoned case justifying the momentous decision, leaving the government vulnerable to charges of high-handedness and in effect handing Labor's opponents the initiative in the vital propaganda war, which they seized to full effect.

Also influential in the 1949 result was Chifley's increasing inflexibility. While consistency and reliability are commendable attributes, he did become too rigid at times. This development was fuelled by his exalted standing in the party; he was so esteemed by his colleagues that his judgment was rarely questioned. (If Curtin had relinquished the leadership before his health became irreparably damaged, Don Rodgers believed, he could have been for Chifley the valuable elder statesman adviser that Scullin had been for him.)

The fierce ongoing struggle within the labour movement concerning communist influence in the unions aggravated Chifley's difficulties in the wake of the 1949 election defeat. Internal party tensions were exacerbated by the advent in caucus of a group of anti-communist zealots. 'Those new Melbourne fellows have a bug', remarked Chifley, 'that's what's wrong with them'.[31] His difficulties intensified when the Menzies government sought to capitalise on Labor's internal problems by introducing legislation to ban the Communist Party. Chifley was opposed to the Bill himself, but in order to fashion a caucus response that all MPs could support he sided with – and publicly advocated – a policy of amending its more obnoxious features. However, the anti-communist crusaders forced the federal executive to direct caucus to allow the Bill through unamended. This was another damaging blow to party cohesion and an ignominious setback for Chifley personally. In caucus he did not hide his dismay, but urged his colleagues in a stirring speech to maintain solidarity: 'Accept your humiliation and we can go forward', he told them, 'recriminate, and we shall split'.[32]

Grappling with these difficulties accelerated the decline in Chifley's health. In November 1950 he suffered a heart attack, but was back in harness for the 1951 double dissolution election, proceeding with a gruelling campaign schedule for his party despite doctor's orders and his personal scepticism about the effectiveness of last-minute appeals to the voters. Labor lost. Six weeks later Chifley made a memorable speech at Labor's NSW state Conference, urging party members to keep 'fighting for what they think is right, whether it brings victory to the party or not'. 'You have to be quite clear about what you believe in, whether popular or unpopular, and you have to fight for it', he declared; 'if I think a thing is worth fighting for, no matter what the penalty may be, I will fight for the right, and truth and justice will always prevail'.[33] On 13 June 1951, three days after this inspiring speech, he suffered a fatal heart attack.

No Australian party leader, no prime minister, has been mourned more deeply. The profound widespread grief derived in large measure from Chifley's attractive personality and leadership style, the sense of comradely solidarity he instilled and personally embodied. He was capable, shrewd and an admirably productive reformer, but what made Chifley special as a leader, especially a Labor one, was that in his everyday dealings with people he genuinely and effortlessly symbolised the ideals of the labour movement more than any other leader in the ALP's entire history. While Curtin was greatly admired by his party, Chifley was greatly loved.

For Menzies' period in office 19 December 1949–26 January 1966, see pages 174–205.

Harold Edward Holt

26 JANUARY 1966 – 19 DECEMBER 1967

Holt's leadership ... marked the transition from [the Liberal government's] internal solidity and outward authority to a period of internecine struggle and leadership uncertainty, accompanied by electoral setbacks and culminating in defeat in 1972.

BY IAN HANCOCK

Harold Holt succeeded Sir Robert Menzies as prime minister on Australia Day 1966. Tony Eggleton, press secretary to both Menzies and Holt, knew that things would now be different. Summoned to meet the new prime minister, he found him dressed in his underclothes.

Holt had served a long apprenticeship. He had been a member of the House of Representatives since 1935, served as a minister between 1939 and 1941 and between 1949 and 1966 and been treasurer for seven years and deputy leader to Menzies for ten. When he finally stepped into the top job the Liberal Party was riding high throughout Australia. It was in government in five of the six states and had been in office in Canberra for just over sixteen consecutive years. A narrow victory in the federal election of 1961 was turned into a comfortable majority in 1963 and, although Holt did not control the Senate, he could feel secure so long as Arthur Calwell remained leader of the Labor Party. Yet within two years and despite a spectacular election victory in December 1966, the federal Liberal government began to develop the unmistakable signs of decline. Holt's leadership, in fact, marked the transition from internal solidity and outward authority to a period of internecine struggle and leadership uncertainty, accompanied by electoral setbacks and culminating in defeat in 1972.

The man who entered Parliament at just twenty-nine years of age did not set out to become a career politician. He was born in Sydney on 5 August 1908, the son of Australian-born parents. Life for him was comfortable if mundane in the early years. As a boy, he attended the Randwick state school, then boarded at Abbotsholme, Killara, where he first encountered William McMahon. But when his father Tom left school-teaching to run a hotel in Adelaide, Harold's world became very unsettled, and especially after Tom left the hotel trade to be a travelling theatrical manager. To salvage some degree of stability, Harold, then aged eleven, was sent with his elder brother Cliff to board at Wesley preparatory school in Melbourne.

Unlike Menzies, who had attended Wesley before him, the young Harold was not outstandingly clever. But he was very good at two things: sport and theatre. And he did manage to win a scholarship to Queen's College at Melbourne University, helped no doubt by the 50 per cent weighting in the selection criteria given to athleticism and character. At university, where he studied law, he played cricket, Australian Rules football and tennis, debated regularly, won a college metal for oratory, and became president of the Law Students' Society. Graduating in 1930, Holt set his sights on the bar, but the Great Depression forced him to leave chambers in 1933 to become a solicitor.

The law was not, however, his sole option for a career. His widowed father had linked up with a Melbourne entrepreneur, F. W. Thring, the father of the actor Frank Thring, to form a company that made feature films. In 1935 Tom managed Radio 3XY in Melbourne, Harold's brother Cliff had become the publicity director for Hoyts Theatres, and an aunt was playing comedy in British theatres. Not surprisingly, Harold had many film and theatre connections, and he was probably tempted to join the business. Indeed, in 1935 he was appointed Secretary of the Cinematographic Exhibitors' Association. By now he had a modest income and a widening circle of companions. It was just as well. His showman father had never given him a sense of security or of belonging, and hurt him deeply by marrying Thring's daughter, whom Harold had been dating.

Holt's friends and mentors included Robert Menzies and Mabel Brookes, the Melbourne socialite and charity worker whose husband Norman was the first non-Briton to win Wimbledon. Together, they were instrumental in turning the young man's mind to politics. Holt joined the Young Nationalists and stood for the United Australia Party against James Scullin in the Labor stronghold of Yarra in 1934. Unperturbed by the inevitable defeat, he put himself forward for another safe Labor seat, this time in the Victorian Parliament. Beaten again, Holt was preselected for the blue ribbon UAP seat of Fawkner following the death of the sitting member. He won in 1935.

But he had no intention of forsaking the law. Opening an office in Collins Street with Jack Graham, an old Geelong Grammarian, Holt paid his partner a retainer to look after his cinema, theatrical and political connections. Holt's own political involvement meant that, although he remained a partner until 1963, his role was very limited. Whether, in the late 1930s, Holt foresaw a long-term career in politics is uncertain. What is clear is that this dashing figure of a man was making a mark in Melbourne society. His charm and ready smile, his good looks and well-tailored clothes, and his ability to mix, made him a welcome guest at society dinner tables. Inwardly, however, the eligible bachelor was deeply unhappy. Zara Dickins, whom he had known since university, had grown tired of waiting for him. She met and married someone else because Holt felt he was too poor to support her.

Politics was a useful diversion. In Canberra Lyons was still prime minister, Menzies was his attorney-general and the UAP, which had been elected with a large majority in 1931 and lost seats in 1934 and 1937, was looking even more like a coalition whose sole bond was opposition to Labor. The new backbencher sponsored the formation of the National Fitness Council to which he was elected as the Parliament's representative. When Menzies, his patron and friend, became prime minister on Lyons' death in 1939, he promoted 'Young Harold' to minister without portfolio assisting the minister for supply and later to the portfolio of trade and customs. Holt served briefly as acting minister for air but had to stand aside when the Country Party rejoined the Coalition in March 1940. Holt enlisted in the second AIF and trained as a gunner, but Menzies recalled him to the ministry following the death of three senior ministers in an aeroplane crash in August 1940. When the UAP scraped home in the 1940 election and governed with the support of two independents, Holt took on the new portfolio of labour and national service – a portfolio suited to one of his tact and easygoing disposition – and introduced child endowment, thus earning him the epithet 'godfather of a million children'.

Cabinet ministers and the UAP backbench grew restless during 1941. Menzies was overseas on the business of war, and he left behind some who detested or feared his arrogance and others who wondered whether he was an electoral liability. The supposedly loyal Holt was absorbed into the opposition by the sheer weight of its numbers. Returning, Menzies was tapped on the shoulder and resigned. Arthur Fadden replaced him and Holt remained in the Cabinet, but after the independents deserted the government he was to spend the next eight years on the Opposition frontbench as spokesman for industrial relations.

Holt was not one of the principal founders of the Liberal Party that emerged after the demise of the UAP in the 1943 election. And though he had become a fulltime politician by the end of World War II, he had some personal matters on his mind. His father died in October 1945 and in

October 1946, one month after the Liberal Party lost the first federal election it contested, he married Zara Dickins, whose first marriage had failed. Occasional encounters with Harold might have led to the birth of her twin boys; she also had an older son, so Holt was presented with an instant family. Assured and secure, he could now give his full attention to the anti-socialist cause. And when the Coalition won so handsomely in 1949 Holt returned as minister for labour and national service with the strong support of Albert Monk, president of the Australian Council of Trade Unions. He also took the immigration portfolio.

The 1950s were Holt's best years in government. For all his achievements in launching the postwar migration program, his predecessor Arthur Calwell had lacked warmth and flexibility in dealing with hardship cases. Holt's human touch and his enthusiasm for non-British migration made him popular with the growing ethnic communities. The NSW division of the Liberal Party recognised his enhanced standing by enlisting him to win the 'New Australian' vote during election campaigns. Although Holt himself wanted to maintain the levels of British migration, he met opposition from his party's grassroots as the British proportion of the migrant intake continued to decline. On one issue, he was adamant: the White Australia Policy. Whereas in 1966 as prime minister he was to preside over a significant breach, he was a stout defender of it in the 1950s, convinced that it caused no resentment in Asia and that tactful administration would suffice.

An instinctive conciliator, Holt as labour minister established such a good relationship with Monk and moderate union leaders that members of his own party accused him of excessive fraternisation and damned him as an appeaser. Holt's methods contributed to the trend where, despite the increase in the number of industrial disputes in the 1950s, the number of working days lost substantially declined. He also introduced significant legislation: most notably, making secret ballots in union elections mandatory(1951), and separating the conciliation and arbitration processes from the exercise of judicial functions (1956), thus establishing the modern form of the federal arbitration system.

Holt's middle years were probably his happiest. Success at home was matched by fun and prominence abroad. Harold discovered a liking for overseas travel and for the Commonwealth Parliamentary Association. He was an enthralled guest for the coronation in 1953, attended the

Commonwealth Conference in London in 1957 and in the same year chaired an International Labour Organisation conference in Geneva. All these trips, involving many stopovers and much sightseeing, brought him new political and social contacts as well as opportunities to swim, to dine and to party.

In 1956 Holt succeeded Sir Eric Harrison as deputy leader of the Parliamentary Liberal Party. Expecting to win easily, he barely prevailed; several party members doubted his substance and mental toughness. Others, mainly from New South Wales, did not want a Victorian. Once in position, however, Holt was well placed to follow Menzies. As leader of the House, he was considered on all sides to be an outstanding success. Appointed treasurer on 10 December 1958 following Sir Arthur Fadden's retirement, he sensibly obeyed his department officials, who better understood the fundamentals of his job. He legislated to separate the functions of the Commonwealth Bank, joined the board of governors of the International Monetary Fund and the International Finance Corporation, chaired the annual meetings of these organisations in 1960 and made several trips to the United States and Europe to deliver speeches and raise loans, a workload that tested even his endurance without noticeably reducing his social round.

In 1960 Holt followed Treasury's line on the need for stricter fiscal and monetary control. In November he imposed a 'credit squeeze' that drove the economy into a recession and saw unemployment rise to more than 2 per cent by January 1962. Again, on Treasury's advice, Holt argued against early remedial action, with the result that the government was almost defeated in the 1961 federal election. Business leaders and senior Liberals demanded Holt's head, and during 1962–63 his prospects of succession as leader looked doomed. Holt was rescued, however, by the gradual restoration of boom conditions and by Liberal resentment at hints that John McEwen, the leader of the Country Party, might eventually succeed Menzies.

So Holt was the unanimous choice of the party room when Menzies announced his retirement in January 1966. He could legitimately boast that he had won the job without stepping over a single dead body. He could also claim to be much more in touch with the times than Menzies. Although fifty-seven years of age, he seemed to be, in the language of the later 1960s, 'with it'. Silver-haired, still fit and good-looking, the prime minister was later famously photographed in a wetsuit alongside his three bikini-clad daughters-in-law. He looked the perfect choice to carry the Liberal Party into and beyond the 'Swinging Sixties'. But he remained a cautious politician, adding only Annabelle Rankin and Malcolm Fraser to the Menzies ministry, and presided over an inner Cabinet whose average age was nearly fifty-nine. The one significant change was in style: the new prime minister behaved more as a chairman of a committee, he included the press in his overseas tours and appeared far more open and informal than his predecessor.

In general, Holt had a very good first year in office, helped by the continuing economic boom and despite a prolonged drought and reduced consumer spending. He won plaudits for the government's decision to relax the White Australia Policy by encouraging non-European immigration on a selected, individual basis, and by reducing the fifteen-year rule to enable non-Europeans to apply for permanent residence and naturalisation on the five-year basis enjoyed by European applicants. These changes, however, were hedged with qualifications. Non-Europeans would be admitted only if they could be easily integrated and had special knowledge, experience or skills that could contribute to Australia's economic, social or cultural progress. Manual workers, even skilled ones, were excluded. Asian students already in Australia would not be considered. The minister for immigration was required to avoid 'unacceptable increases' and to report regularly on the number of non-European admissions, while Cabinet emphasised its commitment to the existing 'social homogeneity' and to the basic principles of immigration policy. Alarmed Labor speakers warned against any fundamental changes. Nevertheless, with Holt's support, an important breach had been made, with far-reaching consequences for the White Australia Policy.

Holt set out to forge a closer relationship between Australia and Asia. He frequently visited Asian capitals during 1966–67, meeting neutrals as well as friends. Paul Hasluck, his minister for external affairs, wrote dismissively of Holt's personal diplomacy but Gough Whitlam later pointed out that he 'made Australia better known in Asia and he made Australians more aware of Asia than ever before'. Exuding confidence over the outcome in Vietnam, Holt in 1966 plunged into defending American and Australian actions, fired in part by what his wife Zara called 'Harry's most spectacular friendship' with President Lyndon

Johnson. His off-the-cuff remark at the White House in July – assuring Johnson that Australia would go 'all the way with LBJ' – might have caused him embarrassment back home, but for Holt such expressions of loyalty did not denote servility. Rather, they reflected both an appreciation of Australia's real interests and the genuine, unsparing relationship between two men who shared many characteristics and who fortified each other in the face of growing domestic criticism. The hostile demonstrations, usually involving university students, distressed Holt personally. Once in Perth he had to escape a crowd by hailing a taxi, and his press secretary was forced to climb into the moving cab through a window. Yet nothing affected the Prime Minister's resolve. He firmly believed that the conflict resulted from China's thrust into South-East Asia, that Australia was in South Vietnam to repel communist aggression and to honour treaty obligations, and that the Asian dominoes would fall if South Vietnam collapsed, thereby endangering Australia. Holt also accepted that Britain's impending withdrawal east of Suez meant Australia must secure the effective presence of the United States in Asia and the Pacific. An increased armed involvement in South Vietnam seemed the appropriate insurance premium.

America's leaders came to Australia during 1966 to reinforce Holt's resolve. Hubert Humphrey, the vice-president, visited just after Holt succeeded Menzies, and told Cabinet that the Vietnam war represented just one of China's offensives in Asia. Johnson himself arrived in October to reward Holt with a barnstorming, folksy, goodwill visit. Labor, understandably , regarded the exercise as a political gimmick, coming as it did one month before the federal election. Holt fought that election on the issue of Australia's participation in the Vietnam war. While Calwell conducted his own crusade against conscription, it was soon evident that the fear factor would overwhelm the Opposition. The Coalition won nearly 50 per cent of the vote on 26 November (its best result since 1951) and an overall majority of 39 in the House of Representatives (its largest ever, to that point). But Holt's obvious pleasure at victory did not translate into authoritative leadership. He exercised characteristic restraint by forming another lacklustre ministry, though he did find room for one name of future importance – Don Chipp.

Whereas 1966 was a good year, 1967 was calamitous. The death of his brother Cliff in March – 'a terrible blow' – unsettled the Prime Minister, though he could now handle personal sadness. The political blows were harder to repel. Tensions within the Coalition over tariff policies did not help. Nor did further embarrassing news about the escalating cost of the American-built strike aircraft, the F-111s, or a politically ill-timed attempt to raise postal charges. The swollen backbench became increasingly restless, and it achieved one notable victory. A reluctant government was forced to revisit Australia's worst peacetime naval disaster, the *Voyager–Melbourne* collision of 1964, and to appoint a second Royal Commission, largely to mollify backbench claims that an injustice had been done by the first Commission to the captain of the *Melbourne*.

But the VIP aircraft issue did the most harm, not least because the damage was partly self-inflicted. After questioning the cost of the recently purchased fleet and alleging private abuse of the privilege, a hostile Senate in October demanded a full disclosure of passenger manifests. Holt and Peter Howson, the minister for air, had insisted that manifests were not kept beyond a few weeks. John Gorton, the government leader in the Senate, than tabled the full information. Had Howson and Holt lied to Parliament? Returning from a conference in Uganda, Howson confessed to negligence. Holt protected his friend, retained him in the ministry, and bore much of the opprobrium.

In March–April Holt received further bad news from London. The British Labour government decided that there would be an immediate reduction in its commitment east of Suez, a 50 per cent reduction by 1970 and a complete withdrawal by 1975. Given that Australian forward defence strategy was based on an American presence in Indo-China and on the British remaining in Malaysia–Singapore, this decision caused a flurry, even though Canberra had been forewarned. Holt marshalled several counter-arguments: Britain's presence was essential to security and stability; 'white faces' would continue to be acceptable in Asia, contrary to London's opinion; withdrawal would be a blow to the progressive Asian nations and harm SEATO's credibility; Hanoi would take succour from the proposal; and American opinion would be affected. While claiming to understand Britain's economic predicament and the renewed desire to enter the Common Market, Holt even resorted to anachronistic appeals for Britain to retain her world power status.

The stark facts behind the rhetoric were that Australia's own forces were stretched and that the country was deeply mired in the Vietnam war. Already the vote-winning war of 1966 was threatening to become a political and financial liability. Recognising the growing strength of domestic opposition, the government now hoped to contain the size of its Vietnam commitment. Going 'all the way with LBJ' would not mean large-scale human and material support. Yet after some dithering, Holt reluctantly agreed to a United States request for a further battalion. He knew that an additional battalion would make no difference militarily, that Treasury was worried about defence costs, that there would be repercussions for economic development and the balance of payments and that public support was no longer guaranteed. But Australia's 'first and lasting consideration' was its position as an American ally, a position which 'must be hardened up at each opportunity'. Even so, Holt wanted to stress that Australia had reached 'the practical sheer limit of contribution', and he told Johnson in October that to go further would be 'publicly unacceptable in the existing climate of opinion'. In any case, by then he wanted to focus Johnson's attention on Malaysia–Singapore as a means of maintaining American interest in the general security and stability of South-East Asia. One thing was now very clear. With the British leaving South-East Asia and the war in Vietnam dragging on, the confident predictions and certainties of 1966 sounded hollow.

A setback of a different kind occurred in May. The government lost a referendum proposal to break the nexus between the size of the Senate and the House of Representatives. Another proposal did pass: Aboriginal people could now be counted in the census and the Commonwealth could legislate outside federal territory on Aboriginal affairs. There were two principal arguments for this proposal. One was that by counting Aborigines in the census, the population figures for Queensland and Western Australia would be sufficiently enhanced to retain their existing representation in the Lower House. The other objective was to counter irritating criticisms of Australian policies towards Aboriginal people. But the Cabinet documents reveal that Holt himself had no great interest in Aboriginal issues. His attitude was that Australia did not have the race problems of other countries: there were 'occasional and unrelated acts of discrimination' that – when publicised – disappeared. Any discrimination that did exist was social rather than racial and would dissolve when 'the habits, manners and education of the race more nearly approached general community standards'.

There was no need, therefore, for any constitutional guarantee against racial discrimination, a step advocated by Bill Wentworth, one of Holt's backbenchers. Nor did Holt see any necessity for the Commonwealth to use its new powers to interfere in the states' administration of Aboriginal affairs. He endorsed his minister's judgment that there were 'practical and political disadvantages' in the Commonwealth entering the Aboriginal field. At most, the government would co-ordinate and consult and, in Holt's words, seek not to 'magnify the Aborigine problem out of its true reality'.

Holt had one major triumph at the end of a difficult second year in office. Treasury had advised against devaluing the dollar in line with the devaluation of the British pound. Holt agreed, knowing that the Australian economy would survive any short-term fall in rural exports. During 1967 there had been a simultaneous increase in consumer spending, public authority outlays and private capital expenditure, and despite a balance of payments deficit and a fall in overseas reserves from $1672 million to $1200 million, Holt and McMahon, the latter now treasurer, were confident about the country's economic future. So when John McEwen, who had been overseas when the decision was made, objected very publicly, Holt confronted him with an ultimatum. Either McEwen and the Country Party accepted the Cabinet decision or Holt would break the Coalition and govern alone. An angry McEwen, accustomed to winning the tough fights, capitulated. The supposedly easygoing, even weak, Liberal leader had won a critical battle.

Unfortunately for Holt, the good news did not cancel out the bad. Labor, which had regrouped federally, was on an upward electoral curve, easily winning two by-elections in July–August, one for the Liberal seat of Corio. Moreover, leader of the Opposition Gough Whitlam clearly had the measure of the often-flustered Prime Minister on the floor of the House. The government suffered a stunning reverse in the half Senate election of November when it managed just 43.3 per cent of the vote against Labor's 47 per cent. By then, Dudley Erwin, the chief government whip, was taking soundings about support for the Prime Minister's leadership, at least one senior minister was questioning Holt's political longevity and there were unfounded rumours abroad in the party that Holt had suffered a heart attack.

A worn-out and grey-looking prime minister left Canberra for the last time on Friday 15 December for a weekend at the family seaside home in Portsea, on Victoria's Mornington Peninsula. Zara remained in the Lodge while her husband sought Portsea's habitual cure for his tiredness. Harold played tennis and relaxed with friends and on Sunday morning he collected Marjorie Gillespie, a neighbour, her daughter, and two young men, and together they watched the lone English yachtsman, Alec Rose, sail through the heads. The five then went to Cheviot Beach, where Holt slipped into his swim trunks and entered, alone, what had become a fierce and high surf. He swam freely out to sea when turbulent water suddenly built up around him and he disappeared. The alarm was sounded and a major rescue operation was mounted but, well before Zara and the immediate family could arrive, no one expected to find him alive. No trace of him was ever found, although the search for his body continued until 5 January 1968. In the meantime a service was held in St Paul's Anglican Cathedral in Melbourne on 22 December 1967, attended by some 2000 mourners, including a tearful President Johnson, British Prime Minister Harold Wilson, Prince Charles and senior representatives of twelve Asian nations.

Every summer Australians of all ages do foolish things in the water and drown. Holt was not a strong swimmer, he had a sore shoulder, probably wanted to 'show off' in front of two women, and had entered a dangerous sea displaying his customary fearlessness. He might have been stunned or dragged down by debris. He almost certainly miscalculated. Yet the obvious explanations were not sufficiently momentous to match the gravity of the event. The conspiracy theorists explained that Holt had been distracted by his political troubles, especially when it became known that his briefcase contained material relating to a feud between McEwen and McMahon, in part over the latter's propensity to leak Cabinet secrets. There were rumours about the marriages of his three sons and speculation that he was troubled by the death of his brother Cliff. Perhaps he wanted to fulfil his premonition of not living beyond sixty, perhaps he committed suicide. Yet those best placed to judge his state of mind remained adamant that Harold Holt, the life-affirmer, was in good spirits. He had laid plans for ministerial changes in the New Year and wanted to make a major statement announcing a switch in foreign policy emphasis to European affairs. In all probability, the Prime Minister was just another statistic of the Australian summer surf.

Harold Holt was very much an *Australian* prime minister. Over the years he might have regarded the Savoy Hotel in London as his 'second home', or thought longingly of Venice as 'an uninterrupted joy to the tourist'. His reaction, however, in London in 1957, on seeing a performance of Ray Lawler's *The Summer of the Seventeenth Doll,* says much about him. 'Expecting the worst', he and Zara 'were thrilled by the play – weeping, both of us, through most of the first act – proud of the Australian author, proud of the all-Australian cast, and proud of the country which had produced the types in the play and the types who played them'. His pride in Australia merely increased through the years. Like Menzies before him, Holt was pro-American because he was pro-Australian. Unlike Menzies, he was prepared to loosen the British connection. After all, it was a Holt government that decided in May 1967 to end High Court appeals to the Privy Council in matters of federal jurisdiction and, the following August, to drop the word 'British' from the cover of Australian passports (with plans to amend the Nationality and Citizenship Act to change the designation 'British subject' on the inside).

He had astonishing stamina. Needing only four hours' sleep a night, he could stay up late on overseas trips, attend to his papers before dawn and then undertake a heavy load of official engagements. Harold liked parties, dancing, restaurants, women, spearfishing and gambling, and found time to sample them all without failing in his public duties. A diary entry for 1962 – that his dinner companion 'is still a very lovely woman, but like a very ripe peach which should be eaten without delay' – attests to his special feeling for women. He was fortunate, therefore, to have the feisty Zara as a partner. She tolerated his occasional roaming, kept the family finances in order, led her own life and stood by him.

Holt was no conceptual or visionary thinker. Paul Hasluck's generally negative estimate included the observation that he had never known Holt say anything 'which revealed any wide range of thought or understanding, or even occasional wisdom'. Judging him to be a good politician, Hasluck nonetheless criticised Holt's tendency, as he saw it, to assess and deal with situations 'with himself in the centre'. Hasluck attributed this characteristic not to vanity but to Holt possibly being 'the product of a simple nature'. Perhaps his simplicity explains the greatest mistake he made in Asia (leaving aside differing views about Australia's Vietnam commitment) – the decision to open an embassy in Taiwan. Curiously, Hasluck ignored this error of judgment in his memoir *The Chance of Politics*. Holt had a lucky escape from another potentially foolhardy gesture, namely his invitation to Air Vice-Marshal Ky, the prime minister of South Vietnam, to visit Australia. Ky arrived in January 1967 but, despite the efforts of Arthur Calwell and a diminishing number of demonstrators to depict him as a fascist butcher, the visit proved to be a public relations success. A relieved Holt owed much to the acute, smiling and dignified Ky, and his photogenic wife.

If Harold Holt was not the deep thinker Hasluck so admired in himself, he had other virtues. He was a team player who neither denigrated his colleagues nor attempted to lord it over the party organisation. He was gregarious, had friends on both sides of the House and was a thoroughly decent man of considerable integrity. When the times were favourable – that is, for most of 1966 – he was a capable prime minister. When they were not – that is, for most of 1967 – his weaknesses were readily apparent: he was not ruthless, he was nice to opponents, loyal to friends, sensitive to criticism, and too cautious and indecisive to anticipate or respond to change.

As a man, he was perhaps too self-absorbed and private to reveal much about himself. He might, in fact, have been just an ordinary bloke wanting approval. For one, however, who seemed to be so 'right' for the times, he was actually nearer in mindset to postwar Australia than to the Australia he did not live to see. Yet he did give Australians a necessary and relatively rare experience: a prime minister who was personal and open, less lofty and remote, closer to the people, and genuinely likeable.

Sir John McEwen

19 DECEMBER 1967 – 10 JANUARY 1968

'Black Jack' McEwen was one of the toughest and most able politicians Australia has ever seen.

BY PETER GOLDING

History may record John McEwen as an accidental prime minister of Australia. And in a sense history would be correct: but for the presumed death by drowning of Harold Holt six days before Christmas in 1967 McEwen would never have achieved the highest political office in the land, and then only for twenty-three days. If, on the other hand, such an historical assertion were to imply that McEwen's brief tenure was all that he deserved, it would be very wrong.

'Black Jack' McEwen, a 'tall, wiry, broad-shouldered, jaw-jutting man' as Jim Killen described him,[1] was one of the toughest and most able politicians Australia has ever seen. Few would doubt that only his membership of the minority Country Party and his refusal to compromise his principles by switching to the Liberal Party prevented him from achieving the national leadership by right instead of by tragedy. Fewer still, even his political enemies, would doubt that, had that happened, he would have been one of Australia's great prime ministers.

For twenty-two years, the last thirteen as deputy prime minister, he was a potent influence on government in Australia; more dominant, many would argue, than anyone except perhaps Menzies; 'perhaps' because for most of the time Menzies was prime minister his government danced to McEwen's tune. For the whole of that time McEwen was Australia's minister of trade – his occupancy of the portfolio was the longest ever – and he built it into a power base so strong that it was capable of directly challenging the supremacy of Treasury in the nation's economic management. Trade's feuding with Treasury, and McEwen's with Holt and McMahon during their terms as treasurer. were among the more notorious episodes in Australia's political history.

When McEwen followed Arthur Fadden as leader of the Country Party in 1958 he could have succeeded him also as treasurer, but the job never interested him. His vision was to play a leadership role in guiding not just the rural industries but also the 'wealth-creating industries' – manufacturing and mining. He reasoned that he could do this as trade minister; he could never do it a treasurer. Trade he saw as the producers, Treasury as the bookkeepers.

The respected journalist Paul Kelly wrote in 1986, fifteen years after McEwen had left the Parliament and six years after his death:

27. *Curtin and his friend and Treasurer, Ben Chifley, walk from the Hotel Kurrajong to Parliament House. The two men had much in common and Curtin relied heavily on Chifley's support.*

28. *In December 1941 Curtin announced that 'Australia looks to America, free of any pangs as to our traditional links or kinship with the United Kingdom'. In March 1942 US General Douglas MacArthur, pictured at his first meeting with Curtin, arrived in Australia. 'Mr Prime Minister,' MacArthur reportedly told Curtin, 'we two, you and I, will see this thing through together … You take care of the rear and I will handle the front.'*

29. Acrimonious disputes between Winston Churchill and John Curtin, seen here at the Dominion Prime Ministers' Conference in May 1944 in London, led to a strained relationship between the two men.

30. In May 1944 on a visit to a RAAF Lancaster Squadron in Leicestershire, England, Curtin gives the thumbs up to Australian crewmen taking off on a bombing mission to France. Curtin's concern for Australian troops caused him many sleepless nights in Canberra and the burden of the war effort affected his health. Little over a year later, in July 1945, Curtin, aged 60, would be dead.

31. On the death of Curtin, his deputy, Frank Forde, stepped briefly into the prime ministership. As Army Minister, Forde had shared the exhausting burden of conducting the war, and as Minister for Defence in the Chifley government, he supervised the demobilisation of the armed forces. Here, on arrival for an inspection tour at Lae airstrip in early 1946, Forde meets RAAF troops stationed in New Guinea.

32. Within a week of Curtin's death, the Labor Party had voted Treasurer and former locomotive driver Ben Chifley to replace the caretaker prime minister, Frank Forde. For Chifley, seen here in front of Parliament House with his trademark pipe, it was a brighter inheritance than Curtin's as war gave way to peace. Within weeks of assuming office, he was able to announce Japan's surrender.

33. The Chifley government embarked on an ambitious program of postwar reconstruction with a talented group of senior public service advisers, foremost among them the economist and Director-General of the Department of Postwar Reconstruction, Dr H.C. 'Nugget' Coombs, seen here with Chifley at Kew Gardens, London, in 1946.

34. Prime Minister Chifley greets a newly arrived migrant while his Minister for Immigration, Arthur Calwell, centre, looks on. The Chifley government, and its energetic immigration minister pioneered the great wave of postwar migration to Australia from 1947.

35. *The 1949 federal election was a watershed. As the Cold War deepened, Menzies played his anti-communism/free-enterprise card promising wealth and expansion while depicting Labor as socialist and backward-looking. In one of the great political comebacks, the Liberal-Country Party coalition swept into power, consigning Chifley to defeat and Labor to almost a quarter of a century in the political wilderness.*

"GOING MY WAY—ON A FULL PETROL-TANK?"

36. *The only serving Member of Parliament in the 1950s who had been a member of the first federal Parliament, Billy Hughes celebrated his 90th birthday in September 1952 at a testimonial dinner. Here Hughes shares a joke with Senator Dorothy Tangney, one of the first two women elected to Parliament. To his left, former prime minister, Sir Earle Page, looks on. Far right (obscured) is Dr Bert Evatt and fourth from right, is the Speaker of the House of Representatives, Archie Cameron. Within a month, one of the most controversial prime ministers in Australian history would be dead.*

37. Prime Minister Menzies in Churchillian mode in 1953 during a tour of Durban, South Africa, while en route to Australia from attending the coronation of Queen Elizabeth in London.

38. Menzies' affable Deputy Prime Minister and long-serving Treasurer, Country Party leader Sir Arthur 'Artie' Fadden, centre, brought down a record 11 budgets before retirement in 1958. He is shown here in 1957 on his way to deliver one of his last Budget speeches, flanked by his successor as Treasurer, Harold Hold, left, Senator Ivy Wedgwood, government Whip Hubert Opperman and Senator John Marriott.

39. Menzies progressively came to terms with criticism of his neglect of Asia, and began a more active diplomatic program. In December 1959 he became the first Australian prime minister to visit Indonesia. Here, during a six-day goodwill visit, he looks on as President Sukarno introduces his daughter, Sukmawati Sukarnaputri, to Dame Pattie.

40. In April 1960, Time *magazine's cover featured a specially commissioned portrait of Menzies by Sir William Dobell. Its cover story enthusiastically reported that, thanks to Menzies' leadership, 'Australia … is savoring a real prosperity and discovering a national maturity … no longer a back-water, but confident of its dynamism and independence'.*

41. Menzies demonstrated his affection for the British monarchy in his welcoming speech to Queen Elizabeth II in King's Hall, Parliament, on 18 February 1963, when, quoting an Elizabethan poet, he declared 'I did but see her passing by, and yet I love her till I die'.

42. The end of an era: Australia's longest-serving prime minister – Menzies, 71, had more than 18 years in office – arrives at Yarralumla in January 1966, to give the Governor-General his resignation.

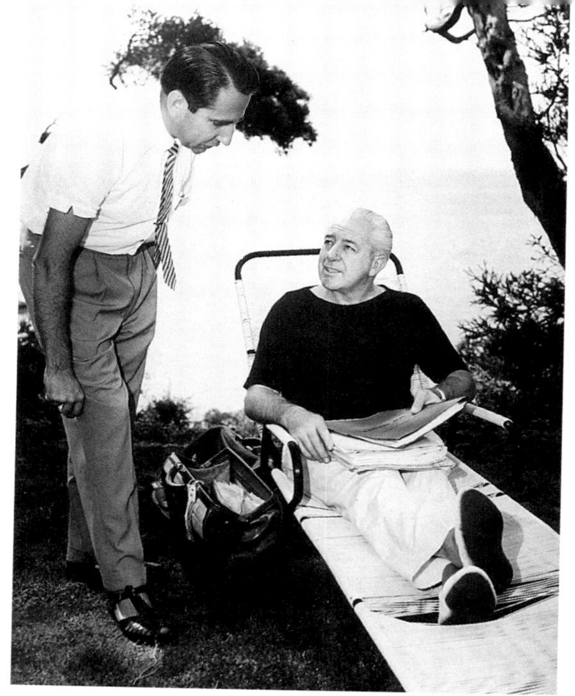

43. Menzies' successor, Harold Holt, brought a change in style more in tune with the 'Swinging Sixties' in his openness and informality. Here, Holt, right, is at his seaside home in Portsea, on Melbourne's Mornington Peninsula, with his press secretary, Tony Eggleton, in 1966.

44. Holt, and his high-profile wife, Dame Zara, on a visit to Asia in 1967. As prime minister, he set out to forge a closer relationship between Australia and Asia and made frequent trips there.

45. As Australian involvement in the Vietnam War deepened, in October 1966, US President Lyndon Baines Johnson, centre right, became the first American president to visit Australia. On an earlier trip to the US, Holt had famously declared his support for the US, in the phrase, 'All the way with LBJ'. Little more than a year later, Johnson would return for a second time, in tragic circumstances.

46. On 17 December 1967, Holt disappeared while swimming at Cheviot Beach near Portsea. At his memorial service in Melbourne a week later, a grim-faced caretaker Prime Minister John McEwen, right, accompanies US President Johnson.

"I do not think there will be any opposition to Mr Gorton . . . !"

47. The bitter antagonism between the formidable, long-serving Minister for Trade, John 'Black Jack' McEwen, and Holt's natural successor, Treasurer William McMahon, led McEwen to veto McMahon's appointment to the prime ministership after Holt's death.

48. John Gorton, sworn in as prime minister in January 1968, was less than enthusiastic about Australia's Vietnam commitment. Here the popular and down-to-earth Gorton, centre, meets Australian troops at Nui Dat on a trip to South Vietnam in mid-1968.

49. Prime Minister Gorton at a press conference in late 1969 after an unsuccessful leadership challenge by William McMahon, left. Shortly afterwards, Gorton relieved McMahon of his Treasury portfolio and moved him to External Affairs.

50. On 8 March 1971, a growing leadership crisis came to a head when the Minister for Defence, Malcolm Fraser, seen here as Army Minister in 1966, resigned from Cabinet alleging Prime Minister Gorton had been disloyal to him. Two days later, after a party-room coup, Gorton surrendered his leadership.

51. William McMahon, right, at Government House on 10 March 1971 after his swearing-in as prime minister by the Governor-General, Sir Paul Hasluck, left. The deposed prime minister, John Gorton, brings up the rear as McMahon's new deputy.

52. Prime Minister McMahon and his wife, Sonia, attend a State dinner hosted by President Richard Nixon at the White House in November 1971. Sonia McMahon's dress made headlines in Australian newspapers of the day; it was described in press reports as 'slit to the thighs, with continuing side-panels filled with flesh-coloured material'.

53. The election of December 1972 saw a revitalised Labor Party, under the leadership of Gough Whitlam and with a well-orchestrated 'It's Time' campaign, emerge victorious to become the first Labor government in Australia since 1949. Whitlam marked a new breed of Labor prime minister. He had not risen from working-class origins through trade-union ranks but had been a barrister from an affluent, middle-class background.

> He was gaunt, gigantic. An old-fashioned Australian who embodied some of the older virtues – courage, vision, pitiless determination.
>
> More influential than most of the prime ministers he served, Sir John McEwen was a cunning manipulator whose scale of operation encompassed the central elements of the Australian economy. McEwen is a forgotten figure: the ghost of an older age before vacuous lucidity became the test for television politicians. But it is McEwen's imprint that remains indelible upon the nation today. The economic structures created by post World War 11 governments were carved by McEwen. Not Menzies, Holt or Gorton. They were merely the Liberal prime ministers he served and who in turn impinged upon but never challenged his own economic domain.[2]

Kelly's next words captured the essence of McEwen. 'There are two types of politicians,' he wrote, 'those who wait on history and those who make history.' The first group abound and the second are in scarce supply. John McEwen's character and intelligence always destined him for the second camp – the men big enough to become the heroes and villains.'

McEwen's destiny was fashioned in a difficult childhood and youth. He was born thirty-nine weeks before Federation, on 29 March 1900 at Chiltern in north-east Victoria – today not much more than a speck on the map but then a bustling gold mining town with thirty-two hotels and a population of 20,000 – the son of David James McEwen, the local pharmacist who, in 1889 aged twenty-five, had migrated with his first wife Saidie from Mountnorris, County Armagh, Ireland. David McEwen had left Ireland with the name of MacEwen but probably because of a misspelling in his documents he entered Australia as McEwen. Saidie died in 1893 of a 'lung ailment', as in 1901 did David's second wife, Amy (née Porter), whom he had married in 1898 – a shade ironic considering that the *Chiltern Federal Standard* regularly carried advertisements for McEwen's Cough Emulsion 'offering instant relief for coughs, bronchitis and all diseases of the chest, through the lungs and arising from colds'.[3] Amy was John McEwen's mother.

Motherless at two, McEwen was to be orphaned at seven when in 1907 his father, meanwhile having married a third time, collapsed while visiting suppliers in Melbourne and returned home to Chiltern in a coffin. Thereafter McEwen and his sister Amy were brought up by Ellen Porter, his maternal grandmother, first at Wangaratta and then at

Dandenong. 'Nellie' Porter obviously had high hopes for her grandson as well as a degree of prescience. When he was a young boy she impressed upon him the need always to strive for the top. 'If you go into the church,' she once said, 'become an archbishop. If you go into the army, become a general. If you go into politics, become a prime minister.'[4]

McEwen left school reluctantly at thirteen ('I realised that we were so hard up it was time I began to keep myself,' he said[5]) and got a job with Rocke Tompsitt & Co, wholesale druggists and chemists. Still hungry for education, he attended classes most nights at a college in Prahran run by a man named Paddy Hassett and eventually passed the entrance examination for the Commonwealth public service. This got him a position with the crown solicitor's office where his immediate boss was Fred Whitlam, whose son Gough would also become an Australian prime minister.

When he turned eighteen McEwen, attracted to a military career, thought about attending the newly opened Duntroon Military College but instead joined the AIF and was in camp awaiting posting when World War I ended. Because he had volunteered for overseas service he was entitled to apply for a soldier-settlement block even though he had never left Australia. He had no farming experience, so to qualify he worked as a labourer on various properties around Victoria. After a few months he managed to convince the authorities that he was capable of farming and was granted thirty-four hectares of untilled ground at Stanhope, its only embellishment four corner posts and a lean-to shanty in which he lived mostly on the rabbits that infested his and his neighbours' land. He was nineteen, his worldly possessions a horse, a gig and fifty shillings. Later in life McEwen, by then a formidable debater in the Parliament, would attribute his exceptional vocabulary to the many lonely nights he spent in his shanty reading from cover to cover a dictionary, the only literature available, into the small hours by the light of a kerosene lamp. He would also attribute a loathing of rabbits to his monotonous diet.

This was a formative time for McEwen. He had to buy farm equipment, fence and stock his property, build barns and put down drains for irrigation. The imperative, therefore, was to make money. This took him to Melbourne's waterfront where, using another man's name, he got a job as a wharf labourer and had his first exposure to the power of organised labour. It was hard work, McEwen recalled, often involving twenty-hour shifts, but it gave him the stake he needed to turn his unstocked bare land into a dairy farm. Many soldier-settlers were less fortunate. Their blocks were too small to be viable and in any case most lacked the capital to improve and stock their land. Then milk prices collapsed. So all around him, as he laboured from dawn to dark, McEwen watched the trailing dust as they walked off their farms. It hurt him and carved deeply into his mind and his makeup.

It also produced the first sinews and guts of a politician. McEwen was still in his teens when he joined the Farmers' Union that in 1917 had been the Victorian sponsoring body of the Australian Farmers' Federal Organisation and thus of the Australian Country Party that replaced it in 1926. He was an activist from the start. Soon he was entreating his fellow soldier-settlers to stand up for their rights, and despite his youth (he was only twenty) he persuaded them to unite to form their own dairy co-operative – putting up £25 and becoming its first chairman – rather than accept the poor milk prices on offer from the Kyabram butter factory.

Menzies' first meeting with him was as Victorian attorney-general, when he received a deputation of soldier-settlers protesting against their living conditions. 'The great advocate of the deputation was a dark-haired eager-looking young man called John McEwen,' Menzies related many years later. 'It was my first contact with him and I've reminded him of it many times since and said, "You know, you were terrifying even when you were quite young"!'[6] It was Menzies who gave McEwen the sobriquet 'Black Jack', ostensibly because he reminded him of a legendary Scottish warrior but more likely because of his dark visage and the blackness of his mood when crossed.

That first meeting of the two men who were to become partners in Australia's most successful and enduring coalition government occurred during the Depression in one of the darkest periods in Australia's history. McEwen never forgot the dreadful effects of unemployment or the bank foreclosures on soldier-settlers who had somehow survived the struggle to get started but were finally overwhelmed by butter fat prices dropping to sixpence a pound and lambs selling at the market for little more than it took to get them there, let alone raise them. Neither did he forget or forgive the banks. Years afterwards, a strong man not easily given to tears, he wept when he remembered a neighbouring settler whose child had died. 'He drove the child's body to the cemetery in his buggy, dug a grave and buried her himself because he couldn't afford a funeral. Next year that soldier was put off his piece of land because he couldn't pay.'[7]

This then was the backdrop to McEwen deciding to become a politician: memories of farmers battling the odds, of ordinary folk battling for jobs, of exploitation, hunger, dole queues – and a burning determination to do something about it.

In 1932 he stood for and won Country Party preselection for the Victorian Legislative Assembly seat of Waranga. He doubled the party's vote – not enough to win, but more than enough to ensure that he was the party's candidate for Echuca at the 1934 federal election, which he did win. He was to retain the seat – it became Indi when Echuca was abolished in 1937 and then Murray in 1949 – in all the following thirteen elections before he retired in 1971.

McEwen was a minister for more than twenty-four of his thirty-seven years in Parliament. His first portfolio – ministry of the interior in the Lyons government – ran from November 1937 to April 1939. He then served under Menzies as minister for external affairs from March to October 1940 and as minister for air and civil aviation until Menzies lost the United Australia Party leadership in October 1941 and stepped down as prime minister. McEwen was back in the Cabinet after the 1949 election, when Menzies appointed him minister for commerce and agriculture, and he remained in charge of trade until his retirement in 1971. He also served for three years and ten months from 1941–45 as a member of the Australian Advisory War Council and for a year in Curtin's War Cabinet (1940–41). He was prime minister from 19 December 1967 to 10 January 1968. His acquaintance with the backbench, therefore, was slight.

The measure of the man was manifest in his maiden speech in Parliament during the Budget debate on 15 November 1934. McEwen canvassed a lot of ground that day, ground that he would revisit again and again throughout his parliamentary career: the scourge of unemployment, the plight of farmers, Australia's trade balance, foreign debt, defence, the need for self-sufficiency in production, protection of Australian industry. And his concern about the banks.

It is unlikely that the banks would have taken much notice of the earnest young soldier-settler's criticism of them at the time. They should have. The following April he was again on his feet in the House calling for a Royal Commission into the banking and monetary system. Prime Minister Lyons did take notice. On 5 October 1935 he announced that there would be an inquiry, naming Joseph Benedict Chifley among the commissioners, thus triggering the chain of events that led in 1947 to Chifley, by then a Labor prime minister, legislating to nationalise the banks, the issue on which Menzies – with McEwen, of course – was swept into power in the 1949 election.

McEwen was a model of consistency throughout his life except, curiously, on the issue of protection, the issue with which his name is most closely linked. He came to be – and still is – derided as the arch-protectionist, but it is clear from his maiden speech that, then at least. he was not overly concerned about the Country Party's opposition to the tariff. One must assume that McEwen hadn't yet sorted out his own thinking on it because it was totally out of character for him to believe one thing and say another or to kowtow blindly to party dogma. Nor was he ever afraid to buck the system, as he was to prove many times – including in December 1937 when he was expelled from the Country Party for defying its prohibition on federal members becoming ministers in a coalition government.

Once McEwen did espouse the cause of protection, however, he pursued it unswervingly, relentlessly, without regard for personal or any other consideration and in the face of fierce opposition from Treasury, to the very day that he left politics. His reason, quite simply, was his certainty that Australia's manufacturers could not survive without protection from imports, and that only they could provide the number of jobs that the country needed. He argued that the cost of losing manufacturing industry would be that of sustaining the unemployed from those industries, and this would be greater than the cost of sustaining the industries with tariff protection. To deny people the dignity of work, he pleaded, was the ultimate obscenity. McEwen also believed that it was wrong for one sector of the economy to be advantaged at the expense of another so, because protection of manufacturers would push up costs to farmers, he reasoned that they should be compensated by subsidies and bounties. Hence what became known derisively as McEwen's policy of 'all-round protection'.

McEwen might at times have been dismayed by his legion of critics, especially when they came, as they did increasingly, from the Country Party's own constituency, but he was never daunted. His first consideration was always his country. If he believed what he was doing was right and to Australia's benefit nothing else mattered; not the interests of his party, not even those of his beloved farmers and certainly not his own. He never courted popularity. In many ways he was an unlikely politician.

It follows that McEwen was no stranger to controversy, and although he was always loyal – sometimes remarkably so – to his three Coalition partners, Menzies, Holt and Gorton, all of them at one time or another had cause to curse him for his unbending adherence to some point at issue or because of his just plain pigheadedness. He could be infuriatingly obdurate and obsessively determined if he judged the cause to be right.

In 1956 lesser men would have shrunk from the task of loosening the bonds that tied Australia's trade to Britain in the Ottawa Agreement, particularly as McEwen's prime minister, Robert Menzies, was a professed anglophile, and knowing that alternative markets for our wheat and wool and meat and fruit and dairy produce would be desperately hard to find. Few, too, would have accepted the political risk a year later of negotiating a trade agreement with Japan when memories of prisoner-of-war camp atrocities were still fresh in the minds of the Australian people and hatred for the Japanese was deep in every town and village in the country; when even to think of reconciliation was anathema. For McEwen the risk was also personal. Malcolm Fraser recalled: 'Menzies would not give him the authority to negotiate in the name of the government because he regarded the political risk as being too great. If it had gone wrong Menzies could have disowned him up to the moment the government accepted the agreement. That is the measure of the man's greatness.'[8]

McEwen's most contentious act, however – and the one that will certainly inscribe his name in history even if his real attainments do not – was to veto William McMahon's first bid to become prime minister after Holt's death in 1967. This was McEwen at his most lethal and determined – and breathtakingly audacious. McMahon, as deputy leader of the Liberal Party, was Holt's natural successor and it was generally assumed that when the party came to elect a new leader McMahon would be chosen. McEwen had different ideas. He detested McMahon – his self-promotion often at the expense of his ministerial colleagues, his disloyalty to his staff when things went wrong, his calculated 'leaking' of Cabinet information to the media. So he promptly informed Richard Casey, the governor-general, and then McMahon himself, that neither he nor the Country Party would serve under him. When McMahon asked him for his reason, he said simply, 'Because I do not trust you.'[9]

After the 1961 election, in which the Coalition government had survived only by the flimsiest of margins, placing strain on Menzies' leadership, there had been moves in the Liberal Party to persuade McEwen to participate in a move to unseat Menzies as prime minister but because this would have meant his leaving the Country Party he was never seriously tempted.

Concern about the Liberal Party leadership surfaced again after Holt's death, especially among Liberals who shared McEwen's reservations about McMahon. The fact that Holt had not been doing well for some time was another factor. As a consequence, the possibility of approaching McEwen to take over the leadership, at least in the medium term, even if this meant his remaining as the leader of the Country Party, was seriously canvassed at a secret meeting of federal and state presidents and secretaries of the Liberal Party at Menzies hotel in Melbourne immediately after Holt's funeral, and there were independent soundings also from members of the parliamentary party.

There is little doubt that McEwen coveted the prospect of crowning his long political career by attaining the prime ministership in his own right, and of course he was well aware that there was precedence for the head of the junior party in the Coalition to do this. Page and Fadden had both done it. Moreover, McEwen was tormented by doubts about the unpredictable Gorton's suitability to be prime minister, even though it had been his own refusal to accept McMahon that had opened the door to Gorton. But there was more to it than that. The fact is that McEwen wasn't sure that he still had it in him to do the job well. He was just short of sixty-eight, tired and far from well. And if he did allow his name to go forward, how long would it be, he wondered, before rank and file Liberals began to resent his leadership? So it was a sizeable dilemma.

In the end he was spared the need to make a decision. A few Liberals – particularly Senator Bob Cotton – protested that, if for no other reason than pride, a leader had to be found within the party.[10] The pro-McEwen movement withered, the ranks closed behind Gorton and he was elected.

McEwen's twenty-three days as prime minister were at an end. Brief though it was, his was not the shortest term; Earle Page occupied the position for twenty days and Frank Forde for eight. Six more prime ministers served for less than a year. Nor was it the only time that a prime minister had come to office in tragic circumstances; Chifley became prime minister because of Curtin's death in office.

It is highly improbable, however, that any Australian prime minister concluded his period in office more abruptly. After his party room victory on 10 January 1968 Gorton strolled up the corridor to McEwen's office and casually reported the result of the ballot. It was 12.30pm. McEwen congratulated Gorton and offered to provide any assistance he needed, reminding him that he had made a commitment to step aside as prime minister once the Liberals had elected a new leader. 'When would you like me to do that, John?' he asked. Gorton looked at his watch. 'Say, half past two?' he said.[11]

Sir John Grey Gorton

10 JANUARY 1968 - 10 MARCH 1971

The essential problem with John Gorton as prime minister is that, apart from exuding a nationalist ethos, he did not really know what he wanted to achieve in a policy sense.

BY GERARD HENDERSON

On Saturday 3 July 1999 the Liberal Party brought John Gorton home. He had been out in the political cold for close to a quarter of a century. In 1975 the former Liberal leader took a series of actions that would not have been contemplated by his predecessors – or his successors. He quit the Liberal Party, urged Australian electors to vote for Labor and against Malcolm Fraser's Coalition government and stood (unsuccessfully) as an independent for one of the Australian Capital Territory's Senate vacancies. Later he admitted that he had voted ALP in December 1975.[1] The public rationale for all of this turned on John Gorton's disagreement with Malcolm Fraser's decision, when Opposition leader, to block supply in the Senate – and the subsequent dismissal of Gough Whitlam's Labor government by the governor-general Sir John Kerr.

However, it is also likely that, circa 1975, John Gorton still deeply resented the fact that he had been dumped by his Liberal colleagues while incumbent prime minister. Moreover, he always wanted to do it his way – both as Liberal leader and backbencher. John Gorton was often independent, invariably stubborn and always a hater. He never forgave Malcolm Fraser for destroying his prime ministership or the late William McMahon for taking over his job. On such matters John Gorton never bothered to 'do the hypocrisies'. On 12 November 1997 he participated in the 'Prime Ministers on Prime Ministers' lecture series at Old Parliament House. In his talk, which was run in full on ABC-TV, Sir John Gorton declared that he could not say 'anything nice' about two of his Liberal predecessors – meaning McMahon and Fraser. Fortunately for Sir John, such animosity was not always reciprocated. He was knighted in 1977, during Malcolm Fraser's time as prime minister.

No one spoke about John Gorton's very personal war with the Liberals at the July 1999 Liberal Party Federal Council's gala dinner at Old Parliament House, Canberra. Guests seated in the historic dining room, which had hosted many an international dignitary in its day, first viewed a video. There were film clips of Gorton as farmer, wartime pilot (including details of the facial injuries suffered when his fighter plane crashlanded while he was on active service in the Pacific), shire counsellor, politician, minister and prime minister. But there was not one mention of the dark side of John Gorton's relationship with the Liberal Party. It was as if Gorton and the Liberals had been as one for aeons. John

Howard led the Liberal cheers. He commented that John Gorton 'was, in every sense of the word, the genuine article as far as a dinkum Australian was concerned. He was direct. He was laconic ... On all occasions John Gorton was a man who had a clear-eyed view of the Australian national interest and he was a passionate nationalist above everything else.'

In response, the guest of honour was also graciously forgetful. On two occasions he referred to the prime minister as 'Sir John Howard'. But he did comment briefly on his time in the (Liberal) political wilderness. John Gorton told Federal Council delegates and invited guests (who included his former chief of staff Ainsley Gotto) that he never really regarded himself as outside the Liberal Party and that it was good that everyone 'can all be together once more'.[2] He received a standing ovation. How times had changed since the early 1990s, when then Liberal leader John Hewson had announced to his party room that he had encouraged Gorton to rejoin the Liberal Party. Some years after the event Dr Hewson wrote that 'half the room was euphoric; half was bitter and twisted'.[3]

It was much the same on Wednesday 10 March 1971 when the federal Liberals gathered in the government members' room to discuss the crises that had been devastating the party. In the event two Gorton supporters – Victorian backbenchers Alan Jarman and Len Reid – formally moved a vote of confidence in their prime minister. It is invariably unwise for a politician's supporters to adopt such a tactic. Far better to force a leader's opponent to move a vote of no confidence – that way, any tied result means that the motion has not passed. In any event, Gorton accepted the motion. The result was a 33/33 tie with one informal vote. According to Neil Brown, who was a young backbencher at the time: '... Gorton took it upon himself to say, "Well that is not a vote of confidence, so the Party will have to elect a new leader".'[4]

From this action grew the myth that Gorton had effectively voted himself out of office by exercising a casting vote against himself. In *Inside Australian Politics* James Killen ran this line, maintaining that 'Gorton gave a casting vote against himself'.[5]As Neil Brown has demonstrated, there is no evidence that the Federal Liberal leader at the time actually had a casting vote in the event of a tied result. There was no such vote and Gorton did not attempt to initiate one. He just stepped down.

As John Gorton acknowledged when I interviewed him in his (then) Narrabundah home in Canberra on 11 May 1990, there was no alternative:

> Gerard Henderson: *There's the current proposition that says when the vote was tied you voluntarily stepped down. There was another ... namely that you had no option because there was a group of about six who indicated that they were so firmly against you that they would have crossed the floor and brought down the government.*
>
> John Gorton: *In my view, I didn't have any option because they were evenly divided. The party room was evenly divided and it was impossible for me to lead ... There were six people in the party who were constantly – no matter what we said – they were constantly against us.*

During our discussion, the former Liberal leader named five of the six backbench colleagues who were 'constantly against' him: Peter Howson, John Jess, Kevin Cairns, Henry ('Harry') Turner and Les Irwin. David Fairbairn should be added to this group, and probably Jeff Bate and Malcolm Mackay. After the October 1969 election, the Coalition's majority in the House of Representatives was a mere 7.

How did it come to this – that the Liberal prime minister realised he had no option but to surrender when half his colleagues voted against him? How was it that the third leader of the federal Liberal Party was rolled so readily – and so suddenly? Perhaps the answer lies in the reported exchange between Senator Vince Gair and John Gorton when the latter was about to leave Australia for an official tour of the United States. Gair said: 'Good luck; behave yourself.' To which an arrogant prime minister replied: 'John Grey Gorton will bloody well behave precisely as John Grey Gorton bloody well decides he wants to behave.'[6] That, in a sense, was the problem.

Anyone in the 1960s with ready access to *Who's Who In Australia* knew that John Grey Gorton was born in Melbourne on 9 September 1911, the son of John Rose Gorton. At the time, mothers' names were rarely listed in *Who's Who*. No doubt it was assumed that John Grey was born to John Rose's wife Kathleen. Not so – as became evident in November 1969 with the publication of Alan Trengrove's *John Grey Gorton: An Informal Biography.*[7] In an author's note, Trengrove acknowledged his subject's 'co-operation in gathering material' and commented: 'Mr Gorton, who read the final manuscript, did not try to effect any suppression or make any major changes ...' Quite the contrary, it seems. Clearly it was the biography's subject who advised the author about the circumstances of his birth. It turned out that the John Rose/Kathleen 'marriage had been a mistake' but the latter refused a divorce. There was, however, a judicial separation. Kathleen went to live in Sydney while her husband remained in business in Melbourne. According to family lore, John Rose had made most of his money in South Africa before coming to Australia as a young man. In 1920 he invested in an orange orchard at Kangaroo Lake, near Kerang in northern Victoria. Both John Rose and his wife were born in England.

John Rose Gorton came to meet Alice Sinn – who is described by Trengrove as 'the Australian-born daughter of a poor Irish railway worker who lived at Port Melbourne'. He added: 'And she was a Roman Catholic.' Kathleen continued her refusal to agree to divorce, so John Rose and Alice set up home in Melbourne, later moving to Sydney. There were two children of this union – a daughter Ruth and then a son who, as Alan Trengrove put it, was 'destined to become the nineteenth Prime Minister of the Commonwealth of Australia'. If destiny was involved in this evolution, it sure got a nudge from ambition and hubris.

Three decades ago an announcement that someone prominent was born out of wedlock was treated differently than it would be now. Today it would be of little moment. Then it was a big story. Clearly John Gorton briefed his biographer about the John Rose/Alice union and its issue. The book was published soon after the October 1969 federal election and sparked considerable attention.

Why did Gorton choose to reveal something he had never mentioned in public before? Including details of Alice's early death, when her only son was seven years old, and the fact that John Rose prevailed on his wife (Kathleen) to bring up Ruth and John at Killara on Sydney's north shore? In 1927 Kathleen sailed to Europe with Ruth and never returned to Australia. Perhaps an answer to why John Gorton decided to tell all can be found on page 29 of Alan Trengrove's text, where the author wrote:

> It is generally accepted these days that environment and experiences in the first years of life play a large part in forming the kernel of a personality. In his tender years Gorton was moved from one environment to another, and now at seven years at age he was passed from the control of one woman to another ... The effect on him surely must have been one of insecurity, and if this is so, it perhaps explains his innate suspiciousness and his nonchalant cynicism of a man who has known deep hurt and needs a tough shell.

So there you have it. John Grey Gorton was born free but acquired an insecurity due to his personal circumstances. In short, don't blame John Gorton for any perceived faults. His (inherited) insecurity explains all. Maybe John Gorton wanted Australians to know more about his past so they would identify more readily with him. And attribute any 'innate suspiciousness' or 'nonchalant cynicism' to the insecurity of his youth and, consequently, come to understand his 'tough shell'. If so, it was a big ask.

In fact, compared with many of his generation, John Gorton did not have a tough life. When living in Killara with Kathleen, he was educated at the Anglican Headford preparatory school. Later he went to board at Sydney Church of England Grammar School (Shore) in North Sydney. According to legend, one of his dormitory companions was the Australian actor Errol Flynn (1909–59) who, in time, was expelled. Such, alas, was the fate of quite a few private school types. When Kathleen left Sydney, John Grey returned to Victoria to be under the care of his father. John Rose was a genuine 'Collins Street farmer', choosing to live at Clivden Mansions in East Melbourne and, later, in a flat on Collins Street, with only occasional visits to Kerang.

After a brief period on the farm at Kangaroo Flat, John Grey recommenced his schooling – this time at Geelong Grammar, one of Australia's wealthiest private schools, where he remained until the end of 1930. Then he worked again on his father's property. Soon after, John Rose took out an overdraft to send his son to Oxford, where he arrived in early 1932. There were many less expensive options, including Melbourne University. John Grey returned to Australia with a Master of Arts in history, economics and political science.

On arrival in Britain in 1932, Gorton had learned to fly. Two years later, while holidaying in Spain, he met Bettina Brown – an eighteen-year-old from Bangor, Maine, who was studying French at the Sorbonne in Paris. They married at St Giles church Oxford on 16 February 1935 and visited Bettina's family in the United States before returning to Australia and the hard life of irrigation farming at Kangaroo Flat. They had a girl and two boys – Joanna (born 1937), Michael (born 1938) and Robin (born 1941). Bettina Gorton, an intelligent woman, effectively ran the farm during her husband's war service and after he entered federal politics.

John Gorton was a real charmer. As a student at Melbourne University in the mid 1960s I well remember a campus performance where he exuded charisma and, occasionally, humour. He had the air of an Aussie larrikin but was a minister of the Crown. This blokey demeanour continued into his retiring years. He told dinner guests at the 'Prime Ministers on Prime Ministers' lecture that, in his day, the atmosphere in Old Parliament House's members' bar had been of 'good humour'. Following a suitable pause he added: 'Only once did they come to blows – when I socked somebody, which was a great mistake.' There followed much laughter. After he became prime minister, John Gorton maintained that he was 'not of or in the establishment'. But his *Who's Who* entry suggested otherwise: MA Oxon.; educated Geelong Grammar and Brasenose College, Oxford; orchardist; pilot RAAF 1940–45; president Kerang Shire 1949–50; Melbourne Club. It was later revealed that Brother Gorton was a Mason.[8]

Perhaps his anti-establishment demeanour exhibited a sense of insecurity. For, clearly, he was not without establishment connections. John Gorton was elected as a Liberal senator for Victoria at the December 1949 federal election that saw the Coalition sweep to office and the defeat of Ben Chifley's Labor government. He was among a number of ex-servicemen who entered Parliament at the time. The former RAAF pilot was strongly anti-communist. Moreover, he was but one of many Australians who were politicised in reaction to the attempts by Labor Prime Minister Ben Chifley to nationalise the private trading banks. Like many Liberals in the 1940s and 1950s, John Gorton did not articulate a coherent political position – except that he was opposed to communism, socialism and Labor. This was sufficient motive for seeking a parliamentary career. Along with, perhaps, the opportunity to escape the drudgery of orchard farming in the Mallee.

Robert Menzies, for one, did not succumb immediately to the Gorton charm. Despite being one of the Coalition's better performers in the Senate, John Gorton was overlooked by Menzies for promotion to the ministry for almost a decade. It is not clear why his talents were ignored at the time. It is likely that the Liberal Party founder disliked Gorton's irreverence and independence. He had crossed the floor in the Senate and voted with the Labor Opposition and was known to be less than deferential to his leader in the Liberal party room. In April 1974, when in retirement, Menzies described Gorton as a 'mischief maker'.[9]

John Gorton was appointed minister for the navy in December 1958. He was moved sideways in December 1963 – becoming minister for works and also minister assisting the prime minister in Commonwealth activities relating to education and research. In this latter role, Gorton was responsible for implementing the Coalition's 1963 election promise to provide financial assistance (by means of science grants) to non-government schools. This represented a victory for Australian Catholics in their long campaign to obtain state aid for Catholic denominational schools.

Harold Holt became prime minister on 26 January 1966, following Sir Robert Menzies' retirement. Gorton retained his ministerial positions, also taking over as deputy leader of the government in the Senate. After the Coalition's landslide victory in December 1966, he was appointed minister for education and science. In October 1967 Denham Henty stepped down as government Senate leader and Gorton took his place. It was in this capacity that he tabled the manifests detailing those who had travelled on the RAAF VIP flights. Previously, acting on departmental advice, the existence of such documentation had been denied by Prime Minister Holt and Peter Howson (the minister for air). The existence of manifests provided evidence that the RAAF VIP squadron had flown passengers other than those who were entitled to such perks – including politicians' family members and friends. This became a political scandal. John Gorton's will to resolve the issue – and his evident frankness – won him political kudos.

Then on Sunday 17 December 1967 Harold Holt drowned at Cheviot beach near Portsea, Victoria. Soon after, John McEwen (deputy prime minister and Country Party leader) declared that he would not enter into coalition with a government headed by deputy Liberal leader William McMahon. John Gorton contested and won the Liberal leadership, defeating Paul Hasluck, Leslie Bury and Billy Snedden in a party room ballot. The result in the final Gorton/Hasluck runoff was never released officially but was probably 43 to 38 – with most of the ministry supporting external affairs minister Hasluck and most of the backbench (including many senators) voting for Gorton. There was a widespread view among Liberal backbench parliamentarians that John Gorton was the best equipped of the available talent to take on Gough Whitlam, a highly skilled parliamentary performer who was in the process of reforming and modernising the Labor Party. William McMahon remained deputy leader. John Gorton was sworn in as prime minister of Australia on 10 January 1968. On 24 February he contested, and won, Harold Holt's seat of Higgins in Melbourne and entered the House of Representatives. In early 1968 John Gorton was a very popular prime minister. He looked fresh and spoke like a true nationalist with a genuine touch. It was not long, however, before he began to stumble and his communications skills deserted him.

For all his time in parliament, John Gorton was inexperienced. As at 10 January 1968 he had never held one of the key portfolios (Treasury, External Affairs, Trade, Defence) and had never sat in the House of Representatives. His accession to the prime ministership was organised by (then) junior minister Malcolm Fraser and (then) backbenchers Malcolm Scott and Dudley Erwin. The leadership ballot was delayed by the fact that Harold Holt's body was not found and it was regarded as proper to allow a decent period to elapse before conducting a ballot to determine his successor. John McEwen had been sworn in as (temporary) prime minister on 19 December 1967. After the Holt memorial service, the four leadership aspirants took part in a number of television appearances. John Gorton was the best performer by far – which assisted those running his campaign within the party. He also hit the phones to lobby on his own behalf and received significant support from within the media. Paul Hasluck, on the other hand, formally wrote to his colleagues and left it at that, and his television performances were somewhat wooden. It was clear that Gorton wanted the job more than Hasluck. He prevailed in the Liberal party room on 9 January 1968. As far as Liberal leaders went, we had not seen anything yet.

On 30 September 1968 John Gorton addressed the West Australian Chamber of Manufacturers in Perth. By then he had been prime minister for just on nine months. As if to celebrate the occasion, Gorton told his audience: 'You ain't seen nothing yet.' By then, however, those who were watching the Gorton government had witnessed plenty – with much more to come.

'You ain't seen nothing yet' was the title given to Maximilian Walsh's analysis of Gorton published in the November–December 1968 issue of *Quadrant* magazine.[10] The author predicted that 'even in this early stage ... Gortonism is going to be exceedingly difficult for the traditional Liberal Party to digest'. During the first year of his prime ministership Gorton indicated that he was a centralist with respect to Commonwealth–state financial relations and something of a foreign policy isolationist who was less than enthusiastic about Australia's Vietnam commitment. He was also cynical about the merits of foreign investment – quite an extraordinary policy position for the leader of Australia's main pro-free enterprise party.

The party established by Robert Menzies had a federal structure with weak central administration and proclaimed states' rights as a value. After the Labor Split of the mid 1950s, the Menzies government had sought to keep the anti-communist breakaway Democratic Labor Party on side, especially with respect to foreign policy matters. In turn, the DLP gave its first preferences to the Coalition. Traditionally the Australian business community, which generally supported foreign investment, had bankrolled the Liberal Party. John Gorton's disputes with the states, the DLP and business put all these key relationships under strain – for no considered or clearly enunciated reason. Yet Gorton held on to publicly stated positions for as long as possible with stubbornness and a dismissive attitude to his critics. The evident arrogance was counterproductive – if only because successful politicians have to make alliances and negotiate. It's part of the craft.

That was just for starters. There was also the question of style. Gorton replaced Peter Bailey (who had worked for Holt) as the prime ministerial private secretary with Ainsley Gotto. Gotto was in her very early twenties. She was able but inexperienced in policy and untested for so senior an appointment. Gorton also removed Sir John Bunting, the head of the Prime Minister's department, replacing him with Sir Lenox Hewitt. At the time, permanent heads were regarded as having what the title suggested – that is, tenure. This upset the Commonwealth public service which, traditionally, had been a key – perhaps the key – provider of policy advice to successive Coalition governments. A compromise was reached, with Bunting heading the newly created Cabinet office. But relations with the public service were never quite the same.

As with most politicians, Gorton had his political friends and enemies. Sir Alexander Downer described himself as one of the former – but was not an uncritical admirer. In *Six Prime Ministers* he wrote that Gorton 'sometimes exuberantly flirted with other men's wives'.[11] Peter Howson fell into the political enemy category. In his diaries, titled *The Life of Politics*, Howson recorded that one evening Bill Aston told him that Gorton 'was not in any condition to have spoken' in the House following a personal attack on him by ALP backbencher Bert James.[12] In the parlance of the day, Ashton was implying that the Prime Minister was 'tired and emotional'. There was a certain bipartisanship about the critics of the public face of the prime ministerial lifestyle. It was not that John Gorton's behaviour was dramatically unusual or untoward – just that he paraded his unorthodoxy, even as prime minister. The Sydney-based Liberal backbencher Edward St John took these criticisms to the floor of the House and later into book form.[13] He objected strongly to Gorton's personal behaviour – in particular his decision to take a young female journalist, after the press gallery dinner, on a late night visit to the United States ambassador in Canberra where US policy in Vietnam was discussed. St John resigned from the Liberal Party and sat as an independent until his defeat at the 1969 election.

John Gorton had wanted to go to an early election in 1968 but was prevented by the DLP's threat to give its preferences to the ALP in a few selected seats. At the time, DLP leader Vince Gair and anti-communist National Civic Council president B. A. Santamaria were in dispute with Gorton over his ambivalence about Australia's overseas commitments – in Vietnam and concerning Malaysia and Singapore. The Cabinet deliberations of 1968 (which were released under the thirty years' rule on 1 January 1999) demonstrated the Gorton government's indecision over Australia's Vietnam commitment. By the time the election was held on 25 October 1969 the government's relationship with the DLP had been patched up somewhat. However, Gorton was still rowing with the state premiers – most notably Liberal Bob Askin in New South Wales and Liberal Henry Bolte in Victoria – over Commonwealth-state financial relations. This was not clever politics for the leader of what was essentially a federalist party.

Harold Holt had led the Coalition to a landslide victory in December 1966. John Gorton could not be expected to match this three years later, especially since he was opposed by a fresh Labor leader, Gough Whitlam. Yet few anticipated the size of the anti-government swing of close to seven per cent. The Coalition lost 15 seats to Labor at a time when the Australian economy was growing strongly with low inflation. Certainly the Gorton government inherited a difficult foreign affairs environment, with the United States uncertain about its commitment in Vietnam and Britain intent on withdrawing from most of the Asia–Pacific region. It was just that, as in so many areas, John Gorton stumbled on foreign policy – due to a lack of coherent policies, poor communication and undisciplined preparation.[14] Australia's Vietnam commitment had been quite popular in 1966; this was much less the case three years later. However, the Gorton government's central foreign policy problem was that it did not have an unequivocal position. As prime minister, John Gorton was not sure whether Australian forces should remain in Vietnam or be withdrawn. And it showed. In the event, in December 1969 the Gorton government announced an in-principle decision to withdraw Australian military forces from Vietnam.

After the election John Gorton was re-elected Liberal leader, defeating challenges by David Fairbairn and William McMahon. For a while it looked as if he might hold on despite ongoing indecision on foreign policy and continuing disagreements with the (mainly Liberal) state premiers. But in March 1971 defence minister Malcolm Fraser resigned from the Cabinet, alleging that the prime minister had been disloyal to him. This was a devastating blow, coming as it did virtually without warning. Within a few days John Gorton surrendered his leadership, following a party room coup. The Gorton/Fraser dispute was not of a kind that should have led to a leadership change. But by then, many a Liberal had had enough. So much so that they were even prepared to vote for William McMahon, knowing that, this time around, the Country Party under its new leader Doug Anthony would not object.

The Gorton government was not without initiative. For example, it set up the National Film and Television Training School and the Australia Council for the Arts. Nevertheless, when in August 1971 John Gorton penned his 'I Did It My Way' apologia for the *Sunday Australian*, his stated list of achievements was, well, slim, unless you count opposition to overseas investment, expanding the government-owned Australian National Line to include shipping operations in international waters and the establishment of the Australian Industry Development Commission as substantial policy initiatives. John Gorton did. He also mentioned some social welfare and environment initiatives (including protection of the Great Barrier Reef), rejoiced in having brought about cheaper petrol prices and claimed to have contributed to 'the creation of an Australian identity and national feeling'. The message was much the same at his 1997 'Prime Ministers on Prime Ministers' address.

Yet for a prime minister who held office in good economic times, there were very few real achievements. The essential problem with John Gorton as prime minister is that, apart from exuding a nationalist ethos, he did not really know what he wanted to achieve in a policy sense. But then policy had never been Gorton's forte. Interviewed by Alan Trengrove just after he had lost Australia's top job, John Gorton concluded: 'I probably wasn't a good politician, or something.'[15] Well, yes. But experienced politicians are expected to be good at politics and on top of policy issues. John Gorton did it his way – with charm and hubris, indecision and arrogance, stubbornness and occasional initiative. He was different. But not constructively so.

Postscript

John Gorton died in Sydney on 19 May 2002, shortly after the publication of Ian Hancock's authorised biography *John Gorton: He Did It His Way.* Hancock concluded that 'Gorton could have been a great Prime Minister, only by ceasing to be himself' and wrote that Gorton had acknowledged that he drank too much when prime minister. Ainsley Gotto addressed The Sydney Institute on 25 March 2002 – it was to be her only public comment on her former employer. She concluded that Australians owed Gorton a 'huge debt'. Tom Hughes QC, Gorton's one-time colleague, spoke at the memorial service in St Andrews Cathedral, with Malcolm Fraser in attendance. Hughes criticised Fraser, saying 'The judgment of history upon John Gorton will be kinder than upon those who conspired to bring him down.' Former Liberal MP Michael Baume described Hughes' address as 'the 13th round of a 12-round championship bout'.

Sir William McMahon

10 MARCH 1971 – 5 DECEMBER 1972

He was the last of Menzies' unbroken line, vainly trying to hold together the remnants of the most enduring political dynasty of the century.

BY PETER SEKULESS

Persistence' is the word that most often recurs in the obituaries of the late Right Honourable Sir William McMahon, CH, LLB, BEc. Friend and foe alike praised this quality in him, if little else. The particular foe who coined the much-repeated description was Gough Whitlam who, as leader of the Australian Labor Party, brought McMahon's twenty-month prime ministership to an end at the December 1972 election. Some of those on his own side of politics were less generous. 'Disloyal, devious, dishonest, untrustworthy, petty, cowardly,' wrote his Liberal Party parliamentary contemporary and rival for office Paul Hasluck.[1]

That McMahon's posthumous reputation has been defined by his enemies was largely his own fault. He frustrated attempts to publish his memoirs and closed access to his personal papers. He deserves, however, a different epitaph; not necessarily more favourable, but different.

Anyone who rises to the peak of his or her profession is remembered mainly for that achievement. Hence McMahon, who liked to be known as 'Bill' but was more often referred to as 'Billy', is recalled for his short but turbulent prime ministership. In McMahon's case the skills of industriously mastering the economy and many ministerial briefs deserted him in the highest office. He was the last of Menzies' unbroken line, vainly trying to hold together the remnants of the most enduring political dynasty of the century. The 1960s was a decade of change worldwide which found political expression in Australia in the federal elections of 1969 and 1972. In the end the traditionalist McMahon could not match Gough Whitlam, the icon of change.

The Liberal–Country Party coalition held power for nearly a quarter of the century but McMahon played a significant role in the defining economic struggle of the entire century; free trade versus protection. History is written by the victors, and the free traders were in the ascendancy at the end of the century. Beside the military exploits of Gallipoli and Kokoda, bureaucratic battles over tariffs and bounties seem like small beer, but the politics of protection have been the most divisive economic issue of the century, particularly for the free-enterprise and rural-based parties.

Protectionist differences between New South Wales and Victoria bedevilled the Federation debate just as fears of globalisation and national competition policy threatened political stability a hundred years later. Honours went to the free traders in the last quarter, but only after the arch-protectionist John McEwen dominated the third quarter. Even the word 'McEwenism' is a term of derision in the free traders' lexicon. McMahon was his principal opponent and McEwen's biography by Peter Golding has a chapter entitled, 'The feud of the giants: McEwen and McMahon'.[2]

In an effort to damn McMahon with faint praise, Paul Hasluck wrote, '... if I allow a busy industry and pertinacity in a cause, I cannot forget that it is the industry and persistence of a man applying himself to mean purpose'. Challenging McEwen at the height of his powers was not a mean purpose, although the means employed by both sides were often less than honourable. In the process McMahon was publicly humiliated. He suffered the most outrageous slings and arrows of political fortune; McMahon was a martyr to the cause of free trade and free market economics. In the end he did not achieve very much, certainly not as prime minister, but he did suffer grievously at the hands of the protectionists. For all his faults, and they were manifold, McMahon should be remembered as one of the martyrs of the free trade movement, because few (if any) suffered more, personally and politically, for their beliefs.

Part of the traditional rivalry between Sydney and Melbourne is based on differences over economic policy. The Victorians favoured those protecting their manufacturing industries while the trading centre of Sydney has always wanted less restrictive policies under which the free flow of goods and services could flourish. Not surprisingly, therefore, the free trader McMahon was born (on 23 February 1908) and bred in Sydney into a wealthy, if not genteel, family. His mother died when he was four years old and his father when he was in his teens. Following his mother's death, he and his siblings were brought up by relatives and guardians, most prominent among them being his mother's politically active brother Samuel Walder, later Sir Samuel, Lord Mayor of Sydney and member of the NSW Legislative Council.

McMahon's education and early career were conventionally upper-middle-class. Sydney Grammar School was followed by study at the University of Sydney, where he boarded at St Paul's College. He followed his father into the law as a matter of course. Both his father and uncle had been active in the United Australia Party, one of the precursors of the Liberal Party. Political activity in the conservative interest was as much part of the Sydney life McMahon indulged in as racing at Randwick and swimming at Bondi.

His progression was not entirely preordained. Although he became a solicitor like his father and joined the leading firm of Allen Allen & Hemsley, he had been originally attracted to a different branch of the law. He told a National Library of Australia oral history interviewer, 'I wanted to become a barrister but my hearing went very bad on me and for a time I found it was difficult for me to hear a person speak unless they spoke rather loudly ... that stopped me from going to the Bar.'[3]

In view of his later political career, McMahon's attraction to the more flamboyant and higher-profile life of a barrister is consistent. His approach to ministerial and legislative duties was that of a barrister mastering every brief and arguing every case vigorously. He carried a brief more successfully in his political career than most of the senior counsel who tried their hands at politics after careers at the Bar, such as Sir Garfield Barwick and Tom Hughes.

In 1939 McMahon enlisted in the army and rose to the rank of major, although his hearing problem precluded operational command or overseas service. After the war he spent sixteen months travelling in England, France, Canada and the United States. On his return he went back to the University of Sydney, where he completed an economics degree, graduating with distinction and winning a prize for proficiency and the Public Service Award for public administration.

The 1949 poll resulted in the election of the first Menzies government and a generation of new Liberal politicians. McMahon was returned as the member for the western Sydney suburban electorate of Lowe, centred on Strathfield. He held Lowe for the Liberal Party until he retired from Parliament in 1982. As one of the 'Forty-niners', as they were known, he was initially unexceptional. His early contributions to parliamentary proceedings, including his maiden speech. were heavily larded with par-for-the-course attacks on communism and socialism.

He advanced quickly, becoming a junior defence minister – navy and air – in 1951, followed by the ministry of social services after the 1954 election. His rapid advancement was probably more a result of his strong connections with the NSW Liberal Party than recognition of his latent abilities. The crucial appointment was as Minister for Primary Industry in 1956. Apart from losing their mothers in early childhood McMahon and John McEwen, leader of the Country Party, had little in common. Until 1956, the slight, suede-shoed (considered a sign of loucheness), garrulous Sydney socialite was beneath the gaze of the dour, depression-scarred minister for the newly created ministry for trade.

According to McEwen's biographer, 'The reality is that for most of the twenty-two years they were in Parliament together the only thing they seemed to share was distaste for each other. It is hard to be sure precisely when it all started but it seems that the spark that ignited their mutual antagonism was McMahon's appointment as Minister for Primary Industry, although its effect was not immediate ... McMahon was generally regarded as a good minister. Once he set his mind on throwing off his playboy image and becoming a career politician he quickly demonstrated a capacity to absorb the detail of his portfolio and to argue his department's case forcibly and well in the Cabinet room.'[2]

Alan Reid, generally more sympathetic to McMahon, described the genesis of the feud differently. 'McMahon was to McEwen what McEwen had been to a procession of Liberal and Country Party leaders: an irritant that gradually developed into a full-sized pain in the neck which, despite all remedial measures, persisted naggingly and irremovably.'[3] The irony of the situation was that McMahon's appointment as minister for primary industry was supposed to ensure that agriculture stayed within the Country Party sphere of influence. Parliamentary wits suggested that McMahon's knowledge of livestock did not extend beyond the saddling enclosure at Royal Randwick racecourse. The appointment gave McMahon a setting in which to demonstrate intelligence, toughness, and a hitherto unsuspected virtuosity: 'He was not satisfied, as the Country Party had mistakenly judged he would be satisfied, with the trappings of authority: he wanted the authority of office, as well as the office. Applying himself with the nervy intensity that was at once a strength and the source of much of his unpopularity with easier going, less-nakedly ambitious colleagues, he concentrated on acquiring a working knowledge of the complexities of Australia's major primary industries.'[4]

After the next election in 1958 McMahon was promoted out of primary industry to the considerably more senior portfolio of Labour and National Service, where he remained until the major reshuffle following Menzies' resignation at the start of 1966. Struggles with the union movement, particularly the Waterside Workers' Federation, enhanced his reputation. There was little doubt he was positioning himself for the Treasury when Menzies stepped down. He took opportunities such as the annual debate on the Budget to showcase his expertise in matters economic. In 1965, then aged fifty-seven, he married Sonia Hopkins, some years his junior, and their union attracted considerable publicity.

In the Liberal Party election for positions following Menzies' resignation, McMahon canvassed his colleagues vigorously, narrowly defeating Hasluck, who did not, for the deputy leadership. Hence early in 1966 McMahon followed Holt's ministerial spoor from Labour and National Service to the Treasury. Only twenty men had become federal treasurer since Federation, and ten had also been prime ministers. McMahon had good qualifications for both jobs: he was the first to have a university degree in economics, he was the ranking Liberal from New South Wales and he was a devoted family man.

The coming clash between McMahon, free trade flagwaver, and McEwen, the champion of protection, can only be understood in the light of the history of the Country Party, particularly McEwen's plans for its expansion. Faced with the inevitable urbanisation of the population, the junior party in the governing coalition faced consequent declining parliamentary representation, fewer ministries and hence less power. McEwen's master plan was to defy the historical forces of declining rural population by broadening the base of his political party to embrace urban manufacturing. It was a bold strategy, necessary for the subsequent continuing survival and significance of what was renamed the National Party. The vital tactic in the strategy of building a bridge between city manufacturing and the bush was industry protection, particularly tariffs.

The bureaucratic vehicle for dispensing protection to Australian industry – both indigenous and branches of foreign companies – was the Department of Trade. In contrast to previous Country Party leaders, McEwen established his own economic bureaucracy to challenge the policymaking role of the Treasury. The officials of the Treasury naturally resented any challenge to their economic supremacy, but McEwen's onslaught was especially offensive in their eyes. Treasury's mission, like that of any accountant, is to balance the books; any expenditure must be questioned and justified. Tariffs much beloved by McEwen offended against Treasury's economic orthodoxy because they were an indirect form of industry assistance.

At the heart of McEwen's strategy was a paradox. His objective was to build the farmers' political party into an enduring national force by forging an alliance with the manufacturing sector. This was to be achieved by using government money to protect secondary industry. Government support meant that the prices of goods such as chemicals, clothing, motor vehicles and machinery were higher than the same goods directly imported without tariffs and other forms of protection. The inherent weakness for McEwen, and the paradox of his strategy, was that those he was supposed to be helping were paying more for the essentials they needed to run their farms, such as machinery, motor vehicles and chemicals. Despite the best efforts of McEwen and his lieutenants to educate their rural constituency about the need for higher prices, dissatisfaction grew within the farming community, particularly among grazier interests and large pastoralists with links to the Liberal and Country parties.

For almost four years, between January 1966 and November 1969, McMahon was treasurer. He delivered four Budgets, then brought down in the August of each year. This period was the pinnacle of his political career, the role for which he had so assiduously prepared himself. His critics point out that the excellent reputation he earned was due more to self-promotion and a benign economy than to skill in handling the economy. The treasurer was the beneficiary, not the cause, of Australia's economic prosperity, and he was further charged with failing to withstand political pressure to be over-generous with taxpayers' money before the 1967 Senate and 1969 general elections. However, no one gainsaid the barrister-like tenacity with which he mastered his new and most challenging ministerial brief. Two incidents above all – the decision not to devalue fully the Australian dollar and his successful opposition to the establishment of the Australian Industry Development Corporation – were crucial.

Both devaluation and 'McEwen's bank', as it was known, went to the heart of the tension between the two men and their respective parties. To maintain the loyalty of its farming base, the Country Party needed to ensure that the price of primary products did not become too high for overseas buyers. A devaluation of sterling late in 1967 threatened just such a crisis. With McEwen overseas, Cabinet adopted McMahon's submission that the Australian dollar should only partially follow the pound. Holt, with McMahon's help, had asserted himself over the Country Party. On his return McEwen unsuccessfully tried to have consideration of the devaluation reopened, but had to be content with compensation for devaluation-affected industries.

Fear of foreign investment leading to overseas control of national assets was another McMahon–McEwen battleground. The Treasury line favoured the free flow of capital, whereas the protectionists wanted to prevent the sale of land and assets to overseas interests, an attitude that found popular expression in emotive terms such as 'selling off the farm' and 'selling the family silver'. One of McEwen's responses was to establish a financial institution capable of keeping assets in Australian hands. His proposal was to establish a lender of the first resort, to be known as the Australian Industry Development Corporation. Such a government-owned investment bank was anathema to Treasury and McMahon who, between them, mounted such an effective counter-attack that McEwen, with maximum bad grace, was forced to withdraw his submission to Cabinet.

In McMahon the free trade interest had such an effective advocate that the arch-protectionist could not risk his becoming prime minister. Following Holt's sudden disappearance late in 1967 McEwen assumed the prime ministership, which arguably should have gone to McMahon as deputy leader of the majority Coalition partner. McEwen then played the ultimate Country Party card. He effectively threatened to end the Coalition by vetoing McMahon as the Liberal's choice for prime minister. The Country Party would not serve in a Coalition government led by McMahon. Adopting smear tactics that even his biographer found dubious, McEwen blackballed McMahon on the unconvincing grounds of his alleged association with journalist and newsletter publisher Maxwell Newton who, in turn, had links with the pro-free trade agricultural lobby, the Basic Industries Group. All leads, however tenuous, led to the end of protectionism, and the one man who as prime minister could thwart McEwen's grand design before he could confidently allow his younger colleagues to succeed him.

Despite the considerable temptation to do otherwise, McMahon behaved with restraint both in his own interest and in that of Coalition unity. As a result he was re-elected Liberal Party deputy leader when the untested John Gorton became prime minister. Following the 1969 election, McMahon unsuccessfully contested the leadership. Gorton moved him to the ministry of external affairs, renamed foreign affairs during his term. Before he retired in 1970 McEwen gained approval for the establishment of the Australian Industry Development Corporation. Although the 1969 election resulted in a huge swing – 7.5 per cent – against the Coalition government, Gorton persisted with his individualistic style of ruling that so antagonised his colleagues in Canberra and the state premiers, provoking a leadership crisis early in 1971.

On 10 March, after Gorton failed to win a vote of confidence of his colleagues, the Liberal Party elected William McMahon as its leader. He was commissioned as prime minister, with Gorton surprisingly elected as deputy, later that day. Gorton also became minister for defence.

'From that day onward, many people myself included, believed that McMahon didn't have a chance electorally unless some cataclysmic event tore the Opposition apart,' wrote Alan Reid nine years later. 'McMahon would have needed the wisdom of a Solomon and the diplomatic skill of a Talleyrand to re-establish the Coalition as a united, coherent fighting force. Half his Cabinet and half his party resented his leadership from the outset, believing that Gorton had been unjustly treated.'[5]

An air of disorganisation at times verging on panic permeated the new government, its first parliamentary session ending in May with seventeen pieces of legislation being rushed through in fifteen hours. Although the focus of government and public attention was primarily domestic, the increasing unpopularity of Australia's involvement in the Vietnam war assisted the Opposition, and the government was unlucky with its China policy. While making secret overtures to the People's Republic of China, the government criticised the Opposition for accepting an invitation for a party led by Whitlam to visit the country. When it became known that US President Nixon was to visit China, signalling the beginning of normalisation of relations with the West, the government's criticism of the Opposition rang hollow. The China incident reinforced in the minds of the Australian electorate the image of an Opposition more in touch with the realities of foreign policy than the government.

McMahon did, however, begin to restore normal relations with the Australian states strained under Gorton. At the first Premiers' Conference of his administration the state leaders were pleased with the increased share of revenues on offer and the foreshadowing of repeal of

Gorton's controversial offshore minerals legislation. Otherwise there was little comfort for the government in 1971.

After less than six months Gorton resigned as minister for defence, ostensibly over his comments in a series of newspaper articles. He and his supporters continued to destabilise the Liberal Party, weakening it in relation to both the Labor Party and the Country Party. At the end of the year, in a bitter reprise of the Holt–McMahon–McEwen currency crisis of 1967, the deteriorating Vietnam War-induced world economic adjustment led to a devaluation battle with McEwen's successor, Country Party leader Doug Anthony and his two colleagues in Cabinet, Ian Sinclair and Peter Nixon. Anthony threatened to take the Country Party out of the Coalition unless the Australian dollar followed the US currency downward. McMahon was forced to compromise.

1972 began with McMahon's economic credentials – previously his strength – undermined. Inflation was running at its highest rate for twenty years and with 130,000 people out of work, unemployment was at its highest for nearly ten years. Even his closest political allies were privately dismayed. 'Bill McMahon is not an easy Prime Minister with whom to work. How often one would like to be firm and tell him what one thinks, but then one has to remember that we put him there, that he's got to be supported. Half the time one spends trying to help him over his own foibles and weakness to character. He is not good at building up a team spirit; he doesn't really know how to delegate; he likes to feel that he's doing everything himself.' Thus wrote McMahon minister and party supporter Peter Howson in his diary entry for 6 January 1972.[6]

Howson's portfolio epitomised the McMahon government's ineffectual attempts to match the broad-ranging comprehensive policies developed by Labor. Howson was minister for Aborigines, arts and the environment, a grab-bag ministry seeking to pre-empt Labor's policies, which were resonating with the electorate. McMahon's piecemeal approach to emerging national issues appears optimistic against Whitlam's sound vision of universal health schemes, renovating the cities and sweeping social welfare reform.

In March, a year after McMahon succeeded Gorton, the Labor Party had a clear lead in the opinion polls over the Coalition and Democratic Labor Party combined, and the prime minister's personal rating continued to slide. By the time Parliament resumed for the Budget session in August, the government's prospects had improved. Generous income tax cuts and pension increases were introduced in a mid-year 'mini' Budget, the states were placated with the restoration of their rights over offshore minerals and the prime minister acted decisively to end a potentially serious oil industry strike.

The August Budget itself did little to restore McMahon's standing as a sound economic manager, but did contain more social welfare handouts, further income tax cuts and new defence spending. The benefits of the Budget were not consolidated, however, and the final months to the 2 December election saw a return to the earlier crisis-ridden administration. A generous assessment of McMahon is provided by Whitlam staffer Graham Freudenberg who, perhaps surprisingly, contradicts the view that his prime ministership was a failure notable for little more than his wife exposing more of her person than was customary at the time. 'Had he been nothing more than that, the Labor victory of 1972 would have been vastly greater than it was, and the Liberal resurgence after 1972 would have taken much longer than it did.' The swing to Labor in 1972 was only 2.5 per cent overall, one-third of the swing against the Gorton government in 1969.

'For Liberals, at the parliamentary, organisation and electorate levels, the fact that McMahon commanded nothing more than nominal loyalty as Menzies' vestigial heir, eased their passage towards defeat. On the Liberals' part, it was never a question of genuine goodwill towards Labor. There was none. But there was, in 1972, a widespread absence of active ill-will, scarcely any of the hatred and fear which disfigured the 1950s. For this condition, McMahon was largely, if indirectly, responsible; and though it was essentially a negative achievement, it is not the worst thing to be said of a Prime Minister that he presided over one of the happiest years of his country's history.'[7]

William McMahon remained the member for Lowe for a decade after the election defeat of 1972. He died in 1988, survived by his wife, a son and two daughters.

Edward Gough Whitlam

5 DECEMBER 1972 – 11 NOVEMBER 1975

Whitlam set the political and policy agendas for Australian federal government over more than a decade.

BY CLEM LLOYD

In 1990, the *Chambers Biographical Dictionary* published a ten-line entry on Edward Gough Whitlam, Australia's nineteenth prime minister. It noted his year of birth (1916), his education at Sydney University, war service in the RAAF, his career as a barrister, election as federal MP for Werriwa in 1952, his leadership of the ALP in 1967, the period of his prime ministership (1972–75), and that he was foreign minister in 1973. The remainder merits quotation:

> [Whitlam] resigned as MP to take up a visiting appointment at the Australian National University. His many publications, chiefly political and constitutional, also include *The Italian Inspiration in English Literature* (1980).[1]

Something missing? What about the constitutional crisis and the dismissal of 1975? Surely these deserve a passing reference in even the skimpiest of biographies? In conveying a sense of career, it's a bit like an entry on Abraham Lincoln concluding: 'American President (1861–65); made keynote address, Gettysburg 1863; pursued theatrical interests.'

As a succinct summary of the Whitlam phenomenon this is, of course, asinine. Yet, inadvertently, it also exposes a kernel of truth. The political crisis and the Dismissal of late 1975 have diminished important themes and exceptional achievements in Whitlam's long public life. It is easy to forget that Whitlam lived for fifty-nine years before the dismissal and more than a quarter of a century after it. The flourishing Whitlam industry has concentrated obsessively on the twenty-five days between 16 October and 15 November 1975. The following account does not diminish the Whitlam government or the Dismissal; far from it. But it is designed to set these transforming events in the narrative dimensions of a whole career, not to let them be its all-consuming denouement.

When Gough Whitlam was born, on 11 July 1916, Billy Hughes was Australian prime minister and all his predecessors were still alive (Barton, Deakin, Reid, Watson, Fisher, Cook). Thus, Whitlam lived during the lives of all Australian prime ministers, and through the prime ministership of seventeen of them, including, of course, himself. His father, Harry Frederick Ernest Whitlam, joined the Victorian public service in 1901, the year of Federation. He transferred to the

Commonwealth public service in 1911 and provided distinguished public service as a senior legal officer, including twelve years as Commonwealth Crown solicitor. His public career overlapped with the political career of his son Gough. Together the Whitlams, father and son, were involved directly in public life and public service through the entire century of the Australian Commonwealth. This constitutes a dynastic accomplishment without peer in the Australian experience. The only conjunction that springs to mind is that of the Earl of Chatham (Pitt the Elder) and William Pitt (Pitt the Younger) in the public life of eighteenth-century England.

Gough Whitlam was a federal parliamentarian for twenty-six years. Of the Australian prime ministers, only a handful served longer in Parliament. He was party leader, deputy leader and prime minister for eighteen years, a record exceeded only by Menzies and McEwen among Australian prime ministers. He has been the only Australian prime minister to use the Constitution to call a joint sitting of both parliamentary Houses to pass deadlocked legislation. For a fortnight in December 1972, Whitlam and his deputy Lance Barnard administered the entire Australian government in a creative and audacious dispensation unique in Australian history and probably also in the annals of democratic government.

Whitlam, as Australian political leader and theorist, worked squarely in the traditions and practice of social democracy. His 25 per cent tariff reduction September 1973 also put Australia in the forefront of market reform. Over twenty years he was largely responsible for devising and collating a massive reformist agenda known in Whitlamism simply as the Program. Between 1972 and 1975 he presided obdurately over a single-minded attempt to implement it in full. The Program was much frustrated by parliamentary opposition and much dismantled after his dismissal. Even so, in Whitlam's estimate, more than half the Program was implemented by legislative and executive means. Even in 2000 an important residue remained. Whitlam set the political and policy agendas for Australian federal government over more than a decade and brought sophistication of structure and process to the moribund party machinery of the Australian Labor Party, which he set out to reform in the early 1960s. This involved a display of raw political courage unwaveringly sustained over a decade, contemptuous of even the most basic tenets of political self-preservation. The ALP's successes over twenty-five years were anchored in the bedrock of the Whitlam-driven reform of the administration and political process.

Whitlam may have been a compound or condensation of a place name, possibly Middle English in origin. The given name, *Gough*, more common as a surname, was a sobriquet from the Welsh *Gogh* or *Coch*, meaning *red*.[2] Gough Whitlam's great-grandfather, Henry George Whitlam, was an officer in the British army in India. He fought in the Sikh wars of the late 1840s and came to colonial Victoria in the 1850s after his British fiancee died. Frederick Whitlam worked on the goldfields, then as a storekeeper and sheriff's officer. He settled in Castlemaine, where he supervised jail work gangs in building the town gardens.[3]

Henry Whitlam's son Henry Hugh Gough Whitlam owed his reverberant name to Viscount Hugh Gough, his father's old commander. Henry moved his family to Melbourne, where he ran a successful fruit and vegetable business. His son Harry Frederick Ernest (Fred) Whitlam, born in 1884, was Gough's father. Fred Whitlam trained as an accountant, and did a law degree by evening study. He joined the Victorian public service in 1901, moving in 1911 to the Federal Land Tax Office, where he administered the Fisher government's federal land tax. Promoted to the Commonwealth Crown solicitor's office in 1913, among his staff was a young clerk, John McEwen, who became Country Party leader and Australian prime minister in 1967.

On 11 September 1914 Fred Whitlam married Martha Maddocks, of a Shropshire family in England's west country. They set up house in Kew, where Edward Gough Whitlam was born on 11 July 1916. His sister Freda was born four years later. Among his earliest memories was being in hospital with his mother during the Spanish influenza pandemic of 1919. In 1921, Fred Whitlam was appointed deputy Crown solicitor in Sydney, where he took his young family. Gough attended Knox Grammar, a private boys' school at Warrawee on Sydney's north shore. Fred became assistant Crown solicitor in Canberra in 1927, moving his family to a house close to Parliament and administration in the rudimentary capital. He was appointed Commonwealth Crown solicitor in 1936, assuming responsibility for the legal advisings of federal government. Paul Hasluck has extolled his civic virtues: 'Any educational or cultural activity in those days in Canberra depended a good deal on Fred Whitlam. I came to know him as a public-spirited, meticulous and dutiful man with an inquiring but cautious mind, who was always very concerned to make sure that whatever was done was right, both in the sense of being legally unexceptionable but soundly based on principle. He was kindly and modest.'[4]

Both Fred and Martha Whitlam were pious church-goers, but accepted with good grace their son's early withdrawal from religious observance while still at high school. In later years Gough Whitlam described himself as a 'fellow traveller' with Christianity, having an intense interest in the Judaeo-Christian tradition but not establishing a working relationship with God.

Gough Whitlam's education was marked by institutional diversity: private prep school; Sydney private school; Canberra state school; Canberra private school. In subjects such as Latin and English he excelled, finishing high in state seniority lists. Complying with his father's wish that he should do Greek, he studied the language on Saturday mornings with Professor L. H. Allen of Canberra University College. The standard biographical studies of Whitlam refer to waywardness, but his childhood and schooldays seem to have been fulfilling.

In 1935, he went to Sydney University to do arts, joining St Pauls, an Anglican college on campus. He won a blue for rowing, reorganised the college library, served as chapel warden, edited *Hermes*, the 'Varsity students' magazine, and *The Pauline*, the college journal. He wrote passable satirical verse after Alexander Pope and did memorable skits on Noel Coward and Neville Chamberlain in university reviews. Gough studied Latin, Greek, English and some psychology. In a 'lounge lizard' role, he appeared briefly in *Broken Melody*, a minor Australian movie. Off campus, Whitlam participated enthusiastically in Sydney's accessible cafe life. He dallied in a well-publicised though short-lived romance with Guila Bustabo, a nineteen-year-old concert violinist from Europe. Says Laurie Oakes: 'The incident was not typical of Whitlam, who was not the lady-killer type, and Guila appears to be the only girl in whom he took any real interest until he met Margaret Dovey a year later ... Margaret Dovey was the daughter of a prominent barrister, Mr Wilfred Dovey, who later became a Supreme Court judge. Unlike Whitlam she was a good mixer and was at home in any group.'[5] He courted Margaret Dovey for more than two years, eventually marrying her on 2 April 1942.

According to Edward St John, a close university friend, Whitlam was popular, although 'there might have been disapproval from some who thought he was too big for his boots'. Edward St John found Whitlam bright, knowledgeable and amusing, but failed to discern leadership qualities: 'I thought he would be a most excellent lieutenant for someone else who had the leadership quality. He would provide all the diplomacy and the knowledge and the background and the finesse and all that sort of thing while someone else might do the leading.'[6]

Whitlam embarked on law studies tardily, saying later that there was 'no urgent inclination'. He joined the Sydney University Regiment, an infantry outfit of sorts, when war broke out in Europe. After Pearl Harbor in late 1941 he enlisted in the RAAF, qualifying for air crew and eventual promotion as a flight lieutenant. Choice of service might have been based on the rationale that fate in the air was mostly quick, clean and decisive compared with war on land and sea. He was a navigator of Ventura bombers on reconnaissance and bombing sorties, based mostly at Gove, in northern Australia. During the 1943 federal elections, Whitlam distributed ALP literature in RAAF messes and barracks. He became keenly involved in the Fourteen Powers referendum of 1944, aimed at giving the federal government powers to implement postwar reconstruction programs. To the consternation of his commanding officer, Whitlam campaigned for a 'Yes' vote in his squadron. The referendum was defeated easily, but Whitlam's teeming political sensibility had been activated. When the war ended, while still in uniform, he joined the ALP in Sydney in August 1945. He was then twenty-nine.

Whitlam resumed his legal studies, completed his Bachelor of Laws and was admitted to the federal and NSW bars in 1947. He was eligible for war service housing, and he used his loan to build a house at Cronulla, a well-established seaside resort south of Sydney. Surrounding country was mostly bush, with miners, small farmers, and families who had sought cheaper living during the Great Depression. The region was ripe for massive urban development: 'Suddenly the war was over, the ex-servicemen wanted somewhere to live, land was £50–$60 a block and out you came.'[7] Whitlam's migration from plush inner Sydney to raw suburbia has been seen as political opportunism by both ALP supporters and political opponents. According to Hasluck, Whitlam had picked both his party and his seat as 'the best bet'. He could see his way to the top in the Labor Party, but not in the Liberal Party. Undoubtedly, Whitlam saw opportunities in the new suburbs for his expanding vision of reformism based on federal constitutional powers. The area was known in Labor Party parlance as the 'Red Belt', no place for a blatant political opportunist, particularly a 'silvertail' from inner Sydney. Realistically, Whitlam set his immediate sights on local government and possibly state government.

Whitlam's task on entering the cabalistic world of Labor branch politics was to convince a dubious branch membership of his Labor sympathies. His remorseless didacticism aroused incredulity among traditional Laborites steeped in class struggle and militant socialism. According to Les Johnson, branch members jumped on chairs to scream abuse at Whitlam. Some threatened to 'belt him up': 'If you'd go to a fund-raising function in a pub or one of the few clubs ... as the night went on they'd all turn on Whitlam and there'd be a bit of a scurry around him and people trying to plant a punch onto him because they saw him as something they didn't comprehend, it wasn't their Labor Party that he was advocating at all. The man was talking about the constitution all the time, not confrontation.'[8]

The old militant socialist Labor Party, anti-boss and anti-establishment, was feeling the 'winds of Whitlam reformism' for the first time: 'He was even talking about [state government's] abolition and widening of local government powers ... and that they'd be funded with special grants from the constitution, whatever that was you see ... People thought this was pie in the sky.'[9]

Whitlam prevailed through a combination of persistence, patience, intelligence, geniality and ubiquity. His opponents had no answer to his vitality, consuming presence and perpetual advocacy. From its very beginnings, Whitlam's success was founded on the willingness of the initially sceptical to recognise his intellectual merit and political appeal. Thus Labor people were prepared to cross factional lines to support him because of his political talent.

Whitlam stood for Sutherland Shire Council in 1948 and was soundly defeated. In 1950 he stood for Labor in the state elections on the principle that 'if you say no in that sort of situation, you may not be asked again'.[10]

He made ground, but lost. A further Council bid also failed. In 1951–52 Whitlam took a prestigious and well-publicised role as junior barrister in a Royal Commission on the liquor trade. This primed him for his big chance when Bert Lazzarini stood down after holding the federal seat of Werriwa for more than thirty years. Whitlam won a difficult preselection. When Lazzarini died almost two years before the scheduled federal election, Whitlam won the by-election in late 1952 by six thousand votes. For him, said Hasluck, 'the trumpets had begun to blow on the steps of heaven'.[11]

Whitlam joined a federal caucus still basking in the warm glow of leader H. V. [Bert] Evatt's defeat of Menzies' proposed outlawing of the Communist Party in the 1951 constitutional referendum. His colleagues were impressed by Whitlam's commanding presence and energy, despite 'silvertail' attributes. His meticulous, finicky approach to his duties prompted both awe and amusement: 'The assiduous Whitlam had files on everything, on defence and housing and health and environment and sewerage ... He'd push everything into these files and on the front of every manilla folder there'd be a summary of the housing scene, the ten salient points, how many people there were waiting for Housing Commission homes in each state of Australia, and the young assiduous lawyer was getting his speechmaking material together under all these topics.'[12]

It was an era when the database of the typical Labor MP typically comprised a few stained folders mostly containing tattered, yellowing press clippings. Whitlam was exemplary in his avoidance of bar and billiard room, the traditional Mecca of political lucubration and lubrication. His disposition was essentially solitary, very much absorbed in his work and making few close friends. The exasperation aroused by Whitlam's oddities and vast height was embodied in a sobriquet coined by veteran left-winger Les Haylen: 'the Young Brolga'.

The optimism and harmony of the Labor caucus were shattered in 1954, firstly by the Petrov Russian spy case on the eve of the May federal elections which Menzies won narrowly. Evatt embarked on a tragic crusade to expose, then destroy, Catholic-action-linked 'industrial groupers' from the ALP. This detonated the great Labor Split of 1954–55, involving more than a decade of purge, schism, and lost opportunity. A breakaway Democratic Labor Party frustrated the ALP's government aspirations for almost twenty years.

Whitlam greatly admired Evatt and supported him staunchly during the Split and its aftermath. In the early years at least, he had some affinity with the traditional Left, which broadly covered about 60 per cent of the caucus, and its fiery leader Eddie Ward. He gradually drifted to a centre position, broadly supporting Evatt's social democracy but without specific factional affiliation. This enabled him to establish support among his colleagues on the basis of perceived merit unaffected by factional loyalty. Thus he made his pitch to his colleagues on leadership and electoral plausibility. His campaign style impressed because he moulded it to specific regional interests and needs. Labor politicians intent on holding their seats and winning government were convinced by this custom-made approach. Labor candidates enlisted his support to get them into Parliament. Progressive leadership in the party machines looking desperately for vote-winners became converts to his style and persona. Evatt was in evident decline. The other senior leadership figures – the deputy leader, Arthur Calwell, Eddie Ward, and Reg Pollard – were in their sixties. Whitlam was in his early forties, in the prime of life, exuberant in mind and body.

Whitlam also picked up caucus support in less unorthodox ways. He disliked Alan Dalziel, a member of Evatt's staff. Tony Mulvihill, an officer in the NSW branch, also loathed Dalziel, who wrote wounding comment about Whitlam and Mulvihill in *Century*, a weekly political newspaper. Mulvihill decided to have it out with him: 'So I went down to the Commonwealth Offices and I thumped [Dalziel] in the ear and Bert Evatt was very upset about it ... A voice came on the phone and it was Edward Gough Whitlam, he was the relatively young member out in the Werriwa electorate. He said, "Tony, you were magnificent." I said, "Well, thanks, Gough." And he said, "Tony, if there is a court case, I'll defend you for free." And from then on, I was a Whitlam man through and through.'[13] Mulvihill became an influential member of the NSW state machine, and then a Senator for NSW, ever a staunch Whitlam supporter.

By the late 1950s, Whitlam's chances began to come. After the 1958 federal elections he was elected to the caucus executive. When Evatt resigned in early 1960, Whitlam emerged as a viable candidate for deputy leader. With three candidates left in the ballot, Ward led Whitlam 32–28, with 12 remaining preference votes expected to favour Ward. Astoundingly, Whitlam secured 10 of these preferences, giving him victory by 38–34. According to scrutineers, several left-wing preferences went to Whitlam on the reasoning: 'Well I couldn't win my electorate with Eddie Ward so I'll vote for Whitlam.'[14] As another backbencher, Gordon Bryant put it, 'I voted for Gough because I recognised his talents ...'[15] A majority of the caucus now saw him as most likely to lead Labor out of the wilderness.

The Calwell–Whitlam leadership was generally accepted in the caucus as a reasonable blending of the traditional Labor politician and the modern. While they were never close, Whitlam and Calwell worked together well enough in the early years. Whitlam was able to expand and refine the Program, assisted by additional staff drawn from his leadership entitlements. With a deepening economic crisis through 1960–61 because of a stringent credit squeeze, and two years of constructive policy development and internal harmony, the ALP almost won a stunning victory in the federal elections of October 1961. It lost by only a seat, and Whitlam nearly became deputy prime minister at his first attempt.

Between 1961 and 1963, Menzies bent his prodigious political skills to the political revival of his frayed government. As a means of electoral redemption, he singled out state aid for non-government schools, a sticky area for Labor policymakers. The increasing dominance of television in political communication told against the rugged Calwell, who had made his supreme effort in 1961. With superb timing, Menzies called a snap election in November 1963, exploiting rumbles within the ALP over a projected US naval communications base in northern Australia. Labor plodded in the campaign, failing to rekindle the flair and competence of 1961. Calwell's campaign was unhinged in some degree by the assassination of American President John F. Kennedy, and Menzies won a comfortable victory.

Whitlam had been content to leave the execution of the 1961 and 1963 campaigns largely to Calwell. As Calwell would be seventy by the next expected election, in 1966, it was reasonable that he would stand down so Whitlam, his assured successor, could establish his leadership. Calwell, however, made it plain that he expected another turn, just as Evatt had been given three turns. Soon after the election, Whitlam made a blistering attack on the leadership, policy and organisation of the ALP, not absolving himself: 'There is something basically faulty in a party which failed to win in the circumstances of the 1961 election, or make up a minute leeway in the 1963 elections ... in 1963, the Liberals won 10 seats because in the meantime they had improved more than Labor ... the party 's failure to devise modern, relevant and acceptable methods of formulating and publicising policy is the fault of members in all sections and at all levels of the party, including leaders and members of the Federal Parliamentary Party.'[16]

Whitlam launched a pitched battle to reform the party machine, policies and election campaigning. His principal target was the dominant hardliners in the Victorian branch, a memorable struggle unfurling across four major issues: unity tickets; institutional reform of the party; state aid to independent schools and Labor policy on Australian participation in the Vietnam war. Unity tickets enabled ALP members to run for trade union office in joint tickets with Communist Party members. The ALP had formally condemned the practice but it persisted, particularly in Victoria. Whitlam tackled the issue squarely as deputy leader, but could not root it out. At the party's Federal Conference in 1965 the Victorian Branch was forced to accept stricter rules against unity tickets, a clear victory for Whitlam.[17]

Whitlam's wrath over fossilised administrative and publicity processes had been stirred particularly by the '36 faceless men' gibe used by Menzies to flail the ALP in the 1963 election campaign. In March 1963, the ALP Federal Conference of thirty-six delegates (six from each state) had met *in camera* to determine Labor policy on the proposed North West Cape naval base in Western Australia. The party leaders, Calwell and Whitlam, were not delegates at the meeting. They were photographed waiting powerless and politically infirm outside the Conference, awaiting instruction from what Menzies called '... the famous "36 faceless men" whose qualifications are unknown, who have no responsibility to you'.[18] Labor's federal secretary, Cyril Wyndham, sought to dispel the 'faceless men' aura by enlarging the federal executive and Federal Conference, by including the federal leaders on both bodies, and by opening the plenary Federal Conference to press and public. Whitlam supported Wyndham's proposed reforms enthusiastically, but they were buried in a party committee.

Menzies' spectacular success with direct state aid in the 1963 election forced the Labor Party to confront the issue. There was support for direct assistance, particularly at state level, where responsibility for education largely resided. Now Menzies had brought the issue irrevocably into the Commonwealth domain. This suited Whitlam's evolving education policies, which proposed direct Commonwealth assistance for schooling based on need, whether schools were state or private. Broadly, the party's position in the mid 1960s was that further assistance should stop but existing benefits should remain.

In early 1966, the ALP's federal executive contemplated a possible High Court challenge to the constitutional legality of state aid. Federal members were directed not to support any move to extend existing assistance to non-government schools. Whitlam was deeply involved in a by-election in the federal seat of Dawson in northern Queensland where he played a large part in developing a northern development program. He denounced the federal executive on the television program, *Seven Days*: 'I can only say that we've only just got rid of the 36 faceless men stigma to be faced with the 12 witless men [of the Federal executive].'[19]

Vaingloriously Whitlam also said that it was his 'destiny' to lead the Labor Party as soon as there was a ballot for the position. His tenuous hold on the deputy leadership following this excoriation of party colleagues was strengthened by a slashing victory in the Dawson by-election. This did not deter swift retribution from the executive, which summoned him before it charged with 'gross disloyalty'. The numbers were there for the executive to expel him for at least a year. Fatalistically Whitlam prepared for suspension, angrily repudiating any suggestion that he would form a breakaway party or join the Liberals. Again, his ability to attract crucial backing at decisive points in his career was his salvation. The Queensland branch, triumphant after the Dawson victory, which they largely attributed to Whitlam, instructed its two federal executive delegates to vote against Whitlam's expulsion. He escaped with a reprimand. A special Federal Conference in May 1966 approved some additional state aid to private schools, taking the heat out of the issue. Calwell's defection from the Victorian delegation broke a deadlock, getting this decision through by a single vote.

The Labor Party's quandary over Vietnam was to find a policy that was not politically damaging while keeping faith with strong party opposition to the war. A workable resolution eluded the ALP for almost five years. Whitlam, sceptical about the politics of the Australian commitment, was sensitive to Australia's alliance with the United States. In the 1966 federal election campaign in November, Calwell pledged the withdrawal of all

Australian troops by Christmas 1966. Whitlam tried to soften this by indicating that if further participation were necessary, the regular Army, not conscripts, would provide it. This was closer to formal caucus policy, but brought the two leaders into conflict in a Vietnam-dominated election. Labor was badly defeated after a campaign that crumbled rapidly from an inauspicious start. Calwell resigned and in February 1967 Whitlam comfortably defeated Jim Cairns for the leadership. Whitlam's ally, Lance Barnard, narrowly defeated Cairns for the deputy leadership.

The first year of Whitlam's leadership passed tranquilly enough. He shaped the amorphous caucus executive into an effective shadow Cabinet, each member having designated policy responsibilities. Policy development was organised coherently in the general ambit of Whitlam's Program, emphasising particularly health, education, urban development, foreign and defence policy.Whitlam sought to reform the representation, control and administration of the Victorian branch, with tactics ranging from sweet persuasion to abrasive confrontation. He was jeered during a stormy session at the Victorian State Conference in April 1967: 'He began by referring to Labor's consistently low vote in Victoria, and complained that ALP people "construct a philosophy of failure which saw in defeat a form of justification and a proof of the purity of our principles". He added scornfully, "Certainly the impotent are pure."'[20]

More fruitfully, Whitlam and Wyndham pursued the significant expansion of the party's sovereign Federal Conference. Their proposals to extend direct representation of the membership, adding state and federal leaders and opening the Conference to media and public, were supported by three state branches. At the Adelaide Federal Conference in May 1967, however, the Wyndham reforms were deadlocked. Whitlam accepted a compromise, adding the four parliamentary leaders and territory representation to the federal executive and all federal and state leaders and territory representatives to the Federal Conference.

If 1967 was progressive for the ALP, the next eighteen months were marked by pandemonium and regression. In April 1968 the federal executive blew up in a welter of bellicose recrimination. The left-wing majority declined to accept the credentials of a newly appointed Tasmanian delegate, Brian Harradine, perceived as a right-wing extremist. This galvanised Whitlam into resigning and re-contesting his leadership. He called on his parliamentary colleagues to confirm his leadership or replace him: 'The actions of the Federal Executive ... were totally destructive of all my efforts to assure the people that our party could in fact accommodate with good-will, tolerance, and commonsense the views of about half the people ... These great gains and immense labours over 14 months were nullified in two days.'[21] Whitlam was returned, but it was close. He defeated Cairns, his only opponent, by 38–32, the vote firmly establishing Cairns as an alternative leader.

A degree of factional equanimity was achieved at the Federal Conference of August 1969. The Conference declined to admit Harradine as a delegate and the party hastily regrouped for an imminent federal election. Vietnam slowly receded in electoral importance as the war wound down. The Federal Conference endorsed substantial changes in policy following the Whitlam agenda, and he performed impressively on the conference floor. The Coalition government of the mercurial John Gorton had become increasingly erratic and prone to embarrassment. Labor's main problem was what its new federal secretary, Mick Young, described as its 'pathetic' campaign organisation: 'However, we did the best we could. We patched things up and struggled through that period only to witness an election night beyond our wildest dreams. If we had been prepared in 1969 as we were in 1972, Whitlam might have been Prime Minister three years earlier than he was. So, after the 1969 election, there was a realisation that we were on the threshold of a victory.'[22]

The ALP won 17 seats, four short of winning government. With the Labor Party so close to office, the key to clinching government remained Victoria, where Labor made no electoral gain.

With a Victorian state election due in May 1970, state aid policy surfaced again. The Victorian central executive directed the state parliamentary party to phase out existing state aid programs. This was clearly in breach of federal policy to retain existing programs. Whitlam threatened to withdraw his electoral participation and poured scalding criticism on the Victorian branch. The ALP polled poorly. The Victorian State Conference suspended for a year the party membership of its Legislative Council leader, Jack Galbally, who had criticised the 'phasing out' policy. Squabbling over state aid policy came to the boil when the party's Federal Executive met at Broken Hill early in August.

The state aid issue was on the executive agenda because Galbally had appealed against his suspension. Through maladroitness the Victorian branch delegates lost control of the agenda, and its structure and conduct came under critical review. In memorable meetings in August–September, 1970, the Federal Executive invoked its plenary powers to investigate the Victorian branch. The investigation was conducted in scrupulous adherence with party rules and the law, leaving little opportunity for appeal. Overturning, then reforming, a major branch in this way was unique in the ALP's federal history. The initial response of the ousted controllers of the Victorian branch was mutinous. They threatened disaffiliation, a split, and creation of a new Industrial Labor Party. The ferment eventually simmered down and, over the following year, the branch was gradually dismantled and reconfigured. It was an impeccable exercise in political reform and rejuvenation. One masterly *coup à tout* resolved for Whitlam state aid and the laggard Victorian branch.

Following the successful intervention in Victoria, the lead-up to the election in December 1972 was straightforward. Whitlam conducted two prestigious international exercises that redounded to his credit. A controversial visit to Papua New Guinea in late 1969 cleared the way for the independence of the territories under Whitlam's Labor government. In mid 1971 Whitlam led a timely ALP delegation to China to discuss trade policy. The visit turned into a political triumph when it became known that US President Richard Nixon was visiting China. The Program was burnished into its final form. A highly personalised strategy focusing on Whitlam was devised for the election campaign. The combination of the Program, merging prosaic reformism with the gaudy panoply of contemporary 'stateside' electioneering was innovatory, but incongruous. Whitlam accepted the format with enthusiasm, but was not always comfortable in execution.

> ... It has never been easy to reconcile the painstakingly developed program solidly in the Fabian style with the California-style campaign in which entertainers displayed their passionate convictions in favour of the 'new', and euphoric crowds joined in an orgy of television glamour. These seemed neither to belong to the Labor Party nor to express the Whitlam program of institutional renovation, educational quality, and so on. And how could Whitlam himself have generated such excitement? Rationalist, professorial, political and hardly Kennedy-like in his personal life, Whitlam looked as surprised by the hoopla, and almost as out of place as any other Australian politician.[23]

In the post-election triumphalism, the slenderness of the 1972 victory was largely overlooked. The victory celebrated was the glorious one anticipated, not the unexceptionable majority that actually materialised. But for the delivery of seats from the revitalised Victorian branch, Labor's victory would have been slender. Even Whitlam never claimed more for it than a 'sound mandate' once the exaltation subsided.

There was a strong whiff of determinism about the fate of the Whitlam government. The long ascendancy of Menzies coincided with most of the twenty years of the postwar 'long boom'. This began in the early 1950s and began to taper off in the late 1960s. Labor muffed its great opportunity for social and economic reform as postwar reconstruction because the Chifley Labor government failed politically in 1949. Other opportunities were missed either through the Split or wretched luck in 1954, 1961 and 1969. As the 'long boom' waned, social democracy was also starting to fade: '... it must be remembered that the [Whitlam] program was developed in the context of the economic buoyancy of the late sixties, the very climax of the post-war triumph of Keynesianism ... That the program would be financed from growth was never seriously questioned.'[24]

How time caught up with the Whitlam government is encapsulated in the contrast between its three Budgets. The first in 1973 was the only one formulated successfully on the basis that growth would deliver spending power. The 1974 Budget was a conceptual mess. The Treasury lost control and the Budget Cabinet devolved into what treasurer Frank Crean described as a 'lunatic asylum'.[25] The 1975 Budget pointed the way towards reform of economic policy and changing ideology.

In essence, Whitlam's Program was one of reform along standard social democratic lines, achievable within the Constitution, and of contemporary relevance. What Whitlam sought to do was commonplace in countries where social democracy was accustomed: the United Kingdom, Canada, Scandinavia, Austria, the German Federal Republic, New Zealand. The United States had the liberal reformism of Kennedy and Johnson. The Program remained relevant because reform based on social democracy and the Constitution had not been attempted in Australia. What was pilloried as revolutionary by Labor's political opponents would have been labelled as well-thumbed convention in comparable countries.

An aura of borrowed time and consequent haste pervaded the parliamentary politics of the Whitlam government. Whitlam had to battle from the beginning to get his legislation through a Parliament without a workable majority in the Senate. There is abundant evidence that the Coalition Opposition resisted his electoral mandate from the first day of sitting. According to Opposition leader Billy Mackie Snedden: '... we were very rowdy in the Opposition, very rowdy, and [Speaker Jim Cope] just couldn't handle us ...'[26]

Cope agreed: 'I'd say that everything possible was done to undermine my authority ... [Whitlam and Snedden] ... detested one another and they were cross firing across the table practically all day at one another ... they were saying gah gah and goof goof and all this business across the table at one another, like two children at times.'[27]

Snedden observed that Whitlam pouted in Parliamentary exchanges: 'He would pull himself up and his chest would go out and his mouth would go out and his lips would turn in a sort of circle and then he would make a woofing noise, you know "woof" and then start to talk. So I used to say to him,"woof, woof", and it upset him, which was good.'[28]

It wasn't good for Billy Mackie Snedden in the long run. Whitlam's demolition job on Snedden in the Parliament destroyed his leadership. The other victim of the parliamentary rowdyism was the hapless Speaker Jim Cope, ruthlessly forced out of his job by Whitlam on the parliamentary floor. Cope considered naming Whitlam for intimidating the chair. Instead, he decided to just take it on the chin and resign as Speaker.

Although Whitlam trounced Snedden in the Parliament, Snedden did well in electoral politics. Whitlam instantly took up Snedden's decision to impose conditions on government money bills in May 1974. Snedden was responding to pressures from within his party, intent on forcing Whitlam to an election at the earliest possible opportunity: 'I think some of them were in favour of it rather recklessly, feeling "Let's give the bastards a go, we'll win." You know, let's kick them out. You know, they were gung ho.'[29]

Another factor was the 'Gair affair', an attempt by Whitlam to improve Labor's numbers in the Senate by appointing the DLP leader Senator Vince Gair as ambassador to Ireland. Snedden saw this as interfering with the expressed will of the electors, and 'the more basic response of terrible conspiracy between Whitlam and this seedy fellow, Gair'. Whitlam won the election in what he saw as reaffirmation of the 'sound mandate' given in 1972. Snedden whittled away Labor's margins in several seats and slightly increased the aggregate Coalition vote. Tragically for Whitlam and his party, Labor failed by a bare margin to win the Senate.

The turbulent parliamentary politics did not reflect the relative stability of much of the administration. Generally, caucus served the Labor government well, rarely overturning or interfering with executive and Cabinet process. The effectiveness of Cabinet government was variable. Caucus had decided that all twenty-seven ministers should be members of Cabinet, with no smaller inner Cabinet and outer ministry. This arrangement frustrated Whitlam and made the effective co-ordination of government more difficult. The most common complaints about Whitlam's leadership among his ministers were failure to co-ordinate government machinery and failure to use the Cabinet as a strategic instrument. They recalled Cabinet processes as stressful, with ministers slaving to meet Whitlam's unrelenting determination to give effect to the program.

Les Johnson recalled a Cabinet meeting where three ministers, Gordon Bryant, Al Grassby and Rex Patterson, tried to initiate a 'little informal talk about the state of things generally': 'And Whitlam turned on the three of them and told them that they weren't going to be allowed to capitulate like that, and we had a program and we were going to give effect to that program. And he threw some ministerial papers across the floor and said to them with great indignation, "Now we'll proceed with the agenda." And the next agenda item was the state of the ball-bearing industry. It was quite symbolical.'[30] As with much anecdotal material about Whitlam, it's a story that probably doesn't lose much in the telling. Even so, there is consensus among ministers that what Kim Beazley (the elder) epitomised as 'government by tantrum' was part of Whitlam's administrative style.

Whitlam very much left his ministers alone to administer their portfolios and public policy areas. Some years after the Dismissal, he speculated that he had been too much of a team man and thought that he should have been more autocratic. The 'boiler room ministers', with little exception, did their jobs competently and without attracting public controversy. Even so, it has been claimed that Whitlam alienated at least five of these ministers.[31] Another, Gordon Bryant, was shifted from his Aboriginal Affairs portfolio because, according to Whitlam, 'You are running it as your own empire.'[32]

The broad capability of the ministerial majority has been buried in the welter of altercation and public rumpus involving a key group of senior ministers. In every case, the relevant minister had been either a rival of Whitlam in Opposition or a dedicated ally. As prime minister, Whitlam was unable to strike a viable balance between personal baggage inherited from Opposition and an enduring working relationship in government. These crucial figures were successive deputy prime ministers Lance Barnard, Jim Cairns and Frank Crean, minerals and energy minister Rex Connor, industrial relations minister Clyde Cameron and Senate leader Lionel Murphy.

Barnard had been Whitlam's deputy leader from 1967 to late 1972, when he became deputy prime minister. After the 1974 election Jim Cairns defeated Barnard for the deputy prime ministership. Barnard was chagrined at what he saw as lack of support from Whitlam. Sensing that the 25 per cent tariff cut would cost him his north Tasmanian seat, Barnard resigned in May 1975 and, with Whitlam's approval, took a diplomatic post. At the by-election in late June, Labor was routed, with a swing against it of 12 per cent. This alerted the Opposition and its driving new leader, Malcolm Fraser, to Labor's electoral vulnerability.

Subtle and persuasive, Murphy's election as Opposition Senate leader in 1967 had put Whitlam under pressure in the leadership and the Senate. Murphy had worked skilfully to aggrandise his role both within the party and Parliament: 'Lionel was quite unabashed in his belief that Gough Whitlam was not a great success and he should be the leader and took advantage of every opportunity to win notoriety and approval from the parliamentary Labor Party.'[33]

By the 1972 election, Whitlam largely had Murphy's measure, but he remained a potential rival. After a shaky start, Murphy had generally proved a creative attorney-general. He certainly had the qualifications for the High Court and he accepted Whitlam's proposal to appoint him there in early 1975. Murphy was replaced by a non-Labor senator, the NSW Liberal premier breaking with convention dictating a Labor replacement. This cost Labor another Senate vote, although the new Senator, Cleaver Bunton, scrupulously voted with the government during the political crisis of late 1975. Murphy's departure, however, meant that he was not available to assist the government when the Loans Affair burst over the Parliament in May 1975. (Murphy had provided the constitutional and legal justification for the attempted loan raisings – see below.) Murphy's legal experience and tactical skills would also have been helpful when the government came under 'endgame' pressure in late 1975.

Clyde Cameron had been predominant in the complex machinations which delivered Victorian branch reform for Whitlam in 1970. Cameron was shifted from his prized Industrial Relations portfolio because Whitlam found his wages policies increasingly unpalatable. With characteristic pugnacity, Cameron resisted the removal, creating further evidence of ruction within the government.

Rex Connor had been closely aligned with Whitlam in Opposition. He was elected to the Cabinet in December 1972 and appointed to the portfolio of Minerals and Energy, well down the chain of seniority. As a minister, he beguiled caucus with his assertion of Australian ownership of resources, his grandiose developmental schemes and his contempt for conventional 'hillbilly' capitalism. After the 1974 elections, Connor soared to third rank in Cabinet, junior only to Whitlam and Cairns. A massive yet subtle figure, Connor gave little away. As Crean put it dryly, 'He was a bit of a legend in the party, but legends are always pretty difficult to explain.'[34]

At the zenith of his influence in late 1974, Connor devised a scheme to raise $4 billion in overseas loans for minerals and energy projects in Australia. A small Cabinet group of Whitlam, Cairns, Murphy and Connor managed the project, which was approved by the governor-general in Council. Thus originated the infamous Loans Affair. Although not an orthodox borrowing, it was legal and probably constitutional. The Treasury opposed it, but other senior public servants were compliant. Most ministers were ignorant of the proposed loan, but were supportive, if somewhat bewildered, as the details dribbled out, as Gordon Bryant confirmed: 'What [Connor] was on about would have had perhaps substantial support in the Cabinet. I'm not convinced that I'd have supported the borrowing of large sums from overseas, but if it would have assisted us to get on with the job I would have done so.'[35]

Tony Mulvihill got to the pith of the matter: '... if you could have got the money in quickly and then been able to achieve Connor's vast dreams, things would have happened, people would have lived with it ... But they had the innuendo and yet the money wasn't coming into Australia.'[36] Thus, the loan proposals dragged on for months beyond any plausible prospect of fulfilment; the innuendo built up into a crescendo; Connor's activities drifted beyond Whitlam's control and Whitlam sacked him for misleading the Parliament.

Gracefully, Jim Cairns had conceded after the 1969 election that Whitlam had restored his legitimacy as Labor leader, and that he would not challenge him again. His performance as senior minister had been impressive, and he had got on well enough with Whitlam as deputy prime minister. Following the virtual collapse of routine Budget process in 1974, Whitlam decided that Cairns should accept responsibility for its implementation as treasurer. With some reluctance the treasurer, Frank Crean, agreed to stand aside for Cairns. As Gordon Bryant put it, 'We didn't get round to a Budget when Jim was treasurer.' [37]

As the Loans Affair spiralled beyond command, a spreading contagion threatened to stain the honour and judgment of Jim Cairns. This was the so-called 'Morosi affair'. (As Gordon Bryant observed, the Labor Party had 'affairs'; the Liberals had blunders.) Cairns employed an attractive Eurasian woman, Junie Morosi, to run his office. Morosi proved neither politically astute nor administratively competent, but there was no evident basis for the innuendo abounding about her relationship with Cairns. Whitlam at first was disposed to be sympathetic, resenting the imputations of sexual impropriety against a colleague he considered honourable. Unfortunately, the Morosi affair hurtled beyond his charge, as he later acknowledged: 'I should have put an end to the Cairns-Morosi nonsense early in 1975 ... The silly statements that Cairns made [that he felt a 'kind of love' for Morosi] ... should have produced a decisive reaction from me ... [It was] grossly misleading and damaging ... It was my fault and my job to call [Cairns] into line and I didn't ... Cairns ... I regret to say seemed to revel in the publicity.'[38]

A distracted Cairns was involved in a series of statements which amounted to misleading the Parliament. Whitlam demoted him first from the deputy prime ministership and Treasury portfolio, and then from Cabinet altogether. Caucus approved Whitlam's drastic if belated response. The cumulative impact of the Loans Affair and the Morosi affair formed the basis for the 'reprehensible circumstances' that justified the Opposition's refusal of supply in October 1975. Snedden, replaced as leader by Malcolm Fraser, acknowledged this: 'It was the Opposition's continual questioning and the feeding out of little bits of information that built it up to scandalising proportions ... we were contemptuous of the Labor Party and the Crean affair and the Cairns affair and Barnard had made a mess of it and Connor, and they were all in terrible trouble.'[39]

Thus ministerial malaise, heavily influenced by relationships established between Whitlam and a key group of ministers in Opposition, was a crucial factor in the fate of the Whitlam government. It lasted from about August–September, when the 1974–75 Budget was framed and presented, until mid October 1975, when Malcolm Fraser decided to block the Budget and force an election. In short, it dominated the core years of the Whitlam government, the period when it should have been in its policy prime. Of course there were remissions, where government was relatively sedate and it seemed that an even keel had been set at last. Invariably, these hopes were blasted by another revelation, another misleading statement to the Parliament or another media scandal. It proved impossible for Whitlam to shape an unwieldy Cabinet into what he wanted, to place the ministers with whom he had no debts or grudges in senior positions, or to appoint younger Labor parliamentarians who cut their political teeth on his Program. In later years, Whitlam claimed that he had been too much of a team man, too lenient in managing his Cabinet. There is some truth in this. It is doubtful, however, whether his proposed solution, that he should have been more autocratic, would have worked either in the volatility of 1974–75.

Whitlam was right to resist the crushing pressure imposed by the Opposition decision to withhold supply. In the short term, a spirited resistance improved the government's political credibility and standing. It was a political crisis that could and should have been resolved by political means. It did not become a constitutional crisis until Sir John Kerr intervened and dismissed the government. The political crisis lasted from October 16 until just after midday on 11 November when Kerr handed Whitlam the notice of dismissal in his study at Government House. The constitutional crisis lasted only a few hours, from the Dismissal just before 1pm on 11 November until the dissolution of the Parliament late that afternoon. The distinction between *political* and *constitutional* in the context of crisis is crucial to understanding Whitlam's responses. The political or parliamentary crisis provoked in Whitlam a full-blooded onslaught of a concentrated political passion, corrosive irony, and stinging logic unsurpassed in Australian parliamentary history. Beyond the Parliament, in the constitutional forum of the governor-general's study, Whitlam's caucus reposed in him total responsibility for the crucial interplay with Sir John Kerr. This was not done without some misgiving, as Tony Mulvihill recalled.

> Whitlam used to come back to each Caucus meeting and say, 'I saw His Excellency and he noted it and no sign. No worry. He's got to do it his way' ... there was no indication that Kerr would have said, 'Well look, Mr PM, if you don't do this, I'll do that.' Now they were the words that I waited for and at no time did Whitlam ever suggest them ... He'd simply say, 'I reported to his Excellency what we were doing.' At no time did he ever hint that the Governor-General was frowning and that's what was such a surprise.'[40]

Whitlam believed that the Opposition Senators would crack under pressure and withdraw the majority for withholding supply. He was within a whisker of being right. At 9am on 11 November, Whitlam was poised to win a stunning victory. He was about to seek the governor-general's approval for a half Senate election in December. The Opposition leaders had rejected any compromise. Scuttlebutt around the corridors indicated that enough Opposition senators were wavering to grant supply. The Opposition parties were about to meet in circumstances of some apprehension.

Senator Alan Missen was the most prominent of a handful of Opposition Senators thought most likely, under pressure, to concede supply. Missen said years later that his group of dissenters would probably have held. At the crucial party meeting on the morning of 11 November he sensed that the Opposition was crumbling:

> We [Senators] did not ever expect that the Governor General would dismiss Whitlam. We, in fact, expected that our House of Representatives colleagues would ultimately give in on this issue ... on [11 November] I think a debate could well have broken out [in the party room] because people were getting very worried as to how their constituents were feeling ... I was surprised at the number ... who were very concerned at the way it was going ... consequently I thought there was likelihood that the crisis would only go for a few days and that party discussion [might] well have led to [us] having to climb down. But in fact, as we know what happened ... the Governor General acted that day ...[41]

As the Duke of Wellington said after Waterloo, 'it was a near run thing!' Whitlam had won everywhere except in the intimate recesses of Sir John Kerr's constitutional and political sensibilities.

If Whitlam's party lauded his conduct of the political crisis, his handling of the constitutional crisis was much criticised. This is very largely for two reasons; Whitlam should not have let Kerr seduce his judgment as he did and he failed to lead in the aftermath of the Dismissal. In his subsequent writings, Whitlam admitted the consequences of his gullibility when dealing with Kerr. Certainly, during the brief but eventful constitutional crisis, Whitlam showed little of the parliamentary élan that so richly animated the political crisis. He returned to the Lodge and ate the famous steak, then he summoned his advisers. The mood was sombre but functional. The group drafted a motion to re-establish Labor control of the House of Representatives and restore it to constitutional government. Questioned years later about the steak, Whitlam responded; 'Life goes on.'[42] This platitude encapsulates Whitlam's response to the constitutional crisis.

Whitlam returned to the Parliament, and a motion of 'no confidence' in the Opposition that had begun before the Dismissal continued after it. The motion was a nonsense, because the previous Opposition was then the government and the previous government was the Opposition. No urgent caucus meeting was called, and more than an hour after the Dismissal, most ministers and members did not know that their government had been liquidated. Kerr announced the Dismissal in a press statement just before 1pm. Even the news reports took time to percolate among the ejected government. At the High Court, Lionel Murphy was phoned by his daughter about radio reports that Kerr had dismissed the government. His immediate response was, 'He can't do that.' Murphy rang Senator Jim McClelland, the industrial relations minister at Parliament House to see if he had been sacked.

> Jim said, "I don't think so. I'm still here." "Are you administering still?" says Lionel, and Jim says. "Well I think so. I'm still here signing papers." And in fact, that's how it went, and it was such an idiotic exercise on the part of the Governor General. [43]

Some Labor ministers in the House of Representatives noted that Whitlam was flushed and agitated when he entered at 2pm.

> He came in florid faced, and obviously agitated, and [for] everyone a sort of sixth sense prevailed although the rumours went around. 'We've been

> sacked, we've been sacked.' ... You're sacked. We're all sacked. Who's sacked? I'm sacked. Why?' And the next thing the whole episode started in the House.[44]

When Fraser stood up and said that he was the prime minister, Frank Crean thought, 'Now, where are all the inkwells we'd throw if this was a Balkan Parliament?'[45] There is an old saw expressing the uncertainty and frequent brevity of political life: 'A peacock today, a feather duster tomorrow.' As the futile attempt to restore the lost government unfolded in the chamber, Les Johnson reworded the bromide: 'It wasn't a matter of tomorrow. It was a peacock today, a feather duster today, it was as quick as that.'[46]

What more could Whitlam have done once the crisis passed from the political to the constitutional realm? Should he have returned immediately to the Parliament and fired up the caucus to defy the governor-general? Many of his colleagues thought so. Most caucus members had gone into the chambers not knowing what they faced. A number thought it advantageous to Labor to keep the Parliament sitting, to filibuster to the national broadcasts while they were on the air. Above all, it was argued that the crucial supply Bills should have been delayed in the Senate. Kerr had appointed Fraser prime minister on guarantee that Fraser could get supply through the Parliament. This was technically feasible because the Coalition was using its Senate majority to block the Bills. If the Bills were presented again, it could approve them and Fraser would obtain supply. That is what happened. The Bills went through the Senate without debate at about 2.15pm. Fraser could then announce in the House of Representatives that he was prime minister and he could tell Kerr he had supply. Labor Senators could not have blocked supply, but they might have deferred it and perhaps frustrated Kerr.

Why wasn't this done? Because the Labor senators, including the leaders, did not know about the Dismissal when the supply Bills went through the Senate. The Labor senators acted on the basis that the Whitlam government was still governing. Ignoring the absurdity of the situation and who was to blame for not telling the Senators, would it have made any difference?

Whitlam's actions might have been interpreted in two ways. Put simply, he was 'gobsmacked' by Kerr and failed to respond aggressively and tactically. The more plausible explanation is that Whitlam was coming to terms with the inevitable. The political crisis had ended. Circumstances and arguments changed utterly once the crisis moved from politics to the Constitution. Kerr had used his reserve powers to dismiss the government. Ultimately he could do this. Whitlam's misjudgment had been that Kerr would not use the reserve powers to override the advice of his elected ministers. The political struggle had been waged to assert the supremacy of the House of Representatives as the chamber where government was won and lost. Government should be freed forever from the threat that a Senate majority could destroy an elected government. The fate of the Whitlam government, therefore, should be determined in the House of Representatives. It would be hypocritical for the Labor Party to use for its immediate benefit Senate processes that it had fought resolutely to overturn. This was essentially Whitlam's argument; in terms of the Constitution, it was logical and consistent.

With the wisdom of retrospect, it appears chimerical to have held any hope that Kerr would have changed his mind if supply for his caretaker government had been blocked. It might even have inflamed him. There were genuine fears early on the afternoon of 11 November that Kerr might invoke his constitutional position as head of the armed forces had he been frustrated. This possibility certainly occurred to Whitlam and some of his ministers.

Les Johnson recalled Whitlam leaning over him to ask defence minister Bill Morrison: 'Who's got Army?'. Johnson felt at first he was being facetious, but quickly changed his mind: 'He was probably examining all the options, what would happen if we refused to relinquish government, would the Army come and throw us out of Parliament House or something. And Morrison said, "They do", or words to that effect.'[47]

Whitlam made it plain in his book *The Truth of the Matter* that be believed Kerr would have called out the troops if the sittings had been maintained. Dissolution of the Parliament constituted an insurmountable constitutional impediment. Even the remotest possibility of a blockaded Parliament or intervention of troops or police was too horrible to contemplate. The Labor Party had to swallow its pride and 'take it on the chin', as Jim Cope had said. It had fought a great political and constitutional battle by the rules. Now, it must die by the rules, at least for a time. 'What humbugs we would have been if, after condemning the Liberals for refusing to vote on the Budget, we ourselves had delayed a vote on the

Budget. We had fought a great fight by the rules. We stuck by the rules to the end.'[48]

Whitlam did agree, however, that it would have been a legitimate and effective tactic to have retained the signed and approved supply bills in the Parliament. The Bills had been sent routinely to the governor-general after formal legislative processes were complete. Kerr was able to dissolve the Parliament when he received the signed documentation. When Kerr finally saw Speaker Gordon Scholes late in the afternoon, he could dismiss the no-confidence motion in the caretaker government passed by the Labor majority in the House of Representatives as irrelevant because he had already dissolved the Parliament. He could do this because Fraser's guarantee of supply had been met, although largely by sheer luck, not constitutional process.

Whitlam's famous address on the parliamentary steps after dissolution of the Parliament was fiery and vituperative. It was not an incitement to ignore or transgress constitutional process. Whitlam pointed unflinchingly to the ultimate right of the electorate to decide the issue:

> Well may we say 'God save the Queen' because nothing will save the governor general. The proclamation which you have just heard read was counter-signed by Malcolm Fraser who will undoubtedly go down in Australia's history from Remembrance Day 1975 as 'Kerr's cur' ... Maintain your rage and enthusiasm through the campaign for the election now to be held. and until polling day.

Whitlam said that this was no exercise in demagoguery and that in the circumstances it showed remarkable restraint and moderation. Somewhat wistfully, he recalled that it was a beautiful late spring afternoon in Canberra – just the night for a nice walk to Government House. Politics can be fun. Upholding the Constitution must invariably be a duty.

Labor was overwhelmingly defeated in the federal election of December 1975. It returned to the wilderness, led by Whitlam in an action that had a certain political symmetry. There was a brief period of bitterness and divisiveness in Australian politics and society but the wounds healed quickly enough. Labor was unable to make electoral ground under Whitlam in 1977 but came in sight of victory in 1980 and won resoundingly in 1983. Unquestionably Whitlam's assumption on 11 November of the Ciceronian virtues and the mantle of Zeno the Stoic, and not that of Cleon the demagogue, contributed mightily to the restoration of both polity and party.

The Whitlam leadership of 1976–77 was a sad coda to an epic political career. His reputation for sagacity was badly tarnished by revelations that he had participated in an effort to raise electoral funding from Iraqi sources. He struggled unavailingly to re-ignite the old spark. The Program proved beyond regeneration in a climate of rapidly changing economic philosophies and policy agendas. In 1977 he was further humiliated when a mid-term challenge to his continuing leadership by Bill Hayden was defeated by only two votes (32–30). In a snap election at the end of 1977, his Labor Party was hopelessly outgeneralled and outvoted by Malcolm Fraser and his buoyant Coalition government. Thus Whitlam was denied the chance to 'do a Menzies' and establish his political greatness beyond challenge with a triumphal renewal of government.

Whitlam was given, however, the compensation of a rich and diverse life after politics. He has also been blessed with the comforts of an enduring marriage and a thriving family life. In his early 60s when he quit politics, he lives vigorously and fruitfully into the new millennium. When Labor returned to federal office in 1983, he was appointed Australian ambassador to UNESCO, and given other government appointments. Universities offered him visiting professorships. Advertising companies solicited his services, the product sometimes gently lampooning his political life. He has travelled widely, lending his expertise to cultural and historical tourism. Whitlam's writings have been largely directed to defence of his government and advocacy of the enduring merits and relevance of his public policy. He has written no autobiography nor has he provided any substantial oral history record. He showed little sympathy to the Hawke Labor government, which he considered to have abandoned reform and social democracy. For the subsequent Keating Labor government he expressed some admiration, detecting some reformist empathy. The breach with Kerr has never healed but, in later years, he has established an 'elder statesman' rapport with his formidable opponent, Malcolm Fraser, particularly in support of an Australian republic.

In 1971, before he became Prime Minister, Gough Whitlam wrote an introduction to a biography of Edward Granville Theodore, a Labor deputy prime minister and premier of Queensland. In a memorable passage, Whitlam described Theodore's career as a powerful reminder of a persistent feature of Australian political history: its chief men and chief efforts had been singularly associated with failure and frustration. There was, he said, a deep poignancy in the fate of a remarkably long list of the chief figures from the very beginning:

> Phillip embittered and exhausted; Bligh disgraced; Macquarie despised here and discredited at home; Macarthur mad; Wentworth rejecting the meaning of his own achievements; Parkes bankrupt; Deakin outliving his superb faculties in a long twilight of senility; Fisher forgotten; Bruce living in self-chosen exile; Scullin heartbroken; Lyons dying in the middle of relentless intrigue against him; Curtin driven to desperation and to the point of resignation by some of his colleagues at the worst period in the war.[49]

How might Whitlam have portrayed himself in this litany of Australian frustration and failure? Perhaps something like this:

> Whitlam, after twenty-five years dedicated to the Australian Labor Party and public life, to the interpretation and enhancement of the Australian Constitution, at the threshold of his greatest moment, to be duped and frustrated by a governor-general who was not of his style.

John Malcolm Fraser

11 NOVEMBER 1975 – 11 MARCH 1983

His economic policy was falsely hailed as Thatcherite or Reaganite, when he was really a disciplinarian upholding the Australian tradition against the rising tide of pro-market reformers.

BY PAUL KELLY

After R.G. Menzies and until John Howard, Malcolm Fraser was the Liberal Party's longest-serving prime minister. A leader of political turbulence, administrative competence and policy caution, he won three elections, in 1975, 1977 and 1980. Fraser was an impressive politician but a more limited prime minister. His prime ministership, so contentious in his own time, appears less formidable in retrospect.

John Malcolm Fraser was a rich farmer with a nation-building philosophy, an anti-communist ideologue, an aggressive politician ambitious for himself and his country, and a patrician imbued with a sense of public duty. He was widely depicted as a 'born to rule' Liberal who, unlike Sir Robert Menzies, had been born to the purple. Tall, thickset, unsmiling and lethal, Fraser never overcame his own deep reserve to engage the public at an emotional level. His media critics loved to caricature him as a 'crazy grazier', reactionary and dull.[1] Yet viewed from the Howard era, Fraser appears a progressive Liberal leader on multiculturalism, immigration, foreign policy and Aboriginal affairs.

For many Australians Fraser's career is dominated by his brinkmanship in 1975. Aware that Labor was doomed and convinced of his own moral superiority, Fraser blocked supply to force the Whitlam government to an election. After a four-week deadlock between the House of Representatives and the Senate, Governor-General Sir John Kerr dismissed Whitlam and appointed Fraser as caretaker prime minister pending that election. Fraser won a sweeping victory, which he saw as confirmation of his tactics. But he paid a punitive price – the hostility of the pro-Labor vote and of much of the opinion-making elite. The 1975 crisis defined how most people saw Fraser, and perhaps also how he saw himself.

The paradox of Fraser's prime ministership is the gulf between process and performance. Fraser was a master of process. Dominant, relentless and knowledgeable, he believed in the power of government and used the machinery of Cabinet, public service and party to achieve in seven years just under 19,000 Cabinet decisions. To insiders Fraser was an awe-inspiring political executive with a near-unrivalled capacity. Yet his record does not match this potential.[2]

Fraser was a misunderstood prime minister, unable to repair his communications defects. He was, in fact, an economic traditionalist and a modest social reformer. Yet this was not grasped until his prime ministership was far advanced. Fraser's aloof bearing and relentless quest for advantage left the impression of a dogmatic, hard, uncompassionate man. Fraser in fact mellowed late in life, particularly after he left politics. The social conscience so prominent in his retirement persona was disguised for much of his prime ministership behind the stony gaze of an Easter Island face. The study of Fraser's record is akin to a trip through a mirror maze. This political giant killer was an agoniser, reluctant to take decisions that hurt people and ultimately a failure because of his policy timidity.

Fraser has a special place in our history – he was the last prime minister before the age of globalisation forced Australia to break from its introspective economic past. He was a regulator, a protectionist and a champion of state intervention. He believed in a moral order, the separation of labour and capital, the equality of all men and a society based upon hierarchy and responsibility. He was a rural paternalist – suspicious of financial power, comfortable when shouting the workers in a bar and devoid of small talk with women.

His economic policy was falsely hailed as Thatcherite or Reaganite, when he was really a disciplinarian upholding the Australian tradition against the rising tide of pro-market reformers who broke through with Bob Hawke's 1983 victory. In his retirement Fraser was so appalled by the deregulatory pro-market values of the 1980s and 1990s that he often seemed aligned with his former enemies on the Left.

In spirit and chronology, Fraser was closer to Sir Robert Menzies than to John Howard. Fraser became prime minister only nine years after Menzies' retirement and departed a full thirteen years before John Howard's election. He had a reverence for Menzies and a distaste for Howard. Fraser's support for the Menzian benchmarks is striking – free enterprise, social progress, home ownership, a strong welfare net, high immigration, national development, economic stability, ministerial integrity, anti-communism and personal security.

The great differences between Menzies and Fraser lay in projection and pace. Compared with Menzies, the magisterial communicator, Fraser appeared wooden and graceless. But Fraser drove his government with an intensity and passion that had no parallel with the earlier Menzies period. Fraser, a product of the World War II period, was a disciple of self-improvement. His most famous quote – 'life was not meant to be easy' – was an appeal to individual sacrifice in the cause of national progress. Fraser was a patriot and a disciplinarian who drove himself, eventually, beyond the physical limit.

Malcolm Fraser was born in 1930 into a wealthy Victorian political family, his grandfather being a senator in the first Commonwealth Parliament. His early years were lonely, spent on the family's Riverina property outside Deniliquin with his sister. He recalled, 'I remember three years in a row knocking lambs on the head as they dropped, trying to save the ewes. I think I was eight in the last of those particular droughts.' The river had to be traversed to reach the town sixty kilometres distant. It was a life of deep isolation, hard work and duty, and it helped shape a solitary, resolute man.

In the 1940s Fraser's parents purchased Nareen, a magnificent property in Victoria's rich western district, which Fraser would inherit. The adolescent Fraser went to Melbourne Grammar, where the headmaster remembered him as shy and reserved. He followed his father's footsteps to Oxford, winning entry after a written request from his father. Oxford would be the turning point – the place where Fraser became politicised. He learned two enduring lessons – the folly of Britain's prewar appeasement and the limitations of postwar British socialism. The serious-minded Fraser accepted the purist virtues of the British tradition: dedication to public service and resort to rational argument. He left Oxford committed a resolute yet idealistic conservatism.[3]

Upon his return to Australia, the career choice for Fraser was the farm or politics. He joined the Liberal Party, made immediate inquiries about preselection and was eventually elected as the member for Wannon at the 1955 election.

Fraser's maiden speech was a call for a bigger, better, braver Australia. He concluded: 'I was too young to fight in the last war ... but I am not now too young to fight for my faith and belief in the future of this great nation in which the individual is and shall always remain supreme.' The metaphor of war and survival would be a constant in Fraser's career. He had missed World War II but would fight for his country by dedicating his public life to its cause. But the war theme had a further omen – he was a man with aggression in his temperament.

Fraser was only twenty-five, easily the youngest MP in the House. He grew up in Parliament on the backbench, watching Menzies, studying, learning, preparing. After a long eleven-year wait Fraser became minister for the army in 1966, in Harold Holt's first government. He served as minister for education and science, for defence and then once more as education and science minister before the Coalition lost the 1972 election to Labor.

These ministerial years catapulted Fraser into prominence and notoriety. The hallmarks of his character were revealed – a driving executive style, firm policy views, a conviction of the superiority of his own judgments and a political ruthlessness that frightened many of his colleagues.

Fraser was a competent army minister at a difficult time of selective national service and the Vietnam War. In education and science he left his mark through a significant increase in federal funds to private schools and a vast expansion in federal support for tertiary education. As head of the Department of Defence he chose a man strong enough to check his own impulses, the formidable Arthur Tange, whom Fraser called 'the ablest public servant I've met'. Fraser worked to achieve better co-ordination in a defence structure not sufficiently integrated; he argued a losing case for Vietnam better than his colleagues and was a champion of forward defence arrangements in the region; he displayed a tough-minded assertion in dealing with the Americans (a rare quality), in particular in renegotiating the F-111 contract.

But Fraser fell out with John Gorton whom he had backed as Holt's successor. His flaw as a minister was his compulsion to crisis – partly reflecting a sense of his own self-importance – which prompted Tange to tell him on paper to calm down. Fraser's demeanour, even more arrogant when combined with executive power, won him few friends.

Between 1971 and 1975 there were three great eruptions in Fraser's career. They delivered him the prime ministership, extinguished the careers of John Gorton, Billy Snedden and Gough Whitlam, and provoked a polarised debate about Fraser's character. Behind his back people whispered that Fraser was the most divisive leader since Billy Hughes, a claim he was most anxious to repudiate.[4]

Fraser's March 1971 resignation destroyed Prime Minister John Gorton, his former ally. The night before he quit Fraser told Gorton, 'Don't worry about it, boss. Just have a good night's sleep.' Fraser struck the next day. His resignation speech was a methodical and public exercise in destruction in which Fraser accused Gorton of 'intolerable' disloyalty and purported to tell the Liberal Party by what code it should be governed. Gorton resigned the next day in favour of Billy McMahon. Fraser damaged his own career by resort to such political overkill. He spent a brief period on the backbench.

Four years later, in March 1975, facing a declining Whitlam government, Fraser overthrew Liberal leader Bill Snedden in a bitter contest. Fraser presented himself as the genuine Liberal leader – tough, bold and philosophical. Snedden succumbed to the dual attack of Whitlam from the front and Fraser from behind. Whitlam and Fraser then confronted each other. It was a time for titans.

Fraser's October 1975 decision to force an election was his ultimate brinkmanship. He was hungry, resolute and self-righteous. Explaining his decision Fraser said: 'The Opposition now has no choice ... The Labor government 1972–75 has been the most incompetent and disastrous government in the history of Australia.' Fraser referred to Whitlam's economic mismanagement and Labor's 'chain of improprieties'. The depth of Whitlam's incompetence, best revealed in the petrodollar loan scandal, put pressure upon Fraser to defy convention and block supply. Fraser's decision to block the Budget, defy Whitlam's counterattack and wait upon the governor-general's intervention revealed a profound faith in his own leadership authority.

Fraser was lucky that Kerr chose an unusual solution – dismissal of Whitlam by ambush. During the crisis Fraser displayed a remarkable strength and a judgment of Kerr far superior to Whitlam's. He won a record 55-seat majority in the House of Representatives as well as a Senate majority. Yet the Whitlam dismissal undermined Fraser's ability to unite the nation in a fashion implied by such a sweeping mandate.

Fraser was locked into defending Kerr, who became a growing liability. At each subsequent election, 1977, 1980 and 1983, Fraser was forced to defend his 1975 blocking of supply. It is hard not to conclude that Fraser's prime ministership would have been better discharged and better received if he had taken power in the conventional way. The idea that Australia would have barely survived another year of Whitlam government with Bill Hayden as treasurer and Jim McClelland as labour minister was a fanciful rationalisation.

Fraser, aged forty-five, was a young man when he entered the Lodge. Indeed, he was only fifty-two when he left, a year younger than Sir Robert Menzies when he won the 1949 election and began his record term. In retrospect Fraser was too naive. He believed that his strong leadership would disprove the theory he once articulated with disdain that 'men and women are governed by inexorable events beyond their control'. Fraser himself was swept away in 1983 by deep political and economic currents that he failed to control.

Fraser had to confront two revolutions: the end of the postwar economic growth cycle that surrendered to the stagflation of the 1970s and 1980s and the rise of new baby-boomer values seeded in the 1960s that endured beyond Whitlam's demise. These revolutions produced two different constituencies that demonised Fraser. In the 1980s the libertarian Right depicted him as weak for refusing to deregulate the economy, and from 1975 onwards the baby-boomer Left depicted him as a reactionary for taking an axe to its precious public sector programs enshrined by Whitlam.

From the start Fraser's mission was manifest – to restore discipline to the economy, confidence to investors and sound government. In short, to purge the Whitlam excesses from the system. It is easy, in hind-sight, to misjudge the deep appeal of this message. In three years under Whitlam, unemployment had risen from below 2 per cent to 4.6 per cent; inflation rose from 4.5 per cent to 13 per cent (after reaching 19 per cent); the taxation burden was increased overall; federal spending as a portion of GDP leapt from 24 to 30 per cent (evidence of the Whitlam program) and the Budget deficit blew out. To his followers Whitlam was an heroic agent of modernisation, but to a majority of Australians he was a threat to established notions of authority, propriety and economic order. The 1975 vote confirms that the people wanted to terminate the Whitlam revolution. The notion of Fraserism was conceived as a reaction against Whitlam and the serious damage done to the economy.

Three ideas were integral to Fraser's restoration of economic order – a reduction in the role of government, a reduction in the tax burden, and an anti-inflation drive based upon the Treasury's conclusion that unemployment was caused by high inflation and high wage costs. As a result Fraser was preoccupied with spending cuts, taxation relief and a 'beat inflation first' mantra.

The entire Fraser era was dominated by economic policy. But the task proved to be far more intractable than Fraser had imagined. The Liberals' superb 1975 campaign slogan 'turn on the lights' implied a quick return to economic salvation. Sadly, such ideas were misplaced. The new international stagflation – sluggish growth but rampant inflation – would plague Fraser, just as it had ruined Whitlam. The postwar age of full employment was over, though this was not universally apparent when Fraser took office.

In retrospect, Fraser's 1975 policy speech reads like an establishment fantasy – economic growth of 6–7 per cent, full tax and wage indexation, corporate tax breaks, as much protection as industry needed and a tighter Budget. Fraser arrived in office with high expectations based on vast delusions. He believed that sound policy would see fast economic growth, upwards of 6 per cent.

Economic policy under Fraser was dominated by a fluctuating 'love–hate' relationship between Fraser and the Treasury, whose guiding star was the combative John Stone, then its deputy and subsequently its chief. While Fraser and Treasury had a common belief in economic discipline, they were divided by Fraser's penchant for vote-buying, his scepticism about markets and his Country Party instinct for rural economics.

But there was a series of policy dilemmas that Fraser never mastered – how to cut both the Budget deficit and the tax burden; how to reduce inflation and real wages when wage levels were primarily determined by an outside body, the Arbitration Commission; and how to generate a growth economy while opposing the key 'freer market' methods of promoting structural change and more efficient industry. The source of these failures lay in Fraser's character as a traditionalist, and the same description fitted his Cabinet.

At the Cabinet table Fraser relied most upon the famous National Country Party trio – deputy prime minister Doug Anthony, Ian Sinclair and Peter Nixon – with whom he was close and comfortable. He enjoyed loyalty from his two non-threatening deputies, Phillip Lynch and then John Howard, and he patronised but mishandled Andrew Peacock, whom he always saw as his only potential rival. But Fraser was not prepared to tolerate Don Chipp, a frontbencher from the party's progressive wing. His decision to dump Chipp from his first ministry had a lasting consequence – Chipp left the party and used his personality and media skills to create the Australian Democrats.

Fraser built an impressive power structure. He was dominant in Cabinet, the Parliament and the Liberal Party in a fashion that demanded parallels with Menzies. He relied upon his own department, headed by Alan Carmody and then Geoffrey Yeend, for 'across the board' advice; upon his strong private office under David Kemp; and he spoke daily with Liberal director Tony Eggleton, his political touchstone. Fraser refined the technique of prime ministerial government.

A workaholic who excelled at mastering his Cabinet brief, Fraser devoured paper at the office, the Lodge, at Nareen, in cars and planes, at any hour of the day or night. He knew the power of collective responsibility and rarely exposed himself by acting alone. Fraser consulted ministers, advisers and public servants endlessly. He dominated his ministers but hated overruling them. Fraser would usually keep the Cabinet sitting until he got his way. He had a remarkable policy grasp across portfolios – economic, industrial, social, foreign affairs. He was always prepared to intervene; his ministers knew him as intimidating, probing and constructive. The public service creaked, groaned and responded.

But Fraser's mastery over the machinery of government rarely extended to its human components. Driven by the furnace of his own motivation, Fraser tended to take loyalty and performance for granted. He was a patriot who demanded high standards and he led by example; he cloaked his base decisions in high principle; he thrived on debating policy but too often shunned the intimate human dialogue that creates personal understanding; he found more ease in formal relations defined by power than in relations of equals; and tragically, he allowed the legacy of a lonely boyhood and the weight of political authority to obscure the compassion within himself. Some of his ministers fell ill; others couldn't stand the pace; their wives told them to retire to escape him. A manager of Nareen, Russell Paltridge, described Fraser as a man 'who thrives on crises and emergencies ... when it's quiet in Canberra he will come down here and pick out little things to complain about. When the whole world is against him, he is happiest.'[5]

From the start Fraser embarked upon an audacious tax reform – full income tax indexation. His motive was to release the economy from Whitlam's tax straitjacket. Fraser overrode the Treasury for this dramatic initiative (the discounting of higher tax thresholds caused by inflation) which meant an inbuilt tax cut each year. An ebullient Fraser told his party room: 'We promised tax indexation over three years. Would any of you have believed we could do it in six months?' The reform was abolished over the next several years and Fraser concluded the political benefit from such an 'invisible' tax cut was minimal. A similar fate befell the trading stock valuation for companies – a system of company tax indexation – which was introduced quickly and later cancelled.

The media view of Fraser in his early years was that he was an intimidating hardliner. The evidence suggesting a more complex politician rarely fractured the stereotype. Yet it was readily available.[6]

In early 1976 Fraser cut a deal with ACTU president Bob Hawke and abandoned his promise to abolish the Prices Justification Tribunal, a symbolic concession to the unions. The same year Fraser proceeded with a modified version of Whitlam's Aboriginal land rights proposal for the Northern Territory. It was the Commonwealth's first foray into land rights and a dramatic reversal of the Coalition's pre-1972 hostility to the issue. It revealed Fraser's strength as a Coalition leader; a generation later it remained the foundation of the Commonwealth's approach. In May 1976 Fraser introduced family allowances, paid to the mother, to replace the old systems of child endowment and tax rebates. This put family assistance onto a transparent basis and meant a significant redistribution of funds to low-income families and children in need. It became a lasting reform upon which Hawke later built.

Signalling a more sympathetic Coalition stand on the environment, the government withheld export approval of mineral sands from Fraser Island following the report commissioned from the Whitlam government. This ended mining on the island, which became the first place to be listed on the National Estate Register. In 1977, after a report by Mr Justice Fox, the Cabinet approved a balanced policy of uranium development with a strong safeguards regime. This was highly contentious at the time, and was attacked by sections of the ALP opposed to any uranium development. But the safeguards framework – which sought to limit commercial interests by supporting the non-proliferation regime – was retained by the Hawke government.

However, the political priority remained the economy and the first two years were dominated by the rhetoric of restraint. The philosophy was outlined by treasurer Lynch who, in a critique of Whitlam, said that orthodox Keynesianism was 'no longer appropriate; on the contrary it is hopelessly outdated'.[7] In his first Budget Lynch declared that 'pump-priming' policies 'have been tried both here and abroad and they have failed'. Any previous virtues of such policies have 'entirely evaporated under conditions of high inflation, high unemployment and a public sector already bloated beyond belief'. The key to the restoration of 'full employment in Australia' was the eradication of inflation.[8]

The spending reductions provoked great political trauma. The most celebrated was the crossing of the floor by Liberal senators to defeat the abolition of funeral benefits for pensioners. Fraser later lamented his inability to persuade his Cabinet to abolish unemployment benefits for sixteen- and seventeen-year-olds. In the government's first year spending was budgeted to rise by 11 per cent, about half the increase of Labor's final year, a modest but not severe pruning.

A myth later arose that Fraser had squandered an opportunity by rejecting demands for tougher action. In fact, there was no such pressure. The *Financial Review* supported Fraser's approach: 'The budget is what we were led to expect from the election campaign and everything that has been said by the government in the intervening period has prepared the community for it. There is no misrepresentation here.' After surveying the debate, internal and external, over the government's first Budget, Patrick Weller concluded: 'No contemporary observer commented that the Budget represented a lost opportunity ... from a technical economic view he [Fraser] might have been tougher, but it would have been political suicide. The perception at the time was that the government was hard enough.'[9]

In later years, however, Fraser himself expressed regrets. He blamed the Treasury, saying the 'worst advice' he received came from its chief, Sir Frederick Wheeler, in early 1976 that 'the economy's had so many shocks – you don't want to give it another one now by cutting expenditure too quickly'. Fraser's biographer, Philip Ayres, trying to capture the post-Whitlam-dismissal mood, ventured that after November 1975 'Australian society was more polarised than it had been since the conscription debate during the First World War'. This judgment is an exaggeration. The point, though, is that the temper of the nation was a sensitive issue among Canberra insiders.[10]

Tensions between Fraser and the Treasury climaxed in November 1976. Backed by his Country Party ministers, Fraser insisted on a hefty 17.5 per cent devaluation, overriding the purity of Treasury's anti-inflation line. In a display of power politics Fraser not only rejected its advice but split the Treasury by creating a separate Department of Finance, changing irrevocably the economic advisory structure of government.

The logic of Fraser's position had always been a second election in late 1977, given that a Senate election was needed anyway by mid 1978. His huge advantage was that the political framework of 1975 remained in place – Fraser as the authority figure restoring order and Whitlam, the agent of the previous upheaval, still Opposition leader. The Labor Party made a fateful choice in May 1977 when it voted 32–30 to keep Whitlam leader over Bill Hayden, a triumph of sentiment over self-interest.

After two years Fraser had reduced inflation to a shade below 10 per cent, but Lynch admitted that the high level of unemployment was the government's 'major disappointment'. Unemployment rose to 5.2 per cent in 1976–77 and then to 6.2 per cent in 1977–78. But the government's August 1977 'election' Budget was typical of Fraser's overkill. Its centrepiece was a new income tax cut, in addition to tax indexation introduced the previous year, although the indexation factor would be reduced. The seven-step rate scale was reduced to three steps, of 32, 46 and 60 per cent, still high when judged against later marginal rate reductions. The tax cut – the zenith of Fraser's belief that excessive taxation was destroying incentive – was timed for a late 1977 election. Liberal television advertisements during the campaign portrayed the tax cuts as a 'fistful of dollars' – a blatant exercise in vote buying. The truth is that Fraser didn't need the tax cut to win, and the next year the economy was unable to absorb it. It was another example of Fraser's miscalculations.

The 1977 election result saw a repeat of Fraser's 1975 victory, this time a 48-seat majority. Fraser's projection of strength and discipline overcame his meagre economic results, to deliver a second landslide. The public was never enthralled by Fraser; but a majority respected him and saw no reason to alter its sweeping decision of two years earlier.

The middle years of the Fraser era were dominated by the perplexing issues of ministerial propriety and economic recovery. Fraser felt a greater than usual obligation to deliver a government of integrity because his 1975 act of constitutional violence had been perpetrated in its name.

But his ministerial house was plagued from the start. Posts and telecommunications minister Vic Garland had to resign over a bribery charge (later dismissed); Attorney-General Bob Ellicott resigned because of a disagreement over legal proceedings against former ALP ministers; Treasurer Lynch was forced to stand down during the 1977 election; finance minister Eric Robinson had to stand aside and the government's Senate leader, Reg Withers, was sacked over issues of propriety involving the electoral system. Primary industry minister Ian Sinclair resigned pending his trial before the NSW Supreme Court, and in 1982 health minister Michael MacKellar and business and consumer affairs minister John Moore were forced to resign over a customs issue.

These crises were damaging for two reasons – the sheer number suggested a generic problem, and many of them betrayed Fraser's lack of man management. The crises over Lynch and Withers shook the government's foundations, since they involved the most senior Liberals after Fraser himself. Lynch had entered a legal arrangement under which he stood to receive hefty profits from a land deal. His resignation became an electoral necessity but it occurred when he was confined to hospital. Fraser refused to speak to Lynch and threatened him with dismissal, and Lynch later accused Fraser of acting in an 'indecent, uncivilised and ruthless fashion'. After the election a reluctant Fraser allowed Lynch back into the ministry, but he lost the Treasury portfolio to John Howard.

Fraser sacked Withers on the basis of a Royal Commissioner's finding of impropriety but no illegality. A bitter Withers branded Fraser a hypocrite. Fraser, he asserted, had an unmatched record of political violence yet he was utterly obsessed about his own integrity. From this episode Fraser won full marks for principle but few for personnel management.

The tax cuts of the 1977 campaign were delivered on deadline in February 1978, but in a stunning reversal they were negated mid year by a tax hike. Fraser applied a 1.5 per cent income tax surcharge for almost eighteen months from the middle of 1978. Tax indexation was totally abandoned during 1979, another casualty of deficit pressures.

These tax reversals were a body blow for Fraser's credibility, and they constituted a famous chapter in the history of broken promises by Australian governments. But they revealed Fraser's true nature – that he preferred taxing to 'axing'; that he felt it was politically unwise to withdraw benefits from people; that he had misjudged his ability to secure a strong economic recovery; and that the conflict between a lower deficit and a lower tax burden was ultimately resolved in favour of a lower deficit.

But Fraser's second term saw steady economic progress and a more consistent policy application. At its end Fraser and Howard had reduced the budget deficit as a portion of GDP from 4.8 to 1 per cent over the entire five-year period, spending was tighter than before, and unemployment had stabilised at just over 6 per cent, even though inflation was back above 10 per cent. Commonwealth revenues had benefited from the landmark 1978 decision to price local oil at world parity. This allocated a vital resource at its true economic value. It also created a new growth tax which further helped the deficit reduction strategy.

The second OPEC oil shock of 1979 increased the world oil price dramatically, with two impacts upon Australia. First, it provoked a new search for energy substitutes for oil – notably steaming coal for electricity – with Australia a major beneficiary since it was energy rich; this was the origin of Fraser's resources boom. Second, the oil shock meant, further down the line, a recession among industrial nations, including Australia. The resources boom, in fact, was an investment boom to open up new coalmines, coal loaders and ports, the North West Shelf, power stations and aluminium plants. The government estimated the prospective investment at $29 billion. Fraser enshrined the boom and not more tax cuts at the heart of his 1980 policy speech: 'This development promises to be as important to Australia and individual Australians as anything in the last thirty-five years.'

But Fraser had lost his electoral invincibility, and faced a stronger Labor Opposition under Bill Hayden (Whitlam having resigned after his second electoral defeat in 1977). He was forced to resort to a capital gains tax scare in the final week to win the 1980 election. Fraser's majority was reduced to 23 seats, but only a small national swing was needed to beat the Coalition next time. Fraser had lost the Senate to an ALP–Democrat majority from 1 July 1981. The golden years were behind him.

By this stage the achievements for which history, as distinct from his contemporaries, will probably best remember Fraser were being put in place. During a reflective discussion in early 1983 Fraser nominated his support for a multicultural Australia as his government's finest legacy.[11] During another interview sixteen years later his view was the same: 'It [multiculturalism] might have been the most important thing that my government accomplished. Whatever anyone might have said since, the fact that we then accepted a multicultural Australia ... was enormously important in building a cohesive society.'[12] The crises of the 1980s and 1990s over immigration and multiculturalism offer weight to Fraser's assessment – yet this was Fraser's own view before he left the Lodge.

Fraser's migrant policy was dominated by three factors – a strong revival of the immigration program; the successful intake of Vietnamese refugees; and the promotion of multiculturalism as a settlement philosophy. The contrast between Fraser's 1975–83 approach and that adopted by his Liberal prime ministerial successor John Howard in his first term is striking. The immigration program had been slashed under the Whitlam government, a point that has largely been ignored. Over three years immigration numbers were cut from 130,000 to just over 50,000, the lowest since the inauguration of the program in the late 1940s. In 1975–76 net immigration was only 25,000. Under Fraser the program was gradually restored, with the intake in 1982 just under 120,000. While Whitlam put a great emphasis on a non-discriminatory policy, it was Fraser who had faith in immigration as central to Australia's future development.[13]

However, it was the outflow of refugees from Vietnam after the fall of Saigon in 1975 that forced an historic change in Australia's immigration intake. Whitlam had been reluctant to accept another surge of anti-communist and pro-Liberal refugees replicating that from the Baltic states a generation earlier. Fraser's attitude was more constructive.[14] The arrival on Australia's coastline of Vietnamese boat people just a few years after the formal abolition of the White Australia Policy constituted a national challenge. In retrospect, the outstanding feature of much, though not all, of this debate, was its moderate tone and the quality of leadership under Fraser, backed by his immigration ministers Michael MacKellar and Ian Macphee.

Most refugees to Australia came as a result of international agreements on resettlement to ease a crisis afflicting South-East Asia. From 1975–82 a total of 2059 boat people landed in Australia and were accepted as refugees and 55,700 people were settled by regular refugee entry. This meant an annual intake of about 15,000 Vietnamese refugees during the intense period. In per capita terms Australia took the highest number of Indochinese refugees of any nation.[15]

There were several lessons – that Australia had little control over the flow of boat people to its shores; that international refugee agreements were critical for Australia; and that Australia's national interest dictated a generous refugee policy. Fraser was helped by a bipartisan approach between Macphee and his ALP counterpart, Mick Young.

Vietnamese refugees were allowed to sponsor their families under the family reunion category. Overall, in the twenty years from 1975 a total of 190,000 Indochinese arrived. Viewed in the longer run it was the entry of Vietnamese refugees that made Australia's migrant intake multiracial. From this time at least one-third of the annual immigration intake has been Asian, with a broadening range of Asian source countries. Fraser's record shows him as a supporter of immigration, of Asian immigration and of a strong refugee program. It was under his management that Australia first confronted the real consequences of abolishing the White Australia Policy. The Vietnamese refugees were the first major intake of Asians into Australia this century.

Fraser's third migrant initiative was to promote the multicultural ethic. This owed much to the drive of his adviser, Petro Georgiou, later a federal MP. In 1977 Fraser established the Galbally inquiry and implemented its recommendation that created a new framework for migrant settlement. This involved ethnic associations to assist their own people, the creation of migrant resource centres, greater English language provision and teaching, better translator services and the development of ethnic broadcasting and television. The Australian Institute of Multicultural Affairs was created in 1978 to oversee the policy and its philosophy.[16]

The Special Broadcasting Service (SBS) began operating in October 1980. In his speech opening SBS Fraser said: 'We used to have a view that to really be a good Australian, to love Australia, you almost had to cut your links with the country of origin. But I do not think that is right, and it never was right.'[17] Fraser saw multiculturalism as accepting both the legitimacy of ethnic culture and assisting the integration of immigrants into Australia. He presided over the absorption of the multicultural ethos into the organs of government and the migrant communities. Fraser's biographer argued that his multiculturalism was inspired by his grasp of the role of tradition. Fraser, after all, was a proud Scottish-Australian. But there is another factor that, on reflection, must surely be relevant:

Malcolm Fraser only discovered as an adult that his mother, Una Woolf, was Jewish.[18] It is likely that this discovery did influence his outlook. A generation beyond Fraser's rule, his support for immigration and multiculturalism looks distinctly impressive.

Fraser's second term also highlighted the departures he brought to the Coalition's foreign policy. His policy was global in outlook, forceful in execution and an unusual blend of Cold War pessimism and Third World empathy. Despite his differences with Whitlam, Fraser further entrenched the notion of Australia as a robust middle power able to punch above her diplomatic weight. In foreign policy Fraser was a blend of 'tough realism' and principled idealism.

Fraser governed after the fall of South Vietnam, during Vietnam's invasion of Cambodia and the Soviet invasion of Afghanistan. Fraser's analytical foundation was that Soviet military force was dominant and the chief source of global instability; that the West had lost its will to combat the Soviets from strength and that the US lacked a game plan to match the Soviets in the developing world. For Fraser there was a strategic link between the anti-communist cause and the anti-colonial agenda. Fraser was a Cold War warrior for whom the conflict between Soviet communism and Western democracy had reached a dangerous moment. He saw (correctly) that US leadership under presidents Ford and Carter was weak; he believed that detente was largely illusory; and, in the cause of both the West and Australia, he urged in his June 1976 speech a more resolute US stance.

This led him to a critical conclusion: that China, with its anti-Soviet fervour, was a natural strategic ally of Australia and the US. He made a remarkable 1976 visit to China for talks with Premier Hua Kuo-feng. This made Australia's pro-China policy bipartisan; it inaugurated a new long-term Australian objective – the promotion of co-operative US–China ties; and it helped to define Fraser's approach to US – that of a firm but privately critical ally.[19]

The second dramatic revelation of Fraser's policy came at the 1977 London Commonwealth Heads of Government Meeting (CHOGM). Many Commonwealth leaders arrived with the notion that Fraser was an orthodox white conservative leader from the old Menzies party. When he began to thunder that policies based on racial superiority 'are the most flagrant violation of fundamental human decency [and] offend the moral sense of every person, every nation, concerned about the dignity and equally of man', they were alerted. Fraser supported majority rule in Rhodesia, took a hard line against South Africa, backed sporting boycotts against apartheid, sympathised with the African freedom fighters and called for global efforts to address inequality by creating a Common Fund to stabilise commodity prices. This was a new dawn for Liberal foreign policy. It was Fraser's decisive break from the Menzies legacy. Jamaica's prime minister, Michael Manley, exclaimed: 'My God, this man has a mind ... I just liked him.'[20]

Fraser's great diplomatic achievement was his role in promoting the independence of Zimbabwe. This process, achieved through the Commonwealth, involved Fraser as an intermediary between a new conservative British leader, Margaret Thatcher, and African nations demanding genuine majority rule. It meant persuading Thatcher that a new Constitution and elections were needed, and winning the confidence of the African leaders who, in turn, had to persuade Patriotic Front fighters in Rhodesia to abandon a military solution. The first step was the agreement at the 1979 CHOGM in Lusaka when Fraser's role was decisive, a point he made by leaking the communique and provoking Thatcher's ire. This next stage involved negotiations in London that saw an end to the civil war, supervised elections and a new government emerge under Robert Mugabe. It was a fine example, overall, of Fraser's idealism and pragmatism and diplomatic weight. Hawke later appointed him to the Eminent Persons Group set up to try to bring a negotiated end to South Africa's apartheid system.

The 1979 Soviet invasion of Afghanistan saw Fraser's Cold War crusade reach its zenith. He boosted defence spending, encouraged greater Australia–US military co-operation and campaigned for Australia to boycott the 1980 Olympic Games in Moscow. But the Australian Olympic officials and the public put sport before any anti-Soviet protest, delivering Fraser a lesson in Australian values.

Ronald Reagan's election as US president, his rearming of the Pentagon and his triumph over communism also casts Fraser in a different light. As Owen Harries argues: 'Fraser was a pre-Reagan Reagan on the Cold War, insisting there was no alternative to confronting evil.'[21] The collapse of communism and the Soviet Union suggests that Fraser's anti-Soviet line was better judged than his Australian critics ever realised.

Within Asia, Fraser, like Whitlam, saw ASEAN (the Association of South-East Asian Nations) as basic to regional stability. Fraser backed ASEAN opposition to Vietnam's invasion of Cambodia, supported the US security pledges to Japan and South Korea, upheld Australia's defence arrangements with its ASEAN allies and, nearer home, pursued close ties with Suharto's Indonesia. He knew that Australia's regional position was heavily dependent upon its links with Jakarta. He accepted Suharto's late 1975 military incorporation of East Timor and in 1978 recognised the Indonesian incorporation. Australia's core choice was either to tolerate this outcome or to oppose it without any hope of turning Suharto. In the mid 1970s Suharto was seen as an anti-communist strongman who had achieved a degree of internal stability and economic progress in his turbulent nation. Fraser's policy was driven by the national interest, not by morality or appeasement.

Fraser had little success in Europe, which he saw as unsympathetic, protectionist and strategically soft. He exaggerated the value of the Commonwealth with his initiative for regional CHOGMs, a forum that disappeared with his own departure. He invited derision as a hypocrite for pursuing trade liberalisation abroad and protection at home. His anti-racist and agrarian instincts saw him champion the Third World in the 'North-South' debate over development issues, but this had little effect beyond generating diplomatic goodwill and giving Fraser the pose of statesmanship.

The unifying theme behind all Fraser's foreign policy was a pragmatic and independent search for the Australian national interest. When speaking for Australia abroad he was consistently informed, formidable and constructive.

However, during Fraser's 1980–83 third term Australia succumbed to another recession that symbolised his economic failure and cast a pall over his reputation. Fraser was exposed as a leader too reluctant to attack Australia's structural defects and timid rather than courageous in his economic thought.

In the 1983 election campaign Fraser blamed the recession on three factors – the global downturn, the drought, and the early 1980s wage explosion. He was not responsible for the former two factors, but the errors his government made in industrial relations were fatal. Fraser was never able to solve the industrial conundrum at the heart of

Australia's economic underperformance: the combination of a strong trade union movement able to secure unsustainable wage rises and a centralised wage system beyond the control of government or discipline of the market.

After his retirement Fraser said that 'the major mistake we made was not to go for full industrial power for the Commonwealth in 1976'. This option would have helped. The trouble, though, is that Fraser was a hardliner but never a radical – and industrial relations needed a radical approach. It is ironic that Fraser operated within the system of wage indexation advanced by the Whitlam government and implemented by the Arbitration Commission. He was seen as confrontationist but he was more bark than bite and accepted the given industrial framework.[22]

The resources boom, much vaunted by Fraser, signalled a new wage push during 1980 – and Fraser was never able to combat this. The flashpoint came with a 1981 campaign by the Transport Workers' Union. Fraser, anxious to attend the wedding of Prince Charles and Lady Diana Spencer, negotiated a deal with ACTU chief Cliff Dolan to allow greater pay rises within the indexation system. The head of the commission, Sir John Moore, promptly abandoned the system on the grounds that the parties were no longer adhering to its principles. For Fraser it was a humiliation. Having criticised wage indexation for so long without producing any alternative, he now had its abolition imposed upon him. Fraser was left without a wages policy amid a new market-induced wages round. In 1981–82, real wages rose more than 4 per cent while productivity stayed weak. Unemployment, eventually, would rise beyond 9 per cent. Fraser had failed to address the precise issue on which he had attacked Whitlam. The economy, once again, had succumbed to a wages breakout. With each recession the jobless rate leaped upward. This was not just Fraser's failure; it was an Australian systemic failure. It paved the way for Hawke.

In the early 1980s three events would compound Fraser's difficulties – a leadership challenge by Andrew Peacock, the emergence of the free market lobby or 'dries' within the Liberal Party (that would establish the enduring critique of Fraserism) and the arrival in Parliament of Bob Hawke, an invincible opponent.

The Fraser–Peacock rivalry had been long and intense. It erupted in 1981 when Peacock went to the backbench accusing Fraser of 'gross disloyalty'. He challenged the next year but was defeated 54–27 in a process that saw Fraser replace Phillip Lynch with John Howard as deputy leader in a bid to strengthen his own hand.

At the same time a new intellectual force emerged within the Liberal Party. Its flag carrier was the West Australian backbench farmer John Hyde, whose target was Fraser's old-fashioned state interventionism. These economic liberals or 'dries' were crusaders and intellectuals. Disciples of Adam Smith, Friedrich Hayek and Milton Friedman, their demands were epic – an end to the Australian tradition of government regulation and an embrace of genuine economic freedom by the Liberal Party. They pointed to Margaret Thatcher and Ronald Reagan to argue that such audacity would deliver electoral success. Hyde launched the revolt against the old order after the October 1980 election, declaring that the problem was not Fraser's strength but his weakness. For Hyde 'the art of leadership is explaining those things that are necessary to the future well-being of the nation'.[23] Fraser was put on notice. The dries mobilised inside and outside Parliament and fought for industry deregulation, lower tariffs and low inflation. Their institutional ally was the Treasury, and they looked in hope if not confidence towards John Howard within the Cabinet. Against this background some key economic battles were waged which became omens of the future.

In early 1981 the Cabinet, led by Fraser and Anthony, rejected a Howard submission for a broadly based indirect tax, a policy Howard would realise only seventeen years later as prime minister. In 1981–82 the Cabinet was shocked when its protectionist outlook towards the car industry was challenged by the dries. They mobilised thirty-three backbenchers for the low-protection cause. They lost, but the winds of change were blowing. Finally, in mid 1982 Fraser and Howard fought over their last Budget – Fraser wanted an orthodox Keynesian stimulus for a downturn while Howard said the Coalition's entire rationale had been that spending taxpayers' money didn't solve economic problems. An angry John Stone delivered the ultimate insult – he likened Fraser to Whitlam. The final folly of Fraser and Howard was leaving a projected $9.6 billion budget deficit for Hawke's first year, a rhetorical weapon that Labor used against the Coalition for years.

Yet to the very end of his career, Fraser was a formidable politician. In the turmoil of late 1982 politics, with Hawke threatening Hayden's leadership, Fraser, aggressive and impatient, was manoeuvring for an early election. In August 1982 he launched an assault on the tax evasion industry, prompted by a Royal Commission report into the Ship Painters' and Dockers' Union that, in a strange twist, turned into a tax evasion exposure. Fraser was severely embarrassed by the finding that administrative dishonesty and ineptitude had encouraged huge tax fraud. Driven by self-interest and moral outrage, Fraser and Howard backed a tax recoupment law to recover lost revenue. Fraser declared war, not just against the values of the 'new rich,' but also against sections of the Liberal Party that overlapped with the evasion industry. Fraser and Howard prevailed – but the government was damaged overall.

It was the prelude to Fraser's last successful initiative – a wage freeze endorsed by the Arbitration Commission to check the economic downturn. It was classic Fraser 'can-do' politics; it divided the ALP and the unions and it assisted the next Hawke government. But Fraser never got his late 1982 election. After seven years of pressure a sciatic back forced his hospitalisation. It was a fateful illness.

The Fraser era, born amid political drama, died the same way. The Labor Party, fearful that a wounded Fraser might still prevail at the polls, intensified the pressure on Hayden to resign in favour of Hawke. On 3 February 1983 a recovered Fraser called his early election – but the ALP switched leaders on the same day. Hayden announced his resignation a few hours before Fraser was able to announce the election. Fraser, hoping to fight Hayden, found himself facing Hawke. The supreme manipulator of 1975 had been outgunned in 1983. Hawke won a 25-seat majority on a 4 per cent national swing. Fraser shed a tear, accepted 'total responsibility' for the defeat and resigned the leadership.

In the end Fraser was beaten by the most electorally successful Labor leader of the century. Few who saw Fraser at close quarters doubt that he would have devoured most Labor leadership candidates, but he seemed old-fashioned when pitted against Hawke. Fraser had depicted himself as the strong leader who never needed to be loved by the people. Yet Hawke was a political messiah about to consummate his love affair with Australians. Hawke touched hearts, preached reconciliation and promised an economic revival. Fraser was unable to do any of these with conviction. His defeat in 1983 was widely presented and seen by the ALP as the ultimate justice for his 1975 methods.

The Fraser period fell between the more dazzling yet destructive Whitlam era and the more successful Hawke era. Fraser can claim to have restored discipline and order to government decision-making and the economy. In hindsight, his economic policy was less severe and more traditionalist than it seemed and his social and foreign policy had more continuity with Whitlam than either party conceded at the time. His Coalition partner Doug Anthony said: 'Malcolm was by far the most intelligent, broad-based PM this country has ever had ... if he had a fault he tried to do too much.'[24] Fraser was almost too political for his own good. His relentless search for advantage drew him into too many compromises and changes in direction.

Overall, Fraser's economic record was disappointing. Over seven years the average economic growth rate was 2 per cent or 2.3 per cent if the recession at the end is excluded. This is below Australia's long-term performance. Under Fraser the income tax burden rose from 12.6 to 14 per cent of GDP. The size of government was only marginally reduced – from more than 30 per cent of GDP under Whitlam to 28 plus per cent in Fraser's mid term before rising to 30 plus per cent with his Keynesian expansion. The jobs performance was dismal. Unemployment ran at 5.2 per cent in 1976–77, stabilised about 6 per cent and went above 9 per cent with the recession. Inflation was back over 10 per cent in his last years.

Fraser had a political mandate in 1975 so sweeping that it is hard to imagine it being reproduced. Yet he sheltered behind this majority, deceiving himself into thinking he was a decisive man of action. Fraser saw the need for change but he was a man of the 1950s and 1960s and locked into the old Menzies economic model. Howard said: 'Malcolm Fraser and Doug Anthony were people who I guess acquired their political and economic experience at a time when the old paradigm worked and understandably they didn't think a change was necessary.'[25]

Fraser's attitude towards financial reform best reveals this outlook. He was instrumental in setting up an inquiry into the financial system, chaired by Sir Keith Campbell, that produced a blueprint for deregulation. Fraser was prepared to take the initial steps down this path but his suspicion of banks and markets prevented his crossing the Rubicon to a floating dollar. That decision was taken by Hawke in late 1983, the year Fraser lost power.

The float became the dividing line between the old and the new economy. It cast Fraser as a leader of the past and Hawke as the leader of the future. In his final term Fraser saw the defects in Australia's economic system but was unable to break the psychology of the past. He kept protection high, refused to reform the industrial system, shunned any real embrace of privatisation and avoided genuine tax reform. His choice, in effect, was to leave these issues to his successors – Hawke, Keating and Howard. Fraser failed to perceive the nature of the globalised age starting to emerge when he lost power.

Fraser's termination of the so-called golden age of Whitlam progressivism imposed a stereotypical lens through which his actions were viewed. It was the orthodoxy that Fraser must be a social policy conservative. Yet his record forces a different conclusion – Fraser championed multiculturalism, backed Asian immigration in the shadow of white Australia, pioneered Aboriginal land rights, pursued environmental causes and reformed the family support system. Each was a new step for the Liberal Party. In retrospect Fraser appears as a leader who believed in a compassionate conservatism, a notion that would have drawn ridicule in his time.

But he invariably followed the Liberal tradition of state rights. The final proof was his refusal to use Commonwealth powers to override Tasmania and halt (on environmental grounds) the building of the Gordon-below-Franklin dam. It was a touchstone issue at the 1983 election and it was Labor's centralism that secured it the 'greenie' vote.

For Fraser, leadership had both a philosophical and a tactical dimension. Where policy and principle were required he would provide them – but when manipulation and expediency were necessary he possessed them in excess. He was both a conservative and a reformer. His patrician bearing and shyness meant that he would win respect, suffer misunderstanding and rarely inspire affection. Fraser's dominance of his own time is not matched by his imprint upon history.

Robert James Lee Hawke

11 MARCH 1983 – 20 DECEMBER 1991

Hawke as prime minister was corporatist and bureaucratic by instinct and presidential in style.

BY NEAL BLEWETT

All prime ministers need a modicum of luck to achieve office, to survive and to succeed. Robert James Lee Hawke, the twenty-third prime minister of Australia, was perhaps the luckiest. Not for him was there the usual long and arduous parliamentary apprenticeship. Whereas all but two of his predecessors and successors served at least ten years in Parliament – and many over two decades – Hawke's apprenticeship lasted less than three years. Moreover, prime ministers coming to office by election from Opposition, rather than succeeding while their party is in office, have usually spent some years in the most demanding job in federal politics – the leadership of the Opposition. Hawke was Opposition leader for little over a month; the day he became Opposition leader was also the day that the election that was to install him as prime minister was called.

In office his luck held. The Liberal Opposition underwent periodic convulsions so that in his nearly nine years as prime minister he faced three different Opposition leaders, with one of these also recycled. Two of his four election victories – 1987 and 1990 – were close-run things; in 1987 the conservative Coalition outpolled Labor on the primary vote, in 1990 on the two-party-preferred vote.

Luck, however, is an odd word to use of Bob Hawke. If ever there seemed to be a man destined to be prime minister, both in his own eyes and that of many others, it was he. His mother has recorded that while pregnant with the future prime minister, during her daily reading of the Bible the Good Book would frequently fall open at Isaiah, chapter 9 verse vi: 'For unto us a child is born, unto us a son is given; and the government shall be upon his shoulder.'[1] As he grew up it became family lore that young Bob would one day become prime minister. From at least the age of seventeen, after a brush with death in a motor bicycle accident, Hawke came to share this sense of destiny.

Hawke was a child of the manse, with an essentially classless background but a strong Labor tradition – an uncle became premier of Western Australia. He was a member of that gifted postwar generation, the first of their families to go to university, from which so many Australian leaders were to come. However, Hawke's scholarships and academic achievements seem trophies in his progress rather than educationally transforming experiences. A modest record at Perth

Modern School, and good but not outstanding degrees in law and arts at the university of Western Australia were climaxed by the most prestigious of all awards, a Rhodes Scholarship in 1952. Oxford left little imprint on him either intellectually or culturally. This was in part the result of Hawke's pragmatic decision to turn his back on the intellectual challenge of that ancient university and to do in Oxford, of all places, a research degree on an aspect of the Australian arbitration system. He thus missed out on Oxford's distinctive teaching, while his choice of research topic isolated him intellectually from the postgraduate activities of the time. But this decision was typical of Hawke. Learning was for practical purposes, there was no time to waste even amongst the dreaming spires; he very much personified intelligence in action.

The pivotal decision in Hawke's life was his decision to join the ACTU as research officer in 1958. Today a union research office is a well-trodden path for bright young graduates with Labor leanings, but Hawke was a pioneer. He used the opportunity to prove himself to industrial labour and ultimately to seize the leadership of the ACTU. Hawke rose superbly to the social challenge of his new milieu. If he appears to have gained little intellectually from Oxford, at least he had not been tainted with the affectations that afflict so many antipodean Oxonians. Gregarious by nature, he had no pretensions to 'cultcha', and he genuinely shared his trade union colleagues' enthusiasm for football, horses and beer.

He proved an accomplished industrial advocate from the very beginning, notching up a memorable victory in his first major test – the 1959 basic wage decision – and following this up with an immediate success with the metal workers' margins. His grasp of economics left the legal representatives of business floundering in his wake, and at times even left the bench bemused. Although there were setbacks, sometimes attributed to his aggressive and abrasive style, his first wife's verdict is a fair one: 'Bob revolutionised the wage fixing processes in Australia, and was regarded as the best advocate the Court had seen.'[2]

By the late 1960s he was the best known figure in the industrial labour movement and poised to challenge the secretary, Harold Souter, for the presidency of the ACTU on the retirement of Albert Monk. Souter – conservative, fastidious, teetotal – was no personal match for the dynamic and gregarious Hawke, but he had a formidable base in the right wing of the industrial movement. Hawke, conservative in substance but radical in style, formed a purely pragmatic alliance with the trade union Left to wrest control of the ACTU from the traditionalists of the Right. With, as always, astute numbers men to marshal his forces, Hawke first eroded Souter's right-wing majority on the ACTU executive and then, on 10 September 1969, won the presidency by 399 votes to Souter's 350.

Hawke's career as president of the ACTU began with a radical bang – the destruction of retail price maintenance through the partnership with Bourke's department store, backed by union muscle, and ACTU support for a flurry of political actions on pensions, opposition to the Vietnam War and the Springbok rugby tour. But such radicalism did not last. Hawke's natural conservatism, the decline of the Australian economy, the interests of the Whitlam government and the struggle to preserve union authority against Malcolm Fraser's government all muted the early radicalism.

Hawke's enthusiasm for political strikes waned over the decade. The turning point was probably 1975, when – on the sacking of the Whitlam government – it was Hawke's resolute stand that prevented industrial action, which in such turbulent times could easily have turned to violence. Hawke was a resolver, not an instigator, of industrial conflicts, and the 1970s were full of occasions when Hawke parachuted in to resolve apparently intractable disputes. As the decade wore on Hawke increasingly sought to restrain union militancy, so much so that he became known, somewhat derisively, as the 'Fireman'.

He had little success with his ambitious plans for ACTU business partnerships. Many enterprises were mooted but few got off the ground, and those that did had chequered histories. On the other hand, he succeeded in reforming the bureaucracy of the ACTU, enlarging its full-time staff from seven to forty, with a strong emphasis on quality and qualifications. He increased the numbers affiliated with the ACTU from 1.4 million workers to 2 million and in addition secured agreement towards the end of his term for the two major umbrella groups of the white-collar workforce – the Congress of Commonwealth and Government Employees' Association (CAGEO) and the Australian Council of Salaried and Professional Associations (ACSPA) – to affiliate with the ACTU. Despite difficulties in raising fees he increased the annual income of the ACTU from $162,000 to $1million. An accomplished television performer, he gave the ACTU a media profile it had never had before.

54. Prime Minister Whitlam with Chairman Mao Zedong in China in November 1973. The previous Liberal government had refused to recognise its communist government but Whitlam hastened to acknowledge China and to transfer Australia's embassy from Taiwan to Beijing.

55. Whitlam, far right, looks on as his appointee to the office of Governor-General – and the man who would later dismiss him – Sir John Kerr, is sworn in on 11 July 1974.

56. Prime Minister Whitlam with the young Member for Blaxland and future prime minister, Paul Keating, 30, left, in October 1974 ...

57. ... and in the same month with another rising star and future prime minister, ACTU president Bob Hawke at a Labor Party rally in Hyde Park, Sydney.

58. *The dismissal, 11 November 1975: on the steps of Parliament House the Governor-General's secretary, David Smith, with Whitlam behind, reads the proclamation dissolving Parliament.*

59. *Whitlam's dismissal prompted demonstrations across the country. Here, ACTU President Bob Hawke addresses one of the rallies in Canberra.*

60. *Gough Whitlam, with his wife, Margaret, in the national tally room in Canberra on 13 December 1975 after the Liberal's landslide victory.*

61. *Prime Minister Malcolm Fraser with Treasurer John Howard at the Premiers' Conference in 1979. Howard had had a meteoric rise, elevated to Treasury during the 1977 election campaign when Philip Lynch stood down because of controversy about his financial affairs.*

62. Malcolm Fraser's 'Easter Island' face was a gift to cartoonists. The wealthy grazier's aloof bearing gave the impression of a 'born-to-rule Liberal': it disguised a social conscience which became more evident after retirement.

63. Fraser's strong stand on race issues and his achievement in promoting Zimbabwean independence marked his prime ministership. African leaders, like Zambian President Kenneth Kaunda, seen here in Melbourne in 1981, became enthusiastic supporters of the Australian Prime Minister.

64. Bob hawke, left, puts on a smiling face after losing his July 1982 bid for the Labor leadership, but in February 1983 Bill Hayden, right, would be pressured out, leaving Hawke to demolish Malcolm Faser at an election called the day Hawke became Labor leader.

65. Prime Minister Fraser with the British Prime Minister, Margaret Thatcher, at a sheep station near Canberra during a break from the Commonwealth Heads of Government Meeting in 1981. Although they both belonged to the conservative side of politics, Fraser, despite his rhetoric, never embraced dry economic Thatcherism, and the two clashed over policy on southern Africa.

66. Treasurer Keating and Prime Minister Hawke with the Labor government's first Budget papers in August 1983. The Hawke–Keating partnership, described by Hawke as 'the most deadly combination in post-war politics' but later to break down in acrimony, oversaw a dramatic transformation of the Australian economy in the 1980s.

67. John Howard was re-elected leader of the Liberal Party after the 1987 election but would be replaced by Andrew Peacock, left, in a 1989 coup. Rivalry between these two ambitious men dogged the Liberals during the 1980s, helping keep them in Opposition.

68. The first parliamentary session of the House of Representatives in the new Parliament House in August 1988, Australia's bicentennial year.

69. A tearful Hawke embraces a Chinese student representative at the June 1989 service in the wake of the Tiananmen Square killings. Hawke's emotionalism was periodically displayed during his prime ministership.

70. On 30 May 1991, Keating precipitated a long night of number-counting and caucus meetings after announcing to Hawke he was challenging for the leadership. However, the following day the two men had to appear together at a meeting with State Premiers, pictured here. Keating lost the leadership bid on 3 June, resigned as Treasurer and Deputy Prime Minister, and moved to the back bench, promising no further challenge.

71. A triumphant Keating after his successful second challenge to Bob Hawke in December 1991. He had feared he might inherit the 'fag end' of Labor's term, but went on to win the 1993 election on an anti-GST platform.

72. Keating was the master of political invective and the sharp parliamentary riposte but critics attacked him for lacking respect for the parliamentary institution: he labelled the Senate 'unrepresentative swill' and said Question Time was 'a courtesy' extended by the executive to the legislature.

73. Despite his working-class origins, an image of arrogance dogged Prime Minister Keating. His passion for French Empire clocks and talk of 'the Paris option' for departing politics encouraged parody.

74. Howard's perceived deputy sheriff role to America's George Bush Jr proved an irrestible source of inspiration to the nation's cartoonists and comedians.

75. Prime Minster Howard, used the Sir Robert Menzies Lecture in Melbourne in October 1999 to defend Australia's links to Britain. Menzies was a hero for Howard – he had Menzies' desk moved into his office – but his adulation helped critics portray him as a 1950s' man.

76. Issues of race dogged John Howard. The One Nation scare was followed by a bitter dispute over the Prime Minister's refusal to make an apology on behalf of the nation to indigenous people, as captured in Geoff Pryor's May 1997 cartoon.

77. Like Keating, Howard was a consummate parliamentary performer, but was often overshadowed by Treasurer Peter Costello, second from right, whose sharp tongue had more than a touch of the Paul Keating style.

78. Five prime minsters gather on Sorry Day 2008, after the landmark apology to Australia's Aborigines. From left: Bob Hawke, Gough Whitlam, Malcolm Fraser, Paul Keating and Kevin Rudd. John Howard refused the invitation to attend.

79. Kevin Rudd greets East Timor's Prime Minister Xanana Gusmao to show solidarity after an attack wounded East Timor's President, Jose Ramos-Horta. Rudd moved rapidly to establish his foreign affair's credentials and cement the friendly relationship with Australia's newest neighbour.

Hawke was never a left-wing president. Indeed he pursued consensus on the ACTU executive and was adept at cobbling together compromises that secured unanimity. But he shifted his base during the 1970s. His industrial moderation, his bitter conflict with the Socialist Left in Victoria, his sympathy for the Israeli cause and his hostility to the Left's defining shibboleth of the late 1970s – opposition to uranium mining – all pushed him to the right.

Well before he left the ACTU Hawke had become for many people – and most of the media – the alternative Labor leader and Australia's prime minister in waiting. After the initial euphoria over Gough Whitlam had subsided, Hawke became the most popular political figure in Australia throughout the 1970s, perhaps because he was not actually a politician. Hawke's status was endorsed by his being national president of the Labor Party from 1973 to 1978, a position that gave him a formal national party post and enhanced his celebrity status. Yet it was not easy wearing two hats during the Whitlam government years, given the government's rather cavalier attitude towards the ACTU and the frank public appraisals of governmental performance by the party president. It also exacerbated the latent rivalry between Hawke and Whitlam, fuelled by differences over taxation, competitive grandstanding over French nuclear tests in the Pacific and public tensions between Hawke's pro-Israeli stance and Whitlam's pursuit of 'even-handedess' in the Middle East. The rock bottom was reached when the president of the Labor Party campaigned against the Labor government's proposal to acquire power over incomes. On the other hand, in the wilderness years after the 1975 debacle, with the Fraser coalition dominant and the parliamentary Labor Party demoralised, it fell to Hawke to defend Labor interests.

Hawke had pursued high political office via the presidency of the ACTU and, apart from a flirtation with the seat of Corio in the federal election of 1963, had turned his back on the parliamentary path. The dangers of Hawke's approach were obvious. Those bred in the parliamentary system, socialised into its values and with their ambitions defined by that arena, were unlikely to accept an outsider at his own valuation. A greater danger was that the parliamentary party might establish an internal succession that would be difficult for an outsider to overturn. This was the very situation that confronted Hawke when, in late 1977, the caucus elected Bill Hayden parliamentary leader.

Through the 1970s it had been possible to envisage Hawke as Whitlam's heir, but it was difficult to see him as Hayden's – a man three years his junior.

However, Hayden was not the only obstacle to Hawke's ambitions. Hawke's glittering public façade could not mask his drinking and his womanising. The demands of his job, which kept him away from home a lot, as well as the heavy drinking and the adulteries, put great strains on his marriage, and the long-suffering Hazel Hawke seriously contemplated divorce in the late 1970s.

A drunken outburst against Hayden in an Adelaide bar during the 1979 National Labor Conference almost brought his career to an end. This shock, along with the death of his mother and his impending entry into federal Parliament, led him to give up alcohol completely in 1980. He appears never to have touched a drop during his prime ministership. There was never any public renunciation of his womanising, though there were to be public confessions to past sins. But he and Hazel achieved a new modus vivendi and their very public partnership was one of his strengths as Prime Minister. His extraordinary popularity was abetted by the public perception of him as a repentant prodigal.

Hawke had been reluctant to abandon his position in the ACTU without being guaranteed the leadership of the Federal Parliamentary Labor Party. By the late 1970s he dared not wait for the chance of a Hayden defeat. The hunt for a federal seat was complicated in Victoria by the Socialist Left's unrelenting hostility to his candidature and possibilities were canvassed in other states. In late 1979 the decision was taken and Hawke became the candidate for the safe seat of Wills in inner Melbourne, defeating the Socialist Left candidate, the young party organiser Gerry Hand, by 38 votes to 29. He entered Parliament in October 1980, taking his place immediately on the Opposition frontbench as shadow minister for industrial relations, employment and youth.

His arrival in Parliament – an event anticipated for a decade – was an anticlimax. Because expectations were unreal, his parliamentary performance as shadow minister – 'patchy' in John Button's judgment[3] – was disappointing. Hawke himself never found the atmosphere in Parliament congenial and was rather contemptuous of the charade there. Hayden had the numbers – his own rather amorphous centre group plus the battalions of the Left gave him a majority. Even if the Right were Hawke's natural allies there were among them many parliamentary club members impatient with his pretensions and at least one, Paul Keating, who saw his own ambitions threatened by Hawke.

But the polls ran for Hawke. Throughout he was preferred to both Fraser and Hayden; and there was also Hawke's messianic conviction that he and he alone could defeat Fraser. All this could be used to destabilise Hayden, compelled to defend himself against Hawke as well as to struggle against Fraser. Party and private polls were leaked against Hayden, while party officials were tempted by the prospect of victory under Hawke. In addition, there can be little doubt that Hawke's allies in the ACTU white-anted Hayden's efforts to achieve a wages accord as the centrepiece of his economic policy.

Hawke's destabilisation of his rival was so blatant at the party's National Conference in early July 1982 that Hayden was compelled to make a pre-emptive strike, calling a leadership vote in the caucus on 16 July. Hayden had been weakened by policy stumbles and a growing paranoia as well as by courageous stances on federal interventions in state party branches, which made enemies, and on uranium policy, which alienated many in the Left. He fended Hawke off by only five votes. It was insufficient. Hayden's fate was sealed by the Flinders by-election on 4 December, when a miserably small swing to Labor convinced many doubters that only Hawke could guarantee a Labor victory. But how to get Hawke to the leadership without an internal bloodbath that could ruin Labor's prospects even under Hawke?

John Button, Labor's Senate leader and Hayden's closest political ally, now played Brutus to Hayden's Caesar. In a series of meetings and a critical letter in January 1983 Button convinced Hayden to abdicate the leadership. Button, who had survived for years in the bearpit of Victorian Labor politics because of a shrewd perception of his friends and enemies, was not merely counselling Hayden, not merely appealing to Hayden's love of the party to which he had given his life. He was in fact removing the last props to Hayden's self-confidence. If Button no longer believed that Hayden could win, his cause was lost.

On 3 February, at a meeting of the parliamentary shadow Cabinet in Brisbane, Hayden resigned the leadership. The same day Fraser, hoping to capitalise on Labor's feuding, called his early election, only to discover his opponent was to be Hawke, not Hayden. Five days later Hawke was formally elected leader of the party; four weeks after that he was prime minister.

The party that had surrendered to Hawke was immediately rewarded. Confident, authoritative, charismatic, its new leader took control of the campaign, indeed of the election – so much so that he 'stole Fraser's prime ministerial mantle during the campaign itself'.[4] Unifying the party and stitching up the wages accord with the ACTU – which had so long eluded Hayden – Hawke seduced the Canberra press gallery, dominated the television networks and won over the swinging voters. The extraordinary rapport that had always existed between Hawke and the ordinary Australian was displayed on a grand national scale. His charisma – not intellectual like Whitlam's but visceral and emotional – was more like that of a pop star than a middle-aged politician, though the dazzled acolytes were as likely to be staid matrons as teenagers.

The Coalition government simply crumbled before this onslaught. Ill-prepared for the election that they had called, with the worst recession for fifty years, characterised by double-digit unemployment and inflation and an almost entirely negative campaign – wholly ineffective against Hawke – the Liberals were scarcely ever in the running. On Saturday 5 March Hawke won one of the great electoral victories in Australian history, securing a Labor majority in the House of Representatives greater than any since Curtin's triumph in 1943.

But Hawke did not simply bring Labor to power; assisted by a finely tuned party machine he kept it in power by continuing to win elections. In his parting gibe as Opposition leader Hayden had suggested that 'a drover's dog could lead the Labor Party to victory the way the country is'. He was probably right, yet it is most unlikely that Hayden could have won as decisively as Hawke did in 1983, although he might not have dissipated a smaller majority as wantonly as Hawke did in 1984. But it is difficult to see any Labor leader other than Hawke winning four consecutive elections, particularly given the economic turbulence of the 1980s and early 1990s. All this was achieved in an age when the West was dominated by libertarian philosophies and conservative political parties. For a Labor government to exist in such a climate, even if it did somewhat change its spots, was remarkable; that it survived for over a decade is extraordinary. In campaigns that had become increasingly presidential, Hawke was the supreme presidential candidate, with an appeal over and beyond his party. He was probably the greatest electioneering prime minister Australia had yet seen.

Hawke as Prime Minister was corporatist and bureaucratic by instinct and presidential in style. He had little time for Parliament, finding the atmosphere, particularly the adversarial nature of the debates, uncongenial and antipathetic to his consensual approach and his negotiating skills. In his 1979 Boyer Lectures (an annual series of lectures given by a prominent person and broadcast over the ABC) he had mooted the rather fanciful notion of the prime minister recruiting up to half his ministers from distinguished figures outside the Parliament. Under Hawke, Parliament's steady decline as an information forum accelerated – Question Time became more theatrical and less informative than ever – while significant prime ministerial statements were increasingly delivered outside Parliament. Hawke preferred to appeal to the people through the media, the televising of Parliament merely enhancing this communication rather than improving the processes of Parliament. He preferred to work directly with the great civil powers – particularly the trade unions and business. It is symptomatic that his first appearance as prime minister in the parliamentary chamber was at the economic summit of April 1983, very much a corporatist undertaking.

He maintained close links with the leaders of the ACTU, mostly his protégés anyhow. It was said, with some truth, that the shrewd and intelligent ACTU secretary, Bill Kelty, had more influence than many a Cabinet minister. Apart from helping economic management, this intimate relationship contributed to a low level of days lost through industrial disputes, a level unprecedented for a generation. The government had only one major industrial confrontation – a prolonged, bitter but ultimately successful dispute with the airline pilots in 1989 – in which the full resources of the state were used to defeat the pilots, whose claims endangered pay restraint across the community.

Nor was the big end of town neglected. The prime minister's business contacts, built up over twenty years with the ACTU, his charm, his skills as a negotiator, and above all the surprisingly benign attitude of his government to the capitalist order, all muted the traditional hostility of business to Labor governments. In close co-operation with the Cabinet, and backed by a disciplined caucus and party, he bypassed Parliament, negotiating directly with the great and powerful. Every now and then the Senate gave his corporatism a jolt, reminding him of the relevance of Parliament.

While Hawke's charisma contributed to his electoral success, his talent for bureaucracy gave his government cohesion, stability and authority. Hawke possessed an unusual combination of qualities, for the charismatic politician tends usually to be slipshod, relying on wits and charm rather than organisation. Not so Hawke; indeed, his great attention to process has been seen as a substitute for his lack of any political philosophy. His rather empty reconciliation theme, which dominated the opening years of his prime ministership, might well have had presentational merits, but it derived whatever substance it had from the fact that its proponent was the great negotiator of his time – reconciliation as a process of negotiation masterminded by Hawke.

It was soon apparent that this was to be an orderly Labor government, working in co-operation rather than in conflict with the public service, which quickly recognised it had a sympathetic prime minister. Moreover, from the head of the prime minister's department, Sir Geoffrey Yeend, to the prime minister's chauffeur, Noel Hansen, Fraser's appointments were left in place.[5] There was none of the suspicion and friction that marked the Whitlam government's early relations with the service, nor any savage partisan purge of senior public servants as marked the arrival of John Howard. Hawke and the Department of Prime Minister and Cabinet (PM&C) were at one in their concern for process at the highest levels of government. Under him it was not to be the task of PM&C to second-guess ministers on policy. Rather the department was to assist the prime minister in monitoring ministerial performance, advise him on the policy interests central to his strategic concerns and protect the processes of Cabinet government. Nor, under Hawke, was his private office – always headed by a public servant on the way to higher things – ever a hive of anti-bureaucratic activity, as the private office had been under both conservative and Labor predecessors.

In deliberate contrast to the Whitlam regime, Hawke gave process prime place in structuring his government. He used the authority of his 1983 election victory to break with Labor tradition by imposing on caucus an inner Cabinet and outer ministry (the shadow ministry had been moving in this direction before Hawke's accession) and to impose solidarity on Cabinet members. A set of functional and co-ordinating

Cabinet committees was designed to facilitate the participation of all ministers in relevant Cabinet decisions and also to ease the load on Cabinet, and simplify its processes. Only major issues, controversies unresolved by the committees and matters of urgency were to come for debate before Cabinet. Hawke himself paid much attention to these rules and insisted on their observance.

Hawke went on tinkering with the structure of government until his dramatic creation, in July 1987, of a system of sixteen mega-departments. Aimed to achieve advantages of scale and to minimise duplication, it had also for the tidy mind of the prime minister the advantage of making it easier to organise Cabinet by clarifying the demarcation between Cabinet and the outer ministry. With every department represented by a Cabinet minister, there was now much less need for junior ministers to be co-opted into Cabinet meetings.

Hawke's was an outwardly open government. He was an excellent Cabinet chairman, well briefed, disciplined and focused, rarely pre-empting debate by a statement of his own views and usually seeking a Cabinet consensus. Ministers, both senior and junior, were given full opportunities to make their cases and ministers were treated with courtesy. Except in a few key strategic areas ministers were left a relatively free hand to develop and implement their policies, coming to Cabinet for major discussions only when in trouble or when policies antagonised other ministers – and of course for money.

Some commentators have seen this formal picture of the Cabinet under Hawke as an almost ideal prime ministerial/Cabinet relationship. Yet the picture needs qualification. At the heart of the Cabinet there was a group of hard men, who along with the Prime Minister provided the engine room of government. They were mostly members of the Expenditure Review Committee, the most powerful committee of the government; it was a kind of inner Cabinet, possessed of superior knowledge, which vetted all expenditure and prepared the Budget. Although its recommendations were appealable to Cabinet they were rarely challenged and even more rarely overturned, while the Cabinet had neither the time nor the information to revise the Budget.

Hawke's style of management was characterised by a prime ministerial concentration on a few major strategic concerns, while leaving vast swathes of governmental policymaking to individual ministers. This focus is readily apparent from his memoirs. Some 80 per cent of the material on his prime ministership is devoted to just two topics – economic management, broadly defined, and foreign policy. The only other issue given any detailed attention is the environment – in the latter 1980s there were major Cabinet controversies pitting Hawke and his environment minister, Graham Richardson, against most of his old allies on the ERC. In these respects the memoirs closely reflect Hawke's emphases in government.

Ministers were generally on a light rein, neither the prime minister nor his department seeking to involve themselves in policymaking, provided it was not an area in which the prime minister was intimately involved or that was central to the government's survival. His government's qualities then, over vast areas of public administration, tended very much to reflect the qualities of his ministers. Hawke was fortunate in his ministers, most of whom were inherited from his predecessor, indeed often in jobs actually designated by Hayden. Commentators are generally agreed that it was one of the abler ministeries in federal history.

In social security, health, education, defence, and primary industries – where ministers mostly had long tenure – major, long-lasting structural changes were achieved. In communications, however, with four ministers over eight years – the longest term a little over two years – with too many vested interests and possibly too many prime ministerial interventions, policies were somewhat incoherent. Despite a courageous start in overturning the Tasmanian government's proposal for the Gordon-below-Franklin dam and despite the later astute reactive responses of Graham Richardson, environmental policies remained reactive, without clear priorities and long-term goals. In immigration a succession of ministers simply struggled to reduce the immigration intake; while despite the best efforts of three ministers, Aboriginal policy never recovered from the torpedoing of national land rights at the behest of the Burke Labor government in Western Australia. Perhaps most disappointing of all were the minimal achievements in political reform. Apart from an early burst of reforming if opportunistic legislation – dealing with the public funding of political parties, a modified list voting for the Senate and the expansion in the size of the House and Senate – the momentum was not maintained and the record was barren. Of six proposals for constitutional change put to referendum – two in 1984 and four in 1988 – all failed.

Like most Australian prime ministers, Hawke was an activist in foreign affairs, although he was more active than most. He came to office with considerable international experience and many influential overseas contacts as a result of his work with the ILO in Geneva, frequent visits to the United States and the Soviet Union and his involvement with Israel. As Prime Minister he kept abreast of the foreign affairs cable traffic, and his mastery of briefs, plus his ability to establish an intimate and easy rapport in face-to-face conversations, made him a first-class interlocutor.

As in other fields he was assisted by able ministers, first his old rival Hayden and then his protégé, Gareth Evans. Relations with Hayden were never easy, but the two men played complementary rather than competitive roles in foreign affairs. This was facilitated by the fact that in the early years Hawke concentrated on establishing his domestic authority, using his major foreign focus – the relationship with the United States – to sustain Hayden initiatives in Indochina, the South Pacific and the United Nations, often in the face of critical attitudes in Washington. With Evans the personal relationship was much closer, and Evans' intellectual abilities and his appetite for work did much to give structure and coherence to Hawke's foreign policy.

Hawke tended to be the big picture man. The broad thrust of policy, relations with the great powers, participation in arenas in which Australia played a big power role, notably CHOGM and the South Pacific forum, were very much the prime minister's preserves. As Gareth Evans has acknowledged, 'foreign ministers no less than any other ministers take their cue from the prime minister of the day'.[6]

While recognising the curbs imposed by Australia's small population and limited military resources, Hawke wanted Australia to be an activist middle power, opportunities for which grew with the decline and end of the Cold War. Hawke – possibly to distract the Labor Left from abandoned platform commitments – initiated the dialogue between Indochina and the relevant great powers in the search for an international solution to the continuing conflict in Cambodia. This was pursued by Hayden and ultimately realised by Evans. Again the active middle-power role envisaged by Hayden on disarmament issues – prevention of nuclear proliferation, the ending of nuclear testing, the banning of chemical and biological warfare – was endorsed and backed by Hawke, possibly to forestall an anti-nuclear program by the Left along New Zealand lines.

Relations, particularly with the great powers, were very much subject to Hawke's predilections for personal diplomacy. Rarely has an Australian leader so assiduously cultivated the great and the good – and the not so good – of the world. It is easy to satirise Hawke's wooing of the great – Reagan and Bush, Hu Yaobang and Mikhail Gorbachev. Yet his much-vaunted three-and-a-quarter-hours' conversation with Gorbachev, for example, raises doubts, not about Hawke's priorities, but about Gorbachev's. At least Hawke secured exit visas for a number of Jewish refuseniks, thus making up for a humiliating rebuff on the same issue in 1979. In the status-conscious world of international diplomacy these personal contacts by the leader of a relatively small middle power could be usefully deployed to advance Australia's standing and to make it an effective player in the international arena.

Hawke probably did overestimate – his 'egocentric presumption' – the extent to which he could exploit these personal relations 'to fine tune the major trouble spots of the world'.[7] Certainly his personal attempt to resolve the impasse over nuclear-powered or armed ships between the United States and New Zealand came to naught. Likewise, while he proved unexpectedly disciplined and pragmatic on the issue of Israel, his cautious personal venture into peacemaking in the Middle East in 1987 proved premature. His efforts to advance a face-saving formula for Saddam Hussein in the Gulf crisis of 1990 were stillborn. By contrast, it was his initiative – overriding the doubts of Evans – and his international contacts that secured the prohibition of all mining and oil drilling in Antarctica.

Hawke was the most pro-American Labor leader since his hero John Curtin. Throughout the 1980s he travelled to the United States for regular consultations with the American leadership. His stance was such that for the first time since World War II attitudes to the American alliance ceased to differentiate the major parties in Australia. He had good access in Washington, originally facilitated by his long-standing friendship with President Ronald Reagan's secretary of state, George Schultz. Hawke shared the Washington establishment's Cold War assumptions but was flexible in adapting to the rapidly changing conditions of the 1980s. Although his readiness to commit Australia to involvement in the

American MX missile tests led to a party crisis and eventual backdown, and while he was prompt in participating in the Gulf imbroglio, efforts to paint him as an American lackey are a caricature. He defended Hayden's pursuit of peace in Indochina despite much American disquiet; he argued against punitive measures against New Zealand as desired by influential American figures; he was strident in condemning American protective policies in agriculture; he defended South Pacific interests against both American nuclear 'hawks' and American fishing interests; and his original version of APEC (Asia–Pacific Economic Co-operation) seems not to have involved the United States out of deference to Asian sensibilities.

Engagement with Asia was a second major aim of Hawke's foreign policy, though this appears much less personalised. The only East Asian leaders cultivated in a sustained way were the Chinese, and that rapprochement ended in tears with Tiananmen Square. He was contemptuous of New Zealand Prime Minister David Lange and his nuclear-free policy on American ships. Surprisingly, in his memoirs there is no mention of President Suharto, only two fleeting references to Indonesia and none to East Timor. Nevertheless, under the influence of his first economics adviser, Ross Garnaut, he quickly recognised the implications for Australia of East Asia's industrial revolution. His assiduous cultivation of the Chinese leaders stemmed less from strategic and security concerns than from the benefits Australia might reap from a resurgent Chinese economy. The establishment of APEC in 1989 was his crowning achievement in this area and sprang very much from personal initiatives. This Asian engagement was linked closely with structural reforms in Australia – the fostering of an export culture with Asia as its target.

The third major theme of his foreign policy – liberalising international trade and enmeshing Australia in a free trading world – was likewise linked to the thrust of domestic economic reform. Aided by a series of capable trade ministers, Hawke became an international spokesman for a successful resolution to the latest and most ambitious negotiations of the General Agreement on Tariffs and Trade (GATT) – the Uruguay round launched in 1986. Australia, through the formation of the Cairns Group of agricultural free-trading nations, became the leading advocate for ending the corruption of international agricultural markets through export subsidies.

At the Commonwealth Heads of Government Meeting (CHOGM) he was one of the major players – with Brian Mulroney of Canada and Rajiv Gandhi of India – in seeking an end to apartheid in South Africa; his abhorrence of racism was never subject to his characteristic pragmatism. He played a key role in establishing the Eminent Persons' Group – magnanimously securing a place for Malcolm Fraser – and the development of a graduated escalation of sanctions against South Africa, as well as in outflanking Margaret Thatcher's opposition to this program.

The South Pacific forum was another arena in which Australia played a major role. Hawke began as a conventional Cold War warrior with an emphasis on security – on Australia's traditional task of keeping the South Pacific free of infiltration by the Soviet Union and its numerous surrogates. But through personal engagement he became open to a much broader set of ideas and became active on a range of questions: the defence of South Pacific fishing interests, decolonisation in New Caledonia, the South Pacific nuclear-free zone and opposition to French nuclear testing in the South Pacific.

However, this activism was not without its problems, for it tended to fuel natural resentment of Australia as the dominant power in the South Pacific region, and also fed suspicions that it was an agent for the United States. Australia's rather alarmist concerns about Libyan infiltration met with negative reactions among some South Pacific nations, and Hawke's 1987 efforts to use the forum to influence developments in post-coup Fiji were rebuffed.

Hawke's last but not least achievement in foreign affairs was his management of Australia's intervention in the Gulf crisis of 1990–91. He committed Australia to participate in the multi-nation force early, some would say prematurely. But recognising the harsh reality of global politics he believed that early action would secure an appreciation that the size of Australia's contribution could not. When war eventually came in January 1991, he managed the inevitable tensions within the Labor Party, and his authoritative public rhetoric commanded widespread support for Australian participation.

The reputation of the Hawke government will ultimately rest on its massive if incomplete transformation of Australian economic life. The Hawke government faced two major economic challenges. One was immediate – the cyclical downturn of the early 1980s that confronted the new government with high levels of inflation and unemployment; the other was long-term and deep-rooted – the structural malaise in the Australian economy that rendered it increasingly uncompetitive in a globalising world. Solving the immediate problems simply brought the long-term ones to the fore.

There was not much help from the past. The economic model that had sustained social democracy since World War II – Keynesian demand management – had been shattered in Australia, as elsewhere, by stagflation. Nor was there much comfort in the present. Ideologically the Labor Party was not a natural vehicle for confronting the competitive imperatives of globalisation, which focused on the dead hand of protective tariffs, the distortions produced by industry subsidies, inefficient public enterprises, the sclerotic grip of financial regulation and the rigidities of the labour market.

In these unpropitious circumstances Hawke was an ideal leader. For one thing, he was a supreme optimist, with an unquenchable faith in his ability to negotiate a way through intractable problems. Though it is easy to dismiss his optimism as naïve, it helped sustain the government through many a dark hour. He was also a complete pragmatist, with only a few passions and less ideology. The ease with which he dumped the fiscally expansive program on which he had been elected in 1983, when he discovered the extent of the budgetary deficit left by Fraser, demonstrated both his pragmatism and his authority.

His experience as ACTU president, his service on the board of the Reserve Bank from 1974 to 1980 and his membership both of the original Committee of Inquiry into Australia's manufacturing industry and the follow-up Crawford Committee all ensured that he was thoroughly conversant with the elite consensus on the structural flaws in the Australian economy and the need to create a more open, competitive, less regulated market economy. In 1983 Hawke was more fully across these issues than any figure in his government.

Neither Hawke nor his party had any comprehensive or coherent plan for tackling the economy. The result was a policy of pragmatic improvisations responding to a series of constantly shifting crises. A trimmed-back but still expansionary policy restored economic growth, though this was much helped by Fraser's fiscal largesse and his pay pause, the ending of the drought and international recovery. Increasingly tight fiscal policies were imposed, providing substantial budgetary surpluses by the end of the 1980s.

One thing the government did have – in many ways the most distinctive feature of its economic management – was the Accord. This was essentially a trade-off: the unions agreeing to voluntary wage restraint in return for social wage gains provided through government. The Accord provided the voluntary restraint, including cuts in real wages, that permitted economic growth without inflation for nearly seven years. Some of the pay-offs, particularly the income tax cuts, might have added to the difficulties of managing the economy, and the Accord relationship might have inhibited the speed of micro-economic reform. But its virtues far outweighed its flaws for most of the period.

The floating of the dollar in December 1983 – the recognition that in a globalising world a trading nation like Australia could not effectively insulate its currency – ushered in a host of financial deregulations. Most controls on the operations of financial markets were removed and foreign banks were admitted. Taxation reform in 1985, despite the treasurer's lament that his tax cart lost a wheel – a consumption tax – was still the most comprehensive since World War II. Taxation on capital gains and fringe benefits was introduced, tax shelters were shut off, dividend imputation was brought in and the top marginal rate of tax was reduced from 62 cents in the dollar to 49.

The overthrow of the old protectionist order came with two major statements in 1988 and 1991. These promised the gradual phasing out of effective tariff protection for all industries by the year 2000 except for motor cars and textiles and footwear, although even here the reductions were to be substantial. At the same time Australia's exports became more diversified and the move into Asian markets accelerated. Tentative beginnings were made to improve infrastructure, particularly in the ports, to open up telecommunications to duopolistic competition, to privatise the domestic airline and the Commonwealth Bank. A first hesitant step was taken to support enterprise bargaining in industrial relations.

Despite the government's achievement of sustained economic growth without inflation, by the late 1980s the economy was growing too fast. Despite significant wage restraint delivered by the Accord, inflation was growing again; despite massive budget surpluses the deficit on the balance of payments was again dangerously high. In a novel environment the old economic verities did not seem to hold. Monetary discipline applied too late – partly because of the uncertainty caused by the international stockmarket crash of October 1987 – turned out to be too severe, and plunged the economy into a downturn. Tragically for the country and fatally for Hawke, his period as prime minister ended in a recession longer, though not deeper, than that which had ushered in his government.

Nevertheless the Hawke government's transformation of the Australian economy marks a watershed in Australian history. Hawke inherited a cosseted economy characterised by all-round protection with an associated rent-seeking culture: it was an economy that was uncompetitive internationally and overly dependent on commodity exports, with little diversification in its export base, inefficient public enterprises, a rigid labour market and low productivity. The Hawke government did not, of course, cure these ills, but it did tackle most of them, and gave Australia an entirely new development trajectory. It left the hope, though not the certainty, that Australia might ultimately be able to pay its way in a globalising world.

Possibly Hawke's greatest achievement was to oversee such profound shifts without any serious fracture within the ALP. Power and the continuing retention of power bred acquiescence, but Hawke was never afraid to teach his party and tackle its shibboleths – indeed he took a certain pleasure in culling sacred cows. The alliance at the heart of his government – between the Right and Centre Left on economic policy – gave him dominance of the party forums. Close liaison with the leadership of all factions, plus subtle and not-so-subtle use of patronage and rewards, enabled him to pilot the party through potentially disastrous shoals. Though he was occasionally rebuffed, as in his first efforts to privatise the airlines and telecommunications in 1988, defeats were rarely permanent, and in the special conference of September 1990 he secured approval for selling equity in both Qantas and Australian Airlines and for a competitive reshaping of telecommunications.

The recession put at risk Hawke's ability to manage the party, for not only did it imperil public support for the modernisation of the Australian economy but it also heightened the disillusionment of Labor voters with their own government. For the recession highlighted an imbalance in the Hawke prospectus. Income tax reform had been unnecessarily regressive, because of both the massive cuts at the top and the emphasis on shaving rates rather than shifting thresholds.[8] Despite significant achievements in the human services, for example the family assistance supplement that extended social security benefits to the children of poorer working families and the Medicare health scheme, Budgets had been very tight. Australia remained one of the meaner social welfare states in the industrialised world, although this was partly a result of the better targeting of resources. Succour for the inevitable victims of modernisation was too tardy and limited and the recession merely stressed these inadequacies.

None of this is to suggest that Hawke's basic priorities were not the right ones. Building a successful competitive economy would in the long run bring lasting benefits to the less well off, providing more employment as well as greater resources for welfare. But the balance in the short run was askew. The human services seem never to have been high on his list of priorities: as a result there was unnecessary sacrifice of social democratic values in pursuit of economic modernity.

While Hawke himself was intimately involved in the making of economic policy, there has been much dispute as to whether he or his treasurer, Paul Keating, led the revolution. Disentangling each man's contribution is perhaps pointless, as it was very much a partnership, in Hawke's words, 'the most deadly combination in postwar politics'. As the government aged, Keating tended to provide the policy detail, Hawke the acute political assessments. Increasingly, for instance, monetary management became the province of the treasurer, advised by Treasury and the Reserve Bank and insulated from the Cabinet, the ERC and to an extent from the prime minister.

Many of the original initiatives appear to have come from Hawke. It was he, with Ralph Willis, who secured the Accord. He was probably the more influential in the dollar float, although this is complicated by the fact that Keating had a more sophisticated operation to carry through, namely the outflanking of his own departmental secretary on the issue. Hawke had 'flagged tax reform ... from the very outset'[9] and certainly determined the process by pre-empting Cabinet discussion with a commitment to a tax summit on talkback radio. Hawke was the first to publicly push for privatisation and his leadership was necessary to give the crucial push to the dismantling of tariffs.

Over time it was Keating's enthusiasm for policymaking, his mastery of detail, his eloquence in argument and above all his overweening confidence in the rightness of his policy prescriptions that came to dominate economic policy development. A sceptic on the Accord to begin with, Keating became its most enthusiastic proponent and tended to take over its management. It was he and Kelty who stitched up the various deals and trade-offs that marked the history of the Accord. Once bitten by deregulation he developed the whole spate of policies that followed. On tax reform his was the 'chariot' and he the charioteer. No one became a more enthusiastic and ingenious privatiser than Keating; no one more staunch for the abolition of tariffs.

Yet Hawke remained the master of his government, however light a leash Keating worked on. Hawke chaired the ERC for most of the life of his government. It was Hawke who pulled the plug on a consumption tax – thereby probably saving his government. It was Hawke who scotched notions of a new summit after Keating's 'banana republic' rhetoric. It was Hawke who broke with his economic ministers to ensure triumphs for Graham Richardson on a series of environmental issues in a strategy designed to maximise the green vote. It was Hawke who, with Beazley, stopped Keating's imperial pretensions in telecommunications in 1990. It was Hawke who took charge of the last great economic statement of his government – that on tariff dismantling in March 1991.

Hawke's overthrow was dramatic enough – it was the first time a Labor prime minister had been toppled by his own party. It is given an almost Shakespearean quality by the ironic parallels with Hawke's overthrow of Hayden nine years before. In both cases the leader is stalked for some years by his rival; in both cases a first strike wounds but does not bring down the leader; in both cases opinion polls are used to denigrate the leader; in both cases the mistakes of the leader are exaggerated and exploited; in both cases party and trade union apparatchiks undermine the leader; in both cases there is a sense that if the challenger is not successful continuing destabilisation is inevitable.

The parallels of course should not be pushed too far. The denouement differs. In 1983 Hayden surrendered to the challenge rather than wreck the party; in 1991 Hawke defied his enemies to vote him from office. Moreover Hayden and Hawke were never a partnership; Hawke and Keating formed one of the great alliances in Australian politics. However, it was essentially a political relationship. In John Button's opinion 'neither of them ever liked the other much', Keating the quintessential parliamentary insider disdaining Hawke as 'an interloper', the older Hawke considering his young rival 'an opinionated upstart', at least in the early 1980s.[10] Given the vanity of one and the pretensions of the other, and given the extraordinary ambition of both men, what is remarkable is not that the relationship eventually broke down, but that it endured for so long.

Keating's impatience to hold the highest office had grown with the years, and by 1988 it threatened the very stability of the government. Keating believed that his massive contribution deserved to be rewarded, a formal recognition of his personal conviction that he was 'the real leader of the government'. What Keating feared was that, as Hawke clung to office year after year, the heritage would be dust and ashes before he secured it. Naturally the prime minister did not see things in quite the same light. Until his judgment was distorted in the final stages of the struggle, Hawke never seems to have doubted that Keating should be his successor. But not yet. He himself was in no sense an old man – not yet sixty in 1988 – he was physically and mentally fit, he enjoyed being prime minister and he was an election winner without equal. Keating would just have to wait.

Many in the government accepted the need for a transition process – a luxury never needed before by a federal Labor government – and the more blunt or foolhardy expressed such views to the prime minister. But few believed the point of actual transition had been reached; even Keating's own base, the New South Wales Right, refused to support his aspirations. What the great bulk of ministers and caucus wanted was the continuation of the successful partnership – Hawke as prime minister, Keating as treasurer. The reality of the situation was that Keating could not oust the most successful of Labor prime ministers, but on the other hand Hawke feared the government could not survive the 1990 election without Keating.

This was the background to the secret agreement between Hawke and Keating drawn up at Kirribilli House on 25 November 1988 in the presence of businessman Sir Peter Abeles and ACTU secretary Bill Kelty. In it Hawke agreed to hand over the prime ministership at some stage after the 1990 election. The agreement secured for Hawke his immediate objectives: it put off any decision on a transition until after the next election, which had yet to be won; it placated Keating, thereby keeping him on board for the election. Keating's acceptance of Hawke's procrastination was a recognition of the weakness of his own position: he could not defeat the prime minister; any withdrawal by him from the government might well imperil its election chances and end his prospects of ever becoming prime minister. Nevertheless, Hawke had mortgaged his future.

The Kirribili pact was never honoured. After much procrastination, Hawke used Keating's perversely provocative off-the-cuff, off-the-record speech at the Canberra press club on 7 December 1990 as the excuse, if not the cause, to repudiate the Kirribilli pact. The speech, which Hawke described as 'an act of treachery', made no explicit mention of Hawke, but a comment on leadership being more than 'tripping over television cables in shopping centres' could have but one referent.

By now both men had been much damaged by the recession. It had severely eroded the credibility of the treasurer who, brazenly refusing to admit error and determined to maintain a resolute fiscal stance, finally proclaimed, in an unwise fit of hyperbole, that 'it was the recession that Australia had to have'. Under the stress of economic failure the treasurer's behaviour was arrogant and erratic: berating colleagues in public, petulantly walking out of a Cabinet meeting and caught out in personal slips and indulgences.

Hawke had responded to the recession with a mixture of contrition and helplessness. His inertia in the face of recession confirmed for many the need for change. While the government remained active on many fronts, it appeared lethargic, even paralysed, before the mounting toll of the recession. Even the sympathetic Stephen Mills noted that Hawke's last term 'lacked the overarching sense of cohesion and relevance, of purpose and direction and dynamism, which animated his first period of government'.[11] Hawke too often in these last years was backward-looking, lacking the drive that had been so characteristic of his career. His successful managerial style of government had become a habit inhibiting innovation; his administrative instincts undermined his political sensibilities; and his personal office had become less politically adept than before. He lacked the resources to galvanise his party in the face of an economic failure that called into question all his achievements.

With the Kirribilli agreement repudiated, a challenge from Keating was now inevitable. Delayed by the Gulf War and then by the NSW state election, it came on 3 June 1991. But Hawke's coalition was too powerful for Keating. The NSW Right had deserted to its favourite, if not exactly lovable, son and the centre-left leadership, whose key figures had worked closely with Keating on the ERC, had long been less than enamoured of Hawke. But the battalions of the Right in Queensland, Victoria and elsewhere were marshalled by their local and national bosses behind Hawke. The Left, whom he had gradually integrated into his government, stayed firm for him, apart from a handful of the disgruntled. In addition Tasmanians, regardless of faction, rallied to his side, as did a majority of the unaligned, and a number of the foot soldiers of the centre left. Hawke saw off the challenge by 66 votes to 44. The challenger retired to the backbench.

Hawke made few changes in his government, refusing to punish those Cabinet colleagues who had voted against him. The times were too desperate for bloodletting. The only two critical changes were the result of Keating's resignation. Brian Howe became deputy prime minister, a reward for the solidarity of the Left, and John Kerin was made treasurer. Neither was an adequate substitute for the charismatic figure they replaced.

The authority of the Hawke government dwindled away during the last months of 1991. Keating contributed by outbidding the government on its responses to the recession and by subverting Hawke's creative scheme for tackling federal/state finances by appealing to caucus' instinctual centralism. But the decisive flaws lay within the government itself: its failure to respond imaginatively to the recession, more intractable than predicted; Kerin's disappointing performance as treasurer; and above all its paralysis when confronted with Opposition leader John Hewson's imaginative and massive economic plan known as Fightback!, launched on 17 November. With a tentative treasurer and a managerial prime minister, both awaiting Treasury analyses to mount a convincing attack on Fightback!, control of the agenda passed to the Opposition. The virtual refusal to debate Fightback! by a government that had lived off Opposition woes for much of its life demoralised the parliamentary party.

Kerin was sacked as treasurer without warning on 6 December, allegedly for his inability to communicate. Hawke survived his treasurer by less than a fortnight. His greatest political weapon had always been his standing in the polls. In December 1991 that standing perished irretrievably, and with it the most powerful of his arguments for resisting Paul Keating. On the eve of the second challenge his personal rating was down to 26 per cent – its lowest ever – and he was now behind Hewson as preferred prime minister. Keating might not be able to retrieve the situation, but he could scarcely do worse.

The astute leaders of both the Left and the loyalist Right could read the writing on the wall, and for a week sought a face-saving retirement. This crippled Hawke's leadership, since virtually his whole Cabinet, for one reason or another, now wanted him to go. Hawke, however, remained obdurate. With a determination at once self-indulgent and admirable, he would defy caucus to oust its most successful prime minister. This they did on the evening of 19 December by 56 votes to 52. Later that evening, in a ceremony tinged with irony and amidst Christmas festivities at Government House, Hawke resigned his commission to the governor-general, the man he had deposed as leader of the Labor party eight years, ten months and sixteen days before.

Hawke's post-prime ministerial activities tarnished his reputation. His rancour against his successor, which mars his impressive memoirs,[12] his sometimes tawdry parlaying of his status, experience and connections into commercial coinage, and above all, his repudiation of his wife of forty years, Hazel, for the younger Blanche d'Alpuget, ended forever his love affair with the Australian people.

He is unlikely ever to achieve the iconic stature of Gough Whitlam, who triumphed over great difficulties to transform the Labor Party and make it electable and who, even amongst the ruins of his government, remained a giant, and a martyred giant to boot. More controversially perhaps, his contribution to policymaking may be seen as of less substance than that of his treasurer and successor, Paul Keating. But judged simply as a prime minister, he is likely to surpass them both. His was one of the great watershed administrations of Australian history, one that changed the ways Australians live and see their world. His government towers above the administrations of the last generation, which can best be defined in the shadow of his. Whitlam's government was a cautionary if inspiring prologue; Fraser's was a hesitant and disappointing conservative interregnum; Keating's a turbulent if creative epilogue.

Moreover, despite much revisionist writing, it was Hawke's government. Its survival, though abetted by conservative instability, owed more to his electoral skills than to any other figure. A great party manager assisted by astute lieutenants, he brought a historically fractious party through a period of profound change without any serious split. He was served by able ministers and he gave them an easy rein, but there was never any question as to who ran the government. His political weight and skills gave him a mastery over his ministers unchallenged until the final months. His imprimatur, or at least his acquiescence, was necessary for every major act of government.

Given the achievement of his government and his central role in that achievement, he must be rated the greatest prime minister since Menzies. For those of radical bent, who look for creativity in their governments rather than a steady conserving hand, he is possibly the greatest since Chifley. In any event, he is likely to be reckoned among the half dozen great prime ministers of the first century of Australian Federation.

Paul Keating

20 DECEMBER 1991 – 11 MARCH 1996

Keating used his eight years as treasurer and four as prime minister to introduce radical changes that would allow Australia to meet the new economic challenges of the 1980s and 1990s. In doing so, he embraced many of the policies that even his conservative opponents had not dared to introduce and overturned long-held Labor shibboleths.

BY DAVID DAY

Few prime ministers have provoked such strong public reactions as Paul Keating. Even fewer have presided over such dramatic changes to Australia's economy and society. A self-professed 'big picture' person, a breeder of budgerigars and collector of fine antiques, Keating used his eight years as treasurer and four as prime minister to introduce radical changes that would allow Australia to meet the new economic challenges of the 1980s and 1990s. In doing so, he embraced many of the open market policies that even his conservative opponents had not dared to introduce and overturned long-held Labor shibboleths. But he will probably be remembered more for embracing closer ties with Asia, promoting Aboriginal land rights and championing the cause of an Australian republic.

Paul Keating was born in Bankstown, a semi-rural suburb twenty kilometres west of Sydney, on 18 January 1944. He was the eldest child of Irish Catholic parents who had moved there from the inner suburbs after their marriage in 1942. Part of Bankstown had been known as Irishtown in the nineteenth century and it retained a sizeable Irish component when the Keatings took up residence in a simple, tiled-roofed house clad with asbestos cement. Bankstown was a closeknit community that provided the young child, along with his two younger sisters and brother, with a secure environment, as did being part of the local Catholic community. However, the population of the district tripled to more than 120,000 in the first twelve years after the war. This great expansion led to an almost insatiable demand for building materials. When Keating was just nine years old, his father Matt used his experience as a boilermaker and welding inspector to become a partner in a business that made ready-mix concrete mixers. From being a minor union representative, Matt Keating became an employer of some two hundred workers, allowing the family eventually to move to a bigger house in a better part of Bankstown.

From an early age, Keating trained as a swimmer and also did long-distance running, but without much success. His educational achievements were also unremarkable. The principal of De La Salle College, where Keating completed his Intermediate Certificate, suggests that he would have been 'about number ten' out of the thirty students in the class. Rather than continuing with high school past the age of fourteen, Keating followed most of his fellow students into the world of work. This would have satisfied his practical, 'knockabout' father, who dismissed university graduates as 'bums'. But it would not have satisfied the expectations of his determined mother and the ambitions she harboured for her son. As a teenager, Keating was afflicted with disfiguring carbuncles on his arms and body, including his eyelids. They left him with no lower eyelashes and chronic problems with his tear ducts that made sustained reading difficult. The problem was caused by an inflamed appendix that had been poisoning his bloodstream.

With his father, Keating had been delivering Labor Party pamphlets to Bankstown letterboxes from a young age. When he turned fifteen his father took him along to the local branch to join up. According to Keating, he was 'the only person under forty [in the branch] and remained that way for quite some time'. It was just after the acrimonious split in the Labor Party that saw many Catholic members leave to form the stridently anti-communist Democratic Labor Party. The political passions of those times left an abiding mark on the impressionable Keating, who soon found that, unlike swimming or running, he could be a winner by dint of careful organisation and persuasive argument. He quickly made his mark, becoming president of the ALP's State Youth Council at the age of eighteen.

Apart from the influence of his father, Keating was also encouraged by the elderly and embittered Labor man and former NSW premier, Jack Lang. During the early years of his political apprenticeship Keating visited Lang regularly for lunchtime discussions on Labor history and the practice of politics. Lang had been a hero of Keating's father and the young Keating was keen to learn the tricks of the political trade from the old demagogue. But there was no certainty that Lang's tutoring of his protégé would be put to a political purpose. Keating's night school studies in electrical engineering could have seen his life take a very different turn. His seven years as a clerk with the Sydney City Council might also have led on to a solid if unspectacular career. His life still lacked focus. In his spare time he took to share-farming with friends on a wheat property in southern New South Wales. And there was his attempt to make the big time in the world of rock music, when he encouraged an upcoming band, the Ramrods, to take him on as manager. Despite Keating's faith in them, the group could not produce a hit record; he later recalled that he led them 'from nowhere to obscurity'. The band's break-up in 1966 allowed him to focus single-mindedly on a political future.

There was an opportunity close at hand, with the safe Labor seat of Banks, centred on Bankstown, being up for grabs. It was a mark of Keating's ambition and self-confidence at the age of twenty-three that he could consider himself sufficiently qualified and experienced to become its member. For two years Keating mounted a campaign to secure the nomination, and he had it all sewn up by 1967, a year before the preselection contest was due. Problems arose when a redistribution of electoral boundaries saw him and many of his supporters suddenly living in the seat of Blaxland, with an elderly and often absent sitting member keen to retain it. Other candidates also declared their intention to stand. Undaunted, and now with the support of the state executive, he began anew to amass the numbers. When the preselection contest was held in October 1968, Keating won by twenty votes. Although an internal party report several years later revealed serious irregularities in the voting, it was then too late. The brash young man was in Parliament.

Despite standing in a safe Labor seat, Keating took nothing for granted in the election campaign of October 1969. Drawing on the successful experience of US President John Kennedy, the twenty-five-year-old candidate styled his campaign accordingly. Instead of the usual round of stolid town hall meetings, Keating decorated a bus with campaign slogans and took his bold message to all corners of the electorate, handing out bumper stickers and badges. His energetic campaigning was rewarded with a 7 per cent swing. Keating was the youngest member in the new Parliament, joining the confident crush on the Opposition benches behind Labor leader Gough Whitlam.

Lang had advised Keating that when he arrived in Canberra 'they will all say you have plenty of time. The truth is you haven't a second to spare.' He seems to have taken the advice to heart. Political columnist Alan Ramsey later recalled how Keating 'wasn't in the place five minutes before he was running in Caucus ballots, twisting arms, organising numbers, and generally operating like a political Sammy Glick who'd pick your pocket while he wheedled your vote'. For his first three years in Canberra's old Parliament House, Keating shared a small basement office with Lionel Bowen, a former NSW state politician and a powerful figure in the NSW Right. Keating also grew close to another NSW MP, the formidable Rex Connor, who was shadow minister for minerals and energy and known in Caucus as 'the strangler'. He later claimed that it was Connor who taught him 'how to think big'. Back home in Sydney, he continued to live with his parents in their Bankstown home, where his father remained his staunchest supporter, advising Keating at one stage that, if he kept his head down, he would 'go through this mob'.

Keating had come to Parliament as mineral developments provided a new engine for Australia's economic growth, and Rex Connor schooled him in the technical details of the mining industry. 'When everyone else was obsessively interested in Medibank and social security,' recalled Keating, 'we were interested in oil and gas and trade.' His grasp of these issues was crucial in establishing his credentials within the Labor Caucus and, just as importantly, within the business community. It also gave him the confidence, at the age of twenty-eight, to stand for the ministry when Whitlam led Labor into government in December 1972.

Although not successful at his first attempt, Keating stood for the ministry at every opportunity during Whitlam's government. His persistence finally paid off in October 1975, following Whitlam's sacking of Connor for misleading Parliament. In the subsequent poll, the thirty-one-year-old Keating beat his main opponent, Mick Young, by 47 votes to 42 and was sworn in on 21 October as the minister for northern Australia, becoming the second-youngest person ever to be made a minister.

Keating's new wife Annita looked on proudly as the snowy-haired governor-general Sir John Kerr swore in her carefully attired husband. Keating had met his wife on board an Alitalia flight, where he eagerly engaged the tall and statuesque flight attendant in conversation. Beguiled by the Dutch-born beauty, Keating pursued her around the world until she consented to marry him. They were married in Holland in January 1975, with Keating dressed in top hat and tails and his proud parents looking on. Only then, at the age of thirty-one, did he move out of his parents' Bankstown house. He did not need a furniture removalist. The couple's new home was just two doors away.

It was not the most propitious time to be elevated to the ministry. But Keating exuded confidence, predicting that he would be a minister for 'quite some time'. To his great chagrin, he was out just three weeks later when Kerr sacked the Labor government and installed Malcolm Fraser as caretaker prime minister. With Labor being trounced at the subsequent poll, Keating and his colleagues were sent back to the Opposition benches. The chastening experience of the Whitlam government had important effects on his subsequent outlook. After twenty-three years of conservative rule, there had been a public expectation of change that had driven the Whitlam government forward. Now, argued Keating, it was time for Labor 'to present a stable face and stable policies to the electorate'. It was a lesson he would later forget.

The Whitlam government had also coincided with a huge rise in the price of oil and a drop in demand for Australian exports as the Vietnam war wound down. After enjoying three decades of mostly low inflation and full employment, Australia was now confronted with the twin ogres of inflation and unemployment. Unfazed, Keating argued that Australia could be 'lucky' once more if it turned to what he called 'our long suit' – minerals, wool and wheat – and also made its secondary industries competitive on world markets. Australia, he argued, had no future as 'a little European enclave in the Pacific' and had to 'trade its way into the South-East Asian community'. Instead of redistributing wealth, governments had to help create wealth and thereby improve the living standards of Labor's traditional constituency.

In the diminished ranks of his Labor colleagues after the crushing defeat of 1975, Keating now stood tall. He was still young and it was obvious to onlookers that, unlike many of his colleagues on the Opposition benches, his best years were before him. Keating made sure that message was understood, assiduously courting the journalists of the Canberra press gallery and the magnates of the mining industry. Within caucus, Keating was one of those who told Whitlam after the 1977 election that it was time for the twice-defeated leader to go. In the subsequent spill of positions in December 1977, Bill Hayden was elected leader. Keating's enhanced standing in the councils of Labor was shown when he stood for the deputy leadership and came close to winning it. Then, in September 1979, he was elected president of Labor's NSW branch.

Keating's accession to the NSW presidency coincided with an announcement by the popular ACTU leader Bob Hawke of his intention to enter Parliament with a view to challenging Hayden for the leadership, thereby threatening Keating's own hopes of being Hayden's successor. Keating continued to back Hayden as leader until a run of poor polls suggested that Labor would have more certainty of winning under Hawke. As a result, Keating did a deal with left-wing leader Tom Uren in July 1982 to support a Hawke challenge. Although the deal came undone when Uren's left-wing colleagues forced him to recant, Keating maintained his support for Hawke despite the challenger now lacking the numbers and losing by five votes.

Desperate to protect his position, Hayden turned to Keating for support, offering him the position of shadow treasurer in January 1983. With an election in the offing and John Howard facing him as treasurer, Keating had a steep learning curve if he was to succeed in his new position. As it happened, Fraser seized the opportunity provided by Labor's disarray to call an early election on 3 February 1983. But he was trumped that same day when the Labor Party forced Hayden to step down in favour of Hawke. Public attention focused on the popular new Labor leader as he flourished a deal with the unions that would cap wage increases and end the inflationary spiral that had bedevilled both Whitlam and Fraser. Holding out the prospect of a new national consensus, Hawke led his team to a solid victory at the polls.

At the age of thirty-nine, Keating was suddenly treasurer, and he struggled to cope with the newfound responsibility. Australia was in a deep recession, marked by unemployment of 10 per cent and inflation of 11 per cent, while Fraser had bequeathed Labor a deficit of nearly $10 billion. Keating surmounted his initial crisis of confidence with the political support of Hawke and the technical support of Treasury officials, including its plain-speaking head, John Stone. By June 1983, he was sufficiently confident to accompany Hawke and Stone on a visit to the United States, where he impressed American policymakers with his grasp of economics.

Keating planned to restore business confidence by reducing inflation and containing labour costs, thereby dragging Australia out of recession. In Keating's view, wages had grown to unsustainable proportions under the Whitlam and Fraser governments and now had to be pegged back to allow profits to grow. An election agreement between the trade unions and the Labor Party allowed for an Accord that would stop the inflation-chasing growth of wages while protecting their real value. The government now privately abandoned this commitment to maintaining the real value of wages while at the same time ditching its expansionary election program in favour of cutting the ballooning deficit.

By the end of 1983, some 130,000 new jobs had been created, confirming the recovery that had begun under the previous government.

But there was still much to do if this economic growth was to be sustained. The most dramatic move came in December 1983, when Keating announced the floating of the Australian dollar. It was a landmark decision that set the tone for the coming decade, having the effect of allowing financial markets to be more influential in setting the parameters of economic policy. Because it was done against the advice of his Treasury secretary John Stone, it stamped Keating's authority on that department while also establishing his authority within the government. He would increasingly be regarded as the heir apparent to Hawke.

With his appointment as treasurer and the onerous workload that it brought, Keating moved his family, now with three children, into a rented house in Canberra. As treasurer, the immaculately attired Keating, with 'a very sleek 1966 Mercedes Benz coupe' in the garage, found that his activities and views now received greater public scrutiny. He presented a puzzling contrast. As Michelle Grattan observed, Keating was a mixture of 'old and new Labor, street-smart Sydney and the sort of sophistication you'd find in a merchant banker'. He was a politician who hankered for the style and refinement of Europe but whose combative language, in private, included such terms as 'in and out of the cat's arse'. In earlier years Keating had conceded that it was 'no good pretending' that he was working class, claiming instead that he was now 'lower middle class' after having 'made the move up' which was 'what we're all after'. By 1985, he was conceding that his lifestyle was now 'upper middle class' but that he was still in politics 'to help working people' and 'to make the country a bit better'.

A federal election in December 1984 saw Labor suffer a swing of 1.4 per cent against it, reducing its majority in the expanded House from 25 seats to 16. The result challenged the accepted belief about Hawke being a certain vote-winner for Labor after the new Liberal leader, Andrew Peacock, proved to be a more formidable opponent than most observers had expected. The result sparked speculation about when Keating would take over the top job, particularly after an international business magazine had voted him finance minister of the year. Many of the government's initiatives were in the economic area and much of the credit for them accrued to Keating.

After the election victory Keating opened up the banking system to foreign banks and set about reforming the unwieldy taxation system by proposing a broad-based consumption tax. While not winning trade union approval for such a regressive taxation measure at the 1985 tax summit, he was widely seen as being, as Alan Ramsey observed, 'the political achiever' of 1985. Keating's political ascendancy not only made Hawke more resentful of his treasurer, thereby threatening their successful political partnership, but also set off alarm bells in the Opposition, now led by John Howard, who sensed that Keating might rob him of his own chance to be prime minister. When parliament gathered in 1986, a hard-hitting Liberal from Western Australia, Wilson Tuckey, was deployed to try and rattle Keating. During the heat of a parliamentary exchange, Tuckey raised an old breach of promise case involving Keating which provoked him to describe Tuckey as a 'stupid foul-mouthed grub' and to accuse Howard of being the author of Tuckey's gutter tactics. 'From this day onward,' declared Keating, 'Mr Howard will wear his leadership like a crown of thorns [and] I will do everything I can to crucify him.' However, rather than the Liberal tactics becoming the issue, it was Keating's vituperative response that evoked most comment.

The brouhaha was the start of a bitter and ongoing vendetta between Keating and Howard. It was also the start of a bad year for Keating, as commentators began to question his fitness for the top job and his political opponents probed at the sensitivities revealed by Tuckey. A report in the *National Times* raised allegations about Keating's relationship with a wealthy property developer; he was attacked by the Opposition for claiming a living away from home allowance while in Canberra, although his family now lived there; and there was further political embarassment when it was disclosed that Keating was being pursued by the taxation department for the tardy submission of his income tax return. Instead of eating humble pie, Keating simply announced that he had been too busy to submit his return. He rebutted charges about his friendship with the property developer, who he described as 'a major achiever'; and he pointed out that his living away from home allowance was in accordance with official guidelines and had been granted to Liberal MPs in similar circumstances. While there was little of substance in any of the issues, they collectively created an impression of arrogance that would dog Keating's political career. Already the *Financial Review* was wondering whether he was 'on the slippery slope to political oblivion'.

It was left to Hawke to spring to Keating's defence, suggesting that the slump in his popularity was unfair. Hawke ascribed it to Keating becoming isolated from the concerns of ordinary people. Colleagues suggested that Keating's 'withdrawal from reality' could be dated from his move to Canberra, while Hawke suggested that Keating should 'get to the shopping centres, go around and meet people so that he can have the two-way exchange'. Keating had already instructed that his official car in Sydney should have anonymous NSW number plates, rather than Commonwealth plates. According to the *National Times*, he also had instructed that his windows be 'dark enough to ensure that he cannot be seen', an allegation that Keating later denied. While dismissing the idea of glad-handing shoppers, he agreed to pay more attention to the popular media.

It nearly brought him undone in May 1986 when he made a comment on the popular John Laws radio program that sparked a political and economic crisis. The worsening trade imbalance had prompted Keating to warn of Australia becoming a banana republic if corrective action was not taken. Although this comment had the desired effect of shocking Australians out of their relative complacency and allowed corrective measures to be introduced, Hawke was furious. He forced Keating to reassure people that the government was bringing the trade crisis under control. Despite this reassurance, the comment would pursue Keating for the remainder of his political career.

Talk of Keating's elevation to the prime ministership became more muted after the July 1987 election when Hawke won his third consecutive poll, an unprecedented achievement for a Labor prime minister. Although Keating was referred to in the press as 'Our prime minister in waiting', the polls revealed little public support for him. Indeed, one of the biggest swings against Labor was in Keating's own seat. 'The message here cannot be ignored,' said Keating, conceding that Labor voters believed there was 'something "un-Labor" about our policies'. There certainly was, claimed one commentator, arguing that Keating's 'ideas for social change can be counted on the toes of one hand'. Of course, as treasurer it was not his role to initiate social policy. But it would be if he became prime minister. To try and broaden his political appeal and defend his more controversial policies, Keating worked the popular media even more assiduously.

While Hawke continued to block his path to the top, Keating's standing as heir apparent was given a huge boost in early 1988 when

Mick Young and Bill Hayden retired and another possible competitor, Kim Beazley, acknowledged Keating as Hawke's successor. John Howard stirred up the subsequent leadership speculation by suggesting that Hawke was in the 'twilight' of his term. When tackled by Howard, Keating turned on the embattled Liberal leader, likening him to a 'dead carcass swinging in the breeze'. For his part, Hawke, revelling in that year's Bicentenary celebrations and the opening of the new and grandiose Parliament House, responded to the increasing speculation by suggesting that Keating was dispensable and that he (Hawke) might stay on as prime minister for another six years. Disheartened by these developments, Keating dallied with the idea of leaving politics altogether, but could not bring himself to do it.

With the Hawke/Keating government now seen as better economic managers than the Liberals, Howard attempted to shift the political debate to other issues, criticising the increase in Asian immigrants and attacking the government for 'apologising to Aboriginals about our past'. Labor, he said, had 'become obsessed with apologising for being authentic Australians'. It gave Keating a new reason for staying on. Warning that Howard was 'the worst thing that's come our way in Australian public life in a long, long time', Keating predicted that, under Howard, there would be 'nothing that is fundamentally important or decent which would be sacrosanct from his opportunism'.

To prevent further damaging speculation about the leadership, Keating announced in October 1988 that he would not seek the leadership before the next election. Unbeknown to journalists, he had done a secret deal with Hawke in which he agreed to stay on as treasurer in return for a commitment from Hawke to retire following the next election. Not trusting Hawke to keep his promise, Keating had then forced him to repeat it in front of two witnesses, Hawke's businessman friend Peter Abeles and Keating's strong supporter, ACTU leader Bill Kelty. This Hawke did at his Sydney residence, Kirribilli House, in November 1988. Labor could now go forward united into the next election.

Keating's ambition to replace Hawke had been helped by polls that showed him to be more popular than Howard. Those polls, together with Howard's appeals to racism, caused the Liberal leader's replacement in May 1989 by Andrew Peacock, the man Keating had written off as a soufflé who would not rise twice. Now he had. What was more worrying for Keating was the deteriorating state of the Australian economy. Ever since the 1988 Budget, some of his Treasury advisers had been warning that the economy was overheating. But interest rates were kept down by the Reserve Bank, while Keating kept fiscal policy in an expansionary mode. As a result, the eventual interest rate rise was much steeper than might otherwise have been necessary and the consequent crash that much more catastrophic. By January 1990 mortgage interest rates had risen to 18 per cent, while overdraft rates were more than 20 per cent and unemployment was creeping back up. With things only likely to get worse, Hawke called an election in March 1990 and, despite the conditions, managed to scrape back in, winning a fourth term for Labor with the crucial help of Green Party preferences.

In the wake of the election, Keating was elected to replace Lionel Bowen as deputy prime minister. On the conservative side, Peacock was replaced by the stony-faced Dr John Hewson, an economics professor and business consultant. With his academic training, Hewson would be a formidable opponent for Keating as the economy slid inexorably into a deep recession. It was only in November 1990, after official figures put it beyond doubt, that Keating finally admitted that it was a recession. Then, in what was to prove the most disastrous remark of his career, he tried to put a positive spin on the poor economic news by remarking that it was 'a recession that Australia had to have'. Only later, after sustained criticism, did Keating say that he was 'sorry' for the pain that it had caused. The recession had at least one positive outcome for Keating, allowing him to get caucus approval for the partial privatisation of the Commonwealth Bank. He signalled that other iconic Labor enterprises, from Qantas to Telecom, were in the pipeline for privatisation.

With the worsening economic conditions making the likelihood of a Labor victory at the 1993 election more remote, and with Hawke showing no sign of moving aside, Keating vented his frustration in an off-the-record address to a press gallery dinner in December 1990. He was speaking in the immediate wake of the sudden death from a heart attack of his Treasury chief and close friend Chris Higgins. He was a year younger than Keating and his death came as a great shock. His own family history suggested that he might not live such a long life himself. As he later told his biographer, John Edwards, 'Dad had a stroke at 49, a coronary at 50 and died at 60. I don't know if I'm like him, but ... That's why I'm cranky with Bob; he slowed my schedule.' This address would help to get his schedule back on track.

Without mentioning Hawke specifically, Keating bemoaned the lack of outstanding political leaders in Australian history. No one was immune from his critical assessment, not even such venerated Labor heroes as John Curtin and Ben Chifley, the former being a particular hero of Hawke's. Calling himself the Placido Domingo of Australian politics, Keating suggested that only he was capable of providing the leadership that Australia needed. When the address leaked into the press, it was seen as being Keating's first shot across Hawke's prime ministerial bows at a time when polls had support for Labor as low as 33 per cent. At a subsequent meeting with Hawke, Keating denied that he was intending to destabilise his leadership, while Hawke declared that he would stay as prime minister for at least five more years.

Hawke's position was boosted after Christmas when the Gulf War caused a surge in support for him. Strengthened by the conflict, he informed Keating at the end of January that his Placido Domingo speech was an act of treachery and that henceforth 'all bets were off'. But the turnaround in the polls was quickly succeeded by a further slide as unemployment crept past 10 per cent. By April 1991, the question of the succession was once more being discussed by the Labor factions. Perhaps to steel the nerve of wavering MPs, Keating suggested that he might not stay on to fight the next election with Hawke. While the financial markets reacted by dumping the Australian dollar, Hawke showed no sign that he would resign in the interests of the party. Either Keating would have to give up on his ambition, or do what he had always said he would not do – mount a direct challenge. Keating finally announced at the end of May that he would do just that, at the same time doing serious damage to Hawke's standing in the caucus by making public the terms of the Kirribilli House agreement.

Although many newspaper editorials favoured a change to Keating, opinion polls confirmed that Hawke was overwhelmingly more popular than his treasurer. The caucus vote reflected this, giving Keating just 44 of the 110 votes. Still, Michelle Grattan was not alone in suggesting that the challenge had mortally wounded the prime minister, predicting that 'Hawke, one way or another, will be gone later this year'. As promised, Keating resigned as treasurer and headed for the backbench, where his political shadow remained over Hawke's leadership. As a fallback position in case his political rise had ended, Keating bought into a piggery business, an investment that would come to haunt him.

By mid July Keating had emerged from a self-enforced silence on the backbench to make well-publicised speeches on urban planning and superannuation, sparking stories that a further challenge to Hawke was in the making. At the same time, opinion polls showed a reversal in Keating's rating now that he was no longer treasurer. Growing more confident, Keating began attacking the government's handling of the economic recovery. By October a poll found that Keating outranked Hawke on a range of measures concerned with leadership and economic management. As press speculation intensified, Keating was forced in early November to announce that he would not be making a further challenge during the life of the present parliament. He still did not have sufficient numbers in caucus. A triumphant Hawke exulted: 'It's over.' But it wasn't. Not by a long shot.

Without Keating, the government fumbled as it tried to attack the Opposition's radical economic program, dubbed Fightback!, that included a proposal for a goods and services tax. Opinion polls showed the approval rating of the increasingly irascible Hawke slumping to just 31 per cent, its lowest level since 1983. It helped focus the minds of wavering MPs on the issue of the succession. One by one they began to declare their support for Keating. The knock on the door of the beleaguered prime minister came on 12 December 1991, when six of his ministers advised him to resign. Hawke preferred to be pushed. A week later, caucus summoned up the courage to depose by five votes a prime minister who had won four elections in a row, causing Hawke to resign soon after from the Parliament as well. Keating's narrow win, said one hopeful Labor official, would add 'a touch of magic to the Labor Party'. It would take all the magic he could muster for Keating to give Labor any chance of winning the next election.

On taking up office, Keating announced that he would target unemployment and interest rates as he moved to 'get the country cracking'. There was little bloodletting among Hawke's former ministry, with Keating making few dramatic changes, the main ones being to shift John Dawkins to the Treasury and making Graham Richardson minister for transport and communications. Keating was in the office he had hankered after, but he seemed slow to adjust to its new demands. Almost immediately he had to host a visit from the US president, George Bush, with whom Keating seemed ill at ease. Keating's confidence would not have been helped by the appearance in mid January of opinion polls that gave him an approval rating of just 17 per cent.

Keating was blamed for the recession and, while being respected for his strong leadership, he was also disliked for his arrogance. Moreover, the economic rationalism he had championed throughout the 1980s was undermining some of the traditional values and institutions that Australians held dear. With the historian Don Watson appointed as speechwriter, Keating addressed these popular concerns in his Australia Day address, arguing that the best aspects of 'old Australia' would survive. Rejecting calls for a halt to the changes, Keating declared that they would have to continue if Australia was to become 'a more dynamic, more efficient and cohesive society'. Then he unsettled the electorate still further by refusing to fly the customary Australian flag on his official car and suggesting that it might be time to drop the Union Jack from the flag's design.

When Queen Elizabeth began a visit to Australia a few days later, Keating's welcoming speech reflected the pro-republican policy that had been accepted by the previous year's Labor Party Conference. The British press were upset when Keating then placed his hand on the Queen's back as he guided her towards official guests and were further distraught when Annita declined to curtsey. No sooner was the Queen out of the country than Keating launched a stinging attack on Britain for having deserted Australia during World War II, prompting a British tabloid to dub him the 'Lizard of Oz'. He then accused Hewson and Howard of being the men of yesteryear, wedded to the Anglophile Australia of the 1950s. It was all part of a strategy to dominate the Parliament and bring his divided troops in behind his leadership. And it worked. By the end of that first week in Parliament, Keating was judged by one journalist to be 'absolutely dominant'. His Labor colleagues were heartened by his aggressive leadership and encouraged by an economic statement that Keating released at the end of February, titled 'One Nation', which was designed to create 800,000 new jobs over four years. Its title emphasised the inclusiveness of Labor policies compared to the retrogressive divisiveness of the Liberal policies.

Keating had reversed the party's slide in the polls and was neck and neck with Hewson as preferred prime minister. Having established an ascendancy over his opponent on economic issues, Keating turned to several other issues that would, in time, come to define his prime ministership. The first issue concerned Australia's relations with Asia. Keating was not the first prime minister to focus on the trade and security possibilities of Asia. But he was the first to make it a defining characteristic of his government and the first to argue the primacy of Asian links over Australia's traditional links with Britain and the United States. He called for acceptance by Australians that 'Asia is where our future lies'. As if to emphasise this new direction, Keating's first overseas visit was to Indonesia, a country he had never visited before. It was the first visit to Jakarta by an Australian prime minister since 1983.

Central to Keating's vision was an upgrading of the Asia-Pacific Economic Co-operation forum (APEC) to allow for regular meetings of heads of government. Australia's future as a trading nation relied upon a general lowering of world tariff levels and an opening up of markets, many in Asia. Keating wanted to realise APEC's full potential by linking Australia to the tremendous growth of the Asian 'tigers' and the economic strength of the United States, Japan and China. Although he had received a lukewarm response from President Bush in January, he pressed ahead with it when he met with President Soeharto in Jakarta, where he was given a much warmer reception. A visit to Japan in October 1992 saw him gain Japanese support, while the election in November of the new US President Bill Clinton provided an opportunity for Keating to bring the United States on board. He would have a more difficult time convincing the Australian public of APEC's potential.

Transforming the Australian economy into an open and internationally competitive one had cost some sectors very dearly. Globalisation seemed to bring only empty factories and lengthening dole queues. The political reaction saw the independent Labor candidate Phil Cleary elected to Hawke's old seat of Wills in Melbourne's industrial north on a platform of restoring tariff protection. There was also Australia's traditional fear of Asia, which made many Australians wary of tying their economic future to a region they had regarded with a combination of disdain, fear and hostility.

Throughout 1992, Keating used a succession of ceremonies commemorating various events of 1942 to sketch out a new national story. He used an Anzac Day visit to New Guinea to argue that the victorious battle of the Kokoda Track, when Australians had stood alone against the Japanese, rather than the World War I defeat at Gallipoli, should be celebrated by Australians. Then, in a flying visit to Kokoda, Keating kissed the earth that so many Australians had died defending. It was, declared Keating, the 'most moving day of my public life'. These attempts to remould Australian identity caused conservatives to rush to defend the historic symbols of the nation's British past. It came just as a more fundamental question of Australian identity was about to erupt with the High Court's favourable decision on Aboriginal land rights in what became known as the Mabo case.

Keating welcomed the Mabo decision, claiming that the establishment of this new legal concept of native title removed the greatest barrier to reconciliation with Aborigines and finally quashed 'the outrageous notion of *terra nullius*', the legal notion that had allowed the original dispossession of the Aborigines. At the same time he reassured Australians that the decision posed no threat to private property. Pastoralists on leasehold properties, as well as mining companies, were not convinced, fearing (correctly) that the decision would have implications for their activities. The Opposition played on these fears, finally forcing Keating in October to announce that he would hold consultations with Aboriginal and industry groups to clarify the implications of the Mabo case and establish a legislative framework for native title.

For most of the electorate, the questions of native title, a republic and ties with Asia were distractions from what they regarded as being the main game – the economy. And the fitful state of the world economy was hampering the recovery in Australia. In July, the jobless rate passed 11 per cent, pushing up Keating's disapproval rating to a daunting 68 per cent. To try to retrieve the situation, he announced plans to cut drastically the numbers of long-term unemployed young people by the creation of training opportunities and a youth training wage. He also backed off from plans to change the flag, promising not to move before the next election. And he launched stinging attacks on the Liberals' plans for a consumption tax, zero tariffs and harsh industrial relations laws. Hewson helped Keating's cause with a series of gaffes, including a derogatory attack on people who rented their houses. Despite desperate television advertisements during September and October attacking

Keating for his arrogance, the Liberals surrendered their previous advantage in the opinion polls. With a federal election in sight, both sides were anxious to keep their heads in front.

When the national accounts for the September quarter showed the third successive quarter of growth, Keating declared that the recession had ended. However, when the growth figures were followed by worsening unemployment figures, Hewson rounded on Keating, claiming that Labor had 'stuffed' Australia. With Keating being perceived in the polls as arrogant and untrustworthy, the Liberals mounted a sustained series of attacks on his integrity, focusing particularly on his investment in the piggery. With no evidence of misdeeds to support their attacks, the Liberals relied on innuendo and used the Senate, where Keating could not respond, to raise their allegations. Frustrated and angered, Keating overreacted to their questioning of what he considered to be his private affairs. The NSW government also intervened, alleging breaches of its pollution laws, while local residents protested at plans for the piggery's expansion. It seemed that the piggery would never be out of the news. But Keating stubbornly kept his investment, convinced that the electorate would judge him on the 'big things'.

As unemployment continued its inexorable climb, hitting 11.4 per cent by December, the highest rate since the 1930s Depression, Keating continued to claim success for his economic policies. At the same time, he pushed ahead with other issues that would redefine what it meant to be Australian. As a step on the road to the republic, Keating called for references to the Queen to be removed from the oath of allegiance. Then, in an address to the Aboriginal community in the Sydney suburb of Redfern, Keating made the most open and frank acknowledgment by an Australian prime minister of the historic injustices that had been perpetrated on Aborigines: 'We took the traditional lands and smashed the traditional way of life. We brought the diseases and the alcohol. We committed the murders. We took the children from their mothers. We practised discrimination and exclusion.' While the speech was welcomed by Aboriginal groups and by many non-indigenous Australians, it was denounced by conservative commentators.

At year's end, journalists wrote with some amazement of Keating's achievement in turning around Labor's fortunes. As the *Canberra Times* observed, Keating's demolition of Hewson's retrogressive economic and social policies had 'brought his team to within sight of victory'. However, achieving such an unprecedented victory remained a difficult task, with Labor losing state elections in Victoria and Western Australia. Hoping that the anger of the electorate had been vented during the state elections, Keating finally called an election for 13 March, declaring that Australia's 'traditions of fairness and opportunity for all' were at stake. To try to appease the hostility of many women, he announced an extension of childcare, while the hostility of business was addressed by offering a substantial reduction in the rate of company tax, from 39 per cent to 33 per cent. He also pointed to promised income tax cuts that had been enshrined in law to reassure the sceptical electorate. The republic was also put on the election agenda. But, after ten years in power, there was a mood for change, with most commentators predicting that Keating would lose. His chances were not helped by the unemployment statistics for January passing the one million mark.

During the final week of campaigning, a late surge in the opinion polls held out hope of Labor snatching a narrow victory. With his fate in the hands of swinging voters, Keating hosted an election eve dinner where he told his staff that he had 'a sneaking suspicion we might get back'. If they did, said Keating, and with 'the authority of a national election behind us, we can really do some very interesting things in world terms'. Within an hour of the polls closing, it was clear that Keating had not only stemmed the anti-Labor tide but turned it back against the Liberals. John Hewson had managed to lose what many considered to be the unlosable election.

Keating declared that it was a victory 'for the true believers', for 'the people who in difficult times have kept the faith'. He hosted a celebratory dinner for 650 of these 'true believers' in the Great Hall of Parliament House. The exclusive celebration, played out against the background of a million unemployed, would be seen in retrospect to have set an unfortunate tone for the new government that had the 'historic chance', wrote Glenn Milne, 'to dominate the 1990s just as it controlled the 1980s'.

The only problem with Milne's assessment was that the economic recovery remained patchy at best and, as Keating was advised in a post-election briefing, the government was heading for a massive deficit that would put paid to him implementing his more expensive election promises. Although Keating used his newfound authority to select his own ministry, the continuing economic problems ensured that his government was embattled from the beginning, despite an initial 'honeymoon' period in the opinion polls. And he made his position worse by ending his formerly close relationship with the members of the press gallery. The advisers who had sustained him through the dark days of his challenge against Hawke and helped his accession to prime minister now became a tight circle, restricting access to Keating even by Cabinet ministers.

After the election, Keating moved to place his stamp on the prime ministership, pledging to achieve gender equality by 2000 and to bring the republic referendum forward. But the year would be marked more by the Mabo decision than by anything else. With mining companies and pastoralists warning of the uncertainty created by the High Court decision, and Aboriginals using it to claim large swathes of land across Australia, Keating was forced to act. However, talks with state premiers in June 1993 revealed the almost intractable difficulties of this problem when the conservative premiers of Western Australia and Victoria refused to accept the legitimacy of the Mabo decision and, as a result, would not even discuss Keating's suggestions for legal clarification.

Keating's vision for Australia rested on it being reconciled with its past, confident about its future and engaged with its region. To advance the cause of APEC, upon which this closer engagement largely rested, Keating dispatched his closest adviser, Don Russell, as ambassador to Washington in June, while another close adviser was sent off as ambassador to Japan. Keating then visited China and South Korea, where he argued for closer trade co-operation and the strengthening of APEC. The Americans were the key to this, and Keating's efforts were rewarded in early July, when Clinton invited the leaders of APEC countries to join him in Seattle for the next meeting in November. It was a political triumph for Keating. But it was diminished by an announcement that same day that unemployment had crept past 11 per cent again.

The government's ability to deal with unemployment was constrained by conflicting election promises that had the government reducing the deficit at the same time as it was implementing substantial tax cuts. Keating tried to resolve the problem by bringing the first stage of the tax cuts forward, while postponing the second stage beyond the term of the present Parliament. It meant that Treasurer John Dawkins' August

Budget contained unpalatable spending cuts that were rejected by sections of the Labor Party, together with the Democrats and the Greens, who held the balance of power in the Senate. It would take weeks of discussions to resolve the issue. In the meantime, Labor's standing in the opinion polls, and Keating's standing as leader, slumped alarmingly. A successful visit to the United States and Britain in September helped to retrieve some of this lost ground, particularly when he rounded off his trip by arriving in Monte Carlo as Sydney's success in its bid to host the Olympic Games was announced. As the celebrations continued, he returned to Australia rejuvenated and refocused.

During an interview with Irish television, Keating had reflected on his approach to politics. 'I'm a punter,' he said. 'I tend to take political risks and I don't mind risking my own hide from time to time because I've always said to my colleagues, the worst thing that can happen to you in this game is to lose your job. So why be a mouse?' Some of his colleagues would have preferred a more mouselike approach to Mabo. But Keating told his Cabinet that an agreement on Mabo would 'warm the soul of the Labor Party for two generations' and would stop Australia from becoming 'marginalised as South Africa was marginalised'. Such an agreement was achieved in October 1993, after protracted negotiations with the major stakeholders were brokered by Keating. With the contentious Budget also passed through the Senate, Labor's stocks rose from their former slump.

The APEC meeting in Seattle in November should have been equally triumphant, but it was marred by an angry Keating jibe at the Malaysian prime minister, Dr Mahathir, who had refused to attend. Pressed by journalists, Keating dismissed Mahathir as 'a recalcitrant'. This offhand comment provoked a diplomatic spat that came to overshadow the success of the Seattle meeting. The dispute was just the latest in a series of incidents where Keating descended to the level of the political street fighter in a way that endangered his standing as prime minister. He was the despair of advisers who were unable to soften his streetfighting persona which, after all, allowed him to exert dominance on the floor of the Parliament. Unfortunately, Keating's pungent language and aggressive demeanour had a negative effect on many voters, who also continued to fear the changes he was forcing upon them. At the end of 1993, Keating promised that Labor would govern during the remaining two years of his term 'with all the energy and gusto we can summon'. Many would have regarded that more as a threat than a promise. Fearing that his aggressive behaviour in the Parliament was having a negative impact on viewers watching snippets of Question Time on the nightly news, Keating limited his appearances in Question Time to twice a week. It simply confirmed the aloof and autocratic image that many people had of him.

Despite the public resentment, Keating's political dominance seemed set to continue for many years as the economic recovery gathered pace. The political and economic cycles seemed finally to be synchronised. In late January 1994 he declared that the recession was 'way behind us'. With annual inflation down to 1.9 per cent, he predicted that growth was likely to be '4 per cent or more for a number of years', a rate of growth that would gradually reduce the level of unemployment. Despite the continuing high levels of unemployment, the resignation of John Dawkins as treasurer and calls for his sports minister Ros Kelly to resign for political incompetence and mismanagement, the Newspoll showed Keating extending his lead over Hewson as preferred prime minister.

While Keating was making an historic visit to the countries of Indochina in April 1994, Hewson tried to retrieve his position by announcing that he was dropping the consumption tax. It was a last desperate bid to beat off the vultures that were circling him. On his return, Keating tried to recapture the political initiative by releasing a White Paper on unemployment that held out the promise of spending $6.5 million over five years to create 2 million jobs and get the unemployment rate down to 5 per cent. The financial markets reacted negatively to the likely inflationary effects of the plan, while the Liberals reacted by dumping Hewson as Opposition leader in late May and replacing him with Alexander Downer, the well-spoken son of an established South Australian family.

It was a mark of Keating's relatively poor public standing that even Downer enjoyed a honeymoon period with the voters. This was despite encouraging economic news that revealed the economy to have been growing at a rate of 5 per cent for the year to March. Keating's standing in the polls was not helped by the publication of Bob Hawke's memoirs, with his predecessor alleging, among many other things, that Keating had described Australia as 'the arse end of the world'. But Downer proved incapable of pressing home any advantage he might have gained from this, finding instead that his own leadership was destabilised by the republic issue. The issue had disconcerted a succession of Liberal leaders, who had difficulty responding to it. For a republican referendum to succeed, bipartisan support was essential. But Keating made no serious attempt to achieve such support. The issue was too valuable as a way of dividing the Opposition.

Further efforts were made to strengthen APEC's regional role. In June 1994 Keating visited Soeharto again, concentrating on trade and improving relations between the two neighbours. He had a vision of Australia, Indonesia and a strengthened Vietnam providing a future security troika covering South-East Asia and acting as a counterbalance to China. More immediately, Soeharto's support was crucial for Keating's APEC aspirations, which also rested on the support of Tokyo and Washington. A visit to Tokyo in September saw further progress being made in Keating's promotion of free trade and Australia's claim to participate in regional groupings. When the APEC leaders met in November in Indonesia, the APEC leaders committed their countries to achieving free trade over the next twenty-five years.

While Keating pursued his long-term vision, a devastating drought was wreaking economic havoc across much of northern New South Wales and Queensland. Keating dismissed it as a normal occurrence to which farmers had to become attuned. His response confirmed the widespread impression of him being distant from the concerns of ordinary Australians, particularly those in the bush. As the drought wore on Keating was finally forced to act, touring southern Queensland in mid September and announcing increased government assistance for the hard-hit farmers. The following week, in an address to the ALP National Conference, Keating nominated the bush and the information revolution as the government's new policy frontiers. To a standing ovation from delegates, Keating claimed that only Labor had 'the courage, the love, the labour and the imagination' to lead Australia into the twenty-first century. Only Labor, he declared, could deliver 'efficiency and equity'.

But Labor's credentials as economic managers were not helped by the recession and the subsequent slow recovery. And the widening gap between Australia's rich and poor raised questions about its credentials as a promoter of greater equity. Keating's own business interests did not help in this regard. His investment in the piggery had been a political disaster and he had sold his interests in 1994, using the proceeds to purchase a $2.2 million house in Sydney. In the Senate, Michael Baume, who had led the Liberal innuendos about the piggery, used the occasion of its sale to raise new questions, again without any supporting evidence. Baume's muckraking had the desired effect of provoking Keating into blasting Baume as 'parliamentary filth'. Liberal polling continued to find that Keating was regarded as remote and arrogant and their parliamentary tactics played to those perceptions. Increasingly, he was depicted in the press by cartoonists and journalists as a Roman emperor.

In October 1994, Keating celebrated his twenty-fifth year in Parliament. His hopes for re-election rested on the recovery proceeding apace, which it did. By November 1994, unemployment had been reduced by 2 per cent to 9.3 per cent, inflation was just 2 per cent and the economy was growing at a rapid 6.4 per cent. With just over a year to the next election, Keating could be relatively confident about the likely result. When Parliament adjourned for the Christmas recess, Keating waved goodbye to Downer, describing him as the Christmas turkey. The Liberals seemed incapable of settling on a leader who could pose a credible alternative. With no clear way forward, the Liberals went backwards, returning on 30 January 1995 to their passed-over leader, John Howard, whose earlier leadership had ended in the self-made mire of racial politics. Facing his third Liberal leader within a year, and a man he had helped defeat before, Keating remained confident that he could do it again. But this was a more canny John Howard, who quickly disowned his previous views on Asian immigration and promised that a GST would 'never, ever' be part of Liberal policy. Howard also neutralised the republic issue by promising, if elected, to hold a convention to consider the issue. He was determined to ensure that the electorate's antipathy towards Keating was not deflected by any suspicions about himself.

That antipathy towards Keating was given full vent in March 1995 in a by-election for the Canberra seat of Ros Kelly who had finally been forced to resign. In a sign of things to come, Labor suffered a massive 16 per cent swing against it. The following month, health minister Carmen Lawrence, widely tipped as a future Labor leader, was targeted in a WA Royal Commission for acts allegedly committed when premier of that state. Keating denounced the Commission as politically biased and stood by Lawrence. The succession of crippled ministers had a debilitating effect on his government and helped boost Howard's rating in the polls. Even the economy became a negative issue for Keating.

The much-vaunted economic recovery was not proceeding to plan. Although economic growth had been gathering strength since 1991, unemployment had remained relatively high. In a memorable phrase, Howard claimed that Keating had only been able to produce 'five minutes of economic sunshine' before the storm clouds once again threatened the economy. A blowout in the current account in May gave added force to the Liberal charges of incompetence. A strong swing in June against the popular Labor government of Wayne Goss during the Queensland state election gave Keating another foretaste of what awaited him. With the Liberals refusing to release their policies for Keating to attack, the consistently bad opinion polls proved impossible to reverse.

With inflation passing 5 per cent in October, and business and consumer confidence retreating, the recovery was becoming increasingly difficult to find. Keating's position was further undermined when the WA Royal Commission report suggested that Carmen Lawrence had committed perjury during her evidence before it. Her acquittal on this charge came too late to save her. Despite this, Keating managed to pare back Howard's lead as preferred prime minister during the final months of 1995. However, while the electorate was no longer embracing Howard, it was clear that it remained keen for the government to go.

In a dramatic attempt to turn the tide, Keating flew off in mid December with a clutch of his senior ministers to Jakarta to sign a security pact with Indonesia. Declaring that no country was more important to Australia than Indonesia, Keating said that the pact was designed to indicate that 'the long-term strategic interests of Australia and Indonesia coincide'. Like a rabbit out of the hat, the move was acclaimed as a triumph that could win the election for Labor. But the support for Labor stayed stubbornly low. In a final swing through the region, Keating visited Malaysia in mid January, the first visit by an Australian prime minister since 1984. Despite their earlier falling out, he was met warmly by Mahathir. He returned home to find that the opinion polls remained sour as the electorate welcomed the belated release by Howard of some details of the Liberal policies. There was no point in holding off the election any longer.

On 28 January 1996, Keating finally announced the election, declaring that it was 'an election about leadership'. Not just his leadership but the 'strong team of leaders' on the Labor side. There was also, argued Keating, 'a profound philosophical gulf between the Government and the Coalition about what kind of society Australia should be'. If there was such a gulf, most Australians seemed not to acknowledge it. They responded instead to the Liberal slogan, 'Enough is enough'. It would take all of Keating's political skills to make them focus on the possible ill-effects of a Liberal victory. But that was made difficult by the Liberal strategy of releasing their policy detail at the last minute, leaving little time for it to be analysed. Labor's tactics became more desperate and as a result more counterproductive.

As the votes started to come into the tally room on 3 March, it was clear that Labor was facing a rout. By the time counting finished, Labor had suffered a swing of 5 per cent and the Liberals emerged with a 40-seat majority. As always, Keating watched the result in the familiar surrounds of the Bankstown Sports Club and conceded defeat before a crowd of his loyal supporters. He defended the record of his government, reminding his television audience of how the country had been transformed for the better. Defending his pursuit of the 'big picture' policies that ultimately helped to bring him undone, Keating was unrepentant: 'In the end it's the big picture which changes nations and, whatever our opponents may say, Australia has changed inexorably for the good, for the better.'

The central idea of Keating's career had been the pursuit of economic growth as a means of lifting living standards and securing the nation's future. During his time as treasurer, he embraced economic rationalism and globalisation, convincing the labour movement to forego wage rises in return for greater superannuation, lower taxation and other social benefits. Some argued that Labor's policies had also been responsible for increasing the gap between rich and poor, something that Keating strongly disputed. Whatever the statistics could be shown to prove, many of those who historically looked to Labor for protection, and for the enhancement of their lives, were left feeling insecure by the radical changes Keating was making to the Australian economy. And they were hurt by the prolonged and ruinous interest rates. As prime minister, Keating responded to the growing anger of the electorate by returning partially to policies that he had earlier disparaged. Despite this hesitant retreat, his economic policies had transformed the Australian economy and financial system, making it more able to meet the international changes of the 1990s. It was more efficient and internationally competitive, more confident and outward-looking. That alone would have been sufficient to guarantee his place in Australia's political history.

By radically reorienting Australian foreign policy towards Asia, by embracing Aboriginal land rights and by calling for a republic, Keating went on to sketch out a new national story that could sustain Australia in the twenty-first century just as its attachment to Britain and then America had sustained it in the twentieth century. Ironically, the political strengths that enabled him to push through his economic reforms and dominate the Parliament were not those that secured the affections of the electorate. Unsettled by the changes he had forced through, and sceptical of his promises, the electorate was unwilling to embrace the future that Keating held out for them. Instead, old prejudices resurfaced as Australians returned under John Howard to the apparent certainties of the past.

Keating took his defeat calmly. Without waiting for Parliament to reassemble, he submitted his resignation to the governor-general. In a last appearance before the Labor Caucus, he thanked his colleagues for the 'pleasure, the excitement, the thrills and spills – I wouldn't have missed it for quids'. Over the succeeding years, there were occasional political pronouncements as his fears about a Howard government were borne out. In November 1996, he attacked the racial politics of Pauline Hanson and made an impassioned plea for Australia not to turn its back on its future and 'retreat to a past that never was'. While his new role as a business consultant proved successful, his private life went through the turmoil of a separation from Annita. In March 2000, he published a book, *Engagement: Australia faces the Asia-Pacific*, which summed up the political and economic direction of his government, arguing its continuing relevance for Australia's future and warning that 'whatever happens in human history from now on, rapid change will be its permanent feature'. It had been the mark of his prime ministership and the cause of his downfall.

John Winston Howard

11 MARCH 1996 – 3 DECEMBER 2007

Circumstances, his own energy and his passion for politics prevented him from walking away from a career that would have been judged better if it had ended a little earlier.

BY MICHELLE GRATTAN

John Winston Howard was Australia's second-longest serving prime minister and only the second to lose his own seat. Those two facts capture the contradictions of a formidable career that ended in a defeat that meant the Liberal Party was out of office everywhere in Australia. Howard was the great survivor who ultimately misjudged his exit so that he failed in his ambition to emulate his hero Robert Menzies and leave on top. Inevitably, the manner in which a political career finishes affects how its whole is viewed, especially in the near term. The Howard story is a cautionary tale in changing perceptions and fortunes. In his final term he went from appearing impregnable to becoming unelectable. He and his party failed to do what a successful company would think necessary: resolve the succession.

Howard's personal political story had mostly been that of someone who defied the odds. He was the man who never gave up. At times – in his darkest days after he lost the Opposition leadership in the late 1980s to his long term rival Andrew Peacock – Howard genuinely believed, as he professed, that the 'Lazarus with a triple bypass' miracle needed for a major comeback would not happen. The leadership seemed to have passed decisively to a new generation … but Howard stayed around and eventually – when that generation was found wanting – the party had little choice but to turn back to him.

It was a desperate but inspired move. Howard led the Coalition to a sweeping victory in 1996, although the extreme unpopularity of the Keating government made that election something of a cakewalk. His 1998 win was another story. Howard campaigned on a bold and risky platform: if his government was returned, it would introduce a new tax, the GST. Labor cut heavily into the government's big majority and indeed won the popular vote, but Howard pulled the election off. By early 2001, it looked as if the electorate might turn its back on him. He regrouped doggedly, then along came the Tampa affair and the September 11 terrorist attacks, which transformed the political climate in Australia. In 2004 the polls again indicated that voters were inclined to change, but the flaws of Labor leader Mark Latham became a shield for Howard. In winning both his third and fourth terms Howard actually achieved a swing towards the government, reinforcing his reputation as a great campaigner.

So, it was perhaps unsurprising that many Liberals felt a certain complacency when signs of trouble started to arise in the fourth term. They believed the previous pattern would be repeated – that when it came to the point, things could be turned around, never mind that Howard himself in 2007 warned the government faced 'annihilation' and said he did not have any rabbits to pull out of the hat. Several factors had broken the mould. The government and the Prime Minister were that much older; hubris had overtaken leader and team; Howard's obsession with industrial relations reform had produced unpopular measures and given Labor powerful ammunition. On other fronts the government had run out of ideas. And from December 2006 Howard was facing a new Labor leader who appealed to voters and was seen as responsible.

Ironically, the seeds of Howard's 2007 defeat were sown in one of his greatest triumphs: winning control of the Senate in the 2004 election. Howard was unable to resist using – to the limit – the power he acquired to promote the most radical change yet contemplated on the issue that had, since the 1980s, been closest to his political heart – industrial relations. His usually well-honed political instincts deserted him as his core ideology reasserted itself.

It was a similar story with the leadership succession. In 2000, on his 61st birthday, he flagged he would review his future when he was 64 (so setting himself up). When that time came, he decided to stay on, and did so again in 2006 and 2007, always infuriating the heir apparent, Peter Costello. Howard's judgement, so good for much of his prime ministership, in the end failed him both on policy and politics.

Central to Howard's political persona was a commitment to the cause of economic reform, spliced with pragmatism, a usually acute sense of tactics and an ordinariness that, while ridiculed by critics, enabled him to tap into 'mainstream' voters. By the mid to late 1990s he had turned his 'ordinariness' into a political virtue and claimed, as had Bob Hawke before him, a special relationship with the Australian people.

The touchstones for Howard's prime ministership were three other prime ministers. Robert Menzies was a revered figure while Malcolm Fraser and Paul Keating, in their separate ways, were models against which he reacted. Fraser taught him how not to run a Cabinet – Howard's cabinet had well ordered meetings. He also thought Fraser wasted his mandate. Howard saw his 1996 victory as a putdown of those in the nation's 'elites' who had supported Keating and a rejection of political correctness. However, in office Howard proved, if not elitist, certainly highly tribal, vetting government appointments carefully for Labor associations, stacking the ABC board, making lots of political appointments overseas. On ministerial standards, he started with a high-sounding code that soon brought down several in his team; eventually he put solidarity before standards, ignoring the code, then softening it.

Howard was a 'conviction politician', certain of his views, driven by long-held values. He was not a self-doubter or agoniser. As journalist Craig McGregor wrote in 1987, he didn't 'ever feel the need to unburden himself to anyone, like Hawke used to, because the distance between his interior and exterior is nil'.[1] He had a clear ideal of what the nation should look like – materially prosperous, socially at one; a diverse economy in a cohesive community. While his economic reformism was often highlighted, he wanted to leave a social legacy as well. His 'modern conservatism' was based on the notion of a 'social coalition' and policies requiring 'mutual obligation'.

While wanting to get out in front on some issues, he also took cues from the electorate. He believed in the 'mainstream' at the levels of philosophy and survival. One academic commentator observed: 'The key to the Howard government ... relates to Howard's characteristic persistence and possession of "a decent amount of ticker" that imparts a hard underbelly to his political pragmatism.'[2] The leader who won power with a least-risk strategy held it at his next election by running on a maximum-risk one, then sold himself as the politician who listens.

On economic issues, Howard was a quick learner and innovative doer throughout most of his career. He fought, far-sightedly though unsuccessfully, for a broad-based indirect tax when he was treasurer in the Fraser government and, from opposition in the 1980s, he vigorously led the argument that Australia's labour market system needed freeing up. On sensitive social issues involving race, however, he was often caught in the rut of his own narrow experience, repeating earlier mistakes. His slow and inadequate response in government to the racist face of Pauline Hanson's One Nation party echoed his flirtation a decade before with a discriminatory position on immigration and he never could simply say 'sorry' to the Aborigines on behalf of the nation.

Deep into his prime ministership, Howard appeared increasingly to see and seek parallels with Menzies who, with Churchill, had always been high on his heroes list and was, indeed, a sort of political benchmark. In 1989

Howard told Gerard Henderson, 'I think of the Menzies period as a golden age in terms of people. Australia had a sense of family, social stability and optimism ... '[3] Was Howard's 1996 wish to make Australia 'comfortable and relaxed' his hoped-for version of such a golden age? In 1999 he boasted that Australia had a stronger economy than at the end of the Menzies era.

Menzies' extraordinary political longevity and his role in creating the Liberal Party ensured that comparisons between the two men would always be limited (despite, as time went on, some colleagues claiming Howard was the Liberals' best prime minister). Still, there were similarities – their grit in the face of adversity for one. Reading in 1999 the second volume of Allan Martin's biography of Menzies, Howard identified with the travails of Menzies' struggle out of disaster. He had already despatched the office desk he inherited from Prime Minister Keating and installed the one Menzies had worked at. Like Menzies, Howard was a traditionalist, not a 'modern' man in his time, yet a promoter of 'modern' policy (Menzies pushed economic development and adopted state aid for non-government schools; Howard embraced free-market reforms relatively early). Menzies tapped into his 'forgotten people'; Howard found 'the battlers'. They both discovered and exploited the potency of radio as a way of communicating with voters.

Menzies' 'forgotten people' talk was one of many radio broadcasts when he was fighting his way back into government in the 1940s; Howard's punishing regular round of the nation's talkback presenters was based on the belief that it is the best way of getting straight to the people. Menzies in his glory days displayed plenty of political nous, a quality shared by Howard for most of the prime ministerial years. Howard's weak spot on issues of race even echoes Menzies: changes to the White Australia Policy had to wait until the Holt government, which also successfully put the referendum to give the federal government power to make policy for Aborigines in the states.

According to David Barnett, the prime minister's first biographer, John Winston (after Churchill) Howard, born in July 1939, the youngest of four sons, set his eye on a parliamentary career 'by the time he reached first year at Canterbury Boys High School'.[4] Howard's politics bore the indelible imprint of his family and its circumstances. A straight line ran from father Lyall, small business owner of a service station in Sydney's Dulwich Hill, to the attitudes and approaches of his son John, prime minister.

Author Paul Kelly describes Howard as 'a recruit to the Liberals from the small capitalist class, a perfect fit into the 1950s Liberal hegemony based on anti-communism, the US alliance, free enterprise rhetoric and family values'.[5]

Unlike his brother Bob, who started Liberal, but veered left and joined the ALP over Vietnam, Howard was not even temporarily radicalised. 'He was always appalled at any challenge to authority and tradition,' said Bob Howard.[6] John, who had joined the Earlwood branch of the Young Liberals as a teenager, was a hawk on Vietnam. In general, Howard seems to have been very certain of his views from a young age.

His formative years had seen the fall of the Chifley government and the accession of the Menzies Liberals, with their rhetoric attuned to the aspirant middle class - people like the Howards. In an interview immediately after becoming a minister in 1975 Howard harked back to the galvanising impact of the 1949 election; the slogan 'Empty out the Chifley socialists and fill up the bowsers' had particular resonance for the Howards. Howard later remembered his father having 'a very strong property sense. What you would generally call the Protestant work ethic was very strong in our family.'[7] Brother Bob recalled: 'My father was a classic small business man. Union activity was perceived as being a nuisance. And John imbibed all that. He believes unions are a problem for the Australian economy. It's the view he grew up with.' Bob also felt Howard imbibed his belief in the importance of competitiveness from his youth: 'He did quite well from the competitive school system of the forties and fifties.' One competitive skill he honed was debating; he would become one of his generation's best performers on the floor of Parliament.

Howard grew up with a strong Methodist background, although he came to attend the Anglican Church. In a 1996 interview he said that Methodism had instilled in him 'a sensitivity to social justice - a sort of social justice streak - I'm a fierce believer in individual dignity and individual self-fulfilment. I'm a strong believer in [the] free enterprise competitive economy, but I am not laissez faire, devil-take-the-hindmost. I do think the government must provide a proper safety net. I guess I'm dryish rather than flintish.'[8]

His Methodism carried through into concern for the social damage caused by excessive gambling; in its second term the Howard government unveiled measures designed to limit the spread of gambling. More controversially, journalist David Marr argued that Howard's approach to Aboriginal affairs was deeply affected by 'the [Methodist] missionary values that seeped into [him] as an adolescent believer and lay dormant in him for over 30 years'.[9] Howard rejected Marr's analysis of his views as 'twaddle'.[10] Some around Howard – when he was PM – saw his personal work ethic as derived from his Methodism. One source said he found it 'hard to see [relaxation] as an end in itself', approaching the job as 'ceaseless activity.'

Lyall Howard (a World War I veteran, like his father) died of a stroke when John was 16. With his older brothers leaving the family nest, John stayed at home with mother Mona. The maternal influence appears to have been very strong in him and he in turn took a lot of the family responsibility for his mother. She became highly supportive of his ambitions. When he ran for a state seat, she moved their household into the electorate.

Howard studied law but, because the Sydney University Law School was physically separated from the university, he did not have an all-round experience of university life.[11] According to his brother Bob, 'He discussed [doing] arts. Then he said there was nothing to be learned from that, that it was a waste of time.' In John Howard's mind, law was always only a prelude to politics. 'With the benefit of hindsight, I probably [also] should have done an arts or economics degree', he said when PM.[12]

He had an extensive trip overseas in his mid twenties, but was still living at home when in 1971 he married Janette Parker, who shared his Young Liberal background. Her ambitions for him matched his own. Her determination that he should have the prime ministerial prize became more steely with the reverses of the 1980s, especially the 1989 'coup' that stripped him of his party's leadership. Howard and his wife are philosophical soulmates, but she sees the world in more black and white terms. She has strong views about people – Howard later said to colleagues he should have listened to her advice not to trust Fred Chaney, one of the 1989 plotters against him.[13] He did heed her advice when the pressure was on him to quit in 2007. He revealed he had consulted his family 'at length' and 'they want me to continue to contribute''. When, however, his comment sparked controversy about Janette's role, he regretted it and backtracked, saying the suggestion she had convinced him to stay was 'unfair to my wife'. After things went bad in the 2007 campaign, there were complaints from players that Janette Howard had interfered. As usual when his wife was criticised, Howard was outraged. Previously, Janette told Howard's biographers Wayne Errington and Peter van Onselen, 'I have my bib in', although she played down her influence.[14]

Howard's early political career was deceptively easy: an example of good fortune combined with the shrewd pursuit of ambition. From the start he grasped the importance of the party's organisational wing and by 1972 he was metropolitan vice-president, with close links to senior Liberal figures. That year he took time off his legal work to help embattled Prime Minister William McMahon, whose defeat ended 23 years of Coalition rule. A year later Howard was preselected for the Sydney North Shore seat of Bennelong, where he and Janette had settled; he entered Parliament at the 1974 election.

The replacement of leader Billy Snedden by Malcolm Fraser in 1975 elevated Howard, a Fraser supporter, to the front bench as spokesman on consumer affairs and commerce. Less than two years after becoming a Member of Parliament, Howard, aged 36, was minister for business and consumer affairs in the Fraser government. He mightn't have had the sort of glowing 'prime minister of the future' reviews that Peacock enjoyed from the start, but he was being spotted as a bright talent on the make. A journalist who interviewed him immediately after his appointment observed: 'John Howard should not be underrated as a young, inexperienced politician. He has a great weight of political experience.' He was also 'a pragmatist with little taste for dogma. He handles issues very much in terms of specifics and with commendable attention to detail.'[15]

He would always retain that pragmatic streak, but his views on economic questions would change considerably. Looking back two decades later, he told Barnett, 'It would be wrong to say I was a free-trader [then]. Some of the decisions I took were, in retrospect, protectionist.'[16] Although he was some years off his commitment to radical labour-market deregulation, Howard as business and consumer affairs minister sponsored tough amendments to the Trade Practices Act that outlawed union black bans. (These were removed from the Act by Labor – and reinstated by the Howard government.)

He came to be seen as a 'can do' man. Fraser gave him oversight of the brief wage-price freeze in April 1977 and appointed him minister assisting the prime minister in May 1977, in addition to his portfolio. In July that year – with Australia pushing for a better deal with Europe for agricultural exports – he was promoted to the newly created job of minister for special trade negotiations.

He was well-placed to step into treasurer Phillip Lynch's shoes when the latter was forced to stand down in the 1977 election campaign because of a row over a land development in which he had an interest. Lynch returned to the Cabinet after the election, but not to the treasurership. Howard inherited, with the job, Lynch's economic adviser Professor John Hewson (a Liberal leader in the 1990s), whose influence was significant in Howard's promotion of measures towards financial deregulation and his advocacy of a broad-based indirect tax. His attempt to secure government backing for the latter failed on two occasions. Prime Minister Fraser, like Prime Minister Hawke subsequently, feared it would spell electoral death. As treasurer, Howard took a firm line against tax rorts – the infamous bottom-of-the - harbour scams were being revealed – including making certain measures retrospective. This earned the enmity of some powerful Liberal party figures, especially in Western Australia, who would help undermine him when he became Opposition leader.

Howard became progressively 'drier', for several reasons. Economic rationalism was becoming the dominant credo; Howard's views were being shaped by Hewson, Treasury and the growing band of vocal dries on the Liberal backbench; and he was positioning himself politically. The still-young treasurer was feeling his oats and distinguishing himself from his leader. He would never be a challenger to Fraser, but he had the succession in mind. As Howard's economics dried out and he gained increasing political confidence, he and Fraser diverged. Howard cast himself as the reformer, compared with his more economically conservative leader. They fell out dramatically before the August 1982 Budget over Fraser's insistence – driven by a plummeting economy and looming election – on a more expansionary policy than Howard and Treasury favoured: Howard contemplated resignation.

For Fraser, however, the advancement of Howard was a useful counterweight to the swelling ambitions of Andrew Peacock. In April 1982 Lynch was persuaded to stand down from the Liberal deputy leadership to allow Howard to run successfully for it. It was a Fraser gesture to the powerful dry backbench ginger group. The day that Howard became deputy, Fraser decisively put down a Peacock challenge to his leadership.

At the end of 1982, with Fraser in hospital with a bad back, Howard led the by-election campaign for the marginal seat of Flinders in Victoria, prompted by the resignation of an ailing Lynch. The triumph in retaining Flinders, however, presaged disaster for the government; it helped undermine Labor leader Bill Hayden. With a severe recession bearing down, the Fraser government was doomed when the prime minister called a premature election in early 1983 and Labor simultaneously installed the electorally-popular Bob Hawke as leader.

Howard was impossibly placed for Opposition leadership in his post-election contest with Andrew Peacock. Not only had he been deputy leader and treasurer in the government that had just lost, but the revelation of a $9.6 billion looming deficit – which the Fraser government had not disclosed, despite Howard's worry about the concealment – was a blow to his reputation. Fraser, leaving Parliament, did not take part in the vote, but by this time he had swung to believing that Peacock rather than Howard would be the better leader. Howard was defeated 20–36 but became deputy and shadow treasurer. Those positions would enable him to be a policy driving force in the party and would also pave the way for a destabilising relationship between the two men. As deputy he had freedom to speak on issues beyond his economic portfolio and he used it, in the process 'getting up the nostrils of his colleagues'.[17]

His advocacy of a deregulatory industrial relations policy, calling for pioneer wage-setter, Justice Higgins, to be turned 'on his head', challenged the continued support of centralised wage fixing preferred by spokesman Ian Macphee and set the course that ended with the Howard government's industrial relations legislation. Later, as Opposition leader, Howard would be undermined by opinion polls, but as deputy his approval ratings outstripped those of Peacock. Also ironic in view of the damage Howard subsequently incurred over comments on Asian immigration, was his much-praised 1984 parliamentary speech calling for a bipartisan approach.

An unexpectedly good showing by Peacock at the 1984 election precluded the opportunity for Howard to challenge. But he kept his future options open when Peacock and he were re-elected unopposed, by avoiding an unqualified pledge of loyalty. Immediately after the election he had told a journalist (whom he had mistaken for a frontbench colleague when the journalist rang) 'I am not certain that [Peacock] won't fall over next year.'[18] The private prediction, not published at the time, proved correct. Continued leadership speculation, a good performance from Howard as deputy and Peacock's failure of nerve led to him falling on his sword in September 1985, handing the leadership to Howard.

Howard's tenure was ill-starred from the first. The Peacock forces undermined him, quickly psyching him into an earlier and more negative response to the Hawke government's 1985 tax reform package than he had wanted to make. Faced with the challenge of a divided party, Howard, who had looked so impressive as deputy, was unequal to his task. Internal schisms, leaks, blunders, a bad press and the government's skilful exploitation of his problems weakened him. Then came the improbable bid by ageing Queensland Premier Joh Bjelke-Petersen to storm to Canberra. In retrospect, Bjelke-Petersen's 'Joh for Canberra' campaign was inevitably doomed, but it was taken seriously enough at the time, including most damagingly by the media, to split the Coalition, distract the Liberals, undermine policymaking and leave the Howard Opposition in disarray going into the 1987 election.

Poor preparation extracted its toll when Labor revealed a big arithmetic hole in the Opposition's tax package, the centrepiece of its election policy. Despite this disaster, Howard personally campaigned competently. He was already identifying himself as a man of the battlers, although he would not use that term until his second campaign as leader, then almost a decade away. In the 1987 election he told journalist Craig McGregor that if he won he 'certainly wouldn't be seeking to run an ostentatious style of government, because I'm not by nature an ostentatious person. It's just going to be what you might call Average Australian, because that's what I am. I think I have more empathy with people who live in the suburbs of Australia than any political leader in the last twenty years.'[19] But the Opposition was too discredited to defeat Labor; an earlier prediction by Howard – that 'the times will suit me' – had turned sour. Post election, Howard held off a Peacock challenge. Peacock became deputy and shadow treasurer.

In 1988 Howard's conservative, indeed illiberal, positions on various social issues, including Aborigines, multiculturalism and the composition of the immigration intake, were highlighted. In response to government talk of a treaty or compact with Australia's Aboriginal people Howard said, 'It will spawn a form of apartheid.' He was critical of multiculturalism, preferring the concept 'One Australia'. In January 1989 he explained, 'The objection I have to multiculturalism is that multiculturalism is in effect saying that it is impossible to have a common Australian culture.'[20]

Politically, Howard saw multiculturalism as a concept owned by Labor – part of a coalition of interest groups, which also included the environmental lobby, that the ALP government cultivated electorally. This attitude worked against Howard in the late 1980s, but in 1996 he reaped the benefit of voter discontent with Labor's interest-group politics.

The 1988 issue that most wounded his leadership was Asian immigration. Howard's problem was one of both attitude and a stubborn refusal to admit a mistake. On 31 July he said: 'I don't think Asian immigration as such is a problem ... I would never get into an election campaign on anything that could be remotely related to racial issues.' But by the following day, in response to a radio question on whether the rate of Asian immigration was too fast, he was saying, 'I do believe that if in the eyes of some in the community, it's too great, it would be in our immediate-term interest and supportive of social cohesion if it were slowed down a little, so that the capacity of the community to absorb was greater.' Although Howard's leadership was also undermined by his mishandling of the party, especially of factional opponents, it did not recover from the furore that followed this comment, which alienated many Liberals. In 1989 the Peacock forces, in a plot prepared by a small group of senior Liberals with the utmost secrecy, overthrew Howard and reinstalled Peacock. The new leader, however, was unable to capitalise on the opportunity at the 1990 election. Howard's observation of this time was, 'I became leader by accident and I lost it by ambush.'[21] It was an ambush his own faults had made possible.

When Hewson succeeded Peacock as leader after the election, he made Howard industrial relations spokesman. Howard prepared the deregulatory Jobsback policy that accompanied Fightback!, the Opposition's radical economic blueprint which proposed establishing a 15 per cent goods and services tax, slashing tariffs and making big spending cuts. Barnett reports that 'Howard regarded his industrial relations proposals, rather than the taxation reforms drawn up around a goods and services tax, as the central element of the policy package which Hewson was drawing up for the 1993 elections.'[22] Howard's hierarchy of issues was clear. 'When I became Leader of the Opposition in 1985 I specified labour market reform as the most crucial economic challenge facing Australia. That remains my view,' he said in 1991; the following year he said that if there were only one thing a future Coalition government could do, 'by far the most important reform is to change Australia's industrial relations system'.

After Hewson lost the 'unlosable' 1993 election and decided – against much advice – that he wanted to remain leader, Howard ran against him, losing 30-47. Peacock was no longer a contestant, but he organised the Hewson numbers (as he had organised Hewson as his successor in 1990). The Liberals preferred a lame-duck leader who had lost the election against all odds to a recycled Howard. The Peacock-Howard rivalry was still keeping Howard out of the leadership and would continue to do so until Peacock, by quitting Parliament in 1994, removed the curse. This enabled Howard to capitalise on the situation after the leadership of Alexander Downer had all but collapsed in a series of blunders. Howard could force Downer into ceding the job to him in early 1995, facilitating a 'draft' of Howard a year before an election was due. He could not know that his negotiations to get the job uncontested would come back to bite him spectacularly in 2006.

The John Howard who shaped up for the 1996 poll was tougher, wilier, better positioned and much more confident than Howard as Opposition leader a decade before. He had reason for confidence. The Keating government had become highly vulnerable, accused of arrogance and being in the sway of sectional interests.

Howard led a united party, determined to do what it took to get to office. His strategy was to keep the focus on the government and make himself – and the Coalition, minimal targets. He had already sought to lighten his own baggage by expressing regret and apologising to the Asian community for his 1988 remarks. Now he downplayed immigration policy generally. Health policy – another danger area for the Liberals – was fireproofed by pledging that Medicare, of which the Coalition had been a stern critic, would be retained. Although a strong monarchist, Howard neutralised Keating's pro-republic stance (which did not seem a plus anyway) by adopting Downer's promise that a Liberal government would hold a constitutional convention and give the people a vote on whether Australia should change its system.

All round, Howard was presenting a soft face for a leader who was by nature a policy radical in several critical areas. Even the industrial relations platform had its harsher edge sanded off and Howard was adamant that a Liberal government would not introduce a GST. When he let his guard slip at a business function in 1995, leaving the possibility of a GST in the indefinite future, he quickly rectified his lapse by declaring there would 'never, ever' be a GST under the Coalition. This would become his most spectacularly broken promise – though mitigated by his taking the revived GST plan to an election.

Detailed policies were held back for the campaign. Howard had learned from the Hewson experience: his release of Fightback! some 18 months before the election had given the government plenty of time to destroy it. Unveiling a plethora of (non-threatening) policies during the campaign itself would both minimise time and opportunity for government and media to attack and ensure that the Opposition had something new to talk about each day. The campaign's most dramatic initiative was the plan to sell one-third of Telstra with the 'carrot' for the green constituency that $1 billion of the proceeds would be spent on the environment.

Howard arrived in power with a 40 seat majority and a legitimate claim to an electoral mandate, but a limited brief for reform and a Senate minority. Perhaps the biggest story of the first term and a half of his prime ministership was the way he sharpened the reform edge of his agenda. The GST that he had ruled out absolutely was in the pipeline by mid 1997 and two years later became one of his biggest achievements.

One subtext of the Howard government's story in its earlier years was the combination of luck and skill that enabled it to get most of its program through a reluctant Senate (with the obvious exception, in the second term, of the sale of the remaining 50.1 per cent of Telstra). Another was Howard's continued personal difficulty, just as in Opposition days a decade before, when confronted with certain touchy issues, notably involving race. A third was the way in which he was able to take up and turn dramatic and unforeseen issues to political advantage. In the first term it was gun control in the wake of the Port Arthur massacre (a hard test for the Coalition, especially the National Party); in the second it was Australia's push for, and later leadership of, a peacekeeping force in East Timor, which also prompted Howard to review and redefine Australia's foreign and defence policies.

In his first term as prime minister, Howard started strongly, even ruthlessly. In the greatest single purge ever seen by the Commonwealth public service, one-third of the existing departmental heads were sacked. In this Howard was a total contrast to his model, Menzies, who kept and used to advantage leading officials he inherited from the Chifley government. Howard's view was coloured by his wider 'them and us' mentality, with the bureaucrats being regarded, for the most part, in the 'them' category. Brother Bob puts much of Howard's anti-public service attitude down to his upbringing. 'Our family in the 1940s and 1950s was very anti-public service. It was a typical Protestant family of the time – it saw the public service as Catholic or somewhere where people didn't want to work much. If he has a grudge against two groups, it's the public service and academics.'[23] The position of senior bureaucratic advisers, already weakened under Labor's public service changes, including a new contract system, was further eroded by the Coalition's public service policies. Howard was suspicious of statutory appointments and independent inquiries. Some say he was influenced by memories of the Fraser government being 'bitten' by such external critics. He and his government were also impatient with niceties on such matters as publicly-funded advertising: the taxpayers shelled out huge amounts over the years for the government to deluge them with propaganda; before the 2007 election it desperately threw money at advertising WorkChoices.

The government's initial priority in 1996 was an attack on the Budget deficit. Treasurer Peter Costello announced – with what had by now become a familiar flourish of governments – that there was a 'black hole' ($8 billion, which expanded to $10 billion) left by Labor. A rigorous program of cuts over two years headed the government into a Budget surplus, a major fiscal achievement and vital to its capacity later to deliver the big income tax cuts that had to sweeten the GST. In those early days the government wasn't afraid to alienate sections of the electorate with its decisions; later, it would become risk-averse, more inclined to the pork barrel than the razor.

The most robust legislative policies of the new government were the part sale of Telstra and the proposed industrial relations changes, which considerably freed up the wages system, introduced statutory individual contracts called Australian Workplace Agreements and reduced the power of unions. Parliamentary support for the industrial legislation was obtained, with extensive amendments, in a deal with the Democrats, then led by Cheryl Kernot. In opposition, Howard had influenced the debate; now he had tangible achievements. Later in his first term, employers and the government would confront union power on the waterfront, suffering legal reverses but changing the stevedoring industry forever.

The Telstra part sale, together with the passage of a number of other measures, was made possible by the defection of a Labor senator, Mal Colston, to become an independent; the government encouraged him to jump by offering him the Senate deputy presidency. From August 1996 to June 1999 the Senate was controlled by two independents, Brian Harradine and Colston; in the latter stages – because Colston was tainted by an expense rorts scandal – mainly by Harradine. (Harradine and Colston would not countenance the industrial relations legislation, hence the deal with the Democrats.) Harradine's eventual willingness to compromise – because he feared a race-based election – gave Howard most of his Wik legislation, which dealt with native title in relation to pastoral leases.

One year into power, the hard budget decisions had been taken, the workplace reforms were in place, and the economy was steaming along. But soon flaws in leadership started to show up, prompting criticisms that would continue until the 1998 election and generate speculation that Howard could face a challenge from the ambitious Peter Costello after the poll. Some of the fault lines that emerged exposed the old weaknesses that had dogged Howard in the 1980s.

The Independent Pauline Hanson, who articulated the growing economic and social discontent of regional and rural Australia, but with racist overtones, presented a challenge that Howard found extraordinarily difficult to meet. He had been happy enough to have the Liberals strip Hanson of endorsement during the 1996 election for her anti-Aboriginal comments. After her September 1996 maiden speech in which she condemned the 'Aboriginal industry' and its funding, multiculturalism and immigration and claimed 'we are in danger of being swamped by Asians', Howard hung back from the attack that many colleagues wanted him to make. Instead he spoke about the 'pall of censorship on certain issues' being lifted since the Coalition's election: 'I welcome the fact that people can now talk about certain things without living in fear of being branded as a bigot or as a racist,' he told the Queensland Liberal state council. Later Howard strongly insisted this point was not made in reference to Hanson. 'It was always wrong that that speech was some kind of benediction,' he said.[24]

His inability to respond decisively to Hanson and his shillyshallying on what stand should be taken on the question of preferences to her in the next election were damaging for him at home and for Australia's image abroad. As in 1988, his stance involved a combination of personal attitude, stubbornness and the sniffing of possible political advantage. Howard knew that some of those Hanson spoke for had supported him in 1996. Calls from those he regarded as the 'politically correct' brigade, including Labor, the media and even many in his own party, for a tough attack on Hanson only dug him in further. On preferences Howard inclined to a seat-by-seat approach, although eventually party pressure forced him into a 'put-Hanson-last' stance.

If Howard grappled unconvincingly with making a principled response to Hansonism, he picked up on the wider political message she represented – the pain and anger of regional and rural Australia. Trying to deal with this alienation became a preoccupation of the Howard government, increasing in its second term.

His problems with just saying 'No' to Hansonism seriously eroded his credibility on the social front with many opinion leaders. Meanwhile, a growing perception in the business community that he did not have a sweeping enough reform program had by mid 1997 started to weaken his economic credentials. Howard understood and responded to this challenge much better than to the Hanson one. He had told a business function in early 1997, 'Can I assure you that I have not lost interest in the cause of taxation reform. The long-term cause of tax reform is still a very important one.' Some months before, the message from the prime minister's office to business pressure for tax overhaul was: 'go build a constituency' for the tax reform cause.

Nevertheless, Howard did not take his big step until he was looking for a boost for his frayed leadership. When he and his government came under heavy attack from business for lack of vision in May 1997 he responded, quickly and without reference to senior colleagues, by putting the whole tax question on the agenda; by August a task force was appointed to prepare a report. A year later the government produced the extensive package, with its 10 per cent GST and big income tax cuts, on which it went to the October 1998 election (winning, on a minority of the total vote, with its majority reduced to 12). While many saw Howard's tax strategy as a reaction to pressure – which at one level it was – the problems he faced provided an opportunity to revive a policy that, given his long commitment to tax reform, he would have brought forward eventually.

Following the election Harradine, after much to-ing and fro-ing, announced he could not support the proposed new tax. This forced Howard to turn to the Democrats, by then led by Meg Lees, who on 1 July 1999 were to assume the Senate balance of power. A deal with the minor party enabled Howard to secure his tax reform package; he became the flexible compromiser, acceding to the Democrats' demand that basic food must not have the 10 per cent GST applied to it. In reality Howard had little choice; a double dissolution election on the GST would almost certainly have swept the government out. On the other hand, if he had let the GST lapse, he would very likely not have survived long as leader, so much did his authority depend on the tax package.

The stamp of Howard's core values was strong on his prime ministership. The policies he promoted reflected long and deeply held attitudes. 'I believe in the traditional social values of Australia: egalitarianism, strong families, entrepreneurial opportunity, hard work, Protestant work ethic,' he told an interviewer in 1989.[25] He also believed that 'mateship' was a defining characteristic of the Australian people. As Opposition leader Howard had issued a manifesto in late 1988 setting out 'the approach to the policies and directions to be followed by the next Liberal/National Government'. The commitments were to strengthening the family, restoring people's control over their own lives, providing more incentive and choice, ensuring a fair go for all, and building One Australia. The thrust of Future Directions – which went into Howard folklore for its cover illustration of the archetypical family in front of a white picket fence – could be found in the Coalition policies of the following decade. Those aspects of the 1998 tax policy that gave women more choice to stay at home with their young children echoed Future Directions. But as time went on, Howard, reflecting the reality of the dual-income family model, gave more attention to one and a half income families, often using the example of a policeman and a part time nurse.

Howard's 'modern conservatism' had government seeking to forge 'a new social coalition' of government, business, charitable and welfare organisations and other community groups to tackle social problems, including drugs, unemployment, homelessness and youth suicide. It did 'not mean winding back the government's support for individuals and families in need', but rejected the view that more government resources alone are the key to fixing society's ills. Central to Howard's 'modern conservatism' was 'mutual obligation', the notion that 'Just as it is an ongoing responsibility of government to support those in genuine need, so it is also the case that – to the extent that it is within their capacity to do so – those in receipt of such assistance should give something back to society in return, and in the process improve their own prospects for self-reliance.' The beacon 'mutual obligation' policy was the work-for-the-dole scheme.

Social policies became an increasingly important priority for the Howard government's second term as it cast around to replenish its agenda, soften its image and try to chip away at Labor's areas of natural strength. Howard told the Liberals' April 2000 National Convention that the government's economic reform program 'has not been pursued because we want to get an A+ in the exam for economic rationalists. ... Economic reform without a social goal, or a social vision, is an economic reform that is destined to fail and ought not to be embraced.'

The government was developing some fundamental structural changes in social policy. In its first term it replaced the old Commonwealth Employment Service with a competitive and privatised (initially with one government-owned provider) employment services market. The large charities obtained a growing slice of the new market. In its second term it commissioned a review of the income support system for those of working age. The welfare review's recommendations were to encourage and if necessary force a greater level of economic and social participation from those on pensions and benefits, an approach in line with what in the United States was known as the 'new paternalism'. In later years the government toughened its approach to the conditions for income support, pushing single mothers and many people on disability support pensions into the workforce.

On one view, Aboriginal reconciliation could be seen as a brand of 'mutual obligation', in this case the obligation of the society to a section of the people for past misdeeds. But for Howard reconciliation remained a challenge to which he could never rise. Most at home with the practical and the tangible, and highly suspicious of what he saw as the 'guilt industry' and the 'black armband' view of history, Howard found it nearly impossible to understand the symbolism of an apology to Aborigines or even the centrality of land. He lacked that special quality of imaginative empathy that would allow him to enter the minds and souls of those whose experience is totally outside his own. Aboriginal health, housing and education needs were one thing, but he did not grasp the emotional legacy borne by the 'stolen generations'. For Howard the oneness of Australia and Australians was the primary characteristic of the country; the diversity was secondary.

Despite his mainstreaming philosophical stance, Howard initially made reconciliation a priority for his second term. Partly this was born out of failure in the previous term, particularly an incident at the 1997 Reconciliation Convention when he reacted badly, shouting at his audience, after Aborigines interjected on his comments about native title. In his victory speech on election night 1998 he promised 'to commit myself very genuinely to the cause of true reconciliation with the Aboriginal people of Australia by the centenary of federation'. It was an undertaking that later dogged him. Spurred by the relationship he developed with newly-elected Aboriginal Democrat senator Aden Ridgeway, Howard in 1999 moved a parliamentary statement of 'regret' to Aborigines for past wrongs. For him it was a significant step; for critics it was not enough. In early 2000 he walked away from the reconciliation timetable he had set himself in 1998. Yet again the race issue was biting him. Even the moderate Ridgeway insisted a national apology was essential, but Howard – who said an apology would signify intergenerational guilt – stayed adamantly against it, backed by opinion polls. (Less than three months after the 2007 defeat, the Coalition Opposition agreed, under the pressure of political necessity and with considerable agonising, to vote for the Rudd government's apology.)

In the approach to Corroboree 2000, the set-piece event that was the culmination of the work of the Council for Aboriginal Reconciliation which had been established a decade before, Howard actively tried to manage the issue, but his concept of 'practical reconciliation' could not bridge the gap to the nation's indigenous people, and his refusal to join in the 200,000-strong people's walk for reconciliation across Sydney Harbour Bridge brought him more criticism. His dissuasion of Costello's taking part – on the grounds that it would be damaging to the government to have the prime minister and his treasurer at odds – highlighted his sensitivity on both Aboriginal affairs and leadership.[26]

Howard was troubled by his problems in handling the indigenous issue; much later he attempted to explain and account for his thinking. Pledging in October 2007 that if he were re-elected he would hold a referendum to put a 'statement of reconciliation' into the constitution, he admitted that he had struggled with indigenous affairs 'during the entire time I have been Prime Minister'. 'The challenge I have faced around indigenous identity politics is in part an artefact of who I am and the time in which I grew up', he said. 'I have always acknowledged the past mistreatment of Aboriginal people ... yet I have felt and I still feel that the overwhelming balance sheet of Australian history is a positive one. In the end, I could not accept that reconciliation required a condemnation of the Australian heritage that I had always owned. At the same time, I recognise that the parlous position of indigenous Australians does have its roots in history and that past injustices have a real legacy in the present'.

Howard's approach to the republic issue was a case of having things both ways. Almost a century after Australia's political leaders made the bold step to Federation, Howard, in opposing the republic, became the first Australian prime minister to argue against a constitutional referendum he put to the people. He kept his election promise of giving the people their say on a republic, but used his position to urge no change. While Labor was unitedly for a republic, Howard – allowing a free vote to Coalition members – ensured that the opposition to the republic came solidly from the government's own ranks, as well as from monarchists and direct-election republicans outside Parliament. His own position was clear throughout, and as the November 1999 vote neared he stepped up his intervention on the 'no' side. The referendum was overwhelmingly defeated; republic campaign leader Malcolm Turnbull (later an MP and Howard Cabinet minister) immediately said the PM 'broke a nation's heart'. An incidental casualty was the constitutional preamble Howard had put up – after criticism forced him to modify his original draft substantially, including dropping the reference to 'mateship'.

It was always clear that Howard would be a prime minister oriented to economics. It was neither predictable nor predicted that he would undertake the most significant Australian foreign engagements since Vietnam. When he became prime minister his inexperience in international affairs was seen as a limitation. In the 1996 campaign Prime Minister Keating – who had recently concluded a security treaty with Indonesia – portrayed Howard as unacceptable in Asia, claiming the Asians would not deal with him.

Howard was determined to differentiate his line from what he saw as Keating's: 'Our policy is Asia-first or Asia-plus; not Asia-only,' he said. He emphasised that Australia, with its 'profound and enduring' links with

Britain and Europe, its 'close alliance' with the United States, and its Asia-Pacific location and 'strong community, economic, political and security ties' to Asian neighbours, occupied 'a unique intersection of geography, history, culture and economic circumstance'.

Howard's foreign policy interests as prime minister were limited, however, until East Timor galvanised his attention. Australia's dramatic reversal of its policy on East Timor, after two decades of accepting its incorporation in Indonesia, was partly driven by changing international circumstances. The Coalition was also being pushed by domestic politics. Whatever the conjunction of pressures, the government's backing for an act of East Timorese self-determination (although at first hoping it would lead to autonomy within Indonesia) and Howard's mustering of international support for a United Nations-backed peace force (led initially by Australia) thrust the nation into a new regional role.

Although East Timor involved peace-enforcement and peacekeeping, Howard tended to speak as if this was a new war. By extension he appeared to be casting himself in the mould of Australian leaders who had been at the helm in other conflicts. He also saw it as part of a more uncertain regional environment; he sent out confusing signals that Australia stood ready for some sort of regional policing role when required.

Howard oscillated in his public comments about Indonesia. Declaring in 2000 that the relationship would never be the same as before East Timor, he seemed more intent on distancing himself from the past policies of both Coalition and Labor towards Indonesia than on worrying overmuch about the need for rebuilding. The Australian-Indonesian relationship would wane and wax over the Howard years, hitting a massive low when Indonesia's President Megawati Soekarnoputri did not take his call during the Government's attempt to force Indonesia to accept the asylum seeker-laden Tampa in 2001. Later, however, Howard and Indonesian President Susilo Bambang Yudhoyono developed a strong bond. The aftermath of the 2002 Bali bombing, in which 88 Australians were killed, was one factor in strengthening relations between the two countries, as they co-operated more closely in the fight against terrorism, although there continued to be various one off issues that periodically caused tensions. In late 2006 the two countries signed a new treaty of security co-operation, replacing the earlier pact that had been scrapped by the Indonesians during the Timor crisis.

As his bid for a third term loomed, Howard's political fortunes were flagging. The implementation of the new tax system, after starting smoothly in July 2000, was fulfilling Labor's predictions of a 'slow burn', with many small business people angry. The West Australian Coalition government's defeat and Queensland Labor's re-election, both in February 2001, sent reverberations through the Howard government. Even worse was the following month's loss of the 'safe' federal Brisbane seat of Ryan, in a by-election prompted by Howard's December ministerial reshuffle. Electoral fears forced a series of big policy retreats as Howard ditched some baggage: tax reporting arrangements for businesses were simplified, petrol excise cut, a crackdown on trusts shelved. Just as Howard appeared to be clawing back a little ground, the Coalition was knocked afresh by a devastating leak of a memo written by Liberal president Shane Stone, saying the government was seen as mean and tricky, and appearing to target the Treasurer. A furious Costello blamed the Howard office, although the leak's source in fact remained a mystery. The always-brittle feelings between Costello and Howard were further strained.

Howard used the May budget to start rebuilding, with a generous appeal to disillusioned older voters. Another by-election, caused by the death of a Liberal member in the marginal Victorian seat of Aston, was a crucial test for both sides. It should have been easy picking for Labor, but the Liberals hung on. The tide was turning, although Labor was still the better placed for the 2001 poll. Then came the MV Tampa.

The Norwegian container ship picked up 438 asylum seekers – whose ship was sinking off Christmas Island – on 26 August. The Tampa captain headed towards Indonesia, but then, under pressure from the behaviour of those aboard, switched course – but Howard refused the ship permission to land. In the extraordinary stand off that followed, an increasingly desperate captain headed for Christmas Island, prompting the government to have the SAS board the ship. The government held firm; meanwhile it pulled all diplomatic strings to find somewhere to send the people. Eventually it unveiled the "Pacific solution", despatching them to Nauru. From then on new asylum seekers were to be kept offshore. The government received tough criticism locally and internationally. By 2005 the whole area of detention policy would cause Howard enormous problems, with revelations of appalling mistakes and maladministration, a community backlash against the long-term incarceration of people, and a backbench revolt that forced changes. But in 2001 the Tampa paved the way for border security to be a central and successful election issue for Howard who rammed home the line at his policy launch: 'We decide who comes to this country and the circumstances in which they come.'

Later, the 2001 election campaign would become notorious for the 'children overboard' affair. The government declared that asylum seekers on a sinking boat had deliberately thrown their children into the water. The incorrect claims served their immediate purpose, but later, when it became clear some in the government knew they were false, the issue left a scar. By 2007, 'children overboard' was one strand in the distrust many voters felt towards Howard. It had combined with other issues, including the failure to find WMD in Iraq, broken promises and the government's callousness towards Australian Guantanamo Bay prisoner David Hicks to disillusion people, well beyond the elites.

Apart from the Tampa, the other big transforming factor of 2001 was the terrorist attacks in America on September 11. Howard happened to be in Washington; the previous day he had met President George W Bush in person for the first time. Howard immediately pledged Australian solidarity with the Americans: 'we will support actions they take to properly retaliate in relation to these acts of bastardry'; Australia invoked the ANZUS alliance. Howard and Bush had already hit it off, but the terrorist attack was to forge a personal rapport and friendship closer perhaps than that between Harold Holt and LBJ in the Vietnam days. In 2003, Bush, feting the Howards at the President's Crawford, Texas ranch praised the Australian prime minister as a 'man of steel'. Australia followed the Americans into two wars, first Afghanistan (coinciding with the 2001 election) and then Iraq (2003).

September 11 fundamentally changed the Howard prime ministership. The new atmosphere was reinforced by the Bali bombing the following year. Suddenly security, national and international, overshadowed much else. Security measures at home were toughened repeatedly, involving controversial encroachments on civil liberties. The preoccupation with security, broadly defined, tended to crowd out some other issues. It also insulated the Howard government politically for a long time, but finally, like much else, what had been a winning card stopped delivering. In 2007 a security scare about an Indian doctor working in Australia, Mohamed Haneef – whose relatives were implicated in a failed British terrorist attack – backfired on the government.

By his third term, war was central to Howard's Prime Ministerial persona. The Anzac legend was part of his personal psyche and political armoury; he returned to it often. Australia's commitment to Afghanistan was bipartisan, but the government's decision to be part of the Iraq coalition sharply divided politics. Given the close relationship between Bush and Howard and the priority Howard gave to the US alliance, it was inevitable that Australia would commit. Howard insisted, however, the troops would not be there for peace enforcement, a position later abandoned when post war conflict continued. Bush was anxious for Australia's continued presence. The troops remained; Howard could deal with the home politics mainly because there were no Australian combat deaths. Indeed in 2004, the government was able to land a significant blow against Labor leader Mark Latham, then riding high, when Latham out of the blue promised an ALP government would bring the troops home by Christmas.

Presenting a youthful contrast, the 43-year-old Latham posed a major challenge to Howard, who turned 65 in 2004. Latham appeared initially to connect with the community, talking about the importance of reading to children and the like. He was also tactically agile, for example forcing Howard to go along with his populist proposal to cut back politicians' generous superannuation. Nevertheless, 'the character question' eventually undermined Latham – a colourful history and volatile temperament made swinging voters uneasy. Howard, whose credibility was under assault over the failure to find WMD in Iraq and fresh allegations about 'children overboard', boldly called the election on the theme of 'trust', meaning reliability and competence ('Who do you trust to keep interest rates low?') Labor was also running on 'trust' – in the sense of 'honesty' and truth telling – but it had misjudged. Howard might be seen as loose with the truth on some things, but when it came to the crucial issue of economic management, it was Latham whom voters feared was a dodgy proposition. Howard successfully fanned these doubts, insisting interest rates would always be higher under Labor than under the Coalition. He also tactically outfoxed Latham: late in the campaign – after Latham over-reached in his promise to protect Tasmanian forests – Howard materialised as the saviour of forest jobs, to be cheered by the Tasmanian unionists.

The 2004 win was, to use a famous Keating phrase (which would never pass Howard's lips), the sweetest victory of them all for the Prime Minister – another swing to the Coalition (1.79 per cent) and, unexpectedly, control of the Senate. Howard declared the Coalition would use its post 1 July 2005 upper house majority with restraint. Suddenly however, as Howard overtook Hawke in December 2004 to become second longest serving prime minister, the impossible was soon to become possible. Howard was determined not to waste his opportunity. The remaining half of Telstra could now be sold; a radical industrial relations agenda could be pulled together into a massive sweeping reform of the labour market, and changes to media laws could be passed.

The foundations of the government, however, were being undermined – especially by the unresolved issue of leadership. Labor had tried to exploit the Howard-Costello strains in the 2004 campaign, but the issue had not penetrated. After that election, even some close to Howard thought he would retire before the 2007 poll, but Howard was starting to fall victim to triumphalism, to say nothing of his sheer love of the job. In April 2005, in Athens at the end of a trip, he told two News Limited journalists he believed he could beat Beazley (by then Opposition leader again) another time. Costello was furious, but his anger was impotent. Howard's power in the party was such that Costello and his supporters could do nothing, apart from making private threats of a challenge the following year.

Relations between Costello and Howard had steadily deteriorated since Howard failed to retire at 64 years of age in 2003. It was always abundantly clear, even when Howard anointed Costello, that he did not have faith in him as a future leader. He appeared to foster Peter Reith and Tony Abbott, but he would contend he never believed they would be alternatives to Costello, who remained the only credible heir – albeit one who the public did not warm to.

Howard's formula, when asked about his future, became that he would stay as long as his party wanted him to and it was in the party's interests. This got him past his fourth election, but for his fifth it was obviously becoming untenable.

As it went through its fourth term, the government's leadership tensions were now erupting annually. In 2006 journalist Glenn Milne revealed that Ian McLachlan, an ex-minister by then long retired from Parliament, had a note of a 1994 conversation between Howard and Costello in which Howard had said that if he became PM he would hand over to Costello after a term and a half. Costello knew the story was coming; he later confirmed he regarded the discussion as an agreement that had been broken. Howard insisted there had been no deal. Tension flared into a fresh crisis. Costello did not challenge because he could not win – the party had not lost faith in Howard's capacity to deliver victory. Howard, however, was forced to make a decision about his future earlier than he wanted. He took party soundings then announced he would contest the 2007 election. Among those close to Howard, there was a belief that if Costello hadn't pushed so hard, Howard might well have retired at the end of 2006. One Howard intimate says: 'Costello never learned how to play the PM properly'. Others, including Costello, thought Howard would never cede the job willingly.

Entering election year, Howard had in Kevin Rudd a new opponent of untested strength, while his own firepower was diminished. His long-time chief of staff and policy adviser Arthur Sinodinos had gone to the private sector, a blow from which the Howard office did not recover.

Howard knew he had to open the year with a big idea; he announced a $10 billion takeover of the Murray-Darling Basin. (Howard was never a supporter of states' rights – he came to give his centralist bent the high-sounded title of 'aspirational nationalism') Like much else in the next few months, the Murray-Darling initiative quickly ran into a snag – in this case trenchant opposition from Victoria. More seriously WorkChoices, which had commenced in March 2006, was becoming an albatross. The changes, which used the Commonwealth's power over corporations to bring in a national IR system, allowed employers to scrap all but the most basic conditions of workers and removed the right of employees – in companies of 100 employees or less – to pursue unfair dismissal cases. It also abolished the no disadvantage test for Australian Workplace Agreements. The government had overreached, underestimating people's reaction (often the fears were for their children rather than for themselves). It also failed to anticipate the union movement's ability to mount a devastatingly effective counter campaign on the ground, in advertising and through the media, replete with horror stories of workers' experiences. The unions' effort added immensely to Labor's strength. The government did not even have a good grasp on what it had done. Workplace Relations minister Joe Hockey subsequently claimed that when he arrived in the job (early 2007) many cabinet ministers were unaware people could be worse off under WorkChoices. By May of 2007 Howard was forced to announce a fairness test for AWAs to counter the negative publicity – but it was too late.

WorkChoices – which was Howard's ultimate ambition fulfilled in industrial relations reform – had a very bad name and it would stick.

With Rudd and Labor holding a commanding poll lead, Howard tried dramatic gestures and wedges. In mid-year, the government announced its spectacular takeover of Aboriginal communities in the Northern Territory. Whatever the objective merits of the intervention, the days were past when Howard could corner Labor. Rudd simply agreed with this move, as he did to other policies on which he chose not to fight. Meanwhile Howard was constantly on the pre-campaign trail, sprinkling money through increasingly vulnerable marginal electorates, hoping that a seat-by-seat pork barrel strategy might help.

One of Howard's biggest struggles was on the hot button issue of climate change. It became a metaphor for the generation gap. He had been slow to appreciate its electoral importance – initially dismissing former US vice president Al Gore's proselytising as political sour grapes – and was then unable to quickly and adequately make up lost ground.

A long and damaging drought gave extra weight to the issue in the public mind and the media. Howard tried a counter by running the nuclear alternative, setting up an inquiry into the nuclear cycle. In theory it was a classic wedge that would snare Labor; instead many of his own backbenchers became alarmed as their constituents reacted to scares about nuclear reactors in their backyards.

Belatedly the government embraced in principle an emissions-trading system, but there was always the feeling that it didn't really believe its own lines on climate change. Howard still would not ratify Kyoto, despite a last minute push (detail of which leaked embarrassingly during the election campaign) by Environment minister Malcolm Turnbull. Post election, other colleagues, including Costello, admitted Kyoto should have been ratified. In retrospect, Howard's intransigence seemed inexplicable, except in terms of the American connection – Bush was anti Kyoto.

A second Howard biography by academics Wayne Errington and Peter van Onselen, appearing in 2007, packed a big political punch, with awkwardly-timed sharp criticism from Costello, who shrugged off Howard's record when Fraser's treasurer as 'not a success in terms of interest rates and inflation', and complained about Howard's big spending habits as PM.[27]

September 2007 was perhaps the most extraordinary time of the Howard prime ministership. Howard was hosting the Asia-Pacific Economic Co-operation forum in Sydney; Australia had never seen such a weighty gathering of international leaders. Simultaneously, as he considered the prospect of losing both the election and his own seat (where former ABC presenter Maxine McKew was Labor's candidate) Howard was reviewing his leadership situation.

Already a report from the Liberals' consultancy-polling firm Crosby Textor, leaked in August, had presented a bleak picture. Homing in on Howard's disadvantages compared with Rudd, Howard was seen as 'increasingly rattled and not responding well under pressure'. The report said that 'the idea of generational change is now attractive' to voters and Rudd 'looks energetic and enthusiastic'.

Howard turned to Foreign Minister Alexander Downer, his closest cabinet confidant. In his post-election account to the ABC's Four Corners Downer said: 'John Howard and I were of the view that we might lose the election ... it was a reasonable thing that he wanted to sound out the views of his colleagues as to whether we would be better off changing the leadership and I did that'. There was a big qualification by Howard – if he was to go, he had to be pushed. 'John Howard's view was that he wouldn't just stand down ... and run away from a fight and be seen by history as a coward, and secondly that he himself thought that he had higher approval ratings than Peter Costello and a better chance of winning the election ...'

The Liberal cabinet ministers were confused and alarmed at Downer's soundings, which most of them discussed at a late night meeting in Downer's Sydney hotel room on the Thursday of the APEC week. Howard's canvassing suggested to some that the PM had lost his nerve. Ministers assumed Howard was thinking he should step down and they basically believed this would be the best course, although they were doubtful about Costello's chances in such a late changeover. The one thing they would not do, however, was be seen to push him out. So, at its very top level the government was paralysed. 'John Howard took the view that he would leave if he was told to leave by his colleagues and his colleagues took the view that if they blasted John Howard out that would be an electoral disaster ... (Costello's leadership) would be stillborn', said Downer.[28]

The message to Howard, supported by most ministers and conveyed by Downer, was unacceptable to the prime minister: there was a mood for him to go, but he had to fall on his own sword. Howard then made it clear that he was going nowhere. The exercise had become one of confusion and futility and, when it was leaked as part of the pressure on Howard, even more damaging. Yet the positions of both Howard and the ministers were understandable. Howard was not a quitter and did not want to look one, especially when he judged that quitting would not save the government. The ministers believed their reputations, and probably that of the government, would be irreparably damaged if they were cast as executioners.

Howard, having been outgunned by Rudd all year, went into the campaign with the Coalition at least a dozen points behind on a two-party basis in the polls – too much to make up unless Labor had some massive setback. Howard had the added campaign burden of Bennelong, to which he kept dashing back, no doubt having in mind from time to time the precedent of PM Stanley Melbourne Bruce, who lost his seat of Flinders in 1929, when the big issue was industrial relations.

In the national campaign, old pluses had become negatives for Howard. He had seen off Latham in 2004 in part because the Labor leader had lacked credibility on interest rates, but after five rate rises since that election, now Howard wasn't credible. Then the Reserve Bank delivered the ultimate blow of a further rise during the campaign itself.

Howard had also become a lame-duck leader: he'd been forced, after the fiasco of the leadership soundings, to abandon his old formula. He announced in a television interview that if the Australian people were 'good enough and kind enough' to re-elect him; 'I would probably, certainly form the view well into my term, that it makes sense for me to retire'. The theme became the team, but a joint Howard-Costello appearance, where they lauded their relationship, looked like bad comedy. The comparison with Rudd highlighted Howard's age; his morning walk routine, once a symbol of vigour and vitality, turned to farce, with him pursued by the ABC *Chaser* crew and women from the 'John Howard Ladies Auxiliary' dressed in outfits of the 1950s. Even post election Howard thought the walk an electoral asset. The campaign did not run as smoothly as previous ones; Howard retreated into himself, sometimes drifting off message. The travelling team, struggling with the tactics, frustrated campaign headquarters by making decisions late and on the run.

Even in defeat, Howard defied the odds: his government had lost while presiding over a booming economy: and a three-decade low in unemployment. The 24 November election resulted in a two party swing of 5.44 per cent against the government and the loss of 22 seats.

Howard's reform achievements will be seen as concentrated in the earlier part of his term: the first wave of IR changes (made more palatable by forced compromise) and the GST. Later, his biggest domestic successes were political more than substantive – surviving and improving the government's position in 2001 and 2004. In foreign policy his record is mixed: the Timor intervention rates well, although that country now struggles. Howard successfully juggled Australia's relationship with China, a key for Australia's economic future, and the US alliance, the cornerstone of its international security, but went overboard with Bush and the Iraq involvement was a bad decision.

Howard was ideological, pragmatic and ruthless as PM. His doggedness was a virtue, but at times it turned into stubbornness. In some areas he was narrow and blinkered, including in his pursuit of history and culture wars. He was a master at wedge politics and scapegoating. His failure to apologise to indigenous Australia may not have lost him votes, but his inability to appreciate properly the actual and political importance of climate change certainly did. It was, for a time, politically useful to demonise asylum seekers from Afghanistan and Iraq (although it later worked against him) but he found that, when he took on an old foe – the union movement – he had met his match.

He changed the country for the better, economically, and the worse, culturally. As soon as he was gone, it was quickly changing again: the 'Apology' was given to the stolen generations, WorkChoices was being rolled back, Kyoto was ratified, former ministers were recanting or regretting. The Howard legacy looked like a building buffeted by strong winds and we won't know for a while how much of it will stand.

Although he came to power in the 1990s, Howard was in many ways a man not of the 1950s – as his critics asserted – but of the 1980s, when issues of tax, industrial relations (the issue that framed his career) and smaller government were the big debates. By his fourth term, he had completed his old agenda and a new one eluded him. He kept saying he had much left to do, while actually he didn't. Circumstances, his own energy and his passion for politics prevented him from walking away from a career that would have been judged better if it had ended a little earlier.

Kevin Michael Rudd

3 DECEMBER 2007 –

It was clear from the start, indeed from opposition, that Rudd would be hands on in the running of all the important areas of government. He was galvanised by the feeling there was a huge amount to do.

BY MICHELLE GRATTAN

Kevin Rudd's rise to the prime ministership was remarkable. Less than a year after seizing Labor's leadership, he dislodged a government presiding over a strong economy in which unemployment had fallen to its lowest in three decades, defeating a prime minister who, earlier in the parliamentary term, had appeared unassailable. Despite a relatively short time in the Parliament, Rudd started his prime ministerial term with a deep knowledge of how government operates, derived from his years working for former Queensland Labor premier Wayne Goss, including in the state bureaucracy. He is Australia's first 'managerialist' PM, even talking about measuring his ministers' performance against 'benchmarks'. There is also a whiff of the Blairite.

Australia's 26th prime minister was elected on a middle-of-the-road program that included a commitment to an 'education revolution', a new era of co-operative federalism to end the 'blame game', the rollback of the Howard government's harsh industrial relations legislation, a pledge to remove Australia's combat troops from Iraq and a promise to turn Australia from a laggard to a progressive player on climate change, the issue of the decade. His first policy act, on the day he was sworn in, was to begin the process of ratifying the Kyoto Protocol; he then led the delegation to the December Bali climate change conference, where Australia took a significant role in brokering an agreement.

Despite some distinctive initiatives, the 2007 election and the months preceding it had seen much that was dubbed 'me-tooism'. Rudd wanted to join battle on the ground he chose. Labor was also determined not to be 'wedged' by the increasingly desperate Coalition, so it simply adopted slabs of Howard government policy. When Howard announced, for example, after a damning report on child abuse in Northern Territory Aboriginal communities, that the government was taking over responsibility for these, Rudd went along with the plan (and continued it, with some changes, once in power).

By 2007, after more than a decade of Howard, the Australian electorate was clearly wanting a new face. Labor leader Kim Beazley already had the ALP ahead in the polls when Rudd overthrew him in late 2006, although there had been a widespread belief that when it came to the point, voters would not turn to Beazley, whose poor approval ratings showed he was seen as of the past rather than the future. For swinging voters, Rudd had a double attraction: he represented safe change. Here was the prospect of continuity as well as newness – at least continuity in what mattered, economic management and national security. In this he was a contrast to Mark Latham, Labor's leader at the 2004 election, whom the public perceived as too risky.

With less than 12 months as leader to establish himself, Rudd used to the full the authority that a party desperate for office was willing to extend him. One of his boldest moves – in terms of Labor tradition – was to announce that he, rather than caucus or factions, would decide the membership of a Labor ministry. Not since the ALP's first PM, Chris Watson, had a Labor PM had this right, though in practice they had been able to substantially call the tune in recent times.

Kevin Michael Rudd[1] was born on 21 September 1957, youngest of four children. His father, a Country Party member but 'not a particularly active one', – according to Rudd – share farmed a 400-acre dairy property inland from Queensland's Sunshine Coast. Despite the rigours of dairying and earlier hardship, the family was comfortable enough, until tragedy hit when Kevin was 11 years old. His father was seriously injured in a car accident, dying weeks later after contracting septicaemia.

The circumstances and consequences of his father's death dramatically affected the family's position and were still playing out in Rudd's mind in 2007. The family was asked to leave the farm; shuttling between relatives for a time. On at least one night they had nowhere to go and Kevin recalled sleeping in the car. Later Rudd's mother brought her nursing training up to date, found permanent work and their circumstances took a turn for the better.

In 2007 Rudd – whose policies included improvement of hospitals – harked back to the poor medical treatment he believed his father received in the Royal Brisbane Hospital; he also claimed his family had been dealt with harshly by the dairy farm's owner, prompting a sharp rejoinder from the family of the now deceased farmer.

The story line wasn't just for election year. In his 1998 maiden speech Rudd, noting that he had started attending meetings of Young Labor as a school kid, said that when his mother was 'left to rely on the bleak charity of the time to raise a family, it made a young person think'. He talked about the need for a 'decent social security system designed to protect the weak'; recalled seeing people 'unnecessarily die in the appallingly underfunded Queensland hospital system of the 1960s and 1970s'; and said he had thought it 'fundamentally crook' that those he went to school with could not begin to realise their potential because of the abysmally funded school system.

Early on, Rudd came to understand the importance of a good education for his own future. He had become a teenage Sinophile, being fascinated by watching on televison Gough Whitlam in China. As a 15-year-old Nambour High student he wrote to Whitlam, saying he wanted to be a diplomat and asking his advice. Whitlam suggested he acquire a foreign language.

A few years later Rudd was deep into the study of Chinese at the Australian National University, where his teachers were impressed by his diligence and demeanour. Graduating with first class honours (his thesis was on a Chinese dissident) he was accepted into the Foreign Affairs Department, serving in Stockholm and Beijing and regarded by peers and superiors in the department as a man with a glowing future.

Rudd, however, was soon looking to different horizons. In 1988 he saw an advertisement for the position of Chief of Staff to Queensland Opposition Leader Wayne Goss and applied (taking leave of absence from Foreign Affairs). After Goss won in 1989, Rudd initially stayed in the Premier's office, then in 1991 became Director-General of the Cabinet Office. His reputation from these years was for tough (even ruthless) efficiency.[2]

The staffer or top bureaucrat can only be a surrogate politician; Rudd aspired to the real thing. By 1996 he was contesting the federal seat of Griffith, but he couldn't prevail against the anti-Keating swing. Two and a half years later, in the GST election, he won the seat and thereafter honed his local campaigning skills to bed it down, skills that stood him in good stead on hustings around the nation in 2007.

Rudd's vaulting ambition was obvious as soon as he arrived in Canberra, where he immediately became chair of the caucus foreign affairs committee and set his sights on the post of foreign affairs spokesman, then occupied by Laurie Brereton. Relations between the two were tense, with Rudd emerging winner from the undeclared battle. After the 2001 election, Brereton retired to the backbench and Rudd replaced him. Rudd was constantly on the international road, speaking at conferences, visiting trouble spots, meeting world figures and deluging the media. By late 2002 his name was appearing in lists of possible future leadership contenders.

In 2003, Simon Crean's leadership became terminal. When Kim Beazley shaped up for the second of his two challenges that year, Rudd trailed his coat, but this was treated derisively by colleagues and media, and he did not enter the ballot. The Crean forces campaigned frenetically and successfully to get up Latham against Beazley, whom Rudd supported.

Rudd and Latham had had a poisonous relationship, exchanging acrimonious public barbs on various issues. Rudd's talent guaranteed he would continue to rise politically, but Latham as leader would give him no help. Rudd needed experience in a major economic area and after the 2004 defeat, he made a bid to Latham for shadow treasury. Latham wrote in his diary that Rudd 'went into a long explanation of why he's so wonderful. When he finished I put my cards on the table: that I regard him as disloyal and unreliable ... '.[3]

Soon after, Latham imploded, leaving the leadership vacant. Rudd again flirted with running; again he opted out when it was clear he could not win. Beazley made an uncontested return, but Rudd was now regarded by many observers as the natural successor, having by that stage pulled ahead – without even entering a contest – of Julia Gillard, Wayne Swan, Stephen Smith and Lindsay Tanner. A reshuffle by Beazley in mid-2005 added trade to Rudd's responsibilities, after he had declined the domestic job of education. He used this opportunity to make economic speeches; trade would also give him carriage of the attack over AWB's payment of bribes to the Saddam regime to facilitate wheat exports, a rich political lode for Labor.

Although Labor did not claim a ministerial scalp out of AWB, Rudd used the scandal to the full to promote Labor's and his own interests. He fought to ask as many as questions as possible in Parliament. Sometimes the Leader's office had to intervene to ensure the prosecution of the issue was evenly shared between Beazley and Rudd. Rudd's notable attention to detail was reflected in his having a member of his staff sit in on hearings of the commission of inquiry.

Rudd broadened on another front too, writing about his Christian faith and his wider philosophy in major articles for *The Monthly*.[4] In 'Faith in Politics' (Oct 2006), an essay on Dietrich Bonhoeffer, German theologian, pastor and opponent of the Nazis, whom Rudd described as 'the man I admire most in the history of the twentieth century', he argued against 'those who would seek today to traduce Christianity by turning it into the political handmaiden of the conservative political establishment'. This was followed by 'Howard's Brutopia', in which Rudd asserted that Howard's culture war 'is essentially a cover for the real battle of ideas in Australian politics today: the battle between free-market fundamentalism and the social-democratic belief that individual reward can be balanced with social responsibility'. The essay concluded that 'the time has come to restore the balance in Australian politics', a theme that would become central in his election pitch. Meanwhile Rudd did not neglect the populist touch. He countered his 'nerdy' image by taking on a weekly spot on Channel 7's *Sunrise*, sparring with minister Joe Hockey.

Rudd could not afford to appear disloyal to Beazley, but he had to be prepared to strike if opportunity presented. He became more actively engaged with the caucus and cultivated powerful organisational figures, notably NSW ALP general secretary Mark Arbib. During 2006, Beazley was on notice. The stakes were high - another Labor election loss would entrench Howard's pro-employer WorkChoices, which could draw the last teeth of the union movement.

A change would not be possible without Rudd, from the right, and Julia Gillard, a leftwinger and also a leadership aspirant, sinking previous differences and joining forces. By the latter half of 2006 this alliance was in place, facilitated by the Crean forces - who had a raft of old and new gripes against Beazley - and the Arbib influence.

A trivial mistake was the catalyst for all the reservations about Beazley to burst out. Expressing sympathy to entertainer Rove McManus on the day of his wife's funeral, Beazley misspoke (without even realising he had done so), saying 'Karl Rove', the name of George Bush Jr's controversial political adviser. The slip sparked a wave of doubt that would sweep away Beazley's leadership. Rudd challenged on 4 December, winning 49–39; Gillard became deputy unopposed.

Rudd's rise had been spectacular; it had taken him well under a decade to become Opposition leader. This was even more remarkable considering that he had no factional base to speak of - he came from the so-called Queensland 'old guard', a small grouping of the right. In his run for leadership, he had skilfully managed to knit together support from those who were longstanding enemies of Beazley and those Beazley supporters who had come to despair of him. In the earlier parliamentary years many inside and outside Labor ranks had under-estimated Rudd, though acknowledging his intellectual abilities. Some now could not quite believe how fast he adapted to the job. As Opposition leader he had a carefully calibrated strategy to out-manoeuvre the government, involving pre-empting its moves, occupying its territory, avoiding the traps it set and brandmarking distinctive areas.

Rudd moved his party further into the centre than ever before and courted the support of those who had become the 'Howard battlers'. Most of his policies – including trades training centres, improvement of hospitals, early childhood education, child care, housing affordability and even broadband rollout – were aimed at 'working families', whose needs became his mantra.

It quickly became clear that Rudd was tactically fast and astute, constantly wrong-footing Howard on everything from water to welfare. Rudd assembled a climate-change summit, with a video message from the American climate-change campaigner, former U.S. vice president Al Gore. He injected himself into the Sydney Asia-Pacific Economic Co-operation forum (APEC), with a disarming meeting with President Bush and a chat in Mandarin with China's President Hu Jintao. When Howard delayed calling the election, Rudd staged his own 'launch', with all the trappings.

Rudd said of Howard in February 2007, 'I think it will be fun to play with his mind for a while'.[5] The comment smacked of arrogance, but that is exactly what the tyro leader did through 2007. In a stroke of political genius Labor announced that the popular former ABC presenter Maxine McKew would run in Howard's marginal seat of Bennelong, thus tying the PM down on his home turf to an unprecedented extent.[6]

Although winning 16 seats was always going to be difficult and Rudd constantly referred to Howard as 'a clever politician', he was personally confident. Talking to a biographer in 2007, Rudd drew a parallel with Queensland where Labor had faced a 'very tough' fight. The lesson was that 'so long as you've got a band of committed warriors, you can pull anything off'.[7]

The Rudd operation wasn't without hiccups. There was criticism of his earlier contacts with lobbyist and disgraced former West Australian premier Brian Burke; a kerfuffle about his knowledge of plans a television station had to involve him in a fake 'dawn service'; the controversy over his claims about his childhood; revelations of a drunken night at a New York stripclub; a fuss about his wife Therese Rein's large employment business. He had to deal with some outspoken militant unionists and with business angst over Labor's industrial relations policy. Nothing much affected the opinion polls. Labor remained high all year; Rudd's approval set a record for an Opposition leader and he settled in as preferred PM.

By the start of the campaign proper for the 24 November election, it was Rudd's to lose, although Labor remained nervous, because of the number of seats it needed and Howard's reputation. Howard, however, campaigned badly and Rudd well. Labor was caught off guard when the government announced its $34 billion tax package the day after calling the election, but quickly recovered, taking over most of the package (while diverting a portion to a popular policy to give a tax rebate for home computers and a range of school expenses). Rudd outshone Howard in the Debate and outflanked him when Labor's launch dramatically underspent the government's launch, showcasing Rudd as a 'fiscal conservative'.

There was the occasional glitch in the Labor campaign – most notably loose words by environment spokesman Peter Garrett – but errors were few and luck was with Labor, including an unprecedented interest rate rise during the campaign. Labor won with 43.4 per cent of the primary vote and a two-party preferred margin of 52.7–47.3 per cent. Its majority in the House of Representatives was 16. In the Senate the Coalition also lost its majority from 1 July, 2008, but the Labor government would need support from all the minor players to pass bills that the Coalition opposed.

Rudd's 30-member ministry (20 of them in Cabinet) saw Australia's first female deputy prime minister and included seven women (four in Cabinet). The best and brightest of the new Labor MPs, including former union heavyweights Greg Combet and Bill Shorten, and McKew – who had done the unthinkable and unseated Howard – were given parliamentary secretaryships. The average age of the ministers and parliamentary secretaries was 48. Rudd moved into the Lodge, reverting to normal residential practice for PMs. The new government said it would sit five-day parliamentary weeks, rather than its predecessor's four.

It was clear from the start, indeed from opposition, that Rudd would be hands on in the running of all the important areas of government.

He was galvanised by the feeling there was a huge amount to do. 'He's 24/7 – he goes and goes', said one adviser. Rudd watched over the work of his ministers like a diligent headmaster. He had one-on-ones with them, setting priorities and imposed what Finance Minister Lindsay Tanner dubbed 'time discipline' – projects were to have deadlines attached. Rudd's style, Tanner observed, 'is generating a ripple effect' across the government. Rudd's response to a question about holidays for his team – that ministers would have Christmas and Boxing Day off – might have been light-hearted, but only up to a point. The government started at a cracking pace, including a pre-Christmas meeting of the Council of Australian Governments to get action underway in many policy areas. Rudd proclaimed: 'We intend to turn COAG into the workhorse of the nation'.

The economy loomed as the overarching issue of the government's early days. Australia suddenly was caught between unacceptably high domestic inflation and a deteriorating United States economy, which had the potential for serious flow-on effects to the rest of the world. The December quarter figures showed underlying inflation running well above the Reserve Bank's 2–3 per cent target band. The bank raised rates early in 2008.

The government talked up the prospect of a tough budget. In the campaign it had announced $10 billion in cuts – much of it offset by spending initiatives; it now flagged several billion more when, in anticipation of the bad inflation figure, it committed to a surplus for 2008-09 of at least 1.5 per cent of GDP. Rudd warned that 'the biggest economic challenge facing the Australian government today is inflation', on which it had declared 'war'. The war would be fought on the fiscal side with a significant tightening and on the supply side by initiatives to tackle the skills shortage and improve the nation's infrastructure.

The government appealed to employers, workers and unions to exercise restraint, while hoping the decentralised wage system would contain wage pressure. Rudd had the politicians set an example by imposing a freeze on their pay. Labor colleagues were dismayed, in some cases annoyed, but acquiescent. The unions made it clear they did not want their constituents to be the fall guys in the belt tightening. Despite the extensive and expensive union campaign that had been a major contributor to Labor's victory, the union movement had still to clearly define its relationship with the new PM. He was not a union man.

Winding back WorkChoices was a top priority, with initial legislation introduced as soon as Parliament met in February. The first legislative task was to ban new Australian Workplace Agreements (statutory individual contracts) - existing AWAs would be allowed to run their course. There would also be a new transitional statutory contract, with strict conditions, to ease the employers' pain of leaving behind AWAs. Legislation for the rest of the changes would follow after further consultations. While unravelling much of WorkChoices, Labor's model would retain a central feature of it - a single national system.

Rudd began early on his 'education revolution' and health initiatives. His first Cabinet meeting considered a submission on an election promise to provide senior secondary students with access to their own computer at school. Before the election, Labor had said that it would inject $2 billion into the states' health care and hospital systems. In return state governments would have to bring in reforms. If they did not perform by mid-2009, Canberra would seek public support to take over the state systems. One of the early tasks of the new government was to negotiate a new long-term hospital-funding agreement with the states.

Removing the combat troops from Iraq was a key pledge, but Rudd - who was strongly committed to the American alliance - had promised to move slowly; the troops would come out in mid-2008. The Bush administration, which in 2004 had been sharply critical of Labor's Iraq withdrawal commitment, seemed unfazed by the Rudd government's plan. Circumstances were different: Bush was coming to the end of his term, the American political climate had changed and Rudd, unlike Latham, was known to be vigorously pro-American.

On the other hand, Labor had backed fully Australia's troop involvement in Afghanistan and the new government took up with vigour the cause of urging NATO countries to pull their weight to a greater extent. Rudd visited the diggers in East Timor, Iraq and Afghanistan in his first month in office. Labor, before the election, had made it clear that defence spending would not be cut, though efficiencies would be sought within it.

For a new prime minister, Rudd was very well placed to juggle the relationships with the two great powers: America and China. He arrived in power with a better knowledge of China than any previous prime minister (not withstanding Whitlam and his path-breaking policy.).

Rudd was not only sympathetic to the U.S. but - in part through his regular participation in the Australian-American leadership dialogue, an unofficial regular meeting attended by, among many others, government figures from both countries - he had an extensive American network.

The first foreign affairs issue the government faced had a touch of the bizarre, when two anti-whaling activists boarded a Japanese vessel in the Southern Ocean. The government had announced its strong opposition to Japanese whaling and was sending an Australian Customs observational vessel to collect information for possible international legal action. It had not anticipated the awkward incident in which the Customs ship ***Oceanic Viking*** – after discussions between the two governments – had to facilitate the transfer of the protesters back to their vessel.

On a more predictable front, the new government differentiated itself from its predecessor by abandoning the recently-decided Howard policy to allow Australian uranium exports to India, which was not a signatory to the nuclear non-proliferation treaty.

An attack by rebels on the East Timorese leadership that severely injured President Jose Ramos-Horta brought a comprehensive and quick response from Rudd. Australian military and police forces in East Timor were boosted and Rudd flew to Dili to show solidarity with the embattled government.

Fulfilling election promises, big and small, was to be a theme of the early Rudd months. He made it clear that these undertakings, including the tax cuts, were to be sacrosanct.

Despite the me-tooism during the campaign, the new government immediately started to differentiate itself from its predecessor in style and symbolism as well as policy. Rudd started 'community cabinets' (the first in Perth in January 2008) – meetings where people could ask questions of him and his ministers and make appointments to see individuals. It was planned to hold these about monthly, with departmental heads travelling with the ministerial entourage. He committed to take his cabinet to a NT Aboriginal community. On a grander scale, Rudd announced an Australia 2020 Summit to gather a thousand of the best and brightest minds to discuss the long-term future of almost every aspect of the nation.

Labor scrapped Howard's advisory National Indigenous Council, but promised not to return to a model like the old elected and shambolic Aboriginal and Torres Strait Islander Commission. An apology to the stolen generations was made a top priority for Parliament's first week, together with a 'Welcome to Country' ceremony. The long overdue 'Sorry' won Rudd great praise; his speech was well crafted and contained a proposal that he and opposition leader Brendan Nelson head a new bipartisan commission to look at indigenous housing and later, if that was successful, other matters. The move for bipartisanship was politically savvy, and Rudd's deft and dignified handling of the apology had commentators seeing a new side to him. The government insisted, however, that the apology was not to be accompanied by a compensation fund.

Also on the social front, changes were flagged to the questions in the controversial citizenship test to make it easier for refugees unfamiliar with Australian culture, but the test itself was to stay. Contracts with the not-for-profit sector that allegedly gagged critics were to be rewritten. The new government was also committed to changing the electoral laws to make political donations more transparent (after its predecessor had greatly increased the amount that could be donated without disclosure) and it promised a revamp of the freedom of information law.

The signs during his first 100 days, as parts of the Howard legacy began to crumble, were that Rudd would bring major change to Australia – but with caution. He was galvanised by the need for his government to be economically responsible, because on that rested his ability to do everything else. His priorities and modus operandi, however, were very different from those of his predecessor.

The new PM was heavily influenced by his early years, his faith and his Queensland experience. From his youth came his passion for education – he said often in the campaign that he wanted to be Australia's 'education prime minister'. His sense of social justice and community was rooted in both his childhood privations and his religion (his mother's Catholicism morphed into his Anglicanism, but he liked to be agnostic as far as denomination was concerned). One Labor man says: 'His most defining characteristic is his progressive Christianity'. His years as a bureaucrat were obvious in his approach to government with an observer noting that he has 'the notion of a highly professional public service able to drive policy', which in turn can be driven by him.

In April 2007, biographer Nicholas Stuart said Rudd was 'a mystery wrapped inside an enigma – the further you go, the more questions you end up with'.

In his early days of office, there was still a note of mystery about Australia's current prime minister who, it can be argued, came to power as the least known of the country's post war national leaders, but there were also distinctive signposts to how he would operate and what drove him.

Unlike the Howard government in 1996, Rudd did not slice through Canberra's top mandarins – a victory for orderly process, continuity and trust. On his first Boxing Day as PM, Rudd, without media fanfare, served up bacon and eggs to homeless people at a centre in Canberra – a pointer to his values.

Rudd himself flatly rejects the 'enigma' theory of his personality. In interviews to mark the first 100 days following the election victory, he emphasised the importance he placed on keeping trust with the Australian people (hence it was vital to fulfil election promises), and his government's openness to ideas (even from the Opposition). 'What you see with me is what you get,' he said.

In the Prime Ministerial Parliament House office, the Chesterfield club suite and Menzies' desk – that Howard had installed – were removed. On the wall hung a framed picture of Chinese characters, which read, 'Unfurl the flag and move forward to victory'.

A new political era had been proclaimed.

Prime Ministers

PRIME MINISTER	STATE	PARTY	ENTERED OFFICE	LEFT OFFICE
Edmund Barton	NSW	Prot	01 Jan 01	24 Sep 03
Alfred Deakin	Vic	Prot	24 Sep 03	27 Apr 04
John Christian Watson	NSW	ALP	27 Apr 04	17 Aug 04
George Reid	NSW	FT	18 Aug 04	05 Jul 05
Alfred Deakin	Vic	Prot	05 Jul 05	13 Nov 08
Andrew Fisher	Qld	ALP	13 Nov 08	01 Jun 09
Alfred Deakin	Vic	Lib	02 Jun 09	29 Apr 10
Andrew Fisher	Qld	ALP	29 Apr 10	24 Jun 13
Joseph Cook	NSW	Lib	24 Jun 13	17 Sep 14
Andrew Fisher	Qld	ALP	17 Sep 14	27 Oct 15
William Morris Hughes	NSW	ALP	27 Oct 15	14 Nov 16
William Morris Hughes	NSW	NL	14 Nov 16	17 Feb 17
William Morris Hughes	NSW/Vic[d]	Nat	17 Feb 17	09 Feb 23
Stanley Melbourne Bruce	Vic	Nat[b]	09 Feb 23	22 Oct 29
James Henry Scullin	Vic	ALP	22 Oct 29	06 Jan 32
Joseph Aloysius Lyons	Tas	UAP	06 Jan 32	09 Nov 34
Joseph Aloysius Lyons[a]	Tas	UAP[b]	09 Nov 34	07 Apr 39
Earle Page	NSW	CP[b]	07 Apr 39	26 Apr 39
Robert Gordon Menzies	Vic	UAP	26 Apr 39	14 Mar 40
Robert Gordon Menzies	Vic	UAP[b]	14 Mar 40	29 Aug 41
Arthur Fadden	Qld	CP[b]	29 Aug 41	07 Oct 41
John Curtin[a]	WA	ALP	07 Oct 41	05 Jul 45
Francis Michael Forde	Qld	ALP	06 Jul 45	13 Jul 45
Joseph Benedict Chifley	NSW	ALP	13 Jul 45	19 Dec 49
Robert Gordon Menzies	Vic	Lib[b]	19 Dec 49	26 Jan 66
Harold Edward Holt[a]	Vic	Lib[b]	26 Jan 66	19 Dec 67
John McEwen	Vic	CP[b]	19 Dec 67	10 Jan 68
John Grey Gorton	Vic	Lib[b]	10 Jan 68	10 Mar 71
William McMahon	NSW	Lib[b]	10 Mar 71	05 Dec 72
Edward Gough Whitlam	NSW	ALP	05 Dec 72	11 Nov 75
John Malcolm Fraser	Vic	Lib[b]	11 Nov 75	11 Mar 83
Robert James Hawke	Vic	ALP	11 Mar 83	19 Dec 91
Paul John Keating	NSW	ALP	20 Dec 91	11 Mar 96
John Winston Howard	NSW	Lib[c]	11 Mar 96	03 Dec 07
Kevin Michael Rudd	Qld	ALP	03 Dec 07	

a Died in office
b Coalition government of major non-Labor party (Nat, UAP, Lib) and the Country Party.
c Coalition government of major non-Labor party (Nat, Lib).
d Prior to his defection from Labor Hughes represented West Sydney (NSW) in the House of Representatives. However, at the May 1917 election he moved to Bendigo (Vic). At the December 1922 election he moved seat again, to North Sydney (NSW).

This table is from *Australian Political Facts*, I. McAllister, M. Mackerras, C. Brown Boldiston, Macmillan Education Australia Pty Ltd, Melbourne, 2nd edition, 1997, p. 8. Reproduced by permission of Macmillan Education Australia. Please note that dates of the terms in office may vary depending on the source of information.

Length of Service of Former Prime Ministers

Name	Term	Y	M	D
Menzies	1949-66	16	1	8
Howard	1996-2007	11	8	22
Hawke	1983-91	8	9	8
Fraser	1975-83	7	4	
Hughes	1915-23	7	3	14
Lyons	1932-39	7	3	2
Bruce	1923-29	6	8	14
Chifley	1945-49	4	5	7
Keating	1991-96	4	2	24
Curtin	1941-45	3	8	29
Deakin	1905-08	3	4	9
Gorton	1968-71	3	2	
Fisher	1910-13	3	1	26
Whitlam	1972-75	2	11	7
Barton	1901-03	2	8	24
Menzies	1939-41	2	4	4
Scullin	1929-32	2	2	16
Holt	1966-67	1	10	23
McMahon	1971-72	1	8	25
Cook	1913-14	1	2	25
Fisher	1914-15	1	1	11
Deakin	1909-10		10	28
Reid	1904-05		10	18
Deakin	1903-04		7	14
Fisher	1908-09		6	21
Watson	1904		3	21
Fadden	1941		1	9
McEwen	1967-68			23
Page	1939			20
Forde	1945			8

Parties in Government

Party/Parties	Entered office	Left office
Prot	01 Jan 01	27 Apr 04
Labor	27 Apr 04	17 Aug 04
FT-Prot[a]	18 Aug 04	05 Jul 05
Prot	05 Jul 05	13 Nov 08
Lab	13 Nov 08	01 Jun 09
Lib	02 Jun 09	29 Apr 10
Lab	29 Apr 10	24 Jun 13
Lib	24 Jun 13	17 Sep 14
Lab	17 Sep 14	14 Nov 16
National Lab	14 Nov 16	17 Feb 17
Nat	17 Feb 17	09 Feb 23
Nat-CP[a]	09 Feb 23	22 Oct 29
Lab	22 Oct 29	06 Jan 32
UAP	06 Jan 32	09 Nov 34
UAP-CP[a]	09 Nov 34	26 Apr 39
UAP	26 Apr 39	14 Mar 40
UAP-CP[a]	14 Mar 40	07 Oct 41
Lab	07 Oct 41	19 Dec 49
Lib-CP[a]	19 Dec 49	05 Dec 72
Lab	05 Dec 72	11 Nov 75
Lib-CP[a]	11 Nov 75	11 Mar 83
Lab	11 Mar 83	11 Mar 96
Lib-Nat[a]	11 Mar 96	03 Dec 07
Lab	03 Dec 07	

a Coalition

These tables are from *Australian Political Facts*, I. McAllister, M. Mackerras, C. Brown Boldiston, Macmillan Education Australia Pty Ltd, Melbourne, 2nd edition, 1997, p. 9. Reproduced by permission of Macmillan Education Australia.

Name	Birth/place	Father's Occupation	Education	Occupation	Religion	Date and age became PM	Date left office and reason
BARTON	18 January 1849 Glebe, Sydney	Accountant/ stockbroker	Fort Street/Sydney Grammar School; University of Sydney	Lawyer	Church of England	1 January 1901 51 years	24 September 1903 Resigned to become a judge of the High Court
DEAKIN	3 August 1856 Collingwood, Melbourne	Various; later manager of Cobb & Co.	Melbourne Grammar; University of Melbourne	Lawyer, journalist	Church of England/Deist	24 September 1903 47 years	27 April 1904 Resigned after legislation defeated in Parliament
						5 July 1905	13 November 1908 Withdrawal of Labor support
						2 June 1909	29 April 1910 Lost election
WATSON	9 April 1867 Valparaiso, Chile	Ship's officer	State school, Oamaru, NZ (until aged 10)	Compositor, trade unionist	Unitarian	27 April 1904 37 years	18 August 1904 Resigned after legislative defeat in Parliament
REID	25 February 1845 Johnstone, Renfrewshire, Scotland	Presbyterian minister	Scotch College, Melbourne (until aged 13); night study	Public servant, lawyer	Presbyterian	18 August 1904 59 years	5 July 1905 Resigned after defeat in Parliament
FISHER	29 August 1862 Crosshouse, Ayrshire, Scotland	Coalminer	Primary school, Crosshouse (until aged about 10 or 12); night study	Coalminer, trade unionist	Presbyterian	13 November 1908 46 years	2 June 1909 Defeated in Parliament
						29 April 1910	24 June 1913 Lost election
						17 September 1914	27 October 1915 Resigned in poor health, to become High Commissioner in London
COOK	7 December 1860 Silverdale, Staffordshire, England	Coalminer	St Luke's Church of England School (until aged about 9); home study	Coalminer, trade unionist, bookkeeper	Methodist	24 June 1913 52 years	17 September 1914 Lost election

Name	Birth/place	Father's Occupation	Education	Occupation	Religion	Date and age became PM	Date left office and reason
HUGHES	25 September 1862 Pimlico, London	Carpenter	Primary school, Llandudno, North Wales; St Stephen's School, Westminster, London	Various: teacher, store-keeper, trade unionist (he also gained legal qualifications while in Parliament)	Baptist	27 October 1915 53 years	9 February 1923 Resigned after Country Party vetoed his leadership
BRUCE	15 April 1883 St Kilda, Melbourne	Owner of a large import company	Melbourne Grammar; Cambridge University	Businessman, lawyer	Church of England	9 February 1923 39 years	22 October 1929 Lost election
SCULLIN	18 September 1876 Trawalla, Victoria	Railway worker	State schools at Trawalla and Mount Rowan; night school, Ballarat	Grocer, trade unionist, editor	Catholic	22 October 1929 53 years	6 January 1932 Lost election
LYONS	15 September 1879 Stanley, Tasmania	Various, including hotelkeeper	St Joseph's, Ulverstone; Stanley State School; Tasmanian Teachers' Training College	Teacher	Catholic	6 January 1932 52 years	7 April 1939 Died in office
PAGE	8 August 1880 Grafton, NSW	Blacksmith, coachbuilder	Grafton Public School; Sydney Boys' High School; University of Sydney	Surgeon, businessman	Methodist	7 April 1939 58 years	26 April 1939 Caretaker
MENZIES	20 December 1894 Jeparit, Victoria	Storekeeper	State school, Ballarat; Grenville College, Ballarat; Wesley College, Melbourne; University of Melbourne	Lawyer	Presbyterian	26 April 1939 44 years 19 December 1949	29 August 1941 Resigned after loss of party support 26 January 1966 Retired
FADDEN	13 April 1895 Ingham, Queensland	Policeman	State school, Walkerston; correspondence	Accountant	Presbyterian	29 August 1941 46 years	7 October 1941 Resigned after defeat in Parliament

Name	Birth/place	Father's Occupation	Education	Occupation	Religion	Date and age became PM	Date left office and reason
CURTIN	8 January 1885 Creswick, Victoria	Policeman, publican	Various Catholic and state schools in Melbourne and Victoria (until aged 13)	Journalist, trade unionist	Catholic/ agnostic	7 October 1941 56 years	5 July 1945 Died in office
FORDE	18 July 1890 Mitchell, Queensland	Railway foreman	State primary school; Christian Brothers' College, Toowoomba	Teacher, clerk, telegraphist, technician	Catholic	6 July 1945 54 years	13 July 1945 Caretaker
CHIFLEY	22 September 1885 Bathurst, NSW	Blacksmith	Limekilns School; St Patrick's School, Bathurst (until aged 15 years); night classes	Locomotive engine driver, trade unionist	Catholic	13 July 1945 59 years	19 December 1949 Lost election
HOLT	5 August 1908 Stanmore, Sydney	Theatrical entrepreneur	State primary school, Sydney: Wesley College, Melbourne; University of Melbourne	Lawyer	Protestant	26 January 1966 57 years	19 December 1967 Died in office
MCEWEN	29 March 1900 Chiltern, Victoria	Pharmacist	State schools, Wangaratta and Dandenong (until aged 13); night classes	Public servant, farmer	Presbyterian	19 December 1967 67 years	10 January 1968 Caretaker
GORTON	9 September 1911 Melbourne	Orchard owner	Sydney Church of England Grammar School (Shore); Geelong Grammar; Oxford University	Orchardist, pilot	Agnostic	10 January 1968 56 years	10 March 1971 Surrendered leadership after party-room coup

Name	Birth/place	Father's Occupation	Education	Occupation	Religion	Date and age became PM	Date left office and reason
MCMAHON	23 February 1908 Sydney	Lawyer	Sydney Grammar School; University of Sydney	Lawyer	Church of England	10 March 1971 63 years	5 December 1972 Lost election
WHITLAM	11 July 1916 Melbourne	Lawyer	Knox Grammar, Sydney; Canberra Grammar; University of Sydney	Lawyer	Anglican/ agnostic	5 December 1972 56 years	11 November 1975 Dismissed by Governor-General
FRASER	21 May 1930 Melbourne	Grazier	Melbourne Grammar; Oxford University	Grazier	Presbyterian	11 November 1975 45 years	11 March 1983 Lost election
HAWKE	9 December 1929 Bordertown, SA	Congregational minister	Perth Modern School; University of WA; Oxford University	Trade unionist (he also qualified as a lawyer)	Agnostic	11 March 1983 53 years	20 December 1991 Defeated in party room
KEATING	18 January 1944 Sydney	Boilermaker/ welding inspector; part-owner of concrete-mixer busines	De La Salle College; Belmore and Sydney technical colleges (until aged 14); night school	Council clerk	Catholic	20 December 1991 47 years	11 March 1996 Lost election
HOWARD	26 July 1939 Earlwood, Sydney	Service-station owner	Canterbury Boys' High School; University of Sydney	Lawyer	Anglican (raised as a Methodist)	11 March 1996 56 years	03 December 2007 Lost election
RUDD	21 September 1957 Nambour Queensland	dairy share farmer	Eumundi Primary; Marist Brothers College, Brisbane; Nambour High School; Australian National University	Diplomat Public servant	Anglican (raised as a Catholic)	03 December 2007 50 years	

The dates of the terms in office for pages 467-470 have been sourced from the Department of the Parliamentary Library, *Parliamentary Handbook of the Commonwealth of Australia*, 28th edition, 1999.

Footnotes & Bibliography

Introduction

Footnotes

1. Solomon Encel, *Cabinet Government in Australia*, Melbourne University Press, Melbourne, 1974, p. 165

2. Walter Murdoch, *Alfred Deakin*, Bookman Press, Melbourne, 1999, p. 194

3. N. Meaney, *The Search for Security in the Pacific 1901-14*, Sydney University Press, Sydney, 1981, p. 206 as quoted in G. Bebbington, *Pit Boy to Prime Minister*, University of Keele, Staffordshire, 1986, p. 35

4. Deakin, as quoted in John Andrew La Nauze, *Alfred Deakin: A Biography*, Melbourne University Press, Melbourne, 1965, p. 355

5. Donald Horne, *Billy Hughes*, Black Ink, Melbourne, 2000, p. 139

6. John Robertson, *J.H. Scullin: A Political Biography*, University of Western Australia Press, Nedlands, 1974, p. 402

7. Exchange quoted in Gough Whitlam, *The Whitlam Government, 1972-1975*, Viking/Penguin, Victoria, 1985, p. 13

8. Menzies served as PM from: 26 April 1939 - 29 August 1941; 19 December 1949 – 26 January 1966.

9. John Edwards, *Keating: The Inside Story*, Viking Penguin, Ringwood, Victoria, 1996, p. 515

10. Forde, 6 July 1945 – 13 July 1945; Page, 7 April 1939 – 26 April 1939; McEwen, 19 December 1967 – 10 January 1968

11. The Lodge was built as the PM's residence and Bruce was the first to live there when Parliament moved to Canberra in 1927. Scullin lived at the Hotel Canberra to save public expense. Chifley lived at the Kurrajong. Howard lives at Kiribilli, staying at the Lodge when in Canberra

12. Watson served as PM from 27 April 1904 – 17 August 1904

13. Barton, Deakin, Watson, Reid and Fisher variously served as prime minister during the first decade of Federation

14. Deakin served as PM for 3 non-consecutive terms: 24 September 1903 - 27 April 1904; 5 July 1905 - 13 November 1908; 2 June 1909 - 29 April 1910

15. Fisher served as PM for 3 non-consecutive terms: 13 November 1908 - 2 June 1909; 29 April 1910 - 24 June 1913; 17 September 1914 - 27 October 1915

16. Horne, *op. cit.*, p. 182

17. Much of the background information about the nation's leaders as it appears in the following few paragraphs is taken from Joanne Holliman, *Century of Australian Prime Ministers*, Murray David Publishing Pty Ltd, NSW, 1999

18. Watson was born in Valparaíso, Chile on 9 April 1867

19. While Hawke was born in South Australia in 1929, his family settled in WA in 1939

20. L. F. Crisp, *Ben Chifley: A Biography*, Longmans, Victoria, 1963, pp. 11-12

21. Hawke's father was a Congregationalist minister and his mother was also deeply religious. It was due to this connection to the church that Hawke's family relocated so often during his early years

22. Bebbington, *op. cit.*, p. 10

23. Crisp, *op. cit.*, p. 3

24. A study of British prime ministers found a frequently occurring characteristic was the loss of a parent in child-

hood or early adolescence. See Lucille Iremonger, *The Fiery Chariot: A Study of British Prime Ministers and the Search for Love*, Secker & Warburg, London, 1970

25. Warren Denning, *Caucus Crisis: The Rise and Fall of the Scullin Government*, Hale & Iremonger, Sydney, 1982, p. 24

26. Curtin, as quoted in David Day, *John Curtin: A Life*, HarperCollins Publishers, Sydney, 1999, p. 523

27. *Ibid.*, p. 525

28. Patrick Weller, *Malcolm Fraser PM: A Study in Prime Ministerial Power in Australia*, Penguin Books, Victoria, 1989, p. 3

29. Personal conversation

30. The Prime Minister's Department was officially established in 1911. See Department of the Prime Minister & Cabinet, 'History of the Department of the Prime Minister and Cabinet', *Annual Report 1978-79*, AGPS, Canberra, 1979, p. 32

31. *Parliamentary Debates* (Representatives), 12 June 1901, vol. 1, p. 985, as quoted in Dept of PM & C, 'History of the Dept of PM & C', pp. 29-30

32. Reported in the *Sun News Pictorial*, 26 October 1923, as quoted in Dept of PM & C, 'History of the Dept of PM & C', p. 32

33. Clem Lloyd, 'Prime Ministers and the Media', in Patrick Weller (ed), *Menzies to Keating: The Development of the Australian Prime Ministership*, Melbourne University Press, Melbourne, 1992, p. 109

34. Gorton, as cited in Lloyd, *ibid.*, p. 124

35. John Bunting, *R. G. Menzie:. A Portrait*, Allen & Unwin, Sydney, 1988, p. 22

36. *Ibid.*, p. 21

37. Dept of PM & C, 'Development of Cabinet Procedures', *Annual Report 1984*, AGPS, Canberra, 1985, p. 6 as cited in Weller, *Menzies to Keating, op. cit.*, p.19

38. Dept of PM & C, 'History of the Dept of PM & C', p. 35

39. *Ibid.*, p. 36

40. Bunting, *op. cit.*, p. 90

41. James Walter, *The Leader: A political biography of Gough Whitlam*, University of Queensland Press, St Lucia, 1980, p. 54

42. *Ibid.*, p. 53

43. Edwards, *op. cit.*, p. 466

44. *Ibid.*, p. 466

45. Encel, *op. cit.*, p. 166

46. Address by the Right Honourable Sir John Gorton GCMG AC CH, 'Prime Ministers on Prime Ministers Lecture Series', Old Parliament House, Canberra, 12 November 1997

Bibliography

Bebbington, G., *Pit Boy to Prime Minister*, University of Keele, Staffordshire, 1986

Bunting, John, *R. G. Menzies: A Portrait*, Allen & Unwin, Sydney, 1988

Crisp, L. F., *Ben Chifley: A Biography*, Longmans, Victoria, 1963

Day, David, *John Curtin: A Life*, HarperCollins Publishers, Sydney, 1999

Denning, Warren, *Caucus Crisis: The Rise and Fall of the Scullin Government*, Hale & Iremonger, Sydney, 1982

Department of the Prime Minister & Cabinet, 'History of the Department of the Prime Minister and Cabinet', *Annual Report 1978-79*, AGPS, Canberra, 1979

Edwards, John, *Keating: The Inside Story*, Viking/Penguin, Victoria, 1996

Encel, Solomon, *Cabinet Government in Australia*, Melbourne University Press, Melbourne, 1974

Holliman, Joanne, *Century of Australian Prime Ministers*, Murray David Publishing Pty Ltd, NSW, 1999

Horne, Donald, *Billy Hughes*, Black Ink, Melbourne, 2000

Iremonger, Lucille, *The Fiery Chariot: A Study of British Prime Ministers and the*

Search for Love, Secker & Warburg, London, 1970

La Nauze, John Andrew, *Alfred Deakin: A Biography*, Melbourne University Press, Melbourne, 1965

Lloyd, Clem, 'Prime Ministers and the Media', in Patrick Weller (ed), *Menzies to Keating: The Development of the Australian Prime Ministership*, Melbourne University Press, Melbourne, 1992

Murdoch, Walter, *Alfred Deakin*, Bookman Press, Melbourne, 1999

Robertson, John, *J. H. Scullin: A Political Biography*, University of Western Australia Press, Nedlands, 1974

Walter, James, *The Leader: A political biography of Gough Whitlam*, University of Queensland Press, St Lucia, 1980

Weller, Patrick (ed.), *Menzies to Keating: The Development of the Australian Prime Ministership*, Melbourne University Press, Melbourne, 1992

Weller, Patrick, *Malcolm Fraser PM: A Study in Prime Ministerial Power in Australia*, Penguin Books, Victoria, 1989

Whitlam, Gough, *The Whitlam Government, 1972–1975*, Viking/Penguin, Victoria, 1985

Sir Edmund Barton

Further Reading

Bolton, G., *Edmund Barton: The One Man for the Job*, Sydney, 2000

Deakin A., *'And Be One People': Alfred Deakin's Federal Story*, Stuart Macintyre (introd.), Melbourne University Press, Melbourne, 1995

Irving. H., ed., *The Centenary Companion to Australian Federation*, Cambridge 1999

Reynolds, J., *Edmund Barton*, Sydney 1948

Alfred Deakin

Footnotes

1. J.A. La Nauze, *Alfred Deakin: A Biography*, Melbourne University Press, Melbourne, 1965, vol. 2, p. 572
2. *Ibid.*, p. 566
3. *Ibid.*, p. 575
4. *Ibid.*
5. *Ibid.*, pp. 60–7, 609.
6. Al Gabay, *The Mystic Life of Alfred Deakin*, Cambridge University Press, Cambridge, 1992, p. 66
7. Paul Kelly, *The End of Certainty: The Story of the 1980s*, Allen and Unwin, St Leonards, NSW, 1992, p. 1
8. Stuart Macintyre, *A Colonial Liberalism: The Lost World of Three Victorian Visionaries*, Oxford University Press, Melbourne, 1991, p. 6
9. J. A. La Nauze, *Alfred Deakin*, vol. 1, p. 40
10. *Ibid.*, p. 52
11. Macintyre, *A Colonial Liberalism*, pp. 185–6
12. Deakin, A., *'And Be One People': Alfred Deakin's Federal Story*, Stuart Macintyre (introd.), Melbourne University Press, Melbourne, 1995, p. 72
13. *Alfred Deakin, Federated Australia: Selections from Letters to the Morning Post 1900–1910*, ed. J.A. La Nauze (ed), Melbourne University Press, Melbourne, 1968, p. 19
14. La Nauze, *Alfred Deakin*, vol. 1, p. 323
15. *Ibid.*, vol. 1, p. 42
16. *Ibid.*, vol. 2, p. 378
17. Colin White, *Mastering Risk: Environment, Markets and Politics in Australian Economic History*, Oxford University Press, Melbourne, 1992, pp. 223, 231, and Kelly, *op. cit.*, pp. 1, 13
18. Walter Murdoch, *Alfred Deakin, A Sketch*, Constable, London, 1923, pp. 174–5

19. La Nauze, *Alfred Deakin*, vol. 2, p. 598

20. Deakin's message appeared in the *Age* on 19 December 1917 and is quoted in Ernest Scott, *Australia During the War*, Angus & Robertson, Sydney, 1936, p. 426

Further Reading

Birrell, Robert, *A Nation of Our Own: Citizenship and Nation-Building in Federation Australia*, Longman, Melbourne, 1995

Deakin, Alfred, *Federated Australia: Selections from Letters to the Morning Post 1900–1910*, J. A. La Nauze (ed), Melbourne University Press, Melbourne, 1968

Gabay, Al, *The Mystic Life of Alfred Deakin*, Cambridge University Press, Cambridge, 1992

La Nauze, J.A., *Alfred Deakin. A Biography*, Melbourne University Press, Melbourne, 1965

Macintyre, Stuart, *A Colonial Liberalism: The Lost World of Three Victorian Visionaries*, Oxford University Press, Melbourne, 1991

Deakin, A., *'And Be One People': Alfred Deakin's Federal Story*, Macintyre, Stuart (introd.), Melbourne University Press, Melbourne, 1995

Murdoch, Walter, *Alfred Deakin, A Sketch*, Constable, London, 1923

Rickard, John, *A Family Romance: The Deakins at Home*, Melbourne University Press, Melbourne, 1996

John Christian Watson

Footnotes

1. R. McMullin, *The Light on the Hill: The Australian Labor Party 1891–1991*, Oxford University Press, Melbourne, 1991, p. 62

2. *Ibid.*, p. 51

3. J. La Nauze, *Alfred Deakin*, Melbourne University Press, Melbourne, 1965, p. 368

4. N. Palmer, *Henry Bournes Higgins*, Harrap, London, 1931, p. 177

5. La Nauze, *op. cit.*, p. 390

6. McMullin, *op. cit.*, p. 58

7. *Ibid.*, p. 57

8. *Ibid.*, p. 58

9. *Ibid.*, p. 62

Sir George Reid

Footnotes

1. W. G. McMinn, *George Reid*, Melbourne University Press, Melbourne, 1989, p. 187

2. John Cockburn, quoted in Norman Abjorensen, 'George Reid, The Democrat as Equivocator: Piss and Wind, or Principles in Search of a Constituency?', in David Headon and John Williams (eds), *Makers of Miracles: The Cast of the Federation Story*, Melbourne University Press, Melbourne, 2000

3. Gavin Souter, *Acts of Parliament*, Melbourne University Press, Melbourne, 1988, p. 47

4. McMinn, *op. cit.*, p. 183

5. Alfred Deakin, *The Federal Story*, Robertson and Mullens, Melbourne, 1944, pp. 60–62

6. L. E. Fredman, 'Yes–No Reid': A Case for the Prosecution', *Journal of the Royal Australian Historical Society*, vol. 50, pt 2, 1964

7. Scott Brodie, *Statesmen, Leaders and Losers: The Prime Ministers of Australia*, Dreamweaver Books, Sydney, 1984, pp. 190–91

8. Abjorensen, *op. cit.*, p. 56

9. McMinn, *op. cit.*, p. 184

10. Quoted in L. F. Crisp, *Federation Fathers*, Melbourne University Press, Melbourne, 1990, p. 40

11. H.G. Turner, *The First Decade of the Australian Commonwealth*, Mason, Firth & McCutcheon, 1911, p. 76

12. *Ibid.*, p. 42

13. Crisp, *op. cit.*, p. 44

Andrew Fisher

Footnotes

1. Michael Boddy and Bob Ellis, *The Legend of King O'Malley*, Angus & Robertson, Sydney, 1974, Act 2, Scene II, p. 88

2. The legend of Braveheart and the Fisher Family is taken from *My Father at Home*, an unpublished memoir by Andrew Fisher's daughter Margaret (Peggy) Fisher. The manuscript is in the Andrew Fisher papers held in the Denis Murphy Collection, Fryer Library, University of Queensland. Because of pagination inconsistency in the original manuscript, page references are not included here.

3. Arthur W. Jose, 'Andrew Fisher', entry in *Dictionary of National Biography*, Oxford University Press, Melbourne, 1922–1930

4. Family detail in this account is taken largely from Margaret Fisher, *op. cit.*

5. For an historical account of the Ayrshire collieries, see David Bremner, *The Industries of Scotland: Their Rise, Progress and Present Condition*, David and Charles Reprints, Scotland, pp. 1–20 Photocopies of this material are included in the Murphy Collection papers, *op. cit.*

6. Herbert Campbell Jones, 'Cabinet of Captains', unpublished manuscript, Australian National Library, Canberra, chapter 29 'Andrew Fisher', pp. 262ff

7. Fisher, *op. cit.*

8. Campbell Jones, *op. cit.*

9. Malcolm Ellis, 'Andrew Fisher' (no. 5 in series 'Australian Prime Ministers'), *Bulletin*, 22 September 1922

10. Campbell Jones, *op. cit.*

11. Ellis, *op. cit.*

12. Malcolm Shepherd, unpublished memoirs and letters, Australian Archives, Canberra. Shepherd's material is loosely organised and paginated. Most of the material used here is taken from pp. 1–30

13. Campbell Jones, *op. cit.*

14. Ellis, *op. cit.*

15. This compilation draws mainly on Shepherd's listing set out in his unpublished memoirs, but also incorporates elements of a broader description prepared by Malcolm Ellis for his *Bulletin* article, *op. cit.* The capitalisation follows the original.

16. Shepherd, *op. cit.*, p. 161

17. *Ibid.*

18. Ellis, *op. cit.*

19. Shepherd, *op. cit.*, p. 179

20. Margaret Fisher, *op. cit.*

21. Denis Murphy, 'Andrew Fisher' *Australian Dictionary of Biography*, Melbourne University Press, Melbourne, 1981, vol. 8, p. 504

22. Ellis, *op. cit.*

23. *Ibid.*

Sir Joseph Cook

Footnotes

1. La Nauze, J. A., *Alfred Deakin. A Biography*, Melbourne University Press, Melbourne 1965, vol. 2, p. 536; L. F. Fitzhardinge, *William Morris Hughes, A Political Biography: vol. 2, The Little Digger 1914–1952*, Angus & Robertson, Sydney, 1979, p. 267; John Murdoch, *Sir Joe: A Political Biography of Sir Joseph Cook*, Minerva Press, London, 1996, pp. 94, xi; F. K. Crowley, *Australian Dictionary of Biography*, Melbourne University Press, Melbourne, 1981, vol. 8, p. 99

2. *Commonwealth Parliamentary Debates*, vol. 10, p. 13613, 12 June 1902

3. *Commonwealth Parliamentary Debates*, vol. 16, p. 4790, 26 August 1904

4. J. A. La Nauze, *op. cit.*, p. 626

5. Double Dissolution: Correspondence between the late Prime Minister (the Right Honourable Joseph Cook) and his Excellency the Governor-General, 1914 Second Session, p. 8

6. Murdoch, *op. cit.*, p. 115

7. *Ibid.*, p. 130

8. *Commonwealth Parliamentary Debates*, vol. 49, p. 187

9. News cuttings, Biographical file, National Library of Australia

Sources

There are two slim biographies of Cook: G. Bebbington, *Pit Boy to Prime Minister*, Centre of Local and Community History, University of Keele, Staffordshire, 1986; and John Murdoch, *Sir Joe: A Political Biography of Sir Joseph Cook*, Minerva Press, London, 1996

F. K. Crowley's article in the *Australian Dictionary of Biography* (vol. 8) gives a useful summary of his career. There is an authoritative account of the double dissolution crisis in Christopher Cunneen, *King's Men: Australian Governors-General from Hopetoun to Isaacs*, George Allen & Unwin, Sydney, 1983, pp. 110–16.

William Morris Hughes

Footnotes

1. L. F. Fitzhardinge, *William Morris Hughes: A Political Biography*, vol 1, Angus & Robertson, Sydney, 1964, p 111

2. Oral tradition

3. W. Denning, *Caucus Crisis: The Rise and Fall of the Scullin Government*, Sydney 1931, p. 47

4. D. Carboch, 'The fall of the Bruce–Page government', in A. Windavsky and D. Carboch, *Studies in Australian Politics*, Cheshire, Melbourne 1958, p. 178

Further Reading

Booker, M., *The Great Professional: A Study of W. M. Hughes*, Sydney 1980

Carboch, D. 'The fall of the Bruce-Page government' in Wildavsky, A. and Carboch, D., *Studies in Australian Politics*, Cheshire, Melbourne, 1958

Denning, W., *Caucus Crisis: The Rise and Fall of the Scullin Government*, Hale & Ironmonger, Sydney, 1982

Evatt, H. V., *Australian Labor Leader*, Angus & Robertson, Sydney, 1940

Fitzhardinge, L. F., *William Morris Hughes: A Political Biography, Volume I: The Fiery Particle*, Angus & Robertson, Sydney, 1964; *Volume II: The Little Digger*, Sydney, 1979

Horne, D., *In Search of Billy Hughes*, Melbourne, 1979

Stanley Melbourne Bruce

Sources

Australian National Review, National Federation, 1923–1929

Edwards, Cecil, *Bruce of Melbourne: Man of Two Worlds*, Heinemann, London, 1965

Ellis, Ulrich, *A History of the Australian Country Party*, Melbourne University Press, Melbourne, 1963, chapters 7–13

Macintyre, Stuart, *The Oxford History of Australia*, Oxford University Press, Melbourne, 1986, vol 4, 1901–1942, 'The succeeding age'

Nationalist election material in Mitchell Library, State Library of New South Wales and National Library of Australia

Popular Politics, National Federation, Victoria, 1926–1927

Potts, David, 'A Study of Three Nationalists in the Bruce-Page Government of 1923-1929', MA thesis, University of Melbourne, 1972

Radi, Heather, *Australian Dictionary of Biography,* Melbourne University Press, Melbourne, vol 7, pp. 453-61

'1920-29' in Frank Crowley (ed), *New History of Australia,* Heinemann, Melbourne, 1974

Sawer, Geoffrey, *Australian Federal Politics and Law, 1901-1929,* Melbourne University Press, Melbourne, 1956, chapters 10-14

Schedvin, Boris, *Australia and the Great Depression: A Study of Economic Development and Policy in the 1920s and 1930s,* Sydney University Press, 1970, chaps 3-6

James Henry Scullin

Sources

The *Age*, 23 May 1959; 26 April 1975

The *Australian*, 25 May 1975

Scullin, James Henry (1873-1953), *Australian Dictionary of Biography,* ANU Press, Canberra

Robertson, John, *J.H. Scullin: A Political Biography,* University of WA Press, Nedlands, 1974

Sydney Morning Herald, 18 August 1973

Joseph Aloysius Lyons

Footnotes

1. Taken from 'My Father', by Rosemary Lyons; private collection of her daughter Mary Pridmore

2. Sir Earle Page, *Truant Surgeon,* Angus & Robertson, Sydney, 1963, p. 226

3. Quoted in Dame Enid Lyons, *So We Take Comfort,* Heinemann, London, 1965, p. 193

4. Dame Enid Lyons, *Among The Carrion Crows,* Rigby Seal, Adelaide, 1977, p. 71

5. Robert Menzies, *Afternoon Light,* Penguin, Ringwood, 1967, p. 125

6. Anne Henderson's interview with Brendan Lyons, 9 October 1999

7. Allan Martin, 'The Politics of The Depression', in *The Australian Century,* Robert Manne (ed), Text Publishing, Melbourne, 1999, p. 114

8. Quoted in Kate White, *A Political Love Story,* Penguin, Ringwood, 1987, p. 132

9. Philip Hart, 'JA Lyons: A Political Biography', PhD thesis, ANU, 1967, p. 29

10. White, *op. cit.,* p. 31

11. W. J. Hudson, *Casey,* Oxford University Press, 1986, p. 108

12. Michael Hogan, *The Sectarian Strand* Penguin, Ringwood, 1987, p. 187

13. *Ibid.,* p. 182

14. Allan Martin, *Robert Menzies, A Life,* Melbourne University Press, Melbourne, 1993, vol 1, p. 84

15. In March 1931, Lang declared that New South Wales would not be paying the interest owed its London creditors; the money saved would finance dole payments. The Scullin government met the debt owed by NSW. This, however, would reverberate the following year under the Lyons government, which took a more confrontational approach to Lang.

16. Martin, *op. cit.,* p. 85

17. *Ibid.,* p. 88

18. Desmond Zwar, *In Search of Keith Murdoch,* Macmillan, Melbourne, 1980, p. 89

19. Hogan, *op. cit.,* p. 214

20. Lyons to Bruce, 2 November 1932, Lyons Papers, National Library, Canberra

21. Page, *op. cit.,* p. 227

22. Martin, *op. cit.,* p. 122

23. Menzies, *op. cit.,* p. 122

24. Stewart to Lyons, 12 June 1933, Lyons Papers, National Library, Canberra

25. Hart, *op. cit.*, p. 210

26. Martin, *op. cit.*, p. 247

27. Cecil Edwards, *Bruce of Melbourne*, Heinemann, London, 1965, p. 261

28. Hart, *op. cit.*, p. 290

29. Anne Henderson's interview with Barry Lyons and Peter Lyons, 9 October 1999

30. Frank Green, *The Servant of The House*, Heinemann, London, 1969, pp. 115–16

31. Anne Henderson's interview with Barry Lyons and Peter Lyons, 9 October 1999

32. Quoted in Hart, *op. cit.*, p. 224

Sir Earle Page

Footnotes

1. Latham to Page, 25 April 1931, Page to Latham, 16 April 1931, Latham Papers, National Library, Canberra, MS1009/49/20

2. Ellis to Page, 6 December 1931, Ellis Papers, National Library, Canberra, MS 1006/22, Box 4

3. Page to Lyons, Lyons to Page, 3 March 1932, Lyons Papers, National Library, Canberra, MS 4851, Box 1, Folder 9

4. *Melbourne Herald*, 14 October 1932, The *Age*, 17 October, 1932

5. Carl Bridge, 'Earle Christmas Grafton Page', in John Ritchie (ed), *Australian Dictionary of Biography*, Melbourne University Press, Melbourne

6. *Ibid.*, p. 122

7. Gwen Gray, 'Social Policy', in Scott Prasser et al (eds), *The Menzies Era*, Hale & Iremonger, Sydney, 1995, p. 217

Further Reading

Ellis, Ulrich, *A History of the Australian Country Party*, Melbourne University Press, Melbourne, 1963

Golding, Peter, *Black Jack McEwen: Political Gladiator*, Melbourne University Press, Melbourne, 1996

Page, Earle, *Truant Surgeon: The Inside Story of Forty Years of Australian Political Life*, Angus & Robertson, Sydney, 1963

Sir Robert Gordon Menzies

Footnote

1. Janet McMCalman, *Journeyings*, Melbourne, 1993, p. 232

Sources

Allan Martin is the author of *Robert Menzies, A Life*, vols 1 and 2, Melbourne University Press, Melbourne, 1993, 1999. This essay draws on ideas and insights from these books.

Further Reading

Denning, Warren, *Caucus Crisis: The Rise and Fall of the Scullin Government*, Hale & Iremonger, Sydney, 1982

Sir Arthur W Fadden

Footnotes

1. Fadden was to hold the seat of Darling Downs until 1949, and then represented the neighbouring seat of McPherson from 1949–1958

2. See Gavin Souter, *Acts of Parliament*, Melbourne University Press, Melbourne, 1988, p. 322

3. *Ibid.*, p. 331

4. See Sir Arthur Fadden, *They Called Me Artie*, Jacaranda Press, Brisbane, 1969, p. 42

5. *Ibid.*, p. 43.

6. See Gavin Souter, *op. cit.*, pp. 340–41

7. *Ibid.*, p. 340–41

8. *Ibid.*, p. 341

9. See Judith Brett, *Robert Menzies' Forgotten People*, Macmillan Australia, Melbourne, 1992, p. 75. During the 1946 election campaign when Fadden was demanding the banning of the Communist Party, Menzies defended the its right to exist, arguing that in time of peace it is 'a very serious step to prohibit the association of people for the promulgation of any particular views ...' (see Sir Percy Joske, *Sir Robert Menzies*, Angus & Robertson, Sydney, 1978, p. 169), and 'that it must not be thought that they are such a force in political philosophy that we cannot meet them ...' (see *Sydney Morning Herald*, 16 February 1948). 'By 1949 Menzies had changed his mind.' Brett, *op cit.*

10. *Ibid.*, p. 121

11. *Ibid.*, p. 126

12. *Ibid.*, p. 147, 155

13. See H. C. Coombs, *Trial Balance*, Sun Books, Melbourne, 1981, p. 154

14. *Ibid.*, p. 131

Further Reading

Brett, Judith, *Robert Menzies' Forgotten People*, Macmillan Australia, Melbourne, 1992

Coombs, H. C., *Trial Balance*, Sun Books, Melbourne, 1981

Fadden, A., *They Called Me Artie*, Jacaranda Press, Brisbane, 1969

Joske, Sir Percy, *Sir Robert Menzies*, Angus & Robertson, Sydney, 1978

Martin, W. A., *Robert Menzies, A Life*, Melbourne University Press, Melbourne, 1993 (vol.1) , 1999 (vol. 2)

Souter, Gavin, *Acts of Parliament*, Melbourne University Press, Melbourne, 1988

John Curtin

Further Reading

Black, David (ed), *In His Own Words: John Curtin's Speeches and Writings*, Paradigm Books, Perth, 1995

Day, David *John Curtin: A Life*, HarperCollins, Sydney, 1999

Ross, Lloyd, *John Curtin: A Biography*, Melbourne University Press, Melbourne, 1996

John Curtin for Labor and for Australia, Australian National University Press, Canberra, 1971

Francis Michael Forde

Footnotes

1. David Andrew Gibson, 'The Right Hon. Francis M. Forde PC: His Life and Times', BA Honours thesis, Department of History, University of Queensland, 1973, p. 24; Murphy, D. J., *T. J. Ryan: A Political Biography*, University of Queensland Press, St Lucia, 1990, p. 243

2. *Queensland Parliamentary Debates*, vol. CXXVI, 1917, pp. 16–223. Charles Arrowsmith Bernays, *Queensland – Our Seventh Political Decade 1920–1930*, Angus & Robertson, Sydney, 1931, pp. 248–50

4. Graham Shirley and Brian Adams, *Australian Cinema: The First 80 Years*, Angus & Robertson, Sydney, 1983, p. 76

5. Lloyd Ross, *John Curtin: A Biography*, Melbourne University Press, Melbourne, 1996, pp. 147–49; Ross McMullin, *The Light on the Hill: The Australian Labor Party 1891–1991*, Oxford University Press, Melbourne, 1991, pp. 74–76, 185; Colin A. Hughes, *Mr Prime Minister: Australian Prime Ministers 1901–1972*, Oxford University Press, Melbourne, 1976, pp. 122, 13

6. David Horner, *Inside the War Cabinet: Directing Australia's War Effort 1939–45*, Allen and Unwin, Sydney, 1996, pp. 141–47

7. Ross, *op. cit.*, pp. 309–314; McMullin, *op. cit.*, p. 224

8. Kylie Tennant, *Evatt: Politics and Justice*, Angus & Robertson, London, 1981, pp. 159, 164–77, 368–69; P.G. Edwards, *The Making of Australian Foreign Policy 1901–1949*, Oxford University Press, Melbourne, 1983, pp. 164–71; McMullin, *op. cit.*, p. 233; Geoffrey Bolton, 'Herbert Vere Evatt', in *Australian Dictionary of Biography*, Melbourne University Press, Melbourne, vol. 14, p. 111

9. McMullin, *op. cit.*, p. 408

Bibliography

Australian Dictionary of Biography, entries on Curtin, Chifley, Scullin, Evatt, Blamey

Bernays, Charles Arrowsmith, *Queensland – Our Seventh Political Decade 1920–1930*, Angus & Robertson, Sydney, 1931

Queensland Politics during Sixty Years 1859–1919, Government Printer, Brisbane, 1920

Bertrand, Ina (ed), *Cinema in Australia: A Documentary History*, University NSW Press, Kensington, 1989

Carroll, Brian, *From Barton to Fraser: Every Australian Prime Minister*, Cassell Australia, Stanmore, 1978

Edwards, P.G, *The Making of Australian Foreign Policy 1901–1949*, Oxford University Press, Melbourne, 1983

Fricke, Graham, *Profiles of Power: The Prime Ministers of Australia*, Houghton Mifflin, Ferntree Gully, Victoria, 1990

Gibson, David Andrew, 'The Right Hon. Francis M. Forde PC: His Life and Times', BA Hons thesis, Dept of History, University of Queensland, 1973

Horner, David, *Inside the War Cabinet: Directing Australia's War Effort 1939–45*, Allen and Unwin, Sydney, 1996

Hughes, Colin A, *Mr Prime Minister: Australian Prime Ministers 1901–1972*, Oxford University Press, Melbourne, 1976

Johnstone, Robert, *Australian Prime Ministers*, Nelson, Melbourne, 1976

McMullin, Ross, *The Light on the Hill: The Australian Labor Party 1891–1991*, Oxford University Press, Melbourne, 1991

Murphy, D.J., *T.J, Ryan: A Political Biography*, University of Queensland Press, St Lucia, 1990

Page, Michael, *The Prime Ministers of Australia*, Robertsbridge, London, 1988

Parliamentary Handbook and Record of Elections for the Commonwealth of Australia, Commonwealth Government Printer, Canberra, 1936–1953

Prime Ministers of Australia, AGPS, Canberra, 1994

Queensland Parliamentary Debates, vol. CXXVI, 1917

Ross, Lloyd, *John Curtin: A Biography*, Melbourne University Press, Melbourne, 1996

Rydon, Joan, *A Biographical Register of the Commonwealth Parliament, 1901–1972*, Australian National University Press, Canberra, 1975

Shirley, Graham and Adams, Brian, *Australian Cinema: The First 80 Years*, Angus & Robertson, Sydney, 1983

Tennant, Kylie, *Evatt: Politics and Justice*, Angus & Robertson, London, 1981

Waterson, D.B, *A Bibliographical Register of the Queensland Parliament 1860–1929*, Australian National University Press, Canberra, 1972

Joseph Benedict Chifley

Footnotes

1. Except for Gough Whitlam during the fortnight he and his deputy comprised an interim ministry following the 1972 election.

2. L. F. Crisp, *Ben Chifley*, Longman's Green & Co, Melbourne, 1963, p. 5

3. *Ibid.*, p. 12

4. *Ibid.*, p. 11

5. *Ibid.*, p. 8

6. *Ibid.*, p. 9

7. *Ibid.*, p. 24

8. *Ibid.*, p. 22

9. *Ibid.*, p. 30

10. J. Thompson (ed), *Five to Remember*, Lansdowne Press, Melbourne, 1964, pp. 78–79

11. Crisp, *op. cit.*, p. 214

11. *Herald*, 14 June 1951

13. Crisp, *op. cit.*, p. 151

14. *Ibid.*, p. 158, note 4

15. Thompson, *op. cit.*, p. 74

16. H. Breen, 'J.B. Chifley', *Twentieth Century*, March 1974, p. 241

17. Breen, *op. cit.*, p. 241

18. Thompson, *op. cit.*, p. 83

19. *Ibid.*, p. 84

20. *Ibid.*, p. 69

21. *Ibid.*, p. 69

22. *Ibid.*, p. 69

23. Crisp, *op. cit.*, p. 147

24. Thompson, *op. cit.*, p. 79

25. *Canberra Times*, 9 March 1966

26. F. Daly, *From Curtin to Hawke*, Macmillan, Melbourne, 1984, p. 36

27. R. McMullin, *The Light on the Hill: The Australian Labor Party 1891–1991*, Oxford University Press, Melbourne, 1991, pp. 246–47

28. Daly, *op. cit.*, p. 58

29. McMullin, *op. cit.*, epigraph

30. D.B. Waterson, 'Chifley', in J. Ritchie (ed), *Australian Dictionary of Biography*, Melbourne University Press, Melbourne, vol. 13, 1993, p. 419

31. Crisp, *op. cit.*, p. 384

32. *Ibid.*, p. 396

33. McMullin, *op. cit.*, pp. 261–62

Harold Edward Holt

Footnotes

1. This chapter draws heavily upon the author's entry on Holt in John Ritchie (ed), *Australian Dictionary of Biography*, Melbourne University Press, Melbourne, 1996, vol. 14

Other sources used include:

Paul Hasluck, *The Chance of Politics*, Nicholas Hasluck (ed), Text Publishing, Melbourne, 1997

Gerard Henderson, *Menzies' Child: The Liberal Party of Australia 1944–1994*, Allen and Unwin, St Leonards, 1994

Dame Zara Holt, *My Life and Harry: An Autobiography*, The *Herald*, Melbourne, 1968

Peter Howson, *The Howson Diaries:The Life of Politics*, Don Aitkin (ed), Penguin, Ringwood, 1984

D. Langmore, *Prime Ministers' Wives: The Public and Private Lives of Ten Australian Women*, McPhee Gribble, Ringwood, 1992

Don Whitington, *Twelfth Man?*, Jacaranda Press, Milton, 1972

G. Whitwell, *The Treasury Line*, Allen and Unwin, St Leonards, 1986; *Bulletin*, 31 May 1961

L. Broderick, 'Transition and Tragedy', BA thesis, Macquarie University, 1989

Cabinet Records, 1966–67, National Archives of Australia

Andrew Holt Papers (in private hands); Harold Holt Papers, National Archives of Australia

Menzies Papers and Liberal Party of Australia Papers, National Library of Australia

Interviews with Nicholas, the late Andrew and Sam Holt, Peter Bailey, Tony Eggleton, Peter Howson and Jim Short.

Sir John McEwen

Footnotes

1. Sir James Killen, Liberal member for Moreton (Qld) 1955–83, *Killen*, Mandarin Australia, Melbourne, 1989, p. 41

2. Paul Kelly, 'Black Jack: Is he Godfather of the Banana Republic?', *Weekend Australian*, 26–27 July 1986

3. Various issues of *Federal Standard* (Chiltern), 1901–06

4. *John McEwen, His Story*, privately published by his widow, p. 2

5. *Ibid.*

6. Gavin Souter, *Sydney Morning Herald*, 7 November 1970, p. 2

7. Profile of McEwen, *People*, 24 September 1952, p. 32

8. John Malcolm Fraser, prime minister 1975–83, discussion with author 23 February 1994

9. *John McEwen, His Story*, p. 76

10. 0. Sir Robert Cotton, New South Wales president of the Liberal Party 1957–60, Liberal senator 1965–78, statement in *Sydney Morning Herald*, 2 January 1968, p. 1

11. Peter Golding, *Black Jack McEwen: Political Gladiator*, Melbourne University Press, Melbourne, 1996, p. 282

Sir John Grey Gorton

Footnotes

1. Geoff Easdown, 'Liberal PM voted for Whitlam', *Herald-Sun*, 30 December 19982. The federal division of the Liberal Party of Australia has produced a video of the 1998 gala dinner

3. John Hewson, 'Eulogy for a living hero', *Australian Financial Review*, 11 June 1993

4. Neil Brown, *On the Other Hand ... Sketches and Reflections from Political Life*, The Popular Press, 1993, p. 59

5. James Killen, *Inside Australian Politics*, Mandarin, Melbourne, 1989, p. 173

6. Alan Reid, *The Gorton Experiment*, Shakespeare Head Press, Sydney, p. 10. Reid's book is unremittingly critical of John Gorton and all too soft on his main political rival, William McMahon. When Gorton was rolled as prime minister he was elected deputy Liberal leader and appointed minister of defence. On 8 August 1971 the *Sunday Australian* commenced a six-part series, written by Gorton and entitled 'I Did It My Way', which was, in effect, his reply to Alan Reid's *The Gorton Experiment*. Within days Gorton was sacked by McMahon on account of his disclosures – he never returned to the ministry.

7. Alan Trengrove, *John Grey Gorton: An Informal Biography*, Cassell, Melbourne, 1969

8. Grahame Cumming, *Freemasonry: Australia's Prime Ministers*, Masonic Historical Society of New South Wales, Sydney, 1994

9. Quoted in David McNicoll, *Luck's A Fortune*, Wildcat Press, Sydney, 1979, p. 228

10. Maxmilian Walsh, 'You Ain't Seen Nothing Yet', *Quadrant*, November–December 1968, pp. 16–23

11. Alexander Downer, *Six Prime Ministers*, Hill of Content, Melbourne, 1982, p. 110

12. Peter Howson, *The Howson Diaries: The Life of Politics* (edited by Don Aitkin), Viking Press, Melbourne, 1984, p. 499. Bert James' highly personal (and inaccurate) attack on John Gorton was delivered in the House of Representatives on 19 March 1969

13. Edward St John, *A Time to Speak*, Sun Books, Melbourne, 1969

14. Ainsley Gotto does not agree. Speaking (at the invitation of the National Archives of Australia) at the release of 1969 Cabinet records she commented: 'To my personal knowledge, John Gorton never went into a Cabinet meeting without fully reading – and marking where he thought necessary – Cabinet submissions, as well as the accompanying notes on those submissions.' See Ainsley Gotto, 'Notes for Embargoed Release of 1969 Cabinet Papers', 1 December 1999. See also Dr Ian Hancock's comments on the 1968 and 1969 Cabinet Papers at www.naa.gov.au

15. Alan Trengrove, *Sun*, 13 March 1971. Paul Hasluck, John Gorton's principal Liberal opponent in the 1968 leadership contest, reached a not dissimilar conclusion. In a private assessment written in June 1970, Hasluck commented that Gorton lacked 'a clear purpose'. (Paul Hasluck, *The Chance of Politics* [edited by Nicholas Hasluck], Text Publishing, Melbourne, 1997, p. 179)

Sir William McMahon

Footnotes

1. Paul Hasluck, *The Chance of Politics*, Text Publishing, Melbourne, 1991

2. Peter Golding, *Black Jack McEwen Political Gladiator*, Melbourne University Press, Melbourne, 1996

3. Oral History Interview with William McMahon by Ray Acheson, National Library of Australia, TRC 317

4. Alan Reid, T*he Power Struggle*, Shakespeare Head Press, Sydney, 1971

5. Alan Reid, *The Bulletin*, 9 February 1980

6. Peter Howson, *The Life of Politics*, Viking Press, Melbourne, 1984

7. Graham Freudenberg, *A Certain Grandeur*, Macmillan, Melbourne, 1977

Edward Gough Whitlam

Footnotes

1. Magnus Magnusson (ed), *Chambers Biographical Dictionary*, W & R Chambers, Edinburgh, 1990, p. 1554

2. P.H. Reaney, *The Origin of English Surnames*, 1967, pp. 52, 206, 317

3. Biographical information in this and following sections is drawn from Laurie Oakes, *Whitlam PM*, Angus & Robertson, Sydney, 1973, and personal information supplied by Richard Hall.

4. Paul Hasluck, *The Chance of Politics*, Text Publishing, Melbourne, 1997, p. 198

5. Oakes, *op. cit.*, p. 26

6. Edward St John, Australian National Library Oral History, TRC 1900–70

7. Leslie R. Johnson, Australian National Library Oral History, TRC 4900–98

8. *Ibid.*

9. *Ibid.*

10. *Ibid.*

11. Hasluck, *op. cit.*, p. 199

12. Johnson, *op. cit.*

13. Tony Mulvihill, Australian National Library Oral History, TRC 1900–77

14. James Cope, Australian National Library Oral History, TRC 4900–2

15. Gordon Bryant, Australian National Library Oral History, TRC 4900–42

16. Oakes, *op. cit.*

17. *Ibid.*, p. 206

18. *Ibid.*

19. *Ibid.*

20. *Ibid.*, p. 155.

21. *Ibid.*, p. 178

22. M. J. Young, M.J. 'The Build-Up to 1972', in *The Whitlam Phenomenon*, Fabian Papers, Penguin, Melbourne, 1986, p.97.

23. Graham Little, *Whitlam, Whitlamism and the Whitlam Years*, p. 62. *Ibid.*, Fabian Papers

24. Graham Freudenberg, *The Program*, pp. 135–36, Fabian Papers, *Ibid.*

25. Frank Crean, Australian National Library Oral History, TRC not recorded

26. Billie Mackie Snedden, Australian National Library Oral History, TRC 4900-57

27. Cope, *op.cit.*

28. Snedden, *op. cit.*

29. Snedden, *op. cit.*

30. Johnson, *op. cit.*

31. Paul Kelly, *The Unmaking of Gough*, Angus & Robertson, Sydney, 1976, p. 349

32. Bryant, *op. cit.*

33. Johnson, *op. cit.*

34. Crean, *op. cit.*

35. Bryant, *op. cit.*

36. Mulvihill, *op. cit.*

37. Bryant, *op. cit.*

38. Peter Bowers, 'Whitlam reflects on Whitlam', *Sydney Morning Herald*, 3 December, 1982, p. 7.

39. Snedden, *op. cit.*

40. Mulvihill, *op. cit.*

41. Alan Missen, Australian National Library Oral History, TRC 732

42. Bowers, *SMH*, *op. cit.*

43. Bryant, *op. cit.*

44. Johnson, *op. cit.*

45. Crean, *op. cit.*

46. Johnson, *op. cit.*

47. *Ibid.*

48. Gough Whitlam, *The Truth of the Matter*, Penguin, Melbourne, 1979, p. 117

49. Irwin Young, *Theodore*, Preface by Gough Whitlam, 1971, p.viii.

John Malcolm Fraser

Footnotes

1. Journalist Mungo MaCallum popularised the term 'crazy grazier'.

2. Patrick Weller, *Malcolm Fraser PM*, Penguin, Ringwood, 1989, chapters 1, 2 and 10

3. See Philip Ayers, *Malcolm Fraser, A Biography*, William Heinemann Australia, Melbourne, 1987; Paul Kelly, *The Unmaking of Gough*, Angus & Robertson, Sydney, 1976

4. See John Edwards, *Life Wasn't Meant to be Easy*, Mayhem, Sydney, 1977; Paul Kelly, *The Hawke Ascendancy*, Angus & Robertson, Sydney, 1984, chapter 3; and Ayers, *op. cit.*, chapters 7–13

5. Kelly, *The Hawke Ascendancy*, pp. 45–48

6. Ayers, *op. cit.*, chapter 14

7. Greg Whitwell, *The Treasury Line*, Allen and Unwin, Sydney, 1986, chapter 8

8. Budget speech, 17 August 1976

9. Weller, *op. cit.*, p. 231

10. Ayers, *op. cit.*, pp. 306–308

11. Personal discussion with author, February 1983

12. Malcolm Fraser, personal interview, October 1999

13. See James Jupp and Marie Kabala (eds), *The Politics of Australian Immigration*, AGPS, Canberra 1993, chapter 1

14. *Ibid.*, p. 148

15. See Nancy Viviani, *The Indochinese in Australia*, 1975–95, Oxford University Press, chapter 1

16. Jupp and Kabala, *op. cit.*, pp. 149–50

17. Ayers, *op. cit.*, p 374

18. *Ibid.*, p. 6

19. *Ibid.*, pp. 337–41

20. *Ibid.*, p. 347

21. Owen Harries, personal interview, January 2000

22. Ayers *op. cit.*, p. 309

23. Paul Kelly, *The End of Certainty*, Allen and Unwin, Sydney, 1994, p. 37

24. D.M. White and D.A. Kemp (eds), *Malcolm Fraser on Australia*, Hill of Content, Melbourne, 1986, p. 20

25. John Howard, personal interview, December 1999

Robert James Lee Hawke

Footnotes

1. Blanche d'Alpuget, *Robert J. Hawke. A Biography*, Schwartz, Melbourne, 1982, p. 1. This is a superb contemporary biography, sympathetic but not hagiographic, and is the indispensable source for the pre-parliamentary Hawke. John Hurst, *Hawke PM*, Angus & Robertson, Sydney, 1983, and Robert Pullan, *Bob Hawke, A Portrait*, Methuen, Sydney, 1980, are useful supplementary works for much the same period.

2. Hazel Hawke, *My Own Life*, Text Publishing, Melbourne, 1982, p. 69

3. John Button, *As It Happened*, Text Publishing, Melbourne, 1998, p. 221

4. Paul Kelly, *The Hawke Ascendancy*, Angus & Robertson, Sydney, 1984, p. 396. Kelly's major work *The End of Certainty*, Allen and Unwin, Sydney, 1994, is the most important general work on the Hawke period and one of the finest pieces of contemporary history yet written in Australia.

5. Bob Hawke, *The Hawke Memoirs*, Heinemann, Sydney, 1994, p. 154

6. Gareth Evans and Bruce Grant, *Australia's Foreign Relations In the World of the 1990s*, Melbourne University Press, Melbourne, 1991, p. 47

7. Bill Hayden, *Hayden. An Autobiography*, Angus & Robertson, Sydney, 1996, pp. 381, 464

8. See Peter Walsh, *Confessions of a Failed Finance Minister*, Random House, Sydney, 1995, pp. 147, 273

9. Hawke, *op. cit.*, p. 294

10. Button, *op. cit.*, p. 233

11. Stephen Mills, *The Hawke Years. The Story from the Inside*, Viking, Melbourne, 1993, p. 303. This is the best account of Hawke as prime minister.

12. *The Hawke Memoirs* have been unfairly castigated. Despite flaws, they are the best and most readable account of his stewardship yet provided by any Australian prime minister. Admittedly, the competition has not been keen.

Paul John Keating

Further Reading

Aubin, Tracey, *Peter Costello: A Biography*, HarperCollins, Sydney, 1999

Carew, Edna, *Paul Keating: Prime Minister*, Allen and Unwin, Sydney, 1992

Edwards, John, *Keating: The Inside Story*, Penguin, Melbourne, 1996

Gordon, Michael, *A True Believer: Paul Keating*, University of Queensland Press, St Lucia, 1996

Kelly, Paul, *The End of Certainty*, Allen and Unwin, Sydney, 1992

John Winston Howard

Footnotes

1. Craig McGregor, ***Headliners***, University of Queensland Press, Queensland, 1990, p. 155

2. Gwynneth Singleton, 'Introduction: Howard's Way'; in Gwynneth Singleton (ed), *The Howard Government: Australian Commonwealth Administration 1996-1998*, UNSW Press, Sydney, 2000, p. 4

3. Gerard Henderson, *A Howard Government? Inside the Coalition*, HarperCollins Publishers, Sydney, 1995, p. 31

4. David Barnett with Pru Goward, *John Howard: Prime Minister*, Viking/Penguin Books, Victoria, 1997, p. 8

5. Paul Kelly, *The End of Certainty*, Allen and Unwin, Sydney, 1994, p. 101

6. This and other Bob Howard observations are from interviews with the author for the *Australian Financial Review* 1996 and 2000.

7. Robert Haupt, *The National Times*, 25 August 1979

8. Michelle Grattan, *Australian Financial Review Magazine*, November 1996, p. 69

9. David Marr, *The High Price of Heaven*, Allen and Unwin, Sydney, 1999, p. 31

10. Personal conversation, July 2000

11. Henderson, *op. cit.*, p.33

12. Personal conversation, July 2000

13. Kelly, *op. cit.*, p. 485

14. Wayne Errington and Peter van Onselen, *John Winston Howard: The Biography*, Melbourne University Publishing, Victoria, 2007, p.329

15. Tony Thomas, *Adelaide Advertiser*, 26 December 1975

16. Barnett with Goward, *op. cit.*, p. 32

17. *Ibid.*, p. 261

18. *Ibid.*, p. 291

19. McGregor, *op. cit.*, p. 153

20. Henderson, *op. cit.*, p. 27

21. Gerard Henderson, *Menzies' Child: The Liberal Party of Australia: 1944-1994*, Allen and Unwin, Sydney, 1994, p. 289

22. Barnett with Goward, *op. cit.*, p. 604

23. Howard baulks at the implication of anti-Catholicism and points to his government's generous treatment of Catholic schools. Personal conversation, July 2000

24. Personal conversation, July 2000

25. Henderson, *A Howard Government? Inside the Coalition*, p. 31

26. The government decided it would be represented in the walk by only the Minister for Aboriginal Affairs and the Minister Assisting the Prime Minister for Reconciliation. When this decision received publicity, Howard said other ministers could walk if they wished, but only two others did so.

27. Errington and van Onselen, *op. cit.*, p. 387

28. *Howard's End* transcript, 4 Corners, ABC, Monday 18 February 2008.

Bibliography

Barnett, David (with Pru Goward), *John Howard: Prime Minister*, Viking/Penguin Books, Victoria, 1997

Grattan, Michelle, *Australian Financial Review Magazine*, November 1996, pp. 66–73

Hancock, Ian, *National and Permanent? The Federal Organisation of the Liberal Party of Australia 1944–1965*, Melbourne University Press, Melbourne, 2000

Henderson, Gerard, *Menzies' Child: The Liberal Party of Australia: 1944–1994*, Allen and Unwin, Sydney, 1994

Henderson, Gerard, *A Howard Government? Inside the Coalition*, HarperCollins Publishers, Sydney, 1995

Kelly, Paul, *The End of Certainty*, Allen and Unwin, Sydney, 1994.

Marr, David, *The High Price of Heaven*, Allen and Unwin, Sydney, 1999

McGregor, Craig, *Headliners*, University of Queensland Press, Queensland, 1990

Singleton, Gwynneth, 'Introduction: Howard's Way' in Gwynneth Singleton (ed), *The Howard Government: Australian Commonwealth Administration 1996–1998*, UNSW Press, Sydney, 2000

Brett, Judith, *Australian Liberals and the Moral Middle Class: from Alfred Deakin to John Howard*, Cambridge University Press, New York, 2003

***

Brett, Judith, 'Exit Right: The Unravelling of John Howard', *Quarterly Essay*, Black Inc., Issue 28, 2007

Brett, Judith, 'Relaxed and Comfortable: The Liberal Party's Australia', *Quarterly Essay*, Black Inc., Issue 19, 2005

Errington, Wayne and van Onselen, Peter, *John Winston Howard: The Biography*, Melbourne University Publishing, Victoria, 2007

Kelly, Paul, *The Australian Inquirer*, 15 December 2007

Manne, Robert (ed), *The Howard Years*, Black Inc. Agenda, Melbourne, Victoria, 2004

Walter, James and Strangio, Paul , *No, Prime Minister: Reclaiming Politics from Leaders*, UNSW Press, Sydney, NSW, 2007

Weller, Patrick, *Cabinet Government in Australia, 1901-2006: Practice, Principles, Performance.* UNSW Press, Sydney, NSW, 2007

Williams, Pamela, *The Australian Financial Review*, 30 November 2007, 11 December 2007 and 21 December 2007

Kevin Michael Rudd

Footnotes

1. Two biographies of Rudd appeared during 2007, both giving full accounts of his youth:

Robert Mackin, *Kevin Rudd: The Biography*, Viking/Penguin Books, Camberwell, Victoria and Nicholas Stuart, *Kevin Rudd: an unauthorised political biography*, Scribe, Carlton North, Melbourne

Rudd co-operated only with Macklin; Stuart found people had been actively discouraged from talking to him.

2. For a detailed account of Rudd's record in Queensland see Simon Mann, 'The Making of Kevin Rudd', *The Age*, 21 April 2007

3. Mark Latham, *The Latham Diaries, Melbourne* University Press, Carlton, Victoria, 2005, p. 364

4. Kevin Rudd: 'Faith in Politics', *The Monthly*, No. 17, October 2006; 'Howard's Brutopia', *The Monthly*, No. 18, November 2006

5 Christine Jackman, 'The Contender', *The Weekend Australian Magazine*, 10 February 2007

6. For an account of the McKew campaign see Margot Saville, *The Battle for Bennelong: The Adventures of Maxine McKew, Aged 50something*, Melbourne University Press, Carlton, Victoria. 2007.

7. Macklin, op. cit., p. 102

Further Reading

Taylor, Lenore : 'Method Man', *Australian Financial Review Magazine*, 23 February 2007

Kelly, Paul: 'Smart. Casual. Kevin.', *The Australian Magazine*, 27 October 2007

Hartcher, Peter, 'Man on the Move', *Good Weekend*, 5 November 2005

Author biographies

Neal Blewett has been an academic, politician, diplomat and writer. He was a minister in the Hawke and Keating governments from 1983 to 1993, holding in turn the portfolios of Health, Community Services, Trade and Overseas Development and Social Security. From 1994 to 1998 he was Australian High Commissioner in London. He is the author of *A Cabinet Diary*, published in 1999.

Geoffrey Bolton is senior scholar in residence at Murdoch University, having taught history at a number of Australian universities. From 1982 to 1985 he was foundation Professor of the Australian Studies Centre at the University of London. He was the ABC Boyer lecturer for 1992 and general editor of *The Oxford History of Australia*. He is currently engaged on a biography of Sir Paul Hasluck.

Judith Brett is a Professor of Politics at La Trobe University, Melbourne. She is the author of *Robert Menzies' Forgotten People, Australian Liberals and the Moral Middle Class,* and most recently, *Exit Right: The Unravelling of John Howard.*

Elaine Brown wrote a biography of sawmiller William Pettigrew for her PhD at the University of Queensland. She is also the author of *Cooloola Coast, an Environmental History.*

Brian Costar is Professor of Victorian State Parliamentary Democracy in the Institute for Social Research at Melbourne's Swinburne University. A graduate of the University of Queensland, he has published widely on Australian and Victorian party politics and elections. A special area of interest is the National (Country) Party. His most recent book (with Paul Strangio) is The Victorian Premiers 1856-2006.

David Day has been Professor of Australian History at University College Dublin and has twice been Professor of Australian Studies at the University of Tokyo. He is currently an Honorary Associate in the History Program at La Trobe University and a visiting professor at the University of Aberdeen. David Day has written widely on Australian history and the history of the Second World War. His recent books include the prize-winning *Claiming a Continent: A New History of Australia* and *Conquest: how societies overwhelm others*. His political biographies include the best-selling *John Curtin: A life* and *Chifley*. He is currently completing a biography of Andrew Fisher.

Peter Golding has worked extensively as a journalist, including 22 years with the Melbourne *Argus*, and as a public relations executive. He is the author of *Black Jack McEwen: Political Gladiator*, a biography of Sir John McEwen. He was awarded the Order of Australia Medal in 1998.

Michelle Grattan has worked as a federal political reporter and columnist for *The Age, The Australian Financial Review* and the *Sydney Morning Herald*. She was editor of *The Canberra Times* from 1993-1995. She is currently political editor of *The Age. Back on the Wool Track* is her most recent book.

Ian Hancock has published a number of books and chapters on Liberals and the Liberal Party, his most recent being *The Liberals: A History of the NSW Division 1945-2000*. He is presently writing a biography of Sir Frederick Wheeler, the former Chairman of the Public Service Board and Secretary of the Treasury.

Anne Henderson is Deputy Director of The Sydney Institute and edits *The Sydney Papers*. She is the author of *From All Corners: Six Migrant Stories, Educating Johannah, Mary MacKillop's Sisters, Getting Even: Women MPs on Life, Power and Politics, The Killing of Sister Irene McCormack* and *An Angel in the Court – The Life of Major Joyce Harmer*. Her biography of Dame Enid Lyons will be released in 2008. She also wrote the biographical entry on Prime Minister Joe Lyons for the UK's *New Dictionary of National Biography* (OUP).

Gerard Henderson is Executive Director of The Sydney Institute and columnist for the *Sydney Morning Herald* and the *West Australian*. He comments regularly on *ABC Radio National Breakfast* and appears on the ABC television *Insiders* and *Lateline* programs along with Sky News' *Agenda*. Henderson's publications include *Mr Santamaria and the Bishops*; *Australian Answers, Menzies' Child: The Liberal Party of*

Australia, A Howard Government? Inside the Coalition and *Islam in Australia*. In August 1984 he profiled Bob Hawke for the ABC TV *Four Corners* program.

Helen Irving formerly Director of the 1901 Centre at UTS, is Associate Professor in the Faculty of Law at the University of Sydney, where she teaches constitutional law. Her publications include *To Constitute a Nation: A Cultural History of Australia's Constitution*; *Five Things to Know About the Australian Constitution*; and *Gender and the Constitution,* as well as several edited works, including *The Centenary Companion to Australian Federation*.

Paul Kelly is Editor-at-Large of *The Australian* and was previously Editor-in-Chief. He writes on Australian politics, history and public policy and has covered national governments from Whitlam to Howard. He has written six books on Australian politics including *The End of Certainty, the Hawke Ascendancy* and *November 1975*. For the Centenary of Federation he presented a five part television special for the ABC on Australia's political history.

Clem Lloyd AO wrote extensively about Australian politics, political history, public policy, public administration and news media history. He was Foundation Professor of Journalism at the University of Wollongong from 1989 until shortly before his death at the end of 2001.

Stuart Macintyre is the Ernest Scott Professor at the University of Melbourne and has written extensively on Australian history. From 1999 to 2006 he was Dean of the Arts Faculty of Melbourne, and is currently Professor of Australian Studies at Harvard. He is the president of the Academy of the Social Sciences in Australia.

Dr Allan Martin, FAHA, FSSA, AM taught history, chiefly Australian, in the universities of Technology (Sydney), Melbourne and Adelaide. He was Foundation Professor of History, La Trobe University, and subsequently Senior Fellow in History, the Australian National University. His publications include (with Peter Loveday) *The First Thirty Years of Responsible Government in N.S.W.*; (with Peter Loveday and R.S. Parker, eds) *The origins of the Australian Party System*; *Henry Parkes: A*

Biography; *Letters from Menzies*; (with Patsy Hardy) *Dark and Hurrying Days*; *Robert Menzies: A Life*, (vol. 1) *1894-1943*; and (vol. 2) *1944-1978*. He died in 2002.

Ross McMullin is a historian and the author of the commissioned ALP centenary history, *The Light on the Hill: The Australian Labor Party 1891-1991* and another political history *So Monstrous a Travesty: Chris Watson and the World's First National Labour Government*. His biography *Pompey Elliott* won two awards, and his most recent book is *Will Dyson: Australia's Radical Genius.*

John Molony was born in Melbourne in 1927. He has been Professor of History at the Australian National University, the National University of Ireland and the Australian Catholic University. His thirteen books include the *Penguin Bicentennial History of Australia, Partito Popolare, Eureka* and *The Worker Question. Luther's Pine* an autobiography is his most recent work.

John Rickard is an honorary professor at Monash University. His books include *Class and Politics: New South Wales, Victoria and the early Commonwealth, 1890-1910; H.B. Higgins: The Rebel as Judge; Australia: A Cultural History;* and *A Family Romance: The Deakins at Home*. He was also a contributor to the recent *The Victorian Premiers 1856-2006* edited by Paul Strangio and Brian Costar.

Peter Sekuless has written two biographies of notable Australians, feminist Jessie Street and George Cross winner Fred March. He has also written two books about lobbying, at which he has laboured for the past two decades. His business partner, Jonathan Gaul, was Prime Minister McMahon's speech writer. Sekuless was a political journalist during McMahon's prime ministership. He is also the author of *A Handful of Hacks*, about Australian war correspondents, published in 1999.

Peter Vlahos is a graduate from the faculties of Law and Arts, Monash University, with LL.B and B.Juris (1987) and Dipl. International Law (1994) and completed a graduate diploma in politics at Monash. Currently, he is a solicitor in private practice and has been a Councillor for the City of Monash.

Picture Credits

AIS = Australian Information Service
AWM = by permission of the Australian War Memorial
NAA = by permission of the National Archives of Australia
NLA = by permission of the National Library of Australia

Frontispiece
Delegates to England (top), MS1540/14/1074, NLA, Centenary of Federation (bottom), Fairfax Photo Library

Portraits
Sir Edmund Barton, neg 565/f, Ravenscroft album 385, p 4, NLA; Alfred Deakin. 1900, neg 3000, NLA; John Christian Watson, neg 23, Parliamentary Handbook, NLA; Right Honourable Sir George Reid, neg 4261, MS album, NLA; Right Honourable Andrew Fisher, neg 4516, NLA; Sir Joseph Cook, neg 2405, NLA; William Morris Hughes, pl no. NL 32324, NLA; Stanley Melbourne Bruce, neg 1361, plate no 479–492, NLA; James Henry Scullin, plate no 32323, NLA; Joseph Aloysius Lyons, NLA; Sir Earle Page, NAA: A3560, 6053; Sir Robert Gordon Menzies, neg 19, plate no L13044, NLA; Sir Arthur William Fadden, 1940, neg 3911, plate no 782/3, NLA; John Joseph Curtin, neg 5, NLA; Right Honourable Francis Michael Forde, neg 4620, Ravenscroft album, NLA; Joseph Benedict Chifley, neg 1869, NLA; Harold Edward Holt, 1966, NLA; Sir John McEwen, neg 17, NLA; Right Honourable, Sir John Grey Gorton, neg 00000011, NLA; Sir William McMahon, neg 24. NLA; Edward Gough Whitlam, December 1972, neg 24, NLA; John Malcolm Fraser, rec. 12/2/81/9, neg 4749, AIS, NLA; Robert James Lee Hawke, 31/3/83/3, AIS, NLA; Paul John Keating, 1992, P339 Govt. Photographic Service File no 204/5/30, NLA; John Winston Howard, *Canberra Times;* Kevin Michael Rudd, *The Age*

Picture inserts
1. NLA **2.** NLA **3.** NLA: pl no 691/5 **4.** NLA: MS51/1268 from MS4936/2/133f793 **5.** NLA: pl no NL28034 **6.** NLA: pl no 241/1;533/247 and 'Mr Yes-No Reid' cartoon NLA: the *Bulletin*, 17/09/1903, NX252 **7.** NLA: in *The Illustrated London News*, 27/04/1907, p. 649 **8.** NLA: MS2919/12/219 **9.** J A La Nauze, *Alfred Deakin*, Melbourne University Press, 1965, facing page 562 **10.** NLA: pl no 241/1;533/247 **11.** NAA: M3614, 8 **12.** NLA: MD3449, in *Australasian*, 20/9/1919, p 602 **13.** Cecil Edwards, *Bruce of Melbourne*, Heinemann, London, 1965, facing page 87 **14.** NLA: neg 1339 **15.** *Opening of Parliament in Canberra, 1927*, (1927) W B McInnes (1889–1939) Historic Memorials Collection, Courtesy of Parliament House Art Collection, Canberra, ACT **16.** NLA **17.** NLA: the *SA Advertiser*, 11/10/1928, p 18, pl no 25186 **18.** NLA: P1313/19 **19.** NLA: MS4851 **20.** NLA: MS4851 **21.** NLA **22.** Sir Earle Page, *Truant Surgeon*, Angus & Robertson, Sydney, 1963, facing page 145 **23.** NLA: Menzies papers MS4936, neg 4084 **24.** NLA: MS3939/28 **25.** NLA: MS3939/28/9 **26.** NLA: MS 3939/1982 addition, *Pix*, 17/1/1942 **27.** NAA:A1200, L26035 **28.** NAA: A1200, L36449 **29.** NLA **30.** AWM 20/100020, Acc no: SUK12195 **31.** AWM 10/100020, Acc no: 099665 **32.** NAA; Australian Overseas Information Service; A1200/18, L11218 **33.** NAA: M2153/1, 1/6 **34.** NAA: A1200, L21159 **35.** NLA: the *Bulletin*, vol 70, 30/11/1949 **36.** NLA: Dwyer Collection **37.** AP/AAP **38.** NLA: neg 3916 **39.** NAA: AA1972/341, 322/ 88 **40.** Courtesy The Sir William Dobell Art Foundation; *Time* Australia **41.** NLA **42.** the *Canberra Times* **43.** NLA **44.** NLA **45.** NAA: A1200/18, L57452 **46.** Jim Green, the *Canberra Times* **47.** Geoff Hook, *Sun News* pictorial, 30/10/1969, page 8, NX351 **48.** NAA: A1200, L73423 **49.** The *Daily Telegraph* **50.** The *Canberra Times* **51.** The *Daily Telegraph* **52.** UPI **53.** Fairfax Photo Library **54.** NLA: P571/11 **55.** Jim Green, the *Canberra Times* **56.** Michael Porter, the *Canberra Times* **57.** Fairfax Photo Library **58.** Graeme Thomson, the *Canberra Times* **59.** the *Canberra Times* **60.** The *Canberra Times* **61.** Peter Wells, the *Canberra Times* **62.** John Lamb courtesy of the *Age*, H23736/cartoon by Ron Tandberg **63.** The *Canberra Times* **64.** Jim Green, the *Canberra Times* **65.** The *Canberra Times* **66.** Jim Green, the *Canberra Times* **67.** Richard Briggs, the *Canberra Times* **68.** Pool picture courtesy of News Ltd **69.** Graham Tidy, the *Canberra Times* **70.** John Woudstra, the *Age* **71.** The *Canberra Times* **72.** Dean McNicol, *the Canberra Times* **73.** Cartoon by Geoff Pryor **74.** Cartoon by Alan Moir **75.** Graham Crouch, courtesy of News Ltd, ref: 05486278 **76.** Cartoon by Geoff Pryor, the *Canberra Times* **77.** Dean McNicoll, the *Canberra Times* **78.** Alan Porritt, AAP Image **78.** Gary Ramage, AAP Image